The WEIGHT of NUMBERS

SIMON INGS

BLACK CAT

a paperback original imprint of Grove/Atlantic, Inc.
New York

Published simultaneously in Canada
Printed in the United States of America

FIRST EDITION

Library of Congress Cataloging-in-Publication Data
Ings, Simon
    The weight of numbers / Simon Ings.
        p. cm.
ISBN-13: 978-0-8021-7030-9
ISBN-10: 0-8021-7037-7
1. Illegal aliens—Death-fiction.   2. Human smuggling—Fiction. I. Title.
PR6059.N54W45 20076
823.92-dc2   200604276

Black Cat
a paperback original imprint of Grove/Atlantic, Inc.
841 Broadway
New York, NY 10003
Distributed by Publishers Group West
www.groveatlantic.com
07 08 09 10 11 12   10 9 8 7 6 5 4 3 2 1

For Anna

It will be an inhuman, an atrocious performance, but these are the facts.

General Giuilo Douhet, *Il Dominio dell'Aria*

The WEIGHT of NUMBERS

PROLOGUE

Lake Kissimmee, Florida

Monday, 25 October 1965

Marilyn, Jim's wife of thirteen years, pours out his second Coke, takes up her own and clinks his glass with ceremony as though it were champagne. Her eyes are big and black in the candlelight, wet with the unnamable emotions pilots' wives acquire in proximity to Canaveral.

Through the window of the restaurant, the night sky is speckled – had they but eyes to see – with spillage from the afternoon's catastrophe: a fuel explosion massive enough to shred a final stage to so much kitchen foil. For Jim the worst part is that at six minutes past three that afternoon, six minutes after the launch and at the very moment the Agena's engine turned over and choked on six tonnes of liquid fuel, he had been gaping, like some fool kid, eyes upturned on a calm sky.

'It'd have reached orbit,' he says, shaking his head.

'Tonight,' their waiter explains, 'our bass comes with a macadamia nut butter.'

'Well, whoop-de-doo,' says Marilyn.

'Ma-am?'

Marilyn blinks. 'I really have no idea why I said that.' She lays her hand on the boy's arm. 'I do apologize. Really.'

Perhaps she felt it, too, today. At six minutes past three, a wrinkle in things.

When they are alone: 'Marilyn?'

Marilyn giggles. This is the girl he fell in love with in high school. 'No idea at all. Sorry. Odd day today.'

Jim sets about his meal, determined to shake off bad thoughts. 'This fish,' he says.

The fish is really very good.

'Yes,' says Marilyn.

He's been told about this place: the best largemouth bass in the county, the tables small, unfussy, few, the air sweet off Lake Kissimmee – all this barely an hour from the Cape. Come December, Jim Lovell is riding shotgun with Frank Borman in Gemini Seven. An unprecedentedly long mission, two whole weeks, Seven is meant to test the shirt-sleeve environment the engineers have planned for the Apollo spacecraft. There's other, rather more gung-ho business for Frank and Jim to perform – for instance, they'll be demonstrating a new, more accurate form of controlled re-entry – but the core of their mission is 'station-keeping', NASA's word for staying clean and tidy and alive for 200 orbits of the Earth. One of the more damn-fool experiments dreamed up for them requires that Jim weigh every mouthful that enters his system before, during and after the flight. Although there are still six weeks to go before the launch, this will be, for Jim, his last unfussed-up meal for some while. To mark the fact, tonight he has arranged babysitters so he can take his wife out to dinner.

He says, 'I was standing on the crawlerway.' A pause. 'This afternoon. I watched it take off from the crawlerway.'

The main body of the rocket, the launch vehicle proper, was an Atlas, the machine that put John Glenn, America's first astronaut, into space. Today's Atlas worked perfectly, as far as he's aware. It was the final stage, the Agena Target Vehicle that exploded, one minute after separation, the very moment it tried to start its engine. Without a target vehicle for them to pursue, astronauts Wally Schirra and the rookie Thomas Stafford are even now slouching their way through the most disappointed night of their careers: the launch of Gemini Six, scheduled for tomorrow, is scratched.

'What will they do with Tom and Wally?' Marilyn's thoughts are tracking Jim's own with a niceness they had all expected of Gemini Six and its ill-fated target. 'Could they run their mission and yours together in any way that makes sense?'

James Lovell looks out the window at the lake. The sky is clear tonight. The water is so still, he can see the brighter stars reflected in the water. 'Probably,' he says. 'We'd at least be able to practise the alignment manoeuvres.' The Geminis are meant to lead to Apollo, and a bid for the moon. They are the only real practice the crews are going to get before the big push. Every Gemini failure makes Apollo that bit more daunting. 'It's not docking practice, but it'd be something.' Jim turns back to his wife, aware that in his preoccupation he is hardly giving her interest its due.

Every couple caught up in NASA's folly has its own way of dealing with the dangers and disappointments. Each solution is personal, its secrecy carefully guarded. It is impossible to know if Marilyn's careful, intelligent curiosity about Gemini is shared by any of the other wives. In public, and even among themselves, there can be no breach of the women's etiquette. This has less to do with class and custom – though that is part of it – so much as their common need to bootstrap a workable life out of the demands and sacrifices of the Cape. The artificiality of that life – Sunday clambakes in the shadow of the Vertical Assembly Building – is a given. That life *is* artificial, something you have to construct for yourself, like a shed or a car motor or a Thanksgiving dinner, is the great, soon-to-be-forgotten lesson of these days.

'They let you on the crawlerway?' says Marilyn, double-taking his earlier remark.

'That's where I watched it from.'

The crawlerway is, like any construction site, out of bounds. But there was no danger, watching a launch from there.

Practically speaking, the crawlerway is a four-lane highway connecting the launch complexes to the Vertical Assembly Building, where Apollo's colossal Saturn rockets will be built. But the lanes are deceptive. They are built, not for ordinary traffic at all, but for the giant caterpillar tracks of a single vehicle: the 500ft-high mobile launcher.

Standing there today, watching as the Atlas-Agena assembly rose out of its own exhaust cloud, high above Complex 14, Jim felt as though he were standing among giants, in a giant's footprint. He felt smaller than a child and infinitely less significant among these towering machines. He felt more like a rat: something tolerated and expendable.

'It seems to me now that I felt it.' This is something Jim Lovell absolutely will *not* say to his wife. 'It seems to me that there was a wrinkle in things. At six minutes past three this afternoon, and with nothing left to see besides the contrail, all of a sudden I became aware of a wrongness in the sky's fabric; a wrongness so intimate, at first I was afraid there was something the matter with my eyes.'

'What are you thinking?' Marilyn is asking him.

Drawn back to the present, Jim is startled to find himself already behind the wheel of their car. Marilyn is next to him, their meal is done, and Camp Mack Lane is already rumbling beneath their wheels. They are part-way home.

'Wait,' he says. 'Wait a minute.'

'What?'

'This isn't right.'

A wrinkle in things. Surfaces are bent and drawn into accidental contact. A short circuit, and the evening comes apart, skipping and hopping like a scratched record. 'Wait,' he says. He slows the car. 'Hang on.' He checks his rear-view mirror, slows them almost to a stop and turns them around.

He cannot rewind the evening. All those minutes wasted in introspection. He has to do something; this is their last easy evening together.

'What is it?' Marilyn asks. 'Did you forget something?'

'Everything is going to be fine,' he says, and he switches on the radio: a clue for her.

He drives them deeper and deeper into Florida's rural dark, under canopies of post oak and hickory, through pastures abandoned to mesquite. One by one, the stations peter out: WWBC out of Cocoa;

WKGF from Kissimmee. Wayne Fontana and The Mindbenders drift in and away and a silence descends, with an eerie, out-of-range sensation that Marilyn remembers now. 'You old fool,' she laughs, guessing his game. 'You fool, you.'

At a sign for a fishing lodge, he rolls the car down a dirt track. There are no lights, no other vehicles. Woods hug the shore. Between the tree trunks, moonlight glistens on Lake Kissimmee.

She leans over and slips into his arms. 'What about the babysitter?' she asks him.

'What about tomorrow's early start?'

'Did I switch the oven off?'

'Did I lock the door?'

A goofy routine to propitiate the ageing process: they understand that they are too old for this. After their first kiss, Jim draws away and turns off the ignition: it would be just like him to knee the stick into Drive and land them in the lake. The headlights die, the night is blue, they kiss again.

An orphan cloud covers the moon. Blue turns to black. The car's surfaces, tin frame and plastic fascia, close in around them. His scream is silent, wracking him out of her arms. He arches back as though electrocuted and cracks his head against the door column. *'Fuck—'*

'Jim!'

'Shit.'

'Not much better.'

'Sorry. *Darn.*'

She tries to laugh. 'What?'

'Nothing.'

'Jim.'

'Nothing. A rabbit ran over my grave.'

She thinks this over.

'Pesky rabbits,' she says.

She leans over and kisses him again. But the moment has passed. 'I'm going for a smoke,' she says, a minute later. She pecks him on the cheek and climbs from the car. He watches her go. He sits back, lays his hands on the steering wheel and forces himself, by main effort, to calm down. A second cloud hides the moon and the night swallows her. He leans forward and peers up at the sky: what is happening to the weather?

One by one, between the slowly stirring branches, stars are going out.

The waters off Japan, February 1954.

This is shortly after the Korean War and two years into Jim's marriage to Marilyn, effected just a couple of hours after graduating from the Naval Academy at Annapolis. At this point in his career, Jim is just a humble aviator, assigned to the SS *Shangri-La* from Moffet Field. He's flying McDonnell F2H Banshees: brutal turbo-powered monsters that cheerfully nudge the stratosphere.

The airframe wraps around him in the night, the dark itself turned metal, stuffing eyes and mouth, as he takes stock. What he's been following all these hours, burning up his fuel, what he thought was his homing beacon – well, it turns out that it wasn't. He's been following the wrong signal for – how long is it now? – and there are no ground lights, no ships in the vicinity, to help him find his way back on course. Neither are there any stars. He can't afford to waste fuel punching the cloud layer, because any navigation reading he takes will be meaningless by the time he descends again, and anyway he hasn't the fuel. Thank God the instrument lights are working. Without them, how could he be sure which way is up? It is at this point that he thinks to plug in the little geegaw he's made to boost the cockpit illumination – and in doing so, he fuses every light in the cockpit.

In a lonely bubble, bobbing above the Pacific, Jim Lovell, navy pilot, looks out from his blacked-out Banshee at the sky. If it is the sky. There are no stars. His instruments are out and his lights are out and there are no stars and there is no carrier, there is no *Shangri-La*. Where is the goddamn S*hangri-La*?

8

Jim Lovell, astronaut, climbs from the car. He misses the path and pushes through the undergrowth to the shore of Lake Kissimmee. Marilyn is stood at the end of a narrow wooden jetty, facing away from him. A red flare arcs and gutters as she tosses her cigarette into the water.

The screws of the carrier *Shangri-La* agitate the waters of the Pacific. The water, rich in plankton, glows. In the extremity of his failure, Jim Lovell, navy pilot, sees a green light: the wake of a ship. He follows the wake. It leads him home.

He steps onto the jetty. He walks up to his wife. An F2H Banshee stays in the air using two Westinghouse J34-WE-30 turbojets, each rated at 3,150 pounds of thrust. It takes off by means of a rubber catapult. It comes to rest by means of a grappling hook. It is very important for him to control his speed at this point. It is vital that he not overshoot and topple off the end of the jetty into the bass-rich waters of Lake Kissimmee. He bites his lip against laughter. The day has shaken loose so many bits of himself, all the joy and fear of what he does. He touches Marilyn on the shoulder.

She turns. 'Oh,' she says, looking straight into his eyes. 'You again.' She lets his laughter roll on a little way, then stops it with a kiss. 'Time to go home.'

BANSHEE

Beira, Mozambique

—

November 1992

In 1992, Mozambique's seventeen-year-old civil war was ended by the worst drought in living memory. Even fertile Gorongosa, in the interior of the country, found itself dependent on food aid. From trains grinding their way west along the contested Beira–Machipanda rail-line, armed men rolled sacks of grain into the dust. The sacks split. It could be days since the last train and I would still find boys from my class crawling about the embankments, sifting grains from fistfuls of gravel.

With the region in such disarray, I found it relatively easy to desert my post. So I returned to the coast and settled in Beira, Mozambique's second city.

Beira was a port town. It depended for its income on Mozambique's landlocked neighbours to the west, and on the busy overland corridor through which their trade was conducted. Attacks on this corridor by RENAMO, the apartheid-backed faction in this war, had rendered Beira redundant, and today's famine relief effort, shipping grain for onward distribution, was too little and too hesitant to revive the city's fortunes. Consequently, the streets had acquired a timelessness that was not romantic. There was no light, no water, no food, no sanitation. There were only people.

Shelter was at a premium. In my building whole families lived out diagonal lives in the stairwell. There was no electricity to run elevators, so the cheapest apartments in the city were on the upper floors of the tower blocks. None of the blocks was especially high by Western standards, so my tenth-floor eyrie gave me views across the whole city.

It was the piano, rather than the views, which first sold the apartment to me. I hadn't had a piano since I was a child. It was an antique upright from colonial days, shipped from Portugal and abandoned during the exodus. Its lid was locked, so I couldn't try it out, but once I'd established that it came with the apartment, I agreed to take the place, overpriced as it was.

For the most part of each day, I would sit out on my handkerchief-sized balcony and watch the city consume itself. There was no firewood to be had, and since most of the windows in town were mesh, not glass, people had decided that it was an easy and a relatively harmless thing to chip out the window frames for fuel. When that supply was exhausted, people turned on their furniture. Those who had run out of furniture pulled up sections of floor. By evening, the woodsmoke from 10,000 *braiis* made my eyes smart, and I went indoors. Usually I went to bed around this time. There was little else to do. The radio was useless as batteries were hard to come by.

The piano was a different story.

The day I moved in, the first thing I did was break open the keyboard. I sat down to play. The instrument emitted a dreadful dead thumping and wheezing. I pulled off the top and looked in.

The strings had been cut.

The piano came with a piano stool; lifting up the lid, I discovered that it was full of sheet music. Bach's *Well-Tempered Clavier*. I managed, with a deal of effort, to wheel the unstrung piano onto the balcony, and there I sat down and played: clippety-clop, clippety-clop – *bonk*. As the weeks went by, so my coordination improved to the point where I could hear the shape of the music and the pattern of the parts. At last the piano's hammers found their mark, tapping, ever so lightly, the strings inside my head.

I stopped my playing and looked over the city to the old holiday camps sprawled along the seafront. Beach huts were being adapted to accommodate refugees flooding to the coast from the parched interior. It seemed to me that, with this latest influx, Beira would achieve a critical mass. All it had going for it was the size of its population, but maybe this was enough. After twenty years of this bare existence, the city had learned how to feed off its own refuse for ever. I imagined it spreading in a chain reaction across the whole world: a self-sustaining half-life.

Communications were unreliable. The city had decayed to the point where it had learned to do without the outside world. There was little in the way of entertainment. A handful of bottle stores operated out of mud-brick houses along the shore, and it was to these that I thumbed my way, come late afternoon – or drove sometimes, if there was fuel enough for the pick-up.

With transport so hard to come by, every vehicle on the road was an unofficial bus; driving without passengers attracted the attention of the police. One afternoon, out on the coastal road, one of the men I had picked up rapped on the roof of the cabin and pointed me down a track towards a bit of beach I had not explored before. Several others seemed to know of the place, so once I had let off the onward travellers I rolled the pick-up down to the beach. At the tree-line, an enclosure fenced off with rushes marked the site of a new bottle store. The place had an ambitious layout. The tables and benches in the enclosure were cast concrete, but their surfaces were decorated with inset fragments of pottery and mirror. Under a raised veranda, I saw the walls of the store had fresh murals.

Inside, a white kid with a slurred Austrian accent was giving the girl behind the bar a hard time.

'I know every fucking owner on this coast,' he said, more or less, his speech a druggy mishmash of German and Portuguese.

Dumb, impassive, the girl shook her head.

'Fucking *bitch*.'

From out the back a white man – a real bruiser – joined the girl. 'Out,' he said, barely bothering to make eye contact. He and Austrian Boy must have run into each other before, because the kid began straight away to retreat towards the veranda. 'You're *fucked*,' he shouted. 'You'd better watch your back. I know people.'

The barman blinked. He was a big man, clean-shaven, crew-cut, built for a fight. His eyes were mean and set close together. His mouth let him down: small and pursed above a weakling chin. 'What crap was *that*?' he asked no one in particular, in English, when the boy was gone. I was surprised to hear the man's Norfolk burr: I had assumed, from the sheer size of him, that he was a Boer.

By way of conversation, I translated the boy's German.

'Really.'

'Or words to that effect,' I said.

All the other bottle stores were locally run and I wondered what had driven a European to set up in so unrewarding a business. The drinks here were the usual trio – orange Fanta, green-label Carlsberg and *chibuku*, a locally produced granular swill I had never got used to. I supposed he must be, like me, an ideological recruit to FRELIMO, the country's beleaguered socialist government. I couldn't think what else would bring an Englishman to such a miserable pass. He was about my age: a middle-aged drifter for whom home was by now a distant memory. He was happy to talk to a countryman and, when I offered to buy him a beer, he plucked a Carlsberg off the shelf and led me to an outdoor table.

His name was Nick Jenkins. I told him something about myself. I mentioned Gorongosa, and it surprised me how much I was prepared to relive of that time, merely to feed a casual chat.

We talked about the war, and when I explained how, in spite of my politics, I had come to work as a teacher in RENAMO's apartheid-funded heartland – how I had fomented Marxist revolution among my seven- and eight-year-olds under the very noses of the party hierarchy – Jenkins chuckled.

My own life, eventful as it might have appeared from the outside, had been dictated by the sweep of political events. Nick Jenkins, on the other hand, like all true adventurers, had somehow sidestepped the big events of his day. This was his second time in Mozambique. The first, the late sixties, had seen him working the merchant lines out of Maputo when it was still

Lourenço Marques, the colonial capital. From there he'd gone to the Caribbean, where he'd built up a small import-export concern. 'It was my second time there, and all,' he laughed. 'I can't seem to make up my mind.'

I did a quick mental calculation. 'You must have been young the first time, then. Your first time in the Caribbean. When was that? Early sixties?'

'Damn right.' He nodded. 'A bloody kid.'

It was when he told me about Cuba that I began to doubt his tale.

'Six bloody battalions,' he sighed, reminiscing. 'Fifteen hundred men. Christ!'

'You were in the Bay of Pigs landing?'

'Not "in" it. We just happened to be berthed in Puerto Cabezas for a refit. The boat was chartered. We came with the boat. We were deckhands, not squaddies.'

The enormity of this new anecdote, artfully shaped out of hints and hesitations and the occasional buzz-word, took my breath away. That a seventeen-year-old boy from the fens should have washed up on the beaches of Havana in 1961 seemed incredible.

He did not stop there. A couple of years later, he told me, one night in October 1963, he found himself washing glasses in the very nightclub where Yuri Gagarin, hero of the Soviet Union and the first man in space, was celebrating the first leg of yet another world friendship tour. Jenkins had a gift for detail. The motley quality of Gagarin's official retinue – every suit an arms supplier or party dilettante – was lent added spice by the invective he had saved up for their wives: monstrous, shot-putting hags obsessed with translating Neruda and Borges into Russian. He even had it in mind that the Playa Girón – the bay where a band of coral had, he said, been fatally mistaken for seaweed – later gave its name to the national honour the Cuban president Fidel Castro awarded Gagarin during this goodwill trip.

'He showed it to me, right there in the bar. Yuri did. His medal. And I showed him my scar. And Yuri laughed and told me, "You too wear the Order of Playa Girón!"'

17

I was tempted to ask what language they had used, that Jenkins could converse so freely with a Russian cosmonaut. Together with his highbrow literary references, so lovingly mispronounced ('Georgie Borkiss'), his story convinced me that I was in the company of a gifted imposter.

It was night by the time we were done, and the kerosene was running low in the lamp. I waited for Jenkins to lock up, and walked with him to where our vehicles were parked. My deepening silence should have warned him that the evening's game was up, but Jenkins could not resist further embroidery.

'Seaweed!' he laughed. 'Fuckers in American intelligence had it down for seaweed. Fucking *coral*, more like. I felt the deck lurch, the whole bloody boat started to roll, and I didn't hang around, I can tell you. I jumped, and it's a bloody miracle I didn't spit myself on the reef.' He thought about this and added, 'Some did.'

Jenkins's Land Rover was drawn up a few feet from where I had parked the Toyota. The moon came out from behind a cloud, and I saw that the Land Rover was leaning drunkenly to the right. Before I thought to stop him, Jenkins had walked over to investigate. He was still spinning his tale as he vanished into shadow. 'I heard them screaming in the dark. I tasted their blood in the water—'

There then came the sound I imagine a cricket bat makes as it strikes a cabbage, a thud as of a body falling into sand, and Jenkins was silent.

I charged like an idiot into the darkness.

I couldn't see a thing. Arms upraised, I swung about, hoping I might collide usefully with Jenkins's attacker. I stumbled and fell headlong. I tried to get up. Something buried itself in the sand by my right ear. I grabbed it. The stick came free without a struggle. I scrambled to my feet. I was afraid to swing the stick blindly, but then the assailant, disarmed, stumbled out of the vehicle's shadow into the moonlight. Austrian Boy, of course. I ran at him with the stick held point-first. It was a flimsy sort of weapon – the best the boy's fool mind could come up with in all the hours Jenkins and I had been drinking. I did what I could with it, punching him deep under his ribcage. Winded, he fell back another couple of paces. Jenkins was already up on his feet. He blundered past me and swung his clenched fist back and forth in front of the boy's face: his features disappeared in a splash of black blood.

'Jesus,' I said.

Jenkins turned past me. The boy was staggering blindly about the track, hands pressed to his face, holding it together.

I followed Jenkins across the sand. It was a magnificent night, the sky white with stars. At the water's edge, each wave gave a faint burst of greenish light as it rolled into the sand. Jenkins kneeled, oblivious to the water swilling round his knees, and washed the blood off his Stanley knife. He dried it fastidiously on his shirt.

I said to him, 'Don't do things by halves, do you?'

He ignored me, scooped up seawater in handfuls and threw it over his face, washing off the blood dribbling from the scratch on his scalp.

When he was done bathing his head he sank back on the sand. 'We never stood a fucking chance,' he said, his face empty of all feeling. I couldn't tell whether he meant tonight, or 16 April 1961. I didn't much care, either. The war had acclimatized me to Jenkins's brand of cheap violence, but it had not got rid of my distaste.

I helped him up and back towards the vehicles. The boy had vanished again. Once I had got Jenkins into the passenger seat of the Toyota, I turned on the cabin light and examined his cut. There was still blood running behind his ear and into the collar of his shirt, but the cut itself was trivial; the seawater had already begun to staunch the flow. I studied his pupils, and got him to hold out his hands for me. I found no sign of concussion. 'Sit tight,' I said.

Taking the flashlight with me, I went to check what damage the boy had done to his Land Rover. The worst I found were a couple of deflated tyres, but, when I returned to the pick-up, Jenkins had disappeared. I called and, when I got no reply, I seriously considered driving off and leaving him there. Every instinct told me I should leave this evening behind as quickly as possible.

Then I heard Jenkins ranting in bad Portuguese: 'What the bloody hell is the point?' His angry exclamation came to me muffled by distance. 'If I was a burglar you'd be dead by now!' Jenkins was fairly screaming. I turned my flashlight back on and shone it towards the bottle store. He must have gone round the back.

Another, unfamiliar voice replied, '*Eeh? Eeh, chiyani?* What? Where are they? I have a club! Look, I have a club!'

For the second time that evening, it sounded as though my host was being threatened. With a heavy heart, I approached the back of the bottle store. I found Jenkins towering over a small man by the side of a watchman's hut not much bigger than a kennel.

'Why don't you use the bloody *light*?' Jenkins shouted. 'You should be round the *front*.'

His watchman laughed at such absurdity. 'To light the burglar's way? They can't see in the dark, you know.'

'How are you meant to spot them, then? Wait till they trip over you? Look, you fucking idiot, *there's one out there now*. What are you going to do about him, eh?'

'The hut is here! I have my gun! I never sleep, I listen all the time.'

'Get out the front. He won't do you any harm, not now I've done your bloody job for you. Find him and get him to clear off.'

Jenkins noticed me waiting for him, and suddenly lost interest in his watchman. 'Oh, stay where you are, then. Get your throat cut, why should I worry?' Mumbling, nursing his head, Jenkins joined me and together we returned to my truck.

I mentioned his flat tyres, and since there had been no other visible damage to his vehicle, Jenkins, much recovered, took this as good news.

'It was so bloody dark we couldn't see a thing,' he said, as I dug about for my keys. He was picking up where he left off, practically mid-sentence. 'We were running into each other. Knocking each other down. Everyone was screaming. Most of us couldn't swim.'

After all that had happened tonight, I was losing my patience. 'If you were captured after the Bay of Pigs fiasco, if you were a convicted contra, how come a couple of years later you were working in a Havana nightclub?'

'That was the length of my sentence,' he said, surprised, as if the answer were self-evident. 'Twenty-two months in La Cabaña. Come on, I was only a kid, anyone could see that.'

He curled forward and bent his head for me to examine his shorn scalp, presenting me with incontrovertible proof of his story. 'There,' he said, playing his fingers over the cut the boy had dealt him. He wanted me to see something else, something beneath: the scar from a wound inflicted by an oar wielded by an outraged Cuban fisherman, twenty-six years before, on the day CIA-backed Cuban contras came to grief in the Bay of Pigs. 'Tottery old fucker, he was. Found me hiding in his boathouse.' Jenkins laughed, head still bent for my inspection. 'A sinking ship to escape from in the middle of the night, a fucking *reef* to climb over, couldn't see a thing, shells and bullets and God knows what whizzing everywhere, and this is my one and only battle scar.'

I could see that he needed a couple of stitches after tonight. What I couldn't see was any old war wound.

Jenkins sat up too fast, groaned and held his head. 'The shit must have clobbered me in the same place. Bloody feels like it, too – *there* he is...'

I had just that moment turned on my headlights. Austrian Boy was slumped some distance up the track, covered in blood. His eyes shone out of the mess of his face like two blue stones.

I drove towards him. Shock had made him stupid: he just sat there, waiting to be run over. I braked. 'Now what?' I said.

'All right, give me a hand.' We got out and went over to the boy. Jenkins took his arms and I took his feet. We ignored his keening and manhandled him into the bed of the Toyota. There were a couple of NGOs newly opened on the highway into town; if we dumped him in front of the right gate, some well-meaning Swedish doctor would see to him soon enough.

London – Johannesburg

September 1998

Heathrow. The airliner makes a lumbering turn, engages its engines and pushes TV and movie actress Stacey Chavez back in her seat.

The acceleration is oddly comforting, as the upholstery enfolds her stick-thin body, wrapping it away from harm, but the moment the plane leaves the ground, all this is lost and Stacey realizes she has made a terrible mistake.

(*'I wonder how you are,'* her father wrote to her recently, a quarter-century too late. How did he get her email address? *'The clinic didn't tell me anything. They just send me the bills.'* Moisés Chavez – a wanted man.)

Stacey is flying to Mozambique to film a short documentary about landmine clearance. Three years ago there were about three million landmines seeded across the country. How many remain to blow off a farmer's genitals here, an inquisitive toddler's head there, is uncertain; her producer Owen has already conducted interviews with a couple of the half-dozen organizations employed in mine clearance, and they have said that the problem will never entirely go away.

(Stacey claws at the armrests as the plane punches through pocket after pocket of dead air. She is afraid, not of flying, but of this sensation, this lurching and dropping which she associates, after years of illness, with the flutters of her starved heart.)

In twenty-four hours or less, Stacey Chavez will be standing in front of a camera, got up in the sort of protective gear – kevlar tabard, plastic visor – sported just last year in Angola by Princess Diana. Disaster is assured. She can see the tabloids now, feasting on the conjunction between her clothes-hanger body and a continent's starvation. (Her knowledge of Africa hardly extends beyond the Live Aid concert, and she imagines everyone there is chronically short of food.) She can rehearse in her own head, long before they are written, the ugly comparisons that will be drawn between her and Saint Diana. 'Who does she think she is?' they will say and people will snigger.

('I see your name in magazines but I don't believe them, I just look at the pictures. It looks to me like you're better now. Are you?')

There is, after ten years of self-starvation, no possibility of Stacey making a full recovery. If she is careful, her heart will not fail her just yet. But it *will* fail. A neat irony, this: the very moment you decide that you want to live, they tell you how many years you have shaved off your life. Yes, she has made a terrible mistake, and not even the attentions of Ewan McGregor can soothe away the fact.

He touches her wrist for the briefest of moments and gives her one of those how-are-you? smiles. His good looks are an affront. By his touch he has made her aware of her hand, and she rather wishes he hadn't: her hand, this pallid claw that is somehow attached to her and is, for some reason, her responsibility, its nails dug deep in the armrest's plastic padding. She lifts it, turns it, examines it: an unfamiliar domestic implement. McGregor, taking its movements for an invitation, takes her hand in his.

McGregor, the star of *Trainspotting* and tipped to play Obi-Wan Kenobi in Lucas's new *Star Wars* trilogy, is flying with Stacey as far as Johannesburg. Stacey Chavez has a three-hour stopover there before flying South African Airways to Maputo, the capital of Mozambique. Over the next couple of months, nine other celebrities will be flying to locations all over Africa. Their punchy, insistently upbeat documentaries will go to support a popular annual TV appeal.

A week before, Stacey's producer Owen sent her the rushes of their initial to-camera. The footage was worse than she'd feared. Who was that dead-eyed brat with her shock-white hair and her chemical tan? Could this really be her? Could those really be her thoughts? Every opinion she

23

spouted came larded with junk words like 'exclusion' and 'branding'.

Owen's pre-fabricated style of documentary is ruthlessly efficient. Over gin and tonics in Blacks on Dean Street, Owen and Benjamin, their cameraman, have talked her through every shot. Each one of Stacey's sentiments and reactions is to be manufactured according to an already written plan. The technique will save a lot of time but this hurried style of rehearsal reminds her, ironically enough, of *Grange Hill*, the children's school soap opera which first launched her acting career. Stacey had been looking forward to something different.

The clearance programmes have lent a boom-town atmosphere to Manhiça, the town where they are filming. With all these foreigners around, Dutch and English and American, Benjamin wondered aloud, over his second G&T, how he was going to keep them out of his footage.

Stacey was slightly scandalized – she is unused to documentary and its compromises – and wondered aloud if this really mattered.

'One random white face and the whole thing's buggered,' Owen assured her, passing his expenses card to the waitress.

A television set domesticates whatever you happen to be watching. This is his theory. The exotic has to be pointed up, exaggerated, even manufactured, or the foreigness of their location – so obvious to them – will simply not translate to the screen. Neither Owen nor Benjamin expressed the slightest faith in the camera's ability to tell the truth.

The drinks trolley passes. McGregor insists they share one of those mini-bottles of champagne and, making conversation, slides unwisely into shop-talk. He asks her, 'Weren't you doing something for Amiel?'

Jon Amiel: director of *The Singing Detective*, back in the eighties. Look closely during the rendition of 'Dry Bones' in episode three and you will spot Stacey kick-stepping her way out of her five-year *Grange Hill* gig in a nurse's hat, white fishnets and a smile. Now Amiel is reinventing himself as a Hollywood action director. Stacey was his first choice for the part of the insurance investigator in *Entrapment*, a role since snapped up by Catherine Zeta-Jones.

'Events got in the way,' Stacey tells McGregor, fixing him with wide, black, mischievous eyes that, though sunken, have not lost all their glamour.

It is all a terrible, grotesque mistake, her being here, her doing this, and what makes it worse, she can't even blame her agent. Did she not burst into the offices of ICM, days after her return from Los Angeles and the eating disorders clinic, to demand work, exposure, media coverage, face-time? Begging for a second shot at the very life that knocked her down?

Looking back on her oh-so-promising past, Stacey senses its sterility. Even before she went to Hollywood, she had reduced her every passion to an ambition, every ambition to a career plan. By the time of her collapse she had stripped her life down so far it felt as though she had run her every permutation a hundred, a thousand times. No wonder death had seemed a welcome novelty; in that state of mind nothing, least of all success, could ever seem fresh or new or exciting.

(*'I want to be something to you now. You were doing so well before, I was only a liability. I hope you see that. I hope you see that things are different now.'*)

She has to find something else to do with her life. Something less fatuous.

'Who's having the special meal, then?'

The stewardess's interruption is fortunate. It is hard to know, otherwise, what response McGregor could have made to Stacey's candid reference to 'events'. He cannot possibly have remained ignorant of them. From *Variety* to *Hello!*, rags of every hue have anatomized the fall of Stacey Chavez, child star turned gymslip pin-up turned LA wannabe. Her collapse. The half-minute she lay flatlined on the gurney.

'The special? Ooh, that will be me.'

What saved her? If she knew that, then maybe this word 'recovery' would hold more meaning for her. If she had 'recovered her faith', for example. But she is not aware of recovering any sort of faith in anything.

It feels to her as if she simply woke up one day, found herself in hospital and decided that she was, after all, still afraid of death. Everything else – her gains in weight, her improved blood pressure, the ketones vanished from her urine – seem to have followed logically from that reawoken fear.

What kind of victory is that? It does not feel at all as though she is 'winning out over her condition'. It is rather as though she has simply swapped her love of death – so grand, so romantic – for the common-or-garden terror of it.

This sense of anticlimax is, she knows, part of her life now: a necessary consequence of her recovery from addiction. How shameful though, how embarrassing, to have to acknowledge that what she has been hooked on all this time is neither drink nor smack nor sex, but simply the glamour of her own will. Dying to please herself, she was larger than life. Actually having to live with herself, day after day – this is a harder, more humbling proposition.

(*Of course I heard about Deborah. I am truly sorry for everything. Not a day went by I did not think of her and of you.*' Moisés Chavez, absent husband, absent father, playing catch-up after all these years. '*I believe your mother had the very best care. Is there anything I can do for you?*' Though wanted by law enforcement on three continents, Moisés still contrives to pay his family's medical bills.)

'Is it special, then?' McGregor is still trying to get her into conversation.

'I'm sorry?'

'Is it a special meal?'

'Oh...' She cannot think how to respond. She casts around her compartmented plastic plate, looking for clues. She cannot think of a single thing to say that will not either embarrass or discomfort him. For instance, how the food on aeroplanes reminds her of the meals in the hospital, each portion so carefully presented, under foil, under plastic, the way a transplant surgeon might receive a donor's organ.

'Yes,' she says, and tries to laugh.

Her special meal. Stacey's circulation is geared by now to the meagre wants of a five-stone body, and her programme of weight-gain, painfully circumspect as it is, makes difficult demands of her ill-used vital organs. She will eat everything they put in front of her. This is the deal. She will neither toy, nor conceal, nor rearrange. Not that it is likely, so soon after treatment, that she will slide into her old, obsessive-compulsive behaviours.

('Call me. Please.')

It is much more probable, at this point in her recovery, that her shrivelled heart will explode.

Glasgow, UK

Friday, 12 March 1999

The receptionist wore an orange Jimmy-wig, a propeller tie and a big red nose. As I came in the door, he squeezed his nose at me. It squeaked.

I told him, 'I have a room booked. Saul Cogan.' I had gone back to using my real identity. I was beyond aliases.

'I am afraid your room is not quite ready, sir.' He made to squeeze his nose at me again, then thought better of it.

I said to him, 'Is this an airport hotel?'

'I am terribly sorry, sir.'

'Have you any idea how long I have been awake?'

'Your room would normally be ready for you, sir, only the staff are taking a little longer this morning.'

'Let me guess,' I said, 'the maids are wearing gigantic clown shoes.'

'Yes, sir!' he agreed, brightly. 'If you would care to wear a hooter today, sir,' he pointed to a cardboard tray piled with squeaky joke-shop noses, 'we undertake to contribute five per cent of your final bill to—'

'Look at my face.'

'It should only be a matter of minutes, sir. The breakfast bar is now open.'

I had spent almost a year working in places where the only food was *nsima*, a kind of gruel, with – as an occasional treat – Maggi instant noodles ('Asam Laksa Flavour'). I had had twenty hours or so of airline food with which to sate my yearning for all the tastes I had been going without. I had eaten everything the stewardesses had put in front of me. I licked the butter raw out of its tiny plastic ramekin. It was not enough. As soon as I entered that room and saw the laden tables, the fresh fruit, the ten different kinds of cereal, the serving bowls of prunes, dried figs, banana chips, mixed nuts, the cold-meat selection, the cheese-board, the tray of fruit-flavoured yoghurts, plain yoghurt, Greek yoghurt, I knew I was going to have to put all of it, everything, at the very least a little bit of everything, into my mouth.

Afterwards there was no point even trying to sleep, and I looked around for some amusement. There was a swimming pool; I liked the notion of standing about in warm water, relieved of my own weight. I could as easily have gone up to my room, assuming it was ready, and run a bath, but I was afraid I might fall asleep. I pictured myself choking on my own swill.

By the door to the pool area there was a keep-fit franchise. Though the hotel staff were bowed beneath the kosh of Comic Relief's Red Nose Day, the girl serving in the franchise had left her circus gear at home. The only swimming trunks she had left in stock were size XXL. They were fluorescent pink. 'Christ,' I said, handing her my card.

The pool was enclosed in a glass dome, the panes held in place by a complex spider-web of white-painted steel struts. The pool was an amoeboid shape that made 'lengths' impossible and off-putting displays of jock athleticism unlikely. The remaining space was filled with white plastic recliners and potted palms. There was one other guest, sat with her feet up on a recliner at the far end of the space, holding the hotel's standard-issue white terry robe tightly to her chin. Every so often she would take a moment to peck intently, one-handed, at a heavy black laptop computer.

I took a bathsheet from the pile by the door and tossed it onto a recliner far away from hers. Once I had found a deepish-looking corner I slipped into the water. The tiles beneath my feet were pimpled, anti-slip affairs that tickled all my cuts and sore places. Underwater light glanced off my trunks and lent the water a pleasant blush.

The water was so hot – practically bath heat – I could not stay in for long. After a desultory paddle or two I heaved myself none too elegantly out of the water. As I got to my feet I caught my neighbour's eye. The defensive way she was clutching her robe was belied by her smile.

I said, 'I just want to make it clear, these were the only trunks they had.'

She took a moment to study them. 'They do not necessarily reflect your opinions?'

'That's correct.'

'I am reassured.'

'I wouldn't want you to think that these trunks speak for me in any way.'

It began to rain. Raindrops driven against the hexagons and pentagons of the dome caused the structure to ring slightly. It was an exhilarating effect, and one the designers had probably not anticipated. 'I'm going to call for a drink. Do you want anything?'

She shook her head.

When my gin and tonic arrived she raised her eyebrows at me.

'It may be your morning,' I said, 'it certainly isn't mine.' I crossed to the recliner next to hers. The crow's feet at her eyes suggested a woman in her forties, and she had one of those perfectly preserved figures that childlessness gives some women.

She adjusted the fold of her robe and took her hand away from her neck. I set my drink down on the table between us and glimpsed, between her collar-bones, the start of a deep and beautiful scar.

She pretended to concentrate.

'What is that you're working on? Beyond the obvious.'

'As if I would stoop to a cheap gag like that.'

'As if.'

'It's a laptop.'

'You could not resist.'

'I felt a terrible compunction.' She set her laptop down beside my drink, loosened her robe and turned – all this in one fluid action. She headed for the pool and performed a goofy little dive: anything more dramatic, and she would have cracked her head on the bottom. She moved well through the water; her movements were so economical it was hard to see how they managed to propel her. When she was done, she pushed herself out on her arms. Her body had the sallow sheen one gets from regular indoor exercise. She walked back to her chair. The scar extended beyond the cut of her one-piece. It was a well-healed thing, perhaps from childhood. I wanted to trace it.

She dried herself off and belted herself into her terry robe. 'Can I have that back now?'

I was tapping at her keyboard, scrolling through the presentation she had been working on. 'Wait. I've nearly worked it out.'

'Really.'

'What this thing is.'

'Give it back.'

I lifted the laptop into her hands.

She closed the machine down and shut the lid.

I finished my drink. 'My room will be ready now,' I said.

'Is that some sort of invitation?'

'I like your aura of calm authority,' I said. 'I like how you move in water.'

'You want to know me better.'

'I can't ask you out for a drink, it's only ten in the morning. Anyway, you'll be gone in a few hours.' I gestured at the black box on her lap. 'According to your calendar.'

We left for our respective changing areas. I collected my card key from reception and went up to my room. There was a minisystem, but only one CD by Phil Collins. I tried tuning the radio, without success. When I turned on the TV it flashed up a greeting for Saul Coogan, whoever he was. I didn't expect her to knock.

When I found her there outside my door I said, 'You forgot your laptop.'

'I thought it might distract you.' She was dressed for leaving. She told me her luggage was already at the desk. It became clear that she was more practised at these encounters than I was.

She asked me what I did. I told her, with some necessary elisions, about the past year. About the camp at Al Ghahain, in the Yemen. About the Somali refugees I had befriended, and their plight. At some point her hand, which had slid from my knee to the crotch of my pants, ceased to move. She did not understand. Struggling to find some point of connection, she told me, 'In my sports centre, they let asylum-seekers in *for free.*'

'Asylum-seekers are not allowed to work,' I pointed out.

'*Exactly,*' she said.

I moved us onto safer ground. 'Your laptop,' I said, and while she talked I took off her clothes.

'It crawls from connection to connection,' she said. 'It closes the gaps between things.'

It learns who you are, she told me, and intuits the things you most desire. Which bottle of wine. Which book. Which holiday. Which human being. I took off her bra and took each nipple into my mouth.

The thing on her laptop was a search engine. This was her work, her reason for being. The crowning glory of a life of project management. Though she told me the project's name, I never saw it again, and I imagine both it and she fell victim to the stock crash which consumed her industry, just a few months later.

I laid her flat on the bed and lifted her arms above her head to stretch her scar. It ran at a slight diagonal from her throat to a point below her rib-cage. She told me they had cracked her chest when she was a baby, to plug a hole in her heart.

The cut had healed very well: the casual stroke of a tailor's chalk, splitting her in half. I knelt down to taste her, and, when she came, the scar flushed suddenly, a streak of red lightning under her skin. I traced it with my finger.

'The heart's signal,' I said.

She laughed. 'I can never fake.'

'A message from the heart.' I was determined to have my meaningful moment.

She told me some men wouldn't kiss her scar; or they would kiss it in a manner they fancied would not be noticed. Some pretended not to notice it at all. I understood why, when I first saw her, she had held her robe closed so tightly around her throat. It was to attract my attention.

I told her I wanted to pull her scar open. That I had this desire to touch what was inside.

Apparently I was not the first to say that, either.

We played each other like instruments, a finger here, lips there, with very little passion. She drew my foreskin down, wetted me with her mouth, and while she ran the palm of her hand in slow circles over me, she told me about her work and its philosophy. (She wanted me to know her work had a philosophy.) About webs and matrices. How things and people are bound together. About the shadow separating a desire and its satisfaction, and how that shadow is banished in the white glare of modern information technology.

'Now I want to fuck you.'

'Do you, now?' she said.

I reached over to the bedside table and fished a condom out of the packet. 'Make me wet,' I said. I held the back of her head while she did it, and then I put on the rubber and climbed on top of her. I wanted to see that white line go red again. I wanted to see that subtle, subterranean eruption along the old fault line: the halves of her yearning to separate. I slid inside her.

The door to the corridor opened and in walked a maid wearing a green fright-wig, a red nose, striped pantaloons and metre-long plastic overshoes.

'For Christ's sake,' I said.

The maid mumbled something about the door being open and hurried to leave. Her feet wouldn't let her turn around. She kept treading on them. Humiliated, she had to edge backwards through the doorway.

The interruption had ruined any chance that lightning might run through that scar a second time. Patting each other, reassuring each other, we abandoned the attempt. 'I need to freshen up,' I said, and locked myself in the bathroom, hoping that by the time I came out, she would be dressed again.

She was faster than I was: the room was empty when I emerged. I returned to the bed. She had straightened the duvet for me: a gesture with so little redeemable meaning, in the end I had to throw the thing off and lie on the bare sheet, just so I could stop thinking about *what it meant.*

I got out my mobile phone and laid it on the pillow beside me. There was still no call from Nick Jinks – Nick Jenkins, as I had first known him. (By the sixth month of our unlikely and profitable partnership, Jinks had drunkenly revealed his real name to me – but not his reason for changing it. That revelation would come later, and until then I more or less assumed that it was a seafarer's superstition that had made him keep Jinks a secret.)

I looked at my watch: why was I worrying? It was still far too early; the ferry wouldn't even have docked. I closed my eyes and tried a relaxing breathing exercise – something I had picked up, in spite of myself, from my long-haul's wakey-wakey prior-to-landing video.

She had told me how everything is architecture.

People, she had said, are the patterns they make.

People are rhythms, reverberating along the strands of an all-encompassing web.

I imagined myself embedded in her web of global connections, the futile syncopations of my gluey little feet, and fell asleep.

Portsmouth, UK

the same day

Fifty-seven-year-old former merchant seaman Nick Jinks rolls his juggernaut off the ferry and up the narrow causeway – tarmac over steel; the whole structure trembles – to the Portsmouth Harbour customs area. He shuts off the container's ventilation so as not to arouse the officers' suspicion, presents his paperwork, and waits.

Nick Jinks has travelled all over the world. In Havana, he has swapped jokes in bad Spanish with Yuri Gagarin. As he celebrated his twenty-eighth birthday alone in a jazz bar by the docks in Port-au-Prince, a man claiming to be John Kennedy's real assassin stood him a *mojito*, lacing it generously with cocaine from a silver spoon. He was in Port Canaveral, December 1972, closing the deal on a Cuban exile's sport fishing boat, in time to see a Saturn V booster carry Apollo Seventeen, the last ever manned moonshot, into orbit. He was in Auckland harbour in 1985, actually staggering along Marsden Wharf with a beer tin in his hand, the night the French secret service blew up the *Rainbow Warrior*. He has been brushed by newsworthy events. He has had more than his share of luck. But Nick Jinks has never acquired the knack of accumulation. What he earns, he spends.

Now, in his late fifties, Jinks wants an end to his seafaring life. He is weary of hard work and difficult hours, the identikit familiarity of ports, the insincerity of port women. He is nettled by the insolence of the young as they scamper up the merchant marine career ladder ahead of him, who never could be bothered to climb. He wants his boyhood before the mast to come to a stop before it is too late. He wants to put away childish things. He wants a wife. A kid. Even someone else's kid, whatever, he is not fussy. He wants to come home.

Saul Cogan, his long-standing business partner, has seen to it that he can return, without fear of arrest. Saul has even made it possible for him to enter the country under his own name.

The way is open to him, and Nick is beginning to wonder what, exactly, he is coming home to. Last time he was in the UK – trying on his real name for size, after nearly forty years of aliases; of Jenkinses and Jenningses, a Jiggins, a Jeves, a Jessup – he took the time to drive, in a rented car, past his boyhood home. The garage and the tea shop were gone, razed, a greenfield Tesco in their place, and the road that led him to the site of the erasure was itself a new thing: smooth, lit, signed, marked, cambered, mathematically curved, like the race-track on a computer game.

He pulled up in Tesco's car park and tried to get his bearings.

Curses perturb only those who are sensitive to them. It was impossible to believe that Tesco's greengrocery section would ever be troubled, as he and his father Dick had been, by fat, shit-coloured flies, wasps, rats, mysterious white galls. It was a different world.

As evening descends, Nick Jinks drives his juggernaut into the lorry park of a service station outside Carlisle. Three magic letters hang off the back of Jinks's lorry: T.I.R., 'Transport International Routier'. By international agreement, rigs with a T.I.R. certificate are exempt from customs inspections at national borders. It is generally agreed that there is little point chilling expensive foodstuffs down to a tidy minus five, if some bureaucrat with a clipboard is just going to open up the back of the van and let everything spoil in the dusty heat of the Spanish–Portuguese border. 'T.I.R.' is the people smuggler's favourite. Uncomfortable, but effective.

Jinks is practised enough at his business to know that he should not leave his vehicle unattended, so once he's washed and fed himself he leaves the service station, crosses the parking area and climbs back on board. In truth, spending a night on the lorry is not such a hardship. The driver's cabin is fitted for long-haul comfort. Nick turns the heater up full, draws the blinds over the insect-spatted windows and settles back to watch TV. There's a little colour set mounted off to one side of the cab. Reception is surprisingly good. The decent programmes haven't begun yet. It's still *London Tonight*. Nick is too exhausted to read (Juan Rulfo's *Pedro Páramo*; his Spanish has fallen away with disuse and he is finding the going very hard) and there is nothing else to do.

The early-evening magazine programmes offer up the usual mix of crime horror, community news and celebrity froth, and around 7.30 p.m. they segue, with disconcerting ease, into the antics of Red Nose Day's charity programming. On the promise of 'one hundred and one game lads and lasses going starkers for the nation', Nick Jinks holds fast to BBC1. He weathers Richard Wilson, and a Kate Bush medley. He even weathers Stephen Fry and Geri Halliwell in Uganda. After Boyzone's 'When the Going Gets Tough, The Tough Get Going' he is reaching for the off-switch when the screen goes dark for a moment and comes back to life on a place he knows: Manhiça, north of Maputo. He spent a while in hiding here, following the fiasco of 1969. Little seems to have changed, except that some scrawnier-than-usual celebrity is now picking her way along its dirt lanes and fly-ridden market.

Time to sleep.

Nick Jinks snaps off his portable television. He turns the powerful cabin heater down one notch, undresses, turns off the lights and climbs stiffly up into his bunk. He closes his eyes.

Nothing happens.

His eyes open.

His whole body is wired.

This is nothing new. Without a woman, he has never found sleep easy – not since he was struck on the head with an oar, the day he came ashore, a hapless seventeen-year-old, at Playa Girón. With weary resignation, he reaches down. He thinks of Manhiça, and the girls there. He thinks back to a time before his muscle turned to fat. Before fear of disease drew his zipper permanently shut. Before he lost his hair, and before his partnership with Saul expanded to its present, burdensome scale. He thinks about tits, comes, and closes his eyes.

Nothing happens.

Too tired to sleep, he figures. A long day. A rough crossing, and a busy road. Tomorrow shouldn't be so bad.

He closes his eyes.

There is a sound in the cab.

Movement. Scampering.

He struggles up onto his elbows to listen.

Nothing.

He lies back down again.

The sound is gone.

He still can't sleep. He reaches down a second time. His cock is slippery and disgusting. He manages somehow and lies back, waiting for a sour second wave of endorphins to carry him away.

Nothing happens.

He cannot remember when sleep finally overtook him. He wakes from troubled dreams, fingers aside the blind by his head. Sodium orange spills over his pillow. It is still dark out. What time is it? He has his watch on. He turns on the cabin light. Christ. Has he slept at all?

There is a sound in the cab. A scratching. Then, a thumping. Then, a scratching again.

He knows, now, what has kept him awake.

The familiar sound takes him back to his childhood home and his father, the old sea-dog Dick Jinks; back to the accident, and the terrible death at his hands which first drove him into exile.

It is the curse.

Even after all this time, the curse is alive. All these long years of his madcap absence, it has been waiting here for him.

Nick Jinks struggles into his clothes, lifts the blinds and takes his seat at the wheel. He turns the key in the ignition. He has to wait, agonizing seconds, for the diesel to warm. A thready keening fills his head. He stuffs fingers into hirsute ears. The light on the dash goes out. He turns the key, and the rig rumbles into life, drowning out the rat-sound of his curse. Roughly, wrestling the wheel, Nick Jinks hauls his rig back onto the A74. How far is Fort William? Eighty miles; a hundred at most. He will not stop again.

His foot comes down hard on the accelerator, though Nick Jinks should know by now that this is something he cannot outrun.

Chicago, Illinois

2.30 p.m., Saturday, 11 March 2000

Nineteen ninety-nine had been a bad year. Following Jinks's disappearance in March, I had had no choice but to dismantle the British end of the business. This inevitably meant that I owed favours. Relocating to the States, I had hoped to revive the fortunes of my moribund employment agency. But competition had grown fierce and word of my problems had arrived before me.

Blessing and Femi, my housekeepers for the northern states, fell foul of US Immigration at the beginning of March 2000, and there was no one on the books I really trusted to take their place. I debated whether to bring Chisulo and Happiness over from London. But they had their daughter to look after, and I had already asked too much of them.

Until I found somebody new, then, it fell to me to meet the arrivals we had already booked in for the spring. Arrivals like Felix Mutangi: I was there to greet him at the gate. It was a risky business, but no riskier than letting this son of the African soil wander alone through all the snares and brakes of late Western capitalism. I was pleased to hear that the paperwork I had prepared for him had seen him past the desk without a hitch. In the car, driving him to his motel and subjected to his boyish burbling, relief was added to pleasure: if he had had to open his mouth for any extended period he would surely have found himself on the first flight home.

He seemed hearty enough when I left him that evening, but the next morning when I picked him up he sneezed almost the moment he got in the car. I thought nothing of it at first; long-haul travel always leaves you feeling depleted. The sneezes did not stop. He was in his mid-twenties and, according to the medical report I had ordered, he was in good health. Still, even a head-cold could delay, by precious days, what we had planned for him. 'How are you feeling?'

'Fine, fine,' he grinned. He pulled out a packet of 555s and offered me one.

'They didn't tell me you were a smoker,' I said, waving it away. Where he came from, what twenty-something man didn't smoke? But I wanted to disconcert him a little; I wanted him to think about what we were doing, and what it would mean for him. The opportunities it represented. 'I don't know that the clinic's going to like you doing that,' I said.

Felix's smile was irrepressible. He wound down his window to let out the smoke. It was freezing outside. Literally: minus one according to the dashboard. He sneezed, spat and noisily inhaled the gasoline fumes of the promised land. Blood and urine tests were booked for 11 a.m. Assuming the authors of the medical report had not been altogether fraudulent, the operation would take place that night and by Monday Felix would be on a plane home.

The Stevenson expressway had other ideas: after half an hour's driving, just as we were passing under the Gilbert Road flyover, everything ground to a halt. I couldn't believe our ill-luck. The Tri-State Tollway was right ahead of us, straddling the expressway on an inclined curve. The whole arrangement of structures, piles and embankments here looked like something sculpted by the sea. We couldn't get near it. The feedlanes were barely half a mile away, and they might as well have been on the other side of Lake Michigan.

We were there so long we started picking up radio bulletins about the tailback building behind us, stretching far along the canal. It was a clear day, bitterly cold. The radio said something about a spilled load, and a couple of fire trucks, with lights but no sirens, slid sedately past us on the hard shoulder. I got out of the car, found my parka in the back and zipped myself up. I glanced around, looking for newscopters. This close to Chicago Midway it probably wasn't worth their while negotiating such a busy airspace. Domestic jets howled over our heads.

'Hiya.'

The voice seemed to come from above me; it made me start. I turned around. Beside my own rental there was a van. Not a pickup, or a people-mover; an honest-to-God van, with scratched blue panels and a faded campaign sticker: 'Vote John Gridley for US Senate'. Which was ironic, given that Gridley's lawyer was in the clinic even now, paying, in cash, for the senator's life-saving operation.

The woman in the passenger seat leaned out to speak to me. Her shock of short white hair was dazzling, her face was strangely sunken. At first I thought she was young – twenty-five or thirty – then that she was much older.

'I don't suppose you've got a cigarette?'

I leaned in through my window and got Felix to hand me his packet of 555s. I opened the packet and offered it to her.

'What are these?' she said. However unfamiliar she was with the brand, it wasn't going to stop her taking one.

There was a lighter inside the pack so I fired up her cigarette for her, cup-handed, shielding the flame from the wind. I handed it over. She smoked. Where it emerged from the cuff of her coat, her wrist was as thin as a child's. She did not cough, but she certainly changed colour. 'Jesus,' she said. She climbed down from the cab. Now I saw why I had not been able to guess her age. Her bright yellow North Face jacket hung off her as though from a peg. She was terrifyingly thin. It had to be an illness.

I glanced through the windscreen and glimpsed her driver: a porcine woman with a double-chin and dykish hair. I thought to myself: Laurel and Hardy.

'The radio said something spilled,' said the girl.

'Yes,' I said, teeth chattering. I lit a cigarette for myself, breaking a twenty-year pledge.

Felix got out the car and walked around, smiling his smile.

Things were in danger of degenerating into a social occasion. I tried to relax. I looked at my watch. Eleven fifteen.

'You're English,' she said.

Her own accent was a mid-Atlantic thing I couldn't pin down.

My Englishness seemed to fascinate her; I couldn't work out why. Poor Felix didn't get a look-in. She seemed to want me to reciprocate her interest and, since it was a good way of not talking about myself or my passenger, I asked her where she was going. This was all the prompting she needed. She leaned back into the truck and came out again with a couple of flyers for us. 'I'm opening tonight,' she said, 'if we ever bloody get there.'

Was the English swear-word for my benefit?

It was only as she climbed back into her van that it occurred to me: she was familiar for some reason.

The flyer was headed *SCTV02*, and underneath there was a picture of a bubble. There was something odd about that bubble. I unfolded the flyer, revealing the rest of the photograph: a hand was holding a disposable cup, and a trail of misshapen bubbles had spilled from the rim of the cup and were hanging in the air.

The bubbles were water, floating in air.

The photograph had been taken in space.

I went to see her show. There were no films I especially wanted to see, Jonny Lang had sold out at the Rialto Square weeks before and I couldn't think what else to do with my time. Felix was in good hands, and I would be seeing him in the morning.

If the venue for *SCTV02* had been some left-field place I might not have gone, but back at the hotel I read the flyer properly and discovered it was playing early at the Museum of Contemporary Art opposite Jan Svankmeyer's *Alice*. I figured if I didn't like the one I could go and watch the other and still have time to hunt down a decent meal.

The woman's name was Stacey Chavez and I understood why my Englishness had intrigued her. From her potted biography I learned that she had been a British TV star. Hearing my accent, she had expected me to recognize her.

Perhaps this was arrogant of her, perhaps not: I had found her vaguely familiar, after all, even though her active years coincided with my time in Mozambique. I had never seen *The Singing Detective*. I had never seen *The Moth*. I had no idea, come to that – beyond the none-too-subtle clues buried in *SCTV02* – how or why a mainstream actress came to be creating intricate, difficult and (for my money) downright unenjoyable performance art for a Chicago museum.

The premise was simple: in space, everything floats, so it is very difficult to eat and drink. Afterwards I couldn't tell whether Stacey's performance, a weird fusion of mime and dance and gesture, had gone over my head, or whether what I had seen was really all there was to get: the sterile white set, part hospital, part spaceship interior; plates that would slip out from under her hand; cups that hovered above her, just out of reach; the pink 'space food' she squeezed into her mouth from an upended detergent bottle.

I had had a belly-full of art for one evening, and rather than repair to the MCA bar – wall-to-wall twenty-somethings in tea-cosy hats – I braved a snow flurry and walked the couple of blocks to the nearest dive.

There was an old episode of *Cheers* running on a TV above the plasticated bar, as if to emphasize the degree to which this watering hole failed to live up to tourist expectation: characterless beer, sterile wood-effect surroundings, bar staff who bore all the behavioural stigmata – bright smiles, gimlet eyes – of some sort of customer-service boot camp. Everything designed and arranged so as to convince us that nothing bad was going to happen. No wonder the people around us were hardly drinking.

The door opened, letting in the cold. I glanced around, and there was Stacey Chavez. When she got to the bar I pointed to the show on the TV

– Kelsey Grammer sparring with Rhea Perlman – and said to her, 'In Rio, meanwhile, the swimsuit boutiques have "The Girl from Ipanema" on a tape loop.'

It took her a moment to remember me. 'Did you see the show?' she asked me.

'I saw the show.'

'You didn't like it.'

I shrugged. 'Was I supposed to?'

'Oof,' she said, miming a blow to the head.

I was growing used to her thinness. I was able to look beyond it, to fill in the gaps, as it were. To see the skin above the skull. This made her seem more familiar. She had a big-featured face, hawkish, striking more than beautiful. Not very kissable. A TV face – distinctive enough to survive the flattening effect of the lens, symmetrical enough not to repulse.

She said, 'I was walking down Southampton Row – Bloomsbury – you know London at all? I passed this place: "Virginia Woolf's Burgers, Kebabs and Grills".'

'Where's your driver?' I asked her.

'Back at the hotel. We're not a couple.'

'Do people assume that?'

'People have dirty minds.'

I had stolen Felix's pack of cigarettes – I figured he had plenty more – and offered her one.

'I remember these,' she said. 'Aren't they African?'

'Among other places.'

'I tried smoking these in Mozambique one time.'

Had I met her in Mozambique? Surely I would have remembered. But the truth turned out to be more banal. She told me about a documentary she had gone out there to make, a mine-clearance appeal, and I remembered that I had, after all, seen her on TV, exactly a year before, as I lay on my bed in a Glasgow hotel room, draining the mini-bar, waiting for Comic Relief to be over and for Nick Jinks to ring. Not a night to remember with great fondness – though it maybe explained why her image should have lodged with me.

We talked about Chicago, and she explained how she had timed her tour so that she could sort out legal wrangles to do with her mother's estate. 'She was only forty-six,' she told me, out of nowhere. She had things she needed to tell somebody.

I listened, or I appeared to be listening – I had my own troubles at this time – and afterwards I was rewarded with a dinner invitation at a place Stacey had learned about on the internet.

It seemed incongruous, her inviting me out to eat. First there was the age difference: I was nearly sixty by then. Second, there was the whole, vexed business of Stacey and food. Her fingers, curled for support around her whiskey glass, were knobbled and grey. When she gestured, the sleeves of her knitted shrug flapped as though hung off wires. Still, she made the place's huckster style sound inviting. 'Then there's Halley's Comet,' she said.

'Halley's Comet?'

'Gin martini. But I prefer their Super Nova.'

'Which is?'

'Vodka martini. Only they stuff the olive with blue cheese.'

'Jesus Christ.'

So it was, later that same evening, that we made our entrance – a starlet and her sugar-daddy – down the carpeted stairs of Lovell's of Lake Forest.

At the bottom of the stairs a small, athletic man glad-handed the patrons as they arrived. Any urge I might have had to giggle at the restaurant's gen-you-wine NASA memorabilia or its novelty martini menu was hereby instantly quashed: this was James Lovell, in the flesh, the veteran of Apollos Eight and infamous Thirteen.

The Ron Howard film had come out a few years before, the one with Tom Hanks as Lovell. I'd seen it on a long-haul flight someplace –

I don't remember where. Since then, Stacey told me, the locals had been queuing up to gobble down his son Jay's modern American cuisine, in hope of meeting Dad. Lovell, for his part, showed his face every few days so as not to disappoint; as we entered the bar he was guiding a family of Gary Larson characters to a coffee table made out of a relief map of an Apollo landing site. A chore for him, or a pleasure? His laugh was higher pitched than I would have imagined. Infectious. But you can't go by smiles or body language; these men are professionals.

Jim Lovell: the man had survived explosion and asphyxia and risked abandonment and slow death in deep space, but had never set foot on the moon. According to Stacey, the fact still rankled with him, even after all these years. (She had read his book, among many others, doing research for her show, and spoke as though she had some knowledge of him.)

I watched Lovell moving about the room, marrying the man to Stacey's words. Yes, it rang true, that here was a man prepared to admit to a single, defining regret. I did not know what attracted her to this idea, or how true it was. But I approved of it, on principle as it were. To compare Lovell's experiences with mine would be pointless, even laughable. Still, I fancied I too knew something about survival; about the double-edgedness of it, and the hollow feeling that comes over you sometimes, on sleepless nights, that you are living beyond your time.

Lake Forest, Illinois

the same day

In the dining room of Lovell's in Lake Forest, just outside Chicago, an alarmingly thin girl shares a candle-lit dinner with a man old enough to be her father. Jim Lovell has seen her before; is she a model? Her companion, a taciturn Englishman with a weathered face and uneasy eyes, has ordered the trio of pâtés with jellied onions and cornichons followed by sliced duck atop a vivid huckleberry reduction. She has ordered – nothing. She has brought in her own food. There it is on her plate: a muffin, as brown and unappetizing as a turd.

Watching her eat is like watching somebody drown. It's all Jim can do not to go over and shake her. Hard. Snap her out of it somehow. And he can imagine the headlines in the *Sun-Times* if he did: 'APOLLO VETERAN ASSAULT SHOCKER'.

Jim Lovell steers himself out of the restaurant. Let the poor folks eat their meals in peace. He heads for the office and moves his chair from behind the desk, over to the radiator. Just looking at her makes him feel cold. Chilled right through. Not a metaphor. He's really shivering.

Don't anyone tell him it's his age, neither. You don't play the 'You are Old, Father William' card on a man who's only just got back from the Antarctic. Five weeks at -10°F – and that was the temperature *inside* the tent – all to find bugs that might flourish on Mars. Really, he is too old for this shit.

Her shrunken face. Her claw-like hands. Jesus, no, he doesn't want to shake her, they'd be picking pieces of her out of the carpet for weeks. Whatever's holding her together must be as weak as wet cardboard by now. What should be wires under the skin turned to taffy. He doesn't want to think about it.

How does she manage to sleep? The waiter had to bring her a cushion, her rear end was too bony for the chairs. What does she lie on at night, that her bones don't jangle her awake? How does she keep warm?

Jim climbs out of his chair, pushes it away and sits on the floor, leaning his back against the radiator. It's scalding hot, and even through his clothes, the skin of his back puckers. He luxuriates: leans away, settles back, leans away, settles back. Should take a shower, he thinks. Warm up properly. But he can't bear the thought of having to take off his clothes.

He shakes his head. Pathetic. A month ago he was braving white-outs in the Patriot Hills. What is up with him? What has changed in him since he returned, that the cold seems to come at him, not from the outside any more, but from within, from his own bones?

Jay, his son, has a theory. (And incidentally, how on earth did the kid persuade him to buy into the restaurant business? Was there ever an occupation so grinding, so thankless?) Jay reckons he still hasn't got over the corpse they found in the ice.

Jim struggles to his feet. As if this was the worst he had ever faced! Jay should know better than to spout the philosophy of daytime TV at him. Yet...

Jim makes his excuses to the staff, finds his coat, heads outside, gets in his car, turns the heater up full, starts the engine, begins the journey home.

And yet.

(Darkness strobed by streetlights. This might be anywhere. The streetlights stop. No stars. All dark. He is thinking: Where is my ship? Where is the *Shangri-La*?)

Ever since Antarctica, things and people have started to acquire a family resemblance. Nothing is just itself any more; everything suggests an unconnected something else. The last time he experienced this muddy sort of thinking was following a particularly brutal centrifuge exercise. (The memory comes cluttered with medical buzzwords:

carbon dioxide poisoning; G-strain anoxia.) It's like the world is melting around him. Why should a girl with an eating problem remind him of a dead sailor, any more than a dead sailor should remind him of a live sailor, a sailor he met, large as life and definitely living, on the streets of Punta Arenas?

This was their jumping-off point: a sterile little township at Chile's southern tip. The polar microbe hunters had a week in Punta Arenas to arrange their gear, to check and recheck their supplies and equipment; above all, to wait. Jim didn't mind. It felt good to be working towards a target again. Missions are like charmed little lives: their purpose is pre-ordained, they are rich in intense experience and (God willing) they end happily. More happily than real life ever can.

The sailor, muffled against the cold in a threadbare black parka and thin knitted gloves, noticed him from across the snowbound street and recognized him for all his winter clothing. He just shambled right on up to Jim in the street and spoke to him, big-eyed and awestruck.

He was a big man so when Jim shook his hand the feel of it – its smallness and fragility – frightened him. The man's features were small, too. They were a woman's features – no, a doll's. Beautiful and cruel. Jinks, he introduced himself, in an English accent.

Nick Jinks.

They made, to begin with, a sort of over-serious smalltalk typical to extreme places. In Punta Arenas, everybody seems to be making a documentary about everybody else, and even the sportsmen and climbers couch their hiking plans in the rhetoric of the study trip. Jinks knew all the teams, but he didn't seem to belong to any of them. He claimed to have drifted in one day – and he didn't seem in any hurry to leave. The man seemed a throwback to the Antarctic's brutal beginnings, years of whaling and sealing, frostbite and trench foot and filthy cabins lit by penguin oil.

Jinks wanted to know if there were any rats on board Apollo Thirteen.

'Come again?'

How did they keep the rats off the ship?

'Well, I don't think—'

That main B bus undervolt which was the start of all their peril – could it have been the work of a rat?

Jim extricated himself as fast and as pleasantly as he could.

In Ellsworth Land, Antarctica, and especially on the Patriot Hills, you can find bubbles in solid ice, sometimes in strings like a diver's air bubbles, and in the summer, when the sun shines continuously, a liquid film forms on the inside of the bubbles, and things in the water begin to grow.

It is -20°F without windchill and Jim Lovell is out here looking for *bubbles*. He feels as clumsy as an infant in his cheery standard-issue red parka, and his hands, snug in layers of polyfleece and wool and leather, feel as useless as paws, when a sudden, unbelievably chill gust nearly takes him off his feet.

Instinctively the team huddle together like penguins under the onslaught of the wind.

Wind whips snow into the air. It is old snow: Antarctica is a desert, and precipitation falls as rarely here as it falls on the Sahara. The granules, ground against each other over decades, are so tiny they will penetrate the weave of rucksacks and the walls of tents. The team leader has them rope themselves together. Any second now, visibility is going to vanish. Really vanish. (Back in Chile, during their familiarization programme, the instructor had them put white plastic buckets on their heads to simulate the effects of white-out.)

Careful, groping, blind mice, the team edge down the slope towards their camp.

How they missed the body on the way out is no mystery. A thin skein of snow would have been enough to conceal him completely. The fierce wind has revealed ice that would be blue were there any sun. Now it is as black as jet.

There he is, inside the ice.

Jim's cry is inaudible in the gale. Katabatic winds – flash floods of cold thick air, spilling from rocky pockets in the highlands, fierce as waters and unimaginably colder – steal his words away. Finally the rope translates his sudden stop to the others of his team. Careful, purblind, they gather round. Jim kneels.

It makes no sense. This man here in the ice. Each inch of ice is an eon of human time. How can this man be buried here, arms spread as though he were treading water, head straining for the surface, eyes open, a trail of bubbles from his screaming lips?

They have to leave him, then. Nothing they can do in this wind. Nothing they can do, period. The next day, they cannot retrace him. They do not try hard, or for long. No way can they dig him out from under all that ice and anyway, what would be the point? In the fug and fabric-whip of their igloo-like Scott tents, the men talk out what they have seen. It must be the body of some early casualty of exploration, interred now in a grander coffin than any undertaker can provide.

A week later, in the relative warmth and comfort of the Amundsen-Scott station at the Pole, Jim Lovell and Skylab astronaut Owen Garriott sing for their supper; they glad-hand the residents and give talks about their experiences. Shouldering his burden ('veteran astronaut and motivational speaker') Jim stands and, without notes, begins his address.

But to be upright in the ice, one knee up and one knee straight, head tilted back like that, the ice so clear?

Jim, standing there before them all – the ultimate captive audience – falls silent. To cover his confusion, he takes a drink of coffee. Where is he up to? What was he talking about? Apollo Eight? Thirteen? It's Thirteen everybody wants to hear about, not least because of the movie. He doesn't mind. It's a decent movie. Is he so precious that he should look such a gift-horse in the mouth? Heck, no, the film's put him back in demand. Would he be here without Ron Howard? Well, yes, for certain – but the expedition sure wouldn't have gotten a plug from CNN.

They have logged the body, as well as they can, with the search and rescue people, and together they have agreed not to rehash the episode in front of the press. Besides, death and dereliction rarely make it out of the back pages this far south of the sixtieth parallel.

Now where was he?

Apollo Eight? Apollo Thirteen?

His audience wait expectantly.

Jim fakes a cough and takes another sip of coffee.

Gemini Seven maybe. Nobody's very interested in Gemini Seven. Not when the talk is only an hour long and they know that Thirteen, the explosion and NASA's most testing hour is still to come. It's not cynicism that makes him think this. He's been at this racket long enough to know what makes a good story and what doesn't. The sad fact is that it's very hard to make Gemini Seven exciting. The way everything, but everything, started packing up around them. Thrusters. Fuel cells. Poor Frank Borman, with a commander's tunnel vision, just itching to twist that abort handle, and who could blame him? Still, they hung in there, waiting for Stafford and Schirra to turn up in Six. Fourteen days in a capsule that, hour by hour, malfunction after malfunction, came to resemble a floating toilet cubicle.

Gemini Seven. The one he never gets to talk about. The one, therefore, that has come to haunt him more and more.

Rising through a calm black ocean, this steel bubble of ape life.

Winter comes. The sun is gone in now. Blue ice turns black. The film of water round each air bubble freezes solid, killing everything inside. There is no colour anywhere. Life stops.

Hoar-frost on the rations in the *Odyssey* command module. Conditions aren't much better in *Aquarius*. (Is this where he is now? Is this where he is up to – Apollo Thirteen, the lunar module their lifeboat, and nothing to do but wait?) He is speaking. The audience is leaning forward, rapt. Now and again, there is laughter. He wishes he could grasp the meaning of the words as they slide, smooth and practised, out of his mouth.

Nick Jinks, the strange Englishman who had approached him on the street in Punta Arenas, was gone by the time they returned, five weeks later, on the first leg of their long journey home. Nobody in town knew of him or remembered him.

So Jim, unable to find any evidence to contradict it, has had to carry this impossible image around with him ever since, unable to shake it free, unable to discount it: that the man in the ice *was* Nick Jinks. That Nick Jinks somehow fell into the ice. Which is the same as saying, that he fell into time. Jinks's pretty, cruel, close-set eyes stare out at Jim from the unimaginable past. His mouth, in rictus, mimes a ghastly *Eeeee!* In boots that look modern – not seal-skin, but plastic – Nick's right foot is raised to step on a sabre-toothed tiger's tail; the left, toe pointed, tests the warm waters of the Cambrian.

There is no *Shangri-La*. Where is the fucking *Shangri-La*?

Jim fumbles behind the steering wheel for the light switch and fills the unlit Lake Forest road with light. The dashboard comes alive, a soft green glow. Windscreen wipers squeal back and forth. Jim snaps them off with a curse that becomes an instant chuckle: in his eighth decade, he can freely admit that he's never been particularly good around buttons and switches. (He'll never forget the dirty look Frank shot him in Apollo Eight, the time he accidentally inflated his life jacket.)

Beyond the immediate splash of illumination cast by his head-lamps, the world is a ghostly grey, no colour anywhere. But Jim Lovell is a professional. With a set smile and eyes tuned to the colours of the world, the greens and the reds, the instruments and signs, Jim Lovell, bubbled in steel, steers his way home as he has steered his way home before, across unimaginable distances, across oceans of night, through the deep black calm of death.

THE GIFT

1

Summer 1939.

The British government believes that an air war will destroy civilization.

It has forecast the number of casualties likely to be sustained following a Luftwaffe attack on London. The numbers are apocalyptic. Bleaker still is Whitehall's estimate of the city's psychological resilience. Analysts believe the experience of bombardment will send the survivors mad.

Hospitals surrounding the capital have sent home their non-urgent cases. They are making up beds ready for tens of thousands of 'nervous cases'.

The government believes that following an air attack, survivors who make it into the city's tunnels will refuse to emerge; that they will turn their backs on the devastated Overground, preferring to live and breed beneath the earth, a Morlock terror to the Eloi above. In London, the Underground is locked at night against those who would seek shelter, come the raids.

Nineteen-year-old former abattoir clerk Kathleen Hosken knows better. She has inside information. With halting fingers, Kathleen has typed up data which even the government has yet to read. She has worked with the government's own specialist on a project to assess the physiological effects of ground shock waves and blast, a man of such luminous intelligence and charm his associates have nicknamed him 'Sage'.

From Sage, she has learned that if you look into the eye of the thing you most fear, and replace your passion with a rational curiosity, then the horror – he calls it 'funk' – goes away. So Kathleen Hosken has left the rain-swept border country of Darlington, and has boarded a train for London, the soon-to-be-devastated metropolis. This journey to the epicentre of the coming war is not just a journey of necessity – a search for employment and a place to live. It is also a test she has set herself. She believes that if she approaches her life there rationally, carefully interrogating her every assumption, then she can protect herself, even from bombs and fire storms.

The men sharing her train carriage – the crooked teeth their smiles reveal, the Players and Capstan cigarettes they offer her – are objects for observation. From Sage, she has learned something about the scientific method. This novel way of thinking requires her to suppress her emotions and to put herself at a distance from things. Besides, she does not smoke.

Some of the men on the train are in uniform. Most are not: volunteers, they have yet to be received into the service. There is a camaraderie between the two groups which marks them out from the handful of young, scrape-faced commercial travellers who also share the carriage.

'The air's sweeter over here, love.'

'There's room to stretch your feet by me.'

'I'm a Darlington man meself, dearie, come and have a chat.'

They are teasing her. She is being offish with them and she isn't pretty enough, and not nearly well dressed enough, to get away with it.

'Cat got your tongue?'

'He joined up already then, love?'

'Tore himself away, he did, from the sparkling ray-pah-tee.'

They laugh.

Kathleen takes a steadying breath. She thinks up an experiment – and smiles softly, knowingly, to appease them.

A lad with infected acne lets out a cheer. The company of friendly elders has made him boisterous. 'Knew you could do it, love!'

She notes, for future reference, the success of her strategy. She has identified, confronted and resolved a problem in her human relations. For the first time in her life, the boys have not made her cry.

She remains – for all their barracking – in the seat she has chosen for herself, riding backwards, facing west. She is looking her last at the moorland of her childhood. More than that: she is looking out, past barren scarps and low stony ridges, over long-abandoned dry-stone walls and between hawthorns stunted by the wind, for the remains of a series of sheds. Given the lie of the land, it is only by facing backwards to the direction of travel that she will be able to spot them.

That these sheds have been visible from passing trains at all is an error Sage made early on in the project, when he misread the contour lines on his Ordnance Survey map. He spotted the error while studying the map for other sites, and before the sheds were ever erected – a feat of magic which amazed Kathleen at the time. The error was tiny, however, and Solly Zuckerman, Sage's colleague and keeper of the project's top-secret experimental menagerie, persuaded him to let it go.

Kathleen remembers her first train ride with Sage. Since going to work for him, she had persisted in calling him Mr Arven, and he was teasing her, telling her that, since he was a professor, she should call him 'Professor Arven'; that he had letters after his name and, since she was so fond of honorifics, she 'ought to recite them, an' all'. Abruptly, he had broken off his jesting and took out his watch. He paused a moment – he appeared to be counting – then he glanced at the window. He took her hand and pulled her with him onto the seat opposite, facing backwards.

'I feel sick this way,' she protested. He did not reply. She wondered when he would let go of her hand. Instead, he squeezed it, painfully hard, and pointed out the window: 'Watch... watch now... There!'

Far in the distance, Kathleen glimpsed the frameworks of their oh-so-secret sheds.

Mr Zuckerman – *Professor* Zuckerman – was quite right: even as they registered on the eye, they were gone. There was no real risk of discovery.

'Feckit!' Sage exclaimed.

She smiles to think of it. The boy with the infected face comes and sits beside her. Her smile has been misinterpreted as a reply to something he has said, which she has not heard. He flicks a cigarette jauntily into his mouth but fumbles the catch, so for a moment the cigarette hangs precariously between prehensile lips. His erupted face boils over in a blush. He thrusts the cigarette pack under her nose.

'No, thank you,' Kathleen says. She turns back to the window. *Watch... Watch...*

It seems the sheds have been dismantled.

Thick clouds of tobacco smoke press white hands against the window.

School ended for Kathleen when she was fourteen. Working in her uncle's office at the abattoir was undemanding. There were clerks employed to tally the animals brought to slaughter, to calculate the number of different cuts, to calculate wastage, the company's profits, the workers' wages. There was a secretary, a long-nosed woman, no longer middle-aged, who saw to her uncle's business correspondence. For Kathleen, there were files to keep in order; 'to do' lists to type for her uncle; wages to hand to the boys who worked on the cutting floor; errands to run in town. Now she has left, Kathleen understands that her uncle employed her, above all, so that he might see her from time to time. He had played no real role in her childhood – the consequence of some nebulous rift between him and his brother, Kathleen's father.

Shortly after her father walked out for good, her uncle visited her and her mother at home. She has a vague memory of being sent upstairs by her mother; of lying on her bedroom floor and pressing her ear to a crack between the boards. If she heard what her uncle said, she has no memory of it.

She understands, now that she is leaving, that her uncle enjoyed her company, that many of the errands and tasks he set for her were made up so that the two of them might spend time together when by rights they should both have been working.

She remembers making blood puddings with him. 'We waste hundreds of gallons of blood a year, Kathleen. Well, what can we do about this? How can we turn this wastage into profit?' Whatever they were up to – visiting a neighbour's farm, experimenting in the firm's huge galley kitchen, taking drives through the country – he had a way of describing the activity so that it seemed important to his business.

'The blood'll splash my dress,' she protested.

'Nonsense.' Her uncle's dark, friendly features wobbled uncertainly towards what he thought was a 'business-like' expression. He looked as though he were sucking a boiled sweet.

He brought her an apron – a long one, it reached almost to her feet – and helped her lift the bucket. Together they strained the pig's blood through a muslin cloth into a pan, and added spices, oatmeal, fat in tiny dice. He showed her how to fill the casing, how to tie it off. Everything had to be a bravura performance with him, even the making of puddings. 'Here, you try!' She was afraid that she might mark her clothes, her shoes. What would her mother say? He could not persuade her. He shook his head, and did the job himself. She watched him, and though it was a trivial thing, she felt that she had let him down.

When the puddings were done, he lifted one from the boiling water by its string, laid it on a board, and cut it through with a knife. It was light like a soufflé. Delighted, he told her to fry some up for them. She did not know how. He showed her, dripping a knob of lard off a butter knife into a hot pan: 'You cook this at home, surely?'

Tongue-tied, she shook her head. He set places for them. He sat her down, adjusting the chair beneath her, as though she were in a hotel. She blushed.

'Eat up!'

She speared a mouthful with her fork. The black blood melted on her tongue.

*

On the bus home, and as usual, the Bridgeman boys – George and Robert, brothers, apprentice slaughtermen, who lived at the end of her street – came and sat behind her. They sniggered at her, and one of them said something disgusting about her and her uncle. She knew nothing she could say would heal their resentment of her: their boss's favourite, his poor relation.

As the bus rolled over the bridge into the village, the bigger of the boys dug about in the pocket of his trousers and produced a twist of bloody paper. He unwrapped it, leaned over and dropped a pig's eye into Kathleen's lap. Kathleen leapt out of her seat, speechless, pale with disgust. The smaller boy practically fell off his seat for laughing. 'Oh George,' he cried, and patted his brother on the arm, 'th'art a proper one!'

Her mother scolded her. 'I'll never get it out,' she snapped, scrubbing at the bloody mark on Kathleen's dress. 'I never shall. It's quite ruined.'

Kathleen mentioned the puddings and lied about how the stain was made: a splash, she said, an accident. While she talked she wrapped her arms around her body. She was cold without her dress.

'Put your hands by your sides,' her mother said.

Kathleen did as she was told.

'Stand up straight.'

The dress was a good one. The sun had set by the time the surface of the material gave way under her mother's scrubbing brush. Kathleen's mother sat at the kitchen table and cried a while, absently tearing threads from the dress she had ruined.

Kathleen stood with her hands by her sides. She did not move. She did not make a sound.

When she was done destroying the dress, Kathleen's mother began her nightly clean of the kitchen. She boiled water in a pan. She added soap flakes. She scrubbed the stove. She scrubbed the table. She swept the floor and scrubbed it. She boiled up more water in a pan. She scrubbed the pan. Knowing her daughter had handled blood, she scrubbed at Kathleen's hands till they were raw.

Kathleen's mother kept the kitchen clean. The pans and plates shone, then she put them away in deep drawers, and the drawers, too, she kept them clean. Each knife was sharp, unblemished: 'Don't touch.'

That evening, because of the dress, and the time taken to clean it, and the time taken to establish that it was altogether ruined – the time spent mourning it, in fact – there was no supper. Normally, supper consisted of tea, bread and butter.

By morning, however, her mother's mood had improved. Night-time had wrought its necessary revisions upon the events of yesterday. It was the shoddy dress at fault, that would not clean up. It was her uncle's fault, that he was careless: 'Why, you might have been *scalded!*'

Her mother's mood was so solicitous, Kathleen dared to ask her for a second slice of bread. Mother laughed. 'Little piglet,' she said. 'Greedy little piglet ears.' It was true: Kathleen was always hungry.

Rather than give her a second slice, Mother poured her a glass of milk. 'Drink up,' she said, 'it's good for you.' There was a tap in the kitchen. She ran the jug under the tap, thinning the milk out for another day. The milk was never actually bad, but the jug lent it a certain sourness.

'Drink up, love, you'll be late.'

Sometimes there would be jam. Never anything hot.

During the weeks of the experiment, John Arven – the man his friends called 'Sage' – took lunch at an isolated pub, about a mile away from the sheds. He drank weak ale and ate sandwiches: huge doorsteps of white bread crammed with thick strips of baked ham. A piece of ham, ointment pink, fell out the bottom of his sandwich onto the table. 'Pitch in, lovey,' said Arven, handing her a sandwich.

Her blush was deep and prickly like a fever.

Arven was curious-looking. His nose hung down as a continuation of his forehead, like the guard on a helmet. This arrangement gave a certain power to his eyes, which were forever laughing and always focused on you. He had dreadful bouffant hair in which he took great pride; she could smell the dressing he used from where she sat. His clothes were unpressed and he hardly ever wore a tie. He talked incessantly, his voice rising to accommodate the broad Lancashire vowels he had picked up at school.

Kathleen swallowed down slivers of crumbly, juicy ham. She forced herself to eat slowly: first her uncle's pudding, now this ham – her shrunken stomach did not know how to handle it all.

'Mr Hosken says you're good with figures.'

Kathleen folded her hands on her lap and nodded. She expected a test. She was ready.

'Do you see 'em?'

He met her blank look. 'Figures, I mean. Only when a chap is good with figures, quite often – this is my experience – he sees them. As colours, as shapes. It's not a question of thinking. It's a question of looking. The inner eye. You know?'

She shook her head, abashed. Amazing, that he should have guessed, that he should have seen so far inside her, to where her private colours lay. 'No,' she said.

'It's a bloody business,' Arven warned her, walking up the dirt track to where the sheds were now nearly complete. The sound of hammers rose on the air in weird syncopation. 'You'll be used to that, I expect.'

A van rocked past them. Arven took Kathleen's arm and drew her up onto the verge bordering the track. The van had a horse-box on tow, and the box slid and teetered in the ruts of the track.

The sheds were wooden but for one wall, made of different stuff: brick, corrugated tin, sandbags; even a patch of dry-stone wall. Some of the sheds had windows. Others did not. The windows were either left open or fitted with a test material: wire mesh, or a coarsely woven material; glass of various sorts. Some of the panes were taped with a white criss-cross. Windows fitted with ordinary window glass were shielded by curtains of different materials.

The sheds had birdcages fixed at different heights on one interior wall, and a larger, waist-high wire enclosure bolted to the floor.

Arven showed Kathleen what to do; how the sheds were numbered, and the walls too, and the cages on the walls; how to use the record sheets he had prepared.

From inside the van, Arven drew out cage after cage of pigeons. Inside cramped mesh containers, the rat-grey birds broiled over and around each other. Arven carried pigeons into the first shed and released them, one at a time, into cages mounted at different heights on the wall facing the window.

'What are you going to do?' she asked, mystified.

A truck in army livery rolled up, drowning out his answer.

The driver and his mate lifted green metal boxes from the back of the truck and carried them towards the sheds. Kathleen, under Arven's instruction, noted down the distances between the boxes and the sheds. She found it hard to concentrate. She had heard strange sounds coming from the horse-box. Professor Arven had disabused her: 'Not horses. Apes.'

She wanted to see the apes. She had never seen an ape except once in a zoo in York, and then it was sleeping, just a big deflated ball of grey-black fur.

She wondered what their eyes were like; their hands. She imagined a troop of gorillas – huge, taller than a man – scampering out of the horse-box, rolling about, playing rough-and-tumble games. But the horse-box was opened only at the last minute, and the apes were in cages, and the cages were much smaller than she had expected, and draped in coarse cream cloths.

At about four in the afternoon, they gathered behind the army lorry: the two soldiers, Arven, Kathleen and the driver of the van – a happy, snub-nosed man about Arven's age who turned out to be his colleague, Solly Zuckerman.

One of the soldiers was fiddling with a box held close to his chest. Wires trailed from the box. When she stepped out to see where the wires led, Arven pulled her back and took her hand.

The explosion tore the roof right off the shed and blew the inner wall away. The silence which followed was punctuated, first by the clatter of shattered timber, then, from inside the broken shed, by screams. They were like the cries of a child. The driver's mate strode over to the site of the explosion, to where the air had coagulated into wisps of smoke and steam. He turned and waved a flag: all clear.

Arven and Zuckerman slogged over to him. Feeling numb, Kathleen made to follow. Arven gestured her to stay where she was. She found a flattish rock to sit on and listened, with an educated ear, to the screaming. There was more humanity to it than even a pig's cry, or a lamb's. When she saw no one was watching her, she covered her ears.

Arven and Zuckerman picked morosely over the wreckage of the shed, peered inside, then beckoned the driver's mate over.

The flat slap of a pistol shot.

A grey feather fell, smouldering, onto Kathleen's dress. She leapt up and shook it away.

Arven and Zuckerman's eventual findings were to run quite counter to the impressions left on them by that first, calamitous experiment. Back at the abattoir, in a room given over by Mr Hosken to the government scientists, the zoologist Zuckerman would spend far more time studying live, undamaged animals than dead or injured ones.

Arven, meanwhile, went from shed to shed, marking the effects of blast upon different kinds of wall: this was where Kathleen's record sheets came in. Arven read out measurements; Kathleen entered the numbers into boxes.

Back at her uncle's office, Arven showed Kathleen how to move the numbers between the boxes, shifting their values as she went. She followed him. She copied what he did.

He stared at her.

She looked up at him. 'What?' she said.

When he didn't reply, she said, 'Did I do it wrong?'

He laughed, and shook his head. He drew his chair closer to hers. He showed her how to make numbers out of other numbers, making them bloom.

Afterwards – 'to celebrate,' he said – he took her by train to Darlington.

'Mother will wonder where I am,' she protested. She was so insistent that, when they got to the hotel, Arven made a call to her uncle, to see to it that her mother was reassured.

Kathleen knew there would be trouble, but weeks of working for Arven and Zuckerman on important war work had excited her to the point where she felt that she could always use this as her excuse: the deadlines they had been struggling to meet; the fact both men would be leaving the following day – Zuckerman to Oxford, Arven to London.

She had never eaten in a real restaurant before, and they were the only diners in the old-world sitting room, decorated with hunting scenes and large solemn prints of Conservative statesmen.

'We'll survive it,' Arven told her. He was excited. His eyes shone from either side of his helmet-guard nose. 'The air war. The figures that have been keeping us up nights. Whitehall's figures are calculated on the assumption that every bit of explosive that's dropped on us will find a target. It just isn't so.'

A charge has to be shaped to fit a target, or most of its energy vanishes into the air. He drew a figure on his napkin to show her. 'It doesn't matter how much explosive the Huns drop on us, only a tiny fraction of it will do us any harm.' He grew reflective. 'The big danger is fire, of course. But better the devil you know.'

While they ate, he told her how to survive an air raid. 'Wrap yourself in an eiderdown when you go out,' he said. 'It'll absorb the blast and protect your lungs. If bombs are falling, lie face down in the gutter. Gutters give good protection – blast and splinters will almost certainly fly over you. And wear a notice round your neck. Something conspicuous.'

'What for?' Kathleen laughed: it was too absurd.

'In case you do get hurt. Blast pressurizes the lungs. So if, heaven forbid, some oh-so-keen sixteen-stone air-raid warden comes across you and fancies a spot of artificial respiration—'

Kathleen blushed.

'Well, that's you done for. So your notice will say "Weak Chest. Leave Off" – or words to that effect.'

Kathleen was awed. 'Is that what people will do? Is that what you will tell them to do?'

Arven laughed. 'I can't see very many people adopting the eiderdown as evening wear, can you?'

Kathleen smiled a small smile. It made her unhappy to think that people would not adopt good advice; that habit and convention overrode even the desire to survive.

Arven shrugged. 'Just remember the gutter trick,' he told her. 'That one's a cert, and you won't have to look like a ninny until the last possible moment.' He drank off his beer. 'Not that the Germans are likely to come bumbling over this little corner.'

Later that evening, he began to speak of other things.

He said, 'I know you see the numbers.'

Kathleen blushed.

Though he was staying in Darlington that night, John Arven insisted on accompanying her home. 'There's time for me to get back. The trains run until eleven,' he said, shrugging off her protests. 'It's you or the fleshpots of Darlington, and I've made my choice.'

On the train he told her, 'This war isn't going to be a won by bombs or bullets. You've seen that yourself, haven't you? An explosion's nothing unless it's shaped. You know what I'm talking about, Kathleen. You don't think you know. You don't know how to know – not yet. But you know. I understand what you see. How easy it is for you. The numbers...' He struggled for a way to explain this to her. 'For most of the rest of them, figures are a language they have to learn. It's not like that for you. Is it?'

She said, 'I don't know what you mean.'

He knew she was lying. 'Listen, this war isn't going to be won by soldiers, or airmen, or heroes, or generals, or any of them. This war is going to be won by numbers. Numbers, and people who know what to do with numbers. Do you understand?'

She shook her head.

As they came out of her local station and left the lights behind, he said to her, 'I can't offer much. There's not very much that's in my gift. Not directly. A job in Senate House to start with. Admiralty tables, that sort of thing.' In the dusk, he caught her expression. 'Don't look so shocked, it's not a secret! Look, I can teach you. Once you have the basics under your belt, it doesn't matter a damn that you're just a slip of a girl. With a head like yours, you can write your own ticket.'

She was shocked at his language. She wondered if she ought to say something. Her mother would have said something. What should she say?

She said, 'The colours—' and stopped.

'Yes,' he said.

'They mean I'm simple.'

He stared at her. '*Of course not*,' he said. 'What blithering idiot gave you that idea?'

In a small voice: 'Aren't I?'

He tucked her arm firmly under his own. 'If you are, then I am. If you are, then Senate House is a sea of simpletons.'

Kathleen trembled all over. It was like discovering you had a brother. A family.

Outside her house, Sage kissed her. 'Kathleen. Promise me. We need people like you. Working people.'

Her mother must have been watching because as soon as they were alone together in the kitchen she struck her daughter in the face so hard – a shaped charge, every particle of force meeting its target – that Kathleen lost her footing and banged her head on the corner of the kitchen table.

Kathleen lay on the floor. Dimly, she could hear her mother's breathing. Her eyes focused. There was a crust of bread on the floor. Her mother bent down to help her up, but she must have spotted the bread crust then because her hand, which was reaching to cradle her daughter's head, changed course suddenly and snatched up the crust instead. She picked it up and carried it off to the rubbish pail.

She returned to her daughter, helped her up, made her tea, ran bluish milk in after it, and made her daughter sit down. She apologized, after her fashion. 'Look what you made me do!' she sobbed.

Kathleen, dazed, sipped her tea.

'Look what you made me do!'

Kathleen watched as her mother, still weeping, picked up the pail and carried it past her to the back door. She passed close enough that Kathleen could see into the pail. The pail shone. There was nothing in it but the crust of bread. Kathleen sipped her tea and listened to her mother's footsteps receding, up the garden path, to where the compost pile lay. Her mother returned and rinsed out the rubbish pail. She set it down. She drew water into a pan and set it on the stove to boil. She sat at the table. She pressed her hand to the side of the teapot. She got up again and picked up the teapot and poured the dregs of the tea down the sink. She rinsed out the sink. She took the lid off the teapot and washed it. She scooped leaves out of the pot and dropped them into the rubbish pail. She rinsed out the pot. She picked up the rubbish pail. While she was in the garden, the water in the pan began to boil.

From John Arven, Kathleen Hosken has learned to look the thing you most fear straight in the eye, not with passion, with a calculating curiosity.

She is going away because she understands, now, why her uncle valued her company so very much; why he took such an interest in her; and when he was approached by his MP to give a discreet hand to two young men from Whitehall, why he thought to involve his niece in their work.

She is leaving because she understands why her mother trusted him to employ her, even though she despises him. Why he is not welcome in their house. Why her father went away.

It is as John Arven said it would be: a problem that is more or less soluble to an active intellect.

Her mother came back inside and rinsed out the rubbish pail. Kathleen nursed the side of her head. She primed the fuse to her life, and lit it.

She said, 'You married the wrong one.'

2

It was October, the time of the phoney war. Indian summer in the big London parks, a false spring in Highgate and Hampstead, perfect weather for long walks by the Thames in Kew and Barnes; and all of it given poignancy by bad news from far-away places.

The dust in the streets shone. Perfect cones of sand shone in the sun. Piles of sand ready for bagging piled up in empty lots. Sunshine glinted off the buttons on the tunics of the AFS men. Their hair. Their belt buckles. Kathleen walked the parks of the unfamiliar city. She wandered its embankments and craned her neck up at its statues. She meandered in a daze. She sleep-walked through Chelsea and Richmond and dozed open-eyed on benches in Battersea. On the grassy banks of Parliament Hill she lay down and slept, the sunlight blood-red through her eyelids, the grass smelling nonsensically of spring. The sun was like a gas fire, warming only what put itself directly in its way, and to step into a shadow was to feel the chill of the true season. Kathleen stayed in the sun.

She did as John Arven had taught her. She approached everything with an aloof curiosity. She assumed nothing. She tuned her feelings out, became all eyes. She followed the advice she had been given, or most of it. Though she neither walked around the city wrapped in an eiderdown, nor strung a sign about her neck, still, she was prepared, at the first whistle of a descending bomb, to leap face-first into the nearest gutter.

Surrounded by unfamiliar streets and unapproachable people, she made what kind of life she could. She bought milk and bread. She did not know how to cook; her mother had never shown her. Once, she tried to drink milk straight from the jar. It was thick and foamy and it sickened her. She ran water in. It was better. When the bread set hard she hacked off a slice and ran it under the tap in the communal bathroom and wrung it out; then it was all right again. Sometimes she had jam.

The first bombs fell.

There was no outcry, no animosity.

At the Lyons corner house where she was training to be a waitress, as he was guiding the girls into the shelter he had made for them in the basement, the boilerman said, 'Them lads is only doing their job, after all.'

The same night, in the street below Kathleen's garret window, two drunk AFS men walked by. They looked up at the bombers thundering overhead, and waved goodbye to them. 'Goodnight!' they laughed. 'Good night, Jerry!' they cheered. 'Sleep tight!'

Kathleen jerked away from the window. They might see her. They might see her at the window and know by her face, rosy in the light from distant fires, that the window was not covered.

On her first night in this guest-house, she had drawn her bed up under the window so that she could spend her nights looking out across the city. Thanks to the blackout, the stars were often visible above the rooftops. Sometimes they winked out as she watched, and it was only by focusing on the patterns the stars made – winking off, then on again – that she made out the egg-shaped silhouettes of the barrage balloons.

Rather than cover her window, she never made a light or lit a fire. She imagined what would happen if the AFS men spotted her. The strange thing was, in her imagination, the men did not point at her. They did not shout at her. They did not accuse her of anything. In her imagination, they smiled at her: '*Sleep tight*!'

There was a knock on her door. 'Hello?' A woman's voice. Whoever it was, she wasn't going away.

Kathleen opened the door a crack.

'Hello?'

'I'm sorry,' Kathleen said.

'What you sorry for?'

'I—'

'Come on, love, let me in, it's bloody freezing out here.'

Kathleen opened her door.

The girl in the hall was short and dumpy, with a pear-shaped face and hair in a great contrived frizz. She stepped into the room quickly, so Kathleen had to take a step back. The dumpy girl felt around for the light switch. She stared past Kathleen at the uncovered window, and snapped the light off again. 'You're a caution,' she said, impressed.

Kathleen helped her with the felt-backed cardboard shutters they used here in place of blackout blinds. Once the window was covered, they put the light back on. The room was hateful now: a box, brightly lit. Kathleen sat on her hands to control her trembling.

'You need the fire on.' The visitor's name was Margaret. 'Wass the matter, love? You homesick? Blimey,' she said, flapping her arms about herself, 'you'll catch your death in here!' She lit the gas fire and came and sat beside Kathleen on the bed. She put an arm around her. 'Bloody hell, lovey, you're all skin and bone. Are you sick?'

Margaret was the eldest of six. She had time for children. In the weeks that followed, she took Kathleen in hand.

'Don't you know no one? No one at all?'

Kathleen shook her head. She had written to Professor Arven at Birkbeck College asking to meet him, asking what useful work she might do. Concerned not to appear naive or unserious, she had carefully followed every stricture and regulation regarding sensitive correspondence: at the top of the letter, the words 'Same Address'; in the body, no mention of how they had met, or what work they had done. Perhaps she had been too oblique. Perhaps he could not place her in his memory. She had never had a reply.

Margaret had five brothers. She received letters from them every week, the army censor allowing. She read them to Kathleen. She expected Kathleen to respond in kind. She was scandalized. 'No brothers or sisters? No cousins, even? What about your mother?'

Margaret was gregarious and overbearing.

'What size shoes do you take, anyway?'

'Your seams are crooked,' Margaret would say. 'Here, let me.' Her fingers pinched and tickled, as she deftly straightened Kathleen's stockings.

Kathleen, wobbling dangerously on borrowed shoes, learned to study the backs of her legs in the mirror, to check if her seams were straight. She caught herself in the glass, peeking over her shoulder: the coy picture she made. 'Where'd you get these stockings?' she asked her new friend.

'Never you worry. Here.' There was a slip to go with the stockings. 'Mind, it's just for tonight.'

Margaret fed her and dressed her. Kathleen was Margaret's project, her doll, her pet.

Kathleen worried: what could she give Margaret in return for her companionship? What amusement could she afford? She began to see that John Arven's cool curiosity had its limits, that an icy objectivity would not suffice in every situation.

She began to measure how little she knew about being alive.

Then came the awkward moment when Kathleen realized what she was: an amusement afforded Margaret by her latest dry spell. Deep down, and all the time, Margaret wanted men.

When Margaret was seeing a man, Kathleen did not see her from one day to the next.

Moments with men were the measure of Margaret's life: evenings in the cinema or at the pub; furtive whispers on the stairs; nights when she did not come home at all. Then, his furlough done, the intensity of departure: the porter tearing her hand from the handle of the carriage as the train pulled away. The smoke, the steam, the grit. These things only piqued Margaret's appetite – when the sentiment ebbed, in a week or two – for the next glance, the next night out, another arm round her waist.

She was 'no better than she ought to be', as Kathleen's mother would say. She was 'second-hand goods'. From the aloof perspectives of the scientific method, however, such strictures counted for little.

'Want to come down the Four Feathers?' said Margaret.

'Why not?' said Kathleen, with a tremor of wrongdoing.

They got ready. Margaret did Kathleen's make-up for her. Margaret's technique began and ended at the eyes. She larded her own eyes with kohl and mascara in a vain attempt to draw attention away from her discoloured teeth. She tried this look on Kathleen.

'It's lovely,' said Kathleen, captivated by the image in her glass, the Egyptian princess there.

'Oh, cobblers,' Margaret snapped. She unscrewed the lid off a jar of cold cream and ordered Kathleen to wipe it away. 'Let's try something else.'

The Four Feathers was one of those shabby commercial drinking places where scraps of lunchtime bar-shrimp litter the sawdust on the floor of the saloon bar and the sawdust is black and malty and sticks to the heel of your shoe. It was packed. Margaret led Kathleen on, head down, elbows out, a human battering ram. A cross-current parted them. Kathleen called out to her friend. Margaret, intent on reaching the counter, did not notice her. Kathleen thought she would wait where she was, but the milling crowd drove her, like a stick in a millrace, steadily towards the other side of the room. When the current changed course suddenly, she found herself pressed up against the counter. 'What's your name, love?'

The voice was only one component of the din.

A finger jabbed her upper arm. 'Hello. What's your name?'

She turned.

Back home, the timbres of Kathleen's voice spelled property. Here, she might as well be 'the lowest of the low'. Her accent was a thick and bitter Durham: sharp, flaked, a rusted gate squealing in the wind. So she spoke only when spoken to, and very softly.

'Kathleen,' she said, softly, into the widest smile she'd ever seen.

'Katherine?'

She nodded and tried to meet the man's eyes. His jaw was too distracting, so thick and pink and smooth.

The jaw offered to buy Kathleen a drink. She asked it for a pink gin; it was the only drink she could think of by name. A woman in a dress made of tiny mirrors had ordered one at a swank bar in a film she had seen with Margaret the night before.

He handed it to her and their eyes met. His eyes sparkled. They were pretty blue eyes. She liked them. Then he smiled – and her gaze fell, magnetized, back to his jaw again: the cleft chin, the muscular smoothness of it.

She turned away, blushing, as from something obscene. She sipped her drink and tried not to splutter. The drink was bitter, like hedge clippings.

'What do you do, then?'

At this time, she still nursed ambitions for the person John Arven believed she could be. She still held out hopes for the letter she had sent him. So she said: 'I'm a computer.'

'Oh yes?'

'Ask me anything,' she said. Not a lie, she told herself: an experiment in identity.

He smirked. 'What's the square root of a hundred and forty-four, then?'

'Twelve.'

He laughed. 'Very good.'

Wrinkling her nose, she drank off a good mouthful of pink gin. She tightened her throat over the burning liquor, counted to five and risked a breath.

'Ask me another,' she said.

'The square root of a hundred and forty-five?' He said it like it was the easiest calculation in the world.

It certainly wasn't hard. 'Twelve point oh-four-one-five-nine-four-five-seven-eight-eight... what?'

His smile had gone. He folded his arms.

'You're making that up.'

'How would you know?' This from Margaret, sprung from nowhere; she muscled in between them.

'Oh,' he said, coldly. He knew Margaret. 'Friend of yours, is she?' He picked up his pint and moved along the bar, away from them.

Kathleen watched him go, disappointed.

Margaret grabbed Kathleen by the arm and led her off to the other side of the central counter. She hissed in Kathleen's ear, 'Can't you tell a bloody policeman when you see one?'

Kathleen tried to maintain eye contact with the man but he had turned his back, nursing his pint. She had to take Margaret's word that he was a policeman. He could have been anything. Munitions. Railways.

Apparently policemen didn't count. 'A policeman!' Margaret railed. 'Hobnobbing with a bloody policeman!' She parked herself down beside Kathleen on a padded bench near the toilets. Two sailors came up and offered them drinks. 'What'll you have, ladies?' asked the older of the two: he had one of those permanently flushed faces you imagine might bleed if you touch it.

'A pale ale,' said Margaret, 'ta, love.' She glanced at Kathleen. The thought of pink gin made Kathleen queasy, but she didn't know any other drinks. 'Two pale ales,' Margaret said, covering for Kathleen's silence.

The younger sailor went off to the bar. He was exceptionally tall and his straw-coloured hair, though regulation short, grew out at all angles. In the buffet and slew of the crowded bar, he tottered about like a young, well-groomed scarecrow.

With a strange convulsion – a red pocketknife clipping shut – the older sailor bent forward at the hip, then fell back into his chair. 'Oof!' he said. He was short, and squat, and his limbs had no flexibility. As he got comfortable, he moved his arms with convulsive jerks, clicking them into position. His hands were red, too.

His name was Dick. Dick Jinks. A funny name for a sailor. 'What are you drinking?' Kathleen asked him, an experiment in conversation.

'Wallop,' Dick grinned, creasing his swollen red face so that it looked as if it might pop. He meant draught bitter. 'Wallop by name and nature.' He laughed, revealing large, cramped teeth. All evening he came out with these catchphrases. He laughed at them, as at a joke someone else had made.

The sailors had met during the Dunkirk evacuation, and had run into each other again by accident, a couple of nights before. They had stories about Dunkirk. The younger sailor, Donald, went first. Donald seemed nervous, unused to company. He ran his hands through his hair, which ignored him and sprang back into place. His tale began dashingly enough. He was still in civvies at the time of the evacuation. He was one of those gallant yachtsmen who had joined the flotilla out of pure patriotism and fellow feeling. He had borrowed his father's yacht. Kathleen imagined his father waving him off at the jetty. The boy was very well-spoken. Almost BBC. What was he doing in a mere rating's uniform? 'Do you know Hayling Island?' he asked them.

'"Do you know Hayling"!' The elder sailor's laughter boomed around the lounge. Heads turned. Donald blushed. He was really very young. Margaret laid her hand on his arm. 'Go on, love.' But Dick wanted his turn. 'Pissing their pants they was!' He didn't have much of a story, though his description of the strafings was vivid. 'Pissing their pants!' He laughed. Kathleen saw right down his throat.

Dick and Donald walked them home. It was impossibly dark. Kathleen staggered. The paving stones were treacherous in the shoes Margaret had lent her. Dick offered her his arm, and she hung off it, gratefully. It surprised her to notice how short he was: he was barely taller than her. His young friend dawdled, or Margaret was holding him back; she seemed to be having trouble with her heel. Kathleen and Dick got to the door of the hostel first. He took off his cap and braced himself as though for inspection. 'Maybe I can call on you. We can have a drink again sometime,' he said.

'Sometime,' she said.

'You knows what I drink,' he said, and laughed his great red booming laugh. Even his eyes were red.

'Wallop,' she said.

'That's the ticket,' he said, stepping forward, as though she had uttered a password. He took her hands in his. An odd look spread over his face. It was bloated and empty, all at once. No one had looked at Kathleen with need before. She did not understand. 'Spare us a kiss, love – a little kiss.'

The impossibility of it was suddenly, liberatingly funny. She laughed. Surprised, he let her go. She coughed to cover her laughter. 'Frog in my throat,' she said. It was as good a catchphrase as any of the sailor's, but he did not smile. An experiment: she pecked him on the corner of his mouth. He tasted of beer and cigarettes. He ran his hand around her waist, squeezed, and kissed her cheek. She experienced a moment's revulsion towards his flushed face, his too-red lips, as though the lips might leave a mark on her. Then he let go, and she found herself wanting to repeat the kiss.

'Goodnight, then,' Dick said.

That was all.

She went inside and waited for Margaret. The sitting room was empty. She slipped Margaret's shoes off her feet – they had been too big for her, and far too high.

Weary of waiting, she went up to her room in her stockinged feet, carrying Margaret's shoes. She took off Margaret's slip. She unclipped Margaret's stockings and eased them off, ever so carefully.

Margaret was still not back.

Kathleen went to bed.

She lay still, wondering what else there was. What else she did not know.

Margaret knew, but Margaret wasn't telling. She had vanished again.

A week passed, and Kathleen didn't see Margaret once.

She was not worried or put out. She was growing used to Margaret's rhythms. Margaret's men overrode the girls' friendship for only a little while. So this time, while she waited for Margaret's man to depart, Kathleen tried to shake off her loneliness. She braved the sitting room.

The other residents were stenographers from Shepherd's Bush, WAFS from Tottenham, fellow nippies from the Lyons corner houses on the Strand and Oxford Street. They intimidated Kathleen: great iconic hulks of girls. By now, though, she knew how to smile, what to say when she entered or left the room, the gestures she should make. She loved to listen to them. The girls spoke a different language, a Margaret sort of language.

'So I said to her...'

'And he said to me...'

At night, bits of their conversation swirled about her, punctuating her dreams, a sort of verbal shrapnel, highly coloured, piecemeal and surreal. Billy drops leaflets over Berlin and Becky does firemen two at a time. David wants me to do it with him. James bought me a ring.

Each evening, as they got ready for this movie, that meal, this man or that, they gathered to listen to the BBC. The strange names of the cities the Nazis had overrun lent the news an operatic quality. The fall of Norway. In Denmark, something rotten. The names erupted like fantasies through the wireless – a huge mahogany box which took pride of place in the room.

One early evening, as Kathleen sat listening to the radio, breathing in the heady acetone of the other girls' nail polish, there was a knock on the door, and it was for her.

'Remember me?' he boomed, and laughed.

There on the stoop was Dick Jinks, the powerful, squat, red-faced sailor, much older than her, who had walked her home the week before.

Kathleen blinked at him, surprised. She had imagined him in deep Atlantic, shepherding the convoys or whatever it was he did.

'Surprised to see me, baby?' His words, glib and saucy, sat ill with the anxiety in his eyes. He raised his hand towards her – a wave? a handshake? – and stopped mid-gesture. He didn't seem to know what to do with his hand. It trembled. 'Ho, ho,' he sang. 'You're the port in my storm!'

London sunsets were a marvel, since the bombing had begun in earnest: cities of vapour taking leave of a city of stone.

'Dick?'

He sang, 'Yo, ho, ho.'

'Where's your friend?'

Blood darkened Dick Jinks's face; in the sunset, his flushed face appeared polished and hard. 'That poofter? That nancy? That queen? Fuck him, darling.' He blinked. 'Ha, ha,' he added, in mitigation.

'Dick?'

'Will you take a turn with me?' The words struck his funny bone immediately. 'A turn! A turn, Ho!'

'Dick?'

'Will you? I'll stand you a Watney's.' He winked. 'Say you will.'

She looked at him. He was no more ready for a night on the town than she was. He was in uniform of a sort, but so threadbare it looked more like labourer's clothes. Lines of braid hung off the sleeves of his jacket in tatters. The material where the braid had been was crusted white. His bell-bottoms, uncreased and shapeless like a cowboy's chaps, scuffed the steps as she led him inside.

He came forward, flinging a leg out in front of him, then falling onto it. Flinging, falling. As he passed her, she smelled something clean but unappealing, like disinfectant.

She showed him into the sitting room and ran upstairs to dress. She was as quick as she could be. She was nervous of him, afraid of what he might say to the other girls. Every so often his 'Yo, ho, ho!' would shiver the floor under her feet, as though he were directly beneath her, calling to her, his red, wet mouth pressed like a sucker to the ceiling.

When she came downstairs she found him sitting in the armchair by the radio. His grin was fixed and ghastly, his lips as white as his clenched knuckles. 'Dick?' she said, in a small voice. He turned to her. His smile grew more terrible. 'Ah! Ha ha!' It was not laughter so much as a struggle for breath. He sprang open from the waist like a flick knife and rocked upright on heavy, scuffed shoes. He led her outside.

A cab passed them; Dick hailed it. 'Let's paint the town red!'

In the taxi, he tried to relax.

'Oof,' he said.

'Aah.'

'What you been up to, then, baby?' he said.

'A bomb came through Lyons' roof last week,' she told him. 'The ovens were out of action all day.'

'Ha,' he said.

The week before, walking back from the pub, when he asked her what she did for a living, Kathleen had bit her tongue against the disappointment – she had so been looking forward to meeting Sage again – and told the truth. She was training to be a waitress.

'A fireman came to defuse it, then a soldier.'

'Ho—' He opened his mouth to laugh, and there was something shapeless about the set of his lips, something ragged, like a wound.

'There was plaster dust everywhere,' she said, warming to her theme. 'We stayed open, though. We served soup...'

He began humming.

She broke off.

'What?' he said.

'You were saying?'

He shook his head vigorously. 'Ah. No. Tell me,' he said, and just as she was about to speak, 'Soup. Yes. And?'

She drew breath to speak.

'It'll be right again,' he said.

'What will?' said Kathleen.

He blinked at her. 'It will,' he said. 'I will.' He tried to smile – and if it was not quite a smile he made, at least it was not a rictus. 'Ha!' He had surprised another pun. 'I'll *right* myself!'

They turned down St Giles High Street. Dick said to the driver, 'This'll do.'

East of St Giles, the bomb damage was immense. Tall brick terraces straggled towards St Paul's, pale under a biscuit of crumbled plaster. Dick and Kathleen avoided the pavements; walls that had not yet been pulled down slanted dangerously over them. You could see the cathedral sometimes, far in the distance, down long, treeless vistas. She could not imagine where he was taking her. She began to be afraid.

The smell of wet plaster, on the contrary, seemed to give Dick a lift. He swung her hand, back and forth, as though they were walking along a promenade.

'Ow. Dick.'

He let go, grinned at her and skipped ahead.

'Dick?'

He capered in the blacked-out streets.

'Dick, where are we going?' Kathleen's ankle was sore. Her shoe was rubbing it raw. She had not worn walking shoes. Her feet hurt. 'Dick,' she called after him. 'Dick!'

She felt a hand on her arm. Startled, she struggled. There he was – right beside her. 'Easy there, now,' he crooned, stroking her arm. 'Easy!' As though it was she who had slipped ahead of him.

They turned north, then east again, then north – was it north? They could have been anywhere, going anywhere.

'Do you know where we are, Dick?'

'Easy does it,' he said. The word he had used to soothe her stuck to him like a burr. He could not shake it off.

'Easy as pie,' he said.

'Easy virtue, eh?' He laughed, and caught her up in his arms.

Kathleen hung there, looking up at him, afraid of him. There was a moon tonight. His head blocked it out. His head loomed over her, a silhouette, a blank.

'Here,' he said, 'don't cry, baby. Don't cry.'

He set her down without kissing her. He took her hand and stared up the road.

'Dick,' she said, in a small voice, 'that's the way we've just come.'

Dick shrugged. He took her hand, pulling her gently along, retracing their steps, then turned, at random, to the left.

They weren't going anywhere. She understood that now.

The fronts down one side of the street were all torn away, revealing doll's house interiors. Wallpaper shone in the moonlight.

He tightened his grip on her hand. 'Oh, that's better,' he said, 'to be moving, that's better. I feel so tight afterwards. You know? Damned tight. Feel.' He stopped suddenly, snatched her hand and pressed it to his upper arm, the muscles there, the knots. The tremors running beneath his skin.

Plaster crunched under her heel.

'After what?' she said.

'After the shocks,' he said. 'After he shocks me. My pal the trick cyclist. My pal, ha!'

'I don't know what you're talking about,' she sobbed.

'It's new,' he said.

The back of her heel felt cold and damp. It was bleeding. It was hard for her to follow his story. 'Oh, the popping!' he cried. 'The popping in my ears!' Eventually she realized that he was not describing his 'shocks' now. He was telling her about something else. Something for which the 'shocks' were a treatment.

Something terrible had happened to him.

He drew the words out painfully, as though he were drawing his fingernails across a blackboard. He had been involved in an accident at sea. An explosion. The vessel had ruptured. It had sunk. Dick had sunk. Dick was trapped with a young rating in a compartment deep in the bowels of the stricken ship. Dick went down with the ship. As he talked, she could feel the popping in her ears, the liquid iciness of the water rising around her calves, her knees. She was there with him in the compartment. She could barely breathe.

How deep was the stricken vessel by the time Dick fought free of the boy trapped there in the compartment with him? The boy had panicked. The boy was clawing at him. How deep when Dick drove the boy's head back one final time, impaling his skull upon the stanchion? How deep when he took his breath, dived, crawled and, at last, his chest on fire, kicked free of the sinking ship?

'Oh, deep, deep,' he sighed.

You have to scream, he explained. As you rise through water, the air in your lungs expands. You have to scream, otherwise your lungs will burst.

They stood alone in the street: the monochrome dark.

'Like this,' he said.

He let go her hand.

'Dick?'

He had lost the sense of her entirely now. 'Like this,' he said.

She reached up for him. She couldn't see him. She touched his face. She surprised tears.

'*Eeeeee!*'

She fell back, gasping, fingers in her ears.

He walked on, not looking at her. She followed him. She thought he had forgotten her. After a little while, he went on with his story. 'How deep?' The question fascinated him. 'Black it was. Black.' He meant the water. 'It was daylight when we drowned. But we was too deep, you see. By the time I kicked free. Too deep for daylight.'

He stopped again. They had come out into a square. A bomb had fallen in the very centre, and there were gobs of mud over the road. Leaves. They filled the gutters. The trees stood out white in the moonlight. The branches were bare. It was deep midwinter here.

'There was stuff in the sea. Bits of stuff. From the ship. Sinking, floating. A jumper, a Bible, a set of false teeth, a child's teddy-bear. Nothing had any colour. Like here. Like this. Now.' He turned a circle in the middle of the street.

It was true: there was no colour here. Not a spot of colour anywhere. No traffic light. No yellow beam from a warden's torch. They were in the world of the movies now. The world of black and white.

A park bench hung in the fork of a tree. It was quite undamaged. The brass plaque on its back winked white.

Far ahead of her Kathleen glimpsed the silhouetted bulk of St Pancras station. She knew where she was. 'Dick? Dick. Where shall we go?' His stare was vacant, without intelligence. She tried to take his hands in hers but they were fists. She took hold of his arms. 'Dick.'

He swallowed. He was done.

Was that it? She wondered. Was there really nowhere for them to go? 'Dick,' she said, in a small voice. 'Dick, do you want to kiss me?' She thought of his mouth, red like a wound, the suck of it. 'Do you? Dick?' She leaned into him. She ran her hands up his arms.

The braid on his jacket came away in her fingers.

She picked it off.

It was metal foil.

She let go of him.

It was the foil wrappers from slabs of chocolate.

The white stuff sticking it to his sleeve was cow gum. It clung in crumbs to the material of his jacket.

So.

She let go of his arms. She felt calm. Dead calm.

'Dick?' she said. 'Where are you from?'

He gave her an address in Fitzrovia: a road off Gower Street. They were practically there. Perhaps they had been headed there all along.

She asked him, 'Is this where you're taking me?'

He stared into her eyes.

'Do you want me to come with you?'

The bloated look was back: his look of need.

'Dick? Do you want me to come home with you?'

She imagined the sort of place where he might be staying. A bleak furnished room with thin walls.

She looked him in the eye, right in the eye, without passion, with a cool, calculating curiosity. She said, 'It doesn't matter, Dick. I'll come with you.'

She imagined the tightness of his muscles, the tremors coursing under his skin, the nature of the experiment to which she was now committing herself.

Limping now, she led him across Southampton Row and around Bloomsbury Square. The gardens were chained shut. They turned off Gower Street. She counted off the houses, looking for a hotel sign.

'Here we are,' he said.

It wasn't what she'd been expecting. It wasn't a boarding house. It was one of a row of smart Georgian terrace houses. Beside the door, a plaque bore the name of a distinguished-sounding philosophical society.

Dick stood beside her on the polished marble steps, shifting from one foot to another. Out of embarrassment? In anticipation? She said, 'Are you sure this is the place?'

'Aye-aye,' he said, and winked at her, as though the whole evening had been one long, terrific joke.

'Are you going to let us in?'

He sobered up.

'Dick?'

His eyes grew big with need. 'Spare us a kiss, love – a little kiss.'

Did he not understand? 'Inside,' she said. She took hold of his hands. 'Take me in with you.'

The door opened. A young woman appeared, smoking a cigarette. 'Yes?' Kathleen let go of Dick's hands.

'What do you want?' The woman was tall and gawky-looking; her white blouse, trimmed with a dark material, carried an intimidating hint of education. Smoke from the woman's cigarette wafted into Kathleen's face. It was strong and foreign-tasting, and it made Kathleen want to rub her eyes.

Dick was staring at the pavement. He was scuffing his shoes against each other like a shamed schoolboy.

'Come along inside, Mr Jinks,' said the woman, without surprise, without ceremony, grinding her spent cigarette underfoot.

Dick stepped inside the hall.

'Dick?' Kathleen reached out after him.

He did not notice. His eyes were downcast. 'Good evening, Miriam.'

His use of her Christian name made the woman bridle. 'Get along, Mr Jinks,' she said.

Suddenly, Kathleen was afraid. 'Dick!' she cried, sharp, to wake him. 'Dick! You don't have to—'

'That's enough out of you,' said the woman called Miriam.

Kathleen peered past her, looking for Dick.

She saw ornate moulded coving; a chandelier; rich red carpeting on the stairs at the hall's far end; closed doors, painted white. An umbrella stand, heavy with men's mackintoshes.

Dick had vanished.

Miriam stood, her hand on the door, her head inclined at an ironic angle, waiting for Kathleen to be done with her inspection. Kathleen tried to make out her face, but the light from the hall held her in silhouette.

'Goodnight, then.' Miriam swung the door.

'Wait!' Kathleen's words came out in a great rush. 'Is he a sailor, really, I mean, whether what he said, I mean, his uniform, but still he could be, or could have been… I want to know.'

The door was shut, and one by one, the lights in the building were going out.

Kathleen has approached her life objectively. In this way she has protected herself, even from bombs and fire storms.

But her experiments are becoming large and unwieldy. They produce results that have no meaning, or that offer up too many meanings. Her experiments keep colliding. Unfamiliar phenomena peel off and spin away, feelings which vanish the moment she stops to analyse them.

The night following her aborted night with Dick, she went with the girls of her boarding house to the Royal Opera House. The opera house hosts regular dance evenings. Shop girls spin and caper amidst gilt and sumptuous red furniture under a dome of perfect blue, like a blackbird's egg.

There was Margaret, in a red print dress, dancing with the policeman from the pub. The smile she gave Kathleen as she rocked past was all mouth; her eyes had no warmth in them.

Kathleen, seated at the edge of the dance floor, folded her hands in her lap, as unfamiliar feelings exploded and vanished inside her like fireworks. It was not that she had liked the policeman. It was not that she had thought of him since that night in the Four Feathers. It was not, precisely, that Margaret had done anything wrong, when she'd steered her new girlfriend away from him that night in the pub. It was not that Margaret had cheated her or, if she had, it was not as though the cheat was very great. It was not precisely anything. It was simply the wreckage left behind when experiments collide: experiments in men, experiments in friendship. Kathleen wondered what conclusion might be drawn from this result.

Sitting beside her she noticed Hazel, a girl from her rooming house, in a new yellow dress which lent her skin a sallow, yielding quality that men seemed to shun. Margaret wheeled by, her face in the shade of the policeman's massive chin, and Hazel yawned, 'Kath, love, you ought to watch that cheeky cow.'

More sparks! How did Hazel know that Margaret had steered her away from the policeman? What would happen if Kathleen asked Hazel what she meant, straight out?

On and on, like dominoes. The more you experimented, the less you really knew. Kathleen has been looking the world straight in the eye, without passion, as though it were a series of soluble problems. She has been living as though life were a set of coolly posed questions. She had expected answers to her questions, not feelings.

Kathleen told Hazel the story of her night with Jinks.

'Oh my God!' Hazel exclaimed. 'Weren't you frightened?'

Kathleen shook her head.

Hazel said, 'I'd have called a copper.'

This was Hazel's one stock response to things: 'I'll call a copper, I shall.' At first, people were taken aback by such threats: awkward bus conductors; inept waitresses; men who had the misfortune to bump against Hazel on the street. Then, quite quickly, they learned that she was not very bright.

3

The Blitz is in full swing. Loss is common throughout the London herd, and exhaustion is a way of life. At the same time, there is very little terror. The government's conscientious plans to deal with the collapse of civil order seem foolish now, a nanny's unnecessary bothering. The beds in hospitals from Croydon to Middlesex, readied for tens of thousands of shell-shock victims, lie empty. Come the air-raid sirens, Londoners flock to the Underground. Afterwards, they re-emerge from the deepest tunnels quite willingly, they do not shun the light, and H. G. Wells's fearsome, trogloditic Morlocks remain a thing of dreams.

The theatres and cinemas, shut up when the first bombs fell, were re-opened almost immediately. In garret rooms in Plumstead and Elstree, young screenwriters, numbed by the Blitz, stumble gormlessly through the toils of self-expression, and Senate House, kindly and oblivious, polishes their efforts bland again, reducing their screen characters to sanctioned types: broken-spirited airman; sparky shopgirl; callow hero-in-waiting; hard-bitten New York journalist with her too-high heels and racy opinions; dependable, if tipsy, artisan. So every man, passing through the censor's narrow gate, becomes an Everyman, a symbol for the mass, hardly a man at all.

Every night, after work, Kathleen finds herself watching films so similar to each other they may as well be one film: a series of civilized exchanges conducted in more-or-less interchangeable white rooms. Each room is handsomely furnished. There is always a floor-length mirror, a box of cigarettes on a coffee table and, by the window, a man and a woman, smoking.

The handsome couple have reached some sort of emotional crisis. The man opens his mouth to speak. 'Have you any idea what this involves?' Though the man and the woman are in black and white, the inside of the man's mouth is red.

'I could get myself *shot!'*

Kathleen comes awake, trying to scream.

'The cutlets, please,' says the colourless young man, the sole occupant of the table before her.

The pencil in her hand is a complex surgical instrument. She does not know how to operate it. All by themselves, as if by a ponderous magic, letters emerge from under the pencil's tip: t... l... e... t... ...1

Kathleen blinks at the colours around her with eyes still tuned to black and white. She is at work. She is standing by table three. She says, automatically, 'Anything to drink?'

'Yes. A cup of tea, please.'

She writes: T

All day, Kathleen has been falling into dreams. It is happening to them all, and so frequently, almost every conversation drifts to the subject of sleep sooner or later: how much sleep you need, what sort of sleep it is and when you take it. Jenny from the kitchens reckons peeling vegetables for the lunchtime rush gives her a good fifteen minutes of deep sleep, 'no dreams, mind'.

Kathleen envies her. Her waking hours are riddled with dreams. Whenever she closes her eyes, a dream appears. Sometimes it is impossible to distinguish between sleeping and waking. On several occasions she has breakfasted, washed, dressed, run to the station and boarded the tube train to work – only to wake up in bed, dizzy and disorientated, and utterly demoralized at the thought that she will have to go through all this morning's rigmarole again.

Recently, dreams such as these have begun to nest inside each other, so that she finds herself waking up from a dream into another dream, and from that dream into another, and another, each one a little chillier, stiffer and more realistic than the last. Who is to say when the chain of dreams ends and reality begins?

Kathleen remembers John Arven telling her to look things in the eye. Replace your horror with a cool curiosity, he said to her: then the horror goes away. She has followed his advice dutifully enough, but last night she saw something that spoiled her belief in him. It was the opening reel of a film about the agonies of a young conductor of an orchestra of refugees.

An elegant woman in a fur coat and bright heels walks the streets of a ruined city. What city? It is impossible to tell. There are no signs, no advertisements; the headlines on the shredded newspapers which bowl along the street beside her, worrying her feet, are too far away to read. All we can say is that the city is modern, its destruction accomplished only recently, by wave after wave of bombing from the air.

The elegant woman holds the collar of her coat tight around her neck, picking her way with unfeasible ease and steadiness over roads reduced to crumbled stream beds, strands of brick-shingle, dunes of plaster dust. Her heels kick motes of light across the screen...

It was, after all, only a scene from a film. But it has made Kathleen look differently at things. The smooth, calm movements of the woman on the film suggested that the character had blocked reality out altogether, preferring to live among memories of the city before it was bombed. But you could just as easily take the scene to mean the opposite: that the woman had achieved a complete psychic adjustment to the bombing.

Utter denial or total acceptance? Everywhere Kathleen turns now, the London masses are dreaming their way through the Blitz. They are not looking the Blitz in the eye at all. They are coming to a glancing, unconscious accommodation with it. They are trying to work around it, to sidestep it and integrate it into a life they try to make as ordinary as possible. Proudly displayed in every shop window she passes, a sign: 'Business as Usual'. A triumph of fantasy.

She thinks: a city is razed, but we pretend otherwise. We survive *because* we pretend.

Waitressing at Lyons is not a job that Kathleen could just turn up one day and do. They trained her. In an upstairs room, she was taught how to dress a dining table. The idea is that it should look exactly like every other dining table of that size – not just within that restaurant, but in every restaurant Lyons own. Kathleen has learned how to dress a table for two, for four, for eight. She has memorized the place of each glass, plate, fork, knife, spoon and trivet. Precision is called for, and precision is something Kathleen enjoys. The neat creases, the bright, cruel reflections of each glass, bottle, plate and cup, the mathematical creases of the tablecloths: these things have for her a nostalgic appeal. They remind her of the kitchen at home, blistering white, and of her mother.

The idea behind all this precision is that a customer, seated at a four-seater in Piccadilly, might as well be seated at a four-seater in Holborn; that a customer might forget, seated at his table, that the restaurant has an actual location. The idea is that Lyons corner houses might become for their customers a single place, a unique, unmappable location. Behind everyday appearances – this is the idea – lies a better world; the world of the Lyons corner house.

Tonight, in her room, in the dark, by the glow of distant harbour fires, she writes to Sage, Professor Arven, John, whatever it is he calls himself: *'We survive because we pretend. Life is too rich, too complex, too uncertain. Life resists method. Life will not be examined. It will not be picked up and laid down.'*

And wakes up. The beautiful cadences of her letter evaporate on the air.

Grim, determined, she gets up, turns on the light, checks the blackout and writes, for real this time:

'Dear Prof. Arven, I have yet to receive a reply to my letter of 3rd inst.'

The following evening after work, Kathleen finds the buses have been badly disrupted. She does not have money enough for the cinema tonight, so she decides to walk home. She walks along shattered streets, past twisted bicycles and ziggurats of shattered masonry, walls made of sandbags and windows criss-crossed with paper tape. The air, though dry, smells wet, a trick of the plaster dust that already reddens the sky as the day slides towards evening. As she goes, a magnificent sunset builds around her, reviving the city's spirits: green and rose and deepest carmine, indigo and lemon; towers and vistas, cloudy bridges, dusty promenades. A city of spirit hangs over this city of stone.

She passes her neighbourhood library – a handsome Edwardian building – and sees that a bomb has been dropped on it.

The explosion has knocked the roof aside as though it were a lid, and the upper storey has come crashing down over the public rooms. The whole frontage has fallen away. Dislodged joists lie up against the remaining walls like pencils in a jar, confusing the geometry of the once orderly rooms. The walls are lined with books. The bomb has done them no harm, though the upper storey has crushed and buried the centre stacks completely.

Kathleen is surprised to see six or seven men inside the ruined library, browsing the shelves. They are like her: ordinary people returning home from work. They wear hats and coats. They carry satchels and leather bags. They move past each other, abstracted, intent on the titles before them. Business as usual.

A short, ill-favoured old man in a sort of quilted smoking jacket – something that went out of fashion long before she was born – opens his satchel and takes out a book. He surveys the stack. He locates the spot he was after, and slots his book back into its rightful place on the shelf.

She says, 'We survive because we pretend.'

She is among them. She has joined them. She is browsing the books, tilting her head to read titles in the fading light. She is picking her way over loose boards, easing past strangers, murmuring 'excuse me' and 'thank you'. Plaster crumbles underfoot. Index cards stir and flap at her ankles as she edges sideways along the shelves with slow, muted movements. Three tall, book-lined walls surround her, shielding her from too much reality, and slowly the fantasy, the browsers' brave 'as if', takes hold.

She reads: *'Apart from its mode of projection, the construction of the space vessel offers little difficulty since it is essentially the same problem as that of the submarine. Naturally the first space vessels will be extremely cramped and uncomfortable, but they will be manned only by enthusiasts.'*

It is from the entry for the biologist J. B. S. Haldane, in an encyclopaedia of philosophy so large it has been published in two volumes: 'A to K' and 'L to Z'. She glances back at the flyleaf and receives a shock. The editors' names are printed there. J. B. Priestley is one, and underneath his name, in smaller type: J. D. Arven.

A hand settles upon her back. There is someone beside her. She steps forward a little, to let him by, and the pressure on her back is lifted. However, the man does not move by. She senses him there, to her left, not reading, looking at her. She pretends to ignore him. The light is failing. Words swim about, tadpoles in the reticular grey pool of the page.

One by one, visitors are leaving the ruined library. She listens to them: shoe leather against stone and brick; a coat-tail brushed over planks; something dislodged; a hollow, confused sound from within the teepee of broken joists, charred linoleum and ceiling lathe which fills the room.

The hand settles on her back once more. Her heart races. She does not step away.

The man has a scent. It is mild and pleasant. It is the scent of tar soap and aftershave, and sherry after lunch. It is smoky and adult. It is the smell of her uncle, who was so friendly to her, and who, she has guessed, is her real father.

The hand moves down her back, over her rear, to the vent in her coat. The hand moves inside, then out again.

She had said to her mother, 'You married the wrong one,' and after that, there was no going back. Her mother did not even come to the station to wish her well. This was all the confirmation she needed that it was true.

She waits for the hand to settle on her back a third time. Browsing the stack opposite theirs, where the light is still strong enough to read, one or two men still linger. The man – her 'uncle', her real father, her fantasy taking root in the shelter of three tall, book-lined walls – waits, not touching her, but standing close beside her, so she can smell him. The scent of the cigars her uncle smoked behind the wheel of his low-slung car. Their famous 'business trips', so urgent, so important, ending always in a picnic in some pleasant spot, and him so kind and smiling, making conversation. Kathleen eating everything in sight. Falling in love with him.

'Dear Father' she had written: a letter she would never send.

'Dear Uncle': that, too, went in the bin.

Did he know by now, that she had found out who he really was? Did he even know, himself? Had her mother told him? Or, once Kathleen had failed to turn up at the abattoir, had he worked it out?

Has he come after her?

Is it him?

In the shadow of three ruined walls, the fantasy blossoms.

They wait to be alone. The man bends forward and takes a book from the shelf. She turns aside. She does not want to see his face. She does not want to know who he really is – some civil servant, bank clerk, inspector of drains. She does not want to know the truth. She does not need the truth. She needs the dream.

By chance, he has picked up the companion volume to her encyclopaedia. He opens it: 'L to Z'.

He leans in to her.

He runs the edge of his volume against hers, back and forth. She studies his thumb. A clean, square-cut nail. Strong. A tiny scar above the knuckle. It might be her uncle's hand.

Yes, she decides. It is his hand.

It has become too dark to read. Her uncle turns, making sure they are alone.

They are alone.

He closes 'L to Z', steps forward and slips the volume back into its place. Kathleen lets 'A to K' fall into the rubble at her feet. What does it matter?

The man sighs. He bends down. She cannot help but look at him. When she sees that he is wearing a hat, she sighs with relief. He can still be her uncle. She has not seen him. He can still be who she wants him to be.

He slides the volume into the stack, beside its mate. He turns to her.

She turns away.

He takes her arm, turning her to face him.

She pulls away, keeping her back to him.

He takes her arm again.

Again, she pulls away.

She feels his breath, fogging the back of her neck. He takes hold of her again – not her arm this time, her shoulder. His hand is heavy. It squeezes. It knows what she wants, now. It drives her forward, over the rubble, to an open doorway.

It used to be the door to a reading room. The reading room is gone. There is a cluttered nothing beyond the door, a waist-high maze of shattered masonry and scorched timber. He pushes her and pushes her. She staggers, her ankle twists and she loses her balance. She falls to her knees. She stops there, on her knees, swallowing the pain. She gets up. Her knees are bleeding. Her stockings are torn. One of her shoes is missing.

Hands reach around her and draw her coat from her shoulders. Her arms hang loose by her sides. She shivers. She waits. One hand at the back of her neck, one hand in the small of her back, he bends her over. She clasps her legs just above her grazed knees. He reaches up under her dress and pulls.

Her knickers will not tear, however hard he tugs. He curses, lets her go. She stands up. It might all be over now. Dreadful. Mortifying. What if the moment is lost? She hoists up her skirts, hoping to keep him. She runs her hands in and down, pulling her knickers to her ankles with a fluid motion. She kicks off her remaining shoe. She steps out of her underwear. She waits.

He lifts up her dress, higher, higher, around her waist, up over her breasts. He runs his fingers down her back, to the crack of her bottom, and in.

She steps forward, surprised, away from him. There is a piece of wall in front of her. Brick, with something painted on it: letters from an advertisement. She leans against it. It shifts sickeningly under her hands, and she is afraid she will fall. She readjusts her weight. The surface holds under her hands. She spreads her legs.

His fingers run lightly down between her buttocks. He cups her cunt with one hand, runs light fingers over her back with the other.

He parts her lips with fingers that are already wet. He runs a finger between her lips, and finds the weak point, enters, curls. She sobs. He moves forward. The wings of his coat tickle the backs of her calves.

He enters her quickly. It is like he is stubbing out a cigar inside her. She cries out. He leans forward, over her, and his free hand covers her mouth. She smells sherry and cigars and soap, closes her eyes and licks the palm of his hand as he snaps her head back.

She thinks of her mother doing this. Bent over. Bent back. Filled. She tries to imagine her mother, given up to this dream. It is impossible. The mother she knows is a woman who looks things in the eye with a terrible dispassion. A woman who looks beyond every pretty dream to the inevitable rot. Beneath the skin, always the skull. Beyond the dress, a pile of rags.

This, she decides, moaning against the restraining hand, is why Sage's method is not enough. Not *wrong* – but nowhere near enough. Because, after all, there's appetite, the human itch. No method can accommodate it. 'Look what you made me do,' her mother used to say to her. Perhaps, when he was spent, she said it to him, too – her real father.

'*Look what you made me do!*'

The image is so ludicrous, Kathleen laughs out loud.

And wakes up.

The man's hand is gone from her mouth.

How much time has she lost?

She nearly forgets her purpose. She nearly turns around.

The man's hand falls on her just in time, firm across her buttocks, holding her to her intention. This dream she is having. Her daddy inside her. His fingers feeling for the other way in.

He sucks his thumb and presses it between her buttocks, wetting her. He licks it again and brings it back to her bottom again. His thumb stirs the muscle there. His breathing becomes laboured. He withdraws from her cunt, then tugs at her hips, repositions himself, and presses his erection against the rose of her anus. He gasps. There is a wetness coming out of him. He presses harder against the muscle of her bottom, the wet lubricating him, so that he begins to penetrate her there. His thrusts are irregular and wet. Another kind of fire runs through her, and her body fights him, fights him, then suddenly, without her meaning to, surrenders, and his erection splits her.

He holds her very still until she has stopped crying. She feels him inside her. She squeezes him, feeling him there. Little by little, savouring it, she squeezes it out like a turd.

She stands upright. She looks for her shoes. The man's hand curls around her arm.

Shuddering, repulsed, she pulls away.

'All right?' he says.

This is her fantasy, not his. She will not share.

'Shall we have a cup of tea somewhere?'

She needs to shut him up. She needs to get rid of him. Fast. She wishes there was a sign around her neck: 'Keep Off'. She will have to speak to him. What should she say?

She remembers the sailor Dick Jinks, the night he turned up at the guest-house door. What he said about Donald, his friend.

'Poofter,' she says.

She hears the breath catch in the stranger's throat.

'Nancy!'

The electricity between them is palpable. Behind her eyes, she sees his fists begin to curl, the knuckles whitening...

'Queen.'

She screws up her eyes, tight shut, anticipating the blow. She is afraid. What if his fists aren't enough? What if he picks up a brick? It is too late now.

'Fuck you,' she says.

She counts to ten.

She opens her eyes.

She feels that he is gone.

Her coat is lying at her feet. She picks it up and slips it round her shoulders.

Her shoes are nearby. Her knickers. She puts them on.

Dizzy, disorientated, it takes her a moment to recognize the sound of the sirens. How much time has she lost? Where is she? Is she alone?

She turns around.

She sees the bomb. She actually sees it falling, the great mass of it, the unlikely speed, as though it has toppled out of the sky by accident. Surely this is not something anyone could ever mean to happen. The whistle at its nose glints in the moonlight as it bursts through the outstretched branches of a tree and the whistle is a terrible, familiar *'Eeeee!'* as it fists the earth.

Kathleen rises. Idly, she backstrokes the air. Something showers her. She is expecting plaster dust, but no, it is a rain of shredded leaves. Bright birds spin around and around the stripped trees. The birds are very bright. Their wings are on fire.

Kathleen lies back and watches the burning birds.

And wakes up.

She is alone. The street smokes and crackles. She sits up. Ahead of her there is a great crater. She looks down at herself. She is covered with earth. She gets up, and the earth falls away from her, and as above, the burning birds wheel with a great scream towards the moon and vanish in its glare, so below, inside her belly, the stranger's sperm, one flagellant stray, finds its mark.

WHITE MAN'S MAGIC

1

It is 1952 and early in the year: already dark by five.

'So dark out there!' Kathleen wails. She is stood before the rain-beaded lounge window, framed by orange-and-brown geometrically patterned curtains. Her shoulders are hunched and rounded under a shiny blue nylon housecoat.

She and I are the only ones home.

'Saul! What are we going to do?'

William, my father, is late home from work. Driving back from Fratton, it is not unusual for him to run into heavy traffic, especially in bad weather. You might think that the more there are of these unexpected late homecomings, the less frightened my mother would be. You might think that the more often William returns home unscathed, cursing the traffic, the less likely Kathleen is, on the next occasion, to assume the worst: the skid, the collision, the closed coffin. But Kathleen lives in a dangerous world, in which every act is a game of Russian roulette, and William's safe homecomings are as the empty chambers in a pistol barrel which, turning, can only draw the fatal bullet, chamber by chamber, closer to the pin.

Home – since she left London with her husband on one arm and me in the crook of the other – has been this new-build bungalow on a residential street running parallel to the London–Portsmouth trunk road. It is small and snug, though the gardens, front and rear, are huge and wild, as though they belonged to a much grander property. Kathleen reckons that I will have a lovely safe time here as I grow up, playing about in these gardens. I am such a happy, lively child! I am sure to have many friends!

Beside the bungalow is a garage big enough for two cars. A second car is an unimaginable luxury, especially since Kathleen has no desire to learn to drive. More likely they will one day buy a caravan; when not in use they can keep it on the patch of hard-standing, screened by conifers, which William has already prepared. He is so practical. So very organized.

Where will they go in their caravan? The Isle of Wight. The Lake District. Up to Darlington, even; Kathleen would like to visit the North again one day, and show me the landscapes of her childhood.

Kathleen has painted every room of the house white. It is the colour of the starched tablecloths in the Lyons corner houses where she used to work. Also, it is the colour of her mother's kitchen. Neither association is a wholly happy one, but associations, memories, the past – these are not the point. The effect of so much whiteness is clean and bright and aspirational. It is the décor of becoming, not of being. This is what her life is: a crisp new blouse, fresh from the wrapper.

William insists that Kathleen need not go out to work. She is a mother. He, meantime, has a job in Fratton, introducing new breeds of calculating machine to the offices of the Southern Electricity Board. (In 1939, flat feet and childhood rickets saw to it that William waddled, ignominiously rejected, out of the Hackney volunteer station. Soon after, he had stumbled into one of the duller reserved occupations, doing sums for the electricity board. He has been in that line of work ever since.)

In vain, Kathleen tries to talk to her husband about his job, the machines and the calculations they perform. In vain, she tries to engage. 'It is very complicated, Kathleen,' he says. He is tired, after a long day at the office and such a long commute. 'It is too complicated for me to explain.'

In idle moments during the day, while Saul naps or plays in the garden, Kathleen may take one of William's books down from the shelf in the lounge. Flashes of colour light the backs of her eyes as she reads, ragged remains of her synaesthetic gifts.

Binary notation.

Boolean algebra.

Algorithms.

Regret is cheap, she knows that. She has much to be thankful for: a handsome, happy child, a generous and handy husband, a clean new home to treasure. But she is not so much of a Pollyanna that she cannot see the opportunities that have passed her by. The strange gift detected in her at the very beginning of the war – her easiness with numbers, her vivid understanding of them, almost a sixth sense – this gift has never found any outlet, for all the professor's encouragement, for all the hopes he stirred up in her, for all the letters she sent him.

She had wanted to be a computer, back in the days when a computer was still a person. A trained and respected computer, perhaps with her own office. How strange her hopes sound now, as though, with the change in the meaning of one word, some part of history has been erased. These days her wasted talents are worth nothing. Any adding machine can perform as well as she ever could, if not better. Even William could best her, armed with one of his precious machines. ('It really is very complicated, Kathleen,' he says, with an exasperating little smile. She finds herself hating him.)

So it is not good for her to look back. She must look forward. She must always be looking forward, to the bright white future of her Second Chance as Wife and Mother.

By day, the limitations of their new life mean less to Kathleen than her own project of improvements. Every year she repaints the bungalow's interior with paint that, every year, promises an even more intense whiteness, a whiter-than-white whiteness, a whiteness that is (according to the changing fashions of the advertising industry) Chemically, Biologically, even Optically White. She longs for surfaces like shells, for the opalescent shimmer of mother-of-pearl. Surfaces from which would issue, on demand, a kind glow. An early convert to the pleasures of indirect lighting, she has asked William to fit dimmer switches in every room. William grumbles that with the lights turned so low, he cannot see to eat.

As the daylight fades, so the colours of the street begin to leach away, and the bungalows to either side of them – early experiments in prefabrication – seem to flatten themselves out against the grey ground of the evening. The whole street becomes a shoddy simulacrum, and the bright white emptiness of Kathleen's future closes around her like the cold enamel walls of a bath.

'So dark, Saul!' Kathleen wails.

'The traffic is so heavy,' she says, gazing across her road, and up, over the earth embankment and through its screen of trees, to the fleeting red-and-white tracer fire that marks the trunk road proper.

'If only the traffic wasn't so heavy.'

And: 'Please let him be careful in the heavy traffic.'

There is panic in her use of the same image, over and over again, and there is poetry, too. *Heavy traffic*. While trying to find the words to express her fear, she has found that it is best expressed, not by the right word, the apt phrase – which, once uttered, can only leave her dumb – but by the wrong word, the trite phrase, repeated to the point where it acquires the ecstatic mumbo-jumbo of an incantation.

'Why is there so much heavy traffic?'

'This heavy traffic isn't necessary.'

'The traffic's getting even heavier.'

Reason cannot comprehend reality, and fantasy cannot manipulate it. This is the lesson Kathleen has drawn from life. Reason and fantasy are two sides of the same bent key. They unlock nothing. They reveal nothing. Step into the world expecting magic; cause and effect will crush your every expectation. Look at the world objectively, and everything before you turns fantastical and absurd. You only have to look at this place. Our address mentions the village of Horndean, but Horndean, pretty as it sounds, is not a village so much as a line of ribbon development, straggling pointlessly by the side of the trunk road as it carves its way through the South Downs. You drive for miles by lawns of tall dead grass and glimpse, now and again, far away down crazy-paving drives, houses of peeling green pressboard and untreated corrugated iron, sheds on concrete stilts surrounded by fences of rusted chicken wire; sometimes knee-high walls, their bricks Post Office red with a thick poisonous resin, the mortar white, a kitsch criss-cross. Hand-painted. Madness.

Whatever strategy Kathleen picks and puts her trust in, it lets her down. There is no compass in this life, no way to measure latitude or longitude. There is no certainty in Life but Death. She knows this now. So the cold white walls of her Second Chance have risen around her. Within them, imprisoned by them, Kathleen has become bullet-proof. She will never be fooled again.

'Look how heavy the traffic is!'

'Why is the traffic so heavy tonight?'

'I've never seen the traffic so heavy!'

Kathleen stands before the window, chanting. Powerless. She is beginning to frighten even herself. This is what she wants: to be frightened by something other than life, that wellspring of escalating terrors. If she can only frighten herself, then it will be like being frightened by a friend; in other words, hardly frightened at all.

Heavy traffic.

'So many accidents, Saul!'

Heavy traffic.

Evoked by her panic, an image forms behind my eyes. William, my father, sat in his Hillman Minx, jostled from side to side by great juggernauts and tankers. He squeezes his elbows in and straightens his back, as though proper posture might save him. He keeps to his lane and maintains his speed, but this pathetic assertion of will only makes a collision more likely.

I would like to give my mother some comfort – for my sake, as much as hers. God forbid she gets any worse. Her panic is an emotional flash-flood that leaves me winded and trembling. 'Dad will be all right,' I assure her, with all the hard-won authority of my nine years, and – painfully aware of my insufficiency – I hug her waist.

Kathleen's imagination is contagious. I can see, behind my mother's eyes – clearly, as though it were a painted miniature – my father torn to shreds, strung between steering column and door pillar in a cat's cradle of bleeding ribbons in the rain, somewhere outside Cosham, or Waterlooville, or Cowplain – all these wet barnyard names.

Misery loves company. 'What are we going to do?' Kathleen cries.

Ten years later: 1962.

'Everybody makes mistakes,' says William Cogan, the day he takes his final leave of the Southern Electricity Board. Today is the first day of the rest of his life – it says so on his card.

To William Cogan: 'The very best of luck'; 'Be missing you'. No one has had the faintest idea what to write.

A radio, tuned to an easy-listening station, snags the air the way a torn fingernail catches on clothing. The air is hot and chlorinated. A cake. A glass of warm white. For a leaving present, a crystal decanter.

'Everyone makes mistakes,' William says, towards the end of his thank you speech, as though excusing his colleagues for their shoddy performance today.

Acutely aware, in this moment, of the possibility of making one of those inevitable mistakes.

His eyes fixate on a point a few inches above his small, shuffling, distracted audience. 'Everyone makes mistakes. The thing is—' He swallows. 'The thing is, to make as few mistakes as possible.'

Saul, his son, gives a sober nod. Ah, my boy!

The truth is, I'm finding something stirring and tragic about my dad today. Not much thought of by his workmates. Misunderstood ('Relax! Have fun! Travel the world!'). Unacknowledged master of the straight line and sharpened pencil, amidst these messy office girls. ('Look who he's had to work with!' Kathleen sighs in my ear: her sucked-lemon face.)

In a couple of months I'll be leaving home for Trinity College, Cambridge, where I will be studying Russian literature. Product of a sheltered upbringing, denied bicycles and sleepovers and childhood friendships, I have not the remotest conception of the world that is about to hit me.

'Machines will take over what I did there,' William says, with not one hint of regret, when we are home. Machines reduce the world to black and white. To zeros and to ones. Everything is either one thing or the other. Something or nothing. Such a system cannot make mistakes. 'Machines will do this now.' For another few years his pianola chest will labour, gears turning: his hands moving automatically across the paper, drafting a mill, a turbine, the plan of a granary. (To fill his retirement, he has joined a local society set up to encourage an interest in such things. He goes on trips to mills and goods yards and derelict factories to measure and draw for the little pamphlets the society prepares, two or three times a year. His drawings are professional, accurate, useful. Art without mistakes is art reduced to the techniques of draughtsmanship.)

He says: 'I have to get this done.' He says, 'They want me to do this.' And: 'This has to be finished by...' I understand that these are expressions of happiness.

William's retirement means that there is little by which one day might be distinguished from another. Shopping day follows washing day. Gardening follows cleaning follows decorating follows gardening. In such an atmosphere, change becomes synonymous with accident, and novelty brings with it a tremor of fear.

Kathleen, however, finds she cannot heighten her experience of life with the usual anxieties. She no longer has any reason to stand at the living-room window, looking out at the rain, dreaming up accidents.

Now she says, 'Do you have to leave all this everywhere?' She says, 'Do you have to do that at the table?' She says, 'Do you have to have it on so loud?'

Come winter, returning home after my first term at Trinity, I find my father fixing strawberry netting over the garden pond.

'Why are you doing that?' I ask him.

'Your mother is afraid the hedgehogs will drown.'

'Why?'

'We have hedgehogs,' William says. 'They can't swim.'

'Of course they can swim.'

'The netting will keep them away from the water.'

'Everything can swim.'

'If they want a drink they can use the bird bath.'

'You just need to prop something up in the water so they can crawl out. There's nothing in there for them to crawl out on.'

'She has it all arranged.'

'A bit of wood or something.'

'She has it how she likes it.'

'They'll still drown.'

'This is good netting.'

'They'll still drown. They'll still find a way in and then the netting will trap them and they'll drown.'

'I'm fixing this properly,' he says.

'It won't make any difference.'

'It will if I do it properly,' he says.

'No,' I tell him, 'it won't.'

'What's the matter?' Kathleen calls out from the kitchen. 'Saul? What have you done?'

Even now that I have left home, it will be a while before I acquire much mature coloration. I remain, in my dress and manners, that gifted, shy, nineteen-year-old schoolboy. My interests are broadly the interests I had as a child and I make a point, during the vacation, of visiting our neighbour – Mrs Wilson, an old woman, long widowed – so that I can thump about on her bizarre, oversize piano.

'What are the pedals for?' I remember asking her, many years before, confronted by the instrument for the first time.

Mrs Wilson, a diabetic and double amputee, had her little legs on that day: stubby metal legs without joints, paddles in place of feet. They helped keep her upright in her chair. They were pretty useless for walking unless you were simply heaving yourself over from one piece of furniture to another. 'Pedals?' said Mrs Wilson, blinking at her paddles, where they dangled over the edge of her Cintique chair. 'These?'

'No! In there. The piano pedals.'

'Ah,' she said, and smiled. 'The *pedals*.'

'Yes.'

'Well, Saul, as I'm sure you've noticed, they make the piano softer or louder.' Playing a little game with me.

'Not *those* pedals. The *others*.'

'Ah,' said Mrs Wilson.

It was a pianola. Mrs Wilson, perched precariously on the piano stool, directed operations: 'Now turn that catch. There. Yes. Now let it down. Gently, Saul, gently.'

The belly of the instrument lay revealed: a handsome gutwork of rollers and spindles, needles and hammers.

'See over there? In that basket? Get a roll.'

I fetched a roll of paper from the basket. It was heavy, the paper thick like parchment. Mrs Wilson showed me how to string the punched paper roll between the sprockets. 'There. Help me down now,' she said.

'Take a seat,' she said, exhausted, balanced on her little legs. 'You pump them. Those pedals. Like riding a bicycle. Do it hard, they'll be very stiff.'

I sat down before the pianola. I pretty much had to slide off the stool to reach the pedals. I began to pump, hard and heavy, on the wide rails set to either side of the usual *piano* and *forte* pedals.

Within the belly of the pianola, something stirred.

The thing played itself.

Bar after bar, line after line and unfailingly, the pianola realizes its self-idea. As I stood in the Fratton office, sipping Blue Nun with his co-workers, I imagined spoked drums turning in my father's chest. His narrow perfection.

2

'Must enjoy filing,' it said on the card – and a Bloomsbury address. The library of a private society, requiring temporary assistance.

I imagined the place, its pre-war interiors given over to elegant decrepitude. I pictured hallways lined with glass-fronted cabinets, and books and manuscripts in teetering piles. Portraits and small Byronic landscapes, steeped in a thick brown lacquer, lined the faded, silk-panelled walls; and were I to negotiate my way through the complicated, dust-smothered window-dressing in the first-floor drawing room, I would come at last, through the age-rippled glass of a sash window, upon a view of a secret garden contained by high walls, swathed in thick ivy of the deepest green. At first glance, the garden would appear deserted. Then, at the last moment, through the straggling knitwork of budleia and rhododendron, there would come a suggestion of movement, a figure. A young woman in a white dress. Were I to wind up my courage and raise the matter with my shadowy employers, of course they would deny her existence.

'Six shillings an hour,' my temp agent told me. Poodle perm; miniskirt; smooth, sallow thighs; thick ankles; large, unlikely breasts. Whenever she stood over me during my typing training, they hung over my head like a threat.

On Monday morning I climbed the stairs and pressed the buzzer. The door honked angrily. I tested it with my hand. It gave smoothly, and I walked in.

Fluorescent light robbed the hall of shadows. The sand in the fire bucket by the door was littered with fag-ends, all of the same make: the banded white filter of Gauloises Disque Bleu cigarettes.

I moved towards the only open door, at the far end of the corridor. From it issued the sound of an old typewriter, as loud and loose-actioned as a steam loom. It stuttered, clack following clack at a rhythm just slower than a heart's beating. The music of depression.

Her name was Miriam Miller. She was tall and bird-like, her greying hair folded softly into a shapeless bun; fastidiously groomed but with a face so lined, dry-cured in French tobacco, it could not help but look dirty. A white blouse trimmed with navy blue.

'Your attention to specifics is very important.' Miriam's gnomic turn of phrase was less distracting to me than her strangely impeded speech. It sounded as though a tape were stretching inside her, shifting everything vowel-wards. 'S's shushed like waves lapsing on a gravel shore.

What was this place? I wondered. What did it do?

'We service an international clientele,' Miriam said. She made the place sound like a high-class knocking shop.

'We concern ourselves with preservation,' she said.

I supposed at first she was talking about herself.

'We foster Research.'

What kind of research?

The Society's library resembled less an academic collection, more the well-worn core of an underfunded public library. What coherence could there be in a collection that rubbed the nasty blue-edged pages of Robert Heinlein's *Revolt in 2100* against six volumes of rambling theosophist autobiography entitled *Old Diary Leaves*?

'Researchers' came and went: men with unkempt beards and unreliable trouser zips; one or two utter derelicts (baffling hints of public library again); well-groomed women of a certain age. The more flirtatious of them would sometimes ask me, 'What's a handsome young man like you doing here?'

In 1965, my last year at Cambridge, my father suffered his first stroke. Because my mother needed my help, the college authorities agreed to defer my final few semesters. This saved me the trouble and embarrassment of dropping out. It also entailed going home – something I had solemnly sworn never to do.

In the featureless shell Mum had made of our home, Dad's cerebral accident took on a terrible rightness: as though he, too, had been integrated into her vision of interchangeable white walls and wipe-clean surfaces.

Mercifully, the repugnant fact of my father's condition – the obscenity of adult helplessness – took my mind off home's other horrors, at least for a while. His infantile walk, his arms extended, hands interlocked to straighten his paretic arm. The way he slumped in his chair, as though unstrung. The keening sounds he made when my mother and I forced his arm and shoulder through their exercises. The ridiculous bright ruler he used when he read the *Express*, so that his eyes would remember to travel to the left to start a new line.

'He doesn't even try!' Mum cried.

She brandished the word the way a maniac brandishes a blunt instrument.

'Why don't you try?'

'You've got to try.'

'Just try a little.'

'Try just once!'

Sadly, in this instance, she had a point. He did not fight back. He did not speak. He did not walk. Now and again – and according to the nurse this should have come under his control long since – he shat his pants.

The truly grotesque element in all this was the degree to which none of it was novel. It was more like the physical manifestation of a psychological state with which Mum and I were already familiar.

Throughout my childhood, he had depended entirely upon my mother for every bite of food, every drop of drink, every clean sock, every fresh towel; at the same time, he seemed entirely self-sufficient. Our affection left him indifferent, and so did our anger. He could take anything the world threw at him. How do you wound a ghost? How do you make a ghost stay? It was only his own inertia which kept him here with us. Had he had a fraction of the energy of other men, I am certain he would have found a way to leave us; and I would have run across him eventually, pursuing some solitary happiness.

As it was, my father had done little for years but sit in his chair in the corner of the living room, watching the football results. When he rose from his chair, which was rarely, he moved from room to room with an air of muted dissatisfaction, like a commercial traveller, forever delayed, who has decided to eat just one more passable meal with the same reliable but overbearing landlady. Not forgetting her son.

So though I trusted him, and even admired him, as children do, my father had never given me any reason to feel that I was related to him. Year after year we had observed each other through the thick glass of our mutual reserve.

When Dad suffered his first stroke, I found myself bursting with such energy, I couldn't sit still, I had to walk up and down the carriages of the train. By the time I was jogging up the hill out of Guildford towards the big new county hospital – I hadn't the patience to wait for a bus – I could no longer pretend to myself that these feelings were normal. I was excited, but not anxious. I was happy to think of my father gone out of control at last. I wanted to hear him say 'Gah' and 'Wonk'. I wanted to see him dribble.

The fact was, I wanted him to be someone different.

I remember when I got to the hospital, the nurses had only just found him a bed, so for a while we had to wait outside the ward. My mother's face was white as though dusted. She was full of that queer, nervous energy I had dreaded to see in her: an overwound toy, exhausting and useless.

'What have I done!' she wailed. (Six hours into my father's stroke and she had already cast herself in the lead.)

They let us in to see him.

Half his face was missing. Where the left-hand side of his face should have been, there was only a greyish bag of loose skin. Where his eye should have been, there was a slit in the skin, and a black marble swimming inside it. His lips were bleary and thick and very pink. There was something grotesquely sexual about the smear his mouth made.

Home again, and in her gleaming kitchen – impossible to imagine these surfaces have ever been contaminated by food – my mother weaves her web of unenticing possibilities: tea or apple juice, or there's some orange barley water in the pantry; Jaffa Cakes or homemade scones. There are some chocolate biscuits somewhere, only she can't find them, she's been looking everywhere. You bite into a scone and she says, 'Or there's some cake.' You stir your tea and she says, 'Or would you rather have coffee?' You tip strawberry jam onto an edge of a scone and she says: 'Would you rather have honey?' You take a bite of scone, raw flour coats the inside of your mouth and she says, 'Ooh! There's some quiche!'

In the middle of the night, a scream.

'Saul!'

'Saul!' she wailed, and entered my room, my old room, this room she had kept for me, and painted white for me, and which I had sworn never to sleep in.

'Saul, he was such a good man!'

Mum wanted to get her elegy in early.

'He took me in, Saul! He took me in!'

'Go to bed, Mother. Try to get some sleep.'

'No one else would touch me. No one.'

'Is there anything in the bathroom cabinet that would help you sleep?'

'Saul, you don't understand.'

'Some hot milk?' I was baiting her. It was irresistible. I was so tired.

'He's been like a father to you. Hasn't he? Hasn't he been like a father to you? He's given you everything, hasn't he?'

'Yes,' I said. Biting my tongue. Crossing my fingers. 'Yes, of course he has.'

'Not every man would do that, Saul.'

She was calming down now. She was Delivering a Lesson.

'I know that, Mum. He's been a great dad.'

She burst into tears.

I laid my hand on hers.

She clutched it.

'He did know, Saul. I didn't trick him. He knew before we were married. I did tell him.'

'Tell him what?'

She blinked at me. 'That I was pregnant,' she said.

'That you were *what*?'

She tried to get into bed with me.

I eased past her and out of the room, touching her as little as possible.

'What have I done!'

'Kathleen,' I said, from the kitchen, 'shut up.' I filled the kettle. My hands were shaking with excitement. I was filled with a sense of sudden and unexpected freedom.

As soon as my mother had learned how to handle things, so that the spotlight of her anxiety shifted naturally onto me:

'Have you done your university work?'

'Have you got much university work to do today?'

'Don't forget your university work.'

'Leave this – go and do some university work.'

('*Wonk*,' my father added. '*Gah*.')

– then I got the hell out of there. I couldn't face going back to my studies and, without my college grant, I had no money. So I did the only thing left to me. Yet another thing I had sworn never to do. I got a job.

The Society hosted speakers. There were talks on Wednesday evenings, sometimes illustrated by means of slides or an overhead projector. P. J. Mills of Surrey University presented 'Teaching Systems, Present and Future – a Multiple Image Tape/Slide Presentation'. There were poetry readings.

When I first began working here I used to wonder how on earth the Society – this dowdy old maid off Gower Street – survived the modern world. It should surely have perished of its own anachronisms years ago. So much for the arrogance of youth. As I began to understand the Society's past, I began also to understand its strength.

The Society had accreted around the writings of the Polish-born American linguist Alfred Korzybski. In the early 1930s Korzybski had developed a theory of relations that did away with the notion of cause and effect. (He was, like all his generation, besotted with Albert Einstein's recently published General Theory of Relativity, and his misreading of it made him the first and greatest of the century's many quantum quacks.) Korzybski declared that everything exists, not because it acts, not even because it thinks (which is, after all, only another kind of acting), but because it is already related to everything else. Cause and effect are merely special manifestations of a relation that already exists.

But if everything is connected to everything else, then the dimensions that separate things from each other – the three spatial dimensions that place things at a distance, and a fourth dimension, time, which makes that distance meaningful – these have no absolute reality. They are, in fact, contingent upon this higher relation of universal connectedness. That being so (the Society's earliest pamphlets argued) might we not use dimensions to our own advantage? They might not turn out to be barriers at all, but doors...

So the spirit of the times drew the Society away from a dry study of Korzybski, and into a frequently confused relation with the many other societies trying, with varying degrees of rigour, neurosis and faith, to come to terms with the scientific ideas of the time. Madame Blavatsky and Colonel Olcott spoke here, and for a while the Society toyed with the principles of theosophism. Bequests from leading spiritualists sustained the Society during the war years, and after the war, science fiction had a major impact on the Society: files of correspondence with A. E. Van Vogt and Robert Heinlein – both at one time or another devotees of Korzybski – were treasured between sheets of acid-free tissue in a fire-proof safe.

The Society had been gorging itself on the new ever since. The second week into my job, I nearly passed out to discover that John Lennon topped Miriam's wishlist of future speakers. (He never came.)

Sat at the back of the Society's puzzling library with my card indexes, my sharpened pencils and my plastic loose-leaf binder detailing the Society's bizarre scherzo on the Dewey system, I was cut off from anything resembling a lived life. Three years went by while I sleep-walked among the stacks.

In March 1968, I woke to discover I had become one of the Society's less vital internal organs.

A spleen.

A gland.

Something unspecialized as yet. Something barely aware that it served a greater metabolism, that discerned only dimly that it lived in a body at all. Something which, if you excised it and grafted it elsewhere, would survive; and not only survive, but adapt, adopting over time the structure and function of the part to which it was newly joined. (*'Saul, do the books', 'Saul, introduce our speaker', 'Saul, type a letter'.*) The outside world had been coming through to me so thoroughly digested, so strongly flavoured by the Society's guts, I was hardly aware what strange times these were.

It was Noah Hayden who woke me. We ran into each other on the street, one evening at the beginning of March.

'Saul!'

I didn't recognize him at first. An honours student at St John's, the latest in a long line of academics and political players, my old room-mate had exhibited, all the time I had known him, the careless charm and casual irony of a privileged caste. Darling of the left-wing, founder of the New Left Reading Group; wits had it that Noah Hayden put the champagne into socialism. It had never occured to me that he would turn native. Bumping into him three years later on the corner of Frith Street and Old Compton Street, confronted with his beard, cravat and velvet coat, I stepped backwards and practically fell into the road.

We went for coffee to Bar Italia – a brightly lit utilitarian café so long and narrow it was more a sort of corridor. We perched on stools beside a chrome shelf which ran the length of the room. Everything glittered: tiles, mirrors, crockery. The broiling reflections in that place were an open invitation to schizophrenia.

'So what are you doing now?' Hayden asked me.

What was I doing? His lack of self-consciousness amazed me. In that get-up – he looked like a demonic ring-master fallen on hard times – it was surely Noah who owed me the explanation.

I opened my mouth to tell him about the Society, the library – and no words came. This was the moment it dawned on me that maybe three years was a long time to spend treading water. Maybe it was too long. I made some noises eventually, using my father's condition as an excuse for my lack of news. Noah Hayden reached over and squeezed my arm in sympathy, and I felt like a shit.

At college, Hayden's inherited self-confidence had made him class-blind. He would drink himself under the table with a party of hoorays one evening, all political differences suspended for the sake of good companionship; the next day he'd be talking protest tactics with the sons of Jarrow marchers in a little diner in the Backs, stuffing his greenish, hungover jowls with cheap waffles.

I was the petty-bourgeois dullard in the corner, the one who belonged in neither camp, and I was as solemn as an owl. Though the first in the family to go to university, I could hardly pretend to be working class, what with my piano lessons and my Penguin Classics paperbacks for Christmas.

If I had kept to myself, it wouldn't have mattered; no one would have stopped me living an anonymous life. But I had discovered, dragged along to meetings by my room-mate, that politics offered a different sort of anonymity: identification with a tribe.

While student revolt gathered pace in Paris and London and Madrid, in the New Left Reading Group we contented ourselves with organizing sit-ins to protest the college curfews. The rest of the time we spent living up to our name: we read. Because I had the knack of languages, I proved useful to Noah Hayden and his precocious Group when it came to unpicking the gnomic pronouncements of Guy Debord, founder of the Situationist International in Paris. It is possible that I was Debord's first English translator. This was, for my money, a much better thing to be than what I truly was: the passive beneficiary of my parents' graft and saving; the grammar-school-educated child of parents who had had to buy their own education late in life, in church halls and schoolrooms after hours, who believed it was a right and good thing to aspire, to amass everything they could in order to invest it, all of it, in their child.

My parents believed, as no generation since has been able to believe, in the overwhelming moral power of financial generosity. Having lavished so much on me, they took my gratitude as a done deal. Their psychological incompetence was extraordinary. At the end of my first term at university my father sent me a cheque, bailing me out of a debt I'd run up at Heffers bookshop. He signed his accompanying letter, 'Yours sincerely, your Father.'

'Why's he writing "yours sincerely"?' Noah Hayden asked me, when I showed this letter to him. 'That cap "F" is very good, by the way.'

'Because I am known to him,' I replied. 'If I was not known to him he would have written "Yours faithfully".'

I had to tell someone. I had to turn it into a joke. I didn't think I could bear it otherwise. For these first, difficult months Noah Hayden was my lifeline, and he never let on that he knew.

'And what about you?'

He told me the New Left Reading Group had fallen apart not long after I dropped out, stifled by its own inertia. Hayden took his finals, but claimed not to know whether he had even got his degree. 'I'm not bloody going back there again,' he said. His scowl was extraordinary. It was ludicrous. It was pasted on – the worst sort of bad acting.

'St John's?' I said, not really understanding him. 'Cambridge?'

He waved his hand, dismissively. 'Any of that shit.'

For all the fierceness of his political rhetoric and his increasing obsession with the situationists, I had never had Hayden down for a drop-out. But how else was I to interpret his words? Or his clothes? The longer we talked, the more it seemed that Hayden had fallen out the bottom of his political convictions into some hyper-theatrical space of his own.

'Are you coming on the march?' he asked me.

There was a big demonstration planned in Grosvenor Square the next day, a Saturday, to protest the war in Vietnam.

'We'll show those Trot bastards a demo!' he exclaimed, rubbing his hands.

It was a different language he was speaking: a puerile rhetoric of cheap aggression. Vietnam was a distant blur on his radar: he was more interested in the other marchers and how misguided they were.

They weren't his own words, of course. They were something he had learned over three years of drifting and unemployment – what he called 'action'. This was a good time for Svengalis, and just as I had fallen under Hayden's spell at university, Hayden – unexpectedly daunted by the world outside St John's – had found himself someone to believe in.

The real story, such as it was, came out in asides and gestures. It was all 'Josh went to Strasbourg in sixty-six.' 'Did you read Josh's piece in *IT*?' 'Josh is planning this freak-out happening in Selfridges.' (Even his syntax had been torn down and rebuilt in his master's image.) It was all 'Josh's barmy army' and 'Josh's knit-your-own revolution'. Scathing and intimate, Noah's off-hand comments revealed his infatuation.

I don't remember much about the march itself. I only went along to meet up with Hayden, and in the press of people we somehow missed each other. From the Society's top floor, I had got not a hint of how strange the world had become. Now I was in the thick of it, trapped by the press of marchers up against a party of German students, row after row of them, running on the spot, then performing lusty squat thrusts, as though they belonged to some sort of youth movement. There were even a handful of *bona fide* clowns and jugglers. A welter of languages I'd not heard before outside the classroom dissolved, as we paraded along Oxford Street, into one long monotonous chant: 'Ho! Ho! Ho Chi Minh!'

Three men in gorilla suits and straw boaters passed me, howling in reply: 'Hot Chocolate! Drinking Chocolate!' One of them took off his head to grin at me. It was Noah Hayden. The next second, he was gone.

I don't remember much else.

I remember Grosvenor Park; the darkening of the day; the sealing of the exits.

I remember the sky filled with clods of earth, and from this I know I must have been near the embassy, right near the front of the line, because the clods were raining down on us, and they hurt.

I remember someone screaming, and the hooves of the police horses and the sound they made, that non-sound, so unthreatening, like a thousand packets of soft butter falling onto a wooden floor. A great turbulence swept through us, the whole crowd knocked off-balance, and I remember, in that crowd, it felt as though the world itself were dipping and swinging like a passenger plane hitting a pocket of dead air. I remember the crowd scattered, and a white horse reared, and I remember a man with a stick, and the stick coming down.

I remember the taste of earth, and hands under my shoulders, testing my weight. And a gorilla's head, seconds before a boot stoved it in, and another boot, scissoring, kicked it away.

I woke up on a mattress on the floor of a big, tatty room in a house I didn't know. The trees outside the window were orange, and the sky was black. It was night-time. Beside the bed there was a bedside lamp, and a scarf over the bulb, and a smell of scorched linen. I pulled the scarf away. The light lanced my eyes. I groaned and turned away, and found myself facing a door. It was ajar. Beyond the door, a chair dragged; there were footsteps.

A teenage girl with blond hair shorn close to her scalp came in and knelt down beside me. She laid her hand on me: my brow, my hand, my shoulder. Her eyes glittered oddly in the light coming from the lamp. She went out again and came back with a bowl of tinned tomato soup and a cup of tea. While I ate I heard other footsteps; a loud, laughing conversation, curtailed suddenly by the careless slam of a door. Comforted, I slept a while more.

I had a crashing headache when I woke up again, and the room was full of people. I sat up.

My shoulder was red raw: there would be a bruise the size of a plate there tomorrow. But it moved OK. I wondered who had undressed me.

'Hey there,' said the girl, noticing me from where she sat, propped up against the opposite wall. She wasn't much more than a child. The rest of them were hardly older. A boy came in with a bundle of something wrapped up in newspaper. I assumed it was chips, but I couldn't smell them.

'Where's Noah?' the boy asked, glancing round.

'Still in the Rio trying to get served, I'd guess.'

The boy knelt down and unrolled the newspaper, revealing a bundle of cannabis.

There were books propped up on the window ledge. I could tell I was coming to, because the spines began popping into focus. (Colin Wilson. John Braine. No wonder the revolution failed.)

'Hey there.'

It was easier to interrogate the books than the people. I couldn't maintain eye contact with anyone for more than a couple of seconds before their faces began to distort, as though their eyes were little gravity wells.

'Hey.'

The air was spiced suddenly; someone was holding a joint under my nose.

The girl who'd fed me soup went out and came in with a wicker sewing basket under one arm and a bundle of black fur trailing across the carpet behind her.

It was a gorilla suit.

She dropped without ceremony onto the middle of the floor and began unpicking the threads at the gorilla's sides. Without thinking, I took a drag of the joint and handed it over to her.

'How you doing?' she asked me.

'The gorilla suits.'

'That's right.'

'You're urban gorillas.'

She smiled. 'Yes.'

'I don't get it.'

'You just got it.'

'I did?'

'Yes.'

'What's to get?'

'That,' she said, nodding at the gorilla fur spread over her lap.

'The pun?'

'The deconstruction.'

'The what?'

She was really very young, maybe sixteen or so, and wanted to be taken for someone older. I thought about Noah Hayden and his extraordinary transfiguration from political player to anarchist clown.

Was everyone here playing a part?

She pushed the suit aside, crawled over and hunkered down beside me on the mattress. '"The Spectacle is a slave society's nightmare, merely expressing its wish for sleep."'

Guy Debord again: a more elegant rendering of his famous line than any I had ever come up with. 'What's your name?' I asked her.

'Deb,' she said. 'Debbie. Deborah.' She seemed unsure.

Another handful of people walked in and Debbie nudged me over, making room on the mattress. It was then, glancing at her, that I noticed, through her fuzz of blond hair, that her skull had a perfect dent in it, the size of a half-crown. Her brutal hairstyle suddenly took on a new and disturbing meaning for me. What if it wasn't some sort of statement? What if it were something to do with that frightening dent?

About an hour later, Noah came in. He was still in full Jerry Cornelius get-up. Debbie got up and went over to him and kissed him on the mouth. Noah had a black eye and news from Vine Street, where two of their number were spending a night in the cells. 'You know Josh is still bound over?'

'Fuck.'

'That's right.'

'Josh is *fucked*.'

News of Josh's fuckedness rattled around the room like a bean in a can. Underneath their anger, people seemed secretly delighted, as though, of all of them, Josh had made it to the next round.

'Yeah, but what about Saul?' said Noah, when the commotion died down. 'Saul took on a horse.' He gestured broadly, conjuring a beast of great size, and his arms, emerging from the capacious flared cuffs of his Paisley shirt, were as white and shapeless as roots. 'He pulled a pig from his horse.'

'No, I didn't.'

'The nasty fucker had his truncheon drawn. Saul ran straight up to him.'

'No, I didn't.'

'Saul is our hero.'

The whole room cheered me. A fresh joint slipped itself between my fingers; a box of matches.

It was a good-natured joke. They were making me feel welcome. I managed a grin. A tin of beer found its way to me.

When people went off to bed, it was all at once, as though someone had blown a secret whistle. The joint was back with me again; I stubbed it out on the nearest ashtray: Guinnless isn't good for you. Noah and the girl remained in the room. It was their room. They were sleeping in the bed, opposite mine.

'Place is stuffed to the gills tonight,' Debbie explained.

'You OK there?' said Noah.

'Yes,' I said. 'If you're sure—'

'OK, then,' he said, cutting me off. 'Good. Good to have you here.' He hunkered down and gave me a hug. His hair was long and unkempt, but it smelled sweet. Before I could figure out whether to hug him back he was halfway to the light switch.

I had never been hugged by a man before.

I lay back in the dark and listened to them undress.

I woke the next day with an even more painful headache to find the house was already virtually empty. After much stumbling around I found the kitchen. Noah was in there eating toast. 'How're you doing?' he greeted me.

'Where the fuck am I?'

Noah and his friends had manhandled my bloody, semi-conscious form onto a number twelve bus, bearing me like a trophy all the way to Holland Park.

'Great,' I said. 'Thanks.' Now all I had to do was work out where Holland Park was.

'If you've a shilling for the meter I've got eggs for an omelette.'

I fished about in my pockets and came up with a coin.

He took it and pointed to the chair next to me.

'Try that on.'

Lying on the chair was a ball of black fun-fur – a gorilla costume.

'What's this for?'

'Try it on for size. We're going gardening.'

'We're what?'

'Gardening.'

'Where?'

'A garden.'

'What?'

'Parsley? In your omelette. Cheese?'

'OK,' I said.

I liked the Society. I liked its location, five minutes from the British Museum and its eclectic, down-at-heel satellites – a comic shop, a science fiction bookshop, several showrooms of Middle Eastern antiques, a dealer in defunct stringed instruments. To the east, Senate House resembled nothing so much as an outsize version of those Victorian obelisks you find in cemeteries. I liked the regularity of the architecture, the neat terraces, the sober bulk of the institutional buildings, the absence of bustle. Never did I imagine that I would one day be wandering these streets armed with a pair of bolt cutters, let alone a gorilla costume strapped across an old duffel bag stuffed with balloons.

The gardens of some of the smaller squares here were privately owned. Just over the road in King's Cross there were whole housing estates with nowhere for kids to play. Josh, our leader *in absentia* – he was serving a month in Brixton – had a lively idea of what redistribution ought really to be about. The idea – fleshed out and agreed upon well before the VSC march and Josh's arrest – involved bolt-cutters, balloons, a van full of sand and a great deal of sweat.

Noah drove the van; the rest of us had to cart our gear to Tavistock Square on the Underground. This was risky – people were starting to hear about Josh's 'urban gorillas', and were cottoning on – but we arrived at the square with no one following, no whistles blown, untroubled, as yet, by what Josh liked to call, in his understated way, 'uniformed support'.

They expected me to use the bolt-cutters on the gate.

'We could just climb over,' I protested.

'We could, stupid,' said Noah, 'but what about the kids? You expect mums with pushchairs to scale the bloody fence?'

Josh's plan gave us twenty minutes to turn a private ornamental garden into a public play area before the pigs turned up. Frantically, we dug and dug, while another of our number, a dwarvish girl with pigtails and a cut-glass Rodean accent called Nova (a corruption of Veronica), tied balloons to the busted-in gate, the oh-so-private trees, and nearby lampposts. Noah plucked the Do Not signs out of the lawns and beds and ran off with them hidden in a carrier-bag.

When the hole for the sandpit was ready, we laid a scrap of tarpaulin down as a crude liner and ran to the van to fetch the sand. The efficiency of the operation surprised and impressed me, and I could barely lift the sacks Noah carted about so nonchalantly on his shoulder. By the time the sand-pit was half full, the girls were into their gorilla costumes, and little kids who were passing, snared by the sight of balloons, were dragging their mothers over to see what was up.

Nova shouted for help with the swing we'd planned to sling over the park's one serviceable tree-branch. 'I wish Debbie was here,' she said, when we were done. 'She'd love this.'

'Where is she, anyway?'

Nova shrugged. 'Gone.'

'Gone?'

'She and Noah – it's kind of stormy.'

I thought of Debbie, her glittery eyes and damaged head. I thought of her feeding me soup, and the way she had scrambled up to hug Noah when he came in the room, and Noah, in his loud shirt and threadbare velvet jacket, bending down to kiss this child on the mouth. The two of them undressing in the dark. 'She's very young,' I said.

Nova thought I was being critical. 'Hey, you, she's, like, dead sound,' she scowled.

I didn't even know what this meant.

'Where's your head?'

'What?'

'Put your head on.'

'What? Oh.'

Kids were streaming into our freshly liberated park; kids from the Brunswick estate; kids from the expensive terraces round Coram's Fields; kids out shopping with their mothers; latch-key kids, their fingers black with engine oil.

I put on my gorilla head.

'Come play with the kids. Come on. The uniformed support'll be here in a minute.' She let out a couple of comedy pig grunts and ran cheerfully ahead of me to welcome the children.

I handed in my notice at the Society and served out my week as conscientiously as I was able. Then I went to live at Josh's squat in Holland Park.

The house was an anomalous survivor of clearances for the new Westway. The terrace it belonged to had been bulldozed away long since, and the Edwardian building, its weak side-wall supported on a timber frame like a man on crutches, stood in a complicated geographical relationship with the feedlanes and towers of the half-built motorway.

Josh and his friends occupied all but the basement. That remained inviolate: the lair of Mr Sadberk, formerly of Istanbul, the autocratic ruler of his little kingdom. He did not own the house, and he had no special relationship with the company that did, but he was as territorial as any other imprisoned beast, and his intermittent rages, his savage bangs and kicks upon the front door, his haranguing us from the pavement whenever he caught a glimpse of a sign of life, these things kicked up clouds of anxiety in the house, like dust, a pain between the eyes.

For as long as the moonscape beyond the front door promised the advent of something futuristic and exciting, Josh and his band rode easily above the locals' occasional hostility; but it was, after all, only a road, rising to block out the light, and, as work progressed, the mundanity of the future it represented began to bite. The scene Josh knew was moving inexorably East. The *International Times* was put together in Covent Garden now; *Oz* came to replace it, to be a voice for the area, and although many of us wrote for it, it seemed weak by comparison. Experiments in community learning and action foundered on the apathy of the straights. Mr Sadberk continued to live up to the weak jokes we made of his name.

In a big unheated front room cleared of furniture, piled with cushions, we overstated these problems to each other, warming ourselves on the idea of embattlement. We were young and frightened. Rather than occupy the future, we preferred to enshrine the past, and hanker for the good old days of last year, last month, last week. Each one of Josh's friends told me, at one time or another, that I should have moved in earlier; that it was a shame that I had missed this happening, that march; that had I moved in *then*, or *then*, then I would truly know what Josh was all about.

Even in 1968, the sixties was a time we looked back on dreamily: the Past.

Debbie was back with Noah by the time I moved in to the squat. Then she vanished again. Then she was back. I asked Noah where she went when she disappeared. He just shrugged.

'You must have some idea.'

'She's a free agent,' Noah replied.

Everyone here seemed very keen on defending Debbie's freedoms. I wondered if anyone had ever thought to defend Debbie. Noah and Debbie's 'stormy' relationship seemed to consist of Noah not giving a shit and Debbie walking out on him – only to return, three or four days later, invariably famished, and with eyes that were even more glittery than normal. The next day they spent in bed – never a sound from the room, though, not the remotest sigh or stir. After that the whole cycle would repeat.

'What happened to her head?'

'Why don't you ask her?'

'She isn't here.'

'She'll be back.'

'Until she isn't.'

Hayden held my look. 'Meaning what?'

'Where does she go, Noah?'

'How should I know?'

'Where does she go once you've fucked her off?'

Christmas 1968, and in Selfridges department store, eight unsanctioned Santas are working the queue for the grotto, handing out presents, spreading good cheer, and all for free. The parents – Kensington mothers in the main – stand by, nonplussed. They know something is off, but they can't pin it down. The event's not falling into any category. And of course, the kids are enjoying themselves.

From shelves and from boxes, from tissue-wrapping and brown paper: free Christmas gifts for everyone. Dolls, cars and fluffy toys. Bears, tanks, footballs, packets of transfers. Model aeroplanes. Angel costumes. Glitter. We sweat up a storm in our rented Santa outfits: everything must go. A crowd is gathering. Some sort of psychic force is drawing in kids from all over the store, from every floor, tugging reluctant mums and dads into the toy department.

Ladybird and Palitoy, Pedigree and Galt and Waddingtons, everything must go. Meccano, whose mind is pure machinery! Monopoly, whose blood is running money! Action Man, whose fingers are ten armies! Sindy, whose breast is a cannibal dynamo!

'Ho! Ho! Ho!' the Santas cry. 'Ho! Ho! Ho Chi Minh!'

How long have we got? Not long. The pigs are on their way, they must be by now, surely, and what began as children's theatre acquires an air of adult desperation: 'Take it! Take it!'

Blindly we thrust free stuff at whoever will accept it. Mistakes are made. A six-year-old girl brandishes a Roy Rogers pistol thoughtfully in front of her parents. Two boys, brothers in the misery of corduroy, wrestle blindly for possession of a My First Make-Up Kit.

'Take it! Merry Christmas!'

'Do you work here?'

'Take it! Here!'

'Excuse me...'

'Merry Christmas!'

Now that the shop's security staff are bundling in, the kids are not so certain about this giveaway. They are not so eager for the gifts we press into their hands. Parental eyes are narrowing. In prams and pushchairs the youngest children sense a change in the air and fear – without a thing to fear, and in the midst of plenty – rips through everyone.

A baby starts to cry. Then another, then another: gentlemen, our work here is done.

So back to Notting Hill, a quick drink in the Rio and out the back, our grass done up in newspaper like chips.

'What happened to your head?'

Drink has made me forward with my questions. Besides, we are alone in her room. Noah has gone out to stuff his face with toast again; everybody else has gone to bed.

Debbie passes me the joint and touches the side of her head, where the dent is. 'When I was a kid,' she says, 'I was in an accident.'

'What sort of accident?'

'A car accident.'

She is lying.

'What do your parents think of you being here?'

She looks at me, incredulous. 'What have they got to do with anything?'

'It's just a question. It's not like I'm saying you're not a free agent or anything.' (Clumsily, I am adopting the tortured rhetoric of this place.)

'Anyway,' she says, 'Mum's dead.'

'What about Dad?' I say, straight off, refusing to be sidelined by this invitation to pity.

She shakes her head.

'What about him?'

She stands up, running her fingers through her close-cropped hair. 'You know, Saul, you're really doing my head in.'

An unfortunate turn of phrase. I am gripped by sudden inspiration: 'Did he do that?'

'What?'

'Your head. Did your dad – *hit* you or something?'

'For Christ's sake!' Her yell is so loud it brings Noah in from the kitchen. '*Of course not*, you stupid bastard.'

All that night I lay awake in the next-door room, listening to Noah and Debbie argue their way up to their next bust-up. Debbie was furious with me and wanted me thrown out of the squat for being 'an arsehole'. Noah defended me.

I listened as the row built and built. When I couldn't bear it any more, I got dressed.

When the argument finally boiled dry, this is what it reduced to: her or me. Either I went, or she went.

Noah, more exhausted than angry, told her to fuck off, then.

I stood there, forehead pressed to my bedroom door, listening while Debbie got dressed. I heard her leave the room she shared with Noah.

She was crying. I heard her clatter down the hall. The front door opened, and slammed shut again.

I grabbed my jacket and went after her.

We put ourselves on the housing list, Debbie faked a doctor's letter, and we moved out of the squat and got the keys to a big, cold flat in a council block not far from the canal above King's Cross.

Hayden insisted on helping us move in, turning up at half-past seven in the morning in a brand-new white rental van which bore the unnerving legend 'Impact Hire'. He had been up all night scavenging from skips. 'You can make bookshelves with these bricks I nicked.'

'Thanks, Noah.'

Because we were so much taller than she was, Hayden and I stayed out on the road while Debbie lowered things down to us from the back of the van. One moment it was, 'Come on, let me have it! Let go!' The next it was, 'Debbie, love, can you not just drop things? Jesus.'

Then Hayden had to leave and Debbie helped me carry my gear up the communal stairwell and into the flat. She insisted on lifting heavy weights and kept having to set things down on the stairs so I couldn't get past. There was a passive-aggressive quality about Debbie's helpfulness that had me guessing about her motives. 'Debbie, stop – my hand is pinned. Deborah!'

We lived together for about three months. We rubbed along pretty well. We washed up. We cooked. We rowed. We scoured skips for more second-hand furniture. We shared the bathwater and the bed. We were as intimate as it is possible to get without actually having any sex.

Her lack of enthusiasm took me by surprise. I thought at first she just needed time. But the longer we spent together, the more remote the possibility seemed. I was disappointed, but I was also relieved. She was very young.

We hugged and kissed. But the slightest suggestion of sexual interest, intended or not, had her turning away from me and the tremor of her tightly wound body would keep me awake for hours; it was like lying beside an unexploded bomb.

She wanted, none the less, to be part of my life. Her insistence was so great she eventually wore me down enough that I took her by train to Rowland's Castle to meet my parents.

Mum expressed her excitement at the prospect of meeting Debbie in a way uniquely hers, by making a chore of everything. 'What does she eat?' she asked me when I made my weekly phone call.

'Grass, mother. She eats grass.'

'I can defrost a chicken pie.'

'Congratulations.'

'Oh, but it's very small.'

Hours and hours of this.

'How will you get from the station?'

'We'll walk.'

'If you get a taxi I can give you the money.'

'You don't have to give me any money, Mum, I've got money.'

'Oh, but there are never any taxis there!'

'No. That's true.'

'What will you do?'

'We'll walk.'

'You can't walk.'

'Then we'll crawl.'

'She won't want to walk all that way.'

'Then I shall bear her through the burning stubble fields on my back like Anchises.' I was twenty-five years old, and still I was punishing her for my grammar-school education.

Dad was sleeping in the garden when we arrived. Hi, said Debbie, walking up to him. He straightened himself in his deckchair. Debbie was so little, her tits were about level with his face. 'Unh,' he said, greeting them.

Debbie and my mother circled round each other all afternoon. It was impossible to imagine they had anything in common: Debbie, all kohl

143

and bangles and barrow-boy haircut; Mum in her slacks. Debbie was by far the more nervous of the two. She had everything an iconoclast needs except for imagination; this is what I supplied. Every few minutes I heard one of my own sardonic *bon mots* spill, lumpen, from her uncomprehending mouth.

Mum, non plussed, chuntered happily on, partly to herself, partly to me, partly to a young lady of her own invention. As the day wore on she grew more confident. She squeezed Debbie into the mould she had dreamed up in the days prior to our visit. Debbie could no more resist the cascade of my mother's logic than a terminal patient can resist the blandishments of an aggressive oncologist, and by two that afternoon, there was Mum snapping away merrily with her Instamatic camera, and there was Debbie, tottering about the garden in one of Mum's old summer frocks.

'Saul, get in the picture!'

Mum sent me one of these photographs a couple of weeks later. Debbie is standing in our back garden wearing a sleeveless summer dress smothered with brown and yellow flowers. She is trying to show willing and flounce for the camera; as a consequence, one of her legs looks shorter than the other. She is looking down and away, hiving herself off from the world. Sealing herself up. You imagine her staggering away from a car accident. Debbie's combination of shorn hair and this old John Lewis summer dress, at least two sizes too big, makes her look even more like a doll hurled out of a pram.

It amused me, that afternoon, to see Mum's quiet egomania carrying the field. On the train back to London, I fed Debbie the story she needed: how kind and patient she had been, and what a good sport. 'Those bloody dresses!'

Debbie had been made to choose one for herself as a present. As we rattled through Godalming, alone in the second-class carriage, she fished it out of its polythene bag: Mum's gift.

'Jesus,' I said.

Debbie laughed, and spread it out on her lap for me to see.

I covered my eyes. 'Take this abomination away.'

'If I slip it on,' she said, 'will you kiss me?'

With an Oedipal howl, I tore the dress out of her hands, pulled open the window and stuffed the dress through.

And that was the end of that: one more moderately disheartening return to the place of my birth. I remember Debbie looking out of the window, as the orange suburbs of London coagulated around us: Croydon to Clapham, Wandsworth to Waterloo. The flatness of her mood. The empty polythene bag, scrunched up in her hands.

Afterwards, whenever the subject came up, she would talk about our 'ghastly' visit. That 'ghastly' day we had. 'Ooh, do you remember that ghastly dress!' But whatever she might say afterwards, whatever she might tell herself, my taking her home with me that day had represented something. All she had to show for meeting my parents was that dress; and I had thrown it away.

It seems so obvious, this long after the event, the damage I was doing to her. I was leading her on. I was making it possible for her to believe in this calamitous idea she had of herself since moving to the squat in Holland Park: Debbie the contrarian, the under-age radical; Debbie the teenage iconoclast.

She was none of these things. She was, like most children, hungry for life, full of energy, desperate for validation.

'What about your dad?' I was still trying to unpick this – still trying to solve the twin mysteries of her injury and aloneness.

'What about him?'

'What's he like?'

It wasn't his cruelty she had run away from. It was his care. 'He thinks he could have stopped the accident,' she told me, in bed one night. 'He thinks he should have prevented it. He's always trying to make it up to me. The accident – I was eight years old when it happened. Ever since he's been... surrounding me.'

The image of herself she had conjured – a child running away from her father's terrible need – should have been enough for me. I had never been as honest about myself. But like a fool, I took this as my cue to ask her again about the accident.

'Leave me alone,' she said.

She liked the idea of independence. For her, solitude and freedom were the same thing. This made for a frustrating sort of companionship. All I could do was inflate her self-confidence or tear it to rags in front of her eyes. Either, or. There was no middle ground with her. Those who were not with her were against her.

It was astonishing the degree to which even the brute stuff of the domestic world resisted her. The vacuum cleaner didn't need emptying so often, she said; eventually it burst into flames on her. You just need a dash of water in this, she said, preparing the pressure cooker; it took a whole day for the smell of burnt beans to clear.

She was one of those people who never follows a recipe and claims to be able to do things with vegetables and pasta. She made us a cauliflower cheese once, only she reached into the wrong cupboard and ended up using laundry starch instead of cornflour. 'It's the same stuff,' she said, swilling the paste from her teeth. She was sick the next morning, and every morning for a week after that.

She took her push-bike to a shop to have new brakes fitted. When she got home she told me the shop had adjusted them all wrong. She spent the rest of the day tinkering with them, and every so often she would start crying: strange little yelping sounds like a puppy caught in a trap. The next day she rode her bike slap into the back of a number twelve bus.

When I phoned him, Debbie's father thought I was a private detective. He had paid two separate agencies to track down his runaway daughter. He thanked me for calling. When he turned up at the hospital, knowing who I was, the atmosphere was different. He seemed as afraid of me as I was of him; seeing the size of his hands, I was heartily thankful.

Debbie's fits were under control by then: one grand mal seizure every twenty-four hours or so. No one could explain why her messy but hardly life-threatening accident with the bus should have triggered epileptic seizures. I wasn't family.

Then, of course, what with one test and another, they found out she was pregnant. Harold wanted his daughter to have an abortion. One of the few things he actually said to me, that he made very clear, standing with his face just a couple of inches from mine, the air between us thick with his Old Spice aftershave, was how much he wanted his daughter to have an abortion. This had nothing to do with me. But since trying to convince him of this would have been an impossible task, I didn't even try. And when Debbie insisted on keeping the child, I steeled myself for a disappearing act of my own. One of the things that had kept me going throughout my miserable three-month charade with Debbie was the thought that Noah Hayden hadn't got to fuck her either. Discovering otherwise was galling enough; there was no way anyone was going to strong-arm me into fathering his bloody kid.

Nothing happened. No one phoned. No one beat at the door. When I visited the hospital a couple of days later, Debbie was gone. Her father had collected her and driven her away.

There was something fairy-tale about Debbie's abrupt disappearance – her clothes and few belongings abandoned in the flat we had shared. (My flat, I would have to learn to say.) She had broken through into the outside world only to be spirited away again. It was as though she had never existed.

I rang up Miriam at the Society, and I went back to work.

3

'My mother was a passionate believer in education. After my father died, she said to me, "You must learn the white man's magic!"'

General laughter.

That's right. Keep it light. Remember: last week this same audience of well-intentioned whites was over at the Africa Centre in Covent Garden, learning how to make traditional costumes with Sally Mugabe.

White man's magic!

White man's 'lore', he might have said. White man's 'skill'. White man's 'culture'. But he has learned, when addressing Western audiences, not to be too po-faced. When he tells the tale they want him to tell – 'When I was but a simple goatherd, my mammy said to me' – he uses the word 'magic', even if it does make it sound like he crawled out from under a mushroom.

It is Tuesday, 4 March 1969, and in the library of a distinguished philosophical society in a leafy offshoot of Gower Street in central London, Jorge Katalayo, president of FRELIMO, is speaking about Mozambique, the country of his birth, about the revolution he is fomenting there, and about the serious threat that he and his comrades – educated revolutionaries – pose to their own cause.

Under colonialism, he says, bureaucracy is the only career open to the educated black man. Paper-shuffling is the only thing at which he is permitted to excel.

(He has a complex, assymetrical face, kept this side of ugliness by its smile. He is wearing a cheap, neat polyester suit. He looks, ironically enough, like a bureaucrat.)

'When the Europeans have gone, we lift it as a shibboleth: this power, not even of the pen, so much as of the carbon copy. This is why we so often find ourselves – to our consternation, yes, but also to our considerable personal profit – colonial rulers in our own land.'

Even at the back of the room, by a draughty window where his every other word is snatched away by the street, Jorge Katalayo's oratory prickles the back of my neck.

When, on my return to work, I discovered that the Society had developed a curiosity about the politics of anticolonialism, I was pleasantly surprised; no more. The Society was insatiable, and it had the stomach of an ox. It had long since learned how to cram down every crumb of novelty, lick every smear of fat from off the New and, furthermore, how to render this stuff, however intractable – the Black Panther movement, *Nova* magazine, Free Love – into a rich and easy stew on which even its most elderly members might feed.

Mornings, I shuffled paper in the Society's library or typed up little articles for its stream of newsletters. Afternoons, I yawned my way around the arrivals hall of Heathrow airport, holding one sign or another to my chest: Lewis Nkosi; Dennis Brutus.

I was the Society's runner and factotum. I showed our guests the sights of the city. I took them to cafés and paid for their tea with petty cash. I reminded them of their schedules. I got them to the meeting room on time.

Invariably, as we climbed the smart white steps up to the front door, our speaker would pause before that discreet brass plaque, and frown. How the Society managed to attract its speakers mystified me. Not one of them, entering the magnolia-painted hallway, seemed happy to be here. What had they been promised? They followed me up the stairs to the meeting rooms, speechless and staring, as though waking from a spell.

Joshua Nkomo; Agostinho Neto; the ANC leader Oliver Tambo. Holden Roberto cancelled at the last minute. A bout of the flu meant I missed Benedicto Kiwanuka. (Years later, Idi Amin would have him killed for not finding the right people guilty.) Amilcar Cabral, the leader of Guinea-Bissau, spoke so softly that I could not hear him from my place at the back of the room.

Would-be presidents and statesmen-in-exile in sober Methodist ties, the Society's speakers were demonstrably adult in a way Josh and his followers were not.

Katalayo tells his audience that when he was twenty-five, and barely out of elementary school, Swedish missionaries arranged a scholarship, plucking the frustrated student from his obscure province and depositing him in the Douglas Laing Smith Secondary School in Lemana, northern Transvaal. It was here that Katalayo came across a book larger and more impressive than any book he had ever seen before, other than the Bible. It was so big, it came in two volumes – 'A to K' and 'L to Z'.

'I remember learning to read English from this book.'

The English language, from a dictionary of philosophy. Was this possible?

Anarchists are not supposed to be interested in politics. These deadly serious Africans and their wars appalled my Holland Park friends. What possible revolution in human relations could mere politicians bring about, with their antediluvian baggage of ideologies and inter-changeable figureheads? In vain, Josh, Holland Park's *eminence gris*, dispatched Noah to guide me back to the path of righteousness: 'What are our actions, our trespasses, our performances, our carefully staged "situations", if not attacks upon the dialectic between property and privacy, that narcotizing dialectic from which the State itself emerges?' These were the kind of rhetorical sticks he beat me with.

Noah and I both knew time was passing, that dressing up in Santa costumes and causing havoc in Selfridges' toy department would accomplish nothing, that the squat was slowly but steadily falling apart.

Seeing it was hopeless, Noah admitted to me that my shacking up with Deborah had sent a number of long-running residents scurrying to the bathroom mirror for a long, hard look at themselves.

When I asked him why he remained, Noah's windy lecture deflated like a wet bag. 'Change is hard,' he said. 'So we go out in scary clown costumes and we sow a little bit of unease – so what? It just makes the straights even more grateful for their old comforts.'

He was finding a way out of the squat's rhetoric. The buzzwords were still in place but the old debating society grammar was knitting itself round them like a vine. It was good to hear Noah sounding like himself again. At the same time, I knew that our friendship could never be what it was. He had been too much someone else's eager fetcher-and-carrier. I could not look up to him any more and, without that, I couldn't see that there was much else left. Deborah had begged me not to tell Hayden about his baby, and I didn't find it hard to grant her plea. I was only doing the right thing; her wishes had to come first.

Later, of course – too late – even I could see the real motive behind my silence. I had been given a certain power over Noah Hayden, and this enabled me to release myself from his influence. So I deliberately let him down.

Red with embarrassment, Noah Hayden confessed that he was in the process of smartening himself up. Once he had paid off his library fines, the authorities at St John's would be more than happy to hand him his forgotten first-class degree. After that, there was an opening for him in public service. His family had probably had a hand in this, but I reckon he was bright enough to fulfil whatever promises had been made on his behalf. I wished him luck with his mission.

'What?'

'Your secret project to change the system from within,' I explained, with a smile.

Hayden bridled. 'And what about you?' he said. He thought I was being sarcastic. This was a shame; given his talents and background,

Hayden's course of action seemed eminently sound to me. 'Back to that ridiculous drop-in centre, I suppose?'

'That's not fair,' I said.

'Why can't you go to work for somebody sensible, for Christ's sake?'

How was I supposed to answer?

'I mean,' said Hayden, waving his hands about in exasperation, 'what does your outfit actually *do*?'

In order to fund its latest hobby horse – *Africa: a Way Forward?* – the Society had embarked on an operation to 'realize its assets'. This was Miriam's important description for the jumble sales she ran, every month or so, in the building's basement. A small, forbidding sign tied to the railing the week before ('Bring Your Own Bag') was her sole advertisement, but she need hardly have bothered. The same dowdy regulars attended these sales as religiously as they attended the Society's talks, seminars and 'tape/slide presentations'.

The first jumbles were ambitious ('Sale & Auction' the sign announced). There was an old Underwood typewriter. A couple of card-index cabinets from the library – fine examples of the sort of eccentric, looks-useful-but-isn't cabinet-work that these days crawls away to Portobello Market to die. A kilim with a pale-brown stain on it – dried blood? An adjustable couch with brass handles and a smell of horse hair under the perished leather – less like a seat, more like a deluxe operating table.

By the second sale, we were reduced to recycling our waste paper. At the absurdly inflated prices Maureen wanted to charge, the Society's past publications were slow to shift, even among the regulars. There were boxes of old programmes: Dr J. R. Rees lectures on the work of Ugo Cerletti and Lucio Bini for the Drill Hall Open Programme on Mental Infirmity and the Arts. Sir Richard Gregory speaks on 'Science and World Order'. There were little pamphlets on the semantics of Korzybski, the poetry of Mayakovsky, the paintings of Kazemir

Malevich. There was a box, never opened, sealed with tape so brittle it crackled to pieces when you tried to pull it, which turned out to contain mint copies of a wartime spiritualist self-help book called *You Can Speak With Your Dead*.

Miriam's third sale was advertised with a justified baldness: 'Clearance'. The first box I unpacked promised much: a set of padded leather straps and a rubber gat carrying unmistakable bite marks. This was a dimension of the Society's business I had not suspected: I imagined Kinseyite sexual experimentations.

The second box contained framed photographs of a European city between the wars. Looking closer, I saw the shop signs were spelled out in a language I did not recognize: not Vienna, then, as I had at first thought, but a place long since swallowed up into Soviet anonymity.

These were the highlights of the sale; the rest amounted to no more than some bizarre bric-à-brac: a leather hat box; a foot-long stuffed alligator; an able seaman's uniform.

The rest of my time I spent watching as modern Africa invented itself, scribbling itself out on paper napkins in cafeterias all over London. I remember sitting in a greasy spoon on Gray's Inn Road, among squeezy ketchup bottles and mugs of half-drunk orange tea, with Tariq Ali and Vanessa Redgrave. With Joseph Nyrere. Kenneth Kaunda getting drunk with Margaret Feeny in a guest-house kitchen in Gower Street. It sounds strange to recall now, I know. The libretto of a comic opera by Doris Lessing. The future of a free Africa, drawn up on a napkin. These good men, with their fragile dreams: all the ironies of their educated, depatriated condition.

And there, in the corner, trading literary recommendations with Sally's husband Robert, a bald little man in a grey suit – the Soviet negotiant.

You had to admire the man's bulldog determination, the weeks and months he spent making friendly overtures and warm promises to the

153

future masters of Mozambique. But Jorge Katalayo and the FRELIMO council had agreed upon a trenchant policy of non-alignment. This policy, put into action in the cafés of east London, gave Katalayo ample opportunities for mischief. Witness the conversation he started, the day following a party at the Chinese embassy.

'Weren't you invited?'

'No,' replies the Soviet purseholder, sulking already.

'The Chinese ambassador congratulated FRELIMO on its self-reliant approach.'

Guarded: 'Yes?'

'He praised our belief in the people's capacity for autonomous change.'

Big eyes now: 'Really?'

Katalayo smiles his trademark smile.

Sweating now: have his paymasters been gazumped? 'What did you tell him?'

'I told him where to stick it. Much as I keep telling you.'

We laughed.

No one took him seriously.

Miriam's sales had by now taken on a life of their own. No room was spared, no cupboard, no shelf. The atmosphere – the desire to shrive – achieved a Lutheran intensity. Chandeliers vanished from under dusty ceiling roses. The cork message board disappeared from the entrance hall, leaving a bright magnolia square on the tobacco-stained wall. At last, Miriam's Lenten ritual drew near to the Society's holy-of-holies – its library.

Towards the end of every afternoon, Miriam and a couple of elderly regulars combed the shelves of the library for volumes to discard. They were like people eating mussels, who start by picking out the choicest shells and end up consuming the lot. The philosophy behind the Society was itself so smudged by the passage of years that even these old hands had trouble deciding which volumes were necessary to the collection and which were not. If *Winged Love* and *Wellington Wendy* had no place here, what case was there for retaining an incomplete set of John Lehmann's *New Writing*? What did the poetry of Keith Douglas have that the short stories of James Hanley did not? If illustrated catalogues of Henry Moore deserved shelf space, who was Graham Sutherland that he should be excluded? And what kind of philosophical society was it that gave shelf space to Arthur Koestler, while expelling J. B. Priestley and J. D. Arven?

I stopped what I was doing. I took the volumes out of the box again and laid them side by side on the table.

'A to K' and 'L to Z'.

A dictionary of philosophy, in two parts.

By then, Jorge Katalayo had left London for Tanzania. He had given me a forwarding address. I wrote to him on the flyleaf of the first volume: 'You actually learned English from this tosh?'

I posted the dictionary off the same day, and forgot all about it.

Jorge Chivambo Katalayo: former goatherd, former UN researcher, freedom fighter, doctor of anthropology. I never saw him again.

My abiding memory is of the afternoon before his speech at the Women's Institute. We spent it in a greasy spoon on the Roman Road, cramming doughnuts into our faces, hoping that the sugar might substitute for inspiration.

'Before we do anything,' Jorge declaims, 'we have to get our own people working with us.' Ring, jam, chocolate icing: it's all one to him. 'Fragmentation is our biggest problem,' he says. 'At the moment, one village barely knows another.'

I say to him, 'Your audience won't understand that. That won't mean anything to them. How can neighbours not be aware of each other? Roads are like trees to us. Like grass. The idea you have to build a road before you know what's at the end of it – it's not in the Home Counties vocabulary.'

'Home Counties?'

'I mean it won't play to the women of the W.I.'

He makes a note.

'We cannot begin to build' – he tries again – 'while our men and women live in hate and fear of each other.'

'Meaning what?'

'Meaning, on any ordinary day under the Portuguese system, two cattle trucks might pull up in the middle of a work village – an *aldeamento*. The men are told to board one truck, the women are told board the other. The men are driven off to work the fields. The women are going to mend the roads. These men and women, from the same village, married, some of them, sweethearts, brother and sister – they may never see each other again. It's not a deliberate policy, exactly. It's just the soldiers lose track of where they've been. It's a big country. Everybody looks alike. The soldiers don't speak Chichewa and the authorities have made damned certain the locals don't learn Portuguese. So the soldiers can't keep track. In the evening, they drive you to the nearest *aldeamento* and dump you there. Where's your wife? Where's your girlfriend? No one knows. No one cares.'

He looks at me.

'Well?'

I nod.

'What does that mean?'

'Yes.'

He lifts his gaze to the ceiling. 'Help me with this, Saul.'

'I just don't think they're going to believe you,' I tell him. 'They grew up with Kipling. They think law and order is a European invention. Whatever else the Portuguese visited on the black man, they've surely been making the trains run on time.'

Sometimes, when Jorge Katalayo is out of inspiration, when he has drunk too much coffee, and eaten too much sugar, and especially when he is nervous, all you can do is make him angry; see if a spark will catch.

He shouts at me: 'You think we have some sort of enlightened master–servant bond? Mozambique isn't the Raj. Even the Raj wasn't the Raj, but let that go...'

He has an idea: 'In the forties there were only about three thousand whites in Mozambique. Now there's two hundred thousand of these idiots dragging their knuckles across our country, thinking they're better than we are because of the colour of their skin. Which, I might add, is like diarrhoea.'

'Jesus, don't say that.'

'The point is, the junta's bankrupted a generation and robbed them of an education. If it leaves them at home, they will topple the government. So it exports them. It sends them to lord it over us.'

He drains his coffee. He looks pleased.

'I thought this speech was supposed to be about the role of women?'

He shoots me a sour look. Silence while he sluices the dregs of his coffee round his cup. 'Better the devil you know, I suppose,' he sighs. 'When my father died, my mother said to me—'

'That's not about women. That's about you.'

I have pushed him about as far as he will be pushed. 'No,' he says, 'it isn't. Listen. Our educated men do not know what women are. They barely know their own mothers. Like me, they had to leave home to go to school – and I really mean leave, journeying for miles, departing for other countries even, just to get some schooling.'

'Meaning what? For the women?'

Katalayo holds my gaze. In a soft voice: 'Meaning we hate them.'

'God, you're not going to say that, are you? They'll tear out your liver with their teeth. Those that still have them.'

'Why shouldn't I say it? It's true. We hate our women. We blame them. They are our scapegoat. They represent what we would have become, had we not got away. Do you know I have a girlfriend, Saul? A white American girlfriend? Why do you think I have a white American girlfriend, Saul? I know. She knows. We're not stupid. We know what this is.'

'So do I – and it's still about you.'

'For the ones who don't get away,' he goes on, ignoring my interruption, 'what of them? What's the point of falling in love, in trying to start a family, in making any real human connection across the sexual divide, if any given day the trucks can pull up and make your mother, your wife, your daughter, disappear? It's the same for the women, too. Men and women are learning to have nothing to do with each other. We are being taught this. Our children are growing up with this. This is what slavery does. This is what slavery is.'

Finally, we are getting somewhere.

It is not the greatest speech of his career, but from the back of the meeting hall I can feel the audience responding to him.

'The future of our country rests with its women,' he says. The girls of Lourenço Marques, for instance. They have a reputation that runs up and down the entire eastern seaboard of the continent. Now, though, they are running away. Every day, another woman flees into the liberated provinces, through minefields, every once in a while a pretty foot blown off at the ankle. 'We're building them their own barracks,' he says. 'We're putting them to work in the fields. We are teaching them to read.'

I am so proud of him.

The day after his speech at the W.I., very early in the morning, Jorge Katalayo hammers on the door of this little flat I have got for myself over a chip shop near Regent's Canal.

He says the walls of his guest-house in Bloomsbury are so thin you can hear everything that goes on in the neighbouring rooms, every whisper, the sweet and the not-so-sweet, every tear of foil, every condom snap. 'I just need a sit-down,' he says, having walked all the way through Fitzrovia, past King's Cross. 'Can I have a cup of tea?'

I know there is more to this visit than meets the eye, and when he mentions the letter he has received from FRELIMO's Paris office, I figure this is it. Katalayo hands me the letter over the crumb-littered breakfast table. I am teaching myself Portuguese. I have a knack for languages.

Portuguese soldiers have ransacked a mission near Beira which they suspected of harbouring FRELIMO soldiers. They stumbled into an arithmetics class. The pupils were teenagers and young men. The soldiers marched them down the beach and into the sea. They ordered the students to clap their hands. When the students clapped their hands, the soldiers shot them.

Katalayo reminds me that atrocities like these are the last acts of a dying regime. Young conscript officers are returning home to Portugal, broken by what they have seen. You find them in the bars of Lisbon and Porto fomenting revolution under the very noses of the PIDE. The Portuguese army wants out of Africa. The generals saw the writing on the wall back in 1961 when India seized Goa. Dr Salazar didn't listen to them then, and now their poor bloody infantry are paying the price in costly colonial wars in Mozambique and Angola.

Katalayo refuses to be intimidated by force of Portuguese arms. The scourge of colonial might is a theme he leaves to others. He has learned how to turn the brute material of his harassment, imprisonment, and even his torture, upon itself. Each arrest, beating and midnight visitation adds one more blackly hilarious episode to his repertoire of amusing autobiographical tales. He is the David Niven of black power.

This morning, for instance, he tells me about the time a protest by Swedish missionaries got him out of a PIDE gaol in Nampula. By the time he got to South Africa, he tells me, the security forces were waiting for him. The men parked outside his apartment building got so sick of him coming over to bum cigarettes from them, they started dropping full packets into his mail slot each evening.

It was during this strange moment of unlicensed *rapprochement* that a bunch of drunken PIDE men in black-face had burst into his home, gang-raped his wife, surprised his ten-year-old daughter as she returned home and pressed a loaded pistol into her hands.

'"You don't have to kill her," they said, "just aim at her knees."'

I am making toast under the grill when he tells me this. I have my back to him. I am afraid to turn round. 'What happened?'

'After an hour or two of that sort of thing, they persuaded her to put a bullet through Memory's head.'

Memory was his wife.

'My daughter's in Tanzania. She must be nineteen now. Twenty.'

I turn to look at him. He is wearing an expression I have never seen before. He looks utterly helpless.

'She disappeared,' he says. 'She ran away. Now she has come back. She says she wants to see me.' There are tears in his eyes and I know, in that moment, that I am not, and never can be, what I most want to be: Jorge Katalayo's son.

I come to the airport to see him off. 'It will not be long,' he tells me. He means the war of liberation. He wants me to join him, when the time is right. FRELIMO needs educated men. The party has such ambitious plans.

All summer long over plates of doughnuts, over pots of tea, over mugs of instant coffee, Jorge Katalayo, FRELIMO's first president, has been sketching out for me his plans for the future of Mozambique – a colour-blind, gender-blind, ideologically fluid Utopia. A land without hate. A land of total literacy and high levels of general education.

It has not escaped my notice that he has been describing Sweden.

'I'll see you in Maputo!' he says, at the gate.

Maputo is the local name for the capital, Lourenço Marques. In 1968 it is still a Portuguese stronghold.

'Write to me,' he says, and I promise I will. He has given me his daughter's address in Dar es Salaam—

*

'His daughter's address?'

They sat up. They looked at each other. Suddenly the polite, buttoned-down young men of the Mozambican consulate were taking notice of me.

The one nearest me put down his tea mug. 'His *daughter*, did you say?'

On 21 July 1969, details of Apollo Eleven's successful moon landing pushed Jorge Katalayo's assassination deep into the bowels of *The Times*. The half-page article devoted to his killing was short on political analysis, but rich in forensic detail. The explosives used were 'characteristically Japanese', whatever that means. The brown paper wrapper in which the bomb arrived had originated in London. The bomb itself was secreted in a hollow cut into a large reference work.

Someone had intercepted my gift of encyclopaedias.

A to K and L to Z.

Someone had knifed out the knowledge and laid death in its place.

ANNIHILATION THERAPY

1

It is 10.30 a.m. local time in Lourenço Marques, the capital city of colonial Mozambique, and so far this is a morning like any other. The street-sellers are setting out their wares: pyramids of peppers and potatoes, expired medicines and Chinese prints. It is Sunday, 20 July 1969. Today, a man prepares to set foot on the moon, another will have his head blown off by a bomb.

Three floors above the street, in the tiny offices of a cash-strapped educational charity, project director Gregor Dimitryvich is startled by the arrival of his sole remaining employee.

Indeed, Anthony Burden's arrival has so surprised him, Gregor Dimitryvich jumps up from behind the table. Now there is a cloth spread over this table – a fancy, frilly Portuguese lace tablecloth – and on it are arranged a bizarre and evocative assortment of batteries, wires, clock parts and scribbled notes. Gregor has tucked an end of the tablecloth into his trousers, presumably to catch stray parts of the watch mechanism he's dissecting. When he jumps, a spool of wire falls to the floor; a clock, and a pencil. A hand magnifying glass follows, shattering on the bare boards of the room. A notebook slides after; a soldering iron; a spool of solder. Another pencil.

Had he burst into the office brandishing a gun, Anthony Burden could not have made a stronger impression.

'Get in!' Gregor barks.

Anthony closes the door, deposits his walking stick in the antique umbrella bucket and lowers himself gingerly into his customary seat, opposite his employer.

Gregor remains standing with the tablecloth spilling from his trousers like a long, white tongue. 'I am expecting a package. A man will deliver this package. A sailor. When the sailor arrives you can wait in the next room.'

This is the name Gregor gives the toilet. The Institute has no other rooms.

'Or I could simply go,' Anthony offers. 'If it's inconvenient—'

'This would not be best.'

'Oh?'

'Please. Sit down.'

Anthony shrugs – he is already seated. The gesture makes him wince: his back is bad today.

'I mean stay seating. I mean...' Sighing, Gregor gives up his attempt to correct his mangled English, and releases himself from the tablecloth.

All of which is disturbing enough, but not at all surprising.

The moment he hobbled off the plane in Lourenço Marques, Anthony Burden guessed that this 'institute' he was supposed to be working for was nothing more than the cover for yet another moribund KGB field station. There should have been a driver waiting for him at the gate, holding up a cardboard sign with his name on it. But the teenage factotum sent to collect him felt so under-used, he instead approached Burden, *sotto voce*, by the newspaper kiosk, slipping a hand under his arm as he did so.

When, rather angrily, Anthony Burden shook him off, the boy responded as if electrocuted, every muscle tensed for action, his hand already inside his coat. 'You are the teacher, yes? You teach the little nigger kiddies?'

Lubyanka's finest.

Pathetic.

Since 1951, when he left the Migdal Tikvah kibbutz, mathematician and communications expert Anthony Burden has been working within the nascent aid industry. With a CV like his, and omitting mention of his treatments for manic depression, a fifty-two-year-old ex-academic of Anthony's stripe should have been able to carve out for himself a small but profitable niche in a top-flight Western NGO. Instead, Anthony has trodden a steeper, stonier path. In reaction to his unhappy years in Israel – the gulf that opened up between his own socialism and his wife's Zionism; their eventual separation; the company he kept in Haifa; the trouble it got him into; finally, his ignominious expulsion – Anthony's political leanings have slid ever leftwards, condemning him, since the Cold War became truly global, to a life of straitened living and unsatisfying piece-work. The latest of the many half-hearted, left-leaning 'friendly institutions' to have employed Anthony Burden is this Soviet-sponsored and practically penniless 'Institute of Field and Distance Learning'. No doubt his old friend John 'Sage' Arven – wartime scientific guru to Whitehall and a lifelong communist – would appreciate the irony of his situation.

He does not expect to be stuck here much longer. Given the wobbly state of the junta in Lisbon, it is a wonder the police have not closed them down already.

Meanwhile, outside the urban strongholds, the forces of black liberation are gaining strength and reputation. From friendly Tanzania, FRELIMO guerrillas are conducting a successful military campaign against Portugal's conscript forces. Their behaviour towards the imperialists – if you believe the pirate radio stations – is positively ethical. On the front line, revenge attacks are forbidden. Soldiers killing white civilians are trucked back to Tanzania for political re-education. Portuguese land-holdings are not targeted. The soldiers of the liberation are not permitted to confiscate food, and so they eat what the peasants eat – millet, a crop in which the Portuguese have no economic stake.

Unsure how much of this to believe, Anthony turned – not unreasonably, he thought – to his colleagues. But all they cared about were the women who walked the promenades above Maputo Bay. The gaudiest fabrics Macao could supply found their way around the waists of those girls. To Anthony's enthusiastic enquiries about the new socialist independent state, surely just around the corner now, the staffers – deadbeats and fumblers, mice-men with grey flannel trousers and myopic, light-frightened eyes, 'the intelligence community' – well, they simply sneered.

Peeved, he started quoting the pirate broadcasts at them: 'There won't be girls on the bluff much longer.' This caught their interest. 'They're running through the minefields to get to the FRELIMO line. FRELIMO are building them their own barracks. They are putting them to work in the fields.' Acidly: 'They are teaching them to read.'

'What do they need to read for?'

'"Ensure all air is expelled from the teat. Do not re-use."'

The men were too bored and demoralized even to laugh at their own jokes.

Oafs, thought Anthony, steering carefully around the idea that he was like them, one of them, another Comintern discard.

He'd known he was in for a rough ride when he discovered that the office of this 'distance learning institute' had no short-wave radio. There was a telephone, but it rarely worked – the area exchange kept 'borrowing' the line. There was a very limited stock of paper, and when Anthony set to work drawing up some of his ideas for discussion, he was told, in no uncertain terms, to obtain his own supply. His enthusiastic descriptions of distance learning techniques; his suggestion that short-wave radio communications might cast 'nets of political mentorship' across the disadvantaged communities of this huge and empty country: these things were greeted with humourless incomprehension.

So he has sat, day after day, nursing the knot in his ruined back, at this big, heavy antique table, covered with a smutted, ink-stained linen cloth; to his left, a heavy German-Gothic sideboard; to his right, a grandfather clock that would not have looked out of place in a railway station ticket hall; behind him, a wrought-iron safe in which all official papers are kept, and to which he has no access. Such furniture might, in another context, generate a pleasant atmosphere for a gentleman's study. Alas, since the room itself is a featureless concrete cube on the top floor of a recently finished towerblock, these wonderfully heavy, lustrous objects have taken on a dejected aspect, like old lags in a cell.

Talking of which.

'He is a British sailor,' Gregor confides to Anthony, around half-past one. There are bags under his eyes. He hasn't shaved for days.

The men sit facing each other across the table.

They wait.

Silence.

2

'Please don't. I'll be all right.' The words grate and quiver in Anthony Burden's schoolboy throat. At the back of his tongue, the taste of silver foil. 'I promise I won't do it again.'

It is 10 p.m., Valentine's Day 1930, and in the gymnasium of Stonegrove College, a cash-strapped Derbyshire grammar school, twelve-year-old Anthony Burden is struggling to explain away the belt around his throat and his trousers round his ankles.

John Arven, fourteen years old, captain of Anthony's dorm, nurses the side of his head where the younger boy's legs, flailing spastically against the wall bars, delivered their inadvertent kick. 'Who did this to you?'

Choking and blubbering on the floor of Stonegrove College gymnasium, his throat on fire, his thighs wet with piss, how is Anthony Burden to explain that he did this to himself? How is he to put into words that this is what he wants, however much his drab, ungainly boy's body fought to keep him living in this world? Even more daunting: how is he to explain that it is not despair that drives him, but hope?

'Who was it? Tell me. Don't be afraid.'

Little Anthony Burden bursts into tears.

Anthony Burden has a secret. Every few months or so come days of bubbling energy and nervous agitation, days when nothing seems impossible and everything takes too long. Then, with a burst of exhilaration indistinguishable from terror, Anthony receives a vision of Paradise.

Paradise is a city. A municipal fantasia of great public works: fine temples, massive aqueducts, embankments, statuary, formal gardens, parklands, bandstands, amphitheatres and parades. A sunlit urban masterpiece, glittering and fine. In the very centre of the city there is a wooded glade, criss-crossed by geometric paths, where deer graze beneath tall, mathematically perfect trees. A girl in a shimmering cotton pinafore dress plucks flowers. A gardener in a wide-brimmed straw hat, his shears in his hand and a little dog at his feet, stands beside a dark lake whose fountain sends a crystal jet into the air like a glittering whip, spreading coolness all around. Above the treetops rises the ornamental outline of a magnificent castle.

How often has Anthony wished that he could carry his physical body into this land! Alas, since that one farcical schoolboy attempt, Anthony has had to content himself with visiting his Heaven disembodied, a soul *sans* flesh.

Anthony's body, meanwhile, clings to the clay of life with dirty fingernails. It longs to wallow unchecked in the stew of life.

Nine years later, at 6.30 a.m., on 10 July 1939 Anthony Burden, King's scholar, twenty-two years old, wakes up in an unfamiliar room – sheets that are too hot, too damp – and in the presence – close, naked and erect – of Cambridge mathematician Alan Turing.

Anthony lets out a scream and tumbles from the bed. Whimpering, he half runs, half crawls, for the nearest door. He finds himself in a bathroom. He slams the door shut behind him and fumbles with the bolt.

'Anthony?' says Alan.

Anthony Burden presses his back against the bathroom door and sinks to the floor, eyes tight shut. Anthony knows who it is, all right. Alan Turing's lectures have been the highlight of his week since they started: 'The Foundations of Mathematics'. But how on earth—?

'Anthony, sweetheart, what the devil's got into you?'

Anthony covers his face with his hands. If he is very quiet, if he is very small, maybe everything can go back to how it was.

*

Two months later. September 1939. Anthony Burden takes a deep breath and wills the tension out of his tight-wound limbs. How dreadful, that he should be rehearsing these shameful episodes, even as he turns over a new leaf and journeys to a new city!

No possible way he could continue his studies after the Incident, of course. How could he trust himself? It is as his Blessed Mother tearfully predicted. The stresses and strains of the academic life have proved too much for him. He must find some other occupation.

This war could not have come at a better time for him. It is time for Anthony Burden to do something practical for his country, something that might, he hopes, deep in his Fabian soul, improve the lot of the Common Man. His school-friend John Arven has persuaded him not to enlist. 'There is so much you can do on the Home Front,' John insisted, bright bird eyes transfixing him, the day Anthony told him of his decision to quit academia. To prove his point, Sage has arranged for Anthony to be interviewed, later today, by the board of the Post Office Research Station at Dollis Hill.

Visions of paradise have accompanied Anthony Burden ever since puberty. They have shaped his life, his interests and his inventions. They do not frighten him any more. He accepts that they are a gift, like perfect pitch, or a precocious talent with brush and pencil. He sees that they have something to do with his aptitude for mathematics. But he does not understand them, and he is troubled by his own ignorance.

Once he is settled in his London digs, Anthony seeks out the distinguished-sounding philosophical society with rooms off Gower Street, and there, in its curious and ramshackle library, he reads everything that might shed light on his condition, from Mme Blavatsky's accounts of spirit travel to the personal diaries of blind introspectionist T. C. Cutsforth. Nothing he reads undercuts the magic of his visions. The visions themselves are the primary Fact.

Arven, meanwhile, encourages Anthony to spread his wings, now that he is living in the capital. He cannot understand why Anthony won't agree to come and lecture to his students at Birkbeck College. He cannot see why Anthony is so determined to shun academia. 'There is so much you have to offer,' he says, flattering the younger man.

Strange, the bond of care between the two old boys, persisting after all these years.

Twelve-year-old Anthony, sprawled choking and half-naked on the floor of the school gymnasium, did not imagine for a second, fervently as he begged, that his dorm captain would keep his suicide attempt a secret. What had happened, that night, that John had stuck by his side, helped him clean himself up and never said anything to anyone, ever, about that night? What, on passing the gymnasium for an illicit smoke, had the older boy seen? What about Anthony's condition, if anything, did he understand?

For years, Anthony has been too afraid to ask. Because if John Arven saw that night what Anthony saw, and continues to see, every few months – the towers, the parades, the fountain – then...

Why, then, the vision must be true!

And why should we go on living, if it was? If the door to Paradise was always open? If the Way was clear?

'Dear Prof. Arven, I have yet to receive a reply to my letter of 3rd inst.'

Well yes, dear little Kathleen, it is true. I have not replied to you. I have not made good my promises. Consequently, I would lay money that wherever you are, and however you make your living, your talents are being belittled or ignored and your potential value to the nation is going entirely to waste. No, I have not written: a misfortune for you, and a tragedy for the country. Or should that be the other way about? In any event, I have not replied. I have not invited you for any interview or examination. How can I? Perhaps next time you write, instead of heading your letter 'Same Address', you could just tell me *where the bloody hell you are.*

Irritated, Professor John Arven – Whitehall guru and the star of Mountbatten's 'Department of Wild Talents' – screws up Kathleen's letter and drops it neatly into the ashtray.

London. October 1940.

What else is there? Arven glances through the rest of the day's meticulously time-stamped correspondence: letters typed and handwritten; a couple of facsimiles from the War Office; a fuzzy transatlantic telephotograph. Most of this material is not supposed to leave his office, but his workload has forced him to play fast and loose with the regulations. Every couple of seconds a paperclip *pings* and falls to the floor, just out of reach. You could eek out a smallish engine component from the paperclips his secretary gets through in a week.

Another mouthful of beer. At this rate he'll be on his second before Anthony arrives. Every time someone comes labouring up the carpeted stairs, John expects to see his old schoolfriend Anthony Burden. They have agreed to meet in the upper bar of the Wheatsheaf in Fitzrovia for a drink after work. John's already got in a pint of the ghastly porter Anthony prefers, and that was twenty minutes ago. Not that it will make any difference to that muck.

John Arven's lifelong friendship with Anthony Burden has recently become a source of mild but persistent annoyance. Anthony is like an unintelligible relation for whom John is always having to find excuses. Take, as a case in point, this paper he has written. John digs it out of his bag.

'What, after all, is a machine?' Anthony asks, with his trademark demotic flourish. *'Where does the operator stop and the machine begin?'*

Anthony has been urging Arven, in his role as a Birkbeck professor, to referee this paper and advise on the possibilities of publication. This is a rather sad business, John feels. When Anthony quit Cambridge, declaring his intent 'to do something for the Common Man', John was intrigued. He awaited developments with anticipation. What would his old friend become? The last thing he expected or wanted was that Anthony should drift into some nebulous reserved occupation, while at the same time plying him with page after page of amateurish philosophy. Anthony is so obviously wedded to the life of the mind, his ambitions for the fruits of his intellectual labours are so painfully nursed, why the devil did he ever leave the purlieus of King's?

'Take a bus driver, for instance. A bus driver operates a bus.' Anthony maintains this irritating *faux naif* style throughout. *'But in what sense is he an "operator"?'* John correctly identifies the central theme of Anthony's paper. It is a tango. Some rather weakly analysed sentiments regarding free will on the one hand; Bertrand Russell's set theory on the other. *'Certainly he is not a free agent. He cannot freely choose his route and schedule. Not if he wants to keep his job.'* John Arven skims Anthony's folksy phrases with a great weariness, all the way to the end. There. Promise kept. Now all he has to do is think of something to say.

Ever since school, Anthony has exhibited an unfortunate talent for frittering away his gifts on wild goose-chases. John still recalls, with some bitterness, their last summer together at Stonegrove – two halcyon months they might have spent walking, sailing; they might even have visited Europe together, and caught a last glimpse of a way of life now gone for ever, crushed beneath the jack-boot of the Reich.

At the last minute, Anthony had scotched all their plans, for all the world as though their friendship meant nothing. In order to do what, exactly? Why, in order to collect fir-cones from the woods behind his parents' house! All because of that obscure, second-hand book he had picked up, linking maths and nature. Twenty years old, written by a naturalist no one had ever heard of. By the summer's end, poor Anthony still had nothing to show for his obsession. No special insight into the relationship between numbers, birds and bees. No, not even a mathematical bauble to dangle in front of the editors of *Eureka*.

It is not that Anthony Burden is without talent. God knows, John has rarely met his equal. At school, Anthony demonstrated an instinctive grasp of mathematical operations. More recently, he was filling his letters from Cambridge with some really quite extraordinary flights of number theory. It's not his talent that's in question.

It is his common sense. The way he allows himself to be borne away on this hobby-horse or that. His insistence that simple operations, repeated endlessly, mechanically, perhaps using some sort of switching system like a telegraph, will revolutionize the practice of mathematics.

'I would argue that the bus driver is a functional "unit" inside a larger machine, more distributed but no less mechanical – namely, the bus route or system...'

John Arven shuffles the sheets back together and stows them away in his bag. He checks the clock above the bar. Really this is insufferable, where the devil has Anthony got to? John contemplates his own irritation, feeding it until it swells into anger. He does this out of choice, and diligently. He has to. If John doesn't work up some anger now, then all he'll be left with by the end of the evening will be fear, for what might have happened to his friend.

In years past, John has felt an intense duty of care towards Anthony Burden. He has lain awake fearing for his friend. But their friendship is past its best, their destinies have come decoupled, and he does not want these feelings any more. The apprehension and fear and dragging sense of responsibility. It is surely time, John tells himself, that he release himself from memories of that overwhelming evening of their first acquaintance: how Anthony, blubbing, extracted from him an oath of secrecy so solemn and profound that it forged an iron bond between them, a bond which John may regret but which, up to now, he has never been able to break.

All afternoon the streets of Fitzrovia have roiled drunk with every type of London life. Free French have rubbed shoulders with displaced African dignitaries, soldiers on furlough have pursued working girls through crowds of muttering black-clad Jewry. Negro poets from Paris have been flashing their gold-capped teeth at all the pretty computers clipping in, figure-dizzy, from the toils of Senate House. From his vantage point in the shadows, Anthony marvels. It is impossible to tell whether these people are masters of their surroundings or unwitting captives. How can they live, dreaming as they do?

As the daytime noises fade, so the people of the street acquire a cool grey uniform of sameness, and Anthony Burden remarks how self-absorbed everyone has grown. Strange, he thinks, that the day should end like this. Why, he wonders, do we not connect with each other constantly in this extremity of war?

Anthony is on fire tonight, with that occasional energy he exhibits prior to a crisis. It is the manic fervour he displayed the week before he fell into bed with Alan Turing. It is the same fire that lit his eyes, back when he was simply 'A. Burden' (much humour in the quad over that), the new boy at Stonegrove, days before John Arven discovered him.

Anthony has, as a consequence, clean forgotten his evening's arrangement with John Arven. He is, instead, on his way through Soho towards the National Gallery. There is a concert tonight, for the benefit of some refugee group or other, and though the programme is not his usual fare, in the Blitz he has learned to seize what shreds of cultural life he can. The only other entertainment tonight is *The Lion Has Wings* with Merle Oberon, playing at the Haymarket, and Anthony has seen that twice already.

He has paused in a shop doorway, feeling in his pocket for his cigarettes.

'Excuse me, sir,' he calls out to a passer-by, 'have you got a light?'

The man bridles. 'I certainly have not,' he snaps, in a thick, East European accent. 'Goodnight.'

Anthony is confused at first, then blushes, mortified. He didn't mean...

Or did he? What did he want, stood here in the dark? Not a light. More than a light.

Here are the matches, in his hand.

He finds it so hard to understand himself at times. He lights his cigarette with trembling fingers and heads south.

It takes him no time at all to see why the foreign gentleman reacted so badly to his innocent hello. At this provocative hour of the evening, pansies line the streets. Pansies leer at him from first- and second-floor windows. From high windows, rouged pansies lean, leer and whistle. They loiter at street corners, inflaming his imagination with their narrow ties and narrow suits with narrow trousers and pointy shoes.

Sill blushing, Anthony stares straight ahead and clips smartly along, closed off to every imagined disturbance, spiralling deeper into purblind fantasy. One by one the colours vanish from the scene. Soon all is black and white. Buses, robbed of their red, slink past along Shaftesbury Avenue. Furled umbrellas spasm like jellyfish. In Trafalgar Square the lions are pacing. Nelson on his column teeters and hesitates; is there really no way down from here? The National Gallery steps trill and tinkle like piano keys when Anthony treads on them and threaten to buck him into the street below.

He enters the gallery and follows the attendants' directions. The walls of the great galleries are bare. According to *The Times*, their treasures have been borne off for safe-keeping to a disused slate quarry somewhere in North Wales. In each room he passes knots of calm grey figures. Is it his imagination, or are they studying the walls? Are they adopting these contemplative poses out of long habit, or are things hung there that he cannot see?

In the basement room the audience is gathering, grey and silent, everyone exactly like everyone else. Above them, the low ceiling bulges, foams at the corners and rises suddenly to make a vault. The audience make no sign of having seen their surroundings transformed. Are they used to miracles, or blind to them?

Anthony's heart thunders in his chest. He'd hug every man and woman to his bosom if he could. At times like these the Truth peeks through appearances, illuminating everything. How everyone is exactly alike.

The audience is given very little time to settle before the Budapest Municipal Orchestra enters and launches into its premiere. With the first swoop and tremble of strings, Anthony Burden knows this isn't going to be his sort of music.

In the days of his mania, as Paradise trundles closer and closer, music fills the space behind Anthony's eyes with images. Different musics build differently: Benny Goodman and Count Basie string bridges between his ears; Bach and Handel erect Venetian palazzi. From the mushy romanticism and mangled folk idiom of this sorry *Budapest Concerto*, however, Anthony manages to construct very little: a blasted heath, a couple of tumble-down cottages; a pond; a mill. He is, without thinking about it, constructing a kind of pastiche or portmanteau Constable to put in place of the paintings missing from the walls upstairs. The sight of those bare walls shakes Anthony. He imagines the art of the nation turning troglodyte, as Londoners themselves might, were the Underground left open during air-raids. Hiding there for safety, going mad, refusing to surface.

What will the art be like when it re-emerges? Anthony wonders. If it emerges. He thinks of the mine, so dry, so secure: D. G. Rossetti and John Martin pressed promiscuously up against Turner, Gainsborough, Dadd. What sort of Morlock art will it be when we drag it from the comfortable Celtic twilight of the mine?

Will we even find it?

He is deliberately scaring himself now.

Will it *hide*?

A delicious shudder...

Applause wakes him – and what on earth is going on? The audience is going wild. The audience is cheering. The audience is leaping to its feet. He folds his arms and keeps his seat, wishing neither to be one of the herd, nor to let his musical standards drop so far. Only then it dawns on him, poor unworldly technician, that he is surrounded by refugees. He looks at them anew. The calm grey figures surrounding him flicker and snap, thick ham hands a-tremble; the glint of tears.

Shamed, Anthony struggles to his feet and joins in their applause, if not for the music, then for the effort, the extraordinary and brave effort of the plucky Jewish people – and a bowler hat, tossed with more energy than circumspection by a jubilant concert-goer, cracks him on the nose.

Several hours earlier, that same evening – and in the Lyons corner house on the Strand, Rachel Causley sips delicately at her hot chocolate, looks at her watch and says: 'I can't be long, Mummy will be waiting for me. Is it done or not?'

Her Major would pull his hair, if he had any. He beats his skull instead – muted little punches to the frontal lobes. 'Have you any idea,' he says, 'what this involves?'

Rachel sits in silence. They both know the answer to this question. Twenty years old, Rachel already knows her business.

'I could get myself *shot*!' the Major declares in a non-too-subtle stage whisper. Rachel glances to their left, to the gawky, pretty waitress standing there – but she is like the rest of them, asleep on her feet. She has not overheard.

The Major waits for a response. Rachel says nothing. Her eyes drill into him. She is waiting for her answer. God, but the bitch is beautiful! He fumbles a cigarette into his mouth. How wise she is, in return for his services, to offer what she offers without love. The unaffectionate kiss. The indolent and bored caress. He knows that at the slightest show of affection from her he would ruin everything: his marriage, his son at Sandhurst, his dear sister, his savings, the whole petty, cherished edifice of his life. She is wise, his Rachel, his blackout girl, to show no chink of light.

'Is it done?'

He stubs out his cigarette, bites his lip, irritated, and snaps at the waitress, standing gormlessly there: 'Please may we have a clean ashtray?'

'Of course,' says the waitress, shaking herself free of her waking dream. 'I won't be a moment.'

He watches her go.

'I've diverted the shipment through Alexandria,' he says. 'I can't do anything about the ammunition, it's already been dispatched, you'll have to look elsewhere for that. Much good may it do you. Do you really think your people... Where are you going?'

Rachel Causley – Clausen as was, in her family's way-back-when – uses a napkin to wipe the chocolate from her lips. She is a creature of extreme times, party to great plans and terrible intelligence, balanced on a knife-edge between promises of promised land and rumours of extermination, emptied of hope, wired with determination, but when the city's cocoa supply runs out – next week or the week after – she will take to her bed and cry like a baby.

She gives the Major what he wants – Tomorrow? Very well – and gets out of there as quickly as she can.

Tomorrow.

The truth is, the Major frightens her. He is one of those well-meaning bumblers whose frustration with life has never found its proper outlet. Tomorrow in that little rented room, alone with her, an unexploded bomb. In his bluster and abjection she has diagnosed a sentimentalist who, given the right sort of encouragement, might just break a bottle in her face.

She wishes that she did not have this power that is not even hers, but belongs to her body so that, as she steers her way to advantage through the infantile expectations of this or that fellow traveller – *Oh, Princess! Let me kiss it! Oh, go on! Let me hold 'em!* – she is no more in control of the process of seduction than if she were put behind the wheel of a racing car. Sometimes, in her darker moments, she even wonders whether the politics in which she has become embroiled is not a sand-trap or thicket into which she has instinctively swerved in order to slow her body's uncontrollable sexual career.

There is something puritan growing within her; it will not leave her sex alone, but must always be pressing the roses in her cheeks into service for the common good. The truth is, Rachel Causley – Clausen as she will be again, entering Zion – is not the Mata Hari she imagines herself to be. She puts herself in the way of these helpful War Office types – communists, closet and not-so-closet; men whose parentage or upbringing enables them to identify, or at least sympathize, with the Zionist cause. Still, the favours she bestows are not much. Every kiss she blows, every glimpse of knee, every button on her blouse, earns the cause another gun; she herself remains unmoved. Undiminished, unenlightened, she still imagines that love – true love – is something unconnected with erotica, something cuddly and vaguely parental. When she imagines her future husband, she imagines a creature not unlike Flopsy, the rabbit she had as a child and petted through a long and terminal illness.

On the steps of the National Gallery, her mother is waiting for her. This benefit is her doing, her bit for a cause of whose deep dark criminality she is merrily unaware. 'My dear! You are so late!'

There is nothing in her mother's appearance to betray the cruel exigencies this war has put her to. She wears the family's recent internment lightly, as though it were a joke at her captors' expense. Neither is there any sign of the punishing hours she keeps now, fire-watching in the dead of night. Tonight she is dashing as ever in a borrowed evening gown and paste jewels. Though bankrupted at home, yet she walks this foreign soil full of happy expectation. Face to face with her, Rachel feels none of the contempt towards the older generation felt by the other members of her cell. It seems cheap to her, to sneer at her parents' lives. It is not hard for her to imagine why her father, awarded the Iron Cross First Class in the last war, should view the idea of Palestine with incredulity. It is not difficult to see why her mother, with her childhood memories of Johann Strauss and concerts in the Vienna Volksgarten, should treasure the culture of Schiller and Schopenhauer above the socialist experiments of the East.

Come the revolution, it will be up to the young to re-educate their parents.

Rachel takes her mother's arm and walks her back inside. She is overcome with affection for her poor parents; the pride they take, even now, in their assimilation; their innocent reverence for *Bildung*. When the revolution comes, she will be able to make everything clear to them. With humour and compassion, she will show them, step by step, why she is right and they are wrong.

The stiff hat-brim cracks Anthony's nose and somewhere behind his eyes, a tap turns. His nose will not stop bleeding. Blood gathers in his moustache as though it were a sponge. His handkerchief is sodden. He is going to faint.

Through his dizziness he feels sympathetic hands upon him, propelling him across the hall, through a door and along an unlit corridor, to where the musicians of the Budapest Municipal Orchestra have retired to smoke, talk and loosen their ties.

'Come over here to the sink.'

He did not expect a woman here among these heavy, sweaty men. He receives a muddled impression that she is familiar to them. Is she a theatrical agent? She is wearing a pale, figure-hugging dress, the colour indeterminate under the weak light. Her skin is the colour of Greek honey. She beckons him. Her arm is like a polished branch.

His heart tilts. *O my America.* He shies away, afraid that he might bloody her clothing.

'Come on.'

She sits him down by a small china sink and tilts his head back. She pinches his septum. Her fingers are strong and capable. Her hand at his temple reminds him of his mother. He closes his eyes. 'What's your name?' he says. He could hug the whole world.

'Rachel,' she says – and seeing something in him she misses, some childhood thing she has lost – strokes him absent-mindedly behind his ears.

They wake just before dawn the next day, naked, spooned under a blanket of leaves in a hollow hidden by thick undergrowth in a little-frequented corner of Regent's Park.

Rachel shimmies against Anthony's warmth. His arms are curled about her. She takes hold of them, tightening his embrace.

Bliss.

She closes her eyes against the colours of the waking world, trying to hold on to last night's vivid dream. Boulevards and squares, great houses, courtyards – all built of space and light.

The city Anthony showed her as they walked had form but no colour. There was a cloistered air to it, as though every street and channel and staircase, followed far enough, would lead inexorably back into itself. Even the distinction between day and night seemed to be a function of perspective. And all the while, slowly, confidently, his hand was stealing across her back to clinch her waist.

They kissed. His moustache tickled her. She ran her hands through his hair, his widow's peak which made him appear so devilish somehow, his rough cheeks, his slim, hard body. He led her on...

Anthony stirs. He wakes. With a little cry, he lets go of her. He sits up.

Rachel, exposed, wraps her arms around herself and shivers.

'What?' says Anthony.

She turns over, chilled through. Still, in one languorous corner of her mind, she is enjoying the feel and rustle of mould and leaf. She smiles up at her seducer, delivers a chipper 'good morning'.

'Where—?' says Anthony.

He smells of leaf and mushroom, of earth and sweat. She lies back into his lap, braving the morning cold to stretch, lifting her little breasts for him. 'Mmmm,' she says.

Anthony casts around. 'Where are our clothes?'

She gazes round their dell, eyes lazy, slitted with sleep. 'Dunno.'

With anxious, mincing gestures, Anthony slides out from under Rachel. He kneels, hunted, like a dog. 'I can't see our clothes anywhere.'

The urgency in his voice wakes her more fully than the cold has done. She sits up. 'They must be somewhere,' she says, unhelpfully.

Together they explore their grotto. Through the dense undergrowth, Rachel sees a park gardener already hard at work with his sheers. He is tidying the edges of a path. Clip by clip, he moves towards them.

'Ah!' Anthony sighs. Rachel turns to shush him.

He has found her dress and her purse.

'Is that all?'

He nods.

'What shall we do?'

Anthony bites his lip. His penis is hard with fear. She wants to hold it. But the moment is gone. 'Help me on with your dress.'

She blinks at him.

'Come on.'

'Why can't I—?'

'I wouldn't dream of it,' he says, gallantly. He holds up her purse. 'May I borrow halfpence for the phone?'

He looks funny in the dress. He elbows his way through the undergrowth and onto the path. Lightly he runs, bare hairy feet a blur. Rachel lies down and covers herself with leaves.

The ground is not so comfortable now. There are twigs and thorns and crawling things.

She wonders who he is going to call, and how long he will be.

3

Even through the lenticular grey warp of his mania, Anthony Burden sees that, of all the women he has ever been introduced to – a slew of sex rabbits, neurotic amateur poets and surrogate mamas thrust upon him by 'understanding' friends – Rachel alone might serve to draw him into a life that is more keenly felt. Wandering the streets of Paradise with her, he has been struck by her social skill, her appetite for adventures. Waking with her in Regent's Park, aghast at their animalism, he has expected everything to go sour – but who would not be charmed by her perky 'good morning'? It gives him the unaccustomed courage, breathless as he is from the sprint from undergrowth to phone box and back again, and half out of his mind with panic, to ask to see her again. And then and there, stood there in their dell, a bare-chested Rosalind, she says yes.

Against all odds, Anthony's erotic encounter with Rachel leads to another, and another. An understanding blossoms. There is even talk of marriage. When the time comes for Anthony to seek the blessing of Rachel's parents, Rachel takes him home to St John's Wood. There is her father's Iron Cross, framed and hung above a bureau designed by Ernst Freud. Beside it hangs the childhood portrait of Rachel painted by Kurt Schwitters. They have arrived to find Rachel's mother playing four-hand piano with the world-renowned violinist Max Rostal. The polite, strained conversation that ensues is gritted with the names of everyone who is anyone in European music. Lili Kraus, Szymon Goldberg: thanks to Hitler, there's not one of them lives more than half a mile from Lili Montagu's new synagogue in Swiss Cottage. For Anthony, this is a different world, impassioned, fiercely intellectual: he longs to be a part of it.

When, alone with her, Anthony speaks of his intentions, Rachel's mother becomes flustered. She is all too aware, this once, of being in a foreign land, her old rules and niceties swept away. Her first response is to demur to her husband – and this is a complicated business, as Mr Causley – his value to the war effort recognized, at last – has been billetted in some out-of-the-way corner of the West Country, monitoring Nazi broadcasts for the BBC.

Together, Rachel and Anthony board a train for Evesham. There, and greatly to Anthony's surprise, Rachel's father responds to news of the match with an enthusiasm that borders on the unseemly.

The men's conversation, conducted on the lawn of a guest-house in the sleepy hamlet of Wood Norton, is one of the more surreal exchanges thrown up by a surreal time. The business of the wedding quickly packed away, Rachel's father wants to pick Anthony's brains. 'I'd like to know all about matrices,' he says. 'Tensors,' he adds, out of the blue. 'Projective geometry.' He has not wasted his internment, his holiday on the Isle of Man. There are some very clever people sitting on their hands in those camps, and giving and attending lectures – on everything from Byzantine art to marine biology – helps them while away the time. 'So what about this "group theory", then?' The breadth, if not the depth, of the man's recently acquired mathematical knowledge is astounding. Anthony half wonders how he can get interned himself.

It is only as the wedding nears that Anthony learns why Rachel's father is so relieved to have him for a son-in-law.

Rachel is young. She was born the year Versailles was signed; she was fourteen the evening her father returned to their Berlin apartment, ashen and shaking, to report the first of many book burnings; she was with her mother in the audience of the Dresden Opera when Fritz Busch was booed for his Jewish violins; three years later, in the stands of the Olympic Stadium, her father gripped her hand, nails digging in, so she would remember not to cheer so loud when Jesse Owens won.

To meet these betrayals, Rachel says, a new, muscular, socialist Jewry is needed; a self-aware Jewry organized into a modern state, defended with modern weapons! Statements like these, screamed across the breakfast table of the family's genteel, cash-strapped exile in St John's Wood, thoroughly unnerved Rachel's parents long before Anthony came on the scene.

This is why the old man is relieved: his dangerous-minded daughter has settled for a middle-of-the-road Fabian, after all. He has concluded from this that his daughter's revolutionary fervour has been just a phase. On the night of their wedding, Anthony, in a mischievous spirit, points this out to his wife.

Rachel laughs as she mounts her new husband. 'Dad said the same about Hitler,' she says.

May 1942. It is several months since Rachel and Anthony were married, yet this is the first opportunity they have had for a honeymoon.

From Fort William, the Road to the Isles follows the crinkled Highland coastline. It is a road of steep inclines, blind summits and sharp, muddy bends; a road for farm wagons, tractors and clapped-out cars. After a couple of hours' steady driving, confusion is assured. It is virtually impossible for a stranger to read this landscape, where every feature feathers into every other feature, so that to distinguish between a channel and a loch, between mainland and island – between land and sea, even – becomes little more than a game of language. The light here turns seawater gold as furze, and rock to an ocean green. Their minds slide off the landscape constantly.

At moments of dizziness like these, Rachel seizes Anthony's knee. Anthony slows the car. Sometimes, he stops. Whenever they stop, they kiss.

It excites Anthony that he has married a Jew. If every new wife is an unexplored territory, then Rachel is a mysterious land indeed: a heady mix of the cosmopolitan and the exotic; the glass and steel of new money seen through the dust and yellow light of an ancient civilization. At night, if Rachel's sex fails to arouse him (and who, in strict honesty, achieves such direct responses, straight away? After all, thinks Anthony, we are not dogs) then her exoticism serves.

Naturally, he says none of this out loud. Rachel's parents are Austrian aesthetes, Goethe's children; for them, their Jewishness is little more than the stick Hitler and his thugs chose to beat them with, once they decided to expropriate the family's bank. As for Rachel, Anthony has been left in no doubt where she stands. He has gone to public meetings and has sat, squirming with embarrassment, as Rachel makes perfectly clear her abhorrence of what she calls 'the argument from blood'. It is the Jewish faith itself – its aloofness and its quietism – which has failed her people, and the desert realm she dreams of and conspires towards is robustly secular.

Anthony Burden drives them over hills of bare rock, rippled and layered by the ages like old wax, and pulls up at last at the village their RAC map promised them.

The place is a figment. There is nothing here but a pond, reflecting the ruins of a castle. A handful of dairy cattle sit by the pond, chewing the cud. A ramshackle gate hangs open on one hinge, and a fence, all but ruined, leads from the pond to a nearby farm. Beyond the castle lies a wide, calm estuary.

The newlyweds climb from the car. A cobblestone jetty stretches a tentative finger into the water. Lobster pots are stacked high along its left-hand side. Rachel pulls gently from Anthony's embrace – he is nothing if not uxorious – and walks the length of the jetty. He pauses a moment before he follows. She is magnificent, he decides, abandoning himself to the unfamiliar heat of sensual observation. Her buttocks are really very narrow for a girl. He surprises a desire to smack them very hard. To pull. To part. She is his wife, after all.

His nerve fails him, or the smell of the lobster pots cuts through his lust, and by the time he is standing beside her again, his mind has turned to safer, more familiar subjects. He says, looking out across the coast, 'One could write the maths for this.'

He is thinking of the Fibonacci series: one plus one equals two, one plus two equals three, two plus three equals five, each term the sum of the previous two, expanding forever into the arrangements of leaves, the patterns of flowers, the arrangements of fir-cones. D'Arcy Thompson wrote this up in 1917 – how nature is underpinned by mathematics. Nobody since has taken a blind bit of notice. It is only by chance that Anthony stumbled on Thompson's book, the year his friend John left Stonegrove. The field – the mathematics of creation – lies wide open. It spreads out before him. A new-found land, there for the taking.

'With one formula,' he says, trying for an unaccustomed clarity, 'you could generate a billion different valleys.'

She looks up at him with beautiful, big, dark eyes. 'What of?' she asks him.

'What?' Anthony thumbs the wedding band on his finger, turning it around and around.

'What would you build them of? These billion valleys.'

Rachel is a practical woman. Hers is a solid, material world. She wants to know what things are made of. She wants to know what things are for. Rachel is just the sort of companion Anthony needs, for he has spent too much of his life among abstract thoughts. *What of?* Her enquiring smile is a bracing challenge, and he confronts the question as a yachtsman turns his face into the wind.

He would build valleys of light. He would build valleys of numbers. 'It would be like watching a picture show,' he tells his new wife. 'But one where the film has been shot at every angle, from every point in space. As you move your eyes across the screen, as you shift about in your theatre chair, the image adapts to your movements, giving you the sense that you are moving through a real place.'

Rachel says, 'There isn't film stock enough in the world for a film like that.'

But the seamlessness and completeness of the world is an illusion. In fact, the film is short, and composed only of the shots you yourself see. Only your view of the world exists: the rest is darkness. In Anthony's fantastical world of numbers, a tree falling in the quad with no one to witness it would make no sound.

'The time it would take,' she continues. 'The time you would need to make such a film – you would never be able to keep up with your audience.'

This is true. This film needs to be composed, painted and shot, even as it is being watched. This film cannot therefore *be* a film, in the conventional sense, but a series of still images presented at speed enough to trick the eye – fifty-six frames per second or not much less – by some other yet-to-be-invented apparatus: a machine closer in kind to the facsimile machine.

'What's it got to do with telephones?' she asks him.

'Telephones carry pictures, as well as sound,' he says.

You could draw up a place, draft it the way an architect sketches a building. You could send its geometries down phone-lines to people all over the world. 'People all over the world could visit this place from the comfort of their armchairs!'

'Don't call them places,' she says.

There is silence between them. She says, 'If you can't be buried in it, it's not a place.'

And a moment later: 'Don't tell a Jew what a place is.'

He walks back along the cobblestone pier to the car. He gets in and slams the door. It is the old challenge again, the one he loves her for, the mental habit that has drawn him to her – but since they set out together this morning she has been wielding her lack of imagination like a club.

She gets in the car beside him.

'All set?' he says.

'What?'

'What?'

'What's the matter?' she says, as though she had not attacked him.

'Nothing,' he says, as though he is not hurt.

In Anthony's land of light and mathematics, there are no conflicts, because there is an imaginary abundance of everything: sunshine, shelter, space. Space above all. There is space enough in Anthony's land for everyone to be alone. In his land, this is how everyone wants to live.

It is a sort of three-dimensional cartoon, rendered in fine line-work by an army of mechanical draughtsmen. The inhabitants move about its infinite coves and inlets with a calm, myopic tread. In Anthony's imagination, there is a mathematical formula for people, too.

Home again, and sequestered in his study, Anthony thinks and writes, filling red school exercise books with exquisite diagrams, drawings, formulae and commentaries. He uses up every square inch of paper – a habit drummed into him at Stonegrove – and on every fourth or fifth day, he reaches for a fresh exercise book. Each book is tied to its neighbour by trains of thought and even sometimes by single sentences, begun in one book, finished in the next.

Since moving to London, Anthony has formalized his working methods to the point of ritual: always the same brand of exercise book and pencil. The same chair, made stable on the study's uneven, uncarpeted floor with a back-copy of *Eureka*. The sounds of familiar streets through a window opened just so. Rachel knocks before she enters. It is a rule with him.

When Anthony first told her about what he did, it sounded to Rachel as though it would change everything; that it was a tool with which to build a new kind of society, a more open, egalitarian way of being. She has spoken up for Anthony's work among her comrades. She has described in glowing terms his brave new world of teleprinters, television scanning and automatic exchange connections, his new model society, linked by wire and radio-wave. But Stalin's behaviour during the war and his anti-Semitism have thrown Zionism's left flank into chaos.

The Party has too many problems of its own to listen to yet another visionary, or sit patiently through descriptions of glittering tomorrows.

Rachel looks in the mirror, sees her mother, and wonders what has happened to her fire. She remembers Anthony, the night she met him, his nose streaming blood, his smile swallowing the world.

She wonders where he went, the man with whom she fell in love.

A bright Tuesday morning in the summer of 1943.

'Sage, thank you.'

John Arven is not listening. 'Get in the car.'

'You really have done enough—'

John Arven is not interested. 'Will you get in?'

'I'm most terribly sorry to put you to—'

John is blisteringly angry, to the point of spitting and blaspheming, and if Anthony bloody Burden doesn't— 'Anthony! Get in the buggering car!'

Anthony Burden gets in.

It is still only half past nine. It feels like two in the afternoon. John Arven is exhausted. Anthony has had neither the patience nor the good sense to wait till a civilized hour before making his one phone call. He shook his friend out of sleep at half past four this morning. John hasn't been able to sleep a wink since. He's been up most of the night, drinking some ghastly burnt-tasting stuff that stands in place of coffee these days, trying to work out what he can say to the duty officer that will have him drop all charges. However much he racked his brains, the 'war work' card was the only one worth playing. A dangerous ploy. If Anthony's work at the Post Office is so vital to the war effort, surely his employers have a right to know that he has been caught wandering Mayfair without his trousers? After four lengthy phone calls and an appearance in person at the police station in his best suit, John hopes he has managed to flannel the affair to a satisfactory conclusion. If Anthony arrives at work on Monday morning to a stiff note and an awkward meeting with the board – well, it is his own look-out.

Anthony directs John along the southern edge of Regent's Park and into a series of dull, unforgiving streets.

They park up at the entrance to a road closed off by sawhorses. 'Is this it?'

Anthony Burden's whole head is blushing. 'I – I think so.'

'Well, is it the place or not?' John fairly shouts at him – and immediately regrets it. There is no point baiting the man. What's done is done. He is here, as usual, to contain the damage Anthony Burden has done himself. Shouting isn't going to help. 'Come on,' he says. He takes Anthony by the arm in a grip he means to be friendly, but which is probably too tight, and leads him through the ruined street. 'Now, do you remember where you took them off?'

His kindness and patience do what his bad temper couldn't, and Anthony Burden bursts into tears. They sit together, companionably enough, on a stub of wall, and John offers Anthony his handkerchief. 'Why don't you phone Rachel?'

Anthony shakes his head.

'She was out of her mind with worry when I phoned her from the station.'

Anthony looks up at John, aghast. 'You did say I was in a hospital, didn't you? Not a...' He cannot say the words.

'A police station, Anthony.' Acidulated tones break through John's veneer of patience. 'You have spent the night in a police station. Yes, I lied for you. But I want you to understand something.'

Anthony looks up at him, puppy-eyed.

'I am never going to lie for you again, especially not to your wife.'

Anthony is suitably humble. 'Yes, Sage. I quite understand.'

'If I were you I would tell Rachel everything. Everything. Things are bad enough without you acting a lie to the one person who is supposed to stick by you.'

'Well,' says Anthony, without conviction, 'I will try...'

'There is another thing.'

'Yes, Sage?'

'I want you to see a psychiatrist.'

Anthony dares a little laugh. 'Oh, now, Sage—'

'Find one yourself this week, or I will find one for you. I promise you, Anthony, I will walk you into the nearest hospital if you do not agree to this.'

Anthony swallows against a fresh flood of tears. 'All right, Sage,' he says, in a little voice. 'I don't really know about such matters but I suppose I can make some enquiries.'

'You do that.'

'Though in days like these—'

'There are plenty of good medical men sitting on their hands, Anthony. I want you to find one, this week – or it's off to the Maudsley with you.'

The air here is yellow with dust and, though dry, the plaster shivered off all the ruined buildings has given it an odour of mould and rot. John thinks: he might have got up to anything in a place like this. Anything. Afraid of what he might find, John draws Anthony to his feet, and together they set about combing the ruins.

'They are a kind of twill,' Anthony tells him, trying to be helpful.

'How many pairs of trousers are we expecting to find?' says John. The joke's on him: there are whole wardrobes strewn across the rubble, scattered by multiple blasts.

'Are these them?'

Anthony peers. 'I don't think so. No. No, I'm afraid not.'

Well, won't they do? John wonders, irritated. What can be so special about a pair of trousers? In fact, why are we hunting for them at all? If Anthony wants to spin a lie about last night to his wife, all he has to do is invent the sort of accident that would damage a pair of trousers. He could fake a sprained ankle and say that the nurses, fearing to disturb bones that might be broken, cut the damn things off his leg.

Come to think of it, what story does he have it in mind to spin? Does he even have the guile to act a lie?

'I say, Sage,' says Anthony, a little later, as they teeter on the edge of a pile of masonry – any moment now a policeman is going to spot them and blow his whistle – 'you know, I am terribly grateful for these things you've lent me.'

As well he might be. John is all out of rags now. These trousers Anthony's wearing are the bottoms to a perfectly serviceable suit. 'I want them back,' John says, brusquely. He is not in the mood to mend fences – not today and not tomorrow.

'Of course,' says Anthony.

'*Pressed*.'

Silence.

'There is one thing,' says Anthony.

John clenches his fists and drives them into the pockets of his trousers. 'Yes?'

'About Rachel...'

'Yes?'

Anthony lays a hand delicately on John's arm. 'Today, before I go home. Do you think...? I mean, could you...'

'You mean, could I go round there first and smooth the waters?'

'Yes.'

'Make some excuses for you.'

'Well, ye—'

'Tell her that she must not question you too closely. That you remember very little. That you have had a nasty shock.'

'Why, yes!'

It is hopeless. Simply hopeless. Anthony hasn't listened to a single word he's said.

This, it turns out, is not strictly true.

The following week, Anthony calls in sick and retires to the little philosophical society he frequents whenever he is passing Gower Street. There, in the library, he falls into conversation with one of that strange breed of somatic therapist who have taken up lodgings in the society's rooms. This way, Anthony can keep his promise to his dear friend John Arven, without at the same time having to admit that anything is actually wrong. John wants him to see a psychiatrist? Well then, he will see a psychiatrist. They will have a pleasant little chat about philosophy. Anthony's promise will be discharged. And that will be that.

He has not counted upon the zeal and perspicacity of Dr Loránt Pál.

Two years earlier: 15 June 1940.

The British Expeditionary Force is being evacuated from France, and in the foc'sle of the cruiser *Arethusa*, tied up at the mouth of the Gironde, Dr Loránt Pál tunes a borrowed fiddle.

Its owner, first violinist and *prima* of the Budapest Municipal Orchestra, lights a Turkish cigar and lies back on his pallet. 'Come along, then.'

Pál plucks and frowns, frowns and plucks. Shaving off that sharp high E does nothing for the pounding in his head, but he is determined to prove his mettle among his countrymen.

Dr Loránt Pál, psychiatrist and medical pioneer, is coming to Britain at the invitation of a small, well-connected philosophical society, to practise a new form of somatic therapy: a treatment for melancholia and schizophrenia that involves the careful application of electricity. Undaunted by the worsening international situation, Pál has managed to finesse his way across Axis Europe with a medicine bag full of apricot brandy. But who would have thought – after running the gamut of so many greasy *fascisti* – that his heaviest binge and his hardest persuasion would be expended trying to get a berth on this miserable tub? The quartermaster shielding the British Naval Attaché had insides of lead and a brain of pure tin.

'Read the *letter*,' Pál demanded, exasperated. 'The letter, it *says*—'

'What's this?' The quartermaster held the paper at arm's length and squinted. 'Ah, now, you see, here's your problem, this isn't a *chit*. It isn't any use if it isn't a *chit*. (Ooh, ta, don't mind if I do.)'

The final irony came when Pál, several bottles the poorer, was finally able to present his *chit* to the guards officer and climb on board. He couldn't believe his eyes, seeing who had got here before him. How often, blinking from the cheaper seats of the Pesti Vigadó, has he yawned away through evenings of their Mahler? Or, in the early hours, tripped over their sprawled, sausage-stuffed corpses in the Fészek Club or the Café Japan? The Budapest Municipal Orchestra! It really is too rich, a cosmic joke, that he should be entering Britain on this boat full of musical Jews!

Cue a rollicking *csarda* that has even the fussily intellectual *prima* puffing syncopations upon his cigar. What gypsy folk memory must Pál be drawing from that he stirs, electrifies and finally breaks this violin's humble heart? A favourite encampment among wooded hills? Dark tresses in the night-time? Tracing the cool gold chain around a hot fourteen-year-old Romany ankle? A reading of grubby cards, with their intimations of fortune and tragedy?

No, just professional annoyance. Pál, in talking about his work and his plans, has once again allowed himself to be eaten up by the knowledge that the bloody Italians got there first.

Electricity.

Of course.

Why did von Meduna never pursue electricity? Ladislas von Meduna, Hungarian innovator and Pál's first and best teacher, is the true father of convulsive therapy, but a really reliable means of triggering seizures eluded him. Why did he waste so many years casting about for something chemical? Strychnine, caffeine, nikethamide. Even wormwood. (The *csarda* collapses, swooping, outrageous, atonal, as Pál recalls how the great von Meduna returned unexpectedly one night from the *kávéház*, soaked to the skin, a bottle of absinthe under his arm and a dangerous light in his eyes.)

Still, does it really matter that it was the Italians who put the 'e' in ECT? Using electricity to induce the seizures is, when all is said and done, an operational detail. No matter what the trigger, it's the seizure that's the thing: the brain stem's primal *I Am*, ringing through the addled cortex like a bell, setting everything in harmony again.

Speaking of which...

Loránt Pál works his bow across the strings as though he were weaving a rug. Smoke curls appreciatively from the *prima*'s cigar. Racial purists like Kodaly and Bartók can brandish staves all they want at this 'restaurant music'. Authenticity be damned; in a time of crisis and with a sea-crossing only hours away, Pál's gypsy fiddling is as poignant a taste of home as a plate of sausages and *lángosh*.

It is morning, and after a night spent at anchor, the ship is under way. Unescorted, painfully vulnerable to U-boat attack, the SS *Arethusa* zig-zags its way towards Devonport where the WVS are waiting with tea urns.

The hours pass.

Past noon: from her room in her parents' Edwardian terrace in Maida Vale – a room little changed from the one she played in as a child so that her feet dangle from the end of the bed at nights – Miriam Miller, Girton graduate, bluestocking factotum of a small philosophical society off Gower Street, looks up at a sky full of dirty air and ties a perfect blue bow at the neck of her starched white blouse.

The hours pass.

Evening: in a Devonport dock shed echoing with the ghosts of donkeymen and trimmers, Miriam Miller meets Hungarian medical genius Loránt Pál. 'Extend every assistance' the telegram has instructed her.

Pál, true to form, ruins everything, slumping down the gangplank drunk, his clothes drenched in the miasma of apricots, and his mind, what there is of it, stuck like a gramophone needle halfway through a story both incomprehensible and vulgar, something about electric shocks; about how he was gypped by a couple of Italian quacks, and how they 'made a complete balls of everything'. Miriam leads the boy – he seems hardly old enough to drive, let alone offer medical treatment to another human being – to her borrowed car, brushes his hand angrily off her lap and starts the engine.

Miriam is a good driver. Had the Society not acquired an unexpected usefulness to the war effort, she might have spent the war travelling. (Pál is sawing his arms now as though he were playing a fiddle. He starts to sing.) Were it not for the Society, she might be seeing the world from behind the windscreen of a bullet-riddled ambulance. She might be undressing in a room with a bed long enough for her chaste, lanky body, watching a sunset unbloodied by Battersea smoke.

Pál, oblivious to her little tears, accompanies her: dreadful, cod-Verdi recicative, as he lovingly rehearses his Italian competitors' initial, unsuccessful trials...

'Feerst, we feed theese wy-eer intoo thee *mawth*,

'Then wee feed theese wy-eer intoo thee *arsehewl*,

'Then wee FRY-UH THEE *HAART!*'

One year later: 1941. In a pleasant upstairs room belonging to the Society, émigré medical practitioner Dr Loránt Pál assembles his new couch.

It is a robust, extremely heavy piece of engineering. Poor little Miss Miriam Miller: when she opened the door to all those delivery boys, the eyes nearly started out of her head. *More* equipment? *More* noise? *More* interruption? Is it not enough that the lights gutter whenever that nasty little Svengali charges up his self-built therapy unit?

Pál lays out the pieces of the couch over the Persian rug in the centre of the room. The daylight is fading fast. He enjoys the green-brown penumbra of evening – the way the shadows of trees dapple the dark, scratched wood of his desk, and seem to animate the photographs he has hung about the room; photographs he brought with him, stuffed and crumpled in his doctor's bag, all the way from Budapest. Daimlers and horse-drawn *fiacres*. Society women with their little dogs. French and English nannies pushing their sailor-suited charges. Seeing these pictures dapple and shift in the light of evening, Pál fancies he can almost hear the hooves of a *fiacre*'s tired horse on the soaked wooden boards of the pavements below the Corso; the obsequious whisper of the barrel-bellied *Fö-úr*, leading him to his table at the Fészek Club.

Pál shakes off his reverie and tears the brown paper from off a shaped headrest. Oh, but this is splendid. He moulds the handsome red leather block in his hands, and appreciates the neat, discreet stitching: acme of the farrier's art. He can't help a mischievous smile as he recalls poor little Miriam, stood there at the foot of the stairs while the delivery boys paraded up and down. Opening and closing her mouth like a fish. What did she imagine these parcels contained? *Exhibits*?

Eyes straining against the dying light – he hates, and will hold off as long as possible, the yellow claustrophobia of electric light and blackout blinds – Pál slots and bolts the couch together. The piece has been manufactured precisely according to his instructions. How delightful it is, to have his idea come to life like this in his hands. He turns a brass wheel. The back of the couch rises. Another wheel: the pads supporting the legs articulate smoothly downwards; the headrest inches forward. Another: the pads supporting the torso part and curve to accommodate the larger patient. Pál sighs. Bliss. He casts around for the canvas bag containing the restraints.

Though he went along to that mews house in Notting Hill armed with several original ideas regarding the immobilization of his clients, in the end he left these details pretty much to the craftsman's discretion. The chap was astonishingly expert in these matters. In his bright, chilly studio, on high stools beside an angled drafting table, the two men contemplated the design in silence. Pinned to the table, the shape of

Pál's couch-to-be seemed to hover in front of the paper. It had been rendered in an exploded orthographic projection which suggested something sleeker and more streamlined than a mere piece of furniture. A space plane, perhaps, from the *Flash Gordon* serial.

'A sheepskin lining will provide security and comfort,' the craftsman opined. He was a big, liquid man with a big, liquid face.

Pál wasn't sure what to say.

The man bit his lips, then let go; the lips emerged, wet and red, and – has he got this right? – did the man actually *wink* at him?

'Compression fractures of the spine are my biggest concern,' Pál explained, confused.

The man closed his eyes and trembled. 'Yes. Yes.'

'Then there is the matter of the gat.'

The man's eyes sprang open. 'The what?'

'The gat. Or something, normally it is a gat – is this the right word? Excuse me. A rubber piece to bite on. To stop from swallowing the tongue.'

'Oh. Oh, yes. Yes.'

Another silence.

'Why—?' More biting of his lips. 'May I ask what will, ah, *occasion* the, ah—'

'The application of electricity.'

The man's enthusiasm for Pál's work was very gratifying. 'Oh, yes! Yes!'

Pál takes the straps out of the bag and reads the accompanying notes. Eccentric as he was, that strange jelly of a man has done an excellent job. It is no laughing matter, this business of immobilization: there's precious little point to Pál's therapy if his every other client ends up in a wheelchair.

Pál threads a braided calico tape experimentally through metal loops on either side of the headrest. Won't this strap interfere with the placement of the electrodes? Ah, no, he understands now, this part crosses *that*, comes *over* the skull to this attachment point here…

Pál, shaking his head, succumbs to a little light melancholy. Here he is, pioneering the most exciting advance in psychiatry this century, and all he can think about is how to lace these silly straps. How can a mere *couch* excite him, he who has the secrets of the human psyche to explore?

Life is like this, he has found. Petty details moss over and obscure the dramatic features of one's life. Pál puts down the bag – it really is too dark to work now – and climbs on board the couch. It is firm, cool and comfortable. Good. So now, perhaps, it is time to think about other things.

Closing his eyes, he wills himself back to the moment that ought to define him, and which, in dark moments, he replays behind his eyes, reminding himself of who and what he wants to be.

He remembers the morning von Meduna first administered camphor to a human patient.

For four years the man had barely moved. A catatonic stupor had rendered him little better than a vegetable. Extreme measures seemed justified, if not positively welcome: anything to break the tension. The man's mother, ashen-faced, had gravely bestowed her consent.

Pál recalls the forty interminable minutes while they waited for the seizure. The terrible tension in von Meduna's face.

It came, at last, with a terrible violence.

Steadily, von Meduna tested the patient's reflexes, he examined the pupils of his eyes, he spoke as steadily as he could. No one was fooled. Meduna's sweat spattered everyone and everything.

Pál remembers von Meduna's achievement chiefly through the look on the great man's face as the seizure took hold: a look that stared the world straight in the eye and would not look away – no, never – not until the world itself was changed.

As for the patient – what does Pál remember of the patient?

Very little. Only one little memory survives. But such a one! Pál chuckles to recall the chap's friendly little wave, a few days later, as he trotted, fully recovered, down the steps of the hospital in his borrowed clothes and into the arms of his mother.

At the open door of Pál's consulting room, a stifled cry.

Pál sits up.

Another, sharply indrawn breath.

Miriam stands in the doorway. 'I—' she begins, fighting for breath, 'I thought no one...' She is blinking against the last of the daylight. The sun is very low now, it is shining in her eyes.

'Hello, Miriam.' Pál slides smoothly from the couch. Miriam, he has decided, is a good-looking woman, if only she would learn to relax a little. He tries his warmest smile.

Miriam raises her hands to cover the blue bow at her neck. From where she is standing, Pál's smile is invisible. He is reduced to a silhouette. His solid shadow rises and straightens against the blood-red window, the rust-red room. His form is as distinct and mobile as a spillage of ink on a metal plate. Pál indicates the couch. 'Miriam, dear Miriam, would you care to experience my device?'

With a scream she barely bothers to stifle, Miriam runs back to her office and slams the door.

'"Poofter! Nancy! Queen!"'

Mr Anthony Burden shrinks in his chair as he recalls his shame.

A year has passed. It is the summer of 1943, and Pál finds himself engaged in work far different from the sort he expected from his London practice. Arriving in England, he had imagined wards of raving lunatics, bomb neurotics, crazed suicides and padded rooms. The mass panic the authorities expected has never come to pass. The people of London, through a combination of denial and habituation, have turned their backs on the Blitz: 'Business as usual'. Such stray neurotics as pass Pál's way are usually referred to him by interested sponsors at University College Hospital, down the road, and he has an uneasy sense that he is their circus dog; they want to see what tricks he can perform.

At least this chap has referred himself. Still, Pál wonders, who exactly is this Anthony Burden? Does he really want to be expending his professional energies on the sort of frayed intellectual that haunts the Society's library?

From Mr Burden's own account it is impossible to understand why he was never called up. He says that he 'tinkers'. That he is 'a tinkerer'. Eventually the words Dollis Hill crop up in conversation. Pál, a stranger here with no great appetite for general knowledge, does not understand their significance at first. Later, following some phoned enquiries, he establishes that his client works at the Post Office Research Station. So Burden is no mere 'tinkerer'.

'Oh, you know, I have these schemes, good enough that I can flannel my way through meetings. They never get me anywhere, they're not important.' Melancholics churn out this self-abnegating rubbish by the yard. In truth, Burden is an expert in telecommunications, in wireless telegraphy, in switching systems. This is why his occupation is reserved.

Loránt Pál records his enthusiasm in his notes: *'The man is an ASSET.'*

For Pál, no shirker, the treatment of Anthony Burden now acquires a special urgency. Yes, he would like to see more of him. Yes, he will be happy to arrange further appointments. For this will be no mere 'treatment'. This, at long last, will be war work!

Pál writes in his journal:

AB presents the classic symptoms of melancholia. He is agitated. He is underweight. He cannot smile. Already there are manifest signs of the patient's lack of personal care. His appearance is dishevelled beyond even the generous norms of English eccentricity. His face is a mass of razor cuts (first hints of hesitation marks?). His fingernails are black. The hands, sooted, unwashed, tremble in his lap.

Anthony Burden gulps and sobs – a little boy's stereotypical boo-hoo. Impossible to gauge what actual emotions underlie such a display. 'She *knew*!' Really it is very embarrassing. 'She never even saw my face, she never even cared to see my face, and still she *knew*!'

Thrown out of gear by the astonishing lewdness of Mr Burden's tale, the youthful therapist instinctively tries to make it less than it is. 'Perhaps she meant it as a joke,' he offers. A friendly act, and of absolutely no therapeutic use to his client whatsoever. *Concentrate!* Pál admonishes himself. *Concentrate. You are new here. Every client is a test. Even this one.*

'A joke?' Anthony Burden echoes, doubtfully.

'Yes. A joke. Maybe she was teasing you. I mean—' Pál can only plough on, with false jocularity. 'You did in the end decide to try and take her up the, ah, *passage…*' He feels a blush spread across his cheeks, hot enough to prickle. He wishes he felt better prepared for this. It's not as though he wasn't forewarned. When a previously buttoned-down civil servant blunders raving into an ARP patrol in the middle of the night without his trousers…

In a small, intense voice: 'This makes me a faggot, doesn't it?'

Pál weaves his hands about in front of his chest like an Anglican priest explaining the Trinity. 'Um,' he says. He knows next to nothing about the invert personality, and cares even less. 'Ah,' he says.

In fact, Pál feels a great deal of sympathy for Anthony Burden. The man's sexual indiscretion was unpardonable, of course, but to have your co-respondent turn around afterwards and look into your heart's deepest, darkest place! To have her drag that repressed Thing, pallid and blinking, into the harsh light of day: *'Poofter! Nancy! Queen!'*

If only the woman had had the good sense to keep her mouth shut. Then Mr Burden might even have had his little peccadillo with nothing worse to follow. It was a strange time, after all, in a city made stranger by bombing. He could have put his sordid little knee-trembler behind him – or found a more conventional way to satisfy his taste for anonymous encounters. The red-lit room. The sink in the corner. Money on the table. As things stand...

These are wild times for electroconvulsive therapy. It has only just wrestled free, strongest of the litter, from out of that slew of somatic therapies – malarial fever therapy, prolonged sleep therapy, insulin coma therapy – whose false dawns brightened many a psychiatrist's breakfast-table reading during the twenties and thirties. ECT works, but no one knows why. The relative therapeutic benefits of electrical dosage and strength of convulsion have yet to be established. The philosophical foundation is missing.

In this atmosphere, it is inevitable that Pál, though he has no great respect for the work of Lucio Bini, will be influenced by that pioneer's theories. What other resources has he? Following the precedent set by the Italian's 1942 'theory of annihilation', Loránt Pál considers himself a sort of mental hygienist, using electricity as a loofah to slough from the grey enamelled brain the scum of past mistakes and long-held misapprehensions.

It is clear to him, after a few preliminary consultations, that Anthony Burden is a sexual invert. A homosexual, in other words. It takes no *a priori* assumption on Pál's part to establish that this affliction lies at the heart of Burden's spiralling melancholy.

Now ECT's efficacy as a treatment for melancholy is beyond question. Six to eight treatments have, in Pál's experience, always sufficed to bring about an improvement. The sixth session's unclouding effect can be positively miraculous.

Some patients, however, require many more treatments before any improvement is seen. In addition, at the back of Pál's mind there is always the daring possibility that their sessions might eventually root out, by the annihilation method, the inversion that lies at the root of Mr Burden's despair.

Besides, the patient approves. He *encourages*. This is the first time in Pál's career that therapy has taken on the quality of a collaboration, and the doctor is flattered as well as enthused. It is as though the two men have embarked upon an adventure together, at this pioneering and dangerous time, into the mysteries of the sexually deviant personality.

Pál does not think to question his client's enthusiasm. Why should he? Who is he to stand in Mr Burden's way when he begs, tears pouring down his face, that everything – from his first, moist, prep-school fumblings in his best friend's Y-fronts to the close relationship he enjoyed with his mother, from his navy father's frequent absences to the precise sensual recall he has achieved, with the professor's help, of his wife's anus at the moment of penetration ('Does it tighten? Does it suck? Tell me your impressions, Mr Burden, leave out nothing. Does it welcome like a mouth or repel like a tightened fist?') – that everything, the lot of it, the very meat and veg of sex, and everything to do with spit and spew, should go?

Beyond the Society's front door, a sumptuous fitted red carpet lies like a spillage of fur over the entrance hall floor, and a wide staircase leads, with barely a creak, to the upper rooms. The industrious clatter of Miriam Miller at her typewriter rises, greatly muffled, through the rugs lain across the first-floor waiting area.

There, on the landing, a handsome carved mahogany bookcase with glass doors sums up in little the Society's pre-occupations: *Science and Sanity* by Alfred Korzybski; a slim pocket hardback called *You Can Speak With Your Dad*.

Anthony Burden, intrigued, goes to fetch this book – only to discover, with a chuckle, that he has misread the title. This misprision of his is something he might mention to the doctor, a revealing 'Freudian slip' which may afford them a minute or two of entertainment, and perhaps an insight or two, before the paddles are applied.

Dr Loránt Pál is not a psychoanalyst, but in the year he spent in Vienna studying brain-behaviour relationships, he learned a trick or two. Take, for example, his consulting room. Pál has transformed his modest upstairs space at the Society into something which resembles the retreat of an elderly gnostic: antique rugs, shelves crammed with cryptic *objets*; framed photographs of a middle-European city.

The machineries of his therapy, by contrast, are wonderfully explicit. Turning the brass wheels underneath a narrow table, padded with horse hair and upholstered in red leather, adjusts the height and angle of the pads on which Anthony lies down, ready for his seizure. Anthony, seeing this table for the first time, imagines a rack. This impression is not lessened by the rasping tightness of the leather straps with which he is bound, the chill kiss of paddles at his temples – metal paddles, with small wooden handles, like library stamps – and the unforgettable taste of the rubber gat that keeps him from swallowing his tongue.

The spasms he endures exhaust him. Several days, sometimes, may pass before he can move without discomfort. Of course, Rachel is worried.

Sighing, John Arven agrees to do his part, as a friend of the family, to put her mind at rest. 'But for goodness' sake, Anthony, what are you doing to yourself? I never expected – I mean, is all this still necessary? Why do you keep putting yourself through this mill?'

Anthony, sprawled blear-eyed and exhausted across his couch, blinks up at his faithful old friend as, from the very bottom of a surprisingly comfortable warm well, one might blink up at the shaft's daylit opening. 'What mill?' The tiredness brought on by his treatments feels positively healthful. After his spasms it is as if – having never knowingly taken a day's exercise in his life – he has run a heroic distance. He could take any amount of this physical 'punishment'.

He is fascinated by the way Dr Loránt's machine dims certain memories; even, in some happy cases, erasing them. His mind is losing its tackiness. It is losing its purchase on the pure everyday. It is becoming more and more polished, more glossy, more adamantine.

Of course, Dr Loránt's 'massage of his diencephalic centres' doesn't come without its sacrifices. The music Anthony loves is losing its power now. Palaces no longer ascend in handsome etched volutes up to the ceilings of his mind. At the resolution of a particularly difficult modulation, no Brunelleschi dome sphincters at nipple's point. All is flat, a grey landscape, a Friesen island of the mind, where fallow fields dribble off in gorse and dunes towards a spit of sand that slides, with aching slowness, beneath a shallow sea.

Dr Loránt is delighted. 'Our enemy,' he tells Anthony, 'is *evasion*. I see this clearly now. You are *evading* your *inversion*. You are trying to turn it into something that you can control. This is not the solution. Tell me, Mr Burden, do you dance?'

Anthony, fascinated, shakes his head. 'Never could stand it,' he concedes.

'You see?' the doctor laughs. 'You are afraid that if you dance to music, you will take the woman's part. So you turn music into architecture – into something you can control! These gifts of yours are veils, behind which you protect yourself from direct experience. I will go further (I think you are ready for this): I believe your *inversion* is itself an *evasion*! But what is it that you are evading? What are you running from, that the anus makes for you a hiding place? This is what we must discover!'

So Anthony, drunk on an orgy of self-annihilation, waves himself goodbye. His work means nothing to him now. He cannot understand it. He boxes up his exercise books and is carrying them out to the bin when he remembers the Society where Pál has his consulting rooms. The irony of it tickles him. He will donate his books to the Society. Cataloguing them will give Miriam Miller something to do during these long, lonely winter nights.

That same evening, when he returns home, Anthony embraces Rachel and bursts into tears.

All evening he stumbles over what he has to say. That he longs to participate in the muscular future of her people, with its hardships and setbacks. 'Our future lies in Palestine,' he says. 'You have been right all along, my darling. Any life worth living belongs to the land. Land you can grow things in. Land you can be buried in.'

Rachel, dumbfounded, stares down at him, sprawled exhausted on their couch. 'Has this something to do with your accident?'

He opens his mouth, but there are no words.

'Why do you shut me out?' she says.

He can only shake his head.

'Tell me,' she says. 'I will understand.'

Of that he has no doubt. Oh, it is hopeless, hopeless… 'My love,' he sobs, and tells her everything.

Afterwards he closes his eyes, spent, content, and waits for his world to end.

Of course, it does not.

He opens his eyes.

Rachel, her brown eyes full of a terrible love, bends over him and strokes him behind his ears.

Now they have a project to work towards, hand in hand, Anthony and Rachel are able to behave more freely towards each other. The air between them is clear. Rachel does not have to value Anthony's work. Anthony no longer pretends to find Rachel attractive.

Their marriage is empty, and therefore powerful: Anthony's honesty has created a vacuum which the future rushes to fill.

As the war in Europe ends, Rachel's friends are making their way to the Protectorate. They send the couple literature from the United Workers' Party. They send photographs of themselves brandishing guns from the Scda Arms Works in Czechoslovakia.

Anthony says they should go. It is exactly what he needs and wants. 'You see, I used to think we were all just bits of some greater whole, a sort of Leviathan. Maybe that's true. I realize now, though, it is up to each man, how he lives. We each decide what we are a part of, and what we stand apart from. For the first time in my life, I feel ready to make that choice. I feel ready to let go, and live my life at a human scale at last. To dig. To hoe. Think of it! To breed...'

'Once you are better, my love,' Rachel promises, still not quite able to understand him. 'As soon as you're quite, quite well.'

4

In 1950, the Migdal Tikvah kibbutz, founded by the Kibbutz Artzi movement in 1930, consists of two long accommodation buildings, an armoury, a school and a canteen. There are no roads, just gaps between the buildings, tracks of beaten earth, and here and there a puddle of concrete to plug a pot-hole. The concrete is all broken up, making stones which the children kick about, viciously, as though they were harrying small animals.

The kibbutz is built on a hillside some way above the tree-line. There is no natural shade to speak of – only the mathematical trapezoids of darkness cast by the squat buildings. Anthony Burden's dazzled eyes cannot adapt to the darkness of these dangerous metallic shadows. He is afraid to approach them. He imagines children in them, watching him with wide, unblinking eyes made dull by dust.

In the machinery store, the muscular men of the kibbutz work in silence. The middle-aged ones made Aliyah here in the 1920s. The youths, barely pubescent, are their children. An intermediate generation fled here as teenagers during the world war. Anthony imagines the stirring letter he will write this evening to Sage:

… They come from Bucharest, from Krakow, from Berlin and from Pécs. They speak Yiddish, German, Hebrew, whatever tongue will serve. They communicate with each other by means of strong, muscular gestures, miming the actions at which they are habitually engaged: ploughing, hoeing, planting, digging, driving, wrestling, shooting. They are miming out a new life for themselves, all the while expecting Soviet forces to roll in from the north, to help them realize their final vision.

Anthony raises a hand to these sons of toil.

They do not respond.

He gives them an ameliorating little wave.

Nothing.

He will write: *'Give my love to Rachel.'*

He comes to the lip of the ledge on which the kibbutz is built. Fields edge up the lower slopes of the hill opposite in a half-hearted, experimental manner. There is nothing cooling or vegetable about those squares of malarial green. They look more like swatches, trial colours for a better creation. Here and there the earth is reddish orange, in other places it is yellowish-orange. Mostly it is greyish-orange.

He misses his wife.

Oranges are the kibbutz's speciality. The oranges of the Migdal Tikvah kibbutz grow from green pips to rock-hard little fruit the size and weight of limes. Unspeaking and unsmiling, the kibbutzim teach Anthony Burden how to prune and how to tend.

The oranges swell. Ditches are dug, cisterns are cast, sacks of concrete and buckets of sand are lined up ready for mixing. Lorries arrive bearing lengths of clay pipe to feed the new cisterns, and pumps that never work, so that the old men spend the day deep in the metallic shadows, stripping the pumps, while Anthony and men younger than him work under the blazing sun among the parched trees.

Looking around him as he works, Anthony sees that the young kibbutzim tend the trees with the same unsmiling seriousness with which they fire their guns at targets set among the rocks. The faces of his comrades look as though they have been carved out of thorn. They looked oiled, no, *resined*. They look as if the sun might set them alight. Burning, they might crack open like seed-pods revealing new, even more brightly burnished faces. He can no more look at the faces around him than he can look into the sun reflected off a polished metal mask.

At first Anthony supposed that these young, fit, handsome men must resent the sweaty hours they have to spend among the trees – that they would sooner be at target practice. He was wrong about this. When the muscular young men take up their guns and fire at the rocks, they have it in mind to prune the very stone, to tend it with a savage love into the shapes they require, until no stone is left unshaped, and the whole land has the even solidity of the bunkhouses in which they sleep.

He cannot speak to them. His rusty schoolboy German barely allows him to ask directions, never mind converse. On their arrival it was left to Rachel, his wife, the conscientious student who had already picked up the rudiments of Hebrew from night classes in London, to teach the ancient tongue to her husband. Her sudden decision to return to England has left him deaf and mute.

In his infrequent letters to friends, he puts on a brave face.

> ... *In this deserted land the people of Migdal Tikvah are shaping a socialist Eden. Soon the Czechoslovakians will be here themselves, in arms with their comrades the Russians, to realize this latest outpost of edenic Soviet futurity, here in ancient Palestine. For now they send guns and promises, and the muscular young kibbutzim of the Migdal Tikvah kibbutz practise among the orange groves, shooting at targets crudely stencilled on the rocks.*

The inclusiveness of this vision – the rallying call to a common cause – is illusory. These are not and never were his politics. It is just that he has learned to ape his wife's opinions. This is not his battle; it is hers – or was.

Bad enough that she should have abandoned her dreams; did she really have to leave him trapped in their wreckage?

Since Rachel left him, Anthony has learned to resent this nation. He resents the rocks over which he stumbles, and the sunlight which swells and reddens his skin, so that he looks ever more like a sunburnt child. However hard he works, he has a dilettante's face. A soft, exquisite face: he probes and prods its schoolboy redness and hopes in vain for it to acquire a metallic sheen.

He resents, finally and overwhelmingly, the orange trees themselves. This is their first commercially viable fruiting, and the elder settlers, entering the groves, weep to see this sweet fraction of their dreams realized. As he labours and stirs the cement for new cisterns, Anthony wants to dash the men's tears from their eyes with his fists.

Now it is time for the kibbutzim to harvest the oranges; crate them; transport them; worst of all, eat them. For the next month, at the Migdal Tikvah kibbutz, oranges will be the only fruit. Glasses of the corrosive syrup are served at every grainy, garlicky meal. Migdal Tikvah's orange juice eats into Anthony's gums like battery acid. It drills a line of tiny holes across the tip of his tongue and plants a row of ulcers there. It bloats him like a toxin. At night, it bubbles through the lining of his stomach, eating holes in him that he can locate precisely, that he can count. Its colour, drunk out of a tin mug, is as brilliantly artificial as car paint, and it discolours the tin, leaving little black patches that no amount of scrubbing will remove.

Each morning, Anthony rolls his bloated stomach out of the dormitory pallet, the stomach that does not seem to belong to him any more. It has become something apart from him, some unit of production intimately connected with the economy of oranges. He enters the canteen and there, beside every bowl of gruel, sits a plate heaped with oranges. Then he shambles, with the strange crab-like gait he has developed since his therapy, down the hill to the terraces marked with huge boulders that the original settlers, now old men, have spent their youth moving aside – by main force, they would have you believe, by donkey and hemp rope and pulley and finally with their bare hands. He pauses a moment, looking over the rough, rusty land beyond the hill, imagining that every square foot is covered in discarded orange peel, peel gone rusty, peel bleached in the sun and soft and rotten in shadow, so that flecks of green here and there are a thin penicillin-like mould growing over the discarded peel covering the earth. Then, hearing the tractor, he comes away from the edge and goes and takes a corner of tarpaulin and helps spread it over the ground, and then the young men take their hooks and scissors and ladders and they harvest the oranges, which fall to the ground with a soft, complacent thump. These are the poorest of the crop, the bruised runts that he will eat this afternoon, because the kibbutzim, drunk on oranges, these emblems of their success, have stopped the midday bread-making in order to make room for more delicious oranges.

When they are done with the runts, the young men and women take up panniers and climb the trees and snip off fat, shiny, healthy oranges, one by one. Anthony considers this a sign of the kibbutzniks' lack of imagination, that they do not keep the best for themselves, that they prefer to gorge on runts and let the choicest fruits be shipped away.

For lunch he eats an orange, facing away from the others so they will not see the grimaces the acid forces him to pull as it eats his face away from the inside. The others eat oranges as though they were soft rolls. They are monsters of consumption, and he is afraid of them.

In deference to his injured back he spends afternoons helping the women in the packing plant. Packing the oranges means laying them in straw, in crates stamped with the name of the kibbutz in dark, blood-like ink. The time he spends bent over box after box, hardly moving, does his back no good at all. It is only with the greatest pain and difficulty that he is able to sit down to his evening meal, rounded off, as always, with a sharp, pippy orange.

The next morning, the orange crates are driven by truck to the market in Haifa, Red Haifa, where the leaders of the United Workers' Party crowd the cafés and talk of revolution and, looking north, anticipate the day when Soviet tanks will lumber into town, bringing to fulfilment the socialist paradise towards which they work so very hard. The men of Haifa imagine laying palm leaves before the tanks. The women of Haifa dream of throwing garlands of orange blossom up to the boys on the tanks. This constant expectation occasions an atmosphere of permanent festival in Haifa. It is the hysteria of a community living always on the brink of millennium.

Something of this telegraphs itself even to the impassive kibbutzniks of Migdal Tikvah, on the day the lorries leave for Haifa. Women run from the terraces with covered baskets and lift them, smiling, up into the hands of the drivers sitting high up in the cabs of their lorries. Under chequered cloths lies a rich abundance of oranges for the drivers and their mates to eat as they go on their way, the juice spitting and spurting over their rough woollen jumpers, the seats, the dashboard, the windscreen and down their sunburnt cheeks. All the way to Haifa, roadside wasps, launch themselves in desperate dives through cracks in the truck windows, and even through the air vents, to get at the oranges within.

Anthony looks forward to these runs to Haifa, in spite of the market, the tiers of crated oranges, the littorals and dunes of loose oranges, the clouds of wasps.

He looks forward to the cafés most of all: sweet coffee and cakes to soothe his burned and bitten mouth. There is, in spite of the sight of so many muscular sun-loving Jews, an atmosphere, or at any rate a saving shred, of *luxe* about the cafés of Haifa. A feeling conducive to conversation, even to thought.

Anthony remembers thought, what it felt like. He recollects how anxious he was, once, to stop thinking, how treacherous thought had proved. He is beginning to wonder whether his decision to stop thinking was entirely wise.

As a man who has been on vacation too long – a man whose languor has begun to turn to a ponderousness that he cannot enjoy – Anthony, sat outside his favourite café overlooking the market square in Haifa, begins to toy with the idea of ideas.

He writes: *'I used to think the individual was redundant. Groups of people, working in concert, were the future. Together, people knew more, and this made them wiser; this is what I believed. And when at*

*last everyone was joined to everyone else by a length of telegraph wire,
on that day, everything would be known by everyone.'*

He wonders for whom he is writing.

*'I thought this would be a good thing. A coming together. A final
wordless reconciliation between people and their world. An end to
Others, and to the messy business of living.'*

Yes, this is true. He is aware now of his limitations. If nothing else,
Pál's treatments have levelled his moods and cleared his head. He
may not have very much to say any more. Few dreams, and fewer
hopes. What little he has to say, he can say it now. Now that it is too
late.

The fag-end of the war and its aftermath are a grey sea of
disconnected memories.

His back kept giving out, again and again.

He remembers lying in a hospital bed, quite crippled.

He remembers begging his old schoolfriend, John Arven, to take a
compassionate interest in his wife.

He remembers – this must have been in 1948 – waking up after a
delicate operation to correct his fused spine. John Arven was in the
recovery room when he woke from the anaesthetic. He was so sore and
stiff he couldn't show any expression, which was lucky, as there was no
expression he especially wanted to show.

'Shall I pull the blinds?' John asked, already moving to the window.

'God, no,' Anthony croaked.

John looked around him at the curtains, the flowers, the machinery
that kept Anthony's back in torsion. 'Up in no time!' he cried,
desperately. 'Back on your feet!'

As though, by these efforts, he might conceal the fact that Rachel was
not there.

The recollection makes Anthony shudder. A breeze is picking up
around the market square. He smoothes out the paper and writes:

*The War fascinated me. The movements of money and machines
and people, the strategies, the shifts in the global balance of power.
Of course, the longer the war went on, the more innovative it
became, the more scientific, the more apparent it was that no one
was in charge; that the war would have to play itself out across the
world in its own way; that even Churchill was dwarfed by events,
no more, by then, than just another cog in a vast economic
'metabolism'.*

The coldness of these sentiments makes him shiver. He imagines what
Rachel would make of these easy, inadequate abstractions. What any
passing Jew would make of them. Any girl from Terezen with a number
on her wrist.

He puts down his pen and watches the business of the town. The
oranges. A sudden gust blows his paper away. He tries to leap up, to
follow the paper, and his back sings with pain. He falls back into his
seat, gasping. Everything he has written vanishes.

A second later, another breeze blows a paper liner past him – the sort
used to cover orange crates. It wraps itself around a table leg. Gingerly,
Anthony bends down and picks it up. The printed side shows a smiling
buxom girl in a headscarf, plucking big juicy oranges from a tree.
Anthony shudders and turns the paper over. The other side is blank.

Strange, the give and take of the world.

He spreads the paper across his table. He picks up his pen, and
finishes his thought: no matter that the start of it is lost. What does it
signify, after all? Having the idea is what counts.

He writes: *'My life has changed since the war, and I no longer enjoy
the luxury of distance.'*

It is harder, and for that reason more admirable, to think of things at
a human scale. It is difficult to be honest.

He begins: *'In Palestine I have buried my marriage, and I have
uncovered my heart.'*

One of many long letters he is writing to a man he can no longer call his friend.

He remembers the lengths to which John Arven went to explain Rachel's absence. How Rachel had moved to the country, in order to create a separation between herself and her London circle: 'She knows that moving to Palestine will effect a very great change in the pace of her life.'

Such casuistry. Anthony, bedridden, reached inside himself for a sympathetic word or two. He found nothing but bile: 'It seems she has chosen to emigrate by degrees.'

'What she is doing,' Arven said, annoyed at his friend's flippancy, 'is waiting for you.'

Why hadn't she come to see him? Why did she not write?

'Just bite the bullet,' John Arven insisted. 'It's time for you to take up the reins of your marriage again. I'll be there with you, if it helps.'

So he was, standing there on the station platform to meet the London train, scruffy as usual, his shirt-sleeves rolled up to his elbows. He drove them to the cottage – with a nice care, and very slowly – in Rachel's car.

There were rhododendrons in the front garden. The lawn was new, a slightly sickly yellow-green in the weak, overcast light. The house, by contrast, was big and hunched in on itself with honeysuckle over the door and old roses, with wicked thorns. Next door to the cottage stood a hideous, white concrete shell of a garage. There was a lawnmower out, a pair of shears, a fork stuck in the earth with an old tweed jacket draped over the back of it. As they walked up the path, Arven stepped casually over, rescued the jacket, and slipped it on over his shirt.

Anthony could not have said what it was about that moment. Was there something casual or proprietorial about John's action? He did not know. But he sensed it contained a meaning which excluded him.

John led the way through the back door into the kitchen.

Rachel was kneading dough in a large china bowl. Her arms were dusted in flour up to her elbows. She looked up. There was a streak of flour, like war paint, under her right eye. Everything about her had a sheen. She had grown out her hair. Anthony had never seen her looking more beautiful. He couldn't say anything. He couldn't move.

She smiled, seeing John enter the room.

Then she saw Anthony.

'Oh,' she said.

She had not been expecting him. John had not told her.

'So you're here, then,' she said.

Remembering all this, he writes: '*I miss you, Sage, my darling. I hope with all my heart that you have found happiness together. I do not blame you for making love to Rachel. But how I wish you had fallen in love with me!*'

5

It is 20 July 1969, and evening in Lourenço Marques, colonial capital of Mozambique. The street-sellers are packing their wares into suitcases: batteries, handbags and carved hardwood boxes. Toy cars made of cans, random pharmaceuticals, fried cakes, combs, cheap make-up from Hong Kong. Pictures of saints. Pictures of Elvis Presley.

Anthony sees none of this. He is still sat opposite Gregor in the offices of the Institute of Distance and Field Education, and he still has no clue why he is being kept here. Plus, the knot in his back feels like a hot coal wedged in his bones.

The tension in the room has been building up all week. Strangeness has followed strangeness. Anthony has arrived at the office to find the place locked up, while silent figures moved behind the frosted glass door panel, ignoring him and the rap of his stick against the frame. Other times, Gregor has welcomed Anthony into the room with the sort of smothering friendliness a murderer in a stage farce might adopt, desperate to draw attention away from the body in the corner.

On these occasions, Gregor has kept Anthony talking after office hours, long into the night, regaling him with stories drawn from his wartime experiences. Gregor is an explosives expert by training, skilled in defusing enemy ordnance. Earnestly, and at great length, he has described to Anthony how various trigger devices succumbed, one by one, to his craft.

At 3 p.m., with the tension at breaking point, Gregor, trembling, turns on the little Bush radio he keeps on the sill of the window. Slumped, his back turned, he resembles the deputy headmaster of an unsuccessful public school.

As the Junta's power has seeped away, so the station's staffers, one by one, have drifted off. Gregor, by contrast, is a man whose keenness for everything borders on the abject. He has assumed the role of caretaker for the defunct office with the punctilious enthusiasm with which he approaches everything: a piece of paperwork, a telephone call. Why has Gregor remained? Can his energy not be harnessed to more useful work? Perhaps now the mystery will be solved.

The radio is tuned to the local government station but the news, as ever, is focused on a glorified tin can, 240,000 miles away. Anthony struggles to hear the American English of Houston's mission controller over the garbled real-time Portuguese translation:

'... *You might be interested in knowing, since you are already on the way, that a Houston astrologer, Ruby Graham, says that all the signs are right for your trip to the moon. She says that Neil is clever; Mike has good judgement and Buzz can work out intricate problems. She also says that Neil tends to see the world through rose-coloured glasses but he is always ready to help the afflicted or distressed.'*

At twenty minutes past five, a newsflash interrupts the broadcast. 'International black fanatic' Jorge Katalayo has died in an explosion at a 'suspected terrorist cell' on the outskirts of Lourenço Marques.

Gregor makes a sound deep in his throat.

Anthony, annoyed by the announcer's boorish interruption, assumes Gregor is voicing a like frustration. He is about to make some bland remark about the radio station when Gregor falls to his knees.

Anthony's next thought is that Gregor is having a heart attack. When he hurries over and sees that Gregor, far from falling at random, has flung himself down before the institute's fire safe, he is momentarily reassured. Has Gregor remembered something? Something urgent? What? 'Gregor?'

Gregor claws at the safe; his fingers tremble as he rattles through the secret combination.

So many of Gregor's recent actions have left Anthony nonplussed, he hardly sees the importance of this one. It is only as Gregor swings open the great steel door and begins pulling out documents in great handfuls, that Anthony wonders whether his employer's actions might not be connected to the recent newsflash.

As Gregor rifles through the papers, Anthony takes advantage of his absorption, stealing forward to study the institute's secrets.

From a sea of bills, receipts and final demands, Gregor plucks a slim white envelope. He tears it open, and unfolds the contents within. He hands a sheet to Anthony, stuffs another in his trouser pocket, crumples up the remainder and the envelope and throws them back into the safe.

He says, without looking at Anthony, 'Do exactly what it says. Don't ask questions. Don't wait here. Don't go home.'

Anthony scans the paper. Typed on a faded ribbon are the details of an escape route. The name of a shipping company. A telephone number. The accompanying instructions are so infantile, they can only be a kind of code:

If time allows, be sure to obtain a sufficiency of warm clothing.
Do not under any circumstances accept rides from strangers.
Discard your house keys.
Avoid intercourse.
Stout shoes must be worn.

Once the papers are back in the safe, Gregor bends awkwardly, reaches into the top right corner of the safe, and pulls out a metal pineapple.

Anthony blinks.

It is a grenade.

Gregor pulls the pin, tosses the grenade into the safe and heaves the door shut.

The door is heavy. It takes a second to close. In that second, the grenade rolls off the papers piled willy-nilly inside the safe, and falls onto the floor. Anthony gasps. Gregor heaves the door open again on smooth, silent hinges, plucks up the grenade as though it is hot, and places it on the papers, all the while pushing at the door to close it again.

The door slams shut.

The grenade goes off. The safe is well built, and the explosion makes no more impact than if someone had rapped it with a spanner.

Far louder is Gregor's wail as he spins up and away. The stub of his amputated forefinger drizzles blood across the floor, the table, Gregor's trousers, his shoes, Anthony's shoes, the door and the door-handle, leaving a trail for Anthony to follow, as Gregor makes his getaway.

Anthony, mystified, follows Gregor out of the building, only to lose his trail across a busy junction. He wonders where to go. He pulls out his paper and reads: *'If time allows, be sure to obtain a sufficiency of warm clothing… Stout shoes must be worn.'*

He wonders if he shouldn't just go home. He wonders what is going on, and what it has to do with him. Of course he should go home.

And tomorrow?

What should he do tomorrow? Should he come into work? What will he find? Will Gregor be there, his hand in bandages, full of apologies and explanations? Or will the place be locked up, secured by the police, surrounded by military vehicles and PIDE men in dark ill-fitting suits?

Or will the room be empty, unlocked, just as they left it, a chaos of imported newspapers and out-of-date gazetteers? If it is, should he sit down? Should he wait for the phone to ring?

Utterly at sea, Anthony thrusts the mysterious paper into his trouser pocket and sets off at random through the town.

In his rush to follow Gregor, Anthony has forgotten his stick. He wants to go back for it. He wants to return and sit down with a cup of tea and listen some more to the little Bush radio on the office window sill; to hear again the miraculous conversation, conducted over a distance of some quarter of a million miles, with the men who will soon be setting foot on the moon. But he is afraid: Gregor's panic and the strange, minatory instructions in his pocket have taken hold of his imagination. There is no way he can go back.

In the yard beside a rundown hotel two old women stand beneath a fig tree, pounding maize for *nsima*. In the street opposite, another woman stirs a pot of *caril de amendoim* – he can smell it from here. The cook's face is covered with the garish white pan-stick make-up you see women use in Tete, against the sun.

He comes to the bluff overlooking the bay. A woman calls to him from a doorway. He knows that if he looks at her, her smile will break his heart.

There is nothing from which he has to run away. There is no need for him to flee. Flee what? Yet he keeps on walking.

'Do not under any circumstances accept rides from strangers.'

Well, really.

He looks around him. This is not the way home. This is not the way back to the office. It is not that he is consciously walking *away* from these places, exactly. On the contrary, when he analyses what few feelings he can muster in response to these bizarre events, it seems to him that he is walking *towards...*

Towards what he doesn't know: whatever shadowy existence is implied by the strange paper in his hand.

'Christ,' he says aloud, reading his instructions over for the third or fourth time. He is not sure whether to be disgusted or amused; it has just dawned on him that this list could just as well double as an account of his life: *'Discard your house keys... Avoid intercourse.'*

The shipping office occupies the first floor of an old Portuguese villa to the north of the port. The room's shelves are lined with old fabric-bound ledgers, and its heavy furniture swims in a dark, resinous light. Near the window, a white girl pecks at a typewriter. She glances at him, then returns to study the keys before her. Her tongue edges between her lips and glistens in the nicotinic light.

He hands over his paper. The girl's tongue withdraws, leaving a wet trail upon her lower lip. Idly, she waves at a connecting door, lays the paper down on her desk and goes back to her typing. Anthony reaches over for the paper. The girl's hand shoots out and slaps the paper, keeping it from him. He meets the girl's belligerent eyes, but lets his gaze slide away. Asking her a question will force her to speak, and he is afraid of what her voice will sound like.

He opens the connecting door.

The room beyond is lighter, busier, more modern. Fluorescent lights hang from a ceiling stained with damp. The uneven floor is covered with a thin carpet of an indeterminate colour. A big, unhealthy man waves him to a desk. There is a radio playing, tuned to an international station. The voice of Mission Control comes through uncluttered by translation: *'We have loss of signal as Apollo Eleven goes behind the moon. Velocity 7,664 feet per second, weight 96,012 pounds. We're seven minutes and forty-five seconds away from lunar orbit insertion.'*

Seven minutes and forty-five seconds later, the means and timing of Anthony Burden's departure from Lourenço Marques have all been dealt with, quickly and without fuss. The false name on his documents sounds the only unorthodox note. Otherwise he might be any other independent traveller signing aboard a tramp steamer.

'Apollo Eleven, Apollo Eleven, this is Houston, can you read me?'

'The captain will hand you your new passport shortly before your arrival.' The man's patter could only have been acquired by his dealing with a dozen similar requests a day. Burden imagines this stream of men who enter the shipping office, more or less desperate, more or less confused, only to emerge, a few minutes later, rebranded.

He knows of no reason why he should run, much less why he should abandon Mozambique, or why he should make his getaway in so uncomfortable a mode of transport, and under a false name at that. At the same time, he is finding it increasingly difficult to think up reasons why he should stay. Everything about his life here is evaporating like the toils of a dream a minute after waking.

How can he go home? He cannot even remember the name of his road.

Neil Armstrong says: *'We're going over the Messier series of craters right at this time, looking vertically down on them and, hey, we can see good-sized blocks in the bottom of the crater. I don't know what our altitude is now but those are pretty good-sized blocks.'*

Anthony walks reluctantly out of range of the radio, out of the room and the building, and into the eyeblink-short tropical evening, boarding papers crumpled in his hand, and with the dizzying sensation of having been flushed through a gap no wider than a clerk's anonymous smile into a new world.

Back in the office, Buzz Aldrin sighs: *'When a star sets up here, there's just no doubt about it. One instant it's there and the next instant it's just completely gone.'*

PQRD

1

Summer 1944.

Dick Jinks – a merchant seaman long since invalided out of the service – takes apart his customer's starter motor and spreads the pieces across his work table, its surface scarred by years of plier-work, chisel-work, horse-chains mended, bridles restitched, saddles restuffed and invisibly repaired. The table's legs are raised on bricks so that Dick can work standing up. Sitting down, alas, is a fond and ever-dimming memory for him, whose red-faced 'oofs!' and 'aahs!' have given way this past year to more clenched forms of suffering. Dick picks up a piece of the dinky little motor, studies it – what will they think of next? – and pops it into his mouth as though it were a plum. He swills it around his mouth until it is clean, spits it out onto a cleanish rag, dries it and picks up the next.

Alice, Dick's wife of eleven years, threads her way into the covered yard, their new baby in her arms, and tries not to muss up her cotton frock on the gear piled all around: farrier's irons in a rusty tin drum, heavy rubber tyres, some of them inflatable, most the solid sort, huge wooden horse collars, an anvil; a broken tractor wheel, higher than a man. Sunlight shines into Dick's dark nook through her frock, silhouetting thighs grown thick from child-bearing, calves still shapely, and knees – well, knees, as ever, too small; fragile knots of bone. Dick Jinks harbours a secret, wincing fear for her knees.

Their first child, the trigger for their shotgun marriage and young Dick's precipitate flight to sea in 1934, would have been eleven now, had she not died within hours of her birth, leaving Alice, fresh seawidow, heartbroken and alone. For his part, Dick was none the wiser for the longest while, for he was already out in mid-Atlantic and, at the moment of his baby girl's death, only hours away from the engine room explosion and the defining cataclysm of his own life.

So this new arrival, apple of his mother's eye, this little Nicky Jinks, represents an unexpected second chance (cafeteria sign still faced 'Open', gingham-curtained door unlocked, a memorably swift, stiff violation against the serving counter, the only copulatory position of which Dick, her poor spinelocked darling, is now capable).

From 1934 to now, in the interval between their dead child and their live one, between Dick Jinks's running off to sea and his return, what has his life been?

He cannot remember.

Dim impressions of a horsehair couch, leather, like an operating table. Pictures on a wall, a foreign city, nowhere he knew or could imagine. The echo of a name, Pál, as in, 'me and my pal', the pun as hollow as a skull's grin. The taste of rubber.

Nothing coheres.

'*Come along, Mr Jinks.*'

Instructions. Admonitions. Corridors of pale green or mustard yellow. Doors with numbers. Hoses. Beds.

'*Where are we?*' says a voice inside his head. A woman's voice.

He looks around him for an answer. This grotto, filmed with oil. These things – tat for farmers' horses, tyre irons, lifting tackle, all the stuff of a modern blacksmith's trade. It should be colourful in here. Yellow paper wrappers round the tins of engine grease. Wheel jack a cheery red enamel. Saddle leathers tan and butterscotch. The colours here have been first muted, then swallowed up utterly by dust, grit, the sump impurities of his trade.

This is no grotto.

He knows what this is.

This place of black and white.

Fighting for breath, Dick drools the motor part out of his mouth onto the table. It glistens there, grey, like a spent tooth.

Alice, babe-besotted, does not see the panic in her husband's eyes, the hollow tremor of his diaphragm as he fights for air. She says, 'A nice day out. The plums are ready for picking. You can hold the ladder for me when you're done in here.'

Even as he draws breath for his terrible *Eeeee!*, the normal, friendly strains of his wife's voice avert catastrophe. They sever the red wire, disarming the terrible thing inside him, and he is back in the present. He lets go a ragged breath and covers, as he always does, with a big piratical 'Yo! Ho!'

One thing is certain: whatever the other details of his history, Dick, like a pocket-knife rusted open, has seized up to the point where he can be of no imaginable wartime use. So he is cast up here – after many strange and shadowy excursions – like a timber shivered from a wreck. He has much to be grateful for. This blacksmithing business for a start, pride and joy of his lowering father-in-law. And his wife, of course. Above all things, this wife he had practically forgotten. Not for a second had he imagined – returning, like a wounded animal, back to his starting point – that he would find her still living here and, if not exactly waiting for him, still amenable enough to his seaman's bluster, his rough re-wooing and finally, his cap-in-hand suggestion that they take up where they had left off, a dozen years before.

He remembers the ripe eighteen-year-old who'd straddled him in 1933, child that he was, for want of older suitors. This girl he'd had to marry. He remembers feeling proud and ashamed at once of such necessity, afraid of his bride, and at the same time unable to believe his luck, his hair plastered down for the ceremony with a redolent dressing he half-suspects, knowing his mother's humour, was plain lard.

This girl, after such an interval, is grown even more buxom now, and she's not at all the bitter shrew she might have become, the jealous termagant of every sailor's fears.

'Take little Nicky, Father,' says Alice, bending forward over him, cleavage branding a holy Y into each confused eye. 'We've customers.'

The business: this smithy, sliding seamlessly to garage now horse-power has had its day; a clean dirt forecourt with two hand-operated petrol pumps; a tea-house for the haulage trade; round the back of the house, an orchard of plum trees.

Gently, Alice lowers their infant son into Dick's arms. Dick would protest, only the space under his tongue is a tray of grit. Of their own accord his brawny arms, built for furnaces and fisticuffs, arrange themselves into a cradle for twelve pounds of alien life.

Already, Mother is vanished, her frock catching for an oily split-second on a pile of articulated metal plates, once a tractor's treads, now – the tractor done for – bound for the foundry, so that the base metal might be granted a brand-new and deadly incarnation at the hands of de Havilland, Browning, Marconi.

Dick cannot imagine achieving greater happiness than this: he has a new trade, and his old wife; he even has a son. But present pleasures, he has found, do not content the past. The happier his present, the more furiously Dick's past bangs on the gates for his attention. Perhaps this is what happens as you grow old. Or maybe that infernal Professor Pál played one too many shocking tricks. In any event, the slightest thing can set him reeling through time. One careless turn of thought, and he is back there. The explosion. The sick tilt of the deck. Seawater bursting chamber after chamber of their ship, as solid-sounding as a hammer swung by a maniac, scampering from compartment to compartment. The struggle to escape. The things in his way. The young able seaman he killed. The look in the boy's eyes as the metal stanchion oyster-knifed the back of his skull.

Sat there in the monochrome gloom, father and son share a look of mutual horror: for Little Nick Jinks, at four months old, is unmistakably the boy Dick killed, reborn, returned and bent on who knows what subtle revenge.

Dick has said nothing to Alice. It is too absurd. But just look at that nose.

Those little eyes, so close together.

That rosebud mouth.

2

Sixteen years later: 1960, a weekend in late March.

It is a dank, chilly, febrile sort of spring. The sky is overcast, with bands of cloud staining the eastern sky. They are sitting in the garden of the local pub. It is a Saturday. Dad is drinking his pint. Deborah is sucking her lemon-and-lime up through a straw. It is so much nicer than Coke, so much sharper. It is what her mother used to drink.

'For over nine hundred years people have been drawn to visit and admire one of this country's finest towns...'

Deborah Conroy unpicks what she can from the Tourist Board pamphlet. Her father Harry, a retired wrestling promoter, helps her over the few difficult words. They are reading about their home, about the windmill that launched Deborah's first word, 'Win-will!' About the church in whose grounds her mother is buried.

Deborah is eight years old. She opted out of her school trip – her class's wild week away on the Suffolk coast. She feigned an illness, and though Harry saw through her in an instant, he did not say anything. It is a guilty secret they share: since her mother's death, neither one can bear to be parted from the other.

At school, for the handful of children who did not go on the trip – those whose parents could not afford to send them, or whose behaviour was atrocious enough to disqualify them – there is another project. 'Penance' might be a more apt term. While their gadabout friends are exploring the creeks and quicksands of the River Alde and the River Ore, Deborah and the rest of them – the poor, the wicked and the lame – are meant to be exploring 'this place right here'. This is just one of many formulations which, like a fixed grin of embarrassment, convince no one:

'this place we call home'; 'this exciting place we walk past every day'; 'this place we think we know, but we don't'. Thaxted: the English country village as it never was. Such a solid, bumptious place. Until the rain comes. In the rain, the whole place looks hollowed out. Only the frontages on the high road stay solid. Everything else hangs in a weird, contingent relationship with the planes of the rain, the twist of the branches of the few trees, the line of a wall here, a roof angle there, as if in a second it might all screw itself up and tumble away in the wind.

Deborah is thinking a lot about the rain. She is doing 'The Geography of Thaxted' this week. She is writing about rainfall. About weather. Dad is trying to be helpful, he got hold of this pamphlet for her, but he isn't keeping up. History was last week. This week is geography.

The weather improves in time for Easter.

The Saffron Waldon District Children's Biblical Weekend is a big outdoor event: an extravaganza of egg-and-spoon races, jolly Bible songs, competitions and prizes for everyone. It's growing year on year. There are four tents in the field this year – four 'houses' – though how the organizers choose which 'house' a child belongs to is a mystery. They are: Panda House, Penguin House, Pony House and Pigeon House. Nobody wants to be in Pigeon House. Even 'pony' is a bit of a kludge. The boys cavil: 'Father Peter, a pony is only a kind of horse!' But the girls are besotted; they surrender unquestioning to the animal's aura of leather and rhythm, obedience and hot breath.

Of course, a panda is only a kind of shrew, but you don't hear Panda House complaining. Pandas are *endangered*. The kids in Panda House have drunk deep from this particular well. Ennobled by visions of mortality, they have been religiously tattooing bear-outlines into each other's upper arms with sharpened pencils.

Here they were, the organizers of this year's Saffron Walden District Biblical Weekend, looking for neutral house names – names picked purposely so as not to put off the more anti-clerical parents – and now these kids are bootstrapping their own theologies around ponies and pandas, a system of personal ethics around penguins. Pigeon House is the only manageable group of the four, because the name has left everybody feeling uniformly dispirited.

The bald fact is, some animals are religious, and some are not. It is easy to imagine the existence, somewhere, of a Horse Cult, even a Pony Cult. But whoever heard of a Pigeon Cult? Some *things* are religious, and some are not. The Divine pervades precisely half of everything.

In the afternoon of the second day, Sunday, the Lord's Day, Father Peter (Saffron Walden), Father Gerry (Thaxted), Father Richard (Great Chesterford) and Father Neil (Linden) erect a bright white marquee in the centre of their camp. They call this the Big House. Deborah Conroy, eight years old, is filled with quiet certainty: she is going in this year, whatever the flutters in her belly.

It is the final event. Ponies, pandas, pigeons and penguins sit cross-legged and higgledy-piggledy facing the bright, pure white marquee. Their parents perch on tiny tubular school seats at the back, and children and parents alike squirm and shudder. The Big House!

Because God slips in without invitation. God in motley, capering.

Which of you is brave enough to step into the Big House?

Eight-year-old Deborah Conroy rises.

Beside her, another child stands, turns and follows her. And another. Then a great rush of children. They are pressing past Deborah now. They are overtaking her, stepping on her toes. The priests are beside themselves. Hard-shelled old tortoises. Something has wormed its way into them: a gift of tongues. 'Are you ready? Ready! Steady! Are you ready? Ready, steady, go!'

This isn't the way Deborah imagined it. It isn't a solemn procession. It is something rough, a great herding, Jesus's flock mounting the metal ramp into the cramped stink of His lorry.

She nears the great white wall of the house of the Lord, and she sees how it flaps in the wind like a sail. This House does not stay still. If she enters, it will bear her away for ever. Everything will change. She is afraid suddenly. She wants to enter, but even if she changed her mind, she would not be able to evade that great wide rent.

So Deborah lets the crowd bear her towards the bellowing House of the Lord; there, she is filled with a joy so all-consuming, it blasts her awareness clean of everything except itself.

Dick Jinks is dead.

Nick, his surviving son, prises the bedsheet from his frozen grip and pulls it up to cover him. The sheet settles over Dick's face and smoothly idealizes its shape. A hollow forms over the mouth, the jaw dropped open as if to scream.

Nick draws up the room's only chair and waits. There will be no more *Eeeee!* in the night. No more of his father's tongue, weaving molten in the air. Silently Nick sits, scratching absently at his oil-stained corduroys, and plumbs the depths of his relief.

Crossing to the dressing table, Nick leans forward and studies himself in the fly-spotted mirror. Even now, at the narcissistic height of his adolescence, Nick accepts he is no oil painting. His head is too small for his body; his features are too small for his head. But what is there about him to make anyone so afraid?

There is no doubt in Nick's mind that his father died of fear; that over the years fear ate through his guts, caustic as an acid. Nick tried to reassure his father and win his trust, never with much success.

Nick wipes away a tear and turns back into the room. He knows his father loved him. Even as he stumbled away from him, or backed into his room's corner, even as he drooled and shook, there was love.

They had learned to live together, to love each other as father and son, by indirect means: in the empty morning kitchen, a bowl of warm porridge; clean clothes outside the bedroom door; shoes cleaned for the next day, and occasionally polished; a little money on the table and a list made out in one hand (milk, bread, bog roll), that by day's end, unfailingly, was ticked off by the other. So they looked after each other, cooked each other's food, cleaned each other's clothes. They were not happy, they were not friends and they hardly knew each other, but they did love each other.

Nick Jinks walks with heavy tread over to the room's only window – a rattly sash that looks out over the rear of the property.

Their life had not always been like this. Nick can remember a time in his childhood when he and his father were still able to speak together. It is from these dimly remembered, yet dearly cherished conversations that Nick knows of an even more distant time, before memory, when his mother was still alive. From his father's stuttering descriptions, Nick knows that Alice was a beauty. There are snapshots, too, though in the absence of memories pictures can never convey much. The truth is, Nick cannot really envisage her, but thinking of her brings a scent to mind, which he concocts from all Dick's talk of what she did: the cakes she'd bake, the fruit she'd pick, the jams she'd stew, the plum trees she would walk among, tending them, eating the fruit, so that the crimson juice would run down her chin onto her apron – 'Always sinkin' her teeth into a plum!'

Nick shudders to recall his father's story, told and retold to the point where it has become a sort of memory: the ladder's fatal toppling, the way his mother, clinging grimly to the top rung, acquired all the lever's deadly momentum. The tree-trunk and her head in spectacular dry collision. Her mouth a mess of blood and fruit pulp. Soon, leaking from her ears, not blood but something clear. Aqua vitae. It drained away into the orchard earth, leaving her brain parched, her spine hollow. Her seizure. Her shoe coming off, kicked off. In that magic instant, death.

Nick presses his head against the cold window pane, hard, harder.

The pane snaps.

Nick pulls back, surprised. He raises a hand to his forehead. No blood. He focuses on the crack in the glass, a crude Y, then beyond the crack, down, to the ruined lot.

The times have not been kind to businesses like these. Highways have funnelled off all trade, stranding the old trunk roads as surely as a river cuts its coils free, leaving them beached, strange shingle hieroglyphs. Still the faithful tanker comes, once in a blue moon, to top up their reservoir with four-star. The pumps are so old they can barely suck, but there is no money for a refit. The tea-house that was his mother's pride is long gone, the country measled now with Little Chef. As for the smithy, its subtle craftwork, that is all forgotten, leaving nothing for Nick to inherit.

To that extent, the whole is doomed, but the lot at the back of the house where the plum orchard once stood – here a deeper, darker curse is lodged.

A curse is a sequence of operations, each one of which will stand the light of day and reason. A curse never shows its hand. Of course the orchard came to grief, once Nick's mother died; how could it not? She knew these trees and loved them. She had tended them all her life. She knew how to bring them on. They flowered and fruited for her. Naturally, under Dick's uncertain management, they would not perform so well.

Then there was Dick: the man the trees had widowed, whose late happiness they had destroyed. He did his best by them. He pruned. He plucked. He cut away dead branches with a dull and rusty saw. Sickness spread. He snapped and tore. He bared green timber to the filthy air, beneath hot summer's eye.

The seasons cycled. The fruits of his first year's husbandry emerged: hard pips, crisp and healthy. All seemed well. They grew. Dick waited impatiently for them to take on their mature coloration, their dark bloom. For a few, strange, happy days, he forgot what the trees had done to his wife; he remembered only how his wife had taken care of the trees. He watched the fruit, and was proud.

The plums swelled to the size of apricots; then, to the size of pears. Their greenish-yellow skins burst, but if he tried to pluck one, it would resist his fingers, the branch would dip and toss, then the skin would give way, revealing a thready, whitish pulp that smelled of nothing. He did not dare taste it.

His son mewling in his brawny arms, Dick watched the trees, dumbfounded and afraid. Their delicate branches began to sag, dragged down to snapping by the mutant fruit. The skins of the plums split and dropped of their own accord, leaving balls of pulp to drip-dry in the autumn air. The pulp was not white now, but the brownish yellow of diarrhoea, and it was not tasteless; it had the corrupt sweetness of spoiled meat. Wasps gorged on the useless fruit. They smothered each soft dung-ball with a broiling, black-orange carapace. Then, as evening approached, drunk and dying from the season's cold, they would crawl away into the house. A moment's inattention, and they would fill your shoe, your slipper, a fold of your sock. Objects had to be examined from all sides before one dared take hold of them. Dressing of a morning, Dick would shake each piece of his and his son's clothing from his window and Nick, listening carefully, heard the husks of the stricken wasps bursting on the flagstones of the path.

Abortive nests hung from the corners of each room as the wasps, confused and desperate, sought sanctuary from the strange poisons which even now were liquefying them.

Come winter, Dick subjected the trees to a thorough and savage pruning.

The following year, the plums hardly grew at all. They shrivelled to a sort of leathery pouch, lobed like a walnut. Inside, the plum stone was ordinary enough except for its colour, which was white. This year the infection attacked the leaves, too. The leaves grew galls, and the air around the trees that autumn was thick with big hairless flies with pendulous brown bellies. They blundered carelessly about, indifferent to heat or cold or time of day. One could only suppose they were a kind of horsefly, because where they bit a boil would rise, much like a horsefly bite. They were something between a cockroach and a wasp and they never slept. Until well into November Nick spent sleepless nights trying to calculate, from their flatulent buzzing, how many flies had managed to penetrate his bedcovers.

Once its first exuberance was past, the curse grew less inventive. Consistently, the plums would shrivel; every year, piles of the abnormal flies built up in the corners of each bedroom window sill. Every spring for eight years, hardly a day went by when little Nicky did not hear, from the desolate depths of the covered yard, a deep, satisfying rumble of the grinding wheel, followed, now and again, by the abrasive swish as a metal edge came into contact with the spinning stone. He knew, or guessed, from the sheer volume of bright hard sounds, that this was no mere knife his dad was grinding. Dick's pale silence, whenever Nick asked him what he was up to, added to his son's conviction that a special blade was being readied for a primal act.

When his father's fear of him began to escalate, around his eleventh birthday, Nick had nightmares that this axe was being made ready for him.

The Act, whatever it was to be, seemed forever delayed. The axe, which surely had an edge to cut a single hair by now, never saw daylight. Until one day in early summer, Nick, then in his twelfth year, woke early and heard the sizzling of the stone.

He cannot now recall in what way the sound was different that day. What it was about the air, or the light. He got out of bed and went to his window. With fresh eyes, he saw the knobbly branches, amputated by so many prunings, their ends, clubbed like fists, sporting twigs like insect hairs, and from the tip of every hair a leaf, or what he took to be a leaf, but which, to his freshened eye, revealed more gall than leaf, each leaf a greyish sac.

He put on his clothes and left the house by the back door. At ground level the trees looked even stranger, more bone than bark. It came to him that the trees were no longer trees; that something new was growing in their place, which, while it was young, had used the coloration and form of trees to conceal itself. It was older now, and strong. It was shedding its camouflage.

Nick met his dad coming the other way along the path that skirted the old house. Dick was carrying an axe. The sight of it made Nick feel sick, because it seemed to have suffered much the same fate as the trees. It was, after so many years against the wheel, hardly an axe at all any more. The metal head was ground down to a sort of truncated sickle blade. With sightless eyes, Dick strode past his son and in among the trees.

Blindly, stiff-legged, he swung.

The axe blade sank without effort into the flesh of the first tree. Dick paused, his glued back a little bent, the axe still buried in the tree. Uneasy, afraid of frightening his father, Nick stepped forward. He wanted to help. His father was struggling to release the blade. 'Dad?'

Dick, startled, stood upright, yanking at the axe. The tree-trunk crumbled. Man and boy stood by, dumbfounded, as the tree fell and shattered. Two big branches shivered free of the trunk, puffing sawdust as they fell. There was no moisture in the thing, no strength. Silently, Dick dropped his axe and walked up to the next tree. He pushed. The trunk snapped with a soft crack, like a biscuit. The tree toppled. Nick came forward and studied the stump. The wood was pale and crumbly. There did not appear to be anything living in the wood, but Nick was afraid to touch it. Dick must have felt a similar revulsion, because he went and fetched two pairs of work gloves. Then, together – and with the axe quite forgotten, lying there in the long grass – father and son went around the orchard, pushing over trees.

Their victory over the curse seemed suspicious. They waited for a plague of flies. It never came. They watched the trees. The galls, in time, dropped off their little twigs and vanished into the lank grass. The grass grew around the trees. The grass was green.

They did not burn the wood. They were afraid of what it would release. Come winter it simply crumbled and blew away, leaving only the shapes of trees in reddish dust. Rains drove the dust into the earth. The grass fed on the earth. The grass was green, and it grew.

Afraid of what might grow there if they planted something new, Dick let the lot go. He did his best to keep the garage business alive. The work was hard. He was not an old man, exactly, but his back was growing stiffer and more painful as he aged. Though Nick was willing enough to help, Dick's fear of him kept him at bay.

So, inevitably, the space where the orchard had been filled with the waste products of the garage trade. Old tyres. The sagging panels of defunct caravans. Wheel-less farm machinery. Empty cans. Things Dick had not the strength to deal with on his own.

When the rats came, Dick and Nick had no one to blame but themselves. What did they imagine would happen, once they had made the old orchard into such a weather-proof warren of abandoned tarpaulin and machinery? After all, the rats were only rats. Bigger than your average rat, perhaps, but only rats. If they were exactly the colour of the galls which had vanished into the long grass two years before, the coincidence was hardly remarkable: what colour should rats be, if not a pewter grey?

Dick, enfeebled, unable any longer to fight his own battles, was forced to turn to Nick for help. For the boy's fourteenth birthday, he dusted off the ancient farmer's shotgun that had belonged to his wife and passed it over, tight-lipped and trembling. Nick also received a puppy, which Dick had rescued from a nearby ditch: a sly, dead-eyed mongrel Nick never named, thinking of her, always and only, as the Rat Catcher. Nick felt that with the gifts of gun and dog, a bond was now established between him and his father, a circuitous trust that dared not speak its name, or look itself in the eye, but which was tangible enough. It was, for Nick, a happy time. He had acquired a purpose: to defend hearth and home.

Nick turns from the window to his father's bed. He has raised the sheet to cover his father's face, and in so doing he has uncovered his father's feet.

Three toes on the left foot are missing.

There is no blood: the rats waited until he was dead.

Nick's little mouth puckers, and he squints through close-set eyes. This, in Nick's ill-favoured face, is what passes for fury. 'Girl!' he cries.

The Rat Catcher hurls herself up the stairs and lands bodily against the door. She never barks. Nick opens the door. The dog, having made her presence known, is already heading down the stairs. There is no time to waste. She knows what this is. Battle is joined.

Nick goes into the cellar, fetching gun and ammunition. He stuffs his pockets, and wipes the last tears from his eyes.

There will be no such display from the Rat Catcher. No keening or scratching at the door as she pines for her old master. Already she is worrying at the edges of the rubbish heap. There is nothing hang-dog about this dog.

The Rat Catcher is a professional.

Harry Conroy watches with amused pride as Deborah leads the children into the big white marquee.

After a little while – no more than ten minutes by Harry's watch – the children come out again. Whatever went on in the Big House, it has contented, rather than transfigured them. They are quiet, with an inner glow. They are smiling, as though they have each been given a small piece of good-quality milk chocolate.

Harry waits patiently by the mouth of the tent. He recognizes some of the children. One or two say hello to him. Deborah's best friend walks straight past him and does not notice him, even when he waves. Then, when they have all come out, and Deborah has still not emerged, Harry walks around the tent, thinking there may be two exits.

There aren't.

He enters the tent. There is no cross. Bunting decks the fabric walls of the marquee. In the middle of the marquee is a folding table covered in a white tablecloth. The table is bare. The marquee is empty.

*

George Bridgeman's preparations have been meticulous, circumspect and expensive. His plans have been written down, then memorized, and all documentation carefully destroyed. The old concrete air-raid shelter, abandoned since the last war, and swamped long since beneath a cloud of savagely spiked blackthorn – a barrier only George knows how to circumvent – has been damp-proofed and sound-proofed, tamper-proofed and child-proofed throughout.

The moment he brings the padded hammer neatly down upon the little girl's head, George expects everything to go to hell. When it doesn't is when George's problems start.

He drops the hammer, catches the little girl up in his arms as she crumples, and checks the pulse in her neck. Alive enough. Who would have thought it would be so easy? The little kitten walking past him, all alone, oblivious to everything, drunk on everything, 'off with the fairies'...

Life isn't like that. It is very important to him that over the next few days, or weeks, or however long it takes, he shows this little lamb what life is really like. That he rubs her face in it. That he reams her clean of all personality, and shows to her the beast she really is. Because people are so stupid. People pretend so much when really they are no better than beasts. Someone has to show them what they really are. Someone, damn it, has to stand up for the truth.

Among the trees, hidden from the tents, his hands moisten against her thin white dress. He picks her up and bears her to his Ford Consul. A peach. So why is he shaking?

The truth of it is, George Bridgeman does not know how to win. His life to this point has been a series of small, spiteful victories secured in the teeth of universal indifference. If the little moppet had struggled, screamed, kicked him in the balls and run away, or if, after his twenty-odd years in an abattoir, George had failed to judge his blow correctly, and splattered her brains over his shoes – then he could have found a comfort in the way the world had turned reliably against him yet again.

As it is, things have gone swimmingly. He slips her into the boot of his car. She fits the space perfectly. Not too big. Not too small. Pale and pretty. He wonders what she looks like naked. He'll know soon enough. He checks her over. Both shoes still on her feet. Hair clip still in place. He glances back the way he has come. No dropped hanky. No trail of bloody spots. Perfection. He gets in the car, turns the key in the ignition, and–

The car rumbles into life.

He jounces down the rough track, out of the copse and into the little lane which runs so near, yet does not meet, the main road. Any second now a hummock in the track will ground the Ford's chassis, or twist a wheel out of true...

It does not happen.

The world absolutely refuses to slap him down. The only way things can go wrong now is if he messes them up himself. George feels a childish need to pee, and a spot of unusual tenderness at the tip of his penis. His palms upon the steering wheel are wet. It's up to him now. It's up to him.

I must have missed her, Harry Conroy says to himself. He goes in search of Deborah. He bumps into the parents of Sarah, Deborah's best friend. They reassure him, and speak to their daughter. Dumb, wide-eyed, Sarah shakes her head; she has not seen her friend all day. So they lead Harry to another, smaller tent, where the organizers are gathered. Father Peter, Father Neil and Father Gerry sit Harry down. One by one, they join in the search for his daughter. Harry is alone.

Harry waits in the small tent...

... for about half a minute. Then he gets up, goes out, joins the search. There are no parents now, no children. The people running around are people he has never seen before. The sun is brighter than ever, but in the opposite corner of the sky, there is a black line on the horizon – a heavy charcoal smudge.

It is about now that Harry starts shouting. It's an incoherent sound – there aren't even any words. Something is working his mouth with strings. Even if Deborah hears him – even if his daughter is near enough to hear – Harry doubts very much whether she will recognize his cry.

The act of reloading the heavy gun is a balletic blur. After two years of practice Nick no longer has to aim the barrel to score a bloody hit, and his arms and shoulders are strong enough to dampen the gun's most awkward recoil. The Rat Catcher has grown into a machine for covering distance, her jaws scissor unstoppably and her spittle, whipped away like foam from a wave, scorches whatever it lands upon. Where her mouth cannot penetrate, the Rat Catcher reaches into cover with powerful forelimbs, killing rats with single blows, like a cat.

Their revenge for Old Father Jinks's mutilation is swift and thorough. Whole rat families have perished this morning, whole gobshite dynasties. The rats, completely demoralized, are pushing their young out in front of them now, a kind of rattish shield. Nick Jinks and the Rat Catcher will not be blackmailed; blind, mewling infants, dismembered by shot, their innards liquefied by hydrostatic shock, plaster their coward parents' pelts with bright, unmissable blood. Deep within the warren, meanwhile, the old and the infirm, the ones with cracked teeth and lame forepaws, gather in bunkers of rusted wire and perished rubber. One, driven mad with despair, sinks her teeth into the belly of her mate, filling her mouth with foamy yellow fat. A third, infuriated by the squeals of the victim, garrottes himself with a transmission wire. All through the nest, young, lithe, healthy rats lie trembling, shell-shocked, beneath blankets of cardboard, while their doughty mothers, deafened long since to the gun's monotonous and terrible blast, hurl themselves out of the nest and through the lank grass towards the house – a suicidal tactic of diversion.

Straining, cursing, Nick pulls the rubbish heap apart. Slavering and silent, the Rat Catcher watches for movement within. Little by little, the nest is crumbling. Rats pause, quivering, before their transformed surroundings, uncertain where to run. Their familiar warrens are being erased, and new and deadly vistas spread before them. The bright white light of day expunges the warren's old chiaroscuro, turns everything shoddy and contingent, demoralizing the rats still further. So they head down, deep down, into the loamy tunnels beneath the rubbish pile, there to encounter a lost tribe of terrible red-eyed sub-rats who have never seen the sun.

Escaping them, his ear torn to cauliflower shreds, his left hind paw stabbed through, his right eye bleared and bleeding, one rat, a sorry sight, stumbles up into the upper air: a deadly mistake.

The rat hurtles pell-mell between Nick Jinks's legs, heading for the corner of the house. Nick Jinks, startled, cries out. The dog makes no sound. The rat powers on. It rounds the corner of the house. The gun goes off. Brick explodes in a red cloud as the rat, unscathed, hurls itself towards the road. Behind it come the heavy, clumping footfalls of the boy; beneath it the faster, softer, deadlier scratchings of the dog's paws, scrabbling on the flags of the path, building up speed.

The rat reaches the road. The ditch is in sight. Safety beckons. Death comes so suddenly, the rat does not even hear the discharge of the gun. A bundle of unwitting, mangled joy, the rat tumbles, propelled by the shot, into the ditch on the far side of the road.

The Rat Catcher, her blood up, ignores her master's call and pursues the dead rat over the road.

George Bridgeman has driven the route to his magical wartime shelter countless times in preparation for today. He does not need a map as he tacks smoothly from lane to lane, east toward the fens. He does not need to consult, or even navigate in any conscious sense. He knows the way.

All hell inside him now. Time to think means time for doubt. Time in which George can measure his loneliness, and feel the weight of responsibility: only he can mess this up now. It's up to him.

He stops the car. A quiet spot. He gets out, walks round to the boot, opens it up. She's still out cold. He touches her. If she wakes up, if she screams, then he can panic, run back to the glove compartment, take out the hammer and spoil everything.

She does not wake up.

The world absolutely refuses to give him an 'out'. It's up to you now, George. It's up to *you*.

He lifts up the girl's skirt, drags it up, up past her white cotton knickers. He sticks a finger into the band of her knickers and pulls. Her hairlessness there gives him an immediate erection, and it frightens him, this fierce bodily response. Of course he is planning to rape her. He has a room full of objects carefully selected over the years, common household objects, tools purloined from the abattoir, a handful of china souvenirs – 'A Gift From Bridport' – to rape her with. But this sudden – well, what would you call it? Lust?

He pulls her roughly over, so one leg falls free of the boot and dangles, shoe half-off, toes tickling the long grass of the verge. She slumps onto her front, her bottom upraised over the sill of the boot.

He checks her pulse. It ticks back against his finger, slow and strong.

He pulls her knickers down and off – much struggling and slapstick here – and crams them into her mouth.

Now what?

He listens for approaching traffic.

He waits.

Nothing comes.

By now thoroughly demoralized, tremble-kneed, George shoves the girl's leg back in the boot, slams the lid shut, climbs back in the car and drives.

George's mission is, he believes, essentially spiritual. Even his earliest experiments lean in this direction. Since the day he flensed out a lamb's eye and dropped it, still warm, into the lap of that stuck-up neighbour girl, that Hosken girl – what was her name? Katherine?

Kathleen? – it has been his mission to awaken his fellow man to his contingent and temporary nature: his equivalence, in other words, to beasts. In better circumstances, and with a better gene-pool to draw from, Bridgeman might have made small, gloomy contributions to moral philosophy. As it is, he is something more imbecile, more direct. He plans to expunge the little girl's spirit, drag her down into his animal reality. Marry her in darkness on all fours and no more words ever again. An end to meaning, sequence, rule. Only cries, a flash of teeth, the bliss of living without thought, his own pet lamb to warm him in the night. But how does he think he can scrape the girl out of that little animal body? How?

It comes to him that his plans do not extend beyond the first couple of days of the child's suffering. What if a couple of days are not enough? He has this image of her, a few days in, tattered beyond further violation, exhausted – and *still* not an animal.

The tools he has amassed. They'll mortify her flesh, but who's to say they will not leave her girlishness intact? What to do?

In need of comfort now, unnerved by his success, George Bridgeman takes one hand off the steering wheel to knead his groin. Ejaculation is a great comfort. Always has been. He imagined, in his twenties, that this endless, importunate tossing would wear itself out, but here he is, balding, hands chewed to red rags by years of handling raw ice-cold meat, sharp slivers of bone, knives slippy with blood and fat, and still he cannot leave his John Thomas alone. It is his only friend.

The car leaps out from a wooded hollow, jerky and undependable as a foal, as George Bridgeman wrestles with his fly. There is a house ahead, an old garage, hand pumps in the yard. By now, crushed by his own success, Bridgeman has retreated into the sort of thinking a child might employ. He tells himself that if he ejaculates before he reaches the garage, he will persevere with his plan, he will smuggle the little rabbit into his theatre of horrors, he will operate upon her, he will do his very best. If orgasm eludes him, however, the game is up.

George's right foot responds, pressing hard against the accelerator, so all his scary, too-ambitious plans might come to nought. No, no way he will be able to toss himself off in time. Oh well. What a shame. He will just have to dump her somewhere.

He thinks about this.

Of course, he'll have to kill her.

He thinks about this.

Just in case.

Very stiff now.

With the hammer.

He thinks about this.

Glans wet and slippery.

The long, cool, polished shaft of the hammer.

He thinks about this.

A black dog runs across the street ahead of him.

Her beautiful white bottom.

He thinks about her buttocks.

Semen leaps acrobatically to splash the decal of his steering wheel, silver 'Ford' inscribed on shiny black enamel.

The dog runs back across the road, something in its teeth.

George Bridgeman is captivated by the sight of his semen, the F of Ford flecked shut to make a P, the o tailed to a q – Pqrd. As if by magic he is driving a Pqrd.

Before him, unregarded, the dog hunkers down in the surety of death, and its head, impacted at high speed by the car's nearside wheel, absorbs all the forces of the collision, shaping them like a bell, so that the wheel, vulnerable at the point of contact, conducts the energy of the crash back into itself and twists itself out of true. As soon as it is back in contact with the tarmac, the car wobbles like a drunk all over the road, squealing horribly, tyres smoking, before it settles softly, as if relieved, into a ditch, barely fifty yards beyond the dirt forecourt of the garage.

*

Nick Jinks is reloading his weapon when the car runs over his dog. Stunned, he walks over to the body. There is no question that the Rat Catcher is dead. Her head is a rubbery smear.

George Bridgeman raises his head from the steering wheel. He touches his hand to it. The top of his head explodes, like a knife has sliced the cap off his skull. When he can bring himself to look at his fingers, George is surprised to find no blood.

Nick, numb and cold, looks up the road. The car has come to grief in a ditch, just beyond the forecourt. Is the driver all right? Nick drags himself away from the ruined body of his companion.

Something moves in the rear-view mirror. It hurts when George moves his eyes. He moves his whole head instead, and freezes, abject, at the sight that greets him: a man with a gun. What if the girl wakes up now? What if the accident has woken her? He has to do something. He has to take control. He reaches for the door. His spermy fingers slip off the catch, reminding him to fasten his fly. He yanks up the zip.

The man inside the car lets out a scream. How badly is he injured? Will Nick know what to do? Daunted yet determined, Nick hurries towards the car to see how he can help.

Gingerly and gasping, George Bridgeman attempts to ease folds of his foreskin from between the teeth of his trouser fly. The pain is too great. Sobbing, sick, he abandons the attempt. Perhaps the youth will help him. It is a garage, after all. There will be tools. Pliers. Cutters. Saws. He looks up into the rear-view, seeking succour.

Oh my God, the youth is running towards the car. George has killed his dog and now the youth is going to kill him. George stares helpless into the mirror. The gun is getting bigger. There is nothing he can do.

It's all falling apart around him, as he surely knew it would. He's just going to have to make a run for it. He fumbles his door open. Every slightest movement threatens to split him. Keening horribly between gritted teeth, he edges his way out of the car.

The car door opens, and from the cabin comes a terrible squeal. Of their own accord, Nick Jinks's hands perform their ballet, snapping the gun breach shut.

George Bridgeman hobbles into the road, His white, sweating face stretched in an O of agony, arms spread for balance, bloody swollen penis dangling like a fruit. Terrified and helpless, he cannot run; he shuffles round to face his nemesis.

With an efficiency born of long practice, Nick Jinks's eyes rake the scene, hunting out the squealing thing. Astounded, his gaze settles upon the stranger's groin. Never has his enemy been so savagely inventive! The rat dangles there by its teeth, spattered with blood.

A split-second later, and Nick will see things differently. His senses are acute. His powers of reasoning are adequate. It will take him no time at all to shake off his rat obsession and see the man's plight for what it actually is. The whole process of revision will happen so blindingly fast, and unthinkingly, that Nick will not even remember why he fired the gun.

None the less, the gun has gone off.

George Bridgeman sprawls in the road, his groin a bloody mess. A piece of shot has shredded an artery in his thigh. Death is coming very quickly now. It towers over him. George Bridgeman sees that his youthful attacker is Death, and that Death is an angel. It has a small, pursed mouth and a smooth, rounded, cherubic head. It might be any angel, were it not for the eyes. Eyes that bore into him, pitiless and strange. As his consciousness falters, so the eyes seem to move closer and closer together…

Nick Jinks stands above the stranger, helpless. What to do? A chill creeps over him. Was this what his poor dead father feared? Was this something of which he knew his son was capable? Blood pools at his feet. Nick begins to tremble all over. Why did he fire the gun? He has not the remotest idea.

The stranger's eyes glass over. Nick crosses to the car. The garage has a phone, but it has been disconnected. Nick has a confused idea that he will drive the car to the nearest village in order to summon help.

The ditch into which the car has been driven is not deep, and the rear wheels are still in contact with the road, more or less. Nick, at fourteen, has grown up among cars and knows how to drive. Besides, he has his father's confidence with machinery. He wrestles the car back onto the road, shifts into first and wobbles away.

He passes through the first village bolt upright in his seat, buttocks clenched to raise him that vital extra half-inch, afraid someone will notice that a child is driving. He passes through the second village, more confident this time: he is getting away with it. By the time he reaches Ipswich and the first breath of sea air, he can no longer pretend that he is going to be making a clean breast of this appalling incident to the authorities. How can he? He cannot even explain why he pulled the trigger. Perhaps he is a killer, after all.

As he drives he comprehends for the first time just how big the world really is. He can count on his fingers the number of times he has set foot outside the county of his birth. Apart from occasional, lacklustre visits to zoos and seasides – journeys buried so far back in his childhood, he can barely remember them – Nick Jinks has never known another landscape. His whole upbringing has been morbidly inturned.

As Nick cruises the streets of Felixstowe, and sees the port cranes towering over the roofs of the drab terraces, it occurs to him that he is truly free for the first time in his life. Liberty has been thrust upon him. He not only has the opportunity to run away, he has a positive obligation, as fast and as far as he can.

He finds his way to the harbour, parks the car and climbs out. The salt air fills his lungs with energy and hope.

Why not?

The ships, the jetties, the very buildings seem to thrum with unfamiliar and purposeful life.

Why not?

It will only take the slightest nudge, and Nick Jinks's destiny will be set.

It comes.

The faintest scratching. The faintest squealing.

Nick Jinks stiffens where he stands.

The old curse has pursued him. Somewhere in the toils of the motor car, that old grey curse sits, preening – but it has overreached itself. It has become separated from its source. It has no power now. It is just one miserable rat, trapped in the belly of a greasy old car.

One more movement, and Nick will be free of the curse for ever.

He steps away from the car. As he goes he smiles, to hear the curse calling him, a thready squeal, desperate, weak, as piteous in its defeat and final extremity as the pleas of a child.

3

It is 10.30 a.m. on Sunday, 20 July 1969. One man is preparing to set foot on the moon; another is going to die, assassinated by a bomb. For now, though, it's like any other mid-morning in Lourenço Marques, and the street-sellers are setting out their wares. There are toy cars made of cans, random pharmaceuticals and pictures of Elvis Presley. Along the promenade, girls are selling themselves.

Nick Jinks passes by, pondering the choice on offer. The girl he settles on finally is not a typical street-walker. For a start she is a good ten years older than the others. Nick assumes this must be the reason why the competition have gathered around them, hissing. Really hissing: from two dozen rouged and milktoothed Mozambican mouths comes a great long *sssssssssss!*

Nick leads the girl into the doorway of a Sunday-closing barbershop. That he has already forgotten her name is hardly his fault. They all have such nutty names round here. The two he bought before her were called Majesty and Hope...

His line of thought is broken as he feels her hands moving to the straps of his wartime canvas satchel, a satchel he has promised his masters not to remove. This inevitably triggers the first of many minor *contretemps* with which encounters like this are inevitably gritted ('Don't kiss my mouth' – 'Don't touch my feet' – 'You'll put my arm to sleep') so that the satchel remains strapped, as per instructions, to his back, no way he is going to let go of it until he is safely in off the street. He pushes her hands away; they purse instead around his groin like a codpiece while, shoulders drawn back manly by the weight of his burden – what the fuck is *in* this bloody thing? – he cops his feel of her between the folds of her *capulana*: a line of sweat beneath each little tit, a line of fur up her tight tum, from thick-pubed mons, her bush V-d to a clit-bound arrow. Some stubble there, and he thinks about offering to tidy up her topiary with his fancy new Gillette, ask her nicely, say please, winning smile. It is an arrow that might Braille the most insensate fingers, the burned and calloused pads of firemen and dockers, to their mark. Finding it for himself, pressing it cruelly so she squeals, Nick Jinks laughs a hearty seaman's 'Yo ho!' and swells into her hands.

Back home, every once in a while, an ambitious young detective will open the file on Nick Jinks: wanted for murder, wanted for the abduction of a child. Nothing is ever resolved. There is next to no information on the suspect – not even a photograph – and besides, the circumstances of both crimes are so confused, it is hard to see how a prosecution would get past a sceptical judge.

Nick, for his part, keeps a weather-eye on the British press, concerned for the child as well as himself. The story of the little girl's abduction, widely reported at the time, is as horrifying as it is baffling. What child? Was there a child? And how on earth did this story get caught up with his own? The grotesque details trouble him nearly as much as the risk of false accusation.

Eight years have passed since Nick took to the high seas. There is little about him now to remind one of the taciturn rat catcher of his youth. In the time he has been at sea, Nick has grown hardier and happier. He knows something about the world and this has made him less afraid of himself. He knows what stone-cold killers look like, from brawls in Singapore and from one dangerous, ridiculous feud on a container run from Japan to San Francisco. He knows he is not one of them. Knowing this he has begun, over the years, to put the accident behind him. He calls himself Jiggins now, Nick Jiggins, and with the new name comes a sunnier outlook on life.

His father's fear of him was his own affair. No use picking at it now. Loyal as Nick tries to be to his father's memory, he's come to understand the limits of Dick's philosophy. 'Not worth the candle,' Dick Jinks had said of the seaman's life. God knows it was a brutish kind of existence, but who could say it was not worthwhile? If it had been up to his dad, and had it not been for the accident, Nick might never have left the fenland of his birth. Then what would he know of anything? He imagines himself sometimes – when nostalgia and weariness threaten to rain on his parade – crouched in his father's room, loaded shotgun across his lap, listening to the rats scuttling behind the wainscots. Picturing this, his appetite for the sea comes rushing back to him.

Rats, the sound of them paddling in the bilges, the sight of them at dusk, playing tag along the chains and hawsers; rats alone have the power to taint Nick Jinks's happy-go-lucky present. He stays as far away from them as he can. Not for him the flop-house floor, the budget brothel, the knee-shaker in the alley. An inadvertent consequence of this is that Nick has acquired a reputation as a man who conducts his shore leaves with a certain amount of panache. Take, for instance, this woman's well-appointed theatre of delectable operations.

(Her hands move across his tired back, hot and slick and warm from the coconut oil she is working into his skin. He turns his head, sees the old army satchel lying at the foot of the bed, the satchel he must deliver, the brown-wrapped package inside, yes, it is there. What can possibly go wrong?)

This upmarket taste of his requires funding additional to his meagre seaman's wage. Nick's courier work has been relatively smalltime up to now, but his inventiveness and discretion have not gone unremarked. The years he spent with his dad – concealing signs of his presence, so as to minimize the old man's terror of him – have made Nick an unobtrusive operator.

This most recent courier job represents the high-water mark of his career. Afterwards, he intends to lay low for a while. Frankly, the whole business has unnerved him.

To start with, the men he went to see refused to come out of their basement. Then, when he had been persuaded to join them in their cellar, he found himself in the middle of some bizarre musical number. At least, this is the only way he has to interpret what he saw. He's never confronted black-face outside *The Black and White Minstrel Show*, let alone seen it used as a disguise. Impossible to tell even the race of these men under such fairground slap. The ointment smell of the local sunscreen – a crackly white porridge – mingled sickly with the smell of black shoe polish, as he slipped their satchel round his back.

'Item: if you look inside the package, we will know. Item: if you take the satchel from your back in a public place, we will know. Item: if you discuss our arrangement with a third party, we will know. Item: if you fail to deliver the package to the correct address, we will know.'

Overkill enough to make the young seaman grin through his sweat – a rictus of fear to answer their painted white grins. Afterwards, he wrote the address he was meant to memorize ('Item: do not write down or share this address with anyone') in big crayon letters all over the packet, just to make doubly sure he couldn't fuck this up.

He balks at the memory, muscles tensing. Bad enough that he should have been led under the ground, let alone that he should be confronted with this. Fatigues without insignia. Guns. Somewhere in that cellar, unmistakable, the scurry and scratch of rats.

'Shhh,' the prostitute soothes, hot hands working him.

It is not the tension of the moment that will spoil his first day's shore leave here, in infamous Lourenço Marques. Nor even the anxiety he feels about the delivery he must make, a couple of hours from now. What scuppers him is, oddly enough, the tale he decides to tell, his favourite ice-breaker, a tale of derring do on the high seas.

'It's proppant,' he says, his voice muffled by the pillow. '*Proppant.* I'm telling you.'

It's little china beads with a coating, a resin, they use it in drilling, in the offshore industry, on drilling rigs, and he is getting dizzy, all the ways there are to explain this thing, this material, which is frankly the least of his story.

'Not "propellant". I'm telling you. What's *propellant*? What kind of *propellant* do you know comes in *sacks*?'

'Proppant.' The girl tries it on her tongue. Her fingers dig his shoulders, like there are gold coins between his muscles, dubloons between the muscle and the bone, and she is rifling these secret pockets in his flesh, not so much a back rub, more an intimate mugging. The trouble with asking for a massage is you occasionally end up with a real masseuse, whatever else she is, with frightening thumbs, really strong, like her day job is screwing on the lids of jars you can't undo.

'Proppant,' she says, 'OK,' in that tone of voice, how do women do that? Letting him know in four syllables that nothing he says now is she possibly going to take seriously. Discouraged, he recalls that at some point in his story he is going to have to use the word 'phenolic'. Though he hardly looks the part, Nick is wedded to an ethic of accurate *reportage*. Words should fit closely the events and situations they describe. Because the world is big, he needs many words, the more accurately to render the truths around him. Word-power is his unlikely passion. So that the third mate, rigging a vacuum line for their second loading attempt, and still white-faced and shaky-fingered from the explosion, couldn't have been more startled when Nick rose up on his ladder out of the silo – where, anyway, he had no place being – a stained rag held close to his mouth and saying: 'What kind of dust, d'you say? Fen-something? How d'ya spell that, then?' The third mate was unable to take his eyes off the Stanley knife tattooed on Nick's arm, an eye where the shank screw should be and shark teeth for a blade. You could tell it was a Stanley knife because the word 'Stanley' was picked out along the thing in the red of venereal rashes. Without it, it might have been anything. A razor shell. A baby eel. A banana.

'Mmm,' the woman says, over him, behind him, and something brushes him, an unmistakable tantalizing point of rubbery contact that is definitely not a finger and this ought to excite him, only that...

The thing is, he's pretty sure her *capulana* was secure before she started this – he expecting her to strip at his word and she instead wanting to tantalize, oh, very European – and both her hands are on him now, either side of his hips, working the handles there. So assuming this *is* a nipple – well, not that he's ungrateful or anything but O! the mysterious toils of this world – if both her hands have been working the flab above his hips all this time, *how in Hell did she get her tits out?*

And here's its twin, tracking through the oil spread like engine lubricant over his back. He arches his back, kitty-friendly, feels the nipple snub and turn, the half-moon of her tit against him. 'Lie down, now.' She pulls away, then tracks again, with both tits now, no hands, just the nipples against his back, angled perfectly like something mechanical come to read his skin. She must be angling them with her hands to maintain such precise and even contact and then it comes to him, a great wave of mystery and unknowing: *how come she doesn't fall over?* Leaning over him all that way, her tits in her hands, how is she able to balance? Maybe, he thinks, she has climbed up onto the table. Maybe she has hooked her feet around the end of the table. He has lost track of her nipples now, he has completely dropped out the bottom of the whole experience, he is off in the land of levers, the land of weights and measures and GOD DAMN WOMAN WATCH WHERE THE JESUS YOU ARE PUTTING THAT THING – but her hand is deep in the crevice of his freshly washed, sweet-smelling buttocks by now – when in hell did that happen? – fingers questing for his BALLS NOT MY BALLS NOT – AHHHHHHHHHHH and she's PULLING THEM now, she is LIFTING HIM OFF THE TABLE BY HIS BALLS and he is kneeling and he thinks, if I hook my feet to the edge of the table I wouldn't need my hands to balance, and really, it is enough to make him despair sometimes how his mind goes wandering off without him and this is really too fucking homosexual she is actually tonguing his balls and where the hell is her nose all this time? Oh CHRIST, there it is, her lips grazing the hair of his balls as her hand reaches round to his prick and she mumbles,

'Proppant, then, come on,' and she is milking him like a cow so he goes on with his story because this is what you do when some mad bitch has your testicles between her teeth you do *exactly what she says.*

The sunlight that morning was of a sort that has resisted his every subsequent attempt to describe it. The low, even white cloud, far from barring the sunlight, trapped the light and pressed it against the sea's surface, so that everything appeared incredibly bright and reflective and the sea was turned to liquid chrome.

The lensing effect of the clouds extended even to sounds, magnifying them and at the same time stripping them of all reverberation, so that every sound seemed to come from inside the ear. In the early-morning quiet, when they were still a nautical mile off the harbour, Nick swears he could hear the footfalls of the crane man, dawdling on the quay. A car starting on the hill above the harbour. A conversation between two elderly men, one out walking his dogs, the other leaning on his gate.

A Navy helicopter hammered by, rotors clipping the clouds. Even this racket was transformed, each element sounding pure, precise, as intimate as the flob of Antonio Carlos Jobim's spittle on 'The Girl from Ipanema'.

It was a strange sort of landfall. No town, no din of machinery. Just a couple of houses – and the quay itself was an untenanted, industrial thing, thrown up as a handy transfer point for the tons of aggregates and chemicals that would one day be consumed by the rigs.

No real town for twenty miles. No pub. A tea shack for the men. One public telephone on a piece of hard-standing that, for sheer size, dwarfed the quay itself: big enough to land a SeaKing on. Why was the phone-box set slap bang in the middle like that? What use was it meant to serve?

'Houses,' said the second mate. 'It's foundations for houses.' He broke into a weird country-and-western drawl: 'Boom town a'comin'.'

'Fuck that.'

The proppant was waiting for them in sacks, paletted on the quayside. They had spent a day, about six weeks ago, vacuuming the material out of the hold, bagging it for later use. Now, coming to collect it, they had the whole job to do again in reverse. They used a mobile crane – the key, as usual, chewing-gummed to the inside of a wheel rim – to lift a smallish hopper, about a ton weight, over the aft silo. Nick guided the hopper into position over the mouth of the silo, thumbed off the karabiners and waved the crane away.

The operator swung the arm back over the quay to the first sack. Men clipped extra chains to the crane arm and hooked it up. The engine laboured, the whole body of the crane shifted, as the operator raised the sack off the quay and began slowly to swing it over to the hopper.

Nick gawped, for all the world as if this operation had nothing to do with him. It was only as the arm came to rest, the sack swinging with dreadful, pregnant force over the mouth of the hopper, that he remembered what he was supposed to be doing.

He reached into his back pocket for his knife.

It wasn't there.

Cursing, he hurried back to his bunk. It was hidden beneath his tiny pillow, nestled in its own, permanent dent in the cheap foam pallet. Not that Nick expected trouble, this trip or any other, but simply because it had become his talisman: slippy cold body, more like stone than steel, wicked lino-cutter blade. He ran his thumb crosswise over the scimitar edge – ah, a tell-tale roughness there. He dug about in his bag of books – Carpentier, Asturias and Marquez, his passion – and fished out his dad's old tin box. From the box he pulled out a stubby screwdriver. Lovingly he loosened the screw in the knife handle. Gingerly he lifted out the blunted blade and reversed it. He did up the screw again and ran his thumb over the unused edge. There was something thrilling about a razor-sharp blade – how it could cut you and you'd not feel a thing, just a wet burn as you first put pressure on the cut, sliding one surface of the slice against the other, revealing damage slowly, by stages: the sick inevitability of it. Like the cartoon coyote, who falls only *after* he finds he's hanging in mid-air.

By the time Nick had recovered enough of himself to pull himself out of this latest excursion through his own head, the first sack of proppant had already stopped swinging, it was in position, suspended over the hopper, ready for emptying.

'I'm there!' Nick shouted, waving the Stanley knife over his head. 'I'm there!' – flinging and flapping his way across the deck.

Anxious not to lose the highlight of his day to another, he threw himself on the sack as though it were a lover. The bright sliver of Sheffield steel slipped neatly through the coarse plastic weave. With a smooth downward motion, Nick disembowelled the sack and the proppant spilled through the hopper into the silo. The air filled with a dust that was, in its frenzy and iodine smell, a distillation of thunderstorms. The air crackled in his nostrils and laid a sourness on his tongue. Nick danced about by the side of the silo hatch, impatient, his blood up, while men fastened the second sack to the crane.

He slashed the second sack back-handed and casual, as he saw his heroes slash their way to victory in the movies he preferred. 'Thank *you*, Mr Jiggins,' the second mate announced, dryly. A few private smiles among the ratings, quickly hidden, as Nick, brandishing his father's doughty Stanley, frowned them away.

So Nick stood, arms folded, Horatio on the bridge, waiting for more sacks. The crane lifted a third sack over the hopper. Nick, catching the second mate's eye, cut the sack carefully, a five-inch gash, letting the proppant out in a steady stream. He stepped away, patient, waiting for the sack to empty. He rubbed his thumb over the blade and felt already, through long practice, a little dullness there.

Black dust lapped the edge of the silo, busy, a midge-cloud, and fell back again. The sack sagged, the flow of proppant eased. Nick stepped forward.

The explosion blew the hopper right off the top of the silo.

The hopper's dented sill missed Nick's nose by inches.

He felt the air on his face.

He watched the hopper rise.

It tumbled through the air.

He felt a chill as its shadow crossed him.

He was aware, for the first time, of the sound of the blast, the great blunt fact of it, ringing in his ears.

The hopper rose and toppled. He watched it curve through the grey china air.

He saw the crane operator throw up his hands in front of his face.

The hopper hit the quay a yard or so in front of the crane, bounced, bounded along the quay, checked itself, ran off in a new direction, stopped, turned over, and rang – the sounds running always a fraction of a second behind the visuals, as though his brain were experiencing the world too fast to put everything in its proper order. The channels falling out of whack, the sound un-synching, and a mutter from the cheap seats: 'Fuck' and 'Christ'; from the English captain, a 'Christmas Day'.

In his lungs, the taste of the forge.

Nick knew that taste, was sent back twenty years by it. The rotting cars. The carcases of caravans, their plastic and fibreboard walls leant in upon each other like a ruined house of cards. The rats...

'The cause of the explosion,' says Nick, to the head bobbing at his lap (things, at his insistence, taking a more orthodox course now: his hand firm on the back of her head, directing the action), 'was probably a combination of electrostatic charge built up during the loading operation and the volume of phenolic dust free in the silo.'

There is a loud – and in tactile terms, not unpleasant – sputtering, followed by a monosyllable expressive of female incredulity.

'Phenolic,' he insists, succinctly, and his erection softens like a toffee between her teeth. He frowns. *'Phenolic.* What? I am telling you this.'

She shrugs, climbs back on the bed and falls back, lifting her knees to her shoulders. 'Whatever,' she says.

He fucks her once, hard, for her insolence. Twice, for the fun of it. A third time, intensely and with feeling, for romance. A fourth time, all wet eyes and slithering tongue and 'I never knew my mammy' –

– and drifts pathetically to sleep.

He dreams:

The hopper, rising.

He sees it rise, he feels the air stroke his face as the lip of the hopper leans over, as though to touch him, as though to kiss him goodbye.

Up it goes, into the silver sky, and its shadow comes over him then, the hopper a gigantic black hexagon in the sky, rising, rising. The bright sky silhouettes it now, backing it like the satin cushion for a piece of jet. The sky is purest white.

Nick Jinks has always wanted to see a rocket launch. This is what he has most wanted to see, ever since he was a child. And today – the very day a man sets foot for the first time on the Moon – at this moment, in this dream, it occurs to him: the accident he witnessed, and maybe even caused, *was a launch*. A detonation. Dead weight, hurled into the air by gigantic unseen forces. (The men on the quay reported a large blue flame shooting out of the silo; Jinks saw nothing like that.)

So, when he wakes, and without quite being able to work out why, Jinks feels an extraordinary sense of fulfilment. Waves of contentment will continue to wash over him at regular intervals, driving him and sustaining him throughout his peril once he discovers, the moment he sits up, shivering in wet sheets, that

(1) he is alone here

and

(2) his satchel is gone.

4

Apollo Eleven's lunar module lands at 3.17 p.m., Eastern Standard Time, and once it is confirmed that astronauts Armstrong and Aldrin are safely settled on the surface of the Moon, Mo Chavez snaps off his dad's little black-and-white TV.

'Moisés!'

'It's time to go, Papa.' Mo opens the curtains to the blinding Miami sun.

'But men are walking on the Moon, Moisés!'

Mo brushes the cookie crumbs off his father's best shirt and adjusts his tie. The men hardly know each other; there is a nine-year separation dividing them. They connect best in the dumb-show of gesture, the grammer of touch and nudge.

'Come along, Papa, you want to look your best for the St Patrick crowd,' says Moisés, hustling him out of his rundown Collins Avenue apartment. Mo wanted to do better by his father than to install him in this semi-derelict thirties hotel, but Anastasio is happy here. He can walk down the street and smell the ocean and the garbage and drink rum and eat roast pork sandwiches. He picks up a little pin money writing numbers for *bolito*, and around here no cop would ever dream of pressing charges. This place, in all its growing squalor, is a kind of Havana for the old man, now that the original is lost.

'St Patrick's?' Old Anastasio is scandalized. '*St Patrick's?*'

'It's the only church on the Beach, papa. We don't want to go far now.'

It was his father's idea that Man's first steps on the Moon – an event that commands a TV audience of one-fifth of the world's population – might be conveniently combined with an exposition of the Holy

Eucharist. Anastasio's regretting his decision now, of course, in thrall to the mission and its enormity, but he can't be seen to ignore the call of the Holy Hour, not in front of his tearaway American son. He spent nine years battling the revolutionary authorities over his freedom to worship. So, muttering, he follows Mo into the unreliable old Deco lift. 'How long have I waited to receive benediction among my countrymen, and now my son takes me to an *Irish...*'

Mo glances at his father, amused, as they cross the dusty lobby. Heaven only knows where this objection has sprung from. Another piece of Yankee folklore his father has somehow misconstrued. Anastasio only got out of Cuba eight months ago, and his desire to acquire the local US colouring has something desperate about it. A strong man growing old, Anastasio expresses his vigour in anxious, opinionated outbursts. He hasn't the patience to soak up America, no, he must forage for it, he must stitch it out of scraps like a naked Adam covering himself with leaves.

What he ends up with – a motley of overheard conversation, misdirected sentiment and poorly comprehended talk-radio – says less about the old man's American present than about his Cuban past: the way Castro's UMAP labour camps stripped his ordinary human dignity away. When people look at Mo's father, they see what Mo sees: a powerful old man, bullish, a survivor. The camps taught Anastasio to see past all that – past his personality, history and character – to some bare, grub-like, essential man. They taught him to be ashamed of himself, so now he is free, he is trying to be someone different. He is trying to be an American.

'Welcome to Florida, Father,' says Mo, baiting the old man a little. 'The melting pot.' This front of easy sarcasm is Mo's antidote to the pity and anger which would otherwise overwhelm him, thinking of his father, for years shackled to the worst dregs of Havana's lowlife, the winos and the queers. For nine years, in prison and out of it, since the day in 1960 he put his fourteen-year-old son on the boat to freedom,

Anastasio has paid the price for his treason. Mo can never let him know how seriously he honours this debt.

Father and son leave the shadow of the dilapidated Greystone Hotel. Mo's automobile is at the kerb, a Thunderbird with brilliant ice-cream bodywork that contrasts obscenely with its cherry-red leather interior. God forbid his father ever catches wind of its nickname among the blades of the *corporaçion*.

The old man makes a big production of how difficult it is to climb into a car so sporty, so low-slung, *tan desrazonable*, and he is messing with the radio before Mo can get to the ignition. Valuable minutes are wasted while Mo hunts for the station, and they are past Lummus Park and its ocean views before the familiar voice of NASA's public affairs officer returns to the air.

'You see?' says Mo. 'Everything'll be fine.'

The two astronauts are still sat in their Eagle, doing whatever it is spacemen do once they have landed on a new world. All month the TV and the radio have been talking about how much rehearsal has gone into this. There have been talk shows, cinema newsreels, pull-out souvenirs in the magazines. But there must be some element of chance, there has to be, a part of the mission the astronauts make up as they go along. Or why would they bother to volunteer?

Mo and his father are headed for Garden Avenue, a stone's throw from the 195 causeway anchoring Miami Beach to the mainland metropolis. The traffic, normally so heavy, has vanished. Mo takes advantage, and the Thunderbird trembles, roars and (eventually) accelerates.

Anastasio glances at his watch. Exasperated: 'Moisés, we are early. We are much too early. Why didn't we wait? Moisés—'

But Neil Armstrong has come on air:

'It's pretty much without colour,' he says. *'It's grey and it's a very white chalk-grey as you look into the zero phase line, and it's considerably darker grey, more like ashen grey as you look up ninety degrees to the sun.'*

It is the Moon, seen from the surface of the Moon, and it is grey.

'Moisés, we are missing it!'

'Papa, it's fine, it's under control, enjoy the radio, there won't be any TV pictures until they leave the rocket.'

St Patrick's occupies the whole block between West 39th and West 40th Street. There is a church, a rectory, a convent, a school, such an excess of space and ambition that, when Anastasio climbs (grumbling) from the car and sees it all, an actual *mall* of Catholicism, he struggles, unsure what attitude to strike. 'Well, it doesn't *look* Irish,' he allows, as they climb the broad white steps to the door. Mo, in a brief, dissociated moment, wonders just what idea of Irishness a Cuban dissident entertains.

A small, malevolent-looking man in a broad suit is standing by the porch, a portable radio in one hand, listening intently.

'Some of the surface rocks in close here that have been fractured or disturbed by the rocket engine are coated with this light grey on the outside, but when they've been broken they display a dark, very dark grey interior…'

You heard it here first, thinks Mo: the Moon is grey.

Mo isn't too sure where this sarcastic inner voice has sprung from. He wants to lose himself in the poetry and majesty of the day, but this voice keeps tripping him up. This bleak voice reminds him, every time the public affairs officer comes on, that this is the Voice of official America, reporting the Daring Deeds of America, Land of Promises and promises and more promises, a superpower whose reach extends to the very stars, but a power so idle it is unable even to sweep a tin-pot dictator from an island not a hundred miles from its own seaboard. Maybe things will get better now that Nixon is in charge – Dickie Nixon who worked so hard and with such passion to make the Bay of Pigs invasion a working reality – but he is not holding his breath. Neither is the *corporaçion*. Even its CIA handlers – Dick's men all, and veterans with Cuba in their blood – have been muttering mutinously into their shot glasses.

He knows today's Moon landing should outweigh these matters. On a planetary scale his can only be local troubles. But it doesn't. It doesn't mean anything more than this: that three crew-cut middle-class boys are putting their lives on the line for the sake of an extraordinary adventure. And good for them, their bravery and dedication and undoubted skill. He salutes the adventure, Hell, yes. It's the national symbolism that sticks in his throat. In 1961, at fifteen, he was too young to join the Brigade. He missed the sorry hash American planning and intelligence made of the Bay of Pigs landings. He was not martyred, as so many fathers of so many friends were that day in April, on the altar of expedience and deniability.

The astronauts, too, have put their lives in the hands of America, and Mo knows, with some bitterness, how risky this must be for them. He wants to see them walk on the Moon, and when he leads his dad into church, he'll be as glad of the little surprise he's been saving as, hopefully, his dad will be. Because there's a television – the biggest you can rent, booked weeks ago from the biggest rental store in the city – hooked up to an aerial in the church tower. The priest is a rocket nut and plans to slip the Holy Hour into whatever dead space becalms the coverage.

There is another reason Mo chose this church.

A baptism party emerges from the portico. They are a miscellaneous bunch: the men tense, overmuscled; the women young, overdressed and at the same time underconcealed, more likely girlfriends than wives. The little man with the radio goes to join them.

'I told you we were early,' Anastasio grumbles, but Mo isn't listening. Mo is shooting his cuffs, he is running his fingers through his hair. The party passes.

'Señor Conroy!'

The mother, striking but pale under her garish white cake decoration – more of a bridal gown than an outfit for baptism – is walking arm in arm with a balding, heavy-set man, who tenses visibly as Mo calls out his name.

This Conroy was a strong man in his day, old Anastasio sees that. A strong man who has applied his strength against other men: the signature of combat is written indelibly in his poise, his hand reluctantly extended to brush Mo's.

The girl blushes and smiles. 'Very many congratulations, Deborah,' Mo says, and bends to coo over her baby. Anastasio is not so old that he does not notice Mo's attention shift fleetingly to the girl's breasts.

'Mr Conroy is a sports promoter, Papa, he holds cards in all the big venues, the Auditorium, the Convention Center. Mr Conroy, I'd like you to meet my father.' Mo's solicitations are so proper they border on parody. This is obvious to everyone, and Anastasio feels shame on his son's behalf.

Conroy waits patiently, holding Anastasio's hand, until the old man looks at him. When he speaks, his accent is soft, not American – Irish? 'Your son tells me you enjoy Jackie Gleason.'

Anastasio shrugs.

'Come to next Wednesday's match and I'll introduce you.'

Gleason works out of the Auditorium. Anastasio saw him coming out of there once, beaming blindly into the sun, hand half-raised to greet a crowd, or fend it off. Expecting a public that, for that brief anomalous moment, had vanished, the street and sidewalk empty. Gleason dropped his hand, noticed Anastasio looking at him from across the street and mugged up an act for him: a big shrug and a disappointed shamble down the street.

'The Great Malenko versus Wahoo McDaniel,' says Mo.

'What?'

'The match. At the Auditorium next Wednesday. Right, Dad?'

This from the girl, Deborah, and straight away the alarm bells are ringing in Anastasio's head. Because if this is her father, and this bundle in her arms is her baby, then where, in the name of decency, is her husband?

*

Hours pass. It is twenty to ten before Armstrong begins his moonwalk, and Harry is drinking in his usual bar down by Woffard Park. The bar is packed and silent, everyone transfixed before the screen on its shelf above the optics. They are wrapped in an atmosphere more profound and deep-felt than church and his own granddaughter's christening.

Harry raises the beer glass to his lips but forgets to drink.

'Neil, you're lined up nicely... toward me a little bit...'

The restricted environment of the lunar module means that Armstrong will enter the history books arse-first, the way his granddaughter Stacey entered the world.

'OK, down...'

Everyone is moved in some way. Harry feels his jaw tighten, but there are men around him weeping into their beer. The wonder of it is, these are his people, men whose profession it is to beat the living shit out of each other. These Mexican hardcases have so little left to prove they can afford to let themselves be children when the occasion suits. Harry has learned to admire their easy sentiment – but from a distance, Belfast still strong in him. Tears can never be Harry's way, brought up as he was under a strict Falls Road ethic, the rod thrust firmly – as his late wife once so delicately put it – up his Fenian backside.

'Roll to the left... put your left foot to the right a little bit... you're doing fine.'

Still no live picture yet.

Beside Harry, below him – he is only five feet six to Harry's six-two – Benjamin Donoso is making the sign of the cross repeatedly across his chest. Donoso is a former ice-house navvy Harry discovered moonlighting on the Guadalajara circuit. This was just a few weeks after Harry arrived in Mexico, wrestling's new El Dorado, Deborah big-bellied on his arm and the pair of them out to start their lives again as far away as possible from 'swinging London'.

The second time they met, Donoso handed Deborah a charm against the devil, a sugar-and-straw trinket Harry didn't understand and, more than that, suspected. Only the sadness in the little Mexican's eyes prevented him from ramming the little juju thing down his neck.

Over time, Harry has come to understand that Benjamin Donoso's superstitions are real to him, turning his every performance in the wrestling ring into a Mystery he could, if he was put to it, explain to any priest. Every Wednesday Donoso puts on a black cloak, white face-paint and a cardboard half-mask painted like a skull, and climbs into the ring with men a foot and a half taller than he is.

Back in 1969, before Donoso came on board to explain it to him, this sort of caper was a closed book to Harry Conroy. Arriving in Mexico, he'd been dismayed to discover that the wrestling scene there was a circus. Literally: there were costumes. Masks. Capes. There were props. In Tijuana the fights were, if possible, even more brutal than those he remembered from Belfast, but here there was an added grace to every bout, and a kind of fairy-tale logic Harry despaired of ever understanding.

With Donoso's encouragement and Deborah's medical bills to pay, Harry finally cracked it. He gathered together the best wrestlers Donoso knew of and showed them the kind of wrestling *he* knew: the sea-sick rhythms of Submission, the brutal groundworks of Collar-and-Elbow. The Mexican fighters watched, and grew pale.

What can we do with this? This was Harry's question: no angle, no pitch, no promises. What can we do? Can we do anything? Is there anything here?

There was. When they were ready, Harry arranged a tour Stateside, and from the very first night, it was a rout, a massacre, an event to change the sport of wrestling for ever.

Harry's outfit settled finally in Florida, integrating uneasily with the already strong promotion there. There were tensions between the natives and the newcomers, and by persuading both sides to let him exploit these tensions in closely scripted angles, Harry made every match he promoted part of a larger epic – a statewide grudge war with instalments every week in an auditorium or school hall near you. It was the birth of modern wrestling, with its storylines, its flawed heroes and irresistible villians, its catastrophic injuries and superhuman returns from the dead. It was pure gold.

Donoso is the most exciting heel on the Florida circuit and certainly the most unlikely. Whoever heard of a heel who was shorter than his opponent? Who, before Donoso, ever imagined that a crowd could be persuaded to bay for the blood of the little guy? Donoso has a way of lending true terror to his litheness, his odd, asymmetric moves and especially his short stature. He is everyone's childhood nightmare of a puppet come to life. He makes even Harry shudder sometimes, even though Harry writes all the angles and keeps him supplied with rubber teeth.

Donoso the Vampyre, at five feet six the undisputed master of the figure four leg-lock, lays his hand on Harry's arm. 'The boy's a blade,' he murmurs as they wait for pictures, any second now: Armstrong's first steps. 'When Castro gets his joke-shop cigar from Uncle Sam, this boy wants to be there with the lighter.'

Christ. 'What else?' Harry asks. He has been turning cartwheels trying to keep his lovely daughter out of the shit, but the evidence is pretty bloody clear by now, Deborah has an unerring instinct for trouble. He had hopes for Mo, too. 'What does he use his boat for?'

Donoso shrugs.

'Weed? Is he shipping weed?'

'I don't think so.'

Every son of every Cuban martyr plies the coast of Cuba in a borrowed boat. It is like a rite of manhood. They are looking for something to tell their handlers back on shore, men they imagine belong to the Agency. They don't even know what it is they are looking for. They missed their moment in history, too young to get butchered with the 2506, so now they wander the Florida Straits like derelicts foraging for scraps. Six months later the ones who don't manage to drown themselves are tacking into the Keys with packets of emeralds and holds full of marijuana.

Still, this Moisés kid is doing a damn good impression of being smitten, and who else is going to look at Deborah now she has Stacey to look after? He's persistent, too. Harry has made sure of that. He's not given the kid the easiest of rides.

'Thanks, Ben,' he says. Benjamin Donoso shrugs, because thanks are nothing to him, he loves Harry fiercely.

Harry wonders what he has done to deserve such friendship. Without Donoso he would surely be down and out in Tijuana still, and Deborah, poor damaged Deborah, this child, the image of her mother, whose precious life he tries to save, but which pours through his fingers like water–

The balance in the room changes. He feels it, a shift of energies.

Above them, on the television, Armstrong's boot appears.

At the same moment, across town, Moisés Chavez has taken advantage of Harry's absence to steal a couple of hours with his love.

'Careful,' Deborah gasps, 'careful.'

Mo lifts his body higher above her, teasing her, his cock inside her but only a little way.

'Mo.'

His quick, shallow thrusts grow deeper, longer, he lowers himself over her, flicks at her lips with his tongue, and she begins to come.

They are still in the flush of things, still new to each other. Next to them, sleeping in her cot, Deborah's baby Stacey stirs in her sleep, comforted by smells and sounds of human need.

The TV is on but the sound is down. Mo wheeled it in from the sitting room so that they could enjoy the bed together and still not miss the moment: man's first steps on the Moon. Plus if Harry her dad comes home early, being in here rather than the sitting room gives Mo precious seconds in which to leap out the window into the shrubbery.

Mo closes his hand around Deborah's throat, playful but firm, choking her softly to her climax.

He turns her over then, or she turns over for him – they are developing a rhythm now, a mutuality of response, impossible to say who gives, who takes – when events overtake them: on the TV, the news studio has been replaced by grainy grey static.

'Shit.' Mo slides out of her.

'Mo.'

'I need the john,' he says. 'Sorry. Shit.' He scampers out the room and across the hall.

'Hurry,' she calls after him, needlessly.

On the TV, Armstrong's boot appears, feeling for the rung of the ladder...

And Deborah Conroy wakes from her evening with Mo into a blast of pain, trapped in the hollow metal dark with the certainty of having been touched.

She is eight years old and she is seventeen years old and she knows exactly what is happening to her.

Beyond the confines of her hot coffin, the scream of gulls. And Mo's voice from the toilet, telling her some joke or other, something from the day, about his dad.

The uselessness of her limbs; paralysed, she cannot even lift her hands to beat against the tight metal lid, inches above her face. And at the same time, the press of pillows at her back, and the draught of the air-con unit.

The taste of Mo's cigarettes; and in the self-same moment, her mouth is stuffed with her own underwear.

Opening her mouth to scream, eight-year-old Deborah discovers what her seventeen-year-old self knows already from memory and regular repetition: that all her consonants have disappeared, that she can make only idiot sounds so unlike the sounds of distress, neither of her selves will be heard. Mo does not hear her, though he is zipping up his fly only feet away; and it is dark and freezing cold before passers-by, a tow-truck driver and his mate, twig to the truth and pop the boot to reveal eight-year-old abductee Deborah, shivering and spasming in Felixstowe's night air.

Even as Neil Armstrong's boot settles into the lunar dust, she is falling.

Mo enters the bedroom, zipping up his fly, in time to see Deborah topple off the side of the bed, headfirst into her baby's cot. Mo's funny story dies on his lips. The baby, pinned beneath her mother, is silent, little hands spinning as she struggles to inhale. Even the TV is silent, in the split-second before Neil Armstrong delivers his famous line. Yet the room is full of sound. Later, sat with Harry in the emergency room, their ritual hostilities suspended while the doctors fight to reinflate little Stacey's lung, Mo presses his hands to his ears against the memory of that sound: the idiot gurgle in his lover's throat; the spastic thump-thump-thump of her head against the floor.

It is the summer of 1974.

They set sail from the Keys last night, around 9 p.m.: Mo, Deborah, little Stacey; Mo's new business partner is alternating watch. Also onboard is Father Turi, a priest Mo's father knew, himself an escapee from the old country and game for a voyage as charged as this one: dropping old Anastasio's urn into the warm waters of his commandeered home.

It is not a usual thing: to burn a body once washed in baptism, anointed with the oil of salvation, and fed with the bread of life. It is not – the first priest Mo approached made this obnoxiously clear – a practice approved of by the Church. But better old Anastasio returns home as ash than he keeps his flesh to moulder in a foreign grave.

So he is ash now, and free to return home. Here is the water, and Father Turi says, 'Lord God, by the power of your Word you stilled the chaos of the primaeval seas, you made the raging waters of the Flood subside and calmed the storm on the sea of Galilee.'

It is five years since Mo Chavez married Deborah and took baby Stacey for his own. A good and happy time, but also a painful one, because his father naturally did not understand why his son, so full of life and wit and blood, should saddle himself with another man's bastard child. Never mind that the girl he was marrying was sick in the head.

This last objection melted over time as Deborah's seizures tailed away, vanishing as mysteriously as they appeared. But it wasn't until little Stacey started to talk that Anastasio allowed the possibility that he might be charmed. Then, of course, he saw what Mo had seen all along: that there is something wonderful in the electric field humming between mother and daughter that overrides the imperatives of pride and blood.

The last two years of Anastasio's life were good ones, reconciling father and son; bringing a new family into being. Though he never spoke of his own deterioration, perhaps Anastasio knew there was no time left for him to nurse his disapproval, only a headlong rush into a future that would not contain him. Accepting this, how could he not accept the love and games of a little child?

Stacey loves her grandfather. 'Grandpa's an angel now,' Mo told Stacey, the day he came to the hotel and found his father dead, the TV on, and Jackie Gleason cracking weak jokes into his open eyes. Stacey blinked. 'Funny,' she said.

The terrible iconoclasm of children.

'How funny?'

'Funny he didn't say anything,' she said. The abruptness meant more to her than the death. 'Where is he, then?' Looking around.

Ill-health barely grazed Anastasio's final months. Whatever was the matter with his heart erupted, decisive and muscular as the man it killed.

'As we commit the earthly remains of our brother Anastasio to the deep, grant him peace and tranquillity until that day when he and all who believe in you will be raised to the glory of new life promised in the waters of baptism.'

Deborah squeezes Mo's hand. Stacey leans in to him. Mo's business partner appreciates that this is a family occasion and has made himself scarce during the committal. Mo is dimly aware of him straddling the bowsprit, book in hand, as Father Turi draws to a close.

'We ask this through Christ our Lord. Amen.'

Mo steps forward and drops the urn containing his father's ashes into Cuban water.

It was a risky thing to do perhaps, to sail into these waters in broad daylight; with his wife and kid, too, a real provocation to fate. But he owed the old man, and he could not have borne the day without Deborah beside him and five-year-old Stacey hugging his knee. (She is trying to look solemn, but she really doesn't know how; she keeps scowling and wrinkling up her nose. Grandpa's an angel now, and because she believes this, she cannot feel grief.)

Afterwards, hands trembling, the urn still sensate in his fingertips, he takes the wheel and pulls them out of there as quickly as he can, breezing up the Santaren Channel like any other clueless Bahamian tourist, taking the long way home. Deborah sweetens the priest's delay with glasses of home-squeezed guayabana juice and Stacey goes below, playing a private game. His business partner joins him by the wheel, tosses his book – Fuentes, *Cambio de Piel* – onto the wheel housing and, after a little rigmarole of handshakes and commiserations, distracts Mo, as he knows Mo likes to be distracted, with tales of April 1961.

'Seaweed! Some fuckwit Yank pilot looked out the window of his U2 and saw *seaweed*...'

Wednesday, 7 August 1974: for five years Mo has been running his boat charter, running ulcer-making surveillance in the teeth of Castro's shore batteries and trying to believe, against all evidence and logic, that another Bay of Pigs is possible. Now, as of today, he is on his own, the very last shreds of Operation Mongoose thrown away, the *corporaçion* disbanded, its handlers gone without goodbye, exiled to desk-jobs in Langley or to moribund research libraries on the Washington outskirts.

Some are retired; some plain thrown out. Mo sees them mumbling their way along Collins Avenue, big men with wet, disappointed eyes.

Two days ago Nixon released three of the transcripts and admitted he had tried to halt the FBI's inquiry into the Watergate break-in. Is this really the same Dick Nixon Mo cheered at the Republican Nomination, all those years ago? The news is full of conspiracy and cover-up but Mo Chavez, blooded in the hot disorder of Little Havana with its three hundred front companies, its six hundred veterans' groups, knows a cheap fantastist when he sees one. There's no conspiracy here: just Dickie leaving others to wipe his drool off the furniture. He will surely not outlast the week.

This is old news. The real damage occurred when it turned out the campaign office burglars were Cubans. This news has hurt Miami past all hope of healing. Five years Mo has spent in the Agency's service, paying back in effort and in peril the debt he owed his father. There will be no second invasion, no bigger, better Bay of Pigs. It has all been for nothing.

Or if not for nothing then – this is the bitterest pill – merely for this lumbering money-pit of a boat. This little perk by way of the Agency's pursuit of plausible denial. (If he'd been running a print shop, they would have given him the shop.) This boat bought for him by the Melmar Corporation, the CIA's Miami front. This boat which is now his, to do with as he likes.

What does he want with a boat? Where will he sail to, now Fidel has been left to lord it over his home?

'We never stood a fucking chance,' the business partner sighs, in conclusion, and lights up a cigar.

Mo's gut responds as always to the old and much-repeated tale. This first-hand account of the Bay of Pigs fiasco makes a hollow space within him for a cocktail of conflicting emotions: regret, envy, incredulity, admiration. There are just two years between them, but this man fought on the beaches; Mo did not. This man served twenty-two months in La

Cabaña, within earshot of daily executions, 'and Gagarin laughed and told me, "You too wear the Order of Playa Girón!"'

Mo has the boat, but he has no idea what to do with it. An image looms: season after season spent helping lobster-faced tourists fish marlin; not a life so much as an afterlife.

This man knows what to do with his boat. They met two years ago, a Thursday in December, the night the last Apollo rose, plangent, a broken promise, through the star-white skies of Cocoa Beach. They reeled together, drunk, along the boardwalks and watched the lift-off, watched as this little bubble of broken hope became another star. Seventeen. The last men on the moon.

'I thought I'd missed them all,' Nick sighed as they wove from one side of the beach to the other through quiet, manicured streets, from the Banana River to the ocean and back again. Nick was newly arrived from east Africa, an experienced merchant marine. 'I dreamed of seeing this.'

When the rocket had vanished from sight they went and found a bar, but even here, in this resort town where old NASA men come to die in the sun, the patrons were glued to a sports channel.

They threw beer tins into the quay and talked about Apollo, what of it they had seen; they played where-were-you-when. They talked Kennedy and Nixon, about history and the way things end and what if anything comes next.

They talked about the Straits of Florida.

Mo has the seamanship, the CIA training and the boat; Jessup has the contacts and the experience. Watergate has laid waste to Miami, and Jessup knows what comes next. Jessup knows what to do with his boat.

Nick Jessup. This is what he calls himself.

Mo understands, of course, that this is not his real name.

RENAMO MOTO

1

It was towards the end of 1984, the aftermath of Mozambique's droughts, and I was leaving Maputo and heading north to the town of Goliata on the Mozambique–Malawi border.

Were God in His heaven, Mozambique, a thousand-mile-long beach state on the eastern seaboard of southern Africa, would be a paradise. Instead the country has laboured for five hundred years under whimsical Portuguese 'government'. Finally, in 1969, even as they mourned Jorge Katalayo, their assassinated leader, and just in time to tweak everyone's Cold War paranoias, Mozambique's socialist liberators, the Frente de Libertaçao de Moçambique or FRELIMO, declared their country's independence. The sovereign state of Mozambique, they said, would align itself neither with the Warsaw Pact nor with the West.

In choosing this difficult and perilous path, FRELIMO's leaders also chose to disregard certain glaring realities. For instance, the fact that they had land borders with Rhodesia and apartheid South Africa. Or that the sea corridors that passed through their territory were crucial to the economies of their landlocked (and, for that reason, increasingly paranoid) neighbours. If I could see the seeds of disaster in all this, why didn't they? In 1969 I was still in London, far from the action, reading newspapers behind the library counter of my dear little philosophical society. How could they have missed what was so obvious to people like me?

The staff of FRELIMO were, like their fallen comrades, all honourable Western-educated blacks who had spent their formative years in countries like America and Sweden. They imagined post-colonial Africa would submit to the rules of fair play. And they were wrong: retribution for their daring stab at self-government was long and terrible. In 1977, Apartheid-backed RENAMO contras launched a war of terror against the civilian population of Mozambique. The campaign lasted fifteen years, aided first by Rhodesia, then South Africa, then by the two severest droughts in living memory.

When I heard the army had wrested Goliata back from the contras, I thought: Now at least I can get there by plane. But RENAMO still controlled the surrounding countryside and the airstrip was too badly damaged to risk a landing. 'Goliata is free,' a well-meaning apparatchik in the ministry of education told me, 'only that you cannot go in or out.'

I thought about travelling steerage on a cacao boat as far as Beira, taking pot luck after that – only RENAMO's piracy had reached a pitch where anything moving outside Beira's mothballed harbour, regardless of flag, ran a risk of being shelled by nervous government batteries scattered along the shore.

All the big roads in Mozambique were built by the Portuguese to speed up their looting, and they all ran east–west, connecting the coast to the interior. Naively I traced out a course which mazed laboriously northward over dirt tracks and seasonal roads. When I showed it to the officer in charge of the car pool, he nearly fell off his chair laughing. Had I not heard of land mines?

A week or so later, a team of Italian engineers managed to hand-wave their way past the border checkpoint on the Malawian side of the Shire river. They mended the airstrip, and finally I was able to piggy-back a government charter.

The only other passenger – Joseph Lichenya, the new district administrator – met me an hour before dawn on a military airstrip just outside Maputo's city limits, by the tailplane of the ancient pre-war Dakota.

Clean-shaven and in his thirties, wearing sunglasses even in the pre-dawn dark, Captain Lichenya was typical of the careful young men the socialist FRELIMO government turned out of Maputo these days. A few years ago he would have been overseeing Operation Production – the government's catastrophic experiment in collectivized agriculture. These days it was all that men like him could do to gather Mozambique's scattered rural population into temporary villages, safe from RENAMO's predations and in reach of the international aid agencies. The irony, that these safe havens were often built on the foundations of *aldeamentos* – Portuguese work-camps – escaped no one.

I asked Lichenya where he hailed from.

'Oh,' he said, shrugging. 'That's a difficult question. I'm from all over.'

Ah, a man of mystery. I elected to dislike him.

The pilot and his mate – two boisterous Soviet airforcemen – turned up to inspect our aircraft with incredulous fascination, as though it were some sort of exhibit. After some persuasion, the engines turned. There were no seats in the Dakota. The captain and I settled opposite each other on sacks of pinto beans.

'Sit on two sacks,' Lichenya said.

'I'm fine.' At forty-two I was older than him by at least fifteen years, and an experienced traveller. I didn't need him to nanny me.

He turned his hand into a make-believe pistol and pointed it into the air; he pulled the trigger. 'Two sacks will stop a bullet.'

I moved to higher ground. This put me closer to the doorway than I wanted, given the plane had no doors.

We swung a lazy arc over Beira's harbour. The curl prolonged itself, turned full-circle, repeated... The pilots were wasting fuel, and it was not hard to see why. At the horizon the sea was a vivid bluish green, as distant waves caught and refracted light from a sun that had yet to rise. The green spread as though a lush prairie were unfolding itself across the ocean. A couple of seconds later, as the sun's first arc came into view, the prairie burst into flames of red and gold.

Nice to know that even Russian pilots have the souls of poets. Content, they changed course and hurled us inland and up, out of range of RENAMO's heat-seeking missiles, and into the strange, marble world of thunderheads and cloud columns that awaited us, five thousand feet above my adopted country.

Jorge Katalayo's assassination had not fractured the liberation movement, nor did it delay the colonists' inevitable defeat. Victory over the colonial power had been achieved by 1974 – much sooner than expected – when a coup in Lisbon cut the Portuguese imperial project off at the root.

So FRELIMO had found itself in the disconcerting position of a dog that's been chasing after a speeding car: once it's caught it, what on earth is it supposed to do with it?

With tiny resources, few personnel and next to no education, FRELIMO found itself with a country to run. Worse, a *Portuguese* country. Even then, the situation might have been saved, had it not been for the exodus.

Boats arrived from Lisbon and carried whole harvests away. What the settlers couldn't carry, they destroyed. These were acts of pure spite. Tractors were driven into the sea. Job-loads of concrete were poured down the lift-shafts of half-finished beachfront hotels.

Once these moral pygmies had returned to the motherland, burped and bedded, their tummies swollen with home-stewed *bacalhau*, the Africans they had so laughably 'governed' for five hundred years took stock. In the words of Yelena Mlokote, *née* Katalayo, bereaved daughter of FRELIMO's first president:

We have nothing to learn, because there is no one left here to teach us. We have nothing to buy because there is no one here left to sell us anything. We have nothing to do because there is no one who can pay us for our labour. We have nowhere to go because no one here knows how to drive a train. Very soon we shall have nothing to wear. Already in the country you find people weaving jerkins and skirts out of tree bark.

This comes from a standard letter Yelena sent me in the summer of 1975. Well, it was her signature printed on the bottom. How many hundreds of these things must they have posted to contacts and friends in Britain, Sweden, America? In it, she invited me ('dear friend', 'valued colleague') to assist the struggling administration:

> *For as long as anyone can remember, bureaucracy has been the black man's only route to preferment. No one here knows how to operate a seed drill; no one here can afford to buy a seed drill; but everyone with a primary education knows what the requisition form would look like. At the moment of liberation, we have the skills required to operate a tin-pot fascist backwater. These skills, and no others. God protect us from our strengths.*

It didn't take much exegesis to discover, behind her words, the writings of her father. Did she read his speeches now? Did she search out his words in the back numbers of obscure Marxist periodicals? In foreign newspapers, microfiched at the SOAS library in London? In correspondence with helpful, if bemused, journalists from Sweden and Japan?

Though I kept her letter, as you might keep a wisdom tooth or a gall-stone, I figured there was nothing to be gained by replying to her. Then, a couple of weeks later, on a whim, I bought a postcard of a Beefeater and scribbled this on the back: *'A to K or L to Z?'*

It was the most compact, brutal way I could think of to tell her what I knew about her father's assassination. What FRELIMO's serious young men had told me, visiting my flat that day in 1969.

About a month later, a second letter arrived. It was very different from the first: much shorter and entirely personal. Yelena is changing bed-pans in a clinic in Lourenço Marques ('We call it Maputo now'). She spends her nights studying in a rented room by the light of a paraffin lamp: *'My father understood that the greatest threat to black power in post-colonial Africa is the educated black. Home rule that side-steps revolution – he appreciated that threat far better than I did. I realize that now.'*

She was trying to locate herself in history. To present her acts in the light of the complex circumstances. *'It was a mistaken path,'* she wrote. (She had acquired the rhetoric of her father's generation: the road; the path; the long march.) She wrote: *'I believe I took a wrong turning.'*

I took this to be her confession.

'By day, I perform menial duties at the hospital. I dress cuts and bruises. I hand out aspirins, when we have any, to the chronic cases. I empty bed-pans in the fever ward. I study at night.'

She wanted every mistake she had made to yield a valuable life lesson.

'Come to Maputo,' she wrote.

The cold shook Captain Lichenya out of his sleep. He'd looked so vulnerable, curled up on his sacks, that I had laid a blanket across him. Some sort of a blanket, sewn together from burlap relief sacks. He pulled it up around himself and blinked. 'Christ,' he said – the *lingua franca* of blasphemy – and added, in English: 'I hate flying.'

Holding the blanket around himself, he climbed off the sacks and began pacing stiffly back and forth along the hold.

'Do you know Goliata?' I asked him.

'I know Goliata.'

I let the silence – or what passed for silence in a doorless prop aeroplane – drag on for as long as I could stand. 'I'm the new teacher there,' I said.

'I know who you are.'

The view out of the open doorway seemed to mesmerize him: storm clouds over the purple carpet of the earth. He stopped to stare, for all the world as if he were surveying the view from the balcony of a hotel. 'Where have you been working?' he shouted back at me.

'Maputo,' I told him. 'Tete. Beira, a few times.'

I had been doing this kind of work for nearly ten years now: arithmetic, literacy, hygiene, a smattering of *Marxismo-Leninismo*. I was a valuable commodity: an educated foreign worker allied to FRELIMO's socialist administration. A *cooperante*.

'Nampula?'

'No. It's odd.' Nampula was Mozambique's northern capital. 'I've never been.'

'A pity.'

'Yes?'

Engine noise filled the hold, and there was a worrying smell of petrol.

'You've never worked in the countryside before?'

'No.'

He nodded. He had guessed as much.

'Is it safe?' The words were out of my mouth before I could stop them.

The captain turned back to the open doorway, the world of strange currents and inversions giving way now, as we dropped towards cloudbase, to a clearer view of the land.

Looking down, I scoured the landscape for its human component. A smallholding, a field of rice or cassava, a stand of cashew trees: the eye leapt to one, then to another, as to a major landmark. Most of the time, there were no tracks in view and no villages worth the name. Rocky bluffs and acacia trees jumbled the landscape like a deliberate camouflage: an outrageous sculptural scatter-painting in purple, white and yellow-green. People lived here, but this was not an ordinary human landscape. It was not carved out, the way the land in other countries is carved and parcelled, cleared and divided. The human parts of the landscape had not agglomerated, the way they had elsewhere, into the ribbons and clumps – villages, roads – which humans usually make on their nation's petri dish. Down there (we had reached the district of Zambezia) it was as though the humans had been scattered evenly over the land in a fine drizzle, and had made do wherever they landed.

Many of the people didn't even know that their country was called Mozambique. The RENAMO contras were just bandits to them – *matsangas*. Socialism was another word they couldn't spell. If they had heard of South Africa at all, it was as a distant place of fabulous wealth. They tilled their land. They wanted to be left alone. They left each other alone. This was the problem: it was virtually impossible for men like Lichenya to defend them.

Of course it wasn't safe.

2

The T-shirt was frayed. It had been washed many times. Across the front of the blouse, glass and concrete towers reached into a sky that must have been blue once, but time and frequent washes had bleached it to pale green. In front of the towers, a beach stretched away in naive perspective: a distant headland, a bikini-clad sunbather, a parasol, a long iced drink in a glass beaded with sweat. Splashed across the sky in big pink letters: Sunny Beirut.

The sunbather's midriff stretched and tore, the glass broke: the T-shirt's wearer inhaled. 'They burned the school, stole the books and used the children to carry the furniture over the border.' Goliata's FRELIMO administrator was a big woman. It was in her face that the hardships of the two-year drought were written: it was shrunken and bruised-looking, like a fruit that has been left out in the sun too long.

Beirut? The top was older than the children I was here to teach.

'Then they sliced off the boys' noses and fed them to the girls.'

Entering this room, I had feared the worst: 'RENAMO MOTO' smeared on the walls in sump oil. 'Moto' meaning fire. But even as we talked, a boy came in silently, unacknowledged, and began pasting frayed posters of FRELIMO President Chissano over the slogan. (The glue smelled foul – his own concoction?)

'One of the girls, she was eight years old, refused to eat her brother's nose. The captain wanted to make an example out of her so he tried to rape her.'

This was Naphiri Calange's office. Naphiri herself stood facing me across a desk knocked together out of crates. We didn't sit down; there were no chairs. Above our heads, the room's central light was missing, along with the fitment, and a jagged tear in the ceiling plaster, from the middle of the room to just over the door, marked the path of the electrical wire: this too had been torn out. The floor of the room was a crumbling skein of cement.

'She was too small for him, so he widened her with his machete.'

The windows had neither glass, nor the cheaper, more common and practical mesh grilles. More ominous still, the windows had no sills or frames, for these too had been ripped away. Their regular shape distinguished them from the artillery holes which had otherwise colandered the town.

'Welcome to Goliata.'

There were two windows. Naphiri stood with her back to one. The other was to her right. Through the window behind her, no building stood tall enough to look me in the eye. Most had been reduced to stubs and slopes of dusty scree, bound already by weeds and creepers. The ones that remained standing – either roofless, or sporting a recent, disreputable-looking greenish thatch – had fared little better.

I asked, 'What happened to all the roofs?'

'Stolen,' Naphiri replied. She told me how RENAMO had kidnapped villagers to carry zinc roofing sheets out of Goliata, across empty cattle pens and through the bush, to the border crossing with Malawi, where the metal was bartered for motorcycle spares, radio batteries, oil, sugar, salt.

Through the other window, bright afternoon light came into the room dappled and scented by shade trees – flame, jacaranda – which grew in the grounds of the old Portuguese church. These were the last trees in Goliata. The RENAMO guerrillas had not touched the church. It was completely undamaged. To stand with a view of both windows was to see in tableau the recent history of the town: the before and the after.

'Come.' She motioned me over to the window overlooking the ruins.

From this distance it was impossible to tell what building was useable, what was a ruin. She pointed down the street towards what must once have been the pretty end of town. The shops – they must at one time have been shops – still sported pillared arcades, shading their frontages from the sun.

'The new school.'

I wondered whether to thank her.

'If you find any cases of gin hiding there, let me know,' she said. 'It used to be the tea-planters' club-house.'

Naphiri wasn't giving me the whole building, just the veranda – at least, the half of it that had survived RENAMO's occupation. I glanced over the collapsed part. It had not been hit by artillery, as I had thought at first. It had been chopped up by hand, and to such a fineness, only a psychopath would have had the patience.

'Well?'

I quickly adjusted. The location made sense. There was shade; we were separated a little way from the street; we could see who was coming. Elsewhere, the grass grew to the levels of the walls. 'Thank you,' I said.

What could be taken away, RENAMO had taken away: roofing sheets, copper wiring, furniture, vehicles. Even the street signs were gone. What could not be carried had been smashed. Vehicles waiting for repair had been set on fire. Water and drainage pipes had been dug out of the earth and broken open with a hammer. A decorative pavement ran under the frontage of an old barber's shop; every tiny tile had been methodically splintered.

More seriously, every generator and water pump serving the town had been hammered to scrap, set on fire, then laid into with axes: bright flecks showed where metal had met metal.

'All this will be cleared!' Naphiri declared, leading me through the town.

And after the clearance – what? Everyone was calling it an occupation, but the truth was RENAMO had razed the town. There were no pipes to lay in place of the ones that were smashed, no bails of electrical wire to restring the unstrung town. Even the shade trees that had once lined the *avenidas* of the elegant quarter had been cut down and burned.

'All this will be cleared!' Naphiri insisted, with something like desperation. 'With the earth-mover, we will sweep the street. Many streets are cleared now. It is a good vehicle.'

'It's still here?' It was my understanding that the Italians had left the area as soon as they'd finished repairing the airstrip.

Naphiri sucked on her lower lip. 'It broke down,' she said. 'It was most unfortunate.' She caught my eye and smiled. 'Our friends had to leave it behind.'

Every couple of weeks, and at great risk, a truck driver ran the gamut of National Highway Number One to bring fuel to Goliata.

We had little enough use for it. The town blacksmith was still working away at his replacement generator, gathering parts from spoil heaps and burnt-out vehicles; bartering for motorcycle spares across the Malawian border; whittling a flywheel out of wood. So most of the fuel ended up in the belly of the Italians' earth-mover.

It could never have broken down. Had it ground to a halt, who here would have had the resources to fix it? By the little hints she kept dropping – 'Most unfortunate. The damnedest thing. The day they were leaving' – Naphiri let me in on her chicanery. How she had got this valuable item all to herself. She was pleased with her cleverness. It was at this point – with Naphiri revealed as a thief and a cheat – that I began to like her.

I had been suspicious at first, and particularly of the feasts Naphiri held every few evenings by firelight, between reed fences, in Goliata's 'cane town'. Everyone was expected to bring something to the meal: a chicken; a flat basket piled with tomatoes or chard; a woman dressed in a rough red shawl arrived with skewers of what looked like satay, but turned out to be roast field mice. It wasn't the food that disturbed me; it was the money. Naphiri saw to it that everyone, no matter how poor, dropped a donation into her old aluminium paint-can.

My neighbour at the feast was a comparatively old man – I guessed mid-forties – whose lips had been cut off by the RENAMO rebels during the occupation. In halting Chichewa, I asked him what the collection was for. 'For FRELIMO,' he replied, as best he could, sucking the spittle back through his teeth. 'A donation to the party.'

What was Naphiri doing, shaking the tin under the noses of people who had nothing?

The man next to me passed me the pot, and I looked inside. It wasn't Mozambican currency. It was Malawian. 'Why *kwacha*?' I asked him, indicating the pot. 'Why foreign money?'

He shrugged. 'You can buy things in Malawi.' He tilted his head back to swallow, so the food would not fall out of his destroyed mouth. 'There are shops in Malawi.'

Naphiri sat with her arms folded, glowering at me. It occurred to me I had not made a donation. I had some hard currency in a bill-fold. I dropped a ten-dollar bill into the pot, slowly enough that people could see.

Ten dollars was an unimaginable amount of money. Nobody reacted. Nobody cared. Even my neighbour seemed not to notice.

I sensed that, with their circumstances this reduced, money had ceased to mean very much to the people here. The food they had brought to the feast had more value to them than currency they could not spend.

Naphiri jumped to her feet. 'Where is Samuel?' she cried.

Silence fell across the feast.

'Where is he?'

All around me, people were exchanging awkward glances.

'This is our banquet.' Naphiri stretched her arms wide, measuring her magnanimity. 'Why is my brother not eating with us?'

The villagers stared into their dinners. We were using leaves as plates; big and leathery and so practical for the purpose, I had barely registered the oddness of it until now.

'Has he somewhere better to be?'

My Chichewa wasn't nearly good enough to follow this performance.

Happily, my neighbour knew a few scraps of Portuguese and – probably as a way of sidestepping the row that was brewing – he muddled up a translation for me.

'Sam is gone.'

This much I had gathered.

'Sam is gone to the graveyard.'

'Why would anyone be going to a graveyard at this time of night?' I asked.

'Because he is eating with the *matsangas*,' my neighbour replied, and pulled the rough reddish jerkin around his matchstick chest, as against a chill.

We were overheard. Around us, the conversation turned to vampires. Only ghouls and the undead, it was agreed, would break bread in a graveyard.

It was my prissiness that had prevented me from understanding Naphiri. Once that wore off, I even began to admire her. Without Naphiri, there would be no Goliata. Naphiri was the only employer in town. Whatever money you dropped in her paint can one evening, you earned it back the next day, scrubbing RENAMO's slogans from the walls, thatching roofs, lifting rubble into the bucket of the earth-mover. When it wasn't being used to clear the cement town, the Italians' abandoned vehicle was dragging gimcrack ploughs through new fields to the west of the cane town. As far as I could see, Naphiri didn't charge for these services.

She was Goliata's inescapable first principal. She was more than our 'administrator'. She was our chief, our *régulo*.

So, imagine Samuel's feelings.

Imagine Sam, former *régulo* of Goliata under the Portuguese colonial administration. A headman deposed by his own sister.

I grilled my neighbour for information. 'So FRELIMO put Naphiri in charge, in her brother's place?'

He unskewered a field-mouse, necked it and wiped his ruined mouth. 'Why not?' he said, sucking spittle back through his teeth. 'Naphiri can read.'

True, Sam's education at the hands of the Portuguese must have been pitiful, in comparison with the education Naphiri had received from FRELIMO in Dar. Sam had no official status any more, and he didn't know much about *Marxismo-Leninismo*.

What he had, in abundance, was an instinct for small-town life. Ever since I'd got here, he and his cronies had been haunting Goliata like a bad smell. The town's old power-brokers had returned from obscurity: a couple of popular *curandeiros*, a former local agent for the Ford motor company, a local landowner who had made his fortune in the mines of Johannesburg. They were shaking hands, they were building bridges. With a casual cynicism, they stirred the rumour mill against Naphiri and the party: FRELIMO has banned private ownership! FRELIMO is demolishing monuments in the cemeteries!

Had I known nothing of this, the way Sam first approached me would still have got my back up: all glad-hands and pat-heads for the kids I was in the middle of teaching, and a patter of twisted subordinate clauses and long loan-words for me.

'Tell me, sir, what is your specialism?'

It was a slick performance, and the level of polish probably counted for a lot in this land without books, where oratory is everything. It had exactly the opposite effect on me. I replied in my dreadful Chichewa, keeping my distance, letting him know my dislike.

'Why don't you come eat with us tonight?' he asked me, coming straight down to business. No prizes for guessing who 'we' were. RENAMO contras still controlled much of the surrounding countryside. Yet he had delivered his invitation in elegant Portuguese as though offering me supper at the Ritz.

I thought about Goliata's spacious new cemetery, and declined Sam's invitation with a shudder. Sam shrugged. It was all one to him. He had felt the wheel turn beneath him. He knew it was only a matter of time before he wore cotton again.

Sam was not the lean, hungry creature I had been expecting. Though they shared a mother only, the family resemblance between Sam and Naphiri was striking. Sam's face was a more evolved version of Naphiri's; his frame lankier and less clumsy. His eyes, far from burning with a wicked flame, crinkled charmingly with every smile. Should he ever be handed back his old mantle as head-man of the town, I could imagine his response: the modest amusement with which he would rehearse all the twists and turns that had brought him back to power: 'Well I never!'

He lingered on the steps of the veranda, listening to me teach. I made a point of ignoring him, so every couple of minutes he grunted his approval, making sure I knew he was there, a sympathetic presence. How long did he intend to keep this up?

Just then, the earth-mover rounded a corner into the main street. It rattled towards us, wreathed in eddies of smoke. The children leapt up cheering and rushed to the balustrade.

Any minute now they would jump into the street and mob the vehicle and tease the driver – Redson, a man who'd driven machines bigger than this in the mines of South Africa. And Redson, obedient to the rules of their cheerful game, would brake sharply, start off again with a jolt, throw gears, brake, start forward and brake again, shaking kids from the scoop as fast as they could clamber on.

Sam Calange just laughed.

'Have you ever seen such a ridiculous contraption?' he said, appealing to me, tears of mirth in his eyes. He was using Chichewa now, so the children would understand. 'Listen to it! The old rust-bucket! I give it another week.'

The children, mortified, turned to me, awaiting their teacher's spirited defence of the village's earth-mover.

Sam pressed home his attack: 'Still, my sister, she is only a woman.

How can we expect her to know what engine oil is for?'

I stared at the vehicle, lumbering smokily up the road, and hunted furiously for an adequate retort. True enough, it was not the most impressive machine of its sort: a tractor with a detachable scoop bolted onto the front, and the scoop was already badly buckled – but I had been here long enough that it had begun to make an impression on me: a valuable mascot of the party.

'Listen to that engine! It's tearing its guts out! Look!' Sam pointed. 'If someone doesn't align that wheel soon...' Gripping an imaginary steering wheel, he mimed the earth-mover's drunken progress. The kids whooped and applauded as Sam wove across the veranda, his face twisted in comical terror: man on runaway machine. When it came to working an audience, there was no competing with Sam Calange. He leapt from the balcony and capered about in the street, running up to the earth-mover; shying away. Redson had to swerve to avoid him, which only made Sam caper the more.

How the children laughed. Even the ones without noses.

The worst thing was, I couldn't stop him. Sam had succeeded in wrenching me back to a place behind my eyes where I could see the earth-mover for what it was: a dinky little plaything with a life of approximately one more month – if we were lucky – before it seized up for good. That, in its turn, was what made Sam's performance so purely cruel. He wasn't saying, 'I will oil your tractor.' He wasn't saying, 'My friends in the bush can get you spares for that buckled axle.' He wasn't offering us anything. He was simply belittling what he didn't control.

'Redson!'

Redson looked up, harried and red-faced, from the wheel of the earth-mover. Sam's ridiculous ballet had brought his vehicle to a stand-still.

'Redson,' I shouted, at the top of my lungs, seized by a sudden inspiration, '*run him over!*'

The children gasped.

Redson frowned.

'Run him over!' I yelled, scenting an advantage. 'Come on!' I rallied my students. 'Man versus machine: *let's see who wins!*'

Redson was a serious man. Clowning was not his style. Scowling, he climbed down from the tractor and tried to remonstrate with Sam. Naturally, it only took a few seconds before Sam had managed to charm him. What could I do but stand there, powerless, while Redson, arm in arm with Sam, the Old Boss, laughed along with his jokes?

The kids, disappointed and uneasy, sat back down. I did my best to smother the seeds of their doubt. *Amo amas ama; c* is 'kuh' before *a, o, u;* 'sss' before *e* or *i. Eu nasci em mil e novecentos e cinquenta e cinco.* Pay attention in the corner.

And all the while I could feel Samuel's smile boring into the back of my neck.

No one was meant to win this war. It existed for one purpose only: to turn a sovereign nation into a no man's land of burnt schoolhouses and decapitated nurses, mine-littered roads and unharvested crops. In line with the Total Strategy coming out of RENAMO's paymasters in the Transvaal, nothing was to replace what had been destroyed. And just as South Africa had no real intention of letting RENAMO take over Mozambique, so RENAMO's bandits had no intention of handing Goliata over to Samuel Calange.

A couple of weeks before a regrouped RENAMO launched their second big offensive in the region, it dawned on Sam – much, much too late – just who he had been breaking bread with.

'Please come with me to the feast,' he said to me, not for the first time. This time, however, his invitation was not a piece of public show. He had knocked on my door in private, and after dark. 'Please.'

I had been issued a freshly thatched brick blockhouse, more or less intact after hurried repairs, right on the border between the cane town and the cement town. It was a prime location, so Naphiri had given me an AK-47 for protection. The rifle hung off one arm, my lantern swung from the other, as I swaggered back into the living room, leading Sam inside. If he could play-act, so could I.

I was surprised that Sam was moving around the village after sundown. Apart from the obvious risk of attack or a mugging, it was too easy to trip and break your neck on an overcast night like this. Though we were in the middle of the village, no light showed. Even the household fires you'd normally expect to burn on after supper-time were snuffed out early, in case the unwelcome dinner guests hiding out in the bush got ideas. Myself, I kept the windows shuttered tight. To be walking around at night, Sam had to be feeling very desperate.

'Please,' he said.

It was the usual deal. You turn up to the meal with a contribution of food, clothing, money: tribute, in other words.

'No,' I told him. I knew I had him over a barrel. The rebels were relying on him and his friends to bring influential villagers over to their side. The price of failure was likely to be high. I set the lantern down in the middle of the floor and sat myself down in the room's only cane chair – I had been over the Malawi border and bought it for myself – with my AK-47 across my knees.

There was a lot of bluster to begin with. Sam's appeal to nostalgia – to the imaginary 'good old days' before FRELIMO's uppity socialists took over – had served him in good stead in the past, and old habits die hard.

'I think it is important – and I feel sure that an educated man like yourself will agree with me – that we should have the ear of the rebels, if only to barter for our own safety.' All week, stories had been flying around town: how the bandits were increasing in numbers; how they had hammered their way into Yelena Mlokote's house, brazenly, without fear of resistance; that they had taken everything of value away with them: goats, clothes, batteries, even a mirror in a metal frame.

'Stop,' I said. He had become almost painful to watch. 'Whose house, did you say?'

'What?'

I couldn't conceal my irritation. 'The goats and the mirror. Whose house?'

Sam blinked. 'Yelena Mlokote's. What? Do you know her?'

'I thought you said someone else,' I said, waving the matter away. I strung him on a while longer – *Tomorrow night, did you say? What should I bring? What should I wear?* – before kicking him out of my house.

3

The next day I borrowed Naphiri's bicycle and cycled out past parched fields of cassava and pineapples and neglected, overgrown shacks to Yelena Mlokote's house.

By local standards, it was a mansion: a brick house surrounded by cashew trees and mangoes; a paved path lined with herbs. It was isolated, though; much further from town than I had expected. There were other houses nearby, sprawled under the shade of the jacaranda trees, but most had been boarded up. Her neighbours had left, she told me, afraid of what RENAMO might do to them if they stayed. They were sleeping rough now, under the few surviving porticoes of Goliata's cement town.

'And you?'

Yelena shrugged.

We were sitting in her kitchen. Walls of wood and iron sheeting; a cement sink for washing clothes – 'only that I still go to the bathing pool to wash my clothes, so that I meet people.' The weird, finicky rhythms of her Chichewa disguised, for a moment, the fact that she had not answered my question.

She didn't bear much resemblance to her father. Until we got talking, I couldn't be sure it was her. She was attractive, in an ironed-out sort of way. She was pushing forty by then, and the recent famine had taken its toll.

She was damned if she was going to be kicked out of her home.

'They took my radio,' she said. 'I had three goats, they took the goats.'

'For God's sake,' I said.

'They went away,' she shrugged.

'They'll be back.'

'Samuel Calange is talking to them. The *curandeiros* are with them now, treating their injured. They are hungry, out in the bush.'

'What are you saying?'

She was doing the only thing she could do. She was trying to come to terms.

'Look,' I said. 'There's room in my house for you. There's room with me.'

The clumsy fixes of white men: she shook her head and smiled.

It was wash-day, so we walked together to the stream that had once fed Goliata's municipal bathing pool.

While Yelena slapped the screwed whip of a *capulana* against a rock, to agitate it clean, and her baby boy Mateu, indifferent to us both, lay on his rush mat, waving his arms about as though conducting something difficult and modern, I sat dangling my legs over the edge of the old bathing pool, thinking through the chances that had led me to this place and moment. This opportunity.

The pool was dry. The pipe supplying it with stream-water had been smashed, and the pool's every decorative blue tile – fish, shellfish, seaweed, sailing boats, windmills – had been cracked. The bandits had demolished the changing blocks, too, which had once preserved the modesty of the planter and his children, the hairdresser and his family, the driving instructor and his wife: the petty white elite of a bygone Goliata. So that now, sitting here, we had a clear view down the hill, past the stubs of the changing blocks, right across Goliata, to the brown scar of the airstrip – and further yet, the air was so clean and clear today, over the Malawian border to the Mulanje plateau.

I watched Yelena wrap up her son in the *capulana*, which was quite dry now, from the fierce sun of that morning, and seeing her tie her son to her, I noticed the trembling of her hands. She gave Mateu a look of hopeless yearning.

'What is it?'

She shrugged. 'I am remembering a friend of mine,' she said.

I waited for more.

'Come with me,' she said. 'We will visit her grave. I like to visit her, to talk to her.'

She led me down the hill to the cemetery. By day there was nothing to fear. In one part of the cemetery there were stones raised for those whose manner of dying left no body to be buried. Yelena had raised such a stone for her husband:

JOSEPH ALEXANDER MLOKOTE
1951–1983

His dates saddened me. 'He was so young.' He must still have been a teenager when Yelena married him.

'He died driving a truck along the corridor,' she said.

Behind his stone lay a plot full of tiny graves, which I assumed at first must be the graves of stillbirths. Yelena corrected me: 'They're for limbs,' she said.

The graves contained legs. Bits of feet. Knuckles of bone and sinew. There were so many little graves, so many piecemeal burials, I wondered where the cripples were. I had not see them on the streets.

'They work their fields,' Yelena told me, leading me to a larger mound of earth: an adult burial. 'What else can they do?'

'What about the mines?'

'What about them?'

I wondered if any cripples visited their own graves.

Then Yelena led me to the grave of her friend. There was no headstone. 'Kesi,' she said, to the mound, 'this is Saul. He was a friend of my father.'

I looked at Yelena. She smiled at me. 'I do not know why he has come to visit us, but I can guess.'

I had expected to find her unprepared for our meeting; to have the advantage over her.

'Your friend,' I said, so as not to show the hit, 'who was she?'

'A nurse,' she said. 'A citizen. According to her husband, she was six months pregnant when the *matsangas* attacked.'

I steeled myself. I was becoming familiar with the nature of these stories.

'They tore it out of her womb and threw it into her hearth-fire. Saul.'

She took my hand.

From the swaddled shadows of her capulana, Yelena's son blinked at me.

'You know,' she said, 'I received your postcard. I know what brought you here. I know what it is you think I did.'

She walked me out of the cemetery and back up the hill to her house, and, as we climbed, she told me the tale of her brief, fatal involvement in world affairs.

'It was never supposed to go off,' she told me.

A devil's alliance of PIDE men and tribalists opposed to RENAMO were already planning Katalayo's assassination. When news of the attempt filtered through to FRELIMO, Yelena, Jorge's alienated daughter, saw an opportunity to play *agent provocateur* and make a name for herself within the movement. Playing up her alienation from her father, she sent the cabal the encyclopaedias I had sent her, and gave them the idea for the book bomb.

'You did this alone, of course.'

Yelena sighed. Apparently I was being boorish. 'FRELIMO is a big organization. There are factions. Groups.'

This faction of hers figured it would be an easy matter to follow the British seaman entrusted with the device; easy to lift it from him in Lourenço Marques; easy to arrange its disarmament at the hands of an old KGB operative, who for long months now had been twiddling his thumbs in some redundant field station in Lourenço Marques.

'So you were working for the Russians?'

Easy, once the bomb had been disarmed, to deliver it to her father: a present as harmless as it was terrifying.

I couldn't believe what I was hearing. 'Why on earth would you attempt anything so stupid?'

Why? Because, once Jorge Katalayo had *survived* his assassination, FRELIMO's leadership – this was the theory – would have been shaken into a more radical agenda and a more positive alignment with the Soviet Union.

Katalayo's daughter spoke with the melancholy of someone who, after years of interior struggle, has made peace with herself.

The bomb should have been intercepted, she told me. It should have been re-routed and defused, before ever being delivered. Only that, in her haste to get away while her mark was sleeping, the woman they'd hired to steal the bomb from the British sailor forgot where she'd written down the KGB man's address. After an hour's fruitless wandering, in a panic, she abandoned the parcel on a park bench –

– where, seeing the package, an elderly Portuguese man (this is what Yelena wanted me to believe) picked it up. He recognized the address, he lived out that way himself, and that evening he stopped by to deliver it. He must have been taken aback when the addressee turned out to be a black man. Perhaps he thought Jorge was a servant...

I could stand no more. I shut her up: 'You can't possibly know any of this.'

'Not the last part, no. We can't know how the bomb left the bench and ended up in my father's hands. The rest we know.'

'The woman who stole the parcel—'

'She was telling the truth.'

'You don't know that.'

Yelena threw up her hands. 'What is the point of this?'

'What was Jorge's address doing on the package in the first fucking place? It wasn't going in the mail.'

'What is the point?'

The point, as far as Yelena was concerned, was that the bomb was meant to fail. It was supposed to manipulate and to frighten. It was not meant to kill. She touched my hand. 'You know,' she said, 'if I could turn back time, I would.'

Well, let her have her dream of redemption. What does it matter?

From the sheetrock interior wall of a summer house, fifteen miles north of Maputo, a twisted pin untwists.

Damp plaster seals the hair-line crack, as the pin corkscrews its way out of the wall, and takes flight.

It shoots past the door to the kitchen, from which comes the faint but unmistakable smell of leaking bottle-gas – one of those signature smells, inseparable from evenings spent in holiday cottages – past bookshelves stacked with Franz Fanon, Georgette Heyer and yearbooks stretching back a dozen years: *Who's Who in World Trade*; UN Factbooks for this region and that; missionary society directories. The books sit up as the pin passes them, at a speed approaching that of sound, accelerating all the time. The books straighten themselves, lining up on the white-painted shelves. From the second shelf up, a second pin unwinds from out the spine of *The Wretched of the Earth*, and, coming free, flies off.

And another, and another. From out of the twill of the rag rug they come, hurling themselves into the air. From out of the walls and the ceiling. From out of the back of the room's centrepiece. Someone's head: unrecognizable.

Outside, the sand-lions are undigging their traps. Puffs of sand gather and cone in the air, then fling themselves into the hole where each spider frantically unburies itself before the retreating tide. On BOAC's night run from Dar to Nairobi, grain factors and irrigation specialists, bankers and fertilizer salesmen, carefully unblend the tonic from their gin.

The sun has unrisen beneath Zanzibar. To the gathering roar – a great re-threading – shavings of aluminium wire rise in a cloud above the sand. The lethal cloud unshreds everything in its wake, leaf and dragonfly and even bird. It hurls itself at the broken window – and sticks there, blasted and fused into a tight, mosquito-resistant grille, by a flash of pinkish light.

The bird unnotices the dragonfly.

In the room, at its precise mathematical centre, the unrecognizable head is repacking itself. The soft innards refold, suck up and re-smear their spilt lubrication; spit out stray shavings and turnings into the ever-faster, ever-hotter air. The head trembles. Vertebrae click and snap together. The meat within them turns from red to white. Sparks fly.

Julius at the door of his apartment in his slippers: 'What now, Jorge?'

A letter from the Phelps Stokes fund.

His brand-new American girlfriend naked.

His brand-new American girlfriend getting naked.

Samora. Marcelino. Alberto. Joaquim.

The head is not yet whole. It contains many minds.

A to K and L to Z.

The white man's magic!

General laughter.

'And you know, we have a paper shortage here.'

The head and body, of a piece once more, rise up: uncanny forward roll. The head snaps forward, a final, sickening crunch as linkage reconnects, vessels rezip themselves and the eyes, regaining their light, spit nails into the air, firing them with the force of bullets at the parcel there, on the desk before the window.

Within the parcel, a pinkish light.

The man – it is a man – crouches forward, and the chair tucks itself up under him. He reaches for the open box, and the pinkish light within; the smell of plastique.

The window mesh zips itself shut.

Jorge Katalayo sits at his desk, bathed in light.

The light unfingers his eyes, and his final thoughts form.

He knows what this is.

They offered him the north. Let's draw a line, they said. FRELIMO sits above the line, the Portuguese sit south – where all the money is.

So history repeats itself, he thought. Tragedy in Korea; farce in Vietnam; in Mozambique: pantomime.

He told them no. No north and south. No black and white. No rich half and poor half. All his life he has been sealing what should never have been split.

Dr Julius Nyerere in his slippers – they met at the UN – 'What now, Jorge?'

They talked till dawn. Geneva, Stockholm, Kensington Park. The money there for them, the friendly faces – the easy handshakes and their ruinous consequences. How many old friends lived their lives now behind tinted windows, gun-toting relations and foreign contracts?

We kept each other strong, Julius. Together, we kept our hands by our sides.

A Chinese delegate congratulated us on our self-reliant approach to revolution; on our belief in our own people's capacity for autonomous change.

We sent him away, too.

A life spent piecing together what should never have been split. What I could never get that oaf Kavandame to understand.

Kavandame, Mozambique's great resistance leader, now gone cap-in-hand – this according to yesterday's phone call – to Cabo Delgado's fascist governor: *Please sir, let me have my square of earth!*

As if clearing the whites out of his personal back yard will make a difference. Prick, thinks Jorge Katalayo, closing the book he has been sent, and the pink fire withdraws, unblackening his hands.

How funny, how apposite, that it should come in two volumes. That nice boy's present. Dictionaries do, of course. A to K and L to Z. We split things for convenience, then we mislay the half we need. Not a profound flaw. Not a complex human condition. We just bungle things.

Where's the cap to this pen?

Black and white. A split as deep as language. A split on which his early life was built.

'After my father died, my mother said to me: You must learn the white man's magic.'

He thinks: I wish to God I'd never come up with that line.

White man's magic! It's not even true. He'd been nervous – first time in America, big opportunity, the Phelps Stokes fund giving him a shot at the education the Portuguese authorities had tried their damnedest to deprive him of. Even to the point of a PIDE interrogation. *'You vill say uz vot you bin tot!'*

Makes me sound like an elf, he thinks, irritated, tying the string around the box. Wondering what's inside.

His brand-new American girlfriend is taking her clothes off.

His brand-new American girlfriend calls from the bedroom: 'Don't be long.'

Jorge at his desk: 'Just want to see what this is.'

His brand-new American girlfriend: 'Now?'

Jorge: 'Sure.'

His brand-new American girlfriend is on her way to the bedroom: 'You coming to bed?'

This is the house owned by a foreign woman, a friend of Julius Nyrere, where Jorge Katalayo comes in secret, under the very noses of the Portuguese, alone or with his girlfriend, to read, to write his speeches, to swim in the shallows and watch the herons and the bee-catchers. To think. Sometimes, when he can bear it, to remember his wife; which is, of course, to remember what his daughter, tiny and frightened and told what to do, did to his wife; and from there to remember what a ruin it all is, beyond hope of consolation, beyond the healing powers of any girlfriend, beyond the combined healing power of all the girlfriends in America, or even the touch of his grown daughter's hand, as they each grope blindly for a forgiveness neither can provide.

A box of books arrives.

*

Yelena's son was fast asleep by the time we reached the house. Carefully, she tucked him into his wicker crib, then went into the kitchen to make a pot of tea. She set the tray down before me. As she poured, she said, 'I'm glad you answered the call. I mean I'm glad that you're here. That you're helping us. That you came to be a *cooperante.*'

I said, 'The main reason I came was to find you. You hid yourself well.'

She sat opposite me. 'And now you've found me?'

'I don't suppose I was the only person upset by what happened.' If she could be suave, so could I.

'No. I don't suppose you are.' She was not afraid. 'Do you know I have been officially pardoned?'

'Does that make you feel more secure?'

She shook her head. 'No.'

Well, let her have her tragic mistake. What did it matter what she had meant to do? True, FRELIMO had slid more under Soviet influence, but who was to say whether the paranoiacs running South Africa would have treated their upstart neighbour any differently? It wasn't as if the Soviets ever achieved much in the region. They didn't even take Mozambique into their development zone, and the materials they exported in the name of aid were shoddier than even our own meagre home production. So really, in all honesty, what did any of it matter?

'I'm glad,' she said, 'that I've had the chance to tell you what really happened.' She imagined she had given me a gift. These days she'd probably say that she was 'offering me closure'. I was spared that, at least.

I said, 'You know I don't believe you.'

She shrugged.

'Do you want to know why?'

I told her what Jorge Katalayo had told me about her mother.

'He's off gallivanting across Europe, leaving you and Memory to rot in some *aldeamento*. He never mentions you. He has girlfriends. He

318

makes one inflammatory speech too many, and suddenly – half a world away – there's a gun being pressed into your hands. Your mother's lying there on the floor, crippled and bleeding and screaming.'

'You don't know this.'

'I think you blamed him for that, just as much as he blamed you.'

'You're not one of the family. You don't have the right—'

'He made a speech once. About how the men and women of this country hate each other. You see, he understood. This is my gift to you. This is what I came here to tell you. He knew what was coming and he knew, when it came, it would be from you.'

'Samuel Calange says you're plotting to kill him.' I had thought our exchange was done, but I was wrong. As I was about to pedal away, Yelena had this gift for me.

'What?'

Yelena shrugged. 'He says you paid Redson to stage an accident with the earth-mover.'

I didn't know what to say.

'I wouldn't worry about it if I were you. There's nothing you can do.' She closed her door.

Now it was my turn to be creeping around town at sundown, looking for reassurance.

Naphiri's response? 'Never mind. Anyway, there's nothing you can do.'

President Chissano nodded glum agreement from half-a-dozen identical wall posters. Bleeding through the cheap, absorbent paper, like a bad dream resurfacing: 'RENAMO MOTO'.

The party administrator's office boasted seats now, of a sort – old pinto bean sacks stuffed with grass. Together, we demolished a half-bottle of Powers – Malawian cane spirit – paid for with the villagers' hard-earned *kwacha*. Another twist of the Goliata economic cycle.

'How much trouble am I in?' I had a creeping horror of the rural rumour mill. I had heard too many stories, from *cooperantes* and others, of people being driven into the bush on the strength of some stupid calumny.

'Trouble? None at all,' said Naphiri, and grinned. 'If your plan succeeds.'

She screwed the cap back on the bottle. 'First watch,' she reminded me. I fetched my gun and traipsed up the stairs onto the roof. The Italian's earth-mover was kept under constant twenty-four-hour armed guard.

Three hours on my own in the dark was more than enough time to convince me that I might be in serious trouble. Naphiri was complacent, full of crazy, romantic dreams about raising Goliata from the rubble: *All these streets will be cleared!* Sam on the other hand was a clever and experienced provincial politician.

It was a mistake solely to associate Naphiri with the party, Sam with the *matsangas*. If Sam was afraid, then there was something for us all to be afraid of.

Yelena and Naphiri had both told me there was nothing to be done. Of course there was something I could do and, once I had been relieved from my post, I did it.

4

Together, Samuel Calange and I made our silent way, under cover of night, towards our assignation. The crocodile of men following us must have made a strange, naive spectacle: fathers seeking news of missing sons; sons who, seeing the way things were going in this war, were thinking of performing a vanishing act of their own. All of us huddled close against the ghouls and vampires who, they say, haunt the graveyards here, so that a meal eaten in such a place is a kind of Hallowe'en.

Sam and I prepared the *braii*. When I had gone to see him and agreed to this meeting, something had passed between us: mutual cowardice, nothing more, but it was a bridge between us now, and it made talking easier. Sam told me how, when he lost Goliata to Naphiri and the FRELIMO government, he had expected to find a role organizing the political opposition – and while Rhodesia had control of RENAMO, that was still what RENAMO at least claimed to be. Now, though, under Johannesburg's 'Total Strategy', nothing was making very much sense. RENAMO wasn't even an army any more. More of a wrecking crew, commanded by *soldados simples*, grunts, amphetamine psychotics, hopping-mad buggers with silver marbles for eyes and muscular sprinters' thighs. 'So where is all this bouncing powder coming from? I am asking. Are they dishing it out like Navy rum now? Or dropping sackfuls from the air? Have they taken to dusting the jungle?'

I wasn't in much of a mood to discuss politics. The disfigured faces of the children I'd been teaching had taught me all I needed to know about this war. The villagers who had accompanied us had gathered nervously together a few yards off, where the hill fell away a little, giving them a view of Goliata's cane town. Sam called them to eat. They came and sat, his obedient flock. It was a strange reprise of Naphiri's feast and, for a moment or two, the similarities helped me tune out our surroundings: the gravestones, and beyond them, the little unmarked graves.

When they bothered to turn up, the forces of the *Resistência Nacional Moçambicana* proved a disappointing lot. The three adults wore burlap sacks over their heads to protect their identities. The effect was more pathetic than frightening. Half a dozen boys accompanied them; not one looked more than twelve. Presumably they had been press-ganged from other towns. They glared at us with a ferocity and a cynicism so extreme it looked rehearsed.

'Where are your students?' one of the hooded figures shouted. It took me a moment to realize he was talking to me. 'Why didn't you bring your students?'

Before I could answer, the hooded figure to his left piped up: 'His boots! He is wearing boots! He is in the militia!'

'They're my own boots,' I said.

'Where are your students? Why are your students not here?'

I was – absurdly enough – reminded of my mother. *('Have you done your university work? Have you much university work to do?')*

'Is this all?' The third ghoul was pawing over the food we had brought: flat baskets piled with roast chicken, *nsima* and relish, mangoes, tomatoes: 'What is this shit?' He squatted before the feast we had laid, his fingers playing over the dishes as though plucking some big, complicated musical instrument. 'Where is the meat? We told you to bring us *meat.*' His fingers were bony and pale: a skeleton's fingers.

'Where are the minds you have poisoned, teacher?'

I tried to shrug. The muscles wouldn't respond. I was shaking very badly.

One of the bandit children turned to the hooded figures, weeping with frustration.

'Can I kill him?'

'We don't want blood tonight,' said the tallest of the hooded men.

'Please. Just one of them.' There were tears running down his cheeks. 'Just him.' He pointed at me.

One by one, the villagers were running off. They knew what this was. They could see what it was turning into. I watched them kicking up these crazy zig-zags between the monuments, the wooden crosses; they were afraid of being shot in the back. Soon only Sam and I were left. I don't know about Sam, maybe he stayed because he felt responsible. I know why I remained: I didn't have the courage to run.

The boy begged and begged. 'Please let me kill him.'

'No.'

'Please.'

'You can take his boots.'

He stalked up to me.

'Give me your boots,' he said.

I smiled at him, the way you smile at a big, angry dog.

From off his back he pulled an AK half as tall as he was. 'Take off your boots,' he said, his finger tight on the trigger. He drove the muzzle into my windpipe. I grabbed it.

'Let go of the gun,' he screamed.

I raised my hands.

The boy pushed the cold muzzle into my throat a second time, much, much harder. 'If he doesn't give me his boots, can I shoot his head?'

'Of course.'

'What is this shit?' screamed the figure playing with our food. He got up into the middle of the feast and trampled it. He worked his way around every plate until he came to Sam. He did a little dance before Goliata's prospective mayor, kicking gobs of *nsima* porridge into his face. 'Is this all you brought? We will kill them all, you piece of shit! We will crush their skulls!'

A couple of the kids started shooting into the air.

Sam opened his mouth to speak, to excuse himself, to apologize.

With a striker's precision, the hooded man kicked him in the mouth. Sam's head snapped back like a boxer's punch-ball. Bones snapped.

I got my boots off at last. The child kicked them away from me and lifted the AK off my neck.

Sam scrambled to his feet. He staggered about the cemetery, groaning, his hands under his jaw, holding it together.

The child adjusted his grip on the gun and brought it down on my head. He was about ten years old but the gun was heavy. My whole skull flexed. I must have passed out for a couple of seconds. Something wet landed in my ear. It felt as though the blow had torn my scalp away, above my right eye.

There was blood in my eyes, over my face and in my mouth. I had bitten through my tongue. I wiped the blood out of my eyes and caught a glimpse of the boy before the red flow blinded me again. He had rejoined his friends. He had his gun in one hand, my boots in the other. I wiped his spit from out of my ear.

Far behind us, down the hill, in the town, came a scream, then some shouting, and another scream, then some children screaming. The sound didn't stop. It swelled.

The feast in the cemetery had only ever been a ploy, to separate us. By reducing the number of menfolk in the town, they had made Goliata easier to attack.

I took off my shirt, wadded it up and pressed it tenderly to my head. Unable to see, I was forced to listen. There was very little gunfire in the cane town. Whatever the *matsangas* were doing, they were doing it with knives and clubs. The villagers' screams were running into each other now: one long, continuous death-squeal. With a loud concussion that forced my eyes open, an orange fireball rose above the town. I blinked the stickiness away and stood up. Beside the fire, muzzle-flashes illuminated the roof of Naphiri's concrete blockhouse. The earth-mover was on fire. I watched the rooftop guns sputter, and thought of the miserable, dull nights I had spent on that roof, armed with a gun I hated and did not know how to use. One by one, the guns went out. Soon, smoke was pouring from the windows of the blockhouse.

Sam, wailing, blood pouring between his fingers, staggered towards the brow of the hill, fell against a gravestone and crumpled.

The hooded men wandered casually over to him. One grabbed him by the hair and pulled his head over the edge of the stone. Another sat on his legs, pinning him there. The third took out a machete and chopped his neck open. Then, muttering, blaming his tools, he tried to use his machete like a saw. The boys gathered round to watch.

No one was paying any attention to me. I edged away. The men at the gravestone separated and Sam fell to the ground. His head was still attached to his shoulders, but only barely. In the light of the *braii* we had lit together, preparing for the feast, Sam blinked at me. His tongue flapped uselessly. 'Gah,' he said.

They brought him over to me. I turned to run, trod with my bare feet on a sharp stone, fell over and grazed my knees. They dropped Sam in front of me. The boy who had taken my boots fired a clip into Sam's neck to loosen the linkage there. The sound tore through my wounded head.

Once they got it off, they played football with it a while, then passed it to me. 'Carry it,' they said.

By then it didn't look very much like Sam, or a head, or anything.

I picked it up.

'Watch this.'

Two of us ran away in the night, another was shot trying to escape.

'Look at this.'

Three collapsed under the loads they'd been given to carry and were shot through the head where they lay. The *matsangas* used the seventh, Naphiri, for demonstration purposes, working at her strenuously until long after she was dead.

'Pay attention.'

We learned very quickly to obey the *matsangas.*

'Watch. Look at this.'

Whatever else it was, it was undoubtedly an education. Following their attack on the town on 15 October 1984, RENAMO soldiers had walked sixteen prisoners of war out of Goliata. Six weeks later, the nine of us who survived reached our journey's end.

The camp was not isolated. There were other RENAMO camps nearby, and even villages. Soldiers in misbegotten headgear rode downhill into camp on motorbikes, churned the site to a muddy slough and sped off again. Peasants walked uphill into camp, bearing food. Incredibly, once they had delivered their supplies, they were permitted to walk out again. The women weren't always so lucky, but among the girls forcibly 'made women' by the bandits, some seemed to have won back their freedom. They walked out of camp in the morning, and back in again at sundown. I wondered after a while whether I too might not be free to go. They were not even teaching me how to kill any more. Most of my days I spent with about a dozen others in a chicken coop, my hands behind my head. At sundown, we were allowed to take our hands off our heads. An hour after that, we were allowed to lie down. At first light, they made us kneel again and after a breakfast of *nsima*, with occasionally a relish of turnips or rotten fish, they told us to put our hands on our heads again. It was as if, after the initial excitements, our captors had run out of imagination. After a couple of months, they weren't even making us kneel.

I leaned my forehead against the wire of the chicken coop, looking out. No one seemed to be paying the least attention to us. Maybe we were not prisoners at all. It might be all in our heads, now. It was the logic of the place.

It was not too difficult a puzzle, working out where we were. Only Gorongosa boasted so many RENAMO militia. Mount Gorongosa was RENAMO's headquarters in Mozambique, a mountain fastness the overstretched FRELIMO military could not possibly overrun, and dead in the centre of the country, within easy striking range of the Beira Corridor. Only the Corridor could throw up the sort of spoils carried through our camp, uphill, to RENAMO's officer elite. Truck-loads of flour, crates of batteries, barrels of oil. Soldiers rattled back and forth in jeeps, in Toyota trucks, on motorbikes, on bicycles, even. They wore uniforms stolen from dead government troops. The uniforms often had tears in them, and terrible bloodstains. The soldiers grinned and strutted in the dead men's clothes, showing off their 'wounds'.

The RENAMO command proper rarely came down from the mountain, and preferred to communicate by radio. They surrounded themselves with camps of bandits. The bandits, in turn, buffered themselves with kidnapped villagers. The displaced villagers must in their turn have come to some unspecified agreement with the locals living in the shadow of the mountain, because everybody on the mountain got fed sooner or later.

Every few weeks or so a new batch of soldiers would come dancing into the camp and slash at their chests with knives – *zsa! zsa! zsa!* – and a man on stilts and a stylized leopard mask rendered them immune to bullets by splashing their wounds with a secret herbal preparation. Men without hands would enter camp to beg from the men who had mutilated them. The old man who fed the chickens had a scar the width of my thumb running right across his throat. A scalped girl shambled from one side of the compound to the other with her broom, intent, it seemed, on sweeping away the very foundations of the houses.

Then, just as I was getting comfortable, they moved me down the hill and I was placed in one of the villages nestling in the shadow of the mountain. Rather than raze it, RENAMO had decided to control it. I limped after the village's *régulo*, up to a drab cement blockhouse in a dusty, unshaded lot behind the marketplace.

I asked, 'What is this?'

He blinked up at me as though I were stupid. 'It's a school,' he said. He showed me inside.

On the desk at the front of the immaculate room sat an unopened box. 'What's that?' I said.

The *régulo* shrugged. No one told him anything. I opened the box. It was full of brand-new textbooks, printed in Maputo, ferried north at great expense, bound at one time for a place like Goliata. The books were another of RENAMO's spoils, plundered from some hijack on the Corridor.

I studied them. I turned to the *régulo*, incredulous: 'You want me to teach from these?'

The *régulo* shrugged. 'They're books, aren't they?'

Certainly they were books. History books, printed in Sweden, edited by an academic friendly to FRELIMO's socialist cause. There were whole chapters on Marx, Lenin, the evils of apartheid and the glory of the anti-colonial struggle. There was a foreword by FRELIMO's first president and chief political martyr, Jorge Katalayo.

I held my tongue.

Every day for the next seven years, RENAMO sent their children marching into school to have me teach them about Marx, Lenin, the evils of apartheid and the anti-colonial struggle. In all that time, no one ever questioned me or stopped me. Not the *régulo*. Not his minders. Not the dignitaries (RENAMO's honoured guests) who came by, once in a while, to witness the renaissance of learning in this liberated, liberalized, free-market corner of capitalist Mozambique.

They had never met a teacher before. They figured I knew what I was doing.

GLASS

1

The walls of the old iron bathtub rise around her, white and smutted. It is early Tuesday morning, 30 August 1983, and Stacey is getting ready for the funeral of her last grandfather, her mother's father, Harry Conroy.

She lies in the bath, staring down at herself, lost in contemplation of the way the water has split her in two. There is the upper part of her: her knees, her chest and her head, of course, mustn't forget her unseen head; this is the tanned, air-breathing part. Then there is the other part, the bigger part by mass, her back, her bum, her feet and halfway up her calves: the pallid, aquatic part.

She lies there, a little shaky. She is fourteen years old and they are burying her grandfather, the man who stepped in when Mo was incarcerated, who for eight years has been a solid presence in her life. But she is fascinated, none the less, by the way she can will this change in her nature, transforming parts of herself by lowering and raising them in the water.

She dips her hand in, slowly, watching her fingers tilt as they enter this other world. It looks as though her fingers are broken. She knows this is refraction because they have been doing this in class. Light entering water changes course. Light always takes the quickest path, and water, being dense, is slow compared to air. So light changes direction, bends, seeking the quickest way through the water. Light is clever.

Her body is too gross a thing, too meaty and massive, to finesse the water this way. It lumbers through air and water the same, insensate, especially now that the bath has cooled to blood heat. Her fingers can barely detect the difference between the air and the water – only this little tingle as her skin passes from one medium into the other. This trembling line like a blade held sensually, edge on, to the skin.

Her mother calls: 'Are you out of the bath yet, Stace?'

'Hang on!' Stacey shakes out of her reverie and reaches for the soap. Her mum says she spends too much time in the bath. It is one of those things that mothers say, but today is not a day to argue.

Stacey remembers how when she was little, for a special treat, Mo would let the bathwater run until it reached all the way up to her neck. She remembers looking down and thinking: this blue-green thing. It seemed amazing that this swimmy alien body was actually attached to her head.

Her name is Stacey Conroy. This is the name on her birth certificate, her mother's maiden name, the name she goes by at school. She does not like the name, and in her TV work she does not have to use it.

Stacey appears in advertisements, and has been doing so, off and on, since she was about six years old. Money has not been a motivation; Harry's wrestling promotion has expanded through syndication to the point where the two suits he employed to run it full-time don't even bother taking a salary any more. Stacey's own stock options – Christmas and birthday gifts from her granddad, held in trust until her twenty-first – will see her through college and long beyond.

Deborah, her mum, has not been pushy, either. If anything she has tried too hard to manage her daughter's expectations, discouraging her keenness for the camera. The push has come from Stacey herself. She loves dressing up. She has grown up among costumes, among capes and masks, the whirr of sewing machines, the sour flop-sweat smell of trailers and toilets and dressing rooms. She knows, and can identify by smell, every one of a hundred different make-ups, alcohol rubs, unguents and deep-heat preparations; let loose among the caravans on fight night, she has been found, come evening's end, wrapped in bandages like a mummy, in sequinned gloves and a padded sparring helmet several tens of sizes too big for her four-year-old head, weeping with frustration because she has got herself inextricably tangled in some visiting fighter's Stars and Stripes cape.

'The theatre is in my blood.' She says this in front of her bedroom mirror, wondering at this body that has always daunted her, like a boisterous pet she has no idea how to care for, this body, growing in maturity, which seems capable of no end of practical jokes, hair, farts, spots on the end of her nose.

Deborah comes into her bedroom without knocking. This is bad enough, let alone to be caught like this in front of the mirror, not even fully dressed.

'Are you OK, sweetheart?' Deborah wants her daughter to give her a very big hug. This could be made easier on two counts: mum could just relax a bit and stop pretending that She is Comforting her Daughter ('How are you feeling, sweetheart?' 'Are you holding up, pet?' 'Come here, petal, come on, poor lost lamb': all this in the last half-hour); second, she could take the goddamn chopsticks out of her *hair, agh,* that nearly went in my *eye...*

Deborah's kimono is black, or started out that way, though the black is hard to see beneath sequinned dragons and lotus flowers and thewed, half-naked samurai. Her face is panstick white, her eyeliner is red – art following grieving nature. Her fingernails, three-inch stick-ons, will have to wait till they get to St Patrick's because she still has to drive. They live out of Miami now, in Belle Glade, on the southern shores of Lake Okeechobee, well out of the operating range of the funeral home's cars. Deborah claims to be looking forward to the drive, that it will steady her nerves.

No one passing them is going to imagine they are on their way to a funeral. Deborah is dressed as a geisha; Stacey's own get-up is relatively conventional, but her wig is green, and Ben Donoso's charm is hanging on a silver chain around her neck. Pray it holds together for the day.

'Come along then, my poor brave chicken,' says Deborah, releasing her at last. Deborah is running out of endearing animals. In the driveway, waiting for her, a stab at her own father's brand of heartiness: 'Hurry up there, monkeybrains.'

Stacey's surname is Conroy. The name lacks conviction. It lacks truthfulness. It does not capture who she is. It carries no echo of the man she considers her real father, the man her mother married and visited in jail every month until he was released; who filled her first conscious memories, ages two to five, with light, and now is vanished, breaking his parole: the felon Mo Chavez.

In the car, Deborah winds down the window and lights up a joint. She wouldn't normally drive while smoking but it is getting late, the service is at two and she needs time to put her nails on. Also there is the question of dosage and timing: she is fifteen minutes late. Since 1969, when she and Mo stumbled upon its happy side-effects, Deborah has been using cannabis to self-medicate her epilepsy. Fourteen years of trial and error have taught her to respect her body and its rhythms: in excess, or taken at the wrong time of day, her smokes can trigger the very seizures they normally suppress.

Deborah maintains that Mo's marijuana runs were for her, more or less. The weekends he spent on his boat, the nights drinking with Nick Jessup, his so-called business partner; all this in the interests of Deborah's health and well-being, with no eye to the profit or the danger to himself. Stacey knows this is crap: a comfort story for a child who's missing her daddy, OK, maybe, but not a line you can expect to keep on spinning, year after year, into the child's teens. Her mother smokes regularly, it is true, but how much pot can one reasonably together woman be expected to inhale in one lifetime? Deborah forgets that Stacey was there with her in court, listening to the coastguard's testimony. When they lifted the weed out of Mo's hold, the boat rose a good two feet by the waterline.

The journey to the church has the clean lines of a proposition in mathematics: when you leave the town behind you're in farmland. The farms stop and the wetlands begin: an abrupt, engineered transition. A canalized river separates the wetlands from the suburbs. You have taken one road to get this far. The road is straight, the landscape is flat. This whole journey could be re-run in *Turbo* with virtually no loss of definition. *(Turbo* is the new Sega game in their laundromat, and Deborah thinks it weird that Stacey plays it so much.) From here the buildings rise in steps, and at a certain point – a point you have to learn is there, because there is no outward marker, no change of flavour or scene – you are in Miami.

Outside the church stands Michio Barondes, half-Japanese, half-Peruvian, the Yellow Peril, in joke-shop whiskers and a canary-yellow polyester cape, weeping into his embroidered sleeves.

The church is packed. There's Jackie Gleason, sat discreetly near the back. He must be seventy by now; his TV career has pretty much bombed but he still crops up in *Smokey and the Bandit* movies. The Mexican old-guard have turned up in their stage gear, and one or two of the home-grown boys have followed suit; Chuck Ryan, resplendent in his heel's garb, a Northwest Mounted Police parade uniform with white dress gloves, stands just inside the door to conduct the family to the front pews. Donoso the Vampyre delivers the oration, his white-face and blood-dribble ruined by tears, his thick black hair plastered down like lacquer. He leans on his best stick, the knob fashioned like a skull, red glass jewels for eyes.

Ben Donoso is a trainer now; one of the best. His fighting days are behind him. In 1980 a visiting fighter hurled him through a table. This was in the ring, a stunt both fighters had paced out a hundred, a thousand times. The table was mocked up the way it was supposed to be, each joint carefully weakened, the whole thing hefted and swung, tested for weight and balance. No one, least of all Ben, cared much about the prop's appearence. It was bright yellow, it looked good under the lights; no one, in the heat of preparation, thought to wonder what happens to linoleum veneer when it shears.

Donoso hobbles off the podium in tears. Harry was his friend, the man who used his own shirt to staunch the blood when Ben's femoral artery was severed, who rode with him in the ambulance as he faded out of consciousness, who was there with his wife and kids when he woke up. Harry funded the wrestling school he runs now, and from which he turns loose, each year, arguably the best fighters in the country; not just showman wrestlers but shootfighters, too, athletes and innovators.

Stacey hasn't seen Ben Donoso in a while. She has fond memories of him from when she was a little kid. Why else, on this day of all days, would she be wearing this weird mumbo-jumbo charm he gave her, back in Mexico? Since his accident he has not been around so much. He has the school to run. Also, things were not so easy with Grandpa. After the accident, Harry was not such an easy person to be around.

It occurs to Stacey, sat in front with a view of the coffin, that some of what she feels is relief. For a start, there is only one coffin; whereas there had definitely been more than one Grandpa, especially towards the end. There was the absent man, the man depressed by all the misfortunes he had failed to prevent: Deborah's childhood accident, Deborah's marriage, Ben's public and very bloody maiming. Then there was the smiling Harry, who was somehow worse: the man determined to shoulder every burden, prevent every misfortune, reliably accompany everyone he loved through every step of life, padding the world's every blow. The needy man. The drunk.

It's been nine years, following Mo's trial and sentence for marijuana smuggling – and, Stacey wonders, where was the snake Jessup while all this was going on? How slippy did he turn out to be, that all the shit was laid at her daddy's door? – nine years, then, since Harry stepped in to save the day, playing both father and grandfather to little Stacey. His daughter and his granddaughter were his burden, and he shouldered them gladly, dismissing every protest. He never let them down.

Ben settles into the pew a few places to the left of her, and she wonders if, sat before Harry's coffin, he feels the same secret relief she does. Ben was Harry's friend, but it must have been exhausting being friends to so many different versions of the same person. Absent Harry had no friends, had betrayed his friends, was a danger to his friends. He did not deserve them and did not know what to do with them. And needy Harry? The hospital bills, the school, could only be the tip of the iceberg: needy Harry would not have stopped there. Desperately wanting to be wanted, he was a smothering presence, his cheerful manner an unhappy, rum-fuelled fiction. No wonder Ben has been keeping his distance. Between one version of himself and another, Harry's been tearing everyone in two.

At home, at school, her name is Stacey Conroy. The name does not do justice to her Miami tan, and at the television studio, in her acting classes and on the billing for this amateur show, that student revue, Stacey uses the name she intends to adopt permanently when she is old enough, especially now that Harry is no longer around to be hurt by the change. A name to reflect her tan, her memories, hers and her mother's heart.

Stacey Chavez.

The priest's homily is rushed and nervous. Surrounded by wrestlers in wild costumes, perhaps he expects the service to climax in an eruption of spectacular comic-book violence. Stacey loves to watch the fights, not least because Deborah tries to steer her away from them.

Instead, once the service is done, everyone files meekly out of church, the men's costumes tawdry, the bodies beneath them lumpen and stiff and the worse for wear, the women thickened by childbearing, the children, in their best clothes, bored and whining, and one thought hanging over all their heads: is it over?

Have we been dreaming?

This good life: is it all over now?

The funeral tea and the wake are being held at Donoso's wrestling school, one of those white, ship-like Deco properties in Little Havana that the realtors get so excited about these days. Tables are set out front among the trees and flowerbeds. It looks like a rest home more than a place of sweat and strain – and before Harry took over the lease, this is exactly what it was.

The inside looks like some sort of political prison. A *Time* magazine photo special from darkest Latin America. Punchbags dangle from the ceiling, their khaki wrappers sweat-stained: complex, liquid patterns that lend the bags a personality. There are mats and weights. Stacey tries hefting a dumb-bell from its stand. The showers smell.

She has come to think about her grandpa, to lose some of the flipness that has been her armour and support during the service and the funeral; to cry, maybe; and to stay well away from the food Deborah has had catered in, weird English nonfoods made of filo pastry and frozen prawns and spit. Later comes the beer, the key lime pie, the hog-roast – probably in that order. Michio's sweating his guts out round the back of the property now because the kid he left in charge of his fire has let it reduce to smoulder and fizz.

She looks at herself in the wall of mirrored tiles, her hair a green cloud, her body broken, factored into neat squares. Like maps of hill country, flattened, idealized. All those damn bags of potato chips her mother kept forcing into her hands, every recess and pee break: 'Got to keep your strength up, little one.'

Throwing up comes naturally to her. She found that out in the courthouse. It was easy to do. Most of her friends at school use two fingers, three, hell, the entire hand, but she can do it with the tip of one finger: as quick and reliable as pressing an elevator button.

Her whole body trembles when she does it. Not to mention before and after. The tremble seems out of scale with the pleasure, as if her body is getting more out of it than she does. It's the same when she touches herself, and it's the same tremble she gets when she does it, if she has the patience, if she doesn't fall asleep or just get so damn bored and sore and what-really-is-the-point? She doesn't like to touch herself so much, because when it's really good it only reminds her of all the other tricks her body is playing on her.

She really ought to try and eat something, but by the time there's any real food around here, Deborah will have whisked them both through their quick-change routine and off to one damn starchy place or another for pine nuts, edible flowers and *ceviche*. Next week it'll be nuts and dried fruits from a post-Woodstock hole in the wall and the following week, God knows, some ethnic horror. One of the great things about your own sick, Stacey tells her friends, in her best, most urbane style, is the constancy of the flavour.

She walks out through the entrance hall, pausing to study the framed photographs: Harry, Harry's crew, Harry's empire: maybe this is why she cannot cry. It is virtually impossible to imagine that he is dead. There is so much evidence of him.

'Come along, little rabbit, eat a little something.'

Right by the door, there is Deborah, waiting to spring her trap. Stacey plucks a vol-au-vent from off the tray, palms the crumbly, slimy thing and secretes it, when her mother isn't looking, in the fork of a nearby tree.

Yesterday, tickling up her sick, she overdid it and hawked up blood. She didn't even know that this was possible. She wants to eat, but even if there were some real food here, she's too freaked out to put it in her mouth. After all – *blood*.

Who wants to throw up *blood*?

A man is watching the property from across the street. He is leaning against a beat-up cream Thunderbird. She spots him through the chainlink.

'Stacey!' Deborah is calling her. 'Jackie's leaving. Come say goodbye to Jackie.'

Stacey goes off to say goodbye to Jackie, and there is a little flurry as some other acquaintances take their leave. Rod Rodriguez – 'The Rod', another of Harry's early discoveries, rescued from a roadhouse outside Teponahuasco where Harry found him trading bouts for beers – is handing round the bourbon now, driving the event forward: Stacey can only imagine how things will be tonight: the wake's raucous, teary-drunk conclusion. She wants to be a part of it. She deserves to be a part of it. She's *fourteen*, for heaven's sake, she needs release.

Deborah has other ideas.

Everyone who's leaving wants to say goodbye to Stacey and, by the time she returns to her tree, both man and car have gone.

2

Where Harry Conroy led, many have followed. Right now on TV a man in a black cape and mask is driving Hulk Hogan's head repeatedly into a table.

Transfixed before the screen, fingers up to the knuckle in her careful hairdo, Deborah absent-mindedly strokes the bald dent in her skull.

Following Harry's death, Deborah has returned to England with her daughter. She wants Stacey to know the old country. She also had it in the back of her mind that the schools are better here, but as things have panned out, Stacey's first love has won out over her studies; a full-time TV actress at sixteen, she does the very minimum the schoolwork regulations will allow.

Mother and daughter live together in Vauxhall, on a forgotten street, in an old Edwardian terrace house with high moulded ceilings. They have money. Deborah's stock options have seen to that, as well as the numerous financial provisions Harry made for his granddaughter. They have no attachments.

It has been a strange few years for Deborah. Out from under her father's heavy care, thirty-two years old, she had thought she might begin again, acquire a lover, travel; she even entertained a certain nostalgia for her last bid for freedom – the disastrous summer of 1968 when, smothered by her father's difficult affection, she ran away to London, just a kid, and fell in with a succession of unsuitable lovers: men who were never kind.

Four years on, 1986, she realizes that this kind of freedom is no longer possible. She is not a teenager any more. The life she has hankered for does not pertain to who she is now. Besides, the times are different. She is happy on her own, happy not to be travelling, happy to sit and steer, as best she can, her daughter's career.

Now the Hulk has hold of the man in the black cape. He is twirling him around and around, over his head, as though he were spinning dough for a pizza. Even the very worst the world has to offer can be controlled now, with only a small loss of realism. Deborah glances at her watch and lights her joint. Although this ersatz world can never be hers, Deborah is glad Stacey lives surrounded by scenarios and mere appearances.

The Hulk is slamming the man down, head-first into the floor. The man's head connects with the sprung floor of the ring. He sprawls. He does not get up.

For her daughter's sake, Deborah will do everything she can to preserve the illusion that the world is harmless: a place of rules, prepared stories, angles and sleights of hand. Stacey knows that she used a walking frame until she was twelve years old. It is evident too that her life has been dominated by the threat of grand mal seizures. But the cause of it all, the details of the event...

To this day Stacey thinks her mum was in a road traffic accident.

Hulk Hogan stamps on his opponent's chest. Deborah expects the man in black to grab the Hulk's foot – to twist it, to rise, even as the Hulk falls. But the man does not move. A pause. Hulk Hogan steps away. Paramedics clamber into the ring and carry the man in black out on a stretcher. Impossible to tell whether this is part of the scenario or not.

Perhaps there was a time, as Stacey reached her early teens, when Deborah could have told her daughter the truth. How she had woken from a dream of God's white house to a blast of pain, trapped in the hollow metal dark of a car boot. To tell her this now – what would Stacey be able do with this information? She would only use it to psychologize her mother. To her mother's every check and word of reason: 'You only say this because of what some maniac did to you.'

How can Deborah admit her sufferings have no meaning? Her

broken skull; her stroke; her epilepsy. Her tongue bitten half away in excruciating increments, the struggle she had to prove herself a fit mother, baby Stacey so often nearly taken away from her; her husband's incarceration and subsequent disappearance; her father's slide into alcoholism, the way he punished himself to death. The fits themselves, their cruel variety. The way they cluster sometimes round her frontal lobe, twisting her moods. All the times she has sat frozen in her chair, staring into the middle distance, counting down, quite rationally and white with fear, to the end of the world.

Her daughter's early success – the speed with which the school soap *Grange Hill* has propelled her into the teen magazines and even the gossip columns – has robbed Deborah of those few moments when an adult intimacy between mother and daughter might have been possible. There is also the conviction – couched in the back of Deborah's mind, a small but certain voice like tinnitus – that she is not wrong; that the higher her daughter climbs, the more terrible the fiend will be who, with one blow of his hammer, will cast her down into the metal dark.

Hulk Hogan leaves and Captain America enters the ring with a bandaged knee. Even before he has finished acknowledging his fans, a man in a sort of beetle costume has wrestled him to the ground. When, Deborah wonders, did the world cease to be real?

She studies the girls surrounding the ring – the show's lean, muscular eye-candy in their swimsuits and cheerleader gear. It is becoming more and more difficult for her to feel easy with Stacey's looks. Even by these girls' streamlined standards, her daughter is becoming painfully thin. The columnists are whispering. Stacey and the rest of the *Grange Hill* cast are in America this week, singing 'Just Say No' for Nancy Reagan. She hopes someone's on hand to make sure Stacey eats properly.

Now the beetle is jumping up and down on the Captain's wounded knee.

Deborah will not always be here to take care of her daughter, so it is good that this new world has come to trivialize her pain. The world is nanny now. Watching these choreographed atrocities, Deborah has convinced herself that this is how her daughter lives these days: the world scripting every line for her; weakening every table; padding every hammer.

Hands held behind her back to thrust her small bust against the cotton of her white school blouse, Stacey kneels on the tiled floor of the players' toilet cubicle and lets her co-star Darren slide his already rock-hard cock between her teeth.

An over-achiever in all things, she takes him all the way to the back of her throat, then, pulling back, she lifts his penis, pressing it against her face as she tongues his balls with a rapacity that is frankly frightening: he wilts.

It is Darren's dick in her face, but neither of them is in any doubt that Stacey Chavez is out to pleasure herself. She is known for this kind of thing, this athletic approach, as if she has something to prove. It does not take much to make Darren hard again. She dry-kisses the vein running along his shaft, pulls his foreskin back and tongues around the groove, then takes him in again. Darren thrusts a little against the roof of her mouth, unsure how much of this she will let him get away with. Stacey, determined to Win, to ruin him for all the others, grabs his hands, presses them to the back of her head and keeps them there, her hands on his, urging him to fuck her face.

The tiles are cold against her knees; her sensible school shoes pinch her feet. There is indignity in this, and perversity too, dressed as the schoolchild she never was; and Darren, in grey jumper and school tie, baby-faced Darren, at twenty playing fourteen-year-old heroin addict Biff McBain.

This American tour rides on the back of Biff's plot-line, for its poignancy has captured the imagination of a drug-paranoid world. Yesterday, at the White House, they sang for Nancy Reagan – Nancy's big on anti-drugs. Today they're in New York, half an hour away from the game at Yankee Stadium, where they will perform their single 'Just Say No' in front of fifty thousand baseball fans.

When Darren comes finally, he ejaculates so far in the back of her throat, Stacey doesn't even taste his semen, only the musty afterbreath, mixing unappetizingly with the toilet's just-scrubbed smell. Still she sucks and sucks, taking him in, further and further, as he softens, Christ, what is she planning to do? *Bite?* Darren pulls her to her feet – a brave move, given she is a good four inches taller than him. Now he is kissing her, lifting her shirt, trying to wedge his head between her breasts, probably for balance, his whole body a-tremble with the aftershock of what is easily and for all time his best-ever blowjob.

She lifts her shirt for him. She doesn't wear a bra. She doesn't need one. Her breasts are so precise and tiny you can fit them in your mouth.

There you go.

Good boy.

She is eighteen years old – the age her mother was when she gave birth.

Deborah has always expected her daughter to do well. She has demanded it. At the same time, she is afraid that Stacey will make her mother's mistakes. So Deborah has set bounds on what her daughter can reasonably be expected to achieve. She has tried to manage her expectations. It is a strange sort of encouragement that begins 'Are you sure...?' 'Do you really think...?' 'Maybe, but...' 'Do not forget...' and its effects are equally strange.

For Stacey, these minatory utterances are not the soft upholstery Deborah meant them to be. They are chains and prison walls, tying her to her mother, this woman who has no life of her own but lives through her. They are goads, reminding Stacey of her own uselessness, driving her forward from one over-achievement to the next.

'I – I think I love you,' Darren stammers, pleasure-drugged.

Good. Meaningless as the words are to her, this is what Stacey wants to hear. This moment is what she has learned to manufacture. It is her solace; otherwise she drowns, every waking minute, in the ghastly conviction of her own weakness.

A bell rings.

Quickly, they dress.

Stacey is first out of the gents', leaving Darren with his fly still undone, his school tie still askew. There are fifty thousand people out there, at the bright end of that tunnel, waiting to hear her sing. Thousands of men and boys who have yet to fall in love with her.

Nine years later. First-time Hollywood director Jon Amiel orders the crayfish. He has done what he can to persuade Stacey Chavez to order from the menu; Stacey is adamant, and has brought along her own muffin.

She has lost the part. There is no way Amiel is going to present the producers of *Entrapment* with such an obvious insurance risk, especially now he's had Zeta-Jones's agent on the line. But it would be tactless to let Stacey Chavez in on his snap decision during their very first face-to-face meeting. Besides, he likes her showreel, and life is long; he may be able to do something for her if she can get her head sorted out. All Brits go a bit crazy the first time they hit LA.

Tuesday, 9 May 1997. It is eight years since Stacey left *Grange Hill.* She has had her share of bit parts, a starring role in a more-than-dodgy Ken Russell B movie, a walk-on in *The Singing Detective*. The work that's really put her on the map is ITV's explicit reworking of *The Moth* – Catherine Cookson must have choked on her teeth, but enough critics looked beyond the carnal distractions and tissue-thin script to discover Stacey Chavez, her hunger, her fire. If she can only learn to harness it, her energy might make her great one day.

'I need a part that really *stretches* me,' says Stacey, lining up her knife. (Has she looked him in the eye once?)

Stacey has her meal planned. She doesn't need to look at her watch; she can count in her head. Every forty-five seconds she is going to eat a piece of muffin approximately the size of the first joint of her forefinger.

She will not tear this off the body of the muffin with her fingers: this method might suffice at home, but here it is too approximate. She will use her knife. A few seconds before she reaches for her knife, she measures the muffin against her forefinger, planning her attack. The conceit of cutting perfect rectangles from a round muffin is appealingly nonsensical, almost Zen. She maps this muffin's every crumb and bubble. Escape is impossible: this muffin is *going down*. Taking her hand away, she reaches for her knife, brings it over her plate and cuts exactly the shape she measured out. What I need, she thinks – because she is not beyond self-parody; like most anoretics, she knows what she is – is one of those vegetable slicers you find sometimes in Japanese kitchen stores. One stamp and hey presto! Every piece the same! Perfect bite-size muffiny chunks. She can even hear the exact note she'd hit, were she selling such a device, for such a purpose, on local TV, her first love.

Like this:

Per...fect (not too fast, build up slowly. Not too much of a smile; a note of suspense) *bite-size* (crisp and even here: nothing much else you can do. Just play up the consonants, the neatness of those two 'eye' sounds; careful not to drawl the 'z': this is no time to slacken the pace!) *muffiny* (a gift; would that every tag-line boasted such a word. You can really camp up kids' words. Big, big grin: hell, you just can't say 'muffiny' without breaking into a great big mischievous grin! Finally...) *CHUNKS*. (What a kicker! A real stamp-on-the-toes number. Heck, frighten them a little, even. Make them think about that sharp metal template hitting that dough. Not tearing it, not squashing it, not squeezing the life out of it *'which, as we ALL KNOW, happens TIME AND TIME AGAIN with INFERIOR CUTTERS'*. No, my friends, my ensofa-ed brethren, we are here today to talk about taking this muffin and CUTTING IT! Into CHUNKS!)

'Of course, the final decision lies mainly with the producers,' says Amiel, unable to keep up the pretence. He hasn't wanted to hurt her feelings, and because of this he is messing up badly. He knows this is cowardly of him, placing responsibility for her eventual rejection at someone else's door. He knows that she will surely hear, at the back of these words, the most mealy-mouthed of excuses.

But she does not hear him. She cuts another bite of muffin free, places it on her tongue, presses her tongue to the roof of her mouth, and suppresses a groan of guilty pleasure as the morsel paps and melts, oozing between tongue and molars into the cavity below so that she must roll her tongue, gather the sweet bolus together once more, only to crush it, dizzy with pleasure, against her top incisors, then lick it off – another bite – and down!

'And you must meet Sam and Judith,' Amiel says. These are business acquaintances of his. A married couple with two kids and a dog. Or is it a kid and two dogs? Anyway it occurs to him that what she needs is some normal people around her. Ordinary dinner parties. Stuff. Because otherwise the sharks are going to have her. She's been here – what? two weeks? – and already she has an assistant and a personal trainer. She's been telling him, when she hasn't been worrying at that bloody cake of hers, all about her important LA lifestyle, and what began as an audition has degenerated, by this point, into something resembling intervention.

'You really must come,' he says.

Stacey isn't listening. What would make this meal complete is mustard. Lashings of mustard. Stacey loves that hackneyed phrase, *lashings,* so irredeemably naughty. It sums up everything she feels about mustard, the sour tang, the granular fascination of wholegrain, Dijon's fabulous range of shades, the melted-ice-cream texture of your everyday squeeze-bottle American blend.

She grips her hands under the table and counts the bones in her palms as though they were a couple of Chinese calculators.

This is an important meeting and the part is hers, she knows it, she can feel it. She is going to be a star. If she can just hold it together a little longer. She will not ask for mustard. She contents herself – when she thinks Amiel's attention is elsewhere – with another quick sprinkle of salt.

*

Monday 7 August: three months later.

Stacey Chavez has sacked her personal trainer. Instead, each weekday morning at 4 a.m., after a breakfast of celery juice and Fiberall, she drives to the beach and pulls up next door to a deep-bed Dodge with a Stars-and-Stripes on its roof and quarter of a million dollars' worth of gym equipment packed into its guts. For $400 a month, and if she gets there before the others, Neal Krantz, ex-Navy Seal, fitness record-holder for an unprecedented four consecutive years, 1983 to 1987, lets her pull the handle, and the truck, wheezing, unpacks itself like a *Transformers* cartoon: 3000lbs of barbells, two dip bars, four 300lb pull-down stacks, T-bars, pull-up bars, bell-bars, and six inclined press-benches in weatherized aluminium. Add a missile launcher to this arsenal, it would not look more intimidating.

Last week, during the most gruelling two minutes of her life, Stacey managed thirty sit-ups – less than half the number the Navy expects of its recruits. She drooled her way through fifteen push-ups, but Neal passed only three. She should have been able to do fifty-two. The demands of this new regime leave her exhausted and trembling. She dozes off in auditions. There's a phone by her bed and yesterday afternoon she slept through its ring.

Last week she flew around a two-mile course in just over twelve minutes, racking up her score; nevertheless, to be considered fit, she needs to dig inside herself for another fifty points. To begin with, the exhaustion worried her. She wondered how she would be able to juggle the competing physical and practical demands of her career. Now that the telephone calls have petered out, Stacey is beginning to leave these cheap anxieties behind. She has her mobile if her agent wants to talk. There's little point Stacey phoning her, she's always in a meeting.

It is dark and the sand is cold through the soles of her sneakers as she lines up behind the eight others in her group. Neal hands her a 30lb pack – what he calls a 'half-weight'. It is standard armed-services issue, drab, with no waist-belt.

For ten years Stacey has been worrying her way up the career ladder. She has forgotten how to play, how to enjoy herself, even for a moment. She cannot stop. She does not know how.

Whatever she achieves can't, by her own impossible criteria, be worth anything, and so she snatches defeat from the jaws of every success. At twenty-six, faced with the first genuine stall of her career, Stacey feels old – as threadbare as a forty-something career woman grown grey and lined on a diet of *Cosmopolitan*.

Neal blows his whistle and they jog towards the dunes.

It seems to her that she has been dreaming her life: an anxious running-on-the-spot dream of unimaginable satisfactions forever delayed. The agent of this dream is her body, which will not let her be her best. It roots her in time and space, separating her from her goals.

The pack bounces from hip to hip, bending her into what Neal assures her is a sprinter's crouch.

Shed the body, and you shed the dream. So she has begun to rid herself of her body, ounce by difficult ounce, and she feels more awake now than she has ever been. Another whistle and they sprint. Another whistle and they drop into the sand for push-ups. Another: they jog again. The sun rises, and the sky does not brighten so much as gain in intensity, as though veils of atmosphere were being driven away, revealing a purer blue. Under this light, through the pain of new muscle, the intense self-centredness of Stacey's anorexia gives way to a spiritual sensation. It is time to shed the last scrap of her flesh. To distill herself down to the absolute.

They reach the foot of the dunes and Neal throws them each an ice-cold water-bottle from his stash. Beside the water crate there are metal ammunition boxes filled with wet sand. They form a line and pick up boxes, one in each hand. Another whistle and they trudge up the steep dune for a view of the ocean, then down again, no pausing, shoulders screaming, arms gorilla-stretched, around and up again.

The air grows thin and bitter. There is a dirty tin-foilish taste in her mouth, a flavour made from dead cells and stale fluids and chocolate Ex-Lax. Pain quarters her body, revealing its component parts. The arms have no solid connection to the skeleton. The shoulder blades float in a crossply of muscle. The calf muscles bend the leg. The quadriceps kick.

There is something electrical about the sky now, the cyan of a dead video screen, except that it is infinitely deep, a space of absolutes. They are running again. She is running into the wind. The front of her is chilled, the back half hot and clammy.

One mile.

A fever-line separates the two halves of her, a seam that shivers with every footfall, every arm swing, as though the halves of her are coming free of each other.

Two miles.

The halves of her lurch in opposite directions. Her prune-like heart misses a beat. Her joints tremble: she imagines the cartilage shrinking in every joint, rattling about in its sinovial bag so that her whole body becomes a baby's plaything: a tambourine of stretched skin.

Three miles.

She feels a shift inside her, nudging aside her dormant ovaries. Her shrivelled heart misses another beat.

Four miles.

This is it. The moment of departure. The sky is an electric blue. Goodbye, she thinks, expecting no answer from the dumb world of material things.

Goodbye.

Not her voice; someone else's.

Not her thought: *Goodbye.*

Five miles. Six miles. Ten miles.

It occurs to her that she is not going anywhere. She is still tangled in her body like a lobster in a trap. She is not leaving.

She sucks in air against panic and the air ripples around her, sending a shiver around her which seems this time to be no mere hint of anything, but an actual unzipping. Stuff spills out of her like ectoplasm. Weightless, bound to no material law of motion, it ascends in absolute terms through the gridded blue that hangs above her in place of a sky.

'Come back,' she gasps, or thinks she does, but so much of herself has poured out, sound will not carry through her. In her terror she thinks this is what it is to be flesh. In this moment, she understands what has left her.

It is her spirit.

'Chavez!'

She had imagined she was a spirit, trapped in mortal meat.

'Drink this. Come on. Sit up. Chavez?'

But no. The soul is something else. Her soul is free, gone. But *she* is still here, tied to flesh. The irony is so fine – finer even than the cruelty – that she wants to laugh.

'Stacey. Chavez.'

She laughs, or thinks she laughs.

MODERN MEDICINE

1

Saturday, 11 March 2000. A rainy Chicago night. I am pressing my hands into the rucks and wrinkles of the bedsheet, searching for some piece of Stacey Chavez.

The room is in darkness and the curtains are open. Vehicles send ripples of light through the room's shifting blue interior. It feels as though we are coupling in an aquarium. She has pulled the sheet over her and around her like a shroud. There is a flash, a peal of thunder. What if the bedsheet is actually holding her together? I imagine unwrapping it, spilling her across the bed like a child emptying a parcel of presents. Disembodied laughter from a disembodied head.

Over the course of our meal at Lovell's I had expected to get to know her a little. The more we talked, the less of her I saw, the more I was confronted with Stacey Chavez, actress. Stacey Chavez, the fallen star, the recovering anoretic. If her recovery was so far advanced, how come she had turned up at the restaurant with a muffin in her handbag?

It had been my impression, returning from our meal, that we had not liked each other very much. Outside her Michigan Avenue hotel, I leaned forward to give her a perfunctory goodnight peck. She turned her head slightly so her lips met mine. Fold after fold of her coat concertinaed under my palm before I found her tiny waist. My fingers, indifferently splayed, ready for the wall of her back, cupped instead the secrets of her pelvic girdle, rising sharp against her skin. The bone whip of her spine.

After a minute of this she said, 'You can come in if you want.'

Stacey pulls the sheet aside, revealing herself, and bends forward to unbuckle me as I shed my shirt. I can hear her panting with the effort of it, the pain, the mattress stiff against her bones. Her legs are splayed, the knees bent, the feet brought together, making a curious 'O'. When she leans forward to fellate me, her back arcs and her spine stands proud of the skin, a line under tension, and her ribs fan either side, the armature of an umbrella. It is impossible to describe Stacey's body without some resort to metaphor. Its radical thinness has robbed it of all familiarity. It does not look like a body at all. It looks like a hand: a delicate, alien hand with its unexpected points of articulation, its difficult, eloquent gestures.

When I woke up it was already light, and breakfast had been delivered to the room.

'I hope you like eggs,' Stacey said. 'You look to me like somebody who likes eggs.'

I like eggs.

Stacey had ordered a continental breakfast for herself. I watched her eat. She did not pick or slice or arrange or juggle. She did not guzzle everything in sight then run for the toilet. She ate: steadily, sparingly. I wondered how to reconcile her perfectly ordinary breakfast with last night's muffin dinner; was she fighting free of her old anoretic behaviours or re-learning them?

I was waiting on a call from the clinic, wanting to know the outcome of Felix's operation. Stacey, taking my edginess as interest, got talking about herself again. Her work.

SCTV: 'SC' for Stacey Chavez; 'TV' not for television, as I had assumed, but for '*tableau vivant*'. She was a long way from *Grange Hill.*

She had managed to place her work beyond casual notice, in a zone where her private obsessions were indistinguishable from the background: the migranous white-noise of the subsidized arts. She regarded this change in career, her successful dismantling of her celebrity status, as her real artistic achievement. The individual happenings – SCTVs one to four, her performances, *tableaux vivants*, whatever you want to call them – were more or less incidental to the central statement.

Stacey considered herself a conceptual artist who took celebrity as her subject. It was apparent that she had private means, aside from her earnings as an actress, and this was just as well, as her work was expensive to make. Her publicist had demanded two years' salary up-front, for fear of what Stacey's manoeuvrings might do to her professional reputation.

'I was doing everything wrong,' she laughed. 'Protesting outside the Turner Prize. Performances in church crypts in Oval and Hackney. The papers lapped it up.' One notorious performance of hers – it had a short run at the ICA in London – had her shoving fifteen Mars Bars down her throat then vomiting them into a bucket.

The business of erasure was more complicated than she had expected: 'That's why I had to pay through the nose for Vera.' Vera was her publicist; her anti-publicist now, sending carefully crafted details of Stacey's work to the usual diarists and media friends, ensuring that the tabloids became not so much frustrated with Stacey as bored and confused.

In spite of myself, I was intrigued. I too knew something about the business of erasure.

'So what do you do, Saul?' Stacey asked, throwing me a bone.

I saw no harm in spending another half-hour in Stacey's company, and, in order to answer her question safely, I did not have to depart very much from the truth. I had merely to talk as if my US business interests were as healthy as once they had been. I told Stacey that I ran an employment agency and from then on it was easy. Automatic, even.

Throughout the nineties it was expected of foreign aid workers settling in Maputo and Beira that they would fill their houses to the gills with domestic staff. It was the local custom, a useful source of employment and, in a city without labour-saving devices, the only practical solution to life's domestic demands. Anyone uncomfortable or embarrassed about employing servants was told, in no uncertain terms, and usually by the Mozambicans themselves, to get over themselves.

Often, once they were rotated back to desks in Washington, these same staffers found themselves hankering after their old retinue, and this is where I came in. My operation, which was entirely above-board, exploited a legal loophole exempting foreign nationals from US labour law. By this means I was able to supply the apparatchiks of the UN, World Bank and the IMF with cheap domestic labour. Better than that, I was pretty much able to guarantee the servants a goodish standard of living and a range of prospects far exceeding anything they'd find at home.

My eager young sub-Saharan jobseekers had all the right papers, and it amused me that the aid industry itself was the inadvertent conduit for their arrival in America.

It was the summer of 1996 before I let Noah Hayden catch up with me.

Nearly thirty years had passed since my lacklustre translations of Guy Debord's *La Societe du Spectacle* had graced the discussions of his New Left Reading Group, but Hayden was effusive. 'Do you remember those marches?' he exclaimed. This was one of the first things he said to me when we met again. We were both hitting fifty by then, and where I had shrunk and hardened, Hayden had acquired some considerable padding.

We were sitting in the garden of the Mount Soche Hotel in Blantyre, the commercial capital of Malawi, Mozambique's small, landlocked neighbour. I was here arranging domestic servants for the wealthier delegates at the Southern Africa Development Conference.

'Do I remember?' I thought I remembered. Voices like tides. The drunkard's walk we did: one miles-long, mutual jostle all the way to Grosvenor Square: *'Ho! Ho! Ho Chi Minh!'* These are the sorts of memories that manufacture themselves out of photographs, TV dramas, advertisements, celebrity reminiscences on *Desert Island Discs*; that widen the cracks between the flagstones of recall and smother them completely in the end. Cliché is a word we give to memories that don't need us to validate them any more. They have their own life.

I tried to show willing: 'I remember writing admiring articles about "Great Leader and Teacher Jack Straw",' I said. 'As I recall, my magazine was called *Letter Bomb.*'

Hayden grinned. 'Maoist.'

It was all bluster, all nonsense. I was worried we might run dry, anxious in case he mentioned Deborah. I didn't want to have to act out all those old lies again, years after the event. So I was boisterous: 'What the fuck's happened to Jack, anyway? Did he take something?'

'I think the question we are here to discuss,' Hayden said, 'is, have you?'

For years an industrious civil servant, Noah Hayden was now, by way of reward, a middle manager in the Department for International Development, with an impressive list of 'interests' to do with New Labour's foreign aid strategy. I knew what he was doing here. The Third Floor wanted a familiar hand to tug my leash. Noah Hayden was their man.

He was here to close me down, or at least, make a show of closing me down. So it was hardly surprising that I had gone into this meeting with a less than level head, teeth gritted against Hayden's complacency, his cereal-packet convictions, his infallible New Labour ideas about right and wrong.

As I saw it, Mozambique had held out against Rhodesia, then South Africa, and weathered all the blandishments of the Cold War, only to lose its independence at last to a handful of western NGOs. Every move the government made had to be countersigned by them or it risked forfeiting its aid. All around the harbour at Beira, international relief organizations were snapping up cheap real-estate. From inside their gated compounds, Scandinavian engineers, sipping imported beer, looked out upon our devastation with a speculative eye.

Although FRELIMO had clung on to power after the civil war, misfortune had softened it up nicely. In following the advices of the World Bank, it had had to defer indefinitely its promise of free universal education. Marxism-Leninism was abandoned. In Maputo, meanwhile, the UN operation ONUMOZ had revived the local economy so that the daughters of famous Lourenço Marques streetwalkers – girls of fifteen, girls of twelve – were trading out of their mothers' old trysting places along the bay and promenade. When I finally shook myself out of my torpor and took a good, hard look at what my adopted country had become, it seemed obvious what career I should pursue.

For months I had being watching from my glassless tenth-floor window as, one by one, my fellow *cooperantes* had abandoned Katalayo's dream of independence for menial jobs in the aid industry. I wasn't ready to buckle under, but there was obviously no future in education, still less in government service.

The first people Nick Jinks and I ever 'trafficked' were families made homeless when the World Bank insisted on denationalizing Mozambique's rental market.

Hayden had neither the sophistication to understand nor the desire to conceal how angry and disappointed he was over my new line of work. 'Have you?'

'Have I what?' I said, teasing him.

'Taken something.'

'I'm sorry,' I smiled, leaving him shipwrecked on the shoals of metaphor, 'I don't follow you.'

Hayden had his alibi for this 'accidental' meeting already prepared, and when the direct approach guttered out, he treated me to the scenic route: 'The F.O.'s getting rather jittery about the spread of the Congolese mafia. You know they run the bus concessions around here?'

'I didn't know that,' I said. 'No.'

Noah Hayden smiled. 'But you have dealings with them.'

That my work so offended the sensibilities of men like Hayden wearied me. What would he rather I dealt in? Drugs? Diamonds? Ivory? Africa's export markets had been so spectacularly decimated, human beings were one of the few resources we had left to trade.

To trade in people? In Hayden's mind, I had fallen off the map in the most spectacular fashion, abandoning FRELIMO and my principles. He couldn't see why I was so hostile to the charitable intervention he was here to promote. What was I kicking against? The truth – that I was still fighting Katalayo's revolution, shaking off the colonial yoke and flying the flag of liberty and self-determination when half FRELIMO had thrown in the towel – this was something Hayden didn't know how to respond to. If I was such an unreconstructed sixties throwback, how come I was so successful, travelling for business between my home in Beira, Maputo and the northern capital, Nampula; then abroad, as far as Kenya and Nigeria, Mali and the oil states of the Middle East? Or look at it the other way: how could a man claim political principles who provided under-fives as jockeys for camel-races in the United Arab Emirates one day, and rushed an ice-box full of human kidneys air freight to an exclusive clinic in Botswana the next? Of course Hayden didn't understand me. He imagined politics and crime were different things.

It pleased Noah Hayden to show himself to me. (Easy enough to imagine his home: cricket cups on the mantelpiece, music certificates framed in the bathroom.) It pleased him to know, from his extensive and industrious reading of the CIA *Yearbook* and who knew what other dry-as-dust public sources, things about the region that I appeared not to know. In his mid-fifties, Noah Hayden was still a puppy, eager to please, pleased to impress. Was he dangerous? Certainly – as a man is dangerous who is set in motion by others; whose actions are innocent of their effects. A man like that cannot be read.

A waiter passed our table. Hayden waved him over and handed him back his steak sandwich: 'Could you? The meat's a bit underdone. Thank you so much. Thank you.'

Hosting this year's Southern Africa Development Conference – the region's major annual political event – had thrown tiny, poor, lackadaisical Malawi into a tizz. Special SADC numberplates had been issued. Every bank in town had a dedicated SADC window, always open, for the negotiation of local currencies. Police and army helicopters hovered precariously above the streets, trailing convoys of statesmen and dignitaries from the airport. Army checkpoints littered the streets in and out of major towns. In Blantyre, Christmas decorations cheered the only roundabout, and men in orange boilersuits were working around the clock to fill the worst potholes with sand and pitch. The town's hundreds of street traders had been banished to the derelict football ground.

Here we were, drinking gin and tonic in a country where life expectancy was plunging through the mid-thirties and the government had just voted to bury the country's former dictator in a gold coffin, and any minute now Hayden was going to start using words like 'human rights'.

'The trouble with you, Saul,' said Hayden, 'is you're political to just the right degree to excuse your cynicism.'

I blinked at him.

'I imagine you say to yourself: "They're better off where they're going than where they are now."'

'Not really,' I said, determined not to show a hit. Of course they were bloody better off.

'Why then?' It was his big moment. 'Why do you do what you do?'

Did he really think, for one second, that people like me were incapable of philosophy? That we had no idealism?

I didn't answer him. I had no wish to play politics, or to match his belligerence. And how else would it have come over? The world I live in. The world I have had a hand in shaping.

Each moonless night, hulks registered in Cambodia ply the seaways from Lebanon to Syria to Cyprus. Fishing boats from Somalia run aground on the beaches of Mocha. A whole mile from the Spanish shore, snakeheads throw children into the sea first so the women will follow; then they torch the ship.

The waiter came back with Hayden's sandwich; this time there was no steak in it. 'You said you didn't want it,' said the waiter, nonplussed, when Hayden complained.

The waiter was local. The following week the conference got started, and the hotel laid off every waiter, cook, bell-boy and maid, and hired South Africans in their place.

That same week, in the northern Transvaal, irate, unemployed locals were throwing Malawian immigrant miners out of speeding trains. In France, meanwhile, an Iraqi Kurd died after leaping twenty feet from a bridge onto the roof of a goods train, only to slip and fall across an electrified rail; six Russians stole a speedboat from a Calais marina, gunned the engine so brutally it exploded, and found themselves having to row across one of the world's busiest shipping lanes; and a middle-aged Lithuanian couple spent ten hours floundering around in the English Channel on children's toy air mattresses. When the English coastguard picked them up barely five hundred yards from the Kent coast they were still, somehow, in possession of a set of matching luggage.

What Hayden couldn't or didn't want to see was that this 'crime' he is so keen to stem is itself a kind of revolution. The vision of Franz Fanon and Jorge Katalayo is dead. Only has-beens like Mugabe believe in it now. So be it. The Third World's revolution – the *need* in the Third World for revolution – lives on.

This time, we are going to do things differently. There will be no attempt at, or expectation of, fair dealing. From our first meeting in 1992 to the operation's collapse in 1999, Nick Jinks and I arranged cross-border transportation for more than ten thousand men, women and children. Ten thousand pioneers, missionaries, merchant adventurers. Compared to the big distributed family networks, the trans-national combines, not to mention the refugee grapevines themselves, Nick and I were small beer.

Ten thousand mouths. The West wants to play by the market? Then so will we. It doesn't matter how many Noah Haydens there are in the world, chasing myopic agendas across continents they think still belong to them. We are going to eat the West, the way the West ate us.

*

'So what went wrong?'

Stacey was scraping up the remains of a dish of yoghurt. There was a mouthful of eggs benedict left on the plate in front of me. Numbly, I scooped it up, chewed, swallowed. It didn't taste of anything.

Through the plate glass windows of the hotel room, the bright sky was dirtied here and there with scraps of last night's raincloud. For the first time in my life I was making confession.

'Saul?'

I drank my coffee, and I told her. What the hell.

Friday, 12 March 1999. After nearly twenty-four hours of air travel, I booked into a Glasgow airport hotel, only to discover the circus had come to town.

Red Nose Day. For lunch, an unsatisfying encounter, interrupted by the maid. In the evening, Johnny Depp and Dawn French in a *Vicar of Dibley* charity special.

About ten to midnight, Nick Jinks finally phoned me. By his voice – it cracked like a crust of salt – I could tell he was crying.

He'd been supposed to call mid-evening, to tell me our consignment of fifty-eight men, women and children were safely delivered to the tender mercies of the Scottish casual labour market. Instead he was ringing me from a layby outside Carlisle to tell me he had killed them all.

And where the button was, to operate the fan on his T.I.R. trailer.

And where the levers were, to open the vents.

And where the vents were, which he closed before Portsmouth customs and forgot to re-open. On and on, round and around.

'Open the doors.'

Fear had made him stupid.

'Open the doors. Look inside.'

'Fuck,' he said, between inhales. 'Fuck you.'

'The ventilation is on, yes?'

'I'm not fucking looking.'

'Is the ventilation on now?'

'I'm not looking.'

'Tell me you've turned the ventilation on.'

'Fuck off.'

'Nick, turn the ventilation on.' I went to the window with the mobile pressed to my ear, and I looked up into the sky.

'Nick, listen to me, they could still be alive. Nick.'

There was nothing to see. No star shone fiercely enough to penetrate the airport's sodium glare.

Stacey picked up her coffee cup. It was empty. She turned it around in her hands, examining it.

I stood up. I caught the edge of the breakfast trolley with my hip and it rolled away. Cups rattled.

'Saul,' she said.

'I have to go.' I stumbled for the door.

'Saul.'

I rode the elevator down to the garage. I had no memory of where I'd left my hire car, but dumb luck led me to the right corner. I climbed in and locked the door. I dug my phone out of my pocket but my fingers were trembling so much, I kept fudging the numbers. The first available flight to Heathrow was at a quarter past three that afternoon. It would have to do. I booked myself a seat with a credit card, and swung by the hotel for my clothes and passport.

On the plane that afternoon, in the seat beside mine, already settled, fussing with her earphones, sat Stacey Chavez.

2

Stacey's apartment occupied the top three floors of a converted wharf in Wapping, a ten-minute walk from the City of London. White walls, mahogany-stained floorboards. The rooms at the front were shielded from the road behind linen blinds. Windows at the back looked over the Thames. If I leaned out and turned my head to the right, I could see Tower Bridge. The riverbank opposite was dark: a pub, a strip of park, a line of council housing.

Stacey's was the kind of life encapsulated on certain Finnish postage stamps. In the living room, back copies of the art magazine *Parkett* lay neatly stacked on the table by the flatscreen TV. Her bathroom cabinet boasted non-abrasive facial scrub and soapless soap. When I began staying over, she bought me some perquisites. This is what she called them. 'I've bought you some bathroom perquisites,' she said, and laughed. I added her purchases to the shelf she had cleared for me: perfumeless aftershave; scruffing lotion.

The top shelf held her medicines. She took small doses of Zoloft every day to balance her mood. 'I am better than well,' she would say, whenever the rigours of the day grew too much. 'Better than well.' And sometimes we went to bed, even if Jerom was there, tap-tapping at his iBook in the kitchen on the floor below. Jerom was Stacey's assistant. Jerom without an 'e'. He arrived early each morning before we woke. He had his own key.

'Hello, Saul,' he'd say. 'How are you? Sleep well?'

He wanted me to know that he was here.

'Good morning, Saul, how do you want your coffee this morning?'

He let me know, always nicely, that I was in the way.

Jerom had a double first from Oxford. When he spoke to Vera on the phone – Vera Stofsky, Stacey's agent, or anti-agent – he called her Vera. It was all first names with him. Phil was Philip Dodd, who ran the ICA at that time. Jeff was Stacey's New York dealer, Jeffrey Deitch.

It was a strange sort of work they were engaged in together: complex, carefully minuted, mediated through emails, websites, PDFs; there was always a biker at the door, collecting a DVD, delivering a printer's proof. At the same time, and perhaps because so much of this work was conducted in the non-spaces of the internet, I saw virtually no evidence of product – as though the art business were an abstruse strand of international politics.

Sometimes it was necessary for me to manufacture an interest; more often I was left to myself. I had my living to make, after all.

The US businesses were ticking over pretty much regardless of Nick Jinks's disappearance. Occasional work for the Chicago clinic supplemented the trickle of clients passing through my employment agency.

The UK was a different matter. After the accident, I had drastically reined in my operation, and for that reason my work had acquired a pleasing simplicity and immediacy: 'Two navvies this way!' and 'Three navvies that!' and 'Jump in the back of the van!' Each week another batch of new arrivals came to me, looking for cash-in-hand: navvies and hod-carriers, brickies and cement artists. Even for the ones who had no transferable skill – the ones for whom being a brickie meant making your own bricks, for whom lighting was synonymous with kerosene and lunch was bushmeat on a *braii* of stones and rusted cementation rods – I was usually able to find them casual work of one sort or another.

Most weekdays saw me plying the M25 in my 3-series BMW. Stabbing at my handsfree with nicotine-stained fingers, I deployed my network of white vans across the country, from Glencoe (cockles) to Glastonbury (mushrooms), Sussex (salads) to Sheffield (greenhouse produce). Most every labourer travels a long way for the privilege of trimming our leeks and hand-selecting our beetroot. There are Lithuanians and Poles, Bulgarians and Turks. Most are legal, but a handful are not. These few are the invisible people, the wainscot people, the people adapted to live undiscovered up against the edges of things. My people.

It was a wrench, come Friday evening, moving from the brute immediacy of this life back into Stacey's orbit: her life lived between inverted commas. All those dinner parties: catty anecdotes about Vanessa Beecroft and Pipilotti Rist. Entire conversations consisted of nothing but other people's names. I did my best to act like a thug – mobile phone pressed to my ear, tales of congestion on the A3 arterial – but my heart wasn't in it.

I wanted her to stop taking the Zoloft. I wanted to know who she was without that crap in her system.

'No, you don't,' she said, and loosed one of her minatory laughs.

Every Sunday, Jerom insisted on filling the apartment with Sunday newspapers. Stacey never read them, and after a hard week's driving and dealing, I rarely got further than the TV listings. It was by accident that I stumbled, early that summer, upon an article about a little distinguished-sounding philosophical society near Malet Street – my first employer.

I showed Stacey the piece: a fragment of biography for her to play with.

She said, 'That man looks like you.'

I leaned over to see. Accompanying the article was a photograph of one of the Society's former members.

'Look,' she said, 'there's going to be a party.' Stacey's enthusiasm for my past was something I had not predicted and did not want.

The picture was of Anthony Burden, the subject of *The Idealist*. This book – the author's first foray into biography – was, according to the paper, the surprise hit of the literary year. 'This is your chance to take me to something,' she said. She had opened up her life to me, but had seen precious little of mine.

Poised midway between Senate House and the Fitzroy pub, the Society had not only survived the years of my absence; it had flourished. Its combination of academic fustiness and public library had matured into something more eclectic and engaged. Its rooms were washed and repainted, the staircases stripped and stained ink-blue. The basement had been leased to a small juice-and-falafel chain called Open Sesame.

By the time we arrived, the party – to celebrate some literary award or other – had spilled onto the pavement. There was no one there either of us knew, but everyone recognized Stacey Chavez. I introduced her to Miriam Miller, the society's receptionist, secretary and general factotum. It was obvious Miriam did not remember me. When Stacey pointed out the uncanny physical similarity between me and the subject of her biography, Miriam blinked at her as though she was mad. She spoke to us for exactly three minutes, then passed on through the crowd.

I had expected a little happy reminiscence; at the very least, I had imagined wandering between the stacks of the library where I had worked for so long. But the collection had been sold off years before. So I watched with something like admiration as Miriam and Stacey, the two women in my life, the old and the new, worked their different and eccentric orbits around the room. At a loss, I hunted down the table where Miriam's book was piled high.

I read: *'Anthony Burden was as much fascinated by people as he was afraid of them.'* I skimmed ahead, looking for pictures. There were pages and pages of them: faithfully reproduced sketches of shells and ferns and matrices, natural patterns and what looked like, but could not possibly be, computer code. None of it seemed remotely fathomable, and I wondered how on earth Miriam had found a publisher willing to foot the expense of so many plates and photographs.

Miriam's stabs at exegesis seemed as stilted as the articles she used to write for the Society's pamphlets: *'Anthony Burden was as much*

373

fascinated by people as he was afraid of them. The patterns they made as they went about their business daunted him. Their movements seemed very unpredictable to him, and he imagined these movements were more complicated than his own. Society wasn't just bigger than he was. It was More.'

The nostalgia I felt while skimming this tosh was, I imagine, similar to the rush of feeling one experiences for a doughty elderly relative once they are past the point where they can damage anyone. I looked for more pictures of her subject. There were very few, and none which resemble me so closely.

Stacey passed behind me, chatting to a short, swarthy man in a T-shirt too young for him. 'We visited a hospital—'

I recognized, in her earnest cadences, the overture to one of her favourite anecdotes: the documentary she had made for Comic Relief. '... A regional centre for the treatment of landmine injuries.'

Manhiça, north of Maputo, this was. I followed a pace or two behind, listening in.

'... This half-human, half-plastic mass. All the ways they had of moving around. One stick. Two. Wheelbarrows. Skateboards made out of crates.' As though the more Stacey told this story, the more weight it would acquire. The truth, as she had told it to me, was that she had been very little moved by her journey. The suddenness of her arrival and departure, the technical difficulties attending the shoot, never mind her own disorientation, so recently released from the clinic, had conspired to place her at several removes from the things she had seen.

'I never expected it to remind me so vividly of the clinic I had just left. Its head-height mirrors and curtainless showers. But the cupboards stocked with limbs, the injuries, the burns. The little boy without hands.' She was speaking of the experience the way one speaks of a particularly gut-wrenching gallery exhibition. The pair paused to have their glasses filled by a teenage girl in a white smock. 'I was not upset,'

Stacey said. She noticed me. She held her hand out for me, drawing me in. 'I have spent so long among monsters,' she said.

Do Goliata's farmers, crippled by anti-personnel mines, ever visit the graves where their limbs are interred?

As summer wore on, I found it harder and harder to concentrate on my work. I lost whole days sometimes, driving for hours through the spoiled southern countryside of my childhood. When I came to, it was late afternoon, the low sun was dazzling, and the clean, mathematical shapes of the rolling hills stood out dark against the sky. I would take long glances out the side windows and in my mirrors, looking for a glimpse of the walls of this world, and the hills changed shape as I passed between them, remoulding themselves, tightening, relaxing, like graphs representing a series of mathematical formulae.

I can only explain these excursions as an attempt – late in life, and hopelessly – to evoke dim childhood memories: the South Downs above Horndean, their rolling, rain-soaked slopes, their valleys boxed off into tiny irregular rooms by overgrown hedgerows.

My past: my missing limb.

3

Saturday, 13 March 1999. I have not slept. I've tried calling Nick Jinks back but he isn't answering.

Around four this morning I found our lorry, abandoned in a lay-by outside Fort William. There was no sign of Nick Jinks. I hadn't the nerve to break the trailer's TIR seal and look inside. After so many hours, what would be the point? I drove our spoiled shipment south, parked it safely, hired a car and went to drum up some assistance.

Ferrer's Grange. The company name is spelt out in stainless steel letters fused alchemically to the granite. Underneath, scuffed into the stone, a sans-serif assertion: 'We Make a Meal of Farming'. In the yard, a fingerpost in white weather-resistant plastic points the way to reception, where the girls – school-leavers from faceless greenfield conurbations outside Spalding and Stamford – have the sallow patina of high-street travel agents.

From inside the Portakabin, with its cheap, crunchy carpet, I can hear the packing houses: the dentist's-drill syncopations of Lincolnshire light industry, plastic bearings squealing in the rollers of stuttering conveyor belts, the squeak-snap of table-top shrinkwrap machines. Every one a sound of protest, barely an honest rumble or clunk anywhere.

'Have you been here before?' the receptionist asks.

Oh yes, I know these places, these draughty barns stacked high with plastic trays, rolls of corrugated paper, brown, purple, green, reams of colourful print, dusky smiling island women, buxom farmer's daughters, headscarves, shell necklaces, *capulanas* slit to the thigh, cheap, badly registered three-colour pornographies of ripeness and increase; in another corner, industrial-sized bails of Clingfilm, boxes of sticky labels; underfoot a smeared confetti, Class I, Class II, Union Jacks, tricolores, dinky little 'Farm Assured' tractors, *marques regionaux*; and beneath them, ingrained, immune to the twenty-four-hour schedule of broom and vacuum, blue-green crumb of broccoli, shred of carrot top, imprinted yellow leafshape of Brussels sprout, liquefaction smears, tomato pips.

The receptionist hands me a yellow plastic hard-hat, a dayglo jerkin, fluorescent gumboots and a laminated name badge: 'Visitor'. In this motley, nothing can mark me; they can always wipe me clean.

'I need a breath of air. I'll just be outside. All right?'

The fear these words plant on the receptionist's face suggests that hers is the sort of job where you have to account for every toilet break. She starts gabbling the company's safety policy. I might trip. I might slip. I might wander into an Orange Work Zone and, intoxicated into madness by the whirl of industry, hurl myself giggling into the shrink-wrap machine.

'I can surely wait outside the office?'

'Oh,' says the receptionist, and because I am already through the door: 'All right, then. Don't go far.'

Beyond the packing houses lies a crackled criss-cross of tractor and trailer tracks. And there they are, Chisulo and Happiness, picking Sweethearts out of the smashed earth.

Happiness is younger than her husband. Her skin is pale and freckled, her blood bleached by a globe-trotting Danishman, her fly-by-night dad.

Felix, on the other hand, is old and dark, and all his life in this country the *Azungu* – his old-country word for the whites he has grown old among – have congratulated him on his black twistedness. 'Like mahogany,' they say, which proves, he says, they are no carpenters.

Thorn would be a better choice; Felix is as twisted as though a mountain wind has sculpted him. When he sees me, he stands and smiles, because it is the custom of his people to smile. It signifies no friendliness whatsoever.

It is a strange sort of service I have done these two, and nigh-on impossible to explain to the natives of this merrie shopkeepers'

377

England, where making one's voice heard above the din has become the highest good. I have erased them – and as a consequence, there is much that Chisulo and Happiness cannot do. Banks refuse to handle their meagre earnings. Public libraries choose not to lend them books. On the other hand, there is much they cannot be made to do, and this, in their lives, was a welcome novelty – at least at first – for they came from a place where the State gives little, and asks much.

Happiness, working beside her husband, looks up, and though her freckled face is a blank, her eyes are full of stratagems. But this is, in turn, merely the customary look of her people, the people of Djibouti, that hell on earth where people chew leaves incessantly like cows simply in order to have something to do.

I tell them I have a job for them, and I pick a figure to turn their heads, but not too extreme: I don't want to scare them off.

Still they hesitate, for they have good work already here. Come the days of high yield, ordinary human sweat can earn them up to £1.50 an hour.

It's Chisulo who relents, finally: 'I'll go and fetch Asha.'

Asha is their daughter. An unwelcome complication, but I don't want to spook them now by saying she can't come.

Leaving Happiness to her pluck and drop, I follow Chisulo down the hill. The whole valleyside is one huge field, planted everywhere with melons, melons for every taste, here green stripy Sweethearts, there crazed yellow Passports, further down the hill the phallic wrongness of *Caroselli di Polignano*, towards woods the managers keep in the bottom for the shooting of great tribes and nations of grouse. (The company's recreation division call this venture 'The Lucky Brakes', but I doubt whether their city-analyst clientele know enough country lore to pick up on the pun.)

We enter the woods, deep enough so that the light begins to gutter. I can't imagine where their daughter must be, among these tangles and paths criss-crossing, these fallen trees.

Chisulo turns sharp left, past a fallen oak – and there is a caravan, a dilapidated Hurricane, abandoned wheel-less among the furthest brakes, the plastic airstream bubble over its rear window long since smashed away, the trellis skirting round its bottom kicked in at precise intervals, suggesting the tantrum of a strictly governed child.

There has at some point in its history been a half-hearted attempt to paint the sides of the caravan Windsor green. Concrete breeze-blocks make steps up to the door, and from inside comes the laughter of children.

The concrete blocks wobble under Chisulo's feet as he climbs. He opens the door.

From the foot of the steps I glimpse children. One of them, a boy, his skin a curdled Balkan colour, is waving a metal contraption over his head, out of the reach of a black girl in a green polyester party dress with a silver ribbon round her waist, undone now and dangling, the ends scuffed and dull where she, along with everyone else, has trodden on them.

The girl hops, panting. This is a game, she is smiling. No, she is not smiling, she is panting, she is exhausted.

She is hopping. She only has one leg. The boy is swinging the other above his head.

Chisulo says something in a language I don't recognize, and smartly, without a trace of fear or embarrassment, the boy hands him his daughter's leg.

Asha hops to the door and Chisulo gathers her up in his arms and steps backwards, gingerly, down the breeze-block stairs. The boy swings the door shut. I catch a glimpse of the caravan's interior: its wallpaper, its mobiles, the pink tricycle, the space-hopper; empty boxes, piled into a half-hearted den.

Chisulo wants to put Asha's leg on, but there's no time. She wouldn't be able to walk across the field anyway, the ground is so uneven.

'We can put her together again in the car,' I tell him.

We ride the A14 – Happiness and the girl in the back, Chisulo riding shotgun beside me – and half an hour later I pull in 'to rest'.

So here we are now, staring numbly out of the window of the service station, blowing on coffee that is both scalding and tasteless. How am I supposed to say what I have to say with the little girl sitting here between us like this? I am still puzzling this through, muzzy from lack of sleep and too many hours behind the wheel, when Asha says, 'Chipsss. I want chipsss.'

I go and buy her some chips.

Then she says, 'Can I have ketchup with my chipsss?'

'Over there,' I tell her, sitting down again. 'See? Those packets over there.'

Asha returns with a fistful of sachets of tomato ketchup and a woman in a giant dishcloth smock running after her because she has not paid for them. They are seventeen pence each. I hand the woman a pound coin, but she says she has to put the sachets through the till – she means scan them. I tell her to use some initiative, pick a sachet from the can by her till and scan it through a few times, but she says she cannot do this, so I ask for my quid back, but she does not want to give me back my money, so I tell her to fuck off.

The till operator returns with the manager. The manager gives me change from my pound and tells me not to make further purchases from his food hall.

'Chipsss!' says Asha, eating them. Chips vanish without effort, without chewing – even without swallowing, it seems – down the little girl's gullet. Watching her, Chisulo's eyes grow grey and wet: windows on stormy weather. (Two years before, back home, Chisulo was studying law. But they were all something.)

'Carsss!'

Asha is done eating; now she pulls on her mother's sleeve.

'Carsss!'

I ask Happiness, 'What cars?'

'The games,' Happiness replies. 'The games, she means, downstairs, the games with cars. No, Asha.'

'The arcade games,' says Chisulo. He stands.

'Stay where you are. I want to talk to you.'

Chisulo sits but, as he does, Happiness stands: it is like they are being operated off the same pulley.

The girl takes her mother's hand.

'Go with her, then, Happiness,' I tell her, 'It's fine.'

'Carsss!' the girl chirrups, hand in hand with her mum, clunktapping away over the dog-hair-thin industrial carpeting towards the arcades.

'What is it, boss?'

I never expected to charge them so high a price for their freedom. But what can I do? Fifty-eight men, women and children. Imagine. The volume of human flesh. It is too much for one man to manoeuvre, let alone conceal.

Stripping, handling, wrapping, packing. Plastic and tape. After months spent trimming and stacking groceries at Ferrer's Grange, Happiness and Chisulo will find the whole process eerily familiar.

4

My hands frozen to the wheel, heavy with nostalgia, sick with it, I hacked back and forth over the South Downs, through villages with names like Hurtmore and Noning. The hills of my childhood had been scrubbed clean. It was a modern, monochrome landscape now. The soil was so thin, modern ploughs had cut great gobbets out of the chalk bed and left the fields flecked white and grey. From a distance, it was as though someone had gone over the land with sandpaper, revealing a grey primer beneath. The crops, when they came, were a sickly yellow-green, and rounded off the imperfections of the hedgeless hills, leaving them as smooth as the features on a golf course.

I could not go back. I would have to go forward. I thought about that.

I had grown bored of the modern arrangement Stacey and I had fallen into. Its lack of commitment was exhausting. I decided to do something selfless, if only for the sake of the change. I tried to make myself, if not useful, then present: a silent partner, someone for Stacey to turn to, to rely on.

But she already had Jerom, and how could I compete with him? Jerom had all the advantages: education, youth, a sense of humour, a missing 'e'. No sooner did I try to participate in their lives, than Stacey and Jerom set about seeing to my every need, hoping perhaps that I would leave them alone.

When I wrapped my BMW around a bus near St Katherine's Dock, Stacey took me to a showroom in Mayfair and bought me a replacement. 'What do you think?' she asked me as we drove back to Wapping along the Strand. I said something about the positive feel of the controls, the hard ride, the snugness of the seat: anything to paper over my wretchedness.

Just then her phone rang. Jerom dug it out of his pocket; Stacey never took her own calls. 'Well, *hello*, Jeff,' Jerom cooed, wriggling into the leather of the back seat. Since I had decided to be Stacey's best friend, Jerom never seemed to leave her side.

He was not so petty that he did not allow me to make some contribution to the household. I took charge of the coffee machine and the herbal teas. I kept house. I swept and tidied. I threw away newspapers before Jerom was done with them, wanting him to stop me, itching for an excuse. This was how I stumbled on the other key story of my year – though this was harder to miss; John Gridley's worn muzzle splashed across the front of a *Guardian* pull-out.

The senator for Illinois was familiar for his maverick politics: by and large a good Republican, Gridley was, at the same time, outspoken in his determination to get the Bush administration to grasp the nettle of foreign aid. Long before debt relief reached the international agenda, Gridley had advocated a unilateral writing-off of African debt. The terrorist atrocities of September 2001 only strengthened his old-school belief in the importance of winning hearts and minds abroad; above all, in being seen not to rip people off. A year ago, the critically ill senator told a *New York Post* interviewer that he would soldier on – and die in office, if necessary – until this 'vital pillar of national security' was enshrined in policy.

The year since had made a nonsense of the *Post*'s valedictory. Not only had the senator's health improved to an improbable degree; there was now a better-than-evens chance that an international agreement would be struck on forgiving Third World debt.

Gridley's response?

Last week, he had declared his intention not to contest the next Senate race.

I was so nervous about what I would find in the *Guardian*, I couldn't even read the article at first; I had to scan it, hunting for tell-tale words like 'clinic' and 'kidney'.

Gridley was intimate, as few others are, with the economic disparity between rich and poor nations. Right now his only functioning kidney belongs properly to a former RENAMO lieutenant by the name of Felix Mutangi. That Gridley, hopelessly compromised, dared to continue his lobbying was admirable, I thought. The hypocrisy he had shown in buying a poor man's kidney, thereby saving his own life, was small beer by comparison.

The *Guardian* piece, after a lot of hand-waving, excused the Senator's resignation with a mere paraphrase of his own announcement. I could only hope its lengthy, saccharine approach would spike the story for other, more inquisitive editors.

I threw the paper in the bin and tried to forget about it. I emptied the ashtrays. I made a salad. I tried to straighten out the mess Stacey was making of her home.

One whole room was devoted to Stacey's wardrobe. There were shelves, floor to ceiling, stacked with her shoes, all in their original boxes. The contents of the bathroom medicine cabinet were sparing in comparison to the powders and lotions and mascaras and God knows what else cluttering her make-up tables; there were two of them, one in her dressing room and one in the bedroom.

Did I ever see her in the same outfit twice? In the unlikely event she ever ran short of cash she could have opened an agnes b museum.

Though the apartment was airy enough, I could never stay inside for long. I found the presence of all these Staceys hard to handle: Staceys hung up on the backs of doors, Staceys spilled from cupboards, laid out over beds and chairs, stacked in boxes, bottled, jarred. There were so many women Stacey could be. She could be anybody she wanted to be, now that she was nobody. She had rendered herself down to the bone. She was starving her life the way she had starved her body. Jerom's phone log in the morning; Vera's pie-charts in the afternoon; in bed, a man twice her age: what kind of life was this?

Similar thoughts must have crossed Stacey's mind, too, because come October she began to take lovers from among the students she met while delivering guest lectures at Goldsmith's and Central Saint Martin's. They were usually girls. The affairs would last a few days; never more than a couple of weeks. They shouldn't have mattered. Though we sometimes shared a bed, Stacey and I hardly ever fucked any more. Come night-time, we had our separate rooms. Still, it angered me to find myself cast in the role of an infinitely indulgent uncle. Someone who would pick up the pieces afterwards. This, my second experiment at living with a woman, had proved just as sexless as the last.

How could Stacey answer my disappointment? With pity, or with laughter? 'Sometimes I feel too delicate for cock,' she told me once, on her way out to a date. She stroked my cheek. She was trying to titillate me, to make me an accomplice in her adventures. A silent partner indeed.

Even when I hit her it didn't make any difference. The next morning I entered the kitchen, wobbly with remorse, to find Jerom taking photographs of her black eye. I couldn't work out if this was for her art or something to do with insurance.

5

Her tour. Imagine. *SCTV05*.

The walls of the bathtub rise around her, high, grey-white, and smutted. The brine supporting her in the bath is thick enough, salt is precipitating out of the water along the tideline, crystallizing wherever a smut greases the enamel.

Her tour begins late in the year in Milan, at the Inga-Pin gallery. The following week she participates in the closing days of the Venice Biennale. In the new year, the Neue Nationalgalerie in Berlin.

SCTV05. Stacey licks salt from her lips – naked, shrunken, she is not eating any more – as, little by little, the water in which she floats evaporates under the gallery's halogen lights.

The atmosphere at the Inga-Pin is business-like. Franca Sozzani, editor of *Vogue Italia*, arrives a few minutes before the end of the technical run-through. (There will be only two performances of *SCTV05* at each venue: once for the public, and once for the DVD.)

Sozzani has arranged for Helmut Newton to take a snap of Stacey this evening for the magazine; he wants to accompany her in person and write up the meeting.

Stacey nods agreement, shivering and dumb. She is not dressed yet. Fan heaters are going full-blast, three of them, plugged into the same extension lead. They have been arranged in a triangle, an almost-safe distance from the bath, and Stacey stands in the middle, scooping the towel up her outstretched arms in the shaft of hot air.

'The studio is half an hour by car,' Sozzani explains. He is struggling, in this white space and in the vacuum of Stacey's wide-eyed regard, to express his solicitude. His panic is palpable. 'We will be driving *north*.'

Nobody pays any attention to me.

Stacey crosses to the chair where her clothes are piled. Her flesh has retreated so far it has abandoned its defence of her sex. Now the gap at the top of her thighs is so wide, were I to put my fist between them, I doubt we'd even touch.

'Here.' Sozzani offers Stacey his coat and leads her from the gallery.

I wander over to the bath.

I dip my hand into the water. It is stone cold.

A jangle of keys.

Closing time.

This is the pattern of our days. By the time I wake up, Stacey has already left for work at the gallery. I throw on a dressing gown and I wander into the lounge to find the TV on, muted, and a line of orange Tic Tacs lined up, uneaten, on the arm of the hotel's easy chair. The suite is a sea of half-drunk bottles of mineral water. There is no Zoloft in the bathroom. She has decided not to take it any more, and because of all the stupid things I have said against it in the past, there is nothing I can say in favour of it now.

I leave the hotel and I look for something to do. More often than not, this is a waste of time. I am out of joint with Europe. I am too old to learn the tricks of Stacey's generation, these cut-and-paste people with their French-fried philosophy. Even their films leave me cold. There is more to life than entertainment, of course, but, having spent so long in Stacey's apartment, among Stacey's friends, drinking Jerom's coffee and listening to his end of complex, fruity transatlantic telephone conversations, I am not sure I can remember what it is. By the time Stacey gets back from the gallery, I am already slumped in front of the TV, hunting the channels for those game shows where the girls take off their bras. A nice hobby for a sixty-year-old.

The evening Stacey had her photograph taken by Helmut Newton, I found something else to watch instead: *Fox News Live* hosted by Martha MacCallum.

John Gridley, former Illinois senator, was dying of AIDS.

I reached for my phone, decided against it, went out into the street and hunted down a public booth. The lines to the Chicago clinic were engaged; a bad sign. I tried Felix and got his wife. Felix was out at work. She gave me a mobile number but I couldn't get it to work. I tried the clinic again.

There was no one there willing to speak to me.

How long had Gridley been keeping a lid on his HIV status? Was he clean last year, when he went in for his operation?

As he was carried into hospital this evening, Gridley's lawyer had issued a public statement to the effect that the senator's HIV infection had been contracted, not through sexual contact, but during the course of a surgical procedure. No journalist in America could fail to spot the invitation in that. The lazy ones would be waiting for news of a lawsuit. The more ambitious among them might notice, perhaps, that according to his medical notes, the senator, for all his troubled health the past few years, had not gone under the knife since his tonsils were removed in 1966.

His foul blood and failing kidneys – these were a matter of public record, so that the miraculous improvement in his health over the last year had been a source of grudging media celebration. But there was still plenty for him to tell. Gridley must even now be juggling offers for his death-bed confession. With a good ghost, you could probably make a book of it. Part One: the family's vain hunt for an appropriate donor. Part Two: and at last, *in extremis*, through discreet channels, via contacts in the overseas aid industry, certain parties are able to offer the dying man a final stab at life. An operation. A transplant.

What was Felix's HIV status now? What had it been, the day they gave his kidney to John Gridley? How could the clinic not have known?

Whether out of remorse, or to head off blackmail, or simply out of a dying wish to light the blue touch paper, and end his cantankerous career in a blaze of controversy, Gridley was getting ready to talk. The clinic's only hope, and by extension mine, was that the pneumonia would get to him before *ABC News*'s dictaphone clicked on. Except that Gridley was a man of education and foresight; he would have prepared his confession already.

I went back to the hotel and waited for Stacey.

She got back from the photoshoot after two in the morning, knowing full well she was in trouble. She put on the bikini she had worn for Newton. It was leather. Expensive. Tiny. They had given it to her.

'What do you think?'

She tried to prance.

SCTV05.

Every so often, heads appear over the sill of Stacey's giant bath-tub. Imagine: the heads lean down and study her, their faces invisible against the glare of the halogen lamps. Stacey can only guess at their expressions.

Horror?

Desire?

Imagine: the computer-controlled canula at her left wrist releases a little of her blood into the water.

'No,' says a woman, looking down at Stacey, floating in water pinked by her own blood. 'No.' Trembling and tense. Her voice can't find the right register. 'No.' It sounds as though someone were offering her a canapé – something to which she is allergic.

'No, no.'

The head retreats. Poor hapless punter. Doesn't know much about art but she knows what she likes. Quick footsteps lead away, making little ripples in the bathwater that tickle Stacey's ears. Hunger twangs her gut like a piano string, and she struggles against the deadly urge to turn her head and drink the brine.

Everybody can see that she is dying. It isn't in me to save her. I know myself too well by now.

*

The clinic phoned me yesterday. A conference call. At least, they said they were calling from the clinic. Only someone used my real name. I cut the line and threw away the phone.

Today I'm phoning Felix again. Once more I get his wife. 'How are you, Lovemore?'

Anyone else buying a kidney transplant would have flown to South Africa or Pakistan for his operation. Not Gridley. Not in his position: the foreign travels of a gravely ill US Senator would not have gone unremarked. Gridley had insisted on shitting in his own back yard. From his deathbed, slowly murdered by the very kidney that saved him, he is even now giving statements to the FBI.

'How are the kids?'

Last year I set up Felix and Lovemore as my new caretakers for the northern states. I saw to their relocation, freed them from their files and police records, their government numbers and other bureaucratic spoors. In doing so, however, I have become the very world they would escape from. I am every policeman, every government official, every doctor, every care worker, every petty bureaucrat. So as I enquire, with a more than casual insistence, into the health of Felix's family – his wife, his two young sons – I must choose my words carefully.

In a couple of hours, the family's bank cards and mobile phones will cease to function. A couple of hours after that, a van will turn up at their door. I think they will cooperate. In any event their Chicago life is over.

If they phone the newspapers, if they tell their story, it won't make any difference: as of yesterday, my American business interests are not simply terminated; they never were.

The call goes as well as such calls can, and yet another SIM-card joins its fellows in the mud of the Arno. I am good at this, and I like to think I conduct myself professionally. I never resort to bluster or threats. The world is the way it is; Felix and Lovemore surely know better than to throw themselves and their children upon the mercy of US Immigration.

*

Venice in November. In the mornings, high water rises through the pavements.

We teeter along duckboards down flooded alleys, pausing distracted at this church or that, this paper shop, that stand-up patisserie. Rain ricochets off the brick walls of the alleys. Tourists in yellow galoshes huddle under the awnings of the ink-and-paper shops, the Murano glass outlets, the porticos of churches. We slip up like a couple of drunks on stone footbridges, their steps edged in marble slick as soap. Come rain or shine, summer or winter, Stacey tells me, the canals of Venice are always the same colour: the blue-green of plastic garden furniture.

(*SCTV05*. The gallery closes. The halogens go out, their glittery, schizophrenic light curdling for a second before it dies, blue to sepia to the brown-black of ashes.)

At lunchtime, from our table at Quadri, overlooking St Mark's Square, we watch as the lagoon water drains away – a clear foot of it, vanishing in minutes through tiny sink-holes between the flagstones.

In the centre of the piazza, a man and a woman in smart casual clothes trot in circles round and round. Every so often they point at random into the air, as though firing imaginary weapons.

Stacey is playing her 'Come here, go away' game with the staff. She wants the waiter to dry her shoes. She wants the waiter to bring her shoes back. She wants the waiter to bring her some dry shoes. Stacey wants a drink. Stacey wants the waiter to know, me to know, the world to know, that she can't be expected to just sit there with wet feet and no drink.

The couple's gestures are ungainly and unpractised. When I lean back in my chair to examine them, I realize I've been watching them through a flaw in the glass; that they are smaller and nearer than I assumed; that they are children.

Paulo, Eduardo: the names of Felix's sons.

I say to her: 'I don't think I can do this any more.'

MAPS OF THE WORLD

Monday, 17 July 2006

A despairing email from Jerom, Stacey's PA ('former PA', he styles himself), has led Moisés Chavez, criminal mastermind and underworld enforcer, out of his Guatemalan hiding place, across the Atlantic and up to the door of his adopted daughter's apartments in Wapping, near the City of London.

He rings the bell.

Jerom comes to the door. He has his jacket on already, his outdoor shoes. As Mo comes in, Jerom goes out, muttering something about an errand.

Mo knows Jerom won't be back. He can spot a coward by the smell.

Mo climbs the stairs up to Stacey's apartment; they issue directly into the main living space, no walls or doors.

It is a relief to find the room clean and well ordered. Jerom has done this much for her, anyway.

On the floor in front of a wall-mounted flatscreen TV, huddled under a Zambaiti blanket, Stacey Chavez kneads her PlayStation remote, slotting her virtual wheels through impossible gaps in her hunt for the closure of digital sunset in *Gran Turismo 4*.

Mo sinks to the floor beside his adopted daughter. This child twice abandoned. 'Stace,' he whispers. 'Stacey. Stace.'

He tries to look her in the face, but this is not so easy, because there is very little face left. It is all skull, the skin shining over the bone as though embalmed.

'Look at you.' Mo strokes his daughter's head. 'You can't even walk.'

He had not expected it to be like this. He had expected a fight, when Stacey found out about Jerom; the way Mo has been keeping tabs on her condition.

He strokes her head, her sunken cheeks, her neck, as loose and folded as the neck of a chicken. 'Please.'

He expected her to recognize him.

Stacey flexes her torso uselessly. Her head bobs and tosses.

Mo remembers playing with Stacey as a child. Her rough giggle. The way in the mornings she would clamber into bed to hug his head.

'It's a good place, Stace,' Mo urges her. 'Your mother went there,' he says, as if this were an inducement.

Through an anonymous account he will pay Coronation House for Stacey's care, as he paid for Deborah – this other ruin of a beautiful girl, the wife he abandoned, for her good, he thought at the time. For her good, and for the good of her child, because in 1983, with eight years of jail behind him and his youth fading fast, Mo knew there was no way that he could lead a legitimate life.

'They know how to help you,' says Mo, into his daughter's ear.

The truth is, he barely recognizes her. The last time Mo saw Stacey she was fourteen years old, wearing a black dress and a green fright wig on the day of the funeral of her grandfather, Harry Conroy. Mo was new out of jail, spying on the wake from across the street. Trying to come home. For weeks he tried. How many sharply truncated phone calls? How many drive-bys? But how could he come home? Knowing what he was now. Knowing the life he knew now, and what prison had taught him. Knowing what he was going to do.

Mo no longer smuggles marijuana.

'Please,' he says. He is reduced to begging. 'Please,' he says, stroking Stacey's shoulder. What there is of it. The bones.

Stacey whispers something, far too soft to hear. She is glued to the screen.

Mo follows Stacey's gaze, into the television.

Scenery rips past.

Only now does Mo see what his daughter is driving.

Inside the plastic PlayStation housing, inside the machine, a fractal math sculpts trees and mountains, throwing them upon the TV screen with the careless mastery of a potter. Each rock, each leaf, each twisted branch is unique, an effervescent work of mindless art, no sooner glimpsed than gone. Clouds swell, glower, then disperse, revealing a low, late sun. Blue shadows spill from the hoardings and stands and the cheering, screaming onlookers, every one an extemporized original, as Stacey, made whole by games like these, made superfast, pumps the brake with a bony forefinger and thumbs the wheel around.

The world has come a long way since *Turbo*. The viewpoint skids and topples, then rights itself, as the game's forgiving physics bounce her off a wall and back onto the track.

Stacey has never got this far before. Her walnut heart shivers, and the game, sensitive to the moment, slackens its break-neck pace. The road straightens as it enters a beautiful park.

Deer graze beneath tall trees with foliage so rich and thick, it looks more black than green.

A dark lake flashes by.

Stacey hits the brake, turns the cream Thunderbird carefully around and, counter to the spirit of the game, retraces her route.

There are no pursuers now. She has fallen out the bottom of the game.

She wonders where she is now.

In the middle of the lake, a fountain sends a crystal jet into the air like a glittering whip, spreading coolness all around.

Stacey Chavez unclips her seatbelt. The cherry-red leather upholstery sticks to the backs of her legs as she reaches for the door.

The boy at the burger bar counter is sweating from more than chip heat, for he cannot hold medium chips and apple pie in his head without dropping the bacon cheese double. Neither can he operate the till: a twenty-by-twenty grid of buttons, their colour-coded subdivisions long since overridden by wear and spillage.

Fifty years ago, no one would have cared that this boy was dull-witted. Back then, being dim was neither a crime nor a catastrophe.

These days even operating a till requires a degree.

Anthony Burden takes his shopping-day lunch over to a table. He sits. He eats. The mush slides down easily enough. He faces the counter. He watches the boy. He feels something. Something he has no use for, no interest in. Something like compassion.

The net has been cast. Anthony Burden can see this. Though he is old and out of touch, though he has spent most of his life trying and failing to improve the lot of the poorer people of the earth, and though it is only the siren call of free health care and council housing that has convinced him to come back to the UK, he knows enough about the modern world. He knows about these places and how they work: how the till talks to the stock control computer, which talks to the email generator, which talks to the supplier's mainframe, and on and on and on. He can see, as though it were etched on the air, the self-stitching net that has been thrown over the world. He can see the struggles of people trapped within that net. He knows where the dreams of his youth have led.

As the boy struggles through his robot day, Anthony Burden realizes it has been given him, in these final years of his much-travelled and impecunious life, to witness something important. Here now, in a Portsmouth burger bar, he is witnessing the birth struggles of a world he has always dreamed of: a pre-wired, pre-fabricated world that has no need of people. A world already in control of itself.

Anthony Burden finishes his meal and leaves. He cannot remember the way home. Every street is like every other street. Every pavement is like every other pavement. Every hoarding is like every other hoarding. There are more connections in the human brain than there are stars in the sky, yet, by their chatter, all these connections go to make one singular 'I am'. So this city, webbed together with glass fibre and microwave, copper, coherent light and GSM, is one place now, one square foot of earth, and to walk through the streets of the city is to return to that square foot of earth continuously and reaffirm the city's great 'I am'.

Anthony Burden is lost, though there is nothing unfamiliar about his surroundings. On the contrary, everywhere he turns, he sees the same familiar scene. He is lost, and yet there can be no doubt where he is.

He is lost, as a man is lost who never leaves his home.

He walks.

This is the world he dreamed of: infinite trivial variations on a single theme. He walks, and the city rolls beneath his feet like a hamster's wheel, recurring endlessly.

His shopping bag knocks against his shin. Inside, his treasures: a bag of Young's frozen prawns (30 per cent extra free) and a half-price coconut. Anthony is going to weave magic tonight. Tonight, Anthony turns escapologist. He is going to make himself a pot of *caril de amendoim*, and taste his way to younger times and warmer lands.

When you have worked with as many anoretics as Professor Emeritus Loránt Pál, it should be painfully apparent to you that their well-being depends less upon their physical condition as upon their outlook.

'Their *philosophy...*'

Loránt Pál sucks his teeth, savouring his *mot juste*, but neither Stacey nor the man accompanying her seems impressed by his analysis.

He recognizes Stacey. He met her during her numerous visits to see her mother, and even then he had it in the back of his mind, given her radical appearance, that he might see her again – that she might one day self-refer.

Deborah, her mother, died here. They'd been unable to bring her out of her coma. An interesting case, if a harrowing one. Impossible to know for sure what caused the original damage. Stacey had told them it was a car accident, but Pál remembers the dent in Deborah's skull: it looked more like something made with a hammer.

'The anoretic constantly tests her body's limits,' Pál explains, sliding, out of bad habit, into an impersonal, third-person style of address. He spends too much time in the lecture hall these days, playing the Grand

Old Man of organic therapy. He flounders a second, experiments with an ingratiating grin and addresses Stacey Chavez directly: 'At least, while you're pushing your body as far as it can go, you're still engaged with it!'

Of course, the person he should really be trying to convince is her companion, this Spanish-looking gentleman in the ice-cream suit who claims to be the man behind the payments Coronation House received for Deborah. What on earth is his business with them, Pál wonders, that he wants Coronation House to treat yet another generation of the same family?

Once again – and is this by design, or by some malign chance? – he has acted too late. From experience, Pál knows just by looking that Stacey is a hopeless case. With the right treatment and surroundings the expert staff of Coronation House might sustain her for a few months more. But the heart is shrivelled beyond saving; the cold is deep in her bones.

Of course, he would not dream of saying such things to her directly. In fact, what can he say to her? What is he trying to say? One would think, at his great age, that Professor Loránt would have learned by now not to trip over his own professional enthusiasms. But it is his nature to be a bumbler in casual conversation. He prefers the lecture hall, and the freedom it gives him to shape a fully rounded idea.

'It is as well you came when you did, I think,' he says to them, euphemistically.

What he means is: Ms Chavez requires twenty-four-hour hospice care. Ms Chavez has passed the Point of No Return. Ms Chavez is dying. He can't disguise a helpless little shudder as he recalls the other ones – not many of them, but enough – who came to him too late.

Unwisely, he seeks to prepare them a little. He explains that the Point of No Return comes when you start thinking: What lies *beyond* the body's limits? *What happens if I let the body go?*

The couple stare at him.

With a sigh, Pál gives in, at last, to the inevitable. 'Well, perhaps I should explain what treatments we offer here,' he says.

The man's interest wakens straight away, while Stacey's sunken eyes burn with suspicion. Both reactions are predictable.

The working day proceeds as normal and by its end, as usual, Professor Emeritus Loránt Pál is left sitting on his hands, waiting for his taxi. Coronation House is profitable enough that he and his senior staff could each have their own driver if they wanted, but Pál, as senior partner, has set a very different tone for his flagship clinic. Not every client of theirs has a five-figure disposable income, nor is every outpatient immortalized in *Hello!*. One journalistic wit from *Vogue*, intuiting how the clinic used money from celebrity treatments to subsidize more interesting cases, compared the running of the place to an old-style grammar school. Pál and his colleagues sometimes stand accused of cherry-picking the most interesting cases. No one, however, can deny their excellent rates of success.

Pál uses the delay to open the day's non-urgent post. On top of the pile sits a large, heavy, brown padded envelope; Pál's thumb scrubs impotently at the flap. Even opening a letter is hard work, now that he is an old man.

After all his efforts, it is yet another 'courtesy' edition of *The Idealist*, this time with a flash on the cover announcing that Miriam has won the Elizabeth Longford Prize. God, is there no stopping this juggernaut?

Pál's feelings about the book are complicated by the fact that he misses and regrets Anthony Burden. He was as keen as anyone to learn what became of his client in the years following their psychological adventure. What he wasn't prepared for was Miriam's snide character assassination; the way she laid the blame for Anthony Burden's later life squarely, if subtly, at his professional door.

Of course he has regrets. What practitioner doesn't? Miriam is hardly the first biographer to judge the actions of the past by the *mouers* of the present. Young Pál leaps off the pages of *The Idealist* like a character out of early Harold Pinter.

401

Having to reassure people about that bloody book is getting to be an irritating obligation. 'Well, *of course* not!' he had exclaimed, that very morning, to the man in the ice-cream suit, that sinister fixer who would not give his name. 'Anyway, what the hell has ECT got to do with eating disorders?' His brain, catching up with his mouth at last, took over the reins: 'Look, what say you both come over to the clinic and meet our staff and see what we actually get up to here? What? Well, no, of course.' Polite laugh through gritted teeth. 'I won't be her actual *physician*. I am an old man now!'

No, no, no, my son, quite right, God forbid you should entrust your dearest to my hands, sullied as they are by over sixty years of practical experience—

Oh, but what's the use? Pál tosses Miriam's book aside. As if he hasn't memorized the thing already.

The great charm of *The Idealist* – or, depending upon your point of view, its great failing – is that Miriam has been unable to ascertain whether Anthony Burden is alive or dead. Her trail of her subject goes cold after Mozambique. Pál doesn't know whether he wants the book and all the attendant fuss to flush the old man from hiding or not. Obviously the mystery is good for sales. It has turned *The Idealist* into a sort of scientific-political *Donald Crowhurst*: the man goes overboard, leaving his writings to tantalize.

Still, can it be much of an Odyssey that ends so abruptly, and without any homecoming?

Pál wonders: if Anthony Burden was alive and they met again, what would they say to each other? Would Anthony blame him for the warp and weirdness of his life? Pál doubts it. After all, Anthony was there. He knew what happened, and why.

What would I say to him? Pál wonders. Would I say sorry? Certainly he has regrets. Of course he has regrets. He is an old man.

What would I say? Like a boy with a scabbed knee, Pál cannot help himself, but has to pick, pick, pick at his wound. He takes up the book and turns with practised ease and heavy heart to chapter five. Miriam writes:

> *By the end of the Second World War, armed service medical personnel were being taught the fundamentals of 'ECT' – primarily as a palliative for schizophrenia – as part of their general training.*
>
> *Accordingly, in the autumn of 1939, the Society sent letters to the Italians Cerletti and Bini, inviting them to present a paper of their choosing to its Drill Hall open programme on Mental Infirmity and the Arts. The exigencies of war prevented the clinicians from accepting.*
>
> *Undeterred, the Society later played host to some lesser-known promulgators of electro-convulsive therapy.*

The cocksucker. For an old man Pál has surprisingly strong lungs. The stupid, dried-up old *vagina.* He never could stand that jumped-up receptionist. Those stinking cigarettes she used to smoke; those dreadful white blouses with the piping on them, like some kind of overgrown sailor-suit.

Lesser known. All right, so Loránt Pál is not the first name you'll hit when you look up the encyclopaedia entry. But what does that signify?

He closes the book and tosses it onto his desk.

He thinks: She'll outlive the lot of us.

In the driveway below his window, a taxi blows its horn.

The exigencies of war prevented them. How can she write like that and not want to fry her own face?

He eases himself down the stairs to the lobby. No lifts, no escalators for him; well into his eighth decade, he daren't let himself seize up for fear he might never get going again. Halfway down, a sudden convulsion seizes his hip. Frightening, insistent, alien – Good God, is this it? Is this how it ends? He imagines the clot in his thigh shattering into greasy brown shards, the shards racing helter-skelter for his heart and brain…

It is only his mobile phone, which he set to vibrate before this morning's staff meeting, then forgot to reset. Cursing, he wheedles the spiteful silver nugget out of his pants. Damned thing has nearly given him a heart attack.

'Hello?' he says.

This is the gauntlet that Pál runs now: the stuff of articles in the *TLS*; graduate papers on the internet; phone calls from 'freelance researchers'; an uncomfortable lunch or two with some gimlet-eyed bastard from the *New Scientist*, 'just to tease out wheat from chaff'.

Isn't there something, well, *unnatural* about all this? That Miriam Miller of all people, so much the Society's servant and retainer, should suddenly acquire her own voice, and at such a late date, suggests to Pál – a keen reader and re-reader of Dumas, *père* and *fils* – some long-nursed mission of revenge. Is it not treacherous, the way she has turned the Society's dull and muddled papers to her own account?

In any event, Miriam's unexpected foray into biography is stirring up no end of trouble for poor Pál. To begin with it had amused him to see how popular her long and tedious opus became. Whatever its stylistic limitations, *The Idealist* had somehow succeeded in awaking the forces of canonization in this nation that forgives failure so much more readily than success.

Now everyone wants a piece of Anthony Burden, the absentee genius, the prophet whose brain was so cruelly fried, who almost invented the computer, the network, the world-wide web; who set down the theoretical principles of virtual reality in the late forties, in a set of school exercise books that he never gave anyone to read.

Pál's own amusement cooled quickly. Watching this fad – this fascination with what might have been – coagulate in backwater after backwater of the public mind has become about as edifying as watching damp spread across a ceiling.

In response to enquiries, Pál has gone over his original notes again and again. He has reported faithfully and discussed candidly everything he can about the case, in so far as it does not transgress his professional code. After all, Anthony Burden may still be alive. His privacy must be respected.

Nobody really wants to know the reasoning behind Pál's treatments, of course. People just want to believe that it wouldn't happen now, to them, to their children. People want to believe that medicine is *getting better*.

Better! And no sooner do we denigrate the therapies of our fathers, their shocks and surgeries, than we start *feeding amphetamines to schoolchildren*, for fuck's sake! *Better*, indeed! As if medicine could ever *get better*!

Whatever you say to them about what medicine really is – where it sits in the realm of social practice – all they want to hear is that you are sorry for what you have done.

Of course, Pál would not treat a man today as he treated poor Burden then. Then was then. Now is now: the AIDS-riddled, porn-infested Now. Why is this so hard to understand? To forgive? Truly, the past is another country, and old men are merely refugees. Go on, tell us to go back where we came from. Spit at us on the street, if you must. Kick us in the head. *I dare you...'*

A polite cough calls Professor Pál to order. The pleasant young man at the other end of the line experiments with a laugh: 'Perhaps I should call back at another time...'

Pál tries to swallow. Lord, what has he said now? He was never able to make much distinction between thinking and speaking, even at the height of his youth and powers. Old age has hardly improved him.

'I am an old man. I am an old man, do you understand? I am old.'

The fact of it is, he is being haunted by his younger self. 'I was a young man then. I was young. Do you understand? Now I am old. I am an *old man*.'

It is the irony of his life that he wasted his youth in pursuit of a certain notoriety. The best marks in his class? An assured future in provincial medicine? What did he care for trivia like that? No, he had to throw all that up, of course, if he was ever to live a real life, following Cerletti and Bini around Europe, snapping at their heels like a crazy little dog...

'I AM AN OLD MAN!'

You can't end a phone call by slamming your mobile satisfyingly onto a surface. He has tried. Instead, obedient to the limitations of the new technology, Pál monkhouses his juddery thumb over to the little red telephone button. Right a bit... left a bit... up a bit... *there.*

Anthony Burden owns a hammer, but he no longer has the strength to wield it. When he raises it to strike – bones augmented, being extended, reach and strength increased, and every inch Tool-Maker Man – the hammer yanks itself out of his grip and goes clattering across the linoleum.

When his wrist has stopped ringing, he raps his bread knife across the coconut, once, twice, three times. The coconut rolls off the kitchen counter onto the floor – and does not crack.

He drops the coconut out of the window of his eighth-floor council flat. Then he goes to the elevator and presses the call button. What possessed him to buy this stupid fruit in the first place?

Classical music is being piped into the elevator to soothe the troubled spirits who tag the interior each week with yet another, seemingly innocuous one-syllable word: CHUTE, PUFF, VIM, DECK. Last week: BULB.

He is an old man, with an old man's mistrust of things and people, but tags and taggers do not rile him, even when the words appear on his front door. They are decorative enough, in a world that would erode all difference. If, as his neighbours claim, the tags mark some gangland boundary – well, then, so much the better: the old geography has not yet lost its power. When this machinic Eden shakes us off finally – the boy thrown from his till – perhaps we will go primitive again and treat this chrome and concrete mess we've made as just another nature.

The lift stops. The door opens. Anthony explores the purlieus of the tower block, hunting his coconut.

It is lying on the grass, beside a cat turd. It is intact.

Burden picks it up and rides it back to his flat, scrubs it clean and places it on the floor. He tries to balance the leg of the kitchen table on top of the coconut. If he sits down hard on the table, the nut will crack. The nut keeps rolling away. He uses tins from the store cupboard to steady the coconut. The tins are not heavy enough to hold the nut in place, and now his back is singing and he has no strength left to lift the table.

He pauses, panting.

The music has followed him from the lift. A passionate piano; swooping strings. He recognizes it, almost. It jags against his ear, then goes swooping off again on a whim of its own. Rachmaninov? No. Tchaikovsky?

Then it comes to him, and all the mistakes of his life bubble up in his heart and he is crying for the first time in forty years. Poor Anthony, at his life's end, with nothing at all to show for his obsession with numbers, birds and bees.

It is the *Budapest Concerto*. The tears run unchecked down his cheeks as he leans against the table, sobbing, for what he has lost of himself. It is the work performed to extraordinary raptures, the night he first met his wife, Rachel, in the basement of the National Gallery.

What is it doing here? Is the lift stuck outside his door? A little recovered, Burden goes and opens his front door. The lift doors are closed, and the light above them indicates that the car is resting at ground level.

Are they piping music through the corridors, now? Are they piping music into our rooms?

Back in his flat, the music grows predatory: diminished fifths for the left hand scratch at the air.

Angrily, he wipes his face – stupid, stupid, ignominious, teary-eyed old age. I would be Lear, he thinks. I would rage rather than cry. But the piano is weeping and he sees himself for what he is: an old man in his bedsit, drizzling tears, and he knows where the music comes from now. It is in his head.

He goes into the kitchenette and picks up the coconut. He sets it down against the doorframe between the kitchenette and his bed-sitting room. He half closes the door, then stands with his back against it. He lets himself fall against the door. He loses his balance and falls to the floor. He cracks his head against the floor.

When he opens his eyes, he finds that something has gone wrong with the light in the room. Things have been sapped of their colour. A narrow, actinic light shines up into the room from sources far below, lighting ceilings and leaving floors in shadow. Streetlights. It is night-time.

Gingerly, he moves one limb at a time. He moves his head. Incredibly, nothing hurts. His head does not smart when he touches it. He sits up without a struggle. A dozen so-so movies replay themselves in his head: touching comic scenes in which a ghost gets up out of its own corpse, yawns and stretches, unaware of what it is. He thinks, I am dying, and he is filled with relief.

A piano, muted and passionate, sobs out a discordant cadence; minor strings put it out of its misery, then go spinning off.

The coconut.

It lies in two neat halves, one on the thin white carpet of the bed-sitting room, one on the black linoleum of the kitchenette. The husks are black, the flesh is white. Most of the coconut milk has run off into the carpet. A little puddle lingers in each scoop. Burden, crouched on the floor like an old cat, lowers his muzzle, and inhales.

Life's sweetness eddies through him, and away.

Weary, Burden staggers to his feet.

He goes to his chair by the window. Tower blocks rise around him, self-similar, peppered with trivial differences. In the street below, the new primitives are gathered: gangs of boys from Turkmenistan, Havant, Albania, Portsea, Nigeria, Hayling Island, Congo, Cosham, China, Horndean, Iraq, Waterlooville, Afghanistan. They smoke cigarettes. They ride their mountain bikes in circles in the road. They shelter mysteriously in doorways, then wander off, as though grazing.

Burden sighs: these are merely the movements of livestock. He would have tribes in bright colours clashing in the streets! But over the years some vital human thing has been invested in this chrome and concrete nature; something that cannot be retrieved. He is glad he has never had children.

A woman in a mackintosh and a white headscarf appears. She is heading for his tower block. She is old, he thinks, watching from his eighth-floor eyrie. She is as old as he is.

The longer he watches her, straining his eyes, the more she resembles a loop cut from a film. It is as though she were super-imposed: there, but not there. Fascinated, his hands white claws, Anthony watches as the woman nears.

The boys spot her. They agitate around her, vaguely threatening. One of them throws a lit cigarette at her back. It strikes her mackintosh. There are sparks.

Oblivious, she keeps walking. She pulls away from them, and they have not the energy to follow her.

She disappears from sight. He imagines her below him, walking the last few yards along the asphalt path. He imagines her climbing up the stairs to the main entrance. She taps in the entry code. She opens the door. She steps inside. He has seen her somewhere before.

He imagines her rising through the building. In his mind she does not take the lift. She climbs the stairs. Though she is as old as him, she climbs the stairs smoothly, mechanically, as though the stairs were a scale in music. Music surrounds her, as it surrounds him. The *Budapest*

Concerto. The walls, the floors, the ceilings of this structure are made of music.

Of music. Suddenly he knows what this is. He knows what is happening. After all these barren years it is happening again.

The woman leaves the stairwell and passes Burden's open door. She pauses, turns; gingerly, she knocks. 'Hello?'

She waits. When there is no answer, she leans into the room. She sees an old man, weeping with frustration.

'Is everything all right in there? Only I saw the door open. I thought maybe—'

'Hello?'

'It's just me. Don't worry. From eight-oh-three. Are you all right?'

He does not turn round. He watches her in the window's reflection. She steps into the monochrome room. She is out of place here, but so is everything else. Everything is disordered. She is no more absurd than the coconut lying broken on the floor, or the bag of prawns he left to defrost in an empty fruit bowl. Stripped of context, every object shines.

She shines. She does not appear to be moving. She appears instead to be expanding. She fills the glass. She fills the room. He feels the air compress as she steps beside him.

She follows his gaze through the window, beyond the towers, out towards the invisible sea.

'Hello,' she says, patient, insistent. 'Hello. It's Mrs Cogan,' she says. 'Kathleen Cogan, just across the hall in eight-oh-three.' He still does not answer, so, gathering her courage, she takes hold of his hand.

The piano swirls. It capers. Anthony imagines temples, aqueducts, arenas, embankments, kiosks, statuary, railways, theatres, formal gardens, vistas, bandstands, playgrounds, fountains, amphitheatres, parades...

Kathleen shifts her hand in his. With a fingertip she traces the scar across his thumb.

'Hello,' he says, at last. 'Hello. Thank you, Mrs Cogan. Thank you, Kathleen, for looking in on me.'

He turns and takes her by the hands. 'I am quite well,' he says.

Outside, lights play over Portsmouth's last remaining marshes. Helicopters belly in the air.

Grade Seven civil servant Noah Hayden, disappointed, exhausted and soon to retire, comes to a nameless mud track between Portsmouth's few undeveloped reed-beds and climbs with trepidation from his car. Above him, police helicopters quarter and dice the landscape with their floodlights, tearing the hot night to shreds.

Today's anonymous tip-off has disturbed them, the way you might disturb a wasps' nest with a stick.

Hayden steps away from the car, testing his footing at every step. There are old moorings among the reed beds. The oldest have long since vanished from view, leaving only holes behind, where the wooden piles have rotted away. The holes have a petrolish sheen over them where nothing grows.

What fills these holes is an essence of rotted wood and the microscopic carcasses of whatever fed on it, mingled with the liquefied remains of whatever fed on the microbes – and on and on, who knows how long a food chain? Though water covers the holes for much of the day, what fills them has very little to do with water. It has the consistency of porridge. Dogs have been known to disappear into them. One or two children. So Noah Hayden treads carefully, and even though there is a line of plastic police tape to follow, it takes him a good five muddy minutes to cross the fifty feet or so to the burial site. The police team, forewarned, are waiting for him.

He is close. Saul Cogan, who was Hayden's room-mate at Cambridge, and his friend. Who stood him a steak sandwich in the Mount Soche Hotel in Blantyre, Malawi. Saul Cogan: gangmaster and entrepreneur; trafficker (this is known, but not yet proven) in men, women and children.

He is blurred. In the files, the tax records, the police tapes, the depositions of foreign governments and the internal inquiries of international aid agencies, nothing adds up. There is no Saul Cogan, or there are too many Saul Cogans. He is nowhere and everywhere, a ghost in the globalized machine.

The helicopters have their lights trained on the work of recovery. The result is a kind of shifting, multi-angled daylight. Shadows leap about as if with a life of their own. Perspectives wheel and collapse. It is impossible to say what are two reed-stalks nearby and what are four reed-stalks far away. The policemen are dressed in identical waders and paper masks, and Hayden finds it no easier to focus on them. How many men are here? How many holes? How many jetties? How many helicopters? Is he going to faint?

The bodies so far recovered are lying in a row to one side of the burial site. In their anaerobic resting place, they have come to little harm. Through the greasy plastic, each horror is still recognisably human.

Why did they call him out here? To what end? He did not have to see this. He passed on the email, didn't he? He made no fuss when they took away his computer. He answered all their questions. He kept his temper when they insisted on interviewing his wife and even his children.

'Who do you think sent this to you?'

Well, really, it hardly took a genius to answer that one.

'Why?'

'Because he can afford to.'

'Meaning?' They were very excited.

'Either Saul Cogan knows you will find him, or he knows that you will not find him.' Hayden could not resist a little smile as he added, 'I suspect the latter.'

No, they did not have to make him see this. It is spite. Punishment for his smile. The Third Floor is spitting blood. All over Europe, the nets are tightening, the gates are swinging shut. The whole northern hemisphere is swaddled in meshes of infra-red and ultrasound. Still, this one man eludes them. Try as they might, they cannot pin him to their card. Saul Cogan, pooping and farting at the new world order, refusing to fit in their file.

At what point, Noah wonders, did I start to like him again?

He heads back to his car. The reeds before him sway and hiss. They tickle his hands, the back of his head, his groin. Reeds spring up between him and the police tape he must follow, back to dry land and his car.

The tides. He imagines the waters encroaching, the little patch of dry land around him shrinking, shrinking. His footing gives way...

Perhaps he has been here before. The place reminds him of the bilharzia-ridden shallows of the Shire River. He has seen the Shire only once, as a functionary for the Department for International Development, when he toured the camps thrown up to accommodate refugees, Mozambican and Malawian, dispossessed by the 2000 floods. The river, which had marked the border between Malawi and Mozambique, was rife with rumours of Saul Cogan and his operations. Diligently, Hayden reported these back to his friends on MI5's Third Floor.

But it is impossible, at such a remove, to imagine what, if anything, they had made of them. Cogan's men stealing food aid. Cogan's men distributing food aid. Cogan, the lender of tractors and ploughs, collector of tithes and tribute.

Saul Cogan, *régulo*.

Yes, this might be any break along the Shire, where starving skeletons of men cook bushmeat on little fires, wary, as easily put to flight as the animals they hunt.

Might two such different places not be one place, after all? Hayling Island, the Shire River, Mozambique, Malawi, Britain – there is no difference. All places are the same place. How close are the walls of the world? Unnerved, he turns around and returns to the place where Saul Cogan has buried his dead.

Up comes another. A helicopter hovers directly overhead, winch spinning, lifting the corpse free of the mudlark's hole. Noah Hayden, craving company, re-enters the circle of men surrounding the hole. The light and sound of the recovery operation are at their fiercest here. Everything shakes in the downwash, vivid in magnesium light.

Up it comes, through the pink-blue skein, through the interface between worlds: the corpse in its plastic wrapper.

Over fifty dead have already been recovered. Men, women, children. Where are they from? What happened, that there are so many?

The black, poisoned water settles. A metallic film forms over the hole. Pastel colours shoot and swirl across the black water, until the black is hidden.

Hayden knows these colours. They belong on maps of the world. Throw a stone into the water, he thinks, and all these pretty colours will disappear.

This is one for his friend.

Throw a stone.

EPILOGUE

Christmas Eve, 1968

Each time their link with Mission Control hissed out, without drama or fanfare, Apollo Eight command module pilot Jim Lovell was reminded of a journey he and his wife once made, driving their car through lonely Florida countryside to Lake Kissimmee: how the radio stations faded out, one by one.

Apollo Eight has not landed on the moon. It has flown by, tantalizingly close, less than seventy miles above the surface: a reconnaissance mission. Altogether, Borman Anders and Lovell have made ten lunar orbits. Each took two hours, and every other hour – when the moon got in the way of their radio communication with Earth – they spent the time in silence, taking it in turns to look out of the window at the Moon's dark side: a secret face no one had ever seen before.

The first thing Jim Lovell noticed about the Moon, seen this close up, was its lack of colour – though why this should have startled him, this self-evident fact, he cannot say.

Ten orbits; twenty hours. All the while they looked at the Moon, their eyes were tuned to the colours of home. Looking on this other world, they saw nothing but shades of grey. For Jim, it was as if the place was holding something back. As though a vital datum were being withheld.

Apollo Eight's purpose is to prove that the dream can be realized: that men can travel this far away from Earth and come home safe again. When they emerged from behind the Moon for the tenth and final time, Mission Control welcomed the crew back on air with more fanfare, relieved for them and proud of themselves. Now, hours later, the Apollo Eight spacecraft is starting its journey home, and it is time for the astronauts to speak to the waiting world.

Jim says to the world, 'The vast loneliness is awe-inspiring.' He tries not to wince.

'It makes you realize just what you have back there on Earth,' he says, wishing he did not have to listen to the words coming out of his mouth.

Lovell's words are weak. His carefully chosen, utterly inadequate words. They lack fuel. They lack thrust. He launches them and watches, helpless, as they struggle and stall and plummet back to the cold, unmeaning ground.

He has been up here often enough – with Aldrin on Gemini Twelve; before that on Gemini Seven, with Frank Borman – to know that he will never find the words. The words do not exist. All he can do, over the course of his career as an astronaut, is to encourage as many people out here as he can. Floating together, they might think up some new words, unearthly words – divine words, even – to do the job he cannot do like this, the TV camera in his face (another Apollo Eight first) and too little time.

'For all the people on Earth,' Bill Anders says, 'the crew of Apollo Eight has a message we would like to send you.'

Frank Borman sticks the camera in Bill's face.

'In the beginning,' says Bill, 'God created the heaven and the earth. And the earth was without form, and void; and darkness was upon the face of the deep. And the Spirit of God moved upon the face of the waters, and God said, Let there be light: and there was light. And God saw the light, that it was good: and God divided the light from the darkness.'

Jim wonders: How did God divide the light? Did he divide it, like Newton, with a prism? There are no colours here. Jim has looked at the far side of the moon, and he cannot imagine that moonlight contains any colour. Pass it through a prism, every band will shine bright white.

Now the camera is in Jim's face. It is his turn. They have practised this. 'And God called the light Day,' says Jim, 'and the darkness he called Night.'

He takes the camera and points it towards Frank Borman. After the broom-cupboard that was Gemini, the Apollo command module feels as spacious as an ordinary room – until you start throwing TV cameras around.

Frank Borman: 'And God said, Let the waters under the heavens be gathered together unto one place, and let the dry land appear: and it was so.'

And were the waters blue? Jim wonders. Was the land grey, or brown, or sandy yellow? Or green with verdigris, or rusty red from all the iron in the earth? He thinks, there is iron in the Moon, but it cannot rust.

It comes to him that nothing is being withheld them here: it is simply that they have come out here with the wrong sort of eyes – eyes that see the colours of earth. They are blind to the colours of space, whatever they may be.

'And God called the dry land Earth; and the gathering together of the waters called he Seas: and God saw that it was good.'

Jim is thinking back to their last lunar orbit: the way the Earth rose over the Moon as they swung clear of the far side.

Earthrise. Above the grey of the lunar surface, the Earth was a colour. The Earth was many colours. Red and yellow in the blue. The different blues of ice and ocean. Green in there somewhere, too. Colour belonged nowhere else but on that ball.

Jim shifts the camera away – it's in the script, they've practised this – up to the window and in, filling the homes of Earth with the first ever television image of their planet. As he does so, a simple thought strikes him: it is only on the Earth that colour makes any sense. Away from Earth, colour means nothing: neither ripeness, nor rot; neither springtime, nor fall. Of course there is no colour out here. There is no one out here to benefit by it.

He thinks: We have no need of colour now. We must let it go. This kaleidoscope, this bauble of our childhood. We must lay it down, Jim thinks, and look about us at the world as it really is. We must press on into the greater world, the real and terrible world we have found beyond our little corner: the world of black and white.

And he finds himself transported back, imprisoned in that jet again, the Banshee, a lonely dot over the Pacific, and his instruments are out and his lights are out and there are no stars and there is no *Shangri-La* and he knows his fuel is low and it is so dark the sea might as well be above him for all he knows. The sea might be above them, beside them and below them all at once, behind them and in front of them.

Rising in a calm black ocean, this bright little bubble of ape hope.

'And from the crew of Apollo Eight,' says Frank Borman, wrapping up transmission, 'we close with goodnight, good luck, a Merry Christmas and God bless all of you – all of you on the good Earth.'

ACKNOWLEDGEMENTS

For their hospitality and good advice I owe many thanks to Patricia and Chris O'Dell, the Barclay family, Susie Tiso, Rhidian Davis, Geoff Ryman and Nancy Hynes.

Without my agent Peter Tallack and my editor Louisa Joyner, this book would be much the poorer.

OXFORD PAPERBACK REFERENCE

The Concise Oxford Dictionary of
Quotations

Oxford
Paperback
Reference

The most authoritative and up-to-date reference books for both students and the general reader.

The Concise
Oxford Dictionary of

Quotations

THIRD EDITION

Edited by
ANGELA PARTINGTON

Oxford   New York

OXFORD UNIVERSITY PRESS

Oxford University Press, Walton Street, Oxford OX2 6DP

Oxford New York
Athens Auckland Bangkok Bogota Bombay
Buenos Aires Calcutta Cape Town Dar es Salaam
Delhi Florence Hong Kong Istanbul Karachi
Kuala Lumpur Madras Madrid Melbourne
Mexico City Nairobi Paris Singapore
Taipei Tokyo Toronto

and associated companies in
Berlin Ibadan

Oxford is a trade mark of Oxford University Press

Selection and arrangement
© Oxford University Press 1993

First Edition published 1964
Second Edition published 1981
Third Edition first published 1993
First issued as an Oxford University Press paperback 1994
Reissued in new covers 1996

British Library Cataloguing in Publication Data
Data available

Library of Congress Cataloging in Publication Data
Data available
ISBN 0-19-280026-4

10 9 8 7 6 5

Printed in Great Britain by
Biddles Ltd
Guildford and King's Lynn

FOREWORD

The *Oxford Dictionary of Quotations*, which first appeared in 1941, is now in its fourth edition, having been considerably expanded and revised in 1992. From this text the new *Concise Oxford Dictionary of Quotations* is drawn, a slimmed-down but decidedly well-toned version of its more substantial parent.

In making our selection, we have given priority to those quotations which we believe to be the best known, or, in the case of longer quotations—such as the big set pieces from Shakespeare—those parts which are the best known. In so doing, our object has been to make room for as many different quotations as possible, thereby enhancing the Dictionary's role as a key reference tool. To achieve this end, it has been necessary to trim selectively. In general, foreign language originals have been retained only for verse or where the words are known, and quoted, in their original language—'*Per ardua ad astra*', '*Plus ça change, plus c'est la même chose*'; occasionally they have been retained where the translation has proved the subject of dispute. Quotations from classical languages, inevitably, have been pruned back quite hard, as have some of the lengthier source notes which distinguish the more leisurely dimensions of the parent volume.

In their place we have inserted a handful of completely new quotations, which we felt made a case for inclusion in a genuinely contemporary work of reference—for instance 'Only the little people pay taxes', an observation which strikes a particularly mordant note in our times; and a further update on an idea originally put forward by Edmund Burke. We used to be 'economical with the truth', courtesy of Sir Robert Armstrong: now we are 'economical with the *actualité*'.

These are small considerations, however, measured against the ground swell of tradition which such a dictionary necessarily represents and reflects. Like its predecessors, the new *Concise Oxford Dictionary of Quotations* is the cumulative effort of many hands, stretching back in a long chain to that first edition of the *Oxford Dictionary of Quotations* in 1941. An acknowledgement of all those involved in the production of the parent text may be found in the 1992 edition; I should not wish to conclude, even so, without acknowledging here the extent to which this volume is indebted to them.

ANGELA PARTINGTON

Oxford, May 1993

Project Team

Managing Editor	Freda Thornton
Editor	Angela Partington
Assistant Editor	Susan Ratcliffe
Research	Melinda Babcock
Data Capture and Validation	Helen McCurdy Patricia Moore Trish Stableford

HOW TO USE THE DICTIONARY

The sequence of entries is by alphabetical order of author, usually by surname but with occasional exceptions such as imperial or royal titles, authors known by a pseudonym ('Saki') or a nickname (Caligula). In general authors' names are given in the form by which they are best known, so we have George Eliot (not Mary Ann Evans), and T. S. Eliot (not Thomas Stearns Eliot). Collections such as Anonymous, Ballads, the Bible, the Book of Common Prayer, the Missal, and so forth, are included in the alphabetical sequence.

Within each author entry, quotations are arranged by alphabetical order of the titles of the works from which they are taken: books, plays, poems. These titles are given in italic type; titles of pieces which comprise part of a published volume or collection (e.g. essays, short stories, poems not published as volumes in their own right) are given in roman type inside inverted commas. For example, *Paradise Lost*, but 'Ode to Autumn'; often the two forms will be found together, e.g. *Cautionary Tales* (1907) 'Matilda'.

Quotations from diaries, letters, speeches, and so on are given in chronological order, and normally follow the literary or other published works quoted; in the case of political figures, for instance, speeches appear first, just as poetry quotations precede those in prose for poets, and vice versa for writers whose principal work was in prose. Quotations cited from secondary sources—biographies and other writers' works—are found towards the end of an author's entry, in alphabetical order of author, editor, or title of work (newspaper, journal, etc.). 'In' preceding a source, such as *The Times*, indicates that the quotation is cited there; where a reference reads, for instance, '*Guardian* 26 February 1972', this indicates the *origin* of the quotation.

All numbers in source references are given in arabic, with the exception of lower-case roman numerals denoting quotations from prefatory matter, whose page numbering is separate from that of the main text. The numbering itself relates to the beginning of the quotation, whether or not it runs on to another stanza or page in the original. Where possible, chapter numbers have been offered for prose works, since pagination varies from one edition to another. In very long prose works with minimal subdivisions, attempts have been made to provide page references to specified editions.

A date in brackets indicates first publication in volume form of the work cited. Unless otherwise stated, the dates thus offered are intended as chronological guides only and do not necessarily indicate the date of the text cited; where the latter is of significance, this has been stated. Where neither date of publication nor of composition is known, an approximate date (e.g. '*c.*1625') indicates the likely date of composition. Where there is a large discrepancy between date of composition (or performance) and of publication, in most cases the former only has been given (e.g. 'written 1725', 'performed 1622').

Spellings have been Anglicized and modernized except in those cases, such as ballads, where this would have been inappropriate; capitalization has been retained only for personifications; with rare exceptions, verse has been aligned with the left hand margin. Italic type has been used for all foreign-language originals.

The Index

Both the keywords and the entries following each keyword, including those in foreign languages, are in strict alphabetical order. Singular and plural nouns (with their possessive forms) are grouped separately: for 'some old lover's ghost' see 'lover'; for 'at lovers' perjuries' see 'lovers'. Variant forms of common words (honey/hunny, luve/love) are grouped under a single heading: 'honey', 'love'.

The references show the author's name, usually in abbreviated form (SHAK/Shakespeare), followed by the page number and the number of the quotation on that page: 183:15 therefore means quotation 15 on page 183.

Quotations

Dannie Abse 1923–

1 I know the colour rose, and it is lovely,
But not when it ripens in a tumour;
And healing greens, leaves and grass, so
springlike,
In limbs that fester are not springlike.
'Pathology of Colours' (1968)

Accius 170–c.86 BC

2 *Oderint, dum metuant.*
Let them hate, so long as they fear.
From *Atreus*, in Seneca *Dialogues* bks. 3–5 *De
Ira* bk. 1, sect. 20, subsect. 4

Dean Acheson 1893–1971

3 Great Britain has lost an empire and has
not yet found a role.
Speech at the Military Academy, West Point,
5 December 1962, in *Vital Speeches* 1 January
1963, p. 163

4 A memorandum is written not to inform
the reader but to protect the writer.
In *Wall Street Journal* 8 September 1977

Lord Acton 1834–1902

5 Power tends to corrupt and absolute power
corrupts absolutely.
Letter to Bishop Mandell Creighton, 3 April
1887, in L. Creighton *Life and Letters of
Mandell Creighton* (1904) vol. 1, ch. 13.
Cf. 249:4

Giuseppe Adami 1878–1946 and
Renato Simoni 1875–1952

6 *Nessun dorma.*
None shall sleep.
Turandot (1926 opera, music by Puccini) *ad
fin.* (after Gozzi's drama, 1762)

Abigail Adams 1744–1818

7 These are times in which a genius would
wish to live. It is not in the still calm of
life, or the repose of a pacific station, that
great characters are formed ... Great
necessities call out great virtues.
Letter to John Quincy Adams, 19 January
1780, in Butterfield et al. (eds.) *The Book of
Abigail and John Adams* (1975) p. 253

Charles Francis Adams 1807–86

8 It would be superfluous in me to point out
to your lordship that this is war.
Dispatch to Earl Russell, 5 September 1863,
in C. F. Adams *Charles Francis Adams* (1900)
ch. 17

Douglas Adams 1952–

9 The Answer to the Great Question Of ...
Life, the Universe and Everything ... [is]
Forty-two.
The Hitch Hiker's Guide to the Galaxy (1979)
ch. 27

Franklin P. Adams 1881–1960

10 Elections are won by men and women
chiefly because most people vote against
somebody rather than for somebody.
Nods and Becks (1944) p. 206. Cf. 139:18

Henry Brooks Adams 1838–1918

11 Politics ... has always been the systematic
organization of hatreds.
Education of Henry Adams (1907) ch. 1

12 Accident counts for much in
companionship as in marriage.
Education of Henry Adams (1907) ch. 4.
Cf. 336:16

13 All experience is an arch to build upon.
Education of Henry Adams (1907) ch. 6

14 A friend in power is a friend lost.
Education of Henry Adams (1907) ch. 7

15 Chaos often breeds life, when order breeds
habit.
The Education of Henry Adams (1907) ch. 16

16 A teacher affects eternity; he can never tell
where his influence stops.
The Education of Henry Adams (1907) ch. 20

17 They know enough who know how to
learn.
The Education of Henry Adams (1907) ch. 21

18 Morality is a private and costly luxury.
The Education of Henry Adams (1907) ch. 22

19 Practical politics consists in ignoring facts.
The Education of Henry Adams (1907) ch. 22

20 Nothing in education is so astonishing as
the amount of ignorance it accumulates in
the form of inert facts.
The Education of Henry Adams (1907) ch. 25

21 No one means all he says, and yet very few
say all they mean, for words are slippery
and thought is viscous.
The Education of Henry Adams (1907) ch. 31

John Adams 1735–1826

22 A government of laws, and not of men.
Boston Gazette (1774) no. 7, 'Novanglus' papers

23 In politics the middle way is none at all.
Letter to Horatio Gates, 23 March 1776, in R.
J. Taylor (ed.) *Papers of John Adams* 3rd series
(1979) vol. 4

1 The happiness of society is the end of government.
Thoughts on Government (1776)

2 Fear is the foundation of most governments.
Thoughts on Government (1776)

3 You and I ought not to die before we have explained ourselves to each other.
Letter to Thomas Jefferson, 15 July 1813, in L. J. Cappon (ed.) *The Adams–Jefferson Letters* (1959) vol. 2

John Quincy Adams 1767–1848

4 Think of your forefathers! Think of your posterity!
Oration at Plymouth 22 December 1802, p. 6

5 *Fiat justitia, pereat coelum* [Let justice be done, though heaven fall]. My toast would be, may our country be always successful, but whether successful or otherwise, always right.
Letter to John Adams, 1 August 1816, in A. Koch and W. Peden (eds.) *Selected Writings of John and John Quincy Adams* (1946) p. 288. Cf. 115:10, 138:24

Samuel Adams 1722–1803

6 What a glorious morning is this.
On hearing gunfire at Lexington, 19 April 1775; in J. K. Hosmer *Samuel Adams* (1886) ch. 19 (traditionally quoted 'What a glorious morning for America')

7 A nation of shop-keepers are very seldom so disinterested.
Oration in Philadelphia 1 August 1776 (of doubtful authenticity). Cf. 237:7, 308:23

Sarah Flower Adams 1805–48

8 Nearer, my God, to thee.
Title of hymn (1841)

Harold Adamson 1906–80

9 Comin' in on a wing and a pray'r.
Title of song (1943)

Joseph Addison 1672–1719

10 He more had pleased us, had he pleased us less.
An Account of the Greatest English Poets (1694); of Cowley

11 And, pleased th' Almighty's orders to perform,
Rides in the whirl-wind, and directs the storm.
The Campaign (1705) l. 291

12 And those who paint 'em truest praise 'em most.
The Campaign (1705) l. 476

13 'Tis not in mortals to command success,
But we'll do more, Sempronius; we'll deserve it.
Cato (1713) act 1, sc. 2, l. 43

14 The pale, unripened beauties of the north.
Cato (1713) act 1, sc. 4, l. 134

15 The woman that deliberates is lost.
Cato (1713) act 4, sc. 1, l. 31

16　　　　　　What pity is it
That we can die but once to serve our country!
Cato (1713) act 4, sc. 1, l. 258

17 Content thyself to be obscurely good.
When vice prevails, and impious men bear sway,
The post of honour is a private station.
Cato (1713) act 4, sc. 1, l. 319

18 Eternity! thou pleasing, dreadful thought!
Cato (1713) act 5, sc. 1, l. 10

19 From hence, let fierce contending nations know
What dire effects from civil discord flow.
Cato (1713) act 5, sc. 1 *ad fin.*

20 There is nothing more requisite in business than dispatch.
The Drummer (1716) act 5, sc. 1

21 A painted meadow, or a purling stream.
Letter from Italy (1704)

22 In all thy humours, whether grave or mellow,
Thou'rt such a touchy, testy, pleasant fellow;
Hast so much wit, and mirth, and spleen about thee,
There is no living with thee, nor without thee.
The Spectator no. 68 (18 May 1711). Cf. 220:7

23 I have often thought, says Sir Roger, it happens very well that Christmas should fall out in the Middle of Winter.
The Spectator no. 269 (8 January 1712)

24 Mirth is like a flash of lightning that breaks through a gloom of clouds, and glitters for a moment: cheerfulness keeps up a kind of day-light in the mind.
The Spectator no. 381 (17 May 1712)

25 The spacious firmament on high,
With all the blue ethereal sky,
And spangled heavens, a shining frame,
Their great Original proclaim.
The Spectator no. 465 (23 August 1712) 'Ode'

26 In Reason's ear they all rejoice,
And utter forth a glorious voice,
For ever singing, as they shine:
'The hand that made us is divine.'
The Spectator no. 465 (23 August 1712) 'Ode'

27 If we may believe our logicians, man is distinguished from all other creatures by the faculty of laughter.
The Spectator no. 494 (26 September 1712)

28 'We are always doing,' says he, 'something for Posterity, but I would fain see Posterity do something for us.'
The Spectator no. 583 (20 August 1714)

George Ade 1866–1944

1 It is no time for mirth and laughter,
The cold, grey dawn of the morning after.
The Sultan of Sulu (1903) act 2, p. 63

Alfred Adler 1870–1937

2 The truth is often a terrible weapon of
aggression. It is possible to lie, and even to
murder, for the truth.
The Problems of Neurosis (1929) ch. 2

Polly Adler 1900–62

3 A house is not a home.
Title of book (1954)

Æ (George William Russell) 1867–1935

4 In ancient shadows and twilights
Where childhood had strayed,
The world's great sorrows were born
And its heroes were made.
In the lost boyhood of Judas
Christ was betrayed.
'Germinal' (1931)

Herbert Agar 1897–1980

5 The truth which makes men free is for the
most part the truth which men prefer not
to hear.
A Time for Greatness (1942) ch. 7

James Agate 1877–1947

6 My mind is not a bed to be made and
re-made.
Ego 6 (1944) 9 June 1943

Agathon b. c.445 BC

7 Even a god cannot change the past.
In Aristotle *Nicomachaean Ethics* bk. 6, 1139b
(literally 'The one thing which even a god
cannot do is to make undone what has been
done')

Alfred Ainger 1837–1904

8 No flowers, by request.
Summarizing the principle of conciseness
for contributors to the *Dictionary of National
Biography*; in *Supplement 1901–1911* (1912)
p. 27

Arthur Campbell Ainger 1841–1919

9 God is working his purpose out as year
succeeds to year;
God is working his purpose out and the
time is drawing near;
Nearer and nearer draws the time, the
time that shall surely be,
When the earth shall be filled with the
glory of God as the waters cover the sea.
'God is working his purpose out' (1894
hymn)

Max Aitken

See LORD BEAVERBROOK

Zoë Akins 1886–1958

10 The Greeks had a word for it.
Title of play (1930)

Alain (Émile-Auguste Chartier) 1868–1951

11 Nothing is more dangerous than an idea,
when you have only one idea.
Propos sur la religion (1938) no. 74

Edward Albee 1928–

12 Who's afraid of Virginia Woolf?
Title of play (1962)

Scipione Alberti

13 *I pensieri stretti ed il viso sciolto* [Secret
thoughts and open countenance] will go
safely over the whole world.
On being asked how to behave in Rome; in
letter from Sir Henry Wotton to Milton,
13 April 1638; prefixed to Milton's *Comus* in
Poems (1645 ed.)

Alcuin c.735–804

14 *Nec audiendi qui solent dicere, Vox populi, vox
Dei, quum tumultuositas vulgi semper insaniae
proxima sit.*
And those people should not be listened to
who keep saying the voice of the people is
the voice of God, since the riotousness of
the crowd is always very close to madness.
Works (1863) vol. 1, Letter 164

Richard Aldington 1892–1962

15 Patriotism is a lively sense of collective
responsibility. Nationalism is a silly cock
crowing on its own dunghill.
The Colonel's Daughter (1931) pt. 1, ch. 6

Brian Aldiss 1925–

16 Keep violence in the mind
Where it belongs.
Barefoot in the Head (1969) 'Charteris' *ad fin.*

Thomas Bailey Aldrich 1836–1907

17 The fair, frail palaces,
The fading alps and archipelagoes,
And great cloud-continents of sunset-seas.
'Miracles' (1874)

Buzz Aldrin 1930–

18 Houston, Tranquillity Base here. The Eagle
has landed.
In *The Times* 21 July 1969, p. 1

Alexander the Great 356–323 BC

1 If I were not Alexander, I would be
Diogenes.
In Plutarch *Parallel Lives* 'Alexander' ch. 14,
sect. 3

Cecil Frances Alexander 1818–95

2 All things bright and beautiful,
All creatures great and small,
All things wise and wonderful,
The Lord God made them all.
'All Things Bright and Beautiful' (1848)

3 The rich man in his castle,
The poor man at his gate,
God made them, high or lowly,
And ordered their estate.
'All Things Bright and Beautiful' (1848)

4 Once in royal David's city
Stood a lowly cattle-shed,
Where a mother laid her baby
In a manger for his bed.
'Once in royal David's city' (1848)

5 I bind unto myself to-day
The strong name of the Trinity,
By invocation of the same
The Three in One and One in Three.
Translation of 'St Patrick's Breastplate' (1889)

6 There is a green hill far away,
Without a city wall,
Where the dear Lord was crucified,
Who died to save us all.
'There is a green hill far away' (1848)

Sir William Alexander, Earl of Stirling *c.*1567–1640

7 The weaker sex, to piety more prone.
'Doomsday' 5th Hour (1637)

Alfonso 'the Wise', King of Castile 1221–84

8 Had I been present at the Creation, I would
have given some useful hints for the better
ordering of the universe.
On studying the Ptolemaic system
(attributed)

Nelson Algren 1909–

9 A walk on the wild side.
Title of novel (1956)

Muhammad Ali (Cassius Clay) 1942–

10 Float like a butterfly, sting like a bee.
Summary of his boxing strategy, in G.
Sullivan *Cassius Clay Story* (1964) ch. 8
(probably originated by Drew 'Bundini'
Brown)

Abbé d'Allainval 1700–53

11 *L'embarras des richesses.*
The embarrassment of riches.
Title of comedy (1726)

Fred Allen 1894–1956

12 Committee—a group of men who
individually can do nothing but as a group
decide that nothing can be done.
Attributed

Woody Allen 1935–

13 [Sex] was the most fun I ever had without
laughing.
Annie Hall (1977 film, with Marshall
Brickman)

14 Don't knock masturbation. It's sex with
someone I love.
Annie Hall (1977 film, with Marshall
Brickman)

15 Is sex dirty? Only if it's done right.
*Everything You Always Wanted to Know about
Sex* (1972 film)

16 It's not that I'm afraid to die. I just don't
want to be there when it happens.
Death (1975) p. 63

17 On bisexuality: It immediately doubles
your chances for a date on Saturday night.
New York Times 1 December 1975, p. 33

William Allingham 1824–89

18 Up the airy mountain,
Down the rushy glen,
We daren't go a-hunting,
For fear of little men.
'The Fairies' (1850)

St Ambrose *c.*339–97

19 *Ubi Petrus, ibi ergo ecclesia.*
Where Peter is, there must be the Church.
'Explanatio psalmi 40' in *Corpus Scriptorum
Ecclesiasticorum Latinorum* (1919) vol. 64

20 When I go to Rome, I fast on Saturday, but
here [Milan] I do not. Do you also follow
the custom of whatever church you attend,
if you do not want to give or receive
scandal.
In *St Augustine: Letters* vol. 1 (tr. Sister W.
Parsons, 1951) 'Letter 54 to Januarius'
(AD *c.*400); usually quoted 'When in Rome,
do as the Romans do'

Leo Amery 1873–1955

21 Speak for England.
To Arthur Greenwood in the House of
Commons, 2 September 1939; *My Political Life*
(1955) vol. 3, p. 324

Fisher Ames 1758–1808

22 A monarchy is a merchantman which sails
well, but will sometimes strike on a rock,
and go to the bottom; whilst a republic is a
raft which would never sink, but then your
feet are always in the water.
Attributed to Ames, speaking in the House
of Representatives, 1795, and quoted by R.
W. Emerson in *Essays* (2nd series, 1844) no. 7

Kingsley Amis 1922–

1 The delusion that there are thousands of young people about who are capable of benefiting from university training, but have somehow failed to find their way there, is ... a necessary component of the expansionist case ... More will mean worse.
    Encounter July 1960

2 His mouth had been used as a latrine by some small creature of the night, and then as its mausoleum.
    Lucky Jim (1953) ch. 6

3 Alun's life was coming to consist more and more exclusively of being told at dictation speed what he knew.
    The Old Devils (1986) ch. 7

4 Outside every fat man there was an even fatter man trying to close in.
    One Fat Englishman (1963) ch. 3. Cf. 106:28, 241:25

5 Should poets bicycle-pump the human heart
    Or squash it flat?
    Man's love is of man's life a thing apart;
    Girls aren't like that.
    'A Bookshop Idyll' (1956). Cf. 86:4

6 Women are really much nicer than men:
    No wonder we like them.
    'A Bookshop Idyll' (1956)

7 Death has got something to be said for it:
    There's no need to get out of bed for it.
    'Delivery Guaranteed' (1979)

8 The women of that ever-fresh terrain,
    The night after tonight.
    'A Dream of Fair Women' (1956)

Anacharsis 6th century BC

9 Written laws are like spider's webs; they will catch, it is true, the weak and poor, but would be torn in pieces by the rich and powerful.
    Plutarch *Parallel Lives* 'Solon' bk. 5, sect. 2. Cf. 319:19

Anatolius 8th century

10 Fierce was the wild billow,
    Dark was the night;
    Oars laboured heavily,
    Foam glimmered white;
    Trembled the mariners,
    Peril was nigh:
    Then said the God of God,
    'Peace! it is I.'
    'Fierce was the wild billow' (tr. J. M. Neale, 1862)

Hans Christian Andersen 1805–75

11 'But the Emperor has nothing on at all!' cried a little child.
    Danish Fairy Legends and Tales (1846) 'The Emperor's New Clothes'

Maxwell Anderson 1888–1959

12 But it's a long, long while
    From May to December;
    And the days grow short
    When you reach September.
    'September Song' (1938 song)

Maxwell Anderson 1888–1959 and Lawrence Stallings 1894–1968

13 What price glory?
    Title of play (1924)

Robert Anderson 1917–

14 Tea and sympathy.
    Title of play (1957)

Bishop Lancelot Andrewes 1555–1626

15 It was no summer progress. A cold coming they had of it, at this time of the year; just, the worst time of the year, to take a journey, and specially a long journey, in. The ways deep, the weather sharp, the days short, the sun farthest off *in solstitio brumali*, the very dead of Winter.
    Of the Nativity (1622) Sermon 15. Cf. 133:21

16 The nearer the Church the further from God.
    Of the Nativity (1622) Sermon 15

Sir Norman Angell 1872–1967

17 The great illusion.
    Title of book (1910) on the futility of war

Anonymous
English

18 An abomination unto the Lord, but a very present help in time of trouble.
    Definition of a lie, an amalgamation of Proverbs 12.22 and Psalms 46.1, often attributed to Adlai Stevenson

19 Adam
    Had 'em.
    On the antiquity of microbes (claimed to be the shortest poem)

20 All human beings are born free and equal in dignity and rights.
    Universal Declaration of Human Rights (1948) article 1

21 All present and correct.
    King's Regulations (Army) Report of the Orderly Sergeant to the Officer of the Day

22 All this buttoning and unbuttoning.
    18th-century suicide note

23 The almighty dollar is the only object of worship.
    Philadelphia Public Ledger 2 December 1836

1 Along the electric wire the message came:
He is not better—he is much the same.
Parodic poem on the illness of the Prince of
Wales, later King Edward VII, in F. H. Gribble
Romance of the Cambridge Colleges (1913) p. 226;
sometimes attributed to Alfred Austin
(1835–1913)

2 Any officer who shall behave in a
scandalous manner, unbecoming the
character of an officer and a gentleman
shall ... be CASHIERED.
Articles of War (1872) 'Disgraceful Conduct'
Article 79; 'conduct unbecoming the
character of an Officer' in Naval Discipline
Act, 10 August 1860, Article 24

3 Appeal from Philip drunk to Philip sober.
Traditional summary of the words of an
unidentified woman in Valerius Maximus
Facta ac Dicta Memorabilia (AD *c.*32) bk. 6, ch. 2

4 Are we downhearted? No!
Expression much taken up by British
soldiers during the First World War.
Cf. 93:24

5 A-roving! A-roving!
Since roving's been my ru-i-n
I'll go no more a-roving
With you fair maid.
'A-roving' (traditional song)

6 A was an apple-pie;
B bit it;
C cut it.
In J. Eachard *Some Observations* (1671) p. 140

7 A bayonet is a weapon with a worker at
each end.
British pacifist slogan (1940)

8 A beast, but a just beast.
Describing Dr Temple, Headmaster of Rugby
School. See F. E. Kitchener *Rugby Memoir of
Archbishop Temple 1857–1869* (1907) ch. 3

9 Be happy while y'er leevin,
For y'er a lang time deid.
Scottish motto for a house. See *Notes and
Queries* 9th series, vol. 8, 7 December 1901,
p. 469

10 Between a rock and a hard place.
Meaning to be in difficulty without a
satisfactory alternative. See *Dialect Notes*
(1921) no. 5, p. 113

11 Bigamy is having one husband too many.
Monogamy is the same.
In Erica Jong *Fear of Flying* (1973) ch. 1
(epigraph)

12 A bigger bang for a buck.
Charles E. Wilson's defence policy, in
Newsweek 22 March 1954

13 Black is beautiful.
Slogan of American civil rights campaigners,
mid-1960s

14 Burn, baby, burn.
Black extremist slogan; Los Angeles riots,
August 1965

15 Careless talk costs lives.
Second World War security slogan

16 The cloud of unknowing.
Title of mystical prose work (14th century)

17 Collapse of Stout Party.
Standard dénouement in Victorian humour.
See R. Pearsall *Collapse of Stout Party* (1975)
introduction

18 For to-night we'll merry be,
To-morrow we'll be sober.
'Come, Landlord, Fill the Flowing Bowl'
(traditional song)

19 Come lasses and lads, get leave of your
dads,
And away to the Maypole hie,
For every he has got him a she,
And the fiddler's standing by.
'Come Lasses and Lads' (traditional song,
*c.*1670)

20 A committee is a group of the unwilling,
chosen from the unfit, to do the
unnecessary.
Various attributions (origin unknown)

21 A Company for carrying on an undertaking
of Great Advantage, but no one to know
what it is.
The South Sea Company Prospectus (1711);
in V. Cowles *The Great Swindle* (1963) ch. 5

22 Conduct ... to the prejudice of good order
and military discipline.
Army Discipline and Regulation Act (1879)
Section 40

23 Coughs and sneezes spread diseases. Trap
the germs in your handkerchief.
Second World War health slogan (1942)

24 Crisis? What Crisis?
Sun headline, 11 January 1979, summarizing
James Callaghan: 'I don't think other people
in the world would share the view [that]
there is mounting chaos'

25 [Death is] nature's way of telling you to
slow down.
Life insurance proverb; in *Newsweek* 25 April
1960, p. 70

26 Do not fold, spindle or mutilate.
Instruction on punched cards (1950s, and in
differing forms from the 1930s)

27 Early one morning, just as the sun was
rising,
I heard a maid sing in the valley below:
'Oh, don't deceive me; Oh, never leave me!
How could you use a poor maiden so?'
'Early One Morning' (traditional song)

28 Earned a precarious living by taking in one
another's washing.
Attributed to Mark Twain by William Morris,
in *The Commonweal* 6 August 1887

29 The eternal triangle.
Book review title, in *Daily Chronicle*
5 December 1907

30 Every country has its own constitution;
ours is absolutism moderated by
assassination.
'An intelligent Russian' quoted in *Political
Sketches of the State of Europe, 1814–1867* (1868)
p. 19

1 Everyman, I will go with thee, and be thy
  guide,
  In thy most need to go by thy side.
  Everyman (*c*.1509–19) l. 522 (spoken by
  Knowledge)

2 Every picture tells a story.
  Advertisement for Doan's Backache Kidney
  Pills (early 1900s)

3 Expletive deleted.
  *Submission of Recorded Presidential Conversations
  ... by President Richard M. Nixon* 30 April 1974,
  appendix 1, p. 2

4 Exterminate ... the treacherous English,
  walk over General French's contemptible
  little army.
  Annexe to British Expeditionary Force
  Routine Orders, 24 September 1914
  (allegedly quoting Kaiser Wilhelm II but
  probably fabricated by the British); in A.
  Ponsonby *Falsehood in Wartime* (1928) ch. 10

5 Faster than a speeding bullet! ... Look! Up
  in the sky! It's a bird! It's a plane! It's
  Superman! Yes, it's Superman! ...
  who—disguised as Clark Kent, mild-
  mannered reporter for a great
  metropolitan newspaper—fights a never
  ending battle for truth, justice and the
  American way!
  Superman (US radio show, 1940 onwards)
  preamble

6 Frankie and Albert were lovers, O Lordy,
  how they could love.
  Swore to be true to each other, true as the
  stars above;
  He was her man, but he done her wrong.
  'Frankie and Albert', in J. Huston *Frankie and
  Johnny* (1930) p. 95 (later better known as
  'Frankie and Johnny')

7 From ghoulies and ghosties and long-
  leggety beasties
  And things that go bump in the night,
  Good Lord, deliver us!
  'The Cornish or West Country Litany', in F. T.
  Nettleinghame *Polperro Proverbs and Others*
  (1926) 'Pokerwork Panels'

8 From shirtsleeves to shirtsleeves in three
  generations.
  In N. M. Butler *True and False Democracy*
  (1907) ch. 2 (often attributed to Andrew
  Carnegie)

9 A gentleman haranguing on the perfection
  of our law, and that it was equally open to
  the poor and the rich, was answered by
  another, 'So is the London Tavern'.
  Tom Paine's Jests (1794) no. 23; also attributed
  to John Horne Tooke (1736–1812) in W.
  Hazlitt *The Spirit of the Age* (1825) 'Mr Horne
  Tooke'. Cf. 222:7

10 Give me a child for the first seven years,
   and you may do what you like with him
   afterwards.
   Attributed as a Jesuit maxim, in *Lean's
   Collectanea* vol. 3 (1903) p. 472

11 God be in my head,
   And in my understanding;
   God be in my eyes,
   And in my looking;
   God be in my mouth,
   And in my speaking;
   God be in my heart,
   And in my thinking;
   God be at my end,
   And at my departing.
   Sarum Missal (11th century)

12 God gave Noah the rainbow sign,
   No more water, the fire next time.
   Home in that Rock (Negro spiritual)

13 God save our gracious king!
   Long live our noble king!
   God save the king!
   'God save the King', attributed to various
   authors, including Henry Carey
   (*c*.1687–1743). See P. Scholes *God save the King*
   (1942). Cf. 170:7

14 Confound their politics,
   Frustrate their knavish tricks.
   'God save the King'

15 Greensleeves was all my joy,
   Greensleeves was my delight,
   Greensleeves was my heart of gold,
   And who but Lady Greensleeves?
   'A new Courtly Sonnet of the Lady
   Greensleeves', in *A Handful of Pleasant Delights*
   (1584)

16 Happy is that city which in time of peace
   thinks of war.
   Inscription found in the armoury of Venice,
   in Robert Burton *Anatomy of Melancholy*
   (1621–51) pt. 2, sect. 3, member 6. Cf. 337:18

17 Here lies a poor woman who always was
   tired,
   For she lived in a place where help wasn't
   hired.
   Her last words on earth were, Dear friends
   I am going
   Where washing ain't done nor sweeping
   nor sewing,
   And everything there is exact to my
   wishes,
   For there they don't eat and there's no
   washing of dishes ...
   Don't mourn for me now, don't mourn for
   me never,
   For I'm going to do nothing for ever and
   ever.
   Epitaph in Bushey churchyard, before 1860;
   destroyed by 1916

18 Here's tae us; wha's like us?
   Gey few, and they're a' deid.
   Scottish toast (probably 19th-century)

19 Hierusalem, my happy home
   When shall I come to thee?
   When shall my sorrows have an end,
   Thy joys when shall I see?
   'Hierusalem' (*c*.1600 hymn)

1 How different, how very different from the home life of our own dear Queen!

Overheard at a performance by Sarah Bernhardt in the role of Cleopatra, in I. S. Cobb *A Laugh a Day* (1924)

2 I don't like the family Stein!
There is Gert, there is Ep, there is Ein.
Gert's writings are punk,
Ep's statues are junk,
Nor can anyone understand Ein.

1920s rhyme, in R. Graves and A. Hodge *The Long Weekend* (1940) ch. 12

3 I feel no pain dear mother now
But oh, I am so dry!
O take me to a brewery
And leave me there to die.

Parody of 'The Collier's Dying Child'. Cf. 138:13

4 If it moves, salute it; if it doesn't move, pick it up; and if you can't pick it up, paint it.

1940s saying, in P. Dickson *The Official Rules* (1978) p. 21

5 I'll hang my harp on a weeping willow-tree,
And may the world go well with thee.

'There is a Tavern in the Town' (traditional song)

6 I'll sing you twelve O.
Green grow the rushes O.
What is your twelve O?
Twelve for the twelve apostles,
Eleven for the eleven who went to heaven,
Ten for the ten commandments,
Nine for the nine bright shiners,
Eight for the eight bold rangers,
Seven for the seven stars in the sky,
Six for the six proud walkers,
Five for the symbol at your door,
Four for the Gospel makers,
Three for the rivals,
Two, two, the lily-white boys,
Clothed all in green O,
One is one and all alone
And ever more shall be so.

'The Dilly Song'

7 I'm armed with more than complete steel—The justice of my quarrel.

Lust's Dominion (1657) act 4, sc. 3 (attributed to Marlowe, though of doubtful authorship)

8 I married my husband for life, not for lunch.

Origin unknown

9 I met wid Napper Tandy, and he took me by the hand,
And he said, 'How's poor ould Ireland, and how does she stand?'
She's the most disthressful country that iver yet was seen,
For they're hangin' men an' women for the wearin' o' the Green.

'The Wearin' o' the Green' (c.1795 ballad)

10 It became necessary to destroy the town to save it.

Statement issued by US Army, referring to Ben Tre in Vietnam; in *New York Times* 8 February 1968

11 It'll play in Peoria.

Catch-phrase of the Nixon administration (early 1970s) meaning 'it will be acceptable to middle America', but originating in a standard music hall joke of the 1930s

12 It's that man again ... ! At the head of a cavalcade of seven black motor cars Hitler swept out of his Berlin Chancellery last night on a mystery journey.

Headline in *Daily Express* 2 May 1939; the acronym ITMA became the title of a BBC radio show, from September 1939

13 Jacques Brel is alive and well and living in Paris.

Title of musical entertainment (1968–72) which triggered numerous imitations

14 John Brown's body lies a mould'ring in the grave,
His soul is marching on.

Song (1861), variously attributed to Charles Sprague Hall, Henry Howard Brownell, Thomas Brigham Bishop, and inspired by the hanging of John Brown, an abolitionist, on 2 December 1859

15 Just when you thought it was safe to go back in the water.

Jaws 2 (1978 film) advertising copy

16 The King over the Water.

Jacobite toast (18th century)

17 King's Moll Reno'd in Wolsey's Home Town.

US newspaper headline on Wallis Simpson's divorce proceedings in Ipswich; in F. Donaldson *Edward VIII* (1974) ch. 7

18 Let's get out of these wet clothes and into a dry Martini.

Line coined in the 1920s by Robert Benchley's press agent and adopted by Mae West in *Every Day's a Holiday* (1937 film)

19 Liberty is always unfinished business.

Title of 36th Annual Report of the American Civil Liberties Union, 1 July 1955–30 June 1956

20 Life is a sexually transmitted disease.

Graffito found on the London Underground, in D. J. Enright (ed.) *Faber Book of Fevers and Frets* (1989) p. 345

21 Little Englanders.

Westminster Gazette 1 August 1895, p. 2 (describing persons opposed to imperialism)

22 Lizzie Borden took an axe
And gave her mother forty whacks;
When she saw what she had done
She gave her father forty-one!

Popular rhyme in circulation after the acquittal of Lizzie Borden, in June 1893, from the charge of murdering her father and stepmother

1 Lloyd George knew my father,
My father knew Lloyd George.
> Sung to the tune of 'Onward, Christian
> Soldiers'; possibly by Tommy Rhys Roberts
> (1910–75)

2 London, thou art the flower of cities all!
Gemme of all joy, jasper of jocunditie.
> 'London' (unknown authorship, previously
> attributed to William Dunbar, c.1465–c.1530)
> l. 16

3 Lousy but loyal.
> East End (London) slogan at George V's
> Jubilee (1935)

4 Love me little, love me long,
Is the burden of my song.
> 'Love me little, love me long' (1569–70)

5 Mademoiselle from Armenteers,
Hasn't been kissed for forty years,
Hinky, dinky, parley-voo.
> Song of the First World War, variously
> attributed to Edward Rowland and to Harry
> Carlton

6 CHILD: Mamma, are Tories born wicked, or
do they grow wicked afterwards?
MOTHER: They are born wicked, and grow
worse.
> In G. W. E. Russell Collections and Recollections
> (1898) ch. 10

7 The man you love to hate.
> Billing for Erich von Stroheim in the film The
> Heart of Humanity (1918)

8 Matthew, Mark, Luke, and John,
The bed be blest that I lie on.
Four angels to my bed,
Four angels round my head,
One to watch, and one to pray,
And two to bear my soul away.
> Traditional (the first two lines in Thomas
> Ady A Candle in the Dark, 1656)

9 The ministry of all the talents.
> Name given ironically to William Grenville's
> coalition of 1806 in G. W. Cooke The History
> of Party (1837) vol. 3, p. 460

10 Miss Buss and Miss Beale
Cupid's darts do not feel.
How different from us,
Miss Beale and Miss Buss.
> Of the Headmistress of the North London
> Collegiate School and the Principal of the
> Ladies' College, Cheltenham (c.1884)

11 Multiplication is vexation,
Division is as bad;
The Rule of Three doth puzzle me,
And Practice drives me mad.
> In Lean's Collectanea vol. 4 (1904) p. 53
> (possibly 16th century)

12 My name is George Nathaniel Curzon,
I am a most superior person.
> The Masque of Balliol (c.1870), in W. G. Hiscock
> The Balliol Rhymes (1939) p. 19. Cf. 32:6,
> 314:1

13 The nature of God is a circle of which the
centre is everywhere and the
circumference is nowhere.
> Said to have been traced to a lost treatise of
> Empedocles; quoted in the Roman de la Rose,
> and by St Bonaventura in Itinerarius Mentis in
> Deum ch. 5 ad fin.

14 The nearest thing to death in life
Is David Patrick Maxwell Fyfe,
Though underneath that gloomy shell
He does himself extremely well.
> In E. Grierson Confessions of a Country
> Magistrate (1972) p. 35 (current on the
> Northern circuit in the late 1930s)

15 Nil carborundum illegitimi.
> Cod Latin for 'Don't let the bastards grind
> you down', in circulation during the Second
> World War, though possibly of earlier
> origin; often quoted 'nil carborundum' or
> 'illegitimi non carborundum'

16 The noise, my dear! And the people!
> Of the retreat from Dunkirk, May 1940. See
> A. Rhodes Sword of Bone (1942) ch. 22 ad fin.

17 No more Latin, no more French,
No more sitting on a hard board bench.
No more beetles in my tea
Making googly eyes at me;
No more spiders in my bath
Trying hard to make me laugh.
> Children's rhyme for the end of school term,
> in Iona and Peter Opie Lore and Language of
> Schoolchildren (1959) ch. 13 (variants include
> 'No more Latin, no more Greek, / No more
> cares to make me squeak')

18 Nostalgia isn't what it used to be.
> Graffito (taken as title of book by Simone
> Signoret, 1978)

19 Not so much a programme, more a way of
life!
> Title of BBC television series, 1964

20 Now I lay me down to sleep;
I pray the Lord my soul to keep.
If I should die before I wake,
I pray the Lord my soul to take.
> First printed in a late edition of the New
> England Primer (1781)

21 O Death, where is thy sting-a-ling-a-ling,
O grave, thy victory?
The bells of Hell go ting-a-ling-a-ling
For you but not for me.
> 'For You But Not For Me', in S. Louis Guiraud
> (ed.) Songs That Won the War (1930).
> Cf. 55:22

22 O God, if there be a God, save my soul, if I
have a soul!
> Prayer of a common soldier before the battle
> of Blenheim (1704); in Notes and Queries
> vol. 173, no. 15 (9 October 1937) p. 264

23 Once again we stop the mighty roar of
London's traffic.
> In Town Tonight (BBC radio series, 1933–60)
> preamble

1 One Cartwright brought a Slave from Russia, and would scourge him, for which he was questioned: and it was resolved, That England was too pure an Air for Slaves to breathe in.

'In the 11th of Elizabeth' (1568–9); in J. Rushworth *Historical Collections* (1680–1722) vol. 2, p. 468. Cf. 110:7

2 O ye'll tak' the high road, and I'll tak' the low road,
And I'll be in Scotland afore ye,
But me and my true love will never meet again,
On the bonnie, bonnie banks o' Loch Lomon'.

'The Bonnie Banks of Loch Lomon' (traditional song)

3 A place within the meaning of the Act.

Usually taken to be a reference to the Betting Act 1853, sect. 2, which banned off-course betting on horse-races

4 Please do not shoot the pianist. He is doing his best.

Printed notice in a dancing saloon, in Oscar Wilde *Impressions of America* 'Leadville' (c.1882–3)

5 Please to remember the Fifth of November, Gunpowder Treason and Plot.

Traditional rhyme (1605)

6 Power to the people.

Slogan of the Black Panther movement, from c.1968

7 The [*or* A] quick brown fox jumps over the lazy dog.

Used by keyboarders to ensure that all letters of the alphabet are functioning. See R. H. Templeton Jr. *The Quick Brown Fox* (1945) introduction

8 The rabbit has a charming face:
Its private life is a disgrace.
I really dare not name to you
The awful things that rabbits do.

'The Rabbit', in *The Week-End Book* (1925) p. 171

9 See the happy moron,
He doesn't give a damn,
I wish I were a moron,
My God! perhaps I am!

Eugenics Review July 1929

10 Seven wealthy towns contend for HOMER dead
Through which the living HOMER begged his bread.

Epilogue to *Aesop at Tunbridge* By No Person of Quality (1698). Cf. 168:9

11 She was poor but she was honest
Victim of a rich man's game.
First he loved her, then he left her,
And she lost her maiden name ...
It's the same the whole world over,
It's the poor wot gets the blame,
It's the rich wot gets the gravy.
Ain't it all a bleedin' shame?

'She was Poor but she was Honest' (sung by British soldiers in the First World War)

12 The singer not the song.

From a West Indian calypso; title of a novel (1959) by Audrey Erskine Lindop

13 Some talk of Alexander, and some of Hercules;
Of Hector and Lysander, and such great names as these;
But of all the world's brave heroes, there's none that can compare
With a tow, row, row, row, row, row, for the British Grenadier.

'The British Grenadiers' (traditional song)

14 So much chewing gum for the eyes.

Small boy's definition of certain television programmes, in J. B. Simpson *Best Quotes* (1957)

15 Sticks nix hick pix.

Headline on the lack of enthusiasm for farm dramas among rural populations, in *Variety* 17 July 1935

16 Sumer is icumen in,
Lhude sing cuccu!

'Cuckoo Song' (c.1250)

17 Swing low, sweet chariot—
Comin' for to carry me home;
I looked over Jordan and what did I see?
A band of angels comin' after me—
Comin' for to carry me home.

Negro spiritual (c.1850)

18 There is a lady sweet and kind,
Was never face so pleased my mind;
I did but see her passing by,
And yet I love her till I die.

Latin verse by Thomas Naogeorgus, Englished by Barnabe Googe and printed in 1570 (sometimes attributed to Thomas Forde)

19 There is one thing stronger than all the armies in the world; and that is an idea whose time has come.

Nation 15 April 1943. Cf. 176:2

20 There is so much good in the worst of us,
And so much bad in the best of us,
That it hardly becomes any of us
To talk about the rest of us.

Attributed, among others, to E. W. Hoch (1849–1945) on the grounds of it having appeared in his Kansas publication, the *Marion Record*, though in fact disclaimed by him ('behooves' sometimes substituted for 'becomes')

21 There's no such thing as a free lunch.

Colloquial axiom in US economics from the 1960s, much associated with Milton Friedman; first found in printed form in Robert Heinlein *The Moon is a Harsh Mistress* (1966) ch. 11

22 There was a young lady of Riga
Who went for a ride on a tiger;
They returned from the ride
With the lady inside,
And a smile on the face of the tiger.

In R. L. Green (ed.) *A Century of Humorous Verse* (1959)

1 They come as a boon and a blessing to
men,
The Pickwick, the Owl, and the Waverley
pen.

Advertisement by MacNiven and H. Cameron
Ltd. (c.1920); almost certainly inspired by J. C.
Prince 'The Pen and the Press' in E. W. Cole
(ed.) *The Thousand Best Poems in the World*
(1891): 'It came as a boon and a blessing to
men, / The peaceful, the pure, the victorious
PEN!'

2 Thirty days hath September,
April, June, and November;
All the rest have thirty-one,
Excepting February alone,
And that has twenty-eight days clear
And twenty-nine in each leap year.

Stevins MS (c.1555)

3 This is a rotten argument, but it should be
good enough for their lordships on a hot
summer afternoon.

Annotation to a ministerial brief, said to
have been read out inadvertently in the
House of Lords; in Lord Home *The Way the
Wind Blows* (1976) p. 204

4 Though I yield to no one in my admiration
for Mr Coolidge, I do wish he did not look
as if he had been weaned on a pickle.

Anonymous remark, in Alice Roosevelt
Longworth *Crowded Hours* (1933) ch. 21

5 Thought shall be the harder, heart the
keener, courage the greater, as our might
lessens.

The Battle of Maldon (c.1000, tr. R. K. Gordon,
1926)

6 Three acres and a cow.

Associated with Jesse Collings and his land
reform propaganda (*Hansard* 26 January
1886, col. 444), although used earlier by
Joseph Chamberlain in a speech at Evesham
(*The Times* 17 November 1885, p. 10), by
which time it was already proverbial

7 To err is human but to really foul things
up requires a computer.

Farmers' Almanac for 1978 'Capsules of
Wisdom'

8 Too small to live in and too large to hang
on a watch-chain.

Chiswick House described by a guest, in C.
Roberts *And so to Bath* (1940) ch. 4

9 Vote early and vote often.

US election slogan, already current when
quoted by William Porcher Miles in the
House of Representatives; *Congressional Globe*
31 March 1858, appendix, p. 286

10 Wall St lays an egg.

Crash headline, *Variety* 30 October 1929

11 War will cease when men refuse to fight.

Pacifist slogan, from c.1936 (often quoted
'Wars will cease . . . ')

12 We hold these truths to be self-evident,
that all men are created equal, that they
are endowed by their Creator with certain
unalienable rights, that among these are
life, liberty and the pursuit of happiness.

American Declaration of Independence,
4 July 1776. Cf. 180:18

13 We're here
Because
We're here.

Sung to the tune of 'Auld Lang Syne', in J.
Brophy and E. Partridge *Songs and Slang of the
British Soldier 1914–18* (1930)

14 Were you there when they crucified my
Lord?

Title of Negro spiritual (1865)

15 We shall not be moved.

Title of labour and civil rights song (1931)
adapted from an earlier gospel hymn

16 We shall overcome.

Title of song, originating from before the
American Civil War, adapted as a Baptist
hymn ('I'll Overcome Some Day', 1901) by C.
A. Tindley; revived in 1946 as a protest song
by black tobacco workers, and in 1963
during the black Civil Rights Campaign

17 We want eight, and we won't wait.

On the construction of Dreadnoughts. See
George Wyndham's speech in *The Times*
29 March 1909

18 Western wind, when will thou blow,
The small rain down can rain?
Christ, if my love were in my arms
And I in my bed again!

'Western Wind' (16th century)

19 When Israel was in Egypt land,
Let my people go,
Oppressed so hard they could not stand,
Let my people go.
*Go down, Moses,
Way-down in Egypt land,
Tell old Pharaoh
To let my people go.*

'Go Down, Moses' (Negro spiritual). Cf. 39:34

20 Who dares wins.

Motto of the British Special Air Service
regiment, from 1942

21 Whose finger do you want on the trigger?

Daily Mirror 21 September 1951 (referring to
the atom bomb)

22 A willing foe and sea room.

Naval toast in the time of Nelson, in W. N. T.
Beckett *A Few Naval Customs, Expressions,
Traditions, and Superstitions* (1931) 'Customs'

23 With a heart of furious fancies,
Whereof I am commander;
With a burning spear,
And a horse of air,
To the wilderness I wander.

'Tom o' Bedlam'

24 Yankee Doodle came to town
Riding on a pony;
Stuck a feather in his cap
And called it Macaroni.

'Yankee Doodle' (song, 1755 or earlier)

1 You should make a point of trying every experience once, excepting incest and folk-dancing.

> Sir Arnold Bax (1883–1953), quoting 'a sympathetic Scot' in *Farewell My Youth* (1943) p. 17

French

2 *Ça ira.*

Things will work out.

> Refrain of 'Carillon national', popular song of the French Revolution (c. July 1790). See W. Doyle *Oxford History of the French Revolution* (1989) p. 129

3 *Cet animal est très méchant,*
Quand on l'attaque il se défend.

This animal is very bad; when attacked it defends itself.

> 'La Ménagerie' (1868 song) by 'Théodore P. K.'

4 *Chevalier sans peur et sans reproche.*

Fearless, blameless knight.

> Description in contemporary chronicles of Pierre Bayard (1476–1524)

5 *Honi soit qui mal y pense.*

Evil be to him who evil thinks.

> Motto of the Order of the Garter, originated by Edward III, probably on 23 April 1348 or 1349

6 *Ils ne passeront pas.*

They shall not pass.

> Slogan of the French army at the defence of Verdun 1916; variously attributed to Marshal Pétain and to General Robert Nivelle, and taken up by the Republicans in the Spanish Civil War. Cf. 178:2

7 *Je suis Marxiste—tendance Groucho.*

I am a Marxist—of the Groucho tendency.

> Slogan found at Nanterre in Paris, 1968

8 *Il ne faut pas être plus royaliste que le roi.*
Cette phrase n'est pas du moment; elle fut inventée sous Louis XVI: elle enchaîna les mains des fidèles, pour ne laisser libre que le bras du bourreau.

You mustn't be more of a royalist than the king. This expression is not new; it was coined under Louis XVI: it chained up the hands of the loyal, leaving free only the arm of the hangman.

> Chateaubriand *De la monarchie selon la charte* (1816) ch. 81

9 *Laissez-nous-faire.*

Allow us to do [it].

> Dating from c.1664, in *Journal Oeconomique* Paris, April 1751: 'M. Colbert assembled several deputies of commerce at his house to ask what could be done for commerce; the most rational and the least flattering among them answered him in one word: "Laissez-nous-faire"'. Cf. 15:6

10 *Le monde est plein de fous, et qui n'en veut pas voir*
Doit se tenir tout seul, et casser son miroir.

The world is full of fools, and he who would not see it should live alone and smash his mirror.

> Adaptation of an original form attributed to Claude Le Petit (1640–65) in *Discours satiriques* (1686)

11 *Liberté! Égalité! Fraternité!*

Freedom! Equality! Brotherhood!

> Motto of the French Revolution, but of earlier origin. The Club des Cordeliers passed a motion (30 June 1793) 'that owners should be urged to paint on the front of their houses, in large letters, the words: Unity, indivisibility of the Republic, Liberty, Equality, Fraternity or death'; in *Journal de Paris* no. 182 (from 1795 the words 'ou la mort [or death]' were dropped). Cf. 94:5

12 *L'ordre règne à Varsovie.*

Order reigns in Warsaw.

> After the brutal suppression of an uprising, the newspaper *Moniteur* reported (16 September 1831) 'Order and calm are completely restored in the capital'; on the same day Count Sebastiani, minister of foreign affairs, declared: 'Peace reigns in Warsaw'

13 *Nous n'irons plus aux bois, les lauriers sont coupés.*

We'll to the woods no more,
The laurels all are cut.

> Nursery rhyme, quoted by Théodore de Banville in *Les Cariatides, les stalactites* (1842–6); translated by A. E. Housman in *Last Poems* (1922) introductory

14 *Revenons à ces moutons.*

Let us get back to these sheep [i.e. 'Let us get back to the subject'].

> *Maistre Pierre Pathelin* (c.1470) l. 1191 (often quoted 'Retournons à nos moutons [Let us return to our sheep]')

15 *Taisez-vous! Méfiez-vous! Les oreilles ennemies vous écoutent.*

Keep your mouth shut! Be on your guard! Enemy ears are listening to you.

> Official notice in France, 1915

16 *Toujours perdrix!*

Always partridge!

> Attributed to a confessor of Henri IV, who was served nothing but partridge, having rebuked the king for his sexual liaisons; in G. Büchmann *Geflügelte Worte* (1874 ed.) p. 240

17 *Tout passe, tout casse, tout lasse.*

Everything passes, everything perishes, everything palls.

> C. Cahier *Quelques six mille proverbes* (1856) no. 1718

German

1 *Arbeit macht frei.*
Work liberates.
> Words inscribed on the gates of Dachau concentration camp, 1933, and subsequently on those of Auschwitz

2 *Ein Reich, ein Volk, ein Führer.*
One realm, one people, one leader.
> Nazi Party slogan, early 1930s

3 *Kommt der Krieg ins Land*
Gibt's Lügen wie Sand.
When war enters a country
It produces lies like sand.
> Epigraph to A. Ponsonby *Falsehood in Wartime* (1928) p. 11. Cf. 182:12

4 *Vorsprung durch Technik.*
Progress through technology.
> Audi motors (advertising slogan, from 1986)

Greek

5 Know thyself.
> Inscribed on the temple of Apollo at Delphi; in *Protagoras* 343 b, Plato ascribes the saying to the Seven Wise Men

6 Let no one enter who does not know geometry [mathematics].
> Inscription on Plato's door, probably at the Academy at Athens, in Elias Philosophus *In Aristotelis Categorias Commentaria* p. 118, l. 18; in A. Busse (ed.) *Commentaria in Aristotelem Graeca* (1900) vol. 18, pt. 1

7 Nothing in excess.
> Inscribed on the temple of Apollo at Delphi, and variously ascribed to the Seven Wise Men

8 Whenever God prepares evil for a man, He first damages his mind, with which he deliberates.
> Scholiastic annotation to Sophocles' *Antigone* l. 622. Cf. 129:11

Latin

9 *Adeste, fideles.*
O come, all ye faithful.
> 'Adeste, fideles' (*c*.1743); based on F. Oakeley's translation (1841)

10 *Venite, adoremus Dominum.*
O come, let us adore him, Christ the Lord!
> 'Adeste, fideles'

11 *Ad majorem Dei gloriam.*
To the greater glory of God.
> Motto of the Society of Jesus

12 *Ave Caesar, morituri te salutant.*
Hail Caesar, those who are about to die salute you.
> Gladiators saluting the Roman Emperor. See Suetonius *Lives of the Caesars* 'Claudius' ch. 21

13 *Ave Maria, gratia plena, Dominus tecum.*
Hail Mary, full of grace, the Lord is with thee.
> 'Ave Maria', also known as 'The Angelic Salutation' (11th century)

14 *Ave verum corpus,*
natum ex Maria Virgine.
Hail the true body, born of the Virgin Mary.
> Eucharistic hymn (probably 14th century)

15 *Et in Arcadia ego.*
And I too in Arcadia.
> Tomb inscription, of disputed meaning, often depicted in classical paintings

16 *Gaudeamus igitur,*
Juvenes dum sumus
Post jucundam juventutem,
Post molestam senectutem,
Nos habebit humus.
Let us then rejoice,
While we are young.
After the pleasures of youth
And the burdens of old age
Earth will hold us.
> Medieval students' song (18th-century revision of 13th-century original)

17 *Nemo me impune lacessit.*
No one provokes me with impunity.
> Motto of the Crown of Scotland and of all Scottish regiments

18 *Per ardua ad astra.*
Through struggle to the stars.
> Motto of the Mulvany family, as translated by Rider Haggard in *The People of the Mist* (1894) ch. 1 (motto of the R.A.F.)

19 *Post coitum omne animal triste.*
After coition every animal is sad.
> Post-classical saying

20 *Quidquid agis, prudenter agas, et respice finem.*
Whatever you do, do cautiously, and look to the end.
> *Gesta Romanorum* no. 103

21 *Salve, regina, mater misericordiae,*
Vita, dulcedo et spes nostra, salve!
Hail holy queen, mother of mercy, hail our life, our sweetness, and our hope!
> Attributed to various 11th-century authors. See *Analecta Hymnica* vol. 50 (1907) p. 318

22 *Sic transit gloria mundi.*
Thus passes the glory of the world.
> Said at the coronation of a new Pope, while flax is burned; used at the coronation of Alexander V in Pisa, 7 July 1409, but earlier in origin. Cf. 329:28

23 *Si monumentum requiris, circumspice.*
If you seek a monument, gaze around.
> Inscription in St Paul's Cathedral, London, attributed to the son of Sir Christopher Wren, its architect

1 *Te Deum laudamus: Te Dominum confitemur.*
We praise thee, God: we own thee Lord.
'Te Deum'; hymn traditionally attributed to
St Ambrose and St Augustine in AD 387,
though more recently to St Niceta (d. *c*.414).
Cf. 63:18

2 *Tempora mutantur, et nos mutamur in illis.*
Times change, and we change with them.
In William Harrison *Description of Britain*
(1577) bk. 3, ch. 3; attributed to Emperor
Lothar I (795–855) in the form '*Omnia
mutantur* ... [All things change ...]'

3 *Vox et praeterea nihil.*
A voice and nothing more.
Describing a nightingale. See Plutarch
Moralia sect. 233a, no. 15

Jean Anouilh 1910–87

4 God is on everyone's side ... And, in the
last analysis, he is on the side of those
with plenty of money and large armies.
L'Alouette (1953) p. 120. Cf. 83:20, 340:23

5 The spring is wound up tight. It will uncoil
of itself. That is what is so convenient in
tragedy. The least little turn of the wrist
will do the job. Anything will set it going.
Antigone (1944, tr. L. Galantiere, 1957) p. 34

6 Tragedy is clean, it is restful, it is flawless.
Antigone (1944, tr. L. Galantiere, 1957) p. 34

7 There is love of course. And then there's
life, its enemy.
Ardèle (1949) p. 8

8 You know very well that love is, above all,
the gift of oneself!
Ardèle (1949) p. 79

9 Dying is nothing. So start by living. It's less
fun and it lasts longer.
Roméo et Jeannette (1946) act 3

F. Anstey 1856–1934

10 Drastic measures is Latin for a whopping.
Vice Versa (1882) ch. 7

Guillaume Apollinaire 1880–1918

11 *Les souvenirs sont cors de chasse
Dont meurt le bruit parmi le vent.*
Memories are hunting horns
Whose sound dies on the wind.
'Cors de Chasse' (1912)

12 *Sous le pont Mirabeau coule la Seine.
Et nos amours, faut-il qu'il m'en souvienne?
La joie venait toujours après la peine.*
Under Mirabeau Bridge flows the Seine.
And our loves, must I remember them?
Joy always came after pain.
'Le Pont Mirabeau' (1912)

13 *On ne peut pas porter partout le cadavre de son
père.*
One can't carry one's father's corpse about
everywhere.
In *Les peintres cubistes* (1965) 'Méditations
esthétiques: Sur la peinture' pt. 1

Thomas Gold Appleton 1812–84

14 A Boston man is the east wind made flesh.
Attributed

15 Good Americans, when they die, go to
Paris.
In Oliver Wendell Holmes *The Autocrat of the
Breakfast-Table* (1858) ch. 6

Arabian Nights

16 Who will change old lamps for new ones?
... new lamps for old ones?
'The History of Aladdin'

17 Open Sesame!
'The History of Ali Baba'

William Arabin 1773–1841

18 If ever there was a case of clearer evidence
than this of persons acting together, this
case is that case.
In H. B. Churchill *Arabiniana* (1843) p. 9

19 They will steal the very teeth out of your
mouth as you walk through the streets. *I
know it from experience.*
On the citizens of Uxbridge, in Sir W.
Ballantine *Some Experiences of a Barrister's Life*
(1882) vol. 1, ch. 6

20 Prisoner, God has given you good abilities,
instead of which you go about the country
stealing ducks.
See Sir Frederick Pollock *Essays in the Law*
(1922) p. 298, where attribution to a Revd Mr
Alderson is preferred

Louis Aragon 1897–1982

21 *Ô mois des floraisons mois des métamorphoses
Mai qui fut sans nuage et Juin poignardé
Je n'oublierai jamais les lilas ni les roses
Ni ceux que le printemps dans ses plis a gardé.*
O month of flowerings, month of
metamorphoses,
May without cloud and June that was
stabbed,
I shall never forget the lilac and the roses
Nor those whom spring has kept in its
folds.
'Les lilas et les roses' (1940)

Dr Arbuthnot 1667–1735

22 Law is a bottomless pit.
The History of John Bull (1712) title of first
pamphlet

23 Hame's hame, be it never so hamely.
The History of John Bull (1712) 'John Bull Still
in His Senses' ch. 3

24 Curle (who is one of the new terrors of
Death) has been writing letters to every
body for memoirs of his life.
Letter to Jonathan Swift, 13 January 1733, in
H. Williams (ed.) *Correspondence of Jonathan
Swift* vol. 4 (1965). Cf. 212:19, 347:2

Archilochus 7th century BC

1 The fox knows many things—the hedgehog
one *big* one.
E. Diehl (ed.) *Anthologia Lyrica Graeca* (3rd ed.,
1949–52) vol. 1, p. 241, no. 103. Cf. 36:4

Archimedes c.287–212 BC

2 *Eureka!*
I've got it!
In Vitruvius Pollio *De Architectura* bk. 9,
preface, sect. 10

3 Give me but one firm spot on which to
stand, and I will move the earth.
On the action of a lever, in Pappus *Synagoge*
bk. 8, proposition 10, sect. 11

Hannah Arendt 1906–75

4 The fearsome, word-and-thought-defying
banality of evil.
Eichmann in Jerusalem (1963) ch. 15

5 The most radical revolutionary will become
a conservative on the day after the
revolution.
New Yorker 12 September 1970, p. 88

Marquis d'Argenson 1694–1757

6 *Laisser-faire.*
No interference.
Mémoires et Journal Inédit (1858 ed.) vol. 5,
p. 364. Cf. 12:9

Comte d'Argenson 1696–1764

7 DESFONTAINES: I must live.
D'ARGENSON: I do not see the necessity.
On Desfontaines having produced a
pamphlet satirizing D'Argenson, his
benefactor. See Voltaire *Alzire* (1736)
'Discours Préliminaire' in *Oeuvres Complètes
Théâtre* vol. 2 (1877) p. 381

Ludovico Ariosto 1474–1533

8 *Natura il fece, e poi roppe la stampa.*
Nature made him, and then broke the
mould.
Orlando Furioso (1532) canto 10, st. 84

Aristophanes c.450–c.385 BC

9 How about 'Cloudcuckooland'?
Naming the capital city of the Birds in *The
Birds* (414 BC) l. 819

10 This Second Logic then, I mean the Worse
one,
They teach to talk unjustly, and—prevail.
The Clouds (423 BC) l. 113 (tr. B. Rogers).
Cf. 228:23

11 Brekekekex koax koax.
Cry of the Frogs in *The Frogs* (405 BC) l. 209
and *passim*

Aristotle 384–322 BC

12 Every art and every investigation, and
likewise every practical pursuit or
undertaking, seems to aim at some good:
hence it has been well said that the Good
is That at which all things aim.
Nicomachean Ethics bk. 1, 1094a 1–3

13 Therefore, the good of man must be the
end [i.e. objective] of the science of politics.
Nicomachean Ethics bk. 1, 1094b 6–7

14 We make war that we may live in peace.
Nicomachean Ethics bk. 10, 1177b 5–6 (tr. M.
Ostwald). Cf. 337:18

15 Tragedy is thus a representation of an
action that is worth serious attention,
complete in itself and of some amplitude
... by means of pity and fear bringing
about the purgation of such emotions.
Poetics ch. 6, 1449b

16 So poetry is something more philosophical
and more worthy of serious attention than
history.
Poetics ch. 9, 1451b

17 Probable impossibilities are to be preferred
to improbable possibilities.
Poetics ch. 24, 1460a

18 Man is by nature a political animal.
Politics bk. 1, 1253a

19 He who is unable to live in society, or who
has no need because he is sufficient for
himself, must be either a beast or a god.
Politics bk. 1, 1253a

20 Nature does nothing without purpose or
uselessly.
Politics bk. 1, 1256b

21 When he was asked 'What is a friend?' he
said 'One soul inhabiting two bodies.'
In Diogenes Laertius *Lives of Philosophers* bk. 5,
sect. 20

22 *Amicus Plato, sed magis amica veritas.*
Plato is dear to me, but dearer still is
truth.
Latin translation of a Greek original ascribed
to Aristotle

Lewis Addison Armistead
1817–63

23 Give them the cold steel, boys!
Attributed during the American Civil War,
1863

Harry Armstrong 1879–1951

24 There's an old mill by the stream, Nellie
Dean,
Where we used to sit and dream, Nellie
Dean.
And the waters as they flow
Seem to murmur sweet and low,
'You're my heart's desire; I love you, Nellie
Dean.'
'Nellie Dean' (1905 song)

Dr John Armstrong 1709–79

1   Much had he read,
Much more had seen; he studied from the
     life,
And in th'original perused mankind.
     The Art of Preserving Health (1744) bk. 4, l. 231

2 'Tis not too late to-morrow to be brave.
     The Art of Preserving Health (1744) bk. 4, l. 460

Louis Armstrong 1901–71

3 All music is folk music, I ain't never heard
no horse sing a song.
     In *New York Times* 7 July 1971, p. 41

4 If you still have to ask … shame on you.
     When asked what jazz is, in Max Jones et al.
     Salute to Satchmo (1970) p. 25 (sometimes
     quoted 'Man, if you gotta ask you'll never
     know')

Neil Armstrong 1930–

5 That's one small step for a man, one giant
leap for mankind.
     Landing on the moon; In *New York Times*
     21 July 1969, p. 5 (interference in
     transmission obliterated 'a')

Sir Robert Armstrong 1927–

6 It contains a misleading impression, not a
lie. It was being economical with the truth.
     During the 'Spycatcher' trial, Supreme
     Court, New South Wales, in *Daily Telegraph*
     19 November 1986. See Edmund Burke *Two
     letters on Proposals for Peace* (1796) pt. 1, p. 137:
     'Falsehood and delusion are allowed in no
     case whatsoever: But, as in the exercise of
     all the virtues, there is an economy of truth'

Sir Edwin Arnold 1832–1904

7 Nor ever once ashamed
So we be named
Press-men; Slaves of the Lamp; Servants of
Light.
     'The Tenth Muse' (1895) st. 18

George Arnold 1834–65

8 The living need charity more than the
dead.
     'The Jolly Old Pedagogue' (1866)

Matthew Arnold 1822–88

9 And we forget because we must
And not because we will.
     'Absence' (1852)

10 A bolt is shot back somewhere in our
breast,
And a lost pulse of feeling stirs again.
The eye sinks inward, and the heart lies
plain,
And what we mean, we say, and what we
would, we know.
     'The Buried Life' (1852) l. 84

11 The Sea of Faith
Was once, too, at the full, and round
     earth's shore
Lay like the folds of a bright girdle furled.
But now I only hear
Its melancholy, long, withdrawing roar,
Retreating, to the breath
Of the night-wind, down the vast edges
     drear
And naked shingles of the world.
     'Dover Beach' (1867) l. 21

12 And we are here as on a darkling plain
Swept with confused alarms of struggle
     and flight,
Where ignorant armies clash by night.
     'Dover Beach' (1867) l. 35

13 Be neither saint nor sophist-led, but be a
man.
     Empedocles on Etna (1852) act 1, sc. 2, l. 136

14 Is it so small a thing
To have enjoyed the sun,
To have lived light in the spring,
To have loved, to have thought, to have
     done.
     Empedocles on Etna (1852) act 1, sc. 2, l. 397

15 Because thou must not dream, thou needst
not then despair!
     Empedocles on Etna (1852) act 1, sc. 2, l. 426

16 Come, dear children, let us away;
Down and away below!
     'The Forsaken Merman' (1849) l. 1

17 Where great whales come sailing by,
Sail and sail, with unshut eye,
Round the world for ever and aye.
     'The Forsaken Merman' (1849) l. 43

18 Creep into thy narrow bed,
Creep, and let no more be said!
Vain thy onset! all stands fast.
Thou thyself must break at last.
Let the long contention cease!
Geese are swans, and swans are geese.
Let them have it how they will!
Thou art tired; best be still.
     'The Last Word' (1867)

19 He spoke, and loosed our heart in tears.
He laid us as we lay at birth
On the cool flowery lap of earth.
     'Memorial Verses, April 1850' (1852) l. 47 (of
     Wordsworth)

20 Ere the parting hour go by,
Quick, thy tablets, Memory!
     'A Memory Picture' (1849)

21 Say, has some wet bird-haunted English
lawn
Lent it the music of its trees at dawn?
     'Parting' (1852) l. 19

22 Eternal Passion!
Eternal Pain!
     'Philomela' (1853) l. 31

23 Cruel, but composed and bland,
Dumb, inscrutable and grand,
So Tiberius might have sat,
Had Tiberius been a cat.
     'Poor Matthias' (1885) l. 40

1 Her cabined ample Spirit,
It fluttered and failed for breath.
To-night it doth inherit
The vasty hall of death.
  'Requiescat' (1853)

2 Not deep the Poet sees, but wide.
  'Resignation' (1849) l. 214

3 Coldly, sadly descends
The autumn evening. The Field
Strewn with its dank yellow drifts
Of withered leaves, and the elms,
Fade into dimness apace,
Silent;—hardly a shout
From a few boys late at their play!
  'Rugby Chapel, November 1857' (1867)

4 Go, for they call you, Shepherd, from the hill.
  'The Scholar-Gipsy' (1853) l. 1

5 All the live murmur of a summer's day.
  'The Scholar-Gipsy' (1853) l. 20

6 Tired of knocking at Preferment's door.
  'The Scholar-Gipsy' (1853) l. 35

7 Crossing the stripling Thames at Bab-lock-hithe.
  'The Scholar-Gipsy' (1853) l. 74

8 Rapt, twirling in thy hand a withered spray,
And waiting for the spark from heaven to fall.
  'The Scholar-Gipsy' (1853) l. 119

9 The line of festal light in Christ-Church hall.
  'The Scholar-Gipsy' (1853) l. 129

10 Thou waitest for the spark from heaven! and we,
Light half-believers in our casual creeds ...
Who hesitate and falter life away,
And lose to-morrow the ground won to-day.
  'The Scholar-Gipsy' (1853) l. 171

11 O born in days when wits were fresh and clear,
And life ran gaily as the sparkling Thames;
Before this strange disease of modern life,
With its sick hurry, its divided aims,
Its heads o'ertaxed, its palsied hearts, was rife—
Fly hence, our contact fear!
  'The Scholar-Gipsy' (1853) l. 201

12 Still nursing the unconquerable hope,
Still clutching the inviolable shade.
  'The Scholar-Gipsy' (1853) l. 211

13 Resolve to be thyself: and know, that he
Who finds himself, loses his misery.
  'Self-Dependence' (1852) l. 31

14 Others abide our question. Thou art free.
We ask and ask: Thou smilest and art still,
Out-topping knowledge.
  'Shakespeare' (1849)

15 Truth sits upon the lips of dying men.
  'Sohrab and Rustum' (1853) l. 656

16 Wandering between two worlds, one dead,
The other powerless to be born.
  'Stanzas from the Grande Chartreuse' (1855) l. 85

17 That sweet City with her dreaming spires.
  'Thyrsis' (1866) l. 19 (of Oxford)

18 So have I heard the cuckoo's parting cry,
From the wet field, through the vext garden-trees,
Come with the volleying rain and tossing breeze:
The bloom is gone, and with the bloom go I.'
  'Thyrsis' (1866) l. 57

19 Too quick despairer, wherefore wilt thou go?
Soon will the high Midsummer pomps come on,
Soon will the musk carnations break and swell.
  'Thyrsis' (1866) l. 61

20 Who saw life steadily, and saw it whole:
The mellow glory of the Attic stage;
Singer of sweet Colonus, and its child.
  'To a Friend' (1849) (of Sophocles)

21 France, famed in all great arts, in none supreme.
  'To a Republican Friend—Continued' (1849)

22 Yes! in the sea of life enisled,
With echoing straits between us thrown,
Dotting the shoreless watery wild,
We mortal millions live *alone*.
  'To Marguerite—Continued' (1852) l. 1

23 The unplumbed, salt, estranging sea.
  'To Marguerite—Continued' (1852) l. 24

24 Our society distributes itself into Barbarians, Philistines, and Populace; and America is just ourselves, with the Barbarians quite left out. and the Populace nearly.
  Culture and Anarchy (1869) preface

25 The pursuit of perfection, then, is the pursuit of sweetness and light ... He who works for sweetness and light united, works to make reason and the will of God prevail.
  Culture and Anarchy (1869) ch. 1. Cf. 319:18

26 When I want to distinguish clearly the aristocratic class from the Philistines proper, or middle class, [I] name the former, in my own mind *the Barbarians*.
  Culture and Anarchy (1869) ch. 3

27 Marching where it likes, meeting where it likes, bawling what it likes, breaking what it likes—to this vast residuum we may with great propriety give the name of Populace.
  Culture and Anarchy (1869) ch. 3

1 Hebraism and Hellenism—between these two points of influence moves our world.
  Culture and Anarchy (1869) ch. 4

2 Whispering from her towers the last enchantments of the Middle Age ... Home of lost causes, and forsaken beliefs.
  Essays in Criticism First Series (1865) preface (of Oxford)

3 The gloom, the smoke, the cold, the strangled illegitimate child! ... And the final touch,—short, bleak and inhuman: *Wragg is in custody*.
  Essays in Criticism First Series (1865) 'The Function of Criticism at the Present Time'

4 In poetry, no less than in life, he is 'a beautiful and ineffectual angel, beating in the void his luminous wings in vain'.
  Essays in Criticism Second Series (1888) 'Shelley' (quoting from his own essay on Byron in the same work)

5 The difference between genuine poetry and the poetry of Dryden, Pope, and all their school, is briefly this: their poetry is conceived and composed in their wits, genuine poetry is conceived and composed in the soul.
  Essays in Criticism Second Series (1888) 'Thomas Gray'

6 Poetry is at bottom a criticism of life.
  Essays in Criticism Second Series (1888) 'Wordsworth'

7 I am past thirty, and three parts iced over.
  H. F. Lowry (ed.) *Letters of Matthew Arnold to Arthur Hugh Clough* (1932) 12 February 1853

8 The true meaning of religion is thus not simply morality, but morality touched by emotion.
  Literature and Dogma (1873) ch. 1

9 Conduct is three-fourths of our life and its largest concern.
  Literature and Dogma (1873) ch. 1

10 But there remains the question: what righteousness really is. The method and secret and sweet reasonableness of Jesus.
  Literature and Dogma (1873) ch. 12

11 So we have the Philistine of genius in religion—Luther; the Philistine of genius in politics—Cromwell; the Philistine of genius in literature—Bunyan.
  Mixed Essays (1879) 'Lord Falkland'

12 Of these two literatures [French and German], as of the intellect of Europe in general, the main effort, for now many years, has been a *critical* effort ... to see the object as in itself it really is.
  On Translating Homer (1861) Lecture 2

13 Have something to say, and say it as clearly as you can. That is the only secret of style.
  In G. W. E. Russell *Collections and Recollections* (1898) ch. 13

Samuel James Arnold

14 England, home and beauty.
  'The Death of Nelson' (1811 song)

Dr Thomas Arnold 1795–1842

15 My object will be, if possible, to form Christian men, for Christian boys I can scarcely hope to make.
  Letter to Revd John Tucker, 2 March 1828, on his appointment to the Headmastership of Rugby School; in A. P. Stanley *Life and Correspondence of Thomas Arnold* (1844) vol. 1, ch. 2

16 As for rioting, the old Roman way of dealing with that is always the right one; flog the rank and file, and fling the ringleaders from the Tarpeian rock.
  From an unpublished letter written before 1828, quoted by Matthew Arnold in *Cornhill Magazine* August 1868 'Anarchy and Authority'

George Asaf 1880–1951

17 What's the use of worrying?
  It never was worth while,
  So, pack up your troubles in your old kit-bag,
  And smile, smile, smile.
  'Pack up your Troubles' (1915 song)

Roger Ascham 1515–68

18 I said ... how, and why, young children, were sooner allured by love, than driven by beating, to attain good learning.
  The Schoolmaster (1570) preface

19 There is no such whetstone, to sharpen a good wit and encourage a will to learning, as is praise.
  The Schoolmaster (1570) bk. 1

Daisy Ashford 1881–1972

20 Mr Salteena was an elderly man of 42.
  The Young Visiters (1919) ch. 1

21 You look rather rash my dear your colors dont quite match your face.
  The Young Visiters (1919) ch. 2

22 Not kind sir he muttered quite usual.
  The Young Visiters (1919) ch. 5

23 Oh I see said the Earl but my own idear is that these things are as piffle before the wind.
  The Young Visiters (1919) ch. 5

24 My life will be sour grapes and ashes without you.
  The Young Visiters (1919) ch. 8

25 Take me back to the Gaierty hotel.
  The Young Visiters (1919) ch. 9

Isaac Asimov 1920–92

1 The three fundamental Rules of Robotics ... One, a robot may not injure a human being, or, through inaction, allow a human being to come to harm ... Two ... a robot must obey the orders given it by human beings except where such orders would conflict with the First Law ... three, a robot must protect its own existence as long as such protection does not conflict with the First or Second Laws.

I, Robot (1950) 'Runaround'

Herbert Asquith 1852–1928

2 We had better wait and see.

Referring, in 1910, to the rumour that the House of Lords was to be flooded with new Liberal peers to ensure the passage of the Finance Bill. See Roy Jenkins *Asquith* (1964) ch. 14

3 It is fitting that we should have buried the Unknown Prime Minister [Bonar Law] by the side of the Unknown Soldier.

In R. Blake *The Unknown Prime Minister* (1955) p. 531

4 [The War Office kept three sets of figures:] one to mislead the public, another to mislead the Cabinet, and the third to mislead itself.

In A. Horne *Price of Glory* (1962) ch. 2

Margot Asquith 1864–1945

5 Kitchener is a great poster.

More Memories (1933) ch. 6

6 The *t* is silent, as in *Harlow*.

To Jean Harlow, who had mispronounced her name; in T. S. Matthews *Great Tom* (1973) ch. 7

Mary Astell 1668–1731

7 If all men are born free, how is it that all women are born slaves?

Some Reflections upon Marriage (1706 ed.) preface

Sir Jacob Astley 1579–1652

8 O Lord! thou knowest how busy I must be this day: if I forget thee, do not thou forget me.

Prayer before the Battle of Edgehill, in Sir Philip Warwick *Memoires* (1701) p. 229

Nancy Astor 1879–1964

9 I married beneath me, all women do.

In *Dictionary of National Biography 1961–1970*

Brooks Atkinson 1894–1984

10 After each war there is a little less democracy to save.

Once Around the Sun (1951) 7 January

E. L. Atkinson 1882–1929 and Apsley Cherry-Garrard 1882–1959

11 Hereabouts died a very gallant gentleman, Captain L. E. G. Oates of the Inniskilling Dragoons. In March 1912, returning from the Pole, he walked willingly to his death in a blizzard to try and save his comrades, beset by hardships.

Epitaph on cairn erected in the Antarctic, 15 November 1912; in Cherry-Garrard's *Worst Journey in the World* (1922) p. 487

Clement Attlee 1883–1967

12 The voice we heard was that of Mr Churchill but the mind was that of Lord Beaverbrook.

Speech on radio, 5 June 1945, in F. Williams *A Prime Minister Remembers* (1961) ch. 6

13 [Russian Communism is] the illegitimate child of Karl Marx and Catherine the Great.

Speech at Aarhus University, 11 April 1956, in *The Times* 12 April 1956

14 Democracy means government by discussion, but it is only effective if you can stop people talking.

Speech at Oxford, 14 June 1957, in *The Times* 15 June 1957

Henriette Auber 1773–1862

15 He came in tongues of living flame,
To teach, convince, subdue;
All-powerful as the wind he came,
As viewless too.

'Our blest Redeemer, ere he breathed' (1829 hymn)

John Aubrey 1626–97

16 How these curiosities would be quite forgot, did not such idle fellows as I am put them down.

Brief Lives 'Venetia Digby'

17 He was wont to say that if he had read as much as other men, he should have known no more than other men.

Brief Lives 'Thomas Hobbes'

18 And when he saw the cheese-cakes:—'What have we here, *crinkum crankum*?'

Brief Lives 'Ralph Kettel'

19 His harmonical and ingenious soul did lodge in a beautiful and well proportioned body. He was a spare man.

Brief Lives 'John Milton'

20 Oval face. His eye a dark grey. He had auburn hair. His complexion exceeding fair—he was so fair that they called him *the lady of* Christ's College.

Brief Lives 'John Milton'

21 He pronounced the letter R (*littera canina*) very hard—a certain sign of a satirical wit.

Brief Lives 'John Milton'

1 Sciatica: he cured it, by boiling his buttock.
   Brief Lives 'Sir Jonas Moore'

2 He was a handsome, well-shaped man: very
   good company, and of a very ready and
   pleasant smooth wit.
   Brief Lives 'William Shakespeare'

Auctoritates Aristotelis

*A compilation of medieval propositions drawn
from diverse classical and other sources (ed. J.
Hamesse, 1974)*

3 *Consuetudo est altera natura.*
   Habit is second nature.

4 *Contra negantem principia non est
   disputandum.*
   You cannot argue with someone who
   denies the first principles.

5 *Deus et natura nihil faciunt frustra.*
   God and nature do nothing in vain.

6 *Omnes homines naturaliter scire desiderant.*
   All men naturally desire to know.

7 *Parentes plus amant filios quam e converso.*
   Parents love their children more than
   children love their parents.

8 *Tempus est mensura motus rerum mobilium.*
   Time is the measure of movement.

W. H. Auden 1907–73

9 Sob, heavy world,
   Sob as you spin
   Mantled in mist, remote from the happy.
   The Age of Anxiety (1947) pt. 4 'The Dirge'

10 Blessed Cecilia, appear in visions
   To all musicians, appear and inspire:
   Translated Daughter, come down and
      startle
   Composing mortals with immortal fire.
   Anthem for St Cecilia's Day (1941) pt. 1

11 I'll love you, dear, I'll love you
   Till China and Africa meet
   And the river jumps over the mountain
   And the salmon sing in the street,

   I'll love you till the ocean
   Is folded and hung up to dry
   And the seven stars go squawking
   Like geese about the sky.
   'As I Walked Out One Evening' (1940)

12 The glacier knocks in the cupboard,
   The desert sighs in the bed,
   And the crack in the tea-cup opens
   A lane to the land of the dead.
   'As I Walked Out One Evening' (1940)

13 At the far end of the enormous room
   An orchestra is playing to the rich.
   'At the far end of the enormous room' (1933)

14 August for the people and their favourite
   islands.
   Title of poem (1936)

15 The desires of the heart are as crooked as
      corkscrews
   Not to be born is the best for man.
   'Death's Echo' (1937). Cf. 311:13

16 Happy the hare at morning, for she cannot
      read
   The Hunter's waking thoughts.
   Dog beneath the Skin (with Christopher
   Isherwood, 1935) act 2, sc. 2

17 To save your world you asked this man to
      die:
   Would this man, could he see you now, ask
      why?
   'Epitaph for the Unknown Soldier' (1955)

18 When he laughed, respectable senators
      burst with laughter,
   And when he cried the little children died
      in the streets.
   'Epitaph on a Tyrant' (1940). Cf. 236:1

19 Altogether elsewhere, vast
   Herds of reindeer move across
   Miles and miles of golden moss,
   Silently and very fast.
   'The Fall of Rome' (1951)

20 To us he is no more a person
   now but a whole climate of opinion.
   'In Memory of Sigmund Freud' (1940) st. 17

21 The mercury sank in the mouth of the
      dying day.
   What instruments we have agree
   The day of his death was a dark cold day.
   'In Memory of W. B. Yeats' (1940) pt. 1

22 You were silly like us; your gift survived it
      all:
   The parish of rich women, physical decay,
   Yourself. Mad Ireland hurt you into poetry.
   'In Memory of W. B. Yeats' (1940) pt. 2

23 For poetry makes nothing happen: it
      survives
   In the valley of its saying where executives
   Would never want to tamper.
   'In Memory of W. B. Yeats' (1940) pt. 2

24 Earth, receive an honoured guest:
   William Yeats is laid to rest.
   Let the Irish vessel lie
   Emptied of its poetry.
   'In Memory of W. B. Yeats' (1940) pt. 3

25 I see it often since you've been away:
   The island, the veranda, the fruit;
   The tiny steamer breaking from the bay;
   The literary mornings with its hoot;
   Our ugly comic servant; and then you,
   Lovely and willing every afternoon.
   'I see it often since you've been away' (1933)

26 Look, stranger, at this island now.
   Title of poem (1936)

27 Lay your sleeping head, my love,
   Human on my faithless arm.
   'Lullaby' (1940)

28 But in my arms till break of day
   Let the living creature lie,
   Mortal, guilty, but to me
   The entirely beautiful.
   'Lullaby' (1940)

1 About suffering they were never wrong,
The Old Masters.
'Musée des Beaux Arts' (1940)

2 Even the dreadful martyrdom must run its
course
Anyhow in a corner, some untidy spot
Where the dogs go on with their doggy life
and the torturer's horse
Scratches its innocent behind on a tree.
'Musée des Beaux Arts' (1940)

3 To the man-in-the-street, who, I'm sorry to
say,
Is a keen observer of life,
The word 'Intellectual' suggests straight
away
A man who's untrue to his wife.
New Year Letter (1941) l. 1277 n.

4 This is the Night Mail crossing the Border,
Bringing the cheque and the postal order,
Letters for the rich, letters for the poor,
The shop at the corner, the girl next door.
'Night Mail' (1936) pt. 1

5 And make us as Newton was, who in his
garden watching
The apple falling towards England, became
aware
Between himself and her of an eternal tie.
'O Love, the interest itself' (1936)

6 Private faces in public places
Are wiser and nicer
Than public faces in private places.
Orators (1932) dedication

7 Out on the lawn I lie in bed,
Vega conspicuous overhead.
'Out on the lawn I lie in bed' (1936)

8 Some thirty inches from my nose
The frontier of my Person goes,
And all the untilled air between
Is private *pagus* or demesne.
Stranger, unless with bedroom eyes
I beckon you to fraternize,
Beware of rudely crossing it:
I have no gun, but I can spit.
'Prologue: the Birth of Architecture' (1966)
postscript

9 My Dear One is mine as mirrors are lonely.
'The Sea and the Mirror' (1944) pt. 2
(Miranda)

10 I and the public know
What all schoolchildren learn,
Those to whom evil is done
Do evil in return.
'September 1, 1939' (1940)

11 All I have is a voice
To undo the folded lie,
The romantic lie in the brain
Of the sensual man-in-the-street
And the lie of Authority
Whose buildings grope the sky:
There is no such thing as the State
And no one exists alone;
Hunger allows no choice
To the citizen or the police;
We must love one another or die.
'September 1, 1939' (1940)

12 A shilling life will give you all the facts.
Title of poem (1936)

13 A poet's hope: to be,
like some valley cheese,
local, but prized elsewhere.
'Shorts II' (1976)

14 Harrow the house of the dead; look
shining at
New styles of architecture, a change of
heart.
'Sir, No Man's Enemy' (1930)

15 The stars are dead; the animals will not
look: ·
We are left alone with our day, and the
time is short and
History to the defeated
May say Alas but cannot help or pardon.
'Spain 1937' (1937) st. 23

16 To ask the hard question is simple.
Title of poem (1933)

17 Was he free? Was he happy? The question
is absurd:
Had anything been wrong, we should
certainly have heard.
'The Unknown Citizen' (1940)

18 When I find myself in the company of
scientists, I feel like a shabby curate who
has strayed by mistake into a drawing
room full of dukes.
The Dyer's Hand (1963) 'The Poet and the City'

19 What do you think about England, this
country of ours where nobody is well?
The Orators (1932) 'Address for a Prize-Day'

20 Art is born of humiliation.
In Stephen Spender *World Within World*
(1951) ch. 2

Émile Augier 1820–89

21 *La nostalgie de la boue!*
Longing to be back in the mud!
Le Mariage d'Olympe (1855) act 1, sc. 1

St Augustine of Hippo AD 354–430

22 Give me chastity and continency—but not
yet!
Confessions (AD 397–8) bk. 8, ch. 7

23 *Tolle lege, tolle lege.*
Take up and read, take up and read.
Confessions (AD 397–8) bk. 8, ch. 12

24 *Sero te amavi, pulchritudo tam antiqua et tam
nova, sero te amavi!*
Too late came I to love thee, O thou Beauty
both so ancient and so fresh, yea too late
came I to love thee.
Confessions (AD 397–8) bk. 10, ch. 27

25 You command continence; and command what you
command, and command what you will.
Confessions (AD 397–8) bk. 10, ch. 29

26 There is no salvation outside the church.
De Baptismo contra Donatistas bk. 4, ch. 17,
sect. 24. Cf. 113:12, 113:14

1 *Audi partem alteram.*
 Hear the other side.
  De Duabus Animabus contra Manicheos ch. 14

2 *Dilige et quod vis fac.*
 Love and do what you will.
  In Epistolam Joannis ad Parthos (AD 413)
  tractatus 7, sect. 8 (often quoted '*Ama et fac
  quod vis*')

3 To many, total abstinence is easier than
 perfect moderation.
  On the Good of Marriage (AD 401) ch. 21

4 *Cum dilectione hominum et odio vitiorum.*
 With love for mankind and hatred of sins.
  Letter 211 in J.-P. Migne (ed.) *Patrologiae
  Latinae* (1845) vol. 33 (often quoted 'Love the
  sinner but hate the sin')

5 *Roma locuta est; causa finita est.*
 Rome has spoken; the case is concluded.
  Traditional summary of words found in
  Sermons (Antwerp, 1702) no. 131, sect. 10

Emperor Augustus 63 BC–AD 14

6 *Festina lente.*
 Make haste slowly.
  In Suetonius *Lives of the Caesars* 'Divus
  Augustus' sect. 25

7 He could boast that he inherited it brick
 and left it marble.
  Of the city of Rome; Suetonius *Lives of the
  Caesars* 'Divus Augustus' sect. 28

Marcus Aurelius AD 121–80

8 Time is a violent torrent; no sooner is a
 thing brought to sight than it is swept by
 and another takes its place.
  Meditations bk. 4, sect. 43

9 Nothing happens to anybody which he is
 not fitted by nature to bear.
  Meditations bk. 5, sect. 18

10 Every instant of time is a pinprick of
 eternity.
  Meditations bk. 6, sect. 36

11 To change your mind and to follow him
 who sets you right is to be nonetheless the
 free agent that you were before.
  Meditations bk. 8, sect. 16

12 Mankind have been created for the sake of
 one another. Either instruct them,
 therefore, or endure them.
  Meditations bk. 8, sect. 59

Jane Austen 1775–1817

13 An egg boiled very soft is not
 unwholesome.
  Emma (1816) ch. 3

14 One half of the world cannot understand
 the pleasures of the other.
  Emma (1816) ch. 9

15 The sooner every party breaks up the
 better.
  Emma (1816) ch. 25

16 Surprises are foolish things. The pleasure
 is not enhanced, and the inconvenience is
 often considerable.
  Emma (1816) ch. 26

17 One has no great hopes from Birmingham.
 I always say there is something direful in
 the sound.
  Emma (1816) ch. 36

18 There is not one in a hundred of either sex
 who is not taken in when they marry ... it
 is, of all transactions, the one in which
 people expect most from others, and are
 least honest themselves.
  Mansfield Park (1814) ch. 5

19 We do not look in great cities for our best
 morality.
  Mansfield Park (1814) ch. 9

20 A large income is the best recipe for
 happiness I ever heard of. It certainly may
 secure all the myrtle and turkey part of it.
  Mansfield Park (1814) ch. 22

21 Let other pens dwell on guilt and misery. I
 quit such odious subjects as soon as I can.
  Mansfield Park (1814) ch. 48

22 'Oh! it is only a novel! ... only Cecilia, or
 Camilla, or Belinda:' or, in short, only some
 work in which the most thorough
 knowledge of human nature, the happiest
 delineation of its varieties, the liveliest
 effusions of wit and humour are conveyed
 to the world in the best chosen language.
  Northanger Abbey (1818) ch. 5

23 Where people wish to attach, they should
 always be ignorant. To come with a well-
 informed mind, is to come with an
 inability of administering to the vanity of
 others, which a sensible person would
 always wish to avoid. A woman especially,
 if she have the misfortune of knowing any
 thing, should conceal it as well as she can.
  Northanger Abbey (1818) ch. 14

24 From politics, it was an easy step to
 silence.
  Northanger Abbey (1818) ch. 14

25 Every man is surrounded by a
 neighbourhood of voluntary spies.
  Northanger Abbey (1818) ch. 34

26 She had been forced into prudence in her
 youth, she learned romance as she grew
 older—the natural sequel of an unnatural
 beginning.
  Persuasion (1818) ch. 4

27 Men have had every advantage of us in
 telling their own story. Education has been
 theirs in so much higher a degree; the pen
 has been in their hands.
  Persuasion (1818) ch. 23

28 All the privilege I claim for my own sex ...
 is that of loving longest, when existence or
 when hope is gone.
  Persuasion (1818) ch. 23

1 It was, perhaps, one of those cases in which advice is good or bad only as the event decides.
Persuasion (1818) ch. 23

2 It is a truth universally acknowledged, that a single man in possession of a good fortune, must be in want of a wife.
Pride and Prejudice (1813) ch. 1. Cf. 81:17

3 Mr Collins had only to change from Jane to Elizabeth—and it was soon done—done while Mrs Bennet was stirring the fire.
Pride and Prejudice (1813) ch. 15

4 Marriage had always been her object; it was the only honourable provision for well-educated young women of small fortune, and however uncertain of giving happiness, must be their pleasantest preservative from want.
Pride and Prejudice (1813) ch. 22

5 Are the shades of Pemberley to be thus polluted?
Pride and Prejudice (1813) ch. 56

6 For what do we live, but to make sport for our neighbours, and laugh at them in our turn?
Pride and Prejudice (1813) ch. 57

7 An annuity is a very serious business.
Sense and Sensibility (1811) vol. 1, ch. 2

8 On every formal visit a child ought to be of the party, by way of provision for discourse.
Sense and Sensibility (1811) vol. 2, ch. 6

9 3 or 4 families in a country village is the very thing to work on.
Letter to Anna Austen, 9 September 1814, in R. W. Chapman (ed.) *Jane Austen's Letters* (1952)

10 The little bit (two inches wide) of ivory on which I work with so fine a brush, as produces little effect after much labour?
Letter to J. Edward Austen, 16 December 1816, in R. W. Chapman (ed.) *Jane Austen's Letters* (1952)

11 Single women have a dreadful propensity for being poor—which is one very strong argument in favour of matrimony.
Letter to Fanny Knight, 13 March 1817, in R. W. Chapman (ed.) *Jane Austen's Letters* (1952)

12 Pictures of perfection as you know make me sick and wicked.
Letter to Fanny Knight, 23 March 1817, in R. W. Chapman (ed.) *Jane Austen's Letters* (1952)

Earl of Avon

See SIR ANTHONY EDEN

Revd Awdry 1911–

13 You've a lot to learn about trucks, little Thomas. They are silly things and must be kept in their place. After pushing them about here for a few weeks you'll know almost as much about them as Edward. Then you'll be a Really Useful Engine.
Thomas the Tank Engine (1946) p. 46

Alan Ayckbourn 1939–

14 My mother used to say, Delia, if S-E-X ever rears its ugly head, close your eyes before you see the rest of it.
Bedroom Farce (1978) act 2

Pam Ayres 1947–

15 Medicinal discovery,
It moves in mighty leaps,
It leapt straight past the common cold
And gave it us for keeps.
'Oh no, I got a cold' (1976)

W. E. Aytoun 1813–65

16 The grim Geneva ministers
With anxious scowl drew near,
As you have seen the ravens flock
Around the dying deer.
'The Execution of Montrose' (1849) st. 17

17 The deep, unutterable woe
Which none save exiles feel.
'The Island of the Scots' (1849) st. 12

18 The earth is all the home I have,
The heavens my wide roof-tree.
'The Wandering Jew' (1867) l. 49

Charles Babbage 1792–1871

19 Every moment dies a man,
Every moment $1\frac{1}{16}$ is born.
Parody of Tennyson's 'Vision of Sin' in an unpublished letter to the poet. See *New Scientist* 4 December 1958, p. 1428. Cf. 328:26

Francis Bacon 1561–1626

20 If a man will begin with certainties, he shall end in doubts; but if he will be content to begin with doubts, he shall end in certainties.
The Advancement of Learning (1605) bk. 1, ch. 5, sect. 8

21 Antiquities are history defaced, or some remnants of history which have casually escaped the shipwreck of time.
The Advancement of Learning (1605) bk. 2, ch. 2, sect. 1

22 They are ill discoverers that think there is no land, when they can see nothing but sea.
The Advancement of Learning (1605) bk. 2, ch. 7, sect. 5

23 Words are the tokens current and accepted for conceits, as moneys are for values.
The Advancement of Learning (1605) bk. 2, ch. 16, sect. 3

24 A dance is a measured pace, as a verse is a measured speech.
The Advancement of Learning (1605) bk. 2, ch. 16, sect. 5

1 But men must know, that in this theatre of man's life it is reserved only for God and angels to be lookers on.
The Advancement of Learning (1605) bk. 2, ch. 20, sect. 8

2 All good moral philosophy is but an handmaid to religion.
The Advancement of Learning (1605) bk. 2, ch. 22, sect. 14

3 It is in life as it is in ways, the shortest way is commonly the foulest, and surely the fairer way is not much about.
The Advancement of Learning (1605) bk. 2, ch. 23, sect. 45

4 That all things are changed, and that nothing really perishes, and that the sum of matter remains exactly the same, is sufficiently certain.
Cogitationes de Natura Rerum Cogitatio 5 in J. Spedding (ed.) *Works* vol. 5 (1858) p. 426

5 Ancient times were the youth of the world.
De Dignitate et Augmentis Scientiarum (1623) bk. 1 (tr. Gilbert Watts, 1640)

6 Riches are a good handmaid, but the worst mistress.
De Dignitate et Augmentis Scientiarum (1623) bk. 6, ch. 3, pt. 3 'The Antitheta of Things' no. 6 (tr. Gilbert Watts, 1640)

7 No term of moderation takes place with the vulgar.
De Dignitate et Augmentis Scientiarum (1623) bk. 6, ch. 3, pt. 3 'The Antitheta of Things' no. 30 (tr. Gilbert Watts, 1640)

8 Silence is the virtue of fools.
De Dignitate et Augmentis Scientiarum (1623) bk. 6, ch. 3, pt. 3 'The Antitheta of Things' no. 31 (tr. Gilbert Watts, 1640)

9 I hold every man a debtor to his profession.
The Elements of the Common Law (1596) preface

10 He is the fountain of honour.
An Essay of a King (1642)

11 Prosperity doth best discover vice, but adversity doth best discover virtue.
Essays (1625) 'Of Adversity'

12 A little philosophy inclineth man's mind to atheism, but depth in philosophy bringeth men's minds about to religion.
Essays (1625) 'Of Atheism'

13 Virtue is like a rich stone, best plain set.
Essays (1625) 'Of Beauty'

14 There is no excellent beauty that hath not some strangeness in the proportion.
Essays (1625) 'Of Beauty'

15 He said it that knew it best.
Essays (1625) 'Of Boldness' (referring to Demosthenes)

16 Mahomet called the hill to come to him again and again; and when the hill stood still, he was never a whit abashed, but said, 'If the hill will not come to Mahomet, Mahomet will go to the hill.'
Essays (1625) 'Of Boldness' (proverbially 'If the mountain will not come ... ')

17 Books will speak plain when counsellors blanch.
Essays (1625) 'Of Counsel'

18 In things that are tender and unpleasing, it is good to break the ice by some whose words are of less weight, and to reserve the more weighty voice to come in as by chance.
Essays (1625) 'Of Cunning'

19 I knew one that when he wrote a letter he would put that which was most material in the postscript, as if it had been a bymatter.
Essays (1625) 'Of Cunning'

20 Men fear death as children fear to go in the dark; and as that natural fear in children is increased with tales, so is the other.
Essays (1625) 'Of Death'

21 Revenge triumphs over death; love slights it; honour aspireth to it; grief flieth to it.
Essays (1625) 'Of Death'

22 It is as natural to die as to be born; and to a little infant, perhaps, the one is as painful as the other.
Essays (1625) 'Of Death'

23 A crowd is not company, and faces are but a gallery of pictures, and talk but a tinkling cymbal, where there is no love.
Essays (1625) 'Of Friendship'

24 It redoubleth joys, and cutteth griefs in halves.
Essays (1625) 'Of Friendship'

25 Cure the disease and kill the patient.
Essays (1625) 'Of Friendship'

26 God Almighty first planted a garden; and, indeed, it is the purest of human pleasures.
Essays (1625) 'Of Gardens'

27 Men in great place are thrice servants: servants of the sovereign or state, servants of fame, and servants of business.
Essays (1625) 'Of Great Place'

28 It is a strange desire to seek power and to lose liberty.
Essays (1625) 'Of Great Place'

29 All rising to great place is by a winding stair.
Essays (1625) 'Of Great Place'

30 As the births of living creatures at first are ill-shapen, so are all innovations, which are the births of time.
Essays (1625) 'Of Innovations'

31 He that will not apply new remedies must expect new evils; for time is the greatest innovator.
Essays (1625) 'Of Innovations'

32 It has been well said that 'the arch-flatterer with whom all the petty flatterers have intelligence is a man's self.'
Essays (1625) 'Of Love'

1 He that hath wife and children hath given hostages to fortune; for they are impediments to great enterprises, either of virtue or mischief.
   Essays (1625) 'Of Marriage and the Single Life'. Cf. 211:26

2 Wives are young men's mistresses, companions for middle age, and old men's nurses.
   Essays (1625) 'Of Marriage and the Single Life'

3 He was reputed one of the wise men that made answer to the question when a man should marry? 'A young man not yet, an elder man not at all.'
   Essays (1625) 'Of Marriage and the Single Life'. Cf. 256:5

4 New nobility is but the act of power, but ancient nobility is the act of time.
   Essays (1625) 'Of Nobility'

5 Nobility of birth commonly abateth industry.
   Essays (1625) 'Of Nobility'

6 Children sweeten labours, but they make misfortunes more bitter.
   Essays (1625) 'Of Parents and Children'

7 Fame is like a river, that beareth up things light and swollen, and drowns things weighty and solid.
   Essays (1625) 'Of Praise'

8 Age will not be defied.
   Essays (1625) 'Of Regimen of Health'

9 Revenge is a kind of wild justice, which the more man's nature runs to, the more ought law to weed it out.
   Essays (1625) 'Of Revenge'

10 Money is like muck, not good except it be spread.
   Essays (1625) 'Of Seditions and Troubles'

11 The remedy is worse than the disease.
   Essays (1625) 'Of Seditions and Troubles'

12 The French are wiser than they seem, and the Spaniards seem wiser than they are.
   Essays (1625) 'Of Seeming Wise'

13 Studies serve for delight, for ornament, and for ability.
   Essays (1625) 'Of Studies'

14 Some books are to be tasted, others to be swallowed, and some few to be chewed and digested.
   Essays (1625) 'Of Studies'

15 Reading maketh a full man; conference a ready man; and writing an exact man.
   Essays (1625) 'Of Studies'

16 Histories make men wise; poets, witty; the mathematics, subtle; natural philosophy, deep; moral, grave; logic and rhetoric, able to contend.
   Essays (1625) 'Of Studies'

17 Travel, in the younger sort, is a part of education; in the elder, a part of experience. He that travelleth into a country before he hath some entrance into the language, goeth to school, and not to travel.
   Essays (1625) 'Of Travel'

18 What is truth? said jesting Pilate; and would not stay for an answer.
   Essays (1625) 'Of Truth'. Cf. 54:1

19 All colours will agree in the dark.
   Essays (1625) 'Of Unity in Religion'

20 It was prettily devised of Aesop, 'The fly sat upon the axletree of the chariot-wheel and said, what a dust do I raise.'
   Essays (1625) 'Of Vain-Glory'

21 Be so true to thyself as thou be not false to others.
   Essays (1625) 'Of Wisdom for a Man's Self'. Cf. 274:23

22 Lucid intervals and happy pauses.
   History of King Henry VII (1622) para. 3 in J. Spedding (ed.) *Works* vol. 6 (1858) p. 32

23 I have taken all knowledge to be my province.
   'To My Lord Treasurer Burghley' (1592) in J. Spedding (ed.) *Letters and Life* vol. 1 (1861) p. 109

24 Opportunity makes a thief.
   'A Letter of Advice to the Earl of Essex ... ' (1598) in J. Spedding (ed.) *Letters and Life* vol. 2 (1862) p. 99

25 For also knowledge itself is power.
   Meditationes Sacrae (1597) 'Of Heresies'

26 The end of our foundation is the knowledge of causes, and secret motions of things; and the enlarging of the bounds of human Empire, to the effecting of all things possible.
   New Atlantis (1627)

27 That great mother of sciences [natural philosophy].
   Novum Organum (1620) bk. 1, Aphorism 80 (tr. J. Spedding)

28 Printing, gunpowder, and the magnet [Mariner's Needle] ... these three have changed the whole face and state of things throughout the world.
   Novum Organum (1620) bk. 1, Aphorism 129 (tr. J. Spedding). Cf. 90:9

29 Anger makes dull men witty, but it keeps them poor.
   J. Spedding (ed.) *Works* vol. 7 (1859) 'Baconiana' (often attributed to Queen Elizabeth I)

30 The world's a bubble; and the life of man Less than a span.
   The World (1629)

31 What then remains, but that we still should cry,
   Not to be born, or being born, to die?
   The World (1629)

Lord Baden-Powell 1857–1941

1 The scouts' motto is founded on my initials, it is: BE PREPARED.

  Scouting for Boys (1908) pt. 1

Walter Bagehot 1826–77

2 A constitutional statesman is in general a man of common opinion and uncommon abilities.

  Biographical Studies (1881) 'The Character of Sir Robert Peel'

3 In such constitutions [as England's] there are two parts ... first, those which excite and preserve the reverence of the population—the *dignified* parts ... and next, the *efficient* parts—those by which it, in fact, works and rules.

  The English Constitution (1867) 'The Cabinet'

4 The Crown is, according to the saying, the 'fountain of honour'; but the Treasury is the spring of business.

  The English Constitution (1867) 'The Cabinet'. Cf. 24:10

5 A cabinet is a combining committee—a *hyphen* which joins, a *buckle* which fastens, the legislative part of the state to the executive part of the state.

  The English Constitution (1867) 'The Cabinet'

6 It has been said that England invented the phrase, 'Her Majesty's Opposition'; that it was the first government which made a criticism of administration as much a part of the polity as administration itself. This critical opposition is the consequence of cabinet government.

  The English Constitution (1867) 'The Cabinet'

7 *The Times* has made many ministries.

  The English Constitution (1867) 'The Cabinet'

8 It has been said, not truly, but with a possible approximation to truth, that in 1802 every hereditary monarch was insane.

  The English Constitution (1867) 'Checks and Balances'

9 Nations touch at their summits.

  The English Constitution (1867) 'The House of Lords'

10 As soon as we see that England is a disguised republic we must see too that the classes for whom the disguise is necessary must be tenderly dealt with.

  The English Constitution (1867) 'Its History'

11 Women—one half the human race at least—care fifty times more for a marriage than a ministry.

  The English Constitution (1867) 'The Monarchy'

12 Royalty is a government in which the attention of the nation is concentrated on one person doing interesting actions. A Republic is a government in which that attention is divided between many, who are all doing uninteresting actions. Accordingly, so long as the human heart is strong and the human reason weak, Royalty will be strong because it appeals to diffused feeling, and Republics weak because they appeal to the understanding.

  The English Constitution (1867) 'The Monarchy'

13 We must not let in daylight upon magic.

  The English Constitution (1867) 'The Monarchy (continued)'

14 The Sovereign has, under a constitutional monarchy such as ours, three rights—the right to be consulted, the right to encourage, the right to warn.

  The English Constitution (1867) 'The Monarchy (continued)'

15 Writers, like teeth, are divided into incisors and grinders.

  Estimates of some Englishmen and Scotchmen (1858) 'The First Edinburgh Reviewers'

16 He describes London like a special correspondent for posterity.

  National Review 7 October 1858 'Charles Dickens'

17 Wordsworth, Tennyson and Browning; or, pure, ornate, and grotesque art in English poetry.

  National Review November 1864 (essay title)

Philip James Bailey 1816–1902

18 We should count time by heart-throbs.

  Festus (1839) sc. 5

19 America, thou half-brother of the world;
  With something good and bad of every land.

  Festus (1839) sc. 10

Bruce Bairnsfather 1888–1959

20 Well, if you knows of a better 'ole, go to it.

  Fragments from France (1915) p. 1

Sir Henry Williams Baker 1821–77

21 Perverse and foolish oft I strayed,
  But yet in love he sought me,
  And on his shoulder gently laid,
  And home, rejoicing, brought me.

  'The King of love my shepherd is' (1868 hymn)

Michael Bakunin 1814–76

22 The urge for destruction is also a creative urge!

  Jahrbuch für Wissenschaft und Kunst (1842) 'Die Reaktion in Deutschland' (under the pseudonym 'Jules Elysard')

1 From each according to his faculties, to each according to his needs.

Declaration signed by forty-seven anarchists on trial after the failure of their uprising at Lyons in 1870, in J. Morrison Davidson *The Old Order and the New* (1890). Cf. 221:9

James Baldwin 1924–87

2 Anyone who has ever struggled with poverty knows how extremely expensive it is to be poor.

Nobody Knows My Name (1961) 'Fifth Avenue, Uptown: a letter from Harlem'

3 Money, it turned out, was exactly like sex, you thought of nothing else if you didn't have it and thought of other things if you did.

Esquire May 1961 'Black Boy looks at the White Boy'

4 If they take you in the morning, they will be coming for us that night.

New York Review of Books 7 January 1971 'Open Letter to my Sister, Angela Davis'

Stanley Baldwin 1867–1947

5 The bomber will always get through. The only defence is in offence, which means that you have to kill more women and children more quickly than the enemy if you want to save yourselves.

Speech, *Hansard* 10 November 1932, col. 632

6 Since the day of the air, the old frontiers are gone. When you think of the defence of England you no longer think of the chalk cliffs of Dover; you think of the Rhine.

Speech, *Hansard* 30 July 1934, col. 2339

7 I shall be but a short time tonight. I have seldom spoken with greater regret, for my lips are not yet unsealed. Were these troubles over I would make a case, and I guarantee that not a man would go into the lobby against us.

Speech, *Hansard* 10 December 1935, col. 856, on the Abyssinian crisis (usually quoted 'My lips are sealed')

8 Do not run up your nose dead against the Pope or the NUM!

In Lord Butler *The Art of Memory* (1982) 'Iain Macleod'. Cf. 215:19

9 They [parliament] are a lot of hard-faced men who look as if they had done very well out of the war.

In J. M. Keynes *Economic Consequences of the Peace* (1919) ch. 5

10 There are three classes which need sanctuary more than others—birds, wild flowers, and Prime Ministers.

In *Observer* 24 May 1925

Arthur James Balfour 1848–1930

11 Christianity, of course ... but why journalism?

Replying to Frank Harris's remark that 'all the faults of the age come from Christianity and journalism'; in Margot Asquith *Autobiography* (1920) vol. 1, ch. 10

12 I thought he was a young man of promise, but it appears he is a young man of promises.

Describing Churchill, in Winston Churchill *My Early Life* (1930) ch. 17

Ballads

13 O mother, mother, make my bed,
O make it saft and narrow:
My love has died for me to-day,
I'll die for him to-morrow.

'Barbara Allen's Cruelty'

14 Ye Highlands and ye Lawlands,
O where hae ye been?
They hae slain the Earl of Murray,
And hae laid him on the green.

'The Bonny Earl of Murray'

15 O lang will his Lady
Look owre the Castle Downe,
Ere she see the Earl of Murray
Come sounding through the town!

'The Bonny Earl of Murray'

16 She hadna sailed a league, a league,
A league but barely three,
Till grim, grim grew his countenance
And gurly grew the sea.

'The Daemon Lover'

17 I am a man upon the land,
I am a selkie in the sea;
When I am far and far from land,
My home it is the Sule Skerry.

'The Great Selkie of Sule Skerry'

18 Where are your eyes that looked so mild
When my poor heart you first beguiled?
Why did you run from me and the child?
Och, Johnny, I hardly knew ye!

'Johnny, I hardly knew Ye'

19 'What gat ye to your dinner, Lord Randal,
my Son?
What gat ye to your dinner, my handsome
young man?'
'I gat eels boil'd in broo'; mother, make my
bed soon,
For I'm weary wi' hunting, and fain wald
lie down.'

'Lord Randal'

20 This ae nighte, this ae nighte,
—*Every nighte and alle,*
Fire and fleet and candle-lighte,
And Christe receive thy saule.

'Lyke-Wake Dirge'

1 When captains courageous whom death
 could not daunt,
 Did march to the siege of the city of
 Gaunt,
 They mustered their soldiers by two and by
 three,
 And the foremost in battle was Mary
 Ambree.
 'Mary Ambree'

2 Yestreen the Queen had four Maries,
 The night she'll hae but three;
 There was Marie Seaton, and Marie Beaton,
 And Marie Carmichael, and me.
 'The Queen's Maries'

3 Fight on, my men, sayes Sir Andrew
 Bartton,
 I am hurt but I am not slain;
 Ile lay mee downe and bleed a while
 And then Ile rise and fight againe.
 'Sir Andrew Bartton'

4 The king sits in Dunfermline town
 Drinking the blude-red wine.
 'Sir Patrick Spens'

5 I saw the new moon late yestreen
 Wi' the auld moon in her arm;
 And if we gang to sea master,
 I fear we'll come to harm.
 'Sir Patrick Spens'

6 Half-owre, half-owre to Aberdour,
 'Tis fifty fathoms deep;
 And there lies good Sir Patrick Spens,
 Wi' the Scots lords at his feet!
 'Sir Patrick Spens'

7 And see ye not yon braid, braid road,
 That lies across the lily leven?
 That is the Path of Wickedness,
 Though some call it the Road to Heaven.
 'Thomas the Rhymer'

8 It was mirk, mirk night, there was nae
 starlight,
 They waded thro' red blude to the knee;
 For a' the blude that's shed on the earth
 Rins through the springs o' that countrie.
 'Thomas the Rhymer'

9 And naebody kens that he lies there
 But his hawk, his hound, and his lady fair.
 'The Twa Corbies'

10 O waly, waly, gin love be bonnie
 A little time while it is new!
 But when 'tis auld it waxeth cauld,
 And fades awa' like morning dew.
 'Waly, Waly'

11 Tom Pearse, Tom Pearse, lend me your
 grey mare,
 All along, down along, out along, lee.
 For I want for to go to Widdicombe Fair,
 Wi' Bill Brewer, Jan Stewer, Peter Gurney,
 Peter Davey, Dan'l Whiddon, Harry Hawk,
 Old Uncle Tom Cobbleigh and all.
 'Widdicombe Fair'

Whitney Balliett 1926–

12 A critic is a bundle of biases held loosely
 together by a sense of taste.
 Dinosaurs in the Morning (1962) introductory
 note

13 The sound of surprise.
 Title of book on jazz (1959)

Richard Bancroft 1544–1610

14 Where Christ erecteth his Church, the
 devil in the same churchyard will have his
 chapel.
 Sermon at Paul's Cross, 9 February 1588.
 Cf. 31:17, 212:9

John Barbour c.1320–95

15 Storys to rede ar delitabill,
 Suppos that thai be nocht bot fabill.
 The Bruce (1375) bk. 1, l. 1

16 A! fredome is a noble thing!
 Fredome mayse man to haiff liking.
 The Bruce (1375) bk. 1, l. 225

Alexander Barclay c.1475–1552

17 The lords will alway that people note and
 see
 Between them and servants some diversity,
 Though it to them turn to no profit at all;
 If they have pleasure, the servant shall
 have small.
 Eclogues (1514) no. 2, l. 791

Revd R. H. B. Barham ('Thomas Ingoldsby') 1788–1845

18 And six little Singing-boys,—dear little
 souls!
 In nice clean faces, and nice white stoles.
 The Ingoldsby Legends (First Series, 1840) 'The
 Jackdaw of Rheims'

19 Never was heard such a terrible curse!
 But what gave rise
 To no little surprise,
 Nobody seemed one penny the worse!
 The Ingoldsby Legends (First Series, 1840) 'The
 Jackdaw of Rheims'

20 Heedless of grammar, they all cried, 'That's
 him!'
 The Ingoldsby Legends (First Series, 1840) 'The
 Jackdaw of Rheims'

21 Here's a corpse in the case with a sad
 swelled face,
 And a 'Crowner's Quest' is a queer sort of
 thing!
 The Ingoldsby Legends (First Series, 1840) 'A
 Lay of St Gengulphus' (in later editions: 'a
 Medical Crowner's a queer sort of thing!')

22 A servant's too often a negligent elf;
 —If it's business of consequence, DO IT
 YOURSELF!
 The Ingoldsby Legends (Second Series, 1842)
 'The Ingoldsby Penance!—Moral'

Revd Sabine Baring-Gould
1834–1924

1 Onward, Christian soldiers,
   Marching as to war,
   With the cross of Jesus
   Going on before.
   'Onward, Christian Soldiers' (1864 hymn)

2 Through the night of doubt and sorrow
   Onward goes the pilgrim band,
   Singing songs of expectation,
   Marching to the Promised Land.
   'Through the night of doubt and sorrow'
   (1867 hymn); translated from the Danish of
   B. S. Ingemann (1789–1862)

Frederick R. Barnard

3 One picture is worth ten thousand words.
   Printers' Ink 10 March 1927

Julian Barnes 1946–

4 The land of embarrassment and breakfast?
   Flaubert's Parrot (1984) ch. 7 (of England)

5 Books say: she did this because. Life says:
   she did this. Books are where things are
   explained to you; life is where things
   aren't.
   Flaubert's Parrot (1984) ch. 13

6 Does history repeat itself, the first time as
   tragedy, the second time as farce? No,
   that's too grand, too considered a process.
   History just burps, and we taste again that
   raw-onion sandwich it swallowed centuries
   ago.
   A History of the World in 10½ Chapters (1989)
   'Parenthesis'. Cf. 221:10

Richard Barnfield 1574–1627

7 The waters were his winding sheet, the sea
   was made his tomb;
   Yet for his fame the ocean sea, was not
   sufficient room.
   The Encomion of Lady Pecunia (1598) 'To the
   Gentlemen Readers' (on the death of Sir John
   Hawkins)

8 My flocks feed not, my ewes breed not,
   My rams speed not, all is amiss:
   Love in dying, Faith is defying,
   Heart's renying, causer of this.
   'The Unknown Shepherd's Complaint' in
   Nicholas Ling (ed.) *England's Helicon* (1600)

Phineas T. Barnum 1810–91

9 There's a sucker born every minute.
   Attributed

J. M. Barrie 1860–1937

10 His lordship may compel us to be equal
   upstairs, but there will never be equality in
   the servants' hall.
   The Admirable Crichton (performed 1902) act 1

11 When the first baby laughed for the first
   time, the laugh broke into a thousand
   pieces and they all went skipping about,
   and that was the beginning of fairies.
   Peter Pan (1928) act 1

12 Every time a child says 'I don't believe in
   fairies' there is a little fairy somewhere
   that falls down dead.
   Peter Pan (1928) act 1

13 To die will be an awfully big adventure.
   Peter Pan (1928) act 3. Cf. 146:6

14 Do you believe in fairies? Say quick that
   you believe! If you believe, clap your hands!
   Peter Pan (1928) act 4

15 That is ever the way. 'Tis all jealousy to the
   bride and good wishes to the corpse.
   Quality Street (performed 1901) act 1

16 Charm . . . it's a sort of bloom on a woman.
   If you have it, you don't need to have
   anything else; and if you don't have it, it
   doesn't much matter what else you have.
   What Every Woman Knows (performed 1908)
   act 1

17 There are few more impressive sights in
   the world than a Scotsman on the make.
   What Every Woman Knows (performed 1908)
   act 2

18 The tragedy of a man who has found
   himself out.
   What Every Woman Knows (performed 1908)
   act 4

Roland Barthes 1915–80

19 I think that cars today are almost the exact
   equivalent of the great Gothic cathedrals:
   I mean the supreme creation of an era,
   conceived with passion by unknown
   artists, and consumed in image if not in
   usage by a whole population which
   appropriates them as a purely magical
   object.
   Mythologies (1957) 'La nouvelle Citroën' (tr. A.
   Lavers, 1972)

Bernard Baruch 1870–1965

20 We are today in the midst of a cold war.
   Speech to South Carolina Legislature
   16 April 1947, in *New York Times* 17 April
   1947, p. 21 ('cold war' was suggested to him
   by H. B. Swope, former editor of the *New York
   World*)

21 Vote for the man who promises least; he'll
   be the least disappointing.
   In M. Berger *New York* (1960)

Jacques Barzun 1907–

22 If it were possible to talk to the unborn,
   one could never explain to them how it
   feels to be alive, for life is washed in the
   speechless real.
   The House of Intellect (1959) ch. 6

Edgar Bateman and George Le Brunn

1 Wiv a ladder and some glasses,
  You could see to 'Ackney Marshes,
  If it wasn't for the 'ouses in between.
    'If it wasn't for the 'Ouses in between' (1894
    song)

Katherine Lee Bates 1859–1929

2 America! America!
  God shed His grace on thee
  And crown thy good with brotherhood
  From sea to shining sea!
    'America the Beautiful' (1893)

Charles Baudelaire 1821–67

3 *Hypocrite lecteur,—mon semblable,—mon frère.*
  Hypocrite reader—my likeness—my
  brother.
    Les fleurs du mal (1857) 'Au Lecteur'

4 *Là, tout n'est qu'ordre et beauté,*
  Luxe, calme et volupté.
  Everything there is simply order and
  beauty, luxury, peace and sensual
  indulgence.
    Les fleurs du mal (1857) 'L'Invitation au
    voyage'—'Spleen et idéal' no. 56

5 *Quelle est cette île triste et noire? C'est Cythère,*
  Nous dit-on, un pays fameux dans les chansons,
  Eldorado banal de tous les vieux garçons.
  Regardez, après tout, c'est un pauvre terre.
  What sad, black isle is that? It's Cythera, so
  they say, a land celebrated in song, the
  banal Eldorado of all the old fools. Look,
  after all, it's a land of poverty.
    Les fleurs du mal (1857) 'Un voyage à
    Cythère'—'Les fleurs du mal' no. 121

6 *Au fond de l'Inconnu pour trouver du nouveau!*
  Through the unknown, we'll find the new.
    Les fleurs du mal (1857) 'Le voyage' no. 126 (tr.
    Robert Lowell)

7 *Il y a dans tout changement quelque chose*
  d'infâme et d'agréable à la fois, quelque chose
  qui tient de l'infidelité et du déménagement.
  Cela suffit à expliquer la Révolution Française.
  There is in all change something at once
  sordid and agreeable, which smacks of
  infidelity and household removals. This is
  sufficient to explain the French Revolution.
    Journaux intimes (1887) 'Mon coeur mis à nu'
    no. 4 (tr. Christopher Isherwood)

8 *La croyance au progrès est une doctrine de*
  paresseux, une doctrine de Belges. C'est
  l'individu qui compte sur ses voisins pour faire
  sa besogne.
  Belief in progress is a doctrine of idlers
  and Belgians. It is the individual relying
  upon his neighbours to do his work.
    Journaux intimes (1887) 'Mon coeur mis à nu'
    no. 9 (tr. Christopher Isherwood)

9 *Il faut épater le bourgeois.*
  One must astonish the bourgeois.
    Attributed. Also attributed to Privat
    d'Anglemont (*c.*1820–59) in the form '*Je les ai*
    épatés, les bourgeois [I flabbergasted them, the
    bourgeois]'

L. Frank Baum 1856–1919

10 The road to the City of Emeralds is paved
   with yellow brick.
    The Wonderful Wizard of Oz (1900) ch. 2
    ('Follow the yellow brick road' in the 1939
    screenplay)

Vicki Baum 1888–1960

11 Marriage always demands the finest arts of
   insincerity possible between two human
   beings.
    Zwischenfall in Lohwinckel (1930) (tr. M.
    Goldsmith as *Results of an Accident* (1931)
    p. 140)

Sir Beverley Baxter 1891–1964

12 Beaverbrook is so pleased to be in the
   Government that he is like the town tart
   who has finally married the Mayor!
    In Sir Henry Channon *Chips: the Diaries* (1967)
    12 June 1940

James Beattie 1735–1803

13 Some deemed him wondrous wise, and
   some believed him mad.
    The Minstrel bk. 1 (1771) st. 16

Lord Beatty 1871–1936

14 There's something wrong with our bloody
   ships today.
    At the Battle of Jutland, 1916; in Winston
    Churchill *The World Crisis 1916–1918* (1927)
    pt. 1, p. 129

Pierre-Augustin Caron de Beaumarchais 1732–99

15 Today if something is not worth saying,
   people sing it.
    The Barber of Seville (1775) act 1, sc. 2

16 Drinking when we are not thirsty and
   making love all year round, madam; that is
   all there is to distinguish us from other
   animals.
    The Marriage of Figaro (1785) act 2, sc. 21

17 Because you are a great lord, you believe
   yourself to be a great genius! ... You took
   the trouble to be born, but no more.
    The Marriage of Figaro (1785) act 5, sc. 3

Francis Beaumont 1584–1616

18   What things have we seen,
   Done at the Mermaid!
    'Letter to Ben Jonson'

Francis Beaumont 1584–1616 and John Fletcher 1579–1625

1 Those have most power to hurt us that we love.
The Maid's Tragedy (written 1610–11) act 5

2 PHILASTER: Oh, but thou dost not know
What 'tis to die.
BELLARIO: Yes, I do know, my Lord:
'Tis less than to be born; a lasting sleep;
A quiet resting from all jealousy,
A thing we all pursue; I know besides,
It is but giving over of a game,
That must be lost.
Philaster (written 1609) act 3

3 It would talk: Lord how it talk't!
The Scornful Lady (1616) act 4

Lord Beaverbrook (Max Aitken) 1879–1964

4 Now who is responsible for this work of development on which so much depends? To whom must the praise be given? To the boys in the back rooms. They do not sit in the limelight. But they are the men who do the work.
Listener 27 March 1941

5 With the publication of his Private Papers in 1952, he committed suicide 25 years after his death.
Men and Power (1956) p. xviii (of Earl Haig)

6 Our cock won't fight.
Of Edward VIII, during the abdication crisis of 1936; in F. Donaldson *Edward VIII* (1974) ch. 22

Samuel Beckett 1906–89

7 It is suicide to be abroad. But what is it to be at home, Mr Tyler, what is it to be at home? A lingering dissolution.
All That Fall (1957) p. 10

8 We could have saved sixpence. We have saved fivepence. (*Pause*) But at what cost?
All That Fall (1957) p. 25

9 CLOV: Do you believe in the life to come?
HAMM: Mine was always that.
Endgame (1958) p. 35

10 Nothing to be done.
Waiting for Godot (1955) act 1

11 One of the thieves was saved. (*Pause*) It's a reasonable percentage.
Waiting for Godot (1955) act 1

12 Nothing happens, nobody comes, nobody goes, it's awful!
Waiting for Godot (1955) act 1

13 VLADIMIR: That passed the time.
ESTRAGON: It would have passed in any case.
VLADIMIR: Yes, but not so rapidly.
Waiting for Godot (1955) act 1

14 We all are born mad. Some remain so.
Waiting for Godot (1955) act 2

15 They give birth astride of a grave, the light gleams an instant, then it's night once more.
Waiting for Godot (1955) act 2

16 Habit is a great deadener.
Waiting for Godot (1955) act 2

Thomas Becon 1512–67

17 For commonly, wheresoever God buildeth a church, the devil will build a chapel just by.
Catechism (1560, ed. J. Ayre, 1844) p. 361.
Cf. 28:14, 212:9

18 When the wine is in, the wit is out.
Catechism (1560, ed. J. Ayre, 1844) p. 375

Thomas Lovell Beddoes 1803–49

19 If there were dreams to sell,
What would you buy?
'Dream-Pedlary' (written 1830)

The Venerable Bede AD 673–735

20 'Such,' he said, 'O King, seems to me the present life of men on earth, in comparison with that time which to us is uncertain, as if when on a winter's night you sit feasting with your ealdormen and thegns,—a single sparrow should fly swiftly into the hall, and coming in at one door, instantly fly out through another'.
Ecclesiastical History of the English People (tr. B. Colgrave, 1969) bk. 2, ch. 13

Harry Bedford and Terry Sullivan

21 I'm a bit of a ruin that Cromwell knocked about a bit.
'It's a Bit of a Ruin that Cromwell Knocked about a Bit' (1920 song, written for Marie Lloyd)

Barnard Elliott Bee 1823–61

22 There is Jackson with his Virginians, standing like a stone wall. Let us determine to die here, and we will conquer.
Referring to General T. J. ('Stonewall') Jackson at the battle of Bull Run, 21 July, 1861 (in which Bee himself was killed); in B. Perley Poore *Perley's Reminiscences* (1886) vol. 2, ch. 7

Sir Thomas Beecham 1879–1961

23 There are two golden rules for an orchestra: start together and finish together. The public doesn't give a damn what goes on in between.
In H. Atkins and A. Newman *Beecham Stories* (1978) p. 27

1 Two skeletons copulating on a corrugated tin roof.

 Describing the harpsichord, in H. Atkins and A. Newman *Beecham Stories* (1978) p. 34

2 A kind of musical Malcolm Sargent.

 Of Herbert von Karajan, in H. Atkins and A. Newman *Beecham Stories* (1978) p. 61

3 Too much counterpoint; what is worse, Protestant counterpoint.

 Of J. S. Bach, in *Guardian* 8 March 1971

4 Madam, you have between your legs an instrument capable of giving pleasure to thousands—and all you can do is scratch it.

 To a cellist (attributed)

Revd H. C. Beeching 1859–1919

5 Not when the sense is dim,
But now from the heart of joy,
I would remember Him:
Take the thanks of a boy.

 'Prayers' (1895)

6 First come I; my name is Jowett.
There's no knowledge but I know it.
I am Master of this college:
What I don't know isn't knowledge.

 The Masque of Balliol (c.1870) in W. G. Hiscock (ed.) *The Balliol Rhymes* (1939). Cf. 9:12, 314:1

Max Beerbohm 1872–1956

7 They so very indubitably *are*, you know!

 Christmas Garland (1912) 'Mote in the Middle Distance'

8 I was not unpopular [at school] ... It is Oxford that has made me insufferable.

 More (1899) 'Going Back to School'

9 Enter Michael Angelo. Andrea del Sarto appears for a moment at a window. Pippa passes.

 Seven Men (1919) 'Savonarola Brown' act 3

10 The fading signals and grey eternal walls of that antique station, which, familiar to them and insignificant, does yet whisper to the tourist the last enchantments of the Middle Age.

 Zuleika Dobson (1911) ch. 1. Cf. 18:2

11 Women who love the same man have a kind of bitter freemasonry.

 Zuleika Dobson (1911) ch. 4

12 The Socratic manner is not a game at which two can play.

 Zuleika Dobson (1911) ch. 15

13 Fate wrote her a most tremendous tragedy, and she played it in tights.

 The Yellow Book (1894) vol. 3, p. 260 (of Queen Caroline of Brunswick)

Ethel Lynn Beers 1827–79

14 All quiet along the Potomac to-night,
No sound save the rush of the river,
While soft falls the dew on the face of the dead—
The picket's off duty forever.

 'The Picket Guard' (1861) st. 6. Cf. 214:14

Mrs Beeton 1836–65

15 A place for everything and everything in its place.

 Book of Household Management (1861) ch. 2, sect. 55 (often attributed to Samuel Smiles)

Brendan Behan 1923–64

16 PAT: He was an Anglo-Irishman.
MEG: In the blessed name of God what's that?
PAT: A Protestant with a horse.

 Hostage (1958) act 1

17 Meanwhile I'll sing that famous old song, 'The Hound that Caught the Pubic Hare'.

 Hostage (1958) act 1

18 When I came back to Dublin, I was courtmartialled in my absence and sentenced to death in my absence, so I said they could shoot me in my absence.

 Hostage (1958) act 1

19 There's no such thing as bad publicity except your own obituary.

 In Dominic Behan *My Brother Brendan* (1965) p. 158

Aphra Behn 1640–89

20 Oh, what a dear ravishing thing is the beginning of an Amour!

 The Emperor of the Moon (1687) act 1, sc. 1

21 Love ceases to be a pleasure, when it ceases to be a secret.

 The Lover's Watch (1686) 'Four o' Clock. General Conversation'

22 Come away; poverty's catching.

 The Rover pt. 2 (1681) act 1

23 Money speaks sense in a language all nations understand.

 The Rover pt. 2 (1681) act 3

24 The soft, unhappy sex.

 The Wandering Beauty (1698) para. 1

John Hay Beith

See IAN HAY

Hilaire Belloc 1870–1953

25 Child! do not throw this book about;
Refrain from the unholy pleasure
Of cutting all the pictures out!

 A Bad Child's Book of Beasts (1896) dedication

1 I shoot the Hippopotamus
  With bullets made of platinum,
  Because if I use leaden ones
  His hide is sure to flatten 'em.
  A Bad Child's Book of Beasts (1896) 'The
  Hippopotamus'. Cf. 143:14

2 And mothers of large families (who claim
    to common sense)
  Will find a Tiger well repay the trouble and
    expense.
  A Bad Child's Book of Beasts (1896) 'The Tiger'

3 Believing Truth is staring at the sun.
  Title of poem (1938)

4 Physicians of the Utmost Fame
  Were called at once; but when they came
  They answered, as they took their Fees,
  'There is no Cure for this Disease.'
  Cautionary Tales (1907) 'Henry King'

5 And always keep a-hold of Nurse
  For fear of finding something worse.
  Cautionary Tales (1907) 'Jim'

6 In my opinion, Butlers ought
  To know their place, and not to play
  The Old Retainer night and day.
  Cautionary Tales (1907) 'Lord Lundy'

7 Sir! you have disappointed us!
  We had intended you to be
  The next Prime Minister but three:
  The stocks were sold; the Press was
    squared;
  The Middle Class was quite prepared.
  But as it is! ... My language fails!
  Go out and govern New South Wales!
  Cautionary Tales (1907) 'Lord Lundy'

8 Matilda told such Dreadful Lies,
  It made one Gasp and Stretch one's Eyes.
  Cautionary Tales (1907) 'Matilda'

9 For every time She shouted 'Fire!'
  They only answered 'Little Liar!'
  Cautionary Tales (1907) 'Matilda'

10 A Trick that everyone abhors
   In Little Girls is slamming Doors.
   Cautionary Tales (1907) 'Rebecca'

11 She was not really bad at heart,
   But only rather rude and wild:
   She was an aggravating child.
   Cautionary Tales (1907) 'Rebecca'

12 I said to Heart, 'How goes it?' Heart
     replied:
   'Right as a Ribstone Pippin!' But it lied.
   'The False Heart' (1910)

13 I'm tired of Love: I'm still more tired of
     Rhyme.
   But Money gives me pleasure all the time.
   'Fatigued' (1923)

14 Strong brother in God and last companion,
     Wine.
   'Heroic Poem upon Wine' (1926)

15 The moral is (it is indeed!)
   You mustn't monkey with the Creed.
   Ladies and Gentlemen (1932) 'The Example'

16 Remote and ineffectual Don
   That dared attack my Chesterton.
   'Lines to a Don' (1910)

17 Dons admirable! Dons of Might!
   Uprising on my inward sight
   Compact of ancient tales, and port
   And sleep—and learning of a sort.
   'Lines to a Don' (1910)

18 Whatever happens we have got
   The Maxim Gun, and they have not.
   The Modern Traveller (1898) pt. 6

19 The Llama is a woolly sort of fleecy hairy
     goat,
   With an indolent expression and an
     undulating throat
   Like an unsuccessful literary man.
   More Beasts for Worse Children (1897) 'The
   Llama'

20 The Microbe is so very small
   You cannot make him out at all.
   More Beasts for Worse Children (1897) 'The
   Microbe'

21 Oh! let us never, never doubt
   What nobody is sure about!
   More Beasts for Worse Children (1897) 'The
   Microbe'

22 Lord Finchley tried to mend the Electric
     Light
   Himself. It struck him dead: And serve him
     right!
   It is the business of the wealthy man
   To give employment to the artisan.
   More Peers (1911) 'Lord Finchley'

23 Like many of the Upper Class
   He liked the Sound of Broken Glass.
   New Cautionary Tales (1930) 'About John'.
   Cf. 343:18

24 And even now, at twenty-five,
   He has to WORK to keep alive!
   Yes! All day long from 10 till 4!
   For half the year or even more;
   With but an hour or two to spend
   At luncheon with a city friend.
   New Cautionary Tales (1930) 'Peter Goole'

25 The accursed power which stands on
     Privilege
   (And goes with Women, and Champagne,
     and Bridge)
   Broke—and Democracy resumed her reign:
   (Which goes with Bridge, and Women and
     Champagne).
   'On a Great Election' (1923)

26 I am a sundial, and I make a botch
   Of what is done much better by a watch.
   'On a Sundial' (1938)

27 When I am dead, I hope it may be said:
   'His sins were scarlet, but his books were
     read.'
   'On His Books' (1923)

28 Pale Ebenezer thought it wrong to fight,
   But Roaring Bill (who killed him) thought
     it right.
   'The Pacifist' (1938)

1 Do you remember an Inn,
   Miranda?
   Do you remember an Inn? . . .
   And the fleas that tease in the High
      Pyrenees
   And the wine that tasted of the tar?
   'Tarantella' (1923)

2 Balliol made me, Balliol fed me,
   Whatever I had she gave me again:
   And the best of Balliol loved and led me.
   God be with you, Balliol men.
   'To the Balliol Men Still in Africa' (1910)

3 From quiet homes and first beginning,
   Out to the undiscovered ends,
   There's nothing worth the wear of
      winning,
   But laughter and the love of friends.
   Verses (1910) 'Dedicatory Ode'

Saul Bellow 1915–

4 If I am out of my mind, it's all right with
   me, thought Moses Herzog.
   Herzog (1961) opening sentence

De Belloy 1727–75

5 The more foreigners I saw, the more I
   loved my homeland.
   Le Siège de Calais (1765) act 2, sc. 3

Robert Benchley 1889–1945

6 STREETS FLOODED. PLEASE ADVISE.
   Telegraph message on arriving in Venice, in
   R. E. Drennan (ed.) *Wits End* (1973) 'Robert
   Benchley'

Julien Benda 1867–1956

7 *La trahison des clercs.*
   The treachery of the intellectuals.
   Title of book (1927)

Stephen Vincent Benét 1898–1943

8 I have fallen in love with American names,
   The sharp, gaunt names that never get fat.
   'American Names' (1927)

9 Bury my heart at Wounded Knee.
   'American Names' (1927)

George Bennard 1873–1958

10 I will cling to the old rugged cross,
    And exchange it some day for a crown.
    'The Old Rugged Cross' (1913 hymn)

Alan Bennett 1934–

11 I don't want to give you the idea I'm trying
    to hide anything, or that anything
    unorthodox goes on between my wife and
    me. It doesn't. Nothing goes on at all . . .
    No foreplay. No afterplay. And fuck all in
    between.
    Enjoy (1980) act 1

12 I have never understood this liking for
    war. It panders to instincts already catered
    for within the scope of any respectable
    domestic establishment.
    Forty Years On (1969) act 1

13 Memories are not shackles, Franklin, they
    are garlands.
    Forty Years On (1969) act 2

14 Standards are always out of date. That is
    what makes them standards.
    Forty Years On (1969) act 2

15 We started off trying to set up a small
    anarchist community, but people wouldn't
    obey the rules.
    Getting On (1972) act 1

16 Here I sit, alone and sixty,
    Bald, and fat, and full of sin,
    Cold the seat and loud the cistern,
    As I read the Harpic tin.
    'Place Names of China'

Arnold Bennett 1867–1931

17 The price of justice is eternal publicity.
    Things that have Interested Me (2nd series,
    1923) 'Secret Trials'

18 A cause may be inconvenient, but it's
    magnificent. It's like champagne or high
    heels, and one must be prepared to suffer
    for it.
    The Title (1918) act 1

Jill Bennett 1931–90

19 Never marry a man who hates his mother,
    because he'll end up hating you.
    In *Observer* 12 September 1982 'Sayings of the
    Week'

A. C. Benson 1862–1925

20 Land of Hope and Glory, Mother of the
       Free,
    How shall we extol thee who are born of
       thee?
    Wider still and wider shall thy bounds be
       set;
    God who made thee mighty, make thee
       mightier yet.
    'Land of Hope and Glory' written to be sung
    as the Finale to Elgar's *Coronation Ode* (1902)

Stella Benson 1892–1933

21 Call no man foe, but never love a stranger.
    This is the End (1917) p. 63

Jeremy Bentham 1748–1832

22 Natural rights is simple nonsense: natural
    and imprescriptible rights, rhetorical
    nonsense—nonsense upon stilts.
    Anarchical Fallacies in J. Bowring (ed.) *Works*
    vol. 2 (1843) p. 501

1 The greatest happiness of the greatest
number is the foundation of morals and
legislation.
   Commonplace Book in J. Bowring (ed.) *Works*
   vol. 10 (1843) p. 142, where Bentham claims
   that either Joseph Priestley (1733–1804) or
   Cesare Beccaria (1738–94) passed on 'the
   sacred truth'. Cf. 177:2

2 All punishment is mischief: all
punishment in itself is evil.
   Principles of Morals and Legislation (1789)
   ch. 13, para. 2

3 Prose is when all the lines except the last
go on to the end. Poetry is when some of
them fall short of it.
   In M. Packe *Life of John Stuart Mill* (1954) bk. 1,
   ch. 2

4 He rather hated the ruling few than loved
the suffering many.
   Of James Mill, in H. N. Pym (ed.) *Memories of
   Old Friends* (1882) 7 August 1840

Edmund Clerihew Bentley
1875–1956

5 The Art of Biography
Is different from Geography.
Geography is about Maps,
But Biography is about Chaps.
   Biography for Beginners (1905) introduction

6 What I like about Clive
Is that he is no longer alive.
There is a great deal to be said
For being dead.
   'Clive' (1905)

7 George the Third
Ought never to have occurred.
One can only wonder
At so grotesque a blunder.
   'George the Third' (1929)

8 Sir Humphrey Davy
Abominated gravy.
He lived in the odium
Of having discovered Sodium.
   'Sir Humphrey Davy' (1905)

9 Sir Christopher Wren
Said, 'I am going to dine with some men.
If anybody calls
Say I am designing St Paul's.'
   'Sir Christopher Wren' (1905)

Richard Bentley 1662–1742

10 It would be port if it could.
   Describing claret, in R. C. Jebb *Bentley* (1902)
   ch. 12

Pierre-Jean de Béranger
1780–1857

11 *Nos amis, les ennemis.*
Our friends, the enemy.
   'L'Opinion de ces demoiselles' (written 1815)
   in *Chansons de De Béranger* (1832)

Lord Charles Beresford 1846–1919

12 Very sorry can't come. Lie follows by post.
   Telegraphed message to the Prince of Wales,
   on being summoned to dine at the eleventh
   hour. See R. Nevill *World of Fashion 1837–1922*
   (1923) ch. 5

Henri Bergson 1859–1941

13 The present contains nothing more than
the past, and what is found in the effect
was already in the cause.
   L'Évolution créatrice (1907) ch. 1

14 *L'élan vital.*
The vital spirit.
   L'Évolution créatrice (1907) ch. 2 (section title)

Bishop George Berkeley
1685–1753

15 They are neither finite quantities, or
quantities infinitely small, nor yet nothing.
May we not call them the ghosts of
departed quantities?
   The Analyst (1734) sect. 35 (on Newton's
   infinitesimals)

16 [Tar water] is of a nature so mild and
benign and proportioned to the human
constitution, as to warm without heating,
to cheer but not inebriate.
   Siris (1744) para. 217. Cf. 110:11

17 Truth is the cry of all, but the game of the
few.
   Siris (1744) para. 368

18 We have first raised a dust and then
complain we cannot see.
   *A Treatise Concerning the Principles of Human
   Knowledge* (1710) introduction, sect. 3

19 Westward the course of empire takes its
way;
The first four acts already past,
A fifth shall close the drama with the day
Time's noblest offspring is the last.
   'On the Prospect of Planting Arts and
   Learning in America' (1752) st. 6. See John
   Quincy Adams *Oration at Plymouth* (1802):
   'Westward the star of empire takes its way'

Irving Berlin 1888–1989

20 There's no business like show business.
   'Annie Get Your Gun' (1946)

21 God bless America,
Land that I love,
Stand beside her and guide her
Thru the night with a light from above.
From the mountains to the prairies,
To the oceans white with foam,
God bless America,
My home sweet home.
   'God Bless America' (1939)

22 There may be trouble ahead,
But while there's moonlight and music and
love and romance,
Let's face the music and dance.
   'Let's Face the Music and Dance' (1936)

1 A pretty girl is like a melody
  That haunts you night and day.
  'A Pretty Girl is like a Melody' (1919)

2 The song is ended (but the melody lingers
  on).
  Title of song (1927)

3 I'm dreaming of a white Christmas,
  Just like the ones I used to know.
  'White Christmas' (1942)

Sir Isaiah Berlin 1909–

4 There exists a great chasm between those,
  on one side, who relate everything to
  a single central vision ... and, on the other
  side, those who pursue many ends, often
  unrelated and even contradictory ... The
  first kind of intellectual and artistic
  personality belongs to the hedgehogs, the
  second to the foxes.
  The Hedgehog and the Fox (1953) ch. 1. Cf. 15:1

5 [Rousseau] is the first militant lowbrow of
  history.
  Unpublished lecture (1952); National Sound
  Archive T10145W

6 Liberty is liberty, not equality or fairness
  or justice or human happiness or a quiet
  conscience.
  Two Concepts of Liberty (1958) p. 10

Georges Bernanos 1888–1948

7 The wish for prayer is a prayer in itself.
  Journal d'un curé de campagne (1936) ch. 2

8 Hell, madam, is to love no more.
  Journal d'un curé de campagne (1936) ch. 2

Bernard of Chartres d. *c.*1130

9 We are like dwarfs on the shoulders of
  giants, so that we can see more than they,
  and things at a greater distance, not by
  virtue of any sharpness of sight on our
  part, or any physical distinction, but
  because we are carried high and raised up
  by their giant size.
  In John of Salisbury *The Metalogicon* (1159)
  bk. 3, ch. 4. Cf. 239:2

Eric Berne 1910–70

10 Games people play: the psychology of
   human relationships.
   Title of book (1964)

John Berryman 1914–72

11   People will take balls,
   Balls will be lost always, little boy,
   And no one buys a ball back.
   'The Ball Poem' (1948)

12 We must travel in the direction of our fear.
   'A Point of Age' (1942)

13 Life, friends, is boring. We must not
   say so ...
   And moreover my mother taught me as
   a boy
   (repeatingly) 'Ever to confess you're bored
   means you have no
   Inner Resources.'
   77 Dream Songs (1964) no. 14

14 I seldom go to films. They are too exciting,
   said the Honourable Possum.
   77 Dream Songs (1964) no. 53

Theobald von Bethmann Hollweg 1856–1921

15 Just for a word 'neutrality'—a word which
   in wartime has so often been
   disregarded—just for a scrap of paper,
   Great Britain is going to make war on
   a kindred nation who desires nothing
   better than to be friends with her.
   Summary of a report by Sir Edward Goschen
   to Sir Edward Grey in *British Documents on
   Origins of the War 1898–1914* (1926) vol. 11,
   p. 351

Sir John Betjeman 1906–84

16 He sipped at a weak hock and seltzer
   As he gazed at the London skies
   Through the Nottingham lace of the
   curtains
   Or was it his bees-winged eyes?
   'The Arrest of Oscar Wilde at the Cadogan
   Hotel' (1937)

17 And girls in slacks remember Dad,
   And oafish louts remember Mum,
   And sleepless children's hearts are glad,
   And Christmas-morning bells say 'Come!'
   'Christmas' (1954)

18 And is it true? And is it true,
   This most tremendous tale of all,
   Seen in a stained-glass window's hue,
   A Baby in an ox's stall?
   'Christmas' (1954)

19 Oh! Chintzy, Chintzy cheeriness,
   Half dead and half alive!
   'Death in Leamington' (1931)

20 Spirits of well-shot woodcock, partridge,
   snipe
   Flutter and bear him up the Norfolk sky.
   'Death of King George V' (1937)

21 Old men who never cheated, never
   doubted,
   Communicated monthly, sit and stare
   At the new suburb stretched beyond the
   run-way
   Where a young man lands hatless from the
   air.
   'Death of King George V' (1937)

22 Whist upon whist upon whist upon whist
   drive, in Institute, Legion and Social Club.
   Horny hands that hold the aces which this
   morning held the plough.
   'Dorset' (1937)

1 Oh shall I see the Thames again?
   The prow-promoted gems again,
   As beefy ATS
   Without their hats
   Come shooting through the bridge?
   And 'cheerioh' or 'cheeri-bye'
   Across the waste of waters die
   And low the mists of evening lie
   And lightly skims the midge.
   'Henley-on-Thames' (1945)

2 Phone for the fish-knives, Norman
   As Cook is a little unnerved;
   You kiddies have crumpled the serviettes
   And I must have things daintily served.
   'How to get on in Society' (1954)

3 The Church's Restoration
   In eighteen-eighty-three
   Has left for contemplation
   Not what there used to be.
   'Hymn' (1931)

4 Think of what our Nation stands for,
   Books from Boots' and country lanes,
   Free speech, free passes, class distinction,
   Democracy and proper drains.
   'In Westminster Abbey' (1940)

5 In the licorice fields at Pontefract
   My love and I did meet
   And many a burdened licorice bush
   Was blooming round our feet.
   'The Licorice Fields at Pontefract' (1954)

6 Belbroughton Road is bonny, and pinkly
     bursts the spray
   Of prunus and forsythia across the public
     way.
   'May-Day Song for North Oxford' (1945)

7 Gaily into Ruislip Gardens
   Runs the red electric train,
   With a thousand Ta's and Pardon's
   Daintily alights Elaine;
   Hurries down the concrete station
   With a frown of concentration,
   Out into the outskirt's edges
   Where a few surviving hedges
   Keep alive our lost Elysium—rural
     Middlesex again.
   'Middlesex' (1954)

8 Pam, I adore you, Pam, you great big
     mountainous sports girl,
   Whizzing them over the net, full of the
     strength of five:
   That old Malvernian brother, you zephyr
     and khaki shorts girl,
   Although he's playing for Woking,
   Can't stand up to your wonderful
     backhand drive.
   'Pot Pourri from a Surrey Garden' (1940)

9 Come, friendly bombs, and fall on Slough!
   It isn't fit for humans now,
   There isn't grass to graze a cow.
   Swarm over, Death!
   'Slough' (1937)

10 Miss J. Hunter Dunn, Miss J. Hunter Dunn,
   Furnish'd and burnish'd by Aldershot sun.
   'A Subaltern's Love-Song' (1945)

11 Love-thirty, love-forty, oh! weakness of joy,
   The speed of a swallow, the grace of a boy,
   With carefullest carelessness, gaily you
     won,
   I am weak from your loveliness, Joan
     Hunter Dunn.
   'A Subaltern's Love-Song' (1945)

12 By roads 'not adopted', by woodlanded
     ways,
   She drove to the club in the late summer
     haze.
   'A Subaltern's Love-Song' (1945)

13 Oh! full Surrey twilight! importunate band!
   Oh! strongly adorable tennis-girl's hand!
   'A Subaltern's Love-Song' (1945)

14 The dread of beatings! Dread of being late!
   And, greatest dread of all, the dread of
     games!
   Summoned by Bells (1960) ch. 7

15 Broad of Church and 'broad of Mind',
   Broad before and broad behind,
   A keen ecclesiologist,
   A rather dirty Wykehamist.
   'The Wykehamist' (1931)

16 Ghastly good taste, or a depressing story of
   the rise and fall of English architecture.
   Title of book (1933)

Aneurin Bevan 1897–1960

17 This island is made mainly of coal and
   surrounded by fish. Only an organizing
   genius could produce a shortage of coal
   and fish at the same time.
   Speech at Blackpool, 24 May 1945, in *Daily
   Herald* 25 May 1945

18 No amount of cajolery, and no attempts at
   ethical or social seduction, can eradicate
   from my heart a deep burning hatred for
   the Tory Party . . . So far as I am concerned
   they are lower than vermin.
   Speech at Manchester, 4 July 1948, in *The
   Times* 5 July 1948

19 The language of priorities is the religion of
   Socialism.
   Speech at Labour Party Conference, 8 June
   1949; in *Report of the 48th Annual Conference*
   (1949) p. 172

20 [Winston Churchill] does not talk the
   language of the 20th century but that of
   the 18th. He is still fighting Blenheim all
   over again. His only answer to a difficult
   situation is send a gun-boat.
   Speech at Labour Party Conference,
   2 October 1951, in *Daily Herald* 3 October
   1951

21 I am not going to spend any time
   whatsoever in attacking the Foreign
   Secretary . . . If we complain about the
   tune, there is no reason to attack the
   monkey when the organ grinder is present.
   During a debate on the Suez crisis, *Hansard*
   16 May 1957, col. 680

1 If you carry this resolution you will send Britain's Foreign Secretary naked into the conference chamber.

Speech at Labour Party Conference, 3 October 1957, against a motion proposing unilateral nuclear disarmament by the UK; in *Daily Herald* 4 October 1957

2 I stuffed their mouths with gold.

On his handling of the consultants during the establishment of the National Health Service, in B. Abel-Smith *The Hospitals 1800–1948* (1964) ch. 29

3 Listening to a speech by Chamberlain is like paying a visit to Woolworth's: everything in its place and nothing above sixpence.

In Michael Foot *Aneurin Bevan* (1962) vol. 1, ch. 8

4 Damn it all, you can't have the crown of thorns *and* the thirty pieces of silver.

In Michael Foot *Aneurin Bevan* (1973) vol. 2, ch. 13

5 We know what happens to people who stay in the middle of the road. They get run down.

In *Observer* 6 December 1953

6 I read the newspapers avidly. It is my one form of continuous fiction.

In *The Times* 29 March 1960

William Henry Beveridge
1879–1963

7 Want is one only of five giants on the road of reconstruction ... the others are Disease, Ignorance, Squalor and Idleness.

Social Insurance and Allied Services (1942) pt. 7

Ernest Bevin 1881–1951

8 The most conservative man in this world is the British Trade Unionist when you want to change him.

Speech, 8 September 1927, in *Report of Proceedings of the Trades Union Congress* (1927) p. 298

9 My [foreign] policy is to be able to take a ticket at Victoria Station and go anywhere I damn well please.

In *Spectator* 20 April 1951, p. 514

10 If you open that Pandora's Box, you never know what Trojan 'orses will jump out.

On the Council of Europe, in Sir Roderick Barclay *Ernest Bevin and the Foreign Office* (1975) ch. 3

11 I didn't ought never to have done it. It was you, Willie, what put me up to it.

To Lord Strang, after officially recognizing Communist China; in C. Parrott *Serpent and Nightingale* (1977) ch. 3

The Bible
(Authorized Version, 1611)

12 Upon the setting of that bright Occidental Star, Queen Elizabeth of most happy memory.

The Epistle Dedicatory

Old Testament: Genesis

13 In the beginning God created the heaven and the earth. And the earth was without form, and void; and darkness was upon the face of the deep. And the Spirit of God moved upon the face of the waters. And God said, Let there be light: and there was light.

Genesis ch. 1, v. 1

14 And the evening and the morning were the first day.

Genesis ch. 1, v. 5

15 And God saw that it was good.

Genesis ch. 1, v. 10

16 Male and female created he them.

Genesis ch. 1, v. 27

17 Be fruitful, and multiply, and replenish the earth, and subdue it.

Genesis ch. 1, v. 28

18 And the Lord God planted a garden eastward in Eden.

Genesis ch. 2, v. 8

19 But of the tree of the knowledge of good and evil, thou shalt not eat of it: for in the day that thou eatest thereof thou shalt surely die.

Genesis ch. 2, v. 17

20 It is not good that the man should be alone; I will make him an help meet for him.

Genesis ch. 2, v. 18

21 And the rib, which the Lord God had taken from man, made he a woman.

Genesis ch. 2, v. 22

22 Bone of my bones, and flesh of my flesh.

Genesis ch. 2, v. 23

23 Therefore shall a man leave his father and his mother, and shall cleave unto his wife: and they shall be one flesh.

Genesis ch. 2, v. 24

24 Now the serpent was more subtil than any beast of the field.

Genesis ch. 3, v. 1

25 Ye shall be as gods, knowing good and evil.

Genesis ch. 3, v. 5

26 And they sewed fig leaves together, and made themselves aprons.

And they heard the voice of the Lord God walking in the garden in the cool of the day.

Genesis ch. 3, v. 7 ('and made themselves breeches' in the Geneva ['Breeches'] Bible, 1560)

27 The serpent beguiled me, and I did eat.

Genesis ch. 3, v. 13

1 In sorrow thou shalt bring forth children.
Genesis ch. 3, v. 16

2 In the sweat of thy face shalt thou eat
bread.
Genesis ch. 3, v. 19

3 For dust thou art, and unto dust shalt thou
return.
Genesis ch. 3, v. 19

4 Am I my brother's keeper?
Genesis ch. 4, v. 9

5 And the Lord set a mark upon Cain.
Genesis ch. 4, v. 15

6 And Cain went out from the presence of
the Lord, and dwelt in the land of Nod,
on the east of Eden.
Genesis ch. 4, v. 16

7 There were giants in the earth in those
days.
Genesis ch. 6, v. 4

8 There went in two and two unto Noah into
the Ark, the male and the female.
Genesis ch. 7, v. 9

9 Whoso sheddeth man's blood, by man shall
his blood be shed.
Genesis ch. 9, v. 6

10 I do set my bow in the cloud, and it shall
be for a token of a covenant between me
and the earth.
Genesis ch. 9, v. 13

11 Even as Nimrod the mighty hunter before
the Lord.
Genesis ch. 10, v. 9

12 Thou shalt be buried in a good old age.
Genesis ch. 15, v. 15

13 His [Ishmael's] hand will be against every
man, and every man's hand against him.
Genesis ch. 16, v. 12

14 Now Abraham and Sarah were old and well
stricken in age; and it ceased to be with
Sarah after the manner of women.
Genesis ch. 18, v. 11

15 But his wife looked back from behind him,
and she became a pillar of salt.
Genesis ch. 19, v. 26

16 Behold behind him a ram caught in a
thicket by his horns.
Genesis ch. 22, v. 13

17 Esau selleth his birthright for a mess of
potage.
Genesis ch. 25 (chapter heading in Geneva
Bible, 1560)

18 And he sold his birthright unto Jacob.
Genesis ch. 25, v. 33

19 Behold, Esau my brother is a hairy man,
and I am a smooth man.
Genesis ch. 27, v. 11

20 The voice is Jacob's voice, but the hands
are the hands of Esau.
Genesis ch. 27, v. 22

21 And he dreamed, and behold a ladder set
up on the earth, and the top of it reached
to heaven: and behold the angels of God
ascending and descending on it.
Genesis ch. 28, v. 12

22 And Jacob served seven years for Rachel;
and they seemed unto him but a few
days, for the love he had to her.
Genesis ch. 29, v. 20

23 The Lord watch between me and thee,
when we are absent one from another.
Genesis ch. 31, v. 49

24 Now Israel loved Joseph more than all his
children, because he was the son of his
old age; and he made him a coat of many
colours.
Genesis ch. 37, v. 3

25 Behold, this dreamer cometh.
Genesis ch. 37, v. 19

26 Then shall ye bring down my grey hairs
with sorrow to the grave.
Genesis ch. 42, v. 38

27 Ye shall eat the fat of the land.
Genesis ch. 45, v. 18

28 See that ye fall not out by the way.
Genesis ch. 45, v. 24

Exodus

29 I have been a stranger in a strange land.
Exodus ch. 2, v. 22. See Exodus ch. 18, v. 3

30 Behold, the bush burned with fire, and the
bush was not consumed.
Exodus ch. 3, v. 2

31 Put off thy shoes from off thy feet, for the
place whereon thou standest is holy
ground.
Exodus ch. 3, v. 5

32 A land flowing with milk and honey.
Exodus ch. 3, v. 8

33 I AM THAT I AM.
Exodus ch. 3, v. 14

34 Let my people go.
Exodus ch. 7, v. 16

35 Stretch out thine hand toward heaven, that
there may be darkness over the land of
Egypt, even darkness which may be felt.
Exodus ch. 10, v. 21

36 And they shall eat the flesh in that night,
roast with fire, and unleavened bread;
and with bitter herbs they shall eat it.
Exodus ch. 12, v. 8

37 With your loins girded, your shoes on your
feet, and your staff in your hand; and ye
shall eat it in haste; it is the Lord's
passover.
Exodus ch. 12, v. 11

38 And they spoiled the Egyptians.
Exodus ch. 12, v. 36

39 And the Lord went before them by day in a
pillar of a cloud, to lead them the way;
and by night in a pillar of fire, to give
them light.
Exodus ch. 13, v. 21

1 Would to God we had died by the hand of the Lord in the land of Egypt, when we sat by the flesh pots, and when we did eat bread to the full.
Exodus ch. 16, v. 3

2 I am the Lord thy God, which have brought thee out of the land of Egypt, out of the house of bondage.
Exodus ch. 20, v. 2

3 Thou shalt have no other gods before me.
Exodus ch. 20, v. 3

4 Thou shalt not make unto thee any graven image.
Exodus ch. 20, v. 4

5 I the Lord thy God am a jealous God, visiting the iniquity of the fathers upon the children unto the third and fourth generation of them that hate me.
Exodus ch. 20, v. 5

6 Thou shalt not take the name of the Lord thy God in vain.
Exodus ch. 20, v. 7

7 Remember the sabbath day, to keep it holy.
Exodus ch. 20, v. 8

8 Honour thy father and thy mother.
Exodus ch. 20, v. 12

9 Thou shalt not kill.
Thou shalt not commit adultery.
Thou shalt not steal.
Thou shalt not bear false witness against thy neighbour.
Thou shalt not covet thy neighbour's house, thou shalt not covet thy neighbour's wife, nor his manservant, nor his maidservant, nor his ox, nor his ass, nor any thing that is thy neighbour's.
Exodus ch. 20, v. 13

10 Life for life,
Eye for eye, tooth for tooth.
Exodus ch. 21, v. 23

11 Thou art a stiffnecked people.
Exodus ch. 33, v. 3

12 There shall no man see me and live.
Exodus ch. 33, v. 20

Leviticus

13 Let him go for a scapegoat into the wilderness.
Leviticus ch. 16, v. 10

14 Thou shalt love thy neighbour as thyself.
Leviticus ch. 19, v. 18. See St Matthew ch. 19, v. 19

Numbers

15 The Lord bless thee, and keep thee:
The Lord make his face shine upon thee, and be gracious unto thee:
The Lord lift up his countenance upon thee, and give thee peace.
Numbers ch. 6, v. 24

16 These are the names of the men which Moses sent to spy out the land.
Numbers ch. 13, v. 16

17 He whom thou blessest is blessed, and he whom thou cursest is cursed.
Numbers ch. 22, v. 6

18 God is not a man, that he should lie.
Numbers ch. 23, v. 19

19 What hath God wrought!
Numbers ch. 23, v. 23 (quoted by Samuel Morse in the first electric telegraph message, 24 May 1844)

20 Be sure your sin will find you out.
Numbers ch. 32, v. 23

Deuteronomy

21 For the Lord thy God is a jealous God.
Deuteronomy ch. 6, v. 15. Cf. 40:5

22 If there arise among you a prophet, or a dreamer of dreams ... Thou shalt not hearken.
Deuteronomy ch. 13, v. 1

23 He found him in a desert land, and in the waste howling wilderness; he led him about, he instructed him, he kept him as the apple of his eye.
Deuteronomy ch. 32, v. 10

24 For they are a very froward generation, children in whom is no faith.
Deuteronomy ch. 32, v. 20

25 The eternal God is thy refuge, and underneath are the everlasting arms.
Deuteronomy ch. 33, v. 27

Joshua

26 Be strong and of a good courage; be not afraid, neither be thou dismayed: for the Lord thy God is with thee, whithersoever thou goest.
Joshua ch. 1, v. 9

27 When the people heard the sound of the trumpet, and the people shouted with a great shout, that the wall fell down flat, so that the people went up into the city.
Joshua ch. 6, v. 20

28 Let them live; but let them be hewers of wood and drawers of water unto all the congregation.
Joshua ch. 9, v. 21

29 I am going the way of all the earth.
Joshua ch. 23, v. 14

Judges

30 He delivered them into the hands of spoilers.
Judges ch. 2, v. 14

31 I arose a mother in Israel.
Judges ch. 5, v. 7

32 The stars in their courses fought against Sisera.
Judges ch. 5, v. 20

33 She brought forth butter in a lordly dish.
Judges ch. 5, v. 25

34 Why tarry the wheels of his chariots?
Judges ch. 5, v. 28

35 The Lord is with thee, thou mighty man of valour.
Judges ch. 6, v. 12

1 Faint, yet pursuing.
Judges ch. 8, v. 4

2 Then said they unto him, Say now Shibboleth: and he said Sibboleth: for he could not frame to pronounce it right.
Judges ch. 12, v. 6

3 Out of the eater came forth meat, and out of the strong came forth sweetness.
Judges ch. 14, v. 14

4 He smote them hip and thigh.
Judges ch. 15, v. 8

5 With the jaw of an ass have I slain a thousand men.
Judges ch. 15, v. 16

6 He did grind in the prison house.
Judges ch. 16, v. 21

7 The people arose as one man.
Judges ch. 20, v. 8

Ruth

8 Intreat me not to leave thee, or to return from following after thee: for whither thou goest, I will go; and where thou lodgest, I will lodge: thy people shall be my people, and thy God my God:
Ruth ch. 1, v. 16

I Samuel

9 Speak, Lord; for thy servant heareth.
I Samuel ch. 3, v. 9

10 Quit yourselves like men, and fight.
I Samuel ch. 4, v. 9

11 And she named the child I-chabod, saying, The glory is departed from Israel.
I Samuel ch. 4, v. 21

12 God save the king.
I Samuel ch. 10, v. 24

13 A man after his own heart.
I Samuel ch. 13, v. 14

14 I did but taste a little honey with the end of the rod that was in mine hand, and, lo, I must die.
I Samuel ch. 14, v. 43

15 For the Lord seeth not as man seeth: for man looketh on the outward appearance, but the Lord looketh on the heart.
I Samuel ch. 16, v. 7

16 Now he was ruddy, and withal of a beautiful countenance, and goodly to look to.
I Samuel ch. 16, v. 12

17 I know thy pride, and the naughtiness of thine heart.
I Samuel ch. 17, v. 28

18 And he took his staff in his hand and chose him five smooth stones out of the brook.
I Samuel ch. 17, v. 40

19 Behold, I have played the fool.
I Samuel ch. 26, v. 21

II Samuel

20 The beauty of Israel is slain upon thy high places: how are the mighty fallen!
II Samuel ch. 1, v. 19

21 Tell it not in Gath, publish it not in the streets of Askelon.
II Samuel ch. 1, v. 20

22 Saul and Jonathan were lovely and pleasant in their lives, and in their death they were not divided: they were swifter than eagles, they were stronger than lions.
II Samuel ch. 1, v. 23

23 Thy love to me was wonderful, passing the love of women.
How are the mighty fallen, and the weapons of war perished!
II Samuel ch. 1, v. 26

24 The poor man had nothing, save one little ewe lamb.
II Samuel ch. 12, v. 3

25 Come out, come out, thou bloody man.
II Samuel ch. 16, v. 7

26 And when Ahithophel saw that his counsel was not followed, he saddled his ass, and arose, and gat him home to his house, to his city, and put his household in order, and hanged himself.
II Samuel ch. 17, v. 23

27 O my son Absalom, my son, my son Absalom! would God I had died for thee, O Absalom, my son, my son!
II Samuel ch. 18, v. 33

28 David ... sweet psalmist of Israel.
II Samuel ch. 23, v. 1

I Kings

29 Then will I cut off Israel out of the land which I have given them; and this house, which I have hallowed for my name, will I cast out of my sight; and Israel shall be a proverb and a byword among all people.
I Kings ch. 9, v. 7

30 Behold, the half was not told me.
I Kings ch. 10, v. 7

31 Once in three years came the navy of Tharshish, bringing gold, and silver, ivory, and apes, and peacocks.
I Kings ch. 10, v. 22

32 But king Solomon loved many strange women.
I Kings ch. 11, v. 1

33 My little finger shall be thicker than my father's loins.
I Kings ch. 12, v. 10

34 My father hath chastised you with whips, but I will chastise you with scorpions.
I Kings ch. 12, v. 11

35 An handful of meal in a barrel, and a little oil in a cruse.
I Kings ch. 17, v. 12

36 How long halt ye between two opinions?
I Kings ch. 18, v. 21

1 There is a sound of abundance of rain.
I Kings ch. 18, v. 41

2 There ariseth a little cloud out of the sea, like a man's hand.
I Kings ch. 18, v. 44

3 But the Lord was not in the wind: and after the wind an earthquake; but the Lord was not in the earthquake:
And after the earthquake a fire: but the Lord was not in the fire: and after the fire a still small voice.
I Kings ch. 19, v. 11

4 Elijah passed by him, and cast his mantle upon him.
I Kings ch. 19, v. 19

5 Hast thou found me, O mine enemy?
I Kings ch. 21, v. 20

6 Feed him with bread of affliction and with water of affliction, until I come in peace.
I Kings ch. 22, v. 27

7 And a certain man drew a bow at a venture, and smote the king of Israel between the joints of the harness.
I Kings ch. 22, v. 34

II Kings

8 Go up, thou bald head.
II Kings ch. 2, v. 23

9 Is it well with the child? And she answered, It is well.
II Kings ch. 4, v. 26

10 There is death in the pot.
II Kings ch. 4, v. 40

11 I bow myself in the house of Rimmon.
II Kings ch. 5, v. 18

12 Is thy servant a dog, that he should do this great thing?
II Kings ch. 8, v. 13

13 The driving is like the driving of Jehu, the son of Nimshi; for he driveth furiously.
II Kings ch. 9, v. 20

14 She painted her face, and tired her head, and looked out at a window.
II Kings ch. 9, v. 30

15 Who is on my side? who?
II Kings ch. 9, v. 32

16 Thou trustest upon the staff of this bruised reed, even upon Egypt, on which if a man lean, it will go into his hand, and pierce it.
II Kings ch. 18, v. 21

I Chronicles

17 For we are strangers before thee, and sojourners, as were all our fathers: our days on the earth are as a shadow, and there is none abiding.
I Chronicles ch. 29, v. 15

18 He died in a good old age, full of days, riches, and honour.
I Chronicles ch. 29, v. 28

Esther

19 And if I perish, I perish.
Esther ch. 4, v. 16

20 Thus shall it be done to the man whom the king delighteth to honour.
Esther ch. 6, v. 9

Job

21 And the Lord said unto Satan, Whence comest thou? Then Satan answered the Lord, and said, From going to and fro in the earth, and from walking up and down in it.
Job ch. 1, v. 7

22 The Lord gave, and the Lord hath taken away; blessed be the name of the Lord.
Job ch. 1, v. 21

23 All that a man hath will he give for his life.
Job ch. 2, v. 4

24 Curse God, and die.
Job ch. 2, v. 9

25 Let the day perish wherein I was born, and the night in which it was said, There is a man child conceived.
Job ch. 3, v. 3

26 Kings and counsellors of the earth, which built desolate places for themselves.
Job ch. 3, v. 14

27 There the wicked cease from troubling, and there the weary be at rest.
Job ch. 3, v. 17

28 Then a spirit passed before my face; the hair of my flesh stood up.
Job ch. 4, v. 15

29 Man is born unto trouble, as the sparks fly upward.
Job ch. 5, v. 7

30 My days are swifter than a weaver's shuttle.
Job ch. 7, v. 6

31 He shall return no more to his house, neither shall his place know him any more.
Job ch. 7, v. 10

32 Canst thou by searching find out God?
Job ch. 11, v. 7

33 Man that is born of a woman is of few days, and full of trouble.
He cometh forth like a flower, and is cut down: he fleeth also as a shadow, and continueth not.
Job ch. 14, v. 1. Cf. 66:6

34 Miserable comforters are ye all.
Job ch. 16, v. 2

35 I am escaped with the skin of my teeth.
Job ch. 19, v. 20

36 I know that my redeemer liveth, and that he shall stand at the latter day upon the earth:
Job ch. 19, v. 25

1 But where shall wisdom be found? and where is the place of understanding?
Job ch. 28, v. 12

2 The price of wisdom is above rubies.
Job ch. 28, v. 18

3 I am a brother to dragons, and a companion to owls.
Job ch. 30, v. 29

4 Canst thou bind the sweet influences of Pleiades, or loose the bands of Orion?
Job ch. 38, v. 31

5 He saith among the trumpets, Ha, ha; and he smelleth the battle afar off, the thunder of the captains, and the shouting.
Job ch. 39, v. 25

6 Canst thou draw out leviathan with an hook?
Job ch. 41, v. 1

Proverbs

7 For whom the Lord loveth he correcteth.
Proverbs ch. 3, v. 12

8 Length of days is in her right hand; and in her left hand riches and honour.
Proverbs ch. 3, v. 16

9 Her ways are ways of pleasantness, and all her paths are peace.
Proverbs ch. 3, v. 17

10 Wisdom is the principal thing; therefore get wisdom: and with all thy getting get understanding.
Proverbs ch. 4, v. 7

11 Go to the ant thou sluggard; consider her ways, and be wise.
Proverbs ch. 6, v. 6

12 Yet a little sleep, a little slumber, a little folding of the hands to sleep.
Proverbs ch. 6, v. 10. See Proverbs ch. 24, v. 33

13 He goeth after her straightway, as an ox goeth to the slaughter.
Proverbs ch. 7, v. 22

14 Wisdom hath builded her house, she hath hewn out her seven pillars.
Proverbs ch. 9, v. 1

15 Stolen waters are sweet, and bread eaten in secret is pleasant.
Proverbs ch. 9, v. 17

16 A wise son maketh a glad father: but a foolish son is the heaviness of his mother.
Proverbs ch. 10, v. 1

17 The destruction of the poor is their poverty.
Proverbs ch. 10, v. 15

18 He that is surety for a stranger shall smart for it.
Proverbs ch. 11, v. 15

19 A virtuous woman is a crown to her husband.
Proverbs ch. 12, v. 4

20 A righteous man regardeth the life of his beast: but the tender mercies of the wicked are cruel.
Proverbs ch. 12, v. 10

21 Hope deferred maketh the heart sick: but when the desire cometh, it is a tree of life.
Proverbs ch. 13, v. 12

22 The way of transgressors is hard.
Proverbs ch. 13, v. 15

23 He that spareth his rod hateth his son.
Proverbs ch. 13, v. 24

24 A soft answer turneth away wrath.
Proverbs ch. 15, v. 1

25 A merry heart maketh a cheerful countenance.
Proverbs ch. 15, v. 13

26 Better is a dinner of herbs where love is, than a stalled ox and hatred therewith.
Proverbs ch. 15, v. 17

27 A word spoken in due season, how good is it!
Proverbs ch. 15, v. 23

28 Pride goeth before destruction, and an haughty spirit before a fall.
Proverbs ch. 16, v. 18

29 A wounded spirit who can bear?
Proverbs ch. 18, v. 14

30 There is a friend that sticketh closer than a brother.
Proverbs ch. 18, v. 24

31 Wine is a mocker, strong drink is raging.
Proverbs ch. 20, v. 1

32 It is better to dwell in a corner of the housetop, than with a brawling woman in a wide house.
Proverbs ch. 21, v. 9

33 Look not thou upon the wine when it is red, when it giveth his colour in the cup . . . At the last it biteth like a serpent, and stingeth like an adder.
Proverbs ch. 23, v. 31

34 The heart of kings is unsearchable.
Proverbs ch. 25, v. 3

35 A word fitly spoken is like apples of gold in pictures of silver.
Proverbs ch. 25, v. 11

36 If thine enemy be hungry, give him bread to eat; and if he be thirsty, give him water to drink.
For thou shalt heap coals of fire upon his head, and the Lord shall reward thee.
Proverbs ch. 25, v. 21

37 As cold waters to a thirsty soul, so is good news from a far country.
Proverbs ch. 25, v. 25

38 Answer not a fool according to his folly, lest thou also be like unto him.
Answer a fool according to his folly, lest he be wise in his own conceit.
Proverbs ch. 26, v. 4

1 A continual dropping in a very rainy day and a contentious woman are alike.
Proverbs ch. 27, v. 15

2 A fool uttereth all his mind.
Proverbs ch. 29, v. 11

3 Where there is no vision, the people perish.
Proverbs ch. 29, v. 18

4 There be three things which are too wonderful for me, yea, four which I know not:
The way of an eagle in the air; the way of a serpent upon a rock; the way of a ship in the midst of the sea; and the way of a man with a maid.
Proverbs ch. 30, v. 18

5 Give strong drink unto him that is ready to perish, and wine unto those that be of heavy hearts.
Proverbs ch. 31, v. 6

6 Who can find a virtuous woman? for her price is far above rubies.
Proverbs ch. 31, v. 10

Ecclesiastes

7 Vanity of vanities; all is vanity.
Ecclesiastes ch. 1, v. 2

8 The thing that hath been, it is that which shall be; and that which is done is that which shall be done: and there is no new thing under the sun.
Ecclesiastes ch. 1, v. 9

9 All is vanity and vexation of spirit.
Ecclesiastes ch. 1, v. 14

10 He that increaseth knowledge increaseth sorrow.
Ecclesiastes ch. 1, v. 18

11 To every thing there is a season, and a time to every purpose under the heaven:
A time to be born, and a time to die; a time to plant, and a time to pluck up that which is planted.
Ecclesiastes ch. 3, v. 1

12 A time to weep, and a time to laugh; a time to mourn, and a time to dance.
Ecclesiastes ch. 3, v. 4

13 A time to love, and a time to hate; a time of war, and a time of peace.
Ecclesiastes ch. 3, v. 8

14 A threefold cord is not quickly broken.
Ecclesiastes ch. 4, v. 12

15 The sleep of a labouring man is sweet.
Ecclesiastes ch. 5, v. 12

16 As the crackling of thorns under a pot, so is the laughter of a fool.
Ecclesiastes ch. 7, v. 6

17 There is no discharge in that war.
Ecclesiastes ch. 8, v. 8

18 A man hath no better thing under the sun, than to eat, and to drink, and to be merry.
Ecclesiastes ch. 8, v. 15. Cf. 45:24, 52:18

19 Whatsoever thy hand findeth to do, do it with thy might; for there is no work, nor device, nor knowledge, nor wisdom, in the grave, whither thou goest.
Ecclesiastes ch. 9, v. 10

20 The race is not to the swift, nor the battle to the strong.
Ecclesiastes ch. 9, v. 11

21 He that diggeth a pit shall fall into it.
Ecclesiastes ch. 10, v. 8

22 Woe to thee, O land, when thy king is a child, and thy princes eat in the morning!
Ecclesiastes ch. 10, v. 16

23 Wine maketh merry: but money answereth all things.
Ecclesiastes ch. 10, v. 19

24 Cast thy bread upon the waters: for thou shalt find it after many days.
Ecclesiastes ch. 11, v. 1

25 Remember now thy Creator in the days of thy youth.
Ecclesiastes ch. 12, v. 1

26 And desire shall fail: because man goeth to his long home, and the mourners go about the streets:
Or ever the silver cord be loosed, or the golden bowl be broken, or the pitcher be broken at the fountain, or the wheel broken at the cistern.
Then shall the dust return to the earth as it was: and the spirit shall return unto God who gave it.
Ecclesiastes ch. 12, v. 5

27 Of making many books there is no end; and much study is a weariness of the flesh.
Ecclesiastes ch. 12, v. 12

28 Fear God, and keep his commandments: for this is the whole duty of man.
Ecclesiastes ch. 12, v. 13

Song of Solomon

29 I am black, but comely.
Song of Solomon ch. 1, v. 5

30 A bundle of myrrh is my wellbeloved unto me.
Song of Solomon ch. 1, v. 13

31 I am the rose of Sharon, and the lily of the valleys.
Song of Solomon ch. 2, v. 1

32 The time of the singing of birds is come, and the voice of the turtle is heard in our land.
Song of Solomon ch. 2, v. 12

33 Take us the foxes, the little foxes, that spoil the vines.
Song of Solomon ch. 2, v. 15

34 Behold, thou art fair, my love; behold, thou art fair.
Song of Solomon ch. 4, v. 1

35 Thou art all fair, my love; there is no spot in thee.
Song of Solomon ch. 4, v. 7

1 Set me as a seal upon thine heart, as a seal upon thine arm.
Song of Solomon ch. 8, v. 6

2 Many waters cannot quench love, neither can the floods drown it.
Song of Solomon ch. 8, v. 7

Isaiah

3 The daughter of Zion is left as a cottage in a vineyard, as a lodge in a garden of cucumbers.
Isaiah ch. 1, v. 8

4 Though your sins be as scarlet, they shall be as white as snow.
Isaiah ch. 1, v. 18

5 They shall beat their swords into plowshares, and their spears into pruninghooks: nation shall not lift up sword against nation, neither shall they learn war any more.
Isaiah ch. 2, v. 4. See also Micah ch. 4, v. 3, Joel ch. 3, v. 10

6 What mean ye that ye beat my people to pieces, and grind the faces of the poor?
Isaiah ch. 3, v. 15

7 My well-beloved hath a vineyard in a very fruitful hill.
Isaiah ch. 5, v. 1

8 Woe unto them that join house to house, that lay field to field, till there be no place.
Isaiah ch. 5, v. 8

9 Woe unto them that call evil good, and good evil.
Isaiah ch. 5, v. 20

10 I saw also the Lord sitting upon a throne, high and lifted up, and his train filled the temple.
Above it stood the seraphims: each one had six wings; with twain he covered his face, and with twain he covered his feet, and with twain he did fly.
And one cried unto another, and said, Holy, holy, holy, is the Lord of hosts: the whole earth is full of his glory.
Isaiah ch. 6, v. 1

11 Then said I, Woe is me! for I am undone; because I am a man of unclean lips, and I dwell in the midst of a people of unclean lips.
Isaiah ch. 6, v. 5

12 Whom shall I send, and who will go for us? Then said I, Here am I; send me.
Isaiah ch. 6, v. 8

13 Then said I, Lord, how long?
Isaiah ch. 6, v. 11

14 Behold, a virgin shall conceive, and bear a son, and shall call his name Immanuel.
Isaiah ch. 7, v. 14

15 The people that walked in darkness have seen a great light: they that dwell in the land of the shadow of death, upon them hath the light shined.
Isaiah ch. 9, v. 2. Cf. 269:10

16 For unto us a child is born, unto us a son is given: and the government shall be upon his shoulder: and his name shall be called Wonderful, Counsellor, The mighty God, The everlasting Father, The Prince of Peace.
Isaiah ch. 9, v. 6

17 The zeal of the Lord of hosts will perform this.
Isaiah ch. 9, v. 7

18 And there shall come forth a rod out of the stem of Jesse, and a branch shall grow out of his roots:
And the spirit of the Lord shall rest upon him, the spirit of wisdom and understanding, the spirit of counsel and might, the spirit of knowledge and of the fear of the Lord.
Isaiah ch. 11, v. 1

19 The wolf also shall dwell with the lamb, and the leopard shall lie down with the kid; and the calf and the young lion and the fatling together; and a little child shall lead them.
Isaiah ch. 11, v. 6

20 And the sucking child shall play on the hole of the asp, and the weaned child shall put his hand on the cockatrice' den.
They shall not hurt nor destroy in all my holy mountain: for the earth shall be full of the knowledge of the Lord, as the waters cover the sea.
Isaiah ch. 11, v. 8

21 Dragons in their pleasant palaces.
Isaiah ch. 13, v. 22

22 How art thou fallen from heaven, O Lucifer, son of the morning!
Isaiah ch. 14, v. 12

23 Watchman, what of the night? Watchman, what of the night?
The watchman said, The morning cometh, and also the night.
Isaiah ch. 21, v. 11

24 Let us eat and drink; for to morrow we shall die.
Isaiah ch. 22, v. 13. Cf. 44:18, 52:18

25 He will swallow up death in victory; and the Lord God will wipe away tears from off all faces.
Isaiah ch. 25, v. 8

26 We have as it were brought forth wind.
Isaiah ch. 26, v. 18

27 For precept must be upon precept, precept upon precept; line upon line, line upon line; here a little, and there a little.
Isaiah ch. 28, v. 10

28 We have made a covenant with death, and with hell are we at agreement.
Isaiah ch. 28, v. 15

29 Speak unto us smooth things, prophesy deceits.
Isaiah ch. 30, v. 10

1 The bread of adversity, and the waters of affliction.
Isaiah ch. 30, v. 20

2 This is the way, walk ye in it.
Isaiah ch. 30, v. 21

3 And thorns shall come up in her palaces, nettles and brambles in the fortresses thereof: and it shall be an habitation of dragons, and a court for owls.
Isaiah ch. 34, v. 13

4 The desert shall rejoice, and blossom as the rose.
Isaiah ch. 35, v. 1

5 Strengthen ye the weak hands, and confirm the feeble knees.
Isaiah ch. 35, v. 3

6 Set thine house in order: for thou shalt die, and not live.
Isaiah ch. 38, v. 1

7 Comfort ye, comfort ye my people, saith your God.
Speak ye comfortably to Jerusalem, and cry unto her, that her warfare is accomplished.
Isaiah ch. 40, v. 1

8 The voice of him that crieth in the wilderness, Prepare ye the way of the Lord.
Isaiah ch. 40, v. 3. Cf. 48:13

9 Every valley shall be exalted, and every mountain and hill shall be made low: and the crooked shall be made straight, and the rough places plain:
And the glory of the Lord shall be revealed, and all flesh shall see it together: for the mouth of the Lord hath spoken it.
Isaiah ch. 40, v. 3

10 All flesh is grass, and all the goodliness thereof is as the flower of the field:
The grass withereth, the flower fadeth: because the spirit of the Lord bloweth upon it: surely the people is grass.
Isaiah ch. 40, v. 6. Cf. 57:6

11 He shall feed his flock like a shepherd: he shall gather the lambs with his arm, and carry them in his bosom, and shall gently lead those that are with young.
Isaiah ch. 40, v. 11

12 Have ye not known? have ye not heard? hath it not been told you from the beginning?
Isaiah ch. 40, v. 21

13 They shall mount up with wings as eagles; they shall run, and not be weary; and they shall walk, and not faint.
Isaiah ch. 40, v. 31

14 There is no peace, saith the Lord, unto the wicked.
Isaiah ch. 48, v. 22

15 How beautiful upon the mountains are the feet of him that bringeth good tidings, that publisheth peace; that bringeth good tidings of good, that publisheth salvation.
Isaiah ch. 52, v. 7

16 For they shall see eye to eye, when the Lord shall bring again Zion.
Break forth into joy, sing together, ye waste places of Jerusalem.
Isaiah ch. 52, v. 8

17 He is despised and rejected of men; a man of sorrows, and acquainted with grief.
Isaiah ch. 53, v. 2

18 Surely he hath borne our griefs, and carried our sorrows.
Isaiah ch. 53, v. 3

19 But he was wounded for our transgressions, he was bruised for our iniquities: the chastisement of our peace was upon him; and with his stripes we are healed.
All we like sheep have gone astray; we have turned every one to his own way; and the Lord hath laid on him the iniquity of us all.
Isaiah ch. 53, v. 5

20 He is brought as a lamb to the slaughter.
Isaiah ch. 53, v. 7

21 He was cut off out of the land of the living.
Isaiah ch. 53, v. 8

22 For my thoughts are not your thoughts, neither are your ways my ways, saith the Lord.
Isaiah ch. 55, v. 8

23 Arise, shine; for thy light is come, and the glory of the Lord is risen upon thee.
Isaiah ch. 60, v. 1

24 To bind up the brokenhearted, to proclaim liberty to the captives, and the opening of the prison to them that are bound.
Isaiah ch. 61, v. 1

25 Stand by thyself, come not near to me; for I am holier than thou.
Isaiah ch. 65, v. 5

26 For, behold, I create new heavens and a new earth.
Isaiah ch. 65, v. 17

Jeremiah

27 This people hath a revolting and a rebellious heart.
Jeremiah ch. 5, v. 23

28 They have healed also the hurt of the daughter of my people slightly, saying, Peace, peace; when there is no peace.
Jeremiah ch. 6, v. 14

29 Is there no balm in Gilead?
Jeremiah ch. 8, v. 22

30 Can the Ethiopian change his skin, or the leopard his spots?
Jeremiah ch. 13, v. 23

31 The heart is deceitful above all things, and desperately wicked.
Jeremiah ch. 17, v. 9

Lamentations

32 Is it nothing to you, all ye that pass by? behold, and see if there be any sorrow like unto my sorrow.
Lamentations ch. 1, v. 12

1 Remembering mine affliction and my misery, the wormwood and the gall.
Lamentations ch. 3, v. 19

2 It is good for a man that he bear the yoke in his youth.
Lamentations ch. 3, v. 27

3 O Lord, thou hast seen my wrong: judge thou my cause.
Lamentations ch. 4, v. 59

Ezekiel

4 As is the mother, so is her daughter.
Ezekiel ch. 16, v. 44

5 The fathers have eaten sour grapes, and the children's teeth are set on edge.
Ezekiel ch. 18, v. 2

6 When the wicked man turneth away from his wickedness that he hath committed, and doeth that which is lawful and right, he shall save his soul alive.
Ezekiel ch. 18, v. 27

7 The king of Babylon stood at the parting of the ways.
Ezekiel ch. 21, v. 21

8 The valley which was full of bones.
Ezekiel ch. 37, v. 1

9 Can these bones live?
Ezekiel ch. 37, v. 3

10 O ye dry bones, hear the word of the Lord.
Ezekiel ch. 37, v. 4

Daniel

11 Cast into the midst of a burning fiery furnace.
Daniel ch. 3, v. 6

12 And this is the writing that was written, MENE, MENE, TEKEL, UPHARSIN.
This is the interpretation of the thing: MENE; God hath numbered thy kingdom, and finished it.
TEKEL; Thou art weighed in the balances and art found wanting.
PERES; Thy kingdom is divided, and given to the Medes and Persians.
Daniel ch. 5, v. 25

13 Now, O king, establish the decree, and sign the writing, that it be not changed, according to the law of the Medes and Persians, which altereth not.
Daniel ch. 6, v. 8

14 The Ancient of days did sit, whose garment was white as snow, and the hair of his head like the pure wool.
Daniel ch. 7, v. 9

15 Ten thousand times ten thousand stood before him: the judgement was set, and the books were opened.
Daniel ch. 7, v. 10

16 O Daniel, a man greatly beloved.
Daniel ch. 10, v. 11

Hosea

17 They have sown the wind, and they shall reap the whirlwind.
Hosea ch. 8, v. 7

18 I drew them . . . with bands of love.
Hosea ch. 11, v. 4

Joel

19 I will restore to you the years that the locust hath eaten.
Joel ch. 2, v. 25

20 Your sons and your daughters shall prophesy, your old men shall dream dreams, your young men shall see visions.
Joel ch. 2, v. 28

21 Multitudes, multitudes in the valley of decision.
Joel ch. 3, v. 14

Micah

22 But thou, Bethlehem Ephratah, though thou be little among the thousands of Judah, yet out of thee shall he come forth unto me that is to be ruler in Israel.
Micah ch. 5, v. 2

23 What doth the Lord require of thee, but to do justly, and to love mercy, and to walk humbly with thy God?
Micah ch. 6, v. 8

Nahum

24 Woe to the bloody city!
Nahum ch. 3, v. 1

Zephaniah

25 Woe to her that is filthy and polluted, to the oppressing city!
Zephaniah ch. 3, v. 1

Malachi

26 But unto you that fear my name shall the Sun of righteousness arise with healing in his wings.
Malachi ch. 4, v. 2

Apocrypha

27 Great is Truth, and mighty above all things.
I Esdras ch. 4, v. 41. Cf. 58:23

28 I shall light a candle of understanding in thine heart, which shall not be put out.
II Esdras ch. 14, v. 25

29 And in the time of their visitation they shall shine, and run to and fro like sparks among the stubble.
Wisdom of Solomon ch. 3, v. 7

30 Even so we in like manner, as soon as we were born, began to draw to our end.
Wisdom of Solomon ch. 5, v. 13

31 For the hope of the ungodly . . . passeth away as the remembrance of a guest that tarrieth but a day.
Wisdom of Solomon ch. 5, v. 14

32 We will fall into the hands of the Lord, and not into the hands of men: for as his majesty is, so is his mercy.
Ecclesiasticus ch. 2, v. 18

33 Laugh no man to scorn in the bitterness of his soul.
Ecclesiasticus ch. 7, v. 11

1 Judge none blessed before his death.
Ecclesiasticus ch. 11, v. 28. Cf. 310:27

2 He that toucheth pitch shall be defiled therewith.
Ecclesiasticus ch. 13, v. 1

3 A merchant shall hardly keep himself from doing wrong.
Ecclesiasticus ch. 26, v. 29

4 Leave off first for manners' sake.
Ecclesiasticus ch. 31, v. 17

5 He that sinneth before his Maker, let him fall into the hand of the physician.
Ecclesiasticus ch. 38, v. 15

6 How can he get wisdom ... whose talk is of bullocks?
Ecclesiasticus ch. 38, v. 25

7 Let us now praise famous men, and our fathers that begat us.
Ecclesiasticus ch. 44, v. 1

8 And some there be, which have no memorial ... and are become as though they had never been born ...
But these were merciful men, whose righteousness hath not been forgotten ...

Their seed shall remain for ever, and their glory shall not be blotted out.
Their bodies are buried in peace; but their name liveth for evermore.
Ecclesiasticus ch. 44, v. 9

New Testament: St Matthew

9 There came wise men from the east to Jerusalem,
Saying, Where is he that is born King of the Jews? for we have seen his star in the east, and are come to worship him.
St Matthew ch. 2, v. 1

10 They presented unto him gifts; gold, and frankincense, and myrrh.
St Matthew ch. 2, v. 11

11 In Rama was there a voice heard, lamentation, and weeping, and great mourning, Rachel weeping for her children, and would not be comforted, because they are not.
St Matthew ch. 2, v. 18. See Jeremiah ch. 31, v. 15

12 Repent ye: for the kingdom of heaven is at hand.
St Matthew ch. 3, v. 2

13 The voice of one crying in the wilderness, Prepare ye the way of the Lord, make his paths straight.
St Matthew ch. 3, v. 3. Cf. 46:8

14 O generation of vipers, who hath warned you to flee from the wrath to come?
St Matthew ch. 3, v. 7

15 This is my beloved Son, in whom I am well pleased.
St Matthew ch. 3, v. 17

16 Man shall not live by bread alone, but by every word that proceedeth out of the mouth of God.
St Matthew ch. 4, v. 4. See Deuteronomy ch. 8, v. 3

17 Thou shalt not tempt the Lord thy God.
St Matthew ch. 4, v. 7. See Deuteronomy ch. 6, v. 16

18 Follow me, and I will make you fishers of men.
St Matthew ch. 4, v. 19

19 Blessed are the poor in spirit: for theirs is the kingdom of heaven.
Blessed are they that mourn: for they shall be comforted.
Blessed are the meek: for they shall inherit the earth.
Blessed are they which do hunger and thirst after righteousness: for they shall be filled.
Blessed are the merciful: for they shall obtain mercy.
Blessed are the pure in heart: for they shall see God.
Blessed are the peacemakers: for they shall be called the children of God.
St Matthew ch. 5, v. 3

20 Ye are the salt of the earth: but if the salt have lost his savour, wherewith shall it be salted?
St Matthew ch. 5, v. 13

21 Ye are the light of the world. A city that is set on an hill cannot be hid.
St Matthew ch. 5, v. 14

22 Let your light so shine before men, that they may see your good works.
St Matthew ch. 5, v. 16

23 Resist not evil: but whosoever shall smite thee on thy right cheek, turn to him the other also.
St Matthew ch. 5, v. 39

24 He maketh his sun to rise on the evil and on the good, and sendeth rain on the just and on the unjust.
St Matthew ch. 5, v. 45

25 Be ye therefore perfect, even as your Father which is in heaven is perfect.
St Matthew ch. 5, v. 48

26 When thou doest alms, let not thy left hand know what thy right hand doeth.
St Matthew ch. 6, v. 3

27 After this manner therefore pray ye: Our Father which art in heaven, Hallowed be thy name.
Thy kingdom come. Thy will be done in earth, as it is in heaven.
Give us this day our daily bread.
And forgive us our debts, as we forgive our debtors.
And lead us not into temptation, but deliver us from evil: For thine is the kingdom, and the power, and the glory, for ever. Amen.
St Matthew ch. 6, v. 9. See St Luke ch. 11, v. 2

1 Lay not up for yourselves treasures upon earth, where moth and rust doth corrupt, and where thieves break through and steal:
But lay up for yourselves treasures in heaven.
St Matthew ch. 6, v. 19

2 Where your treasure is, there will your heart be also.
St Matthew ch. 6, v. 21

3 No man can serve two masters ... Ye cannot serve God and mammon.
St Matthew ch. 6, v. 24

4 Consider the lilies of the field, how they grow; they toil not, neither do they spin:
And yet I say unto you, That even Solomon in all his glory was not arrayed like one of these.
St Matthew ch. 6, v. 28

5 Take therefore no thought for the morrow: for the morrow shall take thought for the things of itself. Sufficient unto the day is the evil thereof.
St Matthew ch. 6, v. 34

6 Judge not, that ye be not judged.
St Matthew ch. 7, v. 1

7 Why beholdest thou the mote that is in thy brother's eye, but considerest not the beam that is in thine own eye?
St Matthew ch. 7, v. 3

8 Neither cast ye your pearls before swine.
St Matthew ch. 7, v. 6

9 Ask, and it shall be given you; seek, and ye shall find; knock, and it shall be opened unto you.
St Matthew ch. 7, v. 7

10 Or what man is there of you, whom if his son ask bread, will he give him a stone?
St Matthew ch. 7, v. 9

11 Therefore all things whatsoever ye would that men should do to you, do ye even so to them: for this is the law and the prophets.
St Matthew ch. 7, v. 12

12 Wide is the gate, and broad is the way, that leadeth to destruction, and many there be that go in thereat.
St Matthew ch. 7, v. 13

13 Strait is the gate, and narrow is the way, which leadeth unto life, and few there be that find it.
St Matthew ch. 7, v. 14

14 Beware of false prophets, which come to you in sheep's clothing, but inwardly they are ravening wolves.
St Matthew ch. 7, v. 15

15 By their fruits ye shall know them.
St Matthew ch. 7, v. 20

16 Lord I am not worthy that thou shouldest come under my roof.
St Matthew ch. 8, v. 8

17 I am a man under authority, having soldiers under me: and I say to this man, Go, and he goeth; and to another, Come, and he cometh; and to my servant, Do this, and he doeth it.
St Matthew ch. 8, v. 9

18 But the children of the kingdom shall be cast out into outer darkness: there shall be weeping and gnashing of teeth.
St Matthew ch. 8, v. 12

19 The foxes have holes, and the birds of the air have nests; but the Son of man hath not where to lay his head.
St Matthew ch. 8, v. 20

20 Let the dead bury their dead.
St Matthew ch. 8, v. 22

21 Why eateth your Master with publicans and sinners?
St Matthew ch. 9, v. 11

22 They that be whole need not a physician, but they that are sick.
St Matthew ch. 9, v. 12

23 I am not come to call the righteous, but sinners to repentance.
St Matthew ch. 9, v. 13

24 Neither do men put new wine into old bottles.
St Matthew ch. 9, v. 17

25 Thy faith hath made thee whole.
St Matthew ch. 9, v. 22

26 The maid is not dead, but sleepeth.
St Matthew ch. 9, v. 24

27 Freely ye have received, freely give.
St Matthew ch. 10, v. 8

28 When ye depart out of that house or city, shake off the dust of your feet.
St Matthew ch. 10, v. 14

29 Be ye therefore wise as serpents, and harmless as doves.
St Matthew ch. 10, v. 16

30 The very hairs of your head are all numbered.
St Matthew ch. 10, v. 30

31 I came not to send peace, but a sword.
St Matthew ch. 10, v. 34

32 A man's foes shall be they of his own household.
St Matthew ch. 10, v. 36

33 He that findeth his life shall lose it: and he that loseth his life for my sake shall find it.
St Matthew ch. 10, v. 39

34 What went ye out into the wilderness to see? A reed shaken with the wind?
St Matthew ch. 11, v. 7

35 Come unto me, all ye that labour and are heavy laden, and I will give you rest.
St Matthew ch. 11, v. 28

36 For my yoke is easy, and my burden is light.
St Matthew ch. 11, v. 30

1 He that is not with me is against me.
St Matthew ch. 12, v. 30 and St Luke ch. 11, v. 23

2 Behold, a greater than Solomon is here.
St Matthew ch. 12, v. 42

3 Then he saith, I will return into my house from whence I came out; and when he is come, he findeth it empty, swept, and garnished.
St Matthew ch. 12, v. 44

4 Behold, a sower went forth to sow;
And when he sowed, some seeds fell by the wayside.
St Matthew ch. 13, v. 3

5 The kingdom of heaven is like to a grain of mustard seed.
St Matthew ch. 13, v. 31

6 The kingdom of heaven is like unto a merchant man, seeking goodly pearls:
Who, when he had found one pearl of great price, went and sold all that he had, and bought it.
St Matthew ch. 13, v. 45

7 A prophet is not without honour, save in his own country, and in his own house.
St Matthew ch. 13, v. 57

8 Be of good cheer; it is I; be not afraid.
St Matthew ch. 14, v. 27

9 O thou of little faith, wherefore didst thou doubt?
St Matthew ch. 14, v. 31

10 If the blind lead the blind, both shall fall into the ditch.
St Matthew ch. 15, v. 14

11 The dogs eat of the crumbs which fall from their masters' table.
St Matthew ch. 15, v. 27

12 Can ye not discern the signs of the times?
St Matthew ch. 16, v. 3

13 Thou art Peter, and upon this rock I will build my church.
St Matthew ch. 16, v. 18

14 Get thee behind me, Satan.
St Matthew ch. 16, v. 23

15 Except ye be converted, and become as little children, ye shall not enter into the kingdom of heaven.
St Matthew ch. 18, v. 3

16 Whoso shall offend one of these little ones which believe in me, it were better for him that a millstone were hanged about his neck, and that he were drowned in the depth of the sea.
St Matthew ch. 18, v. 6. See also St Luke ch. 17, v. 2

17 If thine eye offend thee, pluck it out, and cast it from thee.
St Matthew ch. 18, v. 9

18 For where two or three are gathered together in my name, there am I in the midst of them.
St Matthew ch. 18, v. 20

19 Lord, how oft shall my brother sin against me, and I forgive him? till seven times?
Jesus saith unto him I say not unto thee, Until seven times: but Until seventy times seven.
St Matthew ch. 18, v. 21

20 What therefore God hath joined together, let not man put asunder.
St Matthew ch. 19, v. 6

21 If thou wilt be perfect, go and sell that thou hast, and give to the poor, and thou shalt have treasure in heaven.
St Matthew ch. 19, v. 21

22 It is easier for a camel to go through the eye of a needle, than for a rich man to enter into the kingdom of God.
St Matthew ch. 19, v. 24. See also St Luke ch. 18, v. 24

23 With God all things are possible.
St Matthew ch. 19, v. 26

24 But many that are first shall be last; and the last shall be first.
St Matthew ch. 19, v. 30

25 The burden and heat of the day.
St Matthew ch. 20, v. 12

26 I will give unto this last, even as unto thee.
St Matthew ch. 20, v. 14

27 It is written, My house shall be called the house of prayer; but ye have made it a den of thieves.
St Matthew ch. 21, v. 13. See Isaiah ch. 56, v. 7

28 For many are called, but few are chosen.
St Matthew ch. 22, v. 14

29 Render therefore unto Caesar the things which are Caesar's; and unto God the things that are God's.
St Matthew ch. 22, v. 21

30 For in the resurrection they neither marry, nor are given in marriage.
St Matthew ch. 22, v. 30

31 Ye blind guides, which strain at a gnat, and swallow a camel.
St Matthew ch. 23, v. 24

32 Ye are like unto whited sepulchres.
St Matthew ch. 23, v. 27

33 Ye shall hear of wars and rumours of wars.
St Matthew ch. 24, v. 6

34 For nation shall rise against nation, and kingdom against kingdom.
St Matthew ch. 24, v. 7

35 The abomination of desolation, spoken of by Daniel.
St Matthew ch. 24, v. 15. See Daniel ch. 12, v. 11

36 Wheresoever the carcase is, there will the eagles be gathered together.
St Matthew ch. 24, v. 28

37 Heaven and earth shall pass away, but my words shall not pass away.
St Matthew ch. 24, v. 35

38 Watch therefore: for ye know not what hour your Lord doth come.
St Matthew ch. 24, v. 42

1 Well done, thou good and faithful servant.
St Matthew ch. 25, v. 21

2 Lord, I knew thee that thou art an hard
man, reaping where thou hast not sown,
and gathering where thou hast not
strawed.
St Matthew ch. 25, v. 24

3 Unto every one that hath shall be given,
and he shall have abundance: but from
him that hath not shall be taken away
even that which he hath.
St Matthew ch. 25, v. 29

4 And he shall set the sheep on his right
hand, but the goats on the left.
St Matthew ch. 25, v. 33

5 I was a stranger, and ye took me in.
St Matthew ch. 25, v. 35

6 Inasmuch as ye have done it unto one of
the least of these my brethren, ye have
done it unto me.
St Matthew ch. 25, v. 40

7 And they covenanted with him for thirty
pieces of silver.
St Matthew ch. 26, v. 15

8 It had been good for that man if he had
not been born.
St Matthew ch. 26, v. 24

9 Jesus took bread, and blessed it, and brake
it, and gave it to the disciples, and said,
Take, eat; this is my body.
St Matthew ch. 26, v. 26

10 This night, before the cock crow, thou
shalt deny me thrice.
St Matthew ch. 26, v. 34

11 If it be possible, let this cup pass from me.
St Matthew ch. 26, v. 39

12 What, could ye not watch with me one
hour?
St Matthew ch. 26, v. 40

13 Watch and pray, that ye enter not into
temptation: the spirit indeed is willing
but the flesh is weak.
St Matthew ch. 26, v. 41

14 All they that take the sword shall perish
with the sword.
St Matthew ch. 26, v. 52

15 He saved others; himself he cannot save.
St Matthew ch. 27, v. 42

16 Eli, Eli, lama sabachthani? ... My God, my
God, why hast thou forsaken me?
St Matthew ch. 27, v. 46

17 And, lo, I am with you alway, even unto
the end of the world.
St Matthew ch. 28, v. 20

St Mark

18 The sabbath was made for man, and not
man for the sabbath.
St Mark ch. 2, v. 27

19 If a house be divided against itself, that
house cannot stand.
St Mark ch. 3, v. 25

20 He that hath ears to hear, let him hear.
St Mark ch. 4, v. 9

21 My name is Legion: for we are many.
St Mark ch. 5, v. 9

22 I see men as trees, walking.
St Mark ch. 8, v. 24

23 For what shall it profit a man, if he shall
gain the whole world, and lose his own
soul?
St Mark ch. 8, v. 36. See also St Matthew
ch. 16, v. 26

24 Lord, I believe; help thou mine unbelief.
St Mark ch. 9, v. 24

25 Suffer the little children to come unto me,
and forbid them not: for of such is the
kingdom of God.
St Mark ch. 10, v. 14

26 Go ye into all the world, and preach the
gospel to every creature.
St Mark ch. 16, v. 15

St Luke

27 Hail, thou that art highly favoured, the
Lord is with thee: blessed art thou among
women.
St Luke ch. 1, v. 28

28 My soul doth magnify the Lord,
And my spirit hath rejoiced in God my
Saviour.
For he hath regarded the low estate of his
handmaiden: for, behold, from
henceforth all generations shall call me
blessed.
St Luke ch. 1, v. 46 ('Tell out my soul, the
greatness of the Lord' in New English Bible).
Cf. 58:16

29 He hath shewed strength with his arm; he
hath scattered the proud in the
imagination of their hearts.
He hath put down the mighty from their
seats, and exalted them of low degree.
He hath filled the hungry with good
things; and the rich he hath sent empty
away.
St Luke ch. 1, v. 51

30 To give light to them that sit in darkness
and in the shadow of death, to guide our
feet into the way of peace.
St Luke ch. 1, v. 79

31 And it came to pass in those days, that
there went out a decree from Caesar
Augustus, that all the world should be
taxed.
St Luke ch. 2, v. 1

32 She brought forth her firstborn son, and
wrapped him in swaddling clothes, and
laid him in a manger; because there was
no room for them in the inn.
And there were in the same country
shepherds abiding in the field, keeping
watch over their flock by night.
And, lo, the angel of the Lord came upon
them, and the glory of the Lord shone
round about them: and they were sore
afraid.
St Luke ch. 2, v. 7

1 Behold, I bring you good tidings of great
joy.
St Luke ch. 2, v. 10

2 Glory to God in the highest, and on earth
peace, good will toward men.
St Luke ch. 2, v. 14

3 Lord, now lettest thou thy servant depart
in peace, according to thy word.
St Luke ch. 2, v. 29. Cf. 58:17

4 Wist ye not that I must be about my
Father's business?
St Luke ch. 2, v. 49

5 Physician, heal thyself.
St Luke ch. 4, v. 23

6 Love your enemies, do good to them which
hate you.
St Luke ch. 6, v. 27

7 Give, and it shall be given unto you; good
measure, pressed down, and shaken
together, and running over, shall men
give into your bosom.
St Luke ch. 6, v. 38

8 Her sins, which are many, are forgiven; for
she loved much.
St Luke ch. 7, v. 47

9 No man, having put his hand to the
plough, and looking back, is fit for the
kingdom of God.
St Luke ch. 9, v. 62

10 For the labourer is worthy of his hire.
St Luke ch. 10, v. 7

11 A certain man went down from Jerusalem
to Jericho, and fell among thieves.
St Luke ch. 10, v. 30

12 He passed by on the other side.
St Luke ch. 10, v. 31

13 Go, and do thou likewise.
St Luke ch. 10, v. 37

14 But Martha was cumbered about much
serving.
St Luke ch. 10, v. 40

15 No man, when he hath lighted a candle,
putteth it in a secret place, neither under
a bushel.
St Luke ch. 11, v. 33

16 Woe unto you, lawyers! for ye have taken
away the key of knowledge.
St Luke ch. 11, v. 52

17 Are not five sparrows sold for two
farthings, and not one of them is
forgotten before God?
St Luke ch. 12, v. 6. See also St Matthew
ch. 10, v. 29

18 Soul, thou hast much goods laid up for
many years; take thine ease, eat, drink,
and be merry.
St Luke ch. 12, v. 19. Cf. 44:18, 45:24

19 Thou fool, this night thy soul shall be
required of thee.
St Luke ch. 12, v. 20

20 Let your loins be girded about, and your
lights burning.
St Luke ch. 12, v. 35

21 Friend, go up higher.
St Luke ch. 14, v. 10

22 For whosoever exalteth himself shall be
abased; and he that humbleth himself
shall be exalted.
St Luke ch. 14, v. 11. See also St Matthew
ch. 23, v. 12

23 I have married a wife, and therefore I
cannot come.
St Luke ch. 14, v. 20

24 Bring in hither the poor, and the maimed,
and the halt, and the blind.
St Luke ch. 14, v. 21

25 Go out into the highways and hedges, and
compel them to come in.
St Luke ch. 14, v. 23

26 Leave the ninety and nine in the
wilderness.
St Luke ch. 15, v. 4

27 Rejoice with me; for I have found my sheep
which was lost.
St Luke ch. 15, v. 6

28 Joy shall be in heaven over one sinner that
repenteth, more than over ninety and
nine just persons, which need no
repentance.
St Luke ch. 15, v. 7

29 Wasted his substance with riotous living.
St Luke ch. 15, v. 13

30 I will arise and go to my father, and will
say unto him, Father, I have sinned
against heaven, and before thee,
And am no more worthy to be called thy
son: make me as one of thy hired
servants.
St Luke ch. 15, v. 18

31 Bring hither the fatted calf, and kill it.
St Luke ch. 15, v. 23

32 This my son was dead, and is alive again;
he was lost, and is found.
St Luke ch. 15, v. 24

33 The children of this world are in their
generation wiser than the children of
light.
St Luke ch. 16, v. 8

34 The crumbs which fell from the rich man's
table.
St Luke ch. 16, v. 21

35 Between us and you there is a great gulf
fixed.
St Luke ch. 16, v. 26

36 The kingdom of God is within you.
St Luke ch. 17, v. 21

37 Remember Lot's wife.
St Luke ch. 17, v. 32

38 God, I thank thee, that I am not as other
men are.
St Luke ch. 18, v. 11

39 God be merciful to me a sinner.
St Luke ch. 18, v. 13

40 He shall show you a large upper room
furnished.
St Luke ch. 22, v. 12

1 Not my will, but thine, be done.
St Luke ch. 22, v. 42

2 Father, forgive them: for they know not
what they do.
St Luke ch. 23, v. 34

3 To day shalt thou be with me in paradise.
St Luke ch. 23, v. 43

4 Father, into thy hands I commend my
spirit.
St Luke ch. 23, v. 46. Cf. 66:23

5 He was a good man, and a just.
St Luke ch. 23, v. 50

St John

6 In the beginning was the Word, and the
Word was with God, and the Word was
God.
St John ch. 1, v. 1

7 All things were made by him; and without
him was not any thing made that was
made.
St John ch. 1, v. 3

8 And the light shineth in darkness; and the
darkness comprehended it not.
St John ch. 1, v. 5

9 He was not that Light, but was sent to bear
witness of that Light.
St John ch. 1, v. 8

10 He was in the world, and the world was
made by him, and the world knew him
not.
He came unto his own, and his own
received him not.
St John ch. 1, v. 10

11 And the Word was made flesh, and dwelt
among us.
St John ch. 1, v. 14

12 He it is, who coming after me is preferred
before me, whose shoe's latchet I am not
worthy to unloose.
St John ch. 1, v. 27

13 Behold the Lamb of God, which taketh
away the sin of the world.
St John ch. 1, v. 29

14 Can there any good thing come out of
Nazareth?
St John ch. 1, v. 46

15 Behold an Israelite indeed, in whom is no
guile!
St John ch. 1, v. 47

16 Woman, what have I to do with thee? mine
hour is not yet come.
St John ch. 2, v. 4

17 Except a man be born again, he cannot see
the kingdom of God.
St John ch. 3, v. 3

18 The wind bloweth where it listeth.
St John ch. 3, v. 8

19 God so loved the world, that he gave his
only begotten Son, that whosoever
believeth in him should not perish, but
have everlasting life.
St John ch. 3, v. 16

20 Except ye see signs and wonders, ye will
not believe.
St John ch. 4, v. 48

21 Rise, take up thy bed, and walk.
St John ch. 5, v. 8

22 I am the bread of life: he that cometh to
me shall never hunger; and he that
believeth on me shall never thirst.
St John ch. 6, v. 35

23 Him that cometh to me I will in no wise
cast out.
St John ch. 6, v. 37

24 Verily, verily, I say unto you, He that
believeth on me hath everlasting life.
St John ch. 6, v. 47

25 And the scribes and the Pharisees brought
unto him a woman taken in adultery.
St John ch. 8, v. 3

26 He that is without sin among you, let him
first cast a stone at her.
St John ch. 8, v. 7

27 Neither do I condemn thee: go, and sin no
more.
St John ch. 8, v. 11

28 And ye shall know the truth, and the truth
shall make you free.
St John ch. 8, v. 32

29 I am the door.
St John ch. 10, v. 9

30 I am the good shepherd: the good
shepherd giveth his life for the sheep.
St John ch. 10, v. 11

31 Though ye believe not me, believe the
works.
St John ch. 10, v. 38

32 I am the resurrection, and the life.
St John ch. 11, v. 25

33 Jesus wept.
St John ch. 11, v. 35

34 It is expedient for us, that one man should
die for the people, and that the whole
nation perish not.
St John ch. 11, v. 50

35 The poor always ye have with you.
St John ch. 12, v. 8

36 Let not your heart be troubled: ye believe
in God, believe also in me.
St John ch. 14, v. 1

37 In my Father's house are many mansions
... I go to prepare a place for you.
St John ch. 14, v. 2

38 I am the way, the truth, and the life: no
man cometh unto the Father, but by me.
St John ch. 14, v. 6

39 Peace I leave with you, my peace I give
unto you.
St John ch. 14, v. 27

40 Greater love hath no man than this, that a
man lay down his life for his friends.
St John ch. 15, v. 13

1 Pilate saith unto him, What is truth?
St John ch. 18, v. 38

2 Now Barabbas was a robber.
St John ch. 18, v. 40

3 What I have written I have written.
St John ch. 19, v. 22

4 Woman, behold thy son! . . .
Behold thy mother!
St John ch. 19, v. 26

5 It is finished.
St John ch. 19, v. 30. Cf. 58:21

6 Touch me not.
St John ch. 20, v. 17. Cf. 58:22

7 Feed my sheep.
St John ch. 21, v. 16

Acts of the Apostles

8 And suddenly there came a sound from
heaven as of a rushing mighty wind.
Acts of the Apostles ch. 2, v. 2

9 Silver and gold have I none; but such as I
have give I thee.
Acts of the Apostles ch. 3, v. 6

10 Walking, and leaping, and praising God.
Acts of the Apostles ch. 3, v. 8

11 Saul, Saul, why persecutest thou me?
Acts of the Apostles ch. 9, v. 4

12 It is hard for thee to kick against the
pricks.
Acts of the Apostles ch. 9, v. 5

13 The street which is called Straight.
Acts of the Apostles ch. 9, v. 11

14 Dorcas: this woman was full of good
works.
Acts of the Apostles ch. 9, v. 36

15 God is no respecter of persons.
Acts of the Apostles ch. 10, v. 34. See also
Romans ch. 2, v. 11

16 Come over into Macedonia, and help us.
Acts of the Apostles ch. 16, v. 9

17 What must I do to be saved?
Acts of the Apostles ch. 16, v. 30

18 Certain lewd fellows of the baser sort.
Acts of the Apostles ch. 17, v. 5

19 What will this babbler say?
Acts of the Apostles ch. 17, v. 18

20 I found an altar with this inscription, TO
THE UNKNOWN GOD.
Acts of the Apostles ch. 17, v. 23

21 For in him we live, and move, and have our
being.
Acts of the Apostles ch. 17, v. 28

22 It is more blessed to give than to receive.
Acts of the Apostles ch. 20, v. 35

23 But Paul said, I am a man which am a Jew
of Tarsus, a city in Cilicia, a citizen of no
mean city.
Acts of the Apostles ch. 21, v. 39

24 And the chief captain answered, With a
great sum obtained I this freedom. And
Paul said, But I was free born.
Acts of the Apostles ch. 22, v. 28

25 Hast thou appealed unto Caesar? unto
Caesar shalt thou go.
Acts of the Apostles ch. 25, v. 12

26 Paul, thou art beside thyself; much
learning doth make thee mad.
Acts of the Apostles ch. 26, v. 24

27 Almost thou persuadest me to be a
Christian.
Acts of the Apostles ch. 26, v. 28

Romans

28 Patient continuance in well doing.
Romans ch. 2, v. 7

29 Let God be true, but every man a liar.
Romans ch. 3, v. 4

30 Let us do evil, that good may come.
Romans ch. 3, v. 8

31 Where no law is, there is no transgression.
Romans ch. 4, v. 15

32 Who against hope believed in hope.
Romans ch. 4, v. 18 (of Abraham)

33 Shall we continue in sin, that grace may
abound?
Romans ch. 6, v. 1

34 We also should walk in newness of life.
Romans ch. 6, v. 4

35 Christ being raised from the dead dieth no
more; death hath no more dominion over
him.
Romans ch. 6, v. 9

36 The wages of sin is death.
Romans ch. 6, v. 23

37 I had not known sin, but by the law.
Romans ch. 7, v. 7

38 For the good that I would I do not: but the
evil which I would not, that I do.
Romans ch. 7, v. 19. Cf. 243:15

39 To be carnally minded is death.
Romans ch. 8, v. 6

40 All things work together for good to them
that love God.
Romans ch. 8, v. 28

41 If God be for us, who can be against us?
Romans ch. 8, v. 31

42 For I am persuaded, that neither death, nor
life, nor angels, nor principalities, nor
powers, nor things present, nor things to
come,
Nor height, nor depth, nor any other
creature, shall be able to separate us
from the love of God, which is in Christ
Jesus our Lord.
Romans ch. 8, v. 38

43 Present your bodies a living sacrifice, holy,
acceptable unto God.
Romans ch. 12, v. 1

44 Be not wise in your own conceits.
Romans ch. 12, v. 16

45 Vengeance is mine; I will repay, saith the
Lord.
Romans ch. 12, v. 19

1 Let us therefore cast off the works of darkness, and let us put on the armour of light.
Romans ch. 13, v. 12

2 Salute one another with an holy kiss.
Romans ch. 16, v. 16

I Corinthians

3 I have planted, Apollos watered; but God gave the increase.
I Corinthians ch. 3, v. 6

4 Your body is the temple of the Holy Ghost.
I Corinthians ch. 6, v. 19

5 It is better to marry than to burn.
I Corinthians ch. 7, v. 9

6 The fashion of this world passeth away.
I Corinthians ch. 7, v. 31

7 Knowledge puffeth up, but charity edifieth.
I Corinthians ch. 8, v. 1

8 I am made all things to all men.
I Corinthians ch. 9, v. 22

9 For the earth is the Lord's and the fulness thereof.
I Corinthians ch. 10, v. 26. Cf. 66:19

10 Doth not even nature itself teach you, that if a man have long hair, it is a shame unto him?
But if a woman have long hair, it is a glory to her.
I Corinthians ch. 11, v. 14

11 Though I speak with the tongues of men and of angels, and have not charity, I am become as sounding brass, or a tinkling cymbal.
And though I have the gift of prophecy, and understand all mysteries, and all knowledge; and though I have all faith; so that I could remove mountains; and have not charity, I am nothing.
I Corinthians ch. 13, v. 1

12 Charity suffereth long, and is kind; charity envieth not; charity vaunteth not itself, is not puffed up ...
Beareth all things, believeth all things, hopeth all things, endureth all things.
Charity never faileth.
I Corinthians ch. 13, v. 4

13 For we know in part, and we prophesy in part.
I Corinthians ch. 13, v. 9

14 When I was a child, I spake as a child, I understood as a child, I thought as a child: but when I became a man, I put away childish things.
For now we see through a glass, darkly; but then face to face: now I know in part; but then shall I know even as also I am known.
And now abideth faith, hope, charity, these three; but the greatest of these is charity.
I Corinthians ch. 13, v. 11

15 Let all things be done decently and in order.
I Corinthians ch. 14, v. 40

16 Last of all he was seen of me also, as of one born out of due time.
I Corinthians ch. 15, v. 8

17 But now is Christ risen from the dead, and become the first fruits of them that slept.
For since by man came death, by man came also the resurrection of the dead.
For as in Adam all die, even so in Christ shall all be made alive.
I Corinthians ch. 15, v. 20

18 The last enemy that shall be destroyed is death.
I Corinthians ch. 15, v. 26

19 Evil communications corrupt good manners.
I Corinthians ch. 15, v. 33

20 The first man is of the earth, earthy.
I Corinthians ch. 15, v. 47

21 Behold, I shew you a mystery; We shall not all sleep, but we shall all be changed,
In a moment, in the twinkling of an eye, at the last trump; for the trumpet shall sound, and the dead shall be raised incorruptible, and we shall be changed.
I Corinthians ch. 15, v. 51

22 O death, where is thy sting? O grave, where is thy victory?
I Corinthians ch. 15, v. 55

II Corinthians

23 The letter killeth, but the spirit giveth life.
II Corinthians ch. 3, v. 6

24 We have a building of God, an house not made with hands, eternal in the heavens.
II Corinthians ch. 5, v. 1

25 Behold, now is the accepted time; behold, now is the day of salvation.
II Corinthians ch. 6, v. 2

26 God loveth a cheerful giver.
II Corinthians ch. 9, v. 7

27 For ye suffer fools gladly, seeing ye yourselves are wise.
II Corinthians ch. 9, v. 19

28 There was given to me a thorn in the flesh, the messenger of Satan to buffet me.
II Corinthians ch. 12, v. 7

Galatians

29 Ye are fallen from grace.
Galatians ch. 5, v. 4

30 Be not deceived; God is not mocked: for whatsoever a man soweth, that shall he also reap.
Galatians ch. 6, v. 7

Ephesians

31 The unsearchable riches of Christ.
Ephesians ch. 3, v. 8

32 We are members one of another.
Ephesians ch. 4, v. 25

33 Be ye angry and sin not: let not the sun go down upon your wrath.
Ephesians ch. 4, v. 26

1 See then that ye walk circumspectly, not as fools, but as wise,
Redeeming the time, because the days are evil.
Ephesians ch. 5, v. 15

2 Ye fathers, provoke not your children to wrath.
Ephesians ch. 6, v. 4

3 Put on the whole armour of God.
Ephesians ch. 6, v. 11

4 For we wrestle not against flesh and blood, but against principalities, against powers, against the rulers of the darkness of this world, against spiritual wickedness in high places.
Wherefore take unto you the whole armour of God, that ye may be able to withstand in the evil day, and having done all, to stand.
Stand therefore, having your loins girt about with truth, and having on the breastplate of righteousness.
Ephesians ch. 6, v. 12

Philippians

5 At the name of Jesus every knee should bow.
Philippians ch. 2, v. 10

6 Work out your own salvation with fear and trembling.
Philippians ch. 2, v. 12

7 Rejoice in the Lord alway: and again I say, Rejoice.
Philippians ch. 4, v. 4

8 The peace of God, which passeth all understanding, shall keep your hearts and minds through Christ Jesus.
Philippians ch. 4, v. 7

9 Whatsoever things are true, whatsoever things are honest, whatsoever things are just, whatsoever things are pure, whatsoever things are lovely, whatsoever things are of good report; if there be any virtue and if there be any praise, think on these things.
Philippians ch. 4, v. 8

10 I can do all things through Christ which strengtheneth me.
Philippians ch. 4, v. 13

Colossians

11 Husbands, love your wives, and be not bitter against them.
Colossians ch. 3, v. 19

12 Let your speech be alway with grace, seasoned with salt.
Colossians ch. 4, v. 6

I Thesssalonians

13 Remembering without ceasing your work of faith and labour of love.
I Thesssalonians ch. 1, v. 3

14 Prove all things; hold fast that which is good.
1 Thessalonians ch. 5, v. 21

II Thesssalonians

15 If any would not work, neither should he eat.
II Thesssalonians ch. 3, v. 10

I Timothy

16 A bishop then must be blameless, the husband of one wife, vigilant, sober, of good behaviour, given to hospitality, apt to teach;
Not given to wine, no striker, not greedy of filthy lucre; but patient, not a brawler, not covetous.
I Timothy ch. 3, v. 2

17 Refuse profane and old wives' fables.
I Timothy ch. 4, v. 7

18 For we brought nothing into this world, and it is certain we can carry nothing out.
I Timothy ch. 6, v. 7

19 The love of money is the root of all evil.
I Timothy ch. 6, v. 10

20 Fight the good fight of faith, lay hold on eternal life.
I Timothy ch. 6, v. 12

II Timothy

21 I have fought a good fight, I have finished my course, I have kept the faith.
II Timothy ch. 4, v. 7

Titus

22 Unto the pure all things are pure.
Titus ch. 1, v. 15

Hebrews

23 God, who at sundry times and in divers manners spake in time past unto the fathers by the prophets.
Hebrews ch. 1, v. 1

24 Without shedding of blood is no remission.
Hebrews ch. 9, v. 22

25 It is a fearful thing to fall into the hands of the living God.
Hebrews ch. 10, v. 31

26 Faith is the substance of things hoped for, the evidence of things not seen.
Hebrews ch. 11, v. 1

27 Wherefore seeing we also are compassed about with so great a cloud of witnesses, let us lay aside every weight, and the sin which doth so easily beset us, and let us run with patience the race that is set before us,
Looking unto Jesus the author and finisher of our faith.
Hebrews ch. 12, v. 1

28 Whom the Lord loveth he chasteneth.
Hebrews ch. 12, v. 6

29 Be not forgetful to entertain strangers: for thereby some have entertained angels unawares.
Hebrews ch. 13, v. 2

30 Jesus Christ the same yesterday, and to day, and for ever.
Hebrews ch. 13, v. 8

1 For here have we no continuing city, but we seek one to come.
Hebrews ch. 13, v. 14

James

2 Be ye doers of the word, and not hearers only.
James ch. 1, v. 22

3 Faith without works is dead.
James ch. 2, v. 20

4 Ye have heard of the patience of Job.
James ch. 5, v. 11

5 Let your yea be yea; and your nay, nay.
James ch. 5, v. 12

I Peter

6 All flesh is as grass, and all the glory of man as the flower of grass. The grass withereth, and the flower thereof falleth away.
I Peter ch. 1, v. 24. Cf. 46:10

7 As newborn babes, desire the sincere milk of the word, that ye may grow thereby: If so be ye have tasted that the Lord is gracious.
I Peter ch. 2, v. 2

8 But ye are a chosen generation, a royal priesthood, an holy nation, a peculiar people.
I Peter ch. 2, v. 9

9 Honour all men. Love the brotherhood. Fear God. Honour the king.
I Peter ch. 2, v. 17

10 Giving honour unto the wife, as unto the weaker vessel.
I Peter ch. 3, v. 7

11 Charity shall cover the multitude of sins.
I Peter ch. 4, v. 8

12 Be sober, be vigilant; because your adversary the devil, as a roaring lion, walketh about, seeking whom he may devour.
I Peter ch. 5, v. 8

II Peter

13 The dog is turned to his own vomit again.
II Peter ch. 2, v. 22

I John

14 If we say that we have no sin, we deceive ourselves, and the truth is not in us.
I John ch. 1, v. 8

15 He that loveth not knoweth not God; for God is love.
I John ch. 4, v. 8

16 There is no fear in love; but perfect love casteth out fear.
I John ch. 4, v. 18

17 If a man say, I love God, and hateth his brother, he is a liar: for he that loveth not his brother whom he hath seen, how can he love God whom he hath not seen?
I John ch. 4, v. 20

III John

18 He that doeth good is of God: but he that doeth evil hath not seen God.
III John v. 11

Revelation

19 I am Alpha and Omega, the beginning and the ending, saith the Lord.
Revelation ch. 1, v. 8

20 I have somewhat against thee, because thou hast left thy first love.
Revelation ch. 2, v. 4

21 Be thou faithful unto death, and I will give thee a crown of life.
Revelation ch. 2, v. 10

22 Because thou art lukewarm, and neither cold nor hot, I will spew thee out of my mouth.
Revelation ch. 3, v. 16

23 Behold, I stand at the door, and knock.
Revelation ch. 3, v. 20

24 Holy, holy, holy, Lord God Almighty, which was, and is, and is to come.
Revelation ch. 4, v. 8

25 And I looked, and behold a pale horse: and his name that sat on him was Death.
Revelation ch. 6, v. 8

26 These are they which came out of great tribulation, and have washed their robes, and made them white in the blood of the Lamb.
Revelation ch. 7, v. 14

27 They shall hunger no more, neither thirst any more.
Revelation ch. 7, v. 16

28 God shall wipe away all tears from their eyes.
Revelation ch. 7, v. 17. Cf. 58:5

29 And when he had opened the seventh seal, there was silence in heaven about the space of half an hour.
Revelation ch. 8, v. 1

30 And there appeared a great wonder in heaven; a woman clothed with the sun, and the moon under her feet, and upon her head a crown of twelve stars.
Revelation ch. 12, v. 1

31 And there was war in heaven: Michael and his angels fought against the dragon; and the dragon fought and his angels.
Revelation ch. 12, v. 7

32 And that no man might buy or sell, save he that had the mark, or the name of the beast, or the number of his name.
Revelation ch. 13, v. 17

33 Let him that hath understanding count the number of the beast: for it is the number of a man; and his number is Six hundred threescore and six.
Revelation ch. 13, v. 18

34 Babylon is fallen, is fallen, that great city.
Revelation ch. 14, v. 8

1 Behold, I come as a thief.
Revelation ch. 16, v. 15

2 And upon her forehead was a name
written, MYSTERY, BABYLON THE GREAT, THE
MOTHER OF HARLOTS AND ABOMINATIONS
OF THE EARTH.
Revelation ch. 17, v. 5

3 And the sea gave up the dead which were
in it.
Revelation ch. 20, v. 13

4 And I saw a new heaven and a new earth:
for the first heaven and the first earth
were passed away; and there was no
more sea.
And I John saw the holy city, new
Jerusalem, coming down from God out of
heaven, prepared as a bride adorned for
her husband.
Revelation ch. 21, v. 1

5 And God shall wipe away all tears from
their eyes; and there shall be no more
death, neither sorrow, nor crying, neither
shall there be any more pain: for the
former things are passed away.
And he that sat upon the throne said,
Behold, I make all things new.
Revelation ch. 21, v. 4

6 I will give unto him that is athirst of the
fountain of the water of life freely.
Revelation ch. 21, v. 6

7 And the leaves of the tree were for the
healing of the nations.
Revelation ch. 22, v. 2

8 Amen. Even so, come, Lord Jesus.
Revelation ch. 22, v. 20

Vulgate

9 *Dominus illuminatio mea, et salus mea, quem
timebo?*
The Lord is the source of my light and my
safety, so whom shall I fear?
Psalm 26, v. 1

10 *Jubilate Deo, omnis terra; servite Domino in
laetitia.*
Sing joyfully to God, all the earth; serve the
Lord with gladness.
Psalm 99, v. 2 (Psalm 100, v. 2 in the
Authorized Version). Cf. 68:5

11 *Beatus vir qui timet Dominum, in mandatis ejus
volet nimis!*
Happy is the man who fears the Lord, who
is only too willing to follow his orders.
Psalm 111, v. 1 (Psalm 112, v. 1 in the
Authorized Version)

12 *Non nobis, Domine, non nobis; sed nomini tuo
da gloriam.*
Not unto us, Lord, not unto us; but to thy
name give glory.
Psalm 113 (second part), v. 1 (Psalm 115, v. 1
in the Authorized Version). Cf. 68:17

13 *Nisi Dominus custodierit civitatem, frustra
vigilat qui custodit eam.*
Unless the Lord guards the city, the
watchman watches in vain.
Psalm 126, v. 2 (Psalm 127, v. 2 in the
Authorized Version; contracted to 'Nisi
Dominus frustra' for the motto of the city of
Edinburgh). Cf. 68:30

14 *De profundis clamavi ad te, Domine; Domine,
exaudi vocem meam.*
Up from the depths I have cried to thee,
Lord; Lord, hear my voice.
Psalm 129, v. 1 (Psalm 130, v. 1 in the
Authorized Version). Cf. 68:33

15 *Vanitas vanitatum, dixit Ecclesiastes; vanitas
vanitatum, et omnia vanitas.*
Vanity of vanities, said the preacher; vanity
of vanities, and everything is vanity.
Ecclesiastes ch. 1, v. 2. Cf. 44:7

16 *Magnificat anima mea Dominum.*
My soul doth magnify the Lord.
St Luke ch. 1, v. 46. Cf. 51:28

17 *Nunc dimittis servum tuum, Domine, secundum
verbum tuum in pace.*
Lord, now lettest thou thy servant depart
in peace: according to thy word.
St Luke ch. 2, v. 29. Cf. 52:3

18 *Pax Vobis.*
Peace be unto you.
St Luke ch. 24, v. 36

19 *Quo vadis?*
Where are you going?
St John ch. 16, v. 5

20 *Ecce homo.*
Behold the man.
St John ch. 19, v. 5

21 *Consummatum est.*
It is achieved.
St John ch. 19, v. 30. Cf. 54:5

22 *Noli me tangere.*
Do not touch me.
St John ch. 20, v. 17. Cf. 54:6

23 *Magna est veritas, et praevalet.*
Great is truth, and it prevails.
III Esdras ch. 4, v. 41. Cf. 47:27

See also BOOK OF COMMON PRAYER (Psalms)

Isaac Bickerstaffe 1733–c.1808

24 And this the burthen of his song,
For ever used to be,
I care for nobody, not I,
If no one cares for me.
Love in a Village (1762) act 1, sc. 2 'The Miller
of Dee'

E. H. Bickersteth 1825–1906

25 Peace, perfect peace, in this dark world of
sin?
The Blood of Jesus whispers peace within.
Songs in the House of Pilgrimage (1875) 'Peace,
perfect peace'

Georges Bidault 1899–1983

1 The weak have one weapon: the errors of those who think they are strong.
  In Observer *15 July 1962 'Sayings of the Week'*

Ambrose Bierce 1842–c.1914

2 ALLIANCE, *n*. In international politics, the union of two thieves who have their hands so deeply inserted in each other's pocket that they cannot separately plunder a third.
  The Cynic's Word Book (1906) p. 16

3 APPLAUSE, *n*. The echo of a platitude.
  The Cynic's Word Book (1906) p. 19

4 BATTLE, *n*. A method of untying with the teeth a political knot that would not yield to the tongue.
  The Cynic's Word Book (1906) p. 30

5 CONSERVATIVE, *n*. A statesman who is enamoured of existing evils, as distinguished from the Liberal, who wishes to replace them with others.
  The Cynic's Word Book (1906) p. 56

6 HISTORY, *n*. An account, mostly false, of events, mostly unimportant, which are brought about by rulers, mostly knaves, and soldiers, mostly fools.
  The Cynic's Word Book (1906) p. 161

7 PEACE, *n*. In international affairs, a period of cheating between two periods of fighting.
  The Devil's Dictionary (1911) p. 248

8 PREJUDICE, *n*. A vagrant opinion without visible means of support.
  The Devil's Dictionary (1911) p. 264

9 SAINT, *n*. A dead sinner revised and edited.
  The Devil's Dictionary (1911) p. 306

Josh Billings 1818–85

10 Love iz like the meazles; we kant have it bad but onst, and the latter in life we hav it the tuffer it goes with us.
  Josh Billings' Wit and Humour (1874) p. 146

11 Natur never makes enny blunders. When she makes a phool she means it.
  Josh Billings' Wit and Humour (1874) p. 174

Laurence Binyon 1869–1943

12 They shall grow not old, as we that are left grow old.
  Age shall not weary them, nor the years condemn.
  At the going down of the sun and in the morning
  We will remember them.
  'For the Fallen' (1914)

13 Now is the time for the burning of the leaves.
  'The Ruins' (1942)

Nigel Birch 1906–81

14 My God! They've shot our fox!
  On hearing of the resignation of Hugh Dalton, Chancellor of the Exchequer in the Labour Government, 13 November 1947; in Harold Macmillan Tides of Fortune *(1969) ch. 3*

Earl of Birkenhead

See F. E. SMITH

Augustine Birrell 1850–1933

15 That great dust-heap called 'history'.
  Obiter Dicta (1884) 'Carlyle'

Elizabeth Bishop 1911–79

16 The armoured cars of dreams, contrived to let us do
  so many a dangerous thing.
  'Sleeping Standing Up' (1946)

Prince Otto von Bismarck 1815–98

17 Politics is the art of the possible.
  In conversation with Meyer von Waldeck, 11 August 1867, in H. Amelung Bismarck-Worte *(1918) p. 19*

18 I do not regard the procuring of peace as a matter in which we should play the role of arbiter between different opinions ... more that of an honest broker who really wants to press the business forward.
  Speech to the Reichstag, 19 February 1878, in L. Hahn (ed.) Fürst Bismarck. Sein politisches Leben und Wirken *vol. 3 (1881) p. 90*

19 This policy cannot succeed through speeches, and shooting-matches, and songs; it can only be carried out through blood and iron.
  Speech in the Prussian House of Deputies, 28 January 1886, in Fürst Bismarck als Redner. Vollständige Sammlung der parlamentarischen Reden *(1885–91) vol. 15, p. 157. In an earlier speech, 30 September 1862, Bismarck used the form 'iron and blood'*

20 If there is ever another war in Europe, it will come out of some damned silly thing in the Balkans.
  Quoted in the House of Commons; Hansard *16 August 1945, col. 84*

21 A lath of wood painted to look like iron.
  Describing Lord Salisbury; attributed, but vigorously denied by Sidney Whitman in Personal Reminiscences of Prince Bismarck *(1902) ch. 14*

Valentine Blacker 1728–1823

22 Put your trust in God, my boys, and keep your powder dry.
  'Oliver's Advice' in E. Hayes Ballads of Ireland *(1856) vol. 1 (often attributed to Oliver Cromwell himself)*

Sir William Blackstone 1723–80

1 The king never dies.
Commentaries on the Laws of England (1765)
bk. 1, ch. 7

2 That the king can do no wrong, is a
necessary and fundamental principle of the
English constitution.
Commentaries on the Laws of England (1765)
bk. 3, ch. 17

3 It is better that ten guilty persons escape
than one innocent suffer.
Commentaries on the Laws of England (1765)
bk. 4, ch. 27

Eubie Blake 1883–1983

4 If I'd known I was gonna live this long, I'd
have taken better care of myself.
On reaching the age of 100; in *Observer*
13 February 1983 'Sayings of the Week'

William Blake 1757–1827

5 To see a world in a grain of sand
And a heaven in a wild flower
Hold infinity in the palm of your hand
And eternity in an hour.
'Auguries of Innocence' (*c*.1803) l. 1

6 A robin red breast in a cage
Puts all Heaven in a rage.
'Auguries of Innocence' (*c*.1803) l. 5

7 A truth that's told with bad intent
Beats all the lies you can invent.
'Auguries of Innocence' (*c*.1803) l. 53

8 The strongest poison ever known
Came from Caesar's laurel crown.
'Auguries of Innocence' (*c*.1803) l. 97

9 The whore and gambler by the State
Licensed build that nation's fate
The harlot's cry from street to street
Shall weave old England's winding sheet.
'Auguries of Innocence' (*c*.1803) l. 113

10 Does the eagle know what is in the pit?
Or wilt thou go ask the mole:
Can wisdom be put in a silver rod?
Or love in a golden bowl?
The Book of Thel (1789) plate i 'Thel's Motto'

11 The Vision of Christ that thou dost see
Is my vision's greatest enemy
Thine has a great hook nose like thine
Mine has a snub nose like to mine.
The Everlasting Gospel (*c*.1818) (a) l. 1

12 Humility is only doubt
And does the sun and moon blot out
Rooting over with thorns and stems
The buried soul and all its gems
This life's dim windows of the soul
Distorts the heavens from pole to pole
And leads you to believe a lie
When you see with not through the eye.
The Everlasting Gospel (*c*.1818) (d) l. 99

13 Was Jesus chaste or did he
Give any lessons of chastity
The morning blushed fiery red
Mary was found in adulterous bed.
The Everlasting Gospel (*c*.1818) (e) l. 1

14 I am sure this Jesus will not do
Either for Englishman or Jew.
The Everlasting Gospel (*c*.1818) (f) l. 1

15 Truly, my Satan, thou art but a dunce,
And dost not know the garment from the
man;
Every harlot was a virgin once,
Nor can'st thou ever change Kate into Nan.
Tho' thou art worshipped by the names
divine
Of Jesus and Jehovah, thou art still
The Son of Morn in weary Night's decline,
The lost traveller's dream under the hill.
For the Sexes: The Gates of Paradise 'To the
Accuser who is The God of This World'
[epilogue]

16 Mournful ever weeping Paddington.
Jerusalem (1815) 'Chapter 1' (plate 12, l. 27)

17 The fields from Islington to Marybone,
To Primrose Hill and Saint John's Wood
Were builded over with pillars of gold;
And there Jerusalem's pillars stood.
Jerusalem (1815) 'To the Jews' (plate 27, l. 1)
"The fields from Islington to Marybone"

18 For a tear is an intellectual thing;
And a sigh is the sword of an Angel King.
Jerusalem (1815) 'To the Deists' (plate 52, l. 25)
"I saw a Monk of Charlemaine"

19 He who would do good to another, must
do it in minute particulars.
Jerusalem (1815) 'Chapter 3' (plate 55, l. 60)

20 I give you the end of a golden string;
Only wind it into a ball:
It will lead you in at Heaven's gate,
Built in Jerusalem's wall.
Jerusalem (1815) 'To the Christians' (plate 77)
"I give you the end of a golden string"

21 England! awake! awake! awake!
Jerusalem thy sister calls!
Why wilt thou sleep the sleep of death,
And close her from thy ancient walls?
Jerusalem (1815) 'To the Christians' (plate 77)
"England! awake! ... "

22 I care not whether a man is good or evil;
all that I care
Is whether he is a wise man or a fool. Go!
put off holiness
And put on Intellect.
Jerusalem (1815) 'Chapter 4' (plate 91, l. 54)

23 May God us keep
From Single vision and Newton's sleep!
'Letter to Thomas Butts, 22 November 1802'

24 Energy is Eternal Delight.
The Marriage of Heaven and Hell (1790–3) 'The
voice of the Devil'

25 The reason Milton wrote in fetters when
he wrote of Angels and God, and at liberty
when of Devils and Hell, is because he was
a true Poet, and of the Devil's party
without knowing it.
The Marriage of Heaven and Hell (1790–3) 'The
voice of the Devil' (note)

1 The road of excess leads to the palace of
  wisdom.
  The Marriage of Heaven and Hell (1790–3)
  'Proverbs of Hell'

2 Prudence is a rich, ugly, old maid courted
  by Incapacity.
  The Marriage of Heaven and Hell (1790–3)
  'Proverbs of Hell'

3 He who desires but acts not, breeds
  pestilence.
  The Marriage of Heaven and Hell (1790–3)
  'Proverbs of Hell'

4 A fool sees not the same tree that a wise
  man sees.
  The Marriage of Heaven and Hell (1790–3)
  'Proverbs of Hell'

5 Eternity is in love with the productions of
  time.
  The Marriage of Heaven and Hell (1790–3)
  'Proverbs of Hell'

6 If the fool would persist in his folly he
  would become wise.
  The Marriage of Heaven and Hell (1790–3)
  'Proverbs of Hell'

7 Prisons are built with stones of Law,
  brothels with bricks of Religion.
  The Marriage of Heaven and Hell (1790–3)
  'Proverbs of Hell'

8 The tigers of wrath are wiser than the
  horses of instruction.
  The Marriage of Heaven and Hell (1790–3)
  'Proverbs of Hell'

9 Damn braces: Bless relaxes.
  The Marriage of Heaven and Hell (1790–3)
  'Proverbs of Hell'

10 Sooner murder an infant in its cradle than
  nurse unacted desires.
  The Marriage of Heaven and Hell (1790–3)
  'Proverbs of Hell'

11 If the doors of perception were cleansed
  everything would appear to man as it is,
  infinite.
  The Marriage of Heaven and Hell (1790–3) 'A
  Memorable Fancy' plate 14

12 And did those feet in ancient time
  Walk upon England's mountains green?
  And was the holy Lamb of God
  On England's pleasant pastures seen?

  And did the Countenance Divine
  Shine forth upon our clouded hills?
  And was Jerusalem builded here
  Among these dark Satanic mills?

  Bring me my bow of burning gold:
  Bring me my arrows of desire:
  Bring me my spear: O clouds, unfold!
  Bring me my chariot of fire.

  I will not cease from mental fight,
  Nor shall my sword sleep in my hand,
  Till we have built Jerusalem,
  In England's green and pleasant land.
  Milton (1804–10) preface 'And did those feet
  in ancient time'

13 Mock on mock on Voltaire Rousseau
  Mock on mock on tis all in vain
  You throw the sand against the wind
  And the wind blows it back again.
  MS Note-Book p. 7

14 The atoms of Democritus
  And Newton's particles of light
  Are sands upon the Red sea shore
  Where Israel's tents do shine so bright.
  MS Note-Book p. 7

15 Great things are done when men and
  mountains meet
  This is not done by jostling in the street.
  MS Note-Book p. 43

16 He who binds to himself a joy
  Doth the winged life destroy
  But he who kisses the joy as it flies
  Lives in Eternity's sunrise.
  MS Note-Book p. 99 'Several Questions
  Answered'

17 What is it men in women do require
  The lineaments of gratified desire
  What is it women do in men require
  The lineaments of gratified desire.
  MS Note-Book p. 99 'Several Questions
  Answered'

18 Piping down the valleys wild
  Piping songs of pleasant glee
  On a cloud I saw a child.
  Songs of Innocence (1789) introduction

19 Your chimneys I sweep and in soot I sleep.
  Songs of Innocence (1789) 'The Chimney
  Sweeper'

20 To Mercy Pity Peace and Love,
  All pray in their distress.
  Songs of Innocence (1789) 'The Divine Image'

21 For Mercy has a human heart
  Pity a human face:
  And Love, the human form divine,
  And Peace, the human dress.
  Songs of Innocence (1789) 'The Divine Image'

22 Then cherish pity, lest you drive an angel
  from your door.
  Songs of Innocence (1789) 'Holy Thursday'

23 Little Lamb who made thee
  Dost thou know who made thee.
  Songs of Innocence (1789) 'The Lamb'

24 My mother bore me in the southern wild,
  And I am black, but O! my soul is white;
  White as an angel is the English child:
  But I am black as if bereaved of light.
  Songs of Innocence (1789) 'The Little Black Boy'

25 When the voices of children are heard on
  the green
  And laughing is heard on the hill.
  Songs of Innocence (1789) 'Nurse's Song'

26 Hear the voice of the Bard!
  Who present, past, and future, sees.
  Songs of Experience (1794) introduction

1 Love seeketh not itself to please,
  Nor for itself hath any care;
  But for another gives its ease,
  And builds a Heaven in Hell's despair.
    Songs of Experience (1794) 'The Clod and the
    Pebble'

2 Love seeketh only Self to please,
  To bind another to its delight,
  Joys in another's loss of ease,
  And builds a Hell in Heaven's despite.
    Songs of Experience (1794) 'The Clod and the
    Pebble'

3 My mother groaned! my father wept.
  Into the dangerous world I leapt:
  Helpless, naked, piping loud;
  Like a fiend hid in a cloud.
    Songs of Experience (1794) 'Infant Sorrow'

4 O Rose, thou art sick!
  The invisible worm
  That flies in the night,
  In the howling storm:
  Has found out thy bed
  Of crimson joy:
  And his dark secret love
  Does thy life destroy.
    Songs of Experience (1794) 'The Sick Rose'

5 Tiger Tiger, burning bright,
  In the forests of the night;
  What immortal hand or eye,
  Could frame thy fearful symmetry?
    Songs of Experience (1794) 'The Tiger'

6 When the stars threw down their spears
  And watered heaven with their tears:
  Did he smile his work to see?
  Did he who made the Lamb make thee?
    Songs of Experience (1794) 'The Tiger'

7 Cruelty has a human heart,
  And Jealousy a human face;
  Terror the human form divine,
  And Secrecy the human dress.
    'A Divine Image'; etched but not included in
    Songs of Experience (1794)

Susanna Blamire 1747–94

8 I've gotten a rock, I've gotten a reel,
  I've gotten a wee bit spinning-wheel;
  An' by the whirling rim I've found
  How the weary, weary warl goes round.
    'I've Gotten a Rock, I've Gotten a Reel'
    (c.1790) l. 1

Lesley Blanch 1907–

9 The wilder shores of love.
    Title of book (1954)

Philip Paul Bliss 1838–76

10 Hold the fort, for I am coming.
    Gospel Hymns and Sacred Songs (1875) no. 14
    (suggested by a flag message from General
    Sherman near Atlanta, October 1864)

Karen Blixen

See ISAK DINESEN

Gebhard Lebrecht Blücher
1742–1819

11 *Was für Plunder!*
   What rubbish!
    Of London, as seen from the Monument in
    June 1814; in Evelyn Princess Blücher
    Memoirs of Prince Blücher (1932) p. 33 (often
    misquoted '*Was für plündern* [What a place to
    plunder]!')

Edmund Blunden 1896–1974

12 All things they have in common being so
   poor,
   And their one fear, Death's shadow at the
   door.
    'Almswomen' (1920)

13 I am for the woods against the world,
   But are the woods for me?
    'The Kiss' (1931)

14 Dance on this ball-floor thin and wan,
   Use him as though you love him;
   Court him, elude him, reel and pass,
   And let him hate you through the glass.
    'Midnight Skaters' (1925)

15 I have been young, and now am not too
   old;
   And I have seen the righteous forsaken,
   His health, his honour and his quality
   taken.
   This is not what we were formerly told.
    'Report on Experience' (1929)

John Ernest Bode 1816–74

16 O let me hear thee speaking
   In accents clear and still,
   Above the storms of passion,
   The murmurs of self-will.
    'O Jesus, I have promised' (1869 hymn)

Boethius AD c.476–524

17 For in every ill-turn of fortune the most
   unhappy sort of unfortunate man is the
   one who has been happy.
    De Consolatione Philosophiae bk. 2, prose 4

Louise Bogan 1897–1970

18 Women have no wilderness in them,
   They are provident instead,
   Content in the tight hot cell of their hearts
   To eat dusty bread.
    'Women' (1923)

John B. Bogart 1848–1921

19 When a dog bites a man, that is not news,
   because it happens so often. But if a man
   bites a dog, that is news.
    In F. M. O'Brien *Story of the* [New York] *Sun*
    (1918) ch. 10 (often attributed to Charles A.
    Dana)

Niels Bohr 1885–1962

1 One of the favourite maxims of my father was the distinction between the two sorts of truths, profound truths recognized by the fact that the opposite is also a profound truth, in contrast to trivialities where opposites are obviously absurd.

S. Rozental *Niels Bohr* (1967) p. 328

Alan Bold 1943–

2 Scotland, land of the omnipotent No.
'A Memory of Death' (1969)

Henry St John, 1st Viscount Bolingbroke 1678–1751

3 They make truth serve as a stalking-horse to error.
Letters on the Study and Use of History (1752) No. 4, pt. 1

4 Nations, like men, have their infancy.
On the Study of History letter 5, in *Works* (1809) vol. 3, p. 414

5 Truth lies within a little and certain compass, but error is immense.
Reflections upon Exile (1716)

6 What a world is this, and how does fortune banter us!
Letter to Jonathan Swift, 3 August 1714; in H. Williams (ed.) *Correspondence of Jonathan Swift* (1963) vol. 2

7 The greatest art of a politician is to render vice serviceable to the cause of virtue.
Comment (*c.*1728), in Joseph Spence *Observations, Anecdotes, and Characters* (1820, ed. J. M. Osborn, 1966) Anecdote 882

Robert Bolt 1924–

8 It profits a man nothing to give his soul for the whole world ... But for Wales—!
A Man for All Seasons (1960) act 2

Carrie Jacobs Bond 1862–1946

9 When you come to the end of a perfect day,
And you sit alone with your thought,
While the chimes ring out with a carol gay
For the joy that the day has brought,
Do you think what the end of a perfect day
Can mean to a tired heart,
When the sun goes down with a flaming ray,
And the dear friends have to part?
'A Perfect Day' (1910 song)

Sir David Bone 1874–1959

10 It's 'Damn you, Jack — I'm all right!' with you chaps.
Brassbounder (1910) ch. 3

Dietrich Bonhoeffer 1906–45

11 It is the nature, and the advantage, of strong people that they can bring out the crucial questions and form a clear opinion about them. The weak always have to decide between alternatives that are not their own.
Widerstand und Ergebung (1951) p. 255 (tr. R. Fuller)

The Book of Common Prayer 1662

12 Dearly beloved brethren, the Scripture moveth us in sundry places to acknowledge and confess our manifold sins and wickedness.
Morning Prayer Sentences of the Scriptures

13 We have erred, and strayed from thy ways like lost sheep. We have followed too much the devices and desires of our own hearts.
Morning Prayer General Confession

14 We have left undone those things which we ought to have done; And we have done those things which we ought not to have done; And there is no health in us.
Morning Prayer General Confession

15 And grant, O most merciful Father, for his sake; That we may hereafter live a godly, righteous, and sober life.
Morning Prayer General Confession

16 And forgive us our trespasses, As we forgive them that trespass against us.
Morning Prayer The Lord's Prayer. Cf. 48:27

17 Glory be to the Father, and to the Son: and to the Holy Ghost; As it was in the beginning, is now, and ever shall be: world without end. Amen.
Morning Prayer Gloria

18 We praise thee, O God: we acknowledge thee to be the Lord.
All the earth doth worship thee: the Father everlasting.
To thee all Angels cry aloud: the Heavens, and all the Powers therein.
Morning Prayer Te Deum. Cf. 14:1

19 The glorious company of the Apostles: praise thee.
The goodly fellowship of the Prophets: praise thee.
The noble army of Martyrs: praise thee.
Morning Prayer Te Deum. Cf. 14:1

20 When thou hadst overcome the sharpness of death: thou didst open the Kingdom of Heaven to all believers.
Morning Prayer Te Deum. Cf. 14:1

21 Day by day: we magnify thee;
And we worship thy Name: ever world without end.
Morning Prayer Te Deum. Cf. 14:1

22 O Lord, in thee have I trusted: let me never be confounded.
Morning Prayer Te Deum. Cf. 14:1

1 O all ye Green Things upon the Earth, bless ye the Lord.
Morning Prayer Benedicite

2 O ye Whales, and all that move in the Waters, bless ye the Lord.
Morning Prayer Benedicite

3 I believe in the Holy Ghost; The holy Catholic Church; The Communion of Saints; The Forgiveness of sins; The Resurrection of the body, And the life everlasting. Amen.
Morning Prayer The Apostles' Creed. Cf. 65:5

4 Give peace in our time, O Lord.
Morning Prayer Versicle

5 O God, who art the author of peace and lover of concord, in knowledge of whom standeth our eternal life, whose service is perfect freedom; Defend us thy humble servants in all assaults of our enemies.
Morning Prayer The Second Collect, for Peace

6 Grant that this day we fall into no sin, neither run into any kind of danger.
Morning Prayer The Third Collect, for Grace

7 In Quires and Places where they sing.
Morning Prayer rubric following Third Collect

8 Almighty God, the fountain of all goodness.
Morning Prayer Prayer for the Royal Family

9 And that they may truly please thee, pour upon them the continual dew of thy blessing.
Morning Prayer Prayer for the Clergy and People

10 Almighty God, who hast given us grace at this time with one accord to make our common supplications unto thee; and dost promise, that when two or three are gathered together in thy Name thou wilt grant their requests: Fulfil now, O Lord, the desires and petitions of thy servants, as may be most expedient for them.
Morning Prayer Prayer of St Chrysostom

11 O God, from whom all holy desires, all good counsels, and all just works do proceed; Give unto thy servants that peace which the world cannot give.
Evening Prayer Second Collect

12 Lighten our darkness, we beseech thee, O Lord; and by thy great mercy defend us from all perils and dangers of this night.
Evening Prayer Third Collect

13 Have mercy upon us miserable sinners.
The Litany

14 From all blindness of heart; from pride, vain-glory, and hypocrisy; from envy, hatred, and malice, and from all uncharitableness,
Good Lord, deliver us.
The Litany

15 From all the deceits of the world, the flesh, and the devil,
Good Lord, deliver us.
The Litany

16 In the hour of death, and in the day of judgement,
Good Lord, deliver us.
The Litany

17 That it may please thee to defend, and provide for, the fatherless children, and widows, and all that are desolate and oppressed.
The Litany

18 O God, the Creator and Preserver of all mankind, we humbly beseech thee for all sorts and conditions of men.
Prayers . . . upon Several Occasions 'Collect or Prayer for all Conditions of Men'

19 We commend to thy fatherly goodness all those, who are any ways afflicted, or distressed, in mind, body, or estate; that it may please thee to comfort and relieve them, according to their several necessities, giving them patience under their sufferings, and a happy issue out of all their afflictions.
Prayers . . . upon Several Occasions 'Collect or Prayer for all Conditions of Men'

20 O God our heavenly Father, who by thy gracious providence dost cause the former and the latter rain to descend upon the earth.
Thanksgivings For Rain

21 Almighty God, give us grace that we may cast away the works of darkness, and put upon us the armour of light.
Collects 1st Sunday in Advent

22 Blessed Lord, who hast caused all holy Scriptures to be written for our learning; Grant that we may in such wise hear them, read, mark, learn, and inwardly digest them.
Collects 2nd Sunday in Advent

23 The sundry and manifold changes of the world.
Collects 4th Sunday after Easter

24 O God, the protector of all that trust in thee, without whom nothing is strong, nothing is holy.
Collects 4th Sunday after Trinity

25 Lord of all power and might, who art the author and giver of all good things; Graft in our hearts the love of thy Name, increase in us true religion, nourish us with all goodness, and of thy great mercy keep us in the same.
Collects 7th Sunday after Trinity

26 O God, forasmuch as without thee we are not able to please thee.
Collects 19th Sunday after Trinity

27 Grant that those things which we ask faithfully we may obtain effectually.
Collects 23rd Sunday after Trinity

28 Stir up, we beseech thee, O Lord, the wills of thy faithful people.
Collects 25th Sunday after Trinity

29 An open and notorious evil liver.
Holy Communion introductory rubric

1 His former naughty life.
   Holy Communion introductory rubric

2 Almighty God, unto whom all hearts be
   open, all desires known, and from whom
   no secrets are hid.
   Holy Communion The Collect

3 Incline our hearts to keep this law.
   Holy Communion The Ten Commandments
   (response)

4 Thou shalt do no murder.
   Holy Communion The Ten Commandments.
   Cf. 40:9

5 I believe in one God the Father Almighty,
   Maker of heaven and earth, And of all
   things visible and invisible:
   And in one Lord Jesus Christ, the only-
   begotten Son of God, Begotten of his
   Father before all worlds, God of God,
   Light of Light, Very God of very God,
   Begotten, not made, Being of one
   substance with the Father, By whom all
   things were made.
   Holy Communion Nicene Creed. Cf. 64:3,
   231:15

6 And I believe one Catholick and Apostolick
   Church.
   Holy Communion Nicene Creed

7 Let us pray for the whole state of Christ's
   Church militant here in earth.
   Holy Communion Prayer for the Church
   Militant

8 We humbly beseech thee most mercifully
   to accept our alms and oblations.
   Holy Communion Prayer for the Church
   Militant

9 Inspire continually the universal Church
   with the spirit of truth, unity, and concord.
   Holy Communion Prayer for the Church
   Militant

10 Give grace, O heavenly Father, to all
   Bishops and Curates, that they may both
   by their life and doctrine set forth thy true
   and lively Word.
   Holy Communion Prayer for the Church
   Militant

11 We do earnestly repent, And are heartily
   sorry for these our misdoings; The
   remembrance of them is grievous unto us;
   The burden of them is intolerable.
   Holy Communion General Confession

12 Hear what comfortable words our Saviour
   Christ saith unto all that truly turn to him.
   Holy Communion Comfortable Words
   (preamble)

13 Lift up your hearts.
   Holy Communion versicles and responses

14 It is meet and right so to do.
   Holy Communion versicles and responses

15 It is very meet, right, and our bounden
   duty, that we should at all times, and in
   all places, give thanks unto thee.
   Holy Communion Hymn of Praise

16 Who made there (by his one oblation of
   himself once offered) a full, perfect, and
   sufficient sacrifice.
   Holy Communion Prayer of Consecration

17 We beseech thee to accept this our
   bounden duty and service; not weighing
   our merits, but pardoning our offences.
   Holy Communion First Prayer of Oblation

18 Among all the changes and chances of this
   mortal life.
   Holy Communion Collects after the Offertory

19 O merciful God, grant that the old Adam in
   this Child may be so buried, that the new
   man may be raised up in him.
   Public Baptism of Infants Invocation of blessing
   on the child

20 QUESTION: Who gave you this Name?
   ANSWER: My Godfathers and Godmothers in
   my Baptism; wherein I was made a
   member of Christ, the child of God, and
   an inheritor of the kingdom of heaven.
   Catechism

21 I should renounce the devil and all his
   works, the pomps and vanity of this
   wicked world, and all the sinful lusts of
   the flesh.
   Catechism

22 To keep my hands from picking and
   stealing.
   Catechism

23 QUESTION: What meanest thou by this
   word *Sacrament*?
   ANSWER: I mean an outward and visible
   sign of an inward and spiritual grace.
   Catechism

24 Lord, hear our prayers.
   And let our cry come unto thee.
   Order of Confirmation

25 If any of you know cause, or just
   impediment, why these two persons
   should not be joined together in holy
   Matrimony, ye are to declare it. This is the
   first [*second*, or *third*] time of asking.
   Solemnization of Matrimony The Banns

26 Not by any to be enterprised, nor taken in
   hand, unadvisedly, lightly, or wantonly, to
   satisfy men's carnal lusts and appetites,
   like brute beasts that have no
   understanding.
   Solemnization of Matrimony Exhortation

27 If any man can shew any just cause, why
   they may not lawfully be joined together,
   let him now speak, or else hereafter for
   ever hold his peace.
   Solemnization of Matrimony Exhortation

28 Wilt thou love her, comfort her, honour,
   and keep her in sickness and in health;
   and, forsaking all other, keep thee only
   unto her, so long as ye both shall live?
   Solemnization of Matrimony Betrothal

1 To have and to hold from this day forward, for better for worse, for richer for poorer, in sickness and in health, to love, cherish, and to obey, till death us do part.
Solemnization of Matrimony Betrothal

2 With this Ring I thee wed, with my body I thee worship, and with all my worldly goods I thee endow.
Solemnization of Matrimony Wedding ('All that I am I give to you, and all that I have I share with you' in *Alternative Service Book*)

3 Those whom God hath joined together let no man put asunder.
Solemnization of Matrimony Wedding. Cf. 50:20

4 And thereto have given and pledged their troth either to other, and have declared the same by giving and receiving of a Ring, and by joining of hands.
Solemnization of Matrimony Minister's Declaration

5 The Office ensuing is not to be used for any that die unbaptized, or excommunicate, or have laid violent hands upon themselves.
The Burial of the Dead introductory rubric

6 Man that is born of a woman hath but a short time to live, and is full of misery.
The Burial of the Dead First Anthem. Cf. 42:33

7 In the midst of life we are in death.
The Burial of the Dead First Anthem

8 Forasmuch as it hath pleased Almighty God of his great mercy to take unto himself the soul of our dear brother here departed, we therefore commit his body to the ground; earth to earth, ashes to ashes, dust to dust; in sure and certain hope of the Resurrection to eternal life.
The Burial of the Dead Interment

9 Why do the heathen so furiously rage together: and why do the people imagine a vain thing?
Psalm 2, v. 1

10 Out of the mouth of very babes and sucklings hast thou ordained strength, because of thine enemies.
Psalm 8, v. 2

11 Up, Lord, and let not man have the upper hand.
Psalm 9, v. 19

12 The fool hath said in his heart: There is no God.
Psalm 14, v. 1

13 Lord, who shall dwell in thy tabernacle: or who shall rest upon thy holy hill?
Psalm 15, v. 1

14 He that hath not given his money upon usury: nor taken reward against the innocent.
Psalm 15, v. 6

15 The lot is fallen unto me in a fair ground: yea, I have a goodly heritage.
Psalm 16, v. 7 ('The lines are fallen unto me in pleasant places' in the Authorized Version of the Bible, v. 6)

16 They part my garments among them: and cast lots upon my vesture.
Psalm 22, v. 18

17 The Lord is my shepherd: therefore can I lack nothing.
He shall feed me in a green pasture: and lead me forth beside the waters of comfort.
Psalm 23, v. 1. Cf. 269:8

18 Yea, though I walk through the valley of the shadow of death, I will fear no evil: for thou art with me; thy rod and thy staff comfort me.
Thou shalt prepare a table before me against them that trouble me: thou hast anointed my head with oil, and my cup shall be full.
But thy loving-kindness and mercy shall follow me all the days of my life: and I will dwell in the house of the Lord for ever.
Psalm 23, v. 4. Cf. 269:9

19 The earth is the Lord's, and all that therein is.
Psalm 24, v. 1

20 Lift up your heads, O ye gates, and be ye lift up, ye everlasting doors: and the King of glory shall come in.
Psalm 24, v. 7

21 O remember not the sins and offences of my youth.
Psalm 25, v. 6

22 For his wrath endureth but the twinkling of an eye, and in his pleasure is life: heaviness may endure for a night, but joy cometh in the morning.
Psalm 30, v. 4

23 Into thy hands I commend my spirit.
Psalm 31, v. 6. Cf. 53:4

24 Sing unto the Lord a new song: sing praises lustily unto him with a good courage.
Psalm 33, v. 3

25 Keep thy tongue from evil: and thy lips, that they speak no guile.
Eschew evil, and do good: seek peace, and ensue it.
Psalm 34, v. 13

26 Fret not thyself because of the ungodly.
Psalm 37, v. 1

27 I have been young, and now am old: and yet saw I never the righteous forsaken, nor his seed begging their bread.
Psalm 37, v. 25

28 I myself have seen the ungodly in great power: and flourishing like a green bay-tree.
Psalm 37, v. 36

1 Lord, let me know mine end, and the number of my days: that I may be certified how long I have to live.
Psalm 39, v. 3

2 Mine own familiar friend, whom I trusted.
Psalm 41, v. 9

3 Like as the hart desireth the water-brooks: so longeth my soul after thee, O God.
Psalm 42, v. 1 ('As the hart panteth after the water brooks, so panteth my soul after thee, O God' in the Authorized Version of the Bible)

4 One deep calleth another, because of the noise of the water-pipes: all thy waves and storms are gone over me.
Psalm 42, v. 9

5 My heart is inditing of a good matter: I speak of the things which I have made unto the King.
My tongue is the pen: of a ready writer.
Psalm 45, v. 1

6 God is our hope and strength: a very present help in trouble.
Psalm 46, v. 1

7 Be still then, and know that I am God.
Psalm 46, v. 10

8 God is gone up with a merry noise: and the Lord with the sound of the trump.
Psalm 47, v. 5

9 Thou shalt purge me with hyssop, and I shall be clean: thou shalt wash me, and I shall be whiter than snow.
Psalm 51, v. 7

10 Make me a clean heart, O God: and renew a right spirit within me.
Psalm 51, v. 10

11 O that I had wings like a dove: for then would I flee away, and be at rest.
Psalm 55, v. 6

12 It was even thou, my companion: my guide, and mine own familiar friend.
Psalm 55, v. 14

13 They are as venomous as the poison of a serpent: even like the deaf adder that stoppeth her ears;
Which refuseth to hear the voice of the charmer: charm he never so wisely.
Psalm 58, v. 4

14 Moab is my wash-pot; over Edom will I cast out my shoe.
Psalm 60, v. 8

15 Let them fall upon the edge of the sword: that they may be a portion for foxes.
Psalm 63, v. 11

16 That thy way may be known upon earth: thy saving health among all nations.
Psalm 67, v. 2

17 Thou art gone up on high, thou hast led captivity captive.
Psalm 68, v. 18

18 For promotion cometh neither from the east, nor from the west: nor yet from the south.
Psalm 75, v. 7

19 O how amiable are thy dwellings: thou Lord of hosts!
Psalm 84, v. 1

20 Yea, the sparrow hath found her an house, and the swallow a nest where she may lay her young: even thy altars, O Lord of hosts.
Psalm 84, v. 3

21 Blessed is the man whose strength is in thee: in whose heart are thy ways.
Who going through the vale of misery use it for a well: and the pools are filled with water.
Psalm 84, v. 5

22 For one day in thy courts: is better than a thousand.
I had rather be a door-keeper in the house of my God: than to dwell in the tents of ungodliness.
Psalm 84, v. 10

23 Mercy and truth are met together: righteousness and peace have kissed each other.
Psalm 85, v. 10

24 Very excellent things are spoken of thee: thou city of God.
Psalm 87, v. 2

25 For a thousand years in thy sight are but as yesterday: seeing that is past as a watch in the night.
Psalm 90, v. 4

26 The days of our age are threescore years and ten; and though men be so strong that they come to fourscore years: yet is their strength then but labour and sorrow; so soon passeth it away, and we are gone.
Psalm 90, v. 10

27 So teach us to number our days: that we may apply our hearts unto wisdom.
Psalm 90, v. 12

28 For he shall deliver thee from the snare of the hunter.
Psalm 91, v. 3

29 Thou shalt not be afraid for any terror by night: nor for the arrow that flieth by day;
For the pestilence that walketh in darkness: nor for the sickness that destroyeth in the noon-day.
Psalm 91, v. 5

30 For he shall give his angels charge over thee: to keep thee in all thy ways.
They shall bear thee in their hands: that thou hurt not thy foot against a stone.
Psalm 91, v. 11

31 Let us come before his presence with thanksgiving: and shew ourselves glad in him with psalms.
Psalm 95, v. 2

1 To-day if ye will hear his voice, harden not your hearts: as in the provocation, and as in the day of temptation in the wilderness.
Psalm 95, v. 8

2 O worship the Lord in the beauty of holiness: let the whole earth stand in awe of him.
Psalm 96, v. 9

3 O sing unto the Lord a new song: for he hath done marvellous things.
Psalm 98, v. 1

4 With righteousness shall he judge the world: and the people with equity.
Psalm 98, v. 10

5 O be joyful in the Lord, all ye lands: serve the Lord with gladness, and come before his presence with a song.
Be ye sure that the Lord he is God: it is he that hath made us, and not we ourselves; we are his people, and the sheep of his pasture.
Psalm 100, v. 1. Cf. 58:10

6 The Lord is full of compassion and mercy: long-suffering, and of great goodness.
He will not alway be chiding: neither keepeth he his anger for ever.
Psalm 103, v. 8

7 The days of man are but as grass: for he flourisheth as a flower of a field.
For as soon as the wind goeth over it, it is gone: and the place thereof shall know it no more.
Psalm 103, v. 15

8 Man goeth forth to his work, and to his labour: until the evening.
Psalm 104, v. 23

9 The iron entered into his soul.
Psalm 105, v. 18

10 That he might inform his princes after his will: and teach his senators wisdom.
Psalm 105, v. 22

11 Thus were they stained with their own works: and went a whoring with their own inventions.
Psalm 106, v. 38

12 They that go down to the sea in ships: and occupy their business in great waters.
Psalm 107, v. 23

13 They reel to and fro, and stagger like a drunken man: and are at their wit's end.
Psalm 107, v. 27

14 The Lord said unto my Lord: Sit thou on my right hand, until I make thine enemies thy footstool.
Psalm 110, v. 1

15 The fear of the Lord is the beginning of wisdom.
Psalm 111, v. 10

16 The mountains skipped like rams: and the little hills like young sheep.
Psalm 114, v. 4

17 Not unto us, O Lord, not unto us, but unto thy Name give the praise.
Psalm 115, v. 1. Cf. 58:12

18 They have mouths, and speak not: eyes have they, and see not.
They have ears, and hear not: noses have they, and smell not.
They have hands, and handle not: feet have they, and walk not: neither speak they through their throat.
Psalm 115, v. 5

19 The snares of death compassed me round about: and the pains of hell gat hold upon me.
Psalm 116, v. 3

20 Thou hast delivered my soul from death: mine eyes from tears, and my feet from falling.
Psalm 116, v. 8

21 I said in my haste, All men are liars.
Psalm 116, v. 10

22 The same stone which the builders refused: is become the head-stone in the corner.
Psalm 118, v. 22

23 Blessed be he that cometh in the Name of the Lord.
Psalm 118, v. 26

24 Thy word is a lantern unto my feet: and a light unto my paths.
Psalm 119, v. 105

25 I will lift up mine eyes unto the hills: from whence cometh my help.
Psalm 121, v. 1

26 So that the sun shall not burn thee by day: neither the moon by night.
Psalm 121, v. 6

27 The Lord shall preserve thy going out, and thy coming in: from this time forth for evermore.
Psalm 121, v. 8

28 I was glad when they said unto me: We will go into the house of the Lord.
Psalm 122, v. 1

29 They that sow in tears: shall reap in joy.
Psalm 126, v. 6

30 Except the Lord build the house: their labour is but lost that build it.
Except the Lord keep the city: the watchman waketh but in vain.
Psalm 127, v. 1. Cf. 58:13

31 Like as the arrows in the hand of the giant: even so are the young children.
Happy is the man that hath his quiver full of them.
Psalm 127, v. 5

32 Thy wife shall be as the fruitful vine: upon the walls of thine house.
Thy children like the olive-branches: round about thy table.
Psalm 128, v. 3

33 Out of the deep have I called unto thee, O Lord: Lord, hear my voice.
Psalm 130, v. 1. Cf. 58:14

1 O give thanks unto the Lord, for he is gracious: and his mercy endureth for ever.
Psalm 136, v. 1

2 By the waters of Babylon we sat down and wept: when we remembered thee, O Sion.
Psalm 137, v. 1

3 How shall we sing the Lord's song: in a strange land?
Psalm 137, v. 4

4 If I forget thee, O Jerusalem: let my right hand forget her cunning.
Psalm 137, v. 5

5 O Lord, thou hast searched me out, and known me: thou knowest my down-sitting, and mine up-rising.
Psalm 139, v. 1

6 If I take the wings of the morning: and remain in the uttermost parts of the sea; Even there also shall thy hand lead me: and thy right hand shall hold me.
Psalm 139, v. 8

7 I will give thanks unto thee, for I am fearfully and wonderfully made.
Psalm 139, v. 13

8 Let the lifting up of my hands be an evening sacrifice.
Psalm 141, v. 2

9 O put not your trust in princes.
Psalm 146, v. 2

10 He hath no pleasure in the strength of an horse: neither delighteth he in any man's legs.
Psalm 147, v. 10

11 To bind their kings in chains: and their nobles with links of iron.
Psalm 149, v. 8

12 Praise him upon the well-tuned cymbals: praise him upon the loud cymbals.
Psalm 150, v. 5

13 Be pleased to receive into thy Almighty and most gracious protection the persons of us thy servants, and the Fleet in which we serve.
Forms of Prayer to be Used at Sea First Prayer

14 That we may be ... a security for such as pass on the seas upon their lawful occasions.
Forms of Prayer to be Used at Sea First Prayer

15 We therefore commit his body to the deep, to be turned into corruption, looking for the resurrection of the body (when the Sea shall give up her dead).
Forms of Prayer to be Used at Sea At the Burial of their Dead at Sea

16 Come, Holy Ghost, our souls inspire, And lighten with celestial fire. Thou the anointing Spirit art, Who dost thy seven-fold gifts impart.
Ordering of Priests 'Veni, Creator Spiritus' (tr. Bishop John Cosin, 1627, from 9th-century original)

17 Man is very far gone from original righteousness.
Articles of Religion (1562) no. 9

18 It is a thing plainly repugnant to the Word of God, and the custom of the Primitive Church, to have publick Prayer in the Church, or to minister the Sacraments in a tongue not understood of the people.
Articles of Religion (1562) no. 24

19 A Man may not marry his Mother.
A Table of Kindred and Affinity

John Wilkes Booth 1838–65

20 *Sic semper tyrannis!* The South is avenged.
Having shot President Lincoln, 14 April 1865 ('*Sic semper tyrannis* [Thus always to tyrants]'—motto of the State of Virginia). See *New York Times* 15 April 1865

General William Booth 1829–1912

21 The Submerged Tenth.
In Darkest England (1890) pt. 1, title of ch. 2 ('three million men, women, and children, a vast despairing multitude in a condition nominally free, but really enslaved')

Jorge Luis Borges 1899–1986

22 The original is unfaithful to the translation.
Of Henley's translation, in *Sobre el 'Vathek' de William Beckford*; in *Obras Completas* (1974) p. 730

23 For one of those gnostics, the visible universe was an illusion or, more precisely, a sophism. Mirrors and fatherhood are abominable because they multiply it and extend it.
Tlön, Uqbar, Orbis, Tertius (1941) in *Obras Completas* (1974) p. 431

24 The Falklands thing was a fight between two bald men over a comb.
In *Time* 14 February 1983

Cesare Borgia 1476–1507

25 *Aut Caesar, aut nihil.*
Caesar or nothing.
Motto inscribed on his sword. See J. L. Garner *Caesar Borgia* (1912) p. 309

George Borrow 1803–81

26 A losing trade, I assure you, sir: literature is a drug.
Lavengro (1851) ch. 30

27 Youth will be served, every dog has his day, and mine has been a fine one.
Lavengro (1851) ch. 92

Pierre Bosquet 1810–61

28 *C'est magnifique, mais ce n'est pas la guerre.*
It is magnificent, but it is not war.
On the charge of the Light Brigade at Balaclava, 25 October 1854; in C. Woodham-Smith *The Reason Why* (1953) ch. 12

John Collins Bossidy 1860–1928

1 And this is good old Boston,
The home of the bean and the cod,
Where the Lowells talk to the Cabots
And the Cabots talk only to God.

> Verse spoken at Holy Cross College alumni
> dinner in Boston, Massachusetts, 1910; in
> *Springfield Sunday Republican* 14 December
> 1924

Jacques-Bénigne Bossuet 1627–1704

2 *L'Angleterre, ah, la perfide Angleterre, que le
rempart de ses mers rendait inaccessible aux
Romains, la foi du Sauveur y est abordée.*

England, ah, faithless England, which the
protection afforded by its seas rendered
inaccessible to the Romans, the faith of the
Saviour spread even there.

> First sermon on the feast of the
> Circumcision, in *Oeuvres de Bossuet* (1816)
> vol. 11, p. 469. Cf. 358:9

James Boswell 1740–95

3 I am, I flatter myself, completely a citizen
of the world.

> *Journal of a Tour to the Hebrides* (ed. F. A. Pottle,
> 1936) 14 August 1773

4 A page of my Journal is like a cake of
portable soup. A little may be diffused into
a considerable portion.

> *Journal of a Tour to the Hebrides* (ed. F. A. Pottle,
> 1936) 13 September 1773

5 Most vices may be committed very
genteelly: a man may debauch his friend's
wife genteelly: he may cheat at cards
genteelly.

> *Life of Samuel Johnson* (1934 ed.) vol. 2, p. 340
> (6 April 1775)

Gordon Bottomley 1874–1948

6 Your worship is your furnaces,
Which, like old idols, lost obscenes,
Have molten bowels; your vision is
Machines for making more machines.

> 'To Ironfounders and Others' (1912)

Horatio Bottomley 1860–1933

7 What poor education I have received has
been gained in the University of Life.

> Speech at the Oxford Union, 2 December
> 1920; in Beverley Nichols *25* (1926) ch. 7

Dion Boucicault 1820–90

8 Men talk of killing time, while time quietly
kills them.

> *London Assurance* (1841) act 2, sc. 1. Cf. 307:22

Antoine Boulay de la Meurthe 1761–1840

9 *C'est pire qu'un crime, c'est une faute.*

It is worse than a crime, it is a blunder.

> On hearing of the execution of the Duc
> d'Enghien, 1804; in C.-A. Sainte-Beuve
> *Nouveaux Lundis* (1870) vol. 12, p. 52

Sir Harold Edwin Boulton 1859–1935

10 Speed, bonnie boat, like a bird on the wing,
'Onward,' the sailors cry;
Carry the lad that's born to be king,
Over the sea to Skye.

> 'Skye Boat Song' (1908)

Matthew Boulton 1728–1809

11 I sell here, Sir, what all the world desires
to have—POWER.

> Speaking to Boswell of his engineering
> works; in James Boswell *Life of Samuel Johnson*
> (1934 ed.) vol. 2, p. 459 (22 March 1776)

F. W. Bourdillon 1852–1921

12 The night has a thousand eyes,
And the day but one.

> *Among the Flowers* (1878) 'Light'. Cf. 212:18

Lord Bowen 1835–94

13 When I hear of an 'equity' in a case like
this, I am reminded of a blind man in a
dark room—looking for a black
hat—which isn't there.

> In J. A. Foote *Pie-Powder* (1911) p. 25

14 The rain, it raineth on the just
And also on the unjust fella:
But chiefly on the just, because
The unjust steals the just's umbrella.

> In W. Sichel *Sands of Time* (1923) ch. 4

E. E. Bowen 1836–1901

15 Forty years on, when afar and asunder
Parted are those who are singing to-day.

> 'Forty Years On' (Harrow School Song,
> published 1886)

16 Follow up! Follow up! Follow up! Follow up!
Follow up!
Till the field ring again and again,
With the tramp of the twenty-two men.

> 'Forty Years On'

Elizabeth Bowen 1899–1973

17 There is no end to the violations
committed by children on children, quietly
talking alone.

> *The House in Paris* (1935) pt. 1, ch. 2

18 Fate is not an eagle, it creeps like a rat.

> *The House in Paris* (1935) pt. 2, ch. 2

1 Jealousy is no more than feeling alone
against smiling enemies.
The House in Paris (1935) pt. 2, ch. 8

2 A high altar on the move.
Describing Edith Sitwell, in V. Glendinning
Edith Sitwell (1981) ch. 25

Sir Maurice Bowra 1898–1971

3 I'm a man more dined against than dining.
In John Betjeman *Summoned by Bells* (1960)
ch. 9. Cf. 283:10

4 My dear fellow, buggers can't be choosers.
On being told he should not marry anyone
as plain as his fiancée; in H. Lloyd-Jones
Maurice Bowra: a Celebration (1974) p. 150
(possibly apocryphal)

Charles Brackett 1892–1969 and Billy Wilder 1906–

5 JOE GILLIS: You used to be in pictures. You
used to be big.
NORMA DESMOND: I am big. It's the pictures
that got small.
Sunset Boulevard (1950 film, with D. M.
Marshman Jr.)

John Bradford c.1510–55

6 But for the grace of God there goes John
Bradford.
On seeing a group of criminals being led to
their execution; in *Dictionary of National
Biography* (1917–) p. 1067 (usually quoted
'There but for the grace of God go I')

F. H. Bradley 1846–1924

7 Metaphysics is the finding of bad reasons
for what we believe upon instinct.
Appearance and Reality (1893) preface

8 The world is the best of all possible worlds,
and everything in it is a necessary evil.
Appearance and Reality (1893) preface

9 Where everything is bad it must be good
to know the worst.
Appearance and Reality (1893) preface

Omar Bradley 1893–1981

10 We have grasped the mystery of the atom
and rejected the Sermon on the Mount.
Speech on Armistice Day, 1948, in *Collected
Writings* (1967) vol. 1, p. 588

John Bradshaw 1602–59

11 Rebellion to tyrants is obedience to God.
Suppositious epitaph. See H. S. Randall *Life of
Thomas Jefferson* (1865) vol. 3, appendix 4,
p. 585

Anne Bradstreet c.1612–72

12 I am obnoxious to each carping tongue,
Who says my hand a needle better fits.
'The Prologue' (1650)

James Bramston c.1694–1744

13 What's not destroyed by Time's devouring
hand?
Where's Troy, and where's the Maypole in
the Strand?
The Art of Politics (1729) l. 71

Georges Braque 1882–1963

14 Art is meant to disturb, science reassures.
Le Jour et la nuit: Cahiers 1917–52 p. 11.
Cf. 236:11

15 Truth exists; only lies are invented.
Le Jour et la nuit: Cahiers 1917–52 p. 20

Richard Brathwaite c.1588–1673

16 To Banbury came I, O profane one!
Where I saw a Puritane-one
Hanging of his cat on Monday
For killing of a mouse on Sunday.
Barnabee's Journal (1638) pt. 1, st. 4

Bertolt Brecht 1898–1956

17 The resistible rise of Arturo Ui.
Title of play (1941)

18 Oh, the shark has pretty teeth, dear,
And he shows them pearly white.
Just a jack-knife has Macheath, dear
And he keeps it out of sight.
The Threepenny Opera (1928) prologue

19 Food comes first, then morals.
The Threepenny Opera (1928) act 2, sc. 3

20 They have gone too long without a war
here. Where is morality to come from in
such a case, I ask? Peace is nothing but
slovenliness, only war creates order.
Mother Courage (1939) sc. 1

21 Don't tell me peace has broken out, when
I've just bought fresh supplies.
Mother Courage (1939) sc. 8

Jane Brereton 1685–1740

22 The picture, placed the busts between,
Adds to the thought much strength:
Wisdom and Wit are little seen,
But Folly's at full length.
'On Mr Nash's Picture at Full Length,
between the Busts of Sir Isaac Newton and
Mr Pope' (1744)

Nicholas Breton c.1545–1626

23 I wish my deadly foe, no worse
Than want of friends, and empty purse.
'A Farewell to Town' (1577)

Robert Bridges 1844–1930

24 All my hope on God is founded.
Title of hymn (1899)

1 When men were all asleep the snow came
flying,
In large white flakes falling on the city
brown,
Stealthily and perpetually settling and
loosely lying,
Hushing the latest traffic of the drowsy
town.
'London Snow' (1890)

John Bright 1811–89

2 The angel of death has been abroad
throughout the land; you may almost hear
the beating of his wings.
On the effects of the Crimean war; in
Hansard, 23 February 1855, col. 1761

3 I am for 'Peace, retrenchment, and reform',
the watchword of the great Liberal party
30 years ago.
Speech at Birmingham, 28 April 1859, in The
Times 29 April 1859; the 'watchword' may be
found in Samuel Warren's novel Ten
Thousand a Year (1841) bk. 7, ch. 1

4 My opinion is that the Northern States will
manage somehow to muddle through.
During the American Civil War; in J.
McCarthy Reminiscences (1899) vol. 1, ch. 5

5 England is the mother of Parliaments.
Speech at Birmingham, 18 January 1865, in
The Times 19 January 1865

6 Force is not a remedy.
Speech, 16 November 1880, in The Times
17 November 1880

Anthelme Brillat-Savarin
1755–1826

7 Tell me what you eat and I will tell you
what you are.
Physiologie du Goût (1825) 'Aphorismes pour
servir de prolégomènes' no. 4. Cf. 139:1

Alexander Brome 1620–66

8 Come, blessed peace, we once again
implore,
And let our pains be less, or power more.
Songs and Other Poems (1661) 'The Riddle'

Jacob Bronowski 1908–74

9 The world can only be grasped by action,
not by contemplation ... The hand is the
cutting edge of the mind.
The Ascent of Man (1973) ch. 3

10 The essence of science: ask an impertinent
question, and you are on the way to a
pertinent answer.
The Ascent of Man (1973) ch. 4

11 The wish to hurt, the momentary
intoxication with pain, is the loophole
through which the pervert climbs into the
minds of ordinary men.
The Face of Violence (1954) ch. 5

Charlotte Brontë 1816–55

12 Reader, I married him.
Jane Eyre (1847) ch. 38

13 Of late years an abundant shower of
curates has fallen upon the North of
England.
Shirley (1849) ch. 1

14 Be a governess! Better be a slave at once!
Shirley (1849) ch. 13

15 It is rustic all through. It is moorish, and
wild, and knotty as a root of heath.
On the setting of Emily Brontë's Wuthering
Heights, in her own preface to the 1850
edition

Emily Brontë 1818–48

16 No coward soul is mine,
No trembler in the world's storm-troubled
sphere:
I see Heaven's glories shine,
And faith shines equal, arming me from
fear.
'No coward soul is mine' (1846)

17 My love for Heathcliff resembles the
eternal rocks beneath:—a source of little
visible delight, but necessary.
Wuthering Heights (1847) ch. 9

18 I lingered round them, under that benign
sky: watched the moths fluttering among
the heath and hare-bells; listened to the
soft wind breathing through the grass; and
wondered how any one could ever imagine
unquiet slumbers for the sleepers in that
quiet earth.
Wuthering Heights (1847) ad fin.

Patrick Brontë 1777–1861

19 No quailing, Mrs Gaskell! no drawing back!
Apropos her undertaking to write the life of
Charlotte Brontë; in J. A. V. Chapple and A.
Pollard (eds.) Letters of Mrs Gaskell (1966)
no. 257

Rupert Brooke 1887–1915

20 Blow out, you bugles, over the rich Dead!
There's none of these so lonely and poor of
old,
But, dying, has made us rarer gifts than
gold.
These laid the world away; poured out the
red
Sweet wine of youth; gave up the years to
be
Of work and joy, and that unhoped serene,
That men call age; and those that would
have been,
Their sons, they gave, their immortality.
'The Dead' (1914)

21 Honour has come back, as a king, to earth,
And paid his subjects with a royal wage;
And Nobleness walks in our ways again;
And we have come into our heritage.
'The Dead' (1914)

1 ... The cool kindliness of sheets, that soon
Smooth away trouble; and the rough male
kiss
Of blankets.
'The Great Lover' (1914)

2 Fish say, they have their stream and pond;
But is there anything beyond?
'Heaven' (1915)

3 Just now the lilac is in bloom,
All before my little room.
'The Old Vicarage, Grantchester' (1915)

4 Unkempt about those hedges blows
An English unofficial rose.
'The Old Vicarage, Grantchester' (1915)

5 Curates, long dust, will come and go
On lissom, clerical, printless toe;
And oft between the boughs is seen
The sly shade of a Rural Dean.
'The Old Vicarage, Grantchester' (1915)

6 God! I will pack, and take a train,
And get me to England once again!
For England's the one land, I know,
Where men with Splendid Hearts may go.
'The Old Vicarage, Grantchester' (1915)

7 For Cambridge people rarely smile,
Being urban, squat, and packed with guile.
'The Old Vicarage, Grantchester' (1915)

8 Stands the Church clock at ten to three?
And is there honey still for tea?
'The Old Vicarage, Grantchester' (1915)

9 Now, God be thanked Who has matched us
with His hour,
And caught our youth, and wakened us
from sleeping,
With hand made sure, clear eye, and
sharpened power,
To turn, as swimmers into cleanness
leaping.
'Peace' (1914)

10 If I should die, think only this of me:
That there's some corner of a foreign field
That is for ever England. There shall be
In that rich earth a richer dust concealed;
A dust whom England bore, shaped, made
aware,
Gave, once, her flowers to love, her ways to
roam,
A body of England's, breathing English air,
Washed by the rivers, blest by suns of
home.

And think, this heart, all evil shed away,
A pulse in the eternal mind, no less
Gives somewhere back the thoughts by
England given;
Her sights and sounds; dreams happy as
her day;
And laughter, learnt of friends; and
gentleness,
In hearts at peace, under an English
heaven.
'The Soldier' (1914)

Anita Brookner 1938–

11 Good women always think it is their fault
when someone else is being offensive. Bad
women never take the blame for anything.
Hotel du Lac (1984) ch. 7

12 They were reasonable people, and no one
was to be hurt, not even with words.
Hotel du Lac (1984) ch. 9

13 Dr Weiss, at forty, knew that her life had
been ruined by literature.
A Start in Life (1981) ch. 1

Thomas Brooks 1608–80

14 For (*magna est veritas et praevalebit*) great is
truth, and shall prevail.
The Crown and Glory of Christianity (1662)
p. 407. Cf. 58:23

H. Rap Brown 1943–

15 I say violence is necessary. It is as
American as cherry pie.
Speech, 27 July 1967, in *Washington Post*
28 July 1967, p. A7

John Brown 1715–66

16 I have seen some extracts from Johnson's
Preface to his 'Shakespeare' ... No feeling
nor pathos in him! Altogether upon the
high horse, and blustering about Imperial
Tragedy!
Letter to Garrick, 27 October 1765, in *Private
Correspondence of David Garrick* (1831) vol. 1

Lew Brown 1893–1958

17 Life is just a bowl of cherries.
Title of song (1931)

Thomas Brown 1663–1704

18 I do not love thee, Dr Fell.
The reason why I cannot tell;
But this I know, and know full well,
I do not love thee, Dr Fell.
Written while an undergraduate at Christ
Church, Oxford, of which Dr Fell was Dean;
in A. L. Hayward (ed.) *Amusements Serious and
Comical by Tom Brown* (1927) p. xiii.
Cf. 220:4

T. E. Brown 1830–97

19 A garden is a lovesome thing, God wot!
'My Garden' (1893)

20 O blackbird, what a boy you are!
How you do go it!
'Vespers' (1900)

Cecil Browne 1932–

21 But not so odd
As those who choose
A Jewish God,
But spurn the Jews.
Reply to verse by William Norman Ewer.
Cf. 138:2

Sir Thomas Browne 1605-82

1 He who discommendeth others obliquely commendeth himself.
Christian Morals (1716) pt. 1, sect. 34

2 Life itself is but the shadow of death, and souls departed but the shadows of the living.
The Garden of Cyrus (1658) ch. 4

3 Old mortality, the ruins of forgotten times.
Hydriotaphia (Urn Burial, 1658) Epistle Dedicatory

4 Men have lost their reason in nothing so much as their religion, wherein stones and clouts make martyrs.
Hydriotaphia (Urn Burial, 1658) ch. 4

5 The long habit of living indisposeth us for dying.
Hydriotaphia (Urn Burial, 1658) ch. 5

6 Generations pass while some trees stand, and old families last not three oaks.
Hydriotaphia (Urn Burial, 1658) ch. 5

7 Man is a noble animal, splendid in ashes, and pompous in the grave.
Hydriotaphia (Urn Burial, 1658) ch. 5

8 Ready to be any thing, in the ecstasy of being ever.
Hydriotaphia (Urn Burial, 1658) ch. 5

9 Many from ... an inconsiderate zeal unto truth, have too rashly charged the troops of error, and remain as trophies unto the enemies of truth.
Religio Medici (1643) pt. 1, sect. 6

10 As for those wingy mysteries in divinity and airy subtleties in religion, which have unhinged the brains of better heads, they never stretched the *pia mater* of mine; methinks there be not impossibilities enough in religion for an active faith.
Religio Medici (1643) pt. 1, sect. 9

11 I love to lose myself in a mystery, to pursue my reason to an *O altitudo*!
Religio Medici (1643) pt. 1, sect. 9

12 I have often admired the mystical way of Pythagoras, and the secret magic of numbers.
Religio Medici (1643) pt. 1, sect. 12

13 We carry within us the wonders we seek without us: there is all Africa and her prodigies in us.
Religio Medici (1643) pt. 1, sect. 15

14 All things are artificial, for nature is the art of God.
Religio Medici (1643) pt. 1, sect. 16

15 Obstinacy in a bad cause, is but constancy in a good.
Religio Medici (1643) pt. 1, sect. 25

16 Persecution is a bad and indirect way to plant religion.
Religio Medici (1643) pt. 1, sect. 25

17 Certainly there is no happiness within this circle of flesh, nor is it in the optics of these eyes to behold felicity; the first day of our Jubilee is death.
Religio Medici (1643) pt. 1, sect. 44

18 This trivial and vulgar way of coition; it is the foolishest act a wise man commits in all his life, nor is there any thing that will more deject his cooled imagination, when he shall consider what an odd and unworthy piece of folly he hath committed.
Religio Medici (1643) pt. 2, sect. 9

19 We all labour against our own cure, for death is the cure of all diseases.
Religio Medici (1643) pt. 2, sect. 9

20 For the world, I count it not an inn, but an hospital, and a place, not to live, but to die in.
Religio Medici (1643) pt. 2, sect. 11

21 There is surely a piece of divinity in us, something that was before the elements, and owes no homage unto the sun.
Religio Medici (1643) pt. 2, sect. 11

22 We term sleep a death, and yet it is waking that kills us, and destroys those spirits which are the house of life.
Religio Medici (1643) pt. 2, sect. 12

23 That children dream not in the first half year, that men dream not in some countries, are to me sick men's dreams, dreams out of the ivory gate, and visions before midnight.
S. Wilkin (ed.) *Works* (1835) vol. 4, p. 359 'On Dreams'

William Browne *c.*1590-1643

24 Underneath this sable hearse
Lies the subject of all verse;
Sidney's sister, Pembroke's mother,
Death, ere thou hast slain another,
Fair and learn'd, and good as she,
Time shall throw a dart at thee.
'Epitaph on the Countess Dowager of Pembroke' (1623)

Sir William Browne 1692-1774

25 The King to Oxford sent a troop of horse,
For Tories own no argument but force:
With equal skill to Cambridge books he sent,
For Whigs admit no force but argument.
Reply to Trapp's epigram, in J. Nichols *Literary Anecdotes* vol. 3 (1812) p. 330. Cf. 334:3

Elizabeth Barrett Browning 1806-61

26 The devil's most devilish when respectable.
Aurora Leigh (1857) bk. 7, l. 105

27 And kings crept out again to feel the sun.
'Crowned and Buried' (1844) st. 11

1 And lips say, 'God be pitiful,'
Who ne'er said, 'God be praised.'
  'The Cry of the Human' (1844) st. 1

2 I tell you, hopeless grief is passionless.
  'Grief' (1844)

3 Or from Browning some 'Pomegranate',
which, if cut deep down the middle,
Shows a heart within blood-tinctured, of a
veined humanity.
  'Lady Geraldine's Courtship' (1844) st. 41

4 What was he doing, the great god Pan,
Down in the reeds by the river?
  'A Musical Instrument' (1862)

5 How do I love thee? Let me count the ways.
  Sonnets from the Portuguese (1850) no. 43

6 Thou large-brained woman and large-
hearted man.
  'To George Sand—A Desire' (1844)

Sir Frederick Browning
1896–1965

7 I think we might be going a bridge too far.
  Expressing reservations about the Arnhem
  'Market Garden' operation, 10 September
  1944; in R. E. Urquhart Arnhem (1958) p. 4

Robert Browning 1812–89

8 The high that proved too high, the heroic
for earth too hard,
The passion that left the ground to lose
itself in the sky,
Are music sent up to God by the lover and
the bard;
Enough that he heard it once: we shall
hear it by-and-by.
  'Abt Vogler' (1864) st. 10

9 ... I feel for the common chord again ...
The C Major of this life.
  'Abt Vogler' (1864) st. 12

10 Ah, but a man's reach should exceed his
grasp,
Or what's a heaven for?
  'Andrea del Sarto' (1855) l. 97

11 One who never turned his back but
marched breast forward,
Never doubted clouds would break,
Never dreamed, though right were
worsted, wrong would triumph,
Held we fall to rise, are baffled to fight
better,
Sleep to wake.
  Asolando (1889) 'Epilogue'

12 Greet the unseen with a cheer!
  Asolando (1889) 'Epilogue'

13 Just when we are safest, there's a sunset-
touch,
A fancy from a flower-bell, some one's
death,
A chorus-ending from Euripides.
  'Bishop Blougram's Apology' (1855) l. 182

14 The grand Perhaps!
  'Bishop Blougram's Apology' (1855) l. 190

15 Our interest's on the dangerous edge of
things.
  'Bishop Blougram's Apology' (1855) l. 395

16 He said true things, but called them by
wrong names.
  'Bishop Blougram's Apology' (1855) l. 996

17 Boot, saddle, to horse, and away!
  'Boot and Saddle' (1842)

18 And I turn the page, and I turn the page,
Not verse now, only prose!
  'By the Fireside' (1855) st. 2

19 Oh, the little more, and how much it is!
And the little less, and what worlds away!
  'By the Fireside' (1855) st. 39

20 The raree-show of Peter's successor.
  'Christmas-Eve' (1850) l. 1242

21 We loved, sir—used to meet:
How sad and bad and mad it was—
But then, how it was sweet!
  'Confessions' (1864) st. 9

22 Stung by the splendour of a sudden
thought.
  'A Death in the Desert' (1864) l. 59

23 Progress, man's distinctive mark alone,
Not God's, and not the beasts': God is, they
are,
Man partly is and wholly hopes to be.
  'A Death in the Desert' (1864) l. 586

24 Open my heart and you will see
Graved inside of it, 'Italy'.
  'De Gustibus' (1855) pt. 2, l. 39

25 Reads verse and thinks she understands.
  'Dîs Aliter Visum' (1864) st. 4

26 Sure of the Fortieth spare Arm-chair
When gout and glory seat me there.
  'Dîs Aliter Visum' (1864) st. 12

27   'Tis well averred,
A scientific faith's absurd.
  'Easter-Day' (1850) l. 123

28 Beautiful Evelyn Hope is dead!
  'Evelyn Hope' (1855)

29 You will wake, and remember, and
understand.
  'Evelyn Hope' (1855)

30 If you get simple beauty and naught else,
You get about the best thing God invents.
  'Fra Lippo Lippi' (1855) l. 217

31   This world's no blot for us,
Nor blank; it means intensely, and means
good.
  'Fra Lippo Lippi' (1855) l. 313

32 He said, 'What's time? Leave Now for dogs
and apes!
Man has Forever.'
  'A Grammarian's Funeral' (1855) l. 83

33 That low man seeks a little thing to do,
Sees it and does it:
This high man, with a great thing to
pursue,
Dies ere he knows it.
  'A Grammarian's Funeral' (1855) l. 113

1 Oh, to be in England
Now that April's there.
'Home-Thoughts, from Abroad' (1845)

2 That's the wise thrush; he sings each song
twice over,
Lest you should think he never could
recapture
The first fine careless rapture!
'Home-Thoughts, from Abroad' (1845)

3 Nobly, nobly Cape Saint Vincent to the
North-west died away;
Sunset ran, one glorious blood-red, reeking
into Cadiz Bay.
'Home-Thoughts, from the Sea' (1845)

4 Here and here did England help me: how
can I help England?
'Home-Thoughts, from the Sea' (1845)

5 I sprang to the stirrup, and Joris, and he;
I galloped, Dirck galloped, we galloped all
three.
'How they brought the Good News from
Ghent to Aix' (1845) l. 1

6 A man can have but one life and one
death,
One heaven, one hell.
'In a Balcony' (1855) l. 13

7   I count life just a stuff
To try the soul's strength on, educe the
man.
'In a Balcony' (1855) l. 651

8 'You're wounded!' 'Nay,' the soldier's pride
Touched to the quick, he said:
'I'm killed, Sire!' And his chief beside,
Smiling the boy fell dead.
'Incident of the French Camp' (1842) st. 5

9 Ignorance is not innocence but sin.
The Inn Album (1875) canto 5

10 The swallow has set her six young on the
rail,
And looks sea-ward.
'James Lee's Wife' (1864) pt. 3, st. 1

11 Who knows but the world may end
tonight?
'The Last Ride Together' (1855) st. 2

12 'Tis an awkward thing to play with souls,
And matter enough to save one's own.
'A Light Woman' (1855) st. 12

13 Just for a handful of silver he left us,
Just for a riband to stick in his coat.
'The Lost Leader' (1845) (of Wordsworth)

14 We that had loved him so, followed him,
honoured him,
Lived in his mild and magnificent eye,
Learned his great language, caught his
clear accents,
Made him our pattern to live and to die!
Shakespeare was of us, Milton was for us,
Burns, Shelley, were with us—they watch
from their graves!
'The Lost Leader' (1845)

15 Never glad confident morning again!
'The Lost Leader' (1845)

16 Oppression makes the wise man mad.
Luria (1846) act 4, l. 16

17 A tap at the pane, the quick sharp scratch
And blue spurt of a lighted match,
And a voice less loud, through its joys and
fears,
Than the two hearts beating each to each!
'Meeting at Night' (1845)

18 Ah, did you once see Shelley plain,
And did he stop and speak to you
And did you speak to him again?
How strange it seems, and new!
'Memorabilia' (1855)

19   She had
A heart—how shall I say?—too soon made
glad,
Too easily impressed; she liked whate'er
She looked on, and her looks went
everywhere.
'My Last Duchess' (1842) l. 21

20 Never the time and the place
And the loved one all together!
'Never the Time and the Place' (1883)

21   What's come to perfection
perishes.
Things learned on earth, we shall practise
in heaven:
Works done least rapidly, Art most
cherishes.
'Old Pictures in Florence' (1855) st. 17

22 Measure your mind's height by the shade
it casts!
Paracelsus (1835) pt. 3, l. 821

23 Round the cape of a sudden came the sea,
And the sun looked over the mountain's
rim:
And straight was a path of gold for him,
And the need of a world of men for me.
'Parting at Morning' (1849)

24 It was roses, roses, all the way.
'The Patriot' (1855)

25 The air broke into a mist with bells.
'The Patriot' (1855)

26 Rats!
They fought the dogs and killed the cats,
And bit the babies in the cradles ...
And even spoiled the women's chats
By drowning their speaking
With shrieking and squeaking
In fifty different sharps and flats.
'The Pied Piper of Hamelin' (1842) st. 2

27 So munch on, crunch on, take your
nuncheon,
Breakfast, supper, dinner, luncheon!
'The Pied Piper of Hamelin' (1842) st. 7

28 The year's at the spring
And day's at the morn;
Morning's at seven;
The hill-side's dew-pearled;
The lark's on the wing;
The snail's on the thorn:
God's in his heaven—
All's right with the world!
Pippa Passes (1841) pt. 1, l. 221

1 All service ranks the same with God—
With God, whose puppets, best and worst,
Are we: there is no last nor first.
Pippa Passes (1841) epilogue

2 Fear death?—to feel the fog in my throat,
The mist in my face.
'Prospice' (1864)

3 Grow old along with me!
The best is yet to be.
'Rabbi Ben Ezra' (1864) st. 1

4 Fancies that broke through language and
escaped.
'Rabbi Ben Ezra' (1864) st. 25

5 O lyric Love, half-angel and half-bird
And all a wonder and a wild desire.
The Ring and the Book (1868-9) bk. 1, l. 1391

6   So, Pietro craved an heir,
(The story always old and always new).
The Ring and the Book (1868-9) bk. 2, l. 213

7   Go practise if you please
With men and women: leave a child alone
For Christ's particular love's sake!
The Ring and the Book (1868-9) bk. 3, l. 88

8 In the great right of an excessive wrong.
The Ring and the Book (1868-9) bk. 3, l. 1055

9 Faultless to a fault.
The Ring and the Book (1868-9) bk. 9, l. 1175

10 White shall not neutralize the black, nor
good
Compensate bad in man, absolve him so:
Life's business being just the terrible
choice.
The Ring and the Book (1868-9) bk. 10, l. 1235

11 I want to know a butcher paints,
A baker rhymes for his pursuit.
'Shop' (1876) st. 21

12 There's a great text in Galatians,
Once you trip on it, entails
Twenty-nine distinct damnations,
One sure, if another fails.
'Soliloquy of the Spanish Cloister' (1842) st. 7

13 Sidney's self, the starry paladin.
Sordello (1840) bk. 1, l. 69

14 Still more labyrinthine buds the rose.
Sordello (1840) bk. 1, l. 476

15   Any nose
May ravage with impunity a rose.
Sordello (1840) bk. 6, l. 881

16 The unlit lamp and the ungirt loin.
'The Statue and the Bust' (1863 revision)
l. 247

17 Hark, the dominant's persistence till it
must be answered to!
'A Toccata of Galuppi's' (1855) st. 8

18 What of soul was left, I wonder, when the
kissing had to stop?
'A Toccata of Galuppi's' (1855) st. 14

19 Dear dead women, with such hair,
too—what's become of all the gold
Used to hang and brush their bosoms? I
feel chilly and grown old.
'A Toccata of Galuppi's' (1855) st. 15

20 I would that you were all to me,
You that are just so much, no more.
'Two in the Campagna' (1855) st. 8

21   I pluck the rose
And love it more than tongue can speak—
Then the good minute goes.
'Two in the Campagna' (1855) st. 10

Robert Bruce 1554–1631

22 Now, God be with you, my children: I have
breakfasted with you and shall sup with
my Lord Jesus Christ this night.
In Robert Fleming *The Fulfilling of the Scripture*
(3rd ed., 1693) p. 372

Beau Brummell 1778–1840

23 He [Brummell] always liked to have the
morning well-aired before he got up.
C. Macfarlane *Reminiscences of a Literary Life*
(1917) ch. 27

24 No perfumes, but very fine linen, plenty of
it, and country washing.
In *Memoirs of Harriette Wilson* (1825) vol. 1,
p. 42

Frank Bruno 1961–

25 Boxing's just showbusiness with blood.
In *Observer* 29 December 1991 'Sayings of the
Year'

John Buchan (Baron Tweedsmuir) 1875–1940

26 It's a great life if you don't weaken.
Mr Standfast (1919) ch. 5

27 An atheist is a man who has no invisible
means of support.
In H. E. Fosdick *On Being a Real Person* (1943)
ch. 10

Robert Buchanan 1841–1901

28   She just wore
Enough for modesty—no more.
'White Rose and Red' (1873) pt. 1, sect. 5, l. 60

29 The sweet post-prandial cigar.
'De Berny' (1874)

Frank Buchman 1878–1961

30 There is enough in the world for
everyone's need, but not enough for
everyone's greed.
Remaking the World (1947) p. 56

Gene Buck 1885–1957 and Herman Ruby 1891–1959

31 That Shakespearian rag,—
Most intelligent, very elegant.
'That Shakespearian Rag' (1912 song).
Cf. 134:24

George Villiers, 2nd Duke of Buckingham 1628–87

1 The world is made up for the most part of fools and knaves, both irreconcilable foes to truth.
Dramatic Works (1715) vol. 2 'To Mr Clifford On his Humane Reason'

2 Ay, now the plot thickens very much upon us.
The Rehearsal (1672) act 3, sc. 2

H. J. Buckoll 1803–71

3 Lord, dismiss us with Thy blessing, Thanks for mercies past receive. Pardon all, their faults confessing; Time that's lost may all retrieve.
Psalms and Hymns for the Use of Rugby School Chapel (1850) 'Lord, Dismiss us with Thy Blessing'

Eustace Budgell 1686–1737

4 What Cato did, and Addison approved, Cannot be wrong.
Of suicide, in Colley Cibber *Lives of the Poets* (1753) vol. 5 'Life of Eustace Budgell'

Comte de Buffon 1707–88

5 Style is the man.
Discours sur le style (address given to the Académie Française, 25 August 1753)

6 Genius is only a greater aptitude for patience.
In H. de Séchelles *Voyage à Montbar* (1803) p. 15

Arthur Buller 1874–1944

7 There was a young lady named Bright, Whose speed was far faster than light; She set out one day In a relative way And returned on the previous night.
'Relativity' in *Punch* 19 December 1923

Prince Bernhard von Bülow 1849–1929

8 We desire to throw no one into the shade [in East Asia], but we also demand our own place in the sun.
Reichstag, 6 December 1897, in *Graf Bülows Reden* (1903) p. 8. Cf. 350:25

Edward George Bulwer-Lytton (Baron Lytton) 1803–73

9 The brilliant chief, irregularly great, Frank, haughty, rash,—the Rupert of Debate!
Of Edward Stanley, 14th Earl of Derby, in *The New Timon* (1846) pt. 1, sect. 3, l. 203. Cf. 121:8

10 Out-babying Wordsworth and out-glittering Keats.
Of Tennyson, in *The New Timon* (1846) pt. 2, sect. 1, l. 62

11 Beneath the rule of men entirely great The pen is mightier than the sword.
Richelieu (1839) act 2, sc. 2, l. 307. Cf. 83:9

12 There is no man so friendless but what he can find a friend sincere enough to tell him disagreeable truths.
What will he do with it? (1857) vol. 1, bk. 3, ch. 15

Edward Robert Bulwer, Earl of Lytton

See OWEN MEREDITH

Alfred 'Poet' Bunn *c.*1796–1860

13 I dreamed that I dwelt in marble halls With vassals and serfs at my side.
The Bohemian Girl (1843) act 2 'The Gipsy Girl's Dream'

Basil Bunting 1900–85

14 Praise the green earth. Chance has appointed her home, workshop, larder, middenpit. Her lousy skin scabbed here and there by cities provides us with name and nation.
'Attis: or, Something Missing' (1931) pt. 1

15 Dance tiptoe, bull, black against may.
'Briggflatts' (1965) pt. 1

Luis Buñuel 1900–83

16 The discreet charm of the bourgeoisie.
Title of film (1972)

John Bunyan 1628–88

17 As I walked through the wilderness of this world.
The Pilgrim's Progress (1678) pt. 1, opening words

18 The name of the slough was Despond.
The Pilgrim's Progress (1678) pt. 1, p. 12

19 It is an hard matter for a man to go down into the valley of Humiliation ... and to catch no slip by the way.
The Pilgrim's Progress (1678) pt. 1, p. 46

20 A foul Fiend coming over the field to meet him; his name is Apollyon.
The Pilgrim's Progress (1678) pt. 1, p. 46

21 It beareth the name of Vanity-Fair, because the town where 'tis kept, is lighter than vanity.
The Pilgrim's Progress (1678) pt. 1, p. 72

22 Hanging is too good for him, said Mr Cruelty.
The Pilgrim's Progress (1678) pt. 1, p. 79

1 Yet my great-grandfather was but a water-
man, looking one way, and rowing
another.
  The Pilgrim's Progress (1678) pt. 1, p. 81.
  Cf. 83:7

2 They are for religion when in rags and
contempt; but I am for him when he walks
in his golden slippers, in the sunshine and
with applause.
  The Pilgrim's Progress (1678) pt. 1, p. 83

3 Now Giant Despair had a wife, and her
name was Diffidence.
  The Pilgrim's Progress (1678) pt. 1, p. 93

4 Sleep is sweet to the labouring man.
  The Pilgrim's Progress (1678) pt. 1, p. 111.
  Cf. 44:15

5 So I awoke, and behold it was a dream.
  The Pilgrim's Progress (1678) pt. 1, p. 133

6 A man that could look no way but
downwards, with a muckrake in his hand.
  The Pilgrim's Progress (1684) pt. 2, p. 164.
  Cf. 262:18

7 He that is down needs fear no fall,
He that is low no pride.
He that is humble ever shall
Have God to be his guide.
  The Pilgrim's Progress (1684) pt. 2, p. 197
  'Shepherd Boy's Song'

8 Mercy ... laboured much for the poor ...
an ornament to her profession.
  The Pilgrim's Progress (1684) pt. 2, p. 231

9 Who would true valour see,
Let him come hither;
One here will constant be,
Come wind, come weather.
There's no discouragement
Shall make him once relent
His first avowed intent
To be a pilgrim.
  Who so beset him round
With dismal stories,
Do but themselves confound—
His strength the more is.
  The Pilgrim's Progress (1684) pt. 2, p. 247

10 My sword, I give to him that shall succeed
me in my pilgrimage, and my courage and
skill to him that can get it.
  The Pilgrim's Progress (1684) pt. 2, p. 259 (Mr
  Valiant-for-Truth)

11 So he passed over, and the trumpets
sounded for him on the other side.
  The Pilgrim's Progress (1684) pt. 2, p. 260

Samuel Dickinson Burchard
1812–91

12 We are Republicans and don't propose to
leave our party and identify ourselves with
the party whose antecedents are rum,
Romanism, and rebellion.
  Speech, 29 October 1884, in *New York World*
  30 October 1884

Anthony Burgess 1917–93

13 A clockwork orange.
  Title of novel (1962)

14 It was the afternoon of my eighty-first
birthday, and I was in bed with my
catamite when Ali announced that the
archbishop had come to see me.
  Earthly Powers (1980) p. 7

15 He said it was artificial respiration, but
now I find I am to have his child.
  Inside Mr Enderby (1963) pt. 1, ch. 4

Gelett Burgess 1866–1951

16 I never saw a Purple Cow,
I never hope to see one;
But I can tell you, anyhow,
I'd rather see than be one!
  The Burgess Nonsense Book (1914) 'The Purple
  Cow'

John William Burgon 1813–88

17 A rose-red city—half as old as Time!
  Petra (1845) l. 132. Cf. 261:19

Edmund Burke 1729–97

18 The conduct of a losing party never
appears right: at least it never can possess
the only infallible criterion of wisdom to
vulgar judgements—success.
  Letter to a Member of the National Assembly
  (1791) p. 7

19 Tyrants seldom want pretexts.
  Letter to a Member of the National Assembly
  (1791) p. 25

20 You can never plan the future by the past.
  Letter to a Member of the National Assembly
  (1791) p. 73

21 The king, and his faithful subjects, the
lords and commons of this realm,—the
triple cord, which no man can break.
  A Letter to a Noble Lord (1796) p. 54. Cf. 44:14

22 I know many have been taught to think
that moderation, in a case like this, is a
sort of treason.
  Letter to the Sheriffs of Bristol (1777) p. 30

23 Liberty too must be limited in order to be
possessed.
  Letter to the Sheriffs of Bristol (1777) p. 55

24 It is the nature of all greatness not to be
exact; and great trade will always be
attended with considerable abuses.
  On American Taxation (1775) p. 26

25 Falsehood has a perennial spring.
  On American Taxation (1775) p. 30

26 To tax and to please, no more than to love
and to be wise, is not given to men.
  On American Taxation (1775) p. 49

27 The concessions of the weak are the
concessions of fear.
  On Conciliation with America (1775) p. 7

1 The use of force alone is but *temporary*. It may subdue for a moment; but it does not remove the necessity of subduing again; and a nation is not governed, which is perpetually to be conquered.
On Conciliation with America (1775) p. 14

2 I do not know the method of drawing up an indictment against an whole people.
On Conciliation with America (1775) p. 28

3 Instead of a standing revenue, you will have therefore a perpetual quarrel.
On Conciliation with America (1775) p. 57

4 Slavery they can have anywhere. It is a weed that grows in every soil.
On Conciliation with America (1775) p. 61

5 Magnanimity in politics is not seldom the truest wisdom; and a great empire and little minds go ill together.
On Conciliation with America (1775) p. 62

6 By adverting to the dignity of this high calling, our ancestors have turned a savage wilderness into a glorious empire: and have made the most extensive, and the only honourable conquests; not by destroying, but by promoting the wealth, the number, the happiness of the human race.
On Conciliation with America (1775) p. 62

7 No passion so effectually robs the mind of all its powers of acting and reasoning as fear.
On the Sublime and Beautiful (1757) pt. 2, sect. 2

8 Custom reconciles us to everything.
On the Sublime and Beautiful (1757) pt. 4, sect. 18

9 Whenever our neighbour's house is on fire, it cannot be amiss for the engines to play a little on our own.
Reflections on the Revolution in France (1790) p. 10

10 A state without the means of some change is without the means of its conservation.
Reflections on the Revolution in France (1790) p. 29

11 Make the Revolution a parent of settlement, and not a nursery of future revolutions.
Reflections on the Revolution in France (1790) p. 38

12 People will not look forward to posterity, who never look backward to their ancestors.
Reflections on the Revolution in France (1790) p. 47

13 Whatever each man can separately do, without trespassing upon others, he has a right to do for himself; and he has a right to a fair portion of all which society, with all its combinations of skill and force, can do in his favour.
Reflections on the Revolution in France (1790) p. 87

14 The age of chivalry is gone.— That of sophisters, economists, and calculators, has succeeded; and the glory of Europe is extinguished for ever.
Reflections on the Revolution in France (1790) p. 113

15 This barbarous philosophy, which is the offspring of cold hearts and muddy understandings.
Reflections on the Revolution in France (1790) p. 115

16 Kings will be tyrants from policy when subjects are rebels from principle.
Reflections on the Revolution in France (1790) p. 116

17 Society is indeed a contract ... it becomes a partnership not only between those who are living, but between those who are living, those who are dead, and those who are to be born.
Reflections on the Revolution in France (1790) p. 143

18 Superstition is the religion of feeble minds.
Reflections on the Revolution in France (1790) p. 234

19 By hating vices too much, they come to love men too little.
Reflections on the Revolution in France (1790) p. 251

20 We begin our public affections in our families. No cold relation is a zealous citizen.
Reflections on the Revolution in France (1790) p. 286

21 Good order is the foundation of all good things.
Reflections on the Revolution in France (1790) p. 351

22 Your representative owes you, not his industry only, but his judgement; and he betrays, instead of serving you, if he sacrifices it to your opinion.
Speech, 3 November 1774, in *Speeches at his Arrival at Bristol* (1774) p. 14

23 The people are the masters.
Speech, *Hansard* 11 February 1780, col. 67

24 Bad laws are the worst sort of tyranny.
Speech at Bristol, previous to the Late Election (1780)

25 The people never give up their liberties except under some delusion.
Speech at County Meeting of Buckinghamshire, 1784; attributed in E. Latham *Famous Sayings* (1904)

26 An event has happened, upon which it is difficult to speak, and impossible to be silent.
Speech, 5 May 1789, in E. A. Bond (ed.) *Speeches ... in the Trial of Warren Hastings* (1859) vol. 2

27 Dying in the last dyke of prevarication.
Speech, 7 May 1789, in E. A. Bond (ed.) *Speeches ... in the Trial of Warren Hastings* (1859) vol. 2

1 Old religious factions are volcanoes burnt
out.
Speech on the Petition of the Unitarians,
11 May 1792, in *Works* vol. 5 (1812).
Cf. 121:16

2 Dangers by being despised grow great.
Speech on the Petition of the Unitarians,
11 May 1792, in *Works* vol. 5 (1812)

3 And having looked to government for
bread, on the very first scarcity they will
turn and bite the hand that fed them.
Thoughts and Details on Scarcity (1800) p. 31

4 When bad men combine, the good must
associate; else they will fall, one by one, an
unpitied sacrifice in a contemptible
struggle.
Thoughts on the Cause of the Present Discontents
(1770) p. 71

5 So to be patriots, as not to forget we are
gentlemen.
Thoughts on the Cause of the Present Discontents
(1770) p. 77

6 Laws, like houses, lean on one another.
A Tract on the Popery Laws (planned *c.*1765)
ch. 3, pt. 1; in *Works* vol. 5 (1812)

7 All men that are ruined are ruined on the
side of their natural propensities.
*Two Letters on the Proposals for Peace with the
Regicide Directory* (9th ed., 1796) p. 69

8 Well is it known that ambition can creep
as well as soar.
*Third Letter ... on the Proposals for Peace with the
Regicide Directory* (1797) p. 38

9 People crushed by law have no hopes but
from power. If laws are their enemies, they
will be enemies to laws; and those, who
have much to hope and nothing to lose,
will always be dangerous, more or less.
Letter to Charles James Fox, 8 October 1777,
in *Correspondence of Edmund Burke* vol. 3 (1961)

10 The silent touches of time.
Letter to William Smith, 29 January 1795, in
Correspondence of Edmund Burke vol. 8 (1969)

11 Not merely a chip of the old 'block', but
the old block itself.
On the younger Pitt's maiden Speech,
February 1781; in N. W. Wraxall *Historical
Memoirs of My Own Time* (1904 ed.) pt. 2, p. 377

12 The cold neutrality of an impartial judge.
J. P. Brissot *To his Constituents* (1794)
'Translator's Preface' (written by Burke)

13 It is necessary only for the good man to do
nothing for evil to triumph.
Attributed (in a number of forms) to Burke,
but not found in his writings. Cf. 81:4

Johnny Burke 1908–64

14 Every time it rains, it rains
Pennies from heaven.
Don't you know each cloud contains
Pennies from heaven?
'Pennies from Heaven' (1936 song)

15 Like Webster's Dictionary, we're Morocco
bound.
The Road to Morocco (1942 film) title song

Fanny Burney 1752–1840

16 A little alarm now and then keeps life
from stagnation.
Camilla (1796) bk. 3, ch. 11

17 'The whole of this unfortunate business,'
said Dr Lyster, 'has been the result of PRIDE
AND PREJUDICE.'
Cecilia (1782) bk. 10, ch. 10

18 The delusive seduction of martial music.
In J. Hemlow et al. (eds.) *Journals and Letters of
Fanny Burney* vol. 5 (1975) 'Paris Journal'

19 O! how short a time does it take to put an
end to a woman's liberty!
Of a wedding; L. E. Troide (ed.) *Early Journals
and Letters* (1988) vol. 1 (Journal, 20 July 1768)

John Burns 1858–1943

20 The Thames is liquid history.
To an American, who had compared the
Thames disparagingly with the Mississippi;
in *Daily Mail* 25 January 1943

Robert Burns 1759–96

21 Then gently scan your brother man,
Still gentler sister woman;
Tho' they may gang a kennin wrang,
To step aside is human.
'Address to the Unco Guid' (1787)

22 Ae fond kiss, and then we sever;
Ae fareweel, and then for ever!
'Ae fond Kiss' (1792)

23 Flow gently, sweet Afton, among thy green
braes,
Flow gently, I'll sing thee a song in thy
praise.
'Afton Water' (1792)

24 Should auld acquaintance be forgot
And never brought to mind?
'Auld Lang Syne' (1796)

25 We'll tak a cup o' kindness yet,
For auld lang syne.
'Auld Lang Syne' (1796)

26 Freedom and Whisky gang thegither!
'The Author's Earnest Cry and Prayer' (1786)
l. 185

27 Ye banks and braes o' bonny Doon,
How can ye bloom sae fresh and fair;
How can ye chant, ye little birds,
And I sae weary fu' o' care!
'The Banks o' Doon' (1792)

28 Thou minds me o' departed joys,
Departed, never to return.
'The Banks o' Doon' (1792)

29 Gin a body meet a body
Comin thro' the rye,
Gin a body kiss a body
Need a body cry?
'Comin thro' the rye' (1796)

1 They never sought in vain that sought the Lord aright.
  'The Cotter's Saturday Night' (1786) st. 6

2 The healsome porritch, chief of Scotia's food.
  'The Cotter's Saturday Night' (1786) st. 11

3 I wasna fou, but just had plenty.
  'Death and Dr Hornbook' (1787) st. 3

4 On ev'ry hand it will allow'd be,
  He's just—nae better than he shou'd be.
  'A Dedication to G[avin] H[amilton]' (1786) l. 25

5 I waive the quantum o'the sin;
  The hazard of concealing;
  But och! it hardens a' within,
  And petrifies the feeling!
  'Epistle to a Young Friend' (1786) st. 6

6 An atheist-laugh's a poor exchange
  For Deity offended!
  'Epistle to a Young Friend' (1786) st. 9

7 The rank is but the guinea's stamp,
  The man's the gowd for a' that!
  'For a' that and a' that' (1790)

8 A man's a man for a' that.
  'For a' that and a' that' (1790)

9 Green grow the rashes, O,
  Green grow the rashes, O;
  The sweetest hours that e'er I spend,
  Are spent among the lasses, O.
  'Green Grow the Rashes' (1787)

10 There's death in the cup—so beware!
   'Inscription on a Goblet' (published 1834)

11 John Anderson my jo, John,
   When we were first acquent,
   Your locks were like the raven,
   Your bonny brow was brent.
   'John Anderson my Jo' (1790)

12 I once was a maid, tho' I cannot tell when,
   And still my delight is in proper young men.
   'The Jolly Beggars' (1799) l. 57, also known as 'Love and Liberty—A Cantata'

13 Life is all a VARIORUM,
   We regard not how it goes;
   Let them cant about DECORUM,
   Who have characters to lose.
   'The Jolly Beggars' (1799) l. 270

14 Some have meat and cannot eat,
   Some cannot eat that want it:
   But we have meat and we can eat,
   Sae let the Lord be thankit.
   'The Kirkcudbright Grace' (1790), also known as 'The Selkirk Grace'

15 May coward shame distain his name,
   The wretch that dares not die!
   'McPherson's Farewell' (1788)

16 Man's inhumanity to man
   Makes countless thousands mourn!
   'Man was made to Mourn' (1786) st. 7

17 O Death! the poor man's dearest friend,
   The kindest and the best!
   'Man was made to Mourn' (1786) st. 11

18 My heart's in the Highlands, my heart is not here;
   My heart's in the Highlands a-chasing the deer.
   'My Heart's in the Highlands' (1790)

19 O whistle, an' I'll come to you, my lad.
   Title of poem (1788). Cf. 142:6

20 O, my Luve's like a red, red rose
   That's newly sprung in June;
   O my Luve's like the melodie
   That's sweetly play'd in tune.
   'A Red Red Rose' (1796) (derived from various folk-songs)

21 Scots, wha hae wi' Wallace bled,
   Scots, wham Bruce has aften led,
   Welcome to your gory bed,—
   Or to victorie.
   'Robert Bruce's March to Bannockburn' (1799)

22 Liberty's in every blow!
   Let us do—or die!!!
   'Robert Bruce's March to Bannockburn' (1799)

23 As Tammie glowr'd, amaz'd, and curious,
   The mirth and fun grew fast and furious.
   'Tam o' Shanter' (1791) l. 143

24 Fair fa' your honest, sonsie face,
   Great chieftain o' the puddin'-race!
   'To a Haggis' (1787)

25 O wad some Pow'r the giftie gie us
   To see oursels as others see us!
   It wad frae mony a blunder free us,
   And foolish notion.
   'To a Louse' (1786)

26 Wee, sleekit, cow'rin', tim'rous beastie,
   O what a panic's in thy breastie!
   'To a Mouse' (1786)

27 The best laid schemes o' mice an' men
   Gang aft a-gley.
   'To a Mouse' (1786)

28 Fareweel dear, deluding woman.
   'To J. S[mith]' (1786) st. 14

29 Their sighan', cantan', grace-proud faces,
   Their three-mile prayers, and half-mile graces.
   'To the Rev. John M'Math' (1808)

30 Don't let the awkward squad fire over me.
   Shortly before his death, in A. Cunningham Works of Robert Burns vol. 1 (1834) p. 344

William S. Burroughs 1914–

31 The face of 'evil' is always the face of total need.
   The Naked Lunch (1959) introduction

Sir Fred Burrows 1887–1973

32 Unlike my predecessors I have devoted more of my life to shunting and hooting than to hunting and shooting.
   Speech as last Governor of undivided Bengal (1946–7), having been a former President of the National Union of Railwaymen. See Daily Telegraph 24 April 1973, obituary notice

Benjamin Hapgood Burt
1880–1950

1 'You can tell a man who "boozes" by the company he chooses'
And the pig got up and slowly walked away.
'The Pig Got Up and Slowly Walked Away' (1933 song)

2 When you're all dressed up and no place to go.
Title of song (1913)

Nat Burton

3 There'll be bluebirds over the white cliffs of Dover,
Tomorrow, just you wait and see.
'The White Cliffs of Dover' (1941 song)

Sir Richard Burton 1821–90

4 Don't be frightened; I am recalled. Pay, pack, and follow at convenience.
Note to his wife, 19 August 1871, on being replaced as British Consul to Damascus; in Isabel Burton *Life of Captain Sir Richard F. Burton* (1893) vol. 1, ch. 21

Robert Burton 1577–1640

5 All my joys to this are folly,
Naught so sweet as Melancholy.
Anatomy of Melancholy (1621–51) 'The Author's Abstract of Melancholy'

6 A loose, plain, rude writer . . . I call a spade a spade.
Anatomy of Melancholy (1621–51) 'Democritus to the Reader' (p. 31, Everyman ed., 1932)

7 Like watermen, that row one way and look another.
Anatomy of Melancholy (1621–51) 'Democritus to the Reader' (p. 55, Everyman ed., 1932). Cf. 79:1

8 All poets are mad.
Anatomy of Melancholy (1621–51) 'Democritus to the Reader' (p. 112, Everyman ed., 1932). Cf. 356:17

9 The pen is worse than the sword.
Anatomy of Melancholy (1621–51) pt. 1, sect. 2, member 4, subsect. 4. Cf. 78:11

10 What is a ship but a prison?
Anatomy of Melancholy (1621–51) pt. 2, sect. 3, member 4, subsect. 1. Cf. 184:5

11 All places are distant from Heaven alike.
Anatomy of Melancholy (1621–51) pt. 2, sect. 3, member 4, subsect. 1

12 To enlarge or illustrate this power and effect of love is to set a candle in the sun.
Anatomy of Melancholy (1621–51) pt. 3, sect. 2, member 1, subsect. 2. Cf. 306:14, 360:16

13 England is a paradise for women, and hell for horses: Italy a paradise for horses, hell for women, as the diverb goes.
Anatomy of Melancholy (1621–51) pt. 3, sect. 3, member 1, subsect. 2. Cf. 142:13

14 One religion is as true as another.
Anatomy of Melancholy (1621–51) pt. 3, sect. 4, member 2, subsect. 1

15 Be not solitary, be not idle.
Anatomy of Melancholy (1621–51) *ad fin.*

Hermann Busenbaum 1600–68

16 *Cum finis est licitus, etiam media sunt licita.*
The end justifies the means.
Medulla Theologiae Moralis (1650); literally 'When the end is allowed, the means also are allowed'

George Bush 1924–

17 Oh, the vision thing.
Responding to the suggestion that he turn his attention from short-term campaign objectives and look to the longer term; in *Time* 26 January 1987, p. 20

18 Read my lips: no new taxes.
Campaign pledge on taxation, in *New York Times* 19 August 1988

Comte de Bussy-Rabutin 1618–93

19 *L'absence est à l'amour ce qu'est au feu le vent;*
Il éteint le petit, il allume le grand.
Absence is to love what wind is to fire;
It extinguishes the small, it kindles the great.
Histoire Amoureuse des Gaules: Maximes d'Amour (1665) pt. 2. Cf. 145:5, 201:24

20 As you know, God is usually on the side of the big squadrons against the small.
Letter to the Comte de Limoges, 18 October 1677, in *Lettres de . . . Comte de Bussy* (1697) vol. 4. Cf. 14:4, 322:8, 340:23

Nicholas Murray Butler
1862–1947

21 An expert is one who knows more and more about less and less.
Commencement address at Columbia University (attributed)

Samuel ('Hudibras') Butler
1612–80

22 What ever sceptic could inquire for;
For every why he had a wherefore.
Hudibras pt. 1 (1663), canto 1, l. 131

23 He knew what's what, and that's as high As metaphysic wit can fly.
Hudibras pt. 1 (1663), canto 1, l. 149

24 Compound for sins, they are inclined to,
By damning those they have no mind to.
Hudibras pt. 1 (1663), canto 1, l. 213

25 For rhyme the rudder is of verses,
With which like ships they steer their courses.
Hudibras pt. 1 (1663), canto 1, l. 457

1 Cleric before, and Lay behind;
   A lawless linsy-woolsy brother,
   Half of one order, half another.
       Hudibras pt. 1 (1663), canto 3, l. 1226

2 Learning, that cobweb of the brain,
   Profane, erroneous, and vain.
       Hudibras pt. 1 (1663), canto 3, l. 1339

3 Love is a boy, by poets styled,
   Then spare the rod, and spoil the child.
       Hudibras pt. 2 (1664), canto 1, l. 843

4 Oaths are but words, and words but wind.
       Hudibras pt. 2 (1664), canto 2, l. 107

5 What makes all doctrines plain and clear?
   About two hundred pounds a year.
   And that which was proved true before,
   Prove false again? Two hundred more.
       Hudibras pt. 3 (1680), canto 1, l. 1277

6 He that complies against his will,
   Is of his own opinion still.
       Hudibras pt. 3 (1680), canto 3, l. 547

7 For Justice, though she's painted blind,
   Is to the weaker side inclined.
       Hudibras pt. 3 (1680), canto 3, l. 709

8 The law can take a purse in open court,
   Whilst it condemns a less delinquent for't.
       Genuine Remains (1759) 'Miscellaneous
       Thoughts'

Samuel Butler 1835–1902

9 The advantage of doing one's praising for
   oneself is that one can lay it on so thick
   and exactly in the right places.
       The Way of All Flesh (1903) ch. 34

10 The best liar is he who makes the smallest
   amount of lying go the longest way.
       The Way of All Flesh (1903) ch. 39

11 'Tis better to have loved and lost than
   never to have lost at all.
       The Way of All Flesh (1903) ch. 67. Cf. 325:4

12 It was very good of God to let Carlyle and
   Mrs Carlyle marry one another and so
   make only two people miserable instead of
   four.
       *Letters between Samuel Butler and Miss E. M. A.
       Savage 1871–1885* (1935) 21 November 1884

13 Life is one long process of getting tired.
       Notebooks (1912) ch. 1

14 The history of art is the history of revivals.
       Notebooks (1912) ch. 8

15 An apology for the Devil: It must be
   remembered that we have only heard one
   side of the case. God has written all the
   books.
       Notebooks (1912) ch. 14

16 A definition is the enclosing a wilderness
   of idea within a wall of words.
       Notebooks (1912) ch. 14

17 To live is like to love — all reason is
   against it, and all healthy instinct for it.
       Notebooks (1912) ch. 14

18 The three most important things a man
   has are, briefly, his private parts, his
   money, and his religious opinions.
       Further Extracts from Notebooks (1934) p. 93

19 Jesus! with all thy faults I love thee still.
       Further Extracts from Notebooks (1934) p. 117

20 Conscience is thoroughly well-bred and
   soon leaves off talking to those who do not
   wish to hear it.
       Further Extracts from Notebooks (1934) p. 279

21 Yet meet we shall, and part, and meet
   again
   Where dead men meet, on lips of living
   men.
       'Not on sad Stygian shore' (1904)

William Butler 1535–1618

22 Doubtless God could have made a better
   berry, but doubtless God never did.
       On the strawberry, in Izaak Walton *The
       Compleat Angler* (3rd ed., 1661) pt. 1, ch. 5

John Byrom 1692–1763

23 Christians, awake! Salute the happy morn,
   Whereon the Saviour of the world was
   born.
       Hymn (*c.*1750)

24 Some say, that Signor Bononcini,
   Compared to Handel's a mere ninny;
   Others aver, that to him Handel
   Is scarcely fit to hold a candle.
   Strange! that such high dispute should be
   'Twixt Tweedledum and Tweedledee.
       'On the Feuds between Handel and
       Bononcini' (1727)

Lord Byron 1788–1824

25 Year after year they voted cent per cent
   Blood, sweat, and tear-wrung
   millions—why? for rent!
       'The Age of Bronze' (1823) st. 14

26 It glides along the water looking blackly,
   Just like a coffin clapt in a canoe.
       Beppo (1818) st. 19 (a gondola)

27 In short, he was a perfect cavaliero,
   And to his very valet seemed a hero.
       Beppo (1818) st. 33. Cf. 108:9

28 His heart was one of those which most
   enamour us,
   Wax to receive, and marble to retain.
       Beppo (1818) st. 34

29 Our cloudy climate, and our chilly women.
       Beppo (1818) st. 49

30 None are so desolate but something dear,
   Dearer than self, possesses or possessed
   A thought, and claims the homage of a
   tear.
       Childe Harold's Pilgrimage (1812–18) canto 2,
       st. 24

1 Hereditary bondsmen! know ye not
Who would be free themselves must strike
the blow?
Childe Harold's Pilgrimage (1812–18) canto 2,
st. 76

2 There was a sound of revelry by night,
And Belgium's capital had gathered then
Her beauty and her chivalry, and bright
The lamps that shone o'er fair women and
brave men;
A thousand hearts beat happily; and when
Music arose with its voluptuous swell,
Soft eyes looked love to eyes which spake
again,
And all went merry as a marriage bell;
But hush! hark! a deep sound strikes like a
rising knell!
Childe Harold's Pilgrimage (1812–18) canto 3,
st. 21

3 On with the dance! let joy be unconfined;
No sleep till morn, when Youth and
Pleasure meet
To chase the glowing Hours with flying
feet.
Childe Harold's Pilgrimage (1812–18) canto 3,
st. 22

4 Quiet to quick bosoms is a hell.
Childe Harold's Pilgrimage (1812–18) canto 3,
st. 42

5 To fly from, need not be to hate, mankind.
Childe Harold's Pilgrimage (1812–18) canto 3,
st. 69

6 Sapping a solemn creed with solemn sneer.
Childe Harold's Pilgrimage (1812–18) canto 3,
st. 107 (of Edward Gibbon)

7 Italia! oh Italia! thou who hast
The fatal gift of beauty.
Childe Harold's Pilgrimage (1812–18) canto 4,
st. 42

8 Oh Rome! my country! city of the soul!
Childe Harold's Pilgrimage (1812–18) canto 4,
st. 78

9 Of its own beauty is the mind diseased.
Childe Harold's Pilgrimage (1812–18) canto 4,
st. 122

10 *There* were his young barbarians all at play,
There was their Dacian mother— he, their
sire,
Butchered to make a Roman holiday.
Childe Harold's Pilgrimage (1812–18) canto 4,
st. 141

11 While stands the Coliseum, Rome shall
stand;
When falls the Coliseum, Rome shall fall;
And when Rome falls—the World.
Childe Harold's Pilgrimage (1812–18) canto 4,
st. 145

12 There is a pleasure in the pathless woods,
There is a rapture on the lonely shore,
There is society, where none intrudes,
By the deep sea, and music in its roar:
I love not man the less, but nature more.
Childe Harold's Pilgrimage (1812–18) canto 4,
st. 178

13 Roll on, thou deep and dark blue
Ocean—roll!
Ten thousand fleets sweep over thee in
vain;
Man marks the earth with ruin—his
control
Stops with the shore.
Childe Harold's Pilgrimage (1812–18) canto 4,
st. 179

14 Without a grave, unknelled, uncoffined,
and unknown.
Childe Harold's Pilgrimage (1812–18) canto 4,
st. 179

15 The glory and the nothing of a name.
'Churchill's Grave' (1816)

16   The spirit burning but unbent,
May writhe, rebel—the weak alone repent!
The Corsair (1814) canto 2, st. 10

17 Oh! too convincing—dangerously dear—
In woman's eye the unanswerable tear!
The Corsair (1814) canto 2, st. 15

18   And she for him had given
Her all on earth, and more than all in
heaven!
The Corsair (1814) canto 3, st. 17

19 He left a Corsair's name to other times,
Linked with one virtue, and a thousand
crimes.
The Corsair (1814) canto 3, st. 24

20 Slow sinks, more lovely ere his race be run,
Along Morea's hills the setting sun;
Not, as in northern climes, obscurely
bright,
But one unclouded blaze of living light.
'The Curse of Minerva' (1812) l. 1 and *The
Corsair* (1814) canto 3, st. 1

21 A land of meanness, sophistry, and mist.
'The Curse of Minerva' (1812) l. 138 (of
Scotland)

22 The Assyrian came down like the wolf on
the fold,
And his cohorts were gleaming in purple
and gold;
And the sheen of their spears was like
stars on the sea,
When the blue wave rolls nightly on deep
Galilee.
'The Destruction of Sennacherib' (1815) st. 1

23 Married, charming, chaste, and twenty-
three.
Don Juan (1819–24) canto 1, st. 59

24 What men call gallantry, and gods
adultery,
Is much more common where the
climate's sultry.
Don Juan (1819–24) canto 1, st. 63

25 Christians have burnt each other, quite
persuaded
That all the Apostles would have done as
they did.
Don Juan (1819–24) canto 1, st. 83

1 A little still she strove, and much repented,
And whispering 'I will ne'er
   consent'—consented.
   Don Juan (1819–24) canto 1, st. 117

2 Sweet is revenge—especially to women.
   Don Juan (1819–24) canto 1, st. 124

3 Pleasure's a sin, and sometimes sin's a
   pleasure.
   Don Juan (1819–24) canto 1, st. 133

4 Man's love is of man's life a thing apart,
'Tis woman's whole existence.
   Don Juan (1819–24) canto 1, st. 194

5 There's nought, no doubt, so much the
   spirit calms
As rum and true religion.
   Don Juan (1819–24) canto 2, st. 34

6 Let us have wine and women, mirth and
   laughter,
Sermons and soda-water the day after.
   Don Juan (1819–24) canto 2, st. 178

7 Man, being reasonable, must get drunk;
The best of life is but intoxication.
   Don Juan (1819–24) canto 2, st. 179

8 And thus they form a group that's quite
   antique,
Half naked, loving, natural, and Greek.
   Don Juan (1819–24) canto 2, st. 194

9 In her first passion woman loves her lover,
In all the others all she loves is love.
   Don Juan (1819–24) canto 3, st. 3

10 ... Love and marriage rarely can combine,
Although they both are born in the same
   clime.
   Don Juan (1819–24) canto 3, st. 5

11 Think you, if Laura had been Petrarch's
   wife,
He would have written sonnets all his life?
   Don Juan (1819–24) canto 3, st. 8

12 All tragedies are finished by a death,
All comedies are ended by a marriage;
The future states of both are left to faith.
   Don Juan (1819–24) canto 3, st. 9

13 The isles of Greece, the isles of Greece!
Where burning Sappho loved and sung,
Where grew the arts of war and peace,
Where Delos rose, and Phoebus sprung!
Eternal summer gilds them yet,
But all, except their sun, is set!
   Don Juan (1819–24) canto 3, st. 86 (1)

14 The mountains look on Marathon—
And Marathon looks on the sea;
And musing there an hour alone,
I dreamed that Greece might still be free.
   Don Juan (1819–24) canto 3, st. 86 (3)

15 Milton's the prince of poets—so we say;
A little heavy, but no less divine.
   Don Juan (1819–24) canto 3, st. 91

16 A drowsy frowzy poem, called the
   'Excursion',
Writ in a manner which is my aversion.
   Don Juan (1819–24) canto 3, st. 94

17 We learn from Horace, Homer sometimes
   sleeps;
We feel without him: Wordsworth
   sometimes wakes.
   Don Juan (1819–24) canto 3, st. 98. Cf. 173:3

18 Ave Maria! 'tis the hour of prayer!
Ave Maria! 'tis the hour of love!
   Don Juan (1819–24) canto 3, st. 103

19 Now my sere fancy 'falls into the yellow
   Leaf,' and imagination droops her pinion.
   Don Juan (1819–24) canto 4, st. 3. Cf. 288:1

20 That all-softening, overpowering knell,
The tocsin of the soul—the dinner bell.
   Don Juan (1819–24) canto 5, st. 49

21 A lady of a 'certain age', which means
Certainly aged.
   Don Juan (1819–24) canto 6, st. 69

22 That water-land of Dutchmen and of
   ditches.
   Don Juan (1819–24) canto 10, st. 63

23 And, after all, what is a lie? 'Tis but
The truth in masquerade.
   Don Juan (1819–24) canto 11, st. 37

24   Merely innocent flirtation,
Not quite adultery, but adulteration.
   Don Juan (1819–24) canto 12, st. 63

25 Now hatred is by far the longest pleasure;
Men love in haste, but they detest at
   leisure.
   Don Juan (1819–24) canto 13, st. 4. Cf. 106:13

26 The English winter—ending in July,
To recommence in August.
   Don Juan (1819–24) canto 13, st. 42

27 Society is now one polished horde,
Formed of two mighty tribes, the *Bores* and
Bored.
   Don Juan (1819–24) canto 13, st. 95

28 Of all the horrid, hideous notes of woe,
Sadder than owl-songs or the midnight
   blast,
Is that portentous phrase, 'I told you so.'
   Don Juan (1819–24) canto 14, st. 50

29 'Tis strange—but true; for truth is always
   strange;
Stranger than fiction.
   Don Juan (1819–24) canto 14, st. 101

30 How little do we know that which we are!
How less what we may be!
   Don Juan (1819–24) canto 15, st. 99

31 A man must serve his time to every trade
Save censure—critics all are ready made.
Take hackneyed jokes from Miller, got by
   rote,
With just enough of learning to misquote.
   English Bards and Scotch Reviewers (1809) l. 63

32 The petrifactions of a plodding brain.
   English Bards and Scotch Reviewers (1809) l. 416

33 Then let Ausonia, skilled in every art
To soften manners, but corrupt the heart,
Pour her exotic follies o'er the town,
To sanction Vice, and hunt Decorum down.
   English Bards and Scotch Reviewers (1809) l. 618

1 Friendship is Love without his wings!
'L'Amitié est l'amour sans ailes' (written
1806)

2 Old man! 'tis not so difficult to die.
Manfred (2nd ed., 1819) act 3, sc. 4, l. 151

3   You have deeply ventured;
But all must do so who would greatly win.
Marino Faliero (1821) act 1, sc. 2

4 The Cincinnatus of the West.
'Ode to Napoleon Bonaparte' (1814) st. 19 (of
George Washington)

5 My hair is grey, but not with years,
Nor grew it white
In a single night,
As men's have grown from sudden fears.
The Prisoner of Chillon (1816) st. 1

6 She walks in beauty, like the night
Of cloudless climes and starry skies;
And all that's best of dark and bright
Meet in her aspect and her eyes.
'She Walks in Beauty' (1815) st. 1

7 Eternal spirit of the chainless mind!
Brightest in dungeons, Liberty! thou art.
'Sonnet on Chillon' (1816)

8 So, we'll go no more a-roving
So late into the night,
Though the heart be still as loving,
And the moon be still as bright.
'So we'll go no more a-roving' (written 1817)

9 There's not a joy the world can give like
that it takes away.
'Stanzas for Music' (1816)

10 Oh, talk not to me of a name great in
story;
The days of our youth are the days of our
glory;
And the myrtle and ivy of sweet two-and-
twenty
Are worth all your laurels, though ever so
plenty.
'Stanzas Written on the Road between
Florence and Pisa, November 1821'

11 I knew it was love, and I felt it was glory.
'Stanzas Written on the Road between
Florence and Pisa, November 1821'

12 Still I can't contradict, what so oft has
been said,
'Though women are angels, yet wedlock's
the devil.'
'To Eliza' (1806)

13   Satan met his ancient friend
With more hauteur, as might an old
Castilian
Poor noble meet a mushroom rich civilian
The Vision of Judgement (1822) st. 36

14 When we two parted
In silence and tears,
Half broken-hearted
To sever for years,
Pale grew thy cheek and cold,
Colder thy kiss.
'When we two parted' (1816)

15 My Princess of Parallelograms.
Of Annabella Milbanke, a keen amateur
mathematician, in a letter to Lady
Melbourne, 18 October 1812; in L. A.
Marchand (ed.) *Letters and Journals* vol. 2
(1973)

16 What is hope? nothing but the paint on
the face of Existence; the least touch of
truth rubs it off, and then we see what a
hollow-cheeked harlot we have got hold of.
Letter to Thomas Moore, 28 October 1815, in
L. A. Marchand (ed.) *Letters and Journals* vol. 4
(1975)

17 Love in this part of the world is no
sinecure.
Letter to John Murray from Venice,
27 December 1816, in L. A. Marchand (ed.)
Letters and Journals vol. 5 (1976)

18 Pure invention is but the talent of a liar.
Letter to John Murray, 2 April 1817; in L. A.
Marchand (ed.) *Letters and Journals* vol. 5
(1976)

19 Is it not *life*, is it not *the thing*?
Of *Don Juan*, in a letter to Douglas Kinnaird,
26 October 1819; in L. A. Marchand (ed.)
Letters and Journals vol. 6 (1978)

20 The reading or non-reading a book—will
never keep down a single petticoat.
Letter to Richard Hoppner, 29 October 1819,
in L. A. Marchand (ed.) *Letters and Journals*
vol. 6 (1978)

21 I awoke one morning and found myself
famous.
On the instantaneous success of *Childe
Harold*, in Thomas Moore *Letters and Journals
of Lord Byron* (1830) vol. 1, p. 346

22 You should have a softer pillow than my
heart.
To his wife, who had rested her head on his
breast, in E. C. Mayne (ed.) *Life and Letters of
Anne Isabella, Lady Noel Byron* (1929) ch. 11

James Branch Cabell 1879–1958

23 The optimist proclaims that we live in the
best of all possible worlds; and the
pessimist fears this is true.
The Silver Stallion (1926) bk. 4, ch. 26

Augustus Caesar
See AUGUSTUS

Julius Caesar 100–44 BC

24 *Gallia est omnis divisa in partes tres.*
Gaul as a whole is divided into three parts.
De Bello Gallico bk. 1, sect. 1

25 Caesar's wife must be above suspicion.
Oral tradition, based on Plutarch *Parallel Lives*
'Julius Caesar' ch. 10, sect. 9

26 [Caesar] had rather be first in a village
than second at Rome.
Francis Bacon *Advancement of Learning* pt. 2,
ch. 23, sect. 36 (based on Plutarch *Parallel
Lives* 'Julius Caesar' ch. 11)

1 The die is cast.

At the crossing of the Rubicon, in Suetonius *Lives of the Caesars* 'Divus Julius' sect. 32 (often quoted '*Iacta alea est*' but originally spoken in Greek)

2 *Veni, vidi, vici.*

I came, I saw, I conquered.

Inscription displayed in Caesar's Pontic triumph, according to Suetonius *Lives of the Caesars* 'Divus Julius' sect. 37; or, according to Plutarch *Parallel Lives* 'Julius Caesar' ch. 50, sect. 2, written in a letter by Caesar, announcing the victory of Zela which concluded the Pontic campaign

3 *Et tu, Brute?*

You too, Brutus?

Traditional rendering of Suetonius *Lives of the Caesars* 'Divus Julius' sect. 82 Cf. 281:10

John Cage 1912–92

4   I have nothing to say
and I am saying it   and that is
poetry.

'Lecture on nothing' (1961)

Callimachus c.305–c.240 BC

5 A great book is like great evil.

In R. Pfeiffer (ed.) *Callimachus* (1949–53) Fragment 465 (proverbially 'Great book, great evil')

Charles Alexandre de Calonne 1734–1802

6 Madam, if a thing is possible, consider it done; the impossible? that will be done.

In J. Michelet *Histoire de la Révolution Française* (1847) vol. 1, pt. 2, sect. 8; better known as the US Armed Forces' slogan: 'The difficult we do immediately; the impossible takes a little longer.'

C. S. Calverley 1831–84

7 The farmer's daughter hath soft brown hair;
(*Butter and eggs and a pound of cheese*)
And I met with a ballad, I can't say where,
Which wholly consisted of lines like these.

'Ballad' (1872)

8 O Beer! O Hodgson, Guinness, Allsopp, Bass!
Names that should be on every infant's tongue!

'Beer' (1861)

9 Life is with such all beer and skittles;
They are not difficult to please
About their victuals.

'Contentment' (1872)

10 For king-like rolls the Rhine,
And the scenery's divine,
And the victuals and the wine
Rather good.

'Dover to Munich' (1861)

Pierre, Baron de Cambronne 1770–1842

11 *La Garde meurt, mais ne se rend pas.*

The Guards die but do not surrender.

Attributed to Cambronne when called upon to surrender at Waterloo, 1815, but later denied by him. See H. Houssaye *La Garde meurt et ne se rend pas* (1907)

William Camden 1551–1623

12 Betwixt the stirrup and the ground
Mercy I asked, mercy I found.

Remains Concerning Britain (1605) 'Epitaphs' (for a man who fell from his horse)

Jane Montgomery Campbell 1817–78

13 We plough the fields, and scatter
The good seed on the land,
But it is fed and watered
By God's almighty hand.

'We plough the fields, and scatter' (1861 hymn); translated from the German of Matthias Claudius (1740–1815)

Mrs Patrick Campbell 1865–1940

14 It doesn't matter what you do in the bedroom as long as you don't do it in the street and frighten the horses.

In Daphne Fielding *Duchess of Jermyn Street* (1964) ch. 2

15 The deep, deep peace of the double-bed after the hurly-burly of the chaise-longue.

On her recent marriage, in Alexander Woollcott *While Rome Burns* (1934) 'The First Mrs Tanqueray'

Roy Campbell 1901–57

16 You praise the firm restraint with which they write—
I'm with you there, of course:
They use the snaffle and the curb all right,
But where's the bloody horse?

'On Some South African Novelists' (1930)

Thomas Campbell 1777–1844

17 O leave this barren spot to me!
Spare, woodman, spare the beechen tree.

'The Beech-Tree's Petition' (1800). Cf. 235:13

18 To-morrow let us do or die!

'Gertrude of Wyoming' (1809) pt. 3, st. 37

19 'Tis distance lends enchantment to the view,
And robes the mountain in its azure hue.

Pleasures of Hope (1799) pt. 1, l. 7

20 What millions died—that Caesar might be great!

Pleasures of Hope (1799) pt. 2, l. 174

1 Now Barabbas was a publisher.
   Attributed, in Samuel Smiles *A Publisher and his Friends* (1891) vol. 1, ch. 14; also attributed, wrongly, to Byron. See *Notes and Queries* 11th series, vol. 2, 30 July 1910, p. 92. Cf. 54:2

Thomas Campion 1567–1620

2 My sweetest Lesbia let us live and love,
   And though the sager sort our deeds reprove,
   Let us not weigh them: Heav'n's great lamps do dive
   Into their west, and straight again revive,
   But soon as once set is our little light,
   Then must we sleep one ever-during night.
   A Book of Airs (1601) no. 1 'My sweetest Lesbia' (translation of Catullus *Carmina* no. 5). Cf. 93:2

3 Good thoughts his only friends,
   His wealth a well-spent age,
   The earth his sober inn
   And quiet pilgrimage.
   A Book of Airs (1601) no. 18

Albert Camus 1913–60

4 An intellectual is someone whose mind watches itself.
   Notebooks 1935–42 (1963) p. 15

5 You know what charm is: a way of getting the answer yes without having asked any clear question.
   The Fall (1957) p. 43

6 I'll tell you a big secret, *mon cher*. Don't wait for the last judgement. It takes place every day.
   The Fall (1957) p. 83

7 What is a rebel? A man who says no.
   The Rebel (1953) p. 19

8 All modern revolutions have ended in a reinforcement of the State.
   The Rebel (1953) p. 148

Elias Canetti 1905–

9 All the things one has forgotten scream for help in dreams.
   Die Provinz der Menschen (1973) p. 269

George Canning 1770–1827

10 In matters of commerce the fault of the Dutch
   Is offering too little and asking too much.
   The French are with equal advantage content,
   So we clap on Dutch bottoms just twenty per cent.
   Dispatch, in cipher, to the English ambassador at the Hague, 31 January 1826; in Sir Harry Poland *Mr Canning's Rhyming 'Dispatch' to Sir Charles Bagot* (1905)

11 A steady patriot of the world alone,
   The friend of every country but his own.
   Of the Jacobin, in 'New Morality' (1821) l. 113. Cf. 121:17, 243:8

12 Give me the avowed, erect and manly foe;
   Firm I can meet, perhaps return the blow;
   But of all plagues, good Heaven, thy wrath can send,
   Save me, oh, save me, from the candid friend.
   'New Morality' (1821) l. 207

13 Away with the cant of 'Measures not men'!—the idle supposition that it is the harness and not the horses that draw the chariot along. If the comparison must be made, if the distinction must be taken, men are everything, measures comparatively nothing.
   Speech on the Army estimates, 8 December 1802, in *Speeches* (1828) vol. 2, p. 61. 'Measures not men' appears as early as 1742 (in a letter from Chesterfield to Dr Chevenix, 6 March); also Goldsmith *The Good Natured Man* (1768) act 2, sc. 1

14 I called the New World into existence, to redress the balance of the Old.
   Speech on the affairs of Portugal, in *Hansard* 12 December 1826, col. 397

Truman Capote 1924–84

15 Other voices, other rooms.
   Title of novel (1948)

Al Capp 1907–79

16 A product of the untalented, sold by the unprincipled to the utterly bewildered.
   On abstract art, in *National Observer* 1 July 1963. Cf. 361:1

Francesco Caracciolo 1752–99

17 In England there are sixty different religions, and only one sauce.
   Attributed. See *Notes and Queries* December 1968

Richard Carew 1555–1620

18 Will you have all in all for prose and verse? Take the miracle of our age, Sir Philip Sidney.
   In William Camden *Remains concerning Britain* (1614) 'The Excellency of the English Tongue'

Thomas Carew c.1595–1640

19 Here lies a king, that ruled as he thought fit
   The universal monarchy of wit.
   'An Elegy upon the Death of Dr John Donne' (1640)

20 Ask me no more where Jove bestows,
   When June is past, the fading rose.
   'A Song' (1640)

Henry Carey *c.*1687–1743

1 Let the verse the subject fit,
Little subject, little wit.
'Namby-Pamby' (1725)

2 Of all the girls that are so smart
There's none like pretty Sally,
She is the darling of my heart,
And she lives in our alley.
'Sally in our Alley' (1729)

Jane Carlyle 1801–66

3 I am not at all the sort of person you and I
took me for.
Letter to Thomas Carlyle, 7 May 1822, in C. R.
Sanders et al. (eds.) *Collected Letters of Thomas
and Jane Welsh Carlyle* (1970) vol. 2

Thomas Carlyle 1795–1881

4 In epochs when cash payment has become
the sole nexus of man to man.
Chartism (1839) ch. 6

5 The foul sluggard's comfort: 'It will last my
time.'
Critical and Miscellaneous Essays (1838) 'Count
Cagliostro. Flight Last'

6 History is the essence of innumerable
biographies.
Critical and Miscellaneous Essays (1838) 'On
History'

7 A well-written Life is almost as rare as a
well-spent one.
Critical and Miscellaneous Essays (1838) 'Jean
Paul Friedrich Richter'

8 To the very last he [Napoleon] had a kind
of idea; that, namely, of *La carrière ouverte
aux talents*, The tools to him that can
handle them.
Critical and Miscellaneous Essays (1838) 'Sir
Walter Scott'. Cf. 237:6

9 The three great elements of modern
civilization, Gunpowder, Printing, and the
Protestant Religion.
Critical and Miscellaneous Essays (1838) 'The
State of German Literature'. Cf. 25:28

10 'Genius' (which means transcendent
capacity of taking trouble, first of all).
History of Frederick the Great (1858–65) bk. 4,
ch. 3. Cf. 78:6

11 A whiff of grapeshot.
History of the French Revolution (1837) vol. 1,
bk. 5, ch. 3

12 History [is] a distillation of rumour.
History of the French Revolution (1837) vol. 1,
bk. 7, ch. 5

13 The seagreen Incorruptible.
History of the French Revolution (1837) vol. 2,
bk. 4, ch. 4 (of Robespierre)

14 France was long a despotism tempered by
epigrams.
History of the French Revolution (1837) vol. 3,
bk. 7, ch. 7

15 Aristocracy of the Moneybag.
History of the French Revolution (1837) vol. 3,
bk. 7, ch. 7

16 The true University of these days is a
collection of books.
On Heroes, Hero-Worship, and the Heroic (1841)
'The Hero as Man of Letters'

17 A Parliament speaking through reporters
to Buncombe and the twenty-seven
millions mostly fools.
Latter-Day Pamphlets (1850) 'Parliaments'.
Cf. 341:6

18 The Dismal Science.
Latter-Day Pamphlets (1850) 'The Present Time'
(of political economy)

19 Transcendental moonshine.
Life of John Sterling (1851) pt. 1, ch. 15 (on the
influence of a romantic imagination in
motivating Sterling to enter the priesthood)

20 Captains of industry.
Past and Present (1843) bk. 4, ch. 4 (title)

21 Man is a tool-using animal ... Without
tools he is nothing, with tools he is all.
Sartor Resartus (1834) bk. 1, ch. 5

22 The everlasting No.
Sartor Resartus (1834) bk. 2, ch. 7 (title)

23 'Gad! she'd better!'
On hearing that Margaret Fuller 'accept[ed]
the universe'; in William James *Varieties of
Religious Experience* (1902) lecture 2, p. 41

24 Macaulay is well for a while, but one
wouldn't *live* under Niagara.
In R. M. Milnes *Notebook* (1838) p. 157

25 Cobden is an inspired bagman, who
believes in a calico millennium.
In T. W. Reid *Life, Letters and Friendships of
Richard Monckton* (1890) vol. 1, ch. 10

26 If Jesus Christ were to come to-day, people
would not even crucify him. They would
ask him to dinner, and hear what he had
to say, and make fun of it.
In D. A. Wilson *Carlyle at his Zenith* (1927)
p. 238

Andrew Carnegie 1835–1919

27 The man who dies ... rich dies disgraced.
North American Review June 1889 'Wealth'

Dale Carnegie 1888–1955

28 How to win friends and influence people.
Title of book (1936)

Julia A. Carney 1823–1908

29 Little drops of water,
Little grains of sand,
Make the mighty ocean
And the beauteous land.
'Little Things' (1845)

J. L. Carr 1912–

30 *You* have not had thirty years' experience
... *You* have had one year's experience 30
times.
The Harpole Report (1972) p. 128

Lewis Carroll 1832–98

1 'What is the use of a book,' thought Alice, 'without pictures or conversations?'
Alice's Adventures in Wonderland (1865) ch. 1

2 'Curiouser and curiouser!' cried Alice.
Alice's Adventures in Wonderland (1865) ch. 2

3 How doth the little crocodile
Improve his shining tail,
And pour the waters of the Nile
On every golden scale!
Alice's Adventures in Wonderland (1865) ch. 2.
Cf. 343:5

4 'You are old, Father William,' the young man said,
'And your hair has become very white;
And yet you incessantly stand on your head—
Do you think, at your age, it is right?'
Alice's Adventures in Wonderland (1865) ch. 5.
Cf. 312:1

5 Speak roughly to your little boy,
And beat him when he sneezes;
He only does it to annoy,
Because he knows it teases.
Alice's Adventures in Wonderland (1865) ch. 6

6 'Then you should say what you mean,' the March Hare went on. 'I do,' Alice hastily replied; 'at least—at least I mean what I say—that's the same thing, you know.' 'Not the same thing a bit!' said the Hatter. 'Why, you might just as well say that "I see what I eat" is the same thing as "I eat what I see!"'
Alice's Adventures in Wonderland (1865) ch. 7

7 Twinkle, twinkle, little bat!
How I wonder what you're at!
Up above the world you fly!
Like a teatray in the sky.
Alice's Adventures in Wonderland (1865) ch. 7.
Cf. 323:3

8 'Take some more tea,' the March Hare said to Alice, very earnestly. 'I've had nothing yet,' Alice replied in an offended tone, 'so I can't take more.' 'You mean you can't take *less*,' said the Hatter: 'it's very easy to take *more* than nothing.'
Alice's Adventures in Wonderland (1865) ch. 7

9 Take care of the sense, and the sounds will take care of themselves.
Alice's Adventures in Wonderland (1865) ch. 9.
Cf. 211:21

10 'That's the reason they're called lessons,' the Gryphon remarked: 'because they lessen from day to day.'
Alice's Adventures in Wonderland (1865) ch. 9

11 'Will you walk a little faster?' said a whiting to a snail,
'There's a porpoise close behind us, and he's treading on my tail.'
Alice's Adventures in Wonderland (1865) ch. 10

12 Will you, won't you, will you, won't you, will you join the dance?
Alice's Adventures in Wonderland (1865) ch. 10

13 'Begin at the beginning,' the King said, gravely, 'and go on till you come to the end: then stop.'
Alice's Adventures in Wonderland (1865) ch. 12

14 No! No! Sentence first—verdict afterwards.
Alice's Adventures in Wonderland (1865) ch. 12

15 'Twas brillig, and the slithy toves
Did gyre and gimble in the wabe;
All mimsy were the borogoves,
And the mome raths outgrabe.

'Beware the Jabberwock, my son!
The jaws that bite, the claws that catch!'
Through the Looking-Glass (1872) ch. 1

16 O frabjous day! Callooh! Callay!'
Through the Looking-Glass (1872) ch. 1

17 Curtsey while you're thinking what to say. It saves time.
Through the Looking-Glass (1872) ch. 2

18 Now, *here*, you see, it takes all the running *you* can do, to keep in the same place. If you want to get somewhere else, you must run at least twice as fast as that!
Through the Looking-Glass (1872) ch. 2

19 Speak in French when you can't think of the English for a thing.
Through the Looking-Glass (1872) ch. 2

20 If it was so, it might be; and if it were so, it would be: but as it isn't, it ain't. That's logic.
Through the Looking-Glass (1872) ch. 4

21 The Walrus and the Carpenter
Were walking close at hand;
They wept like anything to see
Such quantities of sand:
'If this were only cleared away,'
They said, 'it would be grand!'

'If seven maids with seven mops
Swept it for half a year,
Do you suppose,' the Walrus said,
'That they could get it clear?'
Through the Looking-Glass (1872) ch. 4

22 'The time has come,' the Walrus said,
'To talk of many things:
Of shoes—and ships—and sealing wax—
Of cabbages—and kings—
And why the sea is boiling hot—
And whether pigs have wings.'
Through the Looking-Glass (1872) ch. 4

23 The rule is, jam to-morrow and jam yesterday—but never jam today.
Through the Looking-Glass (1872) ch. 5

24 Why, sometimes I've believed as many as six impossible things before breakfast.
Through the Looking-Glass (1872) ch. 5

25 They gave it me,—for an un-birthday present.
Through the Looking-Glass (1872) ch. 6

26 'When *I* use a word,' Humpty Dumpty said in a rather scornful tone, 'it means just what I choose it to mean—neither more nor less.'
Through the Looking-Glass (1872) ch. 6

1 'The question is,' said Humpty Dumpty,
'which is to be master—that's all.'
Through the Looking-Glass (1872) ch. 6

2 You see it's like a portmanteau—there are
two meanings packed up into one word.
Through the Looking-Glass (1872) ch. 6

3 He's an Anglo-Saxon Messenger—and those
are Anglo-Saxon attitudes.
Through the Looking-Glass (1872) ch. 7

4 It's as large as life, and twice as natural!
Through the Looking-Glass (1872) ch. 7

5 No admittance till the week after next!
Through the Looking-Glass (1872) ch. 9

6 What I tell you three times is true.
The Hunting of the Snark (1876) 'Fit the First:
The Landing'

7 'What's the good of *Mercator's* North Poles
and Equators,
Tropics, Zones and Meridian lines?'
So the Bellman would cry: and the crew
would reply,
'They are merely conventional signs!'
The Hunting of the Snark (1876) 'Fit the
Second: The Bellman's Speech'

8 But oh, beamish nephew, beware of the
day,
If your Snark be a Boojum! For then
You will softly and suddenly vanish away,
And never be met with again!
The Hunting of the Snark (1876) 'Fit the Third:
The Baker's Tale'

9 They sought it with thimbles, they sought
it with care;
They pursued it with forks and hope;
They threatened its life with a railway-
share;
They charmed it with smiles and soap.
The Hunting of the Snark (1876) 'Fit the Fifth:
The Beaver's Lesson'

William Herbert Carruth
1859–1924

10 Some call it evolution,
And others call it God.
'Each In His Own Tongue' (1908)

Edward Carson 1854–1935

11 My only great qualification for being put at
the head of the Navy is that I am very
much at sea.
In I. Colvin *Life of Lord Carson* (1936) vol. 3,
ch. 23

Henry Carter d. 1806

12 True patriots we; for be it understood,
We left our country for our country's good.
Prologue, written for, but not recited at, the
opening of the Playhouse, Sydney, New
South Wales, 16 January 1796, when the
actors were principally convicts. See A. W.
Jose and H. J. Carter (eds.) *The Australian
Encyclopaedia* (1927) p. 139. Previously
attributed to George Barrington (b. 1755).
Cf. 140:3

Sydney Carter 1915–

13 Dance then wherever you may be,
I am the Lord of the Dance, said he,
And I'll lead you all, wherever you may be
And I'll lead you all in the dance, said he.
'Lord of the Dance' (1967)

John Cartwright 1740–1824

14 One man shall have one vote.
The People's Barrier Against Undue Influence
(1780) ch. 1 'Principles, maxims, and primary
rules of politics' no. 68

Ted Castle 1907–79

15 In place of strife.
Title of Labour Government White Paper,
17 January 1969. See Barbara Castle *Diaries*
(1984) 15 January 1969

Fidel Castro 1926–

16 History will absolve me.
Title of pamphlet (1953)

Edward Caswall 1814–78

17 Jesu, the very thought of Thee
With sweetness fills the breast.
'Jesu, the very thought of thee' (1849 hymn);
translation of 'Jesu dulcis memoria', usually
attributed to St Bernard (1090–1153)

18 Hail, thou ever-blessèd morn!
Hail, redemption's happy dawn!
'See, amid the winter's snow' (1858 hymn)

19 When morning gilds the skies.
Title of hymn (1854)

A Catechism of Christian Doctrine ('Penny Catechism')
1898

20 Who made you? God made me.
Why did God make you? God made me to
know Him, love him, and serve Him in
this world, and to be happy with Him for
ever in the next.
Ch. 1

Empress Catherine the Great
1729–96

21 I shall be an autocrat: that's my trade. And
the good Lord will forgive me: that's his.
Attributed. Cf. 165:3

Cato the Elder 234–149 BC

22 *Delenda est Carthago.*
Carthage must be destroyed.
In Pliny the Elder *Naturalis Historia* bk. 15,
ch. 74

23 *Rem tene; verba sequentur.*
Grasp the subject, the words will follow.
In Caius Julius Victor *Ars Rhetorica* 'De
inventione'

Catullus c.84–c.54 BC

1 *Lugete, O Veneres Cupidinesque,*
Et quantum est hominum venustiorum.
Passer mortuus est meae puellae,
Passer, deliciae meae puellae.
Mourn, you powers of Charm and Desire,
and all you who are endowed with charm.
My lady's sparrow is dead, the sparrow
which was my lady's darling.
Carmina no. 3

2 *Vivamus, mea Lesbia, atque amemus.*
Let us live, my Lesbia, and let us love.
Carmina no. 5. Cf. 89:2

3 *Paene insularum, Sirmio, insularumque*
Ocelle.
Sirmio, bright eye of peninsulas and
islands.
Carmina no. 31

4 *Nam risu inepto res ineptior nulla est.*
For there is nothing sillier than a silly
laugh.
Carmina no. 39

5 *Difficile est longum subito deponere amorem.*
It is difficult suddenly to lay aside a long-
cherished love.
Carmina no. 76

6 *Si vitam puriter egi.*
If I have led a pure life.
Carmina no. 76

7 *Odi et amo: quare id faciam, fortasse requiris.*
Nescio, sed fieri sentio et excrucior.
I hate and I love: why I do so you may well
ask. I do not know, but I feel it happen and
am in agony.
Carmina no. 85

8 *Atque in perpetuum, frater, ave atque vale.*
And so, my brother, hail, and farewell
evermore!
Carmina no. 101

Charles Causley 1917–

9 Timothy Winters comes to school
With eyes as wide as a football-pool,
Ears like bombs and teeth like splinters:
A blitz of a boy is Timothy Winters.
'Timothy Winters' (1957)

Constantine Cavafy 1863–1933

10 When you set out for Ithaka
Ask that your way be long.
'Ithaka' (1911) (tr. E. Keeley and P. Sherrard)

11 And now, what will become of us without
the barbarians?
Those people were a kind of solution.
'Waiting for the Barbarians' (1904) (tr. E.
Keeley and P. Sherrard)

Edith Cavell 1865–1915

12 Patriotism is not enough. I must have no
hatred or bitterness towards anyone.
On the eve of her execution, in *The Times*
23 October 1915

Margaret Cavendish (Duchess of Newcastle) c.1624–74

13 Marriage is the grave or tomb of wit.
Plays (1662) 'Nature's Three Daughters' pt. 2,
act 5, sc. 20

Count Cavour 1810–61

14 We are ready to proclaim throughout Italy
this great principle: a free church in a free
state.
Speech, 27 March 1861, in William de la Rive
*Reminiscences of the Life and Character of Count
Cavour* (1862) ch. 13

Susannah Centlivre c.1669–1723

15 Nothing to be done without a bribe I find,
in love as well as law.
The Perjured Husband (1700) act 3, sc. 2

Cervantes 1547–1616

16 The Knight of the Doleful Countenance.
Don Quixote (1605) pt. 1, ch. 19

17 Hunger is the best sauce in the world.
Don Quixote (1605) pt. 2, ch. 5

18 There are only two families in the world,
as a grandmother of mine used to say: the
haves and the have-nots.
Don Quixote (1605) pt. 2, ch. 20

19 Patience, and shuffle the cards.
Don Quixote (1605) pt. 2, ch. 23

20 Good painters imitate nature, bad ones
spew it up.
El Licenciado Vidriera in *Novelas Ejemplares*
(1613)

21 With one foot already in the stirrup.
Apprehending his own, imminent death; *Los
Trabajos de Persiles y Sigismunda* (1617) preface

Joseph Chamberlain 1836–1914

22 Provided that the City of London remains,
as it is at present, the clearing-house of the
world, any other nation may be its
workshop.
Speech at the Guildhall, London, 19 January
1904; in *The Times* 20 January 1904

23 The day of small nations has long passed
away. The day of Empires has come.
Speech at Birmingham, 12 May 1904, in *The
Times* 13 May 1904

24 We are not downhearted. The only trouble
is we cannot understand what is
happening to our neighbours.
Speech at Smethwick, 18 January 1906
(referring to a constituency which had
remained unaffected by an electoral
landslide); in *The Times* 19 January 1906

Neville Chamberlain 1869–1940

25 In war, whichever side may call itself the
victor, there are no winners, but all are
losers.
Speech at Kettering, 3 July 1938, in *The Times*
4 July 1938

1 How horrible, fantastic, incredible it is that we should be digging trenches and trying on gas-masks here because of a quarrel in a far away country between people of whom we know nothing.
   On Germany's annexation of the Sudetenland; radio broadcast, 27 September 1938, in *The Times* 28 September 1938

2 This is the second time in our history that there has come back from Germany to Downing Street peace with honour. I believe it is peace for our time.
   Speech from 10 Downing Street, 30 September 1938, in *The Times* 1 October 1938. Cf. 121:18, 265:6

3 [Hitler] missed the bus.
   Speech at Central Hall, Westminster, 4 April 1940, in *The Times* 5 April 1940

Nicolas-Sébastien Chamfort 1741–94

4 The poor are Europe's blacks.
   Maximes et Pensées (1796) ch. 8

5 *Sois mon frère, ou je te tue.*
   Be my brother, or I kill you.
   His interpretation of '*Fraternité ou la mort* [Fraternity or death]', in P. R. Anguis (ed.) *Oeuvres Complètes* (1824) vol. 1 'Notice Historique sur la Vie et les Écrits de Chamfort'. Cf. 12:11

John Chandler 1806–76

6 Conquering kings their titles take.
   Title of hymn (1837)

Raymond Chandler 1888–1959

7 It was a blonde. A blonde to make a bishop kick a hole in a stained glass window.
   Farewell, My Lovely (1940) ch. 13

8 A big hard-boiled city with no more personality than a paper cup.
   The Little Sister (1949) ch. 26 (Los Angeles)

9 Down these mean streets a man must go who is not himself mean, who is neither tarnished nor afraid.
   Atlantic Monthly December 1944 'The Simple Art of Murder'

10 If my books had been any worse, I should not have been invited to Hollywood, and if they had been any better, I should not have come.
   Letter to Charles W. Morton, 12 December 1945, in D. Gardiner and K. S. Walker *Raymond Chandler Speaking* (1962) p. 126

11 When I split an infinitive, God damn it, I split it so it will stay split.
   Letter to Edward Weeks, 18 January 1947; in F. MacShane *Life of Raymond Chandler* (1976) ch. 7

Charlie Chaplin 1889–1977

12 All I need to make a comedy is a park, a policeman and a pretty girl.
   My Autobiography (1964) ch. 10

Arthur Chapman 1873–1935

13 Out where the handclasp's a little stronger,
   Out where the smile dwells a little longer,
   That's where the West begins.
   Out Where the West Begins (1916) p. 1

George Chapman *c.*1559–1634

14 An Englishman,
   Being flattered, is a lamb; threatened, a lion.
   Alphonsus, Emperor of Germany (1654) act 1

15 Man is a torch borne in the wind; a dream But of a shadow, summed with all his substance.
   Bussy D'Ambois (1607–8) act 1, sc. 1

16 Who to himself is law, no law doth need, Offends no law, and is a king indeed.
   Bussy D'Ambois (1607–8) act 2, sc. 1

17 We have watered our houses in Helicon.
   May-Day (1611) act 3, sc. 3; occasionally misread 'We have watered our horses in Helicon'. See A. Holaday (ed.) *Plays of George Chapman: Comedies* (1970) p. 383

18 I am ashamed the law is such an ass.
   Revenge for Honour (1654) act 3, sc. 2. Cf. 119:20

19 A poem, whose subject is not truth, but things like truth.
   The Revenge of Bussy D'Ambois (1613) dedication

20 Danger, the spur of all great minds.
   The Revenge of Bussy D'Ambois (1613) act 5, sc. 1

21 And let a scholar all Earth's volumes carry, He will be but a walking dictionary.
   The Tears of Peace (1609) l. 530

Charles I 1600–49

22 Never make a defence or apology before you be accused.
   Letter to Lord Wentworth, 3 September 1636, in Sir Charles Petrie (ed.) *Letters of King Charles I* (1935)

23 I see all the birds are flown.
   In the House of Commons, 4 January 1642, after attempting to arrest the Five Members; *Hansard Parliamentary History to the year 1803* vol. 2 (1807) col. 1010

24 You manifestly wrong even the poorest ploughman, if you demand not his free consent.
   The King's Reasons for declining the jurisdiction of the High Court of Justice, 21 January 1649; in S. R. Gardiner *Constitutional Documents of the Puritan Revolution* (1906 ed.) p. 375

25 A subject and a sovereign are clean different things.
   Speech on the scaffold, 30 January 1649. See J. Rushworth *Historical Collections* pt. 4, vol. 2 (1701) p. 1429

Charles II 1630–85

1 It is upon the navy under the good
Providence of God that the safety, honour,
and welfare of this realm do chiefly
depend.
> 'Articles of War' preamble, in Sir Geoffrey
> Callender *The Naval Side of British History*
> (1952) pt. 1, ch. 8

2 This is very true: for my words are my
own, and my actions are my ministers'.
> Reply to Lord Rochester's epitaph on him, in
> *Thomas Hearne: Remarks and Collections*
> (1885–1921) 17 November 1706. Cf. 261:4

3 Better than a play.
> On the debates in the House of Lords on
> Lord Ross's Divorce Bill, 1670; in A. Bryant
> *King Charles II* (1931) p. 209

4 Let not poor Nelly starve.
> Of Nell Gwyn, his mistress, in Bishop Gilbert
> Burnet *History of My Own Time* (1724) vol. 1,
> bk. 3, p. 609

5 Never *in* the way, and never *out* of the way.
> Of Lord Godolphin, who had been raised as
> page to the king; in *Dictionary of National
> Biography* (1917–) vol. 8, p. 43

6 He had been, he said, an unconscionable
time dying; but he hoped that they would
excuse it.
> Lord Macaulay *History of England* (1849) vol. 1,
> ch. 4

Emperor Charles V 1500–58

7 To God I speak Spanish, to women Italian,
to men French, and to my horse—German.
> Attributed. See Lord Chesterfield *Letters to his
> Son* (ed. Dobrée, 1932) vol. 4, p. 1497

Charles, Prince of Wales 1948–

8 A monstrous carbuncle on the face of a
much-loved and elegant friend.
> Speech on the proposed extension to the
> National Gallery, London, 30 May 1984; in
> *The Times* 31 May 1984. Cf. 312:22

Pierre Charron 1541–1603

9 The true science and study of man is man.
> *De la Sagesse* (1601) bk. 1, preface. Cf. 252:17

Geoffrey Chaucer c.1343–1400

10 Whan that Aprill with his shoures soote
The droghte of March hath perced to the
roote.
> *The Canterbury Tales* 'General Prologue' l. 1

11 And smale foweles maken melodye,
That slepen al the nyght with open ye
(So priketh hem nature in hir corages),
Thanne longen folk to goon on
pilgrimages.
> *The Canterbury Tales* 'General Prologue' l. 9

12 He was a verray, parfit gentil knyght.
> *The Canterbury Tales* 'General Prologue' l. 72

13 He was as fressh as is the month of May.
> *The Canterbury Tales* 'General Prologue' l. 92

14 Curteis he was, lowely, and servysable,
And carf biforn his fader at the table.
> *The Canterbury Tales* 'General Prologue' l. 99

15 And Frenssh she spak ful faire and fetisly,
After the scole of Stratford atte Bowe,
For Frenssh of Parys was to hire unknowe.
> *The Canterbury Tales* 'General Prologue' l. 124

16 And theron heng a brooch of gold ful
sheene,
On which ther was first write a crowned A,
And after *Amor vincit omnia*.
> *The Canterbury Tales* 'General Prologue' l. 160.
> Cf. 340:4

17 A Clerk there was of Oxenford also,
That unto logyk hadde longe ygo.
> *The Canterbury Tales* 'General Prologue' l. 285

18 And gladly wolde he lerne and gladly teche.
> *The Canterbury Tales* 'General Prologue' l. 308

19 Nowher so bisy a man as he ther nas,
And yet he semed bisier than he was.
> *The Canterbury Tales* 'General Prologue' l. 321

20 Housbondes at chirche dore she hadde
fyve,
Withouten oother compaignye in youth.
> *The Canterbury Tales* 'General Prologue' l. 460

21 This noble ensample to his sheep he yaf,
That first he wroghte, and afterward he
taughte.
> *The Canterbury Tales* 'General Prologue' l. 496

22 If gold ruste, what shall iren do?
> *The Canterbury Tales* 'General Prologue' l. 500

23 His walet, biforn him in his lappe,
Bretful of pardoun, comen from Rome al
hoot.
> *The Canterbury Tales* 'General Prologue' l. 686

24 O stormy peple! Unsad and evere untrewe!
> *The Canterbury Tales* 'The Clerk's Tale' l. 995

25 Love wol nat been constreyned by
maistrye.
When maistrie comth, the God of Love
anon
Beteth his wynges, and farewel, he is gon!
> *The Canterbury Tales* 'The Franklin's Tale' l. 764

26 The bisy larke, messager of day.
> *The Canterbury Tales* 'The Knight's Tale' l. 1491

27 The smylere with the knyf under the cloke.
> *The Canterbury Tales* 'The Knight's Tale' l. 1999

28 And what is bettre than wisedoom?
Womman. And
what is bettre than a good womman?
Nothyng.
> *The Canterbury Tales* 'The Tale of Melibee'
> l. 1107

29 Mordre wol out; that se we day by day.
> *The Canterbury Tales* 'The Nun's Priest's Tale'
> l. 3052

30 O wombe! O bely! O stynkyng cod
Fulfilled of dong and of corrupcioun!
> *The Canterbury Tales* 'The Pardoner's Tale'
> l. 534

1 And lightly as it comth, so wol we spende.
The Canterbury Tales 'The Pardoner's Tale'
l. 781

2 The gretteste clerkes been noght wisest
men.
The Canterbury Tales 'The Reeve's Tale' l. 4054

3 So was hir joly whistle wel ywet.
The Canterbury Tales 'The Reeve's Tale' l. 4155

4 'By God,' quod he, 'for pleynly, at a word,
Thy drasty rymyng is nat worth a toord!'
The Canterbury Tales 'Sir Thopas' l. 929

5 Experience, though noon auctoritee
Were in this world, is right ynogh for me
To speke of wo that is in mariage.
The Canterbury Tales 'The Wife of Bath's
Prologue' l. 1

6 A likerous mouth moste han a likerous
tayl.
The Canterbury Tales 'The Wife of Bath's
Prologue' l. 466

7 But yet I hadde alwey a coltes tooth.
Gat-tothed I was, and that bicam me weel.
The Canterbury Tales 'The Wife of Bath's
Prologue' l. 602

8 Wommen desiren to have sovereynetee
As wel over hir housbond as hir love.
The Canterbury Tales 'The Wife of Bath's Tale'
l. 1038

9 Farewel my bok and my devocioun!
The Legend of Good Women 'The Prologue' l. 39

10 That wel by reson men it calle may
The 'dayesye,' or elles the 'ye of day,'
The emperice and flour of floures alle.
The Legend of Good Women 'The Prologue'
l. 183

11 And she was fayr as is the rose in May.
The Legend of Good Women 'Cleopatra' l. 613

12 That lyf so short, the craft so long to lerne.
The Parliament of Fowls l. 1. Cf. 168:19

13 O blynde world, O blynde entencioun!
How often falleth al the effect contraire
Of surquidrie and foul presumpcioun.
Troilus and Criseyde bk. 1, l. 211

14 But love a womman that she woot it
nought,
And she wol quyte it that thow shalt nat
fele;
Unknowe, unkist, and lost, that is
unsought.
Troilus and Criseyde bk. 1, l. 807

15 So longe mote ye lyve, and alle proude,
Til crowes feet be growe under youre yë.
Troilus and Criseyde bk. 2, l. 402

16 For I have seyn of a ful misty morwe
Folowen ful ofte a myrie someris day.
Troilus and Criseyde bk. 3, l. 1060

17 Right as an aspes leef she gan to quake.
Troilus and Criseyde bk. 3, l. 1200

18 For of fortunes sharpe adversitee
The worst kynde of infortune is this,
A man to han ben in prosperitee,
And it remembren, whan it passed is.
Troilus and Criseyde bk. 3, l. 1625. Cf. 62:17,
113:21

19 Oon ere it herde, at tother out it wente.
Troilus and Criseyde bk. 4, l. 434

20 Go, litel bok, go, litel myn tragedye.
Troilus and Criseyde bk. 5, l. 1786

21 And down from thennes faste he gan avyse
This litel spot of erthe, that with the se
Embraced is.
Troilus and Criseyde bk. 5, l. 1814

22 O yonge, fresshe folkes, he or she,
In which that love up groweth with youre
age.
Troilus and Criseyde bk. 5, l. 1835

23 O moral Gower, this book I directe
To the.
Troilus and Criseyde bk. 5, l. 1856

Anton Chekhov 1860–1904

24 If a lot of cures are suggested for a disease,
it means that the disease is incurable.
The Cherry Orchard (1904) act 1 (tr. E. Fen)

25 MEDVEDENKO: Why do you wear black all
the time?
MASHA: I'm in mourning for my life, I'm
unhappy.
The Seagull (1896) act 1

26 Women can't forgive failure.
The Seagull (1896) act 2

27 I'm a seagull. No, that's wrong. Remember
you shot a seagull? A man happened to
come along, saw it and killed it, just to
pass the time. A plot for a short story.
The Seagull (1896) act 4

28 A woman can become a man's friend only
in the following stages—first an
acquaintance, next a mistress, and only
then a friend.
Uncle Vanya (1897) act 2

29 When a woman isn't beautiful, people
always say, 'You have lovely eyes, you have
lovely hair.'
Uncle Vanya (1897) act 3

30 Medicine is my lawful wife and literature
is my mistress. When I get tired of one I
spend the night with the other.
Letter to A. S. Suvorin, 11 September 1888, in
L. S. Friedland (ed.) *Anton Chekhov: Letters on
the Short Story . . .* (1964)

31 Brevity is the sister of talent.
Letter to Alexander Chekhov, 11 April 1889,
in L. S. Friedland (ed.) *Anton Chekhov: Letters on
the Short Story . . .* (1964)

1 In *Anna Karenina* and *Onegin* not a single problem is solved, but they satisfy you completely just because all their problems are correctly presented. The court is obliged to submit the case fairly, but let the jury do the deciding, each according to its own judgement.

Letter to Alexei Suvorin, 27 October 1888, in L. Hellman (ed.) *Selected Letters of Anton Chekhov* (1955, tr. S. Lederer)

Lord Chesterfield 1694–1773

2 Unlike my subject will I frame my song,
It shall be witty and it sha'n't be long.

Epigram on 'Long' Sir Thomas Robinson, in *Dictionary of National Biography* (1917–)
vol. 17, p. 51

3 Religion is by no means a proper subject of conversation in a mixed company.

Letters . . . to his Godson and Successor (1890)
Letter 142

4 Cunning is the dark sanctuary of incapacity.

Letters . . . to his Godson and Successor (1890)
'Letter . . . to be delivered after his own death'

5 An injury is much sooner forgotten than an insult.

Letters to his Son (1774) 9 October 1746

6 Courts and camps are the only places to learn the world in.

Letters to his Son (1774) 2 October 1747

7 Take the tone of the company that you are in.

Letters to his Son (1774) 16 October 1747

8 I recommend to you to take care of minutes: for hours will take care of themselves.

Letters to his Son (1774) 6 November 1747.
Cf. 211:21

9 Advice is seldom welcome; and those who want it the most always like it the least.

Letters to his Son (1774) 29 January 1748

10 Wear your learning, like your watch in a private pocket: and do not merely pull it out and strike it, merely to show that you have one.

Letters to his Son (1774) 22 February 1748

11 Women, then, are only children of a larger growth.

Letters to his Son (1774) 5 September 1748.
Cf. 127:25

12 It must be owned, that the Graces do not seem to be natives of Great Britain; and I doubt, the best of us here have more of rough than polished diamond.

Letters to his Son (1774) 18 November 1748

13 Idleness is only the refuge of weak minds.

Letters to his Son (1774) 20 July 1749

14 Putting moral virtues at the highest, and religion at the lowest, religion must still be allowed to be a collateral security, at least, to virtue; and every prudent man will sooner trust to two securities than to one.

Letters to his Son (1774) 8 January 1750

15 It is commonly said, and more particularly by Lord Shaftesbury, that ridicule is the best test of truth.

Letters to his Son (1774) 6 February 1752.
Cf. 270:21, 270:22

16 Knowledge may give weight, but accomplishments give lustre, and many more people see than weigh.

Maxims, in *Letters to his Son* (3rd ed., 1774)
vol. 4, p. 304

17 The chapter of knowledge is a very short, but the chapter of accidents is a very long one.

Letter to Solomon Dayrolles, 16 February 1753, in M. Maty (ed.) *Miscellaneous Works*
vol. 2 (1778) no. 79

18 The pleasure is momentary, the position ridiculous, and the expense damnable.

Of sex (attributed)

G. K. Chesterton 1874–1936

19 I tell you naught for your comfort,
Yea, naught for your desire.

The Ballad of the White Horse (1911) bk. 1, p. 18

20 For the great Gaels of Ireland
Are the men that God made mad,
For all their wars are merry,
And all their songs are sad.

The Ballad of the White Horse (1911) bk. 2, p. 35

21 The thing on the blind side of the heart,
On the wrong side of the door,
The green plant groweth, menacing
Almighty lovers in the Spring;
There is always a forgotten thing,
And love is not secure.

The Ballad of the White Horse (1911) bk. 3, p. 52

22 Fools! For I also had my hour;
One far fierce hour and sweet:
There was a shout about my ears,
And palms before my feet.

'The Donkey' (1900)

23 They died to save their country and they only saved the world.

'English Graves' (1922)

24 From all that terror teaches,
From lies of tongue and pen,
From all the easy speeches
That comfort cruel men,
From sale and profanation
Of honour and the sword,
From sleep and from damnation,
Deliver us, good Lord!

'A Hymn' (1915)

25 Strong gongs groaning as the guns boom far,
Don John of Austria is going to the war.

'Lepanto' (1915)

1 Before the Roman came to Rye or out to
  Severn strode,
  The rolling English drunkard made the
  rolling English road.
  'The Rolling English Road' (1914)

2 A merry road, a mazy road, and such as we
  did tread
  The night we went to Birmingham by way
  of Beachy Head.
  'The Rolling English Road' (1914)

3 For there is good news yet to hear and fine
  things to be seen,
  Before we go to Paradise by way of Kensal
  Green.
  'The Rolling English Road' (1914)

4 Smile at us, pay us, pass us; but do not
  quite forget.
  For we are the people of England, that
  never have spoken yet.
  'The Secret People' (1915)

5 They haven't got no noses,
  The fallen sons of Eve.
  'The Song of Quoodle' (1914)

6 And goodness only knowses
  The Noselessness of Man.
  'The Song of Quoodle' (1914)

7 And Noah he often said to his wife when
  he sat down to dine,
  'I don't care where the water goes if it
  doesn't get into the wine.'
  'Wine and Water' (1914)

8 An adventure is only an inconvenience
  rightly considered. An inconvenience is
  only an adventure wrongly considered.
  All Things Considered (1908) 'On Running after
  one's Hat'

9 Literature is a luxury; fiction is a necessity.
  The Defendant (1901) 'A Defence of Penny
  Dreadfuls'

10 Bigotry may be roughly defined as the
  anger of men who have no opinions.
  Heretics (1905) ch. 20

11 Thieves respect property. They merely wish
  the property to become their property that
  they may more perfectly respect it.
  The Man who was Thursday (1908) ch. 4

12 Democracy means government by the
  uneducated, while aristocracy means
  government by the badly educated.
  New York Times 1 February 1931, pt. 5, p. 1

13 Tradition means giving votes to the most
  obscure of all classes, our ancestors. It is
  the democracy of the dead.
  Orthodoxy (1908) ch. 4

14 Democrats object to men being
  disqualified by the accident of birth;
  tradition objects to their being disqualified
  by the accident of death.
  Orthodoxy (1908) ch. 4

15 The Christian ideal has not been tried and
  found wanting. It has been found difficult;
  and left untried.
  What's Wrong with the World (1910) pt. 1 'The
  Unfinished Temple'

16 The prime truth of woman, the universal
  mother . . . that if a thing is worth doing, it
  is worth doing badly.
  What's Wrong with the World (1910) pt. 4 'Folly
  and Female Education'

Rufus Choate 1799–1859

17 Its constitution the glittering and
  sounding generalities of natural right
  which make up the Declaration of
  Independence.
  Letter to the Maine Whig State Central
  Committee, 9 August 1856, in S. G. Brown
  Works of Rufus Choate (1862) vol. 1, p. 215.
  Cf. 137:2

Noam Chomsky 1928–

18 Colourless green ideas sleep furiously.
  Syntactic Structures (1957) ch. 2 (illustrating
  that grammatical structure is independent
  of meaning)

Chuang-tzu (or Zhuangzi)
c.369–286 BC

19 I do not know whether I was then a man
  dreaming I was a butterfly, or whether I
  am now a butterfly dreaming I am a man.
  Chuang Tzu (1889) ch. 2 (tr. H. A. Giles)

Charles Churchill 1731–64

20 The danger chiefly lies in acting well;
  No crime's so great as daring to excel.
  An Epistle to William Hogarth (1763) l. 51

21   Be England what she will,
  With all her faults, she is my country still.
  The Farewell (1764) l. 27. Cf. 110:8

22 And adepts in the speaking trade
  Keep a cough by them ready made.
  The Ghost (1763) bk. 2, l. 545

23 Just to the windward of the law.
  The Ghost (1763) bk. 3, l. 56

24 Old-age, a second child, by Nature cursed
  With more and greater evils than the first,
  Weak, sickly, full of pains; in ev'ry breath
  Railing at life, and yet afraid of death.
  Gotham (1764) bk. 1, l. 215

25 Keep up appearances; there lies the test;
  The world will give thee credit for the rest.
  Outward be fair, however foul within;
  Sin if thou wilt, but then in secret sin.
  Night (1761) l. 311

26 Grave without thought, and without
  feeling gay.
  The Prophecy of Famine (1763) l. 60 (on
  pretentious poets)

27 Apt Alliteration's artful aid.
  The Prophecy of Famine (1763) l. 86

28 A pert, prim prater of the northern race.
  The Rosciad (1761) l. 71

29 Learned without sense, and venerably dull.
  The Rosciad (1761) l. 592

Lord Randolph Churchill 1849–94

1 The forest laments in order that Mr Gladstone may perspire.

On Gladstone's fondness for felling trees; speech in Blackpool, 24 January 1884, in F. Banfield (ed.) *Life and Speeches of Lord Randolph Churchill* (1884)

2 Ulster will fight; Ulster will be right.

Public letter, 7 May 1886, in R. F. Foster *Lord Randolph Churchill* (1981) p. 258

3 An old man in a hurry.

Of Gladstone, in an address to the electors of South Paddington, 19 June 1886; in W. S. Churchill *Lord Randolph Churchill* (1906) vol. 2, p. 491

Sir Winston Churchill 1874–1965

4 It cannot in the opinion of His Majesty's Government be classified as slavery in the extreme acceptance of the word without some risk of terminological inexactitude.

Speech, *Hansard* 22 February 1906, col. 555

5 He [Lord Charles Beresford] is one of those orators of whom it was well said, 'Before they get up, they do not know what they are going to say; when they are speaking, they do not know what they are saying; and when they have sat down, they do not know what they have said.'

Speech, *Hansard* 20 December 1912, col. 1893

6 Business carried on as usual during alterations on the map of Europe.

Speech at Guildhall, 9 November 1914, in *Complete Speeches* (1974) vol. 3 (on the self-adopted 'motto' of the British people)

7 The whole map of Europe has been changed ... but as the deluge subsides and the waters fall short we see the dreary steeples of Fermanagh and Tyrone emerging once again.

Speech, *Hansard* 16 February 1922, col. 1270

8 I have waited 50 years to see the boneless wonder [Ramsay Macdonald] sitting on the Treasury Bench.

Speech, *Hansard* 28 January 1931, col. 1021

9 [The Government] go on in strange paradox, decided only to be undecided, resolved to be irresolute, adamant for drift, solid for fluidity.

Speech, *Hansard* 12 November 1936, col. 1107

10 I cannot forecast to you the action of Russia. It is a riddle wrapped in a mystery inside an enigma.

Radio broadcast, 1 October 1939, in *Into Battle* (1941) p. 131

11 I have nothing to offer but blood, toil, tears and sweat.

Speech, *Hansard* 13 May 1940, col. 1502

12 What is our policy? ... to wage war against a monstrous tyranny, never surpassed in the dark, lamentable catalogue of human crime.

Speech, *Hansard* 13 May 1940, col. 1502

13 We shall not flag or fail. We shall go on to the end. We shall fight in France, we shall fight on the seas and oceans, we shall fight with growing confidence and growing strength in the air, we shall defend our island, whatever the cost may be. We shall fight on the beaches, we shall fight on the landing grounds, we shall fight in the fields and in the streets, we shall fight in the hills; we shall never surrender.

Speech, *Hansard* 4 June 1940, col. 796

14 Let us therefore brace ourselves to our duty, and so bear ourselves that, if the British Empire and its Commonwealth lasts for a thousand years, men will still say, 'This was their finest hour.'

Speech, *Hansard* 18 June 1940, col. 60

15 Never in the field of human conflict was so much owed by so many to so few.

Speech, *Hansard* 20 August 1940, col. 1166 (on the Battle of Britain)

16 Give us the tools and we will finish the job.

Radio broadcast, 9 February 1941, in *Complete Speeches* (1974) vol. 6 (addressing President Roosevelt)

17 When I warned them [the French Government] that Britain would fight on alone whatever they did, their generals told their Prime Minister and his divided Cabinet, 'In three weeks England will have her neck wrung like a chicken.' Some chicken! Some neck!

Speech to Canadian Parliament, 30 December 1941, in *Complete Speeches* (1974) vol. 6

18 Now this is not the end. It is not even the beginning of the end. But it is, perhaps, the end of the beginning.

Speech at the Mansion House, London, 10 November 1942, in *The End of the Beginning* (1943) p. 214 (on the Battle of Egypt)

19 We make this wide encircling movement in the Mediterranean, having for its primary object the recovery of the command of that vital sea, but also having for its object the exposure of the under-belly of the Axis, especially Italy, to heavy attack.

Speech, *Hansard* 11 November 1942, col. 28 (often misquoted 'the soft under-belly of the Axis')

20 National compulsory insurance for all classes for all purposes from the cradle to the grave.

Radio broadcast, 21 March 1943, in *Complete Speeches* (1974) vol. 7

21 There is no finer investment for any community than putting milk into babies.

Radio broadcast, 21 March 1943, in *Complete Speeches* (1974) vol. 7

1 From Stettin in the Baltic to Trieste in the
  Adriatic an iron curtain has descended
  across the Continent.
    Speech at Westminster College, Fulton,
    Missouri, 5 March 1946, in *Complete Speeches*
    (1974) vol. 7. 'Iron curtain' previously had
    been applied by others to the Soviet Union
    or her sphere of influence, e.g. Ethel
    Snowden *Through Bolshevik Russia* (1920), Dr
    Goebbels *Das Reich* (25 February 1945), and by
    Churchill himself in a cable to President
    Truman (4 June 1945)

2 Democracy is the worst form of
  Government except all those other forms
  that have been tried from time to time.
    Speech, *Hansard* 11 November 1947, col. 206

3 To jaw-jaw is always better than to war-
  war.
    Speech at White House, 26 June 1954, in *New
    York Times* 27 June 1954, p. 1

4 In war: resolution. In defeat: defiance. In
  victory: magnanimity. In peace: goodwill.
    The Second World War vol. 1 (1948) epigraph

5 This is the sort of English up with which I
  will not put.
    In Ernest Gowers *Plain Words* (1948)
    'Troubles with Prepositions'

6 Don't talk to me about naval tradition. It's
  nothing but rum, sodomy, and the lash.
    In Sir Peter Gretton *Former Naval Person*
    (1968) ch. 1

7 A sheep in sheep's clothing.
    Of Clement Attlee, in Lord Home *The Way the
    Wind Blows* (1976) ch. 6. Cf. 155:25

8 Take away that pudding — it has no
  theme.
    In Lord Home *The Way the Wind Blows* (1976)
    ch. 16

9 In defeat unbeatable: in victory unbearable.
    Of Viscount Montgomery, in E. Marsh
    Ambrosia and Small Beer (1964) ch. 5

10 The candle in that great turnip has gone
   out.
    Of Stanley Baldwin, in *Harold Nicolson: Diaries
    and Letters 1945–62* (1968) Diary 17 August
    1950

11 I have taken more out of alcohol than
   alcohol has taken out of me.
    In Quentin Reynolds *By Quentin Reynolds*
    (1964) ch. 11

Count Galeazzo Ciano 1903–44

12 *La vittoria trova cento padri, e nessuno vuole
   riconoscere l'insuccesso.*
   Victory has a hundred fathers, but defeat is
   an orphan.
    Diary (1946) vol. 2, 9 September 1942 (literally
    'no-one wants to recognize defeat as his
    own')

Colley Cibber 1671–1757

13 Oh! how many torments lie in the small
   circle of a wedding-ring!
    The Double Gallant (1707) act 1, sc. 2

14 One had as good be out of the world, as
   out of the fashion.
    Love's Last Shift (1696) act 2

15 Off with his head—so much for
   Buckingham.
    Richard III (1700) act 4 (adapted from
    Shakespeare)

16 Perish the thought!
    Richard III (1700) act 5 (adapted from
    Shakespeare)

17 Conscience avaunt, Richard's himself
   again.
    Richard III (1700) act 5 (adapted from
    Shakespeare)

18 Stolen sweets are best.
    The Rival Fools (1709) act 1, sc. 1

Cicero 106–43 BC

19 There is nothing so absurd but some
   philosopher has said it.
    De Divinatione bk. 2, ch. 119

20 *Salus populi suprema est lex.*
   The good of the people is the chief law.
    De Legibus bk. 3, ch. 8

21 *'Ipse dixit.' 'Ipse' autem erat Pythagoras.*
   'He himself said,' and this 'himself' was
   Pythagoras.
    De Natura Deorum bk. 1, ch. 10

22 *Summum bonum.*
   The highest good.
    De Officiis bk. 1, ch. 5

23 Let war yield to peace, laurels to paeans.
    De Officiis bk. 1, ch. 77

24 Never less idle than when wholly idle, nor
   less alone than when wholly alone.
    De Officiis bk. 3, ch. 1

25 *O tempora, O mores!*
   Oh, the times! Oh, the manners!
    In Catilinam Speech 1, ch. 1

26 *Abiit, excessit, evasit, erupit.*
   He departed, he withdrew, he strode off, he
   broke forth.
    In Catilinam Speech 2, ch. 1

27 *Civis Romanus sum.*
   I am a Roman citizen.
    In Verrem Speech 5, ch. 147

28 *Quod di omen avertant.* May the gods avert
   this omen.
    Third Philippic ch. 35

29 *Nervos belli, pecuniam infinitam.*
   The sinews of war, unlimited money.
    Fifth Philippic ch. 5

30 Laws are silent in time of war.
    Pro Milone ch. 11

31 *Cui bono?*
   To whose profit?
    Pro Roscio Amerino ch. 84 and *Pro Milone* ch. 12,
    sect. 32 (quoting L. Cassius Longinus Ravilla)

32 *Cum dignitate otium.*
   Leisure with honour.
    Pro Sestio ch. 98

1 I would rather be wrong, by God, with
Plato ... than be correct with those men.
Tusculanae Disputationes bk. 1, ch. 39 (of
Pythagoreans)

2 O happy Rome, born when I was consul!
In Juvenal *Satires* poem 10, l. 122

John Clare 1793–1864

3 He could not die when the trees were
green,
For he loved the time too well.
'The Dying Child'

4 My life hath been one chain of
contradictions,
Madhouses, prisons, whore-shops.
'Child Harold' (written 1841) l. 146

5 Hopeless hope hopes on and meets no end,
Wastes without springs and homes
without a friend.
'Child Harold' (written 1841) l. 1018

6 A quiet, pilfering, unprotected race.
'The Gipsy Camp' (1841)

7 I long for scenes where man hath never
trod
A place where woman never smiled or
wept
There to abide with my Creator God
And sleep as I in childhood sweetly slept,
Untroubling and untroubled where I lie
The grass below, above, the vaulted sky.
'I Am' (1848)

8 The present is the funeral of the past,
And man the living sepulchre of life.
'The present is the funeral of the past'
(written 1845)

Edward Hyde, Earl of Clarendon 1609–74

9 Without question, when he first drew the
sword, he threw away the scabbard.
History of the Rebellion (1703, ed. W. D. Macray,
1888) vol. 3, bk. 7, sect. 84 (of Hampden)

10 He had a head to contrive, a tongue to
persuade, and a hand to execute any
mischief.
History of the Rebellion (1703, ed. W. D. Macray,
1888) vol. 3, bk. 7, sect. 84 (of Hampden).
Cf. 150:12

11 So enamoured on peace that he would
have been glad the King should have
bought it at any price.
History of the Rebellion (1703, ed. W. D. Macray,
1888) vol. 3, bk. 7, sect. 233 (of Falkland)

12 He will be looked upon by posterity as a
brave bad man.
History of the Rebellion (1703, ed. W. D. Macray,
1888) vol. 6, bk. 15, *ad fin.* (of Cromwell)

Alan Clark 1928–

13 Our old friend economical ... with the
actualité.
Under cross-examination at the Old Bailey
during the Matrix Churchill case; in
Independent 10 November 1992, p. 1. Cf. 16:6

Arthur C. Clarke 1917–

14 If an elderly but distinguished scientist
says that something is possible he is
almost certainly right, but if he says that it
is impossible he is very probably wrong.
In *New Yorker* 9 August 1969

John Clarke d. 1658

15 Home is home, though it be never so
homely.
Paraemiologia Anglo-Latina (1639) 'Domi vivere'

Karl von Clausewitz 1780–1831

16 War is nothing but a continuation of
politics with the admixture of other
means.
Vom Kriege (1832–4) bk. 8, ch. 6, sect. B
(commonly rendered 'War is the
continuation of politics by other means')

Henry Clay 1777–1852

17 The gentleman [Josiah Quincy] can not
have forgotten his own sentiment, uttered
even on the floor of this House, 'peaceably
if we can, forcibly if we must'.
Speech in Congress, 8 January 1813, in C.
Colton (ed.) *Works of Henry Clay* (1904) vol. 1,
p. 197. Cf. 257:9

18 I had rather be right than be President.
To Senator Preston of South Carolina, 1839.
See S. W. McCall *Life of Thomas Brackett Reed*
(1914) ch. 14

Eldridge Cleaver 1935–

19 You're either part of the solution or you're
part of the problem.
Speech in San Francisco, 1968, in R. Scheer
*Eldridge Cleaver, Post Prison Writings and
Speeches* (1969) p. 32

John Cleland 1710–89

20 Truth! stark naked truth, is the word.
Memoirs of a Woman of Pleasure (also known as
Fanny Hill, 1749) vol. 1

Georges Clemenceau 1841–1929

21 War is too serious a matter to entrust to
military men.
Attributed to Clemenceau, e.g. in Hampden
Jackson *Clemenceau and the Third Republic*
(1946) p. 228, but also to Briand and
Talleyrand

1 My home policy: I wage war; my foreign
   policy: I wage war. All the time I wage war.
   Speech to French Chamber of Deputies,
   8 March 1918, in *Discours de Guerre* (1968)
   p. 172

2 It is easier to make war than to make
   peace.
   Speech at Verdun, 20 July 1919, in *Discours de
   Paix* (1938) p. 122

Pope Clement XIII 1693–1769

3 *Sint ut sunt aut non sint.*
   Let them be as they are or not be at all.
   Replying to a request for changes in the
   constitutions of the Society of Jesus, in J. A.
   M. Crétineau-Joly *Clément XIV et les Jésuites*
   (1847) p. 370 n.

Grover Cleveland 1837–1908

4 I have considered the pension list of the
   republic a roll of honour.
   Veto of Dependent Pension Bill, 5 July 1888,
   in *Compilation of the Messages and Papers of the
   Presidents* vol. 11 (1897) p. 5269

Bill Clinton 1946–

5 I experimented with marijuana a time or
   two. And I didn't like it, and I didn't inhale.
   In *Washington Post* 30 March 1992, p. A1

Lord Clive 1725–74

6 By God, Mr Chairman, at this moment I
   stand astonished at my own moderation!
   During Parliamentary cross-examination,
   1773, in G. R. Gleig *Life of Robert, First Lord
   Clive* (1848) ch. 29

Arthur Hugh Clough 1819–61

7 Am I prepared to lay down my life for the
   British female?
   Really, who knows? . . .
   Ah, for a child in the street I could strike;
   for the full-blown lady—
   Somehow, Eustace, alas! I have not felt the
   vocation.
   Amours de Voyage (1858) canto 2, pt. 4

8 I do not like being moved: for the will is
   excited; and action
   Is a most dangerous thing.
   Amours de Voyage (1858) canto 2, pt. 11

9 Mild monastic faces in quiet collegiate
   cloisters.
   Amours de Voyage (1858) canto 3, pt. 9

10 Sesquipedalian blackguard.
   The Bothie of Tober-na-Vuolich (1848) pt. 2, l. 223

11 Grace is given of God, but knowledge is
   bought in the market.
   The Bothie of Tober-na-Vuolich (1848) pt. 4, l. 159

12 Afloat. We move: Delicious! Ah,
   What else is like the gondola?
   Dipsychus (1865) sc. 5

13 This world is bad enough may-be;
   We do not comprehend it;
   But in one fact can all agree
   God won't, and we can't mend it.
   Dipsychus (1865) sc. 5

14 My pleasure of thought is the pleasure of
   thinking
   How pleasant it is to have money, heigh
   ho!
   How pleasant it is to have money.
   Dipsychus (1865) sc. 5

15 And almost every one when age,
   Disease, or sorrows strike him,
   Inclines to think there is a God,
   Or something very like Him.
   Dipsychus (1865) sc. 6

16 Thou shalt have one God only; who
   Would be at the expense of two?
   'The Latest Decalogue' (1862)

17 Thou shalt not kill; but need'st not strive
   Officiously to keep alive.
   'The Latest Decalogue' (1862)

18 Do not adultery commit;
   Advantage rarely comes of it.
   'The Latest Decalogue' (1862)

19 Thou shalt not steal; an empty feat,
   When it's so lucrative to cheat.
   'The Latest Decalogue' (1862)

20 Thou shalt not covet; but tradition
   Approves all forms of competition.
   'The Latest Decalogue' (1862)

21 'Tis better to have fought and lost,
   Than never to have fought at all.
   'Peschiera' (1854). Cf. 325:4

22 Say not the struggle naught availeth,
   The labour and the wounds are vain,
   The enemy faints not, nor faileth,
   And as things have been, things remain.
   'Say not the struggle naught availeth' (1855)

23 If hopes were dupes, fears may be liars.
   'Say not the struggle naught availeth' (1855)

24 In front the sun climbs slow, how slowly,
   But westward, look, the land is bright.
   'Say not the struggle naught availeth' (1855)

William Cobbett 1762–1835

25 The slavery of the tea and coffee and other
   slop-kettle.
   Advice to Young Men (1829) letter 1, sect. 31

26 The great wen of all.
   Rural Rides: The Kentish Journal in *Cobbett's
   Weekly Political Register* 5 January 1822,
   vol. 40, col. 1609 (of London)

Alison Cockburn 1713–94

27 O fickle Fortune, why this cruel sporting?
   Why thus torment us poor sons of day?
   Nae mair your smiles can cheer me, nae
   mair your frowns can fear me,
   For the flowers of the forest are a' *wade*
   away.
   'The Flowers of the Forest' (1765); *wade*
   weeded (often quoted 'For the flowers of the
   forest are withered away')

Claud Cockburn 1904–81

1 Small earthquake in Chile. Not many dead.
   Winning entry for a dullest headline
   competition at *The Times*; *In Time of Trouble*
   (1956) ch. 10

Jean Cocteau 1889–1963

2 Life is a horizontal fall.
   Opium (1930) p. 37

3 Victor Hugo was a madman who thought
   he was Victor Hugo.
   Opium (1930) p. 77

4 Being tactful in audacity is knowing how
   far one can go too far.
   Le Rappel à l'ordre (1926) 'Le Coq et l'Arlequin'
   p. 2

George M. Cohan 1878–1942

5 I'm a Yankee Doodle Dandy,
   A Yankee Doodle, do or die;
   A real live nephew of my Uncle Sam's,
   Born on the fourth of July.
   'Yankee Doodle Boy' (1904 song). Cf. 11:24

Desmond Coke 1879–1931

6 As the race wore on ... his oar was dipping
   into the water nearly *twice* as often as any
   other.
   Sandford of Merton (1903) ch. 12 (usually
   misquoted 'All rowed fast, but none so fast
   as stroke')

Sir Edward Coke 1552–1634

7 How long soever it hath continued, if it be
   against reason, it is of no force in law.
   First Part of the Institutes of the Laws of England
   (1628) bk. 1, ch. 10, sect. 80, p. 62 recto

8 For a man's house is his castle, *et domus
   sua cuique est tutissimum refugium* [and each
   man's home is his safest refuge].
   Third Part of the Institutes of the Laws of England
   (1628) ch. 73

9 They [corporations] cannot commit
   treason, nor be outlawed, nor
   excommunicate, for they have no souls.
   Reports of Sir Edward Coke (1658) vol. 5, pt. 10
   'The case of Sutton's Hospital' p. 32 verso.
   Cf. 332:19

10 Magna Charta is such a fellow, that he will
   have no sovereign.
   On the Lords' Amendment to the Petition of
   Right, 17 May 1628, in J. Rushworth *Historical
   Collections* (1659) vol. 1, p. 562

Hartley Coleridge 1796–1849

11 But what is Freedom? Rightly understood,
   A universal licence to be good.
   'Liberty' (1833)

Samuel Taylor Coleridge 1772–1834

12 Behold! her bosom and half her side—
   A sight to dream of, not to tell!
   'Christabel' (1816) pt. 1, l. 252

13 A little child, a limber elf,
   Singing, dancing to itself.
   'Christabel' (1816) pt. 2, conclusion, l. 656

14 I see them all so excellently fair,
   I see, not feel, how beautiful they are!
   'Dejection: an Ode' (1802) st. 2

15 But oh! each visitation
   Suspends what nature gave me at my
   birth,
   My shaping spirit of imagination.
   'Dejection: an Ode' (1802) st. 6. Cf. 104:24

16 And the Devil did grin, for his darling sin
   Is pride that apes humility.
   'The Devil's Thoughts' (1799)

17 What is an Epigram? a dwarfish whole,
   Its body brevity, and wit its soul.
   'Epigram' (1809)

18 The frost performs its secret ministry,
   Unhelped by any wind.
   'Frost at Midnight' (1798) l. 1

19 With all the numberless goings-on of life,
   Inaudible as dreams!
   'Frost at Midnight' (1798) l. 12

20 Only that film, which fluttered on the
   grate,
   Still flutters there, the sole unquiet thing.
   'Frost at Midnight' (1798) l. 15

21 At this moment he was unfortunately
   called out by a person on business from
   Porlock.
   'Kubla Khan' (1816) preliminary note

22 In Xanadu did Kubla Khan
   A stately pleasure-dome decree:
   Where Alph, the sacred river, ran
   Through caverns measureless to man
   Down to a sunless sea.
   So twice five miles of fertile ground
   With walls and towers were girdled round.
   'Kubla Khan' (1816)

23 A savage place! as holy and enchanted
   As e'er beneath a waning moon was
   haunted
   By woman wailing for her demon-lover!
   And from this chasm, with ceaseless
   turmoil seething,
   As if this earth in fast thick pants were
   breathing,
   A mighty fountain momently was forced.
   'Kubla Khan' (1816)

24 It was a miracle of rare device,
   A sunny pleasure-dome with caves of ice.
   'Kubla Khan' (1816)

25 And 'mid this tumult Kubla heard from far
   Ancestral voices prophesying war!
   'Kubla Khan' (1816)

1 And all should cry, Beware! Beware!
His flashing eyes, his floating hair!
Weave a circle round him thrice,
And close your eyes with holy dread,
For he on honey-dew hath fed,
And drunk the milk of Paradise.
'Kubla Khan' (1816)

2 With Donne, whose muse on dromedary trots,
Wreathe iron pokers into true-love knots.
'On Donne's Poetry' (1818)

3 It is an ancient Mariner,
And he stoppeth one of three.
'By thy long grey beard and glittering eye,
Now wherefore stopp'st thou me?'
'The Rime of the Ancient Mariner' (1798)
pt. 1

4 And ice, mast-high, came floating by,
As green as emerald.
'The Rime of the Ancient Mariner' (1798)
pt. 1

5 We were the first that ever burst
Into that silent sea.
'The Rime of the Ancient Mariner' (1798)
pt. 2

6 As idle as a painted ship
Upon a painted ocean.
'The Rime of the Ancient Mariner' (1798)
pt. 2

7 Water, water, everywhere,
And all the boards did shrink;
Water, water, everywhere,
Nor any drop to drink.
'The Rime of the Ancient Mariner' (1798)
pt. 2

8 The Night-mare LIFE-IN-DEATH was she,
Who thicks man's blood with cold.
'The Rime of the Ancient Mariner' (1798)
pt. 3

9 The Sun's rim dips; the stars rush out;
At one stride comes the dark.
'The Rime of the Ancient Mariner' (1798)
pt. 3

10 The hornèd Moon, with one bright star
Within the nether tip.
'The Rime of the Ancient Mariner' (1798)
pt. 3

11 I fear thee, ancient Mariner!
I fear thy skinny hand!
And thou art long, and lank, and brown,
As is the ribbed sea-sand.
'The Rime of the Ancient Mariner' (1798)
pt. 4

12 And a thousand thousand slimy things
Lived on; and so did I.
'The Rime of the Ancient Mariner' (1798)
pt. 4

13 Oh Sleep! it is a gentle thing,
Beloved from pole to pole.
'The Rime of the Ancient Mariner' (1798)
pt. 5

14 We were a ghastly crew.
'The Rime of the Ancient Mariner' (1798)
pt. 5

15 Like one, that on a lonesome road
Doth walk in fear and dread,
And having once turned round walks on,
And turns no more his head;
Because he knows, a frightful fiend
Doth close behind him tread.
'The Rime of the Ancient Mariner' (1798)
pt. 6

16 No voice; but oh! the silence sank
Like music on my heart.
'The Rime of the Ancient Mariner' (1798)
pt. 6

17 I pass, like night, from land to land;
I have strange power of speech.
'The Rime of the Ancient Mariner' (1798)
pt. 7

18 He prayeth well, who loveth well
Both man and bird and beast.
He prayeth best, who loveth best
All things both great and small.
'The Rime of the Ancient Mariner' (1798)
pt. 7

19 A sadder and a wiser man,
He rose the morrow morn.
'The Rime of the Ancient Mariner' (1798)
pt. 7

20 So for the mother's sake the child was dear,
And dearer was the mother for the child.
'Sonnet to a Friend Who Asked How I Felt
When the Nurse First Presented My Infant to
Me' (1797)

21   When the last rook
Beat its straight path along the dusky air.
'This Lime-Tree Bower my Prison' (1800) l. 68

22 Work without hope draws nectar in a sieve,
And hope without an object cannot live.
'Work without Hope' (1828)

23 He who begins by loving Christianity
better than Truth will proceed by loving
his own sect or church better than
Christianity, and end by loving himself
better than all.
Aids to Reflection (1825) 'Moral and Religious
Aphorisms' no. 25

24 That willing suspension of disbelief for the
moment, which constitutes poetic faith.
Biographia Literaria (1817) ch. 14

25 To see him act, is like reading Shakespeare
by flashes of lightning.
Table Talk (1835) 27 April 1823 (on Edmund
Kean)

26 Prose = words in their best order;—poetry
= the best words in the best order.
Table Talk (1835) 12 July 1827

27 The man's desire is for the woman; but the
woman's desire is rarely other than for the
desire of the man.
Table Talk (1835) 23 July 1827

28 In politics, what begins in fear usually
ends in folly.
Table Talk (1835) 5 October 1830

1 Youth and Hope—those twin realities of this phantom world!

Table Talk (1835) 10 July 1834

2 Summer has set in with its usual severity.

Letter to Vincent Novello, 9 May 1826, in A. Ainger (ed.) *Letters of Charles Lamb* (1888) vol. 2

William Collingbourne d. 1484

3 The Cat, the Rat, and Lovell our dog
Rule all England under a hog.

Referring to Sir William Catesby (d. 1485), Sir Richard Ratcliffe (d. 1485), Lord Lovell (1454–*c*.1487), whose crest was a dog, and King Richard III, whose emblem was a wild boar. See Robert Fabyan *Concordance of Chronicles* (ed. H. Ellis, 1811) p. 672

Admiral Collingwood 1748–1810

4 Now, gentlemen, let us do something today which the world may talk of hereafter.

Before the Battle of Trafalgar, 21 October 1805; in G. L. Newnham Collingwood (ed.) *Selection from the Correspondence of Lord Collingwood* (1828) vol. 1, p. 168

R. G. Collingwood 1889–1943

5 Perfect freedom is reserved for the man who lives by his own work and in that work does what he wants to do.

Speculum Mentis (1924) p. 25. Cf. 153:1

Charles Collins

6 Any old iron, any old iron,
Any any old iron?
You look neat
Talk about a treat,
You look dapper from your napper to your feet.
Dressed in style, brand new tile,
And your father's old green tie on,
But I wouldn't give you tuppence for your old watch chain;
Old iron, old iron?

'Any Old Iron' (1911 song, with E. A. Sheppard and Fred Terry); the second line often sung 'Any any any old iron?'

7 My old man said, 'Follow the van,
Don't dilly-dally on the way!'
Off went the cart with the home packed in it,
I walked behind with my old cock linnet.
But I dillied and dallied, dallied and dillied,
Lost the van and don't know where to roam.
You can't trust the 'specials' like the old time 'coppers'
When you can't find your way home.

'Don't Dilly-Dally on the Way' (1919 song, with Fred Leigh); popularized by Marie Lloyd

Michael Collins 1890–1922

8 Early this morning I signed my death warrant.

On signing the treaty establishing the Irish Free State; letter, 6 December 1921, in T. R. Dwyer *Michael Collins and the Treaty* (1981) ch. 4

William Collins 1721–59

9 To fair Fidele's grassy tomb
Soft maids and village hinds shall bring
Each opening sweet of earliest bloom,
And rifle all the breathing spring.

'Dirge' (1744); occasionally included in 18th-century performances of Shakespeare's *Cymbeline*

10 Now air is hushed, save where the weak-eyed bat,
With short shrill shriek flits by on leathern wing.

'Ode to Evening' (1747)

11 How sleep the brave, who sink to rest,
By all their country's wishes blest!

'Ode Written in the Year 1746' (1748)

George Colman, the Elder 1732–94 and David Garrick 1717–79

12 Love and a cottage! Eh, Fanny! Ah, give me indifference and a coach and six!

The Clandestine Marriage (1766) act 1

George Colman, the Younger 1762–1836

13 Oh, London is a fine town,
A very famous city,
Where all the streets are paved with gold,
And all the maidens pretty.

The Heir at Law (performed 1797) act 1, sc. 2

14 Says he, 'I am a handsome man, but I'm a gay deceiver.'

Love Laughs at Locksmiths (1808) act 2

15 Johnson hewed passages through the Alps, while Gibbon levelled walks through parks and gardens.

Random Records (1830) vol. 1, p. 122

Charles Caleb Colton c.1780–1832

16 When you have nothing to say, say nothing.

Lacon (1820) vol. 1, no. 183

17 Examinations are formidable even to the best prepared, for the greatest fool may ask more than the wisest man can answer.

Lacon (1820) vol. 1, no. 322

18 If you would be known, and not know, vegetate in a village; if you would know, and not be known, live in a city.

Lacon (1820) vol. 1, no. 334

1 Man is an embodied paradox, a bundle of contradictions.
Lacon (1820) vol. 1, no. 408

Betty Comden 1919– **and Adolph Green** 1915–

2 The party's over, it's time to call it a day.
'The Party's Over' (1956 song)

Ivy Compton-Burnett 1884–1969

3 Well, of course, people are only human ... But it really does not seem much for them to be.
A Family and a Fortune (1939) ch. 2

4 People don't resent having nothing nearly as much as too little.
A Family and a Fortune (1939) ch. 4

5 There are different kinds of wrong. The people sinned against are not always the best.
The Mighty and their Fall (1961) ch. 7

William Congreve 1670–1729

6 Retired to their tea and scandal, according to their ancient custom.
The Double Dealer (1694) act 1, sc. 1

7 See how love and murder will out.
The Double Dealer (1694) act 4, sc. 6

8 I came upstairs into the world; for I was born in a cellar.
Love for Love (1695) act 2, sc. 7

9 I know that's a secret, for it's whispered every where.
Love for Love (1695) act 3, sc. 3

10 'Tis well enough for a servant to be bred at an University. But the education is a little too pedantic for a gentleman.
Love for Love (1695) act 5, sc. 3

11 Music has charms to soothe a savage breast.
The Mourning Bride (1697) act 1, sc. 1

12 Heaven has no rage, like love to hatred turned,
Nor Hell a fury, like a woman scorned.
The Mourning Bride (1697) act 3, sc. 8

13 SHARPER: Thus grief still treads upon the heels of pleasure:
Married in haste, we may repent at leisure.
SETTER: Some by experience find those words mis-placed:
At leisure married, they repent in haste.
The Old Bachelor (1693) act 5, sc. 1

14 Courtship to marriage, as a very witty prologue to a very dull play.
The Old Bachelor (1693) act 5, sc. 10

15 They come together like the Coroner's Inquest, to sit upon the murdered reputations of the week.
The Way of the World (1700) act 1, sc. 1

16 Say what you will, 'tis better to be left than never to have been loved.
The Way of the World (1700) act 2, sc. 1. Cf. 325:4

17 Here she comes i' faith full sail, with her fan spread and streamers out, and a shoal of fools for tenders.
The Way of the World (1700) act 2, sc. 4

18 WITWOUD: Madam, do you pin up your hair with all your letters?
MILLAMANT: Only with those in verse, Mr Witwoud. I never pin up my hair with prose.
The Way of the World (1700) act 2, sc. 4

19 A little disdain is not amiss; a little scorn is alluring.
The Way of the World (1700) act 3, sc. 5

20 Let us be very strange and well-bred: Let us be as strange as if we had been married a great while, and as well-bred as if we were not married at all.
The Way of the World (1700) act 4, sc. 5

21 These articles subscribed, if I continue to endure you a little longer, I may by degrees dwindle into a wife.
The Way of the World (1700) act 4, sc. 5

22 For 'tis some virtue, virtue to commend.
'To Sir Godfrey Kneller'

James M. Connell 1852–1929

23 Then raise the scarlet standard high!
Within its shade we'll live or die.
Tho' cowards flinch and traitors sneer,
We'll keep the red flag flying here.
'The Red Flag' (1889) in H. E. Piggott *Songs that made History* (1937) ch. 6

Cyril Connolly 1903–74

24 Whom the gods wish to destroy they first call promising.
Enemies of Promise (1938) ch. 13

25 There is no more sombre enemy of good art than the pram in the hall.
Enemies of Promise (1938) ch. 14

26 The Mandarin style ... is beloved by literary pundits, by those who would make the written word as unlike as possible to the spoken one.
Enemies of Promise (1938) ch. 20

27 It is closing time in the gardens of the West and from now on an artist will be judged only by the resonance of his solitude or the quality of his despair.
Horizon December 1949—January 1950, p. 362

28 Imprisoned in every fat man a thin one is wildly signalling to be let out.
The Unquiet Grave (1944) pt. 2. Cf. 241:25

29 The true index of a man's character is the health of his wife.
The Unquiet Grave (1944) pt. 2

1 Our memories are card-indexes consulted, and then put back in disorder by authorities whom we do not control.
The Unquiet Grave (1944) pt. 3

2 Perfect fear casteth out love.
In *Observer* 1 December 1974; obituary notice by Philip Toynbee, to whom Connolly addressed the remark during the Blitz

James Connolly 1868–1916

3 The worker is the slave of capitalist society, the female worker is the slave of that slave.
The Re-conquest of Ireland (1915) p. 38

Joseph Conrad 1857–1924

4 Exterminate all the brutes!
Heart of Darkness (1902) ch. 2

5 The horror! The horror!
Heart of Darkness (1902) ch. 3

6 Mistah Kurtz—he dead.
Heart of Darkness (1902) ch. 3

7 To the destructive element submit yourself.
Lord Jim (1900) ch. 20

8 Action is consolatory. It is the enemy of thought and the friend of flattering illusions.
Nostromo (1904) pt. 1, ch. 6

9 The terrorist and the policeman both come from the same basket.
The Secret Agent (1907) ch. 4

Shirley Conran 1932–

10 Life is too short to stuff a mushroom.
Superwoman (1975) p. 15

John Constable 1776–1837

11 *I never saw an ugly thing in my life*: for let the form of an object be what it may,—light, shade, and perspective will always make it beautiful.
In C. R. Leslie *Memoirs of the Life of John Constable* (1843) ch. 17

12 In Claude's landscape all is lovely—all amiable—all is amenity and repose;—the calm sunshine of the heart.
Lecture, 2 June 1836, in C. R. Leslie *Memoirs of the Life of John Constable* (1843) ch. 18

Benjamin Constant 1767–1834

13 Art for art's sake, with no purpose, for any purpose perverts art. But art achieves a purpose which is not its own.
Journal intime 11 February 1804, in *Revue Internationale* 10 January 1887 p. 96. Cf. 108:17

Emperor Constantine
AD *c*.288–337

14 *In hoc signo vinces.*
In this sign shalt thou conquer.
Traditional form of Constantine's vision (AD 312); in Eusebius *Life of Constantine* bk. 1, ch. 28

A. J. Cook 1885–1931

15 Not a penny off the pay, not a second on the day.
Speech at York, 3 April 1926, as Secretary of the Miners' Federation of Great Britain; in *The Times* 5 April 1926 (often quoted with 'minute' substituted for 'second')

Dan Cook

16 The opera ain't over 'til the fat lady sings.
In *Washington Post* 3 June 1978. See *Concise Oxford Dictionary of Proverbs* under 'opera'

Eliza Cook 1818–89

17 Better build schoolrooms for 'the boy', Than cells and gibbets for 'the man'.
'A Song for the Ragged Schools' (1853)

Calvin Coolidge 1872–1933

18 Civilization and profits go hand in hand.
Speech in New York, 27 November 1920, in *New York Times* 28 November 1920, p. 20

19 The chief business of the American people is business.
Speech in Washington, 17 January 1925, in *New York Times* 18 January 1925, p. 19

20 They hired the money, didn't they?
On war debts incurred by England and others; in J. H. McKee *Coolidge: Wit and Wisdom* (1933) p. 118

Duff Cooper 1890–1954

21 Your two stout lovers frowning at one another across the hearth rug, while your small, but perfectly formed one kept the party in a roar.
Letter to Lady Diana Manners, later his wife, October 1914; in Artemis Cooper *Durable Fire* (1983) p. 17

Wendy Cope 1945–

22 Bloody men are like bloody buses—You wait for about a year And as soon as one approaches your stop Two or three others appear.
'Bloody Men' (1992)

Bishop Richard Corbet 1582–1635

23 Farewell, rewards and Fairies, Good housewives now may say, For now foul sluts in dairies Do fare as well as they.
'The Fairies' Farewell'

Pierre Corneille 1606–84

1 When there is no peril in the fight, there is no glory in the triumph.
   Le Cid (1637) act 2, sc. 2

2 Do your duty, and leave the outcome to the Gods.
   Horace (1640) act 2, sc. 8

3 A first impulse was never a crime.
   Horace (1640) act 5, sc. 3. Cf. 234:1

Bernard Cornfeld 1927–

4 Do you sincerely want to be rich?
   Stock question to salesmen. See C. Raw et al. *Do You Sincerely Want to be Rich?* (1971) p. 67

Frances Cornford 1886–1960

5 How long ago Hector took off his plume,
   Not wanting that his little son should cry,
   Then kissed his sad Andromache
   goodbye—
   And now we three in Euston waiting-room.
   'Parting in Wartime' (1948)

6 O fat white woman whom nobody loves,
   Why do you walk through the fields in
   gloves ...
   Missing so much and so much?
   'To a Fat Lady seen from the Train' (1910)

7 A young Apollo, golden-haired,
   Stands dreaming on the verge of strife,
   Magnificently unprepared
   For the long littleness of life.
   'Youth' (1910) (of Rupert Brooke)

Francis M. Cornford 1874–1943

8 Every public action, which is not customary, either is wrong, or, if it is right, is a dangerous precedent. It follows that nothing should ever be done for the first time.
   Microcosmographia Academica (1908) ch. 7

Mme Cornuel 1605–94

9 No man is a hero to his valet.
   In *Lettres de Mlle Aïssé à Madame C* (1787) Letter 13 'De Paris, 1728'

Coronation Service

10 Here is wisdom; this is the royal Law; these are the lively Oracles of God.
   The Presenting of the Holy Bible. See L. G. Wickham Legge *English Coronation Records* (1901) p. 334

William Cory 1823–92

11 Jolly boating weather,
   And a hay harvest breeze,
   Blade on the feather,
   Shade off the trees
   Swing, swing together
   With your body between your knees.
   'Eton Boating Song' in *Eton Scrap Book* (1865)

12 Nothing in life shall sever
   The chain that is round us now.
   'Eton Boating Song' (1865)

13 They told me, Heraclitus, they told me you
   were dead,
   They brought me bitter news to hear and
   bitter tears to shed.
   I wept as I remembered how often you
   and I
   Had tired the sun with talking and sent
   him down the sky.
   'Heraclitus' (1858); translation of Callimachus 'Epigram 2' in R. Pfeiffer (ed.) *Callimachus* (1949–53)

14 Your chilly stars I can forgo,
   This warm kind world is all I know.
   'Mimnermus in Church' (1858)

Baron Pierre de Coubertin 1863–1937

15 The important thing in life is not the victory but the contest; the essential thing is not to have won but to have fought well.
   Speech in London, 24 July 1908; in T. A. Cook *Fourth Olympiad* (1909) p. 793

Émile Coué 1857–1926

16 Every day, in every way, I am getting better and better.
   To be said 15 to 20 times, morning and evening, in *De la suggestion et de ses applications* (1915) p. 17

Victor Cousin 1792–1867

17 We must have religion for religion's sake, morality for morality's sake, as with art for art's sake ... the beautiful cannot be the way to what is useful, or to what is good, or to what is holy; it leads only to itself.
   Du Vrai, du beau, et du bien [Sorbonne lecture, 1818] (1853) pt. 2, p. 197. Cf. 107:13

Thomas Coventry 1578–1640

18 The dominion of the sea, as it is an ancient and undoubted right of the crown of England, so it is the best security of the land ... The wooden walls are the best walls of this kingdom.
   Speech to the Judges, 17 June 1635, in J. Rushworth *Historical Collections* (1680) vol. 2, p. 297 (*wooden walls* ships). See Herodotus *Histories* bk. 7, ch. 141–3

Noël Coward 1899–1973

19 Dance, dance, dance, little lady!
   Leave tomorrow behind.
   'Dance, Little Lady' (1928 song)

20 Don't let's be beastly to the Germans
   When our Victory is ultimately won.
   'Don't Let's Be Beastly to the Germans' (1943 song)

1 I believe that since my life began
The most I've had is just
A talent to amuse.
'If Love Were All' (1929 song)

2 I'll see you again,
Whenever spring breaks through again.
'I'll See You Again' (1929 song)

3 Mad about the boy.
Title of song (1932)

4 Mad dogs and Englishmen
Go out in the midday sun.
The Japanese don't care to,
The Chinese wouldn't dare to,
The Hindus and Argentines sleep firmly
from twelve to one,
But Englishmen detest a siesta.
'Mad Dogs and Englishmen' (1931 song)

5 Don't put your daughter on the stage, Mrs
Worthington,
Don't put your daughter on the stage.
'Mrs Worthington' (1935 song)

6 Poor little rich girl
You're a bewitched girl,
Better beware!
'Poor Little Rich Girl' (1925 song)

7 Someday I'll find you,
Moonlight behind you,
True to the dream I am dreaming.
'Someday I'll Find You' (1930 song)

8 The Stately Homes of England,
How beautiful they stand,
To prove the upper classes
Have still the upper hand.
'The Stately Homes of England' (1938 song).
Cf. 165:10

9 Very flat, Norfolk.
Private Lives (1930) act 1

10 Extraordinary how potent cheap music is.
Private Lives (1930) act 1

11 Certain women should be struck regularly,
like gongs.
Private Lives (1930) act 3

12 Two wise acres and a cow.
Describing the Sitwells, in J. Pearson Façades
(1978) ch. 10. Cf. 11:6

Abraham Cowley 1618–67

13 God the first garden made, and the first
city Cain.
Essays, in Verse and Prose (1668) 'The Garden'.
Cf. 110:6

14 In all her outward parts Love's always
seen;
But, oh, he never went within.
The Mistress (1647) 'The Change'

15 The world's a scene of changes, and to be
Constant, in Nature were inconstancy.
The Mistress (1647) 'Inconstancy'

16 Lukewarmness I account a sin
As great in love as in religion.
The Mistress (1647) 'The Request'

17 Life is an incurable disease.
'To Dr Scarborough' (1656) st. 6

Hannah Cowley 1743–1809

18 Five minutes! Zounds! I have been five
minutes too late all my life-time!
The Belle's Stratagem (1780) act 1, sc. 1

19 Vanity, like murder, will out.
The Belle's Stratagem (1780) act 1, sc. 4

William Cowper 1731–1800

20 We perished, each alone:
But I beneath a rougher sea,
And whelmed in deeper gulfs than he.
'The Castaway' (written 1799) l. 61

21 Pernicious weed! whose scent the fair
annoys,
Unfriendly to society's chief joys.
'Conversation' (1782) l. 251 (of tobacco)

22 His wit invites you by his looks to come,
But when you knock it never is at home.
'Conversation' (1782) l. 303

23 John Gilpin was a citizen
Of credit and renown,
A train-band captain eke was he
Of famous London town.
'John Gilpin' (1785) l. 1

24 My sister and my sister's child,
Myself and children three,
Will fill the chaise; so you must ride
On horseback after we.
'John Gilpin' (1785) l. 13

25 God moves in a mysterious way
His wonders to perform;
He plants his footsteps in the sea,
And rides upon the storm.
Olney Hymns (1779) 'Light Shining out of
Darkness'

26 Behind a frowning providence
He hides a smiling face.
Olney Hymns (1779) 'Light Shining out of
Darkness'

27 Oh! for a closer walk with God,
A calm and heav'nly frame;
A light to shine upon the road
That leads me to the Lamb!
Olney Hymns (1779) 'Walking with God'

28 Toll for the brave—
The brave! that are no more:
All sunk beneath the wave,
Fast by their native shore.
'On the Loss of the Royal George' (written
1782)

29 I shall not ask Jean Jacques Rousseau,
If birds confabulate or no.
'Pairing Time Anticipated' (1795)

30 The poplars are felled, farewell to the
shade
And the whispering sound of the cool
colonnade.
The Poplar-Field' (written 1784)

1 Oh, laugh or mourn with me the rueful jest,
A cassocked huntsman and a fiddling priest!
'The Progress of Error' (1782) l. 110

2 Remorse, the fatal egg by pleasure laid.
'The Progress of Error' (1782) l. 239

3 Thou god of our idolatry, the press ...
Thou fountain, at which drink the good and wise;
Thou ever-bubbling spring of endless lies;
Like Eden's dread probationary tree,
Knowledge of good and evil is from thee.
'The Progress of Error' (1782) l. 461

4 The disencumbered Atlas of the state.
'Retirement' (1782) l. 394 (of the statesman)

5 Admirals extolled for standing still,
Or doing nothing with a deal of skill.
'Table Talk' (1782) l. 192

6 God made the country, and man made the town.
The Task (1785) bk. 1 'The Sofa' l. 749.
Cf. 109:13

7 Slaves cannot breathe in England, if their lungs
Receive our air, that moment they are free;
They touch our country, and their shackles fall.
The Task (1785) bk. 2 'The Timepiece' l. 40.
Cf. 10:1

8 England, with all thy faults, I love thee still—
My country!
The Task (1785) bk. 2 'The Timepiece' l. 206.
Cf. 98:21

9 Variety's the very spice of life,
That gives it all its flavour.
The Task (1785) bk. 2 'The Timepiece' l. 606

10 Studious of laborious ease.
The Task (1785) bk. 3 'The Garden' l. 361

11 Now stir the fire, and close the shutters fast,
Let fall the curtains, wheel the sofa round,
And, while the bubbling and loud-hissing urn
Throws up a steamy column, and the cups,
That cheer but not inebriate, wait on each,
So let us welcome peaceful evening in.
The Task (1785) bk. 4 'The Winter Evening' l. 34. Cf. 35:16

12 I crown thee king of intimate delights,
Fire-side enjoyments, home-born happiness.
The Task (1785) bk. 4 'The Winter Evening' l. 139

13 Public schools 'tis public folly feeds.
'Tirocinium' (1785) l. 250

14 The parson knows enough who knows a duke.
'Tirocinium' (1785) l. 403

15 A priest,
A piece of mere church furniture at best.
'Tirocinium' (1785) l. 425

16 Tenants of life's middle state,
Securely placed between the small and great.
'Tirocinium' (1785) l. 807

17 He has no hope that never had a fear.
'Truth' (1782) l. 298

18 I am monarch of all I survey,
My right there is none to dispute.
'Verses Supposed to be Written by Alexander Selkirk' (1782)

George Crabbe 1754–1832

19 The Town small-talk flows from lip to lip;
Intrigues half-gathered, conversation-scraps,
Kitchen-cabals, and nursery-mishaps.
The Borough (1810) Letter 3 'The Vicar' l. 70

20 Habit with him was all the test of truth,
'It must be right: I've done it from my youth.'
The Borough (1810) Letter 3 'The Vicar' l. 138

21 Lo! the poor toper whose untutored sense,
Sees bliss in ale, and can with wine dispense;
Whose head proud fancy never taught to steer,
Beyond the muddy ecstasies of beer.
'Inebriety' (in imitation of Pope, 1775) pt. 1, l. 132. Cf. 252:13

22 With awe, around these silent walks I tread;
These are the lasting mansions of the dead.
'The Library' (1808) l. 105

23 Coldly profane and impiously gay.
'The Library' (1808) l. 265

24 The murmuring poor, who will not fast in peace.
'The Newspaper' (1785) l. 158

25 A master passion is the love of news.
'The Newspaper' (1785) l. 279

26 That all was wrong because not all was right.
Tales (1812) 'The Convert' l. 313

27 He tried the luxury of doing good.
Tales of the Hall (1819) 'Boys at School' l. 139

28 'The game,' said he, 'is never lost till won.'
Tales of the Hall (1819) 'Gretna Green' l. 334

29 The face the index of a feeling mind.
Tales of the Hall (1819) 'Lady Barbara' l. 124

30 The cold charities of man to man.
The Village (1783) bk. 1, l. 245

Hart Crane 1899–1932

31 Stars scribble on our eyes the frosty sagas,
The gleaming cantos of unvanquished space.
'Cape Hatteras' (1930)

32 We have seen
The moon in lonely alleys make
A grail of laughter of an empty ash can.
'Chaplinesque' (1926)

1 Ah, madame! truly it's not right
When one isn't the real Gioconda,
To adapt her methods and deportment
For snaring the poor world in a blue funk.
'Locutions des Pierrots' (1933)

2   So the 20th Century—so
whizzed the Limited—roared by and left
three men, still hungry on the tracks,
ploddingly
watching the tail lights wizen and
converge, slipping
gimleted and neatly out of sight.
'The River' (1930)

Stephen Crane 1871–1900

3 The red badge of courage.
Title of novel (1895)

Thomas Cranmer 1489–1556

4 This was the hand that wrote it [his
recantation], therefore it shall suffer first
punishment.
At the stake, 21 March 1556; in J. R. Green
Short History of the English People (1874) ch. 7,
sect. 2

Richard Crashaw c.1612–49

5 Lord, what is man, that thou hast
overbought
So much a thing of nought?
'Caritas Nimia, or The Dear Bargain' (1648)

6 Nympha pudica Deum vidit, et erubuit.
The conscious water saw its God, and
blushed.
Epigrammata Sacra (1634) 'Aquae in vinum
versae' (Dryden's translation; literally 'the
chaste nymph saw . . . ')

7 Love's passives are his activ'st part.
The wounded is the wounding heart.
'The Flaming Heart upon the Book of Saint
Teresa' (1652) l. 73

8 By all the eagle in thee, all the dove.
'The Flaming Heart upon the Book of Saint
Teresa' (1652) l. 95

9 Love, thou art absolute sole Lord
Of life and death.
'Hymn to the Name and Honour of the
Admirable Saint Teresa' (1652) l. 1

10 Poor World (said I) what wilt thou do
To entertain this starry stranger?
'Hymn of the Nativity' (1652)

11 Welcome, all wonders in one sight!
Eternity shut in a span.
'Hymn of the Nativity' (1652)

12 Lo here a little volume, but large book.
'On a Prayer book' (1646)

13 I would be married, but I'd have no wife,
I would be married to a single life.
'On Marriage' (1646)

14 Two walking baths; two weeping motions;
Portable, and compendious oceans.
'Saint Mary Magdalene, or The Weeper'
(1652) st. 19

15 And when life's sweet fable ends,
Soul and body part like friends;
No quarrels, murmurs, no delay;
A kiss, a sigh, and so away.
'Temperance' (1652)

16 That not impossible she
That shall command my heart and me.
'Wishes to His (Supposed) Mistress' (1646)

James Creelman 1901–41 and Ruth Rose

17 Oh no, it wasn't the aeroplanes. It was
Beauty killed the Beast.
King Kong (1933 film)

Bishop Mandell Creighton 1843–1901

18 No people do so much harm as those who
go about doing good.
In Life and Letters of Mandell Creighton by his
wife (1904) vol. 2, p. 503

Francis Crick 1916–

19 Almost all aspects of life are engineered at
the molecular level, and without
understanding molecules we can only have
a very sketchy understanding of life itself.
What Mad Pursuit (1988) ch. 5

Quentin Crisp 1908–

20 There was no need to do any housework at
all. After the first four years the dirt
doesn't get any worse.
The Naked Civil Servant (1968) ch. 15

21 An autobiography is an obituary in serial
form with the last instalment missing.
The Naked Civil Servant (1968) ch. 29

Julian Critchley 1930–

22 The only safe pleasure for a
parliamentarian is a bag of boiled sweets.
Listener 10 June 1982

Richmal Crompton 1890–1969

23 I'll thcream and thcream and thcream till
I'm thick.
Still—William (1925) ch. 8 (Violet Elizabeth)

Oliver Cromwell 1599–1658

24 I would rather have a plain russet-coated
captain that knows what he fights for, and
loves what he knows, than that which you
call 'a gentleman' and is nothing else.
Letter to Sir William Spring, September
1643, in Thomas Carlyle Oliver Cromwell's
Letters and Speeches (2nd ed., 1846)

1 Cruel necessity.
   On the execution of Charles I, in Joseph
   Spence *Anecdotes* (1820) p. 286

2 I beseech you, in the bowels of Christ,
   think it possible you may be mistaken.
   Letter to the General Assembly of the Kirk of
   Scotland, 3 August 1650, in Thomas Carlyle
   Oliver Cromwell's Letters and Speeches (1845)

3 The dimensions of this mercy are above
   my thoughts. It is, for aught I know, a
   crowning mercy.
   Letter to William Lenthall, Speaker of the
   Parliament of England, 4 September 1651, in
   Thomas Carlyle *Oliver Cromwell's Letters and
   Speeches* (1845)

4 You have sat too long here for any good
   you have been doing. Depart, I say, and let
   us have done with you. In the name of
   God, go!
   Addressing the Rump Parliament, 20 April
   1653 (oral tradition; quoted by Leo Amery,
   Hansard 7 May 1940, col. 1150). See Bulstrode
   Whitelock *Memorials of the English Affairs*
   (1732 ed.) p. 529

5 Take away that fool's bauble, the mace.
   At the dismissal of the Rump Parliament,
   20 April 1653, in Bulstrode Whitelock
   Memorials of the English Affairs (1732 ed.)
   p. 529 (often quoted 'Take away these
   baubles')

6 Necessity hath no law. Feigned necessities,
   imaginary necessities ... are the greatest
   cozenage that men can put upon the
   Providence of God, and make pretences to
   break known rules by.
   Speech to Parliament, 12 September 1654, in
   Thomas Carlyle *Oliver Cromwell's Letters and
   Speeches* (1845). Cf. 256:2

7 Remark all these roughnesses, pimples,
   warts, and everything as you see me;
   otherwise I will never pay a farthing for it.
   To Lely, on the painting of his portrait; in
   Horace Walpole *Anecdotes of Painting in
   England* vol. 3 (1763) ch. 1 (commonly quoted
   'warts and all')

8 My design is to make what haste I can to
   be gone.
   Last words, in J. Morley *Oliver Cromwell* (1900)
   bk. 5, ch. 10

Bing Crosby 1903–77

9 Where the blue of the night meets the
   gold of the day.
   Title of song, with Roy Turk and Fred Ahlert
   (1931)

Douglas Cross

10 I left my heart in San Francisco
   High on a hill it calls to me.
   To be where little cable cars climb half-way
   to the stars,
   The morning fog may chill the air—
   I don't care!
   'I Left My Heart in San Francisco' (1954 song)

Richard Assheton, Viscount Cross 1823–1914

11 I hear a smile.
   When the House of Lords laughed at his
   speech in favour of Spiritual Peers, in G. W.
   E. Russell *Collections and Recollections* (1898)
   ch. 29

Richard Crossman 1907–74

12 The Civil Service is profoundly deferential
   — 'Yes, Minister! No, Minister! If you wish
   it, Minister!'
   Diaries of a Cabinet Minister vol. 1 (1975)
   22 October 1964

Samuel Crossman 1624–83

13 My song is love unknown,
   My saviour's love for me,
   Love to the loveless shown,
   That they might lovely be.
   O, who am I,
   That for my sake
   My Lord should take
   Frail flesh and die?
   'My song is love unknown' (1664)

Aleister Crowley 1875–1947

14 Do what thou wilt shall be the whole of
   the Law.
   Book of the Law (1909) l. 40. Cf. 257:12

Bishop Richard Cumberland 1631–1718

15 It is better to wear out than to rust out.
   In George Horne *The Duty of Contending for the
   Faith* (1786) p. 21 n.

e. e. cummings 1894–1962

16 anyone lived in a pretty how town
   (with up so floating many bells down)
   spring summer autumn winter
   he sang his didn't he danced his did.
   50 Poems (1949) no. 29

17 'next to of course god america i
   love you land of the pilgrims' and so forth.
   is 5 (1926) p. 62

18 a politician is an arse upon
   which everyone has sat except a man.
   1 x 1 (1944) no. 10

19 plato told
        him: he couldn't
   believe it (jesus
        told him; he
   wouldn't believe
        it).
   1 x 1 (1944) no. 13

20 pity this busy monster, manunkind,
   not. Progress is a comfortable disease.
   1 x 1 (1944) no. 14

1 We doctors know
a hopeless case if—listen: there's a hell
of a good universe next door; let's go.
   1 x 1 (1944) no. 14

2 when man determined to destroy
himself he picked the was
of shall and finding only why
smashed it into because.
   1 x 1 (1944) no. 26

3 nobody, not even the rain, has such small
hands.
   'somewhere I have never travelled' (1931)

4 i like my body when it is with your
body. It is so quite new a thing.
Muscles better and nerves more.
   'Sonnets–Actualities' no. 8 (1925)

5 the Cambridge ladies who live in furnished
souls
are unbeautiful and have comfortable
minds.
   'Sonnets–Realities' no. 1 (1923)

William Thomas Cummings
1903–45

6 There are no atheists in the foxholes.
   In C. P. Romulo *I Saw the Fall of the Philippines*
   (1943) ch. 15

Allan Cunningham 1784–1842

7 A wet sheet and a flowing sea,
A wind that follows fast
And fills the white and rustling sail
And bends the gallant mast.
   'A Wet Sheet and a Flowing Sea' (1825)

John Philpot Curran 1750–1817

8 The condition upon which God hath given
liberty to man is eternal vigilance.
   Speech on the right of election of the Lord
   Mayor of Dublin, 10 July 1790; in T. Davis
   (ed.) *Speeches* (1845) p. 94

9 Like the silver plate on a coffin.
   Describing Sir Robert Peel's smile; quoted by
   Daniel O'Connell, *Hansard* 26 February 1835,
   col. 397

Michael Curtiz 1888–1962

10 Bring on the empty horses!
   While directing *The Charge of the Light Brigade*
   (1936 film); in David Niven *Bring on the Empty
   Horses* (1975) ch. 6

Lord Curzon 1859–1925

11 Gentlemen do not take soup at luncheon.
   In E. L. Woodward *Short Journey* (1942) ch. 7

St Cyprian *c.*AD 200–258

12 He cannot have God for his father who has
not the church for his mother.
   De Ecclesiae Catholicae Unitate sect. 6. Cf. 21:26

13 *Fratres nostros non esse lugendos arcessitione
dominica de saeculo liberatos, cum sciamus non
amitti sed praemitti.*
Our brethren who have been freed from
the world by the summons of the Lord
should not be mourned, since we know
that they are not lost but sent before.
   De Mortalite ch. 20 (ed. M. L. Hannam, 1933)

14 There cannot be salvation for any, except
in the Church.
   Epistle Ad Pomponium, De Virginibus sect. 4.
   Cf. 21:26, 113:12

Samuel Daniel 1563–1619

15 Care-charmer Sleep, son of the sable Night,
Brother to Death, in silent darkness born.
   Delia (1592) Sonnet 54

16   But years hath done this
wrong,
To make me write too much, and live too
long.
   Philotas (1605) 'To the Prince' (dedication)
   l. 108

Dante Alighieri 1265–1321

17 *Nel mezzo del cammin di nostra vita.*
Midway along the path of our life.
   Divina Commedia 'Inferno' canto 1, l. 1

18 LASCIATE OGNI SPERANZA VOI CH'ENTRATE!
Abandon all hope, you who enter!
   Divina Commedia 'Inferno' canto 3, l. 1
   (inscription at the entrance to Hell)

19 *Non ragioniam di lor, ma guarda, e passa.*
Let us not speak of them, but look, and
pass on.
   Divina Commedia 'Inferno' canto 3, l. 51

20 *Il gran rifiuto.*
The great refusal.
   Divina Commedia 'Inferno' canto 3, l. 60

21 *... Nessun maggior dolore,
Che ricordarsi del tempo felice
Nella miseria.*
There is no greater pain than to remember
a happy time when one is in misery.
   Divina Commedia 'Inferno' canto 5, l. 121.
   Cf. 62:17

22 *E'n la sua volontate è nostra pace.*
In His will is our peace.
   Divina Commedia 'Paradiso' canto 3, l. 85

23 *Tu proverai sì come sa di sale
Lo pane altrui, e com'è duro calle
Lo scendere e'l salir per l'altrui scale.*
You shall find out how salt is the taste of
another man's bread, and how hard is the
way up and down another man's stairs.
   Divina Commedia 'Paradiso' canto 17, l. 58

24 *L'amor che muove il sole e l'altre stelle.*
The love that moves the sun and the other
stars.
   Divina Commedia 'Paradiso' canto 33, l. 145

Georges Jacques Danton 1759–94

1 *De l'audace, et encore de l'audace, et toujours de l'audace!*

Boldness, and again boldness, and always boldness!

Speech to the Legislative Committee of General Defence, 2 September 1792; in *Le Moniteur* 4 September 1792

Joe Darion 1917–

2 Dream the impossible dream.
'The Quest' (1965 song)

Charles Darwin 1809–82

3 I have called this principle, by which each slight variation, if useful, is preserved, by the term of Natural Selection.
On the Origin of Species (1859) ch. 3

4 We will now discuss in a little more detail the Struggle for Existence.
On the Origin of Species (1859) ch. 3

5 What a book a devil's chaplain might write on the clumsy, wasteful, blundering, low, and horridly cruel works of nature!
Letter to J. D. Hooker, 13 July 1856; in *Correspondence of Charles Darwin* vol. 6 (1990)

6 Animals, whom we have made our slaves, we do not like to consider our equal.
Notebook B (1837–8) in P. H. Barrett et al. (eds.) *Charles Darwin's Notebooks 1836–1844* (1987) p. 228

Sir Francis Darwin 1848–1925

7 In science the credit goes to the man who convinces the world, not to the man to whom the idea first occurs.
Eugenics Review April 1914 'Francis Galton'

Charles D'Avenant 1656–1714

8 Custom, that unwritten law,
By which the people keep even kings in awe.
Circe (1677) act 2, sc. 3

Sir William D'Avenant 1606–68

9 In every grave make room, make room!
The world's at an end, and we come, we come.
The Law against Lovers (1673) act 3, sc. 1
'Viola's Song'

10 The lark now leaves his wat'ry nest
And, climbing, shakes his dewy wings.
'Song: The Lark' (1638)

John Davidson 1857–1909

11 A runnable stag, a kingly crop.
'A Runnable Stag' (1906)

12 The race is to the swift,
The battle to the strong.
'War Song' (1899) st. 1

Sir John Davies 1569–1626

13 Wedlock, indeed, hath oft compared been
To public feasts where meet a public rout,
Where they that are without would fain go in
And they that are within would fain go out.
'A Contention Betwixt a Wife, a Widow, and a Maid for Precedence' (1608) l. 193

14 I know my life's a pain and but a span,
I know my sense is mocked in every thing;
And to conclude, I know myself a man,
Which is a proud and yet a wretched thing.
'Nosce Teipsum' (1599) st. 45

15 This wondrous miracle did Love devise,
For dancing is love's proper exercise.
'Orchestra, or a Poem of Dancing' (1596) st. 18

Scrope Davies *c.*1783–1852

16 Babylon in all its desolation is a sight not so awful as that of the human mind in ruins.
Letter to Thomas Raikes, May 1835, in *A Portion of the Journal kept by Thomas Raikes* (1856) vol. 2, p. 113. Addison, in *The Spectator* no. 421 (3 July 1712), also remarked of 'a distracted person' that 'Babylon in ruins is not so melancholy a spectacle'

W. H. Davies 1871–1940

17 And hear the pleasant cuckoo, loud and long—
The simple bird that thinks two notes a song.
'April's Charms' (1916)

18 A rainbow and a cuckoo's song
May never come together again;
May never come
This side the tomb.
'A Great Time' (1914)

19 It was the Rainbow gave thee birth,
And left thee all her lovely hues.
'Kingfisher' (1910)

20 What is this life if, full of care,
We have no time to stand and stare.
'Leisure' (1911)

21 Come, lovely Morning, rich in frost
On iron, wood and glass.
'Silver Hours' (1932)

22 Sweet Stay-at-Home, sweet Well-content,
Thou knowest of no strange continent:
Thou hast not felt thy bosom keep
A gentle motion with the deep.
'Sweet Stay-At-Home' (1913)

Sammy Davis Jnr. 1925–90

23 Being a star has made it possible for me to get insulted in places where the average Negro could never *hope* to go and get insulted.
Yes I Can (1965) pt. 3, ch. 23

Thomas Davis 1814–45

1 Come in the evening, or come in the
    morning,
  Come when you're looked for, or come
    without warning.
  'The Welcome' (1846)

Richard Dawkins 1941–

2 [Natural selection] has no vision, no
  foresight, no sight at all. If it can be said to
  play the role of watchmaker in nature, it is
  the *blind* watchmaker.
  The Blind Watchmaker (1986) ch. 1

3 However many ways there may be of being
  alive, it is certain that there are vastly
  more ways of being dead.
  The Blind Watchmaker (1986) ch. 1

4 The essence of life is statistical
  improbability on a colossal scale.
  The Blind Watchmaker (1986) ch. 11

Lord Dawson of Penn 1864–1945

5 The King's life is moving peacefully
  towards its close.
  Bulletin, 20 January 1936; in K. Rose *King
  George V* (1983) ch. 10

C. Day-Lewis 1904–72

6 It is the logic of our times,
  No subject for immortal verse—
  That we who lived by honest dreams
  Defend the bad against the worse.
  'Where are the War Poets?' (1943)

Percy Dearmer 1867–1936

7 Jesu, good above all other,
  Gentle Child of gentle Mother,
  In a stable born our Brother,
  Give us grace to persevere.
  'Jesu, good above all other' (1906 hymn)

Simone de Beauvoir 1908–86

8 One is not born a woman: one becomes
  one.
  The Second Sex (1949) vol. 2, pt. 1, ch. 1

Eugene Victor Debs 1855–1926

9 While there is a lower class, I am in it;
  while there is a criminal element, I am of
  it; while there is a soul in prison, I am not
  free.
  Speech at his trial for sedition in Cleveland,
  Ohio, 14 September 1918; in *Liberator*
  November 1918, p. 12

Stephen Decatur 1779–1820

10 Our country! In her intercourse with
  foreign nations, may she always be in the
  right; but our country, right or wrong.
  Toast at Norfolk, Virginia, April 1816; in A. S.
  Mackenzie *Life of Stephen Decatur* (1846) ch. 14

Daniel Defoe 1660–1731

11 Pleasure is a *thief* to business.
  The Complete English Tradesman (1725) vol. 1,
  ch. 9

12 Vice came in always at the door of
  necessity, not at the door of inclination.
  Moll Flanders (1721, ed. G. A. Starr, 1971)
  p. 128

13 Give me not poverty lest I steal.
  Review vol. 8, no. 75 (15 September 1711);
  later incorporated into *Moll Flanders* (1721)

14 He told me ... that mine was the middle
  state, or what might be called the upper
  station of low life, which he had found by
  long experience was the best state in the
  world, the most suited to human
  happiness.
  Robinson Crusoe (1719, ed. J. D. Crowley, 1972)
  p. 4

15 My man Friday.
  Robinson Crusoe (1719, ed. J. D. Crowley, 1972)
  p. 207

16 Necessity makes an honest man a knave.
  The Serious Reflections of Robinson Crusoe (1720)
  ch. 2

17 The best of men cannot suspend their fate:
  The good die early, and the bad die late.
  'Character of the late Dr S. Annesley' (1697)

18 We loved the doctrine for the teacher's
  sake.
  'Character of the late Dr S. Annesley' (1697)

19 Actions receive their tincture from the
    times,
  And as they change are virtues made or
    crimes.
  A Hymn to the Pillory (1703) l. 29

20 Nature has left this tincture in the blood,
  That all men would be tyrants if they
    could.
  The History of the Kentish Petition (1712–13)
  addenda, l. 11

21 Fools out of favour grudge at knaves in
  place.
  The True-Born Englishman (1701) introduction,
  l. 7

22 Wherever God erects a house of prayer,
  The Devil always builds a chapel there;
  And 'twill be found, upon examination,
  The latter has the largest congregation.
  The True-Born Englishman (1701) pt. 1, l. 1.
  Cf. 28:14, 212:9

23 In their religion they are so uneven,
  That each one goes his own by-way to
  heaven.
  The True-Born Englishman (1701) pt. 1, l. 104

24 Your Roman-Saxon-Danish-Norman
  English.
  The True-Born Englishman (1701) pt. 1, l. 139

25 And of all plagues with which mankind are
    curst,
  Ecclesiastic tyranny's the worst.
  The True-Born Englishman (1701) pt. 2, l. 299

1 Titles are shadows, crowns are empty
   things,
   The good of subjects is the end of kings.
   The True-Born Englishman (1701) pt. 2, l. 315

Edgar Degas 1834–1917

2 Art is vice. You don't marry it legitimately,
   you rape it.
   In P. Lafond *Degas* (1918) p. 140

Charles de Gaulle 1890–1970

3 France has lost a battle. But France has not
   lost the war!
   Proclamation, 18 June 1940, in *Discours,
   messages et déclarations du Général de Gaulle*
   (1941) p. 15

4 Treaties, you see, are like girls and roses:
   they last while they last.
   Speech at Elysée Palace, 2 July 1963, in A.
   Passeron *De Gaulle parle 1962–6* (1966) p. 340

5 Authority doesn't work without prestige,
   or prestige without distance.
   Le Fil de l'épée (1932) 'Du caractère' sect. 2

6 The sword is the axis of the world and its
   power is absolute.
   Vers l'armée de métier (1934) 'Comment?'
   Commandement 3

7 How can you govern a country which has
   246 varieties of cheese?
   In E. Mignon *Les Mots du Général* (1962) p. 57

Thomas Dekker 1570–1641

8 That great fishpond (the sea).
   The Honest Whore (1604) pt. 1, act 1, sc. 2

9 Honest labour bears a lovely face.
   Patient Grissil (1603) act 1, sc. 1

10 Golden slumbers kiss your eyes,
   Smiles awake you when you rise:
   Sleep, pretty wantons, do not cry,
   And I will sing a lullaby.
   Patient Grissil (1603) act 4, sc. 2

Walter de la Mare 1873–1956

11 Ann, Ann!
   Come! quick as you can!
   There's a fish that *talks*
   In the frying-pan.
   'Alas, Alack' (1913)

12 Oh, no man knows
   Through what wild centuries
   Roves back the rose.
   'All That's Past' (1912)

13 He is crazed with the spell of far Arabia,
   They have stolen his wits away.
   'Arabia' (1912)

14 Beauty vanishes; beauty passes.
   'Epitaph' (1912)

15 Look thy last on all things lovely,
   Every hour.
   'Fare Well' (1918)

16 Nought but vast Sorrow was there —
   The sweet cheat gone.
   'The Ghost' (1918)

17 Three jolly gentlemen,
   In coats of red,
   Rode their horses
   Up to bed.
   'The Huntsmen' (1913)

18 'Is there anybody there?' said the Traveller,
   Knocking on the moonlit door.
   'The Listeners' (1912)

19 'Tell them I came, and no one answered,
   That I kept my word,' he said.
   'The Listeners' (1912)

20 And how the silence surged softly
   backward,
   When the plunging hoofs were gone.
   'The Listeners' (1912)

21 Softly along the road of evening,
   In a twilight dim with rose,
   Wrinkled with age, and drenched with
   dew,
   Old Nod, the shepherd, goes.
   'Nod' (1912)

22 Slowly, silently, now the moon
   Walks the night in her silver shoon.
   'Silver' (1913)

23 Behind the blinds I sit and watch
   The people passing—passing by;
   And not a single one can see
   My tiny watching eye.
   'The Window' (1913)

Walter de Leon and Paul M. Jones

24 It's a funny old world—a man's lucky if he
   gets out of it alive.
   You're Telling Me (1934 film); spoken by W. C.
   Fields

Jack Dempsey 1895–1983

25 Honey, I just forgot to duck.
   To his wife, on losing the World
   Heavyweight title, 23 September 1926, in J.
   and B. P. Dempsey *Dempsey* (1977) p. 202.
   After a failed attempt on his life in 1981,
   Ronald Reagan quipped 'I forgot to duck'

Sir John Denham 1615–69

26 Youth, what man's age is like to be doth
   show;
   We may our ends by our beginnings know.
   'Of Prudence' (1668) l. 225

Lord Denman 1779–1854

27 Trial by jury itself, instead of being a
   security to persons who are accused, will
   be a delusion, a mockery, and a snare.
   Speech in the House of Lords, 4 September
   1844; in E. W. Cox (ed.) *Reports of Cases in
   Criminal Law* (1846) vol. 1, p. 519

John Dennis 1657–1734

1 A man who could make so vile a pun
would not scruple to pick a pocket.
The Gentleman's Magazine (1781) p. 324
(editorial note)

2 Damn them! They will not let my play run,
but they steal my thunder!
On hearing his new thunder effects used at
a performance of *Macbeth*, following the
withdrawal of one of his own plays after
only a short run; in W. S. Walsh *Handy-Book
of Literary Curiosities* (1893) p. 1052

Thomas De Quincey 1785–1859

3 Oxford Street, stony-hearted stepmother,
thou that listenest to the sighs of orphans,
and drinkest the tears of children.
Confessions of an English Opium Eater (1822,
ed. 1856) pt. 1

4 A duller spectacle this earth of ours has
not to show than a rainy Sunday in
London.
Confessions of an English Opium Eater (1822,
ed. 1856) pt. 2

5 Murder considered as one of the fine arts.
Blackwood's Magazine February 1827 (essay
title)

Edward Stanley, 14th Earl of Derby 1799–1869

6 The duty of an Opposition [is] very simple
... to oppose everything, and propose
nothing.
Quoting 'Mr Tierney, a great Whig
authority', in *Hansard* 4 June 1841, col. 1188

7 Meddle and muddle.
Summarizing Earl Russell's foreign policy, in
Speech on the Address, *Hansard* (Lords)
4 February 1864, col. 28

René Descartes 1596–1650

8 Common sense is the best distributed
commodity in the world, for every man is
convinced that he is well supplied with it.
Le Discours de la méthode (1637) pt. 1

9 *Cogito, ergo sum.*
I think, therefore I am.
Le Discours de la méthode (1637) pt. 4

Philippe Néricault Destouches 1680–1754

10 The absent are always in the wrong.
L'Obstacle imprévu (1717) act 1, sc. 6

Robert Devereux, Earl of Essex

See ESSEX

Bernard De Voto 1897–1955

11 The proper union of gin and vermouth is a
great and sudden glory; it is one of the
happiest marriages on earth, and one of
the shortest lived.
Harper's Magazine December 1949, p. 70

Peter De Vries 1910–

12 The value of marriage is not that adults
produce children but that children produce
adults.
The Tunnel of Love (1954) ch. 8

Sir James Dewar 1842–1923

13 Minds are like parachutes. They only
function when they are open.
Attributed

Lord Dewar 1864–1930

14 [There are] only two classes of pedestrians
in these days of reckless motor traffic—the
quick, and the dead.
In George Robey *Looking Back on Life* (1933)
ch. 28

Sergei Diaghilev 1872–1929

15 *Étonne-moi.*
Astonish me.
To Jean Cocteau, in W. Fowlie (ed.) *Journals of
Jean Cocteau* (1956) ch. 1

Porfirio Diaz 1830–1915

16 Poor Mexico, so far from God and so close
to the United States.
Attributed

Charles Dibdin 1745–1814

17 Did you ever hear of Captain Wattle?
He was all for love, and a little for the
bottle.
'Captain Wattle and Miss Roe' (1797)

18 In every mess I finds a friend,
In every port a wife.
'Jack in his Element' (1790)

19 Here, a sheer hulk, lies poor Tom Bowling,
The darling of our crew.
'Tom Bowling' (1790)

Thomas Dibdin 1771–1841

20 Oh! what a snug little Island,
A right little, tight little Island!
'The Snug Little Island' (1833)

Charles Dickens 1812–70

21 There are strings ... in the human heart
that had better not be wibrated.
Barnaby Rudge (1841) ch. 22 (Mr Tappertit)

1 Jarndyce and Jarndyce still drags its dreary length before the Court, perennially hopeless.
   Bleak House (1853) ch. 1

2 This is a London particular ... A fog, miss.
   Bleak House (1853) ch. 3

3 'It is,' says Chadband, 'the ray of rays, the sun of suns, the moon of moons, the star of stars. It is the light of Terewth.'
   Bleak House (1853) ch. 25

4 The one great principle of the English law is, to make business for itself.
   Bleak House (1853) ch. 39

5 O let us love our occupations,
   Bless the squire and his relations,
   Live upon our daily rations,
   And always know our proper stations.
   The Chimes (1844) 'The Second Quarter'

6 'Bah,' said Scrooge. 'Humbug!'
   A Christmas Carol (1843) stave 1

7 'God bless us every one!' said Tiny Tim, the last of all.
   A Christmas Carol (1843) stave 3

8 I am a lone lorn creetur ... and everythink goes contrairy with me.
   David Copperfield (1850) ch. 3 (Mrs Gummidge)

9 Barkis is willin'.
   David Copperfield (1850) ch. 5

10 I live on broken wittles—and I sleep on the coals.
   David Copperfield (1850) ch. 5 (The Waiter)

11 I have known him come home to supper with a flood of tears, and a declaration that nothing was now left but a jail; and go to bed making a calculation of the expense of putting bow-windows to the house, 'in case anything turned up,' which was his favourite expression.
   David Copperfield (1850) ch. 11 (of Mr Micawber)

12 Annual income twenty pounds, annual expenditure nineteen nineteen six, result happiness. Annual income twenty pounds, annual expenditure twenty pounds ought and six, result misery.
   David Copperfield (1850) ch. 12 (Mr Micawber)

13 We live in a numble abode.
   David Copperfield (1850) ch. 16 (Uriah Heep)

14 We are so very 'umble.
   David Copperfield (1850) ch. 17 (Uriah Heep)

15 I only ask for information.
   David Copperfield (1850) ch. 20 (Miss Rosa Dartle)

16 Accidents will occur in the best-regulated families.
   David Copperfield (1850) ch. 28 (Mr Micawber)

17 It's only my child-wife.
   David Copperfield (1850) ch. 44 (of Dora)

18 I'm Gormed—and I can't say no fairer than that!
   David Copperfield (1850) ch. 63 (Mr Peggotty)

19 None of your live languages for Miss Blimber. They must be dead—stone dead—and then Miss Blimber dug them up like a Ghoul.
   Dombey and Son (1848) ch. 11

20 In the Proverbs of Solomon you will find the following words, 'May we never want a friend in need, nor a bottle to give him!' When found, make a note of.
   Dombey and Son (1848) ch. 15 (Captain Cuttle)

21 If you could see my legs when I take my boots off, you'd form some idea of what unrequited affection is.
   Dombey and Son (1848) ch. 48 (Mr Toots)

22 'He calls the knaves, Jacks, this boy,' said Estella with disdain.
   Great Expectations (1861) ch. 8

23 In the little world in which children have their existence, whosoever brings them up, there is nothing so finely perceived and so finely felt, as injustice.
   Great Expectations (1861) ch. 8

24 Her bringing me up by hand, gave her no right to bring me up by jerks.
   Great Expectations (1861) ch. 8

25 It is a most miserable thing to feel ashamed of home.
   Great Expectations (1861) ch. 14

26 On the Rampage, Pip, and off the Rampage, Pip; such is Life!
   Great Expectations (1861) ch. 15 (Joe Gargery)

27 Now, what I want is, Facts ... Facts alone are wanted in life.
   Hard Times (1854) bk. 1, ch. 1 (Mr Gradgrind)

28 People mutht be amuthed.
   Hard Times (1854) bk. 3, ch. 8 (Mr Sleary)

29 Whatever was required to be done, the Circumlocution Office was beforehand with all the public departments in the art of perceiving—HOW NOT TO DO IT.
   Little Dorrit (1857) bk. 1, ch. 10

30 I revere the memory of Mr F. as an estimable man and most indulgent husband, only necessary to mention Asparagus and it appeared or to hint at any little delicate thing to drink and it came like magic in a pint bottle it was not ecstasy but it was comfort.
   Little Dorrit (1857) bk. 1, ch. 24 (Flora Finching)

31 As to marriage on the part of a man, my dear, Society requires that he should retrieve his fortunes by marriage. Society requires that he should gain by marriage. Society requires that he should found a handsome establishment by marriage. Society does not see, otherwise, what he has to do with marriage.
   Little Dorrit (1857) bk. 1, ch. 33 (Mrs Merdle)

1 Father is rather vulgar, my dear. The word Papa, besides, gives a pretty form to the lips. Papa, potatoes, poultry, prunes, and prism, are all very good words for the lips: especially prunes and prism.
Little Dorrit (1857) bk. 2, ch. 5 (Mrs General)

2 Affection beaming in one eye, and calculation shining out of the other.
Martin Chuzzlewit (1844) ch. 8 (Mrs Todgers)

3 Here's the rule for bargains: 'Do other men, for they would do you.' That's the true business precept.
Martin Chuzzlewit (1844) ch. 11 (Jonas Chuzzlewit)

4 Brought reg'lar and draw'd mild.
Martin Chuzzlewit (1844) ch. 25 (Mrs Gamp on her 'half a pint of porter')

5 He'd make a lovely corpse.
Martin Chuzzlewit (1844) ch. 25 (Mrs Gamp)

6 We never knows wot's hidden in each other's hearts; and if we had glass winders there, we'd need keep the shutters up, some on us, I do assure you!
Martin Chuzzlewit (1844) ch. 29 (Mrs Gamp)

7 Howls the sublime, and softly sleeps the calm Ideal, in the whispering chambers of Imagination.
Martin Chuzzlewit (1844) ch. 34

8 His 'owls was organs.
Martin Chuzzlewit (1844) ch. 49 (Mrs Gamp)

9 The words she spoke of Mrs Harris, lambs could not forgive ... nor worms forget.
Martin Chuzzlewit (1844) ch. 49 (Mrs Gamp)

10 EDUCATION.—At Mr Wackford Squeers's Academy, Dotheboys Hall, at the delightful village of Dotheboys, near Greta Bridge in Yorkshire, Youth are boarded, clothed, booked, furnished with pocket-money, provided with all necessaries, instructed in all languages living and dead ... Terms, twenty guineas per annum. No extras, no vacations, and diet unparalleled.
Nicholas Nickleby (1839) ch. 3

11 He had but one eye, and the popular prejudice runs in favour of two.
Nicholas Nickleby (1839) ch. 4 (Mr Squeers)

12 Here's richness!
Nicholas Nickleby (1839) ch. 5 (Mr Squeers)

13 C-l-e-a-n, clean, verb active, to make bright, to scour. W-i-n, win, d-e-r, der, winder, a casement. When the boy knows this out of the book, he goes and does it.
Nicholas Nickleby (1839) ch. 8 (Mr Squeers)

14 As she frequently remarked when she made any such mistake, it would be all the same a hundred years hence.
Nicholas Nickleby (1839) ch. 9 (Mrs Squeers)

15 There are only two styles of portrait painting; the serious and the smirk.
Nicholas Nickleby (1839) ch. 10 (Miss La Creevy)

16 Language was not powerful enough to describe the infant phenomenon.
Nicholas Nickleby (1839) ch. 23

17 All is gas and gaiters.
Nicholas Nickleby (1839) ch. 49 (The Gentleman in the Small-clothes)

18 Please, sir, I want some more.
Oliver Twist (1838) ch. 2 (Oliver)

19 I only know two sorts of boys. Mealy boys, and beef-faced boys.
Oliver Twist (1838) ch. 14 (Mr Grimwig)

20 'If the law supposes that ... the law is a ass—a idiot.'
Oliver Twist (1838) ch. 51 (Bumble). Cf. 94:18

21 A literary man—with a wooden leg.
Our Mutual Friend (1865) bk. 1, ch. 5 (Mr Boffin, of Silas Wegg)

22 There is in the Englishman a combination of qualities, a modesty, an independence, a responsibility, a repose, combined with an absence of everything calculated to call a blush into the cheek of a young person, which one would seek in vain among the Nations of the Earth.
Our Mutual Friend (1865) bk. 1, ch. 11 (Mr Podsnap)

23 A slap-up gal in a bang-up chariot.
Our Mutual Friend (1865) bk. 2, ch. 8

24 He'd be sharper than a serpent's tooth, if he wasn't as dull as ditch water.
Our Mutual Friend (1865) bk. 3, ch. 10 (Fanny Cleaver)

25 I want to be something so much worthier than the doll in the doll's house.
Our Mutual Friend (1865) bk. 4, ch. 5 (Bella)

26 Kent, sir—everybody knows Kent—apples, cherries, hops, and women.
Pickwick Papers (1837) ch. 2 (Jingle)

27 I wants to make your flesh creep.
Pickwick Papers (1837) ch. 8 (The Fat Boy)

28 'It's always best on these occasions to do what the mob do.' 'But suppose there are two mobs?' suggested Mr Snodgrass. 'Shout with the largest,' replied Mr Pickwick.
Pickwick Papers (1837) ch. 13

29 Battledore and shuttlecock's a wery good game, vhen you an't the shuttlecock and two lawyers the battledores, in which case it gets too excitin' to be pleasant.
Pickwick Papers (1837) ch. 20 (Mr Weller)

30 Poverty and oysters always seem to go together.
Pickwick Papers (1837) ch. 22 (Sam Weller)

31 Dumb as a drum vith a hole in it, sir.
Pickwick Papers (1837) ch. 25 (Sam Weller)

32 A double glass o' the inwariable.
Pickwick Papers (1837) ch. 33 (Mr Weller)

33 'Do you spell it with a "V" or a "W"?' ... 'That depends upon the taste and fancy of the speller, my Lord.'
Pickwick Papers (1837) ch. 34 (Sam Weller)

34 'You must not tell us what the soldier, or any other man, said, sir,' interposed the judge; 'it's not evidence.'
Pickwick Papers (1837) ch. 34

1 A good uniform must work its way with
the women, sooner or later.
> *Pickwick Papers* (1837) ch. 37 (The Gentleman
> in Blue)

2 'And a bird-cage, sir,' says Sam. 'Veels
vithin veels, a prison in a prison.'
> *Pickwick Papers* (1837) ch. 40

3 The have-his-carcase, next to the perpetual
motion, is vun of the blessedest things as
wos ever made.
> *Pickwick Papers* (1837) ch. 43 (Sam Weller)

4 'Never ... see ... a dead postboy, did you?'
inquired Sam ... 'No,' rejoined Bob, 'I never
did.' 'No!' rejoined Sam triumphantly. 'Nor
never vill; and there's another thing that
no man never see, and that's a dead
donkey.'
> *Pickwick Papers* (1837) ch. 51

5 Minerva House ... where some twenty girls
... acquired a smattering of everything,
and a knowledge of nothing.
> *Sketches by Boz* (1839) Tales, ch. 3 'Sentiment'

6 It was the best of times, it was the worst
of times.
> *A Tale of Two Cities* (1859) bk. 1, ch. 1

7 It is a far, far better thing that I do, than I
have ever done; it is a far, far better rest
that I go to, than I have ever known.
> *A Tale of Two Cities* (1859) bk. 3, ch. 15

Emily Dickinson 1830–86

8 After great pain, a formal feeling comes.
> Title of poem (1862)

9 Because I could not stop for Death—
He kindly stopped for me—
The Carriage held but just Ourselves—
And Immortality.
> 'Because I could not stop for Death' (c.1863)

10 The Bustle in a House
The Morning after Death
Is solemnest of industries
Enacted upon Earth—

The Sweeping up the Heart
And putting Love away
We shall not want to use again
Until Eternity.
> 'The Bustle in a House' (c.1866)

11 My life closed twice before its close;
It yet remains to see
If Immortality unveil
A third event to me.
> 'My life closed twice before its close'

12 Parting is all we know of heaven,
And all we need of hell.
> 'My life closed twice before its close'

13 Success is counted sweetest
By those who ne'er succeed.
To comprehend a nectar
Requires sorest need.
> 'Success is counted sweetest' (1859)

14 There's a certain Slant of light,
Winter Afternoons—
That oppresses like the Heft
Of Cathedral Tunes.
> 'There's a certain Slant of light' (c.1861)

15 They shut me up in prose—
As when a little girl
They put me in the closet—
Because they liked me 'still'.
> 'They shut me up in prose' (c.1862)

16 This is my letter to the world.
> Title of poem (c.1862)

17 This quiet Dust was Gentlemen and Ladies
And Lads and Girls—
Was laughter and ability and Sighing
And Frocks and Curls.
> 'This quiet Dust was Gentlemen and Ladies'
> (c.1864)

John Dickinson 1732–1808

18 By uniting we stand, by dividing we fall.
> 'The Liberty Song' (1768), in *Writings of John
> Dickinson* vol. 1 (1895) p. 421

Paul Dickson 1939–

19 Rowe's Rule: the odds are five to six that
the light at the end of the tunnel is the
headlight of an oncoming train.
> *Washingtonian* November 1978. Cf. 211:18

Denis Diderot 1713–84

20 *L'esprit de l'escalier.*
Staircase wit.
> The witty riposte one thinks of only when
> one has left the drawing-room and is already
> on the way downstairs; in *Paradoxe sur le
> Comédien* (written 1773–8)

Joan Didion 1934–

21 Was there ever in anyone's life span a
point free in time, devoid of memory, a
night when choice was any more than the
sum of all the choices gone before?
> *Run River* (1963) ch. 4

Wentworth Dillon, Earl of Roscommon c.1633–1685

22 Choose an author as you choose a friend.
> *Essay on Translated Verse* (1684) l. 96

23 Immodest words admit of no defence,
For want of decency is want of sense.
> *Essay on Translated Verse* (1684) l. 113

24 The multitude is always in the wrong.
> *Essay on Translated Verse* (1684) l. 183

Ernest Dimnet

25 Architecture, of all the arts, is the one
which acts the most slowly, but the most
surely, on the soul.
> *What We Live By* (1932) pt. 2, ch. 12

Isak Dinesen (Karen Blixen)
1885–1962

1 A herd of elephant ... pacing along as if
they had an appointment at the end of the
world.
   Out of Africa (1937) pt. 1, ch. 1

2 What is man, when you come to think
upon him, but a minutely set, ingenious
machine for turning, with infinite
artfulness, the red wine of Shiraz into
urine?
   Seven Gothic Tales (1934) 'The Dreamers'

Diogenes *c.*400–*c.*325 BC

3 Alexander ... asked him if he lacked
anything. 'Yes,' said he, 'that I do: that you
stand out of my sun a little.'
   Plutarch *Parallel Lives* 'Alexander' ch. 14,
   sect. 4 (tr. T. North, 1579)

Dionysius of Halicarnassus
fl. 30–7 BC

4 History is philosophy from examples.
   Ars Rhetorica ch. 11, sect. 2

Benjamin Disraeli 1804–81

5 Though I sit down now, the time will come
when you will hear me.
   Maiden speech in the House of Commons;
   Hansard 7 December 1837, col. 807

6 The Continent will [not] suffer England to
be the workshop of the world.
   Speech, *Hansard* 15 March 1838, col. 940

7 Thus you have a starving population, an
absentee aristocracy, and an alien Church,
and in addition the weakest executive in
the world. That is the Irish Question.
   Speech, *Hansard* 16 February 1844, col. 1016

8 The noble Lord is the Prince Rupert of
Parliamentary discussion.
   Speech, *Hansard* 24 April 1844, col. 248 (of
   Lord Stanley). Cf. 78:9

9 The right hon. Gentleman caught the
Whigs bathing, and walked away with
their clothes.
   Speech, *Hansard* 28 February 1845, col. 154
   (on Sir Robert Peel's abandoning protection
   in favour of free trade, traditionally the
   policy of the [Whig] Opposition)

10 Protection is not a principle, but an
expedient.
   Speech, *Hansard* 17 March 1845, col. 1023

11 A Conservative Government is an
organized hypocrisy.
   Speech, *Hansard* 17 March 1845, col. 1028

12 Justice is truth in action.
   Speech, *Hansard* 11 February 1851, col. 412

13 England does not love coalitions.
   Speech, *Hansard* 16 December 1852, col. 1666

14 Party is organized opinion.
   Speech at Oxford, 25 November 1864, in *The
   Times* 26 November 1864

15 Is man an ape or an angel? Now I am on
the side of the angels.
   Speech at Oxford, 25 November 1864, in *The
   Times* 26 November 1864

16 You behold a range of exhausted volcanoes.
   Speaking of the Treasury Bench at
   Manchester, 3 April 1872; in *The Times* 4 April
   1872. Cf. 81:1

17 Cosmopolitan critics, men who are the
friends of every country save their own.
   Speech at Guildhall, 9 November 1877, in *The
   Times* 10 November 1877. Cf. 89:11, 243:8

18 Lord Salisbury and myself have brought
you back peace—but a peace I hope with
honour.
   Speech on returning from the Congress of
   Berlin, 16 July 1878, in *The Times* 17 July
   1878. Cf. 94:2, 265:6

19 A series of congratulatory regrets.
   Describing Lord Harrington's Resolution on
   the Berlin Treaty, 27 July 1878; in *The Times*
   29 July 1878

20 A sophistical rhetorician, inebriated with
the exuberance of his own verbosity.
   Of Gladstone, in *The Times* 29 July 1878

21 One of the greatest of Romans, when asked
what were his politics, replied, *Imperium et
Libertas*. That would not make a bad
programme for a British Ministry.
   Speech, 10 November 1879, paraphrasing
   Tacitus *Agricola* ch. 3. See *Notes and Queries*
   (8th series) vol. 10, p. 453

22 The key of India is London.
   Speech, *Hansard* 4 March 1881, col. 299

23 No Government can be long secure
without a formidable Opposition.
   Coningsby (1844) bk. 2, ch. 1

24 A government of statesmen or of clerks?
Of Humbug or Humdrum?
   Coningsby (1844) bk. 2, ch. 4

25 'A sound Conservative government,' said
Taper, musingly. 'I understand: Tory men
and Whig measures.'
   Coningsby (1844) bk. 2, ch. 6

26 Youth is a blunder; Manhood a struggle;
Old Age a regret.
   Coningsby (1844) bk. 3, ch. 1

27 It seems to me a barren thing this
Conservatism—an unhappy cross-breed,
the mule of politics that engenders
nothing.
   Coningsby (1844) bk. 3, ch. 5

28 Read no history: nothing but biography,
for that is life without theory.
   Contarini Fleming (1832) pt. 1, ch. 23.
   Cf. 136:22

29 His Christianity was muscular.
   Endymion (1880) ch. 14

1 Said Waldershare, 'Sensible men are all of the same religion.' 'And pray what is that?' ... 'Sensible men never tell.'
Endymion (1880) ch. 81. Cf. 270:20

2 The sweet simplicity of the three per cents.
Endymion (1880) ch. 91. Cf. 318:9

3 Time is the great physician.
Henrietta Temple (1837) bk. 6, ch. 9

4 The blue ribbon of the turf.
Lord George Bentinck (1852) ch. 26 (of the Derby)

5 London: a nation, not a city.
Lothair (1870) ch. 27

6 'Two nations; between whom there is no intercourse and no sympathy; who are as ignorant of each other's habits, thoughts, and feelings, as if they were dwellers in different zones, or inhabitants of different planets ... ' 'You speak of—' said Egremont, hesitatingly, 'THE RICH AND THE POOR.'
Sybil (1845) bk. 2, ch. 5. Cf. 144:8

7 That fatal drollery called a representative government.
Tancred (1847) bk. 2, ch. 13

8 The East is a career.
Tancred (1847) bk. 2, ch. 14

9 Experience is the child of Thought, and Thought is the child of Action. We cannot learn men from books.
Vivian Grey (1826) bk. 5, ch. 1

10 All power is a trust.
Vivian Grey (1826) bk. 6, ch. 7

11 'The age of chivalry is past,' said May Dacre. 'Bores have succeeded to dragons.'
The Young Duke (1831) bk. 2, ch. 5

12 We came here for fame.
To John Bright, in the House of Commons; in R. Blake *Disraeli* (1966) ch. 4

13 The school of Manchester.
Describing the free trade politics of Cobden and Bright; in R. Blake *Disraeli* (1966) ch. 10

14 I will not go down to posterity talking bad grammar.
Correcting proofs of his last Parliamentary speech, 31 March 1881; in R. Blake *Disraeli* (1966) ch. 32

15 Damn your principles! Stick to your party.
Attributed to Disraeli and believed to have been said to Edward Bulwer-Lytton; in E. Latham *Famous Sayings and their Authors* (1904) p. 11

16 Pray remember, Mr Dean, no dogma, no Dean.
In Monypenny and Buckle *Life of Disraeli* vol. 4 (1916) ch. 10

17 I have climbed to the top of the greasy pole.
On becoming Prime Minister, in Monypenny and Buckle *Life of Disraeli* vol. 4 (1916) ch. 16

18 I am dead; dead, but in the Elysian fields.
To a peer, on his elevation to the House of Lords; in Monypenny and Buckle *Life of Disraeli* vol. 5 (1920) ch. 13

19 Never complain and never explain.
In J. Morley *Life of Gladstone* (1903) vol. 1, p. 123. Cf. 139:24, 175:13

20 Everyone likes flattery; and when you come to Royalty you should lay it on with a trowel.
To Matthew Arnold, in G. W. E. Russell *Collections and Recollections* (1898) ch. 23

21 There are three kinds of lies: lies, damned lies and statistics.
Attributed to Disraeli in Mark Twain *Autobiography* (1924) vol. 1, p. 246

22 She would only ask me to take a message to Albert.
On his death-bed, declining the proposal of a visit from Queen Victoria; in R. Blake *Disraeli* (1966) ch. 32

Isaac D'Israeli 1766–1848

23 He wreathed the rod of criticism with roses.
Curiosities of Literature (9th ed., 1834) vol. 1, p. 20 (of Pierre Bayle)

William Chatterton Dix 1837–98

24 As with gladness men of old
Did the guiding star behold,
As with joy they hailed its light,
Leading onward, beaming bright.
'As with gladness men of old' (1861 hymn)

Henry Austin Dobson 1840–1921

25 All passes. Art alone
Enduring stays to us;
The Bust outlasts the throne,—
The Coin, Tiberius.
'Ars Victrix' (1876); translation of Théophile Gautier's 'L'Art'

26 Fame is a food that dead men eat,—
I have no stomach for such meat.
'Fame is a Food' (1906)

27 The ladies of St James's!
They're painted to the eyes;
Their white it stays for ever,
Their red it never dies.
'The Ladies of St James's' (1883)

28 Time goes, you say? Ah no!
Alas, Time stays, we go.
'The Paradox of Time' (1877)

Ken Dodd 1931–

29 The trouble with Freud is that he never had to play the old Glasgow Empire on a Saturday night after Rangers and Celtic had both lost.
Guardian 30 April 1991, p. 19 (quoted in many forms since the mid-1960s)

Philip Doddridge 1702–51

30 Ye servants of the Lord,
Each in his office wait,
Observant of his heavenly word
And watchful at his gate.
Hymns (1755) 'The active Christian'

Aelius Donatus 4th century

1 Confound those who have said our
  remarks before us.
  > In St Jerome *Commentary on Ecclesiastes* bk 1;
  > J.-P. Migne *Patrologiae Latinae* vol. 23, col. 1019

J. P. Donleavy 1926–

2 When you don't have any money, the
  problem is food. When you have money,
  it's sex. When you have both, it's health.
  > *The Ginger Man* (1955) ch. 5

John Donne 1572–1631

3 Love built on beauty, soon as beauty, dies.
  > *Elegies* 'The Anagram' (c.1595)

4 Whoever loves, if he do not propose
  The right true end of love, he's one that
  goes
  To sea for nothing but to make him sick.
  > *Elegies* 'Love's Progress' (c.1600)

5 Our first strange and fatal interview.
  > *Elegies* 'On His Mistress' (c.1600)

6 Licence my roving hands, and let them go,
  Behind, before, above, between, below.
  O my America, my new found land,
  My kingdom, safeliest when with one man
  manned.
  > *Elegies* 'To His Mistress Going to Bed' (c.1595)

7 At the round earth's imagined corners,
  blow
  Your trumpets, angels, and arise, arise
  From death, you numberless infinities
  Of souls, and to your scattered bodies go.
  > *Holy Sonnets* (1609) no. 4 (ed. J. Carey, 1990)

8 Death be not proud, though some have
  called thee
  Mighty and dreadful, for thou art not so.
  > *Holy Sonnets* (1609) no. 6 (ed. J. Carey, 1990)

9 One short sleep past, we wake eternally,
  And death shall be no more; Death thou
  shalt die.
  > *Holy Sonnets* (1609) no. 6 (ed. J. Carey, 1990)

10 Batter my heart, three-personed God; for,
  you
  As yet but knock, breathe, shine, and seek
  to mend.
  > *Holy Sonnets* (after 1609) no. 10 (ed. J. Carey,
  > 1990)

11 Take me to you, imprison me, for I
  Except you enthral me, never shall be free,
  Nor ever chaste, except you ravish me.
  > *Holy Sonnets* (after 1609) no. 10 (ed. J. Carey,
  > 1990)

12 I am a little world made cunningly
  Of elements, and an angelic sprite.
  > *Holy Sonnets* (after 1609) no. 15 (ed. J. Carey,
  > 1990)

13 What if this present were the world's last
  night?
  > *Holy Sonnets* (after 1609) no. 19 (ed. J. Carey,
  > 1990)

14   As thou
  Art jealous, Lord, so I am jealous now,
  Thou lov'st not, till from loving more, thou
  free
  My soul; who ever gives, takes liberty.
  > 'A Hymn to Christ, at the Author's last going
  > into Germany' (1619)

15 Seal then this bill of my divorce to all.
  > 'A Hymn to Christ, at the Author's last going
  > into Germany' (1619)

16 Since I am coming to that holy room,
  Where, with thy choir of saints for
  evermore,
  I shall be made thy music; as I come
  I tune the instrument here at the door,
  And what I must do then, think now
  before.
  > 'Hymn to God my God, in my Sickness'
  > (1623)

17 Wilt thou forgive that sin where I begun,
  Which is my sin, though it were done
  before?
  Wilt thou forgive those sins, through
  which I run
  And do them still: though still I do
  deplore?
  When thou hast done, thou hast not done,
  For, I have more.
  > 'A Hymn to God the Father' (1623)

18 Immensity cloistered in thy dear womb,
  Now leaves his well-beloved imprisonment.
  > *La Corona* (1609) 'Nativity'

19 Think then, my soul, that death is but a
  groom,
  Which brings a taper to the outward room.
  > *Of the Progress of the Soul: The Second
  > Anniversary* (1612) l. 85

20 Nature's great masterpiece, an elephant,
  The only harmless great thing.
  > 'The Progress of the Soul' (1601) st. 39

21   Just such disparity
  As is 'twixt air and angels' purity,
  'Twixt women's love, and men's will ever
  be.
  > *Songs and Sonnets* 'Air and Angels'

22 All other things, to their destruction draw,
  Only our love hath no decay;
  This, no tomorrow hath, nor yesterday,
  Running it never runs from us away,
  But truly keeps his first, last, everlasting
  day.
  > *Songs and Sonnets* 'The Anniversary'

23 Come live with me, and be my love,
  And we will some new pleasures prove
  Of golden sands, and crystal brooks,
  With silken lines, and silver hooks.
  > *Songs and Sonnets* 'The Bait'. Cf. 219:3, 253:20

24 For God's sake hold your tongue, and let
  me love.
  > *Songs and Sonnets* 'The Canonization'

1 Dear love, for nothing less than thee
   Would I have broke this happy dream,
   It was a theme
   For reason, much too strong for fantasy.
   Songs and Sonnets 'The Dream' ('Dear love, for
   nothing less than thee')

2 Where, like a pillow on a bed,
   A pregnant bank swelled up, to rest
   The violet's reclining head,
   Sat we two, one another's best.
   Songs and Sonnets 'The Ecstasy'

3 But O alas, so long, so far
   Our bodies why do we forbear?
   They're ours, though they're not we, we
   are
   The intelligencies, they the sphere.
   Songs and Sonnets 'The Ecstasy'

4 So must pure lovers' souls descend
   T'affections, and to faculties,
   Which sense may reach and apprehend,
   Else a great prince in prison lies.
   Songs and Sonnets 'The Ecstasy'

5 I wonder by my troth, what thou, and I
   Did, till we loved, were not weaned till
   then?
   But sucked on country pleasures,
   childishly?
   Or snorted we in the seven sleepers den?
   Songs and Sonnets 'The Good-Morrow'

6 Love is a growing or full constant light;
   And his first minute, after noon, is night.
   Songs and Sonnets 'A Lecture in the Shadow'

7 'Tis the year's midnight, and it is the day's.
   Songs and Sonnets 'A Nocturnal upon St Lucy's
   Day'

8 The world's whole sap is sunk:
   The general balm th'hydroptic earth hath
   drunk.
   Songs and Sonnets 'A Nocturnal upon St Lucy's
   Day'

9 When my grave is broke up again
   Some second guest to entertain,
   (For graves have learnt that woman-head
   To be to more than one a bed)
   And he that digs it, spies
   A bracelet of bright hair about the bone,
   Will he not let us alone?
   Songs and Sonnets 'The Relic'

10 Go, and catch a falling star,
   Get with child a mandrake root,
   Tell me, where all past years are,
   Or who cleft the Devil's foot.
   Songs and Sonnets 'Song: Go and catch a
   falling star'

11 Busy old fool, unruly sun,
   Why dost thou thus,
   Through windows, and through curtains
   call on us?
   Songs and Sonnets 'The Sun Rising'

12 Love, all alike, no season knows, nor clime,
   Nor hours, days, months, which are the
   rags of time.
   Songs and Sonnets 'The Sun Rising'

13 This bed thy centre is, these walls thy
   sphere.
   Songs and Sonnets 'The Sun Rising'

14 I am two fools, I know,
   For loving, and for saying so
   In whining poetry.
   Songs and Sonnets 'The Triple Fool'

15 So let us melt, and make no noise,
   No tear-floods, nor sigh-tempests move,
   'Twere profanation of our joys
   To tell the laity our love.
   Songs and Sonnets 'A Valediction: forbidding
   mourning'

16   O more than moon,
   Draw not up seas to drown me in thy
   sphere,
   Weep me not dead, in thine arms, but
   forbear
   To teach the sea what it may do too soon.
   Songs and Sonnets 'A Valediction: of Weeping'

17 Sir, more than kisses, letters mingle souls.
   'To Sir Henry Wotton' (1597–8)

18 But I do nothing upon my self, and yet I
   am mine own *Executioner*.
   Devotions upon Emergent Occasions (1624)
   'Meditation XII'

19 No man is an Island, entire of it self.
   Devotions upon Emergent Occasions (1624)
   'Meditation XVII'

20 Any man's death diminishes me, because I
   am involved in Mankind; And therefore
   never send to know for whom the bell
   tolls; it tolls for thee.
   Devotions upon Emergent Occasions (1624)
   'Meditation XVII'

21 I throw myself down in my Chamber, and I
   call in, and invite God, and his Angels
   thither, and when they are there, I neglect
   God and his Angels, for the noise of a fly,
   for the rattling of a coach, for the whining
   of a door.
   LXXX Sermons (1640) 12 December 1626 'At
   the Funeral of Sir William Cokayne'

22 Poor intricated soul! Riddling, perplexed,
   labyrinthical soul!
   LXXX Sermons (1640) 25 January 1628/9

23 John Donne, Anne Donne, Un-done.
   In a letter to his wife, on being dismissed
   from the service of his father-in-law, Sir
   George More; in Izaak Walton *Life of Dr Donne*
   (first printed in *LXXX Sermons*, 1640)

Sir Reginald Dorman-Smith
1899–1977

24 Dig for victory
   Radio broadcast as Minister of Agriculture
   and Fisheries, 3 October 1939; in *The Times*
   4 October 1939

Fedor Dostoevsky 1821–81

1 If you were to destroy in mankind the belief in immortality, not only love but every living force maintaining the life of the world would at once be dried up.

The Brothers Karamazov (1879–80) bk. 2, ch. 6

2 Beauty is mysterious as well as terrible. God and devil are fighting there, and the battlefield is the heart of man.

The Brothers Karamazov (1879–80) bk. 3, ch. 3

3 If the devil doesn't exist, but man has created him, he has created him in his own image and likeness.

The Brothers Karamazov (1879–80) bk. 5, ch. 4

4 Too high a price is asked for harmony; it's beyond our means to pay so much to enter. And so I hasten to give back my entrance ticket ... It's not God that I don't accept, Alyosha, only I most respectfully return Him the ticket.

The Brothers Karamazov (1879–80) bk. 5, ch. 4

5 Money is coined liberty.

House of the Dead (1862) pt. 1, ch. 1 (tr. Constance Garnett)

Lord Alfred Douglas 1870–1945

6 I am the Love that dare not speak its name.

'Two Loves' (1896)

James Douglas, 4th Earl of Morton c.1516–81

7 Here lies he who neither feared nor flattered any flesh.

Of John Knox, said as he was buried, 26 November 1572; in G. R. Preedy *Life of John Knox* (1940) ch. 7

Keith Douglas 1920–44

8 And all my endeavours are unlucky explorers
come back, abandoning the expedition.

'On Return from Egypt, 1943–4' (1946)

9 Remember me when I am dead
And simplify me when I'm dead.

'Simplify me when I'm Dead' (1941)

10 For here the lover and killer are mingled
who had one body and one heart.
And death, who had the soldier singled
has done the lover mortal hurt.

'Vergissmeinnicht, 1943'

Lorenzo Dow 1777–1834

11 You will be damned if you do—And you will be damned if you don't.

Reflections on the Love of God (1836) ch. 6 (on 'the doctrine of Particular Election')

Ernest Dowson 1867–1900

12 I have forgot much, Cynara! gone with the wind,
Flung roses, roses, riotously, with the throng,
Dancing, to put thy pale, lost lilies out of mind;
But I was desolate and sick of an old passion,
Yea, all the time, because the dance was long:
I have been faithful to thee, Cynara! in my fashion.

'Non Sum Qualis Eram' (1896). Cf. 173:30

13 They are not long, the days of wine and roses.

'Vitae Summa Brevis' (1896)

Sir Arthur Conan Doyle 1859–1930

14 Singularity is almost invariably a clue. The more featureless and commonplace a crime is, the more difficult is it to bring it home.

Adventures of Sherlock Holmes (1892) 'The Boscombe Valley Mystery'

15 It is quite a three-pipe problem.

Adventures of Sherlock Holmes (1892) 'The Red-Headed League'

16 You see, but you do not observe.

The Adventures of Sherlock Holmes (1892) 'Scandal in Bohemia'

17 Matilda Briggs ... was a ship which is associated with the giant rat of Sumatra, a story for which the world is not yet prepared.

Case-Book of Sherlock Homes (1927) 'The Sussex Vampire'

18 Good old Watson! You are the one fixed point in a changing age.

His Last Bow (1917) title story

19 'Excellent,' I cried. 'Elementary,' said he.

Memoirs of Sherlock Holmes (1894) 'The Crooked Man'. 'Elementary, my dear Watson' is not found in any book by Conan Doyle, although a review of the film *The Return of Sherlock Holmes* in *New York Times* 19 October 1929, p. 22, states: 'In the final scene Dr Watson is there with his "Amazing, Holmes", and Holmes comes forth with his "Elementary, my dear Watson, elementary" '

20 Ex-Professor Moriarty of mathematical celebrity ... is the Napoleon of crime.

Memoirs of Sherlock Holmes (1894) 'The Final Problem'

21 'The curious incident of the dog in the night-time.'
'The dog did nothing in the night-time.'
'That was the curious incident.

Memoirs of Sherlock Holmes (1894) 'Silver Blaze'

1 When you have eliminated the impossible, whatever remains, *however improbable*, must be the truth.
   The Sign of Four (1890) ch. 6

2 You know my methods. Apply them.
   The Sign of Four (1890) ch. 6

3 It is the unofficial force—the Baker Street irregulars.
   The Sign of Four (1890) ch. 8

4 London, that great cesspool into which all the loungers and idlers of the Empire are irresistibly drained.
   A Study in Scarlet (1888) ch. 1

5 It is a capital mistake to theorize before you have all the evidence. It biases the judgement.
   A Study in Scarlet (1888) ch. 3

6 Where there is no imagination there is no horror.
   A Study in Scarlet (1888) ch. 5

7 The vocabulary of 'Bradshaw' is nervous and terse, but limited.
   The Valley of Fear (1915) ch. 1

8 Mediocrity knows nothing higher than itself, but talent instantly recognizes genius.
   The Valley of Fear (1915) ch. 1

Margaret Drabble 1939–

9 England's not a bad country ... It's just a mean, cold, ugly, divided, tired, clapped-out, post-imperial, post-industrial slag-heap covered in polystyrene hamburger cartons.
   A Natural Curiosity (1989) p. 308

Sir Francis Drake c.1540–96

10 There must be a beginning of any great matter, but the continuing unto the end until it be thoroughly finished yields the true glory.
   Dispatch to Sir Francis Walsingham, 17 May 1587, in *Navy Records Society* vol. 11 (1898) p. 134

11 The singeing of the King of Spain's Beard.
   On the expedition to Cadiz, 1587, in Francis Bacon *Considerations touching a War with Spain* (1629)

12 I must have the gentleman to haul and draw with the mariner, and the mariner with the gentleman ... I would know him, that would refuse to set his hand to a rope, but I know there is not any such here.
   In J. S. Corbett *Drake and the Tudor Navy* (1898) vol. 1, ch. 9

13 There is plenty of time to win this game, and to thrash the Spaniards too.
   Attributed, in *Dictionary of National Biography* (1917–) vol. 5, p. 1342

Milton Drake et al.

14 Mares eat oats
   And does eat oats
   And little lambs eat ivy.
   'Mairzy Doats' (1943 song)

Michael Drayton 1563–1631

15 Ill news hath wings, and with the wind doth go,
   Comfort's a cripple and comes ever slow.
   The Barons' Wars (1603) canto 2, st. 28

16 Since there's no help, come let us kiss and part,
   Nay, I have done: you get no more of me,
   And I am glad, yea glad with all my heart,
   That thus so cleanly, I myself can free,
   Shake hands for ever, cancel all our vows,
   And when we meet at any time again,
   Be it not seen in either of our brows,
   That we one jot of former love retain.
   Idea (1619) Sonnet 61

17 That shire which we the Heart of England well may call.
   Poly-Olbion (1612–22) Song 13, l. 2 (of Warwickshire)

18 And thus began th'exordium of our woes,
   The fatal dumb-show of our misery.
   The Shepherd's Garland (1593) Eclogue 8

19 For that fine madness still he did retain
   Which rightly should possess a poet's brain.
   'To Henry Reynolds, of Poets and Poesy' (1627) l. 109 (of Marlowe)

20 Next these, learn'd Jonson, in this list I bring,
   Who had drunk deep of the Pierian spring.
   'To Henry Reynolds, of Poets and Poesy' (1627) l. 129. Cf. 251:28

21 These poor half-kisses kill me quite.
   'To His Coy Love' (1619)

22 Fair stood the wind for France
   When we our sails advance,
   Nor now to prove our chance
   Longer will tarry.
   To the Cambro-Britons (1619) 'Agincourt'

William Drennan 1754–1820

23 Nor one feeling of vengeance presume to defile
   The cause, or the men, of the Emerald Isle.
   Erin (1795) st. 3

John Drinkwater 1882–1937

24   Deep is the silence, deep
   On moon-washed apples of wonder.
   'Moonlit Apples' (1917)

Thomas Drummond 1797–1840

25 Property has its duties as well as its rights.
   Letter to the Earl of Donoughmore, 22 May 1838; in R. B. O'Brien *Thomas Drummond ... Life and Letters* (1889) p. 284

William Drummond of Hawthornden 1585–1649

1 Phoebus, arise,
And paint the sable skies,
With azure, white, and red.
'Song: Phoebus, arise' (1614)

John Dryden 1631–1700

2 In pious times, ere priestcraft did begin,
Before polygamy was made a sin.
Absalom and Achitophel (1681) pt. 1, l. 1

3 Then Israel's monarch, after Heaven's own heart,
His vigorous warmth did, variously, impart
To wives and slaves: and, wide as his command,
Scattered his Maker's image through the land.
Absalom and Achitophel (1681) pt. 1, l. 7

4 Plots, true or false, are necessary things,
To raise up commonwealths and ruin kings.
Absalom and Achitophel (1681) pt. 1, l. 83

5 Of these the false Achitophel was first,
A name to all succeeding ages curst.
Absalom and Achitophel (1681) pt. 1, l. 150

6 A fiery soul, which working out its way,
Fretted the pigmy body to decay:
And o'er informed the tenement of clay.
Absalom and Achitophel (1681) pt. 1, l. 156

7 Great wits are sure to madness near allied,
And thin partitions do their bounds divide.
Absalom and Achitophel (1681) pt. 1, l. 163

8 Bankrupt of life, yet prodigal of ease.
Absalom and Achitophel (1681) pt. 1, l. 168

9 And all to leave what with his toil he won
To that unfeathered two-legged thing, a son.
Absalom and Achitophel (1681) pt. 1, l. 169

10 All empire is no more than power in trust.
Absalom and Achitophel (1681) pt. 1, l. 411

11 But far more numerous was the herd of such
Who think too little and who talk too much.
Absalom and Achitophel (1681) pt. 1, l. 533

12 A man so various that he seemed to be
Not one, but all mankind's epitome.
Stiff in opinions, always in the wrong;
Was everything by starts, and nothing long.
Absalom and Achitophel (1681) pt. 1, l. 545

13 In squandering wealth was his peculiar art:
Nothing went unrewarded, but desert.
Absalom and Achitophel (1681) pt. 1, l. 559

14 And pity never ceases to be shown
To him, who makes the people's wrongs his own.
Absalom and Achitophel (1681) pt. 1, l. 725

15 Nor is the people's judgement always true:
The most may err as grossly as the few.
Absalom and Achitophel (1681) pt. 1, l. 781

16 Never was patriot yet, but was a fool.
Absalom and Achitophel (1681) pt. 1, l. 968

17 Beware the fury of a patient man.
Absalom and Achitophel (1681) pt. 1, l. 1005

18 Free from all meaning, whether good or bad,
And in one word, heroically mad.
Absalom and Achitophel (1681) pt. 2, l. 416

19 None but the brave deserves the fair.
Alexander's Feast (1697) l. 7

20 Sweet is pleasure after pain.
Alexander's Feast (1697) l. 60

21 War, he sung, is toil and trouble;
Honour but an empty bubble.
Never ending, still beginning,
Fighting still, and still destroying,
If the world be worth thy winning,
Think, oh think, it worth enjoying.
Alexander's Feast (1697) l. 97

22 Sighed and looked, and sighed again.
Alexander's Feast (1697) l. 120

23 Errors, like straws, upon the surface flow;
He who would search for pearls must dive below.
All for Love (1678) prologue

24 My love's a noble madness.
All for Love (1678) act 2, sc. 1

25 Men are but children of a larger growth;
Our appetites as apt to change as theirs,
And full as craving too, and full as vain.
All for Love (1678) act 4, sc. 1. Cf. 97:11

26 I am as free as nature first made man,
Ere the base laws of servitude began,
When wild in woods the noble savage ran.
The Conquest of Granada (1670) pt. 1, act 1, sc. 1

27 Thou strong seducer, opportunity!
The Conquest of Granada (1670) pt. 2, act 4, sc. 3

28 Bold knaves thrive without one grain of sense,
But good men starve for want of impudence.
Constantine the Great (1684) epilogue

29 My manhood, long misled by wandering fires,
Followed false lights.
The Hind and the Panther (1687) pt. 1, l. 72

30 Either be wholly slaves or wholly free.
The Hind and the Panther (1687) pt. 2, l. 285

31 Much malice mingled with a little wit.
The Hind and the Panther (1687) pt. 3, l. 1

32 For present joys are more to flesh and blood
Than a dull prospect of a distant good.
The Hind and the Panther (1687) pt. 3, l. 364

33 And love's the noblest frailty of the mind.
The Indian Emperor (1665) act 2, sc. 2.
Cf. 270:18

34 Repentance is the virtue of weak minds.
The Indian Emperor (1665) act 3, sc. 1

35 For all the happiness mankind can gain
Is not in pleasure, but in rest from pain.
The Indian Emperor (1665) act 4, sc. 1

1 War is the trade of kings.
   King Arthur (1691) act 2, sc. 2

2 Fairest Isle, all isles excelling,
   Seat of pleasures, and of loves;
   Venus here will choose her dwelling,
   And forsake her Cyprian groves.
   King Arthur (1691) act 5 'Song of Venus'

3 Ovid, the soft philosopher of love.
   Love Triumphant (1694) act 2, sc. 1

4 All human things are subject to decay,
   And, when fate summons, monarchs must
   obey.
   MacFlecknoe (1682) l. 1

5 The rest to some faint meaning make
   pretence,
   But Shadwell never deviates into sense.
   Some beams of wit on other souls may fall,
   Strike through and make a lucid interval;
   But Shadwell's genuine night admits no
   ray,
   His rising fogs prevail upon the day.
   MacFlecknoe (1682) l. 19

6 And torture one poor word ten thousand
   ways.
   MacFlecknoe (1682) l. 208

7 I am to be married within these three
   days; married past redemption.
   Marriage à la Mode (1672) act 1, sc. 1

8 But treason is not owned when 'tis
   descried;
   Successful crimes alone are justified.
   The Medal (1682) l. 207

9 But love's a malady without a cure.
   Palamon and Arcite (1700) bk. 2, l. 110

10 Antony, who lost the world for love.
   Palamon and Arcite (1700) bk. 2, l. 607

11 Repentance is but want of power to sin.
   Palamon and Arcite (1700) bk. 3, l. 813

12 Like pilgrims to th'appointed place we
   tend;
   The world's an inn, and death the journey's
   end.
   Palamon and Arcite (1700) bk. 3, l. 887

13 A virgin-widow, and a *mourning bride*.
   Palamon and Arcite (1700) bk. 3, l. 927

14 And this unpolished rugged verse I chose
   As fittest for discourse and nearest prose.
   Religio Laici (1682) l. 453

15 A very merry, dancing, drinking,
   Laughing, quaffing, and unthinking time.
   The Secular Masque (1700) l. 39

16 For secrets are edged tools,
   And must be kept from children and from
   fools.
   Sir Martin Mar-All (1667) act 2, sc. 2

17 What passion cannot Music raise and
   quell?
   A Song for St Cecilia's Day (1687) st. 2

18 The soft complaining flute.
   A Song for St Cecilia's Day (1687) st. 4

19　　　　　There is a pleasure sure,
   In being mad, which none but madmen
   know!
   The Spanish Friar (1681) act 1, sc. 1

20 Mute and magnificent, without a tear.
   Threnodia Augustalis (1685) st. 2

21　　　　　Wit will shine
   Through the harsh cadence of a rugged
   line.
   'To the Memory of Mr Oldham' (1684)

22 All delays are dangerous in war.
   Tyrannic Love (1669) act 1, sc. 1

23 I can enjoy her while she's kind;
   But when she dances in the wind,
   And shakes the wings, and will not stay,
   I puff the prostitute away.
   Translation of Horace *Odes* bk. 3, no. 29 (of
   Fortune)

24 She knows her man, and when you rant
   and swear,
   Can draw you to her *with a single hair*.
   Translation of Persius *Satires* no. 5, l. 246

25 Arms, and the man I sing, who, forced by
   fate,
   And haughty Juno's unrelenting hate,
   Expelled and exiled, left the Trojan shore.
   Translation of Virgil *Aeneid* (*Aeneis*, 1697)
   bk. 1, l. 1. Cf. 338:23

26 We must beat the iron while it is hot, but
   we may polish it at leisure.
   Aeneis (1697) dedication

27 A thing well said will be wit in all
   languages.
   Essay of Dramatic Poesy (1668)

28 He is many times flat, insipid; his comic
   wit degenerating into clenches, his serious
   swelling into bombast. But he is always
   great.
   Essay of Dramatic Poesy (1668) of Shakespeare

29 He invades authors like a monarch; and
   what would be theft in other poets, is only
   victory in him.
   Essay of Dramatic Poesy (1668) of Ben Jonson

30 'Tis sufficient to say [of Chaucer], according
   to the proverb, that here is God's plenty.
   Fables Ancient and Modern (1700) preface

Alexander Dubček 1921–92

31 In the service of the people we followed
   such a policy that socialism would not lose
   its human face.
   In *Rudé Právo* 19 July 1968

Joachim Du Bellay 1522–60

32 *France, mère des arts, des armes et des lois.*
   France, mother of arts, of warfare, and of
   laws.
   Les Regrets (1558) Sonnet 9

33 *Heureux qui comme Ulysse a fait un beau
   voyage.*
   Happy he who like Ulysses has made a
   great journey.
   Les Regrets (1558) Sonnet 31

Mme Du Deffand 1697–1780

1 The distance is nothing; it is only the first step that is difficult.

Commenting on the legend that St Denis, carrying his head in his hands, walked two leagues: letter to Jean Le Rond d'Alembert, 7 July 1763, in G. Maugras *Trois mois à la cour de Frédéric* (1886) p. 28

John Foster Dulles 1888–1959

2 The ability to get to the verge without getting into the war is the necessary art ... We walked to the brink and we looked it in the face.

In *Life* 16 January 1956

Alexandre Dumas 1802–70

3 *Cherchons la femme.*
Let us look for the woman.

Les Mohicans de Paris (1854–5) *passim*; attributed to Joseph Fouché (1763–1820) in the form 'Cherchez la femme'

4 *Tous pour un, un pour tous.*
All for one, one for all.

Les Trois Mousquetaires (1844) ch. 9

Daphne Du Maurier 1907–89

5 Last night I dreamt I went to Manderley again.

Rebecca (1938) ch. 1

General Dumouriez 1739–1823

6 The courtiers who surround him have forgotten nothing and learnt nothing.

Of Louis XVIII, in *Examen impartial d'un Écrit intitulé Déclaration de Louis XVIII* (1795) p. 40

Paul Lawrence Dunbar 1872–1906

7 I know why the caged bird sings!

'Sympathy' st. 3. Cf. 344:27

William Dunbar *c.*1465–*c.*1513

8 *Timor mortis conturbat me.*
The fear of death disquiets me.

'Lament for the Makaris [poets]'

Ian Dunlop 1925–

9 The shock of the new.

Title of book about modern art (1972)

John Dunning, Baron Ashburton 1731–83

10 The influence of the Crown has increased, is increasing, and ought to be diminished.

Resolution passed in the House of Commons, 6 April 1780; in *Parliamentary History of England* (T. C. Hansard, 1814) vol. 21, col. 347

James Duport 1606–79

11 *Quem Jupiter vult perdere, dementat prius.*
Whom God would destroy He first sends mad.

Homeri Gnomologia (1660) p. 282. Cf. 13:8

Richard Duppa 1770–1831

12 In language, the ignorant have prescribed laws to the learned.

Maxims (1830) no. 252

Leo Durocher 1906–91

13 Nice guys. Finish last.

Casual remark at a baseball ground, July 1946; in *Nice Guys Finish Last* (as the remark generally is quoted, 1975) pt. 1, p. 14

Ian Dury 1942–

14 Sex and drugs and rock and roll.

Title of song (1977)

Sir Edward Dyer d. 1607

15 Silence augmenteth grief, writing increaseth rage,
Staled are my thoughts, which loved and lost, the wonder of our age.

'Elegy on the Death of Sir Philip Sidney' (1593) (formerly attributed to Fulke Greville, 1554–1628)

16 My mind to me a kingdom is.
Such perfect joy therein I find
That it excels all other bliss
That world affords or grows by kind.
Though much I want which most would have,
Yet still my mind forbids to crave.

'In praise of a contented mind' (1588)

John Dyer 1700–58

17 But transient is the smile of fate:
A little rule, a little sway,
A sunbeam in a winter's day,
Is all the proud and mighty have
Between the cradle and the grave.

Grongar Hill (1726) l. 88

John Dyer

18 And he that will this health deny,
Down among the dead men let him lie.

'Down among the Dead Men' (*c.*1700)

Bob Dylan 1941–

19 How many roads must a man walk down
Before you can call him a man? ...
The answer, my friend, is blowin' in the wind,
The answer is blowin' in the wind.

'Blowin' in the Wind' (1962 song)

20 And Ezra Pound and T. S. Eliot
Fighting in the captain's tower.

'Desolation Row' (1965 song)

1 Don't think twice, it's all right.
Title of song (1963)

2 A hard rain's a gonna fall.
Title of song (1963)

3 Money doesn't talk, it swears.
'It's Alright, Ma (I'm Only Bleeding)' (1965 song)

4 She knows there's no success like failure
And that failure's no success at all.
'Love Minus Zero / No Limit' (1965 song)

5 Hey! Mr Tambourine Man, play a song for me.
I'm not sleepy and there is no place I'm going to.
'Mr Tambourine Man' (1965 song)

6 Ah, but I was so much older then,
I'm younger than that now.
'My Back Pages' (1964 song)

7 Señor, señor, do you know where we're headin'?
Lincoln County Road or Armageddon?
'Señor (Tale of Yankee Power)' (1978 song)

8 All that foreign oil controlling American soil.
'Slow Train' (1979 song)

9 Come mothers and fathers,
Throughout the land
And don't criticize
What you can't understand.
'The Times They Are A-Changing' (1964 song)

Sir Arthur Eddington 1882–1944

10 I shall use the phrase 'time's arrow' to express this one-way property of time which has no analogue in space.
The Nature of the Physical World (1928) ch. 4

11 If your theory is found to be against the second law of thermodynamics I can give you no hope; there is nothing for it but to collapse in deepest humiliation.
The Nature of the Physical World (1928) ch. 14

12 I ask you to look both ways. For the road to a knowledge of the stars leads through the atom; and important knowledge of the atom has been reached through the stars.
Stars and Atoms (1928) Lecture 1

13 Science is an edged tool, with which men play like children, and cut their own fingers.
Attributed in R. L. Weber *More Random Walks in Science* (1982) p. 48

Sir Anthony Eden (Earl of Avon) 1897–1977

14 We are in an armed conflict; that is the phrase I have used. There has been no declaration of war.
Speech, *Hansard* 1 November 1956, col. 1641 (on the Suez crisis)

Marriott Edgar 1880–1951

15 There's a famous seaside place called Blackpool,
That's noted for fresh air and fun,
And Mr and Mrs Ramsbottom
Went there with young Albert, their son.
'The Lion and Albert' (1932)

Maria Edgeworth 1768–1849

16 Well! some people talk of morality, and some of religion, but give me a little snug property.
The Absentee (1812) ch. 2

17 Business was his aversion; pleasure was his business.
The Contrast (1804) ch. 2

18 Man is to be held only by the *slightest* chains, with the idea that he can break them at pleasure, he submits to them in sport.
Letters for Literary Ladies (1795) 'Letters of Julia and Caroline' no. 1

Thomas Alva Edison 1847–1931

19 Genius is one per cent inspiration, ninety-nine per cent perspiration.
Said *c*.1903, in *Harper's Monthly Magazine* September 1932. Cf. 78:6

John Maxwell Edmonds 1875–1958

20 When you go home, tell them of us and say,
'For your tomorrows these gave their today.'
Inscriptions Suggested for War Memorials (1919)

Edward III 1312–77

21 Also say to them, that they suffre hym this day to wynne his spurres, for if god be pleased, I woll this journey be his, and the honoure therof.
Speaking of the Black Prince at Crécy, 1345 (commonly quoted 'Let the boy win his spurs'); in *Chronicle of Froissart* (tr. Sir John Bourchier, Lord Berners, 1523–5) ch. 130

Edward VII 1841–1910

22 I thought everyone must know that a *short* jacket is always worn with a silk hat at a private view in the morning.
To Sir Frederick Ponsonby, who had proposed accompanying him in a tail-coat; in Sir Philip Magnus *Edward VII* (1964) ch. 19

Edward VIII (Duke of Windsor)
1894–1972

1 These works brought all these people here. Something should be done to get them at work again.
   > Speaking at the derelict Dowlais Iron and Steel Works, 18 November 1936; in *Western Mail* 19 November 1936 (generally quoted 'Something must be done')

2 At long last I am able to say a few words of my own ... you must believe me when I tell you that I have found it impossible to carry the heavy burden of responsibility and to discharge my duties as King as I would wish to do without the help and support of the woman I love.
   > Radio broadcast following his abdication, 11 December 1936; in *The Times* 12 December 1936

Jonathan Edwards 1703–58

3 I ... once saw a very large spider to my surprise swimming in the air ... and others have assured me that they often have seen spiders fly, the appearance is truly very pretty and pleasing.
   > *The Flying Spider—Observations by Jonathan Edwards when a boy* 'Of Insects'; in *Andover Review* vol. 13 (1890) p. 5

4 The bodies of those that made such a noise and tumult when alive, when dead, lie as quietly among the graves of their neighbours as any others.
   > Sermon on procrastination (*Miscellaneous Discourses*) in *Works* (1834) vol. 2, p. 241

Oliver Edwards 1711–91

5 I have tried too in my time to be a philosopher; but, I don't know how, cheerfulness was always breaking in.
   > In James Boswell *Life of Samuel Johnson* (1934 ed.) vol. 3, p. 305 (17 April 1778)

6 For my part now, I consider supper as a turnpike through which one must pass, in order to get to bed.
   > In James Boswell *Life of Samuel Johnson* (1934 ed.) vol. 3, p. 306 (17 April 1778)

John Ehrlichman 1925–

7 I think we ought to let him hang there. Let him twist slowly, slowly in the wind.
   > Speaking of Patrick Gray (regarding his nomination as director of the FBI); in *Washington Post* 27 July 1973, p. A27

Albert Einstein 1879–1955

8 God is subtle but he is not malicious.
   > Remark made at Princeton University, May 1921; in R. W. Clark *Einstein* (1973) ch. 14

9 I am convinced that *He* [God] does not play dice.
   > Letter to Max Born, 4 December 1926; in *Einstein und Born Briefwechsel* (1969) p. 130

10 If A is a success in life, then A equals x plus y plus z. Work is x; y is play; and z is keeping your mouth shut.
   > In *Observer* 15 January 1950

11 Science without religion is lame, religion without science is blind.
   > *Science, Philosophy and Religion* (1941) ch. 13

12 Equations are more important to me, because politics is for the present, but an equation is something for eternity.
   > In Stephen Hawking *A Brief History of Time* (1988) p. 178. See also C. P. Snow 'Einstein' in M. Goldsmith et al. (eds.) *Einstein* (1980)

13 I never think of the future. It comes soon enough.
   > In an interview, given on the *Belgenland*, December 1930

Dwight D. Eisenhower 1890–1969

14 This world in arms is not spending money alone. It is spending the sweat of its labourers, the genius of its scientists, the hopes of its children.
   > Speech in Washington, 16 April 1953; in *Public Papers of Presidents 1953* (1960) p. 182

15 You have broader considerations that might follow what you might call the 'falling domino' principle. You have a row of dominoes set up. You knock over the first one, and what will happen to the last one is that it will go over very quickly.
   > Speech at press conference, 7 April 1954; in *Public Papers of Presidents 1954* (1960) p. 383

16 I think that people want peace so much that one of these days governments had better get out of the way and let them have it.
   > Broadcast discussion, 31 August 1959; in *Public Papers of Presidents 1959* (1960) p. 625

Sir Edward Elgar 1857–1934

17 To my friends pictured within.
   > *Enigma Variations* (1899) dedication

18 There is music in the air.
   > In R. J. Buckley *Sir Edward Elgar* (1905) ch. 4

George Eliot (Mary Ann Evans)
1819–80

19 We hand folks over to God's mercy, and show none ourselves.
   > *Adam Bede* (1859) ch. 42

20 Gossip is a sort of smoke that comes from the dirty tobacco-pipes of those who diffuse it: it proves nothing but the bad taste of the smoker.
   > *Daniel Deronda* (1876) bk. 2, ch. 13

1 A difference of taste in jokes is a great
strain on the affections.
Daniel Deronda (1876) bk. 2, ch. 15

2 There is a great deal of unmapped country
within us which would have to be taken
into account in an explanation of our
gusts and storms.
Daniel Deronda (1876) bk. 3, ch. 24

3 Half the sorrows of women would be
averted if they could repress the speech
they know to be useless; nay, the speech
they have resolved not to make.
Felix Holt (1866) ch. 2

4 An election is coming. Universal peace is
declared, and the foxes have a sincere
interest in prolonging the lives of the
poultry.
Felix Holt (1866) ch. 5

5 A woman can hardly ever choose ... she is
dependent on what happens to her. She
must take meaner things, because only
meaner things are within her reach.
Felix Holt (1866) ch. 27

6 'Abroad', that large home of ruined
reputations.
Felix Holt (1866) epilogue

7 Debasing the moral currency.
The Impressions of Theophrastus Such (1879)
essay title

8 A woman dictates before marriage in order
that she may have an appetite for
submission afterwards.
Middlemarch (1871–2) bk. 1, ch. 9

9 He said he should prefer not to know the
sources of the Nile, and that there should
be some unknown regions preserved as
hunting-grounds for the poetic
imagination.
Middlemarch (1871–2) bk. 1, ch. 9

10 If we had a keen vision and feeling of all
ordinary human life, it would be like
hearing the grass grow and the squirrel's
heart beat, and we should die of that roar
which lies on the other side of silence.
Middlemarch (1871–2) bk. 2, ch. 20

11 We do not expect people to be deeply
moved by what is not unusual. That
element of tragedy which lies in the very
fact of frequency, has not yet wrought
itself into the coarse emotion of mankind.
Middlemarch (1871–2) bk. 2, ch. 20

12 Anger and jealousy can no more bear to
lose sight of their objects than love.
The Mill on the Floss (1860) bk. 1, ch. 10

13 The dead level of provincial existence.
The Mill on the Floss (1860) bk. 5, ch. 3

14 The happiest women, like the happiest
nations, have no history.
The Mill on the Floss (1860) bk. 6, ch. 3.
Cf. 233:22

15 'Character' says Novalis, in one of his
questionable aphorisms—'character is
destiny.'
The Mill on the Floss (1860) bk. 6, ch. 6.
Cf. 240:12

16 In every parting there is an image of
death.
Scenes of Clerical Life (1858) 'Amos Barton'
ch. 10

17 Oh may I join the choir invisible
Of those immortal dead who live again
In minds made better by their presence.
'Oh May I Join the Choir Invisible' (1867)

T. S. Eliot 1888–1965

18 Because I do not hope to turn again
Because I do not hope
Because I do not hope to turn.
Ash-Wednesday (1930) pt. 1

19 Teach us to care and not to care
Teach us to sit still.
Ash-Wednesday (1930) pt. 1

20 Lady, three white leopards sat under a
juniper-tree
In the cool of the day.
Ash-Wednesday (1930) pt. 2

21 What is hell?
Hell is oneself,
Hell is alone, the other figures in it
Merely projections.
The Cocktail Party (1950) act 1, sc. 3. Cf. 267:4

22 Over buttered scones and crumpets
Weeping, weeping multitudes
Droop in a hundred A.B.C.'s.
'Cooking Egg' (1920)

23 Success is relative:
It is what we can make of the mess we
have made of things.
The Family Reunion (1939) pt. 2, sc. 3

24 Round and round the circle
Completing the charm
So the knot be unknotted
The cross be uncrossed
The crooked be made straight
And the curse be ended.
The Family Reunion (1939) pt. 2, sc. 3

25 Time present and time past
Are both perhaps present in time future,
And time future contained in time past.
Four Quartets 'Burnt Norton' (1936) pt. 1

26 Footfalls echo in the memory
Down the passage which we did not take
Towards the door we never opened
Into the rose-garden.
Four Quartets 'Burnt Norton' (1936) pt. 1

27 Human kind
Cannot bear very much reality.
Four Quartets 'Burnt Norton' (1936) pt. 1.

28 At the still point of the turning world.
Four Quartets 'Burnt Norton' (1936) pt. 2

1   Words strain,
Crack and sometimes break, under the
     burden,
Under the tension, slip, slide, perish,
Decay with imprecision, will not stay in
     place,
Will not stay still.
Four Quartets 'Burnt Norton' (1936) pt. 5

2 In my beginning is my end.
Four Quartets 'East Coker' (1940) pt. 1.
Cf. 221:16

3   The intolerable wrestle
With words and meanings.
Four Quartets 'East Coker' (1940) pt. 2

4 The houses are all gone under the sea.
The dancers are all gone under the hill.
Four Quartets 'East Coker' (1940) pt. 2

5 The wounded surgeon plies the steel
That questions the distempered part;
Beneath the bleeding hands we feel
The sharp compassion of the healer's art
Resolving the enigma of the fever chart.
Four Quartets 'East Coker' (1940) pt. 4

6   Each venture
Is a new beginning, a raid on the
     inarticulate
With shabby equipment always
     deteriorating
In the general mess of imprecision of
     feeling.
Four Quartets 'East Coker' (1940) pt. 5

7   I think that the river
Is a strong brown god.
Four Quartets 'The Dry Salvages' (1941) pt. 1

8 Ash on an old man's sleeve
Is all the ash the burnt roses leave.
Four Quartets 'Little Gidding' (1942) pt. 2

9   Speech impelled us
To purify the dialect of the tribe.
Four Quartets 'Little Gidding' (1942) pt. 2

10 And the end of all our exploring
Will be to arrive where we started
And know the place for the first time.
Four Quartets 'Little Gidding' (1942) pt. 5

11 What we call the beginning is often the
     end
And to make an end is to make a
     beginning.
The end is where we start from.
Four Quartets 'Little Gidding' (1942) pt. 5

12   So, while the light fails
On a winter's afternoon, in a secluded
     chapel
History is now and England.
Four Quartets 'Little Gidding' (1942) pt. 5

13 And all shall be well and
All manner of thing shall be well
When the tongues of flame are in-folded
Into the crowned knot of fire
And the fire and the rose are one.
Four Quartets 'Little Gidding' (1942) pt. 5.
Cf. 188:21

14 Here I am, an old man in a dry month
Being read to by a boy, waiting for rain.
'Gerontion' (1920)

15 After such knowledge, what forgiveness?
'Gerontion' (1920)

16 Tenants of the house,
Thoughts of a dry brain in a dry season.
'Gerontion' (1920)

17 We are the hollow men
We are the stuffed men
Leaning together
Headpiece filled with straw. Alas!
'The Hollow Men' (1925)

18 Here we go round the prickly pear
Prickly pear prickly pear.
'The Hollow Men' (1925)

19 Between the idea
And the reality
Between the motion
And the act
Falls the Shadow.
'The Hollow Men' (1925)

20 This is the way the world ends
Not with a bang but a whimper.
'The Hollow Men' (1925)

21 A cold coming we had of it,
Just the worst time of the year
For a journey, and such a long journey:
The ways deep and the weather sharp,
The very dead of winter.
'Journey of the Magi' (1927). Cf. 5:15

22   I had seen birth and death
But had thought they were different.
'Journey of the Magi' (1927)

23 An alien people clutching their gods.
'Journey of the Magi' (1927)

24 Let us go then, you and I,
When the evening is spread out against
     the sky
Like a patient etherized upon a table.
'Love Song of J. Alfred Prufrock' (1917)

25 In the room the women come and go
Talking of Michelangelo.
'Love Song of J. Alfred Prufrock' (1917)

26 The yellow fog that rubs its back upon the
     window-panes.
'Love Song of J. Alfred Prufrock' (1917)

27 I have measured out my life with coffee
     spoons.
'Love Song of J. Alfred Prufrock' (1917)

28 I should have been a pair of ragged claws
Scuttling across the floors of silent seas.
'Love Song of J. Alfred Prufrock' (1917)

29 I have seen the moment of my greatness
     flicker,
And I have seen the eternal Footman hold
     my coat, and snicker,
And in short, I was afraid.
'Love Song of J. Alfred Prufrock' (1917)

1 No! I am not Prince Hamlet, nor was
   meant to be;
   Am an attendant lord, one that will do
   To swell a progress, start a scene or two,
   Advise the prince.
   'Love Song of J. Alfred Prufrock' (1917)

2 I grow old ... I grow old ...
   I shall wear the bottoms of my trousers
   rolled.
   'Love Song of J. Alfred Prufrock' (1917)

3 Shall I part my hair behind? Do I dare to
   eat a peach?
   'Love Song of J. Alfred Prufrock' (1917)

4 I am aware of the damp souls of
   housemaids
   Sprouting despondently at area gates.
   'Morning at the Window' (1917)

5 The sapient sutlers of the Lord.
   'Mr Eliot's Sunday Morning Service' (1919)

6 Yet we have gone on living,
   Living and partly living.
   Murder in the Cathedral (1935) pt. 1

7 The last temptation is the greatest treason:
   To do the right deed for the wrong reason.
   Murder in the Cathedral (1935) pt. 1

8 Clear the air! clean the sky! wash the wind!
   Murder in the Cathedral (1935) pt. 2

9 He always has an alibi, and one or two to
   spare:
   At whatever time the deed took place—
   MACAVITY WASN'T THERE!
   Old Possum's Book of Practical Cats (1939)
   'Macavity: the Mystery Cat'

10 The winter evening settles down
   With smell of steaks in passageways.
   Six o'clock.
   The burnt-out ends of smoky days.
   'Preludes' (1917)

11 Midnight shakes the memory
   As a madman shakes a dead geranium.
   'Rhapsody on a Windy Night' (1917)

12 Where is the wisdom we have lost in
   knowledge?
   Where is the knowledge we have lost in
   information?
   The Rock (1934) pt. 1

13 ... Here were decent godless people:
   Their only monument the asphalt road
   And a thousand lost golf balls.
   The Rock (1934) pt. 1

14 Birth, and copulation, and death.
   That's all the facts when you come to brass
   tacks.
   Sweeney Agonistes (1932) 'Fragment of an
   Agon'

15 Any man has to, needs to, wants to
   Once in a lifetime, do a girl in.
   Sweeney Agonistes (1932) 'Fragment of an
   Agon'

16 I gotta use words when I talk to you.
   Sweeney Agonistes (1932) 'Fragment of an
   Agon'

17 The nightingales are singing near
   The Convent of the Sacred Heart,

   And sang within the bloody wood
   When Agamemnon cried aloud
   And let their liquid siftings fall
   To stain the stiff dishonoured shroud.
   'Sweeney among the Nightingales' (1919)

18 April is the cruellest month, breeding
   Lilacs out of the dead land.
   The Waste Land (1922) pt. 1

19 I read, much of the night, and go south in
   the winter.
   The Waste Land (1922) pt. 1

20 I will show you fear in a handful of dust.
   The Waste Land (1922) pt. 1

21 A crowd flowed over London Bridge, so
   many,
   I had not thought death had undone so
   many.
   The Waste Land (1922) pt. 1

22 And still she cried, and still the world
   pursues,
   'Jug Jug' to dirty ears.
   The Waste Land (1922) pt. 2. Cf. 212:17

23 I think we are in rats' alley
   Where the dead men lost their bones.
   The Waste Land (1922) pt. 2

24 O O O O that Shakespeherian Rag—
   It's so elegant
   So intelligent.
   The Waste Land (1922) pt. 2. Cf. 77:31

25 Hurry up please it's time.
   The Waste Land (1922) pt. 2

26 O the moon shone bright on Mrs Porter
   And on her daughter
   They wash their feet in soda water.
   The Waste Land (1922) pt. 3

27 At the violet hour, when the eyes and back
   Turn upward from the desk, when the
   human engine waits
   Like a taxi throbbing waiting.
   The Waste Land (1922) pt. 3

28 I Tiresias, old man with wrinkled dugs.
   The Waste Land (1922) pt. 3

29 One of the low on whom assurance sits
   As a silk hat on a Bradford millionaire.
   The Waste Land (1922) pt. 3

30 Bats with baby faces in the violet light.
   The Waste Land (1922) pt. 5

31 These fragments I have shored against my
   ruins.
   The Waste Land (1922) pt. 5

32 Webster was much possessed by death
   And saw the skull beneath the skin.
   'Whispers of Immortality' (1919)

33 Uncorseted, her friendly bust
   Gives promise of pneumatic bliss.
   'Whispers of Immortality' (1919)

1 The only way of expressing emotion in the form of art is by finding an 'objective correlative'; in other words, a set of objects, a situation, a chain of events which shall be the formula of that *particular* emotion; such that when the external facts, which must terminate in sensory experience, are given, the emotion is immediately evoked.

> *The Sacred Wood* (1920) 'Hamlet and his Problems'

2 Immature poets imitate; mature poets steal.

> *The Sacred Wood* (1920) 'Philip Massinger'

3 Poets in our civilization, as it exists at present, must be *difficult*.

> *Selected Essays* (1932) 'The Metaphysical Poets' (1921)

4 [*The Waste Land*] was only the relief of a personal and wholly insignificant grouse against life; it is just a piece of rhythmical grumbling.

> *The Waste Land* (ed. Valerie Eliot, 1971) epigraph

Elizabeth I 1533–1603

5 I know what it is to be a subject, what to be a Sovereign, what to have good neighbours, and sometimes meet evil-willers.

> Speech, 12 November 1586, in Sir John Neale *Elizabeth I and her Parliaments 1584–1601* (1957) p. 118. The traditional version concludes: 'In trust I have found treason'

6 I know I have the body of a weak and feeble woman, but I have the heart and stomach of a king, and of a king of England too.

> Speech to the troops at Tilbury on the approach of the Armada, 1588; in Lord Somers *A Third Collection of Scarce and Valuable Tracts* (1751) p. 196

7 Though God hath raised me high, yet this I count the glory of my crown: that I have reigned with your loves.

> The Golden Speech, 1601, in *Journals of All the Parliaments . . . Collected by Sir Simonds D'Ewes* (1682) p. 659

8 I will make you shorter by the head.

> To the leaders of her Council, who were opposing her course towards Mary Queen of Scots; in F. Chamberlin *Sayings of Queen Elizabeth* (1923)

9 If thy heart fails thee, climb not at all.

> Lines after Sir Walter Ralegh, written on a window-pane; in Thomas Fuller *Worthies of England* vol. 1, p. 419. Cf. 257:24

10 Must! Is *must* a word to be addressed to princes? Little man, little man! thy father, if he had been alive, durst not have used that word.

> To Robert Cecil, on his saying she must go to bed; in J. R. Green *A Short History of the English People* (1874) ch. 7

11 God may pardon you, but I never can.

> To the dying Countess of Nottingham, in David Hume *History of England under the House of Tudor* (1759) vol. 2, ch. 7

12 The queen of Scots is this day leichter of a fair son, and I am but a barren stock.

> To her ladies, in Sir James Melville *Memoirs of His Own Life* (1827 ed.) p. 159

13 The daughter of debate, that eke discord doth sow.

> Of Mary Queen of Scots, in George Puttenham (ed.) *Art of English Poesie* (1589) bk. 3, ch. 20

14 I would not open windows into men's souls.

> Oral tradition, in J. B. Black *Reign of Elizabeth 1558–1603* (1936) p. 19 (the words possibly originating in a letter drafted by Bacon). See J. Spedding (ed.) *Works of Francis Bacon* (1862) vol. 8, p. 98

15 All my possessions for a moment of time.

> Last words (attributed, probably apocryphal)

Elizabeth II 1926–

16 I think everybody really will concede that on this, of all days, I should begin my speech with the words 'My husband and I'.

> Speech at Guildhall, London, on her 25th wedding anniversary; in *The Times* 21 November 1972

17 In the words of one of my more sympathetic correspondents, it has turned out to be an 'annus horribilis'.

> Speech at Guildhall, London, 24 November 1992; in *The Times* 25 November 1992, p. 3

Queen Elizabeth, the Queen Mother 1900–

18 I'm glad we've been bombed. It makes me feel I can look the East End in the face.

> To a London policeman, 13 September 1940; in J. Wheeler-Bennett *King George VI* (1958) pt. 3, ch. 6

19 The Princesses would never leave without me and I couldn't leave without the King, and the King will never leave.

> On the suggestion that the royal family be evacuated during the Blitz; in P. Mortimer *Queen Elizabeth* (1986) ch. 25

Alf Ellerton

20 Belgium put the kibosh on the Kaiser.

> Title of song (1914)

John Ellerton 1826–93

21 The day Thou gavest, Lord, is ended, The darkness falls at Thy behest.

> Hymn (1870)

Emily Elizabeth Steele Elliot
1836–97

1 O come to my heart, Lord Jesus!
There is room in my heart for thee.
'Thou didst leave thy throne and thy kingly crown' (1870 hymn)

Charlotte Elliott 1789–1871

2 Just as I am, without one plea.
Invalid's Hymn Book (1834) 'Just as I am'

Ebenezer Elliott 1781–1849

3 What is a communist? One who hath yearnings
For equal division of unequal earnings.
'Epigram' (1850)

George Ellis 1753–1815

4 Snowy, Flowy, Blowy,
Showery, Flowery, Bowery,
Hoppy, Croppy, Droppy,
Breezy, Sneezy, Freezy.
'The Twelve Months'

Havelock Ellis 1859–1939

5 What we call 'progress' is the exchange of one nuisance for another nuisance.
Impressions and Comments (1914) 31 July 1912

6 All civilization has from time to time become a thin crust over a volcano of revolution.
Little Essays of Love and Virtue (1922) ch. 7

Friar Elstow

7 With thanks to God we know the way to heaven, to be as ready by water as by land, and therefore we care not which way we go.
When threatened with drowning by Henry VIII; in John Stow *Annals of England* (1615) p. 543. Cf. 151:3

Paul Éluard 1895–1952

8 *L'espoir ne fait pas de poussière.*
Hope raises no dust.
'Ailleurs, ici, partout' (1946)

9 *Adieu tristesse*
Bonjour tristesse.
Farewell sadness
Good-day sadness.
'À peine défigurée' (1932)

Ralph Waldo Emerson 1803–82

10 If the red slayer think he slays,
Or if the slain think he is slain,
They know not well the subtle ways
I keep, and pass, and turn again.
'Brahma' (1867)

11 I am the doubter and the doubt.
'Brahma' (1867)

12 By the rude bridge that arched the flood,
Their flag to April's breeze unfurled,
Here once the embattled farmers stood,
And fired the shot heard round the world.
'Concord Hymn' (1837)

13 Things are in the saddle,
And ride mankind.
'Ode' Inscribed to W. H. Channing (1847)

14 I like a church; I like a cowl;
I love a prophet of the soul.
'The Problem' (1847)

15 He builded better than he knew;—
The conscious stone to beauty grew.
'The Problem' (1847)

16 The frolic architecture of the snow.
'The Snowstorm' (1847)

17 Make yourself necessary to someone.
The Conduct of Life (1860) 'Considerations by the way'

18 All sensible people are selfish, and nature is tugging at every contract to make the terms of it fair.
The Conduct of Life (1860) 'Considerations by the way'

19 Art is a jealous mistress.
The Conduct of Life (1860) 'Wealth'

20 The louder he talked of his honour, the faster we counted our spoons.
The Conduct of Life (1860) 'Worship'. Cf. 184:11, 301:23

21 The only reward of virtue is virtue; the only way to have a friend is to be one.
Essays (1841) 'Friendship'

22 There is properly no history; only biography.
Essays (1841) 'History'. Cf. 121:28

23 The faith that stands on authority is not faith.
Essays (1841) 'The Over-Soul'

24 A foolish consistency is the hobgoblin of little minds.
Essays (1841) 'Self-Reliance'

25 To be great is to be misunderstood.
Essays (1841) 'Self-Reliance'

26 To fill the hour—that is happiness.
Essays. Second Series (1844) 'Experience'

27 Every man is wanted, and no man is wanted much.
Essays. Second Series (1844) 'Nominalist and Realist'

28 Language is fossil poetry.
Essays. Second Series (1844) 'The Poet'

29 What is a weed? A plant whose virtues have not been discovered.
Fortune of the Republic (1878) p. 3

30 Every hero becomes a bore at last.
Representative Men (1850) 'Uses of Great Men'

31 Hitch your wagon to a star.
Society and Solitude (1870) 'Civilization'

32 We boil at different degrees.
Society and Solitude (1870) 'Eloquence'

1 America is a country of young men.
Society and Solitude (1870) 'Old Age'

2 Glittering generalities! They are blazing ubiquities.
On Rufus Choate (attributed). Cf. 98:17

3 If a man write a better book, preach a better sermon, or make a better mouse-trap than his neighbour, tho' he build his house in the woods, the world will make a beaten path to his door.
Attributed to Emerson in Sarah Yule *Borrowings* (1889), but claimed also by Elbert Hubbard

William Empson 1906–84

4 Waiting for the end, boys, waiting for the end.
'Just a smack at Auden' (1940)

5 You don't want madhouse and the whole thing there.
'Let it Go' (1955)

6 Slowly the poison the whole blood stream fills.
It is not the effort nor the failure tires.
The waste remains, the waste remains and kills.
'Missing Dates' (1935)

7 Seven types of ambiguity.
Title of book (1930)

Friedrich Engels 1820–95

8 *Der Staat wird nicht 'abgeschafft', er stirbt ab.*
The State is not 'abolished', *it withers away.*
Anti-Dühring (1878) pt. 3, ch. 2
See also KARL MARX and FRIEDRICH ENGELS

Julius J. Epstein 1909– et al.

9 Of all the gin joints in all the towns in all the world, she walks into mine.
Casablanca (1942 film)

10 If she can stand it, I can. Play it!
Casablanca (1942 film). Spoken by Humphrey Bogart and usually quoted 'Play it again, Sam'

11 Here's looking at you, kid.
Casablanca (1942 film)

12 Major Strasser has been shot. Round up the usual suspects.
Casablanca (1942 film)

Olaudah Equiano c.1745–c.1797

13 A nation of dancers, singers and poets.
Narrative of the Life of Olaudah Equiano (1789) ch. 1 (the Ibo people)

Erasmus c.1469–1536

14 *In regione caecorum rex est luscus.*
In the country of the blind the one-eyed man is king.
Adages bk. 3, century 4, no. 96

Susan Ertz 1894–1985

15 Millions long for immortality who don't know what to do with themselves on a rainy Sunday afternoon.
Anger in the Sky (1943) p. 137

Robert Devereux, 2nd Earl of Essex 1566–1601

16 Reasons are not like garments, the worse for wearing.
Letter to Lord Willoughby, 4 January 1599; in *Notes and Queries* 10th Series, vol. 2 (1904) p. 23

Henri Estienne 1531–98

17 *Si jeunesse savait; si vieillesse pouvait.*
If youth knew; if age could.
Les Prémices (1594) bk. 4, epigram 4

Sir George Etherege (or Etheredge) c.1635–91

18 I walk within the purlieus of the Law.
Love in a Tub (1664) act 1, sc. 3

Euclid fl. c.300 BC

19 *Quod erat demonstrandum*
Which was to be proved.
Latin translation from the Greek of *Elementa* bk. 1, proposition 5 and *passim*

20 A line is length without breadth.
Elementa bk. 1, definition 2

21 There is no 'royal road' to geometry.
Addressed to Ptolemy I, in Proclus *Commentary on the First Book of Euclid's Elementa* prologue, pt. 2

Euripides c.485–c.406 BC

22 My tongue swore, but my mind's unsworn.
Hippolytus l. 612 (lamenting the breaking of an oath)

Abel Evans 1679–1737

23 Under this stone, Reader, survey
Dead Sir John Vanbrugh's house of clay.
Lie heavy on him, Earth! for he
Laid many heavy loads on thee!
'Epitaph on Sir John Vanbrugh, Architect of Blenheim Palace'

David Everett 1769–1813

24 Large streams from little fountains flow,
Tall oaks from little acorns grow.
'Lines Written for a School Declamation' (aged 7)

Viscount Eversley

See CHARLES SHAW-LEFEVRE

William Norman Ewer 1885–1976

1 I gave my life for freedom—This I know:
  For those who bade me fight had told me
  so.
    'Five Souls' (1917)

2 How odd
  Of God
  To choose
  The Jews.
    In Week-End Book (1924) p. 117. Cf. 73:21

F. W. Faber 1814–63

3 My God, how wonderful Thou art!
  Thy Majesty how bright!
    'The Eternal Father' (1854 hymn)

4 The music of the Gospel leads us home.
    'The Pilgrims of the Night' (1854 hymn)

5 There's a wideness in God's mercy
  Like the wideness of the sea.
    'Souls of men, why will ye scatter' (1854
    hymn)

Robert Fabyan d. 1513

6 Finally he paid the debt of nature.
    New Chronicles of England and France (1516)
    vol. 1, ch. 41

7 Ranulphe says he took a surfeit by eating
  of a lamprey, and thereof died.
    New Chronicles of England and France (1516)
    vol. 1, ch. 229 (of Henry I)

8 The Duke of Clarence … then being a
  prisoner in the Tower, was secretly put to
  death and drowned in a barrel of
  Malmesey wine.
    New Chronicles of England and France (1516)
    vol. 2 ('1478')

Clifton Fadiman 1904–

9 Milk's leap toward immortality.
    Any Number Can Play (1957) p. 105 (of cheese)

10 The mama of dada.
    Party of One (1955) p. 90 (of Gertrude Stein)

Lucius Cary, Viscount Falkland 1610–43

11 When it is not necessary to change, it is
   necessary not to change.
    Discourses of Infallibility (1660) 'A Speech
    concerning Episcopacy' (1641)

Eleanor Farjeon 1881–1965

12 Morning has broken
   Like the first morning,
   Blackbird has spoken
   Like the first bird.
    'A Morning Song (for the First Day of
    Spring)' (1957)

Edward Farmer c.1809–76

13 I have no pain, dear mother, now;
   But oh! I am so dry:
   Just moisten poor Jim's lips once more;
   And, mother, do not cry!
    'The Collier's Dying Child'. Cf. 8:3

King Farouk 1920–65

14 Soon there will be only five Kings left—the
   King of England, the King of Spades, the
   King of Clubs, the King of Hearts and the
   King of Diamonds.
    In Lord Boyd-Orr As I Recall (1966) ch. 21
    (Cairo, 1948)

George Farquhar 1678–1707

15 There is no scandal like rags, nor any
   crime so shameful as poverty.
    The Beaux' Stratagem (1707) act 1, sc. 1

16 No woman can be a beauty without a
   fortune.
    The Beaux' Stratagem (1707) act 2, sc. 2

17 Crimes, like virtues, are their own rewards.
    The Inconstant (1702) act 4, sc. 2

18 Money is the sinews of love, as of war.
    Love and a Bottle (1698) act 2, sc. 1. Cf. 100:29

19 Poetry's a mere drug, Sir.
    Love and a Bottle (1698) act 3, sc. 2. Cf. 211:3

20 Hanging and marriage, you know, go by
   Destiny.
    The Recruiting Officer (1706) act 3, sc. 2

21 A lady, if undressed at Church, looks silly,
   One cannot be devout in dishabilly.
    The Stage Coach (1704) prologue

Guy Fawkes 1570–1606

22 A desperate disease requires a dangerous
   remedy.
    6 November 1605. See Dictionary of National
    Biography (1917–) vol. 6, p. 1132. Cf. 276:27

James Fenton 1949–

23 It is not what they built. It is what they
   knocked down.
   It is not the houses. It is the spaces
   between the houses.
   It is not the streets that exist. It is the
   streets that no longer exist.
    German Requiem (1981) p. 1

Emperor Ferdinand I 1503–64

24 Fiat justitia et pereat mundus.
   Let justice be done, though the world
   perish.
    Motto. See Johannes Manlius Locorum
    Communium Collectanea (1563) vol. 2 'De Lege:
    Octatum Praeceptum'. Cf. 342:25

Ludwig Feuerbach 1804–72

1 *Der Mensch ist, was er isst.*
Man is what he eats.
In Jacob Moleschott *Lehre der Nahrungsmittel:*
Für das Volk (1850) 'Advertisement'. Cf. 72:7

Eugene Field 1850–95

2 Wynken, Blynken, and Nod one night
Sailed off in a wooden shoe—
Sailed on a river of crystal light,
Into a sea of dew.
'Wynken, Blynken, and Nod' (1889)

3 He played the King as though under
momentary apprehension that someone
else was about to play the ace.
Of Creston Clarke as King Lear; review
attributed to Field, in *Denver Tribune* c.1880

Henry Fielding 1707–54

4 One fool at least in every married couple.
Amelia (1751) bk. 9, ch. 4

5 The dusky night rides down the sky,
And ushers in the morn;
The hounds all join in glorious cry,
The huntsman winds his horn:
And a-hunting we will go.
Don Quixote in England (1733) act 2, sc. 5
'A-Hunting We Will Go'

6 Oh! The roast beef of England,
And old England's roast beef.
The Grub Street Opera (1731) act 3, sc. 3

7 He in a few minutes ravished this fair
creature, or at least would have ravished
her, if she had not, by a timely compliance,
prevented him.
Jonathan Wild (1743) bk. 3, ch. 7

8 Public schools are the nurseries of all vice
and immorality.
Joseph Andrews (1742) bk. 3, ch. 5

9 Love and scandal are the best sweeteners
of tea.
Love in Several Masques (1728) act 4, sc. 11

10 What is commonly called love, namely the
desire of satisfying a voracious appetite
with a certain quantity of delicate white
human flesh.
Tom Jones (1749) bk. 6, ch. 1

11 His designs were strictly honourable, as
the phrase is; that is, to rob a lady of her
fortune by way of marriage.
Tom Jones (1749) bk. 11, ch. 4

12 That monstrous animal, a husband and
wife.
Tom Jones (1749) bk. 15, ch. 9

13 All Nature wears one universal grin.
Tom Thumb the Great (1731) act 1, sc. 1

Dorothy Fields 1905–74

14 A fine romance with no kisses.
A fine romance, my friend, this is.
'A Fine Romance' (1936 song)

15 Grab your coat, and get your hat,
Leave your worry on the doorstep,
Just direct your feet
To the sunny side of the street.
'On the Sunny Side of the Street' (1930 song)

W. C. Fields 1880–1946

16 Never give a sucker an even break.
Title of a W. C. Fields film (1941); the catch-
phrase (Fields's own) is said to have
originated in the musical comedy *Poppy*
(1923)

17 It ain't a fit night out for man or beast.
Adopted by Fields but claimed by him not to
be original. See Letter, 8 February 1944, in
W. C. Fields by Himself (1974) pt. 2

18 Hell, I never vote *for* anybody. I always vote
against.
In R. L. Taylor *W. C. Fields* (1950) p. 228.
Cf. 1:10

See also LEO ROSTEN

Ronald Firbank 1886–1926

19 I remember the average curate at home as
something between a eunuch and a
snigger.
The Flower Beneath the Foot (1923) ch. 4

20 There was a pause—just long enough for
an angel to pass, flying slowly.
Vainglory (1915) ch. 6

21 All millionaires love a baked apple.
Vainglory (1915) ch. 13

H. A. L. Fisher 1856–1940

22 Europe is a continent of energetic
mongrels.
A History of Europe (1935) ch. 1

Lord Fisher 1841–1920

23 Sack the lot!
Letter to *The Times*, 2 September 1919 (on
government overmanning and overspending)

24 Never contradict. Never explain. Never
apologize.
Letter to *The Times*, 5 September 1919.
Cf. 122:19, 175:13

25 Yours till Hell freezes.
Attributed to Fisher, but not original. See F.
Ponsonby *Reflections of Three Reigns* (1951)
p. 131

Marve Fisher

26 I like Chopin and Bizet, and the voice of
Doris Day,
Gershwin songs and old forgotten carols.
But the music that excels is the sound of
oil wells
As they slurp, slurp, slurp into the barrels.
'An Old-Fashioned Girl' (1954 song)

1 I want an old-fashioned house
With an old-fashioned fence
And an old-fashioned millionaire.
'An Old-Fashioned Girl' (1954 song)

Albert H. Fitz

2 You are my honey, honeysuckle, I am the
bee.
'The Honeysuckle and the Bee' (1901 song)

Charles Fitzgeffrey c.1575–1638

3 And bold and hard adventures t' undertake,
Leaving his country for his country's sake.
Sir Francis Drake (1596) st. 213

Edward Fitzgerald 1809–83

4 Awake! for Morning in the bowl of night
Has flung the stone that puts the stars to
flight:
And Lo! the Hunter of the East has caught
The Sultan's turret in a noose of light.
The Rubáiyát of Omar Khayyám (1859) st. 1

5 Each morn a thousand roses brings, you
say;
Yes, but where leaves the rose of
yesterday?
The Rubáiyát of Omar Khayyám (4th ed., 1879)
st. 9

6 Here with a loaf of bread beneath the
bough,
A flask of wine, a book of verse—and Thou
Beside me singing in the wilderness—
And wilderness is paradise enow.
The Rubáiyát of Omar Khayyám (1859) st. 11. 'A
book of verses underneath the bough, / A
jug of wine, a loaf of bread—and Thou /
Beside me singing in the wilderness— / Oh,
wilderness were paradise enow!' in 4th ed.
(1879) st. 12

7 Ah, take the cash in hand and waive the
rest;
Oh, the brave music of a distant drum!
The Rubáiyát of Omar Khayyám (1859) st. 12.
'Ah, take the cash and let the credit go, / Nor
heed the rumble of a distant drum!' in 4th
ed. (1879) st. 13

8 I sometimes think that never blows so red
The rose as where some buried Caesar
bled.
The Rubáiyát of Omar Khayyám (1859) st. 18

9 Dust into dust, and under dust, to lie,
Sans wine, sans song, sans singer,
and—sans End!
The Rubáiyát of Omar Khayyám (1859) st. 23

10 One thing is certain, and the rest is lies;
The flower that once hath blown for ever
dies.
The Rubáiyát of Omar Khayyám (1859) st. 26

11 Ah, fill the cup:—what boots it to repeat
How time is slipping underneath our feet:
Unborn TO-MORROW, and dead YESTERDAY,
Why fret about them if TO-DAY be sweet!
The Rubáiyát of Omar Khayyám (1859) st. 37

12 'Tis all a chequer-board of nights and days
Where Destiny with Men for pieces plays:
Hither and thither moves, and mates, and
slays,
And one by one back in the closet lays.
The Rubáiyát of Omar Khayyám (1859) st. 49.
'But helpless pieces of the game he plays /
Upon this chequer-board of nights and
days; / Hither and thither moves, and
checks, and slays, / And one by one back
in the closet lays' in 4th ed. (1879) st. 69

13 The ball no question makes of Ayes and
Noes,
But here or there as strikes the player
goes;
And he that tossed you down into the field,
He knows about it all—HE knows—HE
knows!
The Rubáiyát of Omar Khayyám (4th ed., 1879)
st. 70

14 The moving finger writes; and, having writ,
Moves on: nor all thy piety nor wit
Shall lure it back to cancel half a line,
Nor all thy tears wash out a word of it.
The Rubáiyát of Omar Khayyám (1859) st. 51

15 That inverted bowl we call The Sky.
The Rubáiyát of Omar Khayyám (1859) st. 52

16 'Who is the potter, pray, and who the pot?'
The Rubáiyát of Omar Khayyám (1859) st. 60

17 Indeed the idols I have loved so long
Have done my credit in this world much
wrong:
Have drowned my glory in a shallow cup
And sold my reputation for a song.
The Rubáiyát of Omar Khayyám (4th ed., 1879)
st. 93

18 Alas, that spring should vanish with the
rose!
The Rubáiyát of Omar Khayyám (1859) st. 72

19 Taste is the feminine of genius.
To J. R. Lowell, October 1877, in A. and A.
Terhune (eds.) Letters (1980) vol. 4

F. Scott Fitzgerald 1896–1940

20 Let me tell you about the very rich. They
are different from you and me.
All the Sad Young Men (1926) 'Rich Boy' (to
which Ernest Hemingway replied, 'Yes, they
have more money')

21 Her voice is full of money.
The Great Gatsby (1925) ch. 7 (of Daisy)

22 In a real dark night of the soul it is always
three o'clock in the morning.
'Handle with Care' in Esquire March 1936.
'Dark night of the soul' being a translation
of the Spanish title of a work (1578–80) by
St John of the Cross

23 There are no second acts in American lives.
Edmund Wilson (ed.) The Last Tycoon (1941)
'Hollywood, etc.'

Robert Fitzsimmons 1862–1917

1 The bigger they are, the further they have
to fall.
  Prior to a boxing match, in *Brooklyn Daily
  Eagle* 11 August 1900 (similar forms found in
  proverbs since the 15th century)

Bud Flanagan 1896–1968

2 Underneath the Arches,
I dream my dreams away,
Underneath the Arches,
On cobble-stones I lay.
  'Underneath the Arches' (1932 song)

Michael Flanders 1922–75 and Donald Swann 1923–

3 Have Some Madeira, M'dear.
  Title of song (c.1956)

4 Mud! Mud! Glorious mud!
Nothing quite like it for cooling the blood.
  'The Hippopotamus' (1952)

5 Eating people is wrong!
  'The Reluctant Cannibal' (1956 song)

6 That monarch of the road,
Observer of the Highway Code,
That big six-wheeler
Scarlet-painted
London Transport
Diesel-engined
Ninety-seven horse power
Omnibus!
  'A Transport of Delight' (c.1956 song)

Gustave Flaubert 1821–80

7 Human speech is like a cracked kettle on
which we tap crude rhythms for bears to
dance to, while we long to make music
that will melt the stars.
  Madame Bovary (1857) pt. 1, ch. 12 (tr. F.
  Steegmuller)

8 You can calculate the worth of a man by
the number of his enemies, and the
importance of a work of art by the harm
that is spoken of it.
  Letter to Louise Colet, 14 June 1853, in M.
  Nadeau (ed.) *Correspondence 1853–56* (1964)

9 Poetry is a subject as precise as geometry.
  Letter to Louise Colet, 14 August 1853, in M.
  Nadeau (ed.) *Correspondence 1853–56* (1964)

10 Style is life! It is the very life-blood of
thought!
  Letter to Louise Colet, 7 September 1853, in
  M. Nadeau (ed.) *Correspondence 1853–56* (1964)

11 The artist must be in his work as God is in
creation, invisible and all-powerful; one
must sense him everywhere but never see
him.
  Letter to Mlle Leroyer de Chantepie,
  18 March 1857, in M. Nadeau (ed.)
  Correspondence 1857–64 (1965)

12 Books are made not like children but like
pyramids ... and they're just as useless!
and they stay in the desert! ... Jackals piss
at their foot and the bourgeois climb up
on them.
  Letter to Ernest Feydeau, November/
  December 1857, in M. Nadeau (ed.)
  Correspondence 1857–64 (1965)

13 Human life is a sad show, undoubtedly:
ugly, heavy and complex. Art has no other
end, for people of feeling, than to conjure
away the burden and bitterness.
  Letter to Amelie Bosquet, July 1864, in M.
  Nadeau (ed.) *Correspondence 1857–64* (1965)

James Elroy Flecker 1884–1915

14 West of these out to seas colder than the
Hebrides
I must go
Where the fleet of stars is anchored and
the young
Star captains glow.
  'The Dying Patriot' (1913)

15 The dragon-green, the luminous, the dark,
the serpent-haunted sea.
  'The Gates of Damascus' (1913)

16 We who with songs beguile your
pilgrimage
And swear that beauty lives though lilies
die.
  The Golden Journey to Samarkand (1913)
  'Prologue'

17 For lust of knowing what should not be
known,
We take the Golden Road to Samarkand.
  The Golden Journey to Samarkand (1913) pt. 1,
  'Epilogue'

18 I have seen old ships sail like swans asleep
Beyond the village which men still call
Tyre,
With leaden age o'ercargoed, dipping deep
For Famagusta and the hidden sun
That rings black Cyprus with a lake of fire.
  'Old Ships' (1915)

19 A ship, an isle, a sickle moon—
With few but with how splendid stars
The mirrors of the sea are strewn
Between their silver bars!
  'A Ship, an Isle, and a Sickle Moon' (1913)

20 O friend unseen, unborn, unknown,
Student of our sweet English tongue,
Read out my words at night, alone.
  'To a Poet a Thousand Years Hence' (1910)

Ian Fleming 1908–64

21 A medium Vodka dry Martini—with a slice
of lemon peel. Shaken and not stirred.
  Dr No (1958) ch. 14

Marjory Fleming 1803–11

22 The most devilish thing is 8 times 8 and 7
times 7 it is what nature itselfe cant
endure.
  Journals, Letters and Verses (ed. A. Esdaile, 1934)
  p. 47

1 His noses cast is of the roman
He is a very pretty weoman
I could not get a rhyme for roman
And was obildged to call it weoman.
'Sonnet'

Robert, Marquis de Flers
1872–1927 **and Arman de Caillavet** 1869–1915

2 Democracy is the name we give the people whenever we need them.
L'habit vert act 1, sc. 12

Andrew Fletcher of Saltoun
1655–1716

3 If a man were permitted to make all the ballads, he need not care who should make the laws of a nation.
Political Works (1732) pt. 7 'Account of a Conversation concerning a Right Regulation of Government for the Good of Mankind ... ' (1704)

John Fletcher 1579–1625

4 Death hath so many doors to let out life.
The Custom of the Country (with Massinger) act 2, sc. 2. Cf. 222:6, 270:8

5 Care-charming Sleep, thou easer of all woes,
Brother to Death.
Valentinian (performed c.1610–14) act 5, sc. 7 'Song'

6 Whistle and she'll come to you.
Wit Without Money act 4, sc. 4. Cf. 82:19

7 Charity and beating begins at home.
Wit Without Money act 5, sc. 2

See also FRANCIS BEAUMONT and JOHN FLETCHER, SHAKESPEARE Henry VIII

Phineas Fletcher 1582–1650

8 Drop, drop, slow tears,
And bathe those beauteous feet,
Which brought from Heaven
The news and Prince of Peace.
'An Hymn'(1633)

9 Love's tongue is in the eyes.
Piscatory Eclogues (1633) no. 5, st. 13

10 Love is like linen often changed, the sweeter.
Sicelides (performed 1614) act 3, sc. 5

11 The coward's weapon, poison.
Sicelides (performed 1614) act 5, sc. 3

Jean-Pierre Claris de Florian
1755–94

12 Plaisir d'amour ne dure qu'un moment,
Chagrin d'amour dure toute la vie.
Love's pleasure lasts but a moment; love's sorrow lasts all through life.
Célestine (1784) Cf. 217:2

John Florio c.1553–1625

13 England is the paradise of women, the purgatory of men, and the hell of horses.
Second Frutes (1591) ch. 12

Ferdinand Foch 1851–1929

14 My centre is giving way, my right is retreating, situation excellent, I am attacking.
Message during the first Battle of the Marne, September 1914; in R. Recouly Foch (1919) ch. 6

15 This is not a peace treaty, it is an armistice for twenty years.
At the signing of the Treaty of Versailles, 1919; in P. Reynaud Mémoires (1963) vol. 2, p. 457

J. Foley 1906–1970

16 Old soldiers never die,
They simply fade away.
'Old Soldiers Never Die' (1920 song)

Michael Foot 1913–

17 Think of it! A second Chamber selected by the Whips. A seraglio of eunuchs.
Speech, Hansard 3 February 1969, col. 88

18 It is not necessary that every time he rises he should give his famous imitation of a semi-house-trained polecat.
Speech, Hansard 2 March 1978, col. 668 (of Norman Tebbit)

Samuel Foote 1720–77

19 Born in a cellar ... and living in a garret.
The Author (1757) act 2

20 So she went into the garden to cut a cabbage-leaf to make an apple-pie; and at the same time a great she-bear coming up the street, pops its head into the shop. 'What! no soap?' So he died, and she very imprudently married the barber; and there were present the Picninnies, and the Joblillies, and the Garyulies, and the grand Panjandrum himself, with the little round button at top; and they all fell to playing the game of catch as catch can, till the gun powder ran out at the heels of their boots.
Nonsense composed to test the vaunted memory of the actor Charles Macklin; in Maria Edgeworth Harry and Lucy (1825) vol. 2, p. 152. See Quarterly Review (1854) vol. 95, p. 516

1 He is not only dull in himself, but the cause of dullness in others.
Of a dull law lord, in James Boswell *Life of Samuel Johnson* (1934 ed.) vol. 4, p. 178 (1783). Cf. 278:16

Miss C. F. Forbes 1817–1911

2 The sense of being well-dressed gives a feeling of inward tranquillity which religion is powerless to bestow.
In R. W. Emerson *Letters and Social Aims* (1876) p. 79

Gerald Ford 1909–

3 I am a Ford, not a Lincoln.
On taking the vice-presidential oath, 6 December 1973; in *Washington Post* 7 December 1973

4 Our long national nightmare is over.
On being sworn in as President, 9 August 1974; in G. J. Lankevich *Gerald R. Ford* (1977)

5 If the Government is big enough to give you everything you want, it is big enough to take away everything you have.
In J. F. Parker *If Elected* (1960) p. 193

Henry Ford 1863–1947

6 History is more or less bunk.
In *Chicago Tribune* 25 May 1916

7 Any colour—so long as it's black.
On the choice of colour for the Model T Ford, in A. Nevins *Ford* (1957) vol. 2, ch. 15

8 What we call evil is simply ignorance bumping its head in the dark.
In *Observer* 16 March 1930

John Ford 1586–after 1639

9 I am ... a mushroom
On whom the dew of heaven drops now and then.
The Broken Heart (1633) act 1, sc. 3

10 He hath shook hands with time.
The Broken Heart (1633) act 5, sc. 2

11   Why, I hold fate
Clasped in my fist, and could command the course
Of time's eternal motion, hadst thou been
One thought more steady than an ebbing sea.
'Tis Pity She's a Whore (1633) act 5, sc. 4

Lena Guilbert Ford 1870–1916

12 Keep the Home-fires burning,
While your hearts are yearning,
Though your lads are far away
They dream of Home.
There's a silver lining
Through the dark cloud shining;
Turn the dark cloud inside out,
Till the boys come Home.
'Till the Boys Come Home!' (1914 song); music by Ivor Novello

Howell Forgy 1908–83

13 Praise the Lord and pass the ammunition.
At Pearl Harbor, 7 December 1941, while sailors passed ammunition by hand to the deck; in *New York Times* 1 November 1942 (later title of song by Frank Loesser, 1942)

E. M. Forster 1879–1970

14 American women shoot the hippopotamus with eyebrows made of platinum.
Abinger Harvest (1936) 'Mickey and Minnie'. Cf. 33:1

15 They go forth into it [the world] with well-developed bodies, fairly developed minds, and undeveloped hearts.
Abinger Harvest (1936) 'Notes on English Character' (of public-school men)

16 Yes—oh dear yes—the novel tells a story.
Aspects of the Novel (1927) ch. 2

17 The test of a round character is whether it is capable of surprising in a convincing way. If it never surprises, it is flat. If it does not convince, it is flat pretending to be round.
Aspects of the Novel (1927) ch. 4

18 A dogged attempt to cover the universe with mud, an inverted Victorianism, an attempt to make crossness and dirt succeed where sweetness and light failed.
Aspects of the Novel (1927) ch. 6 (of James Joyce's *Ulysses*)

19 Railway termini. They are our gates to the glorious and the unknown. Through them we pass out into adventure and sunshine, to them, alas! we return.
Howards End (1910) ch. 2

20 Personal relations are the important thing for ever and ever, and not this outer life of telegrams and anger.
Howards End (1910) ch. 19

21 Only connect! ... Only connect the prose and the passion.
Howards End (1910) ch. 22

22 There is much good luck in the world, but it is luck. We are none of us safe. We are children, playing or quarrelling on the line.
The Longest Journey (1907) ch. 12

23 Very notable was his distinction between coarseness and vulgarity (coarseness, revealing something; vulgarity, concealing something).
The Longest Journey (1907) ch. 26

24 The so-called white races are really pinko-grey.
A Passage to India (1924) ch. 7

25 Pathos, piety, courage—they exist, but are identical, and so is filth. Everything exists, nothing has value.
A Passage to India (1924) ch. 14

26 Where there is officialism every human relationship suffers.
A Passage to India (1924) ch. 24

1 Like all gossip—it's merely one of those half-alive things that try to crowd out real life.

   A Passage to India (1924) ch. 31

2 If I had to choose between betraying my country and betraying my friend, I hope I should have the guts to betray my country.

   Two Cheers for Democracy (1951) 'What I Believe'

3 So Two cheers for Democracy: one because it admits variety and two because it permits criticism. Two cheers are quite enough: there is no occasion to give three. Only Love the Beloved Republic deserves that.

   Two Cheers for Democracy (1951) 'What I Believe' ('Love, the beloved republic' borrowed from Swinburne's poem 'Hertha')

Venantius Fortunatus AD
c.530–c.610

4 *Pange, lingua, gloriosi*
   Proelium certaminis.
   Sing, my tongue, of the battle in the glorious struggle.

   'Pange lingua gloriosi' (Passiontide hymn: 'Sing, my tongue, the glorious battle')

5 *Vexilla regis prodeunt,*
   Fulget crucis mysterium.
   The banners of the king advance, the mystery of the cross shines bright.

   'Vexilla Regis' (hymn: 'The royal banners forward go')

Charles Foster 1828–1904

6 Isn't this a billion dollar country?

   At the 51st Congress, responding to a Democratic gibe about a 'million dollar Congress'; also attributed to Thomas B. Reed, who reported the exchange in *North American Review* March 1892, vol. 154, p. 319

Sir George Foster 1847–1931

7 These somewhat troublesome days when the great Mother Empire stands splendidly isolated in Europe.

   In *Official Report of the Debates of the House of Commons of the Dominion of Canada* (1896) vol. 41, col. 176 (16 January 1896). On 22 January 1896, *The Times* referred to this speech under the heading 'Splendid Isolation'

John Foster 1770–1843

8 But the two classes [the educated and the uneducated] so beheld in contrast, might they not seem to belong to two different nations?

   Essay on the Evils of Popular Ignorance (1820) p. 277. Cf. 122:6

Stephen Collins Foster 1826–64

9 Beautiful dreamer, wake unto me,
   Starlight and dewdrop are waiting for thee.

   'Beautiful Dreamer' (1864 song)

10 Gwine to run all night!
   Gwine to run all day!
   I'll bet my money on de bobtail nag—
   Somebody bet on de bay.

   'De Camptown Races' (1850) chorus

11 I dream of Jeanie with the light brown hair,
   Floating, like a vapour, on the soft summer air.

   'Jeanie with the Light Brown Hair' (1854)

12 Way down upon the Swanee River,
   Far, far, away,
   There's where my heart is turning ever;
   There's where the old folks stay.

   'The Old Folks at Home' (1851)

13 All the world is sad and dreary
   Everywhere I roam,
   Oh! darkies, how my heart grows weary,
   Far from the old folks at home.

   'The Old Folks at Home' (1851) chorus

Charles Fourier 1772–1837

14 The extension of women's rights is the basic principle of all social progress.

   Théorie des Quatre Mouvements (1808) vol. 2, ch. 4

Charles James Fox 1749–1806

15 He was uniformly of an opinion . . . that the right of governing was not property but a trust.

   On the younger Pitt's scheme of Parliamentary Reform, 1785; in J. L. Hammond *Charles James Fox* (1903) ch. 4

16 How much the greatest event it is that ever happened in the world! and how much the best!

   On the fall of the Bastille; letter to R. Fitzpatrick, 30 July 1789, in Lord John Russell *Life and Times of C. J. Fox* vol. 2 (1859) p. 361

George Fox 1624–91

17 I saw also that there was an ocean of darkness and death, but an infinite ocean of light and love, which flowed over the ocean of darkness.

   Journal 1647 (ed. J. L. Nickalls, 1952) p. 19

18 Walk cheerfully over the world, answering that of God in every one.

   Journal 1656 (ed. J. L. Nickalls, 1952) p. 263

Henry Fox
See 1ST LORD HOLLAND

Anatole France 1844–1924

1 In every well-governed state, wealth is a sacred thing; in democracies it is the only sacred thing.
L'Île des pingouins (1908) pt. 6, ch. 2

2 They [the poor] have to labour in the face of the majestic equality of the law, which forbids the rich as well as the poor to sleep under bridges, to beg in the streets, and to steal bread.
Le Lys rouge (1894) ch. 7

3 The good critic is he who relates the adventures of his soul in the midst of masterpieces.
La Vie littéraire (1888) dedicatory letter

Francis I 1494–1547

4 De toutes choses ne m'est demeuré que l'honneur et la vie qui est saulve.
Of all I had, only honour and life have been spared.
Letter to his mother following his defeat at Pavia, 1525; in Collection des Documents Inédits sur l'Histoire de France (1847) vol. 1, p. 129 (usually quoted 'Tout est perdu fors l'honneur [All is lost save honour]')

St Francis de Sales 1567–1622

5 Big fires flare up in a wind, but little ones are blown out unless they are carried in under cover.
Introduction à la vie dévote (1609) pt. 3, ch. 34. Cf. 83:19, 201:24

6 Quantum ore dixerimus, sane cor cordi loquitur, lingua non nisi aures pulsat.
It has been well said, that heart speaks to heart, whereas language only speaks to the ears.
Latin translation of a letter to the Archbishop of Bourges, 5 October 1604, paraphrased for his motto by John Henry Newman as 'cor ad cor loquitur [heart speaks to heart]'

St Francis of Assisi 1181–1226

7 Lord, make me an instrument of Your peace!
Where there is hatred let me sow love;
Where there is injury, pardon;
Where there is doubt, faith;
Where there is despair, hope;
Where there is darkness, light;
Where there is sadness, joy.
'Prayer of St Francis' (attributed)

Benjamin Franklin 1706–90

8 Remember that time is money.
Advice to a Young Tradesman (1748)

9 Some are weather-wise, some are otherwise.
Poor Richard's Almanac (1735) February

10 Necessity never made a good bargain.
Poor Richard's Almanac (1735) April

11 He that lives upon hope will die fasting.
Poor Richard's Almanac (1758) preface

12 A little neglect may breed mischief ... for want of a nail, the shoe was lost; for want of a shoe the horse was lost; and for want of a horse the rider was lost.
Poor Richard's Almanac (1758) preface

13 We must indeed all hang together, or, most assuredly, we shall all hang separately.
At the Signing of the Declaration of Independence, 4 July 1776 (possibly not original). See P. M. Zall Ben Franklin (1980) p. 154

14 There never was a good war, or a bad peace.
Letter to Josiah Quincy, 11 September 1783, in Works (1882) vol. 10, p. 11

15 In this world nothing can be said to be certain, except death and taxes.
Letter to Jean Baptiste Le Roy, 13 November 1789, in Works (1817) ch. 6.

16 Man is a tool-making animal.
In James Boswell Life of Samuel Johnson (1934 ed.) vol. 3, p. 245 (7 April 1778)

17 What is the use of a new-born child?
When asked what was the use of a new invention; in J. Parton Life and Times of Benjamin Franklin (1864) pt. 4, ch. 17

Frederick the Great 1712–86

18 Drive out prejudices through the door, and they will return through the window.
Letter to Voltaire, 19 March 1771, in Oeuvres Complètes (1790) vol. 12

19 My people and I have come to an agreement which satisfies us both. They are to say what they please, and I am to do what I please.
His interpretation of benevolent despotism (attributed)

20 Rascals, would you live for ever?
To hesitant Guards at Kolin, 18 June 1757 (attributed)

E. A. Freeman 1823–92

21 History is past politics, and politics is present history.
Methods of Historical Study (1886) p. 44

John Hookham Frere 1769–1846

22 The feathered race with pinions skim the air—
Not so the mackerel, and still less the bear!
'The Progress of Man' (1798) canto 1, l. 34

Sigmund Freud 1856–1939

23 Anatomy is destiny.
Collected Writings (1924) vol. 5, p. 210

1 The interpretation of dreams is the royal road to a knowledge of the unconscious activities of the mind.
   The Interpretation of Dreams (2nd ed., 1909) ch. 7, sect. E (often quoted 'Dreams are the royal road to the unconscious')

2 'Itzig, where are you riding to?' 'Don't ask me, ask the horse.'
   Letter to W. Fliess, 7 July 1898, in *Origins of Psychoanalysis* (1950) p. 275

3 What does a woman want?
   Letter to Marie Bonaparte, in E. Jones *Sigmund Freud* (1955) vol. 2, pt. 3, ch. 16

4 All that matters is love and work.
   Attributed

Max Frisch 1911–

5 Technology ... the knack of so arranging the world that we need not experience it.
   Homo Faber (1957) pt. 2

Charles Frohman 1860–1915

6 Why fear death? It is the most beautiful adventure in life.
   Last words before drowning in the *Lusitania*, 7 May 1915; in I. F. Marcosson and D. Frohman *Charles Frohman* (1916) ch. 19. Cf. 29:13

Erich Fromm 1900–80

7 In the nineteenth century the problem was that *God is dead*; in the twentieth century the problem is that *man is dead*.
   The Sane Society (1955) ch. 9

Robert Frost 1874–1963

8 ... Earth's the right place for love:
   I don't know where it's likely to go better.
   'Birches' (1916)

9 Most of the change we think we see in life
   Is due to truths being in and out of favour.
   'The Black Cottage' (1914)

10 Forgive, O Lord, my little jokes on Thee
   And I'll forgive Thy great big one on me.
   'Cluster of Faith' (1962)

11 'Home is the place where, when you have to go there,
   They have to take you in.'
   'I should have called it
   Something you somehow haven't to deserve.'
   'The Death of the Hired Man' (1914)

12 Some say the world will end in fire,
   Some say in ice.
   'Fire and Ice' (1923)

13 The land was ours before we were the land's.
   'The Gift Outright' (1942)

14 Happiness makes up in height for what it lacks in length.
   Title of poem (1942)

15 Something there is that doesn't love a wall.
   'Mending Wall' (1914)

16 My apple trees will never get across
   And eat the cones under his pines, I tell him.
   He only says, 'Good fences make good neighbours.'
   'Mending Wall' (1914)

17 Before I built a wall I'd ask to know
   What I was walling in or walling out,
   And to whom I was like to give offence.
   'Mending Wall' (1914)

18 I never dared be radical when young
   For fear it would make me conservative when old.
   'Precaution' (1936)

19 Two roads diverged in a wood, and I—
   I took the one less travelled by,
   And that has made all the difference.
   'The Road Not Taken' (1916)

20 We dance round in a ring and suppose,
   But the Secret sits in the middle and knows.
   'The Secret Sits' (1942)

21 Pressed into service means pressed out of shape.
   'The Self-Seeker' (1914)

22 The best way out is always through.
   'A Servant to Servants' (1914)

23 The woods are lovely, dark and deep.
   But I have promises to keep,
   And miles to go before I sleep.
   'Stopping by Woods on a Snowy Evening' (1923)

24 The figure a poem makes. It begins in delight and ends in wisdom.
   Collected Poems (1939) 'The Figure a Poem Makes'

25 Like a piece of ice on a hot stove the poem must ride on its own melting. A poem may be worked over once it is in being, but may not be worried into being.
   Collected Poems (1939) 'The Figure a Poem Makes'

26 I'd as soon write free verse as play tennis with the net down.
   In E. Lathem *Interviews with Robert Frost* (1966) p. 203

27 Poetry is a way of taking life by the throat.
   In E. S. Sergeant *Robert Frost* (1960) ch. 18

28 Poetry is what is lost in translation. It is also what is lost in interpretation.
   In L. Untermeyer *Robert Frost* (1964) p. 18

Christopher Fry 1907–

29 The dark is light enough.
   Title of play (1954)

30   What after all
   Is a halo? It's only one more thing to keep clean.
   The Lady's not for Burning (1949) act 1

1 Where in this small-talking world can I
   find
   A longitude with no platitude?
   The Lady's not for Burning (1949) act 3

2   The best
   Thing we can do is to make wherever we're
   lost in
   Look as much like home as we can.
   The Lady's not for Burning (1949) act 3

Roger Fry 1866–1934

3 Art is significant deformity.
   In Virginia Woolf *Roger Fry* (1940) ch. 8

R. Buckminster Fuller 1895–1983

4 God, to me, it seems,
   is a verb
   not a noun,
   proper or improper.
   No More Secondhand God (1963) p. 28 (untitled
   poem written in 1940). Cf. 175:24

Thomas Fuller 1608–61

5 Anger is one of the sinews of the soul.
   The Holy State and the Profane State bk. 3 'Of
   Anger'

6 Light (God's eldest daughter) is a principal
   beauty in building.
   The Holy State and the Profane State bk. 3 'Of
   Building'

Thomas Fuller 1654–1734

7 We are all Adam's children but silk makes
   the difference.
   Gnomologia (1732) no. 5425

Alfred Funke b. 1869

8 *Gott strafe England!*
   God punish England!
   Schwert und Myrte (1914) p. 78

Sir David Maxwell Fyfe 1900–67

See LORD KILMUIR

Rose Fyleman 1877–1957

9 There are fairies at the bottom of our
   garden!
   Fairies and Chimneys (1918) 'The Fairies'

Thomas Gainsborough 1727–88

10 We are all going to Heaven, and Vandyke is
   of the company.
   Attributed last words, in W. B. Boulton
   Thomas Gainsborough (1905) ch. 9

Hugh Gaitskell 1906–63

11 There are some of us ... who will fight and
   fight and fight again to save the Party we
   love.
   Speech at Labour Party Conference,
   5 October 1960; in *Report of 59th Annual
   Conference* p. 201

12 It means the end of a thousand years of
   history.
   On a European federation; Speech at Labour
   Party Conference, 3 October 1962, in *Report of
   61st Annual Conference* p. 159

Gaius (or Caius) AD *c.*110–*c.*180

13 *Damnosa hereditas.*
   Ruinous inheritance.
   The Institutes bk. 2, ch. 163

J. K. Galbraith 1908–

14 These are the days when men of all social
   disciplines and all political faiths seek the
   comfortable and the accepted ... in minor
   modification of the scriptural parable, the
   bland lead the bland.
   The Affluent Society (1958) ch. 1, sect. 3

15 The greater the wealth, the thicker will be
   the dirt.
   The Affluent Society (1958) ch. 18, sect. 2

Galileo Galilei 1564–1642

16 *Eppur si muove.*
   But it does move.
   Attributed to Galileo after his recantation,
   that the earth moves around the sun, in
   1632

John Galsworthy 1867–1933

17 He was afflicted by the thought that where
   Beauty was, nothing ever ran quite
   straight, which, no doubt, was why so
   many people looked on it as immoral.
   In Chancery (1920) pt. 1, ch. 13

18 A man of action forced into a state of
   thought is unhappy until he can get out of
   it.
   Maid in Waiting (1931) ch. 3

John Galt 1779–1839

19 From the lone shieling of the misty island
   Mountains divide us, and the waste of
   seas—
   Yet still the blood is strong, the heart is
   Highland,
   And we in dreams behold the Hebrides!
   'Canadian Boat Song', attributed to Galt and
   translated from the Gaelic in *Blackwoods
   Edinburgh Magazine* September 1829 'Noctes
   Ambrosianae' no. 46

Greta Garbo 1905–90

1 I want to be alone.
Grand Hotel (1932 film)

Federico García Lorca 1899–1936

2 *A las cinco de la tarde.*
Eran las cinco en punto de la tarde.
Un niño trajo la blanca sábana
a las cinco de la tarde.
At five in the afternoon.
It was exactly five in the afternoon.
A boy brought the white sheet
at five in the afternoon.
Llanto por Ignacio Sánchez Mejías (1935) 'La
Cogida y la muerte'

3 *Verde que te quiero verde.*
Verde viento. Verdes ramas.
El barco sobre la mar
y el caballo en la montaña.
Green how I love you green.
Green wind.
Green boughs.
The ship on the sea
and the horse on the mountain.
Romance sonámbulo (1924–7)

Richard Gardiner b. c.1533

4 Sowe Carrets in your Gardens, and humbly
praise God for them, as for a singular and
great blessing.
*Profitable Instructions for the Manuring, Sowing
and Planting of Kitchen Gardens* (1599)

Ed Gardner 1901–63

5 Opera is when a guy gets stabbed in the
back and, instead of bleeding, he sings.
In *Duffy's Tavern* (US radio programme, 1940s)

James A. Garfield 1831–81

6 Fellow-citizens: God reigns, and the
Government at Washington lives!
Speech on the assassination of President
Lincoln, 1865. See *Death of President Garfield*
(1881) p. 24

John Nance Garner 1868–1967

7 The vice-presidency isn't worth a pitcher of
warm piss.
In O. C. Fisher *Cactus Jack* (1978) ch. 11

David Garrick 1717–79

8 Heart of oak are our ships,
Heart of oak are our men:
We always are ready;
Steady, boys, steady;
We'll fight and we'll conquer again and
again.
Harlequin's Invasion (1759) 'Heart of Oak'
(song)

9 Here lies Nolly Goldsmith, for shortness
called Noll,
Who wrote like an angel, but talked like
poor Poll.
'Impromptu Epitaph' (written 1773/4).
Cf. 155:1

10 A fellow-feeling makes one wond'rous
kind.
'An Occasional Prologue on Quitting the
Theatre' 10 June 1776

11 Heaven sends us good meat, but the Devil
sends cooks.
'On Doctor Goldsmith's Characteristical
Cookery' (1777)

See also GEORGE COLMAN and DAVID GARRICK

William Lloyd Garrison 1805–79

12 I am in earnest—I will not equivocate—I
will not excuse—I will not retreat a single
inch—and I will be heard!
The Liberator 1 January 1831 'Salutatory
Address'

13 The compact which exists between the
North and the South is 'a covenant with
death and an agreement with hell'.
Resolution adopted by the Massachusetts
Anti-Slavery Society, 27 January 1843; in A.
H. Grimke *William Lloyd Garrison* (1891)
ch. 16. Cf. 45:28

Sir Samuel Garth 1661–1719

14 Hard was their lodging, homely was their
food;
For all their luxury was doing good.
'Claremont' (1715) l. 148

15 A barren superfluity of words.
The Dispensary (1699) canto 2, l. 82

Elizabeth Gaskell 1810–65

16 A man ... is *so* in the way in the house!
Cranford (1853) ch. 1

17 Bombazine would have shown a deeper
sense of her loss.
Cranford (1853) ch. 7

18 I'll not listen to reason ... Reason always
means what someone else has got to say.
Cranford (1853) ch. 14

19 We donnot want dainties, we want bellyfulls.
Mary Barton (1848) ch. 16

20 That kind of patriotism which consists in
hating all other nations.
Sylvia's Lovers (1863) ch. 1

Gavarni 1804–66

21 *Les enfants terribles.*
The little terrors.
Title of a series of prints (1842)

John Gay 1685–1732

1 O ruddier than the cherry,
  O sweeter than the berry.
  Acis and Galatea (performed 1718) pt. 2

2 How, like a moth, the simple maid
  Still plays about the flame!
  The Beggar's Opera (1728) act 1, sc. 4, air 4

3 Do you think your mother and I should
  have lived comfortably so long together, if
  ever we had been married?
  The Beggar's Opera (1728) act 1, sc. 8

4 The comfortable estate of widowhood, is
  the only hope that keeps up a wife's
  spirits.
  The Beggar's Opera (1728) act 1, sc. 10

5 If with me you'd fondly stray
  Over the hills and far away.
  The Beggar's Opera (1728) act 1, sc. 13, air 16

6 Youth's the season made for joys;
  Love is then our duty.
  The Beggar's Opera (1728) act 2, sc. 4, air 22

7 How happy could I be with either,
  Were t'other dear charmer away!
  The Beggar's Opera (1728) act 2, sc. 13, air 35

8 She who has never loved, has never lived.
  The Captives (1724) act 2, sc. 2

9 She who trifles with all
  Is less likely to fall
  Than she who but trifles with one.
  'The Coquet Mother and the Coquet
  Daughter' (1727)

10 And when a lady's in the case,
  You know, all other things give place.
  Fables (1727) 'The Hare and Many Friends'
  l. 41

11 An open foe may prove a curse,
  But a pretended friend is worse.
  Fables (1727) 'The Shepherd's Dog and the
  Wolf' l. 33

12 Studious of elegance and ease,
  Myself alone I seek to please.
  Fables (1738) 'The Man, the Cat, the Dog, and
  the Fly' l. 127

13 Give me, kind heaven, a private station,
  A mind serene for contemplation.
  Fables (1738) 'The Vulture, the Sparrow, and
  Other Birds' l. 69

14 Behold the bright original appear.
  'A Letter to a Lady' (1714) l. 85

15 Life is a jest; and all things show it.
  I thought so once; but now I know it.
  'My Own Epitaph' (1720)

16 An inconstant woman, tho' she has no
  chance to be very happy, can never be very
  unhappy.
  'Polly' (1729) act 1, sc. 14

17 All in the Downs the fleet was moored,
  The streamers waving in the wind,
  When black-eyed Susan came aboard.
  'Sweet William's Farewell to Black-Eyed
  Susan' (1720)

Noel Gay 1898–1954

18 I'm leaning on a lamp-post at the corner of
  the street,
  In case a certain little lady comes by.
  'Leaning on a Lamp-Post' (1937); sung by
  George Formby

Sir Eric Geddes 1875–1937

19 The Germans ... are going to be squeezed
  as a lemon is squeezed—until the pips
  squeak.
  Speech at Cambridge, 10 December 1918, in
  Cambridge Daily News 11 December 1918

George I 1660–1727

20 I hate all Boets and Bainters.
  In John Campbell *Lives of the Chief Justices*
  (1849) 'Lord Mansfield'

George II 1683–1760

21 *Non, j'aurai des maîtresses.*
  No, I shall have mistresses.
  When Queen Caroline, on her deathbed,
  urged him to marry again; in J. Hervey
  Memoirs of the Reign of George II (1848) vol. 2.
  The Queen replied, '*Ah! mon dieu! cela
  n'empêche pas* [Oh, my God! That won't make
  any difference]'

22 Mad, is he? Then I hope he will *bite* some
  of my other generals.
  Replying to the Duke of Newcastle, who had
  complained that General Wolfe was a
  madman; in H. B. Willson *Life and Letters of
  James Wolfe* (1909) ch. 17

George III 1738–1820

23 Born and educated in this country, I glory
  in the name of Briton.
  The King's Speech on Opening the Session in
  Hansard 18 November 1760, col. 942

24 Was there ever such stuff as great part of
  Shakespeare? Only one must not say so!
  In *Diary and Letters of Madame d'Arblay* [Fanny
  Burney] vol. 2 (1842) Diary, 19 December
  1785

George V 1865–1936

25 The Old Country must wake up if she
  intends to maintain her old position of
  pre-eminence in her Colonial trade against
  foreign competitors.
  Speech at Guildhall, 5 December 1901, in *The
  Times* 6 December 1901; reprinted in 1911
  with the title 'Wake up, England'

26 No more coals to Newcastle, no more
  Hoares to Paris
  Following Samuel Hoare's resignation as
  Foreign Secretary on 18 December 1935; in
  Earl of Avon *Facing the Dictators* (1962) pt. 2,
  ch. 1

1 After I am dead, the boy will ruin himself
  in twelve months.
> Of his son, the future Edward VIII; in K.
> Middlemas and J. Barnes *Baldwin* (1969)
> ch. 34

2 Bugger Bognor.
> Possibly on his deathbed. See K. Rose *King
> George V* (1983) ch. 9

3 How's the Empire?
> To his private secretary on the morning of
> his death; in K. Rose *King George V* (1983)
> ch. 10

George VI 1895–1952

4 Abroad is bloody.
> In W. H. Auden *A Certain World* (1970)
> 'Royalty'. Cf. 232:10

5 I feel happier now that we have no allies
  to be polite to and to pamper.
> To Queen Mary, 27 June 1940; in J. Wheeler-
> Bennett *King George VI* (1958) pt. 3, ch. 6

Daniel George

6 O Freedom, what liberties are taken in thy
  name!
> *The Perpetual Pessimist* (1963) p. 58. Cf. 262:3

David Lloyd George

See LLOYD GEORGE

Ira Gershwin 1896–1983

7 In time the Rockies may crumble,
  Gibraltar may tumble,
  They're only made of clay,
  But our love is here to stay.
> 'Love is Here to Stay' (1938 song)

8 Holding hands at midnight
  'Neath a starry sky,
  Nice work if you can get it,
  And you can get it if you try.
> 'Nice Work If You Can Get It' (1937 song)

Giuseppe Giacosa 1847–1906 and Luigi Illica 1857–1919

9 *Che gelida manina.*
  Your tiny hand is frozen.
> *La Bohème* (1896) act 1 (Rodolfo to Mimi);
> music by Puccini

Edward Gibbon 1737–94

10 The various modes of worship, which
   prevailed in the Roman world, were all
   considered by the people as equally true;
   by the philosopher, as equally false; and by
   the magistrate, as equally useful. And thus
   toleration produced not only mutual
   indulgence, but even religious concord.
> *Decline and Fall of the Roman Empire* (1776–88)
> ch. 2

11 History ... is, indeed, little more than the
   register of the crimes, follies, and
   misfortunes of mankind.
> *Decline and Fall of the Roman Empire* (1776–88)
> ch. 3. Cf. 340:20

12 In every deed of mischief he had a heart to
   resolve, a head to contrive, and a hand to
   execute.
> *Decline and Fall of the Roman Empire* (1776–88)
> ch. 48 (of Comnenus). Cf. 101:10

13 To the University of Oxford I acknowledge
   no obligation; and she will as cheerfully
   renounce me for a son, as I am willing to
   disclaim her for a mother. I spent fourteen
   months at Magdalen College: they proved
   the fourteen months the most idle and
   unprofitable of my whole life.
> *Memoirs of My Life* (1796) ch. 3

14 I sighed as a lover, I obeyed as a son.
> *Memoirs of My Life* (1796) ch. 4 n.

15 Crowds without company, and dissipation
   without pleasure.
> *Memoirs of My Life* (1796) ch. 5

16 My English text is chaste, and all licentious
   passages are left in the obscurity of a
   learned language.
> *Memoirs of My Life* (1796) ch. 8 (parodied as
> 'decent obscurity' in the *Anti-Jacobin*, 1797–8)

Stella Gibbons 1902–89

17 Something nasty in the woodshed.
> *Cold Comfort Farm* (1932) ch. 10

Wolcott Gibbs 1902–58

18 Backward ran sentences until reeled the
   mind.
> *New Yorker* 28 November 1936 'Time ...
> Fortune ... Life ... Luce' (satirizing the style
> of *Time* magazine)

Kahlil Gibran 1883–1931

19 Your children are not your children.
   They are the sons and daughters of Life's
   longing for itself.
   They came through you but not from you
   And though they are with you yet they
   belong not to you.
> *The Prophet* (1923) 'On Children'

20 Work is love made visible.
> *The Prophet* (1923) 'On Work'

21 An exaggeration is a truth that has lost its
   temper.
> *Sand and Foam* (1926) p. 59

Wilfrid Wilson Gibson 1878–1962

22 But we, how shall we turn to little things
   And listen to the birds and winds and
   streams
   Made holy by their dreams,
   Nor feel the heart-break in the heart of
   things?
> 'Lament' (1918)

André Gide 1869–1951

1 The great secret of Stendhal, his great
shrewdness, consisted in writing *at once* ...
thought charged with emotion.
Journal (1939) vol. 3, 3 September 1937 (tr. J.
O'Brien)

2 Hugo—alas!
When asked who was the greatest 19th-
century poet; in C. Martin *La Maturité d'André
Gide* (1977) p. 502

Sir Humphrey Gilbert *c.*1537–83

3 We are as near to heaven by sea as by
land!
In Richard Hakluyt *Third and Last Volume of
the Voyages ... of the English Nation* (1600)
p. 159. Cf. 136:7

W. S. Gilbert 1836–1911

4 That celebrated,
Cultivated,
Underrated
Nobleman,
The Duke of Plaza Toro!
The Gondoliers (1889) act 1

5 Of that there is no manner of doubt—
No probable, possible shadow of doubt—
No possible doubt whatever.
The Gondoliers (1889) act 1

6 But the privilege and pleasure
That we treasure beyond measure
Is to run on little errands for the Ministers
of State.
The Gondoliers (1889) act 2

7 Take a pair of sparkling eyes.
The Gondoliers (1889) act 2

8 When every one is somebodee,
Then no one's anybody.
The Gondoliers (1889) act 2

9 Bow, bow, ye lower middle classes!
Bow, bow, ye tradesmen, bow, ye masses.
Iolanthe (1882) act 1

10 The Law is the true embodiment
Of everything that's excellent.
It has no kind of fault or flaw,
And I, my Lords, embody the Law.
Iolanthe (1882) act 1

11 Hearts just as pure and fair
May beat in Belgrave Square
As in the lowly air
Of Seven Dials.
Iolanthe (1882) act 1

12 I often think it's comical
How Nature always does contrive
That every boy and every gal,
That's born into the world alive,
Is either a little Liberal,
Or else a little Conservative!
Iolanthe (1882) act 2

13 The prospect of a lot
Of dull MPs in close proximity,
All thinking for themselves is what
No man can face with equanimity.
Iolanthe (1882) act 2

14 The House of Peers, throughout the war,
Did nothing in particular,
And did it very well.
Iolanthe (1882) act 2

15 When you're lying awake with a dismal
headache, and repose is taboo'd by
anxiety,
I conceive you may use any language you
choose to indulge in, without
impropriety.
Iolanthe (1882) act 2

16 For you dream you are crossing the
Channel, and tossing about in a steamer
from Harwich—
Which is something between a large
bathing machine and a very small second
class carriage.
Iolanthe (1882) act 2

17 A wandering minstrel I—
A thing of shreds and patches.
Of ballads, songs and snatches,
And dreamy lullaby!
The Mikado (1885) act 1. Cf. 276:21

18 I can trace my ancestry back to a
protoplasmal primordial atomic globule.
Consequently, my family pride is
something in-conceivable. I can't help it. I
was born sneering.
The Mikado (1885) act 1

19 As some day it may happen that a victim
must be found,
I've got a little list—I've got a little list
Of society offenders who might well be
under ground
And who never would be missed—who
never would be missed!
The Mikado (1885) act 1

20 The idiot who praises, with enthusiastic
tone,
All centuries but this, and every country
but his own.
The Mikado (1885) act 1. Cf. 89:11, 121:17,
243:8

21 Three little maids from school are we.
The Mikado (1885) act 1

22 Life is a joke that's just begun.
The Mikado (1885) act 1

23 Three little maids who, all unwary,
Come from a ladies' seminary.
The Mikado (1885) act 1

24 Modified rapture!
The Mikado (1885) act 1

25 Awaiting the sensation of a short, sharp
shock,
From a cheap and chippy chopper on a big
black block.
The Mikado (1885) act 1

26 Here's a how-de-doo!
The Mikado (1885) act 2

27 Here's a state of things!
The Mikado (1885) act 2

1 My object all sublime
  I shall achieve in time—
  To let the punishment fit the crime—
  The punishment fit the crime.
    The Mikado (1885) act 2

2 And there he plays extravagant matches
  In fitless finger-stalls
  On a cloth untrue
  With a twisted cue
  And elliptical billiard balls.
    The Mikado (1885) act 2

3 I have a left shoulder-blade that is a
  miracle of loveliness. People come miles to
  see it. My right elbow has a fascination
  that few can resist.
    The Mikado (1885) act 2

4 Something lingering, with boiling oil in it,
  I fancy.
    The Mikado (1885) act 2

5 Merely corroborative detail, intended to
  give artistic verisimilitude to an otherwise
  bald and unconvincing narrative.
    The Mikado (1885) act 2

6 The flowers that bloom in the spring,
  Tra la,
  Have nothing to do with the case.
    The Mikado (1885) act 2

7 On a tree by a river a little tom-tit
  Sang 'Willow, titwillow, titwillow!'
    The Mikado (1885) act 2

8 There's a fascination frantic
  In a ruin that's romantic;
  Do you think you are sufficiently decayed?
    The Mikado (1885) act 2

9 If you're anxious for to shine in the high
  aesthetic line as a man of culture rare.
    Patience (1881) act 1

10 The meaning doesn't matter if it's only idle
  chatter of a transcendental kind.
    Patience (1881) act 1

11 An attachment à la Plato for a bashful
  young potato, or a not too French French
  bean!
    Patience (1881) act 1

12 Francesca di Rimini, miminy, piminy,
  Je-ne-sais-quoi young man!
    Patience (1881) act 2

13 A greenery-yallery, Grosvenor Gallery,
  Foot-in-the-grave young man!
    Patience (1881) act 2

14 I'm called Little Buttercup—dear Little
  Buttercup,
  Though I could never tell why.
    HMS Pinafore (1878) act 1

15 What, never?
  No, never!
  What, *never*?
  Hardly ever!
    HMS Pinafore (1878) act 1

16 Though 'Bother it' I may
  Occasionally say,
  I never use a big, big D—
    HMS Pinafore (1878) act 1

17 And so do his sisters, and his cousins and
  his aunts!
  His sisters and his cousins,
  Whom he reckons up by dozens,
  And his aunts!
    HMS Pinafore (1878) act 1

18 I cleaned the windows and I swept the
  floor,
  And I polished up the handle of the big
  front door.
  I polished up that handle so carefullee
  That now I am the Ruler of the Queen's
  Navee!
    HMS Pinafore (1878) act 1

19 I always voted at my party's call,
  And I never thought of thinking for myself
  at all.
    HMS Pinafore (1878) act 1

20 Stick close to your desks and never go to
  sea,
  And you all may be Rulers of the Queen's
  Navee!
    HMS Pinafore (1878) act 1

21 For he might have been a Roosian,
  A French, or Turk, or Proosian,
  Or perhaps Ital-ian!
  But in spite of all temptations
  To belong to other nations,
  He remains an Englishman!
    HMS Pinafore (1878) act 2

22 It is, it is a glorious thing
  To be a Pirate King.
    The Pirates of Penzance (1879) act 1

23 In short, in matters vegetable, animal, and
  mineral,
  I am the very model of a modern Major-
  General.
    The Pirates of Penzance (1879) act 1

24 When constabulary duty's to be done,
  A policeman's lot is not a happy one.
    The Pirates of Penzance (1879) act 2

25 Man is Nature's sole mistake!
    Princess Ida (1884) act 2

26 He combines the manners of a Marquess
  with the morals of a Methodist.
    Ruddigore (1887) act 1

27 Some word that teems with hidden
  meaning—like Basingstoke.
    Ruddigore (1887) act 2

28 This particularly rapid, unintelligible
  patter
  Isn't generally heard, and if it is it doesn't
  matter.
    Ruddigore (1887) act 2

29 I was a pale young curate then.
    The Sorcerer (1877) act 1

30 So I fell in love with a rich attorney's
  Elderly ugly daughter.
    Trial by Jury (1875)

31 She may very well pass for forty-three
  In the dusk with a light behind her!
    Trial by Jury (1875)

Eric Gill 1882–1940

1 That state is a state of slavery in which a man does what he likes to do in his spare time and in his working time that which is required of him.

Art-nonsense and Other Essays (1929) 'Slavery and Freedom'. Cf. 105:5

Allen Ginsberg 1926–

2 What if someone gave a war & Nobody came?

'Graffiti' (1972). Cf. 266:16

3 I saw the best minds of my generation destroyed by madness, starving hysterical naked.

Howl (1956) p. 9

George Gipp d. 1920

4 Win just one for the Gipper.

Gipp being an American football legend, the catch-phrase later became associated with Ronald Reagan, who uttered the immortal words in the 1940 film *Knute Rockne, All American*

Jean Giraudoux 1882–1944

5 As soon as war is declared it will be impossible to hold the poets back. Rhyme is still the most effective drum.

La Guerre de Troie n'aura pas lieu (1935) act 2, sc. 4 (translated by Christopher Fry as *Tiger at the Gates*, 1955)

6 No poet ever interpreted nature as freely as a lawyer interprets the truth.

La Guerre de Troie n'aura pas lieu (1935) act 2, sc. 5 (tr. Christopher Fry)

W. E. Gladstone 1809–98

7 Finance is, as it were, the stomach of the country, from which all the other organs take their tone.

Article on finance, 1858, in H. C. G. Matthew *Gladstone 1809–1874* (1986) ch. 5

8 You cannot fight against the future. Time is on our side.

Speech on the Reform Bill, in *Hansard* 27 April 1866, col. 152

9 We have been borne down in a torrent of gin and beer.

Letter to his brother, 6 February 1874, in J. Morley *Life of Gladstone* (1903) vol. 2, ch. 14

10 [The Turks] one and all, bag and baggage, shall I hope clear out from the province they have desolated and profaned.

Bulgarian Horrors and the Question of the East (1876) p. 61

11 Our first site in Egypt, be it by larceny or be it by emption, will be the almost certain egg of a North African Empire.

Aggression on Egypt and Freedom in the East (1884) p. 16

12 The resources of civilization against its enemies are not yet exhausted.

Speech, 7 October 1881, in H. W. Lucy (ed.) *Speeches of . . . Gladstone* (1885) p. 57

13 All the world over, I will back the masses against the classes.

Speech in Liverpool, 28 June 1886, in *The Times* 29 June 1886

14 It is not a Life at all. It is a Reticence, in three volumes.

On J. W. Cross's *Life of George Eliot*; in E. F. Benson *As We Were* (1930) ch. 6

15 I absorb the vapour and return it as a flood.

On public speaking, in Lord Riddell *Some Things That Matter* (1927 ed.) p. 69

Hannah Glasse fl. 1747

16 Take your hare when it is cased.

The Art of Cookery Made Plain and Easy (1747) ch. 1 (*cased* skinned). The proverbial 'First catch your hare' dates from *c.*1300

Duke of Gloucester 1743–1805

17 Another damned, thick, square book! Always scribble, scribble, scribble! Eh! Mr Gibbon?

In Henry Best *Personal and Literary Memorials* (1829) p. 68 (also attributed to the Duke of Cumberland and George III)

Jean-Luc Godard 1930–

18 Photography is truth. The cinema is truth 24 times per second.

Le Petit Soldat (1960 film)

19 'Movies should have a beginning, a middle and an end,' harrumphed French film maker Georges Franju . . . 'Certainly,' replied Jean-Luc Godard. 'But not necessarily in that order.'

Time 14 September 1981

A. D. Godley 1856–1925

20 What is this that roareth thus?
Can it be a Motor Bus?
Yes, the smell and hideous hum
Indicat Motorem Bum!

Letter, 10 January 1914, in *Reliquiae* (1926) vol. 1, p. 292

Joseph Goebbels 1897–1945

21 If we are attacked we can only defend ourselves with guns not with butter.

Speech in Berlin, 17 January 1936, in *Deutsche Allgemeine Zeitung* 18 January 1936. Cf. 153:22

Hermann Goering 1893–1946

22 Would you rather have butter or guns? . . . preparedness makes us powerful. Butter merely makes us fat.

Speech at Hamburg, 1936, in W. Frischauer *Goering* (1951) ch. 10. Cf. 153:21

1 I herewith commission you to carry out all preparations with regard to … a *total solution* of the Jewish question in those territories of Europe which are under German influence.

 Instructions to Heydrich, 31 July 1941; in W. L. Shirer *Rise and Fall of the Third Reich* (1962) bk. 5, ch. 27

Johann Wolfgang von Goethe
1749–1832

2 Elective affinities.

 Title of novel (1809)

3 *Es irrt der Mensch, so lang er strebt.*
Man will err while yet he strives.

 Faust pt. 1 (1808) 'Prolog im Himmel'

4 *Entbehren sollst Du! sollst entbehren!*
Das ist der ewige Gesang.
Deny yourself! You must deny yourself!
That is the song that never ends.

 Faust pt. 1 (1808) 'Studierzimmer'

5 *Grau, teurer Freund, ist alle Theorie*
Und grün des Lebens goldner Baum.
All theory, dear friend, is grey, but the golden tree of actual life springs ever green.

 Faust pt. 1 (1808) 'Studierzimmer'

6 *Meine Ruh' ist hin,*
Mein Herz ist schwer.
My peace is gone,
My heart is heavy.

 Faust pt. 1 (1808) 'Gretchen am Spinnrad'

7 *Die Tat ist alles, nichts der Ruhm.*
The deed is all, the glory nothing.

 Faust pt. 2 (1832) 'Hochgebirg'

8 *Das Ewig-Weibliche zieht uns hinan.*
Eternal Woman draws us upward.

 Faust pt. 2 (1832) 'Hochgebirg' *ad fin.*

9 In art the best is good enough.

 Italienische Reise (1816–17) 3 March 1787

10 *Der Aberglaube ist die Poesie des Lebens.*
Superstition is the poetry of life.

 Maximen und Reflexionen (1819) 'Literatur und Sprache' no. 908

11 *Es bildet ein Talent sich in der Stille,*
Sich ein Charakter in dem Strom der Welt.
Talent develops in quiet places, character in the full current of human life.

 Torquato Tasso (1790) act 1, sc. 2

12 *Über allen Gipfeln*
Ist Ruh'.
Over all the mountain tops is peace.

 Wanderers Nachtlied (1821)

13 *Kennst du das Land, wo die Zitronen blühn?*
Know you the land where the lemon-trees bloom?

 Wilhelm Meisters Lehrjahre (1795–6) bk. 3, ch. 1

14 I do not know myself, and God forbid that I should.

 J. P. Eckermann *Gespräche mit Goethe* (1836–48) 10 April 1829. Cf. 13:5

15 More light!

 Attributed dying words (actually 'Open the second shutter, so that more light can come in')

Isaac Goldberg 1887–1938

16 Diplomacy is to do and say
The nastiest thing in the nicest way.

 The Reflex October 1927, p. 77

Oliver Goldsmith 1730–74

17 Sweet Auburn, loveliest village of the plain.

 The Deserted Village (1770) l. 1

18 Ill fares the land, to hast'ning ills a prey,
Where wealth accumulates, and men decay;
Princes and lords may flourish, or may fade;
A breath can make them, as a breath has made;
But a bold peasantry, their country's pride,
When once destroyed, can never be supplied.

 The Deserted Village (1770) l. 51

19 How happy he who crowns in shades like these,
A youth of labour with an age of ease.

 The Deserted Village (1770) l. 99

20 The loud laugh that spoke the vacant mind.

 The Deserted Village (1770) l. 122

21 A man he was to all the country dear,
And passing rich with forty pounds a year.

 The Deserted Village (1770) l. 141

22 Truth from his lips prevailed with double sway,
And fools, who came to scoff, remained to pray.

 The Deserted Village (1770) l. 179

23 Well had the boding tremblers learned to trace
The day's disasters in his morning face.

 The Deserted Village (1770) l. 199

24 And still they gazed, and still the wonder grew,
That one small head could carry all he knew.

 The Deserted Village (1770) l. 215

25   How wide the limits stand
Between a splendid and a happy land.

 The Deserted Village (1770) l. 267

26 In all the silent manliness of grief.

 The Deserted Village (1770) l. 384

27 Man wants but little here below,
Nor wants that little long.

 'Edwin and Angelina, or the Hermit' (1766). Cf. 360:22

28 The man recovered of the bite,
The dog it was that died.

 'Elegy on the Death of a Mad Dog' (1766)

1 Our Garrick's a salad; for in him we see
Oil, vinegar, sugar, and saltness agree.
Retaliation (1774) l. 11

2 Too nice for a statesman, too proud for a
wit.
Retaliation (1774) l. 32 (of Edmund Burke)

3 An abridgement of all that was pleasant in
man.
Retaliation (1774) l. 93 (of Garrick)

4 Such is the patriot's boast, where'er we
roam,
His first, best country ever is, at home.
The Traveller (1764) l. 73

5 Laws grind the poor, and rich men rule the
law.
The Traveller (1764) l. 386

6 Friendship is a disinterested commerce
between equals; love, an abject intercourse
between tyrants and slaves.
The Good-Natured Man (1768) act 1

7 Silence is become his mother tongue.
The Good-Natured Man (1768) act 2

8 Let schoolmasters puzzle their brain,
With grammar, and nonsense, and
learning,
Good liquor, I stoutly maintain,
Gives genius a better discerning.
She Stoops to Conquer (1773) act 1, sc. 1 'Song'

9 The very pink of perfection.
She Stoops to Conquer (1773) act 1

10 This is Liberty-Hall, gentlemen.
She Stoops to Conquer (1773) act 2

11 I ... chose my wife, as she did her wedding
gown, not for a fine glossy surface, but
such qualities as would wear well.
The Vicar of Wakefield (1766) ch. 1

12 All our adventures were by the fire-side,
and all our migrations from the blue bed
to the brown.
The Vicar of Wakefield (1766) ch. 1

13 When lovely woman stoops to folly
And finds too late that men betray,
What charm can soothe her melancholy,
What art can wash her guilt away?
The Vicar of Wakefield (1766) ch. 29

14 There is no arguing with Johnson; for
when his pistol misses fire, he knocks you
down with the butt end of it.
In James Boswell *Life of Samuel Johnson* (1934
ed.) vol. 2, p. 100 (26 October 1769)

Barry Goldwater 1909–

15 I would remind you that extremism in the
defence of liberty is no vice! And let me
remind you also that moderation in the
pursuit of justice is no virtue!
Accepting the presidential nomination,
16 July 1964, in *New York Times* 17 July 1964,
p. 1

Sam Goldwyn 1882–1974

16 Gentlemen, include me out.
Resigning from the Motion Picture
Producers and Distributors of America,
October 1933; in M. Freedland *The Goldwyn
Touch* (1986) ch. 10

17 A verbal contract isn't worth the paper it
is written on.
In A. Johnston *The Great Goldwyn* (1937) ch. 1

18 Pictures are for entertainment, messages
should be delivered by Western Union.
In A. Marx *Goldwyn* (1976) ch. 15

Ivan Goncharov 1812–91

19 No devastating or redeeming fires have
ever burnt in my life ... My life began by
flickering out.
Oblomov (1859) pt. 2, ch. 4 (tr. D. Magarshack)

20 You lost your ability for doing things in
childhood ... It all began with your
inability to put on your socks and ended by
your inability to live.
Oblomov (1859) pt. 4, ch. 2 (tr. D. Magarshack)

Adam Lindsay Gordon 1833–70

21 Life is mostly froth and bubble,
Two things stand like stone,
Kindness in another's trouble,
Courage in your own.
Ye Wearie Wayfarer (1866) 'Fytte 8'

Mack Gordon 1904–59

22 Dinner in the diner nothing could be finer
Than to have your ham'n eggs in Carolina.
'Chattanooga Choo-choo' (1941 song)

Stuart Gorrell 1902–63

23 Georgia, Georgia, no peace I find,
Just an old sweet song keeps Georgia on
my mind.
'Georgia on my Mind' (1930 song)

Lord Goschen 1831–1907

24 I have the courage of my opinions, but I
have not the temerity to give a political
blank cheque to Lord Salisbury.
Speech, *Hansard* 19 February 1884, col. 1420

Edmund Gosse 1849–1928

25 A sheep in sheep's clothing.
Of the 'woolly-bearded poet' Sturge Moore,
in F. Greenslet *Under the Bridge* (1943) ch. 10.
Cf. 100:7

Edward Meyrick Goulburn
1818–97

26 Let the scintillations of your wit be like the
coruscations of summer lightning, lambent
but innocuous.
Sermon at Rugby School, in W. Tuckwell
Reminiscences of Oxford (2nd ed., 1907) p. 272

Goya 1746–1828

1 The dream of reason produces monsters.
   Los Caprichos (1799) plate 43 (title)

D. M. Graham 1911–

2 That this House will in no circumstances
   fight for its King and Country.
   Motion worded by Graham for a debate at
   the Oxford Union, 9 February 1933

Harry Graham 1874–1936

3 'There's been an accident,' they said,
   'Your servant's cut in half; he's dead!'
   'Indeed!' said Mr Jones, 'and please,
   Send me the half that's got my keys.'
   Ruthless Rhymes for Heartless Homes (1899) 'Mr
   Jones' (attributed to 'G.W.')

4 Billy, in one of his nice new sashes,
   Fell in the fire and was burnt to ashes;
   Now, although the room grows chilly,
   I haven't the heart to poke poor Billy.
   Ruthless Rhymes for Heartless Homes (1899)
   'Tender-Heartedness'

Kenneth Grahame 1859–1932

5 There is *nothing*—absolutely nothing—half
   so much worth doing as simply messing
   about in boats.
   The Wind in the Willows (1908) ch. 1

6 The poetry of motion! The *real* way to
   travel! The *only* way to travel! Here
   today—in next week tomorrow!
   The Wind in the Willows (1908) ch. 2. Cf. 190:5

James Grainger c.1721–66

7 What is fame? an empty bubble;
   Gold? a transient, shining trouble.
   'Solitude' (1755) l. 96

Sir Robert Grant 1785–1838

8 O worship the King, all-glorious above;
   O gratefully sing his power and his love:
   Our Shield and Defender, the Ancient of
   Days,
   Pavilioned in splendour, and girded with
   praise.
   'O worship the King, all glorious above' (1833
   hymn)

Ulysses S. Grant 1822–85

9 I know no method to secure the repeal of
   bad or obnoxious laws so effective as their
   stringent execution.
   Inaugural Address, 4 March 1869, in P. C.
   Headley *Life and Campaigns of General U. S.
   Grant* (1869) ch. 29

George Granville, Baron Lansdowne 1666–1735

10 Bright as the day, and like the morning,
   fair,
   Such Cloe is ... and common as the air.
   'Cloe' (1712)

11 Cowards in scarlet pass for men of war.
   The She Gallants (1696) act 5

John Woodcock Graves 1795–1886

12 D'ye ken John Peel with his coat so grey?
   D'ye ken John Peel at the break of the day?
   D'ye ken John Peel when he's far far away
   With his hounds and his horn in the
   morning?
   'Twas the sound of his horn called me
   from my bed,
   And the cry of his hounds has me oft-times
   led;
   For Peel's view-hollo would waken the
   dead,
   Or a fox from his lair in the morning.
   'John Peel' (1820)

Robert Graves 1895–1985

13 Children are dumb to say how hot the day
   is,
   How hot the scent is of the summer rose.
   'The Cool Web' (1927)

14 There's a cool web of language winds us in,
   Retreat from too much joy or too much
   fear.
   'The Cool Web' (1927)

15 Truth-loving Persians do not dwell upon
   The trivial skirmish fought near Marathon.
   'The Persian Version' (1945)

16 As you are woman, so be lovely:
   As you are lovely, so be various.
   'Pygmalion to Galatea' (1927)

17 Goodbye to all that.
   Title of autobiography (1929)

John Chipman Gray 1839–1915

18 Dirt is only matter out of place; and what
   is a blot on the escutcheon of the Common
   Law may be a jewel in the crown of the
   Social Republic.
   Restraints on the Alienation of Property (2nd ed.,
   1895) preface

Patrick, 6th Lord Gray d. 1612

19 A dead woman bites not.
   Oral tradition, Gray being said to have
   pressed hard for the execution of Mary
   Queen of Scots in 1587, with the words
   '*Mortua non mordet* [Being dead, she will bite
   no more]'; in A. Darcy's 1625 translation of
   William Camden's *Annals of the Reign of Queen
   Elizabeth* (1615) vol. 1, p. 196

Thomas Gray 1716–71

1 Ruin seize thee, ruthless King!
Confusion on thy banners wait,
Tho' fanned by Conquest's crimson wing
They mock the air with idle state.
The Bard (1757) l. 1

2 Weave the warp, and weave the woof,
The winding-sheet of Edward's race.
Give ample room, and verge enough
The characters of hell to trace.
The Bard (1757) l. 49

3 In gallant trim the gilded vessel goes;
Youth on the prow, and Pleasure at the
helm.
The Bard (1757) l. 73

4 The curfew tolls the knell of parting day,
The lowing herd wind slowly o'er the lea,
The ploughman homeward plods his weary
way,
And leaves the world to darkness and to
me.

Now fades the glimmering landscape on
the sight,
And all the air a solemn stillness holds,
Save where the beetle wheels his droning
flight,
And drowsy tinklings lull the distant folds.
Elegy Written in a Country Churchyard (1751)
l. 1

5 Save that from yonder ivy-mantled tow'r,
The moping owl does to the moon
complain.
Elegy Written in a Country Churchyard (1751)
l. 9

6 Beneath those rugged elms, that yew-tree's
shade,
Where heaves the turf in many a
mouldering heap,
Each in his narrow cell for ever laid,
The rude forefathers of the hamlet sleep.
Elegy Written in a Country Churchyard (1751)
l. 13

7 Let not ambition mock their useful toil,
Their homely joys, and destiny obscure;
Nor grandeur hear with a disdainful smile,
The short and simple annals of the poor.

The boast of heraldry, the pomp of pow'r,
And all that beauty, all that wealth e'er
gave,
Awaits alike th' inevitable hour,
The paths of glory lead but to the grave.
Elegy Written in a Country Churchyard (1751)
l. 29

8 Can storied urn or animated bust
Back to its mansion call the fleeting
breath?
Can honour's voice provoke the silent dust,
Or flatt'ry soothe the dull cold ear of
death?
Elegy Written in a Country Churchyard (1751)
l. 41

9 Full many a gem of purest ray serene,
The dark unfathomed caves of ocean bear:
Full many a flower is born to blush
unseen,
And waste its sweetness on the desert air.
Some village-Hampden, that with dauntless
breast
The little tyrant of his fields withstood;
Some mute inglorious Milton here may
rest,
Some Cromwell guiltless of his country's
blood.
Elegy Written in a Country Churchyard (1751)
l. 53

10 Far from the madding crowd's ignoble
strife,
Their sober wishes never learned to stray;
Along the cool sequestered vale of life
They kept the noiseless tenor of their way.
Elegy Written in a Country Churchyard (1751)
l. 73

11 Ye distant spires, ye antique towers,
That crown the wat'ry glade.
Ode on a Distant Prospect of Eton College (1747)
l. 1

12 Alas, regardless of their doom,
The little victims play!
No sense have they of ills to come,
Nor care beyond to-day.
Ode on a Distant Prospect of Eton College (1747)
l. 51

13 To each his suff'rings, all are men,
Condemned alike to groan;
The tender for another's pain,
Th' unfeeling for his own.
Ode on a Distant Prospect of Eton College (1747)
l. 91

14   Where ignorance is bliss,
'Tis folly to be wise.
Ode on a Distant Prospect of Eton College (1747)
l. 99

15 Not all that tempts your wand'ring eyes
And heedless hearts, is lawful prize;
Nor all, that glisters, gold.
'Ode on the Death of a Favourite Cat' (1748)

16 In thy green lap was Nature's darling laid.
The Progress of Poesy (1757) l. 84 (of
Shakespeare)

17 He saw; but blasted with excess of light,
Closed his eyes in endless night.
The Progress of Poesy (1757) l. 95 (of Milton)

18 Thoughts, that breathe, and words, that
burn.
The Progress of Poesy (1757) l. 110

19 Beyond the limits of a vulgar fate,
Beneath the good how far—but far above
the great.
The Progress of Poesy (1757) l. 122

Horace Greeley 1811–72

20 Go West, young man, and grow up with
the country.
Hints toward Reforms (1850). Cf. 311:17

Hannah Green

1 I never promised you a rose garden.
Title of novel (1964)

Graham Greene 1904–91

2 Catholics and Communists have
committed great crimes, but at least they
have not stood aside, like an established
society, and been indifferent. I would
rather have blood on my hands than water
like Pilate.
The Comedians (1966) pt. 3, ch. 4

3 He gave her a bright fake smile; so much
of life was a putting-off of unhappiness for
another time. Nothing was ever lost by
delay.
The Heart of the Matter (1948) bk. 1, pt. 1, ch. 1

4 They had been corrupted by money, and he
had been corrupted by sentiment.
Sentiment was the more dangerous,
because you couldn't name its price. A
man open to bribes was to be relied upon
below a certain figure, but sentiment
might uncoil in the heart at a name, a
photograph, even a smell remembered.
The Heart of the Matter (1948) bk. 1, pt. 1, ch. 2

5 He felt the loyalty we all feel to
unhappiness—the sense that that is where
we really belong.
The Heart of the Matter (1948) bk. 2, pt. 2, ch. 1

6 There is always one moment in childhood
when the door opens and lets the future
in.
The Power and the Glory (1940) pt. 1, ch. 1

7 Innocence always calls mutely for
protection, when we would be so much
wiser to guard ourselves against it:
innocence is like a dumb leper who has
lost his bell, wandering the world meaning
no harm.
The Quiet American (1955) pt. 1, ch. 3

Robert Greene c.1560–92

8 Hangs in the uncertain balance of proud
time.
Friar Bacon and Friar Bungay (1594) act 3, sc. 1

9 Ah! what is love! It is a pretty thing,
As sweet unto a shepherd as a king.
'The Shepherd's Wife's Song' (1590)

Germaine Greer 1939–

10 You can now see the Female Eunuch the
world over ... spreading herself wherever
blue jeans and Coca-Cola may go.
Wherever you see nail varnish, lipstick,
brassieres, and high heels, the Eunuch has
set up her camp.
The Female Eunuch (20th anniversary ed.,
1991) foreword

11 I didn't fight to get women out from
behind the vacuum cleaner to get them
onto the board of Hoover.
In *Guardian* 27 October 1986

Pope Gregory the Great
AD c.540–604

12 *Non Angli sed Angeli.*
Not Angles but Angels.
Oral tradition. See Bede *Historia Ecclesiastica*
bk. 2, sect. 1

Pope Gregory VII c.1020–85

13 I have loved justice and hated iniquity:
therefore I die in exile.
Last words, in J. W. Bowden *Life and
Pontificate of Gregory VII* (1840) vol. 2, bk. 3,
ch. 20

Stephen Grellet 1773–1855

14 I expect to pass through this world but
once; any good thing therefore that I can
do, or any kindness that I can show to any
fellow-creature, let me do it now; let me
not defer or neglect it, for I shall not pass
this way again.
Attributed. See John o' London *Treasure Trove*
(1925) p. 48 for some of the many other
claimants to authorship

Joyce Grenfell 1910–79

15 So gay the band,
So giddy the sight,
Full evening dress is a must,
But the zest goes out of a beautiful waltz
When you dance it bust to bust.
'Stately as a Galleon' (1978 song)

Julian Grenfell 1888–1915

16 And Life is Colour and Warmth and Light
And a striving evermore for these;
And he is dead, who will not fight;
And who dies fighting has increase.
'Into Battle' in *The Times* 28 May 1915

Frances Greville c.1724–89

17 Far as distress the soul can wound
'Tis pain in each degree;
Bliss goes but to a certain bound,
Beyond is agony.
'A Prayer for Indifference' (1759)

Fulke Greville 1554–1628

18 Life is a top which whipping Sorrow
driveth.
Caelica (1633) 'The earth with thunder torn,
with fire blasted'

19 O wearisome condition of humanity!
Born under one law, to another bound;
Vainly begot, and yet forbidden vanity;
Created sick, commanded to be sound.
Mustapha (1609) act 5, sc. 4

Lord Grey of Fallodon 1862–1933

1 The lamps are going out all over Europe;
we shall not see them lit again in our
lifetime.
25 Years (1925) vol. 2, ch. 18 (on the eve of the
First World War)

Mervyn Griffith-Jones 1909–79

2 Is it a book you would even wish your wife
or your servants to read?
Of D. H. Lawrence's *Lady Chatterley's Lover*,
while appearing for the prosecution at the
Old Bailey; in *The Times* 21 October 1960

George and Weedon Grossmith
1847–1912, 1854–1919

3 What's the good of a home if you are never
in it?
Diary of a Nobody (1894) ch. 1

4 I left the room with silent dignity, but
caught my foot in the mat.
Diary of a Nobody (1894) ch. 12

Philip Guedalla 1889–1944

5 Any stigma, as the old saying is, will serve
to beat a dogma.
Masters and Men (1923) 'Ministers of State'

6 The little ships, the unforgotten Homeric
catalogue of *Mary Jane* and *Peggy IV*, of
Folkestone Belle, *Boy Billy*, and *Ethel Maud*, of
Lady Haig and *Skylark* … the little ships of
England brought the Army home.
Mr Churchill (1941) ch. 7 (on the evacuation of
Dunkirk)

7 The work of Henry James has always
seemed divisible by a simple dynastic
arrangement into three reigns: James I,
James II, and the Old Pretender.
Supers and Supermen (1920) 'Some Critics'

Hervé Guibert 1955–91

8 [AIDS was] an illness in stages, a very long
flight of steps that led assuredly to death,
but whose every step represented a unique
apprenticeship. It was a disease that gave
death time to live and its victims time to
die, time to discover time, and in the end
to discover life.
To the Friend who did not Save my Life (1991)
ch. 61 (tr. Linda Coverdale)

Texas Guinan 1884–1933

9 Fifty million Frenchmen can't be wrong.
In *New York World–Telegram* 21 March 1931,
p. 25, which asserts that Guinan used the
phrase at least six or seven years previously;
it was the title of a 1927 song by Billy Rose
and Willie Raskin

Dorothy Frances Gurney
1858–1932

10 The kiss of the sun for pardon,
The song of the birds for mirth,
One is nearer God's Heart in a garden
Than anywhere else on earth.
'God's Garden' (1913)

John Hampden Gurney 1802–62

11 My soul, bear thou thy part,
Triumph in God above,
And with a well-tuned heart
Sing thou the songs of love.
'Ye holy angels bright' (1838 hymn)

Woody Guthrie 1912–67

12 This land is your land, this land is my land,
From California to the New York Island.
From the redwood forest to the Gulf
Stream waters
This land was made for you and me.
'This Land is Your Land' (1956 song)

Nell Gwyn 1650–87

13 Pray, good people, be civil. I am the
Protestant whore.
At Oxford, during the Popish Terror, 1681; in
B. Bevan *Nell Gwyn* (1969) ch. 13

Emperor Hadrian AD 76–138

14 *Animula vagula blandula,*
Hospes comesque corporis.
Ah! gentle, fleeting, wav'ring sprite,
Friend and associate of this clay!
In J. W. Duff (ed.) *Minor Latin Poets* (1934)
p. 445 (translated by Byron as 'Adrian's
Address to His Soul When Dying')

Rider Haggard 1856–1925

15 She who must be obeyed.
She (1887) ch. 6 and *passim*

Earl Haig 1861–1928

16 A very weak-minded fellow I am afraid,
and, like the feather pillow, bears the
marks of the last person who has sat on
him!
Describing the 17th Earl of Derby in a letter
to Lady Haig, 14 January 1918; in R. Blake
Private Papers of Douglas Haig (1952) ch. 16

17 Every position must be held to the last
man: there must be no retirement. With
our backs to the wall, and believing in the
justice of our cause, each one of us must
fight on to the end.
Order to British troops, 12 April 1918; in A.
Duff Cooper *Haig* (1936) vol. 2, ch. 23

Lord Hailsham (Quintin Hogg)
1907–

1 A great party is not to be brought down because of a scandal by a woman of easy virtue and a proved liar.
> BBC television interview on the Profumo affair; in *The Times* 14 June 1963

J. B. S. Haldane 1892–1964

2 Now, my own suspicion is that the universe is not only queerer than we suppose, but queerer than we *can* suppose.
> *Possible Worlds* (1927) title essay

3 The Creator, if He exists, has a special preference for beetles.
> Observing that there are 400,000 species of beetle; in *Journal of the British Interplanetary Society* (1951) vol. 10, p. 156

Edward Everett Hale 1822–1909

4 'Do you pray for the senators, Dr Hale?' 'No, I look at the senators and I pray for the country.'
> Van Wyck Brooks *New England Indian Summer* (1940) p. 418 n.

Sir Matthew Hale 1609–76

5 Christianity is part of the laws of England.
> Sir William Blackstone's summary of Hale's words (Taylor's case, 1676) in *Commentaries* (1769) vol. 4, p. 59

Nathan Hale 1755–76

6 I only regret that I have but one life to lose for my country.
> Prior to his execution by the British for spying, 22 September 1776; in H. P. Johnston *Nathan Hale, 1776* (1914) ch. 7. Cf. 2:16

Sarah Josepha Hale 1788–1879

7 Mary had a little lamb,
Its fleece was white as snow,
And everywhere that Mary went
The lamb was sure to go.
> *Poems for Our Children* (1830) 'Mary's Little Lamb'

George Savile, Marquess of Halifax 1633–95

8 Malice is of a low stature, but it hath very long arms.
> *Political, Moral, and Miscellaneous Thoughts* (1750) 'Of Malice and Envy'

9 When the people contend for their liberty, they seldom get anything by their victory but new masters.
> *Political, Moral, and Miscellaneous Thoughts* (1750) 'Of Prerogative, Power and Liberty'

10 Power is so apt to be insolent and Liberty to be saucy, that they are very seldom upon good terms.
> *Political, Moral, and Miscellaneous Thoughts* (1750) 'Of Prerogative, Power and Liberty'

11 Men are not hanged for stealing horses, but that horses may not be stolen.
> *Political, Moral, and Miscellaneous Thoughts* (1750) 'Of Punishment'

12 [Halifax] had heard of many kicked down stairs, but never of any that was kicked up stairs before.
> Gilbert Burnet *History of My Own Time* vol. 1 (1724) p. 592

Bishop Joseph Hall 1574–1656

13 Perfection is the child of Time.
> *Works* (1625) p. 670

Radclyffe Hall 1883–1943

14 You're neither unnatural, nor abominable, nor mad; you're as much a part of what people call nature as anyone else; only you're unexplained as yet—you've not got your niche in creation.
> *The Well of Loneliness* (1928) bk. 2, ch. 20, sect. 3

Friedrich Halm 1806–71

15 Zwei Seelen und ein Gedanke,
Zwei Herzen und ein Schlag!
Two souls with but a single thought,
Two hearts that beat as one.
> *Der Sohn der Wildnis* (1842) act 2 *ad fin.*

Alex Hamilton 1936–

16 Those who stand for nothing fall for anything.
> 'Born Old' (radio broadcast), in *Listener* 9 November 1978

Sir William Hamilton 1788–1856

17 Truth, like a torch, the more it's shook it shines.
> *Discussions on Philosophy* (1852) title page (epigram)

18 On earth there is nothing great but man; in man there is nothing great but mind.
> *Lectures on Metaphysics and Logic* (ed. Mamsel and Veitch, 1859) vol. 1, p. 24; attributed in a Latin form to Favorinus (2nd century AD)

Oscar Hammerstein II 1895–1960

19 Fish got to swim and birds got to fly
I got to love one man till I die,
Can't help lovin' dat man of mine.
> 'Can't Help Lovin' Dat Man of Mine' (1927 song)

1 The last time I saw Paris
Her heart was warm and gay,
I heard the laughter of her heart in ev'ry
street café.
'The Last Time I saw Paris' (1941 song)

2 The corn is as high as an elephant's eye,
An' it looks like it's climbin' clear up to the
sky.
'Oh, What a Beautiful Mornin' ' (1943 song)

3 Ol' man river, dat ol' man river,
He must know sumpin', but don't say
nothin',
He jus' keeps rollin',
He jus' keeps rollin' along.
'Ol' Man River' (1927 song)

4 I'm as corny as Kansas in August,
High as a flag on the Fourth of July!
'A Wonderful Guy' (1949 song)

Christopher Hampton 1946–

5 A definition of capitalism ... the process
whereby American girls turn into
American women.
Savages (1974) sc. 16

Minnie Hanff 1880–1942

6 High o'er the fence leaps Sunny Jim
'Force' is the food that raises him.
Advertising slogan for breakfast cereal
(1903)

Kate Hankey 1834–1911

7 Tell me the old, old story.
Title of hymn (1867)

Brian Hanrahan 1949–

8 I counted them all out and I counted them
all back.
On the number of British aeroplanes joining
the raid on Port Stanley; BBC broadcast
report, 1 May 1982, in *Battle for the Falklands*
(1982) p. 21

Edmond Haraucourt 1856–1941

9 *Partir c'est mourir un peu,*
C'est mourir à ce qu'on aime.
To go away is to die a little, to that which
one loves it is to die.
Seul (1891) 'Rondel de l'Adieu'

Otto Harbach 1873–1963

10 Now laughing friends deride tears I cannot
hide,
So I smile and say 'When a lovely flame
dies,
Smoke gets in your eyes.'
'Smoke Gets in your Eyes' (1933 song)

E. Y. ('Yip') Harburg 1898–1981

11 Brother can you spare a dime?
Title of song (1932)

12 Say, it's only a paper moon,
Sailing over a cardboard sea.
'It's Only a Paper Moon' (1933 song, with
Billy Rose)

13 Wanna cry, wanna croon.
Wanna laugh like a loon.
It's that Old Devil Moon in your eyes.
'Old Devil Moon' (1946 song)

14 Somewhere over the rainbow
Way up high,
There's a land that I heard of
Once in a lullaby.
'Over the Rainbow' (1939 song)

Sir William Harcourt 1827–1904

15 We are all socialists now.
During the passage of the 1894 budget,
which equalized death duties on real and
personal property (attributed). See H. Bland
'The Outlook' in G. B. Shaw (ed.) *Fabian Essays
in Socialism* (1889)

D. W. Harding 1906–

16 Regulated hatred.
Title of an article on the novels of Jane
Austen, in *Scrutiny* March 1940

Philip Yorke, Earl of Hardwicke 1690–1764

17 His doubts are better than most people's
certainties.
Of *Dirleton's Doubts*, in James Boswell *Life of
Samuel Johnson* (1934 ed.) vol. 3, p. 205

Godfrey Harold Hardy 1877–1947

18 Beauty is the first test: there is no
permanent place in the world for ugly
mathematics.
A Mathematician's Apology (1940) p. 25

Thomas Hardy 1840–1928

19 A local thing called Christianity.
The Dynasts (1904) pt. 1, act 1, sc. 6

20 War makes rattling good history; but Peace
is poor reading.
The Dynasts (1904) pt. 1, act 2, sc. 5

21 A lover without indiscretion is no lover at
all.
The Hand of Ethelberta (1876) ch. 20

22 Done because we are too menny.
Jude the Obscure (1896) pt. 6, ch. 2

23 Dialect words—those terrible marks of the
beast to the truly genteel.
The Mayor of Casterbridge (1886) ch. 20

24 Happiness was but the occasional episode
in a general drama of pain.
The Mayor of Casterbridge (1886) ch. 45 *ad fin.*

25 'Justice' was done, and the President of the
Immortals (in Aeschylean phrase) had
ended his sport with Tess.
Tess of the D'Urbervilles (1891) ch. 59

1 Good, but not religious-good.
  Under the Greenwood Tree (1872) ch. 2

2 When the Present has latched its postern
    behind my tremulous stay,
  And the May month flaps its glad green
    leaves like wings,
  Delicate-filmed as new-spun silk, will the
    neighbours say,
  'He was a man who used to notice such
    things'?
  'Afterwards' (1917)

3 The bower we shrined to Tennyson,
    Gentlemen,
  Is roof-wrecked; damps there drip upon
  Sagged seats, the creeper-nails are rust,
  The spider is sole denizen.
  'An Ancient to Ancients' (1922)

4 After two thousand years of mass
  We've got as far as poison-gas.
  'Christmas: 1924' (1928)

5 The Immanent Will that stirs and urges
    everything.
  'Convergence of the Twain' (1914)

6 An aged thrush, frail, gaunt, and small,
  In blast-beruffled plume.
  'The Darkling Thrush' (1902)

7 So little cause for carollings
  Of such ecstatic sound
  Was written on terrestrial things
  Afar or nigh around,
  That I could think there trembled through
  His happy good-night air
  Some blessed Hope, whereof he knew
  And I was unaware.
  'The Darkling Thrush' (1902)

8 If way to the Better there be, it exacts a full
    look at the worst.
  'De Profundis' (1902)

9 Well, World, you have kept faith with me,
    Kept faith with me;
  Upon the whole you have proved to be
  Much as you said you were.
  'He Never Expected Much' (1928)

10 I am the family face;
   Flesh perishes, I live on,
   Projecting trait and trace
   Through time to times anon,
   And leaping from place to place
   Over oblivion.
   'Heredity' (1917)

11 Only a man harrowing clods
   In a slow silent walk
   With an old horse that stumbles and nods
   Half asleep as they stalk.
   'In Time of "The Breaking of Nations" '
   (1917)

12 Yonder a maid and her wight
   Come whispering by:
   War's annals will cloud into night
   Ere their story die.
   'In Time of "The Breaking of Nations" '
   (1917)

13 Yes; quaint and curious war is!
   You shoot a fellow down
   You'd treat if met where any bar is,
   Or help to half-a-crown.
   'The Man he Killed' (1909)

14 In the third-class seat sat the journeying
     boy
   And the roof-lamp's oily flame
   Played down on his listless form and face,
   Bewrapt past knowing to what he was
     going,
   Or whence he came.
   'Midnight on the Great Western' (1917)

15 Woman much missed, how you call to me,
     call to me.
   'The Voice' (1914)

16 This is the weather the cuckoo likes,
   And so do I.
   'Weathers' (1922)

17 And drops on gate-bars hang in a row,
   And rooks in families homeward go.
   'Weathers' (1922)

18 When I set out for Lyonnesse,
   A hundred miles away,
   The rime was on the spray,
   And starlight lit my lonesomeness.
   'When I set out for Lyonnesse' (1914)

Maurice Evan Hare 1886–1967

19 There once was an old man who said,
     'Damn!
   It is borne in upon me I am
   An engine that moves
   In determinate grooves,
   I'm not even a bus, I'm a tram.'
   'Limerick' (1905)

W. F. Hargreaves 1846–1919

20 I'm Burlington Bertie
   I rise at ten thirty and saunter along like
     a toff,
   I walk down the Strand with my gloves on
     my hand,
   Then I walk down again with them off.
   'Burlington Bertie from Bow' (1915 song)

21 I acted so tragic the house rose like magic,
   The audience yelled 'You're sublime.'
   They made me a present of Mornington
     Crescent
   They threw it a brick at a time.
   'The Night I Appeared as Macbeth' (1922
   song)

Sir John Harington 1561–1612

22 Treason doth never prosper, what's the
     reason?
   For if it prosper, none dare call it treason.
   Epigrams (1618) bk. 4, no. 5

Lord Harlech 1918–85

1 Britain will be honoured by historians
more for the way she disposed of an
empire than for the way in which she
acquired it.
In New York Times 28 October 1962, sect. 4,
p. 11

Jimmy Harper et al.

2 The biggest aspidistra in the world.
Title of song (1938); popularized by Gracie
Fields

Joel Chandler Harris 1848–1908

3 All by my own-alone self.
Nights with Uncle Remus (1883) ch. 36

4 I'm sickly but sassy.
Nights with Uncle Remus (1883) ch. 50

5 Bred en bawn in a brier-patch!
Uncle Remus and His Legends ... (1881) 'How
Mr Rabbit was too Sharp for Mr Fox'

6 Tar-baby ain't sayin' nuthin', en Brer Fox,
he lay low.
Uncle Remus and His Legends ... (1881) 'The
Wonderful Tar-Baby Story'

Lorenz Hart 1895–1943

7 Bewitched, bothered, and bewildered am I.
'Bewitched' (1941 song)

8 When love congeals
It soon reveals
The faint aroma of performing seals.
'I Wish I Were in Love Again' (1937 song)

9 I get too hungry for dinner at eight.
I like the theatre, but never come late.
I never bother with people I hate.
That's why the lady is a tramp.
'The Lady is a Tramp' (1937 song)

10 In a mountain greenery
Where God paints the scenery—
Just two crazy people together.
'Mountain Greenery' (1926 song)

11 Thou swell! Thou witty!
Thou sweet! Thou grand!
Wouldst kiss me pretty?
Wouldst hold my hand?
'Thou Swell' (1927 song)

Bret Harte 1836–1902

12 If, of all words of tongue and pen,
The saddest are, 'It might have been,'
More sad are these we daily see:
'It is, but hadn't ought to be!'
'Mrs Judge Jenkins' (1867). Cf. 349:1

13 And he smiled a kind of sickly smile, and
curled up on the floor,
And the subsequent proceedings interested
him no more.
'The Society upon the Stanislaus' (1868) st. 7

L. P. Hartley 1895–1972

14 The past is a foreign country: they do
things differently there.
The Go-Between (1953) prologue. Cf. 235:7

F. W. Harvey b. 1888

15 From troubles of the world
I turn to ducks
Beautiful comical things.
'Ducks' (1919)

Minnie Louise Haskins 1875–1957

16 And I said to the man who stood at the
gate of the year: 'Give me a light that I may
tread safely into the unknown.' And he
replied: 'Go out into the darkness and put
your hand into the Hand of God. That shall
be to you better than light and safer than
a known way.'
Desert (1908) 'God Knows' (quoted by George
VI in his Christmas broadcast, 1939)

R. S. Hawker 1803–75

17 And have they fixed the where and when?
And shall Trelawny die?
Here's twenty thousand Cornish men
Will know the reason why!
'The Song of the Western Men' (last three
lines traditional since the 17th century)

Stephen Hawking 1942–

18 If we find the answer to that [why it is that
we and the universe exist], it would be the
ultimate triumph of human reason—for
then we would know the mind of God.
A Brief History of Time (1988) ch. 11

Nathaniel Hawthorne 1804–64

19 Dr Johnson's morality was as English an
article as a beefsteak.
Our Old Home (1863) 'Lichfield and Uttoxeter'

Ian Hay 1876–1952

20 What do you mean, funny? Funny-peculiar
or funny ha-ha?
The Housemaster (1938) act 3

J. Milton Hayes 1884–1940

21 There's a one-eyed yellow idol to the north
of Khatmandu,
There's a little marble cross below the
town,
There's a broken-hearted woman tends the
grave of Mad Carew,
And the Yellow God forever gazes down.
'The Green Eye of the Yellow God' (1911)

William Hazlitt 1778–1830

22 His sayings are generally like women's
letters; all the pith is in the postscript.
Conversations of James Northcote (1826–7) (of
Charles Lamb)

1 He talked on for ever; and you wished him to talk on for ever.
Lectures on the English Poets (1818) 'On the Living Poets' (of Coleridge)

2 I have wanted only one thing to make me happy, but wanting that have wanted everything.
Literary Remains (1836) 'My First Acquaintance with Poets'

3 There is nothing good to be had in the country, or if there is, they will not let you have it.
The Round Table (1817) 'Observations on … The Excursion'

4 Of all footmen the lowest class is *literary footmen.*
Sketches and Essays (1839) 'Footmen'

5 Rules and models destroy genius and art.
Sketches and Essays (1839) 'On Taste'

6 His worst is better than any other person's best.
The Spirit of the Age (1825) 'Sir Walter Scott'

7 We can scarcely hate any one that we know.
Table Talk vol. 2 (1822) 'On Criticism'

8 Give me the clear blue sky over my head, and the green turf beneath my feet, a winding road before me, and a three hours' march to dinner—and then to thinking! It is hard if I cannot start some game on these lone heaths.
Table Talk vol. 2 (1822) 'On Going a Journey'

9 Well, I've had a happy life.
Last words, in W. C. Hazlitt *Memoirs of William Hazlitt* (1867)

Denis Healey 1917–

10 Like being savaged by a dead sheep.
On being criticized by Sir Geoffrey Howe in the House of Commons; *Hansard* 14 June 1978, col. 1027

Seamus Heaney 1939–

11   The famous
Northern reticence, the tight gag of place
And times.
'Whatever You Say Say Nothing' (1975)

Edward Heath 1916–

12 The unpleasant and unacceptable face of capitalism.
Hansard 15 May 1973, col. 1243 (on the Lonrho affair)

John Heath-Stubbs 1918–

13 Venerable Mother Toothache
Climb down from the white battlements,
Stop twisting in your yellow fingers
The fourfold rope of nerves.
'A Charm Against the Toothache' (1954)

Bishop Reginald Heber 1783–1826

14 Brightest and best of the sons of the morning,
Dawn on our darkness and lend us thine aid.
'Brightest and best' (1827 hymn)

15 From Greenland's icy mountains,
From India's coral strand,
Where Afric's sunny fountains
Roll down their golden sand.
'From Greenland's icy mountains' (1821 hymn)

16 What though the spicy breezes
Blow soft o'er Ceylon's isle;
Though every prospect pleases,
And only man is vile:
In vain with lavish kindness
The gifts of God are strown;
The heathen in his blindness
Bows down to wood and stone.
'From Greenland's icy mountains' (1821 hymn). 'Ceylon' later altered to 'Java'. Cf. 196:10

17 Holy, Holy, Holy! all the saints adore thee,
Casting down their golden crowns around the glassy sea,
Cherubim and Seraphim falling down before thee,
Which wert, and art, and evermore shalt be.
'Holy, Holy, Holy! Lord God Almighty!' (1826 hymn)

G. W. F. Hegel 1770–1831

18 What experience and history teach is this—that nations and governments have never learned anything from history, or acted upon any lessons they might have drawn from it.
Lectures on the Philosophy of World History: Introduction (1830, tr. H. B. Nisbet)

19 Only in the state does man have a rational existence … Man owes his entire existence to the state, and has his being within it alone.
Lectures on the Philosophy of World History: Introduction (1830, tr. H. B. Nisbet) p. 94

20 When philosophy paints its grey on grey, then has a shape of life grown old. By philosophy's grey on grey it cannot be rejuvenated but only understood. The owl of Minerva spreads its wings only with the falling of the dusk.
Philosophy of Right (1821, tr. T. M. Knox) p. 13

Heinrich Heine 1797–1856

21   *Dort, wo man Bücher*
Verbrennt, verbrennt man auch am Ende Menschen.
Wherever books will be burned, men also, in the end, are burned.
Almansor (1823) l. 245

1 *Auf Flügeln des Gesanges.*
 On wings of song.
 Title of song (1823)

2 Maximilien Robespierre was nothing but
 the hand of Jean Jacques Rousseau, the
 bloody hand that drew from the womb of
 time the body whose soul Rousseau had
 created.
 *Zur Geschichte der Religion und Philosophie in
 Deutschland* (1834) bk. 3, para. 3

3 *Dieu me pardonnera, c'est son métier.*
 God will pardon me, it is His trade.
 On his deathbed, in A. Meissner *Heinrich
 Heine. Erinnerungen* (1856) ch. 5. Cf. 92:21

Werner Heisenberg 1901–76

4 An expert is someone who knows some of
 the worst mistakes that can be made in his
 subject and who manages to avoid them.
 Der Teil und das Ganze (1969) ch. 17 (tr. A. J.
 Pomerans as *Physics and Beyond*, 1971)

Joseph Heller 1923–

5 There was only one catch and that was
 Catch-22, which specified that a concern
 for one's own safety in the face of dangers
 that were real and immediate was the
 process of a rational mind ... Orr would be
 crazy to fly more missions and sane if he
 didn't, but if he was sane he had to fly
 them. If he flew them he was crazy and
 didn't have to; but if he didn't want to he
 was sane and had to.
 Catch-22 (1961) ch. 5

6 Some men are born mediocre, some men
 achieve mediocrity, and some men have
 mediocrity thrust upon them. With Major
 Major it had been all three.
 Catch-22 (1961) ch. 9. Cf. 298:3

Lillian Hellman 1905–84

7 I cannot and will not cut my conscience to
 fit this year's fashions.
 Letter to John S. Wood, 19 May 1952, in *US
 Congress Committee Hearing on Un-American
 Activities* (1952) pt. 8, p. 3546

Leona Helmsley c.1920–

8 Only the little people pay taxes.
 Addressed to her housekeeper in 1983, and
 reported at her trial for tax evasion; in *New
 York Times* 12 July 1989, p. B2

Felicia Hemans 1793–1835

9 The boy stood on the burning deck
 Whence all but he had fled;
 The flame that lit the battle's wreck
 Shone round him o'er the dead.
 'Casabianca' (1849)

10 The stately homes of England,
 How beautiful they stand!
 'The Homes of England' (1849)

John Heming 1556–1630 and Henry Condell d. 1627

11 His mind and hand went together: And
 what he thought, he uttered with that
 easiness, that we have scarce received from
 him a blot.
 First Folio Shakespeare (1623) preface.
 Cf. 187:32, 252:30

Ernest Hemingway 1899–1961

12 But did thee feel the earth move?
 For Whom the Bell Tolls (1940) ch. 13

13 Paris is a movable feast.
 A Movable Feast (1964) epigraph

14 The sun also rises.
 Title of novel (1926)

15 Grace under pressure.
 When asked what he meant by 'guts' in an
 interview with Dorothy Parker; in *New Yorker*
 30 November 1929
 See also F. SCOTT FITZGERALD

Arthur W. D. Henley

16 Nobody loves a fairy when she's forty.
 Title of song (1934)

W. E. Henley 1849–1903

17 Under the bludgeonings of chance
 My head is bloody, but unbowed.
 'Invictus. In Memoriam R.T.H.B.' (1888)

18 I am the master of my fate:
 I am the captain of my soul.
 'Invictus. In Memoriam R.T.H.B.' (1888)

19 What have I done for you,
 England, my England?
 'Pro Rege Nostro' (1900)

Henri IV 1553–1610

20 I want there to be no peasant in my
 kingdom so poor that he is unable to have
 a chicken in his pot every Sunday.
 In Hardouin de Péréfixe *Histoire de Henri le
 Grand* (1681)

21 Paris is well worth a mass.
 Attributed to Henri IV; alternatively to his
 minister Sully, in conversation with him

22 The wisest fool in Christendom.
 Of James I of England (attributed both to
 Henri IV and Sully)

Henry II 1133–89

23 Will no one rid me of this turbulent
 priest?
 Of Thomas Becket, Archbishop of
 Canterbury, murdered in Canterbury
 Cathedral, December 1170 (oral tradition,
 conflating a number of variant forms)

Henry VIII 1491-1547

1 The King found her [Anne of Cleves] so different from her picture ... that ... he swore they had brought him a Flanders mare.

Tobias Smollett *Complete History of England* (3rd ed., 1759) vol. 6, p. 68

Matthew Henry 1662-1714

2 The better day, the worse deed.

Exposition on the Old and New Testament (1710) Genesis ch. 3, v. 6, gloss 2

3 They that die by famine die by inches.

Exposition on the Old and New Testament (1710) Psalm 59, v. 15, gloss 5 (referring incorrectly to v. 13)

O. Henry 1862-1910

4 It was beautiful and simple as all truly great swindles are.

Gentle Grafter (1908) 'Octopus Marooned'

Patrick Henry 1736-99

5 Caesar had his Brutus—Charles the First, his Cromwell—and George the Third—('Treason,' cried the Speaker) ... *may profit by their example*. If *this* be treason, make the most of it.

Speech in the Virginia assembly, May 1765; in W. Wirt *Patrick Henry* (1818) sect. 2, p. 65

6 I know not what course others may take; but as for me, give me liberty, or give me death!

Speech, 23 March 1775; in W. Wirt *Patrick Henry* (1818) sect. 4, p. 123

Philip Henry 1631-96

7 All this, and heaven too!

In Matthew Henry *Life of Mr Philip Henry* (1698) ch. 5

Heraclitus c.540-c.480 BC

8 You can't step twice into the same river.

In Plato *Cratylus* 402a

9 A man's character is his fate.

On the Universe fragment 121 (tr. W. H. S. Jones) Cf. 132:15, 240:12

10 The road up and the road down are one and the same.

In H. Diels and W. Kranz *Die Fragmente der Vorsokratiker* (7th ed., 1954) fragment 60

A. P. Herbert 1890-1971

11 The Farmer will never be happy again;
He carries his heart in his boots;
For either the rain is destroying his grain
Or the drought is destroying his roots.

'The Farmer' (1922)

12 As my poor father used to say
In 1863,
Once people start on all this Art
Goodbye, moralitee!

'Lines for a Worthy Person' (1930)

13 Other people's babies—
That's my life!
Mother to dozens,
And nobody's wife.

'Other People's Babies' (1930)

14 This high official, all allow,
Is grossly overpaid;
There wasn't any Board, and now
There isn't any Trade.

'The President of the Board of Trade' (1922)

15 Nothing is wasted, nothing is in vain:
The seas roll over but the rocks remain.

Tough at the Top (operetta c.1949)

16 Holy deadlock.

Title of novel (1934)

17 People must not do things for fun. We are not here for fun. There is no reference to fun in any Act of Parliament.

Uncommon Law (1935) 'Is it a Free Country?'

18 The critical period in matrimony is breakfast-time.

Uncommon Law (1935) 'Is Marriage Lawful?'

Lord Herbert of Cherbury 1583-1648

19 Now that the April of your youth adorns
The garden of your face.

'Ditty: Now that the April' (1665)

George Herbert 1593-1633

20 Let all the world in ev'ry corner sing
My God and King.

'Antiphon' (1633)

21 A verse may find him, who a sermon flies,
And turn delight into a sacrifice.

'The Church Porch' (1633) st. 1

22 I struck the board, and cried, 'No more.
I will abroad.'

'The Collar' (1633)

23 But as I raved and grew more fierce and wild
At every word,
Methought I heard one calling, 'Child';
And I replied, 'My Lord.'

'The Collar' (1633)

24 I got me flowers to strew Thy way.

'Easter' (1633)

25 Teach me, my God and King,
In all things Thee to see,
And what I do in any thing
To do it as for Thee.

'The Elixir' (1633)

26 A servant with this clause
Makes drudgery divine:
Who sweeps a room as for Thy laws
Makes that and th' action fine.

'The Elixir' (1633)

1 Who says that fictions only and false heir
  Become a verse? Is there in truth no
    beauty?
  Is all good structure in a winding stair?
    'Jordan (1)' (1633)

2 Love bade me welcome: yet my soul drew
    back,
  Guilty of dust and sin.
    'Love: Love bade me welcome' (1633)

3 'You must sit down,' says Love, 'and taste
    my meat.'
  So I did sit and eat.
    'Love: Love bade me welcome' (1633)

4 The land of spices; something understood.
    'Prayer the Church's banquet' (1633)

5 When God at first made man,
  Having a glass of blessings standing by;
  Let us (said he) pour on him all we can:
  Let the world's riches, which dispersed lie,
  Contract into a span.
    'The Pulley' (1633)

6 But who does hawk at eagles with a dove?
    'The Sacrifice' (1633) l. 91

7 Bibles laid open, millions of surprises.
    'Sin: Lord, with what care Thou hast begirt
    us round!' (1633)

8 Sweet spring, full of sweet days and roses,
  A box where sweets compacted lie.
    'Virtue' (1633)

9 He that makes a good war makes a good
  peace.
    Outlandish Proverbs (1640) no. 420

10 He that lives in hope danceth without
  music.
    Outlandish Proverbs (1640) no. 1006

Robert Herrick 1591–1674

11 Here a little child I stand,
  Heaving up my either hand;
  Cold as paddocks though they be,
  Here I lift them up to Thee,
  For a benison to fall
  On our meat, and on us all. Amen.
    'Another Grace for a Child' (1647)

12 I sing of brooks, of blossoms, birds, and
    bowers:
  Of April, May, of June, and July-flowers.
  I sing of May-poles, Hock-carts, wassails,
    wakes,
  Of bride-grooms, brides, and of their
    bridal-cakes.
    'The Argument of his Book' from Hesperides
    (1648)

13 Cherry-ripe, ripe, ripe, I cry,
  Full and fair ones; come and buy:
  If so be, you ask me where
  They do grow? I answer, there,
  Where my Julia's lips do smile;
  There's the land, or cherry-isle.
    'Cherry-Ripe' (1648)

14 So when or you or I are made
  A fable, song, or fleeting shade;
  All love, all liking, all delight
  Lies drowned with us in endless night.
    'Corinna's Going a-Maying' (1648)

15 A sweet disorder in the dress
  Kindles in clothes a wantonness:
  A lawn about the shoulders thrown
  Into a fine distraction ...
  A careless shoe-string, in whose tie
  I see a wild civility:
  Do more bewitch me, than when Art
  Is too precise in every part.
    'Delight in Disorder' (1648)

16 It is the end that crowns us, not the fight.
    'The End' (1648)

17 In prayer the lips ne'er act the winning
    part,
  Without the sweet concurrence of the
    heart.
    'The Heart' (1647)

18 Night makes no difference 'twixt the Priest
    and Clerk;
  Joan as my Lady is as good i' th' dark.
    'No Difference i' th' Dark' (1648)

19 Made us nobly wild, not mad.
    'An Ode for him [Ben Jonson]' (1648)

20 Fain would I kiss my Julia's dainty leg,
  Which is as white and hairless as an egg.
    'On Julia's Legs' (1648)

21 Praise they that will times past, I joy to see
  My self now live: this age best pleaseth me.
    'The Present Time Best Pleaseth' (1648)

22 A little saint best fits a little shrine,
  A little prop best fits a little vine,
  As my small cruse best fits my little wine.
    'A Ternary of Littles, upon a Pipkin of Jelly
    sent to a Lady' (1648)

23 Fair daffodils, we weep to see
  You haste away so soon.
    'To Daffodils' (1648)

24 Gather ye rosebuds while ye may,
  Old Time is still a-flying:
  And this same flower that smiles to-day,
  To-morrow will be dying.
    'To the Virgins, to Make Much of Time'
    (1648)

25 Then be not coy, but use your time;
  And while ye may, go marry:
  For having lost but once your prime,
  You may for ever tarry.
    'To the Virgins, to Make Much of Time'
    (1648)

26 Whenas in silks my Julia goes,
  Then, then (methinks) how sweetly flows
  That liquefaction of her clothes.
    'Upon Julia's Clothes' (1648)

Lord Hervey 1696–1743

27 Whoever would lie usefully should lie
  seldom.
    Memoirs of the Reign of George II (ed. J. W.
    Croker, 1848) vol. 1, ch. 19

1 I am fit for nothing but to carry candles
and set chairs all my life.
> Letter to Sir Robert Walpole, 1737, in
> *Memoirs of the Reign of George II* (ed. J. W.
> Croker, 1848) vol. 2, ch. 40

Hesiod *c.*700 BC

2 The half is greater than the whole.
> *Works and Days* l. 40

Hermann Hesse 1877–1962

3 If you hate a person, you hate something
in him that is part of yourself. What isn't
part of ourselves doesn't disturb us.
> *Demian* (1919) ch. 6

Lord Hewart 1870–1943

4 Justice should not only be done, but should
manifestly and undoubtedly be seen to be
done.
> Rex v Sussex Justices, 9 November 1923, in
> *Law Reports King's Bench Division* (1924) vol. 1,
> p. 259

Du Bose Heyward 1885–1940 and Ira Gershwin 1896–1983

5 It ain't necessarily so,
De t'ings dat yo' li'ble
To read in de Bible
It ain't necessarily so.
> 'It ain't necessarily so' (1935 song)

6 Summer time an' the livin' is easy,
Fish are jumpin' an' the cotton is high.
> 'Summertime' (1935 song)

7 A woman is a sometime thing.
> Title of song (1935)

John Heywood *c.*1497–*c.*1580

8 All a green willow, willow;
All a green willow is my garland.
> 'The Green Willow'. Cf. 292:26

Thomas Heywood *c.*1574–1641

9 Seven cities warred for Homer, being dead,
Who, living, had no roof to shroud his
head.
> 'The Hierarchy of the Blessed Angels' (1635).
> Cf. 10:10

J. R. Hicks 1904–

10 The best of all monopoly profits is a quiet
life.
> *Econometrica* (1935) 'The Theory of Monopoly'

Aaron Hill 1685–1750

11 Tender-handed stroke a nettle,
And it stings you for your pains;
Grasp it like a man of mettle,
And it soft as silk remains.
> 'Verses Written on a Window in Scotland'

Joe Hill 1879–1915

12 Work and pray, live on hay,
You'll get pie in the sky when you die.
> 'Preacher and the Slave' in *Songs of the
> Workers* (Industrial Workers of the World,
> 1911)

13 I will die like a true-blue rebel. Don't waste
any time in mourning—organize.
> Farewell telegram prior to his death by
> firing squad; in *Salt Lake* (Utah) *Tribune*
> 19 November 1915

Rowland Hill 1744–1833

14 He [Hill] did not see any reason why the
devil should have all the good tunes.
> E. W. Broome *Rowland Hill* (1881) ch. 7

Sir Edmund Hillary 1919–

15 Well, we knocked the bastard off!
> On conquering Mount Everest; in *Nothing
> Venture, Nothing Win* (1975) ch. 10. Cf. 216:22

Fred Hillebrand 1893–

16 Home James, and don't spare the horses.
> Title of song (1934)

Lady Hillingdon 1857–1940

17 When I hear his steps outside my door I lie
down on my bed, close my eyes, open my
legs, and think of England.
> *Journal* 1912, in J. Gathorne-Hardy *The Rise
> and Fall of the British Nanny* (1972) ch. 3

James Hilton 1900–54

18 Nothing really wrong with him—only anno
domini, but that's the most fatal complaint
of all, in the end.
> *Goodbye, Mr Chips* (1934) ch. 1

Hippocrates *c.*460–357 BC

19 Life is short, the art long.
> *Aphorisms* sect. 1, para. 1; often quoted 'Ars
> longa, vita brevis'. See Seneca *De Brevitate Vitae*
> sect. 1. Cf. 96:12

Alfred Hitchcock 1899–1980

20 Television has brought back murder into
the home—where it belongs.
> In *Observer* 19 December 1965

Adolf Hitler 1889–1945

21 The night of the long knives.
> Referring to the massacre of Ernst Roehm
> and his associates by Hitler on 29–30 June
> 1934 (subsequently associated with Harold
> Macmillan's Cabinet dismissals of 13 July
> 1962). See S. H. Roberts *The House Hitler Built*
> (1937) pt. 2, ch. 3

1 I go the way that Providence dictates with the assurance of a sleepwalker.

Speech in Munich, 15 March 1936; in M. Domarus (ed.) *Hitler: Reden und Proklamationen 1932–1945* (1962) p. 606

2 It is the last territorial claim which I have to make in Europe.

On the Sudetenland; Speech in Berlin, 26 September 1938, in M. Domarus (ed.) *Hitler: Reden und Proklamationen 1932–1945* (1962) p. 927

3 The broad mass of a nation ... will more easily fall victim to a big lie than to a small one.

Mein Kampf (1925) vol. 1, ch. 10

4 Is Paris burning?

25 August 1944, in L. Collins and D. Lapierre *Is Paris Burning?* (1965) ch. 5

Thomas Hobbes 1588–1679

5 True and False are attributes of speech, not of things. And where speech is not, there is neither Truth nor Falsehood.

Leviathan (1651) pt. 1, ch. 4

6 Words are wise men's counters, they do but reckon by them.

Leviathan (1651) pt. 1, ch. 4

7 They that approve a private opinion, call it opinion; but they that mislike it, heresy: and yet heresy signifies no more than private opinion.

Leviathan (1651) pt. 1, ch. 11

8 During the time men live without a common power to keep them all in awe, they are in that condition which is called war; and such a war as is of every man against every man.

Leviathan (1651) pt. 1, ch. 13

9 For as the nature of foul weather, lieth not in a shower or two of rain; but in an inclination thereto of many days together: so the nature of war consisteth not in actual fighting, but in the known disposition thereto during all the time there is no assurance to the contrary.

Leviathan (1651) pt. 1, ch. 13

10 No arts; no letters; no society; and which is worst of all, continual fear and danger of violent death; and the life of man, solitary, poor, nasty, brutish, and short.

Leviathan (1651) pt. 1, ch. 13

11 I am about to take my last voyage, a great leap in the dark.

Last words. See John Watkins *Anecdotes of Men of Learning* (1808) p. 276

John Cam Hobhouse 1786–1869

12 When I invented the phrase 'His Majesty's Opposition' [Canning] paid me a compliment on the fortunate hit.

Recollections of a Long Life (1865) vol. 2, ch. 12

Ralph Hodgson 1871–1962

13 'Twould ring the bells of Heaven
The wildest peal for years,
If Parson lost his senses
And people came to theirs,
And he and they together
Knelt down with angry prayers
For tamed and shabby tigers
And dancing dogs and bears,
And wretched, blind, pit ponies,
And little hunted hares.

'Bells of Heaven' (1917)

14 Reason has moons, but moons not hers,
Lie mirrored on her sea,
Confounding her astronomers,
But, O! delighting me.

'Reason Has Moons' (1917)

15 Time, you old gipsy man,
Will you not stay,
Put up your caravan
Just for one day?

'Time, You Old Gipsy Man' (1917)

August Heinrich Hoffman 1798–1874

16 *Deutschland über alles.*
Germany above all.

Title of poem (1841)

Max Hoffman 1869–1927

17 Lions led by donkeys.

Of British soldiers during the First World War; in Alan Clark *The Donkeys* (1961) epigraph (from Falkenhayn's *Memoirs*)

Heinrich Hoffmann 1809–94

18 O take the nasty soup away!
I won't have any soup today.'

Struwwelpeter (1848) 'Augustus'

19 But fidgety Phil,
He won't sit still;
He wriggles
And giggles,
And then, I declare,
Swings backwards and forwards,
And tilts up his chair.

Struwwelpeter (1848) 'Fidgety Philip'

20 Look at little Johnny there,
Little Johnny Head-In-Air!

Struwwelpeter (1848) 'Johnny Head-In-Air'

21 The door flew open, in he ran,
The great, long, red-legged scissor-man.

Struwwelpeter (1848) 'The Little Suck-a-Thumb'

22 Snip! Snap! Snip! They go so fast
That both his thumbs are off at last.

Struwwelpeter (1848) 'The Little Suck-a-Thumb'

1 The hare sits snug in leaves and grass,
  And laughs to see the green man pass.
  Struwwelpeter (1848) 'The Man Who Went Out
  Shooting'

2 And now she's trying all she can,
  To shoot the sleepy, green-coat man.
  Struwwelpeter (1848) 'The Man Who Went Out
  Shooting'

3 The hare's own child, the little hare.
  Struwwelpeter (1848) 'The Man Who Went Out
  Shooting'

4 Anything to me is sweeter
  Than to see Shock-headed Peter.
  Struwwelpeter (1848) 'Shock-Headed Peter'
  (title poem)

Gerard Hoffnung 1925–59

5 Standing among savage scenery, the hotel
  offers stupendous revelations. There is
  a French widow in every bedroom,
  affording delightful prospects.
  Supposedly quoting a letter from a Tyrolean
  landlord; in speech at the Oxford Union,
  4 December 1958

Lancelot Hogben 1895–1975

6 This is not the age of pamphleteers. It is
  the age of the engineers. The spark-gap is
  mightier than the pen.
  Science for the Citizen (1938) epilogue

James Hogg 1770–1835

7 Where the pools are bright and deep
  Where the grey trout lies asleep,
  Up the river and o'er the lea
  That's the way for Billy and me.
  'A Boy's Song' (1838)

8 God bless our lord the king!
  God save our lord the king!
  God save the king!
  Make him victorious,
  Happy, and glorious,
  Long to reign over us:
  God save the king!
  'The King's Anthem' in *Jacobite Relics of
  Scotland* Second Series (1821) p. 50. Cf. 7:13

Paul Henri, Baron d'Holbach 1723–89

9 If ignorance of nature gave birth to the
  Gods, knowledge of nature is destined to
  destroy them.
  Système de la Nature (1770) pt. 2, ch. 1

Billie Holiday 1915–59

10 Mama may have, papa may have,
  But God bless the child that's got his own!
  'God Bless the Child' (1941 song, with Arthur
  Herzog Jnr.)

Henry Fox, 1st Lord Holland 1705–74

11 If Mr Selwyn calls again, shew him up: if I
  am alive I shall be delighted to see him;
  and if I am dead he would like to see me.
  During his last illness; in J. H. Jesse *George
  Selwyn and his Contemporaries* (1844) vol. 3,
  p. 50

Henry Scott Holland 1847–1918

12 Death is nothing at all; it does not count. I
  have only slipped away into the next room.
  Sermon preached on Whitsunday, 1910; *Facts
  of the Faith* (1919) 'The King of Terrors'

John H. Holmes 1879–1964

13 This, now, is the judgement of our
  scientific age—the third reaction of man
  upon the universe! This universe is not
  hostile, nor yet is it friendly. It is simply
  indifferent.
  The Sensible Man's View of Religion (1932) ch. 4

Oliver Wendell Holmes 1809–94

14 The axis of the earth sticks out visibly
  through the centre of each and every town
  or city.
  The Autocrat of the Breakfast-Table (1858) ch. 6

15 It is the province of knowledge to speak
  and it is the privilege of wisdom to listen.
  The Poet at the Breakfast-Table (1872) ch. 10

16 Lean, hungry, savage anti-everythings.
  'A Modest Request' (1848)

17 Man wants but little drink below,
  But wants that little strong.
  'A Song of other Days' (1848). Cf. 154:27

John Home 1722–1808

18 My name is Norval; on the Grampian hills
  My father feeds his flocks; a frugal swain,
  Whose constant cares were to increase his
  store
  And keep his only son, myself, at home.
  Douglas (1756) act 2, sc. 1

19 Like Douglas conquer, or like Douglas die.
  Douglas (1756) act 5

Homer 8th century BC

20 Winged words.
  The Iliad bk. 1, l. 201

21 Like that of leaves is a generation of men.
  The Iliad bk. 6, l. 146

22 Smiling through her tears.
  The Iliad bk. 6, l. 484

23 It lies in the lap of the gods.
  The Iliad bk. 17, l. 514 and *passim*

1 Tell me, Muse, of the man of many devices,
who wandered far and wide after he had
sacked Troy's sacred city, and saw the
towns of many men and knew their mind.
The Odyssey bk. 1, l. 1 (of Odysseus)

2 Rosy-fingered dawn.
The Odyssey bk. 2, l. 1 and *passim*

3 I would rather be tied to the soil as
another man's serf, even a poor man's,
who hadn't much to live on himself, than
be King of all these the dead and
destroyed.
The Odyssey bk. 11, l. 489

Thomas Hood 1799–1845

4 Ben Battle was a soldier bold,
And used to war's alarms:
But a cannon-ball took off his legs,
So he laid down his arms!
'Faithless Nelly Gray' (1826)

5 For here I leave my second leg,
And the Forty-second Foot!
'Faithless Nelly Gray' (1826)

6 The love that loves a scarlet coat
Should be more uniform.
'Faithless Nelly Gray' (1826)

7 His death, which happened in his berth,
At forty-odd befell:
They went and told the sexton, and
The sexton tolled the bell.
'Faithless Sally Brown' (1826)

8 I remember, I remember,
The house where I was born,
The little window where the sun
Came peeping in at morn.
'I Remember' (1826)

9 No sun—no moon!
No morn—no noon
No dawn—no dusk—no proper time of
day.
'No!' (1844)

10 No shade, no shine, no butterflies, no bees,
No fruits, no flowers, no leaves, no birds,—
November!
'No!' (1844)

11 She stood breast high amid the corn,
Clasped by the golden light of morn.
'Ruth' (1827). Cf. 192:5

12 Stitch! stitch! stitch!
In poverty, hunger, and dirt.
And still with a voice of dolorous pitch
She sang the 'Song of the Shirt'.
'The Song of the Shirt' (1843)

13 Oh! God! that bread should be so dear,
And flesh and blood so cheap!
'The Song of the Shirt' (1843)

14 The sedate, sober, silent, serious, sad-
coloured sect.
Comic Annual (1839) 'The Doves and the
Crows' (of Quakers)

Richard Hooker *c.*1554–1600

15 Alteration though it be from worse to
better hath in it inconveniences, and those
weighty.
Of the Laws of Ecclesiastical Polity (1593) bk. 4,
ch. 14, sect. 1. Cf. 182:3

Ellen Sturgis Hooper 1816–41

16 I slept, and dreamed that life was beauty;
I woke, and found that life was duty.
'Beauty and Duty' (1840)

Herbert Hoover 1874–1964

17 The American system of rugged
individualism.
Speech, 22 October 1928, in *New Day* (1928)
p. 154

18 The grass will grow in the streets of
a hundred cities, a thousand towns.
Speech, 31 October 1932, in *State Papers of
Herbert Hoover* (1934) vol. 2 (on proposals 'to
reduce the protective tariff to a competitive
tariff for revenue')

Anthony Hope 1863–1933

19 Economy is going without something you
do want in case you should, some day,
want something you probably won't want.
The Dolly Dialogues (1894) no. 12

20 His foe was folly and his weapon wit.
Inscription for W. S. Gilbert's memorial on
the Victoria Embankment, London (1915)

21 Oh, for an hour of Herod!
At the first night of *Peter Pan* (1904); in D.
Mackail *Story of JMB* (1941) ch. 17

Laurence Hope (Adela Florence Nicolson) 1865–1904

22 Pale hands I loved beside the Shalimar,
Where are you now? Who lies beneath
your spell?
The Garden of Kama (1901) 'Kashmiri Song'

23 Less than the dust, beneath thy Chariot
wheel,
Less than the rust, that never stained thy
Sword . . .
Less than the need thou hast in life of me.
Even less am I.
The Garden of Kama (1901) 'Less than the
Dust'

Gerard Manley Hopkins 1844–89

24 Ten or twelve, only ten or twelve
Strokes of havoc únselve.
'Binsey Poplars' (written 1879)

25 Not, I'll not, carrion comfort, Despair, not
feast on thee;
Not untwist—slack they may be—these
last strands of man
In me or, most weary, cry *I can no more.* I
can;
Can something, hope, wish day come, not
choose not to be.
'Carrion Comfort' (written 1885)

1   That night, that year
Of now done darkness I wretch lay
  wrestling with (my God!) my God.
    'Carrion Comfort' (written 1885)

2 Towery city and branchy between towers.
    'Duns Scotus's Oxford' (written 1879)

3 The world is charged with the grandeur of
  God.
    'God's Grandeur' (written 1877)

4 And all is seared with trade; bleared,
  smeared with toil;
And wears man's smudge and shares
  man's smell.
    'God's Grandeur' (written 1877)

5 Elected Silence, sing to me
And beat upon my whorlèd ear.
    'The Habit of Perfection' (written 1866)

6 Palate, the hutch of tasty lust,
Desire not to be rinsed with wine.
    'The Habit of Perfection' (written 1866)

7 I have desired to go
  Where springs not fail,
To fields where flies no sharp and sided
  hail
And a few lilies blow.
    'Heaven-Haven' (written 1864)

8 What would the world be, once bereft
Of wet and wildness? Let them be left,
O let them be left, wildness and wet;
Long live the weeds and the wilderness yet.
    'Inversnaid' (written 1881)

9 No worst, there is none. Pitched past pitch
  of grief,
More pangs will, schooled at forepangs,
  wilder wring.
Comforter, where, where is your
  comforting?
    'No worst, there is none' (written 1885)

10 O the mind, mind has mountains; cliffs of
   fall
Frightful, sheer, no-man-fathomed.
    'No worst, there is none' (written 1885)

11   All
Life death does end and each day dies with
  sleep.
    'No worst, there is none' (written 1885)

12 Glory be to God for dappled things.
    'Pied Beauty' (written 1877)

13 All things counter, original, spare, strange;
Whatever is fickle, freckled (who knows
  how?)
With swift, slow; sweet, sour; adazzle, dim;
He fathers-forth whose beauty is past
  change:
  Praise him.
    'Pied Beauty' (written 1877)

14 Márgarét, áre you gríeving
Over Goldengrove unleaving?
    'Spring and Fall: to a young child' (written
    1880)

15 Though worlds of wanwood leafmeal lie.
    'Spring and Fall: to a young child' (written
    1880)

16 Look at the stars! look, look up at the
  skies!
O look at all the fire-folk sitting in the air!
The bright boroughs, the circle-citadels
  there!
    'The Starlight Night' (written 1877)

17 This piece-bright paling shuts the spouse
Christ home, Christ and his mother and all
  his hallows.
    'The Starlight Night' (written 1877)

18 Thou art indeed just, Lord, if I contend
With thee; but, sir, so what I plead is just.
Why do sinners' ways prosper? and why
  must
Disappointment all I endeavour end?
    'Thou art indeed just, Lord' (written 1889)

19 Birds build—but not I build; no, but strain,
Time's eunuch, and not breed one work
  that wakes.
    'Thou art indeed just, Lord' (written 1889)

20 I caught this morning morning's minion,
  kingdom of daylight's dauphin, dapple-
  dawn-drawn Falcon.
    'The Windhover' (written 1877)

21   My heart in hiding
Stirred for a bird,—the achieve of, the
  mastery of the thing!
    'The Windhover' (written 1877)

22 To lift up the hands in prayer gives God
glory, but a man with a dungfork in his
hand, a woman with a slop-pail, give him
glory too.
    G. Roberts (ed.) *Gerard Manley Hopkins. Selected
    Prose* (1980) 'The Principle or Foundation'
    (1882) *ad fin.*

Horace 65–8 BC

23 *Inceptis gravibus plerumque et magna professis
Purpureus, late qui splendeat, unus et alter
Adsuitur pannus.*
Works of serious purpose and grand
promises often have a purple patch or two
stitched on, to shine far and wide.
    Ars Poetica l. 14

24   *Brevis esse laboro,*
Obscurus fio.
I strive to be brief, and I become obscure.
    Ars Poetica l. 25

25 *Grammatici certant et adhuc sub iudice lis est.*
Scholars dispute, and the case is still
before the courts.
    Ars Poetica l. 78

26 *Proicit ampullas et sesquipedalia verba.*
He throws aside his paint-pots and his
words a foot and a half long.
    Ars Poetica l. 97

27 *Parturient montes, nascetur ridiculus mus.*
Mountains will go into labour, and a silly
little mouse will be born.
    Ars Poetica l. 139

1 *Semper ad eventum festinat et in medias res*
Non secus ac notas auditorem rapit.
He always hurries to the main event and
whisks his audience into the middle of
things as though they knew already.
Ars Poetica l. 148

2 *Difficilis, querulus, laudator temporis acti.*
Tiresome, complaining, a praiser of past
times.
Ars Poetica l. 173

3 *Indignor quandoque bonus dormitat Homerus.*
I'm aggrieved when sometimes even
excellent Homer nods.
Ars Poetica l. 359

4 *Ut pictura poesis.*
A poem is like a painting.
Ars Poetica l. 361

5 *Nullius addictus iurare in verba magistri,*
Quo me cumque rapit tempestas, deferor hospes.
Not bound to swear allegiance to any
master, wherever the wind takes me I
travel as a visitor.
Epistles bk. 1, no. 1, l. 14. 'Nullius in verba' is
the motto of the Royal Society

6 *Si possis recte, si non, quocumque modo rem.*
If possible honestly, if not, somehow, make
money.
Epistles bk. 1, no. 1, l. 66

7 *Nos numerus sumus et fruges consumere nati.*
We are just statistics, born to consume
resources.
Epistles bk. 1, no. 2, l. 27

8 *Dimidium facti qui coepit habet: sapere aude.*
To have begun is half the job: be bold and
be sensible.
Epistles bk. 1, no. 2, l. 40

9 *Ira furor brevis est.*
Anger is a short madness.
Epistles bk. 1, no. 2, l. 62

10 *Nil admirari prope res est una, Numici,*
Solaque quae possit facere et servare beatum.
To marvel at nothing is just about the one
and only thing, Numicius, that can make a
man happy and keep him that way.
Epistles bk. 1, no. 6, l. 1

11 *Naturam expelles furca, tamen usque recurret.*
You may drive out nature with a pitchfork,
yet she'll be constantly running back.
Epistles bk. 1, no. 10, l. 24

12 *Concordia discors.*
Discordant harmony.
Epistles bk. 1, no. 12, l. 19

13 *Et semel emissum volat irrevocabile verbum.*
And once sent out, a word takes wing
beyond recall.
Epistles bk. 1, no. 18, l. 71

14 *Nam tua res agitur, paries cum proximus ardet.*
For it is your business, when the wall next
door catches fire.
Epistles bk. 1, no. 18, l. 84

15 *O imitatores, servum pecus.*
O imitators, you slavish herd.
Epistles bk. 1, no. 19, l. 19

16 *Scribimus indocti doctique poemata passim.*
Skilled or unskilled, we all scribble poems.
Epistles bk. 2, no. 1, l. 117. Cf. 252:29

17 *Atque inter silvas Academi quaerere verum.*
And seek for truth in the groves of
Academe.
Epistles bk. 2, no. 2, l. 45

18 *Multa fero, ut placem genus irritabile vatum.*
I have to put up with a lot, to please the
touchy breed of poets.
Epistles bk. 2, no. 2, l. 102

19 *Nil desperandum.*
Never despair.
Odes bk. 1, no. 7, l. 27

20   *Dum loquimur, fugerit invida*
Aetas: carpe diem, quam minimum credula
postero.
While we're talking, envious time is
fleeing: seize the day, put no trust in the
future.
Odes bk. 1, no. 11, l. 7

21 *Integer vitae scelerisque purus.*
Wholesome of life and free of crimes.
Odes bk. 1, no. 22, l. 1

22 *Auream quisquis mediocritatem*
Diligit.
Someone who loves the golden mean.
Odes bk. 2, no. 10, l. 5

23 *Eheu fugaces, Postume, Postume,*
Labuntur anni.
Ah me, Postumus, Postumus, the fleeting
years are slipping by.
Odes bk. 2, no. 14, l. 1

24 *Credite posteri.*
Believe me, you who come after me!
Odes bk. 2, no. 19, l. 2

25 *Post equitem sedet atra Cura.*
Black Care sits behind the horseman.
Odes bk. 3, no. 1, l. 40

26 *Dulce et decorum est pro patria mori.*
Lovely and honourable it is to die for one's
country.
Odes bk. 3, no. 2, l. 13

27 *Splendide mendax et in omne virgo*
Nobilis aevum.
Gloriously deceitful and a virgin renowned
for ever.
Odes bk. 3, no. 11, l. 35 (of the Danaid
Hypermestra)

28 *Exegi monumentum aere perennius.*
I have erected a monument more lasting
than bronze.
Odes bk. 3, no. 30, l. 1

29 *Non omnis moriar.*
I shall not altogether die.
Odes bk. 3, no. 30, l. 6

30 *Non sum qualis eram bonae*
Sub regno Cinarae.
I am not as I was when good Cinara was
my queen.
Odes bk. 4, no. 1, l. 3

1 *Misce stultitiam consiliis brevem:*
  Dulce est desipere in loco.
  Mix a little foolishness with your
  prudence: it's good to be silly at the right
  moment.
    Odes bk. 4, no. 12, l. 27

2 *Est modus in rebus.*
  There is moderation in everything.
    Satires bk. 1, no. 1, l. 106

3 *Etiam disiecti membra poetae.*
  Even though broken up, the limbs of a
  poet.
    Satires bk. 1, no. 4, l. 62 (of Ennius)

4 *Hoc erat in votis: modus agri non ita magnus,*
  Hortus ubi et tecto vicinus iugis aquae fons
  Et paulum silvae super his foret.
  This was among my prayers: a piece of
  land not so very large, where a garden
  should be and a spring of ever-flowing
  water near the house, and a bit of
  woodland as well as these.
    Satires bk. 2, no. 6, l. 1

Bishop Samuel Horsley 1733–1806

5 In this country ... the individual subject
  ... 'has nothing to do with the laws but to
  obey them.'
    Hansard (Lords) 13 November 1795, col. 268
    (defending a maxim he had earlier used in
    committee)

A. E. Housman 1859–1936

6 And wherefore is he wearing such
  a conscience-stricken air?
  Oh they're taking him to prison for the
  colour of his hair.
    Collected Poems (1939) 'Additional Poems'
    no. 18

7 Mud's sister, not himself, adorns my legs.
    Fragment of a Greek Tragedy (*Bromsgrovian*
    vol. 2, no. 5, 1883)

8 The Grizzly Bear is huge and wild;
  He has devoured the infant child.
  The infant child is not aware
  He has been eaten by the bear.
    'Infant Innocence' (1938)

9 Pass me the can, lad; there's an end of
  May.
    Last Poems (1922) no. 9

10 But men at whiles are sober
   And think by fits and starts,
   And if they think, they fasten
   Their hands upon their hearts.
    Last Poems (1922) no. 10

11 I, a stranger and afraid
   In a world I never made.
    Last Poems (1922) no. 12

12 The candles burn their sockets,
   The blinds let through the day,
   The young man feels his pockets
   And wonders what's to pay.
    Last Poems (1922) no. 21

13 Their shoulders held the sky suspended;
   They stood, and earth's foundations stay;
   What God abandoned, these defended,
   And saved the sum of things for pay.
    Last Poems (1922) no. 37 'Epitaph on an Army
    of Mercenaries'

14 For nature, heartless, witless nature,
   Will neither care nor know
   What stranger's feet may find the meadow
   And trespass there and go,
   Nor ask amid the dews of morning
   If they are mine or no.
    Last Poems (1922) no. 40

15 The rainy Pleiads wester,
   Orion plunges prone.
    More Poems (1936) no. 11

16 Loveliest of trees, the cherry now
   Is hung with bloom along the bough,
   And stands about the woodland ride
   Wearing white for Eastertide.
    A Shropshire Lad (1896) no. 2

17 And since to look at things in bloom
   Fifty springs are little room,
   About the woodlands I will go
   To see the cherry hung with snow.
    A Shropshire Lad (1896) no. 2

18 Clay lies still, but blood's a rover;
   Breath's a ware that will not keep.
   Up, lad: when the journey's over
   There'll be time enough to sleep.
    A Shropshire Lad (1896) no. 4

19 A neck God made for other use
   Than strangling in a string.
    A Shropshire Lad (1896) no. 9

20 In summertime on Bredon
   The bells they sound so clear;
   Round both the shires they ring them
   In steeples far and near,
   A happy noise to hear.
   Here of a Sunday morning
   My love and I would lie,
   And see the coloured counties,
   And hear the larks so high
   About us in the sky.
    A Shropshire Lad (1896) no. 21

21 The lads for the girls and the lads for the
       liquor are there,
   And there with the rest are the lads that
       will never be old.
    A Shropshire Lad (1896) no. 23

22 On Wenlock Edge the wood's in trouble.
    A Shropshire Lad (1896) no. 31

23 To-day the Roman and his trouble
   Are ashes under Uricon.
    A Shropshire Lad (1896) no. 31

24 What are those blue remembered hills,
   What spires, what farms are those?
   That is the land of lost content,
   I see it shining plain,
   The happy highways where I went
   And cannot come again.
    A Shropshire Lad (1896) no. 40

25 The beautiful and death-struck year.
    A Shropshire Lad (1896) no. 41

1 Clunton and Clunbury,
Clungunford and Clun,
Are the quietest places
Under the sun.
A Shropshire Lad (1896) no. 50 (epigraph)

2 By brooks too broad for leaping
The lightfoot boys are laid.
A Shropshire Lad (1896) no. 54

3 Say, for what were hop-yards meant,
Or why was Burton built on Trent?
A Shropshire Lad (1896) no. 62

4 And malt does more than Milton can
To justify God's ways to man.
A Shropshire Lad (1896) no. 62. Cf. 228:9

5 Mithridates, he died old.
A Shropshire Lad (1896) no. 62

6 This great College, of this ancient
University, has seen some strange sights. It
has seen Wordsworth drunk and Porson
sober. And here am I, a better poet than
Porson, and a better scholar than
Wordsworth, betwixt and between.
Speech at Trinity College, Cambridge, in G.
K. Chesterton *Autobiography* (1936) ch. 12

Julia Ward Howe 1819–1910

7 Mine eyes have seen the glory of the
coming of the Lord:
He is trampling out the vintage where the
grapes of wrath are stored;
He hath loosed the fateful lightning of his
terrible swift sword:
His truth is marching on.
'Battle Hymn of the Republic' (1862)

James Howell c.1593–1666

8 Some hold translations not unlike to be
The wrong side of a Turkey tapestry.
Familiar Letters (1645–55) bk. 1, no. 6

9 One hair of a woman can draw more than
a hundred pair of oxen.
Familiar Letters (1645–55) bk. 2, no. 4

Mary Howitt 1799–1888

10 Buttercups and daisies,
Oh, the pretty flowers;
Coming ere the springtime,
To tell of sunny hours.
'Buttercups and Daisies' (1838)

11 'Will you walk into my parlour?' said a
spider to a fly:
''Tis the prettiest little parlour that ever
you did spy.'
'The Spider and the Fly' (1834)

Edmond Hoyle 1672–1769

12 When in doubt, win the trick.
Hoyle's Games Improved (ed. Charles Jones,
1790) 'Twenty-four Short Rules for Learners'
(possibly Jones's addition)

Elbert Hubbard 1859–1915

13 Never explain—your friends do not need it
and your enemies will not believe you
anyway.
The Motto Book (1907) p. 31. Cf. 352:21

14 Life is just one damned thing after
another.
Philistine December 1909, p. 32 (often
attributed to Frank Ward O'Malley)

15 Editor: a person employed by a newspaper,
whose business it is to separate the wheat
from the chaff, and to see that the chaff is
printed.
The Roycroft Dictionary (1914) p. 46

See also RALPH WALDO EMERSON

Frank McKinney ('Kin') Hubbard 1868–1930

16 Classic music is th'kind that we keep
thinkin'll turn into a tune.
Comments of Abe Martin and His Neighbors
(1923)

17 It's no disgrace t'be poor, but it might as
well be.
Short Furrows (1911) p. 42

Jimmy Hughes and Frank Lake

18 Bless 'em all! Bless 'em all! The long and
the short and the tall.
'Bless 'Em All' (1940 song)

Langston Hughes 1902–67

19 I, too, sing America.
'I, Too' in *Survey Graphic* March 1925

Ted Hughes 1930–

20 It took the whole of Creation
To produce my foot, my each feather:
Now I hold Creation in my foot.
'Hawk Roosting' (1960)

21 Adam ate the apple.
Eve ate Adam.
The serpent ate Eve.
This is the dark intestine.
'Theology' (1967)

22 Grape is my mulatto mother
In this frozen whited country.
'Wino' (1967)

Thomas Hughes 1822–96

23 It's more than a game. It's an institution.
Tom Brown's Schooldays (1857) pt. 2, ch. 7 (of
cricket)

Victor Hugo 1802–85

24 The word is the Verb, and the Verb is God.
Contemplations (1856) bk. 1, no. 8

1 If suffer we must, let's suffer on the heights.

> *Contemplations* (1856) bk. 5, no. 26 'Les Malheureux'

2 A stand can be made against invasion by an army; no stand can be made against invasion by an idea.

> *Histoire d'un Crime* (written 1851–2, published 1877) pt. 5, sect. 10

David Hume 1711–76

3 Custom, then, is the great guide of human life.

> *An Enquiry Concerning Human Understanding* (1748) sect. 5, pt. 1

4 If we take in our hand any volume; of divinity or school metaphysics, for instance; let us ask, *Does it contain any abstract reasoning concerning quantity or number?* No. *Does it contain any experimental reasoning, concerning matter of fact and existence?* No. Commit it then to the flames: for it can contain nothing but sophistry and illusion.

> *Enquiry Concerning Human Understanding* (1748) sect. 12, pt. 3

5 Avarice, the spur of industry.

> *Essays: Moral and Political* (1741–2) 'Of Civil Liberty'

6 Money ... is none of the wheels of trade: it is the oil which renders the motion of the wheels more smooth and easy.

> *Essays: Moral and Political* (1741–2) 'Of Money'

7 A little miss, dressed in a new gown for a dancing-school ball, receives as complete enjoyment as the greatest orator, who ... governs the passions and resolutions of a numerous assembly.

> *Essays: Moral and Political* (1741–2) 'The Sceptic'

8 In all ages of the world, priests have been enemies of liberty.

> *Essays, Moral, Political, and Literary* (ed. Green and Grose, 1875) 'Of the Parties of Great Britain' (1741–2)

9 Beauty is no quality in things themselves. It exists merely in the mind which contemplates them.

> *Essays, Moral, Political, and Literary* (ed. Green and Grose, 1875) 'Of the Standard of Taste' (1757)

10 Never literary attempt was more unfortunate than my Treatise of Human Nature. It fell *dead-born from the press.*

> *My Own Life* (1777) ch. 1

11 It is not contrary to reason to prefer the destruction of the whole world to the scratching of my finger.

> *A Treatise upon Human Nature* (1739) bk. 2, pt. 3

Leigh Hunt 1784–1859

12 Abou Ben Adhem (may his tribe increase!) Awoke one night from a deep dream of peace.

> 'Abou Ben Adhem' (1838)

13 Write me as one that loves his fellow-men.

> 'Abou Ben Adhem' (1838)

14 The laughing queen that caught the world's great hands.

> 'The Nile' (1818); of Cleopatra

15 Jenny kissed me when we met, Jumping from the chair she sat in; Time, you thief, who love to get Sweets into your list, put that in.

> 'Rondeau' (1838)

16 Stolen sweets are always sweeter, Stolen kisses much completer, Stolen looks are nice in chapels, Stolen, stolen, be your apples.

> 'Song of Fairies Robbing an Orchard' (1830)

17 The two divinest things this world has got, A lovely woman in a rural spot!

> 'The Story of Rimini' (1816) canto 3, l. 257

18 A mere gossiping entertainment: a few child's squalls, a few mumbled amens, and a few mumbled cakes, and a few smirks accompanied by a few fees.

> Of a christening; letter to Marianne Kent, February 1806, in T. L. Hunt *Correspondence of Leigh Hunt* (1862) vol. 1

Anne Hunter 1742–1821

19 My mother bids me bind my hair With bands of rosy hue, Tie up my sleeves with ribbons rare, And lace my bodice blue.

> 'A Pastoral Song' (1794)

Herman Hupfeld 1894–1951

20 You must remember this, a kiss is still a kiss, A sigh is just a sigh; The fundamental things apply, As time goes by.

> 'As Time Goes By' (1931 song)

John Huss c.1372–1415

21 *O sancta simplicitas!* O holy simplicity!

> At the stake, seeing an aged peasant bringing a bundle of twigs to throw on the pile; in J. W. Zincgreff and J. L. Weidner *Apophthegmata* (Amsterdam, 1653) pt. 3, p. 383. Cf. 181:6

Saddam Hussein 1937–

22 The mother of battles.

> Popular interpretation of his description of the approaching Gulf War, given in a speech in Baghdad, 6 January 1991; *The Times*, 7 January 1991, reported that he was ready for the 'mother of all wars'

Francis Hutcheson 1694–1746

1 Wisdom denotes the pursuing of the best ends by the best means.
Inquiry into the Original of our Ideas of Beauty and Virtue (1725) Treatise 1, sect. 5, subsect. 16

2 That action is best, which procures the greatest happiness for the greatest numbers.
Inquiry into the Original ... (1725) Treatise 2, sect. 3, subsect. 8. Cf. 35:1

Aldous Huxley 1894–1963

3 There are few who would not rather be taken in adultery than in provincialism.
Antic Hay (1923) ch. 10

4 The saxophones wailed like melodious cats under the moon.
Brave New World (1932) ch. 5

5 The proper study of mankind is books.
Crome Yellow (1921) ch. 28. Cf. 252:17

6 Consistency is contrary to nature, contrary to life. The only completely consistent people are the dead.
Do What You Will (1929) 'Wordsworth in the Tropics'

7 Chastity—the most unnatural of all the sexual perversions.
Eyeless in Gaza (1936) ch. 27

8 I can sympathize with people's pains, but not with their pleasures. There is something curiously boring about somebody else's happiness.
Limbo (1920) 'Cynthia'

9 Several excuses are always less convincing than one.
Point Counter Point (1928) ch. 1

10 Brought up in an epoch when ladies apparently rolled along on wheels, Mr Quarles was peculiarly susceptible to calves.
Point Counter Point (1928) ch. 20

11 A million million spermatozoa,
All of them alive:
Out of their cataclysm but one poor Noah
Dare hope to survive.

And among that billion minus one
Might have chanced to be
Shakespeare, another Newton, a new Donne—
But the One was Me.
'Fifth Philosopher's Song' (1920)

12   When the wearied Band
Swoons to a waltz, I take her hand,
And there we sit in peaceful calm,
Quietly sweating palm to palm.
'Frascati's' (1920)

13 Beauty for some provides escape,
Who gain a happiness in eyeing
The gorgeous buttocks of the ape
Or Autumn sunsets exquisitely dying.
'Ninth Philosopher's Song' (1920)

Sir Julian Huxley 1887–1975

14 Operationally, God is beginning to resemble not a ruler but the last fading smile of a cosmic Cheshire cat.
Religion without Revelation (1957 ed.) ch. 3

T. H. Huxley 1825–95

15 The great tragedy of Science—the slaying of a beautiful hypothesis by an ugly fact.
Collected Essays (1893–4) 'Biogenesis and Abiogenesis'

16 Science is nothing but trained and organized common sense, differing from the latter only as a veteran may differ from a raw recruit: and its methods differ from those of common sense only as far as the guardsman's cut and thrust differ from the manner in which a savage wields his club.
Collected Essays (1893–4) 'The Method of Zadig'

17 If a little knowledge is dangerous, where is the man who has so much as to be out of danger?
Collected Essays vol. 3 (1895) 'On Elementary Instruction in Physiology' (written 1877)

18 It is the customary fate of new truths to begin as heresies and to end as superstitions.
Science and Culture and Other Essays (1881) 'The Coming of Age of the Origin of Species'

19 Irrationally held truths may be more harmful than reasoned errors.
Science and Culture and Other Essays (1881) 'The Coming of Age of the Origin of Species'

20 Logical consequences are the scarecrows of fools and the beacons of wise men.
Science and Culture and Other Essays (1881) 'On the Hypothesis that Animals are Automata'

21 A man has no reason to be ashamed of having an ape for his grandfather. If there were an ancestor whom I should feel shame in recalling it would rather be a *man*—a man of restless and versatile intellect—who, not content with an equivocal success in his own sphere of activity, plunges into scientific questions with which he has no real acquaintance, only to obscure them by an aimless rhetoric, and distract the attention of his hearers from the real point at issue by eloquent digressions and skilled appeals to religious prejudice.
Replying to Samuel Wilberforce in a debate on Darwin's theory of evolution at Oxford, 30 June 1860. See L. Huxley (ed.) *Life and Letters of T. H. Huxley* (1900) vol. 1, p. 185. Cf. 349:7

22 I am too much of a sceptic to deny the possibility of anything.
Letter to H. Spencer, 22 March 1886, in L. Huxley (ed.) *Life and Letters of T. H. Huxley* (1900) vol. 2, ch. 8

Edward Hyde
See EARL OF CLARENDON

Dolores Ibarruri ('La Pasionaria')
1895–1989

1 It is better to die on your feet than to live on your knees.
Speech in Paris, 3 September 1936; in *L'Humanité* 4 September 1936 (also attributed to Emiliano Zapata)

2 *No pasarán.*
They shall not pass.
Radio broadcast, Madrid, 19 July 1936, in *Speeches and Articles 1936–38* (1938) p. 7. Cf. 12:6

Henrik Ibsen 1828–1906

3 You should never have your best trousers on when you go out to fight for freedom and truth.
An Enemy of the People (1882) act 5

4 Mother, give me the sun.
Ghosts (1881) act 3

5 But good God, people don't do such things!
Hedda Gabler (1890) act 4

6 Castles in the air—they are so easy to take refuge in. And easy to build, too.
The Master Builder (1892) act 3

7 Take the life-lie away from the average man and straight away you take away his happiness.
The Wild Duck (1884) act 5

St Ignatius Loyola 1491–1556

8 Teach us, good Lord, to serve Thee as Thou deservest:
To give and not to count the cost;
To fight and not to heed the wounds;
To toil and not to seek for rest;
To labour and not to ask for any reward
Save that of knowing that we do Thy will.
'Prayer for Generosity' (1548)

Ivan Illich 1926–

9 In a consumer society there are inevitably two kinds of slaves: the prisoners of addiction and the prisoners of envy.
Tools for Conviviality (1973) ch. 3

Dean Inge 1860–1954

10 The enemies of Freedom do not argue; they shout and they shoot.
End of an Age (1948) ch. 4

11 The effect of boredom on a large scale in history is underestimated. It is a main cause of revolutions, and would soon bring to an end all the static Utopias and the farmyard civilization of the Fabians.
End of an Age (1948) ch. 6

12 To become a popular religion, it is only necessary for a superstition to enslave a philosophy.
Idea of Progress (Romanes Lecture, 27 May 1920) p. 9

13 Many people believe that they are attracted by God, or by Nature, when they are only repelled by man.
More Lay Thoughts of a Dean (1931) pt. 4, ch. 1

14 A man may build himself a throne of bayonets, but he cannot sit on it.
Philosophy of Plotinus (1923) vol. 2, Lecture 22 (quoted by Boris Yeltsin at the time of the failed military coup in Russia, August 1991)

Robert G. Ingersoll 1833–99

15 An honest God is the noblest work of man.
The Gods (1876) pt. 1, p. 2. Cf. 252:22

16 In nature there are neither rewards nor punishments—there are consequences.
Some Reasons Why (1881) pt. 8 'The New Testament'

J. A. D. Ingres 1780–1867

17 *Le dessin est la probité de l'art.*
Drawing is the true test of art.
Pensées d'Ingres (1922) p. 70

Weldon J. Irvine

18 Young, gifted and black.
Title of song (1969)

Washington Irving 1783–1859

19 A ... sharp tongue is the only edged tool that grows keener with constant use.
The Sketch Book (1820) 'Rip Van Winkle'

20 There is a certain relief in change, even though it be from bad to worse ... it is often a comfort to shift one's position and be bruised in a new place.
Tales of a Traveller (1824) 'To the Reader'

Christopher Isherwood 1904–86

21 The common cormorant (or shag)
Lays eggs inside a paper bag,
You follow the idea, no doubt?
It's to keep the lightning out.
But what these unobservant birds
Have never thought of, is that herds
Of wandering bears might come with buns
And steal the bags to hold the crumbs.
'The Common Cormorant' (written *c*.1925)

22 I am a camera with its shutter open, quite passive, recording, not thinking.
Goodbye to Berlin (1939) 'Berlin Diary' Autumn 1930

Alec Issigonis (1906–88)

23 A camel is a horse designed by a committee.
On his dislike of working in teams, in *Guardian* 14 January 1991 'Notes and Queries' (attributed)

Holbrook Jackson 1874–1948

24 Pedantry is the dotage of knowledge.
Anatomy of Bibliomania (1930) vol. 1, p. 150

Joe Jacobs 1896–1940

1 We was robbed!

After Jack Sharkey beat Max Schmeling (of whom Jacobs was manager) in the heavyweight title fight, 21 June 1932; in P. Heller *In This Corner* (1975) p. 44

2 I should of stood in bed.

After leaving his sick-bed to attend the World Baseball Series in Detroit, 1935, and betting on the losers; in J. Lardner *Strong Cigars* (1951) p. 61

Jacopone da Todi c.1230–1306

3 *Stabat Mater dolorosa,*
Iuxta crucem lacrimosa.

At the cross her station keeping,
Stood the mournful Mother weeping.
'Stabat Mater dolorosa' (tr. E. Caswall 1849); also attributed to Pope Innocent III and others

Mick Jagger 1943– and Keith Richard 1943–

4 Get off of my cloud.

Title of song (1966)

5 And though she's not really ill,
There's a little yellow pill:
She goes running for the shelter
Of a mother's little helper.
'Mother's Little Helper' (1966 song)

6 I can't get no satisfaction
I can't get no girl reaction.
'(I Can't Get No) Satisfaction' (1965 song)

7 Ev'rywhere I hear the sound of marching, charging feet, boy.
'Street Fighting Man' (1968 song)

Richard Jago 1715–81

8 With leaden foot time creeps along
While Delia is away.
'Absence'

James I (James VI of Scotland) 1566–1625

9 A custom loathsome to the eye, hateful to the nose, harmful to the brain, dangerous to the lungs, and in the black, stinking fume thereof, nearest resembling the horrible Stygian smoke of the pit that is bottomless.

A Counterblast to Tobacco (1604)

10 The king is truly *parens patriae*, the polite father of his people.

Speech to Parliament, 21 March 1610, in *Works* (1616) p. 529

11 No bishop, no King.

To a deputation of Presbyterians from the Church of Scotland, seeking religious tolerance in England; in W. Barlow *Sum and Substance of the Conference* (1604) p. 82

12 I will govern according to the common weal, but not according to the common will.

December, 1621, in J. R. Green *History of the English People* vol. 3 (1879) bk. 7, ch. 4

13 Dr Donne's verses are like the peace of God; they pass all understanding.

Remark recorded by Archdeacon Plume (1630–1704)

James V 1512–42

14 It came with a lass, and it will pass with a lass.

Of the crown of Scotland, on learning of the birth of Mary Queen of Scots, December 1542; in Robert Lindsay of Pitscottie (c.1500–65) *History of Scotland* (1728) p. 176

Henry James 1843–1916

15 The historian, essentially, wants more documents than he can really use; the dramatist only wants more liberties than he can really take.

The Aspern Papers (1909 ed.) preface

16 Most English talk is a quadrille in a sentry-box.

The Awkward Age (1899) bk. 5, ch. 19

17 Vereker's secret, my dear man—the general intention of his books: the string the pearls were strung on, the buried treasure, the figure in the carpet.

The Figure in the Carpet (1896) ch. 11

18 It takes a great deal of history to produce a little literature.

Hawthorne (1879) ch. 1

19 He was ... worse than provincial—he was parochial.

Hawthorne (1879) ch. 4 (of H. D. Thoreau)

20 The black and merciless things that are behind the great possessions.

The Ivory Tower (1917) notes p. 287

21 I could come back to America ... to die—but never, never to live.

Letter to Mrs William James, 1 April 1913, in Leon Edel (ed.) *Letters* vol. 4 (1984) p. 657

22 Cats and monkeys—monkeys and cats—all human life is there!

The Madonna of the Future (1879) vol. 1, p. 59 ('All human life is there' became the slogan of the *News of the World* from the late 1950s)

23 We work in the dark—we do what we can—we give what we have. Our doubt is our passion and our passion is our task. The rest is the madness of art.

'The Middle Years' (short story, 1893)

24 What is character but the determination of incident? What is incident but the illustration of character?

Partial Portraits (1888) 'The Art of Fiction'

25 The house of fiction has in short not one window, but a million ... but they are, singly or together, as nothing without the posted presence of the watcher.

The Portrait of a Lady (1908 ed.) preface

1 The note I wanted; that of the strange and sinister embroidered on the very type of the normal and easy.
Prefaces (1909) 'The Altar of the Dead'

2 The fatal futility of Fact.
The Spoils of Poynton (1909 ed.) preface

3 We were alone with the quiet day, and his little heart, dispossessed, had stopped.
The Turn of the Screw (1898) p. 169

4 Of course, of course.
On hearing that Rupert Brooke had died on a Greek island; in C. Hassall *Rupert Brooke* (1964) ch. 14

5 Summer afternoon—summer afternoon ... the two most beautiful words in the English language.
In Edith Wharton *A Backward Glance* (1934) ch. 10

6 So here it is at last, the distinguished thing!
On experiencing his first stroke; in Edith Wharton *A Backward Glance* (1934) ch. 14

William James 1842–1910

7 The moral flabbiness born of the exclusive worship of the bitch-goddess *success*.
Letter to H. G. Wells, 11 September 1906, in *Letters* (1920) vol. 2

8 There is no more miserable human being than one in whom nothing is habitual but indecision.
Principles of Psychology (1890) vol. 1, ch. 4

9 The art of being wise is the art of knowing what to overlook.
Principles of Psychology (1890) vol. 2, ch. 22

10 There is no worse lie than a truth misunderstood by those who hear it.
Varieties of Religious Experience (1902) p. 355

11 Hogamus, higamus
Man is polygamous
Higamus, hogamus
Woman monogamous.
In *Oxford Book of Marriage* (1990) p. 195

Randall Jarrell 1914–65

12 To Americans, English manners are far more frightening than none at all.
Pictures from an Institution (1954) pt. 1, ch. 4

13 It is better to entertain an idea than to take it home to live with you for the rest of your life.
Pictures from an Institution (1954) pt. 1, ch. 4

Douglas Jay 1907–

14 Fair shares for all, is Labour's call.
Change and Fortune (1980) ch. 7 (slogan for the North Battersea by-election, 1946)

15 In the case of nutrition and health, just as in the case of education, the gentleman in Whitehall really does know better what is good for people than the people know themselves.
The Socialist Case (1939) ch. 30

Jean Paul
See JOHANN PAUL FRIEDRICH RICHTER

Sir James Jeans 1877–1946

16 Life exists in the universe only because the carbon atom possesses certain exceptional properties.
The Mysterious Universe (1930) ch. 1

17 From the intrinsic evidence of his creation, the Great Architect of the Universe now begins to appear as a pure mathematician.
The Mysterious Universe (1930) ch. 5

Thomas Jefferson 1743–1826

18 We hold these truths to be sacred and undeniable; that all men are created equal and independent, that from that equal creation they derive rights inherent and inalienable, among which are the preservation of life, and liberty, and the pursuit of happiness.
'Rough Draft' of the American Declaration of Independence, in J. P. Boyd et al. *Papers of Thomas Jefferson* vol. 1 (1950) p. 423. Cf. 11:12

19 Peace, commerce, and honest friendship with all nations—entangling alliances with none.
Speech [First Inaugural Address] ... on the 4th of March, 1801

20 A little rebellion now and then is a good thing.
Letter to James Madison, 30 January 1787, in *Papers* vol. 11 (1955)

21 The tree of liberty must be refreshed from time to time with the blood of patriots and tyrants. It is its natural manure.
Letter to W. S. Smith, 13 November 1787, in *Papers* vol. 12 (1955)

22 If a due participation of office is a matter of right, how are vacancies to be obtained? Those by death are few; by resignation none.
Letter to E. Shipman and others, 12 July 1801 (usually quoted 'Few die and none resign'); in P. L. Ford (ed.) *Writings of T. Jefferson* vol. 8 (1897)

23 To attain all this [universal republicanism], however, rivers of blood must yet flow, and years of desolation pass over; yet the object is worth rivers of blood, and years of desolation.
Letter to John Adams, 4 September 1823, in P. L. Ford *Writings of T. Jefferson* vol. 10 (1899). Cf. 255:3, 339:11

24 Indeed I tremble for my country when I reflect that God is just.
Notes on the State of Virginia (1781–5) Query 18

25 We have the wolf by the ears; and we can neither hold him, nor safely let him go. Justice is in one scale, and self-preservation in the other.
On slavery, in a letter to John Holmes, 22 April 1820; in A. Lipscome and A. Berg (eds.) *Writings of T. Jefferson* (1903) vol. 15

1 When a man assumes a public trust, he
should consider himself as public property.
  To Baron von Humboldt, 1807, in B. L.
  Rayner *Life of Jefferson* (1834) p. 356

Francis, Lord Jeffrey 1773–1850

2 This will never do.
  On Wordsworth's *The Excursion* (1814) in
  Edinburgh Review November 1814

David Jenkins, Bishop of Durham 1925–

3 An imported, elderly American.
  Referring to Ian MacGregor, Chairman of the
  National Coal Board; in *The Times*
  22 September 1984

4 I am not clear that God manoeuvres
physical things … After all, a conjuring
trick with bones only proves that it is as
clever as a conjuring trick with bones.
  On the Resurrection, in 'Poles Apart' (BBC
  radio, 4 October 1984)

Paul Jennings 1918–89

5 Resistentialism is concerned with what
Things think about men.
  Even Oddlier (1952) 'Developments in
  Resistentialism'

St Jerome AD c.342–420

6 *Venerationi mihi semper fuit non verbosa
rusticitas, sed sancta simplicitas.*
  I have revered always not crude verbosity,
  but holy simplicity.
  Letter 'Ad Pammachium' in *Patrologiae
  Latinae* vol. 22 (1864) col. 579

Jerome K. Jerome 1859–1927

7 It is impossible to enjoy idling thoroughly
unless one has plenty of work to do.
  Idle Thoughts of an Idle Fellow (1886) 'On Being
  Idle'

8 I want a house that has got over all its
troubles; I don't want to spend the rest of
my life bringing up a young and
inexperienced house.
  They and I (1909) ch. 11

William Jerome 1865–1932

9 Any old place I can hang my hat is home
sweet home to me.
  Title of song (1901)

Douglas Jerrold 1803–57

10 Religion's in the heart, not in the knees.
  The Devil's Ducat (1830) act 1, sc. 2

11 The best thing I know between France and
England is—the sea.
  Wit and Opinions (1859) 'The Anglo-French
  Alliance'

12 Earth is here so kind, that just tickle her
with a hoe and she laughs with a harvest.
  Wit and Opinions (1859) 'A Land of Plenty'
  (Australia)

13 Love's like the measles—all the worse
when it comes late in life.
  Wit and Opinions (1859) 'Love'

Bishop John Jewel 1522–71

14 In old time we had treen chalices and
golden priests, but now we have treen
priests and golden chalices.
  *Certain Sermons Preached Before the Queen's
  Majesty* (1609) p. 176

C. E. M. Joad 1891–1953

15 It all depends what you mean by …
  Replying to questions on 'The Brains Trust'
  (formerly 'Any Questions'), BBC radio
  (1941–8)

St John of the Cross 1542–91

16 *Muero porque no muero.*
  I die because I do not die.
  'Coplas del alma que pena por ver a Dios'
  (c.1578); also in St Teresa of Ávila 'Versos
  nacidos del fuego del amor de Dios'
  (c.1571–3)

Lionel Johnson 1867–1902

17 Alone he rides, alone,
  The fair and fatal king.
  'By the Statue of King Charles I at Charing
  Cross' (1895)

18 I know you: solitary griefs,
  Desolate passions, aching hours.
  'The Precept of Silence' (1895)

Lyndon Baines Johnson 1908–73

19 I am a free man, an American, a United
States Senator, and a Democrat, in that
order.
  Texas Quarterly Winter 1958

20 I don't want loyalty. I want *loyalty*. I want
him to kiss my ass in Macy's window at
high noon and tell me it smells like roses.
I want his pecker in my pocket.
  In D. Halberstam *The Best and the Brightest*
  (1972) ch. 20 (discussing a prospective
  assistant)

21 Better to have him inside the tent pissing
out, than outside pissing in.
  Of J. Edgar Hoover, in D. Halberstam *The Best
  and the Brightest* (1972) ch. 20

22 So dumb he can't fart and chew gum at
the same time.
  Of Gerald Ford, in R. Reeves *A Ford, not
  a Lincoln* (1975) ch. 2

Philander Chase Johnson
1866–1939

1 Cheer up! the worst is yet to come!
Everybody's Magazine May 1920

Philip Johnson 1906–

2 Architecture is the art of how to waste space.
New York Times 27 December 1964, p. 9

Samuel Johnson 1709–84

3 Change is not made without inconvenience, even from worse to better.
Dictionary of the English Language (1755) preface. Cf. 171:15

4 I am not yet so lost in lexicography as to forget that words are the daughters of earth, and that things are the sons of heaven. Language is only the instrument of science, and words are but the signs of ideas.
Dictionary of the English Language (1755) preface. Cf. 216:14

5 Every quotation contributes something to the stability or enlargement of the language.
Dictionary of the English Language (1755) preface (on citations of usage in a dictionary)

6 *Dull.* To make dictionaries is dull work.
Dictionary of the English Language (1755) 'dull' (8th definition)

7 *Excise.* A hateful tax levied upon commodities.
Dictionary of the English Language (1755)

8 *Lexicographer.* A writer of dictionaries, a harmless drudge.
Dictionary of the English Language (1755)

9 *Oats.* A grain, which in England is generally given to horses, but in Scotland supports the people.
Dictionary of the English Language (1755)

10 *Patron.* Commonly a wretch who supports with insolence, and is paid with flattery.
Dictionary of the English Language (1755)

11 When two Englishmen meet, their first talk is of the weather.
The Idler no. 11 (24 June 1758)

12 Among the calamities of war may be jointly numbered the diminution of the love of truth, by the falsehoods which interest dictates and credulity encourages.
The Idler no. 30 (11 November 1758); possibly the source of 'When war is declared, Truth is the first casualty', epigraph to Arthur Ponsonby's *Falsehood in Wartime* (1928); attributed also to Hiram Johnson, speaking in the US Senate, 1918

13 Promise, large promise, is the soul of an advertisement.
The Idler no. 40 (20 January 1759)

14 A Scotchman must be a very sturdy moralist, who does not love Scotland better than truth.
A Journey to the Western Islands of Scotland (1775) 'Ostig in Sky'

15 Grief is a species of idleness.
Letter to Mrs Thrale, 17 March 1773, in R. W. Chapman (ed.) *Letters* (1952) vol. 1

16 He is gone, and we are going.
Letter to Mrs Thrale on the death of her son, Harry, 25 March 1776; in R. W. Chapman (ed.) *Letters* (1952) vol. 3

17 When I rise my breakfast is solitary, the black dog waits to share it, from breakfast to dinner he continues barking, except that Dr Brocklesby for a little keeps him at a distance.
Letter to Mrs Thrale, 28 June 1783, in R. W. Chapman (ed.) *Letters* (1952) vol. 3 (on his melancholia; Winston Churchill later used the words 'black dog' to refer to his own bouts of depression)

18 The true genius is a mind of large general powers, accidentally determined to some particular direction.
Lives of the English Poets (1779–81) 'Cowley'

19 Language is the dress of thought.
Lives of the English Poets (1779–81) 'Cowley'. Cf. 252:2, 346:18

20 The father of English criticism.
Lives of the English Poets (1779–81) 'Dryden'

21 In the character of his Elegy I rejoice to concur with the common reader; for by the common sense of readers uncorrupted with literary prejudices ... must be finally decided all claim to poetical honours.
Lives of the English Poets (1779–81) 'Gray'

22 An exotic and irrational entertainment.
Lives of the English Poets (1779–81) 'Hughes' (of Italian opera)

23 I am disappointed by that stroke of death, which has eclipsed the gaiety of nations and impoverished the public stock of harmless pleasure.
Lives of the English Poets (1779–81) 'Edmund Smith' (on the death of Garrick)

24 Nothing can please many, and please long, but just representations of general nature.
Plays of William Shakespeare ... (1765) preface (Yale ed., p. 61)

25 Love is only one of many passions.
Plays of William Shakespeare ... (1765) preface (Yale ed., p. 63)

26 I have always suspected that the reading is right, which requires many words to prove it wrong; and the emendation wrong, that cannot without so much labour appear to be right.
Plays of William Shakespeare ... (1765) preface (Yale ed., p. 108)

27 This world where much is to be done and little to be known.
Prayers and Meditations (1785) no. 170 'Against inquisitive and perplexing Thoughts' 12 August 1784

1 No place affords a more striking conviction of the vanity of human hopes, than a public library.
The Rambler no. 106 (23 March 1751)

2 The business of a poet, said Imlac, is to examine, not the individual, but the species; to remark general properties and appearances.
Rasselas (1759) ch. 10

3 He [the poet] must write as the interpreter of nature, and the legislator of mankind.
Rasselas (1759) ch. 10. Cf. 305:19

4 Human life is everywhere a state in which much is to be endured, and little to be enjoyed.
Rasselas (1759) ch. 11

5 Marriage has many pains, but celibacy has no pleasures.
Rasselas (1759) ch. 26

6 Example is always more efficacious than precept.
Rasselas (1759) ch. 30

7 I consider this mighty structure [the pyramids] as a monument of the insufficiency of human enjoyments.
Rasselas (1759) ch. 32

8 Here falling houses thunder on your head,
And here a female atheist talks you dead.
London (1738) l. 17

9 This mournful truth is ev'rywhere confessed,
Slow rises worth, by poverty depressed.
London (1738) l. 176

10 The stage but echoes back the public voice.
The drama's laws the drama's patrons give,
For we that live to please, must please to live.
'Prologue spoken at the Opening of the Theatre in Drury Lane' (1747)

11 Let observation with extensive view,
Survey mankind, from China to Peru.
The Vanity of Human Wishes (1749) l. 1

12 There mark what ills the scholar's life assail,
Toil, envy, want, the patron, and the jail.
The Vanity of Human Wishes (1749) l. 159

13 A frame of adamant, a soul of fire,
No dangers fright him, and no labours tire.
The Vanity of Human Wishes (1749) l. 193 (Charles XII of Sweden)

14 He left the name, at which the world grew pale,
To point a moral, or adorn a tale.
The Vanity of Human Wishes (1749) l. 221 (Charles XII of Sweden)

15 Hides from himself his state, and shuns to know,
That life protracted is protracted woe.
The Vanity of Human Wishes (1749) l. 257

16 Must helpless man, in ignorance sedate,
Roll darkling down the torrent of his fate?
The Vanity of Human Wishes (1749) l. 345

17 A lawyer has no business with the justice or injustice of the cause which he undertakes, unless his client asks his opinion, and then he is bound to give it honestly. The justice or injustice of the cause is to be decided by the judge.
In James Boswell *Journal of a Tour to the Hebrides* (1785) 15 August 1773

18 I am always sorry when any language is lost, because languages are the pedigree of nations.
In ... *Tour to the Hebrides* (1785) 18 September 1773

19 A cucumber should be well sliced, and dressed with pepper and vinegar, and then thrown out, as good for nothing.
In ... *Tour to the Hebrides* (1785) 5 October 1773

20 I am sorry I have not learned to play at cards. It is very useful in life: it generates kindness and consolidates society.
In ... *Tour to the Hebrides* (1785) 21 November 1773

The Life of Samuel Johnson (1791) by James Boswell (references are to G. B. Hill's edition, 1934, revised by L. F. Powell, 1964)

21 [JOHNSON] I had no notion that I was wrong or irreverent to my tutor.
[BOSWELL] That, Sir, was great fortitude of mind.
[JOHNSON] No, Sir; stark insensibility.
Boswell *Life* vol. 1, p. 60 (31 October 1728)

22 Sir, we are a nest of singing birds.
Boswell *Life* vol. 1, p. 75 (1730) of Pembroke College, Oxford

23 He was a vicious man, but very kind to me. If you call a dog *Hervey*, I shall love him.
Boswell *Life* vol. 1, p. 106 (1737)

24 I'll come no more behind your scenes, David; for the silk stockings and white bosoms of your actresses excite my amorous propensities.
Boswell *Life* vol. 1, p. 201 (1750)

25 I had done all that I could; and no man is well pleased to have his all neglected, be it ever so little.
Boswell *Life* vol. 1, p. 261 (7 February 1755) letter to Lord Chesterfield

26 Is not a Patron, my Lord, one who looks with unconcern on a man struggling for life in the water, and, when he has reached ground, encumbers him with help?
Boswell *Life* vol. 1, p. 262 (7 February 1755) letter to Lord Chesterfield

27 A fly, Sir, may sting a stately horse and make him wince; but one is but an insect, and the other is a horse still.
Boswell *Life* vol. 1, p. 263, n. 3 (1754)

28 This man [Lord Chesterfield] I thought had been a Lord among wits; but, I find, he is only a wit among Lords.
Boswell *Life* vol. 1, p. 266 (1754)

1 They [the *Letters* of Lord Chesterfield] teach the morals of a whore, and the manners of a dancing master.
Boswell *Life* vol. 1, p. 266 (1754)

2 Ignorance, madam, pure ignorance.
Boswell *Life* vol. 1, p. 293 (1755); on being asked why he had defined *pastern* as the 'knee' of a horse

3 Dictionaries are like watches, the worst is better than none, and the best cannot be expected to go quite true.
Boswell *Life* vol. 1, p. 293, n. 3 (letter to Francesco Sastres, 21 August 1784)

4 If a man does not make new acquaintance as he advances through life, he will soon find himself left alone. A man, Sir, should keep his friendship in constant repair.
Boswell *Life* vol. 1, p. 300 (1755)

5 No man will be a sailor who has contrivance enough to get himself into a jail; for being in a ship is being in a jail, with the chance of being drowned ... A man in a jail has more room, better food, and commonly better company.
Boswell *Life* vol. 1, p. 348 (16 March 1759). Cf. 83:10

6 [BOSWELL:] I do indeed come from Scotland, but I cannot help it ...
[JOHNSON:] That, Sir, I find, is what a very great many of your countrymen cannot help.
Boswell *Life* vol. 1, p. 392 (16 May 1763)

7 You *may* abuse a tragedy, though you cannot write one. You may scold a carpenter who has made you a bad table, though you cannot make a table. It is not your trade to make tables.
Boswell *Life* vol. 1, p. 409 (25 June 1763); on literary criticism

8 He never passes a church without pulling off his hat. This shows that he has good principles.
Boswell *Life* vol. 1, p. 418 (1 July 1763)

9 The noblest prospect which a Scotchman ever sees, is the high road that leads him to England!
Boswell *Life* vol. 1, p. 425 (6 July 1763)

10 A man ought to read just as inclination leads him; for what he reads as a task will do him little good.
Boswell *Life* vol. 1, p. 428 (14 July 1763)

11 But if he does really think that there is no distinction between virtue and vice, why, Sir, when he leaves our houses, let us count our spoons.
Boswell *Life* vol. 1, p. 432 (14 July 1763)

12 Truth, Sir, is a cow, that will yield such people [sceptics] no more milk, and so they are gone to milk the bull.
Boswell *Life* vol. 1, p. 444 (21 July 1763)

13 Your levellers wish to level *down* as far as themselves; but they cannot bear levelling *up* to themselves.
Boswell *Life* vol. 1, p. 448 (21 July 1763)

14 Why, Sir, Sherry [Thomas Sheridan] is dull, naturally dull; but it must have taken him a great deal of pains to become what we now see him. Such an excess of stupidity, Sir, is not in Nature.
Boswell *Life* vol. 1, p. 453 (28 July 1763)

15 It is burning a farthing candle at Dover, to shew light at Calais.
Boswell *Life* vol. 1, p. 454 (28 July 1763); on Thomas Sheridan's influence on the English language. Cf. 360:16

16 A woman's preaching is like a dog's walking on his hinder legs. It is not done well; but you are surprised to find it done at all.
Boswell *Life* vol. 1, p. 463 (31 July 1763)

17 I refute it *thus*.
Boswell *Life* vol. 1, p. 471 (6 August 1763); kicking a large stone by way of refuting Bishop Berkeley's theory of the non-existence of matter

18 Sir John, Sir, is a very unclubbable man.
Boswell *Life* vol. 1, p. 480 n. 1 (Spring 1764)

19 It was not for me to bandy civilities with my Sovereign.
Boswell *Life* vol. 2, p. 35 (February 1767)

20 We *know* our will is free, and *there's* an end on't.
Boswell *Life* vol. 2, p. 82 (16 October 1769)

21 In the description of night in Macbeth, the beetle and the bat detract from the general idea of darkness,—inspissated gloom.
Boswell *Life* vol. 2, p. 90 (16 October 1769)

22 Most schemes of political improvement are very laughable things.
Boswell *Life* vol. 2, p. 102 (26 October 1769)

23 That fellow seems to me to possess but one idea, and that is a wrong one.
Boswell *Life* vol. 2, p. 126 (1770)

24 The triumph of hope over experience.
Boswell *Life* vol. 2, p. 128 (1770); of a man who remarried immediately after the death of a wife with whom he had been unhappy

25 He has, indeed, done it very well; but it is a foolish thing well done.
Boswell *Life* vol. 2, p. 210 (3 April 1773); on a public apology for assault issued by Goldsmith

26 [ELPHINSTON:] What, have you not read it through?
[JOHNSON:] No, Sir, do *you* read books *through*?
Boswell *Life* vol. 2, p. 226 (19 April 1773)

27 Read over your compositions, and where ever you meet with a passage which you think is particularly fine, strike it out.
Boswell *Life* vol. 2, p. 237 (30 April 1773); quoting a college tutor

28 He was dull in a new way, and that made many people think him *great*.
Boswell *Life* vol. 2, p. 327 (28 March 1775); of Thomas Gray

1 The full tide of human existence is at Charing-Cross.
   Boswell *Life* vol. 2, p. 337 (2 April 1775)

2 It is wonderful, when a calculation is made, how little the mind is actually employed in the discharge of any profession.
   Boswell *Life* vol. 2, p. 344 (6 April 1775)

3 A man will turn over half a library to make one book.
   Boswell *Life* vol. 2, p. 344 (6 April 1775)

4 Patriotism is the last refuge of a scoundrel.
   Boswell *Life* vol. 2, p. 348 (7 April 1775)

5 Knowledge is of two kinds. We know a subject ourselves, or we know where we can find information upon it.
   Boswell *Life* vol. 2, p. 365 (18 April 1775)

6 In lapidary inscriptions a man is not upon oath.
   Boswell *Life* vol. 2, p. 407 (1775)

7 Nothing odd will do long. *Tristram Shandy* did not last.
   Boswell *Life* vol. 2, p. 449 (20 March 1776)

8 There is nothing which has yet been contrived by man, by which so much happiness is produced as by a good tavern or inn.
   Boswell *Life* vol. 2, p. 452 (21 March 1776)

9 We would all be idle if we could.
   Boswell *Life* vol. 3, p. 13 (3 April 1776)

10 No man but a blockhead ever wrote, except for money.
   Boswell *Life* vol. 3, p. 19 (5 April 1776)

11 [BOSWELL:] Sir, what is poetry?
   [JOHNSON:] Why Sir, it is much easier to say what it is not. We all *know* what light is; but it is not easy to *tell* what it is.
   Boswell *Life* vol. 3, p. 38 (12 April 1776)

12 To Oliver Goldsmith, A Poet, Naturalist, and Historian, who left scarcely any style of writing untouched, and touched none that he did not adorn.
   Boswell *Life* vol. 3, p. 82 (22 June 1776); translation of his Latin epitaph on Goldsmith

13 If I had no duties, and no reference to futurity, I would spend my life in driving briskly in a post-chaise with a pretty woman.
   Boswell *Life* vol. 3, p. 162 (19 September 1777)

14 Depend upon it, Sir, when a man knows he is to be hanged in a fortnight, it concentrates his mind wonderfully.
   Boswell *Life* vol. 3, p. 167 (19 September 1777)

15 When a man is tired of London, he is tired of life.
   Boswell *Life* vol. 3, p. 178 (20 September 1777)

16 John Wesley's conversation is good, but he is never at leisure. He is always obliged to go at a certain hour. This is very disagreeable to a man who loves to fold his legs and have out his talk, as I do.
   Boswell *Life* vol. 3, p. 230 (31 March 1778)

17 The more contracted that power is, the more easily it is destroyed. A country governed by a despot is an inverted cone.
   Boswell *Life* vol. 3, p. 283 (14 April 1778)

18 So it is in travelling; a man must carry knowledge with him, if he would bring home knowledge.
   Boswell *Life* vol. 3, p. 302 (17 April 1778)

19 Sir, the insolence of wealth will creep out.
   Boswell *Life* vol. 3, p. 316 (18 April 1778)

20 All censure of a man's self is oblique praise. It is in order to shew how much he can spare.
   Boswell *Life* vol. 3, p. 323 (25 April 1778)

21 Were it not for imagination, Sir, a man would be as happy in the arms of a chambermaid as of a Duchess.
   Boswell *Life* vol. 3, p. 341 (9 May 1778)

22 Claret is the liquor for boys; port, for men; but he who aspires to be a hero (smiling) must drink brandy.
   Boswell *Life* vol. 3, p. 381 (7 April 1779)

23 All tricks are either knavish or childish.
   Boswell *Life* vol. 3, p. 396 (letter, 9 September 1779)

24 Worth seeing, yes; but not worth going to see.
   Boswell *Life* vol. 3, p. 410 (12 October 1779); of the Giant's Causeway

25 If you are idle, be not solitary; if you are solitary, be not idle.
   Boswell *Life* vol. 3, p. 415 (letter to Boswell, 27 October 1779). Cf. 83:15

26 Every man has a right to utter what he thinks truth, and every other man has a right to knock him down for it. Martyrdom is the test.
   Boswell *Life* vol. 4, p. 12 (1780)

27 They are forced plants, raised in a hot-bed; and they are poor plants; they are but cucumbers after all.
   Boswell *Life* vol. 4, p. 13 (1780); of Thomas Gray's *Odes*

28 This merriment of parsons is mighty offensive.
   Boswell *Life* vol. 4, p. 76 (March 1781)

29 We are not here to sell a parcel of boilers and vats, but the potentiality of growing rich, beyond the dreams of avarice.
   Boswell *Life* vol. 4, p. 87 (6 April 1781); at the sale of Thrale's brewery. Cf. 234:5

30 Classical quotation is the *parole* of literary men all over the world.
   Boswell *Life* vol. 4, p. 102 (8 May 1781)

31 Resolve not to be poor: whatever you have, spend less. Poverty is a great enemy to human happiness; it certainly destroys liberty, and it makes some virtues impracticable, and others extremely difficult.
   Boswell *Life* vol. 4, p. 157 (letter to Boswell, 7 December 1782)

1 I hate a fellow whom pride, or cowardice, or laziness drives into a corner, and who does nothing when he is there but sit and *growl*; let him come out as I do, and *bark*.
   Boswell *Life* vol. 4, p. 161, n. 3 (10 October 1782)

2 Sir, there is no settling the point of precedency between a louse and a flea.
   Boswell *Life* vol. 4, p. 192 (1783) on the relative merits of two minor poets

3 My dear friend, clear your *mind* of cant ... You may *talk* in this manner; it is a mode of talking in Society: but don't *think* foolishly.
   Boswell *Life* vol. 4, p. 221 (15 May 1783)

4 Milton, Madam, was a genius that could cut a Colossus from a rock; but could not carve heads upon cherry-stones.
   Boswell *Life* vol. 4, p. 305 (13 June 1784); to Hannah More, who had expressed a wonder that the poet who had written *Paradise Lost* should write such poor sonnets

5 Sir, I have found you an argument; but I am not obliged to find you an understanding.
   Boswell *Life* vol. 4, p. 313 (June 1784)

6 No man is a hypocrite in his pleasures.
   Boswell *Life* vol. 4, p. 316 (June 1784). Cf. 251:21

7 Sir, I look upon every day to be lost, in which I do not make a new acquaintance.
   Boswell *Life* vol. 4, p. 374 (November 1784)

8 We shall receive no letters in the grave.
   Boswell *Life* vol. 4, p. 413 (December 1784)

9 Love is the wisdom of the fool and the folly of the wise.
   In W. Cooke *Life of Samuel Foote* (1805) vol. 2, p. 154

10 Of music Dr Johnson used to say that it was the only sensual pleasure without vice.
   In *European Magazine* (1795) p. 82

11 Fly fishing may be a very pleasant amusement; but angling or float fishing I can only compare to a stick and a string, with a worm at one end and a fool at the other.
   Attributed, in Hawker *Instructions to Young Sportsmen* (1859) p. 197; attributed to Jonathan Swift in *The Indicator* 27 October 1819, p. 44

12 Corneille is to Shakespeare ... as a clipped hedge is to a forest.
   In Hester Lynch Piozzi *Anecdotes of ... Johnson* (1786) p. 59

13 If the man who turnips cries,
   Cry not when his father dies,
   'Tis a proof that he had rather
   Have a turnip than his father.
   In Hester Lynch Piozzi *Anecdotes of ... Johnson* (1786) p. 67

14 Abstinence is as easy to me, as temperance would be difficult.
   In W. Roberts (ed.) *Memoirs of ... Mrs Hannah More* (1834) vol. 1, p. 251

15 What is written without effort is in general read without pleasure.
   In W. Seward *Biographia* (1799) p. 260

16 Difficult do you call it, Sir? I wish it were impossible.
   On the performance of a celebrated violinist, in W. Seward *Supplement to the Anecdotes of Distinguished Persons* (1797) p. 267

John Benn Johnstone 1803–91

17 I want you to assist me in forcing her on board the lugger; once there, I'll frighten her into marriage.
   The Gipsy Farmer (performed 1845); since quoted 'Once aboard the lugger and the maid is mine'

Hanns Johst 1890–1978

18 Whenever I hear the word culture ... I release the safety-catch of my Browning!
   Schlageter (1933) act 1, sc. 1 (often attributed to Hermann Goering, and quoted 'Whenever I hear the word culture, I reach for my pistol!')

Al Jolson 1886–1950

19 You think that's noise—you ain't heard nuttin' yet!
   In a café, competing with the din from a neighbouring building site; in M. Abramson *Real Story of Al Jolson* (1950) p. 12 (later title of a Jolson song, 'You Ain't Heard Nothing Yet')

Henry Arthur Jones 1851–1929 and Henry Herman 1832–94

20 O God! Put back Thy universe and give me yesterday.
   The Silver King (1907) act 2, sc. 4

John Paul Jones 1747–92

21 I have not yet begun to fight.
   As his ship was sinking, 23 September 1779, having been asked whether he had lowered his flag; in Mrs Reginald De Koven *Life and Letters of John Paul Jones* (1914) vol. 1, p. 455

Ben Jonson c.1573–1637

22 Fortune, that favours fools.
   The Alchemist (1610) prologue

23   Think
   What a young wife and a good brain may do:
   Stretch age's truth sometimes, and crack it too.
   The Alchemist (1610) act 5, sc. 2

24 The very womb and bed of enormity.
   Bartholomew Fair (1614) act 2, sc. 1 (of Ursula, the 'pig-woman')

25 Neither do thou lust after that tawney weed tobacco.
   Bartholomew Fair (1614) act 2, sc. 6

1 The voice of Rome is the consent of
   heaven!
   Catiline his Conspiracy (1611) act 3, sc. 1

2 Slow, slow, fresh fount, keep time with my
   salt tears.
   Cynthia's Revels (1600) act 1, sc. 1

3 Queen and huntress, chaste and fair,
   Now the sun is laid to sleep,
   Seated in thy silver chair,
   State in wonted manner keep:
   Hesperus entreats thy light,
   Goddess, excellently bright.
   Cynthia's Revels (1600) act 5, sc. 3

4 This is Mab, the Mistress-Fairy
   That doth nightly rob the dairy.
   The Entertainment at Althorpe (1603)

5 Lady, it is to be presumed,
   Though art's hid causes are not found,
   All is not sweet, all is not sound.
   Epicene (1609) act 1, sc. 1

6 Such sweet neglect more taketh me,
   Than all the adulteries of art;
   They strike mine eyes, but not my heart.
   Epicene (1609) act 1, sc. 1

7 And to these courteous eyes oppose a
   mirror,
   As large as is the stage whereon we act;
   Where they shall see the time's deformity
   Anatomised in every nerve, and sinew.
   Every Man out of His Humour (1600) Induction

8   Blind Fortune still
   Bestows her gifts on such as cannot use
   them.
   Every Man out of His Humour (1599) act 2, sc. 2

9 Ramp up my genius, be not retrograde;
   But boldly nominate a spade a spade.
   The Poetaster (1601) act 5, sc. 1

10 Detraction is but baseness' varlet;
   And apes are apes, though clothed in
   scarlet.
   The Poetaster (1601) act 5, sc. 1

11 'Twas only fear first in the world made
   gods.
   Sejanus (1603) act 2, sc. 2

12   I glory
   More in the cunning purchase of my
   wealth
   Than in the glad possession.
   Volpone (1606) act 1, sc. 1

13 I have been at my book, and am now past
   the craggy paths of study, and come to the
   flowery plains of honour and reputation.
   Volpone (1606) act 2, sc. 1

14 Calumnies are answered best with silence.
   Volpone (1605) act 2, sc. 2

15 Suns, that set, may rise again;
   But if once we lose this light,
   'Tis with us perpetual night.
   Volpone (1605) act 3, sc. 5. Cf. 89:2

16 Come, my Celia, let us prove,
   While we can, the sports of love.
   Volpone (1605) act 3, sc. 5. Cf. 93:2

17 You have a gift, sir, (thank your education),
   Will never let you want, while there are
   men,
   And malice, to breed causes.
   Volpone (1605) act 5, sc. 1 (to a lawyer)

18 The voice so sweet, the words so fair,
   As some soft chime had stroked the air;
   And though the sound were parted thence,
   Still left an echo in the sense.
   'Eupheme' (1640) no. 4 'The Mind'

19 Rest in soft peace, and, asked, say here
   doth lie
   Ben Jonson his best piece of poetry.
   'On My First Son' (1616)

20 This figure that thou here seest put,
   It was for gentle Shakespeare cut,
   Wherein the graver had a strife
   With Nature, to out-do the life.
   'On the Portrait of Shakespeare' (1623)

21   Reader, look
   Not on his picture, but his book.
   'On the Portrait of Shakespeare' (1623)

22 So court a mistress, she denies you;
   Let her alone, she will court you.
   Say, are not women truly then
   Styled but the shadows of us men?
   'That Women are but Men's Shadows' (1616)

23 Drink to me only with thine eyes,
   And I will pledge with mine;
   Or leave a kiss but in the cup,
   And I'll not look for wine.
   'To Celia' (1616)

24 In small proportions we just beauty see,
   And in short measures life may perfect be.
   'To the Immortal Memory [of] Sir Lucius
   Carey and Sir H. Morison' (1640)

25   Soul of the Age!
   The applause, delight, the wonder of our
   stage!
   'To the Memory of My Beloved, the Author,
   Mr William Shakespeare' (1623)

26   How far thou didst our Lyly
   outshine,
   Or sporting Kyd, or Marlowe's mighty line.
   'To the Memory of … Shakespeare' (1623)

27 Thou hadst small Latin, and less Greek.
   'To the Memory of … Shakespeare' (1623)

28 He was not of an age, but for all time!
   'To the Memory of … Shakespeare' (1623)

29 Sweet Swan of Avon!
   'To the Memory of … Shakespeare' (1623)

30 The blushing apricot and woolly peach
   Hang on thy walls, that every child may
   reach.
   'To Penshurst' (1616) l. 43

31 Donne, for not keeping of accent, deserved
   hanging … Shakespeare wanted art.
   In *Conversations with William Drummond of
   Hawthornden* (written 1619) no. 3

32 Whatsoever he [Shakespeare] penned, he
   never blotted out a line. My answer hath
   been 'Would he had blotted a thousand'.
   Timber (1641) l. 658. Cf. 165:11, 252:30

John Jortin 1698–1770

1 *Palmam qui meruit, ferat.*
Let him who has won it bear the palm.
Lusus Poetici (3rd ed., 1748) 'Ad Ventos' (motto
of Lord Nelson)

Benjamin Jowett 1817–93

2 The lie in the soul is a true lie.
Introduction to his translation (1871) of
Plato's *Republic* bk. 2

James Joyce 1882–1941

3 riverrun, past Eve and Adam's, from
swerve of shore to bend of bay, brings us
by a commodious vicus of recirculation
back to Howth Castle and Environs.
Finnegans Wake (1939) pt. 1, p. 3

4 All moanday, tearsday, wailsday,
thumpsday, frightday, shatterday till the
fear of the Law.
Finnegans Wake (1939) pt. 2, p. 301

5 Three quarks for Muster Mark!
Finnegans Wake (1939) pt. 2, p. 383

6 Once upon a time and a very good time it
was there was a moocow coming down
along the road and this moocow that was
down along the road met a nicens little boy
named baby tuckoo.
A Portrait of the Artist as a Young Man (1916)
ch. 1

7 Ireland is the old sow that eats her farrow.
A Portrait of the Artist as a Young Man (1916)
ch. 5

8 The artist, like the God of the creation,
remains within or behind or beyond or
above his handiwork, invisible, refined out
of existence, indifferent, paring his
fingernails.
A Portrait of the Artist as a Young Man (1916)
ch. 5

9 The only arms I allow myself to use,
silence, exile, and cunning.
A Portrait of the Artist as a Young Man (1916)
ch. 5

10 By an epiphany he meant a sudden
spiritual manifestation, whether in
vulgarity of speech or of gesture or in a
memorable phase of the mind itself.
Stephen Hero (1944) ch. 25

11 The snotgreen sea. The scrotumtightening
sea.
Ulysses (1922) p. 5

12 It is a symbol of Irish art. The cracked
lookingglass of a servant.
Ulysses (1922) p. 7

13 I fear those big words, Stephen said, which
make us so unhappy.
Ulysses (1922) p. 31

14 History, Stephen said, is a nightmare from
which I am trying to awake.
Ulysses (1922) p. 34

15 Lawn Tennyson, gentleman poet.
Ulysses (1922) p. 50

16 [He] saw the dark tangled curls of his bush
floating, floating hair of the stream around
the limp father of thousands.
Ulysses (1922) p. 83

17 Plenty to see and hear and feel yet. Feel
live warm beings near you ... Warm beds:
warm full blooded life.
Ulysses (1922) p. 102

18 Greater love than this, he said, no man
hath that a man lay down his wife for his
friend.
Ulysses (1922) p. 375

19 The heaventree of stars hung with humid
nightblue fruit.
Ulysses (1922) p. 651

Emperor Julian the Apostate

AD *c.*332–63

20 *Vicisti, Galilaee.*
You have won, Galilean.
Supposed dying words, though in fact a late
embellishment of Theodoret *Ecclesiastical
History* (AD *c.*450) bk. 3, ch. 25

Julian of Norwich 1343–after 1416

21 Sin is behovely, but all shall be well and all
shall be well and all manner of thing shall
be well.
Revelations of Divine Love (the long text) ch. 27,
Revelation 13

Carl Gustav Jung 1875–1961

22 A man who has not passed through the
inferno of his passions has never overcome
them.
Memories, Dreams, Reflections (1962) ch. 9

23 As far as we can discern, the sole purpose
of human existence is to kindle a light in
the darkness of mere being.
Memories, Dreams, Reflections (1962) ch. 11

24 Every form of addiction is bad, no matter
whether the narcotic be alcohol or
morphine or idealism.
Memories, Dreams, Reflections (1962) ch. 12

'Junius' 18th century

25 The liberty of the press is the *Palladium* of
all the civil, political, and religious rights
of an Englishman.
Letters of Junius (1772 ed.) 'Dedication to the
English Nation'

26 There is a holy mistaken zeal in politics as
well as in religion. By persuading others,
we convince ourselves.
Public Advertiser 19 December 1769, Letter 35

Sir John Junor 1919–

27 Pass the sick bag, Alice.
Catch-phrase; in *Sunday Express* 28 December
1980 and elsewhere

Juvenal AD c.60–c.130

1 Honesty is praised and left to shiver.
   Satires no. 1, l. 74 (tr. G. Ramsay)

2 Even if nature says no, indignation makes
   me write verse.
   Satires no. 1, l. 79

3 No one ever suddenly became depraved.
   Satires no. 2, l. 83

4 The misfortunes of poverty carry with
   them nothing harder to bear than that it
   makes men ridiculous.
   Satires no. 3, l. 152

5 They do not easily rise out of obscurity
   whose talents straitened circumstances
   obstruct at home.
   Satires no. 3, l. 164

6 ... *Omnia Romae*
   Cum pretio.
   Everything in Rome has its price.
   Satires no. 3, l. 183

7 *Rara avis in terris nigroque simillima cycno.*
   A rare bird on this earth, like nothing so
   much as a black swan.
   Satires no. 6, l. 165

8 *Hoc volo, sic iubeo, sit pro ratione voluntas.*
   I will have this done, so I order it done; let
   my will replace reasoned judgement.
   Satires no. 6, l. 223

9 *Quis custodiet ipsos custodes?*
   Who is to guard the guards themselves?
   Satires no. 6, l. 347

10 Many suffer from the incurable disease of
   writing, and it becomes chronic in their
   sick minds.
   Satires no. 7, l. 51

11 Travel light and you can sing in the
   robber's face.
   Satires no. 10, l. 22

12 ... *Duas tantum res anxius optat,*
   Panem et circenses.
   Only two things does he [the modern
   citizen] anxiously wish for—bread and the
   big match.
   Satires no. 10, l. 80 (usually quoted 'bread and
   circuses')

13 *Mens sana in corpore sano.*
   A sound mind in a sound body.
   Satires no. 10, l. 356

14 ... *Prima est haec ultio, quod se*
   Iudice nemo nocens absolvitur.
   This is the first of punishments, that no
   guilty man is acquitted if judged by
   himself.
   Satires no. 13, l. 2

15 A child is owed the greatest respect; if you
   ever have something disgraceful in mind,
   don't ignore your son's tender years.
   Satires no. 14, l. 47

Franz Kafka 1883–1924

16 When Gregor Samsa awoke one morning
   from uneasy dreams he found himself
   transformed in his bed into a gigantic
   insect.
   The Metamorphosis (1915) ch. 1

17 You may object that it is not a trial at all;
   you are quite right, for it is only a trial if I
   recognize it as such.
   The Trial (1925) ch. 2

18 It's often better to be in chains than to be
   free.
   The Trial (1925) ch. 8

Gus Kahn 1886–1941 and Raymond B. Egan 1890–1952

19 There's nothing surer,
   The rich get rich and the poor get children.
   'Ain't We Got Fun' (1921 song)

Bert Kalmar et al. 1884–1947

20 Remember, you're fighting for this
   woman's honour ... which is probably
   more than she ever did.
   Duck Soup (1933 film); spoken by Groucho
   Marx

21 If you can't leave in a taxi you can leave in
   a huff. If that's too soon, you can leave in
   a minute and a huff.
   Duck Soup (1933 film); spoken by Groucho
   Marx

Immanuel Kant 1724–1804

22 Two things fill the mind with ever new and
   increasing wonder and awe, the more
   often and the more seriously reflection
   concentrates upon them: the starry heaven
   above me and the moral law within me.
   Critique of Practical Reason (1788) p. 2

23 There is an imperative which commands a
   certain conduct immediately, without
   having as its condition any other purpose
   to be attained by it. This imperative is
   Categorical ... This imperative may be
   called that of Morality.
   *Fundamental Principles of the Metaphysics of
   Ethics* (1785) sect. 2 (tr. T. K. Abbott)

24 Happiness is not an ideal of reason but of
   imagination.
   *Fundamental Principles of the Metaphysics of
   Ethics* (1785) sect. 2 (translated by T. K.
   Abbott)

25 Out of the crooked timber of humanity no
   straight thing can ever be made.
   *Idee zu einer allgemeinen Geschichte in
   weltbürgerlicher Absicht* (1784) Proposition 6

Alphonse Karr 1808–90

1 *Si l'on veut abolir la peine de mort en ce cas, que MM les assassins commencent.*
In that case, if we are to abolish the death penalty, let the murderers take the first step.
Les Guêpes January 1849 (6th series, 1859) p. 304

2 *Plus ça change, plus c'est la même chose.*
The more things change, the more they are the same.
Les Guêpes January 1849 (6th series, 1859) p. 305

George S. Kaufman 1889–1961

3 Satire is what closes Saturday night.
In Scott Meredith *George S. Kaufman and his Friends* (1974) ch. 6

Gerald Kaufman 1930–

4 The longest suicide note in history.
On the Labour Party's *New Hope for Britain* (1983); in Denis Healey *The Time of My Life* (1989) ch. 23

Paul Kaufman and Mike Anthony

5 Poetry in motion.
Title of song (1960). Cf. 156:6

Christoph Kaufmann 1753–95

6 *Sturm und Drang.*
Storm and stress.
Title suggested by Kaufmann for a romantic drama by F. M. Klinger (1775)

Patrick Kavanagh 1905–67

7 But the weak, washy way of true tragedy—
A sick horse nosing around the meadow for a clean place to die.
'The Great Hunger' (1947)

Paul Keating 1944–

8 Even as it [Great Britain] walked out on you and joined the Common Market, you were still looking for your MBEs and your knighthoods, and all the rest of the regalia that comes with it. You would take Australia right back down the time tunnel to the cultural cringe where you have always come from.
Addressing Conservative supporters of Great Britain, 27 February 1992; *House of Representatives Weekly Hansard* [Australia] (1992) no. 1, p. 374

9 These are the same old fogies who doffed their lids and tugged the forelock to the British establishment.
Of Britain's Conservative supporters in Australia, 27 February 1992; *House of Representatives Weekly Hansard* (1992) no. 1, p. 374

John Keats 1795–1821

10 The moving waters at their priestlike task
Of pure ablution round earth's human shores.
'Bright star, would I were steadfast as thou art' (written 1819)

11 A thing of beauty is a joy for ever:
Its loveliness increases; it will never Pass into nothingness.
Endymion (1818) bk. 1, l. 1

12 They alway must be with us, or we die.
Endymion (1818) bk. 1, l. 33

13 Their smiles,
Wan as primroses gathered at midnight By chilly fingered spring.
Endymion (1818) bk. 4, l. 969

14 St Agnes' Eve—Ah, bitter chill it was!
The owl, for all his feathers, was a-cold;
The hare limped trembling through the frozen grass,
And silent was the flock in woolly fold.
'The Eve of St Agnes' (1820) st. 1

15 The sculptured dead, on each side, seem to freeze,
Emprisoned in black, purgatorial rails.
'The Eve of St Agnes' (1820) st. 2

16 The silver, snarling trumpets 'gan to chide.
'The Eve of St Agnes' (1820) st. 4

17 And soft adorings from their loves receive
Upon the honeyed middle of the night.
'The Eve of St Agnes' (1820) st. 6

18 By degrees
Her rich attire creeps rustling to her knees.
'The Eve of St Agnes' (1820) st. 26

19 Trembling in her soft and chilly nest.
'The Eve of St Agnes' (1820) st. 27

20 As though a rose should shut, and be a bud again.
'The Eve of St Agnes' (1820) st. 27

21 And still she slept an azure-lidded sleep,
In blanchèd linen, smooth, and lavendered.
'The Eve of St Agnes' (1820) st. 30

22 And the long carpets rose along the gusty floor.
'The Eve of St Agnes' (1820) st. 40

23 And they are gone: aye, ages long ago
These lovers fled away into the storm.
'The Eve of St Agnes' (1820) st. 42

24 Fanatics have their dreams, wherewith they weave
A paradise for a sect.
'The Fall of Hyperion' (written 1819) l. 1

25 The poet and the dreamer are distinct,
Diverse, sheer opposite, antipodes.
The one pours out a balm upon the world,
The other vexes it.
'The Fall of Hyperion' (written 1819) l. 199

26 Ever let the fancy roam,
Pleasure never is at home.
'Fancy' (1820) l. 1

1 O aching time! O moments big as years!
   'Hyperion: A Fragment' (1820) bk. 1, l. 64

2 Knowledge enormous makes a god of me.
   'Hyperion: A Fragment' (1820) bk. 3, l. 113

3 I had a dove and the sweet dove died;
   And I have thought it died of grieving:
   O, what could it grieve for? Its feet were tied,
   With a silken thread of my own hand's weaving.
   'I had a dove and the sweet dove died' (written 1818)

4   'For cruel 'tis,' said she,
   'To steal my Basil-pot away from me.'
   'Isabella; or, The Pot of Basil' (1820) st. 62

5 A little noiseless noise among the leaves,
   Born of the very sigh that silence heaves.
   'I stood tip-toe upon a little hill' (1817) l. 11

6 Here are sweet peas, on tip-toe for a flight.
   'I stood tip-toe upon a little hill' (1817) l. 57

7 Oh, what can ail thee knight at arms
   Alone and palely loitering?
   'La belle dame sans merci' (1820) st. 1

8 I see a lily on thy brow
   With anguish moist and fever dew,
   And on thy cheeks a fading rose
   Fast withereth too.
   'La belle dame sans merci' (1820) st. 3

9 I met a lady in the meads
   Full beautiful, a faery's child
   Her hair was long, her foot was light
   And her eyes were wild.
   'La belle dame sans merci' (1820) st. 4

10 ... La belle dame sans merci
   Thee hath in thrall.
   'La belle dame sans merci' (1820) st. 10

11 Love in a hut, with water and a crust,
   Is—Love, forgive us!—cinders, ashes, dust.
   'Lamia' (1820) pt. 2, l. 1

12 That purple-linèd palace of sweet sin.
   'Lamia' (1820) pt. 2, l. 31

13 In pale contented sort of discontent.
   'Lamia' (1820) pt. 2, l. 135

14   Do not all charms fly
   At the mere touch of cold philosophy?
   'Lamia' (1820) pt. 2, l. 229

15 Philosophy will clip an Angel's wings.
   'Lamia' (1820) pt. 2, l. 234

16 Souls of poets dead and gone,
   What Elysium have ye known,
   Happy field or mossy cavern,
   Choicer than the Mermaid Tavern?
   'Lines on the Mermaid Tavern' (1820)

17 Thou still unravished bride of quietness,
   Thou foster-child of silence and slow time.
   'Ode on a Grecian Urn' (1820) st. 1

18 What men or gods are these? What maidens loth?
   What mad pursuit? What struggle to escape?
   'Ode on a Grecian Urn' (1820) st. 1

19 Heard melodies are sweet, but those unheard
   Are sweeter.
   'Ode on a Grecian Urn' (1820) st. 2

20 For ever piping songs for ever new.
   'Ode on a Grecian Urn' (1820) st. 3

21 For ever warm and still to be enjoyed,
   For ever panting, and for ever young.
   'Ode on a Grecian Urn' (1820) st. 3

22 O Attic shape! Fair attitude!
   'Ode on a Grecian Urn' (1820) st. 5

23 Thou, silent form, dost tease us out of thought
   As doth eternity: Cold Pastoral!
   'Ode on a Grecian Urn' (1820) st. 5

24 'Beauty is truth, truth beauty,'—that is all
   Ye know on earth, and all ye need to know.
   'Ode on a Grecian Urn' (1820) st. 5

25 No, no, go not to Lethe, neither twist
   Wolf's-bane, tight-rooted, for its poisonous wine.
   'Ode on Melancholy' (1820) st. 1

26 Then glut thy sorrow on a morning rose,
   Or on the rainbow of the salt sand-wave,
   Or on the wealth of globèd peonies;
   Or if thy mistress some rich anger shows,
   Emprison her soft hand, and let her rave,
   And feed deep, deep upon her peerless eyes.
   'Ode on Melancholy' (1820) st. 2

27 She dwells with Beauty—Beauty that must die;
   And Joy, whose hand is ever at his lips
   Bidding adieu.
   'Ode on Melancholy' (1820) st. 3

28 My heart aches, and a drowsy numbness pains
   My sense, as though of hemlock I had drunk,
   Or emptied some dull opiate to the drains.
   'Ode to a Nightingale' (1820) st. 1

29 O, for a draught of vintage! that hath been
   Cooled a long age in the deep-delvèd earth,
   Tasting of Flora and the country green.
   'Ode to a Nightingale' (1820) st. 2

30 O for a beaker full of the warm South,
   Full of the true, the blushful Hippocrene,
   With beaded bubbles winking at the brim,
   And purple-stainèd mouth.
   'Ode to a Nightingale' (1820) st. 2

31 Fade far away, dissolve, and quite forget
   What thou among the leaves hast never known,
   The weariness, the fever, and the fret.
   'Ode to a Nightingale' (1820) st. 3

32 Where youth grows pale, and spectre-thin, and dies.
   'Ode to a Nightingale' (1820) st. 3

1 Away! away! for I will fly to thee,
Not charioted by Bacchus and his pards,
But on the viewless wings of Poesy,
Though the dull brain perplexes and
   retards:
Already with thee! tender is the night.
   'Ode to a Nightingale' (1820) st. 4

2 And mid-May's eldest child,
The coming musk-rose, full of dewy wine,
The murmurous haunt of flies on summer
   eves.
   'Ode to a Nightingale' (1820) st. 5

3 Darkling I listen; and, for many a time
I have been half in love with easeful Death,
Called him soft names in many a musèd
   rhyme,
To take into the air my quiet breath;
Now more than ever seems it rich to die,
To cease upon the midnight with no pain.
   'Ode to a Nightingale' (1820) st. 6

4 Thou wast not born for death, immortal
   bird!
   'Ode to a Nightingale' (1820) st. 7

5 Perhaps the self-same song that found a
   path
Through the sad heart of Ruth, when, sick
   for home,
She stood in tears amid the alien corn;
The same that oft-times hath
Charmed magic casements, opening on the
   foam
Of perilous seas, in faery lands forlorn.
   'Ode to a Nightingale' (1820) st. 7

6 Forlorn! the very word is like a bell
To toll me back from thee to my sole self!
   'Ode to a Nightingale' (1820) st. 8

7 Was it a vision, or a waking dream?
Fled is that music:—do I wake or sleep?
   'Ode to a Nightingale' (1820) st. 8

8 Nor virgin-choir to make delicious moan
Upon the midnight hours.
   'Ode to Psyche' (1820) st. 2

9 A bright torch, and a casement ope at
   night,
To let the warm Love in!
   'Ode to Psyche' (1820) st. 4

10 Much have I travelled in the realms of
   gold,
And many goodly states and kingdoms
   seen.
   'On First Looking into Chapman's Homer'
   (1817)

11 Then felt I like some watcher of the skies
When a new planet swims into his ken;
Or like stout Cortez when with eagle eyes
He stared at the Pacific—and all his men
Looked at each other with a wild
   surmise—
Silent, upon a peak in Darien.
   'On First Looking into Chapman's Homer'
   (1817)

12 And they shall be accounted poet kings
Who simply tell the most heart-easing
   things.
   'Sleep and Poetry' (1817) l. 267

13 Turn the key deftly in the oilèd wards,
And seal the hushèd casket of my soul.
   'Sonnet to Sleep' (written 1819)

14 Season of mists and mellow fruitfulness,
Close bosom-friend of the maturing sun;
Conspiring with him how to load and bless
With fruit the vines that round the thatch-
   eaves run.
   'To Autumn' (1820) st. 1

15 Where are the songs of Spring? Ay, where
   are they?
Think not of them, thou hast thy music
   too.
   'To Autumn' (1820) st. 3

16 Then in a wailful choir the small gnats
   mourn
Among the river sallows, borne aloft
Or sinking as the light wind lives or dies.
   'To Autumn' (1820) st. 3

17 How soon the film of death obscured that
   eye,
Whence genius wildly flashed.
   'To Chatterton' (written 1815)

18   It is a flaw
In happiness, to see beyond our bourn.
   'To J. H. Reynolds, Esq.' (written 1818)

19 When I have fears that I may cease to be
Before my pen has gleaned my teeming
   brain.
   'When I have fears that I may cease to be'
   (written 1818)

20 When I behold, upon the night's starred
   face
Huge cloudy symbols of a high romance.
   'When I have fears that I may cease to be'
   (written 1818)

21   Then on the shore
Of the wide world I stand alone and think
Till love and fame to nothingness do sink.
   'When I have fears that I may cease to be'
   (written 1818)

22 A long poem is a test of invention which I
take to be the polar star of poetry, as fancy
is the sails, and imagination the rudder.
   Letter to Bailey, 8 October 1817, in H. E.
   Rollins (ed.) Letters (1958) vol. 1

23 I am certain of nothing but the holiness of
the heart's affections and the truth of
imagination—what the imagination seizes
as beauty must be truth—whether it
existed before or not.
   Letter to Bailey, 22 November 1817, in H. E.
   Rollins (ed.) Letters (1958) vol. 1. Cf. 191:24

24 O for a life of sensations rather than of
thoughts!
   Letter to Bailey, 22 November 1817, in H. E.
   Rollins (ed.) Letters (1958) vol. 1

1 The excellence of every art is its intensity,
capable of making all disagreeables
evaporate, from their being in close
relationship with beauty and truth.
   Letter to George and Thomas Keats,
   21 December 1817, in H. E. Rollins (ed.)
   Letters (1958) vol. 1

2 Negative Capability, that is when man is
capable of being in uncertainties,
mysteries, doubts, without any irritable
reaching after fact and reason.
   Letter to George and Thomas Keats,
   21 December 1817, in H. E. Rollins (ed.)
   Letters (1958) vol. 1

3 There is nothing stable in the
world—uproar's your only music.
   Letter to George and Thomas Keats,
   13 January 1818, in H. E. Rollins (ed.) *Letters*
   (1958) vol. 1

4 If poetry comes not as naturally as the
leaves to a tree it had better not come at
all.
   Letter to Taylor, 27 February 1818, in H. E.
   Rollins (ed.) *Letters* (1958) vol. 1

5 Scenery is fine—but human nature is finer.
   Letter to Bailey, 13 March 1818, in H. E.
   Rollins (ed.) *Letters* (1958) vol. 1

6 It is impossible to live in a country which
is continually under hatches ... Rain! Rain!
Rain!
   Letter to Reynolds from Devon, 10 April
   1818, in H. E. Rollins (ed.) *Letters* (1958) vol. 1

7 I am in that temper that if I were under
water I would scarcely kick to come to the
top.
   Letter to Bailey, 25 May 1818, in H. E. Rollins
   (ed.) *Letters* (1958) vol. 1

8 The Wordsworthian or egotistical sublime.
   Letter to Woodhouse, 27 October 1818, in
   H. E. Rollins (ed.) *Letters* (1958) vol. 1

9 The roaring of the wind is my wife and the
stars through the window pane are my
children.
   Letter to George and Georgiana Keats,
   24 October 1818, in H. E. Rollins (ed.) *Letters*
   (1958) vol. 1

10 Call the world if you please 'The vale of
soul-making'.
   Letter to George and Georgiana Keats,
   21 April 1819, in H. E. Rollins (ed.) *Letters*
   (1958) vol. 2

11 I have met with women whom I really
think would like to be married to a poem
and to be given away by a novel.
   Letter to Fanny Brawne, 8 July 1819, in H. E.
   Rollins (ed.) *Letters* (1958) vol. 2

12 Fine writing is next to fine doing the top
thing in the world.
   Letter to Reynolds, 24 August 1819, in H. E.
   Rollins (ed.) *Letters* (1958) vol. 2

13 All clean and comfortable I sit down to
write.
   Letter to George and Georgiana Keats,
   17 September 1819, in H. E. Rollins (ed.)
   Letters (1958) vol. 2

14 'Load every rift' of your subject with ore.
   Letter to Shelley, August 1820, in H. E.
   Rollins (ed.) *Letters* (1958) vol. 2 (Spenser
   Faerie Queen (1596) bk. 2, canto 7, st. 28: 'And
   with rich metal loaded every rift')

15 Here lies one whose name was writ in
water.
   Epitaph for himself, in R. Monckton Milnes
   Life, Letters and Literary Remains of John Keats
   (1848) vol. 2, p. 91. Cf. 280:22

John Keble 1792–1866

16 New every morning is the love
Our wakening and uprising prove;
Through sleep and darkness safely
brought,
Restored to life, and power, and thought.
   The Christian Year (1827) 'Morning'

17 The trivial round, the common task,
Would furnish all we ought to ask;
Room to deny ourselves; a road
To bring us, daily, nearer God.
   The Christian Year (1827) 'Morning'

18 The voice that breathed o'er Eden,
That earliest wedding-day.
   'Holy Matrimony' (1857 hymn)

Thomas Kelly 1769–1855

19 The head that once was crowned with
thorns
Is crowned with glory now;
A royal diadem adorns
The mighty Victor's brow.
   'The head that once was crowned with
   thorns' (1820 hymn)

Thomas à Kempis

See THOMAS

Bishop Thomas Ken 1637–1711

20 Awake, my soul, and with the sun
Thy daily stage of duty run.
Shake off dull sloth, and joyful rise
To pay thy morning sacrifice.
   'Morning Hymn' in Winchester College
   Manual of Prayers (1695)

21 Redeem thy mis-spent time that's past,
And live this day as if thy last.
   'Morning Hymn' (1709 ed.) v. 2

22 Teach me to live, that I may dread
The grave as little as my bed.
   'Evening Hymn' (1695) v. 3

Jimmy Kennedy and Michael Carr

23 We're gonna hang out the washing on the
Siegfried Line.
   Title of song (1939)

John F. Kennedy 1917–63

1 We stand today on the edge of a new
frontier.
  Speech accepting the Democratic
  nomination, 15 July 1960, in *Vital Speeches*
  1 August 1960

2 The torch has been passed to a new
generation of Americans—born in this
century, tempered by war, disciplined by a
hard and bitter peace.
  Inaugural address, 20 January 1961, in *Vital
  Speeches* 1 February 1961

3 We shall pay any price, bear any burden,
meet any hardship, support any friend,
oppose any foe to assure the survival and
the success of liberty.
  Inaugural address, 20 January 1961, in *Vital
  Speeches* 1 February 1961

4 Let us never negotiate out of fear. But let
us never fear to negotiate.
  Inaugural address, 20 January 1961, in *Vital
  Speecnes* 1 February 1961

5 All this will not be finished in the first 100
days. Nor will it be finished in the first
1,000 days, nor in the life of this
Administration, nor even perhaps in our
lifetime on this planet. But let us begin.
  Inaugural address, 20 January 1961, in *Vital
  Speeches* 1 February 1961

6 And so, my fellow Americans: ask not what
your country can do for you—ask what you
can do for your country.
  Inaugural address, 20 January 1961, in *Vital
  Speeches* 1 February 1961

7 There are no 'white' or 'coloured' signs on
the foxholes or graveyards of battle.
  Message to Congress on proposed Civil
  Rights Bill, 19 June 1963; in *New York Times*
  20 June 1963, p. 16

8 *Ich bin ein Berliner.*
  I am a Berliner.
  Speech in West Berlin, 26 June 1963; in *New
  York Times* 27 June 1963, p. 12

9 It was involuntary. They sank my boat.
  On being asked how he became a war hero;
  in A. M. Schlesinger Jnr. *A Thousand Days*
  (1965) ch. 4

Joseph P. Kennedy 1888–1969

10 When the going gets tough, the tough get
going.
  In J. H. Cutler *Honey Fitz* (1962) p. 291 (also
  attributed to Knute Rockne)

William Kethe d. 1594

11 O enter then his gates with praise,
Approach with joy his courts unto.
  'All people that on earth do dwell' (metrical
  Psalm, 1561)

Francis Scott Key 1779–1843

12 'Tis the star-spangled banner; O long may
it wave
O'er the land of the free, and the home of
the brave!
  'The Star-Spangled Banner' (1814)

John Maynard Keynes 1883–1946

13 I work for a Government I despise for ends
I think criminal.
  Letter to Duncan Grant, 15 December 1917,
  in *British Library Add. MSS 57931* fo. 119

14 Lenin was right. There is no subtler, no
surer means of overturning the existing
basis of society than to debauch the
currency.
  Economic Consequences of the Peace (1919) ch. 6

15 I do not know which makes a man more
conservative—to know nothing but the
present, or nothing but the past.
  The End of Laissez-Faire (1926) pt. 1

16 If the Treasury were to fill old bottles with
banknotes, bury them at suitable depths in
disused coalmines which are then filled up
to the surface with town rubbish, and
leave it to private enterprise on well-tried
principles of *laissez-faire* to dig the notes up
again ... there need be no more
unemployment and, with the help of the
repercussions, the real income of the
community, and its capital wealth also,
would probably become a good deal
greater than it actually is.
  General Theory (1936) bk. 3, ch. 10

17 *In the long run* we are all dead.
  A Tract on Monetary Reform (1923) ch. 3

Nikita Khrushchev 1894–1971

18 If anyone believes that our smiles involve
abandonment of the teaching of Marx,
Engels and Lenin he deceives himself.
Those who wait for that must wait until a
shrimp learns to whistle.
  Speech in Moscow, 17 September 1955; in
  New York Times 18 September 1955, p. 19

19 If you don't like us, don't accept our
invitations and don't invite us to come to
see you. Whether you like it or not, history
is on our side. We will bury you.
  Speech to Western diplomats in Moscow,
  18 November 1956; in *The Times* 19 November
  1956

20 If one cannot catch the bird of paradise,
better take a wet hen.
  In *Time* 6 January 1958

21 If you start throwing hedgehogs under me,
I shall throw a couple of porcupines under
you.
  In *New York Times* 7 November 1963

Joyce Kilmer 1886–1918

22 I think that I shall never see
A poem lovely as a tree.
  'Trees' (1914)

1 Poems are made by fools like me,
  But only God can make a tree.
    'Trees' (1914)

Lord Kilmuir (Sir David Maxwell Fyfe) 1900–67

2 Loyalty is the Tory's secret weapon.
    In Anthony Sampson *Anatomy of Britain*
    (1962) ch. 6. Cf. 9:14

Francis Kilvert 1840–79

3 Of all noxious animals, too, the most
  noxious is a tourist. And of all tourists the
  most vulgar, ill-bred, offensive and
  loathsome is the British tourist.
    W. Plomer (ed.) *Selections from the Diary of the
    Revd Francis Kilvert* (1938–40) 5 April 1870

Benjamin Franklin King 1857–94

4 Nothing to do but work,
  Nothing to eat but food,
  Nothing to wear but clothes
  To keep one from going nude.
    'The Pessimist'

Bishop Henry King 1592–1669

5 Sleep on (my Love!) in thy cold bed
  Never to be disquieted.
  My last Good-night! Thou wilt not wake
  Till I thy fate shall overtake:
  Till age, or grief, or sickness must
  Marry my body to that dust
  It so much loves; and fill the room
  My heart keeps empty in thy tomb.
  Stay for me there: I will not fail
  To meet thee in that hollow vale.
    'An Exequy' (1657) l. 81 (written for his wife
    Anne, d. 1624)

6 But hark! My pulse, like a soft drum
  Beats my approach, tells thee I come.
    'An Exequy' (1657) l. 111

Martin Luther King 1929–68

7 I want to be the white man's brother, not
  his brother-in-law.
    In *New York Journal-American* 10 September
    1962, p. 1

8 If a man hasn't discovered something he
  will die for, he isn't fit to live.
    Speech in Detroit, 23 June 1963; in J. Bishop
    The Days of Martin Luther King (1971) ch. 4

9 I have a dream that one day on the red
  hills of Georgia the sons of former slaves
  and the sons of former slave owners will
  be able to sit down together at the table of
  brotherhood.
    Speech at Civil Rights March in Washington,
    28 August 1963; in *New York Times* 29 August
    1963

10 We must learn to live together as brothers
   or perish together as fools.
    Speech at St Louis, 22 March 1964; in *St Louis
    Post-Dispatch* 23 March 1964

11 A riot is at bottom the language of the
   unheard.
    Where Do We Go From Here? (1967) ch. 4

Stoddard King 1889–1933

12 There's a long, long trail awinding
   Into the land of my dreams.
    'There's a Long, Long Trail' (1913 song)

Charles Kingsley 1819–75

13 Be good, sweet maid, and let who will be
   clever.
    'A Farewell' (1858)

14 Do the work that's nearest,
   Though it's dull at whiles,
   Helping, when we meet them,
   Lame dogs over stiles.
    'The Invitation. To Tom Hughes' (1856)

15 'Tis the hard grey weather
   Breeds hard English men.
    'Ode to the North-East Wind' (1858)

16 For men must work, and women must
     weep,
   And there's little to earn, and many to
     keep,
   Though the harbour bar be moaning.
    'The Three Fishers' (1858)

17 When all the world is young, lad,
   And all the trees are green;
   And every goose a swan, lad,
   And every lass a queen;
   Then hey for boot and horse, lad,
   And round the world away:
   Young blood must have its course, lad,
   And every dog his day.
    'Young and Old' (from *The Water Babies*, 1863)

18 We have used the Bible as if it was a
   constable's handbook—an opium-dose for
   keeping beasts of burden patient while
   they are being overloaded.
    Letters to the Chartists no. 2. Cf. 221:8

Hugh Kingsmill 1889–1949

19 What still alive at twenty-two,
   A clean upstanding chap like you?
   Sure, if your throat 'tis hard to slit,
   Slit your girl's, and swing for it.
    'Two Poems, after A. E. Housman' (1933)
    no. 1

20 But bacon's not the only thing
   That's cured by hanging from a string.
    'Two Poems, after A. E. Housman' (1933)
    no. 1

Neil Kinnock 1942–

1 I warn you not to be ordinary, I warn you
not to be young, I warn you not to fall ill,
and I warn you not to grow old.
    On the prospect of a Conservative re-
    election; speech at Bridgend, 7 June 1983, in
    Guardian 8 June 1983

Rudyard Kipling 1865–1936

2 When you've shouted 'Rule Britannia',
    when you've sung 'God save the Queen'—
When you've finished killing Kruger with
your mouth—
Will you kindly drop a shilling in my little
tambourine
For a gentleman in *Kharki* ordered South?
    'The Absent-Minded Beggar' (1899) st. 1

3 England's on the anvil—hear the hammers
ring—
Clanging from the Severn to the Tyne!
    'The Anvil' (1927)

4 Oh, East is East, and West is West, and
never the twain shall meet,
Till Earth and Sky stand presently at God's
great Judgement Seat.
    'The Ballad of East and West' (1892)

5 Four things greater than all things are,—
Women and Horses and Power and War.
    'The Ballad of the King's Jest' (1892)

6 Foot—foot—foot—foot—sloggin' over
Africa—
(Boots—boots—boots—boots—movin' up
and down again!)
    'Boots' (1903)

7 If any question why we died,
Tell them, because our fathers lied.
    'Common Form' (1919)

8 It's clever, but is it Art?
    'The Conundrum of the Workshops' (1892)

9 They've taken of his buttons off an' cut his
stripes away,
An' they're hangin' Danny Deever in the
mornin'.
    'Danny Deever' (1892)

10 The 'eathen in 'is blindness must end
where 'e began.
But the backbone of the Army is the non-
commissioned man!
    'The 'Eathen' (1896). Cf. 164:16

11 What should they know of England who
only England know?
    'The English Flag' (1892)

12 The female of the species is more deadly
than the male.
    'The Female of the Species' (1919)

13 What stands if freedom fall?
Who dies if England live?
    For All We Have and Are (1914) p. 2

14 So 'ere's to you, Fuzzy-Wuzzy, at your 'ome
in the Soudan;
You're a pore benighted 'eathen but a first-
class fightin' man.
    'Fuzzy-Wuzzy' (1892)

15 Gentlemen-rankers out on the spree,
Damned from here to Eternity.
    'Gentlemen-Rankers' (1892)

16 Our England is a garden, and such gardens
are not made
By singing:—'Oh, how beautiful!' and
sitting in the shade.
    'The Glory of the Garden' (1911)

17 Though I've belted you and flayed you,
By the livin' Gawd that made you,
You're a better man than I am, Gunga Din!
    'Gunga Din' (1892)

18 The flannelled fools at the wicket or the
muddied oafs at the goals.
    'The Islanders' (1903)

19 For the Colonel's Lady an' Judy O'Grady
Are sisters under their skins!
    'The Ladies' (1896)

20 Down to Gehenna or up to the Throne,
He travels the fastest who travels alone.
    'L'Envoi' (from *The Story of the Gadsbys*, 1890)

21 Come you back to Mandalay,
Where the old flotilla lay:
Can't you 'ear their paddles chunkin' from
Rangoon to Mandalay?
On the road to Mandalay,
Where the flyin'-fishes play,
An' the dawn comes up like thunder outer
China 'crost the Bay!
    'Mandalay' (1892)

22 A-wastin' Christian kisses on an 'eathen
idol's foot.
    'Mandalay' (1892)

23 Ship me somewheres east of Suez, where
the best is like the worst.
    'Mandalay' (1892)

24 And the epitaph drear: 'A fool lies here
who tried to hustle the East.'
    The Naulahka (1892) ch. 5

25 A Nation spoke to a Nation,
A Throne sent word to a Throne:
'Daughter am I in my mother's house,
But mistress in my own.'
    'Our Lady of the Snows' (1898)

26 The toad beneath the harrow knows
Exactly where each tooth-point goes;
The butterfly upon the road
Preaches contentment to that toad.
    'Pagett, MP' (1886)

27 Brothers and Sisters, I bid you beware
Of giving your heart to a dog to tear.
    'The Power of the Dog' (1909)

28 Five and twenty ponies,
Trotting through the dark—
Brandy for the Parson,
'Baccy for the Clerk;
Laces for a lady, letters for a spy,
Watch the wall, my darling, while the
Gentlemen go by!
    Puck of Pook's Hill (1906) 'A Smuggler's Song'

1 Of all the trees that grow so fair,
Old England to adorn,
Greater are none beneath the Sun,
Than Oak, and Ash, and Thorn.
Puck of Pook's Hill (1906) 'A Tree Song'

2 The tumult and the shouting dies—
The captains and the kings depart—
Still stands Thine ancient Sacrifice,
An humble and a contrite heart.
Lord God of Hosts, be with us yet,
Lest we forget—lest we forget!
'Recessional' (1897). Cf. 43:5

3 Lo, all our pomp of yesterday
Is one with Nineveh, and Tyre!
'Recessional' (1897)

4 Such boasting as the Gentiles use,
Or lesser breeds without the Law.
'Recessional' (1897)

5 If you can keep your head when all about
you
Are losing theirs and blaming it on you.
Rewards and Fairies (1910) 'If—'

6 If you can meet with triumph and disaster
And treat those two imposters just the
same.
Rewards and Fairies (1910) 'If—'

7 If you can talk with crowds and keep your
virtue,
Or walk with Kings—nor lose the common
touch ...
If you can fill the unforgiving minute
With sixty seconds' worth of distance run,
Yours is the Earth and everything that's in
it,
And—which is more—you'll be a Man, my
son!
Rewards and Fairies (1910) 'If—'

8 They shut the road through the woods
Seventy years ago.
Weather and rain have undone it again,
And now you would never know
There was once a road through the woods.
Rewards and Fairies (1910) 'The Way through
the Woods'

9 If blood be the price of admiralty,
Lord God, we ha' paid in full!
'The Song of the Dead' (1896)

10 For the sin ye do by two and two ye must
pay for one by one!
'Tomlinson' (1892)

11 Then it's Tommy this, an' Tommy that, an'
'Tommy 'ow's yer soul?'
But it's 'Thin red line of 'eroes' when the
drums begin to roll.
'Tommy' (1892)

12 A rag and a bone and a hank of hair
(We called her the woman who did not
care).
'The Vampire' st. 1

13 But each for the joy of the working, and
each, in his separate star,
Shall draw the Thing as he sees It for the
God of Things as They are!
'When Earth's Last Picture is Painted' (1896)

14 When 'Omer smote 'is bloomin' lyre,
He'd 'eard men sing by land an' sea;
An' what he thought 'e might require,
'E went an' took—the same as me!
'When 'Omer smote 'is bloomin' lyre' (1896)

15 Take up the White Man's burden—
Send forth the best ye breed—
Go, bind your sons to exile
To serve your captives' need.
'The White Man's Burden' (1899)

16 What the horses o' Kansas think to-day,
the horses of America will think
tomorrow; an' I tell *you* that when the
horses of America rise in their might, the
day o' the Oppressor is ended.
The Day's Work (1898) 'A Walking Delegate'

17 Lalun is a member of the most ancient
profession in the world.
In Black and White (1888) 'On the City Wall'

18 Brother, thy tail hangs down behind!
The Jungle Book (1894) 'Road Song of the
Bandar-Log'

19 Yes, weekly from Southampton,
Great steamers, white and gold,
Go rolling down to Rio
(Roll down—roll down to Rio!).
Just So Stories (1902) 'The Beginning of the
Armadilloes'

20 He walked by himself, and all places were
alike to him.
Just So Stories (1902) 'The Cat that Walked by
Himself'

21 An Elephant's Child—who was full of
'satiable curtiosity.
Just So Stories (1902) 'The Elephant's Child'

22 The cure for this ill is not to sit still,
Or frowst with a book by the fire;
But to take a large hoe and a shovel also,
And dig till you gently perspire.
Just So Stories (1902) 'How the Camel got his
Hump'

23 You must *not* forget the suspenders, Best
Beloved.
Just So Stories (1902) 'How the Whale got his
Throat'

24 He was a man of infinite-resource-and-
sagacity.
Just So Stories (1902) 'How the Whale got his
Throat'

25 Little Friend of all the World.
Kim (1901) ch. 1 (Kim's nickname)

26 The mad all are in God's keeping.
Kim (1901) ch. 2

27 The man who would be king.
Title of story (1888)

28 The silliest woman can manage a clever
man; but it takes a very clever woman to
manage a fool.
Plain Tales from the Hills (1888) 'Three and—an
Extra'

1 Now this is the Law of the Jungle—as old
and as true as the sky;
And the Wolf that shall keep it may
prosper, but the Wolf that shall break it
must die.
Second Jungle Book (1895) 'The Law of the
Jungle'

2 A Flopshus Cad, an Outrageous Stinker, a
Jelly-bellied Flag-flapper.
Stalky & Co. (1899) p. 214

3 Being kissed by a man who *didn't* wax his
moustache was—like eating an egg
without salt.
Story of the Gadsbys (1889) 'Poor Dear Mamma'

4 'Tisn't beauty, so to speak, nor good talk
necessarily. It's just It. Some women'll stay
in a man's memory if they once walked
down a street.
Traffics and Discoveries (1904) 'Mrs Bathurst'

5 Power without responsibility: the
prerogative of the harlot throughout the
ages.
Summing up Lord Beaverbrook's political
standpoint *vis-à-vis* the *Daily Express*; in
Kipling Journal vol. 38, no. 180, December
1971, p. 6 (quoted by Stanley Baldwin,
18 March 1931)

Henry Kissinger 1923–

6 Power is the great aphrodisiac.
In *New York Times* 19 January 1971, p. 12

7 We are the President's men.
In M. and B. Kalb *Kissinger* (1974) ch. 7

Lord Kitchener 1850–1916

8 Do your duty bravely. Fear God. Honour
the King.
Message to soldiers of the British
Expeditionary Force (1914); in *The Times*
19 August 1914

9 I don't mind your being killed, but I object
to your being taken prisoner.
To the Prince of Wales during the First
World War; in *Journals and Letters of Viscount
Esher* vol. 3 (1938) p. 198 (18 December 1914)

Paul Klee 1879–1940

10 Art does not reproduce the visible; rather,
it makes visible.
Inward Vision (1958) 'Creative Credo' (1920)

11 An active line on a walk, moving freely
without a goal. A walk for walk's sake.
Pedagogical Sketchbook (1925) p. 6

Friedrich Klopstock 1724–1803

12 God and I both knew what it meant once;
now God alone knows.
In C. Lombroso *The Man of Genius* (1891) pt. 1,
ch. 2 (also attributed to Browning, apropos
Sordello, in the form 'When it was written,
God and Robert Browning knew what it
meant; now only God knows')

Charles Knight and Kenneth Lyle

13 When there's trouble brewing,
When there's something doing,
Are we downhearted?
No! Let 'em all come!
'Here we are! Here we are again!!' (1914
song). Cf. 6:4

Frank H. Knight 1885–1973

14 Costs merely register competing
attractions.
Risk, Uncertainty and Profit (1921) p. 159

Mary Knowles 1733–1807

15 He gets at the substance of a book directly;
he tears out the heart of it.
Of Johnson, in James Boswell *Life of Samuel
Johnson* (1934 ed.) vol. 3, p. 284 (15 April 1778)

John Knox c.1505–72

16 The First Blast of the Trumpet Against the
Monstrous Regiment of Women.
Title of Pamphlet (1558)

Monsignor Ronald Knox 1888–1957

17 When suave politeness, tempering bigot
zeal,
Corrected *I believe* to *One does feel.*
'Absolute and Abitofhell' (1913)

18 There once was a man who said, 'God
Must think it exceedingly odd
If he finds that this tree
Continues to be
When there's no one about in the Quad.'
In L. Reed *Complete Limerick Book* (1924), to
which came the anonymous reply: 'Dear
Sir, / Your astonishment's odd: / I am
always about in the Quad. / And that's why
the tree / Will continue to be, / Since
observed by / Yours faithfully, / God'

19 The baby doesn't understand English and
the Devil knows Latin.
On being asked to perform a baptism in
English; in Evelyn Waugh *Ronald Knox* (1959)
pt. 1, ch. 5

20 A loud noise at one end and no sense of
responsibility at the other.
Definition of a baby (attributed)

Vicesimus Knox 1752–1821

21 Can anything be more absurd than
keeping women in a state of ignorance,
and yet so vehemently to insist on their
resisting temptation?
In Mary Wollstonecraft *A Vindication of the
Rights of Woman* (1792) ch. 7

Ted Koehler

22 Stormy weather,
Since my man and I ain't together.
'Stormy Weather' (1933 song)

Arthur Koestler 1905–83

1 One may not regard the world as a sort of metaphysical brothel for emotions.
   Darkness at Noon (1940) 'The Second Hearing' pt. 7

2 God seems to have left the receiver off the hook, and time is running out.
   The Ghost in the Machine (1967) ch. 18

3 A writer's ambition should be ... to trade a hundred contemporary readers for ten readers in ten years' time and for one reader in a hundred years.
   In *New York Times Book Review* 1 April 1951, p. 24

Jiddu Krishnamurti d. 1986

4 Religion is the frozen thought of men out of which they build temples.
   In *Observer* 22 April 1928 'Sayings of the Week'

Kris Kristofferson 1936–

5 Freedom's just another word for nothin' left to lose,
   Nothin' ain't worth nothin', but it's free.
   'Me and Bobby McGee' (1969 song, with Fred Foster)

Jeremy Joe Kronsberg

6 Every which way but loose.
   Title of film (1978); starring Clint Eastwood

Stanley Kubrick 1928–

7 The great nations have always acted like gangsters, and the small nations like prostitutes.
   In *Guardian* 5 June 1963

Milan Kundera 1929–

8 The unbearable lightness of being.
   Title of novel (1984)

Thomas Kyd 1558–94

9 Thus must we toil in other men's extremes,
   That know not how to remedy our own.
   The Spanish Tragedy (1592) act 3, sc. 6, l. 1

10 My son—and what's a son? A thing begot Within a pair of minutes, thereabout, A lump bred up in darkness.
   The Spanish Tragedy (1592) act 3, sc. 11, The Third Addition (1602 ed.) l. 5

11 For what's a play without a woman in it?
   The Spanish Tragedy (1592) act 4, sc. 1, l. 97

Henry Labouchere 1831–1912

12 He [Labouchere] did not object to the old man always having a card up his sleeve, but he did object to his insinuating that the Almighty had placed it there.
   On Gladstone's 'frequent appeals to a higher power'; in Earl Curzon *Modern Parliamentary Eloquence* (1913) p. 25

Jean de la Bruyère 1645–96

13 The people have little intelligence, the great no heart ... if I had to choose I should have no hesitation: I would be of the people.
   The Characters, or The Manners of the Age (1688) 'The Great'

14 Man has but three events in his life: to be born, to live, and to die. He is not conscious of his birth, he suffers at his death and he forgets to live.
   The Characters, or The Manners of the Age (1688) 'Of Man'

Nivelle de la Chaussée 1692–1754

15 When everyone is wrong, everyone is right.
   La Gouvernante (1747) act 1, sc. 3

Jean de la Fontaine 1621–95

16 Help yourself, and heaven will help you.
   Fables bk. 6 (1668) 'Le Chartier Embourbé'

17 I bend and I break not.
   Fables bk. 1 (1668) 'Le Chêne et le Roseau'

18 The reason of the strongest is always the best.
   Fables bk. 1 (1668) 'Le Loup et l'Agneau'

19 Death never takes the wise man by surprise; he is always ready to go.
   Fables bk. 8 (1678–9) 'La Mort et le Mourant'. Cf. 233:8

Jules Laforgue 1860–87

20 *Ah! que la vie est quotidienne.*
   Oh, what a day-to-day business life is.
   Complainte sur certains ennuis (1885)

Alphonse de Lamartine 1790–1869

21 *Ô temps! suspend ton vol, et vous, heures propices! Suspendez votre cours.*
   O Time! arrest your flight, and you, propitious hours, stay your course.
   Le Lac (1820) st. 6

Lady Caroline Lamb 1785–1828

22 Mad, bad, and dangerous to know.
   Writing of Byron in her journal, March 1812; in E. Jenkins *Lady Caroline Lamb* (1932) ch. 6

Charles Lamb 1775–1834

23 Ceremony is an invention to take off the uneasy feeling which we derive from knowing ourselves to be less the object of love and esteem with a fellow-creature than some other person is.
   Essays of Elia (1823) 'A Bachelor's Complaint of the Behaviour of Married People'

24 Presents, I often say, endear Absents.
   Essays of Elia (1823) 'A Dissertation upon Roast Pig'

1 The human species, according to the best theory I can form of it, is composed of two distinct races, *the men who borrow*, and *the men who lend*.
  Essays of Elia (1823) 'The Two Races of Men'

2 Your *borrowers of books*—those mutilators of collections, spoilers of the symmetry of shelves, and creators of odd volumes.
  Essays of Elia (1823) 'The Two Races of Men'

3 Not many sounds in life ... exceed in interest a knock at the door.
  Essays of Elia (1823) 'Valentine's Day'

4 Things in books' clothing.
  Last Essays of Elia (1833) 'Detached Thoughts on Books and Reading'

5 A poor relation—is the most irrelevant thing in nature.
  Last Essays of Elia (1833) 'Poor Relations'

6 [A pun] is a pistol let off at the ear; not a feather to tickle the intellect.
  Last Essays of Elia (1833) 'Popular Fallacies' no. 9

7 The man must have a rare recipe for melancholy, who can be dull in Fleet Street.
  Letter to Manning, 15 February 1802, in E. W. Marrs (ed.) *Letters of Charles and Mary Lamb* vol. 2 (1976)

8 An Archangel a little damaged.
  Of Coleridge; letter to Wordsworth, 26 April 1816, in E. W. Marrs (ed.) *Letters of Charles and Mary Lamb* vol. 3 (1978)

9 Fanny Kelly's divine plain face.
  Letter to Mary Wordsworth, 18 February 1818, in H. Harper (ed.) *Letters of Charles Lamb* (1905) vol. 4

10 The ever-haunting importunity
   Of business.
   Letter to Barton, 11 September 1822, in H. Harper (ed.) *Letters of Charles Lamb* (1905) vol. 4

11 The greatest pleasure I know, is to do a good action by stealth, and to have it found out by accident.
   'Table Talk by the late Elia' in *The Athenaeum* 4 January 1834

12   Gone before
   To that unknown and silent shore.
   'Hester' (1803) st. 7

13 I have had playmates, I have had companions,
   In my days of childhood, in my joyful school-days,—
   All, all are gone, the old familiar faces.
   'The Old Familiar Faces'

14 A child's a plaything for an hour.
   'Parental Recollections' (1809); often attributed to Lamb's sister Mary

15 I toiled after it, sir, as some men toil after virtue.
   On being asked 'how he had acquired his power of smoking at such a rate'; in T. Talfourd *Memoirs of Charles Lamb* (1892) p. 262

John George Lambton, 1st Earl of Durham 1792–1840

16 £40,000 a year a moderate income—such a one as a man *might jog on with*.
   In Sir Herbert Maxwell (ed.) *The Creevey Papers* (1903) vol. 2, p. 32 (letter, 13 September 1821)

George Lamming b. 1927

17 In the castle of my skin.
   Title of novel (1953)

Norman Lamont 1942–

18 Rising unemployment and the recession have been the price that we've had to pay to get inflation down. [Labour shouts] That is a price well worth paying.
   Speech in House of Commons, 16 May 1991; in *Independent* 17 May 1991, p. 1

Giuseppe di Lampedusa 1896–1957

19 If we want things to stay as they are, things will have to change.
   The Leopard (1957) p. 33

Sir Osbert Lancaster 1908–86

20 Fan-vaulting ... from an aesthetic standpoint frequently belongs to the 'Last-supper-carved-on-a-peach-stone' class of masterpiece.
   Pillar to Post (1938) 'Perpendicular'

Bert Lance 1931–

21 If it ain't broke, don't fix it.
   In *Nation's Business* May 1977, p. 27

Walter Savage Landor 1775–1864

22 I strove with none; for none was worth my strife;
   Nature I loved, and, next to Nature, Art.
   'Dying Speech of an Old Philosopher' (1853)

23 Ah, what avails the sceptred race!
   Ah, what the form divine!
   'Rose Aylmer' (1806)

24 George the First was always reckoned Vile, but viler George the Second;
   And what mortal ever heard
   Any good of George the Third?
   When from earth the Fourth descended
   God be praised the Georges ended!
   Epigram in *The Atlas*, 28 April 1855

25 Fleas know not whether they are upon the body of a giant or upon one of ordinary size.
   Imaginary Conversations (1824) 'Southey and Porson'

Andrew Lang 1844–1912

1 St Andrews by the Northern sea,
A haunted town it is to me!
'Almae Matres' (1884)

2 *I* am the batsman and the bat,
I am the bowler and the ball,
The umpire, the pavilion cat,
The roller, pitch, and stumps, and all.
'Brahma'. Cf. 136:11

3 They hear like ocean on a western beach
The surge and thunder of the Odyssey.
'The Odyssey' (1881)

Julia Lang 1921–

4 Are you sitting comfortably? Then I'll
begin.
Listen with Mother (BBC radio programme for
children, 1950–82); sometimes 'Then we'll
begin'

William Langland c.1330–c.1400

5 In a somer seson, whan softe was the
sonne.
The Vision of Piers Plowman B text (ed. Schmidt,
1987) prologue l. 1

6 Ac on a May morwenynge on Malverne
hilles
Me bifel a ferly, of Fairye me thoghte.
The Vision of Piers Plowman B text (ed. Schmidt,
1987) prologue l. 5 ('Ac on a May mornyng
on Maluerne hulles / Me biful for to slepe,
for werynesse of-walked' in C text (ed., 1978)
prologue l. 6)

7 A faire feeld ful of folk fond I ther bitwene.
The Vision of Piers Plowman B text (ed. Schmidt,
1987) prologue l. 17

8 Grammer, the ground of al.
The Vision of Piers Plowman B text (ed. Schmidt,
1987) Passus 15, l. 370

9 'After sharpest shoures,' quath Pees 'most
shene is the sonne;
Is no weder warmer than after watry
cloudes.'
The Vision of Piers Plowman B text (ed. Schmidt,
1987) Passus 18, l. 411 (*Pees* Peace)

Stephen Langton d. 1228

10 *Veni, Sancte Spiritus,*
Et emitte coelitus
Lucis tuae radium.
Come, Holy Spirit, and send out from
heaven the beam of your light.
The 'Golden Sequence' for Whit Sunday
(attributed also to Pope Innocent III, among
others)

Lao-tsu c.604–c.531 BC

11 Heaven and Earth are not ruthful;
To them the Ten Thousand Things are but
as straw dogs.
Tao-Tê-Ching ch. 5 (tr. A. Waley in *The Way and
its Power*, 1934)

Philip Larkin 1922–85

12 Sexual intercourse began
In nineteen sixty-three
(Which was rather late for me)—
Between the end of the *Chatterley* ban
And the Beatles' first LP.
'Annus Mirabilis' (1974)

13 What are days for?
Days are where we live.
'Days' (1964)

14 Life is first boredom, then fear.
Whether or not we use it, it goes,
And leaves what something hidden from
us chose,
And age, and then the only end of age.
'Dockery & Son' (1964)

15 Nothing, like something, happens
anywhere.
'I Remember, I Remember' (1955)

16 Perhaps being old is having lighted rooms
Inside your head, and people in them,
acting.
People you know, yet can't quite name.
'The Old Fools' (1974)

17 They fuck you up, your mum and dad.
They may not mean to, but they do.
They fill you with the faults they had
And add some extra, just for you.
'This Be The Verse' (1974)

18 Man hands on misery to man.
It deepens like a coastal shelf.
Get out as early as you can,
And don't have any kids yourself.
'This Be The Verse' (1974)

19 Why should I let the toad *work*
Squat on my life?
Can't I use my wit as a pitchfork
And drive the brute off?
'Toads' (1955)

20 A beginning, a muddle, and an end.
New Fiction no. 15, January 1978 (on the
'classic formula' for a novel)

Duc de la Rochefoucauld 1613–80

21 We are all strong enough to bear the
misfortunes of others.
Maximes (1678) no. 19

22 There are good marriages, but no
delightful ones.
Maximes (1678) no. 113

23 Hypocrisy is a tribute which vice pays to
virtue.
Maximes (1678) no. 218

24 Absence diminishes commonplace passions
and increases great ones, as the wind
extinguishes candles and kindles fire.
Maximes (1678) no. 276. Cf. 83:19, 145:5

25 In most of mankind gratitude is merely a
secret hope for greater favours.
Maximes (1678) no. 298

1 The accent of one's birthplace lingers in the mind and in the heart as it does in one's speech.
Maximes (1678) no. 342

2 In the misfortune of our best friends, we always find something which is not displeasing to us.
Réflexions ou Maximes Morales (1665) maxim 99

Hugh Latimer *c.*1485–1555

3 The drop of rain maketh a hole in the stone, not by violence, but by oft falling.
Second Sermon preached before the King's Majesty (19 April 1549). Cf. 243:12

4 Be of good comfort Master Ridley, and play the man. We shall this day light such a candle by God's grace in England, as (I trust) shall never be put out.
Prior to being burned for heresy, 16 October 1555; in John Foxe *Actes and Monuments* (1570 ed.) p. 1937

Sir Harry Lauder 1870–1950

5 Keep right on to the end of the road,
Keep right on to the end.
Tho' the way be long, let your heart be strong,
Keep right on round the bend.
'The End of the Road' (1924 song)

6 I love a lassie, a bonnie, bonnie lassie,
She's as pure as the lily in the dell.
She's as sweet as the heather, the bonnie bloomin' heather—
Mary, ma Scotch Bluebell.
'I Love a Lassie' (1905 song)

7 Roamin' in the gloamin'.
Title of song (1911)

Stan Laurel 1890–1965

8 Another nice mess you've gotten me into.
Another Fine Mess (1930 film) and many other Laurel and Hardy films; spoken by Oliver Hardy

D. H. Lawrence 1885–1930

9 To the Puritan all things are impure, as somebody says.
Etruscan Places (1932) 'Cerveteri'. Cf. 56:22

10 John Thomas says good-night to Lady Jane, a little droopingly, but with a hopeful heart.
Lady Chatterley's Lover (1928) ch. 19

11 If you try to nail anything down in the novel, either it kills the novel, or the novel gets up and walks away with the nail.
Phoenix (1936) 'Morality and the Novel'

12 Morality in the novel is the trembling instability of the balance. When the novelist puts his thumb in the scale, to pull down the balance to his own predilection, that is immorality.
Phoenix (1936) 'Morality and the Novel'

13 Pornography is the attempt to insult sex, to do dirt on it.
Phoenix (1936) 'Pornography and Obscenity' ch. 3

14 The novel is the one bright book of life.
Phoenix (1936) 'Why the novel matters'

15 Never trust the artist. Trust the tale.
Studies in Classic American Literature (1923) ch. 1

16 Be a good animal, true to your instincts.
The White Peacock (1911) pt. 2, ch. 2

17 Don't you find it a beautiful clean thought, a world empty of people, just uninterrupted grass, and a hare sitting up?
Women in Love (1920) ch. 11

18 How beastly the bourgeois is
Especially the male of the species.
'How Beastly the Bourgeois Is' (1929)

19 While we have sex in the mind, we truly have none in the body.
'Leave Sex Alone' (1929)

20 Men! The only animal in the world to fear!
'Mountain Lion' (1923)

21 I never saw a wild thing
Sorry for itself.
'Self-Pity' (1929)

22 And so, I missed my chance with one of the lords
Of life.
And I have something to expiate:
A pettiness.
'Snake' (1923)

23 Not I, not I, but the wind that blows through me!
'Song of a Man who has Come Through' (1917)

24 When I read Shakespeare I am struck with wonder
That such trivial people should muse and thunder
In such lovely language.
'When I Read Shakespeare' (1929)

25 Tragedy ought really to be a great kick at misery.
Letter to A. W. McLeod, 6 October 1912, in H. T. Moore (ed.) *Collected Letters* (1962) vol. 1

26 The dead don't die. They look on and help.
Letter to J. Middleton Murry, 2 February 1923, in H. T. Moore (ed.) *Collected Letters* (1962) vol. 2

T. E. Lawrence 1888–1935

27 Many men would take the death-sentence without a whimper to escape the life-sentence which fate carries in her other hand.
The Mint (1955) pt. 1, ch. 4

28 The trumpets came out brazenly with the last post ... A man hates to be moved to folly by a noise.
The Mint (1955) pt. 3, ch. 9

1 I loved you, so I drew these tides of men
into my hands and wrote my will across
the sky in stars.
Seven Pillars of Wisdom (1926) dedication

Emma Lazarus 1849–87

2 Give me your tired, your poor,
Your huddled masses yearning to breathe
free.
'The New Colossus' (1883); inscribed on the
Statue of Liberty, New York

Stephen Leacock 1869–1944

3 I am what is called a *professor emeritus*—
from the Latin *e*, 'out', and *meritus*, 'so he
ought to be'.
Here are my Lectures (1938) ch. 14

4 A sportsman is a man who, every now and
then, simply has to get out and kill
something. Not that he's cruel. He
wouldn't hurt a fly. It's not big enough.
My Remarkable Uncle (1942) p. 73

5 Lord Ronald said nothing; he flung himself
from the room, flung himself upon his
horse and rode madly off in all directions.
Nonsense Novels (1911) 'Gertrude the
Governess'

Mary Leapor 1722–46

6 In spite of all romantic poets sing,
This gold, my dearest, is an useful thing.
'Mira to Octavia'

Edward Lear 1812–88

7 On the coast of Coromandel
Where the early pumpkins blow,
In the middle of the woods,
Lived the Yonghy-Bonghy-Bó.
'The Courtship of the Yonghy-Bonghy-Bó'
(1871)

8 When awful darkness and silence reign
Over the great Gromboolian plain.
'The Dong with a Luminous Nose' (1871)

9 When storm-clouds brood on the towering
heights
Of the Hills of the Chankly Bore.
'The Dong with a Luminous Nose' (1871)

10 Far and few, far and few,
Are the lands where the Jumblies live;
Their heads are green, and their hands are
blue,
And they went to sea in a Sieve.
'The Jumblies' (1871)

11 The Owl and the Pussy-Cat went to sea
In a beautiful pea-green boat.
They took some honey, and plenty of
money,
Wrapped up in a five-pound note.
'The Owl and the Pussy-Cat' (1871)

12 They sailed away for a year and a day,
To the land where the Bong-tree grows,
And there in a wood a Piggy-wig stood
With a ring at the end of his nose.
'The Owl and the Pussy-Cat' (1871)

13 They dined on mince, and slices of quince,
Which they ate with a runcible spoon;
And hand in hand, on the edge of the sand,
They danced by the light of the moon.
'The Owl and the Pussy-Cat' (1871)

14 The Pobble who has no toes
Had once as many as we;
When they said, 'Some day you may lose
them all';—
He replied,—'Fish fiddle de-dee!'
'The Pobble Who Has No Toes' (1871)

15 He has gone to fish, for his Aunt Jobiska's
Runcible Cat with crimson whiskers!
'The Pobble Who Has No Toes' (1871)

16 There was an old man of Thermopylae,
Who never did anything properly;
But they said, 'If you choose
To boil eggs in your shoes,
You shall never remain in Thermopylae.'
'There was an old man of Thermopylae'
(1872)

17 There was an Old Man with a beard,
Who said, 'It is just as I feared!—
Two Owls and a Hen,
Four Larks and a Wren,
Have all built their nests in my beard!'
'There was an Old Man with a beard' (1846)

18 When they asked,—'Does it trot?'—
He said, 'Certainly not!
He's a Moppsikon Floppsikon bear.'
'There was an old person of Ware' (1872)

Timothy Leary 1920–

19 Turn on, tune in and drop out.
The Politics of Ecstasy (1968) ch. 21

Mary Elizabeth Lease 1853–1933

20 Kansas had better stop raising corn and
begin raising hell.
In E. J. James et al. *Notable American Women
1607–1950* (1971) vol. 2, p. 381

F. R. Leavis 1895–1978

21 The common pursuit.
Title of book (1952)

22 Like Keats's vulgarity with a Public School
accent.
New Bearings in English Poetry (1932) ch. 2 (of
Rupert Brooke's verse)

23 Self-contempt, well-grounded.
On the foundation of T. S. Eliot's work, in
Times Literary Supplement 21 October 1988,
p. 1177

Fran Lebowitz 1946–

24 There is no such thing as inner peace.
There is only nervousness or death.
Metropolitan Life (1978) p. 6

Stanislaw Lec 1909–66

1 Is it progress if a cannibal uses knife and fork?
Unkempt Thoughts (1962) p. 78

John le Carré 1931–

2 The spy who came in from the cold.
Title of novel (1963)

Le Corbusier 1887–1965

3 A house is a machine for living in.
Vers une architecture (1923) p. ix. Cf. 333:12

Alexandre Auguste Ledru-Rollin 1807–74

4 *Eh! je suis leur chef, il fallait bien les suivre.*
Ah well! I am their leader, I really had to follow them!
In E. de Mirecourt *Les Contemporains* vol. 14 (1857) 'Ledru-Rollin'

Gypsy Rose Lee 1914–70

5 God is love, but get it in writing.
Attributed

Harper Lee 1926–

6 Shoot all the bluejays you want, if you can hit 'em, but remember it's a sin to kill a mockingbird.
To Kill a Mockingbird (1960) ch. 10

Henry Lee ('Light-Horse Harry') 1756–1818

7 A citizen, first in war, first in peace, and first in the hearts of his countrymen.
Funeral Oration on the death of General Washington (1800) p. 14

Nathaniel Lee c.1653–92

8 Then he will talk, Good Gods, How he will talk.
The Rival Queens (1677) act 3

9 When Greeks joined Greeks, then was the tug of war!
The Rival Queens (1677) act 4, sc. 2

10 Philip fought men, but Alexander women.
The Rival Queens (1677) act 4, sc. 2

Robert E. Lee 1807–70

11 It is well that war is so terrible. We should grow too fond of it.
After the battle of Fredericksburg, December 1862 (attributed)

Richard Le Gallienne 1866–1947

12 The cry of the Little Peoples goes up to God in vain,
For the world is given over to the cruel sons of Cain.
'The Cry of the Little Peoples' (1899)

Ernest Lehman 1920–

13 Sweet smell of success.
Title of book and film (1957)

Tom Lehrer 1928–

14 Plagiarize! Let no one else's work evade your eyes,
Remember why the good Lord made your eyes.
'Lobachevski' (1953 song)

Gottfried Wilhelm Leibniz 1646–1716

15 *Nihil est sine ratione.*
There is nothing without a reason.
Studies in Physics and the Nature of Body (1671) in *Leibniz: Philosophical Papers and Letters* (tr. L. E. Loemker, 1969) p. 142

16 *Eadem sunt quorum unum potest substitui alteri salva veritate.*
Two things are identical if one can be substituted for the other without affecting the truth.
'Table de définitions' (1704) in L. Coutourat (ed.) *Opuscules et fragments inédits de Leibniz* (1903)

Fred W. Leigh d. 1924

17 Can't get away to marry you today,
My wife won't let me!
'Waiting at the Church' (1906 song)

18 Why am I always the bridesmaid,
Never the blushing bride?
'Why Am I Always the Bridesmaid?' (1917 song, with Charles Collins and Lily Morris)

Henry Sambrooke Leigh 1837–83

19 The rapturous, wild, and ineffable pleasure Of drinking at somebody else's expense.
Carols of Cockayne (1869) 'Stanzas to an Intoxicated Fly'

Curtis E. LeMay 1906–90

20 We're going to bomb them back into the Stone Age.
On the North Vietnamese, in *Mission with LeMay* (1965) p. 565

Lenin (Vladimir Ilich Ulyanov) 1870–1924

1 Communism is Soviet power plus the electrification of the whole country.
> Report to 8th Congress, 1920, in *Collected Works* (ed. 5) vol. 42, p. 30

2 Imperialism is the monopoly stage of capitalism.
> *Imperialism as the Last Stage of Capitalism* (1916) ch. 7

3 What is to be done?
> Title of pamphlet (1902); originally the title of a novel (1863) by N. G. Chernyshevsky

4 Who? Whom?
> Definition of political science, meaning 'Who will outstrip whom?'; in *Polnoe Sobranie Sochinenii* vol. 44 (1970) p. 161 (17 October 1921) and *passim*

5 A good man fallen among Fabians.
> Of G. B. Shaw, in A. Ransome *Six Weeks in Russia in 1919* (1919) 'Notes of Conversations with Lenin'

6 Liberty is precious—so precious that it must be rationed.
> In Sidney and Beatrice Webb *Soviet Communism* (1936) p. 1036

John Lennon 1940–80

7 Imagine there's no heaven,
It's easy if you try,
No hell below us,
Above us only sky.
> 'Imagine' (1971 song)

8 We're more popular than Jesus now; I don't know which will go first—rock 'n' roll or Christianity.
> Interview in *Evening Standard* 4 March 1966 (of The Beatles)

9 Will the people in the cheaper seats clap your hands? All the rest of you, if you'll just rattle your jewellery.
> At Royal Variety Performance, 4 November 1963; in R. Colman *John Winston Lennon* (1984) pt. 1, ch. 11

John Lennon 1940–80 and Paul McCartney 1942–

10 Back in the USSR.
> Title of song (1968)

11 For I don't care too much for money,
For money can't buy me love.
> 'Can't Buy Me Love' (1964 song)

12 All the lonely people, where do they all come from?
> 'Eleanor Rigby' (1966 song)

13 Give peace a chance.
> Title of song (1969)

14 It's been a hard day's night,
And I've been working like a dog.
> 'A Hard Day's Night' (1964 song)

15 Strawberry fields forever.
> Title of song (1967)

16 She's got a ticket to ride, but she don't care.
> 'Ticket to Ride' (1965 song)

17 Will you still need me, will you still feed me,
When I'm sixty four?
> 'When I'm Sixty Four' (1967 song)

18 Oh I get by with a little help from my friends,
Mm, I get high with a little help from my friends.
> 'With a Little Help From My Friends' (1967 song)

Dan Leno 1860–1904

19 Ah! what is man? Wherefore does he why? Whence did he whence? Whither is he withering?
> *Dan Leno Hys Booke* (1901) ch. 1

Speaker William Lenthall 1591–1662

20 I have neither eye to see, nor tongue to speak here, but as the House is pleased to direct me.
> To Charles I, 4 January 1642, on being asked if he had seen any of the five MPs whom the King had ordered to be arrested; in John Rushworth *Historical Collections. The Third Part* vol. 2 (1692) p. 478

Leonardo da Vinci 1452–1519

21 Life well spent is long.
> E. McCurdy (ed. and trans.) *Leonardo da Vinci's Notebooks* (1906) bk. 1, p. 65

22 In her [Nature's] inventions nothing is lacking, and nothing is superfluous.
> E. McCurdy (ed. and trans.) *Leonardo da Vinci's Notebooks* (1906) bk. 1, p. 171

23 Every man at three years old is half his height.
> I. Richter (ed.) *Selections from the Notebooks of Leonardo da Vinci* (World's Classics, 1952) p. 149

Mikhail Lermontov 1814–41

24 Of two close friends, one is always the slave of the other.
> *A Hero of our Time* (1840) 'Princess Mary' (tr. P. Longworth)

25 I am like a man yawning at a ball; the only reason he does not go home to bed is that his carriage has not arrived yet.
> *A Hero of our Time* (1840) 'Princess Mary' (tr. P. Longworth)

Alan Jay Lerner 1918–86

26 Why can't a woman be more like a man?
Men are so honest, so thoroughly square;
Eternally noble, historically fair.
> *My Fair Lady* (1956) 'A Hymn to Him'

1 In Hertford, Hereford, and Hampshire,
Hurricanes hardly happen.
My Fair Lady (1956) 'The Rain in Spain'

2 Oozing charm from every pore,
He oiled his way around the floor.
My Fair Lady (1956) 'You Did It'

Doris Lessing 1919–

3 What of October, that ambiguous month,
the month of tension, the unendurable
month?
Martha Quest (1952) pt. 4, sect. 1

4 What is charm then? ... something extra,
superfluous, unnecessary, essentially a
power thrown away.
Particularly Cats (1967) ch. 9

G. E. Lessing 1729–81

5 One single grateful thought raised to
heaven is the most perfect prayer.
Minna von Barnhelm (1767) act 2, sc. 7

Ada Leverson 1865–1936

6 He seemed at ease and to have the look of
the last gentleman in Europe.
Letters to the Sphinx (1930) p. 34 (of Oscar
Wilde)

Bernard Levin 1928–

7 The Stag at Bay with the mentality of a fox
at large.
Of Harold Macmillan, in *The Pendulum Years*
(1970) ch. 12

8 Whom the mad would destroy, they first
make gods.
Of Mao Tse-tung in 1967; Levin quoting
himself in *The Times* 21 September 1987.
Cf. 129:11

Duc de Lévis 1764–1830

9 *Noblesse oblige.*
Nobility has its obligations.
Maximes et Réflexions (1812 ed.) 'Morale:
Maximes et Préceptes' no. 73

10 *Gouverner, c'est choisir.*
To govern is to choose.
Maximes et Réflexions (1812 ed.) 'Politique:
Maximes de Politique' no. 19

C. S. Lewis 1898–1963

11 We have trained them [men] to think of
the Future as a promised land which
favoured heroes attain—not as something
which everyone reaches at the rate of sixty
minutes an hour, whatever he does,
whoever he is.
The Screwtape Letters (1942) no. 25

12 She's the sort of woman who lives for
others—you can always tell the others by
their hunted expression.
The Screwtape Letters (1942) no. 26

13 Courage is not simply *one* of the virtues
but the form of every virtue at the testing
point.
In Cyril Connolly *The Unquiet Grave* (1944)
ch. 3

Esther Lewis fl. 1747–89

14 Why are the needle and the pen
Thought incompatible by men?
'A Mirror for Detractors' (1754) l. 149

Sir George Cornewall Lewis 1806–63

15 Life would be tolerable but for its
amusements.
In *The Times* 18 September 1872, p. 4

John Lewis 1885–1963

16 Never knowingly undersold.
Motto (from *c.*1920) of the John Lewis
Partnership; in *Partnership for All* (1948) ch. 29

Sam M. Lewis 1885–1959 and Joe Young 1889–1939

17 How 'ya gonna keep 'em down on the farm
(after they've seen Paree)?
Title of song (1919)

Sinclair Lewis 1885–1951

18 Our American professors like their
literature clear and cold and pure and very
dead.
The American Fear of Literature (Nobel Prize
Address, 12 December 1930)

19 She did her work with the thoroughness of
a mind which reveres details and never
quite understands them.
Babbitt (1922) ch. 18

Robert Ley 1890–1945

20 *Kraft durch Freude.*
Strength through joy.
German Labour Front slogan, from 1933

George Leybourne d. 1884

21 He'd fly through the air with the greatest
of ease,
A daring young man on the flying trapeze.
'The Flying Trapeze' (1868 song)

Liberace 1919–87

22 I cry all the way to the bank.
On bad reviews; *Autobiography* (1973) ch. 2
(from the mid-1950s)

Georg Christoph Lichtenberg
1742–99

1 The journalists have constructed for themselves a little wooden chapel, which they also call the Temple of Fame, in which they put up and make such a hammering you can't hear yourself speak.

In A. Leitzmann *Georg Christoph Lichtenberg Aphorismen* (1904) p. 108

Charles-Joseph, Prince de Ligne
1735–1814

2 *Le congrès ne marche pas, il danse.*
The Congress makes no progress; it dances.

In A. de la Garde-Chambonas *Souvenirs du Congrès de Vienne* (1820) ch. 1

George Lillo 1693–1739

3 There's sure no passion in the human soul, But finds its food in music.

The Fatal Curiosity (1736) act 1, sc. 2

Abraham Lincoln 1809–65

4 To give victory to the right, not bloody bullets, but peaceful ballots only, are necessary.

Speech, 18 May 1858, in R. P. Basler (ed.) *Collected Works of Abraham Lincoln* (1953) vol. 2 (usually quoted 'The ballot is stronger than the bullet')

5 'A house divided against itself cannot stand.' I believe this government cannot endure permanently, half slave and half free.

Speech, 16 June 1858, in R. P. Basler (ed.) *Collected Works* (1953) vol. 2. Cf. 51:19

6 In giving freedom to the slave, we assure freedom to the free—honourable alike in what we give and what we preserve. We shall nobly save, or meanly lose, the last, best hope of earth.

Annual Message to Congress, 1 December 1862, in R. P. Basler (ed.) *Collected Works* (1953) vol. 5

7 With malice toward none; with charity for all; with firmness in the right, as God gives us to see the right, let us strive on to finish the work we are in.

Second Inaugural Address, 4 March 1865, in R. P. Basler (ed.) *Collected Works* (1953) vol. 8

8 Fourscore and seven years ago our fathers brought forth upon this continent a new nation, conceived in liberty, and dedicated to the proposition that all men are created equal ... We here highly resolve that the dead shall not have died in vain, that this nation, under God, shall have a new birth of freedom; and that government of the people, by the people, and for the people, shall not perish from the earth.

Address at the Dedication of the National Cemetery at Gettysburg, 19 November 1863, in R. P. Basler (ed.) *Collected Works* (1953) vol. 7 (the Lincoln Memorial inscription reads 'by the people, for the people')

9 I claim not to have controlled events, but confess plainly that events have controlled me.

Letter to A. G. Hodges, 4 April 1864, in R. P. Basler (ed.) *Collected Works* (1953) vol. 7

10 You may fool all the people some of the time; you can even fool some of the people all the time; but you can't fool all of the people all the time.

In A. McClure *Lincoln's Yarns and Stories* (1904); also attributed to Phineas Barnum

11 The Lord prefers common-looking people. That is why he makes so many of them.

Attributed. See J. Morgan *Our Presidents* (1928) ch. 6

12 People who like this sort of thing will find this the sort of thing they like.

Judgement of a book, in G. W. E. Russell *Collections and Recollections* (1898) ch. 30

13 So you're the little woman who wrote the book that made this great war!

On meeting Harriet Beecher Stowe, author of *Uncle Tom's Cabin* (1852); in C. Sandburg *Abraham Lincoln: The War Years* (1936) vol. 2, ch. 39

14 As President, I have no eyes but constitutional eyes; I cannot see you.

Reply to the South Carolina Commissioners (attributed). Cf. 205:20

R. M. Lindner 1914–56

15 Rebel without a cause.

Title of book (1944) and film (1955) starring James Dean

Vachel Lindsay 1879–1931

16 Booth led boldly with his big bass drum— (Are you washed in the blood of the Lamb?)

'General William Booth Enters into Heaven' (1913). Cf. 57:26

Eric Linklater 1899–1974

17 'There won't be any revolution in America,' said Isadore. Nikitin agreed. 'The people are all too clean. They spend all their time changing their shirts and washing themselves. You can't feel fierce and revolutionary in a bathroom.'

Juan in America (1931) bk. 5, pt. 3

Art Linkletter 1912–

18 The four stages of man are infancy, childhood, adolescence and obsolescence.

A Child's Garden of Misinformation (1965) ch. 8

George Linley 1798–1865

1 Among our ancient mountains,
And from our lovely vales,
Oh, let the prayer re-echo:
'God bless the Prince of Wales!'
  'God Bless the Prince of Wales' (1862 song);
  translated from the Welsh original by J. C.
  Hughes (1837–87)

Richard Littledale 1833–90

2 Let holy charity
Mine outward vesture be,
And lowliness become mine inner clothing.
  'Come down, O Love divine' (1867 hymn);
  translation of 'Discendi, Amor santo' by
  Bianco da Siena (c.1350–1434)

Joan Littlewood 1914– and Charles Chilton 1914–

3 Oh what a lovely war.
  Title of stage show (1963)

Maxim Litvinov 1876–1951

4 Peace is indivisible.
  Note to the Allies, 25 February 1920, in A. U.
  Pope *Maxim Litvinoff* (1943) p. 234

Livy 59 BC–AD 17

5 *Vae victis.*
Down with the defeated!
  Cry (already proverbial) of the Gallic king,
  Brennus, on capturing Rome in 390 BC; in *Ab
  Urbe Condita* bk. 5, ch. 48, sect. 9

Richard Llewellyn 1907–83

6 How green was my valley.
  Title of book (1939)

Robert Lloyd

7 All the art of Imitation,
Is pilf'ring from the first creation.
  'Shakespeare' (1762)

David Lloyd George 1863–1945

8 A mastiff? It is the right hon. Gentleman's
poodle.
  On the House of Lords and Lord Balfour
  respectively; in *Hansard* 26 June 1907,
  col. 1429

9 A fully-equipped duke costs as much to
keep up as two Dreadnoughts; and dukes
are just as great a terror and they last
longer.
  Speech at Newcastle, 9 October 1909, in *The
  Times* 11 October 1909

10 I hope we may say that thus, this fateful
morning, came to an end all wars.
  Speech, *Hansard* 11 November 1918,
  col. 2463. Cf. 345:24

11 What is our task? To make Britain a fit
country for heroes to live in.
  Speech at Wolverhampton, 23 November
  1918, in *The Times* 25 November 1918

12 The world is becoming like a lunatic
asylum run by lunatics.
  In *Observer* 8 January 1933. Cf. 264:1

John Locke 1632–1704

13 New opinions are always suspected, and
usually opposed, without any other reason
but because they are not already common.
  Essay concerning Human Understanding (1690)
  'Dedicatory Epistle'

14 No man's knowledge here can go beyond
his experience.
  Essay concerning Human Understanding (1690)
  bk. 2, ch. 1, sect. 19

15 It is one thing to show a man that he is in
error, and another to put him in
possession of truth.
  Essay concerning Human Understanding (1690)
  bk. 4, ch. 7, sect. 11

16 Reason is natural revelation.
  Essay concerning Human Understanding (1690)
  bk. 4, ch. 19, sect. 4

17 Crooked things may be as stiff and
unflexible as straight: and men may be as
positive in error as in truth.
  Essay concerning Human Understanding (1690)
  bk. 4, ch. 19, sect. 11

18 All men are liable to error; and most men
are, in many points, by passion or interest,
under temptation to it.
  Essay concerning Human Understanding (1690)
  bk. 4, ch. 20, sect. 17

19 Whatsoever ... [man] removes out of the
state that nature hath provided and left it
in, he hath mixed his labour with, and
joined to it something that is his own, and
thereby makes it his property.
  Second Treatise of Civil Government (1690) ch. 5,
  sect. 27

20 The end of law is, not to abolish or
restrain, but to preserve and enlarge
freedom.
  Second Treatise of Civil Government (1690) ch. 6,
  sect. 57

21 This power to act according to discretion
for the public good, without the
prescription of the law, and sometimes
even against it, is that which is called
prerogative.
  Second Treatise of Civil Government (1690)
  ch. 14, sect. 160

Frederick Locker-Lampson 1821–95

22 The world's as ugly, ay, as sin,
And almost as delightful.
  'The Jester's Plea' (1868)

1 And many are afraid of God—
And more of Mrs Grundy.
'The Jester's Plea' (1868)

John Gibson Lockhart 1794–1854

2 It is a better and a wiser thing to be
a starved apothecary than a starved poet;
so back to the shop Mr John, back to
'plasters, pills, and ointment boxes.'
Reviewing Keats's *Endymion* in *Blackwood's
Edinburgh Magazine* August 1818

3 Here lies that peerless paper peer Lord
Peter,
Who broke the laws of God and man and
metre.
Epitaph for Patrick ('Peter'), Lord Robertson;
in *Journal of Sir Walter Scott* (1890) vol. 1,
p. 259, n. 2

David Lodge 1935–

4 Literature is mostly about having sex and
not much about having children. Life is the
other way round.
The British Museum is Falling Down (1965) ch. 4

Frank Loesser 1910–69

5 See what the boys in the back room will
have
And tell them I'm having the same.
'Boys in the Back Room' (1939 song)

6 Isn't it grand! Isn't it fine! Look at the cut,
the style, the line!
The suit of clothes is altogether, but
altogether it's altogether
The most remarkable suit of clothes that I
have ever seen.
'The King's New Clothes' (1952 song)

Jack London 1876–1916

7 The call of the wild.
Title of novel (1903)

Huey Long 1893–1935

8 I can go Mr Wilson one better; I was born
barefoot.
In T. Harry Williams *Huey Long* (1969) p. 250
(replying to the claim that an opponent had
gone barefoot as a boy)

9 The time has come for all good men to rise
above principle.
Attributed

Henry Wadsworth Longfellow
1807–82

10 I shot an arrow into the air,
It fell to earth, I knew not where.
'The Arrow and the Song' (1845)

11 Thou, too, sail on, O Ship of State!
Sail on, O Union, strong and great!
'The Building of the Ship' (1849)

12 Between the dark and the daylight,
When the night is beginning to lower,
Comes a pause in the day's occupations,
That is known as the Children's Hour.
'The Children's Hour' (1859)

13 The cares that infest the day
Shall fold their tents, like the Arabs,
And as silently steal away.
'The Day is Done' (1844)

14 If you would hit the mark, you must aim
a little above it;
Every arrow that flies feels the attraction
of earth.
'Elegiac Verse' (1880)

15 This is the forest primeval.
Evangeline (1847) introduction

16 Sorrow and silence are strong, and patient
endurance is godlike.
Evangeline (1847) pt. 2, l. 60

17 A youth, who bore, 'mid snow and ice,
A banner with the strange device,
Excelsior!
'Excelsior' (1841)

18 Giotto's tower,
The lily of Florence blossoming in stone.
'Giotto's Tower' (1866)

19 I like that ancient Saxon phrase, which
calls
The burial-ground God's-Acre!
'God's-Acre' (1841)

20 The holiest of all holidays are those
Kept by ourselves in silence and apart;
The secret anniversaries of the heart.
'Holidays' (1877)

21 A boy's will is the wind's will
And the thoughts of youth are long, long
thoughts.
'My Lost Youth' (1858)

22 Life is real! Life is earnest!
And the grave is not its goal;
Dust thou art, to dust returnest,
Was not spoken of the soul.
'A Psalm of Life' (1838). Cf. 39:3

23 Lives of great men all remind us
We can make our lives sublime,
And, departing, leave behind us
Footprints on the sands of time.
'A Psalm of Life' (1838)

24 Though the mills of God grind slowly, yet
they grind exceeding small;
Though with patience He stands waiting,
with exactness grinds He all.
'Retribution' (1870); translation of Friedrich
von Logau *Sinngedichte* (1654) no. 3224,
being itself a translation of an anonymous
line in Sextus Empiricus *Adversus
Mathematicos* bk. 1, sect. 287

25 A Lady with a Lamp shall stand
In the great history of the land,
A noble type of good,
Heroic womanhood.
'Santa Filomena' (1857); of Florence
Nightingale

1 By the shore of Gitche Gumee,
  By the shining Big-Sea-Water,
  Stood the wigwam of Nokomis,
  Daughter of the Moon, Nokomis.
  The Song of Hiawatha (1855) 'Hiawatha's
  Childhood'

2 From the waterfall he named her,
  Minnehaha, Laughing Water.
  The Song of Hiawatha (1855) 'Hiawatha and
  Mudjekeewis'

3 Ships that pass in the night, and speak
  each other in passing;
  Only a signal shown and a distant voice in
  the darkness;
  So on the ocean of life we pass and speak
  one another,
  Only a look and a voice; then darkness
  again and a silence.
  Tales of a Wayside Inn pt. 3 (1874) 'The
  Theologian's Tale' pt. 4

4 Under a spreading chestnut tree
  The village smithy stands;
  The smith, a mighty man is he,
  With large and sinewy hands.
  'The Village Blacksmith' (1839)

5 It was the schooner Hesperus,
  That sailed the wintry sea.
  'The Wreck of the Hesperus' (1839)

6 There was a little girl
  Who had a little curl
  Right in the middle of her forehead,
  When she was good
  She was very, very good,
  But when she was bad she was horrid.
  Composed for his second daughter *c*.1850.
  See B. R. Tucker-Macchetta *Home Life of
  Longfellow* (1882) ch. 5

Anita Loos 1893–1981

7 So this gentleman said a girl with brains
  ought to do something with them besides
  think.
  Gentlemen Prefer Blondes (1925) ch. 1

8 She said she always believed in the old
  adage, 'Leave them while you're looking
  good.'
  Gentlemen Prefer Blondes (1925) ch. 1

9 Fun is fun but no girl wants to laugh all of
  the time.
  Gentlemen Prefer Blondes (1925) ch. 4

Frederico García Lorca

See GARCÍA LORCA

Edward N. Lorenz

10 Predictability: Does the flap of a butterfly's
   wings in Brazil set off a tornado in Texas?
   Title of paper given to the American
   Association for the Advancement of Science,
   Washington, 29 December 1979. See James
   Gleick *Chaos* (1988) p. 322

Konrad Lorenz 1903–89

11 It is a good morning exercise for a research
   scientist to discard a pet hypothesis every
   day before breakfast.
   On Aggression (1966) ch. 2 (tr. M. Latzke)

Louis XIV 1638–1715

12 *L'État c'est moi.*
   I am the State.
   Before the Parlement de Paris, 13 April 1655;
   in J. A. Dulaure *Histoire de Paris* (1834) vol. 6,
   p. 298 (probably apocryphal)

13 *J'ai failli attendre.*
   I was nearly kept waiting.
   Attribution queried, among others, by E.
   Fournier in *L'Esprit dans l'Histoire* (1857)
   ch. 48

14 Every time I create an appointment,
   I create a hundred malcontents and one
   ingrate.
   In Voltaire *Siècle de Louis XIV* (1768 ed.) vol. 2,
   ch. 26

15 *Il n'y a plus de Pyrénées.*
   The Pyrenees are no more.
   On the accession of his grandson to the
   throne of Spain in 1700; in Voltaire *Siècle de
   Louis XIV* (1753) ch. 26. Attributed to the
   Spanish Ambassador to France in *Mercure
   Galant* (Paris) November 1700, p. 237

Louis XVIII 1755–1824

16 Remember that there is not one of you
   who does not carry in his cartridge-pouch
   the marshal's baton of the duke of Reggio;
   it is up to you to bring it forth.
   Speech to Saint-Cyr cadets, 9 August 1819, in
   Moniteur Universel 10 August 1819

17 *L'exactitude est la politesse des rois.*
   Punctuality is the politeness of kings.
   In *Souvenirs de J. Lafitte* (1844) bk. 1, ch. 3
   (attributed)

Richard Lovelace 1618–58

18 Lucasta that bright northern star.
   'Amyntor from Beyond the Sea to Alexis'
   (1649)

19 Stone walls do not a prison make,
   Nor iron bars a cage.
   'To Althea, From Prison' (1649)

20 Tell me not, Sweet, I am unkind,
   That from the nunnery
   Of thy chaste breast, and quiet mind,
   To war and arms I fly.
   'To Lucasta, Going to the Wars' (1649)

21 I could not love thee, Dear, so much,
   Loved I not honour more.
   'To Lucasta, Going to the Wars' (1649)

Samuel Lover 1797–1868

22 When once the itch of literature comes
   over a man, nothing can cure it but the
   scratching of a pen.
   Handy Andy (1842) ch. 36

Robert Lowe, Viscount Sherbrooke 1811–92

1 The Chancellor of the Exchequer is a man whose duties make him more or less of a taxing machine. He is intrusted with a certain amount of misery which it is his duty to distribute as fairly as he can.
   Speech, *Hansard* 11 April 1870, col. 1639

Amy Lowell 1874–1925

2 And the softness of my body will be guarded by embrace
   By each button, hook, and lace.
   For the man who should loose me is dead,
   Fighting with the Duke in Flanders,
   In a pattern called a war.
   Christ! What are patterns for?
   'Patterns' (1916)

3 All books are either dreams or swords,
   You can cut, or you can drug, with words.
   'Sword Blades and Poppy Seed' (1914).
   Cf. 138:19

James Russell Lowell 1819–91

4 An' you've gut to git up airly
   Ef you want to take in God.
   The Biglow Papers (First Series, 1848) no. 1 'A Letter'

5 Blessèd are the horny hands of toil!
   'A Glance Behind the Curtain' (1844)

6 Before Man made us citizens, great Nature made us men.
   'On the Capture of Fugitive Slaves' (1854)

7 Once to every man and nation comes the moment to decide.
   'The Present Crisis' (1845)

8 Truth forever on the scaffold, Wrong forever on the throne.
   'The Present Crisis' (1845)

9 New occasions teach new duties: Time makes ancient good uncouth;
   They must upward still, and onward, who would keep abreast of Truth.
   'The Present Crisis' (1845)

10 May is a pious fraud of the almanac.
   'Under the Willows' (1869) l. 21

Robert Lowell 1917–77

11 Terrible that old life of decency without unseemly intimacy
   or quarrels, when the unemancipated woman
   still had her Freudian papa and maids!
   'During Fever' (1959)

12 The aquarium is gone. Everywhere, giant finned cars nose forward like fish;
   a savage servility
   slides by on grease.
   'For the Union Dead' (1964)

13 Their monument sticks like a fishbone in the city's throat.
   'For the Union Dead' (1964)

14 These are the tranquillized *Fifties*, and I am forty.
   'Memories of West Street and Lepke' (1956)

15 At forty-five,
   What next, what next?
   At every corner,
   I meet my Father,
   my age, still alive.
   'Middle Age' (1964)

16   This is death.
   To die and know it. This is the Black Widow, death.
   'Mr Edwards and the Spider' (1950)

17 The Lord survives the rainbow of His will.
   'The Quaker Graveyard in Nantucket' (1950)

18 If we see light at the end of the tunnel, It's the light of the oncoming train.
   'Since 1939' (1977). Cf. 120:19

19 But I suppose even God was born too late to trust the old religion.
   'Tenth Muse' (1964)

20 The present, yes,
   we are in it,
   it's the infection
   of things gone.
   'We Took Our Paradise' (1977)

William Lowndes 1652–1724

21 Take care of the pence, and the pounds will take care of themselves.
   In Lord Chesterfield *Letters to his Son* (1774) 5 February 1750

Malcolm Lowry 1909–57

22 How alike are the groans of love to those of the dying.
   Under the Volcano (1947) ch. 12

Lucan AD 39–65

23 The winning cause pleased the gods, but the losing one pleased Cato.
   Pharsalia bk. 1, l. 126

24 There stands the ghost of a great name.
   Pharsalia bk. 1, l. 135 (of Pompey)

25 Thinking nothing done while anything remained to be done.
   Pharsalia bk. 2, l. 657

26 I have a wife, I have sons: we have given so many hostages to the fates.
   Pharsalia bk. 6, l. 661. Cf. 25:1

George Lucas 1944–

27 The Empire strikes back.
   Title of film (1980)

28 Man your ships, and may the force be with you.
   Star Wars (1977 film)

Lucilius c.180–102 BC

1 *Maior erat natu; non omnia possumus omnes.*
He was older; we cannot all do everything.
In Macrobius *Saturnalia* bk. 6, ch. 1, sect. 35.
Cf. 340:2

Lucretius c.94–55 BC

2 *Tantum religio potuit suadere malorum.*
So much wrong could religion induce.
De Rerum Natura bk. 1, l. 101

3 *... Nil posse creari*
De nilo.
Nothing can be created out of nothing.
De Rerum Natura bk. 1, l. 155

4 *Suave, mari magno turbantibus aequora ventis,*
E terra magnum alterius spectare laborem.
Lovely it is, when the winds are churning
up the waves on the great sea, to gaze out
from the land on the great efforts of
someone else.
De Rerum Natura bk. 2, l. 1

5 *Inque brevi spatio mutantur saecla animantum*
Et quasi cursores vitai lampada tradunt.
And in a short while the generations of
living creatures are changed and like
runners relay the torch of life.
De Rerum Natura bk. 2, l. 7

6 *Vitaque mancipio, nulli datur, omnibus usu.*
And life is given to none freehold, but it is
leasehold for all.
De Rerum Natura bk. 3, l. 971

Fray Luis de León c.1527–91

7 We were saying yesterday ...
On resuming a lecture in 1577, after five
years' imprisonment; in A. Bell *Luis de León*
(1925) ch. 8

Martin Luther 1483–1546

8 Here stand I. I can do no other. God help
me. Amen.
Speech at the Diet of Worms, 18 April 1521
(attributed)

9 For, where God built a church, there the
devil would also build a chapel ... In such
sort is the devil always God's ape.
Colloquia Mensalia (1566) ch. 2 (translated by
H. Bell as *Martin Luther's Divine Discourses*,
1652). Cf. 28:14, 31:17

10 *Eine feste Burg ist unser Gott,*
Ein gute Wehr und Waffen.
A safe stronghold our God is still,
A trusty shield and weapon.
'Eine feste Burg ist unser Gott' (1529, tr.
Thomas Carlyle)

11 Who loves not woman, wine, and song
Remains a fool his whole life long.
Attributed (later inscribed, in German, in the
Luther room in the Wartburg)

Rosa Luxemburg 1871–1919

12 Freedom is always and exclusively freedom
for the one who thinks differently.
Die Russische Revolution (1918) sect. 4

John Lydgate c.1370–c.1451

13 Off oure language he was the lodesterre.
The Fall of Princes (1431–8) prologue l. 252 (of
Chaucer)

14 Comparisouns doon offte gret greuaunce.
The Fall of Princes (1431–8) bk. 3, l. 2188

15 Woord is but wynd; leff woord and tak the
dede.
Secrets of Old Philosophers l. 1224

John Lyly c.1554–1606

16 Cupid and my Campaspe played
At cards for kisses, Cupid paid.
Campaspe (1584) act 3, sc. 5

17 What bird so sings, yet so does wail?
O 'tis the ravished nightingale.
Jug, jug, jug, jug, tereu, she cries,
And still her woes at midnight rise.
Campaspe (1584) act 5, sc. 1

18 Night hath a thousand eyes.
The Maydes Metamorphosis (1600) act 3, sc. 1

Baron Lyndhurst 1772–1863

19 Campbell has added another terror to
death.
On Lord Campbell's *Lives of the Lord
Chancellors* being written without the consent
of heirs or executors; in E. Bowen-Rowlands
Seventy-Two Years At the Bar (1924) ch. 10.
Cf. 14:24, 347:2

Henry Francis Lyte 1793–1847

20 Abide with me: fast falls the eventide;
The darkness deepens; Lord, with me abide:
When other helpers fail, and comforts flee,
Help of the helpless, O abide with me.

Swift to its close ebbs out life's little day;
Earth's joys grow dim, its glories pass
away;
Change and decay in all around I see;
O Thou, who changest not, abide with me.
'Abide with Me' (c.1847)

21 Praise my soul, the King of heaven;
To his feet thy tribute bring.
Ransomed, healed, restored, forgiven,
Who like me his praise should sing?
'Praise, my soul, the King of heaven' (1834
hymn)

E. R. Bulwer, 1st Earl of Lytton

See OWEN MEREDITH

General Douglas MacArthur
1880–1964

1 I came through and I shall return.

On reaching Australia, 20 March 1942, having broken through Japanese lines en route from Corregidor; in *New York Times* 21 March 1942

Rose Macaulay 1881–1958

2 'Take my camel, dear,' said my aunt Dot, as she climbed down from this animal on her return from High Mass.

The Towers of Trebizond (1956) p. 9

Lord Macaulay 1800–59

3 The business of everybody is the business of nobody.

Essays [Edinburgh Review] (1843) vol. 1 'Hallam'

4 The gallery in which the reporters sit has become a fourth estate of the realm.

Essays [Edinburgh Review] (1843) vol. 1 'Hallam'

5 Boswell is the first of biographers.

Essays [Edinburgh Review] (1843) vol. 1 'Samuel Johnson'

6 The gigantic body, the huge massy face, seamed with the scars of disease.

Essays [Edinburgh Review] (1843) vol. 1 'Samuel Johnson'

7 As civilization advances, poetry almost necessarily declines.

Essays [Edinburgh Review] (1843) vol. 1 'Milton'

8 If men are to wait for liberty till they become wise and good in slavery, they may indeed wait for ever.

Essays [Edinburgh Review] (1843) vol. 1 'Milton'

9 We know no spectacle so ridiculous as the British public in one of its periodical fits of morality.

Essays [Edinburgh Review] (1843) vol. 1 'Moore's Life of Lord Byron'

10 We have heard it said that five per cent is the natural interest of money.

Essays [Edinburgh Review] (1843) vol. 1 'Southey's Colloquies'

11 An acre in Middlesex is better than a principality in Utopia.

Essays [Edinburgh Review] (1843) vol. 2 'Lord Bacon'

12 The reluctant obedience of distant provinces generally costs more than it is worth.

Essays [Edinburgh Review] (1843) vol. 2 'The War of Succession in Spain'

13 Every schoolboy knows who imprisoned Montezuma, and who strangled Atahualpa.

Essays [Edinburgh Review] (1843) vol. 3 'Lord Clive'

14 That temple of silence and reconciliation where the enmities of twenty generations lie buried.

Essays [Edinburgh Review] (1843) vol. 3 'Warren Hastings' (of Westminster Abbey)

15 She [the Roman Catholic Church] may still exist in undiminished vigour when some traveller from New Zealand shall, in the midst of a vast solitude, take his stand on a broken arch of London Bridge to sketch the ruins of St Paul's.

Essays [Edinburgh Review] (1843) vol. 3 'Von Ranke'

16 She [the Church of Rome] thoroughly understands what no other church has ever understood, how to deal with enthusiasts.

Essays [Edinburgh Review] (1843) vol. 3 'Von Ranke'

17 Persecution produced its natural effect on them [Puritans and Calvinists]. It found them a sect; it made them a faction.

History of England vol. 1 (1849) ch. 1

18 It was a crime in a child to read by the bedside of a sick parent one of those beautiful collects which had soothed the griefs of forty generations of Christians.

History of England vol. 1 (1849) ch. 2

19 The Puritan hated bear-baiting, not because it gave pain to the bear, but because it gave pleasure to the spectators.

History of England vol. 1 (1849) ch. 2

20 The English Bible, a book which, if everything else in our language should perish, would alone suffice to show the whole extent of its beauty and power.

T. F. Ellis (ed.) *Miscellaneous Writings of Lord Macaulay* (1860) 'John Dryden' (1828)

21 His imagination resembled the wings of an ostrich. It enabled him to run, though not to soar.

T. F. Ellis (ed.) *Miscellaneous Writings* (1860) 'John Dryden' (1828)

22 This province of literature [history] is a debatable line. It lies on the confines of two distinct territories ... It is sometimes fiction. It is sometimes theory.

T. F. Ellis (ed.) *Miscellaneous Writings* (1860) vol. 1 'History' (1828)

23 Thank you, madam, the agony is abated.

Aged four, having had hot coffee spilt over his legs; in G. O. Trevelyan *Life and Letters of Lord Macaulay* (1876) ch. 1

24 The rugged miners poured to war from Mendip's sunless caves.

'The Armada' (1833)

25 Oh, wherefore come ye forth in triumph from the north,
With your hands, and your feet, and your raiment all red?

'The Battle of Naseby' (1824)

1 By those white cliffs I never more must
   see,
   By that dear language which I spake like
   thee,
   Forget all feuds, and shed one English tear
   O'er English dust. A broken heart lies here.
   'A Jacobite's Epitaph' (1845)

2 Lars Porsena of Clusium
   By the nine gods he swore
   That the great house of Tarquin
   Should suffer wrong no more.
   Lays of Ancient Rome (1842) 'Horatius' st. 1

3 To every man upon this earth
   Death cometh soon or late.
   And how can man die better
   Than facing fearful odds,
   For the ashes of his fathers,
   And the temples of his Gods?
   Lays of Ancient Rome (1842) 'Horatius' st. 27

4 Now who will stand on either hand,
   And keep the bridge with me?
   Lays of Ancient Rome (1842) 'Horatius' st. 29

5 Then none was for a party;
   Then all were for the state.
   Lays of Ancient Rome (1842) 'Horatius' st. 32

6 Was none who would be foremost
   To lead such dire attack;
   But those behind cried 'Forward!'
   And those before cried 'Back!'
   Lays of Ancient Rome (1842) 'Horatius' st. 50

7 Oh, Tiber! father Tiber
   To whom the Romans pray,
   A Roman's life, a Roman's arms,
   Take thou in charge this day!
   Lays of Ancient Rome (1842) 'Horatius' st. 59

8 And even the ranks of Tuscany
   Could scarce forbear to cheer.
   Lays of Ancient Rome (1842) 'Horatius' st. 60

General Anthony McAuliffe
1898–1975

9 Nuts!
   Replying to the German demand for
   surrender at Bastogne, Belgium,
   22 December 1944; in *New York Times*
   28 December 1944, p. 4

Mary McCarthy 1912–89

10 Europe is the unfinished negative of which
   America is the proof.
   On the Contrary (1961) 'America the Beautiful'

11 In violence, we forget who we are.
   On the Contrary (1961) 'Characters in Fiction'

12 Every word she writes is a lie, including
   'and' and 'the'.
   Quoting herself on Lillian Hellman in *New
   York Times* 16 February 1980, p. 12

Paul McCartney 1942–

13 Ballads and babies. That's what happened
   to me.
   On reaching the age of fifty; in *Time* 8 June
   1992, p. 84

General George B. McClellan
1826–85

14 All quiet along the Potomac.
   Said at the time of the American Civil War
   (attributed). Cf. 32:14

David McCord 1897–

15 By and by
   God caught his eye.
   'Remainders' (1935); epitaph for a waiter

Horace McCoy 1897–1955

16 They shoot horses don't they.
   Title of novel (1935)

John McCrae 1872–1918

17 In Flanders fields the poppies blow
   Between the crosses, row on row.
   'In Flanders Fields' (1915)

George MacDonald 1824–1905

18 Where did you come from, baby dear?
   Out of the everywhere into here.
   At the Back of the North Wind (1871) ch. 33
   'Song'

William McGonagall *c*.1825–1902

19 Beautiful Railway Bridge of the Silv'ry Tay!
   Alas, I am very sorry to say
   That ninety lives have been taken away
   On the last Sabbath day of 1879,
   Which will be remembered for a very long
   time.
   'The Tay Bridge Disaster'

Roger McGough 1937–

20 You will put on a dress of guilt
   and shoes with broken high ideals.
   'Comeclose and Sleepnow' (1967)

21 Let me die a youngman's death
   Not a clean & in-between-
   The-sheets, holy-water death.
   'Let Me Die a Youngman's Death' (1967)

Jimmy McGregor

22 Oh, he's football crazy, he's football mad
   And the football it has robbed him o' the
   wee bit sense he had.
   And it would take a dozen skivvies, his
   clothes to wash and scrub,
   Since our Jock became a member of that
   terrible football club.
   'Football Crazy' (1960 song)

Niccolò Machiavelli 1469–1527

23 Men should be either treated generously or
   destroyed, because they take revenge for
   slight injuries—for heavy ones they
   cannot.
   The Prince (1513) ch. 3 (tr. A. Gilbert)

1 It is much safer for a prince to be feared than loved, if he is to fail in one of the two.
The Prince (1513) ch. 8 (tr. A. Gilbert)

2 Let no one oppose this belief of mine with that well-worn proverb: 'He who builds on the people builds on mud.'
The Prince (1513) ch. 9 (tr. A. Gilbert)

3 The prince must be a fox, therefore, to recognize the traps and a lion to frighten the wolves.
The Prince (1513) ch. 18 (tr. A. Gilbert)

Fritz Machlup 1902–83

4 Let us remember the unfortunate econometrician who, in one of the major functions of his system, had to use a proxy for risk and a dummy for sex.
In *Journal of Political Economy* July/August 1974, p. 892

Sir James Mackintosh 1765–1832

5 The Commons, faithful to their system, remained in a wise and masterly inactivity.
Vindiciae Gallicae (1791) sect. 1

Alexander Maclaren 1826–1910

6 'The Church is an anvil which has worn out many hammers', and the story of the first collision is, in essentials, the story of all.
Expositions of Holy Scripture: Acts of the Apostles (1907) ch. 4

Don McLean 1945–

7 Something touched me deep inside
The day the music died.
'American Pie' (1972 song, on the death of Buddy Holly)

8 So, bye, bye, Miss American Pie,
Drove my Chevy to the levee
But the levee was dry.
Them good old boys was drinkin' whiskey and rye
Singin' 'This'll be the day that I die.'
'American Pie' (1972 song)

Archibald MacLeish 1892–1982

9 A poem should not mean
But be.
'Ars Poetica' (1926)

Fiona McLeod (William Sharp) 1855–1905

10 My heart is a lonely hunter that hunts on a lonely hill.
'The Lonely Hunter' (1896) st. 6

Marshall McLuhan 1911–80

11 The new electronic interdependence recreates the world in the image of a global village.
The Gutenberg Galaxy (1962) p. 31

12 The medium is the message.
Understanding Media (1964) ch. 1 (title)

Comte de Macmahon 1808–93

13 J'y suis, j'y reste.
Here I am, and here I stay.
At the taking of the Malakoff fortress, 8 September 1855. See G. Hanotaux *Histoire de la France Contemporaine* (1903–8) vol. 2, ch. 1, sect. 1

Harold Macmillan 1894–1986

14 Forever poised between a cliché and an indiscretion.
In *Newsweek* 30 April 1956 (on the life of a Foreign Secretary)

15 Let us be frank about it: most of our people have never had it so good.
Speech at Bedford, 20 July 1957, in *The Times* 22 July 1957 ('You Never Had It So Good' was the Democratic Party slogan during the 1952 US election campaign)

16 I thought the best thing to do was to settle up these little local difficulties, and then turn to the wider vision of the Commonwealth.
Statement at London airport on leaving for a Commonwealth tour, 7 January 1958, following the resignation of the Chancellor of the Exchequer and others; in *The Times* 8 January 1958

17 The wind of change is blowing through this continent, and, whether we like it or not, this growth of [African] national consciousness is a political fact.
Speech at Cape Town, 3 February 1960, in *Pointing the Way* (1972) p. 475

18 I was determined that no British government should be brought down by the action of two tarts.
Comment on the Profumo affair, July 1963; in A. Sampson *Macmillan* (1967) p. 243

19 There are three bodies no sensible man directly challenges: the Roman Catholic Church, the Brigade of Guards and the National Union of Mineworkers.
In *Observer* 22 February 1981. Cf. 27:8

20 First of all the Georgian silver goes, and then all that nice furniture that used to be in the saloon. Then the Canalettos go.
Speech on privatization to the Tory Reform Group, 8 November 1985; in *The Times* 9 November 1985

Louis MacNeice 1907–63

21 Better authentic mammon than a bogus god.
Autumn Journal (1939) p. 49

1 It's no go the merrygoround, it's no go the
rickshaw,
All we want is a limousine and a ticket for
the peepshow.
'Bagpipe Music' (1938)

2 It's no go the picture palace, it's no go the
stadium,
It's no go the country cot with a pot of
pink geraniums,
It's no go the Government grants, it's no
go the elections,
Sit on your arse for fifty years and hang
your hat on a pension.
'Bagpipe Music' (1938)

3 The glass is falling hour by hour, the glass
will fall for ever,
But if you break the bloody glass you won't
hold up the weather.
'Bagpipe Music' (1938)

4 Crumbling between the fingers, under the
feet,
Crumbling behind the eyes,
Their world gives way and dies
And something twangs and breaks at the
end of the street.
'Débâcle' (1941)

5 Time was away and somewhere else,
There were two glasses and two chairs
And two people with the one pulse.
'Meeting Point' (1941)

6 I am not yet born; O fill me
With strength against those who would
freeze my
humanity.
'Prayer Before Birth' (1944)

7 Let them not make me a stone and let
them not spill me,
Otherwise kill me.
'Prayer Before Birth' (1944)

8 The drunkenness of things being various.
'Snow' (1935)

9 Down the road someone is practising
scales,
The notes like little fishes vanish with
a wink of tails,
Man's heart expands to tinker with his car
For this is Sunday morning, Fate's great
bazaar.
'Sunday Morning' (1935)

10 The sunlight on the garden
Hardens and grows cold,
We cannot cage the minute
Within its net of gold.
'Sunlight on the Garden' (1938)

11 By a high star our course is set,
Our end is Life. Put out to sea.
'Thalassa' (1964)

Geoffrey Madan 1895–1947

12 The great tragedy of the classical
languages is to have been born twins.
Geoffrey Madan's Notebooks (1981) p. 67

13 The dust of exploded beliefs may make
a fine sunset.
Livre sans nom: Twelve Reflections (privately
printed 1934) no. 12

Samuel Madden 1686–1765

14 Words are men's daughters, but God's sons
are things.
Boulter's Monument (1745) l. 377. Cf. 182:4

Maurice Maeterlinck 1862–1949

15 Il n'y a pas de morts.
There are no dead.
L'Oiseau bleu (1909) act 4

Magna Carta 1215

16 Except by the lawful judgement of his
peers or by the law of the land.
Clause 39

17 To no man will we sell, or deny, or delay,
right or justice.
Clause 40

Josephe de Maistre 1753–1821

18 Every country has the government it
deserves.
Lettres et Opuscules Inédits (1851) vol. 1, letter
53 (15 August 1811)

John Major 1943–

19 Society needs to condemn a little more and
understand a little less.
Interview with Mail on Sunday 21 February
1993

Stéphane Mallarmé 1842–98

20 La chair est triste, hélas! et j'ai lu tous les livres.
The flesh, alas, is wearied; and I have read
all the books there are.
'Brise Marin' (1887)

David Mallet (or Malloch)
c.1705–65

21 O grant me, Heaven, a middle state,
Neither too humble nor too great;
More than enough, for nature's ends,
With something left to treat my friends.
'Imitation of Horace'. Cf. 174:4

George Leigh Mallory 1886–1924

22 Because it's there.
On being asked why he wanted to climb
Mount Everest; in New York Times 18 March
1923

Sir Thomas Malory d. 1471

23 Whoso pulleth out this sword of this stone
and anvil is rightwise King born of all
England.
Le Morte D'Arthur (finished 1470, printed by
Caxton 1485) bk. 1, ch. 4

1 Ah, my little son, thou hast murdered thy mother! ... When he is christened let call him Tristram, that is as much to say as a sorrowful birth.
Le Morte D'Arthur (1485) bk. 8, ch. 1

2 God defend me, said Dinadan, for the joy of love is too short, and the sorrow thereof, and what cometh thereof, dureth over long.
Le Morte D'Arthur (1485) bk. 10, ch. 56

3 Therefore all ye that be lovers call unto your remembrance the month of May, like as did Queen Guenevere, for whom I make here a little mention, that while she lived she was a true lover, and therefore she had a good end.
Le Morte D'Arthur (1485) bk. 18, ch. 25

André Malraux 1901–76

4 *L'art est un anti-destin.*
Art is a revolt against fate.
Les Voix du silence (1951) pt. 4, ch. 7

Thomas Robert Malthus 1766–1834

5 Population, when unchecked, increases in a geometrical ratio. Subsistence only increases in an arithmetical ratio.
Essay on the Principle of Population (1798) ch. 1

6 The perpetual struggle for room and food.
Essay on the Principle of Population (1798) ch. 3

Lord Mancroft 1914–

7 Cricket—a game which the English, not being a spiritual people, have invented in order to give themselves some conception of eternity.
Bees in Some Bonnets (1979) p. 185

W. R. Mandale

8 Up and down the City Road,
In and out the Eagle,
That's the way the money goes—
Pop goes the weasel!
'Pop Goes the Weasel' (1853 song); also attributed to Charles Twiggs

Winnie Mandela 1934–

9 With that stick of matches, with our necklace, we shall liberate this country.
Speech in black townships, 14 April 1986; in *Guardian* 15 April 1986

Osip Mandelstam 1892–1938

10 The age is rocking the wave
with human grief
to a golden beat, and an adder
is breathing in time with it in the grass.
'The Age' (1923, tr. C. M. Bowra)

11 Perhaps my whisper was already born before my lips.
Selected Poems (1973, tr. D. McDuff) 'Poems Published Posthumously' (written 1934)

Joseph L. Mankiewicz 1909–

12 Fasten your seat-belts, it's going to be a bumpy night.
All About Eve (1950 film); spoken by Bette Davis

Thomas Mann 1875–1955

13 We come out of the dark and go into the dark again, and in between lie the experiences of our life.
The Magic Mountain (1924) ch. 6, sect. 8 (tr. H. T. Lowe-Porter)

14 A man's dying is more the survivors' affair than his own.
The Magic Mountain (1924) ch. 6, sect. 8 (tr. H. T. Lowe-Porter)

Katherine Mansfield 1888–1923

15 Whenever I prepare for a journey I prepare as though for death. Should I never return, all is in order.
Journal (1927) p. 224 (29 January 1922)

Lord Mansfield 1705–93

16 Consider what you think justice requires, and decide accordingly. But never give your reasons; for your judgement will probably be right, but your reasons will certainly be wrong.
In Lord Campbell *Lives of the Chief Justices of England* (1849) vol. 2, ch. 40

Richard Mant 1776–1848

17 Bright the vision that delighted
Once the sight of Judah's seer;
Sweet the countless tongues united
To entrance the prophet's ear.
'Bright the vision that delighted' (1837 hymn)

Mao Tse-tung 1893–1976

18 Politics is war without bloodshed while war is politics with bloodshed.
Lecture, 1938, in *Selected Works* (1965) vol. 2, p. 153

19 Every Communist must grasp the truth, 'Political power grows out of the barrel of a gun'.
Speech, 6 November 1938, in *Selected Works* (1965) vol. 2, p. 224

20 The atom bomb is a paper tiger which the United States reactionaries use to scare people. It looks terrible, but in fact it isn't ... All reactionaries are paper tigers.
Interview, 1946, in *Selected Works* (1961) vol. 4, p. 100

1 Letting a hundred flowers blossom and
a hundred schools of thought contend is
the policy for promoting progress in the
arts and the sciences and a flourishing
socialist culture in our land.

  Speech in Peking, 27 February 1957, in
  Quotations of Chairman Mao (1966) p. 302

William Learned Marcy
1786–1857

2 The politicians of New York ... see nothing
wrong in the rule, that to the victor belong
the spoils of the enemy.

  Speech, 25 January 1832, in J. Parton *Life of
  Andrew Jackson* (1860) vol. 3, ch. 29

Marie-Antoinette 1755–93

3 *Qu'ils mangent de la brioche.*
Let them eat cake.

  On being told that her people had no bread.
  In *Confessions* (1740) Rousseau refers to
  a similar remark being a well-known saying;
  in *Relation d'un Voyage à Bruxelles et à Coblentz
  en 1791* (1823) p. 59, Louis XVIII attributes
  'Why don't they eat pastry?' to Marie-Thérèse
  (1638–83), wife of Louis XIV

Edwin Markham 1852–1940

4 A thing that grieves not and that never
hopes,
Stolid and stunned, a brother to the ox?

  'The Man with the Hoe' (1899)

Sarah, Duchess of Marlborough
1660–1744

5 The Duke returned from the wars today
and did pleasure me in his top-boots.

  Attributed in various forms. See I. Butler
  Rule of Three (1967) ch. 7

Bob Marley 1945–81

6 Get up, stand up
Stand up for your rights
Get up, stand up
Never give up the fight.

  'Get up, Stand up' (1973 song)

7 I shot the sheriff
But I swear it was in self-defence
I shot the sheriff
And they say it is a capital offence.

  'I Shot the Sheriff' (1974 song)

Christopher Marlowe 1564–93

8 I'll have them fly to India for gold,
Ransack the ocean for orient pearl.

  Doctor Faustus (1604) act 1, sc. 1

9 Why, this is hell, nor am I out of it.

  Doctor Faustus (1604) act 1, sc. 3

10 Hell hath no limits nor is circumscribed
In one self place, where we are is Hell,
And to be short, when all the world
dissolves,
And every creature shall be purified,
All places shall be hell that are not heaven.

  Doctor Faustus (1604) act 2, sc. 1

11 Was this the face that launched a thousand
ships,
And burnt the topless towers of Ilium?
Sweet Helen, make me immortal with
a kiss!

  Doctor Faustus (1604) act 5, sc. 1

12 Now hast thou but one bare hour to live,
And then thou must be damned
perpetually.
Stand still, you ever-moving spheres of
heaven,
That time may cease, and midnight never
come.

  Doctor Faustus (1604) act 5, sc. 2

13 *O lente lente currite noctis equi.*
The stars move still, time runs, the clock
will strike,
The devil will come, and Faustus must be
damned.
O I'll leap up to my God: who pulls me
down?
See, see, where Christ's blood streams in
the firmament.
One drop would save my soul, half a drop,
ah my Christ.

  Doctor Faustus (1604) act 5, sc. 2

14 Cut is the branch that might have grown
full straight,
And burnèd is Apollo's laurel bough,
That sometime grew within this learned
man.

  Doctor Faustus (1604) epilogue

15 My men, like satyrs grazing on the lawns,
Shall with their goat feet dance an antic
hay.

  Edward II (1593) act 1, sc. 1

16 Base Fortune, now I see, that in thy wheel
There is a point, to which when men
aspire,
They tumble headlong down.

  Edward II (1593) act 5, sc. 6

17 It lies not in our power to love, or hate,
For will in us is over-ruled by fate.

  Hero and Leander (1598) First Sestiad, l. 167

18 Where both deliberate, the love is slight;
Who ever loved that loved not at first
sight?

  Hero and Leander (1598) First Sestiad, l. 175.
  Cf. 273:7

19 I count religion but a childish toy,
And hold there is no sin but ignorance.

  The Jew of Malta (c.1592) prologue

1 Thus methinks should men of judgement
frame
Their means of traffic from the vulgar
trade,
And, as their wealth increaseth, so enclose
Infinite riches in a little room.
The Jew of Malta (c.1592) act 1, sc. 1

2 BARNARDINE: Thou hast committed—
BARABAS: Fornication? But that was in
another country: and besides, the wench
is dead.
The Jew of Malta (c.1592) act 4, sc. 1

3 Come live with me, and be my love,
And we will all the pleasures prove,
That valleys, groves, hills and fields,
Woods or steepy mountain yields.
'The Passionate Shepherd to his Love'.
Cf. 123:23, 257:20

4 From jigging veins of rhyming mother-
wits,
And such conceits as clownage keeps in
pay,
We'll lead you to the stately tents of war.
Tamburlaine the Great (1590) pt. 1, prologue

5 Our swords shall play the orators for us.
Tamburlaine the Great (1590) pt. 1, act 1, sc. 2

6 His looks do menace heaven and dare the
Gods.
Tamburlaine the Great (1590) pt. 1, act 1, sc. 2

7 Is it not passing brave to be a king,
And ride in triumph through Persepolis?
Tamburlaine the Great (1590) pt. 1, act 2, sc. 5

8 The ripest fruit of all,
That perfect bliss and sole felicity,
The sweet fruition of an earthly crown.
Tamburlaine the Great (1590) pt. 1, act 2, sc. 7

9 Virtue is the fount whence honour springs.
Tamburlaine the Great (1590) pt. 1, act 4, sc. 4

10 Ah fair Zenocrate, divine Zenocrate,
Fair is too foul an epithet for thee.
Tamburlaine the Great (1590) pt. 1, act 5, sc. 5

11 Now walk the angels on the walls of
heaven,
As sentinels to warn th' immortal souls,
To entertain divine Zenocrate.
Tamburlaine the Great (1590) pt. 2, act 2, sc. 4

12 Yet let me kiss my Lord before I die,
And let me die with kissing of my Lord.
Tamburlaine the Great (1590) pt. 2, act 2, sc. 4

13 More childish valorous than manly wise.
Tamburlaine the Great (1590) pt. 2, act 4, sc. 1

14 Holla, ye pampered jades of Asia!
What, can ye draw but twenty miles a day?
Tamburlaine the Great (1590) pt. 2, act 4, sc. 3

Don Marquis 1878–1937

15 procrastination is the
art of keeping
up with yesterday.
archy and mehitabel (1927) 'certain maxims of
archy'

16 an optimist is a guy
that has never had
much experience.
archy and mehitabel (1927) 'certain maxims of
archy'

17 it s cheerio
my deario that
pulls a lady through.
archy and mehitabel (1927) 'cheerio, my deario'

18 I have got you out here
in the great open spaces
where cats are cats.
archy and mehitabel (1927) 'mehitabel has an
adventure'

19 but wotthehell archy wotthehell
jamais triste archy jamais triste
that is my motto.
archy and mehitabel (1927) 'mehitabel sees
paris'

20 boss there is always
a comforting thought
in time of trouble when
it is not our trouble.
archy does his part (1935) 'comforting
thoughts'

21 now and then
there is a person born
who is so unlucky
that he runs into accidents
which started to happen
to somebody else.
archys life of mehitabel (1933) 'archy says'

22 Writing a book of poetry is like dropping
a rose petal down the Grand Canyon and
waiting for the echo.
In E. Anthony *O Rare Don Marquis* (1962)
p. 146

23 The art of newspaper paragraphing is to
stroke a platitude until it purrs like an
epigram.
In E. Anthony *O Rare Don Marquis* (1962)
p. 354

John Marriot 1780–1825

24 Thou, whose eternal Word
Chaos and darkness heard,
And took their flight,
Hear us, we humbly pray,
And, where the Gospel-day
Sheds not its glorious ray,
Let there be light!
'Thou, whose eternal Word' (hymn written
c.1813); 'almighty' substituted for 'eternal'
from 1861

Captain Marryat 1792–1848

25 There's no getting blood out of a turnip.
Japhet, in Search of a Father (1836) ch. 4

26 As savage as a bear with a sore head.
The King's Own (1830) vol. 2, ch. 6

27 If you please, ma'am, it was a very little
one.
Mr Midshipman Easy (1836) ch. 3 (the nurse,
excusing her illegitimate baby)

1 All zeal, Mr Easy.
Mr Midshipman Easy (1836) ch. 9

Arthur Marshall 1910–89

2 What, knocked a tooth out? Never mind, dear, laugh it off, laugh it off; it's all part of life's rich pageant.
The Games Mistress (recorded monologue, 1937)

Thomas R. Marshall 1854–1925

3 What this country needs is a really good 5-cent cigar.
In *New York Tribune* 4 January 1920, pt. 7, p. 1

Martial AD *c*.40–*c*.104

4 *Non amo te, Sabidi, nec possum dicere quare: Hoc tantum possum dicere, non amo te.*
I don't love you, Sabidius, and I can't tell you why; all I can tell you is this, that I don't love you.
Epigrammata bk. 1, no. 32. Cf. 73:18

5 *Laudant illa sed ista legunt.*
They praise those works, but read these.
Epigrammata bk. 4, no. 49

6 *Non est vivere, sed valere vita est.*
Life's not just being alive, but being well.
Epigrammata bk. 6, no. 70

7 *Difficilis facilis, iucundus acerbus es idem: Nec tecum possum vivere nec sine te.*
Difficult or easy, pleasant or bitter, you are the same you: I cannot live with you—or without you.
Epigrammata bk. 12, no. 46 (47)

8 *Rus in urbe.*
Country in the town.
Epigrammata bk. 12, no. 57

Andrew Marvell 1621–78

9 Where the remote Bermudas ride
In the ocean's bosom unespied.
'Bermudas' (*c*.1653)

10 He hangs in shades the orange bright,
Like golden lamps in a green night.
'Bermudas' (*c*.1653)

11 Echo beyond the Mexique Bay.
'Bermudas' (*c*.1653)

12 My love is of a birth as rare
As 'tis for object strange and high:
It was begotten by Despair
Upon Impossibility.

Magnanimous Despair alone
Could show me so divine a thing,
Where feeble Hope could ne'er have flown
But vainly flapped its tinsel wing.
'The Definition of Love' (1681)

13 As lines (so loves) oblique may well
Themselves in every angle greet:
But ours so truly parallel,
Though infinite, can never meet.

Therefore the love which us doth bind,
But Fate so enviously debars,
Is the conjunction of the mind,
And opposition of the stars.
'The Definition of Love' (1681)

14 How vainly men themselves amaze
To win the palm, the oak, or bays.
'The Garden' (1681) st. 1

15 What wondrous life is this I lead!
Ripe apples drop about my head;
The luscious clusters of the vine
Upon my mouth do crush their wine;
The nectarine, and curious peach,
Into my hands themselves do reach;
Stumbling on melons, as I pass,
Ensnared with flowers, I fall on grass.
'The Garden' (1681) st. 5

16 Annihilating all that's made
To a green thought in a green shade.
'The Garden' (1681) st. 6

17 Two paradises 'twere in one
To live in paradise alone.
'The Garden' (1681) st. 8

18 *He* nothing common did or mean
Upon that memorable scene.
'An Horatian Ode upon Cromwell's Return from Ireland' (written 1650) l. 57 (on the execution of Charles I)

19 So much one man can do,
That does both act and know.
'An Horatian Ode upon Cromwell's Return from Ireland' (1650) l. 75

20 Ye living lamps, by whose dear light
The nightingale does sit so late.
'The Mower to the Glow-worms' (1681)

21 Ye country comets, that portend
No war, nor prince's funeral.
'The Mower to the Glow-worms' (1681)

22 Had we but world enough, and time,
This coyness, lady, were no crime.
'To His coy Mistress' (1681) l. 1

23   I would
Love you ten years before the flood:
And you should, if you please, refuse
Till the conversion of the Jews.
My vegetable love should grow
Vaster than empires, and more slow.
'To His coy Mistress' (1681) l. 7

24 But at my back I always hear
Time's wingèd chariot hurrying near:
And yonder all before us lie
Deserts of vast eternity.
'To His coy Mistress' (1681) l. 21

25 The grave's a fine and private place,
But none, I think, do there embrace.
'To His Coy Mistress' (1681) l. 31

1 Let us roll all our strength, and all
Our sweetness, up into one ball:
And tear our pleasures with rough strife,
Thorough the iron gates of life.
Thus, though we cannot make our sun
Stand still, yet we will make him run.
  'To His Coy Mistress' (1681) l. 41

2 'Tis not what once it was, the world,
But a rude heap together hurled.
  'Upon Appleton House' (1681) st. 96

3 But now the salmon-fishers moist
Their leathern boats begin to hoist;
And, like Antipodes in shoes,
Have shod their heads in their canoes.
How tortoise-like, but not so slow,
These rational amphibii go!
  'Upon Appleton House' (1681) st. 97

Holt Marvell 1901–69

4 A cigarette that bears a lipstick's traces,
An airline ticket to romantic places.
  'These Foolish Things Remind Me of You'
  (1935 song)

Groucho Marx 1895–1977

5 PLEASE ACCEPT MY RESIGNATION. I DON'T
WANT TO BELONG TO ANY CLUB THAT WILL
ACCEPT ME AS A MEMBER.
  Groucho and Me (1959) ch. 26

6 Either he's dead, or my watch has stopped.
  In A Day at the Races (1937 film; script by
  Robert Pirosh, George Seaton, and George
  Oppenheimer)

7 I never forget a face, but in your case I'll be
glad to make an exception.
  In Leo Rosten People I have Loved, Known or
  Admired (1970) 'Groucho'
  See also BERT KALMAR

Karl Marx 1818–83

8 Religion ... is the opium of the people.
  A Contribution to the Critique of Hegel's
  Philosophy of Right (1843–4) introduction.
  Cf. 195:18

9 From each according to his abilities, to
each according to his needs.
  Critique of the Gotha Programme (written 1875,
  but of earlier origin). See Morelly Code de la
  nature (1755) pt. 4, p. 190, and J. Blanc
  Organisation du travail (1839) p. 126.
  Cf. 27:1

10 Hegel says somewhere that all great events
and personalities in world history reappear
in one fashion or another. He forgot to
add: the first time as tragedy, the second
as farce.
  Eighteenth Brumaire of Louis Bonaparte (1852)
  sect. 1. Cf. 164:18

11 The philosophers have only interpreted the
world in various ways; the point is to
change it.
  Theses on Feuerbach (written 1845) no. 11

12 The class struggle necessarily leads to the
dictatorship of the proletariat.
  Letter to Weydemeyer, 5 March 1852. Marx
  claimed that 'dictatorship of the proletariat'
  had been coined by Auguste Blanqui
  (1805–81), but it has not been found in his
  work

Karl Marx 1818–83 and Friedrich Engels 1820–95

13 A spectre is haunting Europe—the spectre
of Communism.
  The Communist Manifesto (1848) opening words

14 The history of all hitherto existing society
is the history of class struggles.
  The Communist Manifesto (1848) pt. 1

15 The proletarians have nothing to lose but
their chains. They have a world to win.
WORKING MEN OF ALL COUNTRIES, UNITE!
  The Communist Manifesto (1848) ad fin. (from
  the 1888 translation by Samuel Moore,
  edited by Engels and commonly rendered
  'Workers of the world, unite!')

Mary, Queen of Scots 1542–87

16 En ma fin git mon commencement.
In my end is my beginning.
  Motto. Cf. 133:2

Mary Tudor 1516–58

17 When I am dead and opened, you shall find
'Calais' lying in my heart.
  Holinshed's Chronicles vol. 4 (1808 ed.) p. 137

John Masefield 1878–1967

18 Quinquireme of Nineveh from distant
  Ophir
Rowing home to haven in sunny Palestine,
With a cargo of ivory,
And apes and peacocks,
Sandalwood, cedarwood, and sweet white
  wine.
  'Cargoes' (1903). Cf. 41:31

19 Dirty British coaster with a salt-caked
  smoke stack,
Butting through the Channel in the mad
  March days,
With a cargo of Tyne coal,
Road-rails, pig lead,
Firewood, ironware, and cheap tin trays.
  'Cargoes' (1903)

20 And fifteen arms went round her waist.
(And then men ask, Are Barmaids Chaste?)
  'The Everlasting Mercy' (1911) st. 26

21 I must go down to the sea again, to the
lonely sea and the sky,
And all I ask is a tall ship and a star to
steer her by.
  'Sea Fever' (misprinted 'I must down to the
  seas' in the 1902 original)

1 I must go down to the sea again, for the
   call of the running tide
   Is a wild call and a clear call that may not
   be denied.
   'Sea Fever' (1902)

2 I must go down to the sea again, to the
   vagrant gypsy life,
   To the gull's way and the whale's way
   where the wind's like a whetted knife;
   And all I ask is a merry yarn from
   a laughing fellow-rover,
   And quiet sleep and a sweet dream when
   the long trick's over.
   'Sea Fever' (1902)

Philip Massinger 1583–1640

3 Ambition, in a private man a vice,
   Is in a prince the virtue.
   The Bashful Lover (licensed 1636) act 1, sc. 2

4   Pray enter
   You are learned Europeans and we worse
   Than ignorant Americans.
   The City Madam (licensed 1632) act 3, sc. 3

5 Oh that thou hadst like others been all
   words,
   And no performance.
   The Parliament of Love (1624) act 4, sc. 2

6 Death has a thousand doors to let out life.
   A Very Woman (licensed 1634) act 5, sc. 4.
   Cf. 142:4, 270:8, 344:18

Sir James Mathew 1830–1908

7 In England, justice is open to all—like the
   Ritz Hotel.
   In R. E. Megarry *Miscellany-at-Law* (1955)
   p. 254. Cf. 7:9

W. Somerset Maugham 1874–1965

8 The most useful thing about a principle is
   that it can always be sacrificed to
   expediency.
   The Circle (1921) act 3

9 Impropriety is the soul of wit.
   The Moon and Sixpence (1919) ch. 4

10 A woman can forgive a man for the harm
   he does her, but she can never forgive him
   for the sacrifices he makes on her account.
   The Moon and Sixpence (1919) ch. 41

11 Money is like a sixth sense without which
   you cannot make a complete use of the
   other five.
   Of Human Bondage (1915) ch. 51

12 Few misfortunes can befall a boy which
   bring worse consequences than to have
   a really affectionate mother.
   A Writer's Notebook (1949) p. 27 (written in
   1896)

Bill Mauldin 1921–

13 I feel like a fugitive from th' law of
   averages.
   Cartoon caption in *Up Front* (1945)

James Maxton 1885–1946

14 All I say is, if you cannot ride two horses
   you have no right in the circus.
   Opposing disaffiliation of the Scottish
   Independent Labour Party from the Labour
   Party, in *Daily Herald* 12 January 1931
   (usually quoted ' . . . no right in the bloody
   circus')

Vladimir Mayakovsky 1893–1930

15 If you wish—
   . . . I'll be irreproachably tender;
   not a man, but—a cloud in trousers!
   'The Cloud in Trousers' (1915) (tr. S.
   Charteris)

16 The poet is always indebted to the
   universe, paying interest and fines on
   sorrow.
   'Conversation with an Inspector of Taxes
   about Poetry' (1926) (tr. D. Obolensky)

Shepherd Mead 1914–

17 How to succeed in business without really
   trying.
   Title of book (1952)

Hughes Mearns 1875–1965

18 As I was walking up the stair
   I met a man who wasn't there.
   He wasn't there again today.
   I wish, I wish he'd stay away.
   Lines written for an amateur play *The
   Psycho-ed* (1910) and set to music in 1939 as
   'The Little Man Who Wasn't There'

Dame Nellie Melba 1861–1931

19 Sing 'em muck! It's all they can
   understand!
   Advice to Dame Clara Butt, prior to her
   departure for Australia; in W. H. Ponder
   Clara Butt (1928) ch. 12

Lord Melbourne 1779–1848

20 Now, is it to lower the price of corn, or
   isn't it? It is not much matter which we
   say, but mind, we must all say *the same*.
   Attributed, in Walter Bagehot *The English
   Constitution* (1867) ch. 1, p. 16 n.

21 God help the Minister that meddles with
   art!
   In Lord David Cecil *Lord M* (1954) ch. 3

22 What I want is men who will support me
   when I am in the wrong.
   Replying to a politician who said 'I will
   support you as long as you are in the right';
   in Lord David Cecil *Lord M* (1954) ch. 4

23 Things have come to a pretty pass when
   religion is allowed to invade the sphere of
   private life.
   On hearing an evangelical sermon; in
   G. W. E. Russell *Collections and Recollections*
   (1898) ch. 6

Herman Melville 1819–91

1 Call me Ishmael.
Moby Dick (1851) ch. 1

2 Delight,—top-gallant delight is to him,
who acknowledges no law or lord, but the
Lord his God, and is only a patriot to
heaven.
Moby Dick (1851) ch. 9

3 A whaleship was my Yale College and my
Harvard.
Moby Dick (1851) ch. 24

4 Towards thee I roll, thou all-destroying but
unconquering whale ... from hell's heart I
stab at thee.
Moby Dick (1851) ch. 135

Menander 342–c.292 BC

5 Whom the gods love dies young.
Dis Exapaton fragment 4, in F. H. Sandbach
(ed.) *Menandri Reliquiae Selectae* (1990)

H. L. Mencken 1880–1956

6 Love is the delusion that one woman
differs from another.
Chrestomathy (1949) ch. 30

7 Puritanism. The haunting fear that
someone, somewhere, may be happy.
Chrestomathy (1949) ch. 30

8 Conscience: the inner voice which warns
us that someone may be looking.
A Little Book in C major (1916) p. 42

Johnny Mercer 1909–76

9 You've got to ac-cent-tchu-ate the positive
Elim-my-nate the negative
Latch on to the affirmative
Don't mess with Mister In-between.
'Ac-cent-tchu-ate the Positive' (1944 song)

10 Jeepers Creepers—where you get them
peepers?
'Jeepers Creepers' (1938 song)

11 We're drinking my friend,
To the end of a brief episode,
Make it one for my baby
And one more for the road.
'One For My Baby' (1943 song)

George Meredith 1828–1909

12 A witty woman is a treasure; a witty
beauty is a power.
Diana of the Crossways (1885) ch. 1

13 'Tis Ireland gives England her soldiers, her
generals too.
Diana of the Crossways (1885) ch. 2

14 Cynicism is intellectual dandyism without
the coxcomb's feathers.
The Egoist (1879) ch. 7

15 None of your dam punctilio.
One of Our Conquerors (1891) ch. 1

16 I expect that Woman will be the last thing
civilized by Man.
The Ordeal of Richard Feverel (1859) ch. 1

17 Kissing don't last: cookery do!
The Ordeal of Richard Feverel (1859) ch. 28

18 Speech is the small change of silence.
The Ordeal of Richard Feverel (1859) ch. 34

19 The lark ascending.
Title of poem (1881)

20 She whom I love is hard to catch and
conquer,
Hard, but O the glory of the winning were
she won!
'Love in the Valley' st. 2

21 On a starred night Prince Lucifer uprose.
Tired of his dark dominion swung the
fiend.
'Lucifer in Starlight' (1883)

22 Around the ancient track marched, rank
on rank,
The army of unalterable law.
'Lucifer in Starlight' (1883)

23 'I play for Seasons; not Eternities!'
Says Nature.
Modern Love (1862) st. 13

24 Ah, what a dusty answer gets the soul
When hot for certainties in this our life!
Modern Love (1862) st. 50

Owen Meredith (Earl of Lytton) 1831–91

25 Genius does what it must, and Talent does
what it can.
'Last Words of a Sensitive Second-Rate Poet'
(1868)

Dixon Lanier Merritt 1879–1972

26 Oh, a wondrous bird is the pelican!
His beak holds more than his belican.
He takes in his beak
Food enough for a week.
But I'll be darned if I know how the
helican.
In *Nashville Banner* 22 April 1913

Le Curé Meslier c.1664–1733

27 An ignorant, uneducated man [said he
wished] that all the great men in the world
and all the nobility could be hanged, and
strangled with the guts of priests.
Testament (ed. R. Charles, 1864) vol. 1, ch. 2
(often quoted 'I should like ... the last of the
kings to be strangled with the guts of the
last priest')

Methodist Service Book 1975

28 I am no longer my own, but yours. Put me
to what you will, rank me with whom you
will; put me to doing, put me to suffering.
The Covenant Prayer (based on the words of
Richard Alleine in the First Covenant
Service, 1782)

Prince Metternich 1773–1859

1 The Emperor is everything, Vienna is nothing.
  Letter to Count Bombelles, 5 June 1848, in Aus Metternich's Nachgelassenen Papieren (ed. A. von Klinkowström, 1880) vol. 8, p. 426

2 Error has never approached my spirit.
  Addressed to Guizot in 1848, in F. Guizot *Mémoires* (1858–67) vol. 4, p. 21

3 Italy is a geographical expression.
  Discussing the Italian question with Palmerston in 1847; in Mémoires, Documents, etc. de Metternich publiés par son fils (1883) vol. 7, p. 415

Sir Anthony Meyer 1920–

4 I question the right of that great Moloch, national sovereignty, to burn its children to save its pride.
  Speaking against the Falklands War, 1982; in Listener 27 September 1990, p. 31

Thomas Middleton c.1580–1627

5 Anything for a quiet life.
  Title of play (c.1620, possibly with John Webster)

6 I could not get the ring without the finger.
  The Changeling (with William Rowley, c.1622) act 3, sc. 4

7 Y'are the deed's creature.
  The Changeling (with William Rowley, c.1622) act 3, sc. 4

8 My study's ornament, thou shell of death, Once the bright face of my betrothèd lady.
  The Revenger's Tragedy (1607, previously attributed to Cyril Tourneur, c.1575–1626) act 1, sc. 1

9 Does the silk-worm expend her yellow labours
  For thee? for thee does she undo herself?
  The Revenger's Tragedy (1607) act 3, sc. 5

George Mikes 1912–

10 On the Continent people have good food; in England people have good table manners.
  How to be an Alien (1946) p. 10

11 Continental people have sex life; the English have hot-water bottles.
  How to be an Alien (1946) p. 25

12 An Englishman, even if he is alone, forms an orderly queue of one.
  How to be an Alien (1946) p. 44

John Stuart Mill 1806–73

13 Ask yourself whether you are happy, and you cease to be so.
  Autobiography (1873) ch. 5

14 Detention by the State of the unearned increment of rent.
  Dissertations and Discussions vol. 4 (1875) 'The Right of Property in Land'

15 The only purpose for which power can be rightfully exercised over any member of a civilized community, against his will, is to prevent harm to others. His own good, either physical or moral, is not a sufficient warrant.
  On Liberty (1859) ch. 1

16 The liberty of the individual must be thus far limited; he must not make himself a nuisance to other people.
  On Liberty (1859) ch. 3

17 Liberty consists in doing what one desires.
  On Liberty (1859) ch. 5

18 Everyone who desires power, desires it most over those who are nearest to him, with whom his life is passed, with whom he has most concerns in common, and in whom any independence of his authority is oftenest likely to interfere with his individual preferences.
  The Subjection of Women (1869) ch. 1

19 The laws of most countries are far worse than the people who execute them, and many of them are only able to remain laws by being seldom or never carried into effect. If married life were all that it might be expected to be, looking to the laws alone, society would be a hell upon earth.
  The Subjection of Women (1869) ch. 2

20 The true virtue of human beings is fitness to live together as equals; claiming nothing for themselves but what they as freely concede to everyone else; regarding command of any kind as an exceptional necessity, and in all cases a temporary one.
  The Subjection of Women (1869) ch. 2

Edna St Vincent Millay 1892–1950

21 Childhood is the kingdom where nobody dies.
  Nobody that matters, that is.
  'Childhood is the Kingdom where Nobody dies' (1934)

22 My candle burns at both ends;
  It will not last the night;
  But ah, my foes, and oh, my friends—
  It gives a lovely light.
  A Few Figs From Thistles (1920) 'First Fig'

23 After all, my erstwhile dear,
  My no longer cherished,
  Need we say it was not love,
  Now that love is perished?
  'Passer Mortuus Est' (1921)

Alice Duer Miller 1874–1942

24 I am American bred,
  I have seen much to hate here—much to forgive,
  But in a world where England is finished and dead,
  I do not wish to live.
  The White Cliffs (1940) p. 70

Arthur Miller 1915–

1 A suicide kills two people, Maggie, that's what it's for!
   After the Fall (1964) act 2

2 The world is an oyster, but you don't crack it open on a mattress.
   Death of a Salesman (1949) act 1

3 Willy Loman never made a lot of money. His name was never in the paper. He's not the finest character that ever lived. But he's a human being, and a terrible thing is happening to him. So attention must be paid.
   Death of a Salesman (1949) act 1

4 He's a man way out there in the blue, riding on a smile and a shoeshine. And when they start not smiling back—that's an earthquake ... A salesman is got to dream, boy. It comes with the territory.
   Death of a Salesman (1949) 'Requiem'

5 This is Red Hook, not Sicily ... This is the gullet of New York swallowing the tonnage of the world.
   A View from the Bridge (1955) act 1

6 A good newspaper, I suppose, is a nation talking to itself.
   In *Observer* 26 November 1961

Henry Miller 1891–1980

7 Every man with a bellyful of the classics is an enemy to the human race.
   Tropic of Cancer (1934) p. 280

Jonathan Miller 1934–

8 I'm not really a *Jew*. Just Jew-*ish*. Not the whole hog, you know.
   Beyond the Fringe (1960 review) 'Real Class'

William Miller 1810–72

9 Wee Willie Winkie rins through the town, Up stairs and down stairs in his nicht-gown.
   'Willie Winkie' (1841)

Spike Milligan 1918–

10 You silly twisted boy.
   The Goon Show (BBC radio series) 'The Dreaded Batter Pudding Hurler' (12 October 1954)

11 Money couldn't buy friends but you got a better class of enemy.
   Puckoon (1963) ch. 6

A. J. Mills et al.

12 Take me back to dear old Blighty.
   Title of song (1916)

Henry Hart Milman 1791–1868

13 Ride on! ride on in majesty!
   The wingèd squadrons of the sky
   Look down with sad and wond'ring eyes
   To see the approaching sacrifice.
   'Ride on! ride on in majesty!' (1827 hymn)

A. A. Milne 1882–1956

14 The more he looked inside the more Piglet wasn't there.
   The House at Pooh Corner (1928) ch. 1

15 When you are a Bear of Very Little Brain, and you Think of Things, you find sometimes that a Thing which seemed very Thingish inside you is quite different when it gets out into the open and has other people looking at it.
   The House at Pooh Corner (1928) ch. 6

16 Time for a little something.
   Winnie-the-Pooh (1926) ch. 6

17 My spelling is Wobbly. It's good spelling but it Wobbles, and the letters get in the wrong places.
   Winnie-the-Pooh (1926) ch. 6

18 Owl hasn't exactly got Brain, but he Knows Things.
   Winnie-the-Pooh (1926) ch. 9

19 They're changing guard at Buckingham Palace—
   Christopher Robin went down with Alice.
   Alice is marrying one of the guard.
   'A soldier's life is terrible hard,'
   Says Alice.
   'Buckingham Palace' (1924)

20 James James
   Morrison Morrison
   Weatherby George Dupree
   Took great
   Care of his Mother,
   Though he was only three.
   James James
   Said to his Mother,
   'Mother,' he said, said he;
   'You must never go down to the end of the town, if you don't go down with me.'
   'Disobedience' (1924)

21 There once was a Dormouse who lived in a bed
   Of delphiniums (blue) and geraniums (red),
   And all the day long he'd a wonderful view
   Of geraniums (red) and delphiniums (blue).
   'The Dormouse and the Doctor' (1924)

22 The King asked
   The Queen, and
   The Queen asked
   The Dairymaid:
   'Could we have some butter for
   The Royal slice of bread?'
   'The King's Breakfast' (1924)

23 *What* is the matter with Mary Jane?
   She's perfectly well and she hasn't a pain,
   And it's lovely rice pudding for dinner again!
   What *is* the matter with Mary Jane?
   'Rice Pudding' (1924)

1 Little Boy kneels at the foot of the bed,
Droops on the little hands little gold head.
Hush! Hush! Whisper who dares!
Christopher Robin is saying his prayers.
'Vespers' (1924)

Lord Milner 1854–1925

2 If we believe a thing to be bad, and if we
have a right to prevent it, it is our duty to
try to prevent it and to damn the
consequences.
Speech, 26 November 1909, in *The Times*
27 November 1909

John Milton 1608–74

3 Such sweet compulsion doth in music lie.
'Arcades' (1645) l. 68

4 Blest pair of Sirens, pledges of heaven's joy,
Sphere-born harmonious sisters, Voice, and
Verse.
'At a Solemn Music' (1645)

5 Above the smoke and stir of this dim spot,
Which men call earth.
Comus (1637) l. 5

6 An old and haughty nation proud in arms.
Comus (1637) l. 33

7 And the gilded car of day
His glowing axle doth allay
In the steep Atlantic stream.
Comus (1637) l. 95

8 What hath night to do with sleep?
Comus (1637) l. 122

9 Come, knit hands, and beat the ground,
In a light fantastic round.
Comus (1637) l. 143. Cf. 227:2

10 Sweet Echo, sweetest nymph that liv'st
unseen
Within thy airy shell
By slow Meander's margent green,
And in the violet-embroidered vale.
Comus (1637) l. 230

11 Virtue could see to do what Virtue would
By her own radiant light, though sun and
moon
Were in the flat sea sunk.
Comus (1637) l. 373

12 He that has light within his own clear
breast
May sit i' the centre, and enjoy bright day,
But he that hides a dark soul, and foul
thoughts
Benighted walks under the midday sun;
Himself is his own dungeon.
Comus (1637) l. 381

13 Yet where an equal poise of hope and fear
Does arbitrate the event, my nature is
That I incline to hope, rather than fear,
And gladly banish squint suspicion.
Comus (1637) l. 410

14 'Tis chastity, my brother, chastity:
She that has that, is clad in complete steel.
Comus (1637) l. 420

15 How charming is divine philosophy!
Not harsh and crabbèd, as dull fools
suppose,
But musical as is Apollo's lute.
Comus (1637) l. 475

16 Storied of old in high immortal verse
Of dire chimeras and enchanted isles,
And rifted rocks whose entrance leads to
hell.
Comus (1637) l. 516

17 And filled the air with barbarous
dissonance.
Comus (1637) l. 550

18   Against the threats
Of malice or of sorcery, or that power
Which erring men call chance, this I hold
firm,
Virtue may be assailed, but never hurt,
Surprised by unjust force, but not
enthralled.
Comus (1637) l. 586

19 Those budge doctors of the Stoic fur.
Comus (1637) l. 707

20 Beauty is Nature's brag, and must be
shown
In courts, at feasts, and high solemnities
Where most may wonder at the
workmanship.
Comus (1637) l. 745

21 Sabrina fair,
Listen where thou art sitting
Under the glassy, cool, translucent wave,
In twisted braids of lilies knitting
The loose train of thy amber-dropping hair.
Comus (1637) l. 859 'Song'

22 Hence, vain deluding joys,
The brood of folly without father bred.
'Il Penseroso' (1645) l. 1

23 As thick and numberless
As the gay motes that people the
sunbeams.
'Il Penseroso' (1645) l. 7

24 Come, pensive nun, devout and pure,
Sober, steadfast, and demure.
'Il Penseroso' (1645) l. 31

25 Where glowing embers through the room
Teach light to counterfeit a gloom,
Far from all resort of mirth,
Save the cricket on the hearth.
'Il Penseroso' (1645) l. 79

26 Hide me from day's garish eye.
'Il Penseroso' (1645) l. 141

27 Hence, loathèd Melancholy,
Of Cerberus, and blackest Midnight born,
In Stygian cave forlorn
'Mongst horrid shapes, and shrieks, and
sights unholy.
'L'Allegro' (1645) l. 1

28 So buxom, blithe, and debonair.
'L'Allegro' (1645) l. 24

1 Haste thee nymph, and bring with thee
   Jest and youthful jollity,
   Quips and cranks, and wanton wiles,
   Nods, and becks, and wreathèd smiles.
   'L'Allegro' (1645) l. 25

2 Sport that wrinkled Care derides,
   And Laughter holding both his sides.
   Come, and trip it as ye go
   On the light fantastic toe.
   'L'Allegro' (1645) l. 31. Cf. 226:9

3 Where perhaps some beauty lies,
   The cynosure of neighbouring eyes.
   'L'Allegro' (1645) l. 79

4 And the jocund rebecks sound
   To many a youth, and many a maid,
   Dancing in the chequered shade.
   'L'Allegro' (1645) l. 94

5 Then to the spicy nut-brown ale.
   'L'Allegro' (1645) l. 100

6 Towered cities please us then,
   And the busy hum of men.
   'L'Allegro' (1645) l. 117

7 Such sights as youthful poets dream
   On summer eves by haunted stream.
   'L'Allegro' (1645) l. 129

8 Then to the well-trod stage anon,
   If Jonson's learnèd sock be on,
   Or sweetest Shakespeare fancy's child,
   Warble his native wood-notes wild.
   'L'Allegro' (1645) l. 131

9 Let us with a gladsome mind
   Praise the Lord, for he is kind,
   For his mercies ay endure,
   Ever faithful, ever sure.
   'Let us with a gladsome mind' (1645);
   paraphrase of Psalm 136

10 Yet once more, O ye laurels, and once more
   Ye myrtles brown, with ivy never sere.
   'Lycidas' (1638) l. 1

11 He must not float upon his watery bier
   Unwept, and welter to the parching wind,
   Without the meed of some melodious tear.
   'Lycidas' (1638) l. 12

12 For we were nursed upon the self-same
   hill.
   'Lycidas' (1638) l. 23

13   The woods, and desert caves,
   With wild thyme and the gadding vine
   o'ergrown.
   'Lycidas' (1638) l. 39

14 Were it not better done as others use,
   To sport with Amaryllis in the shade,
   Or with the tangles of Neaera's hair?
   Fame is the spur that the clear spirit doth
   raise
   (That last infirmity of noble mind)
   To scorn delights, and live laborious days.
   'Lycidas' (1638) l. 67

15   Their lean and flashy songs
   Grate on their scrannel pipes of wretched
   straw.
   'Lycidas' (1638) l. 123

16 But that two-handed engine at the door
   Stands ready to smite once, and smite no
   more.
   'Lycidas' (1638) l. 130

17 Look homeward angel now, and melt with
   ruth.
   'Lycidas' (1638) l. 163

18 So sinks the day-star in the ocean bed,
   And yet anon repairs his drooping head,
   And tricks his beams, and with new
   spangled ore,
   Flames in the forehead of the morning sky.
   'Lycidas' (1638) l. 168

19 While the still morn went out with sandals
   grey.
   'Lycidas' (1638) l. 187

20 Tomorrow to fresh woods, and pastures
   new.
   'Lycidas' (1638) l. 193

21 What needs my Shakespeare for his
   honoured bones,
   The labour of an age in pilèd stones.
   'On Shakespeare' (1632)

22 O fairest flower no sooner blown but
   blasted.
   'On the Death of a Fair Infant Dying of a
   Cough' (1673) st. 1

23 For what can war, but endless war still
   breed?
   'On the Lord General Fairfax at the Siege of
   Colchester' (written 1648)

24 The star-led wizards haste with odours
   sweet.
   'On the Morning of Christ's Nativity' (1645)
   st. 4

25 It was the winter wild,
   While the heaven-born-child
   All meanly wrapped in the rude manger
   lies;
   Nature in awe to him
   Had doffed her gaudy trim,
   With her great master so to sympathize.
   'On the Morning of Christ's Nativity' (1645)
   'The Hymn' st. 1

26 No war, or battle's sound
   Was heard the world around.
   'On the Morning of Christ's Nativity' (1645)
   'The Hymn' st. 4

27 Time will run back, and fetch the age of
   gold.
   'On the Morning of Christ's Nativity' (1645)
   'The Hymn' st. 14

28 And hell itself will pass away,
   And leave her dolorous mansions to the
   peering day.
   'On the Morning of Christ's Nativity' (1645)
   'The Hymn' st. 14

29 So when the sun in bed,
   Curtained with cloudy red,
   Pillows his chin upon an orient wave.
   'On the Morning of Christ's Nativity' (1645)
   'The Hymn' st. 26

1 Time is our tedious song should here have
ending.
  'On the Morning of Christ's Nativity' (1645)
  'The Hymn' st. 27

2 New *Presbyter* is but old *Priest* writ large.
  'On the New Forcers of Conscience under the
  Long Parliament' (1646)

3 Fly envious Time, till thou run out thy
race,
Call on the lazy leaden-stepping hours.
  'On Time' (1645)

4 If any ask for him, it shall be said,
Hobson has supped, and's newly gone to
bed.
  'On the University Carrier' (1645)

5 Rhyme being ... but the invention of a
barbarous age, to set off wretched matter
and lame metre.
  Paradise Lost (1667) 'The Verse' (preface, 1668)

6 The troublesome and modern bondage of
rhyming.
  Paradise Lost (1667) 'The Verse' (preface, 1668)

7 Of man's first disobedience, and the fruit
Of that forbidden tree, whose mortal taste
Brought death into the world, and all our
woe,
With loss of Eden.
  Paradise Lost (1667) bk. 1, l. 1

8 Things unattempted yet in prose or rhyme.
  Paradise Lost (1667) bk. 1, l. 16

9   What in me is dark
Illumine, what is low raise and support;
That to the height of this great argument
I may assert eternal providence,
And justify the ways of God to men.
  Paradise Lost (1667) bk. 1, l. 22

10 No light, but rather darkness visible
Served only to discover sights of woe.
  Paradise Lost (1667) bk. 1, l. 63

11 And out of good still to find means of evil.
  Paradise Lost (1667) bk. 1, l. 165

12 The mind is its own place, and in itself
Can make a heaven of hell, a hell of
heaven.
  Paradise Lost (1667) bk. 1, l. 254

13 Better to reign in hell, than serve in
heaven.
  Paradise Lost (1667) bk. 1, l. 263

14 Thick as autumnal leaves that strew the
brooks
In Vallombrosa, where the Etrurian shades
High overarched imbower.
  Paradise Lost (1667) bk. 1, l. 302

15   When night
Darkens the streets, then wander forth the
sons
Of Belial, flown with insolence and wine.
  Paradise Lost (1667) bk. 1, l. 500

16 A shout that tore hell's concave, and
beyond
Frighted the reign of Chaos and old Night.
  Paradise Lost (1667) bk. 1, l. 542

17 In dim eclipse disastrous twilight sheds
On half the nations, and with fear of
change
Perplexes monarchs.
  Paradise Lost (1667) bk. 1, l. 597

18   Who overcomes
By force, hath overcome but half his foe.
  Paradise Lost (1667) bk. 1, l. 648

19 Let none admire
That riches grow in hell; that soil may best
Deserve the precious bane.
  Paradise Lost (1667) bk. 1, l. 690

20   From morn
To noon he fell, from noon to dewy eve,
A summer's day; and with the setting sun
Dropped from the zenith like a falling star.
  Paradise Lost (1667) bk. 1, l. 742

21 ... Pandemonium, the high capital
Of Satan and his peers.
  Paradise Lost (1667) bk. 1, l. 756

22 His trust was with the eternal to be
deemed
Equal in strength, and rather than be less
Cared not to be at all.
  Paradise Lost (1667) bk. 2, l. 46

23 But all was false and hollow; though his
tongue
Dropped manna, and could make the
worse appear
The better reason.
  Paradise Lost (1667) bk. 2, l. 112. Cf. 15:10

24 To perish rather, swallowed up and lost
In the wide womb of uncreated night,
Devoid of sense and motion.
  Paradise Lost (1667) bk. 2, l. 149

25 Unrespited, unpitied, unreprieved,
Ages of hopeless end.
  Paradise Lost (1667) bk. 2, l. 185

26 Our torments also may in length of time
Become our elements.
  Paradise Lost (1667) bk. 2, l. 274

27   With grave
Aspect he rose, and in his rising seemed
A pillar of state; deep on his front
engraven
Deliberation sat and public care;
And princely counsel in his face yet shone,
Majestic though in ruin.
  Paradise Lost (1667) bk. 2, l. 300

28   To sit in darkness here
Hatching vain empires.
  Paradise Lost (1667) bk. 2, l. 377

29 And through the palpable obscure find out
His uncouth way.
  Paradise Lost (1667) bk. 2, l. 406

30   Long is the way
And hard, that out of hell leads up to light.
  Paradise Lost (1667) bk. 2, l. 432

31 Eloquence the soul, song charms the sense.
  Paradise Lost (1667) bk. 2, l. 556

32 Sable-vested Night, eldest of things.
  Paradise Lost (1667) bk. 2, l. 962

1 With ruin upon ruin, rout on rout,
Confusion worse confounded.
Paradise Lost (1667) bk. 2, l. 995

2 So he with difficulty and labour hard
Moved on, with difficulty and labour he.
Paradise Lost (1667) bk. 2, l. 1021

3 Die he or justice must.
Paradise Lost (1667) bk. 3, l. 210

4 Dark with excessive bright.
Paradise Lost (1667) bk. 3, l. 380

5 Hypocrisy, the only evil that walks
Invisible, except to God alone.
Paradise Lost (1667) bk. 3, l. 683

6 Me miserable! which way shall I fly
Infinite wrath, and infinite despair?
Which way I fly is hell; myself am hell.
Paradise Lost (1667) bk. 4, l. 73

7 Farewell remorse! All good to me is lost;
Evil, be thou my good.
Paradise Lost (1667) bk. 4, l. 109

8 Flowers of all hue, and without thorn the
rose.
Paradise Lost (1667) bk. 4, l. 256

9 He for God only, she for God in him.
Paradise Lost (1667) bk. 4, l. 299

10   These two
Emparadised in one another's arms
The happier Eden, shall enjoy their fill
Of bliss on bliss.
Paradise Lost (1667) bk. 4, l. 505

11   Sweet the coming on
Of grateful evening mild, then silent night
With this her solemn bird and this fair
moon,
And these the gems of heaven, her starry
train.
Paradise Lost (1667) bk. 4, l. 646

12   Sleep on
Blest pair; and O yet happiest if ye seek
No happier state, and know to know no
more.
Paradise Lost (1667) bk. 4, l. 773

13   Him there they found
Squat like a toad, close at the ear of Eve.
Paradise Lost (1667) bk. 4, l. 799

14 But wherefore thou alone? Wherefore with
thee
Came not all hell broke loose?
Paradise Lost (1667) bk. 4, l. 917

15 My fairest, my espoused, my latest found,
Heaven's last best gift, my ever new
delight.
Paradise Lost (1667) bk. 5, l. 18

16 Best image of myself and dearer half.
Paradise Lost (1667) bk. 5, l. 95

17   Nor jealousy
Was understood, the injured lover's hell.
Paradise Lost (1667) bk. 5, l. 449

18   What if earth
Be but the shadow of heaven, and things
therein
Each to other like, more than on earth is
thought?
Paradise Lost (1667) bk. 5, l. 574

19   Still govern thou my song,
Urania, and fit audience find, though few.
Paradise Lost (1667) bk. 7, l. 30

20   So absolute she seems
And in herself complete, so well to know
Her own, that what she wills to do or say
Seems wisest, virtuousest, discreetest, best.
Paradise Lost (1667) bk. 8, l. 547

21 And dictates to me slumbering, or inspires
Easy my unpremeditated verse.
Paradise Lost (1667) bk. 9, l. 23

22 The serpent subtlest beast of all the field.
Paradise Lost (1667) bk. 9, l. 86

23 As one who long in populous city pent,
Where houses thick and sewers annoy the
air,
Forth issuing on a summer's morn to
breathe
Among the pleasant villages and farms
Adjoined, from each thing met conceives
delight.
Paradise Lost (1667) bk. 9, l. 445

24 She fair, divinely fair, fit love for gods.
Paradise Lost (1667) bk. 9, l. 489

25 God so commanded, and left that
command
Sole daughter of his voice; the rest, we live
Law to our selves, our reason is our law.
Paradise Lost (1667) bk. 9, l. 652

26 Earth felt the wound, and Nature from her
seat
Sighing through all her works gave signs
of woe
That all was lost.
Paradise Lost (1

27 O fairest of creation, last and best
Of all God's works.
Paradise Lost (1667) bk. 9, l. 896

28   Flesh of flesh,
Bone of my bone thou art, and from thy
state
Mine never shall be parted, bliss or woe.
Paradise Lost (1667) bk. 9, l. 914

29 ... Yet I shall temper so
Justice with mercy.
Paradise Lost (1667) bk. 10, l. 77

30 This novelty on earth, this fair defect
Of nature.
Paradise Lost (1667) bk. 10, l. 891

31 Demoniac frenzy, moping melancholy
And moon-struck madness.
Paradise Lost (1667) bk. 11, l. 485

32 ... The evening star,
Love's harbinger.
Paradise Lost (1667) bk. 11, l. 588

1 In me is no delay; with thee to go,
  Is to stay here; without thee here to stay,
  Is to go hence unwilling.
  Paradise Lost (1667) bk. 12, l. 615

2 The world was all before them, where to
      choose
  Their place of rest, and Providence their
      guide:
  They hand in hand, with wandering steps
      and slow,
  Through Eden took their solitary way.
  Paradise Lost (1667) bk. 12, l. 646

3 Of whom to be dispraised were no small
      praise.
  Paradise Regained (1671) bk. 3, l. 56

4 But on occasion's forelock watchful wait.
  Paradise Regained (1671) bk. 3, l. 173

5 He who seeking asses found a kingdom.
  Paradise Regained (1671) bk. 3, l. 242 (of Saul).
  See Samuel ch. 9, v. 3

6 Athens, the eye of Greece, mother of arts
      And eloquence . . .
  See there the olive grove of Academe,
  Plato's retirement, where the Attic bird
  Trills her thick-warbled notes the summer
      long.
  Paradise Regained (1671) bk. 4, l. 240

7 The first and wisest of them all professed
  To know this only, that he nothing knew.
  Paradise Regained (1671) bk. 4, l. 293.
  Cf. 310:21

8 Deep-versed in books and shallow in
      himself.
  Paradise Regained (1671) bk. 4, l. 327

9 But headlong joy is ever on the wing.
  'The Passion' (1645) st. 1

10 Ask for this great deliverer now, and find
      him
   Eyeless in Gaza at the mill with slaves.
   Samson Agonistes (1671) l. 40

11 O dark, dark, dark, amid the blaze of noon,
   Irrecoverably dark, total eclipse
   Without all hope of day!
   Samson Agonistes (1671) l. 80

12 The sun to me is dark
   And silent as the moon,
   When she deserts the night
   Hid in her vacant interlunar cave.
   Samson Agonistes (1671) l. 86

13 To live a life half dead, a living death.
   Samson Agonistes (1671) l. 100

14 Just are the ways of God,
   And justifiable to men;
   Unless there be who think not God at all.
   Samson Agonistes (1671) l. 293

15 Love-quarrels oft in pleasing concord end.
   Samson Agonistes (1671) l. 1008

16 Lords are lordliest in their wine.
   Samson Agonistes (1671) l. 1418

17   Samson hath quit himself
   Like Samson, and heroically hath finished
   A life heroic.
   Samson Agonistes (1671) l. 1709

18 Nothing is here for tears.
   Samson Agonistes (1671) l. 1721

19 Calm of mind, all passion spent.
   Samson Agonistes (1671) l. 1758

20 Time the subtle thief of youth.
   Sonnet 7 'How soon hath time' (1645)

21 Licence they mean when they cry liberty;
   For who loves that, must first be wise and
      good.
   Sonnet 12 'I did but prompt the age' (1673)

22 When I consider how my light is spent,
   E're half my days, in this dark world and
      wide,
   And that one talent which is death to hide
   Lodged with me useless.
   Sonnet 16 'When I consider how my light is
   spent' (1673)

23 They also serve who only stand and wait.
   Sonnet 16 'When I consider how my light is
   spent' (1673)

24 Methought I saw my late espousèd saint
   Brought to me like Alcestis from the grave.
   Sonnet 19 'Methought I saw my late espousèd
   saint' (1673)

25 But oh as to embrace me she inclined
   I waked, she fled, and day brought back my
      night.
   Sonnet 19 'Methought I saw my late espousèd
   saint' (1673)

26 Cromwell, our chief of men.
   'To the Lord General Cromwell' (written
   1652)

27 . . . Peace hath her victories
   No less renowned than war.
   'To the Lord General Cromwell' (written
   1652)

28 He who would not be frustrate of his hope
   to write well hereafter in laudable things,
   ought himself to be a true poem.
   An Apology for Smectymnuus (1642)
   introduction, p. 16

29 As good almost kill a man as kill a good
   book: who kills a man kills a reasonable
   creature, God's image; but he who destroys
   a good book, kills reason itself, kills the
   image of God, as it were in the eye.
   Areopagitica (1644) p. 4

30 A good book is the precious life-blood of a
   master spirit.
   Areopagitica (1644) p. 4

31 I cannot praise a fugitive and cloistered
   virtue, unexercised and unbreathed, that
   never sallies out and sees her adversary,
   but slinks out of the race, where that
   immortal garland is to be run for, not
   without dust and heat . . . that which
   purifies us is trial, and trial is by what is
   contrary.
   Areopagitica (1644) p. 12

32 If we think to regulate printing, thereby to
   rectify manners, we must regulate all
   recreations and pastimes, all that is
   delightful to man.
   Areopagitica (1644) p. 16

1 And who shall silence all the airs and madrigals, that whisper softness in chambers?
   Areopagitica (1644) p. 16

2 What does he [God] then but reveal Himself to his servants, and as his manner is, first to his Englishmen?
   Areopagitica (1644) p. 31

3 City of refuge, the mansion-house of liberty.
   Areopagitica (1644) p. 31 (of London)

4 Opinion in good men is but knowledge in the making.
   Areopagitica (1644) p. 31

5 Let not England forget her precedence of teaching nations how to live.
   The Doctrine and Discipline of Divorce (1643) 'To the Parliament of England'

6 What I have spoken, is the language of that which is not called amiss *The good old Cause.*
   The Ready and Easy Way to Establish a Free Commonwealth (2nd ed., 1660) p. 106.

7 None can love freedom heartily, but good men; the rest love not freedom, but licence.
   The Tenure of Kings and Magistrates (1649)

Comte de Mirabeau 1749–91

8 War is the national industry of Prussia.
   Attributed to Mirabeau by Albert Sorel (1842–1906), on the basis of Mirabeau's introduction to *De la monarchie prussienne sous Frédéric le Grand* (1788)

The Missal

9 *Dominus vobiscum.*
   Et cum spiritu tuo.
   The Lord be with you.
   And with thy spirit.
   Ordinary of the Mass

10 *In Nomine Patris, et Filii, et Spiritus Sancti.*
   In the Name of the Father, and of the Son, and of the Holy Ghost.
   Ordinary of the Mass

11 *Peccavi nimis cogitatione, verbo, et opere, mea culpa, mea culpa, mea maxima culpa.*
   I have sinned exceedingly in thought, word, and deed, through my fault, through my fault, through my most grievous fault.
   Ordinary of the Mass

12 *Kyrie eleison . . . Christe eleison.*
   Lord, have mercy upon us . . . Christ, have mercy upon us.
   Ordinary of the Mass

13 *Gloria in excelsis Deo, et in terra pax hominibus bonae voluntatis.*
   Glory be to God on high, and on earth peace to men of good will.
   Ordinary of the Mass. Cf. 52:2

14 *Deo gratias.*
   Thanks be to God.
   Ordinary of the Mass

15 *Credo in unum Deum.*
   I believe in one God.
   The Ordinary of the Mass 'The Nicene Creed'. Cf. 65:5

16 *Et homo factus est.*
   And was made man.
   Ordinary of the Mass 'The Nicene Creed'

17 *Sanctus, sanctus, sanctus, Dominus Deus Sabaoth. Pleni sunt coeli et terra gloria tua. Hosanna in excelsis. Benedictus qui venit in nomine Domini.*
   Holy, holy, holy, Lord God of Hosts. Heaven and earth are full of thy glory. Hosanna in the highest. Blessed is he that cometh in the name of the Lord.
   Ordinary of the Mass

18 *Pater noster, qui es in coelis, sanctificetur nomen tuum.*
   Our Father, who art in heaven, hallowed be thy name.
   Ordinary of the Mass. Cf. 48:27

19 *Agnus Dei, qui tollis peccata mundi, miserere nobis.*
   Lamb of God, who takest away the sins of the world, have mercy on us.
   Ordinary of the Mass

20 *Ite missa est.*
   Go, you are dismissed.
   Ordinary of the Mass (commonly interpreted as 'Go, the Mass is ended')

21 *Verbum caro factum est.*
   The word was made flesh.
   Ordinary of the Mass. Cf. 53:11

22 *Requiem aeternam dona eis, Domine: et lux perpetua luceat eis.*
   Grant them eternal rest, O Lord; and let perpetual light shine on them.
   Order of Mass for the Dead

23 *Dies irae, dies illa,*
   Solvet saeclum in favilla,
   Teste David cum Sibylla.
   That day, the day of wrath, will turn the universe to ashes, as David foretells (and the Sibyl too).
   Order of Mass for the Dead 'Sequentia' (commonly known as 'Dies Irae') l. 1 (attributed to Thomas of Celano, c.1190–1260)

24 *Rex tremendae maiestatis,*
   Qui salvandos salvas gratis,
   Salva me, fons pietatis!
   O King of tremendous majesty, who freely saves those who should be saved, save me, O source of pity!
   Order of Mass for the Dead 'Sequentia' l. 22

25 *Requiescant in pace.*
   May they rest in peace.
   Order of Mass for the Dead

1 *O felix culpa, quae talem ac tantum meruit habere Redemptorem.*
O happy fault, which has earned such a mighty Redeemer.
'Exsultet' on Holy Saturday

Adrian Mitchell 1932–

2 Most people ignore most poetry
because
most poetry ignores most people.
Poems (1964) p. 8

Joni Mitchell 1945–

3 I've looked at life from both sides now,
From win and lose and still somehow
It's life's illusions I recall;
I really don't know life at all.
'Both Sides Now' (1967 song)

4 We are stardust,
We are golden,
And we got to get ourselves
Back to the garden.
'Woodstock' (1969 song)

Margaret Mitchell 1900–49

5 Death and taxes and childbirth! There's never any convenient time for any of them.
Gone with the Wind (1936) ch. 38. Cf. 145:15

6 I wish I could care what you do or where you go but I can't ... My dear, I don't give a damn.
Gone with the Wind (1936) ch. 57 (Rhett Butler to Scarlett). 'Frankly, my dear, I don't give a damn!' in Sidney Howard's 1939 screenplay

7 After all, tomorrow is another day.
Gone with the Wind (1936) *ad fin.*

Nancy Mitford 1904–73

8 An aristocracy in a republic is like a chicken whose head has been cut off: it may run about in a lively way, but in fact it is dead.
Noblesse Oblige (1956) 'The English Aristocracy'

9 Wooing, so tiring.
The Pursuit of Love (1945) ch. 4

10 Abroad is unutterably bloody and foreigners are fiends.
The Pursuit of Love (1945) ch. 15. Cf. 150:4

Wilson Mizner 1876–1933

11 Be nice to people on your way up because you'll meet 'em on your way down.
In A. Johnston *The Legendary Mizners* (1953) ch. 4

12 If you steal from one author, it's plagiarism; if you steal from many, it's research.
In A. Johnston *The Legendary Mizners* (1953) ch. 4

13 A trip through a sewer in a glass-bottomed boat.
Of Hollywood, in A. Johnston *The Legendary Mizners* (1953) ch. 4

Molière 1622–73

14 One should eat to live, and not live to eat.
L'Avare (1669) act 3, sc. 1

15 All that is not prose is verse; and all that is not verse is prose.
Le Bourgeois Gentilhomme (1671) act 2, sc. 4

16 Good heavens! For more than forty years I have been speaking prose without knowing it.
Le Bourgeois Gentilhomme (1671) act 2, sc. 4

17 One dies only once, and it's for such a long time!
Le Dépit amoureux (performed 1656) act 5, sc. 3

18 A knowledgeable fool is a greater fool than an ignorant fool.
Les Femmes savantes (1672) act 4, sc. 3

19 GÉRONTE: It seems to me you are locating them wrongly: the heart is on the left and the liver is on the right.
SGANARELLE: Yes, in the old days that was so, but we have changed all that.
Le Médecin malgré lui (1667) act 2, sc. 4

20 What's needed in this world is an accommodating sort of virtue.
Le Misanthrope (1666) act 1, sc. 1

21 Here they hang a man first, and try him afterwards.
Monsieur de Pourceaugnac (1670) act 1, sc. 5

22 Assassination is the quickest way.
Le Sicilien (1668) sc. 12

23 *Le ciel défend, de vrai, certains contentements, Mais on trouve avec lui des accommodements.*
God, it is true, does some delights condemn,
But 'tis not hard to come to terms with Him.
Le Tartuffe (1669) act 4, sc. 5

24 *Le scandale du monde est ce qui fait l'offense, Et ce n'est pas pécher que pécher en silence.*
It is public scandal that constitutes offence, and to sin in secret is not to sin at all.
Le Tartuffe (1669) act 4, sc. 5

25 *L'homme est, je vous l'avoue, un méchant animal.*
Man, I can assure you, is a nasty creature.
Le Tartuffe (1669) act 5, sc. 6

William Cosmo Monkhouse
1840–1901

26 There once was an old man of Lyme
Who married three wives at a time,
When asked 'Why a third?'
He replied, 'One's absurd!
And bigamy, Sir, is a crime!'
Nonsense Rhymes (1902)

Duke of Monmouth 1649–85

1 Do not hack me as you did my Lord Russell.
> To his executioner, in T. B. Macaulay *History of England* vol. 1 (1849) ch. 5

John Samuel Bewley Monsell 1811–75

2 Run the straight race through God's good grace,
Lift up thine eyes and seek his face;
Life with its way before us lies,
Christ is the path and Christ is the prize.
> 'Fight the good fight with all thy might' (1863 hymn)

3 With gold of obedience and incense of lowliness,
Kneel and adore him: the Lord is his name.
> 'O worship the Lord in the beauty of holiness' (1863 hymn)

Lady Mary Wortley Montagu 1689–1762

4 And we meet with champagne and a chicken at last.
> *Six Town Eclogues* (1747) 'The Lover' l. 25

5 Civility costs nothing and buys everything.
> Letter to her daughter, 30 May 1756, in R. Halsband (ed.) *Complete Letters* vol. 3 (1967)

6 People wish their enemies dead—but I do not; I say give them the gout, give them the stone!
> In W. S. Lewis et al. (eds.) *Horace Walpole's Correspondence* vol. 35 (1973) p. 489

C. E. Montague 1867–1928

7 War hath no fury like a non-combatant.
> *Disenchantment* (1922) ch. 16

Montaigne 1533–92

8 One should always have one's boots on, and be ready to leave.
> *Essais* (1580, ed. M. Rat, 1958) bk. 1, ch. 20. Cf. 199:19

9 I want death to find me planting my cabbages, but caring little for it, and even less about the imperfections of my garden.
> *Essais* (1580, ed. M. Rat, 1958) bk. 1, ch. 20

10 The ceaseless labour of your life is to build the house of death.
> *Essais* (1580, ed. M. Rat, 1958) bk. 1, ch. 20

11 It should be noted that children at play are not playing about; their games should be seen as their most serious-minded activity.
> *Essais* (1580, ed. M. Rat, 1958) bk. 1, ch. 23

12 If I am pressed to say why I loved him, I feel it can only be explained by replying: 'Because it was he; because it was me.'
> *Essais* (1580, ed. M. Rat, 1958) bk. 1, ch. 28

13 There is scarcely any less bother in the running of a family than in that of an entire state. And domestic business is no less importunate for being less important.
> *Essais* (1580, ed. M. Rat, 1958) bk. 1, ch. 39

14 A man should keep for himself a little back shop, all his own, quite unadulterated, in which he establishes his true freedom and chief place of seclusion and solitude.
> *Essais* (1580, ed. M. Rat, 1958) bk. 1, ch. 39

15 The greatest thing in the world is to know how to be oneself.
> *Essais* (1580, ed. M. Rat, 1958) bk. 1, ch. 39

16 *Mon métier et mon art c'est vivre.*
Living is my job and my art.
> *Essais* (1580, ed. M. Rat, 1958) bk. 2, ch. 6

17 When I play with my cat, who knows whether she isn't amusing herself with me more than I am with her?
> *Essais* (1580, ed. M. Rat, 1958) bk. 2, ch. 12

18 *Que sais-je?*
What do I know?
> *Essais* (1580, ed. M. Rat, 1958) bk. 2, ch. 12 (on the position of the sceptic)

19 It could be said of me that in this book I have only made up a bunch of other men's flowers, providing of my own only the string that ties them together.
> *Essais* (1580, ed. M. Rat, 1958) bk. 3, ch. 12

Montesquieu 1689–1755

20 Men should be bewailed at their birth, and not at their death.
> *Lettres Persones* (1721) no. 40 (tr. J. Ozell, 1722)

21 If the triangles were to make a God they would give him three sides.
> *Lettres Persones* (1721) no. 59 (tr. J. Ozell, 1722)

22 Happy the people whose annals are blank in history-books!
> Attributed to Montesquieu by Thomas Carlyle in *History of Frederick the Great* bk. 16, ch. 1. Cf. 132:14

Field Marshal Montgomery 1887–1976

23 Rule 1, on page 1 of the book of war, is: 'Do not march on Moscow' ... [Rule 2] is: 'Do not go fighting with your land armies in China.'
> *Hansard* (Lords) 30 May 1962, col. 227

24 I have heard some say ... [homosexual] practices are allowed in France and in other NATO countries. We are not French, and we are not other nationals. We are British, thank God!
> Speaking on the 2nd reading of the Sexual Offences Bill; in *Hansard* (Lords) 24 May 1965, col. 648

Robert Montgomery 1807–55

25 The solitary monk who shook the world.
> *Luther: a Poem* (1842) ch. 3 'Man's Need and God's Supply'

Casimir, Comte de Montrond
1768–1843

1 Have no truck with first impulses for they
  are always generous ones.
  Attributed, in Comte J. d'Estourmel Derniers
  Souvenirs *(1860) p. 319 (where the alternative
  attribution to Talleyrand is denied). Cf. 108:3*

Percy Montrose

2 In a cavern, in a canyon,
  Excavating for a mine,
  Dwelt a miner, Forty-niner,
  And his daughter, Clementine.
  'Clementine' (1884 song)

Clement C. Moore 1779–1863

3 'Twas the night before Christmas, when all
  through the house
  Not a creature was stirring, not even a
  mouse.
  'A Visit from St Nicholas' (December 1823)

Edward Moore 1712–57

4 This is adding insult to injuries.
  The Foundling (1748) act 5, sc. 5

5 I am rich beyond the dreams of avarice.
  The Gamester (1753) act 2, sc. 2. Cf. 185:29

George Moore 1852–1933

6 All reformers are bachelors.
  The Bending of the Bough (1900) act 1

7 A man travels the world in search of what
  he needs and returns home to find it.
  The Brook Kerith (1916) ch. 11

Marianne Moore 1887–1972

8 Imaginary gardens with real toads in them.
  'Poetry' (1935)

9 My father used to say,
  'Superior people never make long visits,
  have to be shown Longfellow's grave
  or the glass flowers at Harvard.'
  'Silence' (1935)

Thomas Moore 1779–1852

10 Though an angel should write, still 'tis
   devils must print.
   The Fudges in England (1835) Letter 3, l. 65

11 Believe me, if all those endearing young
   charms,
   Which I gaze on so fondly today,
   Were to change by tomorrow, and fleet in
   my arms,
   Like fairy gifts fading away!
   Irish Melodies (1807) 'Believe me, if all those
   endearing young charms'

12 'Twas from Kathleen's eyes he flew,
   Eyes of most unholy blue!
   Irish Melodies (1807) 'By that Lake'

13 You may break, you may shatter the vase,
   if you will,
   But the scent of the roses will hang round
   it still.
   Irish Melodies (1807) 'Farewell!—but
   whenever'

14 The harp that once through Tara's halls
   The soul of music shed,
   Now hangs as mute on Tara's walls
   As if that soul were fled.
   Irish Melodies (1807) 'The harp that once
   through Tara's halls'

15 No, there's nothing half so sweet in life
   As love's young dream.
   Irish Melodies (1807) 'Love's Young Dream'

16 The Minstrel Boy to the war is gone,
   In the ranks of death you'll find him;
   His father's sword he has girded on,
   And his wild harp slung behind him.
   Irish Melodies (1807) 'The Minstrel Boy'

17 Rich and rare were the gems she wore,
   And a bright gold ring on her wand she
   bore.
   Irish Melodies (1807) 'Rich and rare were the
   gems she wore'

18 'Tis the last rose of summer
   Left blooming alone;
   All her lovely companions
   Are faded and gone.
   Irish Melodies (1807) ''Tis the last rose of
   summer'

19 I never nursed a dear gazelle,
   To glad me with its soft black eye,
   But when it came to know me well,
   And love me, it was sure to die!
   Lalla Rookh (1817) 'The Fire-Worshippers'
   pt. 1, l. 283

20 Oft, in the stilly night,
   Ere Slumber's chain has bound me,
   Fond Memory brings the light
   Of other days around me.
   National Airs (1815) 'Oft in the Stilly Night'

Thomas Osbert Mordaunt
1730–1809

21 One crowded hour of glorious life
   Is worth an age without a name.
   'A Poem, said to be written by Major
   Mordaunt during the last German War', in
   The Bee 12 October 1791

Hannah More 1745–1833

22 How much it is to be regretted, that the
   British ladies should ever sit down
   contented to polish, when they are able to
   reform; to entertain, when they might
   instruct; and to dazzle for an hour, when
   they are candidates for eternity!
   Essays on Various Subjects . . . for Young Ladies
   (1777) 'On Dissipation'

Sir Thomas More 1478–1535

1 After his head was upon the block, [he] lift it up again, and gently drew his beard aside, and said, *This hath not offended the king.*

Francis Bacon *Apophthegms New and Old* (1625) no. 22

2 Is not this house [the Tower of London] as nigh heaven as my own?

In William Roper *Life of Sir Thomas More* (Everyman ed., 1963) p. 41

3 I pray you, master Lieutenant, see me safe up, and my coming down let me shift for my self.

On mounting the scaffold; in William Roper *Life of Sir Thomas More* p. 50

4 Fare well my dear child and pray for me, and I shall for you and all your friends that we may merrily meet in heaven.

Letter to his daughter Margaret, 5 July 1535, on the eve of his execution; in E. F. Rogers (ed.) *Correspondence of Sir Thomas More* (1947)

Thomas Morell 1703–84

5 See, the conquering hero comes! Sound the trumpets, beat the drums!

Judas Maccabeus (1747) 'A chorus of youths'; also *Joshua* (1748) pt. 3

Robin Morgan 1941–

6 Sisterhood is powerful.

Title of book (1970)

Christopher Morley 1890–1957

7 Life is a foreign language: all men mispronounce it.

Thunder on the Left (1925) ch. 14. Cf. 163:14

Lord Morley 1838–1923

8 The golden Gospel of Silence is effectively compressed in thirty fine volumes.

Critical Miscellanies (1886) 'Carlyle' (on Carlyle's *History of Frederick the Great* (1858–65), Carlyle having written of his subject as 'that strong, silent man')

9 You have not converted a man, because you have silenced him.

On Compromise (1874) ch. 5

Countess Morphy fl. 1930–50

10 The tragedy of English cooking is that 'plain' cooking cannot be entrusted to 'plain' cooks.

English Recipes (1935) p. 17

Charles Morris 1745–1838

11 But a house is much more to my mind than a tree,
And for groves, O! a good grove of chimneys for me.

'Country and Town' (1840)

Desmond Morris 1928–

12 The city is not a concrete jungle, it is a human zoo.

The Human Zoo (1969) introduction

George Pope Morris 1802–64

13 Woodman, spare that tree!
Touch not a single bough!
In youth it sheltered me,
And I'll protect it now.

'Woodman, Spare That Tree' (1830). Cf. 88:17

William Morris 1834–96

14 The idle singer of an empty day.

The Earthly Paradise (1868–70) 'An Apology'

15 Dreamer of dreams, born out of my due time,
Why should I strive to set the crooked straight?

The Earthly Paradise (1868–70) 'An Apology'

16 Forget six counties overhung with smoke,
Forget the snorting steam and piston stroke,
Forget the spreading of the hideous town;
Think rather of the pack-horse on the down,
And dream of London, small and white and clean,
The clear Thames bordered by its gardens green.

The Earthly Paradise (1868–70) 'Prologue: The Wanderers' l. 1

17 Fellowship is heaven, and lack of fellowship is hell.

A Dream of John Ball (1888) ch. 4

18 Have nothing in your houses that you do not know to be useful, or believe to be beautiful.

Hopes and Fears for Art (1882) 'Making the Best of It'

Jim Morrison 1943–71

19 C'mon, baby, light my fire.

'Light My Fire' (1967 song, with Robby Krieger)

20 We want the world and we want it now!

'When the Music's Over' (1967 song)

John Mortimer 1923–

21 No brilliance is needed in the law. Nothing but common sense, and relatively clean finger nails.

A Voyage Round My Father (1971) act 1

22 Champagne socialist.

Description of himself (attributed)

Thomas Morton c.1764–1838

23 Always ding, dinging Dame Grundy into my ears—what will Mrs Grundy zay? What will Mrs Grundy think?

Speed the Plough (1798) act 1, sc. 1

John Lothrop Motley 1814–77

1 As long as he lived, he was the guiding-star of a whole brave nation, and when he died the little children cried in the streets.
   Of William of Orange; in *The Rise of the Dutch Republic* (1856) pt. 6, ch. 7. Cf. 20:18

2 Give us the luxuries of life, and we will dispense with its necessities.
   In Oliver Wendell Holmes *Autocrat of the Breakfast-Table* (1857–8) ch. 6

Peter Anthony Motteux
1660–1718

3 The devil was sick, the devil a monk would be;
   The devil was well, and the devil a monk he'd be.
   Translation of Rabelais *Gargantua and Pantagruel* (1693) bk. 4 (1708 ed.) ch. 24 (variant of a medieval Latin proverb)

Earl Mountbatten of Burma
1900–79

4 The nuclear arms race has no military purpose. Wars cannot be fought with nuclear weapons. Their existence only adds to our perils.
   Speech at Strasbourg, 11 May 1979; in P. Ziegler *Mountbatten* (1985) ch. 52

Malcolm Muggeridge 1903–90

5 He was not only a bore; he bored for England.
   Tread Softly (1966) p. 147 (of Sir Anthony Eden)

Edwin Muir 1887–1959

6 And without fear the lawless roads Ran wrong through all the land.
   Journeys and Places (1937) 'Hölderlin's Journey'

Ethel Watts Mumford et al.
1878–1940

7 In the midst of life we are in debt.
   Altogether New Cynic's Calendar (1907). Cf. 66:7

Lewis Mumford 1895–1982

8 Our national flower is the concrete cloverleaf.
   Quote Magazine 8 October 1961

Iris Murdoch 1919–

9 Dora Greenfield left her husband because she was afraid of him. She decided six months later to return to him for the same reason.
   The Bell (1958) ch. 1

10 One doesn't have to get anywhere in a marriage. It's not a public conveyance.
   A Severed Head (1961) ch. 3

11 Anything that consoles is fake.
   In R. Harries *Prayer and the Pursuit of Happiness* (1985) p. 113. Cf. 71:14

C. W. Murphy and Will Letters

12 Has anybody here seen Kelly?
   Kelly from the Isle of Man?
   'Has Anybody Here Seen Kelly?' (1909 song)

Ed Murrow 1908–65

13 He [Winston Churchill] mobilized the English language and sent it into battle to steady his fellow countrymen and hearten those Europeans upon whom the long dark night of tyranny had descended.
   Broadcast, 30 November 1954, in *In Search of Light* (1967) p. 276

14 Anyone who isn't confused doesn't really understand the situation.
   On the Vietnam War, in Walter Bryan *The Improbable Irish* (1969) ch. 1

Alfred de Musset 1810–57

15 *Je ne puis:—malgré moi l'infini me tourmente.*
   I can't help it:—in spite of myself, infinity torments me.
   'L'Espoir en Dieu' (1838)

16 *Le seul bien qui me reste au monde*
   Est d'avoir quelquefois pleuré.
   The only good thing left to me is that I have sometimes wept.
   'Tristesse' (1841)

17 *Je suis venu trop tard dans un monde trop vieux.*
   I have come too late into a world too old.
   Rollo (1833)

Vladimir Nabokov 1899–1977

18 Lolita, light of my life, fire of my loins. My sin, my soul. Lo-lee-ta: the tip of the tongue taking a trip of three steps down the palate to tap, at three, on the teeth. Lo. Lee. Ta.
   Lolita (1955) ch. 1

19 The cradle rocks above an abyss, and common sense tells us that our existence is but a brief crack of light between two eternities of darkness.
   Speak, Memory (1951) ch. 1

20 I think like a genius, I write like a distinguished author, and I speak like a child.
   Strong Opinions (1973) foreword

Ralph Nader 1934–

21 Unsafe at any speed.
   Title of book (1965)

Napoléon I 1769–1821

1 [The Channel] is a mere ditch, and will be crossed as soon as someone has the courage to attempt it.

Letter to Consul Cambacérès, 16 November 1803, in *Correspondance de Napoléon Ier* (1858–69) vol. 9

2 There is only one step from the sublime to the ridiculous.

Following the retreat from Moscow in 1812; in D. G. De Pradt *Histoire de l'Ambassade dans le grand-duché de Varsovie en 1812* (1815) p. 215. Cf. 244:8

3 Think of it, soldiers; from the summit of these pyramids, forty centuries look down upon you.

Speech before the Battle of the Pyramids 21 July 1798; in G. Gourgaud *Mémoires* (1823) vol. 2

4 As to moral courage, I have very rarely met with two o'clock in the morning courage: I mean instantaneous courage.

In E. A. de Las Cases *Mémorial de Ste-Hélène* (1823) vol. 1, pt. 2, 4–5 December 1815

5 An army marches on its stomach.

Attributed, but probably condensed from a long passage in E. A. de Las Cases *Mémorial de Ste-Hélène* (1823) vol. 4, 14 November 1816

6 *La carrière ouverte aux talents.*
The career open to the talents.

In B. O'Meara *Napoleon in Exile* (1822) vol. 1, p. 103

7 England is a nation of shopkeepers.

In B. O'Meara *Napoleon in Exile* (1822) vol. 2, p. 81. Cf. 2:7, 308:23

8 Not tonight, Josephine.

Attributed, but probably apocryphal. See R. H. Horne *History of Napoleon* (1841) vol. 2, ch. 8

Ogden Nash 1902–71

9 The turtle lives 'twixt plated decks
Which practically conceal its sex.
I think it clever of the turtle
In such a fix to be so fertile.

'Autres Bêtes, Autres Moeurs' (1931)

10 The cow is of the bovine ilk;
One end is moo, the other, milk.

'The Cow' (1931)

11 One would be in less danger
From the wiles of the stranger
If one's own kin and kith
Were more fun to be with.

'Family Court' (1931)

12 Professional men, they have no cares;
Whatever happens, they get theirs.

'I Yield to My Learned Brother' (1935)

13 Beneath this slab
John Brown is stowed.
He watched the ads,
And not the road.

'Lather as You Go' (1942)

14 Do you think my mind is maturing late,
Or simply rotted early?

'Lines on Facing Forty' (1942)

15 Candy
Is dandy
But liquor
Is quicker.

'Reflections on Ice-breaking' (1931)

16 I test my bath before I sit,
And I'm always moved to wonderment
That what chills the finger not a bit
Is so frigid upon the fundament.

'Samson Agonistes' (1942)

17 I think that I shall never see
A billboard lovely as a tree.
Perhaps, unless the billboards fall,
I'll never see a tree at all.

'Song of the Open Road' (1933). Cf. 194:22

18 Sure, deck your lower limbs in pants;
Yours are the limbs, my sweeting.
You look divine as you advance—
Have you seen yourself retreating?

'What's the Use?' (1940)

Thomas Nashe 1567–1601

19 Brightness falls from the air;
Queens have died young and fair;
Dust hath closed Helen's eye.
I am sick, I must die.
Lord have mercy on us.

Summer's Last Will and Testament (1600) l. 1588

James Ball Naylor 1860–1945

20 King David and King Solomon
Led merry, merry lives,
With many, many lady friends,
And many, many wives;
But when old age crept over them—
With many, many qualms!—
King Solomon wrote the Proverbs
And King David wrote the Psalms.

'King David and King Solomon' (1935)

John Mason Neale 1818–66

21 All glory, laud, and honour
To thee, Redeemer, King,
To whom the lips of children
Made sweet hosannas ring.

'All glory, laud, and honour' (1851 hymn)

22 Jerusalem the golden,
With milk and honey blessed,
Beneath thy contemplation
Sink heart and voice oppressed.

'Jerusalem the golden' (1858 hymn); translated from the Latin of St Bernard of Cluny (b. *c.*1100)

Horatio, Lord Nelson 1758–1805

23 Before this time to-morrow I shall have gained a peerage, or Westminster Abbey.

Before the battle of the Nile, in R. Southey *Life of Nelson* (1813) ch. 5

1 I have only one eye,—I have a right to be blind sometimes ... I really do not see the signal!

At the battle of Copenhagen, in R. Southey *Life of Nelson* (1813) ch. 7

2 When I came to explain to them the '*Nelson touch*', it was like an electric shock.

Letter to Lady Hamilton, 1 October 1805, in R. Southey *Life of Nelson* (1813) ch. 9

3 England expects that every man will do his duty.

At the battle of Trafalgar, in R. Southey *Life of Nelson* (1813) ch. 9

4 This is too warm work, Hardy, to last long.

At the battle of Trafalgar, in R. Southey *Life of Nelson* (1813) ch. 9

5 Thank God, I have done my duty.

At the battle of Trafalgar, in R. Southey *Life of Nelson* (1813) ch. 9

6 Kiss me, Hardy.

At the battle of Trafalgar, in R. Southey *Life of Nelson* (1813) ch. 9

Emperor Nero AD 37–68

7 *Qualis artifex pereo!*
What an artist dies with me!

In Suetonius *Lives of the Caesars* 'Nero' sect. 49

Gérard de Nerval 1808–55

8 *Je suis le ténébreux,—le veuf,—l'inconsolé, Le prince d'Aquitaine à la tour abolie.*
I am the darkly shaded, the bereaved, the inconsolate, the prince of Aquitaine, with the blasted tower.

Les Chimères (1854) 'El Desdichado'

Allan Nevins 1890–1971

9 Offering Germany too little, and offering even that too late.

In *Current History* (New York) May 1935, p. 178

Sir Henry Newbolt 1862–1938

10 Take my drum to England, hang et by the shore,
Strike et when your powder's runnin' low;
If the Dons sight Devon, I'll quit the port o' Heaven,
An' drum them up the Channel as we drummed them long ago.

'Drake's Drum' (1897)

11 Drake he's in his hammock till the great Armadas come,
(Capten, art tha sleepin' there below?)

'Drake's Drum' (1897)

12 Now the sunset breezes shiver,
And she's fading down the river,
But in England's song for ever
She's the Fighting Téméraire.

'The Fighting Téméraire' (1897)

13 There's a breathless hush in the Close tonight—
Ten to make and the match to win—
A bumping pitch and a blinding light,
An hour to play and the last man in.
And it's not for the sake of a ribboned coat,
Or the selfish hope of a season's fame,
But his Captain's hand on his shoulder smote—
'Play up! play up! and play the game!'

'Vitaï Lampada' (1897)

Anthony Newley 1931– and Leslie Bricusse 1931–

14 Stop the world, I want to get off.

Title of musical (1961)

Cardinal Newman 1801–90

15 He has attempted (as I may call it) to *poison the wells.*

Apologia pro Vita Sua (1864) 'Mr Kingsley's Method of Disputation'

16 Ten thousand difficulties do not make one doubt.

Apologia pro Vita Sua (1864) 'Position of my Mind since 1845'

17 It is almost a definition of a gentleman to say that he is one who never inflicts pain.

The Idea of a University (1852) 'Knowledge and Religious Duty'

18 If I am obliged to bring religion into afterdinner toasts (which indeed does not seem quite the thing) I shall drink ... to Conscience first, and to the Pope afterwards.

Letter Addressed to the Duke of Norfolk ... (1875) sect. 5

19 Firmly I believe and truly
God is Three, and God is One;
And I next acknowledge duly
Manhood taken by the Son.

The Dream of Gerontius (1865)

20 Praise to the Holiest in the height,
And in the depth be praise;
In all his words most wonderful,
Most sure in all His Ways.

The Dream of Gerontius (1865)

21 Lead, kindly Light, amid the encircling gloom,
Lead thou me on;
The night is dark, and I am far from home,
Lead thou me on.
Keep Thou my feet; I do not ask to see
The distant scene; one step enough for me.

'Lead, kindly Light' (1834)

22 I loved the garish day, and spite of fears,
Pride ruled my will: remember not past years.

'Lead, kindly Light' (1834). Cf. 226:26

1 *We can believe what we choose.* We are
answerable for what we choose to believe.
> Letter to Mrs William Froude, 27 June 1848,
> in C. S. Dessain (ed.) *Letters and Diaries of John
> Henry Newman* vol. 12 (1962)

Sir Isaac Newton 1642–1727

2 If I have seen further it is by standing on
the shoulders of giants.
> Letter to Robert Hooke, 5 February 1676, in
> H. W. Turnbull (ed.) *Correspondence* vol. 1
> (1959) p. 416. Cf. 36:9

3 Every body continues in its state of rest, or
of uniform motion in a right line, unless it
is compelled to change that state by forces
impressed upon it.
> *Principia Mathematica* (1687) Laws of Motion 1
> (tr. A. Motte, 1729)

4 To every action there is always opposed an
equal reaction.
> *Principia Mathematica* (1687) Laws of Motion 3
> (tr. A. Motte, 1729)

5 *Hypotheses non fingo.*
I do not feign hypotheses.
> *Principia Mathematica* (1713 ed.) 'Scholium
> Generale'

6 I don't know what I may seem to the
world, but as to myself, I seem to have
been only like a boy playing on the sea-
shore and diverting myself in now and
then finding a smoother pebble or a
prettier shell than ordinary, whilst the
great ocean of truth lay all undiscovered
before me.
> In Joseph Spence *Anecdotes* (ed. J. Osborn,
> 1966) no. 1259

John Newton 1725–1807

7 Amazing grace! how sweet the sound
That saved a wretch like me!
> *Olney Hymns* (1779) 'Amazing grace'

8 Glorious things of thee are spoken,
Zion, city of our God!
> *Olney Hymns* (1779) 'Glorious things of thee
> are spoken'

9 How sweet the name of Jesus sounds
In a believer's ear!
> *Olney Hymns* (1779) 'How sweet the name of
> Jesus sounds'

Emperor Nicholas I of Russia
1796–1855

10 Turkey is a dying man. We may endeavour
to keep him alive, but we shall not
succeed. He will, he must die.
> In F. Max Müller (ed.) *Memoirs of Baron
> Stockmar* (tr. G. Müller, 1873) vol. 2, p. 107

11 Russia has two generals in whom she can
confide—Generals Janvier [January] and
Février [February].
> Attributed. See *Punch* 10 March 1855

Sir Harold Nicolson 1886–1968

12 We shall have to walk and live a
Woolworth life hereafter.
> Anticipating the aftermath of the Second
> World War, in *Diaries and Letters 1939–45*
> (1967) 4 June 1941

13 For seventeen years he did nothing at all
but kill animals and stick in stamps.
> Of King George V, in *Diaries and Letters
> 1945–62* (1968) 17 August 1949

Reinhold Niebuhr 1892–1971

14 Man's capacity for justice makes
democracy possible, but man's inclination
to injustice makes democracy necessary.
> *Children of Light and Children of Darkness* (1944)
> foreword

Martin Niemöller 1892–1984

15 When Hitler attacked the Jews I was not
a Jew, therefore, I was not concerned. And
when Hitler attacked the Catholics, I was
not a Catholic, and therefore, I was not
concerned. And when Hitler attacked the
unions and the industrialists, I was not
a member of the unions and I was not
concerned. Then, Hitler attacked me and
the Protestant church—and there was
nobody left to be concerned.
> In *Congressional Record* 14 October 1968,
> p. 31636

Friedrich Nietzsche 1844–1900

16 I teach you the superman. Man is
something to be surpassed.
> *Also Sprach Zarathustra* (1883) prologue, sect. 3

17 You are going to women? Do not forget the
whip!
> *Also Sprach Zarathustra* (1883) bk. 1 'Von Alten
> und jungen Weiblein'

18 Woman was God's second blunder.
> *Der Antichrist* (1888) aphorism 48

19 What I understand by 'philosopher': a
terrible explosive in the presence of which
everything is in danger.
> *Ecce Homo* (1908) 'Die Unzeitgemässen' sect. 3

20 Morality is the herd-instinct in the
individual.
> *Die fröhliche Wissenschaft* (1882) bk. 3, sect. 116

21 Believe me! The secret of reaping the
greatest fruitfulness and the greatest
enjoyment from life is *to live dangerously!*
> *Die fröhliche Wissenschaft* (1882) bk. 4,
> sect. 283

22 Master-morality and slave-morality.
> *Jenseits von Gut und Böse* (1886) ch. 9, no. 260

23 Wit is the epitaph of an emotion.
> *Menschliches, Allzumenschliches* (1867–80) vol. 2,
> sect. 1, no. 202

Florence Nightingale 1820–1910

1 Too kind, too kind.
   On the Order of Merit being brought to her
   at her home, 5 December 1907; in E. Cook
   Life of Florence Nightingale (1913) vol. 2, pt. 7,
   ch. 9

Richard Nixon 1913–

2 There can be no whitewash at the White
   House.
   Television speech on Watergate, 30 April
   1973, in *New York Times* 1 May 1973, p. 31

3 People have got to know whether or not
   their President is a crook. Well, I'm not
   a crook.
   Speech, 17 November 1973, in *New York Times*
   18 November 1973, p. 62

4 I brought myself down. I gave them
   a sword. And they stuck it in.
   Television interview, 19 May 1977, in David
   Frost *I Gave Them a Sword* (1978) ch. 10

Thomas Noel 1799–1861

5 Rattle his bones over the stones;
   He's only a pauper, whom nobody owns!
   'The Pauper's Drive' (1841)

Christopher North (John Wilson) 1785–1854

6 His Majesty's dominions, on which the sun
   never sets.
   Blackwood's Magazine (April 1829) 'Noctes
   Ambrosianae' no. 42. Cf. 267:19

7 Laws were made to be broken.
   Blackwood's Magazine (May 1830) 'Noctes
   Ambrosianae' no. 49

Lord Northcliffe 1865–1922

8 The power of the press is very great, but
   not so great as the power of suppress.
   Office message, *Daily Mail* 1918, in R. Rose
   and G. Harmsworth *Northcliffe* (1959) ch. 22

9 When I want a peerage, I shall buy it like
   an honest man.
   In Tom Driberg *Swaff* (1974) ch. 2

Caroline Norton 1808–77

10 And all our calm is in that balm—
   Not lost but gone before.
   'Not Lost but Gone Before'. Cf. 113:13

Jack Norworth 1879–1959

11 Oh, shine on, shine on, harvest moon
   Up in the sky.
   I ain't had no lovin'
   Since April, January, June, or July.
   'Shine On, Harvest Moon' (1908 song)

Novalis (Friedrich von Hardenberg) 1772–1801

12 Fate and character are the same concept.
   Heinrich von Ofterdingen (1802) bk. 2 (often
   quoted 'Character is destiny' or 'Character is
   fate'). Cf. 132:15, 166:9

13 A God-intoxicated man.
   Of Spinoza (attributed)

Alfred Noyes 1880–1958

14 Look for me by moonlight;
   Watch for me by moonlight;
   I'll come to thee by moonlight, though hell
   should bar the way!
   'The Highwayman' (1907)

Bill Nye

15 I have been told that Wagner's music is
   better than it sounds.
   In Mark Twain *Autobiography* (1924) vol. 1,
   p. 338

Charles Edward Oakley 1832–65

16 Hills of the North, rejoice:
   River and mountain-spring,
   Hark to the advent voice!
   Valley and lowland, sing!
   'Hills of the North, rejoice' (1870 hymn)

Captain Lawrence Oates 1880–1912

17 I am just going outside and may be some
   time.
   Last words, in *Scott's Last Expedition* (1913)
   ch. 20 (Scott's diary entry, 16–17 March 1912)

Edna O'Brien 1936–

18 August is a wicked month.
   Title of novel (1965)

Flann O'Brien 1911–66

19 The conclusion of your syllogism, I said
   lightly, is fallacious, being based upon
   licensed premises.
   At Swim-Two-Birds (1939) ch. 1

20 A pint of plain is your only man.
   At Swim-Two-Birds (1939) 'The Workman's
   Friend'

Sean O'Casey 1880–1964

21 He's an oul' butty o' mine—oh, he's
   a darlin' man, a daarlin' man.
   Juno and the Paycock (1925) act 1

22 The whole worl's in a state o' chassis!
   Juno and the Paycock (1925) act 1

23 English literature's performing flea.
   In P. G. Wodehouse *Performing Flea* (1953)
   p. 217 (describing the author)

Adolph S. Ochs 1858–1935

1 All the news that's fit to print.
   Motto of the *New York Times*, from 1896

David Ogilvy 1911–

2 The consumer isn't a moron; she is your
   wife.
   Confessions of an Advertising Man (1963) ch. 5

James Ogilvy, 1st Earl of Seafield
1664–1730

3 Now there's ane end of ane old song.
   As he signed the engrossed exemplification
   of the Act of Union, 1706, in *The Lockhart
   Papers* (1817) vol. 1, p. 223

Theodore O'Hara 1820–67

4 Sons of the dark and bloody ground.
   'The Bivouac of the Dead' (1847) st. 1

John O'Keeffe 1747–1833

5 Amo, amas, I love a lass,
   As a cedar tall and slender;
   Sweet cowslip's grace
   Is her nom'native case,
   And she's of the feminine gender.
   The Agreeable Surprise (1781) act 2, sc. 2

6 Fat, fair and forty were all the toasts of the
   young men.
   The Irish Mimic (1795) sc. 2

Dennis O'Kelly *c.*1720–87

7 Eclipse first, the rest nowhere.
   Comment at Epsom, 3 May 1769, in *Annals of
   Sporting* vol. 2 (1822) p. 271

Laurence Olivier 1907–89

8 The tragedy of a man who could not make
   up his mind.
   Introduction to his 1948 screen adaptation
   of *Hamlet*

Frank Ward O'Malley
See ELBERT HUBBARD

Eugene O'Neill 1888–1953

9 For de little stealin' dey gits you in jail
   soon or late. For de big stealin' dey makes
   you Emperor and puts you in de Hall o'
   Fame when you croaks.
   The Emperor Jones (1921) sc. 1

10 The iceman cometh.
   Title of play (1946)

11 A long day's journey into night.
   Title of play (written 1940–1)

12 The sea hates a coward!
   Mourning becomes Electra (1931) pt. 2, act 4

Yoko Ono 1933–

13 Woman is the nigger of the world.
   Interview for *Nova* magazine (1968); adopted
   by John Lennon as song title (1972)

J. Robert Oppenheimer 1904–67

14 The physicists have known sin; and this is
   a knowledge which they cannot lose.
   Open Mind (1955) ch. 5 (lecture, 1947)

Susie Orbach 1946–

15 Fat is a feminist issue.
   Title of book (1978)

Roy Orbison and Joe Melsom

16 Only the lonely (know the way I feel).
   Title of song (1960)

Baroness Orczy 1865–1947

17 We seek him here, we seek him there,
   Those Frenchies seek him everywhere.
   Is he in heaven?—Is he in hell?
   That demmed, elusive Pimpernel?
   The Scarlet Pimpernel (1905) ch. 12

Meta Orred

18 In the gloaming, Oh my darling!
   When the lights are dim and low,
   And the quiet shadows falling
   Softly come and softly go.
   'In the Gloaming' (1877 song)

Joe Orton 1933–67

19 I'd the upbringing a nun would envy . . .
   Until I was fifteen I was more familiar with
   Africa than my own body.
   Entertaining Mr Sloane (1964) act 1

20 It's all any reasonable child can expect if
   the dad is present at the conception.
   Entertaining Mr Sloane (1964) act 3

21 You were born with your legs apart. They'll
   send you to the grave in a Y-shaped coffin.
   What the Butler Saw (1969) act 1

George Orwell 1903–50

22 Four legs good, two legs bad.
   Animal Farm (1945) ch. 3

23 All animals are equal but some animals
   are more equal than others.
   Animal Farm (1945) ch. 10

24 At 50, everyone has the face he deserves.
   Last words in his notebook, 17 April 1949;
   Collected Essays, Journalism and Letters . . .
   (1968) vol. 4, p. 515

25 I'm fat, but I'm thin inside. Has it ever
   struck you that there's a thin man inside
   every fat man, just as they say there's
   a statue inside every block of stone?
   Coming up For Air (1939) pt. 1, ch. 3. Cf. 5:4

1 Down here it was still the England I had known in my childhood: the railway cuttings smothered in wild flowers ... the red buses, the blue policemen—all sleeping the deep, deep sleep of England, from which I sometimes fear that we shall never wake till we are jerked out of it by the roar of bombs.

Homage to Catalonia (1938) ch. 14

2 Keep the aspidistra flying.

Title of novel (1936)

3 It [England] is a family in which the young are generally thwarted and most of the power is in the hands of irresponsible uncles and bed-ridden aunts. Still, it is a family. It has its private language and its common memories, and at the approach of an enemy it closes its ranks. A family with the wrong members in control.

The Lion and the Unicorn (1941) pt. 1 'England Your England'

4 Probably the battle of Waterloo *was* won on the playing-fields of Eton, but the opening battles of all subsequent wars have been lost there.

The Lion and the Unicorn (1941) pt. 1 'England Your England'. Cf. 345:10

5 It was a bright cold day in April, and the clocks were striking thirteen.

Nineteen Eighty-Four (1949) pt. 1, ch. 1

6 BIG BROTHER IS WATCHING YOU.

Nineteen Eighty-Four (1949) pt. 1, ch. 1

7 War is peace. Freedom is slavery. Ignorance is strength.

Nineteen Eighty-Four (1949) pt. 1, ch. 1

8 Who controls the past controls the future: who controls the present controls the past.

Nineteen Eighty-Four (1949) pt. 1, ch. 3

9 Freedom is the freedom to say that two plus two make four. If that is granted, all else follows.

Nineteen Eighty-Four (1949) pt. 1, ch. 7

10 *Doublethink* means the power of holding two contradictory beliefs in one's mind simultaneously, and accepting both of them.

Nineteen Eighty-Four (1949) pt. 2, ch. 9

11 If you want a picture of the future, imagine a boot stamping on a human face—for ever.

Nineteen Eighty-Four (1949) pt. 3, ch. 3

12 The quickest way of ending a war is to lose it.

Polemic May 1946 'Second Thoughts on James Burnham'

13 To the ordinary working man, the sort you would meet in any pub on Saturday night, Socialism does not mean much more than better wages and shorter hours and nobody bossing you about.

The Road to Wigan Pier (1937) ch. 11

14 We of the sinking middle class ... may sink without further struggles into the working class where we belong, and probably when we get there it will not be so dreadful as we feared, for, after all, we have nothing to lose but our aitches.

The Road to Wigan Pier (1937) ch. 13. Cf. 221:15

15 Political language ... is designed to make lies sound truthful and murder respectable, and to give an appearance of solidity to pure wind.

Shooting an Elephant (1950) 'Politics and the English Language'

16 Advertising is the rattling of a stick inside a swill bucket.

Attributed

Dorothy Osborne 1627–95

17 All letters, methinks, should be free and easy as one's discourse, not studied as an oration, nor made up of hard words like a charm.

Letters of Dorothy Osborne to William Temple (ed. G. C. Moore Smith, 1928) September 1653

John Osborne 1929–

18 Don't clap too hard—it's a very old building.

The Entertainer (1957) no. 7

19 Thank God we're normal,
Yes, this is our finest shower!

The Entertainer (1957) no. 7

20 But I have a go, lady, don't I? I 'ave a go. I do.

The Entertainer (1957) no. 7

21 His knowledge of life and ordinary human beings is so hazy, he really deserves some sort of decoration for it—a medal inscribed 'For Vaguery in the Field'.

Look Back in Anger (1956) act 1

22 Slamming their doors, stamping their high heels, banging their irons and saucepans—the eternal flaming racket of the female.

Look Back in Anger (1956) act 1

23 Reason and Progress, the old firm, is selling out!

Look Back in Anger (1956) act 2, sc. 1

24 They spend their time mostly looking forward to the past.

Look Back in Anger (1956) act 2, sc. 1

25 She's like the old line about justice—not only must be done, but must be seen to be done.

Time Present (1968) act 1

26 Royalty is the gold filling in a mouthful of decay.

'They call it cricket' in T. Maschler (ed.) *Declaration* (1957)

Arthur O'Shaughnessy 1844–81

1 We are the music makers,
We are the dreamers of dreams ...
We are the movers and shakers
Of the world for ever, it seems.
'Ode' (1874)

2 For each age is a dream that is dying,
Or one that is coming to birth.
'Ode' (1874)

Sir William Osler 1849–1919

3 One finger in the throat and one in the
rectum makes a good diagnostician.
Aphorisms from his Bedside Teachings (1961)
p. 104

John L. O'Sullivan 1813–95

4 The best government is that which governs
least.
United States Magazine and Democratic Review
(1837) introduction

5 A torchlight procession marching down
your throat.
Of whisky, in G. W. E. Russell *Collections and
Recollections* (1898) ch. 19

James Otis 1725–83

6 Taxation without representation is
tyranny.
Watchword (coined *c.*1761) of the American
Revolution. See *Dictionary of American
Biography* vol. 14, p. 102

Thomas Otway 1652–85

7 No praying, it spoils business.
Venice Preserved (1682) act 2, l. 87

Sir Thomas Overbury 1581–1613

8 He disdains all things above his reach, and
preferreth all countries before his own.
Miscellaneous Works (1632) 'An Affected
Traveller'. Cf. 89:11, 121:17, 151:20

Ovid 43 BC–AD c.17

9 *Procul hinc, procul este, severae!*
Far hence, keep far from me, you grim
women!
Amores bk. 2, no. 1, l. 3

10 *Iuppiter ex alto periuria ridet amantum.*
Jupiter from on high laughs at lovers'
perjuries.
Ars Amatoria bk. 1, l. 633

11 *Expedit esse deos, et, ut expedit, esse putemus.*
It is convenient that there be gods, and, as
it is convenient, let us believe that there
are.
Ars Amatoria bk. 1, l. 637

12 *Gutta cavat lapidem, consumitur anulus usu.*
Dripping water hollows out a stone, a ring
is worn away by use.
Epistulae Ex Ponto bk. 4, no. 10, l. 5. Cf. 202:3

13 *Medio tutissimus ibis.*
You will go most safely by the middle way.
Metamorphoses bk. 2, l. 137

14 *Inopem me copia fecit.*
Plenty has made me poor.
Metamorphoses bk. 3, l. 466

15 *Video meliora, proboque;
Deteriora sequor.*
I see the better things, and approve; I
follow the worse.
Metamorphoses bk. 7, l. 20

16 *Tempus edax rerum.*
Time the devourer of everything.
Metamorphoses bk. 15, l. 234

John Owen c.1563–1622

17 God and the doctor we alike adore
But only when in danger, not before;
The danger o'er, both are alike requited,
God is forgotten, and the Doctor slighted.
Epigrams. Cf. 256:27

Robert Owen 1771–1858

18 All the world is queer save thee and me,
and even thou art a little queer.
To his partner W. Allen, on severing
business relations at New Lanark, 1828
(attributed)

Wilfred Owen 1893–1918

19 My subject is War, and the pity of War.
The Poetry is in the pity.
Poems (1963) preface (written 1918)

20 All a poet can do today is warn.
Poems (1963) preface (written 1918)

21 What passing-bells for these who die as
cattle?
Only the monstrous anger of the guns.
'Anthem for Doomed Youth' (written 1917)

22 The shrill, demented choirs of wailing
shells;
And bugles calling for them from sad
shires.
'Anthem for Doomed Youth' (written 1917)

23 The pallor of girls' brows shall be their
pall;
Their flowers the tenderness of patient
minds,
And each slow dusk a drawing-down of
blinds.
'Anthem for Doomed Youth' (written 1917)

24 Move him into the sun—
Gently its touch awoke him once,
At home, whispering of fields half-sown.
'Futility' (written 1918)

1 Red lips are not so red
As the stained stones kissed by the English
dead.
'Greater Love' (written 1917)

2 It seemed that out of battle I escaped
Down some profound dull tunnel, long
since scooped
Through granites which titanic wars had
groined.
'Strange Meeting' (written 1918)

3 I am the enemy you killed, my friend.
I knew you in this dark.
'Strange Meeting' (written 1918)

4 Let us sleep now.
'Strange Meeting' (written 1918)

Count Oxenstierna 1583–1654

5 Dost thou not know, my son, with how
little wisdom the world is governed?
Letter to his son, 1648, in J. F. af Lundblad
Svensk Plutark (1826) pt. 2, p. 95. In *Table Talk*
(1689) John Selden quotes 'a certain Pope':
'Thou little thinkest what *a little foolery
governs the whole world!'*

Thomas Paine 1737–1809

6 It is necessary to the happiness of man
that he be mentally faithful to himself.
Infidelity does not consist in believing, or
in disbelieving, it consists in professing to
believe what one does not believe.
The Age of Reason pt. 1 (1794) p. 2

7 Any system of religion that has any thing
in it that shocks the mind of a child
cannot be a true system.
The Age of Reason pt. 1 (1794) p. 39

8 The sublime and the ridiculous are often
so nearly related, that it is difficult to class
them separately. One step above the
sublime, makes the ridiculous; and one
step above the ridiculous, makes the
sublime again.
The Age of Reason pt. 2 (1795) p. 20

9 Government, even in its best state, is but a
necessary evil; in its worst state, an
intolerable one. Government, like dress, is
the badge of lost innocence; the palaces of
kings are built upon the ruins of the
bowers of paradise.
Common Sense (1776) ch. 1

10 As to religion, I hold it to be the
indispensable duty of government to
protect all conscientious professors
thereof, and I know of no other business
which government hath to do therewith.
Common Sense (1776) ch. 4

11 These are the times that try men's souls.
The summer soldier and the sunshine
patriot will, in this crisis, shrink from the
service of their country; but he that stands
it *now*, deserves the love and thanks of
men and women.
The Crisis (December 1776) introduction

12 As he rose like a rocket, he fell like the
stick.
On Edmund Burke losing the debate on the
French Revolution to Charles James Fox, in
the House of Commons; in *Letter to the
Addressers on the late Proclamation* (1792) p. 4

13 When, in countries that are called civilized,
we see age going to the workhouse and
youth to the gallows, something must be
wrong in the system of government.
The Rights of Man pt. 2 (1792, ed. P. S. Foner,
1945) p. 404

14 My country is the world, and my religion is
to do good.
The Rights of Man pt. 2 (1792, ed. P. S. Foner,
1945) p. 414

15 A share in two revolutions is living to
some purpose.
In E. Foner *Tom Paine and Revolutionary
America* (1976) ch. 7

José de Palafox 1780–1847

16 *Guerra a cuchillo.*
War to the knife.
At the siege of Saragossa, 4 August 1808,
replying to the suggestion that he should
surrender (as reported). He actually said
'*Guerra y cuchillo* [War and the knife]'. See
José Gòmez de Arteche y Moro *Guerra de la
Independencia* (1875) vol. 2, ch. 4

William Paley 1743–1805

17 Who can refute a sneer?
Principles of Moral and Political Philosophy
(1785) bk. 5, ch. 9

Lord Palmerston 1784–1865

18 We have no eternal allies and we have no
perpetual enemies. Our interests are
eternal and perpetual, and those interests
it is our duty to follow.
Speech, *Hansard* 1 March 1848, col. 122

19 You may call it combination, you may call
it the accidental and fortuitous
concurrence of atoms.
On a projected Palmerston–Disraeli
coalition, in *Hansard* 5 March 1857, col. 1934

20 What is merit? The opinion one man
entertains of another.
In T. Carlyle *Shooting Niagara: and After?*
(1867) ch. 8

21 [Palmerston] once said that only three men
in Europe had ever understood [the
Schleswig-Holstein question], and of these
the Prince Consort was dead, a Danish
statesman (unnamed) was in an asylum,
and he himself had forgotten it.
In R. W. Seton-Watson *Britain in Europe
1789–1914* (1937) ch. 11

22 Die, my dear Doctor, that's the last thing I
shall do!
Last words, in E. Latham *Famous Sayings and
their Authors* (1904) p. 12

Norman Panama 1914– and Melvin Frank 1913–88

1 The pellet with the poison's in the vessel with the pestle. The chalice from the palace has the brew that is true.

The Court Jester (1955 film); spoken by Danny Kaye

Emmeline Pankhurst 1858–1928

2 The argument of the broken window pane is the most valuable argument in modern politics.

In G. Dangerfield *The Strange Death of Liberal England* (1936) pt. 2, ch. 3, sect. 4

Mitchell Parish d. 1993

3 When the deep purple falls over sleepy garden walls.

'Deep Purple' (1939 song)

Dorothy Parker 1893–1967

4 Oh, life is a glorious cycle of song,
A medley of extemporanea;
And love is a thing that can never go wrong;
And I am Marie of Roumania.

'Comment' (1937)

5 Four be the things I'd been better without:
Love, curiosity, freckles, and doubt.

'Inventory' (1937)

6 Men seldom make passes
At girls who wear glasses.

'News Item' (1937)

7 Why is it no one ever sent me yet
One perfect limousine, do you suppose?
Ah no, it's always just my luck to get
One perfect rose.

'One Perfect Rose' (1937)

8 Guns aren't lawful;
Nooses give;
Gas smells awful;
You might as well live.

'Résumé' (1937)

9 By the time you say you're his,
Shivering and sighing
And he vows his passion is
Infinite, undying—
Lady, make a note of this:
One of you is lying.

'Unfortunate Coincidence' (1937)

10 And I'll stay off Verlaine too; he was always chasing Rimbauds.

Here Lies (1939) 'The Little Hours'

11 Sorrow is tranquillity remembered in emotion.

Here Lies (1939) 'Sentiment'. Cf. 357:12

12 How do they know?

On being told that Calvin Coolidge had died; in M. Cowley *Writers at Work* 1st Series (1958) p. 65

13 *House Beautiful* is play lousy.

New Yorker review (1933), in P. Hartnoll *Plays and Players* (1984) p. 89

14 You can lead a horticulture, but you can't make her think.

In J. Keats *You Might as well Live* (1970) p. 46

15 It serves me right for putting all my eggs in one bastard.

On her abortion; in J. Keats *You Might as well Live* (1970) pt. 2, ch. 3

16 She ran the whole gamut of the emotions from A to B.

Of Katherine Hepburn at a Broadway first night (attributed)

Martin Parker d. c.1656

17 You gentlemen of England
Who live at home at ease,
How little do you think
On the dangers of the seas.

'The Valiant Sailors'. See *Early Naval Ballads* (Percy Society, 1841)

18 But all's to no end, for the times will not mend
Till the King enjoys his own again.

'Upon Defacing of Whitehall' (1671)

Ross Parker 1914–74 and Hugh Charles 1907–

19 There'll always be an England
While there's a country lane,
Wherever there's a cottage small
Beside a field of grain.

'There'll always be an England' (1939 song)

C. Northcote Parkinson 1909–93

20 Expenditure rises to meet income.

The Law and the Profits (1960) ch. 1

21 Work expands so as to fill the time available for its completion.

Parkinson's Law (1958) ch. 1

22 Time spent on any item of the agenda will be in inverse proportion to the sum involved.

Parkinson's Law (1958) ch. 3

Charles Stewart Parnell 1846–91

23 No man has a right to fix the boundary of the march of a nation; no man has a right to say to his country—thus far shalt thou go and no further.

Speech, 21 January 1885, in *The Times* 22 January 1885

Blaise Pascal 1623–62

24 I have made this [letter] longer than usual, only because I have not had the time to make it shorter.

Lettres Provinciales (1657) no. 16

1 When we see a natural style, we are quite
surprised and delighted, for we expected to
see an author and we find a man.
Pensées (1670, ed. L. Brunschvicg, 1909) sect. 1,
no. 29

2 Had Cleopatra's nose been shorter, the
whole face of the world would have
changed.
Pensées (1670) sect. 2, no. 162

3 The eternal silence of these infinite spaces
[the heavens] terrifies me.
Pensées (1670) sect. 2, no. 206

4 We shall die alone.
Pensées (1670) sect. 3, no. 211

5 The heart has its reasons which reason
knows nothing of.
Pensées (1670) sect. 4, no. 277

6 Man is only a reed, the weakest thing in
nature; but he is a thinking reed.
Pensées (1670) sect. 6, no. 347

7 The self is hateful.
Pensées (1670) sect. 7, no. 455

8 Comfort yourself, you would not seek me if
you had not found me.
Pensées (1670) sect. 7, no. 553

Boris Pasternak 1890–1960

9 Man is born to live, not to prepare for life.
Doctor Zhivago (1958) pt. 2, ch. 9, sect. 14

10 Yet the order of the acts is planned
And the end of the way inescapable.
I am alone; all drowns in the Pharisees'
hypocrisy.
To live your life is not as simple as to cross
a field.
Doctor Zhivago (1958) 'Hamlet' (tr. M. Hayward
and M. Harari)

Louis Pasteur 1822–95

11 Where observation is concerned, chance
favours only the prepared mind.
Address, 7 December 1854; in R. Vallery-
Radot *La Vie de Pasteur* (1900) ch. 4

12 There are no such things as applied
sciences, only applications of science.
Address, 11 September 1872, in *Comptes
rendus des travaux du Congrès viticole et séricicole
de Lyon, 9–14 septembre 1872*

Walter Pater 1839–94

13 She is older than the rocks among which
she sits.
Studies in the History of the Renaissance (1873)
'Leonardo da Vinci' (of the *Mona Lisa*)

14 All art constantly aspires towards the
condition of music.
Studies in the History of the Renaissance (1873)
'The School of Giorgione'

15 To burn always with this hard, gemlike
flame, to maintain this ecstasy, is success
in life.
Studies in the History of the Renaissance (1873)
'Conclusion'

'Banjo' Paterson 1864–1941

16 Once a jolly swagman camped by
a billabong,
Under the shade of a coolibah tree;
And he sang as he watched and waited till
his 'Billy' boiled:
'You'll come a-waltzing, Matilda, with me.'
'Waltzing Matilda' (1903 song)

Coventry Patmore 1823–96

17 'I saw you take his kiss!' ''Tis true.'
'O modesty!' ''Twas strictly kept:
He thought me asleep; at least, I knew
He thought I thought he thought I slept.'
The Angel in the House (1854–62) bk. 2, canto 8,
'The Kiss'

18 Some dish more sharply spiced than this
Milk-soup men call domestic bliss.
'Olympus' l. 15

Alan Paton 1903–

19 Cry, the beloved country.
Title of novel (1948)

James Payn 1830–98

20 I had never had a piece of toast
Particularly long and wide,
But fell upon the sanded floor,
And always on the buttered side.
Chambers's Journal 2 February 1884. Cf. 234:19

J. H. Payne 1791–1852

21 Mid pleasures and palaces though we may
roam,
Be it ever so humble, there's no place like
home.
Clari, or, The Maid of Milan (1823 opera)
'Home, Sweet Home'

Thomas Love Peacock 1785–1866

22 Where they [the Greeks] had anything that
exalts, delights, or adorns humanity, we
have nothing but cant, cant, cant.
Crotchet Castle (1831) ch. 7

23 My house has been broken open on the
most scientific principles.
Crotchet Castle (1831) ch. 17

24 Marriage may often be a stormy lake, but
celibacy is almost always a muddy
horsepond.
Melincourt (1817) ch. 7

25 Laughter is pleasant, but the exertion is
too much for me.
Nightmare Abbey (1818) ch. 5

Hesketh Pearson 1887–1964

26 There is no stronger craving in the world
than that of the rich for titles, except
perhaps that of the titled for riches.
The Pilgrim Daughters (1961) ch. 6

George Peele c.1556–96

1 What thing is love for (well I wot) love is a thing.
It is a prick, it is a sting,
It is a pretty, pretty thing.
The Hunting of Cupid (c.1591)

2 When as the rye reach to the chin,
And chopcherry, chopcherry ripe within,
Strawberries swimming in the cream,
And schoolboys playing in the stream,
Then O, then O, then O, my true love said,
Till that time come again,
She could not live a maid.
The Old Wive's Tale (1595) l. 75 'Song'

3 His golden locks time hath to silver turned;
O time too swift, O swiftness never ceasing!
Polyhymnia (1590) *ad fin.* 'Sonnet'

Charles Péguy 1873–1914

4 Tyranny is always better organised than freedom.
Basic Verities (1943) 'War and Peace'

William Herbert, 1st Earl of Pembroke c.1501–70

5 Out ye whores, to work, to work, ye whores, go spin.
In A. Clark (ed.) *'Brief Lives ... by John Aubrey'* (1898) vol. 1 (commonly quoted 'Go spin, you jades, go spin')

Henry Herbert, 2nd Earl of Pembroke c.1534–1601

6 A parliament can do any thing but make a man a woman, and a woman a man.
Quoted by his son, the 4th Earl, in a speech on 11 April 1648; in *Harleian Miscellany* (1745) vol. 5, p. 106

Henry Herbert, 10th Earl of Pembroke 1734–94

7 Dr Johnson's sayings would not appear so extraordinary, were it not for his bow-wow way.
In James Boswell *Life of Samuel Johnson* (1934 ed.) vol. 2, p. 326 n. (27 March 1775)

Vladimir Peniakoff 1897–1951

8 A message came on the wireless for me. It said: 'SPREAD ALARM AND DESPONDENCY' ...
The date was, I think, May 18th, 1942.
Private Army (1950) pt. 2, ch. 5 ('reports calculated to create unnecessary alarm or despondency' derives from the Army Act of 1879)

William Penn 1644–1718

9 No pain, no palm; no thorns, no throne; no gall, no glory; no cross, no crown.
No Cross, No Crown (1669 pamphlet)

10 Men are generally more careful of the breed of their horses and dogs than of their children.
Some Fruits of Solitude (1693) pt. 1, no. 85

Roger Penrose 1931–

11 Consciousness ... is the phenomenon whereby the universe's very existence is made known.
The Emperor's New Mind (1989) ch. 10 'Conclusion'

Samuel Pepys 1633–1703

12 And so to bed.
Diary 20 April 1660

13 I went out to Charing Cross, to see Major-general Harrison hanged, drawn, and quartered; which was done there, he looking as cheerful as any man could do in that condition.
Diary 13 October 1660

14 A good honest and painful sermon.
Diary 17 March 1661

15 I see it is impossible for the King to have things done as cheap as other men.
Diary 21 July 1662

16 My wife, who, poor wretch, is troubled with her lonely life.
Diary 19 December 1662

17 Pretty witty Nell.
Diary 3 April 1665 (of Nell Gwyn)

18 Strange to say what delight we married people have to see these poor fools decoyed into our condition.
Diary 25 December 1665

19 Music and women I cannot but give way to, whatever my business is.
Diary 9 March 1666

20 But it is pretty to see what money will do.
Diary 21 March 1667

21 This day my wife made it appear to me that my late entertainment this week cost me above £12, an expense which I am almost ashamed of, though it is but once in a great while, and is the end for which, in the most part, we live, to have such a merry day once or twice in a man's life.
Diary 6 March 1669

22 And so I betake myself to that course, which is almost as much as to see myself go into my grave—for which, and all the discomforts that will accompany my being blind, the good God prepare me!
Diary 31 May 1669

S. J. Perelman 1904–79

23 Crazy like a fox.
Title of book (1944)

Pericles c.495–429 BC

1 Our love of what is beautiful does not lead
to extravagance; our love of the things of
the mind does not make us soft.
> Funeral Oration, Athens, 430 BC, in
> Thucydides *History of the Peloponnesian War*
> bk. 2, ch. 40, sect. 1 (tr. R. Warner)

2 Famous men have the whole earth as their
memorial.
> In Thucydides *History of the Peloponnesian War*
> bk. 2, ch. 43, sect. 3 (tr. R. Warner)

3 The greatest glory of a woman is to be
least talked about by men.
> In Thucydides *History of the Peloponnesian War*
> bk. 2, ch. 45, sect. 2 (tr. R. Warner)

Edward Perronet 1726–92

4 All hail the power of Jesus' Name;
Let Angels prostrate fall;
Bring forth the royal diadem
To crown Him Lord of all.
> 'All hail the power of Jesus' Name' (1780
> hymn)

Jimmy Perry

5 Who do you think you are kidding, Mister
Hitler?
> Theme song of *Dad's Army*, BBC television
> (1968–77)

Ted Persons

6 Things ain't what they used to be.
> Title of song (1941)

Marshal Pétain 1856–1951

7 To write one's memoirs is to speak ill of
everybody except oneself.
> In *Observer* 26 May 1946

Laurence Peter 1919–

8 In a hierarchy every employee tends to rise
to his level of incompetence.
> *The Peter Principle* (1969) ch. 1

Petronius d. AD 65

9 *Abiit ad plures.*
He's gone to join the majority [the dead].
> *Satyricon* 'Cena Trimalchionis' ch. 42, sect. 5

10 *Foeda est in coitu et brevis voluptas
Et taedet Veneris statim peractae.*
Delight of lust is gross and brief
And weariness treads on desire.
> In A. Baehrens *Poetae Latini Minores* (1882)
> vol. 4, no. 101 (tr. H. Waddell)

Edward John Phelps 1822–1900

11 The man who makes no mistakes does not
usually make anything.
> Speech, 24 January 1889; in *The Times*
> 25 January 1889, p. 10

Kim Philby 1912–88

12 To betray, you must first belong.
> In *Sunday Times* 17 December 1967, p. 2

'Jack' Philip 1840–1900

13 Don't cheer, men; those poor devils are
dying.
> At the Battle of Santiago, 4 July 1898; in
> *Dictionary of American Biography* vol. 14 (1934)
> 'John Woodward Philip'

Ambrose Philips c.1675–1749

14 The flowers anew, returning seasons bring;
But beauty faded has no second spring.
> *The First Pastoral* (1708) 'Lobbin' l. 47

15 There solid billows of enormous size,
Alps of green ice, in wild disorder rise.
> 'A Winter-Piece' in *The Tatler* (7 May 1709)

Stephen Phillips 1864–1915

16 Behold me now
A man not old, but mellow, like good wine.
Not over-jealous, yet an eager husband.
> *Ulysses* (1902) act 3, sc. 2

Eden Phillpotts 1862–1960

17 A little dreamin', a little dyin',
A little lew corner of airth to lie in.
> 'Gaffer's Song' (1942)

Pablo Picasso 1881–1973

18 God is really only another artist. He
invented the giraffe, the elephant, and the
cat. He has no real style. He just goes on
trying other things.
> In F. Gilot and C. Lake *Life With Picasso* (1964)
> pt. 1

19 Every positive value has its price in
negative terms ... The genius of Einstein
leads to Hiroshima.
> In F. Gilot and C. Lake *Life With Picasso* (1964)
> pt. 2

Harold Pinter 1930–

20 If only I could get down to Sidcup! I've
been waiting for the weather to break. He's
got my papers, this man I left them with,
it's got it all down there, I could prove
everything.
> *The Caretaker* (1960) act 1

21 Apart from the known and the unknown,
what else is there?
> *The Homecoming* (1965) act 2, sc. 1

22 The weasel under the cocktail cabinet.
> On being asked what his plays were about,
> in J. Russell Taylor *Anger and After* (1962)
> p. 231

Luigi Pirandello 1867–1936

1 Six characters in search of an author.
Title of play (1921)

Robert M. Pirsig 1928–

2 That's the classical mind at work, runs fine inside but looks dingy on the surface.
Zen and the Art of Motorcycle Maintenance (1974) pt. 3, ch. 26

William Pitt, Earl of Chatham 1708–78

3 The atrocious crime of being a young man ... I shall neither attempt to palliate nor deny.
Speech, *Hansard* 2 March 1741, col. 115

4 Unlimited power is apt to corrupt the minds of those who possess it.
Speech, *Hansard* (Lords) 9 January 1770, col. 665. Cf. 1:5

5 I invoke the genius of the Constitution!
Speech, *Hansard* (Lords) 18 November 1777, col. 369

6 The parks are the lungs of London.
In *Hansard* 30 June 1808, col. 1124 (quoted by William Windham)

William Pitt 1759–1806

7 Necessity is the plea for every infringement of human freedom: it is the argument of tyrants; it is the creed of slaves.
Speech, *Hansard* 18 November 1783, col. 1209

8 England has saved herself by her exertions, and will, as I trust, save Europe by her example.
In R. Coupland *War Speeches of William Pitt* (1915) p. 35 (9 November 1805)

9 Roll up that map; it will not be wanted these ten years.
Of a map of Europe, on hearing of Napoleon's victory at Austerlitz, December 1805; in Earl Stanhope *Life of the Rt. Hon. William Pitt* vol. 4 (1862) ch. 43

10 Oh, my country! how I leave my country!
Last words, in Earl Stanhope *Life of the Rt. Hon. William Pitt* vol. 3 (1879) ch. 43 ('How I love my country' in the 1st ed., vol. 4 (1862) ch. 43). G. Rose *Diaries and Correspondence* (1860) vol. 2, cites 'My country! oh, my country!'; oral tradition reports 'I think I could eat one of Bellamy's veal pies'

Pope Pius VII 1742–1823

11 We are prepared to go to the gates of Hell—but no further.
Attempting to reach an agreement with Napoleon, *c.*1800–1, in J. M. Robinson *Cardinal Consalvi* (1987) p. 66

Max Planck 1858–1947

12 A new scientific truth does not triumph by convincing its opponents and making them see the light, but rather because its opponents eventually die, and a new generation grows up that is familiar with it.
A Scientific Autobiography (1949) p. 33 (tr. F. Gaynor)

Sylvia Plath 1932–63

13 Is there no way out of the mind?
'Apprehensions' (1971)

14 Every woman adores a Fascist,
The boot in the face, the brute
Brute heart of a brute like you.
'Daddy' (1963)

15 Dying,
Is an art, like everything else.
'Lady Lazarus' (1963)

16 Love set you going like a fat gold watch.
'Morning Song' (1965)

17 Widow. The word consumes itself.
'Widow' (1971)

Plato 429–347 BC

18 Socrates, he says, breaks the law by corrupting young men and not recognizing the gods that the city recognizes, but some other new deities.
Apologia 24b

19 Is that which is holy loved by the gods because it is holy, or is it holy because it is loved by the gods?
Euthyphro 10

20 This was the end, Echekrates, of our friend; a man of whom we may say that of all whom we met at that time he was the wisest and justest and best.
Phaedo 118a (on the death of Socrates)

21 What I say is that 'just' or 'right' means nothing but what is in the interest of the stronger party.
Spoken by Thrasymachus in *The Republic* bk. 1, 338c (tr. F. M. Cornford)

Plautus *c.*250–184 BC

22 *Dictum sapienti sat est.*
A sentence is enough for a sensible man.
Persa l. 729 (proverbially '*Verbum sapienti sat est* [A word is enough for the wise]')

Pliny the Elder AD 23–79

23 *Semper aliquid novi Africam adferre.*
Africa always brings [us] something new.
Historia Naturalis bk. 8, sect. 42 (often quoted '*Ex Africa semper aliquid novi* [Always something new out of Africa]')

William Plomer 1903–73

1 With first-rate sherry flowing into second-
rate whores,
And third-rate conversation without one
single pause:
Just like a young couple
Between the wars.

'Father and Son: 1939' (1945)

Plutarch AD c.46–c.120

2 He who cheats with an oath acknowledges
that he is afraid of his enemy, but that he
thinks little of God.

Parallel Lives 'Lysander' ch. 8

Edgar Allan Poe 1809–49

3 I was a child and she was a child,
In this kingdom by the sea;
But we loved with a love which was more
than love—
I and my Annabel Lee.

'Annabel Lee' (1849)

4 Keeping time, time, time,
In a sort of Runic rhyme,
To the tintinnabulation that so musically
wells
From the bells, bells, bells, bells.

'The Bells' (1849) st. 1

5 All that we see or seem
Is but a dream within a dream.

'A Dream within a Dream' (1849)

6 The fever called 'Living'
Is conquered at last.

'For Annie' (1849)

7 Take thy beak from out my heart, and take
thy form from off my door!
Quoth the Raven, 'Nevermore'.

'The Raven' (1845) st. 17

8 Helen, thy beauty is to me
Like those Nicean barks of yore.

'To Helen' (1831)

9 Thy Naiad airs have brought me home,
To the glory that was Greece
And the grandeur that was Rome.

'To Helen' (1831)

Henri Poincaré 1854–1912

10 Science is built up of facts, as a house is
built of stones; but an accumulation of
facts is no more a science than a heap of
stones is a house.

Science and Hypothesis (1905) ch. 9

Madame de Pompadour 1721–64

11 *Après nous le déluge.*
After us the deluge.

In Mme du Hausset *Mémoires* (1824) p. 19

Georges Pompidou 1911–74

12 A statesman is a politician who places
himself at the service of the nation.
A politician is a statesman who places the
nation at his service.

In *Observer* 30 December 1973 'Sayings of the
Year'

Alexander Pope 1688–1744

13 Gentle Dullness ever loves a joke.

The Dunciad (1742) bk. 2, l. 34

14 A brain of feathers, and a heart of lead.

The Dunciad (1742) bk. 2, l. 44

15 Flow Welsted, flow! like thine inspirer,
Beer,
Tho' stale, not ripe; tho' thin, yet never
clear;
So sweetly mawkish, and so smoothly dull;
Heady, not strong; o'erflowing tho' not full.

The Dunciad (1742) bk. 3, l. 169

16 'Till Isis' elders reel, their pupils' sport,
And Alma mater lie dissolved in port!

The Dunciad (1742) bk. 3, l. 337

17 A wit with dunces, and a dunce with wits.

The Dunciad (1742) bk. 4, l. 90

18 The Right Divine of Kings to govern wrong.

The Dunciad (1742) bk. 4, l. 187

19 With the same cement, ever sure to bind,
We bring to one dead level ev'ry mind.

The Dunciad (1742) bk. 4, l. 267

20 Stretched on the rack of a too easy chair.

The Dunciad (1742) bk. 4, l. 342

21 Thy truffles, Perigord! thy hams, Bayonne!

The Dunciad (1742) bk. 4, l. 558

22 Lo! thy dread empire, Chaos! is restored;
Light dies before thy uncreating word:
Thy hand, great Anarch! lets the curtain
fall;
And universal darkness buries all.

The Dunciad (1742) bk. 4, l. 653

23 Is there no bright reversion in the sky,
For those who greatly think, or bravely
die?

'Elegy to the Memory of an Unfortunate
Lady' (1717) l. 9

24 Ambition first sprung from your blest
abodes;
The glorious fault of angels and of gods.

'Elegy to the Memory of an Unfortunate
Lady' (1717) l. 13

25 How shall I lose the sin, yet keep the sense,
And love th'offender, yet detest th'offence?

'Eloisa to Abelard' (1717) l. 191. Cf. 22:4

26 How happy is the blameless Vestal's lot!
The world forgetting, by the world forgot.

'Eloisa to Abelard' (1717) l. 207

27 You beat your pate, and fancy wit will
come:
Knock as you please, there's nobody at
home.

'Epigram: You beat your pate' (1732)

1 I am his Highness' dog at Kew;
  Pray, tell me sir, whose dog are you?
    'Epigram Engraved on the Collar of a Dog
    which I gave to his Royal Highness' (1738)

2 Sir, I admit your gen'ral rule
  That every poet is a fool:
  But you yourself may serve to show it,
  That every fool is not a poet.
    'Epigram from the French' (1732)

3 You think this cruel? take it for a rule,
  No creature smarts so little as a fool.
    'An Epistle to Dr Arbuthnot' (1735) l. 83.

4 The Muse but served to ease some friend,
    not wife,
  To help me through this long disease, my
    life.
    'An Epistle to Dr Arbuthnot' (1735) l. 131

5 And he, whose fustian's so sublimely bad,
  It is not poetry, but prose run mad.
    'An Epistle to Dr Arbuthnot' (1735) l. 187

6 Damn with faint praise, assent with civil
    leer,
  And without sneering, teach the rest to
    sneer.
    'An Epistle to Dr Arbuthnot' (1735) l. 201.
    Cf. 358:6

7 Satire or sense, alas! can Sporus feel?
  Who breaks a butterfly upon a wheel?'
    'An Epistle to Dr Arbuthnot' (1735) l. 307

8 Yet let me flap this bug with gilded wings,
  This painted child of dirt that stinks and
    stings.
    'An Epistle to Dr Arbuthnot' (1735) l. 309

9 Unlearn'd, he knew no schoolman's subtle
    art,
  No language, but the language of the
    heart.
    'An Epistle to Dr Arbuthnot' (1735) l. 398

10 Virtue she finds too painful an endeavour,
   Content to dwell in decencies for ever.
    Epistles to Several Persons 'To a Lady' (1735)
    l. 163

11 See how the world its veterans rewards!
   A youth of frolics, an old age of cards.
    Epistles to Several Persons 'To a Lady' (1735)
    l. 241

12 Woman's at best a contradiction still.
    Epistles to Several Persons 'To a Lady' (1735)
    l. 270

13 Die, and endow a college, or a cat.
    Epistles to Several Persons 'To Lord Bathurst'
    (1733) l. 98

14 The ruling passion, be it what it will,
   The ruling passion conquers reason still.
    Epistles to Several Persons 'To Lord Bathurst'
    (1733) l. 155. Cf. 251:21

15 Consult the genius of the place in all.
    Epistles to Several Persons 'To Lord Burlington'
    (1731) l. 57. Cf. 339:18

16 To rest, the cushion and soft Dean invite,
   Who never mentions Hell to ears polite.
    Epistles to Several Persons 'To Lord Burlington'
    (1731) l. 149

17 Deep harvests bury all his pride has
    planned,
   And laughing Ceres re-assume the land.
    Epistles to Several Persons 'To Lord Burlington'
    (1731) l. 175

18 'Tis use alone that sanctifies expense,
   And splendour borrows all her rays from
    sense.
    Epistles to Several Persons 'To Lord Burlington'
    (1731) l. 179

19 Like following life thro' creatures you
    dissect,
   You lose it in the moment you detect.
    Epistles to Several Persons 'To Lord Cobham'
    (1734) l. 39

20 'Tis from high life high characters are
    drawn;
   A saint in crape is twice a saint in lawn.
    Epistles to Several Persons 'To Lord Cobham'
    (1734) l. 87

21 Search then the Ruling Passion: There,
    alone,
   The wild are constant, and the cunning
    known;
   The fool consistent, and the false sincere.
    Epistles to Several Persons 'To Lord Cobham'
    (1734) l. 174. Cf. 251:14

22 Odious! in woollen! 'twould a saint
    provoke!
    Epistles to Several Persons 'To Lord Cobham'
    (1734) l. 242

23 Old politicians chew on wisdom past,
   And totter on in business to the last.
    Epistles to Several Persons 'To Lord Cobham'
    (1734) l. 248

24 She went, to plain-work, and to purling
    brooks,
   Old-fashioned halls, dull aunts, and
    croaking rooks.
    'Epistle to Miss Blount, on her leaving the
    Town, after the Coronation' (1717)

25 Or o'er cold coffee trifle with the spoon,
   Court the slow clock, and dine exact at
    noon.
    'Epistle to Miss Blount, on her leaving the
    Town ... ' (1717)

26 Nature, and Nature's laws lay hid in night.
   God said, Let Newton be! and all was light.
    'Epitaph: Intended for Sir Isaac Newton'
    (1730). Cf. 314:4

27 Some have at first for wits, then poets
    passed,
   Turned critics next, and proved plain fools
    at last.
    An Essay on Criticism (1711) l. 36

28 A little learning is a dangerous thing;
   Drink deep, or taste not the Pierian spring:
   There shallow draughts intoxicate the
    brain,
   And drinking largely sobers us again.
    An Essay on Criticism (1711) l. 215. Cf. 126:20

29 Whoever thinks a faultless piece to see,
   Thinks what ne'er was, nor is, nor e'er
    shall be.
    An Essay on Criticism (1711) l. 253

1 True wit is Nature to advantage dressed,
  What oft was thought, but ne'er so well
  expressed.
  An Essay on Criticism (1711) l. 297

2 Expression is the dress of thought.
  An Essay on Criticism (1711) l. 318. Cf. 346:18

3   As some to church repair,
  Not for the doctrine, but the music there.
  An Essay on Criticism (1711) l. 342

4 A needless Alexandrine ends the song,
  That, like a wounded snake, drags its slow
  length along.
  An Essay on Criticism (1711) l. 356

5 But let a Lord once own the happy lines,
  How the wit brightens! how the style
  refines!
  An Essay on Criticism (1711) l. 420

6 Some praise at morning what they blame
  at night;
  But always think the last opinion right.
  An Essay on Criticism (1711) l. 430

7 To err is human; to forgive, divine.
  An Essay on Criticism (1711) l. 525

8 Men must be taught as if you taught them
  not,
  And things unknown proposed as things
  forgot.
  An Essay on Criticism (1711) l. 574

9 The bookful blockhead, ignorantly read,
  With loads of learned lumber in his head.
  An Essay on Criticism (1711) l. 612

10 Fools rush in where angels fear to tread.
  An Essay on Criticism (1711) l. 625

11 Eye Nature's walks, shoot Folly as it flies,
  And catch the Manners living as they rise.
  Laugh where we must, be candid where we
  can;
  But vindicate the ways of God to man.
  An Essay on Man Epistle 1 (1733) l. 13.
  Cf. 228:9

12 Hope springs eternal in the human breast:
  Man never Is, but always To be blest.
  An Essay on Man Epistle 1 (1733) l. 95

13 Lo! the poor Indian, whose untutored mind
  Sees God in clouds, or hears him in the
  wind.
  An Essay on Man Epistle 1 (1733) l. 99

14 Why has not man a microscopic eye?
  For this plain reason, man is not a fly.
  An Essay on Man Epistle 1 (1733) l. 193

15 The spider's touch, how exquisitely fine!
  Feels at each thread, and lives along the
  line.
  An Essay on Man Epistle 1 (1733) l. 217

16 And, spite of Pride, in erring Reason's
  spite,
  One truth is clear, 'Whatever IS, is RIGHT.'
  An Essay on Man Epistle 1 (1733) l. 293

17 Know then thyself, presume not God to
  scan;
  The proper study of mankind is man.
  An Essay on Man Epistle 2 (1733) l. 1.
  Cf. 95:9

18 Created half to rise, and half to fall;
  Great lord of all things, yet a prey to all;
  Sole judge of truth, in endless error hurled;
  The glory, jest, and riddle of the world!
  An Essay on Man Epistle 2 (1733) l. 15

19 Behold the child, by Nature's kindly law
  Pleased with a rattle, tickled with a straw.
  An Essay on Man Epistle 2 (1733) l. 275

20 For forms of government let fools contest;
  Whate'er is best administered is best.
  An Essay on Man Epistle 3 (1733) l. 303

21 Thus God and nature linked the gen'ral
  frame,
  And bade self-love and social be the same.
  An Essay on Man Epistle 3 (1733) l. 317. See
  also *An Essay on Man* Epistle 4 (1734) l. 396

22 An honest man's the noblest work of God.
  An Essay on Man Epistle 4 (1734) l. 248

23 All our knowledge is, ourselves to know.
  An Essay on Man Epistle 4 (1734) l. 398

24 For I, who hold sage Homer's rule the best,
  Welcome the coming, speed the going
  guest.
  Imitations of Horace Horace bk. 2, Satire 2
  (1734) l. 159 ('speed the parting guest' in
  Pope's translation of *The Odyssey* (1725–6)
  bk. 15, l. 84)

25 Get place and wealth, if possible, with
  grace;
  If not, by any means get wealth and place.
  Imitations of Horace Horace bk. 1, Epistle 1
  (1738) l. 103. Cf. 173:6

26 Not to admire, is all the art I know,
  To make men happy, and to keep them so.
  Imitations of Horace Horace bk. 1, Epistle 6
  (1738) l. 1. Cf. 173:10

27 The worst of madmen is a saint run mad.
  Imitations of Horace Horace bk. 1, Epistle 6
  (1738) l. 27

28   The people's voice is odd,
  It is, and it is not, the voice of God.
  Imitations of Horace Horace bk. 2, Epistle 1
  (1737) l. 89. Cf. 3:14

29 But those who cannot write, and those
  who can,
  All rhyme, and scrawl, and scribble, to a
  man.
  Imitations of Horace Horace bk. 2, Epistle 1
  (1737) l. 187. Cf. 173:16

30 Ev'n copious Dryden, wanted, or forgot,
  The last and greatest art, the art to blot.
  Imitations of Horace Horace bk. 2, Epistle 1
  (1737) l. 280. Cf. 165:11, 187:32

31 Let humble Allen, with an awkward shame,
  Do good by stealth, and blush to find it
  fame.
  Imitations of Horace Epilogue to the Satires
  (1738) Dialogue 1, l. 135

32 Ask you what provocation I have had?
  The strong antipathy of good to bad.
  Imitations of Horace Epilogue to the Satires
  (1738) Dialogue 2, l. 197

1 Where'er you walk, cool gales shall fan the
glade,
Trees, where you sit, shall crowd into a
shade.
Pastorals (1709) 'Summer' l. 73

2 What dire offence from am'rous causes
springs.
The Rape of the Lock (1714) canto 1, l. 1

3 They shift the moving toyshop of their
heart.
The Rape of the Lock (1714) canto 1, l. 100

4 Fair tresses man's imperial race insnare,
And beauty draws us with a single hair.
The Rape of the Lock (1714) canto 2, l. 27

5 Belinda smiled, and all the world was gay.
The Rape of the Lock (1714) canto 2, l. 52

6 Here thou, great Anna! whom three realms
obey,
Dost sometimes counsel take—and
sometimes tea.
The Rape of the Lock (1714) canto 3, l. 7

7 At ev'ry word a reputation dies.
The Rape of the Lock (1714) canto 3, l. 16

8 The hungry judges soon the sentence sign,
And wretches hang that jury-men may
dine.
The Rape of the Lock (1714) canto 3, l. 21

9 Coffee, (which makes the politician wise,
And see thro' all things with his half-shut
eyes).
The Rape of the Lock (1714) canto 3, l. 117

10 Not louder shrieks to pitying heav'n are
cast,
When husbands or when lapdogs breathe
their last.
The Rape of the Lock (1714) canto 3, l. 157

11 Party-spirit, which at best is but the
madness of many for the gain of a few.
Letter to E. Blount, 27 August 1714, in G.
Sherburn (ed.) *Correspondence of Alexander Pope*
(1956) vol. 1

12 To endeavour to work upon the vulgar
with fine sense, is like attempting to hew
blocks with a razor.
Miscellanies (1727) vol. 2 'Thoughts on Various
Subjects'

13 A man should never be ashamed to own he
has been in the wrong, which is but
saying, in other words, that he is wiser
to-day than he was yesterday.
Miscellanies (1727) vol. 2 'Thoughts on Various
Subjects'

14 Here am I, dying of a hundred good
symptoms.
To Lord Lyttelton, 15 May 1744, in Joseph
Spence *Anecdotes* (ed. J. Osborn, 1966) no. 637

Sir Karl Popper 1902–

15 We may become the makers of our fate
when we have ceased to pose as its
prophets.
The Open Society and its Enemies (1945)
introduction

16 Science must begin with myths, and with
the criticism of myths.
'The Philosophy of Science' in C. A. Mace
(ed.) *British Philosophy in the Mid-Century* (1957)

Cole Porter 1891–1964

17 In olden days a glimpse of stocking
Was looked on as something shocking
Now, heaven knows,
Anything goes.
'Anything Goes' (1934 song)

18 When they begin the Beguine
It brings back the sound of music so
tender,
It brings back a night of tropical
splendour,
It brings back a memory ever green.
'Begin the Beguine' (1935 song)

19 There's no love song finer,
But how strange the change from major to
minor
Every time we say goodbye.
'Every Time We Say Goodbye' (1944 song)

20 I get no kick from champagne,
Mere alcohol doesn't thrill me at all.
'I Get a Kick Out of You' (1934 song)

21 So goodbye dear, and Amen,
Here's hoping we meet now and then,
It was great fun,
But it was just one of those things.
'Just One of Those Things' (1935 song)

22 Birds do it, bees do it,
Even educated fleas do it.
Let's do it, let's fall in love.
'Let's Do It' (1954 song; words added to the
1928 original)

23 Miss Otis regrets (she's unable to lunch
today).
Title of song (1934)

24 My heart belongs to Daddy.
Title of song (1938)

25 Night and day, you are the one,
Only you beneath the moon and under the
sun.
'Night and Day' (1932 song)

Beilby Porteus 1731–1808

26 ... One murder made a villain,
Millions a hero.
Death (1759) l. 154. Cf. 263:12

27 Teach him how to live,
And, oh! still harder lesson! how to die.
Death (1759) l. 319

Francis Pott 1832–1909

28 The strife is o'er, the battle done;
Now is the Victor's triumph won.
Hymn (1861); translation of 'Finita iam sunt
praelia' (c.1695)

Beatrix Potter 1866–1943

1 I am worn to a ravelling ... I am undone and worn to a thread-paper, for I have NO MORE TWIST.

The Tailor of Gloucester (1903) p. 22

2 It is said that the effect of eating too much lettuce is 'soporific'.

The Tale of the Flopsy Bunnies (1909) p. 9

3 Don't go into Mr McGregor's garden: your father had an accident there, he was put into a pie by Mrs McGregor.

The Tale of Peter Rabbit (1902) p. 10

Stephen Potter 1900–69

4 *How to be one up*—how to make the other man feel that something has gone wrong, however slightly.

Lifemanship (1950) p. 14

5 'Yes, but not in the South', with slight adjustments, will do for any argument about any place, if not about any person.

Lifemanship (1950) p. 43

6 A good general rule is to state that the bouquet is better than the taste, and vice versa.

One-Upmanship (1952) ch. 14 (on wine-tasting)

7 The theory and practice of gamesmanship or The art of winning games without actually cheating.

Title of book (1947)

Ezra Pound 1885–1972

8 Winter is icummen in,
Lhude sing Goddamm,
Raineth drop and staineth slop,
And how the wind doth ramm!
Sing: Goddamm.

'Ancient Music' (1917). Cf. 10:16

9 With usura hath no man a house of good stone
each block cut smooth and well fitting.

Cantos (1954) no. 45

10 Tching prayed on the mountain and
WROTE MAKE IT NEW
on his bath tub.

Cantos (1954) no. 53

11 Bah! I have sung women in three cities,
But it is all the same;
And I will sing of the sun.

'Cino' (1908)

12 Hang it all, Robert Browning,
There can be but the one 'Sordello'.

Draft of XXX Cantos (1930) no. 2

13 And even I can remember
A day when the historians left blanks in their writings,
I mean for things they didn't know.

Draft of XXX Cantos (1930) no. 13

14 For three years, out of key with his time,
He strove to resuscitate the dead art
Of poetry; to maintain 'the sublime'
In the old sense. Wrong from the start.

Hugh Selwyn Mauberley (1920) 'E. P. *Ode pour l'élection de son sépulcre*' pt. 1

15 His true Penelope was Flaubert,
He fished by obstinate isles;
Observed the elegance of Circe's hair
Rather than the mottoes on sundials.

Hugh Selwyn Mauberley (1920) 'E. P. *Ode* ... ' pt. 1

16 The age demanded an image
Of its accelerated grimace,
Something for the modern stage,
Not, at any rate, an Attic grace.

Hugh Selwyn Mauberley (1920) 'E. P. *Ode* ... ' pt. 2

17 Christ follows Dionysus,
Phallic and ambrosial
Made way for macerations;
Caliban casts out Ariel.

Hugh Selwyn Mauberley (1920) 'E. P. *Ode* ... ' pt. 3

18 Died some, pro patria,
non 'dulce' non 'et decor' ...
walked eye-deep in hell
believing in old men's lies, the unbelieving
came home, home to a lie.

Hugh Selwyn Mauberley (1920) 'E. P. *Ode* ... ' pt. 4. Cf. 173:26

19 There died a myriad,
And of the best, among them,
For an old bitch gone in the teeth,
For a botched civilization.

Hugh Selwyn Mauberley (1920) 'E. P. *Ode* ... ' pt. 5

20 The apparition of these faces in the crowd;
Petals on a wet, black bough.

'In a Station of the Metro' (1916)

21 Pull down thy vanity
Thou art a beaten dog beneath the hail,
A swollen magpie in a fitful sun,
Half black half white
Nor knowst'ou wing from tail.

pisan Cantos (1948) no. 81

22 Music begins to atrophy when it departs too far from the dance ... poetry begins to atrophy when it gets too far from music.

The ABC of Reading (1934) 'Warning'

23 Literature is news that STAYS news.

The ABC of Reading (1934) ch. 2

24 Poetry must be *as well written as prose.*

Letter to Harriet Monroe, January 1915, in D. Paige (ed.) *Selected Letters* (1950)

Anthony Powell 1905–

25 Books do furnish a room.

Title of novel (1971). Cf. 310:2

26 He's so wet you could shoot snipe off him.

A Question of Upbringing (1951) ch. 1

1 Growing old is like being increasingly penalized for a crime you haven't committed.

Temporary Kings (1973) ch. 1

Enoch Powell 1912–

2 History is littered with the wars which everybody knew would never happen.

Speech, 19 October 1967, in *The Times* 20 October 1967

3 As I look ahead, I am filled with foreboding. Like the Roman, I seem to see 'the River Tiber foaming with much blood'.

Speech, 20 April 1968, in *Observer* 21 April 1968. Cf. 339:11

John O'Connor Power b. 1846

4 The mules of politics: without pride of ancestry, or hope of posterity.

Of the Liberal Unionists, in H. H. Asquith *Memories and Reflections* (1928) vol. 1, ch. 16

Keith Preston 1884–1927

5 Of all the literary scenes
Saddest this sight to me:
The graves of little magazines
Who died to make verse free.

'The Liberators'

Jacques Prévert 1900–77

6 *C'est tellement simple, l'amour.*
It's so simple, love.

Les Enfants du Paradis (1945 film)

J. B. Priestley 1894–1984

7 First you take their faces from 'em by calling 'em the masses and then you accuse 'em of not having any faces.

Saturn Over the Water (1961) ch. 2

8 Our great-grand-children, when they learn how we began this war by snatching glory out of defeat, and then swept on to victory, may also learn how the little holiday steamers made an excursion to hell and came back glorious.

Radio broadcast, 5 June 1940, following the evacuation of Dunkirk; in *Listener* 13 June 1940

Matthew Prior 1664–1721

9 Be to her virtues very kind;
Be to her faults a little blind;
Let all her ways be unconfined;
And clap your padlock—on her mind.

'An English Padlock' (1705) l. 79

10 Nobles and heralds, by your leave,
Here lies what once was Matthew Prior,
The son of Adam and of Eve,
Can Stuart or Nassau go higher?

'Epitaph' (1702)

11 Cured yesterday of my disease,
I died last night of my physician.

'The Remedy Worse than the Disease' (1727)

12 No, no; for my virginity,
When I lose that, says Rose, I'll die:
Behind the elms last night, cried Dick,
Rose, were you not extremely sick?

'A True Maid' (1718)

Adelaide Ann Procter 1825–64

13 Seated one day at the organ,
I was weary and ill at ease,
And my fingers wandered idly
Over the noisy keys.

'A Lost Chord' (1858)

14 But I struck one chord of music,
Like the sound of a great Amen.

'A Lost Chord' (1858)

Protagoras b. c.485 BC

15 Man is the measure of all things.

In Plato *Theaetetus* 160d

Pierre-Joseph Proudhon 1809–65

16 *La propriété c'est le vol.*
Property is theft.

Qu'est-ce que la propriété? (1840) ch. 1

Marcel Proust 1871–1922

17 *A la recherche du temps perdu.*
In search of lost time.

Title of novel (1913–27, translated by C. K. Scott-Moncrieff and S. Hudson, 1922–31, as *Remembrance of things past*). Cf. 299:16

18 And suddenly the memory revealed itself. The taste was that of the little piece of madeleine which ... my aunt Léonie used to give me, dipping it first in her own cup of tea or tisane.

Swann's Way (1913, ed. T. Kilmartin, 1981) 'Overture'

19 One becomes moral as soon as one is unhappy.

Within a Budding Grove (1918, ed. T. Kilmartin, 1981) 'Madame Swann at Home'

20 I have a horror of sunsets, they're so romantic, so operatic.

Cities of the Plain (1922, ed. T. Kilmartin, 1981) pt. 2, ch. 2

21 The true paradises are the paradises that we have lost.

Time Regained (1926, ed. T. Kilmartin, 1981) vol. 3, p. 903

Publilius Syrus 1st century BC

22 A beautiful face is a mute recommendation.

Sententiae no. 199, in J. and A. Duff *Minor Latin Poets* (Loeb ed., 1934); tr. Thomas Tenison in *Baconiana* (1679) 'Ornamenta Rationalia' no. 12

1 *Inopi beneficium bis dat qui dat celeriter.*
He gives the poor man twice as much good
who gives quickly.

> *Sententiae* no. 274, in J. and A. Duff *Minor Latin Poets* (proverbially 'Bis dat qui cito dat [He gives twice who gives soon]')

2 *Necessitas dat legem non ipsa accipit.*
Necessity gives the law without itself
acknowledging one.

> *Sententiae* no. 444, in J. and A. Duff *Minor Latin Poets* (proverbially 'Necessitas non habet legem [Necessity has no law]')

John Pudney 1909–77

3 Do not despair
For Johnny-head-in-air;
He sleeps as sound
As Johnny underground.

> 'For Johnny' (1942)

William Pulteney, Earl of Bath
1684–1764

4 For Sir Ph—p well knows
That innuendos
Will serve him no longer in verse or in
prose,
Since twelve honest men have decided the
cause,
And were judges of fact, tho' not judges of
laws.

> 'The Honest Jury' (1729) st. 3 (on Sir Philip Yorke's unsuccessful prosecution of *The Craftsman*, 1729)

Punch 1841–1992

5 Advice to persons about to marry.—'Don't.'

> vol. 8, p. 1 (1845)

6 You pays your money and you takes your
choice.

> vol. 10, p. 17 (1846)

7 The Half-Way House to Rome, Oxford.

> vol. 16, p. 36 (1849)

8 Never do to-day what you can put off till
to-morrow.

> vol. 17, p. 241 (1849)

9 Who's 'im, Bill?
A stranger!
'Eave 'arf a brick at 'im.

> vol. 26, p. 82 (1854)

10 What is Matter?—Never mind.
What is Mind?—No matter.

> vol. 29, p. 19 (1855)

11 It ain't the 'unting as 'urts 'im, it's the
'ammer, 'ammer, 'ammer along the 'ard
'igh road.

> vol. 30, p. 218 (1856)

12 Mun, a had na' been the-erre abune two
hours when—*bang*—went saxpence!!!

> vol. 54, p. 235 (1868)

13 Go directly—see what she's doing, and tell
her she mustn't.

> vol. 63, p. 202 (1872)

14 There was one poor tiger that hadn't *got* a
Christian.

> vol. 68, p. 143 (1875)

15 It's worse than wicked, my dear, it's vulgar.

> Almanac (1876)

16 I used your soap two years ago; since then
I have used no other.

> vol. 86, p. 197 (1884)

17 Don't look at me, Sir, with—ah—in that
tone of voice.

> vol. 87, p. 38 (1884)

18 Botticelli isn't a wine, you Juggins!
Botticelli's a *cheese*!

> vol. 106, p. 270 (1894)

19 I'm afraid you've got a bad egg, Mr Jones.
Oh no, my Lord, I assure you! Parts of it
are excellent!

> vol. 109, p. 222 (1895)

20 Look here, Steward, if this is coffee, I want
tea; but if this is tea, then I wish for coffee.

> vol. 123, p. 44 (1902)

21 Sometimes I sits and thinks, and then
again I just sits.

> vol. 131, p. 297 (1906)

Alexander Pushkin 1799–1837

22 A tedious season they await
Who hear November at the gate.

> *Eugene Onegin* (1833) ch. 4, st. 40 (tr. B. Deutsch)

23 Moscow: those syllables can start
A tumult in the Russian heart.

> *Eugene Onegin* (1833) ch. 7, st. 36 (tr. B. Deutsch)

Israel Putnam 1718–90

24 Don't one of you fire until you see the
white of their eyes.

> At Bunker Hill, 1775, in R. Frothingham *History of the Siege of Boston* (1873) ch. 5 n. (also attributed to William Prescott, 1726–95)

Mario Puzo 1920–

25 I'll make him an offer he can't refuse.

> *The Godfather* (1969) ch. 1

26 A lawyer with his briefcase can steal more
than a hundred men with guns.

> *The Godfather* (1969) ch. 1

Francis Quarles 1592–1644

27 Our God and soldiers we alike adore
Ev'n at the brink of danger; not before:
After deliverance, both alike requited,
Our God's forgotten, and our soldiers
slighted.

> *Divine Fancies* (1632) 'Of Common Devotion'. Cf. 243:17

1 My soul, sit thou a patient looker-on;
   Judge not the play before the play is done:
   Her plot hath many changes; every day
   Speaks a new scene; the last act crowns
   the play.
   Emblems (1635) bk. 1, no. 15 'Respice Finem'

2 We spend our midday sweat, our midnight
   oil;
   We tire the night in thought, the day in
   toil.
   Emblems (1635) bk. 2, no. 2, l. 33

3 Be wisely worldly, be not worldly wise.
   Emblems (1635) bk. 2, no. 2, l. 46

4 Man is man's A.B.C. There is none that can
   Read God aright, unless he first spell Man.
   Hieroglyphics of the Life of Man (1638) no. 1, l. 1

5 We'll cry both arts and learning down,
   And hey! then up go we!
   The Shepherd's Oracles (1646) Eclogue 11 'Song
   of Anarchus'

Peter Quennell 1905–93

6 An elderly fallen angel travelling incognito.
   The Sign of the Fish (1960) ch. 2 (of André Gide)

Sir Arthur Quiller-Couch
1863–1944

7 The best is the best, though a hundred
   judges have declared it so.
   Oxford Book of English Verse (1900) preface

8 O pastoral heart of England! like a psalm
   Of green days telling with a quiet beat.
   'Ode upon Eckington Bridge' (1896)

Josiah Quincy 1772–1864

9 As it will be the right of all, so it will be
   the duty of some, definitely to prepare for
   a separation, amicably if they can, violently
   if they must.
   Abridgement of Debates of Congress vol. 4, p. 327
   (14 January 1811). Cf. 101:17

François Rabelais c.1494–c.1553

10 The appetite grows by eating.
   Gargantua (1534) bk. 1, ch. 5

11 Nature abhors a vacuum.
   Gargantua (1534) bk. 1, ch. 5 (quoting an
   article of ancient wisdom)

12 *Fais ce que voudras.*
   Do what you like.
   Gargantua (1534) bk. 1, ch. 57

13 I am going to seek a great perhaps ...
   Bring down the curtain, the farce is played
   out.
   Last words (attributed)

Jean Racine 1639–99

14 *Je l'ai trop aimé pour ne le point haïr!*
   I have loved him too much not to feel any
   hatred for him.
   Andromaque (1667) act 2, sc. 1

15 *Elle flotte, elle hésite; en un mot, elle est femme.*
   She floats, she hesitates; in a word, she's a
   woman.
   Athalie (1691) act 3, sc. 3

16 *Ce n'est plus une ardeur dans mes veines cachée:
   C'est Vénus tout entière à sa proie attachée.*
   It's no longer a burning within my veins:
   it's Venus entire latched onto her prey.
   Phèdre (1677) act 1, sc. 3

17 *Point d'argent, point de Suisse, et ma porte était
   close.*
   No money, no service, and my door stayed
   shut.
   Les Plaideurs (1668) act 1, sc. 1

James Rado 1939– and Gerome
Ragni 1942–

18 When the moon is in the seventh house,
   And Jupiter aligns with Mars ...
   This is the dawning of the age of Aquarius.
   Hair (1967) 'Aquarius'

Thomas Rainborowe d. 1648

19 The poorest he that is in England hath a
   life to live as the greatest he.
   During the Army debates at Putney,
   29 October 1647; in C. H. Firth (ed.) *Clarke
   Papers* vol. 1, Camden Society, New Series 49
   (1891) p. 301

Sir Walter Ralegh c.1552–1618

20 If all the world and love were young,
   And truth in every shepherd's tongue,
   These pretty pleasures might me move
   To live with thee, and be thy love.
   'Answer to Marlow'. Cf. 123:23, 219:3

21 Go, Soul, the body's guest,
   Upon a thankless arrant:
   Fear not to touch the best;
   The truth shall be thy warrant:
   Go, since I needs must die,
   And give the world the lie.
   'The Lie' (1608)

22 We die in earnest, that's no jest.
   'On the Life of Man'

23 Give me my scallop-shell of quiet,
   My staff of faith to walk upon,
   My scrip of joy, immortal diet,
   My bottle of salvation,
   My gown of glory, hope's true gage,
   And thus I'll take my pilgrimage.
   'The Passionate Man's Pilgrimage' (1604)

24 Fain would I climb, yet fear I to fall.
   Line written on a window-pane, in Thomas
   Fuller *Worthies of England* (1662) 'Devonshire'
   p. 261. Cf. 135:9

1 Even such is Time, which takes in trust
  Our youth, our joys, and all we have,
  And pays us but with age and dust;
  Who in the dark and silent grave,
  When we have wandered all our ways,
  Shuts up the story of our days:
  And from which earth, and grave, and
  dust,
  The Lord shall raise me up, I trust.
    Written the night before his death. See V. B.
    Heltzel 'Ralegh's "Even such is time" ' in
    Huntingdon Library Bulletin no. 10 (October
    1936)

2 O eloquent, just, and mighty Death! ...
  thou hast drawn together all the
  farstretched greatness, all the pride,
  cruelty, and ambition of man, and covered
  it all over with these two narrow words,
  Hic jacet [Here lies].
    The History of the World (1614) bk. 5, ch. 6

3 'Tis a sharp remedy, but a sure one for all
  ills.
    On feeling the edge of the axe prior to his
    execution, in D. Hume *History of Great Britain*
    (1754) vol. 1, ch. 4

4 So the heart be right, it is no matter which
  way the head lies.
    At his execution, on being asked which way
    he preferred to lay his head; in W. Stebbing
    Sir Walter Raleigh (1891) ch. 30

Sir Walter Raleigh 1861–1922

5 In examinations those who do not wish to
  know ask questions of those who cannot
  tell.
    Laughter from a Cloud (1923) 'Some Thoughts
    on Examinations'

6 I wish I loved the Human Race;
  I wish I loved its silly face;
  I wish I liked the way it walks;
  I wish I liked the way it talks;
  And when I'm introduced to one
  I wish I thought *What Jolly Fun!*
    'Wishes of an Elderly Man' (1923)

Arthur Ransome 1884–1967

7 BETTER DROWNED THAN DUFFERS IF NOT
  DUFFERS WONT DROWN.
    Swallows and Amazons (1930) ch. 1

Terence Rattigan 1911–77

8 You can be in the Horseguards and still be
  common, dear.
    Separate Tables (1954) 'Table Number Seven'
    sc. 1

Sir Herbert Read 1893–1968

9 Art is ... pattern informed by sensibility.
    The Meaning of Art (1955) ch. 1

Charles Reade 1814–84

10 *Courage, mon ami, le diable est mort!*
   Take courage, my friend, the devil is dead!
    The Cloister and the Hearth (1861) ch. 24, and
    passim

11 Sow an act, and you reap a habit. Sow a
   habit and you reap a character. Sow a
   character, and you reap a destiny.
    Attributed. See *Notes and Queries* (9th Series)
    vol. 12 (17 October 1903) p. 309

Ronald Reagan 1911–

12 You can tell a lot about a fellow's character
   by his way of eating jellybeans.
    In *New York Times* 15 January 1981

Erell Reaves

13 Lady of Spain, I adore you.
   Right from the night I first saw you,
   My heart has been yearning for you,
   What else could any heart do?
    'Lady of Spain' (1913 song)

Henry Reed 1914–86

14 As we get older we do not get any younger.
   Seasons return, and today I am fifty-five,
   And this time last year I was fifty-four,
   And this time next year I shall be sixty-two.
    'Chard Whitlow (Mr Eliot's Sunday Evening
    Postscript)' (1946)

15 Today we have naming of parts. Yesterday,
   We had daily cleaning. And tomorrow
   morning,
   We shall have what to do after firing. But
   today,
   Today we have naming of parts.
    'Lessons of the War: 1, Naming of Parts'
    (1946)

16 They call it easing the Spring: it is
   perfectly easy
   If you have any strength in your thumb:
   like the bolt,
   And the breech, and the cocking-piece, and
   the point of balance,
   Which in our case we have not got.
    'Lessons of the War: 1, Naming of Parts'
    (1946)

17   And as for war, my wars
   Were global from the start.
    'Lessons of the War: 3, Unarmed Combat'
    (1946)

18 In a civil war, a general must know—and
   I'm afraid it's a thing rather of instinct
   than of practice—he must know exactly
   when to move over to the other side.
    *Not a Drum was Heard: The War Memoirs of
    General Gland* (unpublished radio play, 1959)

19 And the sooner the tea's out of the way,
   the sooner we can get out the gin, eh?
    Private Life of Hilda Tablet (1954 radio play) in
    Hilda Tablet and Others (1971) p. 60

20 Modest? My word, no ... He was an all-the-
   lights-on man.
    A Very Great Man Indeed (1953 radio play) in
    Hilda Tablet and Others (1971) p. 23

21 I have known her pass the whole evening
   without mentioning a single book, or *in
   fact anything unpleasant*, at all.
    A Very Great Man Indeed (1953 radio play) in
    Hilda Tablet and Others (1971) p. 45

John Reed 1887–1920

1 Ten days that shook the world.
   Title of book (1919)

Max Reger 1873–1916

2 I am sitting in the smallest room of my
   house. I have your review before me. In
   a moment it will be behind me.
   Responding to a savage review by Rudolph
   Louis in *Münchener Neueste Nachrichten*,
   7 February 1906; in N. Slonimsky *Lexicon of
   Musical Invective* (1953) p. 139

Keith Reid 1946–

3 Her face, at first ... just ghostly
   Turned a whiter shade of pale.
   'A Whiter Shade of Pale' (1967 song)

Erich Maria Remarque 1898–1970

4 All quiet on the western front.
   English title of *Im Westen nichts Neues* (1929
   novel). Cf. 32:14, 214:14

Montague John Rendall
1862–1950

5 Nation shall speak peace unto nation.
   Motto of the BBC (1927). Cf. 45:5

Pierre Auguste Renoir 1841–1919

6 I paint with my prick.
   Much quoted, but possibly an inversion of
   'It's with my brush that I make love'; in A.
   André *Renoir* (1919) p. 10

Frederic Reynolds 1764–1841

7 It is better to have written a damned play,
   than no play at all—it snatches a man
   from obscurity.
   The Dramatist (1789) act 1, sc. 1

Sir Joshua Reynolds 1723–92

8 If you have great talents, industry will
   improve them: if you have but moderate
   abilities, industry will supply their
   deficiency.
   Discourses on Art (ed. R. Wark, 1975) no. 2
   (11 December 1769)

9 A mere copier of nature can never produce
   anything great.
   Discourses on Art (ed. R. Wark, 1975) no. 3
   (14 December 1770)

10 Genius ... is the child of imitation.
   Discourses on Art (ed. R. Wark, 1975) no. 6
   (10 December 1774)

Malvina Reynolds 1900–78

11 Little boxes on the hillside ...
   And they're all made out of ticky-tacky
   And they all look just the same.
   'Little Boxes' (1962 song); on the tract
   houses in the hills to the south of San
   Francisco

Cecil Rhodes 1853–1902

12 So little done, so much to do.
   On the day of his death, in L. Michell *Life of
   Rhodes* (1910) vol. 2, ch. 39. Cf. 325:14

Jean Rhys c.1890–1979

13 We can't all be happy, we can't all be rich,
   we can't all be lucky ... Some must cry so
   that others may be able to laugh the more
   heartily.
   Good Morning, Midnight (1939) pt. 1

14 The perpetual hunger to be beautiful and
   that thirst to be loved which is the real
   curse of Eve.
   The Left Bank (1927) 'Illusion'

15 A doormat in a world of boots.
   Describing herself; in *Guardian* 6 December
   1990, p. 24

David Ricardo 1772–1823

16 Rent is that portion of the earth, which is
   paid to the landlord for the use of the
   original and indestructible powers of the
   soil.
   *On the Principles of Political Economy and
   Taxation* (1817) ch. 2

Grantland Rice 1880–1954

17 For when the One Great Scorer comes to
   mark against your name,
   He writes—not that you won or lost—but
   how you played the Game.
   'Alumnus Football' (1941)

18 All wars are planned by old men
   In council rooms apart.
   'The Two Sides of War' (1955)

Sir Stephen Rice 1637–1715

19 I will drive a coach and six horses through
   the Act of Settlement.
   In W. King *State of the Protestants of Ireland*
   (1672) ch. 3, sect. 8, p. 6

Mandy Rice-Davies 1944–

20 He would, wouldn't he?
   At the trial of Stephen Ward, 29 June 1963,
   on hearing that Lord Astor denied her
   allegations, concerning himself and his
   house parties at Cliveden; in *Guardian* 1 July
   1963

Frank Richards 1876–1961

1 The fat greedy owl of the Remove.
'Billy Bunter' in the *Magnet* (1909) vol. 3,
no. 72 'The Greyfriars Photographer'

Samuel Richardson 1689–1761

2 Mine is the most plotting heart in the
world.
Clarissa (1747–8) Letter 171

3 I love to write to the moment.
Clarissa (1747–8) Letter 224

4 His [Fielding's] spurious brat, Tom Jones.
Letter to Thomas Edwards, 21 February 1752,
in J. Carroll (ed.) *Selected Letters* (1964)

Hans Richter 1843–1916

5 Up with your damned nonsense will I put
twice, or perhaps once, but sometimes
always, by God, never.
Attributed

Johann Paul Friedrich Richter ('Jean Paul') 1763–1825

6 Providence has given to the French the
empire of the land, to the English that of
the sea, and to the Germans that of—the
air!
In Thomas Carlyle 'Jean Paul Friedrich
Richter' in *Edinburgh Review* no. 91 (1827)

Rainer Maria Rilke 1875–1926

7 *So leben wir und nehmen immer Abschied.*
We live our lives, for ever taking leave.
Duineser Elegien (tr. J. B. Leishman and
Stephen Spender, 1948) no. 8

Arthur Rimbaud 1854–91

8 . . . *Je me suis baigné dans le Poème
De la Mer.*
I have bathed in the Poem of the Sea.
'Le Bâteau ivre' (1883)

9 *Je regrette l'Europe aux anciens parapets!*
I pine for Europe of the ancient parapets!
'Le Bâteau ivre' (1883)

10 *Ô saisons, ô châteaux!
Quelle âme est sans défauts?*
O seasons, O castles! What soul is without
fault?
'Ô saisons, ô châteaux' (1872)

11 *A noir, E blanc, I rouge, U vert, O bleu: voyelles,
Je dirais quelque jour vos naissances latentes.*
A black, E white, I red, U green, O blue:
vowels, some day I will tell of the births
that may be yours.
'Voyelles' (1870)

Hal Riney 1932–

12 It's morning again in America.
Ronald Reagan's election campaign slogan
(1984); in *Newsweek* 6 August 1984

César Ritz 1850–1918

13 The customer is never wrong.
In R. Nevill and C. E. Jerningham *Piccadilly to
Pall Mall* (1908) p. 94

Antoine de Rivarol 1753–1801

14 *Ce qui n'est pas clair n'est pas français.*
What is not clear is not French.
Discours sur l'Universalité de la Langue Française
(1784)

Lord Robbins 1898–1984

15 Economics is the science which studies
human behaviour as a relationship
between ends and scarce means which
have alternative uses.
*Essay on the Nature and Significance of Economic
Science* (1932) ch. 1, sect. 3

Maximilien Robespierre 1758–94

16 Any law which violates the inalienable
rights of man is essentially unjust and
tyrannical; it is not a law at all.
Déclaration des droits de l'homme 24 April 1793,
article 6

17 Any institution which does not suppose
the people good, and the magistrate
corruptible, is evil.
Déclaration des droits de l'homme 24 April 1793,
article 25

Leo Robin 1900–

18 A kiss on the hand may be quite
continental,
But diamonds are a girl's best friend.
'Diamonds are a Girl's Best Friend' (1949
song); from the film *Gentlemen Prefer Blondes*

19 Thanks for the memory.
Title of song (with Ralph Rainger, 1937)

Edwin Arlington Robinson 1869–1935

20 I shall have more to say when I am dead.
'John Brown' (1920)

Bishop John Robinson 1919–83

21 Honest to God.
Title of book (1963)

Mary Robinson 1758–1800

22 Pavement slippery, people sneezing,
Lords in ermine, beggars freezing;
Titled gluttons dainties carving,
Genius in a garret starving.
'January, 1795'

Sir Boyle Roche 1743–1807

1 Mr Speaker, I smell a rat; I see him
forming in the air and darkening the sky;
but I'll nip him in the bud.
  Attributed

John Wilmot, Earl of Rochester
1647–80

2 Tell me no more of constancy,
that frivolous pretence,
Of cold age, narrow jealousy,
disease and want of sense.
  'Against Constancy' (1676)

3   'Is there then no more?'
She cries. 'All this to love and rapture's
due;
Must we not pay a debt to pleasure too?'
  'The Imperfect Enjoyment' (1680)

4 Here lies a great and mighty king
Whose promise none relies on;
He never said a foolish thing,
Nor ever did a wise one.
  'The King's Epitaph' (alternatively 'Here lies
  our sovereign lord the King'); in C. E. Doble
  et al. *Thomas Hearne: Remarks and Collections*
  (1885–1921) 17 November 1706. Cf. 95:2

5 ... Natural freedoms are but just:
There's something generous in mere lust.
  'A Ramble in St James' Park' (1680)

6 Reason, an *ignis fatuus* of the mind,
Which leaves the light of nature, sense,
behind.
  'A Satire against Mankind' (1679) l. 11

7 All men would be cowards if they durst.
  'A Satire against Mankind' (1679) l. 158

8 A merry monarch, scandalous and poor.
  'A Satire on King Charles II' (1697)

9 Ancient person, for whom I
All the flattering youth defy,
Long be it ere thou grow old,
Aching, shaking, crazy, cold;
But still continue as thou art,
Ancient person of my heart.
  'A Song of a Young Lady to her Ancient
  Lover' (1691)

10 Ere time and place were, time and place
were not;
Where primitive nothing something
straight begot;
Then all proceeded from the great united
what.
  'Upon Nothing' (1680)

John D. Rockefeller 1839–1937

11 The growth of a large business is merely
a survival of the fittest ... The American
beauty rose can be produced in the
splendour and fragrance which bring cheer
to its beholder only by sacrificing the early
buds which grow up around it.
  In W. J. Ghent *Our Benevolent Feudalism* (1902)
  p. 29 ('American Beauty Rose' became the
  title of a 1950 song by Hal David and
  others). Cf. 312:17

Gene Roddenberry 1921–91

12 These are the voyages of the starship
Enterprise. Its five-year mission ... to boldly
go where no man has gone before.
  Star Trek (television series, from 1966)

13 Beam us up, Mr Scott.
  Star Trek 'Gamesters of Triskelion' (usually
  quoted 'Beam me up, Scotty')

Theodore Roethke 1908–63

14 I have known the inexorable sadness of
pencils,
Neat in their boxes, dolour of pad and
paper-weight,
All the misery of manilla folders and
mucilage,
Desolation in immaculate public places.
  'Dolour' (1948)

15 The body and the soul know how to play
In that dark world where gods have lost
their way.
  'Four for Sir John Davies' (1953) no. 2

16   O who can be
Both moth and flame? The weak moth
blundering by.
Whom do we love? I thought I knew the
truth;
Of grief I died, but no one knew my death.
  'The Sequel' (1964)

Samuel Rogers 1763–1855

17 Think nothing done while aught remains
to do.
  'Human Life' (1819) l. 49. Cf. 211:25

18 But there are moments which he calls his
own,
Then, never less alone than when alone,
Those whom he loved so long and sees no
more,
Loved and still loves—not dead—but gone
before,
He gathers round him.
  'Human Life' (1819) l. 755

19 By many a temple half as old as Time.
  Italy (1838 ed.) epilogue. Cf. 79:17

20 It doesn't much signify whom one marries,
for one is sure to find next morning that it
was someone else.
  In A. Dyce (ed.) *Table Talk of Samuel Rogers*
  (1860)

Will Rogers 1879–1935

21 Income Tax has made more Liars out of
the American people than Golf.
  The Illiterate Digest (1924) 'Helping the Girls
  with their Income Taxes'

22 Everything is funny as long as it is
happening to Somebody Else.
  The Illiterate Digest (1924) 'Warning to Jokers:
  lay off the prince'

1 Well, all I know is what I read in the papers.
   New York Times 30 September 1923

2 You can't say civilization don't advance, however, for in every war they kill you in a new way.
   New York Times 23 December 1929

Mme Roland 1754–93

3 O liberty! what crimes are committed in thy name!
   In A. de Lamartine *Histoire des Girondins* (1847) bk. 51, ch. 8

Richard Rolle de Hampole *c.*1290–1349

4 When Adam dalfe and Eve spane ... Where was than the pride of man?
   In G. G. Perry *Religious Pieces* (EETS no. 26, 1914 ed.). Taken in the form 'When Adam delved and Eve span, who was then the gentleman?' by John Ball as the text of his revolutionary sermon on the outbreak of the Peasants' Revolt, 1381

Pierre de Ronsard 1524–85

5 *Quand vous serez bien vieille, au soir, à la chandelle,*
   Assise auprès du feu, dévidant et filant,
   Direz, chantant mes vers, en vous émerveillant,
   Ronsard me célébrait du temps que j'étais belle.
   When you are very old, and sit in the candle-light at evening spinning by the fire, you will say, as you murmur my verses, a wonder in your eyes, 'Ronsard sang of me in the days when I was fair.'
   Sonnets pour Hélène (1578) bk. 2, no. 42

Eleanor Roosevelt 1884–1962

6 No one can make you feel inferior without your consent.
   In *Catholic Digest* August 1960, p. 102

Franklin D. Roosevelt 1882–1945

7 The forgotten man at the bottom of the economic pyramid.
   Radio address, 7 April 1932, in *Public Papers* (1938) vol. 1

8 I pledge you, I pledge myself, to a new deal for the American people.
   Speech, 2 July 1932, accepting the presidential nomination; in *Public Papers* (1938) vol. 1

9 The only thing we have to fear is fear itself.
   Inaugural address, 4 March 1933, in *Public Papers* (1938) vol. 2

10 In the field of world policy I would dedicate this Nation to the policy of the good neighbour.
   Inaugural address, 4 March 1933, in *Public Papers* (1938) vol. 2

11 I see one-third of a nation ill-housed, ill-clad, ill-nourished.
   Second inaugural address, 20 January 1937, in *Public Papers* (1941) vol. 6

12 We must be the great arsenal of democracy.
   Broadcast, 29 December 1940, in *Public Papers* (1941) vol. 9

13 We look forward to a world founded upon four essential human freedoms. The first is freedom of speech and expression—everywhere in the world. The second is freedom of every person to worship God in his own way—everywhere in the world. The third is freedom from want ... The fourth is freedom from fear.
   Message to Congress, 6 January 1941, in *Public Papers* (1941) vol. 9

14 Yesterday, December 7, 1941—a date which will live in infamy—the United States of America was suddenly and deliberately attacked by naval and air forces of the Empire of Japan.
   Address to Congress, 8 December 1941, in *Public Papers* (1950) vol. 10

Theodore Roosevelt 1858–1919

15 I wish to preach, not the doctrine of ignoble ease, but the doctrine of the strenuous life.
   Speech, 10 April 1899, in *Works* (Memorial ed., 1923–6), vol. 15

16 Speak softly and carry a big stick; you will go far.
   Speech, 3 April 1903, in *New York Times* 4 April 1903 (quoting an 'old adage')

17 A man who is good enough to shed his blood for the country is good enough to be given a square deal afterwards.
   Speech, 4 June 1903, in *Addresses and Presidential Messages 1902–4* (1904)

18 The men with the muck-rakes are often indispensable to the well-being of society; but only if they know when to stop raking the muck.
   Speech, 14 April 1906, in *Works* (Memorial ed., 1923–6) vol. 18. Cf. 79:6

19 There is no room in this country for hyphenated Americanism.
   Speech, 12 October 1915, in *Works* (Memorial ed., 1923–6) vol. 20

Lord Rosebery 1847–1929

20 Men who sit still with the fly-blown phylacteries bound round their obsolete policy.
   On certain members of the Liberal Party; speech at Chesterfield, 16 December 1901, in *The Times* 17 December 1901, p. 10

Christina Rossetti 1830–94

21 Because the birthday of my life
   Is come, my love is come to me.
   'A Birthday' (1862)

1 Come to me in the silence of the night;
  Come in the speaking silence of a dream.
    'Echo' (1862)

2 In the bleak mid-winter
  Frosty wind made moan,
  Earth stood hard as iron,
  Water like a stone;
  Snow had fallen, snow on snow,
  Snow on snow,
  In the bleak mid-winter,
  Long ago.
    'Mid-Winter' (1875)

3 Oh roses for the flush of youth,
  And laurel for the perfect prime;
  But pluck an ivy branch for me
  Grown old before my time.
    'Oh roses for the flush of youth' (1862)

4 Better by far you should forget and smile
  Than that you should remember and be
  sad.
    'Remember' (1862)

5 Does the road wind up-hill all the way?
  Yes, to the very end.
  Will the day's journey take the whole long
  day?
  From morn to night, my friend.
    'Up-Hill' (1862)

Dante Gabriel Rossetti 1828–82

6 The blessed damozel leaned out
  From the gold bar of Heaven;
  Her eyes were deeper than the depth
  Of waters stilled at even;
  She had three lilies in her hand,
  And the stars in her hair were seven.
    'The Blessed Damozel' (1870) st. 1

7 A sonnet is a moment's monument,—
  Memorial from the Soul's eternity
  To one dead deathless hour.
    The House of Life (1881) pt. 1, introduction

8 Look in my face; my name is Might-have-
  been;
  I am also called No-more, Too-late,
  Farewell.
    The House of Life (1881) pt. 2 'A Superscription'

9 Sleepless with cold commemorative eyes.
    The House of Life (1881) pt. 2 'A Superscription'

10 I have been here before,
   But when or how I cannot tell:
   I know the grass beyond the door,
   The sweet keen smell,
   The sighing sound, the lights around the
   shore.
    'Sudden Light' (1870)

Gioacchino Rossini 1792–1868

11 Wagner has lovely moments but awful
   quarters of an hour.
    In E. Naumann Italienische Tondichter (1883)
    vol. 4, p. 541 (April 1867)

Jean Rostand 1894–1977

12 Kill a man, and you are an assassin. Kill
   millions of men, and you are a conqueror.
   Kill everyone, and you are a god.
    Pensées d'un biologiste (1939) p. 116. Cf. 253:26,
    360:15

Leo Rosten 1908–

13 Any man who hates dogs and babies can't
   be all bad.
    Of W. C. Fields, and often attributed to him,
    in speech at Masquers' Club dinner,
    16 February 1939. See letter in Times Literary
    Supplement 24 January 1975, p. 85

Philip Roth 1933–

14 A Jewish man with parents alive is
   a fifteen-year-old boy, and will remain
   a fifteen-year-old boy until they die!
    Portnoy's Complaint (1967) p. 111

15 Doctor, my doctor, what do you say, LET'S
   PUT THE ID BACK IN YID!
    Portnoy's Complaint (1967) p. 124

Claude-Joseph Rouget de Lisle 1760–1836

16 Allons, enfants de la patrie,
   Le jour de gloire est arrivé ...
   Aux armes, citoyens!
   Formez vos battaillons!
   Come, children of our country, the day of
   glory has arrived ... To arms, citizens!
   Form your battalions!
    'La Marseillaise' (25 April 1792)

Charles Roupell

17 To play billiards well is a sign of an ill-
   spent youth.
    Attributed, in D. Duncan Life of Herbert
    Spencer (1908) ch. 20

Jean-Jacques Rousseau 1712–78

18 Man was born free, and everywhere he is
   in chains.
    Du Contrat social (1762) ch. 1

Martin Joseph Routh 1755–1854

19 You will find it a very good practice always
   to verify your references, sir!
    In J. W. Burgon Lives of Twelve Good Men (1888
    ed.) vol. 1, p. 73

Nicholas Rowe 1674–1718

20 Is this that haughty, gallant, gay Lothario?
    The Fair Penitent (1703) act 5, sc. 1

Helen Rowland 1875–1950

21 A husband is what is left of a lover, after
   the nerve has been extracted.
    A Guide to Men (1922) p. 19

Richard Rowland c.1881–1947

1 The lunatics have taken charge of the asylum.

On the take-over of United Artists by Charles Chaplin and others, in T. Ramsaye *A Million and One Nights* (1926) vol. 2, ch. 79. Cf. 208:12

Maude Royden 1876–1956

2 The Church [of England] should go forward along the path of progress and be no longer satisfied only to represent the Conservative Party at prayer.

In *The Times* 17 July 1917

Naomi Royde-Smith c.1875–1964

3 I know two things about the horse
And one of them is rather coarse.

Weekend Book (1928) p. 231

Paul Alfred Rubens 1875–1917

4 Oh! we don't want to lose you but we think you ought to go
For your King and your Country both need you so.

'Your King and Country Want You' (1914 song)

Richard Rumbold c.1622–85

5 I never could believe that Providence had sent a few men into the world, ready booted and spurred to ride, and millions ready saddled and bridled to be ridden.

On the scaffold, in T. B. Macaulay *History of England* vol. 1 (1849) ch. 1

Damon Runyon 1884–1946

6 I do see her in tough joints more than somewhat.

Collier's 22 May 1930, 'Social Error'

7 I long ago come to the conclusion that all life is 6 to 5 against.

Collier's 8 September 1934, 'A Nice Price'

8 'My boy,' he says, 'always try to rub up against money, for if you rub up against money long enough, some of it may rub off on you.'

Cosmopolitan August 1929, 'A Very Honourable Guy'

Dean Rusk 1909–

9 We're eyeball to eyeball, and I think the other fellow just blinked.

On the Cuban missile crisis, 24 October 1962, in *Saturday Evening Post* 8 December 1962

John Ruskin 1819–1900

10 I have seen, and heard, much of Cockney impudence before now; but never expected to hear a coxcomb ask two hundred guineas for flinging a pot of paint in the public's face.

Fors Clavigera (1871–84) Letter 79, 18 June 1877 (on Whistler's *Nocturne in Black and Gold*). Cf. 347:13

11 Life without industry is guilt, and industry without art is brutality.

Lectures on Art (1870) Lecture 3 'The Relation of Art to Morals' sect. 95

12 All violent feelings ... produce in us a falseness in all our impressions of external things, which I would generally characterize as the 'Pathetic Fallacy'.

Modern Painters (1856) vol. 3, pt. 4, ch. 12

13 Mountains are the beginning and the end of all natural scenery.

Modern Painters (1856) vol. 4, pt. 5, ch. 20

14 All books are divisible into two classes, the books of the hour, and the books of all time.

Sesame and Lilies (1865) p. 16 'Of Kings' Treasuries'

15 Which of us ... is to do the hard and dirty work for the rest—and for what pay? Who is to do the pleasant and clean work, and for what pay?

Sesame and Lilies (1865) p. 69 n. 'Of Kings' Treasuries'

16 When we build, let us think that we build for ever.

Seven Lamps of Architecture (1849) 'The Lamp of Memory' sect. 10

17 Remember that the most beautiful things in the world are the most useless; peacocks and lilies for instance.

Stones of Venice vol. 1 (1851) ch. 2, sect. 17

18 Labour without joy is base. Labour without sorrow is base. Sorrow without labour is base. Joy without labour is base.

Time and Tide (1867) Letter 5

19 The first duty of a State is to see that every child born therein shall be well housed, clothed, fed and educated, till it attain years of discretion.

Time and Tide (1867) Letter 13

20 There is no wealth but life.

Unto this Last (1862) Essay 4, p. 156

Bertrand Russell 1872–1970

21 Boredom is ... a vital problem for the moralist, since half the sins of mankind are caused by the fear of it.

The Conquest of Happiness (1930) ch. 4

22 To be able to fill leisure intelligently is the last product of civilization.

The Conquest of Happiness (1930) ch. 14

1 Work is of two kinds: first, altering the position of matter at or near the earth's surface relatively to other such matter; second, telling other people to do so. The first kind is unpleasant and ill paid; the second is pleasant and highly paid.
  In Praise of Idleness and Other Essays (1986) title essay (1932)

2 Mathematics may be defined as the subject in which we never know what we are talking about, nor whether what we are saying is true.
  Mysticism and Logic (1918) ch. 4

3 Mathematics, rightly viewed, possesses not only truth, but supreme beauty—a beauty cold and austere, like that of sculpture.
  Philosophical Essays (1910) no. 4

4 It is obvious that 'obscenity' is not a term capable of exact legal definition; in the practice of the Courts, it means 'anything that shocks the magistrate'.
  Sceptical Essays (1928) 'The Recrudescence of Puritanism'

George William Russell
See Æ

Lord John Russell 1792–1878

5 It is impossible that the whisper of a faction should prevail against the voice of a nation.
  Reply to an Address from a meeting of 150,000 persons at Birmingham on the defeat of the second Reform Bill, October 1831; in S. Walpole *Life of Lord John Russell* (1889) vol. 1, ch. 7

6 If peace cannot be maintained with honour, it is no longer peace.
  Speech at Greenock, 19 September 1853, in *The Times* 21 September 1853, p. 7. Cf. 94:2

Sir William Howard Russell 1820–1907

7 They dashed on towards that thin red line tipped with steel.
  Of the Russians charging the British, in *The British Expedition to the Crimea* (1877) p. 156. Russell's original dispatch to *The Times*, 14 November 1854, reads 'That thin red streak tipped with a line of steel'

Ernest Rutherford 1871–1937

8 All science is either physics or stamp collecting.
  In J. B. Birks *Rutherford at Manchester* (1962) p. 108

9 We haven't got the money, so we've got to think!
  In *Bulletin of the Institute of Physics* (1962) vol. 13, p. 102 (as recalled by R. V. Jones)

Gilbert Ryle 1900–76

10 Philosophy is the replacement of category-habits by category-disciplines.
  The Concept of Mind (1949) introduction

11 The dogma of the Ghost in the Machine.
  The Concept of Mind (1949) ch. 1 (on the mental-conduct concepts of Descartes)

Vita Sackville-West 1892–1962

12 The greater cats with golden eyes
  Stare out between the bars.
  The King's Daughter (1929) pt. 2, no. 1

Françoise Sagan 1935–

13 To jealousy, nothing is more frightful than laughter.
  La Chamade (1965) ch. 9

Charles-Augustin Sainte-Beuve 1804–69

14 Et Vigny plus secret,
  Comme en sa tour d'ivoire, avant midi rentrait.
  And Vigny more discreet, as if in his ivory tower, returned before noon.
  Les Pensées d'Août, à M. Villemain (1837) p. 152

Antoine de Saint-Exupéry 1900–44

15 Grown-ups never understand anything for themselves, and it is tiresome for children to be always and forever explaining things to them.
  Le Petit Prince (1943) ch. 1

Saki (H. H. Munro) 1870–1916

16 Waldo is one of those people who would be enormously improved by death.
  Beasts and Super-Beasts (1914) 'The Feast of Nemesis'

17 The people of Crete unfortunately make more history than they can consume locally.
  Chronicles of Clovis (1911) 'The Jesting of Arlington Stringham'

18 The cook was a good cook, as cooks go; and as good cooks go, she went.
  Reginald (1904) 'Reginald on Besetting Sins'

19 I always say beauty is only sin deep.
  Reginald (1904) 'Reginald's Choir Treat'

20 You can't expect a boy to be vicious till he's been to a good school.
  Reginald in Russia (1910) 'The Baker's Dozen'

21 Addresses are given to us to conceal our whereabouts.
  Reginald in Russia (1910) 'Cross Currents'

22 We all know that Prime Ministers are wedded to the truth, but like other married couples they sometimes live apart.
  The Unbearable Bassington (1912) ch. 13

J. D. Salinger 1919–

1 I keep picturing all these little kids playing some game in this big field of rye and all ... I mean if they're running and they don't look where they're going I have to come out from somewhere and catch them. That's all I'd do all day. I'd just be the catcher in the rye.
   The Catcher in the Rye (1951) ch. 22

Lord Salisbury 1830–1903

2 English policy is to float lazily downstream, occasionally putting out a diplomatic boathook to avoid collisions.
   Letter, 9 March 1877; in Lady Gwendolen Cecil *Life of Robert, Marquis of Salisbury* (1921–32) vol. 2, p. 130

3 A great deal of misapprehension arises from the popular use of maps on a small scale ... If the noble Lord would use a larger map—say one on the scale of the Ordnance Map of England—he would find that the distance between Russia and British India is not to be measured by the finger and thumb, but by a rule.
   Speech, *Hansard* 11 June 1877, col. 1565

4 We are part of the community of Europe and we must do our duty as such.
   Speech at Caernarvon, 10 April 1888, in *The Times* 11 April 1888

5 Horny-handed sons of toil.
   Quarterly Review October 1873, p. 543 (later popularized in the US by Denis Kearney, 1847–1907). Cf. 211:5

6 By office boys for office boys.
   Of the *Daily Mail*, in H. Hamilton Fyfe *Northcliffe* (1930) ch. 4

Lord Salisbury 1893–1972

7 Too clever by half.
   Of Iain Macleod, Colonial Secretary; in *Hansard* (Lords) 7 March 1961, col. 307

Sallust 86–35 BC

8 A venal city ripe to perish, if a buyer can be found.
   Jugurtha ch. 35 (of Rome)

9 *Punica fide.*
   With Carthaginian trustworthiness.
   Jugurtha ch. 108, sect. 3 (meaning treachery)

Lord Samuel 1870–1963

10 A library is thought in cold storage.
   A Book of Quotations (1947) p. 10

Paul A. Samuelson 1915–

11 The consumer, so it is said, is the king ... each is a voter who uses his money as votes to get the things done that he wants done.
   Economics (8th ed., 1970) p. 55

Carl Sandburg 1878–1967

12 Hog Butcher for the World,
   Tool Maker, Stacker of Wheat,
   Player with Railroads and the Nation's Freight Handler;
   Stormy, husky, brawling,
   City of the Big Shoulders.
   'Chicago' (1916)

13 The fog comes
   on little cat feet.
   It sits looking
   over harbour and city
   on silent haunches
   and then moves on.
   'Fog' (1916)

14 Pile the bodies high at Austerlitz and Waterloo.
   Shovel them under and let me work—
   I am the grass; I cover all.
   'Grass' (1918)

15 I tell you the past is a bucket of ashes.
   'Prairie' (1918)

16 Little girl ... Sometime they'll give a war and nobody will come.
   The People, Yes (1936). 'Suppose They Gave a War and No One Came?' was the title of a piece by Charlotte Keyes in *McCall's* October 1966; 'Suppose They Gave a War and Nobody Came?' was the title of a 1970 film. Cf. 153:2

17 Poetry is the achievement of the synthesis of hyacinths and biscuits.
   Atlantic Monthly March 1923 'Poetry Considered'

18 Slang is a language that rolls up its sleeves, spits on its hands and goes to work.
   In *New York Times* 13 February 1959, p. 21

Henry 'Red' Sanders

19 Sure, winning isn't everything. It's the only thing.
   In *Sports Illustrated* 26 December 1955 (often attributed to Vince Lombardi)

Martha Sansom 1690–1736

20 Foolish eyes, thy streams give over,
   Wine, not water, binds the lover.
   'Song' (written *c.*1726)

George Santayana 1863–1952

21 Fanaticism consists in redoubling your effort when you have forgotten your aim.
   The Life of Reason (1905) vol. 1, introduction

22 Those who cannot remember the past are condemned to repeat it.
   The Life of Reason (1905) vol. 1, ch. 12

John Singer Sargent 1856–1925

23 Every time I paint a portrait I lose a friend.
   In N. Bentley and E. Esar *Treasury of Humorous Quotations* (1951)

Leslie Sarony 1897–1985

1 Ain't it grand to be blooming well dead?
   Title of song (1932)

Jean-Paul Sartre 1905–80

2 I am condemned to be free.
   L'Être et le néant (1943) pt. 4, ch. 1

3 Man is a useless passion.
   L'Être et le néant (1943) pt. 4, ch. 2

4 Hell is other people.
   Huis Clos (1944) sc. 5. Cf. 132:21

5 I confused things with their names: that is belief.
   Les Mots (1964) 'Écrire'

6 Human life begins on the far side of despair.
   Les Mouches (1943) act 3, sc. 2

7 I hate victims who respect their executioners.
   Les Séquestrés d'Altona (1960) act 1, sc. 1

Siegfried Sassoon 1886–1967

8 If I were fierce, and bald, and short of breath,
   I'd live with scarlet Majors at the Base,
   And speed glum heroes up the line to death.
   'Base Details' (1918)

9 Does it matter?—losing your sight? ...
   There's such splendid work for the blind;
   And people will always be kind,
   As you sit on the terrace remembering
   And turning your face to the light.
   'Does it Matter?' (1918)

10 Soldiers are citizens of death's grey land,
   Drawing no dividend from time's tomorrows.
   'Dreamers' (1918)

11 Everyone suddenly burst out singing.
   'Everyone Sang' (1919)

12 The song was wordless; the singing will never be done.
   'Everyone Sang' (1919)

13 'He's a cheery old card,' grunted Harry to Jack
   As they slogged up to Arras with rifle and pack.
   But he did for them both by his plan of attack.
   'The General' (1918)

14 Here was the world's worst wound.
   'On Passing the New Menin Gate' (1928)

George Savile

See 1ST MARQUESS OF HALIFAX

Dorothy L. Sayers 1893–1957

15 I admit it is better fun to punt than to be punted, and that a desire to have all the fun is nine-tenths of the law of chivalry.
   Gaudy Night (1935) ch. 14

Al Scalpone

16 The family that prays together stays together.
   Motto devised for the Roman Catholic Family Rosary Crusade, 1947

Friedrich von Schelling 1775–1854

17 Architecture in general is frozen music.
   Philosophie der Kunst (1809) in *Werke* (1916) vol. 3, p. 24

Friedrich von Schiller 1759–1805

18 *Freude, schöner Götterfunken,*
   Tochter aus Elysium.
   Joy, beautiful radiance of the gods, daughter of Elysium.
   'An die Freude' (1785)

19 The sun does not set in my dominions.
   Don Carlos (1787) act 1, sc. 6 (Philip II). Cf. 240:6

20 With stupidity the gods themselves struggle in vain.
   Die Jungfrau von Orleans (1801) act 3, sc. 6

21 *Die Weltgeschichte ist das Weltgericht.*
   The world's history is the world's judgement.
   'Resignation' (1786) st. 19

Moritz Schlick

22 The meaning of a proposition is the method of its verification.
   Philosophical Review (1936) vol. 45, p. 341

Artur Schnabel 1882–1951

23 Too easy for children, and too difficult for artists.
   Of Mozart's sonatas, in Nat Shapiro (ed.) *Encyclopaedia of Quotations about Music* (1978) p. 58. In *My Life and Music* (1961) p. 122, Schnabel says: 'Children are given Mozart because of the small *quantity* of the notes; grown-ups avoid Mozart because of the great *quality* of the notes'

Budd Schulberg 1914–

24 I could have had class. I could have been a contender.
   On the Waterfront (1954 film); spoken by Marlon Brando

E. F. Schumacher 1911–77

25 Small is beautiful.
   Title of book (1973)

J. A. Schumpeter 1883–1950

26 The cold metal of economic theory is in Marx's pages immersed in such a wealth of steaming phrases as to acquire a temperature not naturally its own.
   Capitalism, Socialism and Democracy (1942) p. 21

Carl Schurz 1829–1906

1 My country, right or wrong; if right, to be
kept right; and if wrong, to be set right!
Speech, US Senate, 29 February 1872, in
Congressional Globe vol. 45, p. 1287. Cf. 115:10

Kurt Schwitters 1887–1948

2 I am a painter and I nail my pictures
together.
In R. Hausmann Am Anfang war Dada (1972)
p. 63

C. P. Scott 1846–1932

3 Comment is free, but facts are sacred.
Manchester Guardian 5 May 1921

Robert Falcon Scott 1868–1912

4 Great God! this is an awful place.
Of the South Pole; Journal, 17 January 1912,
in Scott's Last Expedition (1913) vol. 1, ch. 18

5 For God's sake look after our people.
Last journal entry, 29 March 1912, in Scott's
Last Expedition (1913) vol. 1, ch. 20

Sir Walter Scott 1771–1832

6 The valiant Knight of Triermain
Rung forth his challenge-blast again,
But answer came there none.
The Bridal of Triermain (1813) canto 3, st. 10

7 Come fill up my cup, come fill up my can,
Come saddle your horses, and call up your
men;
Come open the West Port, and let me gang
free,
And it's room for the bonnets of Bonny
Dundee!
The Doom of Devorgoil (1830) act 2, sc. 2 'Bonny
Dundee'

8 Yet seemed that tone, and gesture bland,
Less used to sue than to command.
The Lady of the Lake (1810) canto 1, st. 21

9 Respect was mingled with surprise,
And the stern joy which warriors feel
In foemen worthy of their steel.
The Lady of the Lake (1810) canto 5, st. 10

10 If thou would'st view fair Melrose aright,
Go visit it by the pale moonlight.
The Lay of the Last Minstrel (1805) canto 2, st. 1

11 It is the secret sympathy,
The silver link, the silken tie,
Which heart to heart, and mind to mind,
In body and in soul can bind.
The Lay of the Last Minstrel (1805) canto 5,
st. 13

12 Breathes there the man, with soul so dead,
Who never to himself hath said,
This is my own, my native land!
The Lay of the Last Minstrel (1805) canto 6, st. 1

13 And, doubly dying, shall go down
To the vile dust, from whence he sprung,
Unwept, unhonoured, and unsung.
The Lay of the Last Minstrel (1805) canto 6, st. 1

14 O Caledonia! stern and wild,
Meet nurse for a poetic child!
The Lay of the Last Minstrel (1805) canto 6, st. 2

15 O! many a shaft, at random sent,
Finds mark the archer little meant!
And many a word, at random spoken,
May soothe or wound a heart that's
broken.
The Lord of the Isles (1813) canto 5, st. 18

16 Had'st thou but lived, though stripped of
power,
A watchman on the lonely tower.
Marmion (1808) introduction to canto 1, st. 8

17 And come he slow, or come he fast,
It is but Death who comes at last.
Marmion (1808) canto 2, st. 30

18 O, young Lochinvar is come out of the
west,
Through all the wide Border his steed was
the best.
Marmion (1808) canto 5, st. 12 ('Lochinvar'
st. 1)

19 So faithful in love, and so dauntless in war,
There never was knight like the young
Lochinvar.
Marmion (1808) canto 5, st. 12 ('Lochinvar'
st. 1)

20 For a laggard in love, and a dastard in war,
Was to wed the fair Ellen of brave
Lochinvar.
Marmion (1808) canto 5, st. 12 ('Lochinvar'
st. 2)

21 O what a tangled web we weave,
When first we practise to deceive!
Marmion (1808) canto 6, st. 17

22 O Woman! in our hours of ease,
Uncertain, coy, and hard to please,
And variable as the shade
By the light quivering aspen made;
When pain and anguish wring the brow,
A ministering angel thou!
Marmion (1808) canto 6, st. 30. Cf. 277:10

23 Still from the sire the son shall hear
Of the stern strife, and carnage drear,
Of Flodden's fatal field,
Where shivered was fair Scotland's spear,
And broken was her shield!
Marmion (1808) canto 6, st. 34

24 Vacant heart and hand, and eye,—
Easy live and quiet die.
The Bride of Lammermoor (1819) ch. 2

25 Touch not the cat but a glove.
The Fair Maid of Perth (1828) ch. 34 (but
without)

26 It's ill taking the breeks aff a wild
Highlandman.
The Fortunes of Nigel (1822) ch. 5

27 The hour is come, but not the man.
The Heart of Midlothian (1818) ch. 4, title

1 Proud Maisie is in the wood,
   Walking so early,
   Sweet Robin sits in the bush,
   Singing so rarely.
   The Heart of Midlothian (1818) ch. 40

2 March, march, Eskdale and Liddesdale,
   All the Blue Bonnets are bound for the
   Border.
   The Monastery (1820) ch. 25

3 But with the morning cool repentance
   came.
   Rob Roy (1817) ch. 12

4 There's a gude time coming.
   Rob Roy (1817) ch. 32

5 The play-bill, which is said to have
   announced the tragedy of Hamlet, the
   character of the Prince of Denmark being
   left out.
   The Talisman (1825) introduction (commonly
   alluded to as 'Hamlet without the Prince')

6 The Big Bow-Wow strain I can do myself
   like any now going; but the exquisite
   touch, which renders ordinary
   commonplace things and characters
   interesting, from the truth of the
   description and the sentiment, is denied to
   me.
   On Jane Austen, in W. Anderson (ed.) *Journals
   of Sir Walter Scott* (1972) 14 March 1826.
   Cf. 247:7

7 Too many flowers ... too little fruit.
   Of Felicia Hemans's literary style; letter to
   Joanna Baillie, 18 July 1823, in *Letters*
   (Centenary ed.) vol. 8

Scottish Metrical Psalms 1650

8 The Lord's my shepherd, I'll not want.
   He makes me down to lie
   In pastures green: he leadeth me
   the quiet waters by.
   Psalm 23, v. 1. Cf. 66:17

9 My head thou dost with oil anoint,
   and my cup overflows.
   Psalm 23, v. 2. Cf. 66:18

10 The race that long in darkness pined
   have seen a glorious light.
   Paraphrase 19. Cf. 45:15

Edmund Hamilton Sears 1810–76

11 It came upon the midnight clear,
   That glorious song of old,
   From Angels bending near the earth
   To touch their harps of gold.
   The Christian Register (1850) 'That Glorious
   Song of Old'

Sir Charles Sedley c.1639–1701

12 Phyllis, without frown or smile,
   Sat and knotted all the while.
   'Phyllis Knotting' (1694)

Alan Seeger 1888–1916

13 I have a rendezvous with Death
   At some disputed barricade.
   'I Have a Rendezvous with Death' (1916)

Pete Seeger 1919–

14 Where have all the flowers gone?
   Title of song (1961)

Sir John Seeley 1834–95

15 We [the English] seem, as it were, to have
   conquered and peopled half the world in a
   fit of absence of mind.
   The Expansion of England (1883) Lecture 1

John Selden 1584–1654

16 *Scrutamini scripturas* [Let us look at the
   scriptures]. These two words have undone
   the world.
   Table Talk (1689) 'Bible Scripture'

17 Ignorance of the law excuses no man; not
   that all men know the law, but because 'tis
   an excuse every man will plead, and no
   man can tell how to confute him.
   Table Talk (1689) 'Law'

18 Take a straw and throw it up into the air,
   you shall see by that which way the wind
   is.
   Table Talk (1689) 'Libels'

19 There never was a merry world since the
   fairies left off dancing, and the Parson left
   conjuring.
   Table Talk (1689) 'Parson'

20 Pleasure is nothing else but the
   intermission of pain.
   Table Talk (1689) 'Pleasure'

21 Syllables govern the world.
   Table Talk (1689) 'Power: State'

Arthur Seldon 1916–

22 Government of the busy by the bossy for
   the bully.
   Capitalism (1990) p. 111 (subheading on over-
   government)

W. C. Sellar 1898–1951 and R. J. Yeatman 1898–1968

23 History is not what you thought. *It is what
   you can remember.*
   1066 and All That (1930) 'Compulsory Preface'

24 The Roman Conquest was, however, a *Good
   Thing*, since the Britons were only natives
   at the time.
   1066 and All That (1930) ch. 1

25 'Honi soie qui mal y pense' ('Honey, your
   silk stocking's hanging down').
   1066 and All That (1930) ch. 24. Cf. 12:5

1 The cruel Queen died and a post-mortem examination revealed the word 'CALLOUS' engraved on her heart.
   1066 and All That (1930) ch. 32. Cf. 221:17

2 The Cavaliers (Wrong but Wromantic) and the Roundheads (Right but Repulsive).
   1066 and All That (1930) ch. 35

3 The Rump Parliament—so called because it had been sitting for such a long time.
   1066 and All That (1930) ch. 35

4 The National Debt is a very Good Thing and it would be dangerous to pay it off, for fear of Political Economy.
   1066 and All That (1930) ch. 38

5 AMERICA was thus clearly top nation, and History came to a .
   1066 and All That (1930) ch. 62

Seneca ('the Younger') c.4 BC–AD 65

6 *Homines dum docent discunt.*
   Even while they teach, men learn.
   Epistulae Morales no. 7, sect. 8

7 If one does not know to which port one is sailing, no wind is favourable.
   Epistulae Morales no. 71, sect. 3

8 Anyone can stop a man's life, but no one his death; a thousand doors open on to it.
   Phoenissae l. 152

Robert W. Service 1874–1958

9 A promise made is a debt unpaid, and the trail has its own stern code.
   'The Cremation of Sam McGee' (1907)

10 Ah! the clock is always slow;
    It is later than you think.
    'It Is Later Than You Think' (1921)

11 This is the law of the Yukon, that only the Strong shall thrive;
    That surely the Weak shall perish, and only the Fit survive.
    'The Law of the Yukon' (1907)

12 When we, the Workers, all demand: 'What are WE fighting for?' ...
    Then, then we'll end that stupid crime, that devil's madness—War.
    'Michael' (1921)

13 Back of the bar, in a solo game, sat Dangerous Dan McGrew,
    And watching his luck was his light-o'-love, the lady that's known as Lou.
    'The Shooting of Dan McGrew' (1907)

Edward Sexby d. 1658

14 Killing no murder briefly discourst in three questions.
    Title of pamphlet (an apology for tyrannicide, 1657)

Anne Sexton 1928–74

15 In a dream you are never eighty.
    'Old' (1962)

James Seymour and Rian James

16 You're going out a youngster but you've *got* to come back a star.
    42nd Street (1933 film)

Thomas Shadwell c.1642–92

17 Words may be false and full of art,
    Sighs are the natural language of the heart.
    Psyche (1675) act 3

18 And wit's the noblest frailty of the mind.
    A True Widow (1679) act 2, sc. 1. Cf. 127:33

Peter Shaffer 1926–

19 The Normal is the good smile in a child's eyes—all right. It is also the dead stare in a million adults. It both sustains and kills—like a God. It is the Ordinary made beautiful; it is also the Average made lethal.
    Equus (1983 ed.) act 1, sc. 19

1st Earl of Shaftesbury 1621–83

20 'Men of sense are really but of one religion.' ... 'Pray, my lord, what religion is that which men of sense agree in?' 'Madam,' says the earl immediately, 'men of sense never tell it.'
    Bishop Gilbert Burnet *History of My Own Time* vol. 1 (1724) bk. 2, ch. 1 n.

3rd Earl of Shaftesbury 1671–1713

21 How comes it to pass, then, that we appear such cowards in reasoning, and are so afraid to stand the test of ridicule?
    A Letter Concerning Enthusiasm (1708) sect. 2

22 Truth ... may bear all lights.
    Sensus Communis (1709) pt. 1, sect. 1

William Shakespeare 1564–1616

The line number is given without brackets where the scene is all verse up to the quotation and the line number is certain, and in square brackets where prose makes it variable. All references are to the Oxford Standard Authors edition in one volume

All's Well that Ends Well (1603–4)

23   It were all one
    That I should love a bright particular star
    And think to wed it, he is so above me.
    All's Well that Ends Well act 1, sc. 1, l. [97]

24 Our remedies oft in ourselves do lie
    Which we ascribe to heaven.
    All's Well that Ends Well act 1, sc. 1, l. [232]

25 It is like a barber's chair that fits all buttocks.
    All's Well that Ends Well act 2, sc. 2, l. [18]

1 A young man married is a man that's
married.
All's Well that Ends Well act 2, sc. 3, l. [315]

2 I know a man that had this trick of
melancholy sold a goodly manor for a
song.
All's Well that Ends Well act 3, sc. 2, l. [8]

Antony and Cleopatra (1606–7)

3 The triple pillar of the world transformed
Into a strumpet's fool.
Antony and Cleopatra act 1, sc. 1, l. 12

4 ANTONY: There's beggary in the love that
can be reckoned.
CLEOPATRA: I'll set a bourn how far to be
beloved.
ANTONY: Then must thou needs find out
new heaven, new earth.
Antony and Cleopatra act 1, sc. 1, l. 15

5 Let Rome in Tiber melt, and the wide arch
Of the ranged empire fall. Here is my
space.
Antony and Cleopatra act 1, sc. 1, l. 33

6 A Roman thought hath struck him.
Antony and Cleopatra act 1, sc. 2, l. [91]

7 There's a great spirit gone!
Antony and Cleopatra act 1, sc. 2, l. [131]

8 In time we hate that which we often fear.
Antony and Cleopatra act 1, sc. 3, l. 12

9 O! my oblivion is a very Antony,
And I am all forgotten.
Antony and Cleopatra act 1, sc. 3, l. 90

10 O happy horse, to bear the weight of
Antony!
Antony and Cleopatra act 1, sc. 5, l. 21

11 Where's my serpent of old Nile?
Antony and Cleopatra act 1, sc. 5, l. 25

12   My salad days,
When I was green in judgement.
Antony and Cleopatra act 1, sc. 5, l. 73

13 I do not much dislike the matter, but
The manner of his speech.
Antony and Cleopatra act 2, sc. 2, l. 117

14 The barge she sat in, like a burnished
throne,
Burned on the water; the poop was beaten
gold,
Purple the sails, and so perfumed, that
The winds were love-sick with them, the
oars were silver,
Which to the tune of flutes kept stroke,
and made
The water which they beat to follow faster,
As amorous of their strokes. For her own
person,
It beggared all description.
Antony and Cleopatra act 2, sc. 2, l. [199]

15 Her gentlewomen, like the Nereides,
So many mermaids, tended her i' the eyes,
And made their bends adornings.
Antony and Cleopatra act 2, sc. 2, l. [214]

16   I saw her once
Hop forty paces through the public street;
And having lost her breath, she spoke, and
panted
That she did make defect perfection,
And, breathless, power breathe forth.
Antony and Cleopatra act 2, sc. 2, l. [236]

17 Age cannot wither her, nor custom stale
Her infinite variety; other women cloy
The appetites they feed, but she makes
hungry
Where most she satisfies; for vilest things
Become themselves in her, that the holy
priests
Bless her when she is riggish.
Antony and Cleopatra act 2, sc. 2, l. [243]

18   Egypt, thou knew'st too well
My heart was to thy rudder tied by th'
strings,
And thou shouldst tow me after.
Antony and Cleopatra act 3, sc. 9, l. 56

19 Let's have one other gaudy night: call to
me
All my sad captains; fill our bowls once
more;
Let's mock the midnight bell.
Antony and Cleopatra act 3, sc. 11, l. 182

20 To business that we love we rise betime,
And go to 't with delight.
Antony and Cleopatra act 4, sc. 4, l. 20

21 O infinite virtue! com'st thou smiling from
The world's great snare uncaught?
Antony and Cleopatra act 4, sc. 8, l. 17

22   The hearts
That spanieled me at heels, to whom I gave
Their wishes, do discandy, melt their
sweets
On blossoming Caesar.
Antony and Cleopatra act 4, sc. 10, l. 33

23 The soul and body rive not more in parting
Than greatness going off.
Antony and Cleopatra act 4, sc. 11, l. 5

24 I am dying, Egypt, dying.
Antony and Cleopatra act 4, sc. 13, l. 18

25   O! see my women,
The crown o' the earth doth melt. My lord!
O! withered is the garland of the war,
The soldier's pole is fall'n; young boys and
girls
Are level now with men; the odds is gone,
And there is nothing left remarkable
Beneath the visiting moon.
Antony and Cleopatra act 4, sc. 13, l. 62

26   What's brave, what's noble,
Let's do it after the high Roman fashion,
And make death proud to take us.
Antony and Cleopatra act 4, sc. 13, l. 86

27   A rarer spirit never
Did steer humanity; but you, gods, will
give us
Some faults to make us men.
Antony and Cleopatra act 5, sc. 1, l. 31

1 My desolation does begin to make
    A better life.
        Antony and Cleopatra act 5, sc. 2, l. 1

2   And it is great
    To do that thing that ends all other deeds,
    Which shackles accidents, and bolts up
        change.
        Antony and Cleopatra act 5, sc. 2, l. 4

3 He words me, girls, he words me.
        Antony and Cleopatra act 5, sc. 2, l. 190

4 Finish, good lady; the bright day is done,
    And we are for the dark.
        Antony and Cleopatra act 5, sc. 2, l. 192

5   Antony
    Shall be brought drunken forth, and I shall
        see
    Some squeaking Cleopatra boy my
        greatness
    I' the posture of a whore.
        Antony and Cleopatra act 5, sc. 2, l. 217

6 I wish you all joy of the worm.
        Antony and Cleopatra act 5, sc. 2, l. [260]

7 Give me my robe, put on my crown; I have
    Immortal longings in me.
        Antony and Cleopatra act 5, sc. 2, l. [282]

8   Come, thou mortal wretch,
    With thy sharp teeth this knot intrinsicate
    Of life at once untie.
        Antony and Cleopatra act 5, sc. 2, l. [305]

9   Peace! peace!
    Dost thou not see my baby at my breast,
    That sucks the nurse asleep?
        Antony and Cleopatra act 5, sc. 2, l. [310]

10 Now boast thee, death, in thy possession
        lies
    A lass unparalleled.
        Antony and Cleopatra act 5, sc. 2, l. [317]

11 She hath pursued conclusions infinite
    Of easy ways to die.
        Antony and Cleopatra act 5, sc. 2, l. [356]

As You Like It (1599)

12 Fleet the time carelessly, as they did in the
    golden world.
        As You Like It act 1, sc. 1, l. [126]

13 Hereafter, in a better world than this,
    I shall desire more love and knowledge of
        you.
        As You Like It act 1, sc. 2, l. [301]

14 Sweet are the uses of adversity,
    Which like the toad, ugly and venomous,
    Wears yet a precious jewel in his head;
    And this our life, exempt from public
        haunt,
    Finds tongues in trees, books in the
        running brooks,
    Sermons in stones, and good in everything.
        As You Like It act 2, sc. 1, l. 12

15 Unregarded age in corners thrown.
        As You Like It act 2, sc. 3, l. 42

16 Therefore my age is as a lusty winter,
    Frosty, but kindly.
        As You Like It act 2, sc. 3, l. 52

17 Thou art not for the fashion of these times,
    Where none will sweat but for promotion.
        As You Like It act 2, sc. 3, l. 59

18 In thy youth thou wast as true a lover
    As ever sighed upon a midnight pillow.
        As You Like It act 2, sc. 4, l. [26]

19 Under the greenwood tree
    Who loves to lie with me,
    And turn his merry note
    Unto the sweet bird's throat,
    Come hither, come hither, come hither:
    Here shall he see
    No enemy
    But winter and rough weather.
        As You Like It act 2, sc. 5, l. 1

20 I can suck melancholy out of a song as a
    weasel sucks eggs.
        As You Like It act 2, sc. 5, l. [12]

21 Who doth ambition shun
    And loves to live i' the sun,
    Seeking the food he eats,
    And pleased with what he gets.
        As You Like It act 2, sc. 5, l. [38]

22 And so, from hour to hour, we ripe and
        ripe,
    And then from hour to hour, we rot and
        rot:
    And thereby hangs a tale.
        As You Like It act 2, sc. 7, l. 26

23 A worthy fool! Motley's the only wear.
        As You Like It act 2, sc. 7, l. 34

24 All the world's a stage,
    And all the men and women merely
        players:
    They have their exits and their entrances;
    And one man in his time plays many parts,
    His acts being seven ages.
        As You Like It act 2, sc. 7, l. 139

25   At first the infant,
    Mewling and puking in the nurse's arms.
    And then the whining schoolboy, with his
        satchel,
    And shining morning face, creeping like
        snail
    Unwillingly to school.
        As You Like It act 2, sc. 7, l. 143

26   A soldier,
    Full of strange oaths, and bearded like the
        pard,
    Jealous in honour, sudden and quick in
        quarrel,
    Seeking the bubble reputation
    Even in the cannon's mouth.
        As You Like It act 2, sc. 7, l. 149

27   The sixth age shifts
    Into the lean and slippered pantaloon,
    With spectacles on nose and pouch on
        side.
        As You Like It act 2, sc. 7, l. 157

28 Second childishness, and mere oblivion,
    Sans teeth, sans eyes, sans taste, sans
        everything.
        As You Like It act 2, sc. 7, l. 165

1 Blow, blow, thou winter wind,
Thou art not so unkind
As man's ingratitude.
As You Like It act 2, sc. 7, l. 174

2 Run, run, Orlando: carve on every tree
The fair, the chaste, and unexpressive she.
As You Like It act 3, sc. 2, l. 9

3 Let us make an honourable retreat; though
not with bag and baggage, yet with scrip
and scrippage.
As You Like It act 3, sc. 2, l. [170]

4 O wonderful, wonderful, and most
wonderful wonderful! and yet again
wonderful, and after that, out of all
whooping!
As You Like It act 3, sc. 2, l. [202]

5 I do desire we may be better strangers.
As You Like It act 3, sc. 2, l. [276]

6   Down on your knees,
And thank heaven, fasting, for a good
man's love.
As You Like It act 3, sc. 5, l. 57

7 Dead shepherd, now I find thy saw of
might:
'Who ever loved that loved not at first
sight?'
As You Like It act 3, sc. 5, l. [81]. Cf. 218:18

8 Come, woo me, woo me; for now I am in a
holiday humour, and like enough to
consent.
As You Like It act 4, sc. 1, l. [70]

9 Men are April when they woo, December
when they wed: maids are May when they
are maids, but the sky changes when they
are wives.
As You Like It act 4, sc. 1, l. [153]

10 It was a lover and his lass,
With a hey, and a ho, and a hey nonino,
That o'er the green cornfield did pass,
In the spring time, the only pretty ring
time,
When birds do sing, hey ding a ding, ding;
Sweet lovers love the spring.
As You Like It act 5, sc. 3, l. [18]

11 A poor virgin, sir, an ill-favoured thing, sir,
but mine own.
As You Like It act 5, sc. 4, l. [60]

12 The retort courteous ... the quip modest
... the reply churlish ... the reproof
valiant ... the countercheck quarrelsome
... the lie circumstantial ... the lie direct.
As You Like It act 5, sc. 4, l. [96] (of the degrees
of a lie)

13 Your 'if' is the only peace-maker; much
virtue in 'if'.
As You Like It act 5, sc. 4, l. [108]

14 He uses his folly like a stalking-horse, and
under the presentation of that he shoots
his wit.
As You Like It act 5, sc. 4, l. [112]

Coriolanus (1608)

15 He's a very dog to the commonalty.
Coriolanus act 1, sc. 1, l. [29]

16   Bid them wash their faces,
And keep their teeth clean.
Coriolanus act 2, sc. 1, l. [65]

17 My gracious silence, hail!
Coriolanus act 2, sc. 1, l. [194]

18 Hear you this Triton of the minnows?
mark you
His absolute 'shall'?
Coriolanus act 3, sc. 1, l. 88

19 What is the city but the people?
Coriolanus act 3, sc. 1, l. 198

20   Despising,
For you, the city, thus I turn my back:
There is a world elsewhere.
Coriolanus act 3, sc. 3, l. 131

21   I'll never
Be such a gosling to obey instinct, but
stand
As if a man were author of himself
And knew no other kin.
Coriolanus act 5, sc. 3, l. 34

22   Thou hast never in thy life
Showed thy dear mother any courtesy;
When she—poor hen! fond of no second
brood—
Has clucked thee to the wars, and safely
home,
Loaden with honour.
Coriolanus act 5, sc. 3, l. 160

Cymbeline (1609–10)

23   Boldness be my friend!
Arm me, audacity.
Cymbeline act 1, sc. 6, l. 18

24 But kiss: one kiss! Rubies unparagoned,
How dearly they do't!
Cymbeline act 2, sc. 2, l. 17

25 Hark! hark! the lark at heaven's gate sings.
Cymbeline act 2, sc. 3, l. [22]

26 Is there no way for men to be, but women
Must be half-workers?
Cymbeline act 2, sc. 5, l. 1

27 Fear no more the heat o' the sun,
Nor the furious winter's rages;
Thou thy worldly task hast done,
Home art gone and ta'en thy wages:
Golden lads and girls all must,
As chimney-sweepers, come to dust.
Cymbeline act 4, sc. 2, l. 258

28 No exorciser harm thee!
Nor no witchcraft charm thee!
Ghost unlaid forbear thee!
Nothing ill come near thee!
Quiet consummation have:
And renowned be thy grave!
Cymbeline act 4, sc. 2, l. 276

Hamlet (1601)

29 You come most carefully upon your hour.
Hamlet act 1, sc. 1, l. 6

30 For this relief much thanks; 'tis bitter cold
And I am sick at heart.
Hamlet act 1, sc. 1, l. 8

1 In the most high and palmy state of Rome,
A little ere the mightiest Julius fell,
The graves stood tenantless and the sheeted dead
Did squeak and gibber in the Roman streets.
Hamlet act 1, sc. 1, l. 113

2 Some say that ever 'gainst that season comes
Wherein our Saviour's birth is celebrated,
The bird of dawning singeth all night long;
And then, they say, no spirit can walk abroad.
Hamlet act 1, sc. 1, l. 158

3 But, look, the morn, in russet mantle clad,
Walks o'er the dew of yon high eastern hill.
Hamlet act 1, sc. 1, l. 166

4 The head is not more native to the heart,
The hand more instrumental to the brain,
Than is the throne of Denmark to thy father.
Hamlet act 1, sc. 2, l. 47

5 A little more than kin, and less than kind.
Hamlet act 1, sc. 2, l. 65

6 Not so, my lord; I am too much i' the sun.
Hamlet act 1, sc. 2, l. 67

7 Seems, madam! Nay, it is; I know not 'seems'.
Hamlet act 1, sc. 2, l. 76

8 But I have that within which passeth show;
These but the trappings and the suits of woe.
Hamlet act 1, sc. 2, l. 85

9 O! that this too too solid flesh would melt,
Thaw, and resolve itself into a dew.
Hamlet act 1, sc. 2, l. 129

10 How weary, stale, flat, and unprofitable
Seem to me all the uses of this world.
Fie on't! O fie! 'tis an unweeded garden,
That grows to seed; things rank and gross in nature
Possess it merely.
Hamlet act 1, sc. 2, l. 133

11 So excellent a king; that was, to this,
Hyperion to a satyr.
Hamlet act 1, sc. 2, l. 139

12 Frailty, thy name is woman!
A little month; or ere those shoes were old
With which she followed my poor father's body,
Like Niobe, all tears; why she, even she,—
O God! a beast, that wants discourse of reason,
Would have mourned longer.
Hamlet act 1, sc. 2, l. 146

13 It is not, nor it cannot come to good;
But break, my heart, for I must hold my tongue!
Hamlet act 1, sc. 2, l. 158

14 A truant disposition, good my lord.
Hamlet act 1, sc. 2, l. 169

15 We'll teach you to drink deep ere you depart.
Hamlet act 1, sc. 2, l. 175

16 Thrift, thrift, Horatio! the funeral baked meats
Did coldly furnish forth the marriage tables.
Would I had met my dearest foe in heaven
Ere I had ever seen that day, Horatio!
Hamlet act 1, sc. 2, l. 180

17 He was a man, take him for all in all,
I shall not look upon his like again.
Hamlet act 1, sc. 2, l. 187

18 But answer made it none.
Hamlet act 1, sc. 2, l. 215

19 A countenance more in sorrow than in anger.
Hamlet act 1, sc. 2, l. 231

20 Do not, as some ungracious pastors do,
Show me the steep and thorny way to heaven,
Whiles, like a puffed and reckless libertine,
Himself the primrose path of dalliance treads,
And recks not his own rede.
Hamlet act 1, sc. 3, l. 47

21 The apparel oft proclaims the man.
Hamlet act 1, sc. 3, l. 72

22 Neither a borrower, nor a lender be.
Hamlet act 1, sc. 3, l. 73

23 This above all: to thine own self be true,
And it must follow, as the night the day,
Thou canst not then be false to any man.
Hamlet act 1, sc. 3, l. 76

24 Ay, springes to catch woodcocks.
Hamlet act 1, sc. 3, l. 115

25 It is a nipping and an eager air.
Hamlet act 1, sc. 4, l. 2

26 But to my mind,—though I am native here,
And to the manner born,—it is a custom
More honoured in the breach than the observance.
Hamlet act 1, sc. 4, l. 14

27 Angels and ministers of grace defend us!
Hamlet act 1, sc. 4, l. 39

28 I do not set my life at a pin's fee.
Hamlet act 1, sc. 4, l. 65

29 Something is rotten in the state of Denmark.
Hamlet act 1, sc. 4, l. 90

30 I could a tale unfold whose lightest word
Would harrow up thy soul, freeze thy young blood,
Make thy two eyes, like stars, start from their spheres.
Hamlet act 1, sc. 5, l. 15

31 Murder most foul, as in the best it is;
But this most foul, strange, and unnatural.
Hamlet act 1, sc. 5, l. 27

32 O my prophetic soul!
My uncle!
Hamlet act 1, sc. 5, l. 40

1 But, soft! methinks I scent the morning air.
Hamlet act 1, sc. 5, l. 58

2 O, horrible! O, horrible! most horrible!
Hamlet act 1, sc. 5, l. 80

3 There are more things in heaven and
earth, Horatio,
Than are dreamt of in your philosophy.
Hamlet act 1, sc. 5, l. 166

4 To put an antic disposition on.
Hamlet act 1, sc. 5, l. 172

5 Rest, rest, perturbèd spirit.
Hamlet act 1, sc. 5, l. 182

6 The time is out of joint; O cursèd spite,
That ever I was born to set it right!
Hamlet act 1, sc. 5, l. 188

7 By indirections find directions out.
Hamlet act 2, sc. 1, l. 66

8 Brevity is the soul of wit.
Hamlet act 2, sc. 2, l. 90

9   To define true madness,
What is't but to be nothing else but mad?
Hamlet act 2, sc. 2, l. 93

10 More matter with less art.
Hamlet act 2, sc. 2, l. 95

11 POLONIUS: What do you read, my lord?
HAMLET: Words, words, words.
Hamlet act 2, sc. 2, l. [195]

12 Though this be madness, yet there is
method in't.
Hamlet act 2, sc. 2, l. [211]

13 HAMLET: Then you live about her waist, or
in the middle of her favours?
GUILDENSTERN: Faith, her privates, we.
HAMLET: In the secret parts of Fortune? O!
most true; she is a strumpet.
Hamlet act 2, sc. 2, l. [240]

14 There is nothing either good or bad, but
thinking makes it so.
Hamlet act 2, sc. 2, l. [259]

15 O God! I could be bounded in a nut-shell,
and count myself a king of infinite space,
were it not that I have bad dreams.
Hamlet act 2, sc. 2, l. [263]

16 What a piece of work is a man! How noble
in reason! how infinite in faculty! in form,
in moving, how express and admirable! in
action how like an angel! in apprehension
how like a god! the beauty of the world!
the paragon of animals! And yet, to me,
what is this quintessence of dust? man
delights not me; no, nor woman neither,
though, by your smiling, you seem to say
so.
Hamlet act 2, sc. 2, l. [323]

17 I am but mad north-north-west; when the
wind is southerly, I know a hawk from a
handsaw.
Hamlet act 2, sc. 2, l. [405]

18 The play, I remember, pleased not the
million; 'twas caviare to the general.
Hamlet act 2, sc. 2, l. [465]

19 Good my lord, will you see the players well
bestowed? Do you hear, let them be well
used; for they are the abstracts and brief
chronicles of the time.
Hamlet act 2, sc. 2, l. [553]

20 Use every man after his desert, and who
should 'scape whipping?
Hamlet act 2, sc. 2, l. [561]

21 O, what a rogue and peasant slave am I.
Hamlet act 2, sc. 2, l. [584]

22 What's Hecuba to him or he to Hecuba
That he should weep for her?
Hamlet act 2, sc. 2, l. [593]

23   He would drown the stage with
tears,
And cleave the general ear with horrid
speech,
Make mad the guilty, and appal the free,
Confound the ignorant, and amaze, indeed,
The very faculties of eyes and ears.
Hamlet act 2, sc. 2, l. [596]

24   The play's the thing
Wherein I'll catch the conscience of the
king.
Hamlet act 2, sc. 2, l. [641]

25 To be, or not to be: that is the question:
Whether 'tis nobler in the mind to suffer
The slings and arrows of outrageous
fortune,
Or to take arms against a sea of troubles,
And by opposing end them? To die: to
sleep;
No more; and, by a sleep to say we end
The heart-ache and the thousand natural
shocks
That flesh is heir to, 'tis a consummation
Devoutly to be wished. To die, to sleep;
To sleep: perchance to dream: ay, there's
the rub;
For in that sleep of death what dreams
may come
When we have shuffled off this mortal coil,
Must give us pause.
Hamlet act 3, sc. 1, l. 56

26 ... The dread of something after death,
The undiscovered country from whose
bourn
No traveller returns, puzzles the will,
And makes us rather bear those ills we
have,
Than fly to others that we know not of?
Thus conscience doth make cowards of us
all;
And thus the native hue of resolution
Is sicklied o'er with the pale cast of
thought.
Hamlet act 3, sc. 1, l. 78

27   Nymph, in thy orisons
Be all my sins remembered.
Hamlet act 3, sc. 1, l. 89

28 Get thee to a nunnery.
Hamlet act 3, sc. 1, l. [124]

29 Be thou as chaste as ice, as pure as snow,
thou shalt not escape calumny.
Hamlet act 3, sc. 1, l. [142]

1 I say, we will have no more marriages.
   Hamlet act 3, sc. 1, l. [156]

2 O! what a noble mind is here o'erthrown:
   The courtier's, soldier's, scholar's, eye,
   tongue, sword;
   The expectancy and rose of the fair state,
   The glass of fashion, and the mould of
   form,
   The observed of all observers, quite, quite,
   down!
   Hamlet act 3, sc. 1, l. [159]

3   O! woe is me,
   To have seen what I have seen, see what I
   see!
   Hamlet act 3, sc. 1, l. [169]

4 Speak the speech, I pray you, as I
   pronounced it to you, trippingly on the
   tongue; but if you mouth it, as many of
   your players do, I had as lief the town-crier
   spoke my lines. Nor do not saw the air too
   much with your hand, thus; but use all
   gently.
   Hamlet act 3, sc. 2, l. 1

5 I would have such a fellow whipped for
   o'erdoing Termagant; it out-herods Herod.
   Hamlet act 3, sc. 2, l. 14

6 Suit the action to the word, the word to
   the action.
   Hamlet act 3, sc. 2, l. [20]

7   Give me that man
   That is not passion's slave, and I will wear
   him
   In my heart's core, ay, in my heart of
   heart,
   As I do thee.
   Hamlet act 3, sc. 2, l. [76]

8 Here's metal more attractive.
   Hamlet act 3, sc. 2, l. [117]

9 The lady doth protest too much, methinks.
   Hamlet act 3, sc. 2, l. [242]

10 Let the galled jade wince, our withers are
   unwrung.
   Hamlet act 3, sc. 2, l. [256]

11 What! frighted with false fire?
   Hamlet act 3, sc. 2, l. [282]

12 Why, let the stricken deer go weep,
   The hart ungalled play;
   For some must watch, while some must
   sleep:
   So runs the world away.
   Hamlet act 3, sc. 2, l. [287]

13 You would play upon me; you would seem
   to know my stops; you would pluck out
   the heart of my mystery; you would sound
   me from my lowest note to the top of my
   compass.
   Hamlet act 3, sc. 2, l. [387]

14 They fool me to the top of my bent.
   Hamlet act 3, sc. 2, l. [408]

15 'Tis now the very witching time of night.
   Hamlet act 3, sc. 2, l. [413]

16 O! my offence is rank, it smells to heaven.
   Hamlet act 3, sc. 3, l. 36

17 Now might I do it pat, now he is praying.
   Hamlet act 3, sc. 3, l. 73

18 My words fly up, my thoughts remain
   below:
   Words without thoughts never to heaven
   go.
   Hamlet act 3, sc. 3, l. 97

19 How now! a rat? Dead, for a ducat, dead!
   Hamlet act 3, sc. 4, l. 23

20 Thou wretched, rash, intruding fool,
   farewell!
   I took thee for thy better.
   Hamlet act 3, sc. 4, l. 31

21 A king of shreds and patches.
   Hamlet act 3, sc. 4, l. 102

22   Mother, for love of grace,
   Lay not that flattering unction to your
   soul.
   Hamlet act 3, sc. 4, l. 142

23 Assume a virtue, if you have it not.
   Hamlet act 3, sc. 4, l. 160

24 I must be cruel only to be kind.
   Hamlet act 3, sc. 4, l. 178

25 For 'tis the sport to have the enginer
   Hoist with his own petar.
   Hamlet act 3, sc. 4, l. 206

26 I'll lug the guts into the neighbour room.
   Hamlet act 3, sc. 4, l. 212

27   Diseases desperate grown,
   By desperate appliances are relieved
   Or not at all.
   Hamlet act 4, sc. 2, l. 9

28 We go to gain a little patch of ground,
   That hath in it no profit but the name.
   Hamlet act 4, sc. 4, l. 18

29 How all occasions do inform against me.
   Hamlet act 4, sc. 4, l. 32

30   Some craven scruple
   Of thinking too precisely on the event.
   Hamlet act 4, sc. 4, l. 40

31   Rightly to be great
   Is not to stir without great argument,
   But greatly to find quarrel in a straw
   When honour's at the stake.
   Hamlet act 4, sc. 4, l. 53

32 How should I your true love know
   From another one?
   By his cockle hat and staff,
   And his sandal shoon.
   Hamlet act 4, sc. 5, l. [23]

33 Lord! we know what we are, but know not
   what we may be.
   Hamlet act 4, sc. 5, l. [43]

34 Come, my coach! Good-night, ladies; good-
   night, sweet ladies; good-night, good-night.
   Hamlet act 4, sc. 5, l. [72]

35 When sorrows come, they come not single
   spies,
   But in battalions.
   Hamlet act 4, sc. 5, l. [78]

1 There's such divinity doth hedge a king,
   That treason can but peep to what it
   would.
   Hamlet act 4, sc. 5, l. [123]

2 There's rosemary, that's for remembrance;
   pray, love, remember: and there is pansies,
   that's for thoughts.
   Hamlet act 4, sc. 5, l. [174]

3 There's rue for you; and here's some for
   me; we may call it herb of grace o'
   Sundays. O! you must wear your rue with a
   difference.
   Hamlet act 4, sc. 5, l. [180]

4 And where the offence is let the great axe
   fall.
   Hamlet act 4, sc. 5, l. [218]

5 A very riband in the cap of youth.
   Hamlet act 4, sc. 7, l. 77

6 There is a willow grows aslant a brook,
   That shows his hoar leaves in the glassy
   stream.
   Hamlet act 4, sc. 7, l. 167

7 There, on the pendent boughs her coronet
   weeds
   Clambering to hang, an envious sliver
   broke,
   When down her weedy trophies and
   herself
   Fell in the weeping brook.
   Hamlet act 4, sc. 7, l. 173

8 Alas, poor Yorick. I knew him, Horatio; a
   fellow of infinite jest, of most excellent
   fancy.
   Hamlet act 5, sc. 1, l. [201]

9 Imperious Caesar, dead, and turned to clay,
   Might stop a hole to keep the wind away.
   Hamlet act 5, sc. 1, l. [235]

10 A ministering angel shall my sister be,
   When thou liest howling.
   Hamlet act 5, sc. 1, l. [260]

11 Sweets to the sweet: farewell!
   Hamlet act 5, sc. 1, l. [265]

12 There's a divinity that shapes our ends,
   Rough-hew them how we will.
   Hamlet act 5, sc. 2, l. 10

13 Not a whit, we defy augury; there's a
   special providence in the fall of a sparrow.
   If it be now, 'tis not to come; if it be not to
   come, it will be now; if it be not now, yet it
   will come: the readiness is all.
   Hamlet act 5, sc. 2, l. [232]

14 A hit, a very palpable hit.
   Hamlet act 5, sc. 2, l. [295]

15   This fell sergeant, death,
   Is swift in his arrest.
   Hamlet act 5, sc. 2, l. [350]

16 I am more an antique Roman than a Dane.
   Hamlet act 5, sc. 2, l. [355]

17 If thou didst ever hold me in thy heart,
   Absent thee from felicity awhile,
   And in this harsh world draw thy breath in
   pain,
   To tell my story.
   Hamlet act 5, sc. 2, l. [360]

18 The rest is silence.
   Hamlet act 5, sc. 2, l. [372]

19 Now cracks a noble heart. Good-night,
   sweet prince,
   And flights of angels sing thee to thy rest!
   Hamlet act 5, sc. 2, l. [373]

20 Rosencrantz and Guildenstern are dead.
   Hamlet act 5, sc. 2, l. [385]

Henry IV, Part 1 (1597)

21 So shaken as we are, so wan with care.
   Henry IV, Part 1 act 1, sc. 1, l. 1

22 Let us be Diana's foresters, gentlemen of
   the shade, minions of the moon.
   Henry IV, Part 1 act 1, sc. 2, l. [28]

23 What, in thy quips and thy quiddities?
   Henry IV, Part 1 act 1, sc. 2, l. [50]

24 The rusty curb of old father antick, the
   law.
   Henry IV, Part 1 act 1, sc. 2, l. [68]

25 If all the year were playing holidays,
   To sport would be as tedious as to work;
   But when they seldom come, they wished
   for come.
   Henry IV, Part 1 act 1, sc. 2, l. [226]

26 To put down Richard, that sweet lovely
   rose,
   And plant this thorn, this canker,
   Bolingbroke.
   Henry IV, Part 1 act 1, sc. 3, l. 175

27 By heaven methinks it were an easy leap
   To pluck bright honour from the pale-faced
   moon,
   Or dive into the bottom of the deep,
   Where fathom-line could never touch the
   ground,
   And pluck up drownèd honour by the
   locks.
   Henry IV, Part 1 act 1, sc. 3, l. 201

28 It would be argument for a week, laughter
   for a month, and a good jest for ever.
   Henry IV, Part 1 act 2, sc. 2, l. [104]

29   Falstaff sweats to death
   And lards the lean earth as he walks along.
   Henry IV, Part 1 act 2, sc. 2, l. [119]

30 Out of this nettle, danger, we pluck this
   flower, safety.
   Henry IV, Part 1 act 2, sc. 3, l. [11]

31 We must have bloody noses and cracked
   crowns.
   Henry IV, Part 1 act 2, sc. 3, l. [98]

32 Fie upon this quiet life! I want work.
   Henry IV, Part 1 act 2, sc. 4, l. [119]

33 Nay that's past praying for.
   Henry IV, Part 1 act 2, sc. 4, l. [214]

1 Banish not him thy Harry's company:
  banish plump Jack and banish all the
  world.
  Henry IV, Part 1 act 2, sc. 4, l. [533]

2 O monstrous! but one half-pennyworth of
  bread to this intolerable deal of sack!
  Henry IV, Part 1 act 2, sc. 4, l. [598]

3 GLENDOWER: I can call spirits from the
  vasty deep.
  HOTSPUR: Why, so can I, or so can any man;
  But will they come when you do call for
  them?
  Henry IV, Part 1 act 3, sc. 1, l. [53]

4 That would set my teeth nothing on edge,
  Nothing so much as mincing poetry:
  'Tis like the forced gait of a shuffling nag.
  Henry IV, Part 1 act 3, sc. 1, l. [132]

5 Now I perceive the devil understands
  Welsh.
  Henry IV, Part 1 act 3, sc. 1, l. [233]

6 He was but as the cuckoo is in June,
  Heard, not regarded.
  Henry IV, Part 1 act 3, sc. 2, l. 75

7 My near'st and dearest enemy.
  Henry IV, Part 1 act 3, sc. 2, l. 123

8 Company, villanous company, hath been
  the spoil of me.
  Henry IV, Part 1 act 3, sc. 3, l. [10]

9 Thou seest I have more flesh than another
  man, and therefore more frailty.
  Henry IV, Part 1 act 3, sc. 3, l. [187]

10 Greatness knows itself.
   Henry IV, Part 1 act 4, sc. 3, l. 74

11 Rebellion lay in his way, and he found it.
   Henry IV, Part 1 act 5, sc. 1, l. 28

12 What is honour? A word. What is that
   word, honour? Air. A trim reckoning! Who
   hath it? He that died o' Wednesday.
   Henry IV, Part 1 act 5, sc. 1, l. [136]

13 Two stars keep not their motion in one
   sphere.
   Henry IV, Part 1 act 5, sc. 4, l. 65

14 But thought's the slave of life, and life
   time's fool;
   And time, that takes survey of all the
   world,
   Must have a stop.
   Henry IV, Part 1 act 5, sc. 4, l. [81]

15   Poor Jack, farewell!
   I could have better spared a better man.
   Henry IV, Part 1 act 5, sc. 4, l. [103]

Henry IV, Part 2 (1597)

16 I am not only witty in myself, but the
   cause that wit is in other men.
   Henry IV, Part 2 act 1, sc. 2, l. [10]

17 It is the disease of not listening, the
   malady of not marking, that I am troubled
   withal.
   Henry IV, Part 2 act 1, sc. 2, l. [139]

18 I am as poor as Job, my lord, but not so
   patient.
   Henry IV, Part 2 act 1, sc. 2, l. [145]

19 I can get no remedy against this
   consumption of the purse: borrowing only
   lingers and lingers it out, but the disease is
   incurable.
   Henry IV, Part 2 act 1, sc. 2, l. [268]

20 Away, you scullion! you rampallion! you
   fustilarian! I'll tickle your catastrophe.
   Henry IV, Part 2 act 2, sc. 1, l. [67]

21   Pack-horses,
   And hollow pampered jades of Asia,
   Which cannot go but thirty miles a day.
   Henry IV, Part 2 act 2, sc. 4, l. [176]. Cf. 219:14

22 Is it not strange that desire should so
   many years outlive performance?
   Henry IV, Part 2 act 2, sc. 4, l. [283]

23 Uneasy lies the head that wears a crown.
   Henry IV, Part 2 act 3, sc. 1, l. 31

24 We have heard the chimes at midnight.
   Henry IV, Part 2 act 3, sc. 2, l. [231]

25 I care not; a man can die but once; we owe
   God a death.
   Henry IV, Part 2 act 3, sc. 2, l. [253]

26 O polished perturbation! golden care!
   Henry IV, Part 2 act 4, sc. 5, l. 22

27 Thy wish was father, Harry, to that
   thought.
   Henry IV, Part 2 act 4, sc. 5, l. 91

28   Commit
   The oldest sins the newest kind of ways.
   Henry IV, Part 2 act 4, sc. 5, l. 124

29 This is the English, not the Turkish court;
   Not Amurath an Amurath succeeds,
   But Harry, Harry.
   Henry IV, Part 2 act 5, sc. 2, l. 47

30 My father is gone wild into his grave.
   Henry IV, Part 2 act 5, sc. 2, l. 123

31 'Tis merry in hall when beards wag all.
   Henry IV, Part 2 act 5, sc. 3, l. [35]

32 How ill white hairs become a fool and
   jester!
   Henry IV, Part 2 act 5, sc. 5, l. [53]

Henry V (1599)

33 O! for a Muse of fire, that would ascend
   The brightest heaven of invention.
   Henry V chorus, l. 1

34   Can this cockpit hold
   The vasty fields of France? or may we cram
   Within this wooden O the very casques
   That did affright the air at Agincourt?
   Henry V chorus, l. 11

35 Consideration like an angel came,
   And whipped the offending Adam out of
   him.
   Henry V act 1, sc. 1, l. 28

36   When he speaks,
   The air, a chartered libertine, is still.
   Henry V act 1, sc. 1, l. 47

1 When we have matched our rackets to
  these balls,
  We will in France, by God's grace, play a
  set
  Shall strike his father's crown into the
  hazard.
  Henry V act 1, sc. 2, l. 261

2 Now all the youth of England are on fire,
  And silken dalliance in the wardrobe lies.
  Henry V act 2, chorus, l. 1

3 He's in Arthur's bosom, if ever man went
  to Arthur's bosom.
  Henry V act 2, sc. 3, l. [9]

4 His nose was as sharp as a pen, and a'
  babbled of green fields.
  Henry V act 2, sc. 3, l. [17]

5 Once more unto the breach, dear friends,
  once more;
  Or close the wall up with our English dead!
  In peace there's nothing so becomes a man
  As modest stillness and humility:
  But when the blast of war blows in our
  ears,
  Then imitate the action of the tiger;
  Stiffen the sinews, summon up the blood,
  Disguise fair nature with hard-favoured
  rage;
  Then lend the eye a terrible aspect.
  Henry V act 3, sc. 1, l. 1

6 I see you stand like greyhounds in the
  slips,
  Straining upon the start. The game's afoot:
  Follow your spirit; and, upon this charge
  Cry 'God for Harry! England and Saint
  George!'
  Henry V act 3, sc. 1, l. 31

7 Now entertain conjecture of a time
  When creeping murmur and the poring
  dark
  Fills the wide vessel of the universe.
  Henry V act 4, chorus, l. 1

8 A little touch of Harry in the night.
  Henry V act 4, chorus, l. 47

9 Discuss unto me; art thou officer?
  Or art thou base, common and popular?
  Henry V act 4, sc. 1, l. 37

10 The king's a bawcock, and a heart of gold,
  A lad of life, an imp of fame,
  Of parents good, of fist most valiant:
  I kiss his dirty shoe, and from my heart-
  string
  I love the lovely bully.
  Henry V act 4, sc. 1, l. 44

11 Though it appear a little out of fashion,
  There is much care and valour in this
  Welshman.
  Henry V act 4, sc. 1, l. [86]

12 I think the king is but a man, as I am: the
  violet smells to him as it doth to me.
  Henry V act 4, sc. 1, l. [106]

13 I am afeard there are few die well that die
  in a battle; for how can they charitably
  dispose of any thing when blood is their
  argument?
  Henry V act 4, sc. 1, l. [149]

14 Every subject's duty is the king's; but every
  subject's soul is his own.
  Henry V act 4, sc. 1, l. [189]

15 And what have kings that privates have
  not too,
  Save ceremony, save general ceremony?
  Henry V act 4, sc. 1, l. [258]

16 'Tis not the balm, the sceptre and the ball,
  The sword, the mace, the crown imperial,
  The intertissued robe of gold and pearl,
  The farcèd title running 'fore the king,
  The throne he sits on, nor the tide of pomp
  That beats upon the high shore of this
  world,
  No, not all these, thrice-gorgeous
  ceremony,
  Not all these, laid in bed majestical,
  Can sleep so soundly as the wretched slave,
  Who with a body filled and vacant mind
  Gets him to rest, crammed with distressful
  bread.
  Henry V act 4, sc. 1, l. [280]

17 If we are marked to die, we are enow
  To do our country loss; and if to live,
  The fewer men, the greater share of
  honour.
  Henry V act 4, sc. 3, l. 20

18 He which hath no stomach to this fight,
  Let him depart; his passport shall be made,
  And crowns for convoy put into his purse:
  We would not die in that man's company
  That fears his fellowship to die with us.
  This day is called the feast of Crispian:
  He that outlives this day and comes safe
  home,
  Will stand a tip-toe when this day is
  named,
  And rouse him at the name of Crispian.
  Henry V act 4, sc. 3, l. 35

19 Old men forget: yet all shall be forgot,
  But he'll remember with advantages
  What feats he did that day.
  Henry V act 4, sc. 3, l. 49

20 And Crispin Crispian shall ne'er go by,
  From this day to the ending of the world,
  But we in it shall be rememberèd;
  We few, we happy few, we band of
  brothers;
  For he to-day that sheds his blood with me
  Shall be my brother; be he ne'er so vile
  This day shall gentle his condition:
  And gentlemen in England, now a-bed
  Shall think themselves accursed they were
  not here,
  And hold their manhoods cheap whiles any
  speaks
  That fought with us upon Saint Crispin's
  day.
  Henry V act 4, sc. 3, l. 57

1   But now behold,
In the quick forge and working-house of
 thought,
How London doth pour out her citizens.
 Henry V act 5, chorus, l. 22

2 ... The naked, poor, and manglèd Peace,
Dear nurse of arts, plenties, and joyful
 births.
 Henry V act 5, sc. 2, l. 34

Henry VI, Part 1 (1592)

3 Expect Saint Martin's summer, halcyon
 days.
 Henry VI, Part 1 act 1, sc. 2, l. 131

4   Unbidden guests
Are often welcomest when they are gone.
 Henry VI, Part 1 act 2, sc. 2, l. 55

5 I owe him little duty and less love.
 Henry VI, Part 1 act 4, sc. 4, l. 34

6 She's beautiful and therefore to be wooed;
She is a woman, therefore to be won.
 Henry VI, Part 1 act 5, sc. 3, l. 78. Cf. 296:25

Henry VI, Part 2 (1592)

7 She bears a duke's revenues on her back,
And in her heart she scorns our poverty.
 Henry VI, Part 2 act 1, sc. 3, l. [83]

8 Thrice is he armed that hath his quarrel
 just.
 Henry VI, Part 2 act 3, sc. 2, l. 233

9 The gaudy, blabbing, and remorseful day
Is crept into the bosom of the sea.
 Henry VI, Part 2 act 4, sc. 1, l. 1

10 The first thing we do, let's kill all the
 lawyers.
 Henry VI, Part 2 act 4, sc. 2, l. [86]

11 And Adam was a gardener.
 Henry VI, Part 2 act 4, sc. 2, l. [146]

12 Away with him! away with him! he speaks
 Latin.
 Henry VI, Part 2 act 4, sc. 7, l. [62]

Henry VI, Part 3 (1592)

13 O tiger's heart wrapped in a woman's hide!
 Henry VI, Part 3 act 1, sc. 4, l. 137

Henry VIII (with John Fletcher, 1613)

14 Go with me, like good angels, to my end;
And, as the long divorce of steel falls on
 me,
Make of your prayers one sweet sacrifice,
And lift my soul to heaven.
 Henry VIII act 2, sc. 1, l. 75

15   Heaven will one day open
The king's eyes, that so long have slept
 upon
This bold bad man.
 Henry VIII act 2, sc. 2, l. [42]. Cf. 313:8

16 Orpheus with his lute made trees,
And the mountain-tops that freeze,
Bow themselves when he did sing.
 Henry VIII act 3, sc. 1, l. 3

17   I shall fall
Like a bright exhalation in the evening,
And no man see me more.
 Henry VIII act 3, sc. 2, l. 226

18 Farewell! a long farewell, to all my
 greatness!
This is the state of man: to-day he puts
 forth
The tender leaves of hope; to-morrow
 blossoms,
And bears his blushing honours thick upon
 him;
The third day comes a frost, a killing frost;
And, when he thinks, good easy man, full
 surely
His greatness is a-ripening, nips his root,
And then he falls, as I do. I have ventured,
Like little wanton boys that swim on
 bladders,
This many summers in a sea of glory,
But far beyond my depth.
 Henry VIII act 3, sc. 2, l. 352

19 Cromwell, I charge thee, fling away
 ambition:
By that sin fell the angels.
 Henry VIII act 3, sc. 2, l. 441

20 Love thyself last: cherish those hearts that
 hate thee;
Corruption wins not more than honesty.
 Henry VIII act 3, sc. 2, l. 444

21 Had I but served my God with half the zeal
I served my king, he would not in mine
 age
Have left me naked to mine enemies.
 Henry VIII act 3, sc. 2, l. 456

22 Men's evil manners live in brass; their
 virtues
We write in water.
 Henry VIII act 4, sc. 2, l. 45

23 Some come to take their ease
And sleep an act or two.
 Henry VIII act 5, epilogue, l. 2

Julius Caesar (1599)

24 You blocks, you stones, you worse than
 senseless things!
O you hard hearts, you cruel men of Rome,
Knew you not Pompey?
 Julius Caesar act 1, sc. 1, l. [39]

25 Beware the ides of March.
 Julius Caesar act 1, sc. 2, l. 18

26 Well, honour is the subject of my story.
I cannot tell what you and other men
Think of this life: but, for my single self,
I had as lief not be as live to be
In awe of such a thing as I myself.
 Julius Caesar act 1, sc. 2, l. 92

27 Why, man, he doth bestride the narrow
 world
Like a Colossus; and we petty men
Walk under his huge legs, and peep about
To find ourselves dishonourable graves.
Men at some time are masters of their
 fates:
The fault, dear Brutus, is not in our stars,
But in ourselves, that we are underlings.
 Julius Caesar act 1, sc. 2, l. 134

1 Let me have men about me that are fat;
Sleek-headed men and such as sleep o'
nights;
Yond Cassius has a lean and hungry look;
He thinks too much: such men are
dangerous.
Julius Caesar act 1, sc. 2, l. 191

2 It is the bright day that brings forth the
adder.
Julius Caesar act 2, sc. 1, l. 14

3 Between the acting of a dreadful thing
And the first motion, all the interim is
Like a phantasma, or a hideous dream.
Julius Caesar act 2, sc. 1, l. 63

4 Let's carve him as a dish fit for the gods,
Not hew him as a carcass fit for hounds.
Julius Caesar act 2, sc. 1, l.173

5 But when I tell him he hates flatterers,
He says he does, being then most flattered.
Julius Caesar act 2, sc. 1, l. 207

6   What! is Brutus sick,
And will he steal out of his wholesome bed
To dare the vile contagion of the night?
Julius Caesar act 2, sc. 1, l. 263

7 PORTIA: Dwell I but in the suburbs
Of your good pleasure? If it be no more,
Portia is Brutus' harlot, not his wife.
BRUTUS: You are my true and honourable
wife,
As dear to me as are the ruddy drops
That visit my sad heart.
Julius Caesar act 2, sc. 1, l. 285

8 CALPHURNIA: When beggars die, there are
no comets seen;
The heavens themselves blaze forth the
death of princes.
CAESAR: Cowards die many times before
their deaths;
The valiant never taste of death but once.
Julius Caesar act 2, sc. 2, l. 30

9 But I am constant as the northern star,
Of whose true-fixed and resting quality
There is no fellow in the firmament.
Julius Caesar act 3, sc. 1, l. 60

10 *Et tu, Brute?*
Julius Caesar act 3, sc. 1, l. 77. Cf. 88:3

11 Ambition's debt is paid.
Julius Caesar act 3, sc. 1, l. 83

12   Live a thousand years,
I shall not find myself so apt to die:
No place will please me so, no mean of
death,
As here by Caesar, and by you cut off,
The choice and master spirits of this age.
Julius Caesar act 3, sc. 1, l. 159

13 O! pardon me, thou bleeding piece of
earth,
That I am meek and gentle with these
butchers.
Julius Caesar act 3, sc. 1, l. 254

14 Cry, 'Havoc!' and let slip the dogs of war.
Julius Caesar act 3, sc. 1, l. 273

15 Not that I loved Caesar less, but that I
loved Rome more.
Julius Caesar act 3, sc. 2, l. [22]

16 As he was valiant, I honour him: but, as he
was ambitious, I slew him.
Julius Caesar act 3, sc. 2, l. [27]

17 Who is here so base that would be a
bondman? If any, speak; for him have I
offended.
Julius Caesar act 3, sc. 2, l. [31]

18 Friends, Romans, countrymen, lend me
your ears;
I come to bury Caesar, not to praise him.
The evil that men do lives after them,
The good is oft interrèd with their bones.
Julius Caesar act 3, sc. 2, l. [79]

19 For Brutus is an honourable man.
Julius Caesar act 3, sc. 2, l. [88]

20 When that the poor have cried, Caesar
hath wept;
Ambition should be made of sterner stuff.
Julius Caesar act 3, sc. 2, l. [97]

21 But yesterday the word of Caesar might
Have stood against the world; now lies he
there,
And none so poor to do him reverence.
Julius Caesar act 3, sc. 2, l. [124]

22 If you have tears, prepare to shed them
now.
Julius Caesar act 3, sc. 2, l. [174]

23 This was the most unkindest cut of all.
Julius Caesar act 3, sc. 2, l. [188]

24 O! what a fall was there, my countrymen;
Then I, and you, and all of us fell down,
Whilst bloody treason flourished over us.
Julius Caesar act 3, sc. 2, l. [195]

25 I am no orator, as Brutus is;
But, as you know me all, a plain, blunt
man,
That love my friend.
Julius Caesar act 3, sc. 2, l. [221]

26   But were I Brutus,
And Brutus Antony, there were an Antony
Would ruffle up your spirits, and put a
tongue
In every wound of Caesar, that should
move
The stones of Rome to rise and mutiny.
Julius Caesar act 3, sc. 2, l. [230]

27 Tear him for his bad verses.
Julius Caesar act 3, sc. 3, l. [34]

28 He shall not live; look, with a spot I damn
him.
Julius Caesar act 4, sc. 1, l. 6

29 Let me tell you, Cassius, you yourself
Are much condemned to have an itching
palm.
Julius Caesar act 4, sc. 3, l. 7

30 Away, slight man!
Julius Caesar act 4, sc. 3, l. 37

1 There is a tide in the affairs of men,
Which, taken at the flood, leads on to
fortune;
Omitted, all the voyage of their life
Is bound in shallows and in miseries.
Julius Caesar act 4, sc. 3, l. 217

2 This was the noblest Roman of them all;
All the conspirators save only he
Did that they did in envy of great Caesar;
He, only, in a general honest thought
And common good to all, made one of
them.
His life was gentle, and the elements
So mixed in him that Nature might stand
up
And say to all the world, 'This was a man!'
Julius Caesar act 5, sc. 5, l. 68

King John (1591–8)

3 And if his name be George, I'll call him
Peter;
For new-made honour doth forget men's
names.
King John act 1, sc. 1, l. 186

4 Mad world! mad kings! mad composition!
King John act 2, sc. 1, l. 561

5 Well, whiles I am a beggar, I will rail,
And say there is no sin, but to be rich;
And, being rich, my virtue then shall be,
To say there is no vice, but beggary.
King John act 2, sc. 1, l. 593

6 Old Time the clock-setter, that bald sexton,
Time.
King John act 3, sc. 1, l. 324

7 Bell, book, and candle shall not drive me
back,
When gold and silver becks me to come
on.
King John act 3, sc. 3, l. 12

8 Grief fills the room up of my absent child,
Lies in his bed, walks up and down with
me,
Puts on his pretty looks, repeats his words,
Remembers me of all his gracious parts,
Stuffs out his vacant garments with his
form:
Then have I reason to be fond of grief.
King John act 3, sc. 4, l. 93

9 Life is as tedious as a twice-told tale,
Vexing the dull ear of a drowsy man.
King John act 3, sc. 4, l. 108

10 To gild refinèd gold, to paint the lily,
To throw a perfume on the violet,
To smooth the ice, or add another hue
Unto the rainbow, or with taper light
To seek the beauteous eye of heaven to
garnish,
Is wasteful and ridiculous excess.
King John act 4, sc. 2, l. 11

11 Another lean unwashed artificer
Cuts off his tale and talks of Arthur's
death.
King John act 4, sc. 2, l. 201

12 How oft the sight of means to do ill deeds
Makes ill deeds done!
King John act 4, sc. 2, l. 219

13 Heaven take my soul, and England keep my
bones!
King John act 4, sc. 3, l. 10

14   I do not ask you much:
I beg cold comfort.
King John act 5, sc. 7, l. 41

15 This England never did, nor never shall,
Lie at the proud foot of a conqueror,
But when it first did help to wound itself.
Now these her princes are come home
again,
Come the three corners of the world in
arms,
And we shall shock them: nought shall
make us rue,
If England to itself do rest but true.
King John act 5, sc. 7, l. 112

King Lear (1605–6)

16 Nothing will come of nothing: speak again.
King Lear act 1, sc. 1, l. [92]

17 LEAR: So young, and so untender?
CORDELIA: So young, my lord, and true.
King Lear act 1, sc. 1, l. [108]

18   I want that glib and oily art
To speak and purpose not.
King Lear act 1, sc. 1, l. [227]

19 Fairest Cordelia, that art most rich, being
poor;
Most choice, forsaken; and most loved,
despised!
King Lear act 1, sc. 1, l. [253]

20   Why bastard? wherefore base?
When my dimensions are as well compact,
My mind as generous, and my shape as
true,
As honest madam's issue?
King Lear act 1, sc. 2, l. 6

21 I grow, I prosper;
Now, gods, stand up for bastards!
King Lear act 1, sc. 2, l. 21

22 This is the excellent foppery of the world,
that, when we are sick in fortune,—often
the surfeit of our own behaviour,— we
make guilty of our own disasters the sun,
the moon, and the stars; as if we were
villains by necessity, fools by heavenly
compulsion, knaves, thieves, and treachers
by spherical predominance, drunkards,
liars, and adulterers by an enforced
obedience of planetary influence.
King Lear act 1, sc. 2, l. [132]

23 Who is it that can tell me who I am?
King Lear act 1, sc. 4, l. 230

24 Ingratitude, thou marble-hearted fiend,
More hideous, when thou show'st thee in a
child,
Than the sea-monster.
King Lear act 1, sc. 4, l. [283]

25 How sharper than a serpent's tooth it is
To have a thankless child!
King Lear act 1, sc. 4, l. [312]

1 O! let me not be mad, not mad, sweet
heaven;
Keep me in temper; I would not be mad!
King Lear act 1, sc. 5, l. [51]

2 Thou whoreson zed! thou unnecessary
letter!
King Lear act 2, sc. 2, l. [68]

3   O, sir! you are old;
Nature in you stands on the very verge
Of her confine.
King Lear act 2, sc. 4, l. [148]

4 O reason not the need! Our basest beggars
Are in the poorest thing superfluous.
King Lear act 2, sc. 4, l. 264

5 I will do such things,—
What they are yet I know not,—but they
shall be
The terrors of the earth.
King Lear act 2, sc. 4, l. [283]

6 Blow, winds, and crack your cheeks! rage!
blow!
You cataracts and hurricanoes, spout
Till you have drenched our steeples,
drowned the cocks!
You sulphurous and thought-executing
fires,
Vaunt-couriers to oak-cleaving
thunderbolts,
Singe my white head! And thou, all-shaking
thunder,
Strike flat the thick rotundity o' the world!
King Lear act 3, sc. 2, l. 1

7 Rumble thy bellyful! Spit, fire! Spout, rain!
Nor rain, wind, thunder, fire, are my
daughters:
I tax not you, you elements, with
unkindness.
King Lear act 3, sc. 2, l. 14

8 There was never yet fair woman but she
made mouths in a glass.
King Lear act 3, sc. 2, l. [35]

9 No, I will be the pattern of all patience; I
will say nothing.
King Lear act 3, sc. 2, l. [37]

10   I am a man
More sinned against than sinning.
King Lear act 3, sc. 2, l. [57]

11 O! that way madness lies; let me shun that.
King Lear act 3, sc. 4, l. 21

12   Take physic, pomp;
Expose thyself to feel what wretches feel.
King Lear act 3, sc. 4, l. 33

13 Keep thy foot out of brothels, thy hand out
of plackets, thy pen from lenders' books,
and defy the foul fiend.
King Lear act 3, sc. 4, l. [96]

14 Thou art the thing itself; unaccommodated
man is no more but such a poor, bare,
forked animal as thou art.
King Lear act 3, sc. 4, l. [109]

15 The green mantle of the standing pool.
King Lear act 3, sc. 4, l. [136]

16 The prince of darkness is a gentleman.
King Lear act 3, sc. 4, l. [148]

17 Poor Tom's a-cold.
King Lear act 3, sc. 4, l. [151]

18 Child Roland to the dark tower came,
His word was still, Fie, foh, and fum,
I smell the blood of a British man.
King Lear act 3, sc. 4, l. [185]

19   Out, vile jelly!
Where is thy lustre now?
King Lear act 3, sc. 7, l. [83]

20   The worst is not,
So long as we can say, 'This is the worst.'
King Lear act 4, sc. 1, l. 27

21 As flies to wanton boys, are we to the gods;
They kill us for their sport.
King Lear act 4, sc. 1, l. 36

22 GLOUCESTER: Is't not the king?
LEAR: Ay, every inch a king.
King Lear act 4, sc. 6, l. [110]

23   Die: die for adultery! No:
The wren goes to't, and the small gilded fly
Does lecher in my sight.
Let copulation thrive.
King Lear act 4, sc. 6, l. [114]

24 GLOUCESTER: O! let me kiss that hand!
LEAR: Let me wipe it first; it smells of
mortality.
GLOUCESTER: O ruined piece of nature! This
great world
Should so wear out to nought.
King Lear act 4, sc. 6, l. [136]

25 Why dost thou lash that whore? Strip
thine own back;
Thou hotly lust'st to use her in that kind
For which thou whipp'st her.
King Lear act 4, sc. 6, l. [166]

26   Get thee glass eyes;
And, like a scurvy politician, seem
To see the things thou dost not.
King Lear act 4, sc. 6, l. [175]

27 When we are born we cry that we are
come
To this great stage of fools.
King Lear act 4, sc. 6, l. [187]

28   Mine enemy's dog,
Though he had bit me, should have stood
that night
Against my fire.
King Lear act 4, sc. 7, l. 36

29 I am a very foolish, fond old man,
Fourscore and upward, not an hour more
or less;
And, to deal plainly,
I fear I am not in my perfect mind.
King Lear act 4, sc. 7, l. 60

30   Men must endure
Their going hence, even as their coming
hither:
Ripeness is all.
King Lear act 5, sc. 2, l. 9

1   Come, let's away to prison;
We two alone will sing like birds i' the
  cage:
When thou dost ask me blessing, I'll kneel
  down,
And ask of thee forgiveness.
  King Lear act 5, sc. 3, l. 8. Cf. 344:27

2 The gods are just, and of our pleasant vices
Make instruments to plague us.
  King Lear act 5, sc. 3, l. [172]

3 The wheel is come full circle.
  King Lear act 5, sc. 3, l. [176]

4 Howl, howl, howl, howl! O! you are men of
  stones:
Had I your tongue and eyes, I'd use them
  so
That heaven's vaults should crack. She's
  gone for ever!
  King Lear act 5, sc. 3, l. [259]

5   Her voice was ever soft,
Gentle and low, an excellent thing in
  woman.
  King Lear act 5, sc. 3, l. [274]

6 And my poor fool is hanged! No, no, no
  life!
Why should a dog, a horse, a rat, have life,
And thou no breath at all? Thou'lt come no
  more,
Never, never, never, never, never!
Pray you, undo this button.
  King Lear act 5, sc. 3, l. [307]

7 Vex not his ghost: O! let him pass; he hates
  him
That would upon the rack of this tough
  world
Stretch him out longer.
  King Lear act 5, sc. 3, l. [314]

8 The oldest hath borne most: we that are
  young,
Shall never see so much, nor live so long.
  King Lear act 5, sc. 3, l. [327]

Love's Labour's Lost (1595)

9 Cormorant devouring Time.
  Love's Labour's Lost act 1, sc. 1, l. 4

10 Study is like the heaven's glorious sun,
That will not be deep-searched with saucy
  looks;
  Love's Labour's Lost act 1, sc. 1, l. 84

11 At Christmas I no more desire a rose
Than wish a snow in May's new-fangled
  mirth;
But like of each thing that in season
  grows.
  Love's Labour's Lost act 1, sc. 1, l. 105

12 Warble, child; make passionate my sense
of hearing.
  Love's Labour's Lost act 3, sc. 1, l. 1

13 This wimpled, whining, purblind, wayward
  boy,
This senior-junior, giant-dwarf, Dan Cupid.
  Love's Labour's Lost act 3, sc. 1, l. [189]

14 A wightly wanton with a velvet brow,
With two pitch balls stuck in her face for
  eyes;
Ay, and, by heaven, one that will do the
  deed
Though Argus were her eunuch and her
  guard.
  Love's Labour's Lost act 3, sc. 1, l. [206]

15 He hath not fed of the dainties that are
bred in a book; he hath not eat paper, as it
were; he hath not drunk ink.
  Love's Labour's Lost act 4, sc. 2, l. [25]

16 From women's eyes this doctrine I derive:
They are the ground, the books, the
  academes,
From whence doth spring the true
  Promethean fire.
  Love's Labour's Lost act 4, sc. 3, l. [302]. See also
  act 4, sc. 3, l. [350]

17 They have been at a great feast of
languages, and stolen the scraps.
  Love's Labour's Lost act 5, sc. 1, l. [39]

18 Taffeta phrases, silken terms precise.
  Love's Labour's Lost act 5, sc. 2, l. 407

19 Henceforth my wooing mind shall be
  expressed
In russet yeas and honest kersey noes.
  Love's Labour's Lost act 5, sc. 2, l. 413

20 A jest's prosperity lies in the ear
Of him that hears it, never in the tongue
Of him that makes it.
  Love's Labour's Lost act 5, sc. 2, l. [869]

21 When daisies pied and violets blue
And lady-smocks all silver-white
And cuckoo-buds of yellow hue
Do paint the meadows with delight,
The cuckoo then, on every tree,
Mocks married men.
  Love's Labour's Lost act 5, sc. 2, l. [902]

22 Cuckoo, cuckoo; O, word of fear,
Unpleasing to a married ear!
  Love's Labour's Lost act 5, sc. 2, l. [909]

23 When icicles hang by the wall,
And Dick the shepherd blows his nail,
And Tom bears logs into the hall,
And milk comes frozen home in pail,
When blood is nipped and ways be foul,
Then nightly sings the staring owl,
  Tu-who;
Tu-whit, tu-who—a merry note,
While greasy Joan doth keel the pot.
  Love's Labour's Lost act 5, sc. 2, l. [920]

24 The words of Mercury are harsh after the
songs of Apollo.
  Love's Labour's Lost act 5, sc. 2, l. [938]

Macbeth (1606)

25 FIRST WITCH: When shall we three meet
    again
  In thunder, lightning, or in rain?
SECOND WITCH: When the hurly-burly's
    done,
  When the battle's lost and won.
  Macbeth act 1, sc. 1, l. 1

1 Fair is foul, and foul is fair:
Hover through the fog and filthy air.
Macbeth act 1, sc. 1, l. 11

2 What bloody man is that?
Macbeth act 1, sc. 2, l. 1

3 'Aroint thee, witch!' the rump-fed ronyon
cries.
Her husband's to Aleppo gone, master o'
the Tiger:
But in a sieve I'll thither sail,
And, like a rat without a tail,
I'll do, I'll do, and I'll do.
Macbeth act 1, sc. 3, l. 6

4 Sleep shall neither night nor day
Hang upon his pent-house lid.
He shall live a man forbid.
Weary se'nnights nine times nine
Shall he dwindle, peak, and pine:
Though his bark cannot be lost,
Yet it shall be tempest-tost.
Macbeth act 1, sc. 3, l. 19

5 The weird sisters, hand in hand,
Posters of the sea and land,
Thus do go about, about.
Macbeth act 1, sc. 3, l. 32

6 So foul and fair a day I have not seen.
Macbeth act 1, sc. 3, l. 38

7 If you can look into the seeds of time,
And say which grain will grow and which
will not.
Macbeth act 1, sc. 3, l. 58

8   Say, from whence
You owe this strange intelligence? or why
Upon this blasted heath you stop our way
With such prophetic greeting?
Macbeth act 1, sc. 3, l. 72

9 What! can the devil speak true?
Macbeth act 1, sc. 3, l. 107

10   Two truths are told,
As happy prologues to the swelling act
Of the imperial theme.
Macbeth act 1, sc. 3, l. 127

11   Present fears
Are less than horrible imaginings.
Macbeth act 1, sc. 3, l. 137

12 Come what come may,
Time and the hour runs through the
roughest day.
Macbeth act 1, sc. 3, l. 146

13   Nothing in his life
Became him like the leaving it.
Macbeth act 1, sc. 4, l. 7

14   There's no art
To find the mind's construction in the face.
Macbeth act 1, sc. 4, l. 11

15 Glamis thou art, and Cawdor; and shalt be
What thou art promised. Yet I do fear thy
nature;

It is too full o' the milk of human kindness
To catch the nearest way; thou wouldst be
great,
Art not without ambition; but without
The illness should attend it; what thou
wouldst highly,
That thou wouldst holily; wouldst not play
false,
And yet wouldst wrongly win.
Macbeth act 1, sc. 5, l. [16]

16   The raven himself is hoarse
That croaks the fatal entrance of Duncan
Under my battlements.
Macbeth act 1, sc. 5, l. [39]

17   Unsex me here,
And fill me from the crown to the toe top
full
Of direst cruelty; make thick my blood,
Stop up the access and passage to remorse,
That no compunctious visitings of nature
Shake my fell purpose.
Macbeth act 1, sc. 5, l. [42]

18   Come to my woman's breasts,
And take my milk for gall, you murdering
ministers.
Macbeth act 1, sc. 5, l. [48]

19   Come, thick night,
And pall thee in the dunnest smoke of hell,
That my keen knife see not the wound it
makes.
Macbeth act 1, sc. 5, l. [51]

20 Your face, my thane, is as a book where
men
May read strange matters.
Macbeth act 1, sc. 5, l. [63]

21   This guest of summer,
The temple-haunting martlet.
Macbeth act 1, sc. 6, l. 3

22 If it were done when 'tis done, then 'twere
well
It were done quickly: if the assassination
Could trammel up the consequence, and
catch
With his surcease success; that but this
blow
Might be the be-all and the end-all here,
But here, upon this bank and shoal of
time,
We'd jump the life to come.
Macbeth act 1, sc. 7, l. 1

23   We but teach
Bloody instructions, which, being taught,
return,
To plague the inventor.
Macbeth act 1, sc. 7, l. 8

24   Besides, this Duncan
Hath borne his faculties so meek, hath
been
So clear in his great office, that his virtues
Will plead like angels trumpet-tongued,
against
The deep damnation of his taking-off.
Macbeth act 1, sc. 7, l. 16

1
        I have no spur
To prick the sides of my intent, but only
Vaulting ambition, which o'erleaps itself,
And falls on the other.
   Macbeth act 1, sc. 7, l. 25

2 He hath honoured me of late; and I have
   bought
Golden opinions from all sorts of people.
   Macbeth act 1, sc. 7, l. 32

3
        Was the hope drunk,
Wherein you dressed yourself?
   Macbeth act 1, sc. 7, l. 35

4 Letting 'I dare not' wait upon 'I would',
Like the poor cat i' the adage.
   Macbeth act 1, sc. 7, l. 44

5 I dare do all that may become a man;
Who dares do more is none.
   Macbeth act 1, sc. 7, l. 46

6 LADY MACBETH: I have given suck, and know
How tender 'tis to love the babe that
   milks me:
I would, while it was smiling in my face,
Have plucked my nipple from his
   boneless gums,
And dash'd the brains out, had I so sworn
   as you
Have done to this.
MACBETH: If we should fail,—
LADY MACBETH: We fail!
But screw your courage to the sticking-
   place,
And we'll not fail.
   Macbeth act 1, sc. 7, l. 54

7 Bring forth men-children only.
   Macbeth act 1, sc. 7, l. 72

8 False face must hide what the false heart
   doth know.
   Macbeth act 1, sc. 7, l. 82

9
        There's husbandry in heaven;
Their candles are all out.
   Macbeth act 2, sc. 1, l. 4

10 Is this a dagger which I see before me,
The handle toward my hand? Come, let me
   clutch thee:
I have thee not, and yet I see thee still.
Art thou not, fatal vision, sensible
To feeling as to sight? or art thou but
A dagger of the mind, a false creation,
Proceeding from the heat-oppressèd brain?
   Macbeth act 2, sc. 1, l. 33

11
        The bell invites me.
Hear it not, Duncan; for it is a knell
That summons thee to heaven or to hell.
   Macbeth act 2, sc. 1, l. 62

12 That which hath made them drunk hath
   made me bold.
   Macbeth act 2, sc. 2, l. 1

13
        The attempt and not the deed,
Confounds us.
   Macbeth act 2, sc. 2, l. 12

14
        Had he not resembled
My father as he slept I had done't.
   Macbeth act 2, sc. 2, l. 14

15 Methought I heard a voice cry, 'Sleep no
   more!
Macbeth does murder sleep,' the innocent
   sleep,
Sleep that knits up the ravelled sleave of
   care.
   Macbeth act 2, sc. 2, l. 36

16 Glamis hath murdered sleep, and therefore
   Cawdor
Shall sleep no more, Macbeth shall sleep
   no more!
   Macbeth act 2, sc. 2, l. 43

17
        Infirm of purpose!
Give me the daggers. The sleeping and the
   dead
Are but as pictures; 'tis the eye of
   childhood
That fears a painted devil.
   Macbeth act 2, sc. 2, l. 53

18 Will all great Neptune's ocean wash this
   blood
Clean from my hand? No, this my hand
   will rather
The multitudinous seas incarnadine,
Making the green one red.
   Macbeth act 2, sc. 2, l. 61

19 A little water clears us of this deed.
   Macbeth act 2, sc. 2, l. 68

20 Here's a farmer that hanged himself on the
   expectation of plenty.
   Macbeth act 2, sc. 3, l. 5

21 Drink, sir, is a great provoker . . .
Lechery, sir, it provokes, and unprovokes; it
   provokes the desire, but it takes away the
   performance.
   Macbeth act 2, sc. 3, l. [28]

22 The labour we delight in physics pain.
   Macbeth act 2, sc. 3, l. [56]

23 Confusion now hath made his masterpiece!
   Macbeth act 2, sc. 3, l. [72]

24 Shake off this downy sleep, death's
   counterfeit,
And look on death itself!
   Macbeth act 2, sc. 3, l. [83]

25 MACDUFF: Our royal master's murdered!
LADY MACBETH: Woe, alas!
   What! in our house?
   Macbeth act 2, sc. 3, l. [95]

26 There's nothing serious in mortality:
All is but toys; renown and grace is dead,
The wine of life is drawn, and the mere
   lees
Is left this vault to brag of.
   Macbeth act 2, sc. 3, l. [100]

27 There's daggers in men's smiles: the near
   in blood,
The nearer bloody.
   Macbeth act 2, sc. 3, l. [147]

28 A falcon, towering in her pride of place,
Was by a mousing owl hawked at and
   killed.
   Macbeth act 2, sc. 4, l. 12

1 BANQUO: Go not my horse the better,
   I must become a borrower of the night
   For a dark hour or twain.
   MACBETH: Fail not our feast.
   Macbeth act 3, sc. 1, l. 26

2 Leave no rubs nor botches in the work.
   Macbeth act 3, sc. 1, l. 134

3 LADY MACBETH: Things without all remedy
   Should be without regard: what's done is
   done.
   MACBETH: We have scotched the snake, not
   killed it:
   She'll close and be herself, whilst our
   poor malice
   Remains in danger of her former tooth.
   Macbeth act 3, sc. 2, l. 11

4 Duncan is in his grave;
   After life's fitful fever he sleeps well;
   Treason has done his worst: nor steel, nor
   poison,
   Malice domestic, foreign levy, nothing,
   Can touch him further.
   Macbeth act 3, sc. 2, l. 22

5 Ere the bat hath flown
   His cloistered flight, ere, to black Hecate's
   summons
   The shard-borne beetle with his drowsy
   hums
   Hath rung night's yawning peal, there
   shall be done
   A deed of dreadful note.
   Macbeth act 3, sc. 2, l. 40

6 Come, seeling night,
   Scarf up the tender eye of pitiful day,
   And with thy bloody and invisible hand,
   Cancel and tear to pieces that great bond
   Which keeps me pale!
   Macbeth act 3, sc. 2, l. 46

7 Now spurs the lated traveller apace
   To gain the timely inn.
   Macbeth act 3, sc. 3, l. 6

8 Ourself will mingle with society
   And play the humble host.
   Macbeth act 3, sc. 4, l. 3

9 ... Now I am cabined, cribbed, confined,
   bound in
   To saucy doubts and fears.
   Macbeth act 3, sc. 4, l. 24

10 Now good digestion wait on appetite,
   And health on both!
   Macbeth act 3, sc. 4, l. 38

11 Thou canst not say I did it: never shake
   Thy gory locks at me.
   Macbeth act 3, sc. 4, l. 50

12 Stand not upon the order of your going.
   Macbeth act 3, sc. 4, l. 119

13 It will have blood, they say; blood will have
   blood.
   Macbeth act 3, sc. 4, l. 122

14 I am in blood
   Stepped in so far that, should I wade no
   more,
   Returning were as tedious as go o'er.
   Macbeth act 3, sc. 4, l. 136

15 Double, double toil and trouble;
   Fire burn and cauldron bubble.
   Macbeth act 4, sc. 1, l. 10

16 Eye of newt, and toe of frog.
   Macbeth act 4, sc. 1, l. 14

17 Liver of blaspheming Jew,
   Gall of goat, and slips of yew.
   Macbeth act 4, sc. 1, l. 26

18 By the pricking of my thumbs,
   Something wicked this way comes.
   Macbeth act 4, sc. 1, l. 44

19 MACBETH: How now, you secret, black, and
   midnight hags!
   What is't you do?
   WITCHES: A deed without a name.
   Macbeth act 4, sc. 1, l. 48

20 Be bloody, bold, and resolute.
   Macbeth act 4, sc. 1, l. 79

21 But yet, I'll make assurance double sure,
   And take a bond of fate.
   Macbeth act 4, sc. 1, l. 83

22 His flight was madness: when our actions
   do not,
   Our fears do make us traitors.
   Macbeth act 4, sc. 2, l. 3

23 He loves us not;
   He wants the natural touch.
   Macbeth act 4, sc. 2, l. 8

24 Stands Scotland where it did?
   Macbeth act 4, sc. 3, l. 164

25 Give sorrow words: the grief that does not
   speak
   Whispers the o'er-fraught heart, and bids it
   break.
   Macbeth act 4, sc. 3, l. 209

26 What! all my pretty chickens and their
   dam,
   At one fell swoop?
   Macbeth act 4, sc. 3, l. 218

27 Out, damned spot!
   Macbeth act 5, sc. 1, l. [38]

28 Who would have thought the old man to
   have had so much blood in him?
   Macbeth act 5, sc. 1, l. [42]

29 The Thane of Fife had a wife: where is she
   now? What! will these hands ne'er be
   clean? No more o' that, my lord, no more
   o' that: you mar all with this starting.
   Macbeth act 5, sc. 1, l. [46]

30 Here's the smell of the blood still: all the
   perfumes of Arabia will not sweeten this
   little hand.
   Macbeth act 5, sc. 1, l. [55]

31 What's done cannot be undone.
   Macbeth act 5, sc. 1, l. [74]

32 Bring me no more reports; let them fly all:
   Till Birnam wood remove to Dunsinane
   I cannot taint with fear.
   Macbeth act 5, sc. 3, l. 1

33 The devil damn thee black, thou cream-
   faced loon!
   Where gott'st thou that goose look?
   Macbeth act 5, sc. 3, l. 11

1 I have lived long enough: my way of life
Is fall'n into the sear, the yellow leaf.
Macbeth act 5, sc. 3, l. 22

2 Canst thou not minister to a mind
diseased?
Macbeth act 5, sc. 3, l. 40

3 Throw physic to the dogs; I'll none of it.
Macbeth act 5, sc. 3, l. 47

4 I have supped full with horrors.
Macbeth act 5, sc. 5, l. 13

5 She should have died hereafter;
There would have been a time for such a
word,
To-morrow, and to-morrow, and to-
morrow,
Creeps in this petty pace from day to day,
To the last syllable of recorded time;
And all our yesterdays have lighted fools
The way to dusty death. Out, out, brief
candle!
Life's but a walking shadow, a poor player,
That struts and frets his hour upon the
stage,
And then is heard no more; it is a tale
Told by an idiot, full of sound and fury,
Signifying nothing.
Macbeth act 5, sc. 5, l. 16

6 I bear a charmèd life.
Macbeth act 5, sc. 7, l. 41

7 Macduff was from his mother's womb
Untimely ripped.
Macbeth act 5, sc. 7, l. 44

8   Lay on, Macduff;
And damned be him that first cries, 'Hold,
enough!'
Macbeth act 5, sc. 7, l. 62

Measure for Measure (1604)
9 And liberty plucks justice by the nose.
Measure for Measure act 1, sc. 3, l. 29

10 I hold you as a thing enskyed and sainted.
Measure for Measure act 1, sc. 4, l. 34

11   A man whose blood
Is very snow-broth; one who never feels
The wanton stings and motions of the
sense.
Measure for Measure act 1, sc. 4, l. 57

12 We must not make a scarecrow of the law.
Measure for Measure act 2, sc. 1, l. 1

13   O! it is excellent
To have a giant's strength, but it is
tyrannous
To use it like a giant.
Measure for Measure act 2, sc. 2, l. 107

14 Man, proud man,
Drest in a little brief authority,
Measure for Measure act 2, sc. 2, l. 117

15 That in the captain's but a choleric word,
Which in the soldier is flat blasphemy.
Measure for Measure act 2, sc. 2, l. 130

16   Ever till now
When men were fond, I smiled and
wondered how.
Measure for Measure act 2, sc. 2, l. 186

17 The miserable have no other medicine
But only hope.
Measure for Measure act 3, sc. 1, l. 2

18 Be absolute for death; either death or life
Shall thereby be the sweeter. Reason thus
with life:
If I do lose thee, I do lose a thing
That none but fools would keep.
Measure for Measure act 3, sc. 1, l. 5

19   A breath thou art
Servile to all the skyey influences.
Measure for Measure act 3, sc. 1, l. 8

20   If I must die,
I will encounter darkness as a bride,
And hug it in mine arms.
Measure for Measure act 3, sc. 1, l. 81

21 CLAUDIO: Death is a fearful thing.
ISABELLA: And shamed life a hateful.
CLAUDIO: Ay, but to die, and go we know
not where;
To lie in cold obstruction and to rot;
This sensible warm motion to become
A kneaded clod; and the delighted spirit
To bathe in fiery floods or to reside
In thrilling region of thick-ribbèd ice.
Measure for Measure act 3, sc. 1, l. 114

22 There, at the moated grange, resides this
dejected Mariana.
Measure for Measure act 3, sc. 1, l. [279]

23 When he makes water his urine is
congealed ice.
Measure for Measure act 3, sc. 2, l. [119]

24 Insensible of mortality, and desperately
mortal.
Measure for Measure act 4, sc. 2, l. [151]

25 I am a kind of burr; I shall stick.
Measure for Measure act 4, sc. 3, l. [193]

26 They say best men are moulded out of
faults,
And, for the most, become much more the
better
For being a little bad: so may my husband.
Measure for Measure act 5, sc. 1, l. [440]

The Merchant of Venice (1596–8)
27 I hold the world but as the world,
Gratiano;
A stage where every man must play a part,
And mine a sad one.
The Merchant of Venice act 1, sc. 1, l. 77

28 They are as sick that surfeit with too
much, as they that starve with nothing.
The Merchant of Venice act 1, sc. 2, l. [5]

29 If to do were as easy as to know what were
good to do, chapels had been churches, and
poor men's cottages princes' palaces.
The Merchant of Venice act 1, sc. 2, l. [13]

30 God made him, and therefore let him pass
for a man.
The Merchant of Venice act 1, sc. 2, l. [59]

31 I will buy with you, sell with you, talk with
you, walk with you, and so following; but I
will not eat with you, drink with you, nor
pray with you. What news on the Rialto?
The Merchant of Venice act 1, sc. 3, l. [36]

1 How like a fawning publican he looks!
The Merchant of Venice act 1, sc. 3, l. [42]

2 If I can catch him once upon the hip,
I will feed fat the ancient grudge I bear
him.
The Merchant of Venice act 1, sc. 3, l. [47]

3 The devil can cite Scripture for his
purpose.
The Merchant of Venice act 1, sc. 3, l. [99]

4 Still have I borne it with a patient shrug,
For sufferance is the badge of all our tribe.
The Merchant of Venice act 1, sc. 3, l. [110]

5 You call me misbeliever, cut-throat dog,
And spit upon my Jewish gabardine,
And all for use of that which is mine own.
The Merchant of Venice act 1, sc. 3, l. [112]

6 Mislike me not for my complexion,
The shadowed livery of the burnished sun,
To whom I am a neighbour and near bred.
The Merchant of Venice act 2, sc. 1, l. 1

7 It is a wise father that knows his own
child.
The Merchant of Venice act 2, sc. 2, l. [83]

8 Truth will come to light; murder cannot be
hid long.
The Merchant of Venice act 2, sc. 2, l. [86]

9 There is some ill a-brewing towards my
rest.
For I did dream of money-bags to-night.
The Merchant of Venice act 2, sc. 5, l. 17

10 Let not the sound of shallow foppery enter
My sober house.
The Merchant of Venice act 2, sc. 5, l. [35]

11 What! must I hold a candle to my shames?
The Merchant of Venice act 2, sc. 6, l. 41

12 My daughter! O my ducats! O my daughter!
The Merchant of Venice act 2, sc. 8, l. 15

13   Like the martlet,
Builds in the weather on the outward wall,
Even in the force and road of casualty.
The Merchant of Venice act 2, sc. 9, l. 28

14 The portrait of a blinking idiot.
The Merchant of Venice act 2, sc. 9, l. 54

15 Let him look to his bond.
The Merchant of Venice act 3, sc. 1, l. [51]

16 Hath not a Jew eyes? hath not a Jew hands,
organs, dimensions, senses, affections,
passions?
The Merchant of Venice act 3, sc. 1, l. [63]

17 If you prick us, do we not bleed? if you
tickle us, do we not laugh? if you poison
us, do we not die? and if you wrong us,
shall we not revenge?
The Merchant of Venice act 3, sc. 1, l. [69]

18 The villainy you teach me I will execute,
and it shall go hard but I will better the
instruction.
The Merchant of Venice act 3, sc. 1, l. [76]

19   He makes a swan-like end,
Fading in music.
The Merchant of Venice act 3, sc. 2, l. 44

20 Tell me where is fancy bred.
Or in the heart or in the head?
The Merchant of Venice act 3, sc. 2, l. 63

21 So may the outward shows be least
themselves:
The world is still deceived with ornament.
The Merchant of Venice act 3, sc. 2, l. 73

22   An unlessoned girl, unschooled,
unpractised;
Happy in this, she is not yet so old
But she may learn; happier than this,
She is not bred so dull but she can learn.
The Merchant of Venice act 3, sc. 2, l. 160

23 I pray thee, understand a plain man in his
plain meaning.
The Merchant of Venice act 3, sc. 5, l. [63]

24 I am a tainted wether of the flock,
Meetest for death: the weakest kind of
fruit
Drops earliest to the ground.
The Merchant of Venice act 4, sc. 1, l. 114

25 I never knew so young a body with so old a
head.
The Merchant of Venice act 4, sc. 1, l. [163]

26 The quality of mercy is not strained,
It droppeth as the gentle rain from heaven
Upon the place beneath: it is twice blessed;
It blesseth him that gives and him that
takes:
'Tis mightiest in the mightiest: it becomes
The thronèd monarch better than his
crown.
The Merchant of Venice act 4, sc. 1, l. [182]

27 Though justice be thy plea, consider this,
That in the course of justice none of us
Should see salvation: we do pray for mercy,
And that same prayer doth teach us all to
render
The deeds of mercy.
The Merchant of Venice act 4, sc. 1, l. [197]

28 Wrest once the law to your authority:
To do a great right, do a little wrong.
The Merchant of Venice act 4, sc. 1, l. [215]

29 A Daniel come to judgement! yea, a Daniel!
The Merchant of Venice act 4, sc. 1, l. [223]

30 He is well paid that is well satisfied.
The Merchant of Venice act 4, sc. 1, l. [416]

31 The moon shines bright: in such a night as
this . . .
Troilus methinks mounted the Troyan
walls,
And sighed his soul toward the Grecian
tents,
Where Cressid lay that night.
The Merchant of Venice act 5, sc. 1, l. 1

32   In such a night
Stood Dido with a willow in her hand
Upon the wild sea-banks, and waft her love
To come again to Carthage.
The Merchant of Venice act 5, sc. 1, l. 9

1 How sweet the moonlight sleeps upon this
bank.
Here will we sit, and let the sounds of
music
Creep in our ears; soft stillness and the
night
Become the touches of sweet harmony.
The Merchant of Venice act 5, sc. 1, l. 54

2   Look, how the floor of heaven
Is thick inlaid with patines of bright gold.
The Merchant of Venice act 5, sc. 1, l. 58

3 The man that hath no music in himself,
Nor is not moved with concord of sweet
sounds,
Is fit for treasons, stratagems, and spoils.
The Merchant of Venice act 5, sc. 1, l. 79

4 How far that little candle throws his
beams!
So shines a good deed in a naughty world.
The Merchant of Venice act 5, sc. 1, l. 90

5 How many things by season seasoned are
To their right praise and true perfection!
The Merchant of Venice act 5, sc. 1, l. 107

6 This night methinks is but the daylight
sick.
The Merchant of Venice act 5, sc. 1, l. 124

The Merry Wives of Windsor (1597)

7 I will make a Star-Chamber matter of it.
The Merry Wives of Windsor act 1, sc. 1, l. 1

8 She has brown hair, and speaks small like
a woman.
The Merry Wives of Windsor act 1, sc. 1, l. [48]

9 Why, then the world's mine oyster,
Which I with sword will open.
The Merry Wives of Windsor act 2, sc. 2, l. 2

10 O, what a world of vile ill-favoured faults
Looks handsome in three hundred pounds
a year!
The Merry Wives of Windsor act 3, sc. 4, l. [32]

11 There is divinity in odd numbers, either in
nativity, chance or death.
The Merry Wives of Windsor act 5, sc. 1, l. 3

A Midsummer Night's Dream (1595–6)

12 To live a barren sister all your life,
Chanting faint hymns to the cold fruitless
moon.
A Midsummer Night's Dream act 1, sc. 1, l. 72

13 The course of true love never did run
smooth.
A Midsummer Night's Dream act 1, sc. 1, l. 134

14 Swift as a shadow, short as any dream,
Brief as the lightning in the collied night.
A Midsummer Night's Dream act 1, sc. 1, l. 144

15 So quick bright things come to confusion.
A Midsummer Night's Dream act 1, sc. 1, l. 149

16 Things base and vile, holding no quantity,
Love can transpose to form and dignity.
Love looks not with the eyes, but with the
mind,
And therefore is winged Cupid painted
blind.
A Midsummer Night's Dream act 1, sc. 1, l. 232

17 Masters, spread yourselves.
A Midsummer Night's Dream act 1, sc. 2, l. [16]

18 I could play Ercles rarely, or a part to tear
a cat in, to make all split.
A Midsummer Night's Dream act 1, sc. 2, l. [31]

19 Over hill, over dale,
Thorough bush, thorough brier,
Over park, over pale,
Thorough flood, thorough fire,
I do wander everywhere.
A Midsummer Night's Dream act 2, sc. 1, l. 2

20 I must go seek some dew-drops here,
And hang a pearl in every cowslip's ear.
A Midsummer Night's Dream act 2, sc. 1, l. 14

21 The wisest aunt, telling the saddest tale.
A Midsummer Night's Dream act 2, sc. 1, l. 51

22 Ill met by moonlight, proud Titania.
A Midsummer Night's Dream act 2, sc. 1, l. 60

23 The seasons alter: hoary-headed frosts
Fall in the fresh lap of the crimson rose.
A Midsummer Night's Dream act 2, sc. 1, l. 107

24 And the imperial votaress passed on,
In maiden meditation, fancy-free.
A Midsummer Night's Dream act 2, sc. 1, l. 163

25 I'll put a girdle round about the earth
In forty minutes.
A Midsummer Night's Dream act 2, sc. 1, l. 175

26 I know a bank whereon the wild thyme
blows,
Where oxlips and the nodding violet grows
Quite over-canopied with luscious
woodbine,
With sweet musk-roses, and with
eglantine.
A Midsummer Night's Dream act 2, sc. 1, l. 249

27 And there the snake throws her enamelled
skin,
Weed wide enough to wrap a fairy in.
A Midsummer Night's Dream act 2, sc. 1, l. 255

28 You spotted snakes with double tongue,
Thorny hedge-hogs, be not seen.
A Midsummer Night's Dream act 2, sc. 2, l. 9

29 Weaving spiders come not here;
Hence you long-legged spinners, hence!
A Midsummer Night's Dream act 2, sc. 2, l. 20

30 Look in the almanack; find out moonshine.
A Midsummer Night's Dream act 3, sc. 1, l. [55]

31 What hempen home-spuns have we
swaggering here?
A Midsummer Night's Dream act 3, sc. 1, l. [82]

32 Lord, what fools these mortals be!
A Midsummer Night's Dream act 3, sc. 2, l. 115

33 She was a vixen when she went to school:
And though she be but little, she is fierce.
A Midsummer Night's Dream act 3, sc. 2, l. 323

34   Ghosts, wandering here and
there,
Troop home to churchyards.
A Midsummer Night's Dream act 3, sc. 2, l. 381

35 Let us have the tongs and the bones.
A Midsummer Night's Dream act 4, sc. 1, l. [33]

1 I have an exposition of sleep come upon
me.
A Midsummer Night's Dream act 4, sc. 1, l. [43]

2 So musical a discord, such sweet thunder.
A Midsummer Night's Dream act 4, sc. 1, l. [121]

3 The lunatic, the lover, and the poet,
Are of imagination all compact.
A Midsummer Night's Dream act 5, sc. 1, l. 7

4 The poet's eye, in a fine frenzy rolling,
Doth glance from heaven to earth, from
earth to heaven;
And, as imagination bodies forth
The forms of things unknown, the poet's
pen
Turns them to shapes, and gives to airy
nothing
A local habitation and a name.
A Midsummer Night's Dream act 5, sc. 1, l. 12

5 Merry and tragical! tedious and brief!
That is, hot ice and wondrous strange
snow.
A Midsummer Night's Dream act 5, sc. 1, l. 58

6   To show our simple skill,
That is the true beginning of our end.
A Midsummer Night's Dream act 5, sc. 1, l. [110]

7 Whereat, with blade, with bloody blameful
blade,
He bravely broached his boiling bloody
breast.
A Midsummer Night's Dream act 5, sc. 1, l. [148]

8 The best in this kind are but shadows, and
the worst are no worse, if imagination
amend them.
A Midsummer Night's Dream act 5, sc. 1, l. [215]

9 The iron tongue of midnight hath told
twelve.
A Midsummer Night's Dream act 5, sc. 1, l. [372]

10   Not a mouse
Shall disturb this hallowed house:
I am sent with broom before,
To sweep the dust behind the door.
A Midsummer Night's Dream act 5, sc. 2, l. 17

Much Ado About Nothing (1598–9)

11 He hath indeed better bettered expectation
than you must expect of me to tell you
how.
Much Ado About Nothing act 1, sc. 1, l. [15]

12 He is a very valiant trencher-man.
Much Ado About Nothing act 1, sc. 1, l. [52]

13 I see, lady, the gentleman is not in your
books.
Much Ado About Nothing act 1, sc. 1, l. [79]

14 In time the savage bull doth bear the yoke.
Much Ado About Nothing act 1, sc. 1, l. [271]

15 Lord! I could not endure a husband with a
beard on his face: I had rather lie in the
woollen.
Much Ado About Nothing act 2, sc. 1, l. [31]

16 Speak low, if you speak love.
Much Ado About Nothing act 2, sc. 1, l. [104]

17 Friendship is constant in all other things
Save in the office and affairs of love.
Much Ado About Nothing act 2, sc. 1, l. [184]

18 There was a star danced, and under that
was I born.
Much Ado About Nothing act 2, sc. 1, l. [348]

19 Sigh no more, ladies, sigh no more,
Men were deceivers ever.
Much Ado About Nothing act 2, sc. 3, l. [65]

20 Sits the wind in that corner?
Much Ado About Nothing act 2, sc. 3, l. [108]

21 He hath a heart as sound as a bell, and his
tongue is the clapper; for what his heart
thinks his tongue speaks.
Much Ado About Nothing act 3, sc. 2, l. [12]

22 Every one can master a grief but he that
has it.
Much Ado About Nothing act 3, sc. 2, l. [28]

23 Comparisons are odorous.
Much Ado About Nothing act 3, sc. 5, l. [18]

24 You have stayed me in a happy hour.
Much Ado About Nothing act 4, sc. 1, l. [283]

25 Patch grief with proverbs.
Much Ado About Nothing act 5, sc. 1, l. 17

26 No, I was not born under a rhyming
planet.
Much Ado About Nothing act 5, sc. 2, l. [40]

27   The gentle day,
Before the wheels of Phoebus, round about
Dapples the drowsy east with spots of grey.
Much Ado About Nothing act 5, sc. 3, l. 25

Othello (1602–4)

28 But I will wear my heart upon my sleeve
For daws to peck at: I am not what I am.
Othello act 1, sc. 1, l. 64

29 Even now, now, very now, an old black ram
Is tupping your white ewe.
Othello act 1, sc. 1, l. 88

30 Your daughter and the Moor are now
making the beast with two backs.
Othello act 1, sc. 1, l. [117]

31 Keep up your bright swords, for the dew
will rust them.
Othello act 1, sc. 2, l. 59

32 The wealthy curlèd darlings of our nation.
Othello act 1, sc. 2, l. 67

33   Rude am I in my speech,
And little blessed with the soft phrase of
peace.
Othello act 1, sc. 3, l. 81

34 I will a round unvarnished tale deliver.
Othello act 1, sc. 3, l. 90

35 She loved me for the dangers I had passed,
And I loved her that she did pity them.
Othello act 1, sc. 3, l. 167

36 I do perceive here a divided duty.
Othello act 1, sc. 3, l. 181

37 The robbed that smiles steals something
from the thief.
Othello act 1, sc. 3, l. 208

38 But words are words; I never yet did hear
That the bruised heart was piercèd
through the ear.
Othello act 1, sc. 3, l. 218

1 The tyrant custom, most grave senators,
Hath made the flinty and steel couch of war
My thrice-driven bed of down.
Othello act 1, sc. 3, l. [230]

2   If I be left behind,
A moth of peace, and he go to the war,
The rites for which I love him are bereft me.
Othello act 1, sc. 3, l. [257]

3 Our great captain's captain.
Othello act 2, sc. 1, l. 74

4 To suckle fools and chronicle small beer.
Othello act 2, sc. 1, l. 163

5   If it were now to die,
'Twere now to be most happy.
Othello act 2, sc. 1, l. [192]

6 A slipper and subtle knave.
Othello act 2, sc. 1, l. [247]

7 Silence that dreadful bell! it frights the isle
From her propriety.
Othello act 2, sc. 3, l. [177]

8 O! I have lost my reputation. I have lost the immortal part of myself, and what remains is bestial.
Othello act 2, sc. 3, l. [264]

9 O! thereby hangs a tail.
Othello act 3, sc. 1, l. [8]

10 Excellent wretch! Perdition catch my soul
But I do love thee! and when I love thee not,
Chaos is come again.
Othello act 3, sc. 3, l. 90

11 Good name in man and woman, dear my lord,
Is the immediate jewel of their souls;
Who steals my purse steals trash; 'tis something, nothing;
'Twas mine, 'tis his, and has been slave to thousands;
But he that filches from me my good name
Robs me of that which not enriches him,
And makes me poor indeed.
Othello act 3, sc. 3, l. 155

12   O! beware, my lord, of jealousy;
It is the green-eyed monster which doth mock
The meat it feeds on.
Othello act 3, sc. 3, l. 165

13 Foh! one may smell in such, a will most rank,
Foul disposition, thoughts unnatural.
Othello act 3, sc. 3, l. 232

14   If I do prove her haggard,
Though that her jesses were my dear heart-strings,
I'd whistle her off and let her down the wind,
To prey at fortune.
Othello act 3, sc. 3, l. 260

15   I am black,
And have not those soft parts of conversation
That chamberers have.
Othello act 3, sc. 3, l. 263

16   I am declined
Into the vale of years.
Othello act 3, sc. 3, l. 265

17 I had rather be a toad,
And live upon the vapour of a dungeon,
Than keep a corner in the thing I love
For others' uses.
Othello act 3, sc. 3, l. 270

18   Trifles light as air
Are to the jealous confirmations strong
As proofs of holy writ.
Othello act 3, sc. 3, l. 323

19 Farewell the tranquil mind; farewell content!
Farewell the plumèd troop and the big wars
That make ambition virtue!
Othello act 3, sc. 3, l. 349

20 Pride, pomp, and circumstance of glorious war.
Othello act 3, sc. 3, l. 355

21 Othello's occupation's gone!
Othello act 3, sc. 3, l. 358

22 Jealous souls will not be answered so;
They are not ever jealous for the cause,
But jealous for they are jealous.
Othello act 3, sc. 4, l. 158

23 But yet the pity of it, Iago! O! Iago, the pity of it, Iago!
Othello act 4, sc. 1, l. [205]

24   But, alas! to make me
The fixèd figure for the time of scorn
To point his slow and moving finger at.
Othello act 4, sc. 2, l. 46

25 Heaven stops the nose at it and the moon winks.
Othello act 4, sc. 2, l. 76

26 The poor soul sat sighing by a sycamore tree.
Sing all a green willow;
Her hand on her bosom, her head on her knee,
Sing willow, willow, willow:
Othello act 4, sc. 3, l. [41]. Cf. 168:8

27   This is the night
That either makes me or fordoes me quite.
Othello act 5, sc. 1, l. 128

28 It is the cause, it is the cause, my soul;
Let me not name it to you, you chaste stars!
It is the cause.
Othello act 5, sc. 2, l. 1

29 Put out the light, and then put out the light.
Othello act 5, sc. 2, l. 7

1   One more, and this the last:
So sweet was ne'er so fatal.
Othello act 5, sc. 2, l. 19

2   Murder's out of tune,
And sweet revenge grows harsh.
Othello act 5, sc. 2, l. 113

3   May his pernicious soul
Rot half a grain a day!
Othello act 5, sc. 2, l. 153

4 Here is my journey's end, here is my butt,
And very sea-mark of my utmost sail.
Othello act 5, sc. 2, l. 266

5 I have done the state some service, and
they know 't;
No more of that. I pray you, in your letters,
When you shall these unlucky deeds relate,
Speak of me as I am; nothing extenuate,
Nor set down aught in malice: then, must
you speak
Of one that loved not wisely but too well;
Of one not easily jealous, but, being
wrought,
Perplexed in the extreme; of one whose
hand,
Like the base Indian, threw a pearl away
Richer than all his tribe.
Othello act 5, sc. 2, l. 338

6 I kissed thee ere I killed thee, no way but
this,
Killing myself to die upon a kiss.
Othello act 5, sc. 2, l. 357

Richard II (1595)

7 The purest treasure mortal times afford
Is spotless reputation; that away,
Men are but gilded loam or painted clay.
Richard II act 1, sc. 1, l. 177

8 Mine honour is my life; both grow in one;
Take honour from me, and my life is done.
Richard II act 1, sc. 1, l. 182

9 We were not born to sue, but to command.
Richard II act 1, sc. 1, l. 196

10 How long a time lies in one little word!
Richard II act 1, sc. 3, l. 213

11 Things sweet to taste prove in digestion
sour.
Richard II act 1, sc. 3, l. 236

12 Must I not serve a long apprenticehood
To foreign passages, and in the end,
Having my freedom, boast of nothing else
But that I was a journeyman to grief?
Richard II act 1, sc. 3, l. 271

13 Teach thy necessity to reason thus;
There is no virtue like necessity.
Richard II act 1, sc. 3, l. 277

14 O, no! the apprehension of the good
Gives but the greater feeling to the worse.
Richard II act 1, sc. 3, l. 300

15 More are men's ends marked than their
lives before.
Richard II act 2, sc. 1, l. 11

16 This royal throne of kings, this sceptred
isle,
This earth of majesty, this seat of Mars,
This other Eden, demi-paradise,
This fortress built by Nature for herself
Against infection and the hand of war,
This happy breed of men, this little world,
This precious stone set in the silver sea,
Which serves it in the office of a wall,
Or as a moat defensive to a house,
Against the envy of less happier lands,
This blessèd plot, this earth, this realm,
this England,
This nurse, this teeming womb of royal
kings,
Feared by their breed and famous by their
birth.
Richard II act 2, sc. 1, l. 40

17 I am a stranger here in Gloucestershire:
These high wild hills and rough uneven
ways
Draw out our miles and make them
wearisome.
Richard II act 2, sc. 3, l. 2

18 Grace me no grace, nor uncle me no uncle.
Richard II act 2, sc. 3, l. 87

19 The caterpillars of the commonwealth.
Richard II act 2, sc. 3, l. 166

20 Things past redress are now with me past
care.
Richard II act 2, sc. 3, l. 171

21 Eating the bitter bread of banishment.
Richard II act 3, sc. 1, l. 21

22 Not all the water in the rough rude sea
Can wash the balm from an anointed king.
Richard II act 3, sc. 2, l. 54

23   If angels fight,
Weak men must fall, for heaven still
guards the right.
Richard II act 3, sc. 2, l. 61

24 O! call back yesterday, bid time return.
Richard II act 3, sc. 2, l. 69

25 The worst is death, and death will have his
day.
Richard II act 3, sc. 2, l. 103

26 Let's talk of graves, of worms, and
epitaphs;
Make dust our paper, and with rainy eyes
Write sorrow on the bosom of the earth.
Let's choose executors, and talk of wills.
Richard II act 3, sc. 2, l. 145

27 For God's sake, let us sit upon the ground
And tell sad stories of the death of kings.
Richard II act 3, sc. 2, l. 155

28   Within the hollow crown
That rounds the mortal temples of a king
Keeps Death his court.
Richard II act 3, sc. 2, l. 160

29 See, see, King Richard doth himself appear,
As doth the blushing discontented sun
From out the fiery portal of the east.
Richard II act 3, sc. 3, l. 62

1 The purple testament of bleeding war.
   Richard II act 3, sc. 3, l. 94

2 What must the king do now? Must he
   submit?
   The king shall do it: must he be deposed?
   The king shall be contented: must he lose
   The name of king? o' God's name, let it go.
   I'll give my jewels for a set of beads,
   My gorgeous palace for a hermitage,
   My gay apparel for an almsman's gown,
   My figured goblets for a dish of wood,
   My sceptre for a palmer's walking staff,
   My subjects for a pair of carved saints,
   And my large kingdom for a little grave,
   A little little grave, an obscure grave.
   Richard II act 3, sc. 3, l. 143

3 Shall we play the wantons with our woes,
   And make some pretty match with
   shedding tears?
   Richard II act 3, sc. 3, l. 164

4 God save the king! Will no man say, amen?
   Am I both priest and clerk? Well then,
   amen.
   Richard II act 4, sc. 1, l. 172

5 You may my glories and my state depose,
   But not my griefs; still am I king of those.
   Richard II act 4, sc. 1, l. 192

6   I am sworn brother, sweet,
   To grim Necessity, and he and I
   Will keep a league till death.
   Richard II act 5, sc. 1, l. 20

7 That were some love but little policy.
   Richard II act 5, sc. 1, l. 84

8   Who are the violets now
   That strew the green lap of the new come
   spring?
   Richard II act 5, sc. 2, l. 46

9 He prays but faintly and would be denied.
   Richard II act 5, sc. 3, l. 103

10 I have been studying how I may compare
   This prison where I live unto the world.
   Richard II act 5, sc. 5, l. 1

11   How sour sweet music is,
   When time is broke, and no proportion
   kept!
   So is it in the music of men's lives.
   Richard II act 5, sc. 5, l. 42

12 I wasted time, and now doth time waste
   me.
   Richard II act 5, sc. 5, l. 49

Richard III (1591)

13 Now is the winter of our discontent
   Made glorious summer by this sun of York.
   Richard III act 1, sc. 1, l. 1

14 In this weak piping time of peace.
   Richard III act 1, sc. 1, l. 24

15 Was ever woman in this humour wooed?
   Was ever woman in this humour won?
   Richard III act 1, sc. 2, l. 229

16 Woe to the land that's governed by a child!
   Richard III act 2, sc. 3, l. 11. Cf. 44:22

17 So wise so young, they say, do never live
   long.
   Richard III act 3, sc. 1, l. 79

18 I am not in the giving vein to-day.
   Richard III act 4, sc. 2, l. 115

19 Harp not on that string.
   Richard III act 4, sc. 4, l. 365

20 The king's name is a tower of strength.
   Richard III act 5, sc. 3, l. 12

21 A horse! a horse! my kingdom for a horse!
   Richard III act 5, sc. 4, l. 7

Romeo and Juliet (1595)

22 From forth the fatal loins of these two foes
   A pair of star-crossed lovers take their life.
   Romeo and Juliet prologue

23 The two hours' traffick of our stage.
   Romeo and Juliet prologue

24 O! then, I see, Queen Mab hath been with
   you ...
   She is the fairies' midwife, and she comes
   In shape no bigger than an agate-stone
   On the forefinger of an alderman,
   Drawn with a team of little atomies
   Athwart men's noses as they lie asleep.
   Romeo and Juliet act 1, sc. 4, l. 53

25 You and I are past our dancing days.
   Romeo and Juliet act 1, sc. 5, l. [35]

26 O! she doth teach the torches to burn
   bright.
   It seems she hangs upon the cheek of
   night
   Like a rich jewel in an Ethiop's ear;
   Beauty too rich for use, for earth too dear.
   Romeo and Juliet act 1, sc. 5, l. [48]

27 We have a trifling foolish banquet towards.
   Romeo and Juliet act 1, sc. 5, l. [126]

28 My only love sprung from my only hate!
   Too early seen unknown, and known too
   late!
   Romeo and Juliet act 1, sc. 5, l. [142]

29 He jests at scars, that never felt a wound.
   But, soft! what light through yonder
   window breaks?
   It is the east, and Juliet is the sun.
   Romeo and Juliet act 2, sc. 2, l. 1

30 O Romeo, Romeo! wherefore art thou
   Romeo?
   Romeo and Juliet act 2, sc. 2, l. 33

31 What's in a name? that which we call a
   rose
   By any other name would smell as sweet.
   Romeo and Juliet act 2, sc. 2, l. 43

32 For stony limits cannot hold love out,
   And what love can do that dares love
   attempt.
   Romeo and Juliet act 2, sc. 2, l. 66

33 O! swear not by the moon, the inconstant
   moon,
   That monthly changes in her circled orb,
   Lest that thy love prove likewise variable.
   Romeo and Juliet act 2, sc. 2, l. 109

1 It is too rash, too unadvised, too sudden.
Romeo and Juliet act 2, sc. 2, l. 118

2 Love goes toward love, as schoolboys from
their books;
But love from love, toward school with
heavy looks.
Romeo and Juliet act 2, sc. 2, l. 156

3 How silver-sweet sound lovers' tongues by
night,
Like softest music to attending ears!
Romeo and Juliet act 2, sc. 2, l. 165

4 Good-night, good-night! parting is such
sweet sorrow
That I shall say good-night till it be
morrow.
Romeo and Juliet act 2, sc. 2, l. 184

5 O flesh, flesh, how art thou fishified!
Romeo and Juliet act 2, sc. 4, l. [41]

6 I am the very pink of courtesy.
Romeo and Juliet act 2, sc. 4, l. [63]

7 No, 'tis not so deep as a well, nor so wide
as a church door; but 'tis enough, 'twill
serve.
Romeo and Juliet act 3, sc. 1, l. [100]

8 A plague o' both your houses!
Romeo and Juliet act 3, sc. 1, l. [112]

9 O! I am Fortune's fool.
Romeo and Juliet act 3, sc. 1, l. [142]

10 Gallop apace, you fiery-footed steeds,
Towards Phoebus' lodging.
Romeo and Juliet act 3, sc. 2, l. 1

11 Spread thy close curtain, love-performing
night!
Romeo and Juliet act 3, sc. 2, l. 5

12   Come, civil night,
Thou sober-suited matron, all in black.
Romeo and Juliet act 3, sc. 2, l. 10

13 Come, night! come, Romeo! come, thou day
in night!
Romeo and Juliet act 3, sc. 2, l. 17

14 Give me my Romeo: and, when he shall
die,
Take him and cut him out in little stars,
And he will make the face of heaven so
fine
That all the world will be in love with
night,
And pay no worship to the garish sun.
Romeo and Juliet act 3, sc. 2, l. 21

15 Affliction is enamoured of thy parts,
And thou art wedded to calamity.
Romeo and Juliet act 3, sc. 3, l. 2

16 Adversity's sweet milk, philosophy.
Romeo and Juliet act 3, sc. 3, l. 54

17 It was the nightingale, and not the lark,
That pierced the fearful hollow of thine
ear.
Romeo and Juliet act 3, sc. 5, l. 1

18 Night's candles are burnt out, and jocund
day
Stands tiptoe on the misty mountain tops.
Romeo and Juliet act 3, sc. 5, l. 9

19 I have more care to stay than will to go.
Romeo and Juliet act 3, sc. 5, l. 23

20 Thank me no thankings, nor proud me no
prouds.
Romeo and Juliet act 3, sc. 5, l. 153

21 Death lies on her like an untimely frost.
Romeo and Juliet act 4, sc. 5, l. 28

22 Tempt not a desperate man.
Romeo and Juliet act 5, sc. 3, l. 59

23 How oft when men are at the point of
death
Have they been merry! which their keepers
call
A lightning before death.
Romeo and Juliet act 5, sc. 3, l. 88

24   Beauty's ensign yet
Is crimson in thy lips and in thy cheeks,
And death's pale flag is not advancèd there.
Romeo and Juliet act 5, sc. 3, l. 94

25   Seal with a righteous kiss
A dateless bargain to engrossing death!
Romeo and Juliet act 5, sc. 3, l. 114

26 Seal up the mouth of outrage for a while,
Till we can clear these ambiguities.
Romeo and Juliet act 5, sc. 3, l. 216

The Taming of the Shrew (1592)

27 Kiss me Kate, we will be married o'
Sunday.
The Taming of the Shrew act 2, sc. 1, l. 318

28 This is the way to kill a wife with kindness.
The Taming of the Shrew act 4, sc. 1, l. [211]

29   O vile,
Intolerable, not to be endured!
The Taming of the Shrew act 5, sc. 2, l. 93

30 A woman moved is like a fountain
troubled,
Muddy, ill-seeming, thick, bereft of beauty.
The Taming of the Shrew act 5, sc. 2, l. 143

The Tempest (1611)

31 He hath no drowning mark upon him; his
complexion is perfect gallows.
The Tempest act 1, sc. 1, l. [33]

32 Now would I give a thousand furlongs of
sea for an acre of barren ground.
The Tempest act 1, sc. 1, l. [70]

33   What seest thou else
In the dark backward and abysm of time?
The Tempest act 1, sc. 2, l. 49

34 The still-vexed Bermoothes.
The Tempest act 1, sc. 2, l. 229

35 You taught me language; and my profit
on't
Is, I know how to curse.
The Tempest act 1, sc. 2, l. 363

36 Come unto these yellow sands,
And then take hands.
The Tempest act 1, sc. 2, l. 375

1 Full fathom five thy father lies;
Of his bones are coral made:
Those are pearls that were his eyes:
Nothing of him that doth fade,
But doth suffer a sea-change
Into something rich and strange.
The Tempest act 1, sc. 2, l. 394

2 The fringèd curtains of thine eye advance,
And say what thou seest yond.
The Tempest act 1, sc. 2, l. 405

3 What's past is prologue.
The Tempest act 2, sc. 1, l. [261]

4 When they will not give a doit to relieve a
lame beggar, they will lay out ten to see a
dead Indian.
The Tempest act 2, sc. 2, l. [33]

5 Misery acquaints a man with strange
bedfellows.
The Tempest act 2, sc. 2, l. [42]

6 Thou deboshed fish thou.
The Tempest act 3, sc. 2, l. [30]

7 Flout 'em, and scout 'em; and scout 'em,
and flout 'em;
Thought is free.
The Tempest act 3, sc. 2, l. [133]

8 He that dies pays all debts.
The Tempest act 3, sc. 2, l. [143]

9 Be not afeard: the isle is full of noises,
Sounds and sweet airs, that give delight,
and hurt not.
The Tempest act 3, sc. 2, l. [147]

10 Our revels now are ended. These our
actors,
As I foretold you, were all spirits and
Are melted into air, into thin air:
And, like the baseless fabric of this vision,
The cloud-capped towers, the gorgeous
palaces,
The solemn temples, the great globe itself,
Yea, all which it inherit, shall dissolve
And, like this insubstantial pageant faded,
Leave not a rack behind. We are such stuff
As dreams are made on, and our little life
Is rounded with a sleep.
The Tempest act 4, sc. 1, l. 148

11 I do begin to have bloody thoughts.
The Tempest act 4, sc. 1, l. [221]

12 But this rough magic
I here abjure.
The Tempest act 5, sc. 1, l. 50

13 I'll break my staff,
Bury it certain fathoms in the earth,
And, deeper than did ever plummet sound,
I'll drown my book.
The Tempest act 5, sc. 1, l. 54

14 Where the bee sucks, there suck I
In a cowslip's bell I lie;
There I couch when owls do cry.
On the bat's back I do fly
After summer merrily.
Merrily, merrily shall I live now
Under the blossom that hangs on the
bough.
The Tempest act 5, sc. 1, l. 88

15 How beauteous mankind is! O brave new
world,
That has such people in't.
The Tempest act 5, sc. 1, l. 183

Timon of Athens (c.1607)

16 'Tis not enough to help the feeble up,
But to support him after.
Timon of Athens act 1, sc. 1, l. 108

17 I wonder men dare trust themselves with
men.
Timon of Athens act 1, sc. 2, l. [45]

18 Like madness is the glory of this life.
Timon of Athens act 1, sc. 2, l. [141]

19 Men shut their doors against a setting sun.
Timon of Athens act 1, sc. 2, l. [152]

20 You fools of fortune, trencher-friends,
time's flies.
Timon of Athens act 3, sc. 6, l. [107]

21 We have seen better days.
Timon of Athens act 4, sc. 2, l. 27

22 Never learned
The icy precepts of respect.
Timon of Athens act 4, sc. 3, l. 258

23 The moon's an arrant thief,
And her pale fire she snatches from the
sun.
Timon of Athens act 4, sc. 3, l. 443

24 Timon hath made his everlasting mansion
Upon the beachèd verge of the salt flood.
Timon of Athens act 5, sc. 1, l. [220]

Titus Andronicus (1590)

25 She is a woman, therefore may be wooed;
She is a woman, therefore may be won.
Titus Andronicus act 2, sc. 1, l. 82. Cf. 280:6

26 More water glideth by the mill
Than wots the miller of.
Titus Andronicus act 2, sc. 1, l. 85

27 Come, and take choice of all my library,
And so beguile thy sorrow.
Titus Andronicus act 4, sc. 1, l. 34

Troilus and Cressida (1602)

28 I have had my labour for my travail.
Troilus and Cressida act 1, sc. 1, l. [73]

29 Things won are done; joy's soul lies in the
doing.
Troilus and Cressida act 1, sc. 2, l. [311]

30 Take but degree away, untune that string,
And, hark! what discord follows; each thing
meets
In mere oppugnancy.
Troilus and Cressida act 1, sc. 3, l. 109

31 An envious fever
Of pale and bloodless emulation.
Troilus and Cressida act 1, sc. 3, l. 129

32 The baby figure of the giant mass
Of things to come at large.
Troilus and Cressida act 1, sc. 3, l. 343

33 Thus to persist
In doing wrong extenuates not wrong,
But makes it much more heavy.
Troilus and Cressida act 2, sc. 2, l. 186

1 I am giddy, expectation whirls me round.
Troilus and Cressida act 3, sc. 2, l. [17]

2 This is the monstruosity in love, lady, that
the will is infinite, and the execution
confined; that the desire is boundless, and
the act a slave to limit.
Troilus and Cressida act 3, sc. 2, l. [85]

3　　　　To be wise, and love,
Exceeds man's might.
Troilus and Cressida act 3, sc. 2, l. [163]

4 Time hath, my lord, a wallet at his back,
Wherein he puts alms for oblivion.
Troilus and Cressida act 3, sc. 3, l. 145

5　　　　Perseverance, dear my lord,
Keeps honour bright.
Troilus and Cressida act 3, sc. 3, l. 150

6 One touch of nature makes the whole
world kin.
Troilus and Cressida act 3, sc. 3, l. 175

7 How my achievements mock me!
Troilus and Cressida act 4, sc. 2, l. [72]

8 What a pair of spectacles is here!
Troilus and Cressida act 4, sc. 4, l. [13]
(Pandarus, of the lovers)

9　　　　Fie, fie upon her!
There's language in her eye, her cheek, her
lip,
Nay, her foot speaks; her wanton spirits
look out
At every joint and motive of her body.
Troilus and Cressida act 4, sc. 5, l. 54

10 What's past, and what's to come is strewed
with husks
And formless ruin of oblivion.
Troilus and Cressida act 4, sc. 5, l. 165

11　　　　The end crowns all,
And that old common arbitrator, Time,
Will one day end it.
Troilus and Cressida act 4, sc. 5, l. 223

12 Words, words, mere words, no matter from
the heart.
Troilus and Cressida act 5, sc. 3, l. [109]

Twelfth Night (1601)

13 If music be the food of love, play on;
Give me excess of it, that, surfeiting,
The appetite may sicken, and so die.
Twelfth Night act 1, sc. 1, l. 1

14 That strain again! it had a dying fall.
Twelfth Night act 1, sc. 1, l. 4

15 I am a great eater of beef, and I believe
that does harm to my wit.
Twelfth Night act 1, sc. 3, l. [92]

16 I would I had bestowed that time in the
tongues that I have in fencing, dancing,
and bear-baiting. O! had I but followed the
arts!
Twelfth Night act 1, sc. 3, l. [99]

17 Is it a world to hide virtues in?
Twelfth Night act 1, sc. 3, l. [142]

18 Many a good hanging prevents a bad
marriage.
Twelfth Night act 1, sc. 5, l. [20]

19 A plague o' these pickle herring!
Twelfth Night act 1, sc. 5, l. [127]

20 He is very well-favoured, and he speaks
very shrewishly: one would think his
mother's milk were scarce out of him.
Twelfth Night act 1, sc. 5, l. [170]

21 Make me a willow cabin at your gate,
And call upon my soul within the house;
Write loyal cantons of contemnèd love,
And sing them loud even in the dead of
night;
Halloo your name to the reverberate hills,
And make the babbling gossip of the air
Cry out, 'Olivia!'
Twelfth Night act 1, sc. 5, l. [289]

22 Not to be a-bed after midnight is to be up
betimes.
Twelfth Night act 2, sc. 3, l. 1

23 O mistress mine! where are you roaming?
O! stay and hear; your true love's coming,
That can sing both high and low.
Trip no further, pretty sweeting;
Journeys end in lovers meeting,
Every wise man's son doth know . . .

What is love? 'tis not hereafter;
Present mirth hath present laughter;
What's to come is still unsure:
In delay there lies no plenty;
Then come kiss me, sweet and twenty,
Youth's a stuff will not endure.
Twelfth Night act 2, sc. 3, l. [42]

24 He does it with a better grace, but I do it
more natural.
Twelfth Night act 2, sc. 3, l. [91]

25 Is there no respect of place, persons, nor
time, in you?
Twelfth Night act 2, sc. 3, l. [100]

26 Dost thou think, because thou art virtuous,
there shall be no more cakes and ale?
Twelfth Night act 2, sc. 3, l. [124]

27 My purpose is, indeed, a horse of that
colour.
Twelfth Night act 2, sc. 3, l. [184]

28 I was adored once too.
Twelfth Night act 2, sc. 3, l. [200]

29 These most brisk and giddy-pacèd times.
Twelfth Night act 2, sc. 4, l. 6

30　　　　Let still the woman take
An elder than herself, so wears she to him,
So sways she level in her husband's heart.
Twelfth Night act 2, sc. 4, l. 29

31 The spinsters and the knitters in the sun.
Twelfth Night act 2, sc. 4, l. 44

32 Come away, come away, death,
And in sad cypress let me be laid.
Twelfth Night act 2, sc. 4, l. 51

33 Now, the melancholy god protect thee, and
the tailor make thy doublet of changeable
taffeta, for thy mind is a very opal.
Twelfth Night act 2, sc. 4, l. [74]

1   She never told her love,
But let concealment, like a worm i' the
bud,
Feed on her damask cheek: she pined in
thought;
And with a green and yellow melancholy,
She sat like patience on a monument,
Smiling at grief.
Twelfth Night act 2, sc. 4, l. [112]

2 I am all the daughters of my father's
house,
And all the brothers too.
Twelfth Night act 2, sc. 4, l. [122]

3 But be not afraid of greatness: some men
are born great, some achieve greatness,
and some have greatness thrust upon
them.
Twelfth Night act 2, sc. 5, l. [158]

4 Remember who commended thy yellow
stockings, and wished to see thee ever
cross-gartered.
Twelfth Night act 2, sc. 5, l. [168]

5 O world! how apt the poor are to be proud.
Twelfth Night act 3, sc. 1, l. [141]

6 O! what a deal of scorn looks beautiful
In the contempt and anger of his lip.
Twelfth Night act 3, sc. 1, l. [159]

7 Love sought is good, but giv'n unsought is
better.
Twelfth Night act 3, sc. 1, l. [170]

8 In the south suburbs, at the Elephant,
Is best to lodge.
Twelfth Night act 3, sc. 3, l. 39

9 Why, this is very midsummer madness.
Twelfth Night act 3, sc. 4, l. [62]

10 If this were played upon a stage now, I
could condemn it as an improbable fiction.
Twelfth Night act 3, sc. 4, l. [142]

11 More matter for a May morning.
Twelfth Night act 3, sc. 4, l. [158]

12 Still you keep o' the windy side of the law.
Twelfth Night act 3, sc. 4, l. [183]

13 Leave thy vain bibble-babble.
Twelfth Night act 4, sc. 2, l. [106]

14 Thus the whirligig of time brings in his
revenges.
Twelfth Night act 5, sc. 1, l. [388]

15 When that I was and a little tiny boy,
With hey, ho, the wind and the rain;
A foolish thing was but a toy,
For the rain it raineth every day.
Twelfth Night act 5, sc. 1, l. [401]

The Two Gentlemen of Verona (1592–3)

16 Home-keeping youth have ever homely
wits.
The Two Gentlemen of Verona act 1, sc. 1, l. 2

17 Fie, fie! how wayward is this foolish love
That, like a testy babe, will scratch the
nurse
And presently all humbled kiss the rod!
The Two Gentlemen of Verona act 1, sc. 2, l. 55

18 O! how this spring of love resembleth
The uncertain glory of an April day.
The Two Gentlemen of Verona act 1, sc. 3, l. 84

19 Who is Silvia? what is she,
That all our swains commend her?
The Two Gentlemen of Verona act 4, sc. 2, l. 40

20   O heaven! were man
But constant, he were perfect.
The Two Gentlemen of Verona act 5, sc. 4, l. 110

The Winter's Tale (1610–11)

21 Two lads that thought there was no more
behind
But such a day to-morrow as to-day,
And to be boy eternal.
The Winter's Tale act 1, sc. 2, l. 63

22 A sad tale's best for winter.
The Winter's Tale act 2, sc. 1, l. 24

23 I have drunk, and seen the spider.
The Winter's Tale act 2, sc. 1, l. 39

24 What's gone and what's past help
Should be past grief.
The Winter's Tale act 3, sc. 2, l. [223]

25 Exit, pursued by a bear.
The Winter's Tale act 3, sc. 3 (stage direction)

26 When daffodils begin to peer,
With heigh! the doxy, over the dale,
Why, then comes in the sweet o' the year;
For the red blood reigns in the winter's
pale.
The Winter's Tale act 4, sc. 2, l. 1

27 A snapper-up of unconsidered trifles.
The Winter's Tale act 4, sc. 2, l. [26]

28 Jog on, jog on the foot-path way,
And merrily hent the stile-a:
A merry heart goes all the day,
Your sad tires in a mile-a.
The Winter's Tale act 4, sc. 2, l. [133]

29 For you there's rosemary and rue; these
keep
Seeming and savour all the winter long.
The Winter's Tale act 4, sc. 3, l. 74

30   I'll not put
The dibble in earth to set one slip of them.
The Winter's Tale act 4, sc. 3, l. 99

31 The marigold, that goes to bed wi' the sun,
And with him rises weeping.
The Winter's Tale act 4, sc. 3, l. 105

32   Daffodils,
That come before the swallow dares, and
take
The winds of March with beauty.
The Winter's Tale act 4, sc. 3, l. 118

33   Pale prime-roses,
That die unmarried, ere they can behold
Bright Phoebus in his strength,—a malady
Most incident to maids.
The Winter's Tale act 4, sc. 3, l. 122

34   Each your doing,
So singular in each particular,
Crowns what you are doing in the present
deed,
That all your acts are queens.
The Winter's Tale act 4, sc. 3, l. 144

1   I'll queen it no inch further,
But milk my ewes and weep.
The Winter's Tale act 4, sc. 3, l. [463]

2 Though I am not naturally honest, I am so
sometimes by chance.
The Winter's Tale act 4, sc. 3, l. [734]

3   Stars, stars!
And all eyes else dead coals.
The Winter's Tale act 5, sc. 1, l. 67

4   O! she's warm.
If this be magic, let it be an art
Lawful as eating.
The Winter's Tale act 5, sc. 3, l. 109

The Passionate Pilgrim (1599, attribution doubtful)

5 Crabbed age and youth cannot live
together:
Youth is full of pleasance, age is full of
care.
The Passionate Pilgrim no. 12

6 Age, I do abhor thee, youth, I do adore
thee.
The Passionate Pilgrim no. 12

The Rape of Lucrece (1594)

7 Beauty itself doth of itself persuade
The eyes of men without an orator.
The Rape of Lucrece l. 29

8 Who buys a minute's mirth to wail a
week?
Or sells eternity to get a toy?
For one sweet grape who will the vine
destroy?
The Rape of Lucrece l. 213

9 And now this pale swan in her watery nest
Begins the sad dirge of her certain ending.
The Rape of Lucrece l. 1611

Sonnets (1609)

10 To the onlie begetter of these insuing
sonnets, Mr. W. H.
Dedication (also attributed to Thomas
Thorpe, the publisher)

11 From fairest creatures we desire increase,
That thereby beauty's rose might never die.
Sonnet 1

12 Shall I compare thee to a summer's day?
Thou art more lovely and more temperate:
Rough winds do shake the darling buds of
May,
And summer's lease hath all too short a
date.
Sonnet 18

13 But thy eternal summer shall not fade.
Sonnet 18

14 Desiring this man's art, and that man's
scope,
With what I most enjoy contented least.
Sonnet 29

15 Haply I think on thee,—and then my state,
Like to the lark at break of day arising
From sullen earth, sings hymns at heaven's
gate.
Sonnet 29

16 When to the sessions of sweet silent
thought
I summon up remembrance of things past.
Sonnet 30

17 Full many a glorious morning have I seen
Flatter the mountain-tops with sovereign
eye,
Kissing with golden face the meadows
green,
Gilding pale streams with heavenly
alchemy.
Sonnet 33

18 What is your substance, whereof are you
made,
That millions of strange shadows on you
tend?
Sonnet 53

19 Not marble, nor the gilded monuments
Of princes, shall outlive this powerful
rhyme.
Sonnet 55

20 So true a fool is love that in your will,
Though you do anything, he thinks no ill.
Sonnet 57

21 Like as the waves make towards the
pebbled shore,
So do our minutes hasten to their end.
Sonnet 60

22 Time doth transfix the flourish set on
youth
And delves the parallels in beauty's brow.
Sonnet 60

23 No longer mourn for me when I am dead
Than you shall hear the surly sullen bell
Give warning to the world that I am fled
From this vile world, with vilest worms to
dwell.
Sonnet 71

24 That time of year thou mayst in me behold
When yellow leaves, or none, or few, do
hang
Upon those boughs which shake against
the cold,
Bare ruined choirs, where late the sweet
birds sang.
Sonnet 73

25 So all my best is dressing old words new,
Spending again what is already spent.
Sonnet 76

26 Time's thievish progress to eternity.
Sonnet 77

27 Farewell! thou art too dear for my
possessing,
And like enough thou know'st thy
estimate:
The charter of thy worth gives thee
releasing;
My bonds in thee are all determinate.
Sonnet 87

28 Thus have I had thee, as a dream doth
flatter,
In sleep a king, but, waking, no such
matter.
Sonnet 87

1 Ah, do not, when my heart hath 'scaped
this sorrow,
Come in the rearward of a conquered woe;
Give not a windy night a rainy morrow,
To linger out a purposed overthrow.
Sonnet 90

2 For sweetest things turn sourest by their
deeds;
Lilies that fester smell far worse than
weeds.
Sonnet 94

3 What freezings have I felt, what dark days
seen!
What old December's bareness everywhere!
Sonnet 97

4 When in the chronicle of wasted time
I see descriptions of the fairest wights,
And beauty making beautiful old rime,
In praise of ladies dead and lovely knights.
Sonnet 106

5 For we, which now behold these present
days,
Have eyes to wonder, but lack tongues to
praise.
Sonnet 106

6 Alas! 'tis true I have gone here and there,
And made myself a motley to the view.
Sonnet 110

7   My nature is subdued
To what it works in, like the dyer's hand.
Sonnet 111

8 Let me not to the marriage of true minds
Admit impediments. Love is not love
Which alters when it alteration finds.
Sonnet 116

9 Love alters not with his brief hours and
weeks,
But bears it out even to the edge of doom.
If this be error, and upon me proved,
I never writ, nor no man ever loved.
Sonnet 116

10 The expense of spirit in a waste of shame
Is lust in action.
Sonnet 129

11 My mistress' eyes are nothing like the sun;
Coral is far more red than her lips' red:
If snow be white, why then her breasts are
dun;
If hairs be wires, black wires grow on her
head.
Sonnet 130

12 Whoever hath her wish, thou hast thy Will,
And Will to boot, and Will in over-plus.
Sonnet 135

13 Two loves I have of comfort and despair,
Which like two spirits do suggest me still:
The better angel is a man right fair,
The worser spirit a woman, coloured ill.
Sonnet 144

14 Why so large cost, having so short a lease,
Dost thou upon thy fading mansion spend?
Sonnet 146

15 So shalt thou feed on Death, that feeds on
men,
And Death once dead, there's no more
dying then.
Sonnet 146

16 For I have sworn thee fair, and thought
thee bright,
Who art as black as hell, as dark as night.
Sonnet 147

Venus and Adonis (1593)

17 Love is a spirit all compact of fire,
Not gross to sink, but light, and will
aspire.
Venus and Adonis l. 145

18 Love comforteth like sunshine after rain.
Venus and Adonis l. 799

19 For he being dead, with him is beauty
slain,
And, beauty dead, black chaos comes again.
Venus and Adonis l. 1019

20 Good friend, for Jesu's sake forbear
To dig the dust enclosed here.
Blest be the man that spares these stones,
And curst be he that moves my bones.
Epitaph on his tomb, probably composed by
himself

21 Item, I give unto my wife my second best
bed, with the furniture.
Will, 1616. See E. K. Chambers *William
Shakespeare* (1930) vol. 2, p. 169

Bill Shankly 1914–81

22 Some people think football is a matter of
life and death . . . I can assure them it is
much more serious than that.
In *Sunday Times* 4 October 1981

George Bernard Shaw 1856–1950

23 All great truths begin as blasphemies.
Annajanska (1919) p. 262

24 Oh, you are a very poor soldier—a
chocolate cream soldier!
Arms and the Man (1898) act 1

25 When a stupid man is doing something he
is ashamed of, he always declares that it is
his duty.
Caesar and Cleopatra (1901) act 3

26 We have no more right to consume
happiness without producing it than to
consume wealth without producing it.
Candida (1898) act 1

27 It is easy—terribly easy— to shake a man's
faith in himself. To take advantage of that
to break a man's spirit is devil's work.
Candida (1898) act 1

28 I'm only a beer teetotaller, not
a champagne teetotaller.
Candida (1898) act 3

29 Martyrdom . . . the only way in which
a man can become famous without ability.
The Devil's Disciple (1901) act 3

1 The British soldier can stand up to anything except the British War Office.
  The Devil's Disciple (1901) act 3

2 Stimulate the phagocytes.
  The Doctor's Dilemma (1911) act 1

3 All professions are conspiracies against the laity.
  The Doctor's Dilemma (1911) act 1

4 The one point on which all women are in furious secret rebellion against the existing law is the saddling of the right to a child with the obligation to become the servant of a man.
  Getting Married (1911) preface 'The Right to Motherhood'

5 Go anywhere in England where there are natural, wholesome, contented, and really nice English people; and what do you always find? That the stables are the real centre of the household.
  Heartbreak House (1919) act 3

6 A man who has no office to go to—I don't care who he is—is a trial of which you can have no conception.
  The Irrational Knot (1905) ch. 18

7 There are only two qualities in the world: efficiency and inefficiency, and only two sorts of people: the efficient and the inefficient.
  John Bull's Other Island (1907) act 4

8 The greatest of evils and the worst of crimes is poverty.
  Major Barbara (1907) preface

9 I am a Millionaire. That is my religion.
  Major Barbara (1907) act 2

10 I can't talk religion to a man with bodily hunger in his eyes.
  Major Barbara (1907) act 2

11 Wot prawce Selvytion nah?
  Major Barbara (1907) act 2

12 Alcohol is a very necessary article ... It enables Parliament to do things at eleven at night that no sane person would do at eleven in the morning.
  Major Barbara (1907) act 2

13 He knows nothing; and he thinks he knows everything. That points clearly to a political career.
  Major Barbara (1907) act 3

14 Nothing is ever done in this world until men are prepared to kill one another if it is not done.
  Major Barbara (1907) act 3

15 But a lifetime of happiness! No man alive could bear it: it would be hell on earth.
  Man and Superman (1903) act 1

16 The more things a man is ashamed of, the more respectable he is.
  Man and Superman (1903) act 1

17 Vitality in a woman is a blind fury of creation.
  Man and Superman (1903) act 1

18 Of all human struggles there is none so treacherous and remorseless as the struggle between the artist man and the mother woman.
  Man and Superman (1903) act 1

19 Hell is full of musical amateurs: music is the brandy of the damned.
  Man and Superman (1903) act 3

20 Englishmen never will be slaves: they are free to do whatever the Government and public opinion allow them to do.
  Man and Superman (1903) act 3

21 An Englishman thinks he is moral when he is only uncomfortable.
  Man and Superman (1903) act 3

22 In the arts of peace Man is a bungler.
  Man and Superman (1903) act 3

23 When the military man approaches, the world locks up its spoons and packs off its womankind.
  Man and Superman (1903) act 3

24 What is virtue but the Trade Unionism of the married?
  Man and Superman (1903) act 3

25 Beauty is all very well at first sight; but who ever looks at it when it has been in the house three days?
  Man and Superman (1903) act 4

26 The art of government is the organization of idolatry.
  Man and Superman (1903) 'Maxims: Idolatry'

27 Democracy substitutes election by the incompetent many for appointment by the corrupt few.
  Man and Superman (1903) 'Maxims: Democracy'

28 Liberty means responsibility. That is why most men dread it.
  Man and Superman (1903) 'Maxims: Liberty and Equality'

29 He who can, does. He who cannot, teaches.
  Man and Superman (1903) 'Maxims: Education'

30 Marriage is popular because it combines the maximum of temptation with the maximum of opportunity.
  Man and Superman (1903) 'Maxims: Marriage'

31 Titles distinguish the mediocre, embarrass the superior, and are disgraced by the inferior.
  Man and Superman (1903) 'Maxims: Titles'

32 If you strike a child take care that you strike it in anger, even at the risk of maiming it for life. A blow in cold blood neither can nor should be forgiven.
  Man and Superman (1903) 'Maxims: How to Beat Children'

33 Beware of the man whose god is in the skies.
  Man and Superman (1903) 'Maxims: Religion'

34 Self-denial is not a virtue: it is only the effect of prudence on rascality.
  Man and Superman (1903) 'Maxims: Virtues and Vice'

1 The reasonable man adapts himself to the world: the unreasonable one persists in trying to adapt the world to himself. Therefore all progress depends on the unreasonable man.
Man and Superman (1903) 'Maxims: Reason'

2 The man who listens to Reason is lost: Reason enslaves all whose minds are not strong enough to master her.
Man and Superman (1903) 'Maxims: Reason'

3 Decency is Indecency's conspiracy of silence.
Man and Superman (1903) 'Maxims: Decency'

4 Home is the girl's prison and the woman's workhouse.
Man and Superman (1903) 'Maxims: Women in the Home'

5 Every man over forty is a scoundrel.
Man and Superman (1903) 'Maxims: Stray Sayings'

6 Youth, which is forgiven everything, forgives itself nothing: age, which forgives itself everything, is forgiven nothing.
Man and Superman (1903) 'Maxims: Stray Sayings'

7 Take care to get what you like or you will be forced to like what you get.
Man and Superman (1903) 'Maxims: Stray Sayings'

8 Beware of the man who does not return your blow: he neither forgives you nor allows you to forgive yourself.
Man and Superman (1903) 'Maxims: Stray Sayings'

9 You will never find an Englishman in the wrong. He does everything on principle ... he supports his king on loyal principles and cuts off his king's head on republican principles.
The Man of Destiny (1898) p. 201

10 Anarchism is a game at which the police can beat you.
Misalliance (1914) p. 85

11 The only way for a woman to provide for herself decently is for her to be good to some man that can afford to be good to her.
Mrs Warren's Profession (1898) act 2

12 A great devotee of the Gospel of Getting On.
Mrs Warren's Profession (1898) act 4

13 You'll never have a quiet world till you knock the patriotism out of the human race.
O'Flaherty V.C. (1919) p. 178

14 A perpetual holiday is a good working definition of hell.
Parents and Children (1914) 'Children's Happiness'

15 There is only one religion, though there are a hundred versions of it.
Plays Pleasant and Unpleasant (1898) vol. 2, preface

16 It is impossible for an Englishman to open his mouth without making some other Englishman hate or despise him.
Pygmalion (1916) preface

17 I don't want to talk grammar, I want to talk like a lady.
Pygmalion (1916) act 2

18 Gin was mother's milk to her.
Pygmalion (1916) act 3

19 Walk! Not bloody likely.
Pygmalion (1916) act 3

20 No Englishman is ever fairly beaten.
Saint Joan (1924) sc. 4

21 Must then a Christ perish in torment in every age to save those that have no imagination?
Saint Joan (1924) epilogue

22 Assassination is the extreme form of censorship.
The Showing-Up of Blanco Posnet (1911) 'Limits to Toleration'

23 The great advantage of a hotel is that it's a refuge from home life.
You Never Can Tell (1898) act 2

24 The younger generation is knocking at the door, and as I open it there steps spritely in the incomparable Max.
Saturday Review 21 May 1898 'Valedictory' (on handing over the theatre column to Max Beerbohm)

25 The trouble, Mr Goldwyn, is that you are only interested in art and I am only interested in money.
Telegraphed version of the outcome of a conversation between Shaw and Sam Goldwyn; in A. Johnson *The Great Goldwyn* (1937) ch. 3

26 [Dancing is] a perpendicular expression of a horizontal desire.
In *New Statesman* 23 March 1962 (attributed)

27 England and America are two countries divided by a common language.
Attributed in this and other forms, but not found in Shaw's published writings

Sir Hartley Shawcross 1902–

28 We are the masters at the moment, and not only at the moment, but for a very long time to come.
Speech, *Hansard* 2 April 1946, col. 1213 (often quoted 'We are the masters now'). Cf. 92:1

Charles Shaw-Lefevre, Viscount Eversley 1794–1888

29 What is that fat gentleman in such a passion about?
As a child, hearing Charles James Fox speak in Parliament; in G. W. E. Russell *Collections and Recollections* (1898) ch. 11

Patrick Shaw-Stewart 1888–1917

1 I saw a man this morning
Who did not wish to die;
I ask and cannot answer
If otherwise wish I.

Poem (1916) in M. Baring *Have You Anything
to Declare?* (1936) p. 39

Percy Bysshe Shelley 1792–1822

2 The cemetery is an open space among the
ruins, covered in winter with violets and
daisies. It might make one in love with
death, to think that one should be buried
in so sweet a place.

Adonais (1821) preface

3 I weep for Adonais—he is dead!
O, weep for Adonais! though our tears
Thaw not the frost which binds so dear a
head!

Adonais (1821) st. 1

4 To that high Capital, where kingly Death
Keeps his pale court in beauty and decay,
He came.

Adonais (1821) st. 7

5 The quick Dreams,
The passion-wingèd Ministers of thought.

Adonais (1821) st. 9

6 She faded, like a cloud which had outwept
its rain.

Adonais (1821) st. 10

7 Ah, woe is me! Winter is come and gone,
But grief returns with the revolving year.

Adonais (1821) st. 18

8 Alas! that all we loved of him should be,
But for our grief, as if it had not been,
And grief itself be mortal!

Adonais (1821) st. 21

9 A pardlike Spirit, beautiful and swift.

Adonais (1821) st. 32

10 And in mad trance, strike with our spirit's
knife
Invulnerable nothings.

Adonais (1821) st. 39

11 He has out-soared the shadow of our night;
Envy and calumny and hate and pain,
And that unrest which men miscall
delight,
Can touch him not and torture not again;
From the contagion of the world's slow
stain
He is secure, and now can never mourn
A heart grown cold, a head grown grey in
vain.

Adonais (1821) st. 40

12 He is a portion of the loveliness
Which once he made more lovely.

Adonais (1821) st. 43

13 The One remains, the many change and
pass;
Heaven's light forever shines, Earth's
shadows fly;
Life, like a dome of many-coloured glass,
Stains the white radiance of Eternity,
Until Death tramples it to fragments.

Adonais (1821) st. 52

14 A widow bird sat mourning for her love
Upon a wintry bough;
The frozen wind crept on above,
The freezing stream below.

Charles the First (1822) sc. 5, l. 9

15 I never was attached to that great sect,
Whose doctrine is that each one should
select
Out of the crowd a mistress or a friend,
And all the rest, though fair and wise,
commend
To cold oblivion.

'Epipsychidion' (1821) l. 149

16 The beaten road
Which those poor slaves with weary
footsteps tread,
Who travel to their home among the dead
By the broad highway of the world, and so
With one chained friend, perhaps a jealous
foe,
The dreariest and the longest journey go.

'Epipsychidion' (1821) l. 154

17 Let there be light! said Liberty,
And like sunrise from the sea,
Athens arose!

Hellas (1822) l. 682

18 The world's great age begins anew,
The golden years return.

Hellas (1822) l. 1060

19 O cease! must hate and death return?
Cease! must men kill and die?

Hellas (1822) l. 1096

20 I love all waste
And solitary places.

'Julian and Maddalo' (1818) l. 14

21 Thou Paradise of exiles, Italy!

'Julian and Maddalo' (1818) l. 57

22 Most wretched men
Are cradled into poetry by wrong:
They learn in suffering what they teach in
song.

'Julian and Maddalo' (1818) l. 544

23 A cloud-encircled meteor of the air,
A hooded eagle among blinking owls.

'Letter to Maria Gisborne' (1820) l. 207 (of
Coleridge)

24 When the lamp is shattered
The light in the dust lies dead—
When the cloud is scattered
The rainbow's glory is shed.
When the lute is broken,
Sweet tones are remembered not;
When the lips have spoken,
Loved accents are soon forgot.

'Lines: When the lamp' (1824)

1 Underneath Day's azure eyes
  Ocean's nursling, Venice lies,
  A peopled labyrinth of walls,
  Amphitrite's destined halls.
    'Lines written amongst the Euganean Hills'
    (1818) l. 94

2 Sun-girt city, thou hast been
  Ocean's child, and then his queen;
  Now is come a darker day,
  And thou soon must be his prey.
    'Lines written amongst the Euganean Hills'
    (1818) l. 115 (of Venice)

3 Nothing in the world is single;
  All things, by a law divine,
  In one spirit meet and mingle.
    'Love's Philosophy' (written 1819)

4 I met Murder on the way—
  He had a mask like Castlereagh.
    'The Mask of Anarchy' (1819) st. 2

5 His big tears, for he wept well,
  Turned to mill-stones as they fell.
    'The Mask of Anarchy' (1819) st. 4

6 O wild West Wind, thou breath of
    Autumn's being,
  Thou, from whose unseen presence the
    leaves dead
  Are driven, like ghosts from an enchanter
    fleeing,
  Yellow, and black, and pale, and hectic red,
  Pestilence-stricken multitudes.
    'Ode to the West Wind' (1819) l. 1

7 The sea-blooms and the oozy woods which
    wear
  The sapless foliage of the ocean.
    'Ode to the West Wind' (1819) l. 39

8 Oh, lift me as a wave, a leaf, a cloud!
  I fall upon the thorns of life! I bleed!
    'Ode to the West Wind' (1819) l. 53

9 Make me thy lyre, even as the forest is.
    'Ode to the West Wind' (1819) l. 57

10   O, Wind,
  If Winter comes, can Spring be far behind?
    'Ode to the West Wind' (1819) l. 69

11 I met a traveller from an antique land
  Who said: Two vast and trunkless legs of
    stone
  Stand in the desert.
    'Ozymandias' (1819)

12 My name is Ozymandias, king of kings:
  Look on my works, ye Mighty, and despair!
    'Ozymandias' (1819)

13 Hell is a city much like London.
    'Peter Bell the Third' (1819) pt. 3, st. 1

14 But from the first 'twas Peter's drift
  To be a kind of moral eunuch,
  He touched the hem of Nature's shift,
  Felt faint—and never dared uplift
  The closest, all-concealing tunic.
    'Peter Bell the Third' (1819) pt. 4, st. 11

15   Ere Babylon was dust,
  The Magus Zoroaster, my dead child,
  Met his own image walking in the garden.
    Prometheus Unbound (1819) act 1, l. 191

16 Grief for awhile is blind, and so was mine.
    Prometheus Unbound (1820) act 1, l. 304

17 The good want power, but to weep barren
    tears.
  The powerful goodness want: worse need
    for them.
  The wise want love; and those who love
    want wisdom.
    Prometheus Unbound (1820) act 1, l. 625

18   Peace is in the grave.
  The grave hides all things beautiful and
    good:
  I am a God and cannot find it there.
    Prometheus Unbound (1820) act 1, l. 638

19 The dust of creeds outworn.
    Prometheus Unbound (1820) act 1, l. 697

20 He gave man speech, and speech created
    thought,
  Which is the measure of the universe.
    Prometheus Unbound (1820) act 2, sc. 4, l. 72

21 My soul is an enchanted boat,
  Which, like a sleeping swan, doth float
  Upon the silver waves of thy sweet singing.
    Prometheus Unbound (1820) act 2, sc. 5, l. 72

22 The loathsome mask has fallen, the man
    remains
  Sceptreless, free, uncircumscribed, but
    man
  Equal, unclassed, tribeless, and nationless.
    Prometheus Unbound (1820) act 3, sc. 4, l. 193

23 Pinnacled dim in the intense inane.
    Prometheus Unbound (1820) act 3, sc. 4, l. 204

24 A traveller from the cradle to the grave
  Through the dim night of this immortal
    day.
    Prometheus Unbound (1820) act 4, l. 551

25 To love, and bear; to hope till Hope creates
  From its own wreck the thing it
    contemplates.
    Prometheus Unbound (1820) act 4, l. 573

26 How wonderful is Death,
  Death and his brother Sleep!
    Queen Mab (1813) canto 1, l. 1

27 That sweet bondage which is freedom's
    self.
    Queen Mab (1813) canto 9, l. 76

28 I dreamed that, as I wandered by the way,
  Bare Winter suddenly was changed to
    Spring.
    'The Question' (1822)

29 Daisies, those pearled Arcturi of the earth,
  The constellated flower that never sets.
    'The Question' (1822)

30 A Sensitive Plant in a garden grew.
    'The Sensitive Plant' (1820) pt. 1, l. 1

31 And the jessamine faint, and the sweet
    tuberose,
  The sweetest flower for scent that blows.
    'The Sensitive Plant' (1820) pt. 1, l. 37

32 Rarely, rarely, comest thou,
  Spirit of Delight!
    'Song' (1824)

1 Men of England, wherefore plough
For the lords who lay ye low?
'Song to the Men of England' (written 1819)

2 Lift not the painted veil which those who
live
Call Life.
'Sonnet' (1824)

3 An old, mad, blind, despised, and dying
king.
'Sonnet: England in 1819' (of George III)

4 Music, when soft voices die,
Vibrates in the memory—
Odours, when sweet violets sicken,
Live within the sense they quicken.
'To—: Music, when soft voices die' (1824)

5 The desire of the moth for the star,
Of the night for the morrow,
The devotion to something afar
From the sphere of our sorrow.
'To—: One word is too often profaned' (1824)

6 Hail to thee, blithe Spirit!
Bird thou never wert,
That from Heaven, or near it,
Pourest thy full heart
In profuse strains of unpremeditated art.
'To a Skylark' (1819)

7 And singing still dost soar, and soaring
ever singest.
'To a Skylark' (1819)

8 Thou art unseen, but yet I hear thy shrill
delight.
'To a Skylark' (1819)

9 Like a Poet hidden
In the light of thought,
Singing hymns unbidden.
'To a Skylark' (1819)

10 Our sincerest laughter
With some pain is fraught;
Our sweetest songs are those that tell of
saddest thought.
'To a Skylark' (1819)

11 Teach me half the gladness
That thy brain must know,
Such harmonious madness
From my lips would flow
The world should listen then—as I am
listening now.
'To a Skylark' (1819)

12 Swiftly walk o'er the western wave,
Spirit of Night!
'To Night' (1824)

13 Death will come when thou art dead,
Soon, too soon.
'To Night' (1824)

14 Art thou pale for weariness
Of climbing heaven, and gazing on the
earth,
Wandering companionless
Among the stars that have a different
birth.
'To the Moon' (1824)

15 And like a dying lady, lean and pale,
Who totters forth, wrapped in a gauzy veil.
'The Waning Moon' (1824)

16 A lovely lady, garmented in light
From her own beauty.
'The Witch of Atlas' (written 1820) st. 5

17 For she was beautiful—her beauty made
The bright world dim, and everything
beside
Seemed like the fleeting image of a shade.
'The Witch of Atlas' (written 1820) st. 12

18 Poetry is the record of the best and
happiest moments of the happiest and best
minds.
A Defence of Poetry (written 1821)

19 Poets are the unacknowledged legislators
of the world.
A Defence of Poetry (written 1821). Cf. 183:3

William Shenstone 1714–63

20 A fool and his words are soon parted.
Works (1764) vol. 2 'On Reserve'

21 The world may be divided into people that
read, people that write, people that think,
and fox-hunters.
Works (1764) vol. 2 'On Writing and Books'

Philip Henry Sheridan 1831–88

22 The only good Indian is a dead Indian.
At Fort Cobb, January 1869 (attributed)

Richard Brinsley Sheridan 1751–1816

23 If it is abuse,—why one is always sure to
hear of it from one damned goodnatured
friend or another!
The Critic (1779) act 1, sc. 1

24 O Lord, Sir—when a heroine goes mad she
always goes into white satin.
The Critic (1779) act 3, sc. 1

25 An oyster may be crossed in love!
The Critic (1779) act 3, sc. 1

26 Illiterate him, I say, quite from your
memory.
The Rivals (1775) act 1, sc. 2

27 'Tis safest in matrimony to begin with a
little aversion.
The Rivals (1775) act 1, sc. 2

28 He is the very pineapple of politeness!
The Rivals (1775) act 3, sc. 3

29 If I reprehend any thing in this world, it is
the use of my oracular tongue, and a nice
derangement of epitaphs!
The Rivals (1775) act 3, sc. 3

30 She's as headstrong as an allegory on the
banks of the Nile.
The Rivals (1775) act 3, sc. 3

31 Too civil by half.
The Rivals (1775) act 3, sc. 4

1 No caparisons, Miss, if you
please!—Caparisons don't become a young
woman.
The Rivals (1775) act 4, sc. 2

2 You are not like Cerberus, three gentlemen
at once, are you?
The Rivals (1775) act 4, sc. 2

3 You shall see them on a beautiful quarto
page where a neat rivulet of text shall
meander through a meadow of margin.
The School for Scandal (1777) act 1, sc. 1

4 Here is the whole set! a character dead at
every word.
The School for Scandal (1777) act 2, sc. 2.
Cf. 253:7

5 I'm called away by particular
business—but I leave my character behind
me.
The School for Scandal (1777) act 2, sc. 2

6 Here's to the maiden of bashful fifteen
Here's to the widow of fifty
Here's to the flaunting, extravagant quean;
And here's to the housewife that's thrifty.
The School for Scandal (1777) act 3, sc. 3

7 An unforgiving eye, and a damned
disinheriting countenance!
The School for Scandal (1777) act 4, sc. 1

8 You write with ease, to show your
breeding,
But easy writing's vile hard reading.
'Clio's Protest' (written 1771)

General Sherman 1820–91

9 There is many a boy here to-day who looks
on war as all glory, but, boys, it is all hell.
Speech at Columbus, Ohio, 11 August 1880;
in L. Lewis *Sherman, Fighting Prophet* (1932)

James Shirley 1596–1666

10 The glories of our blood and state
Are shadows, not substantial things.
The Contention of Ajax and Ulysses (1659) act 1,
sc. 3

11 Only the actions of the just
Smell sweet, and blossom in their dust.
The Contention of Ajax and Ulysses (1659) act 1,
sc. 3

12 How little room
Do we take up in death, that, living know
No bounds?
The Wedding (1629) act 4, sc. 4

The Shorter Catechism (1647)

13 'What is the chief end of man?'
'To glorify God and to enjoy him for ever'.

Algernon Sidney 1622–83

14 'Tis not necessary to light a candle to the
sun.
Discourses concerning Government (1698) ch. 2,
sect. 23. Cf. 83:12, 360:16

Sir Philip Sidney 1554–86

15 My true love hath my heart and I have his,
By just exchange one for the other giv'n.
Arcadia ('Old Arcadia', completed 1581) bk. 3

16 Words came halting forth, wanting
Invention's stay.
Astrophil and Stella (1591) sonnet 1

17 Biting my truant pen, beating myself for
spite,
'Fool,' said my Muse to me; 'look in thy
heart and write.'
Astrophil and Stella (1591) sonnet 1

18 With how sad steps, O Moon, thou climb'st
the skies;
How silently, and with how wan a face.
Astrophil and Stella (1591) sonnet 31

19 O moon, tell me,
Is constant love deemed there but want of
wit?
Astrophil and Stella (1591) sonnet 31

20 Come, sleep, O sleep, the certain knot of
peace,
The baiting place of wit, the balm of woe.
Astrophil and Stella (1591) sonnet 39

21 That sweet enemy, France.
Astrophil and Stella (1591) sonnet 41

22 Dumb swans, not chattering pies, do lovers
prove;
They love indeed who quake to say they
love.
Astrophil and Stella (1591) sonnet 54

23 I am no pick-purse of another's wit.
Astrophil and Stella (1591) sonnet 74

24 Highway, since you my chief Parnassus be.
Astrophil and Stella (1591) sonnet 84

25 If thou praise not, all other praise is
shame.
Astrophil and Stella (1591) sonnet 90

26 Poetry [is] a speaking picture, with this
end: to teach and delight.
The Defence of Poetry (1595)

27 [The poet] cometh unto you, with a tale
which holdeth children from play, and old
men from the chimney corner.
The Defence of Poetry (1595)

28 Comedy is an imitation of the common
errors of our life.
The Defence of Poetry (1595)

29 Delight hath a joy in it either permanent
or present. Laughter hath only a scornful
tickling.
The Defence of Poetry (1595)

30 Thy necessity is yet greater than mine.
On giving his water-bottle to a dying soldier
on the battle-field of Zutphen, 1586; in Sir
Fulke Greville *Life of Sir Philip Sidney* (1652)
ch. 12 (commonly quoted 'thy need is greater
than mine')

Abbé Emmanuel Joseph Sieyès
1748–1836

1 *J'ai vécu.*
I survived.
> When asked what he had done during the French Revolution. See F. Mignet *Notice historique sur la vie et les travaux de M. le Comte de Sieyès* (1836)

Maurice Sigler 1901–61 and Al Hoffman 1902–60

2 Little man, you've had a busy day.
> Title of song (1934)

Alan Sillitoe 1928–

3 The loneliness of the long-distance runner.
> Title of novel (1959)

Georges Simenon 1903–89

4 Writing is not a profession but a vocation of unhappiness.
> Interview in *Paris Review* Summer 1955

Paul Simon 1942–

5 Like a bridge over troubled water
I will lay me down.
> 'Bridge over Troubled Water' (1970 song)

6 And here's to you, Mrs Robinson
Jesus loves you more than you will know.
> 'Mrs Robinson' (1967 song, from the film *The Graduate*)

7 People talking without speaking
People hearing without listening ...
'Fools,' said I, 'You do not know
Silence like a cancer grows.'
> 'Sound of Silence' (1964 song)

8 Improvisation is too good to leave to chance.
> In *Observer* 30 December 1990 'Sayings of the Year'

Simonides *c.*556–468 BC

9 Go, tell the Spartans, thou who passest by,
That here obedient to their laws we lie.
> In Herodotus *Histories* bk. 7, ch. 228 (attributed)

Harold Simpson

10 Down in the forest something stirred:
It was only the note of a bird.
> 'Down in the Forest' (1906 song)

Kirke Simpson

11 [Warren] Harding of Ohio was chosen by a group of men in a smoke-filled room early today as Republican candidate for President.
> News report, filed 12 June 1920 (usually attributed to Harry Daugherty, one of Harding's supporters, who appears merely to have concurred with this version of events, when pressed for comment by Simpson). See W. Safire *New Language of Politics* (1968)

N. F. Simpson 1919–

12 Knocked down a doctor? With an ambulance? How could she? It's a contradiction in terms.
> *One Way Pendulum* (1960) act 1

13 A problem left to itself dries up or goes rotten. But fertilize a problem with a solution—you'll hatch out dozens.
> *A Resounding Tinkle* (1958) act 1, sc. 1

George R. Sims 1847–1922

14 It is Christmas Day in the Workhouse.
> 'In the Workhouse—Christmas Day' (1879)

C. H. Sisson 1914–

15 Here lies a civil servant. He was civil
To everyone, and servant to the devil.
> In *The London Zoo* (1961) p. 29

Dame Edith Sitwell 1887–1964

16 Jane, Jane,
Tall as a crane,
The morning light creaks down again.
> *Façade* (1923) 'Aubade'

17 The fire was furry as a bear.
> *Façade* (1923) 'Dark Song'

18 When
Sir
Beelzebub called for his syllabub in the hotel in Hell
Where Proserpine first fell,
Blue as the gendarmerie were the waves of the sea,
(Rocking and shocking the barmaid).
> *Façade* (1923) 'Sir Beelzebub'

19 Still falls the Rain—
Dark as the world of man, black as our loss—
Blind as the nineteen hundred and forty nails
Upon the Cross.
> 'Still Falls the Rain' (1942)

20 Daisy and Lily,
Lazy and silly,
Walk by the shore of the wan grassy sea.
> 'Waltz' (1948)

Sir Osbert Sitwell 1892–1969

21 The British Bourgeoise
Is not born,
And does not die,
But, if it is ill,
It has a frightened look in its eyes.
> *At the House of Mrs Kinfoot* (1921) p. 8

22 In reality, killing time
Is only the name for another of the multifarious ways
By which Time kills us.
> 'Milordo Inglese' (1958). Cf. 70:8

1 On the coast of Coromandel
Dance they to the tunes of Handel.
'On the Coast of Coromandel' (1943)

John Skelton c.1460–1529

2 With solace and gladness,
Much mirth and no madness,
All good and no badness;
So joyously,
So maidenly,
So womanly,
Her demeaning.
   The Garland of Laurel (1523) 'To Mistress
   Margaret Hussey'

3 ... Merry Margaret,
This midsummer flower,
Gentle as falcon
Or hawk of the tower.
   The Garland of Laurel (1523) 'To Mistress
   Margaret Hussey'

4 I blunder, I bluster, I blow, and I blother,
I make on the one day, and I mar on the
   other.
   Magnificence (1530) l. 1037

B. F. Skinner 1904–90

5 The real question is not whether machines
think but whether men do.
   Contingencies of Reinforcement (1969) ch. 9

6 Education is what survives when what has
been learned has been forgotten.
   New Scientist 21 May 1964

Christopher Smart 1722–71

7 For I will consider my Cat Jeoffry.
For he is the servant of the Living God duly
   and daily serving him.
   Jubilate Agno (c.1758–63) Fragment B, l. 695

8 For he counteracts the powers of darkness
   by his electrical skin and glaring eyes.
For he counteracts the Devil, who is death,
   by brisking about the life.
   Jubilate Agno (c.1758–63) Fragment B, l. 719

9 Nature's decorations glisten
Far above their usual trim;
Birds on box and laurels listen,
As so near the cherubs hymn.
   'The Nativity of Our Lord and Saviour Jesus
   Christ' (1765)

10 Strong is the lion—like a coal
His eye-ball—like a bastion's mole
His chest against his foes.
   A Song to David (1763) st. 76

11 And in the seat to faith assigned,
Where ask is have, where seek is find,
Where knock is open wide.
   A Song to David (1763) st. 77

12 Beauteous the garden's umbrage mild,
Walk, water, meditated wild,
And all the bloomy beds.
   A Song to David (1763) st. 78

13 Glorious the northern lights astream;
Glorious the song, when God's the theme;
Glorious the thunder's roar.
   A Song to David (1763) st. 85

14 And now the matchless deed's achieved,
Determined, dared, and done.
   A Song to David (1763) st. 86

Elizabeth Smart 1913–86

15 By Grand Central Station I sat down and
wept.
   Title of book (1945). Cf. 69:2

Samuel Smiles 1812–1904

16 We each day dig our graves with our teeth.
   Duty (1880) ch. 16

17 The spirit of self-help is the root of all
genuine growth in the individual.
   Self-Help (1859) ch. 1

18 The shortest way to do many things is to
do only one thing at once.
   Self-Help (1859) ch. 9

19 Cheerfulness gives elasticity to the spirit.
Spectres fly before it.
   Self-Help (1859) ch. 12

Adam Smith 1723–90

20 And thus, *Place*, that great object which
divides the wives of aldermen, is the end of
half the labours of human life; and is the
cause of all the tumult and bustle, all the
rapine and injustice, which avarice and
ambition have introduced into this world.
   Theory of Moral Sentiments (1759) pt. 1, sect. 3,
   ch. 2

21 People of the same trade seldom meet
together, even for merriment and
diversion, but the conversation ends in a
conspiracy against the public, or in some
contrivance to raise prices.
   Wealth of Nations (1776) bk. 1, ch. 10, pt. 2

22 The chief enjoyment of riches consists in
the parade of riches.
   Wealth of Nations (1776) bk. 1, ch. 11

23 To found a great empire for the sole
purpose of raising up a people of
customers, may at first sight appear a
project fit only for a nation of shopkeepers.
It is, however, a project altogether unfit for
a nation of shopkeepers; but extremely fit
for a nation whose government is
influenced by shopkeepers.
   Wealth of Nations (1776) bk. 4, ch. 7, pt. 3.
   Cf. 2:7, 237:7

24 Consumption is the sole end and purpose
of production; and the interest of the
producer ought to be attended to only so
far as it may be necessary for promoting
that of the consumer.
   Wealth of Nations (1776) bk. 4, ch. 8

1 There is no art which one government
sooner learns of another than that of
draining money from the pockets of the
people.
Wealth of Nations (1776) bk. 5, ch. 2

Alfred Emanuel Smith 1873–1944

2 All the ills of democracy can be cured by
more democracy.
Speech, 27 June 1933, in *New York Times*
28 June 1933

Sir Cyril Smith 1928–

3 The longest running farce in the West End.
Of the House of Commons, in *Big Cyril* (1977)
ch. 8

Dodie Smith 1896–1990

4 The family—that dear octopus from whose
tentacles we never quite escape.
Dear Octopus (1938) p. 120

Edgar Smith 1857–1938

5 You may tempt the upper classes
With your villainous demi-tasses,
But; Heaven will protect a working-girl!
'Heaven Will Protect the Working-Girl' (1909
song)

F. E. Smith (1st Earl of Birkenhead) 1872–1930

6 The world continues to offer glittering
prizes to those who have stout hearts and
sharp swords.
Rectorial Address, Glasgow University,
7 November 1923; in *The Times* 8 November
1923

7 JUDGE: You are extremely offensive, young
man.
SMITH: As a matter of fact, we both are, and
the only difference between us is that
I am trying to be, and you can't help it.
In 2nd Earl of Birkenhead *Earl of Birkenhead*
(1933) vol. 1, ch. 9

8 JUDGE DARLING: And who is George Robey?
SMITH: Mr George Robey is the Darling of
the music halls, m'lud.
In A. E. Wilson *The Prime Minister of Mirth*
(1956) ch. 1

Ian Smith 1919–

9 I don't believe in black majority rule in
Rhodesia—not in a thousand years.
Broadcast speech, 20 March 1976, in *Sunday
Times* 21 March 1976

Logan Pearsall Smith 1865–1946

10 There is more felicity on the far side of
baldness than young men can possibly
imagine.
Afterthoughts (1931) 'Age and Death'

11 The test of a vocation is the love of the
drudgery it involves.
Afterthoughts (1931) 'Art and Letters'

12 A best-seller is the gilded tomb of
a mediocre talent.
Afterthoughts (1931) 'Art and Letters'

13 People say that life is the thing, but
I prefer reading.
Afterthoughts (1931) 'Myself'

14 Most people sell their souls, and live with
a good conscience on the proceeds.
Afterthoughts (1931) 'Other People'

15 All Reformers, however strict their social
conscience, live in houses just as big as
they can pay for.
Afterthoughts (1931) 'Other People'

Samuel Francis Smith 1808–95

16 My country, 'tis of thee,
Sweet land of liberty,
Of thee I sing.
'America' (1831)

Stevie Smith 1902–71

17 Oh I am a cat that likes to
Gallop about doing good.
'The Galloping Cat' (1972)

18 A good time was had by all.
Title of book (1937)

19 I was much too far out all my life
And not waving but drowning.
'Not Waving but Drowning' (1957)

20 Private Means is dead
God rest his soul, officers and fellow-
rankers said.
'Private Means is Dead' (1962)

21 This Englishwoman is so refined
She has no bosom and no behind.
'This Englishwoman' (1937)

22 If there wasn't death, I think you couldn't
go on.
In *Observer* 9 November 1969, p. 21

Revd Sydney Smith 1771–1845

23 A Curate—there is something which
excites compassion in the very name of a
Curate!!!
'Persecuting Bishops' in *Edinburgh Review*
(1822)

24 What bishops like best in their clergy is a
dropping-down-deadness of manner.
Works (1859) vol. 2 'First Letter to
Archdeacon Singleton, 1837' p. 271 n.

25 I have no relish for the country; it is a kind
of healthy grave.
Letter to Miss G. Harcourt, 1838, in *Letters of
Sydney Smith* (1953)

26 That knuckle-end of England—that land of
Calvin, oat-cakes, and sulphur.
In *Lady Holland Memoir* (1855) vol. 1, ch. 2 (of
Scotland)

1 Take short views, hope for the best, and trust in God.
In Lady Holland *Memoir* (1855) vol. 1, ch. 6

2 No furniture so charming as books.
In Lady Holland *Memoir* (1855) vol. 1, ch. 9. Cf. 254:25

3 Not body enough to cover his mind decently with; his intellect is improperly exposed.
In Lady Holland *Memoir* (1855) vol. 1, ch. 9

4 As the French say, there are three sexes—men, women, and clergymen.
In Lady Holland *Memoir* (1855) vol. 1, ch. 9

5 My definition of marriage ... it resembles a pair of shears, so joined that they cannot be separated; often moving in opposite directions, yet always punishing anyone who comes between them.
In Lady Holland *Memoir* (1855) vol. 1, ch. 11

6 He [Macaulay] has occasional flashes of silence, that make his conversation perfectly delightful.
In Lady Holland *Memoir* (1855) vol. 1, ch. 11

7 Serenely full, the epicure would say,
Fate cannot harm me, I have dined to-day.
In Lady Holland *Memoir* (1855) vol. 1, ch. 11 'Receipt for a Salad'

8 Deserves to be preached to death by wild curates.
In Lady Holland *Memoir* (1855) vol. 1, ch. 11

9 I never read a book before reviewing it; it prejudices a man so.
In H. Pearson *The Smith of Smiths* (1934) ch. 3

10 Minorities ... are almost always in the right.
In H. Pearson *The Smith of Smiths* (1934) ch. 9

11 My idea of heaven is, eating *pâté de foie gras* to the sound of trumpets.
In H. Pearson *The Smith of Smiths* (1934) ch. 10

12 What a pity it is that we have no amusements in England but vice and religion!
In H. Pearson *The Smith of Smiths* (1934) ch. 10

13 What two ideas are more inseparable than Beer and Britannia?
In H. Pearson *The Smith of Smiths* (1934) ch. 11

14 I am just going to pray for you at St Paul's, but with no very lively hope of success.
In H. Pearson *The Smith of Smiths* (1934) ch. 13

Walter Chalmers Smith 1824–1908

15 Unresting, unhasting, and silent as light,
Nor wanting, nor wasting, thou rulest in might.
'Immortal, invisible, God only wise' (1867 hymn)

Tobias Smollett 1721–71

16 What you imagine to be the new light of grace, (said his master) I take to be a deceitful vapour, glimmering through a crack in your upper storey.
Humphry Clinker (1771) vol. 2 (letter from Jery Melford, 10 June)

17 That great Cham of literature, Samuel Johnson.
Letter to John Wilkes, 16 March 1759, in James Boswell *Life of Samuel Johnson* (1934 ed.) vol. 1

C. P. Snow 1905–80

18 The official world, the corridors of power.
Homecomings (1956) ch. 22

19 The two cultures and the scientific revolution.
Title of The Rede Lecture (1959)

Socrates 469–399 BC

20 How many things I can do without!
On looking at a multitude of wares exposed for sale, in Diogenes Laertius *Lives of the Philosophers* bk. 2, sect. 25

21 I know nothing except the fact of my ignorance.
In Diogenes Laertius *Lives of the Philosophers* bk. 2, sect. 32

22 The unexamined life is not worth living.
In Plato *Apology* 38a

23 It is never right to do wrong or to requite wrong with wrong, or when we suffer evil to defend ourselves by doing evil in return.
In Plato *Crito* 49d

24 But, my dearest Agathon, it is truth which you cannot contradict; you can without any difficulty contradict Socrates.
In Plato *Symposium* 201d

25 Crito, we owe a cock to Aesculapius; please pay it and don't forget it.
Last words, in Plato *Phaedo* 118

Solon c.640–after 556 BC

26 I grow old ever learning many things.
T. Bergk (ed.) *Poetae Lyrici Graeci* (1843) no. 18

27 Call no man happy before he dies, he is at best but fortunate.
In Herodotus *Histories* bk. 1, ch. 32. Cf. 48:1

Alexander Solzhenitsyn 1918–

28 You only have power over people as long as you don't take *everything* away from them. But when you've robbed a man of *everything* he's no longer in your power—he's free again.
The First Circle (1968) ch. 17

1 The thoughts of a prisoner—they're not
free either. They keep returning to the
same things.
   One Day in the Life of Ivan Denisovich (1962)
   p. 34 (tr. R. Parker)

William Somerville 1675–1742

2 The chase, the sport of kings;
Image of war, without its guilt.
   The Chase (1735) bk. 1, l. 14. Cf. 319:8

3 Hail, happy Britain! highly favoured isle,
And Heaven's peculiar care!
   The Chase (1735) bk. 1, l. 84

Anastasio Somoza 1925–80

4 You won the elections, but I won the count.
   Replying to an accusation of ballot-rigging,
   in *Guardian* 17 June 1977. Cf. 317:28

Stephen Sondheim 1930–

5 Everything's coming up roses.
   Title of song (1959)

6 Ev'ry day a little death
On the lips and in the eyes,
In the murmurs, in the pauses,
In the gestures, in the sighs.
   'Every Day a Little Death' (1973 song)

7 Isn't it rich?
Are we a pair?
Me here at last on the ground, you in mid-
air.
   'Send in the Clowns' (1973 song)

8 I like to be in America!
OK by me in America!
Ev'rything free in America
For a small fee in America!
   'America' (1957 song)

Susan Sontag 1933–

9 Interpretation is the revenge of the
intellect upon art.
   Evergreen Review December 1964

10 Illness is the night-side of life, a more
onerous citizenship. Everyone who is born
holds dual citizenship, in the kingdom of
the well and in the kingdom of the sick.
   New York Review of Books 26 January 1978

Lord Soper 1903–

11 It is, I think, good evidence of life after
death.
   On the quality of debate in the House of
   Lords, in *Listener* 17 August 1978

Sophocles *c*.496–406 BC

12 There are many wonderful things, and
nothing is more wonderful than man.
   Antigone l. 333

13 Not to be born is, past all prizing, best.
   Oedipus Coloneus l. 1225 (tr. R. C. Jebb)

14 Someone asked Sophocles, 'How is your
sex-life now? Are you still able to have a
woman?' He replied, 'Hush, man; most
gladly indeed am I rid of it all, as though I
had escaped from a mad and savage
master.'
   In Plato *Republic* bk. 1, 329b

Charles Hamilton Sorley 1895–1915

15 We swing ungirded hips,
And lightened are our eyes,
The rain is on our lips,
We do not run for prize.
   'Song of the Ungirt Runners' (1916)

16 When you see millions of the mouthless
dead
Across your dreams in pale battalions go,
Say not soft things as other men have said,
That you'll remember. For you need not so.
Give them not praise. For, deaf, how
should they know
It is not curses heaped on each gashed
head?
   'A Sonnet' (1916)

John L. B. Soule 1815–91

17 Go West, young man, go West!
   Terre Haute [Indiana] *Express* (1851) editorial.
   Cf. 157:20

Robert Southey 1774–1843

18 It was a summer evening,
Old Kaspar's work was done,
And he before his cottage door
Was sitting in the sun.
   'The Battle of Blenheim' (1800)

19 Now tell us all about the war,
And what they fought each other for.
   'The Battle of Blenheim' (1800)

20 'And everybody praised the Duke,
Who this great fight did win.'
'But what good came of it at last?'
Quoth little Peterkin.
'Why that I cannot tell,' said he,
'But 'twas a famous victory.'
   'The Battle of Blenheim' (1800)

21 Curses are like young chickens, they
always come home to roost.
   The Curse of Kehama (1810) motto

22 No stir in the air, no stir in the sea,
The ship was still as she could be.
   'The Inchcape Rock'

23 My name is Death: the last best friend
am I.
   'The Lay of the Laureate' (1816) st. 87

24 We wage no war with women nor with
priests.
   Madoc (1805) pt. 1, canto 15 'The
   Excommunication' l. 65

1 You are old, Father William, the young
man cried,
The few locks which are left you are grey;
You are hale, Father William, a hearty old
man,
Now tell me the reason, I pray.
'The Old Man's Comforts' (1799). Cf. 91:4

2 In the days of my youth I remembered my
God!
And He hath not forgotten my age.
'The Old Man's Comforts' (1799)

3 The arts babblative and scribblative.
Colloquies on the Progress and Prospects of Society
(1829) no. 10, pt. 2

4 The march of intellect.
Colloquies on the Progress and Prospects of Society
(1829) no. 14

5 Men started at the intelligence, and turned
pale, as if they had heard of the loss of a
dear friend.
The Life of Nelson (1813) ch. 9 (on Nelson's
death)

6 She has made me in love with a cold
climate, and frost and snow, with a
northern moonlight.
On Mary Wollstonecraft's letters from
Sweden and Norway; letter, 28 April 1797, in
Charles Southey *Life and Correspondence of
Robert Southey* vol. 1 (1849)

Robert Southwell *c.*1561–95

7 Man's mind a mirror is of heavenly sights,
A brief wherein all marvels summèd lie.
'Look Home' (1595)

8 Good is best when soonest wrought,
Lingered labours come to naught.
'Loss in Delays' (1595)

9 Times go by turns, and chances change by
course,
From foul to fair, from better hap to
worse.
'Times go by Turns' (1595). Cf. 14:2

Muriel Spark 1918–

10 The one certain way for a woman to hold a
man is to leave him for religion.
The Comforters (1957) ch. 1

11 I am putting old heads on your young
shoulders . . . all my pupils are the crème
de la crème.
The Prime of Miss Jean Brodie (1961) ch. 1

12 Give me a girl at an impressionable age,
and she is mine for life.
The Prime of Miss Jean Brodie (1961) ch. 1.
Cf. 7:10

13 One's prime is elusive. You little girls,
when you grow up, must be on the alert to
recognise your prime at whatever time of
your life it may occur.
The Prime of Miss Jean Brodie (1961) ch. 1

John Sparrow 1906–92

14 That indefatigable and unsavoury engine of
pollution, the dog.
Letter to *The Times* 30 September 1975

Herbert Spencer 1820–1903

15 Science is organized knowledge.
Education (1861) ch. 2

16 People are beginning to see that the first
requisite to success in life is to be a good
animal.
Education (1861) ch. 2

17 Survival of the fittest implies
multiplication of the fittest.
Principles of Biology (1865) pt. 3, ch. 12,
sect. 164

18 How often misused words generate
misleading thoughts.
Principles of Ethics (1879) bk. 1, pt. 2, ch. 8,
sect. 152

19 Progress, therefore, is not an accident, but
a necessity . . . It is a part of nature.
Social Statics (1850) pt. 1, ch. 2, sect. 4

20 A clever theft was praiseworthy amongst
the Spartans; and it is equally so amongst
Christians, provided it be on a sufficiently
large scale.
Social Statics (1850) pt. 2, ch. 16, sect. 3

21 No one can be perfectly free till all are
free; no one can be perfectly moral till all
are moral; no one can be perfectly happy
till all are happy.
Social Statics (1850) pt. 4, ch. 30, sect. 16
See also CHARLES ROUPELL

Raine, Countess Spencer 1929–

22 Alas, for our towns and cities. Monstrous
carbuncles of concrete have erupted in
gentle Georgian Squares.
The Spencers on Spas (1983) p. 14. Cf. 95:8

Stephen Spender 1909–

23 After the first powerful plain manifesto
The black statement of pistons, without
more fuss
But gliding like a queen, she leaves the
station.
'The Express' (1933)

24 Born of the sun they travelled a short
while towards the sun,
And left the vivid air signed with their
honour.
'I think continually of those who were truly
great' (1933)

25 My parents kept me from children who
were rough
And who threw words like stones and who
wore torn clothes.
'My parents kept me from children who
were rough' (1933)

1 Never being, but always at the edge of
   Being.
   Title of poem (1933)

2 Hearts wound up with love, like little
   watch springs.
   'The Past Values' (1939)

3 Pylons, those pillars
   Bare like nude, giant girls that have no
   secret.
   'The Pylons' (1933)

Edmund Spenser c.1552–99

4 Vain man, said she, that dost in vain assay,
   A mortal thing so to immortalize.
   Amoretti (1595) sonnet 75

5 Wake now, my love, awake; for it is time.
   The rosy morn long since left Tithones bed,
   All ready to her silver coach to climb,
   And Phoebus gins to shew his glorious
   head.
   'Epithalamion' (1595) l. 74

6 Ah! when will this long weary day have
   end,
   And lend me leave to come unto my love?
   'Epithalamion' (1595) l. 278

7 A gentle knight was pricking on the plain.
   The Faerie Queen (1596) bk. 1, canto 1, st. 1

8 A bold bad man, that dared to call by name
   Great Gorgon, Prince of darkness and dead
   night.
   The Faerie Queen (1596) bk. 1, canto 1, st. 37.
   Cf. 280:15

9 Sleep after toil, port after stormy seas,
   Ease after war, death after life does greatly
   please.
   The Faerie Queen (1596) bk. 1, canto 9, st. 40

10 So double was his pains, so double be his
   praise.
   The Faerie Queen (1596) bk. 2, canto 2, st. 25

11 And all for love, and nothing for reward.
   The Faerie Queen (1596) bk. 2, canto 8, st. 2

12 Gather therefore the rose, whilst yet is
   prime,
   For soon comes age, that will her pride
   deflower.
   The Faerie Queen (1596) bk. 2, canto 12, st. 75

13 And painful pleasure turns to pleasing
   pain.
   The Faerie Queen (1596) bk. 3, canto 10, st. 60

14 Be bold, be bold, and everywhere Be bold.
   The Faerie Queen (1596) bk. 3, canto 11, st. 54

15 O sacred hunger of ambitious minds.
   The Faerie Queen (1596) bk. 5, canto 12, st. 1

16 Of such deep learning little had he need,
   Ne yet of Latin, ne of Greek that breed
   Doubts 'mongst Divines, and difference of
   texts,
   From whence arise diversity of sects,
   And hateful heresies.
   'Prosopopoia or Mother Hubbard's Tale'
   (1591) l. 385

17 With that, I saw two swans of goodly hue,
   Come softly swimming down along the
   Lee.
   Prothalamion (1596) l. 37

18 Sweet Thames, run softly, till I end my
   song.
   Prothalamion (1596) l. 54

19 Uncouth unkist, said the old famous poet
   Chaucer.
   The Shepherd's Calendar (1579) 'Letter to
   Gabriel Harvey'

20 So now they have made our English tongue
   a gallimaufry or hodgepodge of all other
   speeches.
   The Shepherd's Calendar (1579) 'Letter to
   Gabriel Harvey'

Steven Spielberg 1947–

21 Close encounters of the third kind.
   Title of film (1977)

Baruch Spinoza 1632–77

22 *Deus, sive Natura.*
   God, or in other words, Nature.
   Ethics (1677) pt. 1, para. 6

23 I have striven not to laugh at human
   actions, not to weep at them, nor to hate
   them, but to understand them.
   Tractatus Politicus (1677) ch. 1, sect. 4

Revd W. A. Spooner 1844–1930

24 Mr Huxley assures me that it's no farther
   from the north coast of Spitzbergen to the
   North Pole than it is from Land's End to
   John of Gaunt.
   Quoted by Julian Huxley in *SEAC* (Calcutta)
   27 February 1944

25 You will find as you grow older that the
   weight of rages will press harder and
   harder upon the employer.
   In William Hayter *Spooner* (1977) ch. 6

Sir Cecil Spring-Rice 1859–1918

26 I vow to thee, my country—all earthly
   things above—
   Entire and whole and perfect, the service
   of my love,
   The love that asks no question: the love
   that stands the test,
   That lays upon the altar the dearest and
   the best:
   The love that never falters, the love that
   pays the price,
   The love that makes undaunted the final
   sacrifice.
   'I Vow to Thee, My Country' (written on the
   eve of his departure from Washington,
   12 January 1918)

27 Her ways are ways of gentleness and all
   her paths are Peace.
   'I Vow to Thee, My Country' (1918). Cf. 43:9

1 I am the Dean of Christ Church, Sir:
There's my wife; look well at her.
She's the Broad and I'm the High;
We are the University.

 The Masque of Balliol (1870) in W. G. Hiscock
 (ed.) *The Balliol Rhymes* (1939) p. 29
 (unofficially altered to 'I am the Dean, and
 this is Mrs Liddell; / She the first, and I the
 second fiddle'). Cf. 9:12, 32:6

C. H. Spurgeon 1834–92

2 It is well said in the old proverb, 'a lie will
go round the world while truth is pulling
its boots on'.

 Gems from Spurgeon (1859) p. 74

Sir J. C. Squire 1884–1958

3 I'm not so think as you drunk I am.

 'Ballade of Soporific Absorption' (1931)

4 It did not last: the Devil howling 'Ho!
Let Einstein be!' restored the status quo.

 'In continuation of Pope on Newton' (1926).
 Cf. 251:26

Mme de Staël 1766–1817

5 *Tout comprendre rend très indulgent.*
To be totally understanding makes one
very indulgent.

 Corinne (1807) bk. 18, ch. 5

6 A man can brave opinion, a woman must
submit to it.

 Delphine (1802) epigraph

7 Speech happens not to be his language.

 On being asked what she found to talk
 about with her new lover, a hussar
 (attributed)

Joseph Stalin 1879–1953

8 The Pope! How many divisions has *he* got?

 On being asked to encourage Catholicism in
 Russia by way of conciliating the Pope,
 13 May 1935; in W. S. Churchill *The Gathering
 Storm* (1948) ch. 8

Sir Henry Morton Stanley 1841–1904

9 Dr Livingstone, I presume?

 How I found Livingstone (1872) ch. 11

Charles E. Stanton 1859–1933

10 *Lafayette, nous voilà!*
Lafayette, we are here.

 At the tomb of Lafayette in Paris, 4 July
 1917; in *New York Tribune* 6 September 1917

Frank L. Stanton 1857–1927

11 Sweetes' li'l' feller,
Everybody knows;
Dunno what to call him,
But he's mighty lak' a rose!

 'Mighty Lak' a Rose' (1901 song)

John Stark 1728–1822

12 We beat them to-day or Molly Stark's a
widow.

 Before the Battle of Bennington, 16 August
 1777; in *Cyclopaedia of American Biography*
 vol. 5

Christina Stead 1902–83

13 A self-made man is one who believes in
luck and sends his son to Oxford.

 House of All Nations (1938) 'Credo'

Sir Richard Steele 1672–1729

14 The insupportable labour of doing nothing.

 The Spectator no. 54 (2 May 1711)

15 A woman seldom writes her mind but in
her postscript.

 The Spectator no. 79 (31 May 1711). Cf. 24:19

16 To love her is a liberal education.

 The Tatler no. 49 (2 August 1709); of Lady
 Elizabeth Hastings

17 Reading is to the mind what exercise is to
the body.

 The Tatler no. 147 (18 March 1710)

18 It was very prettily said, that we may learn
the little value of fortune by the persons
on whom heaven is pleased to bestow it.

 The Tatler no. 203 (27 July 1710)

Lincoln Steffens 1866–1936

19 I have seen the future; and it works.

 Following a visit to the Soviet Union in 1919,
 in *Letters* (1938) vol. 1, p. 463

Gertrude Stein 1874–1946

20 Remarks are not literature.

 Autobiography of Alice B. Toklas (1933) ch. 7

21 Pigeons on the grass alas.

 Four Saints in Three Acts (1934) act 3, sc. 2

22 Rose is a rose is a rose is a rose.

 Sacred Emily (1913) p. 187

23 You are all a lost generation.

 Of the young who served in the First World
 War; subsequently taken by Ernest
 Hemingway as epigraph to *The Sun Also Rises*
 (1926)

John Steinbeck 1902–68

24 Okie use' ta mean you was from
Oklahoma. Now it means you're a dirty
son-of-a-bitch. Okie means you're scum.
Don't mean nothing itself, it's the way they
say it.

 The Grapes of Wrath (1939) ch. 18

Gloria Steinem 1934–

25 We are becoming the men we wanted to
marry.

 Ms July/August 1982

1 Outrageous acts and everyday rebellions.
   Title of book (1983)

2 A woman without a man is like a fish
   without a bicycle.
   Attributed

Stendhal 1783–1842

3 A novel is a mirror which passes over a
   highway. Sometimes it reflects to your eyes
   the blue of the skies, at others the
   churned-up mud of the road.
   Le Rouge et le noir (1830) bk. 2, ch. 19

J. K. Stephen 1859–92

4 Two voices are there: one is of the deep ...
   And one is of an old half-witted sheep
   Which bleats articulate monotony,
   And indicates that two and one are three.
   'A Sonnet' (1891); of Wordsworth. Cf. 357:6

5 When the Rudyards cease from kipling
   And the Haggards ride no more.
   'To R.K.' (1891)

James Stephens 1882–1950

6 Finality is death. Perfection is finality.
   Nothing is perfect. There are lumps in it.
   The Crock of Gold (1912) bk. 1, ch. 4

7 I hear a sudden cry of pain!
   There is a rabbit in a snare:
   Now I hear the cry again,
   But I cannot tell from where ...
   Little one! Oh, little one!
   I am searching everywhere.
   'The Snare' (1915)

Laurence Sterne 1713–68

8 They order, said I, this matter better in
   France.
   A Sentimental Journey (1768) opening words

9 If ever I do a mean action, it must be in
   some interval betwixt one passion and
   another.
   A Sentimental Journey (1768) 'Montriul'

10 There are worse occupations in this world
   than feeling a woman's pulse.
   A Sentimental Journey (1768) 'The Pulse. Paris'

11 God tempers the wind, said Maria, to the
   shorn lamb.
   A Sentimental Journey (1768) 'Maria' (from a
   French proverb)

12 I wish either my father or my mother, or
   indeed both of them, as they were in duty
   both equally bound to it, had minded what
   they were about when they begot me.
   Tristram Shandy (1759–67) opening words

13 'Pray, my dear,' quoth my mother, 'have
   you not forgot to wind up the
   clock?'—'Good G—!' cried my father,
   making an exclamation, but taking care to
   moderate his voice at the same time,—'Did
   ever woman, since the creation of the
   world, interrupt a man with such a silly
   question?'
   Tristram Shandy (1759–67) bk. 1, ch. 1

14 'Tis known by the name of perseverance in
   a good cause,—and of obstinacy in a bad
   one.
   Tristram Shandy (1759–67) bk. 1, ch. 17

15 Digressions, incontestably, are the
   sunshine;—they are the life, the soul of
   reading.
   Tristram Shandy (1759–67) bk. 1, ch. 22

16 I should have no objection to this method,
   but that I think it must smell too strong of
   the lamp.
   Tristram Shandy (1759–67) bk. 1, ch. 23

17 Writing, when properly managed ... is but
   a different name for conversation.
   Tristram Shandy (1759–67) bk. 2, ch. 11

18 It is the nature of an hypothesis, when
   once a man has conceived it, that it
   assimilates every thing to itself, as proper
   nourishment; and, from the first moment
   of your begetting it, it generally grows the
   stronger by every thing you see, hear, read,
   or understand.
   Tristram Shandy (1759–67) bk. 2, ch. 19

19 Is this a fit time, said my father to himself,
   to talk of Pensions and Grenadiers?
   Tristram Shandy (1759–67) bk. 4, ch. 5

20 'Tis better in battle than in bed,' said my
   uncle Toby.
   Tristram Shandy (1759–67) bk. 5, ch. 3

21 There is a North-west passage to the
   intellectual World.
   Tristram Shandy (1759–67) bk. 5, ch. 42

22 'The poor soul will die:—' 'He shall not die,
   by G—,' cried my uncle Toby.—The
   Accusing Spirit, which flew up to heaven's
   chancery with the oath, blushed as he gave
   it in;—and the Recording Angel, as he
   wrote it down, dropped a tear upon the
   word, and blotted it out for ever.
   Tristram Shandy (1759–67) bk. 6, ch. 8

23 My brother Toby, quoth she, is going to be
   married to Mrs Wadman.Then he will
   never, quoth my father, lie *diagonally* in his
   bed again as long as he lives.
   Tristram Shandy (1759–67) bk. 6, ch. 39

24 And who are you? said he.—Don't puzzle
   me, said I.
   Tristram Shandy (1759–67) bk. 7, ch. 33

25 'A soldier,' cried my Uncle Toby,
   interrupting the corporal, 'is no more
   exempt from saying a foolish thing, Trim,
   than a man of letters.'—'But not so often,
   an' please your honour,' replied the
   corporal.
   Tristram Shandy (1759–67) bk. 8, ch. 19

26 —d! said my mother, 'what is all this story
   about?'— 'A Cock and a Bull,' said Yorick.
   Tristram Shandy (1759–67) bk. 9, ch. 33

27 This sad vicissitude of things.
   Sermons (1767) no. 16 'The character of
   Shimei'

Brooks Stevens

1 Our whole economy is based on planned obsolescence.
> In V. Packard *The Waste Makers* (1960) ch. 6

Jocelyn Stevens 1932–

2 If I were a snob I wouldn't be living with Mrs Duffield, and Mrs Duffield has asked me to tell you that if I were a bore she wouldn't be living with me.
> Telephone conversation with the editor of the *Independent*, which had accused him of being a snob and a bore; in *Independent on Sunday* 15 November 1992, Review p. 3

Wallace Stevens 1879–1955

3 The poet is the priest of the invisible.
> 'Adagia' (1957)

4 Chieftain Iffucan of Azcan in caftan
Of tan with henna hackles, halt!
> 'Bantams in Pine Woods' (1923)

5 Call the roller of big cigars,
The muscular one, and bid him whip
In kitchen cups concupiscent curds.
> 'The Emperor of Ice-Cream' (1923)

6 Let be be finale of seem.
The only emperor is the emperor of ice-cream.
> 'The Emperor of Ice-Cream' (1923)

7 Frogs Eat Butterflies. Snakes Eat Frogs.
Hogs Eat Snakes. Men Eat Hogs.
> Title of poem (1923)

8 Poetry is the supreme fiction, madame.
> 'A High-Toned old Christian Woman' (1923)

9 They said, 'You have a blue guitar,
You do not play things as they are.'
The man replied, 'Things as they are
Are changed upon the blue guitar.'
> 'The Man with the Blue Guitar' (1937)

10 Music is feeling, then, not sound.
> 'Peter Quince at the Clavier' (1923) pt. 1

11 Beauty is momentary in the mind—
The fitful tracing of a portal;
But in the flesh it is immortal.
The body dies; the body's beauty lives.
> 'Peter Quince at the Clavier' (1923) pt. 4

12 Complacencies of the peignoir, and late
Coffee and oranges in a sunny chair,
And the green freedom of a cockatoo
Upon a rug mingle to dissipate
The holy hush of ancient sacrifice.
> 'Sunday Morning' (1923) st. 1

13 I do not know which to prefer,
The beauty of inflections
Or the beauty of innuendoes,
The blackbird whistling
Or just after.
> 'Thirteen Ways of Looking at a Blackbird' (1923)

Adlai Stevenson 1900–65

14 I suppose flattery hurts no one, that is, if he doesn't inhale.
> Television broadcast, 30 March 1952, in N. F. Busch *Adlai E. Stevenson* (1952) ch. 5

15 If they [the Republicans] will stop telling lies about the Democrats, we will stop telling the truth about them.
> Speech during 1952 Presidential campaign; in J. B. Martin *Adlai Stevenson and Illinois* (1976) ch. 8

16 Let's talk sense to the American people. Let's tell them the truth, that there are no gains without pains.
> Speech of Acceptance at the Democratic National Convention, 26 July 1952; in *Speeches* (1952)

17 In America any boy may become President.
> Speech in Indianapolis, 26 September 1952; in *Major Campaign Speeches ... 1952* (1953)

18 A free society is a society where it is safe to be unpopular.
> Speech in Detroit, 7 October 1952; in *Major Campaign Speeches ... 1952* (1953)

19 The young man [Richard Nixon] who asks you to set him one heart-beat from the Presidency of the United States.
> Speech at Cleveland, Ohio, 23 October 1952, in *New York Times* 24 October 1952, p. 14 (commonly quoted 'just a heart-beat away ...')

20 We hear the Secretary of State boasting of his brinkmanship—the art of bringing us to the edge of the abyss.
> Speech in Hartford, Connecticut, 25 February 1956; in *New York Times* 26 February 1956, p. 64 (of John Foster Dulles)

21 She would rather light a candle than curse the darkness, and her glow has warmed the world.
> On learning of Eleanor Roosevelt's death; in *New York Times* 8 November 1962

Anne Stevenson 1933–

22 Blackbirds are the cellos of the deep farms.
> 'Green Mountain, Black Mountain' (1982)

Robert Louis Stevenson 1850–94

23 Every one lives by selling something.
> *Across the Plains* (1892) 'Beggars' pt. 3

24 Politics is perhaps the only profession for which no preparation is thought necessary.
> *Familiar Studies of Men and Books* (1882) 'Yoshida-Torajiro'

25 Am I no a bonny fighter?
> *Kidnapped* (1886) ch. 10

26 I've a grand memory for forgetting, David.
> *Kidnapped* (1886) ch. 18

27 For my part, I travel not to go anywhere, but to go. I travel for travel's sake. The great affair is to move.
> *Travels with a Donkey* (1879) 'Cheylard and Luc'

1 If landscapes were sold, like the sheets of
characters of my boyhood, one penny plain
and twopence coloured, I should go the
length of twopence every day of my life.
   Travels with a Donkey (1879) 'Father
   Apollinaris'

2 Fifteen men on the dead man's chest
Yo-ho-ho, and a bottle of rum!
Drink and the devil had done for the rest—
Yo-ho-ho, and a bottle of rum!
   Treasure Island (1883) ch. 1

3 Tip me the black spot.
   Treasure Island (1883) ch. 3

4 Many's the long night I've dreamed of
cheese—toasted, mostly.
   Treasure Island (1883) ch. 15

5 Old and young, we are all on our last
cruise.
   Virginibus Puerisque (1881) 'Crabbed Age and
   Youth'

6 To travel hopefully is a better thing than
to arrive, and the true success is to labour.
   Virginibus Puerisque (1881) 'El Dorado'

7 Even if we take matrimony at its lowest,
even if we regard it as no more than a sort
of friendship recognised by the police.
   Virginibus Puerisque (1881) title essay, pt. 1

8 Marriage is like life in this—that it is a
field of battle, and not a bed of roses.
   Virginibus Puerisque (1881) title essay, pt. 1

9 The cruellest lies are often told in silence.
   Virginibus Puerisque (1881) title essay, pt. 4

10 What hangs people ... is the unfortunate
circumstance of guilt.
   The Wrong Box (with Lloyd Osbourne, 1889)
   ch. 7

11 Nothing like a little judicious levity.
   The Wrong Box (with Lloyd Osbourne, 1889)
   ch. 7

12 In winter I get up at night
And dress by yellow candle-light.
In summer, quite the other way,—
I have to go to bed by day.
   A Child's Garden of Verses (1885) 'Bed in
   Summer'

13 The world is so full of a number of things,
I'm sure we should all be as happy as
kings.
   A Child's Garden of Verses (1885) 'Happy
   Thought'

14 I was the giant great and still
That sits upon the pillow-hill,
And sees before him, dale and plain,
The pleasant land of counterpane.
   A Child's Garden of Verses (1885) 'The Land of
   Counterpane'

15 Let us arise and go like men,
And face with an undaunted tread
The long black passage up to bed.
   A Child's Garden of Verses (1885) 'North-West
   Passage. Good-Night'

16 A child should always say what's true,
And speak when he is spoken to,
And behave mannerly at table:
At least as far as he is able.
   A Child's Garden of Verses (1885) 'Whole Duty
   of Children'

17 Go, little book, and wish to all
Flowers in the garden, meat in the hall,
A bin of wine, a spice of wit,
A house with lawns enclosing it.
   'Envoy' (1887). Cf. 96:20

18 In the highlands, in the country places,
Where the old plain men have rosy faces.
   'In the highlands ... ' (1896)

19 I will make you brooches and toys for your
delight
Of bird-song at morning and star-shine at
night.
   'I will make you brooches ... ' (1896)

20 Trusty, dusky, vivid, true,
With eyes of gold and bramble-dew,
Steel-true and blade-straight,
The great artificer
Made my mate.
   'My Wife' (1896)

21 Under the wide and starry sky
Dig the grave and let me lie.
   'Requiem' (1887)

22 Home is the sailor, home from sea,
And the hunter home from the hill.
   'Requiem' (1887)

23 Sing me a song of a lad that is gone,
Say, could that lad be I?
Merry of soul he sailed on a day
Over the sea to Skye.
   'Sing me a song of a lad that is gone' (1896)

24 Give to me the life I love,
Let the lave go by me,
Give the jolly heaven above
And the byway nigh me.
   'The Vagabond' (1896)

25 Wealth I seek not, hope nor love,
Nor a friend to know me;
All I seek, the heaven above
And the road below me.
   'The Vagabond' (1896)

Joseph C. Stinson 1947–

26 Go ahead, make my day.
   Sudden Impact (1983 film); spoken by Clint
   Eastwood

Samuel John Stone 1839–1900

27 The Church's one foundation
Is Jesus Christ, her Lord;
She is his new creation
By water and the word.
   'The Church's one foundation' (1866 hymn)

Tom Stoppard 1937–

28 It's not the voting that's democracy, it's
the counting.
   Jumpers (1972) act 1. Cf. 311:4

1 The House of Lords, an illusion to which
I have never been able to subscribe—
responsibility without power, the
prerogative of the eunuch throughout the
ages.
Lord Malquist and Mr Moon (1966) pt. 6.
Cf. 198:5

2 I'm with you on the free press. It's the
newspapers I can't stand.
Night and Day (1978) act 1

3 Comment is free but facts are on expenses.
Night and Day (1978) act 2. Cf. 268:3

4 Eternity's a terrible thought. I mean,
where's it all going to end?
Rosencrantz and Guildenstern are Dead (1967)
act 2

5 The bad end unhappily, the good unluckily.
That is what tragedy means.
Rosencrantz and Guildenstern are Dead (1967)
act 2. Cf. 349:20

6 Life is a gamble at terrible odds—if it was
a bet, you wouldn't take it.
Rosencrantz and Guildenstern are Dead (1967)
act 3

7 War is capitalism with the gloves off.
Travesties (1975) act 1

Harriet Beecher Stowe 1811–96

8 I s'pect I growed. Don't think nobody never
made me.
Uncle Tom's Cabin (1852) ch. 20 (Topsy)

Lord Stowell 1745–1836

9 The elegant simplicity of the three per
cents.
In Lord Campbell *Lives of the Lord Chancellors*
(1857) vol. 10, ch. 212. Cf. 122:2

10 A precedent embalms a principle.
An opinion, while Advocate-General, 1788,
quoted by Disraeli in *Hansard* 22 February
1848, col. 1066

Lytton Strachey 1880–1932

11 He was no striped frieze; he was shot silk.
Elizabeth and Essex (1928) ch. 5 (of Francis
Bacon)

12 The time was out of joint, and he was only
too delighted to have been born to set it
right.
Eminent Victorians (1918) 'Cardinal Manning'
pt. 2 (of Hurrell Froude). Cf. 275:6

13 Her conception of God was certainly not
orthodox. She felt towards Him as she
might have felt towards a glorified sanitary
engineer; and in some of her speculations
she seems hardly to distinguish between
the Deity and the Drains.
Eminent Victorians (1918) 'Florence
Nightingale' pt. 4

14 [CHAIRMAN OF MILITARY TRIBUNAL:] What
would you do if you saw a German
soldier trying to violate your sister?
[STRACHEY:] I would try to get between
them.
In Robert Graves *Good-bye to All That* (1929)
ch. 23 (otherwise rendered 'I should
interpose my body')

15 Discretion is not the better part of
biography.
In M. Holroyd *Lytton Strachey* vol. 1 (1967)
preface

16 If this is dying, then I don't think much of
it.
On his deathbed; in M. Holroyd *Lytton
Strachey* vol. 2 (1968) pt. 2, ch. 6

Jan Struther 1901–53

17 Lord of all hopefulness, Lord of all joy,
Whose trust, ever childlike, no cares could
destroy,
Be there at our waking, and give us, we
pray,
Your bliss in our hearts, Lord, at the break
of the day.
'All Day Hymn' (1931)

G. A. Studdert Kennedy 1883–1929

18 Waste of Blood, and waste of Tears,
Waste of youth's most precious years,
Waste of ways the saints have trod,
Waste of Glory, waste of God,
War!
More Rough Rhymes of a Padre by 'Woodbine
Willie' (1919) 'Waste'

19 When Jesus came to Birmingham they
simply passed Him by,
They never hurt a hair of Him, they only
let Him die.
Peace Rhymes of a Padre (1921) 'Indifference'

Sir John Suckling 1609–42

20 Why so pale and wan, fond lover?
Prithee, why so pale?
Will, when looking well can't move her,
Looking ill prevail?
Aglaura (1637) act 4, sc. 1 'Song'

21 Her feet beneath her petticoat,
Like little mice, stole in and out,
As if they feared the light.
'A Ballad upon a Wedding' (1646) st. 8

22 Love is the fart
Of every heart:
It pains a man when 'tis kept close,
And others doth offend, when 'tis let loose.
'Love's Offence' (1646)

23 Sure beauty's empires, like to greater
states,
Have certain periods set, and hidden fates.
'Sonnet' (1646)

Louis Henri Sullivan 1856–1924

1 Form follows function.

The Tall Office Building Artistically Considered (1896)

Terry Sullivan

2 She sells sea-shells on the sea-shore,
The shells she sells are sea-shells, I'm sure,
For if she sells sea-shells on the sea-shore,
Then I'm sure she sells sea-shore shells.

'She Sells Sea-Shells' (1908 song)

See also HARRY BEDFORD and TERRY SULLIVAN

Maximilien de Béthune, Duc de Sully 1559–1641

3 *Labourage et pâturage sont les deux mamelles dont la France est alimenteé.*

Tilling and grazing are the two breasts by which France is fed.

Mémoires (1638) pt. 1, ch. 15

4 The English take their pleasures sadly after the fashion of their country.

Attributed

Edith Summerskill 1901–80

5 Nagging is the repetition of unpalatable truths.

Speech to the Married Women's Association, 14 July 1960; in *The Times* 15 July 1960

Henry Howard, Earl of Surrey c.1517–47

6 Martial, the things for to attain
The happy life be these, I find:
The riches left, not got with pain;
The fruitful ground, the quiet mind.

'The Happy Life' (1547); translation of Martial *Epigrams* bk. 10, no. 47

R. S. Surtees 1805–64

7 The only infallible rule we know is, that the man who is always talking about being a gentleman never is one.

Ask Mamma (1858) ch. 1

8 'Unting is all that's worth living for—all time is lost wot is not spent in 'unting—it is like the hair we breathe—if we have it not we die—it's the sport of kings, the image of war without its guilt, and only five-and-twenty per cent of its danger.

Handley Cross (1843) ch. 7. Cf. 311:2

9 I'll fill hup the chinks wi' cheese.

Handley Cross (1843) ch. 15

10 It ar'n't that I loves the fox less, but that I loves the 'ound more.

Handley Cross (1843) ch. 16

11 Three things I never lends—my 'oss, my wife, and my name.

Hillingdon Hall (1845) ch. 33

12 Better be killed than frightened to death.

Mr Facey Romford's Hounds (1865) ch. 32

13 Life would be very pleasant if it were not for its enjoyments.

Mr Facey Romford's Hounds (1865) ch. 32. Cf. 206:15

14 Everyone knows that the real business of a ball is either to look out for a wife, to look after a wife, or to look after somebody else's wife.

Mr Facey Romford's Hounds (1865) ch. 56

15 He was a gentleman who was generally spoken of as having nothing a-year, paid quarterly.

Mr Sponge's Sporting Tour (1853) ch. 24

Hannen Swaffer 1879–1962

16 Freedom of the press in Britain means freedom to print such of the proprietor's prejudices as the advertisers don't object to.

In Tom Driberg *Swaff* (1974) ch. 2

Jonathan Swift 1667–1745

17 Satire is a sort of glass, wherein beholders do generally discover everybody's face but their own.

The Battle of the Books (1704) preface

18 Instead of dirt and poison we have rather chosen to fill our hives with honey and wax; thus furnishing mankind with the two noblest of things, which are sweetness and light.

The Battle of the Books (1704). Cf. 17:25

19 Laws are like cobwebs, which may catch small flies, but let wasps and hornets break through.

A Critical Essay upon the Faculties of the Mind (1709). Cf. 5:9

20 I have heard of a man who had a mind to sell his house, and therefore carried a piece of brick in his pocket, which he showed as a pattern to encourage purchasers.

The Drapier's Letters (1724) no. 2

21 And he gave it for his opinion, that whoever could make two ears of corn or two blades of grass to grow upon a spot of ground where only one grew before, would deserve better of mankind, and do more essential service to his country than the whole race of politicians put together.

Gulliver's Travels (1726) 'A Voyage to Brobdingnag' ch. 7

22 He had been eight years upon a project for extracting sun-beams out of cucumbers, which were to be put into vials hermetically sealed, and let out to warm the air in raw inclement summers.

Gulliver's Travels (1726) 'A Voyage to Laputa, etc.' ch. 5

1 He replied that I must needs be mistaken, or that I *said the thing which was not.* (For they have no word in their language to express lying or falsehood.)
Gulliver's Travels (1726) 'A Voyage to the Houyhnhnms' ch. 3

2 We are so fond of one another, because our ailments are the same.
Journal to Stella (in *Works*, 1768) 1 February 1711

3 Will she pass in a crowd? Will she make a figure in a country church?
Journal to Stella (in *Works*, 1768) 9 February 1711

4 Proper words in proper places, make the true definition of a style.
Letter to a Young Gentleman lately entered into Holy Orders (9 January 1720)

5 Not die here in a rage, like a poisoned rat in a hole.
Letter to Bolingbroke, 21 March 1730, in H. Williams (ed.) *Correspondence of Jonathan Swift* vol. 3 (1963)

6 Surely mortal man is a broomstick!
A Meditation upon a Broomstick (1710)

7 She wears her clothes, as if they were thrown on her with a pitchfork.
Polite Conversation (1738) Dialogue 1

8 I always love to begin a journey on Sundays, because I shall have the prayers of the church, to preserve all that travel by land, or by water.
Polite Conversation (1738) Dialogue 2

9 I never saw, heard, nor read, that the clergy were beloved in any nation where Christianity was the religion of the country. Nothing can render them popular, but some degree of persecution.
Thoughts on Religion (1765)

10 We have just enough religion to make us hate, but not enough to make us love one another.
Thoughts on Various Subjects (1711)

11 When a true genius appears in the world, you may know him by this sign, that the dunces are all in confederacy against him.
Thoughts on Various Subjects (1711)

12 The stoical scheme of supplying our wants, by lopping off our desires, is like cutting off our feet when we want shoes.
Thoughts on Various Subjects (1711)

13 Every man desires to live long; but no man would be old.
Thoughts on Various Subjects (1727 ed.)

14 A coming shower your shooting corns presage.
'A Description of a City Shower' (1710) l. 9

15 How haughtily he lifts his nose,
To tell what every schoolboy knows.
'The Journal' (1727) l. 81

16 Convey a libel in a frown,
And wink a reputation down.
'The Journal of a Modern Lady' (1729) l. 192

17 Hail, fellow, well met,
All dirty and wet:
Find out, if you can,
Who's master, who's man.
'My Lady's Lamentation' (written 1728) l. 165

18 Philosophy! the lumber of the schools.
'Ode to Sir W. Temple' (written 1692)

19 Say, Britain, could you ever boast,—
Three poets in an age at most?
Our chilling climate hardly bears
A sprig of bays in fifty years.
'On Poetry' (1733) l. 5

20 As learned commentators view
In Homer more than Homer knew.
'On Poetry' (1733) l. 103

21 So geographers, in Afric-maps,
With savage-pictures fill their gaps;
And o'er unhabitable downs
Place elephants for want of towns.
'On Poetry' (1733) l. 177

22 Hobbes clearly proves, that every creature
Lives in a state of war by nature.
'On Poetry' (1733) l. 319

23 So, naturalists observe, a flea
Hath smaller fleas that on him prey;
And these have smaller fleas to bite 'em,
And so proceed *ad infinitum.*
Thus every poet, in his kind,
Is bit by him that comes behind.
'On Poetry' (1733) l. 337

24 Yet malice never was his aim;
He lashed the vice, but spared the name;
No individual could resent,
Where thousands equally were meant.
'Verses on the Death of Dr Swift' (1731)
l. 512. Cf. 250:25

25 Good God! what a genius I had when I wrote that book.
Of *A Tale of a Tub*, in Sir Walter Scott (ed.) *Works of Swift* (1814) vol. 1, p. 90

26 I shall be like that tree, I shall die at the top.
In Sir Walter Scott (ed.) *Works of Swift* (1814) vol. 1, p. 443

27 *Ubi saeva indignatio ulterius cor lacerare nequit.*
Where fierce indignation can no longer tear his heart.
Swift's epitaph. See S. Leslie *The Skull of Swift* (1928) ch. 15

Algernon Charles Swinburne
1837–1909

28 Maiden, and mistress of the months and stars
Now folded in the flowerless fields of heaven.
Atalanta in Calydon (1865) l. 1

1 When the hounds of spring are on winter's
   traces,
   The mother of months in meadow or plain
   Fills the shadows and windy places
   With lisp of leaves and ripple of rain;
   And the brown bright nightingale amorous
   Is half assuaged for Itylus,
   For the Thracian ships and the foreign
   faces,
   The tongueless vigil and all the pain.
   Atalanta in Calydon (1865) chorus 'When the
   hounds of spring'

2 For winter's rains and ruins are over,
   And all the season of snows and sins;
   The days dividing lover and lover,
   The light that loses, the night that wins;
   And time remembered is grief forgotten,
   And frosts are slain and flowers begotten,
   And in green underwood and cover
   Blossom by blossom the spring begins.
   Atalanta in Calydon (1865) chorus 'When the
   hounds of spring'

3 Before the beginning of years
   There came to the making of man
   Time with a gift of tears,
   Grief with a glass that ran.
   Atalanta in Calydon (1865) chorus 'Before the
   beginning of years'

4 The deep division of prodigious breasts,
   The solemn slope of mighty limbs asleep.
   'Ave atque Vale' (1878) st. 6

5 Villon, our sad bad glad mad brother's
   name.
   'Ballad of François Villon' (1878)

6 We shift and bedeck and bedrape us,
   Thou art noble and nude and antique.
   'Dolores' (1866) st. 7

7   Change in a trice
   The lilies and languors of virtue
   For the raptures and roses of vice.
   'Dolores' (1866) st. 9

8 O splendid and sterile Dolores,
   Our Lady of Pain.
   'Dolores' (1866) st. 9

9 No thorns go as deep as a rose's,
   And love is more cruel than lust.
   'Dolores' (1866) st. 20

10 As a god self-slain on his own strange
   altar,
   Death lies dead.
   'A Forsaken Garden' (1878)

11 Glory to Man in the highest! for Man is the
   master of things.
   'Hymn of Man' (1871)

12 Yea, is not even Apollo, with hair and
   harpstring of gold,
   A bitter God to follow, a beautiful God to
   behold?
   'Hymn to Proserpine' (1866)

13 Thou hast conquered, O pale Galilean; the
   world has grown grey from Thy breath;
   We have drunken of things Lethean, and
   fed on the fullness of death.
   'Hymn to Proserpine' (1866). Cf. 188:20

14 And the best and the worst of this is
   That neither is most to blame,
   If you have forgotten my kisses
   And I have forgotten your name.
   'An Interlude' (1866)

15 Swallow, my sister, O sister swallow,
   How can thine heart be full of the spring?
   A thousand summers are over and dead.
   What hast thou found in the spring to
   follow?
   'Itylus' (1864)

16 Till life forget and death remember,
   Till thou remember and I forget.
   'Itylus' (1864)

17 Blown fields or flowerful closes,
   Green pleasure or grey grief.
   'A Match' (1866)

18 I will go back to the great sweet mother,
   Mother and lover of men, the sea.
   'The Triumph of Time' (1866)

19 There lived a singer in France of old
   By the tideless dolorous midland sea.
   In a land of sand and ruin and gold
   There shone one woman, and none but
   she.
   'The Triumph of Time' (1866)

John Addington Symonds
1840–93

20 These things shall be! A loftier race
   Than e'er the world hath known shall rise,
   With flame of freedom in their souls,
   And light of knowledge in their eyes.
   Hymn

John Millington Synge 1871–1909

21 But we do be afraid of the sea, and we do
   only be drownded now and again.
   The Aran Islands (1907) pt. 2

22 Oh my grief, I've lost him surely. I've lost
   the only Playboy of the Western World.
   The Playboy of the Western World (1907) act 3 *ad
   fin.*

Thomas Szasz 1920–

23 Happiness is an imaginary condition,
   formerly often attributed by the living to
   the dead, now usually attributed by adults
   to children, and by children to adults.
   The Second Sin (1973) 'Emotions'

24 The stupid neither forgive nor forget; the
   naïve forgive and forget; the wise forgive
   but do not forget.
   The Second Sin (1973) 'Personal Conduct'

25 If you talk to God, you are praying; if God
   talks to you, you have schizophrenia. If the
   dead talk to you, you are a spiritualist; if
   God talks to you, you are a schizophrenic.
   The Second Sin (1973) 'Schizophrenia'

1 Formerly, when religion was strong and science weak, men mistook magic for medicine; now, when science is strong and religion weak, men mistake medicine for magic.

   The Second Sin (1973) 'Science and Scientism'

2 Two wrongs don't make a right, but they make a good excuse.

   The Second Sin (1973) 'Social Relations'

Albert von Szent-Györgyi
1893–1986

3 Discovery consists of seeing what everybody has seen and thinking what nobody has thought.

   In I. Good (ed.) *The Scientist Speculates* (1962) p. 15

Tacitus AD *c*.56–after 117

4 They make a wilderness and call it peace.

   Agricola ch. 30

5 It is part of human nature to hate the man you have hurt.

   Agricola ch. 42

6 *Sine ira et studio.*
   With neither anger nor partiality.

   Annals bk. 1, ch. 1

7 *Elegantiae arbiter.*
   The arbiter of taste.

   Annals bk. 16, ch. 18 (of Petronius)

8 *Deos fortioribus adesse.*
   The gods are on the side of the stronger.

   Histories bk. 4, ch. 17. Cf. 83:19

Sir Rabindranath Tagore
1861–1941

9 Bigotry tries to keep truth safe in its hand With a grip that kills it.

   Fireflies (1928) p. 29

Nellie Talbot

10 Jesus wants me for a sunbeam.

   Title of hymn (1921)

Charles-Maurice de Talleyrand
1754–1838

11 *Surtout, Messieurs, point de zèle.*
   Above all, gentlemen, not the slightest zeal.

   In P. Chasles *Voyages d'un critique à travers la vie et les livres* (1868) vol. 2, p. 407

12 *Ils n'ont rien appris, ni rien oublié.*
   They have learnt nothing, and forgotten nothing.

   Oral tradition (attributed to Talleyrand by the Chevalier de Panat, January 1796). See A. Sayons (ed.) *Mémoires et correspondance de Mallet du Pan* (1851) vol. 2, p. 196. Cf. 129:6

13 This is the beginning of the end.

   On hearing the outcome of the battle at Borodino, 1812; in Sainte-Beuve *M. de Talleyrand* (1870) ch. 3 (attributed)

Booth Tarkington 1869–1946

14 There are two things that will be believed of any man whatsoever, and one of them is that he has taken to drink.

   Penrod (1914) ch. 10

Nahum Tate 1652–1715

15 When I am laid in earth my wrongs create. No trouble in thy breast, Remember me, but ah! forget my fate.

   Dido and Aeneas (1689) act 3 ('Dido's Lament')

16 As pants the hart for cooling streams When heated in the chase.

   New Version of the Psalms (1696) Psalm 42 (with Nicholas Brady). Cf. 67:3

17 Through all the changing scenes of life, In trouble and in joy, The praises of my God shall still My heart and tongue employ.

   New Version of the Psalms (1696) Psalm 34 (with Nicholas Brady)

R. H. Tawney 1880–1962

18 Militarism ... is fetish worship. It is the prostration of men's souls and the laceration of their bodies to appease an idol.

   The Acquisitive Society (1921) ch. 4

19 Private property is a necessary institution, at least in a fallen world; men work more and dispute less when goods are private than when they are common.

   Religion and the Rise of Capitalism (1926) ch. 1, sect. 1

20 To take usury is contrary to Scripture; it is contrary to Aristotle; it is contrary to nature, for it is to live without labour; it is to sell time, which belongs to God, for the advantage of wicked men.

   Religion and the Rise of Capitalism (1926) ch. 1, sect. 2

21 What harm have I ever done to the Labour Party?

   On declining the offer of a peerage; in *Evening Standard* 18 January 1962, p. 6

A. J. P. Taylor 1906–90

22 History gets thicker as it approaches recent times.

   English History 1914–45 (1965) bibliography

23 The First World War had begun—imposed on the statesmen of Europe by railway timetables.

   The First World War (1963) ch. 1

1 Like most of those who study history, he [Napoleon III] learned from the mistakes of the past how to make new ones.
Listener 6 June 1963 'Mistaken Lessons from the Past'

2 Crimea: The War That Would Not Boil.
Rumours of Wars (1952) ch. 6 (originally the title of an essay in *History Today* 2 February 1951)

Ann Taylor 1782–1866 and Jane Taylor 1783–1824

3 Twinkle, twinkle, little star,
How I wonder what you are!
Up above the world so high,
Like a diamond in the sky!
Rhymes for the Nursery (1806) 'The Star'

Bayard Taylor 1825–78

4 Till the sun grows cold,
And the stars are old,
And the leaves of the Judgement Book unfold.
'Bedouin Song'

Bishop Jeremy Taylor 1613–67

5 The union of hands and hearts.
XXV Sermons Preached at Golden Grove (1653) 'The Marriage Ring' pt. 1

Norman Tebbit 1931–

6 I grew up in the Thirties with our unemployed father. He did not riot, he got on his bike and looked for work.
Speech, 15 October 1981, in *Daily Telegraph* 16 October 1981

7 The cricket test—which side do they cheer for? ... Are you still looking back to where you came from or where you are?
On the loyalties of Britain's immigrant population; interview in *Los Angeles Times*, reported in *Daily Telegraph* 20 April 1990

Archbishop William Temple 1881–1944

8 Personally, I have always looked on cricket as organized loafing.
Attributed

Sir John Tenniel 1820–1914

9 Dropping the pilot.
Cartoon caption, and title of poem, on Bismarck's departure from office; in *Punch* 29 March 1890

Alfred, Lord Tennyson 1809–92

10 Break, break, break,
On thy cold grey stones, O Sea!
'Break, Break, Break' (1842)

11 And the stately ships go on
To their haven under the hill;
But O for the touch of a vanished hand,
And the sound of a voice that is still!
'Break, Break, Break' (1842)

12 I come from haunts of coot and hern,
I make a sudden sally
And sparkle out among the fern,
To bicker down a valley.
'The Brook' (1855) l. 23

13 For men may come and men may go,
But I go on for ever.
'The Brook' (1855) l. 33

14 Half a league, half a league,
Half a league onward,
All in the valley of Death
Rode the six hundred.
'The Charge of the Light Brigade' (1854)

15 'Forward, the Light Brigade!'
Was there a man dismayed?
Not though the soldier knew
Some one had blundered:
Theirs not to make reply,
Theirs not to reason why,
Theirs but to do and die:
Into the valley of Death
Rode the six hundred.
'The Charge of the Light Brigade' (1854)

16 Cannon to right of them,
Cannon to left of them,
Cannon in front of them
Volleyed and thundered.
'The Charge of the Light Brigade' (1854)

17 Into the jaws of Death,
Into the mouth of Hell.
'The Charge of the Light Brigade' (1854)

18 Sunset and evening star,
And one clear call for me!
And may there be no moaning of the bar,
When I put out to sea.
'Crossing the Bar' (1889)

19 For though from out our bourne of time and place
The flood may bear me far,
I hope to see my pilot face to face
When I have crossed the bar.
'Crossing the Bar' (1889)

20 A daughter of the gods, divinely tall,
And most divinely fair.
'A Dream of Fair Women' (1832) l. 87

21 He clasps the crag with crookèd hands;
Close to the sun in lonely lands,
Ringed with the azure world, he stands.
The wrinkled sea beneath him crawls;
He watches from his mountain walls,
And like a thunderbolt he falls.
'The Eagle' (1851)

22 The mellow lin-lan-lone of evening bells.
'Far-Far-Away' (1889)

23 More black than ashbuds in the front of March.
'The Gardener's Daughter' (1842) l. 28

24 A sight to make an old man young.
'The Gardener's Daughter' (1842) l. 140

1 Wearing the white flower of a blameless
life,
Before a thousand peering littlenesses,
In that fierce light which beats upon a
throne,
And blackens every blot.
Idylls of the King Dedication (1862) l. 24

2 Man's word is God in man.
Idylls of the King 'The Coming of Arthur'
(1869) l. 132

3 Clothed in white samite, mystic,
wonderful.
Idylls of the King 'The Coming of Arthur'
(1869) l. 284; 'The Passing of Arthur' (1869)
l. 199

4 From the great deep to the great deep he
goes.
Idylls of the King 'The Coming of Arthur'
(1869) l. 410

5 Live pure, speak true, right wrong, follow
the King—
Else, wherefore born?
Idylls of the King 'Gareth and Lynette' (1872)
l. 117

6 It was my duty to have loved the highest:
It surely was my profit had I known:
It would have been my pleasure had I seen.
We needs must love the highest when we
see it.
Idylls of the King 'Guinevere' (1859) l. 652

7 Elaine the fair, Elaine the loveable,
Elaine, the lily maid of Astolat.
Idylls of the King 'Lancelot and Elaine' (1859)
l. 1

8 He is all fault who hath no fault at all:
For who loves me must have a touch of
earth.
Idylls of the King 'Lancelot and Elaine' (1859)
l. 132

9 His honour rooted in dishonour stood,
And faith unfaithful kept him falsely true.
Idylls of the King 'Lancelot and Elaine' (1859)
l. 871

10 He makes no friend who never made a foe.
Idylls of the King 'Lancelot and Elaine' (1859)
l. 1082

11 The greater man, the greater courtesy.
Idylls of the King 'The Last Tournament' (1871)
l. 628

12 Our hoard is little, but our hearts are
great.
Idylls of the King 'The Marriage of Geraint'
(1859) l. 352

13 It is the little rift within the lute,
That by and by will make the music mute,
And ever widening slowly silence all.
Idylls of the King 'Merlin and Vivien' (1859)
l. 388

14 And trust me not at all or all in all.
Idylls of the King 'Merlin and Vivien' (1859)
l. 396

15 Man dreams of fame while woman wakes
to love.
Idylls of the King 'Merlin and Vivien' (1859)
l. 458

16 I found Him in the shining of the stars,
I marked Him in the flowering of His
fields,
But in His ways with men I find Him not.
Idylls of the King 'The Passing of Arthur'
(1869) l. 9

17 So all day long the noise of battle rolled
Among the mountains by the winter sea.
Idylls of the King 'The Passing of Arthur'
(1869) l. 170

18 Authority forgets a dying king.
Idylls of the King 'The Passing of Arthur'
(1869) l. 289

19 And the days darken round me, and the
years,
Among new men, strange faces, other
minds.
Idylls of the King 'The Passing of Arthur'
(1869) l. 405

20 The old order changeth, yielding place to
new,
And God fulfils himself in many ways,
Lest one good custom should corrupt the
world.
Idylls of the King 'The Passing of Arthur'
(1869) l. 408

21 If thou shouldst never see my face again,
Pray for my soul. More things are wrought
by prayer
Than this world dreams of.
Idylls of the King 'The Passing of Arthur'
(1869) l. 414

22   I am going a long way
With these thou seëst—if indeed I go
(For all my mind is clouded with a
doubt)—
To the island-valley of Avilion;
Where falls not hail, or rain, or any snow,
Nor ever wind blows loudly.
Idylls of the King 'The Passing of Arthur'
(1869) l. 424

23 Our little systems have their day;
They have their day and cease to be:
They are but broken lights of thee,
And thou, O Lord, art more than they.
In Memoriam A. H. H. (1850) Prologue

24 I held it truth, with him who sings
To one clear harp in divers tones,
That men may rise on stepping-stones
Of their dead selves to higher things.
In Memoriam A. H. H. (1850) canto 1

25   Never morning wore
To evening, but some heart did break.
In Memoriam A. H. H. (1850) canto 6

26 Dark house, by which once more I stand
Here in the long unlovely street,
Doors, where my heart was used to beat
So quickly, waiting for a hand.
In Memoriam A. H. H. (1850) canto 7

1 And ghastly through the drizzling rain
On the bald street breaks the blank day.
In Memoriam A. H. H. (1850) canto 7

2 The last red leaf is whirled away,
The rooks are blown about the skies.
In Memoriam A. H. H. (1850) canto 15

3 I envy not in any moods
The captive void of noble rage,
The linnet born within the cage,
That never knew the summer woods.
In Memoriam A. H. H. (1850) canto 27

4 'Tis better to have loved and lost
Than never to have loved at all.
In Memoriam A. H. H. (1850) canto 27.
Cf. 106:16

5 A solemn gladness even crowned
The purple brows of Olivet.
In Memoriam A. H. H. (1850) canto 31

6 Her eyes are homes of silent prayer.
In Memoriam A. H. H. (1850) canto 32

7 Be near me when my light is low,
When the blood creeps, and the nerves
prick
And tingle; and the heart is sick,
And all the wheels of Being slow.
In Memoriam A. H. H. (1850) canto 50

8 Oh yet we trust that somehow good
Will be the final goal of ill.
In Memoriam A. H. H. (1850) canto 54

9 So runs my dream: but what am I?
An infant crying in the night:
An infant crying for the light:
And with no language but a cry.
In Memoriam A. H. H. (1850) canto 54

10 So careful of the type she seems,
So careless of the single life.
In Memoriam A. H. H. (1850) canto 55 (of
Nature)

11   The great world's altar-stairs
That slope through darkness up to God.
In Memoriam A. H. H. (1850) canto 55

12 Nature, red in tooth and claw.
In Memoriam A. H. H. (1850) canto 56

13 O Sorrow, wilt thou live with me
No casual mistress, but a wife.
In Memoriam A. H. H. (1850) canto 59

14 So many worlds, so much to do,
So little done, such things to be.
In Memoriam A. H. H. (1850) canto 73

15 Laburnums, dropping-wells of fire.
In Memoriam A. H. H. (1850) canto 83

16 God's finger touched him, and he slept.
In Memoriam A. H. H. (1850) canto 85

17   Fresh from brawling courts
And dusty purlieus of the law.
In Memoriam A. H. H. (1850) canto 89.
Cf. 137:18

18 You tell me, doubt is Devil-born.
In Memoriam A. H. H. (1850) canto 96

19 There lives more faith in honest doubt,
Believe me, than in half the creeds.
In Memoriam A. H. H. (1850) canto 96

20 Their meetings made December June,
Their every parting was to die.
In Memoriam A. H. H. (1850) canto 97

21 He seems so near and yet so far.
In Memoriam A. H. H. (1850) canto 97

22 Ring out, wild bells, to the wild sky.
In Memoriam A. H. H. (1850) canto 106

23 Ring out the old, ring in the new,
Ring, happy bells, across the snow:
The year is going, let him go;
Ring out the false, ring in the true.
In Memoriam A. H. H. (1850) canto 106

24 Ring out the want, the care, the sin,
The faithless coldness of the times.
In Memoriam A. H. H. (1850) canto 106

25 Ring out false pride in place and blood,
The civic slander and the spite.
In Memoriam A. H. H. (1850) canto 106

26 Ring out the thousand wars of old,
Ring in the thousand years of peace.
In Memoriam A. H. H. (1850) canto 106

27 Ring in the valiant man and free,
The larger heart, the kindlier hand;
Ring out the darkness of the land;
Ring in the Christ that is to be.
In Memoriam A. H. H. (1850) canto 106

28   Not the schoolboy heat,
The blind hysterics of the Celt.
In Memoriam A. H. H. (1850) canto 109

29 Now fades the last long streak of snow,
Now burgeons every maze of quick
About the flowering squares, and thick
By ashen roots the violets blow.
In Memoriam A. H. H. (1850) canto 115

30 And drowned in yonder living blue
The lark becomes a sightless song.
In Memoriam A. H. H. (1850) canto 115

31   Wearing all that weight
Of learning lightly like a flower.
In Memoriam A. H. H. (1850) canto 131

32 There hath he lain for ages and will lie
Battening upon huge seaworms in his
sleep.
'The Kraken' (1830)

33 Kind hearts are more than coronets,
And simple faith than Norman blood.
'Lady Clara Vere de Vere' (1842) st. 7

34 On either side the river lie
Long fields of barley and of rye,
That clothe the wold and meet the sky;
And through the field the road runs by
To many-towered Camelot.
'The Lady of Shalott' (1832, revised 1842)
pt. 1

35 Willows whiten, aspens quiver,
Little breezes dusk and shiver.
'The Lady of Shalott' (1832, revised 1842)
pt. 1

36 Only reapers, reaping early
In among the bearded barley.
'The Lady of Shalott' (1832, revised 1842)
pt. 1

1 'I am half sick of shadows,' said
  The Lady of Shalott.
  'The Lady of Shalott' (1832, revised 1842)
  pt. 2

2 A red-cross knight for ever kneeled
  To a lady in his shield.
  'The Lady of Shalott' (1832, revised 1842)
  pt. 3

3 She left the web, she left the loom,
  She made three paces through the room,
  She saw the water-lily bloom,
  She saw the helmet and the plume,
  She looked down to Camelot.
  Out flew the web and floated wide;
  The mirror cracked from side to side;
  'The curse is come upon me,' cried
  The Lady of Shalott.
  'The Lady of Shalott' (1832, revised 1842)
  pt. 3

4 Slander, meanest spawn of Hell.
  'The Letters' (1855)

5 Airy, fairy Lilian.
  'Lilian' (1830)

6 In the spring a young man's fancy lightly
  turns to thoughts of love.
  'Locksley Hall' (1842) l. 20

7 He will hold thee, when his passion shall
  have spent its novel force,
  Something better than his dog, a little
  dearer than his horse.
  'Locksley Hall' (1842) l. 49

8 But the jingling of the guinea helps the
  hurt that Honour feels.
  'Locksley Hall' (1842) l. 105

9 Men, my brothers, men the workers, ever
  reaping something new:
  That which they have done but earnest of
  the things that they shall do.
  'Locksley Hall' (1842) l. 117

10 Pilots of the purple twilight, dropping
   down with costly bales.
   'Locksley Hall' (1842) l. 122

11 Heard the heavens fill with shouting, and
   there rained a ghastly dew
   From the nations' airy navies grappling in
   the central blue.
   'Locksley Hall' (1842) l. 123

12 Till the war-drum throbbed no longer, and
   the battle-flags were furled
   In the Parliament of man, the Federation
   of the world.
   'Locksley Hall' (1842) l. 127

13 Science moves, but slowly slowly, creeping
   on from point to point.
   'Locksley Hall' (1842) l. 134

14 Knowledge comes, but wisdom lingers.
   'Locksley Hall' (1842) l. 141

15 I will take some savage woman, she shall
   rear my dusky race.
   'Locksley Hall' (1842) l. 168

16 I the heir of all the ages, in the foremost
   files of time.
   'Locksley Hall' (1842) l. 178

17 Let the great world spin for ever down the
   ringing grooves of change.
   'Locksley Hall' (1842) l. 182

18 Better fifty years of Europe than a cycle of
   Cathay.
   'Locksley Hall' (1842) l. 184

19 Music that gentlier on the spirit lies,
   Than tired eyelids upon tired eyes.
   'The Lotos-Eaters' (1832) Choric Song, st. 1

20   And the clouds are lightly
          curled
   Round their golden houses, girdled with
   the gleaming world.
   'The Lotos-Eaters' (1832) Choric Song, st. 8
   (1842 revision)

21   I saw the flaring atom-streams
   And torrents of her myriad universe,
   Ruining along the illimitable inane.
   'Lucretius' (1868) l. 38

22 Weeded and worn the ancient thatch
   Upon the lonely moated grange.
   She only said, 'My life is dreary,
   He cometh not,' she said;
   She said, 'I am aweary, aweary,
   I would that I were dead!'
   'Mariana' (1830) st. 1. Cf. 288:22

23 Faultily faultless, icily regular, splendidly
   null,
   Dead perfection, no more.
   Maud (1855) pt. 1, sect. 2

24 She came to the village church,
   And sat by a pillar alone;
   An angel watching an urn
   Wept over her, carved in stone.
   Maud (1855) pt. 1, sect. 8

25 The snowy-banded, dilettante,
   Delicate-handed priest.
   Maud (1855) pt. 1, sect. 8

26 One still strong man in a blatant land,
   Whatever they call him, what care I,
   Aristocrat, democrat, autocrat—one
   Who can rule and dare not lie.
   Maud (1855) pt. 1, sect. 10, st. 5

27 Gorgonised me from head to foot
   With a stony British stare.
   Maud (1855) pt. 1, sect. 13, st. 2

28 Come into the garden, Maud,
   For the black bat, night, has flown,
   Come into the garden, Maud,
   I am here at the gate alone;
   And the woodbine spices are wafted
   abroad,
   And the musk of the rose is blown.

   For a breeze of morning moves,
   And the planet of Love is on high,
   Beginning to faint in the light that she
   loves
   On a bed of daffodil sky.
   Maud (1855) pt. 1, sect. 22, st. 1

29 Queen rose of the rosebud garden of girls.
   Maud (1855) pt. 1, sect. 22, st. 9

1 There has fallen a splendid tear
From the passion-flower at the gate.
She is coming, my dove, my dear;
She is coming, my life, my fate;
The red rose cries, 'She is near, she is
near;'
And the white rose weeps, 'She is late.'
Maud (1855) pt. 1, sect. 22, st. 10

2 She is coming, my own, my sweet;
Were it ever so airy a tread,
My heart would hear her and beat,
Were it earth in an earthy bed.
Maud (1855) pt. 1, sect. 22, st. 11

3 O that 'twere possible
After long grief and pain
To find the arms of my true love
Round me once again!
Maud (1855) pt. 2, sect. 4, st. 1

4 But the churchmen fain would kill their
church,
As the churches have killed their Christ.
Maud (1855) pt. 2, sect. 5, st. 2

5 You must wake and call me early, call me
early, mother dear;
Tomorrow 'ill be the happiest time of all
the glad New-year;
Of all the glad New-year, mother, the
maddest merriest day;
For I'm to be Queen o' the May, mother,
I'm to be Queen o' the May.
'The May Queen' (1832)

6 After it, follow it,
Follow The Gleam.
'Merlin and The Gleam' (1889) st. 9

7 God-gifted organ-voice of England,
Milton, a name to resound for ages.
'Milton: Alcaics' (1863)

8 The brooks of Eden mazily murmuring.
'Milton: Alcaics' (1863)

9 Doänt thou marry for munny, but goä
wheer munny is!
'Northern Farmer. New Style' (1869) st. 5

10 The poor in a loomp is bad.
'Northern Farmer. New Style' (1869) st. 12

11 The last great Englishman is low.
'Ode on the Death of the Duke of
Wellington' (1852) st. 3

12 That world-earthquake, Waterloo!
'Ode on the Death of the Duke of
Wellington' (1852) st. 6

13 Who never sold the truth to serve the
hour,
Nor paltered with Eternal God for power.
'Ode on the Death of the Duke of
Wellington' (1852) st. 7

14 I built my soul a lordly pleasure-house,
Wherein at ease for aye to dwell.
'The Palace of Art' (1832) st. 1

15 Vex not thou the poet's mind
With thy shallow wit:
Vex not thou the poet's mind;
For thou canst not fathom it.
'The Poet's Mind' (1830)

16 With prudes for proctors, dowagers for
deans,
And sweet girl-graduates in their golden
hair.
The Princess (1847) 'Prologue' l. 141

17 And blessings on the falling out
That all the more endears,
When we fall out with those we love
And kiss again with tears!
The Princess (1847) pt. 2, song (added 1850)

18 A classic lecture, rich in sentiment,
With scraps of thundrous epic lilted out
By violet-hooded Doctors, elegies
And quoted odes, and jewels five-words-
long,
That on the stretched forefinger of all Time
Sparkle for ever.
The Princess (1847) pt. 2, l. 352

19 Sweet and low, sweet and low,
Wind of the western sea,
Low, low, breathe and blow,
Wind of the western sea!
The Princess (1847) pt. 3, song (added 1850)

20 The splendour falls on castle walls
And snowy summits old in story:
The long light shakes across the lakes,
And the wild cataract leaps in glory.
Blow, bugle, blow, set the wild echoes
flying,
Blow, bugle; answer, echoes, dying, dying,
dying.
The Princess (1847) pt. 4, song (added 1850)

21 O sweet and far from cliff and scar
The horns of Elfland faintly blowing!
The Princess (1847) pt. 4, song (added 1850)

22 Tears, idle tears, I know not what they
mean,
Tears from the depth of some divine
despair
Rise in the heart, and gather to the eyes,
In looking on the happy autumn-fields,
And thinking of the days that are no more.
The Princess (1847) pt. 4, l. 21, song (added
1850)

23 Dear as remembered kisses after death.
The Princess (1847) pt. 4, l. 36, song (added
1850)

24 O tell her, Swallow, thou that knowest
each,
That bright and fierce and fickle is the
South,
And dark and true and tender is the North.
The Princess (1847) pt. 4, l. 78, song (added
1850)

25 Man is the hunter; woman is his game.
The Princess (1847) pt. 5, l. 147

26 Home they brought her warrior dead.
She nor swooned, nor uttered cry:
All her maidens, watching said,
'She must weep or she will die.'
The Princess (1847) pt. 6, song (added 1850)

27 Like summer tempest came her tears.
The Princess (1847) pt. 6, song (added 1850)

1   The woman is so hard
Upon the woman.
The Princess (1847) pt. 6, l. 205

2 I love not hollow cheek or faded eye.
The Princess (1847) pt. 7, song (added 1850)

3 Now sleeps the crimson petal, now the
white;
Nor waves the cypress in the palace walk.
The Princess (1847) pt. 7, l. 161, song (added
1850)

4 Now lies the Earth all Danaë to the stars.
The Princess (1847) pt. 7, l. 167, song (added
1850)

5 Now folds the lily all her sweetness up,
And slips into the bosom of the lake:
So fold thyself, my dearest, thou, and slip
Into my bosom and be lost in me.
The Princess (1847) pt. 7, l. 171, song (added
1850)

6 Come down, O maid, from yonder
mountain height:
What pleasure lives in height?
The Princess (1847) pt. 7, l. 177, song (added
1850)

7 For Love is of the valley, come thou down
And find him.
The Princess (1847) pt. 7, l. 184, song (added
1850)

8 The moan of doves in immemorial elms,
And murmuring of innumerable bees.
The Princess (1847) pt. 7, l. 206, song (added
1850)

9 No little lily-handed baronet he.
The Princess (1847) 'Conclusion' l. 84

10 At Flores in the Azores Sir Richard
Grenville lay.
'The Revenge' (1878) st. 1

11 I should count myself the coward if I left
them, my Lord Howard,
To these Inquisition dogs and the
devildoms of Spain.
'The Revenge' (1878) st. 2

12 Let us bang these dogs of Seville, the
children of the devil,
For I never turned my back upon Don or
devil yet.
'The Revenge' (1878) st. 4

13 Sink me the ship, Master Gunner—sink
her, split her in twain!
Fall into the hands of God, not into the
hands of Spain!
'The Revenge' (1878) st. 11

14 And they praised him to his face with their
courtly foreign grace.
'The Revenge' (1878) st. 13

15 My strength is as the strength of ten,
Because my heart is pure.
'Sir Galahad' (1842)

16 Alone and warming his five wits,
The white owl in the belfry sits.
'Song—The Owl' (1830)

17 The woods decay, the woods decay and fall,
The vapours weep their burthen to the
ground,
Man comes and tills the field and lies
beneath,
And after many a summer dies the swan.
Me only cruel immortality
Consumes: I wither slowly in thine arms,
Here at the quiet limit of the world.
'Tithonus' (1860, revised 1864) l. 1

18 The gods themselves cannot recall their
gifts.
'Tithonus' (1860, revised 1864) l. 49

19 It little profits that an idle king,
By this still hearth, among these barren
crags,
Matched with an agèd wife, I mete and
dole
Unequal laws unto a savage race.
'Ulysses' (1842) l. 1

20   I will drink
Life to the lees: all times I have enjoyed
Greatly, have suffered greatly, both with
those
That loved me, and alone.
'Ulysses' (1842) l. 6

21 Much have I seen and known; cities of men
And manners, climates, councils,
governments,
Myself not least, but honoured of them all;
And drunk delight of battle with my peers,
Far on the ringing plains of windy Troy.
I am a part of all that I have met;
Yet all experience is an arch wherethrough
Gleams that untravelled world, whose
margin fades
For ever and for ever when I move.
How dull it is to pause, to make an end,
To rust unburnished, not to shine in use!
As though to breathe were life.
'Ulysses' (1842) l. 13

22 This is my son, mine own Telemachus.
'Ulysses' (1842) l. 33

23 Death closes all: but something ere the
end,
Some work of noble note, may yet be done,
Not unbecoming men that strove with
gods.
'Ulysses' (1842) l. 51

24 It may be we shall touch the Happy Isles,
And see the great Achilles, whom we knew.
'Ulysses' (1842) l. 63

25   That which we are, we are;
One equal temper of heroic hearts,
Made weak by time and fate, but strong in
will
To strive, to seek, to find, and not to yield.
'Ulysses' (1842) l. 67

26 Every moment dies a man,
Every moment one is born.
'The Vision of Sin' (1842) pt. 4, st. 9. Cf. 23:19

1 A land of settled government,
  A land of just and old renown,
  Where Freedom slowly broadens down
  From precedent to precedent.
  'You ask me, why, though ill at ease' (1842)
  st. 3

2 A louse in the locks of literature.
  Of Churton Collins, in E. Charteris *Life and
  Letters of Sir Edmund Gosse* (1931) ch. 14

Terence *c.*190–159 BC

3 *Hinc illae lacrimae.*
  Hence those tears.
  Andria l. 126

4 I am a man, I count nothing human
  foreign to me.
  Heauton Timorumenos l. 77

5 *Fortis fortuna adiuvat.*
  Fortune assists the brave.
  Phormio l. 203. Cf. 339:20

6 There are as many opinions as there are
  people: each has his own correct way.
  Phormio l. 454

St Teresa of Ávila 1512–82

7 O Lord, to what a state dost Thou bring
  those who love Thee!
  Interior Castle Mansion 6, ch. 11, para. 6 (tr.
  Benedictines of Stanbrook, 1921)

Tertullian AD *c.*160–*c.*225

8 As often as we are mown down by you, the
  more we grow in numbers; the blood of
  Christians is the seed.
  Apologeticus ch. 50, sect. 13 (traditionally 'The
  blood of the martyrs is the seed of the
  Church')

9 *Certum est quia impossibile est.*
  It is certain because it is impossible.
  De Carne Christi ch. 5 (often quoted '*Credo quia
  impossibile* [I believe because it is
  impossible]')

A. S. J. Tessimond 1902–62

10 Cats, no less liquid than their shadows,
   Offer no angles to the wind.
   Cats (1934) p. 20

William Makepeace Thackeray 1811–63

11 'Tis strange what a man may do, and a
   woman yet think him an angel.
   The History of Henry Esmond (1852) bk. 1, ch. 7

12 The *Pall Mall Gazette* is written by
   gentlemen for gentlemen.
   Pendennis (1848–50) ch. 32

13 Business first; pleasure afterwards.
   The Rose and the Ring (1855) ch. 1

14 A woman with fair opportunities and
   without a positive hump, may marry
   whom she likes.
   Vanity Fair (1847–8) ch. 4

15 Whenever he met a great man he grovelled
   before him, and my-lorded him as only a
   free-born Briton can do.
   Vanity Fair (1847–8) ch. 13

16 If a man's character is to be abused, say
   what you will, there's nobody like a
   relation to do the business.
   Vanity Fair (1847–8) ch. 19

17 Them's my sentiments!
   Vanity Fair (1847–8) ch. 21 (Fred Bullock)

18 Darkness came down on the field and city:
   and Amelia was praying for George, who
   was lying on his face, dead, with a bullet
   through his heart.
   Vanity Fair (1847–8) ch. 32

19 Nothing like blood, sir, in hosses, dawgs,
   and men.
   Vanity Fair (1847–8) ch. 35 (James Crawley)

20 How to live well on nothing a year.
   Vanity Fair (1847–8) ch. 36 (title)

21 I think I could be a good woman if I had
   five thousand a year.
   Vanity Fair (1847–8) ch. 36

22 Come, children, let us shut up the box and
   the puppets, for our play is played out.
   Vanity Fair (1847–8) ch. 67

23 Werther had a love for Charlotte
   Such as words could never utter;
   Would you know how first he met her?
   She was cutting bread and butter.
   'Sorrows of Werther' (1855)

Margaret Thatcher 1925–

24 We must try to find ways to starve the
   terrorist and the hijacker of the oxygen of
   publicity on which they depend.
   Speech, 15 July 1985, in *The Times* 16 July
   1985

25 There is no such thing as Society. There
   are individual men and women, and there
   are families.
   In *Woman's Own* 31 October 1987

26 We have become a grandmother.
   In *The Times* 4 March 1989

William Roscoe Thayer 1859–1923

27 Log-cabin to White House.
   Title of biography (1910) of James Garfield
   (1831–81)

Thomas à Kempis *c.*1380–1471

28 *O quam cito transit gloria mundi.*
   Oh how quickly the glory of the world
   passes away!
   De Imitatione Christi bk. 1, ch. 3, sect. 6.
   Cf. 13:22

1 For man proposes, but God disposes.
 De Imitatione Christi bk. 1, ch. 19, sect. 2

2 Would that we had spent one whole day well in this world!
 De Imitatione Christi bk. 1, ch. 23, sect. 2

St Thomas Aquinas *c.*1225–74

3 *Pange, lingua, gloriosi*
 Corporis mysterium.
 Now, my tongue, the mystery telling
 Of the glorious Body sing.
 'Pange Lingua Gloriosi' (Corpus Christi hymn, tr. J. M. Neale, E. Caswall, and others)

4 *Tantum ergo sacramentum*
 Veneremur cernui;
 Et antiquum documentum
 Novo cedat ritui.
 Therefore we, before him bending,
 This great Sacrament revere;
 Types and shadows have their ending,
 For the newer rite is here.
 'Pange Lingua Gloriosi'

Brandon Thomas 1856–1914

5 I'm Charley's aunt from Brazil—where the nuts come from.
 Charley's Aunt (1892) act 1

Dylan Thomas 1914–53

6 Though lovers be lost love shall not;
 And death shall have no dominion.
 'And death shall have no dominion' (1936).
 Cf. 54:35

7 Do not go gentle into that good night,
 Old age should burn and rave at close of day;
 Rage, rage against the dying of the light.
 'Do Not Go Gentle into that Good Night' (1952)

8 Now as I was young and easy under the apple boughs
 About the lilting house and happy as the grass was green.
 'Fern Hill' (1946)

9 Oh as I was young and easy in the mercy of his means,
 Time held me green and dying
 Though I sang in my chains like the sea.
 'Fern Hill' (1946)

10 The force that through the green fuse drives the flower
 Drives my green age.
 'The force that through the green fuse' (1934)

11 The hand that signed the treaty bred a fever,
 And famine grew, and locusts came;
 Great is the hand that holds dominion over Man by a scribbled name.
 'The hand that signed the paper felled a city' (1936)

12 Light breaks where no sun shines;
 Where no sea runs, the waters of the heart
 Push in their tides.
 'Light breaks where no sun shines' (1934)

13 It was my thirtieth year to heaven.
 'Poem in October' (1946)

14 There could I marvel
 My birthday
 Away but the weather turned around.
 'Poem in October' (1946)

15 After the first death, there is no other.
 'A Refusal to Mourn the Death, by Fire, of a Child in London' (1946)

16 To begin at the beginning: It is spring, moonless night in the small town, starless and bible-black.
 Under Milk Wood (1954) p. 1

17 Chasing the naughty couples down the grassgreen gooseberried double bed of the wood.
 Under Milk Wood (1954) p. 7

18 Before you let the sun in, mind it wipes its shoes.
 Under Milk Wood (1954) p. 16

19 Oh, isn't life a terrible thing, thank God?
 Under Milk Wood (1954) p. 30

20 The land of my fathers. My fathers can have it.
 Of Wales, in *Adam* December 1953

Edward Thomas 1878–1917

21 Yes; I remember Adlestrop—
 The name, because one afternoon
 Of heat the express-train drew up there
 Unwontedly. It was late June.
 'Adlestrop' (1917)

22 The past is the only dead thing that smells sweet.
 'Early one morning in May I set out' (1917)

23 If I should ever by chance grow rich
 I'll buy Codham, Cockridden, and Childerditch,
 Roses, Pyrgo, and Lapwater,
 And let them all to my elder daughter.
 'Household Poems: Bronwen' (1917)

24 I have come to the borders of sleep,
 The unfathomable deep
 Forest where all must lose
 Their way.
 'Lights Out' (1917)

25 I see and hear nothing;
 Yet seem, too, to be listening, lying in wait
 For what I should, yet never can, remember.
 'Old Man' (1917)

26 Out in the dark over the snow
 The fallow fawns invisible go.
 'Out in the dark' (1917)

Elizabeth Thomas 1675–1731

1 From marrying in haste, and repenting at
    leisure;
  Not liking the person, yet liking his
    treasure:
  Libera nos.
    'A New Litany, occasioned by an invitation to
    a wedding' (1722). Cf. 106:13

Irene Thomas

2 Protestant women may take the pill.
  Roman Catholic women must keep taking
    The Tablet.
    In *Guardian* 28 December 1990, p. 27

R. S. Thomas 1913–

3   Doctors in verse
  Being scarce now, most poets
  Are their own patients.
    'The Cure' (1958)

4 There is no love
  For such, only a willed
    gentleness.
    'They' (1968)

5 There is no present in Wales,
  And no future;
  There is only the past,
  Brittle with relics …
  And an impotent people,
  Sick with inbreeding,
  Worrying the carcase of an old song.
    'Welsh Landscape' (1955)

Francis Thompson 1859–1907

6 As the run-stealers flicker to and fro,
  To and fro:—
  O my Hornby and my Barlow long ago!
    'At Lord's' (1913)

7 Nothing begins, and nothing ends,
  That is not paid with moan;
  For we are born in other's pain,
  And perish in our own.
    'Daisy' (1913)

8 I fled Him, down the nights and down the
    days;
  I fled Him, down the arches of the years;
  I fled Him, down the labyrinthine ways
  Of my own mind; and in the mist of tears
  I hid from Him, and under running
    laughter.
    'The Hound of Heaven' (1913) pt. 1

9 All things betray thee, who betrayest Me.
    'The Hound of Heaven' (1913) pt. 1

10 I said to Dawn: Be sudden—to Eve:
    Be soon.
    'The Hound of Heaven' (1913) pt. 2

11 Such is: what is to be?
  The pulp so bitter, how shall taste the
    rind?
    'The Hound of Heaven' (1913) pt. 4

12 Lo, all things fly thee, for thou fliest Me!
    'The Hound of Heaven' (1913) pt. 5

13 There is no expeditious road
  To pack and label men for God,
  And save them by the barrel-load.
  Some may perchance, with strange
    surprise,
  Have blundered into Paradise.
    'A Judgement in Heaven' (1913) epilogue

14 O world invisible, we view thee,
  O world intangible, we touch thee,
  O world unknowable, we know thee,
  Inapprehensible, we clutch thee!
    'The Kingdom of God' (1913)

15 'Tis ye, 'tis your estrangèd faces,
  That miss the many-splendoured thing.
    'The Kingdom of God' (1913)

16   And upon thy so sore loss
  Shall shine the traffic of Jacob's ladder
  Pitched betwixt Heaven and Charing Cross.
    'The Kingdom of God' (1913)

17 And lo, Christ walking on the water
  Not of Gennesareth, but Thames!
    'The Kingdom of God' (1913)

18 Look for me in the nurseries of heaven.
    'To My Godchild Francis M.W.M.' (1913)

19 Insculped and embossed,
  With His hammer of wind,
  And His graver of frost.
    'To a Snowflake' (1913)

James Thomson 1700–48

20 When Britain first, at heaven's command,
  Arose from out the azure main,
  This was the charter of the land,
  And guardian angels sung this strain:
  'Rule, Britannia, rule the waves;
  Britons never will be slaves.'
    Alfred: a Masque (1740) act 2

21 A little round, fat, oily man of God.
    The Castle of Indolence (1748) canto 1, st. 69

22 Delightful task! to rear the tender thought,
  To teach the young idea how to shoot.
    The Seasons (1746) 'Spring' l. 1152

23 An elegant sufficiency, content,
  Retirement, rural quiet, friendship, books.
    The Seasons (1746) 'Spring' l. 1161

24 Sighed and looked unutterable things.
    The Seasons (1746) 'Summer' l. 1188

25   For loveliness
  Needs not the foreign aid of ornament,
  But is when unadorned adorned the most.
    The Seasons (1746) 'Autumn' l. 204

26 Welcome, kindred glooms!
  Congenial horrors, hail!
    The Seasons (1746) 'Winter' l. 5

27 Studious let me sit,
  And hold high converse with the mighty
    dead.
    The Seasons (1746) 'Winter' l. 431

James Thomson 1834–82

1 The City is of Night; perchance of Death,
But certainly of Night.
  'The City of Dreadful Night' (written 1870–3)

2 As we rush, as we rush in the train,
The trees and the houses go wheeling
back,
But the starry heavens above that plain
Come flying on our track.
  'Sunday at Hampstead' (written 1863–5)
  st. 10

3 Give a man a horse he can ride,
Give a man a boat he can sail.
  'Sunday up the River' (written 1865) st. 15

Roy Thomson (Lord Thomson of Fleet) 1894–1976

4 Like having your own licence to print
money.
  On the profitability of commercial television
  in Britain; in R. Braddon *Roy Thomson* (1965)
  ch. 32

Henry David Thoreau 1817–62

5 Some circumstantial evidence is very
strong, as when you find a trout in the
milk.
  Journal 11 November 1850, in *Writings* (1906
  ed.) vol. 8, p. 94

6 Not that the story need be long, but it will
take a long while to make it short.
  Letter to Harrison Blake, 16 November 1857,
  in *Writings* (1906 ed.) vol. 6, p. 320. Cf. 245:24

7 I have travelled a good deal in Concord.
  Walden (1854) 'Economy' in *Writings* (1906
  ed.) vol. 2, p. 4

8 As if you could kill time without injuring
eternity.
  Walden (1854) 'Economy' in *Writings* (1906
  ed.) vol. 2, p. 8

9 The mass of men lead lives of quiet
desperation.
  Walden (1854) 'Economy' in *Writings* (1906
  ed.) vol. 2, p. 8

10 The three-o'-clock in the morning courage,
which Bonaparte thought was the rarest.
  Walden (1854) 'Sounds' in *Writings* (1906 ed.)
  vol. 2, p. 131. Cf. 140:22, 237:4

11 Our life is frittered away by detail . . .
Simplify, simplify.
  Walden (1854) 'Where I lived, and what I
  lived for' in *Writings* (1906 ed.) vol. 2, p. 101

12 If a man does not keep pace with his
companions, perhaps it is because he hears
a different drummer. Let him step to the
music which he hears, however measured
or far away.
  Walden (1854) 'Conclusion' in *Writings* (1906
  ed.) vol. 2, p. 358

Jeremy Thorpe 1929–

13 Greater love hath no man than this, that
he lay down his friends for his life.
  On Harold Macmillan sacking seven of his
  Cabinet on 13 July 1962; in D. E. Butler and
  A. King *General Election of 1964* (1965) ch. 1

James Thurber 1894–1961

14 Her own mother lived the latter years of
her life in the horrible suspicion that
electricity was dripping invisibly all over
the house.
  My Life and Hard Times (1933) ch. 2

15 Early to rise and early to bed makes a male
healthy and wealthy and dead.
  'The Shrike and the Chipmunks' in *New
  Yorker* 18 February 1939

16 The war between men and women.
  Cartoon series title in *New Yorker*
  20 January–28 April 1934

17 It's a naïve domestic Burgundy without any
breeding, but I think you'll be amused by
its presumption.
  Cartoon caption in *New Yorker* 27 March 1937

18 Well, if I called the wrong number, why did
you answer the phone?
  Cartoon caption in *New Yorker* 5 June 1937

Edward, 1st Baron Thurlow 1731–1806

19 Corporations have neither bodies to be
punished, nor souls to be condemned, they
therefore do as they like.
  In J. Poynder *Literary Extracts* (1844) vol. 1,
  p. 268 (usually quoted 'Did you ever expect a
  corporation to have a conscience, when it
  has no soul to be damned, and no body to be
  kicked?'). Cf. 103:9

Thomas Tickell 1686–1740

20 There taught us how to live; and (oh! too
high
The price for knowledge) taught us how to
die.
  'To the Earl of Warwick. On the Death of Mr
  Addison' (1721) l. 81

Paul Tillich 1886–1965

21 Neurosis is the way of avoiding non-being
by avoiding being.
  The Courage To Be (1952) pt. 2, ch. 3

Emperor Titus AD 39–81

22 Friends, I have lost a day.
  On reflecting that he had done nothing to
  help anybody all day; in Suetonius *Lives of the
  Caesars* 'Titus' ch. 8, sect. 1

Alexis de Tocqueville 1805–59

1 History is a gallery of pictures in which there are few originals and many copies.

L'Ancien régime (1856, ed. J. P. Mayer, 1951) p. 133 (tr. M. W. Patterson, 1933)

2 Of all nations, those submit to civilization with the most difficulty which habitually live by the chase.

De la Démocratie en Amérique (1835–40, ed. J. P. Mayer, 1951) vol. 1, p. 342 (tr. H. Reeve, 1841)

3 What is understood by republican government in the United States is the slow and quiet action of society upon itself.

De la Démocratie en Amérique (1835–40, ed. J. P. Mayer, 1951) vol. 1, p. 412 (tr. H. Reeve, 1841)

4 The French want no-one to be their *superior*. The English want *inferiors*. The Frenchman constantly raises his eyes above him with anxiety. The Englishman lowers his beneath him with satisfaction.

Voyage en Angleterre et en Irlande de 1835 (ed. J. P. Mayer, 1958) 8 May 1835

5 It is from the midst of this putrid sewer that the greatest river of human industry springs up and carries fertility to the whole world. From this foul drain pure gold flows forth.

Voyage en Angleterre et en Irlande de 1835 (ed. J. P. Mayer, 1958) 2 July 1835 (of Manchester)

Alvin Toffler 1928–

6 Future shock.

Title of book (1970); defined by Toffler as 'the dizzying disorientation brought on by the premature arrival of the future' in *Horizon* Summer 1965

7 Culture shock is what happens when a traveller suddenly finds himself in a place where yes may mean no, where a 'fixed price' is negotiable, where to be kept waiting in an outer office is no cause for insult, where laughter may signify anger.

Future Shock (1970) ch. 1 (the term 'culture shock' appears to have been already in use by the 1940s)

J. R. R. Tolkien 1892–1973

8 In a hole in the ground there lived a hobbit.

The Hobbit (1937) ch. 1

9 Never laugh at live dragons.

The Hobbit (1937) ch. 12

10 One Ring to rule them all, One Ring to find them
One Ring to bring them all and in the darkness bind them.

The Lord of the Rings pt. 1 *The Fellowship of the Ring* (1954) epigraph

Leo Tolstoy 1828–1910

11 All happy families resemble one another, but each unhappy family is unhappy in its own way.

Anna Karenina (1875–7) pt. 1, ch. 1 (tr. A. and L. Maude)

12 Our body is a machine for living. It is organized for that, it is its nature. Let life go on in it unhindered and let it defend itself.

War and Peace (1865–9) bk. 10, ch. 29 (tr. A. and L. Maude). Cf. 204:3

13 I sit on a man's back, choking him and making him carry me, and yet assure myself and others that I am very sorry for him and wish to ease his lot by all possible means—except by getting off his back.

What Then Must We Do? (1886) ch. 16 (tr. A. Maude)

A. M. Toplady 1740–78

14 Rock of Ages, cleft for me,
Let me hide myself in Thee;
Let the water and the blood,
From Thy riven side which flowed,
Be of sin the double cure,
Cleanse me from its guilt and power.

'Rock of Ages, cleft for me' (1776 hymn)

Cyril Tourneur

See THOMAS MIDDLETON

A. Toussenel 1803–85

15 The more one gets to know of men, the more one values dogs.

L'Esprit des bêtes (1847) ch. 3 (attributed to Mme Roland in the form 'The more I see of men, the more I like dogs')

Pete Townshend 1945–

16 Hope I die before I get old.

'My Generation' (1965 song)

Thomas Traherne *c.*1637–74

17 An empty book is like an infant's soul, in which anything may be written. It is capable of all things, but containeth nothing.

Centuries of Meditations 'First Century' opening words

18 The corn was orient and immortal wheat, which never should be reaped, nor was ever sown.

Centuries of Meditations 'Third Century' sect. 3

19 O what venerable creatures did the aged seem! Immortal cherubims! And young men glittering and sparkling angels, and maids strange seraphic pieces of life and beauty!

Centuries of Meditations 'Third Century' sect. 3

1 I within did flow
With seas of life, like wine.
I nothing in this world did know,
But 'twas divine!
   'Wonder'

Henry Duff Traill 1842–1900

2 Look in my face. My name is Used-to-was;
I am also called Played-out and Done-to-
death,
And It-will-wash-no-more.
   'After Dilettante Concetti' (i.e. Dante Gabriel
   Rossetti) st. 8. Cf. 263:8

Joseph Trapp 1679–1747

3 The King, observing with judicious eyes
The state of both his universities,
To Oxford sent a troop of horse, and why?
That learned body wanted loyalty;
To Cambridge books, as very well
   discerning
How much that loyal body wanted
   learning.
   Lines written on George I's donation of the
   Bishop of Ely's library to Cambridge
   University; in J. Nichols *Literary Anecdotes*
   (1812–16) vol. 3, p. 330. Cf. 74:25

Merle Travis 1917–83

4 Sixteen tons, what do you get?
Another day older and deeper in debt.
Say brother, don't you call me 'cause I
   can't go
I owe my soul to the company store.
   'Sixteen Tons' (1947 song)

Sir Herbert Beerbohm Tree
1852–1917

5 He is an old bore. Even the grave yawns for
him.
   Of Israel Zangwill, in Max Beerbohm *Herbert
   Beerbohm Tree* (1920) appendix 4

Herbert Trench 1865–1923

6 Come, let us make love deathless.
   Title of poem (1901)

G. M. Trevelyan 1876–1962

7 Disinterested intellectual curiosity is the
life-blood of real civilization.
   English Social History (1942) introduction

8 If the French noblesse had been capable of
playing cricket with their peasants, their
chateaux would never have been burnt.
   English Social History (1942) ch. 8

9 [Education] has produced a vast population
able to read but unable to distinguish what
is worth reading, an easy prey to
sensations and cheap appeals.
   English Social History (1942) ch. 18

Calvin Trillin

10 The shelf life of the modern hardback
writer is somewhere between the milk and
the yoghurt.
   In *Sunday Times* 9 June 1991 (attributed)

Tommy Trinder 1909–89

11 Overpaid, overfed, oversexed, and over
here.
   Of American troops in Britain during the
   Second World War (associated with Trinder,
   but probably not original)

Anthony Trollope 1815–82

12 Three hours a day will produce as much as
a man ought to write.
   Autobiography (1883) ch. 15

13 Those who have courage to love should
have courage to suffer.
   The Bertrams (1859) ch. 27

14 There is no road to wealth so easy and
respectable as that of matrimony.
   Doctor Thorne (1858) ch. 16

15 It's dogged as does it. It ain't thinking
about it.
   The Last Chronicle of Barset (1867) ch. 61 (Giles
   Hoggett)

16 It is because we put up with bad things
that hotel-keepers continue to give them to
us.
   Orley Farm (1862) ch. 18

17 As for conceit, what man will do any good
who is not conceited? Nobody holds a good
opinion of a man who has a low opinion of
himself.
   Orley Farm (1862) ch. 22

18 She knew how to allure by denying, and to
make the gift rich by delaying it.
   Phineas Finn (1869) ch. 57

19 I doubt whether any girl would be satisfied
with her lover's mind if she knew the
whole of it.
   The Small House at Allington (1864) ch. 4

20 The tenth Muse, who now governs the
periodical press.
   The Warden (1855) ch. 14

21 Love is like any other luxury. You have no
right to it unless you can afford it.
   The Way We Live Now (1875) ch. 84

Leon Trotsky 1879–1940

22 Old age is the most unexpected of all
things that happen to a man.
   Diary in Exile (1959) 8 May 1935

23 Civilization has made the peasantry its
pack animal. The bourgeoisie in the long
run only changed the form of the pack.
   History of the Russian Revolution (1933) vol. 3,
   ch. 1

1 You [the Mensheviks] are pitiful isolated individuals; you are bankrupts; your role is played out. Go where you belong from now on—into the dustbin of history!
History of the Russian Revolution (1933) vol. 3, ch. 10

2 Where force is necessary, there it must be applied boldly, decisively and completely. But one must know the limitations of force; one must know when to blend force with a manoeuvre, a blow with an agreement.
What Next? (1932) ch. 14

Harry S. Truman 1884–1972

3 Wherever you have an efficient government you have a dictatorship.
Lecture at Columbia University, 28 April 1959, in *Truman Speaks* (1960) p. 51

4 A statesman is a politician who's been dead 10 or 15 years.
In *New York World Telegram and Sun* 12 April 1958

5 It's a recession when your neighbour loses his job; it's a depression when you lose yours.
In *Observer* 13 April 1958

6 The buck stops here.
Unattributed motto on Truman's desk
See also HARRY VAUGHAN

Barbara W. Tuchman 1912–89

7 Dead battles, like dead generals, hold the military mind in their dead grip and Germans, no less than other peoples, prepare for the last war.
August 1914 (1962) ch. 2

8 For one August in its history Paris was French—and silent.
August 1914 (1962) ch. 20

Sophie Tucker 1884–1966

9 From birth to 18 a girl needs good parents. From 18 to 35, she needs good looks. From 35 to 55, good personality. From 55 on, she needs good cash.
In M. Freedland *Sophie* (1978) p. 214

Martin Tupper 1810–89

10 A good book is the best of friends, the same to-day and for ever.
Proverbial Philosophy Series I (1838) 'Of Reading'

Ivan Turgenev 1818–83

11 Superfluous, superfluous … A supernumerary—that's all. Nature, obviously, hadn't counted on my showing up and consequently treated me as an unexpected and uninvited guest.
Diary of a Superfluous Man (1850) 23 March (tr. F. Reeve)

12 Nature is not a temple, but a workshop, and man's the workman in it.
Fathers and Sons (1862) ch. 9 (tr. R. Edmonds)

13 I share no one's ideas. I have my own.
Fathers and Sons (1862) ch. 13 (tr. R. Edmonds)

14 Just try and set death aside. It sets you aside, and that's the end of it!
Fathers and Sons (1862) ch. 27 (tr. R. Edmonds)

15 Whatever a man prays for, he prays for a miracle. Every prayer reduces itself to this: Great God, grant that twice two be not four.
Poems in Prose (1881) 'Prayer'

A. R. J. Turgot 1727–81

16 He snatched the lightning shaft from heaven, and the sceptre from tyrants.
Inscription for a bust of Benjamin Franklin, inventor of the lightning conductor

Walter James Redfern Turner 1889–1946

17 When I was but thirteen or so
I went into a golden land,
Chimborazo, Cotopaxi
Took me by the hand.
'Romance' (1916)

Mark Twain 1835–1910

18 There was things which he stretched, but mainly he told the truth.
The Adventures of Huckleberry Finn (1884) ch. 1

19 'Pilgrim's Progress', about a man that left his family it didn't say why … The statements was interesting, but tough.
The Adventures of Huckleberry Finn (1884) ch. 17

20 All kings is mostly rapscallions.
The Adventures of Huckleberry Finn (1884) ch. 23

21 Hain't we got all the fools in town on our side? and ain't that a big enough majority in any town?
The Adventures of Huckleberry Finn (1884) ch. 26

22 Soap and education are not as sudden as a massacre, but they are more deadly in the long run.
A Curious Dream (1872) 'Facts concerning the Recent Resignation'

23 Truth is the most valuable thing we have. Let us economize it.
Following the Equator (1897) ch. 7. Cf. 16:6

24 Man is the Only Animal that Blushes. Or needs to.
Following the Equator (1897) ch. 27

25 It takes your enemy and your friend, working together, to hurt you to the heart: the one to slander you and the other to get the news to you.
Following the Equator (1897) ch. 45

1 They spell it Vinci and pronounce it
Vinchy; foreigners always spell better than
they pronounce.
   The Innocents Abroad (1869) ch. 19

2 Lump the whole thing! say that the Creator
made Italy from designs by Michael
Angelo!
   The Innocents Abroad (1869) ch. 27. Cf. 336:17

3 Familiarity breeds contempt—and children.
   Notebooks (1935) p. 237

4 Cauliflower is nothing but cabbage with
a college education.
   Pudd'nhead Wilson (1894) ch. 5

5 When angry, count four; when very angry,
swear.
   Pudd'nhead Wilson (1894) ch. 10

6 As to the Adjective: when in doubt, strike
it out.
   Pudd'nhead Wilson (1894) ch. 11

7 The report of my death was an
exaggeration.
   New York Journal 2 June 1897 (usually quoted
   'Reports of my death have been greatly
   exaggerated')

Kenneth Tynan 1927–80

8 A critic is a man who knows the way but
can't drive the car.
   In *New York Times Magazine* 9 January 1966,
   p. 27

9 A neurosis is a secret you don't know
you're keeping.
   In Kathleen Tynan *Life of Kenneth Tynan* (1987)
   ch. 19

Ulpian d. 228

10 *Nulla iniuria est, quae in volentem fiat.*
No injustice is done to someone who
wants that thing done.
   In *Corpus Iuris Civilis* Digests bk. 47, ch. 10,
   sect. 1, subsect. 5 (usually quoted '*Volenti non
   fit iniuria*')

Miguel de Unamuno 1864–1937

11 *La vida es duda,*
y la fe sin la duda es sólo muerte.
Life is doubt,
And faith without doubt is nothing but
death.
   Poesías (1907) 'Salmo II'

John Updike 1932–

12 A soggy little island huffing and puffing to
keep up with Western Europe.
   Of England, in *Picked Up Pieces* (1976) 'London
   Life' (written 1969)

13 America is a land whose centre is nowhere;
England one whose centre is everywhere.
   Picked Up Pieces (1976) 'London Life' (written
   1969)

14 America is a vast conspiracy to make you
happy.
   Problems (1980) 'How to love America and
   Leave it at the Same Time'

Sir Peter Ustinov 1921–

15 Laughter ... the most civilized music in
the world.
   Dear Me (1977) ch. 3

16 I do not believe that friends are necessarily
the people you like best, they are merely
the people who got there first.
   Dear Me (1977) ch. 5. Cf. 1:12

17 If Botticelli were alive today he'd be
working for *Vogue*.
   In *Observer* 21 October 1962 'Sayings of the
   Week'. Cf. 336:2

18 At the age of four with paper hats and
wooden swords we're all Generals. Only
some of us never grow out of it.
   Romanoff and Juliet (1956) act 1

19 A diplomat these days is nothing but
a head-waiter who's allowed to sit down
occasionally.
   Romanoff and Juliet (1956) act 1

Paul Valéry 1871–1945

20 Science means simply the aggregate of all
the recipes that are always successful. The
rest is literature.
   Moralités (1932) p. 41. Cf. 337:20

21 God created man and, finding him not
sufficiently alone, gave him a companion to
make him feel his solitude more keenly.
   Tel Quel 1 (1941) 'Moralités'

22 Politics is the art of preventing people
from taking part in affairs which properly
concern them.
   Tel Quel 2 (1943) 'Rhumbs'

Sir John Vanbrugh 1664–1726

23 BELINDA: Ay, but you know we must return
good for evil.
   LADY BRUTE: That may be a mistake in the
   translation.
   The Provoked Wife (1697) act 1, sc. 1

24 When once a woman has given you her
heart, you can never get rid of the rest of
her body.
   The Relapse (1696) act 3, sc. 1

Vivian van Damm c.1889–1960

25 We never closed.
   Of the Windmill Theatre, London, during the
   Second World War; in *Tonight and Every Night*
   (1952) ch. 18

William Henry Vanderbilt
1821–85

1 The public be damned!
   On consulting the public about luxury
   trains; in letter from A. W. Cole to *New York
   Times* 25 August 1918

Harry Vaughan

2 If you can't stand the heat, get out of the
   kitchen.
   In *Time* 28 April 1952 (associated with Harry
   S. Truman, but attributed by him to
   Vaughan, his 'military jester')

Henry Vaughan 1622–95

3 Man is the shuttle, to whose winding quest
   And passage through these looms
   God ordered motion, but ordained no rest.
   Silex Scintillans (1650–5) 'Man'

4 Wise Nicodemus saw such light
   As made him know his God by night.
   Silex Scintillans (1650–5) 'The Night'

5 Dear Night! this world's defeat;
   The stop to busy fools; care's check and
   curb.
   Silex Scintillans (1650–5) 'The Night'

6 My soul, there is a country
   Far beyond the stars,
   Where stands a wingèd sentry
   All skilful in the wars;
   There, above noise and danger,
   Sweet Peace is crowned with smiles,
   And One born in a manger
   Commands the beauteous files.
   Silex Scintillans (1650–5) 'Peace'

7 Happy those early days, when I
   Shined in my angel-infancy.
   Before I understood this place
   Appointed for my second race,
   Or taught my soul to fancy aught
   But a white, celestial thought.
   Silex Scintillans (1650–5) 'The Retreat'

8 And in those weaker glories spy
   Some shadows of eternity.
   Silex Scintillans (1650–5) 'The Retreat'

9 But felt through all this fleshly dress
   Bright shoots of everlastingness.
   Silex Scintillans (1650–5) 'The Retreat'

10 Some men a forward motion love,
   But I by backward steps would move,
   And when this dust falls to the urn,
   In that state I came, return.
   Silex Scintillans (1650–5) 'The Retreat'

11 They are all gone into the world of light,
   And I alone sit lingering here.
   Silex Scintillans (1650–5) 'They are all gone'

12 Dear, beauteous death! the jewel of the
   just,
   Shining nowhere but in the dark.
   Silex Scintillans (1650–5) 'They are all gone'

13 Sure thou didst flourish once! and many
   springs,
   Many bright mornings, much dew, many
   showers
   Passed o'er thy head.
   Silex Scintillans (1650–5) 'The Timber'

14 I saw Eternity the other night,
   Like a great ring of pure and endless light,
   All calm, as it was bright;
   And round beneath it, Time in hours, days,
   years,
   Driv'n by the spheres
   Like a vast shadow moved; in which the
   world
   And all her train were hurled.
   Silex Scintillans (1650–5) 'The World'

Thomas, Lord Vaux 1510–56

15 For age with stealing steps
   Hath clawed me with his clutch.
   'The Aged Lover Renounceth Love' (1557)

Thorstein Veblen 1857–1929

16 Conspicuous consumption of valuable
   goods is a means of reputability to the
   gentleman of leisure.
   Theory of the Leisure Class (1899) ch. 4

17 Conspicuous leisure and consumption . . .
   In the one case it is a waste of time and
   effort, in the other it is a waste of goods.
   Theory of the Leisure Class (1899) ch. 4

Vegetius 4th century

18 *Qui desiderat pacem, praeparet bellum.*
   Let him who desires peace, prepare for
   war.
   Epitoma Rei Militaris bk. 3, prologue (usually
   quoted '*Si vis pacem, para bellum* [If you want
   peace, prepare for war]'). Cf. 7:16, 15:14

Pierre Vergniaud 1753–93

19 There was reason to fear that the
   Revolution, like Saturn, might devour in
   turn each one of her children.
   In A. de Lamartine *Histoire des Girondins*
   (1847) bk. 38, ch. 20

Paul Verlaine 1844–96

20 *Et tout le reste est littérature.*
   All the rest is mere fine writing.
   'Art poétique' (1882). Cf. 336:20

21 *Les sanglots longs*
   Des violons
   De l'automne
   Blessent mon coeur
   D'une langueur
   Monotone.
   The drawn-out sobs of autumn's violins
   wound my heart with a monotonous
   languor.
   'Chanson d'Automne' (1866)

1 *Et, Ô ces voix d'enfants chantants dans la coupole!*

And oh those children's voices, singing beneath the dome!
'Parsifal' A Jules Tellier (1886)

2 *Il pleure dans mon coeur
Comme il pleut sur la ville.*

Tears are shed in my heart like the rain on the town.
Romances sans paroles (1874) 'Ariettes oubliées' no. 3

Emperor Vespasian AD 9–79

3 *Pecunia non olet.*

Money has no smell.
Traditional summary of Suetonius *Lives of the Caesars* 'Vespasian' sect. 23, subsect. 3 (quashing an objection to tax on public lavatories)

4 Woe is me, I think I am becoming a god.
When fatally ill; in Suetonius *Lives of the Caesars* 'Vespasian' sect. 23, subsect. 4

Queen Victoria 1819–1901

5 The danger to the country, to Europe, to her vast Empire, which is involved in having all these great interests entrusted to the shaking hand of an old, wild, and incomprehensible man of 82, is very great!
On Gladstone's last appointment as Prime Minister; letter to Lord Lansdowne, 12 August 1892, in T. Wodehouse Legh *Lord Lansdowne* (1929) p. 100

6 We are not interested in the possibilities of defeat; they do not exist.
On the Boer War during 'Black Week', December 1899; in Lady Gwendolen Cecil *Life of Robert, Marquis of Salisbury* (1931) vol. 3, ch. 6

7 We are not amused.
Attributed, in Caroline Holland *Notebooks of a Spinster Lady* (1919) ch. 21 (2 January 1900)

8 I will be good.
On being shown a chart of the line of succession, 11 March 1830; in Sir Theodore Martin *The Prince Consort* (1875) vol. 1, ch. 2

9 He speaks to Me as if I was a public meeting.
Of Gladstone, in G. W. E. Russell *Collections and Recollections* (1898) ch. 14

10 Dirty, dark, and undevotional.
Of St Paul's Cathedral; attributed in this form, but recorded in her Journal, 27 February 1872, as 'so cold, dreary and dingy'. See G. E. Buckle (ed.) *Letters of Queen Victoria: 2nd Series* vol. 2 (1926)

Gore Vidal 1925–

11 [Commercialism is] doing well that which should not be done at all.
In *Listener* 7 August 1975, p. 168

12 A triumph of the embalmer's art.
Of Ronald Reagan, in *Observer* 26 April 1981

13 Whenever a friend succeeds, a little something in me dies.
In *Sunday Times Magazine* 16 September 1973

14 He will lie even when it is inconvenient: the sign of the true artist.
Attributed

King Vidor 1895–1982

15 Marriage isn't a word ... it's a *sentence!*
The Crowd (1928 film)

José Antonio Viera Gallo 1943–

16 Socialism can only arrive by bicycle.
In Ivan Illich *Energy and Equity* (1974) epigraph

Alfred de Vigny 1797–1863

17 *J'aime le son du cor, le soir, au fond des bois.*
I love the sound of the horn, at night, in the depth of the woods.
'Le Cor' (1826)

18 *Seul le silence est grand; tout le reste est faiblesse.*
Silence alone is great; all else is feebleness.
'La mort du loup' (1843) pt. 3

Philippe-Auguste Villiers de L'Isle-Adam 1838–89

19 Living? The servants will do that for us.
Axël (1890) pt. 4, sect. 2

François Villon b. 1431

20 *Mais où sont les neiges d'antan?*
But where are the snows of yesteryear?
Le Grand Testament (1461) 'Ballade des dames du temps jadis' (tr. D. G. Rossetti)

21 *En cette foi je veux vivre et mourir.*
In this faith I wish to live and to die.
Le Grand Testament (1461) 'Ballade pour prier Nôtre Dame'

St Vincent of Lerins d. AD c.450

22 *Quod ubique, quod semper, quod ab omnibus creditum est.*
What is everywhere, what is always, what is by all people believed.
Commonitorium Primum sect. 2

Virgil 70–19 BC

23 *Arma virumque cano, Troiae qui primus ab oris
Italiam fato profugus Laviniaque venit
Litora, multum ille et terris iactatus et alto
Vi superum, saevae memorem Iunonis ob iram.*
I sing of arms and the man who first from the shores of Troy came destined an exile to Italy and the Lavinian beaches, a man much buffeted on land and on the deep by force of the gods because of fierce Juno's never-forgetting anger.
Aeneid bk. 1, l. 1

1 *O passi graviora, dabit deus his quoque finem.*
O you who have borne even heavier things,
God will grant an end to these too.
Aeneid bk. 1, l. 199

2 *Forsan et haec olim meminisse iuvabit.*
Maybe one day it will be cheering to
remember even these things.
Aeneid bk. 1, l. 203

3 *Et vera incessu patuit dea.*
And her true godhead was evident from
her walk.
Aeneid bk. 1, l. 405

4 *Sunt lacrimae rerum et mentem mortalia
tangunt.*
There are tears shed for things and
mortality touches the heart.
Aeneid bk. 1, l. 462

5   *Equo ne credite, Teucri.*
Quidquid id est, timeo Danaos et dona ferentis.
Do not trust the horse, Trojans. Whatever
it is, I fear the Greeks even when they
bring gifts.
Aeneid bk. 2, l. 48

6 *Una salus victis nullam sperare salutem.*
The only safe course for the defeated is to
expect no safety.
Aeneid bk. 2, l. 354

7 *Dis aliter visum.*
The gods thought otherwise.
Aeneid bk. 2, l. 428

8   *Quid non mortalia pectora cogis,*
Auri sacra fames!
To what do you not drive human hearts,
cursed craving for gold!
Aeneid bk. 3, l. 56

9   *Varium et mutabile semper*
Femina.
Fickle and changeable always is woman.
Aeneid bk. 4, l. 569

10 *Hos successus alit: possunt, quia posse videntur.*
These success encourages: they can
because they think they can.
Aeneid bk. 5, l. 231

11   *Bella, horrida bella,*
Et Thybrim multo spumantem sanguine cerno.
I see wars, horrible wars, and the Tiber
foaming with much blood.
Aeneid bk. 6, l. 86

12   *Facilis descensus Averno:*
Noctes atque dies patet atri ianua Ditis;
Sed revocare gradum superasque evadere ad
auras,
Hoc opus, hic labor est.
Easy is the way down to the Underworld:
by night and by day dark Hades' door
stands open; but to retrace one's steps and
to make a way out to the upper air, that's
the task, that is the labour.
Aeneid bk. 6, l. 126

13 *Procul, o procul este, profani.*
Far off, Oh keep far off, you uninitiated
ones.
Aeneid bk. 6, l. 258

14 *Ibant obscuri sola sub nocte.*
Darkling they went under the lonely night.
Aeneid bk. 6, l. 268

15 *Stabant orantes primi transmittere cursum*
Tendebantque manus ripae ulterioris amore.
They stood begging to be the first to make
the voyage over and they reached out their
hands in longing for the further shore.
Aeneid bk. 6, l. 313

16 *Tu regere imperio populos, Romane, memento*
(Hae tibi erunt artes), pacique imponere morem,
Parcere subiectis et debellare superbos.
You, Roman, make your task to rule
nations by your government (these shall be
your skills), to impose ordered ways upon a
state of peace, to spare those who have
submitted and to subdue the arrogant.
Aeneid bk. 6, l. 851

17 *Manibus date lilia plenis.*
Give me lilies in armfuls.
Aeneid bk. 6, l. 883

18   *Geniumque loci primamque deorum*
Tellurem Nymphasque et adhuc ignota precatur
Flumina.
He prays to the spirit of the place and to
Earth, the first of the gods, and to the
Nymphs and as yet unknown rivers.
Aeneid bk. 7, l. 136

19 *Macte nova virtute, puer, sic itur ad astra.*
Blessings on your young courage, boy;
that's the way to the stars.
Aeneid bk. 9, l. 641

20 *Audentis Fortuna iuvat.*
Fortune assists the bold.
Aeneid bk. 10, l. 284 (often quoted 'Fortune
favours the brave'). Cf. 329:5

21 *Et dulcis moriens reminiscitur Argos.*
And dying remembers his sweet Argos.
Aeneid bk. 10, l. 782

22 *Experto credite.*
Trust one who has gone through it.
Aeneid bk. 11, l. 283

23 *Trahit sua quemque voluptas.*
Everyone is dragged on by their favourite
pleasure.
Eclogues no. 2, l. 65

24 *Latet anguis in herba.*
There's a snake hidden in the grass.
Eclogues no. 3, l. 93

25 *Ultima Cumaei venit iam carminis aetas;*
Magnus ab integro saeclorum nascitur ordo.
Iam redit et virgo, redeunt Saturnia regna,
Iam nova progenies caelo demittitur alto.
Now has come the last age according to
the oracle at Cumae; the great series of
lifetimes starts anew. Now too the virgin
goddess returns, the golden days of
Saturn's reign return, now a new race is
sent down from high heaven.
Eclogues no. 4, l. 4

1 *Ambo florentes aetatibus, Arcades ambo,*
Et cantare pares et respondere parati.
Both in the flower of their youth,
Arcadians both, and matched and ready
alike to start a song and to respond.
   Eclogues no. 7, l. 4

2 *Non omnia possumus omnes.*
We can't all do everything.
   Eclogues no. 8, l. 63. Cf. 212:1

3 *Nam neque adhuc Vario videor nec dicere Cinna*
Digna, sed argutos inter strepere anser olores.
For I don't seem yet to write things as
good either as Varius or as Cinna, but to
be a goose honking amongst tuneful
swans.
   Eclogues no. 9, l. 35

4 *Omnia vincit Amor: et nos cedamus Amori.*
Love conquers all things: let us too give in
to Love.
   Eclogues no. 10, l. 69

5 *Ultima Thule.*
Farthest Thule.
   Georgics no. 1, l. 30

6 *Imponere Pelio Ossam*
Scilicet atque Ossae frondosum involvere
Olympum.
To pile Ossa on Pelion, no less, and to roll
leafy Olympus on top of Ossa.
   Georgics no. 1, l. 281

7 *O fortunatos nimium, sua si bona norint,*
Agricolas!
O farmers excessively fortunate if only
they recognized their blessings!
   Georgics no. 2, l. 458

8 *Felix qui potuit rerum cognoscere causas.*
Lucky is he who has been able to
understand the causes of things.
   Georgics no. 2, l. 490

9 *Sed fugit interea, fugit inreparabile tempus.*
But meanwhile it is flying, irretrievable
time is flying.
   Georgics no. 3, l. 284 (usually quoted 'tempus
   fugit [time flies]')

Voltaire 1694–1778

10 *Dans ce meilleur des mondes possibles ... tout*
est au mieux.
In this best of possible worlds ... all is for
the best.
   Candide (1759) ch. 1 (usually quoted 'All is for
   the best in the best of all possible worlds')

11 *Si nous ne trouvons pas des choses agréables,*
nous trouverons du moins des choses nouvelles.
If we do not find anything pleasant, at
least we shall find something new.
   Candide (1759) ch. 17

12 *Dans ce pays-ci il est bon de tuer de temps en*
temps un amiral pour encourager les autres.
In this country [England] it is thought well
to kill an admiral from time to time to
encourage the others.
   Candide (1759) ch. 23

13 *Il faut cultiver notre jardin.*
We must cultivate our garden.
   Candide (1759) ch. 30

14 [Men] use thought only to justify their
injustices, and speech only to conceal their
thoughts.
   Dialogues (1763) 'Le Chapon et la poularde'

15 *Le mieux est l'ennemi du bien.*
The best is the enemy of the good.
   Contes (1772) 'La Begueule' l. 2 (deriving from
   an Italian proverb quoted in Voltaire's
   Dictionnaire philosophique (1770 ed.) 'Art
   Dramatique')

16 Superstition sets the whole world in
flames; philosophy quenches them.
   Dictionnaire philosophique (1764) 'Superstition'

17 The secret of being a bore ... is to tell
everything.
   Discours en vers sur l'homme (1737) 'De la
   nature de l'homme' l. 172

18 *Si Dieu n'existait pas, il faudrait l'inventer.*
If God did not exist, it would be necessary
to invent him.
   Épîtres no. 96 'A l'Auteur du livre des trois
   imposteurs'. Cf. 243:11

19 This agglomeration which was called and
which still calls itself the Holy Roman
Empire was neither holy, nor Roman, nor
an empire.
   *Essai sur l'histoire générale et sur les moeurs et
   l'esprit des nations* (1756) ch. 70

20 History is nothing more than a tableau of
crimes and misfortunes.
   L'Ingénu (1767) ch. 10. Cf. 150:11

21 Whatever you do, stamp out superstition,
and love those who love you.
   Letter to M. d'Alembert, 28 November 1762;
   in Voltaire Foundation (ed.) *Complete Works*
   vol. 25 (1973)

22 *Le superflu, chose très nécessaire.*
The superfluous, a very necessary thing.
   Le Mondain (1736) l. 22

23 God is on the side not of the big battalions,
but of the best shots.
   'The Piccini Notebooks' (c.1735–50) in T.
   Besterman (ed.) *Voltaire's Notebooks* (2nd ed.,
   1968) vol. 2, p. 547. Cf. 14:4, 83:20

24 We owe respect to the living; to the dead
we owe only truth.
   'Première Lettre sur Oedipe' in *Oeuvres* (1785)
   vol. 1, p. 15 n.

25 The composition of a tragedy requires
testicles.
   On being asked why no woman had ever
   written 'a tolerable tragedy'; letter from
   Byron to John Murray, 2 April 1817, in L. A.
   Marchand (ed.) *Byron's Letters and Journals*
   vol. 5 (1976)

26 The English plays are like their English
puddings: nobody has any taste for them
but themselves.
   In Joseph Spence *Anecdotes* (ed. J. M. Osborn,
   1966) no. 1033

1 I disapprove of what you say, but I will defend to the death your right to say it.
Attributed to Voltaire, but actually S. G. Tallentyre's summary of Voltaire's attitude towards Helvétius following the burning of the latter's *De l'esprit* in 1759; in *The Friends of Voltaire* (1907) p. 199

2 What a fuss about an omelette!
What Voltaire *apparently* said on the burning of *De l'esprit*; in J. Parton *Life of Voltaire* (1881) vol. 2, ch. 25

3 This is no time for making new enemies.
On being asked to renounce the Devil, on his deathbed (attributed)

Alice Walker 1944–

4 Expect nothing. Live frugally on surprise.
'Expect nothing' (1973)

5 The quietly pacifist peaceful always die to make room for men who shout.
'The QPP' (1973)

Felix Walker fl. 1820

6 I'm talking to Buncombe ['bunkum'].
Excusing a long, dull, irrelevant speech in the House of Representatives, *c.*1820 (Buncombe being his constituency). See W. Safire *New Language of Politics* (2nd ed., 1972) p. 80. Cf. 90:17

Edgar Wallace 1875–1932

7 Dreamin' of thee! Dreamin' of thee!
'T. A. in Love' (1900); popularized by Cyril Fletcher in 1930s radio shows

George Wallace 1919–

8 Segregation now, segregation tomorrow and segregation forever!
Inaugural speech as Governor of Alabama, January 1963; in *Birmingham World* 19 January 1963

Henry Wallace 1888–1965

9 The century on which we are entering—the century which will come out of this war—can be and must be the century of the common man.
Vital Speeches (1942) vol. 8, p. 483 (8 May 1942)

William Ross Wallace d. 1881

10 The hand that rocks the cradle Is the hand that rules the world.
'What rules the world' (1865)

Graham Wallas 1858–1932

11 The little girl had the making of a poet in her who, being told to be sure of her meaning before she spoke, said, 'How can I know what I think till I see what I say?'
The Art of Thought (1926) ch. 4

Edmund Waller 1606–87

12 Go, lovely rose!
Tell her, that wastes her time and me,
That now she knows,
When I resemble her to thee,
How sweet and fair she seems to be.
'Go, lovely rose!' (1645)

13 Poets that lasting marble seek Must carve in Latin or in Greek.
'Of English Verse' (1645)

14 Why came I so untimely forth Into a world which, wanting thee, Could entertain us with no worth, Or shadow of felicity?
'To My Young Lady Lucy Sidney' (1645)

15 So all we know Of what they do above, Is that they happy are, and that they love.
'Upon the Death of My Lady Rich' (1645) l. 75

Horace Walpole (4th Earl of Orford) 1717–97

16 Our supreme governors, the mob.
Letter to Sir Horace Mann, 7 September 1743, in *Correspondence* (Yale ed., 1937–83) vol. 18

17 Every drop of ink in my pen ran cold.
Letter to George Montagu, 30 July 1752, in *Correspondence* (Yale ed.) vol. 9

18 One of the greatest geniuses that ever existed, Shakespeare, undoubtedly wanted taste.
Letter to Christopher Wren, 9 August 1764, in *Correspondence* (Yale ed.) vol. 40

19 It is charming to totter into vogue.
Letter to George Selwyn, 2 December 1765, in *Correspondence* (Yale ed.) vol. 30

20 The best sun we have is made of Newcastle coal.
Letter to George Montagu, 15 June 1768, in *Correspondence* (Yale ed.) vol. 10

21 It was easier to conquer it [the East] than to know what to do with it.
Letter to Sir Horace Mann, 27 March 1772, in *Correspondence* (Yale ed.) vol. 23

22 The way to ensure summer in England is to have it framed and glazed in a comfortable room.
Letter to Revd William Cole, 28 May 1774, in *Correspondence* (Yale ed.) vol. 1

23 This world is a comedy to those that think, a tragedy to those that feel.
Letter to Anne, Countess of Upper Ossory, 16 August 1776, in *Correspondence* (Yale ed.) vol. 32

24 It is the story of a mountebank and his zany.
Of Boswell's *Tour of the Hebrides*; letter to Hon. Henry Conway, 6 October 1785, in *Correspondence* (Yale ed.) vol. 39

1 All his own geese are swans, as the swans of others are geese.
> Of Sir Joshua Reynolds; letter to Anne, Countess of Upper Ossory, 1 December 1786, in *Correspondence* (Yale ed.) vol. 33

2 That hyena in petticoats, Mrs Wollstonecraft.
> Letter to Hannah More, 26 January 1795, in *Correspondence* (Yale ed.) vol. 31

3 Virtue knows to a farthing what it has lost by not having been vice.
> In L. Kronenberger *The Extraordinary Mr Wilkes* (1974) pt. 3, ch. 2

Sir Hugh Walpole 1884–1941

4 'Tisn't life that matters! 'Tis the courage you bring to it.
> *Fortitude* (1913) bk. 1, ch. 1

Sir Robert Walpole (1st Earl of Orford) 1676–1745

5 They now ring the bells, but they will soon wring their hands.
> On the declaration of war with Spain, 1739; in W. Coxe *Memoirs of Sir Robert Walpole* (1798) vol. 1, p. 618

6 All those men have their price.
> Of fellow parliamentarians; in W. Coxe *Memoirs of Sir Robert Walpole* (1798) vol. 1, p. 757

7 [Gratitude of place-expectants] is a lively sense of future favours.
> In W. Hazlitt *Lectures on the English Comic Writers* (1819) 'On Wit and Humour'. Cf. 201:25

William Walsh 1663–1708

8 I can endure my own despair,
But not another's hope.
> 'Song: Of All the Torments'

Izaak Walton 1593–1683

9 As no man is born an artist, so no man is born an angler.
> *The Compleat Angler* (1653) 'Epistle to the Reader'

10 I am, Sir, a Brother of the Angle.
> *The Compleat Angler* (1653) pt. 1, ch. 1

11 An excellent angler, and now with God.
> *The Compleat Angler* (1653) pt. 1, ch. 4

12 A good, honest, wholesome, hungry breakfast.
> *The Compleat Angler* (1653) pt. 1, ch. 5

13 In so doing, use him as though you loved him.
> *The Compleat Angler* (1653) pt. 1, ch. 8 (on baiting a hook with a live frog)

14 Look to your health; and if you have it, praise God, and value it next to a good conscience; for health is the second blessing that we mortals are capable of; a blessing that money cannot buy.
> *The Compleat Angler* (1653) pt. 1, ch. 21

15 But God, who is able to prevail, wrestled with him, as the Angel did with Jacob, and marked him; marked him for his own.
> *Life of Donne* (1670 ed.) p. 35

16 The great Secretary of Nature and all learning, Sir Francis Bacon.
> *Life of Herbert* (1670 ed.) p. 26

Bishop William Warburton 1698–1779

17 Orthodoxy is my doxy; heterodoxy is another man's doxy.
> To Lord Sandwich, in Joseph Priestley *Memoirs* (1807) vol. 1, p. 372

Artemus Ward (Charles Farrar Browne) 1834–67

18 Let us all be happy, and live within our means, even if we have to borrer the money to do it with.
> *Artemus Ward in London* (1867) ch. 7

19 Why is this thus? What is the reason of this thusness?
> *Artemus Ward's Lecture* (1869) 'Heber C. Kimball's Harem'

Andy Warhol 1927–87

20 In the future everybody will be world famous for fifteen minutes.
> In *Andy Warhol* (1968) [p. 12]

George Washington 1732–99

21 Let me ... warn you in the most solemn manner against the baneful effects of the spirit of party.
> *President's Address ... retiring from Public Life* (17 September 1796)

22 I can't tell a lie, Pa; you know I can't tell a lie. I did cut it with my hatchet.
> In M. L. Weems *Life of George Washington* (10th ed., 1810) ch. 2

Ned Washington 1901–76

23 Hi diddle dee dee (an actor's life for me).
> Title of song from the film *Pinocchio* (1940)

24 The night is like a lovely tune,
Beware my foolish heart!
How white the ever-constant moon,
Take care, my foolish heart!
> 'My Foolish Heart' (1949 song)

William Watson c.1559–1603

25 *Fiat justitia et ruant coeli.*
Let justice be done though the heavens fall.
> *A Decacordon of Ten Quodlibeticall Questions Concerning Religion and State* (1602). Cf. 138:24

William Watson 1858–1936

26 April, April,
Laugh thy girlish laughter.
> 'April'

1 My hand will miss the insinuated nose,
Mine eyes the tail that wagged contempt at
Fate.
'An Epitaph' (for his dog)

Isaac Watts 1674–1748

2 We are a garden walled around,
Chosen and made peculiar ground;
A little spot enclosed by grace,
Out of the world's wide wilderness.
'The Church the Garden of Christ' (1707)

3 Come, let us join our cheerful songs
With angels round the throne;
Ten thousand thousand are their tongues,
But all their joys are one.
'Come, let us join our cheerful songs' (1707)

4 When I survey the wondrous cross
On which the prince of glory died,
My richest gain I count but loss,
And pour contempt on all my pride.
'Crucifixion to the World, by the Cross of
Christ' (1707)

5 How doth the little busy bee
Improve each shining hour,
And gather honey all the day
From every opening flower!
Divine Songs for Children (1715) 'Against
Idleness and Mischief'

6 For Satan finds some mischief still
For idle hands to do.
Divine Songs for Children (1715) 'Against
Idleness and Mischief'

7 Let dogs delight to bark and bite,
For God hath made them so.
Divine Songs for Children (1715) 'Against
Quarrelling'

8 Birds in their little nests agree.
Divine Songs for Children (1715) 'Love between
Brothers and Sisters'

9 'Tis the voice of the sluggard; I heard him
complain,
'You have waked me too soon, I must
slumber again'.
Divine Songs for Children (1715) 'The Sluggard'

10 Hark! from the tombs a doleful sound.
'Hark! from the Tombs' (1707)

11 There is a land of pure delight,
Where saints immortal reign.
'A Prospect of Heaven makes Death easy'
(1707)

12 Jesus shall reign where'er the sun
Does his successive journeys run;
His kingdom stretch from shore to shore,
Till moons shall wax and wane no more.
Psalms of David Imitated (1719) Psalm 72

13 Our God, our help in ages past
Our hope for years to come,
Our shelter from the stormy blast,
And our eternal home.
Psalms of David Imitated (1719) Psalm 90 ('Our
God' altered to 'O God' by John Wesley, 1738)

14 A thousand ages in Thy sight
Are like an evening gone.
Psalms of David Imitated (1719) Psalm 90

15 Time, like an ever-rolling stream,
Bears all its sons away.
The Psalms of David Imitated (1719) Psalm 90

Evelyn Waugh 1903–66

16 I am not I: thou art not he or she: they are
not they.
Brideshead Revisited (1945) 'Author's Note'

17 Charm is the great English blight. It does
not exist outside these damp islands. It
spots and kills anything it touches. It kills
love, it kills art.
Brideshead Revisited (1945) bk. 3, ch. 2

18 The sound of English county families
baying for broken glass.
Decline and Fall (1928) 'Prelude'. Cf. 33:23

19 I expect you'll be becoming a schoolmaster,
sir. That's what most of the gentlemen
does, sir, that gets sent down for indecent
behaviour.
Decline and Fall (1928) 'Prelude'

20 Any one who has been to an English public
school will always feel comparatively at
home in prison. It is the people brought
up in the gay intimacy of the slums, Paul
learned, who find prison so soul-
destroying.
Decline and Fall (1928) pt. 3, ch. 4

21 You never find an Englishman among the
under-dogs—except in England, of course.
The Loved One (1948) ch. 1

22 He abhorred plastics, Picasso, sunbathing
and jazz—everything in fact that had
happened in his own lifetime.
The Ordeal of Gilbert Pinfold (1957) ch. 1

23 *The Beast* stands for strong mutually
antagonistic governments everywhere . . .
Self-sufficiency at home, self-assertion
abroad.
Scoop (1938) bk. 1, ch. 1

24 Up to a point, Lord Copper.
Scoop (1938) bk. 1, ch. 1

25 Feather-footed through the plashy fen
passes the questing vole.
Scoop (1938) bk. 1, ch. 1

26 News is what a chap who doesn't care
much about anything wants to read. And
it's only news until he's read it. After that
it's dead.
Scoop (1938) bk. 1, ch. 5

27 I will not stand for being called a woman
in my own house.
Scoop (1938) bk. 2, ch. 1

28 Other nations use 'force'; we Britons alone
use 'Might'.
Scoop (1938) bk. 2, ch. 5

29 Punctuality is the virtue of the bored.
M. Davie (ed.) *Diaries of Evelyn Waugh* (1976)
'Irregular Notes 1960–65' (26 March 1962)

1 A typical triumph of modern science to find the only part of Randolph that was not malignant and remove it.
> On hearing that Randolph Churchill's lung, when removed, proved non-malignant; in M. Davie (ed.) *Diaries of Evelyn Waugh* (1976) 'Irregular Notes 1960–65' (March 1964)

2 Impotence and sodomy are socially O.K. but birth control is flagrantly middle-class.
> 'An Open Letter' pt. 3 in Nancy Mitford (ed.) *Noblesse Oblige* (1956)

3 Manners are especially the need of the plain. The pretty can get away with anything.
> In *Observer* 15 April 1962

Frederick Weatherly 1848–1929

4 Where are the boys of the old Brigade, Who fought with us side by side?
> 'The Old Brigade' (1886 song)

5 Roses are flowering in Picardy, But there's never a rose like you.
> 'Roses of Picardy' (1916 song)

Sidney Webb (Baron Passfield) 1859–1947

6 The inevitability of gradualness.
> In *The Labour Party on the Threshold* (Fabian Tract no. 207, 1923) p. 11 (26 June 1923)

Max Weber 1864–1920

7 The protestant ethic and the spirit of capitalism.
> Title of article in *Archiv für Sozialwissenschaft Sozialpolitik* vol. 20 (1904–5)

8 The concept of the 'official secret' is its [bureaucracy's] specific invention.
> 'Politik als Beruf' (1919) in *Gesammelte politische Schriften* (1921) p. 672

Daniel Webster 1782–1852

9 Liberty *and* Union, now and forever, one and inseparable!
> Speech, 26 January 1830, in *Writings and Speeches* vol. 6 (1903)

10 Fearful concatenation of circumstances.
> Argument on the murder of Captain Joseph White, 6 April 1830; in *Writings and Speeches* vol. 11 (1903)

11 The Law: It has honoured us, may we honour it.
> Speech at the Charleston Bar Dinner, 10 May 1847, in *Writings and Speeches* vol. 4 (1903)

12 There is always room at the top.
> On being advised against joining the overcrowded legal profession (attributed)

John Webster c.1580–c.1625

13 Vain the ambition of kings Who seek by trophies and dead things, To leave a living name behind, And weave but nets to catch the wind.
> *The Devil's Law-Case* (1623) act 5, sc. 4

14 Why should only I ... Be cased up, like a holy relic? I have youth And a little beauty.
> *The Duchess of Malfi* (1623) act 3, sc. 2

15 Raised by that curious engine, your white hand.
> *The Duchess of Malfi* (1623) act 3, sc. 2

16 O, that it were possible, We might but hold some two days' conference With the dead!
> *The Duchess of Malfi* (1623) act 4, sc. 2

17 Glories, like glow-worms, afar off shine bright, But looked to near, have neither heat nor light.
> *The Duchess of Malfi* (1623) act 4, sc. 2

18 I know death hath ten thousand several doors For men to take their exits.
> *The Duchess of Malfi* (1623) act 4, sc. 2. Cf. 222:6, 270:8

19 Cover her face; mine eyes dazzle: she died young.
> *The Duchess of Malfi* (1623) act 4, sc. 2

20 Physicians are like kings,—they brook no contradiction.
> *The Duchess of Malfi* (1623) act 5, sc. 2

21 We are merely the stars' tennis-balls, struck and bandied Which way please them.
> *The Duchess of Malfi* (1623) act 5, sc. 4

22 Fortune's right whore: If she give aught, she deals it in small parcels, That she may take away all at one swoop.
> *The White Devil* (1612) act 1, sc. 1

23 'Tis just like a summer birdcage in a garden; the birds that are without despair to get in, and the birds that are within despair, and are in a consumption, for fear they shall never get out.
> *The White Devil* (1612) act 1, sc. 2

24 A rape! a rape! ... Yes, you have ravished justice; Forced her to do your pleasure.
> *The White Devil* (1612) act 3, sc. 2

25 Call for the robin-red-breast and the wren, Since o'er shady groves they hover, And with leaves and flowers do cover The friendless bodies of unburied men.
> *The White Devil* (1612) act 5, sc. 4

26 But keep the wolf far thence that's foe to men, For with his nails he'll dig them up again.
> *The White Devil* (1612) act 5, sc. 4

27 We think caged birds sing, when indeed they cry.
> *The White Devil* (1612) act 5, sc. 4. Cf. 284:1

28 I have caught An everlasting cold; I have lost my voice Most irrecoverably.
> *The White Devil* (1612) act 5, sc. 6

Josiah Wedgwood 1730–95

1 Am I not a man and a brother.
Legend on Wedgwood cameo, depicting a kneeling Negro slave in chains; reproduced in facsimile in E. Darwin *The Botanic Garden* pt. 1 (1791) facing p. 87

Simone Weil 1909–43

2 All sins are attempts to fill voids.
La Pesanteur et la grâce (1948) p. 27

3 What a country calls its vital economic interests are not the things which enable its citizens to live, but the things which enable it to make war.
In W. H. Auden *A Certain World* (1971) p. 384

Johnny Weissmuller 1904–84

4 Me Tarzan, you Jane.
Summing up his role in *Tarzan, the Ape Man* (1932 film). The words occur neither in the film nor the original, by Edgar Rice Burroughs. See *Photoplay Magazine* June 1932

Orson Welles 1915–85

5 In Italy for thirty years under the Borgias they had warfare, terror, murder, bloodshed — they produced Michelangelo, Leonardo da Vinci and the Renaissance. In Switzerland they had brotherly love, five hundred years of democracy and peace and what did that produce ... ? The cuckoo clock.
The Third Man (1949 film); words added by Welles to Graham Greene's screenplay

Duke of Wellington 1769–1852

6 All the business of war, and indeed all the business of life, is to endeavour to find out what you don't know by what you do; that's what I called 'guessing what was at the other side of the hill'.
The Croker Papers (1885) vol. 3 ch. 28

7 As Lord Chesterfield said of the generals of his day, 'I only hope that when the enemy reads the list of their names, he trembles as I do.'
Letter, 29 August 1810, in *Supplementary Despatches* ... (1860) vol. 6, p. 582 (usually quoted 'I don't know what effect these men will have upon the enemy, but, by God, they frighten me')

8 Up Guards and at them!
In *The Battle of Waterloo* by a Near Observer [J. Booth] (1815) p. 57 (later denied by Wellington)

9 I never saw so many shocking bad hats in my life.
On seeing the first Reformed Parliament; in Sir William Fraser *Words on Wellington* (1889) p. 12

10 The battle of Waterloo was won on the playing fields of Eton.
Oral tradition, but not found in this form of words. See C. F. R. Montalembert *De l'avenir politique de l'Angleterre* (1856) ch. 10

11 Hard pounding this, gentlemen; let's see who will pound longest.
At the Battle of Waterloo; in Sir Walter Scott *Paul's Letters* (1816) Letter 8

12 Next to a battle lost, the greatest misery is a battle gained.
In *Diary of Frances, Lady Shelley 1787–1817* (ed. R. Edgcumbe) vol. 1, ch. 9, p. 102

13 I used to say of him [Napoleon] that his presence on the field made the difference of forty thousand men.
In Philip Henry Stanhope *Notes of Conversations with the Duke of Wellington* (1888) 2 November 1831

14 Ours [our army] is composed of the scum of the earth—the mere scum of the earth.
In Philip Henry Stanhope *Notes of Conversations with the Duke of Wellington* (1888) 4 November 1831

15 Publish and be damned.
Replying to a blackmail threat (attributed). See Elizabeth Longford *Wellington: The Years of the Sword* (1969) ch. 10

H. G. Wells 1866–1946

16 He had read Shakespeare and found him weak in chemistry.
Complete Short Stories (1927) 'Lord of the Dynamos'

17 'Sesquippledan,' he would say. 'Sesquippledan verboojuice.'
The History of Mr Polly (1909) ch. 1, pt. 5

18 'I'm a Norfan, both sides,' he would explain, with the air of one who had seen trouble.
Kipps (1905) bk. 1, ch. 6, pt. 1

19 I was thinking jest what a Rum Go everything is.
Kipps (1905) bk. 3, ch. 3, pt. 8

20 The Social Contract is nothing more or less than a vast conspiracy of human beings to lie to and humbug themselves and one another for the general Good. Lies are the mortar that bind the savage individual man into the social masonry.
Love and Mr Lewisham (1900) ch. 23

21 Human history becomes more and more a race between education and catastrophe.
The Outline of History (1920) vol. 2, ch. 41, pt. 4

22 Bah! the thing is not a nose at all, but a bit of primordial chaos clapped on to my face.
Select Conversations with an Uncle (1895) 'The Man with a Nose'

23 The shape of things to come.
Title of book (1933)

24 The war that will end war.
Title of book (1914). Cf. 208:10

1 Moral indignation is jealousy with a halo.
The Wife of Sir Isaac Harman (1914) ch. 9,
sect. 2

Arnold Wesker 1932–

2 Chips with every damn thing. You breed
babies and you eat chips with everything.
Chips with Everything (1962) act 1, sc. 2

Charles Wesley 1707–88

3 Amazing love! How can it be
That thou, my God, shouldst die for me?
'And can it be' (1738 hymn)

4 O for a thousand tongues to sing.
'For the Anniversary Day of one's
Conversion' (1740)

5 Forth in thy name, O Lord, I go,
My daily labour to pursue;
Thee, only thee, resolved to know,
In all I think or speak or do.
'Forth in thy name, O Lord, I go' (1749)

6 Gentle Jesus, meek and mild,
Look upon a little child;
Pity my simplicity,
Suffer me to come to thee.
'Gentle Jesus, Meek and Mild' (1742)

7 Hark! how all the welkin rings,
Glory to the King of kings.
Peace on earth and mercy mild,
God and sinners reconciled.
'Hymn for Christmas' (1739); altered to
'Hark! the herald-angels sing / Glory to the
new born king' by George Whitefield, 1753

8 Jesu, lover of my soul,
Let me to thy bosom fly.
'In Temptation' (1740)

9 Lo! He comes with clouds descending,
Once for favoured sinners slain.
'Lo! He comes' (1758)

10 Love divine, all loves excelling,
Joy of heav'n, to earth come down,
Fix in us thy humble dwelling,
All thy faithful mercies crown.
'Love divine' (1747)

John Wesley 1703–91

11 The Gospel of Christ knows of no religion
but social; no holiness but social holiness.
Hymns and Sacred Poems (1739) Preface

12 I went to America to convert the Indians;
but oh, who shall convert me?
Journal (ed. N. Curnock) 24 January 1738

13 I look upon all the world as my parish.
Journal (ed. N. Curnock) 11 June 1739

14 I design plain truth for plain people.
Sermons on Several Occasions (1746) in *Works*
(Centenary ed.) vol. 1, p. 104

15 Let it be observed, that slovenliness is no
part of religion; that neither this, nor any
text of Scripture, condemns neatness of
apparel. Certainly this is a duty, not a sin.
'Cleanliness is, indeed, next to godliness.'
Sermons on Several Occasions (1788) Sermon 88

16 Though I am always in haste, I am never in
a hurry.
Letter to Miss March, 10 December 1777, in
Letters (ed. J. Telford, 1931) vol. 6

17 Time has shaken me by the hand and
death is not far behind.
Letter to Ezekiel Cooper, 1 February 1791, in
Letters (ed. J. Telford, 1931) vol. 8

Samuel Wesley 1662–1735

18 Style is the dress of thought; a modest
dress,
Neat, but not gaudy, will true critics
please.
'An Epistle to a Friend concerning Poetry'
(1700). Cf. 252:2

Mae West 1892–1980

19 I always say, keep a diary and some day it'll
keep you.
Every Day's a Holiday (1937 film)

20 Beulah, peel me a grape.
I'm No Angel (1933 film)

21 It's not the men in my life that
counts—it's the life in my men.
I'm No Angel (1933 film)

22 'Goodness, what beautiful diamonds!'
'Goodness had nothing to do with it.'
Night After Night (1932 film)

23 Is that a gun in your pocket, or are you
just glad to see me?
In J. Weintraub *Peel Me a Grape* (1975) p. 47
(usually quoted 'Is that a pistol in your
pocket . . . ')

24 Why don't you come up sometime, and see
me?
She Done Him Wrong (1933 film); usually
quoted 'Why don't you come up and see me
sometime?'

Rebecca West 1892–1983

25 The point is that nobody likes having salt
rubbed into their wounds, even if it is the
salt of the earth.
The Salt of the Earth (1935) ch. 2

26 Every other inch a gentleman.
Of Michael Arlen, in Victoria Glendinning
Rebecca West (1987) pt. 3, ch. 5

John Fane, 10th Earl of
Westmorland 1759–1841

27 *Merit*, indeed! . . . We are come to a pretty
pass if they talk of *merit* for a bishopric.
Noted in Lady Salisbury's diary, 9 December
1835; in C. Oman *The Gascoyne Heiress* (1968)
pt. 5, p. 188

R. P. Weston 1878–1936 and Bert Lee 1880–1947

1 Good-bye-ee! — Good-bye-ee!
Wipe the tear, baby dear, from your eye-ee.
Tho' it's hard to part, I know,
I'll be tickled to death to go.
Don't cry-ee — don't sigh-ee!
There's a silver lining in the sky-ee!
Bonsoir, old thing! cheerio! chin-chin!
Nahpoo! Toodle-oo! Good-bye-ee!
'Good-bye-ee!' (c.1915 song)

Sir Charles Wetherell 1770–1846

2 Then there is my noble and biographical
friend who has added a new terror to
death.
Of Lord Campbell, in Lord St Leonards
*Misrepresentations in Campbell's Lives of
Lyndhurst and Brougham* (1869) p. 3. Cf. 14:24,
212:19

Edith Wharton 1862–1937

3 An unalterable and unquestioned law of
the musical world required that the
German text of French operas sung by
Swedish artists should be translated into
Italian for the clearer understanding of
English-speaking audiences.
The Age of Innocence (1920) bk. 1, ch. 1

4 Mrs Ballinger is one of the ladies who
pursue Culture in bands, as though it were
dangerous to meet it alone.
Xingu and Other Stories (1916) 'Xingu'

Thomas, 1st Marquess of Wharton 1648–1715

5 Ho, Brother Teague, dost hear de Decree?
Lilli Burlero Bullena-la.
Dat we shall have a new Debity,
Lilli Burlero Bullena-la.
'A New Song' (written 1687), in *Poems on
Affairs of State* (1704) vol. 3, p. 231 (*debity*
deputy)

Richard Whately 1787–1863

6 Happiness is no laughing matter.
Apophthegms (1854)

7 It is not that pearls fetch a high price
because men have dived for them; but on
the contrary, men dive for them because
they fetch a high price.
Introductory Lectures on Political Economy (1832)
p. 253

William Whewell 1794–1866

8 Hence no force however great can stretch a
cord however fine into a horizontal line
which is accurately straight: there will
always be a bending downwards.
Elementary Treatise on Mechanics (1819) ch. 4,
problem 2 (often cited as an example of
accidental metre and rhyme)

James McNeill Whistler 1834–1903

9 I am not arguing with you—I am telling
you.
The Gentle Art of Making Enemies (1890) p. 51

10 I maintain that two and two would
continue to make four, in spite of the
whine of the amateur for three, or the cry
of the critic for five.
Whistler v. Ruskin. Art and Art Critics (1878) p. 6

11 OSCAR WILDE: How I wish I had said that.
WHISTLER: You will, Oscar, you will.
In R. Ellmann *Oscar Wilde* (1987) pt. 2, ch. 5

12 Yes madam, Nature is creeping up.
To a lady who had been reminded of his
work by an 'exquisite haze in the
atmosphere'; in D. C. Seitz *Whistler Stories*
(1913) p. 9

13 No, I ask it for the knowledge of a lifetime.
In his case against Ruskin, replying to the
question: 'For two days' labour, you ask two
hundred guineas?'; in D. C. Seitz *Whistler
Stories* (1913) p. 40

E. B. White 1899–1985

14 Commuter—one who spends his life
In riding to and from his wife;
A man who shaves and takes a train,
And then rides back to shave again.
'The Commuter' (1982)

15 MOTHER: It's broccoli, dear.
CHILD: I say it's spinach, and I say the hell
with it.
New Yorker 8 December 1928 (cartoon
caption)

H. Kirke White 1785–1806

16 Much in danger, oft in woe,
Onward, Christians, onward go;
Bear the toil, maintain the strife,
Strengthened with the Bread of Life.
'Much in danger, oft in woe' (1812 hymn);
altered to 'Oft in danger' by W. J. Hall, 1836

Patrick White 1912–90

17 Conversation is imperative if gaps are to
be filled, and old age, it is the last gap but
one.
The Tree of Man (1955) ch. 22

T. H. White 1906–64

18 The once and future king.
Title of novel (1958), taken from Sir Thomas
Malory *Le Morte d'Arthur* bk. 21, ch. 7: 'Hic
iacet Arthurus, rex quondam rexque futurus'

Alfred North Whitehead
1861–1947

1 There are no whole truths; all truths are half-truths. It is trying to treat them as whole truths that plays the devil.
Dialogues (1954) prologue

2 Intelligence is quickness to apprehend as distinct from ability, which is capacity to act wisely on the thing apprehended.
Dialogues (1954) 15 December 1939

3 What is morality in any given time or place? It is what the majority then and there happen to like, and immorality is what they dislike.
Dialogues (1954) 30 August 1941

4 Art is the imposing of a pattern on experience, and our aesthetic enjoyment is recognition of the pattern.
Dialogues (1954) 10 June 1943

5 Civilization advances by extending the number of important operations which we can perform without thinking about them.
Introduction to Mathematics (1911) ch. 5

6 The safest general characterization of the European philosophical tradition is that it consists of a series of footnotes to Plato.
Process and Reality (1929) pt. 2, ch. 1

Katharine Whitehorn 1926–

7 I wouldn't say when you've seen one Western you've seen the lot; but when you've seen the lot you get the feeling you've seen one.
Sunday Best (1976) 'Decoding the West'

George Whiting

8 When you're all dressed up and have no place to go.
Title of song (1912)

William Whiting 1825–78

9 Eternal Father, strong to save,
Whose arm doth bind the restless wave,
Who bidd'st the mighty ocean deep
Its own appointed limits keep:
O hear us when we cry to thee,
For those in peril on the sea.
'Eternal Father, Strong to Save' (1869 hymn)

Walt Whitman 1819–92

10 I sing the body electric.
Title of poem (1855)

11 O Captain! my Captain! our fearful trip is done,
The ship has weathered every rack, the prize we sought is won.
'O Captain! My Captain!' (1871)

12 Out of the cradle endlessly rocking,
Out of the mocking-bird's throat, the musical shuttle.
'Out of the cradle endlessly rocking' (1881)

13 Have you your pistols? have you your sharp-edged axes?
Pioneers! O pioneers!
'Pioneers! O Pioneers!' (1881)

14 Camerado, this is no book,
Who touches this touches a man.
'So Long!' (1881)

15 Where the populace rise at once against the never-ending audacity of elected persons.
'Song of the Broad Axe' (1881) pt. 5, l. 12

16 I celebrate myself, and sing myself.
'Song of Myself' (written 1855) pt. 1

17 Urge and urge and urge,
Always the procreant urge of the world.
'Song of Myself' (written 1855) pt. 3

18 I believe a leaf of grass is no less than the journey-work of the stars.
'Song of Myself' (written 1855) pt. 31

19 I think I could turn and live with animals, they are so placid and self-contained,
I stand and look at them long and long.
They do not sweat and whine about their condition,
They do not lie awake in the dark and weep for their sins,
They do not make me sick discussing their duty to God.
'Song of Myself' (written 1855) pt. 32

20 Behold, I do not give lectures or a little charity,
When I give I give myself.
'Song of Myself' (written 1855) pt. 40

21 Do I contradict myself?
Very well then I contradict myself,
(I am large, I contain multitudes.)
'Song of Myself' (written 1855) pt. 51

22 I sound my barbaric yawp over the roofs of the world.
'Song of Myself' (written 1855) pt. 52

23 The earth does not argue,
Is not pathetic, has no arrangements,
'A Song of the Rolling Earth' (1881) pt. 1

24 When lilacs last in the dooryard bloomed,
And the great star early drooped in the western sky in the night,
I mourned, and yet shall mourn with ever-returning spring.
'When lilacs last in the dooryard bloomed' (1881) st. 1

25 The United States themselves are essentially the greatest poem.
Leaves of Grass (1855) preface

John Greenleaf Whittier 1807–92

26 Shoot, if you must, this old grey head,
But spare your country's flag.
'Barbara Frietchie' (1863)

27 Dear Lord and Father of mankind,
Forgive our foolish ways!
Re-clothe us in our rightful mind,
In purer lives thy service find,
In deeper reverence praise.
'The Brewing of Soma' (1872)

1 For of all sad words of tongue or pen,
  The saddest are these: 'It might have been!'
  'Maud Muller' (1854). Cf. 163:12

Robert Whittington

2 As time requireth, a man of marvellous
  mirth and pastimes, and sometime of as
  sad gravity, as who say: a man for all
  seasons.
  Of Sir Thomas More, in *Vulgaria* (1521) pt. 2
  'De constructione nominum'. In his
  prefatory letter to *In Praise of Folly* (1509),
  Erasmus describes More as '*omnium horarum
  hominem* [a man of all hours]'

Charlotte Whitton 1896–1975

3 Whatever women do they must do twice as
  well as men to be thought half as good.
  In *Canada Month* June 1963

Cornelius Whur

4 While lasting joys the man attend
  Who has a faithful female friend.
  'The Female Friend' (1837)

George John Whyte-Melville
1821–78

5 But I freely admit that the best of my fun
  I owe it to horse and hound.
  'The Good Grey Mare' (1933)

Bishop Samuel Wilberforce
1805–73

6 If I were a cassowary
  On the plains of Timbuctoo,
  I would eat a missionary,
  Cassock, band, and hymn-book too.
  Impromptu verse (attributed)

7 Was it through his grandfather or his
  grandmother that he claimed his descent
  from a monkey?
  Addressed to T. H. Huxley in a debate on
  Darwin's theory of evolution at Oxford, June
  1860; in *Macmillan's Magazine* vol. 78 (October
  1898) p. 433. Cf. 177:21

Richard Wilbur 1921–

8 Spare us all word of the weapons, their
  force and range,
  The long numbers that rocket the mind.
  'Advice to a Prophet' (1961)

9 There is a poignancy in all things clear,
  In the stare of the deer, in the ring of a
  hammer in the morning.
  'Clearness' (1950)

10 We milk the cow of the world, and as we
   do
   We whisper in her ear, 'You are not true.'
   'Epistemology' (1950)

11 Mind in its purest play is like some bat
   That beats about in caverns all alone,
   Contriving by a kind of senseless wit
   Not to conclude against a wall of stone.
   'Mind' (1956)

12 The good grey guardians of art
   Patrol the halls on spongy shoes.
   'Museum Piece' (1950)

13 Love is the greatest mercy,
   A volley of the sun
   That lashes all with shade,
   That the first day be mended.
   'Someone Talking to Himself' (1961)

Ella Wheeler Wilcox 1855–1919

14 Laugh and the world laughs with you;
   Weep, and you weep alone;
   For the sad old earth must borrow its
   mirth,
   But has trouble enough of its own.
   'Solitude'

15 So many gods, so many creeds,
   So many paths that wind and wind,
   While just the art of being kind
   Is all the sad world needs.
   'The World's Need'

Oscar Wilde 1854–1900

16 The truth is rarely pure, and never simple.
   The Importance of Being Earnest (1895) act 1

17 In married life three is company and two
   none.
   The Importance of Being Earnest (1895) act 1

18 To lose one parent, Mr Worthing, may be
   regarded as a misfortune; to lose both
   looks like carelessness.
   The Importance of Being Earnest (1895) act 1
   (1948 ed.)

19 All women become like their mothers. That
   is their tragedy. No man does. That's his.
   The Importance of Being Earnest (1895) act 1 (in
   dialogue form in *A Woman of No Importance*
   (1893) act 2)

20 The good ended happily, and the bad
   unhappily. That is what fiction means.
   The Importance of Being Earnest (1895) act 2.
   Cf. 318:5

21 Charity, dear Miss Prism, charity! None of
   us are perfect. I myself am peculiarly
   susceptible to draughts.
   The Importance of Being Earnest (1895) act 2

22 Meredith's a prose Browning, and so is
   Browning.
   Intentions (1891) 'The Critic as Artist' pt. 1

23 A little sincerity is a dangerous thing, and
   a great deal of it is absolutely fatal.
   Intentions (1891) 'The Critic as Artist' pt. 2

24 I can resist everything except temptation.
   Lady Windermere's Fan (1892) act 1

25 We are all in the gutter, but some of us
   are looking at the stars.
   Lady Windermere's Fan (1892) act 3

1 A man who knows the price of everything and the value of nothing.
   Lady Windermere's Fan (1892) act 3 (definition of a cynic)

2 Experience is the name everyone gives to their mistakes.
   Lady Windermere's Fan (1892) act 3

3 There is no such thing as a moral or an immoral book. Books are well written, or badly written.
   The Picture of Dorian Gray (1891) preface

4 There is only one thing in the world worse than being talked about, and that is not being talked about.
   The Picture of Dorian Gray (1891) ch. 1

5 A man cannot be too careful in the choice of his enemies.
   The Picture of Dorian Gray (1891) ch. 1

6 Anybody can be good in the country.
   The Picture of Dorian Gray (1891) ch. 19

7 A thing is not necessarily true because a man dies for it.
   Sebastian Melmoth (1904 ed.) p. 12

8 MRS ALLONBY: They say, Lady Hunstanton, that when good Americans die they go to Paris.
   LADY HUNSTANTON: Indeed? And when bad Americans die, where do they go to?
   LORD ILLINGWORTH: Oh, they go to America.
   A Woman of No Importance (1893) act 1. Cf. 14:15

9 The English country gentleman galloping after a fox—the unspeakable in full pursuit of the uneatable.
   A Woman of No Importance (1893) act 1

10 One should never trust a woman who tells one her real age. A woman who would tell one that, would tell one anything.
   A Woman of No Importance (1893) act 1

11 LORD ILLINGWORTH: The Book of Life begins with a man and a woman in a garden.
   MRS ALLONBY: It ends with Revelations.
   A Woman of No Importance (1893) act 1

12 Children begin by loving their parents; after a time they judge them; rarely, if ever, do they forgive them.
   A Woman of No Importance (1893) act 2

13 GERALD: I suppose society is wonderfully delightful!
   LORD ILLINGWORTH: To be in it is merely a bore. But to be out of it simply a tragedy.
   A Woman of No Importance (1893) act 3

14 You should study the Peerage, Gerald ... It is the best thing in fiction the English have ever done.
   A Woman of No Importance (1893) act 3

15 I never saw a man who looked
   With such a wistful eye
   Upon that little tent of blue
   Which prisoners call the sky.
   The Ballad of Reading Gaol (1898) pt. 1, st. 3

16 Yet each man kills the thing he loves,
   By each let this be heard,
   Some do it with a bitter look,
   Some with a flattering word.
   The coward does it with a kiss,
   The brave man with a sword!
   The Ballad of Reading Gaol (1898) pt. 1, st. 7

17 And the wild regrets, and the bloody sweats,
   None knew so well as I:
   For he who lives more lives than one
   More deaths than one must die.
   The Ballad of Reading Gaol (1898) pt. 3, st. 37

18 I have nothing to declare except my genius.
   At the New York Custom House; in Frank Harris *Oscar Wilde* (1918) p. 75

19 Chaos, illumined by flashes of lightning.
   On Robert Browning's 'style'; in Ada Leverson *Letters to the Sphinx* (1930) pt. 1 'The Importance of Being Oscar'

20 Work is the curse of the drinking classes.
   In H. Pearson *Life of Oscar Wilde* (1946) ch. 12

21 He [Bernard Shaw] hasn't an enemy in the world, and none of his friends like him.
   In Bernard Shaw *Sixteen Self Sketches* (1949) ch. 17

22 Ah, well, then, I suppose that I shall have to die beyond my means.
   At the mention of a huge fee for a surgical operation; in R. H. Sherard *Life of Oscar Wilde* (1906) ch. 18

Billy Wilder 1906–

23 Hindsight is always twenty-twenty.
   In J. R. Columbo *Wit and Wisdom of the Moviemakers* (1979) ch. 7

Thornton Wilder 1897–1975

24 Literature is the orchestration of platitudes.
   In *Time* 12 January 1953

Emperor Wilhelm II 1859–1941

25 We have ... fought for our place in the sun and have won it.
   Speech in Hamburg, 18 June 1901; in *The Times* 20 June 1901. Cf. 78:8

John Wilkes 1727–97

26 [EARL OF SANDWICH:] 'Pon my soul, Wilkes, I don't know whether you'll die upon the gallows or of the pox.
   [WILKES:] That depends, my Lord, whether I first embrace your Lordship's principles, or your Lordship's mistresses.
   In Sir Charles Petrie *The Four Georges* (1935)

Emma Hart Willard 1787–1870

27 Rocked in the cradle of the deep.
   Title of song (1840)

William III (William of Orange)
1650–1702

1 'Do you not see your country is lost?' asked the Duke of Buckingham. 'There is one way never to see it lost' replied William, 'and that is to die in the last ditch.'
   In Bishop Gilbert Burnet *History of My Own Time* (1838 ed.) p. 218

2 Every bullet has its billet.
   In John Wesley *Journal* (1827) 6 June 1765

Isaac Williams 1802–65

3 Be thou my Guardian and my Guide.
   Title of hymn (1842)

Tennessee Williams 1911–83

4 We're all of us guinea pigs in the laboratory of God. Humanity is just a work in progress.
   Camino Real (1953) block 12

5 Mendacity is a system that we live in. Liquor is one way out an' death's the other.
   Cat on a Hot Tin Roof (1955) act 2

6 I have always depended on the kindness of strangers.
   A Streetcar Named Desire (1947) sc. 11

William Carlos Williams
1883–1963

7 Minds like beds always made up,
   (more stony than a shore)
   unwilling or unable.
   Paterson (1946) bk. 1, preface

8 so much depends
   upon

   a red wheel
   barrow

   glazed with rain
   water

   beside the white
   chickens.
   'The Red Wheelbarrow' (1923)

Wendell Willkie 1892–1944

9 The constitution does not provide for first and second class citizens.
   An American Programme (1944) ch. 2

Angus Wilson 1913–91

10 Once a Catholic always a Catholic.
   The Wrong Set (1949) p. 168

Charles E. Wilson 1890–1961

11 For years I thought what was good for our country was good for General Motors and vice versa.
   Testimony to the Senate Armed Services Committee on his proposed nomination for Secretary of Defence, 15 January 1953; in *New York Times* 24 February 1953, p. 8

Harold Wilson 1916–

12 All these financiers, all the little gnomes in Zurich.
   Speech, *Hansard* 12 November 1956, col. 578

13 This party is a moral crusade or it is nothing.
   Speech at the Labour Party Conference, 1 October 1962; in *The Times* 2 October 1962

14 From now the pound abroad is worth 14 per cent or so less in terms of other currencies. It does not mean, of course, that the pound here in Britain, in your pocket or purse or in your bank, has been devalued.
   Ministerial broadcast, 19 November 1967; in *The Times* 20 November 1967

15 A week is a long time in politics.
   Probably first said at the time of the 1964 sterling crisis. See Nigel Rees *Sayings of the Century* (1984) p. 149

Harriette Wilson 1789–1846

16 I shall not say why and how I became, at the age of fifteen, the mistress of the Earl of Craven.
   Memoirs (1825) opening words

John Wilson
See CHRISTOPHER NORTH

Sandy Wilson 1924–

17 We've got to have
   We plot to have
   For it's so dreary not to have
   That certain thing called the Boy Friend.
   The Boyfriend (1954) title song

Woodrow Wilson 1856–1924

18 There is such a thing as a man being too proud to fight.
   Speech in Philadelphia, 10 May 1915, in *Selected Addresses* (1918) p. 88

19 We have stood apart, studiously neutral.
   Speech to Congress, 7 December 1915, in *New York Times* 8 December 1915, p. 4

20 Armed neutrality is ineffectual enough at best.
   Speech to Congress, 2 April 1917, in *Selected Addresses* (1918) p. 190

21 The world must be made safe for democracy.
   Speech to Congress, 2 April 1917, in *Selected Addresses* (1918) p. 195

22 Open covenants of peace, openly arrived at.
   Speech to Congress, 8 January 1918, in *Selected Addresses* (1918) p. 247; first of Fourteen Points

Robb Wilton 1881–1957

23 The day war broke out.
   Customary preamble to radio monologues in the role of a Home Guard, from *c.*1940

Anne Finch, Lady Winchilsea
1661–1720

1 Poetry's the feverish fit,
   Th' o'erflowing of unbounded wit.
   'Enquiry after Peace' (1713) l. 38

2 Now the jonquil o'ercomes the feeble
   brain;
   We faint beneath the aromatic pain.
   'The Spleen' (1701) l. 40

3 My hand delights to trace unusual things,
   And deviates from the known and common
   way;
   Nor will in fading silks compose
   Faintly the inimitable rose.
   'The Spleen' (1701) l. 83

Catherine Winkworth 1827–78

4 Now thank we all our God,
   With heart and hands and voices.
   'Now thank we all our God' (1858)
   (translation of Martin Rinkart's 'Nun danket
   alle Gott', c.1636)

George Wither 1588–1667

5 I loved a lass, a fair one,
   As fair as e'er was seen;
   She was indeed a rare one,
   Another Sheba queen.
   A Description of Love (1620) 'I loved a lass, a
   fair one'

Ludwig Wittgenstein 1889–1951

6 Philosophy is a battle against the
   bewitchment of our intelligence by means
   of language.
   Philosophische Untersuchungen (1953) pt. 1,
   sect. 109

7 What is your aim in philosophy?—To show
   the fly the way out of the fly-bottle.
   Philosophische Untersuchungen (1953) pt. 1,
   sect. 309

8 What can be said at all can be said clearly;
   and whereof one cannot speak thereof one
   must be silent.
   Tractatus Logico-Philosophicus (1922) preface

9 The world is everything that is the case.
   Tractatus Logico-Philosophicus (1922) p. 30

10 The limits of my language mean the limits
   of my world.
   Tractatus Logico-Philosophicus (1922) p. 148

P. G. Wodehouse 1881–1975

11 Chumps always make the best husbands
   . . . All the unhappy marriages come from
   the husbands having brains.
   The Adventures of Sally (1920) ch. 10

12 There was another ring at the front door.
   Jeeves shimmered out and came back with
   a telegram.
   Carry On, Jeeves! (1925) 'Jeeves Takes Charge'

13 He spoke with a certain what-is-it in his
   voice, and I could see that, if not actually
   disgruntled, he was far from being
   gruntled.
   The Code of the Woosters (1938) ch. 1

14 Slice him where you like, a hellhound is
   always a hellhound.
   The Code of the Woosters (1938) ch. 1

15 It is no use telling me that there are bad
   aunts and good aunts. At the core, they are
   all alike. Sooner or later, out pops the
   cloven hoof.
   The Code of the Woosters (1938) ch. 2

16 Roderick Spode? Big chap with a small
   moustache and the sort of eye that can
   open an oyster at sixty paces?
   The Code of the Woosters (1938) ch. 2

17 To my daughter Leonora without whose
   never-failing sympathy and encouragement
   this book would have been finished in half
   the time.
   The Heart of a Goof (1926) dedication

18 I turned to Aunt Agatha, whose
   demeanour was now rather like that of
   one who, picking daisies on the railway,
   has just caught the down express in the
   small of the back.
   The Inimitable Jeeves (1923) ch. 4

19 When Aunt is calling to Aunt like
   mastodons bellowing across primeval
   swamps.
   The Inimitable Jeeves (1923) ch. 16

20 It was my Uncle George who discovered
   that alcohol was a food well in advance of
   medical thought.
   The Inimitable Jeeves (1923) ch. 16

21 It is a good rule in life never to apologize.
   The right sort of people do not want
   apologies, and the wrong sort take a mean
   advantage of them.
   The Man Upstairs (1914) title story. Cf. 175:13

22 She fitted into my biggest armchair as if it
   had been built round her by someone who
   knew they were wearing armchairs tight
   about the hips that season.
   My Man Jeeves (1919) 'Jeeves and the
   Unbidden Guest'

23 Ice formed on the butler's upper slopes.
   Pigs Have Wings (1952) ch. 5

24 The Right Hon. was a tubby little chap who
   looked as if he had been poured into his
   clothes and had forgotten to say 'When!'
   Very Good, Jeeves (1930) 'Jeeves and the
   Impending Doom'

Charles Wolfe 1791–1823

25 Not a drum was heard, not a funeral note,
   As his corse to the rampart we hurried.
   'The Burial of Sir John Moore at Corunna'
   (1817)

26 We buried him darkly at dead of night,
   The sods with our bayonets turning.
   'The Burial of Sir John Moore at Corunna'
   (1817)

1 We carved not a line, and we raised not a
  stone—
  But we left him alone with his glory.
  'The Burial of Sir John Moore at Corunna'
  (1817)

Humbert Wolfe 1886–1940

2 You cannot hope
  to bribe or twist,
  thank God! the
  British journalist.
  But, seeing what
  the man will do
  unbribed, there's
  no occasion to.
  'Over the Fire' (1930)

James Wolfe 1727–59

3 The General ... repeated nearly the whole
  of Gray's Elegy ... adding, as he concluded,
  that he would prefer being the author of
  that poem to the glory of beating the
  French to-morrow.
  J. Playfair *Biographical Account of J. Robinson* in
  Transactions of the Royal Society of Edinburgh
  vol. 7 (1815) p. 499

4 Now God be praised, I will die in peace.
  Dying words, in J. Knox *Historical Journal of
  the Campaigns in North America* (ed. A. G.
  Doughty, 1914) vol. 2, p. 114

Thomas Wolfe 1900–38

5 Most of the time we think we're sick, it's
  all in the mind.
  Look Homeward, Angel (1929) pt. 1, ch. 1

6 'Where they got you stationed now, Luke?'
  ... 'In Norfolk at the Navy base,' Luke
  answered, 'm-m-making the world safe for
  hypocrisy.'
  Look Homeward, Angel (1929) pt. 3, ch. 36.
  Cf. 351:21

Tom Wolfe 1931–

7 The bonfire of the vanities.
  Title of novel (1987); deriving from
  Savonarola's 'burning of the vanities' in
  Florence, 1497

8 Electric Kool-Aid Acid test.
  Title of novel on hippy culture (1968)

9 Radical Chic ... is only radical in Style; in
  its heart it is part of Society and its
  tradition—Politics, like Rock, Pop, and
  Camp, has its uses.
  New York 8 June 1970, p. 56

Mary Wollstonecraft 1759–97

10 To give a sex to mind was not very
  consistent with the principles of a man
  [Rousseau] who argued so warmly, and so
  well, for the immortality of the soul.
  A Vindication of the Rights of Woman (1792)
  ch. 3 (often quoted 'Mind has no sex')

11 I do not wish them [women] to have power
  over men; but over themselves.
  A Vindication of the Rights of Woman (1792)
  ch. 4

12 When a man seduces a woman, it should, I
  think, be termed a *left-handed* marriage.
  A Vindication of the Rights of Woman (1792)
  ch. 4

13 A slavish bondage to parents cramps every
  faculty of the mind.
  A Vindication of the Rights of Woman (1792)
  ch. 11

14 Was not the world a vast prison, and
  women born slaves?
  The Wrongs of Woman: or, Maria (1798, ed. G.
  Kelly, 1976) p. 79

Cardinal Wolsey c.1475–1530

15 Father Abbot, I am come to lay my bones
  amongst you.
  In George Cavendish *Negotiations of Thomas
  Wolsey* (1641) p. 108

16 Had I but served God as diligently as I have
  served the King, he would not have given
  me over in my grey hairs.
  In George Cavendish *Negotiations of Thomas
  Wolsey* (1641) p. 113

Mrs Henry Wood 1814–87

17 Dead! and ... never called me mother.
  East Lynne (dramatized by T. A. Palmer, 1874;
  the words do not occur in the novel of 1861)

Woodbine Willie

See G. A. STUDDERT KENNEDY

Thomas Woodroofe 1899–1978

18 The whole Fleet's lit up. When I say 'lit up',
  I mean lit up by fairy lamps.
  First live outside broadcast, Spithead Review,
  20 May 1937. See Asa Briggs *History of
  Broadcasting in the UK* vol. 2 (1965) pt. 2, ch. 2

Harry Woods

19 Oh we ain't got a barrel of money,
  Maybe we're ragged and funny,
  But we'll travel along
  Singin' a song,
  Side by side.
  'Side by Side' (1927 song)

Virginia Woolf 1882–1941

20 Trivial personalities decomposing in the
  eternity of print.
  The Common Reader (1925) 'The Modern Essay'

21 Examine for a moment an ordinary mind
  on an ordinary day.
  The Common Reader (1925) 'Modern Fiction'

22 Life is not a series of gig lamps
  symmetrically arranged; life is a luminous
  halo, a semi-transparent envelope
  surrounding us from the beginning of
  consciousness to the end.
  The Common Reader (1925) 'Modern Fiction'

1 A woman must have money and a room of
her own if she is to write fiction.
A Room of One's Own (1929) ch. 1

2 Women have served all these centuries as
looking-glasses possessing the magic and
delicious power of reflecting the figure of
a man at twice its natural size.
A Room of One's Own (1929) ch. 2

3 This is an important book, the critic
assumes, because it deals with war. This is
an insignificant book because it deals with
the feelings of women in a drawing-room.
A Room of One's Own (1929) ch. 4

4 So that is marriage, Lily thought, a man
and a woman looking at a girl throwing
a ball.
To the Lighthouse (1927) pt. 1, ch. 13

5 I have lost friends, some by death ...
others through sheer inability to cross the
street.
The Waves (1931) p. 202

6 The scratching of pimples on the body of
the bootboy at Claridges.
Of James Joyce's *Ulysses*; letter to Lytton
Strachey, 24 April 1922, in *Letters* (ed. N.
Nicolson and J. Trautmann, 1976) vol. 2

Alexander Woollcott 1887–1943

7 A broker is a man who takes your fortune
and runs it into a shoestring.
In S. Hopkins Adams *Alexander Woollcott*
(1945) ch. 15

8 All the things I really like to do are either
illegal, immoral, or fattening.
In R. E. Drennan *Wit's End* (1973)

Dorothy Wordsworth 1771–1855

9 A beautiful evening, very starry, the
horned moon.
'Alfoxden Journal' 23 March 1798, in *Journals*
(ed. E. de Selincourt, 1941)

10 I never saw daffodils so beautiful. They
grew among the mossy stones about and
about them; some rested their heads upon
these stones as on a pillow for weariness;
and the rest tossed and reeled and danced,
and seemed as if they verily laughed with
the wind that blew upon them over the
lake.
'Grasmere Journal' 15 April 1802, in *Journals*
(ed. E. de Selincourt, 1941). Cf. 355:4

Elizabeth Wordsworth 1840–1932

11 If all the good people were clever,
And all clever people were good,
The world would be nicer than ever
We thought that it possibly could.
But somehow, 'tis seldom or never
The two hit it off as they should;
The good are so harsh to the clever,
The clever so rude to the good!
'Good and Clever'

William Wordsworth 1770–1850

12 And five times did I say to him
'Why, Edward, tell me why?'
'Anecdote for Fathers' (1798)

13 Action is transitory,—a step, a blow,
The motion of a muscle—this way or
that—
'Tis done, and in the after vacancy
We wonder at ourselves like men betrayed:
Suffering is permanent, obscure and dark,
And shares the nature of infinity.
The Borderers (1842) act 3, l. 1539

14 Who is the happy Warrior? Who is he
Whom every man in arms should wish to
be?
'Character of the Happy Warrior' (1807)

15 Earth has not anything to show more fair:
Dull would he be of soul who could pass
by
A sight so touching in its majesty:
This City now doth like a garment wear
The beauty of the morning; silent, bare,
Ships, towers, domes, theatres, and
temples lie
Open unto the fields, and to the sky;
All bright and glittering in the smokeless
air.
'Composed upon Westminster Bridge' (1807)

16 Dear God! the very houses seem asleep;
And all that mighty heart is lying still!
'Composed upon Westminster Bridge' (1807)

17 The light that never was, on sea or land,
The consecration, and the Poet's dream.
'Elegiac Stanzas' (on a picture of Peele Castle
in a storm, 1807)

18 Not in the lucid intervals of life
That come but as a curse to party-strife ...
Is Nature felt, or can be.
'Evening Voluntaries' (1835) no. 4

19   The good die first,
And they whose hearts are dry as summer
dust
Burn to the socket.
The Excursion (1814) bk. 1, l. 500

20 This dull product of a scoffer's pen.
The Excursion (1814) bk. 2, l. 484 (Voltaire's
Candide)

21 Society became my glittering bride,
And airy hopes my children.
The Excursion (1814) bk. 3, l. 735

22 'To every Form of being is assigned,'
Thus calmly spoke the venerable Sage,
'An *active* Principle.'
The Excursion (1814) bk. 9, l. 1

23 How fast has brother followed brother,
From sunshine to the sunless land!
'Extempore Effusion upon the Death of
James Hogg' (1835)

24 Bliss was it in that dawn to be alive,
But to be young was very heaven!
'The French Revolution, as it Appeared to
Enthusiasts' (1809); also *The Prelude* (1850)
bk. 9, l. 108

1 The moving accident is not my trade;
   To freeze the blood I have no ready arts.
   'Hart-Leap Well' (1800) pt. 2, l. 1

2   All shod with steel
   We hissed along the polished ice, in games
   Confederate.
   'Influence of Natural Objects' (1809); also *The
   Prelude* (1850) bk. 1, l. 414

3 I travelled among unknown men,
   In lands beyond the sea;
   Nor England! did I know till then
   What love I bore to thee.
   'I travelled among unknown men' (1807)

4 I wandered lonely as a cloud
   That floats on high o'er vales and hills,
   When all at once I saw a crowd,
   A host, of golden daffodils;
   Beside the lake, beneath the trees,
   Fluttering and dancing in the breeze.
   'I wandered lonely as a cloud' (1815 ed.).
   Cf. 354:10

5 For oft, when on my couch I lie
   In vacant or in pensive mood,
   They flash upon that inward eye
   Which is the bliss of solitude;
   And then my heart with pleasure fills,
   And dances with the daffodils.
   'I wandered lonely as a cloud' (1815 ed.)

6   The gods approve
   The depth, and not the tumult, of the soul.
   'Laodamia' (1815) l. 74

7   More pellucid streams,
   An ampler ether, a diviner air,
   And fields invested with purpureal gleams.
   'Laodamia' (1815) l. 104

8 That best portion of a good man's life,
   His little, nameless, unremembered, acts
   Of kindness and of love.
   'Lines composed a few miles above Tintern
   Abbey' (1798) l. 35

9   The sounding cataract
   Haunted me like a passion: the tall rock,
   The mountain, and the deep and gloomy
   wood,
   Their colours and their forms, were then
   to me
   An appetite.
   'Lines composed ... above Tintern Abbey'
   (1798) l. 72

10 The still, sad music of humanity,
   Nor harsh nor grating, though of ample
   power
   To chasten and subdue.
   'Lines composed ... above Tintern Abbey'
   (1798) l. 91

11 Milton! thou shouldst be living at this
   hour:
   England hath need of thee: she is a fen
   Of stagnant waters.
   'Milton! thou shouldst be living at this hour'
   (1807)

12   Some happy tone
   Of meditation, slipping in between
   The beauty coming and the beauty gone.
   'Most sweet it is' (1835)

13 My heart leaps up when I behold
   A rainbow in the sky.
   So was it when my life began;
   So is it now I am a man.
   'My heart leaps up when I behold' (1807)

14 The Child is father of the Man.
   'My heart leaps up when I behold' (1807)

15 The Sonnet's scanty plot of ground.
   'Nuns fret not ... ' (1807)

16   With gentle hand
   Touch—for there is a spirit in the woods.
   'Nutting' (1800)

17 There was a time when meadow, grove,
   and stream,
   The earth, and every common sight,
   To me did seem
   Apparelled in celestial light,
   The glory and the freshness of a dream.
   'Ode. Intimations of Immortality' (1807) st. 1

18 The rainbow comes and goes,
   And lovely is the rose.
   'Ode. Intimations of Immortality' (1807) st. 2

19 Whither is fled the visionary gleam?
   Where is it now, the glory and the dream?
   'Ode. Intimations of Immortality' (1807) st. 4

20 Our birth is but a sleep and a forgetting:
   The Soul that rises with us, our life's Star,
   Hath had elsewhere its setting,
   And cometh from afar:
   Not in entire forgetfulness,
   And not in utter nakedness,
   But trailing clouds of glory do we come
   From God, who is our home:
   Heaven lies about us in our infancy!
   Shades of the prison-house begin to close
   Upon the growing boy.
   'Ode. Intimations of Immortality' (1807) st. 5

21 At length the man perceives it die away,
   And fade into the light of common day.
   'Ode. Intimations of Immortality' (1807) st. 5

22 But for those obstinate questionings
   Of sense and outward things,
   Fallings from us, vanishings;
   Blank misgivings of a creature
   Moving about in worlds not realised,
   High instincts before which our mortal
   nature
   Did tremble like a guilty thing surprised.
   'Ode. Intimations of Immortality' (1807) st. 9

23 Though nothing can bring back the hour
   Of splendour in the grass, of glory in the
   flower.
   'Ode. Intimations of Immortality' (1807)
   st. 10

24 To me the meanest flower that blows can
   give
   Thoughts that do often lie too deep for
   tears.
   'Ode. Intimations of Immortality' (1807)
   st. 11

25 Stern daughter of the voice of God!
   'Ode to Duty' (1807)

1 Plain living and high thinking are no
more:
The homely beauty of the good old cause
Is gone.
  'O friend! I know not which way I must look'
  (1807)

2 Once did she hold the gorgeous East in fee,
And was the safeguard of the West.
  'On the Extinction of the Venetian Republic'
  (1807)

3 There's something in a flying horse,
There's something in a huge balloon;
But through the clouds I'll never float
Until I have a little Boat,
Shaped like the crescent-moon.
  Peter Bell (1819) prologue, l. 1

4 Is it some party in a parlour,
Crammed just as they on earth were
crammed—
Some sipping punch, some sipping tea,
But as you by their faces see
All silent, and all damned?
  Peter Bell pt. 1, l. 541 in 1819 MS
  (subsequently deleted so as 'not to offend
  the pious')

5 Physician art thou?—one, all eyes,
Philosopher!—a fingering slave,
One that would peep and botanize
Upon his mother's grave?
  'A Poet's Epitaph' (1800)

6 A reasoning, self-sufficing thing,
An intellectual All-in-all!
  'A Poet's Epitaph' (1800)

7 In common things that round us lie
Some random truths he can impart,—
The harvest of a quiet eye
That broods and sleeps on his own heart.
  'A Poet's Epitaph' (1800)

8 Unprofitably travelling toward the grave.
  The Prelude (1850) bk. 1, l. 267

9 Made one long bathing of a summer's day.
  The Prelude (1850) bk. 1, l. 290

10   The statue stood
Of Newton, with his prism, and silent face:
The marble index of a mind for ever
Voyaging through strange seas of Thought,
alone.
  The Prelude (1850) bk. 3, l. 60

11   Spirits overwrought
Were making night do penance for a day
Spent in a round of strenuous idleness.
  The Prelude (1850) bk. 4, l. 376

12 And, through the turnings intricate of
verse,
Present themselves as objects recognised,
In flashes, and with glory not their own.
  The Prelude (1850) bk. 5, l. 605

13   All things have second birth;
The earthquake is not satisfied at once.
  The Prelude (1850) bk. 10, l. 83

14 Not in Utopia,—subterranean fields,—
Or some secreted island, Heaven knows
where!
But in the very world, which is the world
Of all of us,—the place where in the end
We find our happiness, or not at all!
  The Prelude (1850) bk. 11, l. 140

15   There is
One great society alone on earth,
The noble Living, and the noble Dead.
  The Prelude (1850) bk. 11, l. 393

16 I thought of Chatterton, the marvellous
boy.
  'Resolution and Independence' (1807) st. 7

17 We poets in our youth begin in gladness;
But thereof comes in the end despondency
and madness.
  'Resolution and Independence' (1807) st. 7

18 Still glides the Stream, and shall for ever
glide;
The Form remains, the Function never dies.
  'The River Duddon' (1820) no. 34 'After-
  Thought'

19 Enough, if something from our hands have
power
To live, and act, and serve the future hour.
  'The River Duddon' (1820) no. 34 'After-
  Thought'

20 We feel that we are greater than we know.
  'The River Duddon' (1820) no. 34 'After-
  Thought'

21 Scorn not the Sonnet; Critic, you have
frowned,
Mindless of its just honours; with this key
Shakespeare unlocked his heart.
  'Scorn not the Sonnet' (1827)

22 She dwelt among the untrodden ways
Beside the springs of Dove,
A maid whom there were none to praise
And very few to love.
  'She dwelt among the untrodden ways'
  (1800)

23 She lived unknown, and few could know
When Lucy ceased to be;
But she is in her grave, and, oh,
The difference to me!
  'She dwelt among the untrodden ways'
  (1800)

24 And now I see with eye serene
The very pulse of the machine;
A being breathing thoughtful breath;
A traveller betwixt life and death.
  'She was a phantom of delight' (1807)

25 A slumber did my spirit seal;
I had no human fears:
She seemed a thing that could not feel
The touch of earthly years.

No motion has she now, no force;
She neither hears nor sees;
Rolled round in earth's diurnal course,
With rocks, and stones, and trees.
  'A slumber did my spirit seal' (1800)

1 Behold her, single in the field,
Yon solitary Highland lass!
'The Solitary Reaper' (1807)

2 Will no one tell me what she sings?
Perhaps the plaintive numbers flow
For old, unhappy, far-off things,
And battles long ago.
'The Solitary Reaper' (1807)

3 What, you are stepping westward?
'Stepping Westward' (1807)

4 Surprised by joy—impatient as the wind
I wished to share the transport.
'Surprised by joy—impatient as the wind'
(1815)

5 Our meddling intellect
Mis-shapes the beauteous forms of
things:—
We murder to dissect.

Enough of science and of art;
Close up those barren leaves.
'The Tables Turned' (1798)

6 Two Voices are there; one is of the sea,
One of the mountains; each a mighty
Voice:
In both from age to age thou didst rejoice,
They were thy chosen music, Liberty!
'Thought of a Briton on the Subjugation of
Switzerland' (1807)

7 O blithe new-comer! I have heard,
I hear thee and rejoice.
O Cuckoo! Shall I call thee bird,
Or but a wandering voice?
'To the Cuckoo' (1807)

8 Oft on the dappled turf at ease
I sit, and play with similes,
Loose types of things through all degrees.
'To the Daisy' ('With little here to do or see',
1820 ed.)

9 Type of the wise who soar, but never roam;
True to the kindred points of heaven and
home!
'To a Skylark' ('Ethereal minstrel! pilgrim of
the sky', 1827)

10 The world is too much with us; late and
soon,
Getting and spending, we lay waste our
powers.
'The world is too much with us' (1807)

11   Great God! I'd rather be
A Pagan suckled in a creed outworn;
So might I, standing on this pleasant lea,
Have glimpses that would make me less
forlorn;
Have sight of Proteus rising from the sea;
Or hear old Triton blow his wreathèd horn.
'The world is too much with us' (1807)

12 Poetry is the spontaneous overflow of
powerful feelings: it takes its origin from
emotion recollected in tranquillity.
Lyrical Ballads (2nd ed., 1802) Preface

13 Never forget what I believe was observed
to you by Coleridge, that every great and
original writer, in proportion as he is great
and original, must himself create the taste
by which he is to be relished.
Letter to Lady Beaumont, 21 May 1807, in E.
de Selincourt (ed.) Letters of William and
Dorothy Wordsworth vol. 2 (rev. M. Moorman,
1969)

Sir Henry Wotton 1568–1639

14 And entertains the harmless day
With a religious book, or friend.
'The Character of a Happy Life' (1614)

15 This man is freed from servile bands,
Of hope to rise, or fear to fall:—
Lord of himself, though not of lands,
And having nothing, yet hath all.
'The Character of a Happy Life' (1614)

16 You meaner beauties of the night,
That poorly satisfy our eyes,
More by your number, than your light;
You common people of the skies,
What are you when the moon shall rise?
'On His Mistress, the Queen of Bohemia'
(1624); sometimes 'sun shall rise'

17 He first deceased; she for a little tried
To live without him: liked it not, and died.
'Upon the Death of Sir Albertus Moreton's
Wife' (1651)

18 No man marks the narrow space
'Twixt a prison and a smile.
'Upon the sudden restraint of the Earl of
Somerset' (1651)

19 Well building hath three conditions.
Commodity, firmness, and delight.
Elements of Architecture (1624) pt. 1

20 Critics are like brushers of noblemen's
clothes.
In Francis Bacon Apophthegms New and Old
(1625) no. 64

21 Take heed of thinking, The farther you go
from the church of Rome, the nearer you are to
God.
In Izaak Walton Reliquiae Wottonianae (1651)
'Life of Sir Henry Wotton'

22 An ambassador is an honest man sent to
lie abroad for the good of his country.
Written in the album of Christopher
Fleckmore in 1604. See Izaak Walton
Reliquiae Wottonianae (1651) 'Life of Sir Henry
Wotton'

Frank Lloyd Wright 1867–1959

23 The physician can bury his mistakes, but
the architect can only advise his client to
plant vines—so they should go as far as
possible from home to build their first
buildings.
New York Times 4 October 1953, sect. 6, p. 47

Lady Mary Wroth c.1586–c.1652

1 Love, a child, is ever crying:
Please him and he straight is flying,
Give him, he the more is craving,
Never satisfied with having.
  'Love, a child, is ever crying' (1621)

Sir Thomas Wyatt c.1503–42

2 They flee from me, that sometime did me
  seek
With naked foot, stalking in my chamber.
  'They flee from me' (1557)

3 Throughout the world, if it were sought,
Fair words enough a man shall find.
They be good cheap; they cost right
  naught;
Their substance is but only wind.
But well to say and so to mean—
That sweet accord is seldom seen.
  'Throughout the world, if it were sought'
  (1557)

William Wycherley c.1640–1716

4 A mistress should be like a little country
retreat near the town, not to dwell in
constantly, but only for a night and away.
  The Country Wife (1675) act 1, sc. 1

5 Go to your business, I say, pleasure, whilst
I go to my pleasure, business.
  The Country Wife (1675) act 2

6 You who scribble, yet hate all who write ...
And with faint praises one another damn.
  The Plain Dealer (1677) Prologue (of critics).
  Cf. 251:6

William of Wykeham 1324–1404

7 Manners maketh man.
  Motto (proverbial since the mid-14th
  century)

Xenophon c.428–c.354 BC

8 The sea! the sea!
  Anabasis bk. 4, ch. 7, sect. 24

Augustin, Marquis de Ximénèz
1726–1817

9 *Attaquons dans ses eaux
La perfide Albion!*
Let us attack in her own waters perfidious
Albion!
  'L'Ère des Français' (October 1793) in *Poésies
  Révolutionnaires et contre-révolutionnaires* (1821)
  vol. 1, p. 160. Cf. 70:2

Bishop John Yates 1925–

10 There is a lot to be said in the Decade of
Evangelism for believing more and more in
less and less.
  Gloucester Diocesan Gazette August 1991

Thomas Russell Ybarra b. 1880

11 A Christian is a man who feels
Repentance on a Sunday
For what he did on Saturday
And is going to do on Monday.
  'The Christian' (1909)

W. F. Yeames 1835–1918

12 And when did you last see your father?
  Title of painting (1878) in the Walker Art
  Gallery, Liverpool

W. B. Yeats 1865–1939

13 I said 'a line will take us hours maybe,
Yet if it does not seem a moment's thought
Our stitching and unstitching has been
  naught.'
  'Adam's Curse' (1904)

14 O body swayed to music, O brightening
  glance
How can we know the dancer from the
  dance?
  'Among School Children' (1928)

15 That dolphin-torn, that gong-tormented
  sea.
  'Byzantium' (1933)

16 Now that my ladder's gone
I must lie down where all ladders start
In the foul rag and bone shop of the heart.
  'The Circus Animals' Desertion' (1939) pt. 3

17   There's more enterprise
In walking naked.
  'A Coat' (1914)

18 We were the last romantics — chose for
  theme
Traditional sanctity and loveliness.
  'Coole and Ballylee, 1931' (1933)

19 The intellect of man is forced to choose
Perfection of the life, or of the work.
  'Coole Park and Ballylee, 1932' (1933)

20 A woman can be proud and stiff
When on love intent;
But Love has pitched his mansion in
The place of excrement;
For nothing can be sole or whole
That has not been rent.
  'Crazy Jane Talks with the Bishop' (1932)

21 Nor dread nor hope attend
A dying animal;
A man awaits his end
Dreading and hoping all.
  'Death' (1933)

22 He knows death to the bone—
Man has created death.
  'Death' (1933)

1 Down by the salley gardens my love and
   I did meet;
   She passed the salley gardens with little
   snow-white feet.
   She bid me take love easy, as the leaves
   grow on the tree;
   But I, being young and foolish, with her
   would not agree.
   'Down by the Salley Gardens' (1889)

2 Too long a sacrifice
   Can make a stone of the heart.
   'Easter, 1916' (1921)

3 All changed, changed utterly:
   A terrible beauty is born.
   'Easter, 1916' (1921)

4 The fascination of what's difficult
   Has dried the sap out of my veins, and rent
   Spontaneous joy and natural content
   Out of my heart.
   'The Fascination of What's Difficult' (1910)

5 Never to have lived is best, ancient writers
   say;
   Never to have drawn the breath of life,
   never to have looked into the eye of day;
   The second best's a gay goodnight and
   quickly turn away.
   'From *Oedipus at Colonus*' (1928). Cf. 311:13

6 The ghost of Roger Casement
   Is beating on the door.
   'The Ghost of Roger Casement' (1939)

7 I have spread my dreams under your feet;
   Tread softly because you tread on my
   dreams.
   'He Wishes for the Cloths of Heaven' (1899)

8 The innocent and the beautiful
   Have no enemy but time.
   'In Memory of Eva Gore Booth and Con
   Markiewicz' (1933)

9 My country is Kiltartan Cross;
   My countrymen Kiltartan's poor!
   'An Irish Airman Foresees his Death' (1919)

10 Nor law, nor duty bade me fight,
   Nor public man, nor angry crowds.
   'An Irish Airman Foresees his Death' (1919)

11 The years to come seemed waste of breath,
   A waste of breath the years behind.
   'An Irish Airman Foresees his Death' (1919)

12 I will arise and go now, and go to
   Innisfree,
   And a small cabin build there, of clay and
   wattles made;
   Nine bean rows will I have there, a hive for
   the honey bee,
   And live alone in the bee-loud glade.
   'The Lake Isle of Innisfree' (1893)

13 I hear lake water lapping with low sounds
   by the shore . . .
   I hear it in the deep heart's core.
   'The Lake Isle of Innisfree' (1893)

14 A shudder in the loins engenders there
   The broken wall, the burning roof and
   tower
   And Agamemnon dead.
   'Leda and the Swan' (1928)

15 Like a long-legged fly upon the stream
   His mind moves upon silence.
   'Long-Legged Fly' (1939)

16 We had fed the heart on fantasies,
   The heart's grown brutal from the fare.
   'Meditations in Time of Civil War' no. 6 'The
   Stare's Nest by my Window' (1928)

17 Think where man's glory most begins and
   ends
   And say my glory was I had such friends.
   'The Municipal Gallery Re-visited' (1939)

18 A pity beyond all telling,
   Is hid in the heart of love.
   'The Pity of Love' (1893)

19 Out of Ireland have we come.
   Great hatred, little room,
   Maimed us at the start.
   'Remorse for Intemperate Speech' (1933)

20 That is no country for old men. The young
   In one another's arms, birds in the trees
   Those dying generations   at their song.
   'Sailing to Byzantium' (1928)

21 An aged man is but a paltry thing,
   A tattered coat upon a stick, unless
   Soul clap its hands and sing, and louder
   sing
   For every tatter in its mortal dress.
   'Sailing to Byzantium' (1928)

22 And therefore I have sailed the seas and
   come
   To the holy city of Byzantium.
   'Sailing to Byzantium' (1928)

23 All shuffle there; all cough in ink;
   All wear the carpet with their shoes.
   'The Scholars' (1919)

24 Things fall apart; the centre cannot hold;
   Mere anarchy is loosed upon the world,
   The blood-dimmed tide is loosed, and
   everywhere
   The ceremony of innocence is drowned;
   The best lack all conviction, while the
   worst
   Are full of passionate intensity.
   'The Second Coming' (1921)

25 And what rough beast, its hour come
   round at last,
   Slouches towards Bethlehem to be born?
   'The Second Coming' (1921)

26 Far-off, most secret and inviolate Rose.
   'The Secret Rose' (1899)

27 A woman of so shining loveliness
   That men threshed corn at midnight by
   a tress,
   A little stolen tress.
   'The Secret Rose' (1899)

28 Romantic Ireland's dead and gone,
   It's with O'Leary in the grave.
   'September, 1913' (1914)

29 Oh, who could have foretold
   That the heart grows old?
   'A Song' (1919)

1 And pluck till time and times are done,
   The silver apples of the moon,
   The golden apples of the sun.
   'Song of Wandering Aengus' (1899)

2 Swift has sailed into his rest;
   Savage indignation there
   Cannot lacerate his breast.
   'Swift's Epitaph' (1933). Cf. 320:27

3 But where's the wild dog that has praised
   his fleas?
      'To a Poet, Who would have Me Praise
   certain bad Poets, Imitators of His and of
   Mine' (1910)

4 Red Rose, proud Rose, sad Rose of all my
   days!
   Come near me, while I sing the ancient
   ways.
   'To the Rose upon the Rood of Time' (1893)

5 Michaelangelo left a proof
   On the Sistine Chapel roof,
   Where but half-awakened Adam
   Can disturb globe-trotting Madam.
   'Under Ben Bulben' (1939) pt. 4

6 Irish poets, learn your trade,
   Sing whatever is well made.
   'Under Ben Bulben' (1939) pt. 5

7 Cast your mind on other days
   That we in coming days may be
   Still the indomitable Irishry.
   'Under Ben Bulben' (1939) pt. 5

8 Cast a cold eye
   On life, on death.
   Horseman pass by!
   'Under Ben Bulben' (1939) pt. 6

9 When you are old and grey and full of
   sleep,
   And nodding by the fire, take down this
   book
   And slowly read and dream of the soft look
   Your eyes had once, and of their shadows
   deep.
   'When You Are Old' (1893)

10 We make out of the quarrel with others,
   rhetoric, but of the quarrel with ourselves,
   poetry.
   Essays (1924) 'Anima Hominis' sect. 5

11 In dreams begins responsibility.
   Responsibilities (1914) epigraph

Sergei Yesenin 1895–1925

12 It's always the good feel rotten.
   Pleasure's for those who are bad.
   'Pleasure's for the Bad' (1923) (tr. G. McVay)

Edward Young 1683–1765

13 Some for renown on scraps of learning
   dote,
   And think they grow immortal as they
   quote.
   The Love of Fame (1725–8) Satire 1, l. 89

14   Be wise with speed;
   A fool at forty is a fool indeed.
   The Love of Fame (1725–8) Satire 2, l. 282

15 One to destroy, is murder by the law;
   And gibbets keep the lifted hand in awe;
   To murder thousands, takes a specious
   name,
   'War's glorious art', and gives immortal
   fame.
   The Love of Fame (1725–8) Satire 7, l. 55.
   Cf. 263:12

16 How science dwindles, and how volumes
   swell,
   How commentators each dark passage
   shun,
   And hold their farthing candle to the sun.
   The Love of Fame (1725–8) Satire 7, l. 96.
   Cf. 83:12, 184:15, 306:14

17 Tired Nature's sweet restorer, balmy sleep!
   Night Thoughts (1742–5) 'Night 1' l. 1

18 Death! Great proprietor of all!
   Night Thoughts (1742–5) 'Night 1' l. 204

19 Procrastination is the thief of time.
   Night Thoughts (1742–5) 'Night 1' l. 393

20 At thirty a man suspects himself a fool;
   Knows it at forty, and reforms his plan.
   Night Thoughts (1742–5) 'Night 1' l. 417

21 By night an atheist half believes a God.
   Night Thoughts (1742–5) 'Night 5' l. 176

22 To know the world, not love her, is thy
   point,
   She gives but little, nor that little, long.
   Night Thoughts (1742–5) 'Night 8' l. 1276.
   Cf. 154:27

23 Life is the desert, life the solitude;
   Death joins us to the great majority.
   The Revenge (1721) act 4. Cf. 248:9

George W. Young 1846–1919

24 The lips that touch liquor must never
   touch mine.
   Title of verse (c.1870)

Yevgeny Zamyatin 1884–1937

25 Heretics are the only bitter remedy against
   the entropy of human thought.
   'Literature, Revolution and Entropy' quoted
   in The Dragon and other Stories (1967, tr. M.
   Ginsberg) introduction

Israel Zangwill 1864–1926

26 Scratch the Christian and you find the
   pagan—spoiled.
   Children of the Ghetto (1892) bk. 2, ch. 6

27 America is God's Crucible, the great
   Melting-Pot where all the races of Europe
   are melting and re-forming!
   The Melting Pot (1908) act 1

Frank Zappa 1940–

1 Rock journalism is people who can't write
interviewing people who can't talk for
people who can't read.

In L. Botts *Loose Talk* (1980) p. 177.
Cf. 89:16

Robert Zemeckis and Bob Gale

2 Back to the future.

Title of film (1985)

Ronald L. Ziegler 1939–

3 [Mr Nixon's latest statement] is the
Operative White House Position ... and all
previous statements are inoperative.

At the time of the Watergate Affair; in *Boston
Globe* 18 April 1973

Émile Zola 1840–1902

4 *J'accuse.*
I accuse.

Title of an open letter to the President of the
French Republic, in connection with the
Dreyfus affair; in *L'Aurore* 13 January 1898

Index

act (cont.):

within the meaning of the A.	ANON 10:3
acted: a. so tragic the house	HARG 162:21
acting: a. of a dreadful thing	SHAK 281:3
people in them, a.	LARK 201:16
action: A. is consolatory	CONR 107:8
A. is transitory	WORD 354:13
a. of society upon itself	TOCQ 333:3
and a. is a most dangerous thing	CLOU 102:8
can only be grasped by a.	BRON 72:9
If ever I do a mean a.	STER 315:9
imitate in a. of the tiger	SHAK 279:5
lust in a.	SHAK 300:10
Makes that and th' a. fine	HERB 166:26
man of a. forced into a state	GALS 147:18
Suit the a. to the word	SHAK 276:6
Thought is the child of A.	DISR 122:9
actions: A. receive their tincture	DEFOE 115:19
my a. are my ministers	CHAR 95:2
Only the a. of the just	SHIR 306:11
active: a. line on a walk	KLEE 198:11
a. Principle	WORD 354:22
actor: a.'s life for me	WASH 342:23
actors: These our a.	SHAK 296:10
acts: all your a. are queens	SHAK 298:34
first four a. already past	BERK 35:19
His a. being seven ages	SHAK 272:24
nameless, unremembered, a.	WORD 355:8
no second a. in American lives	FITZ 140:23
who desires but a. not	BLAKE 61:3
actualité: economical with the a.	CLARK 101:13
adage: Like the poor cat i' the a.	SHAK 286:4
Adam: A. ate the apple	HUGH 175:21
A. had 'em	ANON 5:19
A. was a gardener	SHAK 280:11
For as in A. all die	BIBLE 55:17
old A. in this Child	BOOK 65:19
past Eve and A.'s	JOYCE 188:3
When A. dalfe and Eve spane	ROLLE 262:4
Where but half-awakened A.	YEATS 360:5
whipped the offending A.	SHAK 278:35
adamant: a. for drift	CHUR 99:9
frame of a., a soul of fire	JOHN 183:13
adazzle: a., dim	HOPK 172:13
adder: a. that stoppeth her ears	BOOK 67:13
day that brings forth the a.	SHAK 281:2
golden beat, and an a.	MAND 217:10
stingeth like an a.	BIBLE 43:33
addiction: Every form of a. is bad	JUNG 188:24
prisoners of a.	ILL 178:9
Addison: Cato did, and A. approved	BUDG 78:4
addresses: A. are given to us to	SAKI 265:21
adeste: A., fideles	ANON 13:9
adieu: Bidding a.	KEATS 191:27
ad infinitum: so proceed a.	SWIFT 320:23
adjective: As to the A.	TWAIN 336:6
Adlestrop: Yes; I remember A.	THOM 330:21
administered: best a. is best	POPE 252:20
administration: criticism of a.	BAG 26:6
admiral: a. from time to time	VOLT 340:12
admirals: A. extolled for standing still	COWP 110:5
admiralty: blood be the price of a.	KIPL 197:9
admirari: Nil a.	HOR 173:10
admire: Let none a.	MILT 228:19
Not to a., is all the art	POPE 252:26
admittance: No a. till the week after next	CARR 92:5
adolescence: a. and obsolescence	LINK 207:18
Adonais: I weep for A.	SHEL 303:3
adopted: by roads 'not a.'	BETJ 37:12
adorable: a. tennis-girl's hand	BETJ 37:13
adored: I was a. once too	SHAK 297:28
adoremus: Venite, a.	ANON 13:10
adorings: a. from their loves	KEATS 190:17
adorn: none that he did not a.	JOHN 185:12
To point a moral, or a. a tale	JOHN 183:14

adorned: unadorned a. the most	THOM 331:25
adornings: made their bends a.	SHAK 271:15
adorns: a. my legs	HOUS 174:7
ads: He watched the a.	NASH 237:13
adulteration: not adultery, but a.	BYRON 86:24
adulteries: all the a. of art	JONS 187:6
adulterous: found in a. bed	BLAKE 60:13
adultery: a. than in provincialism	HUXL 177:3
die for a.!	SHAK 283:23
Do not a. commit	CLOU 102:18
gallantry, and gods a.	BYRON 85:24
Not quite a., but adulteration	BYRON 86:24
Thou shalt not commit a.	BIBLE 40:9
woman taken in a.	BIBLE 53:25
adults: attributed by a. to children	SZASZ 321:23
children produce a.	DE VR 117:12
advantage: a. of doing one's praising	BUTL 84:9
A. rarely comes of it	CLOU 102:18
French are with equal a.	CANN 89:10
take a mean a. of them	WOD 352:21
undertaking of Great A.	ANON 6:21
advent: Hark to the a. voice	OAKL 240:16
adventure: a. is only an inconvenience	CHES 98:8
most beautiful a. in life	FROH 146:6
out into a. and sunshine	FORS 143:19
to die will be an awfully big a.	BARR 29:13
adventures: a. of his soul	FRAN 145:3
a. were by the fire-side	GOLD 155:12
hard a. t' undertake	FITZ 140:3
adversity: a. doth best discover	BACON 24:11
A.'s sweet milk, philosophy	SHAK 295:16
bread of a.	BIBLE 46:1
For of fortunes sharpe a.	CHAU 96:18
Sweet are the uses of a.	SHAK 272:14
advertisement: soul of an a.	JOHN 182:13
advertisers: prejudices the a. don't object to	SWAF 319:16
advertising: A. is the rattling of a stick	ORW 242:16
advice: a. is good or bad only	AUST 23:1
A. is seldom welcome	CHES 97:9
advise: A. the prince	ELIOT 134:1
STREETS FLOODED. PLEASE a.	BENC 34:6
aere: a. perennius	HOR 173:28
aeroplanes: it wasn't the a.	ROSE 111:17
Aesculapius: we owe a cock to A.	SOCR 310:25
aesthetic: a. enjoyment	WHIT 348:4
shine in the high a. line	GILB 152:9
afar: devotion to something a.	SHEL 305:5
affairs: a. which properly concern	VALE 336:22
tide in the a. of men	SHAK 282:1
affection: A. beaming in one eye	DICK 119:2
affections: holiness of the heart's a.	KEATS 192:23
T'a., and to faculties	DONNE 124:4
affinities: Elective a.	GOET 154:2
affliction: A. is enamoured of thy parts	SHAK 295:15
bread of a.	BIBLE 42:6
Remembering mine a.	BIBLE 47:1
waters of a.	BIBLE 46:1
afflictions: out of all their a.	BOOK 64:19
affluent: A. Society	GALB 147:14
afford: can a. to be good to her	SHAW 302:11
unless you can a. it	TROL 334:21
afloat: A. We move	CLOU 102:12
afraid: a. of his enemy	PLUT 250:2
And in short, I was a.	ELIOT 133:29
And many are a. of God	LOCK 209:1
I, a stranger and a.	HOUS 174:11
it is I; be not a.	BIBLE 50:8
It's not that I'm a. to die	ALLEN 4:16
they were sore a.	BIBLE 51:32
we do be a. of the sea	SYNGE 321:21
Who's a. of Virginia Woolf	ALBEE 3:12
Afric: geographers, in A.-maps	SWIFT 320:21
Where A.'s sunny fountains	HEBER 164:15

Africa: A. and her prodigies — BROW 74:13
foot—sloggin' over A. — KIPL 196:6
something new out of A. — PLINY 249:23
Till China and A. meet — AUDEN 20:11
with A. than my own body — ORTON 241:19
African: [A] national consciousness — MACM 215:17
after: A. long grief and pain — TENN 327:3
a. many a summer — TENN 328:17
A. the first death — THOM 330:15
Or just a. — STEV 316:13
afternoon: At five in the a. — GARC 148:2
Lovely and willing every a. — AUDEN 20:25
summer a. — JAMES 180:5
Afton: Flow gently, sweet A. — BURNS 81:23
again: I'll see you a. — COW 109:2
we'll conquer a. and again — GARR 148:8
against: all life is 6 to 5 a. — RUNY 264:7
hand will be a. every man — BIBLE 39:13
he that is not with me is a. — BIBLE 50:1
I always vote a. — FIEL 139:18
I have somewhat a. thee — BIBLE 57:20
who can be a. us — BIBLE 54:41
Agamemnon: And A. dead — YEATS 359:14
When A. cried aloud — ELIOT 134:17
agate-stone: no bigger than an a. — SHAK 294:24
age: a. according to the oracle — VIRG 339:25
A. cannot wither her — SHAK 271:17
a. demanded an image — POUND 254:16
a. going to the workhouse — PAINE 244:13
A., I do abhor thee — SHAK 299:6
a. in pilèd stones — MILT 227:21
a. is a dream that is dying — O'SH 243:2
a. is as a lusty winter — SHAK 272:16
a. is rocking the wave — MAND 217:10
a. is the most unexpected — TROT 334:22
a. of chivalry is gone — BURKE 80:14
a. of ease — GOLD 154:19
a. of pamphleteers — HOGB 170:6
A. shall not weary them — BINY 59:12
a., which forgives itself — SHAW 302:6
A. will not be defied — BACON 25:8
a. with stealing steps — VAUX 337:15
at your a., it is right — CARR 91:4
buried in a good old a. — BIBLE 39:12
cold a., narrow jealousy — ROCH 261:2
companions for middle a. — BACON 25:2
Crabbed a. and youth — SHAK 299:5
dawning of the a. of Aquarius — RADO 257:18
days of our a. are threescore — BOOK 67:26
fetch the a. of gold — MILT 227:27
hath not forgotten my a. — SOUT 312:2
He died in a good old a. — BIBLE 42:18
He was not of an a. — JONS 187:28
His wealth a well-spent a. — CAMP 89:3
If youth knew; if a. could — EST 137:17
master spirits of this a. — SHAK 281:12
my Father, my a. — LOW 211:15
Old-a., a second child — CHUR 98:24
Old a. should burn — THOM 330:7
serene, That men call a. — BROO 72:20
soon comes a. — SPEN 313:12
Soul of the A. — JONS 187:25
stricken in a. — BIBLE 39:14
then the only end of a. — LARK 201:14
this a. best pleaseth — HERR 167:21
Unregarded a. in corners — SHAK 272:15
who tells one her real a. — WILDE 350:10
with a. and dust — RAL 258:1
With leaden a. o'ercargoed — FLEC 141:18
wonder of our a. — DYER 129:15
worth an a. without a name — MORD 234:21
aged: a. man is but a paltry — YEATS 359:21
Certainly a. — BYRON 86:21
creatures did the a. seem — TRAH 333:19

agenda: a. will be in inverse proportion — PARK 245:22
ages: A. of hopeless end — MILT 228:25
heir of all the a. — TENN 326:16
His acts being seven a. — SHAK 272:24
Our God, our help in a. past — WATTS 343:13
aggravating: She was an a. child — BELL 33:11
Agincourt: affright the air at A. — SHAK 278:34
agnus: A. Dei, qui tollis — MISS 231:19
ago: Hornby and my Barlow long a. — THOM 331:6
agony: a. is abated — MAC 213:23
Beyond is a. — GREV 158:17
agree: sugar, and saltness a. — GOLD 155:1
agreement: blow with an a. — TROT 335:2
death and an a. with hell — GARR 148:13
with hell are we at a. — BIBLE 45:28
a-hold: always keep a. of Nurse — BELL 33:5
a-hunting: a. we will go — FIEL 139:5
We daren't go a. — ALL 4:18
aid: Apt Alliteration's artful a. — CHUR 98:27
ailments: our a. are the same — SWIFT 320:2
aim: at which all things a. — ARIS 15:12
have forgotten your a. — SANT 266:21
you must a. a little above — LONG 209:14
aims: its divided a. — ARN 17:11
ain't: a. a fit night out — FIEL 139:17
A. it all a bleedin' shame — ANON 10:11
A. We Got Fun — KAHN 189:19
It a. necessarily so — GERS 168:5
air: a., a chartered libertine — SHAK 278:36
a. a solemn stillness holds — GRAY 157:4
a. broke into a mist — BROW 76:25
ampler ether, a diviner a. — WORD 355:7
Clear the a. — ELIOT 134:8
conscience-stricken a. — HOUS 174:6
Germans that of—the a. — RICH 260:6
His happy good-night a. — HARDY 162:7
into air, into thin a. — SHAK 296:10
lands hatless from the a. — BETJ 36:21
nipping and an eager a. — SHAK 274:25
Nor do not saw the a. — SHAK 276:4
Now a. is hushed — COLL 105:10
path along the dusky a. — COL 104:21
There is music in the a. — ELGAR 131:18
'twixt a. and angels' purity — DONNE 123:21
with pinions skim the a. — FRERE 145:22
airline: a. ticket to romantic places — MARV 221:4
airly: An' you've gut to git up a. — LOW 211:4
airs: Sounds and sweet a. — SHAK 296:9
airy: A., fairy Lilian — TENN 326:5
aitches: nothing to lose but our a. — ORW 242:14
alarm: little a. now and then — BURN 81:16
SPREAD A. AND DESPONDENCY — PEN 247:8
alarms: confused a. of struggle — ARN 16:12
alas: A., poor Yorick — SHAK 277:8
Hugo—a. — GIDE 151:2
may say A. but cannot help — AUDEN 21:15
Albert: take a message to A. — DISR 122:22
Went there with young A. — EDGAR 130:15
Albion: La perfide A. — XIMÉ 358:9
Alcestis: like A. from the grave — MILT 230:24
alcohol: a. doesn't thrill me — PORT 253:20
A. is a very necessary article — SHAW 301:12
a. or morphine or idealism — JUNG 188:24
a. was a food well in advance — WOD 352:20
taken more out of a. than a. — CHUR 100:11
aldermen: divides the wives of a. — SMITH 308:20
Aldershot: burnish'd by A. sun — BETJ 37:10
ale: no more cakes and a. — SHAK 297:26
Sees bliss in a. — CRAB 110:21
Then to the spicy nut-brown a. — MILT 227:5
Aleppo: husband's to A. gone — SHAK 285:3
Alexander: but A. women — LEE 204:10
If I were not A. — ALEX 4:1
Some talk of A. — ANON 10:13

alexandrine: needless A. POPE 252:4
alibi: He always has an a. ELIOT 134:9
Alice: Pass the sick bag, A. JUNOR 188:27
alien: a. people clutching ELIOT 133:23
aliter: Dis a. visum VIRG 339:7
alive: a. and well and living ANON 8:13
dead, and is a. again BIBLE 52:32
Half dead and half a. BETJ 36:19
if he gets out of it a. JONES 116:24
if I am a. HOLL 170:11
in Christ shall all be made a. BIBLE 55:17
in that dawn to be a. WORD 354:24
Life's not just being a. MART 220:6
noise and tumult when a. EDW 131:4
Officiously to keep a. CLOU 102:17
one of those half-a. things FORS 144:1
ways of being a. DAWK 115:3
What still a. at twenty-two KING 195:19
all: A. before my little room BROO 73:3
A. by my own-alone self HARR 163:3
a. for love, and nothing for SPEN 313:11
A. for one, one for all DUMAS 129:4
a. in all for prose CAREW 89:18
A. passes. Art alone DOBS 122:25
a. shall be well ELIOT 133:13
a. shall be well JUL 188:21
A.'s right with the world BROW 76:28
A. that a man hath BIBLE 42:23
A. that I am I give to you BOOK 66:2
a. that's best of dark BYRON 87:6
A. things bright and beautiful ALEX 4:2
a. things to all men BIBLE 55:8
A. things were made BIBLE 53:7
A. we like sheep BIBLE 46:19
at a. times, and in a. places BOOK 65:15
don't think twice, it's a. right DYLAN 130:1
From a. that terror teaches CHES 97:24
have his a. neglected JOHN 183:25
having nothing, yet hath a. WOTT 357:15
Her a. on earth, and more BYRON 85:18
I'm a. right BONE 63:10
I would that you were a. to me BROW 77:20
man for a. seasons WHIT 349:2
not at all or all in a. TENN 324:14
1066 and A. That SELL 269:23
allegory: headstrong as an a. SHER 305:30
alley: And she lives in our a. CAREY 90:2
I think we are in rats' a. ELIOT 134:23
alliance: A., n. union of two thieves BIER 59:2
alliances: a. with none JEFF 180:19
allies: no a. to be polite to GEOR 150:5
we have no eternal a. PALM 244:18
all-in-all: intellectual A. WORD 356:6
alliteration: Apt A.'s artful aid CHUR 98:27
allons: A., enfants de la patrie ROUG 263:16
allure: how to a. by denying TROL 334:18
Alma mater: A. lie dissolved in port POPE 250:16
almanac: Look in the a. SHAK 290:30
pious fraud of the a. LOW 211:10
Almighty: A. placed it there LAB 199:12
A.'s orders to perform ADD 2:11
almost: A. thou persuadest me BIBLE 54:27
alms: a. and oblations BOOK 65:8
a. for oblivion SHAK 297:4
alone: a. against smiling enemies BOWEN 71:1
A. and palely loitering KEATS 191:7
a. with the quiet day JAMES 180:3
dangerous to meet it a. WHAR 347:4
fastest who travels a. KIPL 196:20
I want to be a. GARBO 148:1
left a. with our day AUDEN 21:15
left him a. with his glory WOLFE 353:1
less a. than when alone ROG 261:18
less alone than when wholly a. CIC 100:24

alone (cont.):
man should be a. BIBLE 38:20
not sufficiently a. VALÉ 336:21
One is one and all a. ANON 8:6
along: All a., down along BALL 28:11
alpha: I am A. and Omega BIBLE 57:19
Alps: A. of green ice PHIL 248:15
fading a. and archipelagoes ALDR 3:17
passages through the A. COLM 105:15
altar: great world's a.-stairs TENN 325:11
high a. on the move BOWEN 71:2
lays upon the a. the dearest SPR 313:26
self-slain on his own strange a. SWIN 321:10
altars: even thy a., O Lord BOOK 67:20
alteram: Audi partem a. AUG 22:1
alteration: A. though it be from worse HOOK 171:15
Which alters when it a. finds SHAK 300:8
alternatives: a. that are not their own BONH 63:11
altitudo: reason to an O a. BROW 74:11
altogether: A. elsewhere AUDEN 20:19
suit of clothes is a. LOES 209:6
alway: They a. must be with us KEATS 190:12
will not a. be chiding BOOK 68:6
always: But he is a. great DRYD 128:28
sometimes a., by God RICH 260:5
There'll be an England CHAR 245:19
am: I think, therefore I a. DESC 117:9
ama: A. et fac quod vis AUG 22:2
Amaryllis: sport with A. in the shade MILT 227:14
amateur: whine of the a. for three WHIS 347:10
amateurs: Hell is full of musical a. SHAW 301:19
amaze: men themselves a. MARV 220:14
amazing: A. grace! NEWT 239:7
A. love! WESL 346:3
ambassador: a. is an honest man sent abroad WOTT 357:22
ambiguities: clear these a. SHAK 295:26
ambiguity: Seven types of a. EMPS 137:7
ambition: a. can creep as well BURKE 81:8
A. first sprung from POPE 250:24
A., in a private man a vice MASS 222:3
a. mock their useful toil GRAY 157:7
A.'s debt is paid SHAK 281:11
A. should be made of sterner SHAK 281:20
Art not without a. SHAK 285:15
avarice and a. SMITH 308:20
fling away a. SHAK 280:19
Vain the a. of kings WEBS 344:13
Vaulting a., which o'erleaps SHAK 286:1
wars that make a. virtue SHAK 292:19
Who doth a. shun SHAK 272:21
ambitious: he was a., I slew him SHAK 281:16
O sacred hunger of a. minds SPEN 313:15
ambo: Arcades a. VIRG 340:1
Ambree: foremost in battle was Mary A. BALL 28:1
ambrosial: Phallic and a.? POUND 254:17
ambulance: With an a.? SIMP 307:12
âme: Quelle â. est sans défauts RIMB 260:10
Amelia: A. was praying for George THAC 329:18
amen: Like the sound of a great A. PROC 255:14
So goodbye dear, and A. PORT 253:21
Will no man say, a. SHAK 294:4
amens: few mumbled a. HUNT 176:18
America: America the beautiful BATES 30:2
A. is a country of young men EMER 137:1
A. is a land whose centre UPD 336:13
A. is a vast conspiracy UPD 336:14
A. is God's Crucible ZANG 360:27
A. is just ourselves ARN 17:24
A. is the proof MCC 214:10
A., thou half-brother BAIL 26:19
A. to convert the Indians WESL 346:12
A. was thus clearly top SELL 270:5
A. will think tomorrow KIPL 197:16
come back to A. to die JAMES 179:21

animals (*cont.*):
A., whom we have made our slaves — DARW 114:6
a. will not look — AUDEN 21:15
could turn and live with a. — WHIT 348:19
distinguish us from other a. — BEAU 30:16
animula: *A. vagula blandula* — HADR 159:14
Ann: A., Ann! — DE L 116:11
Annabel Lee: I and my A. — POE 250:3
annals: a. blank in history-books — MONT 233:22
simple a. of the poor — GRAY 157:7
War's a. will cloud into night — HARDY 162:12
annihilating: A. all that's made — MARV 220:16
anniversaries: secret a. of the heart — LONG 209:20
anno domini: only a. — HILT 168:18
annoy: He only does it to a. — CARR 91:5
annual: A. income twenty pounds — DICK 118:12
annuity: a. is a very serious business — AUST 23:7
annus: a. horribilis — ELIZ 135:17
anointed: a. my head with oil — BOOK 66:18
wash the balm from an a. king — SHAK 293:22
anointing: Thou the a. Spirit art — BOOK 69:16
another: A. fine mess — LAUR 202:8
taste of a. man's bread — DANTE 113:23
that was in a. country — MARL 219:2
We are members one of a. — BIBLE 55:32
answer: A. a fool according — BIBLE 43:38
a. is blowin' in the wind — DYLAN 129:19
a. to a difficult situation — BEVAN 37:20
A. to the Great Question — ADAMS 1:9
But a. came there none — SCOTT 268:6
But a. made it none — SHAK 274:18
more than the wisest man can a. — COLT 105:17
on the way to a pertinent a. — BRON 72:10
soft a. turneth away wrath — BIBLE 43:24
what a dusty a. gets the soul — MER 223:24
why did you a. the phone — THUR 332:18
would not stay for an a. — BACON 25:18
answerable: We are a. — NEWM 239:1
answered: I came, and no one a. — DE L 116:19
persistence till it must be a. — BROW 77:17
answering: a. that of God — FOX 144:18
ant: Go to the a. thou sluggard — BIBLE 43:11
antagonistic: a. governments — WAUGH 343:23
anti: savage a.-everythings — HOLM 170:16
antic: goat feet dance an a. hay — MARL 218:15
rusty curb of old father a. — SHAK 277:24
To put an a. disposition on — SHAK 275:4
anti-destin: *L'art est un a.* — MALR 217:21
antipathy: strong a. of good to bad — POPE 252:32
antipodes: like A. in shoes — MARV 221:3
sheer opposite, a. — KEATS 190:25
antique: group that's quite a. — BYRON 86:8
noble and nude and a. — SWIN 321:6
traveller from an a. land — SHEL 304:11
antiquities: A. are history defaced — BACON 23:21
Antony: And Brutus A. — SHAK 281:26
A. shall be brought — SHAK 272:5
bear the weight of A. — SHAK 271:10
O! my oblivion is a very A. — SHAK 271:9
anvil: Church is an a. — MACL 215:6
England's on the a. — KIPL 196:3
any: A. old iron, any old iron — COLL 105:6
Ready to be a. thing — BROW 74:8
anybody: Is there a. there — DE L 116:18
Then no one's a. — GILB 151:8
anything: A. for a quiet life — MIDD 224:5
A. goes — PORT 253:17
fall for a. — HAM 160:16
apart: of man's life a thing a. — BYRON 86:4
We have stood a., studiously — WILS 351:19
ape: a. for his grandfather — HUXL 177:21
devil always God's a. — LUTH 212:9
gorgeous buttocks of the a. — HUXL 177:13
Is man an a. or an angel — DISR 121:15
apes: And a. are apes — JONS 187:10

apes (*cont.*):
a., and peacocks — BIBLE 41:31
aphrodisiac: Power is the great a. — KISS 198:6
Apollo: harsh after the songs of A. — SHAK 284:24
Yea, is not even A. — SWIN 321:12
young A., golden-haired — CORN 108:7
Apollos: A. watered — BIBLE 55:3
Apollyon: his name is A. — BUNY 78:20
apologies: people do not want a. — WOD 352:21
apologize: Never a. — FISH 139:24
rule in life never to a. — WOD 352:21
apology: a. for the Devil — BUTL 84:15
a. before you be accused — CHAR 94:22
Apostles: A. would have done — BYRON 85:25
glorious company of the A. — BOOK 63:19
Twelve for the twelve a. — ANON 8:6
Apostolick: Catholick and A. Church — BOOK 65:6
apothecary: a. than a starved poet — LOCK 209:2
apparel: a. oft proclaims the man — SHAK 274:21
appear: Cecilia, a. in visions — AUDEN 20:10
appearance: outward a. — BIBLE 41:15
appearances: Keep up a. — CHUR 98:25
appetite: a.; a feeling and a love — WORD 355:9
a. grows by eating — RAB 257:10
a. may sicken, and so die — SHAK 297:13
Now good digestion wait on a. — SHAK 287:10
satisfying a voracious a. — FIEL 139:10
appetites: as apt to change — DRYD 127:25
cloy the a. they feed — SHAK 271:17
applause: A., n. echo of a platitude — BIER 59:3
sunshine and with a. — BUNY 79:2
apple: a. falling towards England — AUDEN 21:5
a. of his eye — BIBLE 40:23
millionaires love a baked a. — FIRB 139:21
young and easy under the a. — THOM 330:8
apple-pie: A was an a. — ANON 6:6
cabbage-leaf to make an a. — FOOTE 142:20
apples: golden a. of the sun — YEATS 360:1
Kent—a., cherries, hops — DICK 119:26
On moon-washed a. of wonder — DRIN 126:24
Ripe a. drop about my head — MARV 220:15
Stolen, stolen, be your a. — HUNT 176:16
apply: a. our hearts unto wisdom — BOOK 67:27
know my methods. A. them — DOYLE 126:2
appointed: Its own a. limits keep — WHIT 348:9
Like pilgrims to th'a. place — DRYD 128:12
appointment: a. at the end of the world — DIN 121:1
a. by the corrupt few — SHAW 301:27
Every time I create an a. — LOUI 210:14
apprehension: a. of the good — SHAK 293:14
approaching: To see the a. sacrifice — MILM 225:13
après: *A. nous le déluge* — POMP 250:11
apricot: blushing a. and woolly peach — JONS 187:30
April: A., April, laugh — WATS 342:26
A. is the cruellest month — ELIOT 134:18
A. of your youth adorns — HERB 166:19
A. with his shoures soote — CHAU 95:10
Men are A. when they woo — SHAK 273:9
Now that A.'s there — BROW 76:1
uncertain glory of an A. day — SHAK 298:18
aprons: made themselves a. — BIBLE 38:26
apt: A. Alliteration's artful aid — CHUR 98:27
find myself so a. to die — SHAK 281:12
aquarium: a. is gone — LOW 211:12
Aquarius: age of A. — RADO 257:18
Aquitaine: prince of A. — NERV 238:8
Arabia: with the spell of far A. — DE L 116:13
Arabs: fold their tents, like the A. — LONG 209:13
Arbeit: *A. macht frei* — ANON 13:1
arbiter: *Elegantiae a.* — TAC 322:7
arbitrate: Does a. the event — MILT 226:13
arbitrator: old common a., Time — SHAK 297:11
Arcades: *A. ambo* — VIRG 340:1
Arcadia: *Et in A. ego* — ANON 13:15
Arcadians: A. both — VIRG 340:1

arch: All experience is an a.	ADAMS 1:13	armoured: a. cars of dreams	BISH 59:16
all experience is an a.	TENN 328:21	arms: a. against a sea of troubles	SHAK 275:25
a.-flatterer with whom	BACON 24:32	A., and the man	DRYD 128:25
wide a. of the ranged empire	SHAK 271:5	a. and the man	VIRG 338:23
archangel: A. a little damaged	LAMB 200:8	a. of a chambermaid	JOHN 185:21
archbishop: a. had come to see me	BURG 79:14	a. went round her waist	MAS 221:20
archer: mark the a. little meant	SCOTT 268:15	But in my a. till break of day	AUDEN 20:28
arches: down the a. of the years	THOM 331:8	Emparadised in one another's a.	MILT 229:10
Underneath the A.	FLAN 141:2	everlasting a.	BIBLE 40:25
archipelagoes: fading alps and a.	ALDR 3:17	every man in a.	WORD 354:14
architect: a. can only advise	WRIG 357:23	haughty nation proud in a.	MILT 226:6
A. of the Universe	JEANS 180:17	if my love were in my a.	ANON 11:18
architecture: A. is frozen music	SCH 267:17	In one another's a.	YEATS 359:20
A. is the art of how to waste	JOHN 182:2	it hath very long a.	HAL 160:8
A., of all the arts	DIMN 120:25	So he laid down his a.	HOOD 171:4
fall of English a.	BETJ 37:16	To find the a. of my true love	TENN 327:3
frolic a. of the snow	EMER 136:16	To war and a. I fly	LOV 210:20
New styles of a.	AUDEN 21:14	army: a. marches on its stomach	NAP 237:5
Arcturi: those pearled A.	SHEL 304:29	a. of unalterable law	MER 223:22
ardeur: a. dans mes veines cachée	RAC 257:16	backbone of the A.	KIPL 196:10
ardua: Per a. ad astra	ANON 13:18	brought the A. home	GUED 159:6
are: Let them be as they a.	CLEM 102:3	contemptible little a.	ANON 7:4
That which we a., we are	TENN 328:25	noble a. of Martyrs	BOOK 63:19
we know what we a.	SHAK 276:33	[our a.] the scum of the earth	WELL 345:14
area: despondently at a. gates	ELIOT 134:4	aroint: A. thee, witch!	SHAK 285:3
Argos: remembers his sweet A.	VIRG 339:21	aroma: a. of performing seals	HART 163:8
argue: a. with someone who denies	AUCT 20:4	aromatic: faint beneath the a. pain	WINC 352:2
earth does not a.	WHIT 348:23	a-roving: I'll go no more a.	ANON 6:5
arguing: I am not a. with you	WHIS 347:9	arrangements: has no a.	WHIT 348:23
argument: a. of the broken window	PANK 245:2	arrayed: a. like one of these	BIBLE 49:4
height of this great a.	MILT 228:9	arrest: Is swift in his a.	SHAK 277:15
I have found you an a.	JOHN 186:5	arrive: better thing than to a.	STEV 317:6
it is the a. of tyrants	PITT 249:7	to a. where we started	ELIOT 133:10
stir without great a.	SHAK 276:31	arrogant: to subdue the a.	VIRG 339:16
This is a rotten a.	ANON 11:3	arrow: Every a. that flies	LONG 209:14
Tories own no a. but force	BROW 74:25	I shot an a. into the air	LONG 209:10
when blood is their a.	SHAK 279:13	nor for the a. that flieth	BOOK 67:29
Whigs admit no force but a.	BROW 74:25	time's a.	EDD 130:10
would be a. for a week	SHAK 277:28	arrows: a. in the hand of the giant	BOOK 68:31
Argus: A. were but eunuch	SHAK 284:14	a. of outrageous fortune	SHAK 275:25
Ariel: Caliban casts out A.	POUND 254:17	Bring me my a. of desire	BLAKE 61:12
arise: A. shine	BIBLE 46:23	ars: A. longa, vita brevis	HIPP 168:19
I will a. and go now	YEATS 359:12	arse: politician is an a.	CUMM 112:18
Let us a. and go like men	STEV 317:15	sit on your a. for fifty years	MACN 216:2
aristocracy: absentee a.	DISR 121:7	arsenal: great a. of democracy	ROOS 262:12
a. in a republic	MITF 232:8	art: All passes. A. alone	DOBS 122:25
a. means government by	CHES 98:12	all the adulteries of a.	JONS 187:6
A. of the Moneybag	CARL 90:15	a. can wash her guilt away	GOLD 155:13
aristocrat: A., democrat, autocrat	TENN 326:26	a. constantly aspires	PATER 246:14
aristocratic: a. class from the Philistines	ARN 17:26	A. does not reproduce	KLEE 198:10
Aristotle: it is contrary to A.	TAWN 322:20	A. for art's sake	CONS 107:13
arithmetical: in an a. ratio	MALT 217:5	a. for art's sake	COUS 108:17
ark: two unto Noah into the A.	BIBLE 39:8	A. has no other end	FLAU 141:13
arm: a. doth bind the restless wave	WHIT 348:9	A. is a jealous mistress	EMER 136:19
seal upon thine a.	BIBLE 45:1	A. is a revolt against fate	MALR 217:4
strength with his a.	BIBLE 51:29	A. is born of humiliation	AUDEN 21:20
Wi' the auld moon in her a.	BALL 28:5	A. is meant to disturb	BRAQ 71:14
arma: A. virumque cano	VIRG 338:23	A. is pattern informed by	READ 258:9
armadas: till the great A. come	NEWB 238:11	A. is significant deformity	FRY 147:3
Armageddon: Lincoln County Road or A.	DYLAN 130:7	A. is the imposing	WHIT 348:4
armchair: Fortieth spare A.	BROW 75:26	A. is vice	DEGAS 116:2
armchairs: a. tight about the hips	WOD 352:22	a. lawful as eating	SHAK 299:4
armed: A. neutrality is ineffectual	WILS 351:20	A. most cherishes	BROW 76:21
a. with more than complete steel	ANON 8:7	a. of the possible	BISM 59:17
Armenteers: Mademoiselle from A.	ANON 9:5	a.'s hid causes	JONS 187:5
armes: Aux a., citoyens	ROUG 263:16	Desiring this man's a.	SHAK 299:14
armies: ignorant a. clash by night	ARN 16:12	Drawing is the true test of a.	INGR 178:17
plenty of money and large a.	ANOU 14:4	Dying is an a.	PLATH 249:15
with your land a. in China	MONT 233:23	enemy of good a. the pram	CONN 106:25
armistice: a. for twenty years	FOCH 142:15	Enough of science and of a.	WORD 357:5
armour: put on the a. of light	BIBLE 55:1	excellence of every a.	KEATS 193:1
Put on the whole a. of God	BIBLE 56:3	glib and oily a.	SHAK 282:18
put upon us the a. of light	BOOK 64:21	good grey guardians of a.	WILB 349:12
whole a. of God	BIBLE 56:4	history of a.	BUTL 84:14

art (*cont.*):

importance of a work of a.	FLAU 141:8
In a. the best is good enough	GOET 154:9
industry without a. is brutality	RUSK 264:11
It's clever, but is it A.	KIPL 196:8
kills love, it kills a.	WAUGH 343:17
Life is short, the a. long	HIPP 168:19
Living is my job and my a.	MONT 233:16
Minister that meddles with a.	MELB 222:21
More matter with less a.	SHAK 275:10
nature is the a. of God	BROW 74:14
next to Nature, A.	LAND 200:22
only interested in a.	SHAW 302:25
people start on all this A.	HERB 166:12
rest is the madness of a.	JAMES 179:23
resuscitate the dead a.	POUND 254:14
revenge of intellect upon a.	SONT 311:9
Rules destroy genius and a.	HAZL 164:5
Shakespeare wanted a.	JONS 187:31
strains of unpremeditated a.	SHEL 305:6
triumph of the embalmer's a.	VIDAL 338:12
when A. is too precise	HERR 167:15

artful: Apt Alliteration's a. aid — CHUR 98:27
Arthur: He's in A.'s bosom — SHAK 279:3
articles: These a. subscribed — CONG 106:21
artifex: *Qualis a. pereo!* — NERO 238:7
artificer: great a. made — STEV 317:20
lean unwashed a. — SHAK 282:11
artificial: All things are a. — BROW 74:14
said it was a. respiration — BURG 79:15
artisan: employment to the a. — BELL 33:22
artist: a., like the God — JOYCE 188:8
a. man and the mother woman — SHAW 301:18
a. must be in his work — FLAU 141:11
a. will be judged — CONN 106:27
God is really only another a. — PIC 248:18
no man is born an a. — WALT 342:9
Portrait of the A. — JOYCE 188:6
sign of the true a. — VIDAL 338:14
trust the a. — LAWR 202:15
What an a. dies with me — NERO 238:7
artistic: intellectual and a. — BERL 36:4
arts: a. babblative and scribblative — SOUT 312:3
cry both a. and learning down — QUAR 257:5
Dear nurse of a. — SHAK 280:2
famed in all great a. — ARN 17:21
France, mother of a. — DU B 128:32
Greece, mother of a. — MILT 230:6
had I but followed the a. — SHAK 297:16
No a.; no letters — HOBB 169:10
as: A. with gladness men of old — DIX 122:24
ascend: a. the brightest heaven — SHAK 278:33
ascending: angels of God a. — BIBLE 39:21
ash: A. on an old man's sleeve — ELIOT 133:8
laughter of an empty a. can — CRANE 110:32
Oak, and A., and Thorn — KIPL 197:1
ashamed: more things a man is a. of — SHAW 301:16
something he is a. of — SHAW 300:25
to feel a. of home — DICK 118:25
ashbuds: More black than a. — TENN 323:23
ashen: By a. roots the violets blow — TENN 325:29
ashes: a. to ashes, dust to dust — BOOK 66:8
a. under Uricon — HOUS 174:23
burnt to a. — GRAH 156:4
For the a. of his fathers — MAC 214:3
past is a bucket of a. — SAND 266:15
sour grapes and a. — ASHF 18:24
splendid in a. — BROW 74:7
turn the universe to a. — MISS 231:23
aside: Just try and set death a. — TURG 335:14
ask: A., and it shall be given — BIBLE 49:9
a. faithfully we may obtain — BOOK 64:7
A. me no more — CAREW 89:20
a. not what your country — KENN 194:6
a. the hard question — AUDEN 21:16

ask (*cont.*):

a. why	AUDEN 20:17
Don't a. me, ask the horse	FREUD 146:2
I a. and cannot answer	SHAW 303:1
Where a. is have	SMART 308:11

asking: and a. too much — CANN 89:10
[or *third*] time of a. — BOOK 65:25
asleep: Half a. as they stalk — HARDY 162:11
men were all a. the snow — BRID 72:1
That sucks the nurse a. — SHAK 272:9
very houses seem a. — WORD 354:16
asp: on the hole of the a. — BIBLE 45:20
asparagus: A. and it appeared — DICK 118:30
aspens: Willows whiten, a. quiver — TENN 325:35
aspes: a. leef she gan to quake — CHAU 96:17
asphalt: only monument the a. road — ELIOT 134:13
aspidistra: biggest a. in the world — HARP 163:2
Keep the a. flying — ORW 242:2
aspire: light, and will a. — SHAK 300:17
ass: jaw of an a. — BIBLE 41:5
kiss my a. in Macy's window — JOHN 181:20
law is a a. — DICK 119:20
law is such an a. — CHAP 94:18
nor his ox, nor his a. — BIBLE 40:9
assassin: you are an a. — ROST 263:12
assassination: absolutism moderated by a. — ANON 6:30
A. is the extreme form — SHAW 302:22
A. is the quickest way — MOL 232:22
if the a. could trammel — SHAK 285:22
assaults: all a. of our enemies — BOOK 64:5
assent: a. with civil leer — POPE 251:6
asses: seeking a. found a kingdom — MILT 230:5
assume: A. a virtue — SHAK 276:23
assurance: make a. double sure — SHAK 287:21
One of the low on whom a. sits — ELIOT 134:29
Assyrian: A. came down — BYRON 85:22
Astolat: lily maid of A. — TENN 324:7
astonish: A. me — DIAG 117:15
astonished: a. at my own moderation — CLIVE 102:6
astonishment: Your a.'s odd — KNOX 198:18
astra: *Per ardua ad a.* — ANON 13:18
sic itur ad a. — VIRG 339:19
astray: sheep have gone a. — BIBLE 46:19
astronomers: Confounding her a. — HODG 169:14
asunder: let no man put a. — BOOK 66:3
let not man put a. — BIBLE 50:20
asylum: a. run by lunatics — LLOY 208:12
taken charge of the a. — ROWL 264:1
atheism: inclineth man's mind to a. — BACON 24:12
atheist: a. half believes a God — YOUNG 360:31
a. is a man who has no — BUCH 77:27
a.-laugh's a poor exchange — BURNS 82:6
female a. talks you dead — JOHN 183:8
atheists: no a. in the foxholes — CUMM 113:6
Athens: A. arose — SHEL 303:17
A., the eye of Greece — MILT 230:8
athirst: a. of the fountain — BIBLE 58:6
Atlantic: In the steep A. stream — MILT 226:7
Atlas: disencumbered A. — COWP 110:4
atom: mystery of the a. — BRAD 71:10
only because the carbon a. — JEANS 180:16
saw the flaring a.-streams — TENN 326:21
stars leads through the a. — EDD 130:12
atomic: primordial a. globule — GILB 151:18
atomies: team of little a. — SHAK 294:24
atoms: a. of Democritus — BLAKE 61:14
fortuitous concurrence of a. — PALM 244:19
attach: Where people wish to a. — AUST 22:23
attachment: a. à la Plato — GILB 152:11
attack: both by his plan of a. — SASS 267:13
dared a. my Chesterton — BELL 33:16
lead such dire a. — MAC 214:6
attacked: when a. it defends itself — ANON 12:3
attacking: situation excellent, I am a. — FOCH 142:14
attempt: a. and not the deed — SHAK 286:13

attempts: sins are a. to fill voids — WEIL 345:2
attendant: Am an a. lord — ELIOT 134:1
attendre: J'ai failli a. — LOUI 210:13
attention: a. of the nation — BAG 26:12
So a. must be paid — MILL 225:3
Attic: mellow glory of the A. stage — ARN 17:20
Not, at any rate, an A. grace — POUND 254:16
O A. shape! Fair attitude — KEATS 191:22
where the A. bird — MILT 230:6
attire: a. creeps rustling to her knees — KEATS 190:18
attitude: O Attic shape! Fair a. — KEATS 191:22
attitudes: Anglo-Saxon a. — CARR 92:3
attorney: rich a.'s elderly ugly daughter — GILB 152:30
attracted: a. by God — INGE 178:13
attraction: feels the a. of earth — LONG 209:14
attractions: register competing a. — KNIG 198:14
attractive: Here's metal more a. — SHAK 276:8
Auburn: Sweet A., loveliest village — GOLD 154:17
auctoritee: Experience, though noon a. — CHAU 96:5
audace: et toujours de l'a. — DANT 114:1
audacity: Arm me, a. — SHAK 273:23
a. is knowing how far — COCT 103:4
a. of elected persons — WHIT 348:15
Auden: smack at A. — EMPS 137:4
audi: A. partem alteram — AUG 22:1
audience: fit a. find, though few — MILT 229:19
whisks his a. into the middle — HOR 173:1
audiences: English-speaking a. — WHAR 347:3
augury: Not a whit, we defy a. — SHAK 277:13
August: A. for the people — AUDEN 20:14
A. is a wicked month — O'BR 240:18
I'm as corny as Kansas in A. — HAMM 161:4
To recommence in A. — BYRON 86:26
auld: For a. lang syne — BURNS 81:25
when 'tis a. it waxeth cauld — BALL 28:10
aunt: A. calling to A. like mastodons — WOD 352:19
A. Jobiska's Runcible Cat — LEAR 203:15
Charley's a. from Brazil — THOM 330:5
wisest a., telling the saddest — SHAK 290:21
aunts: bad a. and good aunts — WOD 352:15
dull a., and croaking rooks — POPE 251:24
his cousins and his a. — GILB 152:17
auri: A. sacra fames — VIRG 339:8
Austerlitz: at A. and Waterloo — SAND 266:14
Australia: you take A. right back — KEAT 190:8
Austria: Don John of A. — CHES 97:25
author: a. and finisher of our faith — BIBLE 56:27
a. and giver of all good things — BOOK 64:25
a. as you choose a friend — DILL 120:22
a. of himself — SHAK 273:21
a. of peace — BOOK 64:5
expect an a. and find a man — PASC 246:1
six characters in search of an a. — PIR 249:1
write like a distinguished a. — NAB 236:20
authority: A. doesn't work without prestige — DE G 116:5
A. forgets a dying king — TENN 324:18
Drest in a little brief a. — SHAK 288:14
Experience, though noon a. — CHAU 96:5
faith that stands on a. — EMER 136:3
I am a man under a. — BIBLE 49:17
independence of his a. — MILL 224:18
lie of A. — AUDEN 21:11
authors: invades a. like a monarch — DRYD 128:29
autobiography: a. is an obituary — CRISP 111:21
autocrat: Aristocrat, democrat, a. — TENN 326:26
I shall be an a. — CATH 92:21
autres: pour encourager les a. — VOLT 340:12
autumn: descends the a. evening — ARN 17:3
happy a.-fields — TENN 327:22
thou breath of A.'s being — SHEL 304:8
avarice: a. and ambition — SMITH 308:20
A., the spur of industry — HUME 176:5
beyond the dreams of a. — JOHN 185:29
beyond the dreams of a. — MOORE 234:5

ave: a. atque vale — CAT 93:8
A. verum corpus — ANON 13:14
Ave Maria: A., gratia plena — ANON 13:13
A.! 'tis the hour of prayer — BYRON 86:18
average: A. made lethal — SHAF 270:19
averages: fugitive from th' law of a. — MAUL 222:13
Averno: Facilis descensus A. — VIRG 339:12
aversion: begin with a little a. — SHER 305:27
manner which is my a. — BYRON 86:16
avis: Rara a. — JUV 189:7
avoiding: way of a. non-being — TILL 332:21
Avon: Sweet Swan of A. — JONS 187:29
awake: A.! for Morning — FITZ 140:4
A., my soul, and with the sun — KEN 193:20
England! a.! — BLAKE 60:21
away: a.! for I will fly to thee — KEATS 192:1
kiss, a sigh, and so a. — CRAS 111:15
awe: in a. of such a thing — SHAK 280:26
increasing wonder and a. — KANT 189:22
aweary: I am a., aweary — TENN 326:22
awful: this is an a. place — SCOTT 268:4
awfully: a. big adventure — BARR 29:13
awkward: a. squad fire over me — BURNS 82:30
awoke: a. one morning from uneasy dreams — KAFKA 189:16
So I a., and behold — BUNY 79:5
axe: let the great a. fall — SHAK 277:4
Lizzie Borden took an a. — ANON 8:22
axes: your sharp-edged a. — WHIT 348:13
axis: a. of the earth sticks out — HOLM 170:14
sword is the a. of the world — DE G 116:6
under-belly of the A. — CHUR 99:19
axle: His glowing a. doth allay — MILT 226:7
ayes: no question makes of A. — FITZ 140:13
Azores: At Flores in the A. — TENN 328:10
azure: from out the a. main — THOM 331:20
With a., white, and red — DRUM 127:1
azure-lidded: slept an a. sleep — KEATS 190:21

B

B: B bit it — ANON 6:6
babblative: arts b. and scribblative — SOUT 312:3
babbled: a' b. of green fields — SHAK 279:4
babbler: What will this b. say — BIBLE 54:19
babe: love the b. that milks me — SHAK 286:6
babes: As newborn b., desire — BIBLE 57:7
very b. and sucklings — BOOK 66:10
babies: Ballads and b. — MCC 214:13
bit the b. in the cradles — BROW 76:26
hates dogs and b. — ROST 263:13
Other people's b. — HERB 166:13
putting milk into b. — CHUR 99:21
Bab-lock-hithe: Thames at B. — ARN 17:7
baby: b. doesn't understand English — KNOX 198:19
b. figure of the giant mass — SHAK 296:32
B. in an ox's stall — BETJ 36:18
b. laughed for the first time — BARR 29:11
Bats with b. faces — ELIOT 134:30
Burn, b., burn — ANON 6:14
Make it one for my b. — MERC 223:11
see my b. at my breast — SHAK 272:9
Where did you come from, b. dear — MACD 214:18
Babylon: B. in all its desolation — DAV 114:16
B. is fallen — BIBLE 57:34
B. THE GREAT, THE MOTHER — BIBLE 58:2
By the waters of B. — BOOK 69:2
Ere B. was dust — SHEL 304:15
Bacchus: charioted by B. and his pards — KEATS 192:1
'baccy: b. for the Clerk — KIPL 196:28
bachelors: All reformers are b. — MOORE 234:6
back: at my b. I always hear — MARV 220:24
B. in the USSR — MCC 205:10

back (cont.):
B. to the future | GALE 361:2
B. to the garden | MITC 232:4
boys in the b. room | LOES 209:5
boys in the b. rooms | BEAV 31:4
I counted them all b. | HANR 161:8
I sit on a man's b. | TOLS 333:13
never turned his b. | BROW 75:11
safe to go b. in the water | ANON 8:15
those before cried 'B.!' | MAC 214:6
backbone: b. of the Army | KIPL 196:10
backhand: wonderful b. drive | BETJ 37:8
backs: beast with two b. | SHAK 291:30
backward: B. ran sentences | GIBBS 150:18
But I by b. steps would move | VAUG 337:10
look b. to their ancestors | BURKE 80:12
bacon: b.'s not the only thing | KING 195:20
bad: animal is very b. | ANON 12:3
b. against the worse | DAY-L 115:6
b. aunts and good aunts | WOD 352:15
b. die late | DEFOE 115:17
b. end unhappily | STOP 318:5
b. things that hotel-keepers | TROL 334:16
b. unhappily | WILDE 349:20
B. women never take the blame | BROO 73:11
brave b. man | CLAR 101:12
can't be all b. | ROST 263:13
For being a little b. | SHAK 288:26
How sad and b. and mad | BROW 75:21
Mad, b., and dangerous | LAMB 199:22
no such thing as b. publicity | BEHAN 32:19
our sad b. glad mad brother's | SWIN 321:5
Pleasure's for those who are b. | YES 360:12
poor in a loomp is b. | TENN 327:10
She was not really b. at heart | BELL 33:11
so much b. in the best of us | ANON 10:20
This bold b. man | SHAK 280:15
When b. men combine | BURKE 81:4
when she was b. | LONG 210:6
Where everything is b. | BRAD 71:9
badge: b. of all our tribe | SHAK 289:4
red b. of courage | CRANE 111:3
badly: it is worth doing b. | CHES 98:16
badness: All good and no b. | SKEL 308:2
bag: b. and baggage | GLAD 153:10
not with b. and baggage | SHAK 273:3
baggage: bag and b. | GLAD 153:10
bagman: Cobden is an inspired b. | CARL 90:25
bah: 'B.,' said Scrooge | DICK 118:6
bainters: I hate all Boets and B. | GEOR 149:20
baker: b. rhymes for his pursuit | BROW 77:11
Baker Street: B. irregulars | DOYLE 126:3
balance: uncertain b. of proud time | GREE 158:8
balances: weighed in the b. | BIBLE 47:12
bald: b., and short of breath | SASS 267:8
Go up, thou b. head | BIBLE 42:8
otherwise b. and unconvincing | GILB 152:5
two b. men over a comb | BORG 69:24
baldness: far side of b. | SMITH 309:10
bales: with costly b. | TENN 326:10
Balkans: silly thing in the B. | BISM 59:20
ball: at a girl throwing a b. | WOOLF 354:4
b. no question makes | FITZ 140:13
like a man yawning at a b. | LERM 205:25
Only wind it into a b. | BLAKE 60:20
real business of a b. | SURT 319:14
sweetness, up into one b. | MARV 221:1
ballad: And I met with a b. | CALV 88:7
ballads: B. and babies | MCC 214:13
Of b., songs and snatches | GILB 151:17
permitted to make all the b. | FLET 142:3
ball-floor: Dance on this b. | BLUN 62:14
Balliol: B. made me | BELL 34:2
balloon: something in a huge b. | WORD 356:3
ballot: b. stronger than the bullet | LINC 207:4

balls: B. will be lost always | BERR 36:11
our rackets to these b. | SHAK 279:1
two pitch b. | SHAK 284:14
balm: b. from an anointed king | SHAK 293:22
general b. th'hydroptic earth | DONNE 124:8
Is there no b. in Gilead | BIBLE 46:29
pours out out a b. upon the world | KEATS 190:25
banality: b. of evil | AREN 15:4
Banbury: To B. came I | BRAT 71:16
band: importunate b. | BETJ 37:13
wearied B. swoons | HUXL 177:12
we b. of brothers | SHAK 279:20
bandied: tennis-balls, struck and b. | WEBS 344:21
bands: drew them with b. of love | BIBLE 47:18
loose the b. of Orion | BIBLE 43:4
who pursue Culture in b. | WHAR 347:4
bandy: b. civilities | JOHN 184:19
bane: Deserve the precious b. | MILT 228:19
baneful: b. effects of the spirit | WASH 342:21
bang: b. these dogs of Seville | TENN 328:12
b.—went saxpence | PUNCH 256:12
bigger b. for a buck | ANON 6:12
Not with a b. but a whimper | ELIOT 133:20
banish: b. plump Jack | SHAK 278:1
banishment: bitter bread of b. | SHAK 293:21
bank: b. whereon the wild thyme | SHAK 290:26
I cry all the way to the b. | LIB 206:22
pregnant b. swelled up | DONNE 124:2
this b. and shoal of time | SHAK 285:22
banknotes: fill old bottles with b. | KEYN 194:16
bankrupt: B. of life | DRYD 127:8
banks: bonnie b. o' Loch Lomon' | ANON 10:2
Ye b. and braes o' bonny Doon | BURNS 81:27
banner: b. with the strange device | LONG 209:17
'Tis the star-spangled b. | KEY 194:12
banners: Confusion on thy b. wait | GRAY 157:1
royal b. forward go | FORT 144:5
banquet: trifling foolish b. | SHAK 294:27
baptism: Godmothers in my B. | BOOK 65:20
bar: if met where any b. is | HARDY 162:13
no moaning of the b. | TENN 323:18
When I have crossed the b. | TENN 323:19
Barabbas: Now B. was a publisher | CAMP 89:1
Now B. was a robber | BIBLE 54:2
barbarians: B., Philistines, and Populace | ARN 17:24
become of us without the b. | CAV 93:11
his young b. all at play | BYRON 85:10
name the former the B. | ARN 17:26
barbaric: b. yawp over the roofs | WHIT 348:22
barbarous: b. dissonance | MILT 226:17
invention of a b. age | MILT 228:5
bard: Hear the voice of the B. | BLAKE 61:26
bare: B. like nude, giant girls | SPEN 313:3
B. ruined choirs | SHAK 299:24
barefoot: I was born b. | LONG 209:8
bargain: dateless b. to engrossing death | SHAK 295:25
Necessity never made a good b. | FRAN 145:10
bargains: Here's the rule for b. | DICK 119:3
barge: b. she sat in | SHAK 271:14
bark: come out as I do, and b. | JOHN 186:1
Though his b. cannot be lost | SHAK 285:4
Barkis: B. is willin' | DICK 118:9
barks: Nicean b. of yore | POE 250:8
barley: among the bearded b. | TENN 325:36
Long fields of b. and of rye | TENN 325:34
Barlow: Hornby and my B. | THOM 331:6
barmaid: shocking the b. | SITW 307:18
barmaids: Are B. Chaste | MAS 221:20
baronet: No little lily-handed b. | TENN 328:9
barrel: drowned in a b. of Malmesey | FABY 138:8
handful of meal in a b. | BIBLE 41:35
Oh we ain't got a b. of money | WOODS 353:19
out of the b. of a gun | MAO T 217:19
barrels: slurp into the b. | FISH 139:26

barren: acre of b. ground	SHAK 295:32
b. sister all your life	SHAK 290:12
Close up those b. leaves	WORD 357:5
I am but a b. stock	ELIZ 135:12
barricade: At some disputed b.	SEEG 269:13
barrow: red wheel b.	WILL 351:8
base: b., common and popular	SHAK 279:9
Labour without joy is b.	RUSK 264:18
Things base and vile	SHAK 290:16
Why bastard? wherefore b.	SHAK 282:20
baseless: b. fabric of this vision	SHAK 296:10
baseness: Detraction is but b.' varlet	JONS 187:10
baser: lewd fellows of the b. sort	BIBLE 54:18
bashful: maiden of b. fifteen	SHER 306:6
basil-pot: To steal my B.	KEATS 191:4
Basingstoke: hidden meaning—like B.	GILB 152:27
Bass: Guinness, Allsopp, B.	CALV 88:8
bastard: all my eggs in one b.	PARK 245:15
Well, we knocked the b. off	HILL 168:15
Why b.? wherefore base	SHAK 282:20
bastards: b. grind you down	ANON 9:15
gods, stand up for b.	SHAK 282:21
bastion: like a b.'s mole	SMART 308:10
bat: beetle and the b.	JOHN 184:21
black b., night, has flown	TENN 326:28
Ere the b. hath flown	SHAK 287:5
On the b.'s back I do fly	SHAK 296:14
purest play is like some b.	WILB 349:11
Twinkle, twinkle, little b.	CARR 91:7
weak-eyed b.	COLL 105:10
bath: I test my b. before I sit	NASH 237:16
bathe: b. those beauteous feet	FLET 142:8
bathing: caught the Whigs b.	DISR 121:9
large b. machine	GILB 151:16
long b. of a summer's day	WORD 356:9
bathroom: revolutionary in a b.	LINK 207:17
baths: Two walking b.	CRAS 111:14
baton: cartridge-pouch the marshal's b.	LOUI 210:16
bats: B. with baby faces	ELIOT 134:30
batsman: I am the b. and the bat	LANG 201:2
battalions: big b.	VOLT 340:23
not single spies, but in b.	SHAK 276:35
your dreams in pale b. go	SORL 311:16
battening: B. upon huge seaworms	TENN 325:32
batter: B. my heart	DONNE 123:10
battle: B. method of untying	BIER 59:4
b. to the strong	DAV 114:12
better in b. than in bed	STER 315:20
die well that die in a b.	SHAK 279:13
drunk delight of b.	TENN 328:21
foremost in b. was Mary Ambree	BALL 28:1
France has lost a b.	DE G 116:3
greatest misery is a b. gained	WELL 345:12
marriage a field of b.	STEV 317:8
my tongue, the glorious b.	FORT 144:4
noise of battle rolled	TENN 324:17
nor the b. to the strong	BIBLE 44:20
No war, or b.'s sound	MILT 227:26
out of b. I escaped	OWEN 244:2
smelleth the b. afar off	BIBLE 43:5
strife is o'er, the b. done	POTT 253:28
When the b.'s lost and won	SHAK 284:25
battledore: B. and shuttlecock	DICK 119:29
battlefield: b. is the heart of man	DOST 125:2
battle-flags: b. were furled	TENN 326:12
battlements: from the white b.	HEAT 164:13
battles: b. long ago	WORD 357:2
b. of all subsequent wars	ORW 242:4
Dead b., like dead generals	TUCH 335:7
mother of b.	HUSS 176:22
baubles: Take away these b.	CROM 112:5
bawcock: king's a b.	SHAK 279:10
bawling: b. what it likes	ARN 17:27
bay: like a green b.-tree	BOOK 66:28

bay (cont.):	
steamer breaking from the b.	AUDEN 20:25
baying: b. for broken glass	WAUGH 343:18
bayonet: b. is a weapon with a worker	ANON 6:7
bayonets: sods with our b. turning	WOLFE 352:26
throne of b.	INGE 178:14
Bayonne: thy hams, B.!	POPE 250:21
bays: oak, or b.	MARV 220:14
sprig of b. in fifty years	SWIFT 320:19
bazaar: Fate's great b.	MACN 216:9
be: And can it b.	WESL 346:3
b.-all and the end-all	SHAK 285:22
b. as they are or not at all	CLEM 102:3
Cared not to b. at all	MILT 228:22
Let b. be finale of seem	STEV 316:6
lief not b. as live to be	SHAK 280:26
poem should not mean but b.	MACL 215:9
that which shall b.	BIBLE 44:8
To b., or not to be	SHAK 275:25
beachèd: b. verge of the salt flood	SHAK 296:24
beaches: We shall fight on the b.	CHUR 99:13
Beachy Head: by way of B.	CHES 98:2
beacons: b. of wise men	HUXL 177:20
beaded: b. bubbles winking	KEATS 191:30
beak: He takes in his b.	MERR 223:26
thy b. from out my heart	POE 250:7
beaker: b. full of the warm South	KEATS 191:30
Beale: Miss Buss and Miss B.	ANON 9:10
beam: B. me up, Scotty	RODD 261:13
b. that is in thine own eye	BIBLE 49:7
beaming: Leading onward, b. bright	DIX 122:24
beamish: b. nephew, beware	CARR 92:8
beams: And tricks his b.	MILT 227:18
bean: home of the b. and the cod	BOSS 70:1
Nine b. rows will I have	YEATS 359:12
not too French French b.	GILB 152:11
bear: B. of Very Little Brain	MILNE 225:15
b. thee in their hands	BOOK 67:30
b. the yoke in his youth	BIBLE 47:2
b. with a sore head	MARR 219:26
Cannot b. very much reality	ELIOT 132:27
Exit, pursued by a b.	SHAK 298:25
fire was furry as a b.	SITW 307:17
fitted by nature to b.	AUR 22:9
Grizzly B. is huge and wild	HOUS 174:8
Moppsikon Floppsikon b.	LEAR 203:18
still less the b.	FRERE 145:22
wounded spirit who can b.?	BIBLE 43:29
bear-baiting: Puritan hated b.	MAC 213:19
beard: grey b. and glittering eye	COL 104:3
husband with a b. on his face	SHAK 291:15
King of Spain's B.	DRAKE 126:11
was an Old Man with a b.	LEAR 203:17
bearded: b. like the pard	SHAK 272:26
beards: merry in hall when b.	SHAK 278:31
beareth: B. all things	BIBLE 55:12
that b. up things light	BACON 25:7
bears: And dancing dogs and b.	HODG 169:13
b. might come with buns	ISH 178:21
tap crude rhythms for b.	FLAU 141:7
beast: And what rough b.	YEATS 359:25
beast, but a just b.	ANON 6:8
B. stands for strong mutually	WAUGH 343:23
b., that wants discourse	SHAK 274:12
Beauty killed the B.	ROSE 111:17
be either a b. or a god	ARIS 15:19
count the number of the b.	BIBLE 57:33
fit night out for man or b.	FIEL 139:17
making the b. with two backs	SHAK 291:30
more subtil than any b.	BIBLE 38:24
or the name of the b.	BIBLE 57:32
regardeth the life of his b.	BIBLE 43:20
serpent subtlest b.	MILT 229:22
terrible marks of the b.	HARDY 161:23
beastie: cow'rin', tim'rous b.	BURNS 82:26

beasties: and long-leggety b.	ANON 7:7
beastly: b. to the Germans	COW 108:20
How b. the bourgeois is	LAWR 202:18
beasts: b. that have no understanding	BOOK 65:26
beat: b. him when he sneezes	CARR 91:5
b. the ground	MILT 226:9
b. their swords into plowshares	BIBLE 45:5
beaten: b. road	SHEL 303:16
No Englishman is ever fairly b.	SHAW 302:20
beating: b. in the void his luminous	ARN 18:4
b. myself for spite	SIDN 306:17
Charity and b. begins at home	FLET 142:7
glory of b. the French	WOLFE 353:3
Is b. on the door	YEATS 359:6
than driven by b.	ASCH 18:18
two hearts b. each to each	BROW 76:17
beatings: dread of b.	BETJ 37:14
Beatles: And the B.' first LP	LARK 201:12
beats: light which b. upon a throne	TENN 324:1
beatus: B. vir qui timet Dominum	BIBLE 58:11
beauté: tout n'est qu'ordre et b.	BAUD 30:4
beauties: unripened b. of the north	ADD 2:14
You meaner b. of the night	WOTT 357:16
beautiful: b. and death-struck year	HOUS 174:25
b. and simple	HENRY 166:4
b. and therefore to be wooed	SHAK 280:6
b. cannot be the way to	COUS 108:17
B. dreamer, wake unto me	FOST 144:9
b. things in the world	RUSK 264:17
b. upon the mountains	BIBLE 46:15
Black is b.	ANON 6:13
deal of scorn looks b.	SHAK 298:6
entirely b.	AUDEN 20:28
innocent and the b.	YEATS 359:8
or believe to be b.	MORR 235:18
Our love of what is b.	PER 248:1
perpetual hunger to be b.	RHYS 259:14
see, not feel, how b. they are	COL 103:14
singing 'Oh, how b.!'	KIPL 196:16
Small is b.	SCH 267:25
When a woman isn't b.	CHEK 96:29
beauty: all that b., all that wealth	GRAY 157:7
be a b. without a fortune	FARQ 138:16
b. and truth	KEATS 193:1
B. both so ancient	AUG 21:24
b. coming and the beauty	WORD 355:12
b. draws us with a single	POPE 253:4
b. faded has no second	PHIL 248:14
B. for some provides escape	HUXL 177:13
B. is all very well at first	SHAW 301:25
B. is momentary in the mind	STEV 316:11
B. is mysterious as well as	DOST 125:2
B. is Nature's brag	MILT 226:20
B. is no quality in things	HUME 176:9
b. is only sin deep	SAKI 265:19
B. is truth, truth beauty	KEATS 191:24
B. itself doth of itself	SHAK 299:7
B. killed the Beast	ROSE 111:17
b. lives though lilies	FLEC 141:16
b. making beautiful old rime	SHAK 300:4
b. of inflections	STEV 316:13
b. of Israel is slain upon	BIBLE 41:20
b. of the good old cause	WORD 356:1
b.'s empires, like to	SUCK 318:23
B.'s ensign	SHAK 295:24
b.'s rose might never die	SHAK 299:11
b. that hath not some strangeness	BACON 24:14
B. that must die	KEATS 191:27
B. too rich for use	SHAK 294:26
B. vanishes; beauty passes	DE L 116:14
body's b. lives	STEV 316:11
conscious stone to b. grew	EMER 136:15
delves the parallels in b.'s	SHAK 299:22
dreamed that life was b.	HOOP 171:16

beauty (cont.):	
England, home and b.	ARN 18:14
fatal gift of b.	BYRON 85:7
Helen, thy b. is to me	POE 250:8
her b. made the bright world	SHEL 305:17
in the b. of holiness	BOOK 68:2
in the b. of holiness	MONS 233:3
Of its own b. is the mind diseased	BYRON 85:9
principal b. in building	FULL 147:6
seizes as b. must be truth	KEATS 192:23
She walks in b., like the night	BYRON 87:6
simple b. and naught else	BROW 75:30
terrible b. is born	YEATS 359:3
thick, bereft of b.	SHAK 295:30
thing of b. is a joy for ever	KEATS 190:11
we just b. see	JONS 187:24
where B. was, nothing ever	GALS 147:17
Where perhaps some b. lies	MILT 227:3
whose b. is past change	HOPK 172:13
with him is b. slain	SHAK 300:19
witty b. is a power	MER 223:12
youth and a little b.	WEBS 344:14
Beaverbrook: mind that of Lord B.	ATTL 19:12
because: B. I do not hope to turn again	ELIOT 132:18
B. it's there	MALL 216:22
B. it was he; b. it was me	MONT 233:12
smashed it into b.	CUMM 113:2
B. we're here	ANON 11:13
becks: Nods, and b.	MILT 227:1
become: B. themselves in her	SHAK 271:17
do all that may b. a man	SHAK 286:5
becomes: nothing so b. a man	SHAK 279:5
bed: And I in my b. again	ANON 11:18
and's newly gone to b.	MILT 228:4
And so to b.	PEPYS 247:12
b. be blest that I lie on	ANON 9:8
better in battle than in b.	STER 315:20
black passage up to b.	STEV 317:15
found in adulterous b.	BLAKE 60:13
get out of b. for it	AMIS 5:7
gooseberried double b.	THOM 330:17
grave as little as my b.	KEN 193:22
Has found out thy b.	BLAKE 62:4
I have to go to b. by day	STEV 317:12
in b. with my catamite	BURG 79:14
I should of stood in b.	JAC 179:2
kneels at the foot of the b.	MILNE 226:1
migrations from the blue b.	GOLD 155:12
mother, make my b. soon	BALL 27:19
mother, mother, make my b.	BALL 27:13
My mind is not a b.	AGATE 3:6
my second best b.	SHAK 300:21
not a b. of roses	STEV 317:8
On a b. of daffodil sky	TENN 326:28
out of his wholesome b.	SHAK 281:6
Out on the lawn I lie in b.	AUDEN 21:7
take up thy b., and walk	BIBLE 53:21
This b. thy centre	DONNE 124:13
thy cold b.	KING 195:5
To be to more than one a b.	DONNE 124:9
Up to b.	DE L 116:17
Were it earth in an earthy b.	TENN 327:2
bedfellows: strange b.	SHAK 296:5
bedroom: French widow in every b.	HOFF 170:5
Stranger, unless with b. eyes	AUDEN 21:8
beds: Minds like b. always made up	WILL 351:7
Warm b.: warm full blooded	JOYCE 188:17
bee: butterfly, sting like a b.	ALI 4:10
honeysuckle, I am the b.	FITZ 140:2
How doth the little busy b.	WATTS 343:5
live alone in the b.-loud glade	YEATS 359:12
Where the b. sucks	SHAK 296:14
beef: I am a great eater of b.	SHAK 297:15
Oh! The roast b. of England	FIEL 139:6
beefsteak: English an article as a b.	HAWT 163:19

beefy: As b. ATS without their hats — BETJ 37:1
Beelzebub: B. called for his syllabub — SITW 307:18
beer: B. and Britannia — SMITH 310:13
b. and skittles — CALV 88:9
chronicle small b. — SHAK 292:4
I'm only a b. teetotaller — SHAW 300:28
like thine inspirer, B. — POPE 250:15
muddy ecstasies of b. — CRAB 110:21
O B.! O Hodgson — CALV 88:8
torrent of gin and b. — GLAD 153:9
bees: Birds do it, b. do it — PORT 253:22
murmuring of innumerable b. — TENN 328:8
beetle: b. and the bat detract — JOHN 184:21
b. wheels his droning flight — GRAY 157:4
b. with his drowsy hums — SHAK 287:5
beetles: special preference for b. — HALD 160:3
before: And those b. cried 'Back!' — MAC 214:6
Broad b. and broad behind — BETJ 37:15
Going on b. — BAR 29:1
have said our remarks b. us — DON 123:1
not lost but sent b. — CYPR 113:13
began: So was it when my life b. — WORD 355:13
begetter: To the onlie b. — SHAK 299:10
beggar: whiles I am a b. — SHAK 282:5
beggared: It b. all description — SHAK 271:14
beggars: Lords in ermine, b. freezing — ROB 260:22
Our basest b. — SHAK 283:4
When b. die — SHAK 281:8
beggary: b. in the love that can be reckoned — SHAK 271:4
there is no vice, but b. — SHAK 282:5
begging: his seed b. their bread — BOOK 66:27
begin: B. at the beginning — CARR 91:13
b. with certainties and end — BACON 23:20
But let us b. — KENN 194:5
Then I'll b. — LANG 201:4
To b. at the beginning — THOM 330:16
When they b. the Beguine — PORT 253:18
beginning: As it was in the b. — BOOK 63:17
Before the b. of years — SWIN 321:3
begin at the b. — THOM 330:16
b., a muddle, and an end — LARK 201:20
b. God created the heaven — BIBLE 38:13
b. of an Amour — BEHN 32:20
b. of any great matter — DRAKE 126:10
end is to make a b. — ELIOT 133:11
even the b. of the end — CHUR 99:18
From quiet homes and first b. — BELL 34:3
In my b. is my end — ELIOT 133:2
In my end is my b. — MARY 221:16
In the b. was the Word — BIBLE 53:6
Is a new b., a raid on — ELIOT 133:6
Lord is the b. of wisdom — BOOK 68:15
Movies should have a b. — GOD 153:19
sequel of an unnatural b. — AUST 22:26
That is the true b. of our end — SHAK 291:6
This is the b. of the end — TALL 322:13
told you from the b. — BIBLE 46:12
beginnings: our ends by our b. know — DENH 116:26
begins: man's glory most b. and ends — YEATS 359:17
world's great age b. anew — SHEL 303:18
begot: were about when they b. me — STER 315:12
what's a son? A thing b. — KYD 199:10
begotten: It was b. by Despair — MARV 220:12
very God, B., not made — BOOK 65:5
beguile: And so b. thy sorrow — SHAK 296:27
beguiled: The serpent b. me — BIBLE 38:27
Beguine: begin the B. — PORT 253:18
begun: have b. is half the job — HOR 173:8
I have not yet b. to fight — JONES 186:21
behaviour: human b. — ROBB 260:15
behind: B., before, above — DONNE 123:6
But those b. cried 'Forward!' — MAC 214:6
Get thee b. me, Satan — BIBLE 50:14

behind (cont.):
in a moment it will be b. me — REGER 259:2
Scratches its innocent b. — AUDEN 21:2
She has no bosom and no b. — SMITH 309:21
behold: B. the man — BIBLE 58:20
being: all the wheels of B. slow — TENN 325:7
always at the edge of B. — SPEN 313:1
darkness of mere b. — JUNG 188:23
move, and have our b. — BIBLE 54:21
non-being by avoiding b. — TILL 332:21
not be worried into b. — FROST 146:25
unbearable lightness of b. — KUND 199:8
Belbroughton: B. Road is bonny — BETJ 37:6
Belgium: B.'s capital — BYRON 85:2
Belgrave Square: May beat in B. — GILB 151:11
Belial: sons of B. — MILT 228:15
belief: that is b. — SART 267:5
beliefs: dust of exploded b. — MADAN 216:13
believe: B. me, you who come after — HOR 173:24
b. what one does not believe — PAINE 244:6
Do you b. in the life to come — BECK 31:9
Firmly I b. and truly — NEWM 238:19
God, b. also in me — BIBLE 53:36
he wouldn't b. it — CUMM 112:19
I b. because it is impossible — TERT 329:9
I b. to One does feel — KNOX 198:17
these little ones which b. — BIBLE 50:16
Though ye b. not me — BIBLE 53:31
We can b. what we choose — NEWM 239:1
believed: what is by all people b. — VINC 338:22
Who against hope b. in hope — BIBLE 54:32
believer: In a b.'s ear — NEWT 239:9
believers: half-b. in our casual creeds — ARN 17:10
believeth: b. all things, hopeth — BIBLE 55:12
b. on me hath everlasting — BIBLE 53:24
whosoever b. in him — BIBLE 53:19
believing: b. more and more in less — YATES 358:10
Belinda: B. smiled — POPE 253:5
bell: B., book, and candle — SHAK 282:7
b. invites me — SHAK 286:11
for whom the b. tolls — DONNE 124:20
heart as sound as a b. — SHAK 291:21
hear the surly sullen b. — SHAK 299:23
Let's mock the midnight b. — SHAK 271:19
merry as a marriage b. — BYRON 85:2
sexton tolled the b. — HOOD 171:7
Silence that dreadful b. — SHAK 292:7
very word is like a b. — KEATS 192:6
Bellamy: B.'s veal pies — PITT 249:10
belle: *du temps que j'étais b.* — RONS 262:5
belli: *Nervos b.* — CIC 100:29
bells: b. of Hell — ANON 9:21
broke into a mist with b. — BROW 76:25
From the b., bells — POE 250:4
lin-lan-lone of evening b. — TENN 323:22
Ring out, wild b. — TENN 325:22
so floating many b. down — CUMM 112:16
They now *ring* the b. — WALP 342:5
'Twould ring the b. of Heaven — HODG 169:13
belly: O wombe! O b.! — CHAU 95:30
bellyful: Rumble thy b.! — SHAK 283:7
bellyfulls: we want b. — GASK 148:19
belong: DON'T WANT TO B. TO ANY CLUB — MARX 221:5
To betray, you must first b. — PHIL 248:12
belongs: in the mind where it b. — ALD 3:16
beloved: bourn how far to be b. — SHAK 271:4
Cry, the b. country — PATON 246:9
O Daniel, a man greatly b. — BIBLE 47:16
suspenders, Best B. — KIPL 197:23
This is my b. Son — BIBLE 48:15
below: above, between, b. — DONNE 123:6
belted: b. you and flayed you — KIPL 196:17
Ben: B. Battle was a soldier bold — HOOD 171:4
bend: I b. and I break not — LA F 199:17
Keep right on round the b. — LAUD 202:5

bending: always be a b. downwards | WHEW 347:8
bends: made their b. adornings | SHAK 271:15
beneath: But I b. a rougher sea | COWP 109:20
benedictus: *B. qui venit in nomine* | MISS 231:17
benighted: B. walks under the midday sun | MILT 226:12
benign: under that b. sky | BRON 72:18
benison: For a b. to fall | HERR 167:11
bent: fool me to the top of my b. | SHAK 276:14
bereaved: black as if b. of light | BLAKE 61:24
Berliner: *Ich bin ein B.* | KENN 194:8
Bermoothes: still-vexed B. | SHAK 295:34
Bermudas: Where the remote B. ride | MARV 220:9
berry: could have made a better b. | BUTL 84:22
  O sweeter than the b. | GAY 149:1
berth: which happened in his b. | HOOD 171:7
beside: B. a field of grain | CHAR 245:19
  thou art b. thyself | BIBLE 54:26
best: best administered is b. | POPE 252:20
  b. and the worst of this is | SWIN 321:14
  b. cannot be expected | JOHN 184:3
  b. ends by the best means | HUTC 177:1
  b. in this kind | SHAK 291:8
  b. is the best | QUIL 257:7
  b. is the enemy of the good | VOLT 340:15
  b. is yet to be | BROW 77:3
  b. lack all conviction | YEATS 359:24
  b. men are moulded out | SHAK 288:26
  b. of all possible worlds | CAB 87:23
  b. of all possible worlds | VOLT 340:10
  b. portion of a good man's | WORD 355:8
  b. thing God invents | BROW 75:30
  b. way out is always through | FROST 146:22
  Fear not to touch the b. | RAL 257:21
  In art the b. is good enough | GOET 154:4
  It was the b. of times | DICK 120:6
  past all prizing, b. | SOPH 311:13
  poetry = the b. words | COL 104:26
  record of the b. | SHEL 305:18
  Sat we two, one another's b. | DONNE 124:2
  Send forth the b. ye breed | KIPL 197:15
  so much bad in the b. of us | ANON 10:20
  than any other person's b. | HAZL 164:6
  Thou art tired; b. be still | ARN 16:18
  virtuousest, discreetest, b. | MILT 229:20
  where the b. is like the worst | KIPL 196:23
  wisest and justest and b. | PLATO 249:20
bestial: what remains is b. | SHAK 292:8
bestride: b. the narrow world | SHAK 280:27
best-seller: b. is the gilded tomb | SMITH 309:12
bet: Somebody b. on bay | FOST 144:10
Bethlehem: B. Ephratah | BIBLE 47:22
  Slouches towards B. | YEATS 359:25
betray: All things b. thee | THOM 331:9
  guts to b. my country | FORS 144:2
  To b., you must first belong | PHIL 248:12
betrayed: like men b. | WORD 354:13
betrothèd: bright face of my b. | MIDD 224:8
better: become much more the b. | SHAK 288:26
  begin to make a b. life | SHAK 272:1
  B. by far you should forget | ROSS 263:4
  b. day, the worse deed | HENRY 166:2
  b. mouse-trap | EMER 137:3
  b. part of biography | STR 318:15
  B. than a play | CHAR 95:3
  b. than a thousand | BOOK 67:22
  b. than light and safer than | HASK 163:16
  b. to be in chains | KAFKA 189:18
  b. to have fought and lost | CLOU 102:21
  b. to have loved and lost | BUTL 84:11
  b. to have loved and lost | TENN 324:8
  b. world than this | SHAK 272:13
  even from worse to b. | JOHN 182:3
  far b. thing that I do now | DICK 120:7
  for b. for worse | BOOK 66:1

better *(cont.)*:
  from b. hap to worse | SOUT 312:9
  from worse to b. | HOOK 171:15
  Gad! she'd b. | CARL 90:23
  getting b. and better | COUÉ 108:16
  have better spared a b. man | SHAK 278:15
  He is not b.—he is much worse | ANON 6:1
  if they had been any b. | CHAN 94:10
  If way to the B. there be | HARDY 162:8
  I see the b. things | OVID 243:15
  I took thee for thy b. | SHAK 276:20
  music is b. than it sounds | NYE 240:15
  nae b. than he shou'd | BURNS 82:4
  Something b. than his dog | TENN 326:7
  things I'd been b. without | PARK 245:5
  We have seen b. days | SHAK 296:21
  where it's likely to go b. | FROST 146:8
  will b. the instruction | SHAK 289:18
  You're a b. man than I am | KIPL 196:17
bettered: b. expectation | SHAK 291:11
between: B. the idea and the reality | ELIOT 133:19
  I would try to get b. them | STR 318:14
  wasn't for the 'ouses in b. | BAT 30:1
betwixt: B. the stirrup and the ground | CAMD 88:12
Beulah: B., peel me a grape | WEST 346:20
beware: And all should cry, B.! | COL 104:1
  Better b. | COW 109:6
  B. my foolish heart | WASH 342:24
  B. of rudely crossing it | AUDEN 21:8
  B. of the man who does not | SHAW 302:8
  B. the ides of March | SHAK 280:25
  Sisters, I bid you b. | KIPL 196:27
bewildered: bothered, and b. | HART 163:7
  unprincipled to the utterly b. | CAPP 89:16
bewitch: Do more b. me | HERR 167:15
bewitched: B., bothered, and bewildered | HART 163:7
bewrapt: B. past knowing | HARDY 162:14
beyond: But is there anything b.? | BROO 73:2
biases: critic is a bundle of b. | BALL 28:12
bibble-babble: Leave thy vain b. | SHAK 298:13
Bible: English B. | MAC 213:20
  starless and b.-black | THOM 330:16
  To read in de B. | GERS 168:5
  used the B. as if it was | KING 195:18
Bibles: B. laid open | HERB 167:7
bicker: b. down a valley | TENN 323:12
bicycle: like a fish without a b. | STEI 315:2
  poets b.-pump the human heart | AMIS 5:5
  Socialism can only arrive by b. | VIER 338:16
bid: She b. me take love easy | YEATS 359:1
bien: *Le mieux est l'ennemi du b.* | VOLT 340:15
bier: float upon his watery b. | MILT 227:11
big: b. battalions | VOLT 340:23
  b. enough to take away | FORD 143:5
  b. squadrons | BUSS 83:20
  By the shining B.-Sea-Water | LONG 210:1
  I am b. It's the pictures | BRAC 71:5
  Thy great b. one on me | FROST 146:10
bigamy: And b., Sir, is a crime | MONK 232:26
  B. is having one husband too | ANON 6:11
bigger: b. bang for a buck | ANON 6:12
  b. they are, the further | FITZ 141:1
bigotry: B. roughly defined | CHES 98:10
  B. tries to keep truth | TAG 322:9
bike: got on his b. | TEBB 323:6
bill: b. of my divorce to all | DONNE 123:15
billboard: b. lovely as a tree | NASH 237:17
billet: Every bullet has its b. | WILL 351:2
billiard: elliptical b. balls | GILB 152:2
billiards: To play b. well is a sign | ROUP 263:17
billow: Fierce was the wild b. | ANAT 5:10
billows: solid b. of enormous size | PHIL 248:15
Billy: B., in one of his nice new sashes | GRAH 156:4
  That's the way for B. and me | HOGG 170:7
  waited till his 'B.' boiled | PAT 246:16

bind: b. their kings in chains — BOOK 69:11
  b. the sweet influences — BIBLE 43:4
  b. up the brokenhearted — BIBLE 46:24
  I b. unto myself to-day — ALEX 4:5
  My mother bids me b. my hair — HUNT 176:19
  To b. another to its delight — BLAKE 62:2
binds: He who b. to himself a joy — BLAKE 61:16
biographers: Boswell is the first of b. — MAC 213:5
biographies: essence of innumerable b. — CARL 90:6
biography: B. is about Chaps — BENT 35:5
  not the better part of b. — STR 318:15
  properly no history; only b. — EMER 136:22
  Read nothing but b. — DISR 121:28
bird: b. of dawning — SHAK 274:2
  b. that thinks two notes — DAV 114:17
  B. thou never went — SHEL 305:6
  born for death, immortal b. — KEATS 192:4
  Both man and b. and beast — COL 104:18
  catch the b. of paradise — KHR 194:20
  I know why the caged b. sings — DUNB 129:7
  It's a b.! It's a plane — ANON 7:5
  It was only the note of a b. — SIMP 307:10
  like a b. on the wing — BOUL 70:10
  O Cuckoo! Shall I call thee b. — WORD 357:7
  rare b. on this earth — JUV 189:7
  Stirred for a b.,—the achieve — HOPK 172:21
  wet b.-haunted English lawn — ARN 16:21
  What b. so sings — LYLY 212:17
  widow b. sat mourning — SHEL 303:14
birdcage: And a b., sir — DICK 120:2
  summer b. in a garden — WEBS 344:23
birds: B. build—but not I — HOPK 172:19
  b. got to fly — HAMM 160:19
  B. in their little nests agree — WATTS 343:8
  b. in the trees — YEATS 359:20
  b. of the air — BIBLE 49:19
  B. on box and laurels listen — SMART 308:9
  b. that are without — WEBS 344:23
  b., wild flowers, and P.M.s — BALD 27:10
  But what these unobservant b. — ISH 178:21
  If b. confabulate or no — COWP 109:29
  I see all the b. are flown — CHAR 94:23
  late the sweet b. sang — SHAK 299:24
  singing of b. is come — BIBLE 44:32
  sing like b. i' the cage — SHAK 284:1
  we are a nest of singing b. — JOHN 183:22
  We think caged b. sing — WEBS 344:27
  When b. do sing, hey ding — SHAK 273:10
bird-song: b. at morning and star-shine — STEV 317:19
Birmingham: B. by way of Beachy Head — CHES 98:2
  no great hopes from B. — AUST 22:17
  When Jesus came to B. — STUD 318:19
Birnam wood: Till B. remove to Dunsinane — SHAK 287:32
birth: All things have second b. — WORD 356:13
  bewailed at their b. — MONT 233:20
  B., and copulation, and death — ELIOT 134:14
  b. commonly abateth industry — BACON 25:5
  disqualified by the accident of b. — CHES 98:14
  give b. astride of a grave — BECK 31:15
  I had seen b. and death — ELIOT 133:22
  not conscious of his b. — LA BR 199:14
  Or one that is coming to b. — O'SH 243:2
  Our b. is but a sleep — WORD 355:20
  Rainbow gave thee b. — DAV 114:19
  that have a different b. — SHEL 305:14
  Wherein our Saviour's b. — SHAK 274:2
birth control: b. is flagrantly middle-class — WAUGH 344:2
birthday: afternoon of my eighty-first b. — BURG 79:14
  Because the b. of my life — ROSS 262:21
  marvel my b. away — THOM 330:14
birthplace: accent of one's b. — LA R 202:1
birthright: b. for a mess of potage — BIBLE 39:17

birthright (cont.):
  sold his b. unto Jacob — BIBLE 39:18
births: b. that may be yours — RIMB 260:11
  plenties, and joyful b. — SHAK 280:2
  which are the b. of time — BACON 24:30
bis: B. dat qui cito dat — PUBL 256:1
biscuits: hyacinths and b. — SAND 266:17
bisexuality: b. doubles your chances — ALLEN 4:17
bishop: b. then must be blameless — BIBLE 56:16
  make a b. kick a hole — CHAN 94:7
  No b., no King — JAM 179:11
bishopric: merit for a b. — WEST 346:27
bishops: all B. and Curates — BOOK 65:10
  b. like best in their clergy — SMITH 309:24
bit: b. by him that comes behind — SWIFT 320:23
  Though he had b. me — SHAK 283:28
bitch: old b. gone in the teeth — POUND 254:19
bitch-goddess: b. success — JAMES 180:7
bite: b. some of my other generals — GEOR 149:22
  b. the hand that fed them — BURKE 81:3
  man recovered of the b. — GOLD 154:28
bites: dead woman b. not — GRAY 156:19
biteth: it b. like a serpent — BIBLE 43:33
bitter: b. God to follow — SWIN 321:12
  be not b. against them — BIBLE 56:11
  b. bread of banishment — SHAK 293:21
  news to hear and b. tears — CORY 108:13
  Some do it with a b. look — WILDE 350:16
  with b. herbs they shall eat — BIBLE 39:36
bitterness: scorn in the b. of his soul — BIBLE 47:33
bivouac: B. of the Dead — O'HARA 241:4
Bizet: I like Chopin and B. — FISH 139:26
blabbing: b., and remorseful day — SHAK 280:9
black: Any colour—so long as it's b. — FORD 143:7
  b. against may — BUNT 78:15
  b. and merciless things — JAMES 179:20
  b. as if bereaved of light — BLAKE 61:24
  b. as our loss — SITW 307:19
  b. chaos comes again — SHAK 300:19
  b. dog — JOHN 182:17
  B. is beautiful — ANON 6:13
  b. majority rule in Rhodesia — SMITH 309:9
  B. Widow, death — LOW 211:16
  devil damn thee b. — SHAK 287:33
  I am b. — SHAK 292:15
  I am b., but comely — BIBLE 44:29
  long b. passage up to bed — STEV 317:15
  more b. than ashbuds — TENN 323:23
  nothing so much as a b. swan — JUV 189:7
  sober-suited matron, all in b. — SHAK 295:12
  Tip me the b. spot — STEV 317:3
  What sad, b. isle — BAUD 30:5
  Who art as b. as hell — SHAK 300:16
  Young, gifted and b. — IRV 178:18
  you wear b. all the time — CHEK 96:25
blackbird: B. has spoken — FARJ 138:12
  b. whistling or just after — STEV 316:13
  O b., what a boy you are — BROWN 73:20
blackbirds: B. are the cellos — STEV 316:22
blackens: And b. every blot — TENN 324:1
black-eyed: b. Susan — GAY 149:17
blackguard: Sesquipedalian b. — CLOU 102:10
blackly: glides along the water looking b. — BYRON 84:26
Blackpool: seaside place called B. — EDGAR 130:15
blacks: poor are Europe's b. — CHAM 94:4
bladders: wanton boys that swim on b. — SHAK 280:18
blade: B. on the feather — CORY 108:11
  Steel-true and b.-straight — STEV 317:20
  with bloody blameful b. — SHAK 291:7
blame: bad women never take the b. — BROO 73:11
  It's the poor wot gets the b. — ANON 10:11
  That neither is most to b. — SWIN 321:14
  what they b. at night — POPE 252:6
blameless: Fearless, b. knight — ANON 12:4
  white flower of a b. life — TENN 324:1

blood-red: sunset ran, one glorious b. — BROW 76:3
bloodshed: politics is war without b. — MAO 217:18
blood-tinctured: heart within b. — BROW 75:3
bloody: Abroad is b. — GEOR 150:4
And sang within the b. wood — ELIOT 134:17
Be b., bold, and resolute — SHAK 287:20
B. instructions — SHAK 285:23
B. men are like bloody buses — COPE 107:22
b. noses and cracked crowns — SHAK 277:31
But where's the b. horse — CAMP 88:16
come out, thou b. man — BIBLE 41:25
I do begin to have b. thoughts — SHAK 296:11
My head is b., but unbowed — HENL 165:17
nearer b. — SHAK 286:27
no right in the b. circus — MAXT 222:14
Not b. likely — SHAW 302:19
Sons of the dark and b. ground — O'HARA 241:4
What b. man is that — SHAK 285:2
with b. blameful blade — SHAK 291:7
Woe to the b. city — BIBLE 47:24
bloom: lilac is in b. — BROO 73:3
look at things in b. — HOUS 174:17
opening sweet of earliest b. — COLL 105:9
sort of b. on a woman — BARR 29:16
with b. along the bough — HOUS 174:16
with the b. go I — ARN 17:18
ye b. sae fresh and fair — BURNS 81:27
blooming: grand to be b. well dead — SAR 267:1
bloomy: And all the b. beds — SMART 308:12
blossom: b. as the rose — BIBLE 46:4
B. by blossom the spring — SWIN 321:2
b. in their dust — SHIR 306:11
b. that hangs on the bough — SHAK 296:14
hundred flowers b. — MAO 218:1
blossoming: Florence b. in stone — LONG 209:18
blossoms: I sing of brooks, of b. — HERR 167:12
to-morrow b. — SHAK 280:18
blot: And blackens every b. — TENN 324:1
b. on the escutcheon — GRAY 156:18
greatest art, the art to b. — POPE 252:30
received from him a b. — COND 165:11
This world's no b. for us — BROW 75:31
blotted: b. it out for ever — STER 315:22
Would he had b. a thousand — JONS 187:32
blow: B., b., thou winter wind — SHAK 273:1
B., bugle, blow — TENN 327:20
B. out, you bugles — BROO 72:20
B., winds, and crack — SHAK 283:6
b. with an agreement — TROT 335:2
does not return your b. — SHAW 302:8
themselves must strike the b. — BYRON 85:1
when will thou b. — ANON 11:18
bloweth: wind b. where it listeth — BIBLE 53:18
blowin': b. in the wind — DYLAN 129:19
blown: no sooner b. but blasted — MILT 227:22
once hath b. for ever dies — FITZ 140:10
rooks are b. about — TENN 325:2
blows: that never b. so red — FITZ 140:8
blue: B. as the gendarmerie — SITW 307:18
b. of the night meets — CROS 112:9
b. remembered hills — HOUS 174:24
drowned in yonder living b. — TENN 325:30
Eyes of most unholy b. — MOORE 234:12
grappling in the central b. — TENN 326:11
Upon that little tent of b. — WILDE 350:15
You have a b. guitar — STEV 316:9
bluebell: Mary, ma Scotch B. — LAUD 202:6
bluebirds: b. over the white cliffs — BURT 83:3
blunder: At so grotesque a b. — BENT 35:7
I b., I bluster, I blow — SKEL 308:4
It wad frae mony a b. free us — BURNS 82:25
Woman was God's second b. — NIET 239:18
worse than a crime, it is a b. — BOUL 70:9
blundered: b. into Paradise — THOM 331:13

blundered (cont.):
Some one had b. — TENN 323:15
blunders: Natur never makes enny b. — BILL 59:11
blunt: plain, b. man — SHAK 281:25
blush: born to b. unseen — GRAY 157:9
calculated to call a b. — DICK 119:22
blushed: water saw its God, and b. — CRAS 111:6
blushes: Only Animal that B. — TWAIN 335:24
blushful: b. Hippocrene — KEATS 191:30
blushing: b. discontented sun — SHAK 293:29
b. honours thick upon him — SHAK 280:18
board: struck the b., and cried — HERB 166:22
There wasn't any B., and now — HERB 166:14
boarded: Youth is b., clothed — DICK 119:10
boast: b. of heraldry — GRAY 157:7
Such is the patriot's b. — GOLD 155:4
boat: Give a man a b. he can sail — THOM 332:3
glass-bottomed b. — MIZN 232:13
My soul is an enchanted b. — SHEL 304:21
Speed, bonnie b. — BOUL 70:10
They sank my b. — KENN 194:9
Until I have a little B. — WORD 356:3
boathook: diplomatic b. — SAL 266:2
boating: Jolly b. weather — CORY 108:11
boats: messing about in b. — GRAH 156:5
bobtail: bet my money on de b. nag — FOST 144:10
bodice: And lace my b. blue — HUNT 176:19
bodies: b. are buried in peace — BIBLE 48:8
b. high at Austerlitz — SAND 266:14
b. of those that made such — EDW 131:4
friendless b. of unburied — WEBS 344:25
Our b. why do we forbear — DONNE 124:3
soul inhabiting two b. — ARIS 15:21
with well-developed b. — FORS 143:15
your b. a living sacrifice — BIBLE 54:43
your scattered b. go — DONNE 123:7
body: b. and the soul know — ROET 261:15
b. continues in its state — NEWT 239:3
b. dies — STEV 316:11
b. filled and vacant mind — SHAK 279:16
b. is a machine for living — TOLS 333:12
b. is the temple — BIBLE 55:4
b. of a weak and feeble — ELIZ 135:6
commit his b. to the deep — BOOK 69:15
commit his b. to the ground — BOOK 66:8
gigantic b., huge massy — MAC 213:6
Gin a body meet a b. — BURNS 81:29
I like my b. when — CUMM 113:4
In b. and in soul can bind — SCOTT 268:11
I should interpose my b. — STR 318:14
I sing the b. electric — WHIT 348:10
John Brown's b. — ANON 8:14
joint and motive of her b. — SHAK 297:9
Marry my b. to that dust — KING 195:5
mind, b., or estate — BOOK 64:19
no b. to be kicked — THUR 332:19
O b. swayed to music — YEATS 358:14
Of the glorious B. sing — THOM 330:3
rid of the rest of her b. — VANB 336:24
sound mind in a sound b. — JUV 189:13
Take, eat; this is my b. — BIBLE 51:9
truly have none in the b. — LAWR 202:19
well proportioned b. — AUBR 19:19
what exercise is to the b. — STEE 314:17
with Africa than my own b. — ORTON 241:19
with my b. I thee worship — BOOK 66:2
young a b. with so old — SHAK 289:25
your b. between your knees — CORY 108:11
boets: hate all B. and Bainters — GEOR 149:20
Bognor: Bugger B. — GEOR 150:2
bogus: mammon than a b. god — MACN 215:21
boil: War That Would Not B. — TAYL 323:2
We b. at different degrees — EMER 136:32
boiling: his b. bloody breast — SHAK 291:7
bois: le soir, au fond des b. — VIGNY 338:17

bois (*cont.*):

Nous n'irons plus aux b.	ANON 12:13
bold: be b. and be sensible	HOR 173:8
be b., and everywhere be b.	SPEN 313:14
b. bad man, that dared	SPEN 313:8
bloody, b., and resolute	SHAK 287:20
drunk hath made me b.	SHAK 286:12
This b. bad man	SHAK 280:15
boldly: b. go where no man	RODD 261:12
boldness: B., and again b.	DANT 114:1
B. be my friend	SHAK 273:23
Bolingbroke: this canker, B.	SHAK 277:26
bolt: b. is shot back	ARN 16:10
like the b., and the breech	REED 258:16
bolts: b. up change	SHAK 272:2
bomb: b. is a paper tiger	MAO T 217:20
b. them back into the Stone Age	LEMAY 204:20
bombazine: B. would have shown	GASK 148:17
bombed: glad we've been b.	ELIZ 135:18
bomber: b. will always get through	BALD 27:5
bombs: Come, friendly b.	BETJ 37:9
Ears like b. and teeth like	CAUS 93:9
bond: And take a b. of fate	SHAK 287:21
Let him look to his b.	SHAK 289:15
pieces that great b.	SHAK 287:6
bondage: b. to parents	WOLL 353:13
b. which is freedom's self	SHEL 304:27
modern b. of rhyming	MILT 228:6
out of the house of b.	BIBLE 40:2
bondman: so base that would be a b.	SHAK 281:17
bonds: b. in thee are all determinate	SHAK 299:27
bondsmen: Hereditary b.!	BYRON 85:1
bone: B. of my bones	BIBLE 38:22
B. of my bone thou art	MILT 229:28
bright hair about the b.	DONNE 124:9
He knows death to the b.	YEATS 358:22
rag and a b. and a hank	KIPL 197:12
boneless: b. wonder	CHUR 99:8
bones: be he that moves my b.	SHAK 300:20
Can these b. live	BIBLE 47:9
conjuring trick with b.	JENK 181:4
dead men lost their b.	ELIOT 134:23
England keep my b.	SHAK 282:13
lay my b. amongst you	WOLS 353:15
Of his b. are coral made	SHAK 296:1
O ye dry b.	BIBLE 47:10
Rattle his b. over the stones	NOEL 240:5
tongs and the b.	SHAK 290:35
valley which was full of b.	BIBLE 47:8
bonfire: b. of the vanities	WOLFE 353:7
bong-tree: land where the B. grows	LEAR 203:12
bonjour: B. tristesse	ELUA 136:9
bonnets: B. are bound for the Border	SCOTT 269:2
b. of Bonny Dundee	SCOTT 268:7
bonnie: b. banks o' Loch Lomon'	ANON 10:2
bonny: Am I no a b. fighter	STEV 316:25
Belbroughton Road is b.	BETJ 37:6
bono: *Cui b.?*	CIC 100:31
bonum: *Summum b.*	CIC 100:22
Boojum: If your Snark be a B.!	CARR 92:8
book: Bell, b., and candle	SHAK 282:7
b. a devil's chaplain	DARW 114:5
b. is like an infant's	TRAH 333:17
b. is the best of friends	TUPP 335:10
b. is the precious life-blood	MILT 230:30
B. of Life begins	WILDE 350:11
b. where men may read	SHAK 285:20
b. would have been finished	WOD 352:17
b. you would wish your wife	GRIF 159:2
Camerado, this is no b.	WHIT 348:14
dainties that are bred in a b.	SHAK 284:15
do not throw this b. about	BELL 32:25
Farewell my b. and my devocioun	CHAU 96:9
Go, litel b.	CHAU 96:20
Go, little b.	STEV 317:17

book (*cont.*):

Great b., great evil	CALL 88:5
I'll drown my b.	SHAK 296:13
leaves of the Judgement B.	TAYL 323:4
library to make one b.	JOHN 185:3
little volume, but large b.	CRAS 111:12
mentioning a single b.	REED 258:21
Not on his picture, but his b.	JONS 187:21
novel is the one bright b.	LAWR 202:14
read a b. before reviewing	SMITH 310:9
reading or non-reading a b.	BYRON 87:20
substance of a b. directly	KNOW 198:15
take down this b.	YEATS 360:9
thick, square b.	GLOU 153:17
this b. I directe	CHAU 96:23
What is the use of a b.	CARR 91:1
when I wrote that b.	SWIFT 320:25
With a religious b., or friend	WOTT 357:14
woman who wrote the b.	LINC 207:13
bookful: b. blockhead, ignorantly read	POPE 252:9
books: b. are either dreams	LOW 211:3
B. are made not like children	FLAU 141:12
B. are well written or badly	WILDE 350:3
B. do furnish a room	POW 254:25
B. from Boots'	BETJ 37:4
b. in the running brooks	SHAK 272:14
B. of the hour	RUSK 264:14
B. say: she did this because	BARN 29:5
b., the academes	SHAK 284:16
b., were opened	BIBLE 47:15
B. will speak plain	BACON 24:17
cannot learn men from b.	DISR 122:9
collection of b.	CARL 90:16
Deep-versed in b.	MILT 230:8
do you read b. *through?*	JOHN 184:26
equal skill to Cambridge b.	BROW 74:25
friendship, b.	THOM 331:23
gentleman is not in your b.	SHAK 291:13
has written all the b.	BUTL 84:15
his b. were read	BELL 33:27
many b. there is no end	BIBLE 44:27
my b. had been any worse	CHAN 94:10
No furniture so charming as b.	SMITH 310:2
proper study of mankind is b.	HUXL 177:15
read all the b. there are	MALL 216:20
Some b. are to be tasted	BACON 25:14
Things in b.' clothing	LAMB 200:4
Wherever b. will be burned	HEINE 164:21
Your *borrowers of b.*	LAMB 200:2
boon: b. and a blessing to men	ANON 11:1
boot: b. in the face, the brute	PLATH 249:14
B., saddle, to horse	BROW 75:17
b. stamping on a human face	ORW 242:11
bootboy: b. at Claridges	WOOLF 356:3
booted: B. and spurred to ride	RUMB 264:5
Booth: B. led boldly	LIND 207:16
boots: always have one's b. on	MONT 233:8
Books from B'.	BETJ 37:4
b.—movin' up and down	KIPL 196:6
carries his heart in his b.	HERB 166:11
doormat in a world of b.	RHYS 259:15
pleasure me in his top-b.	MARL 218:5
see my legs when I take my b.	DICK 118:21
truth is pulling its b. on	SPUR 314:2
boozes: tell a man who b.	BURT 83:1
Border: Bonnets are bound for the B.	SCOTT 269:2
Night Mail crossing the B.	AUDEN 21:4
borders: I have come to the b. of sleep	THOM 330:24
bore: be in it is merely a b.	WILDE 350:3
Every hero becomes a b. at last	EMER 136:30
He is an old b.	TREE 334:5
He was not only a b.	MUGG 236:5
if I was a b.	STEV 316:2
secret of being a b.	VOLT 340:17
bored: Bores and B.	BYRON 86:27

bored (cont.):

Ever to confess you're b.	BERR 36:13
virtue of the b.	WAUGH 343:29

boredom: B. is a vital problem RUSS 264:21

b. on a large scale	INGE 178:11
Life is first b., then fear	LARK 201:14

bores: *B.* and *Bored* BYRON 86:27

B. have succeeded to dragons DISR 122:11

boring: Life, friends, is b. BERR 36:13

born: already b. before my lips MAND 217:11

And to the manner b.	SHAK 274:26
b. free and equal in dignity	ANON 5:20
B. in a cellar	FOOTE 142:19
b. in days when wits were	ARN 17:11
b. King of the Jews	BIBLE 48:9
B. of the sun they travelled	SPEN 312:24
B. of the very sigh	KEATS 191:5
B. on the fourth of July	COHAN 103:5
b. out of my due time	MORR 235:15
b. to set it right	SHAK 275:6
b. to set it right	STR 318:12
b. under a rhyming planet	SHAK 291:26
b. we cry that we are come	SHAK 283:27
b. with your legs apart	ORTON 241:21
British Bourgeoise is not b.	SITW 307:21
But I was free b.	BIBLE 54:24
Else, wherefore b.	TENN 324:5
Every moment one is b.	TENN 328:26
Except a man be b. again	BIBLE 53:17
For we are b. in other's pain	THOM 331:7
house where I was b.	HOOD 171:8
I am not yet b.; O fill me	MACN 216:6
if he had not been b.	BIBLE 51:8
I was b. barefoot	LONG 209:8
I was b. in a cellar	CONG 106:8
I was b. sneering	GILB 151:18
Man is b. to live	PAST 246:9
Man is b. unto trouble	BIBLE 42:29
Man that is b. of a woman	BIBLE 42:33
Man that is b. of a woman	BOOK 66:6
Man was b. free, and everywhere	ROUS 263:18
natural to die as to be b.	BACON 24:22
Not to be b. is, past all	SOPH 311:13
Not to be b. is the best for man	AUDEN 20:15
Not to be b., or being born	BACON 25:31
one b. out of due time	BIBLE 55:16
One is not b. a woman	DE B 115:8
other powerless to be b.	ARN 17:16
perish wherein I was b.	BIBLE 42:25
person b. who is so unlucky	MARQ 219:21
some men are b. great	SHAK 298:3
soon as we were b.	BIBLE 47:30
sucker b. every minute	BARN 29:9
they had never been b.	BIBLE 48:8
those who are to be b.	BURKE 80:17
Thou wast not b. for death	KEATS 192:4
time to be b., and a time to die	BIBLE 44:11
'Tis less than to be b.	FLET 31:2
took the trouble to be b.	BEAU 30:17
under that was I b.	SHAK 291:18
unto us a child is b.	BIBLE 45:16
We all are b. mad	BECK 31:14
We were not b. to sue	SHAK 293:9

borne: b. even heavier things VIRG 339:1

borogoves: mimsy were the b. CARR 91:15

boroughs: bright b., the circle-citadels HOPK 172:16

borrow: b. the money to do it WARD 342:18

men who b. LAMB 200:1

borrower: b. of the night SHAK 287:1

Neither a b., nor a lender be SHAK 274:22

borrowers: Your *b. of books* LAMB 200:2

borrowing: b. only lingers SHAK 278:19

bosom: close b.-friend of the maturing sun
KEATS 192:14

her b. and half her side COL 103:12

bosom (cont.):

He's in Arthur's b.	SHAK 279:3
Into my b. and be lost in me	TENN 328:5
into the b. of the sea	SHAK 280:9
Let me to thy b. fly	WESL 346:8
She has no b. and no behind	SMITH 309:21

bosoms: hang and brush their b. BROW 77:19

stockings and white b. JOHN 183:24

boss: b. there is always MARQ 219:20

bossing: shorter hours and nobody b. ORW 242:13

bossy: by the b. for the bully SELD 269:22

Boston: And this is good old B. BOSS 70:1

B. man is the east wind APPL 14:14

Boswell: B. the first of biographers MAC 213:5

botanize: that would peep and b. WORD 356:5

botch: sundial, and I make a b. BELL 33:26

botches: Leave no rubs nor b. SHAK 287:2

Botticelli: B.'s a *cheese* PUNCH 256:18

if B. were alive today UST 336:17

bottle: little for the b. DIBD 117:17

nor a b. to give him	DICK 118:20
way out of the fly-b.	WITT 352:7

bottles: English have hot-water b. MIKES 224:11

fill old b. with banknotes	KEYN 194:16
put new wine into old b.	BIBLE 49:24

bottom: at the b. of our garden FYL 147:9

forgotten man at the b. ROOS 262:7

bottomless: Law is a b. pit ARB 14:22

smoke of the pit that is b. JAM 179:9

bottoms: b. of my trousers rolled ELIOT 134:2

boue: *La nostalgie de la b.* AUG 21:21

bough: blossom that hangs on the b. SHAK 296:14

bread beneath the b.	FITZ 140:6
Petals on a wet, black b.	POUND 254:20
with bloom along the b.	HOUS 174:16

boughs: b. which shake against the cold SHAK 299:24

bounded: b. in a nut-shell SHAK 275:15

bounden: and our b. duty BOOK 65:15

our b. duty and service BOOK 65:17

bounds: living know no b. SHIR 306:12

wider shall thy b. be set BENS 34:20

bouquet: b. is better than the taste POTT 254:6

bourgeois: b. climb up on them FLAU 141:12

How beastly the b.	LAWR 202:18
One must astonish the b.	BAUD 30:9

bourgeoise: British B. is not born SITW 307:21

bourgeoisie: b. in the long run TROT 334:23

discreet charm of the b. BUÑ 78:16

bourn: b. how far to be beloved SHAK 271:4

country from whose b.	SHAK 275:26
our b. of time and place	TENN 323:19
see beyond our b.	KEATS 192:18

bow: b. myself in the house BIBLE 42:11

B. themselves when he did sing	SHAK 280:16
b., ye tradesmen	GILB 151:9
Bring me my b. of burning gold	BLAKE 61:12
drew a b. at a venture	BIBLE 42:7
every knee should b.	BIBLE 56:5
putting b.-windows to the house	DICK 118:11
set my b. in the cloud	BIBLE 39:10

bowels: b. of Christ CROM 112:2

Have molten b. BOTT 70:6

bower: b. we shrined to Tennyson HARDY 162:3

bowl: Fill the Flowing B. ANON 6:18

golden b. be broken	BIBLE 44:26
inverted b. we call The Sky	FITZ 140:15
Morning in the b. of night	FITZ 140:4

bowler: *I* am the b. and the ball LANG 201:2

bows: B. down to wood and stone HEBER 164:16

bow-wow: B. strain I can do SCOTT 269:6

were it not for his b. way PEMB 247:7

box: b. where sweets compacted HERB 167:8

boxing: B.'s just showbusiness BRUNO 77:25

boy: any b. may become President STEV 316:17
Being read to by a b. ELIOT 133:14
b. brought the white sheet GARC 148:2
b. playing on the sea-shore NEWT 239:6
b. stood on the burning deck HEM 165:9
b.'s will is the wind's will LONG 209:21
b. will ruin himself GEOR 150:1
Cleopatra b. my greatness SHAK 272:5
fifteen-year-old b. until *they die* ROTH 263:14
journeying b. HARDY 162:14
Let the b. win his spurs EDW 130:21
Mad about the b. COW 109:3
misfortunes can befall a b. MAUG 222:12
O blackbird, what a b. BROWN 73:20
purblind, wayward b. SHAK 284:13
schoolrooms for 'the b.' COOK 107:17
Smiling the b. fell dead BROW 76:8
Speak roughly to your little b. CARR 91:5
Take the thanks of a b. BEEC 32:5
to be b. eternal SHAK 298:21
Upon the growing b. WORD 355:20
was and a little tiny b. SHAK 298:15
You silly twisted b. MILL 225:10
boy friend: certain thing called the B. WILS 351:17
boyhood: In the lost b. of Judas Æ 3:4
boys: As flies to wanton b. SHAK 283:21
b. in the back room LOES 209:5
b. in the back rooms BEAV 31:4
b. of the old Brigade WEAT 344:4
b. that swim on bladders SHAK 280:18
By office boys for office b. SAL 266:6
Christian b. ARN 18:15
few b. late at their play ARN 17:3
lightfoot b. are laid HOUS 175:2
Mealy b., and beef-faced DICK 119:19
Till the b. come Home FORD 143:12
bracelet: b. of bright hair DONNE 124:9
braces: Damn b.: Bless relaxes BLAKE 61:9
Bradford: silk hat on a B. millionaire ELIOT 134:29
Bradshaw: 'B.' is nervous and terse DOYLE 126:7
braes: banks and b. o' bonny Doon BURNS 81:27
brag: Beauty is Nature's b. MILT 226:20
Is left this vault to b. SHAK 286:26
braids: twisted b. of lilies MILT 226:21
brain: Bear of Very Little B. MILNE 225:15
b. of feathers POPE 250:14
b. perplexes and retards KEATS 192:1
draughts intoxicate the b. POPE 251:28
dry b. in a dry season ELIOT 133:16
from the heat-oppressèd b. SHAK 286:10
harmful to the b. JAM 179:9
has gleaned my teeming b. KEATS 192:19
instrumental to the b. SHAK 274:4
Owl hasn't exactly got B. MILNE 225:18
petrifications of a plodding b. BYRON 86:32
schoolmasters puzzle their b. GOLD 155:8
should possess a poet's b. DRAY 126:19
young wife and a good b. JONS 186:23
brained: large-b. woman BROW 75:6
brains: And dash'd the b. out SHAK 286:6
gentleman said a girl with b. LOOS 210:7
brambles: b. in the fortresses BIBLE 46:3
branch: b. shall grow out BIBLE 45:18
b. that might have grown MARL 218:14
branchy: Towery city and b. between HOPK 172:2
brandy: B. for the Parson KIPL 196:28
b. of the damned SHAW 301:19
must drink b. JOHN 185:22
brass: become as sounding b. BIBLE 55:11
men's evil manners live in b. SHAK 280:22
brat: spurious b., Tom Jones RICH 260:4
brave: b. bad man CLAR 101:12
b. man with a sword WILDE 350:16
b. new world SHAK 296:15

brave (*cont.*):
Fortune assists the b. TER 329:5
Fortune favours the b. VIRG 339:20
home of the b. KEY 194:12
How sleep the b., who sink COLL 105:11
None but the b. DRYD 127:19
Toll for the b. COWP 109:28
to-morrow to be b. ARMS 16:2
What's b., what's noble SHAK 271:26
brawler: not a b., not covetous BIBLE 56:16
Brazil: Charley's aunt from B. THOM 330:5
breach: More honoured in the b. SHAK 274:26
Once more unto the b. SHAK 279:5
bread: bitter b. of banishment SHAK 293:21
b. and circuses JUV 189:12
b. eaten in secret BIBLE 43:15
b. of adversity BIBLE 46:1
b. of affliction BIBLE 42:6
b. to this intolerable deal SHAK 278:2
Cast thy b. upon the waters BIBLE 44:24
crammed with distressful b. SHAK 279:16
Give us this day our daily b. BIBLE 48:27
I am the b. of life BIBLE 53:22
Jesus took b., and blessed BIBLE 51:9
living HOMER begged his b. ANON 10:10
looked to government for b. BURKE 81:3
Man shall not live by b. BIBLE 48:16
Royal slice of b. MILNE 225:22
shalt thou eat b. BIBLE 39:2
She was cutting b. and butter THAC 329:23
Strengthened with the B. of Life WHITE 347:16
taste of another man's b. DANTE 113:23
that b. should be so dear HOOD 171:13
To eat dusty b. BOGAN 62:18
unleavened b. BIBLE 39:36
when we did eat b. BIBLE 40:1
whom if his son ask b. BIBLE 49:10
break: at the b. of the day STR 318:17
b. a man's spirit is devil's SHAW 300:27
B., break, break TENN 323:10
b. the bloody glass MACN 216:3
But b., my heart SHAK 274:13
can b. them at pleasure EDG 130:18
I bend and I not LA F 199:17
I'll b. my staff SHAK 296:13
Never give a sucker an even b. FIEL 139:16
Thou thyself must b. at last ARN 16:18
breakfast: critical period in matrimony is b. HERB 166:18
embarrassment and b. BARN 29:4
impossible things before b. CARR 91:24
wholesome, hungry b. WALT 342:12
breakfasted: b. with you and shall sup BRUCE 77:22
breaking: b. what it likes ARN 17:27
breaks: something twangs and b. MACN 216:4
breast: boiling bloody b. SHAK 291:7
charms to sooth a savage b. CONG 106:11
eternal in the human b. POPE 252:12
Of thy chaste b. LOV 210:20
stood b. high amid the corn HOOD 171:11
with dauntless b. GRAY 157:9
breastie: what a panic's in thy b. BURNS 82:26
breastplate: b. of righteousness BIBLE 56:4
breasts: b. by which France is fed SULLY 319:3
Come to my woman's b. SHAK 285:18
division of prodigious b. SWIN 321:4
why then her b. are dun SHAK 300:11
breath: And thou no b. at all SHAK 284:6
b. can make them GOLD 154:18
breathing thoughtful b. WORD 356:24
B.'s a ware that will not keep HOUS 174:18
b. thou art SHAK 288:19
have drawn the b. of life YEATS 359:5
mansion call the fleeting b. GRAY 157:8
seemed waste of b. YEATS 359:11

breath (*cont.*):
  world draw thy b. in pain   SHAK 277:17
breathe: As though to b. were life   TENN 328:21
  like the hair we b.   SURT 319:8
  Low, low, b. and blow   TENN 327:19
  on a summer's morn to b.   MILT 229:23
breathes: B. there the man   SCOTT 268:12
breathless: b. hush in the Close   NEWB 238:13
bred: B. en bawn in a brier-patch   HARR 163:5
Bredon: In summertime on B.   HOUS 174:20
breeches: made themselves b.   BIBLE 38:26
breed: b. of their horses   PENN 247:10
  Feared by their b.   SHAK 293:16
  not b. one work   HOPK 172:19
  This happy b. of men   SHAK 293:16
breeding: Burgundy without any b.   THUR 332:17
  with ease, to show your b.   SHER 306:8
breeds: Chaos often b. life   ADAMS 1:15
  Or lesser b. without the Law   KIPL 197:4
breeks: b. aff a wild Highlandman   SCOTT 268:26
breeze: Fluttering and dancing in the b.   WORD 355:4
  For a b. of morning moves   TENN 326:28
  volleying rain and tossing b.   ARN 17:18
breezes: Little b. dusk and shiver   TENN 325:35
breezy: B., Sneezy, Freezy   ELLIS 136:4
brekekekex: B. koax koax   ARIS 15:11
brethren: least of these my b.   BIBLE 51:6
brevis: *Ars longa, vita b.*   HIPP 168:19
brevity: B. is the sister of talent   CHEK 96:31
  B. is the soul of wit   SHAK 275:8
  Its body b., and wit its soul   COL 103:17
brew: b. that is true   FRANK 245:1
brewery: O take me to a b.   ANON 8:3
bribe: b. or twist   WOLFE 353:2
  done without a b. I find   CENT 93:15
bribes: man open to b.   GREE 158:4
brick: 'Eave 'arf a b. at 'im   PUNCH 256:9
  found it b. and left it marble   AUG 22:7
  piece of b. in his pocket   SWIFT 319:20
  They threw it a b. at a time   HARG 162:21
bride: all jealousy to the b.   BARR 29:15
  became my glittering b.   WORD 354:21
  b. adorned for her husband   BIBLE 58:4
  encounter darkness as a b.   SHAK 288:20
  mourning b.   DRYD 128:13
  Never the blushing b.   LEIGH 204:18
  unravished b. of quietness   KEATS 191:17
bridegrooms: Of b., brides   HERR 167:12
brides: Of bridegrooms, b.   HERR 167:12
bridesmaid: always the b.   LEIGH 204:18
bridge: And keep the b. with me   MAC 214:4
  b. too far   BROW 75:7
  Champagne, and B.   BELL 33:25
  Come shooting through the b.   BETJ 37:1
  Like a b. over troubled water   SIMON 307:5
  Railway B. of the Silv'ry Tay   MCG 214:19
brief: B. as the lightning   SHAK 290:14
  b. wherein all marvels   SOUT 312:7
  Drest in a little b. authority   SHAK 288:14
  I strive to be b.   HOR 172:24
  tragical! tedious and b.   SHAK 291:5
brier: Bred en bawn in a b.-patch   HARR 163:5
  Thorough bush, thorough b.   SHAK 290:19
brigade: boys of the old B.   WEAT 344:4
bright: All calm, as it was b.   VAUG 337:14
  All things b. and beautiful   ALEX 4:2
  Behold the b. original appear   GAY 149:14
  b. and fierce and fickle   TENN 327:24
  B. as the day   GRAN 156:10
  b. day is done   SHAK 272:4
  b. day that brings forth   SHAK 281:2
  b. particular star   SHAK 270:23
  B. the vision that delighted   MANT 217:17
  b. things come to confusion   SHAK 290:15
  Dark with excessive b.   MILT 229:4

bright (*cont.*):
  Goddess, excellently b.   JONS 187:3
  look, the land is b.   CLOU 102:24
  northern climes, obscurely b.   BYRON 85:20
  thought thee b.   SHAK 300:16
  was a young lady named B.   BULL 78:7
brightest: B. and best of the sons   HEBER 164:14
  B. in dungeons, Liberty   BYRON 87:7
brightness: B. falls from the air   NASHE 237:19
brillig: 'Twas b., and the slithy toves   CARR 91:15
brim: bubbles winking at the b.   KEATS 191:30
bring: B. me my arrows of desire   BLAKE 61:12
  would b. home knowledge   JOHN 185:18
bringing: B. the cheque and the postal order   AUDEN 21:4
  Her b. me up by hand   DICK 118:24
brink: we walked to the b.   DULL 129:2
brinkmanship: boasting of his b.   STEV 316:20
brisking: by b. about the life   SMART 308:8
Britain: B. a fit country for heroes   LLOY 208:11
  Hail, happy B.!   SOM 311:3
  Say, B., could you ever boast   SWIFT 320:19
  When B. first, at heaven's   THOM 331:20
Britannia: Beer and B.   SMITH 310:13
  Rule, B., rule the waves   THOM 331:20
  you've shouted 'Rule B.'   KIPL 196:2
British: B. Grenadier   ANON 10:13
  life for the B. female   CLOU 102:7
  We are B., thank God   MONT 233:24
  With a stony B. stare   TENN 326:27
Briton: glory in the name of B.   GEOR 149:23
  only a free-born B.   THAC 329:15
Britons: B. never will be slaves   THOM 331:20
  we B. alone use 'Might'   WAUGH 343:36
broad: b. is the way   BIBLE 49:12
  B. of Church   BETJ 37:15
  By brooks too b. for leaping   HOUS 175:2
  She's the B. and I'm the High   SPR 314:1
broccoli: It's b., dear   WHITE 347:15
broke: If it ain't b., don't fix it   LANCE 200:21
broken: baying for b. glass   WAUGH 343:18
  b. open on the most scientific   PEAC 246:23
  cord is not quickly b.   BIBLE 44:14
  He liked the Sound of B. Glass   BELL 33:23
  Laws were made to be b.   NORTH 240:7
  When the lute is b.   SHEL 303:24
brokenhearted: bind up the b.   BIBLE 46:24
broker: b. is a man who   WOOL 354:7
  more that of an honest b.   BISM 59:18
bronze: more lasting than b.   HOR 173:28
brooch: b. of gold ful sheene   CHAU 95:16
brooches: b. and toys for your delight   STEV 317:19
brood: b. of folly without father   MILT 226:22
  fond of no second b.   SHAK 273:22
broods: b. and sleeps on his own   WORD 356:7
brook: Fell in the weeping b.   SHAK 277:7
  willow grows aslant a b.   SHAK 277:6
brooks: b. of Eden mazily murmuring   TENN 327:8
  By b. too broad for leaping   HOUS 175:2
  purling b.   POPE 251:24
broom: I am sent with b. before   SHAK 291:10
broomstick: mortal man is a b.   SWIFT 320:6
brothel: metaphysical b. for emotions   KOES 199:1
brothels: b. with bricks of Religion   BLAKE 61:7
  Keep thy foot out of b.   SHAK 283:13
brother: Am I my b.'s keeper   BIBLE 39:4
  Am I not a man and a b.   WEDG 345:1
  Be my b., or I kill you   CHAM 94:5
  BIG B. IS WATCHING YOU   ORW 242:6
  B. can you spare a dime   HARB 161:11
  B., thy tail hangs down   KIPL 197:18
  b. to the ox   MARK 218:4
  Death and his b. Sleep   SHEL 304:26
  has brother followed b.   WORD 354:23
  hateth his b.   BIBLE 57:17

brother (*cont.*):

I am a b. to dragons	BIBLE 43:3
I am, Sir, a B. of the Angle	WALT 342:10
our sad bad glad mad b.'s	SWIN 321:5
shall my b. sin against me	BIBLE 50:19
sticketh closer than a b.	BIBLE 43:30
Strong b. in God	BELL 33:14
white man's b.	KING 195:7
brotherhood: crown thy good with b.	BATES 30:2
Love the b.	BIBLE 57:9
together at the table of b.	KING 195:9
brother-in-law: brother, not his b.	KING 195:7
brothers: And all the b. too	SHAK 298:2
happy few, we band of b.	SHAK 279:20
together as b. or perish	KING 195:10
brought: b. forth her firstborn	BIBLE 51:32
darkness safely b.	KEBLE 193:16
brow: mighty Victor's b.	KELLY 193:19
wanton with a velvet b.	SHAK 284:14
Your bonny b. was brent	BURNS 82:11
Brown: John B.'s body	ANON 8:14
brown: Jeanie with the light b. hair	FOST 144:11
river is a strong b. god	ELIOT 133:7
Browning: B. knew what it meant	KLOP 198:12
B. some 'Pomegranate'	BROW 75:3
Hang it all, Robert B.	POUND 254:12
Meredith's a prose B.	WILDE 349:22
safety-catch of my B.	JOHST 186:18
Wordsworth, Tennyson and B.	BAG 26:17
bruised: be b. in a new place	IRV 178:20
staff of this b. reed	BIBLE 42:16
was b. for our iniquities	BIBLE 46:19
bruit: *Dont meurt le b. parmi le vent*	APOL 14:11
brush: with my b. that I make love	REN 259:6
brushers: Critics are like b.	WOTT 357:20
brutal: grown b. from the fare	YEATS 359:16
brutality: industry without art is b.	RUSK 264:11
brute: Brute heart of a b. like you	PLATH 249:14
Et tu, B.?	CAES 88:3
Et tu, B.?	SHAK 281:10
brutes: Exterminate all the b.	CONR 107:4
brutish: nasty, b., and short	HOBB 169:10
Brutus: B. is an honourable man	SHAK 281:19
What! is B. sick	SHAK 281:6
You too, B.	CAES 88:3
bubble: Honour but an empty b.	DRYD 127:21
Life is mostly froth and b.	GORD 155:21
Seeking the b. reputation	SHAK 272:26
What is fame? an empty b.	GRAI 156:7
world's a b.	BACON 25:30
bubbles: beaded b. winking at the brim	KEATS 191:30
buck: bigger bang for a b.	ANON 6:12
b. stops here	TRUM 335:6
bucket: past is a b. of ashes	SAND 266:15
stick inside a swill b.	ORW 242:16
Buckingham: changing guard at B. Palace	MILNE 225:19
so much for B.	CIBB 100:15
buckle: b. which fastens	BAG 26:5
bud: be a b. again	KEATS 190:20
I'll nip him in the b.	ROCHE 261:1
budge: b. doctors of the Stoic	MILT 226:19
buds: darling b. of May	SHAK 299:12
bug: this b. with gilded wings	POPE 251:8
bugger: B. Bognor	GEOR 150:2
buggers: b. can't be choosers	BOWRA 71:4
bugle: Blow, b., blow	TENN 327:20
bugles: Blow out, you b.	BROO 72:20
b. calling for them from sad	OWEN 243:22
build: And easy to b., too	IBSEN 178:6
build—but not I b.	HOPK 172:19
b. the house of death	MONT 233:10
Except the Lord b. the house	BOOK 68:30
think that we b. for ever	RUSK 264:16
builders: stone which the b. refused	BOOK 68:22

building: b. hath three conditions	WOTT 357:19
it's a very old b.	OSB 242:18
principal beauty in b.	FULL 147:6
We have a b. of God	BIBLE 55:24
builds: B. in the weather	SHAK 289:13
people b. on mud	MACH 215:2
built: are b. with stones of Law	BLAKE 61:7
b. my soul a lordly pleasure-house	TENN 327:14
It is not what they b.	FENT 138:23
bull: are gone to milk the b.	JOHN 184:12
Cock and a B.	STER 315:26
Dance tiptoe, b.	BUNT 78:15
savage b. doth bear the yoke	SHAK 291:14
bullet: Ballot stronger than the b.	LINC 207:4
b. through his heart	THAC 329:18
Every b. has its billet	WILL 351:2
faster than a speeding b.	ANON 7:5
bullets: b. made of platinum	BELL 33:1
bullocks: whose talk is of b.	BIBLE 48:6
bully: by the bossy for the b.	SELD 269:22
I love the lovely b.	SHAK 279:10
bum: Indicat Motorem B.	GODL 153:20
bump: that go b. in the night	ANON 7:7
bumpy: going to be a b. night	MANK 217:12
Buncombe: talking to B.	WALK 341:6
through reporters to B.	CARL 90:17
bungler: arts of peace Man is a b.	SHAW 301:22
bunk: History is more or less b.	FORD 143:6
buns: bears might come with b.	ISH 178:21
Bunyan: genius in literature—B.	ARN 18:11
burden: any price, bear any b.	KENN 194:3
b. and heat of the day	BIBLE 50:25
b. of them is intolerable	BOOK 65:11
impossible to carry the heavy b.	EDW 131:2
Is the b. of my song	ANON 9:4
my b. is light	BIBLE 49:36
Take up the White Man's b.	KIPL 197:15
bureaucracy: [b.'s] specific invention	WEBER 344:8
Burg: *Eine feste B.*	LUTH 212:10
burgundy: naïve domestic B.	THUR 332:17
buried: be b. in a good old age	BIBLE 39:12
b. him darkly	WOLFE 352:26
b. in so sweet a place	SHEL 303:2
Burlington: I'm B. Bertie	HARG 162:20
burn: better to marry than to b.	BIBLE 55:5
b. always with this hard	PATER 246:15
B., baby, burn	ANON 6:14
b. its children to save	MEYER 224:4
B. to the socket	WORD 354:19
old age should b. and rave	THOM 330:7
burned: B. on the water	SHAK 271:14
men in the end, are b.	HEINE 164:21
burning: boy stood on the b. deck	HEM 165:9
b. of the leaves	BINY 59:13
b. roof and tower	YEATS 359:14
Is Paris b.?	HITL 169:4
Keep the Home-fires b.	FORD 143:12
midst of a b. fiery furnace	BIBLE 47:11
Tiger Tiger, b. bright	BLAKE 62:5
burnish'd: b. by Aldershot sun	BETJ 37:10
Burns: B., Shelley, were with us	BROW 76:14
burnt-out: b. ends of smoky days	ELIOT 134:10
burr: I am a kind of b.	SHAK 288:25
burthen: vapours weep their b.	TENN 328:17
Burton: why was B. built on Trent	HOUS 175:3
bury: B. it certain fathoms	SHAK 296:13
B. my heart at Wounded Knee	BENÉT 34:9
I come to b. Caesar	SHAK 281:18
Let the dead b. their dead	BIBLE 49:20
physician can b. mistakes	WRIG 357:23
We will b. you	KHR 194:19
bus: Can it be a Motor B.	GODL 153:20
[Hitler] missed the b.	CHAM 94:3
I'm not even a b., I'm a tram	HARE 162:19

buses: Bloody men are like bloody b. COPE 107:22
bush: b. was not consumed BIBLE 39:30
Thorough b., thorough brier SHAK 290:19
bushel: neither under a b. BIBLE 52:15
busier: he seemed b. than he was CHAU 95:19
business: be about my Father's b. BIBLE 52:4
b. being just the terrible BROW 77:10
B. carried on as usual CHUR 99:6
B. first; pleasure afterwards THAC 329:13
b. is merely a survival ROCK 261:11
b. of nobody MAC 213:3
b. of the American people COOL 107:19
b. that we love we rise SHAK 271:20
B. was his aversion EDG 130:17
For it is your b. HOR 173:14
go to my pleasure, b. WYCH 358:5
how to succeed in b. MEAD 222:17
importunity of b. LAMB 200:10
It is the b. of the wealthy man BELL 33:22
it's b. of consequence BARH 28:22
Liberty is always unfinished b. ANON 8:19
make b. for itself DICK 118:4
no b. like show business BERL 35:20
No praying, it spoils b. OTWAY 243:7
Pleasure is a thief to b. DEFOE 115:11
requisite in b. than dispatch ADD 2:20
servants of b. BACON 24:27
That's the true b. precept DICK 119:3
their b. in great waters BOOK 68:12
totter on in b. to the last POPE 251:23
Treasury is the spring of b. BAG 26:4
Buss: Miss B. and Miss Beale ANON 9:10
bust: B. outlasts the throne DOBS 122:25
Can storied urn or animated b. GRAY 157:8
Uncorseted, her friendly b. ELIOT 134:33
When you dance it b. to bust GREN 158:15
bustle: b. in a House DICK 120:10
busy: B. old fool, unruly sun DONNE 124:11
Government of the b. by the bossy SELD 269:22
how b. I must be this day ASTL 19:8
Little man, you've had a b. day HOFF 307:2
butcher: Hog B. for the World SAND 266:12
I want to know a b. paints BROW 77:11
butchered: B. to make a Roman holiday BYRON 85:10
butchers: gentle that makes these b. SHAK 281:13
butler: on the b.'s upper slopes WOD 352:23
butlers: B. ought to know their place BELL 33:6
butt: journey's end, here is my b. SHAK 293:4
knocks you down with the b. GOLD 155:14
butter: B. and eggs and a pound of cheese CALV 88:7
Could we have some b. MILNE 225:22
forth b. in a lordly dish BIBLE 40:33
guns not with b. GOEB 153:21
rather have b. or guns GOER 153:22
buttercup: I'm called Little B. GILB 152:14
buttercups: B. and daisies HOW 175:10
buttered: always on the b. side PAYN 246:20
butterflies: Frogs Eat B. STEV 316:7
butterfly: b. dreaming I am a man CHUA 98:19
b. upon the road KIPL 196:26
can a b.'s wings in Brazil LOR 210:10
Float like a b., sting like a bee ALI 4:10
Who breaks a b. upon a wheel POPE 251:7
butting: B. through the Channel MAS 221:19
buttock: by boiling his b. AUBR 20:1
buttocks: chair that fits all b. SHAK 270:25
gorgeous b. of the ape HUXL 177:13
button: By each b., hook, and lace LOW 211:2
little round b. at top FOOTE 142:20
Pray you, undo this b. SHAK 284:6
buttoning: All this b. and unbuttoning ANON 5:22
buttons: taken of his b. off KIPL 196:9
butty: He's an oul' b. o' mine O'CAS 240:21
buxom: b., blithe, and debonair MILT 226:28

buy: For money can't b. me love MCC 205:11
I'll b. Codham, Cockridden THOM 330:23
I will b. with you SHAK 288:31
no man might b. or sell BIBLE 57:32
shall b. it like an honest man NORT 240:9
buyer: if a b. can be found SALL 266:8
buys: b. a minute's mirth SHAK 299:8
Civility costs nothing and b. MONT 233:5
by: B. and by God caught his eye MCC 214:15
bymatter: if it had been a b. BACON 24:19
byway: And the b. nigh me STEV 317:24
goes his own b. to heaven DEFOE 115:23
byword: proverb and a b. BIBLE 41:29
Byzantium: holy city of B. YEATS 359:22

C

C: C cut it ANON 6:6
C Major of this life BROW 75:9
ça: Ç. ira. ANON 12:2
cabbage: c. with a college education TWAIN 336:4
cabbage-leaf: c. to make an apple-pie FOOTE 142:20
cabbages: find me planting my c. MONT 233:9
Of c.—and kings CARR 91:22
cabin: Make me a willow c. SHAK 297:21
small c. build there YEATS 359:12
cabined: Her c. ample Spirit ARN 17:1
Now I am c., cribbed SHAK 287:9
Cabinet: another to mislead the C. ASQ 19:4
c. is a combining committee BAG 26:5
consequence of c. government BAG 26:6
cable: little c. cars climb CROSS 112:10
Cabots: Lowells talk to the C. BOSS 70:1
cad: Flopshus C. KIPL 198:2
cadence: harsh c. of a rugged line DRYD 128:21
Cadiz Bay: reeking into C. BROW 76:3
Caesar: Aut C., aut nihil BORG 69:25
C. had his Brutus HENRY 166:5
C. hath wept SHAK 281:20
C.'s wife must be above suspicion CAES 87:25
Came from C.'s laurel crown BLAKE 60:8
did in envy of great C. SHAK 282:2
Hail C., those who are ANON 13:12
Hast thou appealed unto C. BIBLE 54:25
Imperious C., dead SHAK 277:9
Not that I loved C. less SHAK 281:15
On blossoming C. SHAK 271:22
Render therefore unto C. BIBLE 50:29
that C. might be great CAMP 88:20
where some buried C. FITZ 140:8
yesterday the word of C. SHAK 281:21
café: heart in ev'ry street c. HAMM 161:1
caftan: Iffucan of Azcan in c. STEV 316:4
cage: linnet born within the c. TENN 325:3
Nor iron bars a c. LOV 210:19
We cannot c. the minute MACN 216:10
caged: know why the c. bird sings DUNB 129:7
We think c. birds sing WEBS 344:27
Cain: and the first city C. COWL 109:13
C. went out from the presence BIBLE 39:6
cruel sons of C. LE G 204:12
Lord set a mark upon C. BIBLE 39:5
cake: Let them eat c. MAR 218:3
cakes: no more c. and ale SHAK 297:26
their bridal-c. HERR 167:12
Calais: 'C.' lying in my heart MARY 221:17
shew light at C. JOHN 184:15
calamity: thou art wedded to c. SHAK 295:15
calculation: c. shining out DICK 119:2
calculators: economists, and c. BURKE 80:14
Caledonia: C.! stern and wild SCOTT 268:14
calf: Bring hither the fatted c. BIBLE 52:31
c. and the young lion BIBLE 45:19

Caliban: C. casts out Ariel — POUND 254:17
calico: c. millenium — CARL 90:25
California: C. to the New York Island — GUTH 159:12
call: And one clear c. for me — TENN 323:18
  c. back yesterday — SHAK 293:24
  c. me early, mother dear — TENN 327:5
  C. no man foe — BENS 34:21
  c. of the running tide — MAS 222:1
  c. of the wild — LOND 209:7
  it's time to c. it a day — GREEN 106:2
  they c. you, Shepherd — ARN 17:4
  they come when you do c. — SHAK 278:3
  through curtains c. on us — DONNE 124:11
  you call to me, c. to me — HARDY 162:15
called: c. them by wrong names — BROW 75:16
  Out of the deep have I c. — BOOK 68:33
callous: c. engraved upon her heart — SELL 270:1
calls: High on a hill it c. to me — CROSS 112:10
  If anybody c. — BENT 35:9
calm: All c., as it was bright — VAUG 337:14
  And all our c. is in that balm — NORT 240:10
  still c. of life — ADAMS 1:7
calme: Luxe, c. et volupté — BAUD 30:4
calumnies: C. are answered best — JONS 187:14
calumny: thou shalt not escape c. — SHAK 275:29
calves: peculiarly susceptible to c. — HUXL 177:10
Calvin: land of C., oat-cakes — SMITH 309:26
Cambridge: C. ladies — CUMM 113:5
  For C. people rarely smile — BROO 73:7
  to C. books — BROW 74:25
  To C. books — TRAPP 334:3
came: He c. unto his own — BIBLE 53:10
  I c., I saw, I conquered — CAES 88:2
  I c. through and I shall return — MAC 213:1
  Tell them I c., and no one — DE L 116:19
  where you c. from or where — TEBB 323:7
camel: c. is a horse designed — ISS 178:23
  c. to go through the eye — BIBLE 50:22
  How the C. got his Hump — KIPL 197:22
  swallow a c. — BIBLE 50:31
  Take my c., dear — MAC 213:2
Camelot: many-towered C. — TENN 325:34
camera: I am a c. — ISH 178:22
Camerado: C., this is no book — WHIT 348:14
cammin: mezzo del c. di nostra vita — DANTE 113:17
camps: Courts and c. are the only places — CHES 97:6
can: And c. it be — WESL 346:3
  because they think they c. — VIRG 339:10
  C. something, hope — HOPK 171:25
  He who c., does — SHAW 301:29
  Pass me the c., lad — HOUS 174:9
Canalettos: Then the C. go — MACM 215:20
cancel: c. all our vows — DRAY 126:16
  C. and tear to pieces — SHAK 287:6
  c. half a line — FITZ 140:14
cancer: Silence like a c. grows — SIMON 307:7
candid: be c. where we can — POPE 252:11
  from the c. friend — CANN 89:12
candle: c. by God's grace — LAT 202:4
  c. in that great turnip — CHUR 100:10
  c. of understanding — BIBLE 47:28
  c. shall not drive — SHAK 282:7
  c. than curse the darkness — STEV 316:21
  farthing c. at Dover — JOHN 184:15
  farthing c. to the sun — YOUNG 360:16
  Fire and fleet and c.-lighte — BALL 27:20
  hold a c. to my shames — SHAK 289:11
  Is scarcely fit to hold a c. — BYROM 84:24
  light a c. to the sun — SIDN 306:14
  little c. throws his beams — SHAK 290:4
  My c. burns at both ends — MILL 224:22
  out, brief c. — SHAK 288:5
  set a c. in the sun — BURT 83:12
  when he hath lighted a c. — BIBLE 52:15

candle-light: dress by yellow c. — STEV 317:12
candles: carry c. and set chairs — HERV 168:1
  c. burn their sockets — HOUS 174:12
  extinguishes c. and kindles fire — LA R 201:24
  Night's c. are burnt out — SHAK 295:18
  Their c. are all out — SHAK 286:9
candy: C. is dandy — NASH 237:15
canker: this c., Bolingbroke — SHAK 277:26
  cannibal: progress if c. uses knife — LEC 204:1
cannon: C. to right of them — TENN 323:16
  Even in the c.'s mouth — SHAK 272:26
cannon-ball: But a c. took off his legs — HOOD 171:4
cano: Arma virumque c. — VIRG 338:23
canoe: coffin clapt in a c. — BYRON 84:26
canoes: their heads in their c. — MARV 221:3
cant: clear your mind of c. — JOHN 186:3
  Let them c. about DECORUM — BURNS 82:13
  we have nothing but c. — PEAC 246:22
cantons: loyal c. of contemnèd love — SHAK 297:21
cantos: c. of unvanquished space — CRANE 110:31
cap: riband in the c. of youth — SHAK 277:5
capability: Negative C. — KEATS 193:2
capacity: transcendent c. of taking trouble — CARL 90:10
caparisons: No c., Miss — SHER 306:1
cape: c. of a sudden came — BROW 76:23
  nobly C. Saint Vincent — BROW 76:3
capital: Pandemonium, the high c. — MILT 228:21
  they say it is a c. offence — MARL 218:7
  To that high C., where kingly — SHEL 303:4
capitalism: definition of c. — HAMP 161:5
  ethic and the spirit of c. — WEBER 344:7
  monopoly stage of c. — LENIN 205:2
  unacceptable face of c. — HEATH 164:12
  War is with the gloves off — STOP 318:7
capitalist: slave of c. society — CONN 107:3
captain: train-band c. eke was — COWP 109:23
  c.'s but a choleric word — SHAK 288:15
  Fighting in the c.'s tower — DYLAN 129:20
  I am the c. of my soul — HENL 165:18
  O C.! my Captain — WHIT 348:11
  Our great captain's c. — SHAK 292:3
captains: All my sad c. — SHAK 271:19
  c. and the kings depart — KIPL 197:2
  c. courageous — BALL 28:1
  C. of industry — CARL 90:20
  Star c. glow — FLEC 141:14
  thunder of the c. — BIBLE 43:5
captive: hast led captivity c. — BOOK 67:17
captives: To serve your c.' need — KIPL 197:15
captivity: hast led c. captive — BOOK 67:17
car: And the gilded c. of day — MILT 226:7
  expands to tinker with his c. — MACN 216:9
caravan: Put up your c. — HODG 169:15
carbon: c. atom possesses — JEANS 180:16
carborundum: Nil c. illegitimi — ANON 9:15
carbuncle: monstrous c. — CHAR 95:8
carbuncles: Monstrous c. — SPEN 312:22
carcase: c. fit for hounds — SHAK 281:4
  Wheresoever the c. — BIBLE 50:36
  Worrying the c. of an old song — THOM 331:5
card: having a c. up his sleeve — LAB 199:12
cardboard: Sailing over a c. sea — HARB 161:12
cards: At c. for kisses — LYLY 212:16
  not learned to play at c. — JOHN 183:20
  old age of c. — POPE 251:11
  Patience, and shuffle the c. — CERV 93:19
care: age is full of c. — SHAK 299:5
  And Heaven's peculiar c. — SOM 311:3
  are now with me past c. — SHAK 293:20
  c. and valour in this Welshman — SHAK 279:11
  C. of his Mother — MILNE 225:20
  c.'s check and curb — VAUG 337:5
  C. sits behind the horseman — HOR 173:25
  c. to stay than will to go — SHAK 295:19

care (cont.):
don't c. too much for money	MCC 205:11
I c. for nobody	BICK 58:24
Lord, with what c.	HERB 167:7
Nor c. beyond to-day	GRAY 157:12
ravelled sleeve of c.	SHAK 286:15
she don't c.	MCC 205:16
so wan with c.	SHAK 277:21
Sport that wrinkled C. derides	MILT 227:2
Take c., my foolish heart	WASH 342:24
take c. of minutes	CHES 97:8
taken better c. of myself	BLAKE 60:4
Teach us to c. and not to care	ELIOT 132:19
this life if, full of c.	DAV 114:20

career: c. open to the talents
c. open to the talents	NAP 237:6
East is a c.	DISR 122:8

careful: c. in the choice of his enemies
So c. of the type she seems	TENN 325:10

carefully: most c. upon your hour
	SHAK 273:29

careless: C. talk costs lives
first fine c. rapture	ANON 6:15
So c. of the single life	BROW 76:2
	TENN 325:10

carelessness: lose both looks like c.
With carefullest c.	WILDE 349:18
	BETJ 37:11

cares: c. that infest the day
No more c. to make me squeak	LONG 209:13
Professional men, they have no c.	ANON 9:17
	NASH 237:12

Carew: grave of Mad C.
	HAYES 163:21

carf: c. biforn his fader
	CHAU 95:14

cargo: With a c. of ivory
	MAS 221:18

Carlyle: C. and Mrs. C.
	BUTL 84:12

carnal: satisfy men's c. lusts
	BOOK 65:26

carnally: To be c. minded is death
	BIBLE 54:39

carnations: Soon will the musk c. break
	ARN 17:19

caro: Verbum c. factum est
	MISS 231:21

carol: chimes ring out with a c.
	BOND 63:9

Carolina: ham'n eggs in C.
	GORD 155:22

carollings: So little cause for c.
	HARDY 162:7

carpe: c. diem
	HOR 173:20

carpenter: c. who has made you a bad table
	JOHN 184:7
Walrus and the C.	CARR 91:21

carpet: figure in the c.
wear the c. with their shoes	JAMES 179:17
	YEATS 359:23

carpets: c. rose along the gusty
	KEATS 190:22

carping: obnoxious to each c. tongue
	BRAD 71:12

carriage: c. has not arrived yet
C. held but just Ourselves	LERM 205:25
very small second class c.	DICK 120:9
	GILB 151:16

carrion: c. comfort, Despair
	HOPK 171:25

carrots: Sowe C. in your Gardens
	GARD 148:4

carry: c. within us the wonders
certain we can c. nothing out	BROW 74:13
making him c. me	BIBLE 56:18
must c. knowledge with him	TOLS 333:13
Speak softly and c. a big stick	JOHN 185:18
	ROOS 262:16

cars: c. nose forward like fish
c. today	LOW 211:12
	BART 29:19

Carthage: C. must be destroyed
To come again to C.	CATO 92:22
	SHAK 289:32

carve: c. heads upon cherry-stones
c. him as a dish fit for the gods	JOHN 186:4
c. on every tree the fair	SHAK 281:4
Must c. in Latin or in Greek	SHAK 273:2
	WALL 341:13

carved: Last-supper-c.-on-a-peach-stone
	LANC 200:20

case: And when a lady's in the c.
c. is concluded	GAY 149:10
everything that is the c.	AUG 22:5
Have nothing to do with the c.	WITT 352:9
heard one side of the c.	GILB 152:6
Here's a corpse in the c.	BUTL 84:15
this c. is that case	BARH 28:21
which in our c. we have not got	ARAB 14:18
would have passed in any c.	REED 258:16
	BECK 31:13

cased: c. up, like a holy relic
	WEBS 344:14

casement: c. ope at night
ghost of Roger C.	KEATS 192:9
	YEATS 359:8

casements: Charmed magic c.
	KEATS 192:5

cash: c. in hand and waive the rest
c. payment has become	FITZ 140:7
she needs good c.	CARL 90:4
	TUCK 335:9

casket: hushèd c. of my soul
	KEATS 192:13

casse: tout c., tout lasse
	ANON 12:17

Cassius: C. has a lean and hungry look
	SHAK 281:1

cassock: C., band, and hymn-book
	WILB 349:6

cassocked: c. huntsman
	COWP 110:1

cassowary: If I were a c.
	WILB 349:8

cast: C. a cold eye on life
c. away the works of darkness	YEATS 360:8
c. off the works of darkness	BOOK 64:21
c. pearls before swine	BIBLE 55:1
C. thy bread upon the waters	BIBLE 49:8
C. your mind on other days	BIBLE 44:24
first c. a stone at her	YEATS 360:7
pale c. of thought	BIBLE 53:26
will I c. out my shoe	SHAK 275:26
will in no wise c. out	BOOK 67:14
	BIBLE 53:23

Castilian: as might an old C.
	BYRON 87:13

castle: In the c. of my skin
Look owre the C. Downe	LAMM 200:17
man's house is his c.	BALL 27:15
rich man in his c.	COKE 103:8
splendour falls on c. walls	ALEX 4:3
	TENN 327:20

Castlereagh: had a mask like C.
	SHEL 304:4

castles: C. in the air
	IBSEN 178:6

casualty: force and road of c.
Truth is the first c.	SHAK 289:13
	JOHN 182:12

cat: C. on a Hot Tin Roof
C., the Rat, and Lovell the dog	WILL 351:5
C. with crimson whiskers	COLL 105:3
endow a college, or a c.	LEAR 203:15
For I will consider my C.	POPE 251:13
Had Tiberius been a c.	SMART 308:7
Hanging of his c. on Monday	ARN 16:23
Like the poor c. i' the adage	BRAT 71:16
Oh I am a c. that likes	SHAK 286:4
part to tear a c. in	SMITH 309:17
Touch not the c.	SHAK 290:18
umpire, the pavilion c.	SCOTT 268:25
When I play with my c.	LANG 201:2
	MONT 233:17

cataclysm: c. but one poor Noah
	HUXL 177:11

catalogue: lamentable c. of human crime
	CHUR 99:12

catamite: in bed with my c.
	BURG 79:14

cataract: sounding c.
wild c. leaps in glory	WORD 355:9
	TENN 327:20

cataracts: c. and hurricanes
	SHAK 283:6

catastrophe: I'll tickle your c.
race between education and c.	SHAK 278:20
	WELLS 345:21

catch: catch as c. can
c. him once upon the hip	FOOTE 142:20
First c. your hare	SHAK 289:2
that was C.-22	GLAS 153:16
	HELL 165:5

catcher: c. in the rye
	SAL 266:1

catching: poverty's c.
	BEHN 32:22

categorical: imperative is C.
	KANT 189:23

category-habits: c. by category-disciplines
	RYLE 265:10

caterpillars: c. of the commonwealth
	SHAK 293:19

Cathay: cycle of C.
	TENN 326:18

cathedral: heft of C. Tunes
	DICK 120:14

cathedrals: cars are like Gothic c.
	BART 29:19

Catherine: child of Karl Marx and C. the Great
	ATTL 19:13

Catholic: holy C. Church
Once a C. always a C.	BOOK 64:3
Roman C. Church	WILS 351:10
Roman C. women	MACM 215:19
	THOM 331:2

Catholick: C. and Apostolick Church
	BOOK 65:6

Catholics: C. and Communists
	GREE 158:2

Catholics (cont.):

Hitler attacked the C.	NIEM 239:15

Cato: C. did, and Addison approved — BUDG 78:4
losing one pleased C. — LUCAN 211:23
cats: C. and monkeys — JAMES 179:22
C., no less liquid — TESS 329:10
dogs and killed the c. — BROW 76:26
greater c. with golden eyes — SACK 265:12
melodious c. under the moon — HUXL 177:4
where c. are cats — MARQ 219:18
cattle-shed: Stood a lowly c. — ALEX 4:4
cauldron: Fire burn and c. bubble — SHAK 287:15
cauliflower: C. is nothing but cabbage — TWAIN 336:4
causa: c. finita est — AUG 22:5
causas: potuit rerum cognoscere c. — VIRG 340:8
cause: c. may be inconvenient — BENN 34:18
c. of dullness in others — FOOTE 143:1
c. or just impediment — BOOK 65:25
c. that wit is in other men — SHAK 278:16
effect was already in the c. — BERG 35:13
good old c. — MILT 231:6
good old c. — WORD 356:1
it is the c., my soul — SHAK 292:28
judge thou my c. — BIBLE 47:3
man can shew any just c. — BOOK 65:27
perseverance in a good c. — STER 315:14
Rebel without a c. — LIND 207:15
So little c. for carollings — HARDY 162:7
winning c. pleased — LUCAN 211:23
causer: Heart's renying, c. of this — BARN 29:8
causes: Home of lost c. — ARN 18:2
knowledge of c. — BACON 25:26
malice, to breed c. — JONS 187:17
understand the c. of things — VIRG 340:8
cavaliero: he was a perfect c. — BYRON 84:27
Cavaliers: C. (Wrong but Wromantic) — SELL 270:2
cave: her vacant interlunar c. — MILT 230:12
caverns: c. measureless to man — COL 103:22
in c. all alone — WILB 349:11
caves: Mendip's sunless c. — MAC 213:24
pleasure-dome with c. of ice — COL 103:24
unfathomed c. of ocean bear — GRAY 157:9
caviare: c. to the general — SHAK 275:18
Cawdor: Glamis thou art, and C. — SHAK 285:15
cease: C.! must men kill and die — SHEL 303:19
c. upon the midnight — KEATS 192:3
have fears that I may c. — KEATS 192:19
will not c. from mental fight — BLAKE 61:12
ceased: it c. to be with Sarah — BIBLE 39:14
ceasing: Remembering without c. — BIBLE 56:13
Cecilia: Blessed C., appear in visions — AUDEN 20:10
celestial: And lighten with c. fire — BOOK 69:16
Apparelled in c. light — WORD 355:17
Celia: Come, my C., let us prove — JONS 187:16
celibacy: c. has no pleasures — JOHN 183:5
c. is almost always a muddy pond — PEAC 246:24
cell: narrow c. for ever laid — GRAY 157:6
tight hot c. of their hearts — BOGAN 62:18
cellar: Born in a c. — FOOTE 142:19
I was born in a c. — CONG 106:8
cellos: c. of the deep farms — STEV 316:22
cells: Than c. and gibbets — COOK 107:17
Celt: blind hysterics of the C. — TENN 325:28
cement: same c., ever sure — POPE 250:19
cemetery: c. is an open space — SHEL 303:2
censorship: extreme form of c. — SHAW 302:22
censure: c. of a man's self — JOHN 185:20
centre: c. cannot hold — YEATS 359:24
c. is everywhere — ANON 9:13
May sit i' the c. — MILT 226:12
My c. is giving way — FOCH 142:14
real c. of the household — SHAW 301:5
This bed thy c. — DONNE 124:13
whose c. is everywhere — UPD 336:13
centuries: All c. but this — GILB 151:20

centuries (cont.):
forty c. look down — NAP 237:3
Through what wild c. — DE L 116:12
century: c. of the common man — WALL 341:9
So the 20th C. — CRANE 111:2
Cerberus: Of C., and blackest Midnight — MILT 226:27
You are not like C. — SHER 306:2
ceremony: C. is an invention — LAMB 199:23
c. of innocence is drowned — YEATS 359:24
Save c., save general c. — SHAK 279:15
thrice-gorgeous c. — SHAK 279:16
Ceres: laughing C. re-assume the land — POPE 251:17
certain: c. thing called the Boy Friend — WILS 351:17
dirge of her c. ending — SHAK 299:9
lady of a 'c. age' — BYRON 86:21
One thing is c. — FITZ 140:10
certainties: better than most people's c. — HARD 161:17
hot for c. in this our life — MER 223:24
man will begin with c. — BACON 23:20
cesspool: London, that great c. — DOYLE 126:4
Ceylon: Blow soft o'er C.'s isle — HEBER 164:16
chaff: see that the c. is printed — HUBB 175:15
chagrin: C. d'amour — FLOR 142:12
chain: c. that is round us now — CORY 108:12
chainless: Eternal spirit of the c. mind — BYRON 87:7
chains: better to be in c. than to be free — KAFKA 189:18
everywhere he is in c. — ROUS 263:18
kings in c. — BOOK 69:11
nothing to lose but their c. — ENG 221:15
only by the slightest c. — EDG 130:18
sang in my c. like the sea — THOM 330:9
chair: And tilts up his c. — HOFF 169:19
c. that fits all buttocks — SHAK 270:25
La c. est triste — MALL 216:20
Seated in thy silver c. — JONS 187:3
chairs: carry candles and set c. — HERV 168:1
chaise-longue: hurly-burly of the c. — CAMP 88:15
chalice: c. from the palace — FRANK 245:1
chalices: treen priests and golden c. — JEWEL 181:14
Cham: great C. of literature — SMOL 310:17
chamber: stalking in my c. — WYATT 358:2
chamberers: That c. have — SHAK 292:15
Chamberlain: speech by C. — BEVAN 38:3
chambermaid: c. as of a Duchess — JOHN 185:21
chambers: whisper softness in c. — MILT 231:1
champagne: c. and a chicken at last — MONT 233:4
C., and Bridge — BELL 33:25
C. socialist — MORT 235:22
I get no kick from c. — PORT 253:20
It's like c. or high heels — BENN 34:18
not a c. teetotaller — SHAW 300:28
chance: c. favours only the prepared — PAST 246:11
C. has appointed her home — BUNT 78:14
Give peace a c. — MCC 205:13
I missed my c. — LAWR 202:22
too good to leave to c. — SIMON 307:8
voice to come in as by c. — BACON 24:18
Which erring men call c. — MILT 226:18
Chancellor: C. of the Exchequer — LOWE 211:1
chances: c. change by course — SOUT 312:9
changes and c. of this mortal — BOOK 65:18
change: and bolts up c. — SHAK 272:2
architecture, a c. of heart — AUDEN 21:14
certain relief in c. — IRV 178:20
C. and decay in all around — LYTE 212:20
c. from Jane to Elizabeth — AUST 23:3
c. from major to minor — PORT 253:19
c. Kate into Nan — BLAKE 60:15
C. not made without inconvenience — JOHN 182:3
c. something at once sordid — BAUD 30:7
c. that state by forces — NEWT 239:3
c. we think we see in life — FROST 146:9
c. your mind and follow him — AUR 22:11
Even a god cannot c. the past — AGAT 3:7
more things c. — KARR 190:2

change (*cont.*):

necessary not to c.	FALK 138:11
point is to c. it	MARX 221:11
ringing grooves of c.	TENN 326:17
things will have to c.	LAMP 200:19
we c. with them	ANON 14:2
wind of c.	MACM 215:17
with fear of c.	MILT 228:17
without the means of some c.	BURKE 80:10

changeable: Fickle and c. always is woman — VIRG 339:9

changed: changed, c. utterly — YEATS 359:3
c. upon the blue guitar — STEV 316:9
That all things are c. — BACON 24:4
that it be not c. — BIBLE 47:13
we have c. all that — MOL 232:19
we shall all be c. — BIBLE 55:21

changes: c. and chances of this mortal life — BOOK 65:18
sundry and manifold c. — BOOK 64:23
world's a scene of c. — COWL 109:15

changest: who c. not, abide with me — LYTE 212:20

changing: all the c. scenes of life — TATE 322:17
fixed point in a c. world — DOYLE 125:18
Times They Are A-C. — DYLAN 130:9

Chankly Bore: Hills of the C. — LEAR 203:9

channel: C. is a mere ditch — NAP 237:1
drum them up the C. — NEWB 238:10
you are crossing the C. — GILB 151:16

chanting: C. faint hymns — SHAK 290:12

chaos: bit of primordial c. — WELLS 345:22
black c. comes again — SHAK 300:19
C. and darkness heard — MARR 219:24
C., illumined by flashes of — WILDE 350:19
C. is come again — SHAK 292:10
C. often breeds life — ADAMS 1:15
reign of C. and old Night — MILT 228:16
thy dread empire, C. — POPE 250:22

chapel: devil would also build a c. — LUTH 212:9
will build a c. just — BECON 31:17
will have his c. — BANC 28:14

chapels: c. had been churches — SHAK 288:29
Stolen looks are nice in c. — HUNT 176:16

chaplain: What a book a devil's c. — DARW 114:5

chaps: Biography is about C. — BENT 35:5

chapter: c. of accidents — CHES 97:17

character: c. dead at every word — SHER 306:4
c. in the full current of — GOET 154:11
c. is destiny — ELIOT 132:15
C. is destiny — NOV 240:12
habit and you reap a c. — READE 258:11
I leave my c. behind me — SHER 306:5
man's c. is his fate — HER 166:9
man's c. is to be abused — THAC 329:16
What is c. — JAMES 179:24

characters: c. of hell to trace — GRAY 157:2
from high life high c. — POPE 251:20
Six c. in search of an author — PIR 249:1
Who have c. to lose — BURNS 82:13

charge: angels c. over thee — BOOK 67:30
Take thou in c. this day — MAC 214:7

charged: c. the troops of error — BROW 74:9
thought c. with emotion — GIDE 151:1

charging: marching, c. feet, boy — RICH 179:7

Charing Cross: betwixt Heaven and C. — THOM 331:16
human existence at C. — JOHN 185:1

chariot: Bring me my c. of fire — BLAKE 61:12
slap-up gal in a bang-up c. — DICK 119:23
Swing low, sweet c. — ANON 10:17
Time's winged c. — MARV 220:24

charioted: c. by Bacchus and his pards — KEATS 192:1

chariots: tarry the wheels of his c. — BIBLE 40:34

charities: cold c. of man to man — CRAB 110:30

charity: and have not c. — BIBLE 55:11
C. and beating begins at home — FLET 142:7
C., dear Miss Prism — WILDE 349:21
c. envieth not — BIBLE 55:12

charity (*cont.*):

C. never faileth	BIBLE 55:12
C. shall cover the multitude	BIBLE 57:11
C. suffereth long	BIBLE 55:12
c. vaunteth not itself	BIBLE 55:12
faith, hope, c.	BIBLE 55:14
greatest of these is c.	BIBLE 55:14
lectures or a little c.	WHIT 348:20
Let holy c.	LITT 208:2
need c. more than the dead	ARN 16:8
puffeth up, but c. edifieth	BIBLE 55:7
with c. for all	LINC 207:7

Charlotte: Werther had a love for C. — THAC 329:23

charm: c. can soothe her melancholy — GOLD 155:13
c. he never so wisely — BOOK 67:13
C. is the great English blight — WAUGH 343:17
C...it's a sort of bloom — BARR 29:16
Completing the c. — ELIOT 132:24
discreet c. of the bourgeoisie — BUÑ 78:16
hard words like a c. — OSB 242:17
Oozing c. from every pore — LERN 206:2
What is c. then — LESS 206:4
You know what c. is — CAMUS 89:5

charmed: c. it with smiles and soap — CARR 92:9
I bear a c. life — SHAK 288:6

charmer: voice of the c. — BOOK 67:13
Were t'other dear c. away — GAY 149:7

charming: How c. is divine philosophy — MILT 226:15

charms: all c. fly — KEATS 191:14
c. to sooth a savage breast — CONG 106:11
those endearing young c. — MOORE 234:11

charter: c. of thy worth — SHAK 299:27
This was the c. of the land — THOM 331:20

chase: habitually live by the c. — TOCQ 333:2
When heated in the c. — TATE 322:16

chasing: always c. Rimbauds — PARK 245:10

chassis: worl's in a state o' c. — O'CAS 240:22

chaste: Be thou as c. as ice — SHAK 275:29
c., and twenty-three — BYRON 85:23
huntress, c. and fair — JONS 187:3
men ask, Are Barmaids C. — MAS 221:20
Nor ever c., except you ravish — DONNE 123:11
Was Jesus c. — BLAKE 60:13

chasten: To c. and subdue — WORD 355:10

chasteneth: Whom the Lord loveth he c. — BIBLE 56:28

chastised: c. you with whips — BIBLE 41:34

chastisement: c. of our peace — BIBLE 46:19

chastity: C.—the most unnatural — HUXL 177:7
Give any lessons of c. — BLAKE 60:13
Give me c. and continency — AUG 21:22
'Tis c., my brother, chastity — MILT 226:14

châteaux: *Ô saisons, ô c.* — RIMB 260:10

chats: spoiled the women's c. — BROW 76:26

Chattanooga: C. Choo-choo — GORD 155:22

chatter: c. of a transcendental kind — GILB 152:10

chattering: Dumb swans, not c. pies — SIDN 306:22

Chatterley: end of the C. ban — LARK 201:12

Chatterton: C., the marvellous boy — WORD 356:16

Chaucer: [of C.] here is God's plenty — DRYD 128:30
old famous poet C. — SPEN 313:19

cheap: And flesh and blood so c. — HOOD 171:13
done as c. as other men — PEPYS 247:15
how potent c. music is — COW 109:10
They be good c. — WYATT 358:3

cheaper: c. seats clap your hands — LENN 205:9

cheat: c. at cards genteelly — BOSW 70:5
sweet c. gone — DE L 116:16
When it's so lucrative to c. — CLOU 102:19

cheated: Old men who never c. — BETJ 36:21

cheating: c. between two periods — BIER 59:7

cheats: c. with an oath — PLUT 250:2

checks: moves, and c. and slays — FITZ 140:12

cheek: call a blush into the c. — DICK 119:22
Feed on her damask c. — SHAK 298:1
hangs upon the c. of night — SHAK 294:26

cheek (*cont.*):
hollow c. or faded eye	TENN 328:2
smite thee on thy right c.	BIBLE 48:23
cheeks: And on thy c. a fading rose	KEATS 191:8
crack your c.	SHAK 283:6
cheer: Be of good c.	BIBLE 50:8
c. but not inebriate	BERK 35:16
c. but not inebriate	COWP 110:11
Could scarce forbear to c.	MAC 214:8
Don't c., men	PHIL 248:13
Greet the unseen with a c.	BROW 75:12
cheerful: c. as any man could	PEPYS 247:13
Come, let us join our c. songs	WATTS 343:3
God loveth a c. giver	BIBLE 55:25
maketh a c. countenance	BIBLE 43:25
cheerfulness: C. gives elasticity	SMIL 308:19
c. keeps up a kind of day-light	ADD 2:24
c. was always breaking in	EDW 131:5
cheeriness: Chintzy, Chintzy c.	BETJ 36:19
cheerio: it s c. my deario	MARQ 219:17
cheerioh: And 'c.' or 'cheeri-bye'	BETJ 37:1
cheers: Two c. for Democracy	FORS 144:3
cheese: Botticelli's a c.	PUNCH 256:18
eggs and a pound of c.	CALV 88:7
has 246 varieties of c.	DE G 116:7
I'll fill hup the chinks wi' c.	SURT 319:9
like some valley c.	AUDEN 21:13
night I've dreamed of c.	STEV 317:4
chemistry: weak in c.	WELLS 345:16
cheque: blank c. to Lord Salisbury	GOSC 155:24
c. and the postal order	AUDEN 21:4
chequer-board: c. of nights and days	FITZ 140:12
cherchez: C. la femme	DUMAS 129:3
cherish: c. those hearts that hate	SHAK 280:20
love, c., and to obey	BOOK 66:1
cherished: My no longer c.	MILL 224:23
cherries: apples, c., hops	DICK 119:26
Life is just a bowl of c.	BROWN 73:17
cherry: as American as c. pie	BROWN 73:15
C.-ripe	HERR 167:13
Loveliest of trees, the c. now	HOUS 174:16
O ruddier than the c.	GAY 149:1
To see the c. hung with snow	HOUS 174:17
cherry-stones: carve heads upon c.	JOHN 186:4
cherubim: C. and Seraphim	HEBER 164:17
cherubims: Immortal c.	TRAH 333:19
cherubs: As so near the c. hymn	SMART 308:9
Cheshire: smile of a cosmic C. cat	HUXL 177:14
chest: His c. against his foes	SMART 308:10
men on the dead man's c.	STEV 317:2
Chesterton: dared attack my C.	BELL 33:16
chestnut: Under a spreading c. tree	LONG 210:4
chevalier: C. *sans peur et sans reproche*	ANON 12:4
Chevy: Drove my C. to the levee	MCL 215:8
chew: fart and c. gum	JOHN 181:22
chewing gum: c. for the eyes	ANON 10:14
chic: Radical C.	WOLFE 353:9
chicken: c. in his pot	HENR 165:20
republic like a c.	MITF 232:8
Some c.! Some neck!	CHUR 99:17
with champagne and a c.	MONT 233:4
chickens: beside the white c.	WILL 351:8
Curses are like young c.	SOUT 311:21
pretty c. and their dam	SHAK 287:26
chiding: He will not alway be c.	BOOK 68:6
chief: Cromwell, our c. of men	MILT 230:26
What is the c. end of man	SHOR 306:13
chieftain: C. Iffucan of Azcan	STEV 316:4
Great c. o' the puddin'-race	BURNS 82:24
child: angel is the English c.	BLAKE 61:24
c. born therein shall	RUSK 264:19
C.! do not throw this book	BELL 32:25
c. for the first seven years	ANON 7:10
C. is father of the Man	WORD 355:14
c. is owed the greatest	JUV 189:15

child (*cont.*):
c. of dirt that stinks	POPE 251:8
c. of Karl Marx and Catherine	ATTL 19:13
c.'s a plaything for an hour	LAMB 200:14
c. shall play on the hole	BIBLE 45:20
c. should always say what's	STEV 317:16
c. take care that you strike	SHAW 301:32
Christ, the c. of God	BOOK 65:20
every formal visit a c.	AUST 23:8
father that knows his own c.	SHAK 289:7
find I am to have his c.	BURG 79:15
for a c. in the street I could	CLOU 102:7
For unto us a c. is born	BIBLE 45:16
Get with c. a mandrake root	DONNE 124:10
God bless the c. that's got	HOL 170:10
hare's own c.	HOFF 170:3
heard one calling, 'C.'	HERB 166:23
He has devoured the infant c.	HOUS 174:8
Here a little c. I stand	HERR 167:11
Is it well with the c.	BIBLE 42:9
I speak like a c.	NAB 236:20
It's only my c.-wife	DICK 118:17
I was a c. and she was a c.	POE 250:3
leave a c. alone	BROW 77:7
little c., a limber elf	COL 103:13
little c. shall lead them	BIBLE 45:19
Love, a c., is ever crying	WROTH 358:1
mid-May's eldest c.	KEATS 192:2
my absent c.	SHAK 282:8
On a cloud I saw a c.	BLAKE 61:18
Perfection is the c. of Time	HALL 160:13
right to a c.	SHAW 301:4
She was an aggravating c.	BELL 33:11
shocks the mind of a c.	PAINE 244:7
spoil the c.	BUTL 84:3
that's governed by a c.	SHAK 294:16
There is a man c. conceived	BIBLE 42:25
thou show'st thee in a c.	SHAK 282:24
To have a thankless c.	SHAK 282:25
use of a new-born c.	FRAN 145:17
was the mother for the c.	COL 104:20
When I was a c., I spake	BIBLE 55:14
when thy king is a c.	BIBLE 44:22
childbirth: Death and taxes and c.	MITC 232:5
childhood: And sleep as I in c.	CLARE 101:7
C. is the kingdom where	MILL 224:21
c. when the door opens	GREE 158:6
'tis the eye of c.	SHAK 286:17
Where c. had strayed	Æ 3:4
childish: are either knavish or c.	JOHN 185:23
c. valorous than manly wise	MARL 219:13
I put away c. things	BIBLE 55:14
childishness: Second c.	SHAK 272:28
childlike: Whose trust, ever c.	STR 318:17
children: And airy hopes my c.	WORD 354:21
And oh those c.'s voices	VERL 338:1
be called the c. of God	BIBLE 48:19
become as little c.	BIBLE 50:15
breeds contempt—and c.	TWAIN 336:3
by c. to adults	SZASZ 321:23
C. are dumb to say how	GRAV 156:13
c. are heard on the green	BLAKE 61:25
c. at play are not playing	MONT 233:11
C. begin by loving	WILDE 350:12
c. cried in the streets	MOTL 236:1
c. hath given hostages	BACON 25:1
c. in whom is no faith	BIBLE 40:24
c. like the olive-branches	BOOK 68:32
c. love their parents	AUCT 20:7
c. of a larger growth	CHES 97:11
c. of a larger growth	DRYD 127:25
c. of the devil	TENN 328:12
c. of the kingdom	BIBLE 49:18
c. produce adults	DE VR 117:12
C. sweeten labours	BACON 25:6

children (cont.):
  c. to be always and forever — DE S 265:15
  c. who were rough — SPEN 312:25
  Come, dear c., let us away — ARN 16:16
  dogs than of their c. — PENN 247:10
  even so are the young c. — BOOK 68:31
  fathers upon the c. — BIBLE 40:5
  from c. and from fools — DRYD 128:16
  its c. to save its pride — MEYER 224:4
  little c. died in the streets — AUDEN 20:18
  Men fear death as c. fear — BACON 24:20
  Myself and c. three — COWP 109:24
  not much about having c. — LODGE 209:4
  poor get c. — EGAN 189:19
  provoke not your c. — BIBLE 56:2
  Rachel weeping for her c. — BIBLE 48:11
  sleepless c.'s hearts are glad — BETJ 36:17
  stars are my c. — KEATS 193:9
  Suffer the little c. — BIBLE 51:25
  That is known as the C.'s Hour — LONG 209:12
  thou shalt bring forth c. — BIBLE 39:1
  Too easy for c. — SCHN 267:23
  To whom the lips of c. — NEALE 237:21
  turn each one of her c. — VERG 337:19
  violations committed by c. — BOWEN 70:17
  We are c., playing on the line — FORS 143:22
  which holdeth c. from play — SIDN 306:27
  wiser than the c. of light — BIBLE 52:33
  with which men play like c. — EDD 130:13
  young c., were sooner — ASCH 18:18
  Your c. are not your c. — GIBR 150:19
Chile: small earthquake in C. — COCK 103:1
chill: bitter c. it was — KEATS 190:14
chilly: By c. fingered spring — KEATS 190:13
  I feel c. and grown old — BROW 77:19
  our c. women — BYRON 84:29
  room grows c. — GRAH 156:4
Chimborazo: C., Cotopaxi — TURN 335:17
chime: c. had stroked the air — JONS 187:18
chimeras: dire c. and enchanted isles — MILT 226:16
chimes: c. at midnight — SHAK 278:24
  c. ring out with a carol — BOND 63:9
chimney: old men from the c. — SIDN 306:27
chimneys: c. I sweep — BLAKE 61:19
  good grove of c. for me — MORR 235:11
chimney-sweepers: As c., come to dust — SHAK 273:27
chin: his c. upon an orient wave — MILT 227:29
China: from C. to Peru — JOHN 183:11
  Till C. and Africa meet — AUDEN 20:11
  up like thunder outer C. — KIPL 196:21
  your land armies in C. — MONT 233:23
chinks: fill hup the c. wi' cheese — SURT 319:9
chintzy: C., C. cheeriness — BETJ 36:19
chip: c. of the old 'block' — BURKE 81:11
chips: c. with everything — WESK 346:2
chivalry: age of c. is gone — BURKE 80:14
  age of c. is past — DISR 122:11
  nine-tenths of the law of c. — SAY 267:15
chocolate: c. cream soldier — SHAW 300:24
choice: being just the terrible c. — BROW 77:10
  c. and master spirits — SHAK 281:12
  money and you takes your c. — PUNCH 256:6
choices: all the c. gone before — DID 120:21
choir: c. of saints for evermore — DONNE 123:16
  c. the small gnats mourn — KEATS 192:16
  may I join the c. invisible — ELIOT 132:17
  virgin-c. to make delicious moan — KEATS 192:8
choirs: Bare ruined c. — SHAK 299:24
  demented or wailing shells — OWEN 243:22
  in C. and Places where they sing — BOOK 64:7
choking: c. him and making him carry me — TOLS 333:13
choleric: captain's but a c. — SHAK 288:15
choose: believe what we c. — NEWM 239:1
  C. an author as you choose — DILL 120:22
  c. perfection of the life — YEATS 358:19

choose (cont.):
  not c. not to be — HOPK 171:25
  To govern is to c. — LÉVIS 206:10
  woman can hardly ever c. — ELIOT 132:5
choosers: buggers can't be c. — BOWRA 71:4
chopcherry: c., c. ripe within — PEELE 247:2
Chopin: I like C. and Bizet — FISH 139:26
chopper: c. on a big black block — GILB 151:25
chord: feel for the common c. — BROW 75:9
  I struck one c. of music — PROC 255:14
chorus: c.-ending from Euripides — BROW 75:13
chosen: but few are c. — BIBLE 50:28
  ye are a c. generation — BIBLE 57:8
Christ: And C. receive thy saule — BALL 27:20
  C. erecteth his Church — BANC 28:14
  C. follows Dionysus — POUND 254:17
  C. is the path and Christ — MONS 233:2
  C. perish in torment — SHAW 302:21
  C. risen from the dead — BIBLE 55:17
  C.'s particular love's — BROW 77:7
  C. walking on the water — THOM 331:17
  C. was betrayed — Æ 3:4
  churches have killed their C. — TENN 327:4
  If Jesus C. were to come — CARL 90:26
  in C. shall all be made alive — BIBLE 55:17
  Jesus C. the same yesterday — BIBLE 56:30
  Ring in the C. — TENN 325:27
  shuts the spouse C. home — HOPK 172:17
  through C. which strengtheneth — BIBLE 56:10
  Vision of C. — BLAKE 60:11
  was made a member of C. — BOOK 65:20
Christ-Church: line of festal light in C. — ARN 17:9
Christe: C. eleison — MISS 231:12
Christian: C. boys — ARN 18:15
  C. ideal has not been tried — CHES 98:15
  C. is a man who feels — YBAR 358:11
  C. kisses on an 'eathen — KIPL 196:22
  Onward, C. soldiers — BAR 29:1
  persuadest me to be a C. — BIBLE 54:27
  Scratch the C. and you — ZANG 360:26
  tiger that hadn't got a C. — PUNCH 256:14
Christianity: C. is part of the laws — HALE 160:5
  C., of course, but why journalism — BALF 27:11
  C. was the religion — SWIFT 320:9
  His C. was muscular — DISR 121:29
  local thing called C. — HARDY 161:19
  loving C. better than Truth — COL 104:23
  rock 'n' roll or C. — LENN 205:8
Christians: C., awake! — BYROM 84:23
  C. have burnt each other — BYRON 85:25
  forty generations of C. — MAC 213:18
Christmas: C. Day in the Workhouse — SIMS 307:14
  C. I no more desire a rose — SHAK 284:11
  C.-morning bells — BETJ 36:17
  C. should fall out in the — ADD 2:23
  I'm dreaming of a white C. — BERL 36:3
  'Twas the night before C. — MOORE 234:3
Christopher Robin: C. is saying his prayers — MILNE 226:1
  C. went down with Alice — MILNE 225:19
Christ's College: called him the lady of C. — AUBR 19:20
chronicle: and c. small beer — SHAK 292:4
  When in the c. of wasted time — SHAK 300:4
chronicles: brief c. of the time — SHAK 275:19
chumps: C. make the best husbands — WOD 352:11
church: aristocracy, and an alien C. — DISR 121:7
  As some to c. repair — POPE 252:3
  Broad of C. and 'broad of mind' — BETJ 37:15
  Catholick and Apostolick C. — BOOK 65:6
  Christ erecteth his C. — BANC 28:14
  C. is an anvil — MACL 215:6
  C. militant here in earth — BOOK 65:7
  C. [of E.] Conservative Party at prayer — ROYD 264:2
  C.'s one foundation — STONE 317:27
  C.'s Restoration — BETJ 37:3

church (cont.):

c. without pulling off his hat	JOHN 184:8
fain would kill their c.	TENN 327:4
figure in a country c.	SWIFT 320:3
free c. in a free state	CAV 93:14
if undressed at C.	FARQ 138:21
I like a c.; I like a cowl	EMER 136:14
mere c. furniture at best	COWP 110:15
nearer the C. the further from God	ANDR 5:16
nor so wide as a c. door	SHAK 295:7
not the c. for his mother	CYPR 113:12
salvation outside the c.	AUG 21:26
She came to the village c.	TENN 326:24
Stands the C. clock at	BROO 73:8
there must be the C.	AMBR 4:19
understands [the C. of Rome]	MAC 213:16
upon this rock I will build my c.	BIBLE 50:13
where God built a c.	LUTH 212:9
wheresoever God buildeth a c.	BECON 31:17
churches: chapels had been c.	SHAK 288:29
Churchill: [C.] mobilized the language	MURR 236:13
voice was that of C.	ATTL 19:12
churchyards: Troop home to c.	SHAK 290:34
cigar: really good 5-cent c.	MARS 220:3
sweet post-prandial c.	BUCH 77:29
cigarette: c. that bears a lipstick's traces	MARV 221:4
cigars: Call the roller of big c.	STEV 316:5
Cinara: when good C. was my queen	HOR 173:30
Cincinnatus: C. of the West	BYRON 87:4
cinders: c., ashes, dust	KEATS 191:11
cinema: c. is truth 24 times per second	GOD 153:18
circle: c. of which the centre	ANON 9:13
Round and round the c.	ELIOT 132:24
Weave a c. round him thrice	COL 104:1
circumference: c. is nowhere	ANON 9:13
circumlocution: C. Office	DICK 118:29
circumspectly: See then that ye walk c.	BIBLE 56:1
circumspice: Si monumentum requiris, c.	ANON 13:23
circumstance: c. of glorious war	SHAK 292:20
circumstances: Fearful concatenation of c.	WEBS 344:10
circus: no right in the bloody c.	MAXT 222:14
circuses: bread and c.	JUV 189:12
cistern: Cold the seat and loud the c.	BENN 34:16
citadels: circle-c. there	HOPK 172:16
cities: c. for our best morality	AUST 22:19
c. of men and manners	TENN 328:21
scabbed here and there by c.	BUNT 78:14
Seven c. warred for Homer	HEYW 168:9
streets of a hundred c.	HOOV 171:18
thou art the flower of c.	ANON 9:2
citizen: c., first in war	LEE 204:7
completely a c. of the world	BOSW 70:3
John Gilpin was a c.	COWP 109:23
relation is a zealous c.	BURKE 80:20
To the c. or the police	AUDEN 21:11
citizens: Before Man made us c.	LOW 211:6
first and second class c.	WILL 351:9
Soldiers are c. of death	SASS 267:10
citizenship: c. in the kingdom of the well	SONT 311:10
city: citizen of no mean c.	BIBLE 54:23
c. is not a concrete jungle	MORR 235:12
C. is of Night	THOM 332:1
C. now doth like a garment	WORD 354:15
C. of the Big Shoulders	SAND 266:12
c. that is set on a hill	BIBLE 48:21
c., thus I turn my back	SHAK 273:20
C. with her dreaming spires	ARN 17:17
c. with no more personality	CHAN 94:8
each and every town or c.	HOLM 170:14
fallen, that great c.	BIBLE 57:34
first c. Cain	COWL 109:13
Happy is that c.	ANON 7:16
have we no continuing c.	BIBLE 57:1
Hell is a c. much like London	SHEL 304:13

city (cont.):

I John saw the holy c.	BIBLE 58:4
keep the c.	BOOK 68:30
live in a c.	COLT 105:18
London: a nation, not a c.	DISR 122:5
long in populous c. pent	MILT 229:23
Lord guards the c.	BIBLE 58:13
oppressing c.	BIBLE 47:25
people went up into the c.	BIBLE 40:27
rose-red c. half as old as	BURG 79:17
Sun-girt c., thou hast been	SHEL 304:2
thou c. of God	BOOK 67:24
To the holy c. of Byzantium	YEATS 359:22
Up and down the C. Road	MAND 217:8
venal c. ripe to perish	SALL 266:8
What is the c. but the people	SHAK 273:19
Without a c. wall	ALEX 4:6
Woe to the bloody c.	BIBLE 47:24
civil: dire effects from c. discord	ADD 2:19
Here lies a civil servant	SISS 307:15
Too c. by half	SHER 305:31
civilian: mushroom rich c.	BYRON 87:13
civilities: bandy c. with my Sovereign	JOHN 184:19
civility: C. costs nothing and buys	MONT 233:5
I see a wild c.	HERR 167:15
civilization: As c. advances, poetry	MAC 213:7
can't say c. don't advance	ROG 262:2
C. advances by extending	WHIT 348:5
C. and profits go hand in hand	COOL 107:18
c. has become a thin crust	ELLIS 136:6
C. has made the peasantry	TROT 334:23
c. with the most difficulty	TOCQ 333:2
farmyard c. of the Fabians	INGE 178:11
For a botched c.	POUND 254:19
great elements of modern c.	CARL 90:9
last product of c.	RUSS 264:22
life-blood of real c.	TREV 334:7
resources of c. against	GLAD 153:12
civilized: last thing c. by Man	MER 223:16
Civil Service: C. is profoundly deferential	CROS 112:12
civis: C. Romanus sum	CIC 100:27
clair: pas c. n'est pas français	RIV 260:14
clamavi: De profundis c.	BIBLE 58:14
clanging: C. from the Severn to the Tyne	KIPL 196:3
clap: cheaper seats c.	LENN 205:9
c. your hands	BARR 29:14
Don't c. too hard	OSB 242:18
clapped-out: c., post-imperial slag-heap	DRAB 126:9
clapper: his tongue is the c.	SHAK 291:21
claret: C. is the liquor for boys	JOHN 185:22
Claridges: bootboy at C.	WOOLF 354:6
clasps: c. the crag with crookèd	TENN 323:21
class: c. struggle necessarily	MARX 221:12
free passes, c. distinction	BETJ 37:4
history of c. struggles	ENG 221:14
I could have had c.	SCH 267:24
second c. citizens	WILL 351:9
While there is a lower c.	DEBS 115:9
classes: c. which need sanctuary	BALD 27:10
masses against the c.	GLAD 153:13
classic: C. music is th'kind	HUBB 175:16
classical: c. mind at work	PIRS 249:2
C. quotation is the parole	JOHN 185:30
tragedy of the c. languages	MADAN 216:12
classics: man with a bellyful of the c.	MILL 225:7
claw: Nature, red in tooth and c.	TENN 325:12
clawed: Hath c. me with his clutch	VAUX 337:15
claws: c. that catch	CARR 91:15
Had I been a pair of ragged c.	ELIOT 133:28
clay: associate of this c.	HADR 159:14
c. and wattles made	YEATS 359:12
C. lies still, but blood's	HOUS 174:18
informed the tenement of c.	DRYD 127:6
They're only made of c.	GERS 150:7
clean: And keep their teeth c.	SHAK 273:16

clean (cont.):
c. and comfortable I sit	KEATS 193:13
c. & in-between-the-sheets	MCG 214:21
C-l-e-a-n, c., verb active	DICK 119:13
c. place to die	KAV 190:7
c. the sky	ELIOT 134:8
Make me a c. heart	BOOK 67:10
one more thing to keep c.	FRY 146:30
small and white and c.	MORR 235:16

cleanliness: C. is next to godliness — WESL 346:15
cleanly: thus so c., I myself can free — DRAY 126:16
cleanness: swimmers into c. leaping — BROO 73:9
cleanse: C. me from its guilt and power — TOPL 333:14
clear: c. in his great office — SHAK 285:24
C. the air — ELIOT 134:8
poignancy in all things c. — WILB 349:9
What is not c. is not French — RIV 260:14
clearing-house: c. of the world — CHAM 93:22
cleave: c. the general ear — SHAK 275:23
shall c. unto his wife — BIBLE 38:23
cleft: Rock of Ages, c. for me — TOPL 333:14
Clementine: And his daughter, C. — MONT 234:2
Cleopatra: squeaking C. boy my greatness — SHAK 272:5
clercs: La trahison des c. — BENDA 34:7
clergy: c. is a dropping-down-deadness — SMITH 309:24
c. were beloved — SWIFT 320:9
clergymen: men, women, and c. — SMITH 310:4
cleric: C. before, and Lay behind — BUTL 84:1
clerk: C. there was of Oxenford — CHAU 95:17
'twixt the Priest and C. — HERR 167:18
clerks: c. been noght wisest men — CHAU 96:2
government of statesmen or of c. — DISR 121:24
clever: c. so rude to the good — WORD 354:11
c. theft was praiseworthy — SPEN 312:20
It's c., but is it Art? — KIPL 196:8
let who will be c. — KING 195:10
manage a c. man — KIPL 197:28
Too c. by half — SAL 266:7
cliché: c. and an indiscretion — MACM 215:14
cliffs: chalk c. of Dover — BALD 27:6
c. I never more must see — MAC 214:1
c. of fall frightful — HOPK 172:10
white c. of Dover — BURT 83:3
climate: in love with a cold c. — SOUT 312:6
Our chilling c. hardly bears — SWIFT 320:19
Our cloudy c., and our chilly women — BYRON 84:29
whole c. of opinion — AUDEN 20:20
climb: fails thee, c. not at all — ELIZ 135:9
Fain would I c., yet fear — RAL 257:24
climbing: c. clear up to the sky — HAMM 161:2
c., shakes his dewy wings — D'AV 114:10
Of c. heaven, and gazing — SHEL 305:14
climes: cloudless c. and starry skies — BYRON 87:6
cling: c. to the old rugged cross — BENN 34:10
Clive: What I like about C. — BENT 35:6
cloak: the knyf under the c. — CHAU 95:27
clock: Ah! the c. is always slow — SERV 270:10
Church at ten to three — BROO 73:8
c. will strike, the devil will come — MARL 218:13
Court the slow c., and dine — POPE 251:25
forgot to wind up the c. — STER 315:13
clocks: c. were striking thirteen — ORW 242:5
clockwork: c. orange — BURG 79:13
clod: kneaded c. — SHAK 288:21
clods: Only a man harrowing c. — HARDY 162:11
Cloe: Such C. is — GRAN 156:10
cloisters: quiet collegiate c. — CLOU 102:9
close: c. ebbs out life's little day — LYTE 212:20
C. encounters of the third kind — SPIE 313:21
c. the wall up with our — SHAK 279:5
c. your eyes before you see — AYCK 23:14
Doth c. behind him tread — COL 104:15
fatter man trying to c. in — AMIS 5:4
peacefully towards its c. — DAWS 115:5
She'll c. and be herself — SHAK 287:3

closed: We never c. — VAN D 336:25
closer: Oh! for a c. walk with God — COWP 109:27
sticketh c. than a brother — BIBLE 43:30
closes: Blown fields or flowerful c. — SWIN 321:17
Satire is what c. Saturday night — KAUF 190:3
closet: one by one back in the c. — FITZ 140:12
They put me in the c. — DICK 120:15
closing: c. time in the gardens — CONN 106:27
cloth: On a c. untrue — GILB 152:2
clothed: c., fed and educated — RUSK 264:19
C. in white samite — TENN 324:3
woman c. with the sun — BIBLE 57:30
clothes: been poured into his c. — WOD 352:24
brushers of noblemen's c. — WOTT 357:20
c. that I have ever seen — LOES 209:6
Kindles in c. a wantonness — HERR 167:15
She wears her c., as if — SWIFT 320:7
That liquefaction of her c. — HERR 167:26
walked away with their c. — DISR 121:9
who wore torn c. — SPEN 312:25
clothing: become mine inner c. — LITT 208:2
sheep in sheep's c. — CHUR 100:7
sheep in sheep's c. — GOSSE 155:25
Things in books' c. — LAMB 200:4
cloud: c.-continents of sunset-seas — ALDR 3:17
c. in trousers — MAY 222:15
c. of unknowing — ANON 6:16
c. which had outwept — SHEL 303:6
day in a pillar of a c. — BIBLE 39:39
Don't you know each c. — BURKE 81:14
do set my bow in the c. — BIBLE 39:10
Get off of my c. — JAGG 179:4
great a c. of witnesses — BIBLE 56:27
I wandered lonely as a c. — WORD 355:4
Like a fiend hid in a c. — BLAKE 62:3
little c. out of the sea — BIBLE 42:2
On a c. I saw a child — BLAKE 61:18
Turn the dark c. inside out — FORD 143:12
When the c. is scattered — SHEL 303:24
cloudcuckooland: How about 'C.' — ARIS 15:9
clouded: Shine forth upon our c. hills — BLAKE 61:12
clouds: comes with c. descending — WESL 346:9
Never doubted c. would break — BROW 75:11
O c., unfold — BLAKE 61:12
through the c. I'll never float — WORD 356:3
trailing c. of glory — WORD 355:20
clouts: stones and c. make martyrs — BROW 74:4
cloven: out pops the c. hoof — WOD 352:15
cloverleaf: flower is the concrete c. — MUMF 236:8
clownage: conceits as c. keeps in pay — MARL 219:4
clowns: Send in the C. — SOND 311:7
club: savage wields his c. — HUXL 177:16
DON'T WANT TO BELONG TO ANY C. — MARX 221:5
clucked: Has c. thee to the wars — SHAK 273:22
clue: almost invariably a c. — DOYLE 125:14
Clunton: C. and Clunbury — HOUS 175:1
clusters: luscious c. of the vine — MARV 220:15
clutch: clawed me with his c. — VAUX 337:15
Inapprehensible, we c. thee — THOM 331:14
clutching: alien people c. their gods — ELIOT 133:23
Still c. the inviolable shade — ARN 17:12
coach: c. and six horses through the Act — RICE 259:19
her silver c. to climb — SPEN 313:5
rattling of a c. — DONNE 124:21
coach and six: indifference and a c. — GARR 105:12
coal: c. and surrounded by fish — BEVAN 37:17
made of Newcastle c. — WALP 341:20
Strong is the lion—like a c. — SMART 308:10
With a cargo of Tyne c. — MAS 221:19
coalitions: England does not love c. — DISR 121:13
coals: And all eyes else dead c. — SHAK 299:3
c. of fire upon his head — BIBLE 43:36
I sleep on the c. — DICK 118:10
No more c. to Newcastle — GEOR 149:26

coarse: And one of them is rather c. ROYD 264:3
coarseness: c., revealing something FORS 143:23
coast: On the c. of Coromandel LEAR 203:7
 On the c. of Coromandel SITW 308:1
coaster: Dirty British c. MAS 221:19
coat: c. of many colours BIBLE 39:24
 eternal Footman hold my c. ELIOT 133:29
 Grab your c., and get your hat FIEL 139:15
 John Peel with his c. so grey GRAV 156:12
 riband to stick in his c. BROW 76:13
 tattered c. upon a stick YEATS 359:21
 that loves a scarlet c. HOOD 171:6
coats: In c. of red DE L 116:17
cobble-stones: On c. I lay FLAN 141:2
cobweb: Learning, that c. of the brain BUTL 84:2
cobwebs: Laws are like c. SWIFT 319:19
Coca-Cola: wherever blue jeans and C. GREER 158:10
cock: before the c. crow BIBLE 51:10
 C. and a Bull STER 315:26
 Nationalism is a silly c. ALD 3:15
 Our c. won't fight BEAV 31:6
 owe a c. to Aesculapius SOCR 310:25
cockatoo: green freedom of a c. STEV 316:12
cockatrice: hand on the c.' den BIBLE 45:20
cockle: By his c. hat and staff SHAK 276:32
cockpit: Can this c. hold SHAK 278:34
cocks: drowned the c. SHAK 283:6
cocktail: weasel under the c. cabinet PINT 248:22
cod: bean and the c. BOSS 70:1
 O bely! O stynkyng c. CHAU 95:30
code: trail has its own stern c. SERV 270:9
coeur: Il pleure dans mon c. VERL 338:2
coffee: C. (which makes the politician wise) POPE 253:9
 C. and oranges in a sunny STEV 316:12
 if this is c., I want tea PUNCH 256:20
 measured out my life with c. spoons ELIOT 133:27
 slavery of the tea and c. COBB 102:25
coffin: grave in a Y-shaped c. ORTON 241:21
 like a c. clapt in a canoe BYRON 84:26
 Like the silver plate on a c. CURR 113:9
cogito: C., ergo sum DESC 117:9
cognoscere: qui potuit rerum c. causas VIRG 340:8
cohorts: c. were gleaming in purple BYRON 85:22
coin: The C., Tiberius DOBS 122:25
coition: trivial and vulgar way of c. BROW 74:18
coitum: Post c. omne animal triste ANON 13:19
cold: Aching, shaking, crazy, c. ROCH 261:9
 blow in c. blood SHAW 301:32
 Cast a c. eye on life YEATS 360:8
 C. as paddocks HERR 167:11
 c. charities of man to man CRAB 110:30
 c. coming they had ANDR 5:15
 c. coming we had of it ELIOT 133:21
 c. hearts and muddy understandings BURKE 80:15
 c. metal of economic theory SCH 267:26
 C. Pastoral KEATS 191:23
 c. relation is a zealous citizen BURKE 80:20
 C. the seat and loud the cistern BENN 34:16
 everlasting c. WEBS 344:28
 I beg c. comfort SHAK 282:14
 ink in my pen ran c. WALP 341:17
 in love with a c. climate SOUT 312:6
 midst of a c. war BAR 29:20
 Poor Tom's a-c. SHAK 283:7
 spy who came in from the c. LE C 204:2
 straight past the common c. AYRES 23:15
 'tis bitter c. SHAK 273:30
 To lie in c. obstruction SHAK 288:21
coldly: C., sadly descends ARN 17:3
coldness: faithless c. of the times TENN 325:24
Coliseum: While stands the C. BYRON 85:11
collapse: C. of Stout Party ANON 6:17
collateral: c. security CHES 97:14
collections: those mutilators of c. LAMB 200:2

collects: c. which had soothed MAC 213:18
college: cabbage with a c. education TWAIN 336:4
 Die, and endow a c., or a cat POPE 251:13
collegiate: faces in quiet c. cloisters CLOU 102:9
colonel: C.'s Lady an' Judy O'Grady KIPL 196:19
colonnade: whispering sound of the cool c. COWP 109:30
Colonus: Singer of sweet C. ARN 17:20
Colossus: Like a C. SHAK 280:27
colour: And Life is C. and Warmth GREN 158:16
 Any c.—so long as it's black FORD 143:7
 giveth his c. in the cup BIBLE 43:33
 horse of that c. SHAK 297:27
 I know the c. rose ABSE 1:1
 prison for the c. of his hair HOUS 174:6
coloured: no 'c.' signs on the foxholes KENN 194:7
colourless: C. green ideas CHOM 98:18
colours: All c. will agree in the dark BACON 25:19
 Their c. and their forms WORD 355:9
 your c. dont quite match ASHF 18:21
comb: two bald men over a c. BORG 69:24
combination: You may call it c. PALM 244:19
combine: When bad men c. BURKE 81:4
come: And cannot c. again HOUS 174:24
 believe in the life to c. BECK 31:9
 C., and he cometh BIBLE 49:17
 C. away, come away, death SHAK 297:32
 C., dear children, let us away ARN 16:16
 C. down, O Love divine LITT 208:2
 C., friendly bombs BETJ 37:9
 C. hither, come hither SHAK 272:19
 C., Holy Spirit LANG 201:10
 C. in the speaking silence ROSS 263:1
 C. into the garden, Maud TENN 326:28
 C., let us join our cheerful songs WATTS 343:3
 C., lovely Morning DAV 114:21
 C., my Celia, let us prove JONS 187:16
 c. out, thou bloody man BIBLE 41:25
 C. over into Macedonia BIBLE 54:16
 c. to the end of a perfect day BOND 63:9
 C. unto me, all ye BIBLE 49:35
 C. unto these yellow sands SHAK 295:36
 c. when you do call SHAK 278:3
 C. you back to Mandalay KIPL 196:21
 Even so, c., Lord Jesus BIBLE 58:8
 had better not c. at all KEATS 193:4
 if it be now, 'tis not to come SHAK 298:3
 leave to c. unto my love SPEN 313:6
 let him c. out as I do JOHN 186:1
 men may c. and men may go TENN 323:13
 O c., all ye faithful ANON 13:9
 O c. to my heart, Lord Jesus ELL 136:1
 Of things to c. at large SHAK 296:32
 or c. without warning DAVIS 115:1
 Out of Ireland have we c. YEATS 359:19
 Softly and softly go ORRED 241:18
 Suffer me to c. to thee WESL 346:6
 therefore I cannot c. BIBLE 52:23
 war and nobody will c. SAND 266:16
 What's to c. is still unsure SHAK 297:23
 what's to c. is strewed SHAK 297:10
 where do they all c. from MCC 205:12
 whistle, an' I'll come to you BURNS 82:19
 Why don't you c. up and see me WEST 346:24
 world's at an end, and we c. D'AV 114:9
comedies: All c. ended by a marriage BYRON 86:12
comedy: All I need to make a c. CHAP 94:12
 C. is an imitation SIDN 306:28
 c. to those that think WALP 341:23
comely: I am black, but c. BIBLE 44:29
comes: Nothing happens, nobody c. BECK 31:12
cometh: c. in the Name of the Lord BOOK 68:23
 Him that c. to me BIBLE 53:23
 no man c. unto the Father BIBLE 53:38

comets: there are no c. seen | SHAK 281:8
Ye country c., that portend | MARV 220:21
comfort: beside the waters of c. | BOOK 66:17
carrion c., Despair | HOPK 171:25
C.'s a cripple | DRAY 126:15
c. ye my people | BIBLE 46:7
good c. Master Ridley | LAT 202:4
I beg cold c. | SHAK 282:14
I have of c. and despair | SHAK 300:13
I tell you naught for your c. | CHES 97:19
love her, c. her, honour her | BOOK 65:28
not ecstasy but it was c. | DICK 118:30
That c. cruel men | CHES 97:24
comfortable: c. I sit down to write | KEATS 193:13
c. words our Saviour Christ | BOOK 65:12
comfortably: Are you sitting c.? | LANG 201:4
Speak ye c. to Jerusalem | BIBLE 46:7
comforted: they shall be c. | BIBLE 48:19
would not be c. | BIBLE 48:11
comforters: Miserable c. are ye all | BIBLE 42:34
comforting: c. thought | MARQ 219:20
where is your c.? | HOPK 172:9
comforts: helpers fail, and c. flee | LYTE 212:20
comical: Beautiful c. things | HARV 163:15
coming: am c. to that holy room | DONNE 123:16
cold c. we had of it | ELIOT 133:21
c. down let me shift | MORE 235:3
C. in on a wing and a pray'r | ADAM 2:9
C. thro' the rye | BURNS 81:29
even as their c. hither | SHAK 283:30
Everything's c. up roses | SOND 311:5
She is c., my dove, my dear | TENN 327:1
There's a gude time c. | SCOTT 269:4
they will be c. for us | BALD 27:4
command: c. of any kind | MILL 224:20
give what you c. | AUG 21:25
left that c. sole daughter | MILT 229:25
Less used to sue than to c. | SCOTT 268:8
mortals to c. success | ADD 2:13
not born to sue, but to c. | SHAK 293:9
commandments: Fear God, and keep his c. | BIBLE 44:28
Ten for the ten c. | ANON 8:6
commands: C. the beauteous files | VAUG 337:6
commend: hands I c. my spirit | BIBLE 53:4
Into thy hands I c. my spirit | BOOK 66:23
some virtue, virtue to c. | CONG 106:22
commendeth: obliquely c. | BROW 74:1
comment: C. is free, but facts | SCOTT 268:3
C. is free but facts | STOP 318:3
commentators: As learned c. view | SWIFT 320:20
How c. each dark passage shun | YOUNG 360:16
commerce: c., and honest friendship | JEFF 180:19
c. the fault of the Dutch | CANN 89:10
commercialism: [C. is] doing well | VIDAL 338:11
commit: c. his body to the deep | BOOK 69:15
we therefore c. his body | BOOK 66:8
committee: C.—a group of men who | ALLEN 4:12
c. is a group of the unwilling | ANON 6:20
horse designed by a c. | ISS 178:23
commodious: c. vicus of recirculation | JOYCE 188:3
commodity: C., firmness, and delight | WOTT 357:19
common: according to the c. weal | JAM 179:12
century of the c. man | WALL 341:9
c. and popular | SHAK 279:9
c. cormorant or shag | ISH 178:21
c. pursuit | LEAV 203:21
c. reader | JOHN 182:21
c. where the climate's sultry | BYRON 85:24
fade into the light of c. day | WORD 355:21
have in c. being so poor | BLUN 62:12
He nothing c. did or mean | MARV 220:18
Horseguards and still be c. | RATT 258:8
I feel for the c. chord again | BROW 75:9
In c. things that round us lie | WORD 356:7

common (cont.):
Lord prefers c.-looking people | LINC 207:11
nor lose the c. touch | KIPL 197:7
Such Cloe is. . .and c. as the air | GRAN 156:10
trivial round, the c. task | KEBLE 193:17
You c. people of the skies | WOTT 357:16
commonalty: He's a very dog to the c. | SHAK 273:15
commonplace: featureless and c. a crime | DOYLE 125:14
Commons: The C., faithful to | MACK 215:5
common sense: C. is the best distributed | DESC 117:8
c. and clean finger nails | MORT 235:21
trained and organized c. | HUXL 177:16
commonwealth: caterpillars of the c. | SHAK 293:19
commonwealths: raise up c. | DRYD 127:4
communicated: C. monthly | BETJ 36:21
communications: Evil c. corrupt | BIBLE 55:19
communion: C. of Saints | BOOK 64:3
Communism: C. is Soviet power plus | LENIN 205:1
[C. is] the illegitimate child | ATTL 19:13
spectre of C. | ENG 221:13
Communist: What is a c.? | ELL 136:3
Communists: Catholics and C. | GREE 158:2
community: c. of Europe | SAL 266:4
small anarchist c. | BENN 34:15
commuter: C.—one who spends his life | WHITE 347:14
compact: C. of ancient tales | BELL 33:17
of imagination all c. | SHAK 291:3
compacted: where sweets c. lie | HERB 167:8
companion: c. to make him feel solitude | VALE 336:21
c. to owls | BIBLE 43:3
even thou, my c. | BOOK 67:12
companionless: Wandering c. | SHEL 305:14
company: "boozes" by the c. he chooses | BURT 83:1
C. for carrying on an undertaking | ANON 6:21
company, villanous c. | SHAK 278:8
crowd is not c. | BACON 24:23
in married life three is c. | WILDE 349:17
I owe my soul to the c. store | TRAV 334:4
Take the tone of the c. | CHES 97:7
very good c. | AUBR 20:2
Withouten oother c. in youth | CHAU 95:20
compare: c. thee to a summer's day | SHAK 299:12
c. this prison | SHAK 294:10
comparisons: C. are odorous | SHAK 291:23
C. doon offte gret greuaunce | LYDG 212:14
compass: to the top of my c. | SHAK 276:13
compassed: we also are c. about | BIBLE 56:27
compassion: c. in the very name | SMITH 309:23
full of c. and mercy | BOOK 68:6
sharp c. of the healer's art | ELIOT 133:5
compendious: c. oceans | CRAS 111:14
competing: register c. attractions | KNIG 198:14
competition: Approves all forms of c. | CLOU 102:20
complacencies: C. of the peignoir | STEV 316:12
complain: Never c. and never explain | DISR 122:19
then c. we cannot see | BERK 35:18
complaint: most fatal c. of all | HILT 168:18
complete: And in herself c. | MILT 229:20
complex: ugly, heavy and c. | FLAU 141:13
complexion: Mislike me not for my c. | SHAK 289:6
compliance: by a timely c. | FIEL 139:7
complies: c. against his will | BUTL 84:6
composed: Cruel, but c. and bland | ARN 16:23
composition: mad kings! mad c. | SHAK 282:4
comprehended: darkness c. it not | BIBLE 53:8
comprendre: Tout c. | STAEL 314:5
compulsion: fools by heavenly c. | SHAK 282:22
sweet c. doth in music lie | MILT 226:3
compunctious: c. visitings of nature | SHAK 285:17
computer: requires a c. | ANON 11:7
concatenation: Fearful c. of circumstances | WEBS 344:10
conceal: c. our whereabouts | SAKI 265:21
woman should c. it | AUST 22:23

concealing: hazard of c.	BURNS 82:5
concealment: c., like a worm i' the bud	SHAK 298:1
conceit: wise in his own c.	BIBLE 43:38
conceited: any good who is not c.	TROL 334:17
conceits: Be not wise in your own c.	BIBLE 54:44
current and accepted for c.	BACON 23:23
conceive: virgin shall c.	BIBLE 45:14
concentrates: c. his mind wonderfully	JOHN 185:14
conception: dad is present at the c.	ORTON 241:20
concerned: nobody left to be c.	NIEM 239:15
concessions: c. of the weak	BURKE 79:27
concluded: Rome has spoken; the case is c.	AUG 22:5
conclusions: pursued c. infinite	SHAK 272:11
concord: lover of c.	BOOK 64:5
oft in pleasing c. end	MILT 230:15
travelled a good deal in C.	THOR 332:7
truth, unity, and c.	BOOK 65:9
with c. of sweet sounds	SHAK 290:3
concordia: C. discors	HOR 173:12
concrete: city is not a c. jungle	MORR 235:12
flower is the c. cloverleaf	MUMF 236:8
concupiscent: c. curds	STEV 316:5
concurrence: sweet c. of the heart	HERR 167:17
condemn: does some delights c.	MOL 232:23
needs to c. a little more	MAJOR 216:19
Neither do I c. thee	BIBLE 53:27
condemned: c. to have an itching palm	SHAK 281:29
I am c. to be free	SART 267:2
condition: O wearisome c. of humanity	GREV 158:19
conditions: all sorts and c. of men	BOOK 64:18
conduct: C. is three-fourths	ARN 18:9
c. of a losing party	BURKE 79:18
C. to the prejudice	ANON 6:22
c. unbecoming	ANON 6:2
cone: despot is an inverted c.	JOHN 185:17
cones: c. under his pines	FROST 146:16
confabulate: If birds c. or no	COWP 109:29
confederate: in games C.	WORD 355:2
conference: c. a ready man	BACON 25:15
hold some two days' c.	WEBS 344:16
naked into the c. chamber	BEVAN 38:1
confident: Never glad c. morning	BROW 76:15
confine: verge of her c.	SHAK 283:3
conflict: field of human c.	CHUR 99:15
We are in an armed c.	EDEN 130:14
confound: C. their politics	ANON 7:14
confounded: Confusion worse c.	MILT 229:1
let me never be c.	BOOK 63:22
confounding: C. her astronomers	HODG 169:14
confused: c. doesn't really understand	MURR 236:14
confusion: bright things come to c.	SHAK 290:15
C. now hath made his masterpiece	SHAK 286:23
C. on thy banners wait	GRAY 157:1
C. worse confounded	MILT 229:1
congeals: When love c.	HART 163:8
congratulatory: series of c. regrets	DISR 121:19
congregation: largest c.	DEFOE 115:22
congress: C. makes no progress	LIGNE 207:2
conjecture: entertain c. of a time	SHAK 279:7
conjunction: c. of the mind	MARV 220:13
conjuring: c. trick with bones	JENK 181:4
connect: Only c.	FORS 143:21
conquer: die here, and we will c.	BEE 31:22
easier to c. it than to know	WALP 341:21
hard to catch and c.	MER 223:20
In this sign shalt thou c.	CONS 107:14
conquered: c. and peopled	SEEL 269:15
I came, I saw, I c.	CAES 88:2
perpetually to be c.	BURKE 80:1
Thou hast c., O pale Galilean	SWIN 321:13
conquering: C. kings their titles	CHAN 94:6
See, the c. hero comes	MOR 235:5
conqueror: proud foot of a c.	SHAK 282:15
you are a c.	ROST 263:12

conquest: C.'s crimson wing	GRAY 157:1
conscience: catch the c. of the king	SHAK 275:24
C. avaunt, Richard's himself	CIBB 100:17
c. doth make cowards	SHAK 275:26
C. first, the Pope afterwards	NEWM 238:18
C. is thoroughly well-bred	BUTL 84:20
C.: the inner voice	MENC 223:8
corporation to have a c.	THUR 332:19
good c. on the proceeds	SMITH 309:14
happiness or a quiet c.	BERL 36:6
however strict their social c.	SMITH 309:15
value it next to a good c.	WALT 342:14
will not cut my c.	HELL 165:7
conscious: c. stone to beauty grew	EMER 136:15
consciousness: beginning of c.	WOOLF 353:22
C. is the phenomenon	PENR 247:11
consecration: c., and the Poet's dream	WORD 354:17
consent: inferior without your c.	ROOS 262:6
like enough to c.	SHAK 273:8
Rome is the c. of heaven	JONS 187:1
whispering 'I will ne'er c.'	BYRON 86:1
consented: ne'er consent'—c.	BYRON 86:1
consequence: If it's business of c.	BARH 28:22
trammel up the c.	SHAK 285:22
consequences: damn the c.	MILN 226:2
nor punishments—there are c.	ING 178:16
conservatism: barren thing this C.	DISR 121:27
conservative: C. Government is	DISR 121:11
C., n. A statesman	BIER 59:5
C. Party at prayer	ROYD 264:2
most c. man in this world	BEVIN 38:8
Or else a little C.	GILB 151:12
revolutionary will become a c.	AREN 15:5
sound C. government	DISR 121:25
which makes a man more c.	KEYN 194:15
would make me c. when old	FROST 146:18
consider: c. her ways	BIBLE 43:11
c. how my light is spent	MILT 230:22
C. the lilies of the field	BIBLE 49:4
For I will c. my Cat Jeoffry	SMART 308:7
consideration: C. like an angel	SHAK 278:35
consistency: C. is contrary to nature	HUXL 177:6
c. is the hobgoblin of little minds	EMER 136:24
consistent: c. people are the dead	HUXL 177:6
consoles: Anything that c. is fake	MURD 236:11
conspicuous: C. consumption	VEBL 337:16
Vega c. overhead	AUDEN 21:7
conspiracies: c. against the laity	SHAW 301:3
conspiracy: America is a vast c.	UPD 336:14
c. against the public	SMITH 308:21
Indecency's c. of silence	SHAW 302:3
conspiring: C. with him how to	KEATS 192:14
constabulary: c. duty's to be done	GILB 152:24
constancy: is but c. in a good	BROW 74:15
Tell me no more of c.	ROCH 261:2
constant: But c., he were perfect	SHAK 298:20
c. as the northern star	SHAK 281:9
C., in Nature were inconstancy	COWL 109:15
Friendship is c. in all	SHAK 291:17
One here will c. be	BUNY 79:9
constitution: c. does not provide	WILL 351:9
country has its own c.	ANON 6:30
I invoke the genius of the C.	PITT 249:5
constitutional: no eyes but c. eyes	LINC 207:14
construction: mind's c. in the face	SHAK 285:14
consul: born when I was c.	CIC 101:2
consulted: right to be c.	BAG 26:14
consume: more history than they can c.	SAKI 265:17
consumer: c. isn't a moron	OGIL 241:2
c. is the king	SAM 266:11
In a c. society	ILL 178:9
consummation: c. devoutly to be wished	SHAK 275:25
Quiet c. have	SHAK 273:28
consummatum: C. est	BIBLE 58:21

corruptible: magistrate c.   ROB 260:17
corruption: be turned into c.   BOOK 69:15
  C. wins not more than honesty   SHAK 280:20
  Fulfilled of dong and of c.   CHAU 95:30
corrupts: absolute power c.   ACTON 1:5
cors: Les souvenirs sont c. de chasse   APOL 14:11
corse: c. to the rampart we hurried   WOLFE 352:25
Cortez: like stout C.   KEATS 192:11
coruscations: c. of summer lightning   GOUL 155:26
cosmopolitan: C. critics   DISR 121:17
cost: But at what c.   BECK 31:8
  they c. right naught   WYATT 358:3
  Why so large c.   SHAK 300:14
costs: C. merely register   KNIG 198:14
  c. more than it is worth   MAC 213:12
cot: c. with a pot of pink geraniums   MACN 216:2
Cotopaxi: Chimborazo, C.   TURN 335:17
cottage: he before his c. door   SOUT 311:18
  left as a c. in a vineyard   BIBLE 45:3
  Love and a c.!   GARR 105:12
  Wherever there's a c. small   CHAR 245:19
cotton: an' the c. is high   GERS 168:6
couch: flinty and steel c. of war   SHAK 292:1
  For oft, when on my c. I lie   WORD 355:5
  There I c. when owls do cry   SHAK 296:14
cough: all c. in ink   YEATS 359:23
  Keep a c. by them ready made   CHUR 98:22
coughs: C. and sneezes spread   ANON 6:23
counsel: princely c. in his face   MILT 228:27
  sometimes c. take   POPE 253:6
  spirit of c. and might   BIBLE 45:18
counsellor: Wonderful, C.   BIBLE 45:16
counsellors: Kings and c. of the earth   BIBLE 42:26
  speak plain when c. blanch   BACON 24:17
counsels: all good c.   BOOK 64:11
count: c. the number of the beast   BIBLE 57:33
  I c. it not an inn   BROW 74:20
  I won the c.   SOM 311:4
  Let me c. the ways   BROW 75:5
  let us c. our spoons   JOHN 184:11
  To give and not to c. the cost   IGN 178:8
  when angry, c. four   TWAIN 336:5
counted: c. them all out   HANR 161:8
  faster we c. our spoons   EMER 136:20
countenance: damned disinheriting c.   SHER 306:7
  did the C. Divine   BLAKE 61:12
  Knight of the Doleful C.   CERV 93:16
  Lord lift up his c.   BIBLE 40:15
  maketh a cheerful c.   BIBLE 43:25
  Till grim, care grew his c.   BALL 27:16
  withal of a beautiful c.   BIBLE 41:16
counter: All things c., original   HOPK 172:13
countercheck: c. quarrelsome   SHAK 273:12
counterfeit: Teach light to c. a gloom   MILT 226:25
counterpane: pleasant land of c.   STEV 317:14
counterpoint: Too much c.   BEEC 32:3
counters: Words are wise men's c.   HOBB 169:6
counties: see the coloured c.   HOUS 174:20
  six c. overhung with smoke   MORR 235:16
counting: democracy, it's the c.   STOP 317:28
countries: all c. before his own   OVER 243:8
country: America is a c. of young men   EMER 137:1
  another c.   MARL 219:2
  Anybody can be good in the c.   WILDE 350:6
  ask not what your c. can do   KENN 194:6
  best c. ever is, at home   GOLD 155:4
  betraying my c.   FORS 144:2
  Britain a fit c. for heroes   LLOY 208:11
  By all their c.'s wishes blest   COLL 105:11
  c. continually under hatches   KEATS 193:6
  country for his c.'s sake   FITZ 140:3
  country for our c.'s good   CART 92:12
  c. governed by a despot   JOHN 185:17
  c. has its own constitution   ANON 6:30

country (cont.):
  c. has the government it deserves   MAIS 216:18
  C. in the town   MART 220:8
  c. of the blind the one-eyed   ERAS 137:14
  c. retreat near the town   WYCH 358:4
  c. which has 246 varieties   DE G 116:7
  Cry, the beloved c.   PATON 246:19
  die but once to serve our c.   ADD 2:16
  died to save their c.   CHES 97:23
  die for one's c.   HOR 173:26
  every c. but his own   GILB 151:20
  fight for its King and C.   GRAH 156:2
  For your King and your C.   RUB 264:4
  friend of every c. but his own   CANN 89:11
  friends of every c.   DISR 121:17
  God made the c., and man   COWP 110:6
  good for our c. good for General   WILS 351:11
  good news from a far c.   BIBLE 43:37
  good to be had in the c.   HAZL 164:3
  great deal of unmapped c.   ELIOT 132:2
  grow up with the c.   GREE 157:20
  how I leave my c.   PITT 249:10
  I love thee still—My c.   COWP 110:8
  Indeed I tremble for my c.   JEFF 180:24
  in the c. places   STEV 317:18
  In this frozen whited c.   HUGH 175:22
  I pray for the c.   HALE 160:4
  Isn't this a billion dollar c.   FOST 144:6
  lie abroad for the good of his c.   WOTT 357:22
  may our c. be always successful   ADAMS 2:5
  My c. is Kiltartan Cross   YEATS 359:9
  My c. is the world   PAINE 244:14
  My c., right or wrong   SCH 268:1
  My c., 'tis of thee   SMITH 309:16
  My soul, there is a c.   VAUG 337:6
  no relish for the c.   SMITH 309:25
  one life to lose for my c.   HALE 160:6
  our c., right or wrong   DEC 115:10
  past is a foreign c.   HART 163:14
  quarrel in a far away c.   CHAM 94:1
  she is my c. still   CHUR 98:21
  sucked on c. pleasures   DONNE 124:5
  That is no c. for old men   YEATS 359:20
  this c. of ours where nobody is well   AUDEN 21:19
  While there's a c. lane   CHAR 245:19
countrymen: friends, Romans, c.   SHAK 281:18
county: c. families baying   WAUGH 343:18
couple: Just like a young c.   PLOM 250:1
couples: c. down the grassgreen   THOM 330:17
courage: Blessings on your young c.   VIRG 339:19
  C. in your own   GORD 155:21
  C. is not simply one of the virtues   LEWIS 206:13
  C., mon ami, le diable   READE 258:10
  c. the greater   ANON 11:5
  c. to suffer   TROL 334:13
  c. you bring to it   WALP 342:4
  piety, c.—they exist   FORS 143:25
  red badge of c.   CRANE 111:3
  screw your c. to the sticking-place   SHAK 286:6
  strong and of a good c.   BIBLE 40:26
  three-o'-clock in the morning c.   THOR 332:10
  two o'clock in the morning c.   NAP 237:4
  unto him with a good c.   BOOK 66:24
courageous: captains c.   BALL 28:1
couriers: Vaunt-c. to oak-cleaving   SHAK 283:6
course: betake myself to that c.   PEPYS 247:22
  c. of true love never did run   SHAK 290:13
  I have finished my c.   BIBLE 56:21
  Of c., of course   JAMES 180:4
court: C. him, elude him   BLUN 62:14
  c. in beauty and decay   SHEL 303:4
  c. is obliged to submit   CHEK 97:1
  Let her alone, she will c. you   JONS 187:22
courtesy: greater man, the greater c.   TENN 324:11
  I am the very pink of c.   SHAK 295:6

crimes (cont.):
worst of c. is poverty | SHAW 301:8
criminal: for ends I think c. | KEYN 194:13
while there is a c. element | DEBS 115:9
crimson: c. in thy lips | SHAK 295:24
cringe: cultural c. you came from | KEAT 190:8
cripple: comfort's a c. | DRAY 126:15
crisis: C.? What Crisis? | ANON 6:24
Crispian: called the feast of C. | SHAK 279:18
Crispin: C. Crispian shall ne'er | SHAK 279:20
criterion: c. of wisdom to vulgar | BURKE 79:18
critic: c. is a bundle of biases | BALL 28:12
c. is a man who knows | TYNAN 336:8
c. is he who relates | FRAN 145:3
C., you have frowned | WORD 356:21
cry of the c. for five | WHIS 347:10
important book, the c. assumes | WOOLF 354:3
critical: c. period in matrimony | HERB 166:18
criticism: at bottom a c. of life | ARN 18:6
c. of administration | BAG 26:6
father of English c. | JOHN 182:20
wreathed the rod of c. | D'ISR 122:23
criticize: And don't c. | DYLAN 130:9
critics: c. all are ready made | BYRON 86:31
C. are like brushers | WOTT 357:20
Turned c. next, and proved | POPE 251:27
croaks: c. the fatal entrance | SHAK 285:16
crocodile: How doth the little c. | CARR 91:3
Cromwell: Charles the First, his C. | HENRY 166:5
C. guiltless | GRAY 157:9
C., I charge thee | SHAK 280:19
C., our chief of men | MILT 230:26
genius in politics—C. | ARN 18:11
ruin that C. knocked about | SULL 31:21
crook: their President is a c. | NIXON 240:3
crooked: as c. as corkscrews | AUDEN 20:15
c. be made straight | ELIOT 132:24
c. shall be made straight | BIBLE 46:9
C. things may be as stiff | LOCKE 208:17
c. timber of humanity | KANT 189:25
set the c. straight | MORR 235:15
croon: Wanna cry, wanna c. | HARB 161:13
croppy: Hoppy, C., Droppy | ELLIS 136:4
cross: At the c. her station keeping | JAC 179:3
cling to the old rugged c. | BENN 34:10
inability to the c. the street | WOOLF 354:5
marble c. below the town | HAYES 163:21
mystery of the c. | FORT 144:5
no c., no crown | PENN 247:9
With the c. of Jesus | BAR 29:1
crossed: oyster may be c. in love | SHER 305:25
When I have c. the bar | TENN 323:19
crosses: Between the c., row on row | MCCR 214:17
cross-gartered: see thee ever c. | SHAK 284:8
crossing: C. the stripling Thames | ARN 17:7
crossness: c. and dirt succeed | FORS 143:18
crow: c.'s feet do growe | CHAU 96:15
crowd: c. flowed over London Bridge | ELIOT 134:21
c. is not company | BACON 24:23
Far from the madding c. | GRAY 157:10
try to c. out real life | FORS 144:1
Will she pass in a c. | SWIFT 320:3
crowds: C. without company | GIBB 150:15
If you can talk with c. | KIPL 197:7
Nor public man, nor angry c. | YEATS 359:10
crown: All thy faithful mercies c. | WESL 346:10
c. Him Lord of all | PERR 248:4
c. imperial | SHAK 279:16
C. is the fountain of honour | BAG 26:4
c. of thorns and the thirty | BEVAN 38:4
c. o' the earth doth melt | SHAK 271:25
c. the wat'ry glade | GRAY 157:11
c. thy good with brotherhood | BATES 30:2
exchange it some day for a c. | BENN 34:10
father's c. into the hazard | SHAK 279:1

crown (cont.):
give thee a c. of life | BIBLE 57:21
glory of my c. | ELIZ 135:7
head a c. of twelve stars | BIBLE 57:30
head that wears a c. | SHAK 278:23
influence of the C. | DUNN 129:10
no cross, no c. | PENN 247:9
sweet fruition of an earthly c. | MARL 219:8
throne and thy kingly c. | ELL 136:1
Within the hollow c. | SHAK 293:28
woman is a c. to her husband | BIBLE 43:19
crowned: c. with thorns | KELLY 193:19
crowner: Medical C.'s | BARH 28:21
crowning: c. mercy | CROM 112:3
crowns: c. are empty things | DEFOE 116:1
c. for convoy | SHAK 279:18
end that c. us | HERR 167:5
golden c. around the glassy sea | HEBER 164:17
crucible: America is God's C. | ZANG 360:27
crucified: when they c. my Lord | ANON 11:14
crucify: people would not even c. him | CARL 90:26
cruel: C., but composed and bland | ARN 16:23
C. necessity | CROM 112:1
I must be c. only to be kind | SHAK 276:24
That comfort c. men | CHES 97:24
you c. men of Rome | SHAK 280:24
cruellest: April is the c. month | ELIOT 134:18
cruelty: C. has a human heart | BLAKE 62:7
topfull of direst c. | SHAK 285:17
cruise: all on our last c. | STEV 317:5
crumbling: C. between the fingers | MACN 216:4
crumbs: bags to hold the c. | ISH 178:21
c. which fall | BIBLE 50:11
c. which fell | BIBLE 52:34
crusade: This party is a moral c. | WILS 351:13
cruse: c. best fits my little wine | HERR 167:22
little oil in a c. | BIBLE 41:35
crust: c. over a volcano of revolution | ELLIS 136:6
cry: c. of his hounds | GRAV 156:12
c. of the Little Peoples | LE G 204:12
C., the beloved country | PATON 246:19
cuckoo's parting c. | ARN 17:18
his little son should c. | CORN 108:5
I c. all the way to the bank | LIB 206:22
I hear a sudden c. of pain | STEP 315:7
let our c. come unto thee | BOOK 65:24
Some must c. so that others | RHYS 259:13
that we still should c. | BACON 25:31
Truth is the c. of all | BERK 35:17
when indeed they c. | WEBS 344:27
When we are born we c. | SHAK 283:27
with no language but a c. | TENN 325:9
crying: Love, a child, is ever c. | WROTH 358:1
one c. in the wilderness | BIBLE 48:13
crystal: golden sands and c. brooks | DONNE 123:23
cuckoo: as the c. is in June | SHAK 278:6
c. clock | WELL 345:5
c. then, on every tree | SHAK 284:21
heard the c.'s parting cry | ARN 17:18
hear the pleasant c. | DAV 114:17
Lhude sing c. | ANON 10:16
O C.! Shall I call thee bird | WORD 357:7
rainbow and a c.'s song | DAV 114:18
weather the c. likes | HARDY 162:16
cucumber: c. should be well sliced | JOHN 183:19
cucumbers: lodge in a garden of c. | BIBLE 45:3
sun-beams out of c. | SWIFT 319:22
they are but c. after all | JOHN 185:27
cue: With a twisted c. | GILB 152:2
cui: C. bono? | CIC 100:31
culpa: mea c., mea culpa | MISS 231:11
cultivate: We must c. our garden | VOLT 340:13
cultural: c. cringe you came from | KEAT 190:8
culture: as a man of c. rare | GILB 152:9
C. shock is what happens | TOFF 333:7

damn (*cont.*):
old man who said, 'D.' — HARE 162:19
with a spot I d. him — SHAK 281:28
damnation: deep d. of his taking-off — SHAK 285:24
From sleep and from d. — CHES 97:24
damnations: Twenty-nine distinct d. — BROW 77:12
damned: All silent, and all d. — WORD 356:4
brandy of the d. — SHAW 301:19
D. from here to Eternity — KIPL 196:15
d. lies and statistics — DISR 122:21
Faustus must be d. — MARL 218:13
have written a d. play — REYN 259:7
Life is just one d. thing — HUBB 175:14
must be d. perpetually — MARL 218:12
Out, d. spot — SHAK 287:27
public be d. — VAND 337:1
Publish and be d. — WELL 345:15
will be d. if you don't — DOW 125:11
damning: d. those they have no mind — BUTL 83:24
damnosa: D. hereditas — GAIUS 147:13
damozel: blessed d. leaned out — ROSS 263:6
damp: d. souls of housemaids — ELIOT 134:4
Danaë: Now lies the Earth all D. — TENN 328:4
Danaos: timeo D. et dona ferentis — VIRG 339:5
dance: D., d., d., little lady — COW 108:19
d. is a measured pace — BACON 23:24
D. on this ball-floor — BLUN 62:14
dancer from the d. — YEATS 358:14
d. round in a ring — FROST 146:20
departs too far from the d. — POUND 254:22
I am the Lord of the D. — CART 92:13
Let's face the music and d. — BERL 35:22
On with the d.! — BYRON 85:3
will you join the d. — CARR 91:12
danced: d. by the light of the moon — LEAR 203:13
his didn't he d. his did — CUMM 112:16
dancer: know the d. from the dance — YEATS 358:14
dancers: d. are all gone under the hill — ELIOT 133:4
nation of d., singers — EQUI 137:13
dances: And d. with the daffodils — WORD 355:5
makes no progress; it d. — LIGNE 207:2
danceth: hope d. without music — HERB 167:10
dancing: And d. dogs and bears — HODG 169:13
D. in the chequered shade — MILT 227:4
[D.] a perpendicular expression — SHAW 302:26
d. is love's proper exercise — DAV 114:15
Fluttering and d. in the breeze — WORD 355:4
manners of a d. master — JOHN 184:1
Singing, d. to itself — COL 103:13
You and I are past our d. days — SHAK 294:25
dandy: I'm a Yankee Doodle D. — COHAN 103:5
dandyism: Cynicism is intellectual d. — MER 223:14
Dane: antique Roman than a D. — SHAK 277:16
danger: But only when in d. — OWEN 243:17
d. chiefly lies in acting — CHUR 98:20
d. of her former tooth — SHAK 287:3
D., the spur of all great — CHAP 94:20
d., we pluck this flower — SHAK 277:30
everything is in d. — NIET 239:19
five-and-twenty per cent of its d. — SURT 319:8
oft in d., oft in woe — WHITE 347:16
One would be in less d. — NASH 237:11
run into any kind of d. — BOOK 64:6
dangerous: action is a most d. thing — CLOU 102:8
delays are d. in war — DRYD 128:22
interest's in the d. edge — BROW 75:15
little knowledge is d. — HUXL 177:17
Mad, bad, and d. to know — LAMB 199:22
Nothing more d. than an idea — ALAIN 3:11
so many a d. thing — BISH 59:16
such men are d. — SHAK 281:1
were d. to meet it alone — WHAR 347:4
dangerously: live d. — NIET 239:21
dangers: D. by being despised — BURKE 81:2
No d. fright him — JOHN 183:13

dangers (*cont.*):
On the d. of the seas — PARK 245:17
perils and d. of this night — BOOK 64:12
She loved me for the d. — SHAK 291:35
Daniel: D. come to judgement — SHAK 289:29
desolation, spoken of by D. — BIBLE 50:35
O D., a man greatly beloved — BIBLE 47:16
danket: Nun d. alle Gott — WINK 352:4
Dan McGrew: Dangerous D. — SERV 270:13
Danny: they're hangin' D. Deever — KIPL 196:9
dapper: d. from your napper — COLL 105:6
dappled: Glory be to God for d. things — HOPK 172:12
dapples: D. the drowsy east — SHAK 291:27
dare: Do I d. to eat a peach — ELIOT 134:3
Letting 'I d. not' wait — SHAK 286:4
menace heaven and d. the gods — MARL 219:6
none d. call it treason — HAR 162:22
dared: Determined, d., and done — SMART 308:14
dares: that d. love attempt — SHAK 294:32
Who d. do more is none — SHAK 286:5
Who d. wins — ANON 11:20
Darien: upon a peak in D. — KEATS 192:11
daring: d. young man on the flying — LEYB 206:21
dark: And we are for the d. — SHAK 272:4
At one stride comes the d. — COL 104:9
blind man in a d. room — BOWEN 70:13
children fear to go in the d. — BACON 24:20
colours will agree in the d. — BACON 25:19
d., amid the blaze — MILT 230:11
d. and go into the dark — MANN 217:13
d. and true and tender — TENN 327:24
D. as the world of man — SITW 307:19
d. is light enough — FRY 146:29
d. night of the soul — FITZ 140:22
d. Satanic mills — BLAKE 61:12
D. with excessive bright — MILT 229:4
d. world where gods have — ROET 261:15
day of his death was a d. — AUDEN 20:21
Dirty, d., and undevotional — VICT 338:10
great leap in the d. — HOBB 169:11
hell, as d. as night — SHAK 300:16
I knew you in this d. — OWEN 244:3
Lady is as good i' th' d. — HERR 167:18
murmur and the poring d. — SHAK 279:7
Out in the d. over the snow — THOM 330:26
Shining nowhere but in the d. — VAUG 337:12
Sons of the d. and bloody — O'HARA 241:4
this d. world of sin — BICK 58:25
We work in the d. — JAMES 179:23
What in me is d. — MILT 228:9
darkies: d., how my heart grows — FOST 144:13
darkling: as on a d. plain — ARN 16:12
D. I listen — KEATS 192:3
D. they went under the lonely — VIRG 339:14
darkly: through a glass, d. — BIBLE 55:14
darkness: against the rulers of the d. — BIBLE 56:4
And universal d. buries all — POPE 250:22
between two eternities of d. — NAB 236:19
candle than curse the d. — STEV 316:21
cast off the works of d. — BIBLE 55:1
cast out into outer d. — BIBLE 49:18
Chaos and d. heard — MARR 219:24
D. at Noon — KOES 199:1
d. bind them — TOLK 333:10
d. by his electrical skin — SMART 308:8
D. came down on the field — THAC 329:18
d. comprehended it not — BIBLE 53:8
d. falls at Thy behest — ELL 135:21
D. I wretch lay wrestling — HOPK 172:1
d. of mere being — JUNG 188:23
d. visible — MILT 228:10
d. was upon the face — BIBLE 38:13
Dawn on our d. and lend — HEBER 164:14
even d. which may be felt — BIBLE 39:35
Go out into the d. — HASK 163:16

darkness (*cont.*):
Heart of D. — CONR 107:4
I will encounter d. as a bride — SHAK 288:20
leaves the world to d. — GRAY 157:4
Lighten our d., we beseech — BOOK 64:12
lump bred up in d. — KYD 199:10
people that walked in d. — BIBLE 45:15
pestilence that walketh in d. — BOOK 67:29
Prince of d. and dead night — SPEN 313:8
prince of d. is a gentleman — SHAK 283:16
race that long in d. pined — SCOT 269:10
Ring out the d. of the land — TENN 325:27
silent d. born — DAN 113:15
slope through d. up to God — TENN 325:11
them that sit in d. — BIBLE 51:30
then d. again and a silence — LONG 210:3
there was an ocean of d. — FOX 144:17
To sit in d. here — MILT 228:28
When awful d. and silence — LEAR 203:8
works of d. — BOOK 64:21
darlin': oh, he's a d. man — O'CAS 240:21
darling: d. buds of May — SHAK 299:12
d. of our crew — DIBD 117:19
D. of the music halls — SMITH 309:8
green lap was Nature's d. — GRAY 157:16
She is the d. of my heart — CAREY 90:2
darlings: wealthy curlèd d. — SHAK 291:32
dart: Time shall throw a d. at thee — BROW 74:24
dastard: and a d. in war — SCOTT 268:20
date: d. which will live in infamy — ROOS 262:14
doubles your chances for a d. — ALLEN 4:17
Standards are always out of d. — BENN 34:14
dateless: d. bargain to engrossing — SHAK 295:25
daughter: As is the mother, so is her d. — BIBLE 47:4
D. am I in my mother's house — KIPL 196:25
d. hath soft brown hair — CALV 88:7
d. of debate — ELIZ 135:13
d. of the gods, divinely — TENN 323:20
D. of the Moon, Nokomis — LONG 210:1
Don't put your d. on the stage — COW 109:5
Elderly ugly d. — GILB 152:30
let them all to my elder d. — THOM 330:23
O my ducats! O my d. — SHAK 289:12
Sole of his voice — MILT 229:25
Stern d. of the voice of God — WORD 355:25
daughters: d. of my father's house — SHAK 298:2
thunder, fire, are my d. — SHAK 283:7
Words are men's d. — MADD 216:14
words are the d. of earth — JOHN 182:4
dauntless: and so d. in war — SCOTT 268:19
with d. breast — GRAY 157:9
dauphin: kingdom of daylight's d. — HOPK 172:20
David: D. wrote the Psalms — NAYL 237:20
Once in royal D.'s city — ALEX 4:4
Davy: Sir Humphrey D. — BENT 35:8
dawn: d. comes up like thunder — KIPL 196:21
d. of the morning after — ADE 3:1
D. on our darkness — HEBER 164:14
Hail, redemption's happy d. — CASW 92:18
in that d. to be alive — WORD 354:24
I said to D.: Be sudden — THOM 331:10
music of its trees at d. — ARN 16:21
Rosy-fingered d. — HOMER 171:2
dawning: bird of d. singeth all — SHAK 274:2
d. of the age of Aquarius — RADO 257:18
day: All d. long from 10 till 4 — BELL 33:24
And d.'s at the morn — BROW 76:28
And every dog his d. — KING 195:17
Another d. older and deeper — TRAV 334:4
arrow that flieth by d. — BOOK 67:29
breaks the blank d. — TENN 325:1
bright cold d. in April — ORW 242:5
bright d. is done — SHAK 272:4
burden and heat of the d. — BIBLE 50:25
compare thee to a summer's d. — SHAK 299:12

day (*cont.*):
d. brought back my night — MILT 230:25
D. by day: we magnify thee — BOOK 63:21
d. in a pillar of a cloud — BIBLE 39:39
d. of his death was a dark — AUDEN 20:21
d. of salvation — BIBLE 55:25
d. of small nations — CHAM 93:23
d. of wrath — MISS 231:23
d. once or twice in a man's — PEPYS 247:21
d. o' the Oppressor — KIPL 197:16
d. perish wherein I was born — BIBLE 42:25
d. the music died — MCL 215:7
d. Thou gavest — ELL 135:21
d. war broke out — WILT 351:23
each d. dies with sleep — HOPK 172:11
ebbs out life's little d. — LYTE 212:20
end of a perfect d. — BOND 63:9
Friends, I have lost a d. — TITUS 332:22
Go ahead, make my d. — STIN 317:26
have their d. and cease to be — TENN 324:23
Hide me from d.'s garish eye — MILT 226:26
knell of parting d. — GRAY 157:4
last, everlasting d. — DONNE 123:22
left alone with our d. — AUDEN 21:15
live this d. as if thy last — KEN 193:21
long d.'s journey into night — O'NEI 241:11
long weary d. have end — SPEN 313:6
mansions to the peering d. — MILT 227:28
mind on an ordinary d. — WOOLF 353:21
morning were the first d. — BIBLE 38:14
murmur of a summer's d. — ARN 17:5
night do penance for a d. — WORD 356:11
night of this immortal d. — SHEL 304:24
not a second on the d. — COOK 107:15
one d. in thy courts — BOOK 67:22
remorseful d. — SHAK 280:9
seize the d. — HOR 173:20
So foul and fair a d. — SHAK 285:6
spent one whole d. well — THOM 330:2
This'll be the d. that I die — MCL 215:8
thou d. in night — SHAK 295:13
tomorrow is another d. — MITC 232:7
Underneath D.'s azure eyes — SHEL 304:1
unto the d. is the evil — BIBLE 49:5
upon every d. to be lost — JOHN 186:7
wish d. come, not choose — HOPK 171:25
Without all hope of d. — MILT 230:11
daylight: cheerfulness keeps up a kind of d. — ADD 2:24
kingdom of d.'s dauphin — HOPK 172:20
methinks but the d. sick — SHAK 290:6
must not let in d. upon magic — BAG 26:13
days: all the d. of my life — BOOK 66:18
And the d. grow short — AND 5:12
because the d. are evil — BIBLE 56:1
behold these present d. — SHAK 300:5
burnt-out ends of smoky d. — ELIOT 134:10
Cast your mind on other d. — YEATS 360:7
d. are swifter than a weaver's — BIBLE 42:30
D. are where we live — LARK 201:13
d. darken round me — TENN 324:19
d. of our youth — BYRON 87:10
d. of wine and roses — DOWS 125:13
d. that are no more — TENN 327:22
finished in the first 1,000 d. — KENN 194:5
Length of d. is in her right — BIBLE 43:8
number of my d. — BOOK 67:1
number our d. — BOOK 67:27
of few d. and full of trouble — BIBLE 42:33
our d. on the earth — BIBLE 42:17
seemed unto him but a few d. — BIBLE 39:22
We have seen better d. — SHAK 296:21
day-star: d. in the ocean bed — MILT 227:18
day-to-day: what a d. business life is — LAF 199:20
dazzle: d. for an hour — MORE 234:22
mine eyes d. — WEBS 344:19

dea: *Et vera incessu patuit d.*   VIRG 339:3
dead: After that it's d.   WAUGH 343:26
And he is d., who will not fight   GREN 158:16
And simplify me when I'm d.   DOUG 125:9
Beautiful Evelyn Hope is d.   BROW 75:28
besides, the wench is d.   MARL 219:2
Bivouac of the D.   O'HARA 241:4
blooming well d.   SAR 267:1
character d. at every word   SHER 306:4
charity more than the d.   ARN 16:8
cold and pure and very d.   LEWIS 206:18
converse with the mighty d.   THOM 331:27
D.! and never called me mother   WOOD 353:17
D. battles, like dead generals   TUCH 335:7
d., but in the Elysian fields   DISR 122:18
d. donkey   DICK 120:4
d. don't die   LAWR 202:26
D., for a ducat   SHAK 276:19
d. he would like to see me   HOLL 170:11
d. Indian   SHAK 296:4
d. Indian   SHER 305:22
d. level of provincial   ELIOT 132:13
d. men lost their bones   ELIOT 134:23
d. selves to higher things   TENN 324:24
d. shall be raised   BIBLE 55:21
d. shall not have died in vain   LINC 207:8
d. sinner revised   BIER 59:9
d. we owe only truth   VOLT 340:24
d. woman bites not   GRAY 156:19
d. YESTERDAY   FITZ 140:11
democracy of the d.   CHES 98:13
Down among the d. men   DYER 129:18
Either he's d., or my watch   MARX 221:6
fairy that falls down d.   BARR 29:12
Faith without works is d.   BIBLE 57:3
Fame is a food that d. men   DOBS 122:26
female atheist talks you d.   JOHN 183:8
For being d.   BENT 35:6
For y'er a lang time d.   ANON 6:9
God is d.   FROMM 146:7
healthy and wealthy and d.   THUR 332:15
If the d. talk to you   SZASZ 321:25
In the long run we are all d.   KEYN 194:17
I would that I were d.   TENN 326:22
King of all these the d.   HOMER 171:3
kissed by the English d.   OWEN 244:1
lasting mansions of the d.   CRAB 110:22
Let the d. bury their dead   BIBLE 49:20
Lilacs out of the d. land   ELIOT 134:18
maid is not d.   BIBLE 49:26
millions of the mouthless d.   SORL 311:16
Mistah Kurtz—he d.   CONR 107:6
more to say when I am d.   ROB 260:20
more ways of being d.   DAWK 115:3
noble D.   WORD 356:15
not d.—but gone before   ROG 261:18
Not many d.   COCK 103:1
only consistent people are the d.   HUXL 177:6
our English d.   SHAK 279:5
over the rich D.   BROO 72:20
past is the only d. thing   THOM 330:22
quick, and the d.   DEWAR 117:14
renown and grace is d.   SHAK 286:26
sculptured d.   KEATS 190:15
sea gave up the d.   BIBLE 58:3
Sea shall give up her d.   BOOK 69:15
sheeted d. did squeak   SHAK 274:1
sleeping and the d.   SHAK 286:17
Smiling the boy fell d.   BROW 76:8
their home among the d.   SHEL 303:16
There are no d.   MAET 216:15
They must be d.   DICK 118:19
they told me you were d.   CORY 108:13
This my son was d.   BIBLE 52:32

dead (*cont.*):
those who are d.   BURKE 80:17
two days' conference with the d.   WEBS 344:16
very d. of Winter   ANDR 5:15
very d. of winter   ELIOT 133:21
Weep me not d.   DONNE 124:16
When I am d.   BELL 33:27
Where d. men meet   BUTL 84:21
dead-born: d. *from the press*   HUME 176:10
deadener: Habit is a great d.   BECK 31:16
deadlock: Holy d.   HERB 166:16
deadly: more d. in the long run   TWAIN 335:22
more d. than the male   KIPL 196:12
deaf: For, d., how should they   SORL 311:16
deal: be given a square d.   ROOS 262:17
new d. for the American   ROOS 262:8
dean: cushion and soft D.   POPE 251:16
D. of Christ Church   SPR 314:1
no dogma, no D.   DISR 122:16
sly shade of a Rural D.   BROO 73:5
deans: dowagers for d.   TENN 327:16
dear: After all, my erstwhile d.   MILL 224:23
dangerously d.   BYRON 85:17
D. as remembered kisses   TENN 327:23
D. Lord and Father of mankind   WHIT 348:27
D. One is mine as mirrors   AUDEN 21:9
d. to me as are the ruddy   SHAK 281:7
Fareweel d., deluding woman   BURNS 82:28
Plato is d. to me   ARIS 15:22
that bread should be so d.   HOOD 171:13
too d. for my possessing   SHAK 299:27
dearer: d. still is truth   ARIS 15:22
D. than self   BYRON 84:30
d. was the mother   COL 104:20
little d. than his horse   TENN 326:7
death: abolish the d. penalty   KARR 190:1
added a new terror to d.   WETH 347:2
added another terror to d.   LYND 212:19
afraid of d.   CHUR 98:24
After the first d.   THOM 330:15
All in the valley of D.   TENN 323:14
And D. once dead   SHAK 300:15
And d. shall have no dominion   THOM 330:6
And d., who had the soldier   DOUG 125:10
And make d. proud to take us   SHAK 271:26
bargain to engrossing d.   SHAK 295:25
Be afraid for d.   SHAK 288:18
Be thou faithful unto d.   BIBLE 57:21
Birth, and copulation, and d.   ELIOT 134:14
Black Widow, d.   LOW 211:16
blaze forth the d. of princes   SHAK 281:8
Brother to D.   DAN 113:15
Brother to D.   FLET 142:5
Brought d. into the world   MILT 228:7
build the house of d.   MONT 233:10
captains courageous whom d.   BALL 28:1
citizens of d.'s grey land   SASS 267:10
Come away, come away, d.   SHAK 297:32
day of our Jubilee is d.   BROW 74:17
Dear, beauteous d.   VAUG 337:12
d. after life does greatly   SPEN 313:9
D. and his brother Sleep   SHEL 304:26
d. and taxes   FRAN 145:15
D. and taxes and childbirth   MITC 232:5
D. be not proud   DONNE 123:8
D. closes all   TENN 328:23
D. cometh soon or late   MAC 214:3
d. does end and each day   HOPK 172:11
D., ere thou hast slain   BROW 74:24
D.! Great proprietor of all   YOUNG 360:18
d. had undone so many   ELIOT 134:21
D. has a thousand doors   MASS 222:6
D. has got something to be said   AMIS 5:7
d. hath no more dominion   BIBLE 54:35
D. hath so many doors   FLET 142:4

death (*cont.*):

d. hath ten thousand doors	WEBS 344:18
d. in a blizzard	CHER 19:11
D. is a fearful thing	SHAK 288:21
d. is but a groom	DONNE 123:19
[D. is] nature's way	ANON 6:25
d. is not far behind	WESL 346:17
D. is nothing at all	HOLL 170:12
d. is the cure of all diseases	BROW 74:9
D. joins us to the great majority	YOUNG 360:23
D. lies dead	SWIN 321:10
D. lies on her like	SHAK 295:21
D. never takes the wise	LA F 199:19
d. obscured that eye	KEATS 192:17
d.'s counterfeit	SHAK 286:24
d.'s pale flag	SHAK 295:24
D.'s shadow at the door	BLUN 62:12
d. the journey's end	DRYD 128:12
D.! the poor man's	BURNS 82:17
D. thou shalt die	DONNE 123:9
D. tramples it to fragments	SHEL 303:13
d., where is thy sting	BIBLE 55:22
D., where is thy sting-a-ling	ANON 9:21
D. will come when thou	SHEL 305:13
d. will have his day	SHAK 293:25
disappointed by that stroke of d.	JOHN 182:23
disqualified by the accident of d.	CHES 98:14
doubt is nothing but d.	UNAM 336:11
dread of something after d.	SHAK 275:25
dull cold ear of d.	GRAY 157:8
enormously improved by d.	SAKI 265:16
Ev'ry day a little d.	SOND 311:6
fear d. as children fear	BACON 24:20
Fear d.?—to feel the fog	BROW 77:2
fear of d. disquiets me	DUNB 129:8
fed on the fullness of d.	SWIN 321:13
Finality is d.	STEP 315:6
For since by man came d.	BIBLE 55:17
half in love with easeful D.	KEATS 192:3
heroes up the line to d.	SASS 267:8
His d., which happened	HOOD 171:7
I could not stop for D.	DICK 120:9
If there wasn't d.	SMITH 309:22
I had seen birth and d.	ELIOT 133:22
I have a rendezvous with D.	SEEG 269:13
in d. they were not divided	BIBLE 41:22
In the hour of d.	BOOK 64:16
Into the jaws of D.	TENN 323:17
It is but D. who comes at last	SCOTT 268:17
just, and mighty D.	RAL 258:2
Just try and set d. aside	TURG 335:14
Keeps D. his court	SHAK 293:28
killed than frightened to d.	SURT 319:12
kingly D. keeps his pale court	SHEL 303:4
land of the shadow of d.	BIBLE 45:15
Let me die a youngman's d.	MCG 214:21
life forget and d. remember	SWIN 321:16
life half dead, a living d.	MILT 230:13
lightning before d.	SHAK 295:23
little room do we take up in d.	SHIR 306:12
made a covenant with d.	BIBLE 45:28
make one in love with d.	SHEL 303:2
Man has created d.	YEATS 358:22
man's d. diminishes me	DONNE 124:20
Meetest for d.	SHAK 289:24
midst of life we are in d.	BOOK 66:7
much possessed by d.	ELIOT 134:32
must hate and d. return	SHEL 303:19
My name is D.	SOUT 311:23
nearest thing to d. in life	ANON 9:14
neither d. nor life	BIBLE 54:42
nervousness or d.	LEB 203:24
new terrors of D.	ARB 14:24
no mean of d.	SHAK 281:12
none blessed before his d.	BIBLE 48:1

death (*cont.*):

no one knew my d.	ROET 261:16
no one [stop] his d.	SEN 270:8
not at their d.	MONT 233:20
one life and one d.	BROW 76:6
On life, on d.	YEATS 360:8
or give me d.	HENRY 166:6
overcome the sharpness of d.	BOOK 63:20
perchance of D.	THOM 332:1
prepare as though for d.	MANS 217:15
remembered kisses after d.	TENN 327:23
Reports of my d.	TWAIN 336:7
shadow of d.	BROW 74:2
shall be destroyed is d.	BIBLE 55:18
signed my d. warrant	COLL 105:8
sleep of d. what dreams	SHAK 275:25
sleep the sleep of d.	BLAKE 60:21
snares of d. compassed	BOOK 68:19
some one's d.	BROW 75:13
So shalt thou feed on D.	SHAK 300:15
steps that led assuredly to d.	GUIB 159:8
stories of the d. of kings	SHAK 293:27
suffers at his d.	LA BR 199:14
suicide 25 years after his d.	BEAV 31:5
swallow up d. in victory	BIBLE 45:25
Swarm over, D.	BETJ 37:9
talks of Arthur's d.	SHAK 282:11
that sat on him was D.	BIBLE 57:25
there is an image of d.	ELIOT 132:16
There is d. in the pot	BIBLE 42:10
There's d. in the cup	BURNS 82:10
there shall be no more d.	BIBLE 58:5
This fell sergeant, d.	SHAK 277:15
till d. us do part	BOOK 66:1
To be carnally minded is d.	BIBLE 54:39
tragedies are finished by a d.	BYRON 86:12
traveller betwixt life and d.	WORD 356:24
valiant never taste of d.	SHAK 281:8
vasty hall of d.	ARN 17:1
wast not born for d.	KEATS 192:4
way out an' d.'s the other	WILL 351:5
way to dusty d.	SHAK 288:5
we owe God a d.	SHAK 278:25
Why fear d.?	FROH 146:6
Will keep a league till d.	SHAK 294:6
with d. and an agreement	GARR 148:13
deathless: let us make love d.	TREN 334:6
deaths: More d. than one must die	WILDE 350:17
death-sentence: d. without a whimper	LAWR 202:27
death-struck: beautiful and d. year	HOUS 174:25
debars: Fate so enviously d.	MARV 220:13
debasing: D. the moral currency	ELIOT 132:7
debate: daughter of d.	ELIZ 135:13
Rupert of D.	BULW 78:9
debellare: *subiectis et d. superbos*	VIRG 339:16
debonair: buxom, blithe, and d.	MILT 226:28
deboshed: Thou d. fish	SHAK 296:6
debt: Ambition's d. is paid	SHAK 281:11
he paid the d. of nature	FABY 138:6
midst of life we are in d.	MUMF 236:7
National D. is a very Good	SELL 270:4
older and deeper in d.	TRAV 334:4
pay a d. to pleasure too	ROCH 261:3
promise made is a d.	SERV 270:9
debtor: d. to his profession	BACON 24:9
debts: And forgive us our d.	BIBLE 48:27
He that dies pays all d.	SHAK 296:8
decay: Change and d. in all around	LYTE 212:20
D. with imprecision	ELIOT 133:1
Only our love hath no d.	DONNE 123:22
things are subject to d.	DRYD 128:4
decayed: you are sufficiently d.	GILB 152:8
deceitful: heart is d.	BIBLE 46:31
deceits: all the d. of the world	BOOK 64:15
prophesy d.	BIBLE 45:29

deceive: don't d. me ANON 6:27
we d. ourselves BIBLE 57:14
When first we practise to d. SCOTT 268:21
deceived: d. with ornament SHAK 289:21
deceiver: I'm a gay d. COLM 105:14
deceivers: Men were d. ever SHAK 291:19
December: D.'s bareness SHAK 300:3
D. when they wed SHAK 273:9
From May to D. AND 5:12
Their meetings made D. June TENN 325:20
decencies: dwell in d. for ever POPE 251:10
decency: D. is Indecency's conspiracy SHAW 302:3
Terrible that old life of d. LOW 211:11
want of d. is want of sense DILL 120:23
decently: done d. and in order BIBLE 55:15
decent: d. obscurity GIBB 150:16
decide: comes the moment to d. LOW 211:7
decided: d. only to be undecided CHUR 99:9
decision: in the valley of d. BIBLE 47:21
deck: boy stood on the burning d. HEM 165:9
declaration: no d. of war EDEN 130:14
declare: And then, I d. HOFF 169:19
nothing to d. except my genius WILDE 350:18
decomposing: d. in the eternity of print WOOLF 353:20
decorum: Dulce et d. est HOR 173:26
hunt D. down BYRON 86:33
Let them cant about D. BURNS 82:13
decoyed: these poor fools d. PEPYS 247:18
decree: d. from Caesar Augustus BIBLE 51:31
establish the BIBLE 47:13
deed: attempt and not the d. SHAK 286:13
d. is all, the glory GOET 154:7
d. of dreadful note SHAK 287:5
d. without a name SHAK 287:19
good d. in a naughty world SHAK 290:4
leff woord and tak the d. LYDG 212:15
one that will do the d. SHAK 284:14
right d. for the wrong reason ELIOT 134:7
water clears us of this d. SHAK 286:19
Y'are the d.'s creature MIDD 224:7
deeds: Makes ill d. done SHAK 282:12
sight of means to do ill d. SHAK 282:12
though the sager sort our d. CAMP 89:2
deemed: Some d. him wondrous wise BEAT 30:13
deep: commit his body to the d. BOOK 69:15
D. is the silence DRIN 126:24
d. sleep of England ORW 242:1
d. upon her peerless eyes KEATS 191:26
D.-versed in books MILT 230:8
face of the d. BIBLE 38:13
From the great d. TENN 324:4
gentle motion with the d. DAV 114:22
Not d. the Poet sees, but wide ARN 17:2
often lie too d. for tears WORD 355:24
One d. calleth another BOOK 67:4
one is of the d. STEP 315:4
Out of the d. have I called BOOK 68:33
Rocked in the cradle of the d. WILL 350:27
'tis not so d. as a well SHAK 295:7
deepens: d. like a coastal shelf LARK 201:18
deeper: and d. in debt TRAV 334:4
d. than did ever plummet SHAK 296:13
deer: Around the dying d. AYT 23:16
In the stare of the d. WILB 349:9
let the stricken d. go SHAK 276:12
defeat: Dear Night! this world's d. VAUG 337:5
d. is an orphan CIANO 100:12
In d.: defiance CHUR 100:4
In d. unbeatable CHUR 100:9
possibilities of d. VICT 338:6
defeated: Down with the d. AUDEN 21:15
History to the d. AUDEN 21:15
safe course for the d. VIRG 339:6
defect: did make d. perfection SHAK 271:16

defect (cont.):
this fair d. of Nature MILT 229:30
defence: d. of England BALD 27:6
Never make d. or apology CHAR 94:22
only d. is in offence BALD 27:5
defend: d. ourselves with guns GOEB 153:21
d. to the death your right VOLT 341:1
d. us from all perils BOOK 64:12
D. us thy humble servants BOOK 64:5
defended: God abandoned, these d. HOUS 174:13
defends: when attacked it d. itself ANON 12:3
defiance: In defeat: d. CHUR 100:4
defiled: toucheth pitch shall be d. BIBLE 48:2
definition: d. is the enclosing a wilderness BUTL 84:16
deflower: that will her pride d. SPEN 313:12
deformity: time's d. JONS 187:7
defy: d. the foul fiend SHAK 283:13
degree: exalted them of low d. BIBLE 51:29
Take but d. away SHAK 296:30
degrees: things through all d. WORD 357:8
Dei: Ad majorem D. gloriam ANON 13:11
Vox populi, vox D. ALC 3:14
deities: some other new d. PLATO 249:18
deity: D. and the Drains STR 318:13
For D. offended BURNS 82:6
delay: In d. there lies no plenty SHAK 297:23
In me is no d. MILT 230:1
Nothing was ever lost by d. GREE 158:3
delaying: make the gift rich by d. TROL 334:18
delays: All d. dangerous in war DRYD 128:22
delenda: D. est Carthago CATO 92:22
deleted: Expletive d. ANON 7:3
Delia: While D. is away JAGO 179:8
deliberate: Where both d., the love MARL 218:18
deliberation: D. sat MILT 228:27
delight: And go to 't with d. SHAK 271:20
And turn d. into a sacrifice HERB 166:21
best gift, my ever new d. MILT 229:15
Commodity, firmness, and d. WOTT 357:19
d. and ends in wisdom FROST 146:24
D. hath a joy in it either SIDN 306:29
d. is in proper young men BURNS 82:17
d. of battle with my peers TENN 328:21
D. of lust is gross and brief PETR 248:10
each thing met conceives d. MILT 229:23
Energy is Eternal D. BLAKE 60:24
Let dogs d. to bark and bite WATTS 343:7
phantom of d. WORD 356:24
source of little visible d. BRON 72:17
Spirit of D. SHEL 304:32
Studies serve for d. BACON 25:13
sweet airs, that give d. SHAK 296:9
There is a land of pure d. WATTS 343:11
To bind another to its d. BLAKE 62:2
top-gallant d. is to him MELV 223:2
unrest which men miscall d. SHEL 303:11
yet I hear thy shrill d. SHEL 305:8
delighteth: king d. to honour BIBLE 42:20
neither d. he in any man's BOOK 69:10
delightful: And almost as d. LOCK 208:22
marriages, but no d. ones LA R 201:22
delighting: But, O! d. me HODG 169:14
delights: does some d. condemn MOL 232:23
king of intimate d. COWP 110:12
scorn d., and live laborious MILT 227:14
delinquent: condemns a less d. for't BUTL 84:8
delitabill: Storys to rede ar d. BARB 28:15
deliver: d. us from evil BIBLE 48:27
D. us, good Lord CHES 97:24
Good Lord, d. us BOOK 64:14
delivered: d. them into the hands BIBLE 40:30
d. my soul from death BOOK 68:20
delphiniums: d. blue and geraniums red MILNE 225:21
deluding: Fareweel dear, d. woman BURNS 82:28
déluge: Après nous le d. POMP 250:11

delusion: d., a mockery, and a snare	DENM 116:27
demeaning: So womanly, her d.	SKEL 308:2
demesne: private *pagus* or d.	AUDEN 21:8
demi-paradise: This other Eden, d.	SHAK 293:16
demi-tasses: your villainous d.	SMITH 309:5
democracies: d. it is the only sacred	FRAN 145:1
democracy: capacity for justice makes d.	NIEB 239:14
cured by more d.	SMITH 309:2
D. and proper drains	BETJ 37:4
D. is the name we give	CAIL 142:2
D. is the worst form	CHUR 100:2
D. means government	ATTL 19:14
D. means government	CHES 98:12
D. resumed her reign	BELL 33:25
D. substitutes election	SHAW 301:27
great arsenal of d.	ROOS 262:12
It is the d. of the dead	CHES 98:13
little less d. to save	ATK 19:10
made safe for it	WILS 351:21
Two cheers for D.	FORS 144:3
voting that's d.	STOP 317:28
democrat: Aristocrat, d., autocrat	TENN 326:26
D., in that order	JOHN 181:19
democrats: D. object to	CHES 98:14
demon: wailing for her d.-lover	COL 103:23
demonstrandum: *Quod erat d.*	EUCL 137:19
den: hand on the cockatrice' d.	BIBLE 45:20
made it a d. of thieves	BIBLE 50:27
seven sleepers d.	DONNE 124:5
denied: call that may not be d.	MAS 222:1
faintly and would be d.	SHAK 294:9
denizen: spider is sole d.	HARDY 162:3
Denmark: rotten in the state of D.	SHAK 274:29
deny: Room to d. ourselves	KEBLE 193:17
thou shalt d. me thrice	BIBLE 51:10
denying: how to allure by d.	TROL 334:18
deo: *D. gratias*	MISS 231:14
Jubilate D.	BIBLE 58:10
depart: lettest thou thy servant d.	BIBLE 58:17
thy servant d. in peace	BIBLE 52:3
departed: D., never to return	BURNS 81:28
He d., he withdrew	CIC 100:26
our dear brother here d.	BOOK 66:8
depends: all d. what you mean by	JOAD 181:15
so much d. upon a red wheel	WILL 351:8
deportment: adapt her methods and d.	CRANE 111:1
depraved: suddenly became d.	JUV 189:3
depression: d. when you lose yours	TRUM 335:5
depth: And in the d. be praise	NEWM 238:20
But far beyond my d.	SHAK 280:18
d., and not the tumult	WORD 355:6
depths: Up from the d. I have cried	BIBLE 58:14
derangement: nice d. of epitaphs	SHER 305:29
descending: comes with clouds d.	WESL 346:9
descensus: *Facilis d. Averno*	VIRG 339:12
descent: d. from a monkey	WILB 349:7
description: It beggared all d.	SHAK 271:14
descriptions: d. of the fairest wights	SHAK 300:4
desert: d. shall rejoice	BIBLE 46:4
d. sighs in the bed	AUDEN 20:12
every man after his d.	SHAK 275:20
found him in a d. land	BIBLE 40:23
its sweetness on the d.	GRAY 157:9
Life is the d.	YOUNG 360:23
Stand in the d.	SHEL 304:11
went unrewarded, but d.	DRYD 127:13
deserts: D. of vast eternity	MARV 220:24
When she d. the night	MILT 230:12
deserve: we'll d. it	ADD 2:13
you somehow haven't to d.	FROST 146:11
designs: d. were strictly honourable	FIEL 139:11
from d. by Michael Angelo	TWAIN 336:2
desire: all a wonder and a wild d.	BROW 77:5
And d. shall fail	BIBLE 44:26

desire (*cont.*):	
And weariness treads on d.	PETR 248:10
d. is boundless	SHAK 297:2
d. of the moth	SHEL 305:5
d. should so many years	SHAK 278:22
for the d. of the man	COL 104:27
it provokes the d.	SHAK 286:21
lineaments of gratified d.	BLAKE 61:17
when the d. cometh	BIBLE 43:21
desired: I have d. to go	HOPK 172:7
desires: by lopping off our d.	SWIFT 320:12
consists in doing what one d.	MILL 224:17
d. and petitions of thy	BOOK 64:10
d. of the heart	AUDEN 20:15
devices and d.	BOOK 63:13
from whom all holy d.	BOOK 64:11
hearts are open, all d. known	BOOK 65:2
He who d. but acts not	BLAKE 61:3
nurse unacted d.	BLAKE 61:10
desiring: D. this man's art	SHAK 299:14
desk: Turn upward from the d.	ELIOT 134:27
desks: Stick close to your d.	GILB 152:20
desolate: all that are d.	BOOK 64:17
d. and sick of an old passion	DOWS 125:12
d. places	BIBLE 42:26
desolation: abomination of d.	BIBLE 50:35
D. in immaculate public places	ROET 261:14
My d. does begin to make	SHAK 272:1
years of d. pass over	JEFF 180:23
despair: begins on the far side of d.	SART 267:6
builds a Heaven in Hell's d.	BLAKE 62:1
carrion comfort,	HOPK 171:25
depth of some divine d.	TENN 327:22
Do not d.	PUDN 256:3
have of comfort and d.	SHAK 300:13
I can endure my own d.	WALSH 342:8
It was begotten by D.	MARV 220:12
Magnanimous D. alone	MARV 220:12
Now Giant D. had a wife	BUNY 79:3
or the quality of his d.	CONN 106:27
thou needst not then d.	ARN 16:15
ye Mighty, and d.	SHEL 304:12
despairer: Too quick d.	ARN 17:19
desperandum: *Nil d.*	HOR 173:19
desperate: By d. appliances are relieved	SHAK 276:27
Tempt not a d. man	SHAK 295:22
desperately: d. mortal	SHAK 288:24
desperation: lives of quiet d.	THOR 332:9
despised: Dangers by being d.	BURKE 81:2
d., and dying king	SHEL 305:3
d. and rejected of men	BIBLE 46:17
despite: builds a Hell in Heaven's d.	BLAKE 62:2
Despond: name of the slough was D.	BUNY 78:18
despondency: end d. and madness	WORD 356:17
SPREAD ALARM AND D.	PEN 247:8
despot: country governed by a d.	JOHN 185:17
despotism: France was long a d.	CARL 90:14
destined: Amphitrite's d. halls	SHEL 304:1
destiny: Anatomy is d.	FREUD 145:23
character is d.	ELIOT 132:15
D. with Men for pieces plays	FITZ 140:12
homely joys, and d. obscure	GRAY 157:7
you reap a d.	READE 258:11
destroy: d. in all my holy mountain	BIBLE 45:20
d. in mankind the belief	DOST 125:1
d. the town to save it	ANON 8:10
Doth the winged life d.	BLAKE 61:16
One to d., is murder	YOUNG 360:15
when man determined to d.	CUMM 113:2
Whom God would d. He first	DUP 129:11
Whom the gods wish to d.	CONN 106:24
Whom the mad would d.	LEVIN 206:8
destroyed: d. by Time's devouring	BRAM 71:13
destroyeth: d. in the noon-day	BOOK 67:29
destruction: d. is also a creative	BAK 26:22

destruction (cont.):
d. of the poor | BIBLE 43:17
d. of the whole world | HUME 176:11
Pride goeth before d. | BIBLE 43:28
that leadeth to d. | BIBLE 49:12
to their d. draw | DONNE 123:22
destructive: to the d. element submit | CONR 107:7
detail: frittered away by d. | THOR 332:11
Merely corroborative d. | GILB 152:5
details: mind which reveres d. | LEWIS 206:19
detect: lose it in the moment you d. | POPE 251:19
determinate: My bonds in thee are all d. | SHAK 299:27
determination: character but the d. of incident | JAMES 179:24
determined: D., dared, and done | SMART 308:14
detest: they d. at leisure | BYRON 86:25
detraction: D. is but baseness' varlet | JONS 187:10
Deutschland: D. über alles | HOFF 169:16
deviates: Shadwell never d. into sense | DRYD 128:5
device: banner with the strange d. | LONG 209:17
devices: d. and desires of our own hearts | BOOK 63:13
devil: apology for the D. | BUTL 84:15
book a d.'s chaplain might write | DARW 114:5
D. always builds a chapel | DEFOE 115:22
d. a monk would be | MOTT 236:3
d. and all his works | BOOK 65:21
d. can cite Scripture | SHAK 289:3
d. damn thee black | SHAK 287:33
D. howling 'Ho!' | SQUI 314:4
d. in the same churchyard | BANC 28:14
d. is dead | READE 258:10
D. knows Latin | KNOX 198:19
D. sends cooks | GARR 148:11
d. have all the good tunes | HILL 168:14
d.'s most devilish when | BROW 74:26
D.'s party | BLAKE 60:25
d. understands Welsh | SHAK 278:5
d. will come, and Faustus | MARL 218:13
doubt is D.-born | TENN 325:18
Drink and the d. had done | STEV 317:2
For he counteracts the D. | SMART 308:8
If the d. doesn't exist | DOST 125:3
man's spirit is d.'s work | SHAW 300:27
my back upon Don or d. | TENN 328:12
Old D. Moon | HARB 161:13
Or who cleft the D.'s foot | DONNE 124:10
that d.'s madness—War | SERV 270:12
That fears a painted d. | SHAK 286:17
d. would also build a chapel | LUTH 212:9
What! can the d. speak true | SHAK 285:9
world, the flesh, and the d. | BOOK 64:15
your adversary the d. | BIBLE 57:12
devildoms: d. of Spain | TENN 328:11
devilish: thing is 8 times 8 | FLEM 141:22
devils: still 'tis d. must print | MOORE 234:10
devoid: D. of sense and motion | MILT 228:24
Devon: If the Dons sight D. | NEWB 238:10
devotion: Farewell my bok and my d. | CHAU 96:9
d. to something afar | SHEL 305:5
devour: seeking whom he may d. | BIBLE 57:12
devourer: Time the d. of everything | OVID 243:16
devout: cannot be d. in dishabilly | FARQ 138:21
devoutly: D. to be wished | SHAK 275:25
dew: continual d. of thy blessing | BOOK 64:9
d. of heaven drops now | FORD 143:9
d. of yon high eastern hill | SHAK 274:3
d. will rust them | SHAK 291:31
drenched with d. | DE L 116:21
fades awa' like morning d. | BALL 28:10
resolve itself into a d. | SHAK 274:9
there rained a ghastly d. | TENN 326:11
dewdrop: Starlight and d. | FOST 144:9
dewy: from noon to d. eve | MILT 228:20
shakes his d. wings | D'AV 114:10
diable: le d. est mort | READE 258:10

diadem: A royal d. adorns | KELLY 193:19
Bring forth the royal d. | PERR 248:4
diagnostician: makes a good d. | OSLER 243:3
diagonally: lie d. in his bed | STER 315:23
dialect: D. words | HARDY 161:23
To purify the d. of the tribe | ELIOT 133:9
diamond: Like a d. in the sky | TAYL 323:3
rough than polished d. | CHES 97:12
diamonds: d. are a girl's best friend | ROBIN 260:18
Goodness, what beautiful d. | WEST 346:22
Diana: Let us be D.'s foresters | SHAK 277:22
diary: d. and some day it'll keep you | WEST 346:19
dibble: d. in earth to set one | SHAK 298:30
dice: [God] does not play d. | EINS 131:9
Dick: D. the shepherd | SHAK 284:23
dictates: d. to me slumbering | MILT 229:21
woman d. before marriage | ELIOT 132:8
dictation: at d. speed what he knew | AMIS 5:3
dictatorship: d. of the proletariat | MARX 221:12
government you have a d. | TRUM 335:3
dictionaries: D. are like watches | JOHN 184:3
To make d. is dull work | JOHN 182:6
writer of d., a harmless drudge | JOHN 182:8
dictionary: He will be but a walking d. | CHAP 94:21
did: And d. it very well | GILB 151:14
d. for them both with his plan | SASS 267:13
didn't he danced his d. | CUMM 112:16
Dido: D. with a willow | SHAK 289:32
die: about to d. salute you | ANON 13:12
Americans, when they d. | APPL 14:15
And how can man d. better | MAC 214:3
And yet I love her till I d. | ANON 10:18
back to America to d. | JAMES 179:21
clean place to d. | KAV 190:7
Cowards d. many times | SHAK 281:8
Curse God, and d. | BIBLE 42:24
determine to d. here | BEE 31:22
D., and endow a college | POPE 251:13
d., and go we know not | SHAK 288:21
d. before we have explained | ADAMS 2:3
d. beyond my means | WILDE 350:22
d. but do not surrender | CAMB 88:11
d. but once to serve our | ADD 2:16
d. by famine die by inches | HENRY 166:3
d. for adultery! | SHAK 283:23
d. for one's country | HOR 173:26
D. he or justice must | MILT 229:3
d. in that man's company | SHAK 279:18
d. in the last ditch | WILL 351:1
d. is cast | CAES 88:1
d. like a true-blue rebel | HILL 168:13
D., my dear Doctor | PALM 244:22
d. of that roar which lies | ELIOT 132:10
d. on your feet | IBAR 178:1
d. well that die in a battle | SHAK 279:13
d. when the trees were | CLARE 101:3
d. will be an awfully big | BARR 29:13
d. with kissing of my Lord | MARL 219:12
Easy live and quiet d. | SCOTT 268:24
Few d. and none resign | JEFF 180:22
find myself so apt to d. | SHAK 281:12
For as in Adam all d. | BIBLE 55:17
greatly think, or bravely d. | POPE 250:23
harder lesson! how to d. | PORT 253:27
He shall not d. | STER 315:22
He will, he must d. | NICH 239:10
Hope I d. before I get old | TOWN 333:16
I am sick, I must d. | NASHE 237:19
I die because I do not d. | JOHN 181:16
If I should d. before I wake | ANON 9:20
If I should d., think only | BROO 73:10
If it were now to d. | SHAK 292:5
If we are marked to d. | SHAK 279:17
I'll d. for him to-morrow | BALL 27:13

die (cont.):

I shall d. at the top	SWIFT 320:26
I shall not altogether d.	HOR 173:29
it was sure to d.	MOORE 234:19
I will d. in peace	WOLFE 353:4
Let me d. a youngman's death	MCG 214:21
Let us do—or d.	BURNS 82:22
man can d. but once	SHAK 278:25
must be with us, or we d.	KEATS 190:12
myself to d. upon a kiss	SHAK 293:6
natural to d. as to be born	BACON 24:22
Not d. here in a rage	SWIFT 320:5
not so difficult to d.	BYRON 87:2
not that I'm afraid to d.	ALLEN 4:16
not to live, but to d. in	BROW 74:20
Of easy ways to d.	SHAK 272:11
Old soldiers never d.	FOLEY 142:16
or being born, to d.	BACON 25:31
or like Douglas d.	HOME 170:19
passing-bells for these who d.	OWEN 243:21
pie in the sky when you d.	HILL 168:12
poison us, do we not d.	SHAK 289:17
seems it rich to d.	KEATS 192:3
She must weep or she will d.	TENN 327:26
should d. for the people	BIBLE 53:34
something he will d. for	KING 195:8
taught us how to d.	TICK 332:20
Their every parting was to d.	TENN 325:20
Theirs but to do and d.	TENN 323:15
thereof thou shalt surely d.	BIBLE 38:19
they only let Him d.	STUD 318:19
This'll be the day that I d.	MCL 215:8
time to d.	BIBLE 44:11
To d. and know it	LOW 211:16
To d., to sleep	SHAK 275:25
To go away is to d. a little	HAR 161:9
To-morrow let us do or d.	CAMP 88:18
to morrow we shall d.	BIBLE 45:24
We d. in earnest	RAL 257:22
We must love one another or d.	AUDEN 21:11
We shall d. alone	PASC 246:4
What 'tis to d.	FLET 31:2
When beggars d.	SHAK 281:8
Who did not wish to d.	SHAW 303:1
wish to live and to d.	VILL 338:21
wretch that dares not d.	BURNS 82:15
you asked this man to d.	AUDEN 20:17

died: d. by the hand of the Lord

	BIBLE 40:1
d. last night of my physician	PRIOR 255:11
D. some, pro patria	POUND 254:18
d. to save their country	CHES 97:23
He d. in a good old age	BIBLE 42:18
He that d. o' Wednesday	SHAK 278:12
If any question why we d.	KIPL 196:7
liked it not, and d.	WOTT 357:17
Mithridates, he d. old	HOUS 175:5
she d. young	WEBS 344:19
She should have d. hereafter	SHAK 288:5
thought it d. of grieving	KEATS 191:3
Who d. to save us all	ALEX 4:6
would God I had d. for thee	BIBLE 41:27

diem: carpe d.

	HOR 173:20

dies: d. rich dies disgraced

	CARN 90:27
D. irae, dies illa	MISS 231:23
Every moment d. a man	BABB 23:19
Every moment d. a man	TENN 328:26
hath blown for ever d.	FITZ 140:10
He that d. pays all debts	SHAK 296:8
kingdom where nobody d.	MILL 224:21
little something in me d.	VIDAL 338:13
man happy before he d.	SOLON 310:27
One d. only once	MOL 232:17
true because a man d. for it	WILDE 350:7
Who d. if England live	KIPL 196:13
Whom the gods love d. young	MEN 223:5

diesel: D.-engined	FLAN 141:6
diet: d. unparalleled	DICK 119:10

difference: and, oh, the d. to me

	WORD 356:23
And that has made all the d.	FROST 146:19
d. of forty thousand men	WELL 345:13
Divines, and d. of texts	SPEN 313:16
silk makes the d.	FULL 147:7
wear your rue with a d.	SHAK 277:3

different: because he hears a d. drummer

	THOR 332:12
But had thought they were d.	ELIOT 133:22
clean d. things	CHAR 94:25
d. from the home life of our	ANON 8:1
How d. from us	ANON 9:10
rich are d.	FITZ 140:20
We boil at d. degrees	EMER 136:32

differently: one who thinks d.	LUX 212:12
difficile: D. est longum subito deponere	CAT 93:5

difficult: D. do you call it

	JOHN 186:16
difficult we do immediately	CAL 88:6
fascination of what's d.	YEATS 359:4
first step that is d.	DU D 129:1
It has been found d.	CHES 98:15
Poets must be d.	ELIOT 135:3
'tis not so d. to die	BYRON 87:2
too d. for artists	SCHN 267:23
upon which it is d. to speak	BURKE 80:26

difficulties: d. do not make one doubt

	NEWM 238:16
little local d.	MACM 215:16

difficulty: with d. and labour	MILT 229:2
diffidence: her name was D.	BUNY 79:3

dig: D. for victory

	DORM 124:24
d. till you gently perspire	KIPL 197:22
with his nails he'll d.	WEBS 344:26

digest: inwardly d. them	BOOK 64:22

digestion: good d. wait on appetite

	SHAK 287:10
sweet to taste prove in d.	SHAK 293:11

dignified: d. parts	BAG 26:3
dignitate: Cum d. otium	CIC 100:32

dignity: equal in d. and rights

	ANON 5:20
left the room with silent d.	GROS 159:4

digressions: D. are the sunshine	STER 315:15
dilectione: d. hominum et odio vitiorum	AUG 22:4
dilettante: snowy-banded, d.	TENN 326:25
dilige: D. et quod vis fac	AUG 22:2
dillied: But I d. and dallied	COLL 105:7
dilly-dally: Don't d. on the way	COLL 105:7
dim: bright world d.	SHEL 305:17
d. in the intense inane	SHEL 304:23
dime: Brother can you spare a d.	HARB 161:11
dimensions: When my d. are	SHAK 282:20
diminished: and ought to be d.	DUNN 129:10

dine: d. exact at noon

	POPE 251:25
going to d. with some men	BENT 35:9
hang that jury-men may d.	POPE 253:8

dined: d. against than dining	BOWRA 71:3
I have d. to-day	SMITH 310:7
dining: more dined against than d.	BOWRA 71:3

dinner: D. in the diner

	GORD 155:22
d. of herbs	BIBLE 43:26
I get too hungry for d. at eight	HART 163:9
They would ask him to d.	CARL 90:26
three hours' march to d.	HAZL 164:8
tocsin of the soul—the d. bell	BYRON 86:20

Diogenes: I would be D.	ALEX 4:1
diplomacy: D. is to do and say	GOLD 154:16
diplomat: d. these days is	UST 336:19
diplomatic: d. boathook	SAL 266:2
dipping: age o'ercargoed, d. deep	FLEC 141:18
directions: By indirections find d. out	SHAK 275:7
rode madly off in all d.	LEAC 203:5
direful: something d. in the sound	AUST 22:17
dirge: d. of her certain ending	SHAK 299:9
dirt: d. doesn't get any worse	CRISP 111:20
D. is matter out of place	GRAY 156:18

dirt (cont.):
d. succeed where sweetness — FORS 143:18
In poverty, hunger, and d. — HOOD 171:12
thicker will be the d. — GALB 147:15
dirty: D. British coaster — MAS 221:19
D., dark, and undevotional — VICT 338:10
d. work for the rest — RUSK 264:15
'Jug Jug' to d. ears — ELIOT 134:22
Is sex d.? — ALLEN 4:15
dis: D. aliter visum — VIRG 339:7
disagreeables: making all d. evaporate — KEATS 193:1
disappointed: d. by that stroke of death — JOHN 182:23
Sir! you have d. us — BELL 33:7
disappointing: he'll be the least d. — BAR 29:21
disappointment: D. all I endeavour end — HOPK 172:18
disapprove: I d. of what you say — VOLT 341:1
disaster: meet with triumph and d. — KIPL 197:6
disasters: d. in his morning face — GOLD 154:23
guilty of our own d. the sun — SHAK 282:22
disbelief: willing suspension of d. — COL 104:24
discandy: do d., melt their sweets — SHAK 271:22
discerning: Gives genius a better d. — GOLD 155:8
discharge: no d. in that war — BIBLE 44:17
discipline: good order and military d. — ANON 6:22
disciplines: category-d. — RYLE 265:10
discommendeth: He who d. others — BROW 74:1
discontent: In pale contented sort of d. — KEATS 191:13
Now is the winter of our d. — SHAK 294:13
discord: dire effects from civil d. flow — ADD 2:19
that eke d. doth sow — ELIZ 135:13
what d. follows — SHAK 296:30
discors: Concordia d. — HOR 173:12
discouragement: There's no d. — BUNY 79:9
discourse: d. and nearest prose — DRYD 128:14
that wants d. of reason — SHAK 274:12
discoverers: ill d. that think — BACON 23:22
discovery: D. consists of — SZEN 322:3
Medicinal d. — AYRES 23:15
discreet: d. charm of the bourgeoisie — BUÑ 78:16
discretion: D. is not the better part — STR 318:15
discunt: Homines dum docent d. — SEN 270:6
discussion: government by d. — ATTL 19:14
disdain: little d. is not amiss — CONG 106:19
disease: Cured yesterday of my d. — PRIOR 255:11
Cure the d. and kill — BACON 24:25
D., Ignorance, Squalor — BEV 38:7
d. is incurable — SHAK 278:19
d. of not listening — SHAK 278:17
D., or sorrows strike him — CLOU 102:15
d. requires a dangerous — FAWK 138:22
d. that gave death time — GUIB 159:8
incurable d. of writing — JUV 189:10
Life is an incurable d. — COWL 109:17
Progress is a comfortable d. — CUMM 112:20
remedy is worse than the d. — BACON 25:11
sexually transmitted d. — ANON 8:20
strange d. of modern life — ARN 17:11
that the d. is incurable — CHEK 96:24
There is no Cure for this D. — BELL 33:4
this long d., my life — POPE 251:4
diseased: minister to a mind d. — SHAK 288:2
Of its own beauty is the mind d. — BYRON 85:9
diseases: Coughs and sneezes spread d. — ANON 6:23
death is the cure of all d. — BROW 74:19
D. desperate grown — SHAK 276:27
disgrace: It's no d. t'be poor — HUBB 175:17
Its private life is a d. — ANON 10:8
disgraced: dies rich dies d. — CARN 90:27
disgraceful: something d. in mind — JUV 189:15
disgruntled: if not actually d. — WOD 352:13
disguise: D. fair nature with hard-favoured — SHAK 279:5
dish: Let's carve him as a d. fit — BIBLE 40:33 / SHAK 281:4
dishabilly: cannot be devout in d. — FARQ 138:21
dishes: no washing of d. — ANON 7:17

disinheriting: damned d. countenance — SHER 306:7
disinterested: D. intellectual curiosity — TREV 334:7
dismal: D. Science — CARL 90:18
With d. stories — BUNY 79:9
dismayed: neither be thou d. — BIBLE 40:26
Was there a man d. — TENN 323:15
dismiss: Lord, d. us with Thy blessing — BUCK 78:3
disobedience: man's first d. — MILT 228:7
disorder: green ice, in wild d. rise — PHIL 248:15
sweet d. in the dress — HERR 167:15
disparity: Just such d. 'twixt — DONNE 123:21
dispatch: requisite in business than d. — ADD 2:20
disposes: man proposes, God d. — THOM 330:1
disposition: Foul d., thoughts unnatural — SHAK 292:13
To put an antic d. on — SHAK 275:4
truant d., good my lord — SHAK 274:14
dispraised: d. were no small praise — MILT 230:3
dispute: work more and d. less — TAWN 322:19
disquieted: Never to be d. — KING 195:5
dissect: thro' creatures you d. — POPE 251:19
We murder to d. — WORD 357:5
dissipation: d. without pleasure — GIBB 150:15
dissolution: A lingering d. — BECK 31:7
dissolve: Fade far away, d. — KEATS 191:31
dissonance: with barbarous d. — MILT 226:17
distance: d. between Russia and British — SAL 266:3
d. is nothing — DU D 129:1
d. lends enchantment — CAMP 88:19
or prestige without d. — DE G 116:5
seconds' worth of d. run — KIPL 197:7
distant: d. from Heaven alike — BURT 83:11
d. scene, one step enough — NEWM 238:21
prospect of a d. good — DRYD 127:32
distempered: That questions the d. part — ELIOT 133:5
distillation: History is a d. of rumour — CARL 90:12
distinguished: d. thing — JAMES 180:6
distraction: Into a fine d. — HERR 167:15
distress: All pray in their d. — BLAKE 61:20
distressed: afflicted, or d., in mind — BOOK 64:19
distribute: d. as fairly as he can — LOWE 211:1
ditch: Channel is a mere d. — NAP 237:1
die in the last d. — WILL 351:1
he wasn't as dull as d. water — DICK 119:24
ditches: of Dutchmen and of d. — BYRON 86:22
dive: Heav'n's great lamps do d. — CAMP 89:2
search for pearls must d. — DRYD 127:23
divers: sundry times and in d. places — BIBLE 56:23
diversity: arise d. of sects — SPEN 313:16
them and servants some d. — BARC 28:17
divided: d. by a common language — SHAW 302:27
I do perceive here a d. duty — SHAK 291:36
If a house be d. — BIBLE 51:19
in their death they were 1.ot d. — BIBLE 41:22
sick hurry, its d. aims — ARN 17:11
whole is d. into three — CAES 87:24
dividend: d. from time's tomorrows — SASS 267:10
dividing: by d. we fall — DICK 120:18
days d. lover and lover — SWIN 321:2
divine: Ah, what the form d. — LAND 200:23
All things, by a law d. — SHEL 304:3
And Love, the human form d. — BLAKE 61:21
But 'twas d. — TRAH 334:1
depth of some d. despair — TENN 327:22
hand that made us is d. — ADD 2:26
little heavy, but no less d. — BYRON 86:15
Right D. of Kings to govern — POPE 250:18
To err is human; to forgive, d. — POPE 252:7
You look d. as you advance — NASH 237:18
divinely: And most d. fair — TENN 323:20
divines: Doubts 'mongst D. — SPEN 313:16
divinest: d. things this world has — HUNT 176:17
divinity: d. that shapes our ends — SHAK 277:12
such d. doth hedge a king — SHAK 277:1
surely a piece of d. in us — BROW 74:21

divinity (*cont.*):
There is D. in odd numbers	SHAK 290:11
those wingy mysteries in d.	BROW 74:10

division: D. is as bad — ANON 9:11

divisions: How many d. has *he* got? — STAL 314:8

divorce: d. of steel falls on me — SHAK 280:14

this bill of my d. to all — DONNE 123:15

do: Diplomacy is to d. and say — GOLD 154:6

d. a girl	ELIOT 134:15
D. not fold, spindle	ANON 6:26
d. only one thing at once	SMIL 308:18
D. other men, for they would	DICK 119:3
D. this, and he doeth	BIBLE 49:17
d. were as easy as to know	SHAK 288:29
D. what thou wilt shall be	CROW 112:14
D. what you like	RAB 257:12
d. ye even so to them	BIBLE 49:11
HOW NOT TO D. IT	DICK 118:29
I am to d. what I please	FRED 145:19
I can d. no other	LUTH 212:8
I'll do, I'll do, and I'll d.	SHAK 285:3
Let's d. it, let's fall in love	PORT 253:22
Let us d.—or die	BURNS 82:22
Love and d. what you will	AUG 22:2
So little done, so much to d.	RHOD 259:12
so much to d., so little done	TENN 325:14
Theirs but to d. and die	TENN 323:15
To d. it as for Thee	HERB 166:25
To-morrow let us d. or die	CAMP 88:18
Whatever you d., do cautiously	ANON 13:20

docent: *Homines dum d. discunt* — SEN 270:6

doctor: God and the d. we alike adore — OWEN 243:17

Knocked down a d. — SIMP 307:12

doctors: budge d. of the Stoic fur — MILT 226:19

By violet-hooded D.	TENN 327:18
D. in verse	THOM 331:3
We d. know	CUMM 113:1

doctrine: d. of ignoble ease — ROOS 262:15

d. set forth thy true	BOOK 65:10
loved the d. for the teacher	DEFOE 115:18
Not for the d.	POPE 252:3

doctrines: all d. plain and clear — BUTL 84:5

doers: Be ye d. of the word — BIBLE 57:2

doffed: fogies who d. their lids — KEAT 190:9

dog: beaten d. beneath the hail — POUND 254:21

been working like a d.	MCC 205:14
black d. waits	JOHN 182:17
But if a man bites a d.	BOG 62:19
d. is turned to his own	BIBLE 57:13
d. it was that died	GOLD 154:28
d. that has praised his fleas	YEATS 360:3
engine of pollution, the d.	SPAR 312:14
every d. has his day	BORR 69:27
every d. his day	KING 195:17
giving your heart to a d.	KIPL 196:27
If you call a d. *Hervey*	JOHN 183:23
incident of the d. in the night	DOYLE 125:21
Is thy servant a d.	BIBLE 42:12
jumps over the lazy d.	ANON 10:7
Lovell our d.	COLL 105:3
Mine enemy's d.	SHAK 283:28
misbeliever, cut-throat d.	SHAK 289:5
Something better than his d.	TENN 326:7
very d. to the commonalty	SHAK 273:15
whose d. are you?	POPE 251:1
woman's preaching is like a d.'s	JOHN 184:16

dogged: It's d. as does it — TROL 334:15

dogma: no d., no Dean — DISR 122:16

will serve to beat a d. — GUED 159:5

dogs: bang these d. of Seville — TENN 328:12

d. and killed the cats	BROW 76:26
d. delight to bark	WATTS 343:7
d. go on with their doggy	AUDEN 21:2
d. than of their children	PENN 247:10
hates d. and babies	ROST 263:13

dogs (*cont.*):
Lame d. over stiles	KING 195:14
let slip the d. of war	SHAK 281:14
Mad d. and Englishmen	COW 109:4
more I like d.	TOUS 333:15
Things are but as straw d.	LAO-T 201:11
Throw physic to the d.	SHAK 288:3

doing: joy's soul lies in the d. — SHAK 296:29

next to fine d. the top thing	KEATS 193:12
Patient continuance in well d.	BIBLE 54:28
put me to d.	METH 223:28
see what she's d.	PUNCH 256:13
What was he d., the great	BROW 75:4

doleful: Knight of the D. Countenance — CERV 93:16

doll: doll in the d.'s house — DICK 119:25

dollar: d. is the only object — ANON 5:23

Isn't this a billion d. country — FOST 144:6

Dolores: splendid and sterile D. — SWIN 321:8

dolorous: d. mansions to the peering day — MILT 227:28

dolour: d. of pad and paper-weight — ROET 261:14

dolphin-torn: d., that gong-tormented sea — YEATS 358:15

dome: d. of many-coloured glass — SHEL 303:13

singing beneath the d. — VERL 338:1

domestic: d. business is no less — MONT 233:13

Milk-soup men call d. bliss	PATM 246:18
respectable d. establishment	BENN 34:12

dominant: d.'s persistence — BROW 77:17

dominion: death hath no more d. — BIBLE 54:35

death shall have no d.	THOM 330:6
hand that holds d. over Man	THOM 330:11

dominions: His Majesty's d. — NORTH 240:6

sun does not set in my d. — SCH 267:19

domino: 'falling d.' principle — EIS 131:15

dominus: D. *illuminatio mea* — BIBLE 58:9

D. *vobiscum*	MISS 231:9
Nisi D. custodierit civitatem	BIBLE 58:13

don: my back upon D. or devil — TENN 328:12

Remote and ineffectual D. — BELL 33:16

dona: *timeo Danaos et d. ferentis* — VIRG 339:5

done: decide that nothing can be d. — ALLEN 4:12

Determined, dared, and d.	SMART 308:14
D. because we are too menny	HARDY 161:12
d. the state some service	SHAK 293:5
d. those things which we	BOOK 63:14
d. very well out of the war	BALD 27:9
he d. her wrong	ANON 7:6
Inasmuch as ye have d. it	BIBLE 51:6
much is to be d. and little	JOHN 182:27
must be seen to be d.	OSB 242:25
Nay, I have d.	DRAY 126:16
Nothing to be d.	BECK 31:10
Played-out and D.-to-death	TRAI 334:2
should not be d. at all	VIDAL 338:11
so I order it d.	JUV 189:8
surprised to find it d. at all	JOHN 184:16
that which is d. is that which	BIBLE 44:8
Think nothing d.	LUCAN 211:25
though it were d. before	DONNE 123:17
were d. when 'tis done	SHAK 285:22
What is to be d.	LENIN 205:3
What's d. cannot be undone	SHAK 287:31
what's d. is done	SHAK 287:3
won are d.	SHAK 296:29

dong: D. with a Luminous Nose — LEAR 203:8

donkey: that's a dead d. — DICK 120:4

donkeys: Lions led by d. — HOFF 169:17

Donne: another Newton, a new D. — HUXL 177:11

D., for not keeping of accent	JONS 187:31
D.'s verses are like	JAM 179:13
D., whose muse on dromedary	COL 104:2

dons: D. admirable! D. of Might — BELL 33:17

If the D. sight Devon — NEWB 238:10

don't: persons about to marry.—'D.' — PUNCH 256:5

doom: even to the edge of d. — SHAK 300:9

doom (cont.):

regardless of their d.	GRAY 157:12
Doon: banks and braes o' bonny D.	BURNS 81:27
door: coming in at one d.	BEDE 31:20
Death's shadow at the d.	BLUN 62:12
d. flew open, in he ran	HOFF 169:21
d. opens and lets the future in	GREE 158:6
d. we never opened	ELIOT 132:26
drive an angel from your d.	BLAKE 61:22
I am the d.	BIBLE 53:29
instrument here at the d.	DONNE 123:16
interest a knock at the d.	LAMB 200:3
Is beating on the d.	YEATS 359:6
I stand at the d.	BIBLE 57:23
knocking at Preferment's d.	ARN 17:6
On the wrong side of the d.	CHES 97:21
prejudices through the d.	FRED 145:18
whining of a d.	DONNE 124:21
door-keeper: d. in the house of my God	BOOK 67:22
doormat: d. in a world of boots	RHYS 259:15
doors: d. of perception	BLAKE 61:11
D., where my heart was used	TENN 324:26
In Little Girls is slamming D.	BELL 33:10
many d. to let out life	FLET 142:4
ten thousand several d.	WEBS 344:18
their d. against a setting sun	SHAK 296:19
thousand d. open on to it	SEN 270:8
thousand d. to let out life	MASS 222:6
ye everlasting d.	BOOK 66:20
doorstep: Leave your worry on the d.	FIEL 139:15
dooryard: When lilacs last in the d.	WHIT 348:24
Dorcas: D.: this woman was	BIBLE 54:14
dorma: Nessun d.	ADAMI 1:6
dotage: Pedantry is the d. of knowledge	JACK 178:24
Dotheboys Hall: Squeer's Academy, D.	DICK 119:10
dotting: D. the shoreless watery wild	ARN 17:22
double: Double, d. toil and trouble	SHAK 287:15
so d. be his praise	SPEN 313:10
double-bed: d. after the hurly-burly	CAMP 88:15
doubles: d. your chances of a date	ALLEN 4:17
doublet: tailor make thy d.	SHAK 297:33
doublethink: D. means	ORW 242:10
doubt: do not make one d.	NEWM 238:16
d. is our passion	JAMES 179:23
freckles, and d.	PARK 245:5
Humility is only d.	BLAKE 60:12
Life is d.	UNAM 336:11
mind is clouded with a d.	TENN 324:22
more faith in honest d.	TENN 325:19
night of d. and sorrow	BAR 29:2
No possible d. whatever	GILB 151:5
Oh! let us never, never d.	BELL 33:21
when in d., strike it out	TWAIN 336:6
When in d., win the trick	HOYLE 175:12
wherefore didst thou d.	BIBLE 50:9
You tell me, d. is Devil-born	TENN 325:18
doubter: I am the d. and the doubt	EMER 136:11
doubtless: d. God never did	BUTL 84:22
doubts: D. 'mongst Divines	SPEN 313:16
he shall end in d.	BACON 23:20
His d. are better than	HARD 161:17
To saucy d. and fears	SHAK 287:9
Douglas: Like D. conquer	HOME 170:19
Dove: all the eagle in thee, all the d.	CRAS 111:8
and the sweet d. died	KEATS 191:3
Beside the springs of D.	WORD 356:22
hawk at eagles with a d.	HERB 167:6
that I had wings like a d.	BOOK 67:11
Dover: farthing candle at D.	JOHN 184:15
white cliffs of D.	BURT 83:3
doves: harmless as d.	BIBLE 49:29
dowagers: d. for deans	TENN 327:16
down: D. among the dead men	DYER 129:18
D. and away below	ARN 16:16
D. by the salley gardens	YEATS 359:1

down (cont.):

d. express in the small	WOD 352:18
D. in the forest something	SIMP 307:10
d. needs fear no fall	BUNY 79:7
d. the nights and down	THOM 331:8
D. these mean streets	CHAN 94:9
D. to Gehenna or up to	KIPL 196:20
go d. to the sea again	MAS 221:21
meet 'em on your way d.	MIZN 232:11
quite, quite, d.	SHAK 276:2
thou knowest my d.-sitting	BOOK 69:5
valley, come thou d.	TENN 328:7
downhearted: Are we d.?	KNIG 198:13
Are we d.?	ANON 6:4
We are not d.	CHAM 93:24
downs: All in the D. the fleet	GAY 149:17
downwards: could look no way but d.	BUNY 79:6
dozens: Mother to d.	HERB 166:13
Whom he reckons up by d.	GILB 152:17
dragon: angels fought against the d.	BIBLE 57:31
d.-green, the luminous, the dark	FLEC 141:15
dragons: be an habitation of d.	BIBLE 46:3
Bores have succeeded to d.	DISR 122:11
D. in their pleasant palaces	BIBLE 45:21
I am a brother to d.	BIBLE 43:3
Never laugh at live d.	TOLK 333:9
drain: d. pure gold flows forth	TOCQ 333:5
drains: Deity and the D.	STR 318:13
Democracy and proper d.	BETJ 37:4
some dull opiate to the d.	KEATS 191:28
Drake: D. he's in his hammock	NEWB 238:11
drama: close the d. with the day	BERK 35:19
d.'s laws the drama's patrons	JOHN 183:10
general d. of pain	HARDY 161:24
dramatist: d. only wants more liberties	JAMES 179:15
Drang: Sturm und D.	KAUF 190:6
draughts: peculiarly susceptible to d.	WILDE 349:21
draw: began to d. to our end	BIBLE 47:30
d. but twenty miles a day	MARL 219:14
D. not up seas to drown	DONNE 124:16
d. you to her *with a single* hair	DRYD 128:24
drawers: and d. of water	BIBLE 40:28
drawing: D. is the true test of art	INGR 178:17
Mrs Gaskell! no d. back	BRON 72:19
drawing-room: feelings of women in a d.	WOOLF 354:3
drawn: D. with a team of little atomies	SHAK 294:24
dread: d. of beatings	BETJ 37:14
Nor d. nor hope attend	YEATS 358:21
dreadful: acting of a d. thing	SHAK 281:3
City of D. Night	THOM 332:1
deed of D. note	SHAK 287:5
dreading: D. and hoping all	YEATS 358:21
Dreadnoughts: Duke costs as much as two D.	LLOY 208:9
dream: And slowly read and d.	YEATS 360:9
Because thou must not d.	ARN 16:15
behold it was a d.	BUNY 79:15
d. but of a shadow	CHAP 94:15
d. doth flatter	SHAK 299:28
D. of Fair Women	TENN 323:20
d. of money-bags to-night	SHAK 289:9
d. of reason produces monsters	GOYA 156:1
D. the impossible dream	DAR 114:2
d. within a dream	POE 250:5
d. you are crossing the Channel	GILB 151:16
For each age is a d.	O'SH 243:2
freshness of a d.	WORD 355:17
from a deep d. of peace	HUNT 176:12
glory and the d.	WORD 355:19
I d. my dreams away	FLAN 141:2
I have a d.	KING 195:9
In a d. you are never eighty	SEXT 270:15
love's young d.	MOORE 234:15
perchance to d.	SHAK 275:25
phantasma, or a hideous d.	SHAK 281:3

dream (*cont.*):

quiet sleep and a sweet d.	MAS 222:2
salesman is got to d.	MILL 225:4
short as any d.	SHAK 290:14
So runs my d.	TENN 325:9
speaking silence of a d.	ROSS 263:1
traveller's d. under the hill	BLAKE 60:15
True to the d. I am dreaming	COW 109:7
vision, or a waking d.	KEATS 192:7
Where we used to sit and d.	ARMS 15:24

dreamed: d. that Greece

d. that Greece	BYRON 86:14
d. that I dwelt in marble	BUNN 78:13
night I've d. of cheese	STEV 317:4

dreamer: Beautiful d., wake unto me

Beautiful d., wake unto me	FOST 144:9
Behold, this d. cometh	BIBLE 39:25
D. of dreams, born out of	MORR 235:15
or a d. of dreams	BIBLE 40:22
poet and the d.	KEATS 190:25

dreamers: We are the d. of dreams

We are the d. of dreams	O'SH 243:1

dreamin': D. of thee!

D. of thee!	WALL 341:7
little d., a little dyin'	PHIL 248:17

dreaming: City with her d. spires

City with her d. spires	ARN 17:17
d. on the verge of strife	CORN 108:7
I'm d. of a white Christmas	BERL 36:3
man d. I was a butterfly	CHUA 98:19

dreams: armoured cars of d.

armoured cars of d.	BISH 59:16
As d. are made on	SHAK 296:16
awoke from uneasy d.	KAFKA 189:16
because you tread on my d.	YEATS 359:7
beyond the d. of avarice	JOHN 185:29
beyond the d. of avarice	MOORE 234:5
books are either d. or swords	LOW 211:3
D. are the royal road	FREUD 146:1
d. happy as her day	BROO 73:10
d. out of the ivory gate	BROW 74:23
Fanatics have their d.	KEATS 190:24
forgotten scream for help in d.	CAN 89:9
If there were d. to sell	BEDD 31:19
Inaudible as d.	COL 103:19
In d. begins responsibility	YEATS 360:11
Into the land of my d.	KING 195:12
Made holy by their d.	GIBS 150:22
not that I have bad d.	SHAK 275:15
old men shall dream d.	BIBLE 47:20
quick D., the passion-wingèd	SHEL 303:5
we who lived by honest d.	DAY-L 115:6

dreamt: d. I went to Manderley

d. I went to Manderley	DU M 129:5
d. of in your philosophy	SHAK 275:3

dreary: d. length before the Court

d. length before the Court	DICK 118:1
She only said, 'My life is d.	TENN 326:22

dress: And Peace, the human d.

And Peace, the human d.	BLAKE 61:21
d. by yellow candle-light	STEV 317:12
Expression is the d. of thought	POPE 252:2
Full evening d. is a must	GREN 158:15
Style is the d. of thought	WESL 346:18
sweet disorder in the d.	HERR 167:15
through all this fleshly d.	VAUG 337:9
You will put on a d. of guilt	MCG 214:20

dressed: D. in style, brand new tile

D. in style, brand new tile	COLL 105:6
d. up and have no place	WHIT 348:8
d. up and no place to go	BURT 83:2

dressing: best is d. old words new

best is d. old words new	SHAK 299:25

drew: d. them. . .with bands of love

d. them. . .with bands of love	BIBLE 47:18

Dr Fell: I do not love thee, D.

I do not love thee, D.	BROWN 73:18

drift: adamant for d.

adamant for d.	CHUR 99:9

drifts: Strewn with its dank yellow d.

Strewn with its dank yellow d.	ARN 17:3

drink: d., and be merry

d., and be merry	BIBLE 52:18
D. and the devil had done	STEV 317:2
d., and to be merry	BIBLE 44:18
D. deep, or taste not	POPE 251:28
D., sir, is a great provoker	SHAK 286:21
D. to me only with thine eyes	JONS 187:23
eat and d.; for tomorrow	BIBLE 45:24
eat with you, d. with you	SHAK 288:31
Give strong d. unto him	BIBLE 44:5

drink (*cont.*):

I will d. life to the lees	TENN 328:20
Man wants but little d. below	HOLM 170:17
Nor any drop to d.	COL 104:7
strong d. is raging	BIBLE 43:31
that he has taken to d.	TARK 322:14
We'll teach you to d. deep	SHAK 274:15

drinking: curse of the d. classes

curse of the d. classes	WILDE 350:20
d. at somebody else's expense	LEIGH 204:19
d. largely sobers us again	POPE 251:28
D. when we are not thirsty	BEAU 30:16
very merry, dancing, d.	DRYD 128:15

dripping: electricity was d.

electricity was d.	THUR 332:14

drive: but can't d. the car

but can't d. the car	TYNAN 336:8

driveth: he d. furiously

he d. furiously	BIBLE 42:13

driving: d. briskly in a post-chaise

d. briskly in a post-chaise	JOHN 185:13
like the driving of Jehu	BIBLE 42:13

dromedary: muse on d. trots

muse on d. trots	COL 104:2

droning: beetle wheels his d.

beetle wheels his d.	GRAY 157:4

droop: D. in a hundred A.B.C.'s

D. in a hundred A.B.C.'s	ELIOT 132:22

droopingly: Lady Jane, a little d.

Lady Jane, a little d.	LAWR 202:10

droops: D. on the little hands

D. on the little hands	MILNE 226:1

drop: Drop, d., slow tears

Drop, d., slow tears	FLET 142:8
Nor any drop to drink	COL 104:7
One d. would save my soul	MARL 218:13
Turn on, tune in and d. out	LEARY 203:19

dropping: clergy is a d.-down-deadness

clergy is a d.-down-deadness	SMITH 309:24
d. down with costly bales	TENN 326:10
d. in a very rainy day	BIBLE 44:1
D. the pilot	TENN 323:9

drops: D. earliest to the ground

D. earliest to the ground	SHAK 289:24
d. on gate-bars hang	HARDY 162:17
ruddy d. that visit my sad heart	SHAK 281:7

drought: d. is destroying his roots

d. is destroying his roots	HERB 166:11
d. of March hath perced	CHAU 95:10

drown: I'll d. my book

I'll d. my book	SHAK 296:13

drownded: we do only be d. now and then

we do only be d. now and then	SYNGE 321:21

drowned: And: in yonder living blue

And: in yonder living blue	TENN 325:30
BETTER D. THAN DUFFERS	RANS 258:7
d. in a barrel of Malmesey	FABY 138:8
d. in the depth of the sea	BIBLE 50:16
d. with us in endless night	HERR 167:14

drowning: By d. their speaking

By d. their speaking	BROW 76:26
hath no d. mark upon him	SHAK 295:31
not waving but d.	SMITH 309:19

drowns: d. things weighty and solid

d. things weighty and solid	BACON 25:7

drowsy: Dapples the d. east

Dapples the d. east	SHAK 291:27
d. numbness pains	KEATS 191:28
Vexing the dull ear of a d.	SHAK 282:9

drudge: dictionaries, a harmless d.

dictionaries, a harmless d.	JOHN 182:8

drudgery: Makes d. divine

Makes d. divine	HERB 166:26
vocation is the love of the d.	SMITH 309:11

drug: literature is a d.

literature is a d.	BORR 69:26
or you can d., with words	LOW 211:3
Poetry's a mere d., Sir	FARQ 138:19

drugs: Sex and d. and rock and roll

Sex and d. and rock and roll	DURY 129:14

drum: brave music of a *distant* d.

brave music of a *distant* d.	FITZ 140:7
d. them up the Channel	NEWB 238:10
Dumb as a d. with a hole	DICK 119:31
Not a d. was heard	WOLFE 352:25
pulse, like a soft d.	KING 195:6
still the most effective d.	GIR 153:5
Take my d. to England	NEWB 238:10

drummer: hears a different d.

hears a different d.	THOR 332:12

drums: trumpets, beat the d.

trumpets, beat the d.	MOR 235:5
when the d. begin to roll	KIPL 197:11

drunk: being reasonable, must get d.

being reasonable, must get d.	BYRON 86:7
d. deep of the Pierian spring	DRAY 126:20
d. hath made me bold	SHAK 286:12
I have d., and seen the spider	SHAK 298:23
I'm not so think as you d. I am	SQUI 314:3
Philip d. to Philip sober	ANON 6:3
Was the hope d. wherein	SHAK 286:3
Wordsworth d. and Porson	HOUS 175:6

drunken: d. of things Lethean — SWIN 321:13
Shall be brought d. forth — SHAK 272:5
stagger like a d. man — BOOK 68:13
drunkenness: d. of things being various — MACN 216:8
dry: But oh! I am so d. — FARM 138:13
d. brain in a dry season — ELIOT 133:16
old man in a d. month — ELIOT 133:14
O ye d. bones, hear — BIBLE 47:10
they whose hearts are d. — WORD 354:19
Dryden: Ev'n copious D. — POPE 252:30
poetry of D., Pope — ARN 18:5
ducats: O my d.! O my daughter — SHAK 289:12
duchess: chambermaid as of a D. — JOHN 185:21
duck: Honey, I just forgot to d. — DEMP 116:25
ducks: go about the country stealing d. — ARAB 14:20
I turn to d. — HARV 163:15
duffers: BETTER DROWNED THAN D. — RANS 258:7
dugs: old man with wrinkled d. — ELIOT 134:28
duke: And everybody praised the D. — SOUT 311:20
d. costs as much to keep as — LLOY 208:9
D. of Plaza Toro — GILB 151:4
d.'s revenues on her back — SHAK 280:7
knows enough who knows a d. — COWP 110:14
dukes: drawing room full of d. — AUDEN 21:18
dulce: D. est desipere in loco — HOR 174:1
D. et decorum est pro patria — HOR 173:26
dull: Anger makes d. men witty — BACON 25:29
d. in Fleet Street — LAMB 200:7
d. opiate to the drains — KEATS 191:28
d. product of a scoffer's pen — WORD 354:20
D. would he be of soul — WORD 354:15
He was d. in a new way — JOHN 184:28
How d. it is to pause — TENN 328:21
make dictionaries is d. work — JOHN 182:6
so d. but she can learn — SHAK 289:22
so smoothly d. — POPE 250:15
[Thomas Sheridan] is d. — JOHN 184:14
venerably d. — CHUR 98:29
wasn't as d. as ditch water — DICK 119:24
duller: d. spectacle this earth — DE Q 117:4
dullness: cause of d. in others — FOOTE 143:1
Gentle D. ever loves a joke — POPE 250:13
dumb: Children are d. to say — GRAV 156:13
D. as a drum with a hole — DICK 119:31
D., inscrutable and grand — ARN 16:23
so d. he can't fart and chew — JOHN 181:22
dumb-show: fatal d. of our misery — DRAY 126:18
dummy: proxy for risk and d. for sex — MACH 215:4
dun: then her breasts are d. — SHAK 300:11
Duncan: fatal entrance of D. — SHAK 285:16
dunce: d. with wits — POPE 250:17
thou art but a d. — BLAKE 60:15
dunces: d. are all in confederacy — SWIFT 320:11
Dundee: bonnets of Bonny D. — SCOTT 268:7
Dunfermline: king sits in D. town — BALL 28:4
dung: d. and of corrupcioun — CHAU 95:30
dungeon: Himself is his own d. — MILT 226:12
dungeons: Brightest in d., Liberty — BYRON 87:7
dungfork: man with a d. in his hand — HOPK 172:22
dunghill: cock crowing on its own d. — ALD 3:15
dunnest: d. smoke of hell — SHAK 285:19
Dunsinane: Till Birnam wood remove to D. — SHAK 287:32
dupes: If hopes were d. — CLOU 102:23
dusk: d. a drawing-down of blinds — OWEN 243:23
In the d. with a light behind her — GILB 152:31
dusky: rear my d. race — TENN 326:15
straight path along the d. air — COL 104:21
Trusty, d., vivid, true — STEV 317:20
dust: ashes to ashes, d. to dust — BOOK 66:8
blossom in their d. — SHIR 306:11
chimney-sweepers, come to d. — SHAK 273:27
D. hath closed Helen's eye — NASHE 237:19
D. into dust, and under dust — FITZ 140:9

dust (cont.):
d. of creeds outworn — SHEL 304:19
d. of exploded beliefs — MADAN 216:13
d. return to the earth — BIBLE 44:26
D. thou art, to dust returnest — LONG 209:22
D. was Gentlemen and Ladies — DICK 120:17
English tear o'er English d. — MAC 214:1
fear in a handful of d. — ELIOT 134:20
first raised a d. — BERK 35:18
For d. thou art, and unto d. — BIBLE 39:3
Guilty of d. and sin — HERB 167:2
Hope raises no d. — ELUA 136:8
Less than the d., beneath — HOPE 171:23
Marry my body to that d. — KING 195:5
not without d. and heat — MILT 230:31
richer d. concealed — BROO 73:10
shake off the d. of your feet — BIBLE 49:28
this d. falls to the urn — VAUG 337:10
this quintessence of d. — SHAK 275:16
To dig the d. enclosed here — SHAK 300:20
To sweep the d. behind — SHAK 291:10
voice provoke the silent d. — GRAY 157:8
what a d. do I raise — BACON 25:20
with age and d. — RAL 258:1
dustbin: into the d. of history — TROT 335:1
dust-heap: great d. called 'history' — BIRR 59:15
dusty: d. answer gets the soul — MER 223:24
Dutch: commerce the fault of the D. — CANN 89:10
Dutchmen: water-land of D. and of ditches — BYRON 86:22
duties: occasions teach new d. — LOW 211:9
Property has its d. — DRUM 126:25
duty: bounden d. and service — BOOK 65:17
declares that it is his d. — SHAW 300:25
Do your d., and leave — CORN 108:2
d. of a State is to see — RUSK 264:19
d. to have loved the highest — TENN 324:6
every man will do his d. — NELS 238:3
little d. and less love — SHAK 280:5
Love is then our d. — GAY 149:6
Nor law, nor d. bade me fight — YEATS 359:10
perceive here a divided d. — SHAK 291:36
picket's off d. forever — BEERS 32:14
subject's d. is the king — SHAK 279:14
Thank God, I have done my d. — NELS 238:5
Thy daily stage of d. run — KEN 193:20
whole d. of man — BIBLE 44:28
woke, and found that life was d. — HOOP 171:16
dwarfish: an Epigram? a d. whole — COL 103:17
dwarfs: d. on the shoulders of giants — BERN 36:9
dwell: d. in a corner of the housetop — BIBLE 43:32
d. in the house of the Lord — BOOK 66:18
shall d. in thy tabernacle — BOOK 66:13
they that d. in the land — BIBLE 45:15
Wherein at ease for aye to d. — TENN 327:14
dwellings: how amiable are thy d. — BOOK 67:19
dwells: She d. with Beauty — KEATS 191:27
dwelt: and d. among us — BIBLE 53:11
d. among the untrodden ways — WORD 356:22
d. in the land of Nod — BIBLE 39:6
dwindle: d. into a wife — CONG 106:21
Shall he d., peak, and pine — SHAK 285:4
dyer: like the d.'s hand — SHAK 300:7
dyin': little dreamin', a little d. — PHIL 248:17
dying: And, doubly d., shall go down — SCOTT 268:13
attend a d. animal — YEATS 358:21
d., has made us rarer gifts — BROO 72:20
D. in the last dyke — BURKE 80:27
D. is an art — PLATH 249:15
d. is more the survivors' affair — MANN 217:14
D. is nothing — ANOU 14:9
d. of a hundred good symptoms — POPE 263:14
d. remembers his sweet Argos — VIRG 339:21
echoes, d., dying — TENN 327:20
groans of love to those of the d. — LOWRY 211:22

dying (*cont.*):

I am d., Egypt, dying	SHAK 271:24
If this is d., I don't think much	STR 318:16
it had a d. fall	SHAK 297:14
living indisposeth us for d.	BROW 74:5
mouth of the d. day	AUDEN 20:21
rage against the d. of the light	THOM 330:7
sunsets exquisitely d.	HUXL 177:13
there's no more d. then	SHAK 300:15
Those d. generations	YEATS 359:20
those poor devils are d.	PHIL 248:13
Turkey is a d. man	NICH 239:10
unconscionable time d.	CHAR 95:6
dyke: last d. of prevarication	BURKE 80:27

E

each: e. according to his needs | MARX 221:9

eagle: By all the e. in thee	CRAS 111:8
e. among blinking owls	SHEL 303:23
E. has landed	ALDR 3:18
e. know what is in the pit	BLAKE 60:10
Fate is not an e.	BOWEN 70:18
In and out the E.	MAND 217:8
stout Cortez when with e.	KEATS 192:1
way of an e. in the air	BIBLE 44:4
eagles: hawk at e. with a dove	HERB 167:6
mount up with wings as e.	BIBLE 46:13
there will the e. be gathered	BIBLE 50:36
were swifter than e.	BIBLE 41:22
ear: beat upon my whorlèd e.	HOPK 172:5
cleave the general e.	SHAK 275:23
close at the e. of Eve	MILT 229:13
dull cold e. of death	GRAY 157:8
dull e. of a drowsy man	SHAK 282:9
fearful hollow of thine e.	SHAK 295:17
In Reason's e. they all	ADD 2:26
jewel in an Ethiop's e.	SHAK 294:26
Oon e. it herde	CHAU 96:19
piercèd through the e.	SHAK 291:38
Unpleasing to a married e.	SHAK 284:22
early: E. one morning	ANON 6:27
E. to rise and early to bed	THUR 332:15
Vote e. and vote often	ANON 11:9
you've got to get up e.	LOW 211:4
earn: And there's little to e.	KING 195:16
earnest: e. of the things that they shall do	TENN 326:9
I am in e.—I will not equivocate	GARR 148:12
Life is real! Life is e.	LONG 209:22
earnings: division of unequal e.	ELL 136:3
ears: adder that stoppeth her e.	BOOK 67:13
Creep in our e.	SHAK 290:1
e. are listening to you	ANON 12:15
E. like bombs and teeth like	CAUS 93:9
He that hath e. to hear	BIBLE 51:20
lend me your e.	SHAK 281:18
They have e., and hear not	BOOK 68:18
earth: did thee feel the e. move	HEM 165:12
dust return to the e.	BIBLE 44:26
E. all Danaë to the stars	TENN 328:4
e. a richer dust concealed	BROO 73:10
e. does not argue	WHIT 348:23
E. felt the wound	MILT 229:26
E. has not anything to show	WORD 354:15
e. his sober inn	CAMP 89:3
e. in fast thick pants	COL 103:23
e. is all the home I have	AYT 23:18
e. is full of his glory	BIBLE 45:10
e. is the Lord's	BIBLE 55:9
e. is the Lord's	BOOK 66:19
e. must borrow its mirth	WILC 349:14
E., receive an honoured guest	AUDEN 20:24
e.'s diurnal course	WORD 356:25
e. shall be filled	AING 3:9

earth (*cont.*):

e. shall be full	BIBLE 45:20
E.'s shadows fly	SHEL 303:13
E.'s the right place for love	FROST 146:8
E. stood hard as iron	ROSS 263:2
e. to earth, ashes to ashes	BOOK 66:8
e. was without form	BIBLE 38:13
for e. too dear	SHAK 294:26
general balm th'hydroptic e.	DONNE 124:8
girdle round about the e.	SHAK 290:25
going the way of all the e.	BIBLE 40:29
going to and fro in the e.	BIBLE 42:21
Her all on e., and more	BYRON 85:18
in the deep-delvèd e.	KEATS 191:29
It fell to e., I knew not where	LONG 209:10
I will move the e.	ARCH 15:3
lards the lean e. as he walks	SHAK 277:29
let the whole e. stand	BOOK 68:2
Lie heavy on him, E.	EVANS 137:23
must have a touch of e.	TENN 324:8
new heaven and a new e.	BIBLE 58:4
new heaven, new e.	SHAK 271:4
new heavens and a new e.	BIBLE 46:26
On the cool flowery lap of e.	ARN 16:19
round e.'s human shores	KEATS 190:10
round e.'s imagined corners	DONNE 123:7
round e.'s shore	ARN 16:11
sleepers in that quiet e.	BRON 72:18
Than anywhere else on e.	GURN 159:10
There were giants in the e.	BIBLE 39:7
they shall inherit the e.	BIBLE 48:19
This e. of majesty	SHAK 293:16
this e., this realm	SHAK 293:16
This litel spot of e.	CHAU 96:21
thou bleeding piece of e.	SHAK 281:13
Were it e. in an earthy bed	TENN 327:2
What if e. be but the shadow	MILT 229:18
When I am laid in e.	TATE 322:15
Which men call e.	MILT 226:5
whole e. as their memorial	PER 248:2
Ye are the salt of the e.	BIBLE 48:20
Yours is the E.	KIPL 197:7
earthquake: e. is not satisfied	WORD 356:13
Lord was not in the e.	BIBLE 42:3
Small e. in Chile	COCK 103:1
that's an e.	MILL 225:4
That world-e., Waterloo	TENN 327:12
earthy: man is of the earth, e.	BIBLE 55:20
ease: But for another gives its e.	BLAKE 62:1
doctrine of ignoble e.	ROOS 262:15
E. after war, death after	SPEN 313:9
Joys in another's loss of e.	BLAKE 62:2
labour with an age of e.	GOLD 154:19
Some come to take their e.	SHAK 280:23
Studious of elegance and e.	GAY 149:12
Studious of laborious e.	COWP 110:10
take thine e., eat	BIBLE 52:18
Wherein at e. for aye to dwell	TENN 327:14
easeful: half in love with e. Death	KEATS 192:3
easer: thou e. of all woes	FLET 142:5
easier: e. to make war	CLEM 102:2
easing: call it e. the Spring	REED 258:16
east: Boston man is the e. wind	APPL 14:14
cometh neither from the e.	BOOK 67:18
Dapples the drowsy e.	SHAK 291:27
easier to conquer it [the E.]	WALP 341:21
E. is a career	DISR 122:8
E. is East, and West is West	KIPL 196:4
fiery portal of the e.	SHAK 293:29
hold the gorgeous E. in fee	WORD 356:2
It is the e., and Juliet	SHAK 294:29
look the E. End in the face	ELIZ 135:18
on the e. of Eden	BIBLE 39:6
somewheres e. of Suez	KIPL 196:23
tried to hustle the E.	KIPL 196:24

elective: E. affinities	GOET 154:2
Electra: Mourning becomes E.	O'NEI 241:12
electric: E. Kool-Aid Acid test	WOLFE 353:8
I sing the body e.	WHIT 348:10
tried to mend the E. Light	BELL 33:22
electrical: his e. skin and glaring eyes	SMART 308:8
electricity: e. was dripping invisibly	THUR 332:14
electrification: Soviet power plus the e.	LENIN 205:1
elegance: e. of Circe's hair	POUND 254:15
Studious of e. and ease	GAY 149:12
elegant: e. simplicity of the three per cents	STOW 318:9
e. sufficiency	THOM 331:23
It's so e., so intelligent	ELIOT 134:24
Most intelligent, very e.	RUBY 77:31
elegy: whole of Gray's E.	WOLFE 353:3
eleison: Kyrie e.	MISS 231:12
elementary: E., my dear Watson	DOYLE 125:19
elements: Become our e.	MILT 228:26
e. so mixed in him	SHAK 282:2
world made cunningly of e.	DONNE 123:12
elephant: An E.'s Child	KIPL 197:21
at the E., is best to lodge	SHAK 298:8
corn is as high as an e.'s eye	HAMM 161:2
great masterpiece, an e.	DONNE 123:20
herd of e. pacing along	DIN 121:1
elephants: Place e. for want of towns	SWIFT 320:21
elf: A little child, a limber e.	COL 103:13
too often a negligent e.	BARH 28:22
Elfland: horns of E. faintly blowing	TENN 327:21
Eli: E., lama sabachthani	BIBLE 51:16
Elijah: E. passed by him	BIBLE 42:4
eliminated: e. the impossible	DOYLE 126:1
Eliot: And Ezra Pound and T. S. E.	DYLAN 129:20
Elizabeth: Queen E. of most happy	BIBLE 38:12
Ellen: Was to wed the fair E.	SCOTT 268:20
elms: Behind the e. last night	PRIOR 255:12
Beneath those rugged e.	GRAY 157:6
doves in immemorial e.	TENN 328:8
Of withered leaves, and the e.	ARN 17:3
eloquence: E. the soul, song charms the sense	
	MILT 228:31
mother of arts and e.	MILT 230:6
elsewhere: Altogether e.	AUDEN 20:19
elude: Court him, e. him	BLUN 62:14
Elysian: dead, but in the E. fields	DISR 122:18
Elysium: Keep alive our lost E.	BETJ 37:7
What Elysium have ye known	KEATS 191:16
embalmer: triumph of the e.'s art	VIDAL 338:12
embarrassment: e. of riches	ALL 4:11
land of e. and breakfast	BARN 29:4
embers: glowing e. through the room	MILT 226:25
embossed: Insculped and e.	THOM 331:19
embrace: But none, I think, do there e.	MARV 220:25
But oh as to e. me she inclined	MILT 230:5
e. your Lordship's principles	WILK 350:26
embraced: that with the se e. is	CHAU 96:21
emendation: e. wrong	JOHN 182:26
emerald: As green as e.	COL 104:4
Emerald Isle: men of the E.	DREN 126:23
emeralds: road to the City of E.	BAUM 30:10
emeritus: called a professor e.	LEAC 203:3
emotion: e. recollected in tranquillity	WORD 357:12
morality touched by e.	ARN 18:8
thought charged with e.	GIDE 151:1
tranquillity remembered in e.	PARK 245:11
Wit is the epitaph of e.	NIET 239:23
emotions: metaphysical brothel for e.	KOES 199:1
emparadised: E. in one another's arms	MILT 229:10
emperice: e. and flour of floures	CHAU 96:10
emperor: dey makes you E.	O'NEI 241:9
E. has nothing on at all	AND 5:11
E. is everything	METT 224:1
e. of ice-cream	STEV 316:6
empire: Britain has lost an e.	ACH 1:3

empire (cont.):	
e. is no more than power	DRYD 127:10
E. strikes back	LUCAS 211:27
great e. and little minds	BURKE 80:5
How's the E.	GEOR 150:3
loungers and idlers of the E.	DOYLE 126:4
nor Roman, nor an e.	VOLT 340:19
way she disposed of an e.	HARL 163:1
Westward the course of e.	BERK 35:19
wilderness into a glorious e.	BURKE 80:6
empires: day of E. has come	CHAM 93:23
Hatching vain e.	MILT 228:28
Vaster than e., and more slow	MARV 220:23
employee: e. tends to rise	PETER 248:8
employer: harder upon the e.	SPOO 313:25
employment: give e. to the artisan	BELL 33:22
empress: e. and flour	CHAU 96:10
emprison: E. her soft hand	KEATS 191:26
empty: Bring on the e. horses	CURT 113:10
he findeth it e.	BIBLE 50:3
idle singer of an e. day	MORR 235:14
rich he hath sent e. away	BIBLE 51:29
emulation: pale and bloodless e.	SHAK 296:31
enamoured: e. on peace	CLAR 101:11
enchanted: as holy and e.	COL 103:23
Of dire chimeras and e. isles	MILT 226:16
enchanter: like ghosts from an e.	SHEL 304:6
enchantment: distance lends e.	CAMP 88:19
enchantments: last e. of the Middle Age	ARN 18:2
last e. of the Middle Age	BEER 32:10
encircling: amid the e. gloom	NEWM 238:21
enclosing: a wilderness of idea	BUTL 84:16
encounters: Close e.	SPIE 313:21
encourage: right to e., the right	BAG 26:14
to e. the others	VOLT 340:12
end: Ages of hopeless e.	MILT 228:25
ane e. of ane old song	OGIL 241:3
appointment at the e. of the world	DIN 121:1
began to draw to our e.	BIBLE 47:30
beginning of the e.	TALL 322:13
be the be-all and the e.-all	SHAK 285:22
came to an e. all wars	LLOY 208:10
continuing unto the e.	DRAKE 126:10
e. crowns all	SHAK 297:11
e. for which we live	PEPYS 247:21
e. is where we start from	ELIOT 133:11
e. justifies the means	BUS 83:16
e. of a perfect day	BOND 63:9
e. of a thousand years of history	GAIT 147:12
e. of the beginning	CHUR 99:18
e. of the way inescapable	PAST 246:10
e. that crowns us	HERR 167:16
far e. of the enormous room	AUDEN 20:13
God be at my e.	ANON 7:11
grant an e. to these too	VIRG 339:1
In my beginning is my e.	ELIOT 133:2
In my e. is my beginning	MARY 221:16
let me know mine e.	BOOK 67:1
long weary day have e.	SPEN 313:6
look to the e.	ANON 13:20
loud noise at one e.	KNOX 198:20
on to the e. of the road	LAUD 202:5
only e. of age	LARK 201:14
Our e. is Life. Put out to sea	MACN 216:11
right true e. of love	DONNE 123:4
therefore she had a good e.	MAL 217:3
there's an e. of May	HOUS 174:9
there's an e. on't	JOHN 184:20
till you come to the e.	CARR 91:13
to pause, to make an e.	TENN 328:21
true beginning of our e.	SHAK 291:6
Waiting for the e.	EMPS 137:4
war that will e. war	WELLS 345:24
where's it all going to e.	STOP 318:4
world may e. tonight	BROW 76:11

end (*cont.*):
world will e. in fire — FROST 146:12
endearing: e. young charms — MOORE 234:11
endears: That all the more e. — TENN 327:17
endeavours: all my e. are unlucky explorers — DOUG 125:8
ended: revels now are e. — SHAK 296:10
ending: dirge of her certain e. — SHAK 299:9
Never e., still beginning — DRYD 127:21
quickest way of e. a war — ORW 242:12
ends: best e. by the best means — HUTC 177:1
divinity that shapes our e. — SHAK 277:12
e. and scarce means — ROBB 260:15
e. by our beginnings know — DENH 116:26
e. I think criminal — KEYN 194:13
More are men's e. marked — SHAK 293:15
Out to the undiscovered e. — BELL 34:3
that e. all other deeds — SHAK 272:2
endurance: patient e. is godlike — LONG 209:16
endure: I can e. my own despair — WALSH 342:8
instruct them or e. them — AUR 22:12
nature itselfe cant e. — FLEM 141:22
Youth's a stuff will not e. — SHAK 297:23
endured: Intolerable, not to be e. — SHAK 295:29
much is to be e., and little — JOHN 183:4
endureth: e. all things — BIBLE 55:12
enemies: all assaults of our e. — BOOK 64:5
alone against smiling e. — BOWEN 71:1
by the number of his e. — FLAU 141:8
choice of his e. — WILDE 350:5
e. of Freedom do not argue — INGE 178:10
left me naked to mine e. — SHAK 280:21
Love your e. — BIBLE 52:6
no time for making new e. — VOLT 341:3
Open Society and its E. — POPP 253:15
People with their e. dead — MONT 233:6
priests have been e. of liberty — HUME 176:8
they will be e. to laws — BURKE 81:9
thine e. thy footstool — BOOK 68:14
we have no perpetual e. — PALM 244:18
enemy: bellyful of the classics is an e. — MILL 225:7
better class of e. — MILL 225:11
effect upon the e. — WELL 345:7
e. faints not, nor faileth — CLOU 102:22
e. of good art — CONN 106:25
e. of thought — CONR 107:8
Hast thou found me, O mine e. — BIBLE 42:5
he is afraid of his e. — PLUT 250:2
I am the e. you killed — OWEN 244:3
If thine e. be hungry — BIBLE 43:36
last e. that shall be destroyed — BIBLE 55:18
Mine e.'s dog — SHAK 283:28
My near'st and dearest e. — SHAK 278:7
my vision's greatest e. — BLAKE 60:11
no e. but time — YEATS 359:8
No e. but winter — SHAK 272:19
Our friends, the e. — BÉR 35:11
Shaw hasn't an e. in the world — WILDE 350:21
Sir, No Man's E. — AUDEN 21:14
That sweet e., France — SIDN 306:21
then there's life, its e. — ANOU 14:7
your e. and your friend — TWAIN 335:25
energy: E. is Eternal Delight — BLAKE 60:24
enfants: Allons, e. de la patrie — ROUG 263:16
Les e. terribles — GAV 148:21
engine: e. that moves in determinate grooves — HARE 162:19
human e. waits — ELIOT 134:27
Raised by that curious e. — WEBS 344:15
Really Useful E. — AWDRY 23:13
two-handed e. at the door — MILT 227:16
unsavoury e. of pollution — SPAR 312:14
engineers: It is the age of the e. — HOGB 170:6
engineer: e. hoist with his own petar — SHAK 276:25
engines: e. play a little on our own — BURKE 80:9

England: apple falling towards E. — AUDEN 21:5
Be E. what she will — CHUR 98:21
best thing between France and E. — JERR 181:11
deep, deep sleep of E. — ORW 242:7
E. and America — SHAW 302:27
E.! awake! awake! awake — BLAKE 60:21
E. does not love coalitions — DISR 121:13
E. expects that every man — NELS 238:3
E. forget her precedence — MILT 231:5
E. has saved herself — PITT 249:8
E. hath need of thee — WORD 355:11
E., home and beauty — ARN 18:14
E. is a disguised republic — BAG 26:10
E. is a nation of shopkeepers — NAP 237:7
E. is a paradise for women — BURT 83:13
E. is finished and dead — MILL 224:24
E. is the paradise of women — FLOR 142:13
E. keep my bones — SHAK 282:13
E., my England — HENL 165:19
E.'s green and pleasant land — BLAKE 61:12
E.'s not a bad country — DRAB 126:9
E.'s on the anvil — KIPL 196:3
E.'s the one land, I know — BROO 73:6
E. to be the workshop — DISR 121:6
E. to itself do rest but true — SHAK 282:15
E. was too pure an Air — ANON 10:1
E. will have her neck wrung — CHUR 99:17
E., with all thy faults — COWP 110:8
faithless E. — BOSS 70:2
Gott strafe E.! — FUNKE 147:8
Harry! E. and Saint George — SHAK 279:6
Heart of E. well may call — DRAY 126:17
he bored for E. — MUGG 236:5
Here and here did E. help me — BROW 76:4
History is now and E. — ELIOT 133:12
in E. people have good table manners — MIKES 224:10
in E.'s song for ever — NEWB 238:12
Ireland gives E. her soldiers — MER 223:13
no amusements in E. — SMITH 310:12
Nor E.! did I know till then — WORD 355:3
Oh, to be in E. — BROW 76:1
old E.'s winding sheet — BLAKE 60:9
Our E. is a garden — KIPL 196:16
pastoral heart of E. — QUIL 257:8
road that leads him to E. — JOHN 184:9
Rule all E. under a hog — COLL 105:3
Slaves cannot breathe in E. — COWP 110:7
Speak for E. — AMERY 4:21
stately homes of E. — HEM 165:10
summer in E. — WALP 341:22
That is for ever E. — BROO 73:10
There'll always be an E. — CHAR 245:19
think of E. — HILL 168:17
think of the defence of E. — BALD 27:6
This E. never did — SHAK 282:15
this realm, this E. — SHAK 293:16
thoughts by E. given — BROO 73:10
Wake up, E. — GEOR 149:25
Walk upon E.'s mountains green — BLAKE 61:12
we are the people of E. — CHES 98:4
What do you think about E. — AUDEN 21:19
Who dies if E. live — KIPL 196:13
who only E. know — KIPL 196:15
You gentlemen of E. — PARK 245:17
Englanders: Little E. — ANON 8:21
English: baby doesn't understand E. — KNOX 198:19
breathing E. air — BROO 73:10
Breeds hard E. men — KING 195:15
can't think of the E. for a thing — CARR 91:19
Charm is the great E. blight — WAUGH 343:17
E. have hot-water bottles — MIKES 224:11
E. manners are far more frightening — JARR 180:12
E. plays are like puddings — VOLT 340:26
E. take their pleasures — SULLY 319:4

English (cont.):

E. talk is a quadrille	JAMES 179:16
E. that of the sea	RICH 260:6
E. tongue a gallimaufry	SPEN 313:20
E. unofficial rose	BROO 73:4
E. up with which I will not put	CHUR 100:5
E. want *inferiors*	TOCQ 333:4
game which the E. invented	MANC 217:7
Johnson's morality was as E.	HAWT 163:19
really nice E. people	SHAW 301:5
rolling E. drunkard	CHES 98:1
Roman-Saxon-Danish-Norman E.	DEFOE 115:24
shed one E. tear	MAC 214:1
stones kissed by the E. dead	OWEN 244:1
Student of our sweet E. tongue	FLEC 141:20
This is the E., not the Turkish	SHAK 278:29
white as an angel is the E. child	BLAKE 61:24
words in the E. language	JAMES 180:5

Englishman: Either for E. or Jew

	BLAKE 60:14
E. a combination of qualities	DICK 119:22
E. among the under-dogs	WAUGH 343:21
E., being flattered	CHAP 94:14
E., even if he is alone	MIKES 224:12
E. hate or despise him	SHAW 302:16
E. thinks he is moral	SHAW 301:21
find an E. in the wrong	SHAW 302:9
He remains an E.	GILB 152:21
last great E. is low	TENN 327:11
No E. is ever fairly beaten	SHAW 302:20
religious rights of an E.	JUN 188:25

Englishmen: E. never will be slaves

	SHAW 301:20
first to his E.	MILT 231:2
Mad dogs and E.	COW 109:4
When two E. meet	JOHN 182:11

Englishwoman: E. is so refined

	SMITH 309:21
enigma: e. of the fever chart	ELIOT 133:5
mystery inside an e.	CHUR 99:10
enjoy: I can e. her while she's kind	DRYD 128:23
to e. him forever	SHOR 306:13
enjoyed: all times I have e.	TENN 328:20
little to be e.	JOHN 183:4
warm and still to be e.	KEATS 191:21
enjoying: Think, oh think, it worth e.	DRYD 127:21
enjoyment: e. as the greatest orator	HUME 176:7
e. of riches consists	SMITH 308:22
enjoyments: Fire-side e.	COWP 110:12
if it were not for its e.	SURT 319:13
enlargement: e. of the language	JOHN 182:5
enmities: e. of twenty generations	MAC 213:14
enormity: womb and bed of e.	JONS 186:24
enough: e. in the world	BUCH 77:30
E. that he heard it once	BROW 75:8
enskyed: thing e. and sainted	SHAK 288:10
ensue: seek peace, and e. it	BOOK 66:25
entbehren: *E. sollst Du!*	GOET 154:4
enter: Abandon all hope, you who e.	DANTE 113:18
e. into the kingdom	BIBLE 50:15
e. into the kingdom	BIBLE 50:22
e. who does not know geometry	ANON 13:6
entered: iron e. into his soul	BOOK 68:9
enterprise: There's more e.	YEATS 358:17
voyages of the starship E.	RODD 261:12
enterprised: Not by any to be e.	BOOK 65:26
entertain: better to e. an idea	JARR 180:13
e. us with no worth	WALL 341:14
To e. divine Zenocrate	MARL 219:11
To e. this starry stranger	CRAS 111:10
entertained: e. angels unawares	BIBLE 56:29
entertainment: exotic and irrational e.	JOHN 182:22
mere gossiping e.	HUNT 176:18
entertains: e. the harmless day	WOTT 357:14
enthral: Except you e. me	DONNE 123:11
enthralled: unjust force, but not e.	MILT 226:18
enthusiasts: how to deal with e.	MAC 213:16
entire: E. and whole and perfect	SPR 313:26

entirely: e. beautiful	AUDEN 20:28
entrance: To e. the prophet's ear	MANT 217:17
entrances: their exits and their e.	SHAK 272:24
entropy: e. of human thought	ZAMY 360:25
envelope: semi-transparent e.	WOOLF 353:22
envious: e. fever	SHAK 296:31
envy: did in e. of great Caesar	SHAK 282:2
E. and calumny and hate	SHEL 303:11
e. of less happier lands	SHAK 293:16
from e., hatred, and malice	BOOK 64:14
I e. not in any moods	TENN 325:3
prisoners of e.	ILL 178:9
Toil, e., want	JOHN 183:12
épater: *Il faut é. le bourgeois*	BAUD 30:9
epic: thundrous e. lilted out	TENN 327:18
epicure: Serenely full, the e. would say	SMITH 310:7
epigram: purrs like an e.	MARQ 219:23
What is an E.?	COL 103:17
epigrams: despotism tempered by e.	CARL 90:14
epiphany: By an e. he meant	JOYCE 188:10
episode: e. in a general drama	HARDY 161:24
To the end of a brief e.	MERC 223:11
epitaph: Wit is the e. of an emotion	NIET 239:23
epitaphs: nice derangement of e.	SHER 305:29
worms, and e.	SHAK 293:26
epithet: Fair is too foul an e.	MARL 219:10
epitome: all mankind's e.	DRYD 127:12
eppur: *E. si muove*	GAL 147:16
equal: all men are created e.	JEFF 180:18
all men are created e.	LINC 207:8
e. division of unequal earnings	ELL 136:3
E., unclassed, tribeless	SHEL 304:22
faith shines e.	BRON 72:16
free and e. in dignity	ANON 5:20
some animals are more e.	ORW 241:23
equality: e. in the servants' hall	BARR 29:10
Freedom! E.! Brotherhood	ANON 12:11
not e. or fairness	BERL 36:6
equals: live together as e.	MILL 224:20
equanimity: No man can face with e.	GILB 151:13
equation: e. is something for eternity	EINS 131:12
equators: North Poles and E.	CARR 92:7
equipment: e. always deteriorating	ELIOT 133:6
equity: judge people with e.	BOOK 68:4
equivocate: I will not e.	GARR 148:12
erect: e. and manly foe	CANN 89:12
err: e. as grossly as the few	DRYD 127:15
e. while yet he strives	GOET 154:3
To e. is human but to really	ANON 11:7
To e. is human, to forgive	POPE 252:7
errands: e. for the Ministers	GILB 151:6
erred: We have e., and strayed	BOOK 63:13
error: All men are liable to e.	LOCKE 208:18
charged the troops of e.	BROW 74:9
E. has never approached	METT 224:2
e. is immense	BOL 63:5
in endless e. hurled	POPE 252:18
positive in e. as in truth	LOCKE 208:17
show a man that he is in e.	LOCKE 208:15
stalking-horse to e.	BOL 63:3
errors: common e. of our life	SIDN 306:28
E., like straws	DRYD 127:23
e. of those who think	BID 59:1
more harmful than reasoned e.	HUXL 177:19
erstwhile: my e. dear	MILL 224:23
Esau: E. is a hairy man	BIBLE 39:19
E. selleth his birthright	BIBLE 39:17
hands are the hands of E.	BIBLE 39:20
escalier: *L'esprit de l'e.*	DID 120:20
escape: Beauty for some provides e.	HUXL 177:13
What struggle to e.	KEATS 191:18
escaped: e. with the skin of my teeth	BIBLE 42:35
eschew: E. evil, and do good	BOOK 66:25
escutcheon: blot on the e.	GRAY 156:18

Eskdale: E. and Liddesdale	SCOTT 269:2
espoused: my e., my latest found	MILT 229:15
my late e. saint	MILT 230:24
esprit: L'e. de l'escalier	DID 120:20
essence: e. of innumerable biographies	CARL 90:6
establishment: British e.	KEAT 190:9
estate: become a fourth e.	MAC 213:4
low e. of his handmaiden	BIBLE 51:28
mind, body, or e.	BOOK 64:19
ordered their e.	ALEX 4:3
estimate: know'st thy e.	SHAK 299:27
estranging: unplumbed, salt, e. sea	ARN 17:23
état: L'É. c'est moi	LOUI 210:12
eternal: E. Father, strong to save	WHIT 348:9
e. Footman hold my coat	ELIOT 133:29
e. in the heavens	BIBLE 55:24
E. Passion	ARN 16:22
Grant them e. rest	MISS 231:22
himself and her of an e. tie	AUDEN 21:5
Hope springs e.	POPE 252:12
lay hold on e. life	BIBLE 56:20
our e. home	WATTS 343:13
resembles the e. rocks beneath	BRON 72:17
Thou, whose e. Word	MARR 219:24
thy e. summer shall not fade	SHAK 299:13
to be boy e.	SHAK 298:21
eternities: for Seasons; not E.	MER 223:23
eternity: candidates for e.	MORE 234:22
Damned from here to E.	KIPL 196:15
decomposing in the e. of print	WOOLF 353:20
Deserts of vast e.	MARV 220:24
equation is something for e.	EINS 131:12
e. in an hour	BLAKE 60:5
E. is in love with the productions	BLAKE 61:5
E.'s a terrible thought	STOP 318:4
E. shut in a span	CRAS 111:11
E.! thou pleasing, dreadful thought	ADD 2:18
I saw E. the other night	VAUG 337:14
kill time without injuring e.	THOR 332:8
sells e. to get a toy	SHAK 299:8
some conception of e.	MANC 217:7
Some shadows of e.	VAUG 337:8
teacher affects e.	ADAMS 1:16
time is a pinprick of e.	AUR 22:10
Time's thievish progress to e.	SHAK 299:26
white radiance of E.	SHEL 303:13
ether: ampler e., a diviner air	WORD 355:7
etherized: patient e. upon a table	ELIOT 133:24
Eton: playing fields of E.	WELL 345:10
étonne: É.-moi	DIAG 117:15
eunuch: between a e. and a snigger	FIRB 139:19
Female E.	GREER 158:10
prerogative of the e.	STOP 318:1
Though Argus were her e.	SHAK 284:14
Time's e.	HOPK 172:19
To be a kind of moral e.	SHEL 304:14
eunuchs: seraglio of e.	FOOT 142:17
eureka: E.!	ARCH 15:2
Europe: better fifty years of E.	TENN 326:18
community of E.	SAL 266:4
E. a continent of energetic mongrels	FISH 139:22
E. is the unfinished negative	MCC 214:10
E. of the ancient parapets	RIMB 260:9
glory of E. is extinguished	BURKE 80:14
keep up with Western E.	UPD 336:12
lamps are going out all over E.	GREY 159:1
last gentleman in E.	LEV 206:6
poor are E.'s blacks	CHAM 94:4
save E. by her example	PITT 249:8
Europeans: You are learned E.	MASS 222:4
Euston: in E. waiting-room	CORN 108:5
Eve: E. ate Adam	HUGH 175:21
fallen sons of E.	CHES 98:5
past E. and Adam's	JOYCE 188:3

Eve (cont.):	
real curse of E.	RHYS 259:14
When Adam dalfe and E. spane	ROLLE 262:4
Evelyn: E. Hope is dead	BROW 75:28
even: E. so, come, Lord Jesus	BIBLE 58:8
evening: beautiful e., very starry	WORD 354:9
bright exhalation in the e.	SHAK 280:17
e. and the morning	BIBLE 38:14
e. is spread out	ELIOT 133:24
e. star, love's harbinger	MILT 229:32
hands be an e. sacrifice	BOOK 69:8
It was a summer e.	SOUT 311:18
like an e. gone	WATTS 343:14
Of grateful e. mild	MILT 229:11
sadly descends the autumn e.	ARN 17:3
Softly along the road of e.	DE L 116:21
welcome peaceful e. in	COWP 110:11
winter e. settles down	ELIOT 134:10
event: How much the greatest e.	FOX 144:16
hurries to the main e.	HOR 173:1
only as the e. decides	AUST 23:1
eventide: fast falls the e.	LYTE 212:20
events: e. have controlled me	LINC 207:9
e., mostly unimportant	BIER 59:6
ever: Hardly e.	GILB 152:15
Round the world for e. and aye	ARN 16:17
everlasting: caught an e. cold	WEBS 344:28
hath e. life	BIBLE 53:24
have e. life	BIBLE 53:19
Timon hath made his e. mansion	SHAK 296:24
underneath are the e. arms	BIBLE 40:25
everlastingness: Bright shoots of e.	VAUG 337:9
evermore: and e. shalt be	HEBER 164:17
this time forth for e.	BOOK 68:27
every: E. Day a Little Death	SOND 311:6
E. day, in every way	COUÉ 108:16
e. thing there is a season	BIBLE 44:11
E. time we say goodbye	PORT 253:19
E. which way but loose	KRON 199:6
everyman: E., I will go with thee	ANON 7:1
everyone: E. suddenly burst out singing	SASS 267:11
When e. is wrong	LA CH 199:15
everything: chips with e.	WESK 346:2
e. in its place	BEET 32:15
e. in its place and nothing	BEVAN 38:3
Life, the Universe and E.	ADAMS 1:9
robbed a man of e.	SOLZ 310:28
sans taste, sans e.	SHAK 272:28
smattering of e.	DICK 120:5
we cannot all do e.	LUC 212:1
We can't all do e.	VIRG 340:2
world is e. that is the case	WITT 352:9
everywhere: Out of the e. into here	MACD 214:18
Water, water, e.	COL 104:7
What is e., what is always	VINC 338:22
evidence: before you have all the e.	DOYLE 126:5
circumstantial e. is very strong	THOR 332:5
clearer e. than this	ARAB 14:18
e. of things not seen	BIBLE 56:26
it's not e.	DICK 119:34
evil: all e. shed away	BROO 73:10
banality of e.	AREN 15:4
because the days are e.	BIBLE 56:1
defend ourselves by doing e.	SOCR 310:23
deliver us from e.	BIBLE 48:27
doeth e. hath not seen God	BIBLE 57:18
Do e. in return	AUDEN 21:10
do e., that good may come	BIBLE 54:30
do nothing for e. to triumph	BURKE 81:13
Eschew e., and do good	BOOK 66:25
everything a necessary e.	BRAD 71:8
E., be thou my good	MILT 229:7
E. be to him who evil thinks	ANON 12:5
E. communications corrupt	BIBLE 55:19
e. is simply ignorance	FORD 143:8

evil *(cont.)*:
e. that men do lives after — SHAK 281:18
e. which I would not — BIBLE 54:38
face of 'e.' — BURR 82:31
Government is a necessary e. — PAINE 244:9
Great book, great e. — CALL 88:5
knowing good and e. — BIBLE 38:25
money is the root of all e. — BIBLE 56:19
only e. that walks invisible — MILT 229:5
on the e. and on the good — BIBLE 48:24
open and notorious e. liver — BOOK 64:29
punishment in itself is e. — BENT 35:2
Resist not e. — BIBLE 48:23
return good for e. — VANB 336:23
sometimes meet e.-willers — ELIZ 135:5
still to find means of e. — MILT 228:11
sufficient unto the day is the e. — BIBLE 49:5
them that call e. good — BIBLE 45:9
Whenever God prepares e. — ANON 13:8
withstand in the e. day — BIBLE 56:4
evils: enamoured of existing e. — BIER 59:5
greater e. than the first — CHUR 98:24
greatest of e....poverty — SHAW 301:8
must expect new e. — BACON 24:31
evolution: Some call it e. — CARR 92:10
ewe: tupping your white e. — SHAK 291:29
ewes: my e. breed not — BARN 29:8
exact: greatness not to be e. — BURKE 79:24
writing an e. man — BACON 25:15
exactitude: *L'e. est la politesse* — LOUI 210:17
exaggerated: have been greatly e. — TWAIN 336:7
exaggeration: e. is a truth that has lost its temper — GIBR 150:21
exalted: Every valley shall be e. — BIBLE 46:9
e. them of low degree — BIBLE 51:29
exalteth: e. himself shall be abased — BIBLE 52:22
examinations: E. are formidable — COLT 105:17
In e. those who do not wish to know — RAL 258:5
examine: E. for a moment — WOOLF 353:21
example: E. is always more efficacious — JOHN 183:6
save Europe by her e. — PITT 249:8
examples: philosophy from e. — DION 121:4
exceed: reach should e. his grasp — BROW 75:10
excel: so great as daring to e. — CHUR 98:20
excellent: e. thing in woman — SHAK 284:5
e. things are spoken — BOOK 67:24
O! it is e. — SHAK 288:13
Parts of it are e. — PUNCH 256:19
excellently: Goddess, e. bright — JONS 187:3
I see them all so e. fair — COL 103:14
excelling: Love divine, all loves e. — WESL 346:10
Excelsior: banner with the strange device, E. — LONG 209:17
excelsis: *Gloria in e. Deo* — MISS 231:13
Hosanna in e. — MISS 231:17
except: E. the Lord build the house — BOOK 68:30
exception: I'll be glad to make an e. — MARX 221:7
excess: Give me e. of it — SHAK 297:13
Nothing in e. — ANON 13:7
road of e. leads to the — BLAKE 61:1
Such an e. of stupidity — JOHN 184:14
wasteful and ridiculous e. — SHAK 282:10
excessit: *Abiit, e., evasit, erupit* — CIC 100:26
excessive: Dark with e. bright — MILT 229:4
right of an e. wrong — BROW 77:8
exchange: by just e. one for the other — SIDN 306:15
excise: E. A hateful tax — JOHN 182:7
excite: e. my amorous propensities — JOHN 183:24
exciting: films. They are too e. — BERR 36:14
too e. to be pleasant — DICK 119:29
excrement: place of e. — YEATS 358:20
excursion: poem, called the 'E.' — BYRON 86:16
steamers made an e. to hell — PRIE 255:8
excuse: e. every man will plead — SELD 269:17
I will not e. — GARR 148:12

excuse *(cont.)*:
they make a good e. — SZASZ 322:2
excuses: two e. less convincing than one — HUXL 177:9
execution: and the e. confined — SHAK 297:2
their stringent e. — GRANT 156:9
executioner: I am mine own E. — DONNE 124:18
executioners: victims who respect their e. — SART 267:7
executive: weakest e. in the world — DISR 121:7
executives: e. would never want to tamper — AUDEN 20:23
executors: Let's choose e. — SHAK 293:26
exercise: dancing is love's proper e. — DAV 114:15
mind what e. is to the body — STEE 314:17
exhalation: bright e. in the evening — SHAK 280:17
exhausted: enemies are not yet e. — GLAD 153:12
exile: destined an e. — VIRG 338:23
Go, bind your sons to e. — KIPL 197:15
silence, e., and cunning — JOYCE 188:9
therefore I die in e. — GREG 158:13
exiles: Thou Paradise of e., Italy — SHEL 303:21
Which none save e. feel — AYT 23:17
exist: they e., but are identical — FORS 143:25
existence: e. is but a brief crack — NAB 236:19
paint on the face of E. — BYRON 87:16
Struggle for E. — DARW 114:4
'Tis woman's whole e. — BYRON 86:4
when e. or when hope is gone — AUST 22:28
exists: And no one e. alone — AUDEN 21:11
exit: E., pursued by a bear — SHAK 298:25
exits: For men to take their e. — WEBS 344:18
their e. and their entrances — SHAK 272:24
exorciser: No e. harm thee — SHAK 273:28
exordium: e. of our woes — DRAY 126:18
exotic: e. follies o'er the town — BYRON 86:33
expect: E. nothing. Live frugally — WALK 341:4
people e. most from others — AUST 22:18
expectancy: e. and rose of the fair state — SHAK 276:2
expectation: better bettered e. — SHAK 291:11
e. whirls me round — SHAK 297:1
Singing songs of e. — BAR 29:2
expediency: sacrificed to e. — MAUG 222:8
expedient: as may be most e. for them — BOOK 64:10
e. that one man should die — BIBLE 53:34
not a principle, but an e. — DISR 121:10
expedition: abandoning the e. — DOUG 125:8
expeditious: There is no e. road — THOM 331:13
expenditure: annual e. — DICK 118:12
E. rises to meet income — PARK 245:20
expense: drinking at somebody else's e. — LEIGH 204:19
e. damnable — CHES 97:18
e. of spirit in a waste of shame — SHAK 300:10
repay the trouble and e. — BELL 33:2
use alone that sanctifies e. — POPE 251:18
Would be at the e. of two — CLOU 102:16
expenses: facts are on e. — STOP 318:3
expensive: extremely e. to be poor — BALD 27:2
experience: e. is an arch — ADAMS 1:13
e. is an arch — TENN 328:21
E. is the child of Thought — DISR 122:9
E. is the name everyone gives — WILDE 350:2
E., though noon auctoritee — CHAU 96:5
I know it from e. — ARAB 14:19
in the elder, a part of e. — BACON 25:17
knowledge can go beyond his e. — LOCKE 208:14
never had much e. — MARQ 219:16
triumph of hope over e. — JOHN 184:24
we need not e. it — FRIS 146:5
experiences: in between lie the e. of our life — MANN 217:13
experimental: *any e. reasoning* — HUME 176:4
expert: e. is one who knows more — BUTL 83:21
e. is someone who knows — HEIS 165:4
experto: *E. credite* — VIRG 339:22
expiate: I have something to e. — LAWR 202:22
explain: Never complain and never e. — DISR 122:19

explain (*cont.*):

Never e. Never apologise	FISH 139:24
Never e.—your friends do not	HUBB 175:13
explained: die before we have e.	ADAMS 2:3
explaining: forever e. things	DE S 265:15
expletive: E. deleted	ANON 7:3
explorers: endeavours are unlucky e.	DOUG 125:8
exploring: end of all our e.	ELIOT 133:10
explosive: 'philosopher': a terrible e.	NIET 239:19
exposed: intellect is improperly e.	SMITH 310:3
exposition: e. of sleep	SHAK 291:1
express: down e. in the small of the back	WOD 352:18
expressed: ne'er so well e.	POPE 252:1
expression: E. is the dress of thought	POPE 252:2
exquisite: e. touch	SCOTT 269:6
exquisitely: Autumn sunsets e. dying	HUXL 177:13
extenuate: nothing e.	SHAK 293:5
extenuates: e. not wrong	SHAK 296:33
exterminate: E. all the brutes	CONR 107:4
extol: How shall we e. thee	BENS 34:20
extra: add some e., just for you	LARK 201:17
extras: No e., no vacations	DICK 119:10
extravagance: beautiful does not lead to e.	PER 248:1
extremes: toil in other men's e.	KYD 199:9
extremism: e. in the defence of liberty	GOLD 155:15
eye: Affection beaming in one e.	DICK 119:2
apple of his e.	BIBLE 40:23
beam that is in thine own e.	BIBLE 49:7
bright e. of peninsulas	CAT 93:3
Cast a cold e. on life	YEATS 360:8
custom loathsome to the e.	JAM 179:9
death obscured that e.	KEATS 192:17
E. for eye, tooth for eye	BIBLE 40:10
e. of heaven to garnish	SHAK 282:10
e. sinks inward	ARN 16:10
e. that can open an oyster	WOD 352:16
fringèd curtains of thine e.	SHAK 296:2
God caught his e.	MCC 214:15
harvest of a quiet e.	WORD 356:7
He had but one e.	DICK 119:11
Hide me from day's garish e.	MILT 226:26
If thine e. offend thee	BIBLE 50:17
I have neither e. to see	LENT 205:20
language in her e.	SHAK 297:9
long grey beard and glittering e.	COL 104:3
looked into the e. of day	YEATS 359:5
mild and magnificent e.	BROW 76:14
My tiny watching e.	DE L 116:23
Sail and sail, with unshut e.	ARN 16:17
tender e. of pitiful day	SHAK 287:6
they shall see e. to eye	BIBLE 46:16
through the e. of a needle	BIBLE 50:22
twinkling of an e.	BIBLE 55:21
unforgiving e.	SHER 306:7
with its soft black e.	MOORE 234:19
with not through the e.	BLAKE 60:12
eyeball: His e.—like a bastion's mole	SMART 308:10
We're e. to eyeball	RUSK 264:9
eyebrows: e. made of platinum	FORS 143:14
eyeless: E. in Gaza	MILT 230:10
eyelids: tired e. upon tired eyes	TENN 326:19
eyes: all e. else dead coals	SHAK 299:3
bodily hunger in his e.	SHAW 301:10
Closed his e. in endless night	GRAY 157:17
close my e., open my legs	HILL 168:17
close your e. before you see	AYCK 23:14
Crumbling behind the e.	MACN 216:4
cynosure of neighbouring e.	MILT 227:3
deep upon her peerless e.	KEATS 191:26
Drink to me only with thine e.	JONS 187:23
electrical skin and glaring e.	SMART 308:8
e. are homes of silent prayer	TENN 326:18
e. are nothing like the sun	SHAK 300:11
e. as wide as a football-pool	CAUS 93:9
e. have they, and see not	BOOK 68:18

eyes (*cont.*):

e. of gold and bramble-dew	STEV 317:20
E. of most unholy blue	MOORE 234:12
e. to wonder, but lack tongues	SHAK 300:5
e. were deeper than the depth	ROSS 263:6
her e. were wild	KEATS 191:9
Foolish e., thy streams	SANS 266:20
frightened look in its e.	SITW 307:21
From women's e.	SHAK 284:16
gather to the e.	TENN 327:22
Get thee glass e.	SHAK 283:26
God be in my e.	ANON 7:11
good Lord made your e.	LEHR 204:14
Hath not a Jew e.	SHAK 289:16
lift up thine e.	MONS 233:2
lightened are our e.	SORL 311:15
Love looks not with the e.	SHAK 290:16
Love's tongue is in the e.	FLET 142:9
Mine e. have seen the glory	HOWE 175:7
night has a thousand e.	BOUR 70:12
Night hath a thousand e.	LYLY 212:18
no eyes but constitutional e.	LINC 207:14
one, all e., Philosopher!	WORD 356:5
Or was it his bees-winged e.	BETJ 36:16
our e. the frosty sagas	CRANE 110:31
pearls that were his e.	SHAK 296:1
see the white of their e.	PUTN 256:24
Smoke gets in your e.	HARB 161:10
soft look your e. had once	YEATS 360:9
So much chewing gum for the e.	ANON 10:14
stuck in her face for e.	SHAK 284:14
Take a pair of sparkling e.	GILB 151:7
tempts your wand'ring e.	GRAY 157:15
tended her i' the e.	SHAK 271:15
these e. to behold felicity	BROW 74:17
They strike mine e.	JONS 187:6
with cold commemorative e.	ROSS 263:9
with his half-shut e.	POPE 253:9
with sad and wond'ring e.	MILM 225:13
your e. with holy dread	COL 104:1

F

Fabians: civilization of the F.	INGE 178:11
good man fallen among F.	LENIN 205:5
fable: f., song, or fleeting shade	HERR 167:14
that thai be nocht bot f.	BARB 28:15
fables: profane and old wives' f.	BIBLE 56:17
fabric: baseless f. of this vision	SHAK 296:10
face: Cover her f.	WEBS 344:19
day's disasters in his morning f.	GOLD 154:23
dew on the f. of the dead	BEERS 32:14
dont quite match your f.	ASHF 18:21
f. is a mute recommendation	PUBL 255:22
f. of 'evil'	BURR 82:31
f. of my betrothèd lady	MIDD 224:8
f. of the world would have	PASC 246:2
f. that launched a thousand ships	MARL 218:11
f. the index of a feeling mind	CRAB 110:29
False f. must hide	SHAK 286:8
Fanny Kelly's divine plain f.	LAMB 200:9
garden of your f.	HERB 166:19
has the f. he deserves	ORW 241:24
He hides a smiling f.	COWP 109:26
Her f., at first … just ghostly	REID 259:3
his listless form and f.	HARDY 162:14
his prism, and silent f.	WORD 356:10
huge massy f.	MAC 213:6
I am the family f.	HARDY 162:10
I never forget a f.	MARX 221:7
I wish I loved its silly f.	RAL 258:6
labour bears a lovely f.	DEKK 116:9
Lift up thine eyes and seek his f.	MONS 233:2
Look in my f.	TRAI 334:2

face (cont.):
Lord make his f. shine	BIBLE 40:15
mind's construction in the f.	SHAK 285:14
mist in my f.	BROW 77:2
never f. so pleased my mind	ANON 10:18
never see my f. again	TENN 324:21
night's starred f.	KEATS 192:20
paint in the public's f.	RUSK 264:10
Pity a human f.	BLAKE 61:21
rabbit has a charming f.	ANON 10:8
see my pilot face to f.	TENN 323:19
sing in the robber's f.	JUV 189:11
smile on the f. of the tiger	ANON 10:22
socialism would not lose its human f.	DUBC 128:31
spirit passed before my f.	BIBLE 42:28
stamping on a human f.	ORW 242:11
then f. to face	BIBLE 55:14
they praised him to his f.	TENN 328:14
turning your f. to the light	SASS 267:9
unacceptable f. of capitalism	HEATH 164:12
upon the f. of the deep	BIBLE 38:13
upon the f. of the waters	BIBLE 38:13
with how wan a f.	SIDN 306:18
with twain he covered his f.	BIBLE 45:10
Your f., my thane, is as a book	SHAK 285:20
your honest, sonsie f.	BURNS 82:24
faces: accuse 'em of not having any f.	PRIE 255:7
baby f. in the violet light	ELIOT 134:30
Bid them wash their f.	SHAK 273:16
cantan', grace-proud f.	BURNS 82:29
f. are but a gallery of pictures	BACON 24:23
grind the f. of the poor	BIBLE 45:6
In nice clean f.	BARH 28:18
monastic f. in quiet collegiate	CLOU 102:9
old familiar f.	LAMB 200:13
public f. in private places	AUDEN 21:6
these f. in the crowd	POUND 254:20
facilis: F. descensus Averno	VIRG 339:12
fact: fatal futility of F.	JAMES 180:2
hypothesis by an ugly f.	HUXL 177:15
irritable reaching after f.	KEATS 193:2
judges of f.	PULT 256:4
faction: it made them a f.	MAC 213:17
whisper of a f.	RUSS 265:5
factions: religious f. are volcanoes	BURKE 81:1
facts: F. alone are wanted	DICK 118:27
f. are on expenses	STOP 318:3
f. are sacred	SCOTT 268:3
f. when you come to brass tacks	ELIOT 134:14
form of inert f.	ADAMS 1:20
give you all the f.	AUDEN 21:12
politics consists in ignoring f.	ADAMS 1:19
Science is built up of f.	POIN 250:10
faculties: each according to his f.	BAK 27:1
Hath borne his f. so meek	SHAK 285:24
T'affections, and to f.	DONNE 124:4
very f. of eyes and ears	SHAK 275:23
fade: F. far away, dissolve	KEATS 191:31
f. into the light of common day	WORD 355:21
They simply f. away	FOLEY 142:16
faded: not hollow cheek or f. eye	TENN 328:2
fades: f. awa' like morning dew	BALL 28:10
Now f. the glimmering landscape	GRAY 157:4
fading: in f. silks compose	WINC 352:3
faery: f. lands forlorn	KEATS 192:5
Full beautiful, a f.'s child	KEATS 191:9
faiblesse: tout le reste est f.	VIGNY 338:18
fail: F. not our feast	SHAK 287:1
we'll not f.	SHAK 286:6
We shall not flag or f.	CHUR 99:13
failed: fluttered and f. for breath	ARN 17:1
fails: One sure, if another f.	BROW 77:12
failure: f.'s no success at all	DYLAN 130:4
not the effort nor the f.	EMPS 137:6
Women can't forgive f.	CHEK 96:26

faint: beginning to f. in the light	TENN 326:28
Damn with f. praise	POPE 251:6
f. praises one another damn	WYCH 358:6
F., yet pursuing	BIBLE 41:1
walk, and not f.	BIBLE 46:13
fair: all so excellently f.	COL 103:14
anything to show more f.	WORD 354:15
days when I was f.	RONS 262:5
Dream of F. Women	TENN 323:20
f. as is the rose in May	CHAU 96:11
F. is foul, and foul is fair	SHAK 285:1
F. is too foul an epithet	MARL 219:10
F. shares for all	JAY 180:14
F. stood the wind for France	DRAY 126:22
Fat, f. and forty	O'KEE 241:6
How sweet and f. she seems	WALL 341:12
I have sworn thee f.	SHAK 300:16
noble, historically f.	LERN 205:26
None but the brave deserves the f.	DRYD 127:19
Outward be f.	CHUR 98:25
Sabrina f.	MILT 226:21
She f., divinely fair	MILT 229:24
so foul and f. a day	SHAK 285:6
this f. defect of nature	MILT 229:30
Thou art all f., my love	BIBLE 44:35
thou art f., my love	BIBLE 44:34
With you f. maid	ANON 6:5
fairer: surely the f. way	BACON 24:3
fairest: f. creatures we desire	SHAK 299:11
F. Isle, all isles excelling	DRYD 128:2
O f. of creation, last and best	MILT 229:27
fairies: beginning of f.	BARR 29:11
Do you believe in f.	BARR 29:14
f. at the bottom of our garden	FYL 147:9
Farewell, rewards and F.	CORB 107:23
She is the f.' midwife	SHAK 294:24
since the f. left off dancing	SELD 269:19
fairness: equality or f. or justice	BERL 36:6
fairy: f. somewhere that falls	BARR 29:12
Like f. gifts fading away	MOORE 234:11
loves a f. when she's forty	HENL 165:16
of F. me thoghte	LANG 201:6
wide enough to wrap a f. in	SHAK 290:27
fais: F. ce que voudras	RAB 257:12
faith: author and finisher of our f.	BIBLE 56:27
children in whom is no f.	BIBLE 40:24
easy to shake a man's f.	SHAW 300:27
f., hope, charity	BIBLE 55:14
f. shines equal	BRON 72:16
f. that stands on authority	EMER 136:23
F. the substance of things hoped for	BIBLE 56:26
f. unfaithful kept him falsely	TENN 324:9
f. without doubt is nothing	UNAM 336:11
F. without works is dead	BIBLE 57:3
Fight the good fight of f.	BIBLE 56:20
future states of both are left to f.	BYRON 86:12
I have kept the f.	BIBLE 56:21
in the seat to f. assigned	SMART 308:11
In this f. I wish to live	VILL 338:21
Love in dying, F. is defying	BARN 29:8
more f. in honest doubt	TENN 325:19
My staff of f. to walk upon	RAL 257:23
O thou of little f.	BIBLE 50:9
scientific f.'s absurd	BROW 75:27
Sea of f.	ARN 16:11
simple f. than Norman blood	TENN 325:33
though I have all f.	BIBLE 55:11
Thy f. hath made thee whole	BIBLE 49:25
you have kept f.	HARDY 162:9
your work of f. and labour	BIBLE 56:13
faithful: Be thou f. unto death	BIBLE 57:21
Ever f., ever sure	MILT 227:9
good and f. servant	BIBLE 51:1
I have been f. to thee, Cynara	DOWS 125:12

faithful (*cont.*):

mentally f. to himself	PAINE 244:6
O come, all ye f.	ANON 13:9
So f. in love, and so dauntless	SCOTT 268:19
faithfully: ask f. we may obtain	BOOK 64:27
faithless: f. coldness of the times	TENN 325:24
Human on my f. arm	AUDEN 20:27
fake: Anything that consoles is f.	MURD 236:11
falcon: dapple-dawn-drawn F.	HOPK 172:20
f., towering in her pride	SHAK 286:28
Gentle as f.	SKEL 308:3
Falklands: F. thing was a fight	BORG 69:24
fall: by dividing we f.	DICK 120:18
diggeth a pit shall f. into it	BIBLE 44:21
f. for anything	HAM 160:16
F. into the hands of God	TENN 328:13
f. into the hands of the living God	BIBLE 56:25
f. into the hands of the Lord	BIBLE 47:32
f. not out by the way	BIBLE 39:28
f. out with those we love	TENN 327:17
further they have to f.	FITZ 141:1
hard rain's a gonna f.	DYLAN 130:2
haughty spirit before a f.	BIBLE 43:28
I shall f. like a bright exhalation	SHAK 280:17
it had a dying f.	SHAK 297:14
Life is a horizontal f.	COCT 103:2
needs fear no f.	BUNY 79:7
Things f. apart	YEATS 359:23
Weak men must f.	SHAK 293:23
we f. to rise	BROW 75:11
what a f. was there	SHAK 281:24
yet fear I to f.	RAL 257:24
fallacy: Pathetic F.	RUSK 264:1
fallen: art thou f. from heaven	BIBLE 45:22
Babylon is f.	BIBLE 57:34
good man f. among Fabians	LENIN 205:5
lot is f. unto me	BOOK 66:15
Ye are f. from grace	BIBLE 55:29
falling: apple f. towards England	AUDEN 21:5
'f. domino' principle	EIS 131:15
Go, and catch a f. star	DONNE 124:10
my feet from f.	BOOK 68:20
fallings: F. from us, vanishings	WORD 355:22
falls: And then he f., as I do	SHAK 280:18
F. the Shadow	ELIOT 133:19
false: all was f. and hollow	MILT 228:23
Beware of f. prophets	BIBLE 49:14
by the philosopher, as equally f.	GIBB 150:10
F. face must hide	SHAK 286:8
f. sincere	POPE 251:21
f. witness against thy neighbour	BIBLE 40:9
Followed f. lights	DRYD 127:29
not then be f. to any man	SHAK 274:23
Ring out the f.	TENN 325:23
thou be not f. to others	BACON 25:21
wouldst not play f.	SHAK 285:15
falsehood: express lying or f.	SWIFT 320:1
F. has a perennial spring	BURKE 79:25
neither Truth nor F.	HOBB 169:5
falsehoods: f. which interest	JOHN 182:12
falsely: kept him f. true	TENN 324:9
Falstaff: F. sweats to death	SHAK 277:29
falter: hesitate and f. life away	ARN 17:10
falters: love that never f.	SPR 313:26
Famagusta: F. and the hidden sun	FLEC 141:18
fame: blush to find it f.	POPE 252:31
call the Temple of F.	LICH 207:1
F. is a food that dead men eat	DOBS 122:26
F. is like a river	BACON 25:7
F. is the spur	MILT 227:14
his f. the ocean sea	BARN 29:7
love and f. to nothingness	KEATS 192:21
Man dreams of f.	TENN 324:15
Physicians of the Utmost F.	BELL 33:4
servants of f.	BACON 24:27

fame (*cont.*):

We came here for f.	DISR 122:12
What is f.? an empty bubble	GRAI 156:7
famed: f. in all great arts	ARN 17:21
fames: *Auri sacra f.*	VIRG 339:8
familiar: Mine own f. friend	BOOK 67:2
mine own f. friend	BOOK 67:12
old f. faces	LAMB 200:13
familiarity: F. breeds contempt	TWAIN 336:3
families: All happy f. resemble	TOLS 333:11
and there are f.	THAT 329:25
f. in a country village	AUST 23:9
mothers of large f.	BELL 33:2
occur in the best-regulated f.	DICK 118:16
old f. last not three oaks	BROW 74:6
family: f.—that dear octopus	SMITH 309:4
f. that prays together	SCAL 267:16
f. with the wrong members	ORW 242:3
I am the f. face	HARDY 162:10
left his f. it didn't say why	TWAIN 335:19
running of a f.	MONT 233:13
famine: die by f. die by inches	HENRY 166:3
famous: become f. without ability	SHAW 300:29
f. by their birth	SHAK 293:16
f. for fifteen minutes	WARH 342:20
F. men have the whole earth	PER 248:2
found myself f.	BYRON 87:21
Let us now praise f. men	BIBLE 48:7
fan: F-vaulting	LANC 200:20
with her f. spread	CONG 106:17
fanaticism: F. consists in redoubling	SANT 266:21
fanatics: F. have their dreams	KEATS 190:24
fancies: F. that broke through	BROW 77:4
With a heart of furious f.	ANON 11:3
fancy: Ever let the f. roam	KEATS 190:26
f. is the sails	KEATS 192:22
In the spring a young man's f.	TENN 326:6
of most excellent f.	SHAK 277:8
sweetest Shakespeare f.'s child	MILT 227:8
Tell me where is f. bred	SHAK 289:20
fancy-free: In maiden meditation, f.	SHAK 290:24
fantasies: fed the heart on f.	YEATS 359:16
fantastic: In a light f. round	MILT 226:9
On the light f. toe	MILT 227:2
fantasy: much too strong for f.	DONNE 124:1
far: audacity is knowing how f.	COCT 103:4
bridge too f.	BROW 75:7
f. above the great	GRAY 157:19
F. and few, far and few	LEAR 203:10
F. from the madding crowd	GRAY 157:10
f. gone from original righteousness	BOOK 69:17
f. side of despair	SART 267:6
It is a f., far better thing	DICK 120:7
keep f. from me, you grim women	OVID 243:9
Mexico, so f. from God	DIAZ 117:16
much too f. out all my life	SMITH 309:19
news from a f. country	BIBLE 43:37
Oh keep f. off, you uninitiated	VIRG 339:13
old, unhappy, f.-off things	WORD 357:2
Over the hills and f. away	GAY 149:5
quarrel in a f. away country	CHAM 94:1
so near and yet so f.	TENN 325:21
farce: f. is played out	RAB 257:13
longest running f.	SMITH 309:3
second as f.	MARX 221:10
second time as f.	BARN 29:6
farewell: Ae f., and then for ever	BURNS 81:22
f. content	SHAK 292:19
f., he is gon	CHAU 95:25
F. my bok and my devocioun	CHAU 96:9
F.! thou art too dear	SHAK 299:27
f. to the shade	COWP 109:30
hail, and f. evermore	CAT 93:8
long f., to all my greatness	SHAK 280:18
Too-late, F.	ROSS 263:8

farm: keep 'em down on the f.	YOUNG 206:17	fate (cont.):	
farmer: f. that hanged himself	SHAK 286:20	wagged contempt at F.	WATS 343:1
F. will never be happy	HERB 166:11	when f. summons	DRYD 128:4
farmers: embattled f. stood	EMER 136:12	fates: masters of their f.	SHAK 280:27
f. excessively fortunate	VIRG 340:7	periods set, and hidden f.	SUCK 318:23
farms: cellos of the deep f.	STEV 316:22	father: about my F.'s business	BIBLE 52:4
What spires, what f. are those	HOUS 174:24	brood of folly without f. bred	MILT 226:22
farrow: old sow that eats her f.	JOYCE 188:7	cannot have God for his f.	CYPR 113:12
fart: can't f. and chew gum	JOHN 181:22	Child is f. of the Man	WORD 355:14
Love is the f.	SUCK 318:22	Dear Lord and F. of mankind	WHIT 348:27
farther: f. you go from the church	WOTT 357:21	either my f. or my mother	STER 315:12
farthing: Virtue knows to a f.	WALP 342:3	F., I have sinned against heaven	BIBLE 52:30
farthings: sparrows sold for two f.	BIBLE 52:17	f. is gone wild into his grave	SHAK 278:30
fascination: f. of what's difficult	YEATS 359:4	F. is rather vulgar	DICK 119:1
There's a f. frantic	GILB 152:8	f. of English criticism	JOHN 182:20
Fascist: Every woman adores a F.	PLATH 249:14	f.'s corpse	APOL 14:13
fashion: faithful to thee, Cynara! in my f.	DOWS 125:12	Glory be to the F.	BOOK 63:17
f. of this world passeth	BIBLE 55:6	Honour thy f. and thy mother	BIBLE 40:8
glass of f.	SHAK 276:2	I meet my F., my age	LOW 211:15
not for the f. of these times	SHAK 272:17	limp f. of thousands	JOYCE 188:16
out of the world, as out of the f.	CIBB 100:14	Lloyd George knew my f.	ANON 9:1
fashions: conscience to fit this year's f.	HELL 165:7	My f. feeds his flocks	HOME 170:18
fast: but none so f. as stroke	COKE 103:6	My mother groaned! my f. wept	BLAKE 62:3
come he slow, or come he f.	SCOTT 268:17	no man cometh unto the F.	BIBLE 53:38
earth in f. thick pants	COL 103:23	one God the F. Almighty	BOOK 65:5
F. by their native shore	COWP 109:28	Our F. which art in heaven	BIBLE 48:27
fun grew f. and furious	BURNS 82:23	polite f. of his people	JAM 179:10
Silently and very f.	AUDEN 20:19	rather have a turnip than his f.	JOHN 186:13
Snip! Snap! Snip! They go so f.	HOFF 169:22	resembled my f. as he slept	SHAK 286:14
who will not f. in peace	CRAB 110:24	shall a man leave his f.	BIBLE 38:23
fasten: F. your seat-belts	MANK 217:12	She gave her f. forty-one	ANON 8:22
if they think, they f.	HOUS 174:10	thicker than my f.'s loins	BIBLE 41:33
faster: F. than a speeding bullet	ANON 7:5	When did you last see your f.	YEAM 358:12
fastest: f. who travels alone	KIPL 196:20	wise f. that knows his own child	SHAK 289:7
fasting: lives upon hope will die f.	FRAN 145:11	wise son maketh a glad f.	BIBLE 43:16
thank heaven, f.	SHAK 273:6	wish was f., Harry, to that thought	SHAK 278:27
fat: Butter merely makes us f.	GOER 153:22	You are old, F. William	CARR 91:4
eat the f. of the land	BIBLE 39:27	your F. which is in heaven	BIBLE 48:25
F., fair and forty	O'KEE 241:6	fatherhood: Mirrors and f.	BORG 69:23
f. gentleman in such a passion	SHAW 302:29	fatherless: f. children, and widows	BOOK 64:17
F. is a feminist issue	ORB 241:15	fatherly: thy f. goodness	BOOK 64:19
f., oily man of God	THOM 331:21	fathers: f.-forth whose beauty is past	HOPK 172:13
f. white woman whom nobody	CORN 108:6	f., provoke not your children	BIBLE 56:2
Imprisoned in every f. man	CONN 106:28	iniquity of the f. upon the children	BIBLE 40:5
men about me that are f.	SHAK 281:1	My f. can have it	THOM 330:20
opera ain't over 'til the f. lady	COOK 107:16	our f. brought forth upon this	LINC 207:8
Outside every f. man	AMIS 5:4	sojourners, as were all our f.	BIBLE 42:17
thin man inside every f. man	ORW 241:25	spake in time past unto the f.	BIBLE 56:23
fatal: fair and f. king	JOHN 181:17	Tell them, because our f. lied	KIPL 196:7
f. futility of Fact	JAMES 180:2	Victory has a hundred f.	CIANO 100:12
f. gift of beauty	BYRON 85:7	fathom: f.-line could never touch	SHAK 277:27
great deal of it is absolutely f.	WILDE 349:23	For thou canst not f. it	TENN 327:15
most f. complaint of all	HILT 168:18	Full f. five thy father lies	SHAK 296:1
So sweet was ne'er so f.	SHAK 293:1	fathomed: sheer, no-man-f.	HOPK 172:10
strange and f. interview	DONNE 123:5	fathoms: 'Tis fifty f. deep	BALL 28:6
fate: Art is a revolt against f.	MALR 217:4	fatling: young lion and the f.	BIBLE 45:19
become the makers of our f.	POPP 253:15	fatted: Bring hither the f. calf	BIBLE 52:31
cannot suspend their f.	DEFOE 115:17	fattening: illegal, immoral, or f.	WOOL 354:8
Character is f.	NOV 240:12	fault: all f. who hath no fault	TENN 324:8
down the torrent of his f.	JOHN 183:16	f., dear Brutus	SHAK 280:27
F. cannot harm me	SMITH 310:7	f. of angels and of gods	POPE 250:24
F. is not an eagle	BOWEN 70:18	Good women think it is their f.	BROO 73:11
F.'s great bazaar	MACN 216:9	happy f.	MISS 232:1
F. so enviously debars	MARV 220:13	It has no kind of f. or flaw	GILB 151:10
F. wrote her a most tremendous	BEER 32:13	through my most grievous f.	MISS 231:11
forget my f.	TATE 322:15	What soul is without f.	RIMB 260:10
I am the master of my f.	HENL 165:18	faultless: Faultily f., icily regular	TENN 326:23
I hold f. clasped in my fist	FORD 143:11	F. to a fault	BROW 77:9
limits of a vulgar f.	GRAY 157:19	thinks a f. piece to see	POPE 251:29
man's character is his f.	HER 166:9	faults: Be to her f. a little blind	PRIOR 255:9
over-ruled by f.	MARL 218:17	England, with all thy f.	COWP 110:8
take a bond of f.	SHAK 287:21	Jesus! with all thy f.	BUTL 84:19
Till I thy f. shall overtake	KING 195:5	men are moulded out of f.	SHAK 288:26
transient is the smile of f.	DYER 129:17	Some f. to make us men	SHAK 271:27
		their f. confessing	BUCK 278:3

faults (cont.):
They fill you with the f.	LARK 201:17
vile ill-favoured f.	SHAK 290:10
With all her f., she is my country	CHUR 98:21

Faustus: F. must be damned — MARL 218:13

favour: being in and out of f. — FROST 146:9
| out of f. grudge at knaves | DEFOE 115:21 |

favoured: thou that art highly f. — BIBLE 51:27

favours: lively sense of future f. — WALP 342:7
| middle of her f. | SHAK 275:13 |
| secret hope for greater f. | LA R 201:25 |

fawning: How like a f. publican — SHAK 289:1

fawns: fallow f. invisible go — THOM 330:26

fear: acting and reasoning as f. — BURKE 80:7
by means of pity and f.	ARIS 15:15
concessions of f.	BURKE 79:27
equal poise of hope and f.	MILT 226:13
f. first in the world made gods	JONS 187:11
F. God. Honour the King	BIBLE 57:9
F. God. Honour the King	KITC 198:8
F. God, and keep his commandments	BIBLE 44:28
f. in a handful of dust	ELIOT 134:20
F. is the foundation	ADAMS 2:2
F. no more the heat o' the sun	SHAK 273:27
f. of finding something worse	BELL 33:5
f. of the Law	JOYCE 188:4
f. of the Lord	BIBLE 45:18
f. of the Lord	BOOK 68:15
f. usually ends in folly	COL 104:28
Fly hence, our contact f.	ARN 17:11
For f. of little men	ALL 4:18
freedom from f.	ROOS 262:13
hate, so long as they f.	ACC 1:2
hate that which we often f.	SHAK 271:8
hope that never had a f.	COWP 110:17
hope to rise, or f. to fall	WOTT 357:15
I cannot taint with f.	SHAK 287:32
I f. thee, ancient Mariner	COL 104:11
I f. those big words	JOYCE 188:13
I will f. no evil	BOOK 66:18
Life is first boredom, then f.	LARK 201:14
natural f. in children	BACON 24:20
needs f. no fall	BUNY 79:7
never f. to negotiate	KENN 194:4
Perfect f. casteth out love	CONN 107:2
perfect love casteth out f.	BIBLE 57:16
salvation with f. and trembling	BIBLE 56:6
so whom shall I f.	BIBLE 58:9
their one f., Death's shadow	BLUN 62:12
to f. is fear itself	ROOS 262:9
too much joy or too much f.	GRAV 156:14
travel in the direction of our f.	BERR 36:12
without f. the lawless roads	MUIR 236:6
word of f. unpleasing to a married ear	SHAK 284:22

feared: f. nor flattered any flesh — DOUG 125:7
| prince to be f. than loved | MACH 215:1 |

fearful: f. thing to fall — BIBLE 56:25
| frame thy f. symmetry | BLAKE 62:5 |
| our f. trip is done | WHIT 348:11 |

fearfully: f. and wonderfully made — BOOK 69:7

fearless: F., blameless knight — ANON 12:4

fears: f. his fellowship to die — SHAK 279:18
f. may be liars	CLOU 102:23
f. that I may cease to be	KEATS 192:19
grown from sudden f.	BYRON 87:5
I had no human f.	WORD 356:25
man who f. the Lord	BIBLE 58:11
Our f. do make us traitors	SHAK 287:22
Present f. are less	SHAK 285:11
To saucy doubts and f.	SHAK 287:9

feast: Fail not our f. — SHAK 287:1
| great f. of languages | SHAK 284:17 |
| Paris is a movable f. | HEM 165:13 |

feather: Blade on the f. — CORY 108:11
| F.-footed through the plashy | WAUGH 343:25 |

feather (cont.):
f. to tickle the intellect	LAMB 200:6
my foot, my each f.	HUGH 175:20
Stuck a f. in his cap	ANON 11:24

feathered: f. race with pinions — FRERE 145:22

feats: What f. he did that day — SHAK 279:19

fed: But it is f. and watered — CAMP 88:13
every child f. and educated	RUSK 264:19
f. of the dainties	SHAK 284:15
f. on the fullness of death	SWIN 321:13

federation: F. of the world — TENN 326:12

fee: For a small f. in America — SOND 311:8
| gorgeous East in f. | WORD 356:2 |
| set my life at a pin's f. | SHAK 274:28 |

feeble: confirm the f. knees — BIBLE 46:5
jonquil o'ercomes the f. brain	WINC 352:2
not enough to help the f.	SHAK 296:16
Superstition is the religion of f.	BURKE 80:18

feed: f. deep, deep upon her — KEATS 191:26
f. his flock like a shepherd	BIBLE 46:11
f. me in a green pasture	BOOK 66:17
F. my sheep	BIBLE 54:7
shalt thou f. on Death	SHAK 300:15
will you still f. me	LENN 205:17

feel: believe to One does f. — KNOX 198:17
f. for the common chord	BROW 75:9
f. what wretches feel	SHAK 283:12
see and hear and f.	JOYCE 188:7
thing that could not f.	WORD 356:25
tragedy to those that f.	WALP 341:23

feeling: formal f. comes — DICK 120:8
mess of imprecision of f.	ELIOT 133:6
Music is f., then, not sound	STEV 316:10
petrifies the f.	BURNS 82:5
To f. as to sight	SHAK 286:10
without f. gay	CHUR 98:26

fees: accompanied by a few f. — HUNT 176:13
| they took their F. | BELL 33:4 |

feet: And did those f. — BLAKE 61:12
bathe those beauteous f.	FLET 142:8
die on your f. than to live	IBAR 178:1
f. are always in the water	AMES 4:22
f. have they, and walk not	BOOK 68:18
f. into the way of peace	BIBLE 51:30
f. of him that bringeth good tidings	BIBLE 46:15
Her f. beneath her petticoat	SUCK 318:21
Its f. were tied	KEATS 191:3
Just direct your f.	FIEL 139:15
lantern unto my f.	BOOK 68:24
marching, charging f.	JAGG 179:7
moon under her f.	BIBLE 57:30
my f. from falling	BOOK 68:20
off the dust of your f.	BIBLE 49:28
on little cat f.	SAND 266:13
our f. when we want shoes	SWIFT 320:12
palms before my f.	CHES 97:22
slipping underneath our f.	FITZ 140:11
stranger's f. may find the meadow	HOUS 174:14
Til crowes f. be growe under	CHAU 96:15
To his f. thy tribute bring	LYTE 212:21
wash their f. in soda water	ELIOT 134:26
Wi' the Scots lords at his f.	BALL 28:6
with twain he covered his f.	BIBLE 45:10

felicity: Absent thee from f. — SHAK 277:17
| Or shadow of f. | WALL 341:14 |
| these eyes to behold f. | BROW 74:17 |

felix: F. qui potuit rerum — VIRG 340:8
| O f. culpa | MISS 232:1 |

fell: f. among thieves — BIBLE 52:11
| To noon he f. from noon | MILT 228:20 |

fellow: one that loves his f.-men — HUNT 176:13
| Sweetes' li'l' f. | STAN 314:11 |
| testy, pleasant f. | ADD 2:22 |

fellow-feeling: f. makes one — GARR 148:10

fellowship: F. is heaven — MORR 235:17

female: f. atheist talks you dead	JOHN 183:8
F. Eunuch	GREER 158:10
f. of the species is more deadly	KIPL 196:12
f. worker is the slave	CONN 107:3
flaming racket of the f.	OSB 242:22
into the Ark, the male and the f.	BIBLE 39:8
life for the British f.	CLOU 102:7
Male and f. created he them	BIBLE 38:16
Who has a faithful f. friend	WHUR 349:4
feminine: Taste is the f. of genius	FITZ 140:19
feminist: Fat is a f. issue	ORB 241:15
femme: *Cherchez la f.*	DUMAS 129:3
fen: f. of stagnant water	WORD 355:11
plashy f. passes the questing	WAUGH 343:25
fence: o'er the f. leaps Sunny Jim	HANFF 161:6
fences: f. make good neighbours	FROST 146:16
Fermanagh: steeples of F.	CHUR 99:7
fern: sparkle out among the f.	TENN 323:12
fertile: In such a fix to be so f.	NASH 237:9
twice five miles of f. ground	COL 103:22
fertilize: f. a problem with a solution	SIMP 307:13
festal: f. light in Christ-Church	ARN 17:9
fester: Lilies that f.	SHAK 300:2
limbs that f. are not springlike	ABSE 1:1
festina: *F. lente*	AUG 22:6
fetch: f. the age of gold	MILT 227:27
fetish: Militarism is f. worship	TAWN 322:18
fetters: reason Milton wrote in f.	BLAKE 60:25
feuds: Forget all f.	MAC 214:1
fever: after life's fitful f.	SHAK 287:4
enigma of the f. chart	ELIOT 133:5
f., and the free	KEATS 191:31
f. called 'Living'	POE 250:6
grows to an envious f.	SHAK 296:31
signed the treaty bred a f.	THOM 330:11
feverish: Poetry's the f. fit	WINC 352:1
few: Far and f., far and few	LEAR 203:10
f. are chosen	BIBLE 50:28
f. child's squalls	HUNT 176:18
fit audience find, though f.	MILT 229:19
Gey f., and they're a' deid	ANON 7:18
many for the gain of a f.	POPE 253:11
owed by so many to so f.	CHUR 99:15
rather hated the ruling f.	BENT 35:4
we happy f., we band	SHAK 279:20
fiat: *F. justitia et pereat mundus*	FERD 138:24
F. justitia et ruant coeli	WATS 342:25
fickle: fierce and f. is the South	TENN 327:24
Whatever is f., freckled	HOPK 172:13
fiction: condemn it as an improbable f.	SHAK 298:10
f. is a necessity	CHES 98:9
house of f.	JAMES 179:25
if she is to write f.	WOOLF 354:1
It is sometimes f.	MAC 213:22
one form of continuous f.	BEVAN 38:6
Peerage...best thing in f.	WILDE 350:14
Poetry is the supreme f.	STEV 316:8
Stranger than f.	BYRON 86:29
That is what f. means	WILDE 349:20
fictions: f. only and false heir	HERB 167:1
fiddle: and I the second f.	SPR 314:1
fiddling: huntsman and a f. priest	COWP 110:1
fide: *Punica f.*	SALL 266:9
Fidele: To fair F.'s grassy tomb	COLL 105:9
fideles: *Adeste, f.*	ANON 13:9
fidgety: If Phil, he won't sit still	HOFF 169:19
field: Consider the lilies of the f.	BIBLE 49:4
corner of a foreign f.	BROO 73:10
f. ful of folk fond I ther	LANG 201:7
F. strewn with its dank yellow	ARN 17:3
For Vaguery in the F.	OSB 242:21
From the wet f.	ARN 17:18
lay f. to field	BIBLE 45:8
Man comes and tills the f.	TENN 328:17

field *(cont.)*:	
Never in the f. of human conflict	CHUR 99:15
simple as to cross a f.	PAST 246:10
Till the f. ring again	BOWEN 70:16
fields: Blown f. or flowerful closes	SWIN 321:17
f. invested with purpureal	WORD 355:7
flowering of His f.	TENN 324:16
flowerless f. of heaven	SWIN 320:28
Open unto the f.	WORD 354:15
To f. where flies no sharp	HOPK 172:7
walk through the f. in gloves	CORN 108:6
We plough the f., and scatter	CAMP 88:13
whispering of f. half-sown	OWEN 243:24
fiend: dark dominion swung the f.	MER 223:21
defy the foul f.	SHAK 283:13
foul F. coming over	BUNY 78:20
frightful f. doth close behind	COL 104:15
Like a f. hid in a cloud	BLAKE 62:3
fiends: foreigners are f.	MITF 232:10
fierce: bright and f. and fickle	TENN 327:24
f. light which beats upon	TENN 324:1
F. was the wild billow	ANAT 5:10
though she be but little, she is f.	SHAK 290:33
fiery: burning f. furnace	BIBLE 47:11
f. portal of the east	SHAK 293:29
f. soul, which working	DRYD 127:6
fifteen: famous for f. minutes	WARH 342:20
F. men on the dead man's chest	STEV 317:2
fifth: F. of November	ANON 10:5
fifties: tranquillized F.	LOW 211:14
fig: sewed f. leaves together	BIBLE 38:26
fight: bade me f. had told me so	EWER 138:1
dead, who will not f.	GREN 158:16
end that crowns us, not the f.	HERR 167:16
f. and fight and fight again	GAIT 147:11
f. and not to heed the wounds	IGN 178:8
f. for freedom and truth	IBSEN 178:3
f. for its King and Country	GRAH 156:2
F. on, my men, sayes Sir	BALL 28:3
f. on the beaches	CHUR 99:13
F. the good fight	MONS 233:2
F. the good fight of faith	BIBLE 56:20
fought a good f.	BIBLE 56:21
I have not yet begun to f.	JONES 186:21
Ile rise and f. againe	BALL 28:3
man being too proud to f.	WILS 351:18
must f. on to the end	HAIG 159:17
Never give up the f.	MARL 218:6
no peril in the f.	CORN 108:1
Nor law, nor duty bade me f.	YEATS 359:10
no stomach to this f.	SHAK 279:18
Quit yourselves like men, and f.	BIBLE 41:10
thought it wrong to f.	BELL 33:28
Ulster will f.	CHUR 99:2
when men refuse to f.	ANON 11:11
fighter: Am I no a bonny f.	STEV 316:25
fighting: between two periods of f.	BIER 59:7
consisteth not in actual f.	HOBB 169:9
f. Blenheim all over again	BEVAN 37:20
f. for this woman's honour	KALM 189:20
F. in the captain's tower	DYLAN 129:20
F. still, and still destroying	DRYD 127:21
She's the F. Téméraire	NEWB 238:12
Street F. Man	JAGG 179:7
What are WE f. for?	SERV 270:12
who dies f. has increase	GREN 158:16
fights: knows what he f. for	CROM 111:24
figure: f. a poem makes	FROST 146:24
f. in a country church	SWIFT 320:3
f. in the carpet	JAMES 179:17
f. that thou here seest	JONS 187:20
filches: f. from me my good name	SHAK 292:11
files: Commands the beauteous f.	VAUG 337:6
foremost f. of time	TENN 326:16
fill: Come f. up my cup	SCOTT 268:7

fill (*cont.*):

f. hup the chinks wi' cheese	SURT 319:9
f. the cup	FITZ 140:11
I am not yet born; O f. me	MACN 216:6
To f. the hour	EMER 136:26
filled: they shall be f.	BIBLE 48:19
film: f. of death obscured	KEATS 192:17
Only that f., which fluttered	COL 103:20
films: I seldom go to f.	BERR 36:14
filth: identical, and so is f.	FORS 143:25
filthy: greedy of f. lucre	BIBLE 56:16
that is f. and polluted	BIBLE 47:25
finale: Let be be f. of seem	STEV 316:6
finality: Perfection is f.	STEP 315:6
finance: F. is the stomach of the country	GLAD 153:7
financiers: f., the little gnomes	WILS 351:12
Finchley: Lord F. tried	BELL 33:22
find: do not f. anything pleasant	VOLT 340:11
returns home to f. it	MOORE 234:7
searching f. out God	BIBLE 42:32
Someday I'll f. you	COW 109:7
to f., and not to yield	TENN 328:25
with men I f. Him not	TENN 324:16
findeth: f. his life shall lose it	BIBLE 49:33
finds: Who f. himself, loses	ARN 17:13
fine: Another F. Mess	LAUR 202:8
f. madness	DRAY 126:19
f. romance with no kisses	FIEL 139:14
F. writing is next to fine	KEATS 193:12
first f. careless rapture	BROW 76:2
finer: nothing could be f.	GORD 155:22
fines: interest and f. on sorrow	MAY 222:16
finest: This was their f. hour	CHUR 99:14
Yes, this is our f. shower	OSB 242:19
finger: chills the f. not a bit	NASH 237:16
f. do you want on the trigger	ANON 11:21
f. in the throat	OSLER 243:3
God's f. touched him	TENN 325:16
his slow and moving f.	SHAK 292:24
little f. shall be thicker	BIBLE 41:33
measured by the f. and thumb	SAL 266:3
moving f. writes	FITZ 140:14
ring without the f.	MIDD 224:6
scratching of my f.	HUME 176:11
fingernails: paring his f.	JOYCE 188:8
fingers: Crumbling between the f.	MACN 216:4
cut their own f.	EDD 130:13
Stop twisting in your yellow f.	HEAT 164:13
finger-stalls: In fitless f.	GILB 152:2
finish: Nice guys. F. last	DUR 129:13
start together and f.	BEEC 31:23
tools and we will f. the job	CHUR 99:16
finished: f. in half the time	WOD 352:17
f. in the first 100 days	KENN 194:5
I have f. my course	BIBLE 56:21
It is f.	BIBLE 54:5
world where England is f.	MILL 224:24
finisher: author and f. of our faith	BIBLE 56:27
fire: C'mon, baby, light my f.	MORR 235:19
done while Mrs Bennet was stirring the f.	AUST 23:3
don't one of you f. until you see	PUTN 256:24
dropping-wells of f.	TENN 325:15
every time She shouted 'F.!'	BELL 33:9
extinguishes candles and kindles f.	LA R 201:24
Fell in the f. and was burnt	GRAH 156:4
F. and fleet and candle-lighte	BALL 27:20
f. and the rose are one	ELIOT 133:13
F. burn and cauldron bubble	SHAK 287:15
f. next time	ANON 7:12
f. of my loins	NAB 236:18
f. was furry as a bear	SITW 307:17
frame of adamant, a soul of f.	JOHN 183:13
frighted with false f.	SHAK 276:11
heap coals of f.	BIBLE 43:36
Lord was not in the f.	BIBLE 42:3

fire (*cont.*):

Muse of f.	SHAK 278:33
neighbour's house is on f.	BURKE 80:9
night in a pillar of f.	BIBLE 39:39
nodding by the f.	YEATS 360:9
Now stir the f.	COWP 110:11
pale f.	SHAK 296:23
spirit all compact of f.	SHAK 300:17
Thorough flood, thorough f.	SHAK 290:19
world will end in f.	FROST 146:12
youth of England are on f.	SHAK 279:2
fire-folk: f. sitting in the air	HOPK 172:16
fires: Big f. flare up in a wind	FRAN 145:5
thought-executing f.	SHAK 283:6
fireside: adventures were by the f.	GOLD 155:12
F. enjoyments	COWP 110:12
firewood: F., ironware	MAS 221:19
firm: old f., is selling out	OSB 242:23
firmament: blood streams in the f.	MARL 218:13
no fellow in the f.	SHAK 281:9
spacious f. on high	ADD 2:25
firmly: F. I believe and truly	NEWM 238:19
firmness: Commodity, f., and delight	WOTT 357:19
first: Eclipse f., the rest nowhere	O'KEL 241:7
f. day be mended	WILB 349:13
f. fine careless rapture	BROW 76:2
f. fruits of them	BIBLE 55:17
f. in a village than second	CAES 87:26
f. in the hearts of his	LEE 204:7
f., last, everlasting day	DONNE 123:22
f. man is of the earth	BIBLE 55:20
f. step that is difficult	DU D 129:1
know the place for the f. time	ELIOT 133:10
last shall be f.	BIBLE 50:24
nothing be done for the f. time	CORN 108:8
no truck with f. impulses	MONT 234:1
people who got there f.	UST 336:16
there is no last nor f.	BROW 77:1
We were the f. that ever burst	COL 104:5
firstborn: her f. son	BIBLE 51:32
first-class: f. fightin' man	KIPL 196:14
fish: cars nose forward like f.	LOW 211:12
coal and surrounded by f.	BEVAN 37:17
F. are jumpin'	GERS 168:6
F. got to swim and birds	HAMM 160:19
F. say, they have their stream	BROO 73:2
He replied,—'F. fiddle de-dee!'	LEAR 203:14
like a f. without a bicycle	STEI 315:2
Phone for the f.-knives, Norman	BETJ 37:2
There's a f. that *talks*	DE L 116:11
Thou deboshed f. thou	SHAK 296:6
fishbone: monument sticks like a f.	LOW 211:13
fished: He f. by obstinate isles	POUND 254:15
fishers: will make you f. of men	BIBLE 48:18
fishes: notes like little f.	MACN 216:9
Where the flyin'-f. play	KIPL 196:21
fishified: flesh, how art thou f.	SHAK 295:5
fishing: angling or float f.	JOHN 186:11
fishpond: That great f.	DEKK 116:8
fist: f. most valiant	SHAK 279:18
fit: f. audience find	MILT 229:19
f. for nothing but to carry	HERV 168:1
It isn't f. for humans now	BETJ 37:9
only the F. survive	SERV 270:11
fittest: survival of the f.	ROCK 261:11
Survival of the f.	SPEN 312:17
five: At f. in the afternoon	GARC 148:2
chirche dore she hadde f.	CHAU 95:20
f. miles of fertile ground	COL 103:22
f. minutes too late	COWL 109:13
Full fathom f. thy father lies	SHAK 296:1
Wrapped up in a f-pound note	LEAR 203:11
fix: F. in us thy humble dwelling	WESL 346:10
If it ain't broke, don't f. it	LANCE 200:21
fixed: f. point in a changing world	DOYLE 125:18

fixèd: f. figure for the time	SHAK 292:24
flag: death's pale f.	SHAK 295:24
High as a f. on the Fourth of July	HAMM 161:4
Jelly-bellied F.-flapper	KIPL 198:2
spare your country's f.	WHIT 348:26
We'll keep the red f. flying	CONN 106:23
We shall not f. or fail	CHUR 99:13
flame: Both moth and f.	ROET 261:16
hard, gemlike f.	PATER 246:15
Still plays about the f.	GAY 149:2
tongues of f. are in-folded	ELIOT 133:13
tongues of living f.	AUBER 19:15
When a lovely f. dies	HARB 161:10
Flanders: brought him a F. mare	HENR 166:1
In F. fields the poppies blow	MCCR 214:17
flashes: recognised, in f.	WORD 356:12
occasional f. of silence	SMITH 310:6
flashing: His f. eyes	COL 104:1
flat: divide characters into f. and round	FORS 143:17
Very f., Norfolk	COW 109:3
flats: different sharps and f.	BROW 76:26
flatten: His hide is sure to f. 'em	BELL 33:1
flatter: F. the mountain-tops	SHAK 299:17
flattered: Being f., is a lamb	CHAP 94:14
being then most f.	SHAK 281:5
feared nor f. any flesh	DOUG 125:7
flatterers: f. have intelligence	BACON 24:32
flattering: f. unction to your soul	SHAK 276:22
Some with a f. word	WILDE 350:16
flattery: Everyone likes f.	DISR 122:20
f. soothe the dull cold ear	GRAY 157:8
paid with f.	JOHN 182:10
suppose f. hurts no one	STEV 316:14
Flaubert: true Penelope was F.	POUND 254:15
flea: between a louse and a f.	JOHN 186:2
f. hath smaller fleas	SWIFT 320:23
literature's performing f.	O'CAS 240:23
fleas: dog that has praised his f.	YEATS 360:3
Even educated f. do it	PORT 253:22
F. know not whether	LAND 200:25
f. that tease in the High	BELL 34:1
fled: F. is that music	KEATS 192:7
f. from this vile world	SHAK 299:23
I f. Him, down the nights	THOM 331:8
flee: f. from the wrath to come	BIBLE 48:14
then would I f. away	BOOK 67:11
They f. from me, that sometime	WYATT 358:2
fleece: Its f. was white as snow	HALE 160:7
fleet: All in the Downs the f.	GAY 149:17
Fire and f. and candle-lighte	BALL 27:20
F. in which we serve	BOOK 69:13
f. of stars is anchored	FLEC 141:14
F. the time carelessly	SHAK 272:12
whole F.'s lit up	WOOD 353:18
fleeting: fable, song, or f. shade	HERR 167:14
fleets: f. sweep over thee in vain	BYRON 85:13
Fleet Street: who can be dull in F.	LAMB 200:7
flesh: All f. is as grass	BIBLE 57:6
All f. is grass	BIBLE 46:10
all f. shall see it	BIBLE 46:9
delicate white human f.	FIEL 139:10
east wind made f.	APPL 14:14
eat the f. in that night	BIBLE 39:36
feared nor flattered any f.	DOUG 125:7
f., alas, is wearied	MALL 216:20
f. and blood so cheap	HOOD 171:13
f., how art thou fishified	SHAK 295:5
f. is heir to	SHAK 275:25
F. of flesh	MILT 229:28
f. of my flesh	BIBLE 38:22
F. perishes, I live	HARDY 162:10
Frail f. and die	CROS 112:13
in the f. it is immortal	STEV 316:11
I wants to make your f. creep	DICK 119:27

flesh (cont.):	
more f. than another man	SHAK 278:9
not against f. and blood	BIBLE 56:4
spirit willing but the f. is weak	BIBLE 51:13
they shall be one f.	BIBLE 38:23
thorn in the f.	BIBLE 55:28
too solid f. would melt	SHAK 274:9
world, f., and the devil	BOOK 64:15
Word was made f.	BIBLE 53:11
word was made f.	MISS 231:21
fleshly: through all this f. dress	VAUG 337:9
flesh pots: when we sat by the f.	BIBLE 40:1
flicker: moment of my greatness f.	ELIOT 133:29
flies: As f. to wanton boys	SHAK 283:21
murmurous haunt of f.	KEATS 192:2
fliest: fly thee, for thou f. Me	THOM 331:12
flight: alarms of struggle and f.	ARN 16:12
And took their f.	MARR 219:24
His cloistered f.	SHAK 287:5
His f. was madness	SHAK 287:22
fling: f. the ringleaders	ARN 18:16
flirtation: Merely innocent f.	BYRON 86:24
float: English policy is to f.	SAL 266:2
F. like a butterfly	ALI 4:10
f. upon his watery bier	MILT 227:11
through the clouds I'll never f.	WORD 356:3
floating: his f. hair	COL 104:1
floats: f. on high o'er vales	WORD 355:4
She f., she hesitates	RAC 257:15
flock: feed his f. like a shepherd	BIBLE 46:11
keeping watch over their f.	BIBLE 51:32
silent was the f. in woolly fold	KEATS 190:14
tainted wether of the f.	SHAK 289:24
flocks: father feeds his f.	HOME 170:18
My f. feed not	BARN 29:8
Flodden: Of F.'s fatal field	SCOTT 268:23
flog: f. the rank and file	ARN 18:16
flood: beachèd verge of the salt f.	SHAK 296:24
taken at the f.	SHAK 282:1
ten years before the f.	MARV 220:23
Thorough f., thorough fire	SHAK 290:19
vapour and return it as a f.	GLAD 153:15
flooded: STREETS F. PLEASE ADVISE	BENC 34:6
floods: neither can the f. drown	BIBLE 45:2
floor: curled up on the f.	HARTE 163:13
He oiled his way around the f.	LERN 206:2
Look, how the f. of heaven	SHAK 290:2
rose along the gusty f.	KEATS 190:22
floors: across the f. of silent seas	ELIOT 133:28
Flopshus: F. Cad	KIPL 198:2
Flora: F. and the country green	KEATS 191:29
floraisons: O mois des f.	ARAG 14:21
Flores: At F. in the Azores	TENN 328:10
flotilla: Where the old f. lay	KIPL 196:21
flourish: Princes and lords may f.	GOLD 154:18
Sure thou didst f. once	VAUG 337:13
transfix f. set on youth	SHAK 299:22
flourishing: f. like a green bay-tree	BOOK 66:28
flout: scout 'em, and f. 'em	SHAK 296:7
flow: F. gently, sweet Afton	BURNS 81:23
I within did f.	TRAH 334:1
flower: cometh forth like a f.	BIBLE 42:33
constellated f. that never sets	SHEL 304:20
flourisheth as a f. of a field	BOOK 68:7
f. fadeth	BIBLE 46:10
f. is born to blush unseen	GRAY 157:9
f. no sooner blown	MILT 227:22
f. of a blameless life	TENN 324:1
f. of cities all	ANON 9:2
f. that once hath blown	FITZ 140:10
f. thereof falleth away	BIBLE 57:6
From every opening f.	WATTS 343:5
glory in the f.	WORD 355:23
goodliness thereof is as the f.	BIBLE 46:10
green fuse drives the f.	THOM 330:10

flower (cont.):

meanest f. that blows can give	WORD 355:24
Of learning lightly like a f.	TENN 325:31
same f. that smiles to-day	HERR 167:24
sweetest f. for scent	SHEL 304:31
This midsummer f.	SKEL 308:3
we pluck this f., safety	SHAK 277:30

flowering: About the f. squares — TENN 325:29
f. of His fields — TENN 324:16

flowers: bunch of other men's f. — MONT 233:19

emperice and flour of f.	CHAU 96:10
Ensnared with f., I fall	MARV 220:15
F. in the garden	STEV 317:17
F. of all hue	MILT 229:8
f. of the forest	COCK 102:27
f. that bloom in the spring	GILB 152:6
f. the tenderness of patient minds	OWEN 243:23
frosts are slain and f. begotten	SWIN 321:2
her f. to love	BROO 73:10
hundred f. blossom	MAO T 218:1
I got me f. to strew Thy way	HERB 166:24
of June, and July-f.	HERR 167:12
No f., by request	AING 3:8
Too many f. ... too little fruit	SCOTT 269:7
Where have all the f. gone	SEEG 269:14
wild f., and Prime Ministers	BALD 27:10

flowery: cool f. lap of earth — ARN 16:19

flowing: land f. with milk and honey — BIBLE 39:32

flown: I see all the birds are f. — CHAR 94:23

fluidity: solid for f. — CHUR 99:9

flung: f. himself from the room — LEAC 203:5

flush: roses for the f. of youth — ROSS 263:3

flute: soft complaining f. — DRYD 128:18

flutes: tune of f. kept stroke — SHAK 271:14

flutter: F. and bear him up — BETJ 36:20

fluttered: f. and failed for breath — ARN 17:1

fluttering: F. and dancing — WORD 355:4

flutters: Still f. there, the sole unquiet — COL 103:20

fly: all things f. thee — THOM 331:12

F. envious Time	MILT 228:3
F. fishing	JOHN 186:11
f. from, need not be to hate	BYRON 85:5
F. hence, our contact fear	ARN 17:11
f. may sting a stately horse	JOHN 183:27
f. out through another	BEDE 31:20
f. sat upon the axletree	BACON 25:20
f. the way out of the fly-bottle	WITT 352:7
f. to India for gold	MARL 218:8
He wouldn't hurt a f.	LEAC 203:4
I will f. to thee	KEATS 192:1
long-legged f. upon the stream	YEATS 359:15
man is not a f.	POPE 252:14
noise of a f.	DONNE 124:21
said a spider to a f.	HOW 175:11
seen spiders f.	EDW 131:3
small gilded f. does lecher	SHAK 283:23
Which way I f. is hell	MILT 229:6
with twain he did f.	BIBLE 45:10

fly-blown: f. phylacteries — ROS 262:20

flying: asleep the snow came f. — BRID 72:1

he straight is f.	WROTH 358:1
Keep the aspidistra f.	ORW 242:2

foam: F. glimmered white — ANAT 5:10
opening on the f. — KEATS 192:5

foaming: Tiber f. with much blood — POW 255:3
Tiber f. with much blood — VIRG 339:11

foe: Call no man f. — BENS 34:21

erect and manly f.	CANN 89:12
f. was folly and his weapon wit	HOPE 171:20
friend who never made a f.	TENN 324:10
my dearest f. in heaven	SHAK 274:16
open f. may prove a curse	GAY 149:11
perhaps a jealous f.	SHEL 303:16
willing f. and sea room	ANON 11:22
wolf far thence that's f. to men	WEBS 344:26

foes: man's f. shall be they — BIBLE 49:32

fog: feel the f. in my throat — BROW 77:2

f. comes on little cat feet	SAND 266:13
London particular ... A f.	DICK 118:2
morning f. may chill the air	CROSS 112:10
through the f. and filthy air	SHAK 285:1
yellow f. that rubs its back	ELIOT 133:26

fogies: f. who doffed their lids — KEAT 190:9

fogs: f. prevail upon the day — DRYD 128:5

fold: f., spindle or mutilate — ANON 6:26
like the wolf on the f. — BYRON 85:22
So f. thyself, my dearest — TENN 328:5

folded: To undo the f. lie — AUDEN 21:11

folders: misery of manilla f. — ROET 261:14

folding: little f. of the hands — BIBLE 43:12

folds: spring has kept in its f. — ARAG 14:21
tinklings lull the distant f. — GRAY 157:4

folk: All music is f. music — ARMS 16:3
f. to goon on pilgrimages — CHAU 95:11

folk-dancing: incest and f. — ANON 12:1

folks: Far from the old f. at home — FOST 144:13
O yonge, fresshe f. — CHAU 96:22

follies: f., and misfortunes — GIBB 150:11
Pour her exotic f. o'er — BYRON 86:33

follow: F. me, and I will make — BIBLE 48:18

F. The Gleam	TENN 327:6
F. the yellow brick road	BAUM 30:10
F. up	BOWEN 70:16
I f. the worse	OVID 243:15
I really had to f. them	LEDR 204:4
My old man said, 'F. the van	COLL 105:7
Pay, pack, and f.	BURT 83:4

folly: begins in fear ends in f. — COL 104:28

brood of f. without father	MILT 226:22
foe was f. and his weapon wit	HOPE 171:20
f. he hath committed	BROW 74:18
f. like a stalking-horse	SHAK 273:14
F.'s at full length	BRER 71:22
fool according to his f.	BIBLE 43:38
fool would persist in his f.	BLAKE 61:6
Love the f. of the wise	JOHN 186:9
Public schools 'tis public f.	COWP 110:13
shoot F. as it flies	POPE 252:11
'Tis f. to be wise	GRAY 157:14
When lovely woman stoops to f.	GOLD 155:13

fond: au f. des bois — VIGNY 338:17

reason to be f. of grief	SHAK 282:8
should grow too f. of it	LEE 204:11
so f. of one another	SWIFT 320:2
When men were f., I smiled	SHAK 288:16

fons: Salva me, f. pietatis — MISS 231:24

food: chief of Scotia's f. — BURNS 82:2

Continent people have good f.	MIKES 224:10
discovered that alcohol was a f.	WOD 352:20
Fame is a f. that dead	DOBS 122:26
finds its f. in music	LILLO 207:3
F. comes first, then morals	BREC 71:19
F. enough for a week	MERR 223:26
f. that raises him	HANFF 161:6
homely was their f.	GARTH 148:14
music be the f. of love	SHAK 297:13
problem is f.	DONL 123:2
struggle for room and f.	MALT 217:6

fool: and life time's f. — SHAK 278:14

Behold, I have played the f.	BIBLE 41:19
Busy old f., unruly sun	DONNE 124:11
clever woman to manage a f.	KIPL 197:28
every f. is not a poet	POPE 251:2
f. according to his folly	BIBLE 43:38
f. all the people some of the	LINC 207:10
f. and his words soon parted	SHEN 305:20
f. at forty is a fool indeed	YOUNG 360:14
f. at least in every married	FIEL 139:4
f. consistent and the false	POPE 251:21

fool (*cont.*):

f. hath said in his heart	BOOK 66:12
f. his whole life long	LUTH 212:11
f. lies here who tried	KIPL 196:24
f. may ask more	COLT 105:17
f. me to the top of my bent	SHAK 276:14
'F.,' said my Muse to me	SIDN 306:17
f. sees not the same tree	BLAKE 61:4
f. uttereth all his mind	BIBLE 44:2
f. would persist in his folly	BLAKE 61:6
he is a wise man or a f.	BLAKE 60:22
how ill white hairs become a f.	SHAK 278:32
I am Fortune's f.	SHAK 295:9
knowledgeable f. is a greater f.	MOL 232:18
laughter of a f.	BIBLE 44:16
man suspects himself a f.	YOUNG 360:20
smarts so little as a f.	POPE 251:3
So true a f. is love	SHAK 299:20
Thou f., this night thy soul	BIBLE 52:19
wisest f. in Christendom	HENR 165:22
worm at one end and a f.	JOHN 186:11
foolery: little f. governs the world	OXEN 244:5
foolish: being young and f.	YEATS 359:1
Beware my f. heart	WASH 342:24
f. son is the heaviness	BIBLE 43:16
f. thing was but a toy	SHAK 298:15
f. thing well done	JOHN 184:25
Forgive our f. ways	WHIT 348:27
from saying a f. thing	STER 315:25
He never said a f. thing	ROCH 261:4
I am a very f., fond old man	SHAK 283:29
These F. Things	MARV 221:4
foolishest: it is the f. act	BROW 74:18
foolishness: Mix a little f.	HOR 174:1
fools: flannelled f. at the wicket	KIPL 196:18
f. by heavenly compulsion	SHAK 282:22
f. decoyed into our condition	PEPYS 247:18
F.! For I also had my hour	CHES 97:22
f. in town on our side	TWAIN 335:21
F. out of favour grudge	DEFOE 115:21
F. rush in where angels	POPE 252:10
f., who came to scoff	GOLD 154:22
from children and from f.	DRYD 128:16
I am two f., I know	DONNE 124:14
lighted f. the way to dusty death	SHAK 288:5
Lord, what f. these mortals be	SHAK 290:32
perish together as f.	KING 195:10
proved plain f. at last	POPE 251:27
scarecrows of f.	HUXL 177:20
shoal of f. for tenders	CONG 106:17
Silence is the virtue of f.	BACON 24:8
suffer f. gladly	BIBLE 55:27
To this great stage of f.	SHAK 283:27
world made up of f. and knaves	BUCK 78:1
foot: caught my f. in the mat	GROS 159:4
f. already in the stirrup	CERV 93:21
F.-in-the-grave young man	GILB 152:13
f.—sloggin' over Africa	KIPL 196:6
Forty-second F.	HOOD 171:5
her f. speaks	SHAK 297:9
her f. was light	KEATS 191:9
Now I hold Creation in my f.	HUGH 175:20
on an 'eathen idol's f.	KIPL 196:22
proud f. of a conqueror	SHAK 282:15
thy f. against a stone	BOOK 67:30
football: f. is a matter of life	SHAN 300:22
he's f. crazy, he's f. mad	MCGR 214:22
footfalls: F. echo in the memory	ELIOT 132:26
footman: eternal F. hold my coat	ELIOT 133:29
footmen: lowest class is *literary* f.	HAZL 164:4
footnotes: series of f. to Plato	WHIT 348:6
foot-path: jog on the f. way	SHAK 298:28
footprints: F. on the sands of time	LONG 209:23
footsteps: plants his f. in the sea	COWP 109:25
footstool: make thine enemies thy f.	BOOK 68:14

foppery: excellent f. of the world	SHAK 282:22
sound of shallow f.	SHAK 289:10
for: f. whom the bell tolls	DONNE 124:20
F. you but not for me	ANON 9:21
F. your tomorrows	EDM 130:20
forasmuch: f. as without thee	BOOK 64:26
forbid: He shall live a man f.	SHAK 285:4
forbidden: Of that f. tree	MILT 228:7
force: blend f. with a manoeuvre	TROT 335:2
f. alone is but *temporary*	BURKE 80:1
f. and road of casualty	SHAK 289:13
F. is not a remedy	BRIG 72:6
'F.' is the food that raises	HANFF 161:6
f. maintaining the life	DOST 125:1
f. that through the green fuse	THOM 330:10
may the f. be with you	LUCAS 211:28
No motion has she now, no f.	WORD 356:25
other nations use 'f.'	WAUGH 343:28
own no argument but f.	BROW 74:25
Surprised by unjust f.	MILT 226:18
Who overcomes by f.	MILT 228:18
forced: F. her to do your pleasure	WEBS 344:24
forces: change that state by f.	NEWT 239:3
forcibly: f. if we must	CLAY 101:17
Ford: I am a F., not a Lincoln	FORD 143:3
forefathers: f. of the hamlet sleep	GRAY 157:6
Think of your f.!	ADAMS 2:4
forefinger: stretched f. of all Time	TENN 327:18
forehead: f. of the morning sky	MILT 227:18
foreign: attacking the F. Secretary	BEVAN 37:21
F. Secretary naked into	BEVAN 38:1
Life is a f. language	MORL 235:7
my f. policy: I wage war	CLEM 102:1
past is a f. country	HART 163:14
some corner of a f. field	BROO 73:10
Thracian ships and the f. faces	SWIN 321:1
with their courtly f. grace	TENN 328:14
foreigners: f. always spell better	TWAIN 336:1
f. are fiends	MITF 232:10
more f. I saw	BELL 34:5
forelock: f. to the British establishment	KEAT 190:9
foremost: none who would be f.	MAC 214:6
forepangs: schooled at f.	HOPK 172:9
foreplay: No f. No afterplay	BENN 34:11
forest: clipped hedge is to a f.	JOHN 186:12
Down in the f. something	SIMP 307:10
flowers of the f.	COCK 102:27
f. laments in order	CHUR 99:1
F. where all must lose	THOM 330:24
This is the f. primeval	LONG 209:15
forests: In the f. of the night	BLAKE 62:5
foretold: f. that the heart grows old	YEATS 359:29
forever: Man has F.	BROW 75:32
picket's off duty f.	BEERS 32:14
forge: f. and working-house	SHAK 280:1
forget: but do not quite f.	CHES 98:4
do not thou f. me	ASTL 19:8
F. all feuds	MAC 214:4
F. six counties	MORR 235:16
honour doth f. men's names	SHAK 282:3
If I f. thee, O Jerusalem	BOOK 69:4
I never f. a face	MARX 221:7
In violence, we f. who we	MCC 214:11
Lest we f.—lest we forget	KIPL 197:2
nor worms f.	DICK 119:9
not f. the suspenders	KIPL 197:23
Old men f.	SHAK 279:19
Till thou remember and I f.	SWIN 321:16
we f. because we must	ARN 16:9
wise forgive but do not f.	SZASZ 321:24
you should f. and smile	ROSS 263:4
forgetfulness: Not in entire f.	WORD 355:20
forgetting: grand memory for f.	STEV 316:26
sleep and a f.	WORD 355:20

forgetting (*cont.*):

world f., by the world forgot	POPE 250:26
forgive: allows you to f. yourself	SHAW 302:8
Father, f. them	BIBLE 53:2
F., O Lord, my little jokes	FROST 146:10
F. our foolish ways	WHIT 348:27
f. that sin where I begun	DONNE 123:17
f. us our debts	BIBLE 48:27
f. us our trespasses	BOOK 63:16
good Lord will f. me	CATH 92:21
lambs could not f.	DICK 119:9
rarely, if ever, do they f. them	WILDE 350:12
sin against me, and I f. him	BIBLE 50:19
To err is human; to f., divine	POPE 252:7
wise f. but do not forget	SZASZ 321:24
woman can f. a man the harm	MAUG 222:10
Women can't f. failure	CHEK 96:26
forgiven: ransomed, healed, restored, f.	LYTE 212:21
sins, which are many, are f.	BIBLE 52:8
Youth, which is f. everything	SHAW 302:6
forgiveness: ask of thee f.	SHAK 284:1
F. of sins	BOOK 64:3
such knowledge, what f.	ELIOT 133:15
forgot: by the world f.	POPE 250:26
curiosities would be quite f.	AUBR 19:16
Honey, I just f. to duck	DEMP 116:25
unknown proposed as things f.	POPE 252:8
forgotten: always a f. thing	CHES 97:21
been learned has been f.	SKIN 308:6
f. before God	BIBLE 52:17
f. man	ROOS 262:7
f. nothing and learnt nothing	DUM 129:6
f. scream for help in dreams	CAN 89:9
He hath not f. my age	SOUT 312:2
I am all f.	SHAK 271:9
I have f. your name	SWIN 321:14
injury sooner f. than an insult	CHES 97:5
learned nothing, and f. nothing	TALL 322:12
ruins of f. times	BROW 74:3
forked: f. animal as thou art	SHAK 283:14
forks: pursued it with f. and hope	CARR 92:9
forlorn: F.! the very word	KEATS 192:6
that would make me less f.	WORD 357:11
form: earth was without f.	BIBLE 38:13
F. follows function	SULL 319:1
F. of being is assigned	WORD 354:22
F. remains	WORD 356:18
mould of f.	SHAK 276:2
silent f., dost tease us	KEATS 191:23
take thy f. from off my door	POE 250:7
Terror the human f. divine	BLAKE 62:7
formal: f. feeling comes	DICK 120:8
formed: small, but perfectly f.	COOP 107:21
former: f. and the latter rain	BOOK 64:20
f. things are passed	BIBLE 58:5
formerly: what we were f. told	BLUN 62:15
forms: f. of things unknown	SHAK 291:4
forsaken: never the righteous f.	BOOK 66:27
why hast thou f. me	BIBLE 51:16
forsaking: f. all other	BOOK 65:28
forsan: F. et haec olim	VIRG 339:2
forsythia: Of prunus and f.	BETJ 37:6
fort: Hold the f.	BLISS 62:10
forth: F. in thy name	WESL 346:5
Man goeth f. to his work	BOOK 68:8
fortis: F. fortuna adiuvat	TER 329:5
fortress: f. built by Nature	SHAK 293:16
fortresses: brambles in the f.	BIBLE 46:3
fortunate: farmers excessively f.	VIRG 340:7
he is at best but f.	SOLON 310:27
fortune: arrows of outrageous f.	SHAK 275:25
Base F., now I see	MARL 218:16
beauty without a f.	FARQ 138:16
Blind F. still bestows	JONS 187:8
F. assists the brave	TER 329:5

fortune (*cont.*):

F. favours the brave	VIRG 339:20
F.'s a right whore	WEBS 344:22
f.'s sharpe adversitee	CHAU 96:18
F., that favours fools	JONS 186:22
hostages to f.	BACON 25:1
how does f. banter us	BOL 63:6
I am F.'s fool	SHAK 295:9
leads on to f.	SHAK 282:1
little value of f.	STEE 314:18
man who takes your f.	WOOL 354:7
O fickle F.	COCK 102:27
possession of a good f.	AUST 23:2
You fools of f.	SHAK 296:20
forty: Fat, fair and f.	O'KEE 241:6
fool at f. is a fool indeed	YOUNG 360:14
F. years on	BOWEN 70:15
Knows it at f.	YOUNG 360:20
loves a fairy when she's f.	HENL 165:16
man over f. is a scoundrel	SHAW 302:5
forty-five: At f. what next?	LOW 211:15
forty-three: very well pass for f.	GILB 152:31
forward: hold from this day f.	BOOK 66:1
looking f. to the past	OSB 242:24
marched breast f.	BROW 75:11
not look f. to posterity	BURKE 80:12
Some men a f. motion love	VAUG 337:10
those whom cried 'F.!'	MAC 214:6
fossil: Language is f. poetry	EMER 136:28
foster-child: f. of silence	KEATS 191:17
fou: I wasna f.	BURNS 82:3
fought: f. against Sisera	BIBLE 40:32
f. against the dragon	BIBLE 57:31
f. the dogs and killed the cats	BROW 76:26
f. with us upon Saint Crispin's	SHAK 279:20
I have f. a good fight	BIBLE 56:21
not to have won but to have f.	COUB 108:15
Than never to have f. at all	CLOU 102:21
they f. each other	SOUT 311:19
foul: Fair is foul, and f. is fair	SHAK 285:1
Fair is too f. an epithet	MARL 219:10
f. and fair a day	SHAK 285:6
f. Fiend coming over	BUNY 78:20
f. things up requires a computer	ANON 11:7
however f. within	CHUR 98:25
Murder most f.	SHAK 274:31
foulest: shortest way the f.	BACON 24:3
found: f. Him in the shining	TENN 324:16
f. myself famous	BYRON 87:21
f. my sheep which was lost	BIBLE 52:27
Hast thou f. me, O mine enemy	BIBLE 42:5
he was lost, and is f.	BIBLE 52:32
man who has f. himself out	BARR 29:18
When f., make a note of	DICK 118:20
foundation: f. of most governments	ADAMS 2:2
Good order is the f.	BURKE 80:21
fount: f. whence honour	MARL 219:9
slow, fresh f.	JONS 187:2
fountain: f. momently was forced	COL 103:23
f. of all goodness	BOOK 64:8
f. of goodness	BACON 24:10
f. of honour	BAG 26:4
f. of the water of life	BIBLE 58:6
Thou f., at which drink	COWP 110:3
woman moved is like a f.	SHAK 295:30
fountains: from little f. flow	EVER 137:24
Where Afric's sunny f.	HEBER 164:15
four: F. legs good, two legs bad	ORW 241:22
two plus two make f.	ORW 242:9
fourscore: F. and seven years ago	LINC 207:8
strong that they come to f.	BOOK 67:26
fourth: f. estate of the realm	MAC 213:4
fowls: smale f. maken melodye	CHAU 95:11
fox: ar'n't that I loves the f. less	SURT 319:10
Crazy like a f.	PER 247:23

fox (cont.):

f. from his lair	GRAV 156:12
f. jumps over the lazy dog	ANON 10:7
f. knows many things	ARCH 15:1
gentleman galloping after a f.	WILDE 350:9
mentality of a f. at large	LEVIN 206:7
My God! They've shot our f.	BIRCH 59:14
prince must be a f.	MACH 215:3

foxes: f. have a sincere interest

foxes: f. have a sincere interest	ELIOT 132:4
f. have holes	BIBLE 49:19
little f., that spoil the vines	BIBLE 44:33
portion for f.	BOOK 67:15
second to the f.	BERL 36:4

foxholes: on the f. or graveyards	KENN 194:7
There are no atheists in the f.	CUMM 113:6
fox-hunters: people that think, and f.	SHEN 305:21
frabjous: O f. day!	CARR 91:16
fragments: f. I have shored	ELIOT 134:31
frailty: F., thy name is woman	SHAK 274:12
love's the noblest f.	DRYD 127:33
noblest f. of the mind	SHAD 270:18
therefore more f.	SHAK 278:9
frame: f. of adamant	JOHN 183:13
framed: to have it f. and glazed	WALP 341:22
français: pas clair n'est pas f.	RIV 260:14
France: best thing between F. and England	JERR 181:1
Fair stood the wind for F.	DRAY 126:22
F., famed in all great arts	ARN 17:21
F. has lost a battle	DE G 116:3
F., mother of arts	DU B 128:32
F. was long a despotism	CARL 90:14
order this matter better in F.	STER 315:8
sweet enemy, F.	SIDN 306:21
There lived a singer in F.	SWIN 321:19
two breasts by which F.	SULLY 319:3
vasty fields of F.	SHAK 278:34
will in F., by God's grace	SHAK 279:1
Francesca di Rimini: F., miminy	GILB 152:12
Frankie: F. and Albert were lovers	ANON 7:6
frankincense: f., and myrrh	BIBLE 48:10
frankly: F., my dear	MITC 232:6
frantic: There's a fascination f.	GILB 152:8
fraternité: Liberté! Égalité! F.!	ANON 12:11
fraternize: I beckon you to f.	AUDEN 21:8
fraud: pious f. of the almanac	LOW 211:10
freckled: Whatever is fickle, f.	HOPK 172:13
freckles: curiosity, f., and doubt	PARK 245:5
free: better to be in chains than to be f.	KAFKA 189:18
born f. and equal in dignity	ANON 5:20
Comment is f.	SCOTT 268:3
Ev'rything f. in America	SOND 311:8
f. agent that you were	AUR 22:11
f. as nature first made man	DRYD 127:26
f. society ... safe to be unpopular	STEV 316:18
F. speech, free passes	BETJ 37:4
f. themselves must strike	BYRON 85:1
Greece might still be f.	BYRON 86:14
half slave and half f.	LINC 207:5
he's f. again	SOLZ 310:28
I am a f. man, an American	JOHN 181:19
I am condemned to be f.	SART 267:2
I was f. born	BIBLE 54:24
Man was born f., and everywhere	ROUS 263:18
Mother of the f.	BENS 34:20
nominally f., but enslaved	BOOTH 69:21
no such thing as a f. lunch	ANON 10:21
O'er the land of the f.	KEY 194:12
perfectly f. till all are free	SPEN 312:21
Ring in the valiant man and f.	TENN 325:27
soul in prison, I am not f.	DEBS 115:9
that moment they are f.	COWP 110:7
they are f. to do whatever	SHAW 301:20
Thou art f.	ARN 17:14
Thought is f.	SHAK 296:7
truth shall make you f.	BIBLE 53:28

free (cont.):

truth which makes men f.	AGAR 3:5
Was he f.? Was he happy?	AUDEN 21:17
We know our will is f.	JOHN 184:20
wholly slaves or wholly f.	DRYD 127:30
worth nothin', but it's f.	KRIS 199:5
yearning to breathe f.	LAZ 203:2

freedom: better organised than f.	PÉGUY 247:4
bondage which is f.'s self	SHEL 304:27
enemies of F. do not argue	INGE 178:10
establishes his true f.	MONT 233:14
fight for f. and truth	IBSEN 178:3
flame of f. in their souls	SYM 321:20
F. and Whisky gang thegither	BURNS 81:26
f. for the one who thinks	LUX 212:12
f. is a noble thing	BARB 28:16
F. is slavery	ORW 242:7
F. is the freedom to say	ORW 242:9
F. of the press in Britain	SWAF 319:16
F.'s just another word	KRIS 199:5
giving f. to the slave	LINC 207:6
green f. of a cockatoo	STEV 316:12
I gave my life for f.	EWER 138:1
O F., what liberties	GEOR 150:6
Perfect f. is reserved	COLL 105:5
preserve and enlarge f.	LOCKE 208:20
rest love not f.	MILT 231:7
what is F.?	COL 103:11
What stands if f. fall	KIPL 196:13
Where F. slowly broadens down	TENN 329:1
with a great sum obtained I this f.	BIBLE 54:24
whose service is perfect f.	BOOK 64:5

freedoms: four essential human f.	ROOS 262:13
Natural f. are but just	ROCH 261:5
freehold: life is given to none f.	LUCR 212:6
freely: F. ye have received	BIBLE 49:27
freemasonry: kind of bitter f.	BEER 32:11
freeze: f. my humanity	MACN 216:6
f. thy young blood	SHAK 274:30
To f. the blood	WORD 355:1
freezes: Yours till Hell f.	FISH 139:25
freezings: What f. have I felt	SHAK 300:3
frei: Arbeit macht f.	ANON 13:1
French: F. are wiser than they seem	BACON 25:12
F. are with equal advantage	CANN 89:10
F. noblesse had been capable	TREV 334:8
F. of Parys was to hire	CHAU 95:15
F., or Turk, or Proosian	GILB 152:21
F. the empire of the land	RICH 260:6
F. want no-one to be their	TOCQ 333:4
F. widow in every bedroom	HOFF 170:5
glory of beating the F.	WOLFE 353:3
No more Latin, no more F.	ANON 9:17
not too F. French bean	GILB 152:11
Paris was F.—and silent	TUCH 335:8
Speak in F. when you can't	CARR 91:19
to women Italian, men F.	CHAR 95:7
We are not F.	MONT 233:24
What is not clear is not F.	RIV 260:14
Frenchmen: Fifty million F.	GUIN 159:9
frenzy: Demoniac f.	MILT 229:31
fine f. rolling	SHAK 291:4
frequency: very fact of f.	ELIOT 132:11
frère: mon semblable,—mon f.	BAUD 30:3
fresh: both so ancient and so f.	AUG 21:24
f. as is the month of May	CHAU 95:13
f. lap of the crimson rose	SHAK 290:23
noted for f. air and fun	EDGAR 130:15
O yonge, f. folkes	CHAU 96:22
Tomorrow to f. woods	MILT 227:20
women of that ever-f. terrain	AMIS 5:8
fret: fever, and the f.	KEATS 191:31
F. not thyself	BOOK 66:26
frets: struts and f. his hour	SHAK 288:5
fretted: F. the pigmy body	DRYD 127:6

Freud: trouble with F.	DODD 122:29
Freude: F., *schöner Götterfunken*	SCH 267:18
Freudian: her F. papa and maids	LOW 211:11
Friday: My man F.	DEFOE 115:15
friend: At luncheon with a city f.	BELL 33:24
author as you choose a f.	DILL 120:22
betraying my f.	FORS 144:2
Boldness be my f.	SHAK 273:23
diamonds are a girl's best f.	ROBIN 260:18
faithful female f.	WHUR 349:4
F. and associate of this clay	HADR 159:14
F., go up higher	BIBLE 52:21
f. in power is a friend lost	ADAMS 1:14
f. of every country but his own	CANN 89:11
f. of flattering illusions	CONR 107:8
f. sincere enough to tell	BULW 78:12
f. that sticketh closer	BIBLE 43:30
f. unseen, unborn, unknown	FLEC 141:20
from the candid f.	CANN 89:12
goodnatured f. or another	SHER 305:23
have a f. is to be one	EMER 136:21
homes without a f.	CLARE 101:5
last best f. am I	SOUT 311:23
lay down his wife for his f.	JOYCE 188:18
Little F. of all the World	KIPL 197:25
loss of a dear f.	SOUT 312:5
Mine own familiar f.	BOOK 67:2
mine own familiar f.	BOOK 67:12
mistress or a f.	SHEL 303:15
much-loved and elegant f.	CHAR 95:8
never want a f. in need	DICK 118:20
no f. who never made a foe	TENN 324:10
Nor a f. to know me	STEV 317:25
paint a portrait I lose a f.	SARG 266:23
plain, blunt man that love my f.	SHAK 281:25
pretended f. is worse	GAY 149:11
What is a f.	ARIS 16:21
Whenever a f. succeeds	VIDAL 338:13
With a religious book, or f.	WOTT 357:14
With one chained f.	SHEL 303:16
woman can become a man's f.	CHEK 96:28
your enemy and your f.	TWAIN 335:25
friendless: f. bodies of unburied	WEBS 344:25
friends: book is the best of f.	TUPP 335:10
dear f. have to part	BOND 63:9
f. of every country save	DISR 121:17
f. ... people who got there first	UST 336:16
F., Romans, countrymen	SHAK 281:18
glory was I had such f.	YEATS 359:17
Good thoughts his only f.	CAMP 89:3
How to win f.	CARN 90:28
I have lost f.	WOOLF 354:5
laughter and the love of f.	BELL 34:3
lay down his f. for his life	THOR 332:13
little help from my f.	MCC 205:18
Money couldn't buy f.	MILL 225:11
none of his f. like him	WILDE 350:21
Of two close f., one is	LERM 205:24
Our f., the enemy	BÉR 35:11
something left to treat my f.	MALL 216:21
Soul and body part like f.	CRAS 111:15
To my f. pictured within	ELGAR 131:17
want of f., and empty purse	BRET 71:23
friendship: F. is a disinterested commerce	GOLD 155:6
F. is constant in all other	SHAK 291:17
F. is Love without his wings	BYRON 87:1
f. recognised by the police	STEV 317:7
his f. in constant repair	JOHN 184:4
honest f. with all nations	JEFF 180:19
frieze: striped f.	STR 318:11
frighted: f. with false fire	SHAK 276:11
frighten: by God, they f. me	WELL 345:7
don't f. the horses	CAMP 88:14
frightened: f. look in its eyes	SITW 307:21

frightened *(cont.)*:	
killed than f. to death	SURT 319:12
fringèd: f. curtains of thine eye	SHAK 296:2
frocks: F. and Curls	DICK 120:17
frog: Eye of newt, and toe of f.	SHAK 287:16
frogs: F. Eat Butterflies	STEV 316:7
frolics: youth of f.	POPE 251:11
frontier: f. of my Person goes	AUDEN 21:8
on the edge of a new f.	KENN 194:1
frontiers: old f. are gone	BALD 27:6
frost: F. at Midnight	COL 103:18
f. performs its secret ministry	COL 103:18
f. which binds so dear	SHEL 303:3
His graver of f.	THOM 331:19
like an untimely f.	SHAK 295:21
lovely Morning, rich in f.	DAV 114:21
third day comes a f.	SHAK 280:18
frosts: f. are slain	SWIN 321:2
hoary-headed f.	SHAK 290:23
frosty: F., but kindly	SHAK 272:16
froth: Life is mostly f.	GORD 155:21
froward: very f. generation	BIBLE 40:24
frown: Convey a libel in a f.	SWIFT 320:16
Phyllis, without f. or smile	SEDL 269:12
frowning: Behind a f. providence	COWP 109:26
frowst: f. with a book by the fire	KIPL 197:22
frozen: Architecture is f. music	SCH 267:17
f. wind crept on above	SHEL 303:14
trembling through the f. grass	KEATS 190:14
Your tiny hand is f.	ILL 150:9
fruit: disobedience, and the f.	MILT 228:7
humid nightblue f.	JOYCE 188:19
Too many flowers, too little f.	SCOTT 269:7
veranda, and the f.	AUDEN 20:25
weakest kind of f.	SHAK 289:24
fruitful: Be f., and multiply	BIBLE 38:17
f. ground, the quiet mind	SURR 319:6
shall be as the f. vine	BOOK 68:32
vineyard in a very f. hill	BIBLE 45:7
fruitfulness: mists and mellow f.	KEATS 192:14
fruition: f. of an earthly crown	MARL 219:8
fruits: By their f. ye shall know them	BIBLE 49:15
first f. of them that slept	BIBLE 55:17
frustra: *f. vigilat qui custodit*	BIBLE 58:13
frustrate: F. their knavish tricks	ANON 7:14
frying-pan: fish that talks in the f.	DE L 116:11
fuck: f. all in between	BENN 34:11
They f. you up, your mum	LARK 201:17
fugaces: *Eheu f., Postume*	HOR 173:23
fugit: *f. inreparabile tempus*	VIRG 340:9
fugitive: f. from th' law of averages	MAUL 222:13
Führer: *Ein Reich, ein Volk, ein F.*	ANON 13:2
fulfil: F. now, O Lord, the desires	BOOK 64:10
full: F. fathom five thy father	SHAK 296:1
f. of passionate intensity	YEATS 359:24
f. tide of human existence	JOHN 185:1
Reading maketh a f. man	BACON 25:15
Sea of faith was once, too, at the f.	ARN 16:11
Serenely f., the epicure	SMITH 310:7
fulness: and the f. thereof	BIBLE 55:9
fume: stinking f. thereof	JAM 179:9
fun: Ain't We Got F.	KAHN 189:19
f. in any Act of Parliament	HERB 166:17
F. is fun but no girl wants	LOOS 210:9
f. is nine-tenths of the law	SAY 267:15
It was great f.	PORT 253:21
more f. to be with	NASH 237:11
most f. without laughing	ALLEN 4:13
function: Form follows f.	SULL 319:1
F. never dies	WORD 356:18
fundament: frigid upon the f.	NASH 237:16
fundamental: f. things apply	HUPF 176:20
funeral: f. baked meats	SHAK 274:16
not a f. note	WOLFE 352:25
No war, nor prince's f.	MARV 220:21

funeral (*cont.*):		**gallery** (*cont.*):	
present is the f. of the past	CLARE 101:8	History is a g. of pictures	TOCQ 333:1
funk: poor world in a blue f.	CRANE 111:1	**Gallia:** *G. est omnis divisa*	CAES 87:24
funny: f. as long as it is happening	ROG 261:22	**gallimaufry:** g. or hodgepodge	SPEN 313:20
Funny-peculiar or f. ha-ha	HAY 163:20	**gallop:** G. about doing good	SMITH 309:17
It's a f. old world	JONES 116:24	G. apace, you fiery-footed	SHAK 295:10
furious: fun grew fast and f.	BURNS 82:23	**galloped:** we g. all three	BROW 76:5
furiously: green ideas sleep f.	CHOM 98:18	**gallows:** complexion is perfect g.	SHAK 295:31
heathen so f. rage together	BOOK 66:9	upon the g. or of the pox	WILK 350:26
he driveth f.	BIBLE 42:13	**gamble:** Life is a g. at terrible odds	STOP 318:6
furnace: burning fiery f.	BIBLE 47:11	**gambler:** whore and g.	BLAKE 60:9
furnaces: Your worship is your f.	BOTT 70:6	**game:** Anarchism is a g.	SHAW 302:10
furnish: Books do f. a room	POW 254:25	g. at which two can play	BEER 32:12
Would f. all we ought to ask	KEBLE 193:17	g. is never lost till won	CRAB 110:28
furnished: F. and burnish'd	BETJ 37:10	g.'s afoot	SHAK 279:6
ladies who live in f. souls	CUMM 113:5	giving over of a g.	FLET 31:2
large upper room f.	BIBLE 52:40	hard if I cannot start some g.	HAZL 164:8
furniture: No f. so charming as books	SMITH 310:2	helpless pieces of the g.	FITZ 140:12
piece of mere church f.	COWP 110:15	how you played the G.	RICE 259:17
furry: fire was f. as a bear	SITW 307:17	more than a g.	HUGH 175:23
further: f. from God	ANDR 5:16	play up! and play the g.	NEWB 238:13
fury: blind f. of creation	SHAW 301:17	time to win this g.	DRAKE 126:13
full of sound and f.	SHAK 288:5	Truth the g. of the few	BERK 35:17
f. of a patient man	DRYD 127:17	woman is his g.	TENN 327:25
no f. like a non-combatant	MONT 233:7	**games:** dread of g.	BETJ 37:14
Nor Hell a f., like a woman	CONG 106:12	G. people play	BERNE 36:10
fuse: green f. drives the flower	THOM 330:10	their g. should be seen as	MONT 233:11
fuss: What a f. about an omelette	VOLT 341:2	**gamesmanship:** g. or The art of	POTT 254:7
fustian: f.'s so sublimely bad	POPE 251:5	**gamut:** g. of the emotions	PARK 245:16
futility: fatal f. of Fact	JAMES 180:2	**gang:** may g. a kennin wrang	BURNS 81:21
future: Back to the f.	GALE 361:2	**gangsters:** always acted like g.	KUBR 199:7
cannot fight against the f.	GLAD 153:8	**gap:** it is the last g. but one	WHITE 347:17
door opens and lets the f. in	GREE 158:6	**garde:** *La G. meurt*	CAMB 88:11
F. as a promised land	LEWIS 206:11	**garden:** Almighty first planted a g.	BACON 24:26
f. everybody will be famous	WARH 342:20	Back to the g.	MITC 232:4
F. shock	TOFF 333:6	Come into the g., Maud	TENN 326:28
f. states of both are left to faith	BYRON 86:12	cultivate our g.	VOLT 340:13
I never think of the f.	EINS 131:13	fairies at the bottom of our g.	FYL 147:9
lively sense of f. favours	WALP 342:7	g. is a lovesome thing	BROWN 73:19
once and f. king	WHITE 347:18	g. of your face	HERB 166:19
past controls the f.	ORW 242:8	g.'s umbrage mild	SMART 308:12
picture of the f.	ORW 242:11	g. walled around	WATTS 343:2
plan the f. by the past	BURKE 79:20	Glory of the G.	KIPL 196:16
present in time f.	ELIOT 132:25	God the first g. made	COWL 109:13
put no trust in the f.	HOR 173:20	image walking in the g.	SHEL 304:15
seen the f. and it works	STEF 314:19	imperfections of my g.	MONT 233:9
serve the f. hour	WORD 356:19	land where a g. should be	HOR 174:4
Fuzzy-Wuzzy: 'ere's to you, F.	KIPL 196:14	lodge in a g. of cucumbers	BIBLE 45:3
Fyfe: David Patrick Maxwell F.	ANON 9:14	man and a woman in a g.	WILDE 350:11
		Mr McGregor's g.	POTT 254:3
		nearer God's Heart in a g.	GURN 159:10
G		Our England is a g.	KIPL 196:16
		planted a g. eastward in Eden	BIBLE 38:18
gabardine: spit upon my Jewish g.	SHAK 289:5	rosebud g. of girls	TENN 326:29
gadding: thyme and the g. vine	MILT 227:13	sunlight on the g.	MACN 216:10
Gaels: great G. of Ireland	CHES 97:20	through the vext g.-trees	ARN 17:18
gag: tight as g. of place	HEAN 164:11	unweeded g.	SHAK 274:10
gaiety: eclipsed the g. of nations	JOHN 182:23	walking in the g. in the cool	BIBLE 38:26
Take me back to the G. hotel	ASHF 18:25	**gardener:** Adam was a g.	SHAK 280:11
gaily: G. into Ruislip Gardens	BETJ 37:7	**gardens:** closing time in the g. of the West
gain: g. the whole world	BIBLE 51:23		CONN 106:27
richest I count but loss	WATTS 343:4	g. with real toads in them	MOORE 234:8
gains: no g. without pains	STEV 316:16	Sowe Carrets in your G.	GARD 148:4
gait: forced g. of a shuffling nag	SHAK 278:4	**garish:** Hide me from day's g. eye	MILT 226:26
gaiters: All is gas and g.	DICK 119:17	I loved the g. day	NEWM 238:22
Galatians: great text in G.	BROW 77:12	no worship to the g. sun	SHAK 295:14
Galilean: You have won, G.	JUL 188:20	**garland:** green willow is my g.	HEYW 168:8
Galilee: rolls nightly on deep G.	BYRON 85:22	withered is the g. of the war	SHAK 271:25
gall: take my milk for g.	SHAK 285:18	**garlands:** not shackles ... they are g.	BENN 34:13
wormwood and the g.	BIBLE 47:1	**garment:** g. was white as snow	BIBLE 47:14
gallant: died a very g. gentleman	CHER 19:11	know the g. from the man	BLAKE 60:15
g. trim the gilded vessel	GRAY 157:3	**garmented:** g. in light	SHEL 305:16
gallantry: What men call g.	BYRON 85:24	**garments:** Reasons are not like g.	ESSEX 137:16
galleon: Stately as a G.	GREN 158:15	Stuffs out his vacant g.	SHAK 282:8
gallery: faces are but a g.	BACON 24:23	They part my g. among them	BOOK 66:16

garnished: swept, and g.   BIBLE 50:3
garret: Genius in a g. starving   ROB 260:22
   living in a g.   FOOTE 142:19
Garrick: Our G.'s a salad   GOLD 155:1
gas: All is g. and gaiters   DICK 119:17
   G. smells awful   PARK 245:8
gate: hear November at the g.   PUSH 256:22
   I am here at the g. alone   TENN 326:28
   poor man at his g.   ALEX 4:3
   sings hymns at heaven's g.   SHAK 299:15
   stood at the g. of the year   HASK 163:16
   watchful at his g.   DODD 122:30
   Wide is the g., and broad   BIBLE 49:12
gates: despondently at area g.   ELIOT 134:4
   enter then his g. with praise   KETHE 194:11
   g. to the glorious   FORS 143:19
   go to the g. of Hell   PIUS 249:11
   Lift up your heads, O ye g.   BOOK 66:20
Gath: Tell it not in G.   BIBLE 41:21
gather: G. therefore the rose   SPEN 313:12
   G. ye rosebuds while ye may   HERR 167:24
gathered: when two or three are g.   BOOK 64:10
   where two or three are g.   BIBLE 50:18
gathering: g. where thou hast   BIBLE 51:2
gat-tothed: G. I was   CHAU 96:7
gaudeamus: G. igitur   ANON 13:16
gaudy: doffed her g. trim   MILT 227:25
   g., blabbing, and remorseful day   SHAK 280:9
   one other g. night   SHAK 271:19
Gaul: G. as a whole is divided   CAES 87:24
gay: and without feeling g.   CHUR 98:26
   g. Lothario   ROWE 263:20
   Her heart was warm and g.   HAMM 161:1
   I'm a g. deceiver   COLM 105:1
   impiously g.   CRAB 110:23
   second best's a g. goodnight   YEATS 359:5
   So g. the band   GREN 158:15
Gaza: Eyeless in G.   MILT 230:10
gazelle: I never nursed a dear g.   MOORE 234:19
geese: G. are swans   ARN 16:18
   Like g. about the sky   AUDEN 20:11
   swans of others are g.   WALP 342:1
Gehenna: Down to G.   KIPL 196:20
gem: g. of purest ray serene   GRAY 157:9
gems: prow-promoted g. again   BETJ 37:1
   Rich and rare were the g.   MOORE 234:17
   these the g. of heaven   MILT 229:11
gender: she's of the feminine g.   O'KEE 241:5
general: caviare to the g.   SHAK 275:18
   civil war, a g. must know   REED 258:18
generalities: glittering and sounding g.   CHOA 98:17
   Glittering g.   EMER 137:2
General Motors: good for G.   WILS 351:11
generals: bite some of my other g.   GEOR 149:22
   dead battles, like dead g.   TUCH 335:7
   Russia has two g.   NICH 239:11
   wooden swords we're all G.   UST 336:18
generation: g. destroyed by madness   GINS 153:3
   g. of them that hate me   BIBLE 40:5
   leaves is a g. of men   HOMER 170:21
   O g. of vipers   BIBLE 48:14
   very froward g.   BIBLE 40:24
   ye are a chosen g.   BIBLE 57:8
   You are all a lost g.   STEIN 314:23
generations: all g. shall call me blessed   BIBLE 51:28
   G. pass while some trees   BROW 74:6
   shirtsleeves in three g.   ANON 7:8
   Those dying g.—at their song   YEATS 359:20
generous: first impulses ... always g.   MONT 234:1
   My mind as g., and my shape   SHAK 282:20
   something g. in mere lust   ROCH 261:5
Geneva: grim G. ministers   AYT 23:16
geniumque: G. loci   VIRG 339:18
genius: believe yourself a great g.   BEAU 30:17

genius (cont.):
   G. a greater aptitude for patience   BUFF 78:6
   G. a mind of large general power   JOHN 182:18
   G. ... capacity of taking trouble   CARL 90:10
   G. does what it must   MER 223:25
   g. I had when I wrote   SWIFT 320:25
   G. in a garret starving   ROB 260:22
   G. is one per cent inspiration   EDIS 130:19
   G. is the child of imitation   REYN 259:10
   g. of Einstein leads   PIC 248:19
   g. of its scientists   EIS 131:14
   g. of the Constitution   PITT 249:5
   g. of the place   POPE 251:15
   g. that could cut a Colossus   JOHN 186:4
   Gives g. a better discerning   GOLD 155:8
   I think like a g.   NAB 236:20
   models destroy g. and art   HAZL 164:5
   nothing to declare except my g.   WILDE 350:18
   Philistine of g. in religion   ARN 18:11
   Ramp up my g.   JONS 187:9
   talent instantly recognizes g.   DOYLE 126:8
   Taste is the feminine of g.   FITZ 140:19
   times in which a g. would   ADAMS 1:7
   true g. appears in the world   SWIFT 320:11
   Whence g. wildly flashed   KEATS 192:17
genteelly: committed very g.   BOSW 70:5
gentle: G. as falcon   SKEL 308:3
   G. Child of gentle Mother   DEAR 115:7
   g. into that good night   THOM 330:7
   G. Jesus, meek and mild   WESL 346:6
   g. motion with the deep   DAV 114:22
   g. rain from heaven   SHAK 289:26
   His life was g.   SHAK 282:2
   parfit g. knyght   CHAU 95:12
   shall g. his condition   SHAK 279:20
gentleman: died a very gallant g.   CHER 19:11
   Every inch a g.   WEST 346:26
   'g.' and is nothing else   CROM 111:24
   g. having something a-year   SURT 319:15
   g. in Whitehall does know better   JAY 180:15
   g. is not in your books   SHAK 291:13
   g. never inflicts pain   NEWM 238:17
   last g. in Europe   LEV 206:6
   little too pedantic for a g.   CONG 106:10
   mariner with the g.   DRAKE 126:12
   officer and a g.   ANON 6:2
   prince of darkness is a g.   SHAK 283:16
   talking about being a g.   SURT 319:7
   who was then the gentleman   ROLLE 262:4
gentlemen: Dust was G. and Ladies   DICK 120:17
   G. do not take soup at luncheon   CURZ 113:11
   g. in England, now a-bed   SHAK 279:20
   G. Prefer Blondes   LOOS 210:7
   G.-rankers out on a spree   KIPL 196:15
   not to forget we are g.   BURKE 81:5
   Three jolly g.   DE L 116:17
   what most of the g. does   WAUGH 343:19
   while the G. go by   KIPL 196:28
   written by gentlemen for g.   THAC 329:12
   You g. of England   PARK 245:17
gentleness: only a willed g.   THOM 331:4
   ways are ways of g.   SPR 313:27
geographers: g., in Afric-maps   SWIFT 320:21
geographical: Italy is a g. expression   METT 224:3
geography: G. is about Maps   BENT 35:5
geometrical: in a g. ratio   MALT 217:5
geometry: no-one enter who does not know g.   ANON 13:6
   no 'royal road' to g.   EUCL 137:21
   poetry a subject as precise as g.   FLAU 141:9
George: Amelia was praying for G.   THAC 329:18
   G. the Third ought never   BENT 35:7
   Harry! England and Saint G.   SHAK 279:6
   if his name be G.   SHAK 282:3

George (*cont.*):

Vile, but viler G. the Second	LAND 200:24

Georges: G. ended — LAND 200:24

Georgia: G. on my mind — GORR 155:23

on the red hills of G. — KING 195:9

Georgian: all the G. silver goes — MACM 215:20

geranium: madman shakes a dead g. — ELIOT 134:11

geraniums: and g. (red) — MILNE 225:21

pot of pink g. — MACN 216:2

German: G. soldier trying to violate — STR 318:14

to my horse—G. — CHAR 95:7

Germans: beastly to the G. — COW 108:20

G. are going to be squeezed — GEDD 149:19

to the G.—the air — RICH 260:6

Germany: G. above all — HOFF 169:16

Offering G. too little — NEV 238:9

germs: g. in your handkerchief — ANON 6:23

Gert: G.'s writings are punk — ANON 8:2

Gesang: *Das ist der ewige G.* — GOET 154:4

gestures: In the g., in the sighs — SOND 311:6

get: forced to like what you g. — SHAW 302:7

g. anywhere in a marriage — MURD 236:10

G. out as early as you can — LARK 201:18

g. out of these wet clothes — ANON 8:18

G. thee behind me, Satan — BIBLE 50:14

G. up, stand up — MARL 218:6

governments better g. out of the way — EIS 131:16

you've gut to g. up airly — LOW 211:4

getting: G. and spending — WORD 357:10

Gospel of G. On — SHAW 302:12

ghastly: G. good taste — BETJ 37:16

g. through the drizzling rain — TENN 325:1

We were a g. crew — COL 104:14

ghost: G. in the Machine — RYLE 265:11

g. of a great name — LUCAN 211:24

g. of Roger Casement — YEATS 359:6

G. unlaid forbear thee — SHAK 273:28

Vex not his g. — SHAK 284:7

ghosties: From ghoulies and g. — ANON 7:7

ghostly: Her face, at first just g. — REID 259:3

ghosts: g. from an enchanter fleeing — SHEL 304:6

g. of departed quantities — BERK 35:15

G., wandering here and there — SHAK 290:34

ghoulies: g. and ghosties — ANON 7:7

giant: arrows in the hand of the g. — BOOK 68:31

baby figure of the g. mass — SHAK 296:32

G. Despair had a wife — BUNY 79:3

I was the g. great and still — STEV 317:14

one g. leap for mankind — ARMS 16:5

To have a g.'s strength — SHAK 288:13

upon the body of a g. or — LAND 200:25

giants: g. in the earth in those days — BIBLE 39:7

on the shoulders of g. — BERN 36:9

on the shoulders of g. — NEWT 239:2

Want is one only of five g. — BEV 38:7

gibber: Did squeak and g. — SHAK 274:1

gibbets: cells and g. for 'the man' — COOK 107:17

g. keep the lifted hand in awe — YOUNG 360:15

Gibbon: scribble! Eh! Mr G. — GLOU 153:17

while G. levelled walks — COLM 105:15

Gibraltar: G. may tumble — GERS 150:7

giddy: I am g., expectation whirls — SHAK 297:1

So g. the sight — GREN 158:15

giddy-pacèd: brisk and g. times — SHAK 297:29

gift: g. of oneself — ANOU 14:8

g. rich by delaying it — TROL 334:18

Heaven's last best g. — MILT 229:15

You have a g., sir — JONS 187:17

your g. survived it all — AUDEN 20:22

gifted: Young, g. and black — IRV 178:18

giftie: some Pow'r the g. gie us — BURNS 82:25

gifts: cannot recall their g. — TENN 328:18

even when they bring g. — VIRG 339:5

g. of God are strown — HEBER 164:16

g. on such as cannot use — JONS 187:8

gifts (*cont.*):

They presented unto him g. — BIBLE 48:10

gig: Life is not a series of g. lamps — WOOLF 353:22

gigantic: g. body, huge massy face — MAC 213:6

gilded: g. loam or painted clay — SHAK 293:7

gilding: G. pale streams — SHAK 299:17

Gilead: Is there no balm in G. — BIBLE 46:29

Gilpin: John G. was a citizen — COWP 109:23

gin: g. joints in all the towns — EPST 137:9

G. was mother's milk to her — SHAW 302:18

proper union of g. and vermouth — DE V 117:11

sooner we can get out the g. — REED 258:19

torrent of g. and beer — GLAD 153:9

Gioconda: one isn't the real G. — CRANE 111:1

Giotto: G.'s tower — LONG 209:18

Gipper: Win just one for the G. — GIPP 153:4

gipsy: Time, you old g. man — HODG 169:15

girded: g. with praise — GRANT 156:8

girdle: folds of a bright g. furled — ARN 16:11

g. round about the earth — SHAK 290:25

girdled: g. with the gleaming world — TENN 326:20

girl: diamonds are a g.'s best friend — ROBIN 260:18

g. at an impressionable age — SPARK 312:12

g. needs good parents — TUCK 335:9

g. next door — AUDEN 21:4

g. throwing a ball — WOOLF 354:4

g. with brains ought to do — LOOS 210:7

I can't get no g. reaction — RICH 179:6

no g. wants to laugh all the time — LOOS 210:9

Once in a lifetime, do a g. in — ELIOT 134:15

Poor little rich g. — COW 109:6

pretty g. is like a melody — BERL 36:1

There was a little g. — LONG 210:6

unlessoned g., unschooled — SHAK 289:22

zephyr and khaki shorts g. — BETJ 37:8

girlish: Laugh thy g. laughter — WATS 342:26

girls: At g. who wear glasses — PARK 245:6

G. aren't like that — AMIS 5:5

g. in slacks remember Dad — BETJ 36:17

g. turn into American women — HAMP 161:5

In Little G. is slamming Doors — BELL 33:10

nude, giant g. that have no secret — SPEN 313:3

rosebud garden of g. — TENN 326:29

Treaties are like g. and roses — DE G 116:4

give: freely ye — BIBLE 49:27

G., and it shall be given — BIBLE 52:7

g. and not to count the cost — IGN 178:8

G. him, he the more is craving — WROTH 358:1

G. me your tired, your poor — LAZ 203:2

G. to me the life I love — STEV 317:24

g. to the poor — BIBLE 50:21

G. us this day our daily bread — BIBLE 48:27

g. what you command — AUG 21:25

more blessed to g. than to receive — BIBLE 54:22

never g. up their liberties — BURKE 80:25

such as I have g. I thee — BIBLE 54:9

given: g. me over in my grey hairs — WOLS 353:16

one that hath shall be g. — BIBLE 51:3

giver: author and g. of all good — BOOK 64:25

God loveth a cheerful g. — BIBLE 55:26

gives: gives twice who g. soon — PUBL 256:1

who ever g., takes liberty — DONNE 123:14

giving: not in the g. vein to-day — SHAK 294:18

glacier: g. knocks in the cupboard — AUDEN 20:12

glad: g. me with its soft black eye — MOORE 234:19

I'm g. we've been bombed — ELIZ 135:18

I was g. when they said — BOOK 68:28

Never g. confident morning — BROW 76:15

or are you just g. to see me — WEST 346:23

shew ourselves g. — BOOK 67:31

wise son maketh a g. father — BIBLE 43:16

glade: alone in the bee-loud g. — YEATS 359:12

That crown the wat'ry g. — GRAY 157:11

gladly: g. wolde he lerne — CHAU 95:18

gladness: As with g. men of old — DIX 122:24

gladness (cont.):

serve the Lord with g.	BIBLE 58:10
serve the Lord with g.	BOOK 68:5
solemn g. even crowned	TENN 325:5
Teach me half the g.	SHEL 305:11
gladsome: Let us with a g. mind	MILT 227:9
Gladstone: Mr G. may perspire	CHUR 99:1
Glamis: G. hath murdered sleep	SHAK 286:16
G. thou art, and Cawdor	SHAK 285:15
glance: g. from heaven to earth	SHAK 291:4
O brightening g.	YEATS 358:14
Glasgow: play the old G. Empire	DODD 122:29
glass: baying for broken g.	WAUGH 343:18
double g. o' the inwariable	DICK 119:32
Get thee g. eyes	SHAK 283:26
g. of blessings	HERB 167:5
Grief with a g. that ran	SWIN 321:3
hate you through the g.	BLUN 62:14
Satire is a sort of g.	SWIFT 319:17
she made mouths in a g.	SHAK 283:8
Sound of Broken G.	BELL 33:23
through a g. darkly	BIBLE 55:14
you break the bloody g.	MACN 216:3
glasses: At girls who wear g.	PARK 245:6
Wiv a ladder and some g.	BAT 30:1
glassy: crowns around the g. sea	HEBER 164:17
g., cool, translucent wave	MILT 226:21
gleam: Follow The G.	TENN 327:6
gleaming: girdled with the g. world	TENN 326:20
glee: Piping songs of pleasant g.	BLAKE 61:18
glen: Down the rushy g.	ALL 4:18
glib: I want that g. and oily art	SHAK 282:18
gliding: But g. like a queen	SPEN 312:23
glimmering: fades the g. landscape	GRAY 157:4
glimpses: g. that would make me	WORD 357:11
glittering: g. and sounding generalities	CHOA 98:17
g. in the smokeless air	WORD 354:15
g. prizes	SMITH 309:6
grey beard and g. eye	COL 104:3
gloaming: In the g.	ORRED 241:18
Roamin' in the g.	LAUD 202:7
global: g. village	MCL 215:11
Were g. from the start	REED 258:17
globe: great g. itself	SHAK 296:10
globe-trotting: disturb g. Madam	YEATS 360:5
globule: primordial atomic g.	GILB 151:18
gloom: inspissated g.	JOHN 184:21
light to counterfeit a g.	MILT 226:25
glooms: Welcome, kindred g.	THOM 331:26
gloria: G. in excelsis Deo	MISS 231:13
Sic transit g. mundi	ANON 13:22
gloriam: Ad majorem Dei g.	ANON 13:11
glories: G., like glow-worms	WEBS 344:17
g. of our blood and state	SHIR 306:10
in those weaker g. spy	VAUG 337:8
its g. pass away	LYTE 212:20
my g. and my state depose	SHAK 294:5
glorious: g. and the unknown	FORS 143:19
g. morning for America	ADAMS 2:6
G. the northern lights astream	SMART 308:13
G. things of thee are spoken	NEWT 239:8
worship the King, all-g. above	GRANT 156:8
Mud! Mud! G. mud	SWANN 141:4
Sheds not its g. ray	MARR 219:24
glory: All g., laud, and honour	NEALE 237:21
all the g. of man	BIBLE 57:6
count the g. of my crown	ELIZ 135:7
crowned with g. now	KELLY 193:19
day of g. has arrived	ROUG 263:16
days of our g.	BYRON 87:10
deed is all, the g. nothing	GOET 154:7
drowned my g. in a shallow cup	FITZ 140:17
earth is full of his g.	BIBLE 45:10
finished yields the true g.	DRAKE 126:10
g. and the dream	WORD 355:19

glory (cont.):

g. and the freshness of a dream	WORD 355:17
g. and the nothing of a name	BYRON 85:15
G. be to God for dappled things	HOPK 172:12
G. be to the Father	BOOK 63:17
g. in the name of Briton	GEOR 149:23
g. is departed from Israel	BIBLE 41:11
g. of Europe is extinguished	BURKE 80:14
G. of the Garden	KIPL 196:16
g. of the Lord is risen	BIBLE 46:23
g. of the Lord shall be revealed	BIBLE 46:9
g. of the Lord shone round	BIBLE 51:32
g. of the winning	MER 223:20
g. of the world passes	THOM 329:28
g. shall not be blotted out	BIBLE 48:8
g. that was Greece	POE 250:9
G. to God in the highest	BIBLE 52:2
G. to Man in the highest	SWIN 321:11
G. to the new born king	WESL 346:7
g. was I had such friends	YEATS 359:17
Heaven and earth are full of thy g.	MISS 231:17
I felt it was g.	BYRON 87:11
I g. more in the cunning	JONS 187:12
King of g. shall come in	BOOK 66:20
Land of Hope and G.	BENS 34:20
left him alone with his g.	WOLFE 353:1
long hair, it is a g. to her	BIBLE 55:10
looks on war as all g.	SHER 306:9
madness is the g. of this life	SHAK 296:18
mellow g. of the Attic stage	ARN 17:20
Mine eyes have seen the g.	HOWE 175:7
My gown of g.	RAL 257:23
no g. in the triumph	CORN 108:1
paths of g. lead but to the grave	GRAY 157:7
Solomon in all his g.	BIBLE 49:4
Thus passes the g. of the world	ANON 13:22
To the greater g. of God	ANON 13:11
to thy name give g.	BIBLE 58:12
trailing clouds of g.	WORD 355:20
What price g.	STAL 5:13
When gout and g. seat me there	BROW 75:26
with g. not their own	WORD 356:12
Gloucestershire: stranger here in G.	SHAK 293:17
gloves: capitalism with the g. off	STOP 318:7
through the fields in g.	CORN 108:6
with my g. on my hand	HARG 162:20
glow: her g. has warmed	STEV 316:21
glow-worms: Glories, like g.	WEBS 344:17
glut: g. thy sorrow on a morning	KEATS 191:26
gluttons: Titled g.	ROB 260:22
gnashing: weeping and g. of teeth	BIBLE 49:18
gnat: which strain at a g.	BIBLE 50:31
gnats: small g. mourn	KEATS 192:16
gnomes: little g. in Zurich	WILS 351:12
go: better 'ole, g. to it	BAIR 26:20
boldly g. where no man	RODD 261:12
G. ahead, make my day	STIN 317:26
G., and catch a falling star	DONNE 124:10
G., and do thou likewise	BIBLE 52:13
G., and he goeth	BIBLE 49:17
g., and sin no more	BIBLE 53:27
g. anywhere I please	BEVIN 38:9
g. away is to die a little	HAR 161:9
G. down, Moses	ANON 11:19
G., for they call you	ARN 17:4
g. into the house of the Lord	BOOK 68:28
G., litel bok	CHAU 96:20
G., little book	STEV 317:17
G., lovely rose	WALL 341:12
G. out into the highways	BIBLE 52:25
G. to the ant thou sluggard	BIBLE 43:11
g. we know not where	SHAK 288:21
G. West, young man	GREE 157:20
G. ye into all the world	BIBLE 51:26
G., you are dismissed	MISS 231:20

go (cont.):

How you do g. it	BROWN 73:20
I g. on for ever	TENN 323:13
I have a g., lady	OSB 242:20
In the name of God, g.	CROM 112:4
I will arise and g. now	YEATS 359:12
Let my people g.	BIBLE 39:34
Let us g. then	ELIOT 133:24
no place to g.	WHIT 348:8
shalt thou g. and no further	PARN 245:23
Time stays, we g.	DOBS 122:28
we'll g. no more a-roving	BYRON 87:8
we think you ought to g.	RUB 264:4
with thee to g. is to stay	MILT 230:1
goal: moving freely without a g.	KLEE 198:11
Will be the final g. of ill	TENN 325:8
goals: muddied oafs at the g.	KIPL 196:18
goat: Gall of g., and slips of yew	SHAK 287:17
g. feet dance an antic hay	MARL 218:15
sort of fleecy hairy g.	BELL 33:19
goats: g. on the left	BIBLE 51:4
god: angler, and now with G.	WALT 342:11
attracted by G.	INGE 178:13
best of all G.'s works	MILT 229:27
best thing G. invents	BROW 75:30
bitter G. to follow	SWIN 321:12
bogus g.	MACN 215:21
bring us, daily, nearer G.	KEBLE 193:17
burial-ground G.'s Acre	LONG 209:19
By G.'s almighty hand	CAMP 88:13
by searching find out G.	BIBLE 42:32
Cabots talk only to G.	BOSS 70:1
called the children of G.	BIBLE 48:19
cannot have G. for his father	CYPR 113:12
cannot serve G. and mammon	BIBLE 49:3
charged with the grandeur of G.	HOPK 172:3
closer walk with G.	COWP 109:27
conscious water saw its G.	CRAS 111:6
daughter of the voice of G.	WORD 355:25
discussing their duty to G.	WHIT 348:19
door-keeper in the house of my G.	BOOK 67:22
Ef you want to take in G.	LOW 211:4
either a beast or a g.	ARIS 15:19
even G. was born too late	LOW 211:19
Fear G., and keep his commandments	BIBLE 44:28
Fear G. Honour the King	BIBLE 57:9
For G.'s sake look after our people	SCOTT 268:5
From G., who is our home	WORD 355:20
further than G.	ANDR 5:16
G. Almighty first planted	BACON 24:26
G. and angels to be lookers on	BACON 24:1
G. and devil are fighting	DOST 125:2
G. and I both knew	KLOP 198:12
G. and nature do nothing	AUCT 20:5
G. and the doctor we alike	OWEN 243:17
G. be in my head	ANON 7:11
G. be merciful to me a sinner	BIBLE 52:39
G. be thanked Who has matched	BROO 73:9
G. be with you, Balliol men	BELL 34:2
G. bless America	BERL 35:21
G. bless the child	HOL 170:10
G. bless the Prince of Wales	LINL 208:1
G. bless us every one	DICK 118:7
g. cannot change the past	AGAT 3:7
G. caught his eye	MCC 214:15
G. created man	VALE 336:21
[G.] does not play dice	EINS 131:9
G. does some delights condemn	MOL 232:23
G. disposes	THOM 330:1
G. erects a house of prayer	DEFOE 115:22
G. fulfils himself	TENN 324:20
G. gave Noah the rainbow sign	ANON 7:12
G. has given you good abilities	ARAB 14:20
G. has written all the books	BUTL 84:15
G. hath joined together	BIBLE 50:20

god (cont.):

G. hath joined together	BOOK 66:3
G. hath made them so	WATTS 343:7
G. hath numbered thy kingdom	BIBLE 47:12
G. help me	LUTH 212:8
G. help the Minister	MELB 222:21
G.-intoxicated man	NOV 240:13
G. is beginning to resemble	HUXL 177:14
G. is dead	FROMM 146:7
G. is just	JEFF 180:24
G. is love	BIBLE 57:15
G. is love, but get it in writing	LEE 204:5
G. is no respecter of persons	BIBLE 54:15
G. is not a man	BIBLE 40:18
G. is not mocked	BIBLE 55:30
G. is on everyone's side	ANOU 14:4
G. is on the side of the best shots	VOLT 340:23
G. is on the side of the big squadrons	BUSS 83:20
G. is our hope and strength	BOOK 67:6
G. is really only another artist	PIC 248:18
G. is subtle but he is not malicious	EINS 131:8
G. is Three, and God is One	NEWM 238:19
G. is working his purpose out	AING 3:9
G. made me to know Him	CAT 92:20
G. made the country	COWP 110:6
G. moves in a mysterious way	COWP 109:25
G. must think it exceedingly odd	KNOX 198:18
G. of Things as They are	KIPL 197:13
G., or in other words, Nature	SPIN 313:22
G. prepares evil for a man	ANON 13:8
G. punish England	FUNKE 147:8
G. reigns, and the Government	GARF 148:6
G. save our gracious king	ANON 7:13
G. save the king	BIBLE 41:12
G. save the king	HOGG 170:8
G. save the king	SHAK 294:4
G. save the Queen	KIPL 196:2
G. saw that it was good	BIBLE 38:15
g. self-slain on his own altar	SWIN 321:10
G. shall wipe away all tears	BIBLE 57:28
G. shall wipe away all tears	BIBLE 58:5
G.'s in his heaven	BROW 76:28
G. so loved the world	BIBLE 53:19
G. the first garden made	COWL 109:13
G., to me, it seems, is a verb	FULL 147:4
G. was certainly not orthodox	STR 318:13
G. who made thee mighty	BENS 34:20
G. whom he hath not seen	BIBLE 57:17
G. will pardon me	HEINE 165:3
G. won't, and we can't mend it	CLOU 102:13
good G. prepare me	PEPYS 247:22
good of G. to let Carlyle	BUTL 84:12
hands of the living G.	BIBLE 56:25
hath not seen G.	BIBLE 57:18
Have G. to be his guide	BUNY 79:7
he thinks little of G.	PLUT 250:2
honest G. is the noblest work	ING 178:15
Honest to G.	ROB 260:21
How odd of G.	EWER 138:2
I am G. and cannot find it	SHEL 304:18
I am becoming a g.	VESP 338:4
If G. be for us	BIBLE 54:41
If G. did not exist	VOLT 340:18
if G. talks to you	SZASZ 321:25
if there be a G.	ANON 9:22
in apprehension how like a g.	SHAK 275:16
Inclines think there is a G.	CLOU 102:15
I remembered my G.	SOUT 312:2
Jewish G., and spurn the Jews	BROW 73:21
justify G.'s ways to man	HOUS 175:4
justify the ways of G.	MILT 228:9
know his G. by night	VAUG 337:4
Knowledge enormous makes a g.	KEATS 191:2
know the mind of G.	HAWK 163:18
leaping, and praising G.	BIBLE 54:10

god (*cont.*):

Let G. be true	BIBLE 54:29
Lord G. will wipe	BIBLE 45:25
Man's word is G. in man	TENN 324:2
many are afraid of G.	LOCK 209:1
May G. us keep	BLAKE 60:23
My G. and King	HERB 166:20
my G., why hast thou forsaken me	BIBLE 51:16
nature of G. is a circle	ANON 9:13
nearer you are to G.	WOTT 357:21
neglect G. and his Angels	DONNE 124:21
next to of course g. america	CUMM 112:17
not G. that I don't accept	DOST 125:4
Now G. be praised	WOLFE 353:4
O G., our help in ages past	WATTS 343:13
one G. only	CLOU 102:16
only G. can make a tree	KILM 195:1
others call it G.	CARR 92:10
Our G.'s forgotten	QUAR 256:27
paltered with Eternal G.	TENN 327:13
presume not G. to scan	POPE 252:17
Put on the whole armour of G.	BIBLE 56:3
Put your trust in G.	BLAC 59:22
ranks the same with G.	BROW 77:1
Read G. aright	QUAR 257:4
safe stronghold our G.	LUTH 212:10
served G. as diligently	WOLS 353:16
she for G. in him	MILT 229:9
spirit shall return unto G.	BIBLE 44:26
Strong brother in G.	BELL 33:14
strong brown g.	ELIOT 133:7
Teach me, my G. and King	HERB 166:25
that of G. in every one	FOX 144:18
There but for the grace of G.	BRAD 71:6
There is no G.	BOOK 66:12
they shall see G.	BIBLE 48:19
thou city of G.	BOOK 67:24
three-personed G.	DONNE 123:10
through darkness up to G.	TENN 325:11
thy God is a jealous G.	BIBLE 40:21
thy God my G.	BIBLE 41:8
To glorify G.	SHOR 306:13
To G. I speak Spanish	CHAR 95:7
To the greater glory of G.	ANON 13:11
TO THE UNKNOWN G.	BIBLE 54:20
triangles were to make a G.	MONT 233:21
Verb is G.	HUGO 175:24
Very God of very G.	BOOK 65:5
voice of the people is the voice of G.	ALC 3:14
What G. abandoned	HOUS 174:13
What hath G. wrought	BIBLE 40:19
When G. at first made man	HERB 167:5
when G.'s the theme	SMART 308:13
Where G. paints the scenery	HART 163:10
whom G. would destroy	DUP 129:11
whose g. is in the skies	SHAW 301:33
who think not G. at all	MILT 230:14
will of G. prevail	ARN 17:25
with G. all things are possible	BIBLE 50:23
Woman was G.'s second blunder	NIET 239:18
Word was with G.	BIBLE 53:6
wrestling with my G.	HOPK 172:1
ye believe in G.	BIBLE 53:36
you are a g.	ROST 263:12

Goddamm: Lhude sing G. — POUND 254:8
goddess: G., excellently bright — JONS 187:3
godfathers: G. and Godmothers — BOOK 65:20
godhead: g. was evident — VIRG 339:3
godless: Here were decent g. people — ELIOT 134:13
godliness: cleanliness is next to g. — WESL 346:15
godly: g., righteous, and sober life — BOOK 63:15
godmothers: Godfathers and G. — BOOK 65:20
Godot: Waiting for G. — BECK 31:10
gods: By the nine g. he swore — MAC 214:2
  convenient that there be g. — OVID 243:11

gods (*cont.*):

daughter of the g., divinely tall	TENN 323:20
dish fit for the g.	SHAK 281:4
divinely fair, fit love for g.	MILT 229:24
first in the world made g.	JONS 187:11
g. are on the side of	TAC 322:8
g. that the city recognizes	PLATO 249:18
g. themselves cannot recall	TENN 328:18
g. themselves struggle	SCH 267:20
g. thought otherwise	VIRG 339:7
g. wish to destroy they	CONN 106:24
It lies in the lap of the g.	HOMER 170:23
leave the outcome to the G.	CORN 108:2
loved by the g. because	PLATO 249:19
men that strove with g.	TENN 328:23
nature gave birth to the G.	HOLB 170:9
people clutching their g.	ELIOT 133:23
shalt have no other g.	BIBLE 40:3
So many g., so many creeds	WILC 349:15
they first make g.	LEVIN 206:8
What men or g. are these	KEATS 191:18
where g. have lost their way	ROET 261:15
Whom the g. love dies young	MEN 223:5
Ye shall be as g.	BIBLE 38:25

goest: whithersoever thou g. — BIBLE 40:26
  whither thou g. — BIBLE 41:8
goeth: g. after her straightway — BIBLE 43:13
going: g. down of the sun — BINY 59:12
  g. the way of all the earth — BIBLE 40:29
  g. to and fro in the earth — BIBLE 42:21
  He is gone, and we are g. — JOHN 182:16
  knowing to what he was g. — HARDY 162:14
  Than greatness g. off — SHAK 271:23
  Their g. hence — SHAK 283:30
  upon the order of your g. — SHAK 287:12
  When the g. gets tough — KENN 194:10
goings-on: numberless g. of life — COL 103:19
gold: apples of g. in pictures of silver — BIBLE 43:35
  blue of the night meets the g. — CROS 112:9
  builded over with pillars of g. — BLAKE 60:17
  cursed craving for g. — VIRG 339:8
  fetch the age of g. — MILT 227:27
  fly to India for g. — MARL 218:8
  From the g. bar of Heaven — ROSS 263:6
  gleaming in purple and g. — BYRON 85:22
  g., and frankincense — BIBLE 48:10
  G.?, a transient shining trouble — GRAI 156:7
  g. of obedience and incense — MONS 233:3
  harpstring of g. — SWIN 321:12
  If g. ruste, what shall iren do — CHAU 95:22
  I stuffed their mouths with g. — BEVAN 38:2
  little g. head — MILNE 226:1
  Nor all, that glisters, g. — GRAY 157:15
  rarer gifts than g. — BROO 72:20
  Royalty is the g. filling — OSB 242:26
  sand and ruin and g. — SWIN 321:19
  streets are paved with g. — COLM 105:13
  this foul drain pure g. — TOCQ 333:5
  This g., my dearest — LEAP 203:6
  To gild refinèd g. — SHAK 282:10
  travelled in the realms of g. — KEATS 192:10
  what's become of all the g. — BROW 77:19
  Within its net of g. — MACN 216:10
  with patines of bright g. — SHAK 290:2
golden: as they did in the g. world — SHAK 272:12
  Casting down their g. crowns — HEBER 164:17
  chalices and g. priests — JEWEL 181:14
  girl-graduates in their g. hair — TENN 327:16
  G. lads and girls all must — SHAK 273:27
  g. locks time hath to silver — PEELE 247:3
  G. opinions from all sorts — SHAK 286:2
  G. Road to Samarkand — FLEC 141:17
  g. years return — SHEL 303:18
  I went into a g. land — TURN 335:17
  Jerusalem the g. — NEALE 237:22

golden (*cont.*):

Like g. lamps in a green night	MARV 220:10
Miles and miles of g. moss	AUDEN 20:19
Of g. sands, and crystal	DONNE 123:23
Or love in a g. bowl	BLAKE 60:10
or the g. bowl be broken	BIBLE 44:26
perturbation! g. care	SHAK 278:26
Roll down their g. sand	HEBER 164:15
Someone who loves the g. mean	HOR 173:22
We are stardust, we are g.	MITC 232:4
Goldengrove: Over G. unleaving	HOPK 172:14
Goldsmith: Here lies Nolly G.	GARR 148:9
To Oliver G., A Poet	JOHN 185:12
golf: made more liars than G.	ROG 261:21
thousand lost g. balls	ELIOT 134:13
gondola: What else is like the g.	CLOU 102:12
gone: far g. from original righteousness	BOOK 69:17
g.: aye ages long ago	KEATS 190:23
G. before to that unknown	LAMB 200:12
g. into the world of light	VAUG 337:11
g., the old familiar faces	LAMB 200:13
g. up with a merry noise	BOOK 67:8
g. with the wind	DOWS 125:12
He is g., and we are going	JOHN 182:16
not dead—but g. before	ROG 261:18
Not lost but g. before	NORT 240:10
She's g. for ever	SHAK 284:4
welcomest when they are g.	SHAK 280:4
what haste I can to be g.	CROM 112:8
What's g. and what's past help	SHAK 298:24
gongs: g. groaning as the guns	CHES 97:25
struck regularly, like g.	COW 109:11
gong-tormented: that g. sea	YEATS 358:15
good: And common g. to all	SHAK 282:2
And God saw that it was g.	BIBLE 38:15
apprehension of the g.	SHAK 293:14
be a g. animal	SPEN 312:16
Be g., sweet maid	KING 195:13
Beneath the g. how far	GRAY 157:19
best is the enemy of the g.	VOLT 340:15
be thought half as g.	WHIT 349:3
can be g. in the country	WILDE 350:6
corrupt g. manners	BIBLE 55:19
crown thy g. with brotherhood	BATES 30:2
do evil, that g. may come	BIBLE 54:30
Do g. by stealth, and blush	POPE 252:31
do g. to them which hate	BIBLE 52:6
evil and on the g.	BIBLE 48:24
Evil, be thou my g.	MILT 229:7
evil good, and g. evil	BIBLE 45:9
for the public g.	LOCKE 208:21
Gallop about doing g.	SMITH 309:17
giver of all g. things	BOOK 64:25
g. action by stealth	LAMB 200:11
g. and bad of every land	BAIL 26:19
g. are so harsh to the clever	WORD 354:11
G., but not religious-good	HARDY 162:1
g. deed in a naughty world	SHAK 290:4
g. die early	DEFOE 115:17
g. die first	WORD 354:19
g. ended happily	WILDE 349:20
g. [end] unluckily	STOP 318:5
G. fences make g. neighbours	FROST 146:16
g. for America	WILS 351:11
g. for that man if he had	BIBLE 51:8
g. in everything	SHAK 272:14
G. is best when soonest	SOUT 312:8
g. is oft interrèd	SHAK 281:18
G. is That at which all	ARIS 15:12
g. man to do nothing	BURKE 81:13
g. minute goes	BROW 77:21
g. must associate	BURKE 81:4
g. of man must be the end	ARIS 15:13
g. of subjects is the end	DEFOE 116:1
g. of the people	CIC 100:20

good (*cont.*):

g. old *Cause*	MILT 231:6
g. still to find means of evil	MILT 228:11
g. that I would I do not	BIBLE 54:38
G. *Thing*	SELL 269:24
g. thing come out of Nazareth	BIBLE 53:14
g. thing left to me	MUSS 236:16
g. time was had by all	SMITH 309:18
g. to be had in the country	HAZL 164:3
g. will be the final goal of ill	TENN 325:8
g. will toward men	BIBLE 52:2
g. woman if I had five thousand	THAC 329:21
G. women always think it	BROO 73:11
Hanging is too g. for him	BUNY 78:22
He was a g. man, and a just	BIBLE 53:5
highest g.	CIC 100:22
His own g., either physical	MILL 224:15
hold fast that which is g.	BIBLE 56:14
In art the best is g. enough	GOET 154:9
It's always the g. feel rotten	YES 360:12
I will be g.	VICT 338:8
know better what is g. for people	JAY 180:15
knowing g. and evil	BIBLE 38:25
Knowledge of g. and evil	COWP 110:3
Lady is as g. i' th' dark	HERR 167:18
luxury of doing g.	CRAB 110:27
much g. in the worst of us	ANON 10:20
must return g. for evil	VANB 336:23
Never Had It So G.	MACM 215:15
nor g. compensate bad in men	BROW 77:10
nor it cannot come to g.	SHAK 274:13
nothing either g. or bad but	SHAK 275:14
policy of the g. neighbour	ROOS 262:10
prospect of a distant g.	DRYD 127:32
she needs g. cash	TUCK 335:9
strong antipathy of g. to bad	POPE 252:32
that can afford to be g.	SHAW 302:11
that doeth g. is of God	BIBLE 57:18
their luxury was doing g.	GARTH 148:14
things work together for g.	BIBLE 54:40
those who go about doing g.	CREI 111:18
thou g. and faithful servant	BIBLE 51:1
Time makes ancient g.	LOW 211:9
to be obscurely g.	ADD 2:17
universal licence to be g.	COL 103:11
what g. came of it at last	SOUT 311:20
When she was g.	LONG 210:6
would do g. to another	BLAKE 60:19
goodbye: Every time we say g.	PORT 253:19
G., moralitee	HERB 166:12
G. to all that	GRAV 156:17
good-bye-ee: G.! — Good-bye-ee!	LEE 347:1
goodliness: g. thereof is as the flower	BIBLE 46:10
goodly: g. fellowship of the Prophets	BOOK 63:19
g. to look to	BIBLE 41:16
I have a g. heritage	BOOK 66:15
goodness: And g. only knowses	CHES 98:6
fountain of all g.	BOOK 64:8
G. had nothing to do with it	WEST 346:22
long-suffering, and of great g.	BOOK 68:6
powerful g. want	SHEL 304:17
good-night: gay g. and quickly turn away	YEATS 359:5
g., sweet ladies	SHAK 276:34
G., sweet prince	SHAK 277:19
My last G.!	KING 195:5
goods: when g. are private	TAWN 322:19
with all my worldly g.	BOOK 66:2
goodwill: In peace: good g.	CHUR 100:4
goose: And every g. a swan	KING 195:17
g. honking amongst tuneful	VIRG 340:3
gott'st thou that g. look	SHAK 287:33
gooseberried: g. double bed of the wood	THOM 330:17
Gorgon: Great G., Prince of darkness	SPEN 313:8
gorgonised: G. me from head to foot	TENN 326:27
gormed: I'm G.	DICK 118:18

gory: shake thy g. locks at me	SHAK 287:11
Welcome to your g. bed	BURNS 82:21
gosling: such a g. to obey instinct	SHAK 273:21
gospel: Four for the G. makers	ANON 8:6
G. of Christ knows of no	WESL 346:11
G. of Getting On	SHAW 302:12
music of the G.	FABER 138:4
preach the g.	BIBLE 51:26
gossip: babbling g. of the air	SHAK 297:21
G. is a sort of smoke	ELIOT 131:20
Like all g.—it's merely	FORS 144:1
got: which in our case we have not g.	REED 258:16
Gothic: cars are like great G. cathedrals	BART 29:19
gotta: g. use words when I talk to you	ELIOT 134:16
gout: g. and glory seat me there	BROW 75:26
I say give them the g.	MONT 233:6
govern: Go out and g. New South Wales	BELL 33:7
g. according to the common	JAM 179:12
To g. is to choose	LÉVIS 206:10
governed: nation is not g.	BURKE 80:1
governess: Be a g.! Better be a slave	BRON 72:14
governing: g. was not property	FOX 144:15
government: art of g. is the organization	SHAW 301:26
best g. is that which	O'SUL 243:4
cabinet g.	BAG 26:6
efficient g. you have a dictatorship	TRUM 335:3
forms of g. let fools contest	POPE 252:20
G. and public opinion allow	SHAW 301:20
G. at Washington	GARF 148:6
g. by discussion	ATTL 19:14
g. by the uneducated	CHES 98:12
G., even in its best state	PAINE 244:9
G. is big enough to take	FORD 143:5
g. it deserves	MAIS 216:18
g. of laws, and not of men	ADAMS 1:22
g. of statesmen or of clerks	DISR 121:24
G. of the busy by the bossy	SELD 269:22
g. of the people	LINC 207:8
g. shall be upon his shoulder	BIBLE 45:16
g. to protect all conscientious	PAINE 244:10
It's no go the G. grants	MACN 216:2
land of settled g.	TENN 329:1
No G. secure without	DISR 121:23
representative g.	DISR 122:7
republican g.	TOCO 333:3
rule nations by your g.	VIRG 339:16
society is the end of g.	ADAMS 2:1
work for a g. I despise for ends	KEYN 194:13
worst form of G.	CHUR 100:2
governments: foundation of most g.	ADAMS 2:2
g. had better get out of the way	EIS 131:16
nations and g. have never learned	HEGEL 164:18
governors: Our supreme g., the mob	WALP 341:16
governs: that which g. least	O'SUL 243:4
gowd: man's the g. for a' that	BURNS 82:7
Gower: O moral G.	CHAU 96:23
grace: Amazing g.!	NEWT 239:7
Angels and ministers of g.	SHAK 274:27
be the new light of g.	SMOL 310:16
By the g. of God there goes	BRAD 71:6
does it with a better g.	SHAK 293:18
Give us g. to persevere	DEAR 115:7
G. is given of God	CLOU 102:11
G. me no grace, nor uncle	SHAK 293:18
g. of a boy	BETJ 37:11
g.-proud faces	BURNS 82:29
G. under pressure	HEM 165:15
inward and spiritual g.	BOOK 65:23
speech be alway with g.	BIBLE 56:12
that g. may abound	BIBLE 54:33
their courtly foreign g.	TENN 328:14
through God's good g.	MONS 233:2
Ye are fallen from g.	BIBLE 55:29
graces: G. do not seem to be natives	CHES 97:12

graces (cont.):	
half-mile g.	BURNS 82:29
gracious: be g. unto thee	BIBLE 40:15
Lord, for he is g.	BOOK 69:1
Lord is g.	BIBLE 57:7
Remembers me of all his g. parts	SHAK 282:8
gradualness: inevitability of g.	WEBB 344:6
graduates: And sweet girl-g.	TENN 327:16
graft: G. in our hearts the love	BOOK 64:25
grail: g. of laughter of an empty	CRANE 110:32
grain: like to a g. of mustard	BIBLE 50:5
rain is destroying his g.	HERB 166:11
Rot half a g. a day	SHAK 293:3
see a world in a g. of sand	BLAKE 60:5
which g. will grow	SHAK 285:7
grains: Little g. of sand	CARN 90:29
grammar: G., the ground of al	LANG 201:8
Heedless of g.	BARH 28:20
I don't want to talk a	SHAW 302:17
posterity talking bad g.	DISR 122:14
With g., and nonsense	GOLD 155:8
grand: Dumb, inscrutable and g.	ARN 16:23
g. Perhaps	BROW 75:14
g. to be blooming well dead	SAR 267:1
Grand Canyon: rose petal down the G.	MARQ 219:22
grandeur: And the g. that was Rome	POE 250:9
charged with the g. of God	HOPK 172:3
g. hear with a disdainful smile	GRAY 157:7
grandfather: ape for his g.	HUXL 177:21
through his g. or his	WILB 349:7
grandmother: We have become a g.	THAT 329:26
grange: at the moated g.	SHAK 288:22
Upon the lonely moated g.	TENN 326:22
granites: g. which titanic wars	OWEN 244:2
grape: Beulah, peel me a g.	WEST 346:20
G. is my mulatto mother	HUGH 175:22
g. who will the vine destroy	SHAK 299:8
grapes: fathers have eaten sour g.	BIBLE 47:5
sour g. and ashes without you	ASHF 18:24
vintage where the g. of wrath	HOWE 175:7
grapeshot: whiff of g.	CARL 90:11
grasp: G. it like a man of mettle	HILL 168:11
reach should exceed his g.	BROW 75:10
grass: All flesh is as g.	BIBLE 57:6
days of man are but as g.	BOOK 68:7
g. below, above the vaulted	CLARE 101:7
g. will grow in the streets	HOOV 171:18
g. withereth, the flower	BIBLE 46:10
happy as the g. was green	THOM 330:8
I am the g.; I cover all	SAND 266:14
I fall on g.	MARV 220:15
If we could hear the g. grow	ELIOT 132:10
I know the g. beyond the door	ROSS 263:10
leaf of g. is no less	WHIT 348:18
Pigeons on the g. alas	STEIN 314:21
snake hidden in the g.	VIRG 339:24
splendour in the g.	WORD 355:23
two blades of g. to grow	SWIFT 319:21
uninterrupted g. and a hare	LAWR 202:17
grassy: fair Fidele's g. tomb	COLL 105:9
grate: G. on their scrannel pipes	MILT 227:15
grateful: g. thought raised to heaven	LESS 206:5
gratefully: O g. sing his power	GRANT 156:8
gratias: Deo g.	MISS 231:14
gratified: lineaments of g. desire	BLAKE 61:17
grating: Nor harsh nor g.	WORD 355:10
gratitude: g. is merely a secret hope	LA R 201:25
grave: And renowned be thy g.	SHAK 273:28
And the g. is not its goal	LONG 209:22
Between the cradle and the g.	DYER 129:17
birth astride of a g.	BECK 31:15
But she is in her g., and, oh	WORD 356:23
Dig the g. and let me lie	STEV 317:21
Duncan is in his g.	SHAK 287:4
Even the g. yawns for him	TREE 334:5

grave (cont.):

from the cradle to the g.	CHUR 99:20
from the cradle to the g.	SHEL 304:24
glory lead but to the g.	GRAY 157:7
gone wild into his g.	SHAK 278:30
g. as little as my bed	KEN 193:22
g. hides all things beautiful	SHEL 304:18
g. in a Y-shaped coffin	ORTON 241:2
g. of Mad Carew	HAYES 163:21
g.'s a fine and private place	MARV 220:25
g., whither thou goest	BIBLE 44:19
G. without thought	CHUR 98:26
In every g. make room	D'AV 114:9
It's with O'Leary in the g.	YEATS 359:28
kind of healthy g.	SMITH 309:25
kingdom for a little g.	SHAK 294:2
like Alcestis from the g.	MILT 230:24
Marriage is the g. or tomb	CAV 93:13
O g., where is thy victory	BIBLE 55:22
pompous in the g.	BROW 74:7
receive no letters in the g.	JOHN 186:8
see myself go into my g.	PEPYS 247:22
shown Longfellow's g.	MOORE 234:9
travelling toward the g.	WORD 356:8
Upon his mother's g.	WORD 356:5
When my g. is broke up again	DONNE 124:9
Without a g., unknelled	BYRON 85:14
with sorrow to the g.	BIBLE 39:26

graved: G. inside of it, 'Italy' — BROW 75:24
graven: unto thee any g. image — BIBLE 40:4
graver: Wherein the g. had a strife — JONS 187:20

graves: dig our g. with our teeth — SMIL 308:16

g. of little magazines	PRES 255:5
g. stood tenantless	SHAK 274:1
Let's talk of g., of worms	SHAK 293:26
ourselves dishonourable g.	SHAK 280:27
quietly among the g.	EDW 131:4
they watch from their g.	BROW 76:14

graveyards: signs on the foxholes or g. — KENN 194:7
gravy: Abominated g. — BENT 35:8
It's the rich wot gets the g. — ANON 10:11
Gray: whole of G.'s Elegy — WOLFE 353:3
grazing: Tilling and g. — SULLY 319:3
grease: slides by on g. — LOW 211:12
greasy: top of the g. pole — DISR 122:17

great: All creatures g. and small — ALEX 4:2

All things both g. and small	COL 104:18
between the small and g.	COWP 110:16
But he is always g.	DRYD 128:28
far above the g.	GRAY 157:19
g. deep to the great deep	TENN 324:4
G. hatred, little room	YEATS 359:19
g. illusion	ANG 5:17
G. is the hand that holds	THOM 330:11
G. is Truth, and mighty	BIBLE 47:27
g. is truth, and shall	BROO 73:14
g. life if you don't weaken	BUCH 77:26
g. man he grovelled before	THAC 329:15
g. no heart	LA BR 199:13
it kindles the g.	BUSS 83:19
many people think him g.	JOHN 184:28
our hearts are g.	TENN 324:12
Rightly to be g.	SHAK 276:31
some men are born g.	SHAK 298:3
there is nothing g. but man	HAM 160:18
There's a g. spirit gone	SHAK 271:7
those who were truly g.	SPEN 312:24
thou wouldst be g.	SHAK 285:15
To be g. is to be misunderstood	EMER 136:25

Great Britain: G. has lost an empire — ACH 1:3

greater: G. love hath no man — BIBLE 53:40

G. love than this	JOYCE 188:18
g. man, the greater courtesy	TENN 324:11
g. than Solomon is here	BIBLE 50:2
necessity is yet g. than mine	SIDN 306:30

greater (cont.):

we are g. than we know	WORD 356:20

greatest: g. event it is that ever — FOX 144:16

g. happiness for the greatest	HUTC 177:2
g. happiness of the greatest	BENT 35:1
g. thing in the world	MONT 233:15
hath a life to live as the g. he	RAIN 257:19

greatly: who would g. win — BYRON 87:3
greatness: farewell, to all my g. — SHAK 280:18

G. knows itself	SHAK 278:10
have g. thrust upon them	SHAK 298:3
moment of my g. flicker	ELIOT 133:29
nature of g. not to be exact	BURKE 79:24
squeaking Cleopatra boy my g.	SHAK 272:5
Tell out my soul, the g.	BIBLE 51:28
Than g. going off	SHAK 271:23

Greece: G. might still be free — BYRON 86:13
isles of G.! — BYRON 86:14
greed: enough for everyone's g. — BUCH 77:30
greedy: not g. of filthy lucre — BIBLE 56:16
Greek: loving, natural, and G. — BYRON 86:8

Must carve in Latin or in G.	WALL 341:13
ne of G. that breed doubts	SPEN 313:16
No more Latin, no more G.	ANON 9:17
small Latin, and less G.	JONS 187:27

Greeks: fear G. when they bring gifts — VIRG 339:5

G. had a word for it	AKINS 3:10
When G. joined Greeks	LEE 204:9

green: a' babbled of g. fields — SHAK 279:4

actual life springs ever g.	GOET 154:5
And hae laid him on the g.	BALL 27:14
As g. as emerald	COL 104:4
bordered by its gardens g.	MORR 235:6
By slow Meander's margent g.	MILT 226:10
children are heard on the g.	BLAKE 61:25
Colourless g. ideas sleep	CHOM 98:18
Drives my g. age	THOM 330:10
England's g. and pleasant land	BLAKE 61:12
feed me in a g. pasture	BOOK 66:17
Flora and the country g.	KEATS 191:29
g. days telling with a quiet beat	QUIL 257:8
g.-eyed monster	SHAK 292:12
G. grow the rashes, O	BURNS 82:9
G. grow the rushes O	ANON 8:6
G. how I love you green	GARC 148:3
g. lap was Nature's darling	GRAY 157:16
g. mantle of the standing pool	SHAK 283:15
G. pleasure or grey grief	SWIN 321:17
G. Things upon the Earth	BOOK 64:1
g. thought in a green shade	MARV 220:26
How g. was my valley	LLEW 208:6
laughs to see the g. man pass	HOFF 170:1
Like golden lamps in a g. night	MARV 220:10
Making the g. one red	SHAK 286:18
Praise the g. earth	BUNT 78:14
shoot the sleepy, g.-coat man	HOFF 170:2
There is a g. hill far away	ALEX 4:6
Time held me g. and dying	THOM 330:9
wearin' o' the G.	ANON 8:9
When I was g. in judgement	SHAK 271:12
when the trees were g.	CLARE 101:3

greenery: In a mountain g. — HART 163:10
greenery-yallery: g., Grosvenor Gallery — GILB 152:13
Greenland: From G.'s icy mountains — HEBER 164:15
greens: And healing g. — ABSE 1:1
Greensleeves: G. was all my joy — ANON 7:15
greenwood: Under the g. tree — SHAK 272:19
greet: G. the unseen with a cheer — BROW 75:12
grenadier: British G. — ANON 10:13
grenadiers: talk of Pensions and G. — STER 315:19
Grenville: Sir Richard G. — TENN 328:10
grey: all thoery is g. — GOET 154:5

given me over in my g. hairs	WOLS 353:16
Green pleasure or g. grief	SWIN 321:17
g. and full of sleep	YEATS 360:9

grey (*cont.*):
g. hairs with sorrow — BIBLE 39:26
lend me your g. mare — BALL 28:11
philosophy paints its g. — HEGEL 164:20
this old g. head — WHIT 348:26
world has grown g. — SWIN 321:13
greyhounds: like g. in the slips — SHAK 279:6
grief: acquainted with g. — BIBLE 46:17
After long g. and pain — TENN 327:3
And g. itself be mortal — SHEL 303:8
Every one can master a g. — SHAK 291:22
Green pleasure or grey g. — SWIN 321:17
G. fills the room up — SHAK 282:8
g. flieth to it — BACON 24:21
G. for awhile is blind — SHEL 304:16
G. is a species of idleness — JOHN 182:15
g. returns with the revolving — SHEL 303:7
g. that does not speak — SHAK 287:25
G. with a glass that ran — SWIN 321:3
hopeless g. is passionless — BROW 75:2
journeyman to g. — SHAK 293:12
Of g. I died — ROET 261:16
past help should be past g. — SHAK 298:24
Patch g. with proverbs — SHAK 291:25
Pitched past pitch of g. — HOPK 172:9
Silence augmenteth g. — DYER 129:15
silent manliness of g. — GOLD 154:26
Smiling at g. — SHAK 298:1
time remembered is g. forgotten — SWIN 321:2
griefs: cutteth g. in halves — BACON 24:24
g. of forty generations — MAC 213:18
I know you: solitary g. — JOHN 181:18
my state depose, but not my g. — SHAK 294:5
Surely he hath borne our g. — BIBLE 46:18
grievance: Comparisons doon offte gret g. — LYDG 212:14
grieve: what could it g. for — KEATS 191:3
grieves: thing that g. not — MARK 218:4
grieving: Márgarét, áre you g. — HOPK 172:14
grievous: remembrance of them is g. — BOOK 65:11
through my most g. fault — MISS 231:11
grim: g. grew his countenance — BALL 27:16
grimace: Of its accelerated g. — POUND 254:16
grin: wears one universal g. — FIEL 139:13
grind: bastards g. you down — ANON 9:15
g. the faces of the poor — BIBLE 45:6
He did g. in the prison house — BIBLE 41:6
mills of God g. slowly — LONG 209:24
grinders: incisors and g. — BAG 26:15
groan: Condemned alike to g. — GRAY 157:13
groans: How alike are the g. of love — LOWRY 211:22
groined: which titanic wars had g. — OWEN 244:2
Gromboolian: great G. plain — LEAR 203:8
groom: death is but a g. — DONNE 123:19
grooves: In determinate g. — HARE 162:19
ringing g. of change — TENN 326:17
grope: Whose buildings g. the sky — AUDEN 21:11
gross: Not g. to sink, but light — SHAK 300:17
things rank and g. — SHAK 274:10
Groucho: G. tendency — ANON 12:7
ground: acre of barren g. — SHAK 295:32
Betwixt the stirrup and the g. — CAMD 88:12
Chosen and made peculiar g. — WATTS 343:2
fallen unto me in a fair g. — BOOK 66:15
gain a little patch of g. — SHAK 276:28
Grammer, the g. of al — LANG 201:8
here at last on the g. — SOND 311:7
let us sit upon the g. — SHAK 293:27
lose to-morrow the g. won — ARN 17:10
They are the g., the books — SHAK 284:16
whereon thou standest is holy g. — BIBLE 39:31
grouse: g. against life — ELIOT 135:4
grove: good g. of chimneys for me — MORR 235:11
olive g. of Academe — MILT 230:6
grovelled: met a great man he g. — THAC 329:15

groves: forsake her Cyprian g. — DRYD 128:2
g. of Academe — HOR 173:17
grow: They shall g. not old — BINY 59:12
growed: I s'pect I g. — STOWE 318:8
growl: does nothing but sit and g. — JOHN 186:1
growth: children of a larger g. — CHES 97:11
children of a larger g. — DRYD 127:25
genuine g. in the individual — SMIL 308:17
grudge: ancient g. I bear him — SHAK 289:2
grumbling: piece of rhythmical g. — ELIOT 135:4
Grundy: And more of Mrs G. — LOCK 209:1
What will Mrs G. think — MORT 235:23
gruntled: far from being g. — WOD 352:13
guardian: Be thou my G. and my Guide — WILL 351:3
guardians: good grey g. of art — WILB 349:12
guards: Brigade of G. — MACM 215:19
guard the g. themselves — JUV 189:9
G. die but do not surrender — CAMB 88:11
Up G. and at them — WELL 345:8
guardsman: g.'s cut and thrust — HUXL 177:16
guerre: *mais ce n'est pas la g.* — BOSQ 69:28
guest: Earth, receive an honoured g. — AUDEN 20:24
Go, Soul, the body's g. — RAL 257:21
g. that tarrieth — BIBLE 47:31
Some second g. to entertain — DONNE 124:9
speed the parting g. — POPE 252:24
This g. of summer — SHAK 285:21
unexpected and uninvited g. — TURG 335:11
guests: Unbidden g. — SHAK 280:4
guide: Have God to be his g. — BUNY 79:7
Providence their g. — MILT 230:2
guides: Ye blind g., which strain — BIBLE 50:31
guiding: Did the g. star behold — DIX 122:24
Guildenstern: Rosencrantz and G. are dead — SHAK 277:20
guile: in whom is no g. — BIBLE 53:15
packed with g. — BROO 73:7
that they speak no g. — BOOK 66:25
guilt: Cleanse me from its g. — TOPL 333:14
Image of war, without its g. — SOM 311:2
Life without industry is g. — RUSK 264:11
pens dwell on g. and misery — AUST 22:21
unfortunate circumstance of g. — STEV 317:10
What art can wash her g. away — GOLD 155:13
You will put on a dress of g. — MCG 214:20
guilty: g. man is acquitted if — JUV 189:14
G. of dust and sin — HERB 167:2
g. of our own disasters — SHAK 282:22
g. persons escape — BLAC 60:3
like a g. thing surprised — WORD 355:22
Make mad the g., and appal — SHAK 275:23
Mortal, g., but to me — AUDEN 20:28
guinea: g. helps the hurt — TENN 326:8
g. pigs in the laboratory — WILL 351:4
rank is but the g.'s stamp — BURNS 82:7
Guinness: Hodgson, G., Allsopp — CALV 88:8
guitar: changed upon the blue g. — STEV 316:9
gulf: redwood forest to the G. — GUTH 159:12
there is a great g. fixed — BIBLE 52:35
gulfs: whelmed in deeper g. — COWP 109:20
gullet: g. of New York swallowing — MILL 225:5
gum: can't fart and chew g. — JOHN 181:22
gun: barrel of a g. — MAO 217:19
I have no g., but I can spit — AUDEN 21:8
we have got the Maxim G. — BELL 33:18
gun-boat: send a g. — BEVAN 37:20
Gunga Din: better man than I am, G. — KIPL 196:17
gunpowder: g., and the magnet — BACON 25:28
G., Printing, and the Protestant — CARL 90:9
G. Treason and Plot — ANON 10:5
till the g. ran out — FOOTE 142:20
guns: butter or g. — GOER 153:22
gongs groaning as the g. boom — CHES 97:25
G. aren't lawful — PARK 245:8

guns (cont.):

monstrous anger of the g.	OWEN 243:21
than a hundred men with g.	PUZO 256:26
with g. not with butter	GOEB 153:21
gurly: And g. grew the sea	BALL 27:16
gusts: explanation of our g. and storms	ELIOT 132:2
guts: lug the g. into the neighbour room	SHAK 276:26
strangled with the g. of priests	MESL 223:27
gutta: G. cavat lapidem	OVID 243:12
gutter: We are all in the g.	WILDE 349:25
guys: Nice g. Finish last	DUR 129:13
gypsy: vagrant g. life	MAS 222:2
gyre: g. and gimble in the wabe	CARR 91:15

H

ha: among the trumpets, H., ha	BIBLE 43:5
habit: H. is a great deadener	BECK 31:16
H. is second nature	AUCT 20:3
h. of living indisposeth	BROW 74:5
H. with him was all the test	CRAB 110:20
sow a h. and you reap	READE 258:11
when order breeds h.	ADAMS 1:15
habitation: local h. and a name	SHAK 291:4
habitual: nothing is h. but indecision	JAMES 180:8
hack: do not h. me as you did	MONM 233:1
Hackney: see to H. Marshes	BAT 30:1
Hades: dark H.' door stands open	VIRG 339:12
haggard: If I do prove her h.	SHAK 292:14
Haggards: And the H. ride no more	STEP 315:5
hags: and midnight h.	SHAK 287:19
hail: All h. the power of Jesus' name	PERR 248:4
beaten dog beneath the h.	POUND 254:21
flies no sharp and sided h.	HOPK 172:7
h., and farewell evermore	CAT 93:8
H., fellow, well met	SWIFT 320:17
H. holy queen, mother	ANON 13:21
H. Mary, full of grace	ANON 13:13
H., thou ever-blessèd morn	CASW 92:18
H., thou that art highly	BIBLE 51:27
H. to thee, blithe Spirit	SHEL 305:6
Where falls not h.	TENN 324:22
hair: And the stars in her h.	ROSS 263:6
bright h. about the bone	DONNE 124:9
colour of his h.	HOUS 174:6
draws us with a single h.	POPE 253:4
draw you to her *with a single h.*	DRYD 128:24
h. has become very white	CARR 91:4
h. of a woman can draw	HOW 175:9
h. of his head	BIBLE 47:14
h. of my flesh	BIBLE 42:28
Her h. was long, her foot	KEATS 191:9
like the h. we breathe	SURT 319:8
My h. is grey, but not	BYRON 87:5
My mother bids me bind my h.	HUNT 176:19
never hurt a h. of Him	STUD 318:19
part my h. behind	ELIOT 134:3
pin up my h. with prose	CONG 106:18
She has brown h., and speaks	SHAK 290:8
thy amber-dropping h.	MILT 226:21
with such h., too	BROW 77:19
woman have long h.	BIBLE 55:10
you have lovely h.	CHEK 96:29
hairless: white and h. as an egg	HERR 167:20
hairs: grey h. with sorrow	BIBLE 39:26
h. of your head are numbered	BIBLE 49:30
If h. be wires, black wires	SHAK 300:11
hairy: My brother is a h. man	BIBLE 39:19
halcyon: Martin's summer, h. days	SHAK 280:3
hale: You are h., Father William	SOUT 312:1
half: finished in h. the time	WOD 352:17
h.-angel and half-bird	BROW 77:5
h. as old as Time	BURG 79:17
H. dead and half alive	BETJ 36:19

half (cont.):

h. in love with easeful death	KEATS 192:3
h. is greater than the whole	HES 168:2
h. slave and half free	LINC 207:5
h. that's got my keys	GRAH 156:3
h. to rise, and h. to fall	POPE 252:18
h. was not told me	BIBLE 41:30
hath overcome but h. his foe	MILT 228:18
myself and dearer h.	MILT 229:16
One h. of the world cannot	AUST 22:14
one of those h.-alive things	FORS 144:1
temple h. as old as Time	ROG 261:19
three years old is h. his height	LEON 205:23
Too clever by h.	SAL 266:7
half-a-crown: Or help to h.	HARDY 162:13
half-brother: America, h. of the world	BAIL 26:19
half-way: H. House to Rome, Oxford	PUNCH 256:7
hall: fly swiftly into the h.	BEDE 31:20
vasty h. of death	ARN 17:1
hallowed: H. be thy name	BIBLE 48:27
hallows: his mother and all his h.	HOPK 172:17
halls: Amphitrite's destined h.	SHEL 304:1
I dwelt in marble h.	BUNN 78:13
halo: h.? one more thing to keep clean	FRY 146:30
indignation is jealousy with a h.	WELLS 346:1
life is a luminous h.	WOOLF 353:22
halt: h., and the blind	BIBLE 52:24
h. ye between two opinions	BIBLE 41:36
Of tan with henna hackles, h.	STEV 316:4
halting: Words came h. forth	SIDN 306:16
ham: h.'n eggs in Carolina	GORD 155:22
hame: Hame's h., be it never so	ARB 14:23
Hamlet: H. without the Prince	SCOTT 269:5
I am not Prince H.	ELIOT 134:1
hammer: h. along the 'ard 'igh road	PUNCH 256:11
ring of a h.	WILB 349:9
hammers: anvil which has worn out many h.	MACL 215:6
hammock: Drake he's in his h.	NEWB 238:11
Hampshire: Hertford, Hereford, and H.	LERN 206:1
hams: thy h., Bayonne	POPE 250:21
hand: adorable tennis-girl's h.	BETJ 37:13
bite the h. that fed them	BURKE 81:3
bloody and invisible h.	SHAK 287:6
by Time's devouring h.	BRAM 71:13
cloud, like a man's h.	BIBLE 42:2
curious engine, your white h.	WEBS 344:15
died by the h. of the Lord	BIBLE 40:1
dyer's h.	SHAK 300:7
Emprison her soft h.	KEATS 191:26
every man's h. against him	BIBLE 39:13
h. a needle better fits	BRAD 71:12
h. delights to trace unusual	WINC 352:3
h. in hand, on the edge of the sand	LEAR 203:13
h. in hand, with wandering steps	MILT 230:2
h. is the cutting edge of the mind	BRON 72:9
h. more instrumental	SHAK 274:4
h. of Rousseau	HEINE 165:2
h. of the physician	BIBLE 48:5
h. on the cockatrice' den	BIBLE 45:20
h. that made us is divine	ADD 2:26
h. that rocks the cradle	WALL 341:10
h. that signed the treaty	THOM 330:11
h. to execute	GIBB 150:12
h. to execute any mischief	CLAR 101:10
h. will miss the insinuated nose	WATS 343:1
Have still the upper h.	COW 109:18
Heaving up my either h.	HERR 167:11
Her h. on her bosom	SHAK 292:26
His mind and h.	COND 165:11
infection and the h. of war	SHAK 293:16
it will go into his h.	BIBLE 42:16
kingdom of heaven is at h.	BIBLE 48:12
kiss on the h. may be quite	ROBIN 260:18
larger heart, the kindlier h.	TENN 325:27

hand (cont.):

my sword sleep in my h.	BLAKE 61:12
O! let me kiss that h.	SHAK 283:24
put your h. into the h. of God	HASK 163:16
right h. forget her cunning	BOOK 69:4
shaking h. of an old, wild	VICT 338:5
sweeten this little h.	SHAK 287:30
there also shall thy h. lead me	BOOK 69:6
thine h. toward heaven	BIBLE 39:35
Took me by the h.	TURN 335:17
touch of a vanished h.	TENN 323:11
waiting for a h.	TENN 324:26
wash this blood clean from my h.	SHAK 286:18
was the h. that wrote it	CRAN 111:4
Whatsoever thy h. findeth to do	BIBLE 44:19
what thy right h. doeth	BIBLE 48:26
Wouldst hold my h.?	HART 163:11
Your tiny h. is frozen	ILL 150:9
handclasp: Out where the h.'s	CHAP 94:13
Handel: Compared to H.'s a mere ninny	BYROM 84:24
Dance they to the tunes of H.	SITW 308:1
handful: fear in a h. of dust	ELIOT 134:20
h. of meal in a barrel	BIBLE 41:35
handkerchief: Trap the germs in your h.	ANON 6:23
handle: h. of the big front door	GILB 152:18
handmaid: Riches are a good h.	BACON 24:6
handmaidens: low estate of his h.	BIBLE 51:28
hands: Beneath the bleeding h.	ELIOT 133:5
by joining of h.	BOOK 66:4
caught the world's great h.	HUNT 176:14
clasps the crag with crookèd h.	TENN 323:21
h. are the hands of Esau	BIBLE 39:20
h. from picking and stealing	BOOK 65:22
h. I commend my spirit	BIBLE 53:4
h. I commend my spirit	BOOK 66:23
h. I loved beside the Shalimar	HOPE 171:22
h. that hold the aces	BETJ 36:22
has such small h.	CUMM 113:3
He hath shook h. with time	FORD 143:10
Holding h. at midnight	GERS 150:8
horny h. of toil	LOW 211:5
house not made with h.	BIBLE 55:24
into the h. of spoilers	BIBLE 40:30
into the h. of the living	BIBLE 56:25
knit h., and beat the ground	MILT 226:9
Let the lifting up of my h.	BOOK 69:8
Licence my roving h.	DONNE 123:6
little folding of the h.	BIBLE 43:12
not into the h. of men	BIBLE 47:32
not into the h. of Spain	TENN 328:13
or have laid violent h.	BOOK 66:5
reached out their h. in longing	VIRG 339:15
Shake h. for ever, cancel	DRAY 126:16
Soul clap its h. and sing	YEATS 359:21
spits on its h. and goes to work	SAND 266:18
Strengthen ye the weak h.	BIBLE 46:5
their h. are blue	LEAR 203:10
Their h. upon their hearts	HOUS 174:10
these h. ne'er be clean	SHAK 287:29
They have h., and handle	BOOK 68:18
union of h. and hearts	TAYL 323:5
handsaw: know a hawk from a h.	SHAK 275:17
handsome: h. in three hundred pounds	SHAK 290:10
hang: all h. together	FRAN 145:13
h. a pearl in every cowslip's	SHAK 290:20
H. it all, Robert Browning	POUND 254:12
h. my hat is home sweet home	JER 181:9
h. that jury-men may dine	POPE 253:8
Here they h. a man first	MOL 232:21
let him h. there	EHRL 131:7
on gate-bars h. in a row	HARDY 162:17
hanged: And my poor fool is h.	SHAK 284:6
be h. in a fortnight	JOHN 185:14
h. for stealing horses	HAL 160:11
h. himself	BIBLE 41:26

hanged (cont.):

Here's a farmer that h.	SHAK 286:20
Major-general Harrison h.	PEPYS 247:13
hanging: H. and marriage	FARQ 138:20
h. Danny Deever	KIPL 196:9
H. is too good for him	BUNY 78:22
h. men an' women	ANON 8:9
H. of his cat on Monday	BRAT 71:16
h. prevents a bad marriage	SHAK 297:18
hangs: And thereby h. a tale	SHAK 272:22
H. in the uncertain balance	GREE 158:8
What h. people	STEV 317:10
hank: rag and a bone and a h. of hair	KIPL 197:12
happen: accidents which started to h.	MARQ 219:21
happens: dependent on what h. to her	ELIOT 132:5
Nothing h., nobody comes	BECK 31:12
something h. anywhere	LARK 201:15
happier: happiest if ye seek no h. state	MILT 229:12
happiest: h. and best minds	SHEL 305:18
h. if ye seek no happier state	MILT 229:12
h. time of all the glad New-year	TENN 327:5
h. women, like h. nations	ELIOT 132:14
happiness: best recipe for h.	AUST 22:20
consume h. without producing	SHAW 300:26
flaw in h., to see beyond	KEATS 192:18
For all the h. mankind can gain	DRYD 127:35
great enemy to human h.	JOHN 185:31
h. for the greatest numbers	HUTC 177:2
H. is an imaginary condition	SZASZ 321:23
H. is no laughing matter	WHAT 347:6
H. is not an ideal of reason	KANT 189:24
H. makes up in height	FROST 146:14
h. of society	ADAMS 2:1
h. of the greatest number	BENT 35:1
h. of the human race	BURKE 80:6
h. or a quiet conscience	BERL 36:6
h. produced by a good tavern	JOHN 185:8
H. the occasional episode	HARDY 161:22
home-born h.	COWP 110:12
liberty and the pursuit of h.	ANON 11:12
lifetime of h. would be hell on earth	SHAW 301:15
most suited to human h.	DEFOE 115:14
pursuit of h.	JEFF 180:18
result h.	DICK 118:12
somebody else's h.	HUXL 177:8
To fill the hour—that is h.	EMER 136:26
uncertain of giving h.	AUST 23:4
We find our h., or not at all	WORD 356:14
Who gain a h. in eyeing	HUXL 177:13
you take away his h.	IBSEN 178:7
happy: all h. families resemble	TOLS 333:11
Be h. while y'er leevin	ANON 6:9
call no man h. before he dies	SOLON 310:27
conspiracy to make you h.	UPD 336:14
Farmer will never be h.	HERB 166:11
Hail, redemption's h. dawn	CASW 92:18
h. and keep him that way	HOR 173:10
h. as the grass was green	THOM 330:8
H. field or mossy cavern	KEATS 191:16
h. he who crowns in shades	GOLD 154:19
h. he who like Ulysses	DU B 128:33
h. highways where I went	HOUS 174:24
H. in the arms of a chambermaid	JOHN 185:21
H. in this, she is not yet so old	SHAK 289:22
h. issue out of all their	BOOK 64:19
H. is that city	ANON 7:16
H. is the man who fears	BIBLE 58:11
h. noise to hear	HOUS 174:20
H. the hare at morning	AUDEN 20:16
H. the people whose annals	MONT 233:22
H. those early days	VAUG 337:7
His h. good-night air	HARDY 162:7
How h. could I be with either	GAY 149:7
Is that they h. are	WALL 341:15
Lucid intervals and h. pauses	BACON 25:22

happy (cont.):

needed one thing to make me h.	HAZL 164:2
O h. Rome, born when	CIC 101:2
one who has been h.	BOET 62:17
pain than to remember a h. time	DANTE 113:21
perfectly happy till all are h.	SPEN 312:21
remote from the h.	AUDEN 20:9
should all be as h. as kings	STEV 317:13
someone somewhere, may be h.	MENC 223:7
splendid and a h. land	GOLD 154:25
stayed me in a h. hour	SHAK 291:24
This h. breed of men	SHAK 293:16
to attain the h. life	SURR 319:6
To make men h., and to keep	POPE 252:26
touch the H. Isles	TENN 328:24
'Twere now to be most h.	SHAK 292:5
Was he free? Was he h.?	AUDEN 21:17
We can't all be h.	RHYS 259:13
Well, I've had a h. life	HAZL 164:9
you cease to be h.	MILL 224:13

harbinger: evening star, Love's h. — MILT 229:32

harbour: Though the h. bar be moaning — KING 195:16

hard: ask the h. question — AUDEN 21:16

Between a rock and a h. place	ANON 6:10
Breeds h. English men	KING 195:15
h. rain's a gonna fall	DYLAN 130:2
h. words like a charm	OSB 242:17
It's been a h. day's night	MCC 205:14
Long is the way and h.	MILT 228:30
soldier's life is terrible h.	MILNE 225:19
thou art an h. man	BIBLE 51:2
woman is so h. upon the man	TENN 328:1

hard-faced: lot of h. men — BALD 27:9

hardly: Johnny, I h. knew ye — BALL 27:18

hare: Happy the h. at morning — AUDEN 20:16

h. limped trembling through	KEATS 190:14
h. sits snug in leaves	HOFF 170:1
h. sitting up	LAWR 202:17
h.'s own child, the little hare	HOFF 170:3
Take your h. when it is cased	GLAS 153:16
that Caught the Pubic H.	BEHAN 32:17

hares: And little hunted h. — HODG 169:13

hark: H.! hark! the lark — SHAK 273:25

H.! the heaven-angels — WESL 346:7

harlot: Every h. was a virgin once — BLAKE 60:15

h.'s cry from street to street	BLAKE 60:9
h. we have got hold of	BYRON 87:16
Portia is Brutus' h.	SHAK 281:7
prerogative of the h.	KIPL 198:5

harlots: MOTHER OF H. — BIBLE 58:2

harm: do so much h. as those who — CREI 111:18

forgive a man for the h.	MAUG 222:10
I fear we'll come to h.	BALL 28:5
meaning no h.	GREE 158:7
prevent h. to others	MILL 224:15
that does h. to my wit	SHAK 297:15

harmless: entertains the h. day — WOTT 357:14

h. as doves — BIBLE 49:29

only h. great thing — DONNE 123:20

harmonical: h. and ingenious soul — AUBR 19:19

harmonious: Such h. madness — SHEL 305:11

harmony: Discordant h. — HOR 173:12

price is asked for h.	DOST 125:4
touches of sweet h.	SHAK 290:1

harness: between the joints of the h. — BIBLE 42:7

h. and not the horses — CANN 89:13

harp: clear h. in divers tones — TENN 324:24

H. not on that string	SHAK 294:19
h. on a weeping willow-tree	ANON 8:5
h. that once through Tara's	MOORE 234:14
wild h. slung behind him	MOORE 234:16

Harpic: As I read the H. tin — BENN 34:16

harps: To touch their h. of gold — SEARS 269:11

harrow: H. the house of the dead — AUDEN 21:14

Would h. up thy soul — SHAK 274:30

harrowing: Only a man h. clods — HARDY 162:11

Harry: banish not him thy H.'s company — SHAK 278:1

But H., Harry	SHAK 278:29
Cry 'God for H.!	SHAK 279:6
touch of H. in the night	SHAK 279:8

harsh: Nor h. nor grating — WORD 355:10

hart: h. desireth the water-brooks — BOOK 67:3

h. ungallèd play	SHAK 276:12
pants the h. for cooling streams	TATE 322:16

Harvard: glass flowers at H. — MOORE 234:9

Yale College and my H. — MELV 223:3

harvest: h. of a quiet eye — WORD 356:7

shine on, h. moon	NORW 240:11
she laughs with a h.	JERR 181:12

harvests: Deep h. bury all his pride — POPE 251:17

Harwich: in a steamer from H. — GILB 151:16

haste: I said in my h. — BOOK 68:21

Make h. slowly	AUG 22:6
Men love in h.	BYRON 86:25
they repent in h.	CONG 106:13
Though I am always in h.	WESL 346:16
what h. I can to be gone	CROM 112:8

hasten: So do our minutes h. — SHAK 299:21

hat: hang my h. is home sweet — JER 181:9

hang your h. on a pension	MACN 216:2
looking for a black h.	BOWEN 70:13
without popping off his h.	JOHN 184:8

hatches: continually under h. — KEATS 193:6

hatchet: I did cut it with my h. — WASH 342:22

hatching: H. vain empires — MILT 228:28

hate: cherish those hearts that h. — SHAK 280:20

do good to them which h.	BIBLE 52:6
enough religion to make us h.	SWIFT 320:10
Envy and calumny and h.	SHEL 303:11
generation of them that h.	BIBLE 40:5
h. a fellow whom pride	JOHN 186:1
h. any one that we know	HAZL 164:7
h. something in him	HESSE 168:3
h. that which we often	SHAK 271:8
h. the man you have hurt	TAC 322:5
h. you through the glass	BLUN 62:14
have seen much to h. here	MILL 224:24
I h. all Boets and Bainters	GEOR 149:20
I h. and I love	CAT 93:7
Let them h., so long as they fear	ACC 1:2
man you love to h.	ANON 9:7
must h. and death return	SHEL 303:19
need not be to h. mankind	BYRON 85:5
never bother with people I h.	HART 163:9
sprung from my only h.	SHAK 294:28
time to love, and a time to h.	BIBLE 44:13

hated: h. the ruling few — BENT 35:4

hateful: And shamed life a h. — SHAK 288:21

hates: h. dogs and babies — ROST 263:13

man who h. his mother — BENN 34:19

hateth: h. his brother — BIBLE 57:17

hath: that h. shall be given — BIBLE 51:3

hating: h. all other nations — GASK 148:20

hatless: lands h. from the air — BETJ 36:21

hatred: feel any h. for him — RAC 257:14

from envy, h., and malice	BOOK 64:14
Great h., little room	YEATS 359:19
h. for the Tory Party	BEVAN 37:18
h. is by far the longest	BYRON 86:25
like love to h. turned	CONG 106:12
no h. or bitterness	CAV 93:12
Regulated h.	HARD 161:16
stalled ox and h.	BIBLE 43:26

hatreds: systematic organization of h. — ADAMS 1:11

hats: so many shocking bad h. — WELL 345:9

haughty: h. spirit before — BIBLE 43:28

haunches: on silent h. — SAND 266:13

haunt: h. of flies on summer eves — KEATS 192:2

haunted: h. town it is to me — LANG 201:1

haunts: from h. of coot and hern | TENN 323:12
That h. you night and day | BERL 36:1
have: I h. thee not, and yet | SHAK 286:10
They h. to take you in | FROST 146:11
to h. and to hold | BOOK 66:1
they will not let you h. it | HAZL 164:3
have-his-carcase: h., next to the perpetual | DICK 120:3
haven: their h. under the hill | TENN 323:11
haves: h. and the have-nots | CERV 93:18
having: Never satisfied with h. | WROTH 358:1
havoc: Cry, 'H.!' and let slip | SHAK 281:14
Strokes of h. únselve | HOPK 171:24
hawk: But his h., his hound | BALL 28:9
h. at eagles with a dove | HERB 167:6
know a h. from a handsaw | SHAK 275:17
Or h. of the tower | SKEL 308:3
hay: Work and pray, live on h. | HILL 168:12
hazard: father's crown into the h. | SHAK 279:1
he: H. that is without sin | BIBLE 53:26
H. would, wouldn't he | RIC 259:20
head: bear with a sore h. | MARR 219:26
God be in my h. | ANON 7:11
Go up, thou bald h. | BIBLE 42:8
hairs of your h. are numbered | BIBLE 49:30
hath not where to lay his h. | BIBLE 49:19
h. could carry all he knew | GOLD 154:24
h. grown grey in vain | SHEL 303:11
h. is not more native | SHAK 274:4
h. that once was crowned | KELLY 193:19
h. thou dost with oil anoint | SCOT 269:9
h. to contrive | CLAR 101:10
h. to contrive | GIBB 150:12
heaped on each gashed h. | SORL 311:16
her h. on her knee | SHAK 292:26
If sex ever rears its ugly h. | AYCK 23:14
If you can keep your h. | KIPL 197:5
ignorance bumping its h. | FORD 143:8
incessantly stands on your h. | CARR 91:4
Lay your sleeping h., my love | AUDEN 20:27
learned lumber in his h. | POPE 252:9
make you shorter by the h. | ELIZ 135:8
no matter which way the h. lies | RAL 258:4
Off with his h. | CIBB 100:15
Or in the heart or in the h. | SHAK 289:20
repairs his drooping h. | MILT 227:18
shew his glorious h. | SPEN 313:5
so young a body with so old a h. | SHAK 289:25
Uneasy lies the h. | SHAK 278:23
which binds so dear a h. | SHEL 303:3
headache: awake with a dismal h. | GILB 151:15
headin': you know where we're h. | DYLAN 130:7
head-in-air: Little Johnny H. | HOFF 169:20
headpiece: H. filled with straw | ELIOT 133:17
heads: Its h. o'ertaxed, its palsied | ARN 17:11
Lift up your h. | BOOK 66:20
Their h. are green | LEAR 203:10
head-stone: become the h. in the corner | BOOK 68:22
headstrong: h. as an allegory | SHER 305:30
head-waiter: diplomat nothing but a h. | UST 336:19
heady: H., not strong | POPE 250:15
heal: Physician, h. thyself | BIBLE 52:5
healed: h. also the hurt | BIBLE 46:28
Ransomed, h., restored | LYTE 212:21
with his stripes we are h. | BIBLE 46:19
healer: compassion of the h.'s art | ELIOT 133:5
healing: h. of the nations | BIBLE 58:7
with h. in his wings | BIBLE 47:26
health: And there is no h. in us | BOOK 63:14
h. of his wife | CONN 106:29
His h., his honour | BLUN 62:15
Look to your h. | WALT 342:14
saving h. among all nations | BOOK 67:16
when you have both, it's h. | DONL 123:2
healthy: h. and wealthy and dead | THUR 332:15

heap: rude h. together hurled | MARV 221:2
hear: h. it in the deep heart's core | YEATS 359:13
H. the other side | AUG 22:1
h. the pleasant cuckoo | DAV 114:17
h. the word of the Lord | BIBLE 47:10
H. us, we humbly pray | MARR 219:24
He that hath ears to h. | BIBLE 51:20
I h. a smile | CROSS 112:11
I h. a sudden cry of pain | STEP 315:7
I h. thy shrill delight | SHEL 305:8
Lord, h. our prayers | BOOK 65:24
may in such wise h. them | BOOK 64:22
O h. us when we cry to thee | WHIT 348:9
O let me h. thee speaking | BODE 62:16
see and h. and feel yet | JOYCE 188:17
time will come when you will h. me | DISR 121:5
we shall h. it by-and-by | BROW 75:8
which men prefer not to h. | AGAR 3:5
who do not wish to h. it | BUTL 84:20
heard: And then is h. no more | SHAK 288:5
have ye not h.? | BIBLE 46:12
H., not regarded | SHAK 278:6
h. one side of the case | BUTL 84:15
I will be h.! | GARR 148:12
Oon ere it h., at tother | CHAU 96:19
should certainly have h. | AUDEN 21:17
voice of the turtle is h. | BIBLE 44:32
You Ain't H. Nothing Yet | JOLS 186:19
hearers: not h. only | BIBLE 57:2
hearing: passionate my sense of h. | SHAK 284:12
People h. without listening | SIMON 307:7
hears: She neither h. nor sees | WORD 356:25
hearse: Underneath this sable h. | BROW 74:24
heart: Ancient person of my h. | ROCH 261:9
And I am sick at h. | SHAK 273:30
and the h. is sick | TENN 325:7
And with a well-tuned h. | GURN 159:11
anniversaries of the h. | LONG 209:20
autumn's violins wound my h. | VERL 337:21
Batter my h., three-personed | DONNE 123:10
battlefield is the h. of man | DOST 125:2
Because my h. is pure | TENN 328:15
Beware my foolish h. | WASH 342:24
bicycle-pump the human h. | AMIS 5:5
blind side of the h. | CHES 97:21
broken h. lies here | MAC 214:1
Brute h. of a brute like you | PLATH 249:14
Bury my h. at Wounded Knee | BENÉT 34:9
But break, my h. | SHAK 274:13
'Calais' lying in my h. | MARY 221:17
'CALLOUS' engraved on her h. | SELL 270:1
Can make a stone of the h. | YEATS 359:2
can no longer tear his h. | SWIFT 320:27
corrupt the h. | BYRON 86:33
count time by h.-throbs | BAIL 26:18
cracks a noble h. | SHAK 277:19
desires of the h. as crooked | AUDEN 20:15
false h. doth know | SHAK 286:8
For Mercy has a human h. | BLAKE 61:21
from hell's h. I stab at thee | MELV 223:4
God be in my h. | ANON 7:11
great [have] no h. | LA BR 199:13
hear it in the deep h.'s core | YEATS 359:13
h. and stomach of a king | ELIZ 135:6
h. as sound as a bell | SHAK 291:21
h. be full of the spring | SWIN 321:15
h. expands to tinker | MACN 216:9
h. grown cold, a head | SHEL 303:11
h. grows old | YEATS 359:29
h. has its reasons | PASC 246:5
h. hath 'scaped this sorrow | SHAK 300:1
h. is a lonely hunter | MCL 215:10
h. is deceitful above all | BIBLE 46:31
h. is Highland | GALT 147:19

heart (*cont.*):

h. is inditing	BOOK 67:5
h. is on the left	MOL 232:19
h. is strong and the human	BAG 26:12
h. lies plain	ARN 16:10
H. of Darkness	CONR 107:4
H. of England	DRAY 126:17
h. of kings is unsearchable	BIBLE 43:34
h. of lead	POPE 250:14
H. of oak are our ships	GARR 148:8
h. speaks to heart	FRAN 145:6
H.'s renying, causer of this	BARN 29:8
h. the keener, courage	ANON 11:5
heart to h., and mind to mind	SCOTT 268:11
h. too soon made glad	BROW 76:19
h. to poke poor Billy	GRAH 156:4
h. was piercèd through	SHAK 291:38
h. was to thy rudder tied	SHAK 271:18
h. within blood-tinctured	BROW 75:3
He carries his h. in his boots	HERB 166:11
he had a h. to resolve	GIBB 150:12
Her h. was warm and gay	HAMM 161:1
his little h., dispossessed	JAMES 180:3
holiness of the h.'s affections	KEATS 192:23
Hope deferred maketh the h. sick	BIBLE 43:21
If thy h. fails thee	ELIZ 135:9
I left my h. in San Francisco	CROSS 112:10
In my h.'s core	SHAK 276:7
I said to H. 'How goes it?'	BELL 33:12
larger h., the kindlier hand	TENN 325:27
laughter of her h.	HAMM 161:1
let not your h. be troubled	BIBLE 53:36
let your h. be strong	LAUD 202:5
look in thy h. and write	SIDN 306:17
loosed our h. in tears	ARN 16:19
Lord looketh on the h.	BIBLE 41:15
Make me a clean h.	BOOK 67:10
man after his own h.	BIBLE 41:13
merry h. maketh a cheerful	BIBLE 43:25
mighty h. is lying still	WORD 354:16
mine eyes, but not my h.	JONS 187:6
My h. aches, and a drowsy	KEATS 191:28
My h. and tongue employ	TATE 322:17
My h. belongs to Daddy	PORT 253:24
My h. in hiding stirred	HOPK 172:21
My h. is heavy	GOET 154:6
My h. leaps up when I behold	WORD 355:13
My h.'s in the Highlands	BURNS 82:18
My h. would hear her and beat	TENN 327:2
My true love hath my h.	SIDN 306:15
natural language of the h.	SHAD 270:17
naughtiness of thine h.	BIBLE 41:17
nearer God's H. in a garden	GURN 159:10
no matter from the h.	SHAK 297:12
not more native to the h.	SHAK 274:4
Open my h. and you will see	BROW 75:24
Or in the h. or in the head	SHAK 289:20
pastoral h. of England	QUIL 257:8
plotting h. in the world	RICH 260:2
rag and bone shop of the h.	YEATS 358:16
Religion's in the h.	JERR 181:10
revolting and a rebellious h.	BIBLE 46:27
Rise in the h., and gather	TENN 327:22
seal upon thine h.	BIBLE 45:1
Sink h. and voice oppressed	NEALE 237:22
softer pillow than my h.	BYRON 87:22
some h. did break	TENN 324:25
So the h. be right	RAL 258:4
squirrel's h. beat	ELIOT 132:10
Sweeping up the H.	DICK 120:10
sweet concurrence of the h.	HERR 167:17
tears out the h. of it	KNOW 198:15
That visit my sad h.	SHAK 281:7
There is room in my h. for thee	ELL 136:1
there will your h. be also	BIBLE 49:2

heart (*cont.*):

this h., all evil shed	BROO 73:10
thy beak from out my h.	POE 250:7
tiger's h. wrapped in a woman	SHAK 280:13
waters of the h.	THOM 330:12
wear my h. upon my sleeve	SHAK 291:28
We had fed the h. on fantasies	YEATS 359:16
where my h. is turning ever	FOST 144:12
Whispers the o'er-fraught h.	SHAK 287:25
With a h. of furious fancies	ANON 11:23
With h. and hands and voices	WINK 352:4
woman has given you her h.	VANB 336:24
wound a h. that's broken	SCOTT 268:15
wounded is the wounding h.	CRAS 111:7
your h. to a dog to tear	KIPL 196:27
heartache: h. and the thousand natural shocks	
	SHAK 275:25
heartbeat: just a h. away	STEV 316:19
heartbreak: h. in the heart of things	GIBS 150:22
heart-easing: tell the most h. things	KEATS 192:12
hearth: By this still h.	TENN 328:19
Save the cricket on the h.	MILT 226:25
hearts: cold h. and muddy understandings	
	BURKE 80:15
first in the h. of his countrymen	LEE 204:7
harden not your h.	BOOK 68:1
h. are dry as summer dust	WORD 354:19
H. just as pure and fair	GILB 151:11
h. that spanieled me	SHAK 271:22
H. wound up with love	SPEN 313:2
heedless h.	GRAY 157:15
hidden in each other's h.	DICK 119:6
Incline our h. to keep this law	BOOK 65:3
In h. at peace, under	BROO 73:10
Lift up your h.	BOOK 65:13
our h. are great	TENN 324:12
O you hard h., you cruel	SHAK 280:24
shall keep your h. and minds	BIBLE 56:8
Their hands upon their h.	HOUS 174:10
those that be of heavy h.	BIBLE 44:5
thousand h. beat happily	BYRON 85:2
two h. beating each to each	BROW 76:17
Two h. that beat as one	HALM 160:15
undeveloped h.	FORS 143:15
union of hands and h.	TAYL 323:5
unto whom all h. be open	BOOK 65:2
with Splendid H. may go	BROO 73:6
heartstrings: jesses were my dear h.	SHAK 292:14
heat: burden and h. of the day	BIBLE 50:25
Fear no more the h. o' the sun	SHAK 273:27
if you can't stand the h.	VAUG 337:2
have neither h. nor light	WEBS 344:17
not without dust and h.	MILT 230:31
heated: When h. in the chase	TATE 322:16
heath: Upon this blasted h.	SHAK 285:8
heathen: h. in his blindness	HEBER 164:16
h. in 'is blindness	KIPL 196:10
pore benighted h.	KIPL 196:14
Why do the h. so furiously rage	BOOK 66:9
heather: bonnie bloomin' h.	LAUD 202:6
heaths: some game on these lone h.	HAZL 164:8
heaven: All I seek, the h. above	STEV 317:25
All this, and h. too	HENRY 166:7
And a h. in a wild flower	BLAKE 60:5
And H.'s peculiar care	SOM 311:3
and more than all in h.	BYRON 85:18
betwixt H. and Charing Cross	THOM 331:16
But to be young was very h.	WORD 354:24
call it the Road to H.	BALL 28:7
Can make a h. of hell	MILT 228:12
consent of h.	JONS 187:1
distant from H. alike	BURT 83:11
eleven who went to h.	ANON 8:6
Fellowship is h., and lack of	MORR 235:17
flowerless fields of h.	SWIN 320:28

hellhound: h. is always a h. — WOD 352:14
helmet: She saw the h. and the plume — TENN 326:3
help: cannot h. or pardon — AUDEN 21:15
  can't h. lovin' dat man of mine — HAMM 160:19
  encumbers him with h. — JOHN 183:26
  enough to h. the feeble up — SHAK 296:16
  from whence cometh my h. — BOOK 68:25
  h. and support of the woman — EDW 131:2
  H. of the helpless — LYTE 212:20
  h. thou mine unbelief — BIBLE 51:24
  H. yourself, and heaven — LA F 199:16
  how can I h. England — BROW 76:4
  place where h. wasn't hired — ANON 7:17
  present h. in time of trouble — ANON 5:18
  present h. in trouble — BOOK 67:6
  scream for h. in dreams — CAN 89:9
  Since there's no h. — DRAY 126:16
  They look on and h. — LAWR 202:26
  will make him an h. meet — BIBLE 38:20
  with a little h. from my friends — MCC 205:18
  you can't h. it — SMITH 309:7
  your countrymen cannot h. — JOHN 184:6
helper: mother's little h. — RICH 179:5
helpers: When other h. fail — LYTE 212:20
helping: H., when we meet them — KING 195:14
helpless: H., naked, piping loud — BLAKE 62:3
  Help of the h., O abide with me — LYTE 212:20
hem: h. of Nature's shift — SHEL 304:14
hemlock: though of h. I had drunk — KEATS 191:28
hempen: h. home-spuns — SHAK 290:31
hen: better take a wet h. — KHR 194:20
hence: H., loathèd Melancholy — MILT 226:27
  H., vain deluding joys — MILT 226:22
henna: Of tan with h. hackles — STEV 316:4
Heraclitus: They told me, H. — CORY 108:13
herald: Hark! the h.-angels — WESL 346:7
heraldry: boast of h., the pomp — GRAY 157:7
herb: h. of grace o' Sundays — SHAK 277:3
herbs: dinner of h. — BIBLE 43:26
  with bitter h. they shall eat — BIBLE 39:36
Hercules: and some of H. — ANON 10:13
herd: lowing h. wind slowly — GRAY 157:4
  Morality is the h.-instinct — NIET 239:20
here: H. am I; send me — BIBLE 45:12
  H. and here did England — BROW 76:4
  H. I am, and here I stay — MACM 215:13
  H.'s a how-de-doo — GILB 151:26
  H.'s looking at you, kid — EPST 137:11
  H.'s tae us; wha's like us — ANON 7:18
  H.'s to the widow of fifty — SHER 306:6
  h.'s to you, Mrs Robinson — SIMON 307:6
  H. today—in next week — GRAH 156:6
  I have been h. before — ROSS 263:10
  We're h. because we're here — ANON 11:13
hereditary: H. bondsmen! — BYRON 85:1
hereditas: Damnosa h. — GAIUS 147:13
Hereford: Hertford, H., and Hampshire — LERN 206:1
heresies: And hateful h. — SPEN 313:16
  new truths to begin as h. — HUXL 177:18
heresy: h. signifies no more — HOBB 169:7
heretics: H. are the only bitter remedy — ZAMY 360:25
heritage: I have a goodly h. — BOOK 66:15
  we have come into our h. — BROO 72:21
hermitage: palace for a h. — SHAK 294:2
hern: haunts of coot and h. — TENN 323:12
hero: Every h. becomes a bore — EMER 136:30
  Millions a h. — PORT 253:26
  No man is a h. to his valet — CORN 108:9
  See, the conquering h. comes — MOR 235:5
  very valet seemed a h. — BYRON 84:27
  who aspires to be a h. — JOHN 185:22
Herod: it out-herods H. — SHAK 276:5
  Oh, for an hour of H. — HOPE 171:21
heroes: all the world's brave h. — ANON 10:13

heroes (cont.):
  And its h. were made — Æ 3:4
  Britain a fit country for h. — LLOY 208:11
  glum h. up the line to death — SASS 267:8
  thin red line of h. — KIPL 197:11
heroic: finished a life h. — MILT 230:17
  h. for earth too hard — BROW 75:8
  H. womanhood — LONG 209:25
  One equal temper of h. hearts — TENN 328:25
heroically: in one word, h. mad — DRYD 127:18
heroine: when a h. goes mad — SHER 305:24
herring: plague o' these pickle h. — SHAK 297:19
Hertford: H., Hereford, and Hampshire — LERN 206:1
Hervey: If you call a dog H. — JOHN 183:23
hesitate: h. and falter life away — ARN 17:10
hesitates: She floats, she h. — RAC 257:15
Hesperus: H. entreats thy light — JONS 187:3
  Wreck of the H. — LONG 210:5
heterodoxy: h. is another man's doxy — WARB 342:17
heures: h. propices — LAM 199:21
hew: h. him as a carcass fit — SHAK 281:4
hewers: h. of wood and drawers — BIBLE 40:28
hey: Then h. for boot and horse — KING 195:17
hi: H. diddle dee dee — WASH 342:23
hic: H. jacet — RAL 258:2
hick: Sticks nix h. pix — ANON 10:15
hid: I h. from Him — THOM 331:8
hidden: h. in each other's hearts — DICK 119:6
hide: H. me from day's garish eye — MILT 226:26
  Is it a world to h. virtues — SHAK 297:17
  Let me h. myself in Thee — TOPL 333:14
  wrapped in a woman's h. — SHAK 280:13
hideous: h. notes of woe — BYRON 86:28
hides: he that h. a dark soul — MILT 226:12
  H. from himself his state — JOHN 183:15
Hierusalem: H., my happy home — ANON 7:19
high: get h. with a little help — MCC 205:18
  h. as an elephant's eye — HAMM 161:2
  h. life high characters — POPE 251:20
  h. that proved too high — BROW 75:8
  like champagne or h. heels — BENN 34:18
  She's the Broad and I'm the H. — SPR 314:1
  This h. man, with a great — BROW 75:33
  upon the h. horse — BROWN 73:16
  wickedness in h. places — BIBLE 56:4
  ye'll tak' the h. road — ANON 10:2
higher: Can Stuart or Nassau go h. — PRIOR 255:10
  Friend, go up h. — BIBLE 52:21
  their dead selves to h. things — TENN 324:24
highest: h. good — CIC 100:22
  needs must love the h. — TENN 324:6
highland: heart is H. — GALT 147:19
  Yon solitary H. lass — WORD 357:1
Highlandman: breeks aff a wild H. — SCOTT 268:26
highlands: In the h., in the country — STEV 317:18
  My heart's in the H. — BURNS 82:18
  Ye H. and ye Lawlands — BALL 27:14
highly: what thou wouldst h. — SHAK 285:15
highway: broad h. of the world — SHEL 303:16
  H., since you my chief — SIDN 306:24
highways: happy h. where I went — HOUS 174:24
  out into the h. and hedges — BIBLE 52:25
hill: all gone under the h. — ELIOT 133:4
  city that is set on an h. — BIBLE 48:21
  every mountain and h. — BIBLE 46:9
  High on a h. it calls to me — CROSS 112:10
  hunter home from the h. — STEV 317:22
  laughing is heard on the h. — BLAKE 61:25
  Mahomet will go to the h. — BACON 24:16
  nursed upon the self-same h. — MILT 227:12
  other side of the h. — WELL 345:6
  rest upon thy holy h. — BOOK 66:11
  To their haven under the h. — TENN 323:11
  traveller's dream under the h. — BLAKE 60:15
hills: Along Morea's h. — BYRON 85:20

hills (*cont.*):

blue remembered h.	HOUS 174:24
high wild h.	SHAK 293:17
h. of Georgia	KING 195:9
H. of the Chankly Bore	LEAR 203:9
H. of the North, rejoice	OAKL 240:16
lift up mine eyes unto the h.	BOOK 68:25
little h. like young sheep	BOOK 68:16
Over the h. and far away	GAY 149:5
to the reverberate h.	SHAK 297:21
hill-side: h.'s dew-pearled	BROW 76:28
him: they all cried 'That's h.!'	BARH 28:20
himself: He h. said it	CIC 100:21
hindsight: H. is always twenty-twenty	WILD 350:23
hinky: H., dinky, parley-voo	ANON 9:5
hip: catch him once upon the h.	SHAK 289:2
He smote them h. and thigh	BIBLE 41:4
Hippocrene: blushful H.	KEATS 191:30
hippopotamus: I shoot the H.	BELL 33:1
shoot the h. with eyebrows	FORS 143:14
hips: armchairs tight about the h.	WOD 352:22
We swing ungirded h.	SORL 311:15
hire: labourer is worthy of his h.	BIBLE 52:10
hired: They h. the money	COOL 107:20
Hiroshima: Einstein leads to H.	PIC 248:19
hissed: h. along the polished ice	WORD 355:2
historian: h. wants more documents	JAMES 179:15
historians: h. left blanks	POUND 254:13
historically: Eternally noble, h. fair	LERN 205:26
histories: H. make men wise	BACON 25:16
history: annals are blank in h.-books	MONT 233:22
Antiquities are h. defaced	BACON 23:21
dustbin of h.	TROT 335:1
dust-heap called 'h.'	BIRR 59:15
great deal of h. to produce	JAMES 179:18
happiest nations, have no h.	ELIOT 132:14
h. becomes a race	WELLS 345:21
H. came to a .	SELL 270:5
H. gets thicker	TAYL 322:22
[h.] is a debatable line	MAC 213:22
H. [is] a distillation of rumour	CARL 90:12
H. is a gallery of pictures	TOCQ 333:1
H. is a nightmare	JOYCE 188:14
H. is … a tableau of crimes	VOLT 340:20
H. is littered with the wars	POW 255:2
H. is more or less bunk	FORD 143:6
H. is not what you thought	SELL 269:23
H. is now and England	ELIOT 133:12
h. is on our side	KHR 194:19
H. is past politics	FREE 145:21
H. is philosophy from examples	DION 121:4
H. is the essence of	CARL 90:6
h. is the world's judgement	SCH 267:21
H. just burps	BARN 29:6
H. is little more than the register	GIBB 150:11
H., *n*. An account	BIER 59:6
h. of art is the history of revivals	BUTL 84:14
h. of class struggles	MARX 221:14
H. to the defeated	AUDEN 21:15
H. will absolve me	CAST 92:16
more h. than they can consume	SAKI 265:17
never learned anything from h.	HEGEL 164:18
no h.; only biography	EMER 136:22
Read no h.	DISR 121:28
Thames is liquid h.	BURNS 81:20
thousand years of h.	GAIT 147:12
War makes rattling good h.	HARDY 161:20
worthy of serious attention than h.	ARIS 15:16
hit: hit, a very palpable h.	SHAK 277:14
h. it off as they should	WORD 354:11
hitch: H. your wagon to a star	EMER 136:31
Hitler: H. attacked the Jews	NIEM 239:15
[H.] missed the bus	CHAM 94:3
H. swept out	ANON 8:12
kidding, Mister H.	PERRY 248:5

hive: h. for the honey bee	YEATS 359:12
hoard: Our h. is little	TENN 324:12
Hoares: no more H. to Paris	GEOR 149:26
hoarse: raven himself is h.	SHAK 285:16
Hobbes: H. clearly proves	SWIFT 320:22
hobbit: there lived a h.	TOLK 333:8
hobgoblin: h. of little minds	EMER 136:24
hock: weak h. and seltzer	BETJ 36:16
hodgepodge: gallimaufry or h.	SPEN 313:20
hoe: Man with the H.	MARK 218:4
tickle her with a h.	JERR 181:12
hog: Rule all England under a h.	COLL 105:3
hogamus: H., higamous	JAMES 180:11
hogs: Men Eat H.	STEV 316:7
hoist: H. with his own petar	SHAK 276:25
hold: always keep a-h. of Nurse	BELL 33:5
first cries, 'H., enough'	SHAK 288:8
hereafter for ever h. his peace	BOOK 65:27
h. fast blessed hope	BIBLE 56:14
H. the fort	BLISS 62:10
h. the gorgeous East	WORD 356:2
hole: drop of rain maketh a h.	LAT 202:3
h. in the ground	TOLK 333:8
kick a h. in a stained glass	CHAN 94:7
knows of a better h.	BAIR 26:20
play on the h. of the asp	BIBLE 45:20
poisoned rat in a h.	SWIFT 320:5
holes: foxes have h.	BIBLE 49:19
holiday: Butchered to make a Roman h.	BYRON 85:10
h. is a good working definition	SHAW 302:14
now I am in a h. humour	SHAK 273:8
holidays: all the year were playing h.	SHAK 277:25
holiest of all h.	LONG 209:20
holier: I am h. than thou	BIBLE 46:25
holiest: Praise to the H.	NEWM 238:20
holily: That thou wouldst h.	SHAK 285:15
holiness: beauty of h.	BOOK 68:2
Go! put off h.	BLAKE 60:22
h. of the heart's affections	KEATS 192:23
no holiness but social h.	WESL 346:11
hollow: fearful h. of thine ear	SHAK 295:17
We are the h. men	ELIOT 133:17
Within the h. crown	SHAK 293:28
Hollywood: invited to H.	CHAN 94:10
holy: As proofs of h. writ	SHAK 292:18
coming to that h. room	DONNE 123:16
H. deadlock	HERB 166:16
H. ground	BIBLE 39:31
H., holy, holy	BIBLE 57:24
Holy, Holy, H.	HEBER 164:17
H., holy, holy	MISS 231:17
h. hush of ancient sacrifice	STEV 316:12
h., is the Lord of hosts	BIBLE 45:10
h. loved by the gods	PLATO 249:19
h. nation	BIBLE 57:8
h. simplicity	JER 181:6
h.-water death	MCG 214:21
Made h. by their dreams	GIBS 150:22
nothing is h.	BOOK 64:24
Roman Empire was neither h.	VOLT 340:19
sabbath day, to keep it h.	BIBLE 40:7
with an h. kiss	BIBLE 55:2
Holy Ghost: Come, H.	BOOK 69:16
I believe in the H.	BOOK 64:3
temple of the H.	BIBLE 55:4
homage: claims the h. of a tear	BYRON 84:30
home: ashamed of h.	DICK 118:25
beating begins at h.	FLET 142:7
can't find your way h.	COLL 105:7
comes safe h.	SHAK 279:18
Comin' for to carry me h.	ANON 10:17
difficult is it to bring it h.	DOYLE 125:14
earth is all the h. I have	AYT 23:18
England, h. and beauty	ARN 18:14

home (cont.):

first, best country is at h.	GOLD 155:4
H. art gone and ta'en thy wages	SHAK 273:27
H. is home	CLAR 101:15
H. is the girl's prison	SHAW 302:4
H. is the place where	FROST 146:11
H. is the sailor	STEV 317:22
H. James, and don't spare	HILL 168:16
h. life of our own dear Queen	ANON 8:1
H. of lost causes	ARN 18:2
h. of the bean and the cod	BOSS 70:1
h. of the brave	KEY 194:12
h., rejoicing, brought me	BAKER 26:21
H., Sweet Home	PAYNE 246:21
H. they brought her warrior	TENN 327:26
house is not a h.	ADLER 3:3
hunter h. from the hill	STEV 317:22
I can hang my hat is h.	JER 181:9
it never is at h.	COWP 109:22
Keep the H.-fires burning	FORD 143:12
Look as much like h. as we can	FRY 147:2
man goeth to his long h.	BIBLE 44:26
My h. it is the Sule Skerry	BALL 27:17
points of heaven and h.	WORD 357:9
refuge from h.	SHAW 302:23
their h. among the dead	SHEL 303:16
there's nobody at h.	POPE 250:27
there's no place like h.	PAYNE 246:21
Till the boys come H.	FORD 143:12
what is it to be at h.	BECK 31:7
What's the good of a h.	GROS 159:3
homeland: more I loved my h.	BELL 34:5
homely: h. beauty	WORD 356:1
though it be never so h.	CLAR 101:15
youth have ever h. wits	SHAK 298:16
Homer: even excellent H. nods	HOR 173:3
H. smote 'is bloomin' lyre	KIPL 197:14
H. sometimes sleeps	BYRON 86:17
In Homer more than H. knew	SWIFT 320:20
Seven cities warred for H.	HEYW 168:9
towns contend for H.	ANON 10:10
homes: h. without a friend	CLARE 101:5
quiet h. and first beginning	BELL 34:3
Stately H. of England	COW 109:8
stately h. of England	HEM 165:10
home-spuns: hempen h.	SHAK 290:31
homeward: Look h. angel now	MILT 227:17
rooks in families h. go	HARDY 162:17
homo: Ecce h.	BIBLE 58:20
Et h. factus est	MISS 231:16
honest: buy it like an h. man	NORT 240:9
general h. thought	SHAK 282:2
h. broker	BISM 59:18
h. God is the noblest work	ING 178:15
H. labour bears a lovely face	DEKK 116:9
h. man's the noblest work	POPE 252:22
h., sonsie face	BURNS 82:24
H. to God	ROB 260:21
least h. themselves	AUST 22:18
She was poor but she was h.	ANON 10:11
Though I am not naturally h.	SHAK 299:2
we who lived by h. dreams	DAY-L 115:6
whatsoever things are h.	BIBLE 56:9
honestly: If possible h.	HOR 173:6
honesty: H. is praised and left	JUV 189:1
wins not more than h.	SHAK 280:20
honey: did but taste a little h.	BIBLE 41:14
flowing with milk and h.	BIBLE 39:32
gather h. all the day	WATTS 343:5
hive for the h. bee	YEATS 359:12
H., your silk stocking's	SELL 269:25
is there h. still for tea	BROO 73:8
They took some h.	LEAR 203:11
With milk and h. blessed	NEALE 237:22
honey-dew: he on h. hath fed	COL 104:1

honeyed: h. middle of the night	KEATS 190:17
honeysuckle: h., I am the bee	FITZ 140:2
honi: H. soie qui mal y pense	SELL 269:25
H. soit qui mal y pense	ANON 12:5
honour: air signed with their h.	SPEN 312:24
All is lost save h.	FRAN 145:4
as he was valiant, I h. him	SHAK 281:16
cannot be maintained with h.	RUSS 265:6
drowned h. by the locks	SHAK 277:27
Fear God. H. the King	KITC 198:8
fighting for this woman's h.	KALM 189:20
fountain of h.	BACON 24:10
fountain of h.	BAG 26:4
fount whence h. springs	MARL 219:9
Giving h. unto the wife	BIBLE 57:10
greater share of h.	SHAK 279:17
helps the hurt that H. feels	TENN 326:8
H. all men	BIBLE 57:9
h., and keep her	BOOK 65:28
h., and welfare of this realm	CHAR 95:1
h. aspireth to it	BACON 24:21
H. but an empty bubble	DRYD 127:21
H. has come back	BROO 72:21
h. is the subject of my story	SHAK 280:26
h. rooted in dishonour	TENN 324:9
h.'s voice provoke	GRAY 157:8
H. thy father and thy mother	BIBLE 40:8
Keeps h. bright	SHAK 297:5
king delighteth to h.	BIBLE 42:20
left hand riches and h.	BIBLE 43:8
Leisure with h.	CIC 100:32
louder he talked of his h.	EMER 136:20
Loved I not h. more	LOV 210:21
may we h. it	WEBS 344:11
Mine h. is my life	SHAK 293:8
new-made h. doth forget	SHAK 282:3
Of h. and the sword	CHES 97:24
peace I hope with h.	DISR 121:18
peace with h.	CHAM 94:2
pension list a roll of h.	CLEV 102:4
plains of h. and reputation	JONS 187:13
pluck bright h.	SHAK 277:27
post of h. is a private station	ADD 2:17
prophet is not without h.	BIBLE 50:7
What is h.? A word	SHAK 278:12
When h.'s at the stake	SHAK 276:31
honourable: designs were strictly h.	FIEL 139:11
For Brutus is an h. man	SHAK 281:19
h. provision for well-educated	AUST 23:4
Let us make an h. retreat	SHAK 273:3
honoured: He hath h. me of late	SHAK 286:2
h. in the breach	SHAK 274:26
h. of them all	TENN 328:21
honours: bears his blushing h.	SHAK 280:18
hoofs: plunging h. were gone	DE L 116:20
hook: leviathan with an h.	BIBLE 43:6
hoot: literary mornings with its h.	AUDEN 20:25
hooting: shunting and h.	BURR 82:32
Hoover: onto the board of H.	GREER 158:11
hop: H. forty paces	SHAK 271:16
hope: Abandon all h.	DANTE 113:18
against hope believed in h.	BIBLE 54:32
All my h. on God is founded	BRID 71:24
Beautiful Evelyn H. is dead	BROW 75:28
best h. of earth	LINC 207:6
equal poise of h. and fear	MILT 226:13
faith, h., charity	BIBLE 55:14
H. could ne'er have flown	MARV 220:12
h. danceth without music	HERB 167:10
H. deferred	BIBLE 43:21
h. for greater favours	LA R 201:25
h. for the best	SMITH 310:1
Hopeless h. hopes	CLARE 101:5
h. of the Resurrection	BOOK 66:8

hope (*cont.*):

h. of the ungodly	BIBLE 47:31
H. raises no dust	ELUA 136:8
H. springs eternal	POPE 252:12
h. that keeps up a wife's spirits	GAY 149:4
h. that never had a fear	COWP 110:17
hope till H. creates	SHEL 304:25
h. to rise	WOTT 357:15
h., wish day come	HOPK 171:25
Land of H. and Glory	BENS 34:20
leaves of h.	SHAK 280:18
no other medicine but only h.	SHAK 288:17
Nor dread nor h. attend	YEATS 358:21
not another's h.	WALSH 342:8
nursing the unconquerable h.	ARN 17:12
Our h. for years to come	WATTS 343:13
Some blessed H.	HARDY 162:7
triumph of h. over experience	JOHN 184:24
upon h. will die fasting	FRAN 145:11
Was the h. drunk	SHAK 286:3
What is h.?	BYRON 87:16
when h. is gone	AUST 22:28
Where there is despair, h.	FRAN 145:7
work without h.	COL 104:22
Youth and H.	COL 105:1

hoped: substance of things h. for — BIBLE 56:26
hopefully: To travel h. — STEV 317:6
hopefulness: Lord of all h. — STR 318:17
hopeless: Ages of h. end — MILT 228:25

h. grief is passionless	BROW 75:2
H. hope hopes on	CLARE 101:5
perennially h.	DICK 118:1
We doctors know a h. case	CUMM 113:1

hopes: airy h. my children — WORD 354:21

have no h. but from power	BURKE 81:9
h. of its children	EIS 131:14
If h. were dupes	CLOU 102:23
no great h. from Birmingham	AUST 22:17
partly is and wholly h.	BROW 75:23
vanity of human h.	JOHN 183:1

hopeth: h. all things, endureth — BIBLE 55:12
hoping: Dreading and h. all — YEATS 358:21
hops: cherries, h., and women — DICK 119:26
hop-yards: Say, for what were h. meant — HOUS 175:3
horizontal: h. desire — SHAW 302:26

Life is a h. fall	COCT 103:2

horn: h. called me from my bed — GRAV 156:12

love the sound of the h.	VIGNY 338:17
Triton blow his wreathèd h.	WORD 357:11

Hornby: my H. and my Barlow — THOM 331:6
horned: very starry, the h. moon — WORD 354:9
horns: h. of Elfland — TENN 327:21

Memories are hunting h.	APOL 14:11

horny: H.-handed sons of toil — SAL 266:5

h. hands of toil	LOW 211:5

horrible: less than h. imaginings — SHAK 285:11

O, h.! most horrible	SHAK 275:2

horrid: 'Mongst h. shapes — MILT 226:27

when she was bad she was h.	LONG 210:6

horror: I have a h. of sunsets — PROU 255:20

no imagination there is no h.	DOYLE 126:6
The h.! The horror!	CONR 107:5

horrors: Congenial h., hail — THOM 331:26

I have supped full with h.	SHAK 288:4

horse: And a h. of air — ANON 11:23

behold a pale h.	BIBLE 57:25
Boot, saddle, to h., and away	BROW 75:17
But where's the bloody h.	CAMP 88:14
Do not trust the h.	VIRG 339:5
Don't ask me, ask the h.	FREUD 146:2
for want of a h. the rider	FRAN 145:12
Give a man a h. he can ride	THOM 332:3
heard no h. sing a song	ARMS 16:3
h. designed by a committee	ISS 178:23
h. nosing around the meadow	KAV 190:7

horse (*cont.*):

h. of that colour	SHAK 297:27
h. on the mountain	GARC 148:3
h. that stumbles and nods	HARDY 162:11
I know two things about the h.	ROYD 264:3
I owe it to h. and hound	WHYT 349:5
life and the torturer's h.	AUDEN 21:2
little dearer than his h.	TENN 326:7
my h.—German	CHAR 95:7
my h., my wife, and my name	SURT 319:11
my kingdom for a h.	SHAK 294:21
Ninety-seven h. power	SWANN 141:6
O happy h., to bear the weight	SHAK 271:10
something in a flying h.	WORD 356:3
sting a stately h.	JOHN 183:27
strength of an h.	BOOK 69:10
upon the high h.	BROWN 73:16

horseback: On h. after we — COWP 109:24
Horseguards: H. and still be common — RATT 258:8
horseman: Black Care sits behind the h. — HOR 173:25

H. pass by	YEATS 360:8

horses: breed of their h. and dogs — PENN 247:10

Bring on the empty h.	CURT 113:10
don't frighten the h.	CAMP 88:14
don't spare the h.	HILL 168:16
generally given to h.	JOHN 182:9
harness and not the h.	CANN 89:13
hell of h.	FLOR 142:13
h. of instruction	BLAKE 61:8
h. o' Kansas think to-day	KIPL 197:16
if you cannot ride two h.	MAXT 222:14
nothing like blood in h.	THAC 329:19
Rode their h. up to bed	DE L 116:17
that h. may not be stolen	HAL 160:11
They shoot h. don't they	MCCOY 214:16
watered our h. in Helicon	CHAP 94:17
Women and H. and Power	KIPL 196:5

horticulture: You can lead a h. — PARK 245:14
hosanna: H. in excelsis — MISS 231:17
hosannas: Made sweet h. ring — NEALE 237:21
hospes: *deferor h.* — HOR 173:5
hospital: not an inn, but an h. — BROW 74:20
hospitality: given to h., apt to teach — BIBLE 56:16
host: And play the humble h. — SHAK 287:8
hostages: h. to fortune — BACON 25:1

so many h. to the fates	LUCAN 211:26

hot: beat the iron while it is h. — DRYD 128:26

children are dumb to say how h.	GRAV 156:13
h. for certainties	MER 223:24
h. ice and wondrous strange	SHAK 291:5

hotel: his syllabub in the h. — SITW 307:18

h. is a refuge from home life	SHAW 302:23
h.-keepers	TROL 334:16

hound: his h., and his lady fair — BALL 28:9

H. that Caught the Pubic Hare	BEHAN 32:17
I loves the h. more	SURT 319:10
I owe it to horse and h.	WHYT 349:5

hounds: carcass fit for h. — SHAK 281:4

h. all join in glorious	FIEL 139:5
h. and his horn	GRAV 156:12
h. of spring are on winter's	SWIN 321:1

hour: Awaits alike th' inevitable h. — GRAY 157:7

books of the h.	RUSK 264:14
carefully upon your h.	SHAK 273:29
dazzle for an h.	MORE 234:22
Ere the parting h. go	ARN 16:20
fill the h.	EMER 136:26
h. is come, but not the man	SCOTT 268:27
h. your Lord doth come	BIBLE 50:38
I also had my h.	CHES 97:22
Improve each shining h.	WATTS 343:5
In the h. of death	BOOK 64:16
its h. come round at last	YEATS 359:25
known as the Children's H.	LONG 209:12
matched us with His h.	BROO 73:9

hour (cont.):		how (cont.):	
mine h. is not yet come	BIBLE 53:16	H. do they know	PARK 245:12
Oh, for an h. of Herod	HOPE 171:21	H. NOT TO DO IT	DICK 118:29
One crowded h. of glorious life	MORD 234:21	why and h. I became the mistress	WILS 351:16
shouldst be living at this h.	WORD 355:11	With h. sad steps, O Moon	SIDN 306:18
stayed me in a happy h.	SHAK 291:24	how-de-doo: Here's a h.	GILB 151:26
struts and frets his h.	SHAK 288:5	howl: H., howl, howl	SHAK 284:4
This was their finest h.	CHUR 99:14	howls: His h. was organs	DICK 119:8
Time and the h. runs through	SHAK 285:12	H. the sublime	DICK 119:7
'tis the h. of prayer	BYRON 86:18	Howth: recirculation back to H.	JOYCE 188:3
To one dead deathless h.	ROSS 263:7	hues: all her lovely h.	DAV 114:19
hours: glowing H. with flying feet	BYRON 85:3	huff: leave in a minute and a h.	KALM 189:21
h. will take care	CHES 97:8	hug: And h. it in mine arms	SHAK 288:20
lazy leaden-stepping h.	MILT 228:3	Hugo: H.—alas	GIDE 151:2
Nor h., days, months	DONNE 124:12	H. was a madman	COCT 103:3
propitious h., stay your course	LAM 199:21	hulk: Here, a sheer h.	DIBD 117:19
shorter h. and nobody bossing	ORW 242:13	hum: And the busy h. of men	MILT 227:6
house: as the H. is pleased to direct	LENT 205:20	smell and hideous h.	GODL 153:20
brawling woman in a wide h.	BIBLE 43:32	human: all h. life is there	JAMES 179:22
called a woman in my own h.	WAUGH 343:27	And Peace, the h. dress	BLAKE 61:21
called the h. of prayer	BIBLE 50:27	bounds of h. Empire	BACON 25:26
Dark h., by which once more	TENN 324:26	great guide of h. life	HUME 176:3
dwell in the h. of the Lord	BOOK 66:18	h. existence is at Charing-Cross	JOHN 185:1
Except the Lord build the h.	BOOK 68:30	H. kind cannot bear very much	ELIOT 132:27
Father's h. are many mansions	BIBLE 53:37	h. nature is finer	KEATS 193:5
great h. of Tarquin	MAC 214:2	H. on my faithless arm	AUDEN 20:27
had a mind to sell his h.	SWIFT 319:20	H. speech is like a cracked	FLAU 141:7
Harrow the h. of the dead	AUDEN 21:14	h. things are subject to decay	DRYD 128:4
h. as nigh heaven as my own	MORE 235:2	h. zoo	MORR 235:12
H. Beautiful is play lousy	PARK 245:13	insufficiency of h. enjoyments	JOHN 183:7
h. be divided against itself	BIBLE 51:19	I wish I loved the H. Race	RAL 258:6
h. divided against itself	LINC 207:5	milk of h. kindness	SHAK 285:15
h. is a machine for living	LE C 204:3	nothing h. foreign to me	TER 329:4
h. is much more to my mind	MORR 235:11	people are only h.	COMP 106:3
h. is not a home	ADLER 3:3	robot may not injure a h.	ASIM 19:1
h. not made with hands	BIBLE 55:24	socialism lose its h. face	DUBC 128:31
H. of Peers	GILB 151:14	to err is h. but to really foul	ANON 11:7
h. of Rimmon	BIBLE 42:11	to err is h., to forgive divine	POPE 252:7
h. rose like magic	HARG 162:21	To step aside is h.	BURNS 81:21
h. where I was born	HOOD 171:8	humanity: Did steer h.	SHAK 271:27
man is so in the way in the h.	GASK 148:16	freeze my h.	MACN 216:6
man's h. is his castle	COKE 103:8	H. is just a work in progress	WILL 351:4
My sober h.	SHAK 289:10	of a veined h.	BROW 75:3
return no more to his h.	BIBLE 42:31	O wearisome condition of h.	GREV 158:19
Set thine h. in order	BIBLE 46:6	still, sad music of h.	WORD 355:10
sparrow hath found her an h.	BOOK 67:20	timber of h.	KANT 189:25
spirits which are the h. of life	BROW 74:22	humans: It isn't fit for h. now	BETJ 37:9
that join house to h.	BIBLE 45:8	humble: Be it ever so h.	PAYNE 246:21
We will go into the h.	BOOK 68:28	He that is h. ever shall	BUNY 79:7
What! in our h.	SHAK 286:25	Neither too h. nor too great	MALL 216:21
will return into my h.	BIBLE 50:3	humbleth: he that h. himself	BIBLE 52:22
With usura hath no man a h.	POUND 254:9	humbug: H.!	DICK 118:6
young and inexperienced h.	JER 181:8	H. or Humdrum	DISR 121:24
housed: well h., clothed, fed	RUSK 264:19	humdrum: Humbug or H.	DISR 121:24
household: put his h. in order	BIBLE 41:26	humiliation: Art is born of h.	AUDEN 21:20
real centre of the h.	SHAW 301:5	valley of H.	BUNY 78:19
shall be they of his own h.	BIBLE 49:32	humility: H. is only doubt	BLAKE 60:12
housemaids: damp souls of h.	ELIOT 134:4	modest stillness and h.	SHAK 279:5
houses: h. are all gone under the sea	ELIOT 133:4	pride that apes h.	COL 103:16
h. in between	BAT 30:1	humour: effusions of wit and h.	AUST 22:22
h. that you do not know	MORR 235:18	Every Man out of His H.	JONS 187:7
h. thick and sewers annoy	MILT 229:23	woman in his h. won	SHAK 294:15
h. thunder on your head	JOHN 183:8	humours: In all thy h.	ADD 2:22
live in h. just as big	SMITH 309:15	hump: Camel got his H.	KIPL 197:22
plague o' both your h.	SHAK 295:8	without a positive h.	THAC 329:14
Round their golden h.	TENN 326:20	hundred: h. flowers blossom	MAO T 218:1
spaces between the h.	FENT 138:23	same a h. years hence	DICK 119:14
trees and the h. go wheeling	THOM 332:2	hunger: H. allows no choice	AUDEN 21:11
very h. seem asleep	WORD 354:10	h. and thirst after righteousness	BIBLE 48:19
watered our h. in Helicon	CHAP 94:17	H. is the best sauce	CERV 93:17
housetop: dwell in a corner of the h.	BIBLE 43:32	h. to be beautiful	RHYS 259:14
housewife: h. that's thrifty	SHER 306:6	In poverty, h., and dirt	HOOD 171:12
how: and h. much it is	BROW 75:19	sacred h. of ambitious minds	SPEN 313:15
h. are the mighty fallen	BIBLE 41:20	shall never h.	BIBLE 53:22
H. do I love thee	BROW 75:5	They shall h. no more	BIBLE 57:27

hunger (cont.):
with bodily h. in his eyes	SHAW 301:10

hungry: Cassius has a lean and h. look SHAK 281:1
h. for dinner at eight	HART 163:9
h. with good things	BIBLE 51:29
If thine enemy be h.	BIBLE 43:36
she makes h.	SHAK 271:17

hunted: by their h. expression LEWIS 206:12
hunter: from the snare of the h. BOOK 67:28
h. home from the hill	STEV 317:22
H. of the East has caught	FITZ 140:4
H.'s waking thoughts	AUDEN 20:16
Man is the h.	TENN 327:25
My heart is a lonely h.	MCL 215:10
Nimrod the mighty h.	BIBLE 39:11

Hunter Dunn: Miss J. H. BETJ 37:10
hunting: aint the h. as 'urts 'im PUNCH 256:11
For I'm weary wi' h.	BALL 27:19
h.-grounds for the poetic	ELIOT 132:9
H. is all that's worth living	SURT 319:8
shunting and hooting than to h.	BURR 82:32

huntress: Queen and h. JONS 187:3
huntsman: cassocked h. COWP 110:1
hurled: rude heap together h. MARV 221:2
hurly-burly: h. of the chaise-longue CAMP 88:15
When the h.'s done	SHAK 284:25

hurricanes: H. hardly happen LERN 206:1
hurricanoes: cataracts and h. SHAK 283:6
hurry: An old man in a h. CHUR 99:3
H. up please it's time	ELIOT 134:25
I am never in a h.	WESL 346:16
sick h., its divided aims	ARN 17:11

hurt: hate the man you have h. TAC 322:5
have healed also the h.	BIBLE 46:28
helps the h. that Honour	TENN 326:8
h. nor destroy in all	BIBLE 45:20
h. not thy foot against	BOOK 67:30
h. you to the heart	TWAIN 335:25
I am h. but I am not slain	BALL 28:3
no one was to be h.	BROO 73:12
Those have most power to h.	FLET 31:1
wish to h.	BRON 72:11

husband: bride adorned for her h. BIBLE 58:4
having one h. too many	ANON 6:11
h. for life not for lunch	ANON 8:8
h. what is left when the nerve	ROWL 263:21
left her h. because she was afraid	MURD 236:9
monstrous animal, a h. and wife	FIEL 139:12
most indulgent h.	DICK 118:30
My h. and I	ELIZ 135:16
over hir h. as hir love	CHAU 96:8
over-jealous, yet an eager h.	PHIL 248:16
so may my h.	SHAK 288:26
sways she level in her h.'s	SHAK 297:30
woman is a crown to her h.	BIBLE 43:19

husbandry: h. in heaven SHAK 286:9
husbands: chumps make the best h. WOD 352:11
H. at chirche dore	CHAU 95:20
H., love your wives	BIBLE 56:11
h. or when lapdogs breathe	POPE 253:10

hush: Hush! Whisper who dares MILNE 226:1
There's a breathless h.	NEWB 238:13

hushing: H. the latest traffic BRID 72:1
husks: strewed with h. SHAK 297:10
hustle: who tried to h. the East KIPL 196:24
hut: Love in a h. KEATS 191:11
hutch: Palate, the h. of tasty lust HOPK 172:6
hyacinths: h. and biscuits SAND 266:17
hydroptic: h. earth DONNE 124:8
hyena: That h. in petticoats WALP 342:2
hymn-book: Cassock, band, and h. WILB 349:6
hymns: Chanting faint h. SHAK 290:12
Singing h. unbidden	SHEL 305:9
sings h. at heaven's gate	SHAK 299:15

hyperion: H. to a satyr SHAK 274:11

hyphen: Cabinet is a h. BAG 26:5
hyphenated: h. Americanism ROOS 262:19
hypocrisy: Government is organized h. DISR 121:11
from pride, vain-glory, and h.	BOOK 64:14
H. is a tribute which vice	LA R 201:23
H., the only evil that walks	MILT 229:5
making the world safe for h.	WOLFE 353:6

hypocrite: H. lecteur BAUD 30:3
No man is a h. in his pleasures	JOHN 186:6

hypotheses: H. non fingo NEWT 239:5
hypothesis: beautiful h. by an ugly fact HUXL 177:15
nature of an h.	STER 315:18
scientist to discard a pet h.	LOR 210:11

hyssop: shalt purge me with h. BOOK 67:9
hysterics: blind h. of the Celt TENN 325:28

I

I: I am a camera ISH 178:22
I am a free man, an American	JOHN 181:19
I am fearfully and	BOOK 69:7
I am not I	WAUGH 343:16
I am not what I am	SHAK 291:28
I AM THAT I AM	BIBLE 39:33
I grow old . . . I grow old	ELIOT 134:2
My husband and I	ELIZ 135:16
that can tell me who I am	SHAK 282:23

iam: I. redit et virgo VIRG 339:25
ice: Alps of green i. PHIL 248:15
break the i.	BACON 24:18
emperor of i.-cream	STEV 316:6
hissed along the polished i.	WORD 355:2
his urine is congealed i.	SHAK 288:23
hot i. and wondrous strange	SHAK 291:5
I. formed on the butler's	WOD 352:23
i., mast-high, came floating	COL 104:4
i. on a hot stove the poem	FROST 146:25
pleasure-dome with caves of i.	COL 103:24
region of thick-ribbèd i.	SHAK 288:21
Some say in i.	FROST 146:12
To smooth the i., or add	SHAK 282:10

iced: three parts i. over ARN 18:7
iceman: i. cometh O'NEI 241:10
I-chabod: named the child I. BIBLE 41:11
icicles: i. hang by the wall SHAK 284:23
icumen: Sumer is i. in ANON 10:16
icy: i. precepts of respect SHAK 296:22
id: PUT THE I. BACK IN YID ROTH 263:15
idea: against invasion by an i. HUGO 176:2
better to entertain an i. than	JARR 180:13
Between the i. and the reality	ELIOT 133:19
i. whose time has come	ANON 10:19
i. within a wall of words	BUTL 84:16
possess but one i.	JOHN 184:23
teach the young i. how to shoot	THOM 331:22
to whom the i. first occurs	DARW 114:7
when you have only one i.	ALAIN 3:11

ideal: Christian i. not been tried CHES 98:15
softly sleeps the calm I.	DICK 119:7

idealism: morphine or i. JUNG 188:24
ideals: shoes with broken high i. MCG 214:20
ideas: are but the signs of i. JOHN 182:4
I share no one's i.	TURG 335:13

identical: piety, courage are i. FORS 143:25
i. if one can be substituted	LEIB 204:16

ides: Beware the i. of March SHAK 280:25
idiot: i. who praises GILB 151:20
portrait of a blinking i.	SHAK 289:14
Told by an i., full of sound	SHAK 288:5

idle: be not i. JOHN 185:25
Be not solitary, be not i.	BURT 83:15
For i. hands to do	WATTS 343:6
i. as a painted ship	COL 104:6

idle (*cont.*):

idle than when wholly i.	CIC 100:24
mock the air with i. state	GRAY 157:1
would all be i. if we could	JOHN 185:9

idleness: Grief is a species of i.   JOHN 182:15

I. is only the refuge	CHES 97:13
round of strenuous i.	WORD 356:11

idlers: loungers and i. of the Empire   DOYLE 126:4

idling: progress is a doctrine of i.   BAUD 30:8

idling: enjoy i. thoroughly   JER 181:7

idol: one-eyed yellow i.   HAYES 163:21

idolatry: organization of i.   SHAW 301:26

idols: i. I have loved so long   FITZ 140:17

old i., lost obscenes	BOTT 70:6

if: I. it moves, salute it   ANON 8:4

I. you can keep your head	KIPL 197:5
much virtue in 'i.'	SHAK 273:13

ignis: i. *fatuus* of the mind   ROCH 261:6

ignoble: doctrine of i. ease   ROOS 262:15

ignorance: except the fact of my i.   SOCR 310:21

helpless man, in i. sedate	JOHN 183:16
I. is not innocence but sin	BROW 76:9
I. is strength	ORW 242:7
it accumulates	ADAMS 1:20
Ignorance, madam, pure i.	JOHN 184:2
I. of the law excuses no	SELD 269:17
there is no sin but i.	MARL 218:19
What we call evil is simply i.	FORD 143:8
Where i. is bliss	GRAY 157:14
women in a state of i.	KNOX 198:21

ignorant: Confound the i.   SHAK 275:23

i. armies clash by night	ARN 16:12
i. have prescribed	DUPPA 129:12
they should always be i.	AUST 22:23

ile: *cette i. triste et noire*   BAUD 30:5

ill: he thinks no i.   SHAK 299:20

I. fares the land	GOLD 154:18
i.-favoured thing	SHAK 273:11
I. met by moonlight	SHAK 290:22
Looking i. prevail	SUCK 318:20
means to do i. deeds	SHAK 282:12
Nothing i. come near thee	SHAK 273:28
one-third of a nation i.-housed	ROOS 262:11
though she's not really i.	JAGG 179:5
warn you not to fall i.	KINN 196:1
Will be the final goal of i.	TENN 325:8

illegal: i., immoral, or fattening   WOOL 354:8

illegitimate: strangled i. child   ARN 18:3

illegitimi: *Nil carborundum i.*   ANON 9:15

illimitable: i. inane   TENN 326:21

illiterate: I. him, I say   SHER 305:26

illness: i. in stages   GUIB 159:8

I. is the night-side	SONT 311:10
i. should attend it	SHAK 285:15

ills: i. of democracy   SMITH 309:2

no sense have they of i. to come	GRAY 157:12
rather bear those i. we have	SHAK 275:26

illuminatio: *Dominus i. mea*   BIBLE 58:9

illusion: great i.   ANG 5:17

nothing but sophistry and i.	HUME 176:4

illusions: It's life's i. I recall   MITC 232:3

image: age demanded an i.   POUND 254:16

fleeting i. of a shade	SHEL 305:17
graven i.	BIBLE 40:4
i. of death	ELIOT 132:16
i. of myself and dearer	MILT 229:16
i. walking in the garden	SHEL 304:15
Scattered his Maker's i.	DRYD 127:3

imagination: as i. bodies forth   SHAK 291:4

ideal of reason but of i.	KANT 189:24
if i. amend them	SHAK 291:8
i. droops her pinion	BYRON 86:19
i. resembled the wings	MAC 213:21
i. the rudder	KEATS 192:22
My shaping spirit of i.	COL 103:15

imagination (*cont.*):

no i. there is no horror	DOYLE 126:6
of i. all compact	SHAK 291:3
poetic i.	ELIOT 132:9
save those that have no i.	SHAW 302:21
scattered the proud in the i.	BIBLE 51:29
truth of i.	KEATS 192:23
whispering chambers of I.	DICK 119:7

imagine: I. there's no heaven   LENN 205:7

people i. a vain thing	BOOK 66:9

imaginings: less than horrible i.   SHAK 285:11

imitate: i. the action of the tiger   SHAK 279:5

Immature poets i.	ELIOT 135:2

imitation: All the art of I.   LLOYD 208:7

Genius is the child of i.	REYN 259:10

imitators: O i., you slavish herd   HOR 173:15

immanent: I. Will that stirs   HARDY 162:5

Immanuel: call his name I.   BIBLE 45:14

immemorial: doves in i. elms   TENN 328:8

immense: but error is i.   BOL 63:5

immensity: I. cloistered in thy dear womb

                          DONNE 123:18

immoral: illegal, i., or fattening   WOOL 354:8

moral or an i. book	WILDE 350:3

immorality: i. is what they dislike   WHIT 348:3

nurseries of all vice and i.	FIEL 139:8

immortal: But in the flesh it is i.   STEV 316:11

I have lost the i. part	SHAK 292:8
I., invisible, God only wise	SMITH 310:15
I. longings in me	SHAK 272:7
make me i. with a kiss	MARL 218:11
they grow i. as they quote	YOUNG 360:13
What i. hand or eye	BLAKE 62:5

immortality: belief in i.   DOST 125:1

If I. unveil	DICK 120:11
just ourselves—and I.	DICK 120:9
Me only cruel i. consumes	TENN 328:17
Milk's leap toward i.	FAD 138:9
Millions long for i.	ERTZ 137:15
Their sons, they gave, their i.	BROO 72:20

immortalize: mortal thing so to i.   SPEN 313:4

imp: lad of life, an i. of fame   SHAK 279:10

impartial: neutrality of an i. judge   BURKE 81:12

impediment: cause, or just i.   BOOK 65:25

impediments: admit i.   SHAK 300:8

imperative: it is Categorical   KANT 189:23

imperial: Of the i. theme   SHAK 285:10

imperialism: I. is the monopoly stage   LENIN 205:2

imperium: *I. et Libertas*   DISR 121:21

impertinent: ask an i. question   BRON 72:10

impious: i. men bear sway   ADD 2:17

imponere: *I. Pelio Ossam*   VIRG 340:6

important: i. thing is not the victory   COUB 108:15

importunate for being less i.	MONT 233:13
This is an i. book because	WOOLF 354:3

imported: i., elderly American   JENK 181:3

importunate: i. for being less important   MONT 233:13

importunity: ever-haunting i.   LAMB 200:10

impossibilities: i. enough in religion   BROW 74:10

Probable i. are to be preferred	ARIS 15:17

impossibility: by Despair upon I.   MARV 220:12

impossible: believe because it is i.   TERT 329:9

Dream the i. dream	DAR 114:2
have eliminated the i.	DOYLE 126:1
if he says that it is i.	CLAR 101:14
i. takes a little longer	CAL 88:6
i. things before breakfast	CARR 91:24
i. to be silent	BURKE 80:26
i. to carry the heavy burden	EDW 131:2
I wish it were i.	JOHN 186:10
That not i. she	CRAS 111:16

imposters: two i. just the same   KIPL 197:6

impotence: I. and sodomy   WAUGH 344:2

impotent: And an i. people   THOM 331:5

imprecision: Decay with i.   ELIOT 133:1

influence: tell where his i. stops ADAMS 1:16
  win friends and i. people CARN 90:28
influences: bind the sweet i. BIBLE 43:4
in-folded: tongues of flame are i. ELIOT 133:13
inform: How all occasions do i. SHAK 276:29
information: I only ask for i. DICK 118:15
  knowledge we have lost in i. ELIOT 134:12
ingratitude: As man's i. SHAK 273:1
  I., thou marble-hearted fiend SHAK 282:24
inhale: and I didn't i. CLIN 102:5
  if he doesn't i. STEV 316:14
inherit: i. the vasty hall of death ARN 17:1
  they shall i. the earth BIBLE 48:19
inheritance: Ruinous i. GAIUS 147:13
inherited: i. it brick and left it marble AUG 22:7
inhumanity: Man's i. to man BURNS 82:16
inimitable: Faintly the i. rose WINC 352:3
iniquities: bruised for our i. BIBLE 46:19
iniquity: i. of the fathers BIBLE 40:5
  loved justice and hated i. GREG 158:13
injuries: adding insult to i. MOORE 234:4
  take revenge for slight i. MACH 214:23
injury: i. much sooner forgotten CHES 97:5
injustice: all the rapine and i. SMITH 308:20
  i. is done to someone ULP 336:10
  i. makes democracy necessary NIEB 239:14
  justice or i. of the cause JOHN 183:17
  so finely felt, as i. DICK 118:23
injustices: only to justify their i. VOLT 340:14
ink: all cough in i. YEATS 359:23
  he hath not drunk i. SHAK 284:15
  i. in my pen ran cold WALP 341:17
inlaid: i. with patines of bright SHAK 290:2
inn: by a good tavern or i. JOHN 185:8
  Do you remember an I. BELL 34:1
  earth his sober i. CAMP 89:3
  I count it not an i. BROW 74:20
  room for them in the i. BIBLE 51:32
  To gain the timely i. SHAK 287:7
  world's an i. DRYD 128:12
inner: I. Resources BERR 36:13
Innisfree: and go to I. YEATS 359:12
innocence: badge of lost i. PAINE 244:9
  ceremony of i. is drowned YEATS 359:24
  Ignorance is not i. but sin BROW 76:9
  i. is like a dumb leper GREE 158:7
innocent: i. and the beautiful YEATS 359:8
  reward against the i. BOOK 66:14
  than one i. suffer BLAC 60:3
innocents: I. Abroad TWAIN 336:1
innocuous: lambent but i. GOUL 155:26
innovations: i. are the births of time BACON 24:30
innovator: time is the greatest i. BACON 24:31
innuendoes: i. will serve him no longer PULT 256:4
  Or the beauty of i. STEV 316:13
inoperative: previous statements are i. ZIEG 361:3
Inquisition: I. dogs TENN 328:11
inscriptions: in lapidary i. JOHN 185:6
inscrutable: Dumb, i. and grand ARN 16:23
insculped: I. and embossed THOM 331:19
insect: one is but an i. JOHN 183:27
  transformed into a gigantic i. KAFKA 189:16
insensibility: No, Sir; stark i. JOHN 183:21
inside: i. the tent pissing out JOHN 181:21
insincerity: i. possible between BAUM 30:11
insolence: flown with i. and wine MILT 228:15
  i. of wealth will creep JOHN 185:19
  wretch who supports with i. JOHN 182:10
inspiration: Genius one per cent i. EDIS 130:19
inspire: Holy Ghost, our souls i. BOOK 69:16
inspissated: i. gloom JOHN 184:17
instinct: all healthy i. for it BUTL 84:17
  such a gosling to obey i. SHAK 273:21
  what we believe upon i. BRAD 71:7

instincts: animal, true to your i. LAWR 202:16
  i. before which our mortal WORD 355:22
institute: I., Legion and Social BETJ 36:22
institution: more than a game. It's an i. HUGH 175:23
instruct: i. them or endure them AUR 22:12
instruction: I will better the i. SHAK 289:18
  wiser than the horses of i. BLAKE 61:8
instrument: between your legs an i. BEEC 32:4
  I tune the i. here at the door DONNE 123:16
  make me an i. of Your peace FRAN 145:7
  only the i. of science JOHN 182:4
instrumental: hand more i. to the brain SHAK 274:4
instruments: Make i. to plague us SHAK 284:2
  What i. we have agree AUDEN 20:21
insufferable: Oxford made me i. BEER 32:8
insufficiency: i. of human enjoyments JOHN 183:7
insult: sooner forgotten than an i. CHES 97:5
  This is adding i. to injuries MOORE 234:4
insulted: could never hope to get i. DAVIS 114:23
insurance: i. for all classes CHUR 99:20
intangible: O world i. THOM 331:14
integer: I. vitae scelerisque purus HOR 173:21
intellect: And put on I. BLAKE 60:22
  feather to tickle the i. LAMB 200:6
  i. is improperly exposed SMITH 310:3
  i. of man is forced to choose YEATS 358:19
  march of i. SOUT 312:4
  Our meddling i. WORD 357:5
  revenge of the i. upon art SONT 311:9
intellectual: An i. All-in-all WORD 356:6
  For a tear is an i. thing BLAKE 60:18
  i. and artistic personality BERL 36:4
  i. is someone whose mind CAMUS 89:4
  North-west passage to the i. STER 315:21
  word 'I.' suggests straight away AUDEN 21:3
intellectuals: treachery of the i. BENDA 34:7
intelligence: i. by means of language WITT 352:6
  I. is quickness to apprehend WHIT 348:2
  Men started at the i. SOUT 312:5
  people have little i. LA BR 199:13
intelligencies: we the i. DONNE 124:3
intelligent: Most i., very elegant RUBY 77:31
  so elegant, so i. ELIOT 134:24
intensity: full of passionate i. YEATS 359:24
intent: His first avowed i. BUNY 79:9
  prick the sides of my i. SHAK 286:1
  truth that's told with bad i. BLAKE 60:7
interest: i. and fines on sorrow MAY 222:16
  i.'s on the dangerous edge BROW 75:15
  natural i. of money MAC 213:10
interested: I am only i. in money SHAW 302:25
  proceedings i. him no more HARTE 163:13
interesting: person doing i. actions BAG 26:12
  statements was i. TWAIN 335:19
interests: Our i. are eternal PALM 244:18
interim: i. is like a phantasma SHAK 281:3
intermission: but the i. of pain SELD 269:20
interpose: I should i. my body STR 318:14
interpretation: I. is the revenge of the intellect SONT 311:9
  what is lost in i. FROST 146:28
interpreted: i. the world MARX 221:11
interrèd: good is oft i. SHAK 281:18
interval: make a lucid i. DRYD 128:5
intervals: Lucid i. and happy BACON 25:22
  Not in the lucid i. of life WORD 354:18
interview: first strange and fatal i. DONNE 123:5
intestine: This is the dark i. HUGH 175:21
intimacy: without unseemly i. LOW 211:11
intolerable: burden of them is i. BOOK 65:11
  I., not to be endured SHAK 295:29
intoxicated: A God-i. man NOV 240:13
intoxication: best of life is but i. BYRON 86:7
intricated: Poor i. soul DONNE 124:22

intrigues: I. half-gathered CRAB 110:19
intrinsicate: this knot i. SHAK 272:8
invasion: against i. by an idea HUGO 176:2
invent: necessary to i. him VOLT 340:18
invented: only lies are i. BRAQ 71:15
invention: i. is but the talent BYRON 87:18
i. of a barbarous age MILT 228:5
brightest heaven of i. SHAK 278:33
wanting I.'s stay SIDN 306:16
inventions: in her i. nothing is lacking LEON 205:22
whoring with their own i. BOOK 68:11
inventor: To plague the i. SHAK 285:23
inverse: agenda will be in i. PARK 245:22
inviolable: clutching the i. shade ARN 17:12
inviolate: secret and i. Rose YEATS 359:26
invisible: all things visible and i. BOOK 65:5
Immortal, I., God only wise SMITH 310:15
I., except to God alone MILT 229:5
no i. means of support BUCH 77:27
Oh may I join the choir i. ELIOT 132:17
O world i., we view thee THOM 331:14
priest of the i. STEV 316:3
thy bloody and i. hand SHAK 287:6
invocation: By i. of the same ALEX 4:5
invulnerable: I. nothings SHEL 303:10
inward: i. and spiritual grace BOOK 65:23
They flash upon that i. eye WORD 355:5
inwariable: double glass o' the i. DICK 119:32
ipse: I. dixit CIC 100:21
ira: Ça i. ANON 12:2
Sine i. et studio TAC 322:6
irae: Dies i., dies illa MISS 231:23
Ireland: great Gaels of I. CHES 97:20
How's poor ould I. ANON 8:9
I. gives England her soldiers MER 223:13
I. hurt you into poetry AUDEN 20:22
I. is the old sow that eats her JOYCE 188:7
Out of I. have we come YEATS 359:19
Romantic I.'s dead and gone YEATS 359:28
Irish: I. poets, learn your trade YEATS 360:6
It is a symbol of I. art JOYCE 188:12
Let the I. vessel lie AUDEN 20:24
That is the I. Question DISR 121:7
Irishry: Still the indomitable I. YEATS 360:7
iron: Any old i., any old iron COLL 105:6
beat the i. while it is hot DRYD 128:26
blood and i. BISM 59:19
i. curtain has descended CHUR 100:1
i. entered into his soul BOOK 68:9
nobles with links of i. BOOK 69:11
Nor i. bars a cage LOV 210:19
On i., wood and glass DAV 114:21
painted to look like i. BISM 59:21
Thorough the i. gates of life MARV 221:1
what shall I. do CHAU 95:22
irrational: exotic and i. entertainment JOHN 182:22
irregulars: Baker Street i. DOYLE 126:3
Ishmael: Call me I. MELV 223:1
Isis: 'Till I.' elders reel POPE 250:16
island: i. is made mainly of coal BEVAN 37:17
i., the veranda, and the fruit AUDEN 20:25
Look, stranger, at this i. now AUDEN 20:26
No man is an I. DONNE 124:19
Or some secreted i. WORD 356:14
right little, tight little I. DIBD 117:20
soggy little i. UPD 336:12
islands: eye of peninsulas and i. CAT 93:3
their favourite i. AUDEN 20:14
isle: Fairest I., all isles excelling DRYD 128:2
highly favoured i. SOM 311:3
i. is full of noises SHAK 296:9
it frights the i. SHAK 292:7
ship, an i., a sickle moon FLEC 141:19
this sceptered i. SHAK 293:16

isles: i. of Greece! BYRON 86:13
Islington: from I. to Marybone BLAKE 60:17
isn't: but as it i., it ain't CARR 91:20
isolation: Splendid I. FOST 144:7
Israel: glory is departed from I. BIBLE 41:11
I arose a mother in I. BIBLE 40:31
I. loved Joseph more BIBLE 39:24
I. shall be a proverb BIBLE 41:29
I.'s monarch, after Heaven's own DRYD 127:3
sweet psalmist of I. BIBLE 41:28
Israelite: Behold an I. BIBLE 53:15
issue: i. out of all their afflictions BOOK 64:19
it: It's just I. KIPL 198:4
Italia: I.! oh Italia! BYRON 85:7
Italian: Or perhaps I. GILB 152:21
to women I., to men French CHAR 95:7
Italy: Graved inside of it, 'I.' BROW 75:24
I. a paradise for horses BURT 83:13
I. is a geographical expression METT 224:3
made I. from designs by TWAIN 336:2
Thou Paradise of exiles, I. SHEL 303:21
itch: i. of literature LOVER 210:22
itching: condemned to have an i. palm SHAK 281:29
ite: I. missa est MISS 231:20
Ithaka: When you set out for I. CAV 93:10
iubeo: Hoc volo, sic i. JUV 189:8
ivory: if in his i. tower SAIN 265:14
i. on which I work AUST 23:10
silver, i., and apes BIBLE 41:31
With a cargo of i. MASE 221:18
ivy: pluck an i. branch for me ROSS 263:3
with i. never sere MILT 227:10

J

Jabberwock: Beware the J. CARR 91:15
Jack: banish plump J. SHAK 278:1
It's 'Damn you, J. BONE 63:10
jackals: J. piss at their foot FLAU 141:12
jacket: short j. is always worn EDW 130:22
jack-knife: Just a j. has Macheath BREC 71:18
Jacks: He calls the knaves, J. DICK 118:22
Jackson: J. with his Virginians BEE 31:22
Jacob: Angel did with J. WALT 342:15
J. served seven years BIBLE 39:22
traffic of J.'s ladder THOM 331:16
voice is J.'s voice BIBLE 39:20
jade: Let the galled j. wince SHAK 276:10
jades: Go spin, you j. PEMB 247:5
pampered j. of Asia MARL 219:14
pampered j. of Asia SHAK 278:21
jail: being in a ship is being in a j. JOHN 184:5
patron, and the j. JOHN 183:12
stealin' dey gits you in j. O'NEI 241:9
jam: j. to-morrow CARR 91:23
jamais: j. triste archy MARQ 219:19
James: J. James Morrison MILNE 225:20
J. the old Pretender GUED 159:7
Jane: J., Jane, tall as a crane SITW 307:16
Me Tarzan, you J. WEIS 345:4
January: Generals Janvier [J.] NICH 239:11
Jarndyce: J. and Jarndyce DICK 118:1
jasper: j. of jocunditie ANON 9:2
jaw: j. of an ass have I slain BIBLE 41:5
jaw-jaw: j. better than to war-war CHUR 100:3
jaws: Into the j. of Death TENN 323:17
j. that bite, the claws CARR 91:15
jazz: sunbathing and j. WAUGH 343:22
jealous: Art is a j. mistress EMER 136:19
as thou art j., Lord DONNE 123:14
But jealous for they are j. SHAK 292:22
j. confirmations strong SHAK 292:18
J. in honour, sudden SHAK 272:26

jealous (*cont.*):

Lord thy God am a j. God	BIBLE 40:5
Lord thy God is a j. God	BIBLE 40:21
Not over-j., yet an eager husband	PHIL 248:16
Of one not easily j.	SHAK 293:5

jealousy: And J. a human face | BLAKE 62:7

Anger and j. can no more	ELIOT 132:12
indignation is j. with a halo	WELLS 346:1
J. is no more than	BOWEN 71:1
j. to the bride	BARR 29:15
Nor j. was understood	MILT 229:17
O! beware, my lord, of j.	SHAK 292:12
Of cold age, narrow j.	ROCH 261:2
quiet resting from all j.	FLET 31:2
To j., nothing is more	SAGAN 265:13

Jeanie: J. with the light brown | FOST 144:11

jeans: j. and Coca-Cola | GREER 158:10

jeepers: J. Creepers | MERC 223:10

Jeeves: J. shimmered out | WOD 352:12

jelly: Out, vile j. | SHAK 283:19

jellybeans: way of eating j. | REAG 258:12

je-ne-sais-quoi: J. young man | GILB 152:12

Jenny: J. kissed me when we met | HUNT 176:15

jerks: right to bring me up by j. | DICK 118:24

Jerusalem: Built in J.'s wall | BLAKE 60:20

holy city, new J.	BIBLE 58:4
J. builded here	BLAKE 61:12
J., my happy home	ANON 7:19
J. the golden	NEALE 237:22
J. thy sister calls	BLAKE 60:21
there J.'s pillars stood	BLAKE 60:17

jessamine: And the j. faint | SHEL 304:31

Jesse: out of the stem of J. | BIBLE 45:18

jesses: j. were my dear heart-strings | SHAK 292:14

jest: die in earnest, that's no j. | RAL 257:22

fellow of infinite j.	SHAK 277:8
good j. for ever	SHAK 277:28
J. and youthful jollity	MILT 227:1
j.'s prosperity lies	SHAK 284:20
Life is a j.	GAY 149:15

jests: He j. at scars, that never | SHAK 294:29

Jesu: J., good above all other | DEAR 115:7

J., lover of my soul	WESL 346:8
J., the very thought of Thee	CASW 92:17

Jesus: At the name of J. | BIBLE 56:5

Even so, come, Lord J.	BIBLE 58:8
Gentle J., meek and mild	WESL 346:6
How sweet the name of J. sounds	NEWT 239:9
I am sure this J. will not do	BLAKE 60:14
j. told him; he wouldn't believe	CUMM 112:19
J. came to Birmingham	STUD 318:19
J. Christ the same yesterday	BIBLE 56:30
J. Christ were to come	CARL 90:26
J. loves you more than	SIMON 307:6
J. shall reign where'er the sun	WATTS 343:12
J. the author and finisher	BIBLE 56:27
J. wants me for a sunbeam	TALB 322:10
J. wept	BIBLE 53:33
J.! with all thy faults	BUTL 84:19
more popular than J. now	LENN 205:8
O J., I have promised	BODE 62:16
Was J. chaste	BLAKE 60:13

jeunesse: Si j. savait | EST 137:17

Jew: for Englishman or J. | BLAKE 60:14

Hath not a J. eyes	SHAK 289:16
J.-ish. Not the whole hog	MILL 225:8
Liver of blaspheming J.	SHAK 287:17
which am a J. of Tarsus	BIBLE 54:23

jewel: immediate j. of their souls | SHAK 292:11

j. in the crown	GRAY 156:18
j. of the just	VAUG 337:12
precious j. in his head	SHAK 272:14
rich j. in an Ethiop's ear	SHAK 294:26

jewellery: just rattle your j. | LENN 205:9

jewels: j. five-words-long | TENN 327:18

jewels (*cont.*):

my j. for a set of beads	SHAK 294:2

Jewish: J. man with parents | ROTH 263:14

spit upon my J. gabardine	SHAK 289:5
total solution of the J. question	GOER 154:1

Jews: born King of the J. | BIBLE 48:9

But spurn the J.	BROW 73:21
Hitler attacked the J.	NIEM 239:15
odd of God to choose the J.	EWER 138:2
Till the conversion of the J.	MARV 220:23

Joan: greasy J. doth keel the pot | SHAK 284:23

Job: heard of the patience of J. | BIBLE 57:4

I am as poor as J.	SHAK 278:18

job: Living is my j. and my art | MONT 233:16

neighbour loses his j.	TRUM 335:5
we will finish the j.	CHUR 99:16

Jock: J. became a member | MCGR 214:22

jog: j. on the foot-path way | SHAK 298:28

man might j. on with	LAMB 200:16

John: J. Anderson my jo | BURNS 82:11

J. Peel with his coat so grey	GRAV 156:12
J. Thomas says good-night	LAWR 202:10
Land's End to J. of Gaunt	SPOO 313:24

Johnny: J.-head-in-air | PUDN 256:3

Little J. Head-In-Air	HOFF 169:20
Och, J., I hardly knew ye	BALL 27:18

Johnson: J. hewed passages | COLM 105:15

J.'s morality was as English	HAWT 163:19
There is no arguing with J.	GOLD 155:14

join: j. the choir invisible | ELIOT 132:17

that j. house to house	BIBLE 45:8

joined: j. together in holy Matrimony | BOOK 65:25

What therefore God hath j.	BIBLE 50:20

joint: j. and motive of her body | SHAK 297:9

time is out of j.	SHAK 275:6

joints: Of all the gin j. in all | EPST 137:9

tough j. more than somewhat	RUNY 264:6

joke: Dullness ever loves a j. | POPE 250:13

Life is a j. that's just begun	GILB 151:22

jokes: difference of taste in j. | ELIOT 132:1

hackneyed j. from Miller	BYRON 86:31
my little j. on Thee	FROST 146:10

jollity: Jest and youthful j. | MILT 227:1

jolly: J. boating weather | CORY 108:11

wish I thought What J. Fun!	RAL 258:6

Jonathan: Saul and J. were lovely | BIBLE 41:22

jonquil: j. o'ercomes the feeble | WINC 352:2

Jonson: If J.'s learnèd sock be on | MILT 227:8

J. his best piece of poetry	JONS 187:19
learn'd J., in this list I bring	DRAY 126:20

Jordan: over J. and what did I see | ANON 10:17

Joseph: Now Israel loved J. more | BIBLE 39:24

Josephine: Not tonight, J. | NAP 237:8

jostling: not done by j. in the street | BLAKE 61:15

jot: one j. of former love retain | DRAY 126:16

journal: J. is like a cake of portable | BOSW 70:4

journalism: but why j.? | BALF 27:11

journalist: British j. | WOLFE 353:2

journalists: j. have constructed | LICH 207:1

journey: begin a j. on Sundays | SWIFT 320:8

death the j.'s end	DRYD 128:12
dreariest and the longest j. go	SHEL 303:16
Here is my j.'s end	SHAK 293:4
j. I prepare as for death	MANS 217:15
j. take the whole long day	ROSS 263:5
j.-work of the stars	WHIT 348:18
long day's j. into night	O'NEI 241:11
Ulysses has made a great j.	DU B 128:33
Up, lad: when the j.'s over	HOUS 174:18
worst time of year for a j.	ANDR 5:15
worst time of yeat for a j.	ELIOT 133:21

journeying: sat the j. boy | HARDY 162:14

journeyman: I was a j. to grief | SHAK 293:12

journeys: J. end in lovers meeting | SHAK 297:23

Jowett: First come I; my name is J. | BEEC 32:6

joy: And J., whose hand is ever — KEATS 191:27
Break forth into j. — BIBLE 46:16
good tidings of great j. — BIBLE 52:1
He who binds to himself a j. — BLAKE 61:16
I wish you all j. of the worm — SHAK 272:6
J. always came after pain — APOL 14:12
J., beautiful radiance of the gods — SCH 267:18
j. cometh in the morning — BOOK 66:22
j. is ever on the wing — MILT 230:9
J. of heav'n, to earth — WESL 346:10
j. of love is too short — MAL 217:2
j. of the working — KIPL 197:13
J. shall be in heaven over — BIBLE 52:28
j.'s soul lies in the doing — SHAK 296:29
j. that the day has brought — BOND 63:9
j. the world can give like — BYRON 87:9
kisses the j. as it flies — BLAKE 61:16
Labour without j. is base — RUSK 264:18
let j. be unconfined — BYRON 85:3
Lord of all j. — STR 318:17
much j. or too much fear — GRAV 156:14
My scrip of j., immortal diet — RAL 257:23
Of crimson j. — BLAKE 62:4
shall reap in j. — BOOK 68:29
stern j. which warriors feel — SCOTT 268:9
Strength through j. — LEY 206:20
Such perfect j. therein I find — DYER 129:16
Surprised by j. — WORD 357:4
thing of beauty is a j. for ever — KEATS 190:11
Where there is sadness, j. — FRAN 145:7
joyful: O be j. in the Lord — BOOK 68:5
joyfully: Sing j. to God — BIBLE 58:10
joys: All my j. to this are folly — BURT 83:5
But all their j. are one — WATTS 343:3
Earth's j. grow dim — LYTE 212:20
Hence, vain deluding j. — MILT 226:22
It redoubleth j. — BACON 24:24
j. are more to flesh — DRYD 127:32
J. in another's loss of ease — BLAKE 62:2
Their homely j., and destiny — GRAY 157:7
Thou minds me o' departed j. — BURNS 81:28
Thy j. when shall I see — ANON 7:19
While lasting j. the man attend — WHUR 349:4
Youth's the season made for j. — GAY 149:6
jubilate: J. Deo — BIBLE 58:10
jubilee: day of our J. is death — BROW 74:17
Judah: Once the sight of J.'s seer — MANT 217:17
Judas: In the lost boyhood of J. — Æ 3:4
judge: after a time they j. them — WILDE 350:12
be decided by the j. — JOHN 183:17
J. none blessed before — BIBLE 48:1
J. not, that ye be not judged — BIBLE 49:6
j. thou my cause — BIBLE 47:3
neutrality of an impartial j. — BURKE 81:12
righteousness shall he j. — BOOK 68:4
Sole j. of truth, in endless — POPE 252:18
judged: if j. by himself — JUV 189:14
judgement: Daniel come to j. — SHAK 289:29
day of j. — BOOK 64:16
Don't wait for the last j. — CAMUS 89:6
God's great J. Seat — KIPL 196:4
history is the world's j. — SCH 267:21
It biases the j. — DOYLE 126:5
j. of his peers — MAGN 216:16
j. was set — BIBLE 47:15
j. will probably be right — MANS 217:16
leaves of the J. Book unfold — TAYL 323:4
not his industry only, but his j. — BURKE 80:22
people's j. always true — DRYD 127:15
will replace reasoned j. — JUV 189:8
judges: And were j. of fact — PULT 256:4
hundred j. have declared it so — QUIL 257:7
hungry j. soon the sentence sign — POPE 253:8
judicious: little j. levity — STEV 317:11

Judy O'Grady: Colonel's Lady an' J. — KIPL 196:19
jug: J., jug, jug — LYLY 212:17
'J. Jug' to dirty ears — ELIOT 134:22
j. of wine, a loaf of bread — FITZ 140:6
Julia: kiss my J.'s dainty leg — HERR 167:20
Whenas in silks my J. goes — HERR 167:26
Where my J.'s lips do smile — HERR 167:13
Juliet: J. is the sun — SHAK 294:29
July: Born on the fourth of J. — COHAN 103:5
High as a flag on the Fourth of J. — HAMM 161:4
Jumblies: lands where the J. live — LEAR 203:10
jump: We'd j. the life to come — SHAK 285:22
June: January, J., or July — NORW 240:11
J. that was stabbed — ARAG 14:21
meetings made December J. — TENN 325:20
Unwontedly. It was late J. — THOM 330:21
When J. is past, the fading — CAREW 89:20
jungle: not a concrete j. — MORR 235:12
this is the Law of the J. — KIPL 198:1
juniper: sat under a j-tree — ELIOT 132:20
junk: Ep's statues are j. — ANON 8:2
Juno: J.'s never-forgetting anger — VIRG 338:23
Jupiter: J. from on high laughs — OVID 243:10
jury: j. do the deciding — CHEK 97:1
just: all j. works do proceed — BOOK 64:11
gods are j. — SHAK 284:2
He was a good man, and a j. — BIBLE 53:5
jewel of the j. — VAUG 337:12
j. and on the unjust — BIBLE 48:24
J. are the ways of God — MILT 230:14
j. as I am, without one plea — ELL 136:2
j. one of those things — PORT 253:21
'j.' or 'right' means — PLATO 249:21
j. representations of general — JOHN 182:24
j. when we are safest — BROW 75:13
J. when you thought it was safe — ANON 8:15
land of j. and old renown — TENN 329:1
ninety and nine j. persons — BIBLE 52:28
Only the actions of the j. — SHIR 306:11
rain, it raineth on the j. — BOWEN 70:14
reflect that God is j. — JEFF 180:24
that hath his quarrel j. — SHAK 280:8
Thou art indeed j. — HOPK 172:18
whatsoever things are j. — BIBLE 56:9
justest: wisest and j. and best — PLATO 249:20
justice: Die he or j. must — MILT 229:3
For J., though she's painted — BUTL 84:7
j. be done though the heavens — WATS 342:25
J. is in one scale — JEFF 180:25
j. is open to all — MATH 222:7
J. is truth in action — DISR 121:12
j. makes democracy possible — NIEB 239:14
j. of my quarrel — ANON 8:7
j. or injustice — JOHN 183:17
J. should not only be done — HEW 168:4
'J.' was done — HARDY 161:25
J. with mercy — MILT 229:29
Let j. be done — FERD 138:24
liberty plucks j. by the nose — SHAK 288:9
like the old line about j. — OSB 242:25
loved j. and hated iniquity — GREG 158:13
or j. or human happiness — BERL 36:6
price of j. is eternal publicity — BENN 34:17
pursuit of j. is no virtue — GOLD 155:15
Revenge is a kind of wild j. — BACON 25:9
sell, or deny, or delay, right or j. — MAGN 216:17
Though j. be thy plea — SHAK 289:27
truth, j. and the American way — ANON 7:5
what you think j. requires — MANS 217:16
Yes, you have ravished j. — WEBS 344:24
justifiable: j. to men — MILT 230:14
justifies: end j. the means — BUS 83:16
justify: j. the ways of God to men — MILT 228:9

king (*cont.*):

K. of heaven	LYTE 212:21
k. of infinite space	SHAK 275:15
k. of intimate delights	COWP 110:12
K. of love my shepherd is	BAKER 26:21
k. of shreds and patches	SHAK 276:21
K. of tremendous majesty	MISS 231:24
K. over the Water	ANON 8:16
k.'s a bawcock	SHAK 279:10
k.'s head on republican	SHAW 302:9
K.'s life is moving peacefully	DAWS 115:5
k.'s Moll Reno'd	ANON 8:17
k.'s name is a tower	SHAK 294:20
k. sits in Dunfermline town	BALL 28:4
K. to have things done as cheap	PEPYS 247:15
K. to Oxford sent a troop	BROW 74:25
K. will never leave	ELIZ 135:19
little profits that an idle k.	TENN 328:19
man who would be k.	KIPL 197:27
more royalist than the k.	ANON 12:8
No bishop, no K.	JAM 179:11
not offended the k.	MORE 235:1
once and future k.	WHITE 347:18
one-eyed man is k.	ERAS 137:14
passing brave to be a k.	MARL 219:7
played the K.	FIELD 139:3
Ruin seize thee, ruthless K.	GRAY 157:1
still am I k. of those	SHAK 294:5
subject's duty is the k.'s	SHAK 279:14
What must the k. do now	SHAK 294:2
when thy k. is a child	BIBLE 44:22
your K. and your Country both	RUB 264:4

kingdom: In this k. by the sea | POE 250:3
k. against kingdom	BIBLE 50:34
k. of the well	SONT 311:10
k. stretch from shore	WATTS 343:12
k. where nobody dies	MILL 224:21
large k. for a little grave	SHAK 294:2
my k. for a horse	SHAK 294:21
My k., safeliest when	DONNE 123:6
My mind to me a k. is	DYER 129:16
seeking asses found a k.	MILT 230:5
Thy k. come	BIBLE 48:27
Thy k. is divided	BIBLE 47:12

kingdom of God: fit for the k. | BIBLE 52:9
he cannot see the k.	BIBLE 53:17
k. is within you	BIBLE 52:36
rich man to enter into the k.	BIBLE 50:22
such is the k.	BIBLE 51:25

kingdom of heaven: inheritor of the k. | BOOK 65:20
k. is at hand	BIBLE 48:12
k. is like to a grain	BIBLE 50:5
shall not enter into the k.	BIBLE 50:15
theirs is the k.	BIBLE 48:19
thou didst open the K.	BOOK 63:20

kingdoms: goodly states and k. | KEATS 192:10

kingly: k. crop | DAV 114:11

kings: accounted poet k. | KEATS 192:12
be as happy as k.	STEV 317:13
bind their k. in chains	BOOK 69:11
cabbages—and k.	CARR 91:22
captains and the k. depart	KIPL 197:2
Conquering k. their titles	CHAN 94:6
five K. left	FAR 138:14
good of subjects is the end of k.	DEFOE 116:1
heart of k. is unsearchable	BIBLE 43:34
keep even k. in awe	D'AV 114:8
K. and counsellors	BIBLE 42:26
k. crept out again	BROW 74:27
k. is mostly rapscallions	TWAIN 335:20
k. that privates have not too	SHAK 279:15
K. will be tyrants	BURKE 80:16
mad k.! mad composition!	SHAK 282:4
Physicians are like k.	WEBS 344:20
politeness of k.	LOUI 210:17

kings (*cont.*):

ruin k.	DRYD 127:4
sport of k.	SOM 311:2
sport of k.	SURT 319:8
stories of the death of k.	SHAK 293:27
Vain the ambition of k.	WEBS 344:13
walk with K.	KIPL 197:7
War is the trade of k.	DRYD 128:1

Kipling: Rudyards cease from k. | STEP 315:5

kiss: Ae fond k. | BURNS 81:22
Colder thy k.	BYRON 87:14
come k. me, sweet and twenty	SHAK 297:23
come let us k. and part	DRAY 126:16
coward does it with a k.	WILDE 350:16
die upon a k.	SHAK 293:6
I k. his dirty shoe	SHAK 279:10
I saw you take his k.	PATM 246:17
k. again with tears	TENN 327:17
k., a sigh, and so away	CRAS 111:15
k. is still a kiss	HUPF 176:20
K. me, Hardy	NELS 238:6
K. me Kate	SHAK 295:27
k. my ass in Macy's window	JOHN 181:20
k. my Julia's dainty leg	HERR 167:20
k. of the sun for pardon	GURN 159:10
k. on the hand	ROBIN 260:18
k. the rod	SHAK 298:17
leave a k. but in the cup	JONS 187:23
let me k. that hand	SHAK 283:24
make me immortal with a k.	MARL 218:11
rough male k.	BROO 73:1
with an holy k.	BIBLE 55:2
Wouldst k. me pretty	HART 163:11

kissed: Hasn't been k. for forty years | ANON 9:5
k. by a man who *didn't* wax	KIPL 198:3
k. his sad Andromache	CORN 108:5
k. thee ere I killed thee	SHAK 293:6
righteousness and peace have k.	BOOK 67:23

kisses: At cards for k. | LYLY 212:16
fine romance with no k.	FIEL 139:14
half-k. kill me	DRAY 126:21
If you have forgotten my k.	SWIN 321:14
more than k., letters mingle	DONNE 124:17
remembered k. after death	TENN 327:23
Stolen k. much completer	HUNT 176:16
wastin' Christian k.	KIPL 196:22

kissing: die with k. of my Lord | MARL 219:12
K. don't last: cookery do	MER 223:17
K. with golden face	SHAK 299:17
when the k. had to stop	BROW 77:18

kit-bag: troubles in your old k. | ASAF 18:17

kitchen: get out of the k. | VAUG 337:2
| In k. cups concupiscent curds | STEV 316:5 |
| K-cabals, and nursery-mishaps | CRAB 110:19 |

Kitchener: K. is a great poster | ASQ 19:5

kith: If one's own kin and k. | NASH 237:11

knave: makes an honest man a k. | DEFOE 115:16
| slipper and subtle k. | SHAK 292:6 |

knaves: grudge at k. in place | DEFOE 115:21
| He calls the k., Jacks | DICK 118:22 |
| most part of fools and k. | BUCK 78:1 |

knavish: either k. or childish | JOHN 185:23

knee: every k. should bow | BIBLE 56:5
| kneel: k. and adore him | MONS 233:3 |

kneeled: red-cross knight for ever k. | TENN 326:2

knees: confirm the feeble k. | BIBLE 46:5
creeps rustling to her k.	KEATS 190:18
in the heart, not in the k.	JERR 181:10
than to live on your k.	IBAR 178:1
With your body between your k.	CORY 108:11

knell: curfew tolls the k. | GRAY 157:4
| k. that summons thee | SHAK 286:11 |
| strikes like a rising k. | BYRON 85:2 |

knew: He said it that k. it best | BACON 24:15
| Johnny, I hardly k. ye | BALL 27:18 |

knife: k. see not the wound   SHAK 285:19
progress if a cannibal uses k.   LEC 204:1
smylere with the k.   CHAU 95:27
War to the k.   PAL 244:16
wind's like a whetted k.   MAS 222:2
knight: Fearless, blameless k.   ANON 12:4
K. of the Doleful Countenance   CERV 93:16
k. was pricking on the plain   SPEN 313:7
red-cross k. for ever kneeled   TENN 326:2
verray, parfit gentil k.   CHAU 95:12
knighthoods: looking for your k.   KEAT 190:8
knights: ladies dead and lovely k.   SHAK 300:4
knits: k. up the ravelled sleeve   SHAK 286:15
knitters: k. in the sun   SHAK 297:31
knitting: braids of lilies k.   MILT 226:21
knives: night of the long k.   HITL 168:21
knock: As yet but k., breathe   DONNE 123:10
k., and it shall be opened   BIBLE 49:9
K. as you please   POPE 250:27
k. at the door   LAMB 200:3
k. it never is at home   COWP 109:22
right to k. him down for it   JOHN 185:26
stand at the door, and k.   BIBLE 57:23
Where k. is open wide   SMART 308:11
knocked: K. down a doctor?   SIMP 307:12
ruin that Cromwell k. about   SULL 31:21
we k. the bastard off   HILL 168:15
what they k. down   FENT 138:23
knocking: k. at Preferment's door   ARN 17:6
K. on the moonlit door   DE L 116:18
knocks: k. you down with the butt   GOLD 155:14
knot: certain k. of peace   SIDN 306:20
crowned k. of fire   ELIOT 133:13
political k.   BIER 59:4
So the k. be unknotted   ELIOT 132:24
this k. intrinsicate   SHAK 272:8
knots: pokers into true-love k.   COL 104:2
knotted: Sat and k. all the while   SEDL 269:12
knotty: k. as a root of heath   BRON 72:15
know: all ye need to k.   KEATS 191:24
By their fruits ye shall k. them   BIBLE 49:15
do not k. what they have said   CHUR 99:5
do not wish to k. ask questions   RAL 258:5
do were as easy as to k.   SHAK 288:29
God made me to k. Him   CAT 92:20
hate any one that we k.   HAZL 164:7
He must k. sumpin'   HAMM 161:3
How do they k.   PARK 245:12
I do not k. myself   GOET 154:14
k., and not be known   COLT 105:18
k. enough who know how   ADAMS 1:17
k. how to be oneself   MONT 233:15
k. is what I read in the papers   ROG 262:1
k. nothing except the fact   SOCR 310:21
k. that I am God   BOOK 67:7
k. that which we are   BYRON 86:30
K. then thyself   POPE 252:17
k. the place for the first time   ELIOT 133:10
K. thyself   ANON 13:5
k. to know no more   MILT 229:12
k. what I think till I see what   WALL 341:11
men naturally desire to k.   AUCT 20:6
neither shall his place k. him   BIBLE 42:31
no one to k. what it is   ANON 6:21
now I k. it   GAY 149:15
only thee, resolved to k.   WESL 346:5
others that we k. not   SHAK 275:26
place thereof shall k. it no more   BOOK 68:7
So all we k. of what they do   WALL 341:15
they k. not what they do   BIBLE 53:2
things they didn't k.   POUND 254:13
To k. the world, not love   YOUNG 360:22
To k. this only   MILT 230:7
We k. our will is free   JOHN 184:20

know (cont.):
What do I k.   MONT 233:18
what we would, we k.   ARN 16:10
when it came to k. me well   MOORE 234:19
Whitehall really does k. better   JAY 180:15
knoweth: loveth not k. not God   BIBLE 57:15
knowing: k. to what he was going   HARDY 162:14
k. what should not be known   FLEC 141:17
misfortune of k. any thing   AUST 22:23
knowledge: After such k.   ELIOT 133:15
all k. to be my province   BACON 25:23
all mysteries, and all k.   BIBLE 55:11
All our k. is, ourselves to know   POPE 252:23
ask it for the k. of a lifetime   WHIS 347:13
desire more love and k.   SHAK 272:13
full of the k. of the Lord   BIBLE 45:20
he would bring home k.   JOHN 185:18
increaseth k. increaseth sorrow   BIBLE 44:10
in k. of whom standeth   BOOK 64:5
K. comes, but wisdom lingers   TENN 326:14
K. enormous makes a god of me   KEATS 191:2
k. is bought in the market   CLOU 102:11
K. is of two kinds   JOHN 185:5
k. itself is power   BACON 25:25
K. may give weight   CHES 97:16
k. of causes   BACON 25:26
K. of good and evil   COWP 110:3
k. of nothing   DICK 120:5
K. puffeth up   BIBLE 55:7
k. we have lost in information   ELIOT 134:12
k. which they cannot know   OPP 241:14
light of k. in their eyes   SYM 321:20
little k. is dangerous   HUXL 177:17
No man's k. here can go beyond   LOCKE 208:14
Opinion in good men is but k.   MILT 231:4
Out-topping k.   ARN 17:14
Pedantry is the dotage of k.   JACK 178:24
province of k. to speak   HOLM 170:15
Science is organized k.   SPEN 312:15
spirit of k.   BIBLE 45:18
taken away the key of k.   BIBLE 52:16
There's no k. but I know it   BEEC 32:6
thorough k. of human nature   AUST 22:22
too high the price for k.   TICK 332:20
tree of the k. of good and evil   BIBLE 38:19
known: Have ye not k.?   BIBLE 46:12
If you would be k.   COLT 105:18
know even as also I am k.   BIBLE 55:14
k. and common way   WINC 352:3
k. and the unknown   PINT 248:21
k. no more than other men   AUBR 19:17
k. too late   SHAK 294:28
much to be done and little to be k.   JOHN 182:27
safer than a k. way   HASK 163:16
thy way may be k. upon earth   BOOK 67:16
knows: HE k.—HE knows   FITZ 140:13
He k. nothing   SHAW 301:13
he K. Things   MILNE 225:18
if you k. of a better 'ole   BAIR 26:20
sits in the middle and k.   FROST 146:20
knuckle-end: That k. of England   SMITH 309:26
Kruger: killing K.   KIPL 196:2
Kubla: In Xanadu did K. Khan   COL 103:22
Kurtz: Mistah K.—he dead   CONR 107:6
kyrie: K. eleison   MISS 231:12

L

labor: Hoc opus, hic l. est   VIRG 339:12
laboratory: l. of God   WILL 351:4
laborious: Studious of l. ease   COWP 110:10
labour: done to the L. Party   TAWN 322:21
fair shares for all, is L.'s call   JAY 180:14
Honest l. bears a lovely face   DEKK 116:9

labour (cont.):

I have had my l. for my travail	SHAK 296:28
insupportable l. of doing nothing	STEE 314:14
l. and are heavy laden	BIBLE 49:35
l. and not to ask for any reward	IGN 178:8
l. of love	BIBLE 56:13
l. we delight in physics pain	SHAK 286:22
L. without joy is base	RUSK 264:18
mixed his l. with	LOCKE 208:19
My daily l. to pursue	WESL 346:5
strength then but l. and sorrow	BOOK 67:26
that's the task, that is the l.	VIRG 339:12
their l. is but lost	BOOK 68:30
to his work, and to his l.	BOOK 68:8
true success is to l.	STEV 317:6
usury . . . to live without l.	TAWN 322:20
with difficulty and l.	MILT 229:2
youth of l. with an age of ease	GOLD 154:19
labourage: L. et pâturage	SULLY 319:3
labourer: l. is worthy of his hire	BIBLE 52:10
labouring: Sleep is sweet to the l. man	BUNY 79:4
sleep of a l. man is sweet	BIBLE 44:15
labours: and no l. tire	JOHN 183:13
Children sweeten l.	BACON 23:6
Lingered l. come to naught	SOUT 312:8
laburnums: L., dropping-wells	TENN 325:15
labyrinth: peopled l. of walls	SHEL 304:1
labyrinthical: l. soul	DONNE 124:22
labyrinthine: down the l. ways	THOM 331:8
Still more l. buds the rose	BROW 77:14
lace: Nottingham l. of the curtains	BETJ 36:16
lacerate: Cannot l. his breast	YEATS 360:2
lack: therefore can I l. nothing	BOOK 66:17
lacrimae: Hinc illae l.	TER 329:3
l. rerum	VIRG 339:4
lad: l. that's born to be king	BOUL 70:10
Sing me a song of a l.	STEV 317:23
ladder: l. set up on the earth	BIBLE 39:21
Now that my l.'s gone	YEATS 358:16
Wiv a l. and some glasses	BAT 30:1
ladders: where all l. start	YEATS 358:16
laden: labour and are heavy l.	BIBLE 49:35
ladies: Come from a L.' seminary	GILB 151:23
Dust was Gentlemen and L.	DICK 120:17
l. apparently rolled along	HUXL 177:10
l. dead and lovely knights	SHAK 300:4
l. of St James's	DOBS 122:27
l. should ever sit down	MORE 234:22
lads: Come lasses and l.	ANON 6:19
Golden l. and girls all must	SHAK 273:27
l. that will never be old	HOUS 174:21
lady: certain little l. comes by	GAY 149:18
dying l., lean and pale	SHEL 305:15
full-blown l.	CLOU 102:7
hound, and his l. fair	BALL 28:9
I met a l. in the meads	KEATS 191:9
kneeled to a l. in his shield	TENN 326:2
Laces for a l.	KIPL 196:28
lang will his L. look owre	BALL 27:15
l. doth protest too much	SHAK 276:9
l. is a tramp	HART 163:9
L., it is to be presumed	JONS 187:5
l. of a 'certain age'	BYRON 86:21
l. of Christ's College	AUBR 19:20
L. of Shalott	TENN 326:1
L. of Spain, I adore you	REAV 258:13
L.'s not for Burning	FRY 146:30
l. sweet and kind	ANON 10:18
l. that's known as Lou	SERV 270:13
L. with a Lamp shall stand	LONG 209:25
lovely l., garmented in light	SHEL 305:16
Our L. of Pain	SWIN 321:8
want to talk like a l.	SHAW 302:17
when a l.'s in the case	GAY 149:10
young l. named Bright	BULL 78:7

Lady Jane: good-night to L.	LAWR 202:10
lady-smocks: l. all silver-white	SHAK 284:21
Lafayette: L., nous voilà!	STAN 314:10
laggard: For a l. in love	SCOTT 268:20
laid: He l. us as we lay at birth	ARN 16:19
When I am l. in earth	TATE 322:15
lain: l. for ages and will lie	TENN 325:32
laissez-faire: L.	ARG 15:6
laissez-nous-faire: L.	ANON 12:9
laity: conspiracies against the l.	SHAW 301:3
To tell the l. our love	DONNE 124:15
lake: Cyprus with a l. of fire	FLEC 141:18
into the bosom of the l.	TENN 328:5
l. water lapping	YEATS 359:13
lakes: light shakes across the l.	TENN 327:20
lamb: Behold the L. of God	BIBLE 53:13
blood of the L.	BIBLE 57:26
Did he who made the L.	BLAKE 62:6
holy L. of God	BLAKE 61:12
L. of God, who takest away	MISS 231:19
l. to the slaughter	BIBLE 46:20
leads me to the L.	COWP 109:27
Little L. who made thee	BLAKE 61:23
Mary had a little l.	HALE 160:7
save one little ewe l.	BIBLE 41:24
tempers the wind to the shorn l.	STER 315:11
wolf shall dwell with the l.	BIBLE 45:19
lambent: l. but innocuous	GOUL 155:26
lambs: he shall gather the l.	BIBLE 46:11
l. could not forgive	DICK 119:9
little l. eat ivy	DRAKE 126:14
lamentable: l. catalogue	CHUR 99:12
lamentation: l., and weeping	BIBLE 48:11
lamp: Lady with a L.	LONG 209:25
leaning on a l.-post	GAY 149:18
Slaves of the L.	ARN 16:7
smell too strong of the l.	STER 315:16
unlit l. and the ungirt loin	BROW 77:16
When the l. is shattered	SHEL 303:24
lampada: vitai l.	LUCR 212:5
lamprey: surfeit by eating of a l.	FABY 138:7
lamps: Heav'n's great l. do dive	CAMP 89:2
l. are going out all over	GREY 159:1
old l. for new ones	ARAB 14:16
Ye living l.	MARV 220:20
land: Ceres re-assume the l.	POPE 251:17
England's green and pleasant l.	BLAKE 61:12
French the empire of the l.	RICH 260:6
good and bad of every l.	BAIL 26:19
Ill fares the l., to hast'ning ills	GOLD 154:18
l. flowing with milk and honey	BIBLE 39:32
L. of embarrassment	BARN 29:4
L. of Hope and Glory	BENS 34:20
L. of lost content	HOUS 174:24
l. of meanness, sophistry	BYRON 85:21
l. of my fathers	THOM 330:20
l. of poverty	BAUD 30:5
l. of pure delight	WATTS 343:11
l. of sand and ruin	SWIN 321:19
l. of the living	BIBLE 46:21
l. of the shadow of death	BIBLE 45:15
L. that I love	BERL 35:21
l. was ours before we were	FROST 146:13
l. where the lemon-trees	GOET 154:13
lane to the l. of the dead	AUDEN 20:12
like night, from l. to land	COL 104:17
O'er the l. of the free	KEY 194:12
piece of l. not so very large	HOR 174:4
pleasant l. of counterpane	STEV 317:14
ready by water as by l.	ELST 136:7
splendid and a happy l.	GOLD 154:25
that think there is no l.	BACON 23:22
There's the l., or cherry-isle	HERR 167:13
This l. is your land	GUTH 159:12

land (cont.):

Woe to the l. that's governed	SHAK 294:16
landing: fight on the l. grounds	CHUR 99:13
landlord: L., Fill the Flowing Bowl	ANON 6:18
lands: envy of less happier l.	SHAK 293:16
Lord of himself, though not of l.	WOTT 357:15
landscape: Claude's l.	CONS 107:12
landscapes: If l. were sold	STEV 317:1
Land's End: L. to John of Gaunt	SPOO 313:24
lane: l. to the land of the dead	AUDEN 20:12
lang: y'er a l. time deid	ANON 6:9
language: best chosen l.	AUST 22:22
cool web of l.	GRAV 156:14
divided by a common l.	SHAW 302:27
enlargement of the l.	JOHN 182:5
Fancies that broke through l.	BROW 77:4
In l., the ignorant have	DUPPA 129:12
In such lovely l.	LAWR 202:24
intelligence by means of l.	WITT 352:6
l. he was the lodesterre	LYDG 212:13
L. is fossil poetry	EMER 136:28
L. is only the instrument	JOHN 182:4
L. is the dress of thought	JOHN 182:19
l. of priorities	BEVAN 37:19
l. of the heart	POPE 251:9
l. of the unheard	KING 195:11
L. was not powerful enough	DICK 119:16
l. which I spake like thee	MAC 214:1
Learned his great l.	BROW 76:14
Life is a foreign l.	MORL 235:7
limits of my l. mean	WITT 352:10
mobilised the English l.	MURR 236:13
Money speaks sense in a l.	BEHN 32:23
natural l. of the heart	SHAD 270:17
obscurity of a learned l.	GIBB 150:16
our l. should perish	MAC 213:20
Political l.	ORW 242:15
some entrance into the l.	BACON 25:17
Speech happens not to be his l.	STAËL 314:7
There's l. in her eye	SHAK 297:9
use any l. you choose	GILB 151:15
with no l. but a cry	TENN 325:9
You taught me l.	SHAK 295:35
languages: all l. living and dead	DICK 119:10
great feast of l.	SHAK 284:17
L. are the pedigree of nations	JOHN 183:18
live l. for Miss Blimber	DICK 118:19
wit in all l.	DRYD 128:27
languor: monotonous l.	VERL 337:21
languors: lilies and l. of virtue	SWIN 321:7
lantern: word is a l. unto my feet	BOOK 68:24
lap: flowery l. of earth	ARN 16:19
fresh l. of the crimson rose	SHAK 290:23
It lies in the l. of the gods	HOMER 170:23
l. of the new come spring	SHAK 294:8
lapdogs: when l. breathe	POPE 253:10
lapidary: l. inscriptions	JOHN 185:6
lapidem: *Gutta cavat l.*	OVID 243:12
lapping: lake water l.	YEATS 359:13
lards: l. the lean earth	SHAK 277:29
large: It's as l. as life	CARR 92:4
l-brained woman	BROW 75:6
l-hearted man	BROW 75:6
too l. to hang on a watch-chain	ANON 11:8
lark: bisy l., messager of day	CHAU 95:26
l. ascending	MER 223:19
l. at break of day	SHAK 299:15
l. at heaven's gate	SHAK 273:25
l. becomes a sightless song	TENN 325:30
l. now leaves his wat'ry nest	D'AV 114:10
l.'s on the wing	BROW 76:28
nightingale, and not the l.	SHAK 295:17
larks: Four L. and a Wren	LEAR 203:17
hear the l. so high	HOUS 174:20
Lars Porsena: L. of Clusium	MAC 214:2

lasciate: L. OGNI SPERANZA	DANTE 113:18
lash: dost thou l. that whore	SHAK 283:25
rum, sodomy, and the l.	CHUR 100:6
lashes: That l. all with shade	WILB 349:13
lass: Amo, amas, I love a l.	O'KEE 241:5
every l. a queen	KING 195:17
It came with a l.	JAM 179:14
It was a lover and his l.	SHAK 273:10
l. unparalleled	SHAK 272:10
lasse: *tout casse, tout l.*	ANON 12:17
lasses: Come l. and lads	ANON 6:19
lassie: I love a l.	LAUD 202:6
last: Heaven's l. best gift	MILT 229:15
It will l. my time	CARL 90:5
l. and best of all God's works	MILT 229:27
l. great Englishman is low	TENN 327:11
l. person who has sat on him	HAIG 159:16
l. red leaf is whirled	TENN 325:2
l. romantics	YEATS 358:18
l. shall be first	BIBLE 50:24
l. thing I shall do	PALM 244:22
l. time I saw Paris	HAMM 161:1
live this day as if thy l.	KEN 193:21
Look thy l. on all things lovely	DE L 116:15
Nice guys. Finish l.	DUR 129:13
there is no l. nor first	BROW 77:1
they l. while they last	DE G 116:4
unto this l.	BIBLE 50:26
wait for the l. judgement	CAMUS 89:6
latchet: shoe's l. I am not worthy	BIBLE 53:12
late: Dread of being l.	BETJ 37:14
five minutes too l. all my life	COWL 109:18
offering even that too l.	NEV 238:9
So l. into the night	BYRON 87:8
Too l. came I to love thee	AUG 21:24
too l. into a world too old	MUSS 236:17
Which was rather l. for me	LARK 201:12
white rose weeps, 'She is l.'	TENN 327:1
later: It is l. than you think	SERV 270:10
Latin: carve in L. or in Greek	WALL 341:13
Devil knows L.	KNOX 198:19
he speaks L.	SHAK 280:12
L. for a whopping	ANST 14:10
Ne yet of L., ne of Greek	SPEN 313:16
No more L., no more French	ANON 9:17
small L., and less Greek	JONS 187:27
latrine: mouth used as a l.	AMIS 5:2
latter: former and the l. rain	BOOK 64:20
he shall stand at the l. day	BIBLE 42:36
laudamus: *Te Deum l.*	ANON 14:1
laudator: *l. temporis acti*	HOR 173:2
laugh: atheist-l.'s a poor exchange	BURNS 82:6
L. and the world laughs	WILC 349:14
l. at human actions	SPIN 313:23
l. at them in our turn	AUST 23:6
l. broke into a thousand pieces	BARR 29:11
L. no man to scorn	BIBLE 47:33
l. that spoke the vacant mind	GOLD 154:20
l. the more heartily	RHYS 259:13
L. where we must	POPE 252:11
Never l. at live dragons	TOLK 333:9
no girl wants to l. all the time	LOOS 210:9
nothing sillier than a silly l.	CAT 93:4
tickle us, do we not l.	SHAK 289:17
time to weep, and a time to l.	BIBLE 44:12
Wanna l. like a loon	HARB 161:13
laughed: When he l., respectable	AUDEN 20:18
laughing: Happiness is no l. matter	WHAT 347:6
l. is heard on the hill	BLAKE 61:25
Minnehaha, L. Water	LONG 210:2
most fun I ever had without l.	ALLEN 4:13
laughs: l. to see the green man	HOFF 170:1
she l. with a harvest	JERR 181:12
laughter: faculty of l.	ADD 2:27

laughter (cont.):

grail of l. of an empty ash can	CRANE 110:32
l. and ability and Sighing	DICK 120:17
l. and the love of friends	BELL 34:3
l. for a month	SHAK 277:28
L. holding both his sides	MILT 227:2
L. is pleasant	PEAC 246:25
l., learnt of friends	BROO 73:10
l. of her heart	HAMM 161:1
L. only a scornful tickling	SIDN 306:29
L. . . . the most civilized music	UST 336:15
Laugh thy girlish l.	WATS 342:26
more frightful than l.	SAGAN 265:13
Our sincerest l.	SHEL 305:10
Present mirth hath present l.	SHAK 297:23
so is the l. of a fool	BIBLE 44:16
under running l.	THOM 331:8
where l. may signify anger	TOFF 333:7

laurel: Apollo's l. bough — MARL 218:14
l. for the perfect prime — ROSS 263:3

laurels: Birds on box and l. — SMART 308:9

l. all are cut	ANON 12:13
l. to paeans	CIC 100:23
worth all your l.	BYRON 87:10
Yet once more, O ye l.	MILT 227:10

lave: Let the l. go by me — STEV 317:24

law: army of unalterable l. — MER 223:22

Born under one l.	GREV 158:19
breaks the l. by corrupting	PLATO 249:18
Custom, that unwritten l.	D'AV 114:8
dusty purlieus of the l.	TENN 325:17
end of l. is, not to abolish	LOCKE 208:20
fugitive from th' l. of averages	MAUL 222:13
good of the people is the chief l.	CIC 100:20
Ignorance of the l. excuses	SELD 269:17
I, my Lords, embody the L.	GILB 151:10
Just to the windward of the l.	CHUR 98:23
l. and the prophets	BIBLE 49:11
l. can take a purse	BUTL 84:8
l. is a ass	DICK 119:20
L. is a bottomless pit	ARB 14:22
l. is such an ass	CHAP 94:18
L.: It has honoured us	WEBS 344:11
L. of the Jungle	KIPL 198:1
l. of the Medes and Persians	BIBLE 47:13
l. of the Yukon	SERV 270:11
L. to our selves	MILT 229:25
lesser breeds without the L.	KIPL 197:4
majestic equality of the l.	FRAN 145:2
make a scarecrow of the l.	SHAK 288:12
moral l. within me	KANT 189:22
more ought l. to weed it out	BACON 25:9
Necessity has no l.	PUBL 256:2
Necessity hath no l.	CROM 112:6
No brilliance is needed in the l.	MORT 235:21
Nor l., nor duty bade me fight	YEATS 359:10
not a l. at all	ROB 260:16
not known sin, but by the l.	BIBLE 54:37
of no force in l.	COKE 103:7
old father antick, the l.	SHAK 277:24
People crushed by l.	BURKE 81:9
perfection of our l.	ANON 7:9
prescription of the l.	LOCKE 208:21
principle of the English l.	DICK 118:4
Prisons built with stones of L.	BLAKE 61:7
purlieus of the L.	ETH 137:18
rich men rule the l.	GOLD 155:5
royal L., lively Oracles	COR 108:10
till the fear of the L.	JOYCE 188:4
Where no l. is	BIBLE 54:31
Who to himself is l.	CHAP 94:16
whole of the L.	CROW 112:14
windy side of the l.	SHAK 298:12
Wrest once the l.	SHAK 289:28

lawful: L. as eating — SHAK 299:4

lawful (cont.):

that which is l. and right	BIBLE 47:6
upon their l. occasions	BOOK 69:14

lawn: bird-haunted English l. — ARN 16:21

l. about the shoulders thrown	HERR 167:15
Out on the l. I lie in bed	AUDEN 21:7
twice a saint in l.	POPE 251:20

lawns: house with l. enclosing it — STEV 317:17

laws: Bad l. are the worst sort — BURKE 80:24

Christianity is part of the l.	HALE 160:5
government of l., and not of men	ADAMS 1:22
If l. are their enemies	BURKE 81:9
L. are like cobwebs	SWIFT 319:19
l. are like spider's webs	ANAC 5:9
L. are silent in time of war	CIC 100:30
L. grind the poor	GOLD 155:5
L., like houses, lean	BURKE 81:6
l. of God and man and metre	LOCK 209:3
l. of most countries	MILL 224:19
L. were made to be broken	NORTH 240:7
make the l. of a nation	FLET 142:3
not judges of l.	PULT 256:4
obedient to their l.	SIM 307:9
prescribed l. to the learned	DUPPA 129:12
repeal of bad or obnoxious l.	GRANT 156:9
to do with l. but to obey them	HORS 174:5
Unequal l. unto a savage race	TENN 328:19
warfare, and of l.	DU B 128:32
Who sweeps a room as for Thy l.	HERB 166:26

lawyer: l. has no business — JOHN 183:17

l. interprets the truth	GIR 153:6
l. with his briefcase can steal	PUZO 256:36

lawyers: let's kill all the l. — SHAK 280:10

two l. the battledores	DICK 119:29
Woe unto you, l.!	BIBLE 52:16

lay: Cleric before, and L. behind — BUTL 84:1

l. down his friends for his life	THOR 332:13
l. down his life for his friends	BIBLE 53:40
l. down his wife for his friend	JOYCE 188:18
l. hold on eternal life	BIBLE 56:20
l. mee downe and bleed	BALL 28:3
L. not up for yourselves	BIBLE 49:1
L. on, Macduff	SHAK 288:8
L. your sleeping head, my love	AUDEN 20:27

lazy: L. and silly — SITW 307:20
l. leaden-stepping hours — MILT 228:3

lead: L. kindly Light — NEWM 238:21

l. them the way	BIBLE 39:39
l. those that are with young	BIBLE 46:11
l. us not into temptation	BIBLE 48:27
You can l. a horticulture	PARK 245:14

leaden: With l. foot time creeps — JAGO 179:8

leading: L. onward, beaming bright — DIX 122:24

leaf: last red l. is whirled — TENN 325:2

Right as an aspes l.	CHAU 96:17
sear, the yellow l.	SHAK 288:1

leafmeal: worlds of wanwood l. — HOPK 172:15

league: Half a l. onward — TENN 323:14

She hadna sailed a l.	BALL 27:16
Will keep a l. till death	SHAK 294:6

lean: dying lady, l. and pale — SHEL 305:15

Laws, like houses, l.	BURKE 81:6
l. and hungry look	SHAK 281:1

leap: great l. in the dark — HOBB 169:11

methinks it were an easy l.	SHAK 277:27
one giant l. for mankind	ARMS 16:5

leaping: brooks too broad for l. — HOUS 175:2

l., and praising God	BIBLE 54:10
l. from place to place	HARDY 162:10
swimmers into cleanness l.	BROO 73:9

leaps: It moves in mighty l. — AYRES 23:15

learn: cannot l. men from books — DISR 122:9

craft so long to l.	CHAU 96:12
enough who know how to l.	ADAMS 1:17
Even while they teach, men l.	SEN 270:6

learn (cont.):

gladly wolde he l.	CHAU 95:18
l. in suffering	SHEL 303:22
mark, l., and inwardly digest	BOOK 64:22
not yet so old but she may l.	SHAK 289:22
places to l. the world in	CHES 97:6
so dull but she can l.	SHAK 289:22

learned: been l. has been forgotten SKIN 308:6

grew within this l. man	MARL 218:14
l. lumber in his head	POPE 252:9
L. without sense	CHUR 98:29
prescribed laws to the l.	DUPPA 129:12
Things l. on earth	BROW 76:21

learning: attain good l. ASCH 18:18

deep l. little had he need	SPEN 313:16
encourage a will to l.	ASCH 18:19
enough of l. to misquote	BYRON 86:31
grammar, and nonsense, and l.	GOLD 155:8
grow old ever l. many things	SOLON 310:26
L., that cobweb of the brain	BUTL 84:2
little l. is a dangerous thing	POPE 251:28
loyal body wanted l.	TRAPP 334:3
much l. doth make thee mad	BIBLE 54:26
on scraps of l. dote	YOUNG 360:13
sleep—and l. of a sort	BELL 33:17
wearing all that weight of l.	TENN 325:31
Wear your l., like your watch	CHES 97:10
We'll cry both arts and l. down	QUAR 257:5
written for our l.	BOOK 64:22

learnt: forgotten nothing and l. DUM 129:6

They have l. nothing TALL 322:12

lease: having so short a l. SHAK 300:14

summer's l. hath all too short SHAK 299:12

leasehold: it is l. for all LUCR 212:6

least: l. of these my brethren BIBLE 51:6

man who promises l. BAR 29:21

leathern: Their l. boats MARV 221:3

leave: be ready to l. MONT 233:8

couldn't l. without the King	ELIZ 135:19
for ever taking l.	RILKE 260:7
Intreat me not to l. thee	BIBLE 41:8
l. him for religion	SPARK 312:10
l. his father and his mother	BIBLE 38:23
l. in a minute and a huff	KALM 189:21
l. me there to die	ANON 8:3
L. not a rack behind	SHAK 296:10
L. off first for manners' sake	BIBLE 48:4
l. them while you're looking	LOOS 210:8
l. the outcome to the Gods	CORN 108:2
Oh, never l. me	ANON 6:27

leaves: among the l. hast never known KEATS 191:31

burning of the l.	BINY 59:13
Close up those barren l.	WORD 357:5
glad green l. like wings	HARDY 162:2
l. dead are driven	SHEL 304:6
l. is a generation of men	HOMER 170:21
l. of the tree for the healing	BIBLE 58:7
naturally as the l. to a tree	KEATS 193:4
noiseless noise among the l.	KEATS 191:5
tender l. of hope	SHAK 280:18
Thick as autumnal l.	MILT 228:14
yellow drifts of withered l.	ARN 17:3
yellow l., or none	SHAK 299:24

leaving: Became him like the l. it SHAK 285:21

L. his country for his country's FITZ 140:3

lecher: Does l. in my sight SHAK 283:23

lecherous: l. mouth CHAU 96:6

lechery: L., sir, it provokes SHAK 286:21

lecture: classic l., rich in sentiment TENN 327:18

lectures: l. or a little charity WHIT 348:20

lees: drink life to the l. TENN 328:20

mere l. is left SHAK 286:26

left: better to be l. than never CONG 106:16

heart is on the l. MOL 232:19

l. hand know what thy right BIBLE 48:26

left (cont.):

l. her husband because	MURD 236:9
l. thee all her lovely hues	DAV 114:19
l. thy first love	BIBLE 57:20
let them be l., wildness and wet	HOPK 172:8
something l. to treat my friends	MALL 216:21

left-handed: l. marriage WOLL 353:12

leg: here I leave my second l. HOOD 171:5

kiss my Julia's dainty l. HERR 167:20

lege: Tolle l., tolle lege AUG 21:23

legion: L. and Social Club BETJ 36:22

My name is L. BIBLE 51:21

legislator: l. of mankind JOHN 183:3

legislators: l. of the world SHEL 305:19

legs: adorns my l. HOUS 174:7

between your l. an instrument	BEEC 32:4
born with your l. apart	ORTON 241:21
cannon-ball took off his l.	HOOD 171:4
delighteth he in any man's l.	BOOK 69:10
fold his l. and have out his talk	JOHN 185:16
Four legs good, two l. bad	ORW 241:22
l. when I take my boots off	DICK 118:21
open my l., and think of	HILL 168:17
trunkless l. of stone	SHEL 304:11
Walk under his huge l.	SHAK 280:27

leisure: At l. married, they repent CONG 106:13

Conspicuous l. and consumption	VEBL 337:17
fill l. intelligently	RUSS 264:22
he is never at l.	JOHN 185:16
they detest at l.	BYRON 86:25
we may polish it at l.	DRYD 128:26

lemon: squeezed as a l. is GEDD 149:19

where the l-trees bloom GOET 154:13

lend: l. me your ears SHAK 281:18

men who l. LAMB 200:1

lender: borrower, nor a l. be SHAK 274:22

lenders: thy pen from l.' books SHAK 283:13

lends: Three things I never l. SURT 319:11

length: drags its slow l. along POPE 252:4

L. of days is in her right hand	BIBLE 43:8
still drags its dreary l.	DICK 118:1
what it lacks in l.	FROST 146:14

Lenin: L. was right KEYN 194:14

lente: Festina l. AUG 22:6

O lente l. currite noctis equi MARL 218:13

leopard: l. shall lie down BIBLE 45:19

or the l. his spots BIBLE 46:30

leopards: L. sat under a juniper-tree ELIOT 132:20

leper: innocence is like a dumb l. GREE 158:7

Lesbia: L. let us live and love CAMP 89:2

Vivamus, mea L., atque amemus CAT 93:2

less: believing more and more in l. YATES 358:10

had he pleased us l.	ADD 2:10
How l. what we may be	BYRON 86:30
knows more about less and l.	BUTL 83:21
little l., and what worlds away	BROW 75:19
L. than the dust, beneath	HOPE 171:23
nothing l. than thee	DONNE 124:1
rather than be l.	MILT 228:22
You mean you can't take l.	CARR 91:8

lessen: they l. from day to day CARR 91:10

lesser: l. breeds without the Law KIPL 197:4

lessons: reason they're called l. CARR 91:10

lest: l. we forget KIPL 197:2

let: L. my people go ANON 11:19

L. my people go	BIBLE 39:34
l. them all to my elder daughter	THOM 330:23
L. there be light	BIBLE 38:13
L. us with a gladsome mind	MILT 227:9

Lethe: go not to L. KEATS 191:25

letter: l. killeth BIBLE 55:23

[L.] longer than usual	PASC 245:24
This is my l. to the world	DICK 120:16
thou unnecessary l.	SHAK 283:2

life (cont.):

football a matter of l. and death	SHAN 300:22
force maintaining the l.	DOST 125:1
former naughty l.	BOOK 65:1
found that l. was duty	HOOP 171:16
gave my l. for freedom	EWER 138:1
give thee a crown of l.	BIBLE 57:21
giveth his l. for the sheep	BIBLE 53:30
glory of this l.	SHAK 296:18
great l. if you don't weaken	BUCH 77:26
His l. was gentle	SHAK 282:2
Human l. is a sad show	FLAU 141:13
I bear a charmèd l.	SHAK 288:6
I count l. just a stuff	BROW 76:7
in his pleasure is l.	BOOK 66:22
in the sea of l. enisled	ARN 17:22
I really don't know l. at all	MITC 232:3
iron gates of l.	MARV 221:1
Is it not l.	BYRON 87:19
isn't l. a terrible thing	THOM 330:19
I've had a happy l.	HAZL 164:9
jump the l. to come	SHAK 285:22
lad of l., an imp of fame	SHAK 279:10
lay down his friends for his l.	THOR 332:13
lay down his l. for his friends	BIBLE 53:40
l. began by flickering out	GONC 155:19
l. closed twice before its close	DICK 120:11
l. everlasting	BOOK 64:3
L. exists in the universe	JEANS 180:16
l. forget and death remember	SWIN 321:16
L. for life	BIBLE 40:10
l. for the British female	CLOU 102:7
L., friends, is boring	BERR 36:13
l. had been ruined by literature	BROO 73:13
l. hath been one chain	CLARE 101:4
l. heroic	MILT 230:17
l. in my men	WEST 346:21
L. is a foreign language	MORL 235:7
L. is a gamble at terrible odds	STOP 318:6
L. is a glorious cycle	PARK 245:4
L. is a horizontal fall	COCT 103:2
L. is a jest	GAY 149:15
L. is a joke that's just begun	GILB 151:22
L. is all a VARIORUM	BURNS 82:13
L. is an incurable disease	COWL 109:17
L. is a sexually transmitted	ANON 8:20
L. is as tedious as a twice-told	SHAK 282:9
L. is a top	GREV 158:18
L. is but the shadow of death	BROW 74:2
L. is Colour and Warmth	GREN 158:16
L. is doubt	UNAM 336:11
l. is everywhere a state	JOHN 183:4
L. is first boredom, then fear	LARK 201:14
l. is given to none freehold	LUCR 212:6
L. is just a bowl of cherries	BROWN 73:17
L. is just one damned thing	HUBB 175:14
L. is mostly froth and bubble	GORD 155:21
L. is not a series of gig lamps	WOOLF 353:22
L. is one long process	BUTL 84:13
L. is real! Life is earnest	LONG 209:22
L. is short, the art long	HIPP 168:19
L. is the desert	YOUNG 360:23
L. is the other way round	LODGE 209:4
l. is the thing, but I prefer	SMITH 309:13
L. is too short to stuff	CONR 107:10
l. is washed in the speechless real	BARZ 29:22
l., it's enemy	ANOU 14:7
l., liberty, and the pursuit	ANON 11:12
L., like a dome of many-coloured	SHEL 303:13
l. may perfect be	JONS 187:24
l. of man less than a span	BACON 25:30
l. of sensations	KEATS 192:24
l. protracted is protracted woe	JOHN 183:15
l. ran gaily as the sparkling	ARN 17:11
l.'s a pain and but a span	DAV 114:14

life (cont.):

L. says: she did this	BARN 29:5
L.'s but a walking shadow	SHAK 288:5
l.'s dim windows	BLAKE 60:12
L.'s longing for itself	GIBR 150:19
L.'s not just being alive	MART 220:6
l. so short, the craft so long	CHAU 96:12
L.'s rich pageant	MARS 220:2
L., the Universe and Everything	ADAMS 1:9
l. time's fool	SHAK 278:14
L. well spent is long	LEON 205:21
l. will be sour grapes	ASHF 18:24
L. with its way before us lies	MONS 233:2
L. without industry is guilt	RUSK 264:11
L. would be tolerable	LEWIS 206:15
L. would be very pleasant	SURT 319:13
long disease, my l.	POPE 251:4
looked at l. from both sides	MITC 232:3
many doors to let out l.	FLET 142:4
married my husband for l.	ANON 8:8
measured out my l. with coffee	ELIOT 133:27
midst of l. we are in death	BOOK 66:7
midst of l. we are in debt	MUMF 236:7
Midway along the path of our l.	DANTE 113:17
Mine honour is my l.	SHAK 293:8
more a way of l.	ANON 9:19
mourning for my l.	CHEK 96:25
My l. is dreary	TENN 326:22
nearest thing to death in l.	ANON 9:14
No, no, no l.!	SHAK 284:6
Nothing in his l. became him	SHAK 285:13
Nothing in l. shall sever	CORY 108:12
no wealth but l.	RUSK 264:20
of man's l. a thing apart	BYRON 86:4
One crowded hour of glorious l.	MORD 234:21
one l. and one death	BROW 76:6
one l. to lose for my country	HALE 160:6
On l., on death	YEATS 360:8
Our end is l. Put out to sea	MACN 216:11
our little l. is rounded	SHAK 296:10
out-do the l.	JONS 187:20
outer l. of telegrams and anger	FORS 143:20
Perfection of the l.	YEATS 358:19
present l. of men on earth	BEDE 31:20
preservation of l.	JEFF 180:18
resurrection, and the l.	BIBLE 53:32
seas of l., like wine	TRAH 334:1
secret love does thy l. destroy	BLAKE 62:4
set my l. at a pin's fee	SHAK 274:28
shilling l. will give you	AUDEN 21:12
sketchy understanding of l.	CRICK 111:19
So careless of the single l.	TENN 325:10
spirit giveth l.	BIBLE 55:23
studied from the l.	ARMS 16:1
Style is l.!	FLAU 141:10
such is L.	DICK 118:26
taking l. by the throat	FROST 146:27
thousand doors to let out l.	MASS 222:6
tired of London ... tired of l.	JOHN 185:15
'Tisn't l. that matters	WALP 342:4
To live a l. half dead	MILT 230:13
traveller betwixt l. and death	WORD 356:24
tree of l.	BIBLE 43:21
University of L.	BOTT 70:7
Variety's the very spice of l.	COWP 110:9
walk in newness of l.	BIBLE 54:34
warm full blooded l.	JOYCE 188:17
way, the truth, and the l.	BIBLE 53:38
way which leadeth unto l.	BIBLE 49:13
well-written L. as rare	CARL 90:7
What is this l. if full of care	DAV 114:20
Wholesome of l.	HOR 173:21
Who saw l. steadily	ARN 17:20
will he give for his l.	BIBLE 42:23
life-blood: book is the precious l.	MILT 230:30

life-lie: Take the l. away — IBSEN 178:7
life-sentence: l. which fate carries — LAWR 202:27
lifetime: knowledge of a l. — WHIS 347:13
l. of happiness — SHAW 301:15
lifetimes: series of l. starts anew — VIRG 339:25
lift: l. me as a wave, a leaf — SHEL 304:8
l. up his countenance — BIBLE 40:15
l. up mine eyes — BOOK 68:25
L. up your heads — BOOK 66:20
L. up your hearts — BOOK 65:13
lifting: l. up of my hands — BOOK 69:8
light: against the dying of the l. — THOM 330:7
all know what l. is — JOHN 185:11
armour of l. — BOOK 64:21
As if they feared the l. — SUCK 318:21
bear witness of that L. — BIBLE 53:9
Be near me when my l. is low — TENN 325:7
black as if bereaved of l. — BLAKE 61:24
blasted with excess of l. — GRAY 157:17
certain Slant of l. — DICK 120:14
children of l. — BIBLE 52:33
C'mon, baby, l. my fire — MORR 235:19
dark is l. enough — FRY 146:29
festal l. in Christ-Church — ARN 17:9
fire, to give them l. — BIBLE 39:39
garmented in l. — SHEL 305:16
gone into the world of l. — VAUG 337:11
how my l. is spent — MILT 230:22
infant crying for the l. — TENN 325:9
infinite ocean of l. and love — FOX 144:17
In the dusk with a l. behind her — GILB 152:31
Jeanie with the l. brown hair — FOST 144:11
kindle a l. in the darkness — JUNG 188:23
Lead, kindly L. — NEWM 238:21
let perpetual l. shine on them — MISS 231:22
Let there be l. — BIBLE 38:13
Let there be l. — MARR 219:24
Let there be l.! said Liberty — SHEL 303:17
l., and will aspire — SHAK 300:17
l. at the end of the tunnel — DICK 120:19
l. at the end of the tunnel — LOW 211:18
l. between two eternities — NAB 236:19
L. breaks where no sun shines — THOM 330:12
l. fantastic round — MILT 226:9
l. fantastic toe — MILT 227:2
l. gleams an instant — BECK 31:15
L. God's eldest daughter — FULL 147:6
l. in the dust lies dead — SHEL 303:24
l. of common day — WORD 355:21
l. of Terewth — DICK 118:3
l. of the world — BIBLE 48:21
l. shineth in darkness — BIBLE 53:8
l. so shine before men — BIBLE 48:22
l. that I may tread safely — HASK 163:16
l. that loses, the night that — SWIN 321:2
l. that never was — WORD 354:17
l. through yonder window — SHAK 294:29
l. to counterfeit a gloom — MILT 226:25
l. to shine upon the road — COWP 109:27
l. to them that sit in darkness — BIBLE 51:30
l. unto my paths — BOOK 68:24
l. within his own clear breast — MILT 226:12
mend the Electric L. — BELL 33:22
More l. — GOET 154:15
neither heat nor l. — WEBS 344:17
new l. of grace — SMOL 310:16
Newton's particles of l. — BLAKE 61:14
once set is our little l. — CAMP 89:2
put on the armour of l. — BIBLE 55:1
Put out the l. — SHAK 292:29
ring of pure and endless l. — VAUG 337:14
seen a glorious l. — SCOT 269:10
seen a great l. — BIBLE 45:15
Servants of L. — ARN 16:7

light (cont.):
shew l. at Calais — JOHN 184:15
source of my l. and my safety — BIBLE 58:9
sweetness and l. — ARN 17:25
sweetness and l. — SWIFT 319:18
thy l. is come — BIBLE 46:23
turning your face to the l. — SASS 267:9
turret in a noose of l. — FITZ 140:4
unclouded blaze of living l. — BYRON 85:20
upon them hath the l. shined — BIBLE 45:15
while the l. fails — ELIOT 133:12
Light Brigade: Forward, the L. — TENN 323:15
lighten: L. our darkness — BOOK 64:12
l. with celestial fire — BOOK 69:16
lightly: l. as it comth — CHAU 96:1
l. skims the midge — BETJ 37:1
unadvisedly, L., or wantonly — BOOK 65:26
lightness: unbearable l. of being — KUND 199:8
lightning: Brief as the l. in the collied night — SHAK 290:14
coruscations of summer l. — GOUL 155:26
illumined by flashes of l. — WILDE 350:19
l. before death — SHAK 295:23
l. of his terrible swift sword — HOWE 175:7
Shakespeare by flashes of l. — COL 104:25
snatched the l. shaft — TURG 335:16
to keep the l. out — ISH 178:21
lights: all-the-l.-on man — REED 258:20
broken l. of thee — TENN 324:23
Followed false l. — DRYD 127:29
Glorious the northern l. — SMART 308:13
l. around the shore — ROSS 263:10
tail l. wizen and converge — CRANE 111:2
Truth may bear all l. — SHAF 270:22
When the l. are dim and low — ORRED 241:17
your l. burning — BIBLE 52:20
like: Do what you l. — RAB 257:12
forced to l. what you get — SHAW 302:7
l. this sort of thing — LINC 207:12
none of his friends l. him — WILDE 350:21
No wonder we l. them — AMIS 5:6
shall not look upon his l. again — SHAK 274:17
want it the most l. it least — CHES 97:9
liked: l. it not, and died — WOTT 357:17
l. whate'er she looked on — BROW 76:19
likely: Walk! Not bloody l. — SHAW 302:19
likerous: l. mouth moste han — CHAU 96:6
likewise: Go, and do thou l. — BIBLE 52:13
liking: mayse man to haiff l. — BARB 28:16
Not l. the person — THOM 331:1
lilac: forget the l. and the roses — ARAG 14:21
Just now the l. is in bloom — BROO 73:3
lilacs: l. last in the dooryard — WHIT 348:24
L. out of the dead land — ELIOT 134:18
Lilian: Airy, fairy L. — TENN 326:5
lilies: And a few l. blow — HOPK 172:7
beauty lives though l. die — FLEC 141:16
Consider the l. of the field — BIBLE 49:4
Give me l. in armfuls — VIRG 339:17
l. and languors of virtue — SWIN 321:7
L. that fester smell far worse — SHAK 300:2
pale, lost l. out of mind — DOWS 125:12
peacocks and l. — RUSK 264:17
She had three l. in her hand — ROSS 263:6
Lilli Burlero: L. Bullena-la — WHAR 347:5
lilting: About the l. house — THOM 330:8
lily: Elaine, the l. maid of Astolat — TENN 324:7
folds the l. all her sweetness up — TENN 328:5
gold, to paint the l. — SHAK 282:10
I see a l. on thy brow — KEATS 191:8
lies across the l. leven — BALL 28:7
l. of Florence blossoming — LONG 209:18
l. of the valleys — BIBLE 44:31
She's as pure as the l. — LAUD 202:6
lily-white: Two, two, the l. boys — ANON 8:6

limbs: l. of a poet HOR 174:3
l. that fester ABSE 1:1
slope of mighty l. asleep SWIN 321:4
Yours are the l., my sweeting NASH 237:18
lime-tree: This L. Bower my Prison COL 104:21
limit: act a slave to l. SHAK 297:2
quiet l. of the world TENN 328:17
limited: Liberty too must be l. BURKE 79:23
nervous and terse, but l. DOYLE 126:7
so whizzed the L. CRANE 111:2
limits: l. of my language WITT 352:10
stony l. cannot hold love out SHAK 294:32
limousine: l. and a ticket MACN 216:1
One perfect l. PARK 245:7
limp: l. father of thousands JOYCE 188:16
Lincoln: I am a Ford, not a L. FORD 143:3
L. County Road or Armageddon DYLAN 130:7
line: active l. on a walk KLEE 198:11
cancel half a l. FITZ 140:14
cut, the style, the l. LOES 209:6
horizontal l. WHEW 347:8
l. is length without breadth EUCL 137:20
l. upon line BIBLE 45:27
l. will take us hours maybe YEATS 358:13
lives along the l. POPE 252:15
Marlowe's mighty l. JONS 187:26
quarrelling on the l. FORS 143:22
Thin red l. of 'eroes KIPL 197:11
thin red l. tipped with steel RUSS 265:7
We carved not a l. WOLFE 353:1
lineaments: l. of gratified desire BLAKE 61:17
linen: In blanchèd l. KEATS 190:21
Love is like l. often changed FLET 142:10
very fine l. BRUM 77:24
lines: As l. (so loves) MARV 220:13
consisted of l. like these CALV 88:7
l. are fallen unto me BOOK 66:15
Prose is when all the l. BENT 35:3
town-crier spoke my l. SHAK 276:4
linger: l. out a purposed overthrow SHAK 300:1
lingered: I l. round them BRON 72:18
lingering: I alone sit l. here VAUG 337:11
l. dissolution BECK 31:7
Something l., with boiling oil GILB 152:4
lingua: Pange, l. THOM 330:3
lin-lan-lone: mellow l. TENN 323:22
linnet: l. born within the cage TENN 325:3
linsy-woolsy: lawless l. brother BUTL 84:1
lion: devil, as a roaring l. BIBLE 57:12
l. and the fatling together BIBLE 45:19
l. to frighten the wolves MACH 215:3
Strong is the l.—like a coal SMART 308:10
threatened, a L. CHAP 94:14
lions: L. led by donkeys HOFF 169:17
they were stronger than L. BIBLE 41:22
lips: already born before my l. MAND 217:11
hand is ever at his l. KEATS 191:27
l. ne'er act the winning part HERR 167:17
l. of living men BUTL 84:21
l., that they speak no guile BOOK 66:25
l. that touch liquor YOUNG 360:24
My l. are sealed BALD 27:7
people of unclean l. BIBLE 45:11
Read my l.: no new taxes BUSH 83:18
Red l. are not so red OWEN 244:1
Truth sits upon the l. of dying ARN 17:15
very good words for the l. DICK 119:1
When the l. have spoken SHEL 303:24
lipstick: l.'s traces MARV 221:4
liquefaction: l. of her clothes HERR 167:26
liquid: less l. than their shadows TESS 329:10
let their l. siftings fall ELIOT 134:17
Thames is l. history BURNS 81:20
liquor: But l. is quicker NASH 237:15

liquor (cont.):
Good l., I stoutly maintain GOLD 155:8
lips that touch l. YOUNG 360:24
L. is one way out WILL 351:5
lisp: l. of leaves SWIN 321:1
list: I've got a little l. GILB 151:19
listen: Darkling I l. KEATS 192:3
privilege of wisdom to l. HOLM 170:15
world should l. then SHEL 305:11
listening: disease of not l. SHAK 278:17
People hearing without l. SIMON 307:7
listeth: wind bloweth where it l. BIBLE 53:18
lit: whole Fleet's l. up WOOD 353:18
literary: beloved by l. pundits CONN 106:26
l. man—with a wooden leg DICK 119:21
l. mornings with its hoot AUDEN 20:25
lowest class is l. *footmen* HAZL 164:4
Of all the l. scenes PRES 255:5
quotation is the *parole* of l. men JOHN 185:30
uncorrupted with l. prejudices JOHN 182:21
unsuccessful l. man BELL 33:19
literature: English l.'s performing flea O'CAS 240:23
great Cham of l. SMOL 310:17
history to produce a little l. JAMES 179:18
itch of l. LOVER 210:22
life had been ruined by l. BROO 73:13
l. clear and cold and pure LEWIS 206:18
l. is a drug BORR 69:26
L. is a luxury CHES 98:9
L. is mostly about having sex LODGE 209:4
l. is my mistress CHEK 96:30
L. is news that STAYS news POUND 254:23
l. is the orchestration WILD 350:24
louse in the locks of l. TENN 329:2
Philistine of genius in l. ARN 18:11
Remarks are not l. STEIN 314:20
rest is l. VALE 336:20
littérature: *tout le reste est l.* VERL 337:20
little: But wants that l. strong HOLM 170:17
cry of the L. Peoples LE G 204:12
either a l. Liberal GILB 151:12
Ev'ry day a l. death SOND 311:6
Go, l. bok CHAU 96:20
hare's own child, the l. hare HOFF 170:3
here a l., and there a little BIBLE 45:27
hobgoblin of l. minds EMER 136:24
L. boxes on the hillside REYN 259:11
L. Boy kneels at the foot MILNE 226:1
L. drops of water CARN 90:29
L. Englanders ANON 8:21
l. finger shall be thicker BIBLE 41:33
L. Friend of all the World KIPL 197:25
little l. grave SHAK 294:2
Little man, l. man ELIZ 135:10
L. man, you've had a busy day HOFF 307:2
l. may be diffused into BOSW 70:4
l. more, and how much it is BROW 75:19
L. one! Oh, little one STEP 315:9
l. saint best fits a l. shrine HERR 167:22
L. ships of England GUED 159:6
L. subject, little wit CAREY 90:1
l. volume but large book CRAS 111:12
Man wants but l. here below GOLD 154:27
mother's l. helper RICH 179:5
much to be done and l. to be known JOHN 182:27
nor that l., long YOUNG 360:22
nothing as much as too l. COMP 106:4
offend one of these l. ones BIBLE 50:16
Only the l. people pay taxes HELM 165:8
our l. life is rounded SHAK 296:10
snug l. Island DIBD 117:20
So l. done, so much to do RHOD 259:12
So l. done, such things to be TENN 325:14
this l. world SHAK 293:16

little (*cont.*):

though she be but l.	SHAK 290:33
too l., too late	NEV 238:9
turn to l. things	GIBS 150:22
very l. one	MARR 219:27
littleness: long l. of life	CORN 108:7
littlenesses: thousand peering l.	TENN 324:1
live: Come l. with me	DONNE 123:23
Come l.w ith me	MARL 219:3
Days are where we l.	LARK 201:13
do never l. long	SHAK 294:17
Easy l. and quiet die	SCOTT 268:24
enable its citizens to l.	WEIL 345:3
ended by your inability to l.	GONC 155:20
end for which we l.	PEPYS 247:21
forgets to l.	LA BR 199:14
he isn't fit to l.	KING 195:8
He shall not l.	SHAK 281:28
I cannot l. with you	MART 220:7
I must l.	ARG 15:7
in him we l., and move	BIBLE 54:21
In this faith I wish to l.	VILL 338:21
known I was gonna l. this long	BLAKE 60:4
Let us l., my Lesbia	CAT 93:2
l. alone and smash his mirror	ANON 12:10
l. alone in the bee-loud glade	YEATS 359:12
L. a thousand years	SHAK 281:12
l. *dangerously*	NIET 239:21
L. frugally	WALK 341:4
l. together as brothers	KING 195:10
l. well on nothing a year	THAC 329:20
l. without labour	TAWN 322:20
man desires to l. long	SWIFT 320:13
Man is born to l.	PAST 246:9
mortal millions l. *alone*	ARN 17:22
My self now l.	HERR 167:21
nor l. so long	SHAK 284:8
not l. to eat	MOL 232:14
not to l., but to die	BROW 74:20
Rascals, would you l. for ever	FRED 145:20
shall no man see me and l.	BIBLE 40:12
short time to l.	BOOK 66:6
So longe mote ye l.	CHAU 96:15
taught us how to l.	TICK 332:20
teaching nations how to l.	MILT 231:5
Teach me to l.	KEN 193:22
they sometimes l. apart	SAKI 265:22
To l. is like to love	BUTL 84:17
to l. on your knees	IBAR 178:1
To l. without him	WOTT 357:17
To l. with thee	RAL 257:20
to l. your life is not as simple	PAST 246:10
too small to l. in	ANON 11:8
turn and l. with animals	WHIT 348:19
We l. our lives, for ever	RILKE 260:7
we that l. to please	JOHN 183:10
wouldn't l. under Niagara	CARL 90:24
write too much, and l. too long	DAN 113:16
You might as well l.	PARK 245:8
lived: I have l. long enough	SHAK 288:1
L. in his mild and magnificent	BROW 76:14
never loved, has never l.	GAY 149:8
Never to have l. is best	YEATS 359:5
To have l. light in the spring	ARN 16:14
your mother and I should have l.	GAY 149:3
lively: these are the l. Oracles	COR 108:10
thy true and l. Word	BOOK 65:10
liver: L. of blaspheming Jew	SHAK 287:17
open and notorious evil l.	BOOK 64:29
livery: l. of the burnished sun	SHAK 289:6
lives: Careless talk costs l.	ANON 6:15
ends marked than their l.	SHAK 293:15
l. along the line	POPE 252:15
L. in Eternity's sunrise	BLAKE 61:16
L. of great men all remind us	LONG 209:23

lives (*cont.*):

l. of quiet desperation	THOR 332:9
l. upon hope will die fasting	FRAN 145:11
who lives more l. than one	WILDE 350:17
woman who l. for others	LEWIS 206:12
living: alive and well and l.	ANON 8:13
between those who are l.	BURKE 80:17
bodies a l. sacrifice	BIBLE 54:43
body is a machine for l.	TOLS 333:12
Earned a precarious l.	ANON 6:28
fever called 'L.'	POE 250:6
hands of the l. God	BIBLE 56:25
L. and partly living	ELIOT 134:6
l., had no roof to shroud	HEYW 168:9
L. is my job and my art	MONT 233:16
l. know no bounds	SHIR 306:12
l. need charity more	ARN 16:8
L.? The servants will do that	VILL 338:19
long habit of l. indisposeth	BROW 74:5
noble L., and the noble Dead	WORD 356:15
no l. with thee	ADD 2:22
out of the land of the l.	BIBLE 46:21
Plain l. and high thinking	WORD 356:1
respect to the l.	VOLT 340:24
revolutions is l. to some purpose	PAINE 244:15
shadows of the l.	BROW 74:2
start by l.	ANOU 14:9
Summer time an' the l. is easy	GERS 168:6
thou shouldst be l. at this hour	WORD 355:11
unexamined life is not worth l.	SOCR 310:22
wouldn't be l. with me	STEV 316:2
Livingstone: Dr L., I presume	STAN 314:9
Lizzie Borden: L. took an axe	ANON 8:22
llama: L. is a woolly sort	BELL 33:19
Lloyd George: L. knew my father	ANON 9:1
lo: L.! He comes with clouds	WESL 346:9
L.! the poor Indian	POPE 252:13
load: how to l. and bless	KEATS 192:14
L. every rift with ore	KEATS 193:14
loaf: l. of bread beneath	FITZ 140:6
loafing: cricket as organized l.	TEMP 323:8
local: little l. difficulties	MACM 215:16
L., but prized elsewhere	AUDEN 21:13
l. thing called Christianity	HARDY 161:19
loch: bonnie banks o' L. Lomon'	ANON 10:2
Lochinvar: knight like the young L.	SCOTT 268:19
L. is come out of the west	SCOTT 268:18
loci: *Geniumque* l.	VIRG 339:18
locks: louse in the l. of literature	TENN 329:2
l. which are left you	SOUT 312:1
shake thy gory l. at me	SHAK 287:11
Your l. were like the raven	BURNS 82:11
loco: *Dulce est desipere in* l.	HOR 174:1
locust: years that the l. hath eaten	BIBLE 47:19
locusts: famine grew, and l. came	THOM 330:11
locuta: *Roma l. est*	AUG 22:5
lodesterre: language he was the l.	LYDG 212:13
lodge: Is best to l.	SHAK 298:8
l. in a garden of cucumbers	BIBLE 45:3
thou lodgest, I will l.	BIBLE 41:8
lodged: L. with me useless	MILT 230:22
lodging: Hard was their l.	GARTH 148:14
loftier: l. race	SYM 321:20
log-cabin: L. to White House	THAY 329:27
logic: It is the l. of our times	DAY-L 115:6
l. and rhetoric	BACON 25:16
That's l.	CARR 91:20
This Second L.	ARIS 15:10
logical: L. consequences	HUXL 177:20
logs: Tom bears l. into the hall	SHAK 284:23
loin: unlit lamp and the ungirt l.	BROW 77:16
loins: l. girt about with truth	BIBLE 56:4
shudder in the l. engenders	YEATS 359:14
thicker than my father's l.	BIBLE 41:33
With your l. girded	BIBLE 39:37

loins (cont.):
your l. be girded about	BIBLE 52:20

loitering: Alone and palely l. — KEATS 191:7
Lolita: L., light of my life — NAB 236:18
London: And dream of L. — MORR 235:16
crowd flowed over L. Bridge	ELIOT 134:21
gazed at the L. skies	BETJ 36:16
Hell is a city much like L.	SHEL 304:13
key of India is L.	DISR 121:22
L.: a nation, not a city	DISR 122:5
L. Bridge to sketch the ruins	MAC 213:15
L. doth pour out her citizens	SHAK 280:1
L. is a fine town	COLM 105:13
L. like a special correspondent	BAG 26:16
L. particular	DICK 118:2
L., that great cesspool	DOYLE 126:4
L., thou art the flower	ANON 9:2
L. Transport diesel-engined	FLAN 141:6
parks are the lungs of L.	PITT 249:6
rainy Sunday in L.	DE Q 117:4
tired of L., he is tired of life	JOHN 185:15
lone: I am a l. lorn creetur — DICK 118:8
| l. shieling of the misty island | GALT 147:19 |
loneliness: l. of the long-distance | SILL 307:3 |
| Well of L. | HALL 160:14 |
lonely: All the l. people — MCC 205:12
as mirrors are l.	AUDEN 21:9
heart is a l. hunter	MCL 215:10
l. sea and the sky	MAS 221:21
Only the l.	MELS 241:16
rapture on the l. shore	BYRON 85:12
troubled with her l. life	PEPYS 247:16
lonesome: one, that on a l. road — COL 104:15
lonesomeness: starlight lit my l. — HARDY 162:18
long: Ask that your way be l. — CAV 93:10
as l. as ye both shall live	BOOK 65:28
certified how l. I have to live	BOOK 67:1
gonna live this l.	BLAKE 60:4
I am going a l. way	TENN 324:22
if a man have l. hair	BIBLE 55:10
In the l. run we are all dead	KEYN 194:17
it's for such a l. time	MOL 232:17
l., and lank, and brown	COL 104:11
l. and the short and the tall	HUGH 175:18
l. a time lies in one little word	SHAK 293:10
l. for scenes where man	CLARE 101:7
L. is the way and hard	MILT 228:30
l. littleness of life	CORN 108:7
Long, l. thoughts	LONG 209:21
l., long while	AND 5:12
l. trail awinding	KING 195:12
l., withdrawing roar	ARN 16:11
Lord, how l.	BIBLE 45:13
Love me little, love me l.	ANON 9:4
man goeth to his l. home	BIBLE 44:26
night of the l. knives	HITL 168:21
Nor wants that little l.	GOLD 154:27
Not that the story need be l.	THOR 332:6
So l. mote ye lyve	CHAU 96:15
week is a l. time in politics	WILS 351:15
witty and it sha'n't be l.	CHES 97:2
longa: Ars l., vita brevis — HIPP 168:19
long-distance: l. runner — SILL 307:3
longen: l. folk to goon on pilgrimages — CHAU 95:11
longer: I am no l. my own — METH 223:28
| less fun and it lasts l. | ANOU 14:9 |
longings: Immortal l. in me — SHAK 272:7
longitude: l. with no platitude — FRY 147:1
long-suffering: l., and of great goodness — BOOK 68:6
look: all l. just the same — REYN 259:11
full l. at the worst	HARDY 162:8
know not which way I must l.	WORD 356:1
Let him l. to his bond	SHAK 289:15
l. after our people	SCOTT 268:5
l., and pass on	DANTE 113:19

look (cont.):
L. as much like home as we can	FRY 147:2
L. at the stars	HOPK 172:16
L. at things in bloom	HOUS 174:17
L. for me by moonlight	NOYES 240:14
L. for me in the nurseries	THOM 331:18
L. in my face	TRAI 334:2
l. in thy heart and write	SIDN 306:17
l. no way but downwards	BUNY 79:6
l. shining at new styles	AUDEN 21:14
L., stranger, at this island	AUDEN 20:26
l. the East End in the face	ELIZ 135:18
L. thy last on all things lovely	DE L 116:15
L.! Up in the sky!	ANON 7:5
l. upon his like again	SHAK 274:17
Only a l. and a voice	LONG 210:3
row one way and l. another	BURT 83:7
They l. on and help	LAWR 202:26
looked: more he l. inside — MILNE 225:14
lookers on: God and angels to be l. — BACON 24:1
looketh: l. on the outward — BIBLE 41:15
looking: Here's l. at you, kid — EPST 137:11
Leave them while you're l. good	LOOS 210:8
l. one way, and rowing another	BUNY 79:1
plough, and l. back	BIBLE 52:9
someone may be l.	MENC 223:8
looking-glass: cracked l. — JOYCE 188:12
looks: her l. went everywhere — BROW 76:19
His l. do menace heaven	MARL 219:6
she needs good l.	TUCK 335:9
Stolen l. are nice in chapels	HUNT 176:16
loom: she left the l. — TENN 326:3
looms: passage through these l. — VAUG 337:3
loon: thou cream-faced l. — SHAK 287:33
| Wanna laugh like a l. | HARB 161:13 |
loose: all hell broke l. — MILT 229:14
Every which way but l.	KRON 199:6
l. the bands of Orion	BIBLE 43:4
L. types of things	WORD 357:8
man who should l. me	LOW 211:2
loosed: l. our heart in tears — ARN 16:19
lord: come, l. Jesus — BIBLE 58:8
cometh in the Name of the L.	BOOK 68:23
coming of the L.	HOWE 175:7
dear L. was crucified	ALEX 4:6
die with kissing of my L.	MARL 219:12
earth is the L.'s	BOOK 66:19
glory of the L.	BIBLE 46:9
Great L. of all things	POPE 252:18
I am the L. thy God	BIBLE 40:2
I replied, 'My L.'	HERB 166:23
let the L. be thankit	BURNS 82:14
L. be with you	MISS 231:9
L., dismiss us	BUCK 78:3
L. gave, and the L. hath taken	BIBLE 42:22
L. God made them all	ALEX 4:2
L. guards the city	BIBLE 58:13
L. how it talk't	FLET 31:3
L., how long	BIBLE 45:13
L. is his name	MONS 233:3
L. is my shepherd	BOOK 66:17
L. is the source of my light	BIBLE 58:9
L. looketh on the heart	BIBLE 41:15
L. loveth he chasteneth	BIBLE 56:28
L. make his face shine	BIBLE 40:15
L., now lettest thou thy servant	BIBLE 52:3
L. of all hopefulness	STR 318:17
L. of himself, though not	WOTT 357:15
L. of the Dance	CART 92:13
L. once own the happy lines	POPE 252:5
L. Randal, my Son	BALL 27:19
L. require of thee	BIBLE 47:23
L. shall raise me up	RAL 258:1
L.'s my shepherd	SCOT 269:8
L. survives the rainbow	LOW 211:17

lord (*cont.*):

L. thy God is with thee	BIBLE 40:26
L. watch between me	BIBLE 39:23
L., what fools these mortals be	SHAK 290:32
L., with what care	HERB 167:7
Love, thou art absolute sole L.	CRAS 111:9
mouth of the L. hath spoken	BIBLE 46:9
My L. should take frail flesh	CROS 112:13
O L., to what a state dost	TER 329:7
Prepare ye the way of the L.	BIBLE 46:8
sing the L.'s song	BOOK 69:3
sought the L. aright	BURNS 82:1
thou, O L., art more than they	TENN 324:23
Up to a point, L. Copper	WAUGH 343:24
we own thee L.	ANON 14:1
when they crucified my L.	ANON 11:14
lordliest: Lords are l. in their wine	MILT 230:16
lordly: butter in a l. dish	BIBLE 40:33
lords: For the l. who lay ye low	SHEL 305:1
L. are lordliest in their wine	MILT 230:16
L. in ermine, beggars freezing	ROB 260:22
l. alway that people note	BARC 28:17
one of the l. of life	LAWR 202:22
only a wit among L.	JOHN 183:28
Wi' the Scots L. at his feet	BALL 28:6
lordships: l. on a hot afternoon	ANON 11:3
lose: findeth his life shall l. it	BIBLE 49:33
l. his own soul	BIBLE 51:23
l. itself in the sky	BROW 75:8
lose thee, I do l. a thing	SHAK 288:18
l. to-morrow the ground won	ARN 17:10
nobly save, or meanly l.	LINC 207:6
nothing to l. but our aitches	ORW 242:14
nothing to l. but their chains	MARX 221:15
To l. one parent	WILDE 349:18
we don't want to l. you	RUB 264:4
losers: all are l.	CHAM 93:25
loses: l. his misery	ARN 17:13
losing: conduct of a l. party	BURKE 79:18
Does it matter?—l. your sight	SASS 267:9
l. one pleased Cato	LUCAN 211:23
loss: deeper sense of her l.	GASK 148:17
My richest gain I count but l.	WATTS 343:4
To do our country l.	SHAK 279:17
lost: All is l. save honour	FRAN 145:4
all was l.	MILT 229:26
Balls will be l. always	BERR 36:11
be l. in me	TENN 328:5
better to have fought and l.	CLOU 102:21
better to have loved and l.	BUTL 84:11
better to have loved and l.	TENN 325:4
Britain has l. an empire	ACH 1:3
found my sheep which was l.	BIBLE 52:27
France has not l. the war	DE G 116:3
Friends, I have l. a day	TITUS 332:22
he was l., and is found	BIBLE 52:32
Home of l. causes	ARN 18:2
In search of l. time	PROU 255:17
land of l. content	HOUS 174:24
l. boyhood of Judas	Æ 3:4
L. Chord	PROC 255:13
l. generation	STEIN 314:23
l. in translation	FROST 146:28
l., that is unsought	CHAU 96:14
l. the only Playboy	SYNGE 321:22
make wherever we're l. in	FRY 147:2
never l. till won	CRAB 110:28
never to have l.	BUTL 84:11
Not l. but gone before	NORT 240:10
not l. but sent before	CYPR 113:13
not that you won or l.	RICE 259:17
paradises that we have l.	PROU 255:21
want of a horse the rider was l.	FRAN 145:12
woman that deliberates is l.	ADD 2:15
lot: l. is fallen unto me	BOOK 66:15

lot (*cont.*):

policeman's l. is not	GILB 152:24
Remember L.'s wife	BIBLE 52:37
Lothario: gallant, gay L.	ROWE 263:20
lots: cast l. upon my vesture	BOOK 66:16
Lou: lady that's known as L.	SERV 270:13
loungers: l. and idlers	DOYLE 126:4
louse: between a l. and a flea	JOHN 186:2
l. in the locks of literature	TENN 329:2
lousy: L. but loyal	ANON 9:3
l. skin scabbed here	BUNT 78:14
love: Absence is to l.	BUSS 83:19
all for l.	SPEN 313:11
all for l., and a little for the bottle	DIBD 117:17
All l., all liking, all delight	HERR 167:14
all she loves is l.	BYRON 86:9
All that matters is l. and work	FREUD 146:4
Amazing l.!	WESL 346:3
america i l. you	CUMM 112:17
As great in l. as in religion	COWL 109:16
aside a long-cherished l.	CAT 93:5
bring those who l. Thee	TER 329:7
call a dog *Hervey*, I shall l. him	JOHN 183:23
cantons of contemnèd l.	SHAK 297:21
Christ's particular l.'s sake	BROW 77:7
Come down, O L. divine	LITT 208:2
constant l. deemed there	SIDN 306:19
corner in the thing I l.	SHAK 292:17
course of true l.	SHAK 290:13
dark secret l.	BLAKE 62:4
Dear L., for nothing less	DONNE 124:1
dinner of herbs where l. is	BIBLE 43:26
doesn't l. a wall	FROST 146:15
fit l. for gods	MILT 229:24
God is L., but get it in writing	LEE 204:5
good man's l.	SHAK 273:6
Greater l. hath no man	BIBLE 53:40
greater l. hath no man	THOR 332:13
Greater l. than this	JOYCE 188:18
groans of l. to those of the dying	LOWRY 211:22
half in l. with easeful death	KEATS 192:3
Hearts wound up with l.	SPEN 313:2
Hell, madam, is to l. no more	BERN 36:8
hid in the heart of l.	YEATS 359:18
hir housbond as hir l.	CHAU 96:8
hold your tongue, and let me l.	DONNE 123:24
hour of l.	BYRON 86:18
How do I l. thee	BROW 75:5
How I l. my country	PITT 249:10
How should I your true l. know	SHAK 276:32
I could not l. thee	LOV 210:21
I do not l. thee, Dr Fell	BROWN 73:18
I don't l. you, Sabidius	MART 220:4
I drew them ... with bands of l.	BIBLE 47:18
If music be the food of l.	SHAK 297:13
if my l. were in my arms	ANON 11:18
I got to l. one man till I die	HAMM 160:19
I hate and I l.	CAT 93:7
I knew it was l.	BYRON 87:11
I'll l. you, dear	AUDEN 20:11
I l. all waste and solitary	SHEL 303:20
I l. her till I die	ANON 10:18
I l. not man the less	BYRON 85:12
I l. thee still	COWP 110:8
I l. you, Nellie Dean	ARMS 15:24
I'm tired of L.	BELL 33:13
in l. with a cold climate	SOUT 312:6
in l. with the productions of time	BLAKE 61:5
It kills l., it kills art	WAUGH 343:17
joy of l. is too short	MAL 217:2
labour of l.	BIBLE 56:13
Land that I l.	BERL 35:21
laughter and the l. of friends	BELL 34:3
leave to come unto my l.	SPEN 313:6
left thy first l.	BIBLE 57:20

love (cont.):

less the object of l.	LAMB 199:23
let me sow l.	FRAN 145:7
Let's do it, let's fall in l.	PORT 253:22
little duty and less l.	SHAK 280:5
live is like to l.	BUTL 84:17
live with me, and be my l.	DONNE 123:23
live with me, and be my l.	MARL 219:3
live with thee, and be thy l.	RAL 257:20
lost the world for l.	DRYD 128:10
L., a child, is ever crying	WROTH 358:1
L., all alike, no season	DONNE 124:12
L. alters not	SHAK 300:9
l., an abject intercourse	GOLD 155:6
L. and a cottage	GARR 105:12
L. and do what you will	AUG 22:2
l., and fame to nothingness	KEATS 192:21
l., and life, it's enemy	ANOU 14:7
L. and marriage rarely can	BYRON 86:10
l. and murder will out	CONG 106:7
L. and scandal are the best	FIEL 139:9
l. a womman that she woot	CHAU 96:14
L. bade me welcome	HERB 167:2
L. built on beauty	DONNE 123:3
l. can do that dares l. attempt	SHAK 294:32
L. ceases to be a pleasure	BEHN 32:21
L. comforteth like sunshine	SHAK 300:18
L. conquers all things	VIRG 340:4
L., curiosity, freckles	PARK 245:5
L. divine, all loves excelling	WESL 346:10
l. for Heathcliff resembles	BRON 72:17
l. God whom he hath not seen	BIBLE 57:17
L. goes toward love	SHAK 295:2
L. has pitched his mansion	YEATS 358:20
l. her, comfort her	BOOK 65:28
l. him, and serve Him	CAT 92:20
L. in a golden bowl	BLAKE 60:10
l. indeed who quake to say	SIDN 306:22
L. in dying, Faith is defying	BARN 29:8
L. in this part of the world	BYRON 87:17
L. is a boy, by poets styled	BUTL 84:3
L. is a growing or full	DONNE 124:6
L. is a spirit all compact	SHAK 300:17
L. is a thing. It is a prick	PEELE 247:1
l. is a thing that can never	PARK 245:4
L. is hard to catch	MER 223:20
L. is like any other luxury	TROL 334:21
L. is like linen	FLET 142:10
l. is more cruel than lust	SWIN 321:9
L. is not love which alters	SHAK 300:8
L. is not secure	CHES 97:21
l. is of man's life a thing apart	BYRON 86:4
L. is of the valley	TENN 328:7
L. is only one of many passions	JOHN 182:25
l. is slight	MARL 218:18
L. is the delusion	MENC 223:6
L. is the fart	SUCK 318:22
L. is the gift of oneself	ANOU 14:8
L. is the greatest mercy	WILB 349:13
L. is then our duty	GAY 149:6
L. is the wisdom	JOHN 186:9
L. iz like the meazles	BILL 59:10
L. looks not with the eyes	SHAK 290:16
L. me little, love me long	ANON 9:4
l. men too little	BURKE 80:19
l. of money is the root	BIBLE 56:19
l. of what is beautiful	PER 248:1
L.-quarrels oft in pleasing	MILT 230:15
l's a malady without a cure	DRYD 128:9
l. Scotland better than truth	JOHN 182:14
L. seeketh not itself to please	BLAKE 62:1
L. seeketh only Self to please	BLAKE 62:2
L. set you going	PLATH 249:16
l. should have courage	TROL 334:13

love (cont.):

l. slights it	BACON 24:21
L.'s like the measles	JERR 181:13
L. sought is good	SHAK 298:7
L.'s passives are his activ'st	CRAS 111:7
L.'s pleasure lasts	FLOR 142:12
l.'s the noblest frailty	DRYD 127:33
l.'s young dream	MOORE 234:15
l. that asks no question	SPR 313:26
l. that can be reckoned	SHAK 271:4
l. that dare not speak its name	DOUG 125:6
l. that loves a scarlet coat	HOOD 171:6
l. that moves the sun	DANTE 113:24
L. the Beloved Republic	FORS 144:3
L. the brotherhood	BIBLE 57:9
l. the highest when we see it	TENN 324:6
L., the human form divine	BLAKE 61:21
L. the sinner but hate	AUG 22:4
L.-thirty, love-forty	BETJ 37:11
l. those who love you	VOLT 340:21
L., thou art absolute sole Lord	CRAS 111:9
l. thy neighbour as thyself	BIBLE 40:14
L. thyself last	SHAK 280:20
l. to hatred turned	CONG 106:12
l. up groweth with youre age	CHAU 96:22
L. without his wings	BYRON 87:1
L. wol nat been constreyned	CHAU 95:25
L. you ten years before	MARV 220:23
L. your enemies	BIBLE 52:6
make l. deathless	TREN 334:6
make us l. one another	SWIFT 320:10
making l. all year round	BEAU 30:16
man you l. to hate	ANON 9:7
many waters cannot quench l.	BIBLE 45:2
Men l. in haste	BYRON 86:25
more l. and knowledge of you	SHAK 272:13
my Lesbia, and let us l.	CAT 93:2
My l. and I did meet	BETJ 37:5
my l. and I did meet	YEATS 359:1
My l. and I would lie	HOUS 174:20
My l. has died for me to-day	BALL 27:13
my l. is come to me	ROSS 262:21
My l. is of a birth as rare	MARV 220:12
My l.'s a noble madness	DRYD 127:24
my L.'s like a red, red rose	BURNS 82:20
my only l. sprung from	SHAK 294:28
My song is l. unknown	CROS 112:13
My vegetable l. should grow	MARV 220:23
Need we say it was not l.	MILL 224:23
never l. a stranger	BENS 34:21
office and affairs of l.	SHAK 291:17
O lyric L., half-angel	BROW 77:5
one jot of former l. retain	DRAY 126:16
Only our l. hath no decay	DONNE 123:22
our l. is here to stay	GERS 150:7
outward parts L.'s always seen	COWL 109:14
passing the l. of women	BIBLE 41:23
Perfect fear casteth out l.	CONN 107:2
perfect l. casteth out fear	BIBLE 57:16
planet of L. is on high	TENN 326:28
putting l. away	DICK 120:10
right place for l.	FROST 146:8
right true end of l.	DONNE 123:4
says L.	HERB 167:3
separate us from the l. of God	BIBLE 54:42
She bid me take l. easy	YEATS 359:1
So faithful in l.	SCOTT 268:19
soft philosopher of l.	DRYD 128:3
some l. but little policy	SHAK 294:7
sooner allured by l.	ASCH 18:18
so simple, l.	PRÉV 255:6
So true a fool is l.	SHAK 299:20
sports of l.	JONS 187:16
spring of l. resembleth	SHAK 298:18
that they l.	WALL 341:15

love (cont.):

There is no l. for such	THOM 331:4
Though lovers be lost l. shall not	THOM 330:6
time to l., and a time to hate	BIBLE 44:13
To be wise, and l., exceeds	SHAK 297:3
To let the warm L. in	KEATS 192:9
to l. and rapture's due	ROCH 261:3
to l., cherish, and obey	BOOK 66:1
to l. her is a liberal education	STEE 314:16
Too late came I to l. thee	AUG 21:24
To tell the laity our l.	DONNE 124:15
true l. hath my heart	SIDN 306:15
turns to thoughts of l.	TENN 326:6
'Twixt women's l., and men's	DONNE 123:21
Use him as though you l. him	BLUN 62:14
very few to l.	WORD 356:22
waft her l.	SHAK 289:32
waly, waly, gin l. be bonnie	BALL 28:10
wayward is this foolish l.	SHAK 298:17
We must l. one another or die	AUDEN 21:11
What is commonly called l.	FIEL 139:10
what is l.! It is a pretty thing	GREE 158:9
What is l.? 'tis not hereafter	SHAK 297:23
What l. I bore to thee	WORD 355:3
when I l. thee not	SHAK 292:10
When l. congeals	HART 163:8
wilder shores of l.	BLAN 62:9
woman wakes to l.	TENN 324:15
Work is l. made visible	GIBR 150:20
yet in l. he sought me	BAKER 26:21
your true l.'s coming	SHAK 297:23

loved: And the l. one all together

	BROW 76:20
better to have l. and lost	BUTL 84:11
better to have l. and lost	TENN 325:4
for she l. much	BIBLE 52:8
God so l. the world	BIBLE 53:19
holy l. by the gods	PLATO 249:19
I have l. him too much	RAC 257:14
I l. a lass, a fair one	WITH 352:5
I l. you, so I drew these tides	LAWR 203:1
I wish I l. the Human Race	RAL 258:6
left than never to have been l.	CONG 106:16
l. not at first sight	MARL 218:18
l. not at first sight	SHAK 273:7
l. not wisely but too well	SHAK 293:5
l. the doctrine	DEFOE 115:18
most l., despised	SHAK 282:19
nor no man ever l.	SHAK 300:9
Not that I l. Caesar less	SHAK 281:15
prince to l be feared than l.	MACH 215:1
she l. me for the dangers	SHAK 291:35
She who has never l.	GAY 149:8
thirst to be l.	RHYS 259:14
To have l., to have thought	ARN 16:14
use him as though you l.	WALT 342:13
We l., sir—used to meet	BROW 75:21
We that had l. him	BROW 76:14
what thou and I did till we l.	DONNE 124:5

loveless: Love to the l. shown

	CROS 112:13

loveliness: Its l. increases

	KEATS 190:11
l. needs not the foreign aid	THOM 331:25
portion of the l.	SHEL 303:12
Traditional sanctity and l.	YEATS 358:18
weak from your l.	BETJ 37:11
woman of so shining l.	YEATS 359:27

lovely: As you are woman, so be l.

	GRAV 156:16
Claude's landscape all is l.	CONS 107:12
It gives a l. light	MILL 224:22
Look thy last on all things l.	DE L 116:15
L. and willing every afternoon	AUDEN 20:25
l. is the rose	WORD 355:18
more l. and more temperate	SHAK 299:12
Saul and Jonathan were l.	BIBLE 41:22
That they might l. be	CROS 112:13
whatsoever things are l.	BIBLE 56:9

lovely (cont.):

Which once he made more l.	SHEL 303:12
You have l. eyes	CHEK 96:29

lover: days dividing lover and l.

	SWIN 321:2
done the l. mortal hurt	DOUG 125:10
injured l.'s hell	MILT 229:17
I sighed as a l.	GIBB 150:14
It was a l. and his lass	SHAK 273:10
Jesu, l. of my soul	WESL 346:8
lived she was a true l.	MAL 217:3
l. and killer are mingled	DOUG 125:10
l., and the poet	SHAK 291:3
l.'s mind if she knew	TROL 334:19
l. without indiscretion	HARDY 161:21
thou wast as true a l.	SHAK 272:18
what is left of a l.	ROWL 263:21
Wine, not water, binds the l.	SANS 266:20
woman loves her l.	BYRON 86:9

lovers: Frankie and Albert were l.

	ANON 7:6
Journeys end in l. meeting	SHAK 297:23
l. be lost love shall not	THOM 330:6
l. fled away into the storm	KEATS 190:23
pair of star-crossed l.	SHAK 294:22
Sweet l. love the spring	SHAK 273:10

loves: all she l. is love

	BYRON 86:9
fat white woman whom nobody l.	CORN 108:6
He l. us not	SHAK 287:23
l. the fox less	SURT 319:10
l. what he knows	CROM 111:24
man kills the thing he l.	WILDE 350:16
our l., must I remember them	APOL 14:12
reigned with your l.	ELIZ 135:7
so l. oblique may well	MARV 220:13
who l. me must have a touch	TENN 324:8
who l. that, must first be wise	MILT 230:21

love-sick: winds were l.

	SHAK 271:14

lovesome: garden is a l. thing

	BROWN 73:19

loveth: He prayeth well, who l. well

	COL 104:18
Lord l. he chasteneth	BIBLE 56:28
Lord l. he correcteth	BIBLE 43:7
l. not knoweth not God	BIBLE 57:15

loving: For l., and for saying so

	DONNE 124:14
heart be still as l.	BYRON 87:8
I ain't had no l.	NORW 240:11
l. himself better	COL 104:23
l. longest, when existence	AUST 22:28

loving-kindness: l. and mercy

	BOOK 66:18

low: exalted them of l. degree

	BIBLE 51:29
last great Englishman is l.	TENN 327:11
l. estate of his handmaiden	BIBLE 51:28
l. man seeks a little thing	BROW 75:33
l. on whom assurance sits	ELIOT 134:29
l. sounds by the shore	YEATS 359:13
Sweet and l.	TENN 327:19
upper station of l. life	DEFOE 115:14
what is l. raise and support	MILT 228:9

lowbrow: first militant l.

	BERL 36:5

Lowells: L. talk to the Cabots

	BOSS 70:1

lower: they are l. than vermin

	BEVAN 37:18

lowlands: Ye Highlands and ye L.

	BALL 27:14

lowliness: incense of l.

	MONS 233:3
l. become mine inner clothing	LITT 208:2

lowly: As in the l. air

	GILB 151:11

loyal: Lousy but l.

	ANON 9:3

loyalty: I want l.

	JOHN 181:20
L. is the Tory's secret weapon	KILM 195:2
l. we all feel to unhappiness	GREE 158:5
That learned body wanted l.	TRAPP 334:3

Lucasta: L. that bright northern star

	LOV 210:18

lucid: L. intervals and happy pauses

	BACON 25:22
make a l. interval	DRYD 128:5
Not in the l. intervals of life	WORD 354:18

Lucifer: L., son of the morning

	BIBLE 45:22
starred night Prince L.	MER 223:21

luck: much good l. in the world

	FORS 143:22

luck (cont.):
l. and sends his son to Oxford watching his l. — STEAD 314:13
lucky: l. if he gets out of it alive — SERV 270:13
lucrative: so l. to cheat — JONES 116:24
lucre: filthy l. — CLOU 102:19
Lucy: When L. ceased — BIBLE 56:16
lug: l. the guts — WORD 356:23
lugete: L., O Veneres — SHAK 276:26
lugger: Once aboard the l. — CAT 93:1
lukewarm: Because thou art l. — JOHN 186:17
lukewarmness: L. I account a sin — BIBLE 57:22
lullaby: And dreamy l. — COWL 109:16
And I will sing a l. — GILB 151:17
Once in a l. — DEKK 116:10
lumber: learned l. in his head — HARB 161:14
l. of the schools — POPE 252:9
lump: l. bred up in darkness — SWIFT 320:18
lumps: There are l. in it — KYD 199:10
lunatic: l., the lover — STEP 315:6
lunatics: lunatic asylum run by l. — SHAK 291:3
l. have taken charge — LLOY 208:12
lunch: husband for life, not for l. — ROWL 264:1
no such thing as a free l. — ANON 8:8
she's unable to l. today — ANON 10:21
luncheon: At l. with a city friend — PORT 253:23
Breakfast, supper, dinner, l. — BELL 33:24
do not take soup at l. — BROW 76:27
lungs: dangerous to the l. — CURZ 113:11
parks are the l. of London — JAM 179:9
luscious: l. clusters of the vine — PITT 249:6
lust: Delight of l. is gross — MARV 220:15
love is more cruel than l. — PETR 248:10
l. in action — SWIN 321:9
l. of knowing what should not — SHAK 300:10
Palate, the hutch of tasty l. — FLEC 141:17
something generous in mere l. — HOPK 172:6
lustre: Where is thy l. now — ROCH 261:5
lusts: sinful l. of the flesh — SHAK 283:19
lust'st: l. to use her in that kind — BOOK 65:21
lute: little rift within the l. — SHAK 283:25
Orpheus with his l. made trees — TENN 324:13
When the l. is broken — SHAK 280:16
Luther: genius in religion—L. — SHEL 303:21
lux: l. perpetua luceat eis — ARN 18:11
luxe: L., calme et volupté — MISS 231:22
luxuries: Give us the l. of life — BAUD 30:4
luxury: Love is like any other l. — MOTL 236:2
private and costly l. — TROL 334:21
their l. was doing good — ADAMS 1:8
tried the l. of doing good — GARTH 148:14
lying: express l. or falsehood — CRAB 110:27
listening, l. in wait — SWIFT 320:1
l. awake with a dismal headache — THOM 330:25
One of you is l. — GILB 151:15
smallest amount of l. — PARK 245:9
Lyme: old man of L. — BUTL 84:10
Lyonnesse: When I set out for L. — MONK 232:26
lyre: Make me thy l. — HARDY 162:18
'Omer smote 'is bloomin' l. — SHEL 304:9
— KIPL 197:14

M

Mab: M., the Mistress-Fairy — JONS 187:4
Macaroni: And called it M. — ANON 11:24
Macaulay: [M.] has occasional flashes — SMITH 310:6
M. is well for a while — CARL 90:24
Macavity: M. WASN'T THERE — ELIOT 134:9
Macbeth: Night I appeared as M. — HARG 162:21
Macduff: Lay on, M. — SHAK 288:8
M. was from his mother's womb — SHAK 288:7
Macedonia: Come over into M. — BIBLE 54:16
macerations: Made way for m. — POUND 254:17
Macheath: Just a jack-knife has M. — BREC 71:18

machine: body is a m. for living — TOLS 333:12
Ghost in the M. — RYLE 265:11
house is a m. for living — LE C 204:3
m. for turning the red wine — DIN 121:2
very pulse of the m. — WORD 356:24
machines: M. for making more m. — BOTT 70:6
m. think but whether men do — SKIN 308:5
macht: Arbeit m. frei — ANON 13:1
mackerel: Not so the m. — FRERE 145:22
mad: All poets are m. — BURT 83:8
be nothing else but m. — SHAK 275:9
destroy He first sends m. — DUP 129:11
heroically m. — DRYD 127:18
he's football m. — MCGR 214:22
How sad and bad and m. it was — BROW 75:21
let me not be m. — SHAK 283:1
M. about the boy — COW 109:3
m. all are in God's keeping — KIPL 197:26
M., bad, and dangerous to know — LAMB 199:22
M. dogs and Englishmen — COW 109:4
Made us nobly wild, not m. — HERR 167:19
M., is he? Then I hope — GEOR 149:22
m. March days — MAS 221:19
m. north-north-west — SHAK 275:17
M. world! mad kings — SHAK 282:4
Make m. the guilty — SHAK 275:23
men that God made m. — CHES 97:20
much learning doth make thee m. — BIBLE 54:26
old, m., blind despised — SHEL 305:3
pleasure, sure, in being m. — DRYD 128:19
sad bad glad m. brother's name — SWIN 321:5
some believed him m. — BEAT 30:13
We all are born m. — BECK 31:4
when a heroine goes m. — SHER 305:24
Whom the m. would destroy — LEVIN 206:8
madam: As honest m.'s issue — SHAK 282:20
Can disturb globe-trotting M. — YEATS 360:5
madame: m.! truly it's not right — CRANE 111:1
maddest: m. merriest day — TENN 327:5
madding: Far from the m. crowd — GRAY 157:10
made: All things were m. by him — BIBLE 53:7
Begotten, not m. — BOOK 65:5
Dost thou know who m. thee — BLAKE 61:3
fearfully and wonderfully m. — BOOK 69:7
it is he that hath m. us — BOOK 68:5
Who m. you? God made me — CAT 92:20
Madeira: Have Some M., M'dear — SWANN 141:3
madeleine: little piece of m. — PROU 255:18
mademoiselle: M. from Armenteers — ANON 9:5
madhouse: You don't want m. — EMPS 137:5
madhouses: M., prisons — CLARE 101:4
madman: As a m. shakes a dead geranium
— ELIOT 134:11
Victor Hugo was a m. — COCT 103:3
madmen: which none but m. know — DRYD 128:19
worst of m. is a saint run mad — POPE 252:27
madness: Anger is a short m. — HOR 173:9
despondency and m. — WORD 356:17
devil's m.—War — SERV 270:17
generation destroyed by m. — GINS 153:3
Great wits are sure to m. — DRYD 127:7
His flight was m. — SHAK 287:22
Like m. is the glory — SHAK 296:18
m. of many — POPE 253:11
midsummer m. — SHAK 298:9
moon-struck m. — MILT 229:31
My love's a noble m. — DRYD 127:24
rest is the m. of art — JAMES 179:23
Such harmonious m. — SHEL 305:11
that fine m. — DRAY 126:19
that way m. lies — SHAK 283:11
Though this be m. — SHAK 275:12
To define true m. — SHAK 275:9
magazines: graves of little m. — PRES 255:5

Magdalen: fourteen months at M. College   GIBB 150:13
magic: house rose like m.   HARG 162:21
  If this be m.   SHAK 299:4
  let in daylight upon m.   BAG 26:13
  m. in a pint bottle   DICK 118:30
  mistake medicine for m.   SZASZ 322:1
  secret m. of numbers   BROW 74:12
  this rough m.   SHAK 296:12
magical: purely m. object   BART 29:19
magistrate: m. corruptible   ROB 260:17
  shocks the m.   RUSS 265:4
magna: M. est veritas   BIBLE 58:23
Magna Charta: M. is such a fellow   COKE 103:10
magnanimity: In victory: m.   CHUR 100:4
  M. in politics   BURKE 80:5
magnet: gunpowder, and the m.   BACON 25:28
magnificat: M. anima mea   BIBLE 58:16
magnificent: his mild and m. eye   BROW 76:14
  Mute and m., without a tear   DRYD 128:20
magnifique: C'est m., mais ce n'est pas   BOSQ 69:28
magnify: Day by day: we m. thee   BOOK 63:21
  My soul doth m. the Lord   BIBLE 51:28
  My soul doth m. the Lord   BIBLE 58:16
magpie: swollen m. in a fitful sun   POUND 254:21
magus: M. Zoroaster   SHEL 304:15
Mahomet: M. will go to the hill   BACON 24:16
maid: Be good, sweet m.   KING 195:13
  I once was a m.   BURNS 82:12
  lugger and the m. is mine   JOHN 186:17
  m. is not dead   BIBLE 49:26
  m. sing in the valley below   ANON 6:27
  m. whom there were none   WORD 356:22
  many a youth, and many a m.   MILT 227:4
  She could not live a m.   PEELE 247:2
  way of a man with a m.   BIBLE 44:4
  Yonder a m. and her wight   HARDY 162:12
maiden: In m. meditation   SHAK 290:24
  M., and mistress   SWIN 320:28
  m. of bashful fifteen   SHER 306:6
maidenly: So m., womanly   SKEL 308:2
maidens: all the m. pretty   COLM 105:13
  What m. loth   KEATS 191:18
maids: m. are May   SHAK 273:9
  m. strange seraphic pieces   TRAH 333:19
  malady most incident to m.   SHAK 298:33
  seven m. with seven mops   CARR 91:21
  Three little m. from school   GILB 151:21
maimed: m., and the halt   BIBLE 52:24
  M. us at the start   YEATS 359:19
maintenance: Art of Motorcycle M.   PIRS 249:2
maior: M. erat natu   LUC 212:1
Maisie: Proud M. is in the wood   SCOTT 269:1
majestic: M. though in ruin   MILT 228:27
majestical: laid in bed m.   SHAK 279:16
majesty: as his m., so is his mercy   BIBLE 47:32
  Ride on! ride on in m.   MILM 225:13
  sight so touching in its m.   WORD 354:15
  This earth of m.   SHAK 293:16
  Thy M. how bright   FABER 138:3
major: change from m. to minor   PORT 253:19
  M. Major   HELL 165:6
major-general: modern M.   GILB 152:23
majority: big enough m.   TWAIN 335:21
  Death joins us to the great m.   YOUNG 360:23
  join the m. [the dead]   PETR 248:9
  what the m. happen to like   WHIT 348:3
majors: scarlet M. at the Base   SASS 267:8
make: Go ahead, m. my day   STIN 317:26
  he who made the Lamb m. thee   BLAKE 62:6
  I m. on the one day   SKEL 308:4
  M. me a willow cabin   SHAK 297:21
  no mistakes does not usually m.   PHEL 248:11
  Scotsman on the m.   BARR 29:17
  M. IT NEW   POUND 254:10

maker: M. of heaven and earth   BOOK 65:5
  that sinneth before his M.   BIBLE 48:5
makes: m. me or fordoes me quite   SHAK 292:27
making: came to the m. of man   SWIN 321:3
malady: love's a m. without a cure   DRYD 128:9
  m. of not marking   SHAK 278:17
  m. most incident to maids   SHAK 298:33
male: M. and female created he   BIBLE 38:16
  m. and the female   BIBLE 39:8
  m. of the species   LAWR 202:18
  more deadly than the m.   KIPL 196:12
malice: envy, hatred, and m.   BOOK 64:14
  M. domestic   SHAK 287:4
  M. is of a low stature   HAL 160:8
  m. mingled with a little wit   DRYD 127:31
  m., to breed causes   JONS 187:17
  Nor set down aught in m.   SHAK 293:5
  our poor m. remains   SHAK 287:3
  With m. toward none   LINC 207:7
  Yet m. never was his aim   SWIFT 320:24
malicious: God is subtle but not m.   EINS 131:8
malignant: not m. and remove it   WAUGH 344:1
malmesey: barrel of M. wine   FABY 138:8
malt: m. does more than Milton   HOUS 175:4
Malverne: on M. hilles   LANG 201:6
Malvernian: That old M. brother   BETJ 37:8
mama: M. may have   HOL 170:10
  m. of dada   FAD 138:10
mammon: authentic m.   MACN 215:21
  cannot serve God and m.   BIBLE 49:3
man: all that may become a m.   SHAK 286:5
  Am I not a m. and a brother   WEDG 345:1
  And was made m.   MISS 231:16
  Any m. has to, needs to   ELIOT 134:15
  apparel oft proclaims the m.   SHAK 274:21
  Arms and the m.   DRYD 128:25
  arms and the m.   VIRG 338:23
  bold bad m.   SHAK 280:15
  bold bad m., that dared   SPEN 313:8
  Both m. and bird and beast   COL 104:18
  but be a m.   ARN 16:13
  by m. shall his blood be shed   BIBLE 39:9
  came to the making of m.   SWIN 321:3
  Can't help lovin' dat m.   HAMM 160:19
  century of the common m.   WALL 341:9
  Child is father of the M.   WORD 355:14
  every m. against every man   HOBB 169:8
  Every m. is surrounded by   AUST 22:25
  everyone has sat except a m.   CUMM 112:18
  fat, oily m. of God   THOM 331:21
  fit night out for m. or beast   FIEL 139:17
  garment from the m.   BLAKE 60:15
  gibbets for 'the m.'   COOK 107:17
  God created m.   VALE 336:21
  God is not a m.   BIBLE 40:18
  handsome, well-shaped m.   AUBR 20:2
  helpless m., in ignorance   JOHN 183:16
  He was a m., take him for all   SHAK 274:17
  He was her m., but he done   ANON 7:6
  hour is come, but not the m.   SCOTT 268:27
  I am a m. upon the land   BALL 27:17
  if a m. bites a dog   BOG 62:19
  I know myself a m.   DAV 114:14
  I met a m. who wasn't there   MEAR 222:18
  incomprehensible m. of 82   VICT 338:5
  in m. there is nothing great   HAM 160:18
  I saw a m. this morning   SHAW 303:1
  It's that m. again   ANON 8:12
  large-hearted m.   BROW 75:6
  last thing civilized by M.   MER 223:16
  let him pass for a m.   SHAK 288:30
  let no m. put asunder   BOOK 66:3
  make a m. a woman   PEMB 247:6
  m. after his own heart   BIBLE 41:13

man (cont.):

m. delights not me	SHAK 275:16
m. dreaming I was a butterfly	CHUA 98:19
M. dreams of fame while	TENN 324:15
m. for all seasons	WHIT 349:2
M. goeth forth to his work	BOOK 68:8
m. goeth to his long home	BIBLE 44:26
M. hands on misery to man	LARK 201:18
m. has a right to utter	JOHN 185:26
M. has created death	YEATS 358:22
M. has Forever	BROW 75:32
m.-in-the-street, who, I'm sorry to say	AUDEN 21:3
M. is a nasty creature	MOL 232:25
M. is a noble animal	BROW 74:7
M. is a tool-using animal	CARL 90:21
M. is a useless passion	SART 267:3
M. is born unto trouble	BIBLE 42:29
M. is man's ABC	QUAR 257:4
M. is Nature's sole mistake	GILB 152:25
m. is so in the way in the house	GASK 148:16
M. is something to be surpassed	NIET 239:16
M. is the hunter	TENN 327:25
M. is the master of things	SWIN 321:11
M. is the measure of all things	PROT 255:15
M. is the Only Animal that Blushes	TWAIN 335:24
M. is the shuttle	VAUG 337:3
M. is to be held only	EDG 130:18
m. made the town	COWP 110:6
M. marks the earth	BYRON 85:13
m. not old, but mellow	PHIL 248:16
m. of many devices	HOMER 171:1
m. of restless and versatile	HUXL 177:21
M. over forty is a scoundrel	SHAW 302:5
M. owes his entire existence	HEGEL 164:19
M. partly is and wholly hopes	BROW 75:23
m. proposes, but God disposes	THOM 330:1
M., proud man	SHAK 288:14
m. recovered of the bite	GOLD 154:28
m. remains sceptreless	SHEL 304:22
m.'s a man for a' that	BURNS 82:8
m.'s desire is for the woman	COL 104:27
m.'s first disobedience	MILT 228:7
M. shall not live by bread	BIBLE 48:16
m. should be alone	BIBLE 38:20
M.'s inhumanity to man	BURNS 82:16
m.'s the gowd for a' that	BURNS 82:7
M.'s word is God in man	TENN 324:2
m. that hath no music	SHAK 290:3
M. that is born of a woman	BIBLE 42:33
M. that is born of a woman	BOOK 66:6
M. wants but little here below	GOLD 154:27
m. who has found himself out	BARR 29:18
m. who has no office	SHAW 301:6
m. who should loose me	LOW 211:2
m. who stood at the gate	HASK 163:16
m. who's untrue to his wife	AUDEN 21:3
m. who used to notice such	HARDY 162:2
m. who would be king	KIPL 197:27
M. will err while yet	GOET 154:3
m. write a better book	EMER 137:3
m. you love to hate	ANON 9:7
mortal m. is a broomstick	SWIFT 320:6
my m. and I ain't together	KOEH 198:22
No m., having put his hand	BIBLE 52:9
no m. is wanted much	EMER 136:27
number of a m.	BIBLE 57:33
Once to every m. and nation	LOW 211:7
one small step for a m.	ARMS 16:5
only m. is vile	HEBER 164:16
people arose as one m.	BIBLE 41:7
problem is that m. is dead	FROMM 146:7
reflecting the figure of a m.	WOOLF 354:2
repelled by m.	INGE 178:13
science and study of m.	CHAR 95:9
sensual m.-in-the-street	AUDEN 21:11

man (cont.):

She knows her m.	DRYD 128:24
since by m. came death	BIBLE 55:17
strange what a m. may do	THAC 329:11
This is the state of m.	SHAK 280:18
This was a m.	SHAK 282:2
way of a m. with a maid	BIBLE 44:4
What a piece of work is a m.	SHAK 275:16
what is m., that thou hast	CRAS 111:5
what is m.? Wherefore	LENO 205:19
What is the chief end of m.	SHOR 306:13
when a m. should marry	BACON 25:3
When God at first made m.	HERB 167:5
when I became a m.	BIBLE 55:14
Who's master, who's m.	SWIFT 320:17
Why, m., he doth bestride	SHAK 280:27
woman be more like a m.	LERN 205:26
woman without a m. is like	STEI 315:2
Women who love the same m.	BEER 32:11
Would this m., could he see	AUDEN 20:17
you'll be a M., my son	KIPL 197:7
Manchester: school of M.	DISR 122:13
Mandalay: Come you back to M.	KIPL 196:21
mandarin: M. style	CONN 106:26
Manderley: I dreamt I went to M.	DU M 129:5
mandrake: m. root	DONNE 124:10
manger: In a m. for his bed	ALEX 4:4
laid him in a m.	BIBLE 51:32
One born in a m.	VAUG 337:6
wrapped in the rude m.	MILT 227:25
manhood: M. a struggle	DISR 121:26
M. taken by the Son	NEWM 238:19
My m., long misled by wandering	DRYD 127:29
manhoods: m. cheap	SHAK 279:20
manibus: M. date lilia plenis	VIRG 339:17
manifesto: first powerful plain m.	SPEN 312:23
manifold: m. sins and wickedness	BOOK 63:12
sundry and m. changes	BOOK 64:23
mankind: beauteous m.	SHAK 296:15
in th'original perused m.	ARMS 16:1
legislator of m.	JOHN 183:3
M. have been created	AUR 22:12
need not be to hate, m.	BYRON 85:5
proper study of m. is books	HUXL 177:5
proper study of m. is man	POPE 252:17
ride m.	EMER 136:13
manliness: silent m. of grief	GOLD 154:26
manly: valorous than m. wise	MARL 219:13
manna: Dropped m.	MILT 228:23
manned: with one man m.	DONNE 123:6
manner: All m. of thing	ELIOT 133:13
all m. of thing	JUL 188:21
m. of his speech	SHAK 271:13
m. which is my aversion	BYRON 86:16
to the m. born	SHAK 274:26
manners: catch the M. living	POPE 252:11
corrupt good m.	BIBLE 55:19
English m. more frightening	JARR 180:12
good table m.	MIKES 224:10
Leave off first for m.' sake	BIBLE 48:4
M. maketh man	WYK 358:7
m. of a dancing master	JOHN 184:1
m. of a Marquess	GILB 152:26
M. the need of the plain	WAUGH 344:3
Men's evil m. live in brass	SHAK 280:22
Oh, the times! Oh, the m.	CIC 100:25
thereby to rectify m.	MILT 230:32
To soften m., but corrupt	BYRON 86:33
manoeuvre: blend force with a m.	TROT 335:3
mansion: Love has pitched his m.	YEATS 358:20
made his everlasting m.	SHAK 296:24
m. call the fleeting breath	GRAY 157:8
upon thy fading m. spend	SHAK 300:14
mansion-house: m. of liberty	MILT 231:3
mansions: dolorous m.	MILT 227:28

martyrdom (*cont.*):
M. is the test | JOHN 185:26
M. ... only way to become famous | SHAW 300:29
martyrs: blood of the m. | TERT 329:8
noble army of M. | BOOK 63:19
stones and clouts make m. | BROW 74:4
marvel: There could I m. | THOM 330:14
marvellous: done m. things | BOOK 68:3
m. boy | WORD 356:16
marvels: wherein all m. summèd | SOUT 312:7
Marx: Karl M. and Catherine | ATTL 19:13
Marxist: M.—of the Groucho | ANON 12:7
Mary: Hail M., full of grace | ANON 13:13
M. Ambree | BALL 28:1
M. had a little lamb | HALE 160:7
M. was found in adulterous bed | BLAKE 60:13
What is the matter with M. Jane | MILNE 225:23
mask: loathsome m. has fallen | SHEL 304:22
m. like Castlereagh | SHEL 304:4
masonry: man into the social m. | WELLS 345:20
masquerade: truth in m. | BYRON 86:23
mass: Paris is well worth a m. | HENR 165:21
two thousand years of m. | HARDY 162:4
massacre: not as sudden as a m. | TWAIN 335:22
masses: bow, ye m. | GILB 151:9
calling 'em the m. | PRIE 255:7
m. against the classes | GLAD 153:13
m. yearning to breathe free | LAZ 203:2
massy: huge m. face | MAC 213:6
mast: bends the gallant m. | CUNN 113:7
master: eateth your M. with publicans | BIBLE 49:21
great m. so to sympathize | MILT 227:25
mad and savage m. | SOPH 311:14
Man is the m. of things | SWIN 321:11
m. a grief | SHAK 291:22
M.-morality and slave-morality | NIET 239:22
m. of my fate | HENL 165:18
M. of this college | BEEC 32:6
swear allegiance to any m. | HOR 173:5
which is to be m. | CARR 92:1
Who's m., who's man | SWIFT 320:17
masterpieces: in the midst of m. | FRAN 145:3
masters: m. of their fates | SHAK 280:27
never wrong, the Old M. | AUDEN 21:1
people are the m. | BURKE 80:23
serve two m. | BIBLE 49:3
their victory but new m. | HAL 160:9
We are the m. now | SHAW 302:28
mastery: constreyned by m. | CHAU 95:25
m. of the thing | HOPK 172:21
mastodons: calling to Aunt like m. | WOD 352:19
masturbation: Don't knock m. | ALLEN 4:14
match: blue spurt of a lighted m. | BROW 76:17
colors dont quite m. your face | ASHF 18:21
m. with shedding tears | SHAK 294:3
Ten to make and the m. to win | NEWB 238:13
matched: m. us with His hour | BROO 73:9
matches: he plays extravagant m. | GILB 152:2
With that stick of m. | MAND 217:9
matchless: m. deed's achieved | SMART 308:14
mate: Made my m. | STEV 317:20
mater: *Stabat M. dolorosa* | JAC 179:3
mathematician: pure m. | JEANS 180:17
mathematics: M. may be defined | RUSS 265:2
M. possesses not only truth | RUSS 265:3
m., subtle | BACON 25:16
no place for ugly m. | HARDY 161:18
Matilda: M. told such Dreadful Lies | BELL 33:8
matrimony: argument in favour of m. | AUST 23:11
critical period in m. | HERB 166:18
joined together in holy M. | BOOK 65:25
respectable as that of m. | TROL 334:14
safest in m. to begin | SHER 305:27
take m. at its lowest | STEV 317:7
matron: Thou sober-suited m. | SHAK 295:12

matter: altering the position of m. | RUSS 265:1
beginning of any great m. | DRAKE 126:10
Dirt is only m. out of place | GRAY 156:18
Does it m.?—losing your sight | SASS 267:9
if it is it doesn't m. | GILB 152:28
m. enough to save one's own | BROW 76:12
More m. for a May morning | SHAK 298:11
More m. with less art | SHAK 275:10
not much dislike the m. | SHAK 271:13
order this m. better in France | STER 315:8
sum of m. remains | BACON 24:4
What is M.?—Never mind | PUNCH 256:10
What is the m. with Mary Jane | MILNE 225:23
wretched m. and lame metre | MILT 228:5
matters: Nobody that m. | MILL 224:21
Matthew: M., Mark | ANON 9:8
mattress: crack it open on a m. | MILL 225:2
maturing: my mind is m. | NASH 237:14
Maud: Come into the garden, M. | TENN 326:28
mausoleum: then as its m. | AMIS 5:2
mawkish: So sweetly m. | POPE 250:15
Max: incomparable M. | SHAW 302:24
maxim: we have got the M. Gun | BELL 33:18
maxima: *mea m. culpa* | MISS 231:11
maximum: m. of temptation | SHAW 301:30
May: darling buds of M. | SHAK 299:12
fayr as is the rose in M. | CHAU 96:11
fressh as is the month of M. | CHAU 95:13
From M. to December | AND 5:12
I'm to be Queen o' the M. | TENN 327:5
maids are M. | SHAK 273:9
M. is a pious fraud | LOW 211:10
M. month flaps | HARDY 162:2
M. mornyng on Maluerne hulles | LANG 201:6
M. without cloud | ARAG 14:21
More matter for a M. morning | SHAK 298:11
snow in M.'s new-fangled | SHAK 284:11
there's an end of M. | HOUS 174:9
may: know not what we m. | SHAK 276:33
maypole: away to the M. hie | ANON 6:19
where's the M. in the Strand | BRAM 71:13
maypoles: I sing of M. | HERR 167:12
maze: Now burgeons every m. | TENN 325:29
mazily: m. murmuring | TENN 327:8
MBE: M.s and your knighthoods | KEAT 190:8
McGregor: Mr M.'s garden | POTT 254:3
me: For you but not for m. | ANON 9:21
queer save thee and m. | OWEN 243:18
meadow: painted m. | ADD 2:1
through a m. of margin | SHER 306:3
meadows: m. green | SHAK 299:17
meal: handful of m. in a barrel | BIBLE 41:35
mean: Down these m. streets | CHAN 94:9
He nothing common did or m. | MARV 220:18
It all depends what you m. by | JOAD 181:15
loves the golden m. | HOR 173:22
no m. city | BIBLE 54:23
no m. of death | SHAK 281:12
poem should not m. but be | MACL 215:9
say what you m. | CARR 91:6
They may not m. to | LARK 201:11
what we m., we say | ARN 16:10
meander: M.'s margent green | MILT 226:10
meaner: m. things are within her | ELIOT 132:5
meaning: faint m. make pretence | DRYD 128:5
Free from all m. | DRYD 127:18
m. doesn't matter | GILB 152:10
plain man in his plain m. | SHAK 289:23
teems with hidden m. | GILB 152:27
within the m. of the Act | ANON 10:3
meanings: two m. packed | CARR 92:2
With words and m. | ELIOT 133:3
meanly: m. wrapped | MILT 227:25
means: best ends by the best m. | HUTC 177:1

means (cont.):
between ends and scarce m.	ROBB 260:15
die beyond my m.	WILDE 350:22
end justifies the m.	BUS 83:16
invisible m. of support	BUCH 77:27
live within our m.	WARD 342:18
m. intensely, and m. good	BROW 75:31
m. just what I choose	CARR 91:26
m. to do ill deeds	SHAK 282:12
mercy of his m.	THOM 330:9
No one m. all he says	ADAMS 1:21
politics by other m.	CLAU 101:16
Private M. is dead	SMITH 309:20
without m. of some change	BURKE 80:10
meant: knew what it m. once	KLOP 198:12
measles: Love iz like the m.	BILL 59:10
Love's like the m.	JERR 181:13
measure: good m., pressed down	BIBLE 52:7
Man is the m. of all things	PROT 255:15
m. of the universe	SHEL 304:20
M. your mind's height	BROW 76:22
Time is the m. of movement	AUCT 20:8
measured: dance is a m. pace	BACON 23:24
m. out my life with coffee	ELIOT 133:27
measures: in short m.	JONS 187:24
M. not men	CANN 89:13
meat: eater came forth m.	BIBLE 41:3
m. in the hall	STEV 317:17
Heaven sends us good m.	GARR 148:11
I have no stomach for such m.	DOBS 122:26
On our m., and on us all	HERR 167:11
Some have m. and cannot eat	BURNS 82:14
taste my m.	HERB 167:3
meats: funeral baked m.	SHAK 274:16
méchant: un m. animal	MOL 232:25
meddle: M. and muddle	DERBY 117:7
medias: in m. res	HOR 173:1
medical: in advance of m. thought	WOD 352:20
M. Crowner's a queer sort	BARH 28:21
medicinal: M. discovery	AYRES 23:15
medicine: M. is my lawful wife	CHEK 96:30
men mistake m. for magic	SZASZ 322:1
miserable have no other m.	SHAK 288:17
mediocre: Some men are born m.	HELL 165:6
Titles distinguish the m.	SHAW 301:31
mediocrity: M. knows nothing higher	DOYLE 126:8
m. thrust upon them	HELL 165:6
meditation: In maiden m.	SHAK 290:24
some happy tone of m.	WORD 355:12
medium: m. is the message	MCL 215:12
medley: m. of extemporanea	PARK 245:4
meed: m. of some melodious tear	MILT 227:1
meek: Blessed are the m.	BIBLE 48:19
meet: hoping we m. now and then	PORT 253:21
make him an help m.	BIBLE 38:20
m. and right so to do	BOOK 65:14
m. 'em on your way down	MIZN 232:11
m., right, and our bounden	BOOK 65:15
merrily in. in heaven	MORE 235:4
never the twain shall m.	KIPL 196:4
Though parallel, can never m.	MARV 220:13
To m. thee in that hollow vale	KING 195:5
We loved, sir—used to m.	BROW 75:21
Yet m. we shall, and part	BUTL 84:21
meeting: Journeys end in lovers m.	SHAK 297:23
m. where it likes	ARN 17:27
méfiez-vous: M.! Les oreilles	ANON 12:15
melancholy: green and yellow m.	SHAK 298:1
Hence, loathèd M.	MILT 226:27
m. god protect thee	SHAK 297:33
m., long, withdrawing roar	ARN 16:11
m. out of a song as a weasel	SHAK 272:20
m. sold a goodly manor	SHAK 271:2
moping m.	MILT 229:31
Naught so sweet as M.	BURT 83:5

melancholy (cont.):
rare recipe for m.	LAMB 200:7
What charm can soothe her m.	GOLD 155:13
meliora: Video m.	OVID 243:15
melodies: Heard m. are sweet	KEATS 191:19
melody: m. lingers on	BERL 36:2
my Luve's like the m.	BURNS 82:20
pretty girl is like a m.	BERL 36:1
smale foweles maken m.	CHAU 95:11
melons: Stumbling on m.	MARV 220:15
Melrose: view fair M. aright	SCOTT 268:10
melt: crown o' the earth doth m.	SHAK 271:25
m. with ruth	MILT 227:17
So let us m.	DONNE 124:15
too solid flesh would m.	SHAK 274:9
melted: m. into air	SHAK 296:10
melting-pot: great M. [America]	ZANG 360:27
member: ACCEPT ME AS A M.	MARX 221:5
members: m. one of another	BIBLE 55:32
membra: Etiam disiecti m.	HOR 174:3
même: plus c'est la m. chose	KARR 190:2
meminisse: haec olim m. iuvabit	VIRG 339:2
memoirs: To write one's m.	PÉT 248:7
memorable: Upon that m. scene	MARV 220:18
memorandum: m. is written to	ACH 1:4
memorial: which have no m.	BIBLE 48:8
whole earth as their m.	PER 248:2
memories: m. are card-indexes	CONN 107:1
M. are hunting horns	APOL 14:11
M. are not shackles	BENN 34:13
memory: brings back a m. ever green	PORT 253:18
Fond M. brings the light	MOORE 234:20
Footfalls echo in the m.	ELIOT 132:26
grand m. for forgetting	STEV 316:26
Illiterate him from your m.	SHER 305:26
m. revealed itself	PROU 255:18
Midnight shakes the m.	ELIOT 134:11
Quick, thy tablets, M.	ARN 16:20
Thanks for the m.	ROBIN 260:19
Vibrates in the m.	SHEL 305:4
women'll stay in a man's m.	KIPL 198:4
men: all m. are created equal	ANON 11:12
bloody m. are like bloody buses	COPE 107:22
boon and a blessing to m.	ANON 11:1
Bring forth m.-children only	SHAK 286:7
fishers of m.	BIBLE 48:18
For fear of little m.	ALL 4:18
great Nature made us m.	LOW 211:6
I see m. as trees, walking	BIBLE 51:22
leaves is a generation of m.	HOMER 170:21
life in my men	WEST 346:21
Measures not m.	CANN 89:13
m. also are burned	HEINE 164:21
m. and malice to breed causes	JONS 187:17
M. are April when they woo	SHAK 273:9
M. are but children of a larger	DRYD 127:25
M. are but gilded loam	SHAK 293:7
m. are created equal	JEFF 180:18
M. are so honest	LERN 205:26
m. at whiles are sober	HOUS 174:10
m. decay	GOLD 154:18
M. Eat Hogs	STEV 316:7
M. have had every advantage	AUST 22:27
M. in great place	BACON 24:27
m. in women do require	BLAKE 61:17
m. may be as positive in error	LOCKE 208:17
m. may come and m. may go	TENN 323:13
M. must be taught	POPE 252:8
M. must endure their going	SHAK 283:30
m. must work, and women	KING 195:16
M., my brothers, men	TENN 326:9
m. of stones	SHAK 284:4
M. seldom make passes	PARK 245:6
M.! The only animal	LAWR 202:20
m. were all asleep	BRID 72:1

men (cont.):

M. were deceivers ever	SHAK 291:19
m. we wanted to marry	STEI 314:25
m. with the muck-rakes	ROOS 262:18
m., women, and clergymen	SMITH 310:4
My m., like satyrs grazing	MARL 218:15
need of a world of m.	BROW 76:23
no way for m. to be	SHAK 273:26
Old m. who never cheated	BETJ 36:21
Philip fought m.	LEE 204:10
power over m.	WOLL 353:11
really much nicer than m.	AMIS 5:6
rejected of m.	BIBLE 46:17
schemes o' mice an' m.	BURNS 82:27
see of m., the more I like dogs	TOUS 333:15
Some faults to make us m.	SHAK 271:27
to m. French	CHAR 95:7
trust themselves with m.	SHAK 296:17
war between m. and women	THUR 332:16
We are the hollow m.	ELIOT 133:17
What m. or gods are these	KEATS 191:18
when m. and mountains meet	BLAKE 61:15
Where Destiny with M.	FITZ 140:12
menace: looks do m. heaven	MARL 219:6
mend: God won't, and we can't m. it	CLOU 102:13
shine, and seek to m.	DONNE 123:10
mendacity: M. is a system	WILL 351:5
mendax: Splendide m.	HOR 173:27
mended: That the first day be m.	WILB 349:13
Mendip: from M.'s sunless caves	MAC 213:24
mene: M., TEKEL, UPHARSIN	BIBLE 47:12
mens: M. sana in corpore sano	JUV 189:13
mental: cease from m. fight	BLAKE 61:12
Mercator: M.'s North Poles	CARR 92:7
merchant: m. seeking pearls	BIBLE 50:6
m. shall hardly keep himself	BIBLE 48:3
merchantman: monarchy is a m.	AMES 4:22
mercies: All thy faithful m. crown	WESL 346:10
For his m. ay endure	MILT 227:9
m. of the wicked are cruel	BIBLE 43:20
Thanks for m. past receive	BUCK 78:3
merciful: Blessed are the m.	BIBLE 48:19
But these were m. men	BIBLE 48:8
God be m. to me a sinner	BIBLE 52:39
merciless: black and m. things	JAMES 179:20
mercury: m. sank in the mouth	AUDEN 20:21
words of M. are harsh	SHAK 284:24
mercy: crowning m.	CROM 112:3
deeds of m.	SHAK 289:27
hand folks over to God's m.	ELIOT 131:19
his m. endureth for ever	BOOK 69:1
Justice with m.	MILT 229:29
Lord, have m. upon us	MISS 231:12
Love is the greatest m.	WILB 349:13
love m.	BIBLE 47:23
majesty is, so is his m.	BIBLE 47:32
M. and truth are met together	BOOK 67:23
M. has a human heart	BLAKE 61:21
M. I asked, mercy I found	CAMD 88:12
M. laboured much for the poor	BUNY 79:8
m. of his means	THOM 330:9
m. upon us miserable sinners	BOOK 64:13
quality of m. is not strained	SHAK 289:26
they shall obtain m.	BIBLE 48:19
To M. Pity Peace and Love	BLAKE 61:20
wideness in God's m.	FABER 138:5
Meredith: M.'s a prose Browning	WILDE 349:22
merit: m. for a bishopric	WEST 346:27
What is m.? The opinion	PALM 244:20
merits: not weighing our m.	BOOK 65:17
Mermaid: Choicer than the M. Tavern	KEATS 191:16
Done at the M.	BEAU 30:18
merrily: m. hent the stile-a	SHAK 298:28
Merrily, m. shall I live now	SHAK 296:14
merriment: m. of parsons	JOHN 185:28

merry: all their wars are m.	CHES 97:20
eat, and to drink, and to be m.	BIBLE 44:18
eat, drink, and be m.	BIBLE 52:18
gone up with a m. noise	BOOK 67:8
M. and tragical	SHAK 291:5
m. as a marriage bell	BYRON 85:2
m. heart goes all the day	SHAK 298:28
m. heart maketh a cheerful	BIBLE 43:25
m. in hall when beards	SHAK 278:31
m. world since the fairies	SELD 269:19
to-night we'll be m.	ANON 6:18
merrygoround: no go the m.	MACN 216:1
mess: Another fine m.	LAUR 202:8
birthright for a m. of potage	BIBLE 39:17
m. we have made of things	ELIOT 132:23
m. with Mister In-between	MERC 223:9
message: medium is the m.	MCL 215:12
take a m. to Albert	DISR 122:22
messages: m. should be delivered	GOLD 155:18
messenger: bisy larke, m. of day	CHAU 95:26
m. of Satan to buffet	BIBLE 55:28
messing: m. about in boats	GRAH 156:5
met: Hail, fellow, well m.	SWIFT 320:17
Ill m. by moonlight	SHAK 290:22
know how first he m. her	THAC 329:23
metal: cold m. of economic theory	SCH 267:26
Here's m. more attractive	SHAK 276:8
métamorphoses: mois des m.	ARAG 14:21
metaphysic: As m. wit can fly	BUTL 83:23
metaphysics: M. is the finding	BRAD 71:7
meteor: cloud-encircled m.	SHEL 303:23
method: yet there is m. in't	SHAK 275:12
Methodist: morals of a M.	GILB 152:26
methods: You know my m.	DOYLE 126:2
methought: M. I saw my late espousèd	MILT 230:24
métier: c'est son m.	HEINE 165:3
Mon m. et mon art c'est vivre	MONT 233:16
metre: God and man and m.	LOCK 209:3
wretched matter and lame m.	MILT 228:5
mewling: M. and puking	SHAK 272:25
Mexico: Poor M.	DIAZ 117:16
Mexique Bay: Echo beyond the M.	MARV 220:11
mezzo: m. del cammin	DANTE 113:17
mice: Like little m., stole in	SUCK 318:21
schemes o' m. an' men	BURNS 82:27
Michael: M. and his angels	BIBLE 57:31
Michelangelo: designs by M.	TWAIN 336:2
M. left a proof	YEATS 360:5
Talking of M.	ELIOT 133:25
microbe: M. is so very small	BELL 33:20
microscopic: m. eye	POPE 252:14
mid-air: you in m.	SOND 311:7
middenpit: workshop, larder, m.	BUNT 78:14
middle: by the m. way	OVID 243:13
grant me, Heaven, a m. state	MALL 216:21
In politics the m. way	ADAMS 1:23
mine was the m. state	DEFOE 115:14
sits in the m. and knows	FROST 146:20
stay in the m. of the road	BEVAN 38:5
Tenants of life's m. state	COWP 110:16
middle age: companions for m.	BACON 25:2
enchantments of the M.	ARN 18:2
enchantments of the M.	BEER 32:10
middle class: flagrantly m.	WAUGH 344:2
M. was quite prepared	BELL 33:7
Philistines proper, or m.	ARN 17:26
We of the sinking m.	ORW 242:14
middle classes: bow, ye lower m.	GILB 151:9
Middlesex: acre in M.	MAC 213:11
rural M. again	BETJ 37:7
midge: lightly skims the m.	BETJ 37:1
midnight: a-bed after m.	SHAK 297:22
blackest M. born	MILT 226:27
came upon the m. clear	SEARS 269:11

midnight (*cont.*):

cease upon the m. with no pain	KEATS 192:3
chimes at m.	SHAK 278:24
Frost at M.	COL 103:18
Holding hands at m.	GERS 150:8
iron tongue of m.	SHAK 291:9
m. never come	MARL 218:12
m. oil	QUAR 257:2
M. shakes the memory	ELIOT 134:11
mock the m. bell	SHAK 271:19
sighed upon a m. pillow	SHAK 272:18
still her woes at m. rise	LYLY 212:17
'Tis the year's m.	DONNE 124:7
Upon the m. hours	KEATS 192:8
visions before m.	BROW 74:23

midst: m. of life we are in death — BOOK 66:7
there am I in the m. of them — BIBLE 50:18
midsummer: high M. pomps — ARN 17:19
Why, this is very m. madness — SHAK 298:9
midway: M. along the path of our life — DANTE 113:17
midwife: She is the fairies' m. — SHAK 294:24
mid-winter: In the bleak m. — ROSS 263:2
mieux: *Le m. est l'ennemi du bien* — VOLT 340:15
tout est au m. — VOLT 340:10
might: Britons alone use 'M.' — WAUGH 343:28
do it with thy m. — BIBLE 44:19
Exceeds man's m. — SHAK 297:3
It m. have been — HARTE 163:12
It m. have been — WHIT 349:1
Lord of all power and m. — BOOK 64:25
our m. lessens — ANON 11:5
spirit of counsel and m. — BIBLE 45:18
might-have-been: my name is M. — ROSS 263:8
mightier: make thee m. yet — BENS 34:20
pen is m. than the sword — BULW 78:11
mightiest: 'Tis m. in the mightiest — SHAK 289:26
mighty: how are the m. fallen — BIBLE 41:20
Marlowe's m. line — JONS 187:26
M. and dreadful — DONNE 123:8
m. from their seats — BIBLE 51:29
m. lak' a rose — STAN 314:11
m. roar of London's traffic — ANON 9:23
m. Victor's brow — KELLY 193:19
rushing m. wind — BIBLE 54:8
thou m. man of valour — BIBLE 40:35
migrations: all our m. — GOLD 155:12
mild: draw'd m. — DICK 119:4
his m. and magnificent eye — BROW 76:14
miles: draw but twenty m. a day — MARL 219:14
Draw out our m. — SHAK 293:17
go but thirty m. a day — SHAK 278:21
m. to go before I sleep — FROST 146:23
militant: first m. lowbrow — BERL 36:5
state of Christ's Church m. — BOOK 65:7
militarism: M. is fetish worship — TAWN 322:18
military: hold the m. mind — TUCH 335:7
matter to entrust to m. men — CLEM 101:21
order and m. discipline — ANON 6:22
When the m. man approaches — SHAW 301:23
milk: drunk the m. of Paradise — COL 104:1
find a trout in the m. — THOR 332:5
flowing with m. and honey — BIBLE 39:32
Gin was mother's m. to her — SHAW 302:18
gone to m. the bull — JOHN 184:12
m. and the yoghurt — TRIL 334:10
m. comes frozen home — SHAK 284:23
m. my ewes and weep — SHAK 299:1
m. of human kindness — SHAK 285:15
M.'s leap toward immortality — FAD 138:9
m. the cow of the world — WILB 349:10
m. were scarce out of him — SHAK 297:20
One end is moo, the other, m. — NASH 232:5
putting m. into babies — CHUR 99:21
sincere m. of the word — BIBLE 57:7
take my m. for gall — SHAK 285:18

milk (*cont.*):

With m. and honey blessed — NEALE 237:22
milk-soup: M. men call — PATM 246:18
mill: at the m. with slaves — MILT 230:10
More water glideth by the m. — SHAK 296:26
old m. by the stream — ARMS 15:24
millenium: calico m. — CARL 90:25
miller: hackneyed jokes from M. — BYRON 86:31
M. of Dee — BICK 58:24
Than wots the m. — SHAK 296:26
million: Fifty m. Frenchmen — GUIN 159:9
m. million spermatozoa — HUXL 177:11
millionaire: M. That is my religion — SHAW 301:9
old-fashioned m. — FISH 140:1
silk hat on a Bradford m. — ELIOT 134:29
millionaires: m. love a baked apple — FIRB 139:21
millions: M. long for immortality — ERTZ 137:15
m. of strange shadows — SHAK 299:18
m. of surprises — HERB 167:7
m. of the mouthless dead — SORL 311:16
tear-wrung m. — BYRON 84:25
We mortal m. live *alone* — ARN 17:22
What m. died — CAMP 88:20
mills: dark Satanic m. — BLAKE 61:12
m. of God grind slowly — LONG 209:24
millstone: m. were hanged about — BIBLE 50:16
millstones: Turned to m. — SHEL 304:5
Milton: malt does more than M. — HOUS 175:4
M., a name to resound for ages — TENN 327:7
M., Madam, was a genius — JOHN 186:4
M.'s the prince of poets — BYRON 86:15
M.! thou shouldst be living — WORD 355:11
M. was for us — BROW 76:14
M. wrote in fetters — BLAKE 60:25
mute inglorious M. — GRAY 157:9
mimsy: m. were the borogoves — CARR 91:15
mince: They dined on m. — LEAR 203:13
mind: beauty is the m. diseased — BYRON 85:9
body filled and vacant m. — SHAK 279:16
Cast your m. on other days — YEATS 360:7
concentrates his m. — JOHN 185:14
conjunction of the m. — MARV 220:13
could not make up his m. — OLIV 241:8
cutting edge of the m. — BRON 72:9
dagger of the m. — SHAK 286:10
distressed, in m., body — BOOK 64:19
fool uttereth all his m. — BIBLE 44:2
Georgia on my m. — GORR 155:23
He first damages his m. — ANON 13:8
His m. moves upon silence — YEATS 359:15
how little the m. is actually — JOHN 185:2
human m. in ruins — DAV 114:16
If I am out of my m. — BELL 34:4
index of a feeling m. — CRAB 110:29
it's all in the m. — WOLFE 353:5
Keep violence in the m. — ALD 3:16
know the m. of God — HAWK 163:18
many men and knew their m. — HOMER 171:1
marble index of a m. — WORD 356:10
Measure your m.'s height — BROW 76:22
m. a mirror is of heavenly — SOUT 312:7
m. and hand went together — COND 165:11
m. does not make us soft — PER 248:1
m. has mountains — HOPK 172:10
M. has no sex — WOLL 353:10
M. in its purest play — WILB 349:11
m. is a very opal — SHAK 297:33
m. is clouded with a doubt — TENN 324:22
m. is its own place — MILT 228:12
m. is not a bed to be made — AGATE 3:6
m.'s construction in the face — SHAK 285:14
m. serene for contemplation — GAY 149:3
m. that of Lord Beaverbrook — ATTL 19:12
m. watches itself — CAMUS 89:4
m. which contemplates them — HUME 176:9

mind (cont.):

m. which reveres details	LEWIS 206:19
minister to a m. diseased	SHAK 288:2
my m. forbids to crave	DYER 129:16
my m. is maturing late	NASH 237:14
my m.'s unsworn	EUR 137:22
My m. to me a kingdom is	DYER 129:16
noblest frailty of the m.	SHAD 270:18
nothing great but m.	HAM 160:18
not in my perfect m.	SHAK 283:29
no way out of the m.	PLATH 249:13
one dead level ev'ry m.	POPE 250:19
ordinary m. on an ordinary day	WOOLF 353:21
padlock—on her m.	PRIOR 255:9
Reading is to the m.	STEE 314:17
robs the m. of all its powers	BURKE 80:7
satisfied with her lover's m.	TROL 334:19
sentences until reeled the m.	GIBBS 150:18
sex in the m.	LAWR 202:19
shocks the m. of a child	PAINE 244:7
sound m. in a sound body	JUV 189:13
To change your m.	AUR 22:11
true genius is a m. of large	JOHN 182:18
what a noble m. is here	SHAK 276:2
What is M.?—No matter	PUNCH 256:10

minds: comfortable m.

comfortable m.	CUMM 113:5
fairly developed m.	FORS 143:15
great empire and little m.	BURKE 80:5
marriage of true m.	SHAK 300:8
M. are like parachutes	DEWAR 117:13
M. like beds always made up	WILL 351:7
m. made better by their	ELIOT 132:17
m. of my generation destroyed	GINS 153:3
pervert climbs into the m.	BRON 72:11
spur of all great m.	CHAP 94:20
Thou m. me o' departed joys	BURNS 81:28

mine: but m. own

but m. own	SHAK 273:11
If they are m. or no	HOUS 174:14
m. own familiar friend	BOOK 67:12
she is m. for life	SPARK 312:12
'Twas m., 'tis his	SHAK 292:11

miner: Dwelt a m., Forty-niner	MONT 234:2
mineral: animal, and m.	GILB 152:23
miners: m. poured to war	MAC 213:24
Mineworkers: Union of M.	MACM 215:19
mingle: In one spirit meet and m.	SHEL 304:3
minion: morning's m.	HOPK 172:20
minister: help the M. that meddles	MELB 222:21
m. to a mind diseased	SHAK 288:2
Yes, M.	CROS 112:12
ministering: m. angel shall my sister	SHAK 277:10
m. angel thou	SCOTT 268:22
ministers: Angels and m. of grace	SHAK 274:27
grim Geneva m.	AYT 23:16
little errands for the M.	GILB 151:6
my actions are my m.'	CHAR 95:2
passion-wingèd M. of thought	SHEL 303:5
you murdering m.	SHAK 285:18
ministries: made many m.	BAG 26:7
ministry: marriage than a m.	BAG 26:11
m. of all the talents	ANON 9:9
performs its secret m.	COL 103:18
Minnehaha: M., Laughing Water	LONG 210:2
minnows: Triton of the m.	SHAK 283:16
minor: change from major to m.	PORT 253:19
minorities: M. are almost always in the right	
	SMITH 310:10
minstrel: M. Boy to the war is gone	MOORE 234:16
wandering m. I	GILB 151:17
minute: do it in m. particulars	BLAKE 60:19
his first m., after noon	DONNE 124:6
leave in a m. and a huff	KALM 189:21
Then the good m. goes	BROW 77:21
We cannot cage the m.	MACN 216:10
minutes: famous for fifteen m.	WARH 342:20

minutes (cont.):

five m. too late all my life	COWL 109:18
m. hasten to their end	SHAK 299:21
round the earth in forty m.	SHAK 290:25
take care of m.	CHES 97:8
Mirabeau: Sous le pont M.	APOL 14:12
miracle: he prays for a m.	TURG 335:15
m. of our age	CAREW 89:18
m. of rare device	COL 103:24
Miranda: remember an inn, M.	BELL 34:1
mirk: It was m., mirk night	BALL 28:8
mirror: courteous eyes oppose a m.	JONS 187:7
live alone and smash his m.	ANON 12:10
Man's mind a m. is	SOUT 312:7
m. cracked from side	TENN 326:3
novel is a m. which passes	STEN 315:3
mirrored: Lie m. on her sea	HODG 169:14
mirrors: as m. are lonely	AUDEN 21:9
M. and fatherhood	BORG 69:23
m. of the sea are strewn	FLEC 141:19
mirth: buys a many m.	SHAK 299:8
earth must borrow its m.	WILC 349:14
Far from all resort of m.	MILT 226:25
m. hath present laughter	SHAK 297:23
time for m. and laughter	ADE 3:1
misbeliever: You call me m.	SHAK 289:5
mischief: All punishment is m.	BENT 35:2
For Satan finds some m. still	WATTS 343:6
hand to execute any m.	CLAR 101:10
misdoings: sorry for these our m.	BOOK 65:11
miserable: Me m.! which way shall I fly	MILT 229:6
mercy upon us m. sinners	BOOK 64:13
M. comforters are ye all	BIBLE 42:34
m. have no other medicine	SHAK 288:17
no more m. human being	JAMES 180:8
miserere: m. nobis	MISS 231:19
miseries: in shallows and in m.	SHAK 282:1
misery: certain amount of m.	LOWE 211:1
dwell on guilt and m.	AUST 22:21
fatal dumb-show of our m.	DRAY 126:18
finds himself, loses his m.	ARN 17:13
full of m.	BOOK 66:6
great kick at m.	LAWR 202:25
Man hands on m. to man	LARK 201:18
mine affliction and my m.	BIBLE 47:1
M. acquaints a man	SHAK 296:5
m. of manilla folders	ROET 261:14
result m.	DICK 118:12
vale of m.	BOOK 67:21
misfortune: m. of our best friends	LA R 202:2
misfortunes: m. can befall a boy	MAUG 222:12
m. of mankind	GIBB 150:11
strong enough to bear the m.	LA R 201:21
tableau of crimes and m.	VOLT 340:20
they make m. more bitter	BACON 25:6
misgivings: Blank m. of a creature	WORD 355:22
mislead: one to m. the public	ASQ 19:4
mislike: M. me not	SHAK 289:6
misquote: enough of learning to m.	BYRON 86:31
miss: little m., dressed	HUME 176:7
missa: Ite m. est	MISS 231:20
missed: [Hitler] m. the bus	CHAM 94:3
who never would be m.	GILB 151:19
Woman much m.	HARDY 162:15
missing: M. so much and so much	CORN 108:6
missionary: I would eat a m.	WILB 349:6
mis-spent: Redeem thy m. time	KEN 193:21
mist: broke into a m. with bells	BROW 76:25
sophistry, and m.	BYRON 85:21
m. in my face	BROW 77:2
mistake: Man is Nature's sole m.	GILB 152:25
m. in the translation	VANB 336:23
mistaken: possible you may be m.	CROM 112:2
mistakes: everyone gives to their m.	WILDE 350:2
learned from the m. of the past	TAYL 323:1

mistakes (*cont.*):

man who makes no m.	PHEL 248:11
worst m. that can be made	HEIS 165:4

mistress: acquaintance, next a m.

	CHEK 96:28
Art is a jealous m.	EMER 136:19
crowd a m. or a friend	SHEL 303:15
literature is my m.	CHEK 96:30
m. in my own	KIPL 196:25
m. of the Earl of Craven	WILS 351:16
m. of the months	SWIN 320:28
m. should be like	WYCH 358:4
m. some rich anger shows	KEATS 191:26
No casual m., but a wife	TENN 325:13
O m. mine	SHAK 297:23
Riches, the worst m.	BACON 24:6
So court a m., she denies you	JONS 187:22

mistresses: No, I shall have m.

	GEOR 149:21
or your Lordship's m.	WILK 350:26
Wives are young men's m.	BACON 25:2

mists: low the m. of evening lie

	BETJ 37:1
season of m. and mellow	KEATS 192:14

misty: seyn of a ful m. morwe

	CHAU 96:16

misunderstood: To be great is to be m.

	EMER 136:25
worse lie than a truth m.	JAMES 180:10

misused: m. words

	SPEN 312:18

Mithridates: M., he died old

	HOUS 175:5

mix: M. a little foolishness

	HOR 174:1

Moab: M. is my wash-pot

	BOOK 67:14

moan: of doves

	TENN 328:8
not paid with m.	THOM 331:7
virgin-choir to make delicious m.	KEATS 192:8

moanday: m., tearsday, wailsday

	JOYCE 188:4

moaning: no m. of the bar

	TENN 323:18
Though the harbour bar be m.	KING 195:16

moat: m. defensive to a house

	SHAK 293:16

moated: at the m. grange

	SHAK 288:22
Upon the lonely m. grange	TENN 326:22

mob: do what the m. do

	DICK 119:28
Our supreme governors, the m.	WALP 341:16

mock: How my achievements m. me

	SHAK 297:7
m. on Voltaire Rousseau	BLAKE 61:13
m. the air with idle state	GRAY 157:1

mocked: God is not m.

	BIBLE 55:30

mocker: Wine is a m.

	BIBLE 43:31

mockingbird: Out of the m.'s throat

	WHIT 348:12
to kill a m.	LEE 204:6

mocks: M. married men

	SHAK 284:21

model: m. of a modern Major-General

	GILB 152:23

models: Rules and m. destroy

	HAZL 164:5

moderation: astonished at my own m.

	CLIVE 102:6
easier than perfect m.	AUG 22:3
m. in everything	HOR 174:2
m. in the pursuit of justice	GOLD 155:15
m. is a sort of treason	BURKE 79:22
No term of m. takes place	BACON 24:7

modern: m. Major-General

	GILB 152:23
strange disease of m. life	ARN 17:11

modest: M.? My word, no

	REED 258:20

modesty: Enough for m.

	BUCH 77:28

modified: M. rapture

	GILB 151:24

mois: *m. des floraisons*

	ARAG 14:21

mole: like a bastion's m.

	SMART 308:10

molecules: without understanding m.

	CRICK 111:19

moll: King's M. Reno'd

	ANON 8:17

Molly Stark: or M.'s a widow

	STARK 314:12

Moloch: right of that great M.

	MEYER 224:4

mome: m. raths outgrabe

	CARR 91:15

moment: Every m. dies a man

	BABB 23:19
Every m. dies a man	TENN 328:26
m. of my greatness flicker	ELIOT 133:29

momentary: Beauty is m.

	STEV 316:11
pleasure is m.	CHES 97:18

moments: O m. big as years

	KEATS 191:1
Wagner has lovely m.	ROSS 263:11

monarch: hereditary m. was insane

	BAG 26:8

monarch (*cont.*):

merry m., scandalous	ROCH 261:8
m. better than his crown	SHAK 289:26
m. of all I survey	COWP 110:18
m. of the road	SWANN 141:6

monarchs: m. must obey

	DRYD 128:4
Perplexes m.	MILT 228:17

monarchy: m. is a merchantman

	AMES 4:22
universal m. of wit	CAREW 89:19

monastic: m. faces

	CLOU 102:9

Monday: going to do on M.

	YBAR 358:11

money: barrel of m.

	WOODS 353:19
blessing that m. cannot buy	WALT 342:14
corrupted by m.	GREE 158:4
draining m. from the pockets	SMITH 309:1
given his m. upon usury	BOOK 66:14
goä wheer m. is	TENN 327:9
her voice is full of m.	FITZ 140:21
hired the m.	COOL 107:20
licence to print m.	THOM 332:4
love of m. is the root of all evil	BIBLE 56:19
m. and a room of her own	WOOLF 354:1
m. and large armies	ANOU 14:4
m. answereth all things	BIBLE 44:23
m. can't buy me love	LENN 205:11
M. couldn't buy friends	MILL 225:11
M. doesn't talk, it swears	DYLAN 130:3
M. gives me pleasure all	BELL 33:13
M. has no smell	VESP 338:3
M. is coined liberty	DOST 125:5
M. is like a sixth sense	MAUG 222:11
M. is like muck	BACON 25:10
M. is none of the wheels	HUME 176:6
M. is the sinews of love	FARQ 138:18
M. speaks sense in a language	BEHN 32:23
M. was exactly like sex	BALD 27:3
natural interest of m.	MAC 213:10
No m., no service	RAC 257:17
not spending m. alone	EIS 131:14
only interested in m.	SHAW 302:25
pleasant it is to have m.	CLOU 102:14
pretty to see what m.	PEPYS 247:20
private parts, his m.	BUTL 84:18
rub up against m.	RUNY 264:8
sinews of war, unlimited m.	CIC 100:29
somehow, make m.	HOR 173:6
time is m.	FRAN 145:8
uses his m. as votes	SAM 266:11
way the m. goes	MAND 217:8
We haven't got the m.	RUTH 265:9
we have to borrer the m.	WARD 342:18
When you have m., it's sex	DONL 123:2
wrote, except for m.	JOHN 185:10
Yes, they have more m.	FITZ 140:20
You pays your m.	PUNCH 256:6

moneybag: Aristocracy of the M.

	CARL 90:15

moneybags: dream of m.

	SHAK 289:9

moneys: m. are for values

	BACON 23:23

mongrels: continent of energetic m.

	FISH 139:22

monk: devil a m. he'd be

	MOTT 236:3
m. who shook the world	MONT 233:25

monkey: descent from a m.

	WILB 349:7
m. when the organ grinder	BEVAN 37:21
You mustn't m. with the Creed	BELL 33:15

monkeys: Cats and m.

	JAMES 179:22

monogamous: Woman m.

	JAMES 180:11

monogamy: M. is the same

	ANON 6:11

monopoly: m. profits is a quiet life

	HICKS 168:10
m. stage of capitalism	LENIN 205:2

monotony: bleats articulate m.

	STEP 315:4

monster: green-eyed m.

	SHAK 292:12
pity this busy m., manunkind	CUMM 112:20

monsters: dream of reason produces m.

	GOYA 156:1

monstrous: m. anger of the guns

	OWEN 243:21
m. animal, a husband	FIEL 139:12

monstrous (*cont.*):

m. carbuncle	CHAR 95:8
M. carbuncles	SPEN 312:22
M. Regiment of Women	KNOX 198:16
monstruosity: m. in love	SHAK 297:2
Montezuma: who imprisoned M.	MAC 213:13
month: A little m.	SHAK 274:12
April is the cruellest m.	ELIOT 134:18
August is a wicked m.	O'BR 240:18
fressh as is the m. of May	CHAU 95:13
m. of tension	LESS 206:3
months: fourteen m. the most idle	GIBB 150:13
mother of the m. in meadow	SWIN 321:1
monument: If you seek a m.	ANON 13:23
m. more lasting than bronze	HOR 173:28
m. of the insufficiency	JOHN 183:7
m. sticks like a fishbone	LOW 211:13
only m. the asphalt road	ELIOT 134:13
patience on a m.	SHAK 298:1
sonnet is a moment's m.	ROSS 263:7
monuments: nor the gilded m.	SHAK 299:19
moo: One end is m.	NASH 237:10
moocow: there was a m.	JOYCE 188:6
moon: Beneath the visiting m.	SHAK 271:25
by the light of the m.	LEAR 203:13
cold fruitless m.	SHAK 290:12
Daughter of the M., Nokomis	LONG 210:1
from the pale-faced m.	SHAK 277:27
hornèd m.	COL 104:10
How white the ever-constant m.	WASH 342:24
melodious cats under the m.	HUXL 177:4
minions of the m.	SHAK 277:22
m. be still as bright	BYRON 87:8
m. in lonely alleys	CRANE 110:32
m. is in the seventh house	RADO 257:18
m.'s an arrant thief	SHAK 296:23
m. shines bright	SHAK 289:31
m. shone bright on Mrs Porter	ELIOT 134:26
m. under her feet	BIBLE 57:30
m. winks	SHAK 292:25
neither the m. by night	BOOK 68:26
Old Devil M.	HARB 161:13
O more than m.	DONNE 124:16
only a paper m.	HARB 161:12
Only you beneath the m.	PORT 253:25
owl does to the m. complain	GRAY 157:5
Shaped like the crescent-m.	WORD 356:3
ship, an isle, a sickle m.	FLEC 141:19
silent as the m.	MILT 230:12
silver apples of the m.	YEATS 360:1
Slowly, silently, now the m.	DE L 116:22
swear not by the m.	SHAK 294:33
waning m. was haunted	COL 103:23
when the m. shall rise	WOTT 357:16
Wi' the auld m. in her arm	BALL 28:5
With how sad steps, O M.	SIDN 306:18
moonlight: How sweet the m. sleeps	SHAK 290:1
Ill met by m.	SHAK 290:22
m. and music and love	BERL 35:22
M. behind you	COW 109:7
visit it by the pale m.	SCOTT 268:10
Watch for me by m.	NOYES 240:14
moonlit: Knocking on the m. door	DE L 116:18
moons: m. shall wax and wane	WATTS 343:12
Reason has m.	HODG 169:14
moonshine: find out m.	SHAK 290:30
Transcendental m.	CARL 90:19
moon-struck: m. madness	MILT 229:31
moorish: It is m., and wild	BRON 72:15
moppsikon: M. Floppsikon bear	LEAR 203:18
mops: seven maids with seven m.	CARR 91:21
moral: Debasing the m. currency	ELIOT 132:7
Englishman thinks he is m.	SHAW 301:21
kind of m. eunuch	SHEL 304:14
m. as soon as one is unhappy	PROU 255:19

moral (*cont.*):

m. crusade or it is nothing	WILS 351:13
m. Gower	CHAU 96:23
m., grave	BACON 25:16
M. indignation is jealousy	WELLS 346:1
m. is (it is indeed!)	BELL 33:15
m. law within me	KANT 189:22
m. or an immoral book	WILDE 350:3
m. virtues at the highest	CHES 97:14
perfectly moral till all are m.	SPEN 312:21
point a m., or adorn a tale	JOHN 183:14
moralist: vital problem for the m.	RUSS 264:21
morality: cities for our best m.	AUST 22:19
Goodbye, m.	HERB 166:12
Johnson's m. was as English	HAWT 163:19
imperative may be called M.	KANT 189:23
Master-m. and slave-m.	NIET 239:22
m. for morality's sake	COUS 108:17
m. in any given time	WHIT 348:3
M. in the novel	LAWR 202:12
M. is a private luxury	ADAMS 1:8
M. is the herd-instinct	NIET 239:20
m. touched by emotion	ARN 18:8
periodical fits of m.	MAC 213:9
some people talk of m.	EDG 130:16
morals: Food comes first, then m.	BREC 71:19
teach the m. of a whore	JOHN 184:1
with the m. of a Methodist	GILB 152:26
more: art m. than they	TENN 324:23
believing m. and more in less	YATES 358:10
condemn a little m.	MAJOR 216:19
days that are no m.	TENN 327:22
For, I have m.	DONNE 123:17
knows m. and m. about less	BUTL 83:21
m. equal than others	ORW 241:23
m. Piglet wasn't there	MILNE 225:14
m. than she ever did	KALM 189:20
m. than somewhat	RUNY 264:6
m. things in heaven and earth	SHAK 275:3
M. will mean worse	AMIS 5:1
No m. I will abroad	HERB 166:22
No m. o' that, my lord	SHAK 287:29
O m. than moon	DONNE 124:16
Please, sir, I want some m.	DICK 119:18
take m. than nothing	CARR 91:8
you get no m. of me	DRAY 126:16
mores: O tempora, O m.!	CIC 100:25
mori: pro patria m.	HOR 173:26
moriar: Non omnis m.	HOR 173:29
Moriarty: M. of mathematical	DOYLE 125:20
morituri: m. te salutant	ANON 13:12
morn: From m. to night	ROSS 263:5
m., in russet mantle	SHAK 274:3
still m. went out with sandals	MILT 227:19
Son of M. in weary Night	BLAKE 60:15
morning: beauty of the m.	WORD 354:15
Come, lovely M.	DAV 114:21
disasters in his m. face	GOLD 154:23
Early one m.	ANON 6:27
evening and the m.	BIBLE 38:14
Full many a glorious m.	SHAK 299:17
glorious m. for America	ADAMS 2:6
glut thy sorrow on a m. rose	KEATS 191:26
grey dawn of the m. after	ADE 3:1
joy cometh in the m.	BOOK 66:22
Lucifer, son of the m.	BIBLE 45:22
methinks I scent the m.	SHAK 275:1
m. again in America	RINEY 260:12
m. cometh	BIBLE 45:23
M. has broken	FARJ 138:12
M. in the bowl of night	FITZ 140:4
m. light creaks down again	SITW 307:16
M.'s at seven	BROW 76:28
m.'s minion	HOPK 172:20
m. well-aired	BRUM 77:23

morning (cont.):

Never glad confident m.	BROW 76:15
Never m. wore to evening	TENN 324:25
New every m.	KEBLE 193:16
they take you in the m.	BALD 27:4
thy princes eat in the m.	BIBLE 44:22
To pay thy m. sacrifice	KEN 193:20
When m. gilds the skies	CASW 92:19
wings of the m.	BOOK 69:6

mornings: literary m. with its hoot — AUDEN 20:25
Many bright m. — VAUG 337:13

Mornington: present of M. Crescent — HARG 162:21

Morocco: we're M. bound — BURKE 81:15

moron: consumer isn't a m. — OGIL 241:2
See the happy m. — ANON 10:9

morrow: no thought for the m. — BIBLE 49:5

mortal: m. thing so to immortalize — SPEN 313:4

grief itself be m.	SHEL 303:8
chances of this m. life	BOOK 65:18
desperately m.	SHAK 288:24
every tatter in its m. dress	YEATS 359:21
shuffled off this m. coil	SHAK 275:25
M., guilty, but to me	AUDEN 20:28
We m. millions live alone	ARN 17:22

mortality: Insensible of m. — SHAK 288:24
it smells of m. — SHAK 283:24
m. touches the heart — VIRG 339:4
nothing serious in m. — SHAK 286:26
Old m. — BROW 74:3

mortals: Composing m. — AUDEN 20:10
Lord, what fools these m. be — SHAK 290:32
not in m. to command success — ADD 2:13

mortar: Lies are the m. — WELLS 345:20

mortis: Timor m. conturbat me — DUNB 129:8

morts: Il n'y a pas de m. — MAET 216:15

mortuus: Passer m. est — CAT 93:1

Moscow: Do not march on M. — MONT 233:23
M.: those syllables can start — PUSH 256:23

Moses: Go down, M. — ANON 11:19
M. sent to spy out — BIBLE 40:16

moss: miles of golden m. — AUDEN 20:19

mossy: Happy field or m. cavern — KEATS 191:16
m. stones about and about — WORD 354:10

mote: m. that is in thy brother's — BIBLE 49:7

motes: m. that people the sunbeams — MILT 226:23

moth: Both m. and flame — ROET 261:16
desire of the m. for the star — SHEL 305:5
How, like a m., the simple maid — GAY 149:2
m. and rust doth corrupt — BIBLE 49:1
m. of peace — SHAK 292:2

mother: artist man and m. woman — SHAW 301:18
As is the m., so is her daughter — BIBLE 47:4
Behold thy m. — BIBLE 54:4
Care of his M. — MILNE 225:20
church for his m. — CYPR 113:12
Dead! and never called me m. — WOOD 353:17
either my father or my m. — STER 315:12
gave her m. forty whacks — ANON 8:22
Gentle Child of gentle M. — DEAR 115:7
heaviness of his m. — BIBLE 43:16
Honour thy father and thy m. — BIBLE 40:8
I arose a m. in Israel — BIBLE 40:31
I have no pain, dear m., now — FARM 138:13
Man may not marry his M. — BOOK 69:19
man who hates his m. — BENN 34:19
m. and I should have lived — GAY 149:3
M. and lover of men, the sea — SWIN 321:18
m. bore me in the southern — BLAKE 61:24
M., give me the sun — IBSEN 178:4
m., make my bed — BALL 27:13
m. of arts, of warfare — DU B 128:32
m. of battles — HUSS 176:22
M. OF HARLOTS — BIBLE 58:2
m. of months — SWIN 321:1
m. of Parliaments — BRIG 72:5

mother (cont.):

m. of sciences	BACON 25:27
M. of the Free	BENS 34:20
m.'s little helper	RICH 179:5
m.'s sake the child was dear	COL 104:20
M. to dozens	HERB 166:13
My m. bids me bind my hair	HUNT 176:19
My m. groaned	BLAKE 62:3
my m. taught me as a boy	BERR 36:13
really affectionate m.	MAUG 222:12
There was their Dacian m.	BYRON 85:10
thou hast murdered thy m.	MAL 217:1
thy dear m. any courtesy	SHAK 273:22
Where a m. laid her baby	ALEX 4:4

mothers: Come m. and fathers — DYLAN 130:3
m. of large families — BELL 33:2
women become like their m. — WILDE 349:19

mother-wits: rhyming m. — MARL 219:4

motion: Between the m. and the act — ELIOT 133:19
Devoid of sense and m. — MILT 228:24
dreadful thing and the first m. — SHAK 281:3
gentle m. with the deep — DAV 114:22
God ordered m. — VAUG 337:3
next to the perpetual m. — DICK 120:3
No m. has she now — WORD 356:25
oil which renders the m. — HUME 176:6
Poetry in m. — ANTH 190:5
poetry of m. — GRAH 156:6
their m. in one sphere — SHAK 278:13
This sensible warm m. — SHAK 288:21
time's eternal m. — FORD 143:11
uniform m. in a right line — NEWT 239:3

motions: two weeping m. — CRAS 111:14
secret m. of things — BACON 25:26
stings and m. of the sense — SHAK 288:11

motive: joint and m. of her body — SHAK 297:9

motley: M.'s the only wear — SHAK 272:23
m. to the view — SHAK 300:6

motorcycle: Art of M. Maintenance — PIRS 249:2

motto: that is my m. — MARQ 219:19

mottoes: m. on sundials — POUND 254:15

mould: broke the m. — ARIO 15:8

moulded: men are m. out of faults — SHAK 288:26

mouldering: in many a m. heap — GRAY 157:6

mount: m. up with wings as eagles — BIBLE 46:13
rejected the Sermon on the M. — BRAD 71:10

mountain: every m. and hill — BIBLE 46:9
from yonder m. height — TENN 328:6
He watches from his m. walls — TENN 323:21
If the m. will not come — BACON 24:16
in all my holy m. — BIBLE 45:20
In a m. greenery — HART 163:10
Over all the m. tops is peace — GOET 154:12
river jumps over the m. — AUDEN 20:11
sun looked over the m.'s rim — BROW 76:23
tiptoe on the misty m. tops — SHAK 295:18
Up the airy m. — ALL 4:18

mountains: Among the m. by the winter sea — TENN 324:17
From the m. to the prairies — BERL 35:21
M. are the beginning and the end — RUSK 264:13
m. look on Marathon — BYRON 86:14
m. skipped like rams — BOOK 68:16
M. will go into labour — HOR 172:27
one is of the sea, one of the m. — WORD 357:6
that I could remove m. — BIBLE 55:11
when men and m. meet — BLAKE 61:15

mountain-tops: m. that freeze — SHAK 280:16
Flatter the m. — SHAK 299:17

mountebank: m. and his zany — WALP 341:24

mourir: Partir c'est m. un peu — HAR 161:9

mourn: Blessed are they that m. — BIBLE 48:19
don't m. for me never — ANON 7:17
Makes countless thousands m. — BURNS 82:16
m. for me when I am dead — SHAK 299:23

mourn (cont.):	
m. with ever-returning spring	WHIT 348:24
M., you powers of Charm	CAT 93:1
now can never m.	SHEL 303:11
time to m., and a time to dance	BIBLE 44:12
mourned: Would have m. longer	SHAK 274:12
mournful: M. ever weeping	BLAKE 60:16
mourning: Don't waste any time in m.	HILL 168:13
great m., Rachel weeping	BIBLE 48:11
I'm in m. for my life	CHEK 96:25
M. becomes Electra	O'NEI 241:12
widow bird sat m.	SHEL 303:14
mouse: killing of a m. on Sunday	BRAT 71:16
little m. will be born	HOR 172:27
Not a m. shall disturb	SHAK 291:10
not even a m.	MOORE 234:3
mouse-trap: or make a better m.	EMER 137:3
moustache: didn't wax his m.	KIPL 198:3
mouth: Englishman to open his m.	SHAW 302:16
God be in my m.	ANON 7:11
in the cannon's m.	SHAK 272:26
keeping your m. shut	EINS 131:10
Keep your m. shut	ANON 12:15
m. had been used as a latrine	AMIS 5:2
m. of the Lord hath spoken	BIBLE 46:9
m. of very babes and sucklings	BOOK 66:10
proceedeth out of the m. of God	BIBLE 48:16
purple-stainèd m.	KEATS 191:30
sank in the m. of the dying	AUDEN 20:21
spew thee out of my m.	BIBLE 57:22
mouthful: gold filling in a m.	OSB 242:26
mouths: she made m. in a glass	SHAK 283:8
stuffed their m. with gold	BEVAN 38:2
They have m., and speak not	BOOK 68:18
movable: Paris is a m. feast	HEM 165:13
move: Afloat. We m.	CLOU 102:12
But it does m.	GAL 147:16
feel the earth m.	HEM 165:12
great affair is to m.	STEV 316:27
I will m. the earth	ARCH 15:3
m., and have our being	BIBLE 54:21
M. him into the sun	OWEN 243:24
moved: I do not like being m.	CLOU 102:8
m. by what is not unusual	ELIOT 132:11
m. to folly by a noise	LAWR 202:28
We shall not be m.	ANON 11:15
movement: measure of m.	AUCT 20:8
movers: m. and shakers	O'SH 243:1
moves: If it m., salute it	ANON 8:4
movies: M. should have a beginning	GOD 153:19
moving: m. accident is not my trade	WORD 355:1
m. finger writes	FITZ 140:14
m. toyshop of their heart	POPE 253:3
Mozart: Children are given M.	SCHN 267:23
MPs: dull M. in close proximity	GILB 151:13
much: doesn't seem m. for them to be	COMP 106:3
Missing so m. and so much	CORN 108:6
M. as you said you were	HARDY 162:9
M. have I seen and known	TENN 328:21
m. to be done, little to be known	JOHN 182:27
So little done, so m. to do	RHOD 259:12
So many worlds, so m. to do	TENN 325:14
so m. owed by so many	CHUR 99:15
You that are just so m.	BROW 77:20
muck: Money is like m.	BACON 25:10
Sing 'em m.	MELBA 222:19
muckrake: with a m. in his hand	BUNY 79:6
muckrakes: men with the m.	ROOS 262:18
mud: cover the universe with m.	FORS 143:18
Longing to be back in the m.	AUG 21:21
M.! Mud! Glorious mud	SWANN 141:4
M.'s sister, not himself	HOUS 174:7
on the people builds on m.	MACH 215:2
muddle: beginning, a m.	LARK 201:20
manage somehow to m. through	BRIG 72:4

muddle (cont.):	
Meddle and m.	DERBY 117:7
muddy: celibacy a m. horsepond	PEAC 246:24
m. ecstasies of beer	CRAB 110:21
M., ill-seeming, thick	SHAK 295:30
m. understandings	BURKE 80:15
muero: Muero porque no m.	JOHN 181:16
mulatto: Grape is my m. mother	HUGH 175:22
mule: m. of politics	DISR 121:27
mules: m. of politics	POWER 255:4
multiplication: M. is vexation	ANON 9:11
multiply: Be fruitful, and m.	BIBLE 38:17
multitude: cover the m. of sins	BIBLE 57:11
m. is always in the wrong	DILL 120:24
multitudes: I contain m.	WHIT 348:21
m. in the valley of decision	BIBLE 47:21
Pestilence-stricken m.	SHEL 304:6
Weeping, weeping m.	ELIOT 132:22
mum: fuck you up, your m. and dad	LARK 201:17
oafish louts remember M.	BETJ 36:17
mumbled: few m. cakes	HUNT 176:18
munch: So m. on	BROW 76:27
mundi: cito transit gloria m.	THOM 329:28
Sic transit gloria m.	ANON 13:22
muove: Eppur si m.	GAL 147:16
murder: I met M. on the way	SHEL 304:4
Killing no m. briefly discourst	SEXBY 270:14
love and m. will out	CONG 106:7
Macbeth does m. sleep	SHAK 286:15
m. an infant in its cradle	BLAKE 61:10
m. by the law	YOUNG 360:15
m. cannot be hid long	SHAK 289:8
m. for the truth	ADLER 3:2
M. most foul	SHAK 274:31
M. one of the fine arts	DE Q 117:5
m. respectable	ORW 242:15
M.'s out of tune	SHAK 293:2
M. wol out	CHAU 95:29
One m. made a villain	PORT 253:26
Television has brought back m.	HITC 168:20
Thou shalt do no m.	BOOK 65:4
To m. thousands	YOUNG 360:15
Vanity, like m., will out	COWL 109:19
We m. to dissect	WORD 357:5
murdered: m. reputations	CONG 106:15
thou hast m. thy mother	MAL 217:1
murderers: m. take the first step	KARR 190:1
murdering: you m. ministers	SHAK 285:18
murmur: creeping m.	SHAK 279:7
live m. of a summer's day	ARN 17:5
Seem to m. sweet and low	ARMS 15:24
murmuring: brooks of Eden mazily m.	TENN 327:8
m. of innumerable bees	TENN 328:8
murmurs: In the m., in the pauses	SOND 311:6
m. of self-will	BODE 62:16
Murray: slain the Earl of M.	BALL 27:14
muscle: motion of a m.	WORD 354:13
muscles: M. better and nerves more	CUMM 113:4
muscular: His Christianity was m.	DISR 121:29
muse: M. of fire	SHAK 278:33
tenth M., who now governs	TROL 334:20
whose m. on dromedary trots	COL 104:2
mushroom: I am ... a m.	FORD 143:9
Life is too short to stuff a m.	CONR 107:13
meet a m. rich civilian	BYRON 87:13
music: All m. is folk music	ARMS 16:3
Architecture is frozen m.	SCH 267:17
brave m. of a distant drum	FITZ 140:7
Classic m. is th'kind	HUBB 175:16
danceth without m.	HERB 167:10
Darling of the m. halls	SMITH 309:8
day the m. died	MCL 215:7
Fading in m.	SHAK 289:19
finds its food in m.	LILLO 207:3
Fled is that m.	KEATS 192:7

music (*cont.*):

how potent cheap m. is	COW 109:10
If m. be the food of love	SHAK 297:13
I shall be made thy m.	DONNE 123:16
Let's face the m. and dance	BERL 35:22
let the sounds of m. creep	SHAK 290:1
Like m. on my heart	COL 104:16
make the m. mute	TENN 324:13
man that hath no m.	SHAK 290:3
most civilized m.	UST 336:15
M. and women I cannot	PEPYS 247:19
M. begins to atrophy when	POUND 254:22
M. has charms to soothe	CONG 106:11
m. in its roar	BYRON 85:12
m. in the air	ELGAR 131:18
M. is feeling, then, not sound	STEV 316:10
m. is the brandy of the damned	SHAW 301:19
m. of its trees at dawn	ARN 16:21
m. of men's lives	SHAK 294:11
m. of the Gospel leads	FABER 138:4
m. sent up to God	BROW 75:8
m. that excels is the sound	FISH 139:26
M. that gentlier on the spirit	TENN 326:19
m. the only sensual pleasure	JOHN 186:10
M., when soft voices die	SHEL 305:4
not for the doctrine, but the m.	POPE 252:3
O body swayed to m.	YEATS 358:14
seduction of martial m.	BURN 81:18
softest m. to attending ears	SHAK 295:3
step to the m. which he hears	THOR 332:12
still, sad m. of humanity	WORD 355:10
thou hast thy m. too	KEATS 192:15
thy chosen m., Liberty	WORD 357:6
towards the condition of m.	PATER 246:14
uproar's your only m.	KEATS 193:3
We are the m. makers	O'SH 243:1
What passion cannot M. raise	DRYD 128:17

musical: m. Malcolm Sargent — BEEC 32:2

m. as is Apollo's lute	MILT 226:15
So m. a discord	SHAK 291:2

musk: m. carnations break — ARN 17:19

m. of the rose is blown	TENN 326:28

musk-rose: coming in. — KEATS 192:2

musk-roses: With sweet m. — SHAK 290:26

must: m. a word to be addressed — ELIZ 135:10

we forget because we m.	ARN 16:9

mustard: like to a grain of m. — BIBLE 50:5

mutable: *Varium et m. semper* — VIRG 339:9

mute: M. and magnificent — DRYD 128:20

mutilate: Do not fold, spindle or m. — ANON 6:26

mutiny: Rome to rise and m. — SHAK 281:26

my-lorded: m. him — THAC 329:15

myriad: There died a m. — POUND 254:19

myrrh: frankincense, and m. — BIBLE 48:1

m. is my wellbeloved	BIBLE 44:30

myrtle: m. and ivy — BYRON 87:10

m. and turkey part of it	AUST 22:20

myrtles: Ye m. brown — MILT 227:10

myself: I celebrate m. — WHIT 348:16

I do not know m.	GOET 154:14
In awe of such a thing as I m.	SHAK 280:26
When I give I give m.	WHIT 348:20

mysteries: m. in divinity — BROW 74:10

mysterious: God moves in a m. way — COWP 109:25

mystery: Behold, I shew you a m. — BIBLE 55:21

lose myself in a m.	BROW 74:11

M., BABYLON THE GREAT — BIBLE 58:2

m. inside an enigma	CHUR 99:10
m. of the cross shines	FORT 144:5
Now, my tongue, the m. telling	THOM 330:3
pluck out the heart of my m.	SHAK 276:13

mystic: m., wonderful — TENN 324:3

myths: Science must begin with m. — POPP 253:16

N

nag: gait of a shuffling n. — SHAK 278:4

nagging: N. is the repetition — SUMM 319:5

nail: for want of a n. — FRAN 145:12

n. my pictures together	SCHW 268:2
walks away with the n.	LAWR 202:11

nails: n. he'll dig them up again — WEBS 344:26

nineteen hundred and forty n.	SITW 307:19
relatively clean finger n.	MORT 235:21

naïve: n. domestic Burgundy — THUR 332:17

n. forgive and forget	SZASZ 321:24

naked: Half n., loving, natural — BYRON 86:8

In walking n.	YEATS 358:17
left me n. to mine enemies	SHAK 280:21
n. into the conference chamber	BEVAN 38:1
stark n. truth	CLEL 101:20
starving hysterical n.	GINS 153:3
With n. foot, stalking	WYATT 358:2

nakedness: not in utter n. — WORD 355:20

name: at the n. of Jesus — BIBLE 56:5

cometh in the N. of the Lord	BOOK 68:23
Corsair's n. to other times	BYRON 85:19
coward shame distain his n.	BURNS 82:15
deed without a n.	SHAK 287:19
Democracy is the n.	CAIL 142:2
gathered together in my n.	BIBLE 50:18
ghost of a great n.	LUCAN 211:24
glory in the n. of Briton	GEOR 149:23
Good n. in man and woman	SHAK 292:11
his n. shall be called	BIBLE 45:16
I have forgotten your n.	SWIN 321:14
In the n. of God	CROM 112:4
In the N. of the Father	MISS 231:10
leave a living n. behind	WEBS 344:13
Let men not n. it to you	SHAK 292:28
local habitation and a n.	SHAK 291:4
love that dare not speak its n.	DOUG 125:6
my n. is Jowett	BEEC 32:6
my wife, and my n.	SURT 319:11
n. great in story	BYRON 87:10
n. liveth for evermore	BIBLE 48:8
n. of the Lord thy God	BIBLE 40:6
n. to all succeeding ages	DRYD 127:5
n. to the reverberate hills	SHAK 297:21
n. was writ in water	KEATS 193:15
nothing of a n.	BYRON 85:15
number of his n.	BIBLE 57:32
provides us with n. and nation	BUNT 78:14
spared the n.	SWIFT 320:24
thy n. give glory	BIBLE 58:12
thy N. give the praise	BOOK 68:17
What's in a n.	SHAK 294:31
worth an age without a n.	MORD 234:21
yet can't quite n.	LARK 201:16

nameless: n., unremembered — WORD 355:8

names: confused things with their n. — SART 267:5

gaunt n. that never get fat	BENÉT 34:8
honour doth forget men's n.	SHAK 282:3
n. in many a musèd rhyme	KEATS 192:3
N. that should be on every	CALV 88:8

naming: n. of parts — REED 258:15

Nan: change Kate into N. — BLAKE 60:15

Napoleon: N. of crime — DOYLE 125:20

narrative: unconvincing n. — GILB 152:5

narrow: n. is the way — BIBLE 49:13

O make it saft and n.	BALL 27:13

Nassau: Can Stuart or N. go — PRIOR 255:10

nastiest: n. thing in the nicest way — GOLD 154:16

nasty: Man is a n. creature — MOL 232:25

n., brutish and short	HOBB 169:10
Something n. in the woodshed	GIBB 150:17

nation: against the voice of a n. — RUSS 265:5

nation (*cont.*):

boundary of the march of a n.	PARN 245:23
haughty n. proud in arms	MILT 226:6
holy n., a peculiar people	BIBLE 57:8
Licensed build that n.'s fate	BLAKE 60:9
London: a n., not a city	DISR 122:5
n. is not governed	BURKE 80:1
n. of dancers, singers	EQUI 137:13
n. of shopkeepers	ADAMS 2:7
n. of shopkeepers	NAP 237:7
n. of shopkeepers	SMITH 308:23
n. shall not lift up sword	BIBLE 45:5
n. shall rise against nation	BIBLE 50:34
N. shall speak peace unto	REND 259:5
N. spoke to a Nation	KIPL 196:25
n. talking to itself	MILL 225:6
Once to every man and n.	LOW 211:7
one-third of a n. ill-housed	ROOS 262:11
places the n. at his service	POMP 250:12
provides us with name and n.	BUNT 78:14
this continent a new n.	LINC 207:8
top n.	SELL 270:5
what our N. stands for	BETJ 37:4
whole n. perish not	BIBLE 53:34
national: N. Debt is a very Good	SELL 270:4
nationalism: N. is a silly cock	ALD 3:15
nationless: tribeless, and n.	SHEL 304:22
nations: day of small n.	CHAM 93:23
fierce contending n.	ADD 2:19
friendship with all n.	JEFF 180:19
great n. have always acted	KUBR 199:7
happiest n. have no history	ELIOT 132:14
hating all other n.	GASK 148:20
healing of the n.	BIBLE 58:7
languages are the pedigree of n.	JOHN 183:18
n. have never learned	HEGEL 164:18
N. have their infancy	BOL 63:4
N. touch at their summits	BAG 26:9
Other n. use 'force'	WAUGH 343:28
task to rule n.	VIRG 339:16
teaching n. how to live	MILT 231:5
To belong to other n.	GILB 152:21
two different n.	FOST 144:8
Two n.	DISR 122:6
native: Fast by their n. shore	COWP 109:28
not more n. to the heart	SHAK 274:4
This is my own, my n. land	SCOTT 268:12
natural: He wants the n. touch	SHAK 287:23
I do it more n.	SHAK 297:24
N. rights is simple nonsense	BENT 34:22
N. Selection	DARW 114:3
N. selection has no vision	DAWK 115:2
n. to die as to be born	BACON 24:22
twice as n.	CARR 92:4
nature: Beauty is N.'s brag	MILT 226:20
drive out n. with a pitchfork	HOR 173:11
Eye N.'s walks	POPE 252:11
heartless, witless n.	HOUS 174:14
God and n. do nothing in vain	AUCT 20:5
God, or in other words, N.	SPIN 313:22
Good painters imitate n.	CERV 93:20
great N. made us men	LOW 211:6
great Secretary of N.	WALT 342:16
horridly cruel works of n.	DARW 114:5
I do fear thy n.	SHAK 285:15
in N. were inconstancy	COWL 109:15
interpreter of n.	JOHN 183:3
Is N. felt	WORD 354:18
knowledge of n. is destined	HOLB 170:9
Man is N.'s sole mistake	GILB 152:25
man the less, but n. more	BYRON 85:12
mere copier of n.	REYN 259:9
My n. is subdued	SHAK 300:7
N. abhors a vacuum	RAB 257:11
N. does nothing without purpose	ARIS 15:20

N. from her seat	MILT 229:26
n. gave me at my birth	COL 103:15
N. hadn't counted on	TURG 335:11
N. in awe to him	MILT 227:25
N. in you stands	SHAK 283:3
N. is creeping up	WHIS 347:12
N. is not a temple	TURG 335:12
n. is the art of God	BROW 74:14
n. is tugging at every	EMER 136:18
n. itselfe cant endure	FLEM 141:22
N. made him, and then broke	ARIO 15:8
N. never makes enny blunders	BILL 59:11
n. of God is a circle	ANON 9:13
N., red in tooth and claw	TENN 325:12
N.'s decorations glisten	SMART 308:9
N.'s laws lay hid in night	POPE 251:26
n.'s way of telling you to slow	ANON 6:25
n. there are neither rewards	ING 178:16
N. wears one universal grin	FIEL 139:13
next to N., Art	LAND 200:22
one touch of n.	SHAK 297:6
paid the debt of n.	FABY 138:6
poet interpreted n.	GIR 153:6
priketh hem in hir corages	CHAU 95:11
Progress…a part of n.	SPEN 312:19
ruined piece of n.	SHAK 283:24
state that n. hath provided	LOCKE 208:19
Tired N.'s sweet restorer	YOUNG 360:17
True wit is N. to advantage	POPE 252:1
With N., to out-do the life	JONS 187:20
naught: n. for your comfort	CHES 97:19
Say not the struggle n.	CLOU 102:22
naughtiness: n. of thine heart	BIBLE 41:17
naughty: good deed in a n. world	SHAK 290:4
His former n. life	BOOK 65:1
naval: n. tradition	CHUR 100:6
navies: n. grappling	TENN 326:11
navy: n. under the good Providence	CHAR 95:1
put at the head of the N.	CARS 92:11
Ruler of the Queen's N.	GILB 152:18
nay: your n., nay	BIBLE 57:5
Nazareth: good thing come out of N.	BIBLE 53:14
Neaera: tangles of N.'s hair	MILT 227:14
near: come not n. to me	BIBLE 46:25
He seems so n. and yet so far	TENN 325:21
n. me when my light is low	TENN 325:7
She is n., she is near	TENN 327:1
nearer: N. and nearer draws	AING 3:9
n. bloody	SHAK 286:27
n. God's Heart in a garden	GURN 159:10
N., my God, to thee	ADAMS 2:8
n. the Church the further	ANDR 5:16
n. you are to God	WOTT 357:21
nearest: those who are n. to him	MILL 224:18
To catch the n. way	SHAK 285:15
nearly: I was n. kept waiting	LOUI 210:13
neat: You look n.	COLL 105:6
necessarily: It ain't n. so	GERS 168:5
necessary: government is a n. evil	PAINE 244:9
little visible delight, but n.	BRON 72:17
Make yourself n. to someone	EMER 136:17
n. evil	BRAD 71:8
n. not to change	FALK 138:11
superfluous, a very n. thing	VOLT 340:22
necessities: n. call out great virtues	ADAMS 1:7
will dispense with its n.	MOTL 236:2
necessity: always at the door of n.	DEFOE 115:12
Cruel n.	CROM 112:1
grim N.	SHAK 294:6
I do not see the n.	ARG 15:7
N. has no law	PUBL 256:2
N. hath no law	CROM 112:6
N. is the plea	PITT 249:7
N. makes an honest man a knave	DEFOE 115:16

necessity (cont.):
N. never made a good bargain — FRAN 145:10
no virtue like n. — SHAK 293:13
Progress not an accident, but a n. — SPEN 312:19
neck: n. God made for other use — HOUS 174:19
Some chicken! Some n.! — CHUR 99:17
necklace: matches, with our n. — MAND 217:9
nectar: To comprehend a n. — DICK 120:13
Work without hope draws n. — COL 104:22
nectarine: n., and curious peach — MARV 220:15
need: and all ye n. to know — KEATS 191:24
enough for everyone's n. — BUCH 77:30
face of total n. — BURR 82:31
n. of a world of men — BROW 76:23
people whenever we n. them — CAIL 142:2
Requires sorest n. — DICK 120:13
thy n. is greater than mine — SIDN 306:30
Will you still n. me — MCC 205:17
needle: my hand a n. better fits — BRAD 71:12
through the eye of a n. — BIBLE 50:22
Why are the n. and the pen — LEWIS 206:14
needs: each according to his n. — BAK 27:1
each according to his n. — MARX 221:9
negative: Elim-my-nate the n. — MERC 223:9
N. Capability — KEATS 193:2
n. of which America is the — MCC 214:10
neglect: n. may breed mischief — FRAN 145:12
Such sweet n. more taketh me — JONS 187:6
neglected: to have his all n. — JOHN 183:25
negotiate: never n. out of fear — KENN 194:4
Negro: N. could never hope — DAVIS 114:23
neiges: où sont les n. d'antan? — VILL 338:20
neighbour: I am a n. — SHAK 289:6
love thy n. as thyself — BIBLE 40:14
our n.'s house is on fire — BURKE 80:9
policy of the good n. — ROOS 262:10
shalt not covet thy n.'s wife — BIBLE 40:9
neighbourhood: n. of voluntary spies — AUST 22:25
neighbours: Good fences make good n. — FROST 146:16
make sport for our n. — AUST 23:6
to have good n. — ELIZ 135:5
upon his n. to do his work — BAUD 30:8
what is happening to our n. — CHAM 93:24
will the n. say, 'He was a man — HARDY 162:2
neither: n. death, nor life — BIBLE 54:42
Nell: Pretty witty N. — PEPYS 247:17
Nellie Dean: I love you, N. — ARMS 15:24
Nelly: Let not poor N. starve — CHAR 95:4
Nelson: N. touch — NELS 238:2
nemo: N. me impune lacessit — ANON 13:17
nerve: after the n. has been — ROWL 263:21
Anatomised in every n. — JONS 187:7
nerves: and the n. prick — TENN 325:7
Muscles better and n. more — CUMM 113:4
nervos: N. belli — CIC 100:29
nervous: n. and terse, but limited — DOYLE 126:7
nervousness: only n. or death — LEB 203:24
nessun: N. dorma — ADAMI 1:6
nest: n. of singing birds — JOHN 183:22
her soft and chilly n. — KEATS 190:19
now leaves his wat'ry n. — D'AV 114:10
swallow a n. — BOOK 67:20
nests: Birds in their little n. agree — WATTS 343:8
birds of the air have n. — BIBLE 49:19
built their n. in my beard — LEAR 203:17
nets: n. to catch the wind — WEBS 344:13
nettle: Out of this n., danger — SHAK 277:30
Tender-handed stroke a n. — HILL 168:11
nettles: n. and brambles — BIBLE 46:3
neurosis: n. is a secret — TYNAN 336:9
N. is the way of avoiding — TILL 332:21
neutral: stood apart, studiously n. — WILS 351:19
neutrality: Armed n. — WILS 351:20
Just for a word 'n.' — BETH 36:15
n. of an impartial judge — BURKE 81:12

never: always, by God, n. — RICH 260:5
I n. use a big, big D — GILB 152:16
N. do to-day what you can — PUNCH 256:8
N. explain — FISH 139:24
N. explain — HUBB 175:13
N. glad confident morning — BROW 76:15
N. Had It So Good — MACM 215:15
N. in the field of human conflict — CHUR 99:15
N. in the way — CHAR 95:5
N. knowingly undersold — LEWIS 206:16
N., never, never, never, never — SHAK 284:6
N. the time and the place — BROW 76:20
N. to have lived is best — YEATS 359:5
She who has n. loved — GAY 149:8
than n. to have been loved — CONG 106:16
Than n. to have fought at all — CLOU 102:21
This will n. do — JEFF 181:2
We n. closed — VAN D 336:25
What, n.? No, never! — GILB 152:15
nevermore: Quoth the Raven, 'N.' — POE 250:7
new: dull in a n. way — JOHN 184:28
find something n. — VOLT 340:11
make all things n. — BIBLE 58:5
make a n. acquaintance — JOHN 186:7
MAKE IT N. — POUND 254:10
my n. found land — DONNE 123:6
n. deal for the American — ROOS 262:8
N. every morning is the love — KEBLE 193:16
n. heaven and a new earth — BIBLE 58:4
n. heaven, new earth — SHAK 271:4
new heavens and a n. earth — BIBLE 46:26
n. man may be raised up — BOOK 65:19
n. men, strange faces — TENN 324:19
n. thing under the sun — BIBLE 44:8
n. wine into old bottles — BIBLE 49:24
old lamps for n. — ARAB 14:16
piping songs for ever n. — KEATS 191:20
ring in the n. — TENN 325:23
shock of the n. — DUNL 129:9
sing unto the Lord a n. song — BOOK 68:3
something n. out of Africa — PLINY 249:23
so quite n. a thing — CUMM 113:4
time for making n. enemies — VOLT 341:3
we'll find the n. — BAUD 30:6
new-born: use of a n. child — FRAN 145:17
Newcastle: No more coals to N. — GEOR 149:26
newcomer: O blithe n. — WORD 357:7
newest: oldest sins the n. kind — SHAK 278:28
newness: walk in n. of life — BIBLE 54:34
news: All the n. that's fit to print — OCHS 241:1
bitter n. to hear — CORY 108:13
good n. from a far country — BIBLE 43:37
good n. yet to hear — CHES 98:3
Ill n. hath wings — DRAY 126:15
Literature is n. that STAYS n. — POUND 254:23
man bites a dog, that is n. — BOG 62:19
n. and Prince of Peace — FLET 142:8
only n. until he's read it — WAUGH 343:26
other to get the n. to you — TWAIN 335:25
passion is the love of n. — CRAB 110:25
What n. on the Rialto — SHAK 288:31
New South Wales: govern N. — BELL 33:7
newspaper: good n. is a nation — MILL 225:6
newspapers: I read the n. avidly — BEVAN 38:6
It's the n. I can't stand — STOP 318:2
newt: Eye of n., and toe of frog — SHAK 287:16
Newton: another N., a new Donne — HUXL 177:11
Let N. be — POPE 251:26
make us as N. was — AUDEN 21:5
N.'s particles of light — BLAKE 61:14
Single vision and N.'s sleep — BLAKE 60:23
statue stood of N. — WORD 356:10
New World: N. into existence — CANN 89:14
New York: California to the N. Island — GUTH 159:12

New York (cont.):

N. swallowing the tonnage | MILL 225:5
New Zealand: traveller from N. | MAC 213:15
next: n. to Nature, Art | LAND 200:22
n. to of course god america i | CUMM 112:17
What n., what next | LOW 211:15
nexus: sole n. of man to man | CARL 90:4
Niagara: wouldn't live under N. | CARL 90:24
nice: In n. clean faces | BARH 28:18
N. guys. Finish last | DUR 129:13
n. to people on your way up | MIZN 232:11
N. work if you can get it | GERS 150:8
Too n. for a statesman | GOLD 155:2
nicens: n. little boy named baby | JOYCE 188:6
nicest: nastiest thing in the n. | GOLD 154:16
niche: got your n. in creation | HALL 160:14
Nicodemus: Wise N. saw | VAUG 337:4
nigger: Woman is the n. of the world | ONO 241:13
night: ain't a fit n. out for man | FIEL 139:17
as a watch in the n. | BOOK 67:25
black bat, n. | TENN 326:28
blue of the n. meets the gold | CROS 112:9
borrower of the n. | SHAK 287:1
breath of the n.-wind | ARN 16:11
City is of N. | THOM 332:1
Closed his eyes in endless n. | GRAY 157:17
Come, civil n. | SHAK 295:12
Come, seeling n. | SHAK 287:6
Come, thick n. | SHAK 285:19
come, thou day in n. | SHAK 295:13
dangers of this n. | BOOK 64:12
dark n. of the soul | FITZ 140:22
day brought back my n. | MILT 230:25
Dear N.! this world's defeat | VAUG 337:5
dog in the n.-time | DOYLE 125:21
drowned with us in endless n. | HERR 167:14
dusky n. rides down the sky | FIEL 139:5
evening mild, then silent n. | MILT 229:11
Every n. and alle | BALL 27:20
first minute, after noon, is n. | DONNE 124:6
gentle into that good n. | THOM 330:7
genuine n. admits no ray | DRYD 128:5
go bump in the n. | ANON 7:7
hangs upon the cheek of n. | SHAK 294:26
hard day's n. | LENN 205:14
haunts you n. and day | BERL 36:1
honeyed middle of the n. | KEATS 190:17
ignorant armies clash by n. | ARN 16:12
Illness is the n.-side of life | SONT 311:10
infant crying in the n. | TENN 325:9
in weary N.'s decline | BLAKE 60:15
I pass, like n., from land | COL 104:17
know his God by n. | VAUG 337:4
lightning in the collied n. | SHAK 290:14
long day's journey into n. | O'NEI 241:11
love-performing n. | SHAK 295:11
mirk, mirk n. | BALL 28:8
moonless n. in the small town | THOM 330:16
Morning in the bowl of n. | FITZ 140:4
n. after tonight | AMIS 5:8
N. and day, you are the one | PORT 253:25
n. before Christmas | MOORE 234:3
n. do penance for a day | WORD 356:11
n. has a thousand eyes | BOUR 70:12
n. hath a thousand eyes | LYLY 212:18
n. in a pillar of fire | BIBLE 39:39
n. in her silver shoon | DE L 116:22
n. is like a lovely tune | WASH 342:24
N. Mail crossing the Border | AUDEN 21:4
N. makes no difference | HERR 167:18
n. methinks is but the daylight | SHAK 290:6
n. of the long knives | HITL 168:21
n. of this immortal day | SHEL 304:24
n. of tropical splendour | PORT 253:18
n. of tyranny had descended | MURR 236:13

night (cont.):

N.'s candles are burnt | SHAK 295:18
n. that wins | SWIN 321:2
n. we went to Birmingham | CHES 98:2
only for a n. and away | WYCH 358:4
reign of Chaos and old N. | MILT 228:16
returned on the previous n. | BULL 78:7
rung n.'s yawning peal | SHAK 287:5
Sable-vested N. | MILT 228:32
Ships that pass in the n. | LONG 210:3
sleep one ever-during n. | CAMP 89:2
So late into the n. | BYRON 87:8
sound of revelry by n. | BYRON 85:2
Spirit of N. | SHEL 305:12
such a n. as this | SHAK 289:31
tender is the n. | KEATS 192:1
terror by n. | BOOK 67:29
then it's n. once more | BECK 31:15
This is the n. | SHAK 292:27
Through the n. of doubt | BAR 29:2
tire the n. in thought | QUAR 257:2
'Tis with us perpetual n. | JONS 187:15
touch of Harry in the n. | SHAK 279:8
under the lonely n. | VIRG 339:14
upon the n.'s starred face | KEATS 192:20
very witching time of n. | SHAK 276:15
vile contagion of the n. | SHAK 281:6
Watchman, what of the n. | BIBLE 45:23
world's last n. | DONNE 123:13
What hath n. to do with sleep | MILT 226:8
When n. darkens the streets | MILT 228:15
wide womb of uncreated n. | MILT 228:24
You meaner beauties of the n. | WOTT 357:16
night-gown: down stairs in his n. | MILL 225:9
nightingale: brown bright n. | SWIN 321:1
n., and not the lark | SHAK 295:17
n. does sit so late | MARV 220:20
O 'tis the ravished n. | LYLY 212:17
nightingales: n. are singing | ELIOT 134:17
nightmare: History is a n. | JOYCE 188:14
Our long national n. is over | FORD 143:4
nights: chequer-board of n. and days | FITZ 140:12
down the n. and down the days | THOM 331:8
nihil: Aut Caesar, aut n. | BORG 69:25
N. est sine ratione | LEIB 204:15
Vox et praeterea n. | ANON 14:3
nil: N. admirari | HOR 173:10
N. carborundum illegitimi | ANON 9:15
N. desperandum | HOR 173:19
N. posse creari | LUCR 212:3
Nile: allegory on the banks of the N. | SHER 305:30
pour the waters of the N. | CARR 91:3
Where's my serpent of old N. | SHAK 271:11
Nimrod: N. the mighty hunter | BIBLE 39:11
nine: N. bean rows will I have | YEATS 359:12
ninety: heave the n. and nine | BIBLE 52:26
Nineveh: one with N., and Tyre | KIPL 197:3
ninny: compared to Handel's a mere n. | BYROM 84:24
Niobe: Like N., all tears | SHAK 274:12
nip: I'll n. him in the bud | ROCHE 261:1
nipping: n. and an eager air | SHAK 274:25
nipple: plucked my n. | SHAK 286:6
nisi: N. Dominus custodierit | BIBLE 58:13
nix: Sticks n. hick pix | ANON 10:15
no: citizen of n. mean city | BIBLE 54:23
everlasting N. | CARL 90:22
I am also called N.-more | ROSS 263:8
land of the omnipotent N. | BOLD 63:2
man who says n. | CAMUS 89:7
n. go the merrygoround | MACN 216:1
N.! I am not Prince Hamlet | ELIOT 134:1
N. money, no service | RAC 257:17
N. sun—no moon | HOOD 171:9
Noah: but one poor N. | HUXL 177:11
God gave N. the rainbow sign | ANON 7:12

Noah (*cont.*):
N. he often said — CHES 98:7
nobility: ancient n. — BACON 25:4
N. of birth commonly abateth — BACON 25:5
nobis: *Non n., Domine* — BIBLE 58:12
noble: Eternally n., historically fair — LERN 205:26
fredome is a n. thing — BARB 28:16
My love's a n. madness — DRYD 127:24
n. and nude and antique — SWIN 321:6
n. Living, and the n. Dead — WORD 356:15
n. mind is here o'erthrown — SHAK 276:2
n. savage — DRYD 127:26
Some work of n. note — TENN 328:23
What's brave, what's n. — SHAK 271:26
nobleman: underrated N. — GILB 151:4
nobleness: N. walks in our ways — BROO 72:21
nobler: n. in the mind to suffer — SHAK 275:25
nobles: their n. with links of iron — BOOK 69:11
noblesse: *N. oblige* — LEVIS 206:9
noblest: honest God is the n. work — ING 178:15
honest man's the n. work — POPE 252:22
n. Roman of them all — SHAK 282:2
nobly: n. Cape Saint Vincent — BROW 76:3
nobody: business of n. — MAC 213:3
gave a war & N. came — GINS 153:2
give a war and n. will come — SAND 266:16
n. comes, nobody goes — BECK 31:12
noctis: *lente currite n. equi* — MARL 218:13
Nod: dwelt in the land of N. — BIBLE 39:6
Old N., the shepherd, goes — DE L 116:21
nods: even excellent Homer n. — HOR 173:3
N., and becks — MILT 227:1
noise: gone up with a merry n. — BOOK 67:8
happy n. to hear — HOUS 174:20
melt, and make no n. — DONNE 124:15
moved to folly by a n. — LAWR 202:28
n. at one end and no sense — KNOX 198:20
noiseless n. among the leaves — KEATS 191:5
n., my dear! And the people — ANON 9:16
n. of battle rolled — TENN 324:17
noiseless: n. tenor of their way — GRAY 157:10
noises: isle is full of n. — SHAK 296:9
noli: *N. me tangere* — BIBLE 58:22
nominative: her n. case — O'KEE 241:5
nomine: *In N. Patris* — MISS 231:10
non: *N. nobis, Domine* — BIBLE 58:12
non-being: avoiding n. — TILL 332:21
non-combatant: no fury like a n. — MONT 233:7
non-commissioned: n. man — KIPL 196:10
none: answer came there n. — SCOTT 268:6
answer made it n. — SHAK 274:18
malice toward n. — LINC 207:7
N. but the brave — DRYD 127:19
N. shall sleep — ADAMI 1:6
nonsense: damned n. will I put — RICH 260:5
n., and learning — GOLD 155:8
n. upon stilts — BENT 34:22
noon: amid the blaze of n. — MILT 230:11
first minute, after n., is night — DONNE 124:6
returned before n. — SAIN 265:14
noon-day: destroyeth in the n. — BOOK 67:29
noose: turret in a n. of light — FITZ 140:4
Norfan: I'm a N., both sides — WELLS 345:18
Norfolk: bear him up the N. sky — BETJ 36:20
Very flat, N. — COW 109:9
normal: N. is the good smile — SHAF 270:19
Thank God we're n. — OSB 242:19
type of the n. and easy — JAMES 180:1
Norman: simple faith than N. blood — TENN 325:33
north: triumph from the n. — MAC 213:25
true and tender is the N. — TENN 327:24
unripened beauties of the n. — ADD 2:14
North African: egg of a N. Empire — GLAD 153:11
northern: constant as the n. star — SHAK 281:9
Glorious the n. lights astream — SMART 308:13

northern (*cont.*):
Lucasta that bright n. star — LOV 210:18
N. reticence — HEAN 164:11
prim prater of the n. race — CHUR 98:28
north-west: N. passage — STER 315:21
Norval: My name is N. — HOME 170:18
nose: Any n. may ravage — BROW 77:15
Cleopatra's n. been shorter — PASC 246:2
great hook n. like thine — BLAKE 60:11
hateful to the n. — JAM 179:9
Heaven stops the n. at it — SHAK 292:25
His n.'s cast is of the roman — FLEM 142:1
miss the insinuated n. — WATS 343:1
n. dead against the Pope — BALD 27:8
n. was as sharp as a pen — SHAK 279:4
plucks justice by the n. — SHAK 288:9
ring at the end of his n. — LEAR 203:12
Some thirty inches from my n. — AUDEN 21:8
thing is not a n. at all — WELLS 345:22
noselessness: N. of Man — CHES 98:6
noses: men's n. as they lie asleep — SHAK 294:24
n. have they, and smell not — BOOK 68:18
They haven't got no n. — CHES 98:5
nostalgia: N. isn't what it used — ANON 9:18
nostalgie: *La n. de la boue* — AUG 21:21
noster: *Pater n., qui es in coelis* — MISS 231:18
not: n. I, but the wind — LAWR 202:23
N. so much a programme — ANON 9:19
N. unto us, O Lord — BOOK 68:17
thing which was n. — SWIFT 320:1
note: only the n. of a bird — SIMP 307:10
When found, make a n. of — DICK 118:20
notes: n. like little fishes — MACN 216:9
thick-warbled n. — MILT 230:6
nothing: brought n. into this world — BIBLE 56:18
Did n. in particular — GILB 151:14
doing n. with a deal of skill — COWP 110:5
do n. for ever and ever — ANON 7:17
do n. for evil to triumph — BURKE 81:13
don't resent having n. — COMP 106:4
easy to take *more* than n. — CARR 91:8
everything by starts, and n. long — DRYD 127:12
forgotten n. and learnt nothing — DUM 129:6
gives to airy n. — SHAK 291:4
glory and the n. of a name — BYRON 85:15
have not charity, I am n. — BIBLE 55:11
having n., yet hath all — WOTT 357:15
How to live well on n. a year — THAC 329:20
I have n. to say — CAGE 88:4
individually can do n. — ALLEN 4:12
insupportable labour of doing n. — STEE 314:14
Is it n. to you — BIBLE 46:32
I will say n. — SHAK 283:9
know this only, that he n. knew — MILT 230:7
learnt n., and forgotten n. — TALL 322:12
marvel at n. — HOR 173:10
N. ain't worth nothin' — KRIS 199:5
n. a-year, paid quarterly — SURT 319:15
N. begins, and nothing ends — THOM 331:7
N. can be created out of — LUCR 212:3
n. can be sole or whole — YEATS 358:20
n. could be finer — GORD 155:22
n. done for the first time — CORN 108:8
n. ever ran quite straight — GALS 147:17
n. extenuate — SHAK 293:5
N. happens, nobody comes — BECK 31:12
N. happens to anybody — AUR 22:9
N. in excess — ANON 13:7
N. is ever done in this world — SHAW 301:14
N. is here for tears — MILT 230:31
N. is wasted — HERB 166:15
n. left remarkable — SHAK 271:25
N., like something — LARK 201:15
n. something straight begot — ROCH 261:10
N. to be done — BECK 31:10

O

old (*cont.*):

When you are very o.	RONS 262:5
You are o., Father William	CARR 91:4
You are o., Father William	SOUT 312:1
young a body with so o. a head	SHAK 289:25
young, and now am o.	BOOK 66:27
your o. men shall dream	BIBLE 47:20
older: I was so much o. then	DYLAN 130:6
o. than the rocks among	PATER 246:13
o. we do not get any younger	REED 258:14
oldest: o. hath borne most	SHAK 284:8
o. sins the newest kind	SHAK 278:28
old-fashioned: I want an o. house	FISH 140:1
olive-branches: children like the o.	BOOK 68:32
Olivet: purple brows of O.	TENN 325:5
Olivia: Cry out, 'O.!'	SHAK 297:21
Olympus: leafy O. on top of Ossa	VIRG 340:6
Omega: I am Alpha and O.	BIBLE 57:19
omelette: What a fuss about an o.	VOLT 341:2
omen: *Quod di o. avertant*	CIC 100:28
omitted: O., all the voyage	SHAK 282:1
omnia: *Non o. possumus omnes*	VIRG 340:2
O. vincit Amor	VIRG 340:4
omnibus: horse power O.	FLAN 141:6
omnipotent: land of the o. No	BOLD 63:2
once: himself o. offered	BOOK 65:16
o. and future king	WHITE 347:18
o. in a great while	PEPYS 247:21
O. in royal David's city	ALEX 4:4
O. more unto the breach	SHAK 279:5
O. to every man and nation	LOW 211:7
through this world but o.	GREL 158:14
one: All for one, o. for all	DUMAS 129:4
But the O. was Me	HUXL 177:11
Dear O. is mine as mirrors	AUDEN 21:9
do only o. thing at once	SMIL 308:18
How to be o. up	POTT 254:4
Make it o. for my baby	MERC 223:11
o. by one back in the closet	FITZ 140:12
o. day in thy courts	BOOK 67:22
O. man shall have one vote	CART 92:14
O. remains, the many	SHEL 303:13
O. who never turned	BROW 75:11
she who but trifles with o.	GAY 149:9
Win just o. for the Gipper	GIPP 153:4
one-eyed: o. man is king	ERAS 137:14
o. yellow idol to the north	HAYES 163:21
only: It's the o. thing	SAND 266:19
o. begetter of these	SHAK 299:10
O. connect	FORS 143:21
O. the lonely	MELS 241:16
pint of plain is your o. man	O'BR 240:20
only-begotten: o. Son of God	BOOK 65:5
onset: Vain thy o.	ARN 16:18
onward: O., Christian soldiers	BAR 29:1
O. goes the pilgrim band	BAR 29:2
'O.,' the sailors cry	BOUL 70:10
upward still, and o.	LOW 211:9
oozing: O. charm from every pore	LERN 206:2
oozy: o. woods which wear	SHEL 304:7
opal: thy mind is a very o.	SHAK 297:33
open: great o. spaces	MARQ 219:18
o. and notorious evil liver	BOOK 64:29
O. covenants of peace	WILS 351:22
O. Sesame	ARAB 14:17
o. to the poor and the rich	ANON 7:9
O. unto the fields	WORD 354:15
Secret thoughts and o.	ALB 3:13
slepen al the nyght with o. ye	CHAU 95:11
Where knock is o. wide	SMART 308:11
opened: o. the seventh seal	BIBLE 57:29
opera: o. ain't over 'til	COOK 107:16
O. is when a guy gets stabbed	GARD 148:5
operas: o. sung by Swedish artists	WHAR 347:3
operatic: so romantic, so o.	PROU 255:20

operations: number of o.	WHIT 348:5
opiate: dull o. to the drains	KEATS 191:28
opinion: common o. and uncommon	BAG 26:2
low o. of himself	TROL 334:17
man can brave o.	STAËL 314:6
no more than private o.	HOBB 169:7
of his own o. still	BUTL 84:6
O. in good men	MILT 231:4
o. one man entertains	PALM 244:20
Party is organized o.	DISR 121:14
sacrifices it to your o.	BURKE 80:22
think the last o. right	POPE 252:6
vagrant o. without visible	BIER 59:8
whole climate of o.	AUDEN 20:20
opinions: anger of men who have no o.	CHES 98:10
as many o. as there are people	TER 329:6
Golden o. from all sorts	SHAK 286:2
halt ye between two o.	BIBLE 41:36
New o. are always suspected	LOCKE 208:13
Stiff in o.	DRYD 127:12
opium: o.-dose for keeping	KING 195:18
o. of the people	MARX 221:8
opponents: o. eventually die	PLAN 249:12
opportunity: O. makes a thief	BACON 25:24
Thou strong seducer, o.	DRYD 127:27
with the maximum of o.	SHAW 301:30
oppose: o. everything, and propose	DERBY 117:6
opposing: by o. end them	SHAK 275:25
opposites: o. are obviously absurd	BOHR 63:1
opposition: duty of an O.	DERBY 117:6
Her Majesty's O.	BAG 26:6
His Majesty's O.	HOBH 169:12
o. of the stars	MARV 220:13
without a formidable O.	DISR 121:23
oppressed: Sink heart and voice o.	NEALE 237:22
oppressing: o. city	BIBLE 47:25
oppression: O. makes the wise	BROW 76:16
oppressor: day o' the O. is ended	KIPL 197:16
oppugnancy: In mere o.	SHAK 296:30
optimist: o. is a guy	MARQ 219:16
o. proclaims that we live	CAB 87:23
opus: *Hoc o., hic labor est*	VIRG 339:12
oracles: these are the lively O.	COR 108:10
oracular: use of my o. tongue	SHER 305:29
orange: clockwork o.	BURG 79:13
shades the o. bright	MARV 220:10
oranges: Coffee and o.	STEV 316:12
orantes: *Stabant o.*	VIRG 339:15
oration: not studied as an o.	OSB 242:17
orator: enjoyment as the greatest o.	HUME 176:7
eyes of men without an o.	SHAK 299:7
I am no o.	SHAK 281:25
orators: swords shall play the o.	MARL 219:5
orchestra: o. is playing to the rich	AUDEN 20:13
rules for an o.	BEEC 31:23
orchestration: o. of platitudes	WILD 350:24
order: all is in o.	MANS 217:15
Democrat, in that o.	JOHN 181:19
done decently and in o.	BIBLE 55:15
good o. and military	ANON 6:22
Good o. is the foundation	BURKE 80:21
Half of one o., half another	BUTL 84:1
not necessarily in that o.	GOD 153:19
old o. changeth	TENN 324:20
only war creates o.	BREC 71:20
o. of the acts is planned	PAST 246:10
O. reigns in Warsaw	ANON 12:12
put his household in o.	BIBLE 41:26
Set thine house in o.	BIBLE 46:6
They o. this matter better	STER 315:8
upon the o. of your going	SHAK 287:12
when o. breeds habit	ADAMS 1:15
ordered: o. their estate	ALEX 4:3
ordering: better o. of the universe	ALF 4:8

orders: Almighty's o. to perform	ADD 2:11	outrage: Seal up the mouth of o.	SHAK 295:26
ordinary: I warn you not to be o.	KINN 196:1	outrageous: O. acts and everyday	STEI 315:1
O. made beautiful	SHAF 270:19	outside: o. and may be some time	OATES 240:17
o. mind on an o. day	WOOLF 353:21	O. every fat man	AMIS 5:4
ordre: o. et beauté	BAUD 30:4	o. pissing in	JOHN 181:21
ore: load every rift with o.	KEATS 193:14	out-topping: O. knowledge	ARN 17:14
with new spangled o.	MILT 227:18	outward: Of sense and o. things	WORD 355:22
oreilles: Les o. ennemies	ANON 12:15	O. be fair, however foul	CHUR 98:25
organ: o.-voice of England	TENN 327:7	o. parts Love's always seen	COWL 109:14
Seated one day at the o.	PROC 255:13	o. shows be least themselves	SHAK 289:21
when the o. grinder is present	BEVAN 37:21	over: we o. God a death	SHAK 290:19
organization: o. of idolatry	SHAW 301:26	oversexed, and o. here	TRIN 334:11
systematic o. of hatreds	ADAMS 1:11	O. the hills and far away	GAY 149:5
organize: Don't waste time mourning—o.	HILL 168:13	overbought: that thou hast o.	CRAS 111:5
organized: o. hypocrisy	DISR 121:11	overcome: o. the sharpness of death	BOOK 63:20
Party is o. opinion	DISR 121:14	We shall o.	ANON 11:16
organs: His 'owls was o.	DICK 119:8	overcomes: Who o. by force	MILT 228:18
other o. take their tone	GLAD 153:7	overlook: knowing what to o.	JAMES 180:9
orient: o. and immortal wheat	TRAH 333:18	overpaid: Is grossly o.	HERB 166:14
original: Behold the bright o.	GAY 149:14	oversexed: o., and over here	TRIN 334:11
in th'o. perused mankind	ARMS 16:1	overtake: Till I thy fate shall o.	KING 195:5
o. is unfaithful	BORG 69:22	overthrow: linger out a purposed o.	SHAK 300:1
o. righteousness	BOOK 69:17	overwrought: Spirits o.	WORD 356:11
Their great O. proclaim	ADD 2:25	owe: we o. God a death	SHAK 278:25
originals: few o. and many copies	TOCQ 333:1	owl: fat greedy o. of the Remove	RICH 260:1
Orion: O. plunges prone	HOUS 174:15	nightly sings the staring o.	SHAK 284:23
or loose the bands of O.	BIBLE 43:4	O. and the Pussy-Cat	LEAR 203:11
ornament: My study's o.	MIDD 224:8	O., and the Waverley Pen	ANON 11:1
not the foreign aid of o.	THOM 331:25	o. does to the moon complain	GRAY 157:5
o. to her profession	BUNY 79:8	o., for all his feathers	KEATS 190:14
serve for delight, for o.	BACON 25:13	o. hawked at and killed	SHAK 286:28
still deceived with o.	SHAK 289:21	o. of Minerva spreads	HEGEL 164:20
orphan: defeat is an o.	CIANO 100:12	white o. in the belfry sits	TENN 328:16
I'm an o., both sides	WELLS 345:18	owls: companion to o.	BIBLE 43:3
Orpheus: O. with his lute	SHAK 280:16	court for o.	BIBLE 46:3
orthodoxy: O. is my doxy	WARB 342:17	eagle among blinking o.	SHEL 303:23
Oscar: You will, O., you will	WHIS 347:11	There I couch when o. do cry	SHAK 296:14
Ossa: To pile O. on Pelion	VIRG 340:6	Two O. and a Hen	LEAR 203:17
ostrich: wings of an o.	MAC 213:21	own: his o. received him not	BIBLE 53:10
Othello: O.'s occupation's gone	SHAK 292:21	marked him for his o.	WALT 342:15
other: I am not as o. men	BIBLE 52:38	money and a room of her o.	WOOLF 354:1
o. side of the hill	WELL 345:6	my words are my o.	CHAR 89:21
O. voices, other rooms	CAP 89:15	own-alone: All by my o. self	HARR 163:3
strange faces, o. minds	TENN 324:19	ox: brother to the o.	MARK 218:4
trumpets sounded on the o. side	BUNY 79:11	nor his o., nor his ass	BIBLE 40:9
turn to him the o. also	BIBLE 48:23	o. goeth to the slaughter	BIBLE 43:13
Were t'o. dear charmer away	GAY 149:7	stalled o. and hatred	BIBLE 43:26
others: o. by their hunted expression	LEWIS 206:12	oxen: than a hundred pair of o.	HOW 175:9
otherwise: gods thought o.	VIRG 339:7	Oxenford: Clerk there was of O.	CHAU 95:17
Otis: Miss O. regrets	PORT 253:23	Oxford: Half-Way House to Rome, O.	PUNCH 256:7
otium: Cum dignitate o.	CIC 100:32	King to O. sent a troop	BROW 74:25
ought: It is, but hadn't o. to be	HARTE 163:12	O. that has made me insufferable	BEER 32:8
meritus, 'so he o. to be'	LEAC 203:3	sends his son to O.	STEAD 314:13
o. never to have done it	BEVIN 38:11	To O. I acknowledge no	GIBB 150:13
which we o. to have done	BOOK 63:14	To O. sent a troop of horse	TRAPP 334:3
ourselves: Our remedies oft in o.	SHAK 270:24	Oxford Street: O., stony-hearted	DE Q 117:3
out: at tother o. it wente	CHAU 96:19	oxlips: o. and the nodding violet	SHAK 290:26
best way o. is always through	FROST 146:22	oxygen: o. of publicity	THAT 329:24
Gentlemen, include me o.	GOLD 155:16	oyster: open an o. at sixty paces	WOD 352:16
I counted them all o.	HANR 161:8	o. may be crossed in love	SHER 305:25
Mordre wol o.	CHAU 95:29	world is an o.	MILL 225:2
never o. of the way	CHAR 95:5	world's mine o.	SHAK 290:9
o., brief candle	SHAK 288:5	oysters: Poverty and o.	DICK 119:30
O., damned spot	SHAK 287:27	Ozymandias: My name is O.	SHEL 304:12
o. of Africa	PLINY 249:23		
O. of the deep have I called	BOOK 68:33		
o. of the fashion	CIBB 100:14	**P**	
O. where the handclasp's	CHAP 94:13		
preserve thy going o.	BOOK 68:27	pace: Creeps in this petty p.	SHAK 288:5
See that ye fall not o.	BIBLE 39:28	dance is a measured p.	BACON 23:24
outer: o. life of telegrams	FORS 143:20	paces: open an oyster at sixty p.	WOD 352:16
outgrabe: mome raths o.	CARR 91:15	three p. through the room	TENN 326:3
outlive: o. this powerful rhyme	SHAK 299:19	Pacific: He stared at the P.	KEATS 192:11
outlives: He that o. this day	SHAK 279:18	pacific: repose of a p. station	ADAMS 1:7

pacifist: quietly p. peaceful — WALK 341:5
pack: changed the form of the p. — TROT 334:23
I will p., and take a train — BROO 73:6
p. up your troubles — ASAF 18:17
Pay, p., and follow — BURT 83:4
To p. and label men for God — THOM 331:13
pack-horse: p. on the down — MORR 235:16
pack-horses: P. and hollow pampered jades
— SHAK 278:21

Paddington: ever weeping P. — BLAKE 60:16
paddles: p. chunkin' — KIPL 196:21
paddocks: Cold as p. — HERR 167:11
padlock: clap your p.—on her mind — PRIOR 255:9
paeans: laurels to p. — CIC 100:23
pagan: find the p.—spoiled — ZANG 360:26
P. suckled in a creed outworn — WORD 357:11
page: I turn the p. — BROW 75:18
pageant: insubstantial p. faded — SHAK 296:10
part of life's rich p. — MARS 220:2
pagus: private p. or demesne — AUDEN 21:8
paid: Lord God, we ha' p. in full — KIPL 197:9
So attention must be p. — MILL 225:3
well p. that is well satisfied — SHAK 289:30
pain: After great p. — DICK 120:8
After long grief and p. — TENN 327:3
beneath the aromatic p. — WINC 352:2
born in other's p. — THOM 331:7
Eternal P. — ARN 16:22
general drama of p. — HARDY 161:24
I feel no p. dear mother now — ANON 8:3
I have no p., dear mother, now — FARM 138:13
intermission of p. — SELD 269:20
Joy always came after p. — APOL 14:12
labour we delight in physics p. — SHAK 286:22
life's a p. and but a span — DAV 114:14
midnight with no p. — KEATS 192:3
momentary intoxication with p. — BRON 72:11
not because it gave p. — MAC 213:19
one who never inflicts p. — NEWM 238:17
Our Lady of P. — SWIN 321:8
p. and anguish wring — SCOTT 268:22
pleasure turns to pleasing p. — SPEN 313:13
rest from p. — DRYD 127:35
shall there be any more p. — BIBLE 58:5
she hasn't a p. — MILNE 225:23
Sweet is pleasure after p. — DRYD 127:20
tender for another's p. — GRAY 157:13
tongueless vigil and all the p. — SWIN 321:1
With some p. is fraught — SHEL 305:10
painful: p. pleasure turns — SPEN 313:13
pains: let our p. be less — BROME 72:8
Marriage has many p. — JOHN 183:5
no gains without p. — STEV 316:16
p. a man when 'tis kept close — SUCK 318:22
p. of hell gat hold upon me — BOOK 68:19
So double was his p. — SPEN 313:10
sympathize with people's p. — HUXL 177:8
paint: can't pick it up, p. it — ANON 8:4
flinging a pot of p. — RUSK 264:10
I p. with my prick — REN 259:5
p. 'em truest praise 'em — ADD 2:12
p. on the face of Existence — BYRON 87:16
p. the meadows with delight — SHAK 284:21
refinèd gold, to p. the lily — SHAK 282:10
painted: As idle as a p. ship — COL 104:6
fears a p. devil — SHAK 286:17
gilded loam or p. clay — SHAK 293:7
Lift not the p. veil — SHEL 305:2
p. meadow, or a purling stream — ADD 2:1
She p. her face — BIBLE 42:14
They're p. to the eyes — DOBS 122:27
wood p. to look like iron — BISM 59:21
painter: p. and I nail my pictures — SCHW 268:2
painters: Good p. imitate nature — CERV 93:20

painters (cont.):
I hate all Poets and P. — GEOR 149:20
painting: poem is like a p. — HOR 173:4
paint-pots: throws aside his p. — HOR 172:26
paints: I want to know a butcher p. — BROW 77:11
Where God p. the scenery — HART 163:10
pair: Blest p. of Sirens — MILT 226:4
p. of ragged claws — ELIOT 133:28
Sleep on, blest p. — MILT 229:12
Take a p. of sparkling eyes — GILB 151:7
palace: chalice from the p. — FRANK 245:1
leads to the p. of wisdom — BLAKE 61:1
My gorgeous p. for a hermitage — SHAK 294:2
purple-linèd p. of sweet sin — KEATS 191:12
palaces: Dragons in their pleasant p. — BIBLE 45:21
fair, frail p. — ALDR 3:17
gorgeous p. — SHAK 296:10
Mid pleasures and p. — PAYNE 246:21
paladin: Sidney's self, the starry p. — BROW 77:13
palate: P., the hutch of tasty lust — HOPK 172:6
pale: behold a p. horse — BIBLE 57:25
p. and bloodless emulation — SHAK 296:31
p. cast of thought — SHAK 275:26
p. contented sort of discontent — KEATS 191:13
p. fire she snatches — SHAK 296:23
P. grew thy cheek and cold — BYRON 87:14
P. hands I loved — HOPE 171:22
P. prime-roses — SHAK 298:33
p., unripened beauties — ADD 2:14
p. young curate — GILB 152:29
started at the intelligence, and turned p. — SOUT 312:5
whiter shade of p. — REID 259:3
Which keeps me p. — SHAK 287:6
Why so p. and wan — SUCK 318:20
palely: Alone and p. loitering — KEATS 191:7
paling: piece-bright p. — HOPK 172:17
Palladium: press is the P. — JUN 188:25
pallor: p. of girls' brows — OWEN 243:23
palm: has won it bear the p. — JORT 188:1
Hold infinity in the p. — BLAKE 60:5
itching p. — SHAK 281:29
Quietly sweating p. to palm — HUXL 177:12
To win the p., the oak — MARV 220:14
palms: p. before my feet — CHES 97:22
palmy: high and p. state of Rome — SHAK 274:1
palpable: very p. hit — SHAK 277:14
palsied: o'ertaxed, its p. hearts — ARN 17:11
paltered: p. with Eternal God — TENN 327:13
paltry: aged man is but a p. thing — YEATS 359:21
Pam: P., I adore you — BETJ 37:8
pampered: Holla, ye p. jades of Asia — MARL 219:14
hollow p. jades of Asia — SHAK 278:21
Pan: great god P. — BROW 75:4
pandemonium: P., the high capital — MILT 228:21
Pandora: open that P.'s Box — BEVIN 38:10
pane: tap at the p. — BROW 76:17
pange: P., lingua, gloriosi — FORT 144:4
P., lingua, gloriosi — THOM 330:3
panic: what a p.'s in thy breastie — BURNS 82:26
panjandrum: grand P. himself — FOOTE 142:20
pansies: p., that's for thoughts — SHAK 277:2
pantaloon: lean and slippered p. — SHAK 272:27
panting: For ever p. — KEATS 191:21
pants: earth in fast thick p. — COL 103:23
p. the hart for cooling — TATE 322:16
your lower limbs in p. — NASH 237:18
papa: P., potatoes, poultry — DICK 119:1
paper: age of four with p. hats — UST 336:18
All reactionaries are p. tigers — MAO T 217:20
he hath not eat p. — SHAK 284:15
just for a scrap of p. — BETH 36:15
Make dust our p. — SHAK 293:26
more personality than a p. cup — CHAN 94:8
only a p. moon — HARB 161:12
verbal contract isn't worth the p. — GOLD 155:17

papers: He's got my p., this man   PINT 248:20
  what I read in the p.   ROG 262:1
parachutes: Minds are like p.   DEWAR 117:13
parade: p. of riches   SMITH 308:22
paradise: blundered into P.   THOM 331:13
  cannot catch the bird of p.   KHR 194:20
  drunk the milk of P.   COL 104:1
  England is a p. for women   BURT 83:13
  England is the p. of women   FLOR 142:13
  P. by way of Kensal Green   CHES 98:3
  p. for a sect   KEATS 190:24
  shalt thou be with me in p.   BIBLE 53:3
  Thou P. of exiles, Italy   SHEL 303:21
  wilderness is p. enow   FITZ 140:6
paradises: p. we have lost   PROU 255:21
  Two p. 'twere in one   MARV 220:17
paradox: Man is an embodied p.   COLT 106:1
parallel: But ours so truly p.   MARV 220:13
parallelograms: Princess of P.   BYRON 87:15
parallels: p. in beauty's brow   SHAK 299:22
parapets: Europe of the ancient p.   RIMB 260:9
parcels: she deals it in small p.   WEBS 344:22
parcere: P. subiectis   VIRG 339:16
pardlike: p. Spirit   SHEL 303:9
pardon: Bretful of p.   CHAU 95:23
  but cannot help or p.   AUDEN 21:15
  God may p. you, but I never can   ELIZ 135:11
  God will p. me, it is His trade   HEINE 165:3
  kiss of the sun for p.   GURN 159:10
  P. all, their faults confessing   BUCK 78:3
  With a thousand Ta's and P.'s   BETJ 37:7
pards: by Bacchus and his p.   KEATS 192:1
parens: king is truly p. patriae   JAM 179:10
parent: p. of settlement   BURKE 80:11
  To lose one p., Mr Worthing   WILDE 349:18
parents: At 18 a girl needs good p.   TUCK 335:9
  begin by loving their p.   WILDE 350:12
  Jewish man with p. alive   ROTH 263:14
  Of p. good   SHAK 279:10
  p. kept me from children   SPEN 312:25
  P. love their children more   AUCT 20:7
  slavish bondage to p.   WOLL 353:13
parfit: verray p. gentil knyght   CHAU 95:12
Paris: Americans die they go to P.   WILDE 350:8
  Is P. burning   HITL 169:4
  last time I saw P.   HAMM 161:1
  no more Hoares to P.   GEOR 149:26
  P. is a movable feast   HEM 165:13
  P. is well worth a mass   HENR 165:21
  P. was French—and silent   TUCH 335:8
  when they die, go to P.   APPL 14:15
parish: all the world as my p.   WESL 346:13
  p. of rich women   AUDEN 20:22
park: p., a policeman and a pretty girl   CHAP 94:12
parks: p. are the lungs of London   PITT 249:6
parley-voo: Hinky, dinky, p.   ANON 9:5
parliament: In the P. of man   TENN 326:12
  [p.] are a lot of hard-faced men   BALD 27:9
  p. can do any thing   PEMB 247:6
  P. speaking through reporters   CARL 90:17
  P. to do things at eleven   SHAW 301:12
parliamentarian: only safe pleasure for a p.   CRIT 111:22
parliaments: mother of P.   BRIG 72:5
parlour: some party in a p.   WORD 356:4
  Will you walk into my p.   HOW 175:11
Parnassus: my chief P.   SIDN 306:24
parochial: he was p.   JAMES 179:19
parole: p. of literary men   JOHN 185:30
parson: If P. lost his senses   HODG 169:13
  p. knows enough who knows   COWP 110:14
  P. left conjuring   SELD 269:19
parsons: This merriment of p.   JOHN 185:28
part: come let us kiss and p.   DRAY 126:16

part (cont.):
  every man must play a p.   SHAK 288:27
  My soul, bear thou thy p.   GURN 159:11
  p. to tear a cat in   SHAK 290:18
  p. my garments among them   BOOK 66:16
  p. of all that I have met   TENN 328:21
  Shall I p. my hair behind   ELIOT 134:3
  we know in p.   BIBLE 55:13
  What isn't p. of ourselves   HESSE 168:3
  Yet meet we shall, and p.   BUTL 84:21
parted: fool and his words are soon p.   SHEN 305:20
  P. are those who are singing   BOWEN 70:15
  When we two p.   BYRON 87:14
partiality: neither anger nor p.   TAC 322:6
particles: Newton's p. of light   BLAKE 61:14
particular: bright p. star   SHAK 270:23
  London p. . . . A fog   DICK 118:2
particulars: do it in minute p.   BLAKE 60:19
parting: P. is all we know of heaven   DICK 120:12
  p. is such sweet sorrow   SHAK 295:4
  p. there is an image of death   ELIOT 132:16
  rive not more in p.   SHAK 271:23
  speed the p. guest   POPE 252:24
  stood at the p. of the ways   BIBLE 47:7
  Their every p. was to die   TENN 325:20
partir: P. c'est mourir un peu   HAR 161:9
partly: Living and p. living   ELIOT 134:6
partridge: Always p.   ANON 12:16
parts: dignified and efficient p.   BAG 26:3
  in his time plays many p.   SHAK 272:24
  P. of it are excellent   PUNCH 256:19
  secret of Fortune   SHAK 275:13
  Today we have naming of p.   REED 258:15
parturient: P. montes   HOR 172:27
party: Collapse of Stout P.   ANON 6:17
  conduct of a losing p.   BURKE 79:18
  effects of the spirit of p.   WASH 342:21
  I always voted at my p.'s call   GILB 152:19
  none was for a p.   MAC 214:5
  p. is not to be brought down   HAIL 160:1
  P. is organized opinion   DISR 121:14
  p.'s over   GREEN 106:2
  save the P. we love   GAIT 147:11
  some p. in a parlour   WORD 356:4
  sooner every p. breaks up   AUST 22:15
  Stick to your p.   DISR 122:15
party-spirit: P., which at best   POPE 253:11
pasarán: No p.   IBAR 178:2
pass: I keep, and p., and turn again   EMER 136:10
  I p., like night, from land   COL 104:17
  let him p. for a man   SHAK 284:7
  let him p. for a man   SHAK 288:30
  look, and p. on   DANTE 113:19
  my words shall not p.   BIBLE 50:37
  p. for forty-three   GILB 152:31
  P. into nothingness   KEATS 190:11
  P. me the mustard, lad   HOUS 174:9
  p. the ammunition   FORGY 143:13
  P. the sick bag, Alice   JUNOR 188:21
  p. through this world   GREL 158:14
  p. with a lass   JAM 179:14
  pay us, p. us   CHES 98:4
  Ships that p. in the night   LONG 210:3
  they p. all understanding   JAM 179:13
  They shall not p.   ANON 12:6
  They shall not p.   IBAR 178:2
  Will she p. in a crowd   SWIFT 320:3
passage: long black p. up to bed   STEV 317:15
  North-west p.   STER 315:21
  p. which we did not take   ELIOT 132:26
  p. you think is particularly fine   JOHN 184:27
passageways: smell of steaks in p.   ELIOT 134:10
passe: Tout p., tout casse   ANON 12:17
passed: former things are p.   BIBLE 58:5
  He p. by on the other side   BIBLE 52:12

passed (cont.):

remembren, whan it p.	CHAU 96:18
That p. the time	BECK 31:13
passer: P. mortuus est	CAT 93:1
passeront: Ils ne p. pas	ANON 12:6
passes: beauty p.	DE L 116:14
Everything p.	ANON 12:17
free p., class distinction	BETJ 37:4
Men seldom make p.	PARK 245:6
Thus p. the glory of the world	ANON 13:22
passeth: which p. all understanding	BIBLE 56:8
passi: O p. graviora	VIRG 339:1
passing: I did but see her p.	ANON 10:18
is it not p. brave to be a king	MARL 219:7
p. the love of women	BIBLE 41:23
passing-bells: p. for these	OWEN 243:21
passion: Above the storms of p.	BODE 62:16
all p. spent	MILT 230:19
betwixt one p. and another	STER 315:9
connect the prose and the p.	FORS 143:21
desolate and sick of an old p.	DOWS 125:12
Eternal P.	ARN 16:22
fat gentleman in such a p.	SHAW- 302:29
first p. woman loves	BYRON 86:9
Haunted me like a p.	WORD 355:9
he vows his p.	PARK 245:9
Man is a useless p.	SART 267:3
master p. is the love of news	CRAB 110:25
no p. in the human soul	LILLO 207:3
No p. so effectually robs	BURKE 80:7
not p.'s slave	SHAK 276:7
our p. is our task	JAMES 179:23
p. cannot Music raise	DRYD 128:17
p. that left the ground	BROW 75:8
ruling p. conquers reason	POPE 251:14
Search then the Ruling P.	POPE 251:21
passionate: full of p. intensity	YEATS 359:24
p. my sense of hearing	SHAK 284:12
passion-flower: p. at the gate	TENN 327:1
passionless: hopeless grief is p.	BROW 75:2
passions: Desolate p.	JOHN 181:18
diminishes commonplace p.	LA R 201:24
inferno of his p.	JUNG 188:22
Love is only one of many p.	JOHN 182:25
passives: Love's p.	CRAS 111:7
Passover: it is the Lord's p.	BIBLE 39:37
passport: his p. shall be made	SHAK 279:18
past: funeral of the p.	CLARE 101:8
god cannot change the p.	AGAT 3:7
know nothing but the p.	KEYN 194:15
looking forward to the p.	OSB 242:24
nothing more than the p.	BERG 35:13
p. are condemned to repeat it	SANT 266:22
p. help should be p. grief	SHAK 298:24
p. is a bucket of ashes	SAND 266:15
p. is a foreign country	HART 163:14
p. is the only dead thing	THOM 330:22
plan the future by the p.	BURKE 79:20
present controls the p.	ORW 242:8
Remembrance of things p.	PROU 255:17
remembrance of things p.	SHAK 299:16
There is only the p.	THOM 331:5
Things p. redress	SHAK 293:20
Time present and time p.	ELIOT 132:25
What's p., and what's to come	SHAK 297:10
What's p. is prologue	SHAK 296:3
pastoral: Cold P.	KEATS 191:23
pastors: some ungracious p. do	SHAK 274:20
pasture: feed me in a green p.	BOOK 66:17
sheep of his p.	BOOK 68:5
pastures: fresh woods, and p. new	MILT 227:20
pat: Now might I do it p.	SHAK 276:17
patch: P. grief with proverbs	SHAK 291:25
patches: king of shreds and p.	SHAK 276:1
thing of shreds and p.	GILB 151:17

pâté de foie gras: eating p.	SMITH 310:11
pater: P. noster	MISS 231:18
path: beaten p. to his door	EMER 137:3
p. of gold for him	BROW 76:23
P. of Wickedness	BALL 28:7
pathetic: earth does not argue, is not p.	WHIT 348:23
P. Fallacy	RUSK 264:21
pathless: pleasure in the p. woods	BYRON 85:12
pathos: P., piety, courage	FORS 143:25
paths: all her p. are peace	BIBLE 43:9
all her p. are Peace	SPR 313:27
light unto my p.	BOOK 68:24
make his p. straight	BIBLE 48:13
p. of glory lead	GRAY 157:7
So many p. that wind and wind	WILC 349:15
patience: greater aptitude for p.	BUFF 78:6
P., and shuffle the cards	CERV 93:19
p. of Job	BIBLE 57:4
p. on a monument	SHAK 298:1
p. under their sufferings	BOOK 64:19
pattern of all p.	SHAK 283:9
patient: but not so p.	SHAK 278:18
fury of a p. man	DRYD 127:17
kill the p.	BACON 24:25
P. continuance in well doing	BIBLE 54:28
p. etherized upon a table	ELIOT 133:24
p., not a brawler	BIBLE 56:16
patients: poets are their own p.	THOM 331:3
patines: p. of bright gold	SHAK 290:2
patria: pro p. mori	HOR 173:26
Died some, pro p.	POUND 254:18
patrie: Allons, enfants de la p.	ROUG 263:16
patriot: Never was p. yet	DRYD 127:16
only a p. to heaven	MELV 223:2
steady p. of the world alone	CANN 89:11
Such is the p.'s boast	GOLD 155:4
sunshine p.	PAINE 244:11
patriotism: knock p. out of the human race	
	SHAW 302:13
P. is a lively sense	ALD 3:15
P. is not enough	CAV 93:12
P. is the last refuge	JOHN 185:4
p. which consists in hating	GASK 148:20
patriots: blood of p. and tyrants	JEFF 180:21
So to be p.	BURKE 81:5
True p. we	CART 92:12
patrol: P. the halls	WILB 349:12
patron: Is not a P., my Lord	JOHN 183:26
p., and the jail	JOHN 183:12
P. Commonly a wretch	JOHN 182:10
patter: unintelligible p.	GILB 152:28
pattern: imposing of a p.	WHIT 348:4
our p. to live and to die	BROW 76:14
p. informed by sensibility	READ 258:9
p. of all patience	SHAK 283:9
p. to encourage purchasers	SWIFT 319:20
patterns: What are p. for?	LOW 211:2
pâturage: Labourage et p.	SULLY 319:3
pauper: He's only a p.	NOEL 240:5
pause: How dull it is to p.	TENN 328:21
Must give us p.	SHAK 275:25
p. in the day's occupations	LONG 209:12
pauses: happy p.	BACON 25:22
pauvre: c'est un p. terre	BAUD 30:5
pavement: P. slippery	ROB 260:22
pavilioned: P. in splendour	GRANT 156:8
pax: et in terra p.	MISS 231:13
P. Vobis	BIBLE 58:18
pay: for what p.?	RUSK 264:15
Not a penny off the p.	COOK 107:15
p. for one by one	KIPL 197:10
P., pack, and follow	BURT 83:4
Smile at us, p. us, pass us	CHES 98:4
sum of things for p.	HOUS 174:13

pay (*cont.*):

We shall p. any price	KENN 194:3
wonders what's to p.	HOUS 174:12
paying: price well worth p.	LAM 200:18
pays: p. your money	PUNCH 256:6
peace: all her paths are p.	BIBLE 43:9
all her paths are P.	SPR 313:27
author of p. and lover of	BOOK 64:5
certain knot of p.	SIDN 306:20
chastisement of our p.	BIBLE 46:19
deep dream of p.	HUNT 176:12
for ever hold his p.	BOOK 65:27
Give p. a chance	MCC 205:13
Give p. in our time, O Lord	BOOK 64:4
good war makes a good p.	HERB 167:9
good war, or a bad p.	FRAN 145:14
hard and bitter p.	KENN 194:2
I came not to send p.	BIBLE 49:31
In His will is our p.	DANTE 113:22
In p.: goodwill	CHUR 100:4
in p. there's nothing so becomes	SHAK 279:5
instrument of Your p.	FRAN 145:7
into the way of p.	BIBLE 51:30
Let war yield to p.	CIC 100:23
like the p. of God	JAM 179:13
make war than to make p.	CLEM 102:2
May they rest in p.	MISS 231:25
moth of p.	SHAK 292:2
mountain tops is p.	GOET 154:12
My p. is gone	GOET 154:6
Nation shall speak p. unto	REND 259:5
news and Prince of P.	FLET 142:8
no such thing as inner p.	LEB 203:24
on earth p., good will	BIBLE 52:2
Open covenants of p.	WILS 351:22
P. be unto you	BIBLE 58:18
p. cannot be maintained	RUSS 265:6
P., commerce, and honest	JEFF 180:19
p. for our time	CHAM 94:2
p. has broken out	BREC 71:21
P. hath her victories	MILT 230:27
P. I leave with you	BIBLE 53:39
P. is crowned with smiles	VAUG 337:6
P. is indivisible	LITV 208:4
P. is in the grave	SHEL 304:18
P. is nothing but slovenliness	BREC 71:20
P. is poor reading	HARDY 161:20
P.! it is I	ANAT 5:10
p. Man is a bungler	SHAW 301:22
P., n. In international	BIER 59:7
p. of God, which passeth	BIBLE 56:8
P. on earth and mercy mild	WESL 346:7
P., perfect peace	BICK 58:25
P., retrenchment and reform	BRIG 72:3
P., the human dress	BLAKE 61:21
p. which the world cannot give	BOOK 64:11
p. with honour	CHAM 94:2
p. with honour	DISR 121:18
people want p. so much	EIS 131:16
poor, and manglèd P.	SHAK 280:2
publisheth p.	BIBLE 46:15
righteousness and p. have kissed	BOOK 67:23
seek p., and ensue it	BOOK 66:25
So enamoured on p.	CLAR 101:11
soft phrase of p.	SHAK 291:33
state of p.	VIRG 339:16
that we may live in p.	ARIS 15:14
There is no p., saith the Lord	BIBLE 46:14
This is not a p. treaty	FOCH 142:15
thousand years of p.	TENN 325:26
thy servant depart in p.	BIBLE 52:3
time of p.	BIBLE 44:13
time of p. thinks of war	ANON 7:16
want p., prepare for war	VEG 337:18

peace (*cont.*):

War is p.	ORW 242:7
weak piping time of p.	SHAK 294:14
when there is no p.	BIBLE 46:28
wilderness and call it p.	TAC 322:4
peaceably: p. if we can	CLAY 101:17
peacefully: King's life is moving p.	DAWS 115:5
peacemakers: Blessed are the p.	BIBLE 48:19
peach: apricot and woolly p.	JONS 187:30
Do I dare to eat a p.	ELIOT 134:3
nectarine, and curious p.	MARV 220:15
peacocks: apes and p.	MAS 221:18
apes, and p.	BIBLE 41:31
p. and lilies	RUSK 264:17
peal: rung night's yawning p.	SHAK 287:5
pear: round the prickly p.	ELIOT 133:18
pearl: one p. of great price	BIBLE 50:6
p. in every cowslip's ear	SHAK 290:20
ransack the ocean for orient p.	MARL 218:8
threw a p. away	SHAK 293:5
pearls: p. before swine	BIBLE 49:8
p. fetch a high price *because*	WHAT 347:5
p. that were his eyes	SHAK 296:1
search for p. must dive below	DRYD 127:23
string the p. were strung on	JAMES 179:17
pearly: shows them p. white	BREC 71:18
peasant: rogue and p. slave	SHAK 275:21
peasantry: But a bold p.	GOLD 154:18
Civilization has made the p.	TROT 334:23
peasants: cricket with their p.	TREV 334:8
pebble: p. or a prettier shell	NEWT 239:6
peccavi: P. *nimis cogitatione*	MISS 231:11
pécher: p. *que p. en silence*	MOL 232:24
peck: For daws to p. at	SHAK 291:28
pecker: want his p. in my pocket	JOHN 181:20
peculiar: holy nation, a p. people	BIBLE 57:8
pecunia: P. *non olet*	VESP 338:3
pedantic: too p. for a gentleman	CONG 106:10
pedantry: P. the dotage of knowledge	JACK 178:24
pedestrians: two classes of p.	DEWAR 117:14
pedigree: languages the p. of nations	JOHN 183:18
peel: Beulah, p. me a grape	WEST 346:20
peep: p. and botanize	WORD 356:5
peepers: where you get them p.	MERC 223:10
peepshow: ticket for the p.	MACN 216:1
peer: paper p. Lord Peter	LOCK 209:3
peerage: p. or Westminster Abbey	NELS 237:23
want a p., I shall buy one	NORT 240:9
You should study the P.	WILDE 350:14
peering: mansions to the p. day	MILT 227:28
peers: House of P.	GILB 151:14
peignoir: Complacencies of the p.	STEV 316:12
pelican: wondrous bird is the p.	MERR 223:26
Pelion: To pile Ossa on P.	VIRG 340:6
pellet: p. with the poison's	FRANK 245:1
pellucid: More p. streams	WORD 355:7
Pemberley: P. to be thus polluted	AUST 23:5
pen: Biting my truant p.	SIDN 306:17
From lies of tongue and p.	CHES 97:24
nose was as sharp as a p.	SHAK 279:4
p. has been in their hands	AUST 22:27
p. has gleaned my teeming	KEATS 192:19
p. is mightier than the sword	BULW 78:11
p. is worse than the sword	BURT 83:9
poet's p.	SHAK 291:4
product of a scoffer's p.	WORD 354:20
scratching of a p.	LOVER 210:22
spark-gap mightier than the p.	HOGB 170:6
tongue is the p.	BOOK 67:5
Waverley p.	ANON 11:1
Why are the needle and the p.	LEWIS 206:14
penance: night do p. for a day	WORD 356:11
pence: Take care of the p.	LOWN 211:21
pencils: inexorable sadness of p.	ROET 261:14
Penelope: true P. was Flaubert	POUND 254:15

peninsulas: eye of p. and islands   CAT 93:3
pennies: P. from heaven   BURKE 81:14
penny: Nobody seemed one p. the worse   BARH 28:19
   Not a p. off the pay   COOK 107:15
   p. plain and twopence coloured   STEV 317:1
pens: p. dwell on guilt and misery   AUST 22:21
pension: hang your hat on a p.   MACN 216:2
   p. list of the republic   CLEV 102:4
pensions: talk of P. and Grenadiers   STER 315:19
pensive: In vacant or in p. mood   WORD 355:5
pent-house: Hang upon his p. lid   SHAK 285:4
peonies: wealth of globèd p.   KEATS 191:26
people: All p. that on earth   KETHE 194:11
   August for the p.   AUDEN 20:14
   builds on the p. builds on mud   MACH 215:2
   by the p., for the people   LINC 207:8
   fool all the p. some of the time   LINC 207:10
   good of the p. is the chief law   CIC 100:20
   government of the p., by the p.   LINC 207:8
   indictment against an whole p.   BURKE 80:2
   I would be of the p.   LA BR 199:13
   Let my p. go   ANON 11:19
   Let my p. go   BIBLE 39:34
   look after our p.   SCOTT 268:5
   many opinions as there are p.   TER 329:6
   Most p. ignore most poetry   MITC 232:2
   noise, my dear! And the p.   ANON 9:16
   not suppose the p. good   ROB 260:17
   one man should die for the p.   BIBLE 53:34
   p. are only human   COMP 106:3
   p. are the masters   BURKE 80:23
   p. arose as one man   BIBLE 41:7
   p. don't do such things   IBSEN 178:5
   P. mutht be amuthed   DICK 118:28
   p. that walked in darkness   BIBLE 45:15
   p. went up into the city   BIBLE 40:27
   p. were a kind of solution   CAV 93:11
   p. who got there first   UST 336:16
   p. will always be kind   SASS 267:9
   P. you know, yet can't quite   LARK 201:16
   Power to the p.   ANON 10:6
   surely the p. is grass   BIBLE 46:10
   thy people shall be my p.   BIBLE 41:8
   voice of the p. is the voice of God   ALC 3:14
   we are his p.   BOOK 68:5
   we are the p. of England   CHES 98:4
   What is the city but the p.   SHAK 273:19
peopled: p. half the world   SEEL 269:15
peoples: cry of the Little P.   LE G 204:12
Peoria: It'll play in P.   ANON 8:11
percentage: It's a reasonable p.   BECK 31:11
per cents: simplicity of the three p.   DISR 122:2
   simplicity of the three p.   STOW 318:9
perception: doors of p.   BLAKE 61:11
perdition: P. catch my soul   SHAK 292:10
perdu: Tout est p. fors l'honneur   FRAN 145:4
perennial: Falsehood has a p. spring   BURKE 79:25
peres: p.; Thy kingdom is divided   BIBLE 47:12
perfect: Be ye therefore p.   BIBLE 48:25
   But constant, he were p.   SHAK 298:20
   end of a p. day   BOND 63:9
   Entire and whole and p.   SPR 313:26
   If thou wilt be p.   BIBLE 50:21
   None of us are p.   WILDE 349:21
   Nothing is p.   STEP 315:6
   One p. rose   PARK 245:7
   service is p. freedom   BOOK 64:5
   short measures life may p. be   JONS 187:24
perfection: Dead p., no more   TENN 326:23
   make defect p.   SHAK 271:16
   P. is the child of Time   HALL 160:13
   P. of the life, or of the work   YEATS 358:19
   Pictures of p. as you know   AUST 23:12
   pursuit of p.   ARN 17:25

perfection (cont.):
   right praise and true p.   SHAK 290:5
   very pink of p.   GOLD 155:9
   What's come to p. perishes   BROW 76:21
perfectly: small but p. formed   COOP 107:21
perfide: La p. Albion   XIME 358:9
   la p. Angleterre   BOSS 70:2
perform: Almighty's orders to p.   ADD 2:11
   Lord of hosts will p. this   BIBLE 45:17
performance: all words and no p.   MASS 222:5
   it takes away the p.   SHAK 286:21
   so many years outlive p.   SHAK 278:22
performing: aroma of p. seals   HART 163:8
perfume: throw a p. on the violet   SHAK 282:10
perfumes: all the p. of Arabia   SHAK 287:30
   No p., but very fine linen   BRUM 77:24
perhaps: going to seek a great p.   RAB 257:13
   grand P.   BROW 75:14
Perigord: Thy truffles, P.!   POPE 250:21
peril: For those in p. on the sea   WHIT 348:9
   P. was nigh   ANAT 5:10
   there is no p. in the fight   CORN 108:1
perils: from all p. and dangers   BOOK 64:12
periods: Have certain p. set   SUCK 318:23
perish: And p. in our own   THOM 331:7
   believeth in him should not p.   BIBLE 53:19
   day p. wherein I was born   BIBLE 42:25
   if I p., I perish   BIBLE 42:19
   no vision, the people p.   BIBLE 44:3
   p. together as fools   KING 195:10
   P. the thought   CIBB 100:16
   p. with the sword   BIBLE 51:14
   ready to p.   BIBLE 44:5
   though the world p.   FERD 138:24
   To p. rather   MILT 228:24
perished: We p., each alone   COWP 109:20
perishes: nothing really p.   BACON 24:4
   What's come to perfection p.   BROW 76:21
perjuries: laughs at lovers' p.   OVID 243:10
permanent: Suffering is p.   WORD 354:13
pernicious: May his p. soul   SHAK 293:3
   P. weed   COWP 109:21
perpendicular: p. expression   SHAW 302:26
perpetual: let p. light shine   MISS 231:22
   next to the p. motion   DICK 120:3
perplexed: P. in the extreme   SHAK 293:5
perplexes: dull brain p.   KEATS 192:1
persecutest: why p. thou me   BIBLE 54:11
persecution: P. produced its natural effect   MAC 213:17
   P. a bad way to plant religion   BROW 74:16
   some degree of p.   SWIFT 320:9
Persepolis: in triumph through P.   MARL 219:7
perseverance: P., dear my lord   SHAK 297:5
   p. in a good cause   STER 315:14
persevere: Give us grace to p.   DEAR 115:7
Persians: Truth-loving P.   GRAV 156:15
persist: fool would p. in his folly   BLAKE 61:6
person: frontier of my P. goes   AUDEN 21:8
   I am a most superior p.   ANON 9:12
   p. on business from Porlock   COL 103:21
   p. you and I took me for   CARL 90:3
   To us he is no more a p.   AUDEN 20:20
personal: P. relations   FORS 143:20
personality: From 35 to 55, good p.   TUCK 335:9
   no more p. than a paper cup   CHAN 94:8
perspective: p. will always   CONS 107:11
perspiration: ninety-nine per cent p.   EDIS 130:19
perspire: dig till you gently p.   KIPL 197:22
   that Mr Gladstone may p.   CHUR 99:1
persuading: By p. others   JUN 188:26
pertinent: way to a p. answer   BRON 72:10
perturbation: O polished p.!   SHAK 278:26
Peru: from China to P.   JOHN 183:11
perverse: P. and foolish oft I   BAKER 26:21
perversions: unnatural of all the sexual p.   HUXL 177:7

pervert: p. climbs into the minds	BRON 72:11
pessimist: p. fears this	CAB 87:23
pestilence: acts not, breeds p.	BLAKE 61:3
p. that walketh in darkness	BOOK 67:29
petal: Now sleeps the crimson p.	TENN 328:3
p. down the Grand Canyon	MARQ 219:22
petals: P. on a wet, black bough	POUND 254:20
petar: Hoist with his own p.	SHAK 276:25
Peter: first 'twas P.'s drift	SHEL 304:14
I'll call him P.	SHAK 282:3
raree-show of P.'s successor	BROW 75:20
Shock-headed P.	HOFF 170:4
Thou art P., and upon this rock	BIBLE 50:13
Where P. is, there must	AMBR 4:19
petitions: desires and p.	BOOK 64:10
Petrarch: P.'s drink	BYRON 86:11
petrifactions: p. of a plodding brain	BYRON 86:32
petrifies: p. the feeling	BURNS 82:5
petticoat: Her feet beneath her p.	SUCK 318:21
never keep down a single p.	BYRON 87:20
petticoats: hyena in p.	WALP 342:2
pettiness: to expiate a p.	LAWR 202:22
petty: Creeps in this p. pace	SHAK 288:5
we p. men walk under his huge legs	SHAK 280:27
phagocytes: Stimulate the p.	SHAW 301:2
phallic: P. and ambrosial	POUND 254:17
phantom: She was a p. of delight	WORD 356:6
twin realities of this p. world	COL 105:1
Pharisees: P.' hypocrisy	PAST 246:10
phenomenon: infant p.	DICK 119:16
Phil: fidgety P.	HOFF 169:19
Philip: P. drunk to P. sober	ANON 6:3
P. fought men, but Alexander	LEE 204:10
Philistine: P. of genius	ARN 18:11
Philistines: P., and Populace	ARN 17:24
P. proper, or middle class	ARN 17:26
philosopher: P.!—a fingering slave	WORD 356:5
some p. has said it	CIC 100:19
soft p. of love	DRYD 128:3
tried into my time to be a p.	EDW 131:5
What I understand by 'p.'	NIET 239:19
philosophical: poetry is something more p.	ARIS 15:16
philosophy: Adversity's sweet milk, p.	SHAK 295:16
barbarous p.	BURKE 80:15
dreamt of in your p.	SHAK 275:3
History is p. from examples	DION 121:4
How charming is divine p.	MILT 226:15
little p. inclineth man's mind	BACON 24:12
mere touch of cold p.	KEATS 191:14
natural p., deep	BACON 25:16
P. is a battle against	WITT 352:6
p. is but an handmaid	BACON 24:2
P. is the replacement	RYLE 265:10
p. paints its grey on grey	HEGEL 164:20
p. quenches them	VOLT 340:16
P.! the lumber of the schools	SWIFT 320:18
P. will clip an Angel's wings	KEATS 191:15
superstition to enslave a p.	INGE 178:12
Phoebus: P., arise	DRUM 127:1
P. gins to shew his glorious	SPEN 313:5
phone: P. for the fish-knives	BETJ 37:2
why did you answer the p.	THUR 332:18
photography: P. is truth	GOD 153:18
phrases: Taffeta p., silken terms	SHAK 284:18
phylacteries: fly-blown p.	ROS 262:20
Phyllis: P., without frown	SEDL 269:12
physic: Take p., pomp	SHAK 283:12
Throw p. to the dogs	SHAK 288:3
physician: I died last night of my p.	PRIOR 255:11
into the hand of the p.	BIBLE 48:5
need not a p.	BIBLE 49:22
P. art thou?—one, all eyes	WORD 356:5
p. can bury his mistakes	WRIG 357:23
P., heal thyself	BIBLE 52:5

physician (cont.):	
Time is the great p.	DISR 122:3
physicians: P. are like kings	WEBS 344:20
P. of the Utmost Fame	BELL 33:4
physicists: p. have known sin	OPP 241:14
physics: p. or stamp collecting	RUTH 265:8
pianist: do not shoot the p.	ANON 10:4
Picardy: Roses are flowering in P.	WEAT 344:5
Picasso: P., sunbathing and jazz	WAUGH 343:22
picket: p.'s off duty forever	BEERS 32:14
picking: p. and stealing	BOOK 65:22
pickle: weaned on a p.	ANON 11:4
pick-purse: no p. of another's wit	SIDN 306:23
Pickwick: P., the Owl	ANON 11:1
pictura: Ut p. poesis	HOR 173:4
picture: Earth's Last P.	KIPL 197:13
Every p. tells a story	ANON 7:2
It's no go the p. palace	MACN 216:2
Not on his p., but his book	JONS 187:21
p. is worth ten thousand words	BARN 29:3
Poetry [is] a speaking p.	SIDN 306:26
pictured: my friends p. within	ELGAR 131:17
pictures: Are but as p.	SHAK 286:17
History is a gallery of p.	TOCQ 333:1
It's the p. that got small	WILD 71:5
painter and I nail my p.	SCHW 268:2
P. are for entertainment	GOLD 155:18
P. of perfection	AUST 23:12
without p. or conversations	CARR 91:1
pie: into a p. by Mrs McGregor	POTT 254:3
p. in the sky when you die	HILL 168:12
So, bye, bye, Miss American P.	MCL 215:8
pieces: thirty p. of silver	BIBLE 51:7
pierce: into his hand, and p. it	BIBLE 42:16
pies: Bellamy's veal p.	PITT 249:10
piety: Pathos, p., courage	FORS 143:25
to p. more prone	ALEX 4:7
piffle: p. before the wind	ASHF 18:23
pig: p. got up and slowly walked	BURT 83:1
pigeons: P. on the grass alas	STEIN 314:21
piggy-wig: P. stood	LEAR 203:12
pigmy: Fretted the p. body	DRYD 127:6
pigs: whether p. have wings	CARR 91:22
Pilate: hands than water like P.	GREE 158:2
P. saith unto him	BIBLE 54:1
pile: P. the bodies high	SAND 266:14
To p. Ossa on Pelion	VIRG 340:6
pilfering: p., unprotected race	CLARE 101:8
pilgrim: Onward goes the p. band	BAR 29:2
'P.'s Progress', about a man	TWAIN 335:19
To be a p.	BUNY 79:9
pilgrimage: quiet p.	CAMP 89:3
succeed me in my p.	BUNY 79:10
thus I'll take my p.	RAL 257:23
pilgrimages: to go on on p.	CHAU 95:11
pilgrims: love you land of the p.	CUMM 112:17
p. to th'appointed place	DRYD 128:12
pill: little yellow p.	RICH 179:5
Protestant women may take the p.	THOM 331:2
pillar: day in a p. of a cloud	BIBLE 39:39
p. of state	MILT 228:27
p. of the world transformed	SHAK 271:3
she became a p. of salt	BIBLE 39:15
pillars: hewn out her seven p.	BIBLE 43:14
p. of gold	BLAKE 60:17
Pylons, those p. bare	SPEN 313:3
pillow: like the feather p.	HAIG 159:16
on a p. for weariness	WORD 354:10
sighed upon a midnight p.	SHAK 272:18
sits upon the p.-hill	STEV 317:14
softer p. than my heart	BYRON 87:22
Where, like a p. on a bed	DONNE 124:2
pillows: P. his chin	MILT 227:29
pills: back to 'plasters, p.	LOCK 209:2
pilot: Dropping the p.	TENN 323:9

pilot (cont.):

see my p. face to face	TENN 323:19

pilots: P. of the purple twilight — TENN 326:10
pimpernel: demmed, elusive P. — ORCZY 241:17
pimples: scratching of p. — WOOLF 354:6
pin: life at a p.'s fee — SHAK 274:28
  p. up my hair with prose — CONG 106:18
pineapple: very p. of politeness — SHER 305:28
pinion: imagination droops her p. — BYRON 86:19
pinions: with p. skim the air — FRERE 145:22
pink: very p. of courtesy — SHAK 295:6
  very p. of perfection — GOLD 155:9
pinkly: p. bursts the spray — BETJ 37:6
pinko-grey: white races are really p. — FORS 143:24
pinnacled: P. dim in the intense inane — SHEL 304:23
pinprick: time is a p. of eternity — AUR 22:10
pint: like magic in a p. bottle — DICK 118:30
  p. of plain is your only man — O'BR 240:20
pioneers: P.! O pioneers — WHIT 348:13
pipes: Grate on their scrannel p. — MILT 227:15
piping: For ever p. songs — KEATS 191:20
  Helpless, naked, p. loud — BLAKE 62:3
  P. songs of pleasant glee — BLAKE 61:18
  weak p. time of peace — SHAK 294:14
Pippa: P. passes — BEER 32:9
Pippin: Right as a Ribstone P. — BELL 33:12
pips: until the p. squeak — GEDD 149:19
pirate: To be a P. King — GILB 152:22
piss: worth a pitcher of warm p. — GARN 148:7
pissing: inside the tent p. out — JOHN 181:21
pistol: I reach for my p. — JOHST 186:18
  Is that a p. in your pocket — WEST 346:23
  [pun] is a p. let off at the ear — LAMB 200:6
  when his p. misses — GOLD 155:14
pistols: Have you your p.? — WHIT 348:13
piston: steam and p. stroke — MORR 235:14
pistons: black statement of p. — SPEN 312:23
pit: know what is in the p. — BLAKE 60:10
  Law is a bottomless p. — ARB 14:22
  diggeth a p. shall fall — BIBLE 44:21
pitch: Pitched past p. of grief — HOPK 172:9
  toucheth p. shall be defiled — BIBLE 48:2
pitched: Love has p. his mansion — YEATS 358:20
pitcher: or the p. be broken — BIBLE 44:26
  worth a p. of warm piss — GARN 148:7
pitchfork: drive out nature with a p. — HOR 173:11
  thrown on her with a p. — SWIFT 320:7
  use my wit as a p. — LARK 201:19
pith: p. is in the postscript — HAZL 163:22
pitiful: lips say, 'God be p.' — BROW 75:1
pity: cherish p., lest you — BLAKE 61:22
  loved her that she did p. them — SHAK 291:35
  P. a human face — BLAKE 61:21
  p. and fear bringing about — ARIS 15:15
  p. beyond all telling — YEATS 359:18
  p. never ceases to be shown — DRYD 127:14
  p. of it — SHAK 292:23
  p. of War — OWEN 243:19
  save me, O source of p. — MISS 231:24
  'Tis P. She's a Whore — FORD 143:11
pix: Sticks nix hick p. — ANON 10:15
place: all other things give p. — GAY 149:10
  bourne of time and p. — TENN 323:19
  genius of the p. — POPE 251:15
  Get p. and wealth — POPE 252:25
  great p. is by a winding stair — BACON 24:29
  I go to prepare a p. — BIBLE 53:37
  In p. of strife — CAST 92:15
  keep in the same p. — CARR 91:18
  know the p. for the first time — ELIOT 133:10
  Men in great p. are thrice — BACON 24:27
  neither shall his p. know him — BIBLE 42:31
  Never the time and the p. — BROW 76:20
  no p. to go — WHIT 348:8
  p. for everything — BEET 32:15

place (cont.):

  p. in the sun — BULOW 78:8
  p. in the sun — WILH 350:25
  p. of understanding — BIBLE 43:1
  P., that great object — SMITH 308:20
  p. thereof shall know it no more — BOOK 68:7
  spirit of the p. — VIRG 339:18
  till there be no p. — BIBLE 45:8
  time and p. were not — ROCH 261:10
  To know their p. — BELL 33:6
places: all p. were alike to him — KIPL 197:20
  Proper words in proper p. — SWIFT 320:4
  quietest p. under the sun — HOUS 175:1
  Quires and P. where they sing — BOOK 64:7
  which built desolate p. — BIBLE 42:26
plackets: thy hand out of p. — SHAK 283:13
plagiarism: one author, it's p. — MIZN 232:12
plagiarize: P.! Let no one else's — LEHR 204:14
plague: Make instruments to p. us — SHAK 284:2
  p. o' both your houses — SHAK 295:8
  To p. the inventor — SHAK 285:23
plagues: p. with which mankind — DEFOE 115:25
plain: best p. set — BACON 24:13
  especially the need of the p. — WAUGH 344:3
  great Gromboolian p. — LEAR 203:8
  on a darkling p. — ARN 16:12
  pint of p. is your only man — O'BR 240:20
  p., blunt man — SHAK 281:25
  'p.' cooking — MORP 235:10
  P. living and high thinking — WORD 356:1
  p. man in his plain meaning — SHAK 289:23
  plain truth for p. people — WESL 346:14
  pricking on the p. — SPEN 313:7
  rough places p. — BIBLE 46:9
plains: p. of honour and reputation — JONS 187:13
  ringing p. of windy Troy — TENN 328:21
plaintive: p. numbers flow — WORD 357:2
plaisir: P. d'amour — FLOR 142:12
plan: by his p. of attack — SASS 267:13
plane: It's a bird! It's a p.! — ANON 7:5
planet: born under a rhyming p. — SHAK 291:26
  new p. swims into his ken — KEATS 192:11
  p. of Love is on high — TENN 326:28
planetary: p. influence — SHAK 282:22
planned: p. obsolescence — STEV 316:1
  Yet the order of the acts is p. — PAST 246:10
plant: Sensitive P. in a garden grew — SHEL 304:30
  time to p., and a time to pluck — BIBLE 44:11
  weed is a p. whose virtues — EMER 136:29
planted: I have p., Apollos — BIBLE 55:3
planting: p. my cabbages — MONT 233:9
plants: They are forced p. — JOHN 185:27
plashy: through the p. fen — WAUGH 343:25
plasters: back to 'p., pills — LOCK 209:2
plastics: abhorred p., Picasso — WAUGH 343:22
plate: silver p. on a coffin — CURR 113:9
platinum: bullets made of p. — BELL 33:1
  eyebrows made of p. — FORS 143:14
platitude: echo of a p. — BIER 59:3
  longitude with no p. — FRY 147:1
  stroke a p. until it purrs — MARQ 219:23
platitudes: orchestration of p. — WILD 350:24
Plato: attachment à la P. — GILB 152:11
  P. is dear to me, but dearer — ARIS 15:22
  P.'s retirement — MILT 230:6
  p. told him — CUMM 112:19
  rather be wrong with P. — CIC 101:1
  series of footnotes to P. — WHIT 348:6
play: Better than a p. — CHAR 95:3
  children at p. are not playing — MONT 233:11
  damned p. than no play at all — REYN 259:7
  do not p. things as they are — STEV 316:9
  game at which two can p. — BEER 32:12
  Games people p. — BERNE 36:10
  holdeth children from p. — SIDN 306:27

play (*cont.*):

House Beautiful is p. lousy	PARK 245:13
It'll p. in Peoria	ANON 8:11
our p. is played out	THAC 329:22
p. before the play is done	QUAR 257:1
p. Ercles rarely	SHAK 290:18
P. it again, Sam	EPST 137:10
p.'s the thing	SHAK 275:24
play up! and p. the game	NEWB 238:13
p. without a woman in it	KYD 199:11
prologue to a very dull p.	CONG 106:14
to p. with souls	BROW 76:12
When I p. with my cat	MONT 233:17
Work is x; y is p.	EINS 131:10
You would p. upon me	SHAK 276:13
playboy: P. of the Western World	SYNGE 321:22
played: I have p. the fool	BIBLE 41:19
P.-out and Done-to-Death	TRAI 334:2
p. the King as though under	FIELD 139:3
player: as strikes the p.	FITZ 140:13
poor p., that struts	SHAK 288:5
players: men and women merely p.	SHAK 272:24
see the p. well bestowed	SHAK 275:19
playing: on the p. fields of Eton	WELL 345:10
p. or quarrelling on the line	FORS 143:22
plays: English p. are like	VOLT 340:26
plaything: child's a p. for an hour	LAMB 200:14
plea: Just as I am, without one p.	ELL 136:2
Though justice be thy p.	SHAK 289:27
pleasance: Youth is full of p.	SHAK 299:5
pleasant: abridgement of all that was p.	GOLD 155:3
fallen unto me in p. places	BOOK 66:15
hear the p. cuckoo	DAV 114:17
if we do not find anything p.	VOLT 340:11
Jonathan were lovely and p.	BIBLE 41:22
Life would be very p. if	SURT 319:13
p. it is to have money	CLOU 102:14
too excitin' to be p.	DICK 119:29
Who is to do the p. work?	RUSK 264:15
pleasantness: ways are ways of p.	BIBLE 43:9
please: death after life does greatly p.	SPEN 313:9
I am to do what I p.	FRED 145:19
Love seeketh only Self to p.	BLAKE 62:1
must p. to live	JOHN 183:10
Myself alone I seek to p.	GAY 149:12
Nothing can p. many	JOHN 182:24
P. him and he straight is	WROTH 358:1
p. the touchy breed of poets	HOR 173:18
To tax and to p.	BURKE 79:26
Towered cities p. us then	MILT 227:6
Uncertain, coy, and hard to p.	SCOTT 268:22
we are not able to p. thee	BOOK 64:26
pleased: And p. with what he gets	SHAK 272:21
had he p. us less	ADD 2:10
in whom I am well p.	BIBLE 48:15
P. with a rattle, tickled	POPE 252:19
pleases: Though every prospect p.	HEBER 164:16
pleaseth: this age best p. me	HERR 167:21
pleasing: pleasure turns to p. pain	SPEN 313:13
pleasure: Business first; p. afterwards	THAC 329:13
But the privilege and p.	GILB 151:6
dragged on by their favourite p.	VIRG 339:23
fatal egg by p. laid	COWP 110:2
Forced her to do your p.	WEBS 344:24
gave p. to the spectators	MAC 213:19
greatest p. I know	LAMB 200:11
Green p. or grey grief	SWIN 321:17
his p. is life	BOOK 66:22
If they have p., the servant	BARC 28:17
in general read without p.	JOHN 186:15
Love ceases to be a p.	BEHN 32:21
Love's p. lasts but a moment	FLOR 142:12
must we not pay a debt to p.	ROCH 261:3
my heart with p. fills	WORD 355:5
not in p., but in rest from pain	DRYD 127:35

pleasure (*cont.*):

painful p. turns to pleasing	SPEN 313:13
P. at the helm	GRAY 157:3
p. in the pathless woods	BYRON 85:12
p. in the strength of an horse	BOOK 69:10
P. is a *thief* to business	DEFOE 115:11
p. is momentary	CHES 97:18
p. is not enhanced	AUST 22:16
P. is nothing else but	SELD 269:20
p. me in his top-boots	MARL 218:5
P. never is at home	KEATS 190:26
p. of drinking at somebody else's	LEIGH 204:19
P.'s a sin, and sometimes sin's	BYRON 86:3
P.'s for those who are bad	YES 360:12
p. was his business	EDG 130:17
public stock of harmless p.	JOHN 182:23
suburbs of your good p.	SHAK 281:7
Sweet is p. after pain	DRYD 127:20
There is a p. sure	DRYD 128:19
What p. lives in height	TENN 328:6
when Youth and P. meet	BYRON 85:3
whilst I go to my p.	WYCH 358:5
would have been my p.	TENN 324:6
pleasure-dome: stately p.	COL 103:22
sunny p. with caves of ice	COL 103:24
pleasure-house: I built my soul a lordly p.	TENN 327:14
pleasures: And we will all the p. prove	MARL 219:3
And we will some new p. prove	DONNE 123:23
celibacy has no p.	JOHN 183:5
English take their p. sadly	SULLY 319:4
Mid p. and palaces	PAYNE 246:21
No man is a hypocrite in his p.	JOHN 186:6
purest of human p.	BACON 24:26
understand the p. of the other	AUST 22:14
pledge: And I will p. with mine	JONS 187:23
pledged: p. their troth either	BOOK 66:4
Pleiads: rainy P. wester	HOUS 174:15
plenty: here is God's p.	DRYD 128:30
In delay there lies no p.	SHAK 297:23
I wasna fou, but just had p.	BURNS 82:3
on the expectation of p.	SHAK 286:20
P. has made me poor	OVID 243:14
pleuré: *Est d'avoir quelquefois p.*	MUSS 236:16
pleut: *Comme il p. sur la ville*	VERL 338:2
plot: Her p. hath many changes	QUAR 257:1
p. for a short story	CHEK 96:27
p. thickens very much upon	BUCK 78:2
Sonnet's scanty p.	WORD 355:15
This blessèd p., this earth	SHAK 293:16
plots: P., true or false	DRYD 127:4
plough: Men of England, wherefore p.	SHEL 305:1
put his hand to the p.	BIBLE 52:9
this morning held the p.	BETJ 36:22
We p. the fields, and scatter	CAMP 88:13
ploughman: p. homeward plods	GRAY 157:4
wrong even the poorest p.	CHAR 94:24
ploughshares: swords into p.	BIBLE 45:5
pluck: offend thee, p. it out	BIBLE 50:17
p. bright honour from	SHAK 277:27
p. till time and times	YEATS 360:1
plucked: p. my nipple from	SHAK 286:6
plume: In blast-beruffled p.	HARDY 162:6
plunder: separately p. a third	BIER 59:2
What a place to p.!	BLÜCH 62:11
plunging: When the p. hoofs were gone	DE L 116:11
plures: *Abiit ad p.*	PETR 248:9
plus: *P. ça change*	KARR 190:2
pneumatic: promise of p. bliss	ELIOT 134:33
Pobble: P. who has no toes	LEAR 203:14
pocket: Is that a pistol in your p.	WEST 346:23
not scruple to pick a p.	DENN 117:1
pound in your p.	WILS 351:14
want your pecker in my p.	JOHN 181:20
pockets: young man feels his p.	HOUS 174:12
poem: bathed in the P. of the Sea	RIMB 260:8

poem (cont.):

drowsy frowzy p.	BYRON 86:16
figure a p. makes	FROST 146:24
ice on a hot stove the p.	FROST 146:25
like to be married to a p.	KEATS 193:11
ought himself to be a true p.	MILT 230:28
p. is like a painting	HOR 173:4
p. is a test of invention	KEATS 192:22
p. lovely as a tree	KILM 194:22
p. should not mean but be	MACL 215:9
p. to the glory of beating	WOLFE 353:3
p., whose subject is not truth	CHAP 94:19
United States . . . the greatest p.	WHIT 348:25

poems: P. are made by fools like | KILM 195:1 |
| we all scribble p. | HOR 173:16 |

poesis: *Ut pictura p.* | HOR 173:4 |

poesy: viewless wings of P. | KEATS 192:1 |

poet: All a p. can do today is warn | OWEN 243:20 |

apothecary than a starved p.	LOCK 209:2
because he was a true P.	BLAKE 60:25
better p. than Porson	HOUS 175:6
business of a p.	JOHN 183:2
every fool is not a p.	POPE 251:2
Like a P. hidden	SHEL 305:9
limbs of a p.	HOR 174:3
lover, and the p.	SHAK 291:3
Not deep the P. sees, but wide	ARN 17:2
p. and the dreamer	KEATS 190:25
[p.] cometh unto you with a tale	SIDN 306:27
p. ever interpreted nature	GIR 153:6
p. is always indebted	MAY 222:16
p. is the priest	STEV 316:3
P.'s dream	WORD 354:17
p.'s eye, in a fine frenzy	SHAK 291:4
p.'s hope: to be like some	AUDEN 21:13
shall be accounted p. kings	KEATS 192:12
should possess a p.'s brain	DRAY 126:19
Thus every p., in his kind	SWIFT 320:23
Vex not thou the P.'s mind	TENN 327:15

poetic: Meet nurse for a p. child | SCOTT 268:14 |
| which constitutes p. faith | COL 104:24 |

poetical: claim to p. honours | JOHN 182:21 |

poetry: and that is p. | CAGE 88:4 |

cradled into p. by wrong	SHEL 303:22
Emptied of its p.	AUDEN 20:24
geniune p. is conceived	ARN 18:5
grotesque art in English p.	BAG 26:17
In p., no less than in life	ARN 18:4
In whining p.	DONNE 124:14
Ireland hurt you into poetry	AUDEN 20:22
It is not p., but prose	POPE 251:5
Jonson his best piece of p.	JONS 187:19
Language is fossil p.	EMER 136:28
most p. ignores most people	MITC 232:2
Nothing so much as mincing p.	SHAK 278:4
p. begins to atrophy when	POUND 254:22
p. comes not as naturally	KEATS 193:4
P. in motion	ANTH 190:5
P. [is] a speaking picture	SIDN 306:26
P. is a subject as precise	FLAU 141:9
P. is at bottom a criticism	ARN 18:6
P. is a way of taking life	FROST 146:27
p. is conceived and composed	ARN 18:5
P. is in the pity	OWEN 243:19
p. is like dropping a rose	MARQ 219:22
p. is more philosophical	ARIS 15:16
P. is the record	SHEL 305:18
P. is the spontaneous overflow	WORD 357:12
P. is the supreme fiction	STEV 316:8
P. is the synthesis of hyacinths	SAND 266:17
P. is what is lost in translation	FROST 146:28
P. is when all the lines	BENT 35:3
p. makes nothing happen	AUDEN 20:23
P. must be *as well written*	POUND 254:24
p. necessarily declines	MAC 213:7

poetry (cont.):

p. of motion	GRAH 156:6
P.'s a mere drug, Sir	FARQ 138:19
P.'s the feverish fit	WINC 352:1
p. = the *best* words	COL 104:26
polar star of p.	KEATS 192:22
quarrel with ourselves, p.	YEATS 360:10
resuscitate the dead art of p.	POUND 254:14
Sir, what is p.	JOHN 185:11
Superstition is the p. of life	GOET 154:10

poets: All p. are mad | BURT 83:8 |

first for wits, then p. passed	POPE 251:27
impossible to hold the p. back	GIR 153:5
Irish p., learn your trade	YEATS 360:6
mature p. steal	ELIOT 135:2
Milton's the prince of p.	BYRON 86:15
most p. are their own patients	THOM 331:3
p. bicycle-pump the human	AMIS 5:5
P. in our civilization	ELIOT 135:3
p. in our youth begin	WORD 356:17
P. that lasting marble seek	WALL 341:13
p., witty	BACON 25:16
Souls of p. dead and gone	KEATS 191:16
spite of all romantic p.	LEAP 203:6
Such sights as youthful p. dream	MILT 227:7
theft in other p.	DRYD 128:29
Three p. in an age at most	SWIFT 320:19
touchy breed of p.	HOR 173:18

point: creeping on from p. to point | TENN 326:13 |

in thy wheel there is a p.	MARL 218:16
p. his slow and moving finger	SHAK 292:24
still p. of the turning world	ELIOT 132:28
Surtout, Messieurs, p. de zèle	TALL 322:11
To a p. moral, or adorn a tale	JOHN 183:14
Up to a p., Lord Copper	WAUGH 343:24

poison: coward's weapon, p. | FLET 142:11 |
if you p. us, do we not die	SHAK 289:17
p. the wells	NEWM 238:15
p. the whole blood stream	EMPS 137:6
strongest p. ever known	BLAKE 60:8
We've got as far as p.-gas	HARDY 162:4

poisonous: for its p. wine | KEATS 191:25 |

poke: heart to p. poor Billy | GRAH 156:4 |

pokers: p. into true-love knots | COL 104:2 |

pole: Beloved from pole to p. | COL 104:13 |
| returning from the P. | CHER 91:11 |
| top of the greasy p. | DISR 122:17 |

polecat: semi-house-trained p. | FOOT 142:18 |

police: friendship recognised by the p. | STEV 317:5 |
| game at which the p. can beat you | SHAW 302:10 |
| To the citizen or the p. | AUDEN 21:11 |

policeman: park, a p. and a pretty girl | CHAP 94:12 |
| p.'s lot is not a happy one | GILB 152:24 |
| terrorist and the p. | CONR 107:9 |

policy: My home p.: I wage war | CLEM 102:1 |

my p. is to be able to take	BEVIN 38:9
p. is to float lazily downstream	SAL 266:2
p. of the good neighbour	RÓOS 262:10
some love but little p.	SHAK 294:7
will be tyrants from p.	BURKE 80:5

polish: we may p. it at leisure | DRYD 128:26 |

polished: O p. perturbation! | SHAK 278:26 |
| p. up that handle so carefullee | GILB 152:18 |

polite: have no allies to be p. to | GEOR 150:5 |

politeness: pineapple of p. | SHER 305:28 |
| Punctuality is the p. of kings | LOUI 210:17 |
| When square p., tempering | KNOX 198:17 |

political: fear of P. Economy | SELL 270:4 |

Man is by nature a p. animal	ARIS 15:18
points clearly to a p. career	SHAW 301:13
P. language	ORW 242:15
schemes of p. improvement	JOHN 184:22

politician: like a scurvy p. | SHAK 283:26 |
| p. is a statesman who | POMP 250:12 |
| p. is an arse upon | CUMM 112:18 |

politician (*cont.*):
p. is to render vice serviceable — BOL 63:7
statesman is a p. who's been dead — TRUM 335:4
which makes the p. wise — POPE 253:9
politicians: Old p. chew on wisdom past — POPE 251:23
whole race of p. put together — SWIFT 319:21
politics: Confound their p. — ANON 7:14
continuation of p. by other means — CLAU 101:16
From p., it was an easy step — AUST 22:24
In p., what begins in fear — COL 104:28
Magnanimity in p. is not — BURKE 80:5
mule of p. that engenders — DISR 121:27
mules of p. — POWER 255:4
Philistine of genius in p. — ARN 18:11
p. as well as in religion — JUN 188:26
p. consists in ignoring — ADAMS 1:19
p. is for the present — EINS 131:12
p. is present history — FREE 145:21
P. is the art of preventing — VALE 336:22
P. is war without bloodshed — MAO T 217:18
P., like Rock, Pop — WOLFE 353:9
p. the middle way is none — ADAMS 1:23
P. the only profession for which no — STEV 316:24
P. the organization of hatreds — ADAMS 1:11
science of p. — ARIS 15:13
week is a long time in p. — WILS 351:15
polluted: Pemberley to be thus p. — AUST 23:5
that is filthy and p. — BIBLE 47:25
pollution: unsavoury engine of p. — SPAR 312:14
polygamous: Man is p. — JAMES 180:11
polygamy: Before p. was made a sin — DRYD 127:2
pomegranate: from Browning some P. — BROW 75:3
pomp: heraldry, the p. of pow'r — GRAY 157:7
Lo, all our p. of yesterday — KIPL 197:3
nor the tide of p. — SHAK 279:16
p., and circumstance — SHAK 292:20
Take physic, p. — SHAK 283:12
Pompey: Knew you not P. — SHAK 280:24
pompous: p. in the grave — BROW 74:7
pomps: high Midsummer p. — ARN 17:19
p. and vanity of this wicked — BOOK 65:21
pond: have their stream and p. — BROO 73:2
ponies: Five and twenty p. — KIPL 196:28
wretched, blind, pit p. — HODG 169:13
Pontefract: licorice fields at P. — BETJ 37:5
poodle: right hon. Gentleman's p. — LLOY 208:8
pools: p. are bright and deep — HOGG 170:7
p. are filled with water — BOOK 67:21
poop: p. was beaten gold — SHAK 271:14
poor: And makes me p. indeed — SHAK 292:11
Blessed are the p. in spirit — BIBLE 48:19
Bring in hither the p. — BIBLE 52:24
expensive it is to be p. — BALD 27:2
Give me your tired, your p. — LAZ 203:2
give to the p. — BIBLE 50:21
grind the faces of the p. — BIBLE 45:6
have in common being so p. — BLUN 62:12
It's no disgrace t'be p. — HUBB 175:17
It's the p. wot gets the blame — ANON 10:11
Laws grind the p. — GOLD 155:5
murmuring p. — CRAB 110:24
My countrymen Kiltartan's p. — YEATS 359:9
open to the p. and the rich — ANON 7:9
Plenty has made me p. — OVID 243:14
p. always ye have with you — BIBLE 53:35
p. are Europe's blacks — CHAM 94:4
p. are to be proud — SHAK 298:5
p. get children — EGAN 189:19
p. have cried, Caesar hath wept — SHAK 281:20
p. in a loomp is bad — TENN 327:10
p. is their poverty — BIBLE 43:17
P. little rich girl — COW 109:6
p. man at his gate — ALEX 4:3
p. man had nothing — BIBLE 41:24
p. man's dearest friend — BURNS 82:17

poor (*cont.*):
p. relation is the most irrelevant — LAMB 200:5
p. soul sat sighing — SHAK 292:26
p. to do him reverence — SHAK 281:25
propensity for being p. — AUST 23:11
Resolve not to be p. — JOHN 185:31
RICH AND THE P. — DISR 122:6
rich as well as the p. — FRAN 145:2
She was p. but she was honest — ANON 10:11
simple annals of the p. — GRAY 157:7
poorest: p. he that is in England — RAIN 257:19
wrong even the p. ploughman — CHAR 94:24
pop: P. goes the weasel — MAND 217:8
Pope: against the P. or the NUM — BALD 27:8
Conscience first, the P. afterwards — NEWM 238:18
poetry of Dryden, P. — ARN 18:5
P.! How many divisions — STAL 314:8
poplars: p. are felled, farewell — COWP 109:30
poppies: In Flanders fields the p. — MCCR 214:17
populace: Philistines, and P. — ARN 17:24
propriety give the name of P. — ARN 17:27
popular: base, common and p. — SHAK 279:9
population: P., when unchecked — MALT 217:5
you have a starving p. — DISR 121:7
populi: *Salus p. suprema est lex* — CIC 100:20
Vox p., vox Dei — ALC 3:14
porcupines: couple of p. under you — KHR 194:21
Porlock: person on business from P. — COL 103:21
pornography: P. is the attempt to insult sex — LAWR 202:13
porpoise: p. close behind us — CARR 91:11
porridge: healsome p. — BURNS 82:2
Porson: better poet than P. — HOUS 175:6
port: alma mater lie dissolved in p. — POPE 250:16
ancient tales, and p. — BELL 33:17
I'll quit the p. o' Heaven — NEWB 238:10
In every p. a wife — DIBD 117:18
It would be p. if it could — BENT 35:10
p. after stormy seas — SPEN 313:9
p., for men — JOHN 185:22
to which p. one is sailing — SEN 270:7
portable: P., and compendious oceans — CRAS 111:14
portal: fiery p. of the east — SHAK 293:29
fitful tracing of a p. — STEV 316:11
Porter: moon shone bright on Mrs P. — ELIOT 134:26
portion: p. for foxes — BOOK 67:15
portmanteau: it's like a p. — CARR 92:2
portrait: paint a p. I lose a friend — SARG 266:23
p. of a blinking idiot — SHAK 289:14
P. of the Artist — JOYCE 188:6
two styles of p. painting — DICK 119:15
position: p. must be held — HAIG 159:17
p. of matter at or near — RUSS 265:1
p. ridiculous — CHES 97:18
positive: ac-cent-tchu-ate the p. — MERC 223:9
p. value has its price — PIC 248:19
possessed: limited in order to be p. — BURKE 79:23
Webster was much p. by death — ELIOT 134:32
possessing: too dear for my p. — SHAK 299:27
possession: p. of a good fortune — AUST 23:2
Than in the glad p. — JONS 187:12
possessions: p. for a moment of time — ELIZ 135:15
that are behind the great p. — JAMES 179:20
possibilities: preferred to improbable p. — ARIS 15:17
possibility: deny the p. of anything — HUXL 177:23
possible: effecting of all things p. — BACON 25:26
if a thing is p. — CAL 88:6
Politics is the art of the p. — BISM 59:17
p. you may be mistaken — CROM 112:2
says that something is p. — CLAR 101:14
With God all things are p. — BIBLE 50:23
world is the best of all p. — BRAD 71:8
Possum: said the Honourable P. — BERR 36:14
possumus: *Non omnia p. omnes* — VIRG 340:2
possunt: p., *quia posse videntur* — VIRG 339:10

post: Lie follows by p.	BER 35:12	**power** (cont.):	
P. coitum omne animal triste	ANON 13:19	p. can be rightfully exercised	MILL 224:15
p. of honour is a private station	ADD 2:17	p. grows out of the barrel	MAO 217:19
postal: cheque and the p. order	AUDEN 21:4	p. is apt to corrupt	PITT 249:4
postboy: Never see a dead p.	DICK 120:4	P. is so apt to be insolent	HAL 160:10
post-chaise: driving briskly in a p.	JOHN 185:13	P. is the great aphrodisiac	KISS 198:6
posted: p. presence of the watcher	JAMES 179:25	p. of suppress	NORT 240:8
poster: Kitchener is a great p.	ASQ 19:5	p. thrown away	LESS 206:4
posterity: ancestry, or hope of p.	POWER 255:4	p. to act according	LOCKE 208:21
not look forward to p.	BURKE 80:12	p. to hurt us that we love	FLET 31:1
P. do something for us	ADD 2:28	p. to live, and act	WORD 356:19
p. talking bad grammar	DISR 122:14	P. to the people	ANON 10:6
Think of your p.	ADAMS 2:4	p. which erring men call chance	MILT 226:18
postern: Present has latched its p.	HARDY 162:2	p. which stands on Privilege	BELL 33:25
posters: P. of the sea and land	SHAK 285:5	P. without responsibility	KIPL 198:5
postscript: all the pith is in the p.	HAZL 163:22	responsibility without p.	STOP 318:1
her mind but in her p.	STEE 314:15	Restored to life, and p., and	KEBLE 193:16
most material in the p.	BACON 24:19	seek p. and to lose liberty	BACON 24:28
pot: greasy Joan doth keel the p.	SHAK 284:23	though stripped of p.	SCOTT 268:16
have a chicken in his p.	HENR 165:20	with Eternal God for p.	TENN 327:13
potter pray, and who the p.	FITZ 140:16	witty beauty is a p.	MER 223:12
There is death in the p.	BIBLE 42:10	world desires to have—P.	BOUL 70:11
thorns under a p.	BIBLE 44:16	**powerful:** All-p. as the wind	AUBER 19:15
potage: birthright for a mess of p.	BIBLE 39:17	p. goodness want	SHEL 304:17
potato: bashful young p.	GILB 152:11	**powerless:** p. to be born	ARN 17:16
potent: how p. cheap music is	COW 109:10	**powers:** nor p., nor things present	BIBLE 54:42
Potomac: All quiet along the P.	MCCL 214:14	principalities, against p.	BIBLE 56:4
All quiet along the P.	BEERS 32:9	we lay waste our p.	WORD 357:10
potter: Who *is* the p., pray	FITZ 140:16	**pox:** die upon the gallows or of the p.	WILK 350:26
poultry: prolonging the lives of the p.	ELIOT 132:4	**practice:** And P. drives me mad	ANON 9:11
Pound: And Ezra P. and T. S. Eliot	DYLAN 129:20	**practise:** Go p. if you please	BROW 77:7
pound: p. here in Britain	WILS 351:14	we shall p. in heaven	BROW 76:21
pounding: Hard p. this	WELL 345:11	**praemitti:** *sciamus non amitti sed p.*	CYPR 113:13
pounds: handsome in three hundred p.	SHAK 290:10	**praeterea:** *Vox et p. nihil*	ANON 14:3
passing rich with forty p.	GOLD 154:21	**prairies:** From the mountains to the p.	BERL 35:21
p. will take care	LOWN 211:21	**praise:** all other p. is shame	SIDN 306:25
two hundred p. a year	BUTL 84:5	Damn with faint p.	POPE 251:6
poured: p. into his clothes	WOD 352:24	dispraised were no small p.	MILT 230:3
poverty: by p. depressed	JOHN 183:9	girded with p.	GRANT 156:8
Come away; p.'s catching	BEHN 32:22	Give them not p.	SORL 311:16
crime so shameful as p.	FARQ 138:15	if there be any p.	BIBLE 56:9
destruction of the poor is their p.	BIBLE 43:17	lack tongues to p.	SHAK 300:5
Give me not p. lest I steal	DEFOE 115:13	Let us now p. famous men	BIBLE 48:7
In p., hunger, and dirt	HOOD 171:12	no such whetstone as p.	ASCH 18:19
misfortunes of p.	JUV 189:4	oblique p.	JOHN 185:20
P. and oysters always seem	DICK 119:30	paint 'em truest p. 'em most	ADD 2:12
P. is a great enemy	JOHN 185:31	p. a fugitive and cloistered	MILT 230:31
p. knows how extremely	BALD 27:2	p. and true perfection	SHAK 290:5
she scorns our p.	SHAK 280:7	p. at morning what they	POPE 252:6
worst of crimes is p.	SHAW 301:8	P. him upon the well-tuned	BOOK 69:12
powder: keep your p. dry	BLAC 59:22	P. my soul, the King of heaven	LYTE 212:21
when your p.'s runnin' low	NEWB 238:10	P. the green earth	BUNT 78:14
power: absolute p. corrupts	ACTON 1:5	P. the Lord and pass the	FORGY 143:13
All hail the p. of Jesus' Name	PERR 248:4	P. the Lord, for he is kind	MILT 227:9
All p. is a trust	DISR 122:10	P. they that will times past	HERR 167:21
corridors of p.	SNOW 310:18	P. to the Holiest	NEWM 238:20
Everyone who desires p.	MILL 224:18	so double be his p.	SPEN 313:10
friend in p. is a friend lost	ADAMS 1:14	They p. those works	MART 220:5
good want p.	SHEL 304:17	unto thy Name give the p.	BOOK 68:17
gratefully sing his p.	GRANT 156:8	We p. thee, God	ANON 14:1
have p. over men	WOLL 353:11	We p. thee, O God	BOOK 63:18
Horses and P. and War	KIPL 196:5	Who like me his p. should sing	LYTE 212:21
knowledge itself is p.	BACON 25:25	whom there were none to p.	WORD 356:22
lies not in our p. to love or hate	MARL 218:17	**praised:** everybody p. the Duke	SOUT 311:20
Lord of all p. and might	BOOK 64:25	p. him to his face	TENN 328:14
more contracted that p. is	JOHN 185:17	Who ne'er said, 'God be p.'	BROW 75:1
nobility is but the act of p.	BACON 25:4	**praiser:** p. of past times	HOR 173:2
no hopes but from p.	BURKE 81:9	**praises:** faint p. one another damn	WYCH 358:6
no more than p. in trust	DRYD 127:10	sing p. lustily unto him	BOOK 66:24
only have p. over people as long	SOLZ 310:28	**praising:** doing one's p. for oneself	BUTL 84:9
O wad some P. the giftie gie us	BURNS 82:25	**pram:** p. in the hall	CONN 106:25
pains be less, or p. more	BROME 72:8	**prater:** p. of the northern race	CHUR 98:28
p., and the glory	BIBLE 48:27	**pray:** All p. in their distress	BLAKE 61:20
p. breathe forth	SHAK 271:16	came to scoff, remained to p.	GOLD 154:22
		I p. for the country	HALE 160:4

pray (*cont.*):

More things are wrought by p.	TENN 324:21
nor p. with you	SHAK 288:31
p. for you at St Paul's	SMITH 310:14
Watch and p., that ye enter	BIBLE 51:13
we do p. for mercy	SHAK 289:27
Work and p., live on hay	HILL 168:12

prayer: are homes of silent p.

	TENN 325:6
Ave Maria! 'tis the hour of p.	BYRON 86:18
called the house of p.	BIBLE 50:27
Comin' in on a wing and a p.	ADAM 2:9
Conservative Party at p.	ROYD 264:2
Every p. reduces itself	TURG 335:15
More things are wrought by p.	TENN 324:21
most perfect p.	LESS 206:5
p. the lips ne'er act	HERR 167:17
P. the Church's banquet	HERB 167:4
publick P. in the Church	BOOK 69:18
wish for p. is a p. in itself	BERN 36:7

prayers: Christopher Robin is saying his p.

	MILNE 226:1
have the p. of the church	SWIFT 320:8
Knelt down with angry p.	HODG 169:13
Lord, hear our p.	BOOK 65:24
Their three-mile p.	BURNS 82:29
This was among my p.	HOR 174:4

prayeth: p. well, who loveth well

	COL 104:18
praying: Amelia was p. for George	THAC 329:18
do it pat, now he is p.	SHAK 276:17
Nay that's past p.	SHAK 277:33
No p., it spoils business	OTWAY 243:7

prays: family that p. together

	SCAL 267:16
p. but faintly and would be	SHAK 294:9
preach: p. the gospel	BIBLE 51:26
preached: p. to death by wild curates	SMITH 310:8
preaching: woman's p. is like	JOHN 184:16
precedency: p. between a louse and a flea	JOHN 186:2
precedent: dangerous p.	CORN 108:8
From precedent to p.	TENN 329:1
p. embalms a principle	STOW 318:10
precept: more efficacious than p.	JOHN 183:6
p. must be upon precept	BIBLE 45:27
precepts: icy p. of respect	SHAK 296:22
precious: Deserve the p. bane	MILT 228:19
Liberty is p.	LENIN 205:6
p. stone set in the silver sea	SHAK 293:16
precise: Is too p. in every part	HERR 167:15
precisely: thinking too p. on the event	SHAK 276:30
preference: special p. for beetles	HALD 160:3
preferment: knocking at P.'s door	ARN 17:6
preferred: after me is p. before me	BIBLE 53:12
pregnant: p. bank swelled up	DONNE 124:2
prejudice: popular p. runs in favour	DICK 119:11
P., *n*. A vagrant opinion	BIER 59:8
p. of good order	ANON 6:22
result of PRIDE AND P.	BURN 81:17

prejudices: Drive out p. through the door

	FRED 145:18
p. as the advertisers don't	SWAF 319:16
reviewing it; it p. a man so	SMITH 310:9
premises: based upon licensed p.	O'BR 240:19
prepare: I go to p. a place	BIBLE 53:37
not to p. for life	PAST 246:9
p. to shed them now	SHAK 281:22
P. ye the way of the Lord	BIBLE 46:8
P. ye the way of the Lord	BIBLE 48:13

prepared: BE P.

	BAD 26:1
chance favours only the p.	PAST 246:11
world is not yet p.	DOYLE 125:17
prerogative: p. of the eunuch	STOP 318:1
p. of the harlot	KIPL 198:5
that which is called p.	LOCKE 208:21
presbyter: P. is but old *Priest*	MILT 228:2
presence: before his p. with a song	BOOK 68:5
his p. with thanksgiving	BOOK 67:31
posted p. of the watcher	JAMES 179:25

present: All p. and correct

	ANON 5:21
know nothing but the p.	KEYN 194:15
nor things p., nor things	BIBLE 54:42
p. at the conception	ORTON 241:20
p. contains nothing more	BERG 35:13
P. has latched its postern	HARDY 162:2
p. help in time of trouble	ANON 5:18
p. is the funeral	CLARE 101:8
Present mirth hath p. laughter	SHAK 297:23
p. of Mornington Crescent	HARG 162:21
p. were the world's last night	DONNE 123:13
p., yes, we are in it	LOW 211:20
There is no p. in Wales	THOM 331:5
Time p. and time past	ELIOT 132:25
un-birthday p.	CARR 91:25
very p. help in trouble	BOOK 67:6
Who p., past, and future, sees	BLAKE 61:26

presents: P. endear Absents

	LAMB 199:24
preservative: pleasantest p. from want	AUST 23:4
preserve: shall p. thy going out	BOOK 68:27
preserver: Creator and P.	BOOK 64:18
presidency: P. of the United States	STEV 316:19
president: any boy may become P.	STEV 316:17
As P., I have no eyes	LINC 207:14
P. of the Immortals	HARDY 161:25
rather be right than be P.	CLAY 101:18
their P. is a crook	NIXON 240:3
We are the P.'s men	KISS 198:7
press: fell *dead-born from the p.*	HUME 176:10
Freedom of the p. in Britain	SWAF 319:16
god of our idolatry, the p.	COWP 110:3
governs the periodical p.	TROL 334:20
power of the p.	NORT 240:8
p. is the *Palladium*	JUN 188:25
P.-men; Slaves of the Lamp	ARN 16:7
with you on the free p.	STOP 318:2
pressed: p. into service means	FROST 146:21
pressure: Grace under p.	HEM 165:15
prestige: p. without distance	DE G 116:5
presumed: Lady, it is to be p.	JONS 187:5
presumption: Of surquidrie and foul p.	CHAU 96:13
you'll be amused by its p.	THUR 332:17
pretence: some faint meaning make p.	DRYD 128:5
pretender: James II, and the Old P.	GUED 159:7
pretexts: Tyrants seldom want p.	BURKE 79:19
pretio: *Cum p.*	JUV 189:6
pretty: He is a very p. weoman	FLEM 142:1
It is a p., pretty thing	PEELE 247:1
It is a p. thing	GREE 158:9
policeman and a p. girl	CHAP 94:12
p. can get away with	WAUGH 344:3
p. chickens and their dam	SHAK 287:26
p. girl is like a melody	BERL 36:1
p. to see what money will do	PEPYS 247:20
Puts on his p. looks	SHAK 282:8
prevail: great is truth, and shall p.	BROO 73:14
prevails: Great is truth, and it p.	BIBLE 58:23
prevarication: last dyke of p.	BURKE 80:27
prevent: duty to try to p. it	MILN 226:2
preventing: Politics is the art of p.	VALÉ 336:22
prey: hast'ning ills a p.	GOLD 154:18
thou soon must be his p.	SHEL 304:2
Venus entire latched onto her p.	RAC 257:16
yet a p. to all	POPE 252:2
price: All those men have their p.	WALP 342:6
because they fetch a high p.	WHAT 347:7
blood be the p. of admiralty	KIPL 197:9
Everything in Rome has its p.	JUV 189:6
'fixed p.' is negotiable	TOFF 333:7
have bought it at any p.	CLAR 101:11
her p. is far above rubies	BIBLE 44:6
knows the p. of everything	WILDE 350:1
love that pays the p.	SPR 313:26
one pearl of great p.	BIBLE 50:6

price (cont.):
positive value has its p.	PIC 248:19
p. is asked for harmony	DOST 125:4
p. of justice is eternal	BENN 34:17
p. of wisdom is above rubies	BIBLE 43:2
p. well worth paying	LAM 200:18
What p. glory	STAL 5:13
Wot p. Selvytion nah	SHAW 301:11

prices: contrivance to raise p. — SMITH 308:21
prick: If you p. us, do we not bleed — SHAK 289:17
I paint with my p. — REN 259:6
It is a p., it is a sting — PEELE 247:1
p. the sides of my intent — SHAK 286:1
pricking: By the p. of my thumbs — SHAK 287:18
knight was p. on the plain — SPEN 313:7
prickly: Here we go round the p. pear — ELIOT 133:18
pricks: kick against the p. — BIBLE 54:12
pride: And pour contempt on all my p. — WATTS 343:4
burn its children to save its p. — MEYER 224:4
false p. in place and blood — TENN 325:25
from p., vain-glory — BOOK 64:14
He that is low no p. — BUNY 79:7
I know thy p. — BIBLE 41:17
Is p. that apes humility — COL 103:16
P. goeth before destruction — BIBLE 43:28
p. is something in-conceivable — GILB 151:18
P. ruled my will — NEWM 238:22
result of P. AND PREJUDICE — BURN 81:17
that will her p. deflower — SPEN 313:12
priest: Am I both p. and clerk — SHAK 294:4
Delicate-handed p. — TENN 326:25
huntsman and a fiddling p. — COWP 110:1
Presbyter is but old P. writ — MILT 228:2
p., a piece of mere church — COWP 110:15
p. of the invisible — STEV 316:3
rid me of this turbulent p. — HENR 165:23
'twixt the P. and Clerk — HERR 167:18
priestcraft: ere p. did begin — DRYD 127:2
priesthood: royal p., an holy nation — BIBLE 57:8
priestlike: moving waters at their p. task — KEATS 190:10
priests: p. have been enemies — HUME 176:8
strangled with the guts of p. — MESL 223:27
treen p. and golden chalices — JEWEL 181:14
with women nor with p. — SOUT 311:24
prime: having lost but once your p. — HERR 167:25
laurel for the perfect p. — ROSS 263:3
One's p. is elusive — SPARK 312:13
Prime Minister: buried the Unknown P. — ASQ 19:3
next P. but three — BELL 33:7
Prime Ministers: P. wedded to the truth — SAKI 265:22
wild flowers, and P. — BALD 27:10
prime-roses: Pale p. — SHAK 298:33
primeval: This is the forest p. — LONG 209:15
primordial: p. chaos clapped — WELLS 345:22
protoplasmal p. atomic — GILB 151:18
primrose: p. path of dalliance — SHAK 274:20
To P. Hill and Saint John's Wood — BLAKE 60:17
primroses: Wan as p. — KEATS 190:13
prince: Advise the p. — ELIOT 134:1
Else a great p. in prison lies — DONNE 124:4
God bless the P. of Wales — LINL 208:1
Good-night, sweet p. — SHAK 277:19
Is in a p. the virtue — MASS 222:3
news and P. of Peace — FLET 142:8
On which the p. of glory died — WATTS 343:4
P. of darkness and dead night — SPEN 313:8
p. of darkness is a gentleman — SHAK 283:16
P. of Peace — BIBLE 45:16
princes: blaze forth the death of p. — SHAK 281:8
O put not your trust in p. — BOOK 69:9
P. and lords may flourish — GOLD 154:18
p. are come home again — SHAK 282:15
thy p. eat in the morning — BIBLE 44:22
word to be addressed to p. — ELIZ 135:10
princess: P. of Parallelograms — BYRON 87:15

principalities: against p. — BIBLE 56:4
nor p., nor powers — BIBLE 54:42
principle: An active P. — WORD 354:22
'falling domino' p. — EIS 131:15
good men to rise above p. — LONG 209:9
He does everything on p. — SHAW 302:9
precedent embalms a p. — STOW 318:10
p. can be sacrificed to expediency — MAUG 222:8
Protection is not a p. — DISR 121:10
subjects are rebels from p. — BURKE 80:16
principles: Damn your p.! — DISR 122:15
Lordship's p. or your mistress — WILK 350:26
shows that he has good p. — JOHN 184:8
who denies the first p. — AUCT 20:4
print: All the news that's fit to p. — OCHS 241:1
decomposing in the eternity of p. — WOOLF 353:20
licence to p. money — THOM 332:4
p. such of the proprietor's — SWAF 319:16
still 'tis devils must p. — MOORE 234:10
printemps: p. dans ses plis a gardé — ARAG 14:21
printing: Gunpowder, P. — CARL 90:9
P., gunpowder — BACON 25:28
we think to regulate p. — MILT 230:32
printless: lissom, clerical, p. toe — BROO 73:5
priorities: language of p. — BEVAN 37:19
prism: Of Newton, with his p. — WORD 356:10
prison: Come, let's away to p. — SHAK 284:1
comparatively at home in p. — WAUGH 343:20
Else a great prince in p. lies — DONNE 124:4
He did grind in the p. house — BIBLE 41:6
Lime-Tree Bower my P. — COL 104:21
p. and the woman's workhouse — SHAW 302:4
p. for the colour of his hair — HOUS 174:6
prison in a p. — DICK 120:2
p. to them that are bound — BIBLE 46:24
p. where I live unto the world — SHAK 294:10
Shades of the p.-house — WORD 355:20
Stone walls do not a p. make — LOV 210:19
'Twixt a p. and a smile — WOTT 357:18
was not the world a vast p. — WOLL 353:14
What is a ship but a p. — BURT 83:10
while there is a soul in p. — DEBS 115:9
prisoner: thoughts of a p. — SOLZ 311:1
your being taken p. — KITC 198:9
prisoners: p. of addiction — ILL 178:9
Which p. call the sky — WILDE 350:15
prisons: Madhouses, p. — CLARE 101:4
P. are built with stones — BLAKE 61:7
private: grave's a fine and p. place — MARV 220:25
his p. parts, his money — BUTL 84:18
invade the sphere of p. life — MELB 222:23
Its p. life is a disgrace — ANON 10:8
kind heaven, a p. station — GAY 149:13
post of honour is a p. station — ADD 2:17
P. faces in public places — AUDEN 21:6
P. Means is dead — SMITH 309:20
P. property is a necessary — TAWN 322:19
silk hat at a p. view — EDW 130:22
privates: Faith, her p., we — SHAK 275:13
what have kings that p. — SHAK 279:15
privilege: But the p. and pleasure — GILB 151:6
power which stands on P. — BELL 33:25
p. I claim for my own sex — AUST 22:28
prize: heedless hearts, is lawful p. — GRAY 157:15
is the path and Christ the p. — MONS 233:2
p. we sought is won — WHIT 348:11
We do not run for p. — SORL 311:15
prized: local, but p. elsewhere — AUDEN 21:13
prizes: offer glittering p. — SMITH 309:6
probable: P. impossibilities — ARIS 15:17
probationary: Eden's dread p. tree — COWP 110:3
problem: It is quite a three-pipe p. — DOYLE 125:15
not a single p. is solved — CHEK 97:1
or you're part of the p. — CLEA 101:19

problem (*cont.*):
p. left to itself dries up — SIMP 307:13
proceed: all just works do p. — BOOK 64:11
proceedings: p. interested him no more — HARTE 163:13
proceeds: good conscience on the p. — SMITH 309:14
procession: torchlight p. — O'SUL 243:5
proclaims: apparel oft p. the man — SHAK 274:21
procrastination: p. is the art of — MARQ 219:15
P. is the thief of time — YOUNG 360:19
procreant: p. urge of the world — WHIT 348:17
proctors: With prudes for p. — TENN 327:16
procul: *P. hinc, procul este* — OVID 243:9
Procul, o p. este, profani — VIRG 339:13
prodigal: yet p. of ease — DRYD 127:8
production: sole end and purpose of p. — SMITH 308:24
productions: in love with the p. of time — BLAKE 61:5
profanation: From sale and p. — CHES 97:24
'Twere p. of our joys — DONNE 124:15
profane: Coldly p. and impiously gay — CRAB 110:23
P., erroneous, and vain — BUTL 84:2
To Banbury came I, O p. one — BRAT 71:16
profaned: word is too often p. — SHEL 305:5
profani: *Procul, o procul este, p.* — VIRG 339:13
profession: ancient p. in the world — KIPL 197:17
discharge of any p. — JOHN 185:2
man a debtor to his p. — BACON 24:9
ornament to her p. — BUNY 79:8
professional: P. men, they have no cares — NASH 237:12
professions: p. are conspiracies — SHAW 301:3
professor: called a *p. emeritus* — LEAC 203:3
professors: protect all conscientious p. — PAINE 244:10
profit: no p. but the name — SHAK 276:28
surely was my p. had I known — TENN 324:6
To whose p.? — CIC 100:31
what shall it p. a man — BIBLE 51:23
profits: Civilization and p. — COOL 107:18
It little p. that an idle king — TENN 328:19
monopoly p. is a quiet life — HICKS 168:10
profound: p. truths recognized — BOHR 63:1
profundis: *De p. clamavi ad te* — BIBLE 58:14
programme: Not so much a p. — ANON 9:19
progress: Congress makes no p. — LIGNE 207:2
Humanity is just a work in p. — WILL 351:4
It was no summer p. — ANDR 5:15
principle of all social p. — FOUR 144:14
p. depends on the unreasonable — SHAW 302:1
p. if a cannibal uses knife — LEC 204:1
P. is a comfortable disease — CUMM 112:20
p. is a doctrine of idlers — BAUD 30:8
P. is not an accident — SPEN 312:19
p. is the exchange of one nuisance — ELLIS 136:5
P., man's distinctive mark — BROW 75:23
P. through technology — ANON 13:4
Reason and P., the old firm — OSB 242:23
swell a p., start a scene or two — ELIOT 134:1
Time's thievish p. to eternity — SHAK 299:26
projections: Merely p. — ELIOT 132:21
proletariat: dictatorship of the p. — MARX 221:12
prologue: p. to a very dull play — CONG 106:14
What's past is p. — SHAK 296:3
prologues: happy p. to the swelling act — SHAK 285:10
Promethean: true P. fire — SHAK 284:16
promise: P., large promise — JOHN 182:13
p. made is a debt unpaid — SERV 270:9
Whose p. none relies — ROCH 261:4
promised: Jesus, I have p. — BODE 62:16
Marching to the P. Land — BAR 29:2
never p. you a rose garden — GREEN 158:1
think of the Future as a p. land — LEWIS 206:11
promises: But I have p. to keep — FROST 146:23
he is a young man of p. — BALF 27:12
man who p. least — BAR 29:21
promising: destroy they first call p. — CONN 106:24
promotion: none will sweat but for p. — SHAK 272:17
p. cometh neither from — BOOK 67:18

prone: Orion plunges p. — HOUS 174:15
to piety more p. — ALEX 4:7
pronounce: not frame to p. it right — BIBLE 41:2
spell better than they p. — TWAIN 336:1
pronounced: He p. the letter R — AUBR 19:21
proof: of which America is the p. — MCC 214:10
proofs: As p. of holy writ — SHAK 292:18
Proosian: French, or Turk, or P. — GILB 152:21
propensities: ruined on the side of their
natural p. — BURKE 81:7
proper: know our p. stations — DICK 118:5
my delight is in p. young men — BURNS 82:12
no p. time of day — HOOD 171:9
noun, p. or improper — FULL 147:4
p. study of mankind is books — HUXL 177:5
p. study of mankind is man — POPE 252:17
P. words in proper places — SWIFT 320:4
properly: never did anything p. — LEAR 203:16
property: consider himself public p. — JEFF 181:1
give me a little snug p. — EDG 130:16
governing not p. but a trust — FOX 144:15
Private p. is a necessary — TAWN 322:19
P. has its duties as well as — DRUM 126:25
P. is theft — PROU 255:16
thereby makes it his p. — LOCKE 208:19
Thieves respect p. — CHES 98:11
prophecy: though I have the gift of p. — BIBLE 55:11
prophesy: p. deceits — BIBLE 45:29
we p. in part — BIBLE 55:13
your daughters shall p. — BIBLE 47:20
prophet: I love a p. of the soul — EMER 136:14
p. is not without honour — BIBLE 50:7
there arise among you a p. — BIBLE 40:22
To entrance the p.'s ear — MANT 217:17
prophetic: O my p. soul — SHAK 274:32
With such p. greeting — SHAK 285:8
prophets: Beware of false p. — BIBLE 49:14
ceased to pose as its p. — POPP 253:15
goodly fellowship of the P. — BOOK 63:19
this is the law and the p. — BIBLE 49:11
unto the fathers by the p. — BIBLE 56:23
proportion: broke, and no p. kept — SHAK 294:11
some strangeness in the p. — BACON 24:14
propose: oppose everything, and p. nothing — DERBY 117:6
Whoever loves, if he do not p. — DONNE 123:4
proposes: man p. but God disposes — THOM 330:1
proposition: p. is the method — SCHL 267:22
proprietor: Death! Great p. of all — YOUNG 360:18
propriety: From her p. — SHAK 292:7
prose: all for p. and verse — CAREW 89:18
All that is not p. is verse — MOL 232:15
as well written as p. — POUND 254:24
discourse and nearest p. — DRYD 128:14
Not verse now, only p. — BROW 75:18
pin up my hair with p. — CONG 106:18
p. and the passion — FORS 143:21
P. is when all the lines — BENT 35:3
p. run mad — POPE 251:5
P. = words in their best order — COL 104:26
speaking p. without knowing it — MOL 232:16
They shut me up in p. — DICK 120:15
unattempted yet in p. or rhyme — MILT 228:8
prospect: dull p. of a distant good — DRYD 127:32
Though every p. pleases — HEBER 164:16
prosper: I grow, I p. — SHAK 282:21
Treason doth never p. — HAR 162:22
Why do sinners' ways p. — HOPK 172:18
prosperity: jest's p. lies in the ear — SHAK 284:20
man to han ben in p. — CHAU 96:18
P. doth best discover vice — BACON 24:11
prostitute: I puff the p. away — DRYD 128:23
prostitutes: small nations like p. — KUBR 199:7
protect: Heaven will p. a working girl — SMITH 309:5

protection: Innocence calls mutely for p.	GREE 158:7
P. is not a principle	DISR 121:10
protector: p. of all that trust in thee	BOOK 64:24
protest: lady doth p. too much	SHAK 276:9
Protestant: attacked me and the P. church	NIEM 239:15
Gunpowder, Printing and the P.	CARL 90:9
I am the P. whore	GWYN 159:13
p. ethic and the spirit of	WEBER 344:7
P. with a horse	BEHAN 32:16
worse, P. counterpoint	BEEC 32:3
Proteus: P. rising from the sea	WORD 357:11
protoplasmal: p. primordial	GILB 151:18
protracted: life p. is p. woe	JOHN 183:15
proud: Death be not p.	DONNE 123:8
how apt the poor are to be p.	SHAK 298:5
make death p. to take us	SHAK 271:26
man being too p. to fight	WILS 351:18
nation p. in arms	MILT 226:6
p. and yet a wretched thing	DAV 114:14
p. in the imagination	BIBLE 51:29
p. me no prouds	SHAK 295:20
So longe mote ye lyve, and alle p.	CHAU 96:15
too p. for a wit	GOLD 155:2
woman can be p. and stiff	YEATS 358:20
prove: I could p. everything	PINT 248:20
P. all things	BIBLE 56:14
proved: p. to be much as you said	HARDY 162:9
proverb: shall be a p. and a byword	BIBLE 41:29
proverbs: King Solomon wrote the P.	NAYL 237:20
Patch grief with p.	SHAK 291:25
providence: Behind a frowning p.	COWP 109:26
I go the way that P. dictates	HITL 169:1
I may assert eternal p.	MILT 228:9
P. had sent a few men	RUMB 264:5
p. in the fall of a sparrow	SHAK 277:13
P. their guide	MILT 230:2
provident: They are p. instead	BOGAN 62:18
province: all knowledge my p.	BACON 25:23
provinces: p. generally costs more	MAC 213:12
provincial: dead level of p. existence	ELIOT 132:13
worse than p.—he was parochial	JAMES 179:19
provincialism: adultery than in p.	HUXL 177:3
provocation: as in the p.	BOOK 68:1
Ask you what p. I have had	POPE 252:32
provoker: Drink, sir, is a great p.	SHAK 286:21
provokes: No one p. me with impunity	ANON 13:17
proxy: p. for risk and a dummy	MACH 215:4
prudence: effect of p. on rascality	SHAW 301:34
forced into p. in her youth	AUST 22:26
P. is a rich, ugly, old maid	BLAKE 61:2
prudenter: p. agas	ANON 13:20
prudes: With p. for proctors	TENN 327:16
prunes: especially p. and prism	DICK 119:1
pruninghooks: spears into p.	BIBLE 45:5
prunus: p. and forsythia	BETJ 37:6
Prussia: national industry of P.	MIR 231:8
Prussian: French, or Turk, or P.	GILB 152:21
psalm: like a p. of green days	QUIL 257:8
psalmist: sweet p. of Israel	BIBLE 41:28
psalms: glad in him with p.	BOOK 67:31
King David wrote the P.	NAYL 237:20
pubic: that Caught the P. Hare	BEHAN 32:17
public: as if I was a p. meeting	VICT 338:9
Desolation in immaculate p.	ROET 261:14
forsythia across the p. way	BETJ 37:6
I and the p. know	AUDEN 21:6
man assumes a p. trust	JEFF 181:1
Nor p. man, nor angry crowds	YEATS 359:10
one to mislead the p.	ASQ 19:4
Private faces in p. places	AUDEN 21:6
p. be damned	VAND 337:1
p. doesn't give a damn	BEEC 31:23
publican: How like a fawning p.	SHAK 289:1
publicans: Master with p. and sinners	BIBLE 49:21

publicity: oxygen of p.	THAT 329:24
price of justice is eternal p.	BENN 34:17
p. except your own obituary	BEHAN 32:19
public school: been at an English p.	WAUGH 343:20
Keats's vulgarity with a P. accent	LEAV 203:22
public schools: P. the nurseries of all vice	FIEL 139:8
P. 'tis public folly feeds	COWP 110:13
publish: P. and be damned	WELL 345:15
p. it not in the streets	BIBLE 41:21
publisher: Barabbas was a p.	CAMP 89:1
pudding: p.—it has no theme	CHUR 100:8
puddings: are like their English p.	VOLT 340:26
puddin'-race: Great chieftain o' the p.	BURNS 82:24
puff: I p. the prostitute away	DRYD 128:23
puking: Mewling and p.	SHAK 272:25
pull: P. down thy vanity	POUND 254:21
pulls: p. a lady through	MARQ 219:17
pulp: p. so bitter, how shall taste	THOM 331:11
pulse: My p., like a soft drum	KING 195:6
p. in the eternal mind	BROO 73:10
p. of feeling stirs again	ARN 16:10
than feeling a woman's p.	STER 315:10
two people with the one p.	MACN 216:5
very p. of the machine	WORD 356:24
pumpkins: Where the early p. blow	LEAR 203:7
pun: man who could make so vile a p.	DENN 117:1
p. is a pistol let off at the ear	LAMB 200:6
punch: Some sipping p.	WORD 356:4
punctilio: None of your dam p.	MER 223:15
punctuality: P. is the politeness of kings	LOUI 210:17
P. is the virtue of the bored	WAUGH 343:29
punica: P. fide	SALL 266:9
punishment: All p. is mischief	BENT 35:2
it shall suffer first p.	CRAN 111:4
To let the p. fit the crime	GILB 152:1
punk: Gert's writings are p.	ANON 8:2
punt: p. than to be punted	SAY 267:15
puppets: shut up the box and the p.	THAC 329:22
whose p., best and worst	BROW 77:1
purchase: cunning p. of my wealth	JONS 187:12
pure: Because my heart is p.	TENN 328:15
Blessed are the p. in heart	BIBLE 48:19
chaste as ice, as p. as snow	SHAK 275:29
If I have led a p. life	CAT 93:6
Live p., speak true	TENN 324:5
p. as the lily in the dell	LAUD 202:6
too p. an Air for Slaves	ANON 10:1
truth is rarely p. and never simple	WILDE 349:16
Unto the p. all things are pure	BIBLE 56:22
whatsoever things are p.	BIBLE 56:9
purer: In p. lives thy service find	WHIT 348:27
purest: p. of human pleasures	BACON 24:26
purgatorial: black, p. rails	KEATS 190:15
purge: shalt p. me with hyssop	BOOK 67:9
purify: p. the dialect of the tribe	ELIOT 132:9
puritan: P. hated bear-baiting	MAC 213:19
To the P. all things are impure	LAWR 202:9
Where I saw a P.-one	BRAT 71:16
puritanism: P. The haunting fear	MENC 223:7
purlieus: dusty p. of the law	TENN 325:17
I walk within the p. of the Law	ETH 137:18
purling: painted meadow, or a p. stream	ADD 2:21
to plain work, and to p. brooks	POPE 251:24
purple: And p.-stainèd mouth	KEATS 191:30
deep p. falls over sleepy	PAR 245:3
gleaming in p. and gold	BYRON 85:22
I never saw a P. Cow	BURG 79:16
Pilots of the p. twilight	TENN 326:10
p. brows of Olivet	TENN 325:5
p.-linèd palace of sweet sin	KEATS 191:12
p. patch or two	HOR 172:23
p. testament of bleeding	SHAK 294:1
P. the sails, and so perfumed	SHAK 271:14
purpose: any p. perverts art	CONS 107:13

purpose (*cont.*):

does nothing without p.	ARIS 15:20
God is working his p. out	AING 3:9
Infirm of p.	SHAK 286:17
living to some p.	PAINE 244:15
My p. is, indeed, a horse	SHAK 297:27
p. of human existence	JUNG 188:23
Shake my fell p.	SHAK 285:17
To speak and p. not	SHAK 282:18

purpureal: invested with p. gleams — WORD 355:7

purrs: p. like an epigram — MARQ 219:23

purse: consumption of the p. — SHAK 278:19

law can take a p.	BUTL 84:8
steals my p. steals trash	SHAK 292:11
want of friends, and empty p.	BRET 71:23

pursuing: Faint, yet p. — BIBLE 41:1

pursuit: common p. — LEAV 203:21

p. of happiness	ANON 11:12
p. of happiness	JEFF 180:18
p. of the uneatable	WILDE 350:9
What mad p.	KEATS 191:18

pussy-cat: Owl and the P. — LEAR 203:11

put: I p. away childish things — BIBLE 55:14

Our end is Life. P. out to sea	MACN 216:11
P. me to what you will	METH 223:28
P. on the whole armour of God	BIBLE 56:3
P. out the light, and then	SHAK 292:29
p. upon us the armour of light	BOOK 64:21
up with which I will not p.	CHUR 100:5
what p. me up to it	BEVIN 38:11

puzzle: Don't p. me, said I — STER 315:24

Rule of Three doth p. me — ANON 9:11

pylons: P., those pillars — SPEN 313:3

pyramid: bottom of the economic p. — ROOS 262:7

pyramids: books made like p. — FLAU 141:12

p. a monument of the insufficiency	JOHN 183:7
summit of these p.	NAP 237:3

Pyrenees: P. are no more — LOUI 210:15

tease in the High P. — BELL 34:1

Pythagoras: mystical way of P. — BROW 74:12

this 'himself' was P. — CIC 100:21

Q

quad: no one about in the Q. — KNOX 198:18

quadrille: q. in a sentry-box — JAMES 179:16

quaffing: q., and unthinking time — DRYD 128:15

quailing: No q., Mrs Gaskell — BRON 72:19

quaint: q. and curious war — HARDY 162:13

quake: aspes leef she gan to q. — CHAU 96:17

They love indeed who q. — SIDN 306:22

qualis: *Non sum q. eram bonae* — HOR 173:30

qualities: q. as would wear well — GOLD 155:11

quality: his honour and his q. — BLUN 62:15

q. of mercy is not strained — SHAK 289:26

quantities: ghosts of departed q. — BERK 35:15

quantity: vile, holding no q. — SHAK 290:16

quantum: I waive the q. o'the sin — BURNS 82:5

quarks: Three q. for Muster Mark — JOYCE 188:5

quarrel: find q. in a straw — SHAK 276:31

justice of my q.	ANON 8:7
q. in a far away country	CHAM 94:1
q. with ourselves, poetry	YEATS 360:10
that hath his q. just	SHAK 280:8
therefore a perpetual q.	BURKE 80:3

quarrels: unseemly intimacy or q. — LOW 211:11

quarterly: nothing a-year, paid q. — SURT 319:15

quarto: q. page where a neat rivulet — SHER 306:3

quean: flaunting, extravagant q. — SHER 306:6

queen: Hail holy q. — ANON 13:21

home life of our own dear Q. — ANON 8:1

I'll q. it no inch further — SHAK 299:1

queen (*cont.*):

I'm to be Q. o' the May	TENN 327:5
Ocean's child, and then his q.	SHEL 304:2
Q. and huntress, chaste	JONS 187:3
Q. had four Maries	BALL 28:2
Q. Mab hath been with you	SHAK 294:24
q. of Scots is this day	ELIZ 135:12
Q. rose of the rosebud	TENN 326:29
q. that caught the world's	HUNT 176:14
Ruler of the Q.'s Navee	GILB 152:18
when good Cinara was my q.	HOR 173:30

queens: Q. have died young and fair — NASHE 237:19

That all your acts are q. — SHAK 298:34

queer: q. save thee and me — OWEN 243:18

q. sort of thing — BARH 28:21

queerer: q. than we *can* suppose — HALD 160:2

quest: winding q. and passage — VAUG 337:3

questing: passes the q. vole — WAUGH 343:25

question: ask an impertinent q. — BRON 72:10

having asked any clear q.	CAMUS 89:5
If any q. why we died	KIPL 196:7
Others abide our q.	ARN 17:14
q. is absurd	AUDEN 21:17
such a silly q.	STER 315:13
To ask the hard q. is simple	AUDEN 21:16
To be or not to be: that is the q.	SHAK 275:25

questionings: those obstinate q. — WORD 355:22

questions: ask q. of those who cannot tell — RAL 258:5

That q. the distempered part — ELIOT 133:5

queue: forms an orderly q. of one — MIKES 224:12

quick: Come! q. as you can — DE L 116:11

Now burgeons every maze of q.	TENN 325:29
q., and the dead	DEWAR 117:14
Q., thy tablets, Memory	ARN 16:20
So q. bright things come to	SHAK 290:15
Touched to the q., he said	BROW 76:8

quickly: It were done q. — SHAK 285:22

quiddities: in thy quips and thy q. — SHAK 277:23

quidquid: Q. *agis, prudenter agas* — ANON 13:20

quiet: All q. along the Potomac — BEERS 32:14

All q. along the Potomac	MCCL 214:14
All q. on the western front	REM 259:4
alone with the q. day	JAMES 180:3
Anything for a q. life	MIDD 224:5
Easy live and q. die	SCOTT 268:24
Fie upon this q. life	SHAK 277:32
fruitful ground, the q. mind	SURR 319:6
Give me my scallop-shell of q.	RAL 257:23
lives of q. desperation	THOR 332:9
monopoly profits is a q. life	HICKS 168:10
never have a q. world till	SHAW 302:13
q. limit of the world	TENN 328:17
q., pilfering, unprotected race	CLARE 101:6
Q. to quick bosoms is a hell	BYRON 85:4
telling with a q. beat	QUIL 257:8

quietest: q. places under the sun — HOUS 175:1

quietness: unravished bride of q. — KEATS 191:17

quince: slices of q. — LEAR 203:13

quinquireme: Q. of Nineveh — MAS 221:18

quip: q. modest — SHAK 273:12

quips: thy q. and thy quiddities — SHAK 277:23

quires: Q. and Places where they sing — BOOK 64:7

quis: Q. *custodiet ipsos custodes?* — JUV 189:9

quit: I q. such odious subjects — AUST 22:21

Q. yourselves like men — BIBLE 41:19

quiver: hath his q. full of them — BOOK 68:31

quo: Q. *vadis?* — BIBLE 58:19

quod: Q. *erat demonstrandum* — EUCL 137:19

quotation: every q. contributes — JOHN 182:5

quote: grow immortal as they q. — YOUNG 360:13

quotidienne: Ah! *que la vie est q.* — LAF 199:20

R

rabbit: r. has a charming face ANON 10:8
There is a r. in a snare STEP 315:7
race: avails the sceptred r. LAND 200:23
loftier r. SYM 321:20
lovely ere his r. be run BYRON 85:20
pilfering, unprotected r. CLARE 101:6
r. between education WELLS 345:21
r. is not to the swift BIBLE 44:20
r. is sent down from high VIRG 339:25
r. is to the swift DAV 114:12
r. that is set before us BIBLE 56:27
r. that long in darkness SCOT 269:10
r. through God's good grace MONS 233:2
shall rear my dusky r. TENN 326:15
slinks out of the r. MILT 230:31
till thou run out thy r. MILT 228:3
races: white r. are really pinko-grey FORS 143:24
Rachel: R. weeping for her children BIBLE 48:11
served seven years for R. BIBLE 39:22
rack: Leave not a r. behind SHAK 296:10
r. of a too easy chair POPE 250:20
r. of this tough world SHAK 284:7
racket: flaming r. of the female OSB 242:22
rackets: matched our r. to these balls SHAK 279:1
radiance: white r. of Eternity SHEL 303:13
radical: dared be r. when young FROST 146:18
R. Chic WOLFE 353:9
r. revolutionary will become AREN 15:5
raft: republic is a r. AMES 4:22
rag: O that Shakespeherian R. ELIOT 134:24
r. and a bone and a hank KIPL 197:12
r. and bone shop of the heart YEATS 358:16
rage: captive void of noble r. TENN 325:3
heathen so furiously r. BOOK 66:9
Heaven has no r. CONG 106:12
nature with hard-favoured r. SHAK 279:5
Not die here in a r. SWIFT 320:5
Puts all Heaven in a r. BLAKE 60:6
r. against the dying of the light THOM 330:7
writing increaseth r. DYER 129:15
rages: weight of r. SPOO 313:25
ragged: been a pair of r. claws ELIOT 133:28
rags: when in r. and contempt BUNY 79:2
which are the r. of time DONNE 124:12
raid: r. on the inarticulate ELIOT 133:6
rail: her six young on the r. BROW 76:10
railing: R. at life, and yet afraid CHUR 98:24
rails: black, purgatorial r. KEATS 190:15
railway: imposed by r. timetables TAYL 322:23
R. Bridge of the Silv'ry Tay MCG 214:19
R. termini are our gates FORS 143:19
threatened its life with a r. share CARR 92:9
rain: droppeth as the gentle r. SHAK 289:26
former and the latter r. BOOK 64:20
glazed with r. WILL 351:8
hard r.'s a gonna fall DYLAN 130:2
like sunshine after r. SHAK 300:18
not even the r., has such small CUMM 113:3
R. in Spain LERN 206:1
r. is destroying his grain HERB 166:11
r. is on our lips SORL 311:15
r. it raineth every day SHAK 298:15
r., it raineth on the just BOWEN 70:14
r. maketh a hole LAT 202:3
Rain! R.! KEATS 193:6
sendeth r. on the just BIBLE 48:24
small rain down can r. ANON 11:18
sound of abundance of r. BIBLE 42:1
Spout, r. SHAK 283:7
Still falls the R. SITW 307:19
through the drizzling r. TENN 325:1

rain (cont.):
waiting for r. ELIOT 133:14
which had outwept its r. SHEL 303:6
rainbow: God gave Noah the r. sign ANON 7:12
It was the R. gave thee birth DAV 114:19
Lord survives the r. LOW 211:17
r. and a cuckoo's song DAV 114:18
r. comes and goes WORD 355:18
r. in the sky WORD 355:13
r.'s glory is shed SHEL 303:24
Somewhere over the r. HARB 161:14
raineth: R. drop and staineth slop POUND 254:8
rains: r. pennies from heaven BURKE 81:14
rainy: r. day and a contentious woman BIBLE 44:1
r. Pleiads wester HOUS 174:15
windy night a r. morrow SHAK 300:1
raise: The Lord shall r. me up RAL 258:1
raising: corn and begin r. hell LEASE 203:20
ram: r. caught in a thicket BIBLE 39:16
r. is tupping your white ewe SHAK 291:29
Rama: In R. was there a voice BIBLE 48:11
rampage: On the R., Pip, and off DICK 118:26
rampart: As his corse to the r. WOLFE 352:25
rams: mountains skipped like r. BOOK 68:16
My r. speed not, all is amiss BARN 29:8
Ramsbottom: Mr and Mrs R. EDGAR 130:15
Randal: your dinner, Lord R. BALL 27:19
random: many a word, at r. spoken SCOTT 268:15
rangers: English for the eight bold r. ANON 8:6
Rangoon: from R. to Mandalay KIPL 196:21
rank: flog the r. and file ARN 18:16
my offence is r. SHAK 276:16
r. is but the guinea's stamp BURNS 82:7
r. me with whom you will METH 223:28
things r. and gross SHAK 274:10
track marched, r. on rank MER 223:22
ranks: even the r. of Tuscany MAC 214:8
r. of death you'll find him MOORE 234:16
ransack: R. the ocean for orient pearl MARL 218:8
ransomed: R., healed, restored LYTE 212:21
rape: A r.! a rape WEBS 344:24
you don't marry it, you r. it DEGAS 116:2
rapscallions: All kings is mostly r. TWAIN 335:20
rapture: first fine careless r. BROW 76:2
Modified r. GILB 151:24
r. on the lonely shore BYRON 85:12
raptures: r. and roses of vice SWIN 321:5
rara: R. avis in terris nigroque JUV 189:7
rare: Rich and r. were the gems MOORE 234:17
She was indeed a r. one WITH 352:5
raree-show: r. of Peter's successor BROW 75:20
rarely: Rarely, r., comest thou SHEL 304:32
rarer: r. spirit never did steer SHAK 271:27
rascality: effect of prudence on r. SHAW 301:34
rascals: R., would you live for ever FRED 145:20
rash: It is too r., too unadvised SHAK 295:1
You look rather r. my dear ASHF 18:21
rashes: Green grow the r., O BURNS 82:9
rat: And, like a r. without a tail SHAK 285:3
Cat, the R., and Lovell our dog COLL 105:3
giant r. of Sumatra DOYLE 125:17
How now! a r.? SHAK 276:19
it creeps like a r. BOWEN 70:18
Mr Speaker, I smell a r. ROCHE 261:1
poisoned r. in a hole SWIFT 320:5
rational: These r. amphibii go MARV 221:3
rats: I think we are in r.' alley ELIOT 134:23
R.! They fought the dogs BROW 76:26
rattle: Pleased with a r. POPE 252:19
R. his bones over the stones NOEL 240:5
rattling: Advertising is the r. of a stick ORW 242:6
ravage: r. with impunity a rose BROW 77:15
rave: and let her r. KEATS 191:26
old age should burn and r. THOM 330:7
raved: r. and grew more fierce HERB 166:23

red (cont.):
r. flag flying here	CONN 106:23
R. lips are not so red	OWEN 244:1
r. wheel barrow	WILL 351:8
rose-r. city half as old as time	BURG 79:17
that never blows so r.	BUNY 79:9
Their r. it never dies	DOBS 122:27
Thin r. line of 'eroes	KIPL 197:11
thin r. line tipped with steel	RUSS 265:7
your raiment all r.	MAC 213:25
rede: And recks not his own r.	SHAK 274:20
redeem: R. thy mis-spent time	KEN 193:21
redeemer: I know that my r. liveth	BIBLE 42:36
Our blest R.	AUBER 19:15
To thee, R., King	NEALE 237:21
redeeming: R. the time	BIBLE 56:1
redemption: Hail, r.'s happy dawn	CASW 92:18
married past r.	DRYD 128:7
redress: Things past r.	SHAK 293:20
redwood: r. forest to the Gulf Stream	GUTH 159:12
reed: Man is only a r.	PASC 246:6
r. shaken with the wind	BIBLE 49:34
staff of this bruised r.	BIBLE 42:16
reeds: Down in the r. by the river	BROW 75:4
reeking: r. into Cadiz Bay	BROW 76:3
reel: I've gotten a r.	BLAM 62:8
They r. to and fro	BOOK 68:13
reeled: until r. the mind	GIBBS 150:18
references: verify your r.	ROUTH 263:19
refined: r. out of existence	JOYCE 188:8
This Englishwoman is so r.	SMITH 309:21
reflecting: r. the figure of a man	WOOLF 354:2
reform: retrenchment, and r.	BRIG 72:3
reformers: All r. are bachelors	MOORE 234:6
All R., however strict	SMITH 309:15
refuge: eternal God is thy r.	BIBLE 40:25
last r. of a scoundrel	JOHN 185:4
r. from home life	SHAW 302:23
r. of weak minds	CHES 97:13
so easy to take r. in	IBSEN 178:6
refusal: great r.	DANTE 113:20
refuse: offer he can't r.	PUZO 256:25
r. till the conversion of the Jews	MARV 220:23
refused: stone which the builders r.	BOOK 68:22
refute: I r. it thus	JOHN 184:17
Who can r. a sneer	PALEY 244:17
regalia: r. that comes with it	KEAT 190:8
regard: Should be without r.	SHAK 287:3
regardless: r. of their doom	GRAY 157:12
regiment: Monstrous R. of Women	KNOX 198:16
regina: Salve, r.	ANON 13:21
region: r. of thick-ribbèd ice	SHAK 288:21
register: r. of the crimes	GIBB 150:11
regret: Old Age a r.	DISR 121:26
regrets: Miss Otis r.	PORT 253:23
series of congratulatory r.	DISR 121:19
wild r.	WILDE 350:17
regular: Brought r. and draw'd mild	DICK 119:4
icily r., splendidly null	TENN 326:23
regulate: r. all recreations	MILT 230:32
regulated: R. hatred	HARD 161:16
Reich: Ein R., ein Volk	ANON 13:2
reign: Better to r. in hell	MILT 228:13
Long to r. over us	HOGG 170:8
r. of Chaos and old Night	MILT 228:16
reigned: r. with your loves	ELIZ 135:7
reindeer: Herds of r. move across	AUDEN 20:19
rejected: despised and r. of men	BIBLE 46:17
rejoice: desert shall r.	BIBLE 46:4
Let us then r.	ANON 13:16
R. in the Lord alway	BIBLE 56:7
rejoicing: home, r., brought me	BAKER 26:21
relation: nobody like a r. to do	THAC 329:16
No cold r. is a zealous citizen	BURKE 80:20
poor r.—is the most irrelevant	LAMB 200:5

relations: Personal r.	FORS 143:20
relationship: every human r.	FORS 143:26
relative: In a r. way	BULL 78:7
Success is r.	ELIOT 132:23
relaxes: Damn braces: Bless r.	BLAKE 61:9
relent: Shall make him once r.	BUNY 79:9
relic: cased up, like a holy r.	WEBS 344:14
relief: For this r. much thanks	SHAK 273:30
relieve: comfort and r. them	BOOK 64:19
religio: Tantum r. potuit suadere	LUCR 212:2
religion: all of the same r.	DISR 122:1
As great in love as in r.	COWL 109:16
As to r., I hold it to be	PAINE 244:10
bringeth men's minds to r.	BACON 24:12
brothels with bricks of R.	BLAKE 61:7
enough r. to make us hate	SWIFT 320:10
handmaid to r.	BACON 24:2
increase in us true r.	BOOK 64:25
indirect way to plant r.	BROW 74:16
In their r. they are so uneven	DEFOE 115:23
leave him for r.	SPARK 312:10
men of sense are really but of one r.	SHAF 270:20
Millionaire. That is my r.	SHAW 301:9
my r. is to do good	PAINE 244:14
no amusements but vice and r.	SMITH 310:12
no r. but social	WESL 346:11
not impossibilities enough in r.	BROW 74:10
One r. is as true as another	BURT 83:14
only one r.	SHAW 302:15
Philistine of genius in r.	ARN 18:11
r. allowed to invade the sphere	MELB 222:23
r. at the lowest	CHES 97:14
r. but a childish toy	MARL 218:19
R. by no means a proper subject	CHES 97:3
r. for religion's sake	COUS 108:17
r. into after-dinner toasts	NEWM 238:18
r. is powerless to bestow	FORB 143:2
R. is the frozen thought	KRIS 199:4
R. is the opium of the people	MARX 221:8
r. is thus not simply morality	ARN 18:8
r. of Socialism	BEVAN 37:19
R.'s in the heart	JERR 181:10
r. that has any thing in it	PAINE 244:7
r. to a man with bodily hunger	SHAW 301:10
r. when in rags and contempt	BUNY 79:2
r. without science is blind	EINS 131:11
rum and true r.	BYRON 86:5
science is strong and r. weak	SZASZ 322:1
slovenliness is no part of r.	WESL 346:15
some of r.	EDG 130:16
So much wrong could r. induce	LUCR 212:2
Superstition is the r. of feeble	BURKE 80:18
To become a popular r.	INGE 178:12
too late to trust the old r.	LOW 211:19
zeal in politics as well as in r.	JUNB 188:26
religions: sixty different r.	CAR 89:17
religious: even r. concord	GIBB 150:10
his r. opinions	BUTL 84:18
r. factions are volcanoes	BURKE 81:1
With a r. book, or friend	WOTT 357:14
religious-good: Good, but not r.	HARDY 162:1
rem: R. tene; verba sequentur	CATO 92:23
remain: things r.	CLOU 102:22
remains: r., however improbable	DOYLE 126:1
while aught r. to do	ROG 261:17
remarkable: nothing left r.	SHAK 271:25
remarks: R. are not literature	STEIN 314:20
said our r. before us	DON 123:1
remedies: not apply new r.	BACON 24:31
Our r. oft in ourselves do lie	SHAK 270:24
remedy: Force is not a r.	BRIG 72:6
know not how to r. our own	KYD 199:9
r. against the entropy	ZAMY 360:25
r. is worse than the disease	BACON 25:11

remedy (*cont.*):
requires a dangerous r. — FAWK 138:22
Things without all r. — SHAK 287:3
'Tis a sharp r. — RAL 258:3
remember: Do you r. an Inn — BELL 34:1
I r., I remember — HOOD 171:8
no greater pain than to r. — DANTE 113:21
r. and be sad — ROSS 263:4
r. even these things — VIRG 339:2
R. me, but ah! forget my fate — TATE 322:15
R. me when I am dead — DOUG 125:9
r. not past years — NEWM 238:22
R. now thy Creator — BIBLE 44:25
r. the Fifth of November — ANON 10:5
R. the sabbath day — BIBLE 40:7
r. with advantages — SHAK 279:19
should, yet never can, r. — THOM 330:25
Till thou r. and I forget — SWIN 321:16
wake, and r., and understand — BROW 75:29
We will r. them — BINY 59:12
what you can r. — SELL 269:23
Yes; I r. Adlestrop — THOM 330:21
You must r. this, a kiss — HUPF 176:20
remembered: blue r. hills — HOUS 174:24
my youth I r. my God — SOUT 312:2
r. for a very long time — MCG 214:19
we in it shall be r. — SHAK 279:20
remembering: R. without ceasing — BIBLE 56:13
remembers: R. me of all his gracious — SHAK 282:8
remembrance: R. of things past — PROU 255:17
r. of things past — SHAK 299:16
r. of a guest that tarrieth — BIBLE 47:31
r. of them is grievous — BOOK 65:11
rosemary, that's for r. — SHAK 277:2
remembren: it r., whan it passed — CHAU 96:18
remind: Foolish Things R. Me — MARV 221:4
remission: shedding of blood is no r. — BIBLE 56:24
remorse: access and passage to r. — SHAK 285:17
Farewell r.! — MILT 229:7
R., the fatal egg — COWP 110:2
remote: R. and ineffectual Don — BELL 33:16
removals: household r. — BAUD 30:7
remove: fat greedy owl of the R. — RICH 260:1
not malignant and r. it — WAUGH 344:1
render: doth teach us all to r. — SHAK 289:27
R. therefore unto Caesar — BIBLE 50:29
rendezvous: r. with Death — SEEG 269:13
renew: r. a right spirit — BOOK 67:10
Reno'd: King's Moll R. — ANON 8:17
renown: land of just and old r. — TENN 329:1
r. on scraps of learning — YOUNG 360:13
rent: R. is that portion — RIC 259:16
That has not been r. — YEATS 358:20
unearned increment of r. — MILL 224:14
why? for r. — BYRON 84:25
repair: friendship in constant r. — JOHN 184:2
repay: I will r., saith the Lord — BIBLE 54:45
Will find a Tiger well r. — BELL 33:2
repeat: past are condemned to r. — SANT 266:22
repeats: r. his words — SHAK 282:8
repelled: only r. by man — INGE 178:13
repent: r. at leisure — CONG 106:13
R. ye — BIBLE 48:12
weak alone r. — BYRON 85:16
repentance: R. is but want of power — DRYD 128:11
R. is the virtue of weak minds — DRYD 127:34
R. on a Sunday — YBAR 358:11
sinners to r. — BIBLE 49:23
with the morning cool r. came — SCOTT 269:3
repented: she strove, and much r. — BYRON 86:1
repenting: r. at leisure — THOM 331:1
repetition: r. of unpalatable truths — SUMM 319:5
reply: the r. churlish — SHAK 273:12
report: are of good r. — BIBLE 56:9
reporter: mild-mannered r. — ANON 7:5

reports: Bring me no more r. — SHAK 287:32
R. of my death — TWAIN 336:7
repose: r. is taboo'd by anxiety — GILB 151:15
r. of a pacific station — ADAMS 1:7
representation: Taxation without r. — OTIS 243:6
representations: just r. of a general — JOHN 182:24
representative: r. government — DISR 122:7
Your r. owes you — BURKE 80:22
repress: r. the speech they know — ELIOT 132:3
reproof: r. valiant — SHAK 273:12
republic: England is a disguised r. — BAG 26:10
Love the Beloved R. — FORS 144:3
r. is a raft — AMES 4:22
r. is like a chicken — MITF 232:8
republican: on r. principles — SHAW 302:9
r. government in the United — TOCQ 333:3
Republicans: We are R. — BURC 79:12
republics: R. weak because — BAG 26:12
repugnant: r. to the Word of God — BOOK 69:18
repulsive: Right but R. — SELL 270:2
reputation: At ev'ry word a r. dies — POPE 253:7
I have lost my r. — SHAK 292:8
plains of honour and r. — JONS 187:13
Seeking the bubble r. — SHAK 272:26
sold my r. for a song — FITZ 140:17
spotless r. — SHAK 293:7
wink a r. down — SWIFT 320:16
reputations: home of ruined r. — ELIOT 132:6
sit upon the murdered r. — CONG 106:15
request: No flowers, by r. — AING 3:8
requiem: R. *aeternam dona eis* — MISS 231:22
requiescant: R. *in pace* — MISS 231:25
require: doth the Lord r. of thee — BIBLE 47:23
he thought 'e might r. — KIPL 197:14
What is it men in women do r. — BLAKE 61:17
required: thy soul shall be r. — BIBLE 52:19
requisite: r. in business — ADD 2:20
res: *in medias r.* — HOR 173:1
research: steal from many, it's r. — MIZN 232:12
resent: don't r. having nothing — COMP 106:4
resign: Few die and none r. — JEFF 180:22
resist: r. everything except temptation — WILDE 349:24
R. not evil — BIBLE 48:23
resistentialism: R. is concerned with — JENN 181:5
resistible: r. rise of Arturo Ui — BREC 71:17
resolute: Be bloody, bold, and r. — SHAK 287:20
resolution: In war: r. — CHUR 100:4
native hue of r. — SHAK 275:26
resolve: R. to be thyself — ARN 17:13
resolved: speech they r. not to make — ELIOT 132:3
resource: infinite-r.-and-sagacity — KIPL 197:24
resources: born to consume r. — HOR 173:7
Inner R. — BERR 36:13
r. of civilization — GLAD 153:12
respect: child is owed the greatest r. — JUV 189:15
icy precepts of r. — SHAK 296:22
no r. of place, persons — SHAK 297:25
R. was mingled with surprise — SCOTT 268:9
We owe r. to the living — VOLT 340:24
respectable: more r. he is — SHAW 301:16
most devilish when r. — BROW 74:26
respecter: God is no r. of persons — BIBLE 54:15
respice: r. *finem* — ANON 13:20
respiration: artificial r. — BURG 79:15
responsibility: In dreams begins r. — YEATS 360:11
Liberty means r. — SHAW 301:28
no sense of r. — KNOX 198:20
Power without r. — KIPL 198:5
r. without power — STOP 318:1
rest: far, far better r. that I go to — DICK 120:7
flee away, and be at r. — BOOK 67:11
Grant them eternal r. — MISS 231:22
I will give you r. — BIBLE 49:35
ordained no r. — VAUG 337:3

rest (cont.):
R. in soft peace · JONS 187:19
r. is literature · VALÉ 336:20
r. is mere fine writing · VERL 337:20
r. is silence · SHAK 277:18
R., rest, perturbèd spirit · SHAK 275:5
r. upon thy holy hill · BOOK 66:13
Swift has sailed into his r. · YEATS 360:2
talk about the r. of us · ANON 10:20
Their place of r. · MILT 230:2
weary be at r. · BIBLE 42:27
restless: bind the r. wave · WHIT 348:9
restoration: Church's R. · BETJ 37:3
restored: Ransomed, healed, r. · LYTE 212:21
R. to life, and power · KEBLE 193:16
restorer: Tired Nature's sweet r. · YOUNG 360:17
restraint: r. with which they write · CAMP 88:16
result: r. happiness · DICK 118:12
resurrection: certain hope of the R. · BOOK 66:8
I am the r., and the life · BIBLE 53:32
R. of the body · BOOK 64:3
r. of the dead · BIBLE 55:17
r. they neither marry · BIBLE 50:30
resuscitate: r. the dead art · POUND 254:14
retainer: Old R. night and day · BELL 33:6
reticence: Northern r. · HEAN 164:11
R., in three volumes · GLAD 153:14
retirement: there must be no r. · HAIG 159:17
retort: r. courteous · SHAK 273:12
retreat: honourable r. · SHAK 273:3
I will not r. a single inch · GARR 148:12
retreating: seen yourself r. · NASH 237:18
retrenchment: r., and reform · BRIG 72:3
retrograde: be not r. · JONS 187:9
return: came through and I shall r. · MAC 213:1
In that state I came, r. · VAUG 337:10
r. into my house · BIBLE 50:3
r. no more to his house · BIBLE 42:31
Should I never r. · MANS 217:15
spirit shall r. unto God · BIBLE 44:26
unto dust shalt thou r. · BIBLE 39:3
who does not r. your blow · SHAW 302:8
returned: r. on the previous night · BULL 78:7
returning: R. were as tedious · SHAK 287:14
reveal: r. Himself to his servants · MILT 231:2
revealed: Lord shall be r. · BIBLE 46:9
revelation: Reason is natural r. · LOCKE 208:16
revelations: It ends with R. · WILDE 350:11
offers stupendous r. · HOFF 170:5
revelry: sound of r. by night · BYRON 85:2
revels: Our r. now are ended · SHAK 296:10
revenge: r. for slight injuries · MACH 214:23
R. is a kind of wild justice · BACON 25:9
r. of the intellect · SONT 311:9
R. triumphs over death · BACON 24:21
Sweet is r. · BYRON 86:2
sweet r. grows harsh · SHAK 293:2
wrong us, shall we not r. · SHAK 289:17
revenges: time brings in his r. · SHAK 298:14
revenons: R. à ces moutons · ANON 12:14
revenue: Instead of a standing r. · BURKE 80:3
revenues: She bears a duke's r. · SHAK 280:7
reverence: In deeper r. praise · WHIT 348:27
none so poor to do him r. · SHAK 281:21
reversion: no bright r. in the sky · POPE 250:23
review: have your r. before me · REGER 259:2
reviewing: book before r. it · SMITH 310:9
revivals: art is the history of r. · BUTL 84:14
revolting: r. and a rebellious heart · BIBLE 46:27
revolution: crust over a volcano of r. · ELLIS 136:6
explain the French R. · BAUD 30:7
on the day after the r. · AREN 15:5
R., like Satan, might devour · VERG 337:19
revolutionary: r. in a bathroom · LINK 207:17
r. will become a conservative · AREN 15:5

revolutions: main cause of r. · INGE 178:11
nursery of future r. · BURKE 80:11
r. have ended in a reinforcement · CAMUS 89:8
share in two r. · PAINE 244:15
revolving: returns with the r. year · SHEL 303:7
reward: nothing for r. · SPEN 313:11
r. against the innocent · BOOK 66:14
rewards: Crimes are their own r. · FARQ 138:17
Farewell, r. and Fairies · CORB 107:23
rex: caecorum r. est luscus · ERAS 137:14
R. tremendae maiestatis · MISS 231:24
rhetoric: logic and r., able · BACON 25:16
quarrel with others, r. · YEATS 360:10
rhetorician: sophistical r. · DISR 121:20
Rhine: king-like rolls the R. · CALV 88:10
you think of the R. · BALD 27:6
rhyme: could not get a r. for roman · FLEM 142:1
making beautiful old r. · SHAK 300:4
names in many a musèd r. · KEATS 192:3
outlive this powerful r. · SHAK 299:19
R. being no necessary adjunct · MILT 228:5
R. is still the most effective · GIR 153:5
r. the rudder is of verses · BUTL 83:25
still more tired of R. · BELL 33:13
unattempted yet in prose or r. · MILT 228:8
rhyming: born under a r. planet · SHAK 291:26
modern bondage of r. · MILT 228:6
r. is nat worth a toord · CHAU 96:4
rhythmical: piece of r. grumbling · ELIOT 135:4
rhythms: r. for bears to dance · FLAU 141:7
Rialto: What news on the R. · SHAK 288:31
rib: r., which the Lord · BIBLE 38:21
riband: r. in the cap of youth · SHAK 277:5
r. to stick in his coat · BROW 76:13
ribbon: blue r. of the turf · DISR 122:4
ribboned: sake of a r. coat · NEWB 238:13
Ribstone: Right as a R. Pippin · BELL 33:12
rice: r. pudding for dinner again · MILNE 225:23
rich: dies r. dies disgraced · CARN 90:27
Do you sincerely want to be r. · CORN 108:4
ever by chance grow r. · THOM 330:23
forbids the r. as well as the poor · FRAN 145:2
from the r. man's table · BIBLE 52:34
Isn't it r. · SOND 311:7
most r., being poor · SHAK 282:19
no sin, but to be r. · SHAK 282:5
open to the poor and the r. · ANON 7:9
orchestra is playing to the r. · AUDEN 20:13
parish of r. women · AUDEN 20:22
passing r. with forty pounds · GOLD 154:21
Poor little r. girl · COW 109:6
R. and rare were the gems · MOORE 234:17
R. AND THE POOR · DISR 122:6
r. are different from you and me · FITZ 140:20
r. beyond the dreams of · JOHN 185:29
r. beyond the dreams of · MOORE 234:5
r. get rich and the poor get · KAHN 189:19
r. he hath sent empty away · BIBLE 51:29
r. man in his castle · ALEX 4:3
r. man to enter into · BIBLE 50:22
r. men rule the law · GOLD 155:5
r. wot gets the gravy · ANON 10:11
seems it r. to die · KEATS 192:3
something r. and strange · SHAK 296:1
Richard: R.'s himself again · CIBB 100:17
To put down R. · SHAK 277:26
richer: for r. for poorer · BOOK 66:1
R. than all his tribe · SHAK 293:5
riches: craving of the titled for r. · PEAR 246:26
embarrassment of r. · ALL 4:11
Infinite r. in a little room · MARL 219:1
left hand r. and honour · BIBLE 43:8
Let the world's r. · HERB 167:5
parade of r. · SMITH 308:22

riches (*cont.*):

R. are a good handmaid	BACON 24:6
r. left, not got with pain	SURR 319:6
That r. grow in hell	MILT 228:19
unsearchable r. of Christ	BIBLE 55:31
richness: Here's r.	DICK 119:12
rid: gladly indeed am I r. of it	SOPH 311:14
riddle: r. of the world	POPE 252:18
r. wrapped in a mystery	CHUR 99:10
ride: Haggards r. no more	STEP 315:5
if you cannot r. two horses	MAXT 222:14
r. in triumph through Persepolis	MARL 219:7
r. mankind	EMER 136:13
R. on! ride on in majesty	MILM 225:13
She's got a ticket to r.	MCC 205:16
Who went for a r. on a tiger	ANON 10:22
rider: want of a horse the r. was lost	FRAN 145:12
rides: r. upon the storm	COWP 109:25
ridicule: r. is the best test	CHES 97:15
stand the test of r.	SHAF 270:21
ridiculous: makes men r.	JUV 189:4
no spectacle so r. as the British	MAC 213:9
one step above the r.	PAINE 244:8
position r.	CHES 97:18
sublime to the r.	NAP 237:2
riding: r. on a smile and a shoeshine	MILL 225:4
Ridley: good comfort Master R.	LAT 202:4
rifle: r. all the breathing spring	COLL 105:9
rift: little r. within the lute	TENN 324:13
load every r. with ore	KEATS 193:14
riggish: Bless her when she is r.	SHAK 271:17
right: All's r. with the world	BROW 76:28
because not all was r.	CRAB 110:26
born to set it r.	SHAK 275:6
Damn you Jack — I'm all r.	BONE 63:10
defend to the death your r.	VOLT 341:1
everyone is r.	LA CH 199:15
heaven still guards the r.	SHAK 293:23
if r., to be kept right	SCH 268:1
It must be r.: I've done it	CRAB 110:20
it's all r. with me	BELL 34:4
meet, r., and our bounden duty	BOOK 65:15
Minorities almost always in the r.	SMITH 310:10
my r. is retreating	FOCH 142:14
My r. there is none to dispute	COWP 110:18
no r. in the circus	MAXT 222:14
Only if it's done r.	ALLEN 4:15
our country, r. or wrong	DEC 115:10
rather be r. than be President	CLAY 101:18
renew a r. spirit within me	BOOK 67:10
R. as a Ribstone Pippin	BELL 33:12
R. but Repulsive	YEAT 270:2
r. deed for the wrong reason	ELIOT 134:7
r. little, tight little island	DIBD 117:20
'r.' means nothing	PLATO 249:21
r. of an excessive wrong	BROW 77:8
r. to a fair portion	BURKE 80:13
r. to consume happiness	SHAW 300:26
r. to do wrong or to requite	SOCR 310:23
r. to warn	BAG 26:14
r. wrong, follow the King	TENN 324:5
sell, or deny, or delay, r.	MAGN 216:17
Sit thou on my r. hand	BOOK 68:14
successful or otherwise, always r.	ADAMS 2:5
To do a great r., do a little	SHAK 289:28
two wrongs don't make a r.	SZASZ 322:2
Whatever IS, is R.	POPE 252:16
which is lawful and r.	BIBLE 47:6
with firmness in the r.	LINC 207:7
righteous: not come to call the r.	BIBLE 49:23
r., and sober life	BOOK 63:15
r. man regardeth the life	BIBLE 43:20
saw I never the r. forsaken	BOOK 66:27
seen the r. forsaken	BLUN 62:15
righteousness: breastplate of r.	BIBLE 56:4

righteousness (*cont.*):

hunger and thirst after r.	BIBLE 48:19
r. and peace have kissed	BOOK 67:23
r. arise with healing	BIBLE 47:26
r. shall he judge the world	BOOK 68:4
what r. really is	ARN 18:10
rightful: in our r. mind	WHIT 348:27
rights: duties as well as its r.	DRUM 126:25
equal in dignity and r.	ANON 5:20
extension of women's r.	FOUR 144:14
Natural r. is simple nonsense	BENT 34:22
religious r. of an Englishman	JUN 188:25
r. inherent and inalienable	JEFF 180:18
r. of man	ROB 260:16
rime: r. was on the spray	HARDY 162:18
Rimmon: house of R.	BIBLE 42:11
rind: how shall taste the r.	THOM 331:11
ring: giving and receiving of a R.	BOOK 66:4
One R. to rule them all	TOLK 333:10
only pretty r. time	SHAK 273:10
r. at the end of his nose	LEAR 203:12
r. of pure and endless light	VAUG 337:14
r. on her wand she bore	MOORE 234:17
R. out the false	TENN 325:23
R. out, wild bells	TENN 325:22
r. the bells of Heaven	HODG 169:13
r. without the finger	MIDD 224:6
They now r. the bells	WALP 342:5
With this R. I thee wed	BOOK 66:2
ringed: R. with the azure world	TENN 323:21
ringleaders: fling the r.	ARN 18:16
rings: r. black Cyprus	FLEC 141:18
Rio: Go rolling down to R.	KIPL 197:19
riot: r. is at bottom the language	KING 195:11
riotous: with r. living	BIBLE 52:29
ripe: we r. and ripe	SHAK 272:22
ripeness: R. is all	SHAK 283:30
ripens: not when it r. in a tumour	ABSE 1:1
ripple: r. of rain	SWIN 321:1
rise: Created half to r.	POPE 252:18
Held we fall to r.	BROW 75:11
Ile r. and fight againe	BALL 28:3
men may r. on stepping-stones	TENN 324:24
nation shall r. against nation	BIBLE 50:34
hope to r., or fear to fall	WOTT 357:15
populace r. at once	WHIT 348:15
resistible r. of Arturo Ui	BREC 71:17
r. at ten thirty	HARG 162:20
r. out of obscurity	JUV 189:5
rises: sun also r.	HEM 165:14
rising: r. to great place	BACON 24:29
risk: proxy for r. and a dummy	MACH 215:4
risu: *r. inepto res ineptior*	CAT 93:4
rite: For the newer r. is here	THOM 330:4
rites: r. for which I love him	SHAK 292:2
Ritz: open to all, like the R.	MATH 222:7
rivals: Three for the r.	ANON 8:6
rive: body r. not more in parting	SHAK 271:23
riven: From Thy r. side	TOPL 333:14
river: Among the r. sallows	KEATS 192:16
by a r. a little tom-tit	GILB 152:7
Down in the reeds by the r.	BROW 75:4
Fame is like a r.	BACON 25:7
Ol' man r.	HAMM 161:3
on a r. of crystal light	FIELD 139:2
On either side the r. lie	TENN 325:34
R. and mountain-spring	OAKL 240:16
r. is a strong brown god	ELIOT 133:7
r. jumps over the mountain	AUDEN 20:11
r. of human industry	TOCO 333:5
twice into the same r.	HER 166:8
riverrun: r., past Eve and Adam's	JOYCE 188:3
rivers: r. of blood must yet flow	JEFF 180:23
rivulet: r. of text shall meander	SHER 306:3
road: 'ammer along the 'ard 'igh r.	PUNCH 256:11

road (cont.):

Dreams are the royal r.	FREUD 146:1
Golden R. to Samarkand	FLEC 141:17
keep right on to the end of the r.	LAUD 202:5
light to shine upon the r.	COWP 109:27
Like one, that on a lonesome r.	COL 104:15
merry r., a mazy road	CHES 98:2
middle of the r.	BEVAN 38:5
one more for the r.	MERC 223:11
r. below me	STEV 317:25
r. of excess leads	BLAKE 61:1
r. that leads him to England	JOHN 184:9
r. through the woods	KIPL 197:8
r. to bring us daily nearer	KEBLE 193:17
R. to Heaven	BALL 28:7
r. to the City of Emeralds	BAUM 30:10
r. to wealth so easy	TROL 334:14
r. up and the road down	HER 166:10
r. wind up-hill all the way	ROSS 263:5
rolling English r.	CHES 98:1
Softly along the r. of evening	DE L 116:21
watched the ads, and not the r.	NASH 237:13
winding r. before me	HAZL 164:8
ye'll tak' the high r.	ANON 10:2
yon braid, braid r.	BALL 28:7

roads: By r. 'not adopted' BETJ 37:12
How many r. must a man	DYLAN 129:19
lawless r. ran wrong	MUIR 236:6
Two r. diverged in a wood	FROST 146:19

roam: don't know where to r. COLL 105:7
| Everywhere I r. | FOST 144:13 |
| who soar, but never r. | WORD 357:9 |

roaming: R. in the gloamin' LAUD 202:7
| where are you r. | SHAK 297:23 |

roar: long, withdrawing r. ARN 16:11
| mighty r. of London's traffic | ANON 9:23 |
| we should die of that r. | ELIOT 132:10 |

roareth: What is this that r. thus GODL 153:20

roaring: But R. Bill BELL 33:28
| r. of the wind is my wife | KEATS 193:9 |

rob: r. a lady of her fortune FIEL 139:11

robbed: We was r. JAC 179:1

robber: Now Barabbas was a r. BIBLE 54:2

robe: intertissued r. SHAK 279:16

robes: washed their r. BIBLE 57:26

Robespierre: R. was nothing HEINE 165:2

Robey: R. is the Darling SMITH 309:8

robin: Call for the r.-red-breast WEBS 344:25
| r. red breast in a cage | BLAKE 60:6 |
| Sweet R. sits in the bush | SCOTT 269:1 |

Robinson: here's to you, Mrs R. SIMON 307:6

robot: r. may not injure ASIM 19:1

rock: I've gotten a r. BLAM 62:8
Politics, like R., Pop	WOLFE 353:9
r. and a hard place	ANON 6:10
R. journalism	ZAPPA 361:1
R. of Ages, cleft for me	TOPL 333:14
serpent upon a r.	BIBLE 44:4
Sex and drugs and r. and roll	DURY 129:14
tall r., the mountain	WORD 355:9
upon this r. I will build	BIBLE 50:13

rocked: R. in the cradle of the deep WILL 350:27

rocket: As he rose like a r. PAINE 244:12
| long numbers that r. the mind | WILB 349:8 |

Rockies: R. may crumble GERS 150:7

rocking: endlessly r. WHIT 348:12
| R. and shocking the barmaid | SITW 307:18 |

rocks: eternal r. beneath BRON 72:17
hand that r. the cradle	WALL 341:10
older than the r.	PATER 246:13
rifted r. whose entrance leads	MILT 226:16
r. remain	HERB 166:15
With r., and stones, and trees	WORD 356:25

rod: all humbled kiss the r. SHAK 298:17
| r. and thy staff comfort | BOOK 66:18 |

rod (cont.):

r. out of the stem of Jesse	BIBLE 45:18
spare the r., and spoil the child	BUTL 84:3
spareth his r. hateth his son	BIBLE 43:23
rode: r. madly off in all directions	LEAC 203:5
R. the six hundred	TENN 323:15
rogue: r. and peasant slave am I	SHAK 275:21
Roland: R. to the dark tower	SHAK 283:18
role: and not yet found a r.	ACH 1:3
roll: r. all our strength	MARV 221:1
R. on, thou deep and dark	BYRON 85:13
R. up that map	PITT 249:9
Sex and drugs and rock and r.	DURY 129:14
rolled: r. along on wheels	HUXL 177:10
bottoms of my trousers r.	ELIOT 134:2
roller: r., pitch, and stumps	LANG 201:2
rolling: Go r. down to Rio	KIPL 197:19
jus' keeps r. along	HAMM 161:3
r. English drunkard	CHES 98:1

Roman: after the high R. fashion SHAK 271:26
antique R. than a Dane	SHAK 277:16
Before the R. came to Rye	CHES 98:1
Butchered to make a R. holiday	BYRON 85:10
His noses cast is of the r.	FLEM 142:1
I am a R. citizen	CIC 100:27
nor R., nor an empire	VOLT 340:19
noblest R. of them all	SHAK 282:3
R.'s life, a Roman's arms	MAC 214:7
R. thought hath struck him	SHAK 271:6
To-day the R. and his trouble	HOUS 174:23

Roman Catholic: [R. Church] MAC 213:15

romance: fine r. with no kisses FIEL 139:14
learned r. as she grew older	AUST 22:26
music and love and r.	BERL 35:22
symbols of a high r.	KEATS 192:20

Romanism: R., and rebellion BURC 79:12

Romans: Friends, R., countrymen SHAK 281:18

romantic: airline ticket to r. places MARV 221:4
In a ruin that's r.	GILB 152:8
In spite of all r. poets sing	LEAP 203:6
R. Ireland's dead and gone	YEATS 359:28
r. lie in the brain	AUDEN 21:11
Wrong but R.	SELL 270:2

romantics: We were the last r. YEATS 358:18

Romanus: Civis R. sum CIC 100:27

Rome: comen from R. al hoot CHAU 95:23
Everything in R. has its price	JUV 189:6
go from the church of R.	WOTT 357:21
grandeur that was R.	POE 250:9
high and palmy state of R.	SHAK 274:1
I loved R. more	SHAK 281:15
Let R. in Tiber melt	SHAK 271:5
O happy R., born when	CIC 101:2
Oh R.! my country	BYRON 85:8
R. has spoken	AUG 22:5
second at R.	CAES 87:26
voice of R. is the consent	JONS 187:1
When in R.	AMBR 4:20
when R. falls—the World	BYRON 85:11
you cruel men of R.	SHAK 280:24

Romeo: Come night! come, R.! SHAK 295:13
| Give me my R. | SHAK 295:14 |
| wherefore art thou R. | SHAK 294:30 |

Ronsard: R. sang of me RONS 262:5

roof: no r. to shroud HEYW 168:9
| on a corrugated tin r. | BEEC 32:1 |
| shouldest come under my r. | BIBLE 49:16 |

roofs: barbaric yawp over the r. WHIT 348:22

roof-tree: heavens my wide r. AYT 23:18

roof-wrecked: Is r. HARDY 162:3

rook: When the last r. COL 104:21

rooks: dull aunts, and croaking r. POPE 251:24
| r. are blown about | TENN 325:2 |
| r. in families homeward go | HARDY 162:17 |

room: All before my little r. BROO 73:3

room (*cont.*):

boys in the back r.	LOES 209:5
end of the enormous r.	AUDEN 20:13
Fifty springs are little r.	HOUS 174:17
fill the r. my heart keeps empty	KING 195:5
Great hatred, little r.	YEATS 359:19
How little r. do we take up	SHIR 306:12
In every grave make r.	D'AV 114:9
Infinite riches in a little r.	MARL 219:1
make r. for men who shout	WALK 341:5
no r. for them in the inn	BIBLE 51:32
ocean sea, was not sufficient r.	BARN 29:7
r. at the top	WEBS 344:12
r. grows chilly	GRAH 156:4
r. in my heart for thee	ELL 136:1
r. of her own	WOOLF 354:1
R. to deny ourselves	KEBLE 193:17
sitting in the smallest r.	REGER 259:2
slipped away into the next r.	HOLL 170:12
smoke-filled r.	SIMP 307:11
struggle for r. and food	MALT 217:6
taper to the outward r.	DONNE 123:19
upper r. furnished	BIBLE 52:40

rooms: boys in the back r. | BEAV 31:4
In council r. apart	RICE 259:18
lighted r. inside your head	LARK 201:16
Other voices, other r.	CAP 89:15

roost: always come home to r. | SOUT 311:21

root: knotty as a r. | BRON 72:15
March hath perced to the r.	CHAU 95:10
money is the r. of all evil	BIBLE 56:19
nips his r.	SHAK 280:18

roots: drought is destroying his r. | HERB 166:11
| shall grow out of his r. | BIBLE 45:18 |

rope: fourfold r. of nerves | HEAT 164:13
| set his hand to a r. | DRAKE 126:12 |

Rose: R., were you not extremely | PRIOR 255:12

rose: American beauty r. | ROCK 261:11
As though a r. should dare	KEATS 190:20
beauty's r. might never die	SHAK 299:11
blossom as the r.	BIBLE 46:4
Christmas I no more desire a r.	SHAK 284:11
English unofficial r.	BROO 73:4
fading r.	CAREW 89:20
Faintly the inimitable r.	WINC 352:3
fayr as is the r. in May	CHAU 96:11
fire and the r.	ELIOT 133:13
fresh lap of the crimson r.	SHAK 290:23
Gather therefore the r.	SPEN 313:12
glut thy sorrow on a morning r.	KEATS 191:26
Go, lovely r.	WALL 341:12
I know the colour r.	ABSE 1:1
Into the r.-garden	ELIOT 132:26
labyrinthine buds the r.	BROW 77:14
last r. of summer	MOORE 234:18
lovely is the r.	WORD 355:18
mighty lak' a r.	STAN 314:11
musk of the r.	TENN 326:28
never blows so red the r.	FITZ 140:8
never promised you a r. garden	GREEN 158:1
No thorns go as deep as a r.'s	SWIN 321:9
O, my Luve's like a red, red r.	BURNS 82:20
One perfect r.	PARK 245:7
O R., thou art sick	BLAKE 62:4
ravage with impunity a r.	BROW 77:15
r. by any other name	SHAK 294:31
R. is a rose is a rose	STEIN 314:22
r. of Sharon	BIBLE 44:31
r. of the fair state	SHAK 276:2
r. of yesterday	FITZ 140:5
r.-red city half as old as Time	BURG 79:17
Roves back the r.	DE L 116:12
sad R. of all my days	YEATS 360:4
scent is of the summer r.	GRAV 156:13
secret and inviolate R.	YEATS 359:26

rose (*cont.*):

vanish with the r.	FITZ 140:18
white r. weeps	TENN 327:1
without thorn the r.	MILT 229:8

rosebud: Queen rose of the r. garden | TENN 326:29

rosebuds: Gather ye r. | HERR 167:24

rosemary: r. and rue | SHAK 298:29
| r., that's for remembrance | SHAK 277:2 |

Rosencrantz: R. and Guildenstern | SHAK 277:20

roses: ash the burnt r. leave | ELIOT 133:8
days of wine and r.	DOWS 125:13
Everything's coming up r.	SOND 311:5
Flung r., roses, riotously	DOWS 125:12
forget the lilac and the r.	ARAG 14:21
not a bed of r.	STEV 317:8
raptures and r. of vice	SWIN 321:7
R. are flowering in Picardy	WEAT 344:5
r. for the flush of youth	ROSS 263:3
roses, r., all the way	BROW 76:24
scent of the r.	MOORE 234:13

rosy: old plain men have r. faces | STEV 317:18
| r. morn long since left | SPEN 313:5 |

rosy-fingered: R. dawn | HOMER 171:2

rot: cold obstruction and to r. | SHAK 288:21
| R. half a grain a day | SHAK 293:3 |
| we r. and rot | SHAK 272:22 |

rotted: Or simply r. early | NASH 237:14

rotten: It's always the good feel r. | YES 360:12
| r. in the state of Denmark | SHAK 274:29 |

rotundity: thick r. o' the world | SHAK 283:6

rough: from children who were r. | SPEN 312:25
r. places plain	BIBLE 46:9
r. than polished diamond	CHES 97:12
this r. magic	SHAK 296:12
winter and r. weather	SHAK 272:19

rough-hew: R. them how we will | SHAK 277:12

round: little r., fat, oily man | THOM 331:21
R. and round the circle	ELIOT 132:24
r. earth's imagined corners	DONNE 123:7
R. the world for ever and aye	ARN 16:17
R. up the usual suspects	EPST 137:12
test of a r. character	FORS 143:17

rounded: r. with a sleep | SHAK 296:10

Roundheads: R. (Right but | SELL 270:2

Rousseau: mock on Voltaire R. | BLAKE 61:13
not ask Jean Jacques R.	COWP 109:29
[R.] is the first militant	BERL 36:5
whose soul R. had created	HEINE 165:2

rover: blood's a r. | HOUS 174:18

roves: R. back the rose | DE L 116:12

roving: we'll go no more a-r. | BYRON 87:8

row: gate-bars hang in a r. | HARDY 162:17
| r. one way and look another | BURT 83:7 |

rowed: All r. fast, but none so fast | COKE 103:6

rowing: one way, and r. another | BUNY 79:1

royal: Dreams are the r. road | FREUD 146:1
no 'r. road' to geometry	EUCL 137:21
r. banners forward go	FORT 144:5
r. priesthood	BIBLE 57:8
r. throne of kings	SHAK 293:16
subjects with a r. wage	BROO 72:21
this is the r. Law	COR 108:10

royalist: *more of a r. than the king* | ANON 12:8

royalty: R. is the gold filling | OSB 242:26
| R. . . . lay it on with a trowel | DISR 122:20 |
| R. will be strong | BAG 26:12 |

rub: there's the r. | SHAK 275:25
| r. up against money | RUNY 264:8 |

rubbish: What r.! | BLÜC 62:11

rubies: her price is far above r. | BIBLE 44:6
| price of wisdom is above r. | BIBLE 43:2 |
| R. unparagoned | SHAK 273:24 |

rubs: r. nor botches in the work | SHAK 287:2

rudder: My heart was to thy r. tied | SHAK 271:18

rudder (*cont.*):
rhyme the r. is of verses — BUTL 83:25
ruddier: O r. than the cherry — GAY 149:1
ruddy: Now he was r. — BIBLE 41:16
rude: only rather r. and wild — BELL 33:11
R. am I in my speech — SHAK 291:33
r. heap together hurled — MARV 221:2
Rudyards: R. cease from kipling — STEP 315:5
rue: nought shall make us r. — SHAK 282:15
there's rosemary and r. — SHAK 298:29
There's r. for you — SHAK 277:3
ruffle: Would r. up your spirits — SHAK 281:26
rug: cockatoo upon a r. — STEV 316:12
rugged: cling to the old r. cross — BENN 34:10
harsh cadence of a r. line — DRYD 128:21
system of r. individualism — HOOV 171:17
Ruh: *Meine R.' ist hin* — GOET 154:6
ruin: boy will r. himself — GEOR 150:1
formless r. of oblivion — SHAK 297:10
Majestic though in r. — MILT 228:27
R. seize thee, ruthless King! — GRAY 157:1
r. that Cromwell knocked about — SULL 31:21
r. that's romantic — GILB 152:8
sand and r. and gold — SWIN 321:19
With ruin upon r. — MILT 229:1
ru-i-n: Since roving's been my r. — ANON 6:5
ruined: home of r. reputations — ELIOT 132:6
O r. piece of nature — SHAK 283:24
r. on the side of their natural — BURKE 81:7
ruining: R. along the illimitable inane — TENN 326:21
ruinous: R. inheritance — GAIUS 147:13
ruins: shored against my r. — ELIOT 134:31
human mind in r. — DAV 114:16
Ruislip: Gaily into R. Gardens — BETJ 37:7
rule: little r., a little sway — DYER 129:17
only infallible r. — SURT 319:7
Rowe's R. — DICK 120:19
R. 1, on page 1, of the book of war — MONT 233:23
R., Britannia, rule the waves — THOM 331:20
R. of Three doth puzzle me — ANON 9:11
Who can r. and dare not lie — TENN 326:26
ruler: R. of the Queen's Navee — GILB 152:18
r. in Israel — BIBLE 47:22
rulers: brought about by r. — BIER 59:6
r. of the darkness — BIBLE 56:4
R. of the Queen's Navee — GILB 152:20
rules: fundamental R. of Robotics — ASIM 19:1
golden r. for an orchestra — BEEC 31:23
hand that r. the world — WALL 341:10
people wouldn't obey the r. — BENN 34:15
R. and models destroy genius — HAZL 164:5
rulest: thou r. in might — SMITH 310:15
ruling: r. passion conquers reason — POPE 251:14
Search then the R. Passion — POPE 251:21
rum: r. and true religion — BYRON 86:5
r., Romanism, and rebellion — BURC 79:12
r., sodomy, and the lash — CHUR 100:6
what a R. Go everything is — WELLS 345:19
Yo-ho-ho, and a bottle of r. — STEV 317:2
rumble: r. of a distant drum — FITZ 140:7
R. thy bellyful — SHAK 283:7
rumour: distillation of r. — CARL 90:12
rumours: r. of wars — BIBLE 50:33
rump: R. Parliament — SELL 270:3
run: Gwine to r. all day — FOST 144:10
r., though not to soar — MAC 213:21
R., run, Orlando — SHAK 273:2
r. to and fro like sparks — BIBLE 47:29
They get r. down — BEVAN 38:5
till thou r. out thy race — MILT 228:3
true love never did r. smooth — SHAK 290:13
yet we will make him r. — MARV 221:1
runcible: ate with a r. spoon — LEAR 203:13
R. Cat with crimson whiskers — LEAR 203:15
runic: In a sort of R. rhyme — POE 250:4

runnable: r. stag, a kingly crop — DAV 114:11
runners: Song of the Ungirt R. — SORL 311:15
running: R. it never runs from us — DONNE 123:22
shaken together, and r. over — BIBLE 52:7
she'll be constantly r. back — HOR 173:11
takes all the r. *you* can do — CARR 91:18
Rupert: R. of Debate — BULW 78:9
R. of Parliamentary discussion — DISR 121:8
rural: lovely woman in a r. spot — HUNT 176:17
r. quiet, friendship — THOM 331:23
rus: *R. in urbe* — MART 220:8
rushes: *Green grow the r. O* — ANON 8:6
Green grow the r. O — BURNS 82:9
rushing: r. mighty wind — BIBLE 54:8
russet: r. yeas — SHAK 284:19
russet-coated: r. captain — CROM 111:24
Russia: between R. and British India — SAL 266:3
forecast to you the action of R. — CHUR 99:10
R. has two generals — NICH 239:11
Russian: might have been a R. — GILB 152:21
tumult in the R. heart — PUSH 256:23
rust: moth and r. doth corrupt — BIBLE 49:1
To r. unburnished — TENN 328:21
wear out that to r. out — CUMB 112:15
rusty: r. curb of old father antick — SHAK 277:24
Ruth: Through the sad heart of R. — KEATS 192:5
Rye: Before the Roman came to R. — CHES 98:1
rye: catcher in the r. — SAL 266:1
Comin thro' the r. — BURNS 81:29
fields of barley and of r. — TENN 325:34
r. reach to the chin — PEELE 247:2

S

sabbath: Remember the s. day — BIBLE 40:7
s. was made for man — BIBLE 51:18
sable: paint the s. skies — DRUM 127:1
son of the s. Night — DAN 113:15
sable-vested: S. Night — MILT 228:32
Sabrina: S. fair — MILT 226:21
sack: intolerable deal of s. — SHAK 278:2
S. the lot — FISH 139:23
sacrament: by this word S. — BOOK 65:23
This great S. revere — THOM 330:4
sacraments: S. in a tongue not — BOOK 69:18
sacred: only s. thing — FRAN 145:1
sacrifice: be an evening s. — BOOK 69:8
final s. — SPR 313:26
full, perfect, and sufficient s. — BOOK 65:16
holy hush of ancient s. — STEV 316:12
s. in a contemptible struggle — BURKE 81:4
Still stands Thine ancient S. — KIPL 197:2
Too long a s. — YEATS 359:2
To pay thy morning s. — KEN 193:20
To see the approaching s. — MILM 225:13
turn delight into a s. — HERB 166:21
your deaths a living s. — BIBLE 54:43
your prayers one sweet s. — SHAK 280:14
sacrificed: s. to expediency — MAUG 222:8
sacrifices: forgive him for the s. — MAUG 222:10
sad: All my s. captains — SHAK 271:19
all their songs are s. — CHES 97:20
How s. and bad and mad it was — BROW 75:21
mine a s. one — SHAK 288:27
remember and be s. — ROSS 263:4
s., black isle — BAUD 30:5
s. stories of the death of kings — SHAK 293:27
s. tale's best for winter — SHAK 298:22
s. vicissitude of things — STER 315:27
s. words of tongue or pen — WHIT 349:1
With how s. steps — SIDN 306:18
Your s. tires in a mile-a — SHAK 298:28
sadder: s. and a wiser man — COL 104:19

saddest: tell of s. thought	SHEL 305:10
wisest aunt telling the s. tale	SHAK 290:21
saddle: Boot, s., to horse	BROW 75:17
Come s. your horses	SCOTT 268:7
Things are in the s.	EMER 136:13
saddled: he s. his ass, and arose	BIBLE 41:26
s. and bridled to be ridden	RUMB 264:5
sadly: take their pleasures s.	SULLY 319:4
saeclorum: *integro s. nascitur*	VIRG 339:25
safe: s. course for the defeated	VIRG 339:6
s. for democracy	WILS 351:21
s. to be unpopular	STEV 316:18
s. to go back in the water	ANON 8:15
We are none of us s.	FORS 143:22
world s. for hypocrisy	WOLFE 353:6
safeguard: s. of the West	WORD 356:2
safeliest: s. when with one man manned	DONNE 123:6
safely: most s. by the middle way	OVID 243:13
safer: s. for a prince to be feared	MACH 215:1
s. than a known way	HASK 163:16
safest: Just when we are s.	BROW 75:13
safety: pluck this flower, s.	SHAK 277:30
s., honour, and welfare	CHAR 95:1
source of my light and my s.	BIBLE 58:9
sagacity: infinite-resource-and-s.	KIPL 197:24
sagas: our eyes the frosty s.	CRANE 110:31
sager: s. sort our deeds reprove	CAMP 89:2
said: fool hath s. in his heart	BOOK 66:12
s. the thing which was not	SWIFT 320:1
sail: comes i' faith full s.	CONG 106:17
in a sieve I'll thither s.	SHAK 285:3
S. and sail, with unshut eye	ARN 16:17
s. on, O Ship of State	LONG 209:11
sea-mark of my utmost s.	SHAK 293:4
white and rustling s.	CUNN 113:7
sailed: s. away for a year	LEAR 203:12
s. the seas and come to	YEATS 359:22
She hadna s. a league	BALL 27:16
sailing: which port one is s.	SEN 270:7
sailor: Home is the s.	STEV 317:22
saint: England and S. George	SHAK 279:6
little s. best fits a little shrine	HERR 167:22
neither s. nor sophist-led	ARN 16:13
s. in crape is twice	POPE 251:20
S., *n.* A dead sinner	BIER 59:9
saw my late espousèd s.	MILT 230:24
worst of madmen is a s.	POPE 252:27
sainted: thing enskyed and s.	SHAK 288:10
saints: Communion of S.	BOOK 64:3
pair of carvèd s.	SHAK 294:2
Where s. immortal reign	WATTS 343:11
with thy choir of s.	DONNE 123:16
sais: *Que s.-je?*	MONT 233:18
saisons: *Ô s., ô châteaux*	RIMB 260:10
sake: Christ's particular love's s.	BROW 77:7
country for his country's s.	FITZ 140:3
loseth his life for my s.	BIBLE 49:33
O, who am I, that for my s.	CROS 112:13
salad: My s. days	SHAK 271:12
Our Garrick's a s.	GOLD 155:1
sale: From s. and profanation	CHES 97:24
salesman: Death of a S.	MILL 225:22
s. is got to dream	MILL 225:4
salley: Down by the s. gardens	YEATS 359:1
Sally: S. in our Alley	CAREY 90:2
sally: I make a sudden s.	TENN 323:12
salmon: s. sing in the street	AUDEN 20:11
salt: pillar of s.	BIBLE 39:15
s., estranging sea	ARN 17:23
s. is the taste of another's bread	DANTE 113:23
s. of the earth	BIBLE 48:20
s. of the earth	WEST 346:25
seasoned with s.	BIBLE 56:12
verge of the s. flood	SHAK 296:24

Salteena: Mr S. was an elderly man	ASHF 18:20
salus: *S. populi suprema est lex*	CIC 100:20
s. victis nullam sperare	VIRG 339:6
salute: If it moves, s. it	ANON 8:4
S. one another	BIBLE 55:2
S. the happy morn	BYROM 84:23
who are about to die s. you	ANON 13:12
salva: *S. me, fons pietatis*	MISS 231:24
salvation: My bottle of s.	RAL 257:23
none of us should see s.	SHAK 289:27
no s. outside the church	AUG 21:26
now is the day of s.	BIBLE 55:25
publisheth s.	BIBLE 46:15
s. with fear and trembling	BIBLE 56:6
There cannot be s.	CYPR 113:14
Wot prawce S. nah	SHAW 301:11
salve: *S., regina*	ANON 13:21
Sam: nephew of my Uncle S.'s	COHAN 103:5
Play it again, S.	EPST 137:10
Samarkand: Golden Road to S.	FLEC 141:17
same: Christ the s. yesterday	BIBLE 56:30
he is much the s.	ANON 6:1
I'm having the s.	LOES 209:5
more they are the s.	KARR 190:2
s. a hundred years hence	DICK 119:14
s. the whole world over	ANON 10:11
we must all say the *s.*	MELB 222:20
you are the s. you	MART 220:7
samite: Clothed in white s.	TENN 324:3
Samson: S. hath quit himself	MILT 230:17
sancta: *O s. simplicitas!*	HUSS 176:21
sed s. simplicitas	JER 181:6
sanctuary: dark s. of incapacity	CHES 97:4
three classes which need s.	BALD 27:10
sanctus: *S., sanctus, sanctus*	MISS 231:17
sand: land of s. and ruin	SWIN 321:19
on the edge of the s.	LEAR 203:13
s. against the wind	BLAKE 61:13
Such quantities of s.	CARR 91:21
To see a world in a grain of s.	BLAKE 60:5
sandal: And his s. shoon	SHAK 276:32
sandals: morn went out with s.	MILT 227:19
sandalwood: S., cedarwood	MAS 221:18
sands: Come unto these yellow s.	SHAK 295:36
Footprints on the s. of time	LONG 209:23
s. upon the Red sea shore	BLAKE 61:14
sandwich: raw-onion s.	BARN 29:6
San Francisco: left my heart in S.	CROSS 112:10
sang: s. his didn't he danced	CUMM 112:16
s. in my chains	THOM 330:9
s. within the bloody wood	ELIOT 134:17
sanglots: *Les s. longs*	VERL 337:21
sanitary: glorified s. engineer	STR 318:13
sans: s. End	FITZ 140:9
s. everything	SHAK 272:28
sap: dried the s. out of my veins	YEATS 359:4
world's whole s. is sunk	DONNE 124:8
sapere: *s. aude*	HOR 173:8
sapient: s. sutlers of the Lord	ELIOT 134:5
sapless: s. foliage of the ocean	SHEL 304:7
Sappho: burning S. loved	BYRON 86:13
Sarah: it ceased to be with S.	BIBLE 39:14
Sargent: musical Malcolm S.	BEEC 32:2
sashes: one of his nice new s.	GRAH 156:4
sassy: I'm sickly but s.	HARR 163:4
sat: I s. down and wept	SMART 308:15
S. and knotted all the while	SEDL 269:12
s. too long here	CROM 112:4
upon which everyone has s.	CUMM 112:18
we s. down and wept	BOOK 69:2
when they have s. down	CHUR 99:5
Satan: capital of S. and his peers	MILT 228:21
Get thee behind me, S.	BIBLE 50:14
Lord said unto S.	BIBLE 42:21

Satan (cont.):
messenger of S.   BIBLE 55:28
my S., thou art but a dunce   BLAKE 60:15
S. finds some mischief   WATTS 343:6
S. met his ancient friend   BYRON 87:13
Satanic: dark S. mills   BLAKE 61:12
'satiable: full of s. curtiosity   KIPL 197:21
satin: always goes into white s.   SHER 305:24
satire: S. is a sort of glass   SWIFT 319:17
S. is what closes Saturday   KAUF 190:3
S. or sense, alas   POPE 251:7
satirical: certain sign of a s. wit   AUBR 19:21
satisfaction: I can't get no s.   RICH 179:6
satisfied: Never s. with having   WROTH 358:1
well paid that is well s.   SHAK 289:30
satisfies: Where most she s.   SHAK 271:17
satisfy: That poorly s. our eyes   WOTT 357:16
satisfying: s. a voracious appetite   FIEL 139:10
Saturday: For what he did on S.   YBAR 358:11
Glasgow Empire on a S. night   DODD 122:29
Satire is what closes S. night   KAUF 190:3
Saturn: days of S.'s reign return   VIRG 339:25
Saturnia: redeunt S. regna   VIRG 339:25
satyr: Hyperion to a s.   SHAK 274:11
satyrs: My men, like s. grazing   MARL 218:15
sauce: Hunger is the best s.   CERV 93:17
religions, and only one s.   CAR 89:17
saucy: with s. looks   SHAK 284:10
Saul: S. and Jonathan were lovely   BIBLE 41:22
S., why persecutest thou me   BIBLE 54:11
savage: noble s.   DRYD 127:26
s. place   COL 103:23
s. wields his club   HUXL 177:16
soothe a s. breast   CONG 106:11
take some s. woman   TENN 326:15
Unequal laws unto a s. race   TENN 328:19
savaged: s. by a dead sheep   HEAL 164:10
save: destroy the town to s. it   ANON 8:10
God s. the king   HOGG 170:8
he shall s. his soul alive   BIBLE 47:6
himself he cannot s.   BIBLE 51:15
little less democracy to s.   ATK 19:10
matter enough to s.   BROW 76:12
s. Europe by her example   PITT 249:8
s. me, from the candid friend   CANN 89:12
s. me, O source of pity   MISS 231:24
s. my soul   ANON 9:22
s. them by the barrel-load   THOM 331:13
s. those that have no imagination   SHAW 302:21
To s. your world you asked   AUDEN 20:17
We shall nobly s.   LINC 207:6
saved: could have s. sixpence   BECK 31:8
He s. others   BIBLE 51:15
they only s. the world   CHES 97:23
What must I do to be s.   BIBLE 54:17
saving: thy s. health among all   BOOK 67:16
saviour: S. of the world was born   BYROM 84:23
S.'s birth is celebrated   SHAK 274:2
savour: salt have lost his s.   BIBLE 48:20
Seeming and s. all the winter   SHAK 298:29
saw: Nor do not s. the air   SHAK 276:4
say: all s. *the same*   MELB 222:20
don't s. nothin'   HAMM 161:3
easier to s. what it is not   JOHN 185:11
Have something to s.   ARN 18:13
I have nothing to s.   CAGE 88:4
I s. the hell with it   WHITE 347:15
know what they are going to s.   CHUR 99:5
more to s. when I am dead   ROB 260:20
Need we s. it was not love   MILL 224:23
nothing to say, s. nothing   COLT 105:16
s. what they please   FRED 145:19
s. what you mean   CARR 91:6
s. why and how I became   WILS 351:16
someone else has got to s.   GASK 148:18

say (cont.):
think till I see what I s.   WALL 341:11
We must not s. so   BERR 36:13
Whatever you s., s. nothing   HEAN 164:11
saying: and I am s. it   CAGE 88:4
For loving, and for s. so   DONNE 124:14
not know what they are s.   CHUR 99:5
something is not worth s.   BEAU 30:15
We were s. yesterday   LUIS 212:7
scabbard: he threw away the s.   CLAR 101:9
scaffold: Truth forever on the s.   LOW 211:8
scale: puts his thumb in the s.   LAWR 202:12
scales: someone is practising s.   MACN 216:9
scallop-shell: s. of quiet   RAL 257:23
scan: gently s. your brother man   BURNS 81:21
scandal: love and s. are the best   FIEL 139:9
no s. like rags   FARQ 138:15
Retired to their tea and s.   CONG 106:6
s. by a woman of easy virtue   HAIL 160:1
s. that constitutes offence   MOL 232:24
scandalous: s. and poor   ROCH 261:8
scapegoat: s. into the wilderness   BIBLE 40:13
scarecrow: s. of the law   SHAK 288:12
scarecrows: s. of fools   HUXL 177:20
scarf: S. up the tender eye   SHAK 287:6
scarlet: Cowards in s.   GRAN 156:11
His sins were s.   BELL 33:27
love that loves a s. coat   HOOD 171:6
raise the s. standard high   CONN 106:23
though clothed in s.   JONS 187:10
Though your sins be as s.   BIBLE 45:4
scars: He jests at s.   SHAK 294:29
scattered: he hath s. the proud   BIBLE 51:29
S. his Maker's image   DRYD 127:3
scene: Speaks a new s.   QUAR 257:1
start a s. or two   ELIOT 134:1
scenery: end of all natural s.   RUSK 264:13
S. is fine   KEATS 193:5
s.'s divine   CALV 88:10
Standing among savage s.   HOFF 170:5
Where God paints the s.   HART 163:10
scenes: I long for s. where man   CLARE 101:7
no more behind your s.   JOHN 183:24
scent: I s. the morning air   SHAK 275:1
s. is of the summer rose   GRAV 156:13
s. of the roses   MOORE 234:13
sweetest flower for s.   SHEL 304:31
whose s. the fair annoys   COWP 109:21
sceptic: to much of a s. to deny   HUXL 177:22
What ever s. could inquire   BUTL 83:22
sceptre: s. and the ball   SHAK 279:16
s. for a palmer's walking staff   SHAK 294:2
s. from tyrants   TURG 335:16
sceptred: this s. isle   SHAK 293:16
what avails the s. race   LAND 200:23
sceptreless: S., free   SHEL 304:22
schemes: best laid s. o' mice an' men   BURNS 82:27
s. of political improvement   JOHN 184:22
schizophrenic: you are a s.   SZASZ 321:25
Schleswig-Holstein: S. question   PALM 244:21
scholar: better s. than Wordsworth   HOUS 175:6
ills the s.'s life assail   JOHN 183:12
s. all Earth's volumes carry   CHAP 94:21
scholars: S. dispute   HOR 172:25
school: language, goeth to s.   BACON 25:17
s. of Manchester   DISR 122:13
Three little maids from s.   GILB 151:21
till he's been to a good s.   SAKI 265:20
Unwillingly to s.   SHAK 272:25
vixen when she went to s.   SHAK 290:33
schoolboy: every s. knows   MAC 213:13
Not the s. heat   TENN 325:28
tell what every s. knows   SWIFT 320:15
whining s.   SHAK 272:25
schoolboys: s. from their books   SHAK 295:2

schoolboys (cont.):
s. playing in the stream | PEELE 247:2
schoolchildren: What all s. learn | AUDEN 21:10
schoolman: knew no s.'s subtle art | POPE 251:9
schoolmaster: becoming a s. | WAUGH 343:19
schoolmasters: Let s. puzzle | GOLD 155:8
schoolrooms: build s. for 'the boy' | COOK 107:17
schools: hundred s. of thought | MAO 218:1
lumber of the s. | SWIFT 320:18
schooner: It was the s. Hesperus | LONG 210:5
sciatica: S.: he cured it | AUBR 20:1
science: Dismal S. | CARL 90:18
Enough of s. and of art | WORD 357:5
essence of s. | BRON 72:10
How s. dwindles | YOUNG 360:16
Language the instrument of s. | JOHN 182:4
only applications of s. | PAST 246:12
s. and study of man | CHAR 95:9
S. is an edged tool | EDD 130:13
S. is built up of facts | POIN 250:10
s. is either physics or stamp | RUTH 265:8
S. is nothing but trained | HUXL 177:16
S. is organized knowledge | SPEN 312:15
s. is strong and religion weak | SZASZ 322:1
S. means simply the aggregate | VALÉ 336:20
S. moves, but slowly slowly | TENN 326:13
s. must begin with myths | POPP 253:16
s. of politics | ARIS 15:13
s. reassures | BRAQ 71:14
s. the credit goes to the man | DARW 114:7
S. without religion is lame | EINS 131:11
tragedy of S. | HUXL 177:15
typical triumph of modern s. | WAUGH 344:1
sciences: That great mother of s. | BACON 25:27
scientific: broken open on s. principles | PEAC 246:23
judgement of our s. age | HOLM 170:13
s. faith's absurd | BROW 75:27
s. truth does not triumph | PLAN 249:12
scientist: distinguished s. says | CLAR 101:14
research s. to discard | LOR 210:11
scientists: in the company of s. | AUDEN 21:18
scintillations: s. of your wit | GOUL 155:26
scissor-man: long, red-legged s. | HOFF 169:21
scoff: who came to s. | GOLD 154:22
scoffer: dull product of a s.'s pen | WORD 354:20
scones: Over buttered s. | ELIOT 132:22
scope: and that man's s. | SHAK 299:14
scorer: One Great S. comes | RICE 259:17
scorn: deal of s. looks beautiful | SHAK 298:6
fixed figure for the time of s. | SHAK 292:24
laugh no man to s. | BIBLE 47:33
little s. is alluring | CONG 106:19
S. not the Sonnet | WORD 356:21
scorned: fury, like a woman s. | CONG 106:12
scorpions: chastise you with s. | BIBLE 41:34
Scotch: Mary, ma S. Bluebell | LAUD 202:6
scotched: We have s. the snake | SHAK 287:3
Scotchman: noblest prospect which a S. | JOHN 184:9
Scotia: chief of S.'s food | BURNS 82:2
Scotland: from S. but I cannot help it | JOHN 184:6
I'll be in S. afore ye | ANON 10:2
in S. supports the people | JOHN 182:9
love S. better than truth | JOHN 182:14
S., land of the omnipotent No | BOLD 63:2
shivered are fair S.'s spear | SCOTT 268:23
Stands S. where it did | SHAK 287:24
Scots: S., wha hae | BURNS 82:21
Scotsman: S. on the make | BARR 29:17
Scotty: Beam me up, S. | RODD 261:13
scoundrel: last refuge of a s. | JOHN 185:4
man over forty is a s. | SHAW 302:5
scout: s. 'em, and flout 'em | SHAK 296:7
scouts: s.' motto is founded | BAD 26:1
scowl: With anxious s. drew near | AYT 23:16
scrap: just for a s. of paper | BETH 36:15

scraps: stolen the s. | SHAK 284:17
scratch: all you can do is s. it | BEEC 32:4
quick sharp s. | BROW 76:17
S. the Christian | ZANG 360:26
s. the nurse | SHAK 298:17
scratches: S. its innocent behind | AUDEN 21:2
scratching: s. of a pen | LOVER 210:22
s. of pimples on the body | WOOLF 354:6
world to the s. of my finger | HUME 176:11
scream: s. and s. till I'm thick | CROM 111:23
screw: s. your courage | SHAK 286:6
Turn of the S. | JAMES 180:3
scribblative: babblative and s. | SOUT 312:3
scribble: Always s., scribble | GLOU 153:17
s., to a man | POPE 252:29
we all s. poems | HOR 173:16
scribbled: Man by a s. name | THOM 330:11
scrip: yet with s. and scrippage | SHAK 273:3
scripture: devil can cite S. | SHAK 289:3
S. moveth us in sundry places | BOOK 63:12
usury is contrary to S. | TAWN 322:20
scriptures: caused all Holy S. | BOOK 64:22
Let us look at the s. | SELD 269:16
scruple: Some craven s. | SHAK 276:30
scrutamini: S. scripturas | SELD 269:16
scullion: Away, you s.! | SHAK 278:20
sculpture: austere, like that of s. | RUSS 265:3
sculptured: s. dead | KEATS 190:15
scum: mere s. of the earth | WELL 345:14
Okie means you're s. | STEI 314:24
scuttling: S. across the floors | ELIOT 133:28
sea: afraid of the s. | SYNGE 321:21
against a s. of troubles | SHAK 275:25
all gone under the s. | ELIOT 133:4
As is the ribbed s.-sand | COL 104:11
as near to heaven by s. | GILB 151:3
bathed in the Poem of the S. | RIMB 260:8
boy playing on the s.-shore | NEWT 239:6
But I beneath a rougher s. | COWP 109:20
cold grey stones, O S. | TENN 323:10
crowns around the glassy s. | HEBER 164:17
dominion of the s. | COV 108:18
Down to a sunless s. | COL 103:22
down to the s. again | MAS 221:21
down to the s. in ships | BOOK 68:12
English that of the s. | RICH 260:6
forbear to teach the s. | DONNE 124:16
From s. to shining sea | BATES 30:2
goes to s. for nothing | DONNE 123:4
gong-tormented s. | YEATS 358:15
gurly grew the s. | BALL 27:16
home from s. | STEV 317:22
if we gang to s. master | BALL 28:5
in peril on the s. | WHIT 348:9
in the flat s. sunk | MILT 226:11
in the s. of life enisled | ARN 17:22
Into a s. of dew | FIELD 139:2
Into that silent s. | COL 104:5
Lie mirrored on her s. | HODG 169:14
little cloud out of the s. | BIBLE 42:2
lover of men, the s. | SWIN 321:18
my chains like the s. | THOM 330:9
never go to s. | GILB 152:20
no more s. | BIBLE 58:4
one is of the s. | WORD 357:6
Put out to s. | MACN 216:11
sailed the wintry s. | LONG 210:5
salt, estranging s. | ARN 17:23
scrotumtightening s. | JOYCE 188:11
s.-blooms and the oozy woods | SHEL 304:7
s. gave up the dead | BIBLE 58:3
s. hates a coward | O'NEI 241:12
s.-mark of my utmost sail | SHAK 293:4
S. of Faith | ARN 16:11

sea (*cont.*):

S. shall give up her dead	BOOK 69:15
s.! the sea!	XEN 358:8
s. was made his tomb	BARN 29:7
see nothing but s.	BACON 23:22
serpent-haunted s.	FLEC 141:15
She sells s.-shells	SULL 319:2
ship in the midst of the s.	BIBLE 44:4
shore of the wan grassy s.	SITW 307:20
steady than an ebbing s.	FORD 143:11
sudden came the s.	BROW 76:23
suffer a s.-change	SHAK 296:1
summers in a s. of glory	SHAK 280:18
tideless dolorous midland s.	SWIN 321:19
uttermost parts of the s.	BOOK 69:6
very much at s.	CARS 92:11
water in the rough rude s.	SHAK 293:22
waves on the great s.	LUCR 212:4
wet sheet and a flowing s.	CUNN 113:7
When I put out to s.	TENN 323:18
Where no s. runs	THOM 330:12
why the s. is boiling hot	CARR 91:22
willing foe and s. room	ANON 11:22
with the s. embraced	CHAU 96:21
wrinkled s. beneath him crawls	TENN 323:21

seagreen: s. Incorruptible CARL 90:13
seagull: I'm a s. CHEK 96:27
seal: opened the seventh s. BIBLE 57:29
s. upon thine heart BIBLE 45:1
S. up the mouth of outrage SHAK 295:26
sealed: My lips are s. BALD 27:7
sealing wax: ships—and s. CARR 91:22
sear: fall'n into the s. SHAK 288:1
search: characters in s. of an author PIR 249:1
In s. of lost time PROU 255:17
in s. of what he needs MOORE 234:7
searched: deep-s. with saucy looks SHAK 284:10
thou hast s. me out BOOK 69:5
searching: by s. find out God BIBLE 42:32
I am s. everywhere STEP 315:7
seas: dangers of the s. PARK 245:17
Draw not up s. to drown DONNE 124:16
floors of silent s. ELIOT 133:28
multitudinous s. incarnadine SHAK 286:18
perilous s., in faery lands KEATS 192:5
s. colder than the Hebrides FLEC 141:14
s. roll over but the rocks HERB 166:15
s. upon their lawful occasions BOOK 69:14
therefore I have sailed the s. YEATS 359:22
through strange s. of Thought WORD 356:10
season: all alike, no s. knows DONNE 124:12
by s. seasoned SHAK 290:5
dry brain in a dry s. ELIOT 133:16
every thing there is a s. BIBLE 44:11
In a somer s. LANG 201:5
S. of mists and mellow KEATS 192:14
s. of snows and sins SWIN 321:2
selfish hope of a s.'s fame NEWB 238:13
that in s. grows SHAK 284:11
word spoken in due s. BIBLE 43:27
Youth's the s. made for joys GAY 149:6
seasoned: s. with salt BIBLE 56:12
seasons: I play for S. MER 223:23
man for all s. WHIT 349:2
O s., O castles! RIMB 260:10
we see the s. alter SHAK 290:23
seat: s. to faith assigned SMART 308:11
this s. of Mars SHAK 293:16
seat-belts: Fasten your s. MANK 217:12
seated: S. one day at the organ PROC 255:13
seaworms: Battening upon huge s. TENN 325:32
second: All things have s. birth WORD 356:13
Appointed for my s. race VAUG 337:7
beauty faded has no s. spring PHIL 248:14
Habit is s. nature AUCT 20:3

second (*cont.*):

not a s. on the day	COOK 107:15
s. at Rome	CAES 87:26
s. best bed	SHAK 300:21
s. best's a gay goodnight	YEATS 359:5
S. childishness	SHAK 272:28

secrecy: S. the human dress BLAKE 62:7
secret: bread eaten in s. BIBLE 43:15
Et Vigny plus s. SAIN 265:14
giant girls that have no s. SPEN 313:3
I know that's a s. CONG 106:9
in s. sin CHUR 98:25
most s. and inviolate Rose YEATS 359:26
neurosis is a s. TYNAN 336:9
official s. WEBER 344:8
s. anniversaries LONG 209:20
s., black, and midnight hags SHAK 287:19
S. sits in the middle FROST 146:20
S. thoughts and open countenance ALB 3:13
Vereker's s. JAMES 179:17
when it ceases to be a s. BEHN 32:21
secretary: S. of Nature WALT 342:16
secrets: from whom no s. are hid BOOK 65:2
s. are edged tools DRYD 128:16
sect: attached to that great s. SHEL 303:15
found them a s. MAC 213:17
loving his own s. COL 104:23
paradise for a s. KEATS 190:24
serious, sad-coloured s. HOOD 171:14
sects: diversity of s. SPEN 313:16
secure: He is s. SHEL 303:11
securities: trust to two s. CHES 97:14
security: best s. of the land COV 108:18
sedate: s., sober, silent sect HOOD 171:14
seducer: Thou strong s. DRYD 127:27
seduction: s. of martial music BURN 81:18
see: All that we s. or seem POE 250:5
come up and s. me sometime WEST 346:24
complain we cannot s. BERK 35:18
do not s. the signal NELS 238:1
everywhere but never s. him FLAU 141:11
I'd rather s. than be one BURG 79:16
I eat what I s. CARR 91:6
I'll s. you again COW 109:2
In all things Thee to s. HERB 166:25
I s. and hear nothing THOM 330:25
I s., not feel, how beautiful COL 103:14
I think that I shall never s. NASH 237:17
last s. your father YEAM 358:12
more people s. than weigh CHES 97:16
no man s. me more SHAK 280:17
not worth going to s. JOHN 185:24
S., amid the winter's snow CASW 92:18
s. and hear and feel yet JOYCE 188:17
s. beyond our bourn KEATS 192:18
s. it often AUDEN 20:25
s. the object as in itself ARN 18:12
s. with not through BLAKE 60:12
seem to s. the things SHAK 283:26
Shall never s. so much SHAK 284:8
shall no man s. me and live BIBLE 40:12
they shall s. God BIBLE 48:19
till I s. what I say WALL 341:11
To s. oursels as others see us BURNS 82:25
yet I s. thee still SHAK 286:10
You s., but you do not observe DOYLE 125:16
seed: s. shall remain for ever BIBLE 48:8
garden, that grows to s. SHAK 274:10
good s. on the land CAMP 88:13
s. of the Church TERT 329:8
seeds: look into the s. of time SHAK 285:7
s. fell by the wayside BIBLE 50:4
seeing: Discovery consists of s. SZEN 322:3
seek: All I s., the heaven above STEV 317:25
s., and ye shall find BIBLE 49:9

seek (*cont.*):

s. me if you had not found me	PASC 246:8
that sometime did me s.	WYATT 358:2
To strive, to s., to find	TENN 328:25
We s. him here	ORCZY 241:17
where s. is find	SMART 308:11
seem: Let be be finale of s.	STEV 316:6
seeming: S. and savour	SHAK 298:29
seems: it is; I know not 's.'	SHAK 274:7
seen: evidence of things not s.	BIBLE 56:26
God whom he hath not s.	BIBLE 57:17
Has anybody here s. Kelly	MURP 236:12
Much more had s.	ARMS 16:1
s. further it is by standing	NEWT 239:2
s. one Western you've seen	WHIT 348:7
s. to be done	HEW 168:4
seen what I have s.	SHAK 276:3
Too early s. unknown	SHAK 294:28
What things have we s.	BEAU 30:18
seeth: Lord s. not as man seeth	BIBLE 41:15
segregation: S. now, s. tomorrow	WALL 341:8
seize: s. the day	HOR 173:20
seldom: s. come, they wished for come	SHAK 277:25
selection: Natural S.	DARW 114:3
self: Love seeketh only S. to please	BLAKE 62:2
s. is hateful	PASC 246:7
to thine own s. be true	SHAK 274:23
self-assertion: s. abroad	WAUGH 343:23
self-contempt: S., well-grounded	LEAV 203:23
self-defence: I swear it was in s.	MARL 218:7
self-denial: S. is not a virtue	SHAW 301:34
self-evident: hold these truths to be s.	ANON 11:12
self-help: s. the root of all growth	SMIL 308:17
selfish: sensible people are s.	EMER 136:18
self-love: s. and social be the same	POPE 252:21
self-made: s. man is one who	STEAD 314:13
self-preservation: s. in the other	JEFF 180:25
self-slain: As a god s.	SWIN 321:10
self-sufficiency: S. at home	WAUGH 343:23
self-sufficing: reasoning, s. thing	WORD 356:6
self-will: murmurs of s.	BODE 62:16
selkie: I am a s. in the sea	BALL 27:17
sell: go and s. that thou hast	BIBLE 50:21
If there were dreams to s.	BEDD 31:19
I s. what all the world desires	BOUL 70:11
s. with you, talk with you	SHAK 288:31
that no man might buy or s.	BIBLE 57:32
who had a mind to s. his house	SWIFT 319:20
selling: Every one lives by s.	STEV 316:23
old firm, is s. out	OSB 242:23
sells: Or s. eternity to get a toy	SHAK 299:8
seltzer: weak hock and s.	BETJ 36:16
semblable: *mon s.,—mon frère*	BAUD 30:3
seminary: Come from a ladies' s.	GILB 151:23
semper: *Quod ubique, quod s.*	VINC 338:22
Sic s. tyrannis	BOOTH 69:20
Sempronius: we'll do more, S.	ADD 2:13
senator: S., and a Democrat	JOHN 181:19
senators: look at the s. and pray for	HALE 160:4
respectable s. burst with	AUDEN 20:18
teach his s. wisdom	BOOK 68:10
send: Here am I; s. me	BIBLE 45:12
S. in the Clowns	SOND 311:7
se'nnights: s. nine times nine	SHAK 285:4
sensations: easy prey to s.	TREV 334:9
s. rather than of thoughts	KEATS 192:24
sense: borrows all her rays from s.	POPE 251:24
decency is want of s.	DILL 120:23
Devoid of s. and motion	MILT 228:24
disease and want of s.	ROCH 261:2
Learned without s.	CHUR 98:29
light of nature, s.	ROCH 261:6
men of s. never tell	SHAF 270:20
Money is like a sixth s.	MAUG 222:11
never deviates into s.	DRYD 128:5

sense (*cont.*):

Not when the s. is dim	BEEC 32:5
Of s. and outward things	WORD 355:22
Satire or s., alas	POPE 251:7
s. to the American people	STEV 316:16
stings and motions of the s.	SHAK 288:11
Take care of the s.	CARR 91:9
within the s. they quicken	SHEL 305:4
without one grain of s.	DRYD 127:28
senseless: by a kind of s. wit	WILB 349:11
you worse than s. things	SHAK 280:24
senses: If Parson lost his s.	HODG 169:13
sensibility: pattern informed by s.	READ 258:9
sensible: All s. people are selfish	EMER 136:18
be bold and be s.	HOR 173:8
S. men never tell	DISR 122:1
sensitive: S. Plant in a garden grew	SHEL 304:30
sensual: s. pleasure without vice	JOHN 186:10
sentence: Marriage isn't a word, it's a s.	VIDOR 338:15
S. first—verdict afterwards	CARR 91:14
sentenced: s. to death in my absence	BEHAN 32:18
sentences: Backward ran s.	GIBBS 150:18
sentiment: classic lecture, rich in s.	TENN 327:18
s. might uncoil in the heart	GREE 158:4
sentiments: Them's my s.	THAC 329:17
sentinels: s. to warn th' immortal	MARL 219:11
sentry: Where stands a wingèd s.	VAUG 337:6
sentry-box: quadrille in a s.	JAMES 179:16
separate: s. us from the love	BIBLE 54:42
separately: we shall all hang s.	FRAN 145:13
separation: prepare for a s.	QUIN 257:9
September: Thirty days hath S.	ANON 11:2
When you reach S.	AND 5:12
sepulchre: man the living s. of life	CLARE 101:8
sepulchres: like unto whited s.	BIBLE 50:32
sequel: natural s. of an unnatural	AUST 22:26
seraglio: s. of eunuchs	FOOT 142:17
seraphic: maids strange s. pieces	TRAH 333:19
seraphims: Above it stood the s.	BIBLE 45:10
sere: Now my s. fancy	BYRON 86:19
serene: that unhoped s.	BROO 72:20
serf: soil as another man's s.	HOMER 171:3
sergeant: This fell s., death	SHAK 277:15
serial: obituary in s. form	CRISP 111:21
serious: annuity is a very s. business	AUST 23:7
nothing s. in mortality	SHAK 286:26
s. and the smirk	DICK 119:15
their most s.-minded activity	MONT 233:11
War is too s. a matter	CLEM 101:21
sermon: find him, who a s. flies	HERB 166:21
good honest and painful s.	PEPYS 247:14
rejected the S. on the Mount	BRAD 71:10
sermons: S. and soda-water	BYRON 86:6
S. in stones	SHAK 272:14
serpent: it biteth like a s.	BIBLE 43:33
s. ate Eve	HUGH 175:21
s. beguiled me	BIBLE 38:27
s. subtlest beast of all	MILT 229:22
s. was more subtil	BIBLE 38:24
sharper than a s.'s tooth	DICK 119:24
sharper than a s.'s tooth	SHAK 282:25
way of a s. upon a rock	BIBLE 44:4
Where's my s. of old Nile	SHAK 271:11
serpent-haunted: s. sea	FLEC 141:15
serpents: therefore wise as s.	BIBLE 49:29
servant: become the s. of a man	SHAW 301:4
cracked lookingglass of a s.	JOYCE 188:12
Is thy s. a dog	BIBLE 42:12
Our ugly comic s.	AUDEN 20:25
s. of the Living God	SMART 308:7
s. shall have small	BARC 28:17
s.'s too often a negligent elf	BARH 28:22
s. to be bred at an University	CONG 106:10
s. to the devil	SISS 307:15
s. with this clause	HERB 166:26

servant (*cont.*):

thou good and faithful s.	BIBLE 51:1
thy s. depart in peace	BIBLE 52:3
thy s. depart in peace	BIBLE 58:17
thy s. heareth	BIBLE 41:9
Your s.'s cut in half	GRAH 156:3

servants: equality in the s.' hall — BARR 29:10

one of thy hired s.	BIBLE 52:30
S. of Light	ARN 16:7
s. of the sovereign	BACON 24:27
s. will do that for us	VILL 338:19
wish your wife or your s. to read	GRIF 159:2
Ye s. of the Lord	DODD 122:30

serve: And s. him right — BELL 33:22

Fleet in which we s.	BOOK 69:13
no man can s. two masters	BIBLE 49:3
once to s. our country	ADD 2:16
reign in hell than s. in heaven	MILT 228:13
s. Him in this world	CAT 92:20
s. the future hour	WORD 356:19
s. the Lord with gladness	BIBLE 58:10
s. the Lord with gladness	BOOK 68:5
s. who only stand and wait	MILT 230:23
'tis enough, 'twill s.	SHAK 295:7

served: s. my God with half the zeal — SHAK 280:21

service: All s. ranks the same with God — BROW 77:1

done the state some s.	SHAK 293:5
In purer lives thy s. find	WHIT 348:27
No money, no s.	RAC 257:17
our bounden duty and s.	BOOK 65:17
places the servant at his s.	POMP 250:12
pressed into s. means	FROST 146:21
s. of my love	SPR 313:26
whose s. is perfect freedom	BOOK 64:5

serviettes: kiddies have crumpled the s. — BETJ 37:2

servile: S. to all the skyey influences — SHAK 288:19

servility: savage s. — LOW 211:12

serving: cumbered about much s. — BIBLE 52:14

sesame: Open S. — ARAB 14:17

sesquipedalia: *Proicit ampullas et s. verba* — HOR 172:26

sesquipedalian: S. blackguard — CLOU 102:10

sesquippedlan: S. verboojuice — WELLS 345:17

sessions: s. of sweet silent thought — SHAK 299:16

set: by God's grace, play a s. — SHAK 279:1

s. one slip of them	SHAK 298:30
S. thine house in order	BIBLE 46:6

setting: doors against a s. sun — SHAK 296:19

Hath had elsewhere its s.	WORD 355:20

settlement: Revolution a parent of s. — BURKE 80:11

seven: child for the first s. years — ANON 7:10

hewn out her s. pillars	BIBLE 43:14
His acts being s. ages	SHAK 272:24
If s. maids with seven mops	CARR 91:21
S. types of ambiguity	EMPS 137:8
S. wealthy towns contend	ANON 10:10
thy s.-fold gifts impart	BOOK 69:16
Until seventy times s.	BIBLE 50:19

Seven Dials: lowly air of S. — GILB 151:11

seventh: opened the s. seal — BIBLE 57:29

When the moon is in the s. house	RADO 257:18

seventy: Until s. times seven — BIBLE 50:19

sever: Ae fond kiss, and then we s. — BURNS 81:22

Nothing in life shall s.	CORY 108:12
To s. for years	BYRON 87:14

severae: *procul este, s.* — OVID 243:9

severity: set in with its usual s. — COL 105:2

Severn: from the S. to the Tyne — KIPL 196:3

Seville: bang these dogs of S. — TENN 328:12

sewer: midst of this putrid s. — TOCO 333:5

s. in a glass-bottomed boat	MIZN 232:13

sewers: s. annoy the air — MILT 229:23

sex: attempt to insult s. — LAWR 202:13

Continental people have s. life	MIKES 224:11
How is your s.-life now?	SOPH 311:14
If S. ever rears its ugly head	AYCK 23:14

sex (*cont.*):

Is s. dirty?	ALLEN 4:15
Literature mostly about having s.	LODGE 209:4
Mind has no s.	WOLL 353:10
Money was exactly like s.	BALD 27:3
practically conceal its s.	NASH 237:9
privilege I claim for my own s.	AUST 22:28
proxy for risk and a dummy for s.	MACH 215:4
S. and drugs and rock and roll	DURY 129:14
[S.] the most fun without laughing	ALLEN 4:13
s. with someone I love	ALLEN 4:14
soft, unhappy s.	BEHN 32:24
weaker s., to piety more prone	ALEX 4:7
we have s. in the mind	LAWR 202:19
When you have money, it's s.	DONL 123:2

sexes: there are three s. — SMITH 310:4

sexophones: s. wailed — HUXL 177:4

sexton: that bald s., Time — SHAK 282:6

s. tolled the bell	HOOD 171:7

sexual: most unnatural of s. perversions — HUXL 177:7

S. intercourse began	LARK 201:12

sexually: s. transmitted disease — ANON 8:20

shackles: Memories are not s. — BENN 34:13

their s. fall	COWP 110:7

shade: clutching the inviolable s. — ARN 17:12

Dancing in the chequered s.	MILT 227:4
farewell to the s.	COWP 109:30
fleeting image of a s.	SHEL 305:17
gentlemen of the s.	SHAK 277:22
green thought in a green s.	MARV 220:16
shall crowd into a s.	POPE 253:1
sly s. of a Rural Dean	BROO 73:5
That lashes all with s.	WILB 349:13
whiter s. of pale	REID 259:3
Within its s. we'll live or die	CONN 106:23

shades: S. of the prison-house — WORD 355:20

where the Etrurian s.	MILT 228:14

shadow: Be but the s. of heaven — MILT 229:18

days on the earth are as a s.	BIBLE 42:17
dream but of a s.	CHAP 94:15
Falls the s.	ELIOT 133:19
he fleeth also as a s.	BIBLE 42:33
land of the s. of death	BIBLE 45:15
Life's but a walking s.	SHAK 288:5
Like a vast s. moved	VAUG 337:14
Or s. of felicity	WALL 341:14
out-soared the s. of our night	SHEL 303:11
s. of death	BIBLE 51:30
Swift as a s., short as any dream	SHAK 290:14
valley of the s. of death	BOOK 66:18

shadows: Cats, no less liquid than their s. — TESS 329:10

I am half sick of s.	TENN 326:1
In ancient s. and twilights	Æ 3:4
millions of strange s.	SHAK 299:18
of their s. deep	YEATS 360:9
s., not substantial things	SHIR 306:10
Styled but the s. of us men	JONS 187:22
this kind are but s.	SHAK 291:8
Types and s. have their ending	THOM 330:4

Shadwell: S. never deviates into sense — DRYD 128:5

shaft: many a s., at random sent — SCOTT 268:15

shag: common cormorant (or s.) — ISH 178:21

shake: S. off dull sloth — KEN 193:20

s. off the dust	BIBLE 49:28
those boughs which s. against	SHAK 299:24

shaken: S. and not stirred — FLEM 141:21

So s. as we are, so wan	SHAK 277:21
Time has s. me by the hand	WESL 346:17

shakers: We are the movers and s. — O'SH 241:5

Shakespeare: Corneille is to S. — JOHN 186:12

It was for gentle S. cut	JONS 187:20
Or sweetest S. fancy's child	MILT 227:8
read in S. and found him weak	WELLS 345:16
S., another Newton	HUXL 177:11
S. by flashes of lightning	COL 104:25

Shakespeare (*cont.*):

S. for his honoured bones	MILT 227:21
S. I am struck with wonder	LAWR 202:24
S., undoubtedly wanted taste	WALP 341:18
S. unlocked his heart	WORD 356:21
S. wanted art	JONS 187:31
S. was of us, Milton was	BROW 76:14
such stuff as great part of S.	GEOR 149:24
Shakespearian: That S. rag	RUBY 77:31
Shakespeherian: that S. Rag	ELIOT 134:24
shaking: Aching, s., crazy, cold	ROCH 261:9
Shalimar: loved beside the S.	HOPE 171:22
shall: His absolute 's.'	SHAK 273:18
s. and finding only why	CUMM 113:2
shallow: Deep-versed in books and s.	MILT 230:8
shallows: bound in s. and in miseries	SHAK 282:1
Shalott: Lady of S.	TENN 326:3
shame: Ain't all a bleedin' s.	ANON 10:11
expense of spirit in a waste of s.	SHAK 300:10
if you still have to ask . . . s. on you	ARMS 16:4
shamed: And s. life a hateful	SHAK 288:21
shames: hold a candle to my s.	SHAK 289:11
shape: means pressed out of s.	FROST 146:21
s. of things to come	WELLS 345:23
share: All that I have I s. with you	BOOK 66:2
greater s. of honour	SHAK 279:17
I s. no one's ideas	TURG 335:13
I wished to s. the transport	WORD 357:4
shares: Fair s. for all	JAY 180:14
shark: s. has pretty teeth	BREC 71:18
Sharon: I am the rose of S.	BIBLE 44:31
sharp: 'Tis a s. remedy	RAL 258:3
sharper: s. than a serpent's tooth	DICK 119:24
s. than a serpent's tooth	SHAK 282:25
sharpness: overcome the s. of death	BOOK 63:20
sharps: different s. and flats	BROW 76:26
shatter: you may s. the vase	MOORE 234:13
shaves: man who s. and takes a train	WHITE 347:14
Shaw: S. hasn't an enemy	WILDE 350:21
she: S. must weep or she will die	TENN 327:26
S. sells sea-shells	SULL 319:2
S. went, to plain-work	POPE 251:24
S. who must be obeyed	HAGG 159:15
That not impossible s.	CRAS 111:16
unexpressive s.	SHAK 273:2
shears: resembles a pair of s.	SMITH 310:5
Sheba: Another S. queen	WITH 352:5
shed: prepare to s. them now	SHAK 281:22
shedding: s. of blood is no remission	BIBLE 56:24
sheep: come you in s.'s clothing	BIBLE 49:14
Feed my s.	BIBLE 54:7
found my s. which was lost	BIBLE 52:27
from thy ways like lost s.	BOOK 63:13
get back to these s.	ANON 12:14
giveth his life for the s.	BIBLE 53:30
like s. have gone astray	BIBLE 46:19
little hills like young s.	BOOK 68:16
noble ensample to his s.	CHAU 95:21
old half-witted s.	STEP 315:4
savaged by a dead s.	HEAL 164:10
s. in sheep's clothing	CHUR 100:7
s. in sheep's clothing	GOSSE 155:25
s. on his right hand	BIBLE 51:4
sheet: boy brought the white s.	GARC 148:2
old England's winding s.	BLAKE 60:9
waters were his winding s.	BARN 29:7
sheets: cool kindliness of s.	BROO 73:1
shelf-life: s. of the modern hardback	TRIL 334:10
shell: pebble or a prettier s.	NEWT 239:6
thou s. of death	MIDD 224:8
underneath that gloomy s.	ANON 9:14
Within thy airy s.	MILT 226:10
Shelley: Burns, S., were with us	BROW 76:14
did you once see S. plain	BROW 76:18
shells: choirs of wailing s.	OWEN 243:22

shelter: s. from the stormy blast	WATTS 343:13
shelves: symmetry of s.	LAMB 200:2
shene: most s. is the sonne	LANG 201:9
shepherd: As sweet unto a s. as a king	GREE 158:9
feed his flock like a s.	BIBLE 46:11
I am the good s.	BIBLE 53:30
King of love my s. is	BAKER 26:21
Lord is my s.	BOOK 66:17
Old Nod, the s., goes	DE L 116:21
they call you, S., from the hill	ARN 17:4
shepherds: s. abiding in the field	BIBLE 51:32
sheriff: I shot the s.	MARL 218:7
sherry: s. flowing into second-rate	PLOM 250:1
Shibboleth: Say now S.	BIBLE 41:2
shield: And broken was her s.	SCOTT 268:23
Our S. and Defender	GRANT 156:8
To a lady in his s.	TENN 326:2
trusty s. and weapon	LUTH 212:10
shieling: From the lone s.	GALT 147:19
shift: let me s. for myself	MORE 235:3
shilling: s. in my little tambourine	KIPL 196:2
s. life will give you all	AUDEN 21:12
shimmered: Jeeves s. out	WOD 352:12
shine: Arise, s.	BIBLE 46:23
Let your light so s. before men	BIBLE 48:22
Lord make his face s. upon thee	BIBLE 40:15
not to s. in use	TENN 328:21
s. in the high aesthetic line	GILB 152:9
s. on, harvest moon	NORW 240:11
shiners: Nine for the nine bright s.	ANON 8:6
shingles: naked s. of the world	ARN 16:11
shining: I see it s. plain	HOUS 174:24
s. morning face	SHAK 272:25
S. nowhere but in the dark	VAUG 337:12
woman of so s. loveliness	YEATS 359:27
ship: As idle as a painted s.	COL 104:6
being in a s. is being in a jail	JOHN 184:5
O S. of State	LONG 209:11
s., an isle, a sickle moon	FLEC 141:19
s. has weathered every rack	WHIT 348:11
S. me somewheres east of Suez	KIPL 196:23
s. on the sea and the horse	GARC 148:3
S. was still as she could be	SOUT 311:22
way of a s.	BIBLE 44:4
What is a s. but a prison	BURT 83:10
ships: go down to the sea in s.	BOOK 68:12
launched a thousand s.	MARL 218:11
little s. of England	GUED 159:6
shoes—and s.—and sealing wax	CARR 91:22
s. sail like swans asleep	FLEC 141:18
S. that pass in the night	LONG 210:3
S., towers, domes	WORD 354:15
stately s. go to their haven	TENN 323:11
Thracian s. and the foreign faces	SWIN 321:1
wrong with our bloody s.	BEAT 30:14
shipwreck: escaped the s. of time	BACON 23:21
Shiraz: wine of S. into urine	DIN 121:2
shires: both the s. they ring them	HOUS 174:20
calling for them from sad s.	OWEN 243:22
shirt: sang the 'Song of the S.'	HOOD 171:12
shirtsleeves: s. to s. in three	ANON 7:8
shiver: Little breezes dusk and s.	TENN 325:35
praised and left to s.	JUV 189:1
shoal: this bank and s. of time	SHAK 285:22
shock: And we shall s. them	SHAK 282:15
Future s.	TOFF 333:6
sensation of a short, sharp s.	GILB 151:25
s. of the new	DUNL 129:9
shock-headed: S. Peter	HOFF 170:4
shocking: and s. the barmaid	SITW 307:18
looked on as something s.	PORT 253:17
shocks: s. the mind of a child	PAINE 244:7
s. the magistrate	RUSS 265:4
thousand natural s.	SHAK 275:25

shod: All s. with steel	WORD 355:2
s. their heads in their canoes	MARV 221:3
shoe: cast out my s.	BOOK 67:14
I kiss his dirty s.	SHAK 279:10
Sailed off in a wooden s.	FIELD 139:2
whose s.'s latchet I am	BIBLE 53:12
shoes: mind it wipes its s.	THOM 330:18
Of s.—and ships	CARR 91:22
or ere those s. were old	SHAK 274:12
s. with broken high ideals	MCG 214:20
thy s. from off thy feet	BIBLE 39:31
To boil eggs in your s.	LEAR 203:16
your s. on your feet	BIBLE 39:37
shoeshine: on a smile and a s.	MILL 225:4
shoestring: careless s.	HERR 167:15
fortune and runs it into a s.	WOOL 354:7
shone: There is one woman	SWIN 321:19
shook: He hath s. hands with time	FORD 143:10
monk who s. the world	MONT 233:25
more it's s. it shines	HAM 160:17
Ten days that s. the world	REED 259:1
shoot: could s. me in my absence	BEHAN 32:18
Please do not s. the pianist	ANON 10:4
S., if you must, this old	WHIT 348:26
s. the Hippopotamus	BELL 33:1
s. the hippopotamus	FORS 143:14
teach the young idea how to s.	THOM 331:22
They s. horses don't they	MCCOY 214:16
they shout and they s.	INGE 178:10
To s. the sleepy, green-coat	HOFF 170:2
You s. a fellow down	HARDY 162:13
shooting: than to hunting and s.	BURR 82:32
shop: little back s., all his own	MONT 233:14
rag and bone s. of the heart	YEATS 358:16
s. at the corner	AUDEN 21:4
shopkeepers: nation of s.	ADAMS 2:7
nation of s.	NAP 237:7
nation of s.	SMITH 308:23
shore: By the s. of Gitche Gumee	LONG 210:1
high s. of this world	SHAK 279:16
kingdom stretch from s. to s.	WATTS 343:12
lights around the s.	ROSS 263:10
longing for the further s.	VIRG 339:15
rapture on the lonely s.	BYRON 85:12
s. of the wan grassy sea	SITW 307:20
Stops with the s.	BYRON 85:13
Then on the s. of the wide world	KEATS 192:21
To that unknown and silent s.	LAMB 200:12
with low sounds by the s.	YEATS 359:13
shored: have s. against my ruins	ELIOT 134:31
shores: wilder s. of love	BLAN 62:9
short: be but a s. time tonight	BALD 27:7
hath but a s. time to live	BOOK 66:6
long and the s. and the tall	HUGH 175:18
long while to make it s.	THOR 332:6
lyf so s., the craft so long	CHAU 96:12
nasty, brutish, and s.	HOBB 169:10
s., sharp shock	GILB 151:25
Take s. views, hope for the best	SMITH 310:1
shortage: s. of coal and fish	BEVAN 37:17
shorter: make you s. by the head	ELIZ 135:8
not had the time to make it s.	PASC 245:24
shortest: s. way is commonly	BACON 24:3
shot: he was s. silk	STR 318:11
I s. the sheriff	MARL 218:7
My God! They've s. our fox	BIRCH 59:14
Remember you s. a seagull	CHEK 96:27
s. heard round the world	EMER 136:12
shoulder: And on his s. gently laid	BAKER 26:21
government shall be upon his s.	BIBLE 45:16
shoulder-blade: s. that is a miracle	GILB 152:3
shoulders: City of the Big S.	SAND 266:12
dwarfs on the s. of giants	BERN 36:9
lawn about the s. thrown	HERR 167:15

shoulders (cont.):	
old heads on your young s.	SPARK 312:11
s. held the sky suspended	HOUS 174:13
standing on the s. of giants	NEWT 239:2
shout: hardly a s. from a few boys	ARN 17:3
men who s.	WALK 341:5
shouted with a great s.	BIBLE 40:27
s. that tore hell's concave	MILT 228:16
S. with the largest	DICK 119:28
There was a s. about my ears	CHES 97:22
they s. and they shoot	INGE 178:10
shouting: captains, and the s.	BIBLE 43:5
heavens fill with s.	TENN 326:11
tumult and the s. dies	KIPL 197:2
shovel: S. them under	SAND 266:14
show: ourselves glad in him	BOOK 67:31
s. you fear in a handful of dust	ELIOT 134:20
to s. that you have one	CHES 97:10
showbusiness: no business like s.	BERL 35:20
s. with blood	BRUNO 77:25
shower: s. of curates	BRON 72:13
s. your shooting corns	SWIFT 320:14
showers: After sharpest s.	LANG 201:9
Aprill with his s. soute	CHAU 95:10
much dew, many s.	VAUG 337:13
showery: S., Flowery, Bowery	ELLIS 136:4
shreds: king of s. and patches	SHAK 276:21
thing of s. and patches	GILB 151:17
shrewishly: he speaks very s.	SHAK 297:20
shriek: s. flits by on leathern	COLL 105:10
shrieking: With s. and squeaking	BROW 76:26
shrieks: s. to pitying heav'n	POPE 253:10
shrimp: s. learns to whistle	KHR 194:18
shrine: little saint best fits a little s.	HERR 167:22
shrined: bower we s. to Tennyson	HARDY 162:3
shroud: stiff dishonoured s.	ELIOT 134:17
shudder: s. in the loins	YEATS 359:14
shuffle: All s. there	YEATS 359:23
Patience, and s. the cards	CERV 93:19
shuffled: s. off this mortal coil	SHAK 275:25
shunting: s. and hooting	BURR 82:32
shut: s. their doors against	SHAK 296:19
shutters: close the s. fast	COWP 110:11
we'd need keep the s. up	DICK 119:6
shuttle: Man is the s.	VAUG 337:3
musical s.	WHIT 348:12
swifter than a weaver's s.	BIBLE 42:30
shuttlecock: Battledore and s.	DICK 119:29
sick: And I am s. at heart	SHAK 273:30
Created s., commanded to be	GREV 158:19
I am half s. of shadows	TENN 326:1
I am s., I must die	NASHE 237:19
kingdom of the s.	SONT 311:10
make me s. and wicked	AUST 23:12
night … is but the daylight s.	SHAK 290:6
nothing but to make him s.	DONNE 123:4
O Rose, thou art s.	BLAKE 62:4
Pass the s. bag, Alice	JUNOR 188:27
Ruth, when, s. for home	KEATS 192:5
s. discussing their duty	WHIT 348:19
s. hurry, its divided aims	ARN 17:11
s. of an old passion	DOWS 125:12
s. that surfeit with too much	SHAK 288:28
S. with inbreeding	THOM 331:5
thcream till I'm s.	CROM 111:23
they that are s.	BIBLE 49:22
were you not extremely s.	PRIOR 255:12
sickle: ship, an isle, a s. moon	FLEC 141:19
sicklied: s. o'er with the pale cast	SHAK 275:26
sickly: I'm s. but sassy	HARR 163:4
smiled a kind of s. smile	HARTE 163:13
sickness: in s. and in health	BOOK 65:28
in s. and in health	BOOK 66:1
s. that destroyeth	BOOK 67:29
Till age, or grief, or s. must	KING 195:5

Sidcup: I could get down to S.	PINT 248:20
side: God is on everyone's s.	ANOU 14:4
Hear the other s.	AUG 22:1
her bosom and half her s.	COL 103:12
move over to the other s.	REED 258:18
on the s. of the angels	DISR 121:15
S. by side	WOODS 353:19
This s. the tomb	DAV 114:18
trumpets sounded on the other s.	BUNY 79:11
which s. do they cheer	TEBB 323:7
Who is on my s.	BIBLE 42:15
sides: I'm a Norfan, both s.	WELLS 345:18
looked at life from both s.	MITC 232:3
Sidney: miracle of our age, Sir Philip S.	CAREW 89:18
S.'s self, the starry paladin	BROW 77:13
siege: s. of the city of Gaunt	BALL 28:1
Siegfried: washing on the S. line	KENN 193:23
siesta: Englishmen detest a s.	COW 109:4
sieve: in a s. I'll thither sail	SHAK 285:3
they went to sea in a S.	LEAR 203:10
siftings: let their liquid s. fall	ELIOT 134:17
sigh: nor s.-tempests move	DONNE 124:15
s. is just a sigh	HUPF 176:20
s. is the sword of an Angel	BLAKE 60:18
S. no more, ladies	SHAK 291:19
very s. that silence heaves	KEATS 191:5
sighed: I s. as a lover	GIBB 150:14
S. and looked, and sighed	DRYD 127:22
S. and looked unutterable	THOM 331:24
s. his soul toward	SHAK 289:31
sighing: soul sat s. by a sycamore	SHAK 292:26
Was laughter and ability and S.	DICK 120:17
sighs: In the gestures, in the s.	SOND 311:6
S. are the natural language	SHAD 270:17
sight: And he keeps it out of s.	BREC 71:18
does it matter?—losing your s.	SASS 267:9
gimleted and neatly out of s.	CRANE 111:2
sensible to feeling as to s.	SHAK 286:10
s. so touching in its majesty	WORD 354:15
s. to dream of, not to tell	COL 103:12
s. to make an old man young	TENN 323:24
sights: Her s. and sounds	BROO 73:10
impressive s. in the world	BARR 29:17
Such s. as youthful poets dream	MILT 227:7
sign: In this s. shalt thou conquer	CONS 107:14
s. of inward and spiritual grace	BOOK 65:23
s. of the true artist	VIDAL 338:14
signal: Only a s. shown	LONG 210:3
signed: s. my death warrant	COLL 105:8
signo: In hoc s. vinces	CONS 107:14
signs: discern the s. of the times	BIBLE 50:12
Except ye see s. and wonders	BIBLE 53:20
merely conventional s.	CARR 92:7
words are but the s. of ideas	JOHN 182:4
silence: answered best with s.	JONS 187:14
darkness again and a s.	LONG 210:3
Deep is the s., deep on	DRIN 126:24
easy step to s.	AUST 22:24
Elected S., sing to me	HOPK 172:5
His mind moves upon s.	YEATS 359:15
Indecency's conspiracy of s.	SHAW 302:3
In s. and tears	BYRON 87:14
lies are often told in s.	STEV 317:9
My gracious s., hail	SHAK 273:17
occasional flashes of s.	SMITH 310:6
on the other side of s.	ELIOT 132:10
rest is s.	SHAK 277:18
Seul le s. est grand	VIGNY 338:18
s. all the airs and madrigals	MILT 231:1
S. augmenteth grief	DYER 129:15
s., exile, and cunning	JOYCE 188:9
s. in heaven	BIBLE 57:29
S. is become his mother tongue	GOLD 155:7
S. is effectively compressed	MORL 235:8

silence (cont.):	
S. is the virtue of fools	BACON 24:8
S. like a cancer grows	SIMON 307:7
s. of these infinite spaces	PASC 246:3
s. sank like music	COL 104:16
s. surged softly backward	DE L 116:20
s. that dreadful bell	SHAK 292:7
slowly s. all	TENN 324:13
small change of s.	MER 223:18
Sorrow and s. are strong	LONG 209:16
speaking s. of a dream	ROSS 263:1
Thou foster-child of s.	KEATS 191:17
very sigh that s. heaves	KEATS 191:5
When awful darkness and s.	LEAR 203:8
silenced: because you have s. him	MORL 235:9
silent: All s., and all damned	WORD 356:4
impossible to be s.	BURKE 80:26
Laws are s. in time of war	CIC 100:30
Paris was French—and s.	TUCH 335:8
s. manliness of grief	GOLD 154:26
s. touches of time	BURKE 81:10
S., upon a peak in Darien	KEATS 192:11
that strong, s. man	MORL 235:8
thereof one must be s.	WITT 352:8
t is s., as in Harlow	ASQ 19:6
unhasting, and s. as light	SMITH 310:15
silently: How s., and with how wan	SIDN 306:18
S. and very fast	AUDEN 20:19
silk: And it soft as s. remains	HILL 168:11
he was shot s.	STR 318:11
s. hat at a private view	EDW 130:22
s. hat on a Bradford millionaire	ELIOT 134:29
s. makes the difference	FULL 147:7
silken: s. terms precise	SHAK 284:18
silver link, the s. tie	SCOTT 268:11
With s. lines, and silver hooks	DONNE 123:23
silks: in fading s. compose	WINC 352:3
Whenas in s. my Julia goes	HERR 167:26
silk-worm: s. expend her yellow labours	MIDD 224:9
silliest: s. woman can manage a clever	KIPL 197:28
silly: sillier than a s. laugh	CAT 93:4
s. at the right moment	HOR 174:1
with such a s. question	STER 315:13
You were s. like us	AUDEN 20:22
silver: all the Georgian s. goes	MACM 215:20
apples of gold in pictures of s.	BIBLE 43:35
Between their s. bars	FLEC 141:19
Can wisdom be put in a s. rod	BLAKE 60:10
ever the s. cord be loosed	BIBLE 44:26
golden locks time hath to s.	PEELE 247:3
handful of s. he left us	BROW 76:13
precious stone set in the s. sea	SHAK 293:16
silken lines, and s. hooks	DONNE 123:23
S. and gold have I none	BIBLE 54:9
s. apples of the moon	YEATS 360:1
s. lining in the sky-ee	LEE 347:1
s. link, the silken tie	SCOTT 268:11
s., snarling trumpets	KEATS 190:16
There's a s. lining	FORD 143:12
thirty pieces of s.	BEVAN 38:4
thirty pieces of s.	BIBLE 51:9
Walks the night in her s. shoon	DE L 116:22
silver-sweet: s. sound lovers' tongues	SHAK 295:3
Silvia: Who is S.? what is she	SHAK 298:19
similes: I sit, and play with s.	WORD 357:8
simple: C'est tellement s., l'amour	PRÉV 255:6
It was beautiful and s.	HENRY 166:4
rarely pure, and never s.	WILDE 349:16
To ask the hard question is s.	AUDEN 21:16
simplicity: holy s.	HUSS 176:21
holy s.	JER 181:6
Pity my s.	WESL 346:6
s. of the three per cents	DISR 122:2
s. of the three per cents	STOW 318:9
simplify: s. me when I'm dead	DOUG 125:9

simplify (cont.):

S., simplify	THOR 332:11

sin: And say there is no s.

beauty is only s. deep	SAKI 265:19
Be of s. the double cure	TOPL 333:14
Be ye angry and s. not	BIBLE 55:33
brother s. against me	BIBLE 50:19
By that s. fell the angels	SHAK 280:19
fall into no s., neither run	BOOK 64:6
go, and s. no more	BIBLE 53:27
hate the s.	AUG 22:4
He that is without s.	BIBLE 53:26
How shall I lose the s.	POPE 250:25
If we say that we have no s.	BIBLE 57:14
I had not known s.	BIBLE 54:37
in secret s.	CHUR 98:25
I waive the quantum o'the s.	BURNS 82:5
Lukewarmness I account a s.	COWL 109:16
My s., my soul. Lo-lee-ta	NAB 236:18
no s. but ignorance	MARL 218:19
not innocence but s.	BROW 76:9
physicists have known s.	OPP 241:14
purple-linèd palace of sweet s.	KEATS 191:12
Shall we continue in s.	BIBLE 54:33
S. is behovely	JUL 188:21
s. ye do by two and two	KIPL 197:10
sometimes s.'s a pleasure	BYRON 86:3
this dark world of s.	BICK 58:25
to s. in secret is not to sin	MOL 232:24
wages of s. is death	BIBLE 54:36
want of power to s.	DRYD 128:11
want, the care, the s.	TENN 325:24
Which is my s., though it were	DONNE 123:17
which taketh away the s.	BIBLE 53:13
your s. will find you out	BIBLE 40:20

sincerely: s. want to be rich

	CORN 108:4

sincerity: s. is a dangerous thing

	WILDE 349:23

sinecure: Love . . . is no s.

	BYRON 87:17

sinew: every nerve, and s.

	JONS 187:7

sinews: Money is the s. of love

	FARQ 138:18
s. of war, unlimited money	CIC 100:29
Stiffen the s., summon up	SHAK 279:5

sinewy: With large and s. hands

	LONG 210:4

sing: And I will s. of the sun

	POUND 254:11
Elected Silence, s. to me	HOPK 172:5
I'll s. you twelve O	ANON 8:6
I s. of brooks, of blossoms	HERR 167:12
I s. the body electric	WHIT 348:10
I, too, s. America	HUGH 175:19
Let all the world in ev'ry corner s.	HERB 166:20
never heard no horse s.	ARMS 16:3
O for a thousand tongues to s.	WESL 346:4
Of the glorious Body s.	THOM 330:3
Quires and Places where they s.	BOOK 64:7
S. 'em muck	MELBA 222:19
s. in the robber's face	JUV 189:11
s. like birds i' the cage	SHAK 284:1
S. me a song of a lad	STEV 317:23
s. myself	WHIT 348:16
S., my tongue	FORT 144:4
S. thou the songs of love	GURN 159:11
S. unto the Lord a new song	BOOK 66:24
s. unto the Lord a new song	BOOK 68:3
S. whatever is well made	YEATS 360:6
Soul clap its hands and s.	YEATS 359:21
That can s. both high and low	SHAK 297:23
while I s. the ancient ways	YEATS 360:4
worth saying, people s. it	BEAU 30:15

singe: S. my white head

	SHAK 283:6

singeing: s. of the King of Spain's

	DRAKE 126:11

singer: idle s. of an empty day

	MORR 235:14
lived a s. in France of old	SWIN 321:19
s. not the song	ANON 10:12
S. of sweet Colonus	ARN 17:20

singing: s. still dost soar

	SHEL 305:7

singing (cont.):

six little S.-boys	BARH 28:18

Beside me s. in the wilderness	FITZ 140:6
Everyone suddenly burst out s.	SASS 267:11
silver waves of thy sweet s.	SHEL 304:21
S., dancing to itself	COL 103:13
S. so rarely	SCOTT 269:1
s. will never be done	SASS 267:12
time of the s. of birds	BIBLE 44:32
we are a nest of s. birds	JOHN 183:22

single: Behold her, s. in the field

	WORD 357:1
married to a s. life	CRAS 111:13
Nor grew it white in a s. night	BYRON 87:5
Nothing in the world is s.	SHEL 304:3
s. man in possession of a fortune	AUST 23:2
S. vision and Newton's	BLAKE 60:23
S. women have a dreadful	AUST 23:11
they come not s. spies	SHAK 276:35
Two souls with but a s.	HALM 160:15

sings: he s. each song twice

	BROW 76:2
instead of bleeding, he s.	GARD 148:5
tell me what she s.	WORD 357:2

singular: So s. in each particular

	SHAK 298:34

singularity: S. is almost invariably

	DOYLE 125:14

sinister: strange and s.

	JAMES 180:1

sink: Not gross to s., but light

	SHAK 300:17
raft which would never s.	AMES 4:22
S. me the ship, Master	TENN 328:13

sinned: I have s. against heaven

	BIBLE 52:30
More s. against than sinning	SHAK 283:10
people s. against are not	COMP 106:5
s. exceedingly in thought	MISS 231:11

sinner: dead s. revised

	BIER 59:9
God be merciful to me a s.	BIBLE 52:39
Love the s., but hate the sin	AUG 22:4
over one s. that repenteth	BIBLE 52:28

sinners: God and s. reconciled

	WESL 346:7
Master with publicans and s.	BIBLE 49:21
mercy upon us miserable s.	BOOK 64:13
Once for favoured s. slain	WESL 346:9
s. to repentance	BIBLE 49:23
Why do s.' ways prosper	HOPK 172:18

sinning: sinned against than s.

	SHAK 283:10

sins: Be all my s. remembered

	SHAK 275:27
Compound for s.	BUTL 83:24
half the s. of mankind	RUSS 264:21
Her s., which are many	BIBLE 52:8
His s. were scarlet	BELL 33:27
multitude of s.	BIBLE 57:11
oldest s. the newest kind	SHAK 278:28
s. and offences of my youth	BOOK 66:21
s. are attempts to fill voids	WEIL 345:2
takest away the s. of the world	MISS 231:19
Though your s. be as scarlet	BIBLE 45:4
weep for their s.	WHIT 348:19

sint: S. ut sunt aut non sint

	CLEM 102:3

Sion: remembered thee, O S.

	BOOK 69:2

sir: S., no man's enemy

	AUDEN 21:14

sirens: Blest pair of S.

	MILT 226:4

Sirmio: S., bright eye of peninsulas

	CAT 93:3

Sisera: fought against S.

	BIBLE 40:32

sister: barren s. all your life

	SHAK 290:12
My s. and my sister's child	COWP 109:24
trying to violate your s.	STR 318:14

sisterhood: S. is powerful

	MORG 235:6

sisters: And so do his s.

	GILB 152:17
Are s. under their skins	KIPL 196:19
Sphere-born harmonious s.	MILT 226:4
weird s., hand in hand	SHAK 285:5

Sistine: On the S. Chapel roof

	YEATS 360:5

sit: allowed to s. down

	UST 336:19
Here I s., alone and sixty	BENN 34:16
let us s. upon the ground	SHAK 293:27
May s. i' the centre	MILT 226:12
S. thou on my right hand	BOOK 68:14

sit (cont.):

So I did s. and eat	HERB 167:3
Teach us to s. still	ELIOT 132:19
that s. in darkness	BIBLE 51:30
Though I s. down now	DISR 121:5
we used to s. and dream	ARMS 15:24
sits: Sometimes I s. and thinks	PUNCH 256:21
sitting: Are you s. comfortably	LANG 201:4
Lord s. upon a throne	BIBLE 45:10
s. in the smallest room	REGER 259:2
situation: retreating, s. excellent	FOCH 142:14
six: Rode the s. hundred	TENN 323:14
s. little Singing-boys	BARH 28:18
sixpence: and nothing above s.	BEVAN 38:3
bang—went s.	PUNCH 256:12
We could have saved s.	BECK 31:8
sixteen: S. tons, what do you get	TRAV 334:4
sixth: s. age shifts into the lean	SHAK 272:27
sixty: Here I sit, alone and s.	BENN 34:16
rate of s. minutes an hour	LEWIS 206:11
When I'm s.-four	MCC 205:17
skeletons: s. copulating	BEEC 32:1
skies: And paint the sable s.	DRUM 127:1
some watcher of the s.	KEATS 192:11
whose god is in the s.	SHAW 301:33
You common people of the s.	WOTT 357:16
skill: nothing with a deal of s.	COWP 110:5
To show our simple s.	SHAK 291:6
skin: Ethiopian change his s.	BIBLE 46:30
In the castle of my s.	LAMM 200:17
skull beneath the s.	ELIOT 134:32
throws her enamelled s.	SHAK 290:27
with the s. of my teeth	BIBLE 42:35
skinny: I fear thy s. hand	COL 104:11
skins: Are sisters under their s.	KIPL 196:19
skipped: mountains s. like rams	BOOK 68:16
skirmish: s. fought near Marathon	GRAV 156:15
skittles: all beer and s.	CALV 88:9
skivvies: it would take a dozen s.	MCGR 214:22
skull: s. beneath the skin	ELIOT 134:32
sky: above, the vaulted s.	CLARE 101:7
Above us only s.	LENN 205:7
clean the s.	ELIOT 134:8
clear blue s. over my head	HAZL 164:8
climbin' clear up to the s.	HAMM 161:2
clothe the wold and meet the s.	TENN 325:34
inverted bowl we call The S.	FITZ 140:15
lonely sea and the s.	MAS 221:21
lose itself in the s.	BROW 75:8
On a bed of daffodil s.	TENN 326:28
Open unto the fields, and to the s.	WORD 354:15
pie in the s. when you die	HILL 168:12
sent him down the s.	CORY 108:13
s. changes when they are wives	SHAK 273:9
spread out against the s.	ELIOT 133:24
Their shoulders held the s.	HOUS 174:13
Under the wide and starry s.	STEV 317:21
Which prisoners call the s.	WILDE 350:15
With all the blue ethereal s.	ADD 2:25
wrote my will across the s.	LAWR 203:1
Skye: Over the sea to S.	BOUL 70:10
Over the sea to S.	STEV 317:23
skyey: Servile to all the s. influences	SHAK 288:19
slab: Beneath this s.	NASH 237:13
slacks: girls in s. remember Dad	BETJ 36:17
slag-heap: post-industrial s.	DRAB 126:9
slain: ere thou hast s. another	BROW 74:24
I am hurt but I am not s.	BALL 28:3
jaw of an ass have I s.	BIBLE 41:5
Or if the s. think he is slain	EMER 136:10
slamming: s. Doors	BELL 33:10
S. their doors, stamping	OSB 242:22
slander: civic s. and the spite	TENN 325:25
one to s. you and the other	TWAIN 335:25
S., meanest spawn of Hell	TENN 326:4

slang: S. is a language that rolls	SAND 266:18
slant: certain S. of light	DICK 120:14
slap-up: S. gal in a bang-up chariot	DICK 119:23
slaughter: as a lamb to the s.	BIBLE 46:20
ox goeth to the s.	BIBLE 43:13
slave: accept a s. to limit	SHAK 297:2
Better be a s. at once	BRON 72:14
giving freedom to the s.	LINC 207:6
half s. and half free	LINC 207:5
has been s. to thousands	SHAK 292:11
one is always the s.	LERM 205:24
Philosopher!—a fingering s.	WORD 356:5
rogue and peasant s.	SHAK 275:21
s.-morality	NIET 239:22
slave of that s.	CONN 107:3
soundly as the wretched s.	SHAK 279:16
slavery: wise and good in s.	MAC 213:8
s. in which a man does	GILL 153:1
s. of the tea and coffee	COBB 102:25
S. they can have anywhere	BURKE 80:4
slaves: all women are born s.	AST 19:7
at the mill with s.	MILT 230:10
Britons never will be s.	THOM 331:20
Englishmen never will be s.	SHAW 301:20
it is the creed of s.	PITT 249:7
S. cannot breathe in England	COWP 110:7
S. of the Lamp	ARN 16:7
s. with weary footsteps	SHEL 303:16
sons of former s.	KING 195:9
too pure an Air for S.	ANON 10:1
wholly s. or wholly free	DRYD 127:30
whom we have made our s.	DARW 114:6
women born s.	WOLL 353:14
slavish: O imitators, you s. herd	HOR 173:15
slayer: If the red s. think he slays	EMER 136:10
sleave: knits up the ravelled s. of care	SHAK 286:15
sleek-headed: S. men	SHAK 281:1
sleekit: Wee, s., cow'rin'	BURNS 82:26
sleep: And miles to go before I s.	FROST 146:23
And s. an act or two	SHAK 280:23
azure-lidded s.	KEATS 190:21
Care-charmer S.	DAN 113:15
Care-charming S.	FLET 142:5
come to the borders of s.	THOM 330:24
Death and his brother S.	SHEL 304:26
deep, deep s. of England	ORW 242:1
do I wake or s.	KEATS 192:7
each day dies with s.	HOPK 172:11
Entice the dewy-feathered S.	MILT 229:12
From s. and from damnation	CHES 97:24
Glamis hath murdered s.	SHAK 286:16
green ideas s. furiously	CHOM 98:18
grey and full of s.	YEATS 360:9
have an exposition of s.	SHAK 291:1
How s. the brave, who sink	COLL 105:11
In s. a king, but, waking	SHAK 299:28
in soot I s.	BLAKE 61:19
Is rounded with a s.	SHAK 296:10
lasting s.; a quiet resting	BEAU 31:2
Let us s. now	OWEN 244:4
Macbeth does murder s.	SHAK 286:15
Macbeth shall s. no more	SHAK 286:16
Me biful for to s.	LANG 201:6
None shall s.	ADAMI 1:6
Now I lay me down to s.	ANON 9:20
Oh S.! it is a gentle thing	COL 104:13
One short s. past, we wake	DONNE 123:9
quiet s. and a sweet dream	MAS 222:2
Shake off this downy s.	SHAK 286:24
single vision and Newton's s.	BLAKE 60:23
Sleek-headed men and such as s.	SHAK 281:1
S. on (my Love!)	KING 195:5
S. after toil, port after stormy	SPEN 313:9
s. and a forgetting	WORD 355:20

sleep (*cont.*):

s. and darkness safely brought	KEBLE 193:16
s. as I in childhood sweetly	CLARE 101:7
S. is sweet to the labouring	BUNY 79:4
s. of a labouring man	BIBLE 44:15
s. one ever-during night	CAMP 89:2
S. shall neither night nor day	SHAK 285:4
s. so soundly as the wretched	SHAK 279:16
s., the certain knot of peace	SIDN 306:20
s. the sleep of death	BLAKE 60:21
S. to wake	BROW 75:11
sweet restorer, balmy s.	YOUNG 360:17
There'll be time enough to s.	HOUS 174:18
To s.: perchance to dream	SHAK 275:25
We shall not all s.	BIBLE 55:21
We term s. a death	BROW 74:22
What hath night to do with s.	MILT 226:8
while some must s.	SHAK 276:12

sleepers: in the seven s. den DONNE 124:5
unquiet slumbers for the s. BRON 72:18
sleepeth: maid is not dead, but s. BIBLE 49:26
sleeping: art tha s. there below NEWB 238:11
Lay your s. head, my love AUDEN 20:27
s. and the dead are but as pictures SHAK 286:17
sleepless: S. with cold commemorative ROSS 263:9
sleeps: and s. on his own heart WORD 356:7
Homer sometimes s. BYRON 86:17
Now s. the crimson petal TENN 328:3
softly s. the calm Ideal DICK 119:7
sleepwalker: assurance of a s. HITL 169:1
sleepy: not s. and there is no place DYLAN 130:5
sleeve: Ash on an old man's s. ELIOT 133:8
wear my heart upon my s. SHAK 291:28
sleeves: language that rolls up its s. SAND 266:18
Tie up my s. with ribbons rare HUNT 176:19
slepen: s. al the nyght with open CHAU 95:11
slept: fruits of them that s. BIBLE 55:17
thought he thought I s. PATM 246:17
slew: he was ambitious, I s. him SHAK 281:16
slice: S. him where you like WOD 352:14
slight: Away, s. man SHAK 281:30
slimy: thousand thousand s. things COL 104:12
slings: s. and arrows of outrageous SHAK 275:25
slip: catch no s. BUNY 78:19
let s. the dogs of war SHAK 281:14
s. into my bosom TENN 328:5
s., slide, perish ELIOT 133:1
to set one s. of them SHAK 298:30
slipped: s. away into the next room HOLL 170:12
slipper: s. and subtle knave SHAK 292:6
slippers: walks in his golden s. BUNY 79:2
slipping: s. gimleted CRANE 111:2
slips: like greyhounds in the s. SHAK 279:6
slit: S. your girl's, and swing KING 195:19
sliver: envious s. broke SHAK 277:7
slogged: s. up to Arras with rifle SASS 267:13
slopes: on the butler's upper s. WOD 352:23
slop-kettle: coffee and other s. COBB 102:25
slop-pail: woman with a s. HOPK 172:22
sloth: Shake off dull s. KEN 193:20
slouches: S. towards Bethlehem YEATS 359:25
Slough: bombs, and fall on S. BETJ 37:9
slough: s. was Despond BUNY 78:18
slovenliness: Peace is nothing but s. BREC 71:20
s. is no part of religion WESL 346:15
slow: come he s., or come he fast SCOTT 268:17
cripple and comes ever s. DRAY 126:15
Slow, s., fresh fount JONS 187:2
telling you to s. down ANON 6:25
slowly: angel to pass, flying s. FIRB 139:20
let him twist s. in the wind EHRL 131:7
Science moves, but s. slowly TENN 326:13
sluggard: Go to the ant thou s. BIBLE 43:11
foul s.'s comfort CARL 90:5
'Tis the voice of the s. WATTS 343:9

slumber: Ere S.'s chain has bound	MOORE 234:20
little sleep, a little s.	BIBLE 43:12
s. did my spirit seal	WORD 356:25
slumbers: Golden s. kiss your eyes	DEKK 116:10
unquiet s. for the sleepers	BRON 72:18
slums: gay intimacy of the s.	WAUGH 343:20
slurp: As they s., slurp, slurp	FISH 139:26
sluts: For now foul s. in dairies	CORB 107:23
sly: s. shade of a Rural Dean	BROO 73:5
smack: Just a s. at Auden	EMPS 137:4
small: All things both great and s.	COL 104:18
between the s. and great	COWP 110:16
big squadrons against the s.	BUSS 83:20
day of s. nations	CHAM 93:23
deals it in s. parcels	WEBS 344:22
down express in the s. of the back	WOD 352:18
In s. proportions we just	JONS 187:24
Is it so s. a thing	ARN 16:14
It extinguishes the s.	BUSS 83:19
Microbe is so very s.	BELL 33:20
pictures that got s.	WILD 71:5
s., but perfectly formed	COOP 107:21
s. change of silence	MER 223:18
S. is beautiful	SCH 267:25
s. nations like prostitutes	KUBR 199:7
s. talk flows from lip to lip	CRAB 110:19
speaks s. like a woman	SHAK 290:8
still s. voice	BIBLE 42:3
That's one s. step for a man	ARMS 16:5
Too s. to live in	ANON 11:8
smallest: s. amount of lying	BUTL 84:10
small-talking: this s. world	FRY 147:1
smart: stranger shall s.	BIBLE 43:18
smashed: s. it into because	CUMM 113:2
smattering: s. of everything	DICK 120:5
smell: I s. a rat	ROCHE 261:1
Money has no s.	VESP 338:3
shares man's s.	HOPK 172:4
s. and hideous hum	GODL 153:20
s. of the blood	SHAK 287:30
s. the blood of a British	SHAK 283:18
s. too strong of the lamp	STER 315:16
Sweet s. of success	LEHM 204:13
sweet keen s.	ROSS 263:10
smelleth: he s. the battle afar	BIBLE 43:5
smells: it s. of mortality	SHAK 283:24
rank, it s. to heaven	SHAK 276:16
smile: And s., smile, smile	ASAF 18:17
Cambridge people rarely s.	BROO 73:7
Did he s. his work to see	BLAKE 62:6
I hear a s.	CROSS 112:11
Normal is the good s.	SHAF 270:19
on a s. and a shoeshine	MILL 225:4
S. at us, pay us, pass us	CHES 98:4
smiled a kind of sickly s.	HARTE 163:13
s. dwells a little longer	CHAP 94:13
s. of a cosmic Cheshire	HUXL 177:14
s. on the face of the tiger	ANON 10:22
transient is the s. of fate	DYER 129:17
'Twixt a prison and a s.	WOTT 357:18
Where my Julia's lips do s.	HERR 167:13
you should forget and s.	ROSS 263:4
smiler: s. with the knyf	CHAU 95:27
smiles: becks, and wreathèd s.	MILT 227:1
charmed it with s. and soap	CARR 92:9
Nae mair your s. can cheer me	COCK 102:27
robbed that s. steals something	SHAK 291:37
S. awake you when you rise	DEKK 116:10
Their s., wan as primroses	KEATS 190:13
There's daggers in men's s.	SHAK 286:27
smilest: Thou s. and art still	ARN 17:14
smiling: He hides a s. face	COWP 109:26
S. at grief	SHAK 298:1
S. the boy fell dead	BROW 76:8

smiling (*cont.*):
S. through her tears — HOMER 170:22
smirk: serious and the s. — DICK 119:15
smite: s. thee on thy right cheek — BIBLE 48:23
Stands ready to s. once — MILT 227:16
smithy: The village s. stands — LONG 210:4
smoke: counties overhung with s. — MORR 235:16
Gossip is a sort of s. — ELIOT 131:20
s. and stir of this dim spot — MILT 226:5
S. gets in your eyes — HARB 161:10
s. of the pit that is bottomless — JAM 179:9
smoke-filled: s. room — SIMP 307:11
smokeless: glittering in the s. air — WORD 354:15
smoky: burnt-out ends of s. days — ELIOT 134:10
smooth: I am a s. man — BIBLE 39:19
Speak unto us s. things — BIBLE 45:29
To s. the ice, or add another — SHAK 282:10
smote: He s. them hip and thigh — BIBLE 41:4
s. the king of Israel — BIBLE 42:7
smudge: And wears man's s. — HOPK 172:4
snaffle: s. and the curb all right — CAMP 88:16
snail: creeping like s. — SHAK 272:25
said a whiting to a s. — CARR 91:11
s.'s on the thorn — BROW 76:28
snake: like a wounded s. drags — POPE 252:4
s. hidden in the grass — VIRG 339:24
s. throws her enamelled — SHAK 290:27
We have scotched the s. — SHAK 287:3
snakes: S. Eat Frogs — STEV 316:7
You spotted s. — SHAK 290:28
snapper-up: s. of unconsidered trifles — SHAK 298:27
snare: from the s. of the hunter — BOOK 67:28
mockery, and a s. — DENM 116:27
world's great s. uncaught — SHAK 271:21
snares: s. of death compassed me — BOOK 68:19
snaring: s. the poor world — CRANE 111:1
Snark: If your S. be a Boojum — CARR 92:8
snatched: s. the lightning shaft — TURG 335:16
snatches: s. a man from obscurity — REYN 259:7
sneer: solemn creed with solemn s. — BYRON 85:6
teach the rest to s. — POPE 251:6
Who can refute a s. — PALEY 244:17
sneezes: And beat him when he s. — CARR 91:5
Coughs and s. spread diseases — ANON 6:23
sneezing: Pavement slippery, people s. — ROB 260:22
snicker: hold my coat, and s. — ELIOT 133:29
snigger: eunuch and a s. — FIRB 139:19
snip: S.! Snap! Snip! — HOFF 169:22
snipe: So wet you could shoot s. — POW 254:26
snob: If I were a s. — STEV 316:2
snorted: s. we in the seven sleepers — DONNE 124:5
snotgreen: s. sea — JOYCE 188:11
snow: architecture of the s. — EMER 136:16
asleep the s. came flying — BRID 72:1
last long streak of s. — TENN 325:29
or rain, or any s. — TENN 324:22
Out in the dark over the s. — THOM 330:26
s. in May's new-fangled mirth — SHAK 284:11
S. on snow — ROSS 263:2
wondrous strange s. — SHAK 291:5
snow-broth: very s. — SHAK 288:11
snows: s. of yesteryear — VILL 338:20
snow-white: with little s. feet — YEATS 359:1
snowy: s. summits old in story — TENN 327:20
S., Flowy, Blowy — ELLIS 136:4
snub: s. nose like to mine — BLAKE 60:11
so: And s. do I — HARDY 162:16
S. is it now I am a man — WORD 355:13
S. joyously, so maidenly — SKEL 308:2
soap: charmed it with smiles and s. — CARR 92:9
S. and education — TWAIN 335:22
used your s. two years ago — PUNCH 256:16
What? no s.? — FOOTE 142:20
soar: can creep as well as s. — BURKE 81:8
run, though not to s. — MAC 213:21

soar (*cont.*):
Type of the wise who s. — WORD 357:9
soaring: s. ever singest — SHEL 305:7
sob: S., heavy world — AUDEN 20:9
sober: Be s., be vigilant — BIBLE 57:12
But men at whiles are s. — HOUS 174:10
Philip drunk to Philip s. — ANON 6:3
righteous, and s. life — BOOK 63:15
S., steadfast, and demure — MILT 226:24
To-morrow we'll be s. — ANON 6:18
vigilant, s., of good behaviour — BIBLE 56:16
Wordsworth drunk and Porson s. — HOUS 175:6
sobs: s. of autumn's violins — VERL 337:21
social: knows of no religion but s. — WESL 346:11
Legion and S. Club — BETJ 36:22
self-love and s. be the same — POPE 252:21
S. Contract is nothing — WELLS 345:20
Socialism: religion of S. — BEVAN 37:19
S. can only arrive by bicycle — VIER 338:16
S. does not mean much more — ORW 242:13
s. would not lose its human — DUBC 128:31
socialist: Champagne s. — MORT 235:22
socialists: We are all s. now — HARC 161:15
society: consolidates s. — JOHN 183:20
fair portion of all which s. — BURKE 80:13
No arts; no letters; no s. — HOBB 169:10
no such thing as S. — THAT 329:25
One great s. alone on earth — WORD 356:15
Ourself will mingle with s. — SHAK 287:8
quiet action of s. upon itself — TOCQ 333:3
S. became my glittering bride — WORD 354:21
s. distributes itself — ARN 17:24
S. is indeed a contract — BURKE 80:17
S. is now one polished horde — BYRON 86:27
s. is the end of government — ADAMS 2:1
s. is wonderfully delightful — WILDE 350:13
S. needs to condemn a little — MAJOR 216:19
s. where it is safe to be — STEV 316:18
s., where none intrudes — BYRON 85:12
s. would be a hell upon earth — MILL 224:19
unable to live in s. — ARIS 15:19
sock: If Jonson's learnèd s. be on — MILT 227:8
socket: Burn to the s. — WORD 354:19
sockets: candles burn their s. — HOUS 174:12
socks: inability to put on your s. — GONC 155:20
Socrates: contradict S. — SOCR 310:24
S., he says, breaks the law — PLATO 249:18
Socratic: S. manner is not a game — BEER 32:12
soda water: Sermons and s. — BYRON 86:6
wash their feet in s. — ELIOT 134:26
sodium: Of having discovered S. — BENT 35:8
sodomy: Impotence and s. — WAUGH 344:2
rum, s., and the lash — CHUR 100:6
sods: s. with our bayonets — WOLFE 352:26
sofa: wheel the s. round — COWP 110:11
soft: does not make us s. — PER 248:1
her s. and chilly nest — KEATS 190:19
make it s. and narrow — BALL 27:13
s. answer turneth away wrath — BIBLE 43:24
s. falls the dew — BEERS 32:14
s. parts of conversation — SHAK 292:15
s. phrase of peace — SHAK 291:33
s. under-belly of the Axis — CHUR 99:19
s., unhappy sex — BEHN 32:24
whan s. was the sonne — LANG 201:5
softly: run s., till I end my song — SPEN 313:18
S. along the road of evening — DE L 116:21
S. come and softly go — ORRED 241:18
Tread s. because you tread — YEATS 359:7
softness: s. of my body — LOW 211:2
whisper s. in chambers — MILT 231:1
soil: indestructible powers of the s. — RIC 259:16
rather be tied to the s. — HOMER 171:3
that s. may best deserve — MILT 228:21
sojourners: s., as were our fathers — BIBLE 42:17

solace: With s. and gladness	SKEL 308:2
sold: s. his birthright	BIBLE 39:18
s. my reputation	FITZ 140:17
s. the truth to serve the hour	TENN 327:13
went and s. all	BIBLE 50:6
soldier: Ben Battle was a s. bold	HOOD 171:4
chocolate cream s.	SHAW 300:24
death, who had the s. singled	DOUG 125:10
in the s. is flat blasphemy	SHAK 288:15
not tell us what the s. said	DICK 119:34
s. full of strange oaths	SHAK 272:26
s. is no more exempt	STER 315:25
s.'s life is terrible hard	MILNE 225:19
s.'s pole is fall'n	SHAK 271:25
s. stand up to anything except	SHAW 301:1
summer s. and the sunshine	PAINE 244:11
soldiers: having s. under me	BIBLE 49:17
Ireland gives England her s.	MER 223:13
Old s. never die	FOLEY 142:16
our s. slighted	QUAR 256:27
S. are citizens of death's	SASS 267:10
s. by two and by three	BALL 28:1
s., mostly fools	BIER 59:6
sole: nothing can be s. or whole	YEATS 358:20
solemn: s. bird and this fair moon	MILT 229:11
s. creed with solemn sneer	BYRON 85:6
solid: s. for fluidity	CHUR 99:9
too too s. flesh would melt	SHAK 274:9
solidity: appearance of s. to pure wind	ORW 242:15
solitary: Be not s., be not idle	BURT 83:15
if you are s., be not idle	JOHN 185:25
Through Eden took their s. way	MILT 230:2
waste and s. places	SHEL 303:20
Yon s. Highland lass	WORD 357:1
solitude: Life is the desert, life the s.	YOUNG 360:23
make him feel his s.	VALE 336:21
place of seclusion and s.	MONT 233:14
resonance of his s.	CONN 106:27
Which is the bliss of s.	WORD 355:5
Solomon: greater than S. is here	BIBLE 50:2
King S. wrote the Proverbs	NAYL 237:20
S. in all his glory	BIBLE 49:4
S. loved many strange women	BIBLE 41:32
solution: fertilize a problem with a s.	SIMP 307:13
part of the s. or you're part	CLEA 101:19
Those people were a kind of s.	CAV 93:11
total s. of the Jewish question	GOER 154:1
somebody: When every one is s.	GILB 151:8
someday: S. I'll find you	COW 109:7
someone: s. somewhere may be happy	MENC 223:7
something: S. must be done	EDW 131:1
S. you somehow haven't	FROST 146:11
Time for a little s.	MILNE 225:16
sometime: that s. did me seek	WYATT 358:2
woman is a s. thing	GERS 168:7
sometimes: s. always, by God	RICH 260:5
somewhat: I have s. against thee	BIBLE 57:20
tough joints more than s.	RUNY 264:6
somewhere: want to get s. else	CARR 91:18
S. over the rainbow	hARB 161:14
son: conceive, and bear a s.	BIBLE 45:14
gave his only begotten S.	BIBLE 53:19
keep his only s., myself	HOME 170:18
leichter of a fair s.	ELIZ 135:12
my s., mine own Telemachus	TENN 328:22
O Absalom, my s.	BIBLE 41:27
s. of Adam and of Eve	PRIOR 255:10
s. of his old age	BIBLE 39:24
S. of man hath not where	BIBLE 49:19
S. of Morn in weary Night's	BLAKE 60:15
spareth his rod hateth his s.	BIBLE 43:23
This is my beloved S.	BIBLE 48:15
two-legged thing, a s.	DRYD 127:9
unto us a s. is given	BIBLE 45:16
son (*cont.*):	
what's a s.? A thing begot	KYD 199:10
whom if his s. ask bread	BIBLE 49:10
wise s. maketh a glad father	BIBLE 43:16
Woman, behold thy s.	BIBLE 54:4
worthy to be called thy s.	BIBLE 52:30
your s.'s tender years	JUV 189:15
song: becomes a sightless s.	TENN 325:30
before his presence with a s.	BOOK 68:5
burden of my s.	ANON 9:4
burthen of his s.	BICK 58:24
carcase of an old s.	THOM 331:5
Glorious the s.	SMART 308:13
goodly manor for a s.	SHAK 271:2
my reputation for a s.	FITZ 140:17
My s. is love unknown	CROS 112:13
On wings of s.	HEINE 165:1
play a s. for me	DYLAN 130:5
self-same s. that found a path	KEATS 192:5
Singin' a s., side by side	WOODS 353:19
Sing unto the Lord a new s.	BOOK 66:24
sing unto the Lord a new s.	BOOK 68:3
s. charms the sense	MILT 228:31
s. is ended (but the melody	BERL 36:2
S. of the Shirt	HOOD 171:12
s. that never ends	GOET 154:4
s. was wordless	SASS 267:12
start a s. and to respond	VIRG 340:1
suck melancholy out of a s.	SHAK 272:20
suffering what they teach in s.	SHEL 303:22
That glorious s. of old	SEARS 269:11
that thinks two notes a s.	DAV 114:17
there's ane end of ane old s.	OGIL 241:3
There's no love s. finer	PORT 253:19
till I end my s.	SPEN 313:18
Time is our tedious s. should	MILT 228:1
Unlike my subject will I frame my s.	CHES 97:2
woman, wine, and s.	LUTH 212:11
songs: after the s. of Apollo	SHAK 284:24
And all their s. are sad	CHES 97:20
piping s. for ever new	KEATS 191:20
Piping s. of pleasant glee	BLAKE 61:18
Sing thou the s. of love	GURN 159:11
s. beguile your pilgrimage	FLEC 141:16
sweetest s. are those that tell	SHEL 305:10
Their lean and flashy s.	MILT 227:15
Where are the s. of Spring	KEATS 192:15
sonnet: Scorn not the S.	WORD 356:21
s. is a moment's monument	ROSS 263:7
S.'s scanty plot of ground	WORD 355:15
sonnets: written s. all his life	BYRON 86:11
sons: Bears all its s. away	WATTS 343:15
Brightest and best of the s.	HEBER 164:14
cruel s. of Cain	LE G 204:12
fallen s. of Eve	CHES 98:5
Go, bind your s. to exile	KIPL 197:15
God's s. are things	MADD 216:14
s. and daughters of Life's	GIBR 150:19
s. and your daughters shall	BIBLE 47:20
S. of the dark and bloody	O'HARA 241:4
then wander forth the s.	MILT 228:15
soon: to Eve: Be s.	THOM 331:10
sooner: s. every party breaks up	AUST 22:15
soonest: Good is best when s. wrought	SOUT 312:8
soot: and in s. I sleep	BLAKE 61:19
sophist: neither saint nor s.-led	ARN 16:13
sophistry: s. and illusion	HUME 176:4
soporific: too much lettuce is 's.'	POTT 254:2
Sordello: can be but the one 'S.'	POUND 254:12
sore: bear with a s. head	MARR 219:26
sorrow: And so beguile thy s.	SHAK 296:27
and the s. thereof	MAL 217:2
From the sphere of our s.	SHEL 305:5
Give s. words	SHAK 287:25
glut thy s. on a morning rose	KEATS 191:26

sorrow (cont.):

hairs with s. to the grave	BIBLE 39:26
heart hath 'scaped this s.	SHAK 300:1
in s. thou shalt bring forth	BIBLE 39:1
interest and fines on s.	MAY 222:16
knowledge increaseth s.	BIBLE 44:10
labour and s.	BOOK 67:26
Labour without s. is base	RUSK 264:18
more in s. than in anger	SHAK 274:19
night of doubt and s.	BAR 29:2
Nought but vast S. was there	DE L 116:16
O S., wilt thou live with me	TENN 325:13
parting is such sweet s.	SHAK 295:4
S. and silence are strong	LONG 209:16
S. is tranquillity remembered	PARK 245:11
s. lasts all through life	FLOR 142:12
sorrow like unto my s.	BIBLE 46:32
top which whipping S.	GREV 158:18
Write s. on the bosom	SHAK 293:26
sorrowful: s. birth	MAL 217:1
sorrows: carried our s.	BIBLE 46:18
Disease, or s. strike him	CLOU 102:15
man of s., and acquainted	BIBLE 46:17
s. of women would be averted	ELIOT 132:3
When shall my s. have an end	ANON 7:19
When s. come, they come	SHAK 276:35
world's great s. were born	Æ 3:4
sorry: saw a wild thing s. for itself	LAWR 202:21
s. for these our misdoings	BOOK 65:11
sorts: s. and conditions of men	BOOK 64:18
sought: s. in vain that sought	BURNS 82:1
They s. it with thimbles	CARR 92:9
soul: adventures of his s.	FRAN 145:3
As if that s. were fled	MOORE 234:14
bitterness of his s.	BIBLE 47:33
buried s. and all its gems	BLAKE 60:12
city of the s.	BYRON 85:8
dark night of the s.	FITZ 140:22
depth, and not the tumult, of the s.	WORD 355:6
empty book is like an infant's s.	TRAH 333:17
frame of adamant, a s. of fire	JOHN 183:13
God rest his s., officers	SMITH 309:20
Go, S., the body's guest	RAL 257:21
harmonical and ingenious s.	AUBR 19:19
Heaven take my s.	SHAK 282:13
he shall save his s. alive	BIBLE 47:6
he that hides a dark s.	MILT 226:12
His s. is marching on	ANON 8:14
hushèd casket of my s.	KEATS 192:13
I am the captain of my s.	HENL 165:18
I pray the Lord my s. to keep	ANON 9:20
I pray the Lord my s. to take	ANON 9:20
iron entered into his s.	BOOK 68:9
Jesu, lover of my s.	WESL 346:8
lie in the s. is a true lie	JOW 188:2
life's dim windows of the s.	BLAKE 60:12
lift my s. to heaven	SHAK 280:14
lose his own s.	BIBLE 51:23
man, with s. so dead	SCOTT 268:12
Memorial from the S.'s eternity	ROSS 263:7
Merry of s. he sailed on a day	STEV 317:23
My s., bear thou thy part	GURN 159:11
My s. doth magnify the Lord	BIBLE 51:28
My s. doth magnify the Lord	BIBLE 58:16
my soul, if I have a s.	ANON 9:22
My s. is an enchanted boat	SHEL 304:21
my s. is white	BLAKE 61:24
My s., sit thou a patient	QUAR 257:1
My s., there is a country	VAUG 337:6
my s. within the house	SHAK 297:21
No coward s. is mine	BRON 72:16
no s. to be damned	THUR 332:19
Or taught my s. to fancy aught	VAUG 337:7
Perdition catch my s.	SHAK 292:10
poetry ... composed in the s.	ARN 18:5

soul (cont.):

Poor intricated s.	DONNE 124:22
sighed his s. toward	SHAK 289:31
sinews of the s.	FULL 147:5
so longeth my s. after thee	BOOK 67:3
s. a lordly pleasure-house	TENN 327:14
S. and body part like friends	CRAS 111:15
S. clap its hands and sing	YEATS 359:21
s. inhabiting two bodies	ARIS 15:21
s. of our dear brother	BOOK 66:8
S. of the Age	JONS 187:25
s. shall be required	BIBLE 52:19
S., thou hast much goods	BIBLE 52:18
s. to the company store	TRAV 334:4
S. that rises with us	WORD 355:20
subject's s. is his own	SHAK 279:14
Thou hast delivered my s.	BOOK 68:20
try the s.'s strength	BROW 76:7
two to bear my s. away	ANON 9:8
vale of s.-making	KEATS 193:10
yet my s. drew back	HERB 167:2
souls: damp s. of housemaids	ELIOT 134:4
letters mingle s.	DONNE 124:17
Most people sell their s.	SMITH 309:14
open windows into men's s.	ELIZ 135:14
play with s.	BROW 76:12
prostration of men's s.	TAWN 322:18
So must pure lovers' s.	DONNE 124:4
S. of poets dead and gone	KEATS 191:14
they have no s.	COKE 103:9
times that try men's s.	PAINE 244:11
Two s. with but a single	HALM 160:15
sound: all is not sweet, all is not s.	JONS 187:5
commanded to be s.	GREV 158:9
full of s. and fury	SHAK 288:5
Like the s. of a great Amen	PROC 255:14
Music is feeling, then, not s.	STEV 316:10
sighing s., the lights around	ROSS 263:10
s. me from my lowest note	SHAK 276:13
sound mind in a s. body	JUV 189:13
s. of abundance of rain	BIBLE 42:1
s. of shallow foppery	SHAK 289:10
s. of surprise	BALL 28:13
s. strikes like a rising knell	BYRON 85:2
s. were parted thence	JONS 187:18
Whose s. dies on the wind	APOL 14:11
sounding: Come s. through the town	BALL 27:15
sounds: S. and sweet airs	SHAK 296:9
s. of music	SHAK 290:1
s. will take care	CARR 91:9
Wagner's music better than it s.	NYE 240:15
with concord of sweet s.	SHAK 290:3
soup: I won't have any s. today	HOFF 169:18
like a cake of portable s.	BOSW 70:4
not take s. at luncheon	CURZ 113:11
sour: fathers have eaten s. grapes	BIBLE 47:5
How s. sweet music	SHAK 294:11
life will be s. grapes	ASHF 18:24
source: Lord is the s. of my light	BIBLE 58:9
s. of little visible delight	BRON 72:17
sourest: sweetest things turn s.	SHAK 300:2
south: beaker full of the warm S.	KEATS 191:30
fierce and fickle is the S.	TENN 327:24
gentleman in *Kharki* ordered S.	KIPL 196:2
go s. in the winter	ELIOT 134:19
nor yet from the s.	BOOK 67:18
S. is avenged	BOOTH 69:20
Yes, but not in the S.	POTT 254:5
Southampton: weekly from S.	KIPL 197:19
southern: bore me in the s. wild	BLAKE 61:24
souvenirs: Les s. sont cors de chasse	APOL 14:11
sovereign: bandy civilities with my S.	JOHN 184:19
Here lies our s. lord	ROCH 261:4
servants of the s. or state	BACON 24:27
S. has three rights	BAG 26:14

sovereign (cont.):	
subject and a s. are	CHAR 94:25
that he will have no s.	COKE 103:10
to be a S.	ELIZ 135:5
sovereignty: Wommen desiren to have s.	CHAU 96:8
Soviet: S. power plus	LENIN 205:1
sow: Ireland is the old s.	JOYCE 188:7
sower went forth to s.	BIBLE 50:4
They that s. in tears	BOOK 68:29
sower: s. went forth to sow	BIBLE 50:4
soweth: whatsoever a man s.	BIBLE 55:30
sown: reaped, nor was ever s.	TRAH 333:18
They have s. the wind	BIBLE 47:17
where thou hast not s.	BIBLE 51:2
space: art of how to waste s.	JOHN 182:2
cantos of unvanquished s.	CRANE 110:31
Here is my s.	SHAK 271:5
myself a king of infinite s.	SHAK 275:15
spaces: It is the s. between	FENT 138:23
spacious: s. firmament on high	ADD 2:25
spade: I call a s. a spade	BURT 83:6
nominate a s. a spade	JONS 187:9
Spain: Lady of S., I adore you	REAV 258:13
not into the hands of S.	TENN 328:13
Rain in S.	LERN 206:1
span: Contract into a s.	HERB 167:5
Eternity shut in a s.	CRAS 111:11
Less than a s.	BACON 25:30
life's a pain and but a s.	DAV 114:14
spangled: s. heavens	ADD 2:25
Spaniards: S. seem wiser	BACON 25:12
thrash the S. too	DRAKE 126:13
spanieled: That s. me at heels	SHAK 271:22
Spanish: To God I speak S.	CHAR 95:7
spare: Brother can you s. a dime	HARB 161:11
He was a s. man	AUBR 19:19
likes to do in his s. time	GILL 153:1
s. those who have submitted	VIRG 339:16
S. us all word of the weapons	WILB 349:8
s. your country's flag	WHIT 348:26
Woodman, s. that tree	MORR 235:13
woodman, s. the beechen tree	CAMP 88:17
spared: better s. a better man	SHAK 278:15
spares: man that s. these stones	SHAK 300:20
spareth: s. his rod hateth his son	BIBLE 43:23
spark: s. from heaven	ARN 17:10
s. from heaven to fall	ARN 17:8
spark-gap: s. is mightier	HOGB 170:6
sparkle: s. out among the fern	TENN 323:12
S. for ever	TENN 327:18
sparks: like s. among the stubble	BIBLE 47:29
s. fly upward	BIBLE 42:29
sparrow: My lady's s. is dead	CAT 93:1
providence in the fall of a s.	SHAK 277:13
s. hath found her an house	BOOK 67:20
s. should fly swiftly	BEDE 31:20
sparrows: s. sold for two farthings	BIBLE 52:17
Spartans: Go, tell the S.	SIM 307:9
spawn: meanest s. of Hell	TENN 326:4
speak: dare not s. its name	DOUG 125:6
did you s. to him again	BROW 76:18
difficult to s., and impossible to be	BURKE 80:26
In all I think or s. or do	WESL 346:5
let him now s., or else	BOOK 65:27
Let us not s. of them	DANTE 113:19
province of knowledge to s.	HOLM 170:15
S. for England	AMERY 4:21
s. ill of everybody	PÉT 248:7
S., Lord; for thy servant	BIBLE 41:9
S. low, if you speak love	SHAK 291:16
S. roughly to your little boy	CARR 91:5
S. softly and carry a big stick	ROOS 262:16
S. the speech, I pray you	SHAK 276:4
s. they through their throat	BOOK 68:18
S. unto us smooth things	BIBLE 45:29

speak (cont.):	
s. when he is spoken to	STEV 317:16
S. ye comfortably to Jerusalem	BIBLE 46:7
Though I s. with the tongues	BIBLE 55:11
To s. and purpose not	SHAK 282:18
whereof one cannot s.	WITT 352:8
speaking: adepts in the s. trade	CHUR 98:22
By drowning their s.	BROW 76:26
Parliament s. through	CARL 90:17
People talking without s.	SIMON 307:7
Poetry [is] a s. picture	SIDN 306:26
speaks: Gladstone s. to Me	VICT 338:9
her foot s.	SHAK 297:9
s. small like a woman	SHAK 290:8
When he s., the air	SHAK 278:36
spear: Bring me my s.	BLAKE 61:12
With a burning s.	ANON 11:23
spears: sheen of their s.	BYRON 85:22
stars threw down their s.	BLAKE 62:6
their s. into pruninghooks	BIBLE 45:5
specials: 's.' like the old time	COLL 105:7
species: individual, but the s.	JOHN 183:2
spectacle: s. so ridiculous	MAC 213:9
spectacles: s. on nose	SHAK 272:27
What a pair of s. is here	SHAK 297:8
spectre: s. of Communism	ENG 221:13
spectres: S. fly before it	SMIL 308:19
spectre-thin: youth grows pale, and s.	KEATS 191:32
speech: freedom of s.	ROOS 262:13
I have strange power of s.	COL 104:17
manner of his s.	SHAK 271:13
Rude am I in my s.	SHAK 291:33
Speak the s., I pray you	SHAK 276:4
s. be adorned with grace	BIBLE 56:12
s. by Chamberlain is like	BEVAN 38:3
s. created thought	SHEL 304:20
S. impelled us	ELIOT 133:9
s. is like a cracked kettle	FLAU 141:7
S. is the small change	MER 223:18
S. [is] not his language	STAËL 314:7
s. only to conceal	VOLT 340:14
s. they have resolved not	ELIOT 132:3
verse is a measured s.	BACON 23:24
where s. is not, there is	HOBB 169:5
speeches: From all the easy s.	CHES 97:24
speechless: washed in the s. real	BARZ 29:22
speed: S., bonnie boat	BOUL 70:10
s. glum heroes up the line	SASS 267:8
s. the parting guest	POPE 252:24
s. was far faster than light	BULL 78:7
Unsafe at any s.	NADER 236:21
speeding: Faster than a s. bullet	ANON 7:5
spell: foreigners always s. better	TWAIN 336:1
unless he first s. Man	QUAR 257:4
Who lies beneath your s.	HOPE 171:22
speller: taste and fancy of the s.	DICK 119:33
spelling: My s. is Wobbly	MILNE 225:17
spend: so wol we s.	CHAU 96:1
whatever you have, s. less	JOHN 185:31
spending: Getting and s.	WORD 357:10
S. again what is already spent	SHAK 299:25
speranza: LASCIATE OGNI S.	DANTE 113:18
sperare: salus victis nullam s.	VIRG 339:6
spermatozoa: million million s.	HUXL 177:11
spew: bad ones s. it up	CERV 93:20
s. thee out of my mouth	BIBLE 57:22
sphere: their motion in one s.	SHAK 278:13
these walls thy s.	DONNE 124:13
they the s.	DONNE 124:3
spheres: Driv'n by the s.	VAUG 337:14
spice: Variety's the very s. of life	COWP 110:9
spices: land of s.	HERB 167:4
spicy: s. nut-brown ale	MILT 227:5
What though the s. breezes	HEBER 164:16
spider: drunk, and seen the s.	SHAK 298:23

spider (*cont.*):

laws are like s.'s webs	ANAC 5:9
said a s. to a fly	HOW 176:11
s. is sole denizen	HARDY 162:3
s.'s touch, how exquisitely	POPE 252:15
spiders: No more s. in my bath	ANON 9:17
often have seen s. fly	EDW 131:3
Weaving s. come not here	SHAK 290:29
spies: neighbourhood of voluntary s.	AUST 22:25
spill: let them not s. me	MACN 216:7
spin: Go s., you jades	PEMB 247:5
Let the great world s.	TENN 326:17
neither do they s.	BIBLE 49:4
Sob as you s.	AUDEN 20:9
spinach: I say it's s.	WHITE 347:15
spindle: fold, s. or mutilate	ANON 6:26
spinners: long-legged s.	SHAK 290:29
spinning: evening s. by the fire	RONS 262:5
spinning-wheel: wee bit s.	BLAM 62:8
spinsters: s. and the knitters	SHAK 297:31
spires: dreaming s.	ARN 17:17
What s., what farms are those	HOUS 174:24
Ye distant s.	GRAY 157:11
spirit: And with thy s.	MISS 231:9
Blessed are the poor in s.	BIBLE 48:19
break a man's s.	SHAW 300:27
Come, Holy S.	LANG 201:10
elasticity to the s.	SMIL 308:19
Hail to thee, blithe S.	SHEL 305:6
haughty s. before a fall	BIBLE 43:28
Her cabined ample S.	ARN 17:1
I commend my s.	BIBLE 53:4
I commend my s.	BOOK 66:23
My shaping s. of imagination	COL 103:15
never approached my s.	METT 224:2
no s. can walk abroad	SHAK 274:2
pardlike S.	SHEL 303:9
renew a right s. within me	BOOK 67:10
Rest, rest, perturbèd s.	SHAK 275:5
slumber did my s. seal	WORD 356:25
s. all compact of fire	SHAK 300:17
s. burning but unbent	BYRON 85:16
s. giveth life	BIBLE 55:23
s. hath rejoiced in God	BIBLE 51:28
s. indeed is willing	BIBLE 51:13
S. of Delight	SHEL 304:32
S. of God moved	BIBLE 38:13
s. of party	WASH 342:21
s. of the chainless mind	BYRON 87:7
s. of the Lord shall rest	BIBLE 45:18
s. of the place	VIRG 339:18
s. of truth, unity, and concord	BOOK 65:9
s. passed before my face	BIBLE 42:28
s. shall return unto God	BIBLE 44:26
s. in the woods	WORD 355:16
There's a great s. gone	SHAK 271:7
wounded s. who can bear	BIBLE 43:29
spirits: her wanton s. look out	SHAK 297:9
master s. of this age	SHAK 281:12
ruffle up your s.	SHAK 281:26
s. from the vasty deep	SHAK 278:3
S. of well-shot woodcock	BETJ 36:20
S. overwrought	WORD 356:11
s. which are the house of life	BROW 74:22
spiritu: *Et cum s. tuo*	MISS 231:9
spiritual: inward and s. grace	BOOK 65:23
not being a s. people	MANC 217:7
spiritualist: you are a s.	SZASZ 321:25
spiritus: *Veni, Sancte S.*	LANG 201:10
spit: I have no gun, but I can s.	AUDEN 21:8
s. upon my Jewish gabardine	SHAK 289:5
spite: civic slander and the s.	TENN 325:25
splendid: s. and a happy land	GOLD 154:25
S. Isolation	FOST 144:7
splendide: *S. mendax*	HOR 173:27

splendour: Pavilioned in s.	GRANT 156:8
s. borrows all her rays	POPE 251:18
s. falls on castle walls	TENN 327:20
s. in the grass	WORD 355:23
Stung by the s. of a sudden	BROW 75:22
splendoured: many-s. thing	THOM 331:15
split: to make all s.	SHAK 290:18
s. her in twain	TENN 328:13
When I s. an infinitive	CHAN 94:11
spoil: hath been the s. of me	SHAK 278:8
spoiled: they s. the Egyptians	BIBLE 39:38
spoilers: into the hands of s.	BIBLE 40:30
spoils: victor belong the s.	MARCY 218:2
spoken: Excellent things are s.	BOOK 67:24
mouth of the Lord hath s.	BIBLE 46:9
Rome has s.	AUG 22:5
that never have s. yet	CHES 98:4
When the lips have s.	SHEL 303:24
spongy: on s. shoes	WILB 349:12
spontaneous: S. joy	YEATS 359:4
spoon: ate with a runcible s.	LEAR 203:13
spoons: faster we counted our s.	EMER 136:20
let us count our s.	JOHN 184:11
world locks up its s.	SHAW 301:23
sport: ended his s. with Tess	HARDY 161:25
make s. for our neighbours	AUST 23:6
s. of kings	SOM 311:2
s. of kings	SURT 319:8
S. that wrinkled Care derides	MILT 227:2
To s. with Amaryllis	MILT 227:14
To s. would be as tedious	SHAK 277:25
They kill us for their s.	SHAK 283:21
sporting: why this cruel s.	COCK 102:27
sports: mountainous s. girl	BETJ 37:8
While we can, the s. of love	JONS 187:16
sportsman: s. is a man who	LEAC 203:4
spot: little s. enclosed by grace	WATTS 343:2
Out, damned s.	SHAK 287:27
some untidy s.	AUDEN 21:2
there is no s. in thee	BIBLE 44:35
Tip me the black s.	STEV 317:3
with a s. I damn him	SHAK 281:28
spots: or the leopard his s.	BIBLE 46:30
s. and kills anything	WAUGH 343:17
spotted: s. snakes	SHAK 290:28
spouse: shuts the s. Christ	HOPK 172:17
spout: hurricanoes, s.	SHAK 283:6
sprang: I s. to the stirrup	BROW 76:5
spray: pinkly bursts the s.	BETJ 37:6
rime was on the s.	HARDY 162:18
thy hand a withered s.	ARN 17:8
spread: Masters, s. yourselves	SHAK 290:17
S. ALARM AND DESPONDENCY	PEN 247:8
s. my dreams	YEATS 359:7
spree: out on the s.	KIPL 196:15
spring: Blossom by blossom the s.	SWIN 321:2
can S. be far behind	SHEL 304:10
chilly fingered s.	KEATS 190:13
drunk deep of the Pierian s.	DRAY 126:20
easing the S.	REED 258:16
ever-bubbling s. of endless lies	COWP 110:3
Falsehood has a perennial s.	BURKE 79:25
found in the s. to follow	SWIN 321:1
hounds of s.	SWIN 321:1
In the s. a young man's fancy	TENN 326:6
It is s., moonless night	THOM 330:16
lap of the new come s.	SHAK 294:8
rifle all the breathing s.	COLL 105:9
s. breaks through again	COW 109:2
s. has kept in its folds	ARAG 14:21
s. is wound up tight	ANOU 14:5
s. should vanish	FITZ 140:18
s. summer autumn winter	CUMM 112:16
suddenly was changed to S.	SHEL 304:28

spring (*cont.*):

Sweet lovers love the s.	SHAK 273:10
Sweet s., full of sweet days	HERB 167:8
this s. of love resembleth	SHAK 298:18
To have lived light in the s.	ARN 16:14
Treasury is the s. of business	BAG 26:4
Where are the songs of S.	KEATS 192:15
with ever-returning s.	WHIT 348:24

springes: s. to catch woodcocks   SHAK 274:24
springlike: that fester are not s.   ABSE 1:1
springs: Fifty s. are little room   HOUS 174:17

many s., many bright	VAUG 337:13
s. o' that countrie	BALL 28:8
Wastes without s.	CLARE 101:5
Where s. not fail	HOPK 172:7

sprite: fleeting, wav'ring s.   HADR 159:14
sprouting: S. despondently   ELIOT 134:4
spur: Fame is the s.   MILT 227:14

I have no s.	SHAK 286:1
s. of all great minds	CHAP 94:20

spurious: s. brat, Tom Jones   RICH 260:4
spurs: Let the boy win his s.   EDW 130:21
spy: letters for a s.   KIPL 196:28

sent to s. out the land	BIBLE 40:16
s. who came in from the cold	LE C 204:2

squad: awkward s. fire over me   BURNS 82:30
squadrons: side of the big s.   BUSS 83:20

wingèd s. of the sky	MILM 225:13

square: so thoroughly s.   LERN 205:26

s. deal	ROOS 262:17

squat: s., and packed with guile   BROO 73:7

S. like a toad	MILT 229:13

squawking: seven stars go s.   AUDEN 20:11
squeak: s. and gibber   SHAK 274:1
squeaking: With shrieking and s.   BROW 76:26
squeezed: s. as a lemon is s.   GEDD 149:19
squint: banish s. suspicion   MILT 226:13
squire: Bless the s.   DICK 118:5
stab: from hell's heart I s.   MELV 223:4
stabant: S. orantes   VIRG 339:15
stabat: S. Mater dolorosa   JAC 179:3
stability: s. or enlargement   JOHN 182:5
stable: In a s. born our Brother   DEAR 115:7
stables: s. are the real centre   SHAW 301:5
staff: By his cockle hat and s.   SHAK 276:32

I'll break my s.	SHAK 296:13
s. of this bruised reed	BIBLE 42:16
thy rod and thy s. comfort me	BOOK 66:18
your s. in your hand	BIBLE 39:37

stag: runnable s., a kingly crop   DAV 114:11

S. at Bay with the mentality	LEVIN 206:7

stage: All the world's a s.   SHAK 272:24

daughter on the s.	COW 109:5
drown the s. with tears	SHAK 275:23
played upon a s. now	SHAK 298:10
Something for the modern s.	POUND 254:16
s. where every man must play	SHAK 288:27
this great s. of fools	SHAK 283:27
to the well-trod s. anon	MILT 227:8
two hours' traffick of our s.	SHAK 294:23
wonder of our s.	JONS 187:25

stagger: s. like a drunken man   BOOK 68:13
stagnant: Of s. waters   WORD 355:11
stagnation: keeps life from s.   BURN 81:16
St Agnes: S.' Eve   KEATS 190:14
stain: s. the stiff dishonoured   ELIOT 134:17

world's slow s.	SHEL 303:11

stained: hole in a s. glass window   CHAN 94:7
stains: S. the white radiance   SHEL 303:13
stair: place is by a winding s.   BACON 24:29

structure in a winding s.	HERB 167:1

staircase: S. wit   DID 120:20
stairs: any that was kicked up s.   HAL 160:12

down another man's s.	DANTE 113:23

stale: How weary, s., flat   SHAK 274:10

stale (*cont.*):

Tho' s., not ripe	POPE 250:15

staled: S. are my thoughts   DYER 129:15
stalk: Half asleep as they s.   HARDY 162:11
stalking: s. in my chamber   WYATT 358:2
stalking-horse: s. to error   BOL 63:3

uses his folly like a s.	SHAK 273:14

stall: Baby in an ox's s.   BETJ 36:18
stalled: than a s. ox and hatred   BIBLE 43:26
stamp: physics or s. collecting   RUTH 265:8

rank is but the guinea's s.	BURNS 82:7

stampa: e poi roppe la s.   ARIO 15:8
stamps: kill animals and stick in s.   NIC 239:13
stand: British soldier can s. up to   SHAW 301:1

By uniting we s.	DICK 120:18
firm spot on which to s.	ARCH 15:3
Get up, s. up	MARL 218:6
Here s. I. I can do no other	LUTH 212:8
I s. at the door	BIBLE 57:23
serve who only s. and wait	MILT 230:23
s. and look at them long	WHIT 348:19
s. at the latter day	BIBLE 42:36
S. by thyself	BIBLE 46:25
s. for nothing fall for anything	HAM 160:16
S. not upon the order	SHAK 287:12
s. out of my sun a little	DIOG 121:3
S. still, you ever-moving spheres	MARL 218:12
S. therefore	BIBLE 56:4
s. up for bastards	SHAK 282:21
time to s. and stare	DAV 114:20
who will s. on either hand	MAC 214:4

standard: raise the scarlet s. high   CONN 106:23
standards: S. are always out of date   BENN 34:14
St Andrews: S. by the Northern sea   LANG 201:1
stands: s. about the woodland ride   HOUS 174:16

S. the Church clock	BROO 73:8

star: bright northern s.   LOV 210:18

bright Occidental S.	BIBLE 38:12
bright particular s.	SHAK 270:23
Bright s., would I were	KEATS 190:10
By a high s. our course is set	MACN 216:11
catch a falling s.	DONNE 124:10
constant as the northern s.	SHAK 281:9
each, in his separate s.	KIPL 197:13
great s. early drooped	WHIT 348:24
Hitch your wagon to a s.	EMER 136:31
like a falling s.	MILT 228:20
moth for the s.	SHEL 305:5
one bright s.	COL 104:10
our life's S.	WORD 355:20
seen his s. in the east	BIBLE 48:9
S. captains glow	FLEC 141:14
Sunset and evening s.	TENN 323:18
tall ship and a s. to steer her	MAS 221:21
There was a s. danced	SHAK 291:18
Twinkle, twinkle, little s.	TAYL 323:3
Westward the s. of empire	BERK 35:19
you've got to come back a s.	JAMES 270:16

Star-Chamber: S. matter   SHAK 290:7
star-crossed: s. lovers   SHAK 294:22
stardust: We are s.   MITC 232:4
stare: dead s. in a million adults   SHAF 270:19

In the s. of the deer	WILB 349:9
no time to stand and s.	DAV 114:20
With a stony British s.	TENN 326:27

staring: Truth is s. at the sun   BELL 33:3
stark: No, Sir; s. insensibility   JOHN 183:21
starless: s. and bible-black   THOM 330:16
starlight: S. and dewdrop   FOST 144:9

s. lit my lonesomeness	HARDY 162:18
there was nae s.	BALL 28:8

starred: s. night Prince Lucifer   MER 223:21
starry: heaven, her s. train   MILT 229:11

Sidney's self, the s. paladin	BROW 77:13
To entertain this s. stranger	CRAS 111:10

starry (cont.):
very s., the horned moon	WORD 354:9
stars: climb half-way to the s.	CROSS 112:10
crown of twelve s.	BIBLE 57:30
cut him out in little s.	SHAK 295:14
Far beyond the s.	VAUG 337:6
journey-work of the s.	WHIT 348:18
Look at the s.!	HOPK 172:16
looking at the s.	WILDE 349:25
not in our s.	SHAK 280:27
opposition of the s.	MARV 220:13
puts the s. to flight	FITZ 140:4
seven s. go squawking	AUDEN 20:11
seven s. in the sky	ANON 8:6
shining of the s.	TENN 324:16
s. are dead	AUDEN 21:15
s. are my children	KEATS 193:9
s. are old	TAYL 323:4
s. hung with humid nightblue	JOYCE 188:19
s. in her hair were seven	ROSS 263:6
s. in their courses fought	BIBLE 40:32
s. keep not their motion	SHAK 278:13
s. leads through the atom	EDD 130:12
s. move still	MARL 218:13
s. rush out	COL 104:9
S. scribble on our eyes	CRANE 110:31
Stars, s.! and all eyes else	SHAK 299:3
s. threw down their spears	BLAKE 62:6
sun and the other s.	DANTE 113:24
that's the way to the s.	VIRG 339:19
Through struggle to the s.	ANON 13:18
with how splendid s.	FLEC 141:19
you chaste s.	SHAK 292:28
Your chilly s. I can forgo	CORY 108:14
star-shine: s. at night	STEV 317:19
starship: s. Enterprise	RODD 261:12
start: end is where we s. from	ELIOT 133:11
s. a scene or two	ELIOT 134:1
s. from their spheres	SHAK 274:30
s. together and finish	BEEC 31:23
started: to arrive where we s.	ELIOT 133:10
starting: you mar all with this s.	SHAK 287:29
startle: come down and s.	AUDEN 20:10
starts: Was everything by s.	DRYD 127:12
starve: Let not poor Nelly s.	CHAR 95:4
s. for want of impudence	DRYD 127:28
starved: apothecary than a s. poet	LOCK 209:2
state: all were for the s.	MAC 214:5
done the s. some service	SHAK 293:5
free church in a free s.	CAV 93:14
from thy s. mine never shall	MILT 229:28
glories and my s. depose	SHAK 294:5
glories of our blood and s.	SHIR 306:10
Here's a s. of things	GILB 151:27
I am the S.	LOUI 210:12
In that s. I came, return	VAUG 337:10
life is everywhere a s.	JOHN 183:4
mine was the middle s.	DEFOE 115:14
no such thing as the S.	AUDEN 21:11
Only in the s.	HEGEL 164:19
reinforcement of the S.	CAMUS 89:8
sail on, O Ship of S.	LONG 209:11
servants of the sovereign or s.	BACON 24:27
S. in wonted manner keep	JONS 187:3
S. is not 'abolished'	ENG 137:8
s. without the means of change	BURKE 80:10
to what a s. dost Thou bring	TER 329:7
worl's in a s. o' chassis	O'CAS 240:22
stately: S. as a galleon	GREN 158:15
s. tents of war	MARL 219:4
S. Homes of England	COW 109:8
s. homes of England	HEM 165:10
statement: black s. of pistons	SPEN 312:23
statements: previous s. are inoperative	ZIEG 361:2
s. was interesting	TWAIN 335:19

states: goodly s. and kingdoms	KEATS 192:10
like to greater s.	SUCK 318:23
statesman: constitutional s.	BAG 26:2
s. is a politician	POMP 250:12
s. is a politician	TRUM 335:4
s. who is enamoured	BIER 59:5
Too nice for a s.	GOLD 155:2
statesmen: government of s.	DISR 121:24
station: At the cross her s.	JAC 179:3
By Grand Central S. I sat down	SMART 308:15
Hurries down the concrete s.	BETJ 37:7
private s.	GAY 149:13
she leaves the s.	SPEN 312:23
walls of that antique s.	BEER 32:10
stations: know our proper s.	DICK 118:5
statistical: s. improbability	DAWK 115:4
statistics: damned lies and s.	DISR 122:21
We are just s., born	HOR 173:7
statues: Ep's. are junk	ANON 8:2
status quo: restored the s.	SQUI 314:4
stay: care to s. than will to go	SHAK 295:19
Here I am, and here I s.	MACM 215:13
our love is here to s.	GERS 150:7
S. for me there	KING 195:5
want things to s. as they are	LAMP 200:19
will not s. in place	ELIOT 133:1
without thee here to s.	MILT 230:1
stay-at-home: Sweet S.	DAV 114:22
stayed: s. me in a happy hour	SHAK 291:24
stays: prays together s. together	SCAL 267:16
steadfast: would I were s. as thou art	KEATS 190:10
steady: S., boys, steady	GARR 148:8
thought more s. than an ebbing	FORD 143:11
steaks: smell of s. in passageways	ELIOT 134:10
steal: Give me not poverty lest I s.	DEFOE 115:13
if you s. from many	MIZN 232:12
lawyer can s. more	PUZO 256:26
silently s. away	LONG 209:13
s. my Basil-pot	KEATS 191:4
s. the very teeth	ARAB 14:19
they s. my thunder	DENN 117:2
thieves break through and s.	BIBLE 49:1
Thou shalt not s.	BIBLE 40:9
Thou shalt not s.	CLOU 102:19
stealing: hands from picking and s.	BOOK 65:22
Men are not hanged for s.	HAL 160:11
s. dey gits you in jail	O'NEI 241:9
s. ducks	ARAB 14:20
steals: s. my purse steals trash	SHAK 292:11
s. something from the thief	SHAK 291:37
stealth: do a good action by s.	LAMB 200:11
Do good by s., and blush	POPE 252:31
steamer: in a s. from Harwich	GILB 151:16
s. breaking from the bay	AUDEN 20:25
steamers: Great s., white and gold	KIPL 197:19
s. made an excursion to hell	PRIE 255:8
steaming: s. phrases	SCH 267:26
steamy: Throws up a s. column	COWP 110:11
steed: his s. was the best	SCOTT 268:18
steel: All shod with s.	WORD 355:2
clad in complete s.	MILT 226:14
foemen worthy of their s.	SCOTT 268:9
Give them the cold s., boys	ARM 15:23
long divorce of s.	SHAK 280:14
more than complete s.	ANON 8:7
S.-true and blade-straight	STEV 317:20
thin red line tipped with s.	RUSS 265:7
wounded surgeon plies the s.	ELIOT 133:5
steeples: In s. far and near	HOUS 174:20
s. of Fermanagh and Tyrone	CHUR 99:7
you have drenched our s.	SHAK 283:6
steer: they s. their courses	BUTL 83:25
Stein: I don't like the family S.	ANON 8:2
stem: rod out of the s. of Jesse	BIBLE 45:18

step: one small s. for a man	ARMS 16:5
one s. enough for me	NEWM 238:21
To s. aside is human	BURNS 81:21
stepmother: stony-hearted s.	DE Q 117:3
stepped: in blood s. in so far	SHAK 287:14
stepping: s. westward	WORD 357:3
stepping-stones: rise on s.	TENN 324:24
steps: s. that led assuredly	GUIB 159:8
wandering s. and slow	MILT 230:2
sterner: made of s. stuff	SHAK 281:20
stick: carry a big s.	ROOS 262:16
he fell like the s.	PAINE 244:12
I am a kind of burr; I shall s.	SHAK 288:25
S. close to your desks	GILB 152:20
s. inside a swill bucket	ORW 242:16
tattered coat upon a s.	YEATS 359:21
sticketh: friend that s. closer	BIBLE 43:30
sticking-place: courage to the s.	SHAK 286:6
sticks: S. nix hick pix	ANON 10:15
stiff: S. in opinions	DRYD 127:12
woman can be proud and s.	YEATS 358:20
stiffnecked: Thou art a s. people	BIBLE 40:11
stigma: Any s., as the old saying	GUED 159:5
still: Be s. then, and know	BOOK 67:7
If you s. have to ask	ARMS 16:4
mighty heart is lying s.	WORD 354:16
ship was s. as she could be	SOUT 311:22
sound of a voice that is s.	TENN 323:11
S. falls the Rain	SITW 307:19
S. glides the Stream	WORD 356:18
s. point of the turning world	ELIOT 132:28
s. small voice	BIBLE 42:3
s. they gazed	GOLD 154:24
they liked me 's.'	DICK 120:15
Thou art tired; best be s.	ARN 16:18
stillness: all the air a solemn s.	GRAY 157:4
As modest s. and humility	SHAK 279:5
still-vexed: s. Bermoothes	SHAK 295:34
stilly: Oft, in the s. night	MOORE 234:20
stilts: nonsense upon s.	BENT 34:22
stimulate: S. the phagocytes	SHAW 301:2
sting: It is a prick, it is a s.	PEELE 247:1
s. like a bee	ALI 4:10
where is thy s.	BIBLE 55:22
where is thy s.-a-ling-a-ling	ANON 9:21
stingeth: s. like an adder	BIBLE 43:33
stings: it s. you for your pains	HILL 168:11
s. and motions of the sense	SHAK 288:11
stinker: Outrageous S.	KIPL 198:2
stinks: painted child of dirt that s.	POPE 251:8
stir: Above the smoke and s.	MILT 226:5
No s. in the air	SOUT 311:22
S. up, we beseech thee	BOOK 64:28
s. without great argument	SHAK 276:31
stirred: forest something s.	SIMP 307:10
Shaken and not s.	FLEM 141:21
stirring: while Mrs Bennet was s. the fire	AUST 23:3
stirrup: I sprang to the s.	BROW 76:5
s. and the ground	CAMD 88:12
With one foot already in the s.	CERV 93:21
stirs: lost pulse of feeling s.	ARN 16:10
Will that s. and urges	HARDY 162:5
stitch: S.! stitch! stitch	HOOD 171:12
stitching: s. and unstitching	YEATS 358:13
St James: The ladies of S.'s	DOBS 122:27
stocking: glimpse of s.	PORT 253:17
your silk s.'s hanging	SELL 269:25
stockings: s. and white bosoms	JOHN 183:24
yellow s.	SHAK 298:4
stoic: doctors of the S. fur	MILT 226:19
stolen: Stolen, s., be your apples	HUNT 176:16
S. sweets are best	CIBB 100:18
s. the scraps	SHAK 284:17
S. waters are sweet	BIBLE 43:15

stolen (cont.):	
s. his wits away	DE L 116:13
stoles: nice white s.	BARH 28:18
stolid: S. and stunned	MARK 218:4
stomach: army marches on its s.	NAP 237:5
heart and s. of a king	ELIZ 135:6
no s. for such meat	DOBS 122:26
no s. to this fight	SHAK 279:18
s. of the country	GLAD 153:7
stone: back into the S. Age	LEMAY 204:20
conscious s. to beauty grew	EMER 136:15
Florence blossoming in s.	LONG 209:18
give them the s.	MONT 233:6
hurt not thy foot against a s.	BOOK 67:30
let him first cast a s.	BIBLE 53:26
let them not make me a s.	MACN 216:7
make a s. of the heart	YEATS 359:2
precious s. set in the silver	SHAK 293:16
standing like a s. wall	BEE 31:22
s. that puts the stars to flight	FITZ 140:4
S. walls do not a prison make	LOV 210:19
s. which the builders refused	BOOK 68:22
water hollows out a s.	OVID 243:12
Wept over her, carved in s.	TENN 326:24
we raised not a s.	WOLFE 353:1
will he give him a s.	BIBLE 49:10
stones: man that spares these s.	SHAK 300:20
Sermons in s.	SHAK 272:14
smooth s. out of the brook	BIBLE 41:18
s. and clouts make martyrs	BROW 74:4
s. kissed by the English	OWEN 244:1
s. of Rome to rise	SHAK 281:26
stony: more s. than a shore	WILL 351:7
s. limits cannot hold love	SHAK 294:32
stood: Have s. against the world	SHAK 281:21
I should of s. in bed	JAC 179:2
stop: come to the end: then s.	CARR 91:13
could not s. for Death	DICK 120:9
did he s. and speak to you	BROW 76:18
s. a hole to keep the wind	SHAK 277:9
S. the world, I want to get off	BRIC 238:14
s. to busy fools	VAUG 337:5
stops: would seem to know my s.	SHAK 276:13
storage: library is thought in cold s.	SAM 266:10
storey: crack in your upper s.	SMOL 310:16
storied: S. of old in high immortal	MILT 226:16
stories: S. to rede ar delitabill	BARB 28:15
tell sad s. of the death	SHAK 293:27
With dismal s.	BUNY 79:9
storm: And rides upon the s.	COWP 109:25
directs the s.	ADD 2:11
lovers fled away into the s.	KEATS 190:23
S. and stress	KAUF 190:6
when s.-clouds brood	LEAR 203:9
storms: Above the s. of passion	BODE 62:16
all thy waves and s.	BOOK 67:4
storm-troubled: world's s. sphere	BRON 72:16
stormy: O s. peple	CHAU 95:24
S. weather	KOEH 198:22
story: Every picture tells a s.	ANON 7:2
plot for a short s.	CHEK 96:27
Not that the s. need be long	THOR 332:6
novel tells a s.	FORS 143:16
Shuts up the s. of our days	RAL 258:1
s. always old and always	BROW 77:6
To tell my s.	SHAK 277:17
stout: Collapse of S. Party	ANON 6:17
St Paul's: Say I am designing S.	BENT 35:9
sketch the ruins of S.	MAC 213:15
straight: crooked shall be made s.	BIBLE 46:9
line which is accurately s.	WHEW 347:8
nothing ever ran quite s.	GALS 147:17
stiff and unflexible as s.	LOCKE 208:17
street which is called S.	BIBLE 54:13
timber of humanity no s. thing	KANT 189:25

strain: not I build; no, but s.	HOPK 172:19
That s. again	SHAK 297:14
which s. at a gnat	BIBLE 50:31
Words s.	ELIOT 133:1
strains: s. of unpremeditated art	SHEL 305:6
strait: S. is the gate, and narrow	BIBLE 49:13
straits: With echoing s. between	ARN 17:22
Strand: I walk down the S.	HARG 162:20
where's the Maypole in the S.	BRAM 71:13
strands: these last s. of man	HOPK 171:25
strange: foul, s., and unnatural	SHAK 274:31
Into something rich and s.	SHAK 296:1
Let us be very s. and well-bred	CONG 106:20
Lord's song: in a s. land	BOOK 69:3
millions of s. shadows	SHAK 299:18
s. and sinister embroidered	JAMES 180:1
s. faces, other minds	TENN 324:19
stranger in a s. land	BIBLE 39:29
s. the change from major	PORT 253:19
strangeness: some s. in the proportion	BACON 24:14
stranger: From the wiles of the s.	NASH 237:11
I, a s. and afraid	HOUS 174:11
I was a s., and ye took me in	BIBLE 51:5
Look, s., at this island now	AUDEN 20:26
never love a s.	BENS 34:21
s.! 'Eave 'arf a brick at 'im	PUNCH 256:9
s. here in Gloucestershire	SHAK 293:17
s. in a strange land	BIBLE 39:29
S. than fiction	BYRON 86:29
S., unless with bedroom eyes	AUDEN 21:8
surety for a s. shall smart	BIBLE 43:18
To entertain this starry s.	CRAS 111:10
strangers: kindness of s.	WILL 351:6
forgetful to entertain s.	BIBLE 56:29
For we are s. before thee	BIBLE 42:17
I do desire we may be better s.	SHAK 273:5
strangled: s. with the guts of priests	MESL 223:27
strangling: Than s. in a string	HOUS 174:19
Stratford atte Bowe: scole of S.	CHAU 95:15
straw: Take a s. and throw it up	SELD 269:18
Things are but as s. dogs	LAO-T 201:11
strawberries: S. swimming in the cream	PEELE 247:2
strawberry: S. fields forever	MCC 205:15
strawed: where thou hast not s.	BIBLE 51:2
strayed: s. from thy ways like	BOOK 63:13
stream: have their s. and pond	BROO 73:2
leaves in the glassy s.	SHAK 277:6
long-legged fly upon the s.	YEATS 359:15
On summer eves by haunted s.	MILT 227:7
painted meadow, or a purling s.	ADD 2:21
Still glides the S.	WORD 356:18
There's an old mill by the s.	ARMS 15:24
Time, like an ever-rolling s.	WATTS 343:15
streamers: s. waving in the wind	GAY 149:17
streams: Gilding pale s.	SHAK 299:17
More pellucid s.	WORD 355:7
pants the hart for cooling s.	TATE 322:16
street: breaks at the end of the s.	MACN 216:4
bald s. breaks the blank day	TENN 325:1
done by jostling in the s.	BLAKE 61:15
Here in the long unlovely s.	TENN 324:26
inability to cross the s.	WOOLF 354:5
s. fighting man	JAGG 179:7
s. which is called Straight	BIBLE 54:13
sunny side of the s.	FIEL 139:15
streets: children died in the s.	AUDEN 20:18
Down these mean s.	CHAN 94:9
s. are paved with gold	COLM 105:13
S. FLOODED. PLEASE ADVISE	BENC 34:6
s. of a hundred cities	HOOV 171:18
s. that no longer exist	FENT 138:23
when night darkens the s.	MILT 228:15
strength: full of the s. of five	BETJ 37:8
His s. the more is	BUNY 79:9

strength (cont.):	
king's name is a tower of s.	SHAK 294:20
Let us roll all our s.	MARV 221:1
pleasure in the s. of an horse	BOOK 69:10
shewed s. with his arm	BIBLE 51:29
strength is as the s. of ten	TENN 328:15
s. then but labour and sorrow	BOOK 67:26
S. through joy	LEY 206:20
sucklings hast thou ordained s.	BOOK 66:10
To have a giant's.	SHAK 288:13
strengthen: S. ye the weak hands	BIBLE 46:5
strengtheneth: Christ which s.	BIBLE 56:10
strenuous: doctrine of the s. life	ROOS 262:15
round of s. idleness	WORD 356:11
stress: Storm and s.	KAUF 190:6
stretch: S. him out longer	SHAK 284:7
stretched: things which he s.	TWAIN 335:18
stricken: old and well s. in age	BIBLE 39:14
Why, let the s. deer go weep	SHAK 276:12
stride: At one s. comes the dark	COL 104:9
strife: Bear the toil, maintain the s.	WHITE 347:16
curse to party-s.	WORD 354:18
In place of s.	CAST 92:15
stern s., and carnage dear	SCOTT 268:23
s. is o'er, the battle done	POTT 253:28
Wherein the graver had a s.	JONS 187:20
strike: S. flat the thick rotundity	SHAK 283:6
s. his father's crown	SHAK 279:1
s. it out	JOHN 184:27
that you s. it in anger	SHAW 301:32
when in doubt, s. it out	TWAIN 336:6
striker: no s., not greedy of filthy	BIBLE 56:16
string: end of a golden s.	BLAKE 60:20
Harp not on that s.	SHAK 294:19
s. that ties them together	MONT 233:19
Than strangling in a s.	HOUS 174:19
untune that s.	SHAK 296:30
strings: in the human heart	DICK 117:21
strip: S. thine own back	SHAK 283:25
striped: He was no s. frieze	STR 318:11
stripes: with his s. we are healed	BIBLE 46:19
strive: s. officiously to keep alive	CLOU 102:17
To s., to seek, to find	TENN 328:25
strives: Man will err while yet he s.	GOET 154:3
stroke: none so fast as s.	COKE 103:6
s. a platitude until it purrs	MARQ 219:23
strokes: As amorous of their s.	SHAK 271:14
strong: advantage of s. people	BONH 63:11
battle to the s.	DAV 114:12
but s. in will	TENN 328:25
But wants that little s.	HOLM 170:17
Eternal Father, s. to save	WHIT 348:9
nor the battle to the s.	BIBLE 44:20
only the S. shall thrive	SERV 270:11
river is a s. brown god	ELIOT 133:7
Sorrow and silence are s.	LONG 209:16
s. and of a good courage	BIBLE 40:26
S. brother in God	BELL 33:14
s. came forth sweetness	BIBLE 41:3
s. drink unto him	BIBLE 44:5
S. is the lion—like a coal	SMART 308:10
s. man in a blatant land	TENN 326:26
s. name of the Trinity	ALEX 4:5
s. that they come to fourscore	BOOK 67:26
that s., silent man	MORL 235:8
those who think they are s.	BID 59:1
without whom nothing is s.	BOOK 64:24
stronger: are on the side of the s.	TAC 322:8
interest of the s. party	PLATO 249:21
s. by every thing you see	STER 315:18
they were s. than lions	BIBLE 41:22
strongest: reason of the s.	LA F 199:13
stronghold: safe s. our God is still	LUTH 212:10
strove: A little still she s.	BYRON 86:1
unbecoming men that s. with	TENN 328:23

struck: I s. the board, and cried	HERB 166:22
s. regularly like gongs	COW 109:11
struggle: alarms of s. and flight	ARN 16:12
gods themselves s. in vain	SCH 267:20
perpetual s. for room and food	MALT 217:6
Say not the s. naught availeth	CLOU 102:22
s. between the artist man	SHAW 301:18
S. for Existence	DARW 114:4
What s. to escape	KEATS 191:18
struggles: history of class s.	ENG 221:14
strumpet: Into a s.'s fool	SHAK 271:3
she is a s.	SHAK 275:13
struts: s. and frets his hour upon	SHAK 288:5
Stuart: S. or Nassau go higher	PRIOR 255:10
stubble: like sparks among the s.	BIBLE 47:29
studied: he s. from the life	ARMS 16:1
studies: S. serve for delight	BACON 25:13
studio: Sine ira et s.	TAC 322:6
studious: S. let me sit	THOM 331:27
S. of elegance and ease	GAY 149:12
S. of laborious ease	COWP 110:10
studiously: stood apart, s. neutral	WILS 351:19
study: craggy paths of s.	JONS 187:13
My s.'s ornament, thou shell	MIDD 224:8
proper s. of mankind is books	HUXL 177:5
proper s. of mankind is man	POPE 252:17
science and s. of man	CHAR 95:9
s. is a weariness	BIBLE 44:27
S. is like the heaven's	SHAK 284:10
studying: s. how I may compare	SHAK 294:10
stuff: I count life just a s.	BROW 76:7
should be made of sterner s.	SHAK 281:20
s. as great part of Shakespeare	GEOR 149:24
such s. as dreams are made on	SHAK 296:10
too short to s. a mushroom	CONR 107:10
stuffed: s. their mouths with gold	BEVAN 38:2
We are the s. men	ELIOT 133:17
stuffs: S. out his vacant garments	SHAK 282:8
stumbling: S. on melons, as I pass	MARV 220:15
stumps: pitch, and s., and all	LANG 201:2
stung: S. by the splendour	BROW 75:22
stupid: s. man is doing something	SHAW 300:25
s. neither forgive nor forget	SZASZ 321:24
stupidity: Such an excess of s.	JOHN 184:14
With s. the gods struggle in vain	SCH 267:20
Sturm: S. und Drang	KAUF 190:6
Stygian: In S. cave forlorn	MILT 226:27
S. smoke of the pit	JAM 179:9
style: cut, the s., the line	LOES 209:6
He has no real s.	PIC 248:18
how the s. refines	POPE 252:5
only secret of s.	ARN 18:13
S. is life	FLAU 141:10
S. is the dress of thought	WESL 346:18
S. is the man	BUFF 78:5
true definition of a s.	SWIFT 320:4
When we see a natural s.	PASC 246:1
suave: S., mari magno turbantibus	LUCR 212:4
subdue: It may s. for a moment	BURKE 80:1
replenish the earth, and s. it	BIBLE 38:17
s. the arrogant	VIRG 339:16
To chasten and s.	WORD 355:10
To teach, convince, s.	AUBER 19:15
subdued: My nature is s.	SHAK 300:7
subiectis: Parcere s. et debellare	VIRG 339:16
subject: Grasp the s., the words	CATO 92:23
honour is the s.	SHAK 280:26
I know what it is to be a s.	ELIZ 135:5
Lies the s. of all verse	BROW 74:24
Little s., little wit	CAREY 90:1
s. and a sovereign	CHAR 94:25
s.'s duty is the king's	SHAK 279:14
We know a s. ourselves	JOHN 185:5
subjects: policy when s. are rebels	BURKE 80:16

sublime: audience yelled 'You're s.'	HARG 162:21
Howls the s.	DICK 119:7
My object all s.	GILB 152:1
Of poetry; to maintain 'the s.'	POUND 254:14
One step above the s.	PAINE 244:8
s. to the ridiculous	NAP 237:2
Wordsworthian or egotistical s.	KEATS 193:8
submerged: The S. Tenth	BOOTH 69:21
submission: appetite for s.	ELIOT 132:8
submit: to the destructive element s.	CONR 107:7
Must he s.?	SHAK 294:2
subsistence: S. only increases	MALT 217:5
substance: summed with all his s.	CHAP 94:15
Wasted his s. with riotous	BIBLE 52:29
subterranean: s. fields	WORD 356:14
subtle: God is s. but not malicious	EINS 131:8
more s. than any beast	BIBLE 38:24
slipper and s. knave	SHAK 292:6
suburb: s. stretched beyond	BETJ 36:21
suburbs: In the south s.	SHAK 298:8
s. of your good pleasure	SHAK 281:7
succeed: How to s. in business	MEAD 222:17
succeeds: Whenever a friend s.	VIDAL 338:13
success: bitch-goddess s.	JAMES 180:7
ecstasy, is s. in life	PATER 246:15
If A is a s. in life	EINS 131:10
mortals to command s.	ADD 2:13
s. in life is to be a good	SPEN 312:16
S. is counted sweetest	DICK 120:13
S. is relative	ELIOT 132:23
Sweet smell of s.	LEHM 204:13
there's no s. like failure	DYLAN 130:4
These s. encourages	VIRG 339:10
true s. is to labour	STEV 317:6
very lively hope of s.	SMITH 310:14
vulgar judgements—s.	BURKE 79:18
With his surcease s.	SHAK 285:22
successful: S. crimes alone	DRYD 128:8
successive: his s. journeys run	WATTS 343:12
suck: I have given s., and know	SHAK 286:6
sucked: s. on country pleasures	DONNE 124:5
sucker: give a s. an even break	FIEL 139:16
There's a s. born every minute	BARN 29:9
sucking: s. child shall play	BIBLE 45:20
suckle: s. fools and chronicle	SHAK 292:4
sucklings: babes and s.	BOOK 66:10
sudden: I said to Dawn: Be s.	THOM 331:10
splendour of a s. thought	BROW 75:22
too unadvised, too s.	SHAK 295:1
suddenly: s. became depraved	JUV 189:3
sue: used to s. than to command	SCOTT 268:8
Suez: somewheres east of S.	KIPL 196:23
suffer: For ye s. fools gladly	BIBLE 55:27
let's s. on the heights	HUGO 176:1
should have courage to s.	TROL 334:13
S. the little children	BIBLE 51:25
sufferance: s. is the badge of all	SHAK 289:4
suffering: About s. they were never wrong	AUDEN 21:1
learn in s. what they teach	SHEL 303:22
put me to s.	METH 223:28
S. is permanent, obscure	WORD 354:13
sufferings: patience under their s.	BOOK 64:19
To each his s.	GRAY 157:13
sufficiency: An elegant s.	THOM 331:23
sufficient: perfect and s. sacrifice	BOOK 65:16
S. unto the day	BIBLE 49:5
suicide: longest s. note in history	KAUF 190:4
It is s. to be abroad	BECK 31:7
s. 25 years after his death	BEAV 31:5
s. kills two people	MILL 225:1
suis: J'y s., j'y reste	MACM 215:13
Suisse: point de S.	RAC 257:17
suits: trappings and the s. of woe	SHAK 274:8
suivre: il fallait bien les s.	LEDR 204:4

Sule Skerry: My home it is the S. BALL 27:17
sulphur: oat-cakes, and s. SMITH 309:26
sulphurous: s. and thought-executing fires SHAK 283:6
sultry: where the climate's s. BYRON 85:24
sum: *Cogito, ergo s.* DESC 117:9
s. obtained I this freedom BIBLE 54:24
s. of matter remains exactly BACON 24:4
s. of things for pay HOUS 174:13
Sumatra: giant rat of S. DOYLE 125:17
summer: after many a s. dies the swan TENN 328:17
compare thee to a s.'s day SHAK 299:12
Eternal s. gilds them yet BYRON 86:13
Expect Saint Martin's s. SHAK 280:3
ful ofte a myrie s.'s day CHAU 96:16
In a s. seson, whan softe LANG 201:5
In s., quite the other way STEV 317:12
It was a s. evening SOUT 311:18
long bathing of a s.'s day WORD 356:9
lordships on a hot s. afternoon ANON 11:3
murmur of a s.'s day ARN 17:5
On s. eves by haunted stream MILT 227:7
s. afternoon JAMES 180:5
s. birdcage in a garden WEBS 344:23
s. by this sun of York SHAK 294:13
S. has set in with its usual COL 105:2
s. in England WALP 341:22
S. is icumen in ANON 10:16
s.'s lease hath all too short SHAK 299:12
S. time an' the livin' is easy GERS 168:6
That never knew the s. woods TENN 325:3
This guest of s. SHAK 285:21
thy eternal s. shall not fade SHAK 299:13
'Tis the last rose of s. MOORE 234:18
summers: s. in a sea of glory SHAK 280:18
thousand s. are over and dead SWIN 321:15
summertime: In s. on Bredon HOUS 174:20
summits: Nations touch at their s. BAG 26:9
summons: s. thee to heaven SHAK 286:11
summum: S. *bonum* CIC 100:22
sun: all, except their s., is set BYRON 86:13
And I will sing of the s. POUND 254:11
And loves to live i' the s. SHAK 272:21
Before you let the s. in THOM 330:18
blushing discontented s. SHAK 293:29
bosom-friend of the maturing s. KEATS 192:14
Busy old fool, unruly s. DONNE 124:11
crept out again to feel the s. BROW 74:27
doors against a setting s. SHAK 296:19
farthing candle to the s. YOUNG 360:16
glorious summer by this s. of York SHAK 294:13
going down of the s. BINY 59:12
golden apples of the s. YEATS 360:1
Go out in the midday s. COW 109:4
heaven's glorious s. SHAK 284:10
hidden s. that rings black Cyprus FLEC 141:18
I am too much i' the s. SHAK 274:6
Juliet is the s. SHAK 294:29
knitters in the s. SHAK 297:31
light a candle to the s. SIDN 306:14
Light breaks where no s. THOM 330:12
little window where the s. HOOD 171:8
livery of the burnished s. SHAK 289:6
love that moves the s. DANTE 113:24
more the heat o' the s. SHAK 273:27
most shene in the s. LANG 201:9
Mother, give me the s. IBSEN 178:4
Move him into the s. OWEN 243:24
new thing under the s. BIBLE 44:8
nothing like the s. SHAK 300:11
Now the s. is laid to sleep JONS 187:3
on which the s. never sets NORTH 240:6
our own disasters the s. SHAK 282:22
owes no homage unto the s. BROW 74:21
place in the s. BÜLOW 78:8

sun *(cont.)*:
place in the s. WILH 350:25
short while towards the s. SPEN 312:24
So when the s. in bed MILT 227:29
stand out of my s. a little DIOG 121:3
s. also rises HEM 165:14
s. does not set in my dominions SCH 267:19
s. go down upon your wrath BIBLE 55:33
s. goes down with a flaming BOND 63:9
s. in lonely lands TENN 323:21
s. looked over the mountain's BROW 76:23
S. of righteousness arise BIBLE 47:26
s. shall not burn thee BOOK 68:26
s. shall rise WOTT 357:16
S.'s rim dips COL 104:9
s. to me is dark MILT 230:12
s. to rise on the evil BIBLE 48:24
s. we have is made of Newcastle WALP 341:20
though we cannot make our s. MARV 221:1
Till the s. grows cold TAYL 323:4
tired the s. with talking CORY 108:13
To have enjoyed the s. ARN 16:14
Truth is staring at the s. BELL 33:3
Under the s. HOUS 175:1
volley of the s. WILB 349:13
walks under the midday s. MILT 226:12
Was sitting in the s. SOUT 311:18
whan softe was the s. LANG 201:5
what are you when the s. shall rise WOTT 357:16
woman clothed with the s. BIBLE 57:30
worship to the garish s. SHAK 295:14
sunbathing: s. and jazz WAUGH 343:22
sunbeam: Jesus wants me for a s. TALB 322:10
s. in a winter's day DYER 129:17
sunbeams: motes that people the s. MILT 226:23
s. out of cucumbers SWIFT 319:22
Sunday: For this is S. morning MACN 216:9
Here of a S. morning HOUS 174:20
on a rainy S. afternoon ERTZ 137:15
Repentance on a S. YBAR 358:11
than a rainy S. in London DE Q 117:4
Sundays: begin a journey on S. SWIFT 320:8
sundial: s., and I make a botch BELL 33:26
sundry: s. and manifold changes BOOK 64:23
s. times and in divers manners BIBLE 56:23
sunk: All s. beneath the wave COWP 109:28
sunless: Down to a s. sea COL 103:22
From sunshine to the s. land WORD 354:23
sunlight: s. on the garden MACN 216:10
sunny: leaps S. Jim HANFF 161:6
To the s. side of the street FIEL 139:15
sunrise: Lives in Eternity's s. BLAKE 61:16
suns: blest by s. of home BROO 73:10
S., that set, may rise again JONS 187:15
sunset: beliefs may make a fine s. MADAN 216:13
cloud-continents of s.-seas ALDR 3:17
Now the s. breezes shiver NEWB 238:12
S. and evening star TENN 323:18
there's a s.-touch BROW 75:13
sunsets: I have a horror of s. PROU 255:20
Or Autumn s. exquisitely dying HUXL 177:13
sunshine: calm s. of the heart CONS 107:12
comforteth like s. after rain SHAK 300:18
digressions are the s. STER 315:15
From s. to the sunless land WORD 354:23
out into adventure and s. FORS 143:19
s. and with applause BUNY 79:2
sunt: *Sint ut s. aut non sint* CLEM 102:3
sup: shall s. with my Lord BRUCE 77:22
superbos: *subiectis et debellare s.* VIRG 339:16
superfluity: barren s. of words GARTH 148:15
superfluous: in the poorest thing s. SHAK 283:4
nothing is s. LEON 205:22
s....A supernumerary—that's all TURG 335:11
s., a very necessary thing VOLT 340:22

superfluous (*cont.*):
s. in me to point out — ADAMS 1:8
superior: embarrass the s. — SHAW 301:31
I am a most s. person — ANON 9:12
S. people never make long — MOORE 234:9
want no-one to be their s. — TOCQ 333:4
superman: I teach you the s. — NIET 239:16
It's a plane! It's S. — ANON 7:5
superstition: stamp out s. — VOLT 340:21
S. is the poetry of life — GOET 154:10
S. is the religion of feeble — BURKE 80:18
S. sets the whole world — VOLT 340:16
s. to enslave a philosophy — INGE 178:12
superstitions: to end as s. — HUXL 177:18
supped: Hobson has s. — MILT 228:4
I have s. full with horrors — SHAK 288:4
supper: Last-s.-carved-on-a-peach-stone — LANC 200:20
consider s. as a turnpike — EDW 131:6
supplications: make our common s. — BOOK 64:10
supplied: once destroyed, can never be s. — GOLD 154:18
supplies: I've just bought fresh s. — BREC 71:21
support: But to s. him after — SHAK 296:16
help and s. of the woman — EDW 131:2
no invisible means of s. — BUCH 77:27
s. me when I am in the wrong — MELB 222:22
without visible means of s. — BIER 59:8
supports: s. with insolence — JOHN 182:10
suppress: power of s. — NORT 240:8
supreme: great arts, in none s. — ARN 17:21
sure: Ever faithful, ever s. — MILT 227:9
Most s. in all His ways — NEWM 238:20
What nobody is s. about — BELL 33:21
surety: s. for a stranger — BIBLE 43:18
surface: looks dingy on the s. — PIRS 249:2
surfeit: s. by eating of a lamprey — FABY 138:7
They are as sick that s. — SHAK 288:28
surge: s. and thunder of the Odyssey — LANG 201:3
surgeon: wounded s. plies the steel — ELIOT 133:5
surmise: with a wild s. — KEATS 192:11
surprise: Live frugally on s. — WALK 341:4
Respect was mingled with s. — SCOTT 268:9
sound of s. — BALL 28:13
what gave rise to no little s. — BARH 28:19
surprised: like a guilty thing s. — WORD 355:22
S. by joy—impatient as the wind — WORD 357:4
S. by unjust force — MILT 226:18
surprises: millions of s. — HERB 167:7
S. are foolish things — AUST 22:16
surquidrie: Of s. and foul presumpcioun — CHAU 96:13
surrender: Guards die but do not s. — CAMB 88:11
we shall never s. — CHUR 99:13
survey: I am monarch of all I s. — COWP 110:18
time that takes s. of all — SHAK 278:14
When I s. the wondrous cross — WATTS 343:4
survival: s. of the fittest — ROCK 261:11
S. of the fittest — SPEN 312:17
survive: Noah dare hope to s. — HUXL 177:11
I s. — SIEY 307:1
survives: s. in the valley of its — AUDEN 20:23
survivors: dying is more the s.' affair — MANN 217:14
Susan: black-eyed S. — GAY 149:17
susceptible: peculiarly s. to calves — HUXL 177:10
peculiarly s. to draughts — WILDE 349:21
suspects: Round up the usual s. — EPST 137:12
suspenders: must *not* forget the s. — KIPL 197:23
suspension: willing s. of disbelief — COL 104:24
suspicion: banish squint s. — MILT 226:13
Caesar's wife must be above s. — CAES 87:25
sutlers: sapient s. of the Lord — ELIOT 134:5
swaddling: in s. clothes — BIBLE 51:32
swagman: Once a jolly s. — PAT 246:16
swain: a frugal s. — HOME 170:18
swains: all our s. commend her — SHAK 298:19
swallow: and the s. a nest — BOOK 67:20
come before the s. dares — SHAK 298:32

swallow (*cont.*):
O tell her, S. — TENN 327:24
speed of a s., the grace of a boy — BETJ 37:11
s. a camel — BIBLE 50:31
s. has set her six young — BROW 76:10
S., my sister, O sister — SWIN 321:15
swamps: bellowing across primeval s. — WOD 352:19
swan: He makes a s.-like end — SHAK 289:19
like a sleeping s. — SHEL 304:21
many a summer dies the s. — TENN 328:17
nothing so much as a black s. — JUV 189:7
pale s. in her watery nest — SHAK 299:9
Sweet S. of Avon — JONS 187:29
Swanee: down upon the S. River — FOST 144:12
swans: Dumb s., not chattering — SIDN 306:22
honking amongst tuneful s. — VIRG 340:3
old ships sail like s. — FLEC 141:18
saw two s. of goodly hue — SPEN 313:17
s. are geese — ARN 16:18
s. of others are geese — WALP 342:1
swarm: S. over, Death — BETJ 37:9
sway: A little rule, a little s. — DYER 129:17
sways: s. she level in her husband's — SHAK 297:30
swear: s. not by the moon — SHAK 294:33
when very angry, s. — TWAIN 336:5
swears: Money doesn't talk, it s. — DYLAN 130:3
sweat: blood, toil, tears and s. — CHUR 99:11
s. of its labourers — EIS 131:14
s. of thy face shalt thou — BIBLE 39:2
They do not s. and whine — WHIT 348:19
We spend our midday s. — QUAR 257:2
will s. but for promotion — SHAK 272:17
sweating: Quietly s. palm to palm — HUXL 177:12
sweats: regrets, and the bloody s. — WILDE 350:17
sweep: chimneys I s. and in soot — BLAKE 61:19
To s. the dust behind the door — SHAK 291:10
sweeping: The S. up the Heart — DICK 120:10
sweeps: Who s. a room — HERB 166:26
sweet: All is not s., all is not — JONS 187:5
Amazing grace! how s. the sound — NEWT 239:7
buried in so s. a place — SHEL 303:2
But then, how it was s. — BROW 75:21
come kiss me, s. and twenty — SHAK 297:23
comes in the s. o' the year — SHAK 298:26
dead thing that smells s. — THOM 330:22
full of s. days and roses — HERB 167:8
How s. the name of Jesus — NEWT 239:9
parting is such s. sorrow — SHAK 295:4
Sleep is s. to the labouring — BUNY 79:4
sleep of a labouring man is s. — BIBLE 44:15
So s. was ne'er so fatal — SHAK 293:1
Stolen waters are s. — BIBLE 43:15
s. and fair she seems — WALL 341:12
s. and low — ARMS 15:24
S. and low, sweet and low — TENN 327:19
S. are the uses of adversity — SHAK 272:14
S. is pleasure after pain — DRYD 127:20
S. is revenge — BYRON 86:2
s. reasonableness of Jesus — ARN 18:10
S. smell of success — LEHM 204:13
S. Stay-at-Home — DAV 114:22
s. the countless tongues — MANT 217:17
s. the moonlight sleeps — SHAK 290:1
s. to taste prove in digestion — SHAK 293:11
would smell as s. — SHAK 294:31
sweeten: not s. this little hand — SHAK 287:30
sweeteners: Love and scandal are the best s. — FIEL 139:9
sweeter: O s. than the berry — GAY 149:1
those unheard are s. — KEATS 191:19
sweetest: Success is counted s. — DICK 120:13
s. things turn sourest — SHAK 300:2
sweetness: its s. on the desert air — GRAY 157:9
Our s., up into one ball — MARV 221:1
strong came forth s. — BIBLE 41:3
s. and light — ARN 17:25

sweetness (*cont.*):
where s. and light failed — FORS 143:18
which are s. and light — SWIFT 319:18
With s. fills the breast — CASW 92:17
sweet peas: s., on tip-toe — KEATS 191:6
sweets: bag of boiled s. — CRIT 111:22
box where s. compacted lie — HERB 167:8
discandy, melt their s. — SHAK 271:22
Stolen s. are always sweeter — HUNT 176:16
Stolen s. are best — CIBB 100:18
S. into your list — HUNT 176:15
S. to the sweet — SHAK 277:11
swell: Thou s.! Thou witty — HART 163:11
To s. a progress, start a scene — ELIOT 134:1
swelling: prologues to the s. act — SHAK 285:10
swept: s., and garnished — BIBLE 50:3
S. it for half a year — CARR 91:21
S. with confused alarms — ARN 16:12
Swift: S. has sailed into his rest — YEATS 360:2
swift: race is not to the s. — BIBLE 44:20
race is to the s. — DAV 114:12
swifter: s. than a weaver's shuttle — BIBLE 42:30
they were s. than eagles — BIBLE 41:22
swiftness: O s. never ceasing — PEELE 247:3
swim: boys that s. on bladders — SHAK 280:18
swimmers: s. into cleanness leaping — BROO 73:9
swimming: surprise s. in the air — EDW 131:3
s. down along the Lee — SPEN 313:17
swindles: all truly great s. — HENRY 166:4
swine: pearls before s. — BIBLE 49:8
swing: and s. for it — KING 195:19
S. low, sweet chariot — ANON 10:17
Swing, s. together — CORY 108:11
We s. ungirded hips — SORL 311:15
Switzerland: S. they had brotherly love — WELL 345:5
swoons: S. to a waltz — HUXL 177:12
swoop: At one fell s. — SHAK 287:26
take away all at one s. — WEBS 344:22
sword: brave man with a s. — WILDE 350:16
father's s. he has girded on — MOORE 234:16
his terrible swift s. — HOWE 175:7
I gave them a s. — NIXON 240:4
mightier than the s. — BULW 78:11
My s., I give to him — BUNY 79:10
my s. sleep in my hand — BLAKE 61:12
nation shall not lift up s. — BIBLE 45:5
pen is worse than the s. — BURT 83:9
Of honour and the s. — CHES 97:24
not to send peace, but a s. — BIBLE 49:31
shall perish with the s. — BIBLE 51:14
sigh is the s. of an angel — BLAKE 60:18
s. is the axis of the world — DE G 116:6
s. of this stone and anvil — MAL 216:23
upon the edge of the s. — BOOK 67:15
when he first drew the s. — CLAR 101:9
swords: either dreams or s. — LOW 211:3
Keep up your bright s. — SHAK 291:31
s. into plowshares — BIBLE 45:5
s. shall play the orators — MARL 219:5
swore: My tongue s. — EUR 137:22
sworn: had I so s. as you — SHAK 286:6
sycamore: soul sat sighing by a s. — SHAK 292:26
syllable: last s. of recorded time — SHAK 288:5
syllables: S. govern the world — SELD 269:21
syllabub: s. in the hotel in Hell — SITW 307:18
syllogism: conclusion of your s. — O'BR 240:19
symbol: for the s. at your door — ANON 8:6
symbols: s. of a high romance — KEATS 192:20
symmetry: frame thy fearful s. — BLAKE 62:5
sympathise: s. with people's pains — HUXL 177:8
With her great master so to s. — MILT 227:25
sympathy: It is the secret s. — SCOTT 268:11
Tea and s. — AND 5:14
symptoms: dying of a hundred good s. — POPE 253:14
systems: Our little s. have their day — TENN 324:23

T

T: t. is silent, as in *Harlow* — ASQ 19:6
tabernacle: who shall dwell in thy t. — BOOK 66:13
table: behave mannerly at t. — STEV 317:16
carf biforn his fader at the t. — CHAU 95:14
from their masters' t. — BIBLE 50:11
from the rich man's t. — BIBLE 52:34
patient etherized upon a t. — ELIOT 133:24
prepare a t. before me — BOOK 66:18
though you cannot make a t. — JOHN 184:7
tableau: history nothing more than a t. — VOLT 340:20
Tablet: keep taking The T. — THOM 331:2
tablets: Quick, thy t., Memory — ARN 16:20
tactful: t. in audacity is knowing — COCT 103:4
taffeta: doublet of changeable t. — SHAK 297:33
T. phrases, silken terms — SHAK 284:18
tail: And, like a rat without a t. — SHAK 285:3
he's treading on my t. — CARR 91:11
Improve his shining t. — CARR 91:3
moste han a likerous t. — CHAU 96:6
O! thereby hangs a t. — SHAK 292:9
t. that wagged contempt — WATS 343:1
thy t. hangs down behind — KIPL 197:18
tailor: t. make thy doublet — SHAK 297:33
taint: I cannot t. with fear — SHAK 287:32
tainted: t. wether of the flock — SHAK 289:24
taisez-vous: T.! *Méfiez-vous* — ANON 12:15
take: big enough to t. away — FORD 143:5
O t. the nasty soup away — HOFF 169:18
T. a pair of sparkling eyes — GILB 151:7
t. away all at one swoop — WEBS 344:22
T. away these baubles — CROM 112:5
T., eat, this is my Body — BIBLE 51:9
T. the thanks of a boy — BEEC 32:5
T. up the White Man's burden — KIPL 197:15
they t. you in the morning — BALD 27:4
taken: Lord hath t. away — BIBLE 42:22
not t. in when they marry — AUST 22:18
t. away even that which — BIBLE 51:3
takes: like that it t. away — BYRON 87:9
taketh: t. away the sin — BIBLE 53:13
taking-off: deep damnation of his t. — SHAK 285:24
tale: And thereby hangs a t. — SHAK 272:22
Cuts off his t. and talks of — SHAK 282:11
I could a t. unfold — SHAK 274:30
point a moral, or adorn a t. — JOHN 183:14
sad t.'s best for winter — SHAK 298:22
t. told by an idiot — SHAK 288:5
t. which holdeth children — SIDN 306:27
tedious as a twice-told t. — SHAK 282:9
telling the saddest t. — SHAK 290:21
This most tremendous t. of all — BETJ 36:18
Trust the t. — LAWR 202:15
unvarnished t. deliver — SHAK 291:34
talent: t. to amuse — COW 109:1
Brevity is the sister of t. — CHEK 96:31
gilded tomb of a mediocre t. — SMITH 309:12
invention the t. of a liar — BYRON 87:18
T. develops in quiet places — GOET 154:11
T. does what it can — MER 223:25
t. instantly recognizes — DOYLE 126:8
t. which is death to hide — MILT 230:22
talents: career open to the t. — NAP 237:6
If you have great t. — REYN 259:8
ministry of all the t. — ANON 9:9
talk: Careless t. costs lives — ANON 6:15
English t. is a quadrille — JAMES 179:16
fold his legs and have out his t. — JOHN 185:16
gotta use words when I t. to you — ELIOT 134:16
If you can t. with crowds — KIPL 197:7
If you t. to God — SZASZ 321:25
interviewing people who can't t. — ZAPPA 361:1

talk (*cont.*):

I want to t. like a lady	SHAW 302:17
Money doesn't t., it swears	DYLAN 130:3
t. but a tinkling cymbal	BACON 24:23
t. not to me of a name	BYRON 87:10
t. with you, walk with you	SHAK 288:31
Then he will t., Good Gods	LEE 204:8
think too little and who t. too	DRYD 127:11
To t. about the rest of us	ANON 10:20
To t. of many things	CARR 91:22
world may t. of hereafter	COLL 105:4
wished him to t. on for ever	HAZL 164:1
talked: least t. about by men	PER 248:3
Lord how it t.	BEAU 31:3
not being t. about	WILDE 350:4
t. like poor Poll	GARR 148:9
talking: Had tired the sun with t.	CORY 108:13
nation t. to itself	MILL 225:6
never know what we are t.	RUSS 265:2
People t. without speaking	SIMON 307:7
soon leaves off t.	BUTL 84:20
you can stop people t.	ATTL 19:14
tall: gods, divinely t.	TENN 323:20
Jane, Jane, t. as a crane	SITW 307:16
long and the short and the t.	HUGH 175:18
t. ship and a star to steer	MAS 221:21
tambourine: Hey! Mr T. Man	DYLAN 130:5
tamper: Would never want to t.	AUDEN 20:23
Tandy: I met wid Napper T.	ANON 8:9
tangere: *Noli me t.*	BIBLE 58:22
tangles: of Neaera's hair	MILT 227:14
tantum: *T. ergo sacramentum*	THOM 330:4
T. religio potuit suadere	LUCR 212:2
taper: rainbow, or with t. light	SHAK 282:10
t. to the outward room	DONNE 123:19
tapestry: wrong side of a Turkey t.	HOW 175:8
tar: T.-baby ain't sayin' nuthin'	HARR 163:6
[T. water] is of a nature	BERK 35:16
wine that tasted of the t.	BELL 34:1
Tara: harp that once through T.'s	MOORE 234:14
tarnished: neither t. nor afraid	CHAN 94:9
Tarpeian: ringleaders from the T.	ARN 18:16
tarrieth: guest that t. but a day	BIBLE 47:31
tarry: t. the wheels of his chariots	BIBLE 40:34
You may for ever t.	HERR 167:25
tart: t. who has finally married	BAXT 30:12
tarts: by the action of two t.	MACM 215:18
Tarzan: Me T., you Jane	WEIS 345:4
task: that's the t., that is the labour	VIRG 339:12
Thou thy worldly t. hast done	SHAK 273:27
what he reads as a t.	JOHN 184:10
taste: arbiter of t.	TAC 322:7
bad t. of the smoker	ELIOT 131:20
bouquet is better than the t.	POTT 254:6
difference of t. in jokes	ELIOT 132:1
Ghastly good t.	BETJ 37:16
held together by a sense of t.	BALL 28:12
himself create the t. by which	WORD 357:13
Shakespeare wanted t.	WALP 341:18
t. a little honey	BIBLE 41:14
T. is the feminine of genius	FITZ 140:19
t. my meat	HERB 167:3
Things sweet to t. prove	SHAK 293:11
tasted: Some books are to be t.	BACON 25:14
t. that the Lord is gracious	BIBLE 57:7
tasting: T. of Flora	KEATS 191:29
Tat: *Die T. ist alles*	GOET 154:7
tatter: t. in its mortal dress	YEATS 359:21
taught: afterward he t.	CHAU 95:21
taught as if you t. them not	POPE 252:8
You t. me language	SHAK 295:35
tavern: by a good t. or inn	JOHN 185:8
So is the London T.	ANON 7:9
T. in the Town	ANON 8:5
tax: Excise. A hateful t.	JOHN 182:7

tax (*cont.*):

I t. not you, you elements	SHAK 283:7
To t. and to please	BURKE 79:26
taxation: T. without representation	OTIS 243:6
taxed: world should be t.	BIBLE 51:31
taxes: Death and t.	MITC 232:5
except death and t.	FRAN 145:15
Only the little people pay t.	HELM 165:8
Read my lips: no new t.	BUSH 83:18
taxi: If you can't leave in a t.	KALM 189:21
Like a t. throbbing waiting	ELIOT 134:27
taxing: t. machine	LOWE 211:1
Tay: Bridge of the Silv'ry T.	MCG 214:19
te: T. *Deum laudamus*	ANON 14:1
tea: And is there honey still for t.	BROO 73:8
best sweeteners of t.	FIEL 139:9
counsel take and sometimes t.	POPE 253:6
if this is t., then I want coffee	PUNCH 256:20
Retired to their t. and scandal	CONG 106:6
slavery of the t. and coffee	COBB 102:25
some sipping t.	WORD 356:4
Take some more t.	CARR 91:8
T. and sympathy	AND 5:14
t.'s out of the way	REED 258:19
teach: and gladly t.	CHAU 95:18
apt to t.	BIBLE 56:16
Even while they t., men learn	SEN 270:6
suffering what they t. in song	SHEL 303:22
t. and delight	SIDN 306:26
T. him how to live	PORT 253:27
t. his senators wisdom	BOOK 68:10
T. me, my God and King	HERB 166:25
T. me to live, that I may dread	KEN 193:22
t. the young idea how to	THOM 331:22
T. us to care and not to care	ELIOT 132:19
t. you to drink deep	SHAK 274:15
To t., convince, subdue	AUBER 19:15
teacher: A t. affects eternity	ADAMS 1:16
doctrine for the t.'s sake	DEFOE 115:18
teaches: From all that terror t.	CHES 97:24
He who cannot, t.	SHAW 301:29
teaching: t. nations how to live	MILT 231:5
teacup: crack in the t. opens	AUDEN 20:12
tear: claims the homage of a t.	BYRON 84:30
dropped a t. upon the word	STER 315:22
magnificent, without a t.	DRYD 128:20
meed of some melodious t.	MILT 227:11
shed one English t.	MAC 214:1
t.-floods, nor sigh-tempests	DONNE 124:15
T. him for his bad verses	SHAK 281:27
t. is an intellectual thing	BLAKE 60:18
t. our pleasures with rough	MARV 221:1
There has fallen a splendid t.	TENN 327:1
unanswerable t.	BYRON 85:17
Wipe the t., baby dear	LEE 347:1
tears: And kiss again with t.	TENN 327:17
blood, toil, t. and sweat	CHUR 99:11
Drop, drop, slow t.	FLET 142:8
Hence those t.	TER 329:3
His big t., for he wept well	SHEL 304:5
If you have t., prepare	SHAK 281:22
In silence and t.	BYRON 87:14
keep time with my salt t.	JONS 187:2
Like Niobe, all t.	SHAK 274:12
loosed our heart in t.	ARN 16:19
Lord God will wipe away t.	BIBLE 45:25
match with shedding t.	SHAK 294:3
mine eyes from t.	BOOK 68:20
mist of t.	THOM 331:8
news to hear and bitter t.	CORY 108:13
Nothing is here for t.	MILT 230:18
often lie too deep for t.	WORD 355:24
shall wipe away all t.	BIBLE 57:28
shall wipe away all t.	BIBLE 58:5
Smiling through her t.	HOMER 170:22

tears (*cont.*):

sow in t.	BOOK 68:29
summer tempest came her t.	TENN 327:27
t. I cannot hide	HARB 161:10
T., idle tears, I know	TENN 327:22
t. shed for things	VIRG 339:4
Time with a gift of t.	SWIN 321:3
watered heaven with their t.	BLAKE 62:6

tease: dost t. us out of thought — KEATS 191:23
t. in the High Pyrenees — BELL 34:1
teases: Because he knows it t. — CARR 91:5
teatray: Like a t. in the sky — CARR 91:7
Technik: *Vorsprung durch T.* — ANON 13:4
technology: Progress through t. — ANON 13:4
T. . . . the knack of so arranging — FRIS 146:5
tedious: Returning were as t. — SHAK 287:14
t. and brief — SHAK 291:5
teeming: has gleaned my t. brain — KEATS 192:19
teeth: And keep their t. clean — SHAK 273:16
children's t. are set on edge — BIBLE 47:5
dig our graves with our t. — SMIL 308:16
Ears like bombs and t. like — CAUS 93:9
old bitch gone in the t. — POUND 254:19
set my t. nothing on edge — SHAK 278:4
shark has pretty t. — BREC 71:18
steal the very t. out of your — ARAB 14:19
untying with t. a political knot — BIER 59:4
weeping and gnashing of t. — BIBLE 49:18
with the skin of my t. — BIBLE 42:35
teetotaller: I'm only a beer t. — SHAW 300:28
tekel: t.; Thou art weighed — BIBLE 47:12
telegrams: life of t. and anger — FORS 143:20
Telemachus: mine own T. — TENN 328:22
television: t. brought back murder — HITC 168:20
tell: Go, t. the Spartans — SIM 307:9
men of sense never t. it — SHAF 270:20
t. her she mustn't — PUNCH 256:13
T. it not in Gath — BIBLE 41:21
T. me not, Sweet, I am unkind — LOV 210:20
T. me the old, old story — HANK 161:7
T. me what you eat — BRIL 72:7
T. out my soul — BIBLE 51:28
t. sad stories of the death — SHAK 293:27
T. them I came, and no one — DE L 116:19
t. them of us and say — EDM 130:20
telling: not arguing, I am t. you — WHIS 347:9
pity beyond all t. — YEATS 359:18
Téméraire: Fighting T. — NEWB 238:12
temper: Keep me in t. — SHAK 283:1
One equal t. of heroic hearts — TENN 328:25
t. justice with mercy — MILT 229:29
truth that has lost its t. — GIBR 150:21
temperance: t. would be difficult — JOHN 186:14
temperate: more lovely and more t. — SHAK 299:12
temperature: t. not naturally its own — SCH 267:26
tempered: t. by war, disciplined — KENN 194:2
tempest: Like summer t. came her tears — TENN 327:27
Yet it shall be t.-tost — SHAK 285:4
tempests: nor sigh't. move — DONNE 124:15
temple: his train filled the t. — BIBLE 45:10
t. of silence and reconciliation — MAC 213:14
t. of the Holy Ghost — BIBLE 55:4
temples: And the t. of his Gods — MAC 214:3
solemn t., the great globe — SHAK 296:10
theatres, and t. lie — WORD 354:15
out of which they build t. — KRIS 199:4
tempora: *O t., O mores!* — CIC 100:25
T. mutantur, et nos mutamur — ANON 14:2
temps: *A la recherche du t. perdu* — PROU 255:17
Ô t.! suspend ton vol — LAM 199:21
tempt: not t. the Lord thy God — BIBLE 48:17
T. not a desperate man — SHAK 295:22
temptation: And lead us not into t. — BIBLE 48:27
combines the maximum of t. — SHAW 301:30
insist on their resisting t. — KNOX 198:21

temptation (*cont.*):

resist everything except t.	WILDE 349:24
t. in the wilderness	BOOK 68:1
t. is the greatest treason	ELIOT 134:7
that ye enter not into t.	BIBLE 51:13

temptations: But in spite of all t. — GILB 152:21
tempus: *T. edax rerum* — OVID 243:16
t. fugit — VIRG 340:9
ten: Church clock at t. to three — BROO 73:8
t. or twelve strokes of havoc — HOPK 171:24
1066 and All That — SELL 269:23
T. thousand times t. thousand — BIBLE 47:15
tenantless: graves stood t. — SHAK 274:1
tenants: T. of life's middle state — COWP 110:16
T. of the house — ELIOT 133:16
tendebantque: *T. manus* — VIRG 339:15
tendency: Groucho t. — ANON 12:7
tender: I'll be irreproachably t. — MAY 222:15
t. for another's pain — GRAY 157:13
t. is the night — KEATS 192:1
true and t. is the North — TENN 327:24
tenders: shoal of fools for t. — CONG 106:17
ténébreux: *Je suis le t.* — NERV 238:8
tenement: informed the t. of clay — DRYD 127:6
tennis: t. with the net down — FROST 146:26
tennis-balls: merely the stars' t. — WEBS 344:21
Tennyson: bower we shrined to T. — HARDY 162:3
Lawn T., gentleman poet — JOYCE 188:15
T. and Browning — BAG 26:17
tenor: They kept the noiseless t. — GRAY 157:10
tent: inside the t. pissing out — JOHN 181:21
Upon that little t. of blue — WILDE 350:15
tenth: The Submerged T. — BOOTH 69:21
tents: Israel's t. do shine — BLAKE 61:14
Shall fold their t. — LONG 209:13
stately t. of war — MARL 219:4
t. of ungodliness — BOOK 67:22
termagant: whipped for o'erdoing T. — SHAK 276:5
terminological: t. inexactitude — CHUR 99:4
terms: hard to come to t. with Him — MOL 232:23
terrible: being just the t. choice — BROW 77:10
isn't life a t. thing — THOM 330:19
t. beauty is born — YEATS 359:3
T. that old life of decency — LOW 211:11
that t. football club — MCGR 214:22
Then lend the eye a t. aspect — SHAK 279:5
territorial: last t. claim — HITL 169:2
territory: It comes with the t. — MILL 225:4
terror: added a new t. to death — WETH 347:2
added another t. to death — LYND 212:19
afraid for any t. by night — BOOK 67:29
From all that t. teaches — CHES 97:24
T. the human form divine — BLAKE 62:7
terrorist: t. and the policeman — CONR 107:9
terrors: little t. — GAV 148:21
new t. of Death — ARB 14:24
t. of the earth — SHAK 283:5
terse: nervous and t. — DOYLE 126:7
Tess: ended his sport with T. — HARDY 161:25
test: t. of a vocation — SMITH 309:11
testament: purple t. of bleeding war — SHAK 294:1
testicles: tragedy requires t. — VOLT 340:25
testing: every virtue at the t. point — LEWIS 206:13
text: great t. in Galatians — BROW 77:12
where a neat rivulet of t. — SHER 306:3
Thames: Not of Gennesareth, but T. — THOM 331:17
Oh shall I see the T. again — BETJ 37:1
stripling T. at Bab-lock-hithe — ARN 17:7
Sweet T., run softly — SPEN 313:18
T. bordered by its gardens — MORR 235:16
T. is liquid history — BURNS 81:20
thank: And t. heaven, fasting — SHAK 273:6
Now t. we all our God — WINK 352:4
T. me no thankings — SHAK 295:20
t. thee, that I am not as other men — BIBLE 52:38

thankless: To have a t. child — SHAK 282:25
Upon a t. arrant — RAL 257:21
thanks: for this relief much t. — SHAK 273:30
give t. unto thee — BOOK 65:15
I will give t. unto thee — BOOK 69:7
O give t. unto the Lord — BOOK 69:1
Take the t. of a boy — BEEC 32:5
T. be to God — MISS 231:14
T. for mercies past receive — BUCK 78:3
T. for the memory — ROBIN 260:19
thanksgiving: presence with t. — BOOK 67:31
that: man's a man for a' t. — BURNS 82:8
thatch: vines that round the t.-eaves — KEATS 192:14
Weeded and worn the ancient t. — TENN 326:22
thcream: t. till I'm thick — CROM 111:23
theatre: I like the t., but never — HART 163:9
t. of man's life — BACON 24:1
theatres: t., and temples lie — WORD 354:15
thee: Dreamin' of t.! — WALL 341:7
queer save t. and me — OWEN 243:18
theft: clever t. was praiseworthy — SPEN 312:20
Property is t. — PROU 255:16
would be t. in other poets — DRYD 128:29
theme: It was a t. for reason — DONNE 124:1
pudding — it has no t. — CHUR 100:8
theorize: mistake to t. before — DOYLE 126:5
theory: All t. is grey — GOET 154:5
[biography] is life without t. — DISR 121:28
sometimes fiction, sometimes t. — MAC 213:22
t. is found to be against — EDD 130:11
there: Because it's t. — MALL 216:22
I met a man who wasn't t. — MEAR 222:18
T. but for the grace of God — BRAD 71:6
t. when they crucified — ANON 11:14
thereby: O! t. hangs a tail — SHAK 292:9
therein: and all that t. is — BOOK 66:19
thermodynamics: second law of t. — EDD 130:11
Thermopylae: old man of T. — LEAR 203:16
they: t. are not they — WAUGH 343:16
thick: one can lay it on so t. — BUTL 84:9
thcream till I'm t. — CROM 111:23
t. and numberless as the gay — MILT 226:23
T. as autumnal leaves — MILT 228:14
thicker: History gets t. as — TAYL 322:22
shall be t. than my father — BIBLE 41:33
thicket: ram caught in a t. — BIBLE 39:16
thief: Behold, I come as a t. — BIBLE 58:1
Opportunity makes a t. — BACON 25:24
Pleasure is a t. to business — DEFOE 115:11
Procrastination is the t. of time — YOUNG 360:19
steals something from the t. — SHAK 291:37
Time the subtle t. of youth — MILT 230:20
thieves: fell among t. — BIBLE 52:11
have made it a den of t. — BIBLE 50:27
One of the t. was saved — BECK 31:11
T. respect property — CHES 98:11
union of two t. — BIER 59:2
where t. break through — BIBLE 49:1
thievish: Time's t. progress — SHAK 299:26
thigh: smote them hip and t. — BIBLE 41:4
thimbles: They sought it with t. — CARR 92:9
thin: in every fat man a t. one — CONN 106:28
t. man inside every fat man — ORW 241:25
T. red line of 'eroes — KIPL 197:11
t. red line tipped with steel — RUSS 265:7
tho' t., yet never clear — POPE 250:15
thine: For t. is the kingdom — BIBLE 48:27
thing: do that t. that ends all other — SHAK 272:2
is it not the t. — BYRON 87:19
National Debt a Good T. — SELL 269:24
play's the t. — SHAK 275:24
sort of t. they like — LINC 207:12
T. as he sees It — KIPL 197:13
t. enskyed and sainted — SHAK 288:10

thing (cont.):
Thou art the t. itself — SHAK 283:14
thingish: thing which seemed T. — MILNE 225:15
things: all t. to all men — BIBLE 55:8
as t. have been, t. remain — CLOU 102:22
confused t. with their names — SART 267:5
do all t. through Christ — BIBLE 56:10
earnest of the t. that they — TENN 326:9
excellent t. are spoken — BOOK 67:24
for t. they didn't know — POUND 254:13
God's sons are t. — MADD 216:14
infection of t. gone — LOW 211:20
I will do such t. — SHAK 283:5
just one of those t. — PORT 253:21
More t. are wrought by prayer — TENN 324:21
nor t. to come — BIBLE 54:42
O all ye Green T. — BOOK 64:1
people don't do such t. — IBSEN 178:5
shape of t. to come — WELLS 345:23
So little done, such t. to be — TENN 325:14
tears shed for t. and mortality — VIRG 339:4
These t. shall be! — SYM 321:20
T. ain't what they used to be — PERS 248:6
T. are but as straw dogs — LAO-T 201:11
T. are in the saddle — EMER 136:13
t. are the sons of heaven — JOHN 182:4
T. fall apart — YEATS 359:24
t. to come — SHAK 296:32
t. unknown proposed — POPE 252:8
what T. think about men — JENN 181:5
think: And t. by fits and starts — HOUS 174:10
And t., this heart — BROO 73:10
comedy to those that t. — WALP 341:23
don't t. foolishly — JOHN 186:3
Don't t. twice, it's all right — DYLAN 130:1
For those who greatly t. — POPE 250:23
In all I t. or speak or do — WESL 346:5
I t., therefore I am — DESC 117:9
know what I t. till I see what — WALL 341:11
must do then, t. now before — DONNE 123:16
not so t. as you drunk I am — SQUI 314:3
people that t., and fox-hunters — SHEN 305:21
something with them besides t. — LOOS 210:7
so we've got to t. — RUTH 265:9
then I don't t. much of it — STR 318:16
t. of England — HILL 168:17
T. of your forefathers — ADAMS 2:4
t. only this of me — BROO 73:10
t. on these things — BIBLE 56:9
t. too little and who talk — DRYD 127:11
whether machines t. — SKIN 308:5
you can't make her t. — PARK 245:14
thinking: It ain't t. about it — TROL 334:15
Plain living and high t. — WORD 356:1
t. for themselves is what — GILB 151:13
t. makes it so — SHAK 275:14
t. reed — PASC 246:6
t. what nobody has thought — SZEN 322:3
thought of t. for myself at all — GILB 152:19
thinks: he t. no ill — SHAK 299:20
He t. too much — SHAK 281:1
Sometimes I sits and t. — PUNCH 256:21
t. he knows everything — SHAW 301:13
third: A t. event to me — DICK 120:11
separately plunder a t. — BIER 59:2
thirst: shall never t. — BIBLE 53:22
neither t. any more — BIBLE 57:27
t. after righteousness — BIBLE 48:19
thirsty: As cold waters to a t. soul — BIBLE 43:37
if he be t., give him water — BIBLE 43:36
thirteen: clocks were striking t. — ORW 242:5
thirty: At t. a man suspects himself — YOUNG 360:20
past t., and three parts iced over — ARN 18:7
T. days hath September — ANON 11:2
t. pieces of silver — BEVAN 38:4

thirty (*cont.*):

t. pieces of silver	BIBLE 51:7

thorn: Oak, Ash, and T.

	KIPL 197:1
t. in the flesh	BIBLE 55:28
without t. the rose	MILT 229:8

thorns: crackling of t. under a pot

	BIBLE 44:16
crown of t. *and* the thirty	BEVAN 38:4
fall upon the t. of life	SHEL 304:8
No t. go as deep as a rose's	SWIN 321:3
once was crowned with t.	KELLY 193:19
t. shall come up in her	BIBLE 46:3

thou: t. art not he or she

	WAUGH 343:16
T. shalt have no other	BIBLE 40:3
T. swell! Thou witty	HART 163:11

thought: beautiful clean t.

	LAWR 202:17
does not seem a moment's t.	YEATS 358:13
Expression is the dress of t.	POPE 252:2
father, Harry, to that t.	SHAK 278:27
forced into a state of t.	GALS 147:18
Grave without t.	CHUR 98:26
green t. in a green shade	MARV 220:16
I thought he t. I slept	PATM 246:17
Jesu, the very t. of Thee	CASW 92:17
Language is the dress of t.	JOHN 182:19
library is t. in cold storage	SAM 266:10
men use t. only to justify	VOLT 340:14
no t. for the morrow	BIBLE 49:5
One single grateful t.	LESS 206:5
one t. more steady	FORD 143:11
passion-wingèd Ministers of t.	SHEL 303:5
Perish the t.	CIBB 100:16
rear the tender t.	THOM 331:22
Religion is the frozen t.	KRIS 199:4
Restored to life, and power, and t.	KEBLE 193:16
Roman t. hath struck him	SHAK 271:6
sessions of sweet silent t.	SHAK 299:16
sinned exceedingly in t.	MISS 231:11
speech created t.	SHEL 304:20
Style is the dress of t.	WESL 346:18
t. charged with emotion	GIDE 151:1
T. is free	SHAK 296:7
T. is the child of Action	DISR 122:9
t. is viscous	ADAMS 1:21
T. shall be the harder	ANON 11:5
t.'s the slave of life	SHAK 278:14
thou pleasing, dreadful t.	ADD 2:18
through strange seas of T.	WORD 356:10
to have loved, to have t.	ARN 16:14
very life-blood of t.	FLAU 141:10
What oft was t., but ne'er	POPE 252:1
white, celestial t.	VAUG 337:7
with the pale cast of t.	SHAK 275:26
working-house of t.	SHAK 280:1
you sit alone with your t.	BOND 63:9

thoughts: generate misleading t.

	SPEN 312:18
Good t. his only friends	CAMP 89:3
Hunter's waking t.	AUDEN 20:16
I do begin to have bloody t.	SHAK 296:11
only to conceal their t.	VOLT 340:14
pansies, that's for t.	SHAK 277:2
Secret t. and open countenance	ALB 3:13
sensations rather than of t.	KEATS 192:24
Staled are my t.	DYER 129:15
t. are not your thoughts	BIBLE 46:22
t. by England given	BROO 73:10
t. of a prisoner	SOLZ 311:1
t. of youth are long, long t.	LONG 209:21
T., that breathe, and words	GRAY 157:18
T. that do often lie too deep	WORD 355:24
t. unnatural	SHAK 292:13
Words without t. never	SHAK 276:18

thousand: better than a t.

	BOOK 67:22
difference of forty t. men	WELL 345:13
end of a t. years of history	GAIT 147:12
good woman if I had five t.	THAC 329:21

thousand (*cont.*):

night has a t. eyes	BOUR 70:12
Night hath a t. eyes	LYLY 212:18
not in a t. years	SMITH 309:9
O for a t. tongues to sing	WESL 346:4
Ring in the t. years of peace	TENN 325:26
ten t. t. are their tongues	WATTS 343:3
Ten t. times ten thousand	BIBLE 47:15
t. ages in Thy sight	WATTS 343:14
t. thousand slimy things	COL 104:12
Would he had blotted a t.	JONS 187:32

thousands: limp father of t.

	JOYCE 188:16
Where t. equally were meant	SWIFT 320:24

thrall: Thee hath in t.

	KEATS 191:10

thread: t. of my own hand's weaving

	KEATS 191:3

threatened: t. its life with a railway-share

	CARR 92:9

three: married life t. is company

	WILDE 349:17
quite a t.-pipe problem	DOYLE 125:15
tell you t. times is true	CARR 92:6
Though he was only t.	MILNE 225:20
t. events in his life	LA BR 199:14
t. gentlemen at once	SHER 306:2
T. hours a day will produce	TROL 334:12
T. in One and One in Three	ALEX 4:5
T. little maids from school	GILB 151:21
t. men, still hungry	CRANE 111:2
t. o'clock in the morning	FITZ 140:22
t. o'clock in the morning	THOR 332:10
T. quarks for Muster Mark	JOYCE 188:5
t. years old is half his height	LEON 205:23
When shall we t. meet again	SHAK 284:25
when two or t. are gathered	BOOK 64:10
whole is divided into t.	CAES 87:24
would give him t. sides	MONT 233:21

threescore: t. years and ten

	BOOK 67:26

thrice: T. is he armed that hath

	SHAK 280:8

thrift: Thrift, t., Horatio

	SHAK 274:25

thrive: t. without one grain

	DRYD 127:28

throat: feel the fog in my t.

	BROW 77:2
fishbone in the city's t.	LOW 211:13
taking life by the t.	FROST 146:27
your t. 'tis hard to slit	KING 195:19

throne: Bust outlasts the t.

	DOBS 122:25
Gehenna or up to the T.	KIPL 196:20
light which beats upon a t.	TENN 324:1
like a burnished t.	SHAK 271:14
Lord sitting upon a t.	BIBLE 45:10
royal t. of kings	SHAK 293:16
t. and thy kingly crown	ELL 136:1
t. he sits on, nor the tide of pomp	SHAK 279:16
t. of bayonets	INGE 178:14
t. of Denmark	SHAK 274:4
T. sent word to a Throne	KIPL 196:25

through: best way out is always t.

	FROST 146:22
do *you* read books t.?	JOHN 184:26
T. all the changing scenes	TATE 322:17
T. them we pass out into	FORS 143:19
T. the night of doubt	BAR 29:2

thrown: t. out, as good for nothing

	JOHN 183:19

thrush: aged t., frail, gaunt

	HARDY 162:6
That's the wise t.	BROW 76:2

thrust: guardsman's cut and t.

	HUXL 177:16

Thule: *Ultima T.*

	VIRG 340:5

thumb: puts his t. in the scale

	LAWR 202:12

thumbs: By the pricking of my t.

	SHAK 287:18
his t. are off at last	HOFF 169:22

thunder: like t. outer China

	KIPL 196:21
such sweet t.	SHAK 291:2
Glorious the t.'s roar	SMART 308:13
In t., lightning, or in rain	SHAK 284:25
surge and t. of the Odyssey	LANG 201:3
they steal my t.	DENN 117:2
t. of the captains	BIBLE 43:5

thunderbolt: like a t. he falls

	TENN 323:21

thunderbolts: oak-cleaving t.

	SHAK 283:6

tomorrow: in next week t.   GRAH 156:6
   Leave t. behind   COW 108:19
   no t. hath, nor yesterday   DONNE 123:22
   such a day t. as to-day   SHAK 298:21
   T., and to-morrow   SHAK 288:5
   t. is another day   MITC 232:7
   t. we shall die   BIBLE 45:24
   too late t. to be brave   ARMS 16:2
   Unborn T., and dead YESTERDAY   FITZ 140:11
   you can put off till t.   PUNCH 256:8
tomorrows: dividend from time's t.   SASS 267:10
   For your t. these gave   EDM 130:20
tom-tit: by a river a little t.   GILB 152:7
tone: look at me in that t. of voice   PUNCH 256:17
   t. of the company   CHES 97:7
tones: Sweet t. remembered not   SHEL 303:24
tongs: t. and the bones   SHAK 290:35
tongue: English t. a gallimaufry   SPEN 313:20
   For God's sake hold your t.   DONNE 123:24
   for I must hold my t.   SHAK 274:13
   From lies of t. and pen   CHES 97:24
   his t. dropped manna   MILT 228:23
   his t. is the clapper   SHAK 291:21
   Keep thy t. from evil   BOOK 66:25
   Love's t. is in the eyes   FLET 142:9
   My heart and t. employ   TATE 322:17
   My t. is the pen   BOOK 67:5
   My t. swore, but my mind's   EUR 137:22
   nor t. to speak here   LENT 205:20
   Now, my t., the mystery telling   THOM 330:3
   obnoxious to each carping t.   BRAD 71:12
   on every infant's t.   CALV 88:8
   put a t. in every wound   SHAK 281:26
   Silence is become her mother t.   GOLD 155:7
   Sing, my t., the glorious   FORT 144:4
   t. is the only edged tool   IRV 178:19
   t. not understood   BOOK 69:18
   t. of midnight hath told   SHAK 291:9
   t. taking a trip of three   NAB 236:18
   t. to persuade   CLAR 101:10
   trippingly on the t.   SHAK 276:4
   use of my oracular t.   SHER 305:29
   would not yield to the t.   BIER 59:4
tongueless: t. vigil and all the pain   SWIN 321:1
tongues: Finds t. in trees   SHAK 272:14
   He came in t. of living flame   AUBER 19:15
   lack t. to praise   SHAK 300:5
   O for a thousand t. to sing   WESL 346:4
   silver-sweet sound lovers' t.   SHAK 295:3
   Sweet the countless t. united   MANT 217:17
   Though I speak with the t.   BIBLE 55:11
   thousand thousand are their t.   WATTS 343:3
   time in the t.   SHAK 297:16
tonight: Not t., Josephine   NAP 237:8
tonnage: New York swallowing the t.   MILL 225:5
too: T. kind, too kind   NIGH 240:1
   T. small to live   ANON 11:8
took: 'E went an' t.   KIPL 197:14
   person you and I t. me for   CARL 90:3
   stranger, and ye t. me in   BIBLE 51:5
tool: Science is an edged t.   EDD 130:13
   tongue is the only edged t.   IRV 178:19
tool-making: Man is a t. animal   FRAN 145:16
tools: For secrets are edged t.   DRYD 128:16
   give us the t. and we will   CHUR 99:16
   t. to him that can handle   CARL 90:8
   Without t. he is nothing   CARL 90:21
tooth: danger of her former t.   SHAK 287:3
   Eye for eye, t. for tooth   BIBLE 40:10
   hadde alwey a coltes t.   CHAU 96:7
   Nature, red in t. and claw   TENN 325:12
   sharper than a serpent's t.   SHAK 282:25
   where each t.-point goes   KIPL 196:26
toothache: Venerable Mother T.   HEAT 164:13

top: Life is a t. which whipping   GREV 158:18
   There is always room at the t.   WEBS 344:12
   t. thing in the world   KEATS 193:12
toper: t. whose untutored sense   CRAB 110:21
topless: t. towers of Ilium   MARL 218:11
torch: bright t., and a casement   KEATS 192:9
   runners relay the t. of life   LUCR 212:5
   t. borne in the wind   CHAP 94:15
   t. has been passed   KENN 194:2
   Truth, like a t.   HAM 160:17
torches: teach the t. to burn bright   SHAK 294:26
torchlight: t. procession   O'SUL 243:5
Tories: are T. born wicked   ANON 9:6
   T. own no argument   BROW 74:25
torments: t. also may in length   MILT 228:26
   t. lie in the small circle   CIBB 100:13
tornado: set off a t. in Texas   LOR 210:10
torrent: down the t. of his fate   JOHN 183:16
torrents: t. of her myriad universe   TENN 326:21
tortoise: t.-like, but not so slow   MARV 221:3
torture: t. one poor word   DRYD 128:6
torturer: life and the t.'s horse   AUDEN 21:2
Tory: burning hatred for the T.   BEVAN 37:18
   T. men and Whig measures   DISR 121:25
   T.'s secret weapon   KILM 195:2
tossed: t. you down into the field   FITZ 140:13
tossing: t. about in a steamer   GILB 151:16
total: t. solution of the Jewish   GOER 154:1
totter: charming to t. into vogue   WALP 341:19
totters: Who t. forth, wrapped   SHEL 305:15
touch: Can t. him further   SHAK 287:4
   Do not t. me   BIBLE 58:22
   He wants the natural t.   SHAK 287:23
   One t. of nature makes   SHAK 297:6
   T. me not   BIBLE 54:6
   T. not the cat but a glove   SCOTT 268:25
   t. of a vanished hand   TENN 323:11
   t. of earthly years   WORD 356:25
   t. of Harry in the night   SHAK 279:8
   with gentle hand t.   WORD 355:16
touched: t. none that he did not adorn   JOHN 185:12
   T. to the quick, he said   BROW 76:8
touches: silent t. of time   BURKE 81:10
   t. of sweet harmony   SHAK 290:1
   Who t. this touches a man   WHIT 348:14
toucheth: t. pitch shall be defiled   BIBLE 48:2
tough: t. get going   KENN 194:10
   statements interesting, but t.   TWAIN 335:19
toujours: T. perdrix!   ANON 12:16
tourist: loathsome is the British t.   KILV 195:3
tous: T. pour un, un pour tous   DUMAS 129:4
tout: t. n'est qu'ordre et beauté   BAUD 30:4
toves: slithy t.   CARR 91:15
tow: thou shouldst t. me after   SHAK 271:18
tower: Child Roland to the dark t.   SHAK 283:18
   Fighting in the captain's t.   DYLAN 129:20
   from yonder ivy-mantled t.   GRAY 157:5
   Giotto's t.   LONG 209:18
   name is a t. of strength   SHAK 294:20
   watchman on the lonely t.   SCOTT 268:16
   with the blasted t.   NERV 238:8
towered: T. cities please us then   MILT 227:6
towers: cloud-capped t.   SHAK 296:10
   spires, ye antique t.   GRAY 157:11
   t. the last enchantments   ARN 18:2
   With walls and t. were girdled   COL 103:22
towery: T. city and branchy   HOPK 172:2
town: Come sounding through the t.   BALL 27:15
   Country in the t.   MART 220:8
   destroy the t. to save it   ANON 8:10
   down to the end of the t.   MILNE 225:20
   each and every t. or city   HOLM 170:14
   haunted t. it is to me   LANG 201:1
   man made the t.   COWP 110:6

treasury: T. is the spring   BAG 26:4
 T. were to fill old bottles   KEYN 194:16
treat: Talk about a t.   COLL 105:6
 t. if met where any bar   HARDY 162:13
treaties: T. are like girls   DE G 116:4
treaty: not a peace t., an armistice   FOCH 142:15
 signed the t. bred a fever   THOM 330:11
tree: billboard lovely as a t.   NASH 237:17
 If he finds that this t.   KNOX 198:18
 I shall be like that t.   SWIFT 320:26
 more to my mind than a t.   MORR 235:11
 On a t. by a river a little   GILB 152:7
 only God can make a t.   KILM 195:1
 poem lovely as a t.   KILM 194:22
 t. of actual life springs   GOET 154:5
 t. of liberty must be refreshed   JEFF 180:21
 t. of life   BIBLE 43:21
 t. of the knowledge of good   BIBLE 38:19
 t. that a wise man sees   BLAKE 61:4
 t. were for the healing   BIBLE 58:7
 Under the greenwood t.   SHAK 272:19
 Woodman, spare that t.   MORR 235:13
 woodman, spare the beechen t.   CAMP 88:17
treen: t. priests and golden chalices   JEWEL 181:14
trees: And all the t. are green   KING 195:17
 die when the t. were green   CLARE 101:3
 I see men as t., walking   BIBLE 51:22
 Loveliest of t., the cherry now   HOUS 174:16
 music of its t. at dawn   ARN 16:21
 Orpheus with his lute made t.   SHAK 280:16
 Generations pass while some t.   BROW 74:6
 t. and the houses go wheeling   THOM 332:2
 t. that grow so fair   KIPL 197:1
 T., where you sit   POPE 253:1
 t. will never get across   FROST 146:16
 With rocks, and stones, and t.   WORD 356:25
Trelawny: And shall T. die   HAWK 163:17
tremble: t. for my country   JEFF 180:24
trembled: T. the mariners   ANAT 5:10
tremblers: boding t. learned to trace   GOLD 154:23
trembling: salvation with fear and t.   BIBLE 56:6
 T. in her soft and chilly nest   KEATS 190:19
tremulous: postern behind my t. stay   HARDY 162:2
trencher-friends: t., time's flies   SHAK 296:20
trencher-man: very valiant t.   SHAK 291:12
trespass: And t. there and go   HOUS 174:14
trespasses: And forgive us our t.   BOOK 63:16
tress: A little stolen t.   YEATS 359:27
tresses: t. man's imperial race insnare   POPE 253:4
trial: T. by jury itself   DENM 116:27
 t. if I recognize it as such   KAFKA 189:17
 t. is by what is contrary   MILT 230:31
triangle: The eternal t.   ANON 6:29
triangles: If t. were to make a God   MONT 233:21
tribe: badge of all our t.   SHAK 289:4
 may his t. increase   HUNT 176:12
 purify the dialect of the t.   ELIOT 133:9
 Richer than all his t.   SHAK 293:5
tribeless: t., and nationless   SHEL 304:22
tribulation: came out of great t.   BIBLE 57:26
tribute: To his feet thy t. bring   LYTE 212:21
trick: conjuring t. with bones   JENK 181:4
 dream when the long t.'s over   MAS 222:2
 T. that everyone abhors   BELL 33:10
 When in doubt, win the t.   HOYLE 175:12
tricks: Frustrate their knavish t.   ANON 7:14
 t. are either knavish   JOHN 185:23
tried: Christian ideal not t.   CHES 98:15
 she for a little t.   WOTT 357:17
trifle: t. with the spoon   POPE 251:25
trifles: She who t. with all   GAY 149:9
 snapper-up of unconsidered t.   SHAK 298:27
 T. light as air   SHAK 292:18
trigger: Whose finger do you want on the t.
                                                           ANON 11:21

Trinity: strong name of the T.   ALEX 4:5
trip: Come, and t. it as ye go   MILT 227:2
triple: t. cord, which no man   BURKE 79:21
trippingly: t. on the tongue   SHAK 276:4
triste: jamais t. archy   MARQ 219:19
tristesse: Bonjour t.   ÉLUA 136:9
Tristram: let call him T.   MAL 217:1
 T. Shandy did not last   JOHN 185:7
Triton: this T. of the minnows   SHAK 273:18
 T. blow his wreathèd horn   WORD 357:11
triumph: for evil to t.   BURKE 81:13
 in t. from the north   MAC 213:25
 meet with t. and disaster   KIPL 197:6
 Now is the Victor's t. won   POTT 253:28
 there is no glory in the t.   CORN 108:1
 T. in God above   GURN 159:11
 t. of hope over experience   JOHN 184:24
 t. of modern science   WAUGH 344:1
 t. of the embalmer's art   VIDAL 338:12
trivial: t. people should muse   LAWR 202:24
 T. personalities decomposing   WOOLF 353:20
 t. round, the common task   KEBLE 193:17
trivialities: t. where opposites   BOHR 63:1
Troilus: T. methinks mounted   SHAK 289:31
Trojan: T. 'orses will jump out   BEVIN 38:10
troop: T. home to churchyards   SHAK 290:34
troops: charged the t. of error   BROW 74:9
trophies: her weedy t.   SHAK 277:7
tropical: night of t. splendour   PORT 253:18
trouble: Double, double toil and t.   SHAK 287:15
 few days, and full of t.   BIBLE 42:33
 Gold? a transient, shining t.   GRAI 156:7
 has t. enough of its own   WILC 349:14
 In t. and in joy   TATE 322:17
 it is not our t.   MARQ 219:20
 Man is born unto t.   BIBLE 42:29
 present help in time of t.   ANON 5:18
 There may be t. ahead   BERL 35:22
 To-day the Roman and his t.   HOUS 174:23
 transcendent capacity of taking t.   CARL 90:10
 very present help in t.   BOOK 67:6
 Wenlock Edge the wood's in t.   HOUS 174:22
 When there's t. brewing   LYLE 198:13
troubled: heart be t.   BIBLE 53:36
 Like a bridge over t. water   SIMON 307:5
 t. with her lonely life   PEPYS 247:16
troubles: against a sea of t.   SHAK 275:25
 From t. of the world   HARV 163:15
 your t. in your old kit-bag   ASAF 18:17
troubling: wicked cease from t.   BIBLE 42:27
trousers: bottoms of my t. rolled   ELIOT 134:2
 not a man, but—a cloud in t.   MAY 222:15
 t. on when you go out   IBSEN 178:3
trout: grey t. lies asleep   HOGG 170:7
 you find a t. in the milke   THOR 332:5
trowel: should lay it on with a t.   DISR 122:20
Troy: ringing plains of windy T.   TENN 328:21
 sacked T.'s sacred city   HOMER 171:1
 T. came destined an exile   VIRG 338:23
 Where's T., and where's   BRAM 71:13
truant: t. disposition, good my lord   SHAK 274:14
trucks: lot to learn about t.   AWDRY 23:13
true: And is it t.? And is it true   BETJ 36:18
 as t. a lover as ever sighed   SHAK 272:18
 by the people as equally t.   GIBB 150:10
 dark and t. and tender   TENN 327:24
 England to itself do rest but t.   SHAK 282:15
 He said t. things, but called   BROW 75:16
 in her ear, 'You are not t.'   WILB 349:10
 Let God be t.   BIBLE 54:29
 my shape as t.   SHAK 282:20
 pessimist fears this is t.   CAB 87:23

true *(cont.)*:

ring in the t.	TENN 325:23
should always say what's t.	STEV 317:16
speak t., right wrong	TENN 324:5
tell you three times is t.	CARR 92:6
to thine own self be t.	SHAK 274:23
t. because a man dies for it	WILDE 350:7
t. love hath my heart	SIDN 306:15
t. to thyself as thou be not false	BACON 25:21
unfaithful kept him falsely t.	TENN 324:9
What! can the devil speak t.	SHAK 285:9
Whatsoever things are t.	BIBLE 56:9
what we are saying is t.	RUSS 265:2

truffles: Thy t., Perigord! — POPE 250:21

trump: at the last t.	BIBLE 55:21
with the sound of the t.	BOOK 67:8

trumpet: heard the sound of the t. — BIBLE 40:27

t. shall sound — BIBLE 55:21

trumpets: among the t., Ha, ha	BIBLE 43:5
foie gras to the sound of t.	SMITH 310:11
snarling t. 'gan to chide	KEATS 190:16
Sound the t., beat the drums	MOR 235:5
t. came out brazenly	LAWR 202:28
t. sounded for him	BUNY 79:11

trust: All power is a t. — DISR 122:10

hope for the best, and t. in God	SMITH 310:1
In t. I have found treason	ELIZ 135:5
man assumes a public t.	JEFF 181:1
Never t. the artist	LAWR 202:15
no more than power in t.	DRYD 127:10
O put not your t. in princes	BOOK 69:9
put no t. in the future	HOR 173:20
Put your t. in God	BLAC 59:22
t. me not at all or all in all	TENN 324:14
T. one who has gone through it	VIRG 339:22
t. themselves with men	SHAK 296:17
t. was with the eternal	MILT 228:22
was not property but a t.	FOX 144:15
Whose t., ever childlike	STR 318:17

trusted: familiar friend, whom I t. — BOOK 67:2

in thee have I t. — BOOK 63:22

trustworthiness: Carthaginian t. — SALL 266:9

trusty: T., dusky, vivid, true — STEV 317:20

truth: beauty and t. — KEATS 193:1

Beauty is t., truth beauty	KEATS 191:24
Bigotry tries to keep t.	TAG 322:9
Christianity better than T.	COL 104:23
cinema is t. 24 times per	GOD 153:18
dead we owe only t.	VOLT 340:24
dearer still is t.	ARIS 15:22
diminution of the love of t.	JOHN 182:12
economical with the t.	ARMS 16:6
fight for freedom and t.	IBSEN 178:3
Great is t., and it prevails	BIBLE 58:23
Great is T., and mighty	BIBLE 47:27
great is t., and shall prevail	BROO 73:14
His t. is marching on	HOWE 175:7
improbable, must be the t.	DOYLE 126:1
irreconcilable foes to t.	BUCK 78:1
Is there in t. no beauty	HERB 167:1
It is the light of T.	DICK 118:3
Justice is t. in action	DISR 121:12
lawyer interprets the t.	GIR 153:6
least touch of t.	BYRON 87:16
loins girt about with t.	BIBLE 56:4
love Scotland better than t.	JOHN 182:14
mainly he told the t.	TWAIN 335:18
mathematics possesses not only t.	RUSS 265:3
Mercy and t. are met together	BOOK 67:23
murder, for the t.	ADLER 3:2
neither T. nor Falsehood	HOBB 169:5
never ending battle for t.	ANON 7:5
new scientific t.	PLAN 249:12
not t., but things like t.	CHAP 94:19
plain t. for plain people	WESL 346:14

truth *(cont.)*:

positive in error as in t.	LOCKE 208:17
possession of t.	LOCKE 208:15
Prime Ministers wedded to the t.	SAKI 265:22
ridicule is the best test of t.	CHES 97:15
stark naked t.	CLEL 101:20
stop telling the t. about them	STEV 316:15
Stretch age's t. sometimes	JONS 186:23
T. exists; only lies are invented	BRAQ 71:15
T. forever on the scaffold	LOW 211:8
T. from his lips prevailed	GOLD 154:22
t. in masquerade	BYRON 86:23
t. is always strange	BYRON 86:29
t. is not in us	BIBLE 57:14
t. is pulling its boots on	SPUR 314:2
t. is rarely pure and never	WILDE 349:16
T. is staring at the sun	BELL 33:3
T. is the cry of all	BERK 35:17
T. is the first casualty	JOHN 182:12
T. is the most valuable	TWAIN 335:23
t. lay all undiscovered	NEWT 239:6
T. lies within a little and	BOL 63:5
T., like a torch, the more	HAM 160:17
T. may bear all lights	SHAF 270:22
t. misunderstood	JAMES 180:10
t. of imagination	KEATS 192:23
t. serve as a stalking-horse	BOL 63:3
t. shall be thy warrant	RAL 257:21
t. shall make you free	BIBLE 53:28
T., Sir, is a cow	JOHN 184:12
T. sits upon the lips	ARN 17:15
t. that has lost its temper	GIBR 150:21
t. that's told with bad intent	BLAKE 60:7
t. universally acknowledged	AUST 23:2
t. which makes men free	AGAR 3:5
t. which you cannot contradict	SOCR 310:24
T. will come to light	SHAK 289:8
unto the enemies of t.	BROW 74:9
utter what he thinks t.	JOHN 185:26
was all the test of t.	CRAB 110:20
way, the t., and the life	BIBLE 53:38
What is t.?	BIBLE 54:1
What is t.? said jesting	BACON 25:18
Who never sold the t.	TENN 327:5
with the spirit of t.	BOOK 65:9
would keep abreast of T.	LOW 211:9

truths: all t. are half-truths — WHIT 348:1

hold these t. to be self-evident	ANON 11:12
Irrationally held t.	HUXL 177:19
profound t. recognized by	BOHR 63:1
repetition of unpalatable t.	SUMM 319:5
tell him disagreeable t.	BULW 78:12
t. begin as blasphemies	SHAW 300:23
t. being in and out of	FROST 146:9
t. to begin as heresies	HUXL 177:18
t. to be sacred and undeniable	JEFF 180:18
Two t. are told	SHAK 285:10

try: And you can get it if you t. — GERS 150:8

t. him afterwards	MOL 232:21
t. the soul's strength	BROW 76:7

trying: business without really t. — MEAD 222:17

He just goes on t. other	PIC 248:18
I am t., and you can't help it	SMITH 309:7

tu: *Et t., Brute?* — CAES 88:3

Et t., Brute? — SHAK 281:10

tuberose: sweet t. — SHEL 304:31

tuckoo: little boy named baby t. — JOYCE 188:6

tug: then was the t. of war — LEE 204:9

tumble: They t. headlong down — MARL 218:16

tumour: not when it ripens in a t. — ABSE 1:1

tumult: depth, and not the t. of the soul — WORD 355:6

t. and the shouting dies — KIPL 197:2

tune: keep thinkin'll turn into a t. — HUBB 175:16

That's sweetly play'd in t. — BURNS 82:20

t. the instrument here — DONNE 123:16

U

unbribed: what the man will do u. WOLFE 353:2
unburied: friendless bodies of u. WEBS 344:25
uncertain: U., coy, and hard to please SCOTT 268:22
u. glory of an April day SHAK 298:18
uncharitableness: and from all u. BOOK 64:14
uncircumscribed: Sceptreless, free, u. SHEL 304:22
unclassed: Equal, u., tribeless SHEL 304:22
uncle: O my prophetic soul! My u. SHAK 274:32
nor u. me no uncle SHAK 293:18
unclean: people of u. lips BIBLE 45:11
unclouded: u. blaze of living light BYRON 85:20
unclubbable: very u. man JOHN 184:18
uncoffined: u., and unknown BYRON 85:14
uncomfortable: moral when he is only u. SHAW 301:21
uncommon: and u. abilities BAG 26:2
unconquerable: nursing thy u. hope ARN 17:12
unconscionable: u. time dying CHAR 95:6
unconscious: royal road to the u. FREUD 146:1
unconsidered: snapper-up of u. trifles SHAK 298:27
uncouth: find out his u. way MILT 228:29
U. unkist, said the old poet SPEN 313:19
uncreated: wide womb of u. night MILT 228:24
uncreating: before thy u. word POPE 250:22
unction: Lay not that flattering u. SHAK 276:22
under: U. a spreading chestnut tree LONG 210:4
under-belly: u. of the Axis CHUR 99:19
under-dogs: Englishman among the u. WAUGH 343:21
underground: As Johnny u. PUDN 256:3
underlings: we are u. SHAK 280:27
underneath: U. the Arches FLAN 141:2
undersold: Never knowingly u. LEWIS 206:10
understand: don't criticize what you can't u. DYL 130:9
grown-ups never u. anything DE S 265:15
isn't confused doesn't really u. MURR 236:14
Nor can anyone u. Ein ANON 8:2
nor to hate them but to u. them SPIN 313:23
remember, and u. BROW 75:29
u. a little less MAJOR 216:19
u. what is happening CHAM 93:24
understanded: tongue not u. of the people BOOK 69:18
understanding: not obliged to find you an u. JOHN 186:5
shall light a candle of u. BIBLE 47:28
sketchy u. of life itself CRICK 111:19
spirit of wisdom and u. BIBLE 45:18
they pass all u. JAM 179:13
u. makes one very indulgent STAËL 314:5
where is the place of u. BIBLE 43:1
with all thy getting get u. BIBLE 43:10
understandings: cold hearts and muddy u. BURKE 80:15
understands: Reads verse and thinks she u. BROW 75:25
understood: something u. HERB 167:4
Underworld: way down to the U. VIRG 339:12
undevotional: Dirty, dark, and u. VICT 338:10
undiscovered: u. country from whose bourn SHAK 275:26
undo: for thee does she u. herself MIDD 224:9
To u. the folded lie AUDEN 21:11
undone: death had u. so many ELIOT 134:21
John Donne, Anne Donne, U. DONNE 124:23
u. those things which we BOOK 63:14
Weather and rain have u. KIPL 197:8
What's done cannot be u. SHAK 287:31
Woe is me! for I am u. BIBLE 45:11
undulating: and an u. throat BELL 33:19
unearned: u. increment of rent MILL 224:14
uneasy: U. lies the head that wears SHAK 278:23
uneatable: full pursuit of the u. WILDE 350:9
uneducated: government by the u. CHES 98:12
unemployment: need be no more u. KEYN 194:16
u. and the recession have LAM 200:18
unespied: In the ocean's bosom u. MARV 220:9

unexamined: u. life not worth living SOCR 310:22
unexpected: Old age is the most u. TROT 334:22
unexplained: you're u. as yet HALL 160:14
unexpressive: chaste, and u. she SHAK 273:2
unfaithful: faith u. kept him falsely TENN 324:9
u. to the translation BORG 69:22
unfathomable: The u. deep THOM 330:24
unfeeling: Th' u. for his own GRAY 157:13
unfinished: Liberty is always u. business ANON 8:19
unfit: chosen from the u. ANON 6:20
unforgiving: An u. eye SHER 306:7
If you can fill the u. minute KIPL 197:7
unfortunate: u. man is the one BOET 62:17
ungirt: Song of the U. Runners SORL 311:15
ungodliness: tents of u. BOOK 67:22
ungodly: For the hope of the u. BIBLE 47:31
fret not thyself because of the u. BOOK 66:26
seen the u. in great power BOOK 66:28
unhappily: bad end u., the good STOP 318:5
unhappiness: loyalty we feel to u. GREE 158:5
putting-off of u. GREE 158:3
vocation of u. SIM 307:4
unhappy: can never be very u. GAY 149:16
each u. family is u. in its own way TOLS 333:11
For old, u., far-off things WORD 357:2
in mourning for my life, I'm u. CHEK 96:25
moral as soon as one is u. PROU 255:19
soft, u. sex BEHN 32:24
unhasting: u., and silent as light SMITH 310:15
unheard: language of the u. KING 195:11
those u. are sweeter KEATS 191:19
unholy: shrieks, and sights u. MILT 226:27
unhonoured: u., and unsung SCOTT 268:13
uniform: good u. must work its way DICK 120:1
Should be more u. HOOD 171:6
uninitiated: you u. ones VIRG 339:13
union: Liberty and U. WEBS 344:9
O U., strong and great LONG 209:11
u. of hands and hearts TAYL 323:5
unions: u. and the industrialists NIEM 239:15
unite: Workers of the world, u.! MARX 221:15
United States: so close to the U. DIAZ 117:16
U. . . . the greatest poem WHIT 348:25
uniting: By u. we stand DICK 120:18
unity: truth, u., and concord BOOK 65:9
universal: u. monarchy of wit CAREW 89:19
wears one u. grin FIEL 139:13
universe: better ordering of the u. ALF 4:8
cover the u. with mud FORS 143:18
good u. next door CUMM 113:1
Great Architect of the U. JEANS 180:17
Life, the U. and Everything ADAMS 1:9
Put back thy u. and give me JONES 186:20
This u. is not hostile HOLM 170:13
u. is not only queerer HALD 160:2
u.'s very existence PENR 247:11
visible u. was an illusion BORG 69:23
Which is the measure of the u. SHEL 304:20
university: benefiting from u. AMIS 5:1
gained in the U. of Life BOTT 70:7
servant to be bred at an U. CONG 106:10
U. of these days is a collection CARL 90:16
We are the U. SPR 314:1
unjust: on the just and on the u. BIBLE 48:24
u. steals the just's umbrella BOWEN 70:14
unjustly: They teach to talk u. ARIS 15:10
unkempt: U. about those hedges BROO 73:4
unkind: Tell me not, Sweet, I am u. LOV 210:20
unkindest: most u. cut of all SHAK 281:23
unkindness: you elements, with u. SHAK 283:7
unkist: Uncouth u. SPEN 313:19
Unknowe, u. CHAU 96:14
unknowable: O world u. THOM 331:14
unknowe: U., unkist, and lost CHAU 96:14

unknowing: cloud of u. — ANON 6:16
unknown: glorious and the u. — FORS 143:19
I travelled among u. men — WORD 355:3
known and the u. — PINT 248:21
O friend unseen, unborn, u. — FLEC 141:20
She lived u., and few could — WORD 356:23
Through the u., we'll find — BAUD 30:6
To that u. and silent shore — LAMB 200:12
TO THE U. GOD — BIBLE 54:20
tread safely into the u. — HASK 163:16
uncoffined, and u. — BYRON 85:14
U. Prime Minister — ASQ 19:3
u. regions preserved — ELIOT 132:9
unleavened: u. bread — BIBLE 39:36
unleaving: Over Goldengrove u. — HOPK 172:14
unloose: latchet I am not worthy to u. — BIBLE 53:12
unlovely: in the long u. street — TENN 324:26
unluckily: good [end] u. — STOP 318:5
unlucky: born who is so u. — MARQ 219:21
unmapped: u. country within us — ELIOT 132:2
unmarried: prime-roses that die u. — SHAK 298:33
unnatural: most u. of all the sexual — HUXL 177:7
unnecessary: thou u. letter — SHAK 283:2
unfit, to do the u. — ANON 6:20
unofficial: An English u. rose — BROO 73:4
It is the u. force — DOYLE 126:3
unparagoned: Rubies u. — SHAK 273:24
unparalleled: A lass u. — SHAK 272:10
unpitied: u., unreprieved — MILT 228:25
unpleasing: U. to a married ear — SHAK 284:22
unplumbed: u., salt, estranging sea — ARN 17:23
unpopular: safe to be u. — STEV 316:18
unpremeditated: Easy my u. verse — MILT 229:21
In profuse strains of u. art — SHEL 305:6
unprepared: Magnificently u. — CORN 108:7
unprincipled: sold by the u. — CAPP 89:16
unprofitable: weary, stale, flat, and u. — SHAK 274:10
unprofitably: U. travelling toward the grave — WORD 356:8
unprotected: quiet, pilfering, u. race — CLARE 101:6
unquiet: sole u. thing — COL 103:20
u. slumbers for the sleepers — BRON 72:18
unreasonable: progress depends on the u. man — SHAW 302:1
unregarded: U. age in corners thrown — SHAK 272:15
unremembered: nameless, u., acts — WORD 355:8
unrequited: what u. affection is — DICK 118:21
unrest: u. which men miscall delight — SHEL 303:11
unresting: U., unhasting — SMITH 310:15
unrewarded: Nothing u., but desert — DRYD 127:13
unsad: U. and evere untrewe — CHAU 95:24
unsafe: U. at any speed — NADER 236:21
unsearchable: heart of kings is u. — BIBLE 43:34
u. riches of Christ — BIBLE 55:31
unseen: flower is born to blush u. — GRAY 157:9
Greet the u. with a cheer — BROW 75:12
O friend u., unborn, unknown — FLEC 141:20
Thou art u., but yet I hear — SHEL 305:8
unsex: U. me here — SHAK 285:17
unsought: giv'n u. is better — SHAK 298:7
lost, that is u. — CHAU 96:14
unspeakable: u. in full pursuit — WILDE 350:9
unsuccessful: u. literary man — BELL 33:19
unsung: unhonoured, and u. — SCOTT 268:13
untalented: product of the u. — CAPP 89:16
untender: So young, and so u. — SHAK 282:17
unthinking: u. time — DRYD 128:15
untidy: corner, some u. spot — AUDEN 21:2
untilled: all the u. air between — AUDEN 21:8
untimely: U. ripped — SHAK 288:7
Why came I so u. forth — WALL 341:14
'unting: ain't the u. as 'urts 'im — PUNCH 256:11
U. is all that's worth living — SURT 319:8
unto: For u. us a child is born — BIBLE 45:16

unto (cont.):
u. this last — BIBLE 50:26
untravelled: Gleams that u. world — TENN 328:21
untried: found difficult; and left u. — CHES 98:15
untrodden: dwelt among the u. ways — WORD 356:22
untroubled: and u. where I lie — CLARE 101:7
untrue: man who's u. to his wife — AUDEN 21:3
Unsad and evere u. — CHAU 95:24
untune: u. that string — SHAK 296:30
unusual: moved by what is not u. — ELIOT 132:11
unutterable: looked u. things — THOM 331:24
unwashed: lean u. artificer — SHAK 282:11
unwept: U., and welter to — MILT 227:11
U., unhonoured, and unsung — SCOTT 268:13
unwholesome: boiled very soft is not u. — AUST 22:13
unwilling: committee is a group of the u. — ANON 6:20
u. or unable — WILL 351:7
unwontedly: U. It was late June — THOM 330:21
up: And hey! then u. go we — QUAR 257:5
is to be u. betimes — SHAK 297:22
U. and down the City Road — MAND 217:8
U. Guards and at them — WELL 345:8
U., lad: when the journey's — HOUS 174:18
U., Lord, and let not man — BOOK 66:11
U. to a point, Lord Copper — WAUGH 343:24
upharsin: MENE, TEKEL, U. — BIBLE 47:12
uphill: Does the road wind u. — ROSS 263:5
uplift: Felt faint and never dared u. — SHEL 304:14
upper: large u. room furnished — BIBLE 52:40
let not man have the u. hand — BOOK 66:11
Like many of the u. Class — BELL 33:23
To prove the u. classes — COW 109:8
u. station of low life — DEFOE 115:14
You may tempt the u. classes — SMITH 309:5
uprising: down-sitting, and mine u. — BOOK 69:5
Our wakening and u. prove — KEBLE 193:16
uproar: u.'s your only music — KEATS 193:3
upstairs: came u. into the world — CONG 106:8
upstanding: clean u. chap like you — KING 195:19
upward: u. still, and onward — LOW 211:9
urban: u., squat, and packed with guile — BROO 73:7
urbe: Rus in u. — MART 220:8
urge: Always the procreant u. — WHIT 348:17
u. for destruction is also — BAK 26:22
urges: Will that stirs and u. — HARDY 162:5
Uricon: Are ashes under U. — HOUS 174:23
urine: his u. is congealed ice — SHAK 288:23
wine of Shiraz into u. — DIN 121:2
urn: bubbling and loud-hissing u. — COWP 110:11
Can storied u. or animated bust — GRAY 157:8
us: Not unto u., Lord — BIBLE 58:12
Not unto u., O Lord — BOOK 68:17
use: ring is worn away by u. — OVID 243:12
u. alone sanctifies expense — POPE 251:18
u. a poor maiden so — ANON 6:27
U. every man after his desert — SHAK 275:20
u. him as though you loved — WALT 342:13
U. him as though you love him — BLUN 62:14
u. of a new-born child — FRAN 145:17
u. of that which is mine — SHAK 289:5
We shall not want to u. again — DICK 120:10
What's the u. of worrying — ASAF 18:17
used: My name is U.-to-was — TRAI 334:2
since then I have u. no other — PUNCH 256:16
Things ain't what they u. to be — PERS 248:6
useful: equally u. — GIBB 150:10
Really U. Engine — AWDRY 23:13
u., or believe to be beautiful — MORR 235:18
way to what is u. — COUS 108:17
useless: Lodged with me u. — MILT 230:22
most beautiful things the most u. — RUSK 264:17
USSR: Back in the U. — MCC 205:10
usual: Business carried on as u. — CHUR 99:6
Not kind sir quite u. — ASHF 18:22
usura: u. hath no man a house — POUND 254:9

usury: money upon u. BOOK 66:14
  u. is contrary to Scripture TAWN 322:20
Utopia: Not in U. WORD 356:14
  principality in U. MAC 213:11
Utopias: end all the static U. INGE 178:11
uttermost: u. parts of the sea BOOK 69:6

V

vacancies: how are v. to be obtained JEFF 180:22
vacant: In v. or in pensive mood WORD 355:5
  laugh that spoke the v. mind GOLD 154:20
  V. heart and hand, and eye SCOTT 268:24
vacations: No extras, no v. DICK 119:10
vacuum: Nature abhors a v. RAB 257:11
  women from behind the v. cleaner GREER 158:11
vadis: Quo v.? BIBLE 58:19
vae: V. victis LIVY 208:5
vaguery: For V. in the Field OSB 242:21
vain: name of the Lord thy God in v. BIBLE 40:6
  people imagine a v. thing BOOK 66:9
  Profane, erroneous, and v. BUTL 84:2
  V. man, said she SPEN 313:4
  V. the ambition of kings WEBS 344:13
vain-glory: v., and hypocrisy BOOK 64:14
vainly: V. begot, and yet forbidden GREV 158:19
  v. flapped its tinsel wing MARV 220:12
  v. men themselves amaze MARV 220:14
vale: ave atque v. CAT 93:8
  cool sequestered v. of life GRAY 157:10
  Into the v. of years SHAK 292:16
  To meet thee in that hollow v. KING 195:5
  v. of misery BOOK 67:21
  v. of soul-making KEATS 193:10
valet: his very v. seemed a hero BYRON 84:27
  No man is a hero to his v. CORN 108:9
valiant: As he was v., I honour SHAK 281:16
  Ring in the v. man and free TENN 325:27
  v. never taste of death SHAK 281:8
valley: All in the v. of Death TENN 323:14
  Every v. shall be exalted BIBLE 46:9
  For Love is of the v. TENN 328:7
  heard a maid sing in the v. ANON 6:27
  How green was my v. LLEW 208:6
  into the v. of Humiliation BUNY 78:19
  multitudes in the v. of decision BIBLE 47:21
  To bicker down a v. TENN 323:12
  V. and lowland, sing OAKL 240:16
  v. of its saying AUDEN 20:23
  v. of the shadow of a death BOOK 66:18
  v. which was full of bones BIBLE 47:8
valleys: Piping down the v. wild BLAKE 61:18
  v., groves, hills and fields MARL 219:3
Vallombrosa: brooks in V. MILT 228:14
valorous: childish v. than manly MARL 219:13
valour: thou mighty man of v. BIBLE 40:35
  v. in this Welshman SHAK 279:11
  Who would true v. see BUNY 79:9
valuable: Truth the most v. thing TWAIN 335:23
value: and the v. of nothing WILDE 350:1
  Everything exists, nothing has v. FORS 143:25
  little v. of fortune STEE 314:18
values: moneys are for v. BACON 23:23
van: Follow the v. COLL 105:7
Vanbrugh: V.'s house of clay EVANS 137:23
Vandyke: V. is of the company GAIN 147:10
vanish: should v. with the rose FITZ 140:18
  softly and suddenly v. away CARR 92:8
vanishings: Fallings from us, v. WORD 355:22
vanitas: V. vanitatum BIBLE 58:15
vanities: bonfire of the v. WOLFE 353:7
vanity: administering to the v. of others AUST 22:23
  and yet forbidden v. GREV 158:19

vanity (cont.):
  beareth the name of V.-Fair BUNY 78:21
  pomps and v. of this wicked BOOK 65:21
  Pull down thy v. POUND 254:21
  v. and vexation of spirit BIBLE 44:9
  V., like murder, will out COWL 109:19
  v. of human hopes JOHN 183:1
  V. of vanities; all is vanity BIBLE 44:7
  V. of vanities, said the preacher BIBLE 58:15
vapour: take to be a deceitful v. SMOL 310:16
  upon the v. of a dungeon SHAK 292:17
  v. and return it as a flood GLAD 153:15
vapours: v. weep their burthen TENN 328:17
variable: And v. as the shade SCOTT 268:22
  love prove likewise v. SHAK 294:33
variety: Her infinite v. SHAK 271:17
  V.'s the very spice of life COWP 110:9
variorum: Life is all a v. BURNS 82:13
various: As you are lovely, so be v. GRAV 156:16
  drunkenness of things being v. MACN 216:8
varium: V. et mutabile semper VIRG 339:9
varlet: Detraction is but baseness' v. JONS 187:10
vase: you may shatter the v. MOORE 234:13
vaulting: V. ambition, which o'erleaps SHAK 286:1
vaunt: V.-couriers to oak-cleaving SHAK 283:6
vécu: J'ai v. SIEY 307:1
veels: V. vithin veels DICK 120:2
Vega: V. conspicuous overhead AUDEN 21:7
vegetable: My v. love should grow MARV 220:23
  v., animal, and mineral GILB 152:23
vegetate: v. in a village COLT 105:18
veil: Lift not the painted v. SHEL 305:2
  wrapped in a gauzy v. SHEL 305:15
vein: not in the giving v. today SHAK 294:18
veins: v. of rhyming mother-wits MARL 219:4
venerable: v. creatures did the aged TRAH 333:19
Veneres: O V. Cupidinesque CAT 93:1
vengeance: V. is mine BIBLE 54:45
veni: V., Sancte Spiritus LANG 201:10
  V., vidi, vici CAES 88:2
Venice: Ocean's nursling, V. SHEL 304:1
venite: V., adoremus Dominum ANON 13:10
venomous: v. as the poison of a serpent BOOK 67:13
venture: drew a bow at a v. BIBLE 42:7
  Each v. is a new beginning ELIOT 133:6
ventured: You have deeply v. BYRON 87:3
Venus: V. entire latched onto RAC 257:16
  V. here will choose her DRYD 128:2
veranda: v., and the fruit AUDEN 20:25
verb: God, to me, it seems, is a v. FULL 147:4
  word is the V., and the V. is God HUGO 175:24
verba: Nullius in v. HOR 173:5
  Rem tene; v. sequentur CATO 92:23
verbal: v. contract isn't worth GOLD 155:17
verboojuice: Sesquippledan v. WELLS 345:17
verbosity: exuberance of his own v. DISR 121:20
verbum: V. caro factum est MISS 231:21
  V. sapienti PLAU 249:22
verdict: Sentence first—v. afterwards CARR 91:14
Vereker: V.'s secret JAMES 179:17
verge: Stands dreaming on the v. CORN 108:7
  very v. of her confine SHAK 283:3
verification: method of its v. SCHL 267:22
verify: v. your references ROUTH 263:19
verisimilitude: artistic v. GILB 152:5
veritas: magna est v. BROO 73:14
  Magna est v. BIBLE 58:23
  sed magis amica v. ARIS 15:22
vermin: Tory Party lower than v. BEVAN 37:18
vermouth: union of gin and v. DE V 117:11
verse: all in all for prose and v. CAREW 89:18
  All that is not v. is prose MOL 232:15
  Doctors in v. THOM 331:3
  Easy my unpremeditated v. MILT 229:21
  false heir become a v. HERB 167:1

verse (cont.):

flask of wine, a book of v.	FITZ 140:6
indignation makes me write v.	JUV 189:2
Let the v. the subject fit	CAREY 90:1
Lies the subject of all v.	BROW 74:24
No subject for immortal v.	DAY-L 115:6
Not v. now, only prose	BROW 75:18
Only with those in v.	CONG 106:18
turnings intricate of v.	WORD 356:12
unpolished rugged v. I chose	DRYD 128:14
v. and thinks she understands	BROW 75:25
v. is a measured speech	BACON 23:24
v. may find him	HERB 166:21
Voice, and V.	MILT 226:4
Who died to make v. free	PRES 255:5
write free v. as play tennis	FROST 146:26

verses: rhyme the rudder is of v.

	BUTL 83:25
Tear him for his bad v.	SHAK 281:27

versions: hundred v. of it SHAW 302:15

verum: Ave v. corpus ANON 13:14

very: V. God of very God BOOK 65:5

vessel: gallant trim the gilded v.

	GRAY 157:3
Let the Irish v. lie	AUDEN 20:24
unto the weaker v.	BIBLE 57:10
v. with the pestle	FRANK 245:1
wide v. of the universe	SHAK 279:7

vesture: cast lots upon my v.

	BOOK 66:16
Mine outward v. be	LITT 208:2

veterans: world its v. rewards POPE 251:11

vex: V. not thou the poet's mind TENN 327:15

vexation: Multiplication is v. ANON 9:11

vanity and v. of spirit BIBLE 44:9

vexes: The other v. it KEATS 190:25

vexing: V. the dull ear of a drowsy

	SHAK 282:9

vibrated: had better not be v. DICK 117:21

vibrates: V. in the memory SHEL 305:4

vice: Ambition, in a private man a v. MASS 222:3

Art is v. You don't marry it	DEGAS 116:2
defence of liberty is no v.	GOLD 155:15
distinction between virtue and v.	JOHN 184:11
England but v.	SMITH 310:12
He lashed the v., but spared	SWIFT 320:24
lost by not having been v.	WALP 342:3
Prosperity doth best discover v.	BACON 24:11
Public schools nurseries of all v.	FIEL 139:8
raptures and roses of v.	SWIN 321:7
render v. serviceable	BOL 63:7
say there is no v. but beggary	SHAK 282:5
sensual pleasure without v.	JOHN 186:10
To sanction V., and hunt	BYRON 86:33
tribute which v. pays to virtue	LA R 201:23
V. came in always at the door	DEFOE 115:12
When v. prevails	ADD 2:17

vice-presidency: v. isn't worth a pitcher

	GARN 148:7

vices: By hating v. too much BURKE 80:19

most v. committed very genteelly	BOSW 70:5
our pleasant v.	SHAK 284:2

vicious: expect a boy to be v. till SAKI 265:20

vicissitude: This sad v. of things STER 315:27

vicisti: V., Galilaee JUL 188:20

victim: v. must be found GILB 151:19

v. to a big lie HITL 169:3

victims: its v. time to die GUIB 159:8

little v. play	GRAY 157:12
v. who respect their executioners	SART 267:7

victis: Vae v. LIVY 208:5

victor: to the v. belong the spoils MARCY 218:2

Victoria: ticket at V. Station BEVIN 38:9

victories: Peace hath her v. MILT 230:27

victorious: Make him v. HOGG 170:8

victory: But 'twas a famous v. SOUT 311:20

death in v.	BIBLE 45:25
Dig for v.	DORM 124:24
grave, where is thy v.	BIBLE 55:22
In v.: magnanimity	CHUR 100:4

victory (cont.):

in v. unbearable	CHUR 100:9
is only v. in him	DRYD 128:29
not the v. but the contest	COUB 108:15
V. has a hundred fathers	CIANO 100:12

victuals: About their v. CALV 88:9

And the v. and the wine CALV 88:10

vie: Ah! que la v. est quotidienne LAF 199:20

Vienna: V. is nothing METT 224:1

view: lends enchantment to the v. CAMP 88:19

myself a motley to the v. SHAK 300:6

viewless: As v. too AUBER 19:15

vigil: tongueless v. and all the pain SWIN 321:1

vigilance: liberty to man is eternal v. CURR 113:8

vigilant: Be sober, be v. BIBLE 57:12

Vigny: Et V. plus secret SAIN 265:14

vile: And only man is v. HEBER 164:16

O v., intolerable	SHAK 295:29
Things base and v.	SHAK 290:16
V., but viler George II	LAND 200:24

vilest: v. things become themselves SHAK 271:17

village: families in a country v. AUST 23:9

first in a v. than second	CAES 87:26
image of a global v.	MCL 215:11
loveliest v. of the plain	GOLD 154:17
vegetate in a v.	COLT 105:18
v.-Hampden	GRAY 157:9
v. smithy stands	LONG 210:4

villages: pleasant v. and farms MILT 229:23

villains: we were v. by necessity SHAK 282:22

villainy: v. you teach me I will SHAK 289:18

Villon: V., our sad bad glad mad SWIN 321:5

Vinci: V. and pronounce it Vinchy TWAIN 336:1

vindicate: v. the ways of God to man POPE 252:11

vine: little prop best fits a little v. HERR 167:22

luscious clusters of the v.	MARV 220:15
shall be as the fruitful v.	BOOK 68:32
sweet grape who will the v.	SHAK 299:8
thyme and the gadding v.	MILT 227:13

vines: his client to plant v. WRIG 357:23

v. that round the thatch-eaves KEATS 192:14

vineyard: v. in a very fruitful BIBLE 45:7

vintage: draught of v. KEATS 191:29

v. where the grapes of wrath HOWE 175:7

violations: v. committed by children BOWEN 70:17

violence: In v., we forget who we are MCC 214:11

I say v. is necessary	BROWN 73:15
Keep v. in the mind	ALD 3:16

violent: feelings produce RUSK 264:12

v. hands upon themselves BOOK 66:5

violently: v. if they must QUIN 257:9

violet: At the v. hour ELIOT 134:27

bats with baby faces in the v.	ELIOT 134:30
By v.-hooded Doctors	TENN 327:18
in the v.-embroidered vale	MILT 226:10
oxlips and the nodding v.	SHAK 290:26
To throw a perfume on the v.	SHAK 282:10
v. smells to him as it doth	SHAK 279:12
v.'s reclining head	DONNE 122:7

violets: By ashen roots the v. blow TENN 325:29

When daisies pied and v. blue	SHAK 284:21
Who are the v. now	SHAK 294:8

violins: v. wound my heart VERL 337:21

vipers: O generation of v. BIBLE 48:14

vir: Beatus v. qui timet Dominum BIBLE 58:11

virgin: poor v., sir, an ill-favoured SHAK 273:11

Every harlot was a v. once	BLAKE 60:15
v.-choir to make delicious	KEATS 192:8
v. goddess returns	VIRG 339:25
v. renowned for ever	HOR 173:27
v. shall conceive	BIBLE 45:14

virginity: No, no; for my v. PRIOR 255:12

virgo: Iam redit et v. VIRG 339:25

virtue: accommodating sort of v. MOL 232:20

adversity doth best discover v. BACON 24:11

virtue (*cont.*):

Assume a v.	SHAK 276:23
distinction between v. and vice	JOHN 184:11
fugitive and cloistered v.	MILT 230:31
if there be any v.	BIBLE 56:9
Is in a prince the v.	MASS 222:3
lilies and languors of v.	SWIN 321:7
Linked with one v.	BYRON 85:19
O infinite v.!	SHAK 271:21
Punctuality is the v. of the bored	WAUGH 343:29
pursuit of justice is no v.	GOLD 155:15
Repentance is the v. of weak	DRYD 127:34
reward of v. is virtue	EMER 136:21
Self-denial is not a v.	SHAW 301:34
serviceable to the cause of v.	BOL 63:7
Silence is the v. of fools	BACON 24:8
some men toil after v.	LAMB 200:15
That make ambition v.	SHAK 292:19
There is no v. like necessity	SHAK 293:13
'tis some v., v. to commend	CONG 106:22
tribute which vice pays to v.	LA R 201:23
v. at the testing point	LEWIS 206:13
v. but the Trade Unionism	SHAW 301:24
V. could see to do what V.	MILT 226:11
V. is like a rich stone	BACON 24:13
V. is the fount whence	MARL 219:9
V. knows to a farthing what	WALP 342:3
V. may be assailed	MILT 226:18
V. she finds too painful	POPE 251:10

virtues:

Be to her v. very kind	PRIOR 255:9
his v. will plead like angels	SHAK 285:24
Is it a world to hide v. in	SHAK 297:17
makes some v. impracticable	JOHN 185:31
moral v. at the highest	CHES 97:14
necessities call out great v.	ADAMS 1:7
their v. we write in water	SHAK 280:22
v. made or crimes	DEFOE 115:19
weed? A plant whose v.	EMER 136:29

virtuous:

because thou art v.	SHAK 297:26
v. woman is a crown	BIBLE 43:19
Who can find a v. woman	BIBLE 44:6

virtute: *Macte nova v.* — VIRG 339:19

visible:

darkness v.	MILT 228:10
does not reproduce the v.	KLEE 198:10
things v. and invisible	BOOK 65:5
Work is love made v.	GIBR 150:20

vision:

baseless fabric of this v.	SHAK 296:10
Bright the v. that delighted	MANT 217:17
fatal v., sensible to feeling	SHAK 286:10
Oh, the v. thing	BUSH 83:17
single central v.	BERL 36:4
Single v. and Newton's	BLAKE 60:23
V. of Christ	BLAKE 60:11
Was it a v., or a waking dream	KEATS 192:7
Where there is no v.	BIBLE 44:3
your v. is machines for	BOTT 70:6

visionary: fled the v. gleam — WORD 355:19

visions:

Cecilia, appear in v.	AUDEN 20:10
v. before midnight	BROW 74:23
young men shall see v.	BIBLE 47:20

visit:

every formal v. a child	AUST 23:8
v. it by the pale moonlight	SCOTT 268:10

visitation: But oh! each v. — COL 103:15

visitor: I travel as a v. — HOR 173:5

visits: never make long v. — MOORE 234:9

vita:

Ars longa, v. brevis	HIPP 168:19
del cammin di nostra v.	DANTE 113:17

vitae: *Integer v.* — HOR 173:21

vitai: *v. lampada* — LUCR 212:5

vital: *L'élan v.* — BERG 35:14

vitality: V. in a woman — SHAW 301:17

vitam: *Si v. puriter egi* — CAT 93:6

vivamus: *V., mea Lesbia* — CAT 93:2

vivid: v. air signed with their — SPEN 312:24

vixen: v. when she went to school — SHAK 290:33

vobiscum: *Dominus v.* — MISS 231:9

vocation:

I have not felt the v.	CLOU 102:7
test of a v.	SMITH 309:11
v. of unhappiness	SIM 307:4

vogue:

charming to totter into v.	WALP 341:19
he'd be working for V.	UST 336:17

voice:

against the v. of a nation	RUSS 265:5
All I have is a v.	AUDEN 21:11
And a v. less loud	BROW 76:17
And utter forth a glorious v.	ADD 2:26
Hear the v. of the Bard	BLAKE 61:26
hear the v. of the charmer	BOOK 67:13
Her v. is full of money	FITZ 140:21
Her v. was ever soft	SHAK 284:5
I have lost my v.	WEBS 344:28
inner v. which warns	MENC 223:8
It is, and it is not, the v. of God	POPE 252:28
look at me in that tone of v.	PUNCH 256:17
Lord, hear my v.	BIBLE 58:14
Lord, hear my v.	BOOK 68:33
No v.; but oh! the silence sank	COL 104:16
only a look and a v.	LONG 210:3
Or but a wandering v.	WORD 357:7
Rama was there a v. heard	BIBLE 48:11
sisters, V., and Verse	MILT 226:4
sound of a v. that is still	TENN 323:11
still small v.	BIBLE 42:3
v. and nothing more	ANON 14:3
v. is Jacob's voice	BIBLE 39:20
v. of him that crieth	BIBLE 46:8
v. of one crying	BIBLE 48:13
v. of Rome is the consent	JONS 187:1
v. of the Lord God walking	BIBLE 38:26
v. of the people	ALC 3:14
v. of the sluggard	WATTS 343:9
v. of the turtle is heard	BIBLE 44:32
v. so sweet, the words	JONS 187:18
v. that breathed o'er Eden	KEBLE 193:18
v. we heard was Churchill's	ATTL 19:12

voices:

Ancestral v. prophesying war	COL 103:25
Other v., other rooms	CAP 89:15
Two V. are there	WORD 357:6
Two v. are there	STEP 315:4
v. of children are heard	BLAKE 61:25

void:

captive v. of noble rage	TENN 325:3
without form, and v.	BIBLE 38:13

voids: attempts to fill v. — WEIL 345:2

volcano: v. of revolution — ELLIS 136:6

volcanoes:

range of exhausted v.	DISR 121:16
religious factions are v.	BURKE 81:1

vole: passes the questing v. — WAUGH 343:25

volenti: *V. non fit iniuria* — ULP 336:10

Volk: *ein V., ein Führer* — ANON 13:2

volley: v. of the sun — WILB 349:13

volleyed: V. and thundered — TENN 323:16

volleying: v. rain and tossing breeze — ARN 17:18

volo: *Hoc v., sic iubeo* — JUV 189:8

Voltaire: mock on V. Rousseau — BLAKE 61:13

volume: Lo here a little v. — CRAS 111:12

volumes:

compressed in thirty fine v.	MORL 235:8
creators of odd v.	LAMB 200:2
Reticence, in three v.	GLAD 153:14
scholar all Earth's v. carry	CHAP 94:21

voluntary: neighbourhood of v. spies — AUST 22:25

voluptas: *Trahit sua quemque v.* — VIRG 339:23

volupté: *Luxe, calme et v.* — BAUD 30:4

vomit: dog is turned to his own v. — BIBLE 57:13

Vorsprung: *V. durch Technik* — ANON 13:4

votaress: imperial v. — SHAK 290:24

vote:

I never v. for anybody	FIEL 139:18
One man shall have one v.	CART 92:14
v. against somebody rather	ADAMS 1:10
V. early and vote often	ANON 11:9
V. for the man who promises	BAR 29:21

voted: always v. at my party's call | GILB 152:19
they v. cent per cent | BYRON 84:25
votes: who uses his money as v. | SAM 266:11
voting: v. that's democracy | STOP 317:20
vow: I v. to thee, my country | SPR 313:26
vowels: v., some day I will tell | RIMB 260:11
vows: cancel all our v. | DRAY 126:16
vox: *V. et praeterea nihil* | ANON 14:3
  V. populi, vox Dei | ALC 3:1
voyage: about to take my last v. | HOBB 169:11
  all the v. of their life | SHAK 282:1
  first to make the v. over | VIRG 339:15
voyages: v. of the starship *Enterprise* | RODD 261:12
voyaging: V. through strange seas | WORD 356:10
vulgar: takes place with the v. | BACON 24:7
  work upon the v. with fine sense | POPE 253:12
  worse than wicked, it's v. | PUNCH 256:15
vulgarity: v., concealing something | FORS 143:23

W

wabe: gyre and gimble in the w. | CARR 91:15
waded: w. thro' red blude | BALL 28:8
waft: w. her love to come again | SHAK 289:32
wage: home policy: I w. war | CLEM 102:1
wages: better w. and shorter hours | ORW 242:13
  Home art gone and ta'en thy w. | SHAK 273:27
  w. of sin is death | BIBLE 54:36
Wagner: W. has lovely moments | ROSS 263:11
  W.'s music better than it sounds | NYE 240:15
wagon: Hitch your w. to a star | EMER 136:31
wail: mirth to be a week | SHAK 299:8
wailing: w. for her demon-lover | COL 103:23
waist: arms went round her w. | MAS 221:20
  Then you live about her w. | SHAK 275:13
wait: serve who only stand and w. | MILT 230:23
  Tomorrow, just you w. and see | BURT 83:3
  w. for liberty till | MAC 213:8
  We had better w. and see | ASQ 19:2
  We want eight, and we won't w. | ANON 11:17
waiting: I was nearly kept w. | LOUI 210:13
  So quickly, w. for a hand | TENN 324:26
  W. for Godot | BECK 31:10
  W. for the end, boys | EMPS 137:4
wake: do I w. or sleep | KEATS 192:7
  If I should die before I w. | ANON 9:20
  sleep past, we w. eternally | DONNE 123:9
  W. now, my love, awake | SPEN 313:5
  W. up, England | GEOR 149:25
  You will w., and remember | BROW 75:29
waked: You have w. me too soon | WATTS 343:9
waken: would w. the dead | GRAV 156:12
wakening: Our w. and uprising | KEBLE 193:16
wakes: Hock-cart wassails, w. | HERR 167:12
  not breed one work that w. | HOPK 172:19
  Wordsworth sometimes w. | BYRON 86:17
waking: Be there at our w. | STR 318:17
  it is w. that kills us | BROW 74:22
  w., no such matter | SHAK 299:28
Wales: There is no present in W. | THOM 331:5
  But for W.—! | BOLT 63:8
walk: Doth w. in fear and dread | COL 104:15
  In a slow silent w. | HARDY 162:11
  no spirit can w. abroad | SHAK 274:2
  Oh! for a closer w. with God | COWP 109:27
  Or w. with Kings | KIPL 197:7
  Rise, take up thy bed, and w. | BIBLE 53:21
  talk with you, w. with you | SHAK 288:31
  that ye w. circumspectly | BIBLE 56:1
  This is the way, w. ye in it | BIBLE 46:2
  w. and live a Woolworth life | NIC 239:12
  W. cheerfully over the world | FOX 144:18
  w. for walk's sake | KLEE 198:11
  w. humbly with thy God | BIBLE 47:23

walk (*cont.*):
  w. o'er the western wave | SHEL 305:12
  w. on the wild side | ALGR 4:9
  w. through the fields | CORN 108:6
  w. through the valley | BOOK 66:18
  W. under his huge legs | SHAK 280:27
  W. upon England's mountains | BLAKE 61:12
  W., water, meditated wild | SMART 308:12
  w. within the purlieus | ETH 137:18
  was evident from her w. | VIRG 339:3
  Where'er you w., cool gales | POPE 253:1
  Will you w. a little faster | CARR 91:11
walked: He w. by himself | KIPL 197:20
  people that w. in darkness | BIBLE 45:15
  w. through the wilderness | BUNY 78:17
walkers: Six for the six proud w. | ANON 8:6
walking: from w. up and down | BIBLE 42:21
  I see men as trees, w. | BIBLE 51:22
  W., and leaping, and praising | BIBLE 54:10
  w. in the garden | BIBLE 38:26
  W. so early | SCOTT 269:1
walks: I wish I liked the way it w. | RAL 258:6
  She w. in beauty | BYRON 87:6
  while Gibbon levelled w. | COLM 105:15
wall: Before I built a w. | FROST 146:17
  broken w., the burning roof | YEATS 359:14
  conclude against a w. of stone | WILB 349:11
  Or close the w. up | SHAK 279:5
  serves it in the office of a w. | SHAK 293:16
  standing like a stone w. | BEE 31:22
  that doesn't love a w. | FROST 146:15
  that the w. fell down | BIBLE 40:27
  w. next door catches fire | HOR 173:14
  W. St lays an egg | ANON 11:10
  Watch the w., my darling | KIPL 196:28
  weather on the outward w. | SHAK 289:13
  Without a city w. | ALEX 4:6
Wallace: wi' W. bled | BURNS 82:21
wallet: w. at his back | SHAK 297:4
  w., biforn him in his lappe | CHAU 95:23
walling: w. in or walling out | FROST 146:17
walls: close her from thy ancient w. | BLAKE 60:21
  Stone w. do not a prison make | LOV 210:19
  these w. thy sphere | DONNE 124:13
  walk the angels on the w. | MARL 219:11
  w. and towers were girdled | COL 103:22
  wooden w. are the best | COV 108:18
walrus: W. and the Carpenter | CARR 91:21
waltz: goes out of a beautiful w. | GREN 158:15
  Swoons to a w. | HUXL 177:12
waltzing: come a-w., Matilda | PAT 246:16
waly: W., Waly | BALL 28:10
wan: so w. with care | SHAK 277:21
  Why so pale and w., fond lover | SUCK 318:20
wand: bright gold ring on her w. | MOORE 234:17
wander: w. forth the sons of Belial | MILT 228:15
wandered: I w. lonely as a cloud | WORD 355:4
  who w. far and wide | HOMER 171:1
wandering: Or but a w. voice | WORD 357:7
  W. between two worlds | ARN 17:16
wane: moons shall wax and w. | WATTS 343:12
want: envy, w., the patron | JOHN 183:12
  freedom from w. | ROOS 262:13
  must be in w. of a wife | AUST 23:2
  my shepherd, I'll not w. | SCOT 269:8
  pleasantest preservative from w. | AUST 23:4
  Ring out the w., the care | TENN 325:24
  something you probably won't w. | HOPE 171:19
  those who w. it most | CHES 97:9
  W. is one only of five giants | BEV 38:7
  w. of decency is want of sense | DILL 120:23
  w. of friends and empty purse | BRET 71:23
  want the world and we w. it now | MORR 235:20
  w. which most would have | DYER 129:16

wash (cont.):

tears w. out a word of it	FITZ 140:14
w. the balm from an anointed	SHAK 293:22
w. their feet in soda water	ELIOT 134:26
w. the wind	ELIOT 134:8
washed: have w. their robes	BIBLE 57:26
W. by the rivers, blest by	BROO 73:10
w. in the blood of the Lamb	LIND 207:16
w. in the speechless real	BARZ 29:22
washing: and country w.	BRUM 77:24
taking in one another's w.	ANON 6:28
w. ain't done nor sweeping	ANON 7:17
w. on the Siegfried Line	KENN 193:23
Washington: Government at W.	GARF 148:6
wassails: Hock-carts, w., wakes	HERR 167:12
waste: art of how to w. space	JOHN 182:2
Don't w. any time in mourning	HILL 168:13
I love all w. and solitary places	SHEL 303:20
now doth time w. me	SHAK 294:12
W. of Blood, and waste	STUD 318:18
w. of breath the years behind	YEATS 359:11
w. of goods	VEBL 337:17
w. of shame	SHAK 300:10
w. remains and kills	EMPS 137:6
we lay w. our powers	WORD 357:10
ye w. places of Jerusalem	BIBLE 46:16
wasted: W. his substance	BIBLE 52:29
wastes: W. without springs	CLARE 101:5
wasting: nor wanting, nor w.	SMITH 310:15
watch: as a w. in the night	BOOK 67:25
done much better by a w.	BELL 33:26
like a fat gold w.	PLATH 249:16
like little w. springs	SPEN 313:2
Lord w. between me and thee	BIBLE 39:23
not w. with me one hour	BIBLE 51:12
or my w. has stopped	MARX 221:6
too large to hang on a w.-chain	ANON 11:8
W. and pray, that ye enter	BIBLE 51:13
w. over their flock	BIBLE 51:32
W. therefore: for ye know not	BIBLE 50:38
W. the wall, my darling	KIPL 196:28
w., while some must sleep	SHAK 276:12
Wear your learning like your w.	CHES 97:10
watched: w. the ads, and not the road	NASH 237:13
watcher: like some w. of the skies	KEATS 192:11
posted presence of the w.	JAMES 179:25
watches: He w. from his mountain walls	TENN 323:21
watchful: And w. at his gate	DODD 122:30
on occasion's forelock w. wait	MILT 230:4
watching: BIG BROTHER IS W. YOU	ORW 242:6
My tiny w. eye	DE L 116:23
watchmaker: it is the *blind* w.	DAWK 115:2
watchman: w. on the lonely tower	SCOTT 268:16
w. waketh but in vain	BOOK 68:30
w. watches in vain	BIBLE 58:13
W., what of the night	BIBLE 45:23
water: affliction and with w.	BIBLE 42:6
By w. and the word	STONE 317:27
Christ walking on the w.	THOM 331:17
conscious w. saw its God	CRAS 111:6
don't care where the w. goes	CHES 98:7
ever-flowing w. near the house	HOR 174:4
feet are always in the w.	AMES 4:22
fountain of the w. of life	BIBLE 58:6
hands than w. like Pilate	GREE 158:2
hart desireth the w.-brooks	BOOK 67:3
hewers of wood and drawers of w.	BIBLE 40:28
if I were under w.	KEATS 193:7
King over the W.	ANON 8:16
Let the w. and the blood	TOPL 333:14
Minnehaha, Laughing W.	LONG 210:2
More w. glideth by the mill	SHAK 296:26
noise of the w.-pipes	BOOK 67:4
No more w., the fire next time	ANON 7:12
ready by w. as by land	ELST 136:7

water (cont.):

safe to go back in the w.	ANON 8:15
[Tar w.] is of a nature	BERK 35:16
w. clears us of this deed	SHAK 286:19
w. hollows out a stone	OVID 243:12
w. in the rough rude sea	SHAK 293:22
W. like a stone	ROSS 263:2
W., water, everywhere	COL 104:7
We write in w.	SHAK 280:22
whose name was writ in w.	KEATS 193:15
with w. and a crust	KEATS 191:11
watered: Apollos w.	BIBLE 55:3
w. our horses in Helicon	CHAP 94:17
w. our houses in Helicon	CHAP 94:17
water-lily: She saw the w. bloom	TENN 326:3
Waterloo: at Austerlitz and W.	SAND 266:14
That world-earthquake, W.	TENN 327:12
W. was won on the playing	ORW 242:4
W. was won on the playing	WELL 345:10
waterman: w., looking one way	BUNY 79:1
watermen: w., that row one way	BURT 83:7
waters: Across the waste of w. die	BETJ 37:1
all that move in the W.	BOOK 64:2
And the w. as they flow	ARMS 15:24
beside the w. of comfort	BOOK 66:17
Cast thy bread upon the w.	BIBLE 44:24
cold w. to a thirsty soul	BIBLE 43:37
Many w. cannot quench love	BIBLE 45:2
moving w. at their priestlike	KEATS 190:10
quiet w. by	SCOT 269:8
Stolen w. are sweet	BIBLE 43:15
their business in great w.	BOOK 68:12
w. cover the sea	AING 3:9
w. cover the sea	BIBLE 45:20
w. of affliction	BIBLE 46:1
w. of Babylon we sat down	BOOK 69:2
w. of the heart	THOM 330:12
w. were his winding sheet	BARN 29:7
watery: pale swan in her w. nest	SHAK 299:9
shoreless w. wild	ARN 17:22
warmer than after w. cloudes	LANG 201:9
Watson: Elementary, my dear W.	DOYLE 125:19
Wattle: ever hear of Captain W.	DIBD 117:17
wattles: of clay and w. made	YEATS 359:12
wave: age is rocking the w.	MAND 217:10
chin upon an orient w.	MILT 227:29
cool, translucent w.	MILT 226:21
Oh, lift me as a w.	SHEL 304:8
w. rolls nightly on deep	BYRON 85:22
Waverley: W. pen	ANON 11:1
waves: all thy w. and storms	BOOK 67:4
w. make towards the pebbled	SHAK 299:21
w. of thy sweet singing	SHEL 304:21
waving: not w. but drowning	SMITH 309:19
wax: *didn't* w. his moustache	KIPL 198:3
moons shall w. and wane	WATTS 343:12
W. to receive, and marble	BYRON 84:28
way: Ask that your w. be long	CAV 93:10
broad is the w.	BIBLE 49:12
every one to his own w.	BIBLE 46:19
Every which w. but loose	KRON 199:6
flowers to strew Thy w.	HERB 166:24
God moves in a mysterious w.	COWP 109:25
gull's w. and the whale's w.	MAS 222:2
I am the w., the truth	BIBLE 53:38
Is there no w. out of the mind	PLATH 249:13
known and common w.	WINC 352:3
meet 'em on your w. down	MIZN 232:11
more a w. of life	ANON 9:19
Never *in* the w., and never *out*	CHAR 95:5
Prepare ye the w. of the Lord	BIBLE 46:8
Prepare ye the w. of the Lord	BIBLE 48:13
Rebellion lay in his w.	SHAK 278:11
Their w., however straight	THOM 330:24
they kill you in a new w.	ROG 262:2

way (cont.):

This is the w., walk ye in it	BIBLE 46:2
washy w. of true tragedy	KAV 190:7
W. down upon the Swanee	FOST 144:12
w. is commonly the foulest	BACON 24:3
w. may be known upon earth	BOOK 67:16
w. of all the earth	BIBLE 40:29
w. of a man with a maid	BIBLE 44:4
w. of transgressors is hard	BIBLE 43:22
w. to dusty death	SHAK 288:5
w. to the Better there be	HARDY 162:8
ways: at the parting of the w.	BIBLE 47:7
blood is nipped and w. be foul	SHAK 284:23
her w. to roam	BROO 73:10
in whose heart are thy w.	BOOK 67:21
justify the w. of God to men	MILT 228:9
keep thee in all thy w.	BOOK 67:30
Let all her w. be unconfined	PRIOR 255:9
Let me count the w.	BROW 75:5
more w. of being dead	DAWK 115:3
neither are your w. my ways	BIBLE 46:22
vindicate the w. of God to man	POPE 252:11
w. are ways of pleasantness	BIBLE 43:9
w. deep and the weather sharp	ELIOT 133:21
w. with men I find Him not	TENN 324:16
wayside: some seeds fell by the w.	BIBLE 50:4
wayward: w. is this foolish love	SHAK 298:17
we: W. are the hollow men	ELIOT 133:17
W. shall not be moved	ANON 11:15
W. shall overcome	ANON 11:16
weak: concessions of the w.	BURKE 79:27
found him w. in chemistry	WELLS 345:16
Made w. by time and fate	TENN 328:25
refuge of w. minds	CHES 97:13
Repentance is the virtue of w.	DRYD 127:34
Strengthen ye the w. hands	BIBLE 46:5
surely the W. shall perish	SERV 270:11
w. always have to decide	BONH 63:11
w. alone repent	BYRON 85:16
w. from your loveliness	BETJ 37:11
w. have one weapon	BID 59:1
W. men must fall, for heaven	SHAK 293:23
w. piping time of peace	SHAK 294:14
weaken: great life if you don't w.	BUCH 77:26
weaker: to the w. side inclined	BUTL 84:7
w. sex, to piety more prone	ALEX 4:7
w. vessel	BIBLE 57:10
weakness: oh! w. of joy	BETJ 37:11
weal: according to the common w.	JAM 179:12
wealth: consume w. without producing	SHAW 300:26
cunning purchase of my w.	JONS 187:12
get w. and place	POPE 252:25
greater the w., thicker the dirt	GALB 147:15
His w. a well-spent age	CAMP 89:3
insolence of w. will creep out	JOHN 185:19
promoting the w., the number	BURKE 80:6
There is no road to w.	TROL 334:14
There is no w. but life	RUSK 264:20
w. is a sacred thing	FRAN 145:1
W. I seek not, hope nor love	STEV 317:25
w. was his peculiar art	DRYD 127:13
Where w. accumulates	GOLD 154:18
wealthy: business of the w. man	BELL 33:22
weaned: w. child	BIBLE 45:20
w. on a pickle	ANON 11:4
were we not w. till then	DONNE 124:5
weapon: and his w. wit	HOPE 171:20
bayonet is a w. with a worker	ANON 6:7
Loyalty is the Tory's secret w.	KILM 195:2
trusty shield and w.	LUTH 212:10
weak have one w.	BID 59:1
weapons: Spare us all word of the w.	WILB 349:8
w. of war perished	BIBLE 41:23
wear: w. him in my heart's core	SHAK 276:7
Should so w. out to nought	SHAK 283:24

wear (cont.):

such qualities as would w.	GOLD 155:11
w. out than to rust out	CUMB 112:15
worth the w. of winning	BELL 34:3
weariness: Art thou pale for w.	SHEL 305:14
for w. of-walked	LANG 201:6
much study is a w.	BIBLE 44:27
w., the fever, and the fret	KEATS 191:31
w. treads on desire	PETR 248:10
wearing: w. armchairs tight about	WOD 352:22
w. o' the Green	ANON 8:9
w. such a conscience-stricken	HOUS 174:6
wearisome: and make them w.	SHAK 293:17
wears: so w. she to him	SHAK 297:30
w. man's smudge and shares	HOPK 172:4
weary: Age shall not w. them	BINY 59:12
And I sae w. fu' o' care	BURNS 81:27
For I'm w. wi' hunting	BALL 27:19
How w., stale, flat	SHAK 274:10
shall run, and not be w.	BIBLE 46:13
there the w. be at rest	BIBLE 42:27
w. warl goes round	BLAM 62:8
weasel: w. under the cocktail cabinet	PINT 248:22
weather: but the w. turned around	THOM 330:14
But winter and rough w.	SHAK 272:19
first talk is of the w.	JOHN 182:11
Jolly boating w.	CORY 108:11
Stormy w.	KOEH 198:22
'Tis the hard grey w.	KING 195:15
W. and rain have undone	KIPL 197:8
w. the cuckoo likes	HARDY 162:16
w.-wise, some are otherwise	FRAN 145:9
you won't hold up the w.	MACN 216:3
weave: what a tangled web we w.	SCOTT 268:21
W. the warp	GRAY 157:2
weaver: swifter than a w.'s shuttle	BIBLE 42:30
weaving: thread of my own hand's w.	KEATS 191:3
web: cool w. of language	GRAV 156:14
Out flew the w.	TENN 326:3
O what a tangled w. we weave	SCOTT 268:21
She left the w.	TENN 326:3
webs: laws are like spider's w.	ANAC 5:9
Webster: Like W.'s Dictionary	BURKE 81:15
W. was much possessed by death	ELIOT 134:32
wed: And think to w. it	SHAK 270:23
December when they w.	SHAK 273:9
w. the fair Ellen	SCOTT 268:20
With this Ring I thee w.	BOOK 66:2
wedded: thou art w. to calamity	SHAK 295:15
wedding: small circle of a w.-ring	CIBB 100:13
That earliest w.-day	KEBLE 193:18
wedlock: W., indeed, hath oft compared	DAV 114:13
yet w.'s the devil	BYRON 87:12
Wednesday: He that died o' W.	SHAK 278:12
wee: W., sleekit, cow'rin'	BURNS 82:26
W. Willie Winkie	MILL 225:9
weed: Pernicious w.	COWP 109:21
w. that grows in every soil	BURKE 80:4
What is a w.?	EMER 136:29
weeded: W. and worn the ancient thatch	TENN 326:22
weeds: her coronet w.	SHAK 277:7
smell far worse than w.	SHAK 300:2
w. and the wilderness yet	HOPK 172:8
weedy: w. trophies and herself	SHAK 277:7
week: minute's mirth to wail a w.	SHAK 299:8
No admittance till the w. after	CARR 92:5
w. is a long time in politics	WILS 351:9
weep: But milk my ewes and w.	SHAK 299:1
I w. for Adonais—he is dead	SHEL 303:3
She must w. or she will die	TENN 327:26
That he should w. for her	SHAK 275:22
time to w., and a time to laugh	BIBLE 44:12
W., and you weep alone	WILC 349:14
W. me not dead	DONNE 124:16
women must w.	KING 195:16

weeping: Rachel w. for her children — BIBLE 48:11
w. and gnashing of teeth — BIBLE 49:18
weigh: more people see than w. — CHES 97:16
weighed: w. in the balances — BIBLE 47:12
weight: let us lay aside every w. — BIBLE 56:27
to bear the w. of Antony — SHAK 271:10
w. of rages will press — SPOO 313:25
weird: w. sisters, hand in hand — SHAK 285:5
welcome: Advice is seldom w. — CHES 97:9
Love bade me w. — HERB 167:2
W., all wonders in one sight — CRAS 111:11
W. the coming, speed the — POPE 252:24
W. to your gory bed — BURNS 82:21
welcomest: w. when they are gone — SHAK 280:4
welfare: w. of this realm — CHAR 95:1
welkin: Hark! how all the w. rings — WESL 346:7
well: alive and w. and living in — ANON 8:13
And all shall be w. — ELIOT 133:13
and all shall be w. — JUL 188:21
being alive, but being w. — MART 220:6
danger chiefly lies in acting w. — CHUR 98:20
doing w. that which should — VIDAL 338:11
foolish thing w. done — JOHN 184:25
He does himself extremely w. — ANON 9:14
Is it w. with the child — BIBLE 42:9
It is not done w. — JOHN 184:16
looking w. can't move her — SUCK 318:20
loved not wisely but too w. — SHAK 293:5
misery use it for a w. — BOOK 67:21
spent one whole day w. — THOM 330:2
'tis not so deep as a w. — SHAK 295:7
W. done, thou good and — BIBLE 51:1
W. of Loneliness — HALL 160:14
where nobody is w. — AUDEN 21:19
well-aired: have the morning w. — BRUM 77:23
well-beloved: bundle of myrrh is my w. — BIBLE 44:30
w. hath a vineyard — BIBLE 45:7
well-bred: Conscience is thoroughly w. — BUTL 84:20
w. as if we were not married — CONG 106:20
well-content: Stay-at-Home, sweet W. — DAV 114:22
well-dressed: being w. gives a feeling — FORB 143:2
well-informed: To come with a w. mind — AUST 22:23
wells: poison the w. — NEWM 238:15
well-spent: almost as rare as a w. one — CARL 90:7
well-written: w. Life is almost as rare — CARL 90:7
Welsh: devil understands W. — SHAK 278:5
Welshman: care and valour in this W. — SHAK 279:11
welter: w. to the parching wind — MILT 227:11
Weltgeschichte: Die W. ist das Weltgericht — SCH 267:21
wen: great w. of all — COBB 102:26
wench: besides, the w. is dead — MARL 219:2
Wenlock: On W. Edge the wood — HOUS 174:22
weoman: obliged to call it w. — FLEM 142:1
wept: Babylon we sat down and w. — BOOK 69:2
His big tears, for he w. well — SHEL 304:5
Station I sat down and w. — SMART 308:15
that I have sometimes w. — MUSS 236:16
W. over her, carved in stone — TENN 326:24
wert: Which w., and art, and evermore — HEBER 164:17
Werther: W. had a love for Charlotte — THAC 329:23
Wesley: W.'s conversation — JOHN 185:16
west: Cincinnatus of the W. — BYRON 87:4
closing time in the gardens of the W. — CONN 106:27
East is East, and W. is West — KIPL 196:4
from the east, nor from the w. — BOOK 67:18
Go W., young man — GREE 157:20
Go W., young man — SOULE 311:17
Lochinvar is come out of the w. — SCOTT 268:18
safeguard of the W. — WORD 356:2
That's where the W. begins — CHAP 94:13
W. of these out to seas — FLEC 141:14
wester: rainy Pleiads w. — HOUS 174:15
western: All quiet on the w. front — REM 259:4
delivered by W. Union — GOLD 155:18

western (cont.):
Playboy of the W. world — SYNGE 321:22
Swiftly walk o'er the w. wave — SHEL 305:12
when you've seen one W. — WHIT 348:7
Westminster Abbey: peerage, or W. — NELS 237:23
westward: But w., look, the land — CLOU 102:24
W. the course of empire — BERK 35:19
What, you are stepping w.? — WORD 357:3
wet: so w. you could shoot snipe — POW 254:26
w. clothes and into a dry Martini — ANON 8:18
w. sheet and a flowing sea — CUNN 113:7
wildness and w. — HOPK 172:8
wether: tainted w. of the flock — SHAK 289:24
whacks: gave her mother forty w. — ANON 8:22
whales: O ye W. — BOOK 64:2
Where great w. come sailing by — ARN 16:17
whaleship: w. was my Yale — MELV 223:3
what: from the great united w. — ROCH 261:10
He knew what's w. — BUTL 83:23
W. is the matter with Mary Jane — MILNE 225:23
W. is to be done — LENIN 205:3
W. was he doing, the great — BROW 75:4
whatsoever: W. things are true — BIBLE 56:9
wheat: orient and immortal w. — TRAH 333:18
separate the w. from the chaff — HUBB 175:15
wheel: beneath thy Chariot w. — HOPE 171:23
breaks a butterfly upon a w. — POPE 251:7
depends upon a red w. barrow — WILL 351:8
in thy w. there is a point — MARL 218:16
w. broken at the cistern — BIBLE 44:26
w. is come full circle — SHAK 284:3
w. the sofa round — COWP 110:11
wheels: all the w. of Being slow — TENN 325:7
apparently rolled along on w. — HUXL 177:10
none of the w. of trade — HUME 176:6
tarry the w. of his chariots — BIBLE 40:34
w. within w. — DICK 120:2
when: had forgotten to say 'W.' — WOD 352:24
w. a man should marry — BACON 25:3
w. did you last see your father — YEAM 358:12
W. I am dead, I hope it may be — BELL 33:27
W. shall we three meet again — SHAK 284:25
W. you go home, tell them — EDM 130:20
whence: from w. cometh my help — BOOK 68:25
W. did he whence — LENO 205:19
where: But w.'s the bloody horse — CAMP 88:16
fell earth, I knew not w. — LONG 209:10
they fixed the w. and when — HAWK 163:17
W. did you come from — MACD 214:18
w. do they all come from — MCC 205:12
wherefore: every why he had a w. — BUTL 83:22
w. art thou Romeo — SHAK 294:30
W. does he why — LENO 205:19
whereof: w. one cannot speak — WITT 352:8
whetstone: no such w. to sharpen — ASCH 18:19
whiff: w. of grapeshot — CARL 90:11
Whig: Tory men and W. measures — DISR 121:25
Whigs: caught the W. bathing — DISR 121:9
W. admit no force but argument — BROW 74:25
while: But it's a long, long w. — AND 5:12
whimper: Not with a bang but a w. — ELIOT 133:20
whine: They do not sweat and w. — WHIT 348:19
whining: w. of a door — DONNE 124:21
whip: Do not forget the w. — NIET 239:17
whipped: w. the offending Adam — SHAK 278:35
whipping: top which w. Sorrow — GREV 158:18
who should 'scape w. — SHAK 275:20
whips: hath chastised you with w. — BIBLE 41:34
whirligig: w. of time brings — SHAK 298:14
whirling: by the w. rim I've found — BLAM 62:8
whirls: expectation w. me round — SHAK 297:1
whirlwind: Rides in the w. — ADD 2:11
they shall reap the w. — BIBLE 47:17
whiskers: Runcible Cat with crimson w. — LEAR 203:15
whisky: drinkin' w. and rye — MCL 215:8

whisky *(cont.)*:

Freedom and W.	BURNS 81:26

whisper: Hush! W. who dares | MILNE 226:1
w. of a faction | RUSS 265:5
w. softness in chambers | MILT 231:1
w. was already born | MAND 217:11
whispered: it's w. every where | CONG 106:9
whispering: w. sound of the cool colonnade | COWP 109:30
whispers: W. the o'er-fraught heart | SHAK 287:25
whist: W. upon whist upon whist | BETJ 36:22
whistle: hir joly w. wel ywet | CHAU 96:3
until a shrimp learns to w. | KHR 194:18
W. and she'll come to you | FLET 142:6
w., an' I'll come to you | BURNS 82:19
w. her off and let her down | SHAK 292:14
white: always goes into w. satin | SHER 305:24
be the w. man's brother | KING 195:7
But a w., celestial thought | VAUG 337:7
Clothed in w. samite | TENN 324:3
Nor grew it w. in a single night | BYRON 87:5
no 'w.' or 'coloured' signs | KENN 194:7
see the w. of their eyes | PUTN 256:24
Take up the W. Man's burden | KIPL 197:15
Their w. it stays for ever | DOBS 122:27
Wearing w. for Eastertide | HOUS 174:16
w. and hairless as an egg | HERR 167:20
W. as an angel is the English | BLAKE 61:24
w. hairs become a fool | SHAK 278:32
w. in the blood | BIBLE 57:26
w. races are really pinko-grey | FORS 143:24
W. shall not neutralize | BROW 77:10
whose garment was w. | BIBLE 47:14
whited: like unto w. sepulchres | BIBLE 50:32
Whitehall: gentleman in W. | JAY 180:15
White House: Log-cabin to W. | THAY 329:27
no whitewash at the W. | NIXON 240:2
whiter: I shall be w. than snow | BOOK 67:9
Turned a w. shade of pale | REID 259:3
whitewash: no w. at the White House | NIXON 240:2
whither: W. is he withering | LENO 205:19
w. thou goest | BIBLE 41:8
whiting: said a w. to a snail | CARR 91:11
whizzing: W. them over the net | BETJ 37:8
who: that can tell me w. I am | SHAK 282:23
w. am I, that for my sake | CROS 112:13
W. is on my side? who? | BIBLE 42:15
W. is Silvia? what is she? | SHAK 298:19
W.? Whom? | LENIN 205:4
whole: nothing can be sole or w. | YEATS 358:20
Thy faith hath made thee w. | BIBLE 49:25
wholly: w. slaves or wholly free | DRYD 127:30
whom: Who? W.? | LENIN 205:4
whooping: out of all w. | SHAK 273:4
whopping: Latin for a w. | ANST 14:10
whore: Fortune's a right w. | WEBS 344:22
I am the Protestant w. | GWYN 159:13
I' the posture of a w. | SHAK 272:5
lash that w. | SHAK 283:25
Madhouses, prisons, w.-shops | CLARE 101:4
teach the morals of a w. | JOHN 184:1
'Tis Pity She's a W. | FORD 143:11
w. and gambler by the State | BLAKE 60:9
whores: flowing into second-rate w. | PLOM 250:1
no more w. to Paris | GEOR 149:26
to work, ye w., go spin | PEMB 247:5
whoring: w. with their own inventions | BOOK 68:11
why: and I can't tell you w. | MART 220:4
could he see you now, ask w. | AUDEN 20:17
for every w. he had a wherefore | BUTL 83:22
shall and finding only w. | CUMM 113:2
Their's not to reason w. | TENN 323:15
W., Edward, tell me why | WORD 354:12
wibrated: had better not be w. | DICK 117:21
wicked: and desperately w. | BIBLE 46:31

wicked *(cont.)*:

August is a w. month | O'BR 240:18
make me sick and w. | AUST 23:12
no peace unto the w. | BIBLE 46:14
pomps and vanity of this w. | BOOK 65:21
Something w. this way comes | SHAK 287:18
tender mercies of the w. | BIBLE 43:20
Tories born w., and grow worse | ANON 9:6
w. cease from troubling | BIBLE 42:27
worse than w., it's vulgar | PUNCH 256:15
wickedness: manifold sins and w. | BOOK 63:12
spiritual w. in high places | BIBLE 56:4
That is the Path of W. | BALL 28:7
w. that he hath committed | BIBLE 47:6
wicket: flannelled fools at the w. | KIPL 196:18
Widdicombe Fair: for to go to W. | BALL 28:11
wide: nor so w. as a church | SHAK 295:7
Not deep the Poet sees, but w. | ARN 17:2
w. enough to wrap a fairy in | SHAK 290:27
W. is the gate, and broad | BIBLE 49:12
wideness: w. in God's mercy | FABER 138:5
wider: W. still and wider | BENS 34:20
widow: French w. in every bedroom | HOFF 170:5
Here's to the w. of fifty | SHER 306:6
or Molly Stark's a w. | STARK 314:12
virgin-w., and a *mourning bride* | DRYD 128:13
w. bird sat mourning | SHEL 303:14
W. The word consumes itself | PLATH 249:17
widowhood: comfortable estate of w. | GAY 149:4
widows: fatherless children, and w. | BOOK 64:17
wife: man who's untrue to his w. | AUDEN 21:3
And nobody's w. | HERB 166:13
Brutus' harlot, not his w. | SHAK 281:7
by degrees dwindle into a w. | CONG 106:21
chose my w., as she did her | GOLD 155:11
covet thy neighbour's w. | BIBLE 40:9
debauch his friend's w. | BOSW 70:5
either to look out for a w. | SURT 319:14
Giant Despair had a w. | BUNY 79:3
Giving honour unto the w. | BIBLE 57:10
health of his w. | CONN 106:29
hope that keeps up a w.'s | GAY 149:4
husband of one w. | BIBLE 56:16
isn't a moron; she is your w. | OGIL 241:2
I have a w., I have sons | LUCAN 211:26
I have married a w. | BIBLE 52:23
In every port a w. | DIBD 117:18
In riding to and from his w. | WHITE 347:14
kill a w. with kindness | SHAK 295:28
lay down his w. for his friend | JOYCE 188:18
married, but I'd have no w. | CRAS 111:13
Medicine is my lawful w. | CHEK 96:30
Matched with an agèd w. | TENN 328:19
monstrous animal, husband and w. | FIEL 139:12
must be in want of a w. | AUST 23:2
my w., and my name | SURT 319:11
My w., who, poor wretch | PEPYS 247:16
My w. won't let me | LEIGH 204:17
No casual mistress, but a w. | TENN 325:13
roaring of the wind is my w. | KEATS 193:9
shall cleave unto his w. | BIBLE 38:23
Thane of Fife had a w. | SHAK 287:29
There's my w.; look well on her | SPR 314:1
w. and children hostages to | BACON 25:1
w. must be above suspicion | CAES 87:25
w. or your servants to read | GRIF 159:2
w. shall be as the fruitful | BOOK 68:32
young w. and a good brain | JONS 186:23
wigwam: w. of Nokomis | LONG 210:1
wild: call of the w. | LOND 209:7
gone w. into his grave | SHAK 278:30
I never saw a w. thing | LAWR 202:21
Made us nobly w., not mad | HERR 167:19
O Caledonia! stern and w. | SCOTT 268:14
old, w., and incomprehensible | VICT 338:5

wild (cont.):

walk on the w. side	ALGR 4:9
Walk, water, meditated w.	SMART 308:12
wilder: w. shores of love	BLAN 62:9
wilderness: enclosing a w. of idea	BUTL 84:16
I walked through the w.	BUNY 78:17
Long live the weeds and the w.	HOPK 172:8
ninety and nine in the w.	BIBLE 52:26
one crying in the w.	BIBLE 48:13
out into the w. to see	BIBLE 49:34
Out of the world's wide w.	WATTS 343:2
temptation in the w.	BOOK 68:1
that crieth in the w.	BIBLE 46:8
To the w. I wander	ANON 11:23
waste howling w.	BIBLE 40:23
w. and call it peace	TAC 322:4
w. into a glorious empire	BURKE 80:6
w. is paradise enow	FITZ 140:6
Women have no w. in them	BOGAN 62:18
wildness: left, w. and wet	HOPK 172:8
wiles: cranks, and wanton w.	MILT 227:1
will: according to the common w.	JAM 179:12
And not because we w.	ARN 16:9
boy's will is the wind's w.	LONG 209:21
Immanent W. that stirs	HARDY 162:5
In His w. is our peace	DANTE 113:22
let my w. replace reasoned	JUV 189:8
more care to stay than w. to go	SHAK 295:19
Not my w., but thine, be done	BIBLE 53:1
reason and the w. of God	ARN 17:25
Thy w. be done in earth	BIBLE 48:27
We *know* our w. is free	JOHN 184:20
w. is infinite	SHAK 297:2
w. most rank	SHAK 292:13
wrote my w. across the sky	LAWR 203:1
W. in over-plus	SHAK 300:12
w. in us is over-ruled	MARL 218:17
W. you, won't you	CARR 91:12
You w., Oscar, you will	WHIS 347:11
willed: only a w. gentleness	THOM 331:4
Willie: Wee W. Winkie	MILL 225:9
willing: Barkis is w.	DICK 118:9
Lovely and w. every afternoon	AUDEN 20:25
willow: All a green w.	HEYW 168:8
harp on a weeping w.-tree	ANON 8:5
Make me a w. cabin	SHAK 297:21
Sang 'W., titwillow	GILB 152:7
Sing all a green w.	SHAK 292:26
Stood Dido with a w.	SHAK 289:32
w. grows aslant a brook	SHAK 277:6
willows: W. whiten, aspens quiver	TENN 325:35
wills: executors, and talk of w.	SHAK 293:26
wilt: Do what thou w. shall be	CROW 112:14
win: And yet wouldst wrongly w.	SHAK 285:15
Let the boy w. his spurs	EDW 130:21
so who would greatly w.	BYRON 87:3
When in doubt, w. the trick	HOYLE 175:12
w. and lose and still somehow	MITC 232:3
W. just one for the Gipper	GIPP 153:4
wind: answer is blowin' in the w.	DYLAN 129:19
Blow, blow, thou winter w.	SHAK 273:1
boy's will is the w.'s will	LONG 209:21
brought forth w.	BIBLE 45:26
clean the sky! wash the w.	ELIOT 134:8
east w. made flesh	APPL 14:14
Fair stood the w. for France	DRAY 126:22
fires flare up in a w.	FRAN 145:5
Frosty w. made moan	ROSS 263:2
God tempers the w.	STER 315:11
gone with the w.	DOWS 125:12
how the w. doth ramm	POUND 254:8
impatient as the w.	WORD 357:4
let her down the w.	SHAK 292:14
light w. lives or dies	KEATS 192:16
Lord was not in the w.	BIBLE 42:3

wind (cont.):

nets to catch the w.	WEBS 344:13
Nor ever w. blows loudly	TENN 324:22
not I, but the w.	LAWR 202:23
no w. is favourable	SEN 270:7
Only w. it into a ball	BLAKE 60:20
O wild West W., thou breath	SHEL 304:6
piffle before the w.	ASHF 18:23
reed shaken with the w.	BIBLE 49:34
rushing mighty w.	BIBLE 54:8
sand against the w.	BLAKE 61:13
Sits the w. in that corner	SHAK 291:20
solidity to pure w.	ORW 242:15
Their substance is but only w.	WYATT 358:3
They have sown the w.	BIBLE 47:17
twist slowly in the w.	EHRL 131:7
Unhelped by any w.	COL 103:18
welter to the parching w.	MILT 227:11
Western w., when will thou	ANON 11:18
wherever the w. takes me	HOR 173:5
which way the w. is	SELD 269:18
Whose sound dies on the w.	APOL 14:11
w. and the rain	SHAK 298:15
w. bloweth where it listeth	BIBLE 53:18
w. extinguishes candles	LA R 201:24
w. goeth over it	BOOK 68:7
w. of change	MACM 215:17
W. of the western sea	TENN 327:19
w.'s like a whetted knife	MAS 222:2
w. that follows fast	CUNN 113:7
With His hammer of w.	THOM 331:19
Woord is but w.	LYDG 212:15
words but w.	BUTL 84:4
winding: England's w. sheet	BLAKE 60:9
structure in a w. stair	HERB 167:1
to great place is by a w. stair	BACON 24:29
waters were his w.-sheet	BARN 29:7
w.-sheet of Edward's race	GRAY 157:2
window: argument of the broken w.	PANK 245:2
at a w. Pippa passes	BEER 32:9
house of fiction has not one w.	JAMES 179:25
hole in a stained glass w.	CHAN 94:7
kiss my ass in Macy's w.	JOHN 181:20
light through yonder w.	SHAK 294:29
little w. where the sun	HOOD 171:8
looked out at a w.	BIBLE 42:14
stained-glass w.'s hue	BETJ 36:18
will return through the w.	FRED 145:18
w., a casement	DICK 119:13
windows: life's dim w. of the soul	BLAKE 60:12
open w. into men's souls	ELIZ 135:14
Through w. and through	DONNE 124:11
winds: Blow, w., and crack your	SHAK 283:6
w. of March with beauty	SHAK 298:32
w. were love-sick	SHAK 271:14
windward: w. of the law	CHUR 98:23
windy: w. night a rainy morrow	SHAK 300:1
w. side of the law	SHAK 298:12
wine: And I'll not look for w.	JONS 187:23
And the victuals and the w.	CALV 88:10
best fits my little w.	HERR 167:22
bin of w., a spice of wit	STEV 317:17
can with w. dispense	CRAB 110:21
days of w. and roses	DOWS 125:13
doesn't get into the w.	CHES 98:7
Drinking the blude-red w.	BALL 28:4
flask of w., a book of verse	FITZ 140:6
flown with insolence and w.	MILT 228:15
last companion, W.	BELL 33:14
Let us have w. and women	BYRON 86:6
Lords are lordliest in their w.	MILT 230:16
mellow, like good w.	PHIL 248:16
mouth do crush their w.	MARV 220:15
new w. into old bottles	BIBLE 49:24
Not given to w., no striker	BIBLE 56:16

wine (*cont.*):

not to be rinsed with w.	HOPK 172:6
not woman, w., and song	LUTH 212:11
Sans w., sans song	FITZ 140:9
sweet white w.	MAS 221:18
Sweet w. of youth	BROO 72:20
upon the w. when it is red	BIBLE 43:33
w. is in, the wit is out	BECON 31:18
W. is a mocker	BIBLE 43:31
W. maketh merry	BIBLE 44:23
W., not water, binds the lover	SANS 266:20
w. of life is drawn	SHAK 286:26
w. of Shiraz into urine	DIN 121:2
w. that tasted of the tar	BELL 34:1
w. unto those that be of	BIBLE 44:5
With seas of life, like w.	TRAH 334:1

wing: by Conquest's crimson w.

Comin' in on a w. and a pray'r	GRAY 157:1
flits by on leathern w.	ADAM 2:9
headlong joy is ever on the w.	COLL 105:10
Nor knowst'ou w. from tail	MILT 230:9
vainly flapped its tinsel w.	POUND 254:21
	MARV 220:12

winged: Doth the w. life destroy

W. words	BLAKE 61:16
	HOMER 170:20

wingèd: w. squadrons of the sky

wings: Ill news hath w.	MILM 225:13
Love without his w.	DRAY 126:15
mount up with w. as eagles	BYRON 87:1
On w. of song	BIBLE 46:13
take the w. of the morning	HEINE 165:1
viewless w. of Poesy	BOOK 69:6
void his luminous w. in vain	KEATS 192:1
w. like a dove	ARN 18:4
with healing in his w.	BOOK 67:11
	BIBLE 47:26

wink: And w. a reputation down

winners: no w., but all are losers	SWIFT 320:16
winning: If the world be worth thy w.	CHAM 93:25
lips ne'er act the w. part	DRYD 127:21
nothing worth the wear of w.	HERR 167:17
O the glory of the w.	BELL 34:3
w. cause pleased the gods	MER 223:20
w. isn't everything	LUCAN 211:23
wins: Who dares w.	SAND 266:19
	ANON 11:20

winter: blood reigns in the w.'s pale

English w.—ending in July	SHAK 298:26
go south in the w.	BYRON 86:26
hounds of spring are on w.'s	ELIOT 134:19
If W. comes, can Spring be	SWIN 321:1
In w. I get up at night	SHEL 304:10
It was the w. wild	STEV 317:12
Middle of W.	MILT 227:25
mountains by the w. sea	ADD 2:23
my age is as a lusty w.	TENN 324:17
Nor the furious w.'s rages	SHAK 272:16
Now is the w. of our discontent	SHAK 273:27
sad tale's best for w.	SHAK 294:13
See, amid the w.'s snow	SHAK 298:22
Seeming and savour all the w.	CASW 92:18
very dead of W.	SHAK 298:29
very dead of w.	ANDR 5:15
W. Afternoons	ELIOT 133:21
w. and rough weather	DICK 120:14
W. is come and gone	SHAK 272:19
W. is icummen in	SHEL 303:7
w.'s rains and ruins	POUND 254:8
W. suddenly was changed	SWIN 321:2
	SHEL 304:28

wipe: shall w. away all tears

shall w. away all tears	BIBLE 57:28
	BIBLE 58:5

wire: electric w. the message came

wires: If hairs be w., black wires	ANON 6:1
	SHAK 300:11

wisdom: apply our hearts unto w.

beginning of w.	BOOK 67:27
Can w. be put in a silver rod	BOOK 68:15
delight and ends in w.	BLAKE 60:10
Here is w.; this is the royal Law	FROST 146:24
	COR 108:10

wisdom (*cont.*):

How can he get w.	BIBLE 48:6
infallible criterion of w.	BURKE 79:18
Knowledge comes, but w. lingers	TENN 326:14
leads to the palace of w.	BLAKE 61:1
Love is the w. of the fool	JOHN 186:9
price of w. is above rubies	BIBLE 43:2
privilege of w. to listen	HOLM 170:15
spirit of w. and understanding	BIBLE 45:18
teach his senators w.	BOOK 68:10
those who love want w.	SHEL 304:17
what is bettre than w.?	CHAU 95:28
where shall w. be found	BIBLE 43:1
W. and Wit are little seen	BRER 71:22
W. denotes the pursuing	HUTC 177:1
W. hath builded her house	BIBLE 43:14
W. is the principal thing	BIBLE 43:10
w. we have lost in knowledge	ELIOT 134:12
with how little w. the world	OXEN 244:5

wise: All things w. and wonderful

art of being w.	ALEX 4:2
beacons of w. men	JAMES 180:9
Be not w. in your own conceits	HUXL 177:20
be w. in his own conceit	BIBLE 54:44
Be w. with speed	BIBLE 43:38
consider his ways, and be w.	YOUNG 360:14
deemed him wondrous w.	BIBLE 43:11
he is a w. man or a fool	BEAT 30:13
Nor ever did a w. one	BLAKE 60:22
So w. so young, they say	ROCH 261:4
'Tis folly to be w.	SHAK 294:17
To be w., and love	GRAY 157:14
tree that a w. man sees	SHAK 297:3
valorous than manly w.	BLAKE 61:4
w. as serpents	MARL 219:13
w. forgive but do not forget	BIBLE 49:29
w. men from the east	SZASZ 321:24
w. son maketh a glad father	BIBLE 48:9
w. want love	BIBLE 43:16
word is enough for the w.	SHEL 304:17
	PLAU 249:22

wisely: Be w. worldly

loved not w. but too well	QUAR 257:3
wiser: French w. than they seem	SHAK 293:5
sadder and a w. man	BACON 25:12
w. than the children of light	COL 104:19
w. to-day than he was yesterday	BIBLE 52:33
wisest: gretteste clerkes been noght w.	POPE 253:13
than the w. man can answer	CHAU 96:2
w. and justest and best	COLT 105:17
w. fool in Christendom	PLATO 249:20
w., virtuousest, discreetest	HENR 165:22
	MILT 229:20

wish: If otherwise w. I

I w. I loved the Human Race	SHAW 303:1
Thy w. was father, Harry	RAL 258:6
Whoever hath her w.	SHAK 278:27
w. for prayer is a prayer	SHAK 300:12
wishes: exact to my w.	BERN 36:7
wistful: With such a w. eye	ANON 7:17
wit: and fancy w. will come	WILDE 350:15
and his weapon w.	POPE 250:27
at their w.'s end	HOPE 171:20
baiting place of w.	BOOK 68:13
bin of wine, a spice of w.	SIDN 306:20
brevity, and w. its soul	STEV 317:17
Brevity is the soul of w.	COL 103:17
deemed there but want of w.	SHAK 275:8
grave or tomb of w.	SIDN 306:19
he shoots his w.	CAV 93:13
How the w. brightens	SHAK 273:14
Impropriety is the soul of w.	POPE 252:5
Little subject, little w.	MAUG 222:9
mingled with a little w.	CAREY 90:1
o'erflowing of unbounded w.	DRYD 127:31
only a w. among Lords	WINC 352:1
pick-purse of another's w.	JOHN 183:28
	SIDN 306:23

wit (cont.):

pleasant smooth w.	AUBR 20:2
sharpen a good w.	ASCH 18:19
Staircase w.	DID 120:20
too proud for a w.	GOLD 155:2
universal monarchy of w.	CAREW 89:19
use my w. as a pitchfork	LARK 201:19
wine is in, the w. is out	BECON 31:18
Wisdom and W. are little seen	BRER 71:22
w. and humour are conveyed	AUST 22:22
w. be like the coruscations	GOUL 155:26
w. in all languages	DRYD 128:27
w. invites you by his looks	COWP 109:22
w. is Nature to advantage	POPE 252:1
W. is the epitaph of an emotion	NIET 239:23
w. on other souls may fall	DRYD 128:5
w.'s the noblest frailty	SHAD 270:18
W. will shine	DRYD 128:21
w. with dunces, and a dunce	POPE 250:17
witch: Aroint thee, w.!	SHAK 285:3
witchcraft: Nor no w. charm thee	SHAK 273:28
witching: w. time of night	SHAK 276:15
with: I am w. you alway	BIBLE 51:17
not w. me is against me	BIBLE 50:1
wither: Age cannot w. her	SHAK 271:17
w. slowly in thine arms	TENN 328:17
withered: flowers of the forest are w.	COCK 102:27
w. is the garland	SHAK 271:25
withereth: Fast w. too	KEATS 191:8
withers: it w. away	ENG 137:8
our w. are unwrung	SHAK 276:10
within: are w. would fain go out	DAV 114:13
But, oh, he never went w.	COWL 109:14
that w. which passeth show	SHAK 274:8
without: are w. would fain go in	DAV 114:13
forasmuch as w. thee	BOOK 64:26
How many things I can do w.	SOCR 310:20
live with you—or w. you	MART 220:7
withstand: w. in the evil day	BIBLE 56:4
witness: bear w. of that Light	BIBLE 53:9
shalt not bear false w.	BIBLE 40:9
witnesses: so great a cloud of w.	BIBLE 56:27
wits: composed in their w.	ARN 18:5
Great w. are sure to madness	DRYD 127:7
in days when w. were fresh	ARN 17:11
Some have at first for w.	POPE 251:27
They have stolen his w. away	DE L 116:13
warming his five w.	TENN 328:16
youth have ever homely w.	SHAK 298:16
wittles: I live on broken w.	DICK 118:10
witty: am not only w. in myself	SHAK 278:16
Thou swell! Thou w.	HART 163:11
w. and it sha'n't be long	CHES 97:2
w. beauty is a power	MER 223:12
wives: And many, many w.	NAYL 237:20
changes when they are w.	SHAK 273:9
divides the w. of aldermen	SMITH 308:20
Husbands, love your w.	BIBLE 56:11
profane and old w.' fables	BIBLE 56:17
Who married three w. at a time	MONK 232:26
W. are young men's mistresses	BACON 25:2
wizards: w. haste with odours sweet	MILT 227:24
wobbles: good spelling but it W.	MILNE 225:17
woe: and all our w.	MILT 228:7
deep, unutterable w.	AYT 23:17
discover sights of w.	MILT 228:10
hideous notes of w.	BYRON 86:28
life protracted is protracted w.	JOHN 183:15
Oft in danger, oft in w.	WHITE 347:16
rearward of a conquered w.	SHAK 300:1
signs of w. that all was lost	MILT 229:26
trappings and the suits of w.	SHAK 274:8
wit, the balm of w.	SIDN 306:20
W. is me	BIBLE 45:11
w. that is in mariage	CHAU 96:5

woe (cont.):

W. to her that is filthy	BIBLE 47:25
W. to the bloody city	BIBLE 47:24
W. to thee, O land	BIBLE 44:22
W. to the land that's governed	SHAK 294:16
W. unto them that join	BIBLE 45:8
woes: th'exordium of our w.	DRAY 126:18
wantons with our w.	SHAK 294:3
Woking: playing for W.	BETJ 37:8
wold: clothe the w. and meet the sky	TENN 325:34
wolf: have the w. by the ears	JEFF 180:25
like the w. on the fold	BYRON 85:22
w. also shall dwell	BIBLE 45:19
w. far thence that's foe	WEBS 344:26
W. that shall keep it may	KIPL 198:1
wolf's-bane: W., tight-rooted	KEATS 191:25
Wolsey: Reno'd in W.'s Home Town	ANON 8:17
wolves: lion to frighten the w.	MACH 215:3
woman: artist man and the mother w.	SHAW 301:18
As you are w., so be lovely	GRAV 156:16
bloom on a w.	BARR 29:16
body of a weak and feeble w.	ELIZ 135:6
brawling w. in a wide house	BIBLE 43:32
broken-hearted w. tends	HAYES 163:21
called a w. in my own house	WAUGH 343:27
changeable always is w.	VIRG 339:9
clever w. to manage a fool	KIPL 197:28
contentious w. are alike	BIBLE 44:1
dead w. bites not	GRAY 156:19
end to a w.'s liberty	BURN 81:19
Eternal W. draws us upward	GOET 154:8
Every w. adores a Fascist	PLATH 249:14
excellent thing in w.	SHAK 284:5
Fareweel dear, deluding w.	BURNS 82:28
fat white w. whom nobody	CORN 108:6
Frailty, thy name is w.	SHAK 274:12
from man, made he a w.	BIBLE 38:21
glory of a w. to be least talked	PER 248:3
good w. if I had five thousand	THAC 329:21
heart wrapped in a w.'s hide	SHAK 280:13
help and support of the w. I love	EDW 131:2
if a w. have long hair	BIBLE 55:10
in a word, she's a w.	RAC 257:15
inconstant w.	GAY 149:16
large-brained w.	BROW 75:6
Let us look for the w.	DUMAS 129:3
like a w. scorned	CONG 106:12
love a w. that she woot it not	CHAU 96:14
lovely w. in a rural spot	HUNT 176:17
make a man a w.	PEMB 247:6
man that is born of a w.	BIBLE 42:33
Man that is born of a w.	BOOK 66:6
nor w. neither	SHAK 275:16
One hair of a w. can draw	HOW 175:9
One is not born a w.	DE B 115:8
one w. differs from another	MENC 223:6
O W.! in our hours of ease	SCOTT 268:22
post-chaise with a pretty w.	JOHN 185:13
scandal by a w. of easy virtue	HAIL 160:1
She is a w., therefore may be	SHAK 296:25
She is a w., therefore to be	SHAK 280:6
speaks small like a w.	SHAK 290:8
still able to have a w.	SOPH 311:14
There shone one w.	SWIN 321:19
this w. was full of good works	BIBLE 54:14
'Tis w.'s whole existence	BYRON 86:4
unemancipated w. still had	LOW 211:11
virtuous w.	BIBLE 43:19
virtuous w.	BIBLE 44:6
Vitality in a w.	SHAW 301:17
way for a w. to hold a man	SPARK 312:10
What does a w. want	FREUD 146:3
What Every W. Knows	BARR 29:16
what is bettre than a good w.	CHAU 95:28
what's a play without a w.	KYD 199:11

woman (*cont.*):

When lovely w. stoops to folly	GOLD 155:13
while w. wakes to love	TENN 324:15
Who loves not w., wine	LUTH 212:11
will take some savage w.	TENN 326:15
witty w. is a treasure	MER 223:12
W., behold thy son	BIBLE 54:4
w. be more like a man	LERN 205:26
w. but she made mouths	SHAK 283:8
w. can be a beauty without	FARQ 138:16
w. can become a man's friend	CHEK 96:28
w. can be proud and stiff	YEATS 358:20
w. can forgive a man	MAUG 222:10
w. can hardly ever choose	ELIOT 132:5
w. clothed with the sun	BIBLE 57:30
w. dictates before marriage	ELIOT 132:8
w. has given you her heart	VANB 336:24
w. in this humour wooed	SHAK 294:15
w. is a sometime thing	GERS 168:1
w. is his game	TENN 327:25
w. is so hard upon the woman	TENN 328:1
W. is the nigger of the world	ONO 241:13
w. loves her lover	BYRON 86:9
w. moved is like a fountain	SHAK 295:30
W. much missed	HARDY 162:15
w. must have money	WOOLF 354:1
w. must submit to it	STAËL 314:6
w. never smiled or wept	CLARE 101:7
w. of so shining loveliness	YEATS 359:27
W.'s at best a contradiction	POPE 251:12
w.'s desire is rarely other	COL 104:27
w. seldom writes her mind	STEE 314:15
w.'s eye the unanswerable	BYRON 85:17
w. should conceal it	AUST 22:23
w.'s preaching is like	JOHN 184:16
w.'s workhouse	SHAW 302:4
w. take an elder than herself	SHAK 297:30
w. taken in adultery	BIBLE 53:25
w. that deliberates is lost	ADD 2:15
w. to provide for herself	SHAW 302:11
W. was God's second blunder	NIET 239:18
W., what have I to do	BIBLE 53:16
w. who always was tired	ANON 7:17
w. who did not care	KIPL 197:12
w. who lives for others	LEWIS 206:12
w. who tells her real age	WILDE 350:10
w. who wrote the book	LINC 207:13
W. will be the last thing	MER 223:16
w. with a slop-pail	HOPK 172:22
w. with fair opportunities	THAC 329:14
w. without a man is like	STEI 315:2
w. yet think him an angel	THAC 329:11
worser spirit a w.	SHAK 300:13
woman-head: graves have learnt that w.	DONNE 124:9
womanhood: Heroic w.	LONG 209:25
womankind: packs off its w.	SHAW 301:23
womanly: So w., her demeaning	SKEL 308:2
womb: cloistered in thy dear w.	DONNE 123:18
drew from the w. of time	HEINE 165:2
from his mother's w. untimely	SHAK 288:7
O w.! O bely!	CHAU 95:30
teeming w. of royal kings	SHAK 293:16
very w. and bed of enormity	JONS 186:24
wide w. of uncreated night	MILT 228:24
women: after the manner of w.	BIBLE 39:14
Alexander w.	LEE 204:10
all w. are born slaves	AST 19:7
American w. shoot	FORS 143:14
are not w. truly then	JONS 187:22
apples, cherries, hops, and w.	DICK 119:26
blessed art thou among w.	BIBLE 51:27
Dream of Fair W.	TENN 323:20
England is the paradise of w.	FLOR 142:13
far from me, you grim w.	OVID 243:9
girls turn into American w.	HAMP 161:5

women (*cont.*):

Good w. always think	BROO 73:11
Half the sorrows of w.	ELIOT 132:3
happiest w. have no history	ELIOT 132:14
hell for w., as the diverb	BURT 83:13
In the room the w. come and go	ELIOT 133:25
kill more w. and children	BALD 27:5
Let us have wine and w.	BYRON 86:6
married beneath me, all w. do	ASTOR 19:9
men, w., and clergymen	SMITH 310:4
Monstrous Regiment of W.	KNOX 198:16
Music and w. I cannot but	PEPYS 247:19
other w. cloy the appetites	SHAK 271:17
our chilly w.	BYRON 84:29
passing the love of w.	BIBLE 41:23
revenge—especially to w.	BYRON 86:2
Single w. have a dreadful	AUST 23:11
Solomon loved many strange w.	BIBLE 41:32
Some w.'ll stay in a man's	KIPL 198:4
sung w. in three cities	POUND 254:11
Though w. are angels	BYRON 87:12
to w. Italian, to men French	CHAR 95:7
'Twixt w.'s love, and men's	DONNE 123:21
war between men and w.	THUR 332:16
Whatever w. do	WHIT 349:3
with w. nor with priests	SOUT 311:24
W., and Champagne	BELL 33:25
W. and Horses and Power	KIPL 196:5
W. are in furious secret	SHAW 301:4
W. are really much nicer	AMIS 5:6
w. become like their mothers	WILDE 349:19
w. born slaves	WOLL 353:14
W. can't forgive failure	CHEK 96:26
W. desiren to have sovereynetee	CHAU 96:8
w. do in men require	BLAKE 61:17
w. from behind the vacuum	GREER 158:11
W. have no wilderness	BOGAN 62:18
W. have served all these	WOOLF 354:2
w. in a drawing-room	WOOLF 354:3
w. in a state of ignorance	KNOX 198:21
w. must be half-workers	SHAK 273:26
w. must weep	KING 195:16
w. of that ever-fresh terrain	AMIS 5:8
W.—one half the human race	BAG 26:11
w. should be struck regularly	COW 109:11
w.'s rights	FOUR 144:14
W., then, are only children	CHES 97:11
W. who love the same man	BEER 32:11
work its way with the w.	DICK 120:1
You are going to w.	NIET 239:17
won: ground w. today	ARN 17:10
I w. the count	SOM 311:4
never lost till w.	CRAB 110:28
not that you w. or lost	RICE 259:17
prize we sought is w.	WHIT 348:11
Things w. are done	SHAK 296:29
who has w. it bear the palm	JORT 188:1
woman in this humour w.	SHAK 294:15
woman, therefore may be w.	SHAK 296:25
woman, therefore to be w.	SHAK 280:6
w. but to have fought well	COUB 108:15
wonder: all a w. and a wild desire	BROW 77:5
appeared a great w. in heaven	BIBLE 57:30
Have eyes to w.	SHAK 300:5
I w. by my troth, what thou	DONNE 124:5
may w. at the workmanship	MILT 226:20
One can only w.	BENT 35:7
see the boneless w.	CHUR 99:8
still the w. grew	GOLD 154:24
w. at ourselves like men	WORD 354:13
w. of our age	DYER 129:15
w. of our stage	JONS 187:25
wondered: I smiled and w. how	SHAK 288:16
wonderful: All things wise and w.	ALEX 4:2
most w. wonderful	SHAK 273:4

wonderful (*cont.*):

My God, how w. Thou art	FABER 138:3
name shall be called W.	BIBLE 45:16
nothing is more w. than man	SOPH 311:12
which are too w. for me	BIBLE 44:4
wonderfully: fearfully and w. made	BOOK 69:7
wonders: carry within us the w.	BROW 74:13
Except ye see signs and w.	BIBLE 53:20
His w. to perform	COWP 109:25
Welcome, all w. in one sight	CRAS 111:11
wondrous: What w. life is this	MARV 220:15
When I survey the w. cross	WATTS 343:4
woo: are April when they w.	SHAK 273:9
Come, w. me, woo me	SHAK 273:8
wood: Bows down to w. and stone	HEBER 164:16
deep and gloomy w.	WORD 355:9
hewers of w. and drawers	BIBLE 40:28
On Wenlock Edge the w.'s	HOUS 174:22
Warble his native w.-notes	MILT 227:8
w. painted to look like iron	BISM 59:21
woodbine: luscious w.	SHAK 290:26
w. spices are wafted abroad	TENN 326:28
woodcock: Spirits of well-shot w.	BETJ 36:20
woodcocks: springes to catch w.	SHAK 274:24
wooden: literary man *with* a w. leg	DICK 119:21
this w. O	SHAK 278:34
w. walls are the best	COV 108:18
woodland: and a bit of w.	HOR 174:6
And stands about the w. ride	HOUS 174:16
woodlanded: by w. ways	BETJ 37:12
woodlands: About the w. I will go	HOUS 174:17
woodman: W., spare that tree	MORR 235:13
w., spare the beechen tree	CAMP 88:17
woods: But are the w. for me	BLUN 62:13
pleasure in the pathless w.	BYRON 85:12
road through the w.	KIPL 197:8
there is a spirit in the w.	WORD 355:16
We'll to the w. no more	ANON 12:13
w., and desert caves	MILT 227:13
w. are lovely, dark	FROST 146:23
w. decay and fall	TENN 328:17
woodshed: Something nasty in the w.	GIBB 150:17
wooed: therefore may be w.	SHAK 296:25
therefore to be w.	SHAK 280:6
woof: weave the w.	GRAY 157:2
wooing: my w. mind	SHAK 284:19
W., so tiring	MITF 232:9
wool: his head like the pure w.	BIBLE 47:14
woollen: Odious! in w.!	POPE 251:22
rather lie in the w.	SHAK 291:15
woolly: blushing apricot and w. peach	JONS 187:30
flock in w. fold	KEATS 190:14
Woolworth: like paying a visit to W.'s	BEVAN 38:3
walk and live a W. life	NIC 239:12
word: Be ye doers of the w.	BIBLE 57:2
by every w. that proceedeth	BIBLE 48:16
every w. she writes is a lie	MCC 214:12
Greeks had a w. for it	AKINS 3:10
hear the w. of the Lord	BIBLE 47:10
Man's w. is God in man	TENN 324:2
many a w., at random	SCOTT 268:15
meanings packed up into one w.	CARR 92:2
One w. is too often profaned	SHEL 305:5
sincere milk of the w.	BIBLE 57:7
Suit the action to the w.	SHAK 276:6
That I kept my w.,' he said	DE L 116:19
Thou, whose eternal W.	MARR 219:24
thy tears wash out a w. of it	FITZ 140:14
thy true and lively W.	BOOK 65:10
time for such a w.	SHAK 288:5
time lies in one little w.	SHAK 293:10
torture one poor w.	DRYD 128:6
What is that w., honour	SHAK 278:12
When *I* use a w.	CARR 91:26
w. fitly spoken	BIBLE 43:35

word (*cont.*):

w. is a lantern unto my feet	BOOK 68:24
W. is but wynd	LYDG 212:15
w. is enough for the wise	PLAU 249:22
w. is the Verb	HUGO 175:24
w. of Caesar	SHAK 281:21
w. spoken in due season	BIBLE 43:27
w. takes wing beyond recall	HOR 173:13
w. that teems with hidden	GILB 152:27
W. was made flesh	BIBLE 53:11
w. was made flesh	MISS 231:21
W. was with God	BIBLE 53:6
words: all w. and no performance	MASS 222:5
barren superfluity of w.	GARTH 148:15
But w. are words	SHAK 291:38
dressing old w. new	SHAK 299:25
Fair w. enough a man shall	WYATT 358:3
fool and his w. soon parted	SHEN 305:20
Give sorrow w.	SHAK 287:25
gotta use w. when I talk to you	ELIOT 134:16
Hear what comfortable w.	BOOK 65:12
He w. me, girls, he words me	SHAK 272:3
his paint-pots and his w.	HOR 172:26
hurt, not even with w.	BROO 73:12
idea within a wall of w.	BUTL 84:16
I fear those big w.	JOYCE 188:13
In all his w. most wonderful	NEWM 238:20
mere w., no matter from the heart	SHAK 297:12
my w. are my own	CHAR 95:2
of all sad w. of tongue or pen	WHIT 349:1
of all w. of tongue and pen	HARTE 163:12
poetry = *best* w. in the best order	COL 104:26
Proper w. in proper places	SWIFT 320:4
Read out my w. at night	FLEC 141:20
say a few w. of my own	EDW 131:2
These two w. have undone	SELD 269:16
voice so sweet, w. so fair	JONS 187:18
Winged w.	HOMER 170:20
w. are but the signs of ideas	JOHN 182:4
W. are men's daughters	MADD 216:14
w. are slippery and thought	ADAMS 1:21
W. are the daughters	JOHN 182:4
W. are the tokens current	BACON 23:23
w. are wise men's counters	HOBB 169:6
w. but wind	BUTL 84:4
W. came halting forth	SIDN 306:16
w. generate misleading	SPEN 312:18
w. like stones	SPEN 312:25
W. may be false and full	SHAD 270:17
w. of Mercury are harsh	SHAK 284:24
w. shall not pass away	BIBLE 50:37
W. strain	ELIOT 133:1
w., that burn	GRAY 157:18
w. will follow	CATO 92:25
W. without thoughts	SHAK 276:18
W., words, words	SHAK 275:11
worth ten thousand w.	BARN 29:3
wrestle with w. and meanings	ELIOT 133:3
you can drug, with w.	LOW 211:3
Wordsworth: Out-babying W.	BULW 78:10
W. drunk and Porson	HOUS 175:6
W. sometimes wakes	BYRON 86:17
W., Tennyson and Browning	BAG 26:17
work: All that matters is love and w.	FREUD 146:4
breed one w. that wakes	HOPK 172:19
Did he smile his w. to see	BLAKE 62:6
do the hard and dirty w.	RUSK 264:15
Do the w. that's nearest	KING 195:14
For men must w., and women	KING 195:16
goeth forth to his w.	BOOK 68:8
has plenty of w. to do	JER 181:7
He has to w. to keep alive	BELL 33:24
If any would not w.	BIBLE 56:15
in that w. does what he wants	COLL 105:5
I want w.	SHAK 277:32

work (*cont.*):
Let no one else's w. evade	LEHR 204:14
Nice w. if you can get it	GERS 150:8
Nothing to do but w.	KING 195:4
Old Kaspar's w. was done	SOUT 311:18
Perfection of the life, or of the w.	YEATS 358:19
spits on its hands and goes to w.	SAND 266:18
sport as tedious as to w.	SHAK 277:25
very thing to w. on	AUST 23:9
We w. in the dark	JAMES 179:23
What a piece of w. is a man	SHAK 275:16
Why should I let the toad w.	LARK 201:19
W. and pray, live on hay	HILL 168:12
W. expands so as to fill	PARK 245:21
W. is love made visible	GIBR 150:20
W. is of two kinds	RUSS 265:1
W. is the curse of the drinking	WILDE 350:20
W. is x; y is play	EINS 131:10
W. liberates	ANON 13:1
w. more and dispute less	TAWN 322:19
w. together for good	BIBLE 54:40
W. without hope draws nectar	COL 104:22
worker: weapon with a w. at each end	ANON 6:7
w. is the slave of capitalist	CONN 107:3
workers: men the w., ever reaping	TENN 326:9
W. of the world, unite!	MARX 221:11
workhouse: Christmas Day in the W.	SIMS 307:14
prison and the woman's w.	SHAW 302:4
working: been w. like a dog	MCC 205:14
each for the joy of the w.	KIPL 197:13
Heaven will protect a w.-girl	SMITH 309:5
working class: w. where we belong	ORW 242:14
working-house: forge and w. of thought	SHAK 280:1
workmanship: may wonder at the w.	MILT 226:20
works: believe the w.	BIBLE 53:31
devil and all his w.	BOOK 65:21
Faith without w. is dead	BIBLE 57:3
Look on my w., ye Mighty	SHEL 304:12
seen the future; and it w.	STEF 314:19
they may see your good w.	BIBLE 48:22
W. done least rapidly	BROW 76:21
w. of darkness	BIBLE 55:1
w. of darkness	BOOK 64:21
workshop: may be its w.	CHAM 93:22
not a temple but a w.	TURG 335:12
suffer England to be the w.	DISR 121:6
world: All's right with the w.	BROW 76:28
all the uses of this w.	SHAK 274:10
all the w. as my parish	WESL 346:13
All the w. is sad and dreary	FOST 144:13
All the w.'s a stage	SHAK 272:24
all the w. was gay	POPE 253:5
anarchy is loosed upon the w.	YEATS 359:24
ancient times the youth of the w.	BACON 24:5
And when Rome falls—the W.	BYRON 85:11
appointment at the end of the w.	DIN 121:1
banish all the w.	SHAK 278:1
bestride the narrow w.	SHAK 280:27
blynde w., O blynde entencioun	CHAU 96:13
brave new w.	SHAK 296:15
brought nothing into this w.	BIBLE 56:18
dark w. of sin	BICK 58:25
deceits of the w.	BOOK 64:15
excellent foppery of the w.	SHAK 282:22
fashion of this w. passeth	BIBLE 55:6
fled from this vile w.	SHAK 299:23
foolery governs the whole w.	OXEN 244:5
God so loved the w.	BIBLE 53:19
good deed in a naughty w.	SHAK 290:4
Had we but w. enough	MARV 220:22
Hog Butcher for the W.	SAND 266:12
hold the w. but as the world	SHAK 288:27
If the w. be worth thy winning	DRYD 127:21
in all the towns in all the w.	EPST 137:9
In a w. I never made	HOUS 174:11

world (*cont.*):
I nothing in this w. did know	TRAH 334:1
interpreted the w.	MARX 221:11
Into a w. which, wanting thee	WALL 341:14
Into the dangerous w. I leapt	BLAKE 62:3
Is all the sad w. needs	WILC 349:15
Is it a w. to hide virtues	SHAK 297:17
leaves the w. to darkness	GRAY 157:4
light of the w.	BIBLE 48:21
limits of my w.	WITT 352:10
little w. made cunningly	DONNE 123:12
lost the w. for love	DRYD 128:10
knack of so arranging the w.	FRIS 146:5
Mad w.! mad kings!	SHAK 282:4
My country is the w.	PAINE 244:14
nature makes the whole w. kin	SHAK 297:6
need of a w. of men for me	BROW 76:23
never have a quiet w. till	SHAW 302:13
not what once it was, the w.	MARV 221:2
out of the w. as out of fashion	CIBB 100:14
O w. invisible, we view thee	THOM 331:14
pass through this w. but once	GREL 158:14
peopled half the w.	SEEL 269:15
places to learn the w.	CHES 97:6
poor w. in a blue funk	CRANE 111:1
prefer the destruction of the w.	HUME 175:9
prison where I live unto the w.	SHAK 294:10
quiet limit of the w.	TENN 328:17
rack of this tough w.	SHAK 284:7
shall gain the whole w.	BIBLE 51:23
Sob, heavy w.	AUDEN 20:9
solitary monk who shook the w.	MONT 233:25
still point of the turning w.	ELIOT 132:28
Stop the w., I want to get off	BRIC 238:14
Syllables govern the w.	SELD 269:21
Ten days that shook the w.	REED 259:1
Than this w. dreams of	TENN 324:21
Their w. gives way and dies	MACN 216:4
There is a w. elsewhere	SHAK 273:20
These laid the w. away	BROO 72:20
they only saved the w.	CHES 97:23
thick rotundity o' the w.	SHAK 283:6
This great w. should so wear out	SHAK 283:24
This is the way the w. ends	ELIOT 133:20
This warm kind w. is all	CORY 108:14
This w. is bad enough may-be	CLOU 102:13
This w.'s no blot for us	BROW 75:31
though the w. perish	FERD 138:24
Thus passes the glory of the w.	ANON 13:22
To know the w., not love	YOUNG 360:22
To see a w. in a grain of sand	BLAKE 60:5
triple pillar of the w.	SHAK 271:3
upstairs into the w.	CONG 106:8
very w., which is the w. of all of us	WORD 356:14
want the w. and we want it now	MORR 235:20
What a w. is this	BOL 63:6
What would the w. be	HOPK 172:8
when all the w. dissolves	MARL 218:10
When all the w. is young, lad	KING 195:17
woods against the w.	BLUN 62:13
words have undone the w.	SELD 269:15
w. and all her train were hurled	VAUG 337:14
w. and love were young	RAL 257:20
w. as a brothel for emotions	KOES 199:1
w. empty of people	LAWR 202:17
w. forgetting, by the w. forgot	POPE 250:26
w. has grown grey	SWIN 321:13
w., I count it not an inn	BROW 74:20
w. in arms is not spending	EIS 131:14
w. is a comedy to those	WALP 341:23
w. is an oyster	MILL 225:2
w. is becoming like a lunatic	LLOY 208:12
w. is charged with the grandeur	HOPK 172:3
w. is everything that is the case	WITT 352:9
w. is not yet prepared	DOYLE 125:17

world (*cont.*):

w. is so full of a number — STEV 317:13
w. is still deceived — SHAK 289:21
w. is the best of all possible — BRAD 71:8
w. is too much with us — WORD 357:10
w. knew him not — BIBLE 53:10
w. made safe for democracy — WILS 351:21
w. may end tonight — BROW 76:11
w. only grasped by action — BRON 72:9
w.'s a bubble — BACON 25:30
w. safe for hypocrisy — WOLFE 353:6
w.'s an inn, and death — DRYD 128:12
w.'s as ugly, ay, as sin — LOCK 208:22
w.'s at an end — D'AV 114:9
w.'s great age begins anew — SHEL 303:18
w.'s history is the w.'s judgement — SCH 267:21
w. should be taxed — BIBLE 51:31
w.'s last night — DONNE 123:13
w.'s mine oyster — SHAK 290:9
w. spin for ever down — TENN 326:17
w.'s slow stain — SHEL 303:11
w.'s storm-troubled sphere — BRON 72:16
w.'s whole sap is sunk — DONNE 124:8
w.'s worst wound — SASS 267:14
w. was all before them — MILT 230:2
w. will be in love — SHAK 295:14
w. will end in fire — FROST 146:12
w. without end — BOOK 63:17
W., you have kept faith — HARDY 162:9
worldly: be not w. wise — QUAR 257:3
with all my w. goods — BOOK 66:2
worlds: best of all possible w. — CAB 87:23
best of all possible w. — VOLT 340:10
in w. not realised — WORD 355:22
Wandering between two w. — ARN 17:16
what w. away — BROW 75:19
w. of wanwood leafmeal — HOPK 172:15
worm: I wish you all joy of the w. — SHAK 272:6
like a w. i' the bud — SHAK 298:1
invisible w. that flies — BLAKE 62:4
w. at one end and a fool — JOHN 186:11
worms: nor w. forget — DICK 119:9
with vilest w. to dwell — SHAK 299:23
wormwood: w. and the gall — BIBLE 47:1
worried: w. into being — FROST 146:25
worry: Leave your w. on the doorstep — FIEL 139:15
worrying: What's the use of w. — ASAF 18:17
W. the carcase of an old song — THOM 331:5
worse: better day, the w. deed — HENRY 166:2
Defend the bad against the w. — DAY-L 115:6
even from w. to better — JOHN 182:3
fear of finding something w. — BELL 33:5
greater feeling to the w. — SHAK 293:14
If my books had been any w. — CHAN 94:10
I follow the w. — OVID 243:15
I mean the W. one — ARIS 15:10
It is w. than a crime — BOUL 70:9
More will mean w. — AMIS 5:1
one penny the w. — BARH 28:19
w. appear the better reason — MILT 228:23
w. to better hath in it — HOOK 171:15
worst are no w. — SHAK 291:8
worship: And we w. thy Name — BOOK 63:21
are come to w. him — BIBLE 48:9
earth doth w. thee — BOOK 63:18
only object of w. — ANON 5:23
O w. the King, all-glorious — GRANT 156:8
O w. the Lord in the beauty — BOOK 68:2
O w. the Lord in the beauty — MONS 233:3
various modes of w. — GIBB 150:10
with my body I thee w. — BOOK 66:2
w. God in his own way — ROOS 262:13
Your w. is your furnaces — BOTT 70:6
worshipped: art w. by the names divine — BLAKE 60:15
worst: And the best and the w. — SWIN 321:14

worst (*cont.*):

be good to know the w. — BRAD 71:9
Cheer up! the w. is yet to come — JOHN 182:1
exacts a full look at the w. — HARDY 162:8
it was the w. of times — DICK 120:6
No w., there is none — HOPK 172:9
so much good in the w. of us — ANON 10:20
This is the w. — SHAK 283:20
w. are full of passionate — YEATS 359:24
w. is death — SHAK 293:25
w. is better than any other — HAZL 164:6
w. is better than none — JOHN 184:3
world's w. wound — SASS 267:14
w. time of the year — ANDR 5:15
w. time of the year — ELIOT 133:21
worth: but not w. going to see — JOHN 185:24
calculate the w. of a man — FLAU 141:8
charter of thy w. — SHAK 299:27
it is w. doing badly — CHES 98:16
Slow rises w., by poverty — JOHN 183:9
Worthington: on the stage, Mrs W. — COW 109:5
worthy: labourer is w. of his hire — BIBLE 52:10
latchet I am not w. to unloose — BIBLE 53:12
Lord, I am not w. — BIBLE 49:15
w. to be called thy son — BIBLE 52:30
wotthehell: w. archy — MARQ 219:19
would: and what we w., we know — ARN 16:10
evil which I w. not, that I do — BIBLE 54:38
He w., wouldn't he? — RIC 259:20
wound: Earth felt the w. — MILT 229:26
first did help to w. itself — SHAK 282:15
Hearts w. up with love — SPEN 313:2
In every w. of Caesar — SHAK 281:26
keen knife see not the w. — SHAK 285:19
that never felt a w. — SHAK 294:29
world's worst w. — SASS 267:14
wounded: w. for our transgressions — BIBLE 46:19
w. spirit who can bear — BIBLE 43:29
You're w.! — BROW 76:8
Wounded Knee: Bury my heart at W. — BENÉT 34:9
wounding: wounded is the w. heart — CRAS 111:7
Wragg: W. is in custody — ARN 18:3
wrang: may gang a kennin w. — BURNS 81:21
wrapped: All meanly w. — MILT 227:25
w. him in swaddling clothes — BIBLE 51:32
wrath: day of w. — MISS 231:23
flee from the w. to come — BIBLE 48:14
soft answer turneth away w. — BIBLE 43:24
sun go down upon your w. — BIBLE 55:33
tigers of w. are wiser — BLAKE 61:8
w. endureth but the twinkling — BOOK 66:22
wreathed: w. the rod of criticism — D'ISR 122:23
Wren: Sir Christopher W. — BENT 35:9
wren: Four Larks and a W. — LEAR 203:17
robin-red-breast and the w. — WEBS 344:25
w. goes to't — SHAK 283:23
wrest: W. once the law — SHAK 289:28
wrestle: w. not against flesh — BIBLE 56:4
w. with words and meanings — ELIOT 133:3
wrestling: w. with (my God!) — HOPK 172:1
wretch: w. that dares not die — BURNS 82:15
wretched: and yet a w. thing — DAV 114:14
w. men are cradled into poetry — SHEL 303:22
wretches: feel what we feel — SHAK 283:12
wriggles: He w. and giggles — HOFF 169:19
wring: soon w. their hands — WALP 342:5
writ: and, having w., moves on — FITZ 140:14
I never w., nor no man ever — SHAK 300:9
Presbyter is but old *Priest* w. — MILT 228:2
write: But those who cannot w. — POPE 252:29
comfortable I sit down to w. — KEATS 193:13
I love to w. to the moment — RICH 260:3
I w. like a distinguished — NAB 236:20
look in thy heart and w. — SIDN 306:17
much as a man ought to w. — TROL 334:12

write (cont.):
people that w., people | SHEN 305:21
people who can't w. | ZAPPA 361:1
restraint with which they w. | CAMP 88:16
Though an angel should w. | MOORE 234:10
To make me w. too much | DAN 113:16
W. me as one that loves | HUNT 176:13
W. sorrow on the bosom | SHAK 293:26
yet hate all who w. | WYCH 358:6
You w. with ease | SHER 306:8
writer: every style of w. untouched | WORD 357:13
modern hardback w. | TRIL 334:10
pen: of a ready w. | BOOK 67:5
plain, rude w. | BURT 83:6
to protect the w. | ACH 1:4
w.'s ambition should be | KOES 199:3
writers: W., like teeth, are divided | BAG 26:15
writing: All the rest is mere fine w. | VERL 337:20
any style of w. untouched | JOHN 185:12
God is love, but get it in w. | LEE 204:5
incurable disease of w. | JUV 189:10
sign the w., that it be not | BIBLE 47:13
w. an exact man | BACON 25:15
w. at once | GIDE 151:1
w. increaseth rage | DYER 129:15
w. is next to fine doing | KEATS 193:12
W. is not a profession | SIM 307:4
W., when properly managed | STER 315:17
written: Books are well w. or | WILDE 350:3
in which anything may be w. | TRAH 333:17
poetry should be as well w. as prose | POUND 254:24
What I have written I have w. | BIBLE 54:3
w. without effort | JOHN 186:15
w. word as unlike the spoken | CONN 106:26
wrong: absent are always in the w. | DEST 117:10
called them by w. names | BROW 75:16
customer is never w. | RITZ 260:13
different kinds of w. | COMP 106:5
do a little w. | SHAK 289:28
Eating people is w. | SWANN 141:5
Ebenezer thought it w. to fight | BELL 33:28
Englishman in the w. | SHAW 302:9
gone w., however slightly | POTT 254:4
Had anything been w. | AUDEN 21:17
he done her w. | ANON 7:6
he is very probably w. | CLAR 101:14
I called the w. number | THUR 332:18
idea, and that is a w. one | JOHN 184:23
if w., to be set right | SCH 288:1
keep himself from doing w. | BIBLE 48:3
king can do no w. | BLAC 60:2
Kings to govern w. | POPE 250:18
million Frenchmen can't be w. | GUIN 159:9
multitude is always in the w. | DILL 120:24
On the w. side of the door | CHES 97:21
Ran w. through all the land | MUIR 236:6
rather be w. with Plato | CIC 101:1
requite w. with wrong | SOCR 310:23
right deed for the w. reason | ELIOT 134:7
right of an excessive w. | BROW 77:8
Should suffer w. no more | MAC 214:2
suffering they were never w. | AUDEN 21:1
thou hast seen my w. | BIBLE 47:3
When everyone is w. | LA CH 199:15
when I am in the w. | MELB 222:22
w. because not all was right | CRAB 110:26
W. but Wromantic | SELL 270:2
w. could religion induce | LUCR 212:2
w. extenuates not wrong | SHAK 296:33
W. forever on the throne | LOW 211:8
W. from the start | POUND 254:14
w. side of a Turkey tapestry | HOW 175:8
w. the poorest ploughman | CHAR 94:24
w. with our bloody ships | BEAT 30:14
wrongly: And yet wouldst w. win | SHAK 285:15

wrongs: people's w. his own | DRYD 127:14
Two w. don't make a right | SZASZ 322:2
wrote: ever w. except for money | JOHN 185:10
Who w. like an angel | GARR 148:9
wrought: That first he w. | CHAU 95:21
What hath God w. | BIBLE 40:19
Wykehamist: rather dirty W. | BETJ 37:15
Wynken: W., Blynken, and Nod | FIELD 139:2

X

Xanadu: In X. did Kubla Khan | COL 103:22

Y

Yale: whaleship was my Y. | MELV 223:3
Yankee Doodle: I'm a Y. Dandy | COHAN 103:5
Y. came to town | ANON 11:24
yawning: like a man y. at a ball | LERM 205:25
yawns: grave y. for him | TREE 334:5
yawp: barbaric y. over the roofs | WHIT 348:22
yea: Let your y. be yea | BIBLE 57:5
year: beautiful and death-struck y. | HOUS 174:25
next y. I shall be sixty-two | REED 258:14
one y.'s experience 30 times | CARR 90:30
sailed away for a y. and a day | LEAR 203:12
stood at the gate of the y. | HASK 163:16
thirtieth y. to heaven | THOM 330:13
time of y. thou mayst in me | SHAK 299:24
'Tis the y.'s midnight | DONNE 124:7
y. is going, let him go | TENN 325:23
y.'s at the spring | BROW 76:28
years: breath the y. behind | YEATS 359:11
down the arches of the y. | THOM 331:8
end of a thousand y. of history | GAIT 147:12
fleeting y. are slipping by | HOR 173:23
gave up the y. to be | BROO 72:20
Into the vale of y. | SHAK 292:16
nor the y. condemn | BINY 59:12
remember not past y. | NEWM 238:22
Tell me, where all past y. are | DONNE 124:10
thousand y. in thy sight | BOOK 67:25
threescore y. and ten | BOOK 67:26
touch of earthly y. | WORD 356:25
y. of desolation pass over | JEFF 180:23
y. that the locust hath eaten | BIBLE 47:19
y. to come seemed waste | YEATS 359:11
yeas: russet y. and honest kersey | SHAK 284:19
Yeats: William Y. is laid to rest | AUDEN 20:24
yellow: Come unto these y. sands | SHAK 295:36
fall'n into the sear, the y. leaf | SHAK 288:1
falls into the y. leaf | BYRON 86:19
paved with y. brick | BAUM 30:10
silk-worm expend her y. | MIDD 224:9
When y. leaves, or none | SHAK 299:24
Y., and black, and pale | SHEL 304:6
y. fog that rubs its back | ELIOT 133:26
Y. God forever gazes down | HAYES 163:21
yes: place where y. may mean no | TOFF 333:7
way of getting the answer y. | CAMUS 89:5
Y., but not in the South | POTT 254:5
Y.; I remember Adlestrop | THOM 330:21
Y.; Minister! No, Minister! | CROS 112:12
Y.—oh dear yes, the novel | FORS 143:16
yesterday: art of keeping up with y. | MARQ 219:15
call back y., bid time | SHAK 293:24
in thy sight are but as y. | BOOK 67:25
Jesus Christ the same y. | BIBLE 56:30
universe and give me y. | HERM 186:20
We were saying y. | LUIS 212:7
where leaves the rose of y. | FITZ 140:5
yesterdays: all our y. | SHAK 288:5

yesteryear: where are the snows of y. VILL 338:20
yet: continency—but not y. AUG 21:22
  young man not y., an elder BACON 25:3
yew: Gall of goat, and slips of y. SHAK 287:17
yid: LET'S PUT THE ID BACK IN Y. ROTH 263:15
yield: find, and not to y. TENN 328:25
yoghurt: between the milk and the y. TRIL 334:10
yo-ho-ho: Y., and a bottle of rum STEV 317:2
yoke: bear the y. in his youth BIBLE 47:2
  For my y. is easy BIBLE 49:36
  savage bull doth bear the y. SHAK 291:14
Yonghy-Bonghy-Bó: Lived the Y. LEAR 203:7
Yorick: Alas, poor Y. SHAK 277:8
you: For y. but not for me ANON 9:21
  I cannot live with y. MART 220:7
  through y. but not from you GIBR 150:19
young: America is a country of y. men EMER 137:1
  But to be y. was very heaven WORD 354:24
  crime of being a y. man PITT 249:3
  dared to be radical when y. FROST 146:18
  for ever y. KEATS 191:21
  her six y. on the rail BROW 76:10
  I, being y. and foolish YEATS 359:1
  I have been y., and now BLUN 62:15
  I have been y., and now BOOK 66:27
  let me die a y.-man's death MCG 214:21
  love's y. dream MOORE 234:15
  Old and y., we are all STEV 317:5
  O y., fresshe folkes CHAU 96:22
  sight to make an old man y. TENN 323:24
  So wise so y., they say SHAK 294:17
  So y., and so untender SHAK 282:17
  those that are with y. BIBLE 46:11
  we that are y. shall never SHAK 284:8
  When all the world is y., lad KING 195:17
  Whom the gods love dies y. MEN 223:5
  world and love were y. RAL 257:20
  y. a body with so old a head SHAK 289:25
  y. and easy in the mercy THOM 330:9
  y. and easy under the apple THOM 330:8
  Y., gifted and black IRV 178:18
  y. in one another's arms YEATS 359:20
  y. man not yet, an elder BACON 25:3
  y. men glittering and sparkling TRAH 333:19
  y. men shall see visions BIBLE 47:20
  y. wife and a good brain JONS 186:23
younger: I'm y. than that now DYLAN 130:6
youngman: die a y.'s death MCG 214:21
yours: Y. till Hell freezes FISH 139:25
yourself: DO IT Y. BARH 28:22
youth: After the pleasures of y. ANON 13:16

youth (*cont.*):
  All the flattering y. defy ROCH 261:9
  April of your y. HERB 166:19
  Ancient times the y. of the world BACON 24:5
  bear the yoke in his y. BIBLE 47:2
  Crabbed age and y. SHAK 299:5
  Creator in the days of thy y. BIBLE 44:25
  days of our y. are the days BYRON 87:10
  flourish set on y. SHAK 299:22
  flower of their y. VIRG 340:1
  I do abhor thee, y. SHAK 299:6
  If y. knew; if age could EST 137:17
  I have y. and a little beauty WEBS 344:14
  many a y., and many a maid MILT 227:4
  sign of an ill-spent y. ROUP 263:17
  sins and offences of my y. BOOK 66:21
  spice-islands of Y. and Hope COL 105:1
  thoughts of y. are long LONG 209:21
  Time the subtle thief of y. MILT 230:20
  very riband in the cap of y. SHAK 277:5
  when Y. and Pleasure meet BYRON 85:3
  Where y. grows pale KEATS 191:32
  Y. is a blunder DISR 121:26
  y. of England are on fire SHAK 279:2
  y. of frolics, an old age of cards POPE 251:11
  y. of labour with an age of ease GOLD 154:19
  Y. on the prow, and Pleasure GRAY 157:3
  Y.'s a stuff will not endure SHAK 297:23
  Y.'s the season made for joys GAY 149:6
  y. to the gallows PAINE 244:13
  Y., what man's age is like to be DENH 116:26
  Y., which is forgiven everything SHAW 302:6
  Y. will be served BORR 69:27

Z

zany: mountebank and his z. WALP 341:24
zeal: All z., Mr Easy MARR 220:1
  not the slightest z. TALL 322:11
  tempering bigot z. KNOX 198:17
  z. in politics as well JUN 188:26
  z. of the Lord of hosts BIBLE 45:17
zealous: relation is a z. citizen BURKE 80:20
zed: Thou whoreson z.! SHAK 283:2
Zen: Z. and the Art of Motorcyle PIRS 249:2
zenith: z. like a falling star MILT 228:20
Zenocrate: Ah fair Z. MARL 219:10
zest: z. goes out of a beautiful GREN 158:15
Zion: Z., city of our God NEWT 239:8
zoo: it is a human z. MORR 235:12
Zurich: little gnomes in Z. WILS 351:12

OXFORD

MORE OXFORD PAPERBACKS

This book is just one of nearly 1000 Oxford Paper-backs currently in print. If you would like details of other Oxford Paperbacks, including titles in the World's Classics, Oxford Reference, Oxford Books, OPUS, Past Masters, Oxford Authors, and Oxford Shakespeare series, please write to:

UK and Europe: Oxford Paperbacks Publicity Manager, Arts and Reference Publicity Department, Oxford University Press, Walton Street, Oxford OX2 6DP.

Customers in UK and Europe will find Oxford Paperbacks available in all good bookshops. But in case of difficulty please send orders to the Cash-with-Order Department, Oxford University Press Distribution Services, Saxon Way West, Corby, Northants NN18 9ES. Tel: 01536 741519; Fax: 01536 746337. Please send a cheque for the total cost of the books, plus £1.75 postage and packing for orders under £20; £2.75 for orders over £20. Customers outside the UK should add 10% of the cost of the books for postage and packing.

USA: Oxford Paperbacks Marketing Manager, Oxford University Press, Inc., 200 Madison Avenue, New York, N.Y. 10016.

Canada: Trade Department, Oxford University Press, 70 Wynford Drive, Don Mills, Ontario M3C 1J9.

Australia: Trade Marketing Manager, Oxford University Press, G.P.O. Box 2784Y, Melbourne 3001, Victoria.

South Africa: Oxford University Press, P.O. Box 1141, Cape Town 8000.

OXFORD REFERENCE

THE CONCISE OXFORD COMPANION TO ENGLISH LITERATURE

Edited by Margaret Drabble and Jenny Stringer

Based on the immensely popular fifth edition of the *Oxford Companion to English Literature* this is an indispensable, compact guide to the central matter of English literature.

There are more than 5,000 entries on the lives and works of authors, poets, playwrights, essayists, philosophers, and historians; plot summaries of novels and plays; literary movements; fictional characters; legends; theatres; periodicals; and much more.

The book's sharpened focus on the English literature of the British Isles makes it especially convenient to use, but there is still generous coverage of the literature of other countries and of other disciplines which have influenced or been influenced by English literature.

From reviews of *The Oxford Companion to English Literature*:

'a book which one turns to with constant pleasure . . . a book with much style and little prejudice' Iain Gilchrist, *TLS*

'it is quite difficult to imagine, in this genre, a more useful publication' Frank Kermode, *London Review of Books*

'incarnates a living sense of tradition . . . sensitive not to fashion merely but to the spirit of the age' Christopher Ricks, *Sunday Times*